Dictionary of Nineteenth-Century Journalism

In Great Britain and Ireland

Dictionary of Nineteenth-Century Journalism

In Great Britain and Ireland

General editors

Laurel BRAKE & Marysa DEMOOR

Associate editors

Margaret Beetham, Gowan Dawson, Odin Dekkers, Ian Haywood,
Linda Hughes, Aled Jones, Anne Humpherys, Andrew King, Mark Knight,
Brian Maidment, Joanne Shattock, Elizabeth Tilley, Mark Turner
Assisted by John Wood and Cheryl Law

Academia Press
and
The British Library

First published 2009 by

Academia Press
Eekhout 2
B-9000 Gent
Tel: 0032 (0)9/233 80 88   Fax: 0032 (0)9/233 14 09
Info@academiapress.be   www.academiapress.be

subsidiary of

J. Story Scientia nv Wetenschappelijke boekhandel
Sint Kwintensberg 87
B-9000 Gent
Tel: 0032 (0)9 225 57 57   Fax: 0032 (0)9 233 14 09
Info@Story.be   www.story.be

and

The British Library
96 Euston Road
London NW1 2DB

© 2009 The Contributors

Typeset by Proxess Document Management
Cover: Bobby & Co., London
Printed in Belgium

ISBN 978 90 382 1340 8 (Academia Press)
D/2009/4804/1
U1197

ISBN 978 0 7123 5039 6 (The British Library)

In Memoriam: Dr John Davidson and Lic. Simone Dijck
To new lives: Samuel Knight, Casper Dekkers and Juliette Bombaert

Contents

Acknowledgements

This project has been a real, sometimes even a wild adventure, comparable to that of Don Quixote and his faithful friend Sancho Panza in its almost utopian aims. That unlike Don Quixote we have been able to manage the windmills is due to the financial and intellectual generosity of a large number of people and institutions. We name them in chronological order, as we came to know and rely on them. We hope that we have remembered everyone.

The Royal Flemish Academy for the Arts and the Sciences made it all possible: Professor Niceas Schamp, the scientific board of the Academy, Inez Dua, Kris Brossé and the rest of the staff have been supportive since the start of our collaboration in autumn 2004. Without them, and without the opportunity to collaborate in a financially supported scheme and the intellectual community of the VLAC, this project would never have materialised.

Our loyal and hardworking associate editors from six countries, who stayed with the project over four years, deserve our boundless thanks. The project is also immensely grateful to the advisory board of *DNCJ*, the contributors and the scholarly community (members of RSVP and list members of Victoria). We have relied heavily on all of these groups and their expertise, returning again and again with pressing questions. We also want to thank John North, founder and editor of the *Waterloo Directory*, who opened the electronic edition of *Waterloo* to the editors, ProQuest who afforded our contributors online access to their full-text database British Periodicals, and Louis James, an associate editor during the early stages of the project, and an expert adviser later about comic and juvenile journals. A number of libraries and librarians have generously assisted the editors with knotty research problems, notably the British Library, the Bodleian Library, St Bride Library, the National Library of Scotland and Senate House Library, University of London. The advice and knowledge of individuals – Malcolm Chase, Deian Hopkin, Andrew King, Rohan McWilliam, Michael Slater, Steve Tate and Joel Wiener – who responded to 'urgent'queries was much appreciated and immensely helpful.

Throughout we have been assisted in our efforts by researchers David Lawrence, Cheryl Law, John Davidson, Matthew Taunton, Jolein De Ridder, Koenraad Claes, Alice Burley, Zsuzsanna Varga, Matthew B. Tildesley and Ann De Smaele. Cheryl Law and John Wood provided research assistance to Margaret Beetham and Aled Jones. Koenraad Claes assisted us with his Excel skills to bring order where there was none. Cheryl Law, Matthew Taunton, and Vicky Williams indexed the electronic edition, and Louise Lambe, Anthony Cummins, Patrick Vanleene and Vicky

Williams helped with editing. Olivia Malfait and Isabelle Clairhout were trainee students who helped with the illustrations, the early stages of the list of acronyms and the compilation of the letter files. Brian Maidment and ProQuest have been generous in their supply of illustrations for the *Dictionary*. We have relied especially on Cheryl Law and Matthew Taunton, to whom we are grateful for their unstinting work: Cheryl for her help with the bibliography and general editing of the MS, and Matthew, who was writing 'missing' and 'urgent' entries to the final deadline. It has been a pleasure to work so closely with this generous and able team.

We are also indebted to Canterbury Christ Church University who opened their Blackboard facility to the project, and to Sam MacFarlane for his kind and efficient help with this crucial resource; to Gitte Callaert who created an appropriate and attractive *DNCJ* website, and to Drusilla Calvert and her group who skilfully created an index out of a wilderness of names and titles. Adèle Linderholm, Ed King and Andrew King helped us with proofreading, each bringing their own expertise to the project.

Apart from the Royal Flemish Academy, we have received financial support from the British Academy, the Schools of English and Humanities and Continuing Education at Birkbeck College, the Department of English Language and Literature at King's College London, and ProQuest. We owe sincere thanks to each of those institutions.

Finally we want to thank our publishers, Peter Laroy, Geert Van den Bossche and Pieter Borghart of Academia Press in Ghent and David Way of the British Library. And Proxess Document Management patiently corrected version after version of proof. Their belief in the project, generous tolerance and firm guidance enabled us to survive the long process of gestation and to complete the work.

Introduction

DNCJ is an attempt to provide a snapshot of British and Irish journalism in the nineteenth century, and a gateway to the period. Print journalism both shaped and reflected the complexities of its time, as the internet does now. The *Dictionary* takes its place beside distinguished predecessors and contemporaries, most notably the *Waterloo Directory of English Newspapers and Periodicals 1800-1900* which is the most inclusive of its kind, and the more selective but invaluable *British Literary Magazines* and the *Wellesley Index of Victorian Periodicals*. The scope and remit of *DNCJ* lie somewhere between these landmarks. It is a one-volume, rapid reference work.

In its 1,620 entries *DNCJ*, like *Waterloo,* covers periodical and newspaper titles (37% of the total), treating them as part of a single industry. Other categories of entries include journalists/editors (30%), topics (13%), publishers/ proprietors (8.6%), illustrators (6.6%), printers (2.2%), distributors and inventors and Topics. The topics identify some of the overarching categories to which individual entries may belong or relate such as Imperialism and Journalism, the Missionary press, or Trade Papers; or phenomena of the press such as Magazine Day, Puffing, 'Title changes', or Football Specials. Other topics draw attention to the material culture of media history such as Mastheads, Paper and printing machines. The topics are indicative of how inclusive and diverse the press is, and how profoundly it can augment our understanding of the period from a wide range of disciplinary perspectives, from Art History to Temperance. The list of topics may be perused as a griyo in the Categorised Index of Headwords at the end of the volume.

The number of periodical and newspaper titles in the nineteenth century is prodigious, and it could be argued that the relative importance of books and serials in the period achieves a balance rare in the history of print culture. Serials played a significant part in fostering many of the learned, social and political discourses of the century; they 'made' authors, routinely published whole books serially and disseminated knowledge, both verbal and visual; they also created, investigated, reported and disseminated news, and advertising, thereby playing a vital role in the economy; and of course they entertained, through fiction, cartoons, contests, puzzles, and satire.

DNCJ has aimed to select an array of entries by serial title that fully represents the range of the press. It includes general weeklies for the middle classes (Dickens's *All the Year Round* and *Chambers's Journal*) and the upper classes (*Athenaeum*); monthlies for men (the *Practical Mechanic*) and women (*English Woman's Journal*); illustrated titles such as *Cassell's Illustrated Family Paper,* Cleave's *Police Gazette* and *Punch*; monthly class papers such as the *Workman*, and the *Gardener's*

Magazine, and class weeklies such as the [Church] *Guardian*, the *Builder* and the *Queen*. Some serials such as the *Co-operative Magazine* are primarily organs of groups (here the London Co-operative Society) who use them for internal purposes such as identity formation and policy shaping as well as external dissemination of their ideas. Others, such as the *Nineteenth Century*, use the proceedings of a group (here the Metaphysical Society) to generate copy and format for the journal. Our entries on daily and weekly newspapers provide readers with an array of titles to supplement the ubiquitous *The Times*, and some indication of the great range of sources of news and other content, that fuelled the weeklies, monthlies and quarterlies. The conflation of newspapers and periodicals also provides insight into the exchange between literature and journalism, authors and journalists, books and the newspaper press: Charles Dickens was an early editor of the *Daily News*, as well as editor of the weeklies *Household Words* and *All the Year Round*.

DNCJ also includes entries for a large number of persons involved in nineteenth-century journalism. It covers well-known authors, such as George Eliot, who served their apprenticeship for literary work in the journals; Eliot, quite extraordinarily for the 1850s, acted as editor of the radical and progressive *Westminster Review*, and worked regularly in the office of the journal rather than from the privacy of home. Through her position at the hub of the journal, George Eliot met leading thinkers of the day, from across the disciplines. Her position involved book reviewing and provision of articles on current cultural issues, from which she gained understanding of both the literary world and the publishing industry. These helped her gauge the market for the fiction which she started to write immediately following upon her apprenticeship on the *Westminster*.

Other editors and contributors from a range of professions, from barrister to economist, were so regularly associated with journalism that their primary profession might arguably be designated journalist. Alfred Austin, Poet Laureate, was the founder, proprietor and editor of the monthly *National Review* for a decade; Charles Kains-Jackson, a barrister, edited the *Artist*, a trade paper in which he embedded gay discourse; Robert Giffen, cited as an economist in the *ODNB*, is more credibly a journalist, having contributed prodigiously to dailies, weeklies and monthlies over the entirety of his working life. Robert Chambers, a geologist, contributed so liberally to the press that his primary identity arguably might lie within the fourth estate; Chambers particularly was co-proprietor of a huge publishing firm, sometime editor of *Chambers's Journal,* and a frequent contributor to that weekly as well as to any number of the firm's other serial titles; he also was the anonymous author of the best-selling *Vestiges of Creation*. Harriet Martineau took advantage of anonymity to earn her living as a regular leader writer of the *Daily News*, and Henry James, whose aversion to New Journalism is well known, contributed extensively to the periodical market in the course of his career.

DNCJ has also sought to identify publishers whose lists are closely identified with the press, either through a single title (Sampson Low) or a range of titles such as Cassell & Co. Similarly, some printers, particularly radical printers such as Richard Carlile are notable for their press work, and we have endeavoured to indicate this significant sector of the industry, albeit modestly. Having now read and edited *DNCJ* as a whole, we are confident that is a unique resource for this period, and hopeful that students and scholars will find it useful, and absorbing.

DNCJ has been the product of a collaborative and co-operative process from start to finish. From its base in thirteen associate editors, each of them experts in one or more fields associated with the nineteenth-century press, and an active Advisory Board, we went on to consult the international scholarly community at various stages on websites and in person, initially about selection of entries (*which* journalists, titles, topics) and then to recruit contributors (*who* was expert on *what*). In the event, we have contributors from Australia, Belgium, Canada, Eire, France, Hong Kong, Japan, the Netherlands, New Zealand, the UK and the US. We also talked to publishers and researchers, who were themselves engaged in producing full-text digital databases of historical journals, including the British Library, ProQuest, Gale, Cengage Learning, ncse to which resources *DNCJ* will be a useful Companion.

While the associate editors and editors had devised criteria for selection, and a template for contributors, as entries came in, dialogue ensued among editors, associate editors and contributors about the nature of model entries, and new suggestions were made for inclusion that arose from the copy, correspondence or the web which were then in turn commissioned. The critieria for inclusion that we developed were representativeness (e.g. of genre, region, 'class', or period); distinction of format or contribution, even if 'one-off' titles/articles; extent of influence; duration/longevity of serials or personal careers; breadth of contributions by persons, across titles or subjects; and range/variety of entries in *DNCJ* as a whole, with respect to periodicity, gender, readership type, price and illustration.

Four times each year, progress and further selection were reviewed at well-attended Editorial Board meetings, variously in London, the US, and Belgium, and on occasion, an entire area – e.g. Sport – was identified as missing or poorly represented. The search for printers and publishers of the press was intensified, and we employed paid researchers to help develop these areas, which were outside the research expertise of the Board. As various staged deadlines came and went, we took stock of what had arrived and what had not, and commissioned entries anew, mainly from paid researchers. Editing and indexing have also involved an army of additional expert help, who additionally honed, corrected and augmented entries. We have ended up with three publishers, each of whom has played an important part in the shaping of the *Dictionary*. We are also grateful to two others whom we approached with our proposal, whose feedback and enthusiasm for the project enabled us both to revise the proposal and pursue our plan of simultaneous print and electronic publication. Like print journalism, the *DNCJ* project is the product of many hands and sectors, mediated at every level, and the richer for it.

Other features of the *Dictionary* are designed to augment the alphabetical sequence of entries. To offer an historical perspective on the journalism of the period, we have provided a Chronology, which attempts to interweave the essence of what have often been presented as separate histories, of periodicals and newspapers or of genres. It is an ambitious and risky attempt, that will benefit from further input from scholars. The voluminious Bibliography drawn from the sources of entries represents research to date on the vast range of the nineteenth-century press. We also include some serious Indexes: a diagnostic index of the Headwords, grouped into lists of serial titles, journalists, illustrators, printers, publisher/proprietors and topics, and a detailed Index designed to reveal crossovers among entries, and subjects and names embedded in them, of interest in their own right. The Indexes themselves are an important tool of the *Dictionary*.

DNCJ has been an international project, and unthinkable without the internet and email. This was evident to the would-be editors as we scoped the project in autumn 2004 in the Flemish Academy in Brussels, when we benefited from the coincidence of the first appearance of the online, new *ODNB*, and the riches of the online *Waterloo Directory*, whose editor generously gave us access. It was from these two resources, with their flexible and diverse search engines, that we began building the list of entries. Without *Waterloo* and *ODNB* to augment the opportunity afforded by the Flemish Academy, and without the internet, a project like *DNCJ* would have been far more difficult, and the international input impossible. The electronic edition will also enable updating, augmenting and correction of entries through its online edition, suggestions for which should be sent to the editors.

Although *DNCJ* has been envisaged as a reference work, we hope that some readers of the print edition might be tempted to read it through out of sheer interest and fascination, as readers did the letters of the original *DNB* as it appeared quarterly over a fifteen-year period (1886-1900), more than 100 years ago.

Laurel Brake (l.brake@bbk.ac.uk) and Marysa Demoor (marysa.demoor@ugent.be)
London and Gent, November 2008

Chronology

The Nineteenth-century Press
in Britain and Ireland

Eighteenth-century newspapers that continued into the nineteenth century

1711   *Newcastle Courant*; initially thrice weekly, soon weekly; High Tory; in 1712 to avoid tax presented as a periodical; included fashion after 1750; by nineteenth century, anti Reform; inclusion of sports make it popular.

1718   *Leeds Mercury*; weekly; daily (1861ff); important regional Liberal paper.

1720   *Caledonian Mercury*; weekly; thrice weekly, daily (1859ff) Edinburgh; one of Scotland's oldest papers; politically focused; Whig; literary and cultural content as well.
        Ipswich Journal
        Northampton Mercury

1731   *Gentleman's Magazine*; a model for monthly magazines into the nineteenth century.

1737   *Belfast News-Letter*; weekly; twice weekly (early nineteenth century); daily (1855ff) Belfast's first newspaper; Conservative; Protestant.

1747   *Aberdeen's Journal*; *Aberdeen Journal* (1748ff); *Aberdeen Free Press* (1853ff); weekly until 1876; in 1830s, circulation above that of *Scotsman* and *Glasgow Herald*.
        Jackson's Oxford Journal; weekly; 2d; by early nineteenth century local as well as national politics.

1754   *Leeds Intelligencer*, weekly; from 1866 *Yorkshire Post*, daily; conservative/Tory paper that tried to unite the upper and working classes against the middle classes; anti-Catholic, pro child labour; main competitor *Leeds Mercury*.

1763   *Exeter Mercury, Trewman's Exeter Flying-Post, or Plymouth and Cornish Advertiser* (1770ff); weekly; Conservative and agricultural interests.
        Public Register or the Freeman's Journal; *Freeman's Journal* (1806ff); Dublin; founded by John Lucas, radical Protestant patriot; 5d daily in 1820; significant source for research into nineteenth-century Irish history.

1770	*Morning Chronicle*; daily; Whig organ; leading daily at the beginning of the nineteenth century; first to offer parliamentary reports, which Dickens among others wrote for the *Chronicle*. *Lady's Magazine*; the first journal written for and by 'ladies'.
1772	*Morning Post*; daily; founded by John Bell and others; conservative/Tory by early nineteenth century; published Southey, Wordsworth, Lamb and Coleridge who wrote leaders; throughout the century it continued to publish good writers including Disraeli; later William E. Henley, Andrew Lang and Alfred Austin wrote leaders.
1780	*Morning Herald*; daily; founded by Henry Bates, in opposition to the *Morning Post*, which Bates had formerly owned and edited; one of the first to publish parliamentary reports; penchant for scandal, gossip and attacks on politicians.
1782	*Bury Post*; *Bury and Norwich Post* (1786ff).
1783	*Glasgow Advertiser*, *Glasgow Herald* (1802ff); Tory until 1836; then Whig and national; leading Glasgow paper; technically innovative.
1785	*Daily Universal Register*; becomes *The Times* (1788ff).
1787	*Hull Packet*
1790	*Bristol Mercury*; before 1800, 13 papers started in Bristol, of which this is one
1791	*Observer*; weekly Sunday paper; oldest surviving of its kind.
1795	*Bell's Weekly Dispatch*, 1801ff *Weekly Dispatch*; Sunday paper aimed at working-class readers, initially featuring sport and sensational crime reporting.
1796	*Bell's Weekly Messenger: Country Gentleman and Landowners' Journal*; premier and long-lived rural paper, with focus on agricultural news as well as functioning as family paper.
1799	*Portsmouth Telegraph; or Mottley's Naval and Military Journal*; *Hampshire Telegraph and Sussex Chronicle* (1803ff); weekly; broadsheet; 6d (1800).

Nineteenth-century periodicals and newspapers

1802	*Edinburgh Review*; the first of the nineteenth-century quarterlies; Whig; published by A. Constable; Scottish. *Political Register*; weekly; Cobbett's Saturday paper, initially Tory, was radicalized during the paper's run; in 1816 it appeared in two editions, one excluding news to avoid the stamp; achieving high circulation, Cobbett's 'twopenny trash' prompted rapid development of radical successors.
1803	*Globe*; daily. long-lived evening paper; originally published to promote publishing trade; soon aimed at educated radicals but moved from apolitical to Whig to Tory over the century; known for caustic satire and unscrupulous reporting; quarto printed on pink paper.
1804	*Cambria*; weekly; Swansea; first newspaper in Wales.
1806	First illustration published in *The Times*.

Monthly Repository; serious, weighty monthly journal of radical nonconformist politics and theological controversy; organ of Unitarian movement; initially edited by Robert Aspland, it became more literary under W. J. Fox from 1827.

La Belle Assemblee; an early fashion magazine.

1808   *Examiner*; weekly; edited by Leigh Hunt.

North Wales Gazette, North Wales Chronicle (1827ff); weekly; Bangor; first newspaper in North Wales.

1809   *Quarterly Review*; a Tory quarterly published by John Murray, London.

1811   *Liverpool Mercury*; weekly, daily (1858ff); Liberal; reformist.

1814   *New Monthly Magazine and Universal Register*; conservative monthly published by Henry Colburn and conducted as a house magazine; initially advertised as a political reaction to Richard Phillips's liberal and influential *Monthly Magazine* (1796ff) Steam powered printing on Koenig presses initiated in Britain for *The Times*.

Seren Gomer; Swansea; first Welsh-language newspaper; weekly.

1815   Newspaper Stamp Duty increased to 4d per sheet.

1817   *Blackwood's Magazine*; Tory monthly in a magazine format; publisher William Blackwood; Scottish.

Scotsman; Edinburgh; initially weekly, bi-weekly from 1823; 1d daily from 1855, titled *Daily Scotsman* for next 10 years; initially quarto; impartial news coverage while politically liberal; in 1872 organises first newspaper trains to distribute paper more widely.

Literary Gazette: London weekly, focused on literature.

1819   Peterloo Massacre outside Manchester, reported by Joseph Wroe in his *Manchester Observer*; resultant Six Acts included Newspaper Act which redefined the remit of the already high newspaper taxes (per sheet, on advertising and on paper), and levied a bond on newspaper publishers to run presses; it made any periodical which published within a monthly period eligible for Stamp Duty.

1820   *London Magazine*; an English monthly magazine focused on honest reviewing; its attack against *Blackwood's* scurrilous and personal reviews resulted in its editor's death in a dual 13 months into its run.

John Bull; successful example of scandalous (Tory) weekly, including scurrilous gossip, subject to charges of libel, and its editor's imprisonment; owned by Theodore Hook.

1821   (Feb.)*New Observer*; weekly Sunday paper; *Sunday Times* (1822ff).

(May) *Manchester Guardian*; initially weekly; bi-weekly (1836ff); daily (1855ff). Reform paper published in wake of Peterloo and Six Acts, with their extension of newspaper taxes and bond.

Beacon; Edinburgh; short- lived Tory alternative to the *Scotsman* involved in fatal newspaper war (1821-1822).

1822   *Mirror of Literature*; John Limbird's cheap 2d weekly, mostly of cut and paste journalism, with some engravings; monthly (1846ff) with more original copy; early popular, cheap, long-lived paper.

Bell's Life in London, and Sporting Chronicle; weekly; first title to identify as sporting journal.

1823   *Mechanic's Magazine*; illustrated popular science weekly, with elaborate engravings, maps, diagrams and portraits; antedating *Penny Magazine* illustrations and orientation to science and the useful arts.

Lancet; weekly; a journal campaigning for medical reform, edited by Thomas Wakley; frequently sued in its first decade; with the *British Medical Journal,* one of a number of specialist journals springing up among the ubiquitous general press.

Westminster Review; third of the early nineteenth-century quarterlies; monthly (April 1887ff); Utilitarian/Philosophical Radical; established by Jeremy Bentham and James Mill.

World of Fashion; monthly; an example of a long-lived fashion magazine, famed for its original plates and copy.

1827   *Standard*; daily; initially evening; morning paper (1857ff); Old Tory; edited initially by Stanley Giffard, aided by the high-spirited William Maginn and Alaric Watts; anti-Reform, anti-Catholic emancipation and anti-repeal of the Corn Laws; by mid 1880s, a popular conservative paper.

1828   *Athenaeum*; London-based, long-lived weekly of cultural news, reviews and gossip (art, science, music, literature, drama) but no political content; unstamped. Model for general weeklies throughout century.

Spectator; London-based, long-lived weekly; established by Robert Rintoul; political front and arts back.

Forget-me-Not; first of Victorian literary annuals, including poetry, prose and images. Lavishly bound and printed; expensive; issued at Christmas/New Year; Followed quickly by titles such as *Friendship's Offering* (1824), *Amulet* (1826), *Bijou* and the *Keepsake* (both 1828).

1830   *Fraser's Magazine*; Tory monthly; southern rival/imitation of *Blackwood's* founded by ex-*Blackwood's* staff.

1831-1836   War of the Unstamped Press; multiple prosecutions under the Newspaper Act of 1819.

1831   *Poor Man's Guardian*; Hetherington's radical unstamped London 1d weekly; best known and most important of the illegal unstamped press.

Figaro in London; influential comic weekly with many imitators (*Figaro* in Birmingham, in Sheffield and in Liverpool); London version edited by Gilbert Abbot à Beckett, whose sons continued to work in the same tradition on *Punch* (1841ff) and on *Tomahawk* (1867ff), which they founded.

1832   (Feb.) *Chambers's Edinburgh Journal*; popular weekly at 1½d; published by William Chambers, Edinburgh; unstamped weekly, unillustrated; includes fiction.

(May) *Penny Magazine*; illustrated; edited for SDUK by Charles Knight; many successive alternatives/imitators, including the religious *Saturday Magazine,* from the SPCK.

Tait's Edinburgh Magazine; monthly; liberal Scotland-based alternative to *Blackwood's*.

1833   *Dublin University Magazine*; monthly; initially anti-Catholic; conservative, Tory Protestant, stemming from Trinity College, Dublin, in wake and imitation of Tory *Blackwood's* and *Fraser's*; an early attempt to create an Irish literary magazine, which in its long life retained this key element by publication of a succession of Irish authors, two of whom (Lever and LeFanu) served as editors.
Advertisement duty halved from 3s 6d to 1s 9d

1834   *Weekly Police Gazette*; Cleave's short-lived, illustrated, unstamped paper was racy and cheap at 1d.

1836   *Dublin Review*; Catholic theological quarterly; London-based; fostering Catholic revival; edited by succession of Catholic clergy, initially Nicholas Wiseman; not Irish despite title; Catholic alternative to *Edinburgh Review*.
Newspaper Stamp Duty reduced from 4d to 1d per sheet; paper duty halved.
Provincial Newspaper Society founded by J. Buller.

1837   *Northern Star*; weekly; Chartist broadsheet owned by Feargus O'Connor.; initially Leeds, then London; multiple editions for regions/cities in Britain and Ireland; the *Northern Star* was the most durable and famous of a huge crop of Chartist journals, including Harney's *Red Republican*, which in 1850 published the first English translation of the *Communist Manifesto*.
Publishers' Circular; fortnightly trade paper published for group of publishers by Sampson Low to advertise new books to retail trade and bulk buyers; published annual supplement from 1842, the *English Catalogue*, listing new books with dates of publication; its Education and Christmas Advertising Supplements are informative to book and media historians.
Bentley's Miscellany; a long-lived 6d illustrated monthly launched by Richard Bentley as a light-hearted alternative to the *New Monthly Magazine*; initially edited by Dickens and then Ainsworth, and illustrated by Cruikshank and Leech, it was notable for its employment of remarkable writers and artists, its publication of and reviewing of American writers in the 1840s and 1850s, and an increasingly interpretive and critical stance in its reviews; merged with *Temple Bar* in 1868.

1838   *Era*; longstanding Sunday broadsheet originating in the Licensed Victuallers, distinguished by its coverage of sport, theatre and music hall as well as news.

1839   *Art-Union: a Monthly Journal of the Fine Art*; an early specialist journal dedicated to fine art; *Art Journal* (1849ff); founded and edited by S. Carter Hall.

1840   *Provincial, Medical and Surgical Journal*; weekly/ fortnightly; general medical journal; from 1842, organ of the Provincial, Medical and Surgical Association which in 1856 became the British Medical Association; *British Medical Journal* (1857ff) which under editorship of Ernest Hart (1868ff) rivalled the *Lancet*.
Tablet; London-based Catholic weekly newspaper.

1841   *Punch*: London; illustrated weekly satirical paper that stimulated a trail of imitators throughout the century; radical in the 1840s.
Jewish Chronicle; London fortnightly (then weekly); although not the earliest Jewish paper, it was founded after the reduction of the newspaper taxes 1833-1836, and eventually proved the most robust and long lived among many Jewish interest titles.

1842   *Illustrated London News*; popular weekly founded by Herbert Ingram aimed at the middle classes, beginning at 3d but soon rising to 6d; groundbreaking model of the regular combination of news and pictures, initially woodcuts and later photographs; important role in awarding Paxton contract for Crystal Palace, and powerful supporter and exploiter for copy of Great Exhibition and other events of the capital.

       Lloyd's Weekly Newspaper; a popular Sunday newspaper, which by 1896 announced sales of a million.

       Builder; initially an illustrated penny weekly, this early specialist magazine became the most famous architectural journal of the century, read by general readers as well as architectural professionals.

       Family Herald; first of the quartet of penny fiction weeklies (with *London Journal*, *Reynolds's Miscellany*, *Cassell's Illustrated Family Paper*) that sold hundreds of thousands at mid-century; relatively genteel, unillustrated.

1843   *Pictorial Times*; weekly founded by Vizetelly after row with Ingram as a rival to *Illustrated London News*; folded 1848, but Vizetelly tried again with *Illustrated Times* in 1855.

       Illuminated Magazine; monthly; although short-lived, its high visual quality (including coloured woodcuts) and outstanding artists and engravers laid ground for *Once a Week* and *Good Words*; founded by Ingram to keep Douglas Jerrold (its first editor) and Mark Lemon away from contributing to the new *Pictorial Times*.

       News of the World; weekly Sunday paper; low price of 3d which met appetite of working-class readers for news and information through crime, sensation, and scandal-dominated contents; achieved highest circulation of any British weekly in 1855.

1844   (Aug.) First use of telegraph to report news (the birth of Prince Alfred to Queen Victoria in *The Times*).

1845   *Douglas Jerrold's Shilling Magazine*; liberal reformist political and arts monthly, undercutting the price and conservative politics of *Blackwood's* (2s 6d) and the *New Monthly* (3s 6d) with fiction, poetry and articles on social reform.

       London Journal; racy 1d illustrated fiction weekly; started by George Stiff; combined *Family Herald* and *ILN* to become in the 1850s one of the best-selling titles (500,000 a week); first editor G.W.M. Reynolds.

1846   *Daily News*; edited for a short time by Dickens.

       Mitchell's *Newspaper Press Directory* first appeared, to guide advertisers about the nature of titles into which they might place adverts.

       Guardian; weekly and long-surviving Anglican High Church newspaper formed after closure of Tractarian *British Critic* in 1843. Wide range of contents approached from conservative, High Church perspectives.

       Reynolds's Magazine; from fifth issue, *Reynolds's Miscellany*; illustrated penny fiction weekly founded by G.W.M. Reynolds when he left the *London Journal*.

1847   *Lady's Newspaper*; weekly illustrated 6d broadsheet, later merging with *Queen*.

1848   *Rambler*; weekly, then monthly (Sept. 1848 ff), then bi-monthly (May 1859ff); magazine founded by lay converts to Catholicism, following Oxford movement.

Wide-ranging content, with sharp critical commentary from this perspective divergent from Church approval; editors included Newman (in 1859).

First railway bookstall of W. H. Smith's at Euston station, London.

1850   *Reynolds's Weekly Newspaper*; populist Sunday newspaper from G. W. M. Reynolds, serial novelist/journalist.

Leader; reformist weekly initially edited by G. H. Lewes.

Household Words; first of Charles Dickens's two mid-century cheap, unillustrated weeklies; included social reform and serialised fiction; published by Bradbury and Evans.

Working Man's Friend and Family Instructor; an improving illustrated 1d weekly, designed by John Cassell to wean educated working class readers away from *Reynolds's*; one of several such titles from temperance publishers.

Germ; short-lived collaborative little magazine with letterpress and illustrations of the pre-Raphaelite Brotherhood; model for later aesthetic press of 1890s.

1851   Paul Julius Reuter begins to send financial information by telegraph between London and the Continent; by 1865, Reuter opens Reuter's Telegram Company in London to gather and exchange news.

1852   *Englishwoman's Domestic Magazine*; Samuel and Isabelle Beeton's general illustrated monthly, featuring domestic skills for middle-class women readers.

1853   Repeal of Advertisement duty.

(31 Dec.) *Cassell's Illustrated Family Paper*; broadsheet penny fiction weekly, lavishly illustrated; rival to *Reynolds's Miscellany* and *London Journal* with sales in hundreds of thousands; edited initially by John Tillotson.

1855   (1 July) Repeal of Newspaper Stamp Duty.

Clerkenwell News; weekly; local ½d paper; daily in 1872; title change to *Daily Chronicle* (1872), when Edward Lloyd purchased it and transformed it into a national paper; Henry Massingham's column on the 'Labour Movement' in the 1890s; Henry Nevinson war correspondent (1897-1900).

National Review; quarterly; successor to *Prospective Review*, sharing its Unitarian impetus; edited by friends Walter Bagehot and R. H. Hutton; Bagehot's famous dismissal of the early quarterlies ('The first *Edinburgh* Reviewers') in favour of the present new model appeared in the second issue, announcing the advent of a revitalised genre of quarterlies; Matthew Arnold's 'The Function of Criticism' appeared in its last number, envisaging still further generic developments.

Daily Telegraph; first London morning 1d newspaper.

Saturday Review; robust weekly, including (Tory) politics as well as reviews of art, books, and theatre; update of older generation weeklies *Athenaeum* and *Spectator*, both from 1828; called 'Saturday Reviler' for its polemical style.

Illustrated Times; weekly; edited by Henry Vizetelly to rival the *Illustrated London News*; high circulation and success prompted Ingram to purchase this rival in 1859.

1856   High-speed Hoe press first deployed by *Lloyd's Newspaper*.

1857   *Birmingham Daily Post*; daily1d; weekly sister titles published – *Birmingham Journal* and *Saturday Evening Post* -- to provide wide coverage and large circulation; fostered local civic pride; Liberal.

1858   *Bookseller*; monthly through 1908; then weekly. Whittaker's trade paper for the book trade.
        English Woman's Journal; monthly; first of string of publications from the Langham Place women's group with emphasis on employment, education and work for women; soon published by Emily Faithfull's Victoria Press, which trained and employed women in compositing and other print production skills.

1859   *All the Year Round*; Dickens's revised continuation of *Household Words* removed from its publisher Bradbury & Evans, and now owned by Dickens; weekly; more emphasis on serial fiction, but also information and social reform; not illustrated.
        Once a Week; founded by Bradbury & Evans, former publisher of *Household Words* to compete with *All the Year Round*; fiction, general articles and illustration; editor (Samuel Lucas) former literary editor of *The Times*, to rival authority of Dickens.
        Macmillan's Magazine; house journal from Macmillan; first of new crop of shilling monthlies; literary and political contents; initially Christian socialist.
        Irish Times; daily; Dublin; unionist national conservative 1d alternative to *Freeman's Journal*.
        Baner ac Amserau Cymru; weekly; Denbigh; founded by Thomas Gee; non-conformist Liberal; first Welsh-language paper to effectively cover and reach the whole of Wales.

1860   *Cornhill*; a second shilling monthly/house journal from Smith, Elder; initially edited by Thackeray, then by Leslie Stephen; aimed at family readership, with emphasis on fiction; no politics or religion; lavish get-up and illustrations; much imitated, e.g. by G. A. Sala's similarly London-named *Temple Bar* in same year, and by the *Month* (1864), a Catholic version, also London-based .
        Good Words; Strahan's cheap weekly; religious and illustrated, suitable for Sunday (and daily religious) reading, eventually including fiction, and soon (1861) becoming a monthly.

1861   Repeal of Newsprint Paper duty.
        Queen; long-lived upmarket ladies' weekly broadsheet; founded by Isabella and Samuel Beeton; incorporated *Lady's Newspaper* (1847ff).
        Cambrian Daily Leader; Swansea; first daily in Wales.

1863   *Reader*; weekly literary and scientific review that, reflecting its post-Darwin intellectual origins, briefly rivalled the *Athenaeum*.
        Central Press; Central News (1873ff); news agency; founded by William Saunders; a rival to the Press Association.

1864   *Month*; long lived illustrated monthly covering literature, science and art from a Jesuit perspective, complementing in its frequency the quarterly *Dublin Review* and the weekly *Tablet*.
        Illustrated Police News; weekly newspaper; 1d; first and longest- lived of titles that combined 'police'/crime news with illustration.

1865   *Pall Mall Gazette* (*PMG*); evening metropolitan daily; newspaper and review; originally Tory but from 1870 Liberal; key developer of New Journalism.

         Fortnightly Review; first of new generation of reviews; hybrid of magazine and review; fortnightly frequency soon gave way to monthly publication; initially Comtist, then Liberal; published by Chapman and Hall; political and literary; advocate of signature.

         Sporting Times, lobg-lived weekly which, despite its title ddi not only cover sport.

1866   *Contemporary Review*; one of new generation of reviews; liberal religious heavyweight magazine-review published by Strahan and soon edited by James Knowles.

         Belgravia; shilling monthly fiction paper for the middle classes, edited for 11 years by Mary Elizabeth Braddon; published sensation serial novels, including Braddon's, and much work by G. A. Sala.

1867   *Saint Paul's*; Trollope's attempt at a shilling monthly; included fiction and politics

         Tinsley's Magazine; another shilling monthly fiction paper and a house journal; edited initially by Edmund Yates; favoured sensation, crime, and detective serial novels, and ghost stories.

         Bolton Evening News; daily; first evening paper outside London at ½d; established by Tillotson.

1868   *Echo*; first ½d daily.

         Walter (Hoe) Web Rotary Printing Presses introduced at *The Times*.

         Press Association founded following passage of the Telegraph Bill which empowered the Government to acquire the telegraph system.

1869   *Academy*; monthly until 1871, then weekly; aimed at and written by academics; a specialist journal.

         Nature; weekly; general scientific weekly that became the most prestigious scientific journal in Britain; edited by Norman Lockyer, former scientific editor of the *Reader*; *Nature* resembled the *Reader* and the *Athenaeum* in format.

         Graphic; weekly; daily (1890ff); long-lived and most successful imitator/ rival of *Illustrated London News*, founded by ex-*ILN* staff, notably W. L. Thomas; at 6d, now more expensive than *ILN*, but higher technical quality.

         Western Mail; Cardiff; conservative 1d daily; regional news focus plus crime/sensation.

1870   *Northern Echo*; daily ½d; Darlington. edited by W. T. Stead in the 1870s.

1872   *South Wales Daily News*; Cardiff; liberal alternative to *Western Mail*; in 1892 David Duncan, its proprietor, unsuccessfully argued for admission of its Parliamentary correspondent to the Lobby on the basis that, with the exception of the *Western Mail*, it was 'the only daily paper for the whole of Wales', and thus a national rather than a provincial paper.

1873   Tillotson's Newspaper Literature Syndicate; originating in Tillotson's publication of fiction in the *Bolton Weekly Journal*; the most successful of the fiction bureaux that syndicated fiction in newspapers at home and abroad in the later nineteenth century.

1876 *Mind*; quarterly review of psychology and philosophy, with latter becoming its main element; one of a group of early specialist journals such as *Nature* (1869) and *English Historical Review* (1886).

1877 *Nineteenth Century*; secular heavyweight review; founded by James Knowles when he left the *Contemporary Review,* taking many of its writers and its format with him; exploited signature.

1878 *Magazine of Art*; monthly; up-market and sumptuous fine-art magazine, richly illustrated in Cassell's tradition to appeal to middle-class popular readership, as alternative to intellectually elite *Art Journal*.

1879 *Boy's Own Paper*; popular children's weekly from the Religious Tract Society; designed by RTS to displace cheap morally dangerous rivals.

1880 *Girl's Own Paper*; weekly; 1d; important model for subsequent development of titles for young girls.

   St James' Gazette; daily 1d evening paper; edited by Frederick Greenwood as Tory rival to *Pall Mall Gazette,* from which he has just been ousted as editor;. similar path and project to the *Westminster Gazette,* also set up by disgruntled staff from the *PMG* in 1893.

1881 *Evening News*; daily; London's first popular evening daily; ½d; news accompanied by intensive reporting of sports and murders; printed on coloured paper, first blue, then yellow and green; purchased by Harmsworth brothers in 1894, it was their first daily.

   Tit-Bits; George Newnes's popular penny paper of scissors and paste extracts from other journals; also included jokes, puzzles and material from readers; an example of New Journalism much imitated, as in Harmsworth's *Answers to Correspondents* (1888).

1884 *Financial and Mining News,* then after 6 months, *Financial News*; daily; London's first financial daily, which featured orientation to American markets; aimed in part at American tourists.

   National Association of Journalists founded (Institute of Journalists from 1890).

1888 *Scots Observer, National Observer* (1890 ff); initially a Scottish weekly quarto newspaper; conservative and imperialist; edited by W. E. Henley, who published eminent poets such as Kipling, Stevenson, Swinburne and Yeats, and criticism by J. M Barrie, Andrew Lang, Alice Meynell, George Moore, and Kenneth Grahame.

   Financial Times (published for first month as *London Financial Guide*); three times per week, then after a month, six days per week; competitor to *Financial News,* which it regularly attacked as inaccurate and personal; printed on (cheaper) pink paper from 1893.

   Star; daily; radical evening ½ d paper; edited initially by T. P. O'Connor; exemplified New Journalism; first daily to include regular political cartoons.

1889 *Dial*; first of five irregularly issued numbers of an aesthetic art journal; produced by Charles Ricketts and his partner Charles H. Shannon, the last two of which were published by the Vale Press; one of the earlier little magazines of the 1890s.

1890   *Review of Reviews*; W. T. Stead's monthly review of and excerpts from the previous month's press, and original material from Stead; a New Journalism digest aimed at 'busy readers'.

Strand Magazine; monthly; illustrated; Newnes's bestseller published short fiction, rather than serials, notably the linked series of Sherlock Holmes stories.

Woman, illustrated 1d weekly influenced by New Journalism; initially edited by Fitzroy Gardner, Arnold Bennett took over from 1896; motto in the 1890s 'Forward, but not too fast'.

Comic Cuts; Harmsworth ½d (1d 1890ff) illustrated weekly founded to counteract perceived threat of 'penny dreadfuls'; early comic strips; very successful and much imitated.

1891   *Bookman*; 6d, long-lived literary monthly edited by Robertson Nicoll, which used New Journalism formats (especially interviews; photojournalism; supplements, display advertising) to celebrate literature and authorship.

Daily Graphic; first daily illustrated paper; in 1891 published half-tone picture.

1893   *Westminster Gazette*; daily evening 1d paper printed on green paper; created by liberal staff (including Newnes) from the *Pall Mall Gazette,* which had been sold to a Tory in 1892.

Sketch; weekly; heavily illustrated weekly, edited by C. K. Shorter; titbits and anecdotes rather than in-depth articles; short stories rather than novels; by 1900, about 100 images per issue, mostly photographs, except for cartoons, fashion plates and fiction illustrations; a New Journalism exemplum.

Society of Women Journalists founded by Joseph Snell Wood, editor of the *Gentlewoman.*

1894   *Yellow Book*; quarterly; aesthetic hard-back issues from Elkin Mathews & John Lane initially; editors Henry Harland and Aubrey Beardsley; avant-garde; upmarket, retro in frequency and format; Beardsley ousted from Apr. 1895 due to Wilde scandal.

1895   *Home Chat*; weekly; penny domestic magazine for women.

Woman's Life; weekly; penny domestic magazine for women.

1896   *Savoy*; quarterly, then monthly; decadent magazine published by Leonard Smithers in the wake of the Wilde trials, with ex-*Yellow Book* staff for editors, Arthur Symons and Aubrey Beardsley.

Daily Mail; Harmsworth morning newspaper; maximising New Journalism features, its popular appeal to readers quickly led to sales of over a million in 1900.

Daily Express; title created by Pearson's purchase of the *Morning Herald* renamed *Daily Express and Morning Herald*; news on front page.

Sources: Altick 1957, Beetham and Boardman 2001, Bell 2007, BL Newspaper Library, Brown 1985, *Concise History of the British Newspaper in the Nineteenth Century, DNCJ,* Griffiths 1992, Jones 1993, Linton and Boston 1987, Sullivan, *Waterloo.*

Illustrations

Abbreviations

19CBLN	19C British Library Newspapers
19CUKP	19C UK periodicals
BDMBR	*British Dictionary of Modern British Radicals*
BL Catalogue	British Library
BL e-Collections	British Library Online Collections
Boase	*Modern English Biography*
BritPer	British Periodicals online
C19	Nineteenth Century Index online
CBEL	*Cambridge Bibliography of English Literature*
DLB	*Dictionary of Labour Biography*
DNB	*Dictionary of National Biography*
DNCBP	*Dictionary of Nineteenth-Century British Philosophers*
DSB	*Dictionary of Scientific Biography*
DWB	*Dictionary of Welsh Biography*
Grove	*Grove Dictionary of Music*
Mitchell's	*Mitchell's Newspaper Press Directory*
NA/NRA	National Archives/National Register of Archives
NCBEL	*New Cambridge Bibliography of English Literature*
NCBLN	Nineteenth Century British Library Newspapers
ncse	Nineteenth-Century Serials Edition
New Grove	*New Grove Dictionary of Music and Musicians*
NLS	National Library of Scotland
NSTC	Nineteenth-century Short Title Catalogue
NUJ	National Union of Journalists
ODNB	*Oxford Dictionary of National Biography*
OED	*Oxford English Dictionary*
PGIL *Eirdata*	Princess Grace Irish Library
Poole's	*Poole's Index to Periodical Literature*
RIA	Royal Irish Academy
Sullivan	*British Literary Magazines*
VPR	*Victorian Periodicals Review*

VPN	*Victorian Periodicals Newsletter*
Waterloo	*Waterloo Directory of English Newspapers and Periodicals*
Waterloo Irish	*Waterloo Directory of Irish Newspapers and Periodicals*
Waterloo Scottish	*Waterloo Directory of Scottish Newspapers and Periodicals*
Wellesley	*Wellesely Index to Victorian Periodicals*
WGBLP	*Warwick Guide to British Labour Periodicals*
WWBMP	*Who's Who of British Members of Parliament*
WWW	*Who Was Who*

Contributors and Acronyms

Acronym	Contributor	Affiliation
AA	April Austin	University of Missouri – Kansas City
AAT	Allison A. Twells	Sheffield Hallam University
AB	Adelene Buckland	Newnham College Cambridge University
ABH	Ann Birgit Heilmann	Hull University
AC	Anthony Cummins	Independent scholar
AE	Alana Eastman	University of Pittsburgh
AG	Agnés Gulyás	University of Canterbury
AGJ	Aled Jones	Aberystwyth University
AGT	Angela Thirlwell	Independent scholar
AH	Anne Humpherys	The Graduate Center, CUNY
AJ	Anne Jordan	Independent scholar
AJH	Andrew John Hobbs	University of Central Lancashire
AJM	Arthur Jack Meadows	University of Loughborough
AK	Andrew King	Canterbury Christ Church University
AL	Amy Lloyd	University of Cambridge
ALC	Anya L. Clayworth	St Andrews University
ALH	Anne Linden Helmreich	Case Western Reserve University
AM	Anne-Marie McAllister	University of Central Lancashire
AMB	Alistair Matthew Black	Leeds Metropolitan University
AMcN	Anthony McNicholas	University of Westminster
AMS	Anne Marietta Sebba	Independent scholar
AnE	Anouk Ewalts	Independent scholar
AnJ	Anna Johnston	University of Tasmania
APV	Ana Parejo Vadillo	University of Exeter
AS	Alice Smith	Independent scholar
AU	Arline Usden	Independent scholar
AW	Ashley Wassall	Canterbury Christ Church University
AWe	Alexis Weedon	University of Bedfordshire
BA	Brenda Ayres	Liberty University

BB	Bill Bell	University of Edinburgh
BF	Benjamin Fisher IV	University of Mississippi
BJ	Beth Jensen	Georgia Perimeter College
BM	Brian Maidment	University of Salford
BMO	Barbara Onslow	University of Reading (Emerita)
BP	Beth Palmer	University of Leeds
BZ	Bennett Zon	University of Durham
CAK	Christopher Andrew Kent	University of Saskatchewan
CAS	Catherine Ann Siemann	Columbia University
CB	Claire Brock	University of Leicester
CC	Chris Compton	University of Oxford
CCF	Catherine Clare Feely	University of Manchester
CH	Clare Horrocks	Liverpool John Moores University
ChB	Christopher Mark Banham	University of Leeds
ChK	Chandrika Kaul	University of St Andrews
CJM	Clinton John Machann	Texas A&M University
CK	Claire Kaczmareck	Torres Academy Abderdeen
CL	Cheryl Law	Independent scholar
CLM	Chris L. Manno	Texas Christian University
CMB	Christina Margaret Bashford	University of Illinois
CMF	Constance Marie Fulmer	Pepperdine University
CN	Claudia Nelson	Texas A&M University
CO	Carolyn Oulton	Canterbury Christ Church University
CR	Carolyn Reitz	John Jay College, CUNY
CRS	Caroline Ruth Sumpter	Queen's University, Belfast
CS	Casey Smith	Corcoran School of Art, Washington, D C
CTW	Christian (Tage) Wolmar	Independent scholar
CW	Claire Wintle	University of Sussex
DA	Damian Atkinson	St Edmund's College, Oxford
DD	David Doughan	Independent scholar
DEL	David Eaton Latané Jr.	Virginia Commenwealth University
DeM	Delphine MacFarlane	Independent scholar
DF	David Finkelstein	Queen Margaret University of Edinburgh
DH	Deian Hopkin	London South Bank University
DHL	David Haldane Lawrence	Independent scholar
DIM	David Ian Morphet	Independent scholar
DL	Dallas Liddle	Augsburg College
DM	Deborah Mutch	De Montfort University
DND	Dennis Denisoff	Ryerson University
DS	David Shaw	Independent scholar
DSM	David Magee	National Archives, London
DT	Dale Trela	University of Michigan
DU	Don Ulin	University of Pittsburgh
EB	Eugenio Biagini	University of Cambridge

EC	Ellen Casey	University of Scranton
ED	Ella Dzelzainis	Birkbeck, University of London
EFO	E. Foley O'Connor	Fordham University
EG	Emelyne Godfrey	Independent scholar
EJ	Ellen Jordan	University of Newcastle, Australia
EJJ	Elisabeth J Jay	Oxford Brookes University
EL	Emma Liggins	Manchester Metropolitan University
ET	Elizabeth Tilley	National University of Ireland, Galway
EW	Elyssa Warkentin	Bilkent University Ankara
FB	Francesca Benatti	National University of Ireland, Galway
FCA	Flora Armetta	Columbia University, New York
FD	Fionnuala Dillane	University College Dublin
FM	Frank Murray	University of Salford
FN	Frederick Nesta	Lignan University, Hong Kong
FSB	Florence Saunders Boos	University of Iowa
FSM	Fred Milton	University of Newcastle, UK
GB	Gavin Budge	Birmingham City University
GC	Geoffrey Cantor	University of Leeds
GD	Gowan Dawson	University of Leicester
GL	Graham Law	Waseda University, Japan
GRW	Glenn R. Wilkinson	St. Mary's University College, Calgary
GV	Greg Vargo	Columbia University, New York
GW	George Worth	University of Kansas (Emeritus)
HB	Helen Barlow	Open University
HR	Helen Rogers	Liverpool John Moores University
HVH	Heather V. Haskins	University of Reading
IA	Isobel Armstrong	Birkbeck, University of London (Emerita)
IC	Isabelle Clairhout	Ghent University
JA	Joan Allen	University of Newcastle, UK
JAS	John Stokes	King's College London (Emeritus)
JB	Jacqueline Broome	*Financial Times*
JC	Julie Codell	Arizona State University
JCA	Johanna Claire Anne Archbold	Trinity College Dublin
JCW	Joanne Claire Wilkes	University of Auckland
JDR	Jolein De Ridder	Ghent University
JEJ	Judith E. Johnston	University of Western Australia
JEM	James Mussell	University of Birmingham
JG	John Gardner	Anglia Ruskin University
JH	Jade Hunter	Canterbury Christ Church University
JHW	Joel Howard Wiener	CCNY and the Graduate School, CUNY (Emeritus)
JJ	Julia Jones	Independent scholar
JB	James Barnes	Wabash University (Emeritus)
JJP	Jennifer Jean Phegley	University of Missouri

JK	John Kofron	CCNY, CUNY
JKD	James Keith Diedrick	Agnes Scott College
JMD	John Drew	University of Buckingham
JMS	Johanna Mary Smith	University of Texas at Arlington
JN	Jean Neisius	Independent scholar
JNW	Jennifer N Wunder	Georgia Gwinnett College
JoC	Jonathan Coad	Royal Archaeological Institute
JoS	Josine Schuilenburg	Independent scholar
JP	John S. Partington	Independent scholar
JPP	Joe Patrick Phelan	De Montfort University
JRR	John Robert Reed	Wayne State University
JRT	Jonathan Richard Topham	University of Leeds
JRW	John Richard Wood	Independent scholar
JS	Joanne Shattock	University of Leicester
JSN	John North	University of Waterloo, Canada
JSP	John Stephen Plunkett	University of Exeter
JT	Janet Tanke	The Graduate Center, CUNY
J-YG	Jean-Yves Gilg	The *Solicitors' Journal*
KC	Kery Chez	The Graduate Center, CUNY
KCH	Kyriaki Christakis Hadjiafxeni	University of Exeter
KF	Karen Fang	University of Houston
KI	Keith Ives	Independent scholar
KJH	Katie-Jane Hext	University of Exeter
KL	Kathrin Lang	University of Nijmegen
KLM	Kristine Leslie Moruzi	University of Melbourne
KM	Kate Macdonald	Ghent University
KNC	Koenraad Claes	Ghent University
KNH	Kristin Nicole Huston	University of Missouri-Kansas City
KO'B	Kevin O'Brien	St. Francis Xavier University
LAR	Leah A. Richards	Fordham University, New York
LB	Leora Bersohn	Columbia University, New York
LeL	Leanne Langley	Goldsmith's College, University of London
LG	Lawrence Goldman	Oxford University
LH	Linda K. Hughes	Texas Christian University
LJ	Louis James	University of Kent (Emeritus)
LJK	Lorraine Janzen Kooistra	Ryerson University
LKH	Leslie Kathleen Howsam	University of Windsor
LL	Louise Lee	Roehampton University
LML	Lindsy Michelle Lawrence	Texas Christian University
LR	Lisa Rodensky	Wellesley College
LRB	Laurel Brake	Birkbeck, University of London (Emerita)
MA	Megan Alter	University of Iowa (visiting scholar)
MaK	Martin Keunen	Independent scholar
MaT	Matthew Taunton	Independent scholar

MB	Matthew Bradley	Linacre College, University of Oxford
MBT	Matthew Brinton Tildesley	Durham University
MD	Marysa Demoor	Ghent University
MDB	Megan D. Burke	Fordham University
MDS	Margaret Diane Stetz	University of Delaware
MdW	Marco de Waard	University of Amsterdam
ME	Marie Alexis Easley	University of St Thomas
MEC	Meaghan Emily Clarke	University of Sussex
MF	Maria Frawley	George Washington University
MH	Meirion Hughes	Independent scholar
MiS	Michael Shirley	Eastern Illinois University
MJH	Michael James Huggins	University of Chester
MJM	Matthew McIntyre	Cleveland State University
MJR	Meri-Jane Rochelson	Florida International University
MJW	Michael Jonas Wolff	University of Massachusetts (Emeritus)
MK	Mark Knight	Roehampton University
ML	Marie-Lou Legg	Birkbeck, University of London
MLB	Michelle Buchanan	University of Wolverhampton
MM	Maurice Milne	Independent scholar
MP	Michael Powell	Librarian of Chetham's Library, Manchester
MPT	Michael Philip Thompson	Royal Pharmaceutical Society
MR	Matt Rubery	University of Leeds
MRB	Margaret Rachel Beetham	Manchester Metropolitan University (Affiliate)
MRH	Morgan Rochester Holmes	University of Toronto
MRR	Michelle Renee Robinson	Texas Christian University
MS	Michael Slater	Birkbeck, University of London (Emeritus)
MSC	Malcolm S. Chase	University of Leeds
MT	Meagan Timney	Dalhousie University
MV	Minna Vuohelainen	Edge Hill University
MWT	Mark W. Turner	King's College London
NB	Nicholas Birns	New School, New York
ND	Neil Denny	*The Bookseller*
NG	Nathan Garvey	University of Sidney
NK	Norman Kelvin	CCNY and The Graduate School, CUNY
NM	Nickianne Moody	Liverpool John Moores University
NN	Nathalie Neill	York University
OA	Owen Ashton	Staffordshire University
OD	Odin Dekkers	Radbout University, Nijmegen
OM	Olivia Malfait	Ghent University
PAP	Paul Andrew Pickering	Australian National University
PB	Peter Blake	University of Sussex
PC	Philip Cohen	Independent scholar
PF	Pamela Fletcher	Bowdoin College
PG	Priscilla Glanville	University of South Florida

PJG	Peter James Gurney	University of Essex
PL	Patrick Leary	Independent scholar
PN	Peter Nockles	University of Manchester
PP	Peter Putnis	University of Canberra, Australia
PWB	Peter William Bartrip	University of Oxford
PZ	Patricia Zakreski	University of Exeter
RAA	Robin Alan Agnew	Independent scholar
RC	Richard A. Cosgrove	University of Arizona
RH	Roisin Higgins	Belfast University
RHC	Rosalind Helen Crone	Open University
RKL	Robert Keith Lapp	Mount Allison University
RL	Roger Luckhurst	Birkbeck, University of London
RLA	Rebecca Lucy Arnold	Royal College of Art
RM	Rohan McWilliam	Anglia Ruskin University
RN	Richard Noakes	University of Exeter
RR	Ruth Richardson	University of Hertfordshire
RS	Robert J. Scholnick	William and Mary College
RSB	Rachel Sagner Buurma	Swarthmore College
RTB	Robert Terrell Bledsoe	Texas El Paso University (emeritus)
RV	Rosemary VanArsdel	University of Puget Sound (emerita)
SA	Suzy Anger	University of British Columbia
SB	Scott Banville	Georgia Institute of Technology
SBA	Sari Beth Altschuler	New York University
SC	Stephen Colclough	University of Bangor
SD	Sarah Dewis	Birkbeck, University of London
SdB	Simon deBourcier	Anglia Ruskin University
SFR	Stephen Frederick Roberts	University of Birmingham
SGS	Sara Graga da Silva	Keele University
SH-D	Susan Hoecker-Drysdale	Concordia University (emerita)
SJP	Simon Potter	National University of Ireland, Galway
SM	Susan Matthews	Roehampton University
SMcn	Sarah Mcneely	Texas State University
SMM	Sally M. Mitchell	Temple University
SMR	Sean Michael Ryder	National University of Ireland, Galway
SP	Suzanne Paylor	Independent scholar
SR	Sheshalatha Reddy	University of Michigan
SRS	Shannon Rose Smith	Queen's University
ST	Steve Tate	University of Central Lancashire
SY	Sarah Yoder	Texas Christian University
SYM	Susan Yvonne McGann	Royal College of Nursing
SZ	Susan Zieger	University of California Riverside
TD	Terri Doughty	Vancouver Island University
TG	Tim Grass	Spurgeon's College
TH	Trevor Herbert	Open University

TJ	Timothy Johns	New York University
TL	Timothy Larsen	Wheaton College
TPO	Tom P. O'Malley	Aberystwyth University
TR	Tracy Rosenberg	University of Edinburgh
TT	Thomas Tobin	Independent scholar
TW	Terry Wyke	Manchester Metropolitan University
UW	Usha Wilbers	Radbout University, Nijmegen
VF	Valerie Fehlbaum	University of Geneva
VR	Vanessa Ryan	Harvard University
WA	William J. Astore	Pennsylvania College of Technology
WB	William Brock	University of Leicester (Emeritus)
WHF	W. Hamish Fraser	Strathclyde University
WS	William Scheurle	University of South Florida
WSB	William S. Brockman	Pennsylvania State University
ZV	Zsuzsanna Varga	De Montfort University

Notes on Associate Editors

Margaret Beetham is an Affiliate of the Department of English at Manchester Metropolitan University where she taught for many years. Her major research interests are in periodicals addressed to women, domestic advice manuals, women's popular reading, and the regional press in Manchester and the north-west. Publications include *A Magazine of her Own? Domestic and Desire in the Woman's Magazine 1800-1914* (Routledge 1996) and The *Victorian Women's Magazine* (with Kay Boardman, Manchester 2001).

Laurel Brake is Emeritus Professor of Literature and Print Culture, at Birkbeck, University of London. She directed the *Nineteenth-century Serials Edition* 2008 (www.ncse.ac.uk). Books include *Print in Transition, Studies in Media and Book History* (Palgrave 2001), and *Encounters in the Victorian Press. Editors, Authors, Readers.* (Palgrave 2005), co-edited with Julie Codell. Articles on Scottish periodicals – *Blackwood's* and *Chambers's* – appeared in 2006 and 2007, a third on W. T. Stead's Newspaper Fiction (2007), and a fourth on obituaries in *Life Writing and Victorian Culture,* ed. David Amigoni (Ashgate 2007). She is about to restart her biography of Walter Pater, *Ink Work.*

Gowan Dawson is Senior Lecturer in Victorian Literature at the University of Leicester. He is the author of *Darwin, Literature and Victorian Respectability* (CUP 2007), co-author of *Science in the Nineteenth-Century Periodical: Reading the Magazine of Nature* (CUP 2004), and is currently writing a cultural history of the myth that nineteenth-century palaeontologists needed just a single bone to reconstruct prehistoric creatures.

Odin Dekker is Professor of English Literature and Culture at the Radboud University, Nijmegen. His study of John Mackinnon Robertson appeared in 1998 (Ashgate), and he has since published mainly on Victorian criticism and print culture. Current research interests include the professionalization of authorship and the role of the literary agent. He is also the editor of the international journal *English Studies*.

Marysa Demoor is Professor of English Literature at the University of Ghent and a life member of Clare Hall, Cambridge. She is the author of *Their Fair Share. Women, Power and Criticism in the Athenaeum, from Millicent Garrett Fawcett to Katherine Mansfield, 1870-1920* (2000 Ashgate) and the editor of *Marketing the Author. Authorial Personae, Narrative Selves and Self-fashioning, 1880-1930* (2004 Palgrave). With Laurel Brake she has edited *The Lure of Illustration in the Nineteenth Century. Picture and Press* (Palgrave, forthcoming)

Ian Haywood is Professor of English at Roehampton University, London. His research is primarily concerned with radical and popular literary and visual culture in the eighteenth and nineteenth centuries. His books include *The Revolution in Popular Literature 1790-1860: Print, Politics and the People* (CUP 2004) and *Bloody Romanticism: Spectacular Violence and the Politics of Representation 1776-1832* (Palgrave 2006). He has also edited three volumes of Chartist fiction for Ashgate. One of his current projects is to produce a scholarly edition of the Chartist engraver and poet William James Linton´s illuminated poem *Bob Thin or the Poorhouse Fugitive*. He is a great fan of the radical Victorian journalist, editor and author George W. M. Reynolds.

Linda K. Hughes, Addie Levy Professor of Literature at Texas Christian University in Fort Worth, Texas, specializes in literature and publishing history. Her recent publications include *Graham R.: Rosamund Marriott Watson, Woman of Letters* (Ohio UP 2005), awarded the Robert Colby Scholarly Book Prize, and an edition of *Elizabeth Gaskell's Novellas and Shorter Fiction: 'Cousin Phillis' and other Tales from* All the Year Round *and the* Cornhill Magazine *1859-64* (Pickering & Chatto 2006). A book on Victorian poetry in the context of print culture is forthcoming.

Anne Humpherys is Professor of English at Lehman College and the Graduate Center, City University of New York. She has written on popular literature, the press, the Victorian novel and poetry. She is the author of *Travels into the Poor Man's Country: the Work of Henry Mayhew* (University of Georgia Press 1977) and has published on G. W. M. Reynolds, Dickens, Tennyson and the divorce novel in nineteenth-century Britain. Most recently, she has co-edited *G. W.M. Reynolds: Nineteenth-Century Fiction, Politics and the Press* with Louis James (Ashgate 2008). Her next project is a study of the impact of the marriage and divorce laws on the British novel.

Aled Jones is Sir John Williams Professor of Welsh History at Aberystwyth University. He has published widely on the history of nineteenth and early twentieth-century British newspaper journalism, and is the author of *Powers of the Press. Newspapers, power and the public in nineteenth-century England* (Ashgate 1996). He is currently writing a history of religious and cultural communication between Britain and colonial India, 1840-1947.

Andrew King Andrew King is currently a research fellow at the University of Ghent, Belgium, on leave from Canterbury Christ Church University, UK. Interested in the interplay of theory and hard data, he has written on both nineteenth-century print media, especially the mass market, and on cross-cultural study. His books include *Crossing Cultures* (Cavalliotti and British Council, 1998), *Victorian Print Media: a Reader* (OUP 2005, with John Plunkett) and *The London Journal 1845-1883* (Ashgate 2004). Articles on Ouida's Italian novels are in press and he is preparing an edition of her last novel, The Massarenes. He is also working on the relationships between the professions and the press in the nineteenth century.

Mark Knight is a Reader in English Literature at Roehampton University. His publications include *Chesterton and Evil* (2004), *Nineteenth-Century Religion and Literature: An Introduction* (co-authored with Emma Mason, 2006), *Biblical Religion and the Novel* (co-edited with Thomas Woodman, 2006) and *An Introduction to Religion and Literature* (forthcoming 2009). He has also written on nineteenth-century religion and literature for a number of journals. Currently, he is writing a monograph on Evangelicalism and the nineteenth-century novel, and, with Emma Mason, co-editing a new book series for Continuum entitled *New Directions in Religion and Literature*.

Cheryl Law lectured in women's studies at Birkbeck, University of London. She is the author of *Suffrage and Power: the Women's Movement, 1918-1928* (I. B. Tauris 1998) and *Women: A Modern Political Dictionary* (I. B. Tauris 2000*)*. She is currently researching women's contribution to the growth of London's public institutions from 1660 to the present day.

Brian Maidment is Research Professor in Print History at the University of Salford. He is completing *Comedy, Caricature and the Social Order 1820-1850* for Manchester University Press and editing the Victorian volume of the *Oxford History of Popular Print Culture*. His most recent book is *Dusty Bob - A Cultural History of Dustmen* (Manchester University Press 2007). Other books include *Reading Popular Prints 1790-1870* (Manchester UP 1996, 2001). His essay on G. M. W. Reynolds's 'Text and Illustration' appears in *G W M Reynolds*, edited by Anne Humpherys and Louis James (Ashgate 2008).

Joanne Shattock is Professor of Victorian Literature and Director of the Victorian Studies Centre, University of Leicester. She has published *Politics and Reviewers* (1989) and co-edited, with Michael Wolff, *The Victorian Periodical Press: Samplings and Soundings* (1982). She has recently edited *Elizabeth Gaskell's Journalism, Early Fiction and Personal Writings* (2005) and is currently working on an edition of the journalism of Margaret Oliphant.

Elizabeth Tilley is a Lecturer in English at the National University of Ireland, Galway, where she teaches nineteenth-century literature and book history. Her publications include articles on Irish nineteenth-century bookselling firms and periodicals. A chapter on Irish Victorian antiquarianism and the publications of the Royal Irish Academy is shortly to appear in the fourth volume of the *Oxford History of the Irish Book*. She is at present writing a monograph on selected Irish journals from 1830 to 1870.

Mark W. Turner is Reader in English at King's College London. He has published *Trollope and the Magazines* (2000) and several articles on aspects of nineteenth-century serialization, journalism and periodical culture. He is currently co-editing Oscar Wilde's journalism, is on the project team for the Nineteenth-Century Serials Edition, and is co-editor of the journal *Media History*.

John Wood (MA ,Cantab., MRes, Lond.) has an interest in English modernism and its origins, in particular its nineteenth- and early twentieth- century socialist background, He is currently working on a study of A. R. Orage and Katherine Mansfield. He is a contributor to the Modernist Journals Project (Brown and Tulsa Universities), specifically to its online edition of the New Age. He is a practising lawyer and a Member of the Board of the Charity Commission of England and Wales.

A

À BECKETT, ARTHUR WILLIAM (1844-1909) A humorist and journalist* who was involved at crucial moments with such publications as the *Tomahawk**, and *Punch**, À Beckett was not a hugely gifted writer, but he moved in influential circles and his congeniality facilitated a journalistic career that included some important jobs. His first foray into the profession was as co-editor – with his close friend Francis Burnand* – of *Glow-Worm* (1865-1868), a penny* evening humorous paper. In 1867 he founded a more influential weekly* journal of satire, the *Tomahawk,* which he also edited* and which became the template for Gibson Bowles's* hugely successful *Vanity Fair**. In 1874 he began to contribute to *Punch*, and got a job on the staff in the following year. He became deputy editor shortly after Burnand's appointment as editor in 1880, but in spite of his love for the publication his refusal to change its format or bring in new talent contributed to its decline into mediocrity. His 1903 book *The À Becketts of Punch* rather over-stressed the family connection with the periodical, falsely claiming that his father had been among the founders. He was asked to tender his resignation in 1902.

Alongside his career in comic journalism and satire, he also engaged in serious journalism, acting as a special correspondent to the *Globe** (1803-1922) and the *Standard** reporting on the Franco-Prussian war, and later becoming editor of the *Naval and Military Magazine* (1897-1899). He edited the *Sunday Times** from 1893 to 1895, a demanding job at any time, and one hardly compatible with À Beckett's hands-on role at *Punch*. His short tenure was not a distinguished one. **MaT**
Sources: À Beckett 1903, *ODNB*, Spielmann 1895, *Waterloo*.

ABERDEEN JOURNAL (1748-1922) Founded by the printer James Chalmers* in 1748, the *Aberdeen Journal* is one of the oldest newspapers in the UK. It passed to Chalmers's son, James, and, on his death in 1810, to his third son, David Chalmers. From 1797 (to 1903), it acquired a more general and regional title, the *Aberdeen Journal, and General Advertiser for the North of Scotland*. In 1800 it was a four-page weekly* broadsheet, appearing on Wednesdays. Its six columns* in 1800 (24 in total) were increased in 1841 to 28, with a further increase in size in 1847, due to retooling with 'new and beautiful steam machinery'. In 1800 it cost 6d, and carried foreign*, national, London, Scottish, and local news*, including prices, law, and shipping reports. By 1830 its price* rose to 7d, and in 1860 after the withdrawal of Stamp Duty*, it was reduced to 3 ½d unstamped and 4 ½d stamped. With many advertisements*, even in 1800, it was able to maintain a healthy circulation*, ca. 2,300 in 1832, 2,800 in the 1840s, 3,500 in 1855 and 4,000 in 1870.

By 1830 its four pages were more structured into departments than in 1800, and advertisements* now appeared on page 1. Departments included Foreign Intelligence, Ship News, Domestic Intelligence, Edinburgh News, Births etc, Police Court, Aberdeen Shipping, Correspondence*, Miscellaneous Articles, Postscript and Markets. Facing a challenge from the Liberal *Aberdeen Herald*, it gradually responded with a more attractive layout under the editorship* of John Ramsay in the 1840s. Its principal rival, the *Aberdeen Free Press,* appeared in 1853 aimed at advanced Liberals*, while the *Journal*, edited by William Forsyth from 1848, searched for a middle ground but remained old-fashioned in appearance and tone. In 1876, the Chalmers family were bought out by the Aberdeen and North of Scotland Newspaper and Printing Co. and it became a daily*. Shareholders were mainly Conservative landowners trying to counter the anti-landowner stance of the *Aberdeen Free Press*.

From 1879 the *Journal* was depending on the profits of the *Evening Express* launched for financial survival, and under Forsyth's successor, Archibald Gillies, closure threatened, but a legacy from John G. Chalmers saved the day. With the editorship of David Leith Pressly from 1894, it became aggressively Conservative and an active participant in local politics*. In 1897, in a booklet commemorating its 150th year, it boasted that it was 'the only Conservative morning daily in Scotland'. Now it was the *Free Press* that was struggling and which had to seek a merger in 1922 as the *Aberdeen Press and Journal*. **WHF**
Sources: *Aberdeen Journal* 1882 and 1898, 'The *Aberdeen Journal*' 1897, 'Aberdeen Journal' Headnote 2008, Cormack 1958, Cowan 1946, Harper 1998, *Waterloo Scotland*.

ACADEMY (1869-1916) The *Academy: A Monthly Record of Literature, Learning, Science and Art* was founded by Charles Appleton* in 1869 as a more scholarly, and signed*, version of the *Athenaeum**. Intended as a British counterpart to Germany's *Litterarisches Centralblatt*, it was associated with the Endowment of Research movement that aimed at challenging the amateur spirit prevalent in English universities and promoting the ideal of scholarly professionalism*. Appleton's friend Mark Pattison was prominent both in the movement and as a contributor to the journal, which also featured such distinguished scholars as Henry Sidgwick, T. H. Green and Edward Caird. Appleton took over as proprietor* from John Murray* in 1870, making the journal a fortnightly and then a weekly* by 1874, and reducing its price* from 6d to 4d. He also softened its image of severe erudition, changing *Record* in the sub-title to *Review*.

The journal's distinctive intellectual cosmopolitanism also diminished after Appleton sold it in 1878, though it retained its strong university character. It attracted new talents such as George Saintsbury*, Edmund Gosse*, Andrew Lang*, Grant Allen*, Edith Simcox* and Emilia Strong Pattison (later Dilke*). In 1896 it was jolted out of its somewhat stuffy respectability when the American businessman John Morgan Richards bought it as an editorial vehicle for Charles Lewis Hind, the protégé of his daughter, the novelist 'John Oliver Hobbes' (Mrs Pearl Craigie). Under Hind (1896-1903), it became Britain's liveliest literary journal, providing best-seller lists, readers' contests and short, snappy reviews. In 1902 it absorbed *Literature** but declined amid legal and financial vicissitudes despite a brief, scandalous efflorescence under Lord Alfred Douglas's ownership, and disappeared in 1916. **CAK**

Sources: Brake 1994, Kent 1984, Roll-Hansen 1957.

ACCOUNTANT (1874-1986) The *Accountant* was an important organ of finance in nineteenth-century Britain. Its founder and business editor* was Alfred Gee, whose firm is advertised as an 'Advertising Agent'* in the first number. Gee remains the only named figure associated with the journal to 1895, and the editor remains anonymous* in the publication itself. First issued as a monthly* in October 1874, at the price* of 1s, the *Accountant* quickly flourished and appeared weekly* after three issues from January 1875, now costing 6d, a price which was retained throughout the 1890s. Occasional supplements* raised the price of numbers to 9d or 1s. Preponderantly 16 pages per weekly number, pagination was reduced to eight by 1899. But the amount of advertising* flourished, and although No 1 had two pages of small advertisements on pp. one and 16, No 2 immediately had five pages of adverts, and by 1887, there was an advertising wrapper of eight pages. Being a professional jour-

nal, the *Accountant* was expensive. Its price tended to fluctuate; for example, it cost 1s per monthly number (Oct.-Dec. 1874), and then 6d per week, making a total of 2s a month or 24s a year, a price that seemed to remain constant to pre-payers until 1895. Contents included leaders*, articles (monthly and weekly review* columns*), reports and correspondence 'on all interesting topics' (Mitchell 1900: 68).

Becoming a weekly entailed its registration as a newspaper, which then meant that legally it qualified to publish Statutory Notices for the announcement of bankruptcy, for example. From October to December 1874 it was printed and published* by George Berridge, and from 1875, when a New Series began, by Williams and Strahan. By 1885 the printer* and publisher was Gee and Company, which in 1887 boasted that they were printers and publishers of the *Accountant*, the *Accountant's Journal* and the *Accountant's Diary and Directory*.

From the first issue Alfred Gee resolutely pressed for an Accountants' Charter. He urged the rival accountancy organizations, the Institute of Chartered Accountants (founded in 1870) and the Society of Accountants in England, to lay aside their differences and obtain parliamentary sanction for an association, the membership of which would be a guarantee of reputation. Since many unqualified and disreputable people were claiming to be fully qualified accountants, Gee recommended that members of the Institute of Chartered Accountants should have their qualification initials after their names. However, he became critical of the Council of the Institute, which he suggested was taking a narrow and exclusive view of the profession.

Although the Society of Accountants regularly took full page adverts in the *Accountant* from 1874, the Institute would not advertise because it claimed that its members were the elite of the profession and that it was derogatory and unnecessary to appeal for recruits. In February 1875 Gee begged the Institute to reconsider its policy, and the Council of the Institute consented to advertise spasmodically. Finally, in July 1880 the Council recognized the services of the *Accountant* to the profession, and gave the journal £200 in appreciation. Ten years later, in 1890, it urged its members to become subscribers and submit letters and reports. It also arranged for the paper to extend its coverage of law reports. **DHL**

Sources: Back 1925, Howitt 1984, Layton 1912, *Mitchell's, Waterloo*.

ACTON, JOHN EMERICH EDWARD DALBERG (1834-1902) Proprietor*, editor and contributor to the periodical press, the initial involvement of John Acton with the periodical press resulted from his desire to promulgate a robust continental Catholic discourse in England. In 1858 he became the leading shareholder in a monthly journal, the *Rambler**, initiated by John Moore Capes*, intended for Catholic converts. The *Rambler* espoused a liberal posture encouraging greater freedom of thought, resulting in two of its editors leaving under Cardinal Wiseman's attacks. In 1859 Acton became editor*, entrenching the journal's position. Continued ecclesiastical pressure forced Acton into reinventing the *Rambler* in 1862 as the quarterly*, *Home and Foreign Review**, which informed by Acton's exemplary scholarship gained credence for its interplay of independent intellectual excellence and vision. Acton's pursuit of self-determination for Catholic scholars brought direct condemnation from Rome and to escape compromising his principles, Acton closed the *Review* in 1864.

He then became the Rome correspondent of a new liberal Catholic paper, the *Chronicle*, during its brief existence in 1867 before contributing to the *North British Review**, now a liberal Catholic vehicle but originally founded by adherents of the Free Church of Scotland. Acton went on to write articles and book reviews for the *Quarterly Review** and the *Nineteenth Century** before becoming one of the originators of the *English Historical Review* in 1886, where his learned articles appeared. Appointed Regius Professor of Modern History at Cambridge in 1895 he took on the editorship of the Cambridge Modern History series. CL
Source: *ODNB*.

ACTORS BY DAYLIGHT; OR, PENCILLINGS IN THE PIT (1838-1839) *Actors by Daylight* was an early attempt, among the plethora of unstamped* penny* papers published in London in the 1830s, to create a 'free, impartial and independent' account of London actors, plays and performances. Volume I advertised itself as 'containing correct memoirs of upward of forty of the most celebrated London performances; original tales, poetry* and criticisms; the whole forming a faithful account of the London stage for the last twelve months'. Each week featured a memoir and portrait of an actor or actress, and the series formed two volumes each issued with title page, a coloured woodcut* and index.

Although the contents were anonymous*, their quality indicate someone with close theatrical connections, and an imitation suggests that the journal attracted favourable notice – the lighter-hearted *Actors by Gaslight; or 'Boz' in the Pit* ran for 37 numbers, April-December 1838, when it merged with the *Odd Fellow*. According to a note by its editor, *Actors by Daylight* came to an end due to the illness of the editor. LJ
Sources: Lowe 1970, *Wellesley*.

ADAMS, WILLIAM EDWIN (1832-1906) William Edwin Adams was an important radical journalist* in the north-east of England. Trained as a printer, in the 1850s he worked on W. J. Linton's* *English Republic** and Henry Vizetelly's* newly launched *Illustrated Times**. In the early 1860s he wrote articles under the pseudonym* 'Caractacus' for Charles Bradlaugh's* freethinking* journal, the *National Reformer**. Bradlaugh recommended Adams to fellow radical Joseph Cowen Jnr*, who had just acquired the *Newcastle Chronicle and Northern Counties Advertiser*. Adams contributed over 500 articles for this paper under the pseudonym of 'Ironside'.

In 1864 Adams became editor* of Cowen's newly launched *Newcastle Weekly Chronicle**, a position that he held with distinction until his retirement in 1900. Given virtually a free editorial hand by Cowen, Adams transformed the *Weekly* into one of the most important provincial* radical newspapers of the late Victorian period. The paper's advanced radicalism, support for trade union rights, women's rights*, co-operatives and internationalism, underlined by the content of the 'Ironside' column*, earned it a reputation as the 'pit-men's bible'. Adams also appealed to a 'family'* readership* by including a Children's Corner run by himself as 'Uncle Toby'. In 1885, to accompany the *Weekly*, a *Literary Supplement** was launched; two years later this was joined by an antiquarian magazine, the *Monthly Chronicle of North Country Lore and Legend*. In all three papers Adams campaigned for a range of local issues including the establishment of free libraries, tree planting schemes, bowling greens and parks for the people. An inspiration to his staff, Adams was widely admired for his editorial integrity and dedication. On his death one contemporary described him as 'an honour to the Fourth Estate'. OA
Sources: Ashton 1991, Ashton 1992, Joseph Cowen papers, Saville 1968, Todd 1991, W. E. Adams papers.

ADAMS, WILLIAM HENRY DAVENPORT (1828-1891) Adams began his career as a family tutor on the Isle of Wight. Soon he was editing* a local* newspaper, as well as writing for several London dailies*. He reviewed* books for the *Literary Gazette**, wrote articles for *London Society** and published copious amounts of poetry* in the *London Journal*, for which he also served as editorial assistant to Mark Lemon* during the late 1850s. At the beginning of the next decade, Adams edited the short-lived monthly *Everybody's Journal* and from 1864 he read manuscripts and wrote for the Glasgow publishers* Blackie and Son, as well as until 1870 for Nelson and Sons in Edinburgh. In June 1870 he founded the Episcopalian newspaper the *Scottish Guardian*, which he edited until 1878. Subsequently he launched and edited a series named 'The Whitefriars Library of Wit and Humour'. Before his death he was projecting another series entitled 'The Victoria Library for Gentlewomen'.

During his prolific literary and journalistic career, Adams not only edited periodicals and newspapers, he also wrote stories for boys, edited popular science books, published an annotated edition of Shakespeare and was well known for a number of historic and biographical works. His eldest son, William Davenport Adams, maintained the family involvement in journalism, serving as editor of several provincial* newspapers during the 1880s and then as literary editor and drama critic of the *Globe*. **DHL**

Sources: Boase, *Daily Graphic* 2 Jan. 1892, King 2004, *London Figaro* 6 Jan. 1892, *ODNB*, *The Times* 31 Dec. 1891.

ADULT (1897-1899) The official publication of the Legitimation League, which originally wanted to provide a way for children born in free unions to inherit if parents died intestate, the *Adult* soon became the *Journal of Sex*, in which articles argued for (and occasionally against) free unions, the right of women to seek sexual pleasure and a variety of other topics related to the 'sex question' and the 'marriage debates'. Edited* by George Bedborough, it was a conventional-looking journal, despite its radical agenda, a 16- and then 24-page monthly* priced* 2d and then 3d. It reported on meetings and lectures sponsored by the Legitimation League and had a lively 'Answers to Correspondents'* column*.

The police had the Legitimation League under surveillance, not because of its publication of articles on sexual issues but because their meetings were attended by anarchists whom the police were anxious to contain. But what brought the *Adult* to its end was that its publisher*, Rowland de Villiers (also known as George Singer), was also the publisher of Havelock Ellis. When an undercover police officer found copies of Ellis's *Studies in the Psychology of Sex*, specifically the volume on 'Sexual Inversion', or homosexuality, in the *Adult* office, he

Figure 1: Figure shaping corsets advertised in *Once a Week*, March 1878: 64.

had an excuse to seize all copies of the book, stop the publication of the *Adult* and arrest Bedborough. A Freedom of the Press Defence Committee with an impressive roster of radicals (G.W. Foote, Mona Caird*, Grant Allen*, Edward Carpenter among many) was formed, but Bedborough co-operated with the police to plead guilty to publishing obscene material in order to avoid imprisonment. As Foote said in disgust, the freethinkers had been let down by the free lovers. De Villiers, the publisher of the *Adult* and Ellis's *Studies* as well as other progressive and freethinker* materials, turned out to be something of a shady character, though he treated well all the people he published. He was arrested in 1901 on obscenity charges and died in police custody.

For nine issues after Bedborough was arrested and agreed to have no further connection with the Legitimation League or its publication, the *Adult* was edited by Henry Seymour, an anarchist but sexually conservative. Always underfunded and now having no institutional connection or crusading editor, the journal published its last issue in March 1899. **AH**

Sources: Humpherys 2003, *ODNB*.

ADVERTISEMENTS The boom in serial* publications of all kinds from the second quarter of the nineteenth century is the clearest evidence of the emergence of print capitalism: that is, the shift to the wholesale production of texts as commodities. Thus it is not surprising that newspapers and magazines represent the dominant media for advertising*, contributing massively to the rise of commodity culture.

Long before the abolition of taxes* on advertising in 1853, the income from advertising was a key

Despite the low status of advertising and the refusal of certain professions* such as lawyers to engage in it, published articles that attack it in general, such as Jerdan's* (1869), were rare; the norm was, rather, for advertising to be cautiously celebrated both as a sign of progress and as responsible for the prosperity of the press (e.g. *Edinburgh Review*, vol. 77, Feb. 1843: 1-43; *Quarterly Review*, vol. 97, June 1855: 335-50; Palmer 1897). Even the long chapters on hoaxers and quacks in the first book-form history of advertising (Sampson, 1874) are presented for amusement as individual cases rather than condemnation of advertising *per se*. In fact, most periodicals (or their advertising agents) tried to ensure that advertisers were genuine and reliable, whatever the extravagant assertions of the advertisements themselves. While scams were regularly denounced in the press, they are reported as using the press comparatively rarely. The overall effect was to promote the integrity of advertising in periodicals and newspapers.

From the 1860s onwards, advertising became ever more elaborate and pervasive, aided by technological innovation. It is emblematic that Thomas Smith's annual *Successful Advertising* went from a two-page circular in 1878 to an imaginatively illustrated* 776-page book in 1899. Noticeable throughout the press, the escalation of advertising is especially visible in the narrowly targeted trade papers*, where adverts formed the major part of the periodical, and in women's weeklies* ('One of the axioms of the advertising profession is that advertisements appeal primarily to the woman and not to the man', Stead 1899: 142). While the line between advertising and editorial was always permeable (see Puffing*), at the end of the century there was a perception in the trade that advertising had conquered not just every department of the press but the whole world. **AK**

Sources: Beetham 1996, Curran and Seaton 2003, [Jerdan] 1869, Nevett 1982, Nevett 1994, Palmer 1897.

ADVERTISING AGENCIES Advertising* agencies were vital to nineteenth-century journalism, linking individuals, commercial and manufacturing interests to the national and provincial* press, and often foreign and colonial* papers: already by 1850 there were about 50 agencies in London alone and their number and importance grew throughout the century.

Agents were mainly bulk purchasers of discounted space in periodicals, at first generally provincial newspapers. They then sold the space to advertisers, often passing on some of their discount. In theory, this benefited both advertiser and periodical. Advertisers who wanted wide coverage saved both money and the problem of negotiating with individual periodicals (especially if they wanted credit); periodicals knew both how much advertising space they could depend on selling and that the advertisers themselves were creditworthy and respectable (agents guaranteed to check this). However, agents frequently had exclusive agreements with journals to which they would direct their clientele, a practice known as 'farming'. Although defended by agents as efficient and cost-effective, farming did not always operate in the advertiser's interest. Furthermore, if a periodical were reliant on agents, agents could wield power over content. While this remains a relatively unexplored area in the story of the nineteenth-century press (though see Puffing*, in which agents were certainly involved), it is known that agents persuaded London newspapers to accept illustrated adverts* in the 1860s. It is surely significant that from 1855 they financed new metropolitan* papers such as the *Daily Telegraph*.

High circulation* was early considered likely to generate advertising success and serials claimed it to attract advertisers. Until the optionality of the Stamp Duty in 1855, circulations of the stamped press are well documented, though differentiated rates based on circulation were not common until the twentieth century. With the establishment of mass market* media in the 1840s, the purchasing power and habits of readers* were recognized as important; this is the reason behind the appearance of guides like Lewis and Lowe's (1844) that described periodicals' readership profiles. By 1851, *Mitchell's** even rated the advertising effectiveness of publications by where they were read (although it must be stressed that no market research in a modern, scientific, sense occurred until the early 1920s).

Bishop suggests that advertising agencies originated in the activity of shopkeepers who 'took in' advertisements and other pieces for newspapers, citing the first issue of the *Daily Universal Register* in 1785 which lists several shops through whom contributors could forward their material to the paper. The first known advertising agency, William Taylor, dates from the following year. Others followed, such as James White who opened for business in 1800. Agencies burgeoned after the repeal of the duty on advertising, after a minor flowering in the 1840s. Some published what are in effect annual* house journals, guides for advertisers which are invaluable for study of the press. These include *Mitchell's Newspaper Press Directory**; *May's London Press Directory and Advertiser's Handbook**, *Deacon's Newspaper Handbook and Advertiser's Guide* (1876?-1904), and *Sell's Dictionary of the World's Press* (1883/4-1921), Browne's the *Advertisers' ABC* (1886-1925) and Thomas Smith's annual *Successful Advertising* (1878-1902) and monthly* *Advertising* (Oct. 1891-Jan. 1914).

If Charles Lamb* had provided copy for White as early as 1809, it was only from the 1880s that agencies such as Thomas Smith's added sustained creative design services to media purchasing. Most agencies remained small, employing a handful of staff, but in the economic downturn of the 1890s a few began to offer total communications packages which included everything from product design to the organization of publicity stunts designed to gain non-advertising space in newspapers. The number of employees in such firms as well as their finances grew correspondingly. Although branching out into other media, agents continued to regard the press as the pillar of their activity until well into the twentieth century. Several advertising agencies provided news* services as well. **AK**
Sources: Bishop 1944, Nevett 1982, Nevett 1994, Stead 1899, Treasure 1977.

AGE (1825-1843) The *Age*, under the editorship* of Charles Molloy Westmacott* from 1827 to 1838, became one of the most notorious journals of the 1830s. Founded by Henry Hetherington Richards, this Tory weekly* paper first appeared on 15 May 1825. When Westmacott took over as editor* he retained the conservative politics* of the paper, attacking Whigs, Roman Catholics, the Reform Bill, the anti-Corn Law movement and other radical elements throughout the 1830s. He also published libellous gossip* and abusive remarks about the personal lives, characters and appearances of well-known persons. In addition to 'public men', according to James Grant, the *Age* 'invaded in the most ruthless manner the sanctities of the purely private life of gentlemen and ladies of high social position' (Grant 1871: 21). The paper extorted money from its victims by threatening to publish information which it claimed was in its possession. Evidently Westmacott made £5,000 to £7,000 per year from these tactics (Grant 1871: 14). At the same time the *Age* hypocritically affected shock at corruption, exposing medical quacks, unsteady stock companies, financially greedy bishops and the excesses of the aristocracy. Its readers* were presumed to be 'fast gentlemen' and its scandalous content kept circulation* high, ranging from 8,000 to 10,000 in the mid-1830s.

By 1843 Westmacott was having financial difficulties, and his creditors sold the *Age*. He then started the *Argus* as a competitor. The two journals 'assailed one another with the greatest virulence' (Grant 1871: 21). In 1843 both papers faced dissolution and so merged* as the *Age and the Argus*. The price* of the *Age*, expensive for eight pages, had dropped from 7d in 1836 to 6d in 1842 and 1843. However, scandalous journalism* was losing its popularity, and in 1845 the combined paper became the more conventional Tory *English Gentleman*. The decline of the *Age* and its rivals was, according to James Grant, 'a positive blessing to the better classes of society. No gentleman or lady felt safe against their slanders' (Grant 1871: 21). **DHL**
Sources: Grant 1871, Gray 1982, Kent 1982, *Waterloo*.

AGNOSTIC ANNUAL (1884-1907) Launched by Charles A. Watts soon after leaving the editorship of the *Secular Review** and taking charge of his father's printing company in 1884, the *Agnostic Annual* was the cornerstone of Watt's strategy to utilize the press to bring secularist free thought* to new and more respectable audiences than those attracted by the publications of Charles Bradlaugh's* militant National Secular Society. Although priced* cheaply at 6d for each yearly number, the *Agnostic Annual* was modelled on 2/6 monthly* reviews, with its opening issue featuring a symposium of the sort that James Knowles* had introduced into the *Nineteenth Century** seven years earlier.

Watts also sought to attract contributions from prestigious authors, and in its first decade the *Agnostic Annual* featured articles by Francis Newman, William Benjamin Carpenter*, Eliza Lynn Linton*, Leslie Stephen* and Edward Clodd alongside its regular news* from the secularist world and poems on agnostic themes. One of the main objectives of the *Agnostic Annual*, Watts proclaimed, was 'to aid in uniting all liberal thinkers on one common platform' (Watts 1884: 4). However, there were tensions with other elite exponents of secular views, and Watts angered Thomas Henry Huxley*, who had originally coined the term 'agnosticism', by reprinting a private letter in the opening number's symposium as if it were an official contribution to the new journal. Watts's fellow secularist William Stewart Ross took over as publisher* from H. Chattell in 1887 and remained in the role until 1896 when he was replaced by Watts & Co, who had also served as printers since the opening number. In

Figure 3: A portrait of W. H. Ainsworth in the *Illustrated Review*, Dec. 1871 and a copy of the first page of *Ainsworth's Magazine*, Jan. 1842 featuring one of his own tales.

1901, with the emergence of the ethical movement as an important component of secularism, the journal adopted the new title the *Agnostic Annual and Ethical Review*. **GD**

Sources: Lightman 1989, Royle 1980, *Waterloo*, Watts 1884.

AINSWORTH, WILLIAM HARRISON (1805-1882) Proprietor*, editor*, novelist and journalist, Ainsworth first published in *Arliss's Pocket Magazine* in 1821 while still at school under the pseudonym* 'T. Hall'. Almost simultaneously he contributed to several other periodicals, including the *New Monthly Magazine**, the *London Magazine**, the *European Magazine*, the *Edinburgh Magazine and Literary Miscellany* and *Fraser's**, and published his own small weekly*, the *Boeotian*, which lasted for only six numbers in the spring of 1824. After a volume of poetry and a novel, he edited an annual* called the *Christmas* Box* (1828), to which he persuaded Walter Scott* to contribute; he himself published in annuals, including the *Keepsake*. He finally achieved popularity with his triple-decker *Rookwood* (1834), a Newgate novel published by Bentley*. Because of its success, Bentley asked him to take over the editorship of *Bentley's Miscellany** after Dickens* had left. There he serialized* perhaps his most famous novel, 'Jack Shephard' (1839). He left *Bentley's* after disagreements in 1841 and in 1842 set up the rival *Ainsworth's Magazine**, with illustrations* by Cruik-shank*. He sold *Ainsworth's* to his publisher in 1843, though he continued editing it until 1845 when again he resigned, angry at not being paid his monthly fee of £60. During the following decade he acquired three titles, owning two simultaneously for over 20 years: almost immediately he bought the *New Monthly** and took with him key contributors from *Ainsworth's*. Later that year, he rebought a much diminished *Ainsworth's*, in which he serialized his previously published novels. He retained the *New Monthly* until 1870, and bought *Bentley's* itself in 1854, which he owned until 1868.

During the 1850s his style of historical romances lost favour with the public, although he continued writing them, and his occasional attempts at other forms, including the monthly serial 'Mervyn Clitheroe' (1851), based partly on his youth, similarly failed to recapture his former popularity. Always intensely social, his chief interest from then until his death lay in his 'discovery' of Ouida* and Mrs Henry Wood among others. **AW**

Sources: Ellis 1911, *ODNB*, Sutherland 1995, Sullivan.

AINSWORTH'S MAGAZINE (1842-1854) Chiefly known for the historical novels of its owner-editor*, W. H. Ainsworth*, *Ainsworth's Magazine* was a monthly miscellany* of 'Romance, General Literature and Art' for the entertainment of the early Victorian middle class. Its main competitors were

*Bentley's Miscellany** (1837-1868) and Henry Colburn's* revamped *New Monthly Magazine** (1814-1884).

Founded as a rival to *Bentley's Miscellany*, the editorship of which Ainsworth had testily resigned, *Ainsworth's Magazine* opened with the editor's latest serial*, 'The Miser's Daughter', finely illustrated* by George Cruikshank*, and soon attracted a readership* of 7,000. The magazine* preferred descriptive to prescriptive reviews*, avoided controversy and featured a 'Lady's Page'. Representative early contributions were gothic tales by Eliza Skelton, light essays by Samuel Laman Blanchard* and travel writing by the editor's cousin, W. F. Ainsworth. The editor's own interest in the venture soon waned, however, for he relinquished financial control in late 1843 and later gave up the editorship. Though he regained both by the end of 1845, more of his energies then went into the *New Monthly Magazine**, acquired around the same time. Thereafter, *Ainsworth's Magazine* featured only the proprietor's* reprinted fiction, the standard of contributors declined and the illustrations* evaporated. The magazine folded in late 1854, after Ainsworth had purchased *Bentley's Miscellany** and resumed its editorship. GL
Sources: Ellis 1911, Elwin, 1934, Gettmann 1960, *ODNB*, *Wellesley*.

ALCOCK, CHARLES WILLIAM (1842-1907) Alcock's career illustrates the interaction of sport and sporting news*. His powerful position in the sporting world allowed him unparalleled access and influence in shaping the agendas and successes of football and cricket. As a key member of the Football Association (FA), secretary of the Surrey County Cricket Club (Surrey CCC) and as a journalist*, Charles W. Alcock was the seminal figure in the origins of modern English sport. Strangely, his obituary* in *The Times* ignores his journalism, which he practised for nearly 50 years before his death. Alcock began his career in journalism with the *Sportsman**, serving as the first athletics subeditor* before becoming football subeditor of the *Sportsman** and the *Field**. With the approval of the FA, Alcock established the *Football Annual** in 1868, which he edited for almost 40 years.

With his able and prolific pen, Alcock also covered cricket for the *Sportsman** and, in 1872, the same year he became secretary of the Surrey CCC, he became the first editor* of the 'Red Lilly', *James Lillywhite's Cricketers' Annual*, which he edited until 1900. As Surrey CCC secretary he organized the first test match against Australia, held in England in

1880, and planned the famous 1882 Ashes contest against the Australians at the Oval. Also during 1882, the energetic and enterprising Alcock established his most enduring journalistic legacy, *Cricket*. The 2d weekly*, which he edited until his death in 1907, provided player descriptions, match coverage, gossip* and historical articles. MJM
Sources: Bettesworth 1910, Booth 2002, *Cricket* 1907, *ODNB*, *The Times* 1907.

ALDIN, CECIL CHARLES WINDSOR (1870-1935) Artist and illustrator*, Cecil Aldin trained as an animal painter as well as an anatomist, but his central abiding interest was in the comic depiction of equestrian scenes, especially hunting. His simplified outlines and empathy with his subjects found a ready market in Britain before the First World War, and from his early twenties he was a prolific contributor of comic drawings to journals ranging from specialist sporting magazines like the *Illustrated Sporting and Dramatic News** and topical weeklies* like the *Illustrated London News** to society journals like the *Gentlewoman*. Aldin's backward looking evocation of a vanishing rural squirarchic England, derived from Alken, Leech* and a long tradition of humorous celebration of the countryside, was driven more by nostalgia than caricature*, but proved immensely popular. BM
Source: Houfe 1978.

***ALEXANDRA MAGAZINE AND WOMEN'S SOCIAL AND INDUSTRIAL ADVOCATE* (1864-1865)** Hoping to gain a wider audience, Bessie Parkes*, a member of the Langham Place group, launched and edited the *Alexandra Magazine and Women's Social and Industrial Advocate* as a cheaper alternative at 6d to the *English Woman's Journal**, which she had also edited*. Begun in May 1864, the new monthly* magazine was named after Alexandra, the Princess of Wales and Queen Victoria's daughter-in-law, and was a deliberate attempt to challenge the older *Victoria Magazine**. This feminist magazine included serialized fiction*, poetry*, book reviews, and regular features on benevolent societies and employment for women, as well as a correspondence* section. Some contributions were signed and some anonymous*. Advertising* was primarily focused on books, although some household goods also featured.

The *Magazine* merged* with the *English Woman's Journal* in August 1864 and from September became the *Alexandra Magazine and Englishwoman's Journal*. Subscribers were 'earnestly requested' to support the magazine in late 1864 by introducing it to others. Its final number appeared in August

1865, a consequence of internal differences among the members of the Langham Place group. It was refashioned under Jessie Boucherett's* initiative and editorship from 1866 as the *Englishwoman's Review**, which continued until 1910 under various editors*. KLM

Sources: Diamond 1999, Doughan 1987, Hirsch 1998.

ALFORD, HENRY (1810-1871) The son of an Evangelical clergyman, Henry Alford became a priest in 1834. In 1853 he moved to London to take up the ministry of Quebec Chapel, Marylebone before becoming dean of Canterbury in 1857. With a voracious capacity for work, seemingly limitless talent and energy, he found time to edit and write for the periodical press.

His editorial work began in 1839 for less than a year with a monthly* magazine of literature* and science*, *Dearden's Miscellany,* published in Nottingham and founded by the poet, William Dearden. But his most significant editorship* came as the first editor of Alexander Strahan's* *Contemporary Review** from 1866, a post he shared with Edward H. Plumptre until May 1868, continuing as sole editor until the spring of 1870. Combining scholarly excellence, theological balance and cultural awareness, he seemed ideally suited to the intellectual endeavour underlying the *Contemporary.* Not only an editor, Alford wrote articles for three of Strahan's journals, the *Contemporary Review, Good Words** and the *Sunday Magazine.* In the *Contemporary* he wrote on theological debates and church organization, as well as reviewing books, the latter signed with his initials. His poetry*, praised by Wordsworth, was published in the *Edinburgh Review**, the *Wesleyan-Methodist Magazine**, *St James's Magazine**, and the *Mirror of Literature**. CL

Sources: BritPer, *Encyclopaedia Britannica* 10th edn, *ODNB, Wellesley.*

ALL THE YEAR ROUND (1859-1895) *All the Year Round* was in many ways identical to its predecessor *Household Words**, not least because it remained a 2d. weekly* conspicuously 'Conducted by Charles Dickens*'. In two respects, however, its constitution differed. Its leading article now comprised an instalment of serial fiction*, whose authorship was identified; gone were the investigative reports and satirical broadsides that had characterized leaders* in the earlier incarnation. Dickens and subeditor* W. H. Wills* were now the sole partners in and proprietors of their publication. When Dickens serialized 'A Tale of Two Cities' (1859) and 'Great Expectations' (1860-61) in its pages, he was his own publisher; when he contract-

ed authors such as Wilkie Collins*, Edward Bulwer Lytton*, Charles Reade, Frances Trollope, and Edmund Yates* to contribute novels, he became their publisher* as well as editor*.

Together, these changes were effective in raising the circulation* significantly. The first number clocked 120,000, 'settling down', Wills wrote on 19 May 1859, 'to a steady current sale of 100,000'. Sales of the extra 'Christmas Numbers'* increased exponentially to something approaching 300,000 in 1867 (*No Thoroughfare*, with Wilkie Collins*), but set in the context of rising circulation figures across the sector, and the extra sales and income Dickens could generate by syndicating* single short stories in *All the Year Round* and in American journals, he decided to discontinue this feature.

Improvements in transatlantic* communication and voluntary recognition of international copyright* by various US publishers meant that from its launch, *All the Year Round* appeared almost simultaneously in America. In order to ship the plates in time, the magazine had to be put to bed a week earlier than *Household Words*, with a consequent loss of topicality. Regular contributors noted the difference, and felt, with John Hollingshead, that *All the Year Round* 'was not the same journal, although we had the same chief'. His further complaint that it was 'less personal' seems strange however, given that Dickens's major non-fiction contribution to the journal consisted of three series of familiar essays, advertised as 'Occasional Journeys' by 'The Uncommercial Traveller' (1860, 1863, 1868-1869). Other changes of emphasis involved a notable increase in the frequency of articles on foreign* affairs (Italian, Polish, Turkish), on commerce and individual finance and on science* and natural history; conversely, a reduction of coverage of such topics as emigration, education and industry can be observed.

After 20 bi-annual volumes, Dickens decided to introduce improvements in paper* quality, layout and typography* for the New Series (from 5 Dec. 1868). These included a new boxed masthead* illustrated with flowers and fruit in the four corners, representing the cycle of the seasons. Following Wills's retirement in March that year, Dickens's eldest son Charley was brought in to fill the vacant subeditor's chair. After Dickens's death in June 1870, Charles Dickens Jnr took over the editorship, buying out Wills in 1871, and continuing the magazine 'respectably' (in Percy Fitzgerald's opinion) as managing editor and proprietor until 1895. **JMD**

Sources: Drew 2003, Fitzgerald 1913, Hollingshead 1900, Slater and Drew 2000, Sutherland 1976.

ALLEN, (CHARLES) GRANT BLAIRFINDIE (1848-1899) Both a popular fiction and science* writer, Grant Allen produced a staggering amount of journalism in his 22-year career. He published hundreds of articles and around 200 short stories, as well as dozens of novels, many of which were first published serially*. In addition to fiction, he wrote on biology, psychology, physics, natural history, tourism*, and the anthropology of religion*. The Canadian-born Allen moved to England for his secondary education and an Oxford degree. Following an early position as professor of mental and moral philosophy in Jamaica, he returned to England in 1876 and took up freelancing. His first articles on science were accepted in 1877 by Leslie Stephen* at the *Cornhill Magazine*. Allen also wrote several pieces on perceptual psychology for *Mind*. When he started publishing in the monthly* *Belgravia* in 1878, he adopted the pseudonym* 'J. Arbuthnot Wilson' (acronym 'jaw'), aiming to separate his scholarly essays from his popular writing. He soon also began writing anonymously* for weeklies* and dailies*, such as *London** and the *Daily News**.

Allen began publishing fiction when he discovered that it paid far more than scientific journalism. Although he regarded several of his novels as serious works challenging established mores, particularly the scandal-making *The Woman Who Did* (1895), he spoke bitterly of his pandering to the market. A strong advocate of evolutionary theory (above all, of Herbert Spencer's* contributions), Allen's scientific concerns were integrated into his fiction, largely concerned with atavism, heredity, and eugenics. He wrote on popular science for *St James's Gazette**, the *Popular Science Monthly** and *Knowledge**, among others. Working at a feverish pace – he claimed to write a book review every day before breakfast – Allen eventually earned an excellent income. The need to make a living, he believed, had made impossible the serious scientific writing he aspired to do, and in an anonymous* *Fortnightly Review** article in 1889, 'The Trade of Author', he characteristically described journalism as 'the most hateful of professions'. Allen's extraordinary productivity continued until his early death at the age of 51. **SA**
Sources: Allen 1889, Grant Allen Website, Greenslade and Rodgers 2005, Morton 2005, *ODNB*.

ALLINGHAM, HELEN MARY ELIZABETH (1848-1926) Helen Allingham (née Paterson) was a periodical illustrator* and watercolourist. Related through her mother, Mary Herford, to Elizabeth Gaskell, Bessie Parkes* and Joseph Priestley,

Paterson also gained artistic inspiration from her grandmother, Sarah Smith Herford, an oil painter and her aunt, Laura Herford, the first woman to be admitted to the Royal Academy Schools.

In 1867, having moved to London to study at the Royal Academy Schools, she began work as a freelance magazine illustrator in 1868 to finance herself, beginning with drawing on wood for *Once a Week**. Frederic Walker* was one of her influences. Paterson worked on other juvenile* publications such as *Little Folks* and also supplied Joseph Swain* the London engraver* with illustrations* from 1869, and illustrated three serial stories for *Judy's Magazine**.

Contributing to *London Society** and *Cassell's Magazine** in 1870, Paterson became the only woman and one of the founding staff members on the *Graphic*, a new breed of illustrated magazines where she gained attention for her 'vigorous drawing and excellent composition'. She worked there in 1870-1874 while exhibiting her drawings and attending the Slade's evening classes where she met Kate Greenaway* who became a firm friend. Paterson also began illustrating serialized* fiction including Mrs Oliphant's* *Innocent*, and Thomas Hardy's* *Far From the Madding Crowd* for the *Cornhill* in 1872, 'the best illustrator I ever had' he wrote to Edmund Gosse*. Her work also appeared between 1871 and 1898 in the *Illustrated London News**.

After she married William Allingham* the Irish poet and editor of *Fraser's Magazine** in 1874, she gave up work at the *Graphic* to concentrate on painting the predominantly rural cottage scenes which made her enduring reputation. In 1890, Allingham was the first woman elected to the Royal Society of Painters in Water Colour. **CL**
Sources: Allingham Society, Clayton 1876, *ODNB*, Victorian Web.

ALLINGHAM, WILLIAM (1824-1889) William Allingham, generally known as an Irish poet of the Pre-Raphaelite circle, was also a prolific writer for the periodical press until the end of his literary career in 1880. Since 1843 when Leigh Hunt* helped him into print, he published in periodicals many of his poems, some of which were serialized* (for example, 'Laurence Bloomfield in Ireland' in *Fraser's Magazine** 1862). Allingham usually signed them with his full name. However, when he became editor of *Fraser's* in 1874, after he had been the subeditor* under Anthony Froude* for four years, he used the pseudonym* 'Patricius Walker' or the initials 'P. W.'. Allingham's editorship, which lasted until 1879, marked his change of heart from poetry to prose with the serialization of *Rambles* (1866-1877). What bound together his journalistic and poetic work was his Irish heritage (especially the oral tradition of the old ballads of Ireland), the nature of literary criticism and his attack against atheism. According to his wife, the illustrator Helen Allingham*, his fascination with Irish history is most evident in 'Seven Hundred Years Ago: An Historic Sketch' (1870, *Fraser's*; see Allingham 1911: 138). Allingham associated poetry* with the particular on the basis of which he criticised Byron in his 1870 review for *Fraser's* that he signed as 'One Who Loves and Honours English Poetry'. Allingham also wrote a biographical sketch of William Blake (1849, *Hogg's Weekly Instructor*), two articles on *Hamlet* (1879) and one on Edgar Allan Poe's influence on Baudelaire (1869) for *Fraser's*. His journalistic work, as well his short story 'The Wedding Ring' (1851, *Fraser's*) and the play *Ashby Manor* (1883), are overshadowed by his poems, which, during his life, were anthologized in various poetry collections. KCH

Sources: Aghasy 1984, Allingham 1911, Allingham and Radford 1967, Warner 1971.

ALLY SLOPER'S HALF-HOLIDAY (1884-1916) *Ally Sloper's Half-Holiday* was a popular weekly* 1d comic-illustrated* newspaper which reached a 340,000 circulation*, published* by the Dalziel* Brothers and initially edited* by Gilbert Dalziel. Each issue featured a large black and white cartoon* of Ally Sloper, accompanied by an excerpt from the diary of his daughter, Tootsie. Charles Henry Ross created the character of Ally sometime in the 1860s for the comic paper *Judy**, another Dalziel Brothers' publication. His popularity led to several Sloper books and, in 1884, the launch of his very own eight-page paper, issued every Saturday. Inside each issue were comic stories, snippets of poetry* or verse, and smaller illustrations, often recycled from earlier issues of *Judy*. Ross's wife, 'Marie Duval'*, did most of the early illustration. Ally took his final form under the pen of W. G. Baxter*, but after Baxter's untimely death in 1888, W. F. Thomas became the main illustrator.

Ally Sloper was typically shown with a top hat, tattered umbrella, bottle of gin and in outfits ranging from the shabby genteel to outrageous parodies of aristocratic and middle-class dress. Ally, his family and companions appear in a range of leisure activities where they regularly upset conventional notions of good behaviour, whether at the seaside, the theatre or the Mansion House ball. Ally is shown testifying before the London County Council

dressed as a ballerina, campaigning for a seat in Parliament and greeting luminaries such as Henry Stanley, William Gladstone and the Prince of Wales. The temperance movement and other social reformers were regular targets of the paper's satire*.

As in many mass-market* periodicals at the end of the century, the paper conducted regular contests (the prize being a 'Sloper Pocket Watch') and like *Tit-Bits**, offered railway accident life insurance. The paper was unique in the establishment of a fan club for readers, who joined by sending in coupons from 12 issues. Based on the names and occupations of contest winners, the readership* of *Ally Sloper's* was varied but concentrated among the lower-middle and working classes. Publication ceased in 1916 with a brief revival of less than a year (Nov. 1922-Sept. 1923) when it ceased completely. **SB**

Sources: Bailey 1998b, Gifford 1984, Kunzle 1986, Sabin 2003.

ALPINE JOURNAL (1863-) The quarterly* *Alpine Journal* was circulated within the Alpine Club (fl.1857), whose members were either mountaineers or creators of some artistic or literary achievement related to mountains. Its readership* consisted of 823 men who joined the club (1857-1890), mainly of the professional middle classes*, including John Tyndall*, John Ruskin* and Leslie Stephen*, its editor* (1868-1871), several of whose contributions to the journal were collected into *The Playground of Europe*, regarded as a 'formative' text in 'mountaineering literature'. The club and journal were born out of the mid-century middle-class vogue for mountaineering which partly resulted from Albert Smith's* wildly popular show, 'The Ascent of Mont Blanc'. But they also provided middle-class men, fearing British cultural decline during the military crises of the 1850s and 1860s, with an outlet for public-school athleticism and masculine heroics. As such, the *Journal* often described the first ascents of mountains by its members as military conquests and British triumphs.

The *Journal's* editors in the nineteenth century were often members of a wide range of London learned and scientific societies; and while the club adopted the structure of such societies, the *Journal* expressed itself in similar terms, claiming to expand existing geographical knowledge through narratives of its members' expeditions to unmapped corners of the globe and to untrammelled mountain peaks. Its editors had diverse interests and affiliations, but most often came from the growing ranks of professional* scholars. They included the pioneering military historian Hereford Brooke George (1863-1867), Douglas

W. Freshfield, a key early member of the Royal Geographical Society and president of the Geographical Association (1879-1911), A. B. Coolidge, history tutor at Magdalen College, Oxford (1880-1889), the accomplished Dante scholar A. J. Butler (1890-1893) and the art historian W. M. Conway (1894-1895).

Despite its learned appeal, the *Journal* was much more concerned with the spirit of masculine adventure than with real contributions to scientific knowledge, and its contents reflected this wide range of scholarly interests, containing material on the history of mountains and mountaineering, the representation of mountains in art and classical literature, and narratives of expeditions. Priced* at 18d from 1863, its cost rose to 2s in 1891 and remained so until 1912. The journal contained woodcuts*, lithographs* and by the end of the century included photographs*. Still extant, it is now an annual*. The first volume (1863-1864) was published by Longman, Green, Longman, Roberts and Green*, which changed its name twice before the end of the Victorian period. **AB**

Sources: Hansen 1995, *Literary Encyclopedia*, *ODNB*, *Waterloo*, *Wellesley*.

ALSAGER, THOMAS MASSA (1779-1846) In addition to being a businessman in cloth trading, Thomas Massa Alsager was a financial* journalist*, music* critic and partner in *The Times**. Alsager became the City correspondent for *The Times* under the editorship* of his close friend, Thomas Barnes*, in 1817. Two years later, he bought shares from its chief proprietor*, John Walter*, which led not only to his becoming its joint manager with William Delane* but also to purchasing a partnership in 1827. The paper prospered with his development of exclusive modes of the 'fast' communication of news. His reputation was, however, damaged in 1845 due to accusations of puffery*, which resulted in his leaving the following year.

Nonetheless, his reputation as a music reviewer*, recital organizer and founder of the Beethoven Quartet Society remained unscathed. It is noteworthy that his obituaries* in 1846 concentrate on his musical rather than financial achievements (see for example, *Gentleman's Magazine** 27 1847: 91-92). His reviews of operatic performances, such as *Don Giovanni* (14 and 16 April 1817) and *La Dame Blanche* (10 June 1834) in *The Times*, together with the reviewing of the concerts held at his home at Queen Square in *Musical World**, drew attention not only to Beethoven but also to Haydn, Mendlessohn and Mozart and other less well-known composers. **KCH**

Sources: Levy 1985, *ODNB*, Wickham 1981.

AMALGAMATED SOCIETY OF LITHOGRAPHIC PRINTERS (1880-1968) The Amalgamated Society of Lithographic Printers and Auxiliaries of Great Britain and Ireland was founded in 1880, following a plea for the amalgamation of various lithographic and printing societies. This had come from the two largest organizations in Bradford and Manchester. An organization for lithographic printers, known as the Central Association of Lithographic* and Copper-Plate Printers, had existed as early as 1860. It had argued for the union of various branches, but it was not until 1878 that the first amalgamation conference was held. The subsequent foundation of the Amalgamated Society of Lithographic Printers in 1880 saw gradual improvements made to working conditions in the printing industry. At first it was difficult to persuade all societies to join the union, but by the end of 1881 there was an increase of 100 members. Membership continued to grow gradually, so that at the end of 1884, the Society counted 1,040 members.

One of the main concerns during this period was the large-scale employment of boy labour in the printing presses. Before the Factory Acts came into force, the ASLP fought a long and hard battle against child and sweated labour. Concerned about the numbers of uneducated apprentices in the trade, it urged that only boys with some aptitude should be indentured. The Society also helped with the technical education of lithographers, forming classes in various centres. In the 1890s a major campaign was fought for better wages and the reduction of hours. It also opposed the large amount of lithography done on the Continent for British firms.

In 1902 an attempt was made to publish a paper similar to those of other trade unions. The *Lithographic Gazette* was first issued in July 1902. It had a rather precarious existence and ceased after March 1905. By 1913 a national council of seven members from various parts of the country replaced the governing body of six elected by and from the Manchester branch. During 1913 and 1914, agitation for the improvement of wages made by several branches was generally successful. In 1930 there was an amalgamation with music printers. By this time the Society had become a national organization with ten branches. In 1968 the Society merged with the National Graphical Association. **DHL**

Sources: Gennard 1990, Skingsley 1978-1980, Sproat 1930.

ANALYTICAL REVIEW (1788-1798) The monthly* *Analytical Review, or History of Literature, Domestic and Foreign, on an Enlarged Plan* was an influential reviewing* journal of the late eighteenth century. With its emphasis on a high-quality liberal and 'objective' approach to current literature* and intellectual trends, the *Analytical Review* became an important forum for the discussion of radical literature, and subsequently proved a catalyst for the development of a more conservative reviewing press in the early nineteenth century. Founded by Thomas Christie and the leading liberal bookseller Joseph Johnson, the *Analytical Review* included among its reviewers Henry Fuseli, Mary Wollstonecraft, Alexander Geddes, William Cowper, John Horne Tooke, Anna Letitia Barbauld, Alexander Chalmers and Mary Hays. Though its circulation* peaked at only 1,500 copies per month in 1797, the *Review* nonetheless had a significant impact on the future direction of literary periodicals. The backlash against radical writing which gained strength through the 1790s saw the institution of important conservative reviewing journals, such as the *British Critic** (1793ff) and the *Anti-Jacobin Review** (1798ff). The *Review* was discontinued at the end of 1798 when Johnson was prosecuted on trumped-up charges over his bookselling activities. **NG**
Sources: Braithwaite 2003, Timperley 1839, Tyson 1979.

ANDREWS, GEORGE HENRY (1816-1898) Primarily a painter, nonetheless George Andrews, artist and illustrator, drew extensively for the major illustrated* weeklies*, including the *Illustrated London News**, the *Illustrated Times* and the *Graphic**, from the 1850s to the 1870s. His specialisms included marine subjects and machinery, reflecting his training as an engineer and his interests as a painter. **BM**
Sources: Engen 1990, Houfe 1978.

ANDREWS, WILLIAM EUSEBIUS (1773-1837) William Eusebius Andrews was a writer, editor* and publisher* of English Catholic journals. His career began as a printer's apprentice on the *Norfolk Chronicle*. From 1799 until 1813 he was managing editor of the paper. Andrews moved to London in 1813. He considered it as the best place to advance the Catholic cause through journalism*. In June 1813 he launched the monthly* *Orthodox Journal,* which was devoted to English Catholic affairs. While the journal provided a platform for Catholic debate, Andrews alienated many of his subscribers with belligerent articles and criticism of the establishment. Complaints were made to the

Vatican and the *Orthodox Journal* folded in 1820. Undaunted, Andrews launched the weekly* *Catholic Advocate of Civil and Religious Liberty,* a more overtly political publication, in December 1820, which survived less than a year.

In 1822 Andrews promoted two new publications: the *Catholic Miscellany* was under a nominal editor, while Andrews edited the other paper, the *People's Advocate,* which was exclusively political. This was possibly the first Catholic weekly stamped* newspaper in England. However, it lasted for only seven weeks. Despite financial difficulties, Andrews continued to publish the *Catholic Miscellany* until June 1823, when he placed it in other hands. As the final issues were published, Andrews started the *Truthteller**. This began as a stamped* weekly paper but soon changed to a weekly political pamphlet. Andrews's fierce criticism of Daniel O'Connell caused many readers to withdraw their subscriptions, and the *Truthteller* was forced to close in April 1829. However, a New York* edition of the *Truthteller,* launched by Andrews in 1825, had a much longer life. It was possibly New York's first distinctly Catholic newspaper. After Andrews closed the British edition of the *Truthteller,* he revived the *Orthodox Journal,* which, in 1831, became the *British Liberator* and then *Andrews's Constitutional Preceptor.* From 1835 he also issued a weekly paper, the *Penny Orthodox Journal,* which in 1837 was renamed the *London and Dublin Orthodox Journal,* which his son owned after Andrews's death. Andrews was an incessant promoter of English Catholic affairs, but his dubious radicalism often caused the circulation* of his newspapers and journals to fluctuate, while lack of finance made their existence precarious. **DHL**
Sources: Carter 1988, Fletcher 1936, *ODNB*, Taffe 1907, *Waterloo.*

ANELAY, HENRY (1817-1883) Henry Anelay, a popular illustrator*, 'draughtsman on wood' and landscape artist, was tutored by Stephen Sly* early in his career, and Sly secured for him work on Charles Knight's* publications, *London** and the *Penny Magazine**. He contributed designs to a number of popular* illustrated magazines and journals including the *Illustrated London News**, *Cassell's Illustrated Family Paper** and Arthur Hall's *British Workwoman**. He came out of retirement to work for T. B. Smithies* as one of the principal illustrators of the *Band of Hope Review**, the *British Workman** and numerous other works published by S. W. Partridge and Co. **FM**
Sources: Engen 1990, Houfe 1992, White 1897.

ANGLO-SAXON REVIEW – A QUARTERLY MISCELLANY (1899-1901) Under the editorship of Lady Randolph Spencer Churchill, the *Anglo-Saxon Review* ran for ten quarterly* issues (June 1899-Sept. 1901). Notable for its wealthy and aristocratic subscribers (including the Prince of Wales), the publication was itself very expensive, at 21s per 250-page issue; an illustrated* miscellany*, it primarily addressed the literature, art and history of English-speaking nations, and published drama, poetry*, short stories and criticism as well as articles. Contributors included Max Beerbohm*, Winston Churchill, Stephen Crane, George Gissing, 'John Oliver Hobbes' (Pearl Richards Craigie), 'C. E. Raimond' (Elizabeth Robins), George Bernard Shaw* and Algernon Swinburne* as well as artist John Singer Sargent. Reflecting the transatlantic* interests of its American-born editor, many subscribers were from the USA. John Lane* published the journal in London and New York simultaneously, and the first story in the first volume was Henry James's* 'The Great Condition'.

Interesting from an inter-artistic standpoint, the *Anglo-Saxon Review* contained verbal descriptions of visual works, such as a piece on Gilbert Stuart's portraits of George Washington. The visual element of the publication extended to the opulent, gilded-leather bound volumes themselves, whose covers, on Lane's suggestion, were facsimiles of sixteenth- and seventeenth-century folios. Issues of the journal even included articles on the bindings by Cyril Davenport, the journal's binder. **DND**
Sources: Cevasco 1993, Martin 1971, Tye 1974, Victor 1984, *Waterloo*.

ANNALS AND MAGAZINE OF NATURAL HISTORY (1838-) In 1828, two years after founding the successful *Gardener's Magazine*, John Claudius Loudon* began another venture, the *Magazine of Natural History*, that would extend beyond horticulture and, for the first time in a commercial journal, embrace zoology, botany, mineralogy, geology and meteorology. Published* by Longman* and with an initial circulation* of over 2,000, the response to Loudon's new magazine was sufficiently enthusiastic for it to move, in 1834, from bi-monthly to monthly publication and reduce its price* from 3s 6d to 2s. By this time, however, several rivals had imitated Loudon's profitable formula, and he himself was busy editing the *Architectural Magazine,* devolving much of the responsibility for the *Magazine of Natural History* to his assistant, John Denson.

Denson's inept editorship* lasted until 1836 when Loudon hired Edward Charlesworth, at the extremely generous rate of £25 per number, who gave the journal a more controversial and philosophical tone. This new tenor was appreciated by the young Charles Darwin who became an avid reader of the *Magazine of Natural History* and drew much information for his developing theory of natural selection from articles by the longstanding contributor Edward Blyth. In 1838 Charlesworth bought the proprietorship* from Loudon, although his abrasive style drove many of the original contributors to the rival *Magazine of Zoology and Botany*, which had begun in Edinburgh in the previous year. This Edinburgh journal proved financially disastrous and soon folded, but Richard Taylor* opted to continue it as the *Annals of Natural History*, shifting production to London and adding himself and William Jackson Hooker* to the original panel of editors. Taylor's financial prudence, especially in using lithography* rather than expensive engravings in scientific* illustrations*, made the *Annals of Natural History* a modest success, with a circulation of 500, and in 1840 Charlesworth, by now haemorrhaging subscribers as well as contributors, sold Taylor the copyright of the *Magazine of Natural History* for £100.

The amalgamation of the two titles in 1841 as the *Annals and Magazine of Natural History*, with Taylor and William Jardine as editors and Taylor's illegitimate son William Francis* as subeditor*, generated fresh interest and the initial print run was set at 750. While the circulation soon settled at 500, less than half the combined total of the two titles when published separately, the merger* allowed Taylor to monopolize the market for natural history periodicals, and the more casual and familiar tone adopted in the *Annals and Magazine of Natural History* proved an enduring success, with Francis serving as principal editor (1859-1897). **GD**
Sources: Allen 1976, Brock 1980, Sheets-Pyenson 1981a, Sheets-Pyenson 1981b, *Waterloo*.

ANNALS OF ELECTRICITY, MAGNETISM AND CHEMISTRY AND GUARDIAN OF EXPERIMENTAL SCIENCE (1836-1843) A scientific* journal with a focus on the chemistry and physics of electricity, the *Annals of Electricity* was founded and edited by William Sturgeon, the experimental electrician and lecturer on science who invented the electromagnet. It was in part a response to refusals by other scientific periodicals – including the *Philosophical Magazine** – to publish Sturgeon's work on magnetic electric machines. Costing 1s, the journal began life as a quarterly* and switched to monthly* publication in 1838. It carried detailed scientific papers by many of the leading scientists of the day, including Sturgeon's friend James Prescott Joule, and his enemy Michael Faraday. The journal combined original material, articles reprinted from other publications and cutting-edge papers from the Continent, many of which were suffixed with critical comment and analysis by Sturgeon. Sturgeon's many contributions were sometimes marked by a bitterness about his perceived rejection by London's scientific elite, the Royal Institution and the Royal Society in particular. Despite the usually objective and dispassionate tone of the *Annals*, its attacks on the work of William Snow Harris, John Frederic Daniell and Faraday, though supported with rigorously collected experimental data, were occasionally tinged with a sense of personal slight.

The demise of the *Annals of Electricity* was a product of the economic downturn of the early 1840s, as a result of which Sturgeon suffered heavy personal losses that forced him to stop publishing the periodical. He unsuccessfully sought to replace it with the *Annals of Philosophical Discovery* (1843), which ran to only six issues. **MaT**
Sources: *ODNB, Waterloo.*

ANNALS OF SPORTING AND FANCY GAZETTE (1822-1828) This monthly* magazine* was advertised as being 'entirely appropriated to sporting* subjects and *FANCY* pursuits'. An opening 'Address' stated that in giving the journal 'a decided superiority in *paper*, *printing*, and *illustration** it is intended to place it far above the reach of competition, and render it appropriate for the library of the Country Gentleman, and the Man of Fashion'. (I.i, 1822: 2) It also aimed to contain everything significant on a variety of sporting activities including 'hunting, coursing, racing, fishing, cocking, wrestling, single stick, pedestrianism, cricket, billiards, rowing, sailing etc'. Included were sporting events for the month, 'fancy gazette battles', sports stories, poetry* and articles on field sports*. It was illustrated* by, among others, Samuel Alken and J. J. Henning, with engravings and full-page hand-coloured plates. Published* by Sherwood, Neely and Jones, issues were of 68, 22cm.octavo pages, which appeared on the first day of the month, priced* 2s 6d. **DHL**
Sources: *Annals of Sporting and Fancy Gazette* 1822, *Waterloo.*

ANNUAL MONITOR (1813-1913) In 1813, William Alexander (1768-1841) of York, assisted perhaps by his wife, Ann, began editing* and publishing the *Annual Monitor, or new letter case and memorandum book or obituary of the members of the society of friends*. The following year he dropped all reference to obituary* from the title. The aim of this small volume, 12cm × 8cm at first, then slightly larger, was 'to contribute, either to the moral or the religious improvement of its readers' through articles on religious*, political* and humanitarian topics. In addition, the *Monitor* noted all British Friends deceased during the previous year with selected short biographies. The first series also included three sections of about 75 blank or lined pages for memoranda, bookkeeping and a calendar.

With Alexander's death, the 1841 volume was compiled by his executors before Samuel Tuke took over from 1842 until 1852, when Benjamin Seebohm succeeded. Tuke began a new series under the title *Annual Monitor, or Obituary of the Society of Friends,* devoted primarily to obituaries* and death notices. As editor* from 1868 until his death in 1877, John Newby changed the subtitle in 1876 to '*or Obituary of the Members of the Society of Friends in Great Britain and Ireland*' and the same year compiled a cumulative index to all previous volumes. In 1885 the price* was 1s 6d per volume*. By 1891, the *Annual Monitor* was being edited by William Robinson and published by Edward Hicks of London. In 1894, Hicks published another cumulative index, *Quaker records: being an index to* 'The Annual Monitor', *1813-1892,* edited by Joseph J. Green. After financial difficulties precluded publication in 1912, a final volume was published in 1913 covering the two previous years. **DU**
Sources: Altholz 1989, Isichei 1970, *ODNB, Waterloo.*

ANNUALS Early Victorian annuals were a departure from the publishing tradition of pocket books, diaries and almanacs which stretched back into the eighteenth century. Often called 'Books of Beauty', these lavishly produced volumes were notable for their high-quality engravings* and expensive bindings rather than for the quality of the poetry*, short stories and articles which made up the letterpress. Ackerman's *Forget Me Not*, launched in 1823, began the boom in these volumes which lasted until the 1850s and included the *Keepsake, Fishers' Drawing Room Scrap Book* and *Heath's Book of Beauty* (1833-1847). Scorned by Wordsworth and Thackeray*, who nevertheless contributed to them, the financial rewards and publishing opportunities they offered were also taken up by many women writers* and editors*, including Lady Blessington* (editor of the *Keepsake*, 1841 to 1850), Caroline Norton*, Laetitia Landon, Sarah Ellis, Mary Howitt*,

Adelaide Proctor, Mary Russell Mitford and Felicia Hemans. Often produced at Christmas*, the market for these 'Books of Beauty' dwindled from the mid-century. Some annuals adopted a specific focus, notably the landscape and comic annuals*. Landscape series exploited the popularity of topographical prints, but unlike the 'Books of Beauty' that also utilized prints, the accompanying text belonged to the genre of travel writing rather than those of sentimental poetry* and romantic fiction. The best known of these are *Heath's Picturesque Annual* (1832-1845), for which Leitch Ritchie was a major supplier of the letterpress, and Jenning's *Landscape Annual* series (1830-1839) with letterpress by Thomas Roscoe. Roscoe's sister, Mary Anne Jevons, edited another annual genre, an inexpensive pocket annual of religious* poetry, the *Sacred Offering*, during the 1830s. Of the two important comic annuals of the early period, both of which employed woodcuts* rather than steel engravings, Tom Hood's* *Comic Annual* and Louisa Sheridan's* *Comic Offering*, the former survived, albeit in much more modest format. With some gaps it lasted almost to the end of the century, making it the longest lasting of the original annuals. Hood's son Tom edited later editions.

The early children's* annuals, like the comic annuals, left distinct legacies to Victorian publishing. The children's annuals, usually produced by editors of adult titles, like *Ackermann's Juvenile Keepsake* (Thomas Roscoe, 1829) and the *Juvenile Forget Me Not* (Anna Maria Hall*, 1829-1834) had emulated the adult versions in their elegant bindings and lavish illustrations*. Their legacy was the popularity of Christmas annuals well into the twentieth century. While some later Victorian titles such as the *Girl's Own* Annual were simply attractively bound editions of the year's magazine issues, others were specially produced. *Peter Parley's Annual: a Christmas or New Year's present for young people* (Simpkin, Marshall & Co*) ran from 1842 until 1883. Annuals from the 1860s onwards were usually special Christmas* editions of magazines like *Belgravia*, often with a seasonal flavour, illustrated, though lacking the elegance and extravagant bindings, and priced accordingly. Sam Beeton's* startling advertising* for *Beeton's Annuals* became legendary. By the 1890s, annuals and special Christmas numbers were virtually the same genre. At the end of the century, some local* journals in the north began producing holiday or seaside annuals modelled on the Christmas version, as did the Manchester-based *Ben Brierley's Journal*, for example.

In addition to these, numerous societies, including missionary* societies and church groups, as well as women's groups produced annual reports or calendars in which they gave an account of their work over the year. These sometimes included detailed accounts and reports of annual conferences but were not aimed at the general reader*. **BMO/MRB**
Sources: Boyle 1967, Harris online, Hoagwood and Ledbetter online, Ledbetter and Hoagwood 2005, Renier 1964.

ANONYMITY AND SIGNATURE Inherited from the eighteenth-century periodical, the impersonality of the unsigned article remained the rule well into the Victorian period. By the turn of the twentieth century, however, editorial personality* had become a valued critical and commercial commodity, so that signature already represented the norm. This transformation aroused controversy and there were often animated debates on the subject, with both sides adamant that justice in book reviewing* was impossible with or without the cloak of anonymity. Edward Bulwer-Lytton* attacked journalistic impersonality in the *New Monthly Magazine** in November 1832 ('On Preserving the Anonymous in Periodicals'), while S. C. Hall*, Lytton's successor as editor, defended it in the same magazine in September 1833 ('On the Anonymous in Periodicals'). Anthony Trollope* was roundly against it in the *Fortnightly Review** in June 1865 ('On Anonymous Literature'), but seemed to have second thoughts in his *Autobiography* (1883). The first-person plural of impersonal journalism was defended for its dependence on collective authority and encouragement of judicial impartiality; the first-person singular of personal journalism for its promotion of critical honesty and reliance on individual integrity. Not that signature itself was always a transparent index of authorial identity, especially with literary matter and in popular periodicals: gender*, class* and calling could all be concealed or counterfeited by the imaginative use of initials, pseudonyms* and the like.

The transformation from anonymity to signature was also remarkably uneven, with the transition occurring at a different pace according to both genre of discourse and class of periodical. Before the mid-nineteenth century, verse, fiction*, and other narrative modes were much more likely to be signed than book reviews*, leaders* and other forms of critical writing. Strongly partisan magazines were much more likely to enforce anonymity than papers cultivating diversity of opinion. At the same time, the light monthly* miscellanies* and family* weeklies* were quicker to see the advantages of the named

contributor, while the venerable quarterlies*, weekly* reviews and established daily* newspapers long upheld the tradition of anonymity. (The editors of the first volume of the *Wellesley Index** estimated that, until 1870, around 97 per cent of articles in the periodicals they treated were unsigned.) *Macmillan's Magazine* (1859ff), the *Fortnightly Review* (1865ff), *Contemporary Review** (1866ff), and the *Nineteenth Century** (1877ff) were important pioneers in both the theory and practice of personalized criticism. The *Fortnightly Review* declared: 'Each contributor, in giving his name, will not only give an earnest of his sincerity, but will claim the privilege of perfect freedom of opinion, unbiased by the opinions of the Editor' (Maurer 1948). Later in the century, staunch advocates of the New Journalism* like W. T. Stead* and C. K. Shorter*, helped to promote a new style of journalistic personality with techniques such as the 'celebrity at home' interview* or the editorial crusade. As Stead put it in the *Contemporary Review** in November 1886: 'Impersonal journalism is effete. To influence men you must be a man, not a mock-uttering oracle. The democracy is under no awe of the mystic "We"' ('The Future of Journalism'). **GL**
Sources: Brake 1994, Maurer 1948, *Wellesley.*

ANSTED, DAVID THOMAS (1814-1880) After forging a successful academic career as a geologist, David Ansted was appointed assistant-secretary of the Geological Society in 1844, setting up the *Quarterly Journal of the Geological Society* which began publication in the following year, as well as serving as its editor*. However, in 1847 the Society's Council criticized Ansted for lack of diligence, prompting his resignation from his responsibilities. Throughout his career, Ansted supplemented his income from teaching and, from 1848, as a consulting mining engineer, by writing regularly for general periodicals, from the quarterly* *Analyst* in the late 1830s to the shilling monthlies* *Temple Bar**, *Macmillan's Magazine** and the *Cornhill Magazine** in the 1860s, where he treated subjects as diverse as colour blindness and volcanoes in a lively and accessible way. Ansted also wrote for Henry James Slack's* *Intellectual Observer* and contributed extensively to the *Popular Science Review* during the editorships of James Samuelson* and Henry Lawson in the 1860s and 1870s. **GD**
Sources: Lightman 2004a, *ODNB.*

ANSTIE, FRANCIS EDMUND (1833-1874) Best known for research on alcohol and neuralgia, Anstie's medical* journalism for periodicals such as the *Lancet** and his editorship of the *Practitioner*

influenced broader public health education and reforms. Anstie also wrote for general-interest journals such as *Macmillan's Magazine**; particularly well-received were several unsigned* educational articles on over-eating, corpulence, tobacco and alcohol, which appeared in the *Cornhill Magazine** under the editorship of W. M. Thackeray* in 1862-1863. Anstie was a frequent contributor to the *Lancet*, writing two reports on metropolitan and rural workhouse infirmaries that drew much attention and inspired improvements in Poor law medical services. With Henry Lawson, Anstie founded the *Practitioner* in 1868 to supply the lack of medical journalism on therapeutics; the journal quickly became embroiled in controversy about the administration of alcohol and hypodermic morphine. In 1869 Anstie became sole editor*, authoring virtually all of its reviews*. Anstie supported Sophia Jex-Blake's efforts to found a women's medical school, and would have been its dean but for his premature death. His passing was widely lamented as the loss of an influential public health advocate. **SZ**
Sources: Baldwin 1977, Buzzard 1876, *ODNB*, Rolleston and Thomson 1968, Zieger 2005.

ANSWERS TO CORRESPONDENTS (1888-1955) The first press venture of the youthful Alfred Harmsworth (aged 22), the weekly*, illustrated* *Answers to Correspondents on Every Subject Under the Sun* was partially inspired by the popular 'Answers to Correspondents' departments in the Sunday* weeklies like *Lloyd's** and *Reynolds's**. Even more immediately the new title was intended to compete* with George Newnes's popular *Tit-Bits**, a lively compendium of short interesting stories, jokes and practical information. After five months a distinctive orange cover was added, Harmsworth promised to answer every question by post and publish the interesting ones; however he soon realized that the questions sent in were not very interesting and he changed the name to *Answers: a weekly journal of instruction and jokes* and followed the format* of *Tit-Bits*. Later he wrote in *Answers* that 'we are a sort of Universal Information Provider' (Wiener: 158), and indeed the short lively articles were on every subject imaginable from information about the far-flung colonies to how to ride a bicycle. Contributors included Robert Leighton who with his wife wrote some serial* fiction, William LeQueux and Marie Flora Barbara Connor.

Harmsworth's brother Henry was the financial arm of the project. The initial circulation* was 13,000 and within the first year this quadrupled. But Harmsworth wanted even larger sales, and he introduced the first of what was to be a hallmark of his very successful efforts to increase circulation of all his subsequent publications: a contest. This first one promised a £1 a week to the person who correctly guessed nearest the balance in the Bank of England on a particular day. Further ingenious conditions which functioned as advertising* were attached: each entrant had to clip a coupon from *Answers* and have it signed by at least four persons. The number of contestants was around 718,000. Circulation of the paper increased to 200,000 a week. Within four years of its first issue, circulation was over a million copies a week. This success with *Answers* gave Harmsworth the capital to fund his subsequent ventures – specifically his purchase of the *Evening News* in 1894. AH

Sources: *Columbia Encyclopedia 1983, New York Times 1922, ODNB, Waterloo*, Wiener 1988.

ANSWERS/ADVICE TO READERS Throughout the nineteenth century a column* of 'Answers' to readers' queries was an element in a range of titles. Unlike the letters* pages with their exchange of views, 'Answers columns' usually consisted of didactic advice from an authoritative editorial figure. For most of the century and, in papers ranging from the *Family Friend* to the *Boys' Own Paper**, the questions were not printed, only the answers. It is, therefore, difficult to distinguish these 'Answers' from Advice columns and indeed by the end of the century the two were usually completely integrated, particularly in magazines addressed to women*. Philp's* mid-century *Family Friend* was an important example of a journal which made an 'Answers' section central to its project. Dividing his putative readership* into different family members enabled Philp to provide a range of advice and information, although the context was domestic* and the implicit readership predominantly female. Alfred Harmsworth* remade the tradition of 'Answers' in the context of the New Journalism* when he launched his immensely successful weekly*, *Answers to Correspondents on Every Subject under the Sun* (shortened to *Answers* in 1889), in a bid for the new mass* readership* of men and women who were buying Newnes's* *Tit-Bits**.

It was magazines targeting women and young people that were most enthusiastic about providing space for answers to readers' queries. In the first half of the century ladies' magazines* like *La Belle Assemblée** and the *New Monthly Belle Assemblée* (1834-1870), which encouraged readers to provide copy, used the 'Answers' column' for notes of acceptance and rejection. Both the *Lady's Magazine** (from 1770) and the *Lady's Museum* (1798-1832) ran advice columns by 'The Matron' or 'Mrs. Grey' and 'The Old Woman', purporting to respond to readers, but there was never any evidence of letters. The mid-century middle-class women's magazines, by contrast, made the Answers/ Advice column, on domestic issues, central to their success. Samuel Beeton's* *English Woman's Domestic Magazine** (from 1852) began with two; 'Cupid's Letter Bag' was rapidly absorbed into 'The Englishwoman's Conversazione', which became very popular. Readers' questions were given here but always subsumed into the authoritative voice of the editor, one exception to this being the controversial correspondence about corsets and whipping which Beeton claimed was all written by readers. From the 1850s, 'Advice' in the form of 'Answers' became an element of a whole range of women's magazines* including popular fashion journals* like *Myra's Journal**.

By the 1880s and 1890s, 'Answers and Advice' columns in many women's magazine had become divided into sections on 'Dress', 'Recipes', 'Health and Beauty', 'Home Furnishing', 'the Nursery' and so on. These were a staple of magazines from the 1d *Woman** and *Home Chat** through the more up-market *Hearth and Home**, where Mrs Talbot Coke's* advice became so voluminous that it was published as a supplement*. The persona of the advice giver was important and the emergence of a more sympathetic figure prefiguring the twentieth-century 'agony aunt' was evident in *Woman at Home** where Annie Swan's* advice columns apparently drew thousands of letters. She also exemplified the trend to publish letters from readers rather than simply give answers but this practice was still relatively rare. Equally important and pervasive were 'Answers' and Advice' columns in magazines for young people. In the *Girl's Own Paper**, the 'Answers' column' could take up two of the issues' 16 pages and was divided into sections, headed for example (13 Oct. 1883) 'Educational', 'Housekeeping', 'Work'(mainly fancywork queries), 'Art', 'Cookery', 'Music' and 'Miscellaneous', the latter taking over four of the six columns. The *Boy's Own Paper**, too, made 'Answers', on a range of subjects an important one of its regular features. MRB

Sources: Beetham 1991, Beetham 1996.

ANTI-JACOBIN REVIEW AND MAGAZINE OR MONTHLY POLITICAL AND LITERARY CENSOR (1798-1821) 'John Gifford', the pseudonym* of John Richard Green, instigated and edited* the *Anti-Jacobin Review* when the unrelated William

Gifford's* *Anti-Jacobin, or, Weekly Examiner* folded in 1798. However, 'John Gifford', (editor* until 1818?) (Montluzin's more recent research claims he ceased editing in 1806; the second editor is unknown) confirmed that the 2s 6d monthly *Review* would function in the same vein as its predecessor by evaluating the press, especially the *Monthly, Critical* and *Analytical* Reviews*. The collective hysteria of the Establishment in response to the French Revolution and fears of a similar event in England provided propitious ground for the *Anti-Jacobin Review* to appeal to the prejudices of a Tory, Protestant readership*. What the *Review* interpreted as the Jacobin agenda of atheism, anarchic politics and dissolute morals provided a potent mix for its aggressive sensationalism.

The purported Jacobin threat provided the journal with a rationale for denouncing all radicalism, hence non-conformists, abolitionists, Catholic emancipators, educationists and advocates of the labouring poor were in its sights. Mary Wollstonecraft was no better than a prostitute, the Peterloo Massacre was justified and 'Jacobinical' poets, Byron, Coleridge and their, like were condemned, although its vow to despatch hypocrisy meant that aristocratic excesses were also targeted.

Gifford and Andrew Bissett produced a good deal of its extensive copy, with many unsigned* contributions, while in its early years illustrations* were provided by James Gillray*. With the subtitle *True Churchman's Magazine* appended in 1810, increased numbers of named clergymen boosted its religious* content. From 1816, it was entitled the *Anti-jacobin Review, and Protestant Advocate*. CL
Sources: Montluzin 2003, *ODNB*, Sullivan 1983, *Waterloo*.

APPERLEY, CHARLES JAMES (1778-1843) Charles James Apperley was among the leading sports* journalists* of his day. An ardent sportsman from youth, he began his career as a writer in 1821, contributing to the *Sporting Magazine*. He travelled and reported on hunting tours, horse races, and other events, quickly establishing himself as chief correspondent. From 1822 on, he signed his work 'Nimrod', a pen name that became highly marketable in the field of sporting literature. Insofar as popularity with readers is concerned, 'Nimrod' may be grouped with such nineteenth-century sports writers as Charles Bindley*, and Thomas R. Potter*. According to Apperley's own account, annual circulation* of the *Sporting Magazine* doubled after he became a contributor (Nimrod 1927: 197). His relationship with the publication grew troubled after the

death of the original owner, however, and in 1827 he broke his exclusive contract in order to accept an invitation from the *Quarterly Review** to write a series of articles, later published as *The Chase, the Turf, and the Road*. When a legal battle with the *Sporting Magazine* over unpaid debts forced Apperley to take up residence in France, he began writing for the magazine's rivals, the *New Sporting Magazine** and the *Sporting Review**, as well as the *New Monthly Magazine**, the *Edinburgh Review**, *Fraser's Magazine** and *Encyclopaedia Britannica*. A prolific and energetic journalist*, he also wrote for newspapers, including *The Times**, the *Morning Herald** and the *Country Herald*.

Although Apperley's writing reveals a passion for sport and careful attention to detail, some critics considered his style to be prolix and overburdened with Latin references. In R. S. Surtees's novel *Handley Cross* (1839), the 'classical stableman', Pomponius Ego, is a caricature of Nimrod. Yet it is a testimony to Apperley's popularity that many of his writings were reprinted in book form. His two best known books, *The Life of John Mytton* (1837) and *The Life of a Sportsman* (1842), were both originally published serially in the *New Sporting Magazine*. These works, the former a biography, the latter a 'half-true, half-fictitious' sporting novel are most interesting for their depictions of the lifestyle of the early nineteenth-century gentleman sportsman. Apperley's autobiography, *My Life and Times* (1920), first published in instalments in *Fraser's Magazine* in 1842, likewise sheds light on the sporting world of this period and describes Apperley's negotiations as a professional writer, providing an insight into the world of periodical journalism. NN
Sources: Nimrod 1903, Nimrod 1927, *ODNB*, Surtees 1854.

APPLEGATH, AUGUSTUS (1788-1871), COWPER, EDWARD SHICKLE (1790-1852) In 1816, Augustus Applegath, printer, and his brother-in-law Edward Cowper, a printing engineer and university teacher, founded the firm of Applegath and Cowper for the construction and improvement of printing machinery*. In 1818, the firm was employed by *The Times** to improve the printing machine developed by the German engineer Friedrich Koenig.

Applegath and Cowper began their careers by being apprenticed to the stationer William Cornish, in Covent Garden. In 1813, after the death of Cornish, they took over their master's printing firm with another employee, Henry Mitton, who left the partnership in 1817. Applegath and Cowper's first innovation was in developing a method of printing banknotes so that they could not be forged. Although the Bank of England withdrew its support for the scheme, the partners were employed by Thomas Bensley and John Walter*, proprietors* of *The Times*, to supervise and improve their Koenig printing machine. The partners used some of their own patented devices, removing imperfections and improving the inking mechanism. However, it is uncertain whether Cowper remained in the partnership after the Bank of England episode. William Savage, in his *Dictionary of the Art of Printing* (1841: 465), credits Applegath alone for developing 'the mechanism by which *The Times* is now printed'.

After he had left the partnership, Cowper claimed that he was partly responsible for the improvements and by 1820 he had set up as a consulting engineer with his younger brother, Ebenezer. The firm was based in Manchester, although Cowper continued to live in London. Trading as E. and E. Cowper, they manufactured and installed printing machines throughout Europe. In 1827 they brought out for *The Times* a new steam-powered 'multiple' printing machine. Applegath, meanwhile, continued to develop more productive printing machines. By 1826 he was in financial difficulties, and in the following year gave up printing machine manufacture and concentrated on silk-printing at a factory in Cranford, Kent. He returned to his first interest at the request of *The Times*, producing further improved machines in 1846 and 1847. Despite the success of his machines, Applegath was twice declared bankrupt, in 1826 and 1842, yet the technical improvements made by him and Cowper assisted *The Times* in gaining the largest circulation* of any newspaper in Britain. DHL

Sources: Moran 1973, *ODNB*, Savage 1841.

APPLETON, CHARLES EDWARD CUTTS BIRCHALL (1841-1879) Charles Appleton made his major contribution to history with the founding of the *Academy: A Monthly Record of Literature, Learning, Science and Art**. As Appleton wrote in the 22 October 1870 issue, the purpose of the *Academy* was to be an intellectual endeavour that would 'neither praise indiscriminately nor blame from pique or prejudice'. Initially, John Murray III* was the publisher* and Appleton co-owner and editor*, but in October 1870 after a quarrel between Murray and Appleton over advertisements*, Appleton became sole owner of the journal and remained editor until close to his death, when, in the latter part of

1878, Charles E. Doble became interim editor. By 1874 it was published weekly*.

Prior to and during his editorship of the *Academy*, Appleton also contributed articles to the *Contemporary Review**, the *Spectator** and the *Theological Review**, several dealing with the need and the value of scholarly research in universities and the economic aspect of endowment for research. Also after a four-month visit to the United States and Canada in the fall of 1875, where he was entertained by the American writers Mark Twain, Ralph Waldo Emerson and Oliver Wendell Holmes, Appleton wrote for the *Fortnightly Review** (Feb. 1877) on the question of international copyright.

Breaking with the majority of the nineteenth-century periodicals that adhered to the tradition of anonymity* of contributors, the *Academy* published the full names of all of the reviewers so that, as Appleton wrote in the 22 October 1870 statement, the reader could take into account 'the honesty and competence of the reviewer'. Although the quantity of his periodical contributions is not large, Appleton, through those contributions and his editorship of the *Academy*, demonstrated his devotion to the encouragement of learning and scholarship in the nineteenth century. WS

Sources: Appleton and Sayce 1881, *ODNB*, Roll-Hansen 1957, *Waterloo*.

ARCHAEOLOGICAL JOURNAL (1844-) The *Archaeological Journal* was first published in March 1844 by Longman, Brown, Green and Longman* as the quarterly* organ of the newly formed British Archaeological Association (BAA), its issuing body*. In format it was modelled on the quarterly* reviews; though it was heavily illustrated*, articles were signed* and at 2s 6d, it was cheaper in price*. Its purpose was to spread 'antiquarian information and maintain [...] a constant communication with all persons interested in' archaeology ('Abstract of Proposed Rules' inserted into issue 1). The following year a substantial number of members split from the BAA and formed the Archaeological Institute, later given its royal epithet in 1866. They took with them the rights to the *Journal*. By 1849, the Institute had nearly 1,000 members and the *Archaeological Journal* was rapidly establishing a reputation for wide-ranging and scholarly articles on the antiquities, principally of the British Isles. These might be general surveys of particular types of monuments or detailed examinations of individual sites, studies of standing buildings and monuments or reports of archaeological excavations. Shorter notes and book reviews* were also present from the first. Contributors included William Jerdan*, who stressed that 'the only true republics impervious to "class" doubt and censure' (Dec. 1844: 298) were institutions such as the Association. Until the second half of the twentieth century, the date range spanned from prehistory to the end of the medieval period. Detailed reports of the places visited during the annual Summer Meetings, published in or with the subsequent journals, established and still retain a reputation for providing valuable surveys of the topography, archaeology and building history of the locations visited. JoC

Sources: *Archaeological Journal*, Waterloo.

ARCHER, JOHN WYKEHAM (1808-1864) Engraver, watercolourist and topographical illustrator*, John Wykeham Archer was born in Newcastle, but moved to London in 1820 where he was apprenticed to the animal engraver John Scott. By 1827 he had returned to Newcastle, where he worked as an engraver in partnership with William Collard. Archer appears to have also worked in Edinburgh before returning to London in 1831, when he worked for engravers William and Edward Finden. He remained in London until his death.

Archer's skill in both steel and wood* engraving enabled him to survive the upheavals in the engraving industry during the late 1830s, when steel engraving was largely abandoned in favour of wood. Alongside high-quality illustrated books, Archer contributed engravings to many popular periodicals, most notably the *New Sporting Magazine**, the *Illustrated London News**, *Douglas Jerrold's Shilling Magazine** and the *Gentleman's Magazine**. In later life he favoured watercolours over engraving, becoming an ARWS in 1842. Archer gained a reputation for illustrations of topographical and architectural antiquaries in and around London, and was approached by collector William Twopenny, who commissioned a great many paintings from Archer, as well as illustrations for *William Twopenny's Magazine*. In his final years Archer composed poetry*, and in 1862 he contributed an article on J. M. W. Turner to the magazine *Once a Week**. MBT

Sources: Boase 1965, Houfe 1996, *ODNB*, Pinks 1865.

ARCHIVES A complex material record of the workings of Victorian periodicals can sometimes be found in their literary and commercial archives. This may include: office books or marked copies bearing the names of contributors, files of correspondence* with authors and subscribers, production ledgers listing print runs and paper orders, double-entry account books itemizing costs of pro-

duction and taxation as well as income from advertising* and sales, the minutes of editorial and business meetings, etc. Sadly, few such archives have been preserved and even fewer have been kept in complete form. Records are frequently lost during removal, change of ownership, closure or negligence; they are often destroyed to save space and upkeep, or through lack of appreciation of their value; and they are often destroyed by fire, flood or military action. Luck can also play a part, as with the survival of the invaluable office book revealing the identities of the anonymous* contributors to Charles Dickens's* *Household Words**, but this is not the case with *All the Year Round**.

Archives can be maintained by the proprietors* of the periodical, as with *The Times* of London, in local libraries, such as the *Bolton Evening News*, or in academic institutions which is the case of the *Aberdeen Journal**. Not infrequently with literary publishers* of periodicals such as Bentley*, archival records have been dispersed to a number of different locations. **GL**

Sources: Eliot 1994, Sharpweb, Victorian Research, Weedon 2003.

ARGOSY (1865-1901) Alexander Strahan* of Strahan and Company modelled the *Argosy*, a shilling monthly*, on the successful *Cornhill Magazine**. Its selections were often adventure and travel-oriented in keeping with the theme of an argosy, or ship, filled with a rich cargo. Its high-powered list of contributors included Frances Power Cobbe*, Margaret Oliphant*, Bessie Rayner Parkes*, Christina Rossetti and Anthony Trollope*. After the serialization of Charles Reade's controversial 'Griffith Gaunt' (1866) in the first two volumes, the number of famous contributors declined in volumes three and four and Strahan sold the periodical to Ellen Price (Mrs. Henry) Wood* in 1867. Wood's son Charles published the magazine until 1871 when Bentley and Sons* stepped in.

Wood's public image as a private, domestic woman allowed her to restore propriety to the magazine. Because she balanced womanly restraint with a sense of excitement that came with being known as one of the founders of sensation fiction, Wood could both squelch controversy and generate interest. Her achievement is evident in the *Argosy's* average monthly circulation* of 20,000. This figure exceeded the 16,000 average circulation of Mary Elizabeth Braddon's* *Belgravia Magazine**, with which the *Argosy* directly competed* as an outlet for the fiction of a major sensation novelist. Like Braddon, Wood used her magazine as a vehicle for establishing sensationalism as a respectable literary form.

Wood wrote much of the *Argosy's* contents herself, including the important review* section, 'Our Log-Book'. Wood's most famous contributions are her 'Johnny Ludlow' stories, based on her childhood experiences in Worcestershire and the detective novel 'Roland Yorke' (1869). Julia Kavanagh, Alice King and Hesba Stretton were regular contributors. Charles Wood, who had served as the magazine's business manager, took over editorial duties upon his mother's death in 1887. He published portions of his *Memorials of Mrs. Henry Wood* (1894) in the magazine as well as his own travel writings. JJP

Sources: Ellegård 1957, Elwin 1966, Maunder 2000, Phegley 2005, Wood 1894.

ARNOLD, EDWIN (1832-1904) During his 40-year association with the *Daily Telegraph** Edwin Arnold effected a decisive shift in the newspaper's political affiliations and helped transform British journalism by persuading his proprietors* to fund a series of 'missions' to Africa and the East.

The newspaper Arnold joined on returning from India in 1861 was popular* and liberal; its best-known names were Thornton Leigh Hunt* and Matthew Arnold's* *bête noire* George Augustus Sala*. Both as a leader* writer and later (1873-1889) as editor*, Arnold helped the *Telegraph* 'cross the floor' to the conservative and pro-imperial* side. This reorientation was prompted both by the romantic orientalism apparent in *The Light of Asia* (1879), Arnold's epic poem on the founder of Buddhism, and by his sympathy with adventurers and explorers. He is said to have suggested the idea, later popularized by Cecil Rhodes, of a 'Cape-to-Cairo railway'; and he persuaded Edward Levy-Lawson*, the *Telegraph's* proprietor*, to help fund Henry Morton Stanley's second journey to Africa.

On giving up the post of editor, Arnold became a kind of roving correspondent for the newspaper; his fascination with the East produced several articles on Indian and Japanese life and customs, some of which were eventually republished in book form. JPP

Sources: Arnold 1945, Burnham 1955, *ODNB*, Pebody 1882, Peiris 1970.

ARNOLD, MATTHEW (1822-1888) It is difficult to overestimate the level of Matthew Arnold's engagement with nineteenth-century journalism*, despite the common portrayal of him as a proponent of high culture, completely removed from anything ephemeral. Arnold was a major contributor to a number of influential periodicals, including *Fraser's**, *Macmillan's Magazine**, *Cornhill**, the *Contemporary Review**, the *Quarterly Review** and the *Fortnightly Review**. His essay 'The Function of Criticism at the Present Time' first appeared in the *National Review** (Nov. 1864), and material later reprinted in works such as *Culture and Anarchy* (1869) and *Literature and Dogma* (1873) first appeared in the pages of the *Cornhill**.

Arnold was well aware of the commercial value of printing articles in periodicals first before reproducing them in books. In addition to the numerous articles he published in the periodical press, a number of Arnold's poems* began life in journals. 'Stanzas from the Grande Chartreuse' appeared in *Fraser's** in April 1855, while *Thyrsis* was published in *Macmillan's** in April 1866. As well as contributing to a range of periodicals, Arnold's thought and ideas were the source of much discussion by other critics. His importance as a cultural critic who was thoroughly immersed in the developments of nineteenth-century journalism is epitomized by the role that he played in helping coin the term 'new journalism**. In 'Up to Easter', an essay published in the *Nineteenth Century** in May 1887, Arnold criticized the 'feather-brained' New Journalism of W. T. Stead*. MK

Sources: Bell 2002, Campbell 2004, Hughes 2007a, Sullivan, *Wellesley.*

ART JOURNAL (1839-1912) The *Art Journal* has been described as 'a long-lived mirror of contemporary taste and practice in the graphic arts'. The period's leading art journal was launched as a three-column*, quarto, 16-page monthly* in 1839 as the *Art-Union: A Monthly Journal of the Fine Arts*. Its aim was to make high-quality illustrations* available to the general public at a low price*. It carried a healthy amount of advertising* from the start, four pages out of 16 in its first number. Appearing mid-month until June 1841, it explained its switch to the first of the month as related to poor distribution by booksellers, who failed to remember its anomalous mid-month issue until the end of the month, with the appearance of the other monthlies. Costing 8d at the start, it was 2s 6d by 1851, but then for a longer, profusely illustrated and grander folio issue, which had first appeared in a new series from 1849. In that year it claimed a monthly circulation* of 15,000. By January 1851, the 'Art-Journal Advertiser' was 30 pages.

In the first nine years of its existence, the journal had struggled to survive, but after being renamed the *Art-Journal* in 1849, it finally became a popular success. An important factor in its rising popularity appears to have been the permission granted by the wealthy art collector Robert Vernon to publish engravings* made after items in his collection. Popular images from private owners such as Thomas Williams, George Fox and George McCulloch also frequently provided the sources for engravings, which were always a major feature of the journal until colour plates eventually took over. By 1875 (Vol. 37) it had become simply the *Art Journal,* having lost the hyphen that had invoked its original hyphenated title and issuing body*, which was still advertised in its pages.

The founder and long-time editor*, Samuel Carter Hall* held the firm moral conviction that 'a collection of pictures helps to thin our poorhouses and prisons and men to whom public galleries are open will be seldom found in public houses'. He was a keen promoter of English art – though not of the pre-Raphaelites to whom he was deeply unsympathetic – whose life's work it was to instill a sense of aesthetic awareness in his middle-class* readers*. *Art Journal* regularly featured items on Art in the Provinces, Art in the Continental States and Picture Sales. Between 1850 and 1880, the Victorian taste for the Middle Ages was prominently reflected in the journal in articles written by noted antiquarians such as Thomas Wright, Frederick William Fairholt and Edward Lewes Cutts.

In 1851, a catalogue printed to support the Great Exhibition proved a financial disaster and Hall was forced to sell his interest and accept an editor's salary. His alleged sanctimoniousness made him the model for Dickens's* Pecksniff in *Martin Chuzzlewit*. Hall did not retire until 1880, after which the journal went into a steady decline, as it no longer managed to meet the demand for a wider, international orientation. It finally folded in 1912, having had to give way to more forward-looking publications like the *Burlington Magazine* and *Connoisseur*. **OD**

Sources: Landow 1979, Macleod 1998, Robertson 1978, Sutherland 1990, *Waterloo*.

ARTIST AND JOURNAL OF HOME CULTURE (1880-1902) The *Artist* began as a London-based, 6d trade 'literary' monthly*, targeted at a wide range of artists and artisans; not illustrated*, it retained its low price* until 1894. Its first publisher* and printer was William Reeves, the art supplies retailer. Nurturing a bohemian independence of mainstream art politics, it instantly included women among its readers, reporting on a 'Female School of Art' in the first issue and developing a column*,

'Art in the House', which became the 'Ladies' Column'. This was consolidated in January 1881 by adding to the title *and Journal of Home Culture*. This imbrication in gender* issues was characteristic.

Beside a monthly 'Kalendar', the *Artist* contained news about developments in the art and artisan worlds, obituaries*, features on individual artists in their studios and art gossip*. In 1887-1888 a barrister, Charles Kains-Jackson, began a stint as anonymous* editor* that lasted until 1894, when he was sacked. Consistently embedding articles of interest to male, homosocial readers, he displaced the earlier address to women. Domestic arts were now associated with Wilde*, Frederic Leighton* and Beardsley*. The incidence of poetry* rose under Jackson, who published Horatio Brown, Laurence Housman*, Edward Sayle and H. S. Tuke. Other notable contributors included Alfred Douglas, John Gray, J. G. Nicholson, André Raffalovich, Fr. Rolfe, J. A. Symonds, Gleeson White* and Theodore Wratislaw. The prose of J. A. Symonds and the paintings of Tuke, two 'gay' heroes, were repeatedly featured. In April 1894, Kains-Jackson wrote and published 'The New Chivalry', a prompt response to Grant Allen's* 'The New Hedonism' (*Fortnightly Review,* March 1894). Remarkably explicit in his reasoned advocacy of same-sex culture, Jackson clinched the policy of the *Artist* under his editorship.

From May 1894 a homoerotic purge, a change of ownership and editor (to Viscount Mountmorres, editor May-Sept. 1894), a transformation of format and a turn to the applied arts ensued, which a new title in October demonstrates: '*Artist: Photographer and Decorator. An Illustrated Monthly Journal of Applied Art*. In January 1897 the title change* to the *Artist, an illustrated monthly record of arts, crafts and industries* indicates how crucial illustration was to its continuity, due to new rivals such as the *Studio** and the *Yellow Book**, and the increasing importance of graphics in periodicals. Its formal association with the art schools of England also aided survival. From 1898 the *Artist* blossomed into syndicated* New York and Paris editions. **LRB**

Sources: Brake 2000, Brake 2001, D'Arch Smith 1970, Fletcher 1979, *Waterloo*.

ASSOCIATED PRESS The world's longest-running press agency*, Associated Press began in 1846 when the publisher of the *New York Sun** offered to pool reporting resources of the Mexican war with rival newspapers in order to reduce costs. Four other major newspapers joined the scheme: the *Journal of Commerce*, the *Courier and Enquirer*, the *New*

York Herald and the *Express*. Two years later, these collaborating newspapers formed the Harbour News Association and were shortly joined by two further newspapers, the *New York Tribune* and the *New York Times*, who agreed to formalise arrangements for the joint telegraphic* transmission of news in 1851 under the co-operative title, the New York Associated Press. The American Civil War was the first war to be reported in the US in realtime with reporters using anonymous* AP by-lines to avoid censorship* laws. In July 1866, a telegraph* cable was successfully installed between North America and Europe transmitting eight words a minute and ushering in a bold new age of international news* coverage. LL

Source: Associated Press Archive.

ATALANTA (1887-1898) *Atalanta*, a 6d monthly* illustrated* magazine, was successor to *Every Girl's Magazine* (1877-1888). Under its first editor*, L. T. Meade*, *Atalanta* became an ambitious, advanced periodical for girls and young women. Besides printing her own work, Meade secured serials*, articles and short fiction from writers such as Frances Hodgson Burnett, Grant Allen*, H. Rider Haggard, John Strange Winter*, Amy Levy and Walter Besant*. An educational* feature was the department of the journal called 'Scholarship and Reading Union'; it had articles on literature: Anne Thackeray on Jane Austen, Mary Ward on E. B. Browning, Charlotte Yonge* on John Keble, Andrew Lang* on Walter Scott. Each was followed by essay questions; readers* who paid 5s a year received comments on their essays and competed annually for a £30 scholarship. Authoritative practical advice on careers came from Millicent Garrett Fawcett* on the civil service, Dr Edith Huntley on medicine, Agnes Garrett on house decoration.

The quality declined after Alexander Balfour Symington became editor in December 1892 and incorporated his lady's *Victorian Magazine* (1891-1892) into *Atalanta*. In 1894 the cover changed: Atalanta is seated instead of winning a race. Edwin Oliver, editing the final two volumes, had fewer distinguished contributors, although *Atalanta* authors included Margaret Oliphant*, Evelyn Sharp and Edith Nesbit even then. SMM

Sources: Ashley 2006, Mitchell 1995.

ATHENAEUM (1828-1921) The *Athenaeum, London Literary and Critical Journal* was launched as a cultural weekly* in January 1828 with its professed aim to become 'the resort of the distinguished philosophers, historians, orators and poets of our day'. But the journal only achieved that status when Charles Wentworth Dilke* became its new editor* in 1830. Dilke wanted the *Athenaeum* to take a stand against the practice of puffery* then all-pervasive in literary criticism. He secured experts who would present him with objective reviews* of new books in the fields covered by the subtitle of the journal: *literature*, *science*, *fine arts, music and drama*. Contributors under Dilke were Henry* and John Chorley*, Charles Dance and George Darley (drama), Lady Morgan, Allan Cunningham (art), W. Cooke Taylor (education, religion) and Geraldine Jewsbury*. Among the best-known poets* whose verses he published, one finds Elizabeth Barrett Browning, Christina Rossetti, Felicia Hemans, John Clare and James Hogg.

When T. K. Hervey became the new editor in 1846, the *Athenaeum* had become one of the most influential papers of its day. Under Hervey and his successor Hepworth Dixon* (from 1853), however, the journal lost some of its prestige when certain reviews* seemed to reflect deeply ingrained prejudices and there was evidence of log-rolling. A third Dilke, the politician Sir Charles Wentworth Dilke, inherited the weekly in 1869. He had ambitious plans for it and, indeed, under the editorship of his friend, Norman MacColl*, the journal flourished for the next three decades. One of the remarkable policy changes under the new editor was his effort to draw in such expert women as Augusta Webster, Millicent Garrett Fawcett*, Mathilde Blind*, Rosamund Marriott Watson*, Vernon Lee*, Jane Ellen Harrison*, Marie Stopes, Edith Nesbit, Mary and Mabel Robinson and Katharine De Mattos*. Well-known male reviewers of the period were Andrew Lang*, George Saintsbury*, Theodor Watts-Dunton*, Karl Pearson*, Sidney Low, Sidney Lee and W. M. Rossetti*.

The *Athenaeum* under MacColl also played a major role in contemporary controversies such as the one instigated by Robert Buchanan against the 'Fleshly School of Poetry'* (*Contemporary Review*) when Dante Gabriel Rossetti chose to publish his riposte 'The Stealthy School of Criticism' in the *Athenaeum* in December 1871. It was also the chosen forum for influential scientists such as the archaeologist and discoverer of Troy, Heinrich Schliemann, who published lengthy, signed articles there in 1874.

From 1901 to 1916 the weekly was edited by the fairly unremarkable Vernon Rendall and, again, the weekly went into decline. During the last two years of the war, the *Athenaeum* became a monthly*; then, in 1919, John Middleton Murry*, was

N° 1476, Feb. 9, '56 THE ATHENÆUM 173

ing through the streets, constitutes the whole fun. An Englishman looks with extreme surprise—some contempt, I am afraid, and some little envy, I suspect—at a fellow-creature, come to man's estate, who can manufacture a day's exulting happiness out of half-a-dozen yards of red calico. The streets are now full of a boisterously joyous population of young men and maidens, old men and children, whose entire material of happiness is — calico. Despite troubles of all sorts within doors—short crops and short commons, and all the woes of "*serva Italia di dolore ostello*," out of doors carnival is once more carnival. "Regardless of their doom the little victims play,"—and who would be guilty of a falsehood at once so cruel and so absurd as to "tell them they are men"? T. A. T.

Paris, January.

As you are one of the few persons in England who appear to recollect the abject state of the Press in France, or to feel the slightest sympathy with the crushed intelligence of this country, you must permit me to express my surprise on finding in a former number of your journal decorations or distinctions conferred by the French ruler spoken of as objects worthy the desire or fitted for the acceptance of Englishmen, or, indeed, of men of any country who rate the labours and utterances of the mind of man above the force of armies or the magnificence of palaces or cities.

I would fain hope that you will reconsider this subject. I can assure you that many of the most enlightened and most eminent men in this country are fully alive to the bad effects resulting from the attempt, on the part of Governments, to confer reputation. Governments, when they do not run counter to public opinion in their estimate of individuals, can only confirm it. And how poor is that confirmation compared to the voice of which it is the feeble echo! Some illustrious men have, it is true, had the weakness of coveting these futile distinctions; but, in general, the higher a man's real claims to fame, the less will he value or covet factitious distinctions. Ask Mr. Hallam and Mr. Grote if it ever entered their heads to desire a decoration, or if they would not think it a sort of impertinence to affect to put a stamp on such merit as theirs?

A great objection to Orders of Merit and the like, is, their inevitable tendency to confound and level all degrees of merit. This is strongly felt wherever they are used. It is utterly impossible to have *nuances* of decoration for all the infinite shades and sorts of merit which a cultivated and exercised public opinion could alone discriminate and reward. Even in its present *un*cultivated and unrefined state, public opinion does, as in the case of the eminent men I have just mentioned, award to the highest the highest place, and to lesser stars a feebler glory. This process—so salutary to a people, so honourable to its eminent men—can only be retarded or perverted by the interference of a power so liable to abuse.

A very different thing is the duty, so deplorably neglected by the public and the people of England, of providing for men who devote themselves to severe and unremunerative studies, the means of labouring in peace. This duty has been fully recognized only in Germany, — where, out of small resources, means are found to support men in the pursuit of science. Unfortunately, there, too, the performance of this great national duty is alloyed by the taste for orders and badges. But one would fain believe that Englishmen are not yet so entirely in love with military despotism, or with the triumphant compression of public opinion, as to regard a Government which demeans itself as that of France has done towards the organs of thought, as a fit awarder of judgments and a dispenser of honours in matters of intelligence.

A more melancholy part of the story remains to be stated,—namely, that the free Press is not regretted by the bulk of the French nation. If you talk with the manufacturers, tradesmen, and small proprietors of France, you will almost invariably get the same answer:—"Celà regarde Messieurs les hommes de lettres à Paris."—And then follows the too just remark:—"Ils ont trop abusé de la Presse"—"Ils ont fait beaucoup de mal," &c. &c., — undeniable truths, and well worthy the attention of all who are inclined to set in motion forces which they cannot control. I say it with equal confidence and sorrow, a free press is regarded by the majority of the middle and trading classes in France as a dangerous solvent or irritant of society,—as essentially *frondeur* and incompatible with peace and order. This, of course, relates chiefly to the newspaper press, and in so far is not entirely unjust. Unluckily, its excesses have furnished pretexts for acts of repression which extend into higher and more peaceful regions. Of this you, in England, know little—at least, I hope so;—for, if otherwise, the desertion of the great cause of intellectual freedom is worse than I like to believe it. Curiously enough, it is the most unbridled portion of the English press that has been most lavish in its adulation. The effect that this is calculated to produce here, I need hardly attempt to describe. Would that I could believe it could be transient! But it will not be transient. It has produced, and will leave, a feeling of alienation in the best and highest minds of France, which will certainly not be effaced in the generation now living.

An Anglo-Parisian.

Austin.

OUR WEEKLY GOSSIP.

The policy of founding an Order of Merit is once more occupying many minds. Lord Panmure has signed a warrant for the institution of a new badge "For Valour"—the Victoria Cross. The distinguished persons in London who have lately received honours from the hand of Napoleon the Third are preparing a memorial to the Queen on the subject of that old and wholesome rule which refused to recognize foreign decorations in England. The Lord Provost of Glasgow has caused inquiries to be made of Lord Clarendon whether the honours obtained by eminent Scotchmen at the Paris Exhibition may be worn in this country. Lastly, a Correspondent, who has a right to be heard on this or any other topic, has addressed to us, under the signature of "Anglo-Parisian," a letter of remonstrance against the reception in this country of Napoleonic decorations, which letter we have printed above. All these indications of interest in the subject are noticeable. Government has at length pronounced the words—a new Order of Merit. Its scheme, we must be allowed to say, is meagre. Why pronounce the Victoria Cross inferior to a C.B.? Why restrict it to the reward of valour? Is genius to go unrewarded? Is success to count for nothing? Why, too, omit Civil Service? This new Order is certainly not the decoration for which men of genius and men of distinguished attainments have been waiting. We still need the Order of Victoria—an Order open to all Englishmen. Until such an institution is founded we shall have agitations such as that arising from the award of honours in Paris. Our Correspondent, who writes against the reception of these decorations, feels strongly, and in the fervour of the moment mixes up two questions which are quite distinct:—the utility of Orders of Merit in the abstract, and the value of the Napoleonic decoration in particular. On both points we agree with our Correspondent when the necessary qualification is made. We think that all State Orders are needless, and we rate the Napoleonic decoration as of no value out of France. But we are not in a position to argue against Orders in the abstract. Such Orders exist. We meet them in every street. We find them prized. If the question of establishing a State Order of Merit were before us for the first time—if all men were simple citizens and titles were unknown—we should most assuredly raise our voice against Orders.

The literary public will hear with pleasure that the honour of knighthood has been conferred on Col. Henry Rawlinson. In another column of the *Athenæum* will be found an account of a new discovery—most interesting to the student of sacred history — made by this distinguished Oriental explorer.

The University of Dublin has conferred the honorary degree of LL.D. on Mr. W. H. Russell, the Special Correspondent of the *Times* newspaper in the Crimea.

We understand that the Deputy-Keeper of the Public Records, with a laudable anxiety to prevent improper access to the Records about to be deposited in the new buildings in Chancery Lane, has ordered as many different keys as there are different presses, and that the number amounts to many thousands—it is said, seven thousand. A very ingenious plan is also under consideration, by which the custody of the keys will be placed in different hands, and thus, it being difficult, if not impossible, to know who is the possessor of a particular key, the designs of improper persons will be baffled and their access to the Records rendered almost impracticable.

A Correspondent points out what he conceives to be an error on the part of those who deny that Jeffreys lies in the Tower—as Mr. Macaulay's readers might infer:—

I have not seen the *Times*, and know not therefore what is the exact error charged against Mr. Macaulay; but infer from the notice in other journals that Mr. Macaulay having stated that "the emaciated corpse [of Jeffreys] was laid, with all privacy, next to the corpse of Monmouth in the Chapel of the Tower," the *Times* treats this as an error and says Jeffreys was buried at St. Mary Aldermanbury. Mr. Macaulay is correct:—Jeffreys was buried in the Tower. Three years after burial—20th of September, 1692—a warrant was issued to authorize the Governor of the Tower to deliver up the body "of George, late Lord Jeffreys, to his friends and relations, to bury him as they think fit"; and under that warrant the body was removed, and, on the 2nd of November, re-interred at St. Mary Aldermanbury. D.

—No doubt, Mr. Macaulay is correct in his statement; but his statement, left incomplete, leads to an inference which is false. If a biographer of Blake or Cromwell should describe his hero as buried with regal pomp in Westminster Abbey, he would be quite right as to the literal fact. Yet he would undoubtedly mislead his reader. This, we take it, is the point urged against Mr. Macaulay.

The pictures still remain undisturbed on the walls of Mr. Rogers's house, with the exception of the three removed to the National Gallery. The sale will take place in Messrs. Christie & Manson's rooms, commencing, it is said, on Monday, April 28th. The extreme smallness of the house precludes the possibility of a sale on the spot, or of admitting a select portion of the public to view the collection in its original arrangement, even if the relatives were so disposed. The sale will probably last many days, as the prints and drawings are surprisingly numerous. Drawings by Turner, Stothard, and the old masters are too valuable to be sold in lots; and each object may, to use Mr. Rogers's own words, "become the sun of a little system." Expectation will be disappointed with regard to rare books and editions. Much as their late possessor knew and talked upon these matters, his library is more distinguished for Art-illustrations. Fine copies of large books of engravings, from Continental galleries, will be found in the choicest condition; but it is the Marc Antonios, the Dürers, the illuminated pages, which, hitherto condensed in portfolios, will make the display. Each, singly, must claim at least a line of the Catalogue, and will occupy no small time in the final competition. Among them will be found a series of drawings, by a scholar of Michael Angelo, of the Sistine ceiling, which had belonged to Lely and Reynolds. On the one numbered 37 is a note, signed by Sir Joshua, attributing them to Vasari. It was from these drawings that Ottley engraved the genealogical groups which were destroyed to make way for the painting of 'The Last Judgment.' The plate occurs in his specimens of the old Florentine masters.

The following are the names of the examiners appointed by the Society of Arts for the examination of candidates from classes of Mechanics' Institutions:—The Astronomer Royal, Dr. Bernays, Hon. and Rev. S. Best, Rev. Dr. Booth, Rev. Prof. J. S. Brewer, C. Brooke, Esq., Rev. Prof. W. Browne, Dr. Carpenter, Harry Chester, Esq., Rev. S. Clark, the Dean of Christ Church, Oxford, Viscount Ebrington, M.P., Rev. Dr. Elder, J. Glaisher, Esq., the Dean of Hereford, R. Hunt, Esq., Dr. Bence Jones, Prof. Moseley, Rev. Baden Powell, F. R. Sandford, Esq., J. Simon, Esq., Prof. Edward Solly, Rev. F. Temple,

Figure 4: The 'marked file' of the *Athenaeum* showing Sarah Austin's contribution to the gossip column, *Athenaeum*, 9 Feb. 1856.

appointed as the new editor and the journal reverted to its pre-war character, a weekly that focused on literature. Competition with other specialized journals such as the *Times Literary Supplement* and the *London Mercury* forced it to merge* with the *Nation** first (in 1921) and, finally, to disappear entirely when that merged with the *New Statesman** (1930). **MD**

Sources: Demoor 2000, Marchand 1941.

ATHLETIC NEWS AND CYCLISTS' JOURNAL (1875-1931) The *Athletic News and Cyclists' Journal* and its editors* came to hold a special place in the subculture that evolved around the growth of professional football from the mid-1880s to the 1920s. A comprehensive coverage of matches, gossip* and informed comment were the prime features of the weekly* *Athletic News* during the football season, when circulation* peaked, with a similar treatment of cricket in the summer months. The paper supported the right of sportsmen to make a living from their skills in the face of widespread concerns over the potentially corrupting influence of money in sport. The editors, J. J. Bentley*, James Catton* and Ivan Sharpe were regarded by players and readers alike as wielding influence among football's administrators, with Bentley, in fact, holding high office within both the Football League and the Football Association.

Launched by Edward Hulton*, the 2d Manchester-based sports* paper covered athletics, cycling and rugby, too, but ignored horse racing, the staple diet of the sporting press of the time. Hulton also produced the racing-led *Sporting Chronicle** and the two papers, with national circulations, complemented each other, catering for diverse markets. The paper settled on regular Monday publishing and a 1d cover price* to meet the growing demand among sports-conscious clerks and artisans for news* of the weekend sports fixtures.

The paper's regular columnists* included football administrators, leading referees and sportsmen/journalists such as cricketer C. B. Fry. Its editors reported the leading sports fixtures of the day and also wrote for Hulton's other titles, with the first editor, T. R. Sutton, for example, covering coursing for the *Sporting Chronicle* under the byline, 'Donald'. The paper relaunched as a tabloid in 1925 and merged with the *Sporting Chronicle*'s Monday edition in 1931. **ST**

Sources: *Athletic News Football Annual*, Leary 1896, Mason 1986, Tate 2005.

ATLANTIS: A REGISTER OF LITERATURE AND SCIENCE CONDUCTED BY MEMBERS OF THE CATHOLIC UNIVERSITY OF IRELAND (1858-1870) *Atlantis* was started by John Henry Newman as an outlet for the faculty of the recently founded Catholic University of Ireland, of which he was rector. Newman installed Professor William K. Sullivan as scientific* editor*, the scientific portion of the magazine having a much greater significance for Newman, who saw the literary section – which he edited – as 'padding'. Sullivan, who contributed articles to the literary* section as well as the scientific, also ended up dealing with much of the day-to-day running of the periodical since Newman was dividing his time between Birmingham and Dublin.

In terms of content, the *Atlantis* strenuously attempted to efface the sectarian sympathies of its editors and contributors from its pages by avoiding potentially inflammatory subjects. 'The *Atlantis* will not be anything but literary and scientific – not religious, not ecclesiastical, not political', Newman wrote in 1858. The resulting publication was one in which tough, near-impenetrable academic science and learned but readable literary articles (on Seneca, Hieroglyphics or Alcibiades for example) were rather incongruously yoked together: it strove for the scholarly rigor of a learned journal, but – partly because of the literary talents of Newman and Sullivan – also had at least the potential to appeal to a wider readership*.

Newman resigned as rector of the University towards the end of 1858, and Peter le Page Renouf took over as editor of the literary section, although Newman retained the overall editorship, at least in name, until the appointment of the new rector Bartholomew Woodlock in 1861. Meanwhile the journal – which had heretofore been published biannually – had run into financial difficulties, and from 1860 was published at long and irregular intervals: an issue in March 1860, one in January 1862, another early in 1863, and the eighth and final issue, after a gap of seven years, in February 1870. Despite the notoriety of its editor, the *Atlantis* seems to have been seen as merely a somewhat eccentric journal of its issuing body*, and it never established itself as an influential voice. **MaT**

Sources: *ODNB, Wellesley.*

ATLAS (1826-1869) The *Atlas* promoted itself as being 'a general newspaper and journal of literature* on the largest sheet ever issued from the press'. At 40cm, it was almost double the size* of other weekly papers at the time. Costing 1s, it was also nearly double the general price* of 7d for a similar journal. Founded by Robert Stephen Rintoul*, the *Atlas* was a popular and successful paper. It lasted for almost 35 years, until it became the *Englishman* on 5 July 1862. Three years later, on 18 September 1865, this title reverted to the *Atlas*. From 29 January until 26 February 1869 it was known as the *Atlas and Public Schools Chronicle*. From 5 March 1869 it became the *Public Schools Chronicle*. Its price also fluctuated – by 1828 it had been reduced to 10d; in 1846 it cost 8d; by 1858, with the repeal of Stamp Duty* and competition from other papers which had doubled their size, the *Atlas* dropped its price from 3d to 2d. From the late 1850s, the *Atlas* was issued by Manchester's United Kingdom Alliance, an organization founded in 1853 to promote temperance.

The paper, which was illustrated* by engravings*, covered a number of different departments. These included criticism, reviews*, foreign and British news*, parliamentary* debates, literary correspondence*, music* and theatre sections, scientific* notes and finance. Its political* orientation was Benthamite, liberal and Whig. The *Atlas* was held in high regard. *Mitchell's Newspaper Press Directory* stated as the journal's main strength was that it 'never lost sight' of 'talent': 'the best writers … have always held themselves ready for the *Atlas*'. Well-known contributors included William Hazlitt*, Leigh Hunt*, Louis Kossuth and George Henry Lewes*. **DHL**
Sources: Andrews 1859, Grant 1871, *Mitchell's* 1856, *Waterloo*.

ATTWELL, MABEL LUCIE (1879-1964) Mabel Attwell began life in the Mile End Road, London, and was educated at the Coopers' Company School. Attwell devised stories, and provided drawings to accompany them, the earliest expression of her facility for art and her career as an illustrator*. By the time she was 16 she had accumulated a large enough portfolio of drawings of children and fairies to take to the London art agents, Francis and Mills. Her success was immediate with a clamour for her work.

The money she earned from magazines* paid for her art education at Regent Street and Heatherley's art schools; however, her dislike of the formal aspects of such training led her to abandon her studies and continue with her career. Her early delicate watercolour and fine pen and ink drawings of fairies and children appeared in *Cassell's Christmas Annual*, *Father Tuck's Annual*, *Pearson's Magazine** and *Little Folks*.

Her career gathered momentum and by 1922 her *Lucie Attwell Annual* was the first of a lifetime's series.

A successful business woman, Attwell's prodigious output launched a series of ephemera parading her signature plump children with mass appeal. Her drawings were also famously used by many advertisers, sealing her career and financial success. **CL**
Sources: Eastbourne Heritage Centre, Micklethwaite and Peppin 1983, *ODNB*.

AUCTION REGISTER AND LAW CHRONICLE (1811-1847) This weekly* journal was subtitled *Commercial and Bankruptcy Register*. Its contents included 'accurate, authentic and copious lists of bankrupts, insolvents, dividends &c. and reports of cases bearing on such matters'. As well as bankruptcies, *Auction Register* contained items related to commercial interests such as law reports, information on commissioners' meetings, acts of Parliament, a registry of prize sales, and dissolutions of partnerships. Established in 1811, it probably began publication in 1812. The first extant issue is volume I, number 35, dated 7 January 1813. On 2 March 1815, the title changed to *Law Chronicle and Estate Advertiser* and then from 14 September 1820 until 30 December 1847 it was known as *Law Chronicle, Commercial and Bankruptcy Register*. The publisher and printer in 1813 was Amos Topping. Other publishers and printers were C. Windeyer (1819), Fawcett and Company (1822-1829) and Frederick Griffiths (1830-1847). In 1813 the size of the *Auction Register* was eight pages of 40 cm. It cost 1s in 1813, 1/s 6d in 1821, and 1s 3d in 1846. **DHL**
Sources: *English Historical Review* 1950, *Mitchell's*, *Waterloo*.

AUSTIN, ALFRED (1835-1913) In 1860, the poet Alfred Austin inherited money from the death of his uncle, deserted a law career, and devoted the rest of his life to the writing of poetry* and critical essays and to journalism. From 1863 he was a frequent contributor to the periodicals: e.g., *Academy**, *Blackwood's Magazine**, *Britannia*, *Contemporary Review**, *Cornhill Magazine**, *Eclectic Magazine**, *Fortnightly Review**, *Macmillan's Magazine**, *Quarterly Review**, *Pall Mall Magazine**, *Tomahawk** and *Temple Bar**. In addition he was editorially affiliated with the *National Review** and with the newspaper the *Standard**, a strong rival of *The Times**.

Austin's association with the newspaper started in 1866 and lasted 32 years, with Austin acting as leader* writer from 1866 to 1896 and occasionally travelling as a special foreign correspondent*. Like the *National Review*, the *Standard* was another Tory organ. Founded in 1883 as a conservative journal, the *National Review* was first edited* jointly by Austin and William John Courthope*, but Austin became the sole editor* in 1887 and stayed as such until he retired from the editorship in 1893, although he continued to contribute critical essays to the journal. For example, he covered for the *Standard* the ecumenical council in Rome in 1869-1870, the Prussian headquarters in 1870 during the Franco-Prussian War and the congress of Berlin in 1878. Essentially from 1898, Austin retired from journalistic work for the *National Review* and the *Standard*, although an occasional critical article appeared in the *National Review*, such as that on 'Dante and his Treatment of the Ideal' in July 1900.

Austin was named England's poet laureate on 1 January 1896, four years after Tennyson's death. His first official poem as poet laureate, 'Jameson's Ride', was published in *The Times* ten days after his appointment and was, unfortunately, a failure. Not only was this tribute widely criticized and ridiculed as inferior poetry, but the British government had condemned the military action of the South African statesman Leander Starr Jameson, whom the poem commended. It was widely held that Austin's appointment as poet laureate was based more on his pro-Tory journal articles, his editorship of the *National Review* and his journalistic reporting in the conservative *Standard* than on his poetic ability. **WS**

Sources: Austin 1911, *ODNB*, *Waterloo*, *Wellesley*.

AUSTIN, SARAH (1793-1867) Sarah Austin (née Taylor) was at her most productive as a translator, editor* and journalist* between the mid-1820s and mid-1860s. Many of her notable book publications were translations from German and French – histories by Ranke, Sismondi and Guizot – plus editions of her husband John Austin's works on jurisprudence, the Rev. Sydney Smith's* letters, and the *Letters from Egypt* by her only child, Lucie Duff Gordon. Her numerous contributions to a variety of periodicals encompassed translations, reviews*, memoirs and social commentary. Anxious to support her family while avoiding publicity as an author, Austin preferred translating, editing and exploiting the convention of anonymous* periodical publication which enabled her to adopt on occasion a male persona.

The two related *leitmotifs* of her periodical writing were the fostering of intercultural understanding between Britain and European countries, and the education of the British masses (which she considered would benefit from continental models). The first concern is reflected in her series 'Specimens of German Genius' for the *New Monthly Magazine* (1830-1833), offering extracts from Goethe, Schiller, Tieck, A.W. von Schlegel, Novalis, Lessing and others, and collected in 1841 as *Fragments from German Prose Writers*. It emerges as well in her regular reports from Germany and France published in the *Athenaeum*, 1842-1845; in articles on German politics and culture in the *Edinburgh Review* (1843, 1846) and the *British and Foreign Review* (1842) (later adapted for her *Germany from 1760 to 1814*, 1854), in her translation of François Guizot's article on French religion (*Quarterly Review*, June 1848) and in her review of G. H. Lewes's* biography of Goethe (*Edinburgh Review*, July 1857). The second concern emerges in her *Athenaeum* reports; in her October 1833 review for the *Foreign Quarterly Review* of Victor Cousin's *Report on the Prussian System of Education*, which she republished in 1839 as *On National Education*; and in two *Athenaeum* articles on industrial girls' schools (Nov. 1856 and Jan. 1857). Austin's wide social network among British and continental intellectual, political and artistic circles is reflected in her obituaries* for Felix Mendelssohn (*Fraser's*, April 1848) and MP Charles Buller (*Fraser's*, Jan. 1849), and her articles on French salon leader Juliette Récamier (*Fraser's*, Sept. 1849 and *Edinburgh Review*, Jan. 1860). In 1866, however, outraged at Prussia's policy towards Saxony and Bohemia, she regretted her inability to get articles on this accepted by the *Athenaeum*, *Fraser's* or the *Pall Mall Gazette*. **JCW**

Sources: Demoor 2000, Hamburger 1992, *ODNB*, Ross 1892, *Wellesley*.

AUTHORS' CIRCULAR (1898) A short-lived monthly* publication of 16 pages running from January to April 1898, the *Authors' Circular* was subtitled the *Official Organ of the English School of Journalism*. It aimed to 'foster business relations between those who write and those who publish', reflecting the increasing professionalization* of journalism. Advice on pitching to editors and defending intellectual property, gossip* about the literary scene, insight into the means by which editors* selected copy for publication, and a correspondence* section in which such issues were discussed made up the bulk of the magazine. The syllabus for the English School of Journalism (which prepared students for the examinations of the Institute of Journalists*) was printed in each issue, giving insight into the practical art of journalism* as it was then conceived. Early in 1898, Charles Norris, secretary of the English School of Journalism, who was intimately involved in the

THE
Authors' Circular

(The Official Organ of the English School of Journalism.)

No. 1, Vol. 1.   JANUARY 10, 1898.   By Subscription, Five Shillings p r nnnum.

BEATRICE CARTER,
LOVE STORIES AND NOVELETTES.
To Order Only.
Contributor to the Aldine Press, Complete Stories, etc.

23, Malvern Road, LEYTONSTONE.

ALAN TEMPLE.
ADVENTURE STORIES AND TRAVEL SKETCHES.
To Order Only.
"East View," Chiswick Park, W.

HORACE GRIMWOOD,
SPORTING STORIES AND ADVENTURES.
Contributor to leading Sporting Weeklies.

"Little Heath," Leysters, HEREFORDSHIRE.

FRANCES FRANCIS,
Stories for Children; Articles, Book Notices, &c.
Length up to 5,000 words.

Address—care of AUTHORS' CIRCULAR, 295, Strand, W.C.

MARY MACGREGOR,
SHORT STORIES OR ARTICLES,
From 2,000 to 4,000 words. On hand or to order.

Address—care of AUTHORS' CIRCULAR, 295, Strand, W.C.

SEA STORIES, good, any length, by writer well acquainted with modern sea-faring on steam cargo-boats. Terms from two guineas a thousand words.—H. Vaughan, care of THE AUTHORS' CIRCULAR, 295, Strand, London, W.C.

SOCIETY PARS.—Supplied by a Lady-Journalist, moving in a very good set. — Address, Mrs. Colonel, care of AUTHORS' CIRCULAR, 295, Strand, W.C.

BLACK & WHITE WORK, in line or wash. A capable Artist wants more work.—Address, R. M. B., care of AUTHORS' CIRCULAR, 295, Strand, W.C.

PRESS ILLUSTRATIONS IN BLACK AND WHITE.—A thoroughly capable Artist is open to accept engagement on the Staff of a high class Journal or Magazine. Young, experienced, and thoroughly reliable.—Address, M. T. care of AUTHORS' CIRCULAR, 295, Strand, W.C.

LEADERS, political, social, and general, by a trustworthy writer of considerable Continental and London experience.—Address, Box 121, THE AUTHORS' CIRCULAR, 295, Strand, London, W.C.

SPECIAL London and Continental CORRESPONDENCE for American and Colonial newspapers by a staff of experienced press-men. Instructions minutely followed and promptness and accuracy guaranteed. Moderate terms.—Address, in first instance, " Beaufox," Box 111, THE AUTHORS' CIRCULAR, 295, Strand, London, W.C.

EDITORIAL STAFF.—Experienced editor, thorough sub-editor, and three well-trained, capable writers for interviewing, special reports, etc., will undertake the whole work of a weekly newspaper and supply all copy for five guineas a week.—Box 105, THE AUTHORS' CIRCULAR, 295, Strand, London, W.C.

AUTHOR desirous of obtaining further journalistic experience is willing to act as SPECIAL COMMISSIONER in town, country, or abroad. Good descriptive writer; master of five modern languages; moderate terms to good paper.—Address, Box 101, THE AUTHORS' CIRCULAR, 295, Strand, London, W.C.

BOOK REVIEWING.— Novels, Travels, Sport, general Literature by experienced critic.—"Chort," care of THE AUTHORS' CIRCULAR, 295, Strand, W.C.

TRANSLATIONS.—Literary Man, conversant with modern languages, desires more work, and will be glad to undertake translations—statistical, scientific, mechanical, trade, or other—from French, German, Italian, Spanish, or Portuguese, for mining engineers, company-promoters, patent-owners or agents, &c. N.B.—MSS. revised for Press.—Address, "Traducteur," care of THE AUTHORS' CIRCULAR, 295, Strand, London, W.C.

SUB-EDITOR, OR IN SOLE CHARGE OF WEEKLY.—A Journalist, thoroughly qualified and competent Sub., of wide and varied experience, up-to-date and reliable, desires an engagement. A *bonâ-fide* worker; no "slip-shod;" classical and modern languages; familiar with technical, scientific, and illustrated work; good descriptive writer.—Address, " Vif-Argent," care of THE AUTHORS' CIRCULAR, 295, Strand, London, W.C.

STORY WANTED.—A good class adventure story; modern, exciting, of interest to boys, and capable of being used in monthly instalments. Length up to 100,000 words. — Immediate offers (no MS.), to "Carisbrooke," care of THE AUTHORS' CIRCULAR, 295, Strand, London, W.C.

SERIAL.—First publication of good exciting story, with feminine interest and well worked up situations, wanted AT ONCE for a Daily Newspaper, circulating chiefly among the artisan class.—" Feuilleton," care of THE AUTHORS' CIRCULAR, 295, Strand, London, W.C.

WANTED, High-class SHORT STORIES, 2,000 to 4,000 words, suitable for Magazines.—Write, before sending MSS., Curryer and Baynes, Literary Agents, 441, Strand, London.

A GERMAN GENTLEMAN is desirous of corresponding with an English author, willing to give him the RIGHT to TRANSLATING his WORKS into GERMAN.—Address, L. 3676, care of Rudolf Mosse, Breslau.

WANTED, the ADDRESSES of PUBLISHING HOUSES, supplying fashion blocks, paper patterns, literary matter, &c., for Provincial Monthly Publication. — Address, " Free Press," care of THE AUTHORS' CIRCULAR, 295, Strand, W.C.

WANTED.—Used tone—and line—PROCESS BLOCKS of ornamental designs and figure-subjects from high-class artistic drawings or interesting photographs. Continental subjects preferred, and must be from a book or periodical of which small numbers only have been printed. Can make regularly in large numbers.—" The Binde," care of THE AUTHORS' CIRCULAR, 295, Strand, London.

WANTED, Snap-shot Photos of every-day life at sea on screw-colliers. Particularly: hoisting headlight in rough weather: picture of sailor astride peak-halyards slueing gaff-top-s'l sheet; and of deck-hooks.—" Hotspur," care of THE AUTHORS' CIRCULAR, 295, Strand, London, W.C.

WANTED, a run of the FIELD Newspaper from 1885; also FIRST 10 vols.—OLIVER, 2, Kent Villas, Ealing Dean, W.

SECRETARY-PARTNER wanted for an established TECHNICAL INSTITUTION. A gentleman with £200 or £300, and literary tastes. 'Varsity man preferred. Must have a clear head in matters of business, as he will have entire control of financial department.—Apply care of SECRETARY, Sherwood, Alexandra Road, Norbiton, Surrey.

RESIDENT SECRETARY required for a High School for Boys (under Limited Company). Beautiful home, with good stabling, &c. Small investment necessary.—Address SECRETARY, 60, Chandos Street, Charing Cross, W.C.

ASSISTANT SECRETARY wanted for the London Office of a Limited Company engaged in educational enterprises. Salary, to a really smart and capable man (to commence with), £200 per annum. Must be prepared either to introduce Capital or take up Shares.—Address, " MAGISTER," care of Mr. Norrie, Walbrook Chambers, Walbrook, E.C.

EDITORIAL APPOINTMENT.—The Editorship of an important Literary Periodical is offered to a suitable writer, lady or gentleman, who will accept payment by results. Part time only required for the work, and previous editorial experience unnecessary, as the magazine has competent sub-editors and an adequate staff of contributors. Every assistance will be afforded by the present editor, a well known man of letters, and the post presents unequalled facilities for advancing literary interests and obtaining additional remunerative work. Premium, or the investment of £100 at five per cent.—Address " Editor," care of Curryer and Baynes, Literary Agents, 441, Strand London, W.C.

TO AUTHORS and OTHERS.—The WARWICK PRESS, Limited, 6, WARWICK MANSIONS, HOLBORN, W.C., invite Correspondence from Authors or Compilers of Books on practical subjects.
They are prepared either to purchase the copyright or to publish under an approved and entirely equitable arrangement.
Before sending MSS. an indication of the scope and treatment of the subject should be given.

TO EXPERTS.—Publisher wants occasional re earch work done, particularly in the PRINT ROOM at the British Museum; candidates must also be acquainted with the S.K. and other collections, and know what will and what will not reproduce effectively by zinco process. State qualifications and experience to " HUBERT," care of THE AUTHORS' CIRCULAR, 295, Strand, W.C.

TO NOVELISTS AND PLAYWRIGHTS.—For sale, plot and scenario of a strong drama. Adapted for a short caste; good comedy, unhackneyed incident. The author, a well-known writer, is too busy with other work to make of this the success it merits and will accept the first offer of £10 for ALL RIGHTS. That secrecy will be also void is guaranteed by his agent. Address at once " Fitzwilliam," care of THE AUTHORS' CIRCULAR, 295, Strand, London, W C.

FOR SALE.—Old established technical monthly MAGAZINE, hav'ng a steady circulation and good advertisement revenue. Low price will be accepted if printing remains.—App'y, Box 101, THE AUTHORS' CIRCULAR, 295, Strand, W.C.

FOR DISPOSAL.—An old-established weekly NEWSPAPER devoted exclusively to society, sporting and literary views. It is a periodical of the highest class, patronised by royalty and has a steady circulation in aristocratic circles. The income is steady and as at present manage d yields a fair return upon the capital invested. Although to be sold at once owing to exceptional circumstances only reasonable offers will be entertained. Any person wishing an investment for a large sum should write personally, or by solicitor, to Box 117, THE AUTHORS' CIRCULAR, 295, Strand, London, W.C.

FOR SALE.—A popular weekly PERIODICAL, well established and possessing a large and increasing circulation. Principals, or their solicitors only, write—Box 106, THE AUTHORS' CIRCULAR, 29', Strand.

PARTNER wanted, with £300 for a sound business in non-speculative literary enterprise. No publishing. Pleasant occup tion for whole-or part-time.—Box 90, THE AUTHORS' CIRCULAR, 295, Strand, London, W.C.

NEW PERIODICAL.—A cheap popular monthly, wants printer who will invest in ordinary shares. Several posts open to investors. The venture is well backed, has a field to itself absolutely and excellent prospects.—Address, Box 95, THE AUTHORS' CIRCULAR, 295, Strand. London, W.C.

A YOUNG GENTLEMAN can secure position as secretary and part proprie'or in a unique (private) literary enterprise. Congenial, refined, and influential part-time occupat on. Qualification nominal to entrance. By arrangement.—Address, Fortune, Box 118, THE AUTHORS' CIRCULAR, 295, Strand, London, W.C.

PARTNER WANTED, with £500, to join in a promising literary enterprise, which, from training and long experience, advertiser is well qualified to conduct to a successful issue. Full particulars in confidence.—Address, Box 113, THE AUTHORS' CIRCULAR, 295, Strand, London, W.C.

LITERARY INVESTMENT with occupation desirable by competent writer. Only high-class publication entertained, and it must bear strict investigation, when, if suitable, £1,000 will be offered for a part share and congenial post on literary staff.—Address in first instance, " ASIA," care of Literary Agents, 441, Strand, London, W.C.

AS PUBLISHERS' READER, by experienced scholar and book reviewer, who, for many years, was chief reader to an eminent publisher, now deceased. Moderate terms for permanency.—" Reader," care of THE AUTHORS' CIRCULAR, 295, Strand, London, W.C.

INTERVIEWS, CRITICISM (Literary and Dramatic), SUB-EDITING, &c., wanted by a trained journalist.—Address, OSA, care of AUTHORS' CIRCULAR, 295, Strand, W.C.

Figure 5: Front page of the *Authors' Circular*, 10 Jan. 1898.

production of its journal, died, which destabilized the publication and its continuation. **MaT**
Source: *Waterloo.*

AUTHORSHIP AND THE PRESS Authors of many literary fields are linked to the press throughout the nineteenth century, from the later journalistic endeavours of the poet Coleridge* to the critical works of Walter Pater*, which first appeared in journals. However, as much as any other profession, journalism lies at the heart of prose fiction. Dickens's* early career as a journalist informed much of his novel writing, as well as paving the way for his success as the owner*-editor* of weekly* journals such as *Household Words** and *All the Year Round**. His protégé Wilkie Collins* followed this path from journalist* to novelist, aided greatly by the social and professional* networks opened up by his connection with Dickens's journals. George Eliot* 'found her voice' as a novelist through her journalism for the *Westminster Review**, and indeed many women writers*, such as Margaret Oliphant*, Eliza Lynn Linton*, Mary Baldwin, E. B. Nesbit and Dinah Craik, among others, either began their literary careers in journals or forged dual careers as journalist and novelist. For women who lacked the educational advantages and/or social networks readily available to male novelists, journalism offered financial support for a jobbing writer-novelist, and also provided a more accessible inroad into literary publication for young and new writers, as opposed to expensive volume publication, deemed too much of a risk by publishers.

Serial* publication in journals also had a considerable effect upon authors' shaping of the novel's content and form. As well as a serialized novel, such as Collins's *Woman in White*, reflecting the atmosphere of its publication in *All the Year Round* (for example, the fear of Italian espionage in the surrounding political articles bleeding into the character of Fosco, while the chapter containing Fosco's written confession aped Collins's own journalistic technique for meeting a deadline), a book in weekly instalments must be convincing both as a whole, and as self-contained, coherent parts. Furthermore, serialized fiction is far more economically sensitive to reader* response, as the purchase of a poorly written serial can be dropped by readers part way through in a way that volume publication cannot. Thus, in terms of broadening the opportunities to enter the writing profession across gender and class* divides, and in bringing the process of writing and publishing a work closer to the reading public, journalism and the press played an immensely important role in the democratization of literature during the nineteenth century. **MBT**
Sources: Collins 1860, *ODNB*, Onslow 2000.

B

BABY: THE MOTHERS' MAGAZINE (1887-1915) Subtitled *A Guide to the health, dress, food and general management of children*, this illustrated* monthly* was edited by Ada Ballin* and sold for 4d. It offered to all with 'the sweet responsibility of the care of children' the 'opinions of the highest authorities in medicine, hygiene and education' (1: 13). Many of the signed articles were by medical men and scientists, but along with these were photographs* of Beautiful Babies, advice* to readers from 'Mater', a column* of amusing childish sayings called 'Wit and Wisdom', 'Recipes for the Nursery' and discussions of some of Ballin's particular enthusiasms, including rational dress for babies and the Kindergarten movement associated with Froebel. The magazine consisted of 32 pages plus 20 pages of advertisements* and claimed a circulation* of 10,000 in 1895. **MRB**
Sources: *Baby*, Shuttleworth 2004, *Waterloo*

BACHELORS' BUTTONS (1860) This monthly* journal lasted for five issues, from June to October. It claimed to contain 'a variety of poetry*, prose and essays of many sorts, from scientific to biographical to literary'. In an introductory note, the editor* announced the journal as 'a whim'. Its readership* was probably mainly to be found among London barristers since the editorial offices were located at Lincoln's Inn Fields. *Bachelors' Buttons* was published* in Huntingdon by Robert Edis and printed in London by Simpkin, Marshall and Company*. Its size* was 22 cm, and it contained 32 pages. The price* was 6d. **DHL**
Sources: Turner 2000c, *Waterloo*.

BACHELORS' PAPERS (1870-1871) *Bachelors' Papers* was a short-lived Liverpool monthly magazine, sold in London in Lombard Street, in the City. As the editor* admits, the periodical 'was not instituted as a commercial speculation'. (Editorial Preface, Nov. 1870). As both the title and the site of London distribution* suggest, this was a magazine targeting men that took up the subject of bachelorism in a serious way, in the context of ongoing political* debates about the Woman Question, in the 1860s. Of particular interest in this regard is an exchange of articles about single men who oppose married life (see 'A Spinster's Musing' in 1871 and 'A Quid Pro Quo' in April 1871). *Bachelors' Papers* can usefully be read alongside related material at the time, often more satirical in tone, including *Bachelors' Buttons** (1860) and pamphlets such as *Bachelorism Portrayed* (London 1865). **MWT**
Source: Turner 2000c.

BACON, RICHARD MACKENZIE (1776-1844) Although leader*-writer, editor* and proprietor* of the Whig *Norwich Mercury* (which he took over from his father in 1804, becoming editor in 1816), Richard Bacon is most notable for his contribution to music* journalism*. In the autumn of 1818, inspired by the success of the *Edinburgh Review** and the Leipzig *Allgemeine musikalische Zeitung,* he founded, printed, edited and co-owned (with London music publisher Chappell) one of the first musical journals in Britain to last beyond two years, the *Quarterly Musical Magazine and Review**. Bacon wrote most of the (usually unsigned) pieces, along with his daughters, Louisa and Mary Ann. The latter, like her father, also contributed to the *New Monthly Magazine**, he on music and she on French literature*. Bacon also wrote on music for the *London Magazine** (1820-1825), and on drama and the arts for the *Literary Gazette**, as well as on economics and politics*. While outside the metropolis, Bacon relied on an international circle of correspondents for his information. These included another daughter, Jane, a mezzo-soprano who studied in London and Paris. Bacon saw music as vital to the well-being of society morally, socially and politically and argued that British music and musicians needed both patronage and education if they were to take their rightful places. To that end, he supported concerts of exclusively British music and musicians. **AK**
Sources: Langley 1983, *New Grove*, *ODNB*, RIPM online.

BAGEHOT, WALTER (1826-1877) Walter Bagehot's contribution to the press over 30 years placed him among the most influential commentators on economic and political* questions in the mid-Victorian period. Typically, *The English Constitution* (1867), his defining work, appeared first as a series of articles in the *Fortnightly Review**. They show the strand of constitutional Toryism that combined with his economic liberalism to create Bagehot's characteristic 'cross-bench' political position. Though he trained as a lawyer after graduating from University College, London, and worked in the family bank for a decade, he was grounded in journalism*. His early contributions were to periodicals espousing the Unitarian faith of his father: the weekly* *Inquirer*, the quarterly* *Prospective Review** and its successor, the *National Review**, of

which Bagehot was a founding editor*. His name, however, was most readily associated with the weekly financial* review, the *Economist**, to which he began contributing in 1857, marrying the daughter of the founding editor, James Wilson, the following year. By 1861 he had become editor-in-chief, contributing leading economic and political articles to virtually every issue until his death. **GL**
Sources: Buchan 1959, Kuhn 1996, *ODNB*, St John-Stevas 1986.

***BAILY'S MONTHLY MAGAZINE OF SPORTS AND PASTIMES AND RACING REGISTER* (1860-1926)** *Baily's Monthly Magazine of Sports and Pastimes and Racing Register* is one of a number of titles, including turf, fox-hunting and annual* directories, in the Baily stable. Until 1900 its contents comprised a monthly* sporting diary, a correspondence* column, a summary of results, biographical sketches and illustrations*, consisting of engravings, sketches and photographs*. The contents was then enlarged to feature a sportsman's library, sporting* intelligence and a cricket section.

The magazine appeared under its original title until December 1888. Subsequently *Racing Register* was dropped, and it was sometimes familiarly referred to as *Baily's Magazine of Sports and Pastimes*. Its price* varied from 1s 6d in 1889 to 1s by 1912. Contributors included John A. Doyle, Frederick Gale*, Francis Lawley and Edward Delaval Napier. The publishing* remained within the family until 1900, when Vinton and Company Ltd took over. William Clowes* and Sons Ltd were among its printers. **DHL**
Sources: *Baily's Monthly Magazine* 1889-1900, Layton 1912, *Waterloo*.

BAIN, ALEXANDER (1818-1903) Born in northern Scotland and educated at his local Mechanics' Institute, Alexander Bain published his first article in the *Aberdeen Herald* in 1836. By 1840 he was contributing expository articles on science* to the *Westminster Review**, and, having turned down the vacant editorship* of the *Aberdeen Banner* in 1842, moved to London two years later. Already an unbeliever and political radical, in London Bain encountered John Stuart Mill* and became part of the *Westminster*'s dissident circle. As well as the *Westminster*, Bain also wrote extensively for *Lowe's Edinburgh Magazine*, *Chambers's Journal** and *Fraser's Magazine** on a wide variety of subjects, although increasingly focusing on phrenology – to which he was sympathetic – and psychological associationism.

In 1860 Bain was appointed Professor of Logic at the University of Aberdeen, but even with an aca-

demic post he continued to write widely for the press, particularly *Macmillan's Magazine** and the *Fortnightly Review**. In 1876 Bain used his own money to found *Mind**, undertaking all its publishing risks, appointing George Croom Robertson* as editor, and contributing numerous articles and notes. While *Mind* was subtitled *A Quarterly Review of Psychology and Philosophy*, reflecting Bain's own wide-ranging interests, it was of considerable significance to the development of specialist academic psychology, and Bain's pivotal role in its formation justifies regarding him as the first psychologist. **GD**
Sources: Bain 1904, Lightman 2004a, *ODNB*, Rylance 2000, Sheehy *et al* 1997.

BAINES, EDWARD (1774-1848); BAINES, EDWARD (JNR) (1800-1890); BAINES, THOMAS (1806-1881); BAINES, FREDERICK (1811-1893); BAINES, THOMAS BLACKBURN (1832-1891) The first Edward Baines, reforming newspaper proprietor*, politician and historian, was initially expected to work in his father's cotton works. However his aptitude for study persuaded his father to apprentice him to Thomas Walker, Preston printer and stationer. In 1790. Baines also had the opportunity for editorial work on Walker's new venture, the *Preston Review*, but the paper's radical views upset local Tories and it was forced to close. As a founder member of a debating society and 'newsroom' club, Baines was threatened with prosecution as French Revolution nerves infected the authorities, the first of many such accusations. Baines finished his apprenticeship* in Leeds in 1797 at Binns'* and Brown's *Leeds Mercury**. Joining the Reasoning Society, he again fell under suspicion as a 'Tom Painer'.

The day after qualifying, Baines and John Fenwick started their own printing business. However, Baines was a teetotaller and Fenwick's intemperance caused a rift in 1798. As a Dissenter, Baines began printing works for Non-conformists when, at the invitation of some political reformers and with their financial assistance, he bought the *Leeds Mercury* in 1801. Hard work saw Baines as sole proprietor*, improving the fortunes and influence of the *Mercury* by extending advertising*, introducing new typographical* arrangements, increasing its size and the space for '*matter*'. Circulation* rose from a 750 weekly figure in 1801 to 5,200 by 1829. The titles the firm printed reflected his interests: from the *Teetotal Star, Good Templars and Sunday School Magazine** to the laws and regulations of the *Philosophical and Literary Society of Leeds*.

The *Mercury* became a mouthpiece for parliamentary reform, slave trade abolition, anti-war feeling and religious freedom. Upholding the interests of northern manufacturing, it criticized much government legislation including the Corn Law, an agenda Baines championed as MP for Leeds. He actively exposed corruption, famously investigating* the use of agent provocateurs by Lord Liverpool's government, saving the lives of many falsely accused of insurrection. Actions in the community together with his campaigns in the *Mercury* laid him open to accusations of treason by local Tories.

Edward Baines Jnr joined the paper at 15, subsequently becoming a reporter* and from 1818, editorial assistant. By 1827 he was a partner in the business. As a witness and reporter of the 1819 Peterloo Massacre, like his father before him he prevented innocent people from being transported. Following his father as owner of the *Mercury*, when his elder brother Matthew died in 1860, he was asked to take over Matthew's parliamentary seat for Leeds. Edward was succeeded as editor by his son Thomas Blackburn until 1870 when he left to join the Plymouth Brethren. One of Edward's younger brothers, Frederick, was the paper's business manager. Having a particular interest in education (the *Mercury* took up George Birkbeck's 1823 example of the London Mechanics' Institute for Leeds), Edward Baines Junior supported Forster's 1870 Education Bill and was knighted in 1880. He continued with his journalism until he was 88.

Pursuing the family tradition in another important northern town, Thomas Baines bought the Liverpool newspaper the *Billinge's Advertiser*, remodelling it as the *Liverpool Times* (1829-1856). When the paper folded as a result of the competition heralded by new printing processes, Thomas became Liverpool Council's London agent.

Lauded after his death in 1890 as 'the English Benjamin Franklin', Edward Baines had extended his paper's profile to regional and national visibility, succeeding in his lifetime's commitment to his community and the cause of political and social reform. CL

Sources: Baines 1859, *ODNB*, Reid 1905, *Waterloo*.

BAKEWELL, MRS J. (FL.1845-1864) An Evangelical Christian, Mrs J. Bakewell contributed to the *British Mothers' Magazine* with serialized* fiction such as 'The Second Marriage; or, Prejudice Removed' before becoming its editor* from 1847 to 1864. In her first editorial address in the January 1848 issue she informed her readers that the magazine would continue to support and advise mothers in their important work, and although purely evangelical it would be free from sectarian bias. This was confirmed by having contributions from a variety of clergymen, as well as medical men, hospital matrons, governesses and servants such as nursery maids. There would also be a literary* department catering for both mothers and children, and current affairs especially relating to welfare matters.

Bakewell was well qualified to edit such a magazine having a number of advice books to her credit such as *The Mother's Practical Guide*, *The Lord's Prayer Explained* and *Friendly Hints to Female Servants*. In addition to her publications which were widely advertised and recommended, until 1862 she also ran an 'educational establishment for young ladies' at her home in Notting Hill, London. By December 1863, Bakewell was writing in her editorial column of the changes in the magazine market* and the difficulties caused by increased competition* and was thanking her publisher for his continued support. But by the following December the *British Mother' Family Magazine* as it had been renamed in January 1864, had ceased. CL

Sources: *British Mothers' Magazine*, *Waterloo*.

BALDWIN, HENRY (1734-1813); BALDWIN, CHARLES (1774-1869); BALDWIN, EDWARD (1803-1890) The founder of a London newspaper dynasty, Henry Baldwin's career began in time-honoured fashion as a printer's apprentice. He rapidly became a newspaper proprietor*, buying the *London Spy*, *Read's Weekly Journal* and the *St James's Evening Post* from another printer. In 1761 Baldwin combined the *Spy* and the *Journal* into a Saturday paper and transformed the *Evening Post* into the *St James's Chronicle*, financed by a joint stock company. The *Chronicle* made its reputation on the twin basis of literary merit and politically candid views.

In 1801, the nomenclature of Henry Baldwin & Son recognized the success of Henry's son Charles who had been an apprentice compositor. Using his journalistic knowledge and entrepreneurial flair Charles expanded the business, purchasing the competing* evening paper, the *London Evening Post* in 1806 and achieving sole ownership of the *St James's Chronicle* by 1815. Consolidating its position, he bought the *London Chronicle* in 1819 merging* it with the *St James's Chronicle*.

Unlike his father, who had been arrested for criticising the king and the government, Charles was a staunch Establishment figure, launching the *Standard* at the instigation of the reactionary Tory faction. This proved yet another success and with his ownership of the twice weekly, *London Packet* and the weekly* *London Journal,* by the 1830s he was reputed to have an annual income in excess of £15,000.

When Charles retired in 1844, his son Edward, an Oxford graduate, headed the company and true to family tradition bought another newspaper, the *Morning Herald**. Edward decided to compete with *The Times**, employing top-grade journalists on higher pay rates. His course of action was ameliorated by the *Herald*'s cashing in on advertising revenue engendered by the railway boom and the paper prospered. But when these railway schemes were exposed, the ensuing financial collapse and Edward's refusal to lower wages brought an ignominious end in 1857 to the Baldwins' newspaper holdings. **CL**

Sources: *ODNB, Waterloo.*

BALFOUR, CLARA LUCAS (1808-1878) Clara Balfour (née Lucas) edited* and contributed to a number of Temperance journals for thirty years from 1841. Only receiving formal education from 11 to 14, her subsequent self-education and immersion in the temperance movement after signing the pledge in 1837 transformed her life.

After 1837, Balfour began writing for the temperance cause, becoming friends with Jane and Thomas Carlyle, who became her mentors. She was received into the Baptist chapel in Edgware, London and met the temperance campaigner John Dunlop, who arranged an assistant editorial position for her on the *Temperance Journal* from May 1841 with a salary of £25. This gave her the security to begin temperance lecturing work, but as her sphere enlarged from the drawing-room circuit to the lecture hall, so did her subject matter as she explored issues relating to women's development.

Her writing expanded with frequent contributions to temperance journals* beside the one she co-edited*, to the *British Workman**, the *Band of Hope Review**, the *Church Standard, Hand and Heart,* the *Meliora,* the *Westminster Review** and editorships of two short-lived papers, *Teetotal Magazine* and the *Temperance Messenger.* Additionally, she wrote a significant number of works on temperance, women's issues and social and moral concerns. She became President of the British Women's Temperance Association in 1877. **CL**

Source: *ODNB.*

BALLANTYNE, JAMES (1772-1833) James Ballantyne was a Scottish printer and newspaper editor*. Initially, he studied and practised as a lawyer, but his career in editing and publishing began in 1797 when he was invited to edit the *Kelso Mail,* an anti-radical, weekly* newspaper. As a publisher*

Ballantyne printed work by his friend, the novelist and journalist, Walter Scott* who had recommended Ballantyne's move to Edinburgh. In 1806, Ballantyne, together with Scott and his brother-in-law George Hogarth*, acquired the *Edinburgh Weekly Journal* (founded in 1744). During his editorship, Ballantyne became noted for his theatre reviewing* while his brother, John, was the paper's music* critic. Ballantyne continued to edit the *Edinburgh Weekly Journal* until his death. **DHL**

Sources: Dobson 1909, *ODNB,* Sutherland 1995.

BALLIN, ADA SARAH (1862-1906) Ada Sarah Ballin, magazine proprietor*, editor* and writer on health, established herself as an authority on baby and childcare with a particular interest in dress*. Attending University College, London from the age of 16, Ballin had her first signed article, 'Children's Dress' published in November 1883 in *Health,* to which she began to contribute regularly. In 1885 she wrote a series of articles on healthy dress for the periodical *Queen,* which were published as 'The Science of Dress in Theory and Practice'. With her interest in languages, Ballin wrote a series of articles, 'The Evolution of Languages', published in Proctor's paper, *Knowledge** in 1883.

Contributing to as many as 16 magazines and papers, Ballin turned to journalism full time in 1887 when she founded her first and most successful publication, *Baby: The Mother's Magazine**, an illustrated monthly*.

She also edited the health and beauty departments of the *Lady's Pictorial** until 1894, while throughout the 1890s writing and editing a series of 6d pamphlets in the Mothers' Guide series. In December 1898 Ballin launched a monthly* called *Womanhood** aimed at the 'new woman'. She wrote many of the articles for this as well as continuing to publish a number of books about health, dress and childcare. **AMS**

Sources: Ballin 1887, Ballin 1898, Ballin 1902, *Marylebone Gazette* 1906, *The Times* 1906, *Women's Penny Paper* 1890.

BAMFORD, SAMUEL (1788-1872) Born into the Lancashire working class, Samuel Bamford had already had poems* published in various radical pamphlets when in 1826 he became the Manchester correspondent of the London daily* newspaper the *Morning Herald**. In the late 1820s he also wrote for the *Manchester Guardian** and occasionally *The Times**. Bamford states that he 'ceased newspaper correspondence as a means of subsistence' (*Diary:* 252) in 1839 when he began issuing his autobiographical *Passages in the Life of a Radical*

(1839-1841), but this did not spell the end of his involvement in journalism. Though he was an opponent of Chartism, Bamford had his poem 'God Help the Poor' published in the *Northern Star** in 1843. In 1850 Bamford moved to London where in 1854 he wrote three fictionalized articles on the Preston Cotton Lockout of 1853-1854 for *Cassell's Illustrated Family Paper*. Bamford intended these to be 'corrective of the pernicious writings which Mr Dickens was issuing at that time' (*Diary:* 252). This was a reference to Dickens's* article 'On Strike' (*Household Words**, 11 Feb. 1854) which proclaimed the strike 'a waste of time' (Dickens 1997: 464) and on which Dickens drew for *Hard Times*. **JG**

Sources: Bamford 1864, Bamford 1984, Bamford 2000, Dickens 1997, Garratt 1992, *ODNB*.

BAND OF HOPE REVIEW (1851-1937) The *Band of Hope Review* was established by its editor* of 32 years, Thomas Bywater Smithies*, as a temperance educational journal for working-class children*. It was intended to supplement Sunday-school instruction, providing temperance advice to the young and serving as a resource for religious and moral teaching in the home. In the words of one prominent supporter it was 'Designed under God's blessing to form a breakwater against the fearful influence of the immoral prints which are everywhere flooding the country…' ('Preface', *Band of Hope Review*, I).

Each monthly* number included short stories, anecdotes, biblelessons, Band of Hope intelligence and tales of good Sundayschool scholars and ragged school children. The journal supported many causes that were popular among the urban working classes. It was patriotic, anti-slavery, an advocate for peace and the humane treatment of animals and promoted the principle of self-help among children. There were many stories about the actions of children, 'our readers', who, through their intervention, managed to affect a positive influence on drunkards. Among the contributors were Clara Lucas Balfour* and Harriet Beecher Stowe.

However, the most striking features of the journal were the large, wood-engraved* illustrations*. The *Band of Hope Review* was lavishly illustrated by some of the best artists of the period and Smithies was constantly striving to provide the best possible pictures for his readers. Henry Anelay*, John Gilbert*, Harrison Weir, Robert Barnes, W. J. Webb, John Lawson and William Rainey supplied many of the large pictures that adorned the title page after 1861. There were regular engravings after popular works by

Edwin Landseer, J. F. Herring and Edwin Douglas, used to convey some form of simple moral message through what Smithies referred to as 'eye-lessons'.

A Gratuitous Circulation* Fund helped fund the widespread distribution* of the paper which, 'speedily attained a very large circulation, and greatly encouraged Band of Hope work, especially in Sunday Schools' (Smith 1897: 57) and, from 1862 onwards 250,000 copies per month were issued. From 1856 it became the official organ of the Band of Hope Union and the support of national institutions like the Sunday School and the Bands of Hope ensured that it continued to be published until 1937. **FM**

Sources: *Band of Hope Review*, Smith 1897, *Waterloo*.

BAND OF MERCY ADVOCATE (1879-1934) Catherine Smithies* formed the first *Band of Mercy* children's group in 1875 to promote kindness towards animals. Her work inspired similar groups, prompting her son and publisher*, Thomas Bywater Smithies*, to launch the monthly *Band of Mercy Advocate* in January 1879.

The Royal Society for the Prevention of Cruelty to Animals (RSPCA) lacked a separate children's wing and their Ladies Education Committee assented to Thomas Smithies's request for them to take control of the Band of Mercy with its periodical in 1882. Edited* by the Society's secretary, John Colam, since 1880, rapid growth ensued and a readership* of 100,000 was claimed in 1888. By 1910 there were 527 groups in Britain, with an estimated 75,000 to 145,000 members. Priced at 1s 2d the *Band of Mercy* was often given away at meetings and schools, leading to the periodical being a financial but a necessary loss to the RSPCA.

Produced by the publishing house of S. W. Partridge & Co., the eight-page *Band of Mercy* periodical was visually similar in format to the temperance* *Band of Hope Review**. Under the editorship of Smithies, articles were laced with religiosity leading to complaints from Bands that it was 'rather feeble'. After the RSPCA took control the content became lighter in tone and less reliant on biblical rhetoric. A typical year's issues contained sermonizing addresses to members, pet keeping or animal welfare advice, natural history features, Band of Mercy meeting songs or prayers and a column* of Band news. Contributors to the *Band of Mercy* were largely unknown female writers* although articles were submitted by the naturalist William Percival Westell, Frances Stratton and the devoted Band of Mercy worker Florence Suckling. By the early 1900s the content of the periodical had changed little and looked distinctly dated compared to other contemporary children's* magazines. It was eventually retitled *Animal Ways** in 1935 after the Band of Mercy movement was renamed the RSPCA Junior Division. **FSM**

Sources: Moss 1961, Mountjoy 1985, *ODNB*, Rowe 1884.

BANER AC AMSERAU CYMRU (1859-1971; BANNER AND TIMES OF WALES) Y FANER (1972-1992) A weekly* newspaper owned by Welsh publisher* Thomas Gee*, launched in Denbigh in 1859 following the merger* of his *Baner Cymru* (Denbigh 1857-1859) with William Rees's (Gwilym Hiraethog) *Yr Amserau* (established Liverpool in 1857). By 1861 it was appearing twice weekly, and was extending its network of agents, and its news* coverage throughout Wales, the first Welsh-language* newspaper to do so effectively and with commercial success. Under Gee's management, it also was in the forefront of technological modernization and professionalization*, providing training and employment to such journalists as John Griffiths (Y Gohebydd), the paper's London and parliamentary correspondent. Strongly Nonconformist and Liberal in politics, it supported the early political career of David Lloyd-George and campaigned vigorously on such issues as land reform, the tithe and the disestablishment of the church in Wales during the last three decades of the nineteenth century. The paper continued as a weekly in the twentieth century, undergoing a third and last title change* to *Y Faner* before folding after 135 years. **AGJ**

Sources: 19CBLN, Jones 1977.

BARKER, JOSEPH (1806-1875) During a long public career Joseph Barker edited* a number of interesting journals which reflected his sometimes remarkable changes of opinion on religious* and political* questions. His most successful journalistic venture was the *People* (1848-1849), printed on Barker's own steam press* at Wortley near Leeds. At its peak in 1848 this journal was selling 20,000 copies a week, and a year after its first appearance was still making a good profit. Very egotistical, Barker insisted on writing all the material for the journal himself and discouraged readers from sending in their own articles or poetry*. His journal attacked in strong language the aristocracy and the inheritance laws, and promoted phrenology, vegetarianism and manhood suffrage, though by 1850 Barker, who had never joined the National Charter Association, supported a limited household suffrage.

Barker was already a well-known figure in the north of England when he launched the *People*. This was because his career as a Methodist preacher and editor of the *Christian Investigator and Evangelical Reformer* (published in volumes 1842-1843) had been brought to a dramatic and very public end by his rejection of the divine authority of baptism and his consequent expulsion from the Methodist New Connexion in 1841. This very charismatic man inspired great loyalty. Four thousand Methodists who became known as Christian Brethren left with him and became readers of his new journal called the *Christian* (1844-1848).

An advocate of emigration, Barker himself left for America in 1851. Never a quiet man, his opinions were soon filling the columns of the *Anti-Slavery Bugle* (1845-1861). Declaring himself an atheist in 1858, Barker eventually returned to Christianity and, for a few years, to Britain. The controversies in which he involved himself can be rediscovered in the *National Reformer** , for which in 1860-1861 he wrote the leaders* and the first half of the content, and in *Barker's Review* for 1861-1863. This energetic, passionate and disputatious man died at the age of 69 far from his native Yorkshire in Omaha. **SFR**

Sources: Barker 1880, Fladeland 1984, Larson 2006, *ODNB*, Roberts 1991.

BARNARD, FREDERICK (1846-1896) Adept in both serious and comic black and white illustration*, Frederick Barnard had worked as an illustrator for both the *Illustrated London News** and *Punch** while still a teenager. The quality of his work in magazine reportage is demonstrated by the illustrations he drew for George Sims's* series of London sketches 'How the Poor Live' which appeared in the *Pictorial Times* in 1883. His frequent social-realist contributions to the *Illustrated London News* were among the images that influenced Van Gogh. He also worked for a large range of humorous journals at various times, including a spell at *Judy** (1887-1890), and made occasional contributions to *Punch* into the 1890s. Primarily a black and white illustrator, and working mainly in pen and ink, Barnard's career suggests the range and diversity of commissions that came the way of a successful specialist illustrator in the second half of the nineteenth century, with sustained associations with particular magazines like *Broadway* (1867-1874) and especially the *Illustrated London News* (1863-1896), augmented by one-off commissions from the likes of *Once a Week** (1869). His close friendship with the Dalziel brothers*, who much admired

both his work and his good humour, was also of great service to him. **BM**
Sources: Engen 1990, Houfe 1978, *ODNB*, Spielmann 1895.

BARNES, THOMAS (1785-1841) For 22 years, from 1819, Thomas Barnes was the highly influential editor* of *The Times*. His career with the paper began around 1810 when he succeeded his friend Barron Field as drama critic. Field had introduced Barnes to the editor John Walter* as a possible recruit. In his theatre criticisms, Barnes was more candid than his predecessors and his honest appraisal of performances provoked hostile reactions. He also reported on legal cases and in January 1811 was appointed to the parliamentary staff. Between 1813 and 1814, he assisted Leigh Hunt* with the *Reflector* and the *Weekly Examiner*.

In 1817, Barnes was appointed editor* of *The Times* in succession to Dr John Stoddart, also making a financial investment in the paper. Meanwhile, John Walter was finding being chief editor and manager of *The Times* too arduous for one man. Initially he hesitated to appoint Barnes as his successor because of his radical views, but after others, including Thomas Southey, had turned down the appointment, Barnes was given the post. Barnes was the first editor to use journalism* consistently to influence public opinion. Sublimating his vigorous personality to the public image of his paper, he maintained that anonymous* journalism was the only kind to be read seriously. He changed the layout* of *The Times* by abandoning wood block illustrations*, making it appear more serious in content. Barnes's other innovations included the development of the 'Letters' to the Editor' page. He published reviews* by Thackeray* and commissioned articles from Benjamin Disraeli. As editor-in-chief, Barnes has been credited with creating the nineteenth-century newspaper, making *The Times* a model for serious newspapers at home and abroad. He developed the paper's prestige, which led to an association between *The Times* and the government. By 1840 Barnes's health began to fail, but he continued to edit almost until his death a year later. **DHL**
Sources: Hudson 1943, *ODNB*, Woods and Bishop 1983.

BARRETT, WILLIAM A. (1834-1891) As chief music* critic on the *Morning Post* (1866-1891), editor* of the *Monthly Musical Record* (1877-1887), and editor* of the *Musical Times* (1887-1891), the Oxford-educated Barrett was an influential figure both in the formation of public taste and in the establishment of the British musical canon.

'Essentially a modern man', according to fellow-critic Joseph Bennett*, William Barrett gave a positive reception in the *Morning Post* to the music of those continental composers, like Brahms, who adhered to classical forms, and to those whose music exhibited 'national' traits. His commitment to modernity did not however extend to promoting the work of the leading progressives, Liszt and Wagner. Regarding British music, Barrett was a critic-patriot who backed the 'renaissance' in British music, endorsing the works of Arthur Sullivan, Hubert Parry, Charles Stanford and, especially, Alexander Mackenzie.

As editor of Augener's *Monthly Musical Record*, Barrett ensured that British composers and performers were given substantial and positive coverage despite the journal's avowedly internationalist leanings and priorities. As editor of the *Musical Times*, he maintained that publication's market leadership while keeping it abreast of developments in contemporary music both in Britain and abroad. He was also, briefly, editor of the *Orchestra* (1881).

Barrett's importance, both as critic and editor, lay in the dedication, insight and suave professionalism that he brought to promoting music, especially new native works, to a readership* that lived, by common consent, in a 'land without music'. **MH**
Sources: Brown and Stratton 1976, *Grove's*, Hughes 2002, *Musical Times* 1891, *New Grove*.

BASKET BOYS 'Basket boys' were the newsboys* of the Scottish company of newsagent* and bookseller, John Menzies*, operating from his extensive system of Scottish railway station bookstalls which he gained his first interest in after 1857. Bookstalls on large urban stations would have a manager, frequently a woman, perhaps two assistants and a fleet of 'basket boys' who made their first appearance in the latter part of the century. These boys were a significant element of Menzies' distribution* methods, and as respectability was the key to access and higher sales, basket boys were trained and kitted out in a uniform, carrying identity cards as well as wearing a metal identity tally on their wrists. Their name came from the basket tray they carried in front of them suspended from their shoulders by a leather strap. In these trays they carried newspapers and periodicals; in essence they functioned as mobile bookstalls. Their task was to sell to passengers on the trains that had only a brief stop at a basket boy's allocated platform. On those occasions when there was a sufficient gap between trains, the boys would be expected to stock their baskets, board a train, travel down the line, sell the papers at that station and be back in time at their home station to meet the next train.

There could be problems at large, overcrowded stations such as Edinburgh's Waverley, where at peak times the scruffy itinerant newsboys would cash in on the basket boys' custom. This came at great risk to them for if they were caught by the railway authorities they would be soundly beaten. Protests at such treatment were expressed in letters to the *Edinburgh Evening News* at 'the little ragged fellows' who were giving a service when the official newsboys were 'invariably at the wrong end of the station'. Greater hazards befell the basket boys with frequent reports of accidents as they fell in the path of oncoming trains, when they ran across the tracks between platforms or slipped between the platform and the train.

Menzies' business ingenuity found two further openings for this sales technique. He paid a small fee to station hotels to enable the boys to sell morning and evening papers in the hotels' public rooms. Even on the Clyde steamers, before he had installed his bookstalls, the basket boys would travel the steamers, parading around the upper decks and lounges selling to the passengers. At holiday periods their usual uniform was transformed with beribboned straw boaters boasting the boat's name on the band. The basket boys lasted into the twentieth century, more often as a part-time job for school-age young people. **CL**

Sources: Gardiner 1983, John Menzies online.

BAX, ERNEST BELFORT (1854-1926) A prolific journalist and author of many books, Bax was a prominent Marxist and a key figure in the development of English Socialism, who edited several socialist* journals. As a young man he studied composition at the Stuttgart conservatory, and was for a time music* critic for the London *Star*, where he wrote under the pseudonym* 'Musigena'.

In 1881, after a stint in Berlin as correspondent for the *London Standard*, Bax published an article on Marx in the periodical *Modern Thought* (1879-1884), drawing the praise of Marx himself. After Marx's death in 1883, Bax increasingly deviated from the official line as propounded by Engels, drawing on German Idealism as he sought to develop a Marxism that was not tied to economic determinism, but allowed autonomy to philosophical categories of ethics, aesthetics and even metaphysics.

In 1882 Bax joined Henry Hyndman's* Democratic Federation, and soon began to contribute articles to its organ* *Justice*. He became editor* of *Today* in 1884, establishing it as a resolutely socialist* journal, attracting contributions from Hyndman and William Morris* and serializing George Bernard Shaw's* *An Unsocial Socialist*. Later that year, Bax and Morris – along with Eleanor Marx*, Edward Aveling and Walter Crane* – broke with Hyndman to form the Socialist League, and to launch the *Commonweal* (1885-1894), which Bax edited with Morris. The two collaborated on a series of articles called 'Socialism from the Root Up' in this journal, which also carried Bax's incisive critiques of imperialism.

Bax later rejoined what was now the Social Democratic Federation but continued to defend the purity of revolutionary Marxism, rejecting the reformist tendencies within the Second International and the Fabian movement. In his journalism – notably in articles for *Justice* – as well as in books like *The Legal Subjection of Men* (1908) and *The Fraud of Feminism* (1913), he was a staunch critic of the women's movement. **MaT**

Sources: Bax 1881, Bax 1885, Cowley 1992, *ODNB*.

BAXTER, JOHN (1781-1858) John Baxter was a printer and bookseller, who because of ill health, had left London to settle in Lewes. He was the first printer in England to use the inking roller and his most successful publication was an edition of the Bible which ran into thousands of copies and became known as 'Baxter's Bible'. In 1837, with his youngest son, William Edward Baxter, he founded the *Sussex Agricultural Express*, 'a newspaper which was so successful, that it now enjoys a circulation equal to that of any provincial* paper in the South of England' (Lower: 284). Baxter's second son, George, also gained renown as a lithographer* and colour printer. **DHL**

Sources: Lewis 1908, Lower 1865, *ODNB*.

BAXTER, WILLIAM GILES (1856-1888) While not the originator of 'Ally Sloper', one of the best known graphic comic creations of the nineteenth century, William Baxter, comic artist and illustrator*, was the driving force that rendered Sloper an omnipresent figure in the 1890s and on into the popular collective consciousness of the early twentieth century. Baxter had a formal background in drawing through his architectural training, and had drawn for the Manchester-based magazine *Momus** before working for *Judy** in the early 1880s.

On his move to London, he began to work for *Ally Sloper's Half Holiday** (1884 to 1888), a comic tabloid that exploited the already established comic persona of Sloper, which had been invented and developed by Charles Henry Ross and first appeared in *Judy* in August 1867. Ross had worked with his wife, the cartoonist*, Isabelle Emily de Tessier* ('Marie Duval'), in taking the Ally Sloper idea from an occasional presence in *Judy* to establishing both Sloper's complex comic persona and elaborating a variety of formats* through which his presence might be exploited commercially. Apart from appearances in the magazine, *Judy* reprinted Sloper's exploits in volume form, thus creating the first comic books.

Separate periodical publications also began to emerge, most notably *Ally Sloper's Comic Kalendar*, published annually* as a picture paper between 1875 and 1887. But the Sloper phenomenon only took off after 1884 when Ross sold the rights to Gilbert Dalziel* who launched *Ally Sloper's Half-Holiday* as a weekly* publication on 3 May 1884. Although largely made up of reprints of the *Judy* comic strips, Dalziel brought in Baxter to draw large-scale front page cartoons* for the paper, which was published in tabloid form. Baxter went on in four short years to evolve a whole set of characters which brought Ally Sloper's imagined world into substantial and celebrated being. Baxter died a young man in 1888, but the Sloper cartoons were continued by W. F. Thomas until the final issue of the paper in 1923, with several attempts to revive the Sloper brand well into the twentieth century. BM

Source: *ODNB*.

BAYLEY, FREDERICK WILLIAM NAYLOR (1808-1852) Frederick William Naylor Bayley, poet, author, and first editor of the *Illustrated London News*, was born in Ireland, possibly of mixed race. After accompanying his father to Barbados at age 17 he returned to England in 1829 and around 1831 became music critic* for the *Morning Post*. The same year he founded and edited the penny* *National Omnibus and General Advertiser*. When he became editor* of the *Illustrated London News* in 1842, he set the journal's style and format for the next hundred years with the first number. Throughout his life he published poetry* in newspapers and issued albums such as *Six Sketches of Taglioni* (1831) and *Gems for the Drawing Room* (1852), as well as songs and fiction.

One of the most innovative editors of the 1840s, he became known as 'Omnibus' or 'Alphabet' Bayley. He was forced to relinquish his position with the *Illustrated London News*, however, because of his debts (Richardson: 198). A projected publication, *The Great Gun,* failed. After this, 'Mr. Bayley sunk gradually in the estimation of the learned and unlearned'. (Richardson: 202) DHL
Sources: Boase, *ODNB*, Richardson 1855.

***BEACON* (1821-1822)** Established in Edinburgh in 1821, the Tory *Beacon* was founded in reaction to the Whiggish *Scotsman* by editor* Duncan Stevenson (1776-1867), formerly of the *Edinburgh Weekly Chronicle*. Particularly incendiary in tone, the *Beacon*'s editorial matter was aimed at redressing the 'evil' perpetrated by other newspapers at the time, attacking what it saw as the 'licentiousness of the press'. Alongside attacks on the commercial, immoral and unscrupulous press, there are many articles which assail and lampoon Whiggism in general, as well as specific personal attacks, most notably on the Whig politician James Stuart (1775-1849). This and other similar incidents led to libel suits, personal physical attacks and challenges of duels between Stevenson and his backers and those he had attacked in the paper.

The *Beacon* was a large-format* Saturday weekly* in three columns* rather than a broadsheet, and the first issue was 'Gratis', though from then on the price* was 10d. In 1822, production moved from Edinburgh to London where the *Beacon* was presided over by Walter Scott*, and the price dropped to 7d. Although focusing on heavily biased political* news, it covered national and international news* in general, including several articles reproduced from the national* press such as *The Times*, and carried targeted advertising* on its rear pages. MBT
Sources: *Beacon*, Bell 2007, *ODNB*, Waterloo.

BEARDSLEY, AUBREY VINCENT (1872-1898) Aubrey Beardsley's brief career as an artist, illustrator and writer identified him closely with two avant-garde magazines*, both of which sought to give equal status to visual and written contributions. The first was the *Yellow Book* which Beardsley, already notorious for the sensuality of his drawings for the 1894 John Lane* edition of *Salome*, co-founded with Henry Harland and edited* between April 1894 and May 1895. Although the *Yellow Book* contained illustrations* by such worthies as Frederick Leighton and Robert Anning Bell* as well as several established writers, it was Beardsley's drawings that attracted attention and, generally, outrage and contempt. Yet, despite impressive sales and the mistakenness of the general association of the *Yellow Book* with Oscar Wilde*, Beardsley became a victim of Wilde's arrest and trial, and he was sacked from his editorship by John Lane.

Tubercular from childhood, Beardsley's career might have been in jeopardy at this point but for the intervention of Leonard Smithers*, a bookseller turned publisher*, who proposed to set up a rival to the *Yellow Book*. The *Savoy*, which first appeared in January 1896, paired Beardsley as editor with Arthur Symons*, but the artist had begun to sink into illness and dissipation, and some of his projected illustrations for the *Savoy* were only publishable in an expurgated form. Beardsley also submitted occasional work to the *Pall Mall Budget*, the *Studio* and the *Idler**. Beardsley's provoking use of the grotesque and the menacing, his eroticism and determination to shock, all came at a moment when new reprographic technologies, especially half-tone and photogravure, gave black and white illustration a new charge, and furthered his influence as an avant-garde artist who gave enhanced aesthetic stature to the medium of illustration. The fineness and precision of his line, enabled and enhanced by new photo-reprographic methods, were new and unique in the periodical press. **BM**

Sources: Engen 1990, *ODNB*.

BEAUMONT, THOMAS WENTWORTH (1792-1848) Educated at Eton and St John's College, Cambridge, Thomas Beaumont inherited the Tory parliamentary seat for Northumberland from his father and a vast fortune from his mother. He utilized both political and financial inheritances in his venture as proprietor* and editor*of the *British and Foreign Review; or, European Quarterly Journal**.

The spirit of reform that was sweeping through England and the rest of Europe contributed to the 1832 foundation of the Literary Association of the Friends of Poland. Beaumont was president of the Association and the need for a publication resulted in the launch, in 1835, of the *British and Foreign Review*, the requisite £2,000 provided from the fortune of the MP. As its proprietor, Beaumont only contributed eight articles of editorial and political content, but he clearly outlined in the 'Prospectus' the broader political* and cultural landscape within which the Polish question was set. He made grand claims for his periodical: in 'shaking the throne of the despot', it would seek truth in politics*, science* and literature* to provide 'useful and agreeable entertainment'.

With his hands-on proprietorial style Beaumont found difficulty in relinquishing power to his editors. While officially only named as editor from April to July 1836, he dipped in and out with his interference. Beaumont's editorial hand was supposedly relinquished after July 1836 to John

Kemble* but Beaumont retained control while Kemble operated with the power of a subeditor. By 1844, the *Review* was losing money despite Beaumont spending £3,000 annually on it. Not surprisingly, he baulked at expenditure on a project in which he had, according to Kemble, lost interest, as he spent more time on the Continent. Disagreements between them rumbled on and the end of the *Review* came in July 1844, supposedly as a result of disputes on foreign policy. **CL**

Sources: *ODNB, Wellesley.*

BECKER, LYDIA ERNESTINE (1827-1890) Born in Manchester, Lydia Becker was a pioneer suffragist, who used journalism as a propaganda tool in her activism. After becoming the secretary of the Manchester National Society for Women's Suffrage in 1867, she founded and edited* the monthly* *Journal of the Manchester National Society for Women's Suffrage* first issued in March 1870, which changed its name after a year to the *Women's Suffrage Journal**. She kept the price* at 1d, often having to subsidize its cost, and it ceased publication only with her death.

Her articles were not confined to the *Journal*. Dean Alford*, editor of the *Contemporary Review** and a member of the London Provisional (Suffrage) Petition Committee, had asked Emily Davies to arrange for someone to write an article on women's suffrage* for the *Review*. Becker's article, 'Female Suffrage' appeared in the March 1867 issue. The Manchester Committee then had 10,000 copies of the article printed in pamphlet form for campaigning. Other articles included 'Political Disabilities of Women' (*Westminster Review** Jan. 1872) which was reprinted in the *Englishwoman's Review** in addition to several others for that journal. She also had articles published in *Longman's**, the *Nineteenth Century**, *Women and Work** and the *Journal of the Women's Education Union*.

From 1881, as secretary to the central committee of the National Society for Women's Suffrage and later its parliamentary agent, she undertook lecture tours which were caricatured in press cartoons*. **SBA**

Sources: Crawford 1999, Liddington and Norris 1978, *ODNB*, 19CUKP.

BEE-HIVE (1861-1876) The most influential trade union paper of its time, the *Bee-Hive* began as a 2d weekly* founded and managed by George Potter (1832-1893), a renowned and militant trade unionist. Potter had little experience of journalism*, but installed George Troup* as his editor*. The content was managed to ensure a broad appeal: conventional news* items sat alongside political* comment and reports on union meetings.

Circulation* quickly reached 5,000, but the failure of the unions to back the paper financially soon led it into difficulty. Circulation declined to 2,700 after two years, and by April 1862 the paper was £827 in the red. Troup's backing for the Confederacy in the American Civil War caused friction among the Board of Directors, who insisted that he resign in 1863. Robert Hartwell, a working-class compositor, became editor, bringing the paper's views into line with the majority of the trades union* movement by transferring its allegiance to the North.

The *Bee-Hive* reported on the first meeting of the First International in 1864, and was quickly recognised as its organ. Potter's policy of supporting every strike regardless of circumstances was good for business – circulation exceeded 8,000 during the industrial disputes of 1865 – but it angered advocates of a more considered approach. A group of trade union leaders known as 'the Junta' made concerted efforts to take over.

Financial strain and declining sales forced the *Bee-Hive* to change direction and in 1868 it promised to include 'such lighter matter as will please the females', later assuming the subtitle *A General Family Newspaper*. The paper was saved from bankruptcy by Daniel Pratt, coming under the control of the Liberal MP Samuel Morley (1809-1886). Hartwell left, and when the paper was relaunched as a penny* weekly in 1870, it effectively became a liberal paper for workers. A eulogistic letter to Gladstone pleaded for a 'patient hearing' for the 'working bees'. Potter later returned as editor and the paper swung back to the left. At the end of 1876, complaining of financial difficulties, it became the 2d *Industrial Review*, closing down two years later. **MaT**

Sources: Coltham 1964, Coltham 1965, Harrison 1974, *ODNB*, *Waterloo*.

BEER, RACHEL (1858-1927) Rachel Beer (née Sassoon) arrived in England soon after being born in India. In 1887, she married Frederick Beer who inherited ownership* of the *Observer** newspaper. However, Rachel Beer's involvement in the paper was always much greater than her husband's, and she contributed articles to it before taking over as editor* in 1891.

Rachel Beer purchased the eight-page, 1d *Sunday Times** for £11,000 in October 1894 from its wealthy proprietor*, Alice Cornwell. Beer decided she would largely edit* the paper herself from home in Mayfair and to facilitate this had a telephone

connection set up to the office in Fleet Street*. For the first two years her assistant editor was Arthur A' Beckett*. Beer wrote leaders*, features and book reviews*, and became the first woman to own a national newspaper, and the first person to have editorship of two national papers. She used the *Sunday Times* as a vehicle for her imperialist* views in the leader, 'The World's Work'. As a member of the Society of Women Journalists*, she sometimes hosted the annual meeting at her Mayfair home, and was also a member of the Institute of Journalists*. Beer made her reputation in Fleet Street for her business acumen and the 'equal assurance' with which she wrote articles for both her papers. The news* story for which she gained greatest acclaim was her involvement in the exposure of Esterhazy in the 1898 Dreyfus affair. When her husband died in 1903, she had a breakdown, and in 1904 both newspapers were sold. **CL**

Sources: *Freeman's Journal* 1894, Griffiths 2006, *ODNB*, Onslow 2000.

BEERBOHM, HENRY MAXIMILIAN (1872-1956) Illustrator*, caricaturist* and writer, Max Beerbohm's caricature portraits, as much as Beardsley's* erotically charged, elegant grotesqueries or Phil May's genial London street characters, are entirely characteristic of the 1890s. Derived from the famous mildly satirical* portraits contributed to *Vanity Fair** by Pellegrini* for many years from 1865, Beerbohm's gently satiric images of well-known contemporaries, many of them belonging to London artistic or bohemian circles, gave a more literary and contextualized account of their lives than Pellegrini's images. Beerbohm's first major contribution to periodicals comprised a series of over 30 'club* types' in the *Strand Magazine** in 1892, and he contributed other illustrations to the *Yellow Book**, the *Pall Mall Budget*, the *Savoy** and the *Sketch** over the next decade. As a writer he was a widely published essayist, but his major written contribution to the periodical press was as the theatre critic for the *Saturday Review**, a post he occupied in succession to George Bernard Shaw* without much qualification but with increasing assurance between 1898 and 1910. **BM**

Sources: Houfe 1978, Houfe 1992, *ODNB*.

BEETON, ISABELLA MARY (1836-1865) Mrs Beeton (née Mayson) became a household name because of Beeton's *Book of Household Management*, issued in parts (1859-1861) and subsequently in proliferating volume and part-issues until long after Isabella's death. However, most of her working life was spent as editor*, journalist* and business partner of her husband, Samuel Beeton*. The famous 'Book' grew out of the *Englishwoman's Domestic Magazine** which they jointly edited from their marriage in 1856 until her early death.

Her role in the Beeton publishing* ventures is not clear but was probably considerable. As 'Editress' of the *Englishwoman's Domestic Magazine* she contributed anonymous material on fashion* and domestic* advice. A visit to Paris in 1860 established a French connection which was exploited in a new enlarged series featuring her accounts of the modes and high-quality steel-engraved plates by Jules D-avid. She oversaw much of this, as she did the launch of their ambitious up-market weekly* newspaper, the *Queen**, in 1861. Isabella was also deeply involved in the next Beeton magazine, the *Young Englishwoman**, launched in 1864 just months before her death, aged 28, from puerperal fever. Samuel's subsequent bankruptcy and other difficulties can not be attributed entirely to the absence of her efficiency and influence. However, it is clear that during their brief life as a married couple and business partnership Isabella was crucial to their joint success in opening up the magazine market to new groups of women readers*. **MRB**

Sources: Beetham 1996, *Englishwoman's Domestic Magazine,* Hughes 2005, *ODNB*.

BEETON, SAMUEL ORCHART (1831-1877) Samuel Beeton was a radical and energetic publisher* of books of instruction and useful knowledge, including *The Book of Household Management* edited by his wife, Isabella*. However, his major contribution to Victorian publishing was a variety of pioneering journals. The *Englishwoman's Domestic Magazine** (1852-1879) was a monthly* aimed at middle-class* women with a mixture of serialized fiction*, domestic advice*, fashions* and letters* pages, which was to become the pattern for the woman's magazine* for more than a century. The *Boy's Own Magazine** (1855-1862) pioneered the journal for boys while the *Queen** (1861-1967) was a large-format up-market weekly* full of illustrations*, particularly of fashion, while his final venture was the *Young Englishwoman** (1864-1877). Beeton's advertising* techniques were bold and eye-catching, particularly for the run of Beeton Christmas Annuals*. As well as the normal modes of self-advertisements in his magazines, he offered prizes, special supplements* and other inducements.

From 1856 to her death in 1865 Samuel's wife, Isabella, was his business partner, fellow-editor* and journalist. After her death, Samuel's affairs

spiralled downwards. He became bankrupt and in 1866 sold his name and titles to Ward and Lock (later Ward, Lock and Tyler*). In 1867, the correspondence column of the *Englishwoman's Domestic Magazine* ran a series of controversial letters on tight-lacing and whipping. In 1872, he lost a court case over the use of the Beeton name. Despite these later problems, Beeton made an important contribution to journalism, not only because he opened up new readerships* among middle-class women and young people but also because he helped launch the careers of Frederick and James Greenwood*, Mrs Matilda Browne ('Myra')* and Christopher Weldon*. **MRB**

Sources: Beetham 1996, *Englishwoman's Domestic Magazine,* Hughes 2005.

BELFAST NEWS-LETTER (1737-) Belfast's first newspaper, the bi-weekly *Belfast News-Letter's* most interesting period was perhaps from the 1780s until 1795, when it was a mouthpiece for radical Presbyterianism in the north of Ireland. It was edited* in the 1790s by Henry Joy (cousin of the United Irishman Henry Joy McCracken). Joy was a former Irish Volunteer who had supported Irish legislative independence in the 1780s. After the suppression of the United Irishmen in 1795, new editor George Gordon promised to uphold 'peace, order and the constitution'. Almost immediately the paper became more parochial in outlook. By the time of the rebellion of 1798 it had joined the loyal mainstream, and welcomed the Act of Union of Britain and Ireland (1801) with a leader* urging all Irish people to bury their political* differences within the wider interests of empire.

In 1804, Alfred MacKay became the proprietor*, and it was owned, published* and printed by members of his family for the rest of the century, during which time the paper remained politically Conservative, speaking largely to the Protestant land-owning elite. James Alexander Henderson, MacKay's descendent through the female line, took over in 1844. Its 'ecclesiastical intelligence' reports were confined to the Protestant churches, and in 1829 it vehemently opposed Catholic emancipation.

In 1828 it consisted of four quarto pages five columns* in width, and cost 5d, with the price* dropping to 4d in 1836. It went daily* in 1854, expanding to eight columns, and in 1878 it doubled in size to eight pages and dropped its price to 1d. In 1900 it expanded to 12 pages.

From 1800 until the 1840s, the newspaper almost exclusively reported on news from London and on foreign affairs*. Gradually, from the 1840s onwards, more Irish news was incorporated, and by the 1860s it was reporting in detail on local* events in Belfast. Also, from that date, it dedicated an unusual amount of column inches to literary* matters for a newspaper and printed sports'* reports, articles on horticulture and gardening*, and pieces detailing the latest developments in ladies' fashion*. MJH/MaT

Sources: 19CBLN, *Waterloo Irish.*

BELFAST VINDICATOR (1839-1848) The *Vindicator* was a bi-weekly newspaper published in Belfast on Wednesdays and Saturdays, costing 4d. Founded by a group of Belfast Catholics in response to the growth of the Protestant press, its aim was to represent Catholic opinion and to support Daniel O'Connell's Repeal movement. When consulted, O'Connell suggested journalist Thomas Murray Hughes as editor*, but his refusal led to the appointment of Charles Gavan Duffy*. Besides political coverage, the *Vindicator* included poetry*, often patriotic in theme. Known contributors in this area include T. M. Hughes and James Clarence Mangan *, in addition to verses by Duffy himself.

Duffy relinquished the proprietorship* and editorship of the *Vindicator* in 1842, when he founded the *Nation** in Dublin. He was followed as editor by Kevin T. Buggy, a former contributor to *Tait's Edinburgh Magazine*** and the *Freeman's Journal**. Dying soon afterward, Buggy was succeeded as editor by C. D. Fitzgerald (1843-1846). Young Ireland journalist Thomas MacNevin was a regular contributor during this period. The *Vindicator* was closed in 1848 after a prosecution for libel, and was forced to sell its equipment in order to discharge its debts. **FB**

Sources: Brown 1937, Duffy 1898, *Waterloo Irish.*

BELFAST WEEKLY NEWS (1855-1942) The *Belfast Weekly News* was published from July 1855 as a weekly* companion newspaper to the *Belfast News-Letter*. Editor* and proprietor* James Alexander Henderson promised that the *Weekly News* would be the servant of no political party. However, it adopted the stridently conservative, anti-Catholic tone of the *News-letter* and claimed, in particular, to stand for the rights and interests of the tenant farmers of Ulster.

It covered local* politics* and news* in depth, trade, literature, including serializations* of popular novels, and fashion*. Its pages were replete with reports of the proceedings of Orange Lodges in both Ireland and Britain. The *Weekly News*'s hardline conservatism was apparent in its views on Fenianism. The required response to nationalist

conspiracy, it claimed, was not 'Whig doctoring' but 'smiting, with an unrelenting hand, every man who lifts his head in rebellion'. It portrayed Parnell as an agrarian terrorist in cartoons* reminiscent of *Punch**, before conceding in an obituary* (Oct. 1891) that he had been a statesman and a gentleman compared to his followers.

In the late nineteenth century the *Weekly News* reflected Belfast's growing importance as an industrial city by covering trade and labour relations in some detail. Its view of industrial relations was that labour and capital shared similar interests, which ought to be balanced in the 'commonweal'. **MJH**

Source: *Waterloo Irish.*

BELGRAVIA (1867-1899) *Belgravia,* an illustrated* shilling* monthly edited* by the sensation novelist Mary Braddon* from its foundation in 1867 until 1876, was perhaps the most successful of John Maxwell's* magazine* ventures. In its green cover with an elaborate border, it was launched in a blaze of publicity, and advertised on station hoardings. It reached a circulation* of 18,000 in 1868, averaging 15,000 at its sale to Chatto and Windus* in 1876, when its title changed from *Belgravia: A London Magazine* to *Belgravia: An Illustrated London Magazine. Belgravia*'s commercial success under Braddon owed much to her policy of serializing* her own sensation novels in it, but also to her vigorous, sometimes challenging, editing of a magazine, which, superficially, merely marketed an illusion of intimacy with 'high society' to the middle classes.

Belgravia offered readers a lively mix of poetry*, social satire and topical essays. Scientific articles by Richard Proctor* and others were cleverly linked to concepts of 'sensation'. When her own sensation fiction was attacked in *Blackwood's**, she organized a vigorous and sustained defence by herself and George Augustus Sala*. During her editorship contributors were drawn largely from the interlocking networks of *Temple Bar**, *St James's** and *Dublin University Magazine** writers, Sala being notably prolific. Others included Blanchard Jerrold*, T. H. S. Escott*, Sheridan Le Fanu* and Percy Fitzgerald and Dutton Cook, both of whom continued as contributors for Chatto. Among illustrators* were Mary Ellen Edwards*, Alfred Thompson and Louis Huard. Work by 'Phiz' (Hablot K. Browne)* appeared in the *Belgravia Annuals** of the late 1860s.

After the sale, Andrew Chatto introduced work by Wilkie Collins*, Mark Twain and Charles Reade. Thomas Hardy's* 'Return of the Native', (1878-1879) and W. H. Mallock's 'The New

Republic' (1876) were both serialized in *Belgravia*. Other contributors included Eliza Linton*, Mrs Lovett Cameron, Florence Marryat* and Beatrice Harraden, whose first story was published there. The loss of regular Braddon serials after 'Joshua Haggard's Daughter' finished, however, appears to have resulted in a loss of readers, from which *Belgravia* never recovered. Circulation* declined steadily from 12,000 in August 1876 to 3,500 a year later. From 1886 to 1889 *Belgravia* included fiction only, and in 1888 the word *Illustrated* was dropped from its title. Chatto sold *Belgravia* to F. V. White and Co. in September 1889. From the mid-1880s onwards there was a noticeable reduction in the number of illustrations, although Alfred Rimmer contributed some and T. R. Macquoid illustrated Katherine Macquoid's travel essays, the most consistent of *Belgravia*'s non-fiction genres. Contributors in the final decade included Helen Mathers, Florence Maryatt and Marie Corelli. In this period, advertisements* occupied up to 27 pages. After further changes of ownership (1897-1899) *Belgravia* ceased publication. **BMO**
Sources: Edwards, Sibley and Versteeg 1989, Onslow 2002, Robinson 1995, Sullivan, Wolff 1974, Wolff 1979.

BELL, JOHN (1745-1831) John Bell was a prolific figure in the London printing and book trade during the late eighteenth and early nineteenth centuries, with activities including both book publishing* and newspapers. He founded no fewer than five newspapers, the first of which was the *Morning Post**. Instigated in 1772, Bell was the principal proprietor* for nearly 15 years, contributing a column* two or three times a week. The *Morning Post* continued throughout the nineteenth and early twentieth centuries, merging with the *Daily Telegraph** in 1937. Bell launched several other papers and journals during the late eighteenth century, including the *Oracle*, which amalgamated with the *Daily Advertiser* in 1798. In 1796, the successful *Bell's Weekly Messenger** began its hundred-year run, developing a large circulation at home (circulation* records were broken with 14,405 copies of the Nelson funeral edition sold) and acknowledgement abroad. At the end of the century, Bell established two society journals, containing fashion* plates: the *World, or Fashionable Gazette** in January 1787 and *La Belle Assemblée** in February 1790. As the *World of Fashion*, the former journal continued until 1851, when it became the *Ladies' Monthly Magazine*. The title finally changes to *Le Monde Elegant* until 1891, when it ceased. Among

his other achievements, Bell revolutionized bookbinding enabling the production of cheaper books, as well as being credited with modernizing the typeface of English printing. **DHL**
Sources: Hindle 1937, Morison 1930, *ODNB*, Sullivan.

BELL, ROBERT ANNING (1863-1933) An important figure in the Arts and Crafts design movement, Robert Bell, artist, designer and sculptor, was also an illustrator* using a simplified line derived from the woodcut* tradition, much in the manner of Walter Crane*. He became closely associated with the *Studio**, which began publication in 1893 and gave him an immediate place to publish work, including photographs* of his designs for large-scale panels, stained glass and reliefs. He published little further in periodicals, but did contribute to the *Yellow Book** in 1894-1895. **BM**
Sources: Houfe 1978, *ODNB*.

***BELL'S LIFE IN LONDON, AND SPORTING CHRONICLE* (1822-1886)** *Bell's* was the first newspaper to feature sport* as a major component, from bare-knuckle and other prizefighting to horse racing, cricket and rowing. The paper also published the minutes of sporting organizations, news* about politics*, the royal family, foreign* news, theatre reviews* and the more notorious crimes* of the day. Heavily illustrated*, it featured woodcuts*, engravings, and cartoons*.

First published in January 1822 by Robert Bell*, a printer and newsvendor*, *Bell's Life in London* became known as *Bell's Life in London, and Sporting Chronicle* by March, when it began its official series run as a weekly* newspaper, with the enticing subtitle *combining with the news of the week, a rich repository, of fashion*, wit and humour, and interesting incidents of high and low life*. In 1827, it absorbed *Pierce Egan's Life in London and Sporting Guide*, and it later merged* with the *Sportsman** and in the 1880s with *Penny Bell's Life, or Sporting News*. In 1885 the newspaper was renamed again *Bell's Life in London*, but was absorbed 14 months later by *Sporting Life**.

In 1824 William Innell Clement, publisher* of the *Observer**, bought the newspaper from Bell, and he made Vincent George Dowling* its editor*, a post Dowling held for nearly 30 years until his death. During Dowling's tenure, *Bell's* developed a wide appeal: engaging the respectable and the rough, it prospered by covering the popular sports like pedestrianism, pugilism, cricket and horse racing. The paper became a source of authority in the sporting culture* of nineteenth-century Britain.

Using the technique and style pioneered by Pierce Egan*, *Bell's* made its early reputation covering prize fighting. It could also boast prestigious contributors including Charles Dickens*, 'Frosty Faced' Jack Fogo, Thomas Hood*, William Howitt*, Robert Southey and Robert Surtees*, with high-calibre illustrators* such as George Cruikshank*, John Leech*, Kenny Meadows* and Robert Seymour*. *Bell's* also served as a source of information in the broadest sense, as it published schedules, results, sporting challenges and answers to correspondents'* questions concerning sports and games of all kinds. Dowling's son Frank Louis Dowling* became editor in 1851. Under the guidance of Turf editor, William Ruff*, *Bell's* also provided reliable and up-to-date horse racing intelligence at a price far below monthlies* like the *Sporting Magazine*.

Typically perceived as a publication with a lower-class* audience due to its low cost and its subject matter, *Bell's* was also read by members of the middle and upper classes*, and was highly respected as an institution, even serving as a stakeholder for sporting bets and prizefights. Starting with a circulation* of 3,000, *Bell's* enjoyed a tremendous upsurge in popularity* beginning in the mid-1830s and 1840s, when weekly circulation hovered around 20,000, and peaked in the 1850s at 30,000 per week. It survived for 64 years with 3,799 numbers.

Throughout its run, *Bell's* was published on Saturdays or Sundays, and reprinted on Mondays with updated market* news; the publishers made brief forays into daily* publication in the 1840s and bi-weekly publication in the 1880s. The newspaper's standard format* was 39 cm sheets, three columns* per page, and eight or 12 pages per issue. The only significant deviations from this format were made during the final years of publication, when the newspaper merged with other periodicals and circulation was dropping. Printing information available suggests in-house printing, as the only outside printers named, besides Robert Bell in 1822, are W. R. Macdonald, also in 1822, and Bleakley and Co., in 1886. Costing 7d in 1822, *Bell's* continued as a low-price* weekly, never costing as much as it had initially: in the 1840s, it cost 5d, and in the 1850s, 6d; by the 1870s, the price had again dropped to 5d; increased circulation never altered the total weekly price.

At Ruff's death in 1856, the paper faced competition from the *Field*, and the new 1d sporting papers, which began appearing in 1859. *Bell's* struggled in the transformed market, altering its frequency* and price in the late 1860s and early 1870s, until it was sold in 1883. The new proprietors*, racing reporters Henry Buck and Charles Greenwood, could not save the paper and sold it in 1885 to E. O. Bleackley and Edward Hulton*. They unsuccessfully converted *Bell's* into a daily* before selling the name to the *Sporting Life* in 1886. **LAR/MM**

Sources: Harvey 2004, Knight 1851, Mason 1986, *ODNB*, *Sporting Press* 1856, Vann and Van Arsdel 1994, *Waterloo*, Watson 1899, *Wellesley.*

BELL'S WEEKLY DISPATCH AND SUNDAY DISPATCH See *Weekly Dispatch*

***BELL'S WEEKLY MESSENGER: THE COUNTRY GENTLEMAN AND LANDOWNERS' JOURNAL* (1796-1896)** Started by the renowned London printer and bookseller, John Bell*, who managed the paper until 1819, *Bell's Weekly Messenger* became the premier rural newspaper for many years, providing information necessary to the agricultural community. However, by cleverly expanding its appeal by widening its range of subject matter, it also functioned as a family* paper. By 1832 it consisted of three sections: *Bell's Weekly Messenger*, the *Reviewer* and the *Commercialist & Weekly Advertiser*. Having started life with a strict policy of no advertisements*, it became the first paper to include advertisements as opposed to announcements. The year 1832 also marked an increase in agricultural subject matter and around 1834 the *Messenger* absorbed the *Farmer's Journal*. By the 1870s the paper's significance in the originality and spread of agricultural content made it invaluable, its circulation* having increased from 13,000 in 1837 to 60,000 by 1870.

A moderate Tory paper, it not only covered the predictable sporting and country pursuits, but also the week's news, both home and foreign affairs* cultural matters including theatre reviews*, and by 1837, up to ten book reviews*. This cultural breadth was also reflected in the early 1840s in the brief editorial tenure of the poet and playwright Thomas Wade, surely a surprising candidate for the editorship* of an agricultural journal.

As its format* of eight pages with five broad columns* was larger than other papers, *Bell's Weekly Messenger* was considered to be good value for its early 6d price*. In 1896 it became the *Country Sport and Messenger*, which ceased publication in 1904. **CL**

Sources: *ODNB*, *Waterloo.*

***LA BELLE ASSEMBLÉE* (1806-1847)** *La Belle Assemblée, or Bell's Court and Fashionable Magazine addressed particularly to the Ladies,* was the most important women's fashion* magazine of its day, as well as the most expensive, at 3s an issue. It was launched by John Bell* as a monthly* in 1806, and in addition to sections devoted to London and Paris fashions, with engraved plates (eventually in colour), it included news from foreign courts, papers on politics*, details of places of interest such as museums and galleries, literary offerings including a serial* romance, songs with music* and 'lectures on useful sciences'*, such as astronomy, botany, hydrostatics and cookery. There was also a high-class gossip* column following the activities of various celebrities*. In addition, each issue was accompanied by an advertising* supplement, with advertisements* for clothing, insurance, accommodation and much else. There was also a literary supplement*, containing extracts from recently published novels, poems*, histories and the like. Like other magazines of the period, it often relied on readers to provide copy, especially of social news. In 1832 it changed its title* to the *Court Magazine*, being edited* by Caroline Norton*, and in 1838 it merged with the *Lady's Magazine* and the *Lady's Monthly Museum*. **DD**

Sources: Adburgham 1972, Beetham 1996.

BENBOW, WILLIAM (1784-?1853) In 1817, Benbow was a key figure linking ultra-radicals in London and Lancashire, where he was agent for *Cobbett's Political Register*. William Cobbett* dedicated the first edition (1818) of his *English Grammar* to him. With Cobbett's encouragement, Benbow established a publishing* business in London and between June 1820 and January 1821, Benbow published *Cobbett's Political Register*. However, in the opinion of Cobbett's daughter, Benbow was 'the greatest, ten thousand million times the greatest, villain that Papa ever had to deal with' and they parted acrimoniously.

Alongside a steady stream of bawdy pamphlets, Benbow published first the *Radical Magazine* (1821) and then the daring *Rambler's Magazine: or, Fashionable Emporium of Polite Literature* (1822-1824). Breaking new ground in serialized* translations of French libertine fiction, it was targeted in a failed prosecution for obscenity by the Society for the Suppression of Vice. Despite this lack of publishing respectability, Benbow is principally remembered as a political* agitator and an innovative and forceful advocate of general strike, or 'Grand National Holiday' (the *Poor Man's Guardian** first publicized this in 1831). In January 1832 this was printed in book form by Richard Lee, whose unstamped *Man* (1833-1834), gave extensive space to

followers of Thomas Spence, with whom Benbow associated. Lee also printed Benbow's next periodical, *Tribune of the People* (1832), but peremptorily ceased publication when sales (under 500 an issue) failed to meet creditors' demands. Benbow alleged Cleave* and Hetherington* had turned paper merchants against him 'and in otherways contribute to his injury by spoiling his credit'. His next periodical, *Agitator and Political Anatomist* (1833), was his last. Benbow's career underlines that unstamped* papers were not always politically high-minded. Yet his renown was such that a former employee, Jack Mitford, launched a *New London Rambler's Magazine* (1828-1830), while his mission to expose (as *Agitator* declaimed) 'the profligacy and crimes of the clergy' in turn influenced Cleave's *Weekly Police Gazette** and later G. W. M. Reynolds*. **MSC**

Sources: *DLB*, Hollis 1970, McCalman 1988, *ODNB*.

BENNETT, ALFRED WILLIAM (1833-1902) Bennett's journalism spanned the two areas that dominated his life: Quakerism, including the social issues encompassed by contemporary Quakers, and science*, especially botany. Bennett pursued a career in publishing* (1857-1868), producing a number of books and periodicals relating principally to issues of concern to the Society of Friends, including the *Friend**, which he also edited* (1858-1870), and the temperance *Band of Hope Review** (see also Quaker* periodicals). After selling his publishing business he lectured in Botany at Bedford College and St Thomas's Hospital London, pursued botanical research (which resulted in several books) and wrote for the periodical press. Having served his journalistic apprenticeship working as an editorial assistant to Norman Lockyer* on *Nature** (1869-early 1873), he became a regular contributor, principally on botanical topics, not only to such scientific titles as *Nature*, the *Popular Science Review*, and the *Journal of Botany*, but also to the *Academy**. Writing in the *Friend* and the *Friends' Quarterly Examiner* he addressed a wide range of social issues, including women's education* and poverty, and also frequently commented on questions concerning Quaker faith and practice, including Quaker attitudes to the natural world and to the theory of evolution. **GC**

Sources: *Annual Monitor* 1903, *ODNB*, *Waterloo*, *Wellesley*.

BENNETT, ARNOLD (1867-1931) Born into a middle-class Wesleyan family, Arnold Bennett began his career as a solicitor's clerk but soon rose to prominence as an influential editor*, journalist*, and fiction writer. In the 1890s, he began his journalistic career by contributing articles to the *Staffordshire Knot, Tit-bits** and the *Yellow Book**. In 1893 he was appointed assistant editor of *Woman** and assumed the role of editor-in-chief in 1896. During this period, he wrote the 'Book Chat' feature in *Woman* under the pseudonym* 'Barbara'. At the same time, he published reviews* and fiction in a variety of periodicals, including *Hearth and Home** and the *Academy**. After resigning his post as editor of *Woman* in 1900, Bennett became increasingly prolific and versatile as a writer, publishing a diverse array of novels, plays and periodical articles. He moved to Paris in 1902, where he wrote a regular self-help column* for *T. P.'s Weekly**. After the publication of his novel *The Old Wives Tale* in 1908, Bennett became well known as a fiction writer. At the same time, he continued to publish literary criticism in a variety of journals. From 1908 to 1911, Bennett contributed a series of short reviews to the *New Age** under the pseudonym* 'Jacob Tonson'. He returned to Britain in 1912 and a year later published a series of notable essays on the craft of writing in *Metropolitan Magazine**. Bennett played an important role as a war commentator for the *Daily News and Leader* (1914-1918), and later he wrote a highly regarded literary column for the *Evening Standard* (1926-1931). **ME**

Sources: Miller 1977, *ODNB*.

BENNETT, CHARLES HENRY (1828-1867) Artist, illustrator* and caricaturist*, Charles Bennett was best known as a comic artist who had worked for a number of humorous journals such as *Diogenes* (1855), the *Comic Times* (1855) and the *Comic News* (1863-1865). Bennett established his reputation with humorous illustrations for Henry Vizetelly's* *Illustrated Times* (1856), although he also drew for such mainstream illustrated magazines as *Good Words** (1861) and *London Society** (1862-1865) as well as *Every Boy's Magazine* (1864-1865). He joined the *Punch** staff early in 1865, drawing a series of illustrations for 'Essence of Parliament', and making an immediate impact with a wide range of contributions in the two years up to his death. Bennett's forte was the caricature portrait, produced in an idiom owing much to Regency grotesquerie. **BM**

Sources: de Maré 1980a, Engen 1990, Goldman 2004, Houfe 1978, *ODNB*, Spielmann 1895, White 1897.

BENNETT, JOSEPH (1831-1911) As chief music* critic of the *Daily Telegraph** (1870-1906), Joseph Bennett was a mover of public taste and a shaper of the emerging canon of contemporary British music.

At the *Daily Telegraph* Bennett took full advantage of the paper's huge readership* to enunciate his musical ideology. Regarding continental music, Bennett was a self-styled 'musical conservative' who admired Brahms and excoriated Wagner for being decadent and a destructive influence on musical development. With British music, he was a fervent critic-patriot who promoted composers such as Arthur Sullivan, Hubert Parry, C. V. Stanford and Edward Elgar in his columns, so that they might 'restore' the nation's musical glory and transform the perception that Britons were an unmusical people.

Bennett's early career as a critic began on the *Sunday Times** (1865-1874), the *Graphic** (1869-1874) and the *Pall Mall Gazette** (1867-1874), and he contributed numerous articles to both the *Musical Times** and the *Musical World**. Later, Bennett was founding editor* of *Concordia* (1875-1876), an ambitious and wide-ranging weekly* journal that placed music in the context of the other arts. He likewise served as founding-editor of the *Lute* (1883-1886) and worked as an assistant editor of the *Musical World* (1868-1874), becoming its acting editor in the early 1880s.

Bennett stressed the importance of music as a social and moral force, regarded journalism as much of a calling as a profession*, and relished his role as the people's critic, a journalist* who had his finger on the musical pulse of the nation. He was a key figure in the construction of the 'renaissance' of British music in the nineteenth century, an eminence that Elgar acknowledged when in 1905 he referred to Bennett as 'the patriarch and head of the profession'. **MH**

Sources: Bennett 1908, Hughes 2002, *New Grove*, Obituaries 1911, Young 1968.

BENNETT, THOMAS JEWELL (1852-1925) Journalist, newspaper proprietor*, and Conservative MP, Thomas Bennett began his apprenticeship on the *Ely and Wisbech Advertiser*, moving to the *Western Daily Press* in Bristol as assistant editor* and subsequently to the London *Standard** as a leader* writer. He went to Bombay in western India in 1884 to work on the *Bombay Gazette** as leader writer and associate editor. Bennett's big break came in 1892 when he became editor and co-proprietor* (sole proprietor from 1894) of the *Times of India**. Bennett was responsible for the modernization, and professionalization* of the paper, making it arguably the pre-eminent Anglo-Indian newspaper. He brought over a master printer, F. M.

Coleman, from England and the resultant publishing company, Bennett, Coleman & Co., still operates under that name, though it passed into Indian ownership in 1946. Bennett also invited leader* writers from Britain, the most prominent being Lovat Fraser and Stanley Reed, both of whom subsequently became editors of the *Times of India*. Bennett was a writing editor and championed Indian grievances with regularity and compassion. He left India in 1901 but retained control of the company until his death.

In Parliament he spoke chiefly on India, and occasionally on domestic, Irish and African affairs. Outside Parliament he continued to work on Indian issues, often contributing to the columns of *The Times**. ChK

Source: *ODNB*.

BENTLEY, JOHN JAMES (1860-1918) John James Bentley began his career in journalism in 1877 when, as a member of the Turton association football club, he began writing match reports and even reported on Turton's contests. After moving to Bolton in 1880, Bentley worked as a clerk before becoming an accountant and income tax collector. He also joined the Bolton Wanderers football club and was appointed secretary in 1885. Bentley's acumen as the 'Free Critic'* led to regular contributions under this pseudonym* to Bolton's *Football Field and Sports Telegram*, beginning in 1884. Two years later, in 1886, Bentley moved to Manchester as an assistant editor for England's top football paper, Edward Hulton's* *Athletic News**. He became the chief reporter* for the weekly*, covering football and cricket. Bentley transformed the bland narrative that was characteristic of the sporting* journalism of the 1880s by pioneering the lively, candid, chatty style of the New Journalism*. Bentley succeeded Sutton as editor* (1895-1900). After leaving the paper, the 'Free Critic' continued to contribute to a wide range of periodicals. MJM
Sources: Arnold 1902, Gibson and Pickford 1906, Inglis 1988, Mason 1980, *ODNB*.

BENTLEY, RICHARD (1794-1871) Richard Bentley and his elder brother Samuel, in partnership from 1819, were 'arguably the finest printers in London' (*ODNB*), but the former also played an important role as a publisher* of magazines and promoter of periodical literature in the early and mid-Victorian period. In 1829, Richard went into business with his firm's largest client, Henry Colburn*, and although the relationship soured within months, the 1830s saw a period of successful expansion by Bentley into mass-market* popular*

publishing, of which the most notable success was the 'Standard Novels' series of one-volume 6s reprints of popular authors (126 titles between 1831 and 1855). After splitting with Colburn, who was successfully exploiting the *New Monthly Magazine** to puff* his own authors and titles, Bentley sought a similar vehicle, eventually hitting on an idea for a light-hearted monthly magazine to be called the 'Wits' Miscellany'; this became *Bentley's Miscellany**. Its first editor* and serial* author was Charles Dickens*, hired at the height of his early success with *Pickwick Papers* and *Sketches by Boz*, but many of the other early contributors were also high-profile journalists: notably William Maginn*, Francis Mahony*, Thackeray*, William Jerdan*, Charles Mackay and George Hogarth*. While its later career was chequered, the early *Miscellany* set a new standard in genteel literary journalism*, with its fine illustrations* (many by George Cruikshank*) and light touch.

A staunch Tory, Bentley had good literary judgement but could be prickly and awkward to work for, and the mid-1840s saw a decline in his fortunes, with an ill-judged attempt to float a weekly* political* newspaper called *Young England*. It folded after 14 issues (Jan.-April 1845). Similarly unsuccessful in 1859 was *Bentley's Quarterly Review*, designed to steal a march on the established *Quarterly**. Success with another journal did not come until 1866, when Bentley bought *Temple Bar** from George Augustus Sala*, and installed his eldest son George (soon to take over day-to-day management from his ailing father) as editor. JMD
Sources: Chittick 1990, *ODNB*, Sutherland 1989, *Wellesley*.

BENTLEY'S MISCELLANY (1837-1868) In venturing into magazine* publishing, Richard Bentley* intended to eclipse the *New Monthly Magazine** of his great rival, Henry Colburn*, by commissioning new work by established names, rather than reprinting matter, and by promising a feast of wit and humour, rather than a diet of political and personal scraps. The working title was *Wits' Miscellany*, and as his first editor*, Bentley headhunted Charles Dickens*, then known to an ever-growing public as 'Boz', author of *Pickwick Papers* and various series of popular newspaper sketches. Sales under 'Boz's' editorship (Jan. 1837-Feb. 1839) were excellent for this handsomely-produced periodical of 108 pages, priced* at 2s 6d, printed on Royal octavo and illustrated* (until 1843) with exceptionally fine plates by George Cruikshank*. Thanks in part to the serialization of 'Oliver Twist' (Feb.

1837-April 1839), overlapping with that of 'Jack Sheppard' (Jan. 1839-Feb. 1840), the controversial prison-break thriller by Dickens's successor in the editorial chair, W. Harrison Ainsworth*, circulation* rose from 6,000 per month to over 7,500 at the change of hands, to a high of 8,500. The London-based *Miscellany** was already rivalling well-established monthlies such as *Fraser's** (8,700) and *Blackwood's** (8,000) in terms of sales.

Despite what R. H. Barham called the 'Radicalish tone' of 'Oliver' and the distinct Newgate atmosphere of 'Jack Sheppard', a light touch – conservative if never openly Tory – was provided by other well-known writers of both articles and fiction: Washington Irving, Charles Mackay, Catherine Gore, Willam Jerdan* and James Morier among them. Agreeably apolitical overall, the *Miscellany* courted blandness. Indeed, given that a majority of the contributors were also authors with book contracts for Bentley (e.g. 17 of the 22 fanfared before the first issue), the magazine was perhaps inevitably 'more of a publisher's list' than the product of the kind of *esprit de corps* that secured for some monthlies their market niche (Chittick: 38).

Ainsworth remained as editor until December 1841, when, with sales dropping to below 5,000, Bentley himself became the editor in name as well as *de facto* (both Dickens and Ainsworth had complained bitterly of his interference in the commissioning of articles and make-up of numbers). The decline continued. By 1845, many of the old hands were dead or retired. In 1852, the front-running serial novel made way for short anonymous tales, and the *Miscellany* became, in the words of Mrs Gore, 'too scrappy'. Bentley sold it to Ainsworth in November 1854 for £1,700, and its content briefly revived under the new proprietor* and experienced editor, becoming somewhat more political and topical, with series of articles on India and Russia, while rediscovering its literary distinction, with serials by Ellen (Mrs Henry) Wood* and fast stories of military and fashionable life by 'Ouida*'. Yet competitors*, particularly post 1860, came crowding in, and sales fell, by December 1868, to the nadir of 500, at which point Bentley finally succeeded in repurchasing his quondam flagship publication for £250, in order to absorb it into *Temple Bar**. JMD

Sources: Chittick 1990, Drew 2003, Gettman 1960, Schlicke 1998, Sutherland 1989, *Wellesley*.

BENT'S MONTHLY LITERARY ADVERTISER (1802?-1860) Best known as the rival to the *Publishers' Circular** and *Bookseller** until the latter

bought it out in 1862, *Bent's* was a simple publishers' advertising* sheet. William Bent began his *Literary Advertiser* in 1802, 'under a Committee of London Publishers' according to *Mitchell's Press Directory** to disseminate news of their products among booksellers more efficiently and cheaply. From 10 October 1805, the sixth issue and the earliest in the British Library, its masthead* declares it to be the *Monthly Literary Advertiser*. With what seems a supplement* for August 1805, the whole came to eight pages and cost 6d. Despite rising to 7d in June 1827, the price* and format* hardly changed until its close. It was divided into new publications, last season's works, works in the press and 'Literary Intelligence', the latter a set of very simple announcements of planned and forthcoming works contributed by publishers. Each section* (apart from Literary Intelligence) is divided by publisher (in the first issue, Murray*, Longman*, Rivington* and Hatchard among others are included). After Bent died in 1824, Hurst and then Simpkin* (who was later to start the *Publisher's Circular*) took over the publication for a brief period until Bent's son Robert purchased it. In 1832 he added *Bent's* before the title. From 1857 Thomas Hodgson succeeded Robert, and then Edward Tucker, both keeping the name. Although adding a list of newly published engravings* from August 1828, and later situations vacant or desired, lists of French and American works, lists of books wanted, book auctions, and an annual catalogue of new publications, the format remained almost unchanged to the end, void of the features and commentary its rivals carried. AK

Sources: Growoll and Eames 1903, *Waterloo*.

BERGER, GEORGE (1796?-1868) Berger was an enterprising and occasionally unscrupulous bookseller and publisher* of unstamped* journals, including several radical titles. Based in Hollywell Street by the Strand, he established himself as the biggest newsagent* in London prior to the success of W. H. Smith*.

Berger published political* tracts like 'An Address from H. Hunt Esq. to the Radical Reformers of England, Ireland and Scotland' (1831-1832), which complained of the Reform Bill's failure to deliver universal suffrage. He was also one of the publishers of the Owenite weekly *Crisis** (1832-1834). Apart from radical publications, his output included sensationalist matter such as the *Annals of Crime and Newgate Calendar* – an illustrated* penny* weekly* dramatizing the crimes* and trials of criminals – and miscellaneous fare like *Captain Pidding's*

Chinese Olio and Tea Talk (1844-1855), combining Chinese trivia and stories with weekly updates on the tea market.

He was not above cashing in on the success of others. *Chambers's London Journal* (1844-1845), co-published with John Clements and William Strange* under the fictional name of 'H. H. Chambers', clearly hinted at a non-existent affiliation with the hugely popular *Chambers's Edinburgh Journal* (1832-1956). The short-lived *Penny Lancet* (1832) – trading on the reputation of Thomas Wakley's* *Lancet** – sought to bring medical knowledge* to the masses and 'render it unnecessary to apply to medical men, except in extraordinary circumstances'. Berger assembled it himself, calling on the denizens of Grub Street rather than those of Harley Street to provide copy, and its advice – if followed – was potentially deadly. The opening of the jugular vein, for example, was recommended as a treatment for apoplexy.

He became embroiled in controversy in 1844 when Charles Dickens* sued him along with some of his associates ('vagabonds' and 'pirates' as Dickens called them) for selling a pirated version of his *Christmas Carol* that appeared in *Parley's Penny Library*. **MaT**
Sources: Haywood 2004, Hurwitz and Richardson 2004, James 1963, *Waterloo*, Wiener 1970.

BERTRAM, JAMES GLASS (1824-1892) A Scottish publisher*, editor* and journalist*, Bertram was apprenticed* to William Tait* at the age of 13, and worked on *Tait's Edinburgh Magazine**, where he became head clerk. By 1848, he was printer and publisher of the *North British Express**, and in 1855 he was appointed editor of the *North Briton**, of which he also became proprietor*. He sold the paper in 1872, remaining editor for one further year. He then moved to Glasgow, where he assisted in the establishment of the *Glasgow News*, which he left in 1874. After this date he supported himself by writing freelance journalism.

Throughout his career, he contributed articles to publications such as the *Contemporary Review**, the *Cornhill Magazine**, the *Fortnightly Review**, *Blackwood's Edinburgh Magazine** and *Fraser's Magazine**. The principal themes of his journalism were fishing and horse racing, but he surveyed both sports with the dispassionate eye of a keen businessman. Pisciculture interested him as much as the pursuit of angling, and his valorization of the Scottish 'fisher folk' focused on their diligence and industry. Similarly, his interest in racing was inseparable from his intense fascination with the amount of money that was changing hands: he estimated in 1877 that an average of £10,000 was staked every day in Britain: the turf legislation of 1874 had proved an ineffective deterrent for gamblers.

He wrote numerous books, including *Flagellation & the Flagellants: A History of the Rod in All Countries from the Earliest Period to the Present Time* (1869) (under the pseudonym* 'William M. Cooper'). Two books on horse racing (as 'Henry Louis Curzon'), books on fishing and a posthumous memoir, *Some Memories of Books, Authors and Events* (1893) drew on his journalism. **MaT**
Sources: Bertram 1862, Bertram 1877, Bertram 1882, Bertram 1893, *Scotsman* online, *Scoop, Scottish Book Trade Index, Wellesley*.

BESANT, ANNIE (1847-1933) A radical campaigner and theosophist, she was born Annie Wood and was related to Matthew Wood, a lord mayor of London and supporter of William Cobbett, and Katharine Parnell. In 1872, Thomas Scott, the freethinker published her pamphlet 'On the Deity of Jesus of Nazareth', which led to the breakdown of her marriage to the Rev. Frank Besant. In 1875, Charles Bradlaugh* engaged her to write for the *National Reformer**, the weekly journal of the National Secular Society, and eventually, as 'Ajax', she wrote a weekly column*. In 1877, Bradlaugh and Besant jointly published Charles Knowlton's 'The Fruits of Philosophy', advocating birth control.

In 1879, Besant started, but did not complete, a degree course at Birkbeck, where she met Edward Aveling, who was subsequently to introduce her to socialism. From 1883 to 1888, she published and edited* *Our Corner*, a 6d socialist* and literary monthly*. She was the first to publish work by George Bernard Shaw*, serializing* his novel 'The Irrational Knot' (1886-1887). After joining the Social Democratic Federation and the Law and Liberty League, she and W. T. Stead* jointly published* the *Link*, a ½d weekly*, in which during 1888, Besant campaigned on behalf of the match-girls' strike.

In 1889, she came into contact with Madame Blavatsky, the founder of the Theosophical Society, and became progressively involved with Theosophy, editing its journals, *Lucifer** and the *Theosophical Review**. She succeeded to the presidency of the Society in 1907, and moved to India, where she died. **JRW**
Sources: Banks 1985, *ODNB*.

BESANT, WALTER (1836-1901) Walter Besant began publishing* novels, in collaboration* with

James Rice, editor* of *Once a Week**, in the early 1870s, and by the1880s had established himself as one of the most popular and prolific writers in England. As well as serialized novels, he had previously published short fiction, historical essays and polemical writings in various journals including the *Daily News* (London)*, *Macmillan's Magazine** and the *British Quarterly Review**. Besant and Rice's 'Ready-Money Mortiboy: A Matter-of-Fact Story', a popular novel in which virtue triumphs over greed and selfishness, was serialized* in *Once a Week* (Jan.-June 1872), and had some success. In 1876 Besant and Rice were asked by the editors of *All the Year Round** to write the Christmas number*, and their novel 'The Golden Butterfly', first published in the *World** (Jan.-Oct. 1876), was well received. The two continued to write for *All the Year Round*, as well as collaborating in more than a dozen novels and collections of stories, which brought them both commercial and critical success.

After Rice's death in 1882, Besant achieved his greatest success with two novels about life among the poor in London's East End: *All Sorts and Conditions of Men*, serialized in *Belgravia** (Jan.-Dec. 1882), and *Children of Gibeon*, serialized in *Longman's Magazine** (Jan.-Dec. 1886). Besant's status as a reformer and philanthropist was a major reason for his being knighted in 1895. He was a founder member of the Society of Authors and creator and editor of its organ, the monthly* *Author*. CJM
Sources: *DLB, ODNB, Wellesley.*

BEVINGTON, LOUISA SARAH (1845-1895) Louisa Sarah Bevington, born in Battersea, Surrey and raised as a Quaker, used a range of genres from poetry* to political argument to express her views on science* and politics* and their impact on society, religion* and morality. In addition to poetry, Bevington wrote over half a dozen articles between the late 1870s and early 1880s signed as L. S. Bevington. A two-part piece for the *Nineteenth Century**, 'Modern Atheism and Mr. Mallock' (Oct. and Dec. 1879) was a measured response to Mallock's essay, 'Modern Atheism' (Jan. 1877), with Bevington arguing that morality was not dependent on a belief in God. Bevington's early interest in science and particularly evolution was encouraged by Herbert Spencer who asked her to write for the *Fortnightly Review** in 1881. The resulting piece, 'The Moral Colour of Rationalism' defends scientific philosophy* against the immorality charged by its critics. Her September 1881 essay for the *Nineteenth Century*, 'How to Eat Bread' illustrates the sharpening of her concern for the poor.

She also contributed to the *Modern Review** in 1882.

In 1883 she went to Germany and married, but by the early 1890s she had returned to London alone, more radicalized about anarchist politics* and continued to write under her maiden name. Her later work was largely for anarchist journals such as *Liberty*. She also wrote for *Commonweal** and *Freedom**. Her faith in evolution and disillusion with social organization is evident in a poem, 'The Secret of the Bees', that ran in *Liberty* in 1895, 'What man only talks of, the busy bee does;/ Shares food, and keeps order, with no waste of buzz'. CR
Sources: *ODNB*, Victorian Women Writers Project, Indiana.

***BICYCLING TIMES AND TOURIST'S GAZETTE* (1877-1887)** Promoted as 'an independent weekly* record of bicycling events', this journal underwent a number of title changes* over its run of a decade. In August 1882, it became the *Bicycling Times and Tricycle Record: a Weekly Review of Sport and Trade*, and in January 1884 it finally became the *Cycling Times: a Weekly Review of Sport and Trade*. Edited* in 1882 by Charles James Fox, and printed in 1877 by J. Adlard, it was priced* 2d. From its inception it was intended to be 'a high-class periodical' illustrated* with sketches and engravings*, devoted to this popular pastime. The first issues contained racing reports, club fixtures, and racing appointments; from 1882 a sale and exchange column* was introduced as well as tricycling notes with information on patents. Sections devoted to cycling clubs, police cyclists and coming events appeared from 1884. DHL
Source: *Waterloo.*

BIGGS, CHARLES HENRY WALKER (1845-1923) Charles Biggs's early career was as a schoolmaster and tutor at Reading. In 1870 he contributed a paper on middle-class schools to the British Association for the Advancement of Science and a few years later, in 1876, started to write technical articles and took up journalism, starting the *Journal of Education*, published in Reading. Although not greatly involved with electrical* matters, he was offered the editorship* of the *Electrician**, possibly because of his writing skills and administrative ability. The journal published reports of scientific meetings, accounts of inventions and discoveries, as well as instruction in electrical principles. Biggs remained editor from 1878 until 1887. Recognising the importance of the electrical genius Oliver Heaviside (1850-1925), Biggs published his most advanced theoretical work in the journal and it was possibly Biggs's championship of Heaviside against opposition that cost him his job in October 1887. Biggs subsequently became editor and co-owner of a new paper, the *Electrical Engineer*, and after the death of his partner in the venture, he edited the *Contractor's Record and Municipal Engineering* until his death in 1923. He also collected Heaviside's work on electricity and published it in the two volume *Electrical Papers* (1892). DHL

Sources: Nahin 1988, *ODNB*.

BILLINGTON, MARY FRANCES (1862-1925) A career journalist on national dailies*, Mary Frances Billington specialized in 'descriptive' writing or the vivid evocation of reported events, a feature of New Journalism* in which she was considered by some the equal of Harriet Martineau* and Frances Cobbe*. Billington began her professional life contributing to the *Globe** and then in 1888 helped establish the *Southern Echo* in Southampton, from which she was recruited by John Passmore Edwards* to the London *Echo**.

She joined the new *Daily Graphic** in 1890 as the first female special correspondent on women's interests. Her most striking contribution was securing a commission to visit India and report on the role of women there, producing 28 articles later published as *Women in India* (1895). In 1897 she assumed oversight of the women's department of the *Daily Telegraph** and stayed with this paper until her death in 1925.

Billington contributed to various journals, including the first issue of *Merry England**, *Pearson's Magazine** and *Girl's Own Paper**, writing on women's medical careers and war work. She became president of the Society of Women Journalists* and participated in training women. Her own career was a shining example to 'the ambitious and the independent' women she thought suitable for journalism. BMO

Sources: *ODNB*, Onslow 2000, Ward 1992.

BINDLEY, CHARLES (1795/6-1859) Charles Bindley, whose articles on field sports* appeared regularly in the *Sporting Magazine* from c. October 1843, became widely known by his signature* of 'Harry Hie'over' (or later Hieover). According to his obituary* in the *Sporting Review** Bindley's 'favourite topics' in his books, essays and articles were 'hunting and stable management'. These works 'were all eminently practical and not descriptive'. (*Sporting Review* March 1859: 155)

During his career, Bindley published several compilations of his sporting articles, the first of which was the hefty, two-volume *Stable-Talk and Table-Talk*, or *Spectacles for Young Sportsmen* (1845-1846),

which he obliquely referred to in the Preface as a collection of 'fugitive pieces'. Later, in the Preface to *Sporting Facts and Sporting Fancies* (1853), Bindley openly acknowledged the journalism source of his work, claiming that all of the 'carefully revised' articles republished in his books to date had appeared in one periodical only, the *Sporting Magazine*. This he claimed was more reputable than republication of journalism* that had appeared in *Bell's Life*, which had 'such an extended circulation'. Like the articles, most of his books were published under his pseudonym* 'Harry Hierover'. Bindley also used this name when, in 1852, he edited, with two others, a new and revised edition of Delabere Blaine's *Encyclopaedia of Rural Sports or, Complete account, historical, practical and descriptive of hunting, shooting, fishing, racing &c.* As well as Bindley's sporting journalism, 'a tale' entitled 'The Two Mr. Smiths, or the Double Mistake' appeared in *Bentley's Miscellany** (Dec. 1848: 533-540). Almost until his death in 1859, 'Harry Hieover' continued to contribute articles to the *Sporting Review*, his last piece being 'Riding to the Hounds'. DHL

Sources: Bindley 1853, Boase, *Gentleman's Magazine* 1859, Higginson 1951, *ODNB*, *Sporting Review* 1859.

BINNS, JOHN (1772-1860) An Irish journalist* and Jacobin, Binns arrived in London in 1794 where he worked as a plumber, joining the radical London Corresponding Society and quickly becoming a prominent member. It was here that he began to learn the mechanisms (and the legal pitfalls) of radical periodical publishing. Binns figures in many of the pamphlets published by the society, and contributed to the short-lived *Moral and Political Magazine of the London Corresponding Society* (1796), arguing for universal suffrage. He campaigned against two treason and sedition bills introduced in 1795, and later fell foul of them, being charged with sedition in 1796 – he published the proceedings of this trial himself the following year – and high treason in 1798. Although neither of these charges stuck, he spent two years in Gloucester gaol under a suspension of the habeas corpus act. Binns and his brother Benjamin became members of the United Englishmen, a covert organization closely affiliated with Irish revolutionaries, and he was personally associated with Arthur O'Connor, editor of the *Press* (1797-1798), the Dublin-based organ of the United Irishmen, a sister organization.

Binns left England for America in 1801, where he adopted a more settled mode of life as a political* journalist. Being based initially in Northumberland, Pennsylvania, he contributed to the *Northumberland Gazette* (1790-1817) before beginning his own newspaper – the *Republican Argus* – in 1802. Moving to Philadelphia in 1807, he established the *Democratic Press* (1807-1829), which he worked on until its demise. His autobiography, *Recollections of the Life of John Binns*,was published in Philadelphia in 1854. MaT

Sources: Binns 1854, *The Making of the Modern World* online, *ODNB*, Thompson 1963.

BINSTEAD, ARTHUR MORRIS (1861-1914)
Arthur Morris Binstead learnt the craft of sports* reporting in the early 1880s in a news agency* run by Joe Capp, a doyen of late-Victorian racing journalism. It was a business operating on the edge of respectable journalism and respectable society, with reporters* providing a telegraphed* results service for licensed clubs and the London and provincial* press. He worked his 'apprenticeship' among a coterie of racing writers representing papers such as the *Sporting Life** and *Sportsman**, travelling together by train, working together on the courses, staying in country town hotels and socializing at the theatre or music hall. It was an introduction to popular* journalism that provided a fund of anecdotes and experience that informed Binstead's later humorous sketches in man-about-town titles the *Sporting Times** and *Town Topics*.

Binstead was born in London, his father working as a clerk at the time. Binstead had ambitions to become an illustrator*, but found work in a furniture factory counting house before joining Capp's agency. He later worked for *Sporting Life* as a subeditor* where duties included the provision of rhyming tips for race meetings. In 1884 he moved to the *Sporting Times*, owned and edited* by John Corlett*, where he was to spend 28 years writing of London club life, racing, boxing, barmaids, tipsters and the music hall under the penname 'Pitcher'. He edited Corlett's paper the *Man of the World* from 1891, and also acted as 'press director' at the Alhambra Theatre. Upon the sale of the *Sporting Times* in 1912, Binstead resigned and founded the rival *Town Topics*. His stories of Bohemian London, in newspaper articles and books such as *A Pink 'Un and a Pelican* (1898) and *Pitcher in Paradise* (1903) established him as a popular recorder of a fast-disappearing social scene. ST

Sources: Binstead 1898/1903, Booth 1930, *ODNB*, *Town Topics* 1914.

BIRMINGHAM ARGUS (1818-1819) The *Birmingham Argus* was a weekly* reformist newspaper,

published in Birmingham, and printed as stated on its front page, every Saturday afternoon, at 4 o'clock. Mouthpiece of the radical Birmingham Union Society, the *Argus,* was edited* throughout its short-lived existence by George Ragg, a Birmingham printer, bookseller, and vice-president of the Society. Circulated* within the Midland counties, all eight pages of the *Argus* were used by George Ragg to advocate parliamentary reform. The front page* especially, was devoted to political* issues affecting Birmingham workers, featuring lively comment written by George Edmonds, chairman of the Birmingham Hampden Club. Content included news of other union activities, and articles written by prominent reformists like Thomas Jonathan Wooler*, promoting parliamentary reform, repeal of the Corn Laws and the rights of workers. In addition to news* and comment on politics and regular news stories, the Argus also included county session reports, the London markets*, and a poetry* section* that featured poems of a reformist nature. Government suppression of the Birmingham radicals throughout 1819-1821 resulted in the *Argus* coming to an abrupt end with George Ragg imprisoned for 12 months in a Middlesex house of correction, in December 1818, for selling seditious tracts. MLB

Sources: Briggs 1949, Langford 1871, Wickwar 1928.

BIRMINGHAM DAILY POST (1857-) A daily* broadsheet newspaper, it was founded by the proprietor* of the *Birmingham Journal*, John Frederick Feeney and its editor* John Jaffray in December 1857. Over the next 85 years, the Feeney family established the *Post* as a leading provincial* daily and liberal unionist newspaper, aimed specifically at the business and professional classes* of Birmingham, and the surrounding Midland towns. Jaffray was the first editor of this initially small, four-page paper, priced* 1d. In 1862 Jaffray was replaced by John Thackray Bunce, one of the founders of the National Liberal Federation who edited the *Post* until 1898, ensuring that the paper played a major role in the Reform movement in Birmingham. Leading writer William Harris an ardent radical, devised the plan 'vote as you're told', to defeat the minority clauses of the 1867 Reform Bill, enabling Birmingham to elect three Liberals, and no Tories in the 1868 General Election. Throughout his editorship, Bunce maintained close relations with leaders of the Liberal party, especially Joseph Chamberlain, to whom Bunce provided loyal support throughout Chamberlain's entire career, particularly regarding Home Rule and tariff reform.

This resulted in the *Post* being dubbed by its rivals as 'Chamberlain's organ'. Throughout this period circulation* was between 40,000 to 50,000 copies a week. The *Post* is still published today as the *Birmingham Post*. MLB

Sources: McCulloch 2004, *Mitchell's*, Whates 1957.

BIRMINGHAM JOURNAL (1825-1869) Although best known as a newspaper committed to liberal* politics, the weekly* *Birmingham Journal* came into existence in summer 1825 as the voice of the Birmingham Tories. After being ridiculed by *The Times*, the Tories of the town called a meeting, ceremoniously burnt a copy of the offending newspaper and declared their intention to launch their own organ. The paper was set up by subscriptions, £50 coming from William Hodgetts, who undertook to print it. Two years into its existence, Hodgetts became sole proprietor*. By 1830 circulation* stood at 1,000 copies a week. This was largely due to the decision of the Tory editor*, Jonathan Crowther, to lend support to the Birmingham Political Union. The *Journal* came into the ownership of reformers in September 1832 when it was purchased by Joseph Parkes and other liberals for £2,000. For the next few years the paper was edited by R. K. Douglas, one of the Birmingham delegates to the Chartist Convention in February 1839. An accomplished orator, Douglas unashamedly printed long reports of his own speeches. The *Journal* remained committed to manhood suffrage, often including reports of Chartist meetings. Sales, however, began to decline and in April 1844 Parkes sold the paper to John Frederick Feeney. With his right hand man, John Jaffray, Feeney moderated the paper's politics* and by 1861 the circulation had reached 23,000. The *Birmingham Journal* was merged* with the *Birmingham Daily Post* in 1869. SFR

Sources: Edwards 1877, McCulloch 2004.

BIRRELL, AUGUSTINE (1850-1933) Birrell was a prominent journalist* and writer as well as a Liberal Member of Parliament (1889ff) and Chief Secretary for Ireland (1907-1916). Surveying his life's work in 1922, he wrote that 'I have pursued, as an avocation, the pleasant path of periodical publication', but the record suggests that his journalistic writing was significantly more than a diverting hobby. From 1874 onwards, he contributed articles on literary* topics to (among others) *Atalanta**, the *Cornhill Magazine**, *Contemporary Review**, the *Nation** and *Macmillan's Magazine**. His affectionate portraits of popular literary greats – Dr.

Johnson, Charles Lamb*, Robert Louis Stevenson – were written with the frank congeniality for which he became known in his political life. He republished many of his articles in book form as two volumes of *Obiter dicta* (1884, 1887) – which also incorporated new material – and which were collected again, alongside more journalism, in editions of *Collected Essays* published in 1899 and 1922.

Birrell also produced topical articles dealing with contemporary political* issues, sometimes with an international flavour. One such piece, published in the *Contemporary Review* (July 1900), dealt with Russia's domination of Finland, a 'collision of a small State with a tyrannous idea'. Birrell tellingly contrasted the situation in Finland with that in Ireland, revealing something of his early attitude to the developing political crisis that would come to define his career: Irish independence. In his resignation speech to the House of Commons in 1916, he was to accept the blame for the Easter uprising. MaT

Sources: BL Catalogue, *ODNB*, *The Times* online, *Waterloo*, *Wellesley*.

BLACK, CLEMENTINA MARIA (1853-1922) When Clementina Black's first published short story, 'The Troubles of an Automaton' appeared in the *New Quarterly Magazine** (1876), she was a long way from capitalizing on her emerging literary* talent in the service of the women's trade union* movement and suffragist cause. A further series of short stories appeared in the *Dublin University Magazine** before the focus of her life changed. In an interview with the *Woman's Signal** (1895) she recalled how her social conscience was activated when she moved to London. Research at the British Museum Reading Room brought her into the socialist and literary circle of Eleanor Marx*, Olive Schreiner and Amy Levy, who introduced her to the Fabian Society where she worked with Annie Besant*.

Becoming Secretary of the Women's Trade Union League (1886), Black used articles and letters* in reviews, magazines* and newspapers to disseminate information, enlist public understanding and support, influence, and change government policy and reform legislation. Examples include her proposed Consumers' League to challenge sweating (*Longman's Magazine** 1886), the matchmakers' trade union (*The Times** 1888), her challenge to marriage (*Fortnightly Review** 1890) and her labour theory (*Contemporary Review** 1892). She wrote for the *Women's Union Journal**, *Woman's World** and the *Young Woman**, and edited* the *Women's Industrial News** from 1895 and later the suffragist paper *Common Cause* (1912).

Black also wrote short stories, seven novels and reviews (for example on Gissing's *Odd Women)*, a literary output which complemented her journalism. **CL**
Sources: Beckman 2000, Besant 1893, Glage 1981, Grenier 1986.

BLACK, HELEN C. (1838-?) Helen C. Black (née Spottiswoode), journalist and philanthropist, was brought up in Afghanistan and spent much of her life travelling through the Far East, Australia and North Africa. Returning to England, she founded and managed the St Mary's Cottage Hospital in Southampton, and her writing began as a means of relaxation from the rigours of this work.

Her first article, 'Celebrity at Home', about the actor/manager Johnston Forbes Robertson was accepted by the *World**, launching her on the genre in which she came to specialize, the celebrity* interview*. More interviews for *Queen**, *Black and White** and a series for the *Lady's Pictorial** (1881) followed, the latter of six prominent women, later published in 1893 as *Notable Women Authors of the Day.* 'Two Women's Tramp in South Africa' appeared in the *Sunday Magazine*, and more celebrity articles for the *World* and *London Society*. A series of interviews in *Lloyd's Weekly** was again collected as a book of biographical sketches in 1896 as *Pen, Pencil, Baton and Mask.* In 1898 she began to write regularly for Ada Ballin's* periodical, *Womanhood** still producing interviews, but also on more varied topics such as natural healing. **CL**
Sources: BritPer, *Womanhood* 1899.

BLACK, WILLIAM (1841-1898) Journalist*, novelist, and editor*, William Black was born in Glasgow, the son of a minor businessman. After leaving school at 16 and studying painting at the Glasgow School of Art, he took up journalism, writing short sketches for the *Glasgow Citizen* and acting as subeditor for the *Weekly Citizen*. In 1864 he moved to London and through the influence of fellow Scot and belles-lettrist Robert Buchanan* moved steadily through the journalistic ranks. Alongside contributions to the radical *Morning Star* and the *Examiner**, he wrote extensively for literary* periodicals* and journals: weekly serials for the *Graphic**, serials* and short fiction for *Cornhill Magazine** and *Longman's Magazine**, and prose contributions to *Macmillan's Magazine**, the *North British Review** and *Temple Bar**.

In 1866 the *Morning Star* sent Black to Germany to cover the Austro-Prussian War, also known as the Seven Weeks War*. Briefly imprisoned on suspicion of spying, he later fashioned his experiences in Germany into the successful novel *In Silk Attire* (1869).

Black similarly reutilized his journalistic experiences in other novels produced from the 1860s onwards, collected and published in 26 volumes in 1894. In 1870 Black became assistant editor of the *Daily News** and was also for a short period editor of the *London Review**. By 1876 he had made enough money from writing to retire from journalism. **DF**
Sources: *ODNB*, Reid 1902, Sutherland 1988.

BLACK AND WHITE (1889-1912) *Black and White*, renamed *Black and White: a weekly illustrated record and review* in 1891, blended contemporary news*, politics*, and illustration*. In this it resembled the *Illustrated London News** and other weekly* illustrated newspapers; it also employed a large format* similar to the *Graphic**. Topical in nature, *Black and White* covered 'home and foreign politics [and] social movements of England and abroad', as well as addressing current movements in literature*, art and the sciences*.

Recognizing that engravings and sketches – the primary mode of illustration in the newspaper until 1899 – took time to create, editor* Oswald John F. Crawfurd* wisely decided to illustrate 'subjects likely to be of permanent historical importance' rather than 'passing events of the moment', though 'these too will be depicted when occasion requires'. The weekly included notes on Parliament, politics, current book reviews*, poetry*, stories, a gossip* column, and a fashion* column starting in 1899. Henry Dawson Lowry and Barry Eric Odell Pain both wrote fiction for the magazine, and Charles Samuel Keene*, Walter Crane*, L. Raven-Hill, Linley Sambourne*, Sidney Sime, and Maurice Greiffenhagen contributed illustrations. The magazine absorbed the *Pictorial World* (1874-1892) in 1892 and merged* with the *Sphere* (1900-1964), another weekly illustrated newspaper, in 1912. **LML**
Sources: Ashley 2006, *Waterloo*.

BLACK DWARF (1817-1824) The *Black Dwarf, A London Weekly** *Publication* was a political* journal edited*, printed and published* by T. J. Wooler*. Aimed primarily at a working-class* audience interested in Reform, as well as some middle-class Radicals, the *Black Dwarf* was a mixture of satire*, serious political* polemic, correspondence* and reports of various Reform Societies throughout Britain. In its heyday, in 1819, the *Black Dwarf*'s circulation* was approximately 12,000, but it was more widely read than figures suggest as copies were often shared among workers or members of workingmen's and Radical organizations.

Black Dwarf's popularity rested on Wooler's

surreal imaginative writing, with Wooler signing his satirical pieces as the 'Black Dwarf'. Posters for *Black Dwarf* imitated theatrical playbills while its pages teemed with colourful invention, notably the Black Dwarf himself, but also his Japanese correspondent the 'Yellow Bonze', 'Green Goblin' (Irish affairs), 'Zekiel Strawyard' (bemused rural commentator on metropolitan affairs) and 'Black Neb', advocate 'of the good old cause'. The cabinet ministers Castlereagh, Canning and Sidmouth shuffled on as the comic actors Curseallray, Cunning and Widemouth. Though the paper broke new ground in developing a journalistic style rooted in street culture, it also reflected Wooler's interest in literature* and flair for multi-layered meaning. The title was taken from Scott's novel (1816) of the same name, in which a dwarf of extreme ugliness and vituperative speech nonetheless exercises beneficent influence upon the book's characters; but it also owed something to Thomas Spence's conception of radicals as giant killers (*Giant-Killer* was also a short-lived Spencean weekly*, 1814).

Well-known reform leaders like Major John Cartwright and Henry Hunt published under their own names, and a number of pieces of political poetry* by J. W. Dalby were signed. Reports from corresponding societies were sometimes published with real names, including Joseph Swann, Joseph Harrison, Joseph Taylor and A. Wilson. Other correspondents and contributors appeared anonymously*, under initials, or pseudonyms* like 'Agricola', 'Hibernicus', 'Brutus', 'Cato', and 'Moloch Zoroaster'. Regular departments included 'Letters of the Black Dwarf', and the 'Black Neb', which was a series of miscellaneous relevant extracts from political philosophy and literature. Topics addressed included universal manhood suffrage, the English Constitution, the misuse of sedition laws and the suspension of habeas corpus, the justice system, taxation, Parliament, the use of religion as a panacea for social control, the Peterloo Massacre, the Queen Caroline controversy, Catholic emancipation, the folly of the middle classes* in supporting the present system rather than allying themselves with the working classes and the theories of Thomas Malthus.

In June 1817 Wooler was prosecuted for alleged seditious libels in issues three and ten. The two trials ended in government embarrassment, with one acquittal and a guilty verdict so riddled with procedural irregularities that a retrial was never pursued. These important victories for free speech and Wooler's reputation swelled accordingly. His

15-month imprisonment (1820-1821) for activities linked to the parliamentary reform campaign did not damage the journal as he received generous help from the leading reformer John Cartwright. However, Wooler was more cautious on his release.

The *Black Dwarf* had several different formats. For the first three volumes it was a broadsheet (21cm × 26cm) with eight pages, each column* numbered separately, so 16 numbered 'pages', and cost 2d an issue (with the exceptions of I.1 and I.7, which cost 4d). Beginning in January 1820 it was revised in order to avoid stamp duty on the 2d press. Volumes IV-XII (1820-1824) were published in a smaller size (12cm × 20 7/10cm) with 34 pages in most issues, and were priced* 6d. E. P. Thompson suggests that at its peak the *Black Dwarf* was nearly as influential as Cobbett's *Political Register** and it spawned imitators such as *Yellow Dwarf* (1818) by John Hunt and William Hazlitt. Decreasing momentum in the reform movement, however, led to the publication becoming monthly*, beginning with XII.14, in May 1824, and ceasing altogether after XII.20, which covered the funeral of Major Cartwright in November 1824. CAS/MSC

Sources: Epstein 1994, Hendrix 1976, Thompson 1966, Wiener 1988.

BLACKBURN, HELEN (1842-1903) Helen Blackburn's involvement with campaigning and journalism came relatively late in life. Her interest in the suffrage movement was ignited by J. S. Mill's* 1867 parliamentary speech on women's suffrage, after which she educated herself about the Cause through reading the *Women's Suffrage Journal** before becoming actively involved.

In 1874 she became the secretary of the London-based National Society for Women's Suffrage. At this point she started contributing articles to the feminist *Englishwoman's Review**, the first of which in May 1876, 'The Argument of Custom' demonstrated her knowledge and dialectical powers. Irish by birth, she contributed obituaries* of Irish women to the *Englishwoman's Review*, and from 1881 to 1890, she was both contributor and editor* of that title, then joint editor until 1895 when her father's ill-health forced her to withdraw.

After her father died her contributions to journals resumed, including the first issue of the Paris-based *La Revue de Morale Sociale* (1899). CR

Sources: Banks 1985, Crawford 1999, *Myra's Journal* 1894, *ODNB*.

BLACKWOOD, JOHN (1818-1879) The sixth of William Blackwood's* sons, and the third to enter the family business, John Blackwood most fully combined his father's attributes of vigorous enterprise and literary discrimination, particularly as editor* of *Blackwood's Edinburgh Magazine** from late 1845 to 1879. Between William's death in 1834 and son Alexander's in 1845, the firm was jointly run by Alexander and Robert. John was introduced to the business at the end of 1840 by being entrusted with the running of the firm's newly opened London office. Five years later he returned to Edinburgh to succeed Alexander in the editorship of the *Magazine*. In 1850 Robert ceased to participate in the business, for health reasons, dying in 1852. John was now the head of the firm, being assisted by his brother, Major Blackwood, and then by the major's son, William, who, as 'William Blackwood III', succeeded to the dynastic headship on John's death.

In his London period, John made a number of valuable contacts, helping to make the *Magazine* more fully recognized there. Perhaps his most fruitful friendship in this regard was with J. T. Delane. The two young men were sharing lodgings when Delane, in 1841, became editor of *The Times**. He subsequently provided space in his newspaper for occasional citations of *Blackwood's Magazine*. John Blackwood continued his father's practice of making annual visits to London to meet regular contributors and to effect introductions between them. In this way an *esprit de corps* was sustained, conducive to the cohesion and vitality of the *Magazine*. Further cohesion came from John's staunch Conservatism, although the columns remained open to a wide range of writers. It was under John that *Blackwood's* developed the distinctive strengths that it retained until its dying day in December 1980: military history* and analysis, travel and exploration, and colonial/imperial concerns.

John Blackwood's greatest contribution to the wider field of literature* was the opening he gave to George Eliot*. Her earliest works of fiction were published in the *Magazine*, and Blackwood remained her main publisher. Another woman author regularly published by John Blackwood was Margaret Oliphant*. The third volume of the firm's history was completed by John's daughter, Mrs Gerald Porter. It provides a full account of John's life from the stance of filial piety. A more sophisticated analysis has recently been published by David Finkelstein. **MM**

Sources: Blackwood Papers NLS, Finkelstein 2002, Finkelstein 2006, *ODNB*, Oliphant 1897, Porter 1898, Sullivan, Tredrey 1954, *Wellesley*.

BLACKWOOD, WILLIAM (1776-1834) *Blackwood's Edinburgh Magazine**, proudly characterized in William Blackwood's Edinburgh parlance as 'ma Maga-zine', hence 'Maga', owed much more to him than its name. Already an Edinburgh bookseller and publisher*, he terminated his first periodical venture, the *Edinburgh Monthly Magazine*, founded in April 1817, and replaced it with the infinitely livelier and more forceful *Blackwood's*, from October 1817. Retrospective perception has prolonged the myth that what *became* a first-rate periodical was *originally* (in its April incarnation) founded to challenge Archibald Constable's* *Edinburgh Review**. The first target was Constable's enfeebled *Scots Magazine*. Nor was it the case that Blackwood sought 'vengeance' for Constable's having filched Scott's *Tales of My Landlord* from him. The fifth edition (Constable's first) was not arranged until November 1818, over a year after 'Maga' began.

Blackwood assembled a brilliant team to write for his refounded magazine: John Wilson*, J. G. Lockhart*, James Hogg and William Maginn*. The lack of a formal position of 'Editor*' proved useful in deflecting some of the flak incurred by the notorious first issue of 'Maga'. Thus, excusing himself to Scott for the biblical parody the 'Chaldee Manuscript', Blackwood pleaded, 'The Editor took his own way and I cannot interfere with him'. In truth there was no editor* other than Blackwood himself. The best formulation is to be found on his tombstone: 'Originator and for seventeen years Conductor and Publisher of the Magazine which bears his name'. Blackwood did the hiring and firing, handled a huge volume of correspondence, and paid the libel damages. Even so, he owed much to the exuberant fecundity of Wilson, Lockhart, and the other writers. Blackwood's strong Tory convictions gave another enduring dimension to 'Maga'. In David Robinson* he recruited a forceful political controversialist who made *Blackwood's* the voice of ultra-Toryism. Then, when the Tories fell, Blackwood helped to steer his magazine onto the safer and more permanent ground of Conservatism, as expressed by his chief political* contributor from 1831, Archibald Alison.

Leaving the principal credit for the *Noctes Ambrosianae* to John Wilson, two of Blackwood's other contributions to periodical journalism deserve mention: first, the publication of novels in serial* form, prior to their reissue as volumes from the same house. John Galt's 'The Ayrshire Legatees', from June 1820, initiated the process. Second, particularly through J. G. Lockhart, Blackwood opened the

columns of his magazine to continental literature especially from Germany. At his death, the management of the business passed to his sons, Alexander and Robert, and then to a third son, John*, who most fully inherited his father's qualities of commercial acumen and literary judgement. **MM**
Sources: Blackwood Papers NLS, Mason 2006, *ODNB*, Sullivan, *Wellesley.*

BLACKWOOD'S EDINBURGH MAGAZINE (1817-1980) In October 1817, after a lacklustre six-month start under the editorship* of Thomas Pringle* and James Cleghorn, William Blackwood I* relaunched the monthly* journal *Blackwood's Edinburgh Magazine* at a price of 2s 6d. Blackwood drew on the talents of two members of his literary coterie, John Gibson Lockhart* and John Wilson*, to help him write and edit the new version of his house magazine*. The first few issues of *Blackwood's Magazine* featured sharp attacks on local* and national literary figures, as well as an unusual blend of anonymously* authored literature*, politics*, fiction and poetry*. The ensuing controversy of such contributions as the mock-Biblical poetical satire* on local celebrities, the 'Chaldee Manuscript', the attacks on the 'Cockney School of Poetry' and on Lord Byron, established the reputation of the journal across the English-speaking world.

From its inception in 1817, *Blackwood's Magazine* was used as a showcase for new talent and as a method of attracting potential contributors to the firm's lists. A technique pioneered by William Blackwood I was the publication in book form of works first serialized* in the magazine, predating Henry Colburn's* and Richard Bentley's* use of such marketing strategies by several years. Works featured in this way included John Galt's 'The Ayrshire Legatees' (1820-1821) and Douglas M. Moir's 'The Autobiography of Mansie Wauch' (1824-1828). This innovative pattern of literary publication was continued by William's successors, and in particular by John Blackwood*, whose tenure as editor of *Blackwood's Magazine* (1845-1879), and as head of the firm (1852-1879) was marked by a successful and rapid expansion of the firm's lists and interests. John Blackwood published the work of such mid-century literary figures as R. D. Blackmore, Elizabeth Barrett Browning, Anthony Trollope*, Charles Lever* and Edward Bulwer Lytton, Margaret Oliphant*, Alexander Kinglake, Charles Reade and George Eliot*.

His nephew William Blackwood III, editor from 1879 to 1912, continued the magazine's tradition of nurturing new authors – among those featured

in the journal's pages during these years were John Buchan, Joseph Conrad, Stephen Crane, Jack London, Hugh Clifford and Oscar Wilde*. Yet the journal's conservative literary and political stance particularly during William Blackwood III's tenure would lead it away from a dominant position in mainstream literary culture. By the turn of the twentieth century it would become strongly identified as an essential part of the British colonial social life, the type of magazine George Orwell in the early 1940s characterized as being taken by the 'service' middle class: patriots who 'read *Blackwood's Magazine* and publicly thanked God that [they] were "not brainy"' (Finkelstein, 2006: 13-14). **DF**
Sources: Finkelstein 2002, Finkelstein 2006, *ODNB*, Oliphant 1897-1898, Porter 1898, Tredrey 1954.

BLAKEY, ROBERT (1795-1878) Robert Blakey was introduced to the radical press* of the London *Examiner*, the *Tyne Mercury* and *Cobbett's Political Register* at an early age and at 16 entered into correspondence with the *Tyne Mercury.* By 1815, he was producing articles on issues such as the ballot and the slave trade for the press, particularly the *Newcastle Magazine.* From 1817 he was writing articles for T. J. Wooler's* London paper, *Black Dwarf* which sold well in the North East and was giving considerable annoyance to the Government. His writing increasingly complemented his political activism on poor law reform, and he published essays, letters, articles, satires* and squibs in the *Newcastle Magazine, the Durham Chronicle, Cobbett's Political Register* and *Black Dwarf* (1822-1832). In 1827, a series of political economy* papers for the *Tyne Mercury* analysed the effects of the introduction of machinery to industry. Through his work he was meeting significant figures of the age, the writer Johanna Baillie, Thomas Bewick the artist, philosopher William Godwin and the political reformer, William Cobbett.

Increasing his political work he joined the Northern Political Union in 1832, and in 1838 he became mayor of Morpeth, his home town. In the same year he bought the *Northern Liberator* (1837-1840), the paper of the Newcastle Chartists* and at Cobbett's suggestion merged it with the failing London weekly*, the *Champion*. Through its advertising* revenue and the improvements Blakey made in the production process, he enlarged the paper. Despite its high standard of popular* journalism and creative use of illustrations*, the paper was a short-lived success. As a result of his 'Essay on the National Right of Resistance to Constituted

Authorities' he was charged with seditious libel by the government. Bound over to keep the peace for three years in his own personal recognizance of £500, he was forced to sell the paper at a loss in 1840. In May of that year he moved to London, where he started a new weekly paper, the *Politician* but terminated it after six issues.

Alongside his political work, Blakey wrote literary pieces for the *Newcastle Magazine* (1820-1831) and completed a work on moral philosophy. He left London for the Continent in 1841 to concentrate on philosophy. Briefly, in 1849 he became professor of Logic and Metaphysics at Belfast University, subsequently gaining a reputation for his writing on philosophy. He used the pseudonym* 'Palmer Hackle' when publishing books on his other love, angling. CL

Sources: Miller 1879, *ODNB*, *Waterloo*.

BLANCHARD, (SAMUEL) LAMAN (1803-1845) Blanchard's violent suicide in February 1845, during a depressive fit following his wife's illness and death, shocked an unusually large circle of friends across literary and journalistic London. A versatile writer of verse and humorous articles – compared by admirers to Charles Lamb's* 'Elia' essays – and a hardworking editor* of respected radical and Whig papers, Blanchard was also known for his optimism, charm, good looks and nature, qualities warmly recalled in tributes by Forster*, Ainsworth*, Bulwer Lytton* and Thackeray*.

Growing up in Southwark, the son of a glazier, he excelled at school and developed a passion for Romantic poetry, but limited family finances precluded a university education. He served an apprenticeship as clerk to a proctor in Doctor's Commons, but by the early 1820s was contributing dramatic sketches to *Drama*, reviews* to John Duncombe's *Mirror of the Stage* (making a lifelong friend of Douglas Jerrold*, who was a fellow contributor) and prose and verse to the *Monthly Magazine**. As secretary to the London Zoological Society (1827-1830), he acquired numerous literary friends, among them Ainsworth, who published his *Lyric Offerings* in 1828, to some acclaim. But for the last 15 years of his life, Blanchard found himself sucked into reformist newspaper journalism: subediting the *Monthly*, editing the *True Sun* (1832-1836, during which period Charles Dickens* was one of the auxiliary reporters), the *Constitutional* (1836), the *Court Journal* (1836-1837), the *Courier* (1837-1839), the *New Monthly Magazine**, *George Cruikshank's Omnibus* (1842), and subediting *Ainsworth's Magazine** (1842-1845). He was on the staff

of the *Examiner** from 1841 until his untimely death. JMD

Sources: Davies 1983, House *et al.* 1965-1977, *DNB*, *ODNB*, Slater 2002.

BLATCHFORD, ROBERT PEEL GLANVILLE (1851-1943) The socialist journalist Robert Blatchford began his career in Manchester in 1885 working on the London-based *Bell's Life**, during which time he met future *Clarion** co-founder, Alexander Thompson (1861-1948). He moved to the Manchester *Sunday Chronicle* later in 1885, where he took the pen-name 'Nunquam Dormio' ('I never sleep'). In 1889 Blatchford wrote a series of articles denouncing Manchester's slum housing; his researches convinced him of the necessity of socialism. He left the *Sunday Chronicle* in 1891 after being asked to remove socialist politics* from his column*, and spent two months writing for Joseph Burgess's* *Workman's Times** (1890-1894) before founding the *Clarion* in 1891.

Blatchford's journalism was friendly, chatty and often humorous, having a direct style he described as 'horse-sense in tinker's English'. The series of letters published in the *Clarion* as 'Merrie England' sold a remarkable two million copies when published as a penny pamphlet, and the series was considered one of the most effective pieces of socialist* propaganda in the British labour movement. He also contributed short stories and serialized fiction* to the *Clarion*. He drew criticism from female socialists for his patriarchal views, but he was a generous editor who opened the pages of the *Clarion* to opposing views. When his criticism of organized religion, 'God and My Neighbour', produced an angry response, Blatchford allowed equal space to the secularists and their opponents to air their views without editorial interference. Criticism of the Independent Labour Party and support for the Boer War lost him influence in the British socialist movement, and his support for the British government at the outbreak of the First World War fractured the *Clarion* group. He wrote for the *Sunday Chronicle* and the *Weekly Dispatch** during the war*, and he became a freelance journalist from 1927. DM

Sources: Blatchford 1931, *DLB*.

BLATHWAYT, RAYMOND (1855-1935) Blathwayt started his working life as a clergyman; though he found himself unsuited to religious life, he was summed up by a colleague in 1900 as 'that quaint mixture of ecclesiasticism and journalism' (Forbes cited in Heilmann and Forward: 258). A freelance writer, he made his name by persuading famous people to give him interviews*, 'a mode of publicity then barely heard of in Britain' (Blathwayt 1917: 134). Blathwayt was among the most successful of the 1890s journalists who developed a career based on that still nascent feature of new journalism*, later observing that 'it was as though I had gone into an oil district and started a "gusher"' (Blathwayt: ibid). By the end of the nineteenth century he was a 'major British proponent of the form' (Beegan: 20).

In his early career he had been encouraged by his friend, the romantic novelist Hall Caine, to send his 'chatty little articles' to *Answers to Correspondents*, Alfred Harmsworth's* popular magazine. He was introduced to Edmund Yates* by Lady Colin Campbell*, a regular contributor to Yates's *World* and among Blathwayt's pieces for that paper was the hugely successful 'Celebrities at Home' series. Blathwayt considered the interviewer as the 'the incarnation of the modern zeitgeist'; he must be a well-educated gentleman, up to date on all cultural, political, scientific and social life, and able to mix with all types of men from 'cardinals to caricaturists'. He saw interviews as 'the photographic reproduction of the almost unconscious thought and words and deeds' (Blathwayt 1893, 347-50), though he was modest about his writings: 'indeed I am no stylist, [I] just write about interesting things' (Blathwayt 1935: 29). Some of his most celebrated interviews included encounters with Marie Corelli, Sarah Bernhardt and Thomas Hardy*.

Blathwayt published his work in a number of journals and papers, including *Pall Mall Gazette*, *Daily News*, *Idler*, *Black and White*, *Home Messenger*, and *Fortnightly Review* throughout the 1890s and into the twentieth century. **FD**
Sources: Beegan 2001, Blathwayt 1893, Blathwayt 1917, Heilmann and Forward 2000.

BLESSINGTON, MARGUERITE (1789-1849) The Countess of Blessington (née Gardiner) was one of the most assiduous and prominent editors* of the illustrated* annuals*, to which she was also a major contributor. For Charles Heath she edited *Heath's Book of Beauty* (1834-1847) and the *Keepsake* (1841-1849). At her fashionable salons she gathered prominent men of her day – politicians, aristocrats and writers, including Dickens*, Lytton and Landor. By this means she recruited celebrities* as contributors to the annuals she edited, but she also encouraged younger women writers like Camilla Toulmin*. Blessington also wrote novels and other books of which the best known, *Journal of Conversations with Lord Byron*, was originally published in

instalments in the *New Monthly Magazine* (1832-1833). *Strathern, or, Life at Home or Abroad* also first appeared in serial* form in the *Sunday Times*, and for a short while after its foundation she wrote a society gossip* column for the newly founded *Daily News*. **BMO**
Sources: Madden 1855, *ODNB*, Onslow 2000.

BLIND, MATHILDE (1841-1896) Mathilde Blind (née Cohen), German-born poet, biographer, translator and critic, used journalism to establish and extend her literary reputation. Her 1870 *Westminster Review* article on William Michael Rossetti's* edition of Shelley elevated her status among London's leading aesthetes, especially Algernon Charles Swinburne*. Her review-essay, three poems, and short story shared space with Swinburne in *Dark Blue* (1871-1872). One of several late-century women contributors, Blind also published 20 reviews* and two poems in the *Athenaeum* from 1872-1887.

Her poetry*, articles, reviews and translations appeared in over a dozen journals during her career. All testify to her intellectual and political* range and radicalism. She published a translation of Goethe's 'Maxims and Reflections' in *Fraser's*; personal recollections of the Italian revolutionary Giuseppe Mazzini in the *Fortnightly*; a piece on Mary Wollstonecraft in the *New Quarterly Magazine*; and a two-part biographical article on the Russian painter and proto-New Woman Marie Bashkirtseff, written at Oscar Wilde's* request for the *Woman's World*. Her last published work, a sonnet, appeared in Arthur Symons's* *Savoy*. Her journalistic career illuminates important connections between the 'female aesthetes' of the 1860s and 1870s and the decadent and New Woman writers of the 1880s and 1890s. **JKD**
Sources: Demoor 2000, Diedrick 2003, *ODNB*, Swinburne 1875.

BLUMENFELD, RALPH DAVID (1864-1948) Ralph David Blumenfeld was the son of a professor of literature and history at Nuremberg who emigrated to the United States in 1848, and later founded *Der Weltbürger*, one of the first German newspapers in the Mid-west. Blumenfeld followed his father into the business and joined the *Chicago Herald* in 1884. In 1887 he first arrived in London as a reporter* for the United Press to cover Queen Victoria's jubilee. Having read an impressive dramatic account of a fire that Blumenfeld published in Albert Pulitzer's New York *Morning Journal*, James Gordon Bennett Jnr of the rival *New York Herald* offered him a job. He became the *Herald's* leading special correspondent, where his writing was admired for its 'verve, and a commendable brevity and simplicity' (*ODNB*). He began to take on more managerial and editorial roles at the paper, but resigned in 1892 when he decided to stay in England rather than return as requested to New York.

For the next six years he made and sold typesetting* (linotype) machines* but was persuaded by Albert Harmsworth* to return to journalism in 1900 with the offer of the news* editorship of the *Daily Mail*. Arthur Pearson* secured his services for the *Mail's* new rival, the *Daily Express**, where in 1902 Blumenfeld effectively became editor*. He remained with the *Express* until his retirement in 1932, and though an independent, formidable editor, he had to endure 'considerable editorial interference' from Pearson, who did not withdraw from affairs at the *Express* until 1912 (Koss: 63) and later from Lord Beaverbrook, who took control of the paper from 1917.

Blumenfeld is credited with bringing a new shape to the *Express*, then struggling with stagnant sales and labouring to compete with outdated machinery in the popular daily* market*. He introduced American-style front page news* to the paper (instead of using the space for advertisements*) and innovations in typography and layout, including banner headlines. He is acclaimed as an 'architect of modern, popular journalism' not least for his characteristic punning headlines (*ODNB*). He published articles in New York's *Town and Country* and *Outlook* and wrote a number of books on his life as a newspaper man, including *R.D.B's Diary, 1887-1914* (1930), *What is a Journalist* (1930) and *The Press in My Time* (1933). He was the first journalist elected to the Carlton Club, became a British citizen in 1917 and enjoyed a close friendship with Stanley Baldwin. **FD**
Sources: Blumenfeld 1931, Koss 1973, *ODNB*.

BODICHON, BARBARA LEIGH SMITH (1827-1891) Barbara Leigh Smith, later Bodichon, was a key figure in the emergence of a feminist press* in Britain from the mid-1850s through her own writings and through her personal and professional support of the Langham Place Group that centred around her London residence.

Bodichon's earliest writings for the press signalled some of her life-long concerns: her articles for the *Hastings and St Leonard's News* addressed women's education and needlessly restrictive women's fashion*; she contributed pieces to the *Leader* on the economic reasons behind female prostitution and to the Glasgow-based *Waverley Journal*,

edited by and written for women, on women and the labour market. Her friend and collaborator, Bessie Parkes*, was on the *Waverley* staff and when their attempt to purchase the journal failed, Parkes and Bodichon, who had a 'sophisticated grasp of the importance of the press in influencing public opinion' (*ODNB*), established the *English Woman's Journal* * with Parkes as editor* and Bodichon as the major shareholder. The journal focused on causes espoused by Bodichon.

Radical, direct and pragmatic in the tone and content of her writings, her journalistic pieces were the foundation of important pamphlets calling for equality in law and in the labour market, among which is 'Women and Work' (1857) reprinted from the *Waverly*. Bodichon travelled widely in Europe, the United States and Africa. Spending much of her life in Algiers with her husband Eugene Bodichon, she wrote articles on her travels for *Temple Bar**, *Macmillan's Magazine**, the *Art Journal** and predominantly for the *English Woman's Journal*, including a series of abolitionist articles on the slave trade in America, and, somewhat atypically, a ghost story set in France. **FD**
Sources: Herstein 1985, Hirsch 1998, Lacey 1987, *ODNB*.

BOLSTER'S QUARTERLY (1826-1830) *Bolster's Quarterly* was published* in Cork by John Bolster of Patrick Street and edited by antiquarian John Windele. Its aim was 'to call forth native Irish literary talent'. As such, Irish matter was prominent in its contents. Departments included poetry*, fiction (serial* and non-serial), letters* to the editor*, biographical sketches, drama and excerpts from national newspapers. **FB**
Sources: Clyde 2003, *Concise Oxford Companion to Irish Literature* 2000, *ODNB*, *Waterloo Irish*.

BOLTON WEEKLY JOURNAL (1871-1976) Launched on 4 November 1871, the *Bolton Weekly Journal* was the first in a chain of Liberal weekly* papers issued by the local firm of Tillotson* and Son to serve distinct industrial townships to the northwest of Manchester. These 'Lancashire Journals' included a digest of the main issues of the week both local and national, plus a cornucopia of feature articles, with serial* fiction to the fore. Indeed, after the Bolton firm entered the fiction* syndication business, the Journals were among the most innovative venues for serial novels in the last quarter of the nineteenth century. With stories by both metropolitan* stars such as Mary Elizabeth Braddon* and locals* like the ex-miner Monk Foster, they achieved a collective weekly circulation* over 100,000 copies.

The energy underlying this enterprise came from William Frederic Tillotson*, who persuaded his Nonconformist father to expand the family business beyond bookselling, stationery and job-printing. In 1867 the firm launched the *Bolton Evening News*, one of the first English ½d evening papers, and the following year became a founding member of the Press Association*. The newspaper business remained in family hands until 1971, when it was bought by St Regis Newspapers, who folded the *Journal* in 1976. **GL**
Sources: Johanningsmeier 1997, Law 2000, Singleton 1950, Turner 1968.

BONNER, GEORGE WILMOT (1796-1836)
George Bonner, wood* engraver, belonged to a generation which pre-dated the massive development of wood engraved illustrated* journals in the early 1830s, but he is important as the teacher of a number of key illustrators and entrepreneurs of the early Victorian period, most notably W. J. Linton* and Henry Vizetelly*. **BM**
Sources: Engen 1990, *ODNB*.

BOOK WORLD: A MAGAZINE OF LITERARY AND DRAMATIC NEWS, FICTION AND GENERAL INFORMATION (1890-1899) *Book World* was a house* magazine* for Smith Ainslie and Co of 25 Newcastle St, Strand, who printed and published it. It began as the single-sheet 2d monthly *Book World, a Journal for Publishers, Booksellers and Kindred Trades*, edited by 'Boswell' and ostensibly aimed at 'that ever growing class who take a keen interest in the work and aims of the literary craft'. While it sold its advertising* space at the rate of 3s 6d per column inch, almost all such space throughout its 70 irregular issues was taken by Smith Ainslie themselves. Smith Ainslie was an American book and news supply agency, a business they combined with second-hand book dealing. They used *Book World* to advertise* above all the shilling* *New York Cosmopolitan Illustrated Monthly*, and their 'Books Wanted' and 'Books for Sale'. The number of pages varied, but in 1897 the magazine stabilised under an 'Editress' into 16 pages for a 1d, offering news* of books to a general reader (clearly not the trade) with short stories, poetry*, domestic* information (in a column headed 'Wives and Daughters'), a correspondence column*, brief remarks about the theatre, a few extremely brief reviews* of new books, 'Books Wanted' and two to three pages of advertisements. It claimed to circulate in America and Australia. **AK**
Sources: *Book World, Waterloo*.

BOOKMAN (1891-1934) W. Robertson Nicoll* (1851-1923) founded the *Bookman* in 1891 as an

Figure 6: The American version of the *Bookman*, June 1896.

illustrated* 6d literary journal aimed at working writers, general-interest readers and booksellers. Part trade* journal and part celebrity* magazine, the *Bookman* included up-to-date information about authors and the publishing* industry. This included literary gossip*, book reviews*, best-seller lists, advice for fledgling authors and feature articles on up-and-coming writers. The *Bookman* was one of many editorial assignments Nicoll assumed during his lifelong connection with Hodder and Stoughton* publishers, a partnership that included the *Expositor* and the *British Weekly*. When Nicoll added the *Bookman* to his growing list of editorial projects, he engaged the services of Jane Stoddart*, Annie Macdonell and later J. Ernest Hodder Williams as subeditors. The large, two-column format* of the magazine along with its concise 20-page length and elaborate illustrations* made it attractive to a popular audience.

Indeed, the *Bookman* soon proved to be a financial success. On the first day of publication, it sold 6,000 copies and eventually achieved a circulation* of 10,000 per issue. Like many other periodicals influenced by the New Journalism*, the *Bookman* featured celebrity* interviews and reader competitions. It also published sales figures for recently published books and periodicals. The contributors list, highlighted at the beginning of each number, most likely also served to attract readers. It included Oscar Browning, W. B. Yeats, Thomas Hardy*, J. M. Barrie, and Mary Cholmondeley. From 1893 to 1913 a Christmas* number was published, and selected numbers of the journal were devoted to particular authors, for example the special 1914 edition on the life and works of Charles Dickens*. In 1895, Nicoll formed an alliance with Dodd, Mead, and Co. to publish an American edition of the *Bookman*. ME

Sources: Attenborough 1975, Nicoll 1901, Sullivan, *Waterloo*.

BOOKSELLER (1858-) The *Bookseller* was founded in January 1858 by Joseph Whitaker* as 'a handbook of British and Foreign literature ... intended primarily for the use of booksellers and publishers*, furnishing them with a handy book of references and doing for the Bookselling trade what Bradshaw* does for the Railways, but so conducted that it may be equally useful to the Book-buyer and to the Bookseller' (No. 1: 2). The first issue set the template for this trade* journal. It contained a wide range of trade news*: bankruptcies, insolvencies, news of sales of private libraries, copyrights and bookshops, booksellers changing jobs and a copyright* tussle with American publishers, plus a sizeable list of publications of the month compiled from 129 publishers. This service, listing price*, publisher, author and a brief description of the book, was a staple until 2005, when the *Bookseller* went online.

Issue size* increased throughout its first year and annual subscriptions rose from 3s to 4s. By 1860, when it absorbed *Bent's Literary Advertiser**, the periodical's Christmas issue comprised around 240 pages. In 1862, 4,828 separate new books were listed; and by 1890, 6,490. Accounts of trade celebrities* were regular (e.g. Dickens's* funeral arrangements in 1870) as well as developments in the trade such as the first proposal for a London Book Fair (1889). Key themes, beyond the fortunes of the individual publishing and bookselling companies, were a long-running campaign against underselling (i.e. discounting of books by publishers and booksellers) and attempts to set up what eventually became the net book agreement. In 1874 Joseph Whitaker handed over the editorship* to his eldest son Joseph Vernon*, who occupied the chair until his death in 1895, predeceasing his father by four months. George Herbert Whitaker (1858-1933) then became editor. ND

Sources: *Bookseller* 1908, *Bookseller* 1958, Sullivan.

BORDERLAND (1893-1897) In 1891, the year after he founded the *Review of Reviews**, William Thomas Stead* publicly acknowledged his fervent belief in spiritualism, and the editor's* new interest in the occult provided a wealth of intriguing and eerie journalistic copy that soon began to monopolize the 6d monthly*. The 1891 Christmas* number, devoted to so-called 'Real Ghost Stories', sold over 100,000 copies, but within a year the *Review*'s business manager Edwin H. Stout considered that Stead's preoccupation with spiritualism had become deleterious to circulation*.

In July 1893 Stead launched *Borderland*, a quarterly* costing 18d entirely devoted to various supernatural phenomena, ranging from automatic writing (which Stead apparently used to communicate with his subeditor Ada Goodrich Freer*) and telepathy, to haunted houses and theosophy. As with the *Review of Reviews*, on which it was closely modelled, Stead acted as both editor and proprietor* of *Borderland* and deployed many trademark features of the New Journalism*, including fervent crusades against both the dogmatic hostility of the scientific establishment towards heterodox forms of knowledge and the deliberate exclusivity of the Cambridge-based Society for Psychical Research. Stead acknowledged that 'Borderland is a region which has hitherto been more productive in spectres than subscribers', and, despite its editor's sanguine claims in 1894 that 'the magazine has paid its expenses from the first number', the overtly populist *Borderland* was never able to gain a mass* audience and the journal folded in October 1897. GD

Sources: Baylen 1969, Baylen 1979, Dawson 2004a, Stead 1894b, *Waterloo*.

BOTANICAL MAGAZINE (1787-) The *Botanical Magazine or Flower-Garden Displayed*, was launched by William Curtis (1746-1799), a botanist and entomologist. The magazine* was just one of the means through which Curtis, a Quaker, shared his knowledge. Intended for 'the Use of Such Ladies, Gentlemen and Gardeners*, as wish to become scientifically acquainted with the Plants they cultivate', Curtis's aim was to associate his magazine with the expensive learned quarterlies of the Royal Societies, but for a broader audience. The relatively low price* of this small (14 x 23 cm) publication at 1s per monthly* number, made it more accessible; the first sold approximately 3,000 copies.

The magazine contained three hand-coloured images of 'the most Ornamental Foreign Plants, cultivated in the Open Ground, the Green-House, and the Stove [...] accurately presented in their natural Colours'. The exotic content was largely Curtis's response to low sales of his earlier publication on less colourful local plants, *Flora Londinensis*. The volume of plates in subsequent numbers of his magazine varied, averaging at 45 per year. The origins, properties and methods of cultivation for each plant were given in text accompanying the illustrations*.

By 1808, because of increases in the cost of paper*, the price* of the magazine had risen to 3s 6d and its circulation* fell. Furthermore from 1797 onwards similar periodicals had been launched, rising to at least 15 during the 1830s. However, in 1826 William Jackson Hooker, Professor of Botany at Glasgow University and later director of the recently nationalized gardens at Kew, had become editor*, and 'careful analyses and dissections now gave the work a truly scientific character' (Blunt: 213).

Curtis's Botanical Magazine was the title given to the magazine after its founder's death. Known as *Kew Magazine* from 1984 to 1994, the title subsequently reverted to its origins and has proved to be the longest-running publication of its kind. **SD**
Sources: Blunt 1994, Desmond 1980, Gardham 2004.

BOTTOMLEY, HORATIO WILLIAM (1860-1933) From the humiliating anonymity of being No. 64 in a Birmingham orphanage to a showman's public profile as newspaper proprietor*, journalist*, MP and convicted criminal, Horatio Bottomley's abilities enabled him to accrue unlikely wealth and infamy. After a succession of menial jobs, Bottomley worked at a solicitor's and was soon carrying out tasks far above his office-boy station. His uncle, the freethinker, George Jacob Holyoake*, sent him to Pitman's College, enabling Bottomley to work as a legal shorthand* writer. He gained further experience working as a part-time proofreader for his uncle on his paper the *Secularist* and for the radical, Charles Bradlaugh* on the *National Reformer**.

At the age of 24 he took his first steps as a newspaper proprietor, starting the *Hackney Hansard* (1884) which reported debates in the local council 'Parliaments'; then came the *Battersea Hansard*. He merged* both into the *Debater* when money problems arose. Bottomley launched the weekly* *Municipal Review* and expanded with a trade paper*, the *Draper's Record* and *Baby, or the Mother's Magazine** which formed the basis of the 1885 Catherine Street Publishing Association. His ability to attract advertising* revenue funded his money-making schemes.

In January 1888, he started a four-page journal, the *London Financial Guide*; renamed the *Financial Times** in February, it was printed on pink paper to make it stand out from its competitor, the *Financial News*. Differences with his partner left Bottomley with the printing business and marked the start of his fraudulent activities. Having obtained the contract to print Hansard, he merged his printing* company with four newspaper firms, becoming the Hansard Publishing and Printing Union. As managing director, he recruited prominent figures such as publisher, Kegan Paul* and the lord mayor as company directors to give his venture credibility. In 1889 the company was launched with a £500,000 stock exchange quotation. While announcing massive profits and relieving the company of £200,000, Bottomley faced bankruptcy and accusations of fraud. Conducting his own defence at his trial in 1893, he was acquitted when the judge recommended that Bottomley should train as a barrister.

A millionaire with an extravagant lifestyle, he became MP for Hackney South in 1905. His publishing forays continued in 1902 with the *Sun,* an unsuccessful evening paper, which he had printed on green paper to differentiate it from its rivals. He created a triumph in 1906 with the 1d weekly* *John Bull* editing it from his Pall Mall flat with journalist friends such as Frank Harris* writing for it. There was further success with the *Sunday Illustrated* in 1919, and as a journalist he was reputedly earning £8,000 a year for his column* in Northcliffe's* *Sunday Pictorial*. But his ebullience was scotched in 1922 when he was convicted and imprisoned for fraud. **CL**
Sources: Hyman 1972, *ODNB*, *Waterloo*.

BOUCHERETT, EMILIA JESSIE (1825-1905) Jessie Boucherett was the founder and financial backer of the *Englishwoman's Review**, and its editor* from 1866 to 1871. She was born into a wealthy Lincolnshire landed family, and by the age of 30 had a large private income from which she contributed freely to feminist causes. In 1859 she was inspired by Harriet Martineau's* article 'Female Industry' in the *Edinburgh Review** to make contact with the Langham Place group of feminists, publishers of the *English Woman's Journal**. With their support she founded the Society for Promoting the Employment of Women to open new occupations to women and provide training for them.

Although Boucherett wrote a number of articles on women's employment for feminist* journals, her main contribution to periodical literature was the founding and financing of the *Englishwoman's*

Review to fill the place left when the *English Woman's Journal* folded. From 1866 to 1910 the *Review* provided articles and news items of interest to supporters of the Women's Movement, covering such topics as women's education, employment, emigration, and suffrage. There are no records of any editorial board or shareholders connected to the *Review*, and it seems that Jessie Boucherett subsidized it throughout its existence, and that it ceased publication when the £500 left in her will to the final editor, Antoinette Mackenzie, was exhausted. EJ

Sources: Archives of the Society for Promoting the Training of Women, Crawford 1983, *Englishwoman's Review, Englishwoman's Review of Social and Industrial Questions*, Jordan and Bridger 2006.

BOURNE, HENRY RICHARD FOX (1837-1909) Journalist*, editor*, proprietor* and historian of the press, Fox Bourne was born in Jamaica, the son of Stephen Bourne, stipendary magistrate and founder of the *World* (1826-1832), 'the first nonconformist and exclusively religious journal in England' (Nworah*). The Bournes moved to British Guiana in 1841, and to Britain in 1848. Fox Bourne seems to have begun his long career in journalism in 1858 at the same time as he joined the War Office as a clerk, a post he filled until 1870. A Liberal reformist, Bourne campaigned for support of the welfare of indigenous peoples and against slavery. Meanwhile, he wrote, for Dickens* at *Household Words**, the *Reader**, and for Henry Morley at the *Examiner*, which he bought and edited after his retirement from the War Office (1871-1873).

Having sold the *Examiner*, Bourne took on the editorship of another progressive weekly* (1876-1887), the *Weekly Dispatch**, a popular* penny* paper for working-class readers*. Near the end of his tenure there, he published his compendious and valuable two-volume history *British Newspapers: Chapters in the History of Journalism* in 1886. In 1889 he became Chair of the Aborigines' Protection Society, and edited its organ, the *Colonial Intelligencer and Aborigines' Friend* until his death. LRB

Sources: Nworah 1971, *ODNB*, *Waterloo*.

BOW BELLS (1862-1897) *Bow Bells* was a popular* weekly* 1d magazine* aimed at lower-middle class* readers*, many of them women, as indicated by its fashion* and housekeeping departments. Initially subtitled *a weekly* magazine of general literature and art, for family reading* and illustrated* with numerous engravings*, it subsequently became *a Magazine of General Literature Illustrated*

by Eminent Artists. Published by John Dicks* who said in the initial issue on 12 November that his desire was 'to cultivate a taste for beauty and goodness in humanity', it claimed an 1865 circulation* of 200,000. Edited* for a few years by G. W. M. Reynolds* and later by W. H. Ainsworth*, *Bow Bells* attracted as contributors Wilkie Collins*, Tom Hood*, George August Sala* and Edmund Yates* and a host of lesser-known popular fiction writers like Charlotte Mary Brame and Colin Henry Hazlewood.

In part, the journal was directed towards practical issues encountered by the upwardly mobile. Its pages included advice columns* of various sorts, recipes and guidance on issues of grammar and etiquette, as had *Reynolds's Weekly** which it had absorbed in 1869. In its correspondence* columns much of the material was made up of items lifted from almanacs and household recipe books. A regular and very popular feature was the publication of a piece of sheet music* on the back page, but like most penny* magazines its staple was romantic and sensational fiction. Under the *Bow Bells* name the firm also published the *Bow Bells Almanack* (1877-1897), *Bow Bells Annual** (1885-1892) and a series of *Bow Bells Novelettes*. Dicks died in 1881, but *Bow Bells* continued for another 15 years. AH

Sources: Dicks 2005, *ODNB*, Rosen 1992, *Waterloo*.

BOWLES, THOMAS MILNER-GIBSON (1842-1922) Thomas Bowles, politician and journalist/proprietor*, was the illegitimate son of the Conservative MP Thomas Milner Gibson and a servant, but was treated as her son by his father's wife. Bowles began his journalistic career by contributing to a theatrical paper called the *Glow-Worm*, started by his half-sister, Alice Milner-Gibson, and her husband, William Wybrow-Robertson. He also wrote for the *Owl*, a society magazine launched by Algernon Borthwick, the editor of the *Morning Post**, started a satiric* magazine, the *Tomahawk**, and in 1866 began writing articles and leaders* for the *Morning Post*. Appointing himself Paris correspondent to the paper in 1870, he sent back reports of the siege from a starving Paris.

In 1868, he borrowed £200 to found *Vanity Fair**, 'a weekly show of political*, social and literary wares'. Much of it was written by Bowles himself with characteristic wit, but other contributors included Oscar Wilde's* journalist brother, William, and Charles L Dodgson ('Lewis Carroll'). The magazine became famous for its colour caricatures* of politicians, literary figures, overseas royalty and other notables often drawn by the Italian artist Carlo Pellegrini* who produced 333 cartoons* from 1869-1889.

In 1887 Bowles sold *Vanity Fair* for £20,000 to Arthur H. Evans, but he did not abandon all his journalistic interests. The *Lady*, which he had launched in 1885, continued and Rita Shell, his putative mistress and children's governess, took over the editorship* in 1895 and ensured its continuing success. However, Bowles's energies now were directed towards politics. He launched an anti-corruption journal, the *Candid Quarterly Review*, in February 1914 but it failed almost immediately. **AU**
Source: *ODNB*.

BOWRING, JOHN (1792-1872) Politician, diplomatist and writer, John Bowring was best known as a close associate of the Benthamite radicals and of the group who founded the *Westminster Review* in 1824. He later edited* the *Review*. He also made his name as a linguist and an early popularizer of European literature* in Britain. His contributions to the *Westminster* between 1824-1833 included translations and a series of articles on Russian literature (1824-25), Greek (1824, 1826), Spanish (1829) and Hungarian literature (1829). Each of his articles provided useful introductions to the history and current politics of the country as a background to the evaluation of its literature. In these introductions Bowring challenged the predominant utilitarian unease about the works of imagination, arguing that literature did not lack practical usefulness, rather, its pursuit, and especially knowledge about less well-known literatures, was practical as it added to the common stock of pleasure and knowledge of humanity.

He also wrote on Danish, Norwegian and Dutch literature in the *Foreign Quarterly Review* between 1828 and 1832. His contributions to *Tait's Edinburgh Magazine* focused more intensively on French political* events, and he also published a serialized biography of his mentor Jeremy Bentham in *Tait's* (Jan. 1840-Nov. 1841).

During the 1840s and 1850s, Bowring played an important part in domestic and foreign politics. He was elected MP for Bolton in 1841 as a free-trade candidate. He was offered a consulship in Canton in 1848, which he accepted, and later became the governor of Hong Kong. His experiences in the Far East informed his journalism in the *Cornhill Magazine* (1860-1865) and in the *Fortnightly Review* from 1865 to 1868. **ZV**
Sources: Bowring 2006, *ODNB*, *Wellesley*.

BOY'S JOURNAL (1863-1871) The *Boy's Journal*, also known as *Vickers' Boy's Journal*, was an early juvenile* magazine* in competition* with Samuel Beeton's* *Boy's Own Magazine*. Published by Henry Vickers and conducted by Charles Perry Brown, the *Boy's Journal*, like its rival, was predominantly aimed at a middle-class audience. Costing 3d for each monthly* number at launch, the high-quality publication was enlarged and improved in 1864, at which point its price* rose to 6d.

The *Boy's Journal* was characterized by a stirring concoction of fiction and non-fiction; although similar in content to the *Boy's Own Magazine*, its stories tended to be somewhat fiercer. Contributors included renowned boys' author Captain Mayne Reid, Fleet Street* stalwart Percy B. St John*, and illustrator Robert Prowse. Among the paper's most significant stories were 'The Cloud King, or, the Adventures of Charley Skyflier' and 'Up in the Air and Down in the Sea', both by William Stephens Hayward. These were early science fiction tales which anticipated the invention of aeroplanes and submarines. In 1870 the paper serialized* Jules Verne's 'Journey to the Centre of the Earth', its UK debut.

Although circulation* figures have not survived, it is certain that the *Boy's Journal* proved popular. Demand for the first number was purportedly so great that Vickers's offices in the Strand were crammed to capacity with copies, necessitating that customers were served via the windows.

However, like the *Boy's Own Magazine*, the *Boy's Journal* struggled to compete with the penny* weeklies* of Edwin J. Brett* and the Emmett brothers (1866ff). Consequently, the paper was incorporated into the *Youths' Play Hour* (1870-1872) in 1871. Charles Perry Brown later founded the Aldine Publishing Company, which continued to issue penny fiction well into the twentieth century. **ChB**
Sources: Jay 1918-1921, Rollington 1913, *Waterloo*.

BOYS' MISCELLANY (1863-1864) Edward Harrison's *Boys' Miscellany*, although commercially unsuccessful, is significant for establishing the blueprint for boys' magazines later standardized by Edwin J. Brett* and the Emmett brothers.

While its predecessors, including Samuel Beeton's* *Boy's Own Magazine* (1855-1874), *Kingston's Magazine for Boys* and Henry Vickers's *Boy's Journal*, had sought to cater predominantly for boys of the middle classes, Harrison's *Boys' Miscellany* was aimed squarely at a working* class readership*, and was considerably cheaper at 1d per number. Visually striking, it was larger and more profusely illustrated* than any periodical before it. It was also more thrilling, boasting stirring tales such as 'Sixteen String Jack, the Daring Highwayman: His Daring Exploits and Miraculous Escapes'. Indeed, Harrison was also responsible for publishing numerous penny dreadful serials*, including Edward Viles's 254-part epic *Black Bess* (1866-1868). Yes despite this, the *Boys' Miscellany* balanced its sensational fiction with informative non-fiction tailored to suit working-class tastes, spanning themes such as gardening*, science*, and sports*. With a flair for promotion, Harrison issued free gifts and supplements* to the journal on a regular basis.

Despite its many qualities, Harrison's *Boys' Miscellany* failed to achieve lasting success, and was discontinued in 1864 after 74 numbers. Nevertheless, its impact was considerable. Edwin J. Brett, who worked with Harrison on several publications in the early 1860s, was profoundly impressed by the short-lived weekly*. As chairman of the Newsagents' Publishing Company, the leading purveyor of penny dreadful literature, Brett reprinted several *Boys' Miscellany* stories in the form of weekly serials in the mid-1860s, and adapted the paper's format for his hugely successful *Boys of England**. ChB
Sources: Jay 1918-1921, *Waterloo*.

BOYS OF ENGLAND (1866-1899) *Boys of England* was arguably the most popular and successful of all Victorian boys' magazines*.

Launched by Edwin J. Brett* in 1866, the weekly* paper was lavish and striking, boasting 16 full pages of thrilling fiction and rousing non-fiction, plus a thriving correspondence* column*, all led by a tempting cover illustration*. This format remained the industry standard for decades to come.

In the paper's earliest weeks, editorial duties were delegated to journalist Charles Stevens, after which point Brett himself took charge. The paper became characterized by his convivial style, a marked departure from the rather stuffy dispositions of many editors* of juvenile* periodicals. Although issued initially via the offices of the Newsagents' Publishing Company, renowned for their penny dreadful fiction, in 1869 Brett established his own 'Boys of England Office' in an attempt to distance himself, and his paper, from what the public often perceived to be a disreputable branch of literature.

Boys of England boasted a wide variety of narrative types, the most common being adventure stories, historical fiction, public school stories and tales of the supernatural, penned by a host of authors and journalists, among them the famed Captain Mayne Reid. The paper's non-fiction encompassed anecdotes, biography, history*, hobbies, humour, nature, science* and sports*; although these were often published anonymously*, Brett managed to secure contributions from several personalities* of the day, including horticulturalist G. M. F. Glenny, rower Henry Kelly and conjurer David Prince Miller. Illustrators included numerous Fleet Street* stalwarts, such as Charles Dickens'* principal illustrator 'Phiz'*.

Brett was a skilled marketer. Consequently, *Boys of England* regularly ran extravagant promotional schemes, including a lavish prize draw and a national football league. An agreement with London's Britannia Theatre even led to numerous *Boys of England** serials being performed on the stage. Yet the paper was also remarkably benevolent: £350 donated by readers paid for the launch of Southend's first lifeboat. This went on to save the lives of 23 men, in 1879.

Boys of England was aimed unequivocally at the working classes*; both its fiction and non-fiction were specifically tailored to suit their tastes and beliefs. Moreover, although historians have commonly thought of boys' papers as being closely aligned with hegemonic values, *Boys of England* carried undertones of political* radicalism, borne from the former involvement of Brett himself, and several of his authors, within the Chartist movement.

More transatlantic than imperialistic in its outlook, *Boys of England* was also sold in the USA and Canada from 1874 onwards. In the same year, a reissued edition commencing from the very first number began in the UK.

Costing just one penny*, young readers flocked to *Boys of England*. Within a matter of months, Brett claimed a circulation* of 150,000 copies per week; it is thought that this figure rose to 250,000 in the 1870s, largely due to Bracebridge Hemyng's* popular 'Jack Harkaway' series. However, the paper began to struggle in the 1890s in the wake of stiff competition from Alfred Harmsworth's* halfpenny weeklies; consequently, it was merged* into *Up-To-Date Boys* (1899-1901) in 1899. ChB
Sources: Banham 2006, Boyd 2003, Drotner 1988, Springhall 1989-1990, *Waterloo*.

BOY'S OWN LIBRARY (1861 OR 1862-1866) The *Boy's Own Library*, published in London by Samuel Orchart Beeton*, was the name of both this monthly* publication featuring historical* and travel narratives, and a series of books in which stories from the monthly and from Beeton's *Boy's Own Magazine** were collected. Authors included John Tillotson*, William Dalton and James Greenwood*. The price* of the 22.2cm by 14.2cm paper-covered monthly was 6d. The cloth-bound, gilt-edged books first sold at 5s, peaking at 7s 6d, and continuing at a reduced price after the 1866 sale of Beeton's business to Ward, Lock and Tyler*. Dalton's story 'Phaulcon' and Greenwood's 'Stories of Savage Life' were serialized in 1862. The sole copy of the monthly *Boys' Own Library* held in the Cambridge University Library, volume five number 40, is dedicated to Tillotson's 'Stories of the Wars, being episodes in the struggles for civil and religious freedom in England and the Low Countries from 1574 to 1651'. Tillotson's style mixes Byzantine historical detail, the occasional high-flown classicism, and lurid descriptions of atrocities and mutilations. This number is paginated 241-288, with a four-colour frontispiece, and 15 black and white illustrations* signed W. Thomas, R. Hullula, or unsigned. Each story begins with an illuminated letter; the text is in a single column. Inside front and back covers are advertisements* for other Beeton publications, including *Boy's Own Library* books.

A notice in *Lloyd's Weekly Newspaper** in November 1862 describes Beeton's publications as 'cheap and excellent', and an 1873 review of one of the book-length volumes calls it 'a goodly volume which will be a favourite wherever there are lads'. SdB
Sources: Freeman 1977, Le Pla 2000, 19CBLN, *ODNB, Waterloo.*

BOY'S OWN MAGAZINE (1855-1874) Launched in 1855 by Samuel Beeton*, the *Boy's Own Magazine* was perhaps the first boys' magazine to achieve significant and lasting success, and was a key inspiration behind the later journals of Edwin J. Brett*.

Whereas most juvenile* papers before it had proved rather too instructive, even didactic, for boyish tastes, the pioneering *Boy's Own Magazine* offered a robust combination of stirring tales and enlightening articles. Specializing in historical* fiction, contributors included renowned authors such as W. H. G. Kingston and Captain Mayne Reid, while authorities such as the Rev. J. G. Wood penned non-fiction on a variety of wholesome subjects, spanning biography, nature, puzzles, science* and sports*. While ostensibly Christian in tone, and differing markedly from the gore-laden periodicals of Brett and the Emmett brothers which appeared in later years, the *Boy's Own Magazine* was yet invigorating reading.

Each monthly* number boasted 32 pages of octavo-sized text and illustration*, bound in distinctive orange covers. At 2d per number, its price* was not necessarily prohibitive to lower-class* boys, although the tone of the periodical tended to attract a middle-class audience; annual* bound volumes

were also commonly purchased by parents and teachers as gifts or prizes. Adjustments were made to the paper's format* on regular occasions throughout its lifespan. Notably, in 1863 a markedly enlarged and enhanced new edition commenced, adopting the new title *Boy's Own Volume*, and necessitating a rise in cost to 6d. A second new edition, also known as *Beeton's Boy's Annual*, ran from 1870 to 1874, although much of its content was simply rehashed from the 1863-1870 edition.

In the 1850s and early 1860s, Beeton's *Boy's Own Magazine* managed to maintain a healthy circulation* of 40,000 copies monthly. However, by 1866, periodicals such as Brett's, which had elaborated upon Beeton's formula, offered boys greater thrills, and could command much larger sales. This stiff competition caused the *Boy's Own Magazine* to fall out of favour. After Beeton met financial difficulties in 1866, the paper was sold to Ward and Lock*. It continued to struggle, and its 1874 volume proved its last. Although Beeton himself died in 1877, hardcover author G. A. Henty later revived the once-popular periodical under the title of *Beeton's Boy's Own Magazine* (1888-1890). ChB
Sources: Drotner 1988, Jay 1918-1921, *Waterloo.*

BOY'S OWN PAPER (1879-1967) The *Boy's Own Paper*, fondly dubbed the *BOP*, was a leading Victorian boys' magazine characterized by its high quality of production and its Christian ethos.

Launched by the Religious Tract Society* in 1879, the paper was intended to provide a wholesome alternative to boys' weeklies like Edwin J. Brett's* *Boys of England**, which the middle classes* believed were corrupting Victorian youth. Superficially, the paper resembled any other boys' weekly*, deliberately mimicking the genre's distinguishing characteristics, bloody violence included, in order to covertly spread its Christian message via subtle moralizing.

The *Boy's Own Paper* was conducted by subeditor* George Andrew Hutchison until his death in 1912, although until 1897 the Religious Tract Society board insisted that the elder (though less experienced) James Macaulay exercised official editorial control. Its stories were penned by a great many of the best-known authors of Victorian boys' fiction, including R. M. Ballantyne, G. A. Henty, W. H. G. Kingston, Talbot Baines Reed and Gordon Stables. Non-fiction of a high quality was also to be found in abundance, spanning such subjects as biography, history*, nature, science*, and sports*; contributors included cricketer W. G. Grace and naturalist Rev. J. G. Wood. The paper frequently printed reports and anecdotes by Religious Tract Society missionaries* posted in remote outposts around the globe. Additional weekly features, such as a correspondence* column* and puzzles, were accompanied by occasional competitions and free gifts, including lavish colour illustrations*.

The *Boy's Own Paper* was characterized by its championing of hegemonic values, particularly the endorsement of imperialism*. In this respect it differed markedly from the more subversive publications of Brett and the Emmett brothers.

Priced* competitively at just 1d per weekly number, the *Boy's Own Paper* sought to appeal to boys from across the class* spectrum. However, although the Religious Tract Society claimed a circulation* of 200,000 copies per week in its first year, rising to 500,000 in the late 1880s, 650,000 in the 1890s and even 400,000 during its Edwardian decline, recent scholarship has argued that the paper's true sale may have been considerably lower, perhaps peaking at just 150,000 in 1888. Indeed, autobiographical evidence indicates that many boys, especially working-class boys, found the *Boy's Own Paper*'s moralizing to be rather unpalatable, preferring the less temperate *Boys of England* and its kind. In practice, therefore, the majority of the paper's readers tended to be drawn from the middle class.

The *Boy's Own Paper* was unique among boys' weeklies in that it was financially secure, backed by the considerable financial reserves of the Religious Tract Society. Consequently, it continued to be issued long after it ceased to be profitable, undergoing periodic revision in content and format until its final edition in 1967. **ChB**
Sources: Cox 1982, Dunae 1976, McAleer 1992, Reed 1997.

BRADBURY, WILLIAM (1800-1869) William Bradbury, printer, was one half of the printing and publishing* firm Bradbury and Evans*. In 1824 Bradbury set up a Fleet Street* business as Bradbury and Dent, with his brother-in-law William Dent. The firm lasted six years, later becoming Bradbury, Dent, and Manning. In 1830 Bradbury started a new firm with Southampton printer Frederick Mullett Evans*, with premises in Whitefriars and a state-of-the-art press* suitable for printing newspapers and periodicals. In its first ten years Bradbury and Evans was a printing firm with a special expertise in legal printing.

Bradbury was known as a generous employer, paying unusually high wages to compositors, and he used his early experience on the printing shop floor

to personally supervise the printing work at Whitefriars. After 1842, when the firm became proprietors* of *Punch* and branched into publishing, Bradbury's supervisory role led to friction with several editors*, including Charles Dickens*, editor of the firm's *Daily News*. Dickens resigned from the post following Bradbury's editorial interference and his brusque treatment of Dickens's father. The rift was quickly healed, and Bradbury and Dickens shared a long friendship. Bradbury was also a friend of the gardener Joseph Paxton, editor of the *Horticultural Register* which Bradbury and Evans had printed, and Paxton helped him invest money in railway shares. But Bradbury was never as sociable a character as Evans, and in late years stopped attending the famous weekly dinners the firm hosted for contributors to *Punch* because of nervous fatigue.

Two of Bradbury's sons, Henry Riley and William, followed him into printing, with William taking his share of the firm in 1865. Henry Riley introduced innovations in the practice of nature-printing but committed suicide in September 1860. Increasingly suffering from poor health, Bradbury retired, with Evans, in November 1865. **AB**
Sources: Bourne 1887, Dixon 1991, *ODNB*, Patten 1978, Spielmann 1895.

BRADBURY AND EVANS (1830-1865) The London firm formed by William Bradbury and Frederick Mullett Evans in 1830, was a publisher of high-quality fiction, as well as a printer* and publisher* of newspapers and magazines, including *Punch*, the *Daily News* and *Once a Week*. In its first ten years the firm was a jobbing printer, turning publisher and proprietor* when it took over the fledgling *Punch* in 1842 and transformed the struggling fortunes of the comic weekly*. The profits of *Punch* amounted to over £10,000 a year by the 1860s, one of Bradbury and Evans's most unequivocal triumphs.

The firm's association with Charles Dickens*, however, was equally important. Bradbury and Evans published all Dickens's novels from *Oliver Twist* on, and in 1846 persuaded him to edit a liberal newspaper, the *Daily News*. The collaboration was a disaster and Dickens resigned in February 1846, just 17 issues into his editorship*. Nonetheless, four years later Bradbury and Evans agreed to publish Dickens's weekly* journal *Household Words*. It was a great success, selling 40,000 copies a week and introducing major writers such as Harriet Martineau* and Elizabeth Cleghorn Gaskell to the firm.

But the partnership ended disappointingly for

Bradbury and Evans when, in 1859, it failed to announce Dickens's separation from his wife in *Punch*. Dickens dissolved *Household Words* and launched *All the Year Round**, published by Chapman and Hall*. Bradbury and Evans countered with a rival magazine, *Once a Week**, but the venture was not commercially successful. This disappointment characterized many of the firm's other forays into periodical publishing, such as the *Army and Navy Gazette*. In 1865 the founding partners retired and their sons took over the firm. Its publishing interests declined and the firm reverted to its roots as a printer. **AB**

Sources: Bourne 1887, Dixon 1991, *ODNB*, Patten 1978, Vann 1994.

BRADDON, MARY ELIZABETH (1835-1916)
Best-selling novelist and magazine editor* Mary Elizabeth Braddon was born in London and published her first novel, *Three Times Dead*, in 1860. Publisher John Maxwell reprinted it as *The Trail of the Serpent* a year later and it sold rapidly, spurred on by the success of 'Lady Audley's Secret', which was simultaneously serialized* in Maxwell's magazine *Robin Goodfellow**. When that magazine failed, Maxwell restarted 'Lady Audley' in the *Sixpenny Magazine*. The three-volume version published in 1862 went through eight editions in three months and established Braddon as the matriarch of a new genre, the sensation novel.

Braddon became a regular contributor to Maxwell's periodicals and she was the chief fiction writer for his cheap* periodicals, the *Halfpenny Journal* and the *Welcome Guest**. She would soon be featured in his middlebrow magazines as well. *Aurora Floyd* (1863), *John Marchmont's Legacy* (1863) and *The Doctor's Wife* (1864) were first serialized* in *Temple Bar** and *Only a Clod* (1865) and *The Lady's Mile* (1866) originally appeared in *St James's Magazine**. In 1866 Maxwell named Braddon editor of the new *Belgravia** magazine, which served as the primary vehicle for the publication of her fiction until 1876. Braddon remained a prominent literary figure throughout the rest of the century, editing a Christmas Annual*, the *Mistletoe Bough*, from 1878 to 1887 and continuing to write about two novels per year, many of which were sold to the provincial* newspapers and the foreign press in addition to London venues. Braddon used two pseudonyms* – 'Babington White' and 'Aunt Belinda'. **JJP**

Sources: Carnell 2000, Gilbert et al. 2000, Maunder 2007, Phegley 2006, Wolff 1979b.

BRADLAUGH, CHARLES (1833-1891) Charles Bradlaugh, radical politician, and freethinker, is best known as editor* and proprietor* of the weekly* *National Reformer**.

In 1858, Bradlaugh succeeded George Holyoake* as president of the London Secular Society, working as a national advocate for secularism. His pseudonym* 'Iconoclast' was adopted to protect his professional work in a solicitor's firm, as at first he edited the *Investigator*, a free-thought* journal (Nov. 1858-Aug. 1859), before becoming co-editor of the *National Reformer* in 1860, progressing to editor (1860-1864, 1866-1890). Having been a shareholder in the paper, he became its proprietor (1862). As editor and proprietor he made the *Reformer* a strong voice for propounding atheism, republicanism and neo-Malthusianism.

At the *National Reformer* he was supported by Annie Besant* who had joined the National Secular Society in 1874 and began writing for the journal the following year. Bradlaugh and Besant had a close association over the years, both professional and personal. They were involved in campaigning through many publications such as with their articles for the monthly *Malthusian*. After Charles Watts, who worked with Bradlaugh on the *Reformer*, was prosecuted in 1876 with a Bristol bookseller for publishing and selling Charles Knowlton's birth control pamphlet 'The Fruits of Philosophy', Bradlaugh and Besant established their Freethought Publishing Company to publish* the pamphlet themselves. In 1877, they were prosecuted, tried and convicted, but the case was quashed on appeal on a technicality. This was just another in a long line of skirmishes with the law; in 1868, for instance, as proprietor of the *National Reformer*, he was acquitted on charges of blasphemy and sedition. Other freethought publications he and Besant worked together on were as joint editors of the *National Secular Society's Almanack* (1878), contributors to an essay series, the *International Library of Science and Freethought* (1880-1883), joint printer and contributors for the fortnightly, *Atheistic Platform* (1884) and joint printer for the monthly*, *Our Corner*. Additionally, Bradlaugh contributed to the periodicals, the *Speaker** and *Truth**. **JRW**

Sources: National Secular Society online, *ODNB*.

BRADLEY, EDWARD (1827-1889) Clergyman, illustrator* and writer, 'Cuthbert Bede', Edward Bradley's literary pseudonym*, was first used to accompany some poems* he published in *Bentley's Miscellany** in 1846, but it became celebrated in the

series of 'Verdant Green' novels about Oxford undergraduate life which Bradley subsequently published. These fictions had their origins in some sketches Bradley had produced with *Punch** in mind, but which, under the guidance of Mark Lemon*, eventually appeared in the *Illustrated London News** in December 1851. Bradley continued to illustrate his own works. Acquainted with several of the *Punch* circle, notably Albert Smith*, Bradley published further work in *Punch** as well as in Smith's varied comic magazines, and he became a familiar contributor to many magazines of the 1870s and 1880s, including the *Boy's Own Paper**, not just as an illustrator but, more often, as an author of essays, poems and sketches. He was a stalwart contributor to *Notes and Queries** (1852-1886). Among his many publications, he had the unusual distinction of writing the double acrostics that appeared in the *Illustrated London News*. **BM**
Sources: Engen 1990, Houfe 1978, *ODNB,* Spielmann 1895.

BRADSHAW'S RAILWAY GAZETTE (1845-1846); RAILWAY GAZETTE (1846-1847); RAILWAY GAZETTE AND MINING CHRONICLE (1847-1872); JOINT STOCK COMPANIES' JOURNAL, RAILWAY GAZETTE AND MINING CHRONICLE (1872-1879); JOINT STOCK COMPANIES' AND TRAMWAYS JOURNAL (1879-1882) Published three times a week for the first two years and then weekly*, this 6d journal was geared to the railway trade. It gave news* about the railway building progress for the week, news of the courts*, and parliamentary proceedings in addition to railway news of all sorts: railway share lists, weekly traffic tables and timetables. Its motto was 'Open to all parties – Influenced by none'. Undergoing four subsequent title changes* during its run, the *Railway Gazette* took its brand name from George Bradshaw (1801-1853), who is identified in the *ODNB* as a 'compiler of railway guides'. His first publication was *Bradshaw's Railway Companion* (1839-1845). The most famous title from the Bradshaw list was the yellow-covered *Bradshaw's Monthly Railway Guide* (1841-1961). Other publications under this imprint were *Bradshaw's Railway Almanack* (1848-1849), *Bradshaw's Railway Companion* (1839-1845) and *Bradshaw's Railway Timetables* (1842-1865). **AH**
Sources: *ODNB*, Vann and VanArsdel 1994, *Waterloo*.

BRAITHWAITE, JOHN, THE YOUNGER (1797-1870 An inventor and engineer at the forefront of the development of the British railway system, Braithwaite founded, in conjunction with J. C.

Robertson, the *Railway Times* in 1837, serving as both its editor* and proprietor* until 1845. His editorial in the first issue suggested that while 'a prominence will be given ...to railway matters ...Politics, Science, Art, Literature and the Drama, will each receive its share of attention'. This was probably a sign of a tentative first issue feeling for an audience, and hoping for a general appeal that was never there. As the paper established itself as a major player, it became less embarrassed about its focus on the technicalities of building and running the railway system, and the investment opportunities it offered. Braithwaite switched his energies to a war-of-words with John Herapath's rival *Railway Magazine*, and campaigned against excessive government interference with the railways. His involvement in journalism seems to have ceased after he left the editorship of the *Railway Times* in 1845. **MaT**
Sources: *ODNB, Railway Times.*

BRANDARD, ROBERT (1805-1862), BRANDARD, EDWARD PAXMAN (1819-1898) Robert Brandard was a landscape engraver, etcher, oil and watercolour painter, a pupil of the eminent landscape engraver, Edward Goodall. Born in Birmingham, he moved to London in 1824. Apart from book illustrations*, he contributed engravings to various journals including the *Bijou, Literary Souvenir, Friendship's Offering,* the *Keepsake, Landscape's Annual* and *Heath's Picturesque Annual.* Between 1851 and 1866, 15 of his plates appeared in the *Art Journal**, several of these being copies of paintings by Turner. Examples of his etchings were published in the same journal in 1875. Robert Brandard taught his younger brother, Edward, and apart from vignette illustrations for art and travel books, Edward Brandard contributed etchings to *Portfolio** and 13 of his plates appeared in the *Art Journal* between 1853 and 1887. **DHL**
Sources: Hunisett 1980, *ODNB.*

BRANDE, WILLIAM THOMAS (1788-1866) In 1805, while training as an apothecary, Brande contributed two articles on medical and chemical subjects to *Nicholson's Journal*, and in the following year began publishing original papers on organic chemistry in the *Philosophical Transactions of the Royal Society*. By 1813 he had replaced Sir Humphrey Davy as professor of chemistry at the Royal Institution, and in 1816 began the *Quarterly Journal of Science, Literature, and the Arts,* which, although independently owned and edited by Brande and published by John Murray*, gave precedence to authors associated with the Royal

Institution as well as giving detailed reports of its lectures.

Initially Brande was assisted in his editorial work by his Royal Institution colleague John Millington and then from 1821 by Michael Faraday, who prepared the 'Miscellanea' section and occasionally took charge of the whole journal when Brande was away. Faraday considered that, under Brande's editorship, the *Quarterly Journal of Science* neglected developments in European science*, and in 1830, when the managers of the Royal Institution took over the journal and renamed it the *Journal of the Royal Institution*, Faraday was put in control – although not formally made editor* – and charged with rectifying the deficiency. Without Brande, however, the new journal lasted less than two years. As president of the Chemical Society between 1847 and 1849, Brande also played an important role in the foundation of its *Quarterly Journal*, which began publication in 1849 with Edmund Ronalds as editor. **GD**
Sources: James 1991-, Lightman 2004a, *ODNB*, Spiers 1969.

BRANSTON, ROBERT (1778-1827); BRANSTON, ROBERT EDWARD (1803?-1877); BRANSTON, FREDERICK WILLIAM (1805?-?) A prolific family of wood* engravers, the Branstons were important entrepreneurs in the trade, and between them they trained or collaborated with many influential figures in the development of periodicals including James Henry Vizetelly*, Ebenezer Landells* and W. H. Wills*. They are credited with the establishment of a 'London School' of black line wood engraving which nurtured the talents of several of their apprentices who went on to engrave widely for the new illustrated* magazines of the mid-Victorian period. Of the three main Branstons, Frederick William was the one who contributed most to periodicals, working widely in the 1830s for the French illustrated press as well as such publications as Hood's* *Comic Annual*. **BM**
Sources: Engen 1990, *ODNB*.

BRETT, EDWIN J. (1828-1895) Edwin J. Brett was the foremost publisher* of Victorian boys' magazines, and the proprietor* of the renowned *Boys of England**.

Brett established a reputation for himself through the burgeoning periodical press, illustrating* profusely for several leading journals. Idealistic and politically minded, Brett also became actively involved in the Chartist movement, at that time gathering pace, associating closely with G. W. M. Reynolds*.

In the early 1860s, Brett joined the Newsagents' Publishing Company, a small Fleet Street* venture dedicated to the sale and acquisition of periodicals and copyrights. Under his chairmanship the company became notorious for its penny dreadfuls: high-sale crime* and horror serials* aimed at the juvenile* market. Encouraged by his success, Brett decided to launch a new type of miscellany* aimed at working-class* boys. After failing with the *Boys' Companion and British Traveller* (1865) and the *Boys' Own Reader and Companion* (1866), he realized his ambition in 1866 with *Boys of England*.

Brett's *Boys of England* boasted a heady mix of exciting fiction, informative non-fiction, vivid illustration and free gifts and competitions, the like of which had never been seen before. The paper was expressly tailored to suit the tastes of the young working classes, eager to be entertained yet thirsty for knowledge. It proved enormously popular, achieving a circulation* of 150,000 in its earliest months, rising to 250,000 in the 1870s, securing Brett a reputation as a linchpin of the Victorian periodical press, and making him a household name.

In 1869 Brett left the Newsagents' Publishing Company, setting up his own '*Boys of England* Office' on Fleet Street*. Over the following decades Brett launched many more boys' periodicals, including *Young Men of Great Britain* (1868-1888)*, the *Boys' Favourite* (1870-1871), *Rovers of the Sea* (1872-1873), *Our Boys' Journal* (1876-1882), the *Boys' Sunday Reader* (1879), the *Boys' Weekly Reader* (1880), *Boys of the British Empire* (1882-1883), the *Boys' Comic Journal* (1883-1898) and *Jack Harkaway's Journal for Boys* (1893). While some of these were short lived, many were successful in their own right. Moreover, the financial assurance provided by the high sale of *Boys of England*, which continued to flourish until 1899, allowed Brett to experiment with unconventional periodical formats* – such as the halfpenny *Boys of the World* (1869-1870) and the full-colour *Boys of the Empire* (1888-1893) – safe in the knowledge that failure would not spell bankruptcy. Brett also achieved success with periodicals aimed at other demographics, the most noteworthy being the young ladies journal *Wedding Bells* (1871-1879) and the family* miscellany* *Something to Read* (1881-1909)

Around 1890 Brett began to suffer from a serious illness, and became less involved with the day-to-day management of his company. His empire, which remained strong during his lifetime, was consistently mismanaged following his death, and collapsed in dire financial circumstances in 1909. **ChB**
Sources: Anon. 1880, Banham 2006, Jay 1918-1921, *ODNB*, Springhall 1989-1990.

BREWSTER, DAVID (1781-1868) Although generally known as a natural philosopher*, David Brewster's primary source of income came from editing and contributing to the periodical press, principally on scientific* topics. Brewster wrote principally on optics. Experiencing difficulty with public speaking, he instead wielded the pen as author and editor*. From 1808 to 1830 he undertook the mammoth task of editing the *Edinburgh Encyclopaedia* and contributed many articles both to it and also to its rival, the *Encyclopaedia Britannica*. He also edited or co-edited a string of scientific* periodicals: the *Edinburgh Philosophical Journal* (1819-1824), the *Edinburgh Journal of Science* (1824-1832) and the *Philosophical Magazine** (1832-1868).

A forceful writer and ready controversialist, Brewster contributed to a wide range of both scientific and non-scientific titles. Being a Whig and friend of Henry Brougham* he wrote many articles for the *Edinburgh Review** between 1833 and 1844, but subsequently became closely aligned with the *North British Review** as he shared its evangelicalism and support of the Free Church of Scotland. He often used his journalism to press his own views on such controversial subjects as the nature of light, the decline of British science and the role of natural theology. **GC**

Sources: Brock 1984, Gordon 1869, *ODNB*, *Waterloo*, *Wellesley*.

BRIERLEY, BENJAMIN (1825-1896) Benjamin (Ben) Brierley was born to a poor family of Lancashire weavers. An active Chartist in the 1840s and a life-long autodidact, Brierley's first involvement in the newspaper world came through having short poems* and sketches on Lancashire life accepted for publication in the *Oddfellows' Magazine* (1846-1847), the *Manchester Guardian** (1854), *Manchester Spectator* (1855) and the *Manchester Weekly Times* (1857). By 1861, capitalizing on his newfound reputation, he finished as a silk warper and accepted a post as subeditor of the *Oldham Times*. A year later he abandoned this and set out to make his mark in London. Here the gregarious Brierley became associated with the Bohemian-inspired Savage Club. For their journal, *Colman's Magazine*, he was invited to write more Lancashire-inspired sketches but the magazine* folded after three issues. He returned to Manchester and became a professional writer of articles, poems and short stories. Between 1865-1867 he wrote stories, often in the local dialect, for the Manchester Literary Club's 2d monthly, *Country Words: A North of England Magazine of Literature, Science and Art* (17 issues).

By April 1869 Brierley was sufficiently well established to launch and edit* his own *Ben Brierley's Journal*. Subtitled *Journal of Literature, Science and Art, for the Promotion of Good-will and Good-fellowship among Men*, this 2d monthly* was one of the most successful of the magazines dedicated to healthy and humorous reading. Each issue typically included in Standard English and Lancashire dialect a miscellany of information, amusement and serialized* fiction. Out of the latter two elements the *Journal* became the medium for the development of Brierley's apolitical but shrewd, roguish, fun-loving working-class* character, Ab-o-'th'-Yate (Abraham at the Gate). The pseudonym* reflected Brierley's own first-hand experiences as a cotton weaver. Early circulation* figures were as high as 13,000; the average was about 10,000. Brierley's brother-in-law, James Firth, joined him as a partner in offices in Deansgate in 1874 at which point the *Journal* was turned into an illustrated* 1d weekly. Following the untimely death of his daughter in 1875, the magazine was sold to Abel Heywood* and Son, who continued to publish it successfully – with Ben Brierly remaining as editor – until December 1891. Brierley was a legendary figure in his own lifetime: he was lionised as a writer and journalist who could articulate the thoughts and ideas, hopes and aspirations of the Lancashire cotton weavers. **OA**

Sources: Ashton and Roberts 1989, Beetham 1985, Brierley 1886, Howell 2003, Huk 1995, Maidment 1987.

BRITISH AND FOREIGN CONFECTIONER (1877-1972) When the *British and Foreign Confectioner* was launched in May 1877 as a 6d monthly by S. Straker & Sons, it was dedicated to representing what the previous census had revealed to be a substantial number of tradespeople hitherto deprived of an organ that helped 'in the competitive race of life' (May 1877: 1). The periodical offered the typical ingredients of a trade journal*: market reports, lists of wholesalers, salient technical articles (e.g. recipes, new technological developments), legal issues including bankruptcies, patents and infringements of trademark, accounts of trade meetings and national and international events that affected trade (reports on the weather's effects on crops were frequent). Typical too were the descriptions of how major players organized their bakeries. Linking the field to science* was of particular concern. This extended to illustration* (even in adverts): images of machinery predominate. Though there was always room for cheap 'Situations Vacant', advertisements* quickly grew in number, size and visual complexity, as did the periodical itself.

By the early 1880s, out of 40 pages 18 were consistently adverts* each giving income of £4 a page, and there were numerous smaller adverts* as well. At this stage the journal had a global readership*: subscription prices* are listed for many countries. By 1893 it was so successful that it became a 2d weekly*, but reverted to monthly publication in 1897 (but with a gold title-piece and border, and 80 pages). Its status is indicated by its changes of address: by 1890 it had moved from Jewry St in Aldgate to St Mary Axe, before ending the century in the Strand. In May 1883 it had been silently amalgamated with the *Food Trades Journal* and a year later it became the *British and Foreign Confectioner Baker and Restaurateur*, which title more accurately indicated a readership* that it had targeted since its first year. **AK**

Source: *British and Foreign Confectioner.*

BRITISH AND FOREIGN EVANGELICAL REVIEW (1852-1888) The *British and Foreign Evangelical Review* was initially published under the title of the *Foreign Evangelical Review* (1852-1853) and reproduced papers from denominational quarterly* magazines from the United States* such as the *Biblical Repertory* or the *New Englander*. Produced in Edinburgh, it sought to unite forces from England and the United States in a struggle against 'Romanism' and 'Rationalism'. Within a year, the publication was enlarged to include original articles and it was made available at Mudie's circulating library. The *Review* was aimed at a highly literate clerical audience and would have held most appeal for evangelicals and Presbyterians. It saw itself as cultivating the 'higher departments of Theological Literature' and was interested in keeping its readers abreast of religious* scholarship from Europe as well as Britain and North America. Articles on church history and biographical sketches of religious personalities were fairly frequent elements. The dry and often exacting language frequently assumed detailed theological knowledge and was only occasionally relieved by lighter articles such as 'The Religious Belief of Shakespeare'. *British and Foreign Evangelical Review* was outward looking but simultaneously conservative and orthodox in tone and content. **BP**

Sources: Altholz, 1989, Ellegård 1971, *Waterloo.*

BRITISH AND FOREIGN REVIEW (1835-1844) Following the division and annexation of Poland at the end of the eighteenth century, the Literary Association of the Friends of Poland created the *British and Foreign Review; or, European Quarterly Journal** in 1835 to support the reunification and independence of Poland. The journal published liberal opinions concerning governments throughout Europe. Its proprietor* was Thomas Wentworth Beaumont*, a wealthy Member of Parliament and the president of the Literary Association. William Wallace edited* the first issue (July 1835); subsequent issues were edited by Gilbert Ainslie Young, Beaumont, and Henry Reeve*. John Mitchell Kemble* contributed to the journal and undertook some editorial work in 1835; in December 1836 he accepted the position of editor and remained in post until the journal ended. Besides politics, the *Review* covered diverse topics in economics, philosophy, and the arts, with prestigious contributors such as John Stuart Mill*, Alexis de Tocqueville, George Henry Lewes*, and William Bodham Donne*. By 1838 the paper was losing money and although Mill offered to merge* the paper with the *London and Westminster Review**, Kemble declined and the last issue appeared in December 1844. **BA**

Source: *Wellesley.*

BRITISH ARCHITECT: NATIONAL RECORD OF THE AESTHETIC AND CONSTRUCTIVE ARTS; AND BUSINESS JOURNAL OF THE BUILDING COMMUNITY (1874-1919) The *British Architect* was a lavishly illustrated* 6d folio weekly* founded to take a non-partisan view of the 'Battle of the Styles' by stressing 'facts, data and principles in connection with actual practice' rather than theory. It originated in Manchester, in January 1874 (though within ten years it had moved to London) and borrowed elements of the trade magazine*, seeking to be useful to managers and professionals of the industry both on national and local levels. To this end, in addition to descriptions and illustrations* of new and historical buildings, it regularly featured notices of architectural competitions, reports of both architectural and engineering* societies, the latest news* on labour, wages and legal cases, patents and inventions, relevant parliamentary bills, restoration projects, decorative arts such as mosaics and stained glass, civil engineering, the state of the timber trade, prices for building materials, value of land and property, public health and reviews* of relevant publications. While the price* was reduced to 4½d in 1881 and the look of the periodical changed in line with changes in architectural and advertising fashion, the format* remained the same throughout the century. For most of its life, it was edited* by Thomas Raffles Davison (1853-1937), an architect and artist in his own right as well as a journalist*. He contributed elegant drawings as well as numerous articles. While sustained by abundant advertising* and sales in the US as well as Britain, the shortages of World War I clearly restricted the market so that in April 1919 it was eventually absorbed into the *Builder*. AK

Sources: Plume 1937, Richardson and Thorne 1994, Webb 1927.

BRITISH BANDSMAN (1887-) Initially marketed as 'A monthly magazine for members of military and brass bands', the *British Bandsman* became the *British Bandsman and Orchestral Times* (1888-1890), and the *Orchestral Times and Bandsman* in 1891. However, it reverted to its original title in 1899. Its main sales were always to brass instrument players, particularly the many thousands who populated Victorian amateur brass bands.

The founder and editor* Sam Cope was an evangelist for the brass band movement, which he felt ought to be judged alongside other, longer-standing forms of music*-making. The magazine was published monthly until 8 March 1902, when it became a weekly* (and has remained so ever since). Throughout the nineteenth century it sought to foster a national network of brass band players, to raise standards of playing by providing didactic advice, and, more importantly, to advocate the development of the brass band contest according to common and well understood regulations and high standards of integrity. The *British Bandsman* became the most articulate voice of the brass band, and without it, one suspects, this remarkable indigenous form of music-making would not have gained the coherence it did in the Victorian period. TH

Sources: Hailstone 1987, Herbert 2000.

BRITISH CHESS MAGAZINE (1881-) There is some disagreement about the initial date of the *British Chess Magazine,* as according to Layton's *Handy Newspaper List* (1912) it was established in 1870. The first issues were published in London and New York by the Brentano Brothers, later it was produced in Huddersfield by J. E. Wheatley & Co., finally in London by Kegan, Paul, Trench, Trübner & Co*. Editors* included John Watkinson (1884) and Isaac M. Brown (1898), with contributions from E. Freeborough. G. E. Fulstow and A. G. and Hobart Fellows (1898). A monthly* magazine, it cost 8d (1884-1894), then the price* rose by 1d (1896-1912). Until photographs*

appeared in 1926, the magazine was illustrated* by diagrams and it included chess problems, foreign news*, poems*, obituaries*, replies to correspondents* and games. DHL

Sources: Layton 1912, *Waterloo.*

BRITISH CONTROVERSIALIST (1850-1872) A monthly* magazine that aimed to provide a 'spot on which men of every creed may meet as upon neutral ground, and there engage in calm and deliberate controversy', the *British Controversialist* was premised on the idea that enlightenment rises from the clash of differing opinions. Initially costing 3d, the cover price* rose gradually, reaching 6d in 1862, with the magazine expanding from 32 to 80 pages over the same period. While keeping its core title over the entirety of its run, there were various title changes* of the adjunct after the 'and', in ways that reflect adjustments to its publishing environment and contents: *British Controversialist and Impartial Inquirer* (1850-1853), *British Controversialist and Magazine of Self-Culture* (1854-1855), *British Controversialist and Self-Educator* (1856-1858), *British Controversialist and Literary Magazine* (1859-1872). The *Controversialist's* two core contributors were J. A. Cooper – the Birmingham manufacturer who was both proprietor* and editor* – and Samuel Neil – a lecturer and author of text books on self-education, but its real interest is that many contributions were submitted by (anonymous*) readers.

Its readership* was largely composed of young men from the working class and the lower-middle class* who were deeply concerned about self improvement – indeed were often members of mutual improvement societies – and wanted to learn from and participate in reasoned debate. Readers' submissions appeared mainly in the debates on religion, politics*, history*, literature* and philosophy* which were played out in its pages over the course of 3-15 issues. These debates were composed of short pieces taking differing stances on questions such as 'Is War, under every Circumstance, opposed to Christianity?' (May-Sept. 1850), 'Is Woman Mentally Inferior to Man?' (June-Oct. 1852) and 'Are the Working Classes Qualified for Political Representation?' (Feb.-June 1865). Aside from these debates, there was a regular leader*, which explored a subject or theme such as 'Legislation' or 'The Sophists', or, as in a two-part biographical sketch of Francis Bacon, sought to bring works of genius into the compass of an ordinary mind. Over more than 20 years, the *Controversialist* remained largely unchanged in format, but as time wore on the debates in its pages came increasingly to resemble a discussion among educated men of letters rather than one orientated towards the improvement of the lower classes. MaT/ MJW

Sources: *Waterloo*, Wolff 1968, Wolff 1982.

BRITISH CRITIC (1792-1853) The *British Critic* was founded in 1792 as part of a counterattack by various conservative groups to stem the rise of Jacobinism in Britain. Its aim was 'to obtain criticisms from the eminent persons in every field'. The journal went through three series until it merged with the *Quarterly* Theological Review* in 1826.

The editor* of the first series was Archdeacon Robert Nares (1753-1829), with the Reverend William Beloe (1753-1829), a classicist, as co-proprietor*. They shaped the journal's religious policy. Each owned a third share in the periodical, with the printers Charles and Francis Rivington* owning the other third. The first series appeared monthly*. It consisted of about 25 reviews* occupying 100 pages, a 'British Catalogue' of five pages and eight pages of brief notices. Reviews included Robert Burns's *Poems* and in 1799 a favourable review of Wordsworth's *Lyrical Ballads* appeared. By the end of the eighteenth century the 'British Catalogue' section had increased to 22 pages and there were three pages of reviews of foreign books. There was also a tendency toward longer review articles.

The second series of the journal started in January 1814 under the editorship of T. F. Middleton and William R. Lyall. With shifts in management and changes of format the second series saw drastic changes. These included the elimination of the entire British Catalogue section. By 1816 reviews became longer and short reviews had disappeared. The third series in 1827 saw further changes. The journal became a quarterly* publication, merging with the *Quarterly Theological Review and Ecclesiastical Record*. Each number now contained 15 long articles and averaged about 260 pages. By the fourth series subject matter focused on sermons, essays and letters, ecclesiastical history and philosophy. Between 1838 and 1843 the *British Critic* was edited successively by J. H. Newman and Thomas Mozley, prominent members of the Tractarian or Oxford Movement. Mozley's brother, J. B. Mozley*, was a contributor. Affiliation with the Tractarians led to a drastic decline in circulation*. Opponents of the Oxford Movement tried to halt publication on the grounds that the journal was dividing the church it had been established to defend. In 1844 it became the *English Review or Quarterly Journal of Ecclesiastical and General Literature*. DHL

Sources: De Montluzin 1998, Graham 1930, Sper 1937, Sullivan 1983, *Waterloo*, *Wellesley*.

BRITISH MEDICAL JOURNAL (1857-) The *British Medical Journal* was launched as a general medical* weekly* in 1857. It was a continuation of the *Provincial Medical and Surgical Journal* (1840-1857), which was known as the *Association Medical Journal* (1853-1855) and founded and co-edited* by an Irish paediatrician, Peter Hennis Green. His fellow editor, Robert Streeten, was a member of the council of the Provincial Medical and Surgical Association (British Medical Association from 1856). Other nineteenth-century editors were W. H. Ranking and J. H. Walsh*, Andrew Wynter*, W. O. Markham, Ernest Hart*, Jonathan Hutchinson and Dawson Williams*. From the start, Green aspired to appeal to Provincial Medical and Surgical Association members. Links between the original title and the Association were established during the early 1840s, and from 1842 the *Journal* was supplied weekly (fortnightly 1847-1853) to all Association members as a subscription benefit.

Then, in 1844, the Association ousted Green and placed Streeten in sole editorial charge; it also assumed proprietorship* and transferred printing and publication from London to Worcester. As such, the journal became the first medical weekly published outside the capital. Until the 1860s, Association members repeatedly questioned the value of a journal once termed 'stale, flat and unprofitable' (*PMSJ*, 4 Aug. 1852). Proposals to terminate it were discussed on several occasions and most of the early editors left partly because they could not tolerate the incessant criticism.

Ernest Hart edited* the *British Medical Journal* in 1867-1869 and again in 1870-1898. The gap in his editorial career was probably caused by the discovery that he was using the journal's contributor fund to augment his salary. Something of a prodigy, both as a schoolboy and medical student, Hart joined the editorial staff of the *Lancet** in 1858. Such was his success there that his appointment as editor of the *BMJ* prompted the *Medical Press and Circular* (1866-1961) to observe that the British Medical Association council 'had caught the editorial *Leprechaun*, actually bought up the life and soul of the opposition establishment' (5 May 1869: 375). Although Hart's editorship of the *British Medical Journal* involved scandal, controversy and litigation, he more than anyone else was responsible for transforming a somewhat parochial publication into a thriving, influential weekly covering both national and international issues. It had more pages, more advertising* and a higher circulation* than any other medical journal.

In transforming the fortunes of the *British Medical Journal*, Hart greatly strengthened the Association. Under his editorship the journal took a strong line on many socio-medical issues. It campaigned against baby farming, workhouse conditions and other abuses; it championed such causes as vivisection, the contagious diseases acts and compulsory vaccination against smallpox. It also gained a formidable scientific reputation through publishing original articles by such medical luminaries as Joseph Lister, Patrick Manson and Ronald Ross.

Notwithstanding his successes, Hart acquired many enemies and shortly before his death the BMA was exploring ways of facilitating his resignation. Hart was succeeded by his deputy, Dawson Williams, who had been associated with the *BMJ* since 1881. He remained in post until he reluctantly retired in 1928. **PWB**

Sources: Bartrip 1990, Bynum et al. 1992.

BRITISH MOTHERS' MAGAZINE (1845-1864) This monthly* journal became *Mrs Bakewell's British Mothers' Journal* (1856-1861), the *British Mothers' Journal and Domestic Magazine* (1862-1863) and then was briefly the *British Mothers' Family Magazine*. It was set up and remained as the 'organ of communication' for the Maternal Associations. Like its American counterpart, the *Mothers' Magazine*, it therefore carried articles and letters* from and about these evangelical Christian mothers' meetings on both sides of the Atlantic, as well as reports from missionaries* abroad. Costing 4d in 1845, the price* dropped to 3d by 1855. It was edited by Mrs Bakewell* who also contributed signed articles – as did Eliza Cook*, T. Hood* and 'Charlotte Elizabeth' [Tonna]*, among others. Though it carried a woodcut on the first page, it was otherwise unillustrated and printed in a single column*. The diet which it offered was serious but not without variety, consisting of moral tales (though not novels), poetry* and articles on questions of faith and social issues, as well as the Maternal Association reports. Conservative in tone and appearance, it argued that women should be given mental stimulation and it included book reviews*, mainly of publications of the Religious Tract Society*. **MRB**

Sources: Beetham 1996, *British Mothers' Magazine, Waterloo.*

BRITISH QUARTERLY REVIEW (1845-1886) Following the secession of moderate Congregationalists from the *Eclectic Review**, the *British Quarterly Review* was established in 1845 as a quarterly* periodical. Run by evangelical Nonconformists and initially priced* at 6s, the *Quarterly* covered a range of perspectives and subjects, indicating a breadth to nineteenth-century evangelical nonconformism that other, more sectarian, publications sometimes hide. While several of the articles in the *British Quarterly Review* were on theological topics, most of the space was given over to literature*, science* and politics*. The tone of the writing was set by Robert Vaughan*, the first editor*, who envisioned a serious, earnest and tolerant publication. When Vaughan* retired in 1865, Henry Allon became joint editor with Henry Robert Reynolds, before becoming sole editor from 1874. The ongoing respect that the *British Quarterly Review* enjoyed among leading cultural figures was evident in a letter that Matthew Arnold* sent Allon, praising the *Quarterly's* educational and cultural contribution. Writers in the *British Quarterly Review*, anonymous* until 1870, included G. H. Lewes*, Coventry Patmore, Herbert Spencer*, Walter Besant* and 'Vernon Lee'* (Violet Paget). The journal's circulation* shrank to 500 copies in the 1880s from an earlier height of around 2,500, and the demise of the *British Quarterly Review* reflected a declining interest in quarterly publications towards the end of the nineteenth century. **MJK**

Sources: Altholz 1989, Osbourn, 1950, Sullivan.

BRITISH STAGE AND LITERARY CABINET (1817-1822) This illustrated* stage monthly* was set up as a rival to the popular *Theatrical Inquisitor**. It offered broad coverage of the London and provincial theatre world, in addition to book reviews* and miscellaneous articles. Occasionally, *British Stage* published supplements* containing 'Reprints of Scarce Plays, and tracts relating to the drama'. It contained high-quality illustrations* (some of which were coloured), with George* and Robert Cruikshank being among its most noted illustrators. **OD**

Source: *Waterloo.*

BRITISH WEEKLY (1886-1970) The *British Weekly* was first published as a Nonconformist 1d religious* newspaper for promoting 'Social and Christian Progress'. Founded and edited* by Sir William Robertson Nicoll*, the newspaper was sponsored by Hodder and Stoughton*, who gave Nicoll a free editorial hand and affirmed his unashamed support for the Liberal Party. Nicoll had acquired an extensive knowledge and memory of periodicals and newspapers from his Aberdeenshire home, and his own voracious reading. He was not an originator; instead, he copied successful methods from others. For example, the focus on his leading article* was inspired by W. T. Stead's* *Pall Mall Gazette*, although Nicoll made his leading articles religiously devotional. Nicoll's contribution, which included his own mixture of 'Thrills, News, Sense and Pastimes' and a personable style epitomized in 'Correspondence of Claudius Clear', built the circulation* of the *British Weekly* to over 100,000 in the early 1900s. The *British Weekly* continued for many years after Nicoll died in 1923 before eventually being subsumed by the *Christian Week* from 1970. **KI**

Sources: Attenborough 1975, Darlow 1925.

BRITISH WORKMAN (1855-1921) The *British Workman and Friend of the Sons of Toil* was, 'commenced... to promote the health, wealth and happiness of the working classes'(Feb.1855). It was edited* by T. B. Smithies* and designed to promote temperance*, religious* observance, industry, thrift, kindness to animals and peace among the urban 'industrial classes*' through a combination of short articles and good pictures. Large wood*-engraved images were accompanied by stories about self-made men, the advantages of sobriety, hard-working fathers and good mothers. Each number of the journal contained a variety of poetry*, anecdotes, short stories and serialized fiction*. There were factual items, pieces of statistical information, notices of new publications and correspondence*.

The journal was supported by prominent evangelicals and philanthropists such as the Earl of Shaftesbury, Samuel Gurney and Samuel Morley, and bodies like the Pure Literature Society. From October 1857 it was distributed in large numbers by the London City Mission in the poorest districts of the city. By 1862 the paper was circulating* in excess of 250,000 copies monthly*. A new series was introduced in January 1861 and the full-page wood-engraving became a hallmark of the magazine. Illustrations* were provided by John Gilbert*, Louis Huard, Henry Anelay*, Harrison Weir, John Dawson Watson* and William Rainey. Additionally, engravings after Edwin Landseer, Edwin Douglas, J. F. Herring and Birket Foster; portraits of self-made philanthropists, politicians and members of the aristocracy and the royal family were a regular feature. The contributors of letterpress included Clara Lucas Balfour*, Mrs Ellis, Mary Howitt*, Nelsie Brook, George Mogridge ('Old Humphrey'*), John W. Kirton, the Rev. P. B. Power and Edwin Harcourt Burrage.

Smithies edited the journal for more than 27 years and on his death in1883 the role was taken up by his assistant, Samuel Reeve. After Reeve's death in 1886 there followed a succession of editors* including Edward Step, Jesse Page and Sam Woods, M.P. A new series was issued in January 1892, when ownership of the paper was transferred to the publishers S. W. Partridge & Co. Several changes of format, modifications to the title and the replacement of the wood-engraved image by photomechanical processes, gradually eroded the identity of the journal. From 1901 onwards it went into a slow, steady decline and publication ceased abruptly in September 1921. **FM**

Sources: *British Workman, Waterloo.*

BRITISH WORKWOMAN (1863-1896) A large-sized, three columns*, penny* monthly* magazine aimed at 'workwomen', it had exactly the same format as the *British Workman* and a similar pro-temperance* message though it was published by Richard Willoughby. Like the *British Workman*, it was distinguished by the high-quality illustrations*, especially the full-size woodcut* on its front page, which usually pictured scenes from working-class* life, but it also included smaller illustrations in the text, along with framed mottos. 'Workwomen' were broadly defined and, according to an article in the first number, included the Queen, Florence Nightingale, Jenny Lynd and Miss Burdett-Couts. However, the price* and tone indicated that this improving publication was aimed at working-class* women, including machine operatives. Purchasers were encouraged to buy several copies to give away to deserving poor women. The publication announced that its aim was 'by the exposition of Bible truths and a mixture of anecdote, poetry*, fiction, sketch and essay to encourage women to recognise their importance in the morality of the nation'. **MRB**

Sources: *British Workwoman, Waterloo.*

BROADSIDES AND CHAPBOOKS Broadsides and chapbooks were staples of popular literature aimed at the working class* and date back to the sixteenth century. Literacy was not a barrier to enjoying them as illiterate people would find someone who could read their contents out loud. Chapbooks were cheaply printed, small booklets whose contents and length varied and usually featured cheap woodcuts* for illustration*. Contents varied widely but included political* and religious* tracts, almanacs and abridgements of books such as John Bunyan's the *Pilgrim's Progress* (1678); they also often featured early forms of children's literature with stories derived from mythology or fairy tales. They were sold by 'chapmen' who hawked them on the streets and at fairs.

Broadsides were printed on one side of paper and contained news* about important events. More commonly, they contained ballads, which adopted songs from the oral tradition and fixed them in print. They were frequently love songs or contained patriotic themes that stressed the virtue of the common people. The authors and publishers were usually working-class artisans, using simple presses* with a few decorative blocks to provide illustrations*. They took traditional tunes that everyone knew and added new words on topical themes (broadsides usually presented the words and not the music*). The songs were available from sellers, or patterers, who sang the songs on street corners. Customers listened to the tune and then bought the broadside for the words. Many broadsides were printed in London and spread metropolitan* concerns all over the country, but there were broadside publishers in other cities as well who produced songs or news items that spoke to local* interests. The most successful publisher* was James Catnach, who originally made his fortune from publishing broadsides about the Queen Caroline affair in 1820 and allegedly sold 2,500,000 copies of broadsides about the execution of the murderer James Rush in 1849. Many broadsides were devoted to the 'last dying speech' of criminals, frequently sold at executions.

Both broadsides and chapbooks declined as a popular form after about 1850, replaced by the new popular press*. They are significant not only for generating a form of cultural capital for working* class people but also for developing the demotic language of sensation that the popular press would adopt as its own. **RM**

Sources: Hindley 1871, James 1976, McWilliam 2007, Mayhew 1861, Shepard 1962.

BROOKS, CHARLES WILLIAM SHIRLEY (1816-1874) Best known for his long association with *Punch**, Shirley Brooks was one of Victorian London's most versatile and prolific literary journalists*. For some 30 years, he moved easily among many genres of periodical contributions, including leading* articles, news* items, parliamentary* and investigative reporting*, cartoon* captions, comic tales, serial fiction*, gossip* columns, political* analysis, obituaries*, book and theatre reviews*, and satirical verse. Inspired as a young man by the 'Literary Portrait Gallery' series in *Fraser's Magazine**, Brooks began sending verses and tales to magazines during his 20s while working in his uncle's law office. Beginning a literary career in earnest

in the early 1840s, he soon found a congenial outlet in *Ainsworth's Magazine**, going on to edit the short-lived *Age and Argus* and contributing to a wide assortment of magazines. Brooks's first involvement with the *Punch* circle dates from this period, with contributions to serials* edited by *Punch* mainstay Gilbert Abbott À Beckett*. In the late 1840s he wrote verses satirizing *Punch* for Albert Smith's* *Man in the Moon**, and began a career-long association with the *Illustrated London News** and the *Era**.

In 1848, Angus Bethune Reach* introduced Brooks to John Douglas Cook*, the new editor* of the newly Peelite *Morning Chronicle**, who recruited Brooks to join the staff. For the next five years, in addition to reports and reviews, Brooks wrote the parliamentary* summary for the *Morning Chronicle*, experience that would provide the foundation for much of his later political writing. In 1853, as part of its series on labour and the poor, the paper sent him to southern Russia, Syria and Egypt. When Reach suffered a paralytic seizure in 1854, Brooks took on his friend's assignments for the *Morning Chronicle*, turning the payments over to Reach's wife.

Brooks began writing for *Punch* in 1851, and was soon invited to join the staff, filling the gap left by the departure of William Makepeace Thackeray*. While he continued to contribute regularly to many other periodicals, even serving as editor of the *Literary Gazette** and *Home News*, *Punch* thereafter remained at the centre of his working life. The most distinctive of his myriad contributions was 'The Essence of Parliament', a deftly humorous yet informative summary of the week's political news that proved enormously popular. Equally influential was Brooks's role as 'suggester in chief' of the subject of each week's full-page political cartoon*, normally drawn by John Tenniel*. At the weekly staff meetings, Brooks by the 1860s exercised a dominance even more pronounced than Douglas Jerrold's* had been in the 1840s. A staunch Tory from his earliest days, he played a key part in the magazine's mid-Victorian retreat from its early Radical politics. Brooks succeeded founding editor Mark Lemon* as editor on the latter's death in 1870, and continued to contribute his usual large share of *Punch*'s weekly contents, in addition to his editorial duties, until his own death four years later. **PL**

Sources: Jerrold 1874, Layard 1907, *ODNB*, Spielmann 1895.

BROUGH, JOHN CARGILL (1834-1872) Despite his bohemianism and lack of formal scientific training, Brough's geniality made him socially acceptable among members of the British and European scientific communities. Through his editing and writing he helped to establish scientific* journalism as a respectable occupation. Brough graduated into freelance journalism in the late 1850s after working as an office boy for various newspapers. In 1859 he became founder editor* of the monthly* trade journals* *Ironmonger* (1859-1969) and *Chemist & Druggist* (1859-). By commissioning contributions from members of the scientific community he ensured that both journals served a literary function as well as a mercantile one. In April 1867, supported by his scientific feature writers, Brough launched a weekly* physical science journal *Laboratory* which competed directly with the cheaper *Chemical News* edited by William Crookes*. Brough's belief that there was a sufficiently large international readership* to sustain a high-class weekly journal written by paid experts proved incorrect and the journal collapsed after only 26 weeks. Nevertheless, *Laboratory* became the model for Norman J. Lockyer* when he persuaded Alexander Macmillan* to underwrite the weekly *Nature* in 1869 with Brough as a subeditor*. In 1870 ill health forced Brough to abandon all his journalistic responsibilities. **WB**

Sources: Brock 1980, Lightman 2004a, *ODNB*.

BROUGH, ROBERT BARNABAS (1828-1860) Robert Brough was a novelist and playwright who also made contributions as a satirical poet, illustrator* and essayist to numerous journals and newspapers throughout the 1840s and 1850s, some of which he edited*. His extreme radical tendencies and his dissipated lifestyle made his name synonymous with the bohemian literary milieu of London. Brough began his journalistic career on Merseyside in 1847 when, with assistance from his brother William Brough (1826-1870), he edited, contributed and illustrated a satirical* 3d fortnightly magazine* the *Liverpool Lion* (1847). The success of a burlesque Brough wrote with his brother, entitled *The Enchanted Isle* (1848), based on *The Tempest*, enabled him to relocate to London.

Now a working dramatist in the capital, Brough supplemented his income by contributing satirical and comic essays and poems* to journals seeking to rival the hegemony of *Punch*. These journals included the *Man In The Moon*, *Diogenes* (1853-1855), *Comic Times* (1855-1856) and *Train*. During this period he became acquainted with other bohemian, non-university journalists* and authors, men like George Augustus Sala*, Edmund Yates*

and Albert Smith*. Brough also contributed to more serious ventures, including *Household Words*, *Illustrated Times*, and as Brussels correspondent for the *Sunday Times* *. Briefly he was also editor* of *Atlas* and *Welcome Guest*.

Inextricably linked with Sala, due to their bohemian lifestyle, the two journalists were subjected to scathing attacks by university-educated critics like James Hannay (1827-1873) in the *Idler*, and in 'high-brow' periodicals like the *Saturday Review*. Brough's most acclaimed and biographical novel, *Marston Lynch*, had appeared first in *Train* in 1856 because Sala's dissipation had forced him to abandon the writing of his intended novel, *Fripanelli's Daughter*. Sala repaid the debt by completing *Marston Lynch* in 1860 on Brough's death from alcoholism.

Brough's versatility as a wit and satirist meant that his articles and poetry were constantly in demand. He was held in high regard by his bohemian contemporaries, who particularly favoured his savage satire of the aristocracy in *Songs Of the Governing Classes* (1855), his paraphrases of Victor Hugo's 'Odes et Ballades' in *Train*, and 'The Barlow Papers' in *Comic Times*. **PB**

Sources: Edwards 1997, *ODNB*, Sutherland 1989, *Waterloo*, Yates 1885.

BROUGHAM, HENRY (1778-1868) Henry Brougham, later first Baron Brougham and Vaux, was the fourth of the quartet of Edinburgh-based young professionals who founded the *Edinburgh Review*. Like Francis Jeffrey* and Francis Horner*, two of the co-founders, he was trained for the law but attracted by the world of affairs as well as the world of letters. Unlike Jeffrey and Sydney Smith*, he became more directly involved in the world of Whig politics, rising to the position of Lord Chancellor in Lord Grey's government of 1830. Accounts of the events leading up to the establishment of the *Review* in 1802 differ in detail, but all agree that Brougham was the last member of the group, joining after the early numbers had been published. He proved a difficult colleague, a victim of his own temperament, at times domineering, irascible, peremptory and always self-regarding. Unlike Jeffrey, the first editor*, he was London based, and used his contacts effectively, brokering many of the review's political* articles and writing many of them himself. His relationship with Macvey Napier*, Jeffrey's successor, was more fraught. His position in the government was not secure, and in addition he was jealous of Thomas Babington Macaulay*, a rising star in the *Review*, and also in the Whig Party.

Brougham's influence in *Edinburgh Review* circles waned during the course of Napier's editorship, reflecting his diminishing political influence. He wrote fewer political articles after being excluded from Melbourne's cabinet in 1835. Even his articles on historical* subjects could have a sting in the tail, prompted as he was to settle old scores. His contributions to the *Edinburgh* stopped in 1841, after which he occasionally contributed to the *Quarterly Review** and later to the *Law Magazine and Review**. As the moving force behind the foundation of the Society for the Diffusion of Useful Knowledge* in 1826 he took an active interest in the society's publications, among which was the *Penny Magazine**. JS
Sources: Clive 1957, *ODNB*, Shattock 1989, *Wellesley*.

BROWNE, HABLOT KNIGHT (1815-1882) Under his famous pen name of 'Phiz'* and firmly lodged in the public's mind through his collaborations with Dickens*, Hablot Browne was a hugely prolific, and popular, comic artist and illustrator*. He was, however, limited by his preference for working in the tradition of Regency single plate etchings and engravings rather than the more versatile wood engraving*, which resulted in much of his major work appearing in book form, especially in serialized* novels. His artistic conservatism gave all his work a slightly old-fashioned air with an attenuated and scratchy linearity present in many of his illustrations. Already a well-known illustrator by the late 1830s, Browne's work was published as etched illustrations to the prestigious fiction-led monthlies* of the 1840s including works by such major authors as W. H. Ainsworth* (*Ainsworth's Magazine* 1844).

His preference for an older style of illustration never prevented him, however, from making a major contribution to many diverse periodicals, ranging from the *Illustrated London News** (1844-1861), which had a penchant for commissioning occasional spreads from contemporary comic artists, to such artistically ambitious magazines as the *Illuminated Magazine** (1845). He worked for *Punch** on two separate occasions, and drew its second wrapper design during his first residency there (1842-1844), leaving on that occasion because the magazine could scarcely afford two such stars as Browne and Leech*. But, barely able to hold a pencil after a serious illness, Browne worked again for *Punch* (1861-1869), providing over 60 illustrations. Other overtly comic and caricature* work had appeared in the *Great Gun* in 1844. Browne's eminence meant that he was able to publish occasional work in well-established and popular literary journals such as the *Welcome Guest** and the *New Monthly Magazine**, as well as news*-led journals like the *Illustrated Times**. **BM**
Sources: Engen 1990, Everitt 1893, Houfe 1978, *ODNB*, Spielmann 1895.

BROWNE, MATILDA (?-1936) Matilda Browne's journalistic career, like her personal history, was entwined with that of Samuel Beeton* and his family. When Isabella Beeton* died, aged 28, in 1865, she left behind not only her new-born child but also the various editorial and journalistic ventures in which she was engaged with her husband. These included the well-established *Englishwoman's Domestic Magazine** and the *Young Englishwoman**, launched only months before. Matilda Browne seems to have taken on both tasks, bringing up the two Beeton boys and assuming the roles of 'Editress'* and journalist* in Beeton's office. In the *Englishwoman's Domestic Magazine,* unlike Isabella, she developed a public persona in her regular column*, 'Spinnings', writing under the pseudonym* 'Silkworm'. Here she offered advice on fashion*, personal life and above all on the female pastime of 'shopping'. Encouraged by her success, Beeton and Browne launched *Myra's Journal** in which as 'Myra' she continued to provide advice on fashion, recommending shops in a way which foreshadowed the twentieth-century advertorial. **MRB**.
Sources: Beetham 1996, *Englishwoman's Domestic Magazine,* Hughes 2005, *Myra's Journal*.

BUCHANAN, DAVID (1779-1848) Although David Buchanan first made his name by writing articles on political* theory, and continued writing in economics, it was his career as editor* of various Scottish newspapers which allowed him the greatest latitude in promoting liberal ideas. Born in Montrose in 1779, to a father whose publishing* work included Samuel Johnson's dictionary, Buchanan was an early contributor to the *Edinburgh Review** (1802-1929). His first known publication was a response to William Cobbett's theories on political economy*, and he gained public notice around 1806 with a pamphlet criticizing William Pitt the Younger's volunteer system. Buchanan moved from Montrose to Edinburgh in 1808 after being invited to help found and edit* a liberal newspaper, the *Weekly Register*. Although the paper folded less than a year later, Buchanan then edited the *Caledonian Mercury* from 1810 to 1827, at which point he took over the editorship of the *Edinburgh Evening Courant**, a position he held until his death. Throughout this period, he continued writing, primarily in the field of economics*; he published articles in *Cobbett's Political Register** (1802-1835) and the *Edinburgh Review* on issues such as finance, the Corn Laws, and free trade. He also contributed several articles in the seventh edition of the *Encyclopedia Britannica*, largely on geography and statistics. **TR**

Sources: Anderson 1882, Eatwell 1987, *ODNB*.

BUCKINGHAM, JAMES SILK (1786-1855) Largely self-educated, most of James Silk Buckingham's early life was spent as a sailor in the Atlantic and Mediterranean. He first went to Calcutta around 1815, where, in 1818, he founded the *Calcutta Journal*. Because his newspaper was highly critical of the government of India and the East India Company, it was suppressed. Buckingham was expelled in 1823. He claimed to have invested £23,000 in the venture and that the *Calcutta Journal* was worth £40,000 at the time of its suppression. Buckingham campaigned for many years for its restitution. Finally the East India Company conceded the injustice of its suppression of the paper and granted him a modest annual pension of £200.

On returning to London in 1824, Buckingham published accounts of his travels in the Middle East. He founded the monthly *Oriental Herald and Colonial Review* which he edited* until 1829. In this journal he continued his campaign against the East India Company and advocated colonial self-government. It was replaced in 1830 by the *Oriental Quarterly Review* which lasted for only two issues. In 1827 Buckingham started another journal, the *Sphynx*, a weekly* devoted to politics*, literature* and news*. This survived for barely two years. But before its demise he had founded the *Athenaeum** which became of the most successful literary journals of the nineteenth century. However Buckingham edited the *Athenaeum* for a few weeks after its first issue on 2 January 1828. Handing the journal over to John Sterling, he went on to found a London evening newspaper 'the *Argus*' which survived for only four weeks.

Buckingham also pursued a political career, which was mainly concerned with attempts at social reform. In 1828 he was elected to the first reformed Parliament, where he advocated several reforms. These were met with apathy both from Parliament and the public. In 1843 he founded the British and Foreign Institute and for two years published its transactions in a quarto form. In later years he continued to travel and became president of the London Temperance League in 1851. He also helped to end the East India Company's monopoly on trade in the Far East. In 1855 he died

after completing a four volume autobiography, only two volumes of which were ever published. **DHL**

Sources: *Gentleman's Magazine* Sept. 1855, McKay 1984, *ODNB*.

BUCKLAND, FRANCIS (1826-1880) Francis Buckland, son of the Oxford geologist William Buckland, was a pisciculturalist and natural historian who made regular contributions to the field-sports magazine* *Field** (1856-1865) and set up a rival magazine *Land and Water** in 1866, which he edited* until his death. In 1851 Buckland wrote an article on the muscles of the arm but failed to get it published despite the support of his friend the anatomist Richard Owen*. His first article, on the habits and peculiarities of rats, was published in *Bentley's Miscellany** in August 1852. He also published several articles on natural history topics in Charles Dickens's* weekly* periodical *Household Words** (1853-1857). Many of his articles were revised and republished as *Curiosities of Natural History* (1857, 1860, 1866), *The Log-Book of a Fisherman and Naturalist* (1875) and *Notes and Jottings from Animal Life* (1880). In 1863, while still writing prolifically for *Field**, Buckland made the acquaintance of the natural history collector John Keast Lord and encouraged him to write for the magazine. He later made Lord a staff writer at *Land and Water*. His editorship of the latter magazine, which gave combined practical natural history with the reporting and discussion of country sports*, represented his most important contribution to Victorian journalism*. *Land and Water* achieved a good circulation* and fulfilled Buckland's desire to demonstrate that natural history knowledge could be put to practical use, particularly in order to augment British food supplies (a passion of Buckland's as Inspector of Fisheries from 1867 to 1880), and to diffuse the subject of natural history to a non-specialist public. **AB**

Sources: Bompas 1885, Buckland 1872, *ODNB*, *Wellesley*.

BUCKNILL, JOHN CHARLES (1817-1897) After finding success as an asylum superintendent, Bucknill sought to augment his professional standing by helping to found and then, in 1853, edit* the *Asylum Journal of Mental Science*, which soon superseded Forbes Winslow's *Journal of Psychological Medicine and Mental Pathology* as the principal organ of the nascent mental health profession, both in the public and private sectors. Bucknill's dynamic editorship lasted for nine years during which he used the journal to advocate his own preference for non-restraint in the treatment of the insane as well as emphasizing the interests of public county asylums like the one he superintended in Devon. Often unable to solicit sufficient contributions from colleagues, Bucknill also wrote extensively for the *Asylum Journal*, even penning several articles on madness in literature which were republished in book form as *The Psychology of Shakespeare* (1859).

After moving to a more prominent asylum post in 1862, Bucknill resigned as the journal's editor*, having truncated its title to the *Journal of Mental Science** in 1856; during subsequent decades he wrote on lunacy and alcoholism for general periodicals such as the *Contemporary Review**, stirring up a fervid controversy over private asylums in 1885 with an article in the *Nineteenth Century**. In 1878 Bucknill helped found and edit *Brain*, a new journal that advocated neuropsychiatry. **GD**
Sources: Scull, Mackenzie and Hervey 1996, *ODNB*.

BUILDER (1842-1966) The *Builder* is the most famous architectural periodical of the nineteenth century. While there had been previous attempts in this genre – the *Architectural Magazine* (1834-1839), *Civil Engineer and Architect's Journal* (1837-1869) and the *Surveyor, Engineer and Architect* (1840-1843), the founding editor* of the *Builder*, Joseph Aloysius Hansom, drew more on the *Penny Magazine** and above all on the *Illustrated London News** for his emphasis on illustration* over words. Starting (31 Dec. 1842) as a 16-page quarto penny* weekly* (2d stamped), the periodical grew in price* and size* until it reached 4d in 1848. By that time it was folio-sized* and its illustrations were printed on separate sheets with no letterpress on the reverse, a practice followed by other similar journals such as the *British Architect**. Intended to target workers rather building professionals, it was the latter who actually bought the magazine, although Mitchell's* and Deacon's press directories repeatedly claim that such was its quality that its readership went far beyond architectural professionals. Its circulation* was only 6,600 in 1856 and 8,774 in 1867, but such was its readership* that it garnered abundant and expensive advertising* and made a profit that journals with a higher circulation could not match. Grant indeed calls it 'one of the finest properties in the category of the weekly press'

However, this success did not come early. Hansom was forced to sell in 1843 when Alfred Bartholomew became editor* for a year until forced to resign because of ill health. George Godwin, who had previously contributed to the *Architectural Magazine*, published the monumental *Churches of London* (1837-1838) and had been secretary of the Art Union, then took over and remained in the editor's chair until 1883. It was he who established the journal's identity as a highly regarded champion of housing and sanitary reform (which would therefore, he believed, lead to social transformation), and of both conservation and new technologies. He may well have written most of the copy himself – certainly his staff was very small – but he also attracted luminous contributors such as Pugin and Ruskin*. When Godwin retired, he was succeeded by the reputable but conservative architect, H. H. Statham, who remained ably in charge until 1908. **AK**
Sources: Brooks 1981, Grant 1871, *ODNB*, Richardson and Thorne 1994.

BUILDERS' WEEKLY REPORTER (1856-1886), BUILDERS' REPORTER AND ENGINEERING TIMES (1886-1906) The *Builders' Weekly Reporter*, an illustrated* weekly* for the building trade priced* 2d, was initially a four page paper, but in its sixth issue it doubled in size* to eight pages when T. Blower of Stoke Newington – who also produced other trade journals* such as the *Draper* (1862-1866) – took over its printing and publication. Advertisements* (for materials, equipment, apprenticeships, competitions inviting proposals, and contractors offering their services) were not merely an ancillary source of income, but central to the paper's content. Indeed, it boasted that it was the 'cheapest and most perfect advertising medium in London'. By charging 6d per line for the outer pages, and 4d per line inside the paper, it put advertising* within reach of the small contractor, and it also guaranteed a large and targeted circulation*: it was 'delivered regularly to every Architect, Surveyor, Builder, and Engineer, whose name appears in the Post-Office London Directory'.

Inside, the paper reported on new techniques and technologies – with information on new patents – as well as acting as a price guide, covering auctions of houses, listing market prices of materials and comparing bids tendered for new contracts. There was little in the way of comment or opinion: its function was to circulate costing data within the trade, and as such it comprised a series of lists.

The *Builders' Weekly Reporter* had reached a reported circulation of 8,000 in 1881, and in 1886, it absorbed the more discursive *Building and Engineering Times* to become the *Builders' Reporter and Engineering Times*. With the new remit that came with this merger*, and now spread over 24 pages, the paper incorporated more editorial comment

1889   *THE FORTH BRIDGE.*   37

part is laid from side to side.' Making allowance for difference of material, the preceding work may fairly be looked upon as the true prototype of the present Forth Bridge.

The adaptability of the cantilever system of construction for railway bridges of large span became obvious to ourselves, and no doubt to others, soon after the invention of Bessemer made cheap steel a possibility. In 1865 we designed a steel cantilever bridge of 1,000 feet span for a proposed viaduct across the Severn, near the site of the present tunnel; but it was not until 1881 that the Forth Bridge designs were published in the English and American technical journals. These designs naturally attracted much attention, and with characteristic promptness American engineers realised the advantages of the system, and designed and built the following year a steel cantilever railway bridge on the Canadian Pacific Railway, and have

since followed on with more than half a dozen others of the same type of construction.

Owing to the arched form of the under side of the Forth Bridge cantilevers, many persons visiting the works or seeing the drawings entertain the mistaken notion that the principle of construction is analogous to that of the arch, and that the insertion of a keystone will be required to complete the work. This assumption is entirely wrong. The 1,710 feet spans are traversed by two cantilevers or brackets, each projecting 680 feet from the piers, and connected by a central girder 350 feet in length.

The true principle of construction and the nature of the stresses are well illustrated by a 'living model' of the bridge photographed at the works some time ago (fig. 2). Two men sitting on chairs extended their arms, and supported the same by grasping sticks but—

Figure 7: A living model of a bridge in an article on the Forth bridge for the *Nineteenth century: a monthly review* July 1889: 35.

and opinion, and longer articles on new legal issues, trade union* news and the progress of and controversies surrounding major building works. **MaT**
Sources: Vann and VanArsdel 1994, *Waterloo.*

BUILDING PRESS The building press of the nineteenth century reflects the increasing division of labour involved in the building of houses, churches, bridges, cotton mills, railway stations, town halls and so on. Arguably, the most significant development is the separation of the building trade from the architectural profession, with the founding of the Institute of British Architects in 1834 being a key development in this process. At the earlier stages of this process, periodicals were able to claim both groups as their readership*. The *Architectural Magazine* (1834-1839) was interested in 'Improvement in Architecture, Building, and Furnishing and in the Various Arts and Trades Connected Therewith'. Similarly the Owenite *Builder** (1842-) was a journal 'for the architect, engineer*, archaeologist, constructor, sanitary-

reformer and art lover'. Its radical trade unionism* was underpinned by a sense of the essential unity of these occupations. It reported on the results of architectural competitions, and carried well-informed discussions of new building materials and methods. Specialization – and in particular the professionalization of architecture – made it increasingly difficult to constitute builders and architects as a coherent audience, and it was the fate of the *Builder* (1842-1966) – despite its title – to become a specialist journal for professional architects, gradually losing its radical orientation and much of its working-class* readership in the process. The *Builder* probably retained a small fraction of its audience in the building trade, but there also emerged a number of publications addressed to labourers, an increasingly viable demographic for periodical literature due to the decreasing cost of production and circulation* and increasing literacy among the workers. Such journals were often dedicated to a specialist branch of building – such as ceramics in the *Brick and Tile Gazette* (1885-1892) – but there was also scope for broader publications such as the *Illustrated Carpenter and Builder* (1877-1971).

Even as the class divide between professional and tradesman grew, there was a significant body of complex and rapidly changing information – on the price and availability of materials, new patents, and other technical data – that needed to be disseminated among architects and tradesmen alike if they were to collaborate successfully on building projects. A space for advertising* contracts and services was also required. The *Builders' Weekly Reporter** (1856-1906) became the principal conduit for such information. Journals like the *Building and Engineering Times* (1881-1886) (which eventually merged with the *Builders' Weekly Reporter*) and the *Builder's Journal and Architectural Record* (1895-1906) attempted to bridge the gap with longer comment pieces of interest to architects and better educated builders, while architects were catered for by lavishly illustrated* periodicals such as the *British Architect**. **MaT**
Sources: Brooks 1981, Olsen 1973, Vann and VanArsdel 1995, *Waterloo.*

BULLIONIST, A WEEKLY FINANCIAL AND COMMERCIAL JOURNAL, ETC. (1866-1900) The *Bullionist* began as a 6d 24-page Tory financial* weekly* edited by David Morier Evans, a well-known economic journalist who had previously been financial editor of the *Morning Herald** and *Standard**. After he died in 1874, his son Richard took

over the editorship (he had published it since its inception), followed in 1887 by Richard's son Arthur, erstwhile city editor* of *Vanity Fair*. After the advertisements* (5½ pages already in issue 1), the paper started with a leading* article, often concerned with the demoralising effects of a market devoted to luxury. There followed accounts of joint-stock bank and other meetings, notices of bank and mercantile suspensions, railway and mining news* and produce prices. The money market was of particular concern, the title declaring its Ricardian allegiance in this matter. Never very successful, it was bought some time before 1891 by Henry Thomas Walker, an advertising agent. He reckoned it brought just £100 profit a year. In 1891 he sold it for £1,500 to the Bullionist Publishing Co. and appointed himself managing director at £1,000 a year. In September 1897 he was forced to pay £240 damages for libel for false statements made in the paper. This brought him to bankruptcy and shares in the paper were auctioned off. The paper limped on, finally becoming *Daily Bullionist*, a penny* daily*, in December 1899. Six months after, it stopped appearing and it merged with the *Financier*. **AK**
Sources: Grant 1871, *The Times* 7 Dec. 1898: 13, Vann and VanArsdel 1994.

BULWER LYTTON, EDWARD (1803-1873) Poet, politician and one of the most prominent novelists of his day, Bulwer Lytton also worked for the press both as a journalist* and an editor*. His introduction to the world of periodical publication came when in 1823 W. M. Praed asked him, as a young poet with a burgeoning reputation, to contribute to *Knight's Quarterly Magazine*, which he did under the pseudonym* 'Edmund Bruce'. Bulwer was elected as an independent Radical MP in 1831, and the two major themes of his political* journalism were the campaigns for the Reform Bill (1832) and for the reduction of the newspaper* stamp duty (or 'taxes on knowledge'*), finally repealed in 1855.

He was appointed editor of Henry Colburn's* *New Monthly Magazine*ization in November 1831, and turned the previously rather apolitical (if mildly Whiggish) periodical into a passionate advocate of reform. As well as authoring the regular sections entitled 'Monthly Commentary' and 'The Politician', he contributed many essays, articles and reviews* on political and literary* subjects, some of which were republished in book form as *Asmodeus at Large* (1833) and *The Student* (1835). He claimed to have raised the circulation* of the *New Monthly*, but Samuel Carter Hall* (a Tory who perhaps bore Bulwer a grudge after being displaced by him as editor)

claimed that circulation had declined from 5,000 to 4,000 as a result of Bulwer's politicization of the magazine.

Alongside his political journalism, his notoriety was growing as an author of lurid but portentously philosophical novels bubbling over with the purplest prose in the business. In 1832, the publication of *Eugene Aram* – a Newgate novel that seemed to glamorize the criminal life of its protagonist – provoked a critical onslaught in the periodical press spearheaded by Thackeray*, who prosecuted a personal crusade against Bulwer's perceived immorality in the *Quarterly Review*image and *Fraser's Magazine*. The widespread approbation caused by this furore was largely responsible for the novel's commercial success, but Bulwer nevertheless opted for anonymous* publication in his next novel, and even attempted to lower the critical temperature by writing his own – lukewarm – review of it in the *New Monthly*. He resigned as editor in August 1833 citing ill health.

His next foray into the editorial side of magazine publication came in 1838, when he was appointed editor of the *Monthly Chronicle*. He lasted only a few months in the post – from March to October – but wrote a number of interesting articles for the journal, most notably 'On Art in Fiction'. He continued to write journalism throughout his career contributing to the *Edinburgh Review*, the *Westminster Review* and the *Quarterly Review* among others. His literary productions were also frequently serialized* in periodicals, notably *Blackwood's Edinburgh Magazine*, where appeared his translations of Schiller's poems* (1842-1843), of Horace's *Odes* (1868), and numerous serialized novels, starting with 'The Caxtons' in 1849. Dickens* – the only of Bulwer's contemporaries to outsell him at the newsstand – was a friend and admirer, and serialized 'A Strange Story' in *All the Year Round*izations in 1862. As his career wore on, Bulwer's persistent criticisms of free trade increasingly deviated from Whig and Radical orthodoxy and left him in unfamiliar political company. He eventually sided with the Tories as the party of protection. **MaT**
Sources: *ODNB*, Sullivan, *Waterloo*, *Wellesley*.

BURGESS, JOSEPH (1853-1934) Former millworker Joseph Burgess already had a reputation for dialect poetry* when he joined the Liberal *Oldham Evening Express* (1867-1889) as a reporter* in 1881 where he was soon promoted to editor* in 1882. He resigned from the paper in 1884 over temperance issues and founded the Liberal *Oldham Operative* (1884-1885), priced* at 1d. In March 1885 he was subeditor* for trade union* affairs for the *Cotton Factory Times* (1885-1937), followed by a spell as editor of the *Yorkshire Factory Times* (1889-1913). His period of greatest influence was as editor of the *Workman's Times* (1890-1894). A convert to socialism, Burgess used the paper to campaign for the launch of the Independent Labour Party in 1893, contributing articles under the pseudonym* 'Autolycus' and recruiting Robert Blatchford* to his staff. After the *Workman's Times* folded in 1894, Burgess could only find part-time employment as a journalist* and he had to supplement his income with lecturing. However, he contributed to a wide range of socialist* and mainstream periodicals including the *Cotton Factory Times*, *Manchester Evening Chronicle*, *Scottish Weekly Record*, *People's Journal*, *Yorkshire Factory Times*, *Labour Leader* and *Clarion*. DM

Sources: Barnes 2006, Burgess n.d., McPhilips 2005.

BURNAND, FRANCIS COWLEY (1836-1917) Francis Burnand was a playwright, author and, most notably, editor* for *Punch* from 1880 to 1906, when he was succeeded by Owen Seamen. Educated at Eton and Trinity College Cambridge, he was called to the bar in 1862. However, the following year he moved into comic journalism for *Fun*, and edited the satirical* *Glowworm* (1865-1869) in its first few weeks of production. Burnand's 'Mokeanna', a parody of sensation fiction, was rejected by *Fun*, but proved to be the beginning of a long career with *Punch*. On 21 February 1863 it appeared, and by the end of that year Burnand had become a member of the salaried staff. 'Happy Thoughts', started in 1866, was Burnand's most celebrated serial* and the precursor to the humorous pieces of personal experience and misadventure which he was to create during the years of his *Punch* editorship.

Following its more serious tone under Tom Taylor, *Punch* came to be characterized as 'jolly kindness itself', Burnand toning down political fervour in favour of domestic family fun. Besides the chronicle of personal misadventure, he introduced the book review* section and an increase in the amount of verse. Burnand also introduced new talents to the periodical, including George Augustus Sala*. Though he has been criticized for overworking the pun and making the form mechanical, Burnand's scattered jokes and prose pieces were collected together in the final years of his editorship under the title of 'Charivaria', a new feature section introduced to *Punch* in 1902. Although a prolific play-

wright, it was for his work on *Punch* that Burnand received a knighthood in 1902. CH

Sources: À Beckett 1903, *ODNB*, Prager 1979, Price 1957, Spielmann [1895] 1969.

BURNETT, GEORGE (1822-1890) Burnett was a Scottish journalist*, genealogist and historian. His journalism is grouped around his three principal interests in medieval Scottish history* (with a particular focus on heraldry), genealogy and music*. Burnett was for a long time music critic for the *Scotsman*, where issues of national* identity and pride were a central theme in the coverage of musical events, which were often dominated by English musicians performing continental music.

He was Lyon King of Arms for Scotland from 1866 to his death, and he edited* 12 volumes of the Exchequer Rolls of Scotland, illuminating many previously uncharted areas of Scottish history. Much of his research was brought into the public domain through articles he published in the *Edinburgh Review*, the *North British Review* and *Macmillan's Magazine*. MaT

Sources: Boase, *ODNB*, *The Times* obituary 1890, *Wellesley*.

BUTLER, JOSEPHINE ELIZABETH (1828-1906) Josephine Butler (née Grey), social reformer and women's rights'* campaigner prolifically expounded her arguments in over 90 books and pamphlets as well as through the periodical press, editing* three papers and contributing to many more. As a signatory to the 1866 women's suffrage petition, her earliest contributions seem to have been to the feminist* paper, the *Woman's World* from 1867 and its subsequent titles, the *Kettledrum* and *Now-A-Days*. Leading the campaign against the sexual inequalities inscribed in the Contagious Diseases Act from 1866, she edited* the Association's weekly* paper, the *Shield* from March 1870, later also taking on editorship of the quarterly* *Dawn* (1888-1896), the organ of the General Federation for the Abolition of the State Regulation of Vice. Her third editorship was for the *Storm-Bell* (1898-1900), the monthly paper of the Ladies' Association for the Abolition of the State Regulation of Vice.

As she toured the country lecturing, visiting prostitutes imprisoned in the 'Lock' hospitals and talking to their clients in brothels, she was also promoting education for women, the suffrage campaign, married women's property rights and the temperance movement. Her campaigning articles appeared in, among others, the *Contemporary Review*, the *Link*, the *Methodist Times*, the *Pioneer*, the *Woman's Herald* and its successor the *Woman's*

Signal, as well as the *Liverpool Mercury**. From 1885 Butler was involved in the investigative journalism of W. T. Stead's*, *Pall Mall Gazette**, joining with him against the 'white slave trade' of child prostitution. Shunned by many members of the women's movement in Britain for her involvement in such scandalous subjects, she extended her fight for an equal moral standard across Europe and America, using the press to educate and gain support. **CL**

Sources: 19CUKP online, *Waterloo*.

BUTT, ISAAC (1813-1879) An editor* writer, and politician, Isaac Butt was born into a Protestant family in Co. Donegal. While studying at Trinity College Dublin in 1833, he was among the founders of the *Dublin University Magazine**, personally contributing £15 to the venture. He also wrote articles for the *Dublin Evening Mail**. In 1834 he succeeded Charles Stuart Stanford as editor* of the *Magazine*, until called to the Bar in 1838. Under his editorship the *Magazine* included the foremost Irish authors: poetry* from James Clarence Mangan*, John Francis Waller and James Wills, articles from Samuel Ferguson* and fiction from William Carleton*, Charles Lever*, William Hamilton Maxwell* and Sheridan Le Fanu*. Butt himself contributed tales ('Chapters of College Romance', 1834-1837), poems and leaders* that showed him as staunchly Protestant and Unionist but still critical of aspects of British rule. He founded the *Protestant Guardian* newspaper in 1838, retaining a connection after its amalgamation with the *Warder* in 1842. He embraced nationalist views after the 1840s, leading him to found the Home Rule movement. While Butt's involvement with periodicals is limited to the earlier phase of his career, it demonstrates his early awareness of Irish cultural politics. His capable editorship established the *DUM* as the leading Irish magazine, and one of the most respected of its kind. **FB**

Sources: Hall 1999, *ODNB*, *Waterloo Irish*, *Wellesley*, White 1946.

C

'CAIRD, MONA' (1854-1932) Now considered a radical, *fin de siècle* New Woman novelist, Mona Caird, born Alice Mona Alison, was noted by contemporaries for her bold journalism. Caird's *Westminster Review** article 'Marriage' (1888) was, Annie S. Swan* observed in her autobiography (1934), like a 'flaming bomb' thrown against 'the thoroughly smug and respectable'. In a historically erudite indictment of patriarchy, Caird argued that marriage amounted to 'degradation'. Few journalists could boast of hitting the raw nerve of their time to the same extent: the *Daily Telegraph*'s* invitation to respond resulted in some 27,000 readers' replies subsequently published by Harry Quilter as a selection in *Is Marriage a Failure?* (1888), a title echoed in a series run by the American *Cosmopolitan**.

Caird followed up with other essays, in the *Westminster** and the *Nineteenth Century**, on 'Ideal Marriage' (1888), 'The Emancipation of the Family' (1890), 'Phases of Human Development' (1894) and (responding to Eliza Lynn Linton*) the 'Defence of the So-called "Wild Women"' (1892); her revised articles were collected as *The Morality of Marriage* (1897). Caird offered commentary on current debates, submitting pieces to the women's press – such as a role-reversal parody in response to opinion pieces run by the *Lady's Realm** ('Does Marriage hinder a Woman's Self-development?', 1898-1899) – as well as promoting feminism, suffragism and internationalism in the *Westminster* and the *Fortnightly Review**. She later reported sympathetically on the suffragettes ('Militant Tactics and Woman's Suffrage', 1908), argued against eugenics and promoted internationalism for world peace ('A Ridiculous God', 1906; 'The Greater Community', 1918).

Dubbed a 'priestess of revolt' by Stead*'s *Review of Reviews**, Caird was a 'pioneer of humanity' according to Margaret Shurmer Sibthorp's magazine *Shafts**. Her journalism had a far-reaching impact on a diversity of readers* and gave extensive currency to feminist and radical ideas. In an 1894 *Punch** cartoon* ('Donna Quixote') Caird's writings rightly feature alongside Tolstoy and Ibsen as foundation texts of the New Woman. **ABH**
Sources: Gullette 1980, Heilmann 1998, Heilmann 2004, Pykett 1995, Richardson 2003.

CALCUTTA REVIEW (1844-) The *Calcutta Review** was the brainchild of the noted military historian John William Kaye, who was also its first editor*. Published quarterly*, Kaye noted in the inaugural number that its aim was 'to bring together such useful information, and propagate such sound opinions…as will…conduce, in some small measure, directly or indirectly, to the amelioration of the condition of the people'. He argued that the 'bane' of India was 'ignorance' and not simply among the masses, but also within the ruling classes. The journal reflected variations in opinion while maintaining an overall harmony of sentiment and objectives. The editorial line-up included well-known personalities drawn from the civil, military and missionary* sectors, such as Rev. A. Duff, W. S. Mackay, George Smith*, M. Townsend, Sir R. Temple, W. Heeley, Roper Lethbridge and J. W. Furrell.

The format* allowed in-depth coverage of topics and consisted of articles based on book reviews* and first-hand expertise covering an impressive variety of areas, including philosophy*, social* science, agriculture, law*, religion*, language, arts, literature*, history*, geography, travel and biography. It also reprinted articles published in other journals, both Anglo-Indian and British. For instance, the first numbers covered the social morality of the English in India, the earliest Protestant mission, astronomy of the Hindus, the Kulin Brahmins of Bengal, the war in China, Lord Bentinck's administration, female infanticide and the history of the recently conquered Punjab. The *Review* was extensively quoted in Britain (with editions often collated and republished), thus serving to exert significant influence on opinion on India beyond the shores of the subcontinent. It was taken over by Calcutta University during the twentieth century and published as a monthly. **ChK**
Sources: *Calcutta Review* 1844, *Calcutta Review* Index 1873.

CALDECOTT, RANDOLPH (1846-1886) Although better known today for the series of 16 children's books he published with Edmund Evans*, Randolph Caldecott began his career as a journalist. His first published illustration* appeared in the *Illustrated London News** in 1861. Caldecott moved to London in 1872, after contributing to *London Society** and other papers. Initially, his social satire* was a little too sharp, and some of his artwork had to be rejected. From 1874-1875, Caldecott worked as a 'special reporter*' for the *Graphic** and *Pictorial World*, in which his first attributed work appeared and also as 'London artistic correspondent' for the

New York *Daily Graphic*. Celebrated for his comical pictures of hunting scenes and English leisure pursuits (he was a regular, if infrequent, contributor to *Punch**), Caldecott also illustrated newsworthy events such as political* meetings and trials. Travelling frequently for his health, he reported on English social life abroad, as well. According to editor* Henry Blackburn, Caldecott refused a regular position at *Pictorial World* because he found steady journalistic work too onerous.

Nonetheless, journalistic work remained a constant throughout Caldecott's working life and a key influence on his art. He developed his characteristic strong, simple line from his work as a reporter: the necessity of sketching scenes rapidly helped him move away from the style of heavy cross-hatching. Caldecott experimented with new printing technologies, but most of his illustrations were photographed* onto woodblocks and etched by engravers; Blackburn notes that Caldecott found this process allowed him to draw with greater freedom.

Journalistic work shaped Caldecott's style and also made him contacts with men who would encourage and promote his work: Blackburn, George du Maurier*, engraver Joseph Cooper, and Evans, whose mastery of new techniques of colour printing led to Caldecott's greatest successes as an illustrator. **TD**

Sources: Blackburn 1886, Engen 1976, Joseph 1996, *ODNB*.

CALEDONIAN MERCURY (1720-1867) The *Caledonian Mercury* is one of the oldest Edinburgh newspapers, established as a moderate Jacobite publication. For more than a century the paper was printed and owned by the Allan (Robert and Thomas) family, leaving their hands in 1862 before finally being sold to its competitor* the *Scotsman** in 1867. A broadsheet covering literature*, culture and predominantly politics*, the *Caledonian* was allied to the Church of Scotland and the Whigs initially, though these connections became less pronounced during the 1840s; by the 1860s it was attached to the Edinburgh Radical Group under Duncan MacLaren (1800-1886) and espoused Presbyterian Voluntaryism.

In 1800 the paper was a four-column*, thrice weekly paper costing 6d, and by 1850 a seven-column broadsheet costing 4½d though the Saturday edition was dropped and it appeared only on Mondays and Thursdays. Keeping the seven-column format*, the *Caledonian* was a penny* daily* by 1860, though still retaining its modest four pages throughout the nineteenth century. The final for-

mat* in 1867 had five columns and sold for ½d, and from 1866-1867 the *Caledonian* was an evening newspaper exclusively. William Saunders (1823-1895), proprietor* of the paper for its final year, marketed* the *Caledonian Mercury* as 'the cheapest Evening Newspaper in the United Kingdom' (Bell). **MBT**

Sources: Bell 2007, 19 CBLNP, *ODNB*.

CALENDAR OF HORRORS (1835-1836) The *Calendar of Horrors* was an eight-page weekly* priced* at one penny*. The title page claims that it was edited by Thomas Peckett Prest and printed by George Drake of Clare Market, though recent scholarship has also emphasised the role of Edward Lloyd* in its production. The periodical was liberally illustrated* with wood* engravings and boasted the rather catchy subtitle: 'An interesting collection of the romantic, wild and wonderful'. Over its run, 91 numbers were published and circulated*.

Its contents were designed to shock, horrify and terrify readers, mixing the factual with the imaginative. Serial* fiction, mostly composed in the gothic genre, dominated, the tales being a combination of original works, copies from higher-class magazines or collections and adaptations of German or Celtic folktales. Authors' initials at the conclusion of these stories suggest that the *Calendar* had a number of contributors, with the largest number signed* 'T.P.' If these refer to Thomas Prest, it is significant, as Prest seems to have been much more reluctant in later years to reveal his authorship. Alongside serial fiction were printed shorter articles of extraordinary or bloodthirsty events and customs. Cannibalistic savages frequently appeared, as did descriptions of modes of punishment from around the world. Longer pieces on sensational crimes*, particularly murders, were also included, often as part of a long-running series, such as the 'Criminal Annals'. Thus, in many ways, the *Calendar of Horrors* occupied the space between the Newgate Calendars and the miscellanies of fiction published by Lloyd during the next decade, such as *Lloyd's Penny Atlas**, *Lloyd's Penny Weekly Miscellany** and the *People's Periodical and Family Library*.

Circulation of the *Calendar of Horrors* remains unknown, though at the conclusion of Vol. 1 Prest and Lloyd made reference to the 'extensive circulation our work has experienced'. To survive for two years, the periodical probably did enjoy some success. Evidence of readership* is also elusive. It is likely that the *Calendar of Horrors*, with its cheap* price* and sensational content would have predominantly appealed to the working* and lower-middle classes, at that time desperately in need of exciting reading material, and who seem to have been the main supporters of Lloyd's and Prest's fiction of the 1840s. During a survey of the reading material available to the poor in the parishes of St James, St George and St Anne Soho in 1838, Edgell Wyatt Edgell discovered a copy of the *Calendar of Horrors* in one of the local coffee houses which could be borrowed. **RHC**

Sources: Edgell 1838, James 1963, *Waterloo*.

CAMBRIAN (1804-1930) The first Welsh* weekly* newspaper was established by a group of businessmen in Swansea, then the largest town in Wales. They raised sufficient sums in shares to establish a Cambrian Newspaper Co. and recruited Thomas Jenkins, then working as a printer in Worcester, to be its publisher* and editor*. The first printing machine* and boxes of type were shipped from Bristol on the Phoenix, and were nearly lost at sea. It quickly became an important regional* title, and a model for other early English-language weeklies such as the *North Wales Gazette* in Bangor in 1808 and the *Carmarthen Journal* in 1810. Initially, however, as the title suggests, it sought to cover the whole of the territory of Wales and beyond. Agents were sent to all the Welsh counties and Herefordshire.

Although 40 per cent of its early content consisted of advertisements* it was intended to be, in the words of its publisher, 'a vehicle of refinement, instruction and amusement' that sought to 'multiply the channels of general knowledge' in Wales. A Home Office spy claimed it was also read in three coffee houses in London, including the Jacobin Chapter and George's club. It also signalled its intention to 'promote the advance of Wales' by making its beauty, resources and 'enlightened inhabitants' better known to the outside world, and to 'fan the generous flames of patriotism' during the Napoleonic wars. Its early example led to the launch in Swansea in 1861 of the *Cambrian Daily Leader*, the first daily* newspaper in Wales. The *Cambrian* was discontinued in March 1930 in a merger* with the *Herald of Wales*. **AGJ**

Sources: *Cambrian* Index Online, Jones 1993, Jones and Rees 1998.

CAMBRO-BRITON; AND GENERAL CELTIC DEPOSITORY (1819-1822) The monthly* *Cambro-Briton*, published by Simpkin and Marshall*, was launched with the aim of diffusing 'among strangers a knowledge of the history, manners, the genius of Wales, and to extend beyond her mountain barriers the fame of [her] literary treasures'. At its launch the journal comprised 40 22-cm

pages (later 56) and typically included articles on the language, poetry* and music* of Wales, antiquarian research, biographical sketches of figures prominent in Welsh life and items of cultural news* and comment. In all, 30 issues appeared with publication suspended July-October 1821. The journal was available by subscription only (price* unknown) and did not contain advertising*.

With its Anglo-centric, metropolitan* approach, the *Cambro-Briton* not only promoted Welsh identity within a British unionist context, but also campaigned on several controversial socio-cultural issues, such as the 'defective state' of education in Wales, and the Anglican Church's 'neglect' of the Welsh language. The journal was edited* throughout its existence by John Humffreys Parry and numbered the distinguished music critic John Parry*, 'Bardd Alaw' ['Master of Song'] among its contributors. **MH**

Source: *Waterloo*.

CAMPBELL, LADY COLIN (1857-1911) Although Lady Colin Campbell, née Gertrude Elizabeth Blood, wrote in other genres, most of her work was in journalism and art criticism. She was particularly known for her contributions to the *World* (1888-1906), where she published under various pseudonyms. She began writing the travel column* 'A Woman's Walks' as 'Vera Tsaritsyn', occasionally using 'Fiamma' for European articles. In 1889 she also took over from George Bernard Shaw* as art critic (initially as 'Q.E.D.'), drawing upon her earlier training with painter Frank Duveneck and wide connections in the Victorian art world.

Campbell debuted with a travel article in *Cassell's Family Magazine* (Jan. 1875), but only began writing seriously after estrangement from her husband in 1883. She wrote two or three articles a week for the *Saturday Review* (1883-1888) and many of its foreign language book reviews*. She founded a weekly* journal, the *Realm* (1894-1895), running it as co-editor* with fellow journalist William Earl Hodgson before it folded. She became editor of the *Ladies' Field* (1901-c 1905/1906), but had to resign due to ill health.

Throughout her career she contributed articles to numerous other titles on her favourite subjects of art, music*, travel, women's sports* and etiquette. These appeared mainly in London publications but also in America, Australia and France. **AJ**

Sources: Clarke 2005, *ODNB*, Weintraub 2005.

CAMPBELL, THOMAS (1777-1844) A distinguished Scottish poet and journalist*, Thomas Campbell became a successful magazine* editor*.

Apart from his many articles on literature* and current affairs, his poetry* also appeared in periodicals ranging from the *Edinburgh Review** to the *Mirror of Literature** and *Chambers's Edinburgh Journal**.

In 1820, Campbell became editor of Henry Colburn's* ailing *New Monthly Magazine**. Apart from his personal prestige and his own poetry and prose – his first articles in the magazine were lectures on poetry given at the Royal Institution – he brought vitality and a talented new staff to the title, significantly increasing its circulation*. He became renowned, however, for his slapdash approach to the quotidian duties of editor, leaving much of the spadework to his assistant Cyrus Redding.

A university man – he was rector of Glasgow University from 1826 to 1829 – Campbell's journalism played a role in the formation of University College London. A missive published in *The Times** on 9 February 1825 advocated the establishment of a university in London 'worthy of the times', and in the same year Campbell elaborated on this in a two-part series entitled 'Suggestions Respecting the Plan of an University in London', in the *New Monthly Magazine*.

He left in 1830, going on to edit the *Metropolitan Magazine** (1831-1832). For a long time he had championed the cause of the Poles, and he was deeply affected when in 1831 the Russians captured Warsaw. His poem on the subject was published in the *Metropolitan*, and he formed the Association of the Friends of Poland, where he assisted with the publication of its organ *Polonia* (1832). In Algeria in 1835-1836, he wrote a series of 'Letters From the South', appearing in the *New Monthly Magazine*, which were later collected in book form. **MaT**
Sources: *Encyclopaedia Britannica*, *ODNB*, Sullivan, *Waterloo*, *Wellesley*.

CANNON, GEORGE (1789-1854) Lawyer, editor*, publisher*, pornographer* and Spencean radical, George Cannon is an important figure in the 'radical underworld' in the early nineteenth century. He adopted the pseudonym* of 'Reverend Erasmus Perkins' for most of the work he produced, although he used a number of other pseudonyms to hide behind. His journalism and periodicals made a significant contribution to the development of English deism.

Between December 1814 and April 1815, Cannon (as 'Erasmus Perkins') produced a number of articles based on Baron d'Holbach's *Ecce homo* for William Cobbett's* *Political Register**. Shelley had dealings with him (Feb. 1815) over a proposed monthly paper, the *Theological Inquirer, or, Polemical Magazine*. However,

Shelley found Cannon 'a very foolish man' and a 'vulgar brute' (Holmes,: 280). Nevertheless, Cannon published seven numbers of this paper* from March to September 1815, of 80 pages each, comprising articles on religion*, politics*, philosophy*, freethinking, reviews* and poetry*. Between March and July of that year, again as 'Erasmus Perkins', Cannon published a third of Shelley's *Queen Mab* and all of his *Refutation of Deism* in the *Theological Inquirer*. In 1820 the paper was briefly resurrected as the *Deists Magazine, or Theological Inquirer*, and Cannon defended Robert Wedderburn*, unsuccessfully, during his trial for blasphemous libel. Thereafter Cannon concentrated on publishing French Libertinist works and pornography. **JG**
Sources: Boas 1955, Holmes 1974, McCalman 1988, *ODNB*.

CANONICAL POETRY 'Canonical' literature*, work traditionally regarded as the most notable within its genre, is a construct that shifts according to developments in scholarship (e.g., expanding to include formerly marginalized poets). Many poets recognized as canonical first published their poetry* in periodicals to reach a larger readership* than they would through volumes of poetry. Despite professing an aversion to publishing in magazines* and annuals*, even Tennyson recognized the benefit of such reception: his 'Tithonus' appeared in *Cornhill Magazine** in February 1860, and 'Lucretius' in *Macmillan's Magazine** in May 1868. Other traditionally canonical poets appearing in periodicals include Robert Browning, Elizabeth Barrett Browning, Matthew Arnold*, Thomas Hardy*, George Meredith, Christina Rossetti, Dante Gabriel Rossetti, Charles Algernon Swinburne*, Arthur Hugh Clough and William Morris*.

The inclusion of well-known poets likewise increased a periodical's marketability, enacting a reciprocal commodification through symbolic and literal capital. With an increasingly literate and accessible mass-reading* public developing in the nineteenth century, popular and high culture thus began to converge. Tennyson's name could sell numbers, and rivals *Cornhill* and *Macmillan's* knew it.

Resituating canonical poetry within its original context, as opposed to the anthology (where canons are born and perpetuated), reveals the intertextuality between poetry and contemporary articles, criticism, serial fiction* and even between the periodicals themselves, allowing for a more accurate perspective on nineteenth-century reading culture. **MRR**
Sources: Altick 1957, Hughes 2007b, Ledbetter 2007, *ODNB*, *Waterloo*.

CAPE ARGUS (1857-) Published daily* from 1880, the *Argus* was established in the Cape Colony in 1857. A dynamic commercial enterprise, the newspaper was part of the Argus Company which bought into a number of newspapers across southern Africa including the Johannesburg *Star*. In 1889, the Argus Company expanded to become the Argus Printing and Publishing Company of Johannesburg, Cape Town, Kimberley and London. Having a large circulation* throughout the Cape Colony to enable people in Britain to keep in touch with events, in 1868 it was providing a monthly summary in Britain, post free for 7d.

From 1881 mining interests increased their financial stake until the paper seemed to be their mouthpiece at the Cape. Some believed that, in the interests of mining capital, it helped prepare public opinion for the South African War* of 1899-1902. Yet again, Cecil Rhodes had managed to infiltrate the *Argus* for his own political* ends, as he had done with the *Cape Times**, similarly by befriending the editor*. This time he assisted Francis J. Dormer, the prominent nineteenth-century editor, in 1881, to become the paper's proprietor*. Dormer was succeeded as editor by Edmund Powell, an important member of the Welsh community in Cape Town, who was commended in Wales for the great service he was rendering to the British cause in the Cape. SJP
Sources: Ainslie 1966, Barlow 1988, Potter 1975, Shaw 1999, Tamarkin 1996.

CAPE TIMES (1876-) The *Cape Times* was founded by a former Anglican missionary, Frederick York St Leger, who was also the paper's editor* until 1895. The paper was originally founded for a working-class* readership* and to challenge government corruption, but it has also been represented as championing the new imperialism*. In the early 1890s, the mining tycoon and politician, Cecil Rhodes purchased a minority interest in the paper, using an intermediary. St Leger had retained the controlling interest and in 1895 he appointed Edmund Garrett as his editorial replacement. Garrett had first come to South Africa as a cure for consumption in 1889, having worked as a journalist* on the *Pall Mall Gazette** in London. He returned to London in 1891 to his job at the *Gazette* before working on the *Westminster Gazette** from 1893. St Leger then offered Garrett the post of editor and he returned once more to South Africa.

The *Cape Times* was the principal English newspaper in this part of Africa and Garrett took on the role of a campaigning editor and journalist. He wrote a large number of the paper's articles, push-ing for education rights for all people, better housing and also started a column* giving a voice to the black population. On his previous visit, Garrett had met Rhodes and Sir Alfred Milner (the British high commissioner) and other politicians and supported imperial* expansion. There were those who accused Garrett of helping to precipitate the South African War of 1899-1902, implying that he was being used by the mining interests who had invested in the paper. In 1898, he won a seat in Parliament but his health deteriorated and he was forced to resign as editor in January 1900 before returning to England. Whatever the complexities of his political* entanglements, it was recognized that he had strengthened the position of the *Cape Times* and increased its circulation*.

In the mid-twentieth century, the paper opposed both the Nationalist government and apartheid and in 1996 the paper's first non-white editor was appointed. SJP
Sources: Ainslie 1966, Barlow 1988, *ODNB*, Potter 1975, Shaw 1975, Shaw 1999.

CAPES, JOHN MOORE (1812-1879) John Moore Capes was an editor*, journalist*, proprietor*, clergyman, composer and novelist. He was one of the converts to Roman Catholicism from the Oxford Movement in the 1840s. Seeing the need for a journal for English Catholic lay converts, he founded the *Rambler, A Journal of Home and Foreign Literature, Politics, Science and Art** in 1848. This was a joint venture with his brother Frederick, and a fellow convert, J. Spencer Northcote. As well as Catholic issues, the *Rambler* covered artistic, political* and scientific* topics. Capes wrote the largest part of the journal himself, and determined its policies.

Initially the *Rambler* had the approval of Cardinal John Henry Newman, but it soon came into conflict with the church hierarchy. A series of articles criticizing the English Catholic Church, particularly its policies over education, caused William Ullathorne, the influential Roman Catholic Bishop of Birmingham to fulminate against the journal. Capes declared himself an independent editor, but because of chronic illness found the strain of editing too great. Also his wife was becoming increasingly blind. In 1852 he entrusted the editorship to Northcote, who was not successful and resigned after two years to become a priest. Capes took over once again as editor. At the same time Richard Simpson*, a young convert, joined the magazine and became subeditor* in 1856. His criticism of English Catholicism caused Cardinal Wiseman to attack the *Rambler* in the *Dublin Review** of 1856.

By the following year the *Rambler* had become the journal of the liberal Catholic movement. Under Capes the *Rambler* tended toward 'social Catholicism'. It treated the problems of urban poverty, particularly the Irish immigrants who formed the bulk of the Catholic poor in English cities. In October 1857, being ill, short of money and having an invalid wife, Capes handed over the editorship to Simpson. He sold the journal to his brother, Simpson and Sir John (later Lord) Acton*. The proprietorship* of the magazine was divided into six £50 shares. Capes's reward for all his effort was only £200 and the praise of Cardinal Newman. After the *Rambler* years, Capes was a frequent contributor to the *Fortnightly Review* (1866-1869), the *Contemporary Review* (1871-1876) and the *Quarterly Review* (1874). DHL

Sources: Altholz 1962, Altholz 1989, Boase *etal.*1965, Brown and Stratten 1976, Sullivan, *Wellesley.*

CARICATURE The concept of a periodical devoted solely to caricature preoccupied the comic artists, publishers* and entrepreneurs of print culture in the 1820s and 1830s, but never found much favour with the public. As the single-plate satirical* political print lost its cultural energy, caricaturists launched a wide variety of experimental periodicals built out of elaborate and often large-scale images in the attempt to sustain the caricature mode. William Heath's* *Glasgow Looking Glass* (1825-1826) was the first of these, and was followed in the 1830s by the London-based *Looking Glass* published by the print seller and entrepreneur Thomas McClean, C. J. Grant's* the *Caricaturist*, the *Squib* and several others. Radical periodicals, too, still found room for the caricature as part of their political weaponry, and artists like Robert Seymour* in *Figaro in London* continued to use the idiom of the eighteenth-century personal and political graphic satire*.

But comic art had become increasingly dependent on text, and the new readers* of the early Victorian period preferred miscellanies* of comic images and text like Hood's* *Comic Annual.* The caricature tradition had by this time been adapted to the new medium of small-scale humorous wood* engraving, which, while it drew on the humorous tropes and puns of Regency caricature, was more delicate in its mode and more domestic in its interests. While a whole generation of early Victorian illustrators*, among them Kenny Meadows*, George Cruikshank*, John Leech* and Richard Doyle*, had been trained in the caricature tradition, they turned increasingly either to the linear

simplicities of the cartoon* or to the whimsicalities and quirks of Victorian middle-class* manners for their sources of humour. Caricature elements appeared in the illustrations* to many later Victorian periodicals, the portraits in *Once A Week* in the 1870s for example, with their elaborately finished oversized heads of celebrities* perched on tiny bodies. But the caricature mode as understood in the late eighteenth century largely gave way to the cartoon or the humorous sketch even before the founding of *Punch* in 1841. **BM**

Sources: Altick 1997, Anderson 1991, Fox 1988, James 2002.

CARICATURIST (1831) At the moment in the late 1820s and 1830s when caricature* began to be formulated into periodicals, a number of journals called the *Caricaturist* were projected. The most representative of these was Charles Jameson Grant's* 1831 venture the *Caricaturist* which used a large-page format* drawn from newspapers but with wood* engraved political* caricatures held within the columns* of type. Equally characteristic was the short life of the magazine, a recurrent feature of a mode still frantically searching for its most effective layout. Perhaps only McClean's *Looking Glass* found a proper model for a successful caricature* based periodical from this period. **BM**

Source: Pound 1998.

CARLETON, WILLIAM (1794-1869) William Carleton was an Irish author of short stories and serial* fiction based on Irish themes that appeared regularly in the press. He was born in the north of Ireland to a Catholic family, but converted to Protestantism in 1818. Informally educated, he came to writing after working as a teacher. After a brief stint on the *Westmeath Guardian* around 1824-1825, he published his first short story in 1828 in the Protestant *Christian Examiner*, where his work continued to appear until 1831, when its editor* and Carleton's personal friend, the Rev. Caesar Otway*, left the magazine. In 1830-1831 Carleton also contributed to the *National Magazine*. These Irish-themed tales were collected in the extremely successful *Traits and Stories of the Irish Peasantry* (1830), which Carleton augmented and revised throughout his life. The definitive edition appeared in 23 monthly shilling parts in 1843-1844, with illustrations* by 'Phiz'* and John Gilbert* among others.

Carleton then published numerous tales in the *Dublin University Magazine* (1833-1839), including his first serial novel, 'Fardorougha the Miser' (1837-1838, collected 1839). Disagreements with editor Charles Lever* led him to abandon the *Dublin University Magazine*, and in 1840-1841 he contributed short stories to the weekly* *Irish Penny Journal*, edited by George Petrie*. Despite his militant Protestantism, Carleton then moved closer to the nationalist weekly newspaper the *Nation* (1842-1862) and its editor Charles Gavan Duffy* writing two literary reviews* for it. A change of editorship at the *Dublin University Magazine* saw renewed contributions* (1846-1860) by Carleton, including the serialized novel 'The Black Prophet'.

Other periodicals Carleton contributed to are the *Irish Tribune* in 1848; the *Illustrated London News* (1850-1853); the *Illustrated London Magazine* (1852-1853); *Duffy's Hibernian Magazine* (1860-1862), and the *Shamrock* (1868-1869). Despite the popularity of his short stories and novels in Britain, Carleton published very little original work in British periodicals. He proposed himself as a contributor to *Blackwood's Edinburgh Magazine* in 1829, 1839 and 1848, but was rejected each time. Though often motivated by financial difficulties, Carleton relished his contributions to Irish periodicals and always regarded periodicals as legitimate literature. His decision to publish in Ireland was central to the rise of an Irish reading* and publishing market*. FB

Sources: Carleton and O'Donoghue 1896, Hayley 1985, *ODNB*, PGIL Eirdata.

CARLILE, ELIZABETH SHARPLES See Sharples, Eliza

CARLILE, RICHARD (1790-1843) In 1817 Richard Carlile, an itinerant tinsmith from Devon, began hawking Thomas Wooler's* *Black Dwarf*. Soon after, William Sherwin employed him to assist managing his *Weekly Political Register*, also permitting the use of his Fleet Street* premises for Carlile's own initiatives as a publisher*. These included the ephemeral *Gracchus* (1818, edited* by John Whitehead), the weekly* *Gorgon* and, notably, reprints of Paine. In 1819 Carlile bought the business, relaunching the *Register* as *Republican* (1819-1826).

With a circulation* over 5,000, the 32 pages of the *Republican* were packed with anti-clerical and anti-establishment invective. In October 1819 Carlile was imprisoned for six years for blasphemous libel, but the *Republican* continued to appear, sustained by shopmen like James Watson* and Thomas Davison*, and by Carlile's indomitable wife and their sons Alfred and Thomas. Three new periodicals followed: the short-lived *Deist* (1819-1820) and *Moralist* (1823), and the more

successful *Newgate Monthly Magazine* (1824-1826). Carlile's incarceration attracted many admiring readers, but their loyalty was sorely tried by his criticism of other prominent radicals. When Carlile was finally released from prison (Nov. 1825), the *Republican's* circulation* was already declining and it closed 12 months later.

Carlile now devoted his energies to promoting birth control, but resumed periodical publishing with an anti-clerical monthly*, the *Lion* (1828-1829). It struggled to a peak circulation of 1,000. A broader weekly, the *Prompter* (1830-1831), replaced it with little more success. The *Prompter's* defence of the Swing disturbances of 1830 earned Carlile a further prison sentence, during which the *Prompter* (and its short-lived successor the *Union*, 1831-1832) were largely sustained by Eliza Sharples* (to whom Carlile shortly announced his 'moral marriage'). *Devil's Pulpit* (1831-1832), a weekly conducted by Carlile's other close colleague, the Reverend Robert Taylor, was moderately successful; *Isis*, a weekly Sharples edited on her own account, rather more so. Carlile in turn discreetly supported *Cosmopolite* (1832), the influential unstamped* weekly.

In the final phase of his life, Carlile advocated a distinctive brand of mystical Christian anti-clericalism to a dwindling readership*. Increasingly, Socialism and Chartism dominated the reform agenda but he was hostile to both. Only *Gauntlet* (1833-1834), 'a sound Republican weekly newspaper' recaptured something of his old popularity, boasting a circulation* of 2,500 at its close. *Political Soldier* (1833-1834) collapsed after five issues, *London Star* (1834) after two. *Scourge for the Littleness of 'Great' Men* (1834-1835) appeared erratically. The monthlies *Phoenix* (1837) and *Christian Warrior* (1843) each lasted four issues, the weeklies *Church* (1838) and *Carlile's Political Register* (1839) eight and nine respectively. It was an indifferent conclusion to a towering career devoted to a free press. MSC

Sources: *DLB, ODNB*, Wiener 1983.

CARLYLE, THOMAS (1795-1881) Until the 1840s, the reputation of Thomas Carlyle, historian, critic and Victorian 'Sage' came primarily from periodical writing. From his championing of German literature to his commentary on the second Reform Act, Carlyle skillfully exploited literary*, social or political* trends, maintaining his topicality even in his books. While many writers became 'house'* authors, Carlyle's political and social eclecticism gave him entrée to journals considered conservative, liberal and radical.

Carlyle's apprenticeship writing focused on science* and translations and appeared in the Scottish provincial* press. His first literary article on Joanna Baillie's poetry, for example, appeared in the *New Edinburgh Review* (1821). His pieces on German literature (1822-1833) inaugurated his major writings. Carlyle's first original book, the 'Life of Schiller', was serialized* in the *London Magazine** (1823-1824); and the majority of his essays on Goethe, Jean Paul Friedrich Richter, Herder, Heine and the *Nibelungenlied* appeared in the *Foreign Review.* Concurrently, he published significant articles on Burns (*Edinburgh Review**), Voltaire *(Foreign Review)* and Johnson *(Fraser's**)*; essays on history* and biography; and stunning proto-Victorian social criticism in 'Signs of the Times' (1829) and 'Characteristics' (1831) in the *Edinburgh Review.* 'Sartor Resartus', Carlyle's masterpiece, appeared in *Fraser's (1833-1834).*

After shifting his focus to *The French Revolution* (1837) from 1833-1838, his periodical contributions became offshoots of his research. He published 'Diderot' (*Foreign Quarterly Review** 1833), 'Memoirs of Mirabeau' (*London and Westminster Review** 1837), the classic 'Diamond Necklace' (*Fraser's* 1837), and 'Sir Walter Scott' (*London and Westminster Review** 1838).* In 1839 Carlyle discussed publication of *Chartism* with *both* J. G. Lockhart and John Stuart Mill for the *Quarterly* or *London and Westminster* Reviews. For financial and audience reasons the essay became a book.

After 1843 Carlyle produced less memorable work. He published as genuine 35 forged Oliver Cromwell letters in 1847 (*Fraser's*), then anonymously* assisted in his own defence in the *Examiner**. In December 1849 Carlyle published 'On the Negro Question' (*Fraser's*), later expanded with a racist title. John Stuart Mill's* rejoinder appeared the next month.

More positively, Carlyle wrote articles on Ireland in early 1848 for the *Spectator** and *Examiner** which led to the *Latter-Day Pamphlets* (1850) on British society and politics. His last writings that became books or pamphlets also first appeared as articles: the 1866 'Inaugural Address', after election as Rector of Edinburgh University *(The Times**),* second Reform Act commentary in 'Shooting Niagara: And After?' (*Macmillan's Magazine** 1867)** and 'Early Kings of Norway' (*Fraser's* 1875).

During Carlyle's lifetime, he maintained friendships with editors* and authors and assisted the careers of younger writers including David Masson*, Francis Espinasse*, Gavan Duffy* and Margaret

Oliphant*. After his death in 1881 and swift publication of his *Reminiscences*, his wife Jane Carlyle's letters and Froude's biography, the periodical press engaged in a lively debate about Carlyle's character and the ethics of publishing controversial material about the recently deceased. In death Carlyle proved just as controversial as he had been in life. DT

Sources: Carlyle *Letters* 1970ff, Cumming 2004, *ODNB,* Tarr 1976, Tarr 1989, Vanden Bossche 2002.

CARPENTER, WILLIAM (1797-1874) An autodidact bookbinder, William Carpenter was led by religious conviction to change career in the 1820s. Between 1824 and 1827 he worked, with the philologist William Greenfield, on a monthly* serial *Critica Biblica,* also publishing religious textbooks. Then, in 1828, he became editor* of the *Weekly Free Press* (1828-1831), a London co-operative and labour movement paper, and a continuation of the *Trades Newspaper* (1825-1828). Increasingly, Carpenter concentrated on politics*. A pioneering unstamped* pressman, he sought to evade stamp duty with weekly* *Political Letters & Pamphlets*, each nominally free-standing (1830-1831). His other serial* publications at this time were *Carpenter's Political and Historical Essays* and the *Political Anecdotist & Popular Instructor* (both 1831). Imprisoned for six months in 1831, he resumed publishing just on the right side of the law with *Carpenter's Monthly Political Magazine* (1831-1832) and the deliciously titled *Church Examiner & Ecclesiastical Record* and *Slap at the Church* (both 1832), co-edited with fellow radical John Cleave*. After just two issues, his *Political Unionist* failed and Carpenter became subeditor* of the radical daily* *True Sun* (1832-1837) a post he left in 1833 for a similar job with the rival *Weekly True Sun* (1833-1834). An attempt to resume publishing independently with *Carpenter's London Journal* (1836) failed. He survived on hack work, which included for the *Shipping Gazette* and the *Era.*

Like other London pressmen (Cleave, Hetherington*, O'Brien*), Carpenter was a delegate to the Chartist* Convention (alternative parliament) of 1839. On behalf of the London Working Men's Association he edited *Charter,* a weekly intended to be the paper of record for the Convention. The latter's diminishing prestige, and collapse in September, were reflected in *Charter's* fortunes. Its closure in March 1840 marked the end of Carpenter's political career, except for a brief phase as editor

(1844-1845) of *Lloyd's Weekly Newspaper**, during which he became embroiled in a bruising dispute with Feargus O'Connor*. Carpenter worked for many other papers, including the *Railway Observer, Family Herald**, *Court Journal, Sunday Times** and *Bedfordshire Independent*. Increasingly, however, he refocused his career on the compilation of religious reference works. **MSC**

Sources: Chase 2007, *ODNB*.

CARPENTER, WILLIAM BENJAMIN (1813-1885) After initially training in medicine at Edinburgh, Carpenter opted instead to pursue a more precarious career lecturing and writing on a diverse range of scientific* and medical* subjects, from oceanography to physiological psychology. As well as publishing several successful textbooks, he wrote extensively for the press, especially for the *British and Foreign Medico-Chirurgical Review*, which he edited* for five years from 1847, and more general periodicals like the *Contemporary Review**. In particular, Carpenter's journalism helped popularize new developments in psychology such as the process which he termed 'unconscious cerebration', and many of his articles for *Fraser's Magazine**, the *Quarterly Review** and the *Nineteenth Century** were devoted to exposing the apparently supernatural agencies at work in pseudosciences like phrenology, mesmerism and spiritualism. A staunch Unitarian who envisaged the material world as the product of a beneficent Creator operating in accordance with natural laws, Carpenter wrote important early favourable reviews* of Charles Darwin's *Origin of Species* (1859) for the *National Review** and the *British and Foreign Medico-Chirurgical Review*, and, despite later proclaiming himself 'anti-Darwinian' in the *Athenaeum**, he contributed a touchingly personal obituary* of Darwin to the *Modern Review* in 1882. **GD**

Sources: Carpenter 1888, Lightman, 2004a, *ODNB*.

CARR, JOSEPH WILLIAM COMYNS (1849-1916) J. Comyns Carr embodied the new professional* art critic of the late nineteenth century. In 1873 Carr opted to pursue art journalism to ensure sufficient income as opposed to continuing law. He gained an intimate knowledge of the art world as contributor and critic for serials*, including *Contemporary Review**, *Cornhill Magazine**, *Fortnightly Review**, *Manchester Guardian**, *New Quarterly Magazine**, *Pall Mall Gazette** and *Saturday Review** as well as the French journal *L'Art*.

Putting his experience of the art world gleaned from journalism to good use, he assisted Sir Coutts and Lady Lindsay and Charles Hallé in establishing the Grosvenor Gallery and became co-manager with Hallé in 1878. In 1888 Hallé and Carr broke with the Lindsays over management practices and founded the New Gallery, which survived until 1908.

He reprinted numerous pieces from his journalism, some revised or expanded, in *Essays on Art* (1879), *Art in Provincial France* (1883), and *Ideals of Painting* (1917). A review of the latter published in the *Burlington Magazine* acknowledged him as among 'the pioneers of a literary school of art-critics' (C., L. 1917). Through his critical writing and gallery positions, Carr supported artists affiliated with Aestheticism and Pre-Raphaelitism. However, he broke with James McNeill Whistler* after publication of *Whistler v. Ruskin: Art and Art Critics* (1878). **ALH**

Sources: C., L. 1917, Denney 2000, Merrill 1992, *Oxford Encyclopedia of British Literature 2006*, Prettejohn 1997.

CARTOONS Cartoons became the dominant mode of comic image-making for magazines* after caricature* failed to find a suitable and successful periodical mode for visual satire*. Led by the success of *Punch** in finding a variety of formats* and idioms for both political* and social graphic satire acceptable to genteel sensibilities, and much assisted by the capacity of the wood* engraving to situate itself within the typeset page, the cartoon quickly learnt to exploit linearity, topicality and speed of composition without entirely losing the codes, stereotypes and bluntness of the caricature tradition. Captions, which could again be easily accommodated in the typeset page alongside wood engravings, became the norm, and were important within the highly verbal Victorian consciousness in their ability to explain or comment on complex images.

The exigencies of the wood engraving trade in the 1840s meant that many artists who had started out as caricaturists turned from metal engraving and etching to wood engraving, and began to draw documentary and decorative subjects as well as comic and satirical images for the periodical press. The result in many cases was the hybrid forms of reportage developed by artists like Kenny Meadows*, John Leech* and George Cruikshank* which combined social observation with elements of the cartoon. But increasingly periodicals turned to the cartoon as a central comic mode, and it retained its position as a key mode of political and social commentary right through the century..

Many periodicals became so closely associated with a single cartoonist that the artist's name became a crucial part of the magazine's brand image.

13

CARICATURES OF THE MONTH.

From a photograph by]   [Mayall.
MR. F. CARRUTHERS GOULD.

THE increasing importance of caricature in politics is shown by two notable publications which appeared on the eve of the Election. One is the "Elector's Picture Book," published by the *Pall Mall Gazette*, being compiled from copious contributions which Mr. Gould and a few other caricaturists have contributed to the pages of the *Pall Mall Gazette* and the *Pall Mall Budget*. Mr. Gould is quite in the first rank of our political caricaturists. As an artist he is not in the same category as Mr. Tenniel; but as a caricaturist, especially in hitting off the characteristics of those whom he selects for his victims,

he has a wider range and a much more biting pencil than the Grand Old Man of Mr. *Punch*. There is a tendency in Mr. Gould to harp too much upon one characteristic; for instance, the upper teeth of Mr. W. H. Smith become almost as monotonous as Mr. Chamberlain's eye-glass. Mr. Gould is a good hater, and he takes good care not to spare the objects of his antipathy. Mr. Chamberlain, for instance, who is a favourite subject of Mr. Gould's pencil, is by no means a favourite with Mr. Gould as a politician. On the whole, however, Mr. Gould's humour is playful, and he differs very much from most caricaturists in being a keen politician.

The other publication is by no means as interesting as the "Elector's Picture Book;" it is the "Coming (?) Gladstone," and is the work of a very fervent, not to say bigoted, Unionist. The author is the same who was responsible for the "Irish Green Book," a publication which has now reached its fortieth thousand. The "Coming (?) Gladstone" has reached its twentieth thousand. It is smartly compiled.

From *Kladderadatsch*]   [June 19, 1892.

NANCY AND KIEL.—An Afterword: Russia keeps her relations to France and Germany firmly in view. But things are not looking well.

MR. GOULD'S WORK AT ITS BEST.
(*From the* "Elector's Picture Book.")

Figure 8: 'Caricatures of the Month' in *Review of Reviews*, July 1892: 13.

Punch had the great trio of Leech, Tenniel* and Doyle* in its early days, and its imitators *Fun** and *Judy** also depended on named cartoonists. *Will o' the Wisp** gave John Proctor's name in blocked gold capitals on the volume covers with equal billing to the editor*, and Matt Morgan's* innovative and enormous tinted fold-out plates for the *Tomahawk** were undoubtedly its main commercial attraction. *Ally Sloper's Half Holiday** was every bit as closely associated with Baxter's* drawings.

Artists like Leech were successful enough to be able to publish their cartoons as separate volumes. The appearance of series of comic drawings by named artists was also an incentive to readers in the serious monthlies*, and one used by the *Cornhill** in particular. Cartoons were well served by the scale on which they could be produced, even the double-page weekly* spreads of *Punch** were outdone by the triple-page *Tomahawk* fold-outs, which also used colour to give them even more emphasis, and the spectacular imported American lithographic* centre-folds of *Puck**. Many cartoonists, drawing on Continental models, began to use recurrent motifs and personae for their drawings, and thus to build long-term proto-narratives out of their cartoons, and certainly Doyle's *Manners and Customs of Ye Englyshe* series for *Punch* from 1849, let alone the continuing adventures of Ally Sloper as drawn by Sullivan and Baxter, looked increasingly towards the comic strip. **BM**

Sources: Houfe 1978, Kunzle 1990.

CASSELL, JOHN (1817-1865) As popular publisher*, printer and editor* John Cassell became a household name and archetypal 'self-made man'. After working in boyhood at a Manchester cotton mill, he left a carpentry apprenticeship to move to London in 1835. He soon became a speaker for the National Temperance Movement and his initial business ventures derived from teetotalism. With money from his wife's family in 1843 he founded Cassell & Co*, specialising in tea and coffee and then having bought a small press to print his labels branched into publishing as an offshoot from advertising* with the penny* monthly* *Teetotal Times*, commencing 2 March 1846.

Cassell's publishing reputation began with the four-penny weekly* newspaper the *Standard of Freedom* (July 1848). Cassell aimed at a wide readership*, supporting universal suffrage and advocating religious*, political* and commercial freedom. As a leading campaigner against the newspaper 'taxes on knowledge'*, he gave evidence to the select committee on the newspaper stamps* in 1851. His penny weekly *Working Man's Friend, and Family Instructor**(1850-1853) championed 'the moral and social well-being of the working classes* and stood out from contemporaries in its encouragement of artisan writers. Avoiding the didactic tone of 'namby-pamby literature', *Working Man's Friend* was typical of Cassell's publications in addressing a family* readership* through amusement and instruction. '[E]ach member of a household should have something to interest him' Cassell said of the long-running religious* and literary* journal the *Quiver* (1861ff), which serialized Ellen (Mrs Henry) Wood's* 'The Channings' (Nowell-Smith: 22). His commitment to self-education is evident in the *Popular Educator* (1852) and *John Cassell's Library* (1850-1851), and popular publications in *The Emigrant's Almanak and Directory for 1849*, and the *Illustrated Exhibitor**, a catalogue of the Great Exhibition wood-engravings*. *Cassell's Illustrated Family Paper**, begun in 1853, was probably his greatest success.

Despite his astute appreciation of popular taste, Cassell lacked business acumen. He was bought out by his printers Galpin and Petter in 1854, though they traded under the famous name and retained Cassell as editor*. Under tight financial direction, the firm went from strength to strength and Cassell was made senior partner in 1858. Cassell's papers flourished, eventually reaching a circulation* of 285,000, with distribution* in London, Middlesex, Melbourne, Derbyshire, New York and Paris. The publishing house survived his death in 1865 and the name continues today. **HR**

Sources: Anderson 1991, Haywood 2004, Nowell-Smith 1958, *ODNB*, Pike 1894.

CASSELL AND CO. With the money he came into on marriage, John Cassell* was able to start a tea and coffee business in the City in 1847. Cassell and Co. was informed by its owners' beliefs in universal suffrage, free trade, anti-slavery, working* class* education and temperance.

Cassell's first serious but anonymous*endeavour was fuelled by his temperance* commitment in 1846, the 1d *Teetotal Times* which was taken over by the Temperance Movement's own publication. It was followed by the 4d weekly* *Standard of Freedom* (1848) calling for political*, religious* and commercial freedom. He briefly published the *London Mercury* and, in 1849, the *Emigrant's Almanack and Directory,* their first lucrative annual* before getting into stride with his abiding passion, fostering education partly as an antidote to the lures of drink. The first such title (in 1850), the 1d weekly

Working Man's Friend, and Family Instructor*, achieved a circulation* of 100,000 by the following year and signalled the start of an avalanche of self-improvement magazines. The *John Cassell's Library* (1850-1851) was a monthly* containing history*, geography and biography in a serialized* format*. The *Popular Educator,* which provided economic self-education for artisans, *Cassell's Magazine** and the irregular *Illustrated Magazine of Art,* all started in 1852. These were closely followed by the weekly *Cassell's Illustrated Family Paper**(from 1853) combining entertainment and education targeted at the middle and working class*. The firm's popular publications included the *Illustrated Exhibitor**.

Producing so many publications stretched Cassell's and Co's finances, but disaster was averted in 1854 by its printers, Thomas Dixon Galpin and George William Petter. They took over the company, retaining Cassell as editor* until 1858 when he became a partner; the 1859 Messrs Cassell, Petter, Galpin & Co. eventually became Cassell & Company Ltd in 1883. The company went on to publish large numbers of illustrated* popular educational texts and periodicals, one of which, the *Quiver**, provided religious* articles and serialized novels such as Mrs Henry Wood's, 'The Channings'.

One of the firm's innovations was producing partly printed news-sheets for local and country editors to add their own local* news*. On a wider scale, its commitment to anti-slavery was demonstrated in its status as the first English publisher of Harriet Beecher Stowe's novel, *Uncle Tom's Cabin.* At Cassell's early death in 1865, a flourishing company with 500 employees continued to expand, becoming a leader in illustrated reference works which continued into the twentieth century. In the twenty-first century it is now part of the Orion Publishing Group. **CL**
Sources: Boase 1965, Herd 1952, *ODNB.*

CASSELL'S (ILLUSTRATED) FAMILY PAPER (1853-1867) AND CASSELL'S MAGAZINE (1867-1932) *Cassell's Illustrated Family Paper,* a weekly* that first appeared on 31 December 1853, was the beginning of a series of successful titles that aimed to improve and uplift middle-class* readers and was widely considered, as Margaret Oliphant* put it, as 'a highly moral and edifying publication'.

Distinguished from its competitors not only by its range of content, with articles on topics such as household economy and management, fashion*, popular scientific* news, and famous names of the day, *Cassell's* also contained quality writing. J.M. Barrie, Arnold Bennett*, Mary Elizabeth Braddon*, G.

K. Chesterton, Joseph Conrad, Stephen Crane, Conan Doyle, Catherine (Kate) Greenaway*, Jack London, Baroness Orczy, W. M. Thackeray*, Anthony Trollope* and Rudyard Kipling, whose story 'Kim'' the magazine serialized*, were among the authors who contributed fiction and poetry*. Issues were large* enough (between 26 and 44 cm over the course of the publication's life) to be easily shared during family sessions of reading* aloud, and were plentifully illustrated*, sometimes in colour, with engravings, sketches, etchings, and even photographs*. Illustrators included Mary Ellen Edwards*, Luke Fildes*, H. Furniss*, H. R. Millar, Arthur Rackham and John Dawson Watson*.

As *Cassell's* grew with the times, its successful formula remained essentially the same, though it underwent changes in title*, publication frequency*, and price*. In its first five years the cost went from 1d to 6d. Through March 1867, it was published every Saturday; as *Cassell's Magazine*, it became a monthly* (April 1867-Nov.1874). Its price increased to 7d. It was available monthly as *Cassell's Family Magazine* (Oct. 1847-Nov. 1897). Having become one of the four highest-selling penny-fiction magazines of the mid-nineteenth century, it finally entered its longest incarnation as the monthly *Cassell's Magazine of Fiction,* (Dec. 1897-Dec. 1932). **FCA**
Sources: Altholz 1989, Altick 1957, Dixon 1986a, King and Plunkett 2005, Newsplan BL, Oliphant 1858, *Waterloo.*

CATLING, THOMAS (1838-1920) Thomas Catling is best known for his long employment at and eventual editorship* of *Lloyd's Weekly Newspaper**, a reign which encompassed a number of crucial changes in the mechanics and style of news* reporting*, some of which were driven by Catling himself.

Born in Cambridge to a botanist and his wife, Catling spent a short number of years at a dame school and a private academy before being sent to work for the *Cambridge Chronicle* at 12 to help support the family. As the paper could only be printed on one side at a time, Catling's first job was to take each sheet as it was fed through the machine, though he eventually rose to the position of 'reading boy' for the newspaper. Unable to secure an apprenticeship, Catling left the *Cambridge Chronicle* at 14, supporting himself through 'jobbing' before leaving Cambridge for London in April 1854.

In London Catling very quickly attained a position as a compositor for *Lloyd's Weekly Newspaper**, arriving precisely at the moment when its proprietor* Edward Lloyd* was turning his attention away

from instalment fiction to focus entirely on the publication of his newspaper. Over the next 53 years, Catling successfully rose through the ranks and both witnessed and was involved with several important developments within the industry more generally. In the summer of 1856, when Lloyd installed the first Hoe rotary presses in England at the office, Catling welcomed the change as his fast progress with the machines secured him advancement in the composing room and meant that he was called on to assist in bringing out a special edition of the newspaper devoted to the execution of poisoner William Palmer. In 1866, Catling was promoted to the position of subeditor*, an important post as, although the editor's name appeared on the front page, Catling was responsible for closely supervising the material. Moreover, when Blanchard Jerrold* spent long periods of time in France and the post failed to bring copy for that week's newspaper, Catling had to supply the leaders*. After Jerrold's death in 1884, Catling succeeded him as editor after proving himself capable by gaining an exclusive report on a recent murder in a lawyer's office. Under his editorship, in 1896 *Lloyd's Weekly* achieved the unprecedented circulation* of one million copies. Furthermore, Catling was also credited with being the first to use a motor car in journalistic work which he did in the event of the Moot Farm murder. Finally, Catling also served as president of the British International Association of Journalists. He retired from *Lloyd's Weekly Newspaper* in January 1907. **RHC**
Sources: Catling 1911, *The Times*.

CATTON, JAMES ALFRED HENRY (1860-1936) James Alfred Henry Catton spent 24 years (1900-1924) as editor* of the influential *Athletic News*, a Manchester-based weekly* sports* paper founded by Edward Hulton*. Catton's pseudonym*, 'Tityrus', became synonymous with the reporting of football and cricket, and he was acknowledged as a leading figure in the introduction of elements of the New Journalism* with a lighter, more chatty and informed style of sports journalism, in contrast to the laboured reports common in much of the Victorian and Edwardian press.

Catton, the son of a schoolmaster, was born in Greenwich, Kent and joined the *Preston Herald*, in Lancashire in 1875 as an apprentice reporter*, moving to the *Nottingham Daily Guardian* in 1883 as a reporter, later becoming sporting editor. In 1891, Catton joined the Hulton group of newspapers, reporting sport for the *Sunday Chronicle*, *Sporting Chronicle* and *Athletic News*, a paper with a comprehensive national coverage and a wide circulation*, especially in the north of England and Midlands. He was editor of the *Sporting Chronicle* (1894-1900). Catton had two books published covering the growth of football and the impact of professionalism that drew on his journalism, *The Rise of the Leaguers* (1897) and *The Real Football* (1900).

As *Athletic News* editor, Catton, renowned for his diminutive stature (4 ft 10 ½ in.), reported the leading sports fixtures and commented on important sporting issues in his 'Stray Leaves' column*, where he consistently promoted the integrity of the professional sportsman in the face of widespread concern that paid performers would encourage gambling, partisanship and the will to win at all costs. Catton's memoirs, *Wickets and Goals. Stories of Play*, were published in 1926. Under the byline J. A. H. Catton, he later wrote for a variety of Fleet Street* titles (1924-1936), including the *Observer* and *Evening Standard*, and compiled records for *Wisden* Cricketers' Almanack*. **ST**
Sources: Catton 1926, Tate 2005.

CAUSERIES This term appears to have entered journalistic discourse in the mid-nineteenth century, perhaps through the influence of the celebrated 'Causeries de Lundi' by French literary critic Sainte-Beuve. G. H. Lewes* adopted the term in the *Fortnightly Review* for his editorial address to the reader; his successor John Morley*, a Francophile, continued the practice. A hint of mockery of the term's pretentious foreignness underlies the use of 'causerie' in the satirical* *Anti-Teapot Review* in the 1860s. However the term had become substantially naturalized by the 1880s to describe the sort of free-form book chat best exemplified by Andrew Lang's* monthly 'At the Sign of the Ship' column* in *Longman's Magazine*, where he rambled on genially in short, unbuttoned paragraphs about men and books, avoiding the strictest standards of criticism while entertaining and enlightening his readers* with wide-ranging snippets of information, literary* news*, and gossip* accompanied by the odd puff*, for example of May Kendall. Other examples of this genre* of literary journalism were Arnold Bennett* writing as 'Jacob Tonson' in the *New Age* and W. R. Nicoll* as 'Claudius Clear' in the *British Weekly*. Another type of causerie was the chat column that became a standard feature in women's magazines, establishing a bond of intimacy between the reader and the journalist/editor*. An early example is Matilda Browne's* column

'Spinnings' in the *Englishwoman's Domestic Magazine**; it becomes dominant in later magazines like *Home Chat**. **CAK**
Sources: Beetham 1996, Gross 1969, Maurer 1965, *ODNB*, Waller 2006.

CELEBRITIES OF THE DAY: BRITISH AND FOREIGN (1881-1882) *Celebrities of the Day: British and Foreign,* subtitled *A Monthly Repertoire of Contemporary Biography,* initially published between 15-20 biographical sketches in each issue, though that number dropped to around six per month by spring 1882. Of the variety of accomplished individuals given notice, only two were women, both actresses. While biographical sketches had been a mainstay of journalism* since the eighteenth century, *Celebrities of the Day* is one indication of the shift from biography to personality* and celebrity which was taking place in the last decades of the nineteenth century, in the context of the New Journalism*. The 'Celebrities at Home' series published in Edmund Yates's* The *World** in the 1870s and other periodicals such as *Our Celebrities: A Portrait Gallery* (a more lavish publication at 2s/125 6d, which ran to 12 issues in 1888-1889) are other examples of the new interest in celebrity lives. **MWT**
Sources: Turner 2000c, Wiener 1988b.

CELEBRITY See Personality and the press

CENSORSHIP AND TRIALS That newspapers were, unlike many books, relatively free from external censorship may be attributed to the Regency trials and acquittals for seditious libel of William Hone* and Thomas Wooler* in 1817, after which the press acquired freedom from similar prosecutions.

Hone had been tried three times for what was pretty much the same charge; twice for blasphemous and seditious libel, and once for blasphemous libel, for printing *The Late John Wilkes's Catechism, The Political Litany* and *The Sinecurist's Creed.* Symbolically Hone linked himself with Wilkes's early radicalism. In his publications released after 1816 Hone frequently states that his shop is at '45 Ludgate Hill'. As Robert Southey noted in a footnote to his 'A Vision of Judgement', '45' was a significant number for radicals. Looking back to the unrest of the 1760s, Southey quotes Dr Franklin: 'The mob [... required] gentlemen and ladies of all ranks, as they passed in their carriages, to shout for Wilkes and liberty, marking the same words on all their coaches with chalk, and No. 45 on every door'. Wilkes edited* the counter to the Ultra-Tory *Briton* – the *North Briton,* and, in number 45 of this paper (23 April 1763) he insinuated that the king had lied in a speech from the throne. Hone allied himself with the radicalism of the second half of the eighteenth century that had ferociously attacked Bute's government and the King. Defending himself in court, without the aid of a lawyer, Hone used the unusual defence that his parodies attacked the state, and not the word of God. His acquittal was a great victory for the radical press and is said to have led to the early death of the presiding judge, Lord Ellenborough.

Thomas Wooler*, who had shared a cell with Hone, was arrested in May 1817 and charged with seditious libel for two articles published in the *Black Dwarf*: 'The right of petition' and 'The past – the present – and the future'. His trial before Justice Charles Abbott took place in front of two special juries on 5 June 1817. Like Hone he gave a brilliant defence. Found guilty on the first trial, he was acquitted on the second. The government did not pursue another. Afterwards John Keats wrote, 'Wooler and Hone have done us an essential service'. However Hone's victory in court did not please everyone: Dorothy Wordsworth wrote, 'The acquittal of Hone is enough to make one out of love with English Juries'. The effect of these victories was that successive governments were reluctant to question the freedom of the press. The issue of press freedom was displaced onto the conflict over the 4d newspaper* stamp* duty and the 'taxes on knowledge'*, resulting in the mass defiance of the radical unstamped press in the 1830s. This campaign resulted in the reduction of the stamp duty to 1d in 1836. The next 25 years saw the abolition of remaining taxes: newspaper advertising* (1853), the stamp duty (1855) and paper duty (1861). **JG**
Sources: Hackwood 1970, Haywood 2004.

CENTURY GUILD HOBBY HORSE (1884-1894) Founded in 1884 when it was priced* at 2s, this quarto journal was at first badly received. It was restarted in 1886 with another Volume 1, and 28 issues appeared between then and 1892. In 1893 it was renamed the *Hobby Horse* and three more issues, now published by Elkin Mathews and John Lane* and costing £1, appeared until 1894. Circulation* never exceeded 500 although the contributors included Oscar Wilde*, Ford Madox Ford, William Michael Rossetti*, Lionel Johnson, Ernest Dowson, Laurence Binyon, John Addington Symonds and Richard Le Gallienne*.

The journal was an offshoot of the Century Guild, a small group of young architects committed to Arts and Crafts, who set themselves against the materialistic ideals of mid-Victorian building and who believed that all components of an architectural structure should minister to a single vision. Prominent among them were the designer and poet Herbert Percy Horne and the designers A. H. Mackmurdo and Selwyn Image. Horne, who in a later phase was to become a distinguished art historian, was effectively the editor*. The *Hobby Horse* is of particular interest in that it attempts to enact the concept of 'the unity of the arts', a cornerstone of late nineteenth century aesthetic theory, in both its format* and its contents. Topics ranged from early music* (often contributed by Arnold Dolmetsch), architecture (especially the work of Inigo Jones), painting (particularly the achievements of the Italian Renaissance) as well as most branches of literature* with an especial emphasis on a poetic* tradition stretching from William Blake to Dante Gabriel Rossetti. In the early issues the avowed godfather is clearly Walter Pater* but by the 1890s ideas of 'decadence' begin to infiltrate with features on, for instance, French symbolist poets. The visual styles also begin to move away from Pre-Raphaelite medievalism to the more organic and sinuous shapes of Art Nouveau.

Throughout its career the *Hobby Horse* was printed on handmade paper* with carefully chosen typography*, high quality illustrations* (especially the woodcuts*) and wide margins, making it one of the most elegant, symptomatic and influential artefacts of the *fin-de-siècle*. JAS

Sources: Fletcher 1990, Houfe 1992.

CHALMERS FAMILY (1713-1876) James Chalmers (ca. 1713-1764) a printer in Aberdeen, founded the *Aberdeen Journal*, first issued in December 1747. Establishing his business as printer to the town, the region and both the college and university, he laid the foundations for a dynasty of printers and newspaper publishers* in the Aberdeen region for generations. He became a famous political* journalist* for his articles on the battle of Culloden to which he was an eyewitness in his early career. His son James Chalmers (1742-1810) studied at Marischal College, Aberdeen, and trained as a journalist in London and Cambridge. When his father died in 1764, he took over as proprietor*, editor* and printer of the *Aberdeen Journal*, managing the paper until his death in 1810. It then became the property of his son David Chalmers (1778-1859), who purchased steam presses* for their newspaper printing in the 1830s. The title remained in the family for over a century until 1876. An older son, James Chalmers (1775-1831), became printer of the *Dundee Advertiser*.

Alexander Chalmers (1759-1835), James Chalmers's youngest son, having studied medicine, became a journalist in London, where he worked on the *General Advertiser*, among other titles. In 1783, he married Elizabeth, the widow of John Gillett, a London printer. In the late eighteenth century he became editor of the *Public Ledger* and the *London Packet*, and later the *Morning Herald**. As a political journalist, he wrote numerous essays on the American war of independence under the pseudonym* of 'Senex' for the *St. James's Chronicle*. His more literary* work appeared in the *Critical Review*, the *Analytical Review** and the *Morning Chronicle**, where he published epigrams and satirical* poems*.

In addition to being a newspaper editor and journalist, Alexander Chalmers was renowned as an editor of books, bibliographer and biographer. In 1803 his edition of *The British Essayists* 'not only preserved many periodicals that might otherwise have been lost, but provided valuable analyses in the prefaces' (*ODNB*), and in 1805 he was elected Fellow of the Society of Antiquaries. From 1812 to 1817, he edited his most famous work, which was issued in parts: *The General Biographical Dictionary, containing a Historical and Critical Account of the Lives and Writings of the Most Eminent Men in every Nation, especially the British and the Irish, from the Earliest Accounts to the Present Times*. The *Gentleman's Magazine**, to which he contributed over many years judged him, 'one of the most eminent biographers that Great Britain has ever produced' (*Gentleman's Magazine* 1835: 207). CK

Sources: *Aberdeen Journal, Gentleman's Magazine* 1835, Kenneth 1818, *ODNB, Scottish Book Trade Index*.

CHAMBERS, ROBERT (1802-1871) Robert Chambers is primarily remembered as the author of *Vestiges of the Natural History of Creation* (1844), published anonymously* during his lifetime. However, together with his brother, William Chambers*, he revolutionised popular* literature* in Britain.

Their first joint venture consisted of a magazine series called the *Kaleidoscope*, or *Edinburgh Literary Amusement*, issued fortnightly (6 Oct.1821-12 Jan.1822). This was followed by *Illustrations of the Author of Waverley* (1822), which contained sketches of individuals believed to have been the inspirations for some of the characters in Walter Scott's works. Robert's enthusiasm in researching the history and antiquities of Edinburgh resulted in a personal friendship with Walter Scott, to whom Robert paid tribute after his death with the *Life of Sir Walter Scott* (1832). In 1830 Robert became editor* of the *Edinburgh Advertiser** and, in order to have more time for writing, left his retail business in the hands of his younger brother, David.

When, at the beginning of 1832, William Chambers* invited his brother Robert to join him in creating a low-cost weekly*, a 'shocked' Robert turned him down flat. By 1832, Chambers had written over 20 volumes dealing primarily with Scottish history and literature, and he associated William's proposed *Chambers's Edinburgh Journal** with 'the not very creditable papers [aimed at working-class readers] then current'. However, brotherly affection trumped literary and political misgivings. Beginning with the first number in February, Robert contributed copiously to the *Journal*. Finding an appreciative readership* for his wide-ranging articles, several months later Robert agreed formally to become co-editor of the *Journal* and a partner in the publishing firm, W. & R. Chambers, with William primarily taking responsibility for business development.

An instant success, the pioneering *Journal* sold upwards of 50,000 copies per-week within its first year. Addressing an expanding body of readers* on subjects ranging from public health, literature*, economic inequality, science* and manners, Chambers, a self-styled 'essayist of the middle class', underwent a remarkable transformation. In 1847 he explained that when he joined his brother he was a political conservative and literary 'antiquarian', but weekly journalism changed him into an engaged Utilitarian: 'Wherever human wo [sic] can be lessened, or happiness increased, I would work to that end – wherever intelligence and virtue can be promoted, I would promote them'. Robert's own essays became the weekly's leading feature.

During the 1840s *Chambers's Edinburgh Journal* became arguably the most popular periodical in Britain, with sales approaching 80,000. In the *Journal* Robert explored the scientific concepts that became the building blocks of his most important book, the anonymous *Vestiges of the Natural History of Creation* (1844), the first full treatment of evolution in English. *Chambers's Edinburgh Journal* paved the way for the brothers' immensely profitable publishing firm, which poured forth an ever-increasing volume of books, encyclopedias, educational texts and much else besides – designed to promote literacy and educate and entertain the rising middle class. To be successful, Robert explained in a letter to George Combe, a periodical requires 'at least one constant writer to give it a strong and abiding character'. He claimed justifiably to be the 'constant writer', the 'presiding spirit', of *Chambers's Edinburgh Journal*.

Topping the century's best sellers lists were grammars and encyclopaedias, reflecting the Victorian desire for 'useful knowledge', and Robert published two volumes of the *Cyclopaedia of English Literature* (1840-1843), followed by the *Chambers's Encyclopaedia* (1859-1868), an endeavour carried out by the two brothers with Dr Andrew Findlater as editor. In 1850, Robert obtained the majority of the firm's shares, and began *Chambers's Encyclopaedia of Universal Knowledge for the People* (1860-1960). The *Book of Days* (1864), with detailed descriptions of key historical events, was Chambers's last major publication. The University of St Andrews awarded him the degree of Doctor of Law (1862), and he was also elected a member of the Athenaeum Club, London. Named as a fellow of the Royal Society of Edinburgh, this was a deserved recognition for a man who dedicated his life to the cultivation and dissemination of knowledge.

The impact of W. & R. Chambers remains to be assessed. Although initially 'shocked' by William's proposed weekly*, Robert came to fashion the *Journal* and give the Chambers firm editorial direction. RS/SGS

Sources: Cooney 1970, *ODNB*, Ordish 1883, Scholnick 1999, Secord 2000, Weedon 2003, *Wellesley*.

CHAMBERS, WILLIAM (1800-1883) With his younger brother Robert Chambers*, William was among the most influential popular publishers* and educators of the nineteenth century. Known best for *Chambers's Journal**, a cheap* weekly* family* miscellany*, the Edinburgh firm of W. and R. Chambers also published a wide range of works in the useful knowledge* tradition, typically in economical serial* formats, including school textbooks like *Chambers's Educational Course* (1835-1896), and major works of reference, notably *Chambers's Encyclopaedia: A Dictionary of Universal Knowledge* (1859-1868).

Though Robert Chambers tended to take a more active editor* role in the firm's collective publishing projects, while William managed the business side, the latter was also a prolific writer. He contributed regular articles to the *Journal*, compiled *Introduction to the Sciences* (1836) and other texts for the *Educational Course*. On the death of William Chambers, control of the publishing firm passed to his nephew, Robert Chambers (1832-1888), who had jointly edited the *Journal* with his uncle since 1873. GL

Sources: Anderson and Rose 1991, Chambers 1882, Chambers 1884, *ODNB*.

CHAMBERS'S (EDINBURGH) JOURNAL, 1832-1956 William Chambers*, a Scottish bookseller and printer, began *Chambers's Edinburgh Journal*, one of Britain's first cheap*, general interest weekly* magazines, in February 1832. Priced* at 1 ½ d and unstamped*, it was an eight-page, three-column* broadsheet. In the inaugural issue Chambers wrote, 'the leading principle of this paper is to take advantage of the universal appetite for instruction which at present exists [and] to supply to that appetite food of the best kind'. To this end, the journal contained largely unsigned* or excerpted articles with an emphasis on moral instruction* and uplift on a variety of topics including literature*, history*, science* and religion*, targeted at the lower and middle classes*, particularly young people. Unlike its chief competitor, the shorter-lived *Penny Magazine*, *Chambers's* included fiction and a poem in each issue. Contributors included Walter Besant*, Mrs. Craik, Arthur Conan Doyle, Maria Edgeworth, Elizabeth Gaskell, Thomas Hardy*, James Hogg, George Meredith and Mary Russell Mitford.

Within two months of publication, Chambers reported that circulation* was 31,000 copies each week and this print run severely stretched the resources of the original printer, John Johnstone of Edinburgh, who was quickly replaced by John Ballantyne. Not content to limit the distribution to Scotland, Chambers took advantage of the recent invention of stereotype* plates and had a separate English edition published in London by W. S. Orr starting in May 1832, which resulted in a combined circulation of 50,000 by the end of the year. In 1833 an attempt to expand publication to Dublin was short-lived, as was the magazine's American* edition in New York (1837-1841).

Although Robert Chambers*, William's younger brother and anonymous* author of the controversial *Vestiges of the Natural History of Creation* (1844), was initially only a contributor, he joined William as editor*, proprietor* and publisher* in September 1832. Beginning in 1834, the Chambers brothers took over printing the Edinburgh edition of the magazine themselves but continued to use London printers such as Bradbury & Evans* until 1842 when they opened their own London office. By 1840 the journal reached a peak circulation of 90,000 which fell to a weekly 23,000 in 1855 with an additional 35,000 for the monthly 7d fiction supplement* which began in 1851 and included advertisements*. In January 1844, the journal switched to a 16-page, two-column double crown octavo, although the 1 ½d price remained

static until 1897. Its name changed to *Chambers's Journal of Popular Literature, Science and Arts* in January 1854 and to *Chambers's Journal* in December 1897. The journal's only illustrations* were wood engravings*. The journal was predominantly edited by Robert Chambers between 1832 and 1858, followed by a succession of editors including Leitch Ritchie and James Payn*, Robert Chambers Jr. and Charles E. S. Chambers. **EFO**
Sources: Altick 1957, Bell 2007, Fyfe 2006, Ordish 1883, *Waterloo*.

CHAMPION, HENRY HYDE (1859-1928) The career of this prolific socialist* journalist* and publisher* began in 1883 with the purchase of a large share in the London-based Modern Press, publisher of the Social Democratic Federation, the issuing body* of *Justice*, its mouthpiece. Having financially supported *Justice* by not calling in its debts, the Modern Press stopped publishing the periodical in 1887, when Champion disagreed with Henry Hyndman's* temporary shift to revolutionary socialism. Champion left the SDF and launched two periodicals: *Common Sense* and the more substantial *Labour Elector*. His campaign against working practices at Brunner Mond's chemical factory in the *Labour Elector* was a great success: using Tom Mann's undercover reports, Champion helped to unionise the workers and bring about the eight-hour working day.

A trip to Australia resulted in the winding up of the Modern Press in 1889 and the temporary suspension of the *Labour Elector*, though the periodical was resumed in 1893 with a new editor* Michael Maltman Barry. The same year Champion made an unsuccessful bid for Joseph Burgess's* *Workman's Times*. His attempt to become the socialist MP for Aberdeen in 1892 was supported by the *Fiery Cross* and the *Aberdeen Standard*. Other journalistic ventures included co-editing *To-Day* during 1885 with R. P. B. (Percy) Frost, founding the *Christian Socialist* with James Leigh Joynes and contributing to (and briefly editing) the *Nineteenth Century* (1888-1892). After emigrating to Australia in 1894, he continued to edit socialist journals. **DM**
Sources: Barnes 2006, *DLB*, *ODNB*, Pelling 1952-1953; *Waterloo*, Whitehead 1983.

CHAMPION, A LONDON WEEKLY JOURNAL (1813-1822) Under the editorial guidance of the Aberdonian John Scott, this was a successful and influential newspaper favouring radical causes. In his editorial debut, Scott worked at *Drakard's Paper* in London from 1813, changing the name in 1814 to the *Champion*. Replicating the arrangement of other weeklies*, with its main rival being Leigh Hunt's* *Examiner*, it focused on national and international proceedings with local* news*, significant Parliamentary* topics, law reports, financial* news, obituaries*, criminal* activity, and social events. Initially, the *Champion* published Saturday and Sunday* editions, confining advertisements* to book notices on the front and back pages.

Although John Scott astutely maintained a non-partisan position as editor*, the paper developed an integrity that reputedly made it compulsory reading for cabinet ministers. It had, for instance, protested against the 1817 suspension of *habeas corpus* in relation to the 1816 Luddite Riots; in 1820, it had supported Queen Caroline against the government's attempts to dissolve her marriage to George IV. While Scott wrote the significant portion of the political* articles*, the calibre of writers he attracted increased the paper's success. Horace Smith, Thomas Barnes*, Hazlitt*, Byron, Keats and Charles Wentworth Dilke* all appeared.

In 1816, Scott sold the paper to J. Clayton Jennings, but it was managed by John Hamilton Reynolds* for two years (1815-1817), before being bought and edited by John Thelwall in 1818. Although he had radical credentials and was a poet who had close links with Coleridge*, Wordsworth and Southey, Thelwall was unable to recreate Scott's success and circulation* fell from 1,200 in 1817 to only 500 by 1819. Despite a change* to the *Investigator,* for the last month of its existence, publication ceased in 1822. CL

Source: Sullivan.

CHAPMAN, JOHN (1821-1894) John Chapman, a publisher*, editor*, and physician, had a peripatetic beginning to his working life, selling watches in Australia in his late teens and studying medicine in Paris in his early twenties. He established himself in London in 1844, however, having purchased the business established by the Unitarian publisher and bookseller John Green. Chapman continued Green's engagements as a publisher of periodicals including Emerson's journal the *Dial* and the Unitarian *Christian Teacher** (and its later incarnation, the *Prospective Review**), but his most significant involvement with the periodical press was his purchase in 1851 of one of the leading intellectual of the day, the *Westminster Review.**

In its early years, Chapman was editor of the *Westminster* quarterlies in name only: he had persuaded Marian Evans* later 'George Eliot'* to move from Coventry to 142* The Strand, his London home, boarding house and business premises to deal with the production of each issue of the journal while he managed the finan-cial side and his book-selling business. Chapman paid his contributors well (*GEL* 2: 23), but historically, the journal had a relatively limited number of subscribers and Chapman was not always strict in maintaining separate *Westminster* and bookselling accounts, often to the detriment of the former. That said, he was extremely resourceful in ensuring the radical intellectual elite continued to finance the journal and he used his many contacts in publishing and political life to maintain high-quality articles in the *Westminster* by prominent radical and liberal thinkers including James Martineau*, Harriet Martineau*, George Combe, J. A. Froude*, Thomas Huxley*, Herbert Spencer*, G. H. Lewes* and Marian Evans. His own writings for the *Westminster* include polemical articles on medical* reform and medical advances; health issues related to prostitution and reviews* of George Eliot's early fiction. He was sympathetic to republican movements in Europe, philosophical and religious scepticism, educational and legal reform. The *Westminster* under Chapman's reign maintained its links with the spirit of its original founders by continuing to support such issues in its pages, but crucially he expanded its remit to address a broader political* and intellectual base (Ashton: 298).

The establishment of a distinct contemporary literature* section was another striking and influential innovation, as was the method of classification. Texts from England, Germany, France and America were reviewed in four separate articles implying the existence of distinct national literatures, but also, no doubt, promoting Chapman's own book importing business. These categories were realigned in January 1854 into the subject-based *Belles Lettres*; *Science; Art, etc.,* just before Marian Evans ceased her editorial work, for personal and professional reasons, having become increasingly frustrated with Chapman's business methods and editorial interference. Chapman took over as sole editor following her departure; he sold the publishing business in 1860 but continued to edit the journal until his death in Paris in 1894 where he had also been practising as a doctor. **FD**

Sources: Ashton 2006, *George Eliot Letters* 1954-1978, Haight 1969, *Poole's*, Rosenberg 1982, Rosenberg 2000.

CHAPMAN AND HALL (1830-1938) Originally set up in 1830 in London at 186 Strand by Edward Chapman (1804-1880), and William Hall, printer and publisher (1801-1847), Chapman and Hall quickly built up a reputation as one of the most respected publishing houses, investing largely but not exclusively in bookselling* during its first years. In late 1841, the firm bought the *Foreign Quarterly Review**, to which authors such as William Makepeace Thackeray* contributed. Frederic Chapman (1823-1895), Edward's cousin, joined the firm as an apprentice in 1834, becoming a full partner in 1847, following William Hall's death, and would later become the firm's chairman and chief proprietor* in 1864, after Edward's retirement. In 1852 the firm moved to 193 Piccadilly. Most notably, the company published Charles Dickens's* serials, part-issues and books, with the part-issue publication of *Pickwick Papers*, which they initiated, representing a turning point for the firm's fortunes. In 1838, Dickens was paid £1,500 for the copyright of *Nicholas Nickleby*, and in 1870 Chapman and Hall offered £7,500 for the copyright of the by then still unpublished *Mystery of Edwin Drood*. Dickens also edited* the satirical* weekly* periodical *Master Humphrey's Clock* (1840-1841) for the firm.

By the 1850s, much to the credit of their literary adviser, John Forster* (who was later replaced by George Meredith after his retirement in 1860), the firm continued to publish the works of leading authors, despite Dickens's absence after 1844, when he moved to Bradbury and Evans*. In 1858-1859 Dickens returned to Chapman and Hall, and Frederic revealed his brilliance as a publisher*. Not only did he propose agreements for new serials and various collected editions, and issued a new Dickens periodical, *All the Year Round**, but he also launched new serial fictions, and re-issued older titles and multiple collected editions in new formats.

In 1865, Frederic Chapman founded the initially bi-monthly and later monthly* *Fortnightly Review**, with Anthony Trollope*, personally enlisting George Henry Lewes* as first editor, and John Morley*, as second. Some famous contributors to the *Fortnightly* included George Eliot*, John Herschel*, and George Meredith. Besides the *Fortnightly*, the firm owned, published and/or printed, among others, the *Foreign Quarterly Review* (1841-1846), *New Monthly Magazine** (publisher 1845-1869; proprietor 1879-1884), *Ainsworth's Magazine* (publisher 1846-1854), *Bentley's Miscellany* (proprietor 1854-?1868; printer 1861-1868), the *National Review** (1856-1864), *Journal of Social Science* (1865-1866) and the *Fine Arts Quarterly Review* (1863-1867), cementing its role as a crucial contributor to the Victorian periodical press. Chapman and Hall was merged* with Methuen in 1938. SGS

Sources: DLB 106 1991, Glasgow 1998, *ODNB*, Waugh 1930, *Waterloo, Wellesley.*

CHARTIST PRESS From its inception Chartism developed an extensive and sophisticated periodical press. Taking its title and key organizing concept from the oft-reprinted *People's Charter* (first published May 1838), the nascent movement was fortunate in immediately drawing upon the support of lively regional radical newspapers, notably London's *True Sun*, the *Birmingham Journal**, the Newcastle-based *Northern Liberator**, the *Carlisle Patriot, Sheffield Iris**, the *Scots Times* and *Scotch Reformers' Gazette*. Towering over them all, however, was the *Northern Star & Leeds General Advertiser**, which achieved a mass* national distribution* by autumn 1838. The *Northern Star* was also the most enduring Chartist paper, as regional titles (*Sheffield Iris* excepted) soon shifted political* allegiance to liberalism.

However, the Chartist press was always significantly broader than the *Northern Star*. At least 125 other papers and periodicals designated themselves Chartist for some or all of their publishing history. Some were ephemeral, but most were not. Collectively, their debt to the unstamped* press was considerable. Prominent in that earlier phase of radical journalism were the Chartist pressmen John Cleave*, Joshua Hobson*, Bronterre O'Brien* and Henry Hetherington*. The latter's *London Dispatch* was an important element of continuity, especially influencing the character of the *Northern Star*. The *Star* aside, stamped newspapers were atypical of Chartist titles: this reflected that paper's dominance of the market, but also popular demand both for affordable periodicals and the reflective journalism that the unstamped*, especially Hetherington's *Poor Man's Guardian**, exemplified.

A consistent feature of the Chartist press was small periodicals launched by leading figures in the movement to help sustain their political careers and promulgate their opinions. Notable among these were *Cooper's Journal** (1850), *Democratic Review** (1849-1850) and *Red Republican**, published* by George Julian Harney*, Ernest Jones's* *Notes to the People** and Henry Vincent's *Western Vindicator**, along with journals conducted by O'Brien, William Hill* and John Watkins*. Niche titles of a different kind were the two powerful advocates for combining Chartism and temperance*: Cleave's *English Chartist Circular* (1841-1843) and the Edinburgh-based *True Scotsman* (1838-1841). However, the latter's Glasgow rival *Chartist Circular* outsold all other Chartist newspapers (excepting *Northern Star*). Its issuing body*, the Universal Suffrage Central Committee for Scotland, claimed an average circulation* of over 19,000 during its first two years. In Wales the *Western Vindicator** was the paper of choice, later supplanted by the *Advocate and Merthyr Free Press* and especially, the Welsh*-language *Udgorn Cymru* ('Trumpet of Wales').

The fortunes of the Chartist press reflected those of the broader movement, the periods of peak activity (in terms of titles in circulation) being 1839-1842 and 1848. In 1845 and 1846 there were as few as six titles, compared to a peak of 27 in 1839. The 1848 revival was not followed by a collapse comparable with that after 1842. Although sales of Chartist newspapers were a literal tithe of those achieved in 1839-1842, *Reynolds's Weekly Newspaper** (launched 1850) triumphed over the other main Chartist title, Ernest Jones's *People's Paper** (1852ff), laying the fortunes for a radical-populist paper that endured a further century.

However, *Reynolds's Political Instructor** (1849-1850) was more typical of the Chartist press which, viewed as a whole, was noticeably high-minded. It largely eschewed satire* and sensation in favour of reportage and passionate editorialising. This does not mean that the Chartist press was dour or disconnected from the broader concerns of its readers*. Book reviews* and poetry* columns* were an almost universal feature, serial* fiction appeared in several papers and the press showed considerable flair for reaching out to new readerships*. For example, *McDouall's Chartist & Republican Journal* (1841) ran a mathematics puzzle page to which readers sentin problems and solutions; the *London Dispatch** and *Northern Star* boosted sales through the presentation of engravings to regular readers; and the *Gazette of the* [London] *Working Men's Association* featured a children's corner. **MSC**
Sources: Allen and Ashton 2005, Ashton *et al.* 1995.

CHATTO AND WINDUS (1873-1969) This publishing house had its roots in a firm founded in 1855 by John Camden Hotten (1832-1873) in Piccadilly, primarily as an outlet for books of fiction and poetry. Andrew Chatto (1841-1913), who worked there from 1856, eventually as publications manager, bought the company from Hotten's widow in 1873 for £25,000, transferring Hotten's list which included A. C. Swinburne's* *Poems and Ballads* (1866) to the new firm. Later in 1873 Chatto went into partnership with William Edward Windus, thus creating Chatto and Windus.

In addition to the firm's significant innovations in book publishing – its yellowback series was a path-breaking experiment in the production of cheap editions of novels – under Chatto's direction

it made periodical publication a central plank of its business model. Over the last few decades of the nineteenth century, the firm became involved in various ways in a wide range of periodicals. Its first engagement with the periodical press began in 1876 when Chatto acquired the *Belgravia Annual** and the *Belgravia** (where Thomas Hardy's* *Return of the Native* first appeared), from Mary Elizabeth Braddon*, using them as outlets for serialized* fiction. In 1877 the *New Quarterly Magazine** was bought by Francis Hueffer* who promptly assigned the copyright to Chatto and Windus, who were to shoulder the financial risk and reap a proportion of any rewards. The magazine became more political* in emphasis and more controversial, and quality contributors from the Chatto and Windus stable – including R. L. Stevenson, Thomas Hardy* and Edmund Gosse* – raised the standard. But the firm evidently lost interest and in December 1878 all rights were transferred to Kegan, Paul & Co*. The long-established *Gentleman's Magazine** also began to be published by Chatto and Windus around this time, the first bound volume to bear the company's name being issued in 1877. The affiliation was a longstanding one, lasting into the twentieth century, with Joseph Knight (1829-1905) acting as editor throughout this period. The firm also published the *Idler** (from 1882), and Chatto quickly installed Jerome K. Jerome* and Robert Barr (1850-1912) as joint editors, with Jerome taking over as sole editor around 1895.

In the twentieth century Chatto and Windus continued as a successful publishing house, though books now made up the majority of its business. It is now an imprint of Random House. **MaT/SGS**
Sources: BritPer, Anderson 1991, *DLB*, Eliot 2000, Nash 2003, *ODNB*, Warner 1973, Weedon 2003, *Wellesley*.

CHEAP JOURNALISM The evolution of the cheap periodical – and the concomitant emergence of a working-class* reading public – is of fundamental importance to nineteenth-century culture. The first appearance of an embryonic cheap press was heavily associated with the Jacobin movement in the 1790s and the emergence of such groups as the London Corresponding Society, which circulated radical pamphlets, news-sheets and handbills to subscribers who paid a penny a week. Such organizations were quickly suppressed, and the boom in mass-circulation* cheap periodicals was held off for several years. A number of factors eventually made it impossible to resist.

First, there was a legal obstacle that needed to be circumvented in the form of the punitive 4d Stamp*

Duty on newspapers. In 1816, William Cobbett* exploited a loophole in the Stamp Act to avoid the duty, and produced an affordable 2d digest of *Cobbett's Political Register*, providing a legal template for the production of cheap journalism*. The next key development was technological, with the combined effect of John Gamble's patented paper-making machine and the rotary steam press (both coming into widespread use around 1820) significantly reducing the cost of the mass-production of periodicals. A wave of cheap publications resulted, the most successful of which was the *Mirror of Literature, Amusement and Instruction** (from1822), which provided its predominantly lower middle-class* readership* with a miscellaneous assortment of quality reading material. In the 1820s wake of this success, the *Portfolio**, *Tell-Tale*, *Legends of Horror* and many other cheap periodicals began to exploit the commercial potential of more sensational material.

In 1832, the emergence of *Chambers's Edinburgh Journal**, costing only 1 ½d, and Charles Knight's* *Penny Magazine**, represented another watershed. Rather more highminded than some of their predecessors, these publications placed instruction and improvement on a par with entertainment, and achieved huge readerships*. There is some debate over the extent to which the working class actually purchased these weeklies, but it was axiomatic to William Chambers* that his magazine 'pervade[d] the whole of society'. This should be heavily qualified, as Chambers's core constituency was probably middle class. Despite this ambiguity, the economic implications of the success of these journals for the periodical publishing industry were profound, suggesting a radically new business model based on huge circulations* and low cover prices.

Beyond the wholesome improvement offered by these titles, the cheap journalism of the 1830s provided for every taste, from the pious to the frankly coarse, from true crime to Gothic horror. Moreover, ever since *Cobbett's Political Register*, the history of cheap journalism is in various ways inseparable from that of the radical unstamped press*. Cheap journalism was almost invariably unstamped – right up to the abolition of the Stamp Duty in 1855. Furthermore, many of the publishers who produced cheap periodicals, such as William Strange*, Benjamin Steill, George Purkess and George Berger*, had radical leanings, and produced unashamedly commercial, apolitical penny weeklies* alongside radical tracts.

The repeal of the Stamp Duty in 1855 and then the Paper Duty in 1861 meant that the press was completely free of legally enforced financial restraints for the first time since the reign of Queen Anne. The daily* newspapers responded, with the 1d *Daily Telegraph** released in 1855 (and reaching a record daily circulation* of 200,000 by the 1870s), and the *Standard**, the *Daily News**, the *Pall Mall Gazette** and the *Morning Post** all following suit. The *Echo** appeared in 1868 for the price of ½d, followed 13 years later by the *Evening News**. The extension of the franchise to a large section of the urban working class in 1867 combined with the Education Act of 1870 which made elementary schooling compulsory for all helped to create an increasingly literate working-class readership, whose opinions now counted in the political arena. The trend, however, was towards a media environment that was increasingly driven by apolitical populism. Condemned by critics such as Matthew Arnold*, the New Journalism*, it was argued, fed the masses with sensational and easily digestible fare, and failed to live up to the expectations of those who had seen the repeal of the taxes on knowledge either as the first step to political emancipation, or as an encouragement to temperance and moral improvement among the lower orders. **MaT**

Sources: Altick 1998, Harrison, 1974, James 1963, *ODNB*, Wiener 1970.

CHEMICAL NEWS (1859-1932) While editing the weekly* *Photographic News* (1858-1908), William Crookes* decided to utilize information on chemical developments not relevant to photography in a complementary but independent weekly*. He purchased the copyright of William Francis's* bimonthly *Chemical Gazette* (1842-1859) and relaunched it in December 1859 as the *Chemical News: with which is incorporated the Chemical Gazette. A journal of practical chemistry in all its applications to pharmacy, arts, and manufactures*, price* 3d. Backed by a partnership between Crookes's family, the printer Spottiswoode* & Co. and the publisher* Charles Mitchell, the octavo weekly appeared on Saturdays in 12 pages of double columns* and 4 pages of advertisement. It was bound as two volumes a year with separate wrappers indexes in June and December. A 712 page index to the first hundred volumes (1859-1909) appeared in 1913. A vehicle for Crookes's prolific research, the journal contained lively editorials, reports on chemistry, pharmacy, public health and the proceedings of learned societies, lectures, patent lists, abstracts of foreign journals and readers' queries and letters. This formula remained unchanged during Crookes's lifetime.

Barely profitable initially, the price* rose to 4d in 1861 (6d in 1920) when Crookes changed partners. In 1862 Crookes bought out his partners and became owner, editor* and printer (Chemical News Press). Competition from *Laboratory**, edited by J. C. Brough*, in 1867 led to typographical* and other improvements. By 1900 Crookes was making £400 a year on sales of 10,000 copies. Crookes's former laboratory assistant, James H. Gardiner, assumed the editorship in 1919 when the journal was inherited by Walter Crookes, a solicitor. No longer a lively journal, it was edited by the science school teacher, John F. G. Druce (1924-1930). Its last editor, the egotistic fascist H. C. Blood-Ryan, brought about the journal's bankruptcy. **WB**

Sources: Brock 1992, Brock 2008, *Waterloo*.

CHILD'S COMPANION; OR SUNDAY SCHOLAR'S REWARD (1824-1932) Published by the Religious Tract Society*, an organization dedicated to embedding Christian morals within serialized* stories for young children, the *Child's Companion* was owned and edited* by George Stokes.

A monthly* publication, its text exemplifies the Evangelical revivalist tradition of improving moral stories based on scriptural text. Illustrated* with engravings of children in suitable poses, the text with its assorted tales of missionaries*, natural history and geography, and stories with the unequivocal message that it is better to be a pious child than a rich one, was a classic RTS publication. Priced* at a 1d, its 20,000 monthly circulation* by 1828 testified to rising literacy rates. By 1898, there was more emphasis on storytelling, with a large number of women contributors such as Charlotte Mason – whose work appeared in a number of religious* periodicals*, Ida Lemon, and the American poet – Ella Wheeler Wilcox. The RTS merged* with another group in 1935 soon after the *Child's Companion* ceased its impressive run. **CL**

Sources: Victorian Web, *Waterloo*.

CHILDREN'S COLUMNS In October 1876 the *Newcastle Weekly Chronicle** launched its 'Children's Corner' as the first children's column* in a nineteenth-century British newspaper. Managed by the newspaper's editor* William Edwin Adams*, the column also offered a club, the Dicky Bird Society (DBS), for children to join. There was no subscription fee, but members had to agree a pledge to be considerate towards birds. A measured take-up of children's columns by other newspapers followed, such as the *Leeds Mercury**, and by the 1890s this feature, often replete with a similar club, had become a relatively widespread aspect of other weekly* newspapers. Dundee children could join the Sunbeam Club of the *People's Journal**, young readers of the *Portsmouth Times** enrolled in the League of Love, the *Manchester Weekly Times* offered a Guild of Gentleness and the Sunday* *Weekly Times and Echo** encouraged children to join its Children's Corner. As evidence of their popularity, by 1914 the DBS had enrolled over 300,000 children. A further five clubs had membership lists exceeding six figures. The nomination by the *Newcastle Weekly Chronicle** readers of the DBS as the most popular column* in the newspaper and the enlistment of Florence Nightingale and John Ruskin* to the DBS suggest strong endorsement.

The newspaper clubs had attendant rules insisting on civil behaviour which can be regarded as an attempt to stem the moral decline thought to be sweeping the nation's youth and a reaction against the spectre of animal cruelty thought to be one of the roots of this problem. The promotion of healthy reading material and warnings against insidious literature suggest a panacea to the 'moral panic' induced by the 'penny dreadfuls'*. A more fundamental motivation was to widen circulation* and foster reader loyalty. As New Journalism* took hold, editors* included more 'family* friendly* features including 'supplements'* to reach out to new readers who were then carefully courted. Like the children's magazine press, avuncular titled editors governed these columns. The *Birmingham Weekly Post*'s 'Uncle John' assured his 'dear young friends' that he wanted to befriend his 'nieces and nephews'.

The content of the children's columns varied considerably. In 1900 the *Paddington Chronicle* relied heavily on pasted articles from magazines for its 'Readings for the Young' column in 1900 and made no effort to interact with its readers. In contrast the *Northern Weekly Gazette*'s 'Children's Circle' of the same year took up a full page with children's letters*, stories and its club. The continuation of such columns into the twentieth-century demonstrates that their popularity was not restricted to nineteenth-century journalism; indeed the DBS remained a feature of the *Newcastle Weekly Chronicle* until 1940 when wartime caused the paper to cease production. **FSM**

Sources: Allen 2005a, Allen 2007, Ashton 1991, BL Newspaper Catalogue, Dixon 1986a, Springhall 1998, *Waterloo*.

CHILDREN'S FRIEND (1824-1860; NEW SERIES 1861-1930) The *Children's Friend* was founded by the Rev. William Carus Wilson (1791-1859) as a companion to his magazines* for adults, the *Friendly Visitor* and the *Visitor's Friend*. Together, the three magazines had a circulation* of around 50,000 in 1850. Initially conducted entirely by Wilson, the *Children's Friend*, a 1d monthly, was published in Westmoreland. It was about 24 pages in length and featured a couple of engravings and woodcuts* for visual stimulation. Designed for evangelical young Anglicans, or their well-meaning parents, and featuring sermons, poems*, epitaphs, missionary* stories, hymns, and prayers, the magazine was a competitor of the Religious Tract Society's* *Child's Companion*. In the first series of the *Children's Friend* there was a heavy emphasis on death, a stress on the rewards of the afterlife over pleasures in this life, and the promotion of missionary activity. Wilson had been the inspiration for Rev. Brocklehurst in Jane Eyre.

Wilson died in 1859, and there is some debate as to whether the magazine was briefly continued by Wilson's brother Charles. A new series began in 1861 under the London publisher* S. W. Partridge & Co., known for religious* fiction and magazines. Shorter in length at about 16 pages per issue, it featured a range of contributors. Although it was still religious in content, it had more games, puzzles and other fun elements missing from the original, probably a necessity in the wider market of children's* magazines by that time. **TD**
Sources: Altholz 1989, Carpenter 1984, Drotner 1988, Egoff 1951, *Waterloo*.

CHILDREN'S OWN PAPER (1882-1891; 1893-1895) The *Children's Own Paper* was launched as a 16-page weekly* magazine* costing 1d to support the Band of Kindness Children's Society. This institution was first established by the journalist* Frank Fearneley, known to his readers as 'Uncle George', as a children's column* to foster positive animal welfare in the *Stockport Advertiser* in January 1882. Divorcing the Band of Kindness from the *Advertiser* was acrimonious and was never fully resolved. Several children reported that 'Uncle George' had circulated to them details of the *Children's Own Paper*, leading the *Advertiser* to insist that 'Uncle George' remained firmly affiliated to them. Fearneley retorted that the *Advertiser* limited the ambitions he held for the Band of Kindness and his new *Children's Own Paper* was now the Society's official publication. The style of advertisements* in the *Paper* suggest's it targeted middle class children, although an analysis of Band of Kindness members demonstrates it was generally working class children who supported the Society. The magazine offered a mixture of stories, competitions, and printed children's letters* that

meditated predominantly on humanitarianism. Readers were encouraged to feed the birds and bird nesting was condemned. The Band's business was publicized including meetings and membership lists.

In 1883 Fearneley left Stockport, and the editorship* of the *Children's Own Paper* was taken over by the philanthropist Gilbert Kirlew. The tone of articles increasingly became more evangelical and shifted towards Kirlew's primary concern, charitable childcare. He urged readers to form 'Advance Guards' to distribute the *Paper*, but also severely criticised those who were 'sham' and did not help out. The *Paper* was limited to circulation* in the northwest of England, and suffering financial losses it changed to a monthly* issue in 1890, when Kirlew's sister Marianne, was in control. Complete financial collapse in 1891 led the *Children's Own Paper* to be transferred to the *Christian Worker* magazine. Although it was revived briefly (1893-1895) a final collapse resulted from the fallout of an unfounded accusation of paedophilia against Kirlew by *Spy* magazine in 1895. **FSM**
Sources: Kirlew 1908, Mohr 1991, Mohr 1992.

CHILTON, WILLIAM (1815-1855) A staunch atheist from Bristol where he worked as a longstanding compositor and proofreader for the *Bristol Mercury*, Chilton joined forces with the similarly forthright Charles Southwell* in 1841 to form the provocatively irreligious and crude penny weekly* the *Oracle of Reason*, for which Chilton acted as printer and subeditor*. When, after the fourth number, Southwell was gaoled for blasphemy, Chilton decided he was more valuable in the actual production of the journal and asked George Jacob Holyoake* to become the new editor*, although he finally took on the role himself in June 1843 following the arrest of Holyoake and then his successor Thomas Paterson, under whom the circulation* had fallen sharply from a peak of 4,000 copies a week. Chilton was unable to halt the *Oracle of Reason's* decline and the debt-ridden paper closed later in 1843. In 1844 Chilton joined Holyoake's more moderate replacement 'the *Movement*' and two years later helped manage Holyoake's new venture the *Reasoner*. Chilton's own journalism for such freethought* periodicals was distinctive for employing materialistic and evolutionary science*, often gleaned from *Chambers's Information for the People*, in the cause of popular secularism*. **GD**
Sources: Desmond 1987, *ODNB*, Royle 1974.

CHORLEY, HENRY FOTHERGILL (1808-1872) Starting his working life as a clerk in Liverpool, Chorley was to become one of the most prolific general reviewers* of the nineteenth century as well as one of the most influential and flamboyant

music* critics of his time. Inspired by the work of E. T. A. Hoffman, and encouraged in his musical observations by the conductor James Z. Herrmann and by Felicia Hemans whom he knew (he published the two-volume *Memorials of Mrs Hemans* in 1836), he began to work for the *Athenaeum** in 1833, having already contributed a few pieces. He was to remain on the staff until 1868 having reviewed around 2,500 books. However, he is most notable for his conservative weekly* columns* on musical performances and backstage life in the *Athenaeum, All the Year Round** and the *Orchestra*, in which he celebrated the commercially successful Rossini, Mendelssohn, Meyerbeer and Gounod (*Faust* was first performed in England in his translation), as well as Arthur Sullivan late in his life. He disliked Verdi and execrated what he saw as the decadent Schumann and Wagner. In 1851 he edited* the *Ladies' Companion** with indifferent success. **BZ**
Sources: Bledsoe 1988, Chorley 1873, Grove, *ODNB*.

CHORLEY, JOHN RUTTER (1806-1867) Best remembered as a scholar of Spanish literature and as a collector of Spanish plays, John Rutter Chorley was also a prolific reviewer* of foreign publications. His reticent, unsocial disposition and financial independence, however, prevented him from seeking either a reputation or a large audience for his work. He thus remained a 'gentleman amateur' whose (largely anonymous*) articles were never collected and republished.

Until becoming the beneficiary of a bequest in 1845, Chorley worked for the Liverpool-Birmingham Grand Junction Railway. From 1832-1846 he wrote primarily for *Tait's Edinburgh Magazine**, reviewing German, Italian, English, French and Spanish literature (29 contributions attributed). From 1834 onwards he also wrote occasionally for the *Athenaeum**, where he became principal reviewer of German, Italian and Spanish publications (1846-1854). By the late 1840s Chorley counted as an authority on Spanish Golden Age drama. He was keen to assert his independence when reviewing authors who did not bring his own Romantic sensitivity to Spanish texts. Although he had assisted the American scholar George Ticknor in writing his *History of Spanish Literature*, he reviewed it critically in the *Athenaeum* (2 March 1850). His censorious treatment of Edward FitzGerald's 'free' translations of Spanish playwright Caldéron – he gave FitzGerald merely 18 lines among the briefer notices (*Athenaeum* 10 Sept. 1853) – allegedly discouraged FitzGerald from republishing his work. Chor-

ley's 'Notes on the national drama of Spain', published in four instalments in *Fraser's Magazine** (May-Oct. 1859), is regarded as his most important work of criticism. His friend Thomas Carlyle* regretted that Chorley, who had 'proudly pitched his ideal very high', never produced a book on Spanish literature.

Unlike his younger brother, the music critic Henry Fothergill Chorley*, John Chorley was not a society figure. Had he been more ambitious or better connected he might have published more than his 1865 volume of poetry. By the time of his death, the attitude of the private, disinterested gentleman-scholar which he exemplified had started to appear somewhat old-fashioned. **MdW**
Sources: Marchand 1941, Metford 1948, *ODNB, Wellesley.*

CHRISTIAN EXAMINER AND CHURCH OF IRELAND MAGAZINE (1825-1869) The *Christian Examiner* was founded by Caesar Otway* and Joseph Henderson Singer, two clerics in the Church of Ireland. The journal's aim was to support the evangelical movement in the Church against, according to the Preface in the 1826 volume, 'her incessantly active enemies [and] to advocate the cause of Protestantism against the Roman Catholic, and of Christianity against the Infidel; and to seek to raise to the Gospel level the standard of Christian morals'. Published monthly in Dublin, the single column*, 70-page magazine cost 1s 6d per issue and had a circulation* of about 1,000 copies per month in 1850. Despite its rather forbidding mandate, the *Christian Examiner* did include literary reviews* and poetry*, 'Foreign Religious* Intelligence' and letters from correspondents* at home and abroad. From 1828 the *Christian Examiner* is also responsible for first publishing the work of William Carleton*, a recent convert to Protestantism apparently encouraged by Otway. When Otway ceased editing the journal in 1831, its anti-Catholic stance became more pronounced. Singer went on to become Bishop of Meath and Regius Professor of Divinity at Trinity College and Otway was one of the founders of the *Dublin University Magazine** in 1833. **ET**
Sources: Hayley 1985, *PGIL-Eirdata*, Rafroidi 1980.

CHRISTIAN GLOBE (1874-1918) The *Christian Globe* was founded as the *Christian Glowworm*, a non-denominational 1d monthly newspaper. Its title changed in the *Christian Globe* three months later (Jan. 1875) when it became the property of a limited liability company. Almost 200 investors, including shop assistants and labourers, bought shares in the business. Weekly* publication was established (Oct. 1875) and the paper soon claimed a circulation* approaching 100,000. The *Christian Globe's* founder and first editor* was James Allingham, brother of John Allingham (the children's writer 'Ralph Rollington'*) and father of Herbert Allingham (*London Journal* editor* and writer of mass-market fiction). The paper retained a close commercial connection to the Allingham family and its foundation was later fictionalized by Allingham's granddaughter Margery. Early editions of the paper made use of the techniques of New Journalism* and were technically innovative. Its early success was boosted by public enthusiasm for evangelists such as Dwight Moody and Charles Spurgeon. Celebrity* preacher portraits and weekly sermons by the American T. DeWitt Talmadge were key selling points. Entertainment, not exhortation, was central to the paper's appeal and it devoted large amounts of space to serial* fiction as well as to secular advertising*. When Allingham stood down as editor to found an advertising agency in the early 1880s, the *Christian Globe* began its steady decline. **JJ**

Sources: Allingham Archive, Allingham 1943, Aspden 1930, Jones 2006, National Archives.

CHRISTIAN GUARDIAN AND CHURCH OF ENGLAND MAGAZINE (1802-1852) The *Christian Guardian and Church of England Magazine* began life in 1798 as *Zion's Trumpet; or the penny spiritual magazine*. Started by Thomas T. Biddulph, an English clergyman, the publication became the *Christian Guardian, a theological miscellany* in 1802. In 1809, *Church of England Magazine* was added to the title, until the final two years of the magazine when it was renamed the *Christian Guardian and Churchman's Magazine*. Priced* 6d and published monthly* (1809-1821), the magazine enjoyed considerable success, with a circulation* that varied between 2,000 and 5,500. A quarterly supplement* was available (May 1819-Feb. 1830) at 1s each. In 1809 it declared itself to be 'a cheap* and popular magazine devoted to the cause of vital religion*, as professed and established in the Church of England'. Alarmed by the emergence of the Tractarian Movement, it steadily affirmed and promoted what it held to be the Church of England's position. While the introduction to the 1851 volume acknowledged that the influence of the Tractarians appeared to be in decline, concern continued to be expressed: 'The *Christian Guardian* must, therefore, more than ev-

er, be on the alert to expose, with holy faithfulness, the absurdities and errors of Rome, in its doctrine and ritual'. **CL**

Sources: *Christian Guardian* (1851), Lowndes 1842, *Waterloo*.

CHRISTIAN LADY'S MAGAZINE (1834-1849) *Christian Lady's Magazine* (1834-1849) was edited* by Charlotte Elizabeth Tonna* until her death in 1846. The editor* thereafter is unknown, but without Tonna's crusading energy, the monthly* lost its vigour and folded in 1849. The magazine set out to be 'solidly instructive' and its ideal reader was the 'active, intelligent, useful Christian woman'. It provided a diet of poetry*, letters*, reviews*, tales from Scripture, theological essays and prayers* – mostly unsigned, though much written by Tonna. But its journalistic importance lies in its encouragement of women to adopt a campaigning stance toward causes informed by Tonna's ardent pre-Millenarian Tory evangelicalism* (and that of the magazine's publisher*, R. B. Seeley). The magazine was anti-slavery, virulently anti-Catholic (but not anti-Irish) anti-Chartist* and in favour of factory reform. In the monthly department, 'The Protestant', Tonna used a dialogue between the fictional characters of Uncle and Niece to reassure her evangelical upper and middle-class* female readership* that political* activism (using their influence with their menfolk at elections; petitioning Parliament) was not only compatible with St Paul's teachings on female subordination but also had divine sanction. Serialized* in the magazine from 1839-1841, Tonna's propagandist novel 'Helen Fleetwood', was based on parliamentary* reportage and written in support of a Ten Hours Factory Bill. **ED**

Sources: Altholz 1989, Beetham 1996, Dzelzainis 2003, *ODNB*, *Wellesley*

CHRISTIAN MOTHERS' MAGAZINE (1844-1857) Initially, the articles in the 1/s monthly *Christian Mothers' Magazine* were almost all the sole effort of its founder and editor*, Mary Milner*. The lengthy content, all unsigned*, mirrored her considerable scholarly interest and achievements in history*, theology, natural history and children's education. Milner emphasised her intention for a 'FAMILY* MAGAZINE'* (sic) 'to interest, instruct, attract and amuse' a variety of readers within a 'decidedly religious'* context. It continued in its original format* with no illustrations, and no advertisements*, until 1846 when Milner announced that to abandon the exclusivity of the previous title and increase circulation* with an appeal to a broader readership*, the new series would be entitled, the

Englishwoman's Magazine and Christian Mother's Miscellany. This formula had wider appeal: it was less academic in tone, engravings were introduced with considerably more poetry*, serialized* fiction, short stories* and book reviews*. It began to feature serials: of ecclesiastical buildings; 'Reflections on the art of writing'; 'Biographical Sketches of Celebrated Women', including Hannah More and Elizabeth Fry; and 'The Influence of English Women on English Literature' by Mrs Riley. By the end of 1846, Milner was able to inform her readers that the changes had succeeded.

In 1855 she reverted to a compromise in the format* of the *Christian Lady's Magazine*, the run's last title* change: bound in green covers, it featured contents on the inner front cover, advertisements on inner and outer back cover, more reviews, correspondence and named contributors, while closer in style to the first series. There were occasional articles about women such as 'A Word in Behalf of the Assistants in Dressmaking and Millinery Establishments' supporting the Early Closing Association (March 1857), but in the main it was a return to a more traditional tone. Despite a reduced price* of 6d, the last number of June 1857 carried a closing message from the final publisher (there had been eight others), Partridge and Co., London, intimating that it was the editor's 'great distance from London' (she had lived in Westmoreland all her married life) that had contributed to the *Magazine's* failure, despite her, 'zeal, ability, and perseverance'. **CL**

Sources: *Christian Lady's Magazine, Christian Mothers' Magazine, Englishwoman's Magazine, Waterloo.*

CHRISTIAN OBSERVER (1802-1877) Launched by members of the Clapham Sect, who saw the value of a distinctly Anglican evangelical voice in the rapidly developing world of journalism*, the *Christian Observer* quickly became one of the most important evangelical* periodicals of the nineteenth century. Published monthly*, initially for 6s and edited by Zachary Macaulay (1802-1816), the *Christian Observer* established a good reputation in evangelical circles. The content of the periodical was clearly evangelical but it was also quite moderate and wide-ranging, including, among other things, religious communication, literary, philosophical and scientific* intelligence, a view of public affairs, and obituaries*. In line with its evangelical constituency, the *Christian Observer* was initially suspicious about literature* in general and the novel in particular, but these suspicions decreased as the century went on. Early contributors to the *Chris-*

tian Observer included Hannah More*, William Wilberforce and John Henry Newman, and the editors that followed Macaulay included Samuel Charles Wilks, William Goode, John William Cunningham and John Buxton Marsden. Having enjoyed a long life as an influential evangelical monthly, the *Christian Observer* became the *Christian Observer and Advocate* in 1875 before ceasing publication entirely. **MK**

Sources: Pickering 1976, Sullivan, *Waterloo.*

CHRISTIAN REFORMER (1815-1863) The *Christian Reformer* was a Unitarian review, originally intended by its editor* and chief contributor, Robert Aspland (1782-1845), to be a cheaper and more accessible alternative to the *Monthly Repository*, the main Unitarian publication at that time, which Aspland had begun. In the first number Aspland proclaimed the *Reformer's* purpose as 'diffusing religious* knowledge, promoting scriptural enquiries, and exciting serious reflection particularly among that class of readers* whom more bulky, laboured and expensive works are not likely to reach'. It was characterised by its tolerant editorial stance, a focus on biography and history*, and its scholarly interest in scripture and biblical criticism. A number of external factors affected the *Reformer* through its 18-year history. In 1834, the subtitle was changed from *New Evangelical Miscellany* to *Unitarian Magazine and Review*, part of Aspland's successful repositioning of the periodical as the main organ of Unitarian thought in the wake of the *Repository's* drift away from Unitarianism. Following the death of Aspland in 1845, the periodical was edited by his son Robert Brook Aspland (1805-1869). Publication finally ceased for financial reasons. **MB**

Sources: Altholz 1989, McLachlan 1934, *ODNB.*

CHRISTIAN REMEMBRANCER (1819-1868) Issued* by the Hackney Phalanx, a group of High Church activists, the *Christian Remembrancer* served as the publication of this element within the Church of England. In the 1840s it reinvigorated itself to replace the *British Critic*, which was suppressed for its perceived Romish tendencies. The *Christian Remembrancer* espoused more orthodox and conservative views than its predecessor but continued to welcome contributors associated with the Oxford Movement such as John Henry Newman (1801-1890), J. B. Mozly*, the co-editor* and his sister Anne Mozley*. High Church clergymen were the target audience* of the publication. A section entitled 'Ecclesiastical Intelligence' listed ordinations, preferments and degrees awarded. In 1844 the monthly* became a quarterly* and longer articles gradually subsumed the reports and notices. During its middle to later years it acquired a literary* flavour and its leaders* often tussled with a religious* issue thrown up by recent publications. In its final decade its religiosity seemed muted. This may have been the review's downfall, as its popular successor, the *Church Quarterly Review** (from 1875), proclaimed its High Church allegiance more loudly. For many, though, the *Christian Remembrancer* served as a representative of the conservative High Church in times of religious turbulence. BP

Sources: Altholz, 1989, Ellegård 1971, *ODNB, Waterloo.*

CHRISTIAN TEACHER (1835-1844); CHRISTIAN TEACHER, OR, PROSPECTIVE REVIEW, A QUARTERLY JOURNAL OF THEOLOGY AND LITERATURE (1845-1855) Founded and edited* by John Relly Beard, minister and educational reformer, the *Christian Teacher* was intended to be a practical and devotional religious* paper, stating the principles of Unitarian faith. John Hamilton Thom* followed Beard, editing the *Christian Teacher* from 1838, with other Unitarian ministers (James Martineau*, Charles Wicksteed, and John James Tayler*) contributing. Thom's envisaged the *Christian Teacher* as a Unitarian vehicle but also as a 'produce of a spiritual union among the civilized portion of mankind'. This ecumenical ambition did not find favour among the Unitarian audience and circulation* fell.

Faced with a decline in the journal's popularity, Thom and his team decided to launch a new version: *Christian Teacher, or, Prospective Review.* Their hope was that the relaunched journal 'would be conducted in the confidence that only the free mind, not in bondage to the letter, can receive the living Spirit of Revelation'. The plan was for the new version of the journal, still priced* at 2s 6d, to be published in February, May, August and November, cleverly interleaved between the publication dates of the other 'great Quarterlies'*. This came at the dawn of a tradition of liberal Unitarian journals that engaged with a range of ideas, including politics* at home and abroad, theology, the arts, history*, natural science, sociology and philology. With no payment made for articles, only production costs had to be covered, but even so, there were often financial difficulties, as the periodical's appeal was not clear to its target readership*. Nevertheless, the journal gained respect for its integrity and regular readers included Marian Evans* and her circle.

Over the years, the demands of their vocations meant that the management team had less time for the *Prospective* and in 1852 William Caldwell Roscoe* came in as assistant editor. By June 1854 Wicksteed, Tayler and Thom had departed. A younger team took over and tried to enlarge the *Prospective's* appeal, but in February 1855 its closure was announced. CL

Sources: *ODNB, Wellesley.*

CHRISTIAN WITNESS (1834-1841) The *Christian Witness*, a quarterly*, was one of several religious* journals established c 1830 by evangelicals interested in biblical prophecy, and it was the first periodical to be associated with the (Plymouth) Brethren. The initial proposal may have come from a leader at Plymouth, Benjamin Wills Newton (1807-1899), and the preface to Vol. 1 stated that it was intended as a witness to biblical teaching concerning the church. After the first issues, another leader, the former clergyman John Nelson Darby (1801-1882), urged that it should focus more clearly on Christ's Second Coming. It was edited* by two further ex-clergymen, Henry Borlase (1806-1835) of St Keyne, Cornwall (possibly only a nominal appointment, in view of his serious illness from early 1834), and James Lampen Harris (1793-1870) of Plymstock.

The content comprised biblical expositions, especially on topics relating to church order and prophetic belief, introductions to like-minded groups overseas, analyses of the errors of existing churches and warnings against other new religious movements. Contributions were anonymous*, but copies in several archives have been annotated with contributors' initials. Publication ceased suddenly after January 1841; no explanation was offered, but it was probably a casualty of tension between Newton and Darby. TG

Sources: Altholz 1989, Coad 1976, Grass 2006, Rowdon 1967.

CHRISTIAN WORKER AND CRY OF THE CHILDREN (1882-1895) The *Christian Worker* started life as the *Worker* (1879-1881). As the *Christian Worker and Cry of the Children*, it was variously subtitled, *a monthly record of loving labour amongst the lost little ones* and, from 1893 to 1895, *organ of the Boys' and Girls' Refuges and Homes.* Published monthly* and priced* at 1d, the paper was issued by the Manchester and Salford Boys' and Girls' Refuges and Homes, founded in 1870 by Leonard K. Shaw and Richard Taylor. Sunday School teachers at St Ann's Church in Manchester, Shaw and Taylor were determined to alleviate the shocking destitution of the children and young people they saw living rough on the city's streets. Shaw was an evangelical and businessman and worked with the ragged schools movement before opening the Refuges. He edited* the paper from 1884 until 1895. CL

Sources: Together Trust online, *Waterloo*.

CHRISTIAN WORLD (1857-1961) The *Christian World* was the most successful of the new type of religious* weekly* newspaper which profited from the abolition of the taxes on knowledge* and an increased public appetite for respectable entertainment within Nonconformist family* life. Many similar papers were attempted (1860-1890) but the enduring prosperity of the *Christian World* was due to the journalistic skill and business acumen of its first editor*, and later, proprietor*, publisher* and printer James Clarke. Clarke conceived a paper that would be 'wholly unsectarian but decidedly evangelical'. He broke with the tradition of the denominational monthly* magazine and created a 1d newspaper with as wide an appeal as possible. For many years the *Christian World* claimed that its circulation* exceeded that of all its rivals together. Advertising* revenue was also substantial. Once the core business was established, Clarke used the talents of evangelical journalists such as Emma Jane Worboise (1825-1887) and Marianne Hearn* (1834-1909) to develop other forms of religious entertainment including the *Literary World, Family Circle, Christian World Magazine, Christian World Pulpit, Rosebud, Sunday School Times* and the *English Independent*, as well as books and annuals*. One of Fleet Street's* most dynamic advertising agents*, Henry Sell, started his career with the *Christian World* and wrote of the 'almost personal influence' such papers exerted on their readers*. JJ

Sources: Billington 1986, Grant 1872, Sell 1886.

CHRISTMAS ISSUES Special issues of established periodicals, published during the Christmas period and exploring themes appropriate to the season, can be seen as a development of the Annuals*, fashionable giftbooks, 'Books of Beauty', 'Keepsakes' and so forth that were a regular end-of-year phenomenon by the late 1820s. Individual authors such as Charles Dickens* and W. M. Thackeray*, together with their publishers, were later inspired to publish short, fanciful books at Christmas-time during the so-called Hungry Forties, in which decade the Christmas issues of *Punch** were also popular, such as that in which Thomas Hood's* famous poem 'Song of the Shirt' was first published (16 Dec. 1843).

It was Dickens, however, who most successfully combined these formats of publication and fictional themes as a regular feature of an established periodical. He dubbed the issue of *Household Words** for 21 December 1850 'The Christmas Number', having commissioned a range of popular authors to describe how the festival was kept in different parts of the world (India, the Arctic, Australia) and among different groups of people (the London poor, people in lodgings, in the Navy). The leader* was Dickens's own familiar, largely autobiographical, essay 'A Christmas Tree'. By 1851, the issue had become a 24-page 2d 'Extra Number for Christmas', published separately from the weekly* magazine, and carefully planned since the Autumn: 'something with no detail in it but a tender fancy that shall hit a great many people' was how Dickens described what he was aiming for (To W. H. Wills*, 8 Dec. 1851). Circulation* for the 36-page Christmas issues (1852-1858) suggest he was eminently successful in this ambition, taking the weekly magazine sale of c.40,000 up to and over 100,000 and the bi-annual receipts for the journal show a pattern of surges in the spring, owing largely to the popularity of this innovation.

When *Household Words* merged* into *All the Year Round**, Dickens continued the tradition, increasing the issue to 48 pages, and extending the scope of the subject matter although each issue still had a basic narrative scenario or framework from which individual tales were launched. While the number of contributors and collaborators could be as many as 10 in an individual issue, Dickens's hand is detectable throughout; his most frequent collaborator was Wilkie Collins*. New Year letters through the 1860s celebrate still greater sales figures of 191,000 (1862), 220,000 (1863), 250,000 (1865), 265,000 (1866), and finally reaching to nearly 300,000 with 'No Thoroughfare' in 1867.

Numerous other publications across the spectrum, from the *Gentleman's Magazine** to the *Norwood Post*, had by this time flooded the market with similar offerings, and the novelty was wearing thin. In the 'Extra Double Christmas Number' of *Chambers's Journal** (Dec. 1865), the editor, Leitch Ritchie, professed himself to be wearying of the task. Dickens too felt that this form of collaborative authorship was getting too labour intensive, and when set against the profits to be made from syndicating* a single short story by a celebrity author (notably himself), the return on a sale of even 300,000 was no longer attractive. 'No Thoroughfare' was his last Christmas issue, but the practice of course, however time-worn, has continued down to the present time, with *Punch* commenting satirically on the phenomenon* in articles titled 'A Notion of a Christmas Number' (Vol. 56, 1869), 'A Christmas Number à la Mode' (Vol. 68, 1875), 'A Really New Christmas Number' (Vol. 73, 1877), 'How To Write a Cheap Christmas Number' (Vol. 105, 1893) and 'The Christmas Number Producer's *Vade Mecum*' (Vol. 109, 1895). JMD

Sources: Anon. 1865, Drew 2003, Forster 1872-1874, Patten 1978, Storey 1988, Thomas 1982.

CHURCH OF ENGLAND QUARTERLY REVIEW (1837-1858) The *Church of England Quarterly Review; a journal of theology, art, science* and literature* for the United Church of England and Ireland* was first launched and published* by William Pickering*. It was an example of a remarkable flowering of religious* periodical literature in the first half of the nineteenth century. The 1830s represented a particularly turbulent and competitive decade for religious activity. Theological polarization within the Church of England was symbolized by the rival periodical extremes represented by the ultra-High Church and (after 1838) the Tractarian *British Critic and Quarterly Theological Review* on the one hand, and by the extreme Evangelical *Record* on the other.

The *Church of England Quarterly Review* represented a moderate high church editorial line and readership* at its inception, albeit inclining more towards the *British Critic* than its polar opposite rival. In the first number of 310 pages, the editor* declared that it would fight the 'triple alliance of infidelity, liberalism, and papistry' on old High Church principles. After complaints that in its increasingly strident opposition to Tractarianism, the *Church of England Quarterly Review* was losing its High Church character, the journal was re-established in 1840 under the editorship of Henry Christmas (1811-1868), who had two stints as editor* of the journal, 1840-1843 and 1854-1858 (*ODNB*). Under his editorship, the journal re-established its orthodox High Church credentials but still followed a moderate line between the extremes of Tractarianism and hardline anti-Tractarianism represented by ultra-evangelicals.

Between 1840 and 1843 Christmas simultaneously edited the *Churchman: a monthly magazine in defence of the venerable church and constitution of England*, a sister journal to the *Review*, and similarly from the list of its most consistent publisher (W. E.

Painter, 1839 to 1853), the *British Churchman* (1846-1848). In 1841 the monthly *Churchman* and the *Church of England Quarterly Review* cost respectively 1s and 6s per issue. Christmas can be credited with coining the label 'Evangelical High Churchmanship', the term used to characterize the *Review*'s adherence to the loyal, mainstream Anglicanism represented by the *Book of Common Prayer*, the Thirty-Nine Articles, Richard Hooker, the Caroline Divines and later pre-Tractarian high churchmanship. PN

Sources: Altholz 1989, Nockles 1994, *ODNB*.

CHURCH TIMES (1863-) The *Church Times* began life in February 1863 as a weekly* newspaper for the Church of England. Its founder and initial editor* was George Josiah Palmer (1828-1892), who used the paper to promote the cause of the Anglo-Catholic wing of the Church of England. Palmer remained editor until 1887, when the paper was taken over by his sons.

Initially offering eight pages for a 1d, the success of the *Church Times* forced its chief rival, the *Guardian,* to reduce its price from 6d to 3d. The number of pages in the *Church Times* steadily increased: in 1879 the average size of the paper was 12 pages and by 1895 each issue ran to 32-40 pages. Content included a summary of secular and ecclesiastical news*, foreign* news, notes on art and literature, and leading* articles. Net sales in 1863 averaged 3,976 copies a week; by 1867 circulation* had increased to 10,382; and by 1886 sales had risen to 24,153 copies a week. When two of Palmer's sons retired in 1914 and sold their shares to the other brother, Fred, the circulation was at 64,559 copies a week. MJK

Source: Palmer 1991.

CIGAR AND TOBACCO WORLD (1889-1953); CONFECTIONARY AND TOBACCO NEWS; TOBACCO WORLD (1953-1961) INCORP. INTO CONFECTIONERY AND TOBACCO NEWS (1962-1970); CTN (1970-1999) Initially published by T. C. Aylett, *Cigar and Tobacco World* was a 6d monthly* trade journal* aimed at tobacconists, offering relevant national and international news* such as accounts of regional tobacconists association meetings, reports of strikes amongst dockers and cigarette-makers, how to deal with rivalry from grocers, the state of the economy and its effect on sales. It was a relentlessly good-humoured illustrated* 6d monthly, with anonymous or pseudonymous* contributors – a format* and tone Heywood & Co maintained when they took it over in 1893. When the quantity of advertising* allowed (1900), subscription came down to one shilling a year while the size* and number of pages expanded. In addition to linking tobacconists and confirming their professional* identity, much of the periodical seems intended to improve sales: many of the full-page illustrations* are suitable for display in shops; many verbal items would have been useful for sales patter. An important feature comprised advertisements for jobs in the tobacco trade.

The journal kicked off with a respectable circulation* of over 5,000 nationally and colonially and aggressively maintained its market dominance: it incorporated a new rival (the *Tobacconist*) after only a few months of the latter's existence in 1891 and while from 1896 it competed with a variety of *Cigarette* magazines, all were short-lived. *Tobacco** and the *Tobacco Trade Review** do not seem to be rivals to *Cigar and Tobacco World* as they aimed at a different audience. Of interest to social historians will be the many ways tobacco and its sales techniques were tied into conceptions of gender* and empire*.
AK

Sources: *Cigar and Tobacco World* 1889-1910, *Mitchell's*.

CIRCULAR TO BANKERS (1828-1860) Henry Burgess began his signed *Circular to Bankers* on Friday 25 July 1828 'to diffuse information respecting the general state of the banking interest; to give extracts from acts of parliament and parliamentary proceedings; and to provide a general record to all public matters touching the concern of Bankers'. He charged six guineas per annum, but subscribers did not pay merely for a weekly* eight pages of highly personal if formally expressed views, but 'use of a room at 81 Lombard St [the *Circular*'s office] where they can conduct business out of the ordinary routine of their affairs, and where they may obtain verbal information that may affect the private or the public interest of Bankers'. Unlike many financial* writers, Burgess was opposed to free trade (though allied to no political party). He paid special attention to relaying banking laws. Only the last page had a table – of the English and Foreign Stock market – and thus the *Circular* did not compete with the prices published by stockbrokers such as Atkinson's (1824-1829) or James Wetenhall's bi-weekly *Course of the Exchange* (1803-1908). Nor did Burgess report vulgar matters available elsewhere such as *Perry's Bankrupt and Insolvent Weekly Gazette* (1828-1881).

The formula changed little until 1850 when the paper was bought by Henry Ayres, who added the subtitle *and Gazette of Banking, Agriculture, Commerce and Finance*, printed it on 16 pages of pale blue paper* and added many more tables and short articles, providing a more extensive view of finances and commerce internationally as well as nationally. Regular departments now included produce markets, the money market and commercial intelligence, and a commercial summary. The tone was now far more impersonal and 'professional'*, although Ares was, a cautious free-trade supporter, also repeatedly sought to prick the consciences of his readers* by reminding them of the continued existence of poverty. In 1857 the paper was retitled the *Bankers' Circular*, Gazette of Commerce and Finance and Journal of Political Economy* and on 16 January the following year, in a bid to expand the readership*, the paper became the biweekly *Monetary Times and Bankers' Circular or Chronicle of British and Foreign Finance, Funds, Banks, Railways and Commerce*, although the format* and content otherwise changed little. A year later the paper was bought by H. Brooks, who altered the order of the title to *Bankers' Circular and Monetary Times*. Now very much in support of free trade, the management of the paper laboured under difficulties 'over which [they] have no control'. Its last issue is dated 24 March 1860. **AK**

Sources: *Mitchell's*, Moss 1992, Moss and Hosgood 1994.

CIRCULATING LIBRARIES Circulating libraries, which rented books to readers* for a subscription, first appeared in England in the seventeenth century. But it was not until the nineteenth century that they became indispensable institutions serving as arbiters of national taste and centres of social life. At first they were generally additional businesses for booksellers who loaned books for a fee to those who could not afford them outright, increasing access, as literature* had long been a luxury almost exclusively for the wealthy. Under these conditions circulating libraries, where by one estimate a person could read 26 novels a year for slightly more than it would cost to buy just one, began to flourish. By 1801 there were approximately 1,000 circulating libraries in England. The largest on record, John Lane's* of London, had 20,000 volumes; small country libraries, themselves subscribers to larger libraries, might have as few as 200.

The best known of these libraries was Charles Edward Mudie's famous Mudie's Select Library, opened in 1842 in Bloomsbury, London. Ten years later he moved to larger premises in New Oxford Street. Refusing to stock what he considered immoral books, and charging only a guinea a year for subscription, Mudie offered readers lists of 'the principal New and Choice Books in circulation', with which he assured his customers of the quality of his selections. These became so influential that the popularity of, among others, George Eliot*, Thomas Hardy* and Henry James* has been ascribed to him. The rival to Mudie's was W.H. Smith's*, operating from the Strand and astutely, from his hundreds of railway bookstalls throughout the country. Although the Mudie archive* has not survived, the range of titles which included periodicals, and the ubiquity of its presence may still be seen in the regular adverts* for its lists in the weekly* and monthly press.

Eventually Mudie's declined; cheap single-volume reprints began to be available to buyers within weeks of the library's purchase of three-volume ('three-decker') publications of the same works. Mudie's finally closed in 1937 having also seen the demise of many other circulating libraries, the increase in free public libraries, chain-store lending libraries such as Boots' Booklovers' Library which opened in 1900 and more inexpensive editions of new novels. But demand for these would doubtless never have increased if not for the circulating libraries' encouragement of reading in the first place, and Mudie's introduction of some of the best Victorian literature to a whole new populations of readers. FCA

Sources: Altick 1957, Clark 2005, Erickson 1990, Griest 1965, Landow 1972.

CIRCULATION Although revenue from advertising* was crucial to the economics of periodical publication for most of the nineteenth century, reliable statistics concerning the circulation of individual journals are hard to come by. This is unfortunate since surges, slumps and fluctuations in sales can reveal a good deal about the general impact of formal innovations such as the introduction of illustration*, and the popularity of specific content like a new serial novel*. On the other hand, fascinating qualitative information concerning readership* can often still be gleaned from material in the journals themselves, whether editorial (e.g. correspondence* from subscribers) or advertising* (e.g. the targeting of gender* or social class*).

Between 1836 and 1855, each registered newspaper in Britain had to bear a distinctive stamp, and the official tax returns from this period can therefore be taken as a reliable guide to sales. Be-

fore that period, newspapers purchased sheets bearing a generic stamp through paper* agents, whose often arbitrary records formed the basis of returns. From 1855 to 1870, the newspaper stamp remained as an optional postal charge, and these returns have been used by Ellegård to estimate circulations of a wide range of metropolitan* journals. Until the turn of the twentieth century, when advertisers began to demand audited evidence of sales, circulation figures provided by the periodical proprietors* themselves can be dubious: the exception is sometimes presented as the norm, and inflated claims are often challenged by rivals. Such information on sales was made public in the journals themselves, and/or in newspaper directories such as *Mitchell's**. It can also be hidden in archives, whether files of company records or surviving correspondence. Compilations of such figures can be found in histories such as those by Altick and Law, as well as in reference works like the *Wellesley* Index* or *Waterloo* Directory*. GL

Sources: Altick 1957, Ellegård 1971, Law 2000, House of Commons 1852-1856, Wadsworth 1955.

CITIZEN (1839-1843) The *Citizen* was an Irish nationalist monthly* magazine with varying levels of literary and political content as its title and printer changed over its four-year existence: *from Citizen; a monthly journal of politics literature and art* (Nov. 1839-Feb. 1841), *Citizen; or, Dublin Monthly Magazine* (March-Dec. 1841), *Dublin Monthly Magazine; being a new series of The Citizen* (Jan.-Dec. 1842), to the *Dublin Magazine and Citizen* (Jan.-April 1843). Published in Dublin and London, with a two-column* page, and pagination varying between 42 and 88 pages, it was illustrated* and carried adverts*. It was considered an important literary antecedent to the Young Ireland* movement and particularly to the *Nation* newspaper.

Such connections are strengthened by the networks of its founders, Thomas Clarke Wallis and John Blake Dillon, both friends of Thomas Davis* and Charles Gavin Duffy*, and it was largely subsidized by another friend, William Elliott Hudson, who functioned as the proprietor*. Davis was a regular contributor on various topics of Irish interest; his noted articles 'Udalism and Feudalism' was first published in the *Citizen*. Hudson's expertise in traditional Irish music* was represented by an ongoing series: 'The Native Music of Ireland'. All variations of the *Citizen* published stories, songs, poems and articles about the United Irishmen and material of general Irish interest was a strong feature of the content.

Political* material was most strongly represented in early volumes; for example, in volume 1 issues of national interest prominently discussed included railways, emigration, grand juries, the electoral franchise, corporation reform, Irish foreign policy, science* in Ireland, the commerce of Dublin and medical reform. The second volume continued to discuss matters of political interest with articles such as 'Irish men for Irish offices' (July 1840) and 'The real grievance – Absenteeism' (Oct. 1840).

Literary material from prominent Irish figures began to be more common, though the *Citizen* attacked what it saw as pseudo-national Irish writing by Mr and Mrs Hall*. It admired and published regular contributions from Carleton* and Banim such as 'The Parent's Trial' in June 1840 and Banim's play 'Sylla; A Tragedy' (July/Aug. 1840). Reprintings of poems* by Gerald Griffin and Mary Leadbetter further bolstered the literary reputation of the magazine* and increasing amounts of Irish sheet music included with each issue marked a shift away from political material. Content also included a smattering of ancient writers and literary translations from European writers such as Goethe.

The *Citizen* proved to be a 'journalistic training-ground' for many poets and writers who later contributed to the *Nation,* alongside other periodical publications of the 1830s such as the *Ulster Magazine* (1830-1832), *Irish Rushlight* (1831) and *Irish Monthly Magazine**, it must be considered as a continuation of the journalism by the United Irishmen in the 1790s, through its publication of Irish history*, poetry*, essays and songs. JCA

Sources: Clyde 2003, Hayley 1976, Hayley 1987, Thuente 1994, *Waterloo.*

CITY JACKDAW (1875-1880) *City Jackdaw* advertised itself as being a 'Humorous and Satirical'* magazine. Published weekly* in Manchester by Abel Heywood* and Son, it was a penny* magazine*, 12 pages long, plus two of advertisements*. These were plentiful and elaborately displayed on the covers, both inside and out, and sometimes on other pages as well (see *Waterloo* thumbnail above). *City Jackdaw* was illustrated* with plates, and it included poetry* as well as sections on theatre. DHL

Sources: Gray 1972, *Mitchell's* 1876, *Waterloo.*

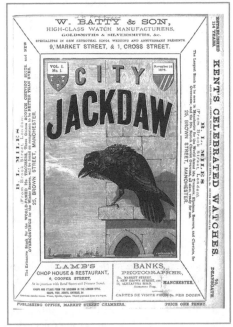

Figure 9: The *City Jackdaw,* Nov. 1875 (Copyright *Waterloo*).

CIVIL ENGINEER AND ARCHITECT'S JOURNAL (1837-1867) A monthly* architectural periodical, the *Civil Engineer and Architect's Journal* was founded by the surveyor William Laxton (1802-1854) as a rival to the *Architectural Magazine* (1834-1839). Edited* and published* by Laxton until his death in 1854, it initially cost 6d unstamped or 7d stamped, a price* that had risen to 2s by 1854, remaining at this level until the magazine ceased publication. It claimed for itself a 'large' circulation*, and achieved international distribution*.

Its primary contents were informative accounts of the latest developments in both architecture and civil engineering, accompanied by helpful illustrations*. For example, it supplied detailed technical descriptions of the building of the railways in the United States (reflecting the preference of the journal to look to America rather than Europe for foreign examples of engineering excellence), of the construction of the bridge across the river Tees (including etchings of plans and elevations) and of the proposed botanical gardens in the inner circle at Regent's Park. Aside from this, it sought to keep its readership* abreast of the latest inventions that might impact on the trade, both by printing descriptive lists of new patents, and by reporting on the proceedings of learned and scientific societies.

Hard data – such as price lists relating to building materials – were included in the magazine, but in a monthly publication these could hardly claim to be authoritative and up-to-date. Publishing weekly*, both the *Builder** (from 1843) and the *Builders' Weekly Reporter** (from 1856) were better adapted to delivering accurate price lists. Though the *Civil Engineer and Architect's Journal* switched to weekly publication when it absorbed the *Architect and Building Operative* (1849-1850) in December 1850, this experiment was short-lived, and it had reverted to monthly publication by 1852. As a monthly, the strength of the journal was in its more discursive articles such as a 'Cursory Glance at the Present State of Architecture in England' (appearing in the first issue), papers on architectural history* (some of which were delivered at the Royal Institute of British Architects), and reviews* of the latest books pertaining to the professions* it covered. Advertisements* were not included in the early years, but by the time it folded in 1867 they took up 12 pages of a total 32. By this time, it had been eclipsed by the *Builder**, which had cemented its position as the principal architectural journal of its day. MaT

Sources: *ODNB*, Richardson and Thorne 1995, *Waterloo*.

CLARION (1891-1934) The *Clarion*, a socialist* journal based in Manchester and London, was not only a source of news* and entertainment among working-class* socialists, but was also at the centre of a popular social movement. The first issue did not portend well: advertising posters were ripped off walls in a ferocious storm and the ink did not hold. But the *Clarion* became the most influential socialist* periodical of the late nineteenth and early twentieth centuries, and the only one to break even financially. The first issue sold 40,000 copies and circulation* settled at around 34,000.

This weekly* 1d broadsheet traded on Robert Blatchford's* journalistic* reputation. The newspaper itself, owned and edited* by Blatchford* (known as 'Nunquam') and Alexander M. Thompson, featured news* summaries and analysis, theatre reviews*, sports* columns, book reviews, poetry*, a children's column*, reader correspondence*, serialized* fiction and fiction excerpts, and 'Our Woman's Letter', with reports of the various Clarion organizations. (The Clarion social organizations existed to provide working-class* socialists with healthy and improving pastimes; among the most prominent were Clarion Clubs: Clarion Cycling Clubs (later motorcycle clubs), the Clarion Scouts (a socialist version of the Boy Scouts), the Cinderella Clubs which provided entertainment and education for slum children, Clarion Vocal Unions and the Clarion vans which toured the country. Participants in these organizations were nicknamed Clarionettes.)

Blatchford, a journalist with the *Manchester Sunday Chronicle*, was drawn to write about the condition of the poor. Inspired by a reader, Joe Waddington, he set out to meet the poor of Manchester and give them their own voice. As a result of his conversion to socialism, he found himself at odds with his editor of the *Chronicle*, Edward Hulton*, and resigned with a number of his fellow workers to found a new paper where they could give voice to their ideals and concerns. The original core group of writers for the *Clarion* included Robert Blatchford, under his own name and as 'Nunquam', as well as Alexander M. Thompson (a.k.a. 'Dangle'), Edward Fay ('the Bounder'), Robert's brother Montague Blatchford ('Mont Blong') and William Palmer ('Whiffly Puncto'). Julia Dawson, Harry Lowerison, Neil Lyons and George Bernard Shaw* were also among the contributors.

The *Clarion* focused primarily on the socialist working classes, but the tone of the paper was light and satirical*, with wry and ironic observations on royalty and the aristocracy, the government, the Church and industrialists. It was illustrated* with black and white engravings, mostly humorous in tone, and also with portraits. Blatchford's influential socialist treatise 'Merrie England' was serialized (March-Sept. 1893). Blatchford's policy was for open debate: during the religious* controversy surrounding 'God and My Neighbour', for example, he allowed first Christians and then Secularists* to respond, without comment from *Clarion* writers. The paper relocated to London in 1895 to secure a larger circulation* and by that time, there were also larger political cartoons*, generally on the subject of the oppression of the people by industrialists, or the mishaps of various government officials. The *Clarion* also featured didactic articles on various socialist topics with excerpts from works by prominent authors such as Walter Savage Landor, 'George Eliot' (see Marian Evans*) and John Ruskin*. Blatchford's own novels were serialized, as were the works of other authors.

Some of Blatchford's and the *Clarion's* nationalistic views of foreign policy, such as support for the Boer War, alienated many of socialist readers. There were also controversies surrounding the serialized tracts 'God and My Neighbour' (1903) and 'Not Guilty'

(1905) which boosted sales, peaking at 83,000 in 1910. Also Blatchford's support for the government at the outbreak of the First World War* lost readers*. Afer the war, Blatchford resigned from the paper and handed over editorial responsibility to his daughter Winnie, and the *Clarion* was published by the Clarion Fellowship as the *New Clarion* (1932-1934). **CR/DM**
Sources: Blatchford 1931, *DLB*, Moore 2001, Osborne 1997, Pye n.d., Thompson 1937, Thompson 1951, *Waterloo*, Waters 1990.

T&T CLARK (1821-1973): CLARK, THOMAS (1846-1865) & CLARK, THOMAS (1823-1900)

After being apprenticed in Edinburgh to David Brown, Thomas Clark (1799-1865) worked for Joseph Butterworth, a London law bookseller in Fleet Street*. Returning to Edinburgh he established his own business as a law bookseller in 1821 before publishing law books. By May 1829 Clark was publishing* the first Scottish law magazine*, the monthly* *Law Chronicle,* but the innovative venture folded within five years. He also planned a theological quarterly*, *Clark's Biblical Magazine and Review,* to promote British theological writing; despite the backing of several eminent professors, it did not progress beyond the planning stage. In the 1830s Clark tended to publish theology, whilst retaining an interest in legal works. The firm also published European literature and English translations of leading theological texts, particularly German ones and established a thriving business.

Clark's nephew, Thomas Clark (1823-1900), who had served an apprenticeship with the wholesaler Hamilton, Adams & Co. in London, joined the firm in 1846 so establishing T.&T. Clark. Clark Jnr was particularly involved in publishing periodicals. Established in 1857, the candid *Journal of Jurisprudence* was so successful a rival to the *Scottish Law Magazine* that it amalgamated with it in 1866. In 1891, edited by John Chisholm, its sales had slumped as contributors' fear of sacrificing promotion by criticizing senior legal figures led to a lacklustre content. Clark Jnr bought the theological but predominantly literary* *North British Review* from W. P. Kennedy; between 1860-1863 edited by W. G. Blaikie, it tried to broaden its appeal. Later, the *Monthly Interpreter* was begun in 1884 but collapsed after 1886 due to editorial failing, and an attempt at distributing the American *Presbyterian Review* also foundered.

Clark Jnr's son John Maurice became a partner in 1880 until his father's retirement in 1886, when he ran the firm until his younger brother Thomas George Clark became a partner in 1894. The business expanded by taking in the American market* while maintaining the tradition of periodical publishing with the monthly *Expository Times,* acquired in 1890 (still published). Between 1890-1899, the quarterly* *Critical Review of Theological and Philosophical Literature* edited by S. D. F. Salmond was also theirs. Value for money was one of their concerns, expressed in type* size and number of pages together with making their publications attractive to an American audience. T.&T. Clark also believed in good contributors who were well paid and in spending money on promotion and advertising*, that appealed to specialist interests. They were prepared to shoulder losses in periodicals, realizing their value to the academic community.

A succession of sons, all called Thomas, upheld the tradition of family control for c./25 years. Although it merged with John Bartholomew & Son, mapmakers, in 1973, T.&T. Clark is still in existence as an imprint of Continuum Books. **CL**
Sources: Centre for the History of the Book online, Dempster 1992, 'Scottish Clarks' online.

CLARKE, CHARLES ALLEN (1863-1935)

Former mill-worker and teacher, Clarke began his career as a journalist* employed on the *Bolton Evening News* in 1884. Converted to socialism by Tom Mann in 1888, Clarke published the unsuccessful *Labour Light* in 1890 followed by the more successful *Bolton Trotter* in 1891. The Trotter was written primarily by Clarke under a series of pseudonyms* including 'Ben Adhem', 'Teddy Ashton' for dialect writing, 'Capanbells' for poetry*, and 'Grandad Grey' for the children's column*. Despite the paper's brief popularity (*ODNB* states that circulation* peaked at around 20,000), he later regretted making the Trotter's style public entertainment rather than political* edification. Clarke joined the *Cotton Factory Times*￼* in 1892, when the *Trotter* was discontinued.

In 1896 he began the *Northern Weekly/Teddy Ashton's Journal*￼* and, having also published his book of verse, *Voices and Other Verses,* through the *Clarion*￼* in 1896, he serialized* his influential text 'Effects of the Factory System' there in 1897-1898; it was later translated into Russian by Tolstoy. After 1909 Clarke contributed to the *Liverpool Weekly Post* and the *Blackpool Gazette.*

Clarke's journalism was less overtly didactic than other socialist* authors of this period, and included accounts of Lancashire places and characters, dialect sketches, serial stories and poetry. A skilled dialect writer, he was most renowned for his 'Bill Spriggs' sketches. **DM**
Sources: Angus-Butterworth 1980, Espinasse 1977, Frow 1971-1972, *ODNB*.

CLARKE, CHARLES COWDEN (1787-1877)
Charles Cowden Clarke is perhaps best known as
the teacher and friend of Keats, who attended the
school run by Clarke's father John. In addition,
Clarke was closely associated with Charles Lamb*
and Leigh Hunt*. From the mid-1820s through the
1830s, however, he was involved in the book trade,
as a publisher*, journalist*, reviewer*, and editor*.
In 1825 he became the partner of Leigh Hunt's
nephew Henry Leigh Hunt in Hunt and Clarke, a
publishing firm, most notably producing William
Hone's* *Every-day Book* and Leigh Hunt's periodical the *Companion*. The firm, however, went bankrupt in 1829. The year before he had wed Mary
Victoria Novello, a writer and daughter of the celebrated musician and musical publisher Vincent
Novello.

Around 1826 he began to write on fine arts for
the *Atlas** newspaper (such as a piece on the Fitzwilliam Museum in 1830) and theatrical and musical*
notices for Leigh Hunt's the *Tatler**. In the mid-
1830s he published essays and fiction in the *Analyst*
monthly* magazine and by 1834 was also contributing theatrical notices to the *Examiner**. In 1836
he became the first editor* of *Musical World**, a
weekly* paper for musical insiders founded by
Novello, his father-in-law.

For 22 years (1834-1856) he made his living
chiefly as a public lecturer but revived his periodical
writing in old age, publishing 'On the Comic Writers of England' in the *Gentleman's Magazine** and
'The Taming of the Shrew' for *Temple Bar** at age
85 in 1872. **DEL**
Sources: Altick 1948, Clarke 1896, *ODNB*.

**CLARKE, JAMES FERNANDEZ (C. 1812-
1875)** Clarke's historical significance is as a medical* journalist and writer associated with several
journals, principally the *Lancet** (1823-). He,
though, regarded medical practice as his life's work;
literature was simply an 'amusement' (Clarke: 142).
In 1834, when still a student, Clarke assisted
Michael Ryan in editing* the *London Medical and
Surgical Journal* (1828-1837). His account for that
journal of an operation to amputate a toe so impressed the surgeon Robert Liston that he gave
Clarke a letter of introduction to the *Lancet's* editor
Thomas Wakley*, who hired him to report hospital
cases, review* books and make himself 'generally
useful' (Clarke: 141-142). 'Clarke of the *Lancet*'
(*British Medical Journal* 24 July 1875: 115) became
a renowned medical journalist. In reflecting on his
career, Clarke deemed himself the *Lancet's* 'main
support' for a 'considerable period' (Clarke: 142).

He remained with the journal until 1864 when 'an
act impossible to be passed over' (*British Medical
Journal* 31 July 1875: 149) led to his dismissal. The
nature of this act is not known. Clarke went on to
contribute to the *Medical Times and Gazette* (1852-
1885). His entertaining and informative 'Autobiographical Recollections of the Medical Profession'
(1874) was serialized* in the *Medical Times and Gazette* before being published in book form. **PWB**
Sources: *British Medical Journal* 31 July 1875,
Clarke 1874, *Lancet* 17 July 1875, *Medical Times
and Gazette* 17 July 1875, *ODNB*.

**CLARKE, MARY VICTORIA COWDEN (1809-
1898)** Daughter of musician and publisher, Vincent
Novello (1781-1861) and wife of writer, Charles Cowden Clarke* (1787-1877), Clarke contributed articles
to a number of publications, and in 1853 became the
first and only female editor* of the Novello publication, the *Musical Times**. That Clarke was helped in
her career by male members of her family is clear. How
she asserted her position as a woman in a male-dominated industry may be hinted at from her ambitious
studies of Shakespeare. Clarke's most important work,
'The Complete Concordance to Shakespeare' was published in monthly parts in 1844-1845 and was immediately recognized as significant: Douglas Jerrold*
sought to critique it in *Punch**, despite *Punch's* usual
reluctance to publish reviews*. Clarke's series of ten articles entitled 'On Shakespeare's Individuality in his
Characters', published in *Sharpe's London Magazine*
1848-1851, consolidated her position as a Shakespeare
scholar and she continued to write on the bard even
when her main publishing activities were in other
spheres. While editing the *Musical Times* she included
a series of articles named 'Music* among the Poets and
Political Writers' and commissioned significant work
from other authors including Leigh Hunt*.

During her editorship, the *Musical Times* received
great acclaim; Novello even volunteered it as a test case
in the appeal against the government's 'taxes on
knowledge'*. In 1858, Clarke released 'World Noted
Women'. On the publication of *Shakespeare's Works,
edited with a scrupulous revision of the text*, she described her 'pride' of becoming the first female to edit
his work (Clarke 1896). Mary and Charles Cowden
Clarke went on to contribute 'Recollection of writers'
to the *Gentlemen's Magazine* (1875-1876). Clarke's
journalistic career included publications outside the
UK with titles including 'Shakespeare's Self, as revealed in his Writings', printed in the American magazine *Shakespeariana* in 1886. **JH**
Sources: Altick 1948, Clarke 1858, Clarke 1896,
Clarke 1902.

CLASS AND THE PRESS As the theme of class was ubiquitous in nineteenth-century society, so it also impinged upon the composition and circulation* of newspapers and periodicals. During the first half of the century the press was strongly divided along class lines, but during the second half such a division took on a different character.

The Stamp Act* of 1815, a deliberate government attempt to suppress political opposition, helped to divide the early nineteenth-century press along class lines. With newspapers at 7d, the working and lower middle classes were excluded from the purchase of stamped (establishment) newspapers. Yet substantial numbers of readers were still able to purchase them, as copies were lent out from public houses and coffee shops, and sharing networks within communities transcended barriers imposed by both high prices* and low levels of literacy. More particularly, however, the Stamp Act encouraged the growth of a radical unstamped* press which gave voice to many dissenting political* groups around the country. Circulation* rates for individual titles were comparatively small, as newspapers were supported by particular occupational or political groups and failed to achieve a more general appeal uniting groups within classes. But their cumulative impact was important, especially after the 1832 Reform Act when a number of unstamped newspapers were able to increase their circulations by mixing radical politics with sensation.

Similarly, the periodicals market during the nineteenth century was determined by class. The high prices of early nineteenth-century titles such as *Blackwood's Edinburgh Magazine*, *Fraser's Magazine** and the critical quarterlies* meant that access for many was limited. By the 1820s, the lack of publications available for working people inspired several publishers to print cheap* periodicals designed to educate and elevate, the most famous being the SDUK's* *Penny Magazine** (1832ff). However, it never reached the class for whom it was intended in any numbers, attracting instead mainly middle-class readers, in large part because Charles Knight* and other printers failed to accommodate the desire for entertaining reading material among the working class. Recognizing this gap, by the 1840s new entrepreneurs in the industry began to publish a number of successful periodicals that appealed precisely to these readers including *Lloyd's Penny Weekly Miscellany** (1842ff), *Lloyd's Penny Atlas** (1842ff), *Reynolds's Miscellany** (1846ff) and the *London Journal** (1845ff).

In the 1850s the relationship between class and the press shifted, most notably because of the emergence of mass* audiences for newspapers and periodicals. The eventual removal of the Stamp Tax and paper duties (1855-1861) meant that a cheap, popular* weekly* press emerged, which, through combining news with sensational content, and by adopting a more moderate political* tone, appealed to a large cross-section of occupational groups within the lower classes. As time progressed and circulation rates grew at a phenomenal rate, these newspapers were able to claim support from a mass audience, thus transcending some class barriers. However, at the same time, a substantial radical fringe popular within the working class persisted, for example visible in *Reynolds's Weekly Newspaper** (1850ff). Also, mass audiences for newspapers tended to come from the working and lower middle classes. The upper class and more affluent and aspirational sections of the middle class continued to purchase newspapers which they perceived to be 'respectable'. Despite this, the rise of the New Journalism* during the latter decades of the nineteenth century ensured that there were as many similarities between these newspapers as differences, as especially demonstrated in the reporting of headline events such as the Ripper murders of 1888.

Furthermore, periodicals, especially those composed of more entertaining material, also began to attract mass audiences. By the late 1850s, the combined circulation of the *London Journal**, the *Family Herald** (1842ff) and *Cassell's Family Paper** (1853ff), had reached 895,000, and in 1897, George Newnes's* *Tit-Bits** (1881ff) had reached 600,000. Again, these mass audiences were largely composed of readers from the working and lower-middle classes, while the intelligentsia continued to support periodicals such as the intellectual *Athenaeum** (1828ff) and the educated middle class flocked to the new *Cornhill Magazine** (1860ff) and *Nineteenth Century** (1877ff), a situation described by Wilkie Collins* in 'The Unknown Public' as early as 1858. At the same time, growing numbers of readers combined with increasing incomes and falling prices meant that there emerged more specialist periodicals concerned with gender* and age as much as with class. Women became a target readership for periodicals offering romantic serial fiction* and recipes, while adolescent males acquired their own, much more robust and strongly flavoured magazines.

Thus, by 1900 newspaper and periodical readership* in general had become much more diverse than it had been at the start of the century, as cheap prices and vastly improved distribution* ensured that most people had access to the press. But, while other forms of identity such as age and gender became influential, class continued to have an impact on patterns of readership as it remained a determining factor of the tone and support of individual newspapers and periodicals. **RHC**

Sources: Altick 1957, Collins 1858, Curtis 2001, Vincent 1989, Wiener 1988a.

'CLASS' PUBLICATIONS Class publication was a legal concept, first codified in 1836. It was key to continuing the operation of the Stamp Duty (see Taxes on Knowledge*) and yet eventually led to its undoing. A 'class' publication was – in theory – a periodical that came out with a frequency greater than 26 days, aimed at a very specific group. So the *Builder** was aimed at those in the building trade, the *Bookseller** at booksellers and so on. A 'class' publication should contain only one kind of information, which could not be considered 'news'* under the legal definition. This meant that it was not obliged to pay the Stamp Duty, although it could do so in order to be distributed free by post. Most 'class' journals offered the consumer an alternative of stamped for the country and unstamped* in town (where distribution* methods alternative to the post were easier to arrange). Whether a periodical could be considered a 'class' publication was always open to debate, and the arbitrary application of the term to certain journals and not others created confusion and resentment: the *Lancet**, *Punch** and the *Racing Times** were so categorised, but the *Dublin Medical Press** was not; *Holt's Army and Navy Despatch* (1854-1877) was silently tolerated (it professed to be a legal 'class' publication, even though it came out weekly* since, when it began, it dealt exclusively with the Crimean war). Taking *Holt's* as their target, the Association for the Repeal of the Stamp Tax started the thrice daily 1d *War Telegraph* to test the legality of *Holt's* position. The government by now, however, could see the utility of news in unifying the nation and no prosecution took place. The term 'class' publication or similar continued in use for some time after the Stamp Tax became optional in 1855, but its once fraught political associations had become commercial or at most moralistic, pointing the way towards ever more subtle market* segmentation. **AK**

Sources: Chandler 1981, Collet 1899.

CLAXTON, FLORENCE A., (FL. 1855-1879); CLAXTON, ADELAIDE, (FL. 1858-C. 1905) Florence Claxton achieved a first for a woman artist by using the technique of drawing on wood* for a weekly* illustrated* paper, making a full-

page 'cut' for the *Illustrated Times*. Her work appeared in the *Illustrated Times* (1855-1867); the *Illustrated London News** (1860); *London Society** (1862); the *Churchman's Family Magazine* (1863), and *Good Words** (1864); in 1860 she illustrated a satirical* poem, 'Married Off', by the unknown, 'H. B.' When she married in 1868 she gave up her magazine work but in 1875 produced the anti-suffrage cartoon* book *The Adventures of a Woman in Search of her Rights. Containing Nearly One Hundred Original Drawings by the Author.*

Adelaide Claxton followed her sister in designing on wood, but was also watercolourist. She worked more extensively, although they collaborated on character subjects. Adelaide specialized in illustrating ghost stories in addition to her weekly* comic drawings in *Bow Bells**, *Judy** (1871-1879), the *Illustrated Times* (1859-1866) and in some illustrated monthlies*. She was one of the principal illustrators at *Judy*. Her subject matter sprang out of observing high society, from the salon to the croquet lawn. Her accomplished illustrations and cartoons can be found in the *Englishwoman's Domestic Magazine**; *Illustrated London News** (1858); *London Society** (1862-1865); *Once a Week** (1862) and the *Boys' Herald*. Her double-page cartoons were also seen in *Echoes* and its successor the *Period*.

Adelaide co-produced a piece of whimsy in 1876 with *Judy's* editor* and illustrator Charles H. Ross*, *A Shillingsworth of Sugar Plums. Containing Several Hundreds of Num-Nums and Nicey-Nicies. And an Equal Number of Mottoes and Labels, and Other Literary Sweetstuff.* A later collection was *Brainy Odds and Ends, annotated by a cheap cynic* (1900). **CL**

Sources: Clayton 1876, Houfe 1978, *ODNB*, Women's Library, Yesterday's Papers.

CLEAVE, JOHN (1795?-1850) Irish-born Londoner John Cleave entered journalism* in the late 1820s as assistant to William Carpenter* on the *Weekly Free Press* (1828-1831), a trade union* and co-operative paper. From 1829 until his death Cleave was a major presence in metropolitan* radicalism and publishing*. Carpenter's unstamped* *Political Letters and Pamphlets* (1830-1831) was equally Cleave's brainchild, as was their *Slap at the Church* (1832). When the latter failed in December 1832, he launched (with James Watson*) and edited* the *Working Man's Friend** (1832-1833).

Cleave was a highly principled political* activist but a ruthless businessman. The turning point in his career was the launch in 1834 of his *Weekly Police Gazette**, which quickly enjoyed the highest circulation*(30,000-40,000) of any un-stamped* paper, forcing Charles Penny's *People's Police Gazette* (on which Cleave had worked) to close. Cleave was twice imprisoned for un-stamped activities, and his printing press* and types seized in 1835. After the reduction of newspaper stamp duty* in 1836, he elected to operate within the law, merging the *Gazette* with Hetherington's* *London Dispatch* and concen-trating on popular publishing and his burgeon-ing newsagent* business.

However, he used his status as a hero of the unstamped press* to cultivate 'brand recogni-tion', notably with *Cleave's London Satirist and Gazette of Variety* (1837-1844). Retitled (from Dec. 1837) *Cleave's Penny Gazette of Variety (and Amusement)*, this spirited weekly* pioneered the deft mingling of romance, sensation and radical politics that Edward Lloyd* and G. W. M. Rey-nolds* would soon make their own. Cleave re-entered political* journalism with the influential *English Chartist Circular and Temperance Record* (1841-1843), closely based on the model of its Glasgow namesake, though never enjoying its profitability. As editor and publisher*, though, Cleave offset its losses against the *Gazette*. He also acted as publisher and distributor* for sever-al socialist* titles, including Robert Owen's* *New Moral World*, while his newsagency was the main southern distributor for the Chartist *Northern Star**. MSC

Sources: *DLB*, Hollis 1970, *ODNB*.

CLEAVE'S WEEKLY POLICE GAZETTE (1834-1836)

Although *Cleave's Weekly Police Gazette* was relatively short-lived, it represents one of several lit-erary* efforts of printer, publisher* and editor* John Cleave*, 'one of the heroes of the unstamped* working-class*press'. Printed at his London book-shop in Shoe Lane with help from Richard Butler and George Henry Davis, the *Police Gazette* was in-stantly successful with a circulation* around 40,000 and a weekly* profit of £30. Its four pages (29 cm) came out on Saturdays, with engravings, sketches and advertisements*, and priced* at 1d. While it did cover crimes* and police news, the *Po-lice Gazette* agitated for radical political* reform in-cluding Chartism, factory reform, a repeal of the newspaper tax* and a repeal of the Poor Law Amendment Act of 1834. Cleave, refusing to pay the stamp duty on papers he published, was con-victed and imprisoned. His fines, as well as those of fellow radical publisher Henry Hetherington*, were in part paid by the Association of Working

Men to Procure a Cheap and Honest Press. This group would later become the Working Men's As-sociation, for which Cleave continued to organize until his death. The *Police Gazette* merged with Hetherington's *London Dispatch* in 1836 and Cleave went on to start *Cleave's London Satirist and Gazette of Variety* the following year. **CR**

Sources: Kunzle 1983, Rose 1897, Rowe 1971, *Waterloo*.

CLEPHAN, JAMES (1804-1888)

James Clephan, journalist*, poet and antiquary, was born into a Unitarian family. When his indentures ex-pired in 1825, he was employed in the offices of the Edinburgh publisher* Messrs. Ballantyne*. Clephan became a journeyman printer for the *Leicester Journal* in 1828, also serving as a sub-ed-itor*. In 1838 he was appointed editor* of the re-cently founded weekly* *Gateshead Observer*, later the organ of the Whig party in North Durham. Af-ter 1840, when the editor-in-chief relinquished his position, Clephan combined the roles of editor, subeditor and reporter*. Until his resignation in 1859 he had almost total control of the paper. By 1861 he was free-lancing for the *Newcastle Daily Chronicle** and the *Newcastle Weekly Chronicle**. In his articles he drew on his literary and antiquarian knowledge, as well as reminiscences of the social and industrial upheavals of his youth. Clephan was a staunch liberal and reformer, opposing capital punishment and advocating sanitary reforms. Early in the 1880s he officially withdrew from journalism but continued to contribute occasional articles to the Unitarian *Christian Life**. **DHL**

Sources: *ODNB*, Temple Patterson 1954, Welford 1895.

CLERKE, AGNES MARY (1842-1907)

Clerke was a prolific contributor to numerous periodicals, from specialist scientific* journals such as the *Ob-servatory* and the *Astrophysical Journal* to staples of Victorian culture such as *Nature** and the *Edin-burgh Review**. She was a close friend both of *Na-ture**'s founder Sir Norman Lockyer* and of Henry Reeve*, editor of the *Edinburgh*. The latter journal published over 50 articles by Clerke over a period of 30 years. The diversity of Clerke's interests was apparent from her very first submissions to the *Ed-inburgh* in 1877: 'Brigandage in Sicily' and 'Coper-nicus in Italy'. Her natural flair for languages al-lowed her to review* books in English, French, German, Greek, Italian and Latin. Although Clerke initially published historical* surveys, she also later became known for her explications of the latest sci-entific developments for wider audiences, especially in the field of astronomy. Additionally, she is now considered to have led the way in introducing photography* into works of popular science, exemplified in 'Sidereal Photography' for the *Edinburgh* in 1888. Clerke's contribution to the wider scientific community has recently been reassessed and her conception of herself as an important interpreter of contemporary discoveries for populace and professionals* alike has been acknowledged. **CB**

Sources: Brück 1994, Brück 2002, Lightman 2000, Lightman 2004, *ODNB*.

CLERKENWELL NEWS (1855-1930) The *Clerkenwell News* was founded, as a ½d weekly* in 1855. Subsequently, it was known as the *Clerkenwell News and London Times*, then the *London Daily Chronicle and Clerkenwell News*, until, in 1872, it became the *Daily Chronicle*. Edward Lloyd*, the founder of *Lloyd's Weekly News*ic, purchased the paper in 1876, converting it from a local* London paper into a major national daily* with special correspondents world-wide. Liberal and radical, it ran a daily column*, 'The Labour Movement', during the 1890s with Henry Massingham* editing the paper with distinction (1895-1899). Another notable journalist was H.W. Nevinson who was its war* correspondent (1897-1900). The paper was taken into the United Newspapers fold in 1918, merging with the *Daily News*ic in 1930 to become the *News Chronicle*. **JRW**

Sources: Brown 1985, Linton en Boston 1987, *ODNB*.

CLIFFORD, WILLIAM KINGDON (1845-1879) Even before entering Cambridge as an undergraduate in 1863, the precociously talented Clifford had already begun contributing to mathematical journals, and he continued to write for specialist scientific* periodicals such as the *Proceedings of the London Mathematical Society* throughout his subsequent career as a non-Euclidean geometer. After moving to London in 1871 as professor of mathematics at University College, Clifford also became known as a highly skilful popularizer of science, although his outspoken atheism made him somewhat controversial. He published numerous articles in leading liberal periodicals like the *Nineteenth Century*ic, the *Academy*ic and *Macmillan's Magazine*ic which informed but also not infrequently outraged their predominantly middle-class* readership*.

By the mid-1870s Clifford had established himself in the public mind as a kind of celebrity* iconoclast, and his swaggering attacks on religion* tested the very boundaries of press tolerance of free speech.

Clifford's acerbic review of *The Unseen Universe* (1875) in the *Fortnightly Review*ic sparked a bitter war-of-words that greatly perturbed the journal's editor* John Morley*, while an article for the *Contemporary Review*ic, on 'The Ethics of Belief', was so strident in its scepticism that it led to the dismissal of the *Contemporary's* editor James Knowles*. Clifford's journalism was generally written in an impromptu manner that took its toll on his delicate health and he died of pulmonary disease in 1879. **GD**

Sources: Dawson 2004c, Lightman 2004a, *ODNB*, Small 2004.

CLIQUE JOURNALISM While most journals in the nineteenth century tended to rely on a core of writers, often drawn from a network of friends or colleagues (see, for example, the formation of the *Nineteenth Century*), clique journalism refers more specifically to a periodical which is overwhelmingly focused around a small coterie of friends who write about each other in the pages of a journal. This was the case with the Jerome K. Jerome* circle in the *Idler*ic and *To-day*ic, and the practice was particularly associated with smaller journals in the 1890s. **MWT**

CLOWES FAMILY William Clowes (1779-1847), born in Chichester, went to London as a journeyman printer, and in 1803 opened a business that eventually became, at its Blackfriars site, 'the largest printing works in the world' (Weedon, *ODNB*). He, his sons and grandsons formed a family firm renowned for its accuracy, speed and output. Over the years the firm printed a significant number of familiar nineteenth-century periodical titles at some point in their runs, including the *Academy*ic, *Argosy*ic, *Aunt Judy*ic, *Belle Assemblée*ic, *Bentley's Quarterly Review*, *Companion to the Newspaper*ic, *Family Herald*ic, *Girl's Own Paper*ic, *Household Words*ic, *Illustrated Messenger*, *Illustrated Newspaper*, *Murray's Magazine*, *Quarterly Review*ic, *Shilling Magazine*ic, *Sylvia's Home Journal*ic, *Temple Bar*ic, *Westminster Review*ic and *Young England*. Less familiar titles include *Articled Clerk's Journal and Examiner*, *Book Binder*, *British Bookmaker*, and *Telephone*. *ODNB* singles out the publication of the gold coronation edition of the *Sun* newspaper in May 1837 as Clowes' finest technical achievement.

A revealing view of the firm in 1839 may be gleaned from F. B. Head's report, 'The Printer's Devil' in the *Quarterly Review* of December 1839. In this account of his visit to the Blackfriars works, he notes that the largest compositor's hall (of five) is 200 feet long, housing 60 compositors, and 19 steam presses*. Later in the century, the firm was chosen as the printers for both the official catalogue to the Great Exhibition in 1851, as well as the *British Museum General Catalogue of Printed Books* in 1859ff.

Having installed an Applegath and Cowper* steam press in 1823, the first William Clowes bought Applegath's premises in Blackfriars and from 1827 printed there. In 1832, Clowes was selected by the SDUK* to print the *Penny Magazine*, which was 'the earliest instance of printing woodcuts* by steam' (Weedon, *ODNB*). The elder Clowes's son, William Clowes (1807-1883) joined the firm, and in 1839 the name of the firm changed to William Clowes and Sons. In 1842 this son, William, began to experiment with a composing machine to print the *Family Herald*, but it was not until 1875 that Hooker's electric typesetting* machines were introduced, and still later when E. A. Clowes (1851-1911) was sent to the United States to investigate and bring back monotype machines. From 1844 the younger William promulgated the Printers' Pension Corporation for which he served as Trustee (from 1844) and Treasurer (1853). **LRB**
Sources: Head 1839, *ODNB*, *Waterloo*, Weedon 2003.

CLUBS Membership in a club was virtually essential for the working journalist, and by the late nineteenth century a considerable number existed to accommodate their needs. Club membership might confer some social status, though most of the prestigious West End gentlemen's clubs were reluctant to admit journalists as members, excepting practitioners of higher journalism in the senior reviews*. An early exception was the Reform Club, which admitted some professional journalists* in recognition of their political* influence, including even the arch-Bohemian G. A. Sala*. The Conservatives later followed suit and became very hospitable to membership of professional* journalists at their more junior clubs like the St Stephen's, Constitutional and Primrose. Lower in the social hierarchy, the more Bohemian Savage and Arundel clubs had large journalist contingents.

Among the amenities clubs offered journalists, besides reasonably priced food and drink, and a place to relax considerably more luxurious than their own dwellings, were access to a wide range of periodicals and books of reference in the club library, and opportunities to network and gossip*. Certain clubs such as the Cosmopolitan and Century existed for the latter purpose alone. The later years of the century saw the foundation of new literary* clubs like the prestigious Savile, whose members were notorious for mutual log-rolling*. Also important were certain dining clubs like the

Rabelais, Omar Khayam and Cemented Bricks. Unique among discussion clubs was the intellectually elite Metaphysical Society. Women journalists, excluded from such clubs, started their own. Among these were the Ladies' Literary Dinner* (later renamed the Women Writers' Dinner), a dining club founded in 1889, the Writers' Club(1892) and the Lyceum(1902). The last two had premises of their own, the Lyceum's being notably palatial. **CAK**
Sources: Escott 1914, Hughes 2007a, Kent 2000, *ODNB*, Waller 2006.

COBBE, FRANCES POWER (1822-1904) During her 45-year working life, Frances Power Cobbe published in at least 69 periodicals with circulations* ranging from under 200 to more than 200,000. Usually promoting social, legal or religious* reforms, her articles and leaders* are marked by impassioned earnestness, concrete details and a biting edge that compelled public attention. They also supplied the income to live comfortably in Kensington from 1865 until 1884. Cobbe's public career began with an 1860 Social Science Association paper. In spring 1861 David Masson* accepted 'Workhouse Sketches' for *Macmillan's Magazine** and *Fraser's Magazine** took her account of a visit to Baalbec. By the following winter she was in Rome as correspondent for the *Daily News**.

The combination of anonymous* work for daily* and weekly* papers, substantial signed essays in both prestige journals and more popular* monthly* magazines*, and occasional unpaid efforts for advocacy organs set the pattern of Cobbe's working life. On the staff of the halfpenny London newspaper the *Echo** (1868-March 1875), she produced two or three leaders* per week on politics, crime*, poverty, cruelty, official malfeasance, religious excess and women's rights. She also wrote regular leaders for the *Day* (a short-lived Tory newspaper) and, in the 1880s, for the *Standard**. She did occasional leaders in the weekly *Examiner** and *Reader**, wrote unsigned articles for Henry Labouchère's* *Truth**, and supplied some 70 columns* and letters* to the *Spectator**. Editors who refused to print a leader sometimes published it as a 'letter' signed with a pseudonym* such as 'Only a Woman' for a very early suffrage appeal in the *Day*.

Cobbe's substantial essays in reviews* and monthly magazines were almost always signed, even in journals where signature was not yet usual. The *Theological Review** published 24 of her articles. There were 20 in *Fraser's**, 17 in *Contemporary Review**, seven each in *Macmillan's**, *Cornhill** and the *New Quarterly Magazine**, five in the *Fortnightly Review**, and smaller numbers in other places that included lighter publications such as *Once a Week** and *Temple Bar** as well as several US magazines. Aside from the writing that paid her bills, Cobbe contributed unpaid work to many feminist journals and created periodicals for the two antivivisection societies (both still active) she founded. Though only briefly editor*, she supplied much content for the *Zoophilist* (1881-1896) and wrote a column* for the *Abolitionist* from 1899 until her death. SMM

Sources: Cobbe Archive, Hamilton 2006, Mitchell 2004.

COBBETT, MARTIN RICHARD (1846-1906) Martin Cobbett of the *Sportsman** magazine reported the England cricket team's tour of Australia in 1882-1883 when, for the first time, they were presented with 'the Ashes'. The *Sportsman* broke new ground by sending its own reporter* to spend seven months with the tourists, rather than rely on the efforts of the cricketers or Australian correspondents. Cobbett's reputation as one of the finest sporting journalists* of his era was said to have been established by his work on the tour. His lengthy travel articles and match reports mailed back to London by sea, with a month's timelag before publication, together with brief but expensive telegraphed* summaries of the more important matches for next-day publication, reveal a journalist making full use of the available technology to satisfy a public appetite for up to date sports news.

Born in Brighton into a middle-class family, Cobbett worked as a timber merchant into his 20s, before an enthusiasm for horse racing saw him begin writing for the *Sporting Life** in the 1870s and the *Sportsman*. He was the *Sporting Life*'s 'Man in the Ring' when, in the 1870s, the two papers first shared responsibility for determining the starting prices of horses at meetings, ensuring a fairer deal for the punter. With the turf his speciality, but turning his hand to all sports*, he wrote for the *Globe**, the *People* as its first sports editor*, the *Penny Illustrated*, *News of the World** and *Tribune*. In 1886 he joined the *Referee*, the Sunday* paper founded by Henry Sampson*, and his contributions under the pseudonym* 'Geraint' continued up until his death. He was a popular writer on the countryside and was the author of four books including *Racing Life and Racing Characters** (1903), with two volumes of his journalism published posthumously. ST

Sources: Cobbett 1896, Cobbett 1906, *Referee* 1906, *Sportsman* 1906, *The Times* 1906.

COBBETT'S POLITICAL REGISTER (1802-1836) *Cobbett's Political Register*, a Saturday weekly*, played a significant role in both the history of popular* journalism and the annals of radical politics*. The magazine earned William Cobbett the epithet, 'a kind of fourth estate in the politics of the country'. Hazlitt's famous phrase was coined not to describe the press generally but the extraordinary impact of one individual. For Cobbett's personality, acerbic, indignant at injustice, occasionally prejudiced, stamped every sheet of the paper. Other authors were not permitted by-lines, and Cobbett's columns* and open letters* developed and popularized an opinionated, editorial kind of journalism*.

Over the years of the *Register*'s publication, Cobbett moved politically from fierce anti-democrat to committed reformer. Indeed, his trajectory was so pronounced that during the Reform Bill crisis the government could publish a satirical* anti-Cobbett pamphlet using only the author's early writing. Known for his scathing satire* and Tory views, the young Cobbett received help founding the *Register*, in the form of a £600 investment from William Windham, the former Secretary at War. In the early issues of the 16-page, octavo-size* journal, Cobbett publicized his sponsor's speeches, focused on Parliament and foreign* affairs and attacked Jacobinism at home and abroad. But by 1805, Cobbett's polemics against the misuse of funds by Melville and Pitt brought him into the orbit of the radicals. For the next three decades, the columns of the journal excoriated sinecures, predatory taxes, military spending and the national debt. Cobbett eventually championed Catholic emancipation, the expansion of suffrage, the maintenance of generous poor relief and the end of Irish coercion.

Though relatively expensive, the *Register* was successful from the beginning. Its circulation* was 4,000 in 1805 and 6,000 in 1810. But in 1816 Cobbett revolutionized the popular press by pioneering a cheap* edition of his paper. To exploit loopholes in the Stamp Act*, Cobbett published* two versions of the *Register*. The second, priced* only 2d, avoided the stamp tax by omitting news* and appearing as a single broadsheet. The effect was electric. Cobbett's familiar idiom, his call for mass political participation and the paper's low price combined with the ferment of the post-war period to transform political* journalism. The *Register*'s circulation climbed to 40,000, and a single issue sold 200,000 copies. By the time the government passed the 1819 Newspaper Stamp Duties Act, which forced Cobbett to cease publishing the cheap edition, a generation of radical journalists had learned the potential of the unstamped* from Cobbett's experiment. In 1830-1832 Cobbett revived his inexpensive edition, now appearing monthly as *Cobbett's Twopenny Trash*, embracing the name conservative critics had dubbed his paper.

Cobbett was twice charged with seditious libel for articles that appeared in the *Register*. In June 1810, along with publishers Richard Bagshaw and John Budd and printer T. C. Hansard*, Cobbett was convicted for a broadside against the flogging of militia members at Ely. For the next two years, Cobbett defiantly dated his editorials 'State Prison, Newgate', even adding a Wednesday edition for a short period. The government failed to obtain a second conviction in 1831 for an article supporting the Swing rioters. Cobbett's legal victory demonstrated the immense popular support he enjoyed, as well as the strength of the radical opposition which he helped to nourish and which, in turn, propelled his career forwards. **GV**

Sources: Altick 1957, Aspinall 1949, Dyck 1992, Hollis 1970, Spater 1982.

COKE, CHARLOTTE H. TALBOT (1843-1922?) Mrs Talbot Coke, (née Fitzgerald) as she was known professionally, was a leading authority on home décor, most closely associated with *Hearth and Home**. According to fellow journalist* Mary Billington* 'many thousands of pounds' were spent every year on her advice. Her stay in Paris when young, travels with her husband, management of 25 houses in as many years, and experience as mother of three sons and four daughters proved invaluable in advising readers. Her early career on the *Queen** in the late 1880s was cut short when her husband, then a colonel, was suddenly sent to Egypt with his battalion. During more than two decades at *Hearth and Home,* of which she was co-proprietor*, she covered everything from redesigning a boudoir to buying furniture via 'the gradual purchase system'. Rather than present herself as the arbiter of style she instead encouraged a sense of 'friendly advice' to individuals and shared her personal preferences. Her 'Answers' column* was eventually so voluminous that replies were published in full as a supplement*.

Mrs Talbot Coke additionally contributed to papers such as *Woman's Life, Home Chat** and *Chambers's Journal** and covered home-related topics such as gardening* and engaging servants. **BMO**

Sources: Beetham 1996, Cohen 2005, Cohen 2006, Talbot Coke 1892.

COLBURN, HENRY (1784/5-1855) Henry Colburn was an innovative book publisher* of the first half of the century who was controversial for using his ownership of two influential journals, the weekly* *Literary Gazette** and the *New Monthly Magazine**, to promote the sale of his popular fiction. He was born in Chelsea, and emerged into publishing from the circulating* library* trade. In 1814, Colburn joined forces with Frederic Shoberl* to found the *New Monthly Magazine and Universal Register*, ostensibly to combat the radical politics of the *Monthly Magazine**. In 1821 'Universal Register' was dropped for 'Literary Journal', and, in an unusual move when editorial anonymity* was the norm, the poet Thomas Campbell* was announced as the editor* and was paid £500 for relatively light services. He was succeeded as a celebrity* editor by Edward Bulwer* (1831-1833), who for a few years turned the *New Monthly* into an intelligent vehicle for reform. When Colburn's ex-partner Richard Bentley* secured Charles Dickens* to edit his own journal, Colburn hired Theodore Hook* (1837-1841), followed by Thomas Hood* (1841-1843). The magazine* was sold to William Harrison Ainsworth* in 1845. Under Colburn's direction the *New Monthly* was a business asset, and profitable in its own right; he correctly gauged the growing public taste for literary* pleasure divorced from politics* and 'personalities'. More important to his business, however, was the magazine's ability to boost book sales through puffing and advertising*.

The *Literary Gazette* (begun 25 Jan. 1817) was the first widely popular* weekly* review* of books, and because its reviews appeared first was reputed to have a powerful impact on sales (Colburn's products were supplied to its reviewers before publication). The *Gazette* appeared on Saturdays and was edited by William Jerdan*, who with Colburn was part-proprietor* (and sole owner after 1841). Jerdan took a weak Tory line in politics but generally kept the paper light and appealing to a growing number of new readers, especially of fiction. Colburn hedged his book-reviewing bets by taking a share in the *Athenæum** when it was founded in 1828. In 1829, he began expanding into niche markets with the *Court Journal*, edited briefly by P. G. Patmore, as well as Laman Blanchard* (1836-1837), and *United Service Journal and Naval and Military Magazine* (1829; *United Service Magazine* after 1841). This was followed by a newspaper, *Naval and Military Gazette: East India and Colonial Chronicle* (1833). Between all of these endeavours (and more) his stable of writers and subeditors* moved freely. His staff was well-known as the writers of a form of puffing*; paid paragraphs* were short reviews of fiction on his list which were placed by Colburn in other journals as *bona fide* reviews. He gave up his business in 1853, and died two years later. DEL

Sources: Ainsworth 1854, Grant 1837, *ODNB*, Sullivan, *Wellesley*.

COLERIDGE, MARY ELIZABETH (1861-1907) Although Coleridge was a poet, novelist, teacher and advocate of women's rights, her longest-term success was as a critic and essayist. In the early 1880s, Coleridge began writing for several periodicals, often using the pseudonym* 'Anodos'. She contributed essays, articles and reviews*, poetry* and fiction, to the *Monthly Packet*, the *Monthly Review, Merry England*, and the *Guardian* (edited* in the 1890s by her distant relation, Christabel Rose Coleridge). Her essays were notable for their dry wit, and as a critic she was an early supporter of modern artists and playwrights, including Renoir, Monet, and Ibsen. In 1895, she began teaching at the Working Women's College while continuing to write for several prestigious periodicals, including, after 1902, the *Times Literary Supplement*. LAR

Sources: Blain 1990, *ODNB*, Sage 1999, Schlueter 1988, Shattock 1993.

COLERIDGE, SAMUEL TAYLOR (1772-1834) Coleridge published journalism throughout his career on literary*, political* and philosophical* topics as well as publishing* and editing* his own journals, and many of his important poems* appeared from 1793 in the *Morning Chronicle** and elsewhere. After canvassing support and obtaining sufficient subscriptions to make his first journal financially viable, he issued the *Watchman* in March 1796. In line with his early radicalism, and reflecting his sympathy for the ideals of the French Revolution, the *Watchman* bore the subtitle *That all may know the Truth; / And that the Truth may make us free!* Containing digests of news* from opposition papers – the *Morning Chronicle, Star* and the *Morning Post** – political leaders* by Coleridge, reviews* and poems, it appeared every eight days to avoid stamp duty* payable on weeklies, and lasted for ten issues.

In 1797 Coleridge began to contribute prose and verse to the *Morning Post*, and moved to London in 1799 to take up a regular job at the *Post*. Its editor* Daniel Stuart* valued Coleridge as a political writer of talent who could criticise Pitt while keeping his distance from Jacobinism. He briefly became parliamentary* reporter,

which he enjoyed, and continued to contribute to the *Post* until Stuart sold it in 1803. Stuart purchased the *Courier* (1792-1804) in 1800 or 1801, and Coleridge was again drafted in. The *Courier* took a patriotic line in the Napoleonic wars and was generally more pro-establishment than the *Post*. Stuart's change in political direction chimed with Coleridge's disaffection with radical politics, and Coleridge's articles for the *Courier* reveal a more conservative mindset, echoed by his turn from Unitarianism to a more orthodox Anglicanism. He continued to write for the *Courier* for many years, with some of these articles recycled subsequently. His savage attacks, reprinted in 1816, on a now forgotten play by C. R. Maturin (which had been preferred at Drury Lane to one of Coleridge's own productions) became a part of *Biographia Literaria*, rather undermining his calls in the same volume for a more reasoned and philosophical criticism that would escape from the partisanship and vindictiveness of contemporary journalism.

In 1808 Coleridge conceived his second journal, the *Friend**, in Grasmere with the Wordsworths. He wrote it mostly by himself, with Sara Hutchinson as amanuensis, and each number was taken by foot to Penrith for printing. Unlike the *Watchman*, it was weekly* and stamped, and its 16 pages were less concerned with reporting on immediate political developments than with elaborating a philosophical position inflected by his reading of Kant. It also expressed his newfound conservatism, and he now attacked Voltaire, Rousseau and the ideologues of the French Revolution freely. The *Friend* ran sporadically to 28 issues (June 1809-March 1810), but generated sufficient interest for later reprints, including a revised three-volume edition in 1818.

Coleridge's continued involvement in journalism occasionally got him into trouble, as when he became involved with the pranksters of *Blackwood's Magazine** from 1819, even offering to become 'London Editor or Curator'. His epistles both to William Blackwood and to the mischievous co-editor* John Gibson Lockhart* offered pompous and earnest advice on how the magazine should be run, but were apparently scoffed at. Lockhart twice embarrassed Coleridge by printing in *Blackwood's* private letters, on one occasion with an openly mocking preface. MaT

Sources: Ashton, 1996, *ODNB*, *Waterloo*.

COLLABORATION Collectively authored contributions, usually appearing serially under disguised authorship, were an intriguing feature of nineteenth-century periodicals. Examples of such series and their most prominent contributors include *Blackwood's** 'Noctes Ambrosianae' (March 1822-Feb. 1835), by John Wilson*, John Gibson Lockhart* and William Maginn*, and which pretended to include James Hogg; the *Examiner's** 'Round Table' (May 1814-Jan. 1817) by William Hazlitt* and Leigh Hunt*; and the *Pall Mall Gazette's** 'Wares of Autolycus' (29 May 1893-28 Dec. 1898) by Alice Meynell*, Violet Hunt, Elizabeth Pennell*, Rosamund Marriott Watson*, 'George Fleming' (Constance Fletcher), Katharine Tynan, Alice Dew-Smith, Edith Nesbit and, near the end of the run, Nathaniel Newnham-Davis.

For authors the appeal of such collaborations lay in the creative energy generated by collective, often competitive composition as well as the freedom afforded by authorial covers; in addition, readers enjoyed detecting or speculating on likely contributors. While such collaborations exemplify the collective nature of periodicals, the practice is particularly interesting because of its playful exception to individual authorship. Indeed, the relative lack of collaborative features towards mid-century perhaps reflects contemporary pressure to stabilize authorship – a practice consecrated in Romantic veneration of the solitary author and, with the attempt to institutionalize verifiable authorial signatures from 1860 as seen in sporadic debates about anonymity* and signature, it was a trend that later acts of dismantling paradoxically only reaffirmed. **KF**

Sources: Parker 2000, Schaffer 2000.

COLLINS FAMILY (FL. 1820-C. 1980) The Collins publishing dynasty was one of the largest and most influential of the nineteenth century. The original firm was founded in 1819, when William Collins (1789-1853) established William Collins & Co. a printing and publishing* business in Glasgow, in partnership with Charles Chalmers*. Collins was a devout Christian, and having taught religion and literacy, founded the first British temperance society in 1829. His involvement with evangelical Christian ethics and education was reflected in his publications. In 1826 Collins bought Chalmers out and went on to establish a company renowned for its prolific output of text books, classics, bibles, religious tracts, reference works and books on education, travel and science, although some links remained as Collins was the Glasgow publisher for the short-lived monthly miscellany*, *Chalmers' Journal of Useful Knowledge* (1827). Under William Collins I, the firm printed and published* a number of journals, including the *Ame-*

thyst or Christian's Annual (1832-1834), the *Theatrical Journal** (1849) and *Lowe's Edinburgh Magazine* (1848). Collins opened a London office in 1840. After 1853 William Collins was succeeded by his son William Collins II (1817-1895) under whose aegis the business expanded adding a paper* mill and a stationers' section. The installation of ten new steam presses in the 1860s made printing more economically viable. It helped Collins become one of the leading publishers of the Bible, and the firm eventually had a monopoly on Bible printing. In 1862 William Collins II was appointed the Queen's printer for Scotland. By 1880 the firm had nearly 2,000 employees, 28 presses with an output in excess of two million books annually. The firm continued producing some periodicals, printing the monthly *British Messenger** in 1858, and also published local* papers such as the *Dudley Weekly Times* (1858), the *Trowbridge Chronicle* (1861) and the almanack, *Collins' Directory of Trowbridge* (1888-1907). In 1874, the monthly 1d illustrated* *School Newspaper* was launched (Jan. 1874-July 1923). *Cheer-Me-Up*, sometimes known as, *Collins' Cheer-Me-Up* (1890-1891) was an illustrated 1d monthly true to its title, containing short stories, amusing anecdotes and other entertaining miscellaneous items. **DHL**

Sources: Bell 2007, *ODNB*, *Waterloo*, *Wellesley*.

COLLINS, WILLIAM (WILKIE) (1824-1889)
Though Wilkie Collins is best known as one of the creators of the sensation novel, his writing rhythm was characteristically that of a journalist*. His fiction was typically written to deadlines for publication in serial* form in magazines* or newspapers both in Britain and overseas, and he contributed over 100 non-fiction pieces to various journals. Of these only about a quarter were reprinted in book form during his lifetime, notably in the two-volume collection *My Miscellanies* (1863). Collins learned the trade of journalism in the early 1850s, turning out art, literature* or theatre reviews* for the monthly *Bentley's Miscellany** and the radical weekly* review the *Leader**. Then partly owned by his friend Edward Pigott (1824-1895), the *Leader* also offered Collins the chance to explore more polemical themes. Collins worked most concertedly in journalism between 1856 and 1862, as staff writer on the miscellanies* of Charles Dickens*, *Household Words** and *All the Year Round**. There his typical approach was to treat serious social issues ironically through humorous dramatic monologue or dialogue, thus blurring the boundaries between journalism and fiction. Later he produced much

less non-fiction, channelling his reformist enthusiasms directly into the later 'missionary' novels of the 1870s and 1880s. **GL**
Sources: Gasson 1998, Law and Maunder 2008, *ODNB*, Peters 1991.

COLONIAL PRESS The colonial press encompasses newspapers published in the British Empire, including Australia, Canada, India, New Zealand, and South Africa, but excluding Great Britain itself, and constitutes one way in which imperialism* and journalism* were linked.

The original mass*-circulation* newspaper produced in India was the *Bengal Gazette*, first published in 1780 followed by hundreds of publications on the South Asian subcontinent during the nineteenth century. These included Anglo-Indian productions such as the *Times of India*, Indian-English productions such as the *Hindu* and Indian-language newspapers such as *Amrita Bazar Patrika*. Similarly, South African periodical culture included both Afrikaner and English-language newspapers. The latter began in the 1820s with the first British settlers and comprised papers such as the *Cape Times*, *Cape Argus*, *Natal Mercury* and the *South African Journal*, which was the subcontinent's first literary journal (1824ff).

In the settler colonies of Canada, New Zealand and Australia, the colonial press began as a result of missionary* involvement and expanded most rapidly in the centres of high population. The long-running *Literary Garland and North American Magazine, A Monthly Repository of Tales, Sketches, Poetry, Music, etc.* (1838-1852) featured lithographic* illustrations*, engraved musical* scores and a number of original pieces by Canadians, including women. The *New Zealand Gazette* printed its first issue in London and the second issue in Wellington Harbor; the first illustrated weekly*, *Illustrated New Zealander*, was printed in 1866. The *Australian Magazine*, the first periodical to appear on the continent in 1821, was edited* by Methodist missionaries. In Australia, women more frequently acted as owners*, editors, and contributors to periodicals* such as the *Spectator: Journal of Literature and Art*.

The distribution* of colonial newspapers was limited by high postal rates, lack of equipment, personnel, capital and low advertising* revenue. From the late 1840s onwards, telegraph* networks allowed the rapid distribution of news*. However, because cable rates and individual subscriptions to news agencies* were prohibitively expensive, most colonial newspapers either collectively purchased news from agencies such as Reuters* or the Associ-

ated Press* (Canada) or continued to receive information from copies of British newspapers arriving by sea. **SR**
Sources: Codell 2003, Lambert 2006, Potter 2003, Raghavan 1994, Vann 1996.

COLUMNS Columns are basic units of graphic design in newspapers and periodicals that distinguish serials from most printed books and predate later additions of page design such as tiered headlines, subheads, font variation and imaginative layout. In large formats* such as broadsheets, the division of pages into multiple columns presents copy in widths that the eye can read. Ruled or unruled, columns impose a vertical reading of broadsheet pages, which were both significantly wider and longer than most book formats* in the nineteenth century. Columns of this sort extend to many weeklies*, the frequency* and topicality of which retain links with news*, but more bookish serials* such as monthlies* and early nineteenth-century quarterlies* often refrained from the use of columns, retaining a more literary appearance. The breakdown of columns, whereby copy spreads across two or more columns, seems to have begun in display advertising* in the latter half of the century, in harbingers of the New Journalism* such as the *Pall Mall Gazette*.

'Column' has a second meaning and function in nineteenth-century journalism, irrespective of whether the item is printed in column format. It is distinguished from other copy in an issue: it may have a recurring title ('Noctes Ambrosianae' in early *Blackwood's* or 'The Old Saloon' in late *Blackwood's*, or 'Over the Teacups' in *Woman at Home*) or a recurring signature, normally a recognizable pseudonym*; it reappears regularly, if not in every number, and it is normally distinguished from other serialized articles by its longevity, not having a foreseeable ending. Columns in this sense accord such copy an apparent freedom from the collective policies of the journal, and may license highjinks apparently unsanctioned by the editor*, and less vulnerable to charges of libel. While 'Noctes Ambrosianae' exemplifies the latter points, it was written by different contributors from number to number.

Columns of this kind can function in a variety of ways: as covert leaders* (eg 'Yellow Dwarf' in the *Yellow Book*); as a form of signature for an author whose pieces are thereby linked and identified, rather than lost in the porridge of anonymity* (e.g. 'Vivian' in the *Leader*); as a mnemonic 'name' whose writing the reader attaches to the title and may look forward to in successive issues. In this way columns

may be seen as one of the strategies of serials to create desire and expectation in readers that will result in reiterated purchase over time. **LRB/AK**
Sources: Beetham 2000, BritPer, Shattock 2000, *Waterloo, Wellesley.*

COLVIN, SIDNEY (1845-1927) A critic, biographer and museum administrator, Sidney Colvin established his reputation as a critic, mainly of fine art. He wrote for *Cornhill Magazine** (1872-1881), *Dark Blue** (1871), *Edinburgh Review**, (1879), *Fortnightly Review** (1867-1887), *Longman's Magazine** (1895), *Macmillan's Magazine** (1872-1888), *Magazine of Art** (1885-1886), *New Quarterly Magazine** (1878), *Nineteenth Century** (1877-1899), *Pall Mall Gazette**, *Portfolio** (1870-1883), and *Westminster Review** (1871).

In 1872 Colvin published two volumes compiled from his journalism, *Children in Italian and English Design* followed by *A Selection from Occasional Writings on Fine Art* (1873). Colvin's journalism established his art credentials and he was elected Slade Professor of Fine Art at Cambridge (1873-1885). His appointment as director of the Fitzwilliam Museum, Cambridge, in 1876 was followed by his selection as Keeper of Prints and Drawings at the British Museum (1884-1912). He continued to produce journalism and books, writing biographies and editing collections of Landor (1881) and Keats (1887) as well as R. L. Stevenson (1899).

As an art critic Colvin was an early advocate of aestheticism (*Fortnightly Review* 1867) and he continued to champion artists associated with this movement and the new Grosvenor Gallery in the ensuing decades. **MEC**
Sources: Colvin 1921, *ONDB, Poole's, Wellesley.*

COMIC ALMANACK (1835-1853) While strictly speaking a serial rather than a periodical, the *Comic Almanack* was projected as a sustained pastiche of the almanac form. Almanacs, with their roots in popular superstition, were in the 1830s a subject of considerable contention, and certainly vulnerable to travesty. Gilbert À Beckett, the editor* of the *Comic Almanack,* assembled a team of outstanding contributors that included Thackeray*, Hood*, Henry Mayhew* and Albert Smith*, but it was the combination of etched plates and wood* engraved textual illustrations* by George Cruikshank*, Ebenezer Landells* and H. G. Hine* superimposed on the traditional almanac format that gave the publication much of its energy and visual appeal. Tied closely to the gift book and Christmas* market, like the many comic annuals* of the 1830s, the *Comic Almanack* survived for

nearly 20 years, providing a source for *Punch's** equally well-known 'Almanack' in the process. An important link between the world of Regency grotesque humorous modes and the more genteel modes quickly adopted by *Punch*, the *Comic Almanack* remains a rich source for understanding the social anxieties of the early Victorian middle classes*. It was popular enough to be reprinted several times in the later nineteenth century. **BM**
Sources: Patten 1992, Vogler 1979.

COMIC ANNUALS Initially a fad of the 1830s, comic illustrated* gift books, usually illustrated by small scale wood* engravings that drew on Regency caricature* tropes, became one of the serial publications that supplied the Christmas* book trade. The most successful, with an annual circulation* according to one source of at least several thousand copies, was the 'anniversary of literary fun' published as the *Comic Annual* and edited by Thomas Hood*(1830-1839; 1842). But the *Comic Offering* (1831-1835), edited by Louisa Sheridan* and illustrated mainly by women artists, and the *New Comic Annual* (n.d.), with cuts by William Brown, also attracted many readers. Robert Seymour* was one of several well-known comic artists who projected annuals* under his own name; he also drew the title pages and frontispieces for the *Comic Offering*.

The use of distinctive publishers'* bindings, illustrated paper boards and the pocketbook size of the comic annuals all contributed to their distinctive presence in the marketplace, and suggested growing awareness of 'brand identity'. Clearly aimed at exploiting the seasonal market and readership* established by the literary annual and gift book in the 1820s, comic annuals also proved a useful way for the fading caricature* tradition to extend its popularity through seriality, targeting family social occasions with a whimsical humour based on the visual/verbal pun and the humorous anecdote rather than on political satire*. There were later attempts to sustain this formula, especially by Tom Hood the Younger, but the more miscellaneous yearly annual supplements* offered cheaply or free by many magazines* and the rising popularity of comic journals like *Punch** rendered the genre* obsolete. **BM**
Sources: British Annuals and Giftbooks (online), SciPer (online).

COMIC CUTS (1890-1953) *Comic Cuts* was founded by the future newspaper tycoons Alfred and Harold Harmsworth* as a light-hearted alternative to the so-called 'penny dreadfuls', which were considered to be a bad influence on working-class boys.

Comic Cuts gave 'One Hundred Laughs for one Halfpenny!'. Its formula of comic strips and snippets was based on the concept pioneered by George Newnes* with his comic magazine *Tit-Bits**. With its low price* of ½ d, *Comic Cuts* was a cheaply produced weekly* paper. Its typeface was tiny, it was printed on poor quality paper* and many of its cartoons* were 'dim and dated'. Although much of the text was lifted from back numbers of Harmsworth's earlier paper *Answers**, (1888). Alfred Harmsworth claimed that *Comic Cuts* employed 'the best artists' and was 'printed on good paper' and it rapidly became Harmsworth's best seller. By 1891 its price rose to 1d, which did not prevent the circulation* from rising to 430,000 one year later.

Comic Cuts was so successful that its first two numbers sold out. Other publishers began to publish halfpenny comics, but Harmsworth was soon producing another comic of his own called *Funny Cuts* (1890). The main attraction of *Comic Cuts* was in its humorous comic strips, while its illustrations* also included sketches and drawings. Most of these were in black and white, but there was occasional colour printing as in the 'Autumn Double Number' of 15 October 1895. Also included were stories, advertisements*, jokes, poetry* and serial* fiction. Harmsworth claimed that it was the first 'halfpenny illustrated' ever to offer 'valuable prizes' for competitions. *Comic Cuts* was published in Australia and South Africa. In September 1953, it became *Funny Wonder*. **DHL**
Sources: Dunae 1979, Egoff 1951, Gifford 1975a, Gifford 1976b, *Waterloo*.

COMMONWEAL (1885-1894) The official publication of the Socialist League, the *Commonweal* was a London penny paper* edited* by William Morris* and subedited* by Edward Aveling. It was published monthly* until 1886 and then weekly* when Ernest Belfort Bax* became subeditor*. Compared to other socialist* periodicals at this time, the *Commonweal* had the most illustrious list of contributors: Morris, Aveling and Bax published a-longside Andreas Scheu, John Sketchley, Pierre Kropotkin, Paul Lafargue (Marx's son-in-law), Eleanor Marx* (Karl Marx's daughter and Aveling's common-law wife) and Friedrich Engels (whose famous 'England in 1845 and in 1885' appeared in 1885). Morris's major radical works appeared in the periodical, including: 'Socialism from the Root Up' (1886-1888), written in collaboration with Bax; 'How We Live and How We Might Live' (1887); 'A Dream of John Ball' (1886-1887); 'The Pilgrims of Hope' (1885-1886); and 'News from Nowhere' (1890). The paper opposed the Sudan War in 1885 and attacked child prostitution when it was exposed by W. T. Stead* in the *Pall Mall Gazette** in 1885. Though the first issue sold 5,000 copies, sales settled at 2,000-3,000 per issue, requiring Morris personally to subsidize the publication.

Poor circulation* coincided with the takeover of both the Socialist League and the paper by the anarchist faction. This change was reflected in *Commonweal*'s subtitles: the original *The Official Organ of the Socialist League* became *A Journal of Revolutionary Socialism* (Dec. 1890) and later *A Revolutionary Journal of Anarchist Communism*. The anarchist faction ousted Morris from his position as editor in 1890, and he was succeeded by David Nicholl (imprisoned in 1892 for using the paper to incite murder) and Thomas Cantwell. From this point *Commonweal* appeared erratically, alternating between monthly and weekly publication. It closed in 1894 without regaining the influence and calibre of its early days. **DM/NK**
Sources: Mutch 2005, *ODNB*, Thompson 1955

COMPANION FOR YOUTH (1858-61) The *Companion for Youth* (1858-1861) was edited* by John and Mary Bennett for the 'boys and girls of England'. The magazine started as a weekly* under the title the *Boys' and Girls' Companion for Leisure Hours*, but as it did not prove very successful it became the *Companion for Youth* in 1858 and was published monthly* instead. The magazine* was intended to be an informative, educational* and most of all entertaining juvenile* paper, whilst retaining a morally uplifting tone throughout. It included educational sections such as 'history* and biography', 'poetry'*, 'science'*, 'natural history', but also entertaining ones such as 'tales and sketches', 'charades and puzzles', 'design in needle-work' and 'the girls' work-table'. It was enriched with many drawings, colour plates, engravings, and wood* engravings.

The *Companion for Youth* offers 12 pages per week for 1d and 28-32 pages per month for 2d. Its editor* John Bennett (1815-1894) was also responsible for the *Dublin University Magazine**, besides writing fiction and working as a journalist. His wife and co-editor Mary Bennett (1813-1899), who wrote novels such as *The Jew's Daughter* and *The Gipsey Bride*, worked as a contributor for the magazine, alongside writers such as Richard Chandler, Edward Cox* and Madame Eugenie. The *Companion for Youth* did not employ its own illustrators, but instead borrowed most of its illustrations* and drawings from other titles. Even

though the magazine initially enjoyed reasonable popularity, it only survived for three years. The fierce competition* of the other boys' magazines contributed to its early demise. **OD**
Sources: Jay 1919, *ODNB*, Rollington 1913, *Waterloo*.

COMPANION TO THE NEWSPAPER; AND JOURNAL OF FACTS IN POLITICS, STATISTICS, AND PUBLIC ECONOMY (1834-1837) was published under the auspices of Charles Knight's* two issuing bodies*, the Society for the Diffusion of Useful Knowledge* and later the Society for the Diffusion of Political Knowledge. It was published monthly* and cheaply (2d initially, though the price* later increased by necessity) as a way of allowing more extended discussion of news* and events than the daily* and weekly* press had space or time to allow, but also as a way of avoiding the stamp* duty. The *Companion* sought to take some of the major political* issues of the day – such as the Poor Laws – and provide more extensive material about them to help readers augment and supplement their daily and weekly reading. There were occasional, single-topic supplements* and annual* news round-ups or 'retrospects'. Off-shoots of the journal include an almanac and the *Printing Machine; A Review for the Many** (edited by George Lillie Craik, 4d, monthly, from 1834). **MWT**
Sources: Gray 2006, *Waterloo*.

COMPETITION Competition shaped an expanding market* for journalism in the nineteenth century, whether one preferred a regulated market* or welcomed a free one. In the first half of the century competition tended to be between classes of newspapers rather than within market niches: it was curbed by the strong party affiliations of the relatively few dailies*, and stimulated between classes of papers by newspaper* taxes which resulted in expensive, news-rich titles, as set against cheaper alternatives that were shorn of political news*, or infrequent or illegal. After the removal of stamp duty in 1855, when titles and readership* proliferated, competition among titles accelerated within niche markets; with the advent of general newspaper access to the telegraph* from 1870 in the UK, the speed of the publication of news* enhanced competition among journalists* as well as among titles for sales in a widely expanded market of cheap* papers.

While many established newspaper proprietors* supported newspaper taxes in the first half of the century as a means of limiting competition and prohibiting the proliferation of cheap papers, some quarterly* reviews and monthly* magazines* exploited it by juicy parodies of their rivals, and in-

Figure 10: 'New Journalism' in competition, *Longman's Magazine*, July 1885: 10.

teractive barbs in order to increase circulation*. Other newspapers similarly exploited what they saw as unfair competition in the ownership and dissemination of news by undercutting the price* of stamped papers in illicitly published, unstamped titles*, which were cheap and accessible to many working-class readers*. As newspaper taxes diminished from 1833, so competition among serial titles across the board increased as cheaper and eventually penny papers* appeared.

Forms of competition were always changing. While it might bite as a result of new or rejuvenated rivals, it might also take the forms of reduction of prices in a price war, the introduction of new technology such as the steam press* or illustration*, the issue of extras or supplements*, or the inclusion of popular fiction by a rival publication. Proprietors*, such as Herbert Ingram*, of successful journals, for instance, the *Illustrated London News**, could target rivals, buy them and merge* or force them to cease publication. Competition might also result from the division of an extant market, exemplified in the succession of the *Nineteenth Century**, the *St James's Gazette** and the *Savoy** to the *Contemporary Review**, the *Pall Mall Gazette**, and the *Yellow Book** respectively; or from the addition of features exploited particularly by New Journalism* such as puzzles, competitions, prizes, interviews*, gossip*, sports'* news, and signature. Among titles carrying news, the speed of newsgathering, its catchy communication and rapid distribution* also became important elements of competition among dailies* and weeklies* in the nineteenth century.

All titles were dynamic in time, with regular changes of price, frequency*, title, proprietor*, editor* and political* affiliation or issuing body*. The effect of competition on these and on sales has been often overlooked, even in individual histories of titles. LRB/AK

Sources: Jackson 1885, Jones 2005, King 2004, Sinnema 1998, *ODNB, Waterloo.*

CONSTABLE, ARCHIBALD (1774-1827) Designated a publisher* 'of uncommon importance to literature*' by Walter Scott*, Archibald Constable first made his name and established his professional reputation as the publisher of the quarterly *Edinburgh Review*. The review's founders, Sydney Smith*, Francis Jeffrey*, and Francis Horner* entrusted its publication to Constable, who put up the money for the first three numbers. Sydney Smith suggested that if he were to pay the editor £200 per annum, and the contributors ten guineas a sheet (of 16 pages), he would 'soon have the best review in Europe'. The stratagem proved highly effective, attracting a wide range of able contributors.

The *Edinburgh* payments, which eventually rose as high as £20 and £25 per sheet were unmatched by most of its competitors*. Constable gave the review's founders a free hand by distancing his own publications from their agenda, unlike the publishers of eighteenth-century monthly reviews* who routinely used them to promote their own lists. The *Edinburgh's* sales of more than 13,000 by its second decade were a tribute not only to clever and often iconoclastic reviewing*, but also to Constable's promotional skills. He had gained experience in journal publishing by setting up the *Farmer's Magazine* in 1800 and in 1801 had purchased the *Scots Magazine* (established in 1739). He later added the *Edinburgh Medical and Surgical Journal*, the *Edinburgh Philosophical Journal* and the publications of learned societies, including the Royal Society of Edinburgh, the Highland Society, the Caledonian Horticultural Society and the Wernerian Society, to his lists. In 1813 he became the publisher of the *Edinburgh Annual Register*.

Constable recognized that sales of the *Edinburgh Review* south of the border could be enhanced by an energetic London partner. This was entrusted to the firm of Thomas Longman*, who later bought a half-share in the review. The relationship of the two firms was not an easy one. As well as the *Edinburgh*, Constable's two other major publishing ventures were the *Encyclopaedia Britannica*, which he purchased in 1812, and the works of Walter Scott. Constable's business affairs were inextricably linked to those of Scott and his partners James and John Ballantyne*. When the latter experienced financial difficulties, exacerbated by the national financial crisis of 1812-1814, Constable's firm was plunged into crisis, only partially remedied by an upturn in the sales of Scott's works. After a protracted period of fluctuation, and precipitated by the financial crisis of 1825-1826, the firm eventually crashed in 1826. Longman purchased the *Edinburgh Review* outright after the bankruptcy. Constable never fully recovered from the disaster, and died the following year. JS

Sources: Bell 2007, Clive 1957, Constable 1873, *ODNB.*

CONSTABLE & CO. (1804-) Multiple publishing* houses and printers incorporating the name 'Constable' existed during the nineteenth century. While they were not all directly connected, they constitute a publishing lineage by virtue of having been owned by members of the same family. Together, the Constables as publishers* and printers are involved with numerous, and some eminent periodical and newspaper titles in the period.

In addition to the prestigious and weighty *Edinburgh Review*, Constable published more bread and butter periodicals such as the *Farmer's Magazine* (1800-1825), the *Scots Magazine* (1801ff), and the *Edinburgh Medical and Surgical Journal* (1805ff), as well as a wide array of books and pamphlets. Constable's bookselling work, a sideline he abandoned in 1815, allowed him to build connections to booksellers, book buyers and authors in London and throughout Scotland. Constable & Co. acquired the *Encyclopedia Britannica* in 1812, but was by then in severe financial difficulties. The house was saved by the return of Scott and the publication of *Waverley* in 1814. Constable purchased all of Scott's copyrights* outright in 1820, but a planned edition of Scott's complete works came to nothing when the house went bankrupt in 1826. In that year the firm had commenced publication of a monthly series of flagship volumes, *Constable's Miscellany: of original and selected works in literature*, art, and science* (1826-1835). Constable & Co. began in 1804, founded by the Scottish publisher* and bookseller Archibald Constable*. Even before its official establishment, the house acquired two significant publishing projects. The *Edinburgh Review** (1802 ff) attracted a high class of contributors thanks to its generous pay. The necessity of having a distribution* partner in southern England caused some instability, but taking this step assured Constable of guaranteed bulk purchases. Also in 1802, Constable became involved in the sales of Walter Scott's work, a relationship which included the purchase of Scott's *Marmion* for the previously unheard of sum of 1,000 guineas. However, after receiving a negative review of the work from Francis Jeffrey* in the firm's own *Edinburgh Review* in April 1808, Scott broke away, forming his own publishing fit in.

The publishing house had long been connected with the printing business of David Willison, and in 1833 Constable's son Thomas took over this business under his own name, becoming King's Printer in 1835 and Printer to the University of Edinburgh four years later. Numerous periodicals were printed, ranging from the *Edinburgh Ladies' Magazine* (1843) to evangelical journals such as the *Children's Missionary Record* (1845), the *British Mother's Magazine** (1845ff), the monthly *Bulwark, or Reformist Journal*, and reports from the Women's Foreign Missionary Society of the Free Church of Scotland. On a different note, the firm printed the first numbers of the quarterly* *North British Review** (1844 ff) and the *Scottish Jurist*. In the late 1840s he began publishing as Thomas Constable & Co. The house's publications included the complete works of Dugald Stewart. Thomas Constable continued as a publisher until 1860, at which point he sold the publishing business to Edmonston & Douglas, though he kept the printing establishment, which was one of the early printers of *Good Words** (1860). In the mid-1860s, Thomas's son Archibald because a partner, and the name was changed to T & A Constable. This imprint is associated in 1890 with the printing of the first numbers of the weekly* *Scots Observer**, and the *Art Review*.

Archibald Constable & Co. was founded in London in 1890, and in 1894-1895 they picked up the printing of the London-based trade* journal the *Artist**: *An illustrated monthly record of arts, crafts & industries*, which had recently experienced a sudden makeover. Soon the firm established itself as publishers of good literature* in editions of George Meredith in both 32-volumes (1896) and in an 18-volume New Popular Edition (1897-1898) and, by the turn of the century, of contemporary drama in the emerging works of George Bernard Shaw. **TR**
Sources: Bell 2007, Constable 1937, Memoir c. 1870 *ODNB*, Rose and Anderson 1991, *Waterloo*.

CONTEMPORARY REVIEW (1866-1988) The Presbyterian publisher* Alexander Strahan* launched the Broad Church* monthly* *Contemporary Review* after popular success with his evangelical miscellany* *Good Words**. A more highbrow venture, it contained no fiction. The *Contemporary* responded to the appearance of the secular *Fortnightly Review** in 1865, aiming to provide the Established Church with a liberal forum for similarly serious, signed essays on theology and philosophy*. The launch editor* was the Anglican Henry Alford* but the *Contemporary Review*'s reputation grew under James Thomas Knowles* editor* (1870-1877). A founder of the Metaphysical Society, Knowles published articles by Society members Matthew Arnold*, W. E. Gladstone, T. H. Huxley* and John Ruskin*. Sacked by Strahan for insufficiently theological contents, Knowles left, with a number of contributors, to found and edit the *Nineteenth Century*. In 1882, editorship of the *Contemporary* passed to Percy Bunting, who devoted greater space to international politics. Under Bunting (who helped to found the National Vigilance Association in 1885), the monthly pursued social reform with zeal. W. T. Stead's* essay 'Government by Journalism' (1886) was characteristic in arguing for the political* power held by the press. Although the departure of Knowles was a setback, the *Contemporary Review* remained a prominent high-cultural journal into the twentieth century. **AC**
Sources: Brake 1994a, *ODNB*, Srebrnik 1986, Sullivan 1984, *Wellesley*.

COODE, HELEN HOPPNER (FL. 1859-1882) Eldest daughter of George Coode, barrister and poor law reformer and Helen Meyer, Helen Coode was an illustrator*, artist and writer.

Between 1859 and 1861, Coode was the first woman to work for *Punch**. However, as her work was signed with a conjoined double H surmounted with a C, the reading public would not have been aware of her gender* from her signature. From 1859, she also worked for *Once a Week**. **CL**
Sources: England's Poor Law Commissioners, Houfe 1978.

COOK, EDWARD TYAS (1857-1919) E.T. Cook joined the Inner Temple in 1881, but turned to journalism* instead of politics or law to become 'one of the most influential journalists' in late Victorian and Edwardian London (*ODNB*).

Initially an occasional contributor to *Truth**, *Pall Mall Gazette**, *Temple Bar**, and the *Oxford Chronicle*, he joined the staff of the *Pall Mall Gazette* at Alfred Milner's* request and in 1888 became assistant editor* to W. T. Stead*. Cook took over as editor following Stead's departure in 1889 and though he learned much from Stead, their styles were very different: Cook 'relied upon quiet, incisive argument, not emphatic assertion and remonstrance' (*ODNB*). He was methodical and effective, with a 'mind in which everything seemed to be indexed' (Spender: 33) and invented a multi-reference index system which he called 'clag books', based on scrap books of clippings. According to H. W. Massingham*, Cook turned the *Gazette* into a 'young man's paper' (Massingham: 188), though it maintained its focus on social issues and liberal imperialism*.

In 1892 when W. W. Astor bought the *Gazette* and reoriented it towards Tory interests, Cook resigned, along with many of his staff. In 1893 he launched the *Westminster Gazette** with the financial support of George Newnes* to continue the *Pall Mall Gazette* traditions. However, he moved to the editorial role at the *Daily News** in 1895, even though Cook had previously dismissed the paper as a mere party mouthpiece (*ODNB*). As editor of the *Daily News*, he believed his duty was to keep 'steadily in view the larger interests and duties of the country', and to ignore 'mere party considerations in the face of national emergency' (Koss: 1.399; cited in *ODNB*). Thus he supported the war in South Africa and entered into conflict with 'Little Englanders' within the Liberal Party, and with staff members of the *News* who had joined the paper before Cook had shifted its politics*. The purchase of the *Daily News* by an anti-imperialist* group that included the Quaker, George Cadbury, in 1901 saw Cook dismissed.

Following his ignominious exit from his high profile press position Cook worked as leader* writer for the *Daily Chronicle** until 1910, but much of his energy was diverted towards his magisterial editing, with Alexander Wedderburn, of John Ruskin's* work in 39 volumes (1903-1911); biographies followed including *Delane of the Times* (1915). Cook went on to play an important role in the press bureau established in 1915 by Winston Churchill to manage media coverage during the First World War and later wrote about the experience. **FD**

Sources: Koss 1981, Massingham 1892, Mills 1921, *ODNB*, Spender 1927.

COOK, ELIZA (1812-1889) In her day, Eliza Cook was regarded first and foremost as a poet as her various obituaries* indicate: the 'popular poetess' is noticed well before the *Journal* bearing her name. She published *Lays of a Wild Harp* in 1835

and poetry anonymously* in various journals including *Metropolitan Magazine** and *New Monthly Magazine**. Her rapid popularity convinced her to publish under her own name. *Melaia and Other Poems* appeared in 1838, the *Athenaeum** declaring the work 'calculated to please the not very select readers of a provincial* newspaper.... Eliza Cook, in her happiest vein, is a sort of 'L.E.L.' for the working classes'*.

In 1849 she began publishing *Eliza Cook's Journal**. She was proprietor* and editor*, contributing both poetry* and articles, the latter evincing a lively, humorous style suggesting a male persona, in an ironic positioning given the female name of the journal and her preference for male-style dress. Her prefatory 'A Word to my Readers' declares that she is not 'anxious to declare myself a mental Joan of Arc'; rather she wishes to aid 'the gigantic struggle for intellectual elevation', and this, with the low cost, 1s ½d, suggests an artisan and lower-middle class readership*, with a focus on women, addressing domestic* and work issues for women, and publishing women's writing. The *Journal* allowed Cook to further the ideals of social and gender* equity broached in her poetry. She ceased publishing the *Journal* in 1854 due to ill-health. Her *Journal* essays were republished in *Jottings from My Journal* (1860). **JEJ**

Sources: Anon *Athenaeum* 1838, Fraser 2003, *DNB* Supplement, *Waterloo*.

COOK, JOHN DOUGLAS (1808?-1868) John Douglas Cook was a newspaper editor* from Aberdeenshire. The date of his birth is uncertain: it was possibly 1808 yet he claimed he was born in 1811. He was rumoured to be the illegitimate son of the author Thomas Hope, making him half-brother to A. J. B. Beresford Hope*, with whom he later collaborated*. Early in his career, he went to India as a clerk, but after a disagreement with his employers Cook returned to London, and lived by his wits doing literary* work. This included indexing early volumes of the *Quarterly Review** for John Murray*. The acceptance of an anonymous* article by *The Times** led to Cook becoming a reporter* and making the acquaintance of the proprietor* John Walter*. In 1841 Cook acted as a canvassing agent for Walter's Tory candidacy, through which he met Lord Lincoln.

When, in 1848, Lincoln with some other Peelites bought the *Morning Chronicle and London Advertiser**, Cook was appointed editor*. Since he had limited editorial experience, he appointed the Unitarian Philip Harwood as co-editor and they worked

together on various titles until Cook's death in 1868. Cook employed several well-known writers and journalists* including William Makepeace Thackeray*, Henry Mayhew* and Eliza Lynn Linton*. Although the *Morning Chronicle** was a literary success, it failed politically* and financially. After it was sold in 1854, Cook went on to plan a new journal with Beresford Hope*. Their joint venture, the weekly *Saturday Review of Politics, Literature, Science and Art**, first appeared on 3 Nov. 1855. Its success was mainly due to the editorial prowess of Cook and its lively articles. Cook was exacting, but he also promoted young talent, and became one of the most efficient newspapermen of his time. DHL
Sources: Bevington 1941, Escott 1911, *ODNB*, Sullivan, *The Times* 1868.

COOKE, MORDECAI CUBITT (1825-1914)
Cooke's journalism was connected with his lifelong interest in natural history, and he contributed to at least 35 periodicals, usually on mycological subjects, and edited* three successful journals: *Hardwicke's Science-Gossip**, the *Journal of the Quekett Microscopical Club**, and *Grevillea*. Cooke's first contributions to the press were for the *School and the Teacher* (1854-1860), written while he was teaching in Lambeth. In 1860 he was introduced to the publisher* Robert Hardwicke*, beginning a productive relationship with his firm. Cooke started publishing his books with Hardwicke and, in 1865, co-founded the long-running natural history monthly* *Hardwicke's Science-Gossip*, editing the journal until 1871. With Hardwicke, Cooke also co-founded the Quekett Microscopical Club and, although already de facto editor of its *Journal*, took over officially in 1869. Cooke fell out with Hardwicke in 1871, leaving *Hardwicke's Science-Gossip* in the same year and the *Journal of the Quekett Microscopical Club* in 1872. His next venture was *Grevillea*, a journal devoted to cryptogamic botany. Initially a monthly, Cooke edited *Grevillea* as a quarterly* until 1892. He sold the journal to his protégé George Massee, but it was not a success and ceased publication in 1894. JEM
Sources: English 1987, Lightman 2004a, *ODNB*.

COOPER, THOMAS (1805-1892) Thomas Cooper was a radical journalist*, lecturer and poet who first became involved in newspaper work in Lincoln in the 1830s. His radical contributions to the *Lincoln, Rutland and Stamford Mercury* increased sales but also made Cooper enemies. Thwarted in his ambition of becoming editor*, he went to London and scraped a meagre living from small journalistic ventures. In 1840 his fortunes improved when he was appointed editor* of the *Kentish Mercury*. His radical leaders* met with the approval of the owner, but there was soon another falling out and Cooper left. He took up a position on the *Leicestershire Mercury*, and this brought him into contact with Chartism*. Under Cooper's leadership, Leicester became a Chartist stronghold and he edited five Chartist* periodicals (Feb. 1841-June 1842). Few other local areas had the level of support to contemplate so many radical publications, though Cooper accepted money from local Tories to sustain the *Midland Counties Illuminator* (Jan.-May 1841) and the *Extinguisher* (July-Nov. 1841). His head full of the poetical, theological and historical writings he had absorbed as a young autodidact, Cooper filled his periodicals with the radicalism of the past. The title of the *Commonwealthsman* (Dec. 1841-June 1842), for example, reflected his admiration for seventeenth-century radicals.

After completing a prison sentence for seditious conspiracy, Cooper resumed his journalistic career in the late 1840s. In 1849 Benjamin Steill, the publisher* of the famous *Black Dwarf**, gave him the opportunity to edit a new radical journal, the *Plain Speaker*. Notable for its letters* to public figures, circulation* in the first weeks reached 5-7,000. *Cooper's Journal** followed in 1850, but this was Cooper's last attempt to edit his own periodical. Numerous Chartist journals of the 1840s and 1850s included contributions from Cooper, and he also wrote for *Douglas Jerrold's Weekly Newspaper** and the *People*. His activities as a journalist came to an end when, in the late 1850s, he devoted his life to lecturing in defence of Christianity. SFR
Sources: Cooper 1971, *ODNB*, Roberts 1993, Roberts 2008.

COOPER'S JOURNAL: OR, UNFETTERED THINKER AND PLAIN SPEAKER FOR TRUTH, FREEDOM AND PROGRESS (5 JANUARY-29 JUNE, 5-26 OCTOBER 1850) Launched as the personal radical journal of Thomas Cooper*, this weekly* penny* periodical of 16 pages was aimed at self-improving working men. Published* by James Watson*, it could also be purchased in monthly and one-volume format*.

Initially Cooper's Journal was a commercial success: after an initial circulation* of 9,000, it regularly sold several thousand copies a week. Cooper closed his journal down for a summer lecturing tour, but when publication was resumed, sales fell to an unsustainable 2,000 a week. That the magazine did so well at first owed much to Cooper's talents as a writer and editor*. His own contributions – advice to studiously-inclined young working men, mocking letters to the Bishop of Exeter – were guaranteed to be lively and interesting. His lectures based on David Friedrich Strauss' Leben Jesu, which at the time was greatly influencing his religious* thinking, also appeared each week. Additionally, Cooper published pieces from other able radical journalists, including the Tory-inclined Samuel Kydd* and Frank Grant, who wrote extensively for the radical press in the 1850s. Cooper also included a great deal of poetry* by artisan poets who would have been known to his readers – Gerald Massey*, J. A. Langford and William Jones. Trying very hard to emulate his radical hero William Cobbett*, Cooper tried to create an intimate relationship with his readers: his frontpage letters* read as though written to them personally, rejected poets were gently encouraged, and queries were answered. This was Cooper's second attempt at editing his own radical journal – the Plain Speaker had appeared in 1849 – but with the failure of this venture he confined himself to contributing to other people's periodicals. SFR

Sources: Cooper 1872, Roberts 1993.

CO-OPERATIVE MAGAZINE AND MONTHLY HERALD (1826-1830)

Owned and produced by the first London Co-operative Society, the *Co-operative Magazine and Monthly Herald* was a shilling* monthly*, octavo 24-page single-column* publication, which until 1828 was the sole periodical organ of metropolitan* co-operation. Published* by Knight* and Lacey*, and then by the firm of Hunt and Clarke, it featured numerous contributions from the co-operative theorist William Thompson (1785-1833). In its pages, Thompson developed a radical critique of competitive individualism, publicized his belief in popular education, calling for the independence of mechanics' institutes from 'middle-class'* control and outlined his plans for sexual equality*.

The *Co-operative Magazine* offered its readers a miscellaneous content including: the lectures of Frances Wright, Robert Owen* and Robert Dale Owen; book reviews*, anecdotes, poetry*, correspondence (including letters from Allen Davenport*) and reports from the Owenite communities at New Lanark, Orbiston and New Harmony. In January 1828, as the *Co-operative Magazine*, it reduced its price* to 6d in an attempt to increase circulation*, but this was raised to 1s when it became a quarterly* in July 1828. In 1828-1829 it was superseded as the voice of co-operation by several other titles* (including the *Co-operator*, the *Weekly Free Press* and the *Associate*), and its reinvention as a 16-page, 6d monthly in January 1830 as the *London Co-operative Magazine* was short-lived. The significance of the *Co-operative Magazine* was as a locus of debate between early co-operative thinkers and as a window into the organization of metropolitan co-operation in the 1820s. DSM

Sources: Harrison 1977, *Waterloo*.

CO-OPERATIVE PRESS

During the 1850s and 1860s there was a dearth of periodicals that recorded the vigorous growth of consumer co-operative societies, which were rapidly becoming a key feature of working-class* culture, especially in the industrial north of England. Both the *Christian Socialist* and G. J. Holyoake's* *Reasoner** devoted space to these developments after mid-century but were mostly concerned with religious* controversy. From 1860 Henry Pitman's journal the *Co-operator* attempted to reach a national audience but it was financially weak and never fulfilled this promise. Leaders of the co-operative movement, including old Owenite educationalists, campaigned for a national newspaper that they believed would be a vital means of propaganda and instruction. Consequently, from 1871 the *Co-operator* was replaced by the *Co-operative News and Journal of Associated Industry*, published weekly* in Manchester by the Co-operative Printing Society, a profit-sharing enterprise established two years earlier. Sold at the 'workingman's price'* of 1d. the initial circulation* of the paper disappointed the hopes of many. The fortunes of the paper improved after Samuel Bamford* took over as editor* in 1875. Climbing gradually from the 10,000 mark when it was first issued, by the turn of the century 50,000 copies were sold each week; this figure doubled by the end of the First World War. Heavily subsidized by local societies, the *News* was a difficult and demanding read with a decidedly improving tone. Scotland was served by the *Scottish Co-operator** from 1894.

A flood of co-operative periodicals appeared during the late nineteenth century. Many consumer societies produced their own monthly* or quarterly* 'records' which were distributed free to members with their groceries; there were at least 32 of these issued in all parts of the country by 1900, with a combined circulation of over 384,000 per month. Some records, such as *Comradeship* published by the Royal Arsenal Co-operative Society, were vital component parts of a vigorous alternative culture at the local level. From 1896 the Co-operative Wholesale Society (CWS) published a monthly entitled the *Wheatsheaf* which eventually supplanted or incorporated these periodicals: the CWS supplied the inner pages and local societies not served by their own journals contributed news*, reports and notices of events. This was by far the most successful journal in this period; by December 1902 over 208,000 copies were distributed to 366 societies. By the end of World War One the circulation of this paper had reached 500,000. The CWS also published *Millgate Monthly* from 1905 which tried to tap into the expanding market for miscellany* periodicals, though it failed to dent the circulation of journals such as Newnes's penny* *Tit-Bits**.

The co-operative press nurtured the talents of many important working-class journalists* and writers including Percy Redfern, James Haslam and Ethel Carnie. It was regarded as a superior alternative to the vulgarity and anti-working-class bias which characterised capitalist productions. Thoroughly didactic in tone, the informal education it furnished was of particular benefit to working-class housewives whose support largely determined the success of the retail stores. Spare time to devote to more formal instruction was a luxury for these women, but the *News* and other co-operative papers made it possible for many of them to learn about the wider movement within their homes. Mrs Wrigley, who joined the Oldham Society in the mid-1870s, was a typically overworked woman who managed to piece together her understanding of co-operation in this way: 'I can't say that I have read many books as I had no time,' she later recalled, although 'I have learnt a great deal through newspapers.' **PJG**

Sources: Cole 1945, Gurney 1996.

COPYRIGHT The British copyright regime in force throughout the Victorian period was confusing even to specialists, particularly with regard to periodical publications. The Copyright Commission, reporting in 1878, stated that the law was 'wholly destitute of any sort of arrangement, incomplete, often obscure, and... in many parts so ill-expressed that anyone who does not give strict study to it cannot expect to understand it', pointing out in particular that 'much doubt appears to exist in consequence of several conflicting legal decisions whether there is any copyright in Newspapers'.

The governing statute, passed before the boom in periodical publishing following the repeal of the 'taxes on knowledge'*, was the 1842 Copyright Act, which remained active until 1911 when extensive changes were introduced under pressure to bring British law into line with the Revised International Copyright Convention of 1908. The 1842 Act was above all concerned 'to afford greater Encouragement to the Production of literary Works of lasting benefit to the World'. It thus centred on copyright in books (the term 'book' being broadly defined to include items such as a volume, pamphlet, map, sheet of music or published drama) which was vested in the author. A separate section dealt with collective works such as encyclopaedias or magazines*, where, with certain exceptions and unless otherwise agreed by prior contract, copyright was vested in the proprietor* for a given period, though an article could only be reprinted with the express permission of its author. Newspapers were not specifically mentioned, and uncertainty remained for a considerable period in case law as to whether newspapers were to be understood as periodicals, as books or whether they were not subject to copyright at all under the act.

Thus the time-honoured practice of 'lifting' articles wholesale from other periodicals with acknowledgement but without authorization continued well after the mid-century, particularly in the newspaper press. For example, reports in *The Times** of Commodore Perry's expedition in 1852-1853 to open Japanese ports to Western trade were culled from the *New York Courier and Enquirer* and the *China Mail*. A judgment in 1881 established that newspapers were to be classed as books under the 1842 Act, but the question of which specific categories of newspaper content were subject to protection was left to a series of subsequent rulings. The extent of copyright in news* material itself was still at issue in the 1890s, when there were important decisions on the protection of press agency information. An article by Sidney Low in the *National Review** in summer 1892, and the lengthy correspondence* it generated, revealed that the legal situation still remained uncertain in many respects.

Regarding international copyright, Article 7 of the 1886 Berne Convention, to which Britain was a signatory, confirmed that authors could prevent the reproduction or translation of literary material appearing as *feuilleton** in newspapers. But in the United States there was zero protection for alien authors until 1891, so that British periodical contents were often appropriated across the Atlantic. **GL**

Sources: Copinger 1904, Low 1892, Nowell-Smith 1968, Saunders 1992, Shortt 1884.

CORBOULD, ASTOR CHANTREY (1853?-1920) A *Punch** regular (1871-1890), sporting* artist and illustrator*, Astor Corbould had been introduced to the magazine by his uncle Charles Keene* at the age of 18. Though never given the staff post he craved, Corbould was a popular

illustrator especially of hunting and equine subjects. He was also a 'Special Artist' for the *Illustrated London News** in 1876, and drew for a range of magazines in the 1890s, extending interests to include social and war* reportage. **BM**
Sources: Houfe 1978, Spielmann 1895.

CORK EXAMINER (1841-1996) Launched by John Francis Maguire as a 4d broadsheet of four pages published on Mondays, Wednesdays and Fridays, the *Cork Examiner* set out its stall as an alternative to the unionist *Cork Constitution.* 'England, or an English Parliament, will never give to Ireland the justice which Ireland has a right to demand', it proclaimed in the first issue. The *Examiner* reflected the politics* of conservative nationalism in the south-west of Ireland, regularly publishing 'Catholic intelligence' and offering little to members of other churches. O'Connell was repeatedly eulogised as Ireland's 'mighty leader' or Ireland's 'glorious leader'. The newspaper encouraged 'the march of peaceable and strictly constitutional agitation', and hoped 'that the spirit of Chartism* should be crushed for ever in this country'. However, when John Mitchel was sentenced to transportation (May 1848) it described him as a martyr, the victim of a British policy to pack juries and to 'stimulate madness into insurrection'. Similarly, the *Examiner* had little sympathy for Fenianism, but said it understood why there were 'misguided people who have allowed themselves to be tempted into this movement'. It provided Justin McCarthy with his first opportunity as a journalist*, and later published his articles on the Irish Famine.

The nationalist split over Parnell demonstrated the *Examiner*'s alignment with the Catholic Church, suggesting that those who attended his funeral in October 1891 had done so 'not because of, but in spite of the unhappy proceedings which darkened the last years of his life'. Aside from its reports on national and regional news* and its often trenchant leaders*, the *Cork Examiner* carried detailed parliamentary reports*, listings of the latest prices of stocks, shares and commodities from Cork, Dublin, Liverpool, London and elsewhere, extensive classified advertisements* and international news*.

The price* had risen to 6d by 1851, and it claimed a circulation* of 161,000 in 1850. It went daily* in 1858, dropping in price to 2d unstamped or 3d stamped* in 1861: by 1871 the cover price had dropped to 1d. Long-time owner John Francis Maguire published the *Cork Examiner* until his death in 1872, when the editor,

Thomas Crosbie, also became the paper's proprietor*. **MJH/MaT**
Sources: *Cork Examiner, Waterloo.*

CORLETT, JOHN (1841-1915) John Corlett was a key figure in the world of sports'* journalism*. Born in Nottinghamshire, he started life as a grocer but having moved to London, he became a contributor to several sporting papers including *Bell's Life**. He was influenced by many turf writers including Henry Hall Dixon* ('The Druid'). By 1867 he was employed at the *Sportsman** writing mainly about horse racing. Then in 1874 Corlett purchased the *Sporting Times** (1865 ff), otherwise known as 'The Pink 'Un' after 1876 because of its tinted pink paper*. The *Sporting Times,* published at 52 Fleet Street* reached a circulation* of 20,000, and became one of England's most popular social journals and horse racing digests. Cultivating a raffish 'Lunchtime O'Booze' image, it was directed towards young men attending club, mess, smoking room and bar, maintaining a bohemian reputation.

Corlett reported politics* from a strong Tory Party* perspective and left social commentary to staff members. But it was for his authoritative racing knowledge that Corlett was most noted. Owners of racehorses trusted Corlett and confided in him, while readers* knew his influence and that he detested gossip*. In race reporting he preferred colourful traditional descriptions to modern exact science and ran the motto 'High Churchism, High Toryism, High Farming, and Old Port for Ever!' In 1882, Corlett published a mock obituary* for England's first ever loss on home soil against Australia during a series cricket match: England's 'Ashes', the title of the now prestigious annual cricket match, were to be shipped to Australia.

Known for his voracious zest for life and sport, Corlett, as proprietor* and editor* was nicknamed 'The Master', and in September 1889 *Vanity Fair** featured a side profile caricature* of 'The Master' in a large cloak. Corlett sold the *Sporting Times* in 1912, the same year he reported on his 50th straight Derby. **AA**
Sources: Booth 1938, *ODNB.*

CORMACK, JOHN ROSE (1815-1882) Cormack, was a prize-winning medical* student at Edinburgh University. In 1841, at the age of 25, he founded the *Edinburgh Monthly Journal of Medical Science,* which he edited*, under three successive titles, until June 1846. In January 1849, while practising as a GP in Putney, he founded the monthly *London Journal of Medicine* (1849-1852). It amalgamated with the *Provincial Medical and Surgical Journal*

(1840-1852) to become the *Association Medical Journal* (1853-1856) and *British Medical Journal** from 1857. The Provincial Medical and Surgical Association (British Medical Association from 1855) appointed Cormack editor* of its journal in August 1852 and relocated it from Worcester to London. The joint editorship of Cormack's predecessors, John Walsh* and William Ranking, had ended acrimoniously and Cormack rightly anticipated a legacy of hostility from the Association members. Although, by common consent, Cormack improved the journal he inherited, he resigned in August 1855, a victim of the internal dissension that then characterized the PMSA.

From 1866 to his death Cormack lived in France. After leaving the *Association Medical Journal* he never resumed editorial work, but during the Franco-Prussian War (1870-1871) he served as the *British Medical Journal*'s war* correspondent in Paris. He received French and British honours soon afterwards. **PWB**

Sources: Bartrip 1990, Boase 1965, *BMJ* 20 May 1882, *Lancet* 20 May 1882, *ODNB*, *The Times* 17 May 1882.

CORNHILL MAGAZINE (1860-1975) The first and most popular of the shilling* monthly* magazines* catering to a broad middle-class audience, the *Cornhill* was published by George Smith* of Smith, Elder, & Company (1860-1901). As the magazine's first editor* (Jan. 1860-May 1862), William Thackeray* lent a tone of respectability and light-heartedness to the magazine with his regularly featured column* 'Roundabout Papers'. Thackeray was followed by a shifting editorial board that included George Smith, Frederick Greenwood*, George Henry Lewes* and Edward Dutton Cook (May 1862-March 1871). Leslie Stephen* once again unified the magazine under a single authority (April 1871- Dec. 1882), initiating the practice of including signed contributions. Stephen was succeeded by James Payn* (June 1883-June 1896), John St Loe Strachey (July 1896-Dec. 1897) and Reginald John Smith (Jan. 1898-Dec. 1900).

Each issue of the *Cornhill* included two high-quality serialized* novels accompanied by lavish illustrations* as well as a wide range of articles on science*, travel, art and items of social and cultural interest. The popularity of the *Cornhill Magazine* is often attributed to its emphasis on entertainment over education and to its avoidance of controversial issues that could have offended women readers; however, the magazine did not completely ignore controversial topics and, indeed, made an effort to cover the important issues of the day in a family* friendly way.

The combination of respected publisher* Smith and editor*-novelist Thackeray was enough to make the magazine the talk of the town. The magazine began with an astonishing circulation* of 110,000 and maintained a readership* of 80,000 for the first two years, but then steadily declined. Smith's strategy for outdoing the magazine's competitors* was to pay contributors generously. Smith, who was accordingly called 'the prince of publishers', offered Anthony Trollope* £1,000 to write *Framley Parsonage* (Jan.-April 1861) and £3,200 for *The Small House at Allington* (Sept.- April 1864). Wilkie Collins* received £5,000 for *Armadale* (Nov. 1864-June 1866) and 'George Eliot'* was offered £10,000 for *Romola* (Jan. 1862 - Aug. 1863), though this amount was eventually reduced. Other important contributors include Elizabeth Gaskell, Edmund Gosse*, Thomas Hardy*, Henry James*, Anne Thackeray Ritchie, G. A. Sala*, Fitzjames Stephen* and Harriet Beecher Stowe.

By the time Stephen resigned his editorship in 1882, the magazine's readership had dwindled to 12,000. However, the *Cornhill* survived well beyond the nineteenth century. The *Cornhill* is significant not only for its role in establishing a new magazine* genre*, but also for its contribution to eliminating part-issue serialization and establishing magazine serialization as the primary publication format for mid-Victorian fiction. **JJP**

Sources: Eddy 1970, Glynn 1986, Houghton 1966, Phegley 2004b, Sullivan.

CORRESPONDENCE: See Letters

COSMOPOLIS: AN INTERNATIONAL REVIEW (1896-98) *Cosmopolis*, a miscellaneous monthly review* priced* at 5s and edited* by F. Ortmans, was launched in 1896 with the idea that print culture might be one way to help counter Europe's increasingly fragmentary, nationalist tendencies. With a view towards inclusion and cultural cohesion, *Cosmopolis* published contributions in three languages – English, French and German – each of which had its own large section within the 300 octavo pages that formed each issue. Contents included fiction, poetry* and drama, alongside articles about literature*, theatre and politics*. The journal relied on a team of regular writers (including Andrew Lang* and Henry Norman* in Britain), and the same topic might be discussed simultaneously by writers in different languages, ensuring a comparative dialogue across languages, cultures and political contexts. Among the writers whose work appeared in the periodical were Henry

James*, George Gissing*, Ouida, Mary Robinson, Rudyard Kipling and W. B. Yeats. Initially a success with a circulation* of 24,000 for the first issue, *Cosmopolis* likely proved too challenging for readers*, even the most ardent and sophisticated internationalists. **MWT**

Sources: Sullivan, *Waterloo*.

Costello, Dudley (1803-1865) and Costello, Louisa (1799-1870) The Costellos are typical in turning to writing out of decayed gentility. Educated at Sandhurst, Dudley Costello served in North America and the West Indies, retiring on half pay aged 25. He went to live with his mother and sister Louisa in Paris where he joined his sister in her work as an artist and copyist until 1833 when he left for London. In 1837 he started publishing in *Bentley's* while Dickens* was editor*. This was a connection he maintained all his life. The following year he began writing for newspapers when he became foreign* correspondent for the *Morning Herald*. Later, he contributed to *Ainsworth's* (1842-1847). He performed in several of Dickens's theatricals from 1845 as well as joined Dickens's Guild of Literature and Art, both of which enabled him to extend his network. Thus in 1846 he became foreign* correspondent for the *Daily News* and from 1845 to his death was subeditor* of Forster's *Examiner*, of which he wrote the major part. Meanwhile he contributed tales and articles to *Household Words* (1850-1859), to *All the Year Round* thereafter and (apart from two isolated earlier pieces) from 1845 to the *New Monthly*.

His sister Louisa had early supported the family by painting miniatures and she gained fame as an artist. Her major breakthrough was the publication in 1835 of *Specimens of the Early Poetry in France* which she edited and (with the aid of her brother) illustrated*. This brought her to the attention of Sir Walter Scott* and thereafter she turned almost exclusively to writing. She contributed regularly to *Bentley's* (1840-1855), and the occasional piece to *Ainsworth's*, the *Dublin University Magazine* and *Fraser's* in the early 1840s. In 1852 she was granted a Civil List pension, the same year she started writing for *Household Words*. Throughout their lives it seems she helped her brother financially. **AK**

Sources: Lohrli 1973, *ODNB*, *Wellesley*.

Cottager and Artisan (1861-1919) Starting publication as the *Cottager in Town and Country*, in 1865 its title changed* to the *Cottager and Artisan*, subtitled the *People's Own Paper*. Costing 1d, it was designed to provide useful family* reading for the working classes*. Each issue contained a number of short, entertaining and educational items, many of which were, like the article on 'American Coal Mines' (Jan. 1879), profusely illustrated*. It was particularly noted for the full-page wood* engravings that adorned the title page of each monthly number. Illustrations were designed by popular artists including Harrison Weir and Davidson Knowles. Issued by the Religious Tract Society* and therefore, overtly evangelical in nature, the departments comprised bible tracts, serial stories, children's-pages printed in large type, poetry* and general fiction. Among the contributors of letterpress were Beatrice Forster and Charles Courtney. In January 1919 the magazine incorporated *Light in the Home* but ceased publication in December of that year. **FM**

Sources: Altholz 1989, Altick 1957, Boardman 2000, *Cottager and Artisan*, *Waterloo*.

Country Life (1897-) *Country Life* began its long period of publication as *Country Life Illustrated*, which was founded and edited by Edward Burgess Hudson* who remained editor* until his death in 1936. In 1897, in collaboration with the publishing* magnate Sir George Newnes* he acquired *Racing Illustrated* which was transformed into *Country Life Illustrated*, subtitled, *The journal for all interested in Country Life and Country Pursuits*. George Newnes was both printer and joint publisher* in association with the firm of Hudson and Kearns. The journal appeared weekly* and cost 6d, or 28s 2d annually*.

Printed on high-quality glossy paper*, it set the tone in content and layout* for the later *Country Life*. Articles were featured on a variety of sporting* and country matters, including hunting, racing, golf, football, angling, cycling and dog breeding. There were also features on stately homes, fashion*, literature* and 'Town Topics', as well as comical short stories accompanied by sketches. The majority of illustrations* in the magazine were photographic* reproductions and another distinguishing mark of the magazine was the inclusion of full-page photographic portraits of royalty, aristocracy and prominent members of county society. A number of advertisements* were also included. *Country Life Illustrated* became *Country Life* in 1903 and continues publication. **DHL**

Sources: *Country Life Illustrated* 1897, Kamen 1981, *Waterloo*.

Country Words; A North of England Magazine (1866-1867) Despite its title, this weekly* magazine* was an urban production which came out of the literary* culture of Manchester, and in particular the Manchester Literary Club. Subtitled *A North of England Magazine of Literature, Science, and Art*, it was edited by Charles Hardwick and published* by Abel Heywood's* brother, John. It was aimed at a readership* simultaneously local and national ('our Countrymen'). Serious, unillustrated, and cheap* (it cost 2 d at first but that dropped to 1 ½ d), the magazine came out of the tradition of improving literature embodied in journals like *Howitt's**. The title poem was by Eliza Cook* and Eliza Meteyard* was also a contributor. Ben Brierley contributed a series about a Lancashire village of 30 years earlier in which he developed the nostalgic yet gritty descriptions of Lancashire life which were to inform the far more successful *Ben Brierley's Journal**. An important article by the dialect poet Joseph Ramsbottom defended the use of dialect in literature. That *Country Words* ran only 17 months suggests the difficulty of making local* literature, including the dialect, appeal also to a national readership*. **MRB**

Sources: Beetham 1985, *Country Words*, Leary 1896.

COURT AND PARLIAMENTARY REPORTING At the beginning of the nineteenth century, there was not a single standard for the reporting of court cases. The common law system, where both statutory and case law together comprise the governing law of the land, ideally requires a thorough and authoritative set of case law reports. However, with the demise of the legal Year Books in the early sixteenth century, law reporting was done privately, where individual jurists or practitioners compiled cases for their own use and subsequently began to publish them. By the late eighteenth century, particular reporters* became 'authorized', which gave their reports special status and meant that the judges who had decided the cases examined and sometimes amended the reports prior to publication. Authorized reports had some difficulties, however; the delays in publication led to the continued existence of unofficial reporters who were of varying levels of reliability, also there was the problem of cost, with authorized reports at £30 annually, and unofficial reporters causing additional expense.

The courts of law and Parliament were the chief arenas reported by the press. Reporters* were permitted to publish verbatim transcripts of most legal trials without interference after the 1790s. Before 1865, law reports were produced by private reporters under their own names. These reporters were of differing quality; Isaac Espinasse, for example, was described by a judge as hearing only half of what

went on in court and reporting the other half. In 1863, a campaign led by W. T. S. Daniel resulted in a meeting of the Bar on the subject of regularizing the system which resulted in the establishment of the General Council of Law Reporting that began to issue the *Law Reports,* a central and official set of case reports in 1865 that have continued to the present day. Certain periodicals carried case reports for either the legal profession such as the *Legal Guide,* the *Legal Record,* the *Law Journal**, and *Gibson's Law Notes* or for members of the general public who needed more specific legal information there were the *Justice of the Peace**, the *Law Times and Journal of Property.* From 1865, the Incorporated Council of Law Reporting began to report cases on a formal basis.

In 1882, the Supreme Court was re-housed in the Victorian Gothic building which it now occupies in the Strand, adjacent to the Inns of Court and Fleet Street*. The proximity of the centres of legal process to the centre of nineteenth century journalism* meant that it was natural that a legal orientated publishing* industry should emerge and that there should be some overlap between the two. The newspaper industry also participated in the production of law reports, *The Times**, for example published a formal set of reports, the *Times Law Reports,* from 1884 to 1952, and still publishes reports of cases today. From this background it is unsurprising to find the law and the courts finding their way into literature. Charles Dickens* started his career as a lawyer's clerk and court reporter, and the cumbersome, lengthy and unreformed early nineteenth-century court process features in *Pickwick Papers* and *Bleak House,* the latter published as a serial* in *Household Words**. Reports of trials were immensely popular in nineteenth-century Britain, and the public followed them eagerly in newspaper reports, particularly when they were notable or notorious. Indeed, many publications used court reports as a bait to increase circulation*. The Sunday* papers in particular attracted large readerships* through their reports of the police courts.

Forbidden entry throughout the eighteenth century by Standing Order, the press was admitted to the House of Commons for parliamentary debates from 1802. After the Houses of Parliament burned to the ground in 1834, the rebuilt Westminster chambers included reporters' galleries, despite occasional efforts by some parliamentarians to limit press access. A 'turn' system was used whereby reporters covered proceedings for a fixed interval of several minutes to several hours before being relieved by a second reporter. The subsequent report was then transmitted to the newspaper offices by courier, telegraph*, or telephone. It was Thomas Hansard* who refined this process with his specifically tailored *Parliamentary Debates*.

Court and parliamentary reporting involved taking notes of speeches that were written up for publication, verbatim. Shorthand* systems devised by Thomas Gurney (1705-1770) and Isaac Pitman (1813-1897) improved the accuracy and speed of writing through the use of an abbreviated, symbolic notation method. While some reporters used longhand, shorthand increasingly became the norm when taking evidence in court or recording parliamentary debates. By the 1870s, longhand was no longer used by reporters. The growth of the mass* press during the second half of the nineteenth century expanded the role of reporting to eyewitness accounts, investigative* reports, and colourful sketches. The efficiency of reporting was improved after mid-century by the invention of the telegraph and the subsequent formation of collective news-gathering agencies such as Reuters* and the Press Association*. **MR/CAS/JRW**
Sources: Brown 1985, Cosgrove 1975, James 1979, Lindley 1885, MacDonagh 1913, *ODNB*, Sparrow 2003, Williams 1963.

COURTHOPE, WILLIAM JOHN (1842-1917) A well-born old Harrovian, Courthope followed a prize-winning undergraduate career in classics at Oxford by entering the education department of the civil service where he eventually rose to the top as first civil commissioner. Meanwhile he pursued a parallel career as a poet, literary* historian, journalist* and editor*.

A frequent writer of letters* to the editor of *The Times**, Courthope regularly contributed to the *Quarterly Review** (1872-1893) on matters of poetry*, taste, culture and conservatism, and later to the *Nineteenth Century** and *Blackwood's**. When Alfred Austin* launched the *National Review** in 1883 as an intellectual organ of the Conservative Party*, he shared its editorship with Courthope, who brought to the journal scholarly prestige as well as his shrewd worldliness. His reputation enabled the *Review* to attract contributors of distinction who might have shied away from the ultra-partisan Austin. The two men formed an effective partnership, collaborating* on 17 articles concerning contemporary affairs, while Courthope contributed a further 18 in his own name, including those later republished as *The Liberal Movement in*

English Literature. The journal had a secure reputation when Courthope retired from the joint editorship in 1887. In some respects a lesser Matthew Arnold*, Courthope illustrates how in Victorian Britain amateurs in higher journalism* filled the space occupied today by academic intellectuals. **CAK**
Sources: *ODNB*, Sladen 1914, Waller 2006, *Waterloo, Wellesley.*

COURTNEY, WILLIAM LEONARD (1850-1928) Courtney was a man with two careers: he was a distinguished philosopher in the 1870s-1880s, with a fellowship at New College, Oxford. While there, he became known for the clarity of his presentations in lectures, and for the role he played in establishing the New Theatre. As well, he was a Fleet Street* journalist* and editor*, who wrote for publications as diverse as the society journal the *World** and the heavyweight quarterly* *Edinburgh Review**. In 1882, while still an Oxford don, he became a reader and general assistant to T. H. S. Escott*, editor of the *Fortnightly Review**, a monthly coustney went on to edit for an impressive 34 years (1894-1928). He officially left his post in Oxford in 1890, when offered a permanent post on the *Daily Telegraph**, where he wrote the weekly 'Book of the Day' review* and became chief dramatic critic and literary editor until 1925. His overlapping work at the *Fortnightly* and the *Telegraph* did not deter him from taking on other prominent positions, as editor of *Murray's Magazine** (1890-1891) and, beginning in 1894, as chairman of the publishing* firm Chapman and Hall*. Courtney's academic and philosophical background seems to have served him well as a professional journalist who was known for his sound judgment, broad range of interests in literature* and drama and seriousness of purpose. **MWT**
Sources: Courtney 1930, *ODNB.*

COWEN, JOSEPH (1829-1900) Like his father before him, Joseph Cowen MP, the famous radical and newspaper entrepreneur was the Senior Liberal member for Newcastle (1874-1886). His ultra radicalism placed him at the heart of the European republican movement and at the centre of democratic politics*. This agenda was given expression in a number of republican journals in the 1850s: he was the financial backer of the *English Republic** that W. J. Linton* published* in the Lake District (1851-1855) and, following the launch of his Newcastle Foreign Affairs Committee which had been set up to monitor the Crimean War, Cowen called upon Linton to publish a second journal, the *Northern Tribune: A Periodical for the People** in January 1854. Both publications had an impact upon the circulation* of progressive ideas but neither survived the competitive climate of the mid-century. In March 1855 Cowen sold the *Tribune* to his close friend George Jacob Holyoake* who incorporated it into his own anti-clerical publication the *Reasoner*. The late 1850s saw the launch of the *Northern Reform Record*, a monthly* journal which attempted to regenerate the Chartist* campaign. By then the climate for hard political journalism has waned and Cowen had concluded that cheap tracts were a better means of promoting democratic ideals. Most of all, Cowen realized that he would need to acquire a mainstream newspaper if he was to proselytize his ideas to the wider public.

In 1859, Cowen bought the *Newcastle Daily Chronicle*, a four-page penny* paper which he transformed from an ailing weekly* into the 'Pitman's Bible', with offices in Paris and New York and a web of agents throughout the British Isles. He spent more than £40,000 on technological and stylistic improvements in a bid to make the *Daily Chronicle* 'The Times of the North' and launched its innovative stablemate the *Newcastle Weekly Chronicle*. No expense was spared as he invested in the new rotary press, private telegraph* and linotype. By 1873 daily sales figures for the second quarter were estimated to be 35,534 and the *Weekly's* circulation* was just slightly less. His command of the region's readership* was complete when he launched the *Evening Chronicle* in 1885. At his death in 1900, Cowen's press empire was renowned not just in Britain but overseas too. **JA**

Sources: Allen 2005a, Allen 2007, Ashton 1991, Cowen Papers (TWAS), Smith 1973, W. E. Adams Papers (AIISH)

COWHAM, HILDA GERTRUDE (1873-1964) In 1894 Hilda Cowham (later Mrs Edgar Lander) won a competition in the *Studio* art periodical, going on to study at Wimbledon College, Lambeth School of Art and the Royal College of Art. During her student days she had cartoons* published in *Pick-Me-Up* and the *Sketch*' (1894-1895) and made her career as an illustrator*.

Characteristically, she used brush and ink in preference to pen, with children figuring frequently as her subject matter, often with trademark thin black legs. She also wrote and illustrated* magazine stories. Her reputation as a leading woman cartoonist paved the way for her being one of the first women to work on *Punch*' with her creation 'the Cowham kid'. She also contributed to *Moonshine*'(1896), the *Sphere*, the *Tatler*', the *Royal Magazine* (1901), *Girl's Realm* (1904), the *Graphic's*' Christmas* supplements* (1902-1905,

1908, 1912), the *Strand*' (1913), *Little Folks, Pearson's*' (1901-1909), the *Queen*' and the *Windsor Magazine*'. **CL**

Sources: Houfe 1978, *ODNB*.

COWIE, GEORGE (B. 1799/1800) A London printer and publisher* of cheap periodicals*, Cowie began his career in 1822 in collaboration with William Strange* (1801-1871), and established a bookselling and publishing* business in Fetter Lane. Cowie and Strange's first periodical was the 3d *London Mechanics' Register* (1824-1826)*. In 1826 they opened a shop at 60 Paternoster Row from where they disseminated a wide range of religious*, literary* and satirical* periodicals, including the shilling *Christian Moderator* (1826-1828), the 4d *Ass; or Weekly Beast of Burden* (1826) and the penny *Casket* (1827-1829). In 1829-1830, trading from 55 Paternoster Row, they became publishers of the popular *Olio; or, Museum of Entertainment* (1828-1833), simultaneously publishing a number of penny co-operative journals, including the *Associate* (1829) and the *Birmingham and Co-operative Herald* (1829-1830) (see Co-operative press*). Cowie also produced a number of trade guides, the most successful of which were the *Bookbinder's manual* (1828) and the *Printer's pocket book* (1829).

Following his bankruptcy in 1830 Cowie relocated to the Strand, and over the next five years became involved in the production of 'unstamped' penny periodicals*, including the *New Casket* (1831-1833), *Figaro in London* (1831-1839)*, the *Political Unionist* (1832), the *Boys' and Girls' Penny Magazine* (1832-1833) and his own *National Omnibus* (1831-1833). In June 1832 he was fined £20 for selling the anti-clerical *Church Examiner* (1832), and this prosecution, combined with his membership of the Society for the Protection of Booksellers, secured his reputation in radical circles as a champion of press freedom. After 1835 Cowie published only a small number of periodicals, the last of which was a Chartist* newspaper, the *Southern Star* (1840). Between 1841 and 1851 he worked as a printer and compositor in Clerkenwell, but details of his later life remain obscure. **DSM**

Sources: Census returns 1841 and 1851, Harrison 1978, Hollis 1970, James 1963, *The Times* 4 Nov. 1829, *Warwick Guide* 1977, *Waterloo*.

COX, EDWARD WILLIAM (1809-1879) The early part of Edward Cox's professional life was as a solicitor in the West Country. Called to the bar in 1843, he became a recorder and ultimately chairman of the second court of the Middlesex sessions. From 1854 he was able to utilize his large personal fortune to begin a complementary career in publishing*.

Cox's publishing venture fell into two categories, legal texts and journals he wrote and edited* plus a diverse range of prestigious periodicals he owned. In 1854 he bought the *Field: a Gentleman's Newspaper Devoted to Sport*, the first country and field sports'* magazine started the previous year. This was complemented by the 1873 *Country: a Journal of Rural Pursuits*. He had also become one of the proprietors* of the *Field's* sister paper, the weekly* *Queen: a Lady's Newspaper* in 1862. The *Critic* and the *Royal Exchange* were also his. Cox's own books had previously been published by John Crockford; in 1853 they jointly published the *Clerical Journal*, from whose separate directory supplements* they compiled the 1860 *Crockford's Clerical Directory*. Cox's gift for locating and creating periodicals which would have popular longevity was demonstrated by his creation of *Exchange and Mart* in 1868.

In the legal field, he started the weekly* *Law Times* in 1843 which made his name and in 1846, the *County Courts Chronicle and Gazette of Bankruptcy*. The *Law Times's* uniqueness and popularity lay in two dimensions: the legal* practice content was politically and culturally contextualized, enlarging the legal perspective. Second, Cox was prescient enough to understand that the new railway network brought an extended audience. Previous publications had a metropolitan* bias; now lawyers in the regions* could access the *Law Times*, its news and information. More than that, Cox understood the implications for engaging this new audience in aspects of legal practice that needed reform. Consequently, the metropolitan* legal community's insularity and professional stronghold were breached. As lawyer and publisher, Cox was well placed to use his paper as a campaigning vehicle which he did to some effect. **CL**
Sources: Boase, *ODNB*.

CRACKANTHORPE, BLANCHE ALETHEA (1847-1928) Blanche Crackanthorpe (also wrote as Cookson-Crackanthorpe) published a novel and several one-act plays, but her journalism made her reputation. She wrote on literature*, theatre and women's issues for the *Woman's World*, the *Fortnightly Review* and the *Contemporary Review* from the late 1880s into the 1900s. Crackanthorpe's most significant work appeared in the *Nineteenth Century*, launching a key New Woman journalistic debate with 'The Revolt of the Daughters' (1894). Though she supported education and work for

women, her title spawned the catch-phrase 'Revolting Daughters'. Crackanthorpe also created controversy with 'Sex in Literature' (1895), defending George Moore and Thomas Hardy. **TD**
Sources: Crackanthorpe 1977, *ODNB* (entry for husband, Montague Hughes Crackanthorpe), *WWW* (entry for husband).

CRAIG, EDWARD HENRY GORDON (1872-1966) Wood-engraving* was only one of the many talents of the theatrical designer, actor, producer and thoroughly bohemian Edward Craig. As a young man he met the artists William Nicholson* and William Pryde who together had brought wood* engraving back into fashion through combining bold linearity, blocked colours and an art nouveau sensibility. In his periodical the *Page* (1898-1901) Craig sought to exploit the aestheticized qualities of black and white illustration*, which he largely focused on theatrical subjects and portraits. He brought modernity to the art of wood engraving through using white line engraving in alliance with his turn of the century aesthetic awareness. A prolific engraver, Craig contributed to the *Dome* in the last two years of the century, although his undoubted influence was mainly on later artists and illustrators*, both through his work with wood engraving groups and societies, especially the Society of Wood Engravers, and through his later periodical projects such as the *Mask* (1908-1929). **BM**
Sources: Engen1990, Houfe 1978, *ODNB*.

CRANE, WALTER (1845-1915) Although Walter Crane did contribute substantially as an illustrator* to a wide variety of late Victorian magazines, his major significance to the history of periodicals is as a theorist of the decorated page. As Houfe has remarked 'it was only in the pioneering work of Walter Crane…that the artist left his allotted page…establishing his right to be considered and consulted over type faces, frontispieces, covers, initial letters and all manner of decoration'. Apprenticed to W. J. Linton*, and always an illustrator rather than a converted artist, Crane came to regard black and white design and illustration as a major popular* art form available easily and cheaply to the mass* of the population especially through periodicals. He saw illustration as a democratic form appropriate to his commitment to the socialist cause. Although he drew on a variety of sources from within the British craft tradition, Crane's designs are less self-consciously allusive than those of contemporaries like William Morris*, and he was not afraid to support the use of mechanized photo-reprographic processes.

He was also an immensely influential figure in the development of art education and craft associations with an interest in print culture. In all these respects, and despite the occasional sentimental nature of his illustrations, Crane foreshadowed modernism in his work, and his influential 1901 treatise *Of the Decorative Illustration of Books* marked the new century in decidedly progressive ways. His superb cover and title page designs for *St George*, the magazine of the Ruskin Society of Birmingham, executed in 1898, characterize Crane's best work, combining art nouveau sinuosity and neo-medieval inking and lettering with a thoroughly modernist setting of design and type on to the open white spaces of the page. BM

Sources: Engen 1990, Houfe 1978, *ODNB*, White 1897.

CRAWFORD, EMILY (1831?-1915) Born in Ireland and educated by her mother, Emily Crawford, née Johnstone and her sister left for Paris with their mother when their father died in 1863. Her career as a journalist and Paris correspondent* began after a friend in Britain reading her letters from Paris suggested she should send a 'Letter from Paris' to an American newspaper. Crawford also sent one to London's *Morning Star* and by 1864 she was making £400 a year from her journalism.

Johnstone married George Morland Crawford, assistant Paris correspondent for the *Daily News** in 1864 and they became a journalistic team until his death in 1885. Emily Crawford then formally inherited her husband's position on the *Daily News* and wrote for the weekly* *Truth*, started in 1877 by Henry Labouchère*, the owner of the *Daily News*. The *Weekly Dispatch*, the *Calcutta Englishman* and the Chicago *Daily News* all employed Crawford as their Paris correspondent while she also wrote for the New York *Tribune*, the New York *Century*, *Macmillan's*, the *Fortnightly Review**, the *Contemporary Review**, the *Lady's World* and the quarterly* *Subjects of the Day*. Crawford largely covered politics* and cultural events. Her impressive network of political and artistic connections informed her own habit of personal study and reflection on daily events which accorded her a reputation for analytical depth in her writing.

She was offered the Légion d'honneur, which she declined, but was made a life fellow of the Institute of Journalists* in 1890 by her colleagues in Britain and president of the Society of Women Journalists* in 1901. CL

Source: *ODNB*.

CRAWFORD, VIRGINIA MARY (1862-1948) Virginia Mary Crawford, journalist*, writer and feminist* is perhaps best known for having named Sir Charles Dilke, 2nd bt, as her lover in the divorce case initiated by her husband, Donald Crawford, in 1885. Her sister introduced Crawford to W. T. Stead*, then editor* of the *Pall Mall Gazette** and a ferocious critic of Dilke; Stead employed Crawford as a journalist though she never wrote about the politician. She was an early practitioner of the still nascent interview* style, and among her first interviews was one with Cardinal Manning in 1888. She converted to Catholicism the following year. Crawford wrote articles on women's issues for a range of journals. In one, on 'Feminism in France' for the *Fortnightly Review** in 1897, she implied that since women were barred from the 'parliamentary arena' they had to carry out their fight in the 'political byways of the press' (Onslow: 170).

Crawford covered a broad spectrum of topics in her work (amounting to over 130 articles and numerous books). She wrote on Italian art, French and Belgian literature*, social work and women's employment for mainstream publications such as *Littell's Living Age*, *Dublin Review**, and the *Contemporary Review** and was a regular writer on more specialized issues for religious journals including the *Month: a Catholic magazine** and *Catholic World**. FD

Sources: C19 online, *ODNB*, Onslow 2000.

CRAWFORD, OSWALD JOHN FREDERICK (1834-1909) A diplomat who served over 24 years as British consul in Portugal, Crawfurd was an energetic journalistic entrepreneur and literary* man-about-town, the author of 13 minor novels, and a contributor to several periodicals including the *Fortnightly Review**, the *Cornhill Magazine**, *Nineteenth Century** and the *New Review**. In 1873 he founded the *New Quarterly Magazine**, an innovative hybrid of magazine* and quarterly* whose intended readership* was 'educated and intelligent persons' of the upper classes*. He also edited* it during its first five years, and indeed wrote much of its gentlemanly contents himself, particularly in the first few issues. His six pseudonyms*, 'John Dangerfield', 'John Latouche', 'Matthew Freke Turner', 'Archibald Banks', 'George Windle Sandys' and 'Joseph Strange', helped to conceal this, as well as insulating his literary activities from his diplomatic career.

The *New Quarterly* was a modestly s-uccessful property by the time he sold it to Francis Hueffer* in November 1877. After retiring from the consular service in 1891 he became editor and director of *Black and White**, managing director of the publishers* Chapman & Hall*, and editor of *Chapman's Magazine of Fiction* 1895-1898. A sociable and well-connected Old Etonian, Crawfurd embodied the gentleman amateur spirit in journalism and letters. In 1891 the newly founded Authors' Club declared its social tone by making him its first president. CAK

Sources: Hughes 2005, *ODNB*, Sladen 1914, Waller 2006, *Wellesley.*

CREED, FREDERICK GEORGE (1871-1957)

Frederick Creed, inventor and manufacturer of telegraph* equipment, was born in eastern Nova Scotia, a remote fishing port where the transatlantic* telegraph cables terminated. Aged 14 Creed became a telegraph operator, eventually moving from Canada to work in the USA, Peru and Chile. The laborious method of transmitting messages by the Morse three-key type perforator damaged Creed's left hand, causing him to invent a more efficient system. By late 1897 he had formulated a typewriter-styled machine which enabled Morse code signals to be punched into tape by operating the corresponding character. In the same year he sailed to Glasgow where he hoped to put his idea into practice. Initially he worked for the *Glasgow Herald** as a Morse operator. Lord Kelvin, the proprietor* was impressed with Creed's invention and offered him facilities to complete his work. However it was not until 1906 that the *Glasgow Herald* adopted Creed's system, which it maintained was three times faster than the earlier Morse apparatus.

Creed resigned from the *Glasgow Herald* in 1904 to start his own telegraphic equipment business. In 1902 the Post Office had bought twelve of Creed's perforators, and in 1909 with his Danish partner, Harald Bille, Creed moved his firm from Glasgow to Croydon, partly to be closer to the Post Office headquarters. He opened a small factory in Croydon, which soon expanded into a flourishing enterprise. After the Great War, the Newspaper Press Association paid Creed £90,000 for his system. In 1928 his company became part of the International Telephone and Telegraph Corporation, but Creed resigned, from the company in 1931 to devote himself to invention. DHL

Sources: *Croydon Advertiser* 1956, Jeremy 1984, *ODNB*, *Private Wire* 1971.

CRIME REPORTING Crime reports were a pervasive, popular, and often controversial feature of the nineteenth-century newspaper and periodical press, and the character of crime reporting was closely related to the growth of the press through the nineteenth century. At the beginning of the period, crime coverage in the press was relatively limited. Many newspapers obtained their crime reports from shorthand* reporters* engaged by the various courts and assizes, with trial transcripts often appearing verbatim in the papers. Though the practice of printing transcripts of important legal* cases as a matter of public record persisted through the nineteenth century, particularly in newspapers like *The Times* (1785-)*, by the 1820s a number of London dailies* had correspondents dedicated to court* reporting, and this development led to a more fulsome and creative approach to the reporting of crime.

The *Morning Chronicle** and the *Morning Herald** were two early exponents of innovative crime reporting, though their styles were dissimilar: whereas the *Chronicle* used its crime reports to editorialize on the need for legal and police reform, the *Herald* concentrated on entertaining crime stories. One of the *Herald's* correspondents, John Wight, specialized in satirical* reports on the proceedings at the Bow Street Public Office in London, helping develop a style of comic journalism that was influential in the rise of humour journals such as *Figaro in London** and *Punch**. Widespread public interest in topical crimes was also met in the early nineteenth century by a prodigious array of broadside news-sheets, chapbooks and ballads – works which typically blended fact and fiction in their treatment of criminal subjects. Crime fiction also became extremely popular, particularly with working-class* and lower middle-class* readers, and from the 1830s weekly unstamped* papers like John Cleave's* *Weekly Police Gazette** and Edward Lloyd's* *Penny Sunday Times and People's Police Gazette* (1840-1843) offered lurid serialized crime stories and fabricated police reports as part of their core attraction.

The growth of the popular press* from the mid-nineteenth century saw a new wave of cheap* newspapers that used the appeal of sensationalised reports on crime and violence as a means of attracting a mass* readership*. Sunday* newspapers with radical leanings, such as *Lloyd's Weekly Newspaper* (1842ff)*, the *News of the World* (1843ff)* and *Reynolds's Weekly Newspaper* (1850 ff)*, gave particular attention to crimes occurring in the upper classes of society, and their formula was substantially imitated in the first penny* daily*, the *Daily Telegraph** (1855 ff). The later nineteenth century also saw the rise of sensationalist 'true crime' journals, notably the *Illustrated Police News** (1864 ff), and in the United States, the *National Police Gazette* (1845 ff). While the popular press was often criticized for reporting crime in a visceral and exaggerated manner, by the 1860s notable crimes excited a similar degree of attention from the more respectable papers, and vivid and copious coverage of particularly shocking or scandalous crimes became a hallmark of the Victorian press.

Throughout the Victorian era there was a fluid interchange between crime reporting and crime fiction (which was often serialized in the newspapers), with novelists employing plotlines derived from newspaper crime reports, and journalists employing speculative techniques where the facts of a case were lacking. Crime reporting remained a maligned aspect of the journalistic profession in the nineteenth century and is rarely discussed in contemporary histories of journalism*. Consequently, little is known about nineteenth-century crime reporters, although anecdotal evidence suggests that many were freelance, 'penny-a-line' writers. Despite its dubious reputation, the popular appeal of crime reporting made it a staple feature in an increasingly commercialised, circulation*-driven press. **NG**
Sources: Altick 1972, Altick 1986, Bourne 1887, Brake *et al.* 2000, Brown 1985, Knelman 1998, Rowbotham and Stevenson eds. 2005.

CRISIS, OR THE CHANGE FROM ERROR AND MISERY, TO TRUTH AND HAPPINESS, (1832-1834), CRISIS AND NATIONAL CO-OPERATIVE TRADES UNION AND EQUITABLE LABOUR EXCHANGE GAZETTE (1833-1834)

An unstamped* radical weekly* established and edited* by Robert Owen* (with his son Robert Dale Owen), *Crisis* boasted in its first issue of its low price* – a penny* (rising to 1 1/2d in 1833) – and that it had gone to press with 8,744 copies already under order from subscribers. 'From this commencement', the announcement went on, 'we augur well of our ultimate success, and feel assured that the great crisis is indeed near at hand'. Owen's concept of 'the crisis' carried a quasi-religious connotation: this was to be a moment of historical rupture, a millennial horizon beyond which lay the promise of a 'new moral world'.

Crisis set out in its motto to 'unite all Hearts', and it was clear that such a unification was to be realized through the institutional mechanisms of organized labour. Indeed, the paper is best seen in the context of Owen's mission of the early 1830s to create a general trades union*. *Crisis* frequently reported the proceedings of various public meetings and labour exchanges, and in Vol. 1 carried in its masthead* an engraving of the Institution of the Industrious Classes on Gray's Inn Road.

In April 1833, *Crisis* became the *Crisis and National Co-operative Trades Union and Equitable Labour Exchange Gazette*. Around this time, circulation* having declined to a reported 1,250, Owen's son made a gift of the paper to B. D. Cousins, who ran it until its demise in August 1834. Although it still claimed, for a while, to be 'under the patronage of Robert Owen', there are signs that Owen's direct involvement was increasingly limited. In a sardonic salvo that appeared in the final number, he distanced himself from what had become 'a compound paper', comprising an incoherent spectrum of opinion, some of which contradicted his ideals. He also announced his *New Moral World**, which launched that year. **MaT**
Sources: *ODNB, Waterloo.*

CRITERION. AN INDEPENDENT ORGAN OF THE INSURANCE, BANKING, COMMERCIAL AND SOCIAL WORLD (1893-1905)

The *Criterion*, which started on 9 August as a 16-page 2d fortnightly quarto published in Liverpool, is interesting as an attempt to fuse a specialist financial* journal with social news* and publication outside the metropolitan commercial and publishing hub (*Insurance World* had been published in London since 1879 and would continue until 1916). Initially the *Criterion's* subtitle was, 'Insurance – Banking – Commercial Social' [sic] but by the second issue longer subtitle was established. It was addressed to all *Insurance readers, who are to be found in every household, either as policy holders, agents, superintendents, managers, or secretaries.* There was the intention to publish announcements of at-homes and dinner parties, presentations and company outings as well as insurance news*. While it had the notion of a mass readership*, the subject matter did not inspire regular purchase beyond specialists. Soon the paper realized its actual readership, beginning a series of biographies of luminaries in the insurance world, with photographic* portraits. At first well supported by advertisements* (7 out of 16 pages for its first issues), it covered events and companies in

Manchester and Liverpool as well as London. While its head office was in Liverpool, in imitation of grander financial journals, it set up branch offices in Manchester, London and Glasgow, though there is little indication that Glasgow had much effect on the contents.

Within a year the paper was obviously undergoing problems: on 27 June 1894 there was a bid to attract readers with a free detachable photo of a country bridge (see Supplements*). The following month its offices moved, and it went bankrupt. Its assets were bought by W. J. Fleming who used them to start up a 2d weekly* (also concerning insurance) called *Commercial Progress*. This appeared on 14 September but lasted only three issues (issue 2 was never forwarded to the British Museum, as explained in a note from the editor bound into the British Library copy). On 7 December the *Criterion* reappeared in a revised format, now monthly* and entirely unillustrated, with the announcement in the masthead* that it had incorporated the *Commercial Progress*. The office moved to Manchester and soon the title changed* to *Criterion: a Business and Pleasure Journal*. It limped on, with fewer and fewer adverts, until it closed on 24 May 1905, announcing its circulation* as 7,000*. **AK**
Sources: *Mitchell's, Waterloo.*

CRITIC (1843-1863) A literary* journal started by Sergeant Edward Cox (1809-1879), the *Critic* was initially a section of Cox's *Law Times* (1843-1965), launching as an independent publication in November 1843. Its readership* was drawn from the wealthy class* of educated professionals, the same people who might have had cause to read the *Law Times*. By 1854, the *Critic* was claiming to have the largest circulation* of all the literary periodicals, although its main competitors, the *Athenaeum** and the *Literary Gazette**, both thought that this claim was not only exaggerated but fraudulent, and to some extent typical of the underhand way in which Cox conducted his business.

The *Critic* was edited* by James Lowe (d. 1865) throughout its 20-year life, but underwent constant changes in other respects. After starting as a monthly*, it shifted to biweekly then weekly* publication and back again, its price* fluctuated between 4d and 9d and its subtitle changed many times. Various regular supplements* were tried, the most successful of which was *Beautiful Poetry* which ran for six years: most of them proved less enduring. These fluctuations probably reflect the journal's struggle – despite its self-confident pronouncements – to establish itself as a major literary journal. Over the

first eight years of the periodical's life £5,000 was invested before it became self-sufficient, and there are indications – such as a proposed merger* with the *Literary Gazette* in 1859 – that it continued to struggle financially.

The backbone of the *Critic* – essays and reviews* on literary, artistic* and scientific* matters – was that of a conventional literary journal of the time, and it drew on some familiar contributors. William Michael Rossetti* and Frederic George Stephens* were, successively, art editors, and Alexander Gilchrist (1828-1861) was also a contributor from around 1858, all three pushing a Pre-Raphaelite agenda. From 1851, George Gilfillan* and Francis Espinasse* – who contributed countless articles, among them a notable series on Victorian periodicals – began to write regularly for the magazine. **MaT**
Sources: *ODNB*, Sullivan, *Waterloo*.

CROKER, JOHN WILSON (1780-1857) In his day – most of the first half of the nineteenth century – John Wilson Croker was known as Secretary to the Admiralty (1809-1830), founder of the Athenaeum Club (1824), a leader of parliamentary opposition to the 1832 Reform Bill, and editor*, among other works, of Boswell's *Life of Johnson* (1831). But his greatest fame was as author of articles in the *Quarterly Review**, which, unyielding in their Tory sentiments, provided, in his words, a 'kind of direction post' to its readers.

He had been involved with the *Quarterly* from its inception in 1809, and wrote occasional articles during his time at the Admiralty, including a review* of Keats' *Endymion* in 1818 (erroneously claimed by Byron to have led to the poet's death). However, it was only after he resigned his parliamentary seat in 1832 that he was engaged by John Murray*, the *Quarterly's* publisher*, to undertake the 'political'* articles which thereafter appeared in almost every issue up to mid-century. In these, he drew on close contacts with key figures such as Wellington and Peel, and his articles were long regarded as authoritative reflections of Tory party policy. This came to an end in 1845-1846, with the repeal of the Corn Laws – the *Quarterly* had earlier led its readers to believe that Peel would do no such thing. In all, Croker published around 270 articles in the *Quarterly*. These included 30 or so on French affairs, sternly warning that radicals in Britain could provoke a revolution similar to that of 1789. His articles on the French Revolution were separately published by John Murray in 1857, and his notable collections of revolutionary pamphlets are in the

British Library. Towards the end of his life, he became deeply suspicious of Louis Napoleon ('the French Autocrat') and broke with the *Quarterly* on its support for coalition with the French in the Crimean War. Disraeli caricatured* him as Rigby in *Coningsby* (1844). **DIM**

Sources: Brightfield 1940, Jennings 1884, *ODNB*, Thomas 2000.

CROOKES, WILLIAM (1832-1919) A flamboyant and controversial figure, Crookes was almost unique among major Victorian scientists* in combining a business career with experimental research. A non-graduate, Crookes earned his daily bread as a working journalist*, chemical consultant, and company director. Working with an assistant in a home laboratory he made important contributions to chemistry, physics, scientific* journalism and popularization, as well as to the development of spiritualism. As a well-known photographic chemist in the 1850s, Crookes was appointed the second editor* of the bimonthly *Liverpool Photographic Journal* (1854-1859, then *British Journal of Photography*) in January 1857. He left this position four months later on appointment as editor of the monthly *Journal of the Photographic Society of London* (1853-1858, then *Photographic Journal*). He was ignominiously sacked in July 1858, ostensibly for financial impropriety, but recovered his career by becoming the first editor of Cassell*, Petter & Galpin's weekly *Photographic News* (1858-1908) in September 1858. He was sacked again in January 1860 when the proprietors* brought a legal action against him. This was partly due to his strident leaders*, but also because of his founding an independent weekly*, *Chemical News**(1859-1932), that caused him to neglect *Photographic News*.

Chemical News, printed on his own presses, became Crookes's principal source of income. In 1864 he joined James Samuelson* in the editorship of the *Quarterly Journal of Science**, in which he published his sensational investigations of spiritualism in 1870 and 1871. He became sole editor from 1870, and remained on its editorial board after selling it as the monthly *Journal of Science* (1878-1885). His venture into publishing a weekly* *Electrical News & Telegraphic Reporter* from July 1875 was a failure and the periodical collapsed after only 20 issues. He remained editor of *Chemical News* and owner of the Chemical News Press until his death. **WB**

Sources: Brock 2004, Brock 2008, D'Albe 1923, *DSB*, *ODNB*.

CRUIKSHANK, GEORGE (1792-1878) As the most celebrated comic artist of the early and mid

Victorian periods, George Cruikshank was frequently commissioned by ambitious editors* to lend his prestige and manifest ability to their periodicals either as an illustrator* of fiction or as a contributor of decorative or comic illustrations. He also used his fame to market popular, if sometimes short-lived, comic* periodicals produced under his own name and edited* by well-known contemporary journalists* like Frank Smedley and Gilbert Abbott À Beckett*. Cruikshank's illustrations, both wood* engravings and etchings, were combined with a variety of articles, anecdotes and short narratives in such monthly miscellanies* as *George Cruikshank's Omnibus* (1841-1842), *George Cruikshank's Table-Book* (1845) and *George Cruikshank's Magazine* (1854). Material from these journals was frequently reprinted in a variety of volume forms in subsequent years.

Perhaps Cruikshank's most substantial serialized work as a comic artist can be found in the 19 annual* volumes of the *Comic Almanack**, a high-spirited pastiche of the almanac form edited by Gilbert À Beckett and illustrated by a riotous assembly of Cruikshank's tiny wood engravings and full- page etchings. In his work for the *Almanack* Cruikshank reveals most clearly his apprenticeship in the caricature* tradition and the effects of his mass of jobbing work in the 1820s for serialised songbooks and comic magazines as disparate as *Bell's Life in London** and the *Universal Songster* (1825-1828). Cruikshank's most prestigious magazine illustrations, however, were published in the form of commissioned illustrations for fiction in the illustrated monthlies of the 1830s and 1840s, most notably *Bentley's Miscellany** (vols. 1-14 1837-1843) and *Ainsworth's Magazine** (1842). Yet such was the reach and versatility of Cruikshank's output that he could be found in journals as varied as the *Illustrated Times**, the *Illustrated London News** and the *British Workman**. **BM**

Sources: Cohn 1924, Houfe 1978, *ODNB*, Patten 1992-1996.

CURRY, WILLIAM JNR. (D. 1870) William Curry, Jnr (fl. 1825-1864) was a Dublin publisher* and bookseller*. The earliest periodicals* he published were the monthly* *Christian Examiner and Church of Ireland Magazine** (edited* by Caesar Otway* 1825-1831), the annual* *Wreath from the Emerald Isle* (1826, edited by P. D. Hardy*) and the weekly* *Dublin Family Magazine* (1829). In the *Christian Examiner* Curry printed William Carleton's* first tale.

Curry's greatest contribution to Irish periodicals was his decision, with partner James McGlashan*, to publish, and later purchase, the monthly *Dublin University Magazine** (1833 - 1846). Curry is reported to have paid contributors £3 per every 16 pages, with editor Charles Lever* receiving £100 per month. The sum included remuneration for Lever's serial* fiction, offered by Curry both within the *Dublin University Magazine* and in monthly parts.

Curry published further religious* magazines, mostly Protestant, such as the *New Irish Pulpit* (1836-1840) and the *Churchman's Almanack* (1841-1859), but including also the monthly *Catholic Layman* (1852-1858). He also published specialist magazines, such as the monthly *Irish Farmer and Gardner's Magazine* (1833-1841). His full catalogue included general, Irish and religious books. Curry retired from business in 1864 and moved to Liverpool. **FB**

Sources: Anderson 1991, Hoey 1878, *Waterloo Irish*.

CUST, HENRY (HARRY) JOHN COCKAYNE (1861-1917) Harry Cust, as he was generally known, was educated at Eton and Cambridge and later called to both the English and French Bars. He never practised, but instead became Unionist (Conservative) MP for Stamford, Lincolnshire, in 1890, and an occasional contributor to the *New Review**, the *National Review** and the *North American Review*.

While an MP he accepted William Waldorf Astor's surprising offer to edit* the *Pall Mall Gazette**, which he did (1892-1896). Before accepting the post Cust took advice from Lord Salisbury and Arthur Balfour, stating that he 'could not be a mere Party hack' and he 'should seek to retain the right of independent criticism' and this he did. He had no experience of editorship and treated the post as yet another exciting and enjoyable experience and a relief from the tedium of parliamentary business. Cust established a group of young contributors at the *Gazette*, among whom were Alice Meynell*, George Warrington Steevens*, H. G. Wells*, R. A. M. Stevenson* and Edith Nesbit. The 'Wares of Autolycus' articles were introduced in May 1893 and, although unsigned, Alice Meynell*, Elizabeth Robins Pennell*, Katharine Tynan and Rosamund Marriott Watson* ('Graham R. Tomson') were among contributors on topics including food, literature* and fashion*. Another feature introduced by Cust was the 'Occasional Verse' or 'Occ. Verse' column* to which he was a contributor.

Cust's editorial style was often pragmatic and he was at times too extravagant in his payments to staff. His relationship with Astor was not of the best and Astor complained of Cust's 'habitual disregard of my instructions'. Cust was also in the habit of rejecting copy from Astor. The incompatibility between them resulted in Astor's abrupt dismissal of Cust in February 1896. Cust's journalism was an interlude in his social and political life. He returned to Parliament in 1900. **DA**

Sources: Hughes 2005, *ODNB*, Scott 1952.

CYCLIST (1879-1902) The *Cyclist and Bicycling, and Tricycling Trades Review* was published in Coventry. Its initial proprietors* were W. I. Iliffe* and one of the sport's leading manufacturers and equipment developers, Henry Sturmey, who edited* the magazine along with C. W. Nairn. The 28 cm, 13 page magazine appeared weekly*, sold for 1d (1884) and contained regular features that helped to define cycling culture including columns*, notes of the week, coming events, what the clubs are doing, general correspondents, the death roll and results of both amateur and professional* championships. The *Cyclist* also featured illustrations* and early club photographs*.

Title changes* between 1902-1905 reflect the development of the sport* at the turn of the century. In 1903, the magazine became known as the *Cycling Trade Review* to reflect the decline in popularity of tricycles following the introduction of the safety bicycle in 1902. The title was expanded in 1905 to the *Cycling and Motor Trades Review* in order to address the rise of the automobile. Other features of the magazine that highlight the development of the sport are advertisements* in a wrapper for a wide array of bicycles, and accessories, drawing attention to the link between the sport of cycling, and the sphere of technology, invention and entrepreneurship characteristic of the times.

Magazines such as the *Cyclist* were a unifying force behind a sport that was still in its early stages of development. The *Cyclist* helped to structure the sport, emphasizing the distinction between professional and amateur participants in its race reporting, reinforcing club identities in feature pieces and, through its advertisements, placing an emphasis on technology and equipment development that is still a part of cycling's culture today. **SRS/JNW**

Sources: Herlihy 2004, *Waterloo*.

D

DADD, FRANK (1851-1929) The illustrator* Frank Dadd used a variety of techniques derived from photo-realist models to provide illustrations for late Victorian and Edwardian magazines ranging from the *Graphic** to the *Cornhill**, from the *Boy's Own Paper** to the *Illustrated London News**. Royal Academy trained, and an accomplished and widely exhibited artist, Dadd's heavily finished and naturalistic drawings used a wide variety of washes that were hard to reproduce through wood* engraving, but his work was better adapted to the photo-reprographic methods introduced by magazines* later in the century. His specialism as an illustrator was the adventure story, where his painterly method proved widely popular. **BM**
Sources: Engen 1990, Houfe 1978.

DAILIES Daily newspapers in Britain originated in the eighteenth century with the *Daily Courant* appearing in 1702, the *Belfast News-Letter** in 1737 and the *Daily Universal Register* of 1785, which became *The Times** in 1788. In the nineteenth century, dailies were established in larger numbers following, or in anticipation of, the abolition of the Stamp* Duty in 1855. There were 17 regional dailies launched in that year, and other important weeklies* such as the *Manchester Guardian**, the *Scotsman** and the *Liverpool Post** switched to daily publication. Others, such as the *Daily Chronicle** followed in 1869, the *Daily Graphic** in 1890 and perhaps most significantly, the *Daily Mail** in 1896. The Press Association* was established as a news agency* to service the increasing demand in 1868, and in 1906 the Newspaper Proprietors'* Association was founded to advance the interests of the British dailies. Evening newspapers such as Bath's *Evening Chronicle* (1877) and Brighton's *Evening Argus* (1880) were aimed at returning commuters and could print more recent items of news, including updated editions. Daily production increased both the volume and pace of news* distribution, but also, crucially, the industry's advertising* income. It also facilitated professionalization* of journalism. **AGJ**
Source: Boyce 1978.

DAILY GRAPHIC (1890-1926) The *Daily Graphic* was started on 4 January 1890 by William Luson Thomas* with his company, H. R. Baines & Co. Thomas was a wood* engraver and, like his friend Charles Dickens*, an advocate for social reform. Thomas understood the power of illustration* as a method of raising social awareness and had previously founded the thriving weekly* *Graphic** in 1869 of which the *Daily Graphic* was an offshoot. Described as 'the first really successful daily picture paper' publishing the first half-tone newspaper picture on 4 November 1891, with illustrators* including Reginald Cleaver and Phil May, it became noted for its images of social conditions. Mary Frances Billington* was engaged as a special correspondent on female interests. The *Daily Graphic* was merged* with the *Daily Sketch* in 1926. **JRW**
Sources: Griffiths 1992, Linton and Boston 1987, *ODNB*.

DAILY MAIL (1896-) The founding of the *Daily Mail* by Kennedy Jones with Harold and Alfred Harmsworth* is considered a major turning point in the history of popular British journalism*. The *Mail* differed from all other newspapers with its short and lively news* stories and its price*, both reflected in its mottoes, 'The Busy Man's Daily Journal' and 'A Penny Newspaper for One Halfpenny'*. It catered to the new class of readers* recently enfranchised by the Third Reform Bill, the lower middle classes. It appealed to men and women, particularly clerical and government employees as Lord Salisbury dismissively asserted, 'a newspaper for office boys written by office boys'. Alfred Harmsworth's formula of human interest stories, comic strips, jokes and large illustrations* was successful to an unprecedented degree. Under his editorial guidance, it offered in its eight sober-looking pages a compact and effective overview of the morning news alongside lighter fare, all mixed with copious advertisements*. The *Daily Mail's* first issue on 4 May 1896 was immensely successful, supposedly numbering 397,213 copies, the highest circulation* ever achieved by a morning newspaper. Sales peaked at 989,255 in 1900, never to fall below 713,000.

While avoiding long parliamentary* speeches familiar in other dailies*, the *Mail's* concise news* stories did cover events such as the Boer War followed by realistic accounts of the conflict. The paper largely avoided partisan politics but was nationalistic* and supportive of the imperialist* project, becoming known as the 'Voice of Empire in London journalism'. Among its departments were City news, American markets*, world affairs, weather, sport*, the woman's page, fashion*, gossip*, church business, finance, parliament*, shipping intelligence, serialized* novels, hints for housewives, and daily menus. In its early years it boasted quality contributors including Max Beerbohm*, Robert Blatchford*, Edward H. Cooper (foreign* correspondent 1903-1906), Robert Dennis, Mary Howarth, Rudyard Kipling, John Mackie, Sir William Maxwell*, Charles E. Hands, George Warrington Steevens*, Edgar Wallace, Sidney Warwick and Lady Sarah Wilson.

The *Daily Mail* took advantage of technological advancements with telegraphic* communication between London and New York, improved distribution* through chartering special newspaper trains to the West and North of England and simultaneous publication in Manchester (1902). Harold Harmsworth, the business brain, invested in machinery that could cut, fold, and count papers as well as printing between 48,000 and 90,000 copies an hour. To court advertisers*, the *Mail* used net sales certificates and to court readers, it engaged in publicity stunts such as offering free insurance to subscribers and sponsoring contests; it was also the first daily* newspaper to become a public company. In its history, the *Mail* also produced different editions, such as the *Continental Daily Mail*, the *Overseas Daily Mail* (weekly)*, a Braille edition, the *Atlantic Daily Mail* (1923) and the *Weekly Transatlantic Edition* (1944). **KC**

Sources: *ODNB,* Pound and Harmsworth 1959, *Waterloo.*

DAILY NEWS (1846-1912) Announced in *Punch* as a 'Morning Newspaper of Liberal Politics and thorough Independence', and intended as a Liberal rival to the *Morning Chronicle,* the *Daily News* was launched on 21 January 1846 under the editorship* of Charles Dickens*. It was published* by Bradbury and Evans* and sold for 5d. In the first issue, Dickens wrote that the *Daily News* would advocate the principles of 'Progress and Improvement; of Education, Civil and Religious Liberty, and Equal Legislation' while seeking to 'elevate the character of the Public Press in England'. Though Dickens lasted only 17 days at the helm before passing the editorship to John Forster* in exhaustion, the paper maintained the principles he laid out in his first leader*. Over the course of its history, the *Daily News* advocated reform in social, political*, and economic legislation, fought for a Free Press in supporting the repeal of the Stamp Act, campaigned for impartial dealings with the natives of India and supported Irish Home Rule.

In 1852, editor Frederick Knight Hunt invited Harriet Martineau* to contribute to the *Daily News,* which she did for 14 years, influencing and strenuously arguing many of the paper's Liberal positions. Martineau was the paper's expert on America, and the *Daily News* adopted her abolitionist, pro-North position at the beginning of the Civil War and held to it. The *Daily News* was nearly alone in siding with the North, but its reporting managed to turn Liberal opinion to its cause. Still, in 1868, its fortunes in decline, the paper was sold and its price* reduced to 1d.

The *Daily News* was as well known for its war* reporting as it was for its role as the mouthpiece of the Liberal Party. Its war correspondents covered every major conflict during the paper's history. Manager John Richard Robinson recognized at the start of the Franco-Prussian War that readers wanted quick as well as detailed reporting. He directed his correspondents to telegraph* rather than post their dispatches, and to give rich descriptions of the war in addition to the hard facts. Robinson obtained the services of such notable contributors as Archibald Forbes* and Januarius Aloysius MacGahan, whose reporting of the Turkish atrocities in Bulgaria during the Russo-Turkish War convinced the public (in opposition to Disraeli) to support the Russians. Part-proprietor* Henry Du Pre Labouchère's* series of letters from Paris during the siege of 1870 helped to boost the ailing paper's circulation* from 50,000 to 150,000 in a single year.

Quaker chocolateer George Cadbury gained a controlling interest in the paper in 1901, in a takeover organized by Lloyd George, in order to oppose the Second African War. Under Cadbury, alcohol and betting advertising* were excluded and the paper continued to express Liberal Party, Nonconformist views under the editorship of A. G. Gardiner.

The *Daily News* merged* with the *Morning Leader* as the *Daily News and Leader* on 13 May 1912, and underwent several more mergers before shutting down 17 October 1960. **JK**

Sources: Koss 1973, McCarthy 1896, *ODNB, Waterloo.*

DAILY TELEGRAPH (1855-) Of all the major London newspapers, the *Daily Telegraph* had the most colourful origin when its first proprietor*, Colonel Arthur Sleigh, founded the paper in June 1855 as the *Daily Telegraph and Courier* in order to pursue a grudge against Prince George, a commander in the Crimean War. However, Sleigh's competitors under priced their newspapers to compete with him, and he also failed to attract sufficient advertising* so his printer, Joseph Moses Levy*, took over the paper in September 1855, pricing it at 1d, half of its original price*. Its editors* were Levy's son, Edward Levy Lawson*, who was also its drama critic, together with Thornton Hunt*, Sleigh's original choice as editor, son of the poet, Leigh Hunt*. From its inception, the paper was directed at a wealthy, educated readership*.

By early 1856 the *Telegraph* had achieved a circulation* of 270,000 and at the end of the decade its size* had doubled from four to eight pages. At this time, the first of the foreign* correspondents, for which it was eventually to be renowned, had been employed, one of these being Charles Dickens's* protégé, George Augustus Sala*, who covered the American Civil War for the paper and became the *Telegraph's* flagship writer. Composing many leaders* and articles, he became the cynosure of the newspaper, attracting both praise for his unmistakable style and censure for a certain excessively populist mentality which some discerned in his writing.

The *Telegraph*, despite its twentieth-century associations with traditional Toryism, was Whig in political tincture, especially in its liberal foreign policy. In general, the paper was liberal to the moderate extent that the rival *Pall Mall Gazette* was conservative. This changed in the late 1870s when the *Telegraph* began to support Disraeli over the Eastern question and though the Levy-Lawsons were among England's most successful Jewish families, the Jewish proprietorship of the *Telegraph* was never really an issue until this time. The paper's circulation had fallen to 240,000 in 1863 and towards the end of the 1860s it was being printed on a rotary press*, originally using the Hoe process until moving to the more efficient Bullock method. The paper had a tightly knit staff led by men of considerable intellectual weight and in 1873, Edwin Arnold*, poet and Orientalist, became editor.

Under Arnold, the *Telegraph* showed an interest not just in imperial* expansion and global politics, as seen in Edward Dicey's writings on foreign affairs, but also in its knowledge of other cultures as with its coverage of the Stanley-Livingstone African expedition which it co-sponsored with James Gordon Bennett's *New York Herald*. The paper also excelled in the arts. Clement Scott's* discursive essays on the theatre went well beyond the mere 'notice' of a play to pioneer the extended newspaper drama review*. Arnold's successor in 1899, William Leonard Courtney*, was a renowned writer on philosophy who continued Arnold's tradition of intellectual seriousness. Under Hunt and Arnold, the *Daily Telegraph* was the essence of the mid-Victorian press, but when Arnold was succeeded by Courtney it had been eclipsed by more populist newspapers such as the Harmsworths'* *Daily Mail*. NB

Sources: Bourne 1887, Brown 1985, Burnham 1955, Griffiths 1992, *Waterloo*.

DALLAS, ENEAS SWEETLAND (1828-1879)

Eneas Sweetland Dallas was a prominent and prolific journalist* who wrote mainly for *The Times*, but whose special literary interests did not prevent him from addressing a varied range of subjects for other papers and periodicals, such as the *Daily News*, *Saturday Review* and the *Pall Mall Gazette*.

In Scotland in the early 1850s, he founded and reviewed* for the *Edinburgh Guardian*. He wrote *Poetics: An Essay on Poetry* in 1852 and marked himself out as an outspoken critic who put the pleasure of the reader* first in his poetic theory. Dallas then moved to London where his first review* for *The Times* controversially attacked Tennyson for encouraging introverted poetry*. From 1855, when he joined the staff of *The Times*, until his death, he contributed regularly on biographical, political, cultural and literary* topics. 'George Eliot's*' words on hearing of Dallas's review of *Adam Bede* may be taken as indicative of his status as a literary critic in the 1850s and 1860s: 'the best news from London hitherto is that Mr Dallas is an enthusiastic admirer of Adam'. Dallas also wrote obituaries*, notably that of Prince Albert, and was the paper's Paris correspondent in the 1860s. While his contributions to *The Times* were anonymous*, he was well known in literary circles, and became a convivial member of the Garrick Club.

Dallas's best-known book, *The Gay Science* (1866), which pioneered the application of psychology to literary criticism, cemented his reputation as an original literary thinker as well as a journalist. It did not sell well, but its boost to his reputation may have facilitated his gaining the editorship* of *Once a Week* in January 1868. The magazine had attracted some celebrity* contributors and its illustrators* included high-profile men who also worked for *Punch*. By the time Dallas acquired the editorship, *Once a Week* was no longer as vibrant as its earliest editions, and he did not manage to recreate its most successful years. After a year and a half, Dallas moved back to working primarily as a journalist but also published more of his own book-length works. **BP**

Sources: Drinkwater 1932, *ODNB*, Taylor 1984, *Waterloo*, *Wellesley*.

DALZIEL FAMILY: DALZIEL, EDWARD (1817-1905); DALZIEL, EDWARD GURDEN (1849-1889); DALZIEL, GEORGE (1815-1902); DALZIEL, GILBERT (1853-1930); DALZIEL, JOHN (1822-1869); DALZIEL, MARGARET (1819-1894); DALZIEL, THOMAS BOLTON GILCHRIST SEPTIMUS (1823-1906) The firm of the Dalziel Brothers was one of the great commercial concerns of Victorian print culture, with the business eventually evolving from its roots in wood* engraving to encompass varied roles: illustration* (Thomas Bolton Dalziel was the most artistically talented of the brothers); art directorships for periodicals and multi-volume editions; printing and publishing*, where it specialised in illustrated books; and general trade work, including catalogues and technical handbooks.

Trained in his native north-east, George Dalziel had come to London in 1835 to serve his apprenticeship, and had subsequently set up his own business in 1840 just at the moment when *Punch** (1841) and the *Illustrated London News** (1842) were being established. The network of contacts built up by George and Edward in the early days of the firm took their work to Charles Knight* as well as Ebenezer Landells*, and they were soon working for a range of London publishers including Cadell, Cundall and Bogue, although the connection formed with Routledge* in 1850 was perhaps the commercially decisive one. While the firm found its metier originally in work for the comic artists of the 1840s like Cruikshank*, Leech*, Doyle* and Meadows*, it moved on to specialize in self-consciously 'artistic' illustration, thus extending the claims of wood engraving to be taken seriously as an aesthetic medium. Such claims were much enhanced by the black and white work of pre-Raphaelite artists like Millais*, Holman Hunt and Rossetti, who all drew for magazines as well as book projects; indeed, many of the Dalziels' publications were cleverly conceived as both series of illustrations for magazines* and as potential books. Over 60 illustrations by a range of well-known artists that were eventually published as *Dalziel's Bible Gallery* (1881) had appeared previously in the best-known illustrated monthlies of the 1860s like *Good Words**, and the Dalziel engravers worked prolifically to turn drawings into illustrations for those magazines which had established the full-page, signed, wood engraving as one of the most admired (and collectable) artistic products of the mid-Victorian period.

By the 1870s the Dalziel Brothers had additionally become the owners and printers of a stable of comic journals including *Fun**, *Judy** and *Hood's*

Comic Annual as well as sustaining their staggering output of engraved illustrations. There was no innovative technological basis for their success. The originality of the firm lay in the scale of its operations, and its willingness to train up an ever-increasing stream of apprentices to the requisite level of technical skill. Thomas Dalziel took the lead in working with the apprentices, who included draughtsmen of the level of Fred Walker* and George Pinwell* as well as many lesser-known but highly competent figures. Few firms can claim to have had the influence over print culture gained by the Dalziel Brothers in the period between 1850 and 1880, and the definition of popular art brought into being by the brothers is widely reflected in the illustrated periodicals and books of the 1860s and given testimony in their own two volume *Record* published in 1901. BM

Sources: Dalziel 1901, de Maré 1980a, Engen 1990, Reid 1928, White 1897, *ODNB*.

DANGERFIELD, EDMUND (1864-1938) Edmund Dangerfield was a printer and magazine* publisher* who launched several sporting and technical magazines at the turn of the century. Dangerfield began his career as a wages' clerk in his father's printing works. Gradually he was put in charge of printing journals such as the *Friendly Companion* and *Gospel Standard*. A keen cyclist at a time when cycling was both fashionable and popular, Dangerfield saw the need for a paper devoted to this sport*. About a dozen cycling periodicals had appeared since 1876, but none was in a truly popular format. *Cycling,* founded in 1891, fulfilled this need, and was far livelier than earlier cycling journals. The success of *Cycling* encouraged Dangerfield to open an office in Birmingham in 1895. His next venture, *Cycling Manufacture and Dealers' Review* was less successful, lasting only until 1899. Also unsuccessful was *Pictorial Life*, which was intended to be a popular illustrated paper. This was launched in 1900, but only had a run of 13 weeks. Despite these set backs, Dangerfield continued to produce new titles, most of which embraced the new technological and sporting developments of the early twentieth century. They included the *Regiment* (1901), *Motor Cycling and Motoring* (1902), the *Motor Boat* (1904), the *Commercial Motor* (1905) and the *Cycle Car* (1912), which became the *Light Car and Cycle Car* in 1913. Another paper, the *Aero*, was registered on 9 November 1901, but never appeared. Dangerfield continued to publish technical magazines until his death. DHL

Sources: Armstrong 1946, *ODNB*.

D'ARCY, ELLA (1857-1937) Ella D'Arcy's eyesight necessitated her switching from a contemplated career as a painter to authorship, and she retained a painter's eye in her fiction and journalism*. Fiction, mainly the short-story form, became her staple. Her stories appeared in the London *Argosy** (1891-1893), *All the Year Round**, *Temple Bar** (1890) and *Blackwood's Edinburgh Magazine** (1891), sometimes under the pseudonym* 'Gilbert H. Page'. However, her story 'Irremediable', published in the first issue of the *Yellow Book** (1894) after rejection by other magazines, established her in the literary world. D'Arcy became, after Henry Harland, the editor*, the most prolific contributor to the *Yellow Book,* providing stories for 10 issues – two in volume 10.

As subeditor* on the *Yellow Book*, a vaguely-defined and poorly-paid post, she proofread, paginated, arranged the pictures, and indexed. She also served as a sort of business-cum-social secretary to Harland, and liaised between him and the publisher*, John Lane*, and his business manager, Frederic Chapman*. When Harland was abroad she was responsible for preparing everything for the press, but had limited authority. In the wake of Oscar Wilde's* arrest, she arrived at Bodley Head to discover that Lane had suppressed Aubrey Beardsley's* drawings without explanation and, subsequently, that the cover and title page were also censored*. Her hopes that her art training would lead to the position of art editor after Beardsley's departure were frustrated. On her return from her visit to France in 1895-96 she saw herself as defending the aesthetic standards of the quarterly* when she unilaterally not only altered Harland's contents list by removing Ethel Colburne Mayne's story but 'expunged her name from the Yellow Dwarf's mistaken eulogies'. This display of independence led to her dismissal, although her fiction continued to be published in the magazine.

Though she attained responsibilities granted to few women, her editorial correspondence reveals scant effort to promote women writers. She championed the poetry of Ralph Hodgson and Charlotte Mew but remained unimpressed by the lapidary style of Henry James*. Having published several articles on art and artists in the *Westminster Review** (1893) and the *Yellow Book* (1894), in the early 1900s she contributed reviews* anonymously* to the London *Daily Chronicle**. Other projected publications – a cookbook, later a biography of Arthur Rimbaud and a selection of his poems – came to nothing. **BF/BMO/CO**
Sources: D'Arcy *Letters* 1990, Fisher 1992, Fisher 1994, Fisher 2006, Mix 1960, *ODNB*, Windholz 1996.

***DARK BLUE* (1871-1873)** When he began *Dark Blue*, with start-up funds contributed by John Ruskin*, John C. Freund envisaged a periodical beyond its Oxford University origins that would 'appeal... to the whole English-speaking public, and hence influence their mode of thought' (Feb. 1872: iv). During its 25-issue run, a broad readership* eluded the shilling* monthly*, but it earned a lasting place in the history of British aestheticism, publishing poetry* and prose by A. C. Swinburne*, D. G. Rossetti, William Morris*, Mathilde Blind*, W. M. Rossetti*, Sheridan LeFanu, Andrew Lang*, Edward Dowden, and W. S. Gilbert, with illustrations* by Ford Madox Brown and Simeon Solomon*. Blind published her first signed works in *Dark Blue*, and Swinburne's 'The End of a Month' appeared there after being rejected by *Fraser's Magazine** for its sexual content. The sexually transgressive nature of many of the works it published – Le Fanu's 'Carmilla', Blind's 'The Song of the Willi', Swinburne's poem and Solomon's accompanying illustration* – illuminate important connections between the aesthetic movement of the 1870s and fin-de-siècle decadence.

Freund's vanity and financial mismanagement doomed *Dark Blue*. 'Edited' by John C. Freund' came off the title page after the issue for January 1873, and two months later the magazine ended. **JKD**
Sources: Freund 1872, Graves 1930, Sims 1917, Swinburne *Letters* 1959, Welby 1929, *Wellesley.*

DARLEY, GEORGE (1795-1846) Poet and writer George Darley was born in Dublin and studied there at Trinity from 1815. In 1821 he moved to London and began life as a writer, contributing regularly to the *London Magazine**. In 1823 Darley published 'Letters to the Dramatists of the Day' as 'John Lacy' in the *London Magazine*, articles which denounced much contemporary theatrical writing and helped establish his name as a 'fine contributor' to the journal. During the early 1830s, Darley travelled extensively in Europe, visiting and studying at most of the major art galleries, his writings on which spawned many perceptive articles for the *Athenaeum**, to which he became a life-long and regular contributor of reviews* and articles, notably on Ruskin's* *Modern Painters* (1844, 1846). Darley also contributed poetry* and short stories to *Bentley's Miscellany** and the *Illuminated Magazine**, though it is his criticism of art that remains his most enduring and praiseworthy contribution to nineteenth-century journalism*. **MBT**
Sources: *ODNB*, Sullivan, *Waterloo*, *Wellesley.*

DAVENPORT, ALLEN (1775-1846) A staunch contributor to London's unstamped press*, Allen Davenport was a self-educated shoemaker. He was a leading promoter of the ideas of the revolutionary agrarian reformer Thomas Spence, whose biography he wrote (1836), extracts from which were widely printed in the radical press. Davenport's autobiography (1845) was similarly circulated, as late even as 1861 in the *National Co-operative Leader.*

Davenport's ventures into journalism* began in 1818 with *Sherwin's Political Register* (1817-1819) and extended over two decades and more than 20 different titles. *Sherwin's* was one of four publications with which he was particularly associated, the others being Carlile's* *Republican* (1819-1926), Hetherington's* *Poor Man's Guardian* and *Working Bee* (1840), the newspaper of the early socialist* community at Manea Fen, Cambridgeshire. He also contributed to Carlile's *Isis* (1832) and *Cosmopolite* (1832), the Owenite *Crisis* and *New Moral World* (1834-1845) and occasionally to the Chartist* press. Much of his work was unsigned or appeared over the pseudonyms* 'Alphus' or 'Economicus'. Davenport emphatically wished to be remembered as a poet (his poetry* was widely printed in the metropolitan radical press), but his easy, conversational style of political journalism* was widely admired, especially by George Julian Harney*. MSC

Sources: *DLB, ODNB.*

DAVIS, THOMAS (1814-1845) A native of Mallow, Co. Cork, but resident for most of his life in Dublin, Thomas Davis was probably the single most influential Irish political* journalist* of the nineteenth century. Son of an English army surgeon and an Irish Protestant mother, Davis attended Trinity College Dublin and trained as a barrister, though he never practised. Instead, supported by family means, he turned to journalism as a way of articulating his evolving views on Irish nationality, under a variety of signatures*: 'T. D.', 'The True Celt' and 'The Celt'.

His first periodical writing appeared in the monthly* liberal magazine the *Citizen* in 1839, where for the next four years he contributed carefully researched articles on themes such as emigration, British imperialism* in Asia and absentee landlordism in Ireland. With his friend John Blake Dillon, Davis took over the editorship* of the Dublin newspaper the *Morning Register* in 1841, but the controversy aroused by Davis's nationalist polemics led to the termination of the arrangement after four months. In October 1842, with John Blake Dillon

and Charles Gavan Duffy*, Davis founded the *Nation* newspaper, which was to become the chief organ of the newly-energized Irish nationalism of the 1840s, especially what came to be known as the Young Ireland* movement. Liberal rather than revolutionary, Davis's writing advocated the fostering of nationality through education and activism, with the ultimate aim of uniting the divided classes, sects and traditions in Ireland, and creating the conditions for cultural and political independence.

His own intellectual interests were eclectic and wide-ranging, and his several hundred contributions to the *Nation* addressed topics as diverse as land reform, imperial* politics, university education, Irish language policy, industrial development, tourism, art, music* and archaeology. He was also one of the paper's most popular writers of poetry*, and believed strongly that nationality must have its source in emotional attachment as well as political principle. An inspiring leader of great personal charisma, Davis's sudden death from scarletina in September 1845 was widely felt as a tragic loss to Irish cultural and political life. His powerful writings shaped Irish nationalist* discourse for more than a century. SMR

Sources: Molony 1995, *ODNB.*

DAVISON, JAMES W. (1813-1885) As chief music critic of *The Times* (1846-1878) and editor* of the *Musical World* (1843-1885), Davison was probably the most influential music journalist of his generation. As editor of the *Musical World*, Davison created a successful template that withstood the test of time, since, until well into the 1860s, the journal dominated its rivals while joyously indulging its editor's opinions and prejudices in countless (anonymous*) articles and reviews*. He also contributed music reviews and articles to a number of other journals and newspapers, most notably the *Musical Examiner* (in the 1840s), the *Saturday Review* (1860s and 1870s), the *Pall Mall Gazette* (1860s) and the *Graphic* (1874-1885).

Davison was the first trained musician to be appointed critic of a London daily* newspaper, and brought a new refreshing range and insight to music* journalism*. A conservative, he venerated the German 'masters' from Handel to Mendelssohn while being dismissive of developments in European music after 1850, especially the emergence of Wagner and the 'music of the future'. Despite his reactionary instincts, he was the first British critic to grasp the importance of Berlioz's music, and even his estimate of Wagner's works was to change by the 1870s. Regarding British music, Davison was a critic-patriot, keen to support the development of an indigenous school of composition. Even so, his reception of native works in *The Times* reflected his long-held prejudices against progressive tendencies, composers being praised or damned according to their adherence to classical precepts and the Mendelssohnian tradition. His style was bold, abrasive and controversial and, in terms of canon formation, he wielded enormous power with his pen. As an editor, he was a key figure in the development of a dedicated musical press and in the evolution of music journalism as a profession* in Britain. **MH**

Sources: Davison 1912, Grove, Hughes 2002, Obituaries *Musical World* 26 March 1885 and *The Times* 28 March 1885, Reid 1984.

DAVISON, THOMAS (1794-1826) Thomas Davison (aka Davidson) flourished briefly in Regency London as an ultra-radical publisher*, printer and journalist*. He was closely associated with the revolutionary Spencean circle, one Home Office spy describing him as a friend of Thomas Thistlewood, leader of the 1820 Cato Street Conspiracy to assassinate the Cabinet. However, Davison's influential mentor was George Cannon*, a freethinker and libertinist publisher, a sponsor shared with Robert Wedderburn*. Cannon introduced Davison to the French deist Volney (whose works Davison published in 1819) and underwrote Davison's business in Duke Street, West Smithfield. From here Davison printed and published three notable unstamped* weeklies*, *Medusa, or Penny Politician* (Feb. 1819-Jan. 1820), *London Alfred, or People's Recorder* at 1 ½d (Aug.-Nov. 1819) and *Cap of Liberty* at 2d (Sept. 1819-Jan. 1820), the first two of which he edited*. To this stable of overtly political* titles*, Davison added the *Deists' Magazine or Theological Inquirer* (1820 – some issues titled *Polemical Magazine*), mainly to recycle Cannon's works.

Medusa, effectively a Spencean journal, was Davison's most significant periodical. A strikingly effective blend of political comment and poetry*, its contributors included Wedderburn and Allen Davenport*. Davison himself was probably responsible for its sustained critique of William Cobbett*, but *Medusa* was most notable for its fierce attacks upon official handling of the Peterloo Massacre (16 Aug. 1819). He launched *London Alfred* expressly to publish detailed accounts of protest meetings against the Manchester incident. Davison also helped manage Richard Carlile's* *Republican** when its editor was imprisoned for blasphemy in October 1819. However, the following year Davison was himself convicted of blasphemous libel and sen-

tenced to two years' imprisonment. Carlile headed an appeal to support his family, as he did six years later when Davison died in poverty, having precariously survived as a bookseller following his release in 1822. **MSC**

Sources: *BDMBR*, McCalman 1988.

DELANE, JOHN THADDEUS (1817-1879) Delane edited* *The Times** (1785-) between 1841 and 1877, where his father, William Delane (1793-1857), was treasurer from 1831. After graduating from Magdalen Hall, Oxford in 1840, he was immediately given a job on the staff by John Walter*, then chief proprietor*, who had recognized Delane's potential. He performed various reporting and editorial tasks until the death of the editor, Thomas Barnes* in 1841, left a vacancy for one of the most prestigious jobs in journalism with no obvious successor in place. That Walter appointed the 23-year-old Delane to the role may have seemed rash – and Delane himself was very surprised – but he went on to hold the position for 36 years, overseeing a tripling in circulation* from 20,000 in 1842 to more than 60,000 in the final decade of his tenure. This, at a time when *The Times* was being undercut by the proliferation of cheaper titles, represented a remarkable achievement.

After the thundering style that *The Times* had adopted under the editorship of Barnes, Delane took the paper in a milder, more conciliatory direction. He had an astute political mind and fostered close links with men in government (especially Peel's foreign secretary, Lord Aberdeen and later Lord Palmerston), providing *The Times* with unrivalled access to invaluable sources of inside information. While the paper was during the period of his editorship associated broadly with Liberalism, Delane fought to ensure it was both well connected in Westminster circles and independent from the political parties*. This meant that while it was generally supportive of the government, *The Times* could criticize its policies when Delane's political instincts dictated it, which it did famously during the Crimean War.

Delane distinguished himself as a loyal and hardworking editor (16-hour working days were common), but he never wrote much for publication, preferring to shape opinion by nurturing leader* writers – who were never forced to write against their consciences – and reporters*. A difficult situation arose in 1847 when his father – who was still treasurer – fell out with the ageing proprietor* John Walter over a misleading financial report. Walter ousted William Delane, and John Delane's position seemed briefly to be in jeopardy. But the younger Delane managed to hang on and, after Walter died, later that year went on to develop a close working relationship with his successor and son, also John Walter (1818-1894). Towards the end of his life, he gradually and tacitly ceded control of many aspects of the paper until his official departure in November 1877. **MaT**

Sources: *ODNB*, *Times* Digital Archive.

DE LA RUE FAMILY (C. 1820-1923) Thomas De La Rue (1793-1866) was the family member most memorably concerned with newspaper publishing*. On 26 September 1812, at St Peter Port, Guernsey he launched the first issue of *Le Publiciste*, a weekly*, in partnership with Tom Greenslade, from Devon. Despite the existence of two rivals, the *Mercury* and the *Star*, the two proprietors* decided that Guernsey could support another newspaper devoted to politics* and literature*. However the two men quarrelled bitterly, and the paper ran under their joint editorship* for only 13 issues until 19 December 1812. By 6 February 1813, De La Rue had set up a rival called *Le Miroir Politique*, priced* 3d. Despite threats from Greenslade, the new title survived and prospered. The last issue with De La Rue as proprietor appeared 18 July 1815. Shortly afterwards he left for London, mainly because of economic problems after the Napoleonic Wars. His brother-in-law John Champion replaced him as sole publisher* of *Le Miroir Politique*.

In London Thomas De La Rue also experimented with different printing techniques* and the use of colour. This resulted in the printing of playing cards. In 1838 his firm was commissioned to gild a special edition of the *Sun** newspaper which celebrated Queen Victoria's coronation. The job took six days to complete, and De La Rue employed 100 staff especially for the task. **DHL**

Sources: Houseman 1968, *ODNB*.

DE MATTOS, KATHARINE (1851-1939) In 1881 Katharine de Mattos moved to London, where she tried to support herself and her two children by writing. Robert Louis Stevenson, a cousin, introduced her to William Ernest Henley* and she started writing for the *Magazine of Art**, edited by Henley, and for the *Saturday Review**. Her poems* were published in *Sylvia's Journal**, the *Windsor Magazine**, and the *Yellow Book**.

In 1888, Henley accused Stevenson's wife, Fanny, of plagiarism for allegedly having published one of De Mattos's stories as her own. This caused a breach between Henley and Stevenson,

as well as between de Mattos and Stevenson. By this time, de Mattos had developed into a professional* writer; producing translations and a few short stories, which she published under the pseudonym* 'Theodor Hertz-Garten', she could stand on her own. With her contribution 'In a Gallery: Portrait of a Lady (Unknown)', written from the perspective of a New Woman, she was one of the first women whose poetry* appeared in the *Yellow Book**. Her most important contribution to journalism and her main source of income were the 1,300 anonymous* book reviews* that she wrote for the *Athenaeum**. In 1908, her name abruptly disappeared from the *Athenaeum's* 'marked file'. **IC**

Sources: Demoor 2000, Hughes 2004, *ODNB*.

DEMOCRATIC REVIEW OF BRITISH AND FOREIGN POLITICS, HISTORY AND LITERATURE (1849-1850) Edited* by George Julian Harney*, the *Democratic Review* was an important mouthpiece for European republican ideas. Harney established his journalistic reputation at the *Northern Star** and when Feargus O'Connor's* grip on the Chartist movement waned, Harney and other republicans such as William James Linton* produced a number of periodicals whose aim was to refocus the radical agenda along democratic-socialism lines. The unstamped* *Democratic Review* was published as a small monthly* journal of 40 pages by Eneas Mackenzie at his Fleet Street* print shop. The format was plain apart from an emblazoned emblem on the frontispiece bearing the words 'Liberty, Equality, Fraternity'.

Harney's opening address 'To the Working Classes' complained that the vast majority of the press had 'misrepresented' European revolutionary movements and he promised to set the record straight. Regular contributors to the *Democratic Review* thus included such European luminaries as Ledru Rollin, Louis Blanc, Friedrich Engels* and 'citizen' Marx*. Just as adventurously, perhaps, Harney published a series of articles on democracy by a female writer, Helen Macfarlane*. Harney's quarrels with the Chartist leadership were played out in the pages of the June 1850 issue and his withdrawal from the *Northern Star* was marked by the launch of a new title, the *Red Republican**, under the guiding hand of his self-styled Jacobin persona 'ami du peuple'. In September 1850 Harney was obliged to offset growing losses by amalgamating the two journals. **JA**

Sources: Allen 2005a, Allen 2007, Black and Black 1969, Finn 1993, Schoyen 1958.

DE QUINCEY, THOMAS PENSON (1785-1859) Known mostly for his *success de scandale*, *Confessions of an English Opium-Eater* (1821), Thomas De Quincey was a largely self-educated and prolific polymath who has proven to be, with the exceptions of Scott* and perhaps Coleridge*, the most influential, if idiosyncratic, of all English prose writers of the early nineteenth century. De Quincey's career as a professional journalist* began in 1818 with the publication of the pamphlet 'Close Comments upon a Straggling Speech', a Tory polemic in opposition to the Radical candidate, Henry Brougham*, in the Westmoreland by-election. The success of this pamphlet, and the support of his friends William Wordsworth and S. T. Coleridge, led to De Quincey's appointment to the editorship* of the newly founded Tory newspaper, the *Westmorland Gazette*.

It was De Quincey's habitual failure to meet deadlines, however, that forced his resignation from the *Westmorland* in 1819. Eventually his penury and his increasing dependence upon opium brought about the 1821 appearance of the auto-biographical Confessions, in Taylor and Hessey's *London Magazine** where he famously detailed his hallucinatory experiences with opiates. De Quincey remained a regular contributor to the *London* until October 1826. The following year, he began to supplement his income by writing for the Tory *Edinburgh Saturday Post* until he resumed contact with his friend John Wilson* of *Blackwood's Edinburgh Magazine**. Here De Quincey published some of his most famous essays such as 'On murder considered as one of the fine arts', 'Suspiria de Profundis' and a 'sequel' to the 'Confessions', and continued as a prominent contributor until 1849.

Tired of having to circulate between London, his family farmhouse at Fox Ghyll, Rydal and Edinburgh, from December 1830 De Quincey and his family henceforth resided in Edinburgh. As a result of accumulating debt and possible imprisonment, De Quincey's existence in Edinburgh became a complex and fugitive one, with many of his articles being clandestinely delivered to his editors by his children. In 1833, friction arose between the author and *Blackwood's* editorial policies, and De Quincey was forced to turn to the liberal *Tait's Edinburgh Magazine** as a market for his work. He was not to return to *Blackwood's* until 1837.

From 1834 to 1839, De Quincey contributed to *Tait's* biographical reminiscences of his long relationship with Wordsworth, Coleridge and the other Lake District Poets, in 'Sketches of Life and Manners; from the autobiography of the English opium-eater', one of the finest examples of nineteenth-century autobiography. Having published 'The English Mail-Coach', his final essay for *Blackwood's* in 1849, De Quincey introduced himself in 1850 to James Hogg, editor and publisher* of a cheap and critically maligned magazine, the *Instructor* which, between 1850 and 1858, printed more than 30 articles by De Quincey, on an immense range of topics. Hogg thus became De Quincey's principal publisher, and in 1852 the publisher of the first British collected edition of De Quincey's works. **CC**

Source: *ODNB*.

DIAL (1889-1897) This art and literature* periodical is notable for being the quintessential little magazine* of the Aesthetic/Decadent avantgarde. The *Dial* was a coterie publication in every sense: an irregular frequency of five issues spread over eight years (1889, 1892, 1893, 1896 and 1897), a small circulation* of a few hundred copies every issue and the constant reappearance of the same few contributors. Its editors* were the versatile artists Charles Ricketts* and Charles H. Shannon*. Ricketts declared in the 'Apology' in issue one: 'The sole aim of this magazine is to gain sympathy with its views. … [W]e are out of date in our belief that the artist's consciousness cannot be controlled by the paying public, and just as far as this notion is prevalent we hope we shall be pardoned our seeming aggressiveness'. The first three issues were published privately; Hacon & Ricketts (the Vale Press) were the publishers of the final two. All issues were printed by the Ballantyne Press*. The first issue, which was a bit smaller in format* than subsequent numbers* was priced* at 7s 6d, and the second probably at 10s 6d; nd while the cover of No 1 pronounces it 'The first number of the series', those of Nos 2-5 add the subtitle *an occasional publication*. At least half of the contents was art work, not only full-page plates of wood* engravings and lithography*, but sumptuous initial letters and tailpieces integrated into the letterpress, itself often related to visual art. Ranging from essays on individual artists and art critics and poetry* inspired by them, to 'notes' on current exhibitions and the art scene, the letterpress is reminiscent of the *Century Guild Hobby Horse**. The *Dial's* large-format*, graphics-oriented design was partly aimed at a connoisseur/collectors market, with 15 copies of No 2 being available with illuminated initial letter pieces for two guineas.

The critical reception was almost unanimously positive, although some reviewers predicted that the *Dial* was not destined to enjoy a long existence, and others complained of the eclecticism of the material included. In the second issue, there is an unsigned defence of the editorial policy, in which it is stated that the editors* sought to offer 'Documents' or 'monuments of moods', and that the eras or schools these came from were irrelevant. In practice this amounted to a preference for French painting and literature* and a distinct influence of the Pre-Raphaelites, both of which clearly herald the aestheticism of the decade to come. The *Dial* published the occasional poem* by Michael Field and Herbert Horne*, and an abundance of work by John Gray and Thomas Sturge Moore*. The latter two also contributed translations of French authors (Verlaine, Rimbaud and De Guérin), as well as articles on Puvis de Chavannes and the Goncourt brothers. The stylish lay-out, for which Ricketts and Shannon were largely responsible, and the faultless printing of the magazine also proved an inspiration to later little magazines. When Ricketts's Vale Press was founded in 1896, the *Dial* to some extent became a prestigious advertisement* scheme for the new publishing house. **KNC**
Source: Watry 2004.

DIAMOND, CHARLES (1858-1934) An Irish press baron* based in Newcastle, Charles Diamond produced a number of popular newspapers which supported Irish nationalism*. His most enduring title was the *Irish Tribune: An Irish Journal for England and Scotland** (1884ff), a paper cheap enough for even the poorest of readers. It offered a lively mixture of educational and entertaining copy combined with support for both Irish nationalism and Roman Catholicism. Circulation* rapidly reached a healthy 20,000 weekly* sales and by the end of 1885 the *Irish Tribune* was published in several separate editions to serve Irish communities in Newcastle, Glasgow, Liverpool, Manchester and London. Diamond's close connections with Catholic elites underpinned both advertising* revenue and circulation rates, enabling him to expand the paper to 12 pages in 1886.

The *Tribune* claimed to reach an astonishing 'four million Irish and Catholic people in England and Scotland', and other titles followed in quick succession including the *Catholic Household: A Weekly Journal for every Catholic Home* (1887), the *Catholic Educator* (1893) and, for London readers, the *Weekly Herald* (1888). Diamond also took over the struggling *Glasgow Observer* (later the *Glasgow*

Observer and Scottish Catholic Herald) and made it the Scottish* sister paper to the *Tribune*, reproducing much of the same copy but also providing a distinctively Scottish agenda on such issues as Catholic School Board representation. Diamond purchased this paper outright in 1894 with the backing of his Scottish Catholic Printing Company. The *Tribune* survived as an independent title until 1897 when it was relaunched as a syndicated* title* the *Catholic Times,* for circulation across most if not all regions of the British Isles. **JA**
Sources: Allen 2005b, Allen 2007, Allen 2008, Cowen Papers (TWAS), *DLB*, Edwards 1979, Edwards and Storey 1985, NRA (Home Office Papers).

DICK, THOMAS (1774-1857) Scottish author, educator, journalist*, editor* and self-styled 'Christian Philosopher', Thomas Dick began as a Secessionist minister, turning to journalism to restore and broaden his reputation after he was defrocked in 1805. While a schoolmaster, he penned a series of articles 'On Literary and Philosophical Societies' for the London *Monthly Magazine** (1814-1815); together, they constituted a detailed proposal for what later became known as Mechanics' Institutes. Seeking a reputation in science*, he also wrote for William Nicholson's* *Journal of Natural Philosophy, Chemistry, and the Arts*, the *Annals of Philosophy* and the *Edinburgh Philosophical Journal*. After the success of his book *The Christian Philosopher* (1823), Dick retired from teaching and wrote eight more books as well as three tracts. In 1835-1836, he edited the first three volumes of the *Educational Magazine and Journal of Christian Philanthropy and of Public Utility*, which promoted education in an evangelical context. Other literary efforts included 24 articles on celestial phenomena written for the *Dundee, Perth and Cupar Advertiser* (1836-1840).

Dick's writings were a heady mix of devotional effusions, imaginative speculation and basic science. Typical articles speculated on the celestial scenery and inhabitants of the rings of Saturn, or called for the reform of the 'pagan' nomenclature of constellations. They were especially popular in the United States, where their transparently devotional and evangelical tone, together with their espousal of 'useful knowledge'* and the plurality of worlds, captured the religious* yearnings and optimism of Americans during the Second Great Awakening. Indeed, all his writings had a decidedly Christian tone. Through them he actively sought to inculcate moral and didactic lessons, counter secularization, advance the millennium and prepare the elect for the afterlife, which he conceived as an extended and rapturous exploration of God's physical universe. Dick's uniqueness was his unparalleled enthusiasm for promoting Christianized natural knowledge in such a way as to lead readers to consider the majesty and beauty of God's handiwork, ultimately precipitating conversions. **WA**

Sources: Astore 2001, Gavine 1974, Smith 1983, *ODNB*.

DICKENS, CHARLES (1812-1870) Dickens served a full newspaper apprenticeship, beginning as a teenage penny-a-liner for the *British Press* (1826). Having taught himself shorthand* in the late 1820s, Dickens practised the craft in the antiquated courts* of Doctors' Commons before moving up to join the select band of parliamentary* reporters, working first for his uncle's voluminous *Mirror of Parliament*, then for the radical *True Sun* during the stormy passage of the Reform Bill through Parliament (1832), and finally securing a coveted reporter's job on the newly reorganised *Morning Chronicle*, under veteran Benthamite editor John Black (1783-1855). There he undertook varied work – theatre reviewing*, election reporting, express reporting of extra-mural political events, as well as enduring the daily grind of parliamentary debates. Given the fluctuating demands for space which the latter placed on a 7-column* broadsheet like the *Chronicle*, room was soon found for Dickens's witty sketches employing, among a wardrobe of other styles, the rhetoric of political journalism* to narrate the world of everyday Londoners. These came to be signed 'Boz', and between 1836 and 1839, together with tales from the *Monthly Magazine** and *Bell's Life in London** they were republished to extensive acclaim, overlapping with the monthly release of 'Boz's' next great success, *The Pickwick Papers* (1836-1837).

Thereafter, Dickens's writing ventures all self-consciously straddled the permeable frontier between journalism and popular literature. He left the daily* press for the more genteel world of monthly* magazines*, with the editorship of *Bentley's Miscellany** (1837-1839), but sought to reconnect with satirical* weekly journalism through editing *Master Humphrey's Clock** for Chapman & Hall* (1840-1841). This was something of a misfire, in journalistic terms, though it bequeathed 'Old Curiosity Shop' and 'Barnaby Rudge' to literature. So too was Dickens's involvement with the *Daily News** (1845-1846); critics note that only 17 issues of the new Liberal broadsheet were published under his watch. Yet Dickens's effectiveness, as celebrity* launch ed-

itor, should not be underestimated; his newsgathering and recruiting arrangements stood the test of time, and he led from the front with a series of inventive contributions on social and cultural issues.

Even while seeking to reposition himself as a serious novelist with *Dombey and Son* (1846-1848), Dickens returned to newsprint, with around 30 anonymous* reviews and irony-laden leaders* for the *Examiner** under John Forster* (1848-1849). These were a prelude to his return to full-time editing and leader*-writing, with *Household Words** and *All the Year Round** – hugely successful enterprises in weekly* magazine journalism which, however, did not prevent Dickens from writing a further eight serial* novels and undertaking punishing tours as a public reader in Britain, France and America. Dickens is now widely recognized – and was during his lifetime – as a crucial contributor both to the popular* appeal and the respectability of the mass-market* newspaper and periodical press. **JMD**

Sources: Drew 2003, Drew 2007, Maurice 1909, Schlicke 2005, Slater 1994-2000.

DICKES, WILLIAM (1815-1892) The career of William Dickes characterises the second generation of London-based wood* engravers who combined their artistic and technical skills with entrepreneurial flare and an evolving awareness of the requirements of the London book and periodical trade. Although he began work as a Royal Academy-trained artist/engraver, and learnt wood engraving technique as one of the Branstons'* apprentices, much of his subsequent work was as a printer and art director for a wide variety of projects, including the magnificent Abbotsford edition of Scott's work (1842-1847) which drew together an outstanding group of wood engravers and did much to establish the aesthetic credentials of the medium.

An expert in colour printing, and a pioneer in the use of oil coloured images drawn from wood blocks, he undertook work for many publications from the Society for the Promotion of Christian Knowledge* as well as for magazines ranging from the *Queen** to the *Gentleman's Journal*. Dickes's work, and that of many jobbing and usually less skilful engravers, played a major role in supplying the illustrations* for the mass of literature, especially periodicals, targeted at a broad reading*public among the lower middle classes*. Highly skilled, inventive, energetic and open to new technology, Dickes, and many lesser known figures, provided the technical means by which the mass market* could be developed in the mid-Victorian period. **BM**

Sources: Engen 1990, Houfe 1978.

THE

ILLUSTRATED REVIEW

No. 1.—Vol. I.　　　FRIDAY, OCTOBER 14, 1870.　　　Price Threepence.

CONTENTS

CHARLES DICKENS.

THE life of Charles Dickens remains yet to be written; and it must take some time before the thread of a life that has run out can be gathered together and worked into a connected story. In the following pages we can only profess to give a rapid sketch of his life—a sketch which may perhaps enable our readers to understand something of the position he occupied in the world of letters, and the influence he exercised on his own generation. Charles Dickens was, in a great measure, the architect of his own fortunes. Born in the year 1812, at Portsmouth, where his father held a Government appointment in the Navy Pay Office, he was, at the conclusion of the war, when his father retired with a pension, brought up to London, where the greater part of his life was afterwards spent. To this we owe, no doubt, in great measure, the intimate knowledge he displays of all parts of the great metropolis—a knowledge which was increased and perfected afterwards; but its reality must have been acquired in early life. At the age of seven he was placed at a school in Chatham, under the Rev. W. Giles, a master for whom he always retained an affectionate remembrance. His education was what is called commercial. The classics were not cultivated, but he received the rudiments of a good sound English education, such as is given to the great bulk of Englishmen who require to turn their knowledge to account at the very earliest period. Charles Dickens was no exception; and whilst quite a boy he entered a lawyer's office. There he acquired some little knowledge of the law; but his literary instincts were too strong, and the law was soon abandoned for work of a more exciting and more congenial character. He was first engaged as reporter for the *True Sun*, and then for the *Mirror of Parliament*, a paper conducted by his uncle, Mr. Barlow. After the short-lived existence of this paper had ceased, through his father's influence, who had become connected with the *Morning Chronicle*, Mr. Dickens was engaged on its staff as a reporter. This

CHARLES DICKENS.
From a Photograph, and by permission, of Messrs. Mason & Co. of New Bond Street.

Figure 11: Homage to Charles Dickens in the *Illustrated Review*, 14 Oct. 1870: 1.

DICKS, JOHN (1818-1881) John Dicks was amongst the foremost publishers* of Victorian popular* periodicals, and a pioneer of cheap* reading for the masses*.

Dicks held jobs in various London printing offices through the 1830s, including a stint at the Queen's Printers, before becoming chief assistant to Peter Perring Thoms, a printer/publisher based in Warwick Square, in 1841. However, it was the late 1840s which saw Dicks's career begin to burgeon with the commencement of what would become a close, lasting, and profitable business relationship with author, publisher and radical G. W. M. Reynolds*. In 1847 Dicks became publisher of *Reynolds's Miscellany**, a popular weekly* which Reynolds had launched the previous year. Setting up his own office on Wellington Street, Dicks continued to publish *Reynolds's Miscellany*, plus companion papers such as *Reynolds's Weekly Newspaper**, along with Reynolds's epic novel *Mysteries of the Court of London* (1849-1856) and a myriad of other periodicals. By the early 1850s Dicks had become Reynolds's official publishing and managing agent. The two men consolidated this relationship by entering into partnership in 1863, around which time their offices were relocated to the Strand. Upon Reynolds's death in 1879, Dicks purchased the copyrights* to all of his colleague's popular works.

Beyond his affiliation with Reynolds, Dicks was a prolific publisher in his own right, issuing a bewildering array of periodicals over several decades. Among the foremost of these were the *Halfpenny Gazette* (1861-1865), a miscellany*, and *Every Week* (1869-1896), a journal of thrilling literature*. He serialized* sensational fiction in penny numbers, for example, *The Dark Woman, or, the Life and Adventures of Sixteen String Jack* (1861) and *Rook the Robber, or, London Fifty Years Ago* (1863) by the renowned James Malcolm Rymer. Reprints of novels and plays were another specialism: *Dicks' Standard Plays* (1864-1907), which offered a complete play for 1d per week, ran to over 1,000 numbers, while *Dicks' Shakespeare* (1866-1884) allowed readers* to purchase editions of the bard's works, again for the small price of 1d each. Like many of his contemporaries, Dicks also attempted to carve himself a share of the boys' periodical market, although neither the *Boy's Herald* (1877-1878) nor the *Boy's Halfpenny Journal* (1878-1879) achieved lasting success.

In 1862 Dicks launched what was perhaps his most significant work, *Bow Bells**. A family* miscellany, *Bow Bells* contained serial* fiction, a diverse range of non-fiction, correspondence* and adver-tisements*. Priced* at one penny* per week, it proved a lasting success, so much so that Dicks took the step of merging* *Reynolds's Miscellany* into *Bow Bells* in 1869.

Dicks retired in the late 1870s, after which point his sons assumed control of his business, and continued to publish well into the twentieth century. ChB

Sources: Dicks 2006, Jay 1918-1921, *ODNB*, *Waterloo*.

DILKE, CHARLES WENTWORTH (1789-1864) In 1817 Charles Wentworth Dilke, an Admiralty clerk, made the acquaintance of the 'cockney school' of poets, including Leigh Hunt*, Thomas Hood* and John Keats. From 1818 he began to contribute anonymously* to the periodical press, acting as drama reviewer* for the *Champion* (1818), and at least once discussing eighteenth-century drama in the *Retrospective Review* (1825). He was an occasional contributor to the *London Magazine** in 1821, and his series 'View of public affairs' (1823ff), became the periodical's dominant public voice. In 1824-1825, he was co-editor* of the *London Magazine*, whilst continuing to work as political* correspondent. His articles endorsed the Greek and the Spanish fight for freedom (Aug. 1823), and pursued liberal issues such as the abolition of slavery (Jan., June and Aug. 1824) and the reform of the penal code in England (July 1824).

His involvement with the *Athenaeum** began in the late 1820s; he became editor* in 1830, continuing until he resigned in 1846. The strength of the periodical consisted in literary and arts reviews* rather than original articles. Dilke consistently commissioned reviews from specialists in every field. As editor he took particular pride in the series 'Foreign Correspondence'* which included criticism and gossip* of all the European capitals and centres of art, from English citizens resident abroad (the Trollopes) or his own staff sent for the purpose (e.g. Sarah Austin*). Dilke's editorial principles and practice represented a complete independence from the book trade. Unlike other periodicals, the *Athenaeum* refused to practise puffing*, and it also carried several anti-puffing articles in 1831 and 1832. It was largely due to Dilke's efforts that the practice had abated by the 1850s. After his retirement from the *Athenaeum*, Dilke returned to it as a contributor of articles in the field of eighteenth-century biographical and textual studies. In a series of reviews* between 1848 and 1853, he attempted to clear up the mystery attached to the highly political 'Letters of Junius' which first appeared in the *Public Advertiser* (1768-1772).

In 1846, Dilke had been asked to assist the *Daily News**, edited* by John Forster* by becoming its managing editor until 1849. Dilke's business policy consisted of cutting the price of the paper and thereby increasing its circulation*; by this means he created a cheap* daily* before the removal of the stamp* duty. From 1854, Dilke's main intellectual focus was Alexander Pope, and he addressed the mysteries of the textual history of Pope's correspondence in several articles, some of which were published in *Notes and Queries** (1854-1863). He also devoted attention to establishing a corpus of Jonathan Swift's work as shown in articles in *Notes and Queries* (1854-1862). Another area of publication in his life was the reform of the Literary Fund. In 1858 he, Dickens and John Forster wrote a pamphlet called 'The case of the Reformers of the Literary Fund', part of which appeared in the *Athenaeum* (6 March 1858). ZV

Sources: *Athenaeum* Index online, Garrett 1982, Marchand 1941, *ODNB*.

DILKE, EMILIA (1840-1904) Art historian, critic, and art editor* of the *Academy** 1873-1883, Emilia Dilke (née Strong) studied at the South Kensington School of Art (1859-1861). Her early writing was published anonymously* or under the signature E. F. S. Pattison, her married name from 1861. In addition to her salaried editorial position on the *Academy*, she contributed reviews* and articles to the *Athenaeum** (1876-1904), *Contemporary Review** (1877), *Cosmopolis**, *Fortnightly Review** (1872-1893), *Gazette des beaux-arts* (1898-1899), *L'Art*, *L'Oeuvre d'Art*, *New Review** (1890-1891), *Universal Review** (1888-1890) and *Westminster Review** (1869-1875). Her articles also document her support of the women's Trade Union* movement.

After 1885 she published under the name Emilia Dilke, having married Charles Wentworth Dilke, 2nd bt., liberal politician and *Athenaeum* proprietor*. She was one of several women contributors appearing regularly in the *Athenaeum*. Emilia Dilke was already by this time an established authority on French art history (having published *The Renaissance of Art in France* in 1879) and a critic of both historical and contemporary art. Her scholarly approach to art history with which her journalism was implicated was also evident in *Art in the Modern State* (1888) and a multi-volume study of eighteenth-century French painters, sculptors, engravers, architects, furniture and decoration (1899-1902). Dilke was a pioneer in art journalism, a profession that opened up for women in the ensuing decades. MEC

Sources: Clarke 2005, Demoor 2000, Israel 1999, Mansfield 2000, *Wellesley*.

DISTRIBUTION Booksellers, coffee shops and street hawkers had served as the principal distribution routes for newspapers and periodicals in the metropolises of the eighteenth century and this held true in the first part of the nineteenth century. When it came to supplying the provinces, the improving state of the roads in the latter part of the eighteenth century had emboldened John Palmer to introduce the mailcoach in 1784, a method of transporting the printed word that proved to be both faster and safer from theft than the horsemail. The Post Office played a central role in the growth of nationally distributed newspapers in the eighteenth century, and by 1790 it delivered 4,650,000 London papers to the country annually. In 1787, the Post Office had set up a separate office for dealing with newspapers, and by 1792 it had begun to distribute all newspapers for free as a result of a governmental decree. Not simply a 'tax on knowledge'*, the Stamp* Duty, as its name suggests, was understood to cover the cost of postage. The centrality of the Post Office to newspaper distribution continued into the nineteenth century and in 1851 it was estimated that each paper was sent through the post an average of three times. When the Stamp Duty was abolished as a compulsory tax in 1855, the option to buy stamped papers and periodicals (at a slightly higher price*) remained, to cover the cost of postage.

While recognizing the importance of the development of formal distribution networks, it should also be noticed that periodical literature continued to circulate* after it had been sold, with many people reading the same copy of a given periodical. This was especially true in the first half of the century. There are reports of the radical *Cobbett's Political Register** and other similar publications being read out loud in pubs, so that their readership* could have included illiterate labourers. Newspapers and periodicals could even be hired by the hour in the street. Following the repeal of the stamp duty in 1855, the wave of cheap* newspapers and periodicals – often costing 1d or even ½d – created financial pressure to encourage a 'buy your own' mentality in their readers. This was helped by the declining quality of newsprint as robust (but expensive) paper* made from rags was replaced by cheaper, less durable wood-pulp-based paper.

Distribution was transformed by the extension of the railway system in mid-century, and the latter played a key role in enabling the speedy and pervasive distribution of national* daily* papers. W. H.

Smith* – whose grandfather Henry Walton Smith had established the family firm's first bookstall in 1792 – was the great innovator here, realizing the potential of the railway to enable the London papers to reach Birmingham on the morning of their publication, and Manchester and Liverpool the day after. Before Smith, Northern cities had to wait until two mornings after publication for London-based newspapers. Though the use of 'Special Newspaper Trains'* was becoming widespread by the end of the century – in 1872 the *Scotsman** began to run its own dedicated train carrying the day's edition from Edinburgh to Glasgow, departing every weekday at around 4am – much of the increased distribution was achieved by using scheduled passenger services. Smith combined the use of trains with a developing system of station book- and news-stalls – starting with Euston in 1848 – providing a radically new business model for the distribution and sale of print. A deal he struck with *The Times** in 1854 gave him a monopoly over the wholesale distribution of the paper outside London in return for an annual payment of £4,000, and is suggestive of the way in which emerging distribution networks were starting to shape the media landscape.

The career of Scotland-based John Menzies* was in many ways analogous to that of Smith. Opening his first bookstall in Edinburgh in 1833, he was innovative in selling the *Scotsman* directly over the counter at a time when newspapers usually sold their product directly to subscribers. He branched into wholesale distribution, obtaining the agency* for *Punch** in 1841. He opened a group of railway station bookstalls in Scotland starting from 1857, employing fleets of basket boys* who would board trains while they idled at the station, passing down the aisle from one end to the other selling newspapers and periodicals. This shows that the train was not only a new way of shifting periodicals and newspapers from one end of the country to the other: it also provided a new location in which to read them, since all previous modes of transport were too bumpy to sustain reading easily. Both Smith and Menzies profited from this fact.

The fast distribution enabled by the railways tended to work to the advantage of the national* London papers and to the detriment of the regional press. In this sense, it is mirrored by the broadcast networks of the twentieth century, during which news became still more centralized in London. But although the new distribution networks in some ways helped to compound the hegemony of a national daily press produced in London, there was still a considerable amount of two-way traffic. The quarterly* reviews based in Edinburgh – such as the *Edinburgh Review** – started to suffer as the century went on, but *Chambers' Edinburgh Journal**, along with a number of other titles, flourished south of the border, achieving a large number of subscribers as well as being distributed wholesale.

Moreover, in the days of stamp duty, regional papers were often particularly adept at reaping the benefit of the postal concessions associated with it. It was by this means that the Leeds-based, Chartist *Northern Star** was able to achieve a large circulation* in the pit towns of Lancashire. Its first edition was also distributed in London, and by the end of 1841 it was claiming to be a national paper. That the *Star* moved its offices to London in 1844 was in part due to a decline in the fortunes of Chartism, but it also reconfirmed the centrality of London to Britain's print distribution network. New communications technology was to change this somewhat. Members of the Provincial* Newspaper Society (1836-1888) – including the *Manchester Guardian**, the *Leeds Intelligencer* *(1777-1883) and the *Sheffield Daily Telegraph** (1855-1934) – increased their circulation in the latter part of the century largely because the Press Association* (in whose formation in 1868 they played a key part) used the telegraph* to transmit national and international news practically instantaneously. The further the newspaper office was from London the better, as this made it easier for the morning edition to hit the newsstand before the London papers arrived by train. On the other hand, some London papers made concessions to regional news by leaving a page or more blank so that local offices could add news from their own area before the issue reached the point of sale.

Compared with daily* and weekly* newspapers, periodicals that went out monthly* were under less time pressure, but the absence of a daily routine for distribution (and therefore of full-time staff and infrastructure given over to this function presented its own problems. By the late 1840s, when monthlies had largely taken over from quarterlies, Magazine Day* had become a national institution. This monthly frenzy of activity involved the hiring of special carriers to transport the journals to agents and publishers in Paternoster Row. Periodicals could also be borrowed from circulating libraries* such as Mudies, which then sent them on to subscribers in the provinces a month late.

Aside from the effects of distribution on the national press (and thereby on the idea of the nation itself), many publications – both newspapers and more general periodicals – were distributed internationally. The biggest market for this was colonial*, and the establishment of regular shipping routes for cargo and for passengers offered a means of delivering print to the empire. *The Times* was the most widely read newspaper, while both *Blackwood's Magazine** and *Chambers's Edinburgh Journal* achieved healthy readerships in the colonies. The latter even adapted its publishing schedule to fit patterns of shipping, producing a monthly number in the mid-1840s in order to cater for the colonies. Mudies offered a service whereby tin trunks of books were sent out by ship to subscribers in the colonies, and it seems highly probable that periodical literature formed a part of this consignment.

Like analogous technological developments in production* – e.g. the printing press*, the mechanization of paper production, the telegraph*, typesetting – the development of the railway system, regular shipping and other distribution networks drove, and in turn were driven by, the growth of mass*-circulation* print media in nineteenth-century Britain and its Empire. One should hesitate before implying a direct causal relationship, but it can safely be said that the one is unimaginable without the other. **MaT**

Sources: Bell 2007, Boyce *et al* 1978, Brown 1985, Cooper 1896, King and Plunkett 2005, ncse, *ODNB*, 'Redivivus' 1899.

DIVORCE NEWS News about divorce cases was an integral part of the British newspaper press, particularly after the Matrimonial Causes Act of 1857 which established the Divorce Court. While there were reports covering divorce since the eighteenth century, the Divorce Court ensured the need for dedicated reporters who covered the cases heard there. News about the Divorce Court usually appeared not in news* columns *– apart from the most sensational divorce cases – but in legal columns, such as the 'Law Report' in *The Times*. While the full range of dailies* and weekly* papers covered divorce news, it was *The Times* that kept the most complete record and reported the largest number of cases. However, divorce news circulated elsewhere as entertaining, sensational narratives about the wealthy, and also provided the opportunity for political* commentary. In the republican *Reynolds's Weekly**, it did both. Arguably, one of the accumulative effects of the regular reporting of divorce news was to make divorce seem more natural,

if not quite normative. The prevalence of divorce coverage in the papers highlighted problems within marriage (violence, for example) and helped provide a context in which debates about equality in marriage could be discussed in serials* and in fiction alike. **MWT**
Source: Humphreys 2005.

DIXIE, FLORENCE CAROLINE DOUGLAS (1855-1905) 'The claims of woman are many, and until they are satisfied she must remain, what she is – a slave'(*Women's Penny Paper** 26 April 1890). These were the uncompromising words of the uncompromising 'Lady Florence Dixie', journalist and the first woman war* correspondent appointed to a daily* newspaper.

Her reputation for independent travel, as a first-class shot and an accomplished horse rider secured her the appointment of war correspondent in the Boer War for the *Morning Post** in 1879. When the news of her appointment became public, articles appeared in the press either acknowledging her fitness for the task or expressing horror, as in the 'Save her from herself' of the *Hampshire Telegraph*. By the time she took passage to South Africa, the fighting had ceased, but she spent six months as a field correspondent; her articles for the *Post* investigated the results of the conflict, espousing the cause of King Cetewayo and the Zulu people.

This spirit of independence found political* expression in her journalism on the cause of women's equality, from issues of dress to legal impediments on marriage and especially the vote. Used to dressing in practical trousers for her travels, she scandalously abandoned the side-saddle in favour of the cross-saddle, writing articles on rational dress* for the *Daily Graphic**, among others. Dixie contributed to the *Publisher and Bookbuyer's Journal, Beauty Queens, Vanity Fair**, *St Stephen's Review*, the *Welsh Review* and the *Pall Mall Gazette**. In the latter, she wrote on women's football and her presidency of the British Ladies' Football Club (1895). Increasingly in the 1890s she wrote for women's* journals such as her series of articles 'Short Papers on Women's Position' for the *Women's Penny Paper** and its successors, the *Woman's Herald* and the *Woman's Signal*. **CL**
Sources: 19CUKP, ODNB, Waterloo.

DIXON, ELLA NORA HEPWORTH (1857-1932) 'Born into journalism' as *The Times** obituary* noted, Ella Hepworth Dixon was the seventh child of William Hepworth Dixon*, long time editor* of the *Athenaeum**. Her entire output, including her famous New Woman novel, *The Story of a Modern Woman* (1894), and her collection of short stories, *One Doubtful Hour, and Other Side-lights on the Feminine Temperament* (1904), first appeared in periodicals. Initially trained as an artist at the Academie Julian in Paris with her sister Marion, she exhibited in London, but on her father's sudden death in 1879 leaving the family in financial difficulties, she took to writing. Helped by family connections, she began contributing short stories, 'Town and Country Tales', travel articles, 'At homes', 'Chats with Celebrities'* and articles of general interest to Edmund Yates's* the *World**, Oscar Wilde's* *Woman's World**, and Arnold Bennett's* *Woman**, usually anonymously*, sometimes signed 'E. H. D'. Her first signature appeared in the *Sunday Times** in 1888. Her first book, *My Flirtations* (1892), a series of satirical* sketches, appeared under the pseudonym 'Margaret Wynman', which she also used for a few short stories until resorting to using only her own name from 1894.

In March 1895 she became editor* of the *Englishwoman** for the first six months of its existence. In June of the same year she began contributing to the *Lady's Pictorial**, writing a weekly* column*, originally entitled 'Pensées de Femme', from 1895-1921 when the *Lady's Pictorial* amalgamated with *Eve*. She contributed a short story, 'The Sweet o' the Year', to the *Yellow Book** in 1896, and contributed short stories to various magazines, including the *Ladies' Field*, the *Lady's Pictorial*, the *Pall Mall Magazine**, *Woman* and the *World* until 1907. Head-hunted to join the staff of the *Daily Mirror* when it began as a daily* paper for women, she contributed short articles in November 1903. From 1907 to 1917 she wrote a weekly column for the *Sketch*. In 1908 she turned her short story 'The World's Slow Stain' into a one-act play, 'The Toyshop of the Heart'. She continued to contribute to periodicals not aimed at women readers, e.g. the *Humanitarian* (1899), the *Idler** (1894), the *Illustrated London News** (1914), and her articles did not always appear on the woman's page, e.g in the *Manchester Daily Despatch* (1921-1923) and the *Westminster Gazette** (1921-1928). Her last pieces appeared in the *Empire Review* (1929-1931). In 1930 she published her memoirs, *As I Knew Them: Sketches of Those I have met on the Way*. Her novels were also published in the USA and she wrote at least one article for the *New York Independent* (29 July 1900). VF

Sources: Dixon 1930, Fehlbaum 2005, *ODNB*, Stead 1894a, *The Times* 13 Jan. 1932, Toye 1950.

DIXON, HENRY HALL (1822-1870) Henry Dixon was unrivalled as a sports* journalist*. Born near Carlisle where his family were cotton manufacturers, his admiration for horses and horse racing was cultivated during his education at Rugby and Trinity College, Cambridge. While still at school and university, he became an avid sports journalist and contributor to *Bell's Life**. Subsequently, he worked in Doncaster training for the law, but spent the majority of his time involved with racing, successfully writing for the *Doncaster Gazette* and becoming its editor*.

In 1850 Dixon moved to London where he began writing for the *Sporting Magazine**, under the pseudonyms* of 'General Chasse' and later, 'the Druid'. In 1852, after Vincent Dowling*, editor of *Bell's Life* had died, Dixon was offered the editorship, but refused it. The following year he was called to the bar. A large amount of Dixon's journal writing appeared in his books which were later to be regarded as classic sports literature*, *Post and Paddock* (1856), *Silk and Scarlett* (1859), and *Scott and Sebright* (1862).

Although a foremost sports' writer, he contributed articles to many journals, including his columns*, 'National sports' and 'The farm' for the *Illustrated London News**, political poetry* for *Punch** and the *Examiner**, leaders* and biographies for the *Sporting Life** *and* articles for the *Daily News** and the *Gentleman's Magazine**. Having written a book on agricultural law, his enthusiasm for agricultural matters was renewed and he contributed a series of pieces to the *Mark Lane Express* on 'The flocks and herds of Great Britain', going on to write more books on cattle herds. Eccentric in both his life and his writing style, Dixon remained unpaid for much of his journalistic work, and was succeeded by his son Henry Sydenham Dixon (1848-1931), another significant sporting writer. AA
Source: *ODNB*.

DIXON, WILLIAM HEPWORTH (1821-1879) A journalist*, editor*, essayist, traveller, and historian, 'one of the most conspicuous working men of letters in the nineteenth century' according to the *Daily Telegraph** obituary*, William Hepworth Dixon originally studied Law, but never practised. He began contributing articles, signed 'W. H. D.', to the *North of England Magazine* (1842-1843), and wrote for Douglas Jerrold's* *Illuminated Magazine** (1843). In 1846 he became editor* of the *Cheltenham Journal* and then moved to London where he started writing for the *Athenaeum** and the *Daily News**. Two series of papers in the latter on 'The Literature of the Lower Orders' and 'London Prisons' brought him a certain notoriety. In 1850 he published *John Howard, and the Prison World of Europe*. His

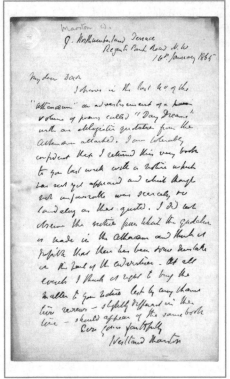

Figure 12: Letter from J. W. Marston (1819-1890), poet, playwright and contributor to the *Athenaeum*, to W. H. Dixon as editor of the *Athenaeum*, 16 Jan. 1865 (Ghent University Library).

daughter Ella* described him as a 'knight of the inkstand' since he often wrote to defend people and causes. He became editor of the *Athenaeum* in January 1853 and resigned in August 1869 when Charles Wentworth Dilke* inherited the journal. The latter's letters, however, indicate that he was dismissed by the new proprietor* (Demoor 2000: 25). 'His life was laborious and he died in harness' declared the above-mentioned *Daily Telegraph* obituary.

Two daughters, Ella* and Marion, also pursued careers in journalism, the latter primarily as an art critic contributing articles to the *Magazine of Art** (1891ff), the *Ladies' Realm** (1899ff) and the *Studio** (1908ff). Marion contributed two short stories to the *Yellow Book** and Ella one, and Marion wrote book reviews* for her sister's *Englishwoman** (1895). **VF**

Sources: *Athenaeum* 3 Jan. 1880, *Daily Telegraph* 29 Dec. 1879, Demoor 2000, Dixon 1930, *DNB*, *ODNB*.

DOHERTY, JOHN (1797/8-1854) An Irish immigrant, John Doherty established himself as a tenacious and talented trade union* leader and po-

litical agitator before his first attempt at journalism. Most of his newspaper ventures were specifically designed to address the needs of the political or industrial struggles that occupied his primary attention at the time. In 1828, for example, following a divisive internal election which saw him become secretary of the spinners' union in Manchester, he established the *Conciliator or Cotton Spinners' Weekly Journal* as an attempt to promote unity in the trade. Similarly his second newspaper, the *United Trades' Co-operative Journal*, was published in 1830 at the height of his involvement in efforts to establish a general union among the trades. By contrast, Doherty's next newspaper, the *Voice of the People**, published during 1830-1831, was a stamped* paper with a broader radical agenda. He resigned his union positions to devote his full attention to it.

Having set up a print and bookshop in Manchester, Doherty published* what was arguably his most important radical newspaper early in 1832: the *Poor Man's Advocate and People's Library*. The *Advocate* provided an extensive catalogue of the horrors of the factory system (including lists of 'Midnight robbers', factory owners operating their establishments at night), combined with news about the trade union*, cooperative and short-time movements, as well as strident comment on the political* news of the day. A similar agenda was to be found in his last newspaper venture, the *Herald of the Rights of Industry* (1834), which also showed a strong Owenite* influence. Doherty's news agency* cum bookshop remained a popular radical haunt in Manchester during the 1830s and early 1840s long after his days as a journalist and newspaper publisher* had ended. **PAP**

Sources: Kirby and Musson 1975, *ODNB*, Wood 1979.

DOME (1897-1900) Notable as the longest running of the little magazines* of the 1890s, the *Dome*'s editor* and proprietor* was Ernest J. Oldmeadow, who published the title at his own Unicorn Press. Although a deluxe edition was available, the standard price* of the *Dome* was 1s, which placed it at the cheap end of the literary and aesthetic periodical market. The *Dome* boasted value for money as well as championing its avant-garde credentials, and expected to sell over 7,000 copies of its first number. Oldmeadow's balance of prudence and experimentalism, self-advertisement and wry self-mockery owed obvious debts to John Lane's* *Yellow Book**.

Oldmeadow's light plays, tongue-in-cheek fictions and art criticism in the *Dome* were not always as imaginative as the aliases he used to write them

('J. E. Woodmeald', 'L. A. Corbeille' and 'Louis Bar-sac'). Yet the magazine offers valuable insights into connections between avant-garde figures and movements in the 1890s, embracing Arts and Crafts, Symbolism and the Irish/Celtic Revivals. The *Dome* was particularly interested in the interplay between visual and verbal arts, and the Arts and Crafts influence was clear in the periodical's subtitles. *A Quarterly* Containing Examples of All the Arts* until spring 1898, the *Dome* then became a monthly, subtitled an *Illustrated* Magazine and Review of Literature*, Music*, Architecture and the Graphic Arts.* It included discussions of Richard Wagner and musical* contributions by Edward Elgar, articles by art critic Gleeson White* (co-editor* of the *Pageant**), and short stories and poetry* by Laurence Housman. Late Pre-Raphaelite and early Symbolist works by Dante Gabriel Rossetti and Edward Burne-Jones were among the *Dome*'s varied and good quality art reproductions. The Symbolist influence was also apparent in literary contexts, in the articles by Arthur Symons* and W. B. Yeats, the plays by the Belgian writer Maurice Maeterlink, and in poems* by Yeats and the Celtic Revivalists Fiona Macleod (William Sharp*) and Nora Hopper.

Oldmeadow (a former Non-conformist minister) cuts rather a curious figure. An occasional contributor to the *Nineteenth Century** and the *Saturday Review**, in the 1920s he became editor* of the *Tablet**. His conversion to Catholicism, bringing him close to the diverse artistic circles that gathered around the writer Alice Meynell*, may be one explanation for the *Dome*'s eclecticism. If it was not the most coherent of the little magazines, the *Dome* nevertheless found a successful formula. It happily accommodated mystics, practitioners of Art for Art Sake, and defenders of use and beauty in art. **CRS**
Sources: Frost 1979, Sullivan, West 1957, Ziegler 1965.

DOMESTIC/HOME One aspect of the history of the nineteenth-century periodical is the increasing privatization of its consumption. Periodicals continued to have multiple readers who were not necessarily in one household, since journals were passed around, swapped and borrowed both privately and from libraries*. However, 'home' and 'the family' were privileged as the ideal sites for reading, as against the coffee house, the tavern or even the reading room. This attitude was underpinned by material factors which made print cheaper and more accessible to individual buyers as the century went on, by middle-class fears that radical politics was nourished by the sharing of print, and

by the ideological privileging of the domestic. Consequently, numerous magazines had the words 'Home', 'Family'* or 'Household' in their title* or subtitle. Names such as that of the popular fiction weekly*, the *Family Herald** or Dickens's* *Household Words** were indicative not so much of the magazine's content as of the target readership* and presumed place of reading.*

However, there were some periodicals which made home and the domestic their subject. Inevitably these were mainly addressed to women*. The emergence of the 'domestic' magazine in this sense can be dated to mid-century with the rise of titles addressed to middle-class women, including the *Ladies' Companion** and Beeton's* *Englishwoman's Domestic Magazine**. These carried recipes and advice on the home and garden* as part of their mix of ingredients. After this, most magazines for women included some domestic advice. The exceptions were the ladies' newspapers like *Queen**, fashion* journals and women's rights papers. In the 1880s and 1890s domestic magazines* for women extended further down-market and advice proliferated into several columns*. Furnishing and home decoration, for example, became more important. Penny* magazines like *Home Notes**, *Home Chat** and *Woman's Life** also carried extensive advertisements* for convenience food, furniture and other domestic items which were sometimes linked with the editorial material surrounding them. In the 1880s and 1890s, interviews* with famous people 'at home', where their rooms and furnishings were described, became a feature of range of magazines, not only those for women. This gave a further twist to the domestic theme. **MRB**
Sources: Altick 1957, Beetham 1996, Fraser *et al.* 2003, Phegley 2004a.

DOMESTIC SERVANTS' JOURNAL (1875) Attempting to solve, 'one of the greatest social problems of the day', the *Domestic Servants' Journal* editor*, Mrs Stannard*, hoped to provide a channel of communication between the mistress and the servant. Published and printed every Wednesday in London by Frederick A. Gosnold at 1d, the paper was ambitious, promising illustrations* by the 'most celebrated artists' together with superlative serials*. Additionally, situations vacant and wanted would be accompanied by society gossip*, comic tales and letters* to the editor in the 51cm, four pages. Despite noting with some displeasure how far servants' wages were being driven up by the pay on offer to factory girls, and how effective the *Journal* would be by intervening in this dilemma, Mrs

Stannard's hopes were shortlived, as the *Journal* only ran for five issues from 23 June until its closure on 21 July. **CL**

Source: *Waterloo.*

DORAN, JOHN (1807-1878) John Doran's journalistic career started as a correspondent from abroad when he published his 'Parisian Sketches and Paris Letters' in the *Athenaeum** in 1828. Unusually gifted at learning foreign languags, he contributed translations from French, German, Latin and Italian to the *Bath Journal* in the 1830s. In that same decade he married and subsequently travelled on the Continent, obtaining a doctor's degree at the faculty of philosophy of the University of Marburg in Prussia. After his return to Britain in 1841 he became the literary editor* of the *Church and State Gazette*. In the mid-1850s Doran became a regular contributor to the *Athenaeum*. This connection reached a climax in 1869 when the proprietor*, Charles Wentworth Dilke, 1st bt, died and his son, Charles Wentworth Dilke, 2nd bt dismissed the then editor* (William Hepworth Dixon*), leaving Doran temporarily in charge. Dilke's college friend Norman MacColl* became the new editor in 1870 and by way of recompense Doran was appointed as editor of *Notes and Queries**, which the young Dilke had bought from William John Thoms around that period. The index to the *Athenaeum* lists more than 1,500 reviews* by Doran for the period 1828-1871, and another 200 for the subsequent period until his death. **MD**

Sources: Demoor 2000, Gwynn and Tuckwell 1917, *ODNB*.

DORÉ, PAUL GUSTAVE LOUIS CHRISTOPHE (1832-1893) Notwithstanding his Europe-wide reputation as a grandiose and somewhat baroque illustrator* of classic texts, Gustave Doré drew for relatively few British periodicals. Yet his many drawings from the mid- and late 1850s for both the *Illustrated London News** (including an epic series of views of the Crimean War*) and the *Illustrated Times** were both celebrated and spectacular. A frustrated painter all his life, Doré began his career working for the Paris-based *Journal de Rire* under the guidance of Charles Philipon (1800-1861), but built his reputation in Britain on his many book illustrations, mostly aimed at the gift book market or the library table. All his work was on a gigantic scale, and the large page of the illustrated weeklies*, as well as the encouragement of eminent proprietors* like Vizetelly* and the historic significance of the events he was depicting, gave Doré's periodical illustrations an epic flamboyance that frequently transcended the conventions of reportage. **BM**

Sources: Engen 1990, Houfe 1978, *ODNB*.

DORRINGTON, WILLIAM. (D.C. 1893.) Printer and journalist*, William Dorrington is trumpeted as being the 'conductor' of the *London, Provincial, and Colonial Press News: A Literary and Business Journal* (1866-1912), of which he was proprietor*, editor*, printer and publisher*. On the early title pages Dorrington is noted as having been the 'Late Editor of "The Printer's Register"', and his contributions to the *Press News* include editorial comment and articles on printing and the press, as well as occasional poetry* during the early years. The subtitle was changed to *A Monthly Literary and Business Journal* in 1867, though the journal had been a monthly publication from inception. However the literary connections were severed and the subtitle dropped altogether in later issues, as the journal focused solely upon 'Trade connected with the Art of Printing'. Early issues of *Press News* also include engraved illustrations by, and an advert for, 'George Dorrington, Artist and Engraver'.

During 1893 the title page changes to 'Founded by Mr William Dorrington, Printer and Journalist', and *Willing's British and Irish Press Guide* marks the change in proprietors from William to 'C. and H. Dorrington'. The final issues of the periodical were presided over by 'Provincial Newspaper Proprietors: Dorrington Bros'. **MBT**

Sources: *London, Provincial, and Colonial Press News, Waterloo, Willing's British and Irish Press Guide.*

DOUBLEDAY, THOMAS (1790-1870) A radical Newcastle activist who was inspired by the example of William Cobbett*, Thomas Doubleday was the principal editor* of the outspoken Chartist* paper the *Northern Liberator**. Hired by the paper's owner Robert Blakey*, the two men complemented each other very well and the paper's notable success was a product of Blakey's command of political economy* and Doubleday's classical education. Between them they produced an unusually entertaining radical journal that blended analysis and satire* to great effect. However, the distinctly anti-semitic overtones of the *Liberator* may have reflected Doubleday's prejudices and similar sentiments appear in some of his later writings. A busy provincial radical, in later life Doubleday was an occasional contributor to Joseph Cowen's* *Newcastle Chronicle**. **JA**

Sources: Allen 2007, BDMBR 1984, Cowen Papers, Hugman 1999, Nossiter 1975, *ODNB*, Welford II 1895.

DOUGLAS JERROLD'S SHILLING MAGAZINE (1845-1848) This monthly* periodical was brought out by Bradbury and Evans*, the publishers of *Punch**, and was named after, and edited* by, its most well-known contributor. As the title, and the illustration of a shilling coin on the front page of each issue made clear, its image tried to persuade readers that it was cheaper than other monthlies. At its height, the *Shilling Magazine* managed to sell 9,000 copies a month, but it was falling sales, as the ever-busy Douglas Jerrold* handed over more and more space to other contributors, that led to its demise. Perhaps the most successful part of the magazine was Jerrold's series of 'Hedgehog Letters' in which a London cabman reflected, in best *Punch* style, on the affairs of the day. Jerrold employed numerous contributors including writers from *Punch*, the communist poet Goodwyn Barmby, the talented labouring-class poet William Thom and the mysterious Edward Youl. The contents were intended to be morally uplifting: Thomas Cooper's* 'Crinkum Crankum' is a typical short story. The magazine reviewed* a wide range of literature including *Sybil*, *Jane Eyre* and the poetry* of R. H. Horne* and Charles Mackay. The moderate reforming tone of the magazine* suggests that its appeal was mainly to disgruntled middle-class* readers. SFR

Source: Slater 2002.

DOUGLAS JERROLD'S WEEKLY NEWSPAPER (1846-1851) This paper was first published on 18 July 1846 at a price* of 6d. It consisted of 26 pages including, on average, four pages of advertisements*. Liberal in sentiment, and strongly pro Free Trade, Douglas Jerrold's *Weekly Newspaper* was aimed squarely at a 'progressive' lower-middle and middle-middle class* readership*. Jerrold's first editorial announced his desire to make the paper a 'powerful instrument' for social reform. Thomas Cooper* contributed a series of 'eye-witness' reports on the harsh lives of industrial and colliery workers in the Midlands and the North, and the paper campaigned strongly on such issues as national education, sanitary reform and the Early Closing Movement, as well as the abolition of corporal punishment in the armed forces and the need for reform of Irish land tenure. A regular column* signed 'Church Mouse' closely scrutinized ecclesiastical affairs, especially the exercise of episcopal power and the scale of episcopal remuneration. Jerrold's 'The Barber's Chair', a regular column* of satirical* commentary on the news* of the day, contributed greatly to the paper's popularity. Other features were full reports of Parliamentary* debates, police news, a gossip* column*, extensive book and theatre reviews*, and at monthly intervals two or three pages of 'Magaziniana' anthologizing extracts from a wide range of contemporary periodicals.

According to G. H. Lewes* (letter 24 Dec. 1849), Jerrold's paper achieved a circulation* of 20,000. In January 1847, Jerrold increased its size* to 32 pages, the maximum pagination permitted by the Stamp Act*, and announced he would greatly extend its news* coverage. It became weighed down, however, by the huge amount of space given to 'Aladdin', an economist writing under that name on currency matters, and it failed to respond adequately to the dramatic foreign events in 1848. At the end of that year Jerrold was forced to sell. The paper became the *Weekly News and Financial Economist* and in 1851 finally merged* with the *Weekly Chronicle*. MS

Sources: Lewes 1995, Slater 2002.

DOWLING, VINCENT GEORGE (1785-1852) During his career as a journalist*, Vincent George Dowling had a tremendous impact shaping the sporting* culture of Britain before 1850. Dowling began his journalism career aiding his father after the latter joined *The Times** at the turn of the century. After a short stint at the *Star* he moved to the *Day* in 1809. He also wrote pieces for the *Observer**, beginning in 1804, where he began his lengthy relationship with proprietor*, William Clement. His early success as a journalist grew in 1812 with his eyewitness account of the assassination of Prime Minister Spencer Percival by John Bellingham. When Queen Caroline sought to return to England from France after the accession of George IV in 1820, Dowling travelled to France to record her journey. After a stormy night crossing the English Channel, the enterprising reporter* was the first journalist back in London with the news*. He also served as a government informer during these years

After Clement acquired *Bell's Life in London and Sporting Chronicle** in 1824, he moved Dowling from the *Observer* into the editor's* chair at *Bell's*, a post he occupied until his death. During Dowling's tenure, *Bell's* introduced a thorough coverage of contests like prize fights, pedestrian races and horse races, by publishing numerous reports of the same event in a single issue. Even as Dowling checked the veracity of the incoming intelligence from his readers and free lance journalists, he also shaped the debate concerning sporting rules and practices. While *Bell's* increasingly criticized the corruption in prize fighting and other sports after 1845, the paper had no power to govern sport. Even when parties asked Dowling to adjudicate sporting disputes, they had the option to disregard his decisions. **MJM**

Sources: Boase 1965, Harvey 2004, *Illustrated London News* 1852, *ODNB*.

DOYLE, RICHARD (1824-1883) The son of the renowned comic artist John Doyle (aka 'HB'), Richard Doyle was something of a prodigy as a child artist (his 1840 *Journal* is an accomplished illustrated text, showing the young Doyle observing the publication and reception of his own work). With John Leech* and John Tenniel*, Doyle was part of the great trio of mid-Victorian *Punch* artists as well as a widely published illustrator* who specialized in fairy tales and fantasy literature. He began working for *Punch* in 1843, and quickly found that the decorative potential of the magazine's double-column* page suited his penchant for delicate whimsicality. He especially liked drawing decorated capital letters and complex borders, and was responsible for establishing a cover design that continued to be used until 1854. His thin line and lack of facility in drawing the human figure worked against Doyle becoming as effective a cartoonist* as Leech or Tenniel, but he was a good enough artist to draw many readers* to *Punch* and to help raise the visual content of *Punch* to an unprecedented and consistent level. In the seven years he drew for the magazine he published well over 800 drawings, but in 1850 he resigned after a famous row with Mark Lemon* and the other *Punch* regulars over their stance on Catholic emancipation, thus, according to Spielmann, 'sacrificing lucrative employment, and condemning him in the result to a life in toil'. Certainly the rest of his career, despite his fluency, failed to fulfil his early promise, although a version of his most famous *Punch* series, the 'Manners and Customs of ye Englishe' re-surfaced in the *Cornhill Magazine** in 1861 and 1862 as 'Bird's Eye Views of English Society' before being reprinted as a successful volume. After *Punch*, Doyle drew very little for the periodicals beyond some decorative elements in the *Illustrated London News** and some full-page plates for the *Cornhill* in 1861 and 1862. **BM**

Sources: Engen 1983, Engen 1990, Everitt 1893, *ODNB*, Spielmann 1895.

DRAMATIC NOTES, AN ILLUSTRATED YEARBOOK OF THE LONDON THEATRES (1879-1893) Intended as a cumulative reference work, the annual* *Dramatic Notes* recorded the major theatrical productions on the London stage, with plentiful illustrations* to add to its attraction for its seasonal readership*. As the years went on, *Dramatic Notes* was extended to embrace provincial theatrical events, as well as Parisian productions and English plays conducted on the rest of the Continent, in New York and even Australia. By 1893, pantomimes were featured in a publication that at its height comprised nearly 300 pages. The first editor Charles Eyre Pascoe, was author of *London of To-Day*; from 1883 to 1887 its editor* was the journalist, biographer, theatre historian and manager, Austin Brereton. **CL**

Source: *Waterloo.*

DRESS AND FASHION At the start of the century, discussion of dress and fashion in journals presented a luxury ideal aimed at the leisured, elite 'Lady'. By the 1840s, the tone was domestic and instructive; dressmaking instructions and patterns showed dress as a practical necessity, although the fashion plates included in, for example, the *Englishwoman's Domestic Magazine** (1852ff), simultaneously represented fashion as a necessary feminine attribute.

The increasing wealth of the middle classes* encouraged larger numbers to seek information on how to become fashionable – in dress and behaviour. Lively reports, fashion plates, correspondence* and advertising* in, for example, *Myra's Journal of Dress and Fashion** (1875ff), provided a template to aspire to, and engaged readers* in consumption of fashion as pleasurable and entertaining.

By the 1870s fashion was established as an essential component of all mainstream magazines addressed to middle-class women, as is evident in journals such as the *Ladies' Cabinet** (1832ff) and the *Ladies' Treasury** (1858ff). It was equally significant to the new upper-class journals, most significant of which was the *Queen** (1861ff). This was a 6d 'ladies' newspaper,' which gave prominence to the latest Paris modes, supported by copious illustrations* and advertisements*. At the other end of the social scale, penny weeklies* and monthlies* targeted lower-middle-class women and were a central feature of 1890s New Journalism*. Titles including *Woman** (1890ff), *Home Notes** (1894ff) and *Home Chat** (1895ff) carried fashion columns*, patterns, and advice on home dressmaking, some with aristocratic-sounding by-lines. Alongside the explosion in such down-market journals, middle-class monthly magazines, such as the *Woman at Home* (1893ff), continued to feature illustrated advice on fashion and even extended this into columns on 'Health and Beauty'. Fashion also

PROMENADE HALF FULL DRESS.

Engraved for the 5th Number, New Series of La Belle Assemblée, June 1 1810.

EVENING FULL DRESS.

Engraved for the 5th Number, New Series of La Belle Assemblée: Published by J. Bell, June 1 1810.

Figure 13: Summer fashion in *La Belle Assemblée*, June 1810.

began to be addressed in 'ladies' pages' in general magazines and papers.

Moral concern about focusing on appearance was widely debated and specifically embodied in minority publications such as the *Rational Dress Society Gazette* (1888-1890), which advocated healthy, functional dress. Fashion was generally represented as a feminine pursuit, although early journals such as *Le Beau Monde* (1806-1810) had included plates of fashionable dress, carriages and accessories for men. In the 1860s there was *Taylor and Cutter**. At the end of the century, alternative magazines such as the *Yellow Book** parodied mainstream fashion, and included essays by Max Beerbohm* on male attire, and Oscar Wilde* wrote in similar vein in the *Pall Mall Magazine,* while general interest magazines largely for men such as the *Strand** (1891) included reference to fashion as part of its interest in social life.

Fashion journalism was part of the burgeoning fashion industry, communicating new styles and ideals of beauty, and reflecting changing gender roles, with the inclusion from the 1880s of articles on sportswear, travel and jobs for women. RLA

Sources: Beetham 1996, Beetham 2001, Brake 1994a, Fraser 2003.

DU MAURIER, GEORGE (1834-1896) Artist and illustrator. George Du Maurier is an unusual, if significant, figure among the major illustrators of the Victorian periodical press. First, although a highly trained artist, he dedicated himself to black and white illustration* early in his career – his famous novels were a late development. Second, his work comprised both drawings in a serious Pre-Raphaelite manner which appeared in most of the prestigious illustrated magazines of the mid-Victorian period, especially the *Cornhill Magazine**, and social satire*, which made him *Punch's** leading artist in succession to John Leech* from 1860 until his death.

For the *Cornhill* Du Maurier specialized in the illustration of serial fiction, and he became closely identified with Elizabeth Gaskell* with his illustrations for *Wives and Daughters* (Aug. 1864-Jan. 1866). His affinity with Gaskell's writing, like that between Trollope* and Millais* in the same journal, resulted in an outstanding moment in the relationship between serialized fiction and black and white illustration. He also drew extensively for *Once a Week** (1860-1863), and, again as an illustrator of fiction, for the *Leisure Hour**. The success of Du Maurier's magazine work was acknowledged through several volume reprints of his *Cornhill* illustrations. Described by Spielmann* as 'one of the

four great pillars on which would rest the artistic reputation of the paper', Du Maurier's work for *Punch** was less concerned with caricature* than with comedy of manners, and his humour was based more on situation than on physical characteristics. He was especially good at satirizing the pretensions of the socially ambitious middle classes, using what Spielmann has called 'polite satire' as his watchword. BM

Sources: Engen 1990, Goldman 1994, Houfe 1978, Spielmann 1895, Suriano 2005.

DUBLIN BUILDER, OR ILLUSTRATED IRISH ARCHITECTURAL, ENGINEERING, MECHANICS' & SANITARY JOURNAL (1859-1866); IRISH BUILDER AND ENGINEERING RECORD (1867-1871), IRISH BUILDER (1872-1899), IRISH BUILDER AND TECHNICAL JOURNAL (1899-1903); IRISH BUILDER AND ENGINEER (1903-1979) The *Dublin Builder* is more commonly referred to as the *Irish Builder*, the generic name it assumed between 1872-1899, with variations before and afterwards (*Irish Builder and Engineering Record* (1867-1871) and *Irish Builder and Technical Journal* (1899-1903). It was a trade journal* intended to serve 'with very few exceptions, all the Architects, Civil Engineers, Surveyors, Builders, Clerks of Works, Foremen, Mechanics, &c.; likewise Reading-rooms, Hotels, Mechanics' Institutes in every town in Ireland, very many throughout the United Kingdom, and in the Colonies'. With such a clientele, the paper was bound to be a success.

Appearing monthly*, and soon twice monthly, the *Irish Builder* began life as a four-page, three-column* general chronicle of the trade. By the end of the first year of production*, the proprietor* and editor* J. J. Lyons was boasting that the subscribers' list had doubled, advertisements* had trebled in value, and the journal had grown to 24 (soon to be 32) pages in length. By 1866 its price* had been reduced from 4d to 3d. One of the great attractions of the paper was the appearance, during its second year, of architectural illustrations*, either woodcuts* or lithographs*, 'proofs suitable for framing' always available from the publisher*. Though precise circulation* figures are not available, there is no doubt that the success of the journal coincided with a relative boom in the building industry in Ireland. A review article in the *Irish Builder*'s Jubilee issue in 1909 chronicles the sorts of changes in building covered in the run: the building of great edifices in 1800, palatial residences in 1830 and city suburbs in 1859. These domestic buildings and the armies of artisans and labourers needed to service them became the main concern of the periodical, along with the class* placement of those involved in the design and building professions. For instance, reporters* from the *Irish Builder* were sent to scientific and cultural events in order to condense and make comprehensible to busy readers information thought essential for them to know.

One of the most interesting features was a 22-part series (July 1877-June 1878) entitled 'Notes on the Rise and Progress of Printing and Publishing in Ireland'. Written by Christopher Clinton Hoey*, the series is full of anecdotal information about Irish printers, publishers and booksellers from the beginning of the industry in Ireland up to the 1860s. Fiercely nationalist*, the series sees its subjects as defenders of intellectual and personal freedom; those known to have been under government patronage (i.e. in the pay of Dublin Castle), are scathingly described. The *Irish Builder* is an invaluable source of information both for book historians, and for those interested in the development of domestic design and manufacture in Ireland. Publication ceased 1979. **ET**

Sources: *Irish Builder, Waterloo Irish.*

DUBLIN EVENING MAIL (1823-1962) Joseph Timothy Haydn* launched the *Dublin Evening Mail* in 1823 as a broadsheet of four pages, priced* 5d. Published on Monday, Wednesday and Friday evenings, it became, under Haydn's direction, the chief Protestant newspaper in Ireland. Although Haydn claimed that the paper's aim was 'to soften all political* asperities, not to provoke the acerbities of party', the paper's raucously conservative unionism at a time when a dynamic and entrepreneurial Catholic middle class* was transforming local politics and print culture in the city, led him to be physically assaulted in 1823, and prosecuted in 1824-1825 for concealing his ownership of the *Mail*. The paper's militant Protestantism was evident in its opposition to the campaign led by Daniel O'Connell for Catholic emancipation (1829). Following the success of the campaign, the tone of the *Evening Mail* became a little calmer, yet it retained its die-hard Ascendancy edge. This was apparent in its opposition to the increase of the grant to the Roman Catholic training college at Maynooth (1845) and to disestablishment of the Church of Ireland (1869).

When the nationalists, William Smith O'Brien and Thomas Francis Meagher, were discharged following allegations of sedition in May 1848, the *Evening Mail* complained bitterly that 'the dissentient voice of one Roman Catholic clergyman' on

the jury had been sufficient to secure the Confederates' release. The following week it made no comment on the widespread allegations that the jury at John Mitchel's trial on similar charges had been packed. For all that it engaged with the bitterly sectarian politics of the Ireland of its day, the paper was far from parochial in its outlook, reporting widely on international news*. The paper also contained reports on shipping, particularly in times of adverse weather conditions, regular updates on the Dublin stocks and commodities markets, legal reports*, fashion* tips, verse parodies and lists of classified advertisements*. In the latter part of the century, sporting* reports, including the latest odds on horse racing, became a feature, and by 1895 there was a regular chess problem, plus some satirical* cartoons*. The paper was also distributed* in England and reached a circulation* of 2,019 in 1850. By 1844, it was available on subscription at £3 per annum, and by 1875 the cover price* had dropped to 1d, falling still further to a ½d by 1895. It absorbed the *Dublin Evening Packet* in 1862 and the *Dublin Evening Standard* in 1870. **MJH/MaT**

Sources: *ODNB, Waterloo.*

DUBLIN EVENING POST (1725-21 AUG. 1875) Though a paper of the same name existed in Dublin at various times since 1719, the *Dublin Evening Post* achieved its greatest influence and fame, first under the proprietorship* of the Presbyterian Magee family from the late 1780s, and then the Anglican Conway family until its demise in 1875. Magee senior was succeeded by his sons, John in 1807 and then James in 1814, who employed Frederick W. Conway as editor*. He was listed as proprietor* (1846-1853), when his son W. A. Conway took over. A broadsheet paper (57 cm 1830; 64 cm 1875), it cost 4d in 1807, but was down to 1d in 1875 after the repeal of stamp* duty. In 1822 it appeared three times a week on Tuesday, Thursday and Saturday, and in 1850 circulation* is reported as ca 1000.

The Magees, though Presbyterian, were 'Whig and Catholic in their sympathies', which cost them dearly, and by 1814, coming under political pressure from successive Tory administrations they reached an accommodation with Government, their paper becoming more like a 'Castle Catholic' journal, (a term used to describe those Catholics who were more sympathetic to the policies emanating from Dublin Castle the seat of English power in Ireland than most of their co-religionists) in the process. The *Dublin Evening Post* never went entirely over to the government side: in the 1820s;

(172-21 Aug. 1875), for example, F. W. Conway became an active member of the Catholic Association, and throughout its career the paper was a consistent opponent of the Orange faction. After Catholic Emancipation in 1829, Magee fell out with Daniel O'Connell over Repeal, which he had earlier briefly supported, and in the words of his *Times* obituary*, their relations 'assumed a new and hostile complexion', though friendly relations were eventually restored. In 1851, the paper was described in *Mitchell's** as advocating 'all the national interests; supports free trade; and in religion, perfect freedom and equality of sects'.

The paper carried news* from Dublin, London and abroad, including a 'Roman Notes' section, for items from the Vatican. Reports of debates from both Houses of Parliament and the assizes appeared, as did military* news*. There were also sections for postscript, poetry* and advertising*. Editorially, the paper argued for representative government and protection in trade. **AMcN**

Sources: Brown 1937, Inglis 1954, *Mitchell's* 1851, *The Times* 26 May 1853, *Waterloo Irish*.

DUBLIN MEDICAL PRESS, A WEEKLY JOURNAL OF MEDICINE (1839-1866); MEDICAL PRESS AND CIRCULAR (1867-1961) In its first issue, the *Dublin Medical Press* claimed to be the first medical journal in Ireland, needed because English journalists were ignorant of the state of society in Ireland (a jibe at the *Lancet's** columnist* on Irish medical matters, 'Erinensis'), and because it was necessary 'to diffuse useful knowledge… to rouse the slumbering energies of the Irish practitioner; to preserve the respectability of the professional character, to instil honourable principles, and foster kind feelings in the breast of the student; and to protect the institutions of the country against the attacks of those interested in their destruction' ('Introductory Address'). Published* by Fannin & Co, a leading instrument and medical bookseller in Dublin, with some success – after three months, circulation* was 1,000 a week – it had been founded as a 6d 16-page stamped* periodical by Arthur Jacob, the Professor of Anatomy and Physiology at the Royal College of Surgeons in Ireland. In 1836 he had edited* a few numbers of the *Dublin Journal of Medical and Chemical Science* (1832-1922, with changes of title), a learned journal concerned with scientific advances. With co-editor Henry Maunsell, also a professor at the Royal College, he worked with Richard Carmichael the founder of the Medical Union – later the Irish Medical Association – and established a close bond between them.

From its inception, the *Press* combined matters medical with the quotidian realities of doctors' lives. There was correspondence*, notice of positions vacant, promotions and appointments, reviews*, translations of foreign-language works, reports of learned societies and many case studies. There were also vigorous attacks on abuses. In the second series from 1860 (when the number of pages was increased to 22, and Jacob's son Archibald took over the editorship), the periodical was much concerned with the effects of poor laws, though its most famous involvement lies in its criticism of Oscar Wilde*'s father when he was publicly accused of rape by a patient during 1864-1865; (the profession was incensed at the Press's disloyalty).

In 1865 *Dublin* was dropped from the title and the following year it purchased the *Medical Circular*, a journal founded by Dr James Yearsley in 1852 and edited* by Dr George Ross from its inception. The two combined to become initially the *Dublin Medical Press and Circular* until again *Dublin* was dropped in 1867. Archibald Jacob remained as editor of the *Medical Press and Circular* until his death in 1901 (though he played a smaller role as time went on). From 1868 it was published and managed by Albert Alfred Tindall, a London publisher, at which point the journal became gradually less concerned with Irish matters, although it continued to publish an Irish supplement* and was linked to the Irish Medical Association until it became the Irish Free State Medical Union in 1935. The journal continued until 1961. **AK**

Sources: Rowlette 1939, *Waterloo*.

DUBLIN PENNY JOURNAL (1832-1836) A direct imitation of Charles Knight's* London *Penny Magazine**, which had begun publication three months previously, the *Dublin Penny Journal* was an unstamped* weekly* journal that offers an interesting comparison in terms of contrasting definitions of national identity*.

Owned and printed by J. S. Folds*, the Dublin title was first edited* by Rev. Caesar Otway*, joined two months later by painter and antiquarian George Petrie*. Each issue contained on average three woodcut* illustrations*. While modelled on the *Penny Magazine**, the *Dublin Penny Journal* also intended to keep 'national as well as useful objects in view', with the editors' fostering 'a national and concordant feeling' among Irish readers of all religious and political persuasions. The Dublin journal focused on topography, ruins and tradition to build an account of Irishness. However, the introduction of the railways in Ireland was greeted by a spate of illustrations and articles, and, in an extremely interesting and self-conscious response to the *Penny*, the *Dublin Penny Journal* also published an illustrated account of its own manufacture, revealing the old technology and labour intensive methods used by the magazine. The inclusion of short fiction was probably due to Otway. The main contributors included Petrie himself (Irish topography, history, antiquities, and related illustrations), Otway (Irish topography), John O'Donovan* (translations from Gaelic historical documents), self-taught schoolmaster Robert Armstrong (Irish topography and illustrations), James Clarence Mangan* and Rev. James Wills (poetry*), Edward Walsh (fiction), and proprietor J. S. Folds (technology). Over half of the articles were signed* with initials.

Sales reached 30,000 in November 1832, but circulation* fell to less than 10,000 in 1833. After 56 issues, Folds sold the title to printer Philip Dixon Hardy*, who dismissed Petrie and Otway, becoming the new editor himself in July 1833. Under him the *Dublin Penny Journal* retained few of its original contributors, and issued most articles anomynausly. Scissors* and paste journalism also became more common. Though the *Journal* retained its original format, including illustrations, under Hardy it shifted to presenting romantic Irish locations for the benefit of tourists. One-third of its 1836 sales of 12,000 were in Britain, and Hardy was forced to close it due to ill-health and disputes with his staff in that year. Samuel Ferguson* reviewed the title in the *Dublin University Magazine** in 1840, emphasizing the differences between the two editorships.

The *Dublin Penny Journal* was the first Irish example of a cheap mass-circulation* periodical and provides evidence of the distinctiveness of the Irish market for print. Petrie and Otway's emphasis on Irish culture as the basis of an inclusive Irish identity made it extremely influential with later Irish cultural nationalism. **FB/BM**

Sources: Clyde 2003, Hayley 1976, *Waterloo*.

DUBLIN REVIEW (1836-1968) Part of the Catholic revival of the first quarter of the nineteenth century, the *Dublin Review* was the idea of an Irish barrister, Michael Quin (1796-1843). He approached Nicholas Wiseman* and the Irish nationalist, Daniel O'Connell (1775-1847), who became joint proprietors* of the journal. Published in London and intended for an English readership*, the *Dublin Review* initially had green covers and 'Eire Go Brath' as its motto. Produced monthly* and priced* at 6s for 278 pages, its early years were

troubled: it failed to attract subscribers, it suffered from a rapid turnover of editors* and its publication dates were erratic. Nevertheless, its influence grew. Wiseman insisted on a moderate editorial line, with a view to securing and articulating the Catholic position, and by acquiring the services of H. R. Bagshawe as editor and Charles William Russell* as a contributor, Wiseman ensured enough stability until he took over executive control from 1840 on his return from Rome.

Controversy over the issue of Catholic converts, Wiseman's overloaded schedule and Bagshawe's uninspiring editorship propelled the *Review* into a precarious position until William George Ward's* editorship and the 'New Series' (July 1863-). Politics*, literature*, history*, and a new supplement* dealing with European ideas and events now characterized the *Dublin Review*. Subsequent editors took a quieter position, offering extended book reviews* and introducing travel, exploration, and science*, with the encouragement of signed articles. **CL**

Sources: *Waterloo, Wellesley.*

DUBLIN UNIVERSITY MAGAZINE: A LITERARY AND POLITICAL JOURNAL (1833-1877); UNIVERSITY MAGAZINE (1878-1880) The *Dublin University Magazine* represented, throughout its long history, the interests of Ireland's Protestant, Anglo-Irish educated class*. Begun by a group of Trinity College Dublin undergraduates, including Caesar Otway* and Isaac Butt*, it was intended to be an Irish *Blackwood's** or *Fraser's**. Like its models, the *Dublin University Magazine* preceded the revolution of the shilling* monthlies* and was relatively expensive at 2s 6d a month, and like them its contributors form a who's who of literary talent in nineteenth-century Ireland: Charles Lever*, William Carleton*, J. S. Le Fanu*, Samuel Lover*, Samuel Ferguson*, J. C. Mangan*, and others less well-known today. By 1833 Reform had already begun to erode the traditional power base of the Protestant Ascendancy; as such, the leaders* and review* essays* in the *Dublin University Magazine* form a remarkable chronicle of the waning of an entire class, one whose demands for equal partnership under the Empire became increasingly anxiety-ridden.

Arguably, the best Irish fiction of the nineteenth-century appeared first in the pages of the *Dublin University Magazine*, and the magazine* made it possible, for the first time, for Irish writers to make a name for themselves without publishing with English firms. Lever's fiction contributed greatly to its early popularity, and circulation* figures are highest during his tenure (approximately 4,000 copies per month). The tone of the literature* during this period is light-hearted, rather nostalgic, balancing the frequently strident denunciations of Catholic emancipation and support of the tithe system in the magazine's political* articles.

After Lever's departure in 1845 the magazine went through a number of editors; it was even published in London for a short time in 1856, much to the fury of the Irish public. LeFanu became the proprietor* in 1861, and his decision to fill its pages with his own fiction, and the work of other sensation novelists such as Rhoda Broughton, brought circulation* up again. When, in 1870, he sold it to a London printer, its quality declined sharply as its resort to scissors and paste journalism* increased. By 1877 it was no longer able to pay its contributors, among them Oscar Wilde*, whose mother Speranza* was also a contributor. The decision of the last proprietor, Keningdale Cook, to drop *Dublin* from the title of the magazine from January 1878 caused a minor furore in Ireland, and in 1880 it ceased publication.

The *Dublin University Magazine* remains the most important organ of conservative, Protestant opinion in nineteenth-century Ireland, and it is credited with aiding in a very significant way the development of Irish literature during a difficult period in the country's history. ET
Sources: Clyde 2003, Hall 1999, McCormack 1991, *ODNB*, Sadleir 1938, *Wellesley.*

DUFFY, CHARLES GAVAN (1816-1903) Charles Gavan Duffy, also known as 'C. G. D.', the 'Black Northern', 'Ben Header' and the 'O'Donnell', was born in Co. Monaghan in the north of Ireland in 1816. He became a journalist in 1836, when he joined the *Dublin Morning Register* as an unpaid trainee, being promoted to subeditor* a year later. In 1839 he became the editor* in Belfast of a biweekly* Catholic newspaper, the *Belfast Vindicator*. In October 1842 Duffy started the weekly newspaper the *Nation** in Dublin with journalists Thomas Davis* and John Blake Dillon. Duffy was sole proprietor* and editor*, though Davis and subsequent recruit John Mitchel* occasionally assisted with editorial duties. Duffy also contributed regular editorial articles, occasional poems, and a lively 'Answers to Correspondents'* column*.

Duffy and the *Nation* supported Daniel O'Connell's Repeal Association, promoted an inclusive Irish nationalism, (comprising Protestants as well as Catholics) and emphasized the role of education and culture in achieving Irish independence. In

1843-1844 Duffy and publisher James Duffy (no relation) collected the poetry* of the *Nation* in *The Spirit of the Nation* and subsequently produced a series of shilling monthly* volumes, the *Library of Ireland*, in 1845-1846. Both proved great editorial successes.

As editor of the *Nation*, Duffy was tried for seditious conspiracy in 1844, and for seditious libel in 1846, being discharged or acquitted both times. In 1846 Duffy became one of the leaders of the Young Ireland* movement and was involved in their plans for armed insurrection in 1848. Arrested on 8 July 1848, he was forced to suspend publication of the *Nation* when its office was seized on 28 July 1848. Duffy was tried for treason-felony five times, but was ultimately discharged in 1849. He struggled to revive the *Nation* in 1849 and use it as an organ for his Tenant Rights League, but it did not prosper as before. Duffy sold a quarter-share of the concern in 1850 for £600. He was elected MP in 1852, left the *Nation* in 1855 and emigrated to Australia the same year. There he continued his parliamentary career, rising to become prime minister of Victoria in 1871-1872. In 1880 he settled in southern Europe, where he wrote numerous books on the history of the Young Ireland movement, dying in Nice in 1903.

Duffy was a talented and innovative editor who made effective use of the press to promote Irish cultural nationalism, and is one of the dominant figures of nineteenth-century Irish journalism. FB
Sources: Duffy 1880-1883, Duffy 1898, *ODNB*.

DUFFY, JAMES (1809-1871) Duffy was one of the most important Catholic publishers*/booksellers in nineteenth-century Ireland. As the designated publisher of the Young Ireland* movement under Thomas Davis* and Charles Gavan Duffy*, and as a prolific producer of Catholic works (prayer books, missals, Catholic biographies and journals) Duffy was well-placed to take advantage of a newfound confidence in home-produced literature. Duffy's premises in Dublin employed about 120 at its height in the 1850s-1860s. The list of Duffy-produced serials is a long one and includes several Irish penny* magazines as well as *Duffy's Irish Catholic Magazine, Duffy's Fireside Magazine*, the *Catholic Guardian, or the Christian Family Library*, the *Catholic University Gazette* (containing Newman's 'Idea of a University'), *Duffy's Hibernian Magazine*, and the *Illustrated Dublin Journal*. None of these journals was particularly long-lived, but many offered contributions from the best-known Irish writers of the day, and their omnipresence under

the Duffy label helped form a strong sense of Irish identity as Catholic and nationalist. The firm of James Duffy & Co. survived until the 1980s. **ET**
Sources: CHC 1878, Hayley 1987, Hogan 1996, *Irish Book Lover* 1930, *PGIL-Eirdata*, Russell 1895, *Waterloo*.

DUFFY'S HIBERNIAN MAGAZINE (1860-1861); DUFFY'S HIBERNIAN SIXPENNY MAGAZINE (1862-1864) *Duffy's Hibernian* was one of a number of cheap*, unillustrated magazines issued from James Duffy's* publishing house in Dublin. Aimed at a domestic* audience, the monthly* magazine cost 9d in 1860 for about 48 pages of fiction (much of it signed), poetry* and articles of general interest, all with an Irish focus. The magazine also frequently reviewed* volumes published by Duffy, and acted in many respects as an in-house* journal, like *Cornhill** or *Macmillan's**.

Longevity was never uppermost in Duffy's mind, and under the 'new is good' principle, the *Hibernian* became *Duffy's Hibernian Sixpenny Magazine* in 1862. The reduced price* was matched by a reduction in paper* size (from quarto to octavo) and from two columns* to one over an average of 80 pages. Condemned by critic Barbara Hayley as one of a series of periodicals catering to a 'new kind of cosy family* Catholicism' (Hayley, 42), *Duffy's Hibernian* did offer an outlet for Irish authors, and did in fact offer works by many of the best writers of the day: William Carleton*, John O'Donovan*, Lady Wilde ('Speranza')*, Julia Kavanagh and others whose names were often prominently displayed on the title page. **ET**
Sources: Anon. *Irish Monthly 1895*, Hayley 1987, Hogan 1996, *Irish Book Lover*, *PGIL-eirdata*.

DUGDALE, WILLIAM (C. 1799-1868) One of the leading publishers* of London's 'radical underworld' in the early nineteenth-century, William Dugdale began his career as a journalist* on James Watson's* *Shamrock, Thistle and Rose* (1818), subsequently finding employment with the radical publisher William Benbow*. In 1822 Dugdale established his own bookselling business in the vicinity of Covent Garden, beginning a long career in the book trade. Like other radical booksellers* of early nineteenth-century London, the 1820s saw Dugdale move into the publication and distribution of obscene and pornographic* works. He used a variety of aliases, and often published reprints or piracies of previously published works, operating a printery on his premises for this purpose.

The journalist Thomas Frost*, who briefly worked in Dugdale's printery, described the 'dirty, cobwebby room' at the rear of the Holywell Street shop where a team of compositors worked in the production of Dugdale's books. The Society for the Suppression of Vice brought a number of successful prosecutions against him, but on at least one occasion he was released early from a prison sentence – possibly, as Thomas Frost imputed, through the influence of wealthy patrons of his shop. A sentence of hard labour in 1868, however, resulted in Dugdale's death in prison the same year. **NG**
Sources: Frost 1886, Marcus 1985, McCalman 1988, Todd 1972.

DUNDEE COURIER (1816-) Originally founded as the *Dundee Weekly Courier and Forfarshire Agricultural and Commercial Advertiser* and established by its publishers* Thomas and Alexander Colville in the Tory interest to rival Robert Rintoul's *Dundee Advertiser*, it quickly became in April 1817 the weekly* broadsheet *Dundee Courier*, priced* 7d. Beside agricultural reports and prices, it carried local* news*, trade information and advertisements*, and letters*. The early editors* were all Church of Scotland clergymen and the paper struggled until adopting the reform line from 1823, under David Hill's editorship, before reverting to Conservatism after 1832. The *Courier* sided with Peel in 1846 and accepted free trade, but struggled to compete with John Leng's* more progressive *Dundee Advertiser*. By the 1850s, circulation* had fallen to a mere 500. After merging* with the new *Dundee Argus* in 1861, it became a daily*, reducing its price* to a 1s 2d in 1866, and over the next decade favoured Liberalism but reverted to Toryism after 1886. In 1829 Hill brought Charles Alexander into partnership and Charles Alexander & Co. owned the paper until the 1870s by which time a local ship owner, William Thomson, had become part owner. In 1886 he and his son, David Couper Thomson*, took complete control. In 1905 the firm of D. C. Thomson and Co. took over its main rival, John Leng & Co. The title remains in circulation today as the *Courier and Argus*. **WHF**
Sources: Cowan 1946, Ferguson 1984, *ODNB*, *Waterloo*.

DUNKIN, ALFRED JOHN (1812-1879) Printer and antiquarian, Alfred Dunkin was born in Islington and educated in Britain and France. In 1831 he joined his father John's printing and stationery business in Bromley, Kent and in 1837 the firm moved to Dartford where he worked as a printer and wholesaler until his death. Dunkin contributed articles on antiquarian subjects to the *Dover Chronicle** and also the *Court Maga-*

zine and Monthly Critic and Lady's Magazine and Museum* in 1842.

His largest contribution to journalism* was the founding of the *Archaeological Mine* in 1853, published by Dunkin and John Russell Smith, which appeared at irregular intervals over the next 10 years. Also known as the *Kentish Magazine*, the journal focused almost exclusively on the county of Kent during Saxon times. Although soliciting a few articles from other writers, the *Archaeological Mine* was largely Dunkin's own work. Prominent among the many archaeological groups to which he belonged was the new British Archaeological Association, for whom he acted as printer during its early years. Dunkin's published work has not found favour with professionals 150 years later, as may be seen in the *ODNB*. **MBT**

Sources: *ODNB, Waterloo, Wellesley.*

DUNN, JAMES NICOL (1856-1919) Born in Scotland, James Nicol Dunn intended to become a lawyer but turned to journalism in his student days. He joined the staff of the *Dundee Advertiser* and later the *Scotsman** in Edinburgh and Glasgow before briefly becoming editor* of the weekly* *Scots Observer* 'Nov.-Dec. 1888'. Dunn was replaced as editor by W. E. Henley* and became managing editor of the journal instead. While at the *National Observer* (as the *Scots Observer* had become in Nov. 1890), Dunn was involved in trying to save the subsequent sale of the paper in 1894.

In 1895 he moved to the weekly* *Black and White** where he stayed for two years as editor and, according to Robertson Scott*, Dunn was simultaneously news* editor under Harry Cust's* editorship* at the daily *Pall Mall Gazette** (1894-1896). His next editorship, in 1897, was the *Morning Post**, which he left in 1905 to join the *Manchester Courier* as editor (1905-1910). In 1903-1904 Dunn was President of the Institute of Journalists* and in February 1911 he sailed to South Africa where he became editor of the Johannesburg *Star*. Returning to England in 1914 on the outbreak of the First World War, he became the London editor of the *Glasgow Evening News*, where he stayed until his death.

Although Dunn's career seems full and varied, he remains a shadowy figure in the history of journalism. **DA**

Sources: *BL Newspaper Catalogue*, Scott 1952, *Waterloo, WWW.*

DUNPHIE, CHARLES JAMES (1820-1908) Irish journalist, critic, essayis and poet, C.J. Dunphie was art and theatre critic for the conservative *Morning Post** for over 50 years (1856-1908).

Dunphie began his career at *The Times**, but in 1853 he declined the post of special correspondent* in the Crimea due to personal commitments (W. H. Russell* went instead!) and eventually moved to the *Morning Post*. During the Crimean War, he co-founded the minor *Patriotic Fund Journal* (1854-1855), a weekly* literary* magazine whose small profits were advertised as being paid to the Patriotic Fund; John Gilbert* and Birket Foster* contributed engravings*, and Dunphie himself prose and poetry* under the pseudonym* 'Melopoyn'.

From 1871-1876 he was affiliated with *Belgravia**, and in 1884 with the American magazines the *Saturday Evening Post* and *Frank Leslie's Popular Monthly*, again as poet and fiction writer. Dunphie also published poems in the *Cornhill Magazine**, articles in the *Observer* signed 'Rambler', and contributed to the *Sunday Times**. **CW**

Sources: *ONDB, The Times* 1 Feb. and 15 Oct. 1855, 10 July 1908, *Wellesley.*

'DUVAL, MARIE' (B.1850/1851-?) Born in Paris, Isabelle Emilie Louisa de Tessier, also known as Mrs Henry Ross, was a governess and an actress before becoming a comic illustrator* best-known under the pseudonym* 'Marie Duval'. As a self-taught artist, her often grotesque caricatures* appeared in French, German and English journals* as well as books, where she frequently chose a different pseudonym* for each publication. For instance, for the Chatto and Windus* children's book *Queens and Kings, and Other Things*, she was 'Princess of Hesse Schartzbourg'. Her most famous work (1869-1880s) was the comic character of Ally Sloper*, portrayed with a mixture of humour and pathos, which she signed 'MD' for 'Marie Duval' in *Judy**.

Married to Charles Henry Ross*, *Judy's* editor, it is thought that she drew many of the illustrations with which he has been credited. Fashion* sketches in *Judy* were also by Tessier under another penname, 'Noir', as she always dressed in black. **CL**

Sources: Clayton 1876, Kunzle 1986, *ODNB.*

E

EAGLES, REV JOHN (1783-1855) Primarily a clergyman, but also an established art critic, essayist, and poet, John Eagles was a regular contributor to *Blackwood's Edinburgh Magazine** (1832-1855). Wellsuited to this Tory journal, his diverse journalism were coloured by his conservative stance on politics, religion and art.

Eagles's journalism included political* commentary on subjects such as the Bristol Riots, rural economy and temperance. He contributed both original and translated poetry* to the *London Saturday Journal* (1839-1842) and *Felix Farley's Bristol Journal* (1752-1853), as well as *Blackwood's Edinburgh Magazine*. Perhaps as a result of his frustrated painting and etching career, Eagles found particular enthusiasm and a reputation as art instructor and critic. His best-known criticism appeared in 'The Sketcher' (*Blackwood's Edinburgh Magazine*, 1833-1835), a series in which Eagles wrote of his countryside rambles, using them to champion the cause of poetic landscape and selecting and describing scenes to appeal to the painter. A critical assessment of J. M. W. Turner in *Blackwood's* in October 1836 sparked the outrage of John Ruskin* and developed into a wider debate between Ruskin and other conservative critics. **CW**
Sources: Adams 1973, *Blackwood's* obituary 1855, Gutch 1857, *ODNB*, Oliphant 1897.

EASTLAKE, ELIZABETH (1809-1893) Elizabeth Eastlake (née Rigby) was a critic, art historian, translator and travel writer who contributed regularly to the *Quarterly Review**, the *Edinburgh Review** and other quarterlies* and monthlies*. Brought up in Norwich, she learned German while in residence abroad in 1827 and translated Johann David Passavant's essay on English art, later published as *Tour of a German Artist in England* (1836). She also wrote her first short story, 'My Aunt in a Salt Mine', which appeared in *Fraser's Magazine**.

Moving to London in 1832 to study, she published an article on Goethe in the *Foreign Quarterly Review* (1836)*. The opportunity to develop her writing came from the publication of her letters, *A Residence on the Shores of the Baltic* (1841), after 18 months spent in Russia. John G. Lockhart*, editor* of the *Quarterly Review**, having read this work invited Eastlake to submit an article in March 1842, with the result that she became the first woman to write regularly for the *Quarterly Review*. At first, she specialised in writing travel pieces, and reviewing* other women travel writers and novelists, while her travel articles also appeared in *Fraser's Magazine*, and John Murray* continued to publish her books.

Eastlake's contributions to the *Quarterly Review* which continued until 1891, were often lengthy, 'Crystal Palace' (1855) being over 50 pages; they were also anonymous*, although in her robust attack on 'Vanity Fair and Jane Eyre' she intimates that the writer of the latter is male! Over the years she covered travel, art and architecture, literature and general topics such as 'The Englishwoman at School'(1878). Sometimes controversial, she published on 'Photography' (1857) early in the appreciation of this new medium. For 11 years from 1872 she also wrote for the *Edinburgh Review** on art history, clearly demonstrating her erudition. In the last two years of her life she published her reminiscences in *Longman's Magazine**, pseudonymously* signed 'Author of *Baltic Letters*'. **CL**
Sources: *BritPer*, *ODNB*, *Wellesley*.

ECCLESIASTICAL GAZETTE (1838-1900) The *Ecclesiastical Gazette* was designed to fill 'the want of a proper medium for communicating to the whole body of the Parochial Clergy authentic intelligence upon ecclesiastical matters', and was first published by John W. Parker*. It was sent gratis* to every parochial clergyman in England and Wales, something that, according to Parker, was only made possible by the recent Stamp Act*. The editors* calculated that in its first year the *Gazette's* circulation* was 11,437 copies monthly*, of which approximately 9,000 were gratis copies. Contributors were unpaid and the newspaper was funded by subscriptions and advertisements*. It contained detailed information on ecclesiastical appointments, preferments, 'parliamentary* intelligence' and reports from various societies such as the Society for Promoting Christian Knowledge (SPCK)*. Undoubtedly, the aim to establish the *Gazette* as a monthly 'record of facts, and a general medium of intelligence' for the Anglican clergy was successful. It remained for many years the newspaper for competitors* in this area to beat, and was consistently profitable despite attracting criticism for its 'dry-as-dust' content. The *Ecclesiastical Gazette* eventually ended as it had begun, through a change in law. When the practice of buying and selling presentations to benefices was restricted, the newspaper lost a large source of advertising, revenue and was discontinued in 1900. **MB**
Source: Altholz 1989.

ECCLESIOLOGIST (1841-1868) The *Ecclesiologist* was initially conceived as a monthly organ costing 4d, through which members of the controversial Cambridge Camden Society could remain in contact after departing from the University. Taking inspiration from the Tractarians, the young men of the Society promoted Gothic principles in all matters of ecclesiastical architecture, building and decoration. The *Ecclesiologist* quickly broadened into a 'magazine of general Ecclesiological intelligence', but the Committee of the Society formed the editorial board and contributed the majority of articles; prominent members/contributors included John Mason Neale (1818-1866), Benjamin Webb (1819-1885), Edward Jacob Boyce and Alexander Beresford Hope*. One of the avowed aims of the *Ecclesiologist* was 'to suggest, where it can be done without unwarrantable interference or presumption, alterations or improvements in the arrangements and decorations of new designs', but this innocuous-sounding goal translated in early issues into excoriating criticism of any ecclesiastical building, restoration work or architecture that did not meet with the editors' approval or, as many thought, their prejudices. Controversy forced the editors* to formally sever ties between the *Ecclesiologist* and the Society in 1845 (although they were later reunited); it went bi-monthly and the periodical's tone substantially softened in later years. Reverting to monthly publication in 1846, it went bi-monthly for its final decade; by 1868, it cost 6d. It did not survive Neale's withdrawal from active involvement in 1868, however, and the final number was issued in October of that year. **MB**
Sources: Webster and Elliott 2000, White 1962.

ECHO (1868-1905) The *Echo* was London's first ½d daily* evening paper. Started by Cassell, Petter & Galpin*, its eight pages were modelled on the successful *Glasgow Evening Citizen*. By 1870, its editor* Arthur Arnold claimed it had achieved a circulation* of 200,000. It was liberal and radical in its politics*, with a reputation for its cultural content, and was aimed at London workers and small tradesmen. Writers who worked under Arnold on the paper included William Black*, Frances Power Cobbe*, who was a regular leader* writer, and George Byrom Curtis, later editor of the *Standard*. From October 1875 its format* changed – its page size was increased and its pagination halved, and it was also published (until May 1876) in a morning edition, but the latter was unsuccessful. It was acquired in 1876 by J. Passmore Edwards*, the liberal philanthropist, who owned it, with a short break,

until 1896. By the turn of the century, it was known for its good City, sports*, and arts coverage. But it refused to print racing tips, which may have contributed to its demise under Frederick Pethick-Lawrence, a Suffragette supporter, and its last proprietor* (1902-1905). **JRW**
Sources: Brown 1985, Griffiths 1992, Jones, 1996, Linton and Boston 1987, *ODNB*.

ECLECTIC REVIEW (1805-1868) The *Eclectic Review* was founded by a group of evangelical leaders, both clergy and laity, as a nonprofit journal with revenues allotted to various missionary* societies. It aspired to be a bridge between evangelicalism and establishment Anglicanism, hence the source of the 'eclectic' of its title. Edited* by Samuel Greenford and published by C. Taylor, it was priced* at 2s 6d a month*, printed in one column*, often with discursive footnotes at the bottom of the page. The length of an individual issue was approximately 90 pages. At first, the editors decided not to include any literary content, but exigencies of available contributors and the proclivities of a potential audience diminished this intention, and the poet*, James Montgomery was among its early contributors. Aimed at the general, educated reader of a moderate evangelical disposition, coverage extended to self-educated lower-middle class* readers but did not particularly cater to this constituency. However, by 1810, it was realized that the middle-to-lower-class appeal of the *Review* meant that establishment support would be lacking.

By 1810, the journal was edited* by Daniel Parken and when Parken stepped down, he was succeeded briefly by Theophilus Williams. Due to financial difficulties the journal was taken over by Josiah Conder, its printer at the time, who quickly became the most influential figure in its history. Diligent and indefatigable, Conder produced up to half the content of each journal, much of it anonymously*, and his farewell letter at the beginning of 1837 protested exhaustion. There followed a number of editors: some short-lived, Thomas Price (main tenure from 1837-1849), William Hendry Stovell (1850-1855) and Edwin Paxton Hood (1861-1868).

The *Eclectic* reviewed the major literary names of the day, but few of them published in it. Its coverage was diverse in content, as well as in religious* disposition: a typical issue included coverage of science*, art, and historical* writing as well as literature*. The *Review* part of the title was honoured with a sizeable proportion of book reviews*, or review articles with books of the genre where science*, history*, religion, and literature* could meet. Travel writing was also included. The 1850s saw an emphasis on more purely scientific topics, whereas the last throes of the journal displayed a shift to literary/historical content with reviews of Carlyle's *Frederick The Great* and Christina Rossetti's *Goblin Market* (June 1862).

From its earliest issues, the *Review* was notable for its inclusion of American contributors such as James Fennimore Cooper and Joel Barlow, with a print run in New York City under the aegis of Foster and Bisbee (Jan.-Dec. 1841). After 1845, with the rise of a new generation of American writers, these links lessened. In England, the growth of the Oxford Movement propelled the *Eclectic Review* toward a more partisan and marginalized position. It continued publication until 1868, known in its last four years as the *Eclectic and Congregational Review*.
NB
Sources: Hiller 1994, *ODNB*, *Waterloo*, *Wellesley*.

ECONOMIST: OR THE POLITICAL, COMMERCIAL, AGRICULTURAL, AND FREE-TRADE JOURNAL (1843-) The *Economist*, one of the world's foremost economics journals, was founded by James Wilson, a passionate believer in the socially improving effects of free trade. He was its first editor* and laid its foundations firmly on the classical economics of Adam Smith, Ricardo, James Mill* and Tooke. Inspired by the success of his friends' *Anti-Corn-Law Circular* (1839-1841), Wilson launched his 9d 'class'* weekly* to counter what he saw as class-based rhetoric around the Corn Laws: as Dudley Edwards put it, he wished 'to secure the triumph of reason' (p.8) among the élite. After the repeal of the Corn Laws in 1846, the *Economist* concentrated on economics in general, politics* and the law. Notable writers such as W. R. Greg* contributed, and Herbert Spencer* was the subeditor (1848-1853); after Wilson, its editors were Richard Holt Hutton* and Wilson's son-in-law Walter Bagehot*. Thereafter, the journal was co-edited by Daniel Lathbury and R. H. I. Palgrave, before Edward Johnstone took over (1883-1907). Initially a commercial failure, the *Economist* eventually yielded a profit with the help of advertising*.

By 1871, Grant (p. 199) was commenting on the exceptionally high price* its advertising* space commanded: five years later, the combined advertising revenue of the weekly with its monthly supplement* was almost £3,500 a year. Its circulation* being less than 4,000, such income suggests the wealth and influence of its readership*. Reliance on advertising did not stop the *Economist* from championing integrity and business transparency, which

became indeed its selling point for the rest of the century. In response to the 1862 Companies Act, in October 1864, Bagehot launched a supplement*, the *Investors' Monthly Manual*, which cost 6d extra to subscribers (in an innovative turn, subscribers had actively to state they did not want it; otherwise they were charged). Developing Bagehot's interest in statistics (which had already resulted in the *Economist* publishing the world's first regular price index), the Manual listed all the stocks and shares.
AK
Sources: Edwards 1993, Grant 1871, Moss and Hosgood 1994, Tener 1975.

EDINBURGH EVENING COURANT (1718-1886) This title seems to have its origins in the *Scots Courant* established in 1710, and indirectly in the *Edinburgh Courant* established in 1705, but this genealogy is not clear. According to one newspaper historian, the insertion of the word 'Evening' into the new title in 1718 was to distinguish it from Daniel Defoe's continuation of the *Evening Courant* in 1710 after its first proprietor* died. In 1800 its four pages (the first of which was taken up with advertising*) cost 6d, rising to 7d by 1832 while retaining the same format*. Throughout its run its frequency varied at different periods between twice and thrice per week. However, in 1860 (until November) it appeared as a morning daily* of four larger pages priced* 1d and under the title the *Daily Courant*, but it then reverted to twice weekly. From 16 December 1871 to its demise, it appeared as the *Edinburgh Courant*, a daily evening paper. By the time of its final issue, it cost 1d and ran to eight pages.

In the early nineteenth century, under the ownership of David Ramsay and his heirs, it was firmly Tory, supporting the repression of reform movements. David Buchanan* served as its editor* (1827-1848), followed by Joseph Robertson when it became Peelite in its politics*. By mid-century it was the best source of London news*, with extensive articles transcribed from leading journals and its readership* was predominantly among the wealthy. After 1855 the paper moved to two supplements* a week, free to subscribers of the weekly. Among its nineteenth-century contributors were George Hogarth (c 1815-1830), the youthful James Barrie (late 1870s-1882) and James Miller Gray (ca 1870s) and *Waterloo* names early nineteenth-century contributors from the Scottish Tory press, notably *Blackwood's*, W. E. Aytoun, James Hogg, J. G. Lockhart and 'Christopher North'*.

The *Courant* went through a lively period under the editorship of James Hannay (1860-1864), determined to counter Liberal influence in Edinburgh. This was followed by a run of relatively short-lived editors, Francis Espinasse*, J. Scott Henderson, James Mure and, finally, W. R. Lawson. It was subsidized with Conservative Party money and, from 1868, was owned by Charles Westcomb. It merged with the Conservative *Glasgow Evening News* in 1886 to form the *Scottish News*, which – the final issue of the *Courant* promised – would devote a 'Larger Space to matters of Non-Political but General Interest. WHF
Sources: Cowan 1946, Espinasse 1893, Ferguson 1984, *ODNB*, *Waterloo Scotland*, Worth 1964.

***EDINBURGH MEDICAL AND SURGICAL JOURNAL* (1805-1855), *EDINBURGH MEDICAL JOURNAL* (1855-1954)** Among the leading medical quarterlies* of the century, the *Edinburgh Medical and Surgical Journal* was a continuation of the *Annals of Medicine* started in 1796 (which itself had forebears that went back to *Medical Essays and Observations* in 1733). Andrew Duncan, a professor of the Institute of Medicine at the University of Edinburgh, was its first editor*, having been co-editor with his father of the *Annals*. The 3s illustrated* house journal of the Edinburgh College of Physicians carefully marked its allegiance in its title (important given the different organization of medical systems in Scotland and England, and how St Andrews and Aberdeen universities would grant MDs to English practitioners for £10). Early in the century, it had a reputation for being both 'studious and gentlemanly' (Clarke 1874: 10) and cliquey, often stressing the superiority of Edinburgh medicine over English. However, the journal was not exclusively local in its coverage, regularly extracting and translating long passages from medical works in French and German. The influence of imperial* enterprises is also very clear in its extensive publication of papers by the East India Company and army medical officers as well as papers from West Africa and the Americas. Varying in price* (4s in 1819 and 6s in 1823), it was originally published* by Constable*, and passed to Black's in 1827 when Constable failed.

As a quarterly*, the journal could not carry up-to-date news*; rather, it specialized in long and detailed articles and reviews*, avoiding reports of societies or hospital practice (which became increasingly prominent in the medical press after the establishment of the *Lancet**). However, 'yield[ing] to the sprit of the age' as the last number of the first version put it (1 April 1855), it incorporated the London *Monthly Journal of Medicine* (1841-; various titles, and itself having absorbed in 1846 the *Northern Journal of Medicine* 1843-1846) and became a 2s monthly, entitled *Edinburgh Medical Journal* (1855-1954) which reported on the meetings of medical societies as well as continuing its reviews and articles. Oliver and Boyd took over publication in 1862 and by 1874 it was widely circulating in England (Clarke 1874: 10). In January 1897 a new series began, published by the medical specialists Young J. Pentland (offices in both Edinburgh and London) and edited by G. A. Gibson, who was later aided by Alexis Thompson. The stress was still on learned papers, with reviews, case studies, statistics and obituaries*. In 1955 it amalgamated with the *Glasgow Medical Journal* to become the *Scottish Medical Journal*. AK
Sources: Bynum 1992, Clarke 1874, Couper 1904, *Waterloo*.

***EDINBURGH REVIEW* (1802-1929)** The establishment of the *Edinburgh Review* in 1802 was a defining moment in the history of periodical literature and in the history of criticism. It was, as Margaret Oliphant* later observed, 'the first-born of modern periodicals'. Its founders, Francis Jeffrey*, Sydney Smith*, Francis Horner* and Henry Brougham* were young professionals with Whig sympathies, three of them lawyers, resident in Edinburgh during an ultra-conservative political regime. Unlike the earlier monthly* reviews* which it supplanted, it was independent of booksellers. Archibald Constable*, its first publisher, paid the reviewers at the generous rate of ten guineas a sheet (of 16 printed pages), setting a precedent which other reviews struggled to match.

The *Edinburgh* was published quarterly*, and sold for 6s. All contributions were published anonymously*, contributors subscribing implicitly to the editorial 'we' of the review's collective voice. It retained its policy of anonymity until 1912. The *Edinburgh's* review* articles were lengthy, often 40 pages, and it selected books for review, rather than producing brief notices of numerous publications, which had previously been the practice of reviews*.

The *Edinburgh* espoused a vigorously Whig position in contrast to the Tory politics* of the *Quarterly Review**, established in opposition to it in 1809, and the radical position of the *Westminster Review**, founded in 1824. Its greatest period of political influence was under Francis Jeffrey's editorship* (1802-1829), during which, for the most part, the Whigs were in opposition. The political power of the *Edinburgh*, like that of other politically aligned quarterlies was eroded from the 1840s with the rise of the daily* newspaper.

The *Edinburgh*, as Walter Bagehot* commented in 1855 'began the system' of reviewing* which prevailed for most of the nineteenth century. One of its innovations was the emphasis placed on political economy* and on contemporary science*. Its early criticism of contemporary literature* was famous for its prejudices, Jeffrey's dismissal of the English 'Lake Poets' being a case in point. But it continued to review literature in all fields responsibly into the twentieth century. Hazlitt's* comment, made in the review's early years, that 'To be an Edinburgh Reviewer is, I suspect, the highest rank in modern literary society', would have prompted general agreement for much of the nineteenth century. Jeffrey was succeeded as editor in 1829 by Macvey Napier* (1829-1847), then by his son-in-law William Empson* (1847-1853), followed briefly by George Cornewall Lewis (1853-1855), Henry Reeve* (1855-1895), and Arthur R. D. Elliot*. **JS**

Sources: Bagehot 1855, Clive 1957, Demata and Wu 2002, Shattock 1989, *Wellesley.*

EDITOR The function of the editor in the nineteenth century varied hugely across different publications and changed fundamentally over time. There is nevertheless a damaging tendency to conflate the diverse roles played by various editors of various publications at various times under a generic job description that limits our understanding of the social, intellectual and economic functioning of the press.

A brief sketch of the development of the role of magazine editor in the nineteenth century might read something like this, though exceptions to this general trend can be found at every level. Early in the century, during the heyday of the Edinburgh quarterlies*, there began to emerge a set of editors who were arguably among the first professional journalists, often producing a great deal of copy but being paid a stipend rather than by the article. This was partly at odds with a prevailing sense that the editor of a distinguished journal should be a 'gentleman amateur'. Francis Jeffrey*, editor of the Edinburgh Review* (1802-1829), initially believed that editors and contributors alike should go unpaid for their labours. Yet while this may have been feasible for the editor of a quarterly publication who could make up the bulk of his salary elsewhere (in Jeffrey's case by practising law) it was close to impossible in the case of the monthly* and weekly* publications that became increasingly prevalent, and these consequently tended to

have professional editors earlier. Nevertheless, despite his objections to the principle of paid editorial work, Jeffrey received generous remuneration, and this increasingly became the rule. According to Walter Bagehot*, Jeffrey transformed the role of the editor from 'bookseller's drudge' to 'distinguished functionary'. Lower down the social spectrum, editors like William Maginn* – a frequent contributor to Blackwood's Magazine* who co-founded Fraser's Magazine* in 1830, becoming its first editor – and William Jerdan* – editor of Henry Colburn's* Literary Gazette* from 1817 to 1850 – were also key in redefining the role. Apart from being hugely influential in shaping the agendas of their respective publications (partly through their own extensive contributions and partly by fostering a stable of regular contributors) men like these were themselves closely connected to the publishers*, contributors, typesetting* and production* of the periodicals concerned.

By mid-century, the role of editor had become an exalted position, dominated by powerful literary personalities. Patten and Finkelstein (2006) note three types of editor in this period: the big name editor, such as Thackeray* at the Cornhill Magazine*, who used his literary connections to attract renowned contributors and left the day-to-day running of the magazine to subordinates; the hands-on editor, who closely managed the content and timing of articles and reviews (like Dickens* at Household Words*); and the publisher-proprietor, like William Blackwood III* at Blackwood's Magazine*, who wrote little or no copy but took an active interest in their business, profiting moreover from republishing noted contributions in book form. These three paradigms are not exhaustive – and many editors straddled or moved between them in their careers – but they are indicative. The shift in the last years of the century – which saw the character of the press transformed by cheaper cover prices*, mass circulation*, and (broadly speaking) a displacement of in-depth essays and reviews* by news* and entertainment – was towards a new, less lofty definition of the editor as an assembler of ephemera.

This broad outline of the development of the magazine editor's role in part reflects shifts in the dominance of different formats, as competition from monthlies edged out the quarterlies, and so on. Connected developments in the editorship of newspapers can be pinned to innovations in the manner and mode of newspaper production. Editing a national daily paper was a key role even in the

Figure 14: 'Some Editors' in the *Review of Reviews*, May 1891: 508. James Payn, Mrs Meade, Jos. Cook, Rev. Dr. Macleod, T. W. Reid, M. H. Spielmann, G. Newnes, P. W. Bunting, A. Kaufmann, Madame Adam, Archibald Grove.

early years of the century, when there were fewer of them. Editors of the most popular and influential papers were in a unique position, using political contacts to beat the competition to the latest story, and – when circumstances allowed – forming the paper in the image of their own political and journalistic values. John Delane's* editorship of The Times* from 1841 to 1877 was a defining one, converting it from the conservative 'thunderer' of his predecessor Thomas Barnes's* editorship into a broadly liberal voice, tripling its circulation* in the process. Later in the century, accompanying the rise of the 'New Journalism'*, a new model emerged with W. T. Stead* of the Northern Echo* and then the Pall Mall Gazette* as its exemplar. A populist social crusader and agitator, Stead's editorship at both papers was characterised by the ample use of illustrations*, sensationalist investigative* journalism* and a more colloquial tone in the support of a radical Liberal agenda, backing Gladstone as well as the Salvation Army and railing against child prostitution and other social problems. Stead relished his ability to shape popular opinion, and described editors as 'the uncrowned kings of an educated democracy', an analogy whose ambiguous poise illustrates some of the contradictory dynamics of the new mass media landscape.

With this in mind, it should be said that in both periodicals and newspapers the extent to which the publication reflected the outlook of its editor varied enormously. Partly this is because of the differing roles played by publishers and/or proprietors*, who – if they were not themselves the editors (like Charles Knight* of the Penny Magazine* or Robert and William Chambers* of Chambers's Edinburgh Journal*) – generally had the power to hire and fire editors if the product did not meet expectations however, changes in editorship frequently occurred without a significant shift in the style or content of the publication. Conversely, major editorial revamps of the look and content of a magazine often merely followed wider fashions. The overhaul of the New Monthly Magazine* carried out by Thomas Campbell*, for example, aped a recent change in format by Blackwood's Magazine, and can therefore hardly be seen as a strong expression of Campbell's editorial personality, though he was undoubtedly the agent of the change. Editors could be highly influential figures, but Stead's assertion that they were 'uncrowned kings' went too far: in many cases, they were in thrall to their paymasters. **MaT**
Sources: ODNB, Patten and Finkelstein 2006, Wiener 1985.

EDITORS AND AUTHORSHIP Literary periodicals throughout the nineteenth century in general forsook named authorship contributions; material published was usually unsigned or credited with a byline referring to other work by the same individual. Partially this was due to a penchant for presenting journal contents under a veil of anonymity* and within parameters of a unified editorial identity. At times pseudonyms were also employed to conceal the extent to which material was produced by a collective, or by different authors at different times. Thus Oliver Yorke, the inebriated figure created to stand as editor* of Fraser's Magazine*, was himself a collaborative* product of the editor William Maginn and his stable of authors that included William Thackeray*, J. G. Lockhart*, Theodore Hook*, Percival Weldon Banks, and D. M. Moir* (Thrall 1934). Equally famous was the collective editorial persona of Mr. Punch, whose squabbling and variable stances reflected the agglomeration of contributors involved in his creation.

But editors did on occasion throughout the first half of the century break the unspoken rule of anonymity to name star author contributions. And from the 1860s onwards journals drew more frequently on the power of celebrity* authors to raise their profiles and increase circulation*. This was due to the impact of the avalanche of shilling* monthlies* founded in the wake of the successful launch in 1859 and 1860 of Macmillan's Magazine* and the Cornhill Magazine*. A plethora of other middle-class, 'light', cheap* and entertaining titles followed, and with competition* came changes to authorship status. From the 1890s onwards, mainstream and popular 'magazines' such as the Strand Magazine* and the Pall Mall Magazine*, dedicated to entertainment, heavily illustrated*, and drawing interest through use of named celebrity authors and personal journalism, also changed the manner in which authorship was editorially conceived. Anonymity as the main strategy of periodical press presentation was used less and less until it remained more the preserve of older, established journals such as Blackwood's Magazine* and the Quarterly Review*. **DF**
Sources: Altick 1997, Brake 1994a, Brake 2001, Brake and Codell 2005, Brake 2006, Brake, Bell and Finkelstein 2001, Demoor 2004a, Finkelstein 2006, Slater 2002, Spielmann 1895, Thrall 1934.

EDWARDS, (SAMUEL JULES) CELESTINE (1857-1894) Celestine Edwards, Methodist evangelist and journal editor*, began his extraordinary journey in the West Indies. The son of slaves, Edwards stowed away on a ship in 1870, and travelled the world before arriving in Britain where he lived briefly in Scotland and the north-east. After joining the Primitive Methodists, he was assigned to work as an evangelist in London, where he attended King's College's theology school and began to write religious pamphlets.

In 1892 he founded and edited a weekly* Christian newspaper, Lux. Provisionally intended to combat the 'poison' of atheism, Lux became more overtly anti-imperialist* in defence of colonized subjects. His lectures on such themes drew vast crowds and he came to the attention of the Society for the Recognition of the Brotherhood of Man (SRBM), who asked Edwards to take on the post of General Secretary for the Society as well as the editorship of Fraternity, its house* journal. Edwards wrote a large amount of its copy, and increased circulation* to 7,000. Simultaneously, he was writing for and editing Lux, whilst supporting himself by lecturing for the Christian Evidence Society. Two years later his exhausting workload resulted in his premature death in Barbados. CL

Source: ODNB.

EDWARDS, JOHN PASSMORE (1823-1911) Edwards left his native Cornwall in 1844 to become the Manchester agent of the Sentinel, a liberal London weekly* involved in agitation against the Corn Laws. Although the Sentinel soon folded, and had failed to pay Edwards a living wage, it gave him a taste for journalism, and from 1845 he lived in London, supporting himself by freelance writing for the press. By 1850 Edwards had earned enough to begin a newspaper of his own, the Public Good, serving as not only its editor* and publisher*, but also its advertising* canvasser, thus ensuring wide sales. However, the eventual failure of the Public Good, as well as of three other journals he began during the early 1850s, left Edwards bankrupt and in poor health.

Strenuous efforts as a freelance journalist allowed him to try again as a publisher, and in 1862 he took over the Building News, which he made into a financial success. A passionate advocate of the Mechanics' Institutes movement, Edwards had also held the lease of the Mechanics' Magazine* since 1857. Restricted in the changes he could make to the now ailing weekly, Edwards returned the lease in 1865 and instead bought the English Mechanic* in 1869. As both publisher and editor, and with the assistance of Ebeneezer Kibblewhite, Edwards transformed the fortunes of the penny* weekly*, which reached a circulation* of 30,000 by 1871 and was affectionately referred to as 'Ours' by editor and readers alike. In 1876 Edwards made Kib-

blewhite editor of the English Mechanic, and he himself took over the daily* newspaper the Echo*, although relinquishing the editorship to Howard Evans in 1878.

As proprietor* of the Echo Edwards steered its political* outlook from the Conservatives to the Liberals, and despite needing substantial investment to renew its infrastructure, the innovatively priced* halfpenny paper soon began to return a profit and was selling 300,000 copies by 1883. In the following year Edwards sold a two-thirds share of the now lucrative paper to Andrew Carnegie and Samuel Storey, but bought it back less than 12 months later and again installed himself as the Echo's editor, enabling him to take a stand on all the major political questions of the period. By the late 1890s Edwards's interests increasingly lay in the philanthropic schemes which he financed with profits from the Echo, and in 1898 he sold the paper to a Liberal syndicate. GD

Sources: Baynes 1994, Brock 1980, Edwards 1906, ODNB, Waterloo.

EDWARDS, MARY ELLEN (1839-C.1910) The prodigious career as a periodical illustrator of Mary Ellen Edwards, pseudonym 'M. E. E.', began in 1855 when she was 16. In 1859 her wood* engraving 'Checkmate' was on the cover of the Illustrated Times*; as a result she was asked to illustrate 'Ordeal for Wives' in London Society* and went on to a staff position at the Graphic*. She drew for the specialist illustrated* journals of the 1860s, notably Good Words* and Once a Week*, the weekly* news* magazines, including the Illustrated London News* to which she contributed over many years, and the fiction bearing journals like the Argosy* and the Quiver*. She was also a book illustrator and her reputation was firmly established by her illustrations for Trollope's* 'The Claverings' which was serialized* in the Cornhill* (1866-1867).

Her illustrations of women, girls and children in idyllic garden scenes are emblematic of the period and are regarded as surprisingly mature and accomplished considering her lack of training. Her work for the Graphic (1869-1880) was among that admired by Van Gogh, an artist much influenced by periodical illustration in Britain. Edwards's work appeared in wide range of titles, including Belgravia* (1855), the Christian Guest (1859); Argosy*, Puck on Pegasus (1862), the Churchman's Family Magazine (1863-1864), Parables from Nature (1861/1867), London Society* (1864-1869), Family Fairy Tales (1864), the Quiver* (1864/1890), Once a Week* (1865-1868), the Sunday Magazine

(1865), *Good Words** (1866), *My Pale Companion* (1866), *Aunt Judy's Magazine** (1867), *Cassell's Magazine** (1867-1870), the *Churchman's Shilling Magazine* (1867), the *Broadway* (1867-1870), *Dark Blue* (1871-1873), *After Work, Mother's Last Word*, and *Girl's Own Paper**. **CL/BM**
Sources: Clayton 1876, Engen 1990, Houfe 1978, Bob Speel online, *Waterloo*, White 1897.

EGAN, PIERCE (1772-1849) Egan is best known as one of the first sports* journalists and as author of the serial *Life in London*. While his earliest sports writing is thought to date from 1804 (*Sporting Anecdotes* 'by an amateur sportman'), Egan was 40 before his first major success, *Boxiana, or, Sketches of Ancient and Modern Pugilism*, in 1812 (more volumes came out in 1818 and 1821). By 1819 he was reporting sports (especially boxing) for the *Weekly Dispatch** and contributed a serial novel 'The Life and Adventures of Samuel Denmore Hayward' in 1821. The monthly serial *Life in London, with its heroes the rustic Tom, the city sophisticate Corinthian Jerry, and the Oxford graduate Bob Logic*, illustrated* by George and (mainly) Robert Cruikshank* and published by Sherwood, Neely and Jones in 36 numbers, began publication in September 1821, and became enormously popular. Delighting both in melodramatic contrasts of high and low life and in the slang of various social groups, it forms a bridge between eighteenth-century scandalous 'Spy' literature and nineteenth-century explorations of the city by Ainsworth*, Eugene Sue, G. W. M. Reynolds*, Dickens* and others.

In early 1824 Egan published a detailed account of the trial of John Thurtell, cashing in on a celebrated murder case, and the same month was fired from the *Dispatch* for unknown reasons. The following month he launched his 8½d Sunday* *Pierce Egan's Life in London and Sporting Guide*, marking out 'Life in London' as his own after *Bell's Life in London** had appropriated it the previous year. Making a feature of sports, Egan's newspaper also focused on crime*, including the trial of Henry Fauntleroy for forgery in 1824 (an account reissued in pamphlet format). However, the circulation* of Egan's paper was never large enough to sustain it, and in 1827 he became bankrupt. In November 1827 *Egan's* merged* with *Bell's Life in London*, to become one of the most important sporting periodicals of the nineteenth century. Thereafter Egan returned to serial* publication with *The Finish to the Adventures of Tom, Jerry and Logic* (1828) before his last attempt to run a Sunday newspaper, the 7d *Pierce Egan's Weekly Courier* (1829). Without the resources of *Bell's* or the *Weekly Dispatch*, the *Courier* lasted only a few months. Later

publications include *Pierce Egan's Book of Sports* (1832, in 25 weekly parts at 3d each) but Egan's heyday was over. He died in 1849, his career plainly showing the overlaps between serial, newspaper and periodical publication of the time. He left his son, Pierce James Egan*, to take mass-market* reading* in new directions. **AK**
Sources: BL catalogue, Reid 1971, *The Times*.

EGAN, PIERCE JAMES (1814-1880) Egan's *Times** obituary* (8 July 1880) called him 'one of the pioneers of cheap* literature'. Son of Pierce Egan I, educated at the Royal Academy as an artist, Egan both wrote and illustrated* the penny* weekly* parts of his novels *Quentin Matsys* (1839), *Robin Hood* (1840) and *Wat Tyler* (1841). By 1842 he was providing illustrations* for the *Illustrated London News** and for Webster's Acting Drama series. Between 1849 and 1854 he edited* *Home Circle** (printed by W. S. Johnson) and returned to penny-part novels before beginning his career in the major mass-market* periodicals of the 1850s, initially for *Reynolds's Miscellany**. In 1857 he began to write for the *London Journal**. He became editor* in 1860 after a brief stint editing the *Journal's* brother newspaper, the *Weekly Times**. He stayed with the *Journal* until his death, contributing a further 23 novels. Many of these were also published in volume form by the *Journal's* proprietor* and printer, W. S. Johnson*. Egan was widely translated into French, Italian and German and was popular in America and Canada. *The Times* obituary notes that 'Besides delighting the toiling millions with his novels, Mr Egan was an earnest politician and a staunch Liberal'. He was succeeded as editor by his son, also Pierce Egan, about whom very little is known. **AK**
Sources: King 2004, *ODNB*, *The Times* 8 July 1888.

ELECTRICAL JOURNALS The rise of telegraphy*, sound recording, electric lighting and telephony from 1850 created a new class of skilled worker who required regular updates in their fields. These technological developments also inspired amateur enthusiasts to take an interest in the rapid evolution of electrical science, and many of the electrical journals of the period are characterized by the attempt to address both audiences at once. This distinguishes them from earlier learned quarterlies* such as the famous *Annals of Electricity, Magnetism and Chemistry* (1836-1843), conducted by the inventor William Sturgeon, or the *Electrical Magazine* (1843-1845), founded by Charles Vincent Walker, which carried detailed scientific* papers addressed exclusively to a specialist readership*.

Figure 15: Humorous reactions to the introduction of electric light in *Fun Almanac*, Jan. 1882: 12.

The *Electrician, A Weekly Journal of Telegraphy, Electricity and Applied Chemistry* (1861-1864) – published by Thomas Piper, who also published photographic* journals including the *Photographic News* (1858-1908) – was a weekly* class* journal priced* 4d. It was designed both to enable 'the Telegraphist to keep *au courant* with the scientific and material progress of his profession' and to 'meet the requirements of the student in the field of knowledge which is every day being extended, and which, in all probability, is destined to solve many of the most important problems connected with the wellbeing of mankind'. Undoubtedly, the material is often of world-historical significance. In the pages of the *Electrician*, Charles Bright and Latimer Clark proposed a standardized system of units – the ohma, farad, galvat and volt (forerunners of the ohms, amps and volts we use today) – and there appeared a paper (and ensuing discussion) on the method for laying the projected transatlantic telegraphic cable, illustrated* with engravings. The exposition was technical and rather dry, however, and the *Electrician* was discontinued in May 1864, promising to reappear that July in a 'new and greatly improved form' as a monthly review, which never materialised.

Its successor – similarly titled the *Electrician, A Weekly Journal of Theoretical and Applied Electricity and Chemical Physics* (1878-1952) – was more enduring. Also costing 4d, and very similar in format* to its earlier namesake, there seems to have been little continuity in terms of personnel, and it did not acknowledge the existence of the earlier paper until it was well established – attaining an international distribution* – when the later title began to claim the 1861-1864 run as its 'First Series'. Its comparative success can probably be attributed to the growth of the professional sector rather than finding much of an audience outside the profession, although the illustrated explanations of newly patented devices become more lucid and accessible as time wore on. Pocket-sized supplements* were periodically included, producing in a portable format 'Hints to Workmen' ('rubber galoshes are useful on wet days') alongside useful tables of resistance and so forth. Advertisements* for the latest equipment and services (telegraph companies, microphones, science text books, carbon batteries and lecture series) were significant for both magazines, but where in the earlier run they had composed 4 pages out of a total 16, by the end of the century – while the cover price rose to 6d – they took up 36 pages of a 56-page magazine.

As the use of electrical appliances became increasingly widespread, their installation and use were much less confined to a coterie of specialists and enthusiasts, and a truly popular market for electrical knowledge opened up. A new monthly*, *Electric Light* (1882-1883) came on the market, but it found success only after dropping its price* to 3d 'to bring it within the reach of all', changing its name to *Electrical Engineering* (1883-1912) and eventually switching to weekly publication. *Electricity, and Electrical Engineering* (1890-1929) was the first penny* weekly* electrical journal, aiming, through its low price and accessible style, 'to spread this knowledge among the people, to popularise our noble science'. **MaT**

Sources: *ODNB, Waterloo*.

ELIAS, JULIUS SALTER (1873-1946) Elias (Viscount Southwood) was a printer and newspaper proprietor*. He worked as an office boy in several printing firms before joining the publisher*, Odhams Brothers, in 1894. With an insatiable appetite for work, he was soon promoted to manager and, in 1898, became a director of the company. He quickly saw the ownership of magazines* both as an outlet for their presses, and as a means of expansion. His first step was to acquire *Table Talk*, the in-house* journal of the Hotel Cecil in the Strand which was a 'little paper' for hotel residents giving information about the hotel and London attractions. In 1896, Elias purchased other titles, including the theatrical journal *Entr'Acte*, which featured programmes for music halls on its middle pages. In 1900 Odhams Brothers became Odhams Limited, and was a private limited company until 1912. After failing to obtain contracts to print the *Tribune* and *The Times*, Elias published the 1d weekly* *John Bull* for Horatio Bottomley* in 1906. This was a hard-hitting popular paper, intended to expose criminality and corruption. Elias's main achievement was to take over the Labourite *Daily Herald* in 1929, but its circulation* was gradually surpassed by the *Daily Express*. Apart from newspapers, Odhams under Elias published many profitable magazines as well as printing Debrett's *Peerage*. **DHL**

Sources: Griffiths 1992, Minney 1954, *ODNB*.

'ELIOT, GEORGE' See Evans, Marian

ELIZA COOK'S JOURNAL (1849-1854) Popular poet Eliza Cook* published the first number of the weekly* *Eliza Cook's Journal* from her office in Fleet Street*, with the avowed intention of assisting 'the people' in 'the gigantic struggle for intellectual elevation now going on'. Readership* is difficult to assess but the journal, priced* 1d and 1 ½d per 16-page issue over its run, appeared to be aimed at the artisan and lower middle classes*, and was polemical with regard to independence for women. In the first year circulation* was 50,000-60,000 per issue. As editor* and proprietor* she told a major contributor, Samuel Smiles, that the publication was her declaration of independence, and there was 'no reason why a *woman* should not possess sufficient brains to be *allowed* to try her luck in the world with kindly help as well as these 'almighty Lords'.

Smiles wrote many of the journal's leaders* anonymously* in support of that polemic, and also claimed 'Notes of the Month', 'Biographies' and the occasional tale or sketch. The list of contributors, including novelist Eliza Meteyard ('Silverpen')*, and writers Julia Kavanagh, Charles Swain and Thomas Hood* shows that male contributors seem to have outnumbered women. While some pieces are anonymous*, signature is also indicated by pen-names, or the author's full name. Cook signed some of her leaders* and articles, and all her poetry*. Poems by others are signed with a full name or initials to differentiate the poems by author. Cook began to reissue her published poetry from November 1850 as a means, she suggests, for subscribers to own all of her poems published prior to the *Journal*'s inception, at a minimal cost. Unlike other journals aimed at the same readership*, *Eliza Cook's* was not illustrated. From August 1854 there are repeated notices that editing is now 'solely in the hands of the Proprietress'. The journal ceased publication late in 1854 due to Cook's ill health. **JEJ**
Sources: Fraser 2003, *ODNB*, Tyrell 2000.

ELLIOT, ARTHUR RALPH DOUGLAS (1846-1923) As an opponent of Home Rule and as an advocate of Free Trade, Elliot wrote over 50 articles from 1879 for the *Edinburgh Review* on parliamentary* matters, and criminal law*, as well as reviews* of the biographies of statesmen. Trained as a barrister, Liberal MP for Roxburghshire (1880-1892), and later for the City of Durham, a writer of political* pamphlets and well-known parliamentary speaker, Elliot was acquainted with the editors of the best journals of the day. In 1895, after the death of Henry Reeve*, Elliot was appointed editor* of the *Edinburgh Review*, a position he occupied until 1912. During his tenure Whig politics* set the tone for the *Review*, and the journal's principle of anonymity* was upheld. His editorship is known for its fierce protection of the *Edingburgh Review's* reputation as the organ of moderate political opinion. **ET**
Sources: *ODNB*, *Wellesley*.

ELLIOT STOCK (1859-1939) An enterprising publisher* of magazines and books who combined high production values with low prices, Elliot Stock (1838-1911) was little-known outside of London bibliographical circles. During the last decades of the century Stock published innovative books and magazines that were both highly conscious of typographical and design history and affordable to a middle-class readership*. However, printing firms for Stock's titles are often a mystery, because Stock did not follow any standard practice; to compound problems, in the position at the end of a book where one would traditionally find a printer's imprint, Stock's products often repeated the firm and its address: 'Elliot Stock, 62 Paternoster Row', even though there is no evidence that Stock operated a printing operation at that address.

The firm started out as primarily a publisher of religious material, much of it related to the Sunday School Movement. In the 1860s Stock was financially interested in many short-lived denominational magazines such as the *Scattered Nation*, edited by C. Schwartz, the *Hive: A Storehouse of Material for Working Sunday School Teachers*, and the *Church: A Monthly Penny Magazine*. Longer running was the *Baptist* (1873-1910). Even after the firm's attention turned away from religious work, it was never abandoned.

Stock's new magazines in the 1880s and 1890s had antiquarian and bookish interests. The *Antiquary* (1879-1915) edited by Edward Walford, was a monthly, crown 4to, priced* 1s; the *Bibliographer* (1881-1884) edited by H. B. Wheatley, was published in the same format*, as was *Book-Lore* (1884-1887) edited by William Azon. The *Book-Worm* (1887-1894) changed its format to 8vo and dropped the price to 6d. All of Stock's bibliographic magazines were typically 32 pages with illustrated* cover and advertisements*. Also during this time, Stock began to publish the monthly *Book-Prices Current* (1886-1956) edited by J. Herbert Slater (1888-1921). The work was issued only to annual subscribers at £1 5s 6d, and quickly became a standard reference work for book dealers and collectors.

Stock corresponded with all of the major figures in London bibliophile society. The public reading room at the firm's office became a meeting place for scholars, collectors and poets, such as Gladstone, William Morris, Bernard Quaritch, William Blades, Kegan Paul*, and Richard Le Gallienne*, among others. In many respects, the design and content of his belles-lettres titles in the 1870s and 1880s prefigured the early years of The Bodley Head. **CS**
Sources: Anderson and Rose 1991, Pantazzi 1971, Prance 1979, Sherbo 1987, Tanselle 1988.

ELMY, ELIZABETH CLARKE WOLSTENHOLME (1833-1918) AND ELMY, BENJAMIN (1838-1906) Born in the Manchester area, Elizabeth Elmy was an indefatigable radical women's rights* campaigner, political journalist* and writer. Denied the university education enjoyed by her brother and largely self-educated, Wolstenholme Elmy forged a career as the head mistress of several girls' boarding schools in Cheshire. Involved in the campaign for secondary and higher education for women and girls she contributed 'The Education of Girls: Its Present and Its Future' to Josephine Butler's *Woman's Work and Woman's Culture* (1869). She also made some of her earliest contributions with Butler and Jessie Boucherett* to the short-lived periodical *Now-a-Days* (1869).

Her commitment to women's suffrage began in 1865 as secretary to the Manchester Committee for the Enfranchisement of Women and in 1872 she founded and became paid secretary of the Vigilance Association for Defence of Personal Rights. From the inception of its *Journal of the Vigilance Association for the Defence of Personal Rights* in 1881, she was a major contributor. From September 1893 she published a regular column* in *Shafts*, 'Practical Work for Women Workers: Bills Before Parliament' and a series, 'Progress at Home and Abroad'; many letters* and articles appeared in newspapers, such as 'A Woman's Plea to Woman' in the *Macclesfield Courier* (1886) which became a pamphlet, in addition to others such as 'Woman's Franchise: The Need of the Hour' for the Independent Labour Party.

Husband and wife collaborated on many writing projects, creating a debate about where the joint pseudonym 'Ellis Ethelmer' began and ended. A number of pieces are thought to have been written jointly, although the advertisements* in newspapers and periodicals offered them as 'Available from Mrs. Wolstenholme Elmy'. Ben Elmy contributed to the *Westminster Review* (1896-1899) using the pseudonym 'Ellis Ethelmer', writing a tribute on his wife, 'A Woman Emancipator' (April 1896) plus articles on the Contagious Diseases Acts and aspects of feminism. Wolstenholme Elmy's articles after 1897 in the *Westminster Review*, that included a series on 'Judicial Sex Bias' and another series on 'Women in Local Administration' as well as pieces on suffrage, some reviews and an obituary* of her husband, 'Pioneers, O Pioneers' (April 1906), all bear her own pseudonym, 'Ignota'. Articles from 1907, after her husband's death, are published under her own name, yet the piece, 'The Married Woman's Property Act, 1882' in the *Englishwoman's*

*Review** (Sept. 1882) was signed E. C. W. Elmy. In 1911, she was contributing to *Votes for Women* and the *New Age** magazine.

She wrote to Sylvia Pankhurst in 1908, 'My writing day begins at 3am and lasts as long as I am too tired to do more'. But it seemed that Mrs Wolstenholme Emy was never too tired to do more. **SBA**
Source: Banks 1985, Crawford 1999, Doughan 1987, *ODNB*.

ELWIN, WHITWELL (1816-1900) Whitwell Elwin was the epitome of a mid-Victorian scholarly clergyman whose literary endeavours often took precedence over theological matters. His 40-year connection with the *Quarterly Review** began in 1843 when John Gibson Lockhart*, then the editor*, published his first article, and continued until 1885. Elwin succeeded Lockhart as editor in 1853, a surprising choice, some thought, given Elwin's apparent other-worldliness. Four times a year he left his parsonage in Booton, Norfolk to go up to London to prepare the *Review* for the press, not a practice which would have commended itself to his predecessors in the heyday of the *Quarterly's* political* influence. The village of Booton did not have a post office when Elwin was appointed to the editorship. One was created, and a post box installed near the rectory gate in order to handle the volume of editorial correspondence. The irony was that Elwin was notoriously dilatory in answering his post.

Although the review's political* agenda was less urgent in the 1850s, Elwin's contributors included Lord Robert Cecil and W. E. Gladstone, and he took care to secure authoritative reviewers on all subjects. He was a remorseless reviser of the work of others, so much so that one irritated contributor returned a cheque, claiming that the article that was printed was not his at all. Elwin was a prolific reviewer, contributing over 40 articles to the review. He described the responsibilities of editorship as going about with 'a clog on my leg'. Eventually, in 1860, he wearied of the task, and John Murray*, the review's publisher, found a successor. Elwin commented, 'I feel like a man who has been transported for seven years and whose time is up'.

Elwin's bookishness was legendary. He spent a great deal of time in bed reading, and perfected a technique of reading large folio volumes while lying down. He continued to combine literary* work with his parochial duties for a further 40 years, continuing his contributions to the *Quarterly* and taking over John Wilson Croker's* edition of Pope, and editing a selection of Byron. G. M. Young suggested that anyone wishing to understand the

Victorian mind should turn away from remembered names, and study three men, among them Whitwell Elwin, 'reflecting... on the breadth of their interests... and the quiet and substantial permanence of what they did'. JS

Sources: Elwin 1902, *ODNB*, Shattock 1985, Young 1948.

EMPSON, WILLIAM (1791-1852) William Empson began to write for the *Edinburgh Review** in 1823 while a practising lawyer and member of Lincoln's Inn. The following year he was appointed Professor of Law at the East India College, Haileybury, where he continued to combine reviewing* with his academic responsibilities. He supported the appointment of Macvey Napier* to succeed Francis Jeffrey* as editor* of the *Edinburgh* in 1829 and became the de facto subeditor*, using his London base and metropolitan connections as a counterweight to Napier's provincial bias and Edinburgh residence.

Empson was a versatile and prolific reviewer*, writing on history*, biography, literature*, law* and politics* over a period of almost 30 years, sometimes contributing two articles to a number. He acted as a conduit for political intelligence, and sounded out likely metropolitan*-based reviewers. In 1838 he cemented his connections with Jeffrey by marrying his only daughter. Empson exuded vagueness and other-worldliness in his personal demeanour but this did not disguise a shrewdness and intelligence which served the *Edinburgh* and both Napier and Jeffrey well. When Napier died in 1847 Empson succeeded to the editorship of the review, moving its operations from Edinburgh to London, and making it, as observers noted, 'Edinburgh in name only'. Harriet Martineau* reported the allegation that both Empson and Napier automatically inserted all articles sent to the review by Whig ministers, even when they contradicted each other. She also alleged that Empson did not keep a sufficient grip on the literary reviewing of the *Edinburgh*, so that its reputation declined under his command. His five-year period as editor ended abruptly with his death. That the *Edinburgh* was no longer the influential journal it once had been owed more to the growing influence of the newspaper press and the establishment of competition* than to Empson's lack of editorial skills. JS

Sources: Cockburn 1852, Martineau 1877, *ODNB*, Shattock 1989.

ENGINEER (1856-) The *Engineer* was a technical and scientific* weekly* journal priced* 5d unstamped or 6d stamped. Its first issue bravely stated that 'it is mainly by the diffusion of knowledge that new knowledge is evolved', and that a periodical like itself dedicated to the dissemination of the latest scientific discoveries – always with an eye to their practical applications – could 'claim to be regarded itself among the aids to advancement'. To this end, it included detailed descriptions of new inventions (illustrated* with high quality engravings), reprinted extracts from scientific journals (often including passages translated from foreign periodicals, reflecting the journal's willingness to look overseas for cutting-edge developments), a 'Note Book' section* that provided synoptic updates on recent discoveries and news* in the various branches of science and 'The Patent Journal', a detailed list of patents applied for and granted complete with the name and sometimes the address of the inventor.

The *Engineer* always insisted on the interdependence of science and technology, and was clearly intended to be of considerable practical use: as well as articles explaining how to use a new lathe or drill, the journal contained price lists for metals, timber and coal. Small columns* detailed the new inventions that pertained to the various branches of industry: transport, agriculture and mining for example. Mining* received especially detailed coverage, with regional* correspondents providing weekly updates, presumably because this was the primary source of raw materials. Classified advertisements*, where engineers* offered their services or sought employees (from steam roller drivers to travelling salesmen) and tools and equipment were bought and sold took their place alongside commercial advertisements, mainly for heavy machinery and raw materials.

Zerah Colburn, the talented American engineer and journalist who had first become editor* in 1858, finally resigned the editorship in 1864 to begin a rival weekly entitled *Engineering**, but this cheaper competition* appears to have had little impact on the *Engineer*. By 1866 (when the price* had risen by 1d to 6d unstamped* and 7d stamped), advertisements* took up around 14 pages while a further 18 or so pages made up the rest of the magazine*. George Leopold Riche had also taken over as publisher* and printer, and was still in place in 1885. Though the magazine continued to grow – especially in terms of the number of advertisements*, which occupied 58 pages from a total of 84 in 1899 (when Sydney White was publisher and printer) – in its format* and approach it remained in essence unchanged, and still cost 6d at the close of the century. The success of the journal perhaps owed something to its ability to assess and explain the rapidly changing technologies of the second half of the nineteenth century within the framework of a familiar format. MaT

Sources: Houghton 1975, *ODNB, Waterloo*.

ENGINEERING, AN ILLUSTRATED WEEKLY JOURNAL (1866-) Founded by the American engineer and journalist* Zerah Colburn (1832-1870), *Engineering* was a weekly* priced* at 4d unstamped and 5d stamped. Initially, it undercut its competitor*, the *Engineer*, though by 1870 its price had risen to 6d and 7d, at which price it remained to the end of the century, matching that of its already well-established rival. Colburn, who had himself previously edited the *Engineer* (resigning as editor* in 1864) and returned from the United States to edit the new title, possessed skills as an editor and journalist that were crucial to the early success of the new journal. Following Colburn's death in 1870, James Dredge (1840-1906) and W. H. Maw – who had previously been subeditor* – became joint editors. Dredge in particular proved to be a worthy successor, and was actively involved in managing the journal until May 1903, when paralysis prevented him from continuing.

Similar in many respects to its rival, *Engineering* was intended to keep readers abreast of the latest inventions and developments that were likely to impact on the profession. Detailed descriptions of the functioning of new machines – usually illustrated* with engravings and later with photographic* reproductions – were designed to be of practical use both to those who might operate them and to those involved in developing and perfecting such machinery. Large-scale building and engineering projects featured (e.g., the works at the Newhaven Harbour or the regular reports on the progress of the Indian railways), and details of new patents. There was also a healthy portion of classified advertisements*, alongside commercial advertisements for heavy machinery and raw materials.

A key difference between *Engineering* and the *Engineer* was that the former contained much less undigested hard science*. Where the *Engineer* asked its readers to engage with developments in science as well as with their technological ramifications, *Engineering* focused on practice at the expense of theory. By boasting that '[i]n no other publication is Engineering and Mechanical Science treated with more strict reference to its commercial results', *Engineering* sought to appeal to the aspiring entrepreneur rather than to the gentleman amateur. MaT

Sources: *ODNB, Waterloo*.

ENGLEFIELD, HENRY CHARLES (1752-1822) Englefield published numerous articles on antiquarian and scientific* subjects. His first, on Reading Abbey, appeared in 1782 in *Archaeologia*. As well as papers published in the transactions* of learned societies, Englefield contributed many articles to William Nicholson's* *Journal of Natural Philosophy* and Alexander Tilloch's* *Philosophical Magazine*. A member of the English Catholic gentry, Englefield's diverse antiquarian and scientific interests earned him election to various learned organisations including the Society of Antiquaries. His controversial defeat in the presidential election of the latter in 1812 was lampooned by George Cruikshank* in his satirical* monthly* the *Scourge*.

Englefield also had a strong interest in the visual arts. His development of a durable red colour from madder earned him the Society for the Encouragement of Arts, Manufactures and Commerce's gold medal and his findings were published in their *Transactions* for 1804. His interest in science led to his devising improved instruments for travellers, including a portable mountain barometer in 1806 that was first announced in the *Journal of Natural Philosophy*, and in 1814 a compact telescope, details of which were revealed in the *Philosophical Magazine*. DHL

Sources: Burton 1909, Evans 1956, Nurse 2000, *ODNB*, Ward 1909.

ENGLISH GENTLEMAN (1824-1827) The *English Gentleman* was a London Sunday paper owned by E. D. Poucheé (receiver of stagecoach duties at Somerset House) and published at 7 Brydges Street, the Strand. The first issue appeared 19 December, edited* initially by Walter Lane, with Charles Molloy Westmacott* and William Maginn* involved by early 1827, when more satiric* and scandalous copy began to be printed. The paper was conservative, invoking the doings of Tory cronies such as John Wilson Croker* and Theodore Hook*, and in the crisis after Lord Liverpool's death supported Canning. In November of 1827 it was sold to Westmacott, who amalgamated it with *Nimrod*, a sporting* paper. The *English Gentleman* served as a proving ground for the pioneering tabloid techniques of the *Age*, which Westmacott had purchased the previous July. DEL

Sources: privately held manuscript letter from Walter Lane to E. D. Poucheé.

ENGLISH ILLUSTRATED MAGAZINE (1883-1913) The *English Illustrated Magazine* began as a shilling* monthly* published* by Macmillan and edited* by J. W. Comyns Carr* (1883-1889),

The English Illustrated Magazine.

OCTOBER, 1883.

THE COURT OF APPEAL.

FROM THE OLD LAW COURTS TO THE NEW.

THERE were some persons perhaps who on the 4th of December last, when the Queen went in pomp to open the new Law Courts, betook themselves not to the new hall, but to the old. Possibly they had no choice but to put up with the less gorgeous of the two pageants, for they were neither jurors in the Belt case nor otherwise persons of mark. Or it may be they preferred to see the end of an old story—a very old story—to the beginning of a new.

No. 1

For such a choice there was something to be said. They may live to see many noteworthy sights in Mr. Street's new Courts; they will hardly see another procession of judges in Westminster Hall, and when the procession had passed, they may have felt that they had seen what was worth remembering. Not that there was any excuse for profound emotion, but still something had happened; the curtain had fallen on a scene which began who shall say how long ago? Possibly some readers may be so far like-minded with these spectators, that having seen through the artist's eye something of the judges as they sit in their new Courts, and being of the sound opinion that a good picture needs no bush of words, they will be willing to throw a glance back on Westminster Hall.

By a little manipulation of definitions it might be proved that the Courts have not left Westminster, and possibly the proof might satisfy a sentimental craving, for Westminster is the capital of England, and

B 2

Figure 16: The front page of the *English Illustrated Magazine*, Oct. 1883.

formerly art critic for the *Pall Mall Gazette**. Its American edition (entitled *New Illustrated Magazine* Feb. 1897-Sept. 1901) challenged *Harper's** and *Century*, while at home it increasingly faced competition from inexpensive and lavishly illustrated* titles that proliferated in the 1890s. Under pressure from the *Strand** and others, the *English Illustrated Magazine* reduced its price* to 6d in 1893, gradually expanded from 64 pages to 112, and moved from publisher to publisher as circulation* declined: 11 months with Edward Arnold, five years with the *Illustrated London News** and on through William Ingram, T. Fisher Unwin and Hutchinson's before settling down with Central Publishing in 1905.

The magazine sought a family* readership: 'we are inundated with letters* if anything appears in its pages to which the "British Matron" finds it possible to take exception', Frederick Macmillan told Margaret Oliphant* in 1892 (Worth 2003). The inaugural serial* by Tractarian Charlotte Yonge* set the tone, and as Siobhan Brownson records, writers more daringly inclined, such as Thomas Hardy*, censored* themselves to sell to *EIM*. Contributors ranged from romantic novelist Stanley Weyman to George Gissing, Edmund Gosse*, Francis Thompson, H. G. Wells*, Henry James* and Stephen Crane. Sharing the earnest tone of some of the fiction were articles on travel, natural history, political* economy*, history*, and popular science*, typically addressing readers* eager to learn but not necessarily well educated. For less intellectual subscribers, the magazine provided celebrity* profiles, such as an 1894 piece on W. E. Gladstone as grandfather, and articles on sport*: cricket, including a contribution by cricketing great W. G. Grace; billiards; fox-hunting (illustrated by Randolph Caldecott*); rowing at Cambridge; and, in 1902, the newly fashionable ping-pong, with diagrams.

As Caldecott's presence on the staff suggests, the *English Illustrated Magazine* was initially not merely profusely but also well illustrated. Headpieces and tailpieces came from Arts and Crafts notables such as Heywood Sumner and Henry Ryland. *Punch* caricaturist* Harry Furniss* was a long-time contributor; work by Hugh Thomson*, George Du Maurier*, Walter Crane*, and Kate Greenaway* could also be found in the *Magazine*'s pages. Carr, its first editor, was co-director of two art galleries and well situated to solicit articles and drawings from prominent artists. After Carr resigned over Macmillan's decision to reduce the number of engravings, his successors Clement King Shorter* and Bruce Ingram both edited* the *Illustrated London News* (among other *ILN* titles) concurrently with *English Illustrated Magazine*.

Arguably, however, the *English Illustrated Magazine* lost something of its vision over time. Circulation*-boosting efforts were initiated, without lasting effect. A *Bookman** article in October 1896 noted that under Shorter 'the magazine is neither strictly literary nor strictly popular' (110). And while the *Magazine* continued to instruct about painters past and present, its own look grew less individual, with photographs* and colour illustrations* increasingly dominant over woodcuts*. As the roster of writers also dimmed in brilliance, ultimately the *English Illustrated Magazine* may have become insufficiently differentiated to hold its audience. **CN**

Sources: Brownson 2000, 'Chronicle and Comment' 1896, Ellis 1993, Magazine Data File, Worth 2003.

***ENGLISH MECHANIC* (1865-1926)** The *English Mechanic* was the first successful scientific* magazine. Founded by publisher George Maddick (1824-1880), its first issue appeared 31 March. The industrial revolution had created an audience for a scientific magazine for the common man: the 'bone and sinew workers' of the country who were actually working with the latest technological innovations. The weekly* magazine* was an instant success and in 1866 the *English Mechanic*'s price rose from 1d to 2d after absorbing Maddick's *Mirror of Science* (1865-1866). The improved magazine was expanded so as to optimize its advertising* potential, with a full eight pages dedicated to adverts.

In 1869 it was sold to John Passmore Edwards*, a clever businessman and philanthropist who earlier had tried to buy the ailing *Mechanics' Magazine**. With the help of his friend Ebeneezer Job Kibblewhite, Edwards made the *English Mechanic* the most popular* scientific magazine of the day. In due course, the magazine absorbed all of its competitors: the *Mechanic* (1868), *World of Science* (1867-1868), *Penny Mechanic* (1868), *Scientific Opinion* (1868-1870) and the *British and Foreign Mechanic* (1869-1870), taking 'the best portions of their animating spirit'. The *English Mechanic* grew in size* to 32 pages and its circulation* rose to an impressive 30,000 copies a week.

The *English Mechanic* was successful mostly because it managed to forge a close bond with its middle-class* readership*. Readers were allowed to send in letters* and articles and could correspond with other readers through the magazine. Sections* such as 'our subscribers', 'notes and queries', 'letters to the editor', 'replies to queries', 'answers* and notices to correspondents and readers', allowed readers to ask or say whatever they wanted. But the *English Mechanic* was also informative because of its articles, reviews*, and explanations of many of the contributors of which most prominent were E. J. Kibblewhite, who later became the editor*, Lord Beckett and Lord Rayleigh; but Captain Sir Andrew Noble, 'A Fellow of the R. A. S.' (pseudonym), Richard Proctor*, William Taylor, Alfred Russel Wallace*, John Hampeden, John T. Sprague and S. Bottone also made major contributions..

The magazine remained very popular until the First World War, which decimated its readership, and the journal went into rapid decline. A title change to *English Mechanics* could not prevent this, and in 1926 the magazine was forced to merge* with the *Amateur Mechanic and Work* and to become *English and Amateur Mechanics,* which in its turn was transformed into *Home Mechanics* in 1940. **AnE**

Sources: Brock 1980, King 2004, Lightman 1994, *Waterloo.*

***ENGLISH REPUBLIC* (1851-1855)** The *English Republic* was the brainchild of the radical engraver and ardent republican, William James Linton*. First published in Leeds, it was distributed with a temperance* paper, the *Truth Seeker and Present Age* (1849-1852). It circulated in various formats later and until its demise, a reflection of the struggle, that Linton had to make the journal pay. Thus in 1852-1853 it was offered as a weekly* series of political* tracts and from 1854-1855 it reverted to its monthly* format* when Linton enlisted the help of the bookseller James Watson*.

By 1854 too Linton was publishing the *Republic* from his new home, Brantwood, in the Lake District (made famous by its next occupant, John Ruskin*) with financial support from the northeast radical Joseph Cowen*, and the assistance of a small coterie of like-minded individuals. These included the Cheltenham Chartist, W. E. Adams*, who later edited* the *Newcastle Weekly Chronicle*. Linton's opening leader* for the *Republic* outlined his vision for reviving the 'earnestness which marked the brief day of our Commonwealth' and the creation of a Republican Party. Linton was no narrow nationalist, however, and the *Republic* offered a platform for the views of prominent European exiles including Ledru Rollin, Arnold Ruge, Alexander Herzen and, most prominently, Giuseppe Mazzini, one of the architects of Italian

reunification. Linton also published Victor Hugo's 'Chatiments' in translation and articles by internationally acclaimed writers such as Wendell Phillips. Commercially unsuccessful, the *Republic* nevertheless played a key role in supporting the incipient republicanism which emerged in Britain in the mid-1850s. In addition, it helped to maintain the momentum for electoral reform after the decline of Chartism. **JA**

Sources: Allen 2007, Ashton 1993, Joseph Cowen Papers, Finn 1993, Smith 1973, W. E. Adams papers.

***ENGLISH WOMAN'S JOURNAL* (1858-1864)**

The *English Woman's Journal* was a monthly* publication begun by the liberal feminist* Langham Place group of women activists and funded by its prominent member, Barbara Bodichon*. The journal promoted, recorded and discussed their activities and those of other feminist enterprises. The magazine* was published* by the English Woman's Journal Co., a concern set up by the Langhamites, and in which several were shareholders. When Emily Faithfull*, another Langham member, initiated the Victoria Press, the only press in the country at that time to be staffed by women, the *English Woman's Journal* moved its printing there from 1860. Bessie Parkes* was the founding editor*, assisted by Matilda Mary Hays*; Emily Davies took charge in 1862.

Parkes wanted the *Journal* to provide a forum that brought together various reform causes in the hope of uniting individual efforts. It was primarily interested in women's employment and education as keys to progress. It reported on the reformist activities of other enterprises such as the Society for Promoting Employment for Women (with which the journal shared an office). The *English Woman's Journal* posited the middle-class* woman as having a special responsibility to further opportunities for women in these spheres. It supported middle-class philanthropy and provided models of work and education from which, it hoped, working-class women might learn. George Eliot had written to Parkes recommending 'the *less* literature the better' but the journal also published short stories and poetry*.

During its first year the magazine collected only a few hundred subscribers, accumulating to 700 by 1859. However, Sheila R. Herstein' argues that women from all around the country used the journal 'to create the country's first effective feminist network' and Margaret Beetham recognizes its importance in terms of the 'development of feminism as a theory and practice'. The example of the Victoria Press was soon followed by the establishment of

the Caledonian Press in Edinburgh in 1862, and its launch of the *Rose, the Shamrock and the Thistle* (1862-1865; see Women's periodicals*). **BP**
Sources: Beetham 1996, Herstein 1985, *ODNB, Waterloo.*

ENGLISHMAN'S MAGAZINE (APRIL-OCT. 1831) The *Englishman's Magazine* though short-lived, was a lively, illustrated*, liberal monthly* significant for publishing the early works of Alfred Tennyson and John Forster*, and interesting as an early venture of Victorian publisher* Edward Moxon (1801-1868). Courtney notes that it formed 'a remarkable bridge between the Romantics and the Victorians' (148), containing some of Lamb's *Last Essays of Elia*, poems* by John Clare and Leigh Hunt, as well as Arthur Hallam's prescient review*-article of Tennyson's *Poems, Chiefly Lyrical*. Launched in the context of the political* upheavals of the first Reform Bill, it was staunchly reformist, taking the editorial persona of 'Daniel Rex' to invoke the libertarian ideals of Daniel Defoe, and adding strong advocacy for the Anti-Slavery Society via contributor Thomas Pringle*, with sympathy for the Polish Revolt of 1830-1831. Other period-defining contexts addressed include the publishing schemes of the 'March of Intellect', and the fears aroused by the spread of cholera across Europe in 1831.

Begun as a collaboration* between Moxon, Thomas Hurst, William Kennedy and Leitch Ritchie (then popular in the literary annuals), Moxon took over sole proprietorship* with the fifth number in August 1831. He assembled, with Lamb's assistance, such contributors as Caroline Norton*, John Banim and William Scargill. The economic pressures of the period, however, made it impossible for the young publisher to compete with other such popular new ventures as *Fraser's Magazine** and the *Metropolitan Magazine**. The series of fine, engraved prints in the first four numbers disappeared, and the monthly 'Journal of Literature*' was replaced by Lamb's 'Epistles of DeFoe'. Unfortunately, there remain no paratextual* records of the magazine; therefore readership* issues and reasons for the journal's demise remain problematic. **RKL**
Sources: Campbell 1889, Courtney 1983, Gilfallan 1909, Lamb 1935, Merriam 1939, *ODNB,* Ostrom 1991, Prance 1982.

ENGLISHWOMAN (1895-1899) 'Number 1 of the *Englishwoman* edited* by Ella Hepworth Dixon'* was widely advertised by the publishers, F. V. White Company, in several periodicals including the *World** and the *Sketch**, as well as on hoardings,

or so Ella Hepworth Dixon* recounts in her memoirs. The advertisements* promised: 'An Illustrated* Magazine of Fiction, Fashion*, Society, and the Home. Stories by the Most Popular Authors of the Day. Articles of General Interest and Interviews with Celebrities*, Profusely Illustrated. Monthly Prize Competitions. Exhaustive Articles on Every Topic Connected with the House and Home. Well received at first, for example in the *Lady's Pictorial**, this 6d monthly did not retain Dixon as editor* for long. As she recounted in an article in *Woman** in September 1896, due to 'circumstances over which I had no control, within half a year, the *Englishwoman* had changed publishers' and, consequently, changed editors. From then on no editor's* or publisher's names were given until the names Simpkin*, Marshall, Hamilton and Kent appeared. The *Englishwoman* continued as a 'high class Illustrated Magazine Published Monthly*', and employed the pens of prestigious writers including Marie Belloc, Rhoda Broughton, Mona Caird*, Violet Hunt, Eliza Lynn Linton*, 'John Strange Winter'. Its primary innovation was the setting up of an employment agency for women from August 1898. **VF**
Sources: Dixon 1896, Dixon 1930, Fehlbaum 2005, *Lady's Pictorial* 23 March 1895, Onslow 2000.

ENGLISHWOMAN'S DOMESTIC MAGAZINE (1852-1879) The *Englishwoman's Domestic Magazine* was launched by Samuel Beeton* as a 2d monthly* with the avowed aim of helping readers 'to make home happy'. Beeton's winning formula (he claimed a circulation* of 50,000 in 1857) brought together elements of the aristocratic lady's journals with those of the new middle-class* press. It included serialized* fiction, fashion* and, after 1860, high-quality fashion plates, together with domestic* advice and lively letters* columns*. On their marriage in 1856 Isabella Beeton* became 'The Editress' and her *Book of Household Management* had its origins in the magazine's recipe columns. The price* went up to 6d, and it changed to a larger, more lavishly illustrated*, format* with extended letters* pages in 1860. Isabella attended the Paris fashion shows and not only provided pictures and detailed accounts of the 'modes' but also paper patterns, an important innovation. After her death in 1865, Matilda Browne* ('Myra') took over her role. However, almost immediately Samuel's bankruptcy forced the sale of the Beeton name and all its titles to Ward, Lock*. The magazine became briefly notorious for a correspondence on tight-lacing and on whipping young women, which Beeton exploited for further publicity.

The success of the *Magazine* can partly be attributed to Beeton's skilful advertising* and use of prizes, special offers and pull-outs. However, it also rested on the development of a successful formula; a mixture of domestic advice, fashion*, fiction, a consistently lively correspondence column and a liberal stance on women's suffrage and women's access to print. This provided a pattern for the middle-class* women's magazine* for the next century. **MRB**

Sources: Beetham 1996, *Englishwoman's Domestic Magazine*, Hughes 2005, *Waterloo*.

ENGLISHWOMAN'S REVIEW OF SOCIAL AND INDUSTRIAL QUESTIONS (1866-1910) The *Englishwoman's Review of Social and Industrial Questions* operated as the monthly *Englishwoman's Review: A Journal of Woman's Work* until 1870, when it changed its frequency* to quarterly* as well as its title. Its founder-editor*, Emilia Jessie Boucherett*, a member of the feminist* Langham Place group, had insisted on her 'intention to follow the plan of the recently defunct *English Woman's Journal*'*, an earlier Langham Place project. Boucherett's absorbing interest in the themes that exercised this group, primarily female education, employment and legal reform, are evidenced in the *Review's* contents. Contributors included the Langhamites, Emily Davies and Barbara Bodichon*, as well as Dinah Mulock and Frances Power Cobbe*.

The *Englishwoman's Review* eschewed fiction and poetry* to move away from a magazine format* and towards that of a bulletin of political activities. Boucherett funded the project, maintaining that the *Review* would lose its integrity if it had to compete commercially. The *Review* was at the centre of a burgeoning feminist network. It printed records of reform groups' meetings, summarized political* debates such as those over married women's property rights, extracted government reports, listed degrees taken by female students, and reported overseas, as well as local, feminist initiatives. The *Englishwoman's Review* was a production very much aware of its own status as the record of a movement in dynamic progress. It maintained an interactive relationship with its readers in its lively 'Letters'* pages and through its tone of encouragement to action.

Boucherett was conscious of the potentially curtailing effects of the *Englishwoman's Review's* limited readership*: circulation* had only reached 2,000 by 1910. However, the longevity of the review affirms the middle-class* woman's ongoing interest in feminist activities even when unleavened by popular or literary features. The magazine lasted until 1910

with, in succession, Caroline Ashurst Biggs, Helen Blackburn*, and Antoinette Mackenzie taking over as competent editors. **BP**

Sources: Doughan and Sanchez 1987, Fraser 2003, Murray and Stark 1985, Onslow 2000, *Waterloo*.

ERA (1838-1939) *Era* was the leading theatrical journal of the Victorian period. It had its unlikely origins in a Sunday paper published, from 30 September 1838 by the Licensed Victuallers' Association, to represent the interests of those in the catering trade. As the profession had connections to the horseracing and theatre communities, both of these interests came to feature prominently in the initial issues. Since the early editors* Leitch Ritchie and Frederick Ledger both had a particular interest in theatre, the magazine had become exclusively concerned with theatre by the 1850s. Its up-to-date, comprehensive reports of metropolitan* and provincial* performances came to make it a register of the contemporary stage, and as music* hall developed, this was included. *Era* also published biographical pieces on actors and actresses, and knowledgeable articles on particular theatres, and on theatrical issues, sometimes with illustrations*. In 1872 James Grant* declared that 'in relation to the amount and accuracy of its theatrical intelligence, it far surpasses every other weekly* journal'. In the 1870s it circulated* 500 copies among the Licensed Victuallers Association, and sold 5,000 to the general public.

From 1868, under the editorship of Edward Ledger, the *Era Almanack* (1868-1913) gathered much of the journal's features into an annual* form, providing an invaluable account of drama in England in the later nineteenth century. **LJ**

Sources: Bourne 1887, Grant 1872, Lowe 1970, *Mitchell's*, *Wellesley*.

ESCOTT, THOMAS HAY SWEET (1844-1924) Although he entered a teaching position at King's College London on graduating from Oxford, Escott began almost immediately to write for the *Saturday Review*￼* in 1865, and soon became one of Britain's most energetic and versatile journalists*. As one of the clever young gentlemen who congregated at the Bohemian Arundel Club, he wrote for *Fun**, the *Glow-Worm* (which he briefly edited*) and *Tomahawk*￼* in the 1860s. He was also a major contributor of articles on light social topics to the middlebrow *Belgravia*￼* and in like vein to *London Society*￼* and *Temple Bar*￼* in the 1860s and 1870s.

In 1866 he became a regular leader* writer for the *Standard*￼*, and continued for over 40 years. He also wrote the political* articles in the *World*￼* (as he informed Gladstone) from its inception into the 1880s at least. He was Thomas Hamber's partner in founding the *Hour*, a Conservative London morning daily* (1873-1876), and he wrote on politics for *Lloyd's Weekly Newspaper**. He reached the zenith of his journalistic career in 1882 when he succeeded John Morley* as editor of the *Fortnightly Review**, on which he had started in 1879. He was now extremely well connected and writing regularly on politics for four periodicals with different readerships* and political complexions. He was close to several ambitious politicians – particularly Joseph Chamberlain, Lord Randolph Churchill and John Morley – who used him as an information source, a back-channel for confidential communication with other politicians, and a media voice. When his health broke down in 1885, Chamberlain and Churchill combined to organize a subscription for him.

Although Escott never regained his political clout, he continued to publish until his death. Journals as various as the *Globe**, *Argosy**, *Fraser's Magazine**, *Blackwood's Magazine**, *Macmillan's Magazine**, the *Eclectic Magazine,* the *New Review**, the *Contemporary Review**, the *National Review** and the *Quarterly Review** shared his remarkable output. He is best remembered as a talented journalist and social historian of his own times. His obituary* in *The Times* (17 June 1924) suggested that his death marked the end of an era: 'With Mr. T. H. S. Escott, the late Editor of the *Fortnightly Review**, who died at Hove on Saturday at the age of 79, there disappears almost the last link with the great period of what may be called "Mid-Victorian" journalism'. **CAK**

Sources: Kent 1998, Koss 1981, *ODNB, Waterloo.*

ESPINASSE, FRANCIS (1823-1912) A journalist of some note in his time, Espinasse worked for most of his career as a freelancer, and contributed to countless periodicals and newspapers including Leigh Hunt's* *London Journal**, *Macmillan's Magazine** and the *Bookman**. From 1851 he became one of the chief contributors to the *Critic**, with his copy appearing either under his own name or under one of three pseudonyms*: 'Herodotus Smith', 'Frank Grave' and 'Lucian Paul'. One of the chief reasons for the continuing interest and importance of his work is the insight it often gives into the nineteenth-century literary* scene, and the press in particular. A notable series of nine articles (signed 'Herodotus Smith') on nineteenth-century periodicals – including the *Quarterly Review**, *Westminster Review**, and the *British Quarterly Review**

– appearing in the *Critic* (1851-1852) remains a useful introduction to the topic. Espinasse's in-depth knowledge of the workings of the press suggests that he was probably involved on the editorial side in some capacity, and his obituary* in *The Times** indicates that he succeeded James Hannay (1827-1873) as editor* of the Tory *Edinburgh Courant**, a post Hannay left in 1864.

Espinasse also specialized in biographical sketches, and he wrote a series of articles on 'Notable Contemporaries' for the *Critic*. His friendships with Wordsworth, Carlyle* and Thackeray* – and many other of the literary celebrities* of his day – provided ample material for his journalism and for his *Literary Recollections*, a book composed partly of material that had been previously published in periodicals. He contributed many lives to the *Imperial Dictionary of Universal Biography* as well as to George Smith's* *Dictionary of National Biography.* **MaT**
Sources: Espinasse 1893, Sullivan, *The Times* 4 Jan. 1912.

EVANGELICAL CHRISTENDOM (1847-1899)
Evangelical Christendom was a monthly* religious* review* with an interdenominational outlook and contributor list. It aimed to promote the interests of the Evangelical Alliance, an umbrella organization formed to bring evangelicals together and promote their interests in society. Profits from the magazine were given to the Alliance, but the magazine was run discretely. It reported the Evangelical Alliance's activities at home and abroad and constructed a community of readers* based on an opposition to 'Romanism' and 'Rationalism'. The combative rhetoric of the magazine encouraged and reported Protestant missions around the world. Biographical sketches outlined lives of religious figures and poetry* also supported the journal's cross-denominational religiosity. Its contributors were mostly clergymen but also included Prince Albert (1819-1861) and Sir Culling Eardley Eardley (1805-1863), the founding president of the Evangelical Alliance. The original papers that held a prominent place in its early years later gave way to shorter pieces of intelligence from around the world and home. 'Home Intelligence' reported meetings of the Religious Tract Society* and events at Exeter Hall. By the 1890s *Evangelical Christendom* was dependent on the Evangelical Alliance for funding. In 1899 the decision was made to replace the monthly with the *Evangelical Alliance Quarterly** in the hope that a new format* would prove more profitable. **BP**
Sources: Bebbington 1989, *Missionary Periodicals Database, ODNB, Waterloo.*

EVANGELICAL MAGAZINE (1793-1904) The *Evangelical Magazine* was founded as an interdenominational Calvinist alternative to the *Arminian Magazine*. Published monthly* and priced* 6d, the *Evangelical Magazine* was established by well-known Congregationalists and Anglicans, with the first editor* being an Anglican, and the second, George Burder, a Congregationalist. The emergence of the *Christian Observer** in 1802 as an organ for Anglican Evangelicals meant that the *Evangelical Magazine* soon became focused on the interests of Non-conformist Evangelicals. This shift was one of a number of changes that took place during the history of the *Evangelical Magazine*, with the periodical seeing the launch of several new series. None of the changes was that radical, however. The preface to the new series of 1823 was typical in its claim that the magazine would continue the work of the past 30 years: 'our aim will be, under the divine blessing, still by the same means to promote the glory of God and the interests of evangelical religion*'. While the *Evangelical Magazine* addressed a range of topics, such as literature*, throughout the nineteenth century, the focus never shifted far from subjects that were clearly and identifiably evangelical. These included missionary* notices and theological articles on doctrines such as justification by faith and the Cross. **MK**

Sources: Altholz 1989, Billington 1986.

EVANS, EDMUND (1826-1905) Edmund Evans was one of the most successful entrepreneurs among those who brought together the roles of engraver*, printer, art editor* and mentor to the engraving trade. His particular expertise lay in colour printing*, and his reputation was established by his development of the 'yellow-back'* format* for publishing* cheap novels mainly at railway bookstalls*. An apprenticeship with Ebenezer Landells* brought Evans into contact with *Punch** and the *Illustrated London News**, and he worked with another of Landells's apprentices Birket Foster* for both magazines in their early years.

He left Landells's employ in 1847 and set up on his own as a jobbing engraver, but struggled to establish himself in a competitive* market. His productive and commercially successful later career was more concerned with the production of illustrated* books than with periodicals. Evans was largely responsible for the development of the illustrated toy book, bringing Walter Crane* and Kate Greenaway* to widespread public attention. His expertise in colour printing techniques, however, did have important ramifications for the periodical

press, especially his early use in the mid-1880s of photo-reprographic* methods for colour illustrations. **BM**

Sources: Engen 1990, Houfe 1978, *ODNB*.

EVANS, FREDERICK MOULE (1832/3-1902) Frederick Moule Evans was the son of Frederick Mullet Evans*, of Bradbury and Evans*, publisher* and printers* for Charles Dickens*, *Punch**, and the *Daily News**. During the early 1860s, he helped his ailing farther to run the firm. After his father and W. H. Bradbury retired in 1865 from the business, and he was left in charge together with Bradbury's son Hardwick, the firm was renamed Bradbury, Evans & Company. When Fred's father died in 1870, he was left in a vulnerable position within the business and was effectively forced to leave.

Subsequently, in partnership with Dickens's eldest son, 'Charley', he started a paper*-making company which went bankrupt. In 1873 Evans and Dickens gained the printing contract for the Crystal Palace at Sydenham (then a venue for popular entertainment), publishing guidebooks, notices and play scripts, with the imprint Charles Dickens and Evans, Crystal Palace Press. Charley was now the editor* of his father's magazine, *All the Year Round** which they printed. Additionally, they undertook reprints from that magazine, work for the publisher Chapman and Hall* and Charley's own London reference books. Dickens and Evans had ceased to operate by 1896 (Berkeley: 283). **DHL**

Sources: Berkeley 1978, *ODNB*.

EVANS, FREDERICK MULLET (1803-1870) After employment as a printer in Southampton, in 1830 Frederick Evans established a partnership in London with William Bradbury* as Bradbury & Evans*. They gradually rose to a prominent position among London printers, and were later able to employ their sons in the firm, including Fred Moule Evans*. With the financial difficulties experienced by a new comic weekly*, *Punch**, they were persuaded by Mark Lemon*, its editor*, to become printers, publishers* and proprietors* from December 1842. In the 1850s they dabbled as publishers and printers with a curious corner of the colonial market, beginning with *Home News* (1851-1852), a monthly for British readers in India, and printing two other monthlies* in relation to Australia, the *Australian Mail* (1859) for readers in Britain, and the *English Mail* (1859-1860) for readers in Australia.

Evans's character was a vital element in the success of *Punch*. Described by one of his authors as 'a round, ruddy, genial, cheery, busy little man' his kindness, good humour and generosity toward the staff working on *Punch* ensured a productive working atmosphere. This harmony and conviviality was further enhanced by the famous weekly* *Punch* lunches. Evans recalled these years as some of the happiest of his life.

Bradbury and Evans replaced Chapman and Hall* as Charles Dickens's publisher in 1844, and in 1850 they became part owners with Dickens of his magazine, *Household Words**. They also published and printed the *Daily News**, a paper which Dickens edited briefly in 1846. This relationship with Dickens was also one of friendship and the families spent a great deal of time together at social events and on holiday. This provided an extra dimension to the rift when their involvement with Dickens ceased in acrimonious circumstances in 1858 after Evans refused to publish, in *Punch*, the author's justification for leaving his wife. The split was never repaired and Bradbury and Evans did not entirely recover from the break with Dickens, financially or emotionally.

In later years Evans suffered financial loss through bad investment in a paper-making venture, bankruptcy and exclusion from the Garrick Club. **DHL**
Sources: Davis 1999, *ODNB*, Patten 1978, Spielmann 1895.

EVANS, JOHN (1774-1828) Although John Evans's main employment was as a printer*, he also took on the proprietorship* and editorship* of several local* Bristol papers, buying for example the *Bristol Mercury* (1790-1909) in June 1808. By 1812, he was jointed by John Grabham. They were partners until 1814, when Evans left the firm to run his own printing business. However, in 1817 he took over as publisher* and editor of a Tory weekly*, the *Bristol Observer and Gloucester, Monmouth, Somerset and Wilts Courier* (1817-1823), for which he wrote numerous articles; when it folded in October 1823 he is listed only as its printer.

The lack of success of his many ventures led Evans to quit printing and take a clerical post. However, with the death of his wife, he left Bristol for London. Early in 1828, in addition to joining the printing firm of J. D. Maurice of Fenchurch Street, he became proprietor* of the Brunswick Theatre, in which he was killed during a rehearsal, when the building collapsed. **DHL**
Sources: Hudleston 1939, *ODNB*.

EVANS, MARIAN (1819-1880) Marian Evans, better known as 'George Eliot' the novelist, was characteristically scathing about the world of journalism. But Marian Evans's persistent distancing from the business in her later career was preceded by almost a decade of direct, intense engagement in the newspaper and periodical industry. She published her first poem* (signed M. A. E.) in the *Christian Observer** in January 1840 and wrote a series of playful, if uneven, pieces* and some brief reviews in the late 1840s for the *Coventry Herald and Observer*, then owned by her friend Charles Bray. Evans broke into metropolitan journalism through the intervention of the radical publisher* John Chapman*, with a review* of R. W. Mackay's *Progress of the Intellect* for the *Westminster Review** in 1851. She went on to edit* that journal (1851-1854) with Chapman, its new owner and publisher. Though Chapman was editor in name, Evans carried out the practical work of seeing each issue to print, introduced important innovations in layout and design, and marshalled the substantial 'review'* section on contemporary literature* for which the *Westminster* earned high praise. She was, in fact, the first woman editor* of a leading British intellectual quarterly*.

In July 1854 Evans left England for Germany but continued her association with the *Westminster*, writing the lengthy 'Belles Lettres' section (July1855-Jan.1857) and review articles, on among other topics, women novelists, the limitations of orthodox religion and developments in social science. Most of her 80 or so published articles appeared within this 18 months period. Evans often wrote on the same material for politically* diverse papers such as the radical *Leader**, and the conservative *Saturday Review**, shaping her work accordingly.

She took on the mantle of a male drama critic when she filled in briefly for G. H. Lewes's* 'Vivian' at the *Leader* in 1854. Also in the guise of a male persona she published her first fiction (the three stories that later comprised *Scenes of Clerical Life*) in eleven monthly parts in John Blackwood's* popular miscellany*, *Blackwood's Magazine** in 1857. Their success brought an end to her dependence on journalism as a career, although George Smith* persuaded her to return to periodical publication with the offer of £10,000 for a serial* for his *Cornhill Magazine**. *Romola*, with illustrations* by Frederic Leighton was published in 14 parts (July 1862-Aug. 1863) for the agreed reduced sum of £7,000.

George Eliot's poems* were published in *Blackwood's*, *Macmillan's Magazine**, the *Atlantic Monthly* and the *Canadian Monthly and National*

Review in the 1860s and 1870s, but despite offers, she never resumed regular work for the periodical press once her success as a fiction writer was established. However, in 1865 she added the weight of her name to the first issue of the *Fortnightly Review**, edited by Lewes, with a long review* essay on William Lecky, and provided four short, light pieces for George Smith's newly launched *Pall Mall Gazette**, under the pen name 'Saccharissa', her only work ever written in a stylized female voice.

Marian Evans was a pragmatic and capable journalist – influential in her introduction of German and French writers (including Heinrich Heine for instance) to an English public, a pioneering (if veiled) woman editor*, and a successful serial* fiction writer (in economic terms at least). She is interesting too for the way her work reveals the constraints imposed on the journalist by the journal but also for the intriguing complexity of tone of her writing that journalistic anonymity* both accommodated and provoked in the early to mid-1850s as the woman journalist negotiated a male-dominated intellectual sphere. **FD**
Sources: Ashton 2006, Baker and Ross 2002, Dillane 2004, *George Eliot Letters* 1954-1978, *Journals of George Eliot* 1998, Martin 1994, Pinney 1963, Rosenberg 1963.

EVENING NEWS (1881-1987)   An evening daily broadsheet, the *Evening News* was started in 1881 by Coleridge Kennard and Harry Marks as a popular London ½d paper. The price separated it from the more serious press, and its more conservative politics from the liberal ½d *Echo*. Edited by Frank Harris* (1882-1886), it was also distinguished by being printed on coloured paper, blue at first, then yellow and green. As an evening publication it depended upon the most up-to-date news* available, and at the beginning printed on its front page a daily 'epitome of news', listing recent events in Britain and abroad, culled from newspapers or news agency* telegrams. This was followed by slightly more detailed reports of events in Parliament*, financial news and a notable preponderance of international affairs. Lead articles and editorials contain discussions of politics* that are intelligent, and to some extent belie the paper's automatic classification (because of its low price*) as mass journalism. Certainly, if one were to measure it by the standards of today's tabloid press, the *News* – in its early years– appears passably serious in its news* coverage. However, its prurient fascination with gory murders and chilling suicides as well as its extensive coverage of sports* – including horse racing

– marked it out from the more upright dailies* of the nineteenth century.

It amalgamated with the *Evening Post* in 1889, to become the *Evening News and Post*, and a leader* in the first issue of the new series hoped that 'the popular style of the *Evening News* will be rendered still more attractive by being blended with the literary crispness and brightness of the *Evening Post*'. It denied any party affiliation, but owned up to 'Conservatively Democratic' sympathies, advocating the 'British Empire one and indivisible' at the same time as 'a fair day's work for a fair day's wage in Whitechapel as well as in Lancashire'. The emphasis of the paper remained on political* news. At this time, up to (and perhaps exceeding) five editions were produced daily: the precise number is difficult to determine because generally – whether in hard copy or on microfilm – only one edition of each issue is preserved. For the same reason, it is difficult to determine how much changed between editions.

As time wore on, trashy, populist material increasingly came to dominate, so that by 1894 the *Evening News* (which in this year dropped the '*Post*', reverting to its original title) was carrying information on forthcoming race meetings – including extensive lists of horses running and their weights – on its front page. A four-page Saturday supplement* entitled *Football* also started up, carrying that evening's, results and match reports for games played that day in the various leagues. A wealth of other sporting information – including the latest racing odds, comment pieces focusing on football, and gossip* about sportsmen – was also included. Political news and comment was increasingly confined to the inside of the paper, and became synoptic and partisan in character.

The *Evening News* was purchased by Alfred Harmsworth* and his brother Harold Harmsworth* in 1894 and was their first daily* newspaper. It claimed the largest circulation* of any London evening paper, and a few months later put the figure at nearly 400,000. A still more populist approach was adopted under the Harmsworths and Kennedy Jones*, who edited the paper 1894-1896, as the paper adopted the style and concerns of the New Journalism*. Short stories, chess puzzles, more illustrations*, gossip* and a 'Woman's World' column* containing fashion* and dressmaking tips, became regular features. Its coverage of sports remained a large part of its appeal, and there was (in 1901, and probably before) a special 'Cricket Edition' containing the latest scores. A blank space was left for these to be added after the rest of the paper had been printed. The paper remained a key component of Associated Newspapers until 1987 when it was incorporated into the *Evening Standard*. MaT

Sources: Evening News, Griffiths 1992, Griffiths 2006, *Waterloo*.

EVERYBODY'S ALBUM AND CARICATURE MAGAZINE (1834) One of several innovative magazines projected by the acerbic caricaturist*, Charles Jameson Grant*, *Everybody's Album* was one of few British magazines to exploit the new medium of lithography*. Only 14 issues were published(Jan.-July 1834), and the periodical was expensive at 6d an issue plain, and 1s coloured. The dramatic impact of the large multi-image page was enhanced by the grotesquerie of Grant's imagination and the sustained disgust of his social vision. The format* seems partly aimed at the scrap album compiler, and Grant's images do appear in many contemporary albums, although quite what his intended audience made of his violent critique of contemporary society is hard to imagine. Grant also published a lengthy series called the *Political Drama* (1833-1835) which used subversively large and crudely drawn woodcuts* to support a radical and alienated analysis of contemporary political* events. He also illustrated* several other radical journals, including Cousins's *Penny Satirist* (1837-1846). A shadowy figure with Chartist* connections, Grant was a major figure in developing the relationship between seriality* and caricature in the 1830s. BM

Sources: *ODNB*, Pound 1998.

EXAMINER (1808-1881) Brothers John and Leigh Hunt* founded the *Examiner*, a highbrow 16-page weekly* with the quixotic aim of using a literary sensibility to reform both government and journalism*. United in their hatred for 'kept journalists' who puffed* their patrons' projects, the Hunts aimed to publish without advertising*, a goal they eventually had to abandon. Literature* was as important to the Hunts as politics* and they named their paper after the eighteenth-century Tory mouthpiece edited by Jonathan Swift, in homage to his 'wit and fine writing'. John, a printer who had already edited the *Statesman*, handled the business side of the magazine, while Leigh, then an obscure young poet and essayist, wrote most of the features. Their younger brother Robert covered art, badly. The magazine's first issue was an immediate success, with circulation* that reached 2,200 in November 1808 and over 7,000 by 1812. In its early days, the *Examiner* made Leigh Hunt and William Hazlitt*, a frequent

contributor, famous. It is credited with 'discovering' John Keats and Percy Bysshe Shelley as well as pioneering Italian opera criticism.

Unfortunately, the brothers' commitment to telling their version of the truth brought them to grief. Having already been charged with libel three times, in December 1812 the Hunts were found guilty of mocking the Prince Regent, fined £500 and sentenced to two years in prison, from which Leigh continued to edit* the *Examiner* and criticize the government. The Hunts were released in 1815, but the hefty fine they had paid created financial problems from which they never fully recovered. After Waterloo, when radicalism became discredited, the *Examiner*'s circulation dwindled and in 1821, Leigh sailed for Italy to join Byron. Meanwhile, John was imprisoned for an additional two years for political libel. When Leigh returned to London in 1825, he wished to return to the *Examiner*, but John refused, leading to an estrangement between them.

John Hunt edited the magazine on his own from 1821 to 1828, when he gave the reins to his son, Henry Leigh Hunt, who mismanaged the paper and ruined his father. John was forced to sell it to the Rev. Dr Fellowes, who resold it within a year to the Benthamite radical Albany Fonblanque. Fonblanque's tenure as editor-proprietor* (1830-1847) was a second glory period, with contributions from John Stuart Mill*, John Forster*, Dickens*, Thackeray*, and significant financial support from Edward Bulwer Lytton* and Benjamin Disraeli. In 1847, Fonblanque handed the editorship* to John Forster, who had been the literary and dramatic editor since 1833. Forster immediately modernized the journal's format* and recruited Walter Savage Landor and Thomas Carlyle* to write for it. M. W. Savage took over from Forster in 1856, and in 1859 Henry Morley, previously of *Household Words*, succeeded him.

From 1865 on, as the *Examiner*'s fortunes waned, it passed through many hands, and although the quality of the writers and editors* remained high, the weekly* was no longer profitable. In 1865, Fonblanque sold it to William McCullough Torrens, M.P., who sold it in 1870 to Henry Richard Fox Bourne*, who in turn sold it in 1873. As for the editorship*, Henry Morley was replaced in 1867 by the novelist William Black*, who was followed by William Minto (1874-1878). In its later years, the paper succumbed to new competition from the *Spectator** and the *Saturday Review**. LB

Sources: Blunden 1967, Bostick 1978, *Encyclopaedia Britannica* 11th ed., *ODNB*, Thompson 1977.

EXQUISITE (1842-1844) With the initial subtitle, *A Collection of Tales, Histories, and Essays, Funny, Fanciful, and Facetious, Interspersed with Andecdotes, Amorous Adventures, Piquant Jests, and Spicey Sayings,* the *Exquisite* was an illustrated* erotic* magazine aimed at men, published by H. Smith in Holywell Street, the centre of the pornographic* and obscene literature trade in London. Each issue was 4d (later rising to 6d), ran to 12 pages, and included full-page illustrations* of women in various poses and states of semi-undress alongside fiction, poetry* and articles such as 'Stray Hints to Young Men' (about how to avoid sexually transmitted diseases), 'On the Necessity which exists for Prostitution' (arguing against contemporary moral crusades), 'The Bridal Pocket Book' (a series covering such issues as puberty and the difference between the sexes) and 'Flagellation' (about *le vice Anglais*). It was less explicitly pornographic than the *Pearl** which came several decades later. **MWT**

Sources: *Equisite* BL, Gray 1982.

F

FAIRPLAY, A JOURNAL FOR THE CONSIDERA-TION OF FINANCIAL, SHIPPING AND COMMERCIAL SUBJECTS, (1883-) The title *Fairplay*, according to the leader* of the first issue (18 May: 3), was derived from the paper's ambition to 'call things by their right names' and to look at them 'with uncoloured spectacles' (a definition repeated in *Mitchell's Press Directory** even after the character of the paper had been transformed). It was initially a chatty general 3d weekly*, founded by Thomas Hope Robinson and published by Ranken & Co from Drury Lane, aimed at businessmen. To that end it not only covered financial* information and trade, but also politics* and the arts (soon corralled into a department called 'Small Talk'). It immediately set itself up against other financial* journals (without naming them) because they supported a free trade which damaged 'home-producers'. The paper at first strongly supported London (not national) businessmen both through its advertisements* and copy.

This narrowness of appeal widened in 1885, when ownership changed along with the subtitle which now became *Fairplay. Trade, Shipping, Finance (and Politics)*. The arts were dropped altogether. Regularly featured were 'Clydeside Cameos' and 'Liverpool Lights', satiric descriptions of business types and (possibly) coded descriptions of real people. They were so popular they were republished in volume format. Gradually, however, the paper became more serious, specializing in shipping news and becoming not only the recognized place to explore disputes between ship owners and the Board of Trade, but (so it claimed) the only paper that dealt with mutual marine insurance companies. In 1892 the price* rose to 6d and another change of subtitle indicated its focus: *Weekly Shipping Journal*. It is still published as *Fairplay International Shipping Weekly*, now owned by Lloyd's Register-Fairplay. **AK**
Sources: *Fairplay* online, *Mitchell's*.

FAITHFULL, EMILY (1835-1895) Emily Faithfull's innovations, as publisher* and editor*, made a practical contribution to, and provided favourable publicity for the early women's rights movement. Though presented at Court, her later relationship with the monarchy reflected, not social status, but her activism as co-founder of the Victoria Press in

1860. She was appointed Printer and Publisher* in Ordinary to Her Majesty (Queen Victoria).

In the late 1850s Faithfull had joined Barbara Bodichon*, Bessie Parkes* and others at Langham Place, London, in organizing the Society for Promoting the Employment of Women. After training as a typesetter* herself, she considered that, though certain printing tasks were beyond women's strength, they were well suited to be compositors. The Victoria Press, established in Great Coram Street, Russell Square, took on young girl apprentices, paid compositors according to the men's recognized scale and gave attention to working conditions. Faithfull courted the support of the Queen with lavish volumes like *Victoria Regia* (1861) in which Tennyson, Arnold and Trollope took shares, and *A Welcome* (1863), commemorating the marriage of the Prince of Wales. Among early periodical publications of the press were the weekly* *Friend of the People*, the quarterly* *Law Magazine* and the *English Woman's Journal** for which it proved the cheapest of the printing firms approached. This relationship with the *English Woman's Journal* provided valuable experience for her launch of the *Victoria Magazine** with its ambitious aim of covering literature*, art and science* and competing with *Fraser's**, *Macmillan's** and *Blackwood's**. Though Emily Davies was appointed editor, financial constraints caused Emily Faithfull to take over the editorship* herself after only a few months. The *Journal** never challenged the likes of *Blackwood's*, butkept its core readership* by providing extensive information on women's issues. Faithfull undertook highly successful lecture tours of America in 1872-1873, and in 1877 she helped found the short-lived *West London Express*, introducing new steam machinery and increasing the number of women compositors. She was a founding member of the Women's Printing Society*. Among her articles writings were contributions to the *Pall Mall Gazette**; she was on the staff of the *Lady's Pictorial* and was still writing its woman's column in the 1890s. **BMO**
Sources: Lacey 1986, *ODNB*, Onslow 2000, Rossetti Archive online.

FAMILY HERALD (1842-1940) One of the most popular cheap*, general interest magazines* of the mid-nineteenth century, *Family Herald or Useful Information and Amusement for the Million* first appeared on 17 December, owned and edited* by James Elishama Smith (known as 'Shepherd Smith'). Spearheaded by publisher and proprietor* George Biggs, the journal was the first journal to be

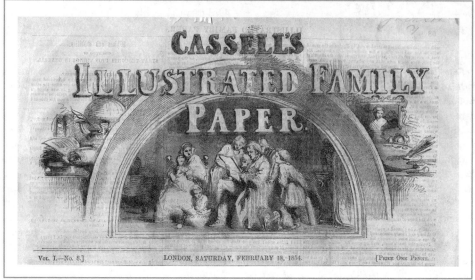

Figure 17: The masthead* of *Cassell's Illustrated Family Paper*, 18 Feb. 1854.

typeset, printed, and bound entirely by machine. Only four folio-sized pages, it was also the first publication worked entirely by female labour. Due in part to labour disputes with union leaders over the employment of women, the journal ceased publication after only 22 weekly* issues. Biggs relaunched the *Family Herald* on 13 May 1843. This new series featured the 16-page, double-column* quarto format* that was to become the magazine's hallmark.

Priced* at only 1d, the journal appealed to a broad readership* that eventually included the petty bourgeoisie and labour aristocracy, as well as shopkeepers' families and servant girls. The editor wrote in the first issue of his intention to provide informative amusement with the *Family Herald's* central focus on complete and serial fiction* pieces. The journal also regularly included poetry*, an article on a historical* topic or a biography, a letters* page and advertisements*. Weekly columns* featured information on natural history, literature*, fashion*, riddles, parlor magic and general advice. In addition to the engraved* masthead*, the magazine contained occasional illustrations*. It avoided news* and politics* in order to circumvent the stamp* tax and keep the price low.

Unlike its chief competition*, the *London Journal*, the *Family Herald* eschewed overly lurid tales in favor of historical romances or family-centred stories that imparted a moral lesson. In the early 1870s the magazine began to publish novelettes* in its Christmas* and summer special numbers. By 1877, they

were published as supplements*, for an additional penny, on the first and third Monday of every month. Many of the *Family Herald's* articles were anonymous* or excerpted from books or other publications. The majority of the authors who were identified were only credited by pseudonyms. As a result, almost all the contributors remain unknown.

Circulation* was high from the journal's inception due mainly to its cheap* price, varied content and broad appeal. In 1849, the *Family Herald* sold 125,000 weekly copies, rising steadily to 300,000 (1855), and falling to 200,000 in 1860. The journal was published by Biggs (1842-1858), Benjamin Blake (1858-1864) and William Stevens, Ltd. (1864-1899), with the printers working on the paper the longest being Bradbury & Evans* (1851-1872) and William Clowes & Sons Ltd.* (1878-1899). **EFO**

Sources: Altick 1957, Mitchell 1981, *Waterloo*.

FAMILY PAPER Though it is possible to find periodicals with a domestic* focus as early as the eighteenth century, Sarah Trimmer's *Family Magazine* (1788-1789) for example, the vogue for cheap* weekly* family journals began after the accession of Queen Victoria, when the cult of domesticity encouraged by the Evangelical revival was reinforced by widespread images in the media of the homelife of the royal family. The term 'family* paper' thus tends to imply not only an extension of readership* to women, children and the workingman, but also a particular ideological orientation with the promotion of Christian virtue, domestic economy and the avoidance of social impropriety and political controversy.

Contents of family papers typically include poetry* and fiction of an uplifting character, articles on popular science* or missionary* work, columns* devoted to domestic and moral advice* and prize competitions in composition or needlework. John Biggs's *Family Herald**, the *Leisure Hour** from the Religious Tract Society* and *Cassell's Illustrated Family Paper** are seminal examples, each circulating* over 100,000 copies at only 1d. Other terms recurring in journal titles to flag this orientation are 'home', 'household', 'domestic' and 'fireside', as reflected in titles such as the *Home Circle**, the *Household Friend* (1850-1851), *the Domestic Messenger* (1859-1867) and *Our Own Fireside* (1864-1905). In its tone as well as its title, Charles Dickens's* *Household Words** is associated with this tradition, though the paper is concerned with the public sphere to a far greater extent. As the longevity of several of these titles suggests, the weekly family paper retained its popularity into the twentieth century, albeit with some diminution of evangelical zeal. At least one example, the Dundee *People's Friend* (1869-) now owned by the D. C. Thomson* organization, still survives. **GL**

Sources: Altholz 1989, Billington 1986, Mitchell 1981.

FARISH, WILLIAM (1818-1896) A self-educated radical from a humble background, William Farish became an important figure in the expanding provincial* press in England. After a spell as editor* of the new weekly* Radical newspaper, the *Cheshire Observer,* in the 1850s, he moved on to work for almost 30 years as a political* columnist* for three Liberal papers: the *Chester Chronicle* (weekly), the *Chester Quil* (quarterly*) and the *Carlisle Journal* (weekly). His incisive and lively reporting for these papers moved beyond purely provincial concerns to a discussion of a wide range of topics, including support for the North (and anti-slavery) in the American Civil War, the Working Men's Club movement, Home Rule for Ireland and an endorsement of the Channel Tunnel scheme. He also contributed articles on local* cultural life and public affairs to Alexander Mackie's *Warrington Guardian* in the mid-1870s. Farish's credentials as a letter* writer also drew acclaim: in *The Times** (23 Dec. 1856); he broke new ground in the debate on effective punishment for felons, by advocating their employment on state-sponsored public works schemes; and in the *Newcastle Weekly Chronicle**

(21 Jan. 1893) he reviewed the illustrious career of G. J. Harney*, one of the last of the Chartist leaders still alive. **OA**

Sources: Ashton and Roberts 1996, Farish 1887, Farish 1890.

FASHION JOURNALS The first British journal devoted to fashion was Heideloff's the *Gallery of Fashion* (1794-1803). However, women's* magazines* had included a high level of such content since the *Lady's Magazine* (1770-1837). Alongside journals that included fashion plates with detailed descriptions, numerous women's magazines followed the lead given by John Bell's *La Belle Assemblée** in extending coverage to reports on London and Paris styles, social commentary, fashion-and beauty-related advice* and correspondence*, and, in the second half of the nineteenth century, dressmaking instructions and patterns. Although Paris led the way in fashion itself and journalism, with many fashion plates reproduced from French magazines, the British market was saturated, with numerous mergers* and name changes (such as the *World of Fashion**). Some titles had a run of many decades with various changes of title or format*, as did for example the *Ladies Fashionable Repository* (1809-1905, called *Pawsey's* (1837-1894) and the *Ladies' Gazette of Fashion* (1834-1894).

The closely allied fashion and women's journals can be divided into three phases: titles such as the *Lady's Magazine* continued eighteenth-century models, addressing readers as 'ladies' and catering to a leisured, fashionable elite; a more domesticated format by the 1840s, targeting middle-class* women with instructive and entertaining content including dressmaking and etiquette articles, embodied by Samuel Beeton's* *Englishwoman's Domestic Magazine**; finally, from the 1870s, a livelier, more engaging style of fashion reporting influenced by the New Journalism* was integrated with an increased amount of imagery, including better quality fashion plates, as epitomized by *Myra's Journal of Dress and Fashion**. The democratization of fashion was extended into home dressmaking with journals like *Weldon's Ladies' Journal**.

Fashion journals, like women's magazines were strongly gendered*, and few were published for men. *Le Beau Monde* (1806-1810) was intended as a male version of *La Belle Assemblée*, but was short-lived and quickly included images of women too. Trade papers*, particularly the *Tailor and Cutter**, included specialist information and fashion engravings*. **MRB/RA**

Sources: Beetham 1996, Beetham 2001, Holland 1988, Onslow 2000, White 1971.

FAWCETT, MILLICENT GARRETT (1847-1929) As an activist and leader of the women's suffrage movement, journalism was an essential component of Millicent Garrett Fawcett's political life. Her father's legacy of civic responsibility, the influence of two elder sisters' feminist intellectual and political engagement, endorsed by studying J. S. Mill*, all fuelled an early interest in women's rights and political economy*. This background ensured a successful literary partnership with her husband, Cambridge academic and Radical Liberal MP, Henry Fawcett.

Encouraged to write by Henry Fawcett and benefiting from his association with Alexander Macmillan*, her first article was on women's education for *Macmillan's Magazine* (1868). Successive articles in *Macmillan's* plus additional essays comprised a joint collection of the Fawcetts, *Essays and Lectures on Social and Political Subjects* (1872), following her own best-selling, *Political Economy for Beginners* (1868).

Her articles on the political*, economic and social emancipation of women embraced the equal moral standard, marriage, divorce and equal pay campaigns, as well as single issues like child marriage in India. Finding writing easier than speaking, she turned lectures into articles, and articles on notable women into books. Ray Strachey marvelled at Fawcett's output, 'crushing replies to antifeminist journalists, serious articles for the quarterlies*...topical letters* to the daily papers...also for real books'. Fawcett's gradualist strategy sought society's transformation through many publications such as reviews in the *Athenaeum* on political economy (1870s), articles on suffrage and education for the *Daily News* (1884), the Factory Acts in the *Echo** (1888) and New Zealand's female franchise for the *Contemporary Review* (1894). As the suffrage struggle intensified, her contributions to the feminist press*, the *Common Cause* (1909-20), the *Englishwoman* (1909-1920) and the *Woman's Leader* (1920-1929), predominated. As an obituary* in the *Glasgow Herald* observed, she 'wielded a vivacious and able pen'. **CL**

Sources: Crawford 2002, Demoor 2000, Fawcett 1924, Strachey 1931.

FEMINIST PRESS Although there were occasional forays by women into feminist journalism* in the early nineteenth century, such as Eliza Sharples's* short-lived *Isis** (1832) and *Eliza Cook's Journal** (1849-1854), feminist publishing really began with the monthly *English Woman's Journal** (1858-1864), edited* by Bessie Rayner Parkes* and Barbara Bodichon*. This contained a mixture of general interest articles, stories and poetry*, but increasingly came to concentrate on feminist issues, notably education and employment. Its successor, the *Englishwoman's Review** (1866ff), although including articles, was really a current-awareness quarterly* for the women's movement. Broader feminist issues were now addressed by Emily Faithfull's* Victoria Press, most notably the *Victoria Magazine** (1863ff). The parliamentary vote became increasingly important, and not only in Lydia Becker's* *Women's Suffrage Journal** (1870ff); another major campaign that had its own periodical was that to repeal the Contagious Diseases Acts, whose organ was the *Shield* (1870ff). A notable new development in feminist publishing was marked by the weekly *Women's Penny Paper** (1888ff), 'conducted' by Henrietta Müller* under the pseudonym* of 'Helena B. Temple', which initially was printed by the Women's Printing Society*. This, and its successors, the *Woman's Herald* (1891ff) and *Woman's Signal* (1894ff), mainly edited by Lady Henry Somerset and subsequently Florence Fenwick-Miller*, provided a valuable source of information on feminist issues and activities for this period. Other feminist periodicals of the 1890s included *Shafts** (1872ff) and the *Young Woman** (1892ff). **DD**

Source: Doughan and Sanchez 1987.

FENNELL, JOHN GREVILLE (1807-1885) The *Athenaeum** described Greville Fennell as being 'an ardent naturalist and angler' (1882: 153), but he started his career as an artist and engraver portraying natural history, especially fish and water birds. His writing helped to increase the popularity of coarse fishing on the Thames, and he was on the staff of the *Field**, *the Country Gentleman's Newspaper* from its inception in 1853, where his articles on angling, signed 'Greville F' were widely read. As 'Creel' he was a frequent contributor to the *Fishing Gazette* as well as to journals such as *Land and Water**, the *Sporting Magazine**, *All the Year Round** and *Bell's Life in London**. His books, signed 'Greville Fennell (of 'The Field')' traded on his name and reputation from the *Field. The Rail and the Rod* (1867), a guidebook to fishing grounds within 60 to 80 miles of London which could be reached by train was published* by the same firm as the *Field,* while the *Book of the Roach* (1870) was published by Longman, which had a small angling list. From 1879 probably until his death in 1885, Fennell also wrote the angling section of Charles Dickens's the younger's annual* *Dictionary of the Thames.* **DHL**

Sources: *Athenaeum* 1885, *Fishing Gazette* 1885, Marston 1885, *ODNB*.

FEUILLETON The *feuilleton* was first used in the French press by the *Journal des Débats*, and was a portion of a page or pages marked off by a line from the rest of the page – frequently appearing in smaller type* – dedicated to either criticism or to light literature*. In 1836, with the serial* publication of Balzac's 'La Vielle Fille' in *La Presse*, the *roman feuilleton* was born. This became a popular form for French novelists of the nineteenth century, and had a significant effect on British popular fiction. In French, the term now generally means simply serialized fiction*, and there was and is a significant gap between what would be considered a *feuilleton* in France and in Britain. The key distinction in Britain is between the *feuilleton* – a low-cultural serial that would appear in a newspaper or periodical – and the novel published in monthly parts, in the way that most – but not all – of Dickens's* novels were published. In practice, the boundary between the two is porous, and the difficulty of translation can cause confusion, since French authors are apt to refer to a novel like *Bleak House* – published in monthly parts – as an example of a *feuilleton*. Dickens would not have so labelled it, though the word was in use in Britain at the time.

In Victorian Britain, the *feuilleton* enjoyed an ambiguous status at best, partly because it remained closely associated with France, and therefore with sexual licentiousness and political machination. On the one hand, *feuilletons* from France were imported and translated, sometimes accompanied by a disclaimer – as in *Chambers's Edinburgh Journal** in January 1851 – about the productions of 'our volatile neighbours'. G. M. W. Reynolds* – who engaged in radical politics early in his life possibly became a French citizen during a period of political ferment – saw the commercial potential of the *feuilleton*, and the *London Journal**, which he edited*, carried translations of the latest serials* from France, alongside illustrations*.

The term increasingly came to be used loosely in Britain to describe a literary squib in a journal or newspaper: one might find a short story or critical article entitled 'A Feuilleton', not necessarily separated from the rest of the text, and often set in or pertaining to France, playing with the scurrility of French literature. The *feuilleton* was frequently disparaged by the serious press for its superficiality, as when R. Y. Tyrrell complained in the *Fortnightly Review** of January 1888 about the practice of 'dignifying … feuilletonism …with the name of scholarship'. **MaT**
Sources: BritPer, Cachin *et al.* 2007, Humpherys and James 2008, Law 2000, *ODNB, OED*.

FFENNELL, WILLIAM JOSHUA (1799-1867) The main journalistic* achievement of William Ffennell, journalist and pisciculturalist, was the founding in 1866 of the weekly* periodical *Land and Water**, started in collaboration with Frank (Francis T.) Buckland*. The purpose of the journal was to bring fishing matters to a wider public, and Ffennell recruited 'many valuable contributors' (*Land and Water* 16 March 1867: 173). Ffennell was born in Ireland and most of his career was concerned with salmon fisheries there and in England. He had the ability to convey to all social levels his knowledge and expertise concerning fishery matters and much of this was done through literary endeavour. **DHL**
Sources: *Field* 1867, *Land and Water* 1867, *ODNB, The Times* 1867.

FICTION SYNDICATION Fiction syndication – the simultaneous serial* publication of novels and tales in a number of journals with discrete readerships* – flourished in the last quarter of the nineteenth century, offering authors major and minor a wider circulation* and increased remuneration. Typical venues were the cheap* weekly* news* miscellanies* circulating in and around provincial* cities. Methods of distribution*, borrowed from the advertising* industry, included stereotypes*, galley proofs and partly printed sheets. The market leader was the 'Fiction Bureau' of Tillotson* & Son, proprietors* of the *Bolton Weekly Journal**, starting up in 1873 through a deal with sensation novelist Mary Elizabeth Braddon*. It quickly attracted newspapers, not only nationwide but also overseas, and authors as distinguished as Thomas Hardy*. The honour of inventing the syndicated newspaper novel*, however, must go to David Pae*, the Scottish journalist who personally arranged the disseminating of over 50 of his own melodramatic works, beginning with 'Lucy, the Factory Girl' in the Edinburgh *North Briton* and the *Glasgow Times* in 1858. Major competitors* were Cassell's General Press in London, W. C. Leng at the *Sheffield Telegraph** and the Northern Newspaper Syndicate in Kendal, Lancashire. Fiction syndication continued well into the twentieth century, though its economic and cultural significance steadily declined. **GL**
Sources: Donaldson 1986, Johanningsmeier 1997, Law 2000, Turner 1968.

FIELD (1853-) The *Field, or Country Gentleman's Newspaper* (1853-1854) began publication as a 'purely pleasurable paper' costing 6d, published on Saturdays and focusing on hunting, shooting and related sports*, an 'advocate of the healthy out-of-door pursuits that its name implies'; while it would furnish its readers with the 'raw material', it would not descend into the contentious tedium that characterized the 'Political Field'. The leader* in its first issue began with the improbable statement (for a newspaper) that 'no very striking events have occurred this week'. Indeed, its news* coverage had a tendency to produce that assumption in the reader, reporting to the country gentleman gossip* about the fashionable goings on in town, in royal, aristocratic and diplomatic circles: a seemingly endless litany of house calls, balls and soirées (liberally peppered with such French vocabulary as befitted the contemporary beau monde).

The bulk of the paper, though, was given over to sports*, in the form of fairly lengthy updates and advice for the amateur on hunting, angling, horse racing (including lists of odds and runners' weights for forthcoming meetings), yachting, coursing, chess (including problems for readers) and cricket. Lists of fixtures for hunts were also given. A weekly* report on agriculture reported on meetings of agricultural societies, gave lists of the latest market prices of farm produce and contained practical and scientific advice for the landowner on how to maximise production. Illustrations*, by John Leech* and H. K. Browne*, among others, were a prominent feature. The journal carried advertisements*, including some for up-market periodicals such as the *New Quarterly Review**, the *Westminster Review**, and the *Athenaeum**, which occupied an increasing proportion of the newspaper as time passed.

In 1854, the paper was purchased by Edward William Cox* and by September of the same year it was maintaining that it had achieved 'an extensive circulation* among the Aristocracy, Gentry and Monied Classes* in this country and its dependencies, and in Europe and America'. Whether or not this was an accurate characterization of the paper's readership* (it seems likely that at least some of its readers came from the aspiring middle class*), it claimed weekly sales of 4,409 based on stamp* returns, beating *John Bull**, the *Leader** and the *Guardian**. In 1855 its title* changed to the *Field, the Farm, the Garden, the Country Gentleman's Newspaper*. Letters* became gradually more prominent, with 'Country-House Notes and Questions' and 'Notes and Questions on Natural History' (with questions and answers supplied by readers*) taking their place alongside longer correspondence. In 1870, the proprietor* Horace Cox (1844-1918) – nephew of Edward – issued a sister publication,

the *Field Quarterly Magazine and Review*, which lasted only until 1872.

Any attempt to provide general news coverage had by 1885 been all but abandoned, and as the *Field*'s reporting of sports (the coverage of which was becoming increasingly more oriented to official and league events) became increasingly extensive and detailed, so its fascination with high society gossip* waned and then vanished. Whether this reflected a shift in readership towards a more downmarket demographic is open to question, but that the *Field* continued its coverage of horse racing (at a time when its disreputability had caused several upright papers to banish the sport from their pages) tends to support this view. However, the coverage of hunting and possibly the 6d price* tag would have been off-putting for punters from the 'lower orders'. The more likely hypothesis, therefore, is that the *Field* provided a context in which racing could retain its aristocratic associations and remain respectable. From 1929, its title became the *Field: the Country Newspaper*. **MaT**

Sources: *ODNB, Waterloo.*

FIGARO IN LONDON (1831-1839) One of the most successful 1d comic* weeklies* of the 1830s, *Figaro in London* (quarto; four pages, eight colums) appeared on Saturdays and boasted a circulation* of over 70,000 by 1832. Derivative of a Parisian prototype, it was produced until 1835 by the publisher William Strange* and his editor*, Gilbert Abbot À Beckett. Combining radical political* comment with irreverent anti-establishment squibs, it mobilized the persona of 'the barber' to expose 'all kinds of quackery, fraud, or oppression, whether it be Social, Literary, Political, or Theatrical'. In format* it comprised a single-page leader* illustrated* with a Robert Seymour* caricature* and subsequent pages entitled 'The Interpreter', 'Brevities' and the 'Drama'. Although ostensibly independent of party, in 1834 À Beckett expressed his 'obligations to Tory, Whig, Radical, Republican, Revolutionary, Destructive and Conservative ... [because] we have been in the habit of treating them all as fair game', 'Anti-Reform' remained the principal target.

Figaro in London drew together the diverse literary*, theatrical, visual and political* periodical genres that had emerged in the 1820s, and a line of continuity can be traced to Strange's earlier satirical* titles, *Paul Pry** (1826) and the *Ass; or Weekly Beast of Burden* (1826). Its impact on the 'unstamped'* market of the early 1830s was nonetheless profound, and À Beckett dubbed the widespread practice of copying its format*

'Figaro-Mania'. The *Patriot, Critical Figaro, Literary Test, English Figaro, Devil's Walk, Giovanni in London* and 'Figaro' titles in Birmingham, Liverpool, Sheffield and Chesterfield were all cited as evidence of this 'cholera'. Henry Mayhew* became editor* in 1835 and the title survived for the rest of the decade. It was in its early years, however, that *Figaro in London* made its greatest impact, identifying and exploiting an inclusive 'populist' readership* later targeted by comic serials such as *Punch**. In this, as in its content and format*, it was simultaneously a product and shaper of London's cheap* periodical market. BM

Sources: Harrison 1977, Haywood 2004, *Waterloo*.

FILDES, SAMUEL LUKE (1844-1927) The contributions to periodicals of Luke Fildes, artist and illustrator*, appeared in the late 1860s in monthlies* like *Good Words** and the *Quiver** long known for their ambitious artwork. But he was of a generation and worked in a style that had moved on from the moment of imaginative intensity characteristic of the illustrated magazines of the early 1860s. The market*, too, had changed, and Fildes, acknowledging the extent to which spiralling costs were eating into the aesthetic pretensions of the established fiction bearing monthlies, was willing to work for more mundane journals like the *Cottager and Artisan**, a large format* paper that allowed him to produce spectacular cover illustrations. More naturalistic and journalistic than Millais* and his pre-Raphaelite contemporaries, Fildes's social realist images for the *Graphic**, most notably 'Houseless and Hungry' (4 Dec. 1869), combined moral outrage and journalistic know-how to telling effect. BM

Sources: Engen 1990, Goldman 1994, Houfe 1978, *ODNB*, Reid 1928, Suriano 2005, White 1897.

FINANCIAL AND COMMERCIAL RECORD (1818-1845) The *Financial and Commercial Record* (of which issues survive only from no.612, 2 Nov. 1824) was a bi-weekly 2-page sheet consisting only of lists of government funds and foreign stocks, the price of corn and sugar, shares in canals, docks, waterworks, insurance and gaslight companies, mines, railways, bridges, roads, and, interestingly, 'literary institutions'– which come to include University College and King's College – and 'Miscellaneous' (e.g. theatres). Subscriptions cost 2 guineas per annum. It was published* until 1835 by the stockbrokers Jonah Smith Wells & Son and thereafter by Wells, Westropp & Prinsep, also stockbrokers. The format*

did not vary until it closed (30 Dec. 1845), although by this time exchange rates for currencies had been added and the page size had grown from 40 cm to 51 cm. The publication ceased evidently because the firm was not doing well, the exchange now dealing 'almost wholly in shares of railways and in stocks' rather than in canals and insurance companies. The periodical is interesting for how it demonstrates that the Taxes on Knowledge* constrained the growth of the Stock Exchange as well as the press. For example, the *Record* was not allowed to give notice of shareholders' meetings or dividends as these were all classed as advertisements* and taxed accordingly. All Wells and his associates could do was announce that such news was available every day from their offices, effectively thereby limiting participants in the stock market to local residents and personal contacts, a restriction visible also in the early years of the *Circular to Bankers**. AK

Source: *Waterloo*.

FINANCIAL JOURNALS While prices of produce and shipping lists began to be published* in the eighteenth century (*Lloyd's List*, starting in 1726, is traditionally said to be the first), these multiplied and included lists published by stockbrokers such as James Wetenhall's *Course of the Exchange* (1803-1908) or Jonah Smith Wells & Son's *Financial and Commercial Record**. Advice and comment papers such as the *Circular to Bankers** and the *Magnet** arose with the increasing complexity of the City and its legal regulation (e.g. the repeal in 1825 of the 1720 Bubble Act and the subsequent proliferation of chartered joint-stock railway companies). Interestingly, such papers were hampered by the Taxes on Knowledge*. Meanwhile, periodicals such as the *Economist** were set up to debate the continuation of the Corn Laws. Initially containing little financial* news, the *Economist* nonetheless soon felt its sway, even publishing a specialist *Railway Monitor* from 1845. Its primary concern was not the day-to-day specifics of the City, however, so much as economics in general, a field where it was seriously rivalled as a specialist periodical only by the *Statist** from 1878.

The 1857 and 1862 Companies Acts proved turning points by legally codifying the concept of limited liability. This opened the market* to smaller (but still wealthy) investors by rendering investment safer. It thus meant a wider market for financial papers. This new readerships is what the Saturday *Money Market Review** targeted from 1860, supplemented from 1870 by its daily* sibling, the *Financier*. The *Bullionist** from 1866 was aimed at

a similar 'Tory' audience. But financial journals such as we know them today are very much a product of the last two decades of the nineteenth century. If by 1884 British industrial supremacy had been seriously challenged by Germany and the USA, the City had continued to flourish: over 2,500 brokers and jobbers were trading in around 2000 securities. The stage was set for the rivals that would hold a duopoly until they merged in 1945, the New Journalist* *Financial News* and the more sober and practical *Financial Times*. Other papers tried to enter the market (e.g. *Financial Truth* 1889-1904; *Financial Post* 1895-1898), but the *Financial News* and *Financial Times* took over City-related advertising* and news*, and either crushed or absorbed effective opposition, or forced it to specialise in specific areas (e.g. *Fairplay*, *Criterion*).
AK

Sources: Baskin and Miranti 1997, Dudley Edwards 1993, Kynaston 1988, Micklethwait and Woolridge 2003, Moss and Hosgood 1994.

***FINANCIAL NEWS* (1884-1940)** The *Financial News* was London's first financial* daily*. It transformed the financial press. Begun by Harry Hananel Marks (backed by the American engineer Colonel Edward McMurdo) as the penny* *Financial and Mining News* on 23 January, with plentiful adverts from its first day, it claimed to be the London edition of a New York analogue (probably the *Daily Mining News,* which Marks had edited from 1880). It targeted wealthy Americans residing in Europe, claiming to be the only paper that made use of the telegraph* to permit simultaneous publication on both sides of the Atlantic. Originally published* by Andrew Faunch and edited* by Marks, the manager of the paper (who dealt with subscriptions and correspondence) was C. F. Tombs. From 1 July 1884 the paper was renamed the *Financial News* but otherwise changed not at all.

The *Financial News* always maintained close attention to finances and trade with the Americas. Later it had correspondents* in the Transvaal as well, with branch offices in Paris, New York and Rome. At the Paris office there was even a reading room* where subscribers (£ 1 12 s per annum, post free anywhere in the world) could write and receive letters, and consult files of the paper. Unusually, the *Financial News* featured lists of 'Strangers in London' – arrivals (not only American) at prestigious hotels such as the Langham, Morley's and Long's. The influence of American and New Journalism* is very clear. Besides elegantly chatty financial and commercial articles, crossheads and short paragraphs, there was a regular department called 'Personalities'* which comprised celebrity gossip*. In the first week alone there were interviews* with the American financiers William H. Vanderbilt and Jay Gould. There was also 'Answers to Correspondents'* which gave advice on financial matters, as well as the usual tables of stocks and shares. This format* continued for the rest of the century. Like other financial journals, including its main rival the *Financial Times*, it championed honesty while Marks and his journalists were involved in shady dealing, several times landing in court. The Financial News Ltd had been floated in March 1885 (50,000 shares at £1 each) and in 1898, when it was reconstructed, it raised £100,000. Marks continued to hold the majority of shares until his death in 1916. It was this company that bought the *Financial Times* in 1945 when the latter absorbed the *Financial News*. AK

Sources: Edwards 1993, Kynaston 1988, *ODNB*, Porter 1986.

***FINANCIAL TIMES* (1888-)** Now the leading financial daily*, the *Financial Times* did not have a promising start. Launched on 9 January as the thrice-weekly *London Financial Guide* by James Sheridan and his brother (about whom little is known), it entered a crowded market with powerful competitors, above all the *Financial News*. In its first issue the *Guide* announced that it would follow *The Times* and (by implication) would distance itself from the *Financial News* by refusing both Personalities* and 'the clearing out of any Augean stables' that the *Financial News* claimed it wanted to do. It also announced its famous strapline 'Without Fear and Without Favour' under its masthead*. Within a month the Sheridans were forced to sell out to their printer, Douglas Gordon MacRae* who changed the name to the *Financial Times*, brought it out six times a week and created a public limited company. MacRae (who also owned the highly profitable *Draper's Record*) laid the foundations of success through a combination of persistence in the face of initial losses and aggressive attacks on its main rival the *Financial News* for inaccuracy and deceit (though like the *Financial News* it also was perfectly capable of printing an advert* for a company on one page and puffing* it on the other). Leopold Graham was the first editor* (1888-1889) but MacRae himself took over in 1889, to be followed by W. R. Lawson (1890-1892; a defector from the *FN*), Sydney Murray (1892-1895) and A. E. Murray (1896-1909).

On 2 January 1893, the *Financial Times* turned pink (pink paper* being cheaper) - a daring move for a financial* paper when other coloured newspapers included popular titles such as the *Sporting Times** and *Evening News**, and by 31 January the *Westminster Gazette**. At the same time MacRae started to pay Reuters* £400 for their general service, including New York commercial and financial information, and introduced an epitome of the general news* designed to be read on the train. There was also a new masthead and a sharper use of headlines. Despite economic difficulties in 1893, three years later when FT Ltd was reconstructed, it raised capital of £200,000. The paper itself made a profit of £14,600 in the second half of the year alone. In 1911, the *Financial Times* incorporated the *Financier and Bullionist** and in 1919 became a property of the press barons William and Gomer Berry. In 1945, it was itself taken over by Financial News Ltd, which nevertheless retained the *Financial Times* title and merged* its fiercest rival into it. **AK**

Sources: Kynaston 1988, *ODNB*.

FINLAY, FRANCIS DALZELL (1793-1857)
Francis Finlay, a radical printer from Newtownards, was the apprentice of Samuel Archer of Belfast. In 1808 Finlay began to print the radical *Belfast Monthly Magazine* (1808-1814), founded and edited* by William Drennan, a United Irishmen member, and in 1815 Finlay opened his own printing works in Joy Street, with Drennan's assistance. He established a reputation for the high standard of his letterpress work, and Drennan's poems*, *Fugitive Pieces* (1815) was the first thing he printed.

Finlay was involved in radical politics* and supported the key issues of his day – Catholic emancipation, the disestablishment of the Irish Church and parliamentary* and land reform. In 1824 he extended his ambitions and turned to journalism himself. Supported by Drennan, Hamilton Rowan, secretary of the United Irishmen and others, he started his own radical newspaper, the *Northern Whig**, named from a club* opened in Belfast in 1791 by the Society of United Irishmen. The paper was a pioneer of the Liberal press, advocating civil and religious equality, as well as free trade. But he was repeatedly charged with libel, his newspaper was suspended, he was imprisoned twice and fined for championing cases of tenants' rights and giving voice to the injustices of the day. However, his radicalism does not appear to have extended to his own employees. **CL**

Sources: Crone 1928, Newmann 1993, *ODNB*, Ulster History Circle online.

***FISHING GAZETTE* (1865-1966).** In 1900 *Mitchell's Newspaper Press Directory* described the *Fishing Gazette* as 'a gentleman's paper, devoted to angling, river, lake and sea-fishing and fish culture'. The high-quality weekly* *Gazette* maintained its original name until July 1962, when it became the *Fishing Gazette and Sea Angler*. The original proprietor* was Sampson Low* and nineteenth-century editors* included George Harvey Howard and R. B. Marston. Among its publishers* were E. W. Allen (1877) and Harvey Bell (1877), and Horace Cox (1895) who were also its printers. The price* of 2d seems to have been consistent for 35 years (1877-1912). The journal contained 'special articles on all fresh and salt-water fish and fishing; state of rivers; where to fish; angling notes and queries' (*Mitchell's* 1900), as well as information on angling clubs and correspondence columns*. It was illustrated* with engravings, as well as carrying advertisements*, although an advertisement in the *British Fisheries Directory* (1883-1884) belied *Mitchell's* description by claiming that the *Gazette* was a magazine with a wide appeal for all classes*. **DHL**

Sources: Layton 1912, *Mitchell's* 1900, *Waterloo*.

FLEET STREET Fleet Street, which runs from the Strand to Ludgate Circus in London, takes its name from the Fleet River, a tributary of the Thames, now underground. The connection with printing dates from 1500, when William Caxton's assistant, Wynkyn de Worde, moved his printing press next to St Bride's Church and, gradually, other printers established workrooms in the district largely serving the legal profession. In addition, Fleet Street has literary associations with Shakespeare, Ben Jonson, Pepys and Samuel Johnson. All this, coupled with its location on the main thoroughfare linking the political district of Westminster, the financial heart of the City of London and the legal centre of the Inns of Court, and later the High Court, made it fertile ground for the emergence of journalism. On 11 March 1702, the first daily* newspaper, the *Daily Courant*, was issued from 'next Door to the King's Arms Tavern' in Fleet Street. By the last half of the nineteenth century, all the significant London-based national papers and a myriad of periodicals and their attendant services, had offices and printing presses on or in the streets close to Fleet Street. The expression 'Fleet Street' became synonymous with the national press itself. Despite the logistical difficulties of producing newspapers from a dense

Figure 18: An anonymous drawing of Fleet Street in *Fun*, 17 Nov. 1866: 102.

and congested area of central London, Fleet Street continued to be the centre of the British newspaper industry until the 1980s. **JRW**
Sources: Griffiths 2006.

FLINDELL, THOMAS (1767-1824) Thomas Flindell was a Cornish editor*, printer and publisher* whose early career seems to have been peripatetic. Apprenticed to a printer in Falmouth who died, Flindell then moved between Bath, Edinburgh, London and Doncaster. In 1790 he became editor of the *Doncaster Gazette*, but eight years later he returned to Cornwall to establish the Stannary Press at Helston. At Falmouth, in 1801, he launched the first Cornish newspaper, the *Cornwall Gazette and Falmouth Packet,* but the paper failed after a year and Flindell was imprisoned for debt. However, in 1803, with the assistance of local clergy and gentry who saw the need for a Cornish newspaper, Flindell moved to Truro where his debts were paid and he was provided with sufficient capital to start another paper. Flindell launched the weekly* *Royal Cornwall Gazette and Western Advertiser* in July 1803, published on Saturdays* at the price* of 7d. To begin with, the paper was politically* impartial, but by 1809 it had become the organ of the Tory Party. A rival newspaper, the *West Briton,* appeared in 1810 and a bitter feud between

himself and its editor, Edward Budd, forced Flindell to sell his interest in the *Royal Cornwall Gazette* and move to Exeter where, in 1813, he established the *Western Luminary*, another weekly* with a Tory bias. Further trouble awaited Flindell when he was imprisoned in 1821 for printing derogatory remarks about Queen Caroline in his newspaper. After his death in 1824 proprietorship* of the *Western Luminary* was continued by his widow, Mary. As well as printing newspapers, Flindell also printed and published the only known Cornish edition of the Bible. **DHL**
Sources: *ODNB*, Potts 1963.

FOLDS, JOHN S. (FL. 1830s-1840s) A printer with a thriving business in Dublin in the 1830s and 1840s, John S. Folds was the first proprietor* of the *Dublin Penny Journal*. In 1841 his premises in Dublin was destroyed by fire, taking with it the sheets of Charles Lever's* *Charles O'Malley*. In 1845 Folds tried the newspaper business with the publication of the *Dublin Times*; the paper failed and Folds, bankrupt, emigrated to America. J. S. Le Fanu* is reported as purchasing some of his stock. Folds is likely to be the author of an article on 'Printing and Publishing* in Ireland' in the *Dublin Penny Journal* (23 March 1833). **ET**
Sources: 'CHC' 1877, Kinane 1994.

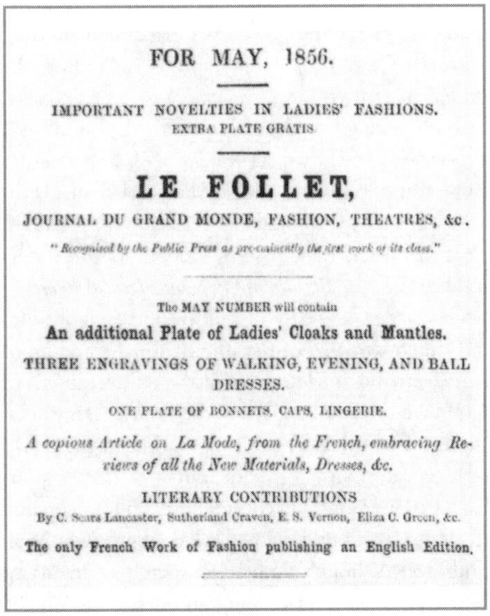

FOR MAY, 1856.

IMPORTANT NOVELTIES IN LADIES' FASHIONS.
EXTRA PLATE GRATIS

LE FOLLET,

JOURNAL DU GRAND MONDE, FASHION, THEATRES, &c.

" *Recognised by the Public Press as pre-eminently the first work of its class.*"

The MAY NUMBER will contain
An additional Plate of Ladies' Cloaks and Mantles.

THREE ENGRAVINGS OF WALKING, EVENING, AND BALL
DRESSES.

ONE PLATE OF BONNETS, CAPS, LINGERIE.

A copious Article on La Mode, from the French, embracing Reviews of all the New Materials, Dresses, &c.

LITERARY CONTRIBUTIONS
By C. Scars Lancaster, Sutherland Craven, E. S. Vernon, Eliza C. Green, &c.

The only French Work of Fashion publishing an English Edition.

Figure 19: An advert for *Le Follet* in the *Musical World*,
5 April 1856.

LE FOLLET (1846-1900) *Le Follet: Journal du Grand Monde, Fashion, Polite Literature, Beaux Arts, &c.* was the English edition of the leading French fashion* magazine by the same title. It promised its upper-class* female readers* the convenience of easier access to 'La Mode Parisienne'. A central place in each issue was occupied by full-page fashion plates (three per number, sometimes coloured), but there was also a literary* department, offering original prose and verse alongside the occasional translation. The journal was lavishly produced, and its price* varied between 1s and 1s 6d during its run. Its juxtaposition of fashion and literature in a woman's journal positioned it within the on-going process of emancipation. OD
Sources: Beetham 2001, *Waterloo.*

FOOTBALL ANNUAL (1868-1908) The *Football Annual*, published for its first year as *John Lilywhite's Football Annual*, was the first of what was to become a crowded market for football yearbooks and directories as the winter game grew in popularity. 'Published with the sanction of the Football Association', it was edited* by Charles W. Alcock*, FA honorary secretary, journalist*and leading amateur footballer. Both association and rugby codes were covered in its early years. In 1873 it was published* by Virtue & Co. and included summaries of matches 'by Chief Schools and Leading Clubs', rules of the Football Association and the Rugby Union, lists of football clubs in England, biographies of major Eng-

lish players and articles on football in public schools abroad, and in Scotland, Wales and Ireland. A. E. Guillemand, Vice President of the Rugby Union, was a contributor, who also collaborated with Alcock. The *Football Annual* carried advertisements* for football clubs, as well as for items such as sports' gear. An invaluable reference book for soccer enthusiasts and club administrators, the *Football Annual* provided tips on how to master the game, promoted discussion on the sport's* rules and commented on the game's development. ST
Sources: Booth 2002, *Football Annual* 1873, Fulton 1985, Russell 2002, *Waterloo.*

FOOTBALL SPECIALS Papers designated 'football specials' emerged in the Midlands, the North, and Glasgow during the 1880s, and provided up-to-the minute rugby and association football results and match summaries on Saturday evenings. In most cases, local evening papers exploited the growing popularity of football to fashion these innovative editions. Perhaps the first of these specials was the four-page* *Saturday Night*, which started in Birmingham for ½d on 30 September 1882. *Saturday Night* established the formula for the football special, offering readers news of the large local* clubs, Aston Villa and West Bromwich Albion and scores from throughout Britain, as well as some general news* and local gossip*. Other towns soon followed with their own football specials, including Blackburn (1883), Bolton (1884), Glasgow (1884), Sheffield (1886), Derby (1888) and London (1889). By 1900, these journals, whose pages often were coloured blue, green, or pink, had spread throughout Britain.

Football specials depended on technology for their success. In order to obtain the latest results the papers first utilized telegraphy* and then telephones to transmit news as soon as possible after the referee's last whistle. Reporters* and press agencies*, however, could not fulfil all of the news needs of the football special. Clubs, especially small amateur ones, were often responsible for furnishing their fixture lists and reporting their match results. Contemporary observers noted the significance of Saturday football editions as these papers enabled individuals to experience the game in print, whether they had attended a match or not. With the creation of leagues, football specials supplied the information by which readers could not only follow their club's performance but also the results of their rivals and the subsequent effects on the league-tables. Unfortunately, copies of some of these editions no longer exist. MJM
Sources: Edwards 1892, Gibson and Pickford 1906, Mason 1980, Murray 2000.

FORBES, ARCHIBALD (1838-1900)   Archibald Forbes was one of the late nineteenth-century's most experienced and famous war* correspondents. His father intended him for the ministry, but Forbes led a directionless life until he joined the first Royal Dragoons. Serving from 1859-1864, he spent much of his time 'reading military* theory and publishing pseudonymous* articles on military subjects', and attributed much of his later success as a war journalist* to insights developed during this period (*ODNB*).

Forbes held a series of journalistic posts (1864-1870) on the *Morning Advertiser, Morning Star*, the *Evening Star*, and the unsuccessful weekly* *London Scotsman*, which he also edited*. The *Advertiser*'s owner, James Grant* sent Forbes to Paris as war correspondent in 1870 at the outbreak of the Franco-Prussian war; his dispatches caught the attention of J. R. Robinson at the *Daily News** and when Grant sacked Forbes, following cutbacks at his paper, Robinson secured his services for the *News*. An inventive, resourceful and effective writer, Forbes famously managed to scoop a number of stories for his new employer (using the still new telegraph* to get reports to London ahead of his rivals) and became the *Daily News*'s leading war reporter. The 1870s was a busy decade for war reporters, and Forbes secured his formidable reputation reporting from the decade's numerous wars across Europe, India and Africa, as well as the famine in Bengal. Between wars, he was special correspondent for the *News,* reporting on topics as diverse as shipwrecks, the Vienna Exhibition and royal visits, He continued to work as an embedded journalist (he had accompanied the German forces in Paris and remained a life-long admirer of their military methods) until failing health forced him to leave the battlefields in 1883.

This direct field engagement brought him not only professional success but fame as a courageous and somewhat romantic figure who braved dangerous territory to ensure his news reports made it to press as swiftly as possible. His critics were more skeptical, suggesting that he exaggerated, over-dramatized and occasionally falsified reports, and sometimes took credit for other correspondents' stories (*ODNB*). His confrontational reporting style made him an effective 'crusading journalist' in addition to supporting, among other issues, agriculture trade unionism* (*ODNB*). He published numerous works of fiction and non-fiction, the latter drawing heavily on his journalism, including the well regarded *Memories and Studies of War and Peace* (1895). **FD**
Sources: *ODNB*, Stearn 1992, Thorold 1913, Yates 1885.

FORBES, JOHN (1787-1861)   After studying medicine in Edinburgh, Forbes began contributing articles to a variety of periodicals, including the *Transactions of the Provincial and Surgical Association*. He collaborated in the publication of a monthly*, *Cyclopaedia of Practical Medicine* (1832-1835), and alone compiled a chronological and alphabetical bibliography of its contents, the first of its kind, in 1835. In 1836 he and John Conolly began a new publication, the *British and Foreign Medical Review**, which was read widely in Europe and America and did much to enhance the international standing of British medicine. They shared the editorship* until 1839, when Conolly left, and the *Review*'s continued success established Forbes's reputation in the world of medical* journalism. In 1846 the *Review* published anonymously* a commentary on homeopathy to which the London medical establishment took umbrage. Although Forbes was merely acting as an impartial editor and keeping an open mind on the doctrine of 'like cures like', he was almost certainly the author of the article, and was clearly interested in fringe subjects like magnetism in medicine, while totally shunning quackery. Forbes resigned his editorship in 1847 and the *Review* amalgamated with the *Medical-Chirurgical Review* in 1848. **RAA**
Sources: Agnew 2002, *ODNB*.

FOREIGN CORRESPONDENT   Foreign correspondents were initially, as the name suggests, letter* writers who sent 'newsy' letters to friends and relatives, which would subsequently be published in the local* newspaper. Many started as 'stringers' for various newspapers, a term said to be derived from the lengths of string used to measure column* inches and determine pay scales, acting as part-time or occasional suppliers of stories from their locale. James Perry is usually regarded as the first modern foreign correspondent as he reported events from Paris during the Revolution for the *Morning Chronicle**, but others followed in increasing numbers in the early nineteenth century. Another early foreign correspondent, Henry Crabb Robinson, reported from Spain during the Peninsular War, later becoming the first foreign news editor for *The Times**, employing numerous in stringers of his own across Europe. The importance of the foreign correspondent was highlighted by the career of William Howard Russell*, who became the first internationally famous foreign correspondent through his reporting of the Crimean War and other conflicts for *The Times*.

Foreign correspondents were fundamentally different from their domestic journalist counterparts in significant ways. British journalists tended to start their vocation straight from school, be more mobile, and rise to the top of their profession, usually for the same paper. Foreign correspondents would generally remain in one place, have specialized language and other skills, engage local contacts at all levels and be likely to change newspaper employer when the time suited. They would also generally be older, have good connections with the local social and political elite, and possibly be émigrés from other countries. *The Times* actively sought out potential correspondents who had connections with the diplomatic service who would generally relay information from personal contacts rather than initiate independent investigations. These reports from around the world were relayed to both the large and influential newspapers as well as to smaller local* and provincial* newspapers through news agencies* – organizations which were to become increasingly significant in the second half of the nineteenth century.

More established foreign correspondents emerged with the development of the permanent bureau, most famously *The Times* bureau in Paris established in 1848. Bureaus in Berlin, Madrid, Florence, Vienna, Constantinople, Rome and other centres were soon founded. The regularized and permanent characteristic of the foreign correspondent differed a great deal from the itinerant and irregular nature of the war correspondent*.

While the vast majority of foreign correspondents were men, the nature of the despatches from foreign correspondents was that they were usually anonymous*, credited to 'Our Own Correspondent', 'Special Correspondent' or sometimes accompanied by just the author's initials. This enabled women* to play a role as foreign correspondents in a way that would have been more difficult in other parts of the profession outside of those areas reserved for 'women's journalism'*. Women such as Margaret Fuller, who became America's first female foreign correspondent in 1846 and Harriet Ward, a British woman said to be the first female war* correspondent who wrote about conflicts in Southern Africa in the 1840s and 1850s for the *United Service Magazine*, and Flora Shaw*, the first woman on the permanent staff of *The Times* in 1892, sent in that year to South Africa. GRW

Sources: Brown 1985, Chambers *et al.* 2004, Collins 2007, Dell'Orto 2002, Desmond 1978.

FOREIGN NEWS Early-nineteenth century foreign news* was essentially the exchange of newspapers and periodicals between regions or nations

with stories culled from their pages and reprinted. Agents were sent out to ports in order to gather written news reports, newspapers and gossip* from passengers and sailors, either waiting for ships to dock or rowing out to meet them. Overseas information was despatched overland in a variety of ways: postal services; river or coastal steamboats* after 1813 in Britain; railways* in Britain from the 1820s and in the United States from the 1830s and organized rider-relays such as the one introduced by the *New York Herald* in 1838 to connect New York and Washington. *The Times** even used carrier pigeons to convey news from the continent in 1837, a somewhat risky innovation instituted later in France and the United States.

By the 1830s, the industrial revolution had provided new and quicker means to convey information. Steam power had revolutionized both industry and communication. The railway* was perhaps the single most important contribution to nineteenth-century development and its importance to the gathering and diffusion of foreign news cannot be over stated. In addition, the dissemination of transatlantic* news was enhanced by the use of steam-powered ocean-going vessels, such as the *Sirius* and the *Great Western,* both of which crossed the Atlantic in 1838 in 15 days. While Claude Chappe's system of semaphore telegraphy was in use in France from 1794, the invention of the electric telegraph* was the most profound development in the timely conveyance of news over long distances. Samuel Morse in the United States, whose name was applied to the famous 'Morse Code', demonstrated his telegraph in 1836, gaining a patent in 1844. Charles Wheatstone and William Fothergill Cooke in England developed their own means of telegraphy in the 1830s, being the first to patent (1837) and then commercially use (1838) the telegraph. The submarine cable, first used successfully in 1851 to connect Dover and Calais and then across the Atlantic in 1866, enabled the world-wide use of telegraphic communication to convey foreign news. The relay of foreign news was greatly enhanced by Thomas Edison's invention of the duplex telegraph in 1868, enabling the transmission of telegraphic signals in both directions over the same wire.

As the telegraph was inordinately expensive, very few newspapers could use it to communicate with their own correspondents and 'stringers' overseas, and even then only very sparingly. The news agency* allowed foreign news to be distributed to subscribing newspapers who shared the cost of the service. News agencies that were crucial to the explosion of foreign news included the Paris-based *Agence Havas*, founded in 1832; the New York Associated Press, formed in 1848; Berlin's *Wolff'sche Telegraphen Büro* established in 1849; Reuter's* Telegram Company Ltd., founded 1851 and based in London; and Turin's *Agenzia Telegrafica Stefani*, created in 1853.

In Britain, the London-based Press Association* was formed in 1868 to gather and disseminate foreign news for the provincial press. It also successfully lobbied the government to nationalise the telegraph network through the Electric Telegraph Acts and to put the system under the auspices of the General Post Office in 1870. In addition, the Press Association had an arrangement with Reuter's to provide the news agency with provincial news and to relay Reuter's reports of foreign news to British subscribers outside of London. **GRW**
Sources: Bray 2002, Brown 1985, Collins 2007, Desmond 1978, Nalbach 2003, Noll 2001.

***FOREIGN QUARTERLY REVIEW* (1827-1846)** Published over 20 years in 37 volumes, the *Foreign Quarterly Review* was the longest-running nineteenth-century review principally devoted to foreign ideas and literature*, with contributors as varied as the topics covered. The *Foreign Quarterly* published pieces by lawyers, clergymen, scholars, professors, Benthamite reviewers such as John Bowring* and Henry Southern, and economists of the capacity of John Ramsey McCulloch, originator of the wage-fund theory. During its initial years it offered a predominantly liberal tone with occasional conservative voices through a mixture of literary reviews,* topographical approaches to whole bodies of literature*, and traditional essays.

In its first years, the *Foreign Quarterly* sought with some success to emulate the quality of the *Edinburgh** and *Quarterly* reviews*. Although its founder, Robert Pearse Gillies,* was the nominal editor* until February 1830, John George Cochrane* was the actual editor from the second issue to June 1830. Gillies, with William Fraser as unofficial co-editor, produced the first volume and subsequently avoided editorial duties, leaving to found the rival *Foreign Review*, taking contributors such as Thomas Carlyle* with him. In spite of this initial setback, under Cochrane the *Foreign Quarterly* flourished, reaching a steady circulation* of 1,500. Its goal was to introduce the English to foreign ideas and to this end the journal reviewed books not yet available in English translation, published essays and literary reviews as well as summaries of

whole bodies of national literature predominantly French and German. Articles from the *Foreign Quarterly* were even translated into French, German and Dutch.

The *Foreign Quarterly Review*'s initial success was not to last and in 1830 it merged* with the *Foreign Review*, but soon encountered financial problems that led to Cochrane's departure in 1834 to establish a short-lived rival, *Cochrane's* or the *New Foreign Quarterly Review*. The new editor from March 1835 to January 1838 was Frederic Shoberl* which led to the *Foreign Quarterly* losing its balanced content and treatment, as he emphasized the pro-Turkish, anti-Russian school of David Urquhart, leaning towards Toryism. There were two new contributors, John Stuart Blackie* on German literature, and on medieval subjects, Thomas Wright*. There was also a new rival to contend with, the *British and Foreign Review**, which contributed to declining circulation*.

The journal fell into the hands of editor Benjamin Edward Pote, known as the 'mad editor', between April 1838 and January 1840 with unfortunate results. The periodical became ultra-Tory in tone and the erratic editing led to contemporaries deriding the incoherent prose, the apparent lack of proofreading and the evidence of Pote's inexpert meddling as he used the journal to publish his own articles on antiquarian topics. After Pote's departure, the *Foreign Quarterly*'s editorship passed to the Rev. Dr James Worthington in April 1840 with a continuation of the Tory tone seasoned with a strong Church of England bias. Worthington's editing was superior to Pote's, but the journal continued to decline, and maintaining the tradition of former editors, Worthington founded a short-lived rival, the *Foreign and Colonial Quarterly*, later the *New Quarterly**, when he left.

John Forster* was selected (over Thackeray*) as the new editor*, and in a brief stint (July 1842-Oct. 1843), Forster temporarily restored the quality of the *Foreign Quarterly* by cajoling his own powerful circle of literary* contacts to contribute. His first issue included Edward Bulwer Lytton, John Sterling, Walter Savage Landor, George Stovin Venables, Frazer Corkran, John Oxenford*, Thackeray* and Robert Browning. Final editorial control was in the hands of Walter Keating Kelly for two years from 1844, maintaining the respectability re-established by Forster and retaining many of the old contributors such as George Henry Lewes*, Thomas A. Trollope, J. A. and Bayle St. John*, Andrew Valentine Kirwan, J. S. Blackie, Jane Sinnett and

Thomas Wright. Nevertheless, July 1846 saw the final issue, after which it merged* with the *Westminster Review*.* KC

Sources: Sullivan 1983, *Wellesley*.

FORMAT See Size and format

FORRESTER, ALFRED HENRY (1804-1872) Alfred Forrester was as much a writer as an illustrator* and also a significant stage designer. His career suggests a versatile talent, and his best-remembered work comprises comic books and children's books, with his own illustrations. His early career was as a contributor to the illustrated* information-based miscellanies* emerging in the 1820s, and most famously represented by John Timbs's*, *Mirror of Literature*. He did, however, contribute drawings to a number of major magazines with full-page designs during the early 1840s, most notably *Punch** (1842-1844) and wrote in the same period for *Bentley's Miscellany**. Using the pseudonym*, 'Crowquill', his later graphic work for magazines was confined to occasional full-page designs for the *Illustrated London News** and the *Illustrated Times**. He also provided the text that in 1841 turned R. Seymour's* *Sketches* from a graphic into a literary work. BM

Sources: Engen 1990, Everitt 1893, Houfe 1978, *ODNB*, Spielmann 1895.

FORSTER, JOHN (1812-1876) John Forster abandoned a legal career to become a writer and journalist*. His first published article appeared in the *Newcastle Magazine* in 1829. He contributed to the *New Monthly Magazine** and in 1831 edited* the short-lived *Reflector*. In 1832, after publishing an undistinguished volume of verse, he became drama critic of the radical *True Sun*. A series of articles on Commonwealth leaders in the *Englishman's Magazine** led to a commission to contribute to Dionysius Lardner's* multi-volume *Cabinet Cyclopaedia* (1836-1839). In 1833 Forster became drama critic of the *Examiner**, a weekly* journal to which he contributed regular reviews until 1855. In 1847 he succeeded Albany Fonblanque as editor. He also wrote political* articles and edited and contributed to the *Foreign Quarterly Review**.

Forster was friendly with several noted writers and actors, but his closest friendship was with Charles Dickens*. Forster became Dickens's adviser, literary executor and first biographer. Their association also led to journalistic opportunities. After Dickens resigned from the *Daily News** in 1846, Forster took over as editor. When Dickens's *Household Words** was founded in 1850, Forster became joint proprietor* with William Bradbury, Frederick Mullet Evans and W. H. Wills. He also contributed

articles to the journal. In later years Forster had differences with Dickens and there was a rift in their relationship. Nevertheless, Dickens made Forster executor of his will and bequeathed important manuscripts to him. Two years after the author's death, Forster published his three-volume *Life of Charles Dickens*. DHL

Sources: Davies 1983, Fenstermaker 1984, Harle 1888, *ODNB*, *The Times* 1876.

FORSTER, THOMAS IGNATIUS MARIA (1789-1860) Following a Rousseauan education that emphasized a love of nature, Forster began contributing articles to the *Philosophical Magazine** even before becoming a medical student at Cambridge. His first article in 1808, on swallow migration, was signed 'Philochelidon', a pseudonym* he was still using when writing for the *Magazine of Natural History** two decades later. Forster continued to write for the *Philosophical Magazine*, as well as the occasional journal the *Pamphleteer*, on an eclectic range of sometimes eccentric scientific* subjects, including vegetarianism – which he considered man's natural state – and animal immortality. In 1806 he had been attracted to Franz Joseph Gall's theories of the relation between brain and character, probably after reading a favourable account in the *Medical and Physical Journal*, and in January 1815 he coined the term 'phrenology' to describe them in an article for the *Philosophical* Magazine (reprinted a month later in the Pamphleteer). In the following year he helped set up a famous lecture in Edinburgh in which Johann Gaspar Spurzheim, with a copy of the periodical in his hand, refuted John Gordon's critical account of phrenology in the *Edinburgh Review**. Forster continued to publish fulsome accounts of the controversial new science in the *Philosophical Magazine;* indeed the partiality of his articles suggests that the journal's editor Alexander Tilloch* was himself sympathetic to phrenology. GD

Sources: Cooter 1984, Lightman 2004a, *ODNB*.

***FORTNIGHTLY REVIEW* (1865-1954)** Modelled on the French *Revue des Deux Mondes*, the *Fortnightly Review* was in the vanguard of change in mid-century periodical publishing*. Founded in 1865 by a proprietorial* collective – including Anthony Trollope*, Frederic and Edward Chapman*, E. S. Beesly and James Cotter Morison, who together invested £9,000 initially – the magazine sought to create a new middle-class* reading market, one that would accept serial* fiction alongside weighty articles and reviews*. G. H. Lewes* was the first editor* and he sought to combine the opinion-forming, serious journalism of the quarter-lies*, with the more responsive criticism of the weeklies, together with the entertainment value of a shilling monthly*. And it sought to do so fort-nightly, in a hitherto untested periodical rhythm in the publishing schedule. Alas, its innovative hy-bridity was never appreciated fully by the reading public and after 20 months, the 'Fortnightly' be-came a monthly, though its name stuck.

The politics* of the periodical was equally exper-imental, outward-looking and offering a challenge to overly partisan journals, as the prospectus (15 May 1865, inside front cover) indicates: 'we propose to remove all those restrictions of party and of edi-torial 'consistency' which in other journals hamper the full and free expression of opinion; and we shall ask each writer to express his own views and senti-ments with all the force of sincerity…He will be asked to say what he really thinks and really feels; to say it on his own responsibility, and to leave its ap-preciation to the public'. In short, contributors were free to adopt a range of political positions and to do so under the sign of their own name. It was here that the *Fortnightly* was particularly making a stand, since anonymous* journalism was an unspoken rule in virtually all levels of periodical culture, though this was waning by the early 1860s. What the signed journal hoped to do was enable robust debate across issues, though in fact the *Fortnightly* became known as a Liberal, free-thinking journal, and the conserv-ative point of view was infrequently adopted.

Lewes left the journal at the end of 1866, and was succeeded by John Morley*, who cemented the *Fortnightly*'s reputation as a serious, often reformist, journal of intellectual opinion, for example cham-pioning women's rights and education reform. He also published poetry* by Swinburne, Rossetti and Morris*, unusual for an opinion-led journal. Among the other frequent and well-known con-tributors during Morley's editorship were Walter Pater*, T. H. Huxley*, Matthew Arnold*, Andrew Lang* and George Saintsbury*. Morley was suc-ceeded by T. H. S. Escott*, who edited for four years, making the journal more conservative than it had ever been, but when Frank Harris* took over in 1886, it became more radical. William Leonard Courtney* edited from 1894 to 1928, during which time the *Fortnightly* returned to its broad church of intellectual enquiry. MWT
Sources: Everett 1929, Sullivan, *Wellesley.*

FOSTER, MYLES BIRKET (1825-1899) De-spite a brilliant initial career as a wood* engraver, Foster became famous as a book illustrator* and

painter of the English pastoral scene, and his tech-nically innovative watercolours of the countryside were immensely popular. His pedigree as a wood engraver was impeccable. He was one of Ebenezer Landells's* many successful apprentices*, and the Landells connection put him in a direct line of ar-tistic descent from Thomas Bewick. It also gave him access to Landells's publications, especially the *Illustrated London News**, for which he drew a series of illustrations of English watering places that gave clear evidence of the magazine's commitment to ex-ploiting the artistic and technical ambitions of the wood engraving. The engraver Edmund Evans* was a fellow apprentice to Landells, and engraved many of Foster's early drawings. Foster drew occasionally for the *Illustrated London News* for a decade (1847-1857) and also contributed a few capital letters to *Punch** (1841-1843), thus again emphasising the precocious youthfulness of many Victorian illustra-tors. By the late 1840s Foster had become inde-pendent of Landells's influence and turned his at-tention to book illustration, which he developed through the 1850s before his late and extended suc-cess as a painter. BM
Sources: Engen 1990, Houfe 1978, *ODNB.*

FOX, WILLIAM JOHNSON (1786-1864) A controversial Unitarian preacher and politician, and later radical journalist and lecturer, Fox was largely self-educated. He moved from the plebeian radical culture of Norwich to London, where he be-longed to an influential network of dissenting intel-lectuals. From 1817-1836 he was the minister of the Unitarian chapel, South Place, Finsbury. His most creative phase as a journalist was the nine-year period when he owned and edited* the Unitarian *Monthly Repository** (1827-1836), a formative time in the history of British radicalism.

He transformed the *Repository* from a theological organ to a speculative and campaigning journal that developed a unique fusion of Unitarian and Benthamite thought. John Stuart Mill*, Thomas Southwood Smith, Crabb Robinson and William Bridges Adams wrote for it. Its feminism – Harriet Martineau*, Harriet Taylor and Sarah Flower were contributors – and extensive attention to literary and aesthetic questions, modern poetry* in partic-ular, distinguished it from the philosophical radi-calism of the *Westminster**, though Fox wrote the lead article for that journal's first issue.

But his radicalism was aggressive. In the crucial year 1832 his January editorial (Vol. 6) demanded funda-mental changes in the law, abolition of taxes on knowledge, state education and universal suffrage.

The forms of society, he argued, no longer realized 'the desires of the community'. He attacked the handling of the Bristol riots ('Who killed Colonel Brereton?': 130-134), and celebrated the dissection of Bentham's body (450-451). Later he campaigned for Chartism and the Anti-Corn Law League.

While MP for Oldham from 1847-1862 he contributed to journals that belonged to an important radical-liberal formation. Dickens's* editorial in the first number of the *Daily News** (1846), for which Fox was a leader* writer, echoed Fox's 1832 demands: 'Improvement of Education, Civil and Religious Liberty and Equal Legislation' (No.1: 4). He was co-owner of the *True Sun* (1832-1837), to which Mill, Dickens and Henry Hunt contributed. With Mill and G. W. M. Reynolds* he contributed to the *Weekly Dispatch**, and with Thomas Attwood and Henry Mayhew* to the *Morning Chronicle** and the liberal *Sunday Times**. IA
Sources: Fox 1845-1849, Garnett 1910, Hodgson and Slack 1865-1868, Mineka 1944, Parnaby 1979.

FRANCIS, JOHN (1811-1882) Publisher* of the literary* weekly *Athenaeum** for over 50 years, Francis was a leading opponent of the newspaper advertising* and paper duties collectively known as the 'taxes on knowledge*.' Born in London to a family of artisans, he attended a nonconformist free school to the age of 14. In 1823 he was apprenticed to a London news agency*, Marlborough's, doing strenuous delivery work until he completed his term and was hired by Charles Dilke* in September 1831 as junior clerk for the *Athenaeum*. He became the weekly's* sole business manager and publisher a month later in October 1831, and remained its publisher until his death in 1882. Francis assisted Dilke in 1846 to sustain Charles Dickens's* struggling *Daily News**, taking over its subscription list and using newsvendors to both deliver and promote the paper in the three years Dilke was editor*. With both liberal and radical political* tendencies, he became interested in the 'taxes on knowledge' in 1830. He founded and helped lead a campaign* in 1849 to repeal the duty of 1s 6d on newspaper advertisements*, which succeeded in 1853.

Francis went on to combat successively the newspaper Stamp Duty* of 1d per sheet (repealed 1855) and the paper* duty of 1 ½ d per pound (repealed 1861), travelling around Britain, serving on committees, addressing meetings and personally lobbying members of Parliament in their homes at all hours. The last of his committees, the Society for Promoting the Repeal of the Paper Duty, enrolled

100 members of Parliament as its vice-presidents. In 1872 he also took charge of the business side of *Notes and Queries** (1849-). Deeply religious and personally disciplined, he was said to have missed only one day of work for illness in his first 30 years at the *Athenaeum*. Contemporaries considered his successful half-century stewardship of the paper remarkable and unprecedented. DL
Sources: *Athenaeum* 1882, Boase, Francis 1888, Marchand 1941, *ODNB*, *Waterloo*.

FRANCIS, WILLIAM (1817-1904) Francis, the natural son of Richard Taylor* under whom he served a printing apprenticeship, was educated in Germany where he studied zoology and took his doctorate in chemistry in 1842 as well as developing an interest in natural history. While on the continent, he began to translate important chemical and biological papers for publication in his father's monthly *Philosophical Magazine**. On returning to London in 1842, he became an editor* of Taylor's monthly* *Annals of Natural History** and he and Henry Croft founded the bimonthly *Chemical Gazette* (1842-1859) which contained translations and abstracts of British and foreign literature*. In 1852, when Francis joined the editorial board of the *Philosophical Magazine*, he was made a partner in his father's large printing and publishing* house in Red Lion Court. On Taylor's death in 1858, Francis became sole proprietor* of the firm, Taylor & Francis. He continued to sustain and enlarge the firm's portfolio of learned society periodicals printing contracts, as well as scientific* textbooks. The firm also printed a number of titles such as the monthly trade* paper *Chemist and Druggist* (1859ff). He resigned from *Annals* in 1897 on taking a son into partnership but continued to co-edit the *Philosophical Magazine* until his death. WB
Sources: Brock and Meadows 1998, Lightman 2004.

***FRASER'S MAGAZINE FOR TOWN AND COUNTRY* (1830-1882)** *Fraser's*, founded by the exuberant, witty Irishman William Maginn* and his friend Henry Fraser, with funds from the publisher* James Fraser (no relation), was at the forefront of monthly* miscellanies* in the nineteenth century. If its early years possess something of the cheeky Regency period, its subsequent period was stolidly, soundly Victorian. Less literary* than some later monthlies, *Fraser's* was known particularly for its progressive stance in politics* and social matters, though it espoused Toryism early on and broadly took the conservative *Blackwood's** as its model and, as a result, chief competitor*.

Fraser's was thoroughly miscellaneous, with a strikingly diverse, even playfully wide range of articles on everything from Horace to the High Church, from ancient Rome to Scottish rationalism. Maginn, who wrote for nearly every issue until 1836 when he and the magazine parted company, was the presiding genius who ensured its lively, eclectic tone. His 'Gallery of Illustrious Literary Characters' was a high-point of the early years, providing pithy, sharply delineated sketches of contemporary figures accompanied by drawings by Daniel Maclise; the series was a milestone in the gradual shift towards personality journalism in the nineteenth century.

Alongside Maginn was a formidable group of writers who published important work in the magazine – most notably, Thomas Carlyle* ('Sartor Resartus', 1833-1834 and many significant essays) and William Makepeace Thackeray* ('Yellowplush Papers', 1838 and 'Barry Lyndon', 1844 among many other writings), but also figures including John Galt, James Hogg and Francis Mahoney. The influence of Maginn and his 'Fraserians' lasted far longer than Maginn's editorship*, and it wasn't until 1847, when John William Parker* and his son became publisher and editor, that a real shift in tone takes place. *Fraser's* relied less on brilliant wit and more on distinguished liberal thinking, with writers such as G. H. Lewes*, Charles Kingsley and J. A. Froude*, who took over the editorship in 1860. The magazine continued broadly in the same vein under Froude's direction, sometimes despite his own conservative politics, ensuring that *Fraser's* provided open discussion of politics and religion. By the 1870s, *Fraser's* best days were behind it, not least due to increasing competition from a range of new shilling monthlies* in the 1860s, including Thackeray's *Cornhill*, though *Fraser's* managed to survive into the 1880s. **MWT**
Sources: Fisher 2006, Leary 1994, *Wellesley.*

FREE REVIEW (1893-1897) John M. Robertson, a future M.P., founded and edited* this freethought* monthly* journal to replace Charles Bradlaugh's* the *National Reformer*which ceased publication after Bradlaugh's death. Costing a shilling and published by the firm of Swan and Sonnenschein, the journal had articles on the radical subjects of the 1890s such as the woman question, marriage and sex as well as religion* and secularism*. As the address to readers in the first issue declared: 'It is primarily an attempt to make a platform for opinions which are more or less unlikely to get a hearing in even the more advanced and established reviews'.

Contributors to the *Free Review* included in addition to Robertson, D. H. Balfour, Ernest Newman, W. Renton, Henry S. Salt, Mrs. H. D. Webb.

Robertson sold the *Free Review* to Roland de Villiers, who was the publisher of the *Adult** and Havelock Ellis's *Studies in Psychology of Sex: Sexual Inversion.* In 1897 the title was changed to the *University Magazine and Free Review* and the publication moved to The Watford University Press. Robertson continued to contribute to the journal under its new ownership until it failed in 1900 in the aftermath of its publishers arrest and death. **AH**
Sources: *ODNB*, Humphreys 2006, *Waterloo.*

FREEDOM; A JOURNAL OF ANARCHIST SOCIALISM (1886-1927) Co-founded by Peter Kropotkin and Charlotte Wilson*, this monthly* eight-page journal costing 1s was modelled on the French-language anarchist papers that Kropotkin had edited in Switzerland. The journal featured editorial comments against government interference in all areas of life, news* from labour movements and listed planned events and protests. It covered political* events both in Britain and abroad, and gave voice to Kropotkin's principle of mutual aid. As the first issue announced, 'We claim for each and all the personal right and social obligation to be free'. The subtitle of the journal changed to *A Journal of Anarchist Communism* in 1889. Until January 1895 Wilson was publisher*, editor* and main contributor, and remained associated with the paper until 1901. She published 'A Short History of *Freedom*' in the journal in December 1900.

According to *Waterloo**, *Freedom* was incorporated with *Fighting Call* in 1936, and *Freedom,* an extant anarchist paper (1936ff), positions itself as a continuation of Kropotkin and Wilson's journal. **AH**
Sources: Anarchy Archives online, *ODNB*, *Waterloo.*

FREEMAN'S JOURNAL (1763-1924) The *Public Register or the Freeman's Journal* was first published in Dublin in 1763 by Charles Lucas, the radical Protestant 'patriot'. In April 1806 it was renamed the *Freeman's Journal and Daily Commercial Advertiser* and retained this title throughout the nineteenth century, until 1924. A four-page daily* costing 5d in 1820, its price* dropped subsequently (4d in 1840 and 1d by 1860), and from 1872, daily issues were eight pages. Given its provenance, it is unsurprising that it supported the establishment of Henry Grattan's [Irish] parliament (1782-1783). From 1783 to 1802 the government paid *Journal* owner Francis Higgins to support its policies and actions. However, for much of the nineteenth century the *Journal* reflected mainstream moderate nationalist opinion, describing the approach of Catholic emancipation (1829) as 'the triumph of freedom' but opposing Young Ireland in the 1840s and Fenianism in the 1860s.

The Protestant John Gray (1807-1875), a moderate nationalist, became co-owner and political* editor* from 1841, and sole proprietor from 1850. He gave the title a more distinctly Liberal flavour, advocating Church disestablishment and the reform of local government, education and landholding. Gray became an MP in 1865, enhancing the power of his paper. Success enabled him to expand it from four to eight pages in 1872, while maintaining the penny* cover price*. His son, Edmund Dwyer Gray (1845-1888), a Catholic convert, took over as proprietor* in 1875, and the *Journal* followed its new editor's conversion to Catholicism. He also became an MP in 1877.

Considered by some to be the most significant newspaper for research into nineteenth-century Irish history, the *Journal* was at the heart of the country's political and cultural life throughout the period. When the Irish parliamentary party split in 1890, the *Journal* supported the Catholic opponents of Charles Parnell. Having previously supported Parnell, the about turn was for partly commercial, partly political reasons. Parnell had planned to publish a more radical nationalist newspaper and was seeking to lure staff from the *Journal* to his new venture. The successor to Parnell's *Irish Daily Independent*, the *Irish Independent**, absorbed the *Freeman's Journal* in 1924. **MJH/AGJ**
Sources: Brown 1937, *NCBLN*, *ODNB*, *Waterloo Irish*.

FREEMANTLE, GEORGE (1833-1894)   As chief music* critic of the *Manchester Guardian**, Freemantle was an influential figure in the musical life of northern Britain. At the *Manchester Guardian*, Freemantle worked closely with the editor*, C. P. Scott, to make music coverage an integral part of the paper's policy of promoting progress in the arts. Central to this endeavour was Freemantle's interplay with the conductor, Charles Hallé, and his mission to bring the best in music to Manchester and beyond. As an ally of Hallé's for a quarter of a century, Freemantle helped transform Manchester into a major musical centre, where orchestral music would be permanently resident, affordable by the many and where only the best music would be performed to the highest performance standards. Not only did he provide the Hallé Orchestra with comprehensive, informed, balanced and lively reviews*, but he also furnished its Free Trade Hall concerts

with free advance publicity, and even helped to write the programme notes so vital to Victorian audiences. Regarding continental music, although Freemantle found Hallé's 'progressivism' and emphasis on 'foreign' music often hard to bear, he was supportive of the works of several leading contemporary composers, such as Berlioz (invariably), Brahms (eventually), Wagner, Grieg and Dvorøák. As a staunch critic-patriot, he gave British composers, such as Hubert Parry, Charles Stanford and Arthur Sullivan, his consistent and wholehearted backing in his Guardian columns.

Journalism was an avocation for Freemantle: away from it, he was a millowner (Messrs Vernon & Freemantle) and sometime director both of the Free Trade Hall Co. and the Carl Rosa Opera Co. **MJH**
Sources: Ayerst 1971, Brown and Stratton 1971, Gunn 2000, *Manchester Evening News* 1894.

FREER, ADA GOODRICH (1857-1931)   Freer, who wrote under the pseudonym 'Miss X', was a psychic, psychical researcher and folklorist. With the support of co-founder Frederic Myers, she joined the Society for Psychical Research and contributed a number of articles to the Society's *Proceedings**. It was her work for the Society on subjects such as crystal-gazing and visionary experience which attracted the interest of William Thomas Stead*, who made her co-editor of *Borderland**. Stead claimed he conducted their editorial meetings through automatism, whereby Freer used Stead's hand to write reports as a 'writing telephone without wires', as Stead put it. Unlike Stead, however, Freer was not always convinced of the apparent products of her own hand. She did defend the hereditary psychic though, seeking to discredit trance-like states instigated by artificial means. Scandal dogged Freer in the later 1890s after she was disowned by the Society over the allegedly haunted Ballechin House in Perthshire, exposed as a fraudulent set-piece in *The Times** on 8 June 1897 by J. Callendar Ross. From 1897 she wrote for *Folklore** about the pagan superstitions and second sight of the inhabitants of the Hebrides but exaggerated her own contribution to the detriment of the folklorist Father Allan McDonald. **CB**
Sources: Luckhurst 2002, *ODNB*, Oppenheim 1985.

FREETHINKER (1881-)   The longest surviving secularist journal, the *Freethinker* was founded in 1881 as a 1d weekly* by George William Foote, one of the best-known and most combative secularists of the nineteenth century, The journal was closely linked with the National Secular Society though not an official organ of the group. In the first issue Foote declared, 'The Freethinker is an anti-Christian organ, and must therefore be chiefly aggressive. It will wage relentless war against superstition in general, and against Christian superstition in particular'. In an unusual move, given the contents and its aggressive anti-religious* agenda, articles in the journal were signed.

Foote wrote a weekly leader*, but its combination of humour, puns, cartoons* and fake advertisements* with articles debating and debunking religion* and related subjects is probably one reason for its popularity*. It had sales of 10,000 in 1882 and circulation* never fell below 4,000, a fascinating phenomenon given the emphatic place of religion in Victorian society. In its second year, Foote went too far with the mix of humour and anti-religious argument and following publication of anti-religious cartoons in the Christmas* 1882 edition, he was prosecuted for blasphemy and sentenced to 12 months' imprisonment with hard labour. However, in the judgment, Lord Chief Justice Coleridge ruled that it was the manner and not the content of an alleged blasphemy that mattered, a fundamental change in the law. Foote, however, still went to jail for the manner of his attacks on Christianity and Edward Aveling, the socialist campaigner, kept the magazine in production to the annoyance of the Home Office. Foote was editor* until his death in 1915 when Chapman Cohen, who had been assistant editor since 1898, became editor.

The journal continued throughout the twentieth and into the twenty-first centuries. In 2006 its masthead* was changed from Secular Humanist Monthly to The Voice of Atheism since 1881 and since 1998 its editor has been Barry Duke. **AH** Sources: Marsh 1998, ODNB.

FREETHOUGHT PRESS The campaign for freedom of thought required freedom of expression, on the platform and in print. For freethinkers, therefore, the press was both the medium and the message and their leaders were invariably publishers* and editors* of the press. Freethinking in the eighteenth century had been a popularised offshoot of enlightenment coffee-house society propagated through pamphlet literature. This began to change in the 1790s when Thomas Paine in The Age of Reason (1793-1794) attacked both the political structure of monarchy and its ideological underpinnings in revealed religion. Freethought in the nineteenth century was cast in this image, promoting through the press a twin critique of established politics* and religion*. The nature of this press also began to

change as the single reasoned argument of the pamphlet was supplemented by the monthly* or weekly* periodical. The latter was usually shorter and cheaper, containing several articles together with announcements, news* of meetings and advertisements* – usually for in-house* publications*. Frequently a leader would work up a theme in lectures, then publish them in serial form for his or (occasionally) her periodical, and eventually rescue the text from the periodical's ephemera to issue it, suitably revised and developed, as a pamphlet. Occasionally, especially when original copy was short, the process might be reversed and a longer and perhaps expensive freethought 'classic' might be extracted and serialized in the periodical. This remained the basic format throughout the nineteenth century. The content was serious, even dull, and illustrations* were few until deliberately exploited for propagandist purposes in the 1880s. Sales were from a few hundred to, at most, around 10,000. At first they were only octavo or quarto in size*, running to eight or 16 pages and consuming no more than one sheet of highly-taxed paper. With the success of the campaign against the 'Taxes on Knowledge'*, in which freethinkers took a prominent part in the 1830s and 1850s, the periodical became larger, usually 16 pages of foolscap folio. There was even briefly an attempt, with the first issues of the National Reformer* in 1860, to put out a weekly broadsheet newspaper but this was abandoned on practical grounds in 1864.

Throughout the century, freethought editors and publishers were prepared to challenge the law against blasphemous libel. This marked them out from the general run of radical publishers as they maintained an atheistic equivalent of the apostolic succession, beginning with Richard Carlile* whose Republican (1819ff)* set the pattern until the 1850s. One of those attracted to help Carlile in the 1820s was James Watson*, a publisher whose business poured into general circulation cheap freethought and radical literature, linking the post-war radical agitations after 1815 with Chartism and beyond. Another pioneer, Charles Southwell*, a discontented Owenite* lecturer, was the first freethought editor to be imprisoned for blasphemy in the periodical press when his Oracle of Reason (1841-1843) was prosecuted in 1842. Among those drawn into freethought from Owenism by Southwell was G. J. Holyoake*, who from 1854 distributed Watson's stock from the printing and publishing house he had established with his brother Austin in Fleet Street*. Holyoake made several attempts to create a national freethought movement organized around his weekly periodical, the *Reasoner** (1846ff), before Secularism caught on in the 1850s. It was not until 1866, though, by which time Charles Bradlaugh* had displaced Holyoake as the leading Secularist, that a truly national organization, the National Secular Society, succeeded, based on Bradlaugh's periodical, the *National Reformer* (1860ff).

At its height in the 1880s, Secularism was able to support three major weekly periodicals but, since freethought attracted the independently minded, it was always prone to fissure, leading to a proliferation of many more minor and ephemeral papers. The three main periodicals and associated publishing ventures were: the *National Reformer* edited by Bradlaugh and, for a time, Annie Besant*; the *Secular Review**, later the *Agnostic Journal**, edited first by Charles Watts (1836-1906) and then W. Stewart Ross (1844-1906); and the *Freethinker** (1881ff), edited by George William Foote (1850-1915). Foote was an innovator, adding to the usual contents a weekly anti-Christian 'Bible' cartoon*, for which he was censored* by imprisonment for blasphemy in 1882. The three main publishing firms in the 1880s were the Freethought Publishing Company, owned by Bradlaugh and Besant; Foote's Progressive Publishing Company and its successors; and Charles Watts's business at 17 Johnson's Court, incorporating the Watson and Holyoake concerns. Under Watts's son, Charles Albert (1858-1946) this latter took a new turn in the 1890s as Secularism and its periodicals faltered and the nature of the publishing world and the reading market* changed, and in 1899 he launched the Rationalist Press Association based on the innovatory idea of a subscription book club. **ER**

Sources: Royle 1974, Royle 1980.

FRENCH PRESS Although the history of the press in nineteenth-century France shows structural similarities with the British situation (i.e. a growth and intensification of journalistic discourses in step with increasing literacy), France's diverging political* history also yielded conspicuous differences. France saw much greater restrictions placed upon the freedom of expression, in conjunction with a greater level of politicisation of the population. As a result, its press was more changeable, more polarised, and characterized by strategies to by-pass or subvert censorship*.

The restoration of 1814 formally instituted liberty of the press in an attempt to reconcile revolutionary France with the return of the monarch.

This liberty was curtailed, however, by press bills, stamp duties and legislation against libel and 'defamation'. Only with the July Monarchy (1830-1848) did something like a free press develop. The Guizot Law of 1833 gave all French males access to elementary education, raising literacy levels considerably and ensuring the proper conditions for mass* newspapers to emerge. In 1836, Girardin began the first commercial daily*, *La Presse*, inventing the 'roman-feuilleton'* at one sweep as a sales strategy to guarantee financial independence. *La Presse* placed popular education above political partisanship; if it became politically colourless, this did not discourage idealistic expectations.

When all press controls were abolished in the wake of the 1848 revolution, a massive number of newspapers sprang up, their daily run growing almost overnight from 50,000 to 400,000 copies. Under Napoleon III, however, there was a crackdown and reduction that lasted from his 1851 *coup d'état* until 1871. Transgressions of censorial laws were heavily fined (newspapers paid deposits beforehand), and reviews* printed blank spaces or descriptions of rejected illustrations* when censored. Yet in response to so much state interference, the French satirical* tradition thrived (e.g. in the *Charivari*, started in 1832; in England it was emulated by *Punch**). The press was normalized with the fall of the Second Empire in 1870 and the subsequent establishment of a republican parliamentary democracy. If the decade of 1871 to 1880 saw 'la fin des notables' in France, this applied to journalism as well.

Important cultural transfers with the English-speaking world can be found in the *Journal des Débats*, distinguished by John Lemoinne's pieces on English politics and culture; the *Revue Brittanique* (edited by English translator Amédée Pichot from 1840), largely comprised of translated articles from the larger British and American monthlies and quarterlies* and the bi-monthly *Revue des Deux Mondes*, which took the advancement of French-European and French-American relations and understanding as its constitutive goal. **MdW**

Sources: Bellanger 1969 and 1972, Collins 1959, De la Motte and Przyblyski 1999, Ferenczi 1993, Martin and Chartier 1985.

FREQUENCY Temporality defines the periodical press and should be integral to the ways we think about it. The press operates according to different rhythms and schedules, each of which, arguably, produces different sorts of meanings culturally. The quarterly* review* requires extended periods of time for reading, enabling a reader* to read through the often 50 pages or more of a single article, whereas the daily cycle of the morning newspaper* is designed to be consumed more quickly, with less time for pause and reflection. In the nineteenth century, there were many frequencies – morning, evening, daily*, weekly*, fortnightly, monthly*, quarterly and annual*. Not all of these temporal rhythms were popular, either with the industry or with readers. As Anthony Trollope* wrote of the *Fortnightly Review**, 'we found that a fortnightly issue was not popular with the trade through whose hands the work must reach the public; and, as our periodical had not become sufficiently popular itself to bear down such opposition, we succumbed, and brought it out once a month'. Similarly, the short-lived *Monday Review* (1862), in a bid to challenge the dominance of the *Saturday Review**, argued that a weekly review published on a Monday could provide 'an honest comment upon its events, at once turning back a comprehensive glance at the six days gone, and casting forward a prescient gaze at those which are to come', but it folded after a few months. The frequency of a periodical generally needed to be synchronic with the established publication schedules of other titles. Magazine Day*, that day at end of the month when virtually all monthlies were published*, was something of an event – certainly a significant, recurring moment in both the publication cycle and in lives of readers. Magazine Day provides a useful example of how frequency comes to be integrated into the social frameworks of everyday life. **MWT**

Source: Turner 2002.

FRIEDERICHS, HULDA (C. 1856-1927) Hulda Friederichs (1856/7-1927), journalist, editor*, writer, born in Ronsdorf, Prussia, studied English literature in London in her early twenties under a scheme run by the University of St Andrews to help open up higher education for women. She passed the first part of its higher certificate in 1883 (*ODNB*) and that year began her life long career in the London press.

Her first break came from the editor* of *Pall Mall Gazette**, W. T. Stead*. An influential advocate of New Journalism* and sympathetic to the cause of women's rights, Stead initially employed Friederichs as his private secretary. She eventually became the *Gazette's* 'chief interviewer' (Waller, 411), employed on the same terms: and conditions as male reporters, a move highly unusual for the time, and the cause, along with her close relationship with Stead, of some antagonism from fellow *Pall Mall Gazette* colleagues: Robertson Scott* called her 'The Friederichs' and 'The Prussian Governess' (*ODNB*). Friederichs, 'probably the best known woman interviewer of her day' (Onslow: 225) was a pioneering journalist of the mainstream press: she specialized in serious women's issues, usually eschewed in such publications, and followed the turn of New Journalism towards more investigative* research, including first-person accounts, and advocated social reform.

She was among the group of journalists that left the *Pall Mall Gazette* with its then editor, E. T. Cook,* following the surprise sale of the paper to W. W. Astor. She joined Cook's team at the evening penny* paper *Westminster Gazette**, newly founded in 1893 by Cook and subsidized by Sir George Newnes,* in order to continue her engagement with liberal reformist politics*. She became editor of the illustrated* weekly family* magazine, *Westminster Budget** at Newnes's request, following a stint as a section manager at the paper, where she was left 'entirely free' to dictate subject and tone of the section. (Friederichs: 229-231; Onslow: 112, 150). Friederichs took advantage of this 'landmark appointment' (*ODNB*) to set the political agenda of this mainstream publication for nine years, from 1896-1905. She later worked as deputy to J. A. Spender* on the *Saturday Westminster.**

A linguist and biographer, Friederichs translated poems from Russian, Swedish, Spanish and French into English and German, and among her biographical studies are a seminal work on Newnes (1911), a study of women in the Salvation Army (1907) and a collection of pieces on Gladstone, complied from her journalism. **FD**

Sources: Friederichs 1911, *ODNB*, Onslow 2000, Waller 2006.

FRIEND (1843-) AND BRITISH FRIEND (1843-1914) The *Friend, a Religious and Literary Journal for the Society of Friends* and the *British Friend* emerged in 1843 to replace William Bell's *Irish Friend* (1837-1842) as the principal voice of the Society of Friends (Quakers)*. In January, William and Robert Smeal, of Glasgow began distributing* the *British Friend* to Bell's subscribers. The following month, a group of prominent London Friends organized the *Friend* with Charles Tylor as editor*.

The two monthlies were of the same size (21 cm by 27.5 cm), with the *Friend* printed in double columns* and the *British Friend* in triple until 1846, when it switched to double. The number of pages was highly variable, ranging from 16 in the first

DIFFICULTIES AND DELIGHTS OF INTERVIEWING.

By HULDA FRIEDERICHS.

PATERFAMILIAS had died. The mother, whom her husband had never initiated into the mystery of cheque books, asked her son—to whom I am indebted for this story—to write out a cheque for her. While he was doing this the tearful mother stood silently by his side. Presently she said with a look of unbounded admiration, "It is quite wonderful how you do it."

I have sometimes been reminded of this incident when people—"outsiders," of course, for to a fellow journalist these things are no mystery—have said to me after a little cross-examination about some interview I may have been doing, "It is perfectly amazing how you manage it." As a matter of fact, it is not amazing at all. Indeed, interviewing, besides being one of the most interesting parts of journalists' work, is the most natural thing in the world. For after all, what are the eternal "what?" and "why?" and "wherefore?" of childhood but the first efforts by little 'prentice-hands in the art of interviewing? Or what is human life from first to last but a long series of interviews?

Still, from the journalistic point of view, interviewing is partly an acquired art, or rather a matter of habit, and familiarity with it breeds—no, certainly not contempt, but facility. It is nearly ten years since I first began to practice this art, clumsily enough, I dare say, and certainly with fear and trembling. If I remember rightly, it was somewhere in the Midland counties, where I had been sent to interview the women working on board the canal-boats; viragos they were, almost every one of them, with loud voices, red, weather-beaten faces, and a look of grim determination which was anything but inviting. Through the long rainy day I had been tramping along the canals, accompanied by Mr. George Smith of Coalville and of canal-boat children fame, or sitting in the small cabins of canal-boats, or breathing the thick air in the darkness of some long canal tunnel. And all the while interviewing, cross-questioning the women, who gave inarticulate replies in a dialect which I did not understand.

Now the night had come, a night in an old, old farmhouse. To-morrow morning, so ran my orders, the first batch of "copy" must be despatched to town. But what, in heaven's name, was I to say, I asked myself in utter wretchedness when, long after 10 P.M, I was at last alone in my room. It was true I had gathered a great deal of information about the women by picking up this detail of their hard lives on one barge, another on the next, and a third while making friends for a few minutes with one of the poor women on the towing path; but all the information was a chaotic mass in my head, and absolutely nothing seemed clear except the one feeling of infinite pity for the poor creatures whose lives are spent on the canals—and for the poor lady journalist who was sent to write about them. If this was what interviewing meant, then interviewing was distinctly distasteful. However, I was not going to "say die" so soon, and sat down to write. The room was so large, the candles so dim, and the dark corners so uncanny that I

Figure 20: Hulda Friederichs on the art of interviewing* in the *English Illustrated Magazine*, Feb. 1893: 338.

[235]

year to as many as 58 pages later in the century. Both were wrapped with 10-20 pages of advertising*, largely for Quaker businesses and schools, religious publications, and employment wanted. Priced* 6s per annum and delivered by post, the *Friend* and *British Friend* both offered news of the Society of Friends along with general articles on religious* and social reform, poetry*, and reviews* of recent publications of interest to Quakers. The *British Friend* represented the more conservative elements in the Society of Friends, with its appeal to 'inner light' as a surer guide than scripture and its support for Friends' 'peculiarities' of dress, speech, worship and marriage rules. In contrast, the *Friend* represented the more evangelical elements with its greater emphasis on scripture and salvation through Christ's atonement.

The editorial history of the two publications was radically different. While the *British Friend* remained in the hands of the Smeal family until 1892, the *Friend* went through numerous editors and proprietors*. Charles Gilpin owned and sometimes edited the paper from 1849 until 1857, when he was elected as MP for Northampton. In 1861, the *Friend* began a new series and moved to Bristol. Page size* was reduced slightly to imperial 8vo., the subtitle was changed to a *Religious, Literary, and Miscellaneous Journal* without reference to the Society of Friends, and a motto appeared, 'In Essentials, Unity; in Non-essentials, Liberty; in All Things, Charity', a Restoration slogan usually attributed, falsely, to St Augustine. In 1892, missionary* and evangelical Henry Stanley Newman took over editorship of the *Friend* from Joseph Sewell and began weekly* publication, still with the advertising* wrappers, at 1d per issue.

In 1892, the *British Friend* began a new series at 6s 6d annually for 13 issues, including an extra annual issue covering the Yearly Meetings in London and Dublin. The new editors, William Edward Turner and William Pollard, co-authors of the anti-evangelical *A Reasonable Faith* (1884), represented a new, liberal Quakerism. The Old Testament motto (added in 1861), 'Stand ye in the ways, and ask for the old paths, where is the good way, and walk therein' was replaced with two less conservative ones. In stating their intention 'to present and apply the *principles* of *primitive Quakerism* to the needs of our time,' the new editors rejected both the quietist tendencies of conservative Friends and what they saw as the sacerdotal innovations of the evangelicals. Although the *Friend*, with its evangelical outlook may have more accurately reflected the dominant position among Victorian Quakers, the

British Friend was the first of the two to advocate the sort of liberal Quakerism that would define British Quakerism in the next century. The *Friend* also became more liberal and in 1914 absorbed its long-time rival. **DU**

Sources: Altholz 1989, Bronner 1990, Cantor 2001, Isichei 1970, Kennedy 2001.

FRIEND OF INDIA (1818-1883) The *Statesman and Friend of India* (1883-1894) established in Serampore, a Danish enclave near Calcutta, by Baptist missionaries* William Carey, journalist, orientalist and linguist, the printer William Ward and the teacher, linguist and outstanding second editor* Joshua Marshman, the *Friend of India** bore the distinct imprint of its Christian proselytizing background. Begun as a monthly* and continued as a weekly* from January 1835, it was sold in 1875 to the radical journalist Robert Knight and moved to Calcutta. It continued to be published as a weekly, incorporating the overseas edition of Knight's newspaper, the *Statesman*, till 1883, in which year it was amalgamated and published as the *Statesman and Friend of India*, continuing to exist today as the *Statesman* (1909ff.).

Of independent and liberal proclivities, the paper was aimed at educating Indians in Western religion*, literature* and the arts and informing the British about India. As its name implied, it was also conceived as a vehicle to befriend and enfranchise the ordinary man by publicizing what the missionaries considered negative aspects of Indian culture and society. Its campaigns for the abolition of *sati* (widow immolation), female infanticide and thugs (dacoits) – as well as, paradoxically, given its support for Oriental languages, the propagation of English education for Indians – received the backing of the East India Company government and bear testimony to this zeal. The only editorial shift from this policy occurred temporarily from 1852, under Marshman's nephew, the conservative Meredith Townsend, when the paper reflected his militant missionary zeal, and belief in the army and militarism* as the bedrock of British imperial* policy. Importantly, the *Friend* was part of an overall mission which witnessed the establishment of a school and the first Indian newspaper in Bengali, and later papers in Urdu. As such it has a seminal place in the history of Anglo-Indian journalism. **ChK**

Source: Kaul 2003.

FRIENDS' QUARTERLY EXAMINER (1867-) The semi-annual *Friends' Examiner*, which became the *Friends' Quarterly* Examiner, a Religious, Social, & Miscellaneous Review* after the first issue, was begun in 1867 by William C. Westlake in response to the rise of liberal theology. Although evangelical articles dominated under Westlake's editorship*, the *Examiner* contributed to the liberalization of British Quakerism by printing longer articles than other Quaker* periodicals and by its policy of openness to divergent positions on Quaker doctrine and practice.

Content and price* (2s initially, 1s 6d by 1880) indicate an audience of the better educated and more affluent members of the Society of Friends. Typical of reviews*, the *Examiner* was printed without columns* on pages 14cm by 21cm. In 1872, Westlake claimed a readership* of 1,000 British households. Although neither editors* nor contributors were paid, contributions (always signed or initialed) came from some of the most prominent Friends, including Joseph Bevan Brathwaite, Francis Frith and John Wilhelm Rowntree. With William Westlake's death in 1887, his brother Richard Westlake took over as editor until 1899, when he was replaced by George Newman (son of Henry Stanley Newman, evangelical editor of the *Friend**), although Westlake continued to contribute. Publication has continued to this day under the title *Friends' Quarterly*, and the commencement of a new series in January 1947. DU
Sources: Altholz 1989, Bronner 1990, Isichei 1970, Kennedy 2001.

FRINGE MEDICAL PRESS See Medical press (alternative/complementary/fringe)

FROST, THOMAS (1821-1908) A radical journalist* and novelist from a working-class background in Croydon, Thomas Frost made a living as a writer although he was often plagued by money problems. In the 1840s, Frost was active in both the Chartist* and the Owenite* socialist movements. With only a small amount of capital, he managed to revive and publish the *Communist Chronicle*, and after a dispute with John Goodwyn Barmby, the paper's editor*, Frost then issued the short-lived *Communist Journal*. With the end of Chartism, and unable to make a living out of fiction, he worked as a journalist and editor for numerous Liberal periodicals and newspapers including the (Liverpool) *Albion*, *Birmingham Journal*, *Northern Star** and *Shrewsbury Chronicle*. In 1882 he edited the *Barnsley Times*, one of the rare occasions he worked for a pro-Tory paper. Frost's two volumes of memoirs have become key sources for understanding journalism, literary life and popular politics in the mid-nineteenth century. RM
Sources: Frost 1880, Frost 1886, Gurney 2006.

FROUDE, JAMES ANTHONY (1818-1894) After a turbulent early career as the young rebel writer of notorious theological novels, Froude became prolific as a historian, editor* of *Fraser's Magazine**, and Thomas Carlyle's* controversial biographer. Froude's first articles appeared in the *Westminster Review**; the most notable being 'England's forgotten Worthies' (July 1852). Despite the growing reputation of his 12-volume *History of England from the Fall of Wolsey to the Death of Elizabeth*, Froude was frequently the target of coruscating criticism in literary reviews*, particularly from historian E. A. Freeman in the *Saturday Review**. As editor of *Fraser's Magazine* from 1860 to 1874, Froude was motivated by the issues of the day, yet open-minded, with the ability 'of encompassing many sides of the same subject'. Believing that 'free discussion through a free press' was the best instrument of the truth, he published many articles with which he did not personally agree, including a career-boosting reappraisal of Robert Browning. During the American Civil War he carried opinion in *Fraser's* from both abolitionist and Confederate sides. A natural controversialist, Froude once described himself as having the propensity of always 'laying hold of the stick by the burnt end'. This gave him a fascinating relationship with the world of print media: a martyr's desire to publicly tell the truth, as he saw it, in spite of the painful consequences. LL
Sources: Markus 2005, *ODNB*, *Wellesley*.

FUN (1861-1901) One of several successful imitators of the *Punch** format* – a squarish double columned* page with illustrations* dropped into the text as well as forming full-page, or even double-page, spreads – *Fun*, edited* for over a decade from its founding by Tom Hood* the younger, is nonetheless a distinctive journal for a number of reasons.

First, it pioneered the simple linear story strip as a comic form, drawing on Continental precedents, especially the work of the German cartoonist Wilhelm Busch.

The key artist was James Frank Sullivan, brother of the better known and prolific Edmund Joseph Sullivan, who drew for *Fun* between 1878-1901, contributing both large-scale cartoons* and a series of strips in which he depicted the trials of everyday life, especially as experienced by the 'British Working Man', a stereotypical persona extensively developed by Sullivan over many years. The misadventures of Sullivan's 'British Working Man' offered an interesting alternative to Baxter's knowing

Figure 21: The cover of the first number of *Fun*, Sept. 1861.

provincial* 'Ally Sloper'* as a means of formulating a comic but not unsympathetic middle-class* response to the lives of the working classes. Second, Fun presupposed a considerable level of political* awareness and understanding from its readers* as it drew heavily on pastiche and travesty of well known periodical columns* like the 'Court Circular' for its humour. Third, *Fun* was extremely successful in reprinting its cartoons* in volume form and thus consolidating its 'brand image'.

As well as volumes drawn from work by Sullivan and George Thomson, *Fun* also offered a yearly 'Almanack'* with illustrations* by artists of the high stature of Small*, Pinwell* and Houghton*, doubtless brought in by the magazine's endlessly entrepreneurial owners, the Dalziel Brothers*. J. Don Vann has described *Fun* as 'perhaps the second most important comic periodical in the Victorian period', and, despite its obvious debts to *Punch**, it was able to sustain a combination of serious political commentary and innovative graphic modes over several decades. **BM.**

Sources: Houfe 1978, Kunzle 1986, Sullivan.

***FUNNY FOLKS* (1874-1894)** This was the first English 'comic' paper, the culmination of a tradition rooted in the English caricatures* of Hogarth, Gillray and the Cruikshanks, melding the Eng-

lish periodical with *Punch* in the 1840s. James Henderson published* *Funny Folks, A Weekly Budget of Funny Pictures – Funny Notes – Funny Jokes – Funny Stories* weekly* from 12 December at 1d. Its form was innovative in that its miscellaneous contents were divided equally between cartoons* and text and printed as large octavo: a newspaper in format*, light entertainment in content. Cartoons remained individual items – the strip cartoon developed later. With his paper Henderson targeted the better-educated working/lower-middle class* reader by offering them superior illustrations*, including reprints from German and French sources, employing artists of the calibre of John Proctor and aiming for intelligent satire*, and lively text. It was designed for adults: the first 'comic' specifically written for children* was William Long's *Jack and Jill** in 1885, but within two years this had been relaunched as *Jack's Journal. An Illustrated Weekly Miscellany for Everybody.*

One of Henderson's freelance contributors to *Funny Folks* was the young Alfred Charles William Harmsworth*, who drew on this apprenticeship when designing his halfpenny *Comic Cuts** (1890-1953). By 1892 this was selling 430,000 copies a week, and launched the major 'comic boom' of the 1890s. *Funny Folks* initiated the format of the British 'comic' that flourished until well into the middle of the next century. **LJ**

Sources: Carpenter 1983, Gifford 1975a, Gray 1972, *Wellesley*.

FURNISS, HENRY (1854-1925) One of the most prolific and respected illustrators* of the late nineteenth century, the Irish-born Furniss was an artist for *Punch** (1880-1894). Although to some extent classically trained, Furniss preferred to draw from life, and regarded the facility and speed of his draughtsmanship as the product of his talent rather than his education. A relentless promoter of his own interests in spite of a generally goodhumoured approach to life, Furniss's seemingly boundless energy brought him immediate work on his move to London in 1873. He always valued his documentary work for major journals like the *Illustrated London News** (1876-1886), and his book illustrations (Furniss illustrated nearly 30 of his own books as well as a run of 500 drawings for Dickens* among much else) above his caricature* and comic drawings. Yet during his 14 years at *Punch*, first as a freelance and then on a retainer after 1884, he produced over 2,500 images, many of them full page cartoons*.

Building on his rapidly made reputation, Furniss

THE TALK OF THE TOWN. 11

him a smile of welcome, but at the same time she moved a little towards the top of the table, so as to leave a space for him on the other side of her, an invitation which he lost no time in accepting.

A scornful poet, whose appetite was considerably jaded, has expressed his disgust at seeing women eat; but women, I have

noticed, take great pleasure in seeing men, for whom they have any regard, relish a hearty meal. The new-comer ate as only a young gentleman who has travelled for hours on a coach-top can eat, and Margaret so enjoyed the spectacle that she neglected her own opportunities in that way, to watch him. 'The ardour with

Figure 22: A drawing by Henry Furniss for the serialisation of James Payn's 'The Talk of the Town' in *Cornhill Magazine*, July 1884: 11.

worked as well for most of the well-known late Victorian illustrated journals, the *Graphic**, *Black and White** and *Good Words** in particular. After leaving *Punch* in 1894 after a row over the reuse of one of his images for advertising* purposes, he still found time to found several short-lived but not unsuccessful humorous magazines of his own. Furniss's speed and energy were an ideal combination for topical magazines like the *Illustrated London News*, especially as Furniss taught himself to engrave his own images to help him to meet pressing deadlines. He was also well disposed to the technical innovations of the late Victorian reprographic trades, and willingly used photo-reprographic* methods to give even more pace to his furious output. Furniss's two-volume *The Confessions of a Caricaturist* (1901) give something of a sense of the diversity of his many interests and achievements. **BM**

Sources: Engen 1990, Furniss 1901, Houfe 1978, *ODNB,* Spielmann 1895.

G

GALE, FREDERICK (1823-1904)   Frederick Gale was a solicitor, parliamentary agent and writer on sport, especially cricket under the pseudonym* the 'Old Buffer'. The exact division of his activities, in terms of the call upon his time and the level of remuneration associated with his journalism is difficult to gauge, as is the case with many occasional writers for the Victorian sporting* press. Born in Wiltshire, the son of a clergyman, Gale attended Winchester College where he developed an enthusiasm for cricket, later representing Kent in 1845, and captaining club side Mitcham, in Surrey, playing his last match in 1883. Articled to a London firm of solicitors, he worked as a Westminster clerk and later, independently as a parliamentary agent, as his sporting journalism* developed to take up more of his time. His work appeared in the sporting press, including *Sporting Life** and *Bell's Life**, specialist weeklies such as *Cricket* and *Baily's Magazine**, where he was a contributor up to 1903, and in a variety of periodicals including *Punch** and the *Cornhill Magazine**. Gale was described in his obituary* in *Wisden Cricketers' Almanack** as a 'prolific' writer on the sport, with 'a high ideal of the way in which cricket should be played'. James Catton*, editor* of the *Athletic News**, noted the 'charm' of Gale's sporting journalism.

Typically of sportswriters of this period, he collected his journalism in a number of books, which included *The Public School Matches and Those We Meet There* (1853), *Echoes from Old Cricket Fields* (1871), *Modern English Sports: Their Use and Their Abuse* (1885), *The Game of Cricket* (1887) and *Sports and Recreations in Town and Country* (1888)*. ST
Sources: Obituary *The Times* 1904, Obituary *Wisden* 1905, *ODNB*.

GALIGNANI, GIOVANNI ANTONIO (1757-1821); GALIGNANI, (JOHN) ANTHONY (1796-1873); GALIGNANI, WILLIAM (1798-1882)
Family of Parisian booksellers, newspaper proprietors and publishers* notable for their dissemination of English-language material throughout Europe and often referred to in accounts of nineteenth-century Paris. Giovanni was born in Brescia and moved to London (via Paris) in the early 1790s. There he married the daughter of a printer and had two sons, whereupon the entire family moved to Paris. In

1800 he opened a bookshop in the rue Vivienne aimed at English tourists and four years later began publishing mainly pirated reprints. Anthony and William both expanded their father's business on his death and rendered it respectable by entering into alliance with British publishers such as Colburn* and Bentley*, whose lists they reprinted. Amongst their many joint Anglo-French activities, they co-published the periodicals of G.W.M. Reynolds* in the 1840s. Under them, the English-language newspaper *Galignani's Messenger* (1814-1895) – for which Thackeray* worked in the 1830s 'for 10 francs a day very cheerfully' (Thackeney *Letters* II: 475) – became very popular with British residents and tourists, as did the Galignani reading room*, which moved to a premier address (224 rue de Rivoli) in 1856, where it still remains. AK
Sources: King 2004, *ODNB*, Thackeray 1945-1946.

GARDENER'S CHRONICLE AND AGRICULTURAL GAZETTE (1841-) The *Gardeners' Chronicle and Agricultural Gazette* was a weekly* founded and edited* by Joseph Paxton (1801-1865) and John Lindley (1799-1865). It prided itself on the quality of its journalism, original illustrations*, respectability and affordability. It used a larger format* to emulate a newspaper, reporting broadly on topics of rural economy, but including a digest of domestic* and political news*. The first leader* described the project as a 'record of everything that bears upon Horticultural, or Garden Botany, and to introduce Natural History as has a relation to Gardening*, together with Notices and Criticisms of every work of importance on the subject which may appear'.

Paxton and Lindley were significant members of the scientific* community and experienced horticultural journalists. Paxton objected to the tone and manner of George Glenny's editorship of the *Gardeners' Gazette* (1837-1844) and conceived a new publication which would be 'a highly respectable paper for the Gardening world, to be conducted in a gentlemanly manner'. Glenny (1793-1876) was ousted by his publishers and replaced by John Loudon*, who was also the editor of the *Chronicle's* original rival, the *Gardener's Magazine**. Nevertheless, Paxton continued with the launch of the publication which dominated horticultural journalism in the nineteenth century.

It was immediately successful. Paxton acted as general editor while Lindley assumed responsibility for all the botanical contributions and wrote the majority of the leaders*. The content was extremely varied, with reports on plant hunting expeditions, plans for the Crystal Palace, reviews*, descriptions of gardens, natural history observations, biographies and obituaries* of gardeners*, reports of flower shows and campaigns often in the context of national rather then domestic economy. One significant example is Lindley's announcement and response to the potato famine in Ireland. Its advertising* columns* became the main location for gardeners seeking employment.

The botanist Maxell T. Masters took over editorship in 1863 and retained the position until the early twentieth century. He was another active Royal Horticultural Society official and maintained a close connection with learned societies and the research community. The publication also continued to feature the work of professional gardeners on country estates, making increasing use of photographs* to enhance illustration*. NM
Sources: Colquhoun 2002, Desmond 1977, Tjaden 1983, *Waterloo*.

GARDENER'S MAGAZINE AND REGISTER OF RURAL AND DOMESTIC IMPROVEMENT (1826-1844)

This periodical was the first illustrated* horticultural journal published for a general readership*. The editor* and founder, John Claudius Loudon*, drew upon his popular *Encyclopaedia of Gardening* (1822) for a publication that aimed to provide a forum for gardeners* outside scientific and learned societies. Loudon's intention was to use the magazine 'to disseminate new and important information on all topics connected with horticulture and to raise the intellect and the character of those engaged in this art'. His first leader* declared that the magazine was for all garden lovers regardless of social rank, offered praise and criticism for the Horticultural Society and began his campaign for better education and pay for labourers and gardeners within the profession.

The publication was originally a pocket-sized quarterly* sold at 5s. The price* was kept relatively low by relying on uncoloured wood engravings* for its illustrations. Loudon's commitment to increasing the readership* and its popular cross-cultural appeal meant that it became bi-monthly in 1827 (at 3s 6d) and monthly* in 1831. The price was reduced until it sold at 1s 6d in 1835. The magazine was the first in this genre* to have advertisements; it also included news* pages alongside horticultural reports and journalism.

Loudon wrote extensively about his own travels, garden design, planting and cultivation, and his proposals for social and technical innovation. The publication reviewed* a variety of books and new horticultural inventions. To accompany his own writing, he assembled a team of knowledgeable contributors which included gentleman members of the Horticultural Society, overseas university researchers, members of regional horticultural societies, and amateur and professional* gardeners. The magazine encouraged controversy through replies to correspondence, and critical articles about current scientific and practical horticultural debates. Loudon commented on the activities of the Horticultural Society and reprinted extensive sections about the experimental gardens taken from its high-quality journal *Transactions* of the Horticultural Society* (1807-1848). When he was accused of plagiarism in 1827, he explained that he was making scientific* knowledge available to a wider public. The magazine ceased publication on Loudon's death. NM
Sources: Desmond 1977, Drower 2006.

GARDENING JOURNALISM By the 1830s, horticultural journalism had established itself as a commercial genre* catering for different professional*, class* and scientific* interests. The first gardening periodical was *A General Treatise of Husbandry and Gardening* (1721-1724), founded and edited* by Richard Bradley, Professor of Botany at Cambridge. Nineteenth-century publications evolved through the desire to promote scientific knowledge, e.g. : *Transactions of the Horticultural Society of London* (1807-1848). There was also the recognition of fashionable interest in gardening met by William Curtis's monthly* *Botanical Magazine** (1787). Each edition of Curtis's magazine had three coloured plates and the quality of illustrations* for later publications would become a distinguishing feature. The development of the gardening industry was also significant. The *Botanical Cabinet* (1817-1833) was a quarto-sized* illustrated catalogue for Conrad Loddiges's nursery, accompanied by plant descriptions and notes on cultivation.

Editors and contributors for these publications were largely drawn from the emerging profession. Chief among these was John Claudius Loudon*, who founded the *Gardener's Magazine*. Edward Beck, the editor of the *Florist* (1848-1861), was a nurseryman. Joseph Harrison, editor of the *Florist Magazine* (1833-1916), was a head gardener who achieved sales of 10,000 copies for this magazine in the 1840s. Robert Marnock, who launched the *Floriculture Magazine* (1836-1842), was the designer and curator of the Sheffield Botanical Garden.

Joseph Paxton (1801-1865) was associated with a number of magazines*. The *Horticultural Register* *and General Magazine* (1841-1848) had the same broad coverage and interest in expanding the readership* as Loudon's and many other publications launched in the 1840s. Jane Loudon's* *Ladies' Magazine of Gardening* (1841) was published for the use of those who were 'neither regular gardeners nor professional florists'. The *Cottage Gardener* (1848-1915), edited by George W. Johnson, introduced several innovations, including weekly garden planners.

The magazine which dominated the field was Paxton and John Lindley's *Gardeners' Chronicle and Agricultural Gazette**, founded in response to George Glenny's editorship of the *Gardeners' Gazette* (1837-1844). Glenny's publication followed the format* of a weekly newspaper with its front and rear pages covered in advertisements* and copy arranged in six columns* without illustrations. The content focused on show reports, correspondence and the forthright opinions of its editor.

Periodicals in the 1860s addressed the suburban gardener. James Shirley Hibberd launched and edited the *Floral World and Garden Guide* (1858-1886) entirely for this burgeoning market. In the 1880s several magazines printed photographic* images on special supplementary* pages, and publications such as Lovell Reeve's *Floral Magazine* (1866-1881) were dedicated to illustrating new varieties of ornamental garden plants. Hibberd's editorship of *Amateur Gardening* (1884-) resumed an emphasis on correspondence, gardening opinion and advice for and from readers. The overall trend in the nineteenth century was the increasing divide between audiences for lifestyle magazines featuring gardens and those seeking practical advice and information, both of which drew on a group of distinguished garden writers featured by the publications of William Robinson. The success of *Country Life** exemplifies this trend, although, while it featured gardening journalism, it has no claim to being called a horticultural magazine. **NM**
Sources: Desmond 1977, Tjaden 1983, Uglow 2005.

GARDNER, W. BISCOMBE (1849?-1919) W. Biscombe Gardner's speciality as an engraver* and illustrator* was the large double-page images that gave weight and spectacular visuality to the late Victorian illustrated* press. Like many engravers, he became an accomplished professional draughtsman and then a wood* engraver at an early age. By the early 1870s he was contributing substantially to magazines like the *Graphic**, and he produced much of his work in the form of admired engravings taken either from paintings by leading contemporary artists or produced as portraits. His magazine work showed a technical

mastery of the range of available techniques for reproducing the tonality and textures of paintings, a level of accomplishment acknowledged by many commissions for large-scale, highly finished illustrations from the *Illustrated London News** in the 1870s and the *English Illustrated Magazine** (1887-1892). He also contributed engravings of art works to the *Magazine of Art** and the *Pictorial World*. Unlike many less accomplished contemporaries, Gardner adapted well to the introduction of the process block, which had threatened to eliminate traditional if laborious engraving skills, but his later career both as an illustrator and a painter was undermined by drink. **BM**
Sources: Engen 1990, Houfe 1978.

GARNETT, JEREMIAH (1793-1870) Versatility was the hallmark of Jeremiah Garnett's career on the *Manchester Guardian**, and over the 40 years he worked as editor*, leader writer*, reporter, printer, as well as publisher* and manager*, and often the roles overlapped. He was central to the paper's success as it developed from a weekly* launched in 1821 with circulation* under 2,000, to a daily* in 1855, with average sales of 23,000 three years later.

The son of a paper* manufacturer in Otley, West Yorkshire, Garnett was apprenticed* to a printer in Barnsley. In about 1814 he joined the *Manchester Chronicle* as a journeyman printer, later also acting as a reporter*. He stayed until 1821, apart from a brief spell editing the *West Riding Gazette**, Huddersfield. He was recruited to help launch the *Manchester Guardian*, named in the prospectus for the 7d paper as printer and publisher. In fact, his role was that of printer, business manager and reporter on a salary of £120.

Garnett was a familiar figure on the Manchester Exchange, gathering news* and opinion, travelling widely on news assignments. He claimed to have occasionally set his own reporting notes in print, helped work the printing presses* and aided in the paper's distribution*, and he was credited with the design of print room improvements. In 1826 he became a partner in the business, with a third share of the profits. On the death in 1844 of *Manchester Guardian* founder and editor John Edward Taylor, Garnett became sole editor, a position he held until retirement in 1861. His support for libertarian causes through the columns of the *Guardian** may have given rise to a challenge to a duel by a Tory newspaper rival, which he declined, although he was later assaulted in the street. **ST**
Sources: Ayerst 1971, *Manchester Guardian 1870*, Mills 1922, *ODNB*.

GATTY, MARGARET (1809-1873) Margaret Gatty, née Scott, a respected scientific writer, prolific children's author, and editor* of *Aunt Judy's Magazine* began her career in journalism after a late marriage and in the course of bearing ten children. In 1848, forced to rest for five months in a seaside town, she was inspired to write *Parables from Nature* (1855) by a borrowed copy of Dr William Harvey's* *Phycologia Britannica* on algae; in contrast to her serious scientific* publications, she continued to publish much-admired children's stories, some of which had appeared in a volume from George Bell (1851). These provided the impetus for Bell to found the successful monthly *Aunt Judy's Magazine* (1866-1885), which Gatty edited and wrote for until her death. Her children, particularly Juliana, contributed stories to the magazine* along with others such as Lewis Carroll. When their mother died, Juliana continued to write in addition to co-editing the magazine with her sister, Horatia, until at Juliana's death in 1885, Horatia closed the magazine. **FCA**

Sources: Le-May Sheffield 2001, *ODNB,* Onslow 2000.

GAVARNI, H. G. S. CHEVALIER (1804-1866) H. G. S. Chevalier Gavarni emerged into the English periodical press on his arrival in London from Paris in 1847. He had become a comic artist after working in various roles as a designer and artist: initially designing machinery, then as an architectural draughtsman and illustrator* before working on fashion plates and for the theatre, finally turning to the comic representation of urban life. He worked for *Charivari*, the Paris equivalent of *Punch**, before he came to London where he was immediately taken up by the *Illustrated London News**, a journal always ready to give space to leading French graphic artists. Between 1848 and 1855 he produced illustrations* for serial fiction*, sketches of urban characters and robust if somewhat rococo images of the political upheavals in France during 1848 for that title. A versatile and adaptable artist, Gavarni worked in lithography* and metal engraving as well as wood*. His four-year stay in London coincided with his moment of greatest popularity, and he was a key figure in the development of the urban sketch as a graphic mode. **BM**

Sources: Engen 1990, Houfe 1978, Lauster 2007.

GEE, THOMAS (1815-1898) The reputation of Thomas Gee is largely determined by his political* influence and vision for Welsh autonomy and like many newspaper proprietors* of this era, he used his publications to disseminate his political*

message. Apprenticed to his father's printing works in Denbigh, he subsequently spent two years working in London at the publishers* Eyre & Spottiswoode*. In 1845 at his father's early death his ambition to fulfil a religious calling had to be abandoned when he took over the business.

He published a Welsh-language quarterly* in 1845, *Y Traethodydd* (the *Essayist),* edited* by the writer and theologian Lewis Edwards. This periodical was similar in style to the *Edinburgh Review** and continued until 1854. But his biggest success and most influential publication was his delivery of a Welsh-language* newspaper launched in 1857, *Baner Cymru* (*Welsh Banner).* It was merged with the Liverpool *Yr Amserau* (the *Times)* in 1859 to become *Baner ac Amserau Cymru** (the *Banner and Times of Wales).* An indicator of its significance was its employment of its own London correspondent, John Griffith, who also travelled worldwide reporting for the paper. With its Liberal politics combined with Gee's informed editorial control, *Baner* championed the Liberal cause.

A political radical, Gee's supported tithe reform, the disestablishment of the Anglican Church in Wales, voting by ballot, land nationalization and Welsh home rule, which put him in the forefront of Liberal politics in Wales. An adherent of Calvinist Methodism, his roots in the religious life of the community coupled with his political involvement gave him a powerful platform from which to expand and entrench his publishing business. Supplying Welsh language editions and all manner of religious printed matter demonstrated his marketing adroitness. Gee's success was founded on his ability to exploit every avenue of his trade, 'publisher – wholesaler, printer, binder, newspaper proprietor*, stationer and retail book-seller'. **CL**

Sources: *ODNB,* Welsh Biography Online.

GENDER AND THE PERIODICALS Gender, which, like class* and race, is one of our primary social determinants, can be read in the nineteenth-century press in a number of ways. Increasingly throughout the century, gendered reading became more strictly demarcated than ever before. If we take the example of juvenile* periodicals* from about the 1860s, a far greater number of boys' magazines were launched than in any previous decade, and numbers would continue to increase later in the century. The idea that boys should read different material from girls took hold at precisely the same moment that debates about women's rights and about manliness were taking place in the serious reviews*. The growth of women's* periodicals of all sorts in the mid-/late-nineteenth century – from the feminist* *English Woman's Journal** to the more domestic and conventional *Lady's Pictorial** – similarly suggests a gendered construction of reading and the press.

Alongside these somewhat overt constructions of gender in the press, it is important to think about how gender is constructed *within* the pages of the periodical itself. Through looking at the topics chosen for discussion in each title, the inclusion of serial fiction* (and what kind), the contributors who wrote, the range of fiction and non-fiction, the inclusion of poetry*, etc. – in short, through content analysis – we can determine a great deal about the way gender figures in the textual space of a title. Consider the innovative and liberal *Fortnightly Review** in 1865: in its early years under the editorship* of G. H. Lewes, of 131 different contributors listed in the *Wellesley Index*, only four were women, and they wrote a total of seven articles. While these figures don't tell us everything about gender in the *Fortnightly*, they do suggest the overwhelming way in which non-fiction journalism of serious opinion was largely written by men at the time, and with an intended male reader.

The *Cornhill Magazine**, launched in 1860 with Thackeray* as editor, sought to construct a periodical which kept the woman reader always in mind. This meant that overtly controversial subjects to do with politics* and religion* were not given space. 'There are points on which agreement is impossible', Thackeray writes, 'and on these we need not touch. At our social table, we shall suppose the ladies and children always present; we shall not set up rival politicians by the ears…' In short, the contents of Thackeray's *Cornhill* were circumscribed by a definition of gendered reading – controversy was for men, not for women – and the contents were edited accordingly. By the time Oscar Wilde* came to edit *Woman's World** in 1887, he was hoping to challenge assumptions about both gendered reading and gendered textual space, but his forward-thinking venture was somewhat ahead of its time and never made to pay. Determining the readership* of a periodical and unpacking the constructions of gender within its pages is not always straightforward, but it surely tells us something significant about how gender was understood by and shaped in the press. **MWT**

Sources: Brake 1994a, Demoor 2000, Fraser 2003, Hughes 1995, Turner 2000b.

GENRE AND JOURNALISM Although it seems a commonplace, the nineteenth-century press is characterized by a number of distinct genres beyond that of the usual distinction between periodicals and newspapers. At its most basic level, their generic contents, formal conventions and price* range are related to frequency of publication, but explanation of distinctions among genres does not entirely reside there: dailies* are both broadsheet and quarto, and weeklies* include popular Sunday* newspapers such as *Reynolds's Weekly**, hybrid titles that combine news* with reviewing* such as the *Spectator** and *Saturday Review** and regional newspapers that appear once (or twice) a week. Monthlies* include magazines*, by definition with a miscellany* of contents, and reviews, such as the *Fortnightly Review**, which tend to be weighty, more intellectual and far more expensive. Earlier in the century, reviews were almost all quarterly*, and that descriptor referred to their salient characteristic – their contents consisted entirely of book reviews, which, given their girth and number, could occupy readers over three months. In the 1890s a magazine such as the avant-garde and retro *Yellow Book** chose to appear quarterly, in order to distance itself from the monthly frequency of the by now popular* monthly press. Other generic descriptors in the nineteenth century include 'class'* journalism, which refers to specialist papers (e.g., the *Lancet**) as opposed to the default miscellany, 'clique'* journalism which comprises titles written by friends, family* papers, fiction papers, illustrated* papers, shilling monthlies, the penny* press*, police gazettes, society papers and the unstamped* press, to name but a few. Each type has its own set of conventions and discourses, pertinent to readers and later press analysts. **LRB**

Sources: Berridge 1978, Bevington 1941, Brake 2001, Mason 1978, Phegley 2004a, Shattock 1989.

GENTLEMAN'S MAGAZINE (1731-1907) The *Gentleman's Magazine,* possibly the first magazine, is certainly the longest running literary periodical. Appearing monthly for over 175 years, it served as a model of format* and contents for early nineteenth-century titles such as the *Monthly Magazine* (1796ff), the *New Monthly Magazine* (1814ff) and the *Edinburgh Monthly Magazine* (April-Sept. 1817). Between 1800 and 1900, the *Gentleman's Magazine* attracted a number of well-known writers, including R. D. Blackmore, Samuel Taylor Coleridge*, Charles Dickens*, William Hazlitt*, Henry Kingsley*, Charles Lamb*, E. Lynn Linton*, John Murray and John Ruskin*.

Founded by Edward Cave as a social 'intelligencer' under the title the *Gentleman's Magazine or Monthly Intelligencer,* it soon changed its title to the *Gentleman's Magazine and Historical Chronicle*

(1736-1833) to draw attention to its substantial Register section*, in which information about the preceding month was recorded. The size* of the journal varied between 96 and 108 pages. The price* also changed from 2s 6d to 1s (in 1868 – 1870, and in 1894), and to 1s 6d. A circulation* of 10,000 in 1870 had dropped to 850 by 1898.

The magazine was originally designed to appeal to a middle-to upper-class* town and country readership*, as indicated by Cave's pseudonym* as editor*, 'Sylvanus Urban', which appeared on the title page until 1856, and was later used by Joseph Knight when he became editor (1874-1906). Cave pioneered a number of innovations including parliamentary* reports, letter* columns* and poetry*. He introduced reports of military campaigns, complete with maps and charts. Other important subjects were antiquities, genealogy, history*, economics, agriculture, astronomy, physics, chemistry and items of interest to female readers such as cookery receipts and conundrums. Among the most notable of eighteenth-century contributors was Samuel Johnson. In 1754 Cave's brother-in-law David Henry became joint publisher*, and after Cave's death in 1766, Henry took over as sole publisher. In 1778 he introduced John Nichols (1745-1826) as his partner. Nichols took control in 1791, and the Nichols family* ran the *Gentleman's Magazine* until 1856.

Nichols doubled the size of the journal, which had originally been issued on seven octavo half sheets. He included longer reviews* and involved readers by giving considerable space to their contributions on literary* and antiquarian matters. He also gave more prominence to obituary* columns. In 1826 John Nichols was succeeded by his son John Bowyer Nichols who became associated with the magazine for the rest of his working life. After purchasing the remaining shares from the descendents of Edward Cave and David Henry when he became proprietor* in 1833, he gradually transferred the property to the publisher William Pickering*. In 1834 the subtitle was dropped, and for 34 years it was known simply as the *Gentleman's Magazine*. John Bowyer's son John Gough Nichols was assistant editor (1828-1851) and editor (1851-1856). In 1850 John Bowyer Nichols bought back Pickering's share and in 1856 sold the *Gentleman's Magazine* property to J. H. Parker* of Oxford. It continued to publish serious historical and antiquarian articles until 1868 when the new editor Joseph Hatton* introduced drastic changes. The subtitle was resumed in 1869 – the *Gentleman's Magazine and Historical Review* – to broaden its appeal in the face of competition from the shilling monthlies*. The magazine became less literary and its specialized features were dropped. It began to publish popular* light literature and serialized* novels. Hatton reduced the price from 2s 6d to one shilling. In 1877 the journal was acquired by the publishing firm Chatto & Windus*. Illustrations*, which included engravings and woodcuts*, ceased in 1880, and serialized novels were dispensed with in the mid-1880s. With increasing competition*, the *Gentleman's Magazine* became unsure of its direction. The last 50 years of its run saw a decline in its prosperity, and this longstanding title ceased publication in September 1907. DHL

Sources: Graham 1930, Griffiths 1992, *ODNB*, Sullivan, Sutherland 1988, *Waterloo*.

GERM: THOUGHTS TOWARDS NATURE IN POETRY, LITERATURE, AND ART (1850)

A monthly* magazine of art and literature* launched in January 1850 by a group of artists, writers and critics associated with the Pre-Raphaelites, the *Germ* foundered after four numbers, having sold fewer than 300 copies in its entire print run. Its importance, however, should not be measured in its unprepossessing form or immediate readership*, but rather in the originality of its conception and contents and the influence it exerted over the Arts and Crafts movement and fin-de-siècle magazines that followed. Also, it has been considered as the first 'little magazine' (Hosman, Demoor).

The *Germ* was a modest magazine printed by G. F. Tupper and published* by Aylott and Jones. No number exceeded 50 pages of letterpress plus the single illustration* that acted as frontispiece and a few pages of advertisements*; the table of contents was printed on the verso of the cover sheet. The title page duplicated the pale yellow wrappers' cover design: a sonnet in black letter surrounded by a gothic border, with title and publishing information likewise printed in gothic font. The interior contents were similarly severe, with black-letter titles printed over single-column* texts on thinly calendered paper*. Its price* of 1s may have seemed unreasonably high to the common reader, and the periodical was a commercial failure, with the loss principally borne by the printer. But this was no common periodical: rather than a wood-engraver's* interpretation of an artist's design, the *Germ* offered original artists' etchings; 50 copies of the first number printed the etching on India paper. In a material instance of the Pre-Raphaelite emphasis on the sister arts, each original etching was connected to the leading poem* of the issue.

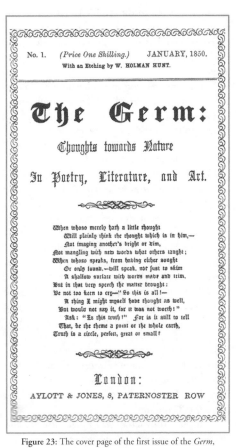

Figure 23: The cover page of the first issue of the *Germ*, Jan. 1850.

Dante Gabriel Rossetti initiated the idea of a monthly magazine of art and literature and the venture was supported by most of the initial Pre-Raphaelite circle. William Michael Rossetti, who went on to become the regular art critic of the *Spectator* later that year, was the *Germ's* editor*; he also contributed the sonnet for each cover. After the first number the anonymity* policy was relaxed and all contributions were signed, although some under pseudonyms. Christina Rossetti, the only female contributor to the magazine, published her poetry* under the name 'Ellen Alleyn', and Frederick George Stephens published his essays on art variously as 'John Seward' and 'Laura Savage'. A new title of the magazine – *Art and Poetry* – was introduced in its third number; it clarifies the focus of the magazine on poetry and visual art, while the subtitle – *Being Thoughts towards Nature Conducted Principally by Artists* – underscores its unique managerial approach, as it was 'conducted principally by artists'. The *Germ* thus unites the collaborative

aesthetic of the early Pre-Raphaelites with a nascent Arts and Crafts emphasis on the artist-practitioner.

Although Robert Buchanan called the *Germ* 'an unwholesome periodical' in his vitriolic 'The Fleshly School of Poetry', its contents were in fact conducted on an elevated plane. The dominant concerns of its prose contributions include art's moral purpose, the connection between medieval religious painting and contemporary artistic practice, and the importance of truth to nature in representation. Poetry was central to the magazine in both literary reviews and original contributions. Romances of love and death, celebrations of the natural world and imagined scenes from the medieval or Shakespearean past are the characteristic topoi of the *Germ's* poetry. Of the four etchings, two (by Ford Madox Brown and Walter Deverell) illustrate scenes from Shakespeare, one (by James Collinson) takes the Child Jesus as its subject and one (by William Holman Hunt*) represents a medieval diptych of love and loss.

The influence of the *Germ* on later periodicals of art and literature was profound. The lead artists of Pre-Raphaelitism's second phase, William Morris and Edward Burne-Jones, launched the *Oxford and Cambridge Magazine* in deliberate imitation. The first magazine of art and literature to emerge out of the Arts and Crafts movement, the *Century Guild Hobby Horse**, likewise took its inspiration from the early example of the *Germ*. Fin-de-siècle magazines like the *Dial**, the *Yellow Book**, the *Savoy**, the *Quarto*, the *Evergreen*, the *Pageant** and the *Dome** owe their late flowering to the seed planted by the *Germ*. LJK/TT

Sources: Buchanan 1871, Demoor 2008, Fredeman 1972, Hosmon 1970, Hunt 1913, Noble 1882, Radford 1898, Rose 1992, Rossetti 1975, Rossetti 1992, Rossetti Archive online.

GIFFORD, WILLIAM (1756-1826) When William Gifford was appointed editor* of the *Anti-Jacobin or Weekly Examiner** in 1797, he published the satirical writings of George Canning and George Ellis, both of whom were instrumental in the foundation in 1809 of the *Quarterly Review**, and in securing him as its editor. For the next 15 years, until 1824, he conducted the *Quarterly* on a determinedly partisan and politically* motivated basis. In 1818, *Blackwood's Magazine** noted that the 'temper of his mind' was 'scornful and intolerant', and the notorious review* in that year of Keats's *Endymion* was published by him. Hazlitt*, attacked in the *Quarterly* of July 1819, countered in his 'Letter to Gifford', 'It is your business to keep a strict eye over all writers

who differ in opinion with His Majesty's Ministers … you mind only the distinction between Whig and Tory ….You have been well called an Ultra-Crepidarian …. There is an innate littleness and vulgarity in all you do'. Hazlitt extended his attack in *The Spirit of the Age*, describing Gifford's *Quarterly* as 'a depository for every species of political sophistry and personal calumny'. Gifford was notorious for redrafting the work of contributors – Southey and others complained about this, but to no avail. **DIM**
Sources: Hazlitt 1819, Hazlitt 1825, *ODNB*, Shattock 1989, Shine 1942.

GILBERT, JOHN (1817-1897) John Gilbert was, 'the most prolific black and white artist of his time' (Reid : 20), draughtsman on wood and painter of historical subjects. He contributed some 30,000 wood engravings* to the *Illustrated London News*, including many popular double-page engravings, and from 1845 his illustrations* regularly appeared in the *London Journal*. He intermittently produced designs for *Punch** and provided most of the wood illustrations for weekly* magazines such as Vizetelly's* rival papers to the *Illustrated London News*, the *Pictorial Times,* (later the *Illustrated Times**) and *Once a Week**. In order to meet the deadlines imposed by the weeklies, he drew directly on to the block sometimes producing 12 blocks an hour. His skill and draughtsmanship enabled him to command 'enormous sums' for his sketches and the opportunity to work with some of the most prominent engravers like the Dalziel Brothers*.

Gilbert was also credited with being associated with '…the most beautiful books emanating from the London press…'(*Bow Bells* 4 Feb. 1874: 65), illustrating some 150 books and producing illustrations for works by Cervantes and Sir Walter Scott*. Some of the best examples of this aspect of his work can be found in S. C. Hall's* *Book of English Ballads* (1842), Longfellow's *Poetical Works* (1856) and Staunton's three-volume edition of *Shakespeare's Works* (1856-1858) for which Gilbert produced some 750 illustrations. As well as producing designs for some of the more popular, well-established magazines and journals of the nineteenth century, and for numerous books, John Gilbert produced large and vigorous engravings for less well known religious* and temperance journals such as the *Band of Hope Review**, *Leisure Hour**, and the *British Workman**. Gilbert was knighted in 1872 in recognition of his, 'lasting impression on the pictorial records of his own time' (*Bow Bells* 4 Feb. 1874). **FM**
Sources: *Bow Bells* 1874, Engen 1985, Goldman 1994, *ODNB,* Reid 1975, Victoria Research Web, White 1897.

GILFILLAN, GEORGE (1813-1878) The 'literary portraits' of George Gilfillan, literary critic, anthologist and reformist theologian, introduced literary and historical figures to a wide Victorian audience.

A minister of religion and an unstinting advocate of the poor and oppressed, Gilfillan also published* many books and more than 100 articles and literary reviews in the *Critic**, *Hogg's Instructor, Eclectic Review**, *Palladium, Celtic Magazine, Scottish Review** and other mostly Scottish periodicals from 1845 to 1878. His articles were reprinted in three widely read *Galleries of Literary Portraits* (1845, 1849 and 1855), in which he sketched the 'genius' and sensibilities of a wide range of predecessors and contemporaries, among them younger poets such as Sydney Dobell, Gerald Massey and Alexander Smith.

In 1854, W. E. Aytoun followed a hostile *Blackwood's** review of the 'spasmodics' Smith, Dobell, and others with a verse-epic *Firmilian*, in which he parodied Gilfillan as a too enthusiastic promoter of the works of neophytes. The assault damaged Gilfillan's reputation, but he continued to publish literary reviews*, many of which formed introductions to his 48-volume *Library of British Poets* (1853-1860) or called attention to the work of little-known Scottish writers such as working-class poet Janet Hamilton.

Itself little known today, Gilfillan's literary and religious* journalism merits more sustained attention. **FSB**
Sources: Boos 2004, Cronin 2002, Fennell 1968, Pursglove 1994, Watson and Watson 1892.

GILL, MICHAEL HENRY (1794-1879) Gill was a well-known master printer and later publisher* in nineteenth-century Dublin, apprenticed to the Dublin University Press (Trinity College) in 1813, and becoming 'Printer to the University' in 1842. In 1855 Gill purchased the stock, copyrights, (including those of the *Dublin University Magazine**) and Dublin offices of publisher James McGlashan* after the latter's retirement from business. Gill retained McGlashan's name, setting up the firm of McGlashan and Gill, no doubt trading on 20 years of public familiarity with the business. The new firm published a host of journals, from *Catholic Ireland* ('a monthly memorial of our country's consecration to the heart of Jesus') to the papers of the *Kilkenny Archaeological Society,* and *Now-A-Days,* concerned wholly with the publication of serial* novels and short stories. The purchase made Gill the most powerful printer/publisher in Dublin, a position he retained until 1874,

when he left the University Press. In 1875 Gill changed the name of the firm to M. H. Gill and Son and gradually passed the business over to his son Henry. Until 1965 the firm retained its own printing plant. It continues trading today as Gill and Macmillan, having formed an association with Macmillan of London in 1968. **ET**
Sources: Boylan 1998, Kinane 1994, *Waterloo*.

GIRL'S OWN PAPER (1880-1956) The *Girl's Own Paper* (*GOP*) was launched in January 1880 by the Religious Tract Society* as a companion to the *Boy's Own Paper*, intended likewise to combat the 'pernicious' influence of penny* papers. A 16-page weekly, the *GOP* (by which it was affectionately known) reached a circulation* of 250,000, eventually outstripping the *Boy's Own* and becoming one of the most successful girls' magazines* of the period. The paper was also issued in a 6d monthly edition, which included advertisements* on the end papers.

Editor* Charles Peters introduced the *Girl's Own Paper* as 'a Counsellor, Playmate, Guardian, Instructor, Companion, and Friend', offering information and entertainment without evangelical rigor. It comprised fiction, competitions, answers to correspondents*, music*, poetry*, and articles on topics such as household management, self-culture, hobbies, conduct, health and recreation. Fiction contributors included Rosa Nouchette Carey and Evelyn Everett Green. Regular non-fiction contributors included Emma Brewer, Sophia F. A. Caulfeild and Gordon Stables. The non-fiction was more progressive than the fiction: into the 1890s articles on education, work and independent living flourished. The *Girl's Own Paper* also had visual appeal, with spot illustrations* and half- and full-page engravings by artists like Frank Dadd* and Mary Ellen Edwards*.

The *GOP's* audience was mostly middle and lower-middle-class* young women between the schoolroom and marriage, though older women also read the magazine. This led to Peters's successor, Flora Klickmann*, to change the title to the *Girl's Own Paper and Woman's Magazine* in 1908. Under Klickmann the then monthly* magazine devoted greater attention to fashion* and domesticity. In 1928 the title changed* briefly to the *Woman's Magazine and Girl's Own Paper* before it was split into separate magazines. The *Girl's Own Paper* had renewed success in the 1930s but suffered after the Second World War, becoming *Girl's Own Paper and Heiress* in 1947, then *Heiress* in 1951, which folded in 1956. **TD**
Sources: Doughty 2004, Drotner 1988, Forrester 1980, Ward 1992.

GIRLS' MAGAZINES An early attempt at a magazine* designed for girls, the *Young Ladies' Magazine of Theology, History and General Knowledge* (1838), was short lived, but after 1850 successful examples of the genre* emerged. The distinction between juvenile*, girls' and women's* magazines in terms of readership* is not clear cut. The lively and resilient *Girl's Own Paper*, which lasted over three-quarters of a century and reached a circulation* of 250,000, and Charlotte Yonge's* *Monthly Packet* were both read by women in their twenties as well as girls in their teens. These older readers were also directly targeted by Beeton's* *Young Englishwoman* (1864-1877), then *Sylvia's Journal* – 1894)* and Edward Harrison's *Young Ladies' Journal* (1864-1920). *Aunt Judy's Magazine for Young People* targeted children of various ages, but its correspondence* columns suggest a predominantly female readership* and show evidence of over-18s still reading it.

Aunt Judy's (1866-1885) was published* by George Bell on the back of Margaret Gatty's* *Aunt Judy's Tales* (1859) and *Aunt Judy's Letters* (1862). In the opening number Gatty promised stories as a 'staple commodity' but also natural history, indoor amusements and the occasional 'talk about new books', reassuring parents that they 'need not fear an overflowing of mere amusement'. As a noted expert on seaweeds and zoophytes, she ensured scientific* articles of high quality, but her most innovative contribution was the 'Emblems', allegorical pictures illustrating 'some moral truth'.

Aunt Judy's was a family effort. Almost all of her daughter Juliana Ewing's (1841-1885) fiction first appeared there, which also published fairy stories by Hans Andersen and Lewis Carroll's 'Bruno's Revenge' (1867). Following their mother's death, Juliana and her sister Horatia jointly edited it until 1876 when Horatia took sole charge. Despite – or perhaps because of – its high cultural standards, *Aunt Judy's* circulation* was small, a labour of love rather than a profitable venture, but its core of loyal readers were enthusiastic correspondents and keen supporters of its sponsored children's hospital cot.

Though the *Girl's Own Paper*, published by the Religious Tract Society*, remained the most popular* girls' paper in the changing market of the 1890s, a rival publication was *Atalanta**, edited solely or in collaboration until 1894, by L. T. (Elizabeth Thomasina) Meade*. It aimed at an intellectually high level, with contributors like Millicent Fawcett*, Margaret Oliphant* and R. L. Stevenson, and actively promoted higher education and careers for girls.

Figure 24: Detail of the 'Answers to Correspondents'* page in the *Girl's Own Paper*, 20 Jan. 1883.

A number of new girls' magazines were launched in the late 1890s and early twentieth century, including the 6d monthly *Girl's Realm* (1898-1915), published by Hutchinson, and the ½d romantic fiction magazines such as the *Girl's Best Friend* (1898-1899, then *Girl's Friend* to 1931) aimed at working-class* girls. BMO

Sources: Drotner 1988, Ewing 1885, *ODNB*, Onslow 2000.

GLASGOW HERALD (1783-) Launched as the *Glasgow Advertiser** by the printer John Mennons, it became the *Herald and Advertiser* in 1802, priced* 6d, before being abbreviated to the *Glasgow Herald* in August 1805. Samuel Hunter edited* and published* it from 1803 for the next 34 years. Its four pages carried classified advertisements* and *London Gazette* announcements, shipping news*, London, foreign and local* news, Parliamentary* reports, prices and advertising. In 1820, it was a five-column* broadsheet, costing 7d. Twice weekly, it projected Hunter's Tory politics*, rejecting the demands for parliamentary reform but critical of the Corn Laws. Hunter's successor, after a brief interregnum under Francis Weir, was George Outram who edited it from 1837 to 1856; he followed a moderate Toryism in shaping his editorial comments and stood firmly on the side of the established Church.

Challenged from 1847, when it cost 4 ½d, by the first Scottish daily, the *North British Daily Mail*, a Wednesday edition was added in July 1855 to the existing Monday and Friday issues, but it was not until January 1859 that it became a 1d daily*, with seven columns*, eight pages Monday and Friday, four pages Tuesday to Thursday and enhanced contents. After Outram's longstanding assistant, James Pagan, assumed editorial control (1856-1870), a new professionalism* was apparent and circulation* rose to 25,000 by the end of the 1860s. Always responsive to Glasgow business views it initially supported the Confederacy in the American Civil War. Under William Jack (1870-1875), the paper became more sympathetic to Liberalism and more national* in its coverage. But, after 1886, Jack's successor, James H. Stoddart (1875-1888), placed the paper behind Liberal Unionism, a position maintained by his successor, Charles C. Russell (1888-1907). From 1837 the proprietors* were the heirs of the early partners, under the name of George Outram & Co., which became a private limited company in 1903. **WHF**

Sources: Cowan 1956, Ewing 1948, 19CBLN, *ODNB*, Phillips 1982, Sinclair 1896, *Waterloo Scotland*.

GLASGOW LOOKING GLASS (1825) AND NORTHERN LOOKING GLASS (1825-1826) Only 17 issues of the *Glasgow Looking Glass* and its immediate successor the *Northern Looking Glass* were ever published, but the periodical has enormous historical importance as the first magazine entirely devoted to caricature*. Produced fortnightly from 11 June 1825 until 3 April 1826, with a couple of later numbers, the title was changed after the first five issues to draw in a broader readership*. Its contents mainly comprised caricatures by William Heath*, but the large-page multi-image format* shifted from lithography* into etched plates after seven issues, and by issue nine had also begun to incorporate letterpress. Centred on traditional caricature tropes drawn from contemporary manners, the two magazines nonetheless had a lot to say on other topics, especially the abuses of the medical profession. One important feature of the magazine*, which was in any form expensive, was the publication of a 'beautifully coloured' edition which cost 6s against the 1s for the 'common' edition. In its use of lithography, (Twyman notes that there was only one lithographic press in Glasgow at this time), its recognition of the significance of seriality in the production of comic images, its use of an increasingly complex multi-mode page incorporating both words and images and its ability to transcend local gossip*, the *Glasgow Looking Glass* opened the way for Thomas McClean's London-based *Looking Glass** of 1830 and the consequent flood of caricature based and illustrated comic magazines. **BM**

Sources: Glasgow University Library Special Collections website, Twyman 2001.

GLASGOW SENTINEL (1850-1877) Owned by Alexander Gardner (1821-1882), the Owenite* socialist later to become a renowned photographer of the American Civil War, and edited* (1850-1860) from its inception by the activist Owenite Robert Buchanan*, this Chartist then Radical, anti-clerical, freethinking weekly*, priced* initially at 4 ½d was the principle working-class* paper in the west of Scotland in its day. Gardner wrote the leaders* and supported socialism* and reforms, such as those in the Charter, to benefit the working class*. As he said in the initial issue, he had purchased the paper 'as a means of enlightening the public on the great political, educational, and social questions of the times and of guiding right the popular mind of this country on all matters of state policy whatever advice was necessary or important'. Published every Saturday, the weekly reported on national and international news*. Within three months of Gardner taking control, circulation* had grown to 6,500.

Over its run, it changed its publisher*, size*, pagination and title in various permutations. In 1856 Gardner moved to the United States and eventually in the 1860s the editorship passed to the veteran trade unionist, Alexander Campbell, who had worked on the *Glasgow Chronicle*. Beginning as a 16-page broadsheet printed by George MacKay & Co, and entitled simply the *Glasgow Sentinel,* it expanded to the *Glasgow Sentinel and Scottish Banner* (1864-1868) when it merged* with the *Scottish Banner*, and finally to the *Glasgow Sentinel and Journal of the Industrial Interests* (1868-1877).

Larger in size but down to eight pages in 1862, and switching to four still larger pages in 1868, it cost 1 ½d in 1863, dropping to 1d in 1864 when James Watt was publisher. It was still priced at a penny* when it ceased publication. Circulation* in 1854 was reportedly 4,500 per week, and the paper claimed a guaranteed figure of 15,000 in 1868. Multiple editions were a feature, and in 1868 for example it typically produced a 'Town Edition', a 'Country Edition' and a 'Second Edition'. Breaking news could be added to later editions. It featured full coverage of trade union and labour news*, along with national, local, and foreign news, parliamentary reports*, trade information including market* prices, railway timetables, mining intelligence and shipping news, serial* fiction, literature* and art. At best classified advertisements* made up 25 per cent of the paper. Besides the writing of Buchanan, leader articles were allegedly contributed by Lloyd Jones, writing as 'Cromwell'.

Two earlier newspapers with this title appeared in Glasgow in the nineteenth century. The first (1809-1811), bore on its front page the Glasgow coat-of-arms. It supported electoral reform, attacked sinecures, praised William Cobbett and was succeeded by the *Glasgow Chronicle* (1811-1857).The second *Sentinel* (1821-1823) was owned by William Borthwick and edited by Robert Alexander; it was a militant Tory paper supported by the government, though its style 'was lively, its readers' correspondence* copious and its arrangement and type as attractive as any contemporary's' (Cowan: 63). This version of the *Sentinel* came to an end when a duel fought over some material published in the paper resulted in the death of Sir Alexander Boswell, alleged to be the author of the offending copy. LRB/AH

Sources: Aspinall 1949, *Chambers Biographical Dictionary,* Cowan 1946, Fraser 1971, Jack 1855, *ODNB,* Spartacus International (online), *Waterloo Scotland*, Webb 1896.

GLOBAL JOURNALISM Coverage of events and people in far away lands varied greatly between newspapers but in general was more limited than today. However, by 1850 foreign* news* had become a staple of national daily* titles, supported by the rapidly developing international transport* and communication infrastructure. Though steamships* and railways were important for bulkier and less topical items such as fiction serials and feuilletons* distributed by Fiction Bureaux, the telegraph* proved key for news. For instance, a letter posted in England could take five to eight months to reach India in the 1830s, while a telegram could reach Bombay in five hours in the 1870s (Thompson 1995: 154). Demand for financial* information was a driving force as burgeoning international trade and investment required a constant supply of up-to-date reliable data (see Financial Journals*). Furthermore, colonization and empire building, as Thussu (2000: 13) reminds us, required a constant source of information to establish and maintain political alliances and military* security (see also Imperialism* and Journalism*). Population migration as a result of industrialization and colonization was also an important source of demand for information about places overseas: readers wanted to find out about countries to which their relatives had emigrated or they themselves were about to embark. A pecking order of which countries were covered in the news became established, forming a system of news values and news construction that has not changed significantly since. Countries with the most economic and political power and those with the closest ties to Britain were featured, while other states were hardly ever covered.

If not all countries were represented in the press, many could not themselves access international information flow, and in this respect global journalism in the nineteenth century was not really global. Even more than now, 'the dominant powers of the world made and remade global interconnections, controlled the infrastructures that supported them and devised and controlled the institutions that regulated them' (Held *et al.* 1999: 423). The early telegraph was dominated by British and other Western commercial interests, and the content of the information flow reflected that. Inequalities in information flow were also reinforced by the structures of international news provision.

By the mid-nineteenth century international news flow was controlled and dominated by three European news agencies* which formed a cartel and marketed 'news' as commodity. The first news agency was established in Paris by Charles Havas in 1835, followed in 1849 by Wolff in Berlin and in 1851 by Reuter's* in London. Competition* was at first fierce among them (Reuter and Wolff were both former employees of Havas), but they soon agreed to divide the world into mutually exclusive territories. Reuters obtained the British Empire and the Far East; Havas acquired the French Empire, Italy, Spain and Portugal; Wolff was granted the exclusive rights to operate in German, Austrian, Scandinavian and Russian territories (Thompson 1995: 155). Each agency was a commercial enterprise, but worked closely with the political and commercial elites of their own country and received subsidies from their governments.

Most media organizations relied on news agencies for their foreign news. Very few had their own foreign correspondents* and then only a handful in a very limited number of places (e.g. *Morning Post**, *Daily News**). Indeed, until the 1860s, 'only *The Times** was willing and able to meet the expense of an extensive network of correspondents and stringers to telegraph news from around the world' (Allan 1999: 20). Other British newspapers relied almost entirely on Reuters for their foreign news, a more cost effective option than maintaining an expensive network of correspondents, an important factor during the drive to form a cheap* daily press after 1850. News agencies were not only important as the main definers of foreign news, but they also altered the process of news dissemination and contributed to changing perceptions of 'news' and 'objectivity' by taking pride in providing the essential facts of 'hard' news, leaving 'opinions' and 'interpretations' to their client newspapers (Allan 1999: 18), a division of labour which gradually led the profession, and the public, to distinguish between the two. News agencies also contributed to a change in the news values of media organiZations in relation to timeliness, with a more emphatic and constant focus on 'dailyness' and the immediate present, generating a habitual expectation of (and desire for) the world in constant crisis, very different from financial journals earlier in the century which were regularly content to print 'there is nothing to report'. **AG**

Sources: Allan 1999, Chapman 2005, Held *et al.* 1999, Rantanen 1997, Thompson 1995, Thussu 2000.

GLOBE (1803-1921) During its 118-year history, the evening daily* the *Globe* (named *Globe and Traveller* from 1823 on) shifted from apolitical to Whig to Tory*, and caused enough stir with its caustic satire* and unscrupulous reporting to be suppressed at least twice, while retaining a reputation as a 'good-humoured,' 'sarcastic and stinging,' 'lively' and 'bitter' source of entertainment. Readers were generally of the middle to upper educated classes*, and numbered 3,500 in 1855 rising to 7,000 in 1870. A general coverage newspaper, originally started to promote the interests of the publishing* trade, its departments included national news*, foreign policy, notes of the day, men and matters, to-day in America (beginning in 1900), sporting* intelligence, crime* reports, murder and execution coverage and fashion*. Contributors over the years included Arthur William À Beckett* as a war* correspondent*, William Cobbett, Wilkie Collins*, the illustrator* George Cruikshank* and Thornton Hunt*. Walter Coulson became editor* in 1823 and Sir George Armstrong in 1871. According to Hamilton Fyfe, its 'small size*, its pink paper*, its agreeable print and lay-out gave its appearance distinctive character'.

Shortly after its inception, the *Globe* became, according to Mitchell, 'the organ of the educated Radicals', publishing pieces by Whig party members and parliamentarians. Among such radical contributors was John Stuart Mill*. After 1866, the *Globe* lowered its price*; beginning at 6d, it fell to1d in 1869 and transferred its support to the conservatives. Having absorbed the *Statesman*, the *Evening Chronicle*, the *Nation** and the *Argus*, the *Globe* was in turn taken over by the *Pall Mall Gazette** in 1921. At that time it was the oldest evening newspaper in England. **KC**

Sources: Fyfe 1949, Mitchell 1846, *Waterloo*, National Archives Learning Curve online.

GLOVER, WILLIAM HOWARD (1819-1875) William Glover was music critic of the *Morning Post** (1850-1865). Like many music* critics of the period, Glover was an eminent practitioner as well as a journalist, having a successful career as a tenor, composer and conductor.

During Richard Wagner's visit to London in 1855 – mainly in the capacity of conductor – Glover was among the few critics who were initially receptive to performances given by the Old Philharmonic under Wagner's direction, in particular renditions of selections from Haydn, Beethoven and Mendelssohn which had 'never, in our recollection, been so well played in this country'. Later concerts, which included sections of Wagner's *Lohengrin*, met with a cooler reception from Glover.

In 1864, he wrote a piece complaining that the Covent Garden programme was 'pompous', 'pretentious' and above all dominated by foreign operatic talent. As for many music critics of the day, the relation of music* to national identity was a central theme. Ultimately, the authorities were to be blamed for failing to seek out worthy English composers. **MaT**

Sources: *Grove Music Online*, *Morning Post*, *ODNB*, Sessa 1979.

GOLF (1890-2005) Beginning in 1890 as a weekly* journal of 16 pages costing 2d and published on Fridays, *Golf: A Weekly Record of 'Ye Royal and Ancient' Game* (1890-1899) was a light-hearted sports* journal covering all elements of the game. Its first issue claimed that while golf had long been Scotland's national game, its popularity had extended in recent years to all of Britain and its colonies. The journal's readership* was seemingly composed of amateur golf enthusiasts, who might be members of their local golf club and occasionally participate in competitions. It carried fixture lists, detailed reports on recent matches, humorous verse on golfing matters and occasional coverage of other sports including tennis, curling and bowls. Secretaries of golf clubs forwarded reports on competitions and other golfing news, which were printed with lists of scores. A section entitled 'Tee Shots' contained a series of short comic vignettes, taking advantage of the game and its mores as a source for observational humour. Letters* from readers – generally asking advice about technique or equipment, quibbling over the rules or boasting about improbably long drives – were printed in a correspondence section.

Golf flirted for a time with bi-weekly publication (certainly by 1894), coming out on Tuesdays and Fridays and briefly changing its subtitle accordingly, but it had reverted to weekly* publication by 1899. By 1894 it was carrying reviews* of relevant books, and a series on eminent golfers which featured a photograph of the (usually dead) golfer in question and a short hagiography. Photography* began to play an increasingly important role in the journal, and by 1899 it was issuing a regular invitation to its readers to send in their photographs of pretty golf courses for publication. It also began to cater for female golfers, with an 'On the Ladies' Links' section dedicated to women's golf, including biographies and portraits of eminent female golfers. It grew in size*, incorporating extra pages in order to provide complete coverage of recent competitions (in the form of rather boring lists of scores).

Apart from this, it remained very similar in appearance until it announced, 9 June 1899, a new format* for the following issue: an enlarged size, better quality paper*, 'sumptuously illustrated*', and containing a new series of articles by the celebrated golf writer Horace G. Hutchinson. *Golf Illustrated* (1899-1989), whose 36 pages appeared the next week at the higher price* of 6d, persisted with the light-hearted approach that had served its predecessor well, and kept many of the same departments, but was noticeably more luxurious, with its larger size, glossy paper and well-reproduced photographs, which were perfectly adapted for demonstrating variations in stance and grip. The publication lasted throughout the twentieth century, changing its name to *Golf Illustrated Weekly* (1989-1991) and then *Golf Weekly* (1992-2005), finally ceasing publication in April 2005. **MaT**
Sources: BL Catalogue, *Waterloo*.

GOOD WORDS (1860-1911) *Good Words* was an illustrated* monthly magazine that was the brainchild of the young Scottish publisher Alexander Strahan*. Intended to be a magazine for reading throughout the week, it combined a religious* outlook with diverse content, publishing sermons, stories and articles. Strahan chose as his first editor* Norman Macleod, a prominent minister in the Church of Scotland. The first issue appeared as a 16-page weekly* priced* 3 ½d. By January 1861, it had been transformed into a 6d, 64-page monthly. When Macleod died in 1872, his brother Donald became editor* and he maintained continuity in practice and policy. During its best years, in the 1860s and 1870s, circulation* achieved between 80,000 and 130,000

copies per issue. It attracted many contributions from prominent figures, such as fiction* by Anthony Trollope* and Thomas Hardy, poetry* by Lord Alfred Tennyson, articles by William Gladstone (1809-1898) and J. A. Froude* and illustrations* by J. E. Millais*. By 1900, however, *Good Words* had lost the prominent position it had once held and was sold in 1905 to Harmsworth (the Amalgamated Press), merged* with the *Sunday Magazine* and changed into a 1d weekly*, surviving until 1911. **AL**
Sources: Macleod 1876, Srebrnik 1986, Sullivan, Sutherland 1988, Turner 2000c.

GOOD WORDS FOR THE YOUNG (1868-1877) *Good Words for the Young* was an illustrated* monthly magazine for children* published* by Alexander Strahan*, a companion to Strahan's* successful *Good Words*. It contained wholesome literature* for children with a broad Christian outlook. Priced* at 6d, it attracted a middle-class* readership* and was intended for children of both sexes. Although the editor* of *Good Words*, the ailing Norman Macleod*, was initially advertised as the editor of *Good Words for the Young*, the poet and novelist, George MacDonald (1824-1905) edited the magazine at first.

In 1872, Strahan, deeply in debt to his creditors, was forced out of the firm. He retained copyright to only two of his many magazines, one of which was *Good Words for the Young*. Now separated from *Good Words*, it was duly renamed *Good Things for the Young of All Ages*. A year later, MacDonald resigned from the struggling magazine and Strahan took over as editor. The magazine had never been very successful and it eventually stopped publication in the autumn of 1877. Prominent writers included Charles Kingsley (1819-1875), W. S. Gilbert (1836-1911), Dinah Craik (1826-1887) and its first editor, George MacDonald. Illustrators included Arthur Hughes*, G. J. Pinwell* and Arthur Boyd Houghton*. **AL**
Sources: Drotner 1988, Egoff 1951, *ODNB*, Srebrnik 1986, Triggs 1986.

GORDON, ALICE MARY (C. 1850/1851-1929) Alice Gordon, née Brandreth, wrote a number of articles in the 1890s, which, in conjunction with the book for which she is best known, *Decorative Electricity* (1891), assessed the domestic implications of the new electrical technology. As the wife of inventor and engineer J. E. H. Gordon, Alice Gordon was aware of the contemporary public scepticism about electricity and sought to allay the fears and concerns felt especially by women readers of late nineteenth-century periodicals. In the *Fortnightly Review** (Feb. 1891), Gordon recommended decorative shading as a means of softening the effects of unforgiving electric light upon the female complexion, but also noted the ways in which the home could be made aesthetically pleasing through the considered use of electricity.

Gordon was also interested in female education. In 1895 she wrote 'The After-Careers of University Educated Women' for the *Nineteenth Century** which, after deploying statistics, concluded that marriage was neither desired nor attained by highly educated women. Unlike *Decorative Electricity* where she styled herself as 'Mrs J. E. H. Gordon', she appeared as 'Alice M. Gordon' when she wrote periodical articles, seeking recognition under her own name in this particular genre* and without the aid of her husband's scientific authority. **CB**
Sources: Gooday 2004a, Gooday 2004b, Kaiser 2005, Levine 1989.

GORGON (1818-1819) In just 49 weekly* penny* issues over a year, (March 1818-April 1819) *Gorgon: A Weekly Political Publication* significantly developed political* journalism and can be regarded as the first trade unionist* periodical. Printed and published* by Richard Carlile*, it was the creation of John Wade (1788-1875), a woolsorter who rose to prominence through trade politics. Wade was sponsored by the veteran radical Francis Place* and received financial backing from the utilitarian philosopher Jeremy Bentham. Though its title and format* owed something to *Black Dwarf**, *Gorgon* had no real precursor. It was a pioneering, campaigning journal, aimed at organized labour with the intention of building nationwide awareness of labour issues. Factual content and editorial line were tailored to skilled workers.

Gorgon covered trade politics and industrial disputes across England and was especially influential in developing a campaign to repeal the anti-trade union Combination Acts. Francis Place wrote extensively for it and circulated copies among MPs to influence parliamentary opinion. In Place's opinion *Gorgon* was 'the only' periodical to carry this 'considerable effect'. Wade, however, was no establishment toady. *Gorgon* editorials denounced employers for 'trading in the blood and bones' of workers. Wade went out on a limb to support Lancashire cotton workers during their bruising 1818 strike; he denounced 'that detestable paper' *The Times** as 'howling like a starved and blood-thirsty wolf at the Manchester Spinners'. When *Gorgon*

closed, Wade compiled the *Black Book; or Corruption Unmasked!,* the many editions of which provided material and column-fillers for generations of radical journalists. His direct involvement in journalism continued as a leader* writer for Robert Rintoul's *Spectator**. The genre* he initiated continued with a flurry of papers aimed at artisan readers*, for example the *Labourer's Friend & Handicrafts Chronicle* (1821-1825), the *Mechanic's Magazine** (1823ff) and the *Trades Newspaper & Weekly Free Press** (1825-1831). **MSC**
Sources: Chase 2000, *ODNB*.

GOSSE, EDMUND WILLIAM (1849-1928) Much of Gosse's fame and name was built on periodical contributions, which were often collected subsequently for book publication. Born in 1849, and brought up as a member of the strict puritan Plymouth Brethren, young Gosse was fed on a diet of purely devotional works. Yet in spite of that, he made literature his career. His first article, published in 1871 in *Fraser's Magazine** and devoted to his trip to the Lofoden Islands, was indicative of a life-long interest in Scandinavian languages and literature. Subsequently he became a regular contributor to many of the most influential journals of his day, such as the *Spectator**, the *Academy**, the *Saturday Review**, the *Contemporary Review** and the *Pall Mall Gazette** and he slowly made his mark as a critic. Much of his reputation rested and still rests on his championship of Scandinavian literature, especially Ibsen.

Gosse earned a living first as a clerk in the cataloguing section of the British Library, and then from 1875 as a translator to the Board of Trade. By 1884, his prestige as a literary critic was such that he was appointed Clark lecturer at Cambridge University. His lectures, published as *From Shakespeare to Pope* (1885), provoked one of the most painful attacks on a literary critic of the period when John Churton Collins splenetically reviewed* them in the *Quarterly Review**, attacking Gosse's scholarship and exposing many errors. Gosse recovered, not least because of his immense network and his exquisitely developed social skills. The regular Sunday 'At Homes', at 29 Delamere Terrace, included the cultural elite as guests. In 1906 Gosse became director of the literary supplement* of the *Daily Mail** for 18 months, he wrote sporadically for the *Athenaeum**, regularly for the *Daily Chronicle** and, from 1919 until his death, for the *Sunday Times**. **MD**
Sources: Brugmans 1959, Demoor 1989, *ODNB*, Thwaite 1985.

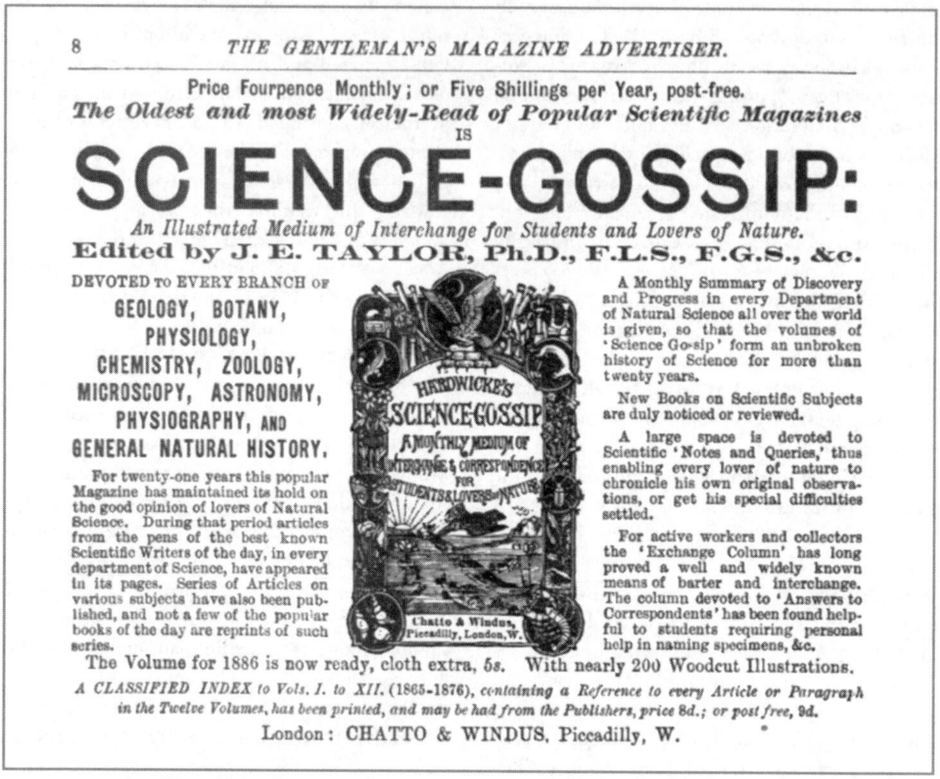

Figure 25: An advertisement for *Science-Gossip* in the *Gentleman's Magazine*, Sep. 1887.

GOSSIP A new style of gossip column* appeared in the mid-Victorian press that was less racy and abusive than those in earlier scandal sheets such as the *Age** (1825ff) and the *Town** (1832ff), aiming at a wider readership* than the would-be fast man-about-town. Leading examples in the 1850s and 1860s were Edmund Yates's* 'The Lounger at the Clubs' in the *Illustrated Times**, 'Le Flâneur' in the *Morning Star*, Shirley Brooks's* 'Nothing in the Papers' and G. A. Sala's* 'Echoes of the Week' column* in the *Illustrated London News**.

With the 1870s, personality* journalism proliferated in the society papers where gossip ran to several pages and became the papers' chief feature. Leading the way was T. G. Bowles's high-end *Vanity Fair** with its gossip aimed at the smart set, followed by Edmund Yates's the *World** and Henry Labouchere's* *Truth**. Although largely anodyne one-sentence paragraphs reporting the movements of celebrities*, led by the Prince of Wales, such gossip sometimes had a definite edge that could lead to physical violence or the courts. Yates the journalist was famously expelled from the Garrick Club* for sniping at a fellow member, Thackeray*. Gossip hinting at scandal in high places could have even more serious consequences for editors*. Labouchere and Bowles were both assaulted by aggrieved subjects of gossip, and Yates went to prison for criminal libel.

Less risky, yet influential for careers, was the gossip that featured significantly in the fine arts, science*, and literary* sections*, particularly the causeries*, of many periodicals, including the *Athenaeum** since the 1830s. **CAK**

Sources: Demoor 1996, Hirshfield 1984, Kent 1985, Naylor 1965, Waller 2006, Wiener 1985.

***GOVERNESS* (1882-1884)** The cover of the *Governess, a Ladies' Literary and Educational Monthly* (1882) proclaimed Friedrich Froebel's 'Let us live for our children', and his theory of the kindergarten and active learning was expounded in a regular column*. Teaching methodology, curriculum lesson plans, some explanatory diagrams, sheet music*, annotated Shakespeare extracts and examination questions formed the core of its contents. Broader interests were addressed by articles on women's higher education, book reviews*, professional news* and women's civil service examinations, and a supplement* on employment, the *Governess Advertiser.*

After a hiatus of a month, it resumed publication in February 1883 as the *Governess, a Weekly Journal for School Mistresses,* but in September 1883 it changed its title* for a third time, in an attempt to broaden its readership* to *Governess and Head-Mistress, a Weekly Journal for Certificated and High School Teachers,* with its own distinctive front cover, contents and advertisements*. Inspectors' reports, an editorial and extra news* could not prevent closure on 12 January 1884 from 'financial failure' as publisher* and editor*, Joseph Hughes explained. Regular contributors, such as Margaret Lorne and Mrs Mortimer, hoped to continue writing in the *Practical Teacher.* **CL**

Sources: *Governess, Waterloo.*

'GRAND, SARAH' (1854-1943) The author of *The Heavenly Twins* (1893), whose writings acted as a 'bomb of dynamite' (W. T. Stead*) in projecting the New Woman onto 1890s culture, was born Frances Elizabeth Bellenden Clarke. After the uncongenial schooling later explored in the *Lady's Magazine** (1901), and marriage when she became Frances McFall, she began writing short stories, traveller's impressions and her first novels while stationed in China. After early setbacks, her stories, which appeared in *Aunt Judy's Magazine for Young People**, and later in *Phil May's Illustrated Winter Annual**, *Temple Bar** and the *Idler** helped provide an independent income. After abandoning the marriage, she launched her public career as 'S-arah Grand' in 1893.

Though publications like the *Women's Herald** had used the term 'New Woman', it was Grand's exchange with 'Ouida'* in the *North American Review** in 1894 which established the concept in the cultural imagination. Skilfully manipulating class* papers like *Lady's Realm**, *Woman at Home**, *Young Woman**, and more general titles such as the *Canadian Magazine** and *Pall Mall Magazine**, Grand marketed the New Woman as a model of stylish femininity concerned as much with fashion* as public health and morality. Offering middle-class women keen to engage in personal development a diluted feminism ('Is It Ever Justifiable to Break off an Engagement?', 'Should Married Women Follow Professions?'), she also outlined the New Woman's socio-political concerns in the *Fortnightly Review**, the *Humanitarian**, the *Ludgate** and the *New Review**. Grand's journalism complemented her novels' radicalism in tackling taboos like syphilis and castigated the medical, military and religious estab-

lishment's complicity in sexual exploitation and moral degeneration. **ABH**

Sources: Beetham 1996, Heilmann and Forward 2000, Heilmann 2004, Huddleston 1979, Kersley 1983, Mangum 1998, Richardson 2003, Tusan 1998.

GRANT, CHARLES JAMESON (FL.1830-1852) Whether driven by a radical social critique, financial necessity or entrepreneurial restlessness, the caricaturist* Charles Jameson Grant was an inventive and prolific figure in the development of graphic journalism. His output, like that of the Heath brothers*, shifted from single plate caricature through multi-image plates organized largely around single themes towards serial publication*. Grant used the full range of available reprographic techniques with considerable inventiveness, and two of his periodicals are especially noteworthy for their progressive formal qualities. *Everybody's Album and Caricature Magazine** extended the idea of the lithographed* caricature magazine, invented a decade before by the *Glasgow Looking Glass**, into a new market*, combining a sceptical view of contemporary politics* with multi-image pages aimed at the scrapbook compiler.

Grant's relentless and subversive sense of the grotesque, as well as his contempt for the political and social establishment, also informed his most sustained serial publication, the spectacular set of 131 large-scale woodcuts* that comprised the *Political Drama* (1833-1835). By the late 1830s, Grant seems to have abandoned publishing* on his own account and is largely visible as a contributor of often crudely powerful wood engravings* to a variety of unstamped* radical journals published by the likes of Cleave* and Cousins. Despite his decline into obscurity and the little known about his life, Grant was a uniquely powerful presence in the development of visual culture between 1830 and 1840. **BM**

Source: *ODNB.*

GRANT, JAMES (1802-1879) James Grant, a Scot, became a contributor to the *Statesman* (1806-1824) and other newspapers from the age of 19. In 1827, with others, he helped to launch the *Elgin Courier,* serving as its editor* until 1833, when he left Scotland to try his luck in London. His first job in the metropolis was as a reporter* on the recently founded *Standard** (1827ff). He then worked for a number of titles including the *Morning Chronicle** and the *Morning Advertiser;* among other stints he did parliamentary* reporting. In these years he also edited the *London Saturday Journal* in 1839 and

Grant's London Journal in 1840. In 1850 he was appointed editor of the *Morning Advertiser*, the organ of the Licensed Victuallers' Association, where he remained until 1871. As editor of the *Morning Advertiser* Grant helped to establish Reuters's long association with British national* newspapers: in 1858 he accepted their telegrams free for a fortnight's trial and then paid £30 per month for a full service, which was £10 less than their competitors (*ODNB*). In 1872 Grant became editor of the *Christian Standard*.

Apart from journalism Grant wrote books, those on theological subjects being published anonymously*, according to fellow journalist George Augustus Sala*. His classic of its day, *The Newspaper Press: its Origins, Progress and Present Position,* appeared in three volumes in 1871-1872. In his autobiography, Sala wrote that Grant's 'pluck, his hardheadedness, his intelligence, his unswerving truthfulness and integrity raised him to an important position in the world of journalism of which he was to be afterwards historian'. **DHL**
Sources: Griffiths 1992, *ODNB*, Sala 1895.

GRANT, ROBERT (1814-1892) Largely self-taught in astronomy, Grant produced a successful *History of Physical Astronomy* (1848-1852) that brought him to the attention of the Royal Astronomical Society, and in 1852 he was appointed editor* of its *Monthly Notices* (1827ff). Under Grant's editorship, the *Monthly Notices* emphasized physical astronomy and, for the first time, supplemented its regular accounts of the Royal Astronomical Society's meetings and correspondence* from its members with abstracts of the latest astronomical intelligence from foreign scientific periodicals such as *Astronomische Nachrichten* and the *Comptes Rendus de l'Académie des Sciences,* to which Grant also contributed. In 1860 Grant became professor of astronomy at the University of Glasgow and resigned the editorship of the *Monthly Notices*, which was taken up by Arthur Cayley who pushed it more in the direction of mathematical astronomy, although Grant continued to contribute numerous astronomical observations to its pages. In a controversy in *The Times** in 1867 over the publication of forged papers in the *Comptes Rendus* Grant showed an acute awareness of how a scientific society's reputation often rested on the conduct of its official periodicals. **GD**
Sources: Crilly 2006, Higgit 2003, *ODNB*.

GREENAWAY, CATHERINE (1846-1901) Kate Greenaway, an illustrator*, having been one of the earliest students at the South Kensington Art Training School followed by the Slade and Heatherly

School, was formally trained as an artist. She began her career by illustrating greetings cards, and in 1869 her first commission for a book illustration* came through contacts of her father John Greenaway*, a wood engraver* for the *Illustrated London News* and *Punch*. Her magazine work can be found in the *People's Magazine* (1868), *Little Folks* (1873-1880), *Little Wide-Awake*, *Cassell's Magazine**(1874ff), *Illustrated London News** (1874-1882), *Kate Greenaway's Almanack* (1883ff), *Harper's Young People*, *St Nicholas*, the *Graphic**, the *American Queen*, *Every Girl's Annual* (1882), *Girl's Own Paper**(1879-1890), *Girl's Own Annual* and the *English Illustrated Magazine*. She consistently contributed illustrations to periodicals, but it was her children's books that brought her recognition, a lasting reputation and financial success. **CL**
Sources: Houfe 1978, *ODNB*, *Waterloo*, *Women Children's Book Illustrators online*.

GREENAWAY, JOHN (1816-1890) John Greenaway's career was characteristic of the little known but significant artist/engravers who supplied the periodical press with the necessary mass of rapidly produced, technically highly competent wood* engravings* it required. His apprenticeship was exemplary: he worked first with Robert Branston* and then with Ebenezer Landells*, thus coming into regular contact with the such stalwarts of the trade as Edmund Evans* and Birket Foster*, and his early work was for the two most celebrated publications of Landells, *Punch** and the *Illustrated London News**.

Greenaway then established his own business in partnership with W. Wright which was not immediately prosperous enough to ensure independence, forcing Greenaway to become a freelance engraver, later establishing a workshop in central London. From here he maintained his business and gained a reputation for reliability that led to many commissions, especially for children's books. His most substantial contribution to the periodical press was the work he undertook for the *Illustrated London News* over many years, especially in the 1860s and 1870s, which comprised topographical illustrations*, reproductions of paintings and other art works and reportage. Greenaway was occasionally one of the 'specials' sent by the *Illustrated London News* to cover important public events. Now perhaps most remembered for teaching and mentoring his famous daughter, the writer and artist Kate Greenaway*, he was nonetheless a representative and respected figure among the ever increasing body of able wood engravers who contributed to the periodical market. **BM**
Source: Engen 1990.

GREENWOOD, FREDERICK (1830-1909) Frederick Greenwood was one of the most prominent, prolific, and influential journalists* and editors* of the nineteenth century. From a very early age, he earned his living by writing for a variety of newspapers and journals. The first periodical he was closely associated with was Henry Vizetelly's* *Illustrated Times*, to which he made regular contributions from 1855 onwards, and which he eventually came to edit. In 1861, he established himself more firmly as a professional editor with the weekly* *Queen*, for which he had formerly acted as dramatic critic. When the journal was combined with the *Lady's Newpaper** in 1863, and acquired a more pronounced feminine slant, he resigned. In 1862, he was appointed editor* of the monthly* *Cornhill Magazine** by its proprietor* George Smith*, with whom Greenwood had established close relations. Greenwood did not stay with the *Cornhill* for long. He found Smith prepared to back a new and daring publishing venture, and on 7 February 1865, the first edition of an evening daily*, the *Pall Mall Gazette**, saw the light, with Greenwood as editor. Leslie Stephen* famously dubbed it 'Greenwood's incarnation', and for 15 years, his editorial dominance remained unchallenged. He acquired a reputation as 'the perfect editor', finding and fostering new writing talent, and thereby leaving a permanent mark on the Victorian literary scene. As Greenwood became more Conservative and anti-Gladstonian/pro-Disraeli in his views, so his political* influence grew: Disraeli's purchase of the Suez Canal shares of the Khedive of Egypt in 1875 was Greenwood's suggestion.

When the *Pall Mall* changed owners in 1880, and Greenwood was faced with having to take the paper in a Liberal direction, he angrily resigned and shortly afterwards retaliated by launching the *St James's Gazette**, another evening daily that he also edited, and modelled closely on its predecessor. Its editor's hard-line Conservative views did not endear it the general public, and a dispute about editorial control with the owner, Henry Hucks Gibbs, caused Greenwood to give up the editorship of *St James's Gazette* in 1888. The weekly *Anti-Jacobin* (31 Jan. 1891ff), which Greenwood then started, never got off the ground properly and lasted less than a year. This was his final editorship, but he continued to write prolifically on social and political issues and journalism itself in *Blackwood's Edinburgh Magazine**, *Contemporary Review**, *Cornhill Magazine**, *New Review**, *Nineteenth Century**, *Saturday Review**, and *Westminster Gazette**. Two articles by his hand even graced the pages of the *Yellow Book**. In addition to his journalistic work, Greenwood published fiction and poetry, but it is as one of the century's great editors that he will mostly be remembered. **OD**

Sources: *ODNB*, Scott 1950, *Waterloo, Wellesley*.

GREENWOOD, JAMES (1832-1929) James Greenwood (1832-1929), younger brother of Frederick Greenwood*, first editor of the *Pall Mall Gazette**, achieved fame as a pioneering reporter of New (investigative*) Journalism* through his brother's influence: disguised as a beggar with his friend Blackstone, his undercover accounts of an overnight stay in a casual ward of a London workhouse caused a sensation in 1865. Frederick persuaded a reluctant James, then a contributor to *Welcome Guest**, to take on the project for £30 or £40 down, and 'more if it turned out well' (Scott: 166). Their account, 'The Amateur Casual', appeared in the *Gazette* over three issues. Immediately effective, the story invigorated sluggish sales, increasing circulation* by 1,200 issues per day. Greenwood and Blackstone were lionised for what was presented as extraordinary courage and daring. The story appeared in *The Times** and as a pamphlet, republished many times, along with Greenwood's follow-up reports on the underbelly of London life entitled *The Seven Curses of London* (1869). W. T. Stead later credited 'the storm of indignation' over 'that one night in a casual ward' with the beginning of Poor Law reform (Scott: 168). William Hardman, editor of the *Morning Post** called it 'an act of bravery' that should earn the reporter 'the V.C.'. The melodramatic responses, as Robertson Scott observed, highlighted the enormous gap between rich and poor at the time and the pervasive ignorance of the actual conditions in which the poorest classes lived (Robertson Scott: 168).

Described by Hall Richardson as 'a short, squarish, good-humoured man, dressed in a long black frock-coat...the cut of a slum missionary' (cited in Robertson-Scott: 170), James Greenwood alienated his brother by moving from the *Pall Mall Gazette* to work for the *Daily Telegraph**, though he maintained an interest in London life, writing articles on the problem of employed adolescents and initiating the *Telegraph's* Children's Country Outings fund. As author of the popular 'One of the Crowd' columns*, he contributed articles and fiction throughout the late 1860s and 1870s, mostly based on London, to a range of British and American journals, including *Hours at Home, Eclectic Magazine* and *Saint Paul's**. In addition to his journalism,

Greenwood wrote a number of books for children in the 1860s (*CBEL*) and non-fiction works said to be based on first-hand experiences in the manner that brought his initial fame. **FD**

Sources: *CBEL*, Greenwood 1869, Robertson Scott 1950.

GREG, WILLIAM RATHBONE (1809-1881) Apprenticed as manager of one of his father's cotton mills, Gregg became a partner in 1830, went on the grand tour and in the 1830s began writing on social and economic issues. During the 1840s his articles appeared in the *Edinburgh Review**. An April 1849 review* of Elizabeth Gaskell's *Mary Barton* followed his anonymous* letter to the *Manchester Guardian** (1848) criticizing Gaskell's inaccurate portrayal of the industrial masters. In his review, the workers were allegedly agents of their own misfortune, and his solution for them was to follow the example of their masters: to 'imitate their prudence and worldly wisdom, their unresting diligence, their unflagging energy, their resolute and steady economy'. Most of his contributions in the 1840s were to the *Westminster Review** under the signature* 'G.,W.R.' A series of family illnesses together with his inadequacy as a businessman resulted in the sale of the mill in 1850 and for the next six years he made his living by writing. His work continued in the *Edinburgh* and *Westminster* reviews*, and he also covered politics* and foreign policy in the *North British Review** and *National Review**. During the 1850s he was also manager and columnist on the *Economist**.

In 1856, a civil servant post in the south provided security until his retirement in 1877. His output was sustained. He added the *Quarterly Review** and *Fraser's Magazine** to his existing outlets and wrote occasional pieces in *St Paul's** and the *Cornhill Magazine**, the *Academy**, the *Pall Mall Gazette** and *Under the Crown* (1869). The span of his interests – the world of Empire, science and discovery and a brief correspondence with Darwin, his contemporary at Edinburgh – marked him out as a product of his time. His love of intellectual expression through literature* and philosophy* contrasted with an industrial heritage and social position which provided an arrogant assurance of 'solving' economic and social problems with his pen, as with the single woman problem ('Why are women redundant?' *National Review* April 1863). In the 1870s, with Ireland being *the* question of the day, he added the *Fortnightly Review* to the titles for which he wrote. In his work, Greg tried to make sense of 'the various forms of wrong, of error, and

of wretchedness which multiply around us'('The social sores of Britain' *NBR* 1867) in a style suitable for the pulpit despite his religious cynicism. **CL**

Sources: BritPer online; *ODNB, Waterloo, Wellesley.*

GREGORY, BARNARD (1796-1852) Man of many parts: schoolteacher, travelling preacher, drug dispenser and, latterly, newspaper proprietor*, editor*, writer, blackmailer, defamer, dramatist and actor, Barnard Gregory was a drama in himself. His colourful life as a journalist emanated from the contents of his weekly* paper, the *Satirist, or, the Censor of the Times** started in April 1831. Politically, anti-Tory, yet first and foremost a weapon of exposure and intimidation, perhaps only because of its London base could it boast a breathtaking circulation* of 10,000 at 7d a copy.

Gregory played a dangerous game and one, which, noting the number of times he was convicted, imprisoned, fined or impugned for libel, he ultimately lost. He would frequently send the pre-publication libel to the intended victim together with the amount required for suppression. Many people paid, but the rich could afford to call his bluff and take him to court. Gregory's political pathology meant inevitably that his exposures frequently fell on the aristocracy and too often they took their revenge. He also edited the *Penny Satirist** 1837-1846.

The author of four plays, he made his theatrical presentations both on and off the stage, but sometimes they would collide. Performances were then at their most dazzling when appearing on stage in his own play he would be mobbed by an incensed victim, such as the Duke of Brunswick for whom he kept a special place in the *Satirist's* pages. Yet the spectacle could not be sustained and the *Satirist* took its final bow in 1849. **CL**

Sources: Boase, *ODNB.*

GREGORY, RICHARD ARMAN (1864-1952) Gregory, science* journalist* and editor* of *Nature**, was the son of a cobbler in Bristol, who won a scholarship to the Normal School of Science at South Kensington in the mid-1880s. There he was a fellow-student of H. G. Wells*, who became a lifelong friend. Gregory was subsequently appointed an assistant to Norman Lockyer*, and began writing articles and reviews for *Nature**. In the early 1890s, he became a freelance lecturer and journalist, with a special interest in scientific education. He soon produced a series of popular and educational science books, one written jointly with Wells. In 1893, Lockyer appointed him assistant editor of *Nature*. This brought Gregory into close contact with the journal's publishers, Macmillan & Co.*, and he later became their scientific editor. In 1899, Gregory helped found the journal *School World* (incorporated into the *Journal of Education* in 1918). Two years later, he played an important part in the formation of a new section of the British Association devoted to education. Gregory succeeded Lockyer as editor of *Nature* in 1919, and continued in charge until almost the Second World War. He was recognized from quite early on in his career as one of the leading science* journalists in Britain, and was – exceptionally – elected to the Royal Society for his activities. AJM

Sources: Armytage 1957, Lightman 2004, *ODNB*.

GRIMSTONE, MARY LEMAN (c.1800-c.1851 OR?1796-1869) Mary Leman Grimstone (later Gillies) was one of the most outspoken, widely published and commonly cited feminists of the first half of the nineteenth century. Little is known of her life and biographers disagree over dates of birth and death (c. 1800-c.1851 [ODNB] or 1796-1869 [Roe]). Born Mary Leman Rede into an impecunious literary family, from 1815 she contributed to the ladies' magazine *La Belle Assemblée* often anonymously*, under the male pseudonym 'Oscar'. Between 1834 and 1836 Grimstone contributed to *Tait's Edinburgh Magazine*,* the *Tatler*, and most, significantly, to the radical Unitarian *Monthly Repository*,* where she became the most forthright and advanced writer of the day on the Woman Question. She demanded women's political emancipation as well as improvements in education and employment. Like Wollstonecraft, Grimstone was interested in female manners as much as rights and emphasised women's nurturing and moral qualities. Her advocacy of the rights of the poor, like her feminism, drew upon a dialogue with Owenism*, and her essays on subjects like 'Universal Co-operation' and poems* like 'The Mechanic's Wife' were reprinted in *New Moral World*.*

In the mid-1830s Grimstone remarried and for a while seems to have retired from writing, but between 1846 and 1848 she returned as 'Mrs Gillies' in John Saunders's *People's Journal*.* There she expressly wrote for a cross-class* readership*, addressing 'The People' and especially the operative classes on political* and domestic economy. Though she championed the social advancement of the working classes, her support for 'self-government' and 'self-culture' was essentially radical-liberal in outlook. She did not align herself with the contemporary Chartist movement, though some of her work appeared in Chartist papers like the *National Association Gazette* (1841-

1842). Her advocacy of female equality was part of a wider project of domestic reform and 'fireside attractions' which she saw as imperative for national improvement. Consequently, her writings of the 1830s and 1840s became transatlantic*; they were republished on both sides of the Atlantic in a surprisingly eclectic range of radical, religious* and improvement publications. There are no records of any writings after the close of the *People's Journal* in 1848. HR

Sources: Gleadle 1995, Haywood 2004, *ODNB*, Roe 2005, Rogers 2000, *Wellesley*.

GROCER AND OIL TRADE REVIEW (1862-) Catering to a populous demographic in the nineteenth century, the *Grocer* is one of the longest-lasting trade* periodicals. In September 1860 a 2d weekly* dedicated to the reform of the sugar duties appeared, the *Grocer's Journal*, published* by R. Barrett. It was short lived but revealed a gap in the market filled in January 1862 by H. S. Simpson and William Reed with the *Grocer and Oil Trade Review*. A 4d 16-page weekly, it launched itself (correctly) as the only organ devoted to the interests of 'the connecting link' between 'the Merchant Prince... and the great body of consumers'. In particular it was concerned to educate grocers on 'the great "Adulteration" question' and to that end included a large number of essays on the properties, origins and manufacture of sugar, tea, coffee, spices and so on so that grocers might recognize the genuine article. Contributors, when not anonymous, included scientists* such as Noad (Professor of Chemistry at St George's Hospital), John Scoffern, J.C. Braithwaite and the editor of the *Mechanic's Magazine*,* R. A. Brooman, for his expertise on patents. Further regular ingredients comprised current bulk prices of goods, reports on stocks, shares and British and 'Foreign' markets for commodities. Court cases involving the trade were also regularly reported, including bankruptcies. The publication of letters* soon became weekly.

That the periodical was quickly successful is marked by a piece celebrating its first quarter (vol. I : 212) and by the appearance of large advertising* supplements* every week; from the 1890s these became far larger than the periodical itself even though it had grown to 34 or more pages while the price* remained steady. In 1877 publication had been taken over by C. E. Mackadam. A monthly supplement 'The Oil Trade Review' was incorporated into the title in November 1886. Later interesting additions include reviews* of relevant books and profiles of prominent grocers. AK

Sources: *Mitchell's*, *Grocer* 1860-1902.

GROSVENOR, JOHN (1742-1823) Born in Oxford, John Grosvenor was a printer and editor*. Trained as a surgeon, he gained a post at the University as a surgeon at Christ Church. When in 1795 the University printer William Jackson died, Grosvenor became editor and printer of the weekly* *Jackson's Oxford Journal,* Oxford's only newspaper at the time. Having started the *Journal* in 1753 under the title, *News, Boys, News or the Electioneering Journal,* Jackson left his estate, including the *Journal,* to his servant and friend Mary Jones, who continued to work at the High Street office. It was not until 1816, after Mary's death* that Grosvenor & Hall, joint printers of the paper, became proprietors* of the *Journal.* Grosvenor then retired from his post as surgeon in 1817.CL

Sources: *ODNB,* Jenkins online accessed 11 July 2008.

GROVE, ARCHIBALD NEWCOMEN (1885-1920) Grove's single claim to journalistic fame is as the founder of the *New Review** (1889-1897), of which he was the proprietor* (1889 – Dec. 1893) and editor* (until Dec. 1894). He modelled his journal closely on the *Contemporary Review**, attempting to offer similar quality at a much lower price* of 6d. When Grove started the *New Review,* he had little or no previous experience as a journalist. In fact, even during his time as editor, Grove's attention appears to have been focused mainly on his political career, and he failed to leave a distinctive mark on his brainchild. He was a Liberal MP for West Ham North (1892-1895), and he later went on to take the seat for South Northamptonshire (1906-1910).

Grove was a close friend of Edmund Gosse*, who temporarily took over the editorship when Grove was on honeymoon at the end of 1889, and was instrumental in enlisting major contributors like Tennyson, Henry James* and Andrew Lang*. Their presence did not prevent the journal's financial decline, which Grove attempted to counteract to no avail by raising its price twice; in 1894 it reached 1s. In January 1894, he relinquished the ownership to a 'little company' of friends, which included publisher* William Heinemann, who used the journal as a testbed for his own company's publications. Arthur Waugh – who later became general manager at Chapman & Hall* – acted as Grove's subeditor during 1894, and he remembers him as a 'smart, dapper little man' who was bitterly harassed 'by the lack of pence which vexes public men'. In January 1895, Grove made way for the flamboyant William Ernest Henley*. There are no records of any jour-

nalistic activities on Grove's part after this. OD

Sources: *WWW, Who's Who of British Members of Parliament.*

GROVE, GEORGE (1820-1900) Although George Grove entered journalism having first worked as a civil engineer and public servant, he rapidly became a major figure in periodical publishing in Britain as editor* of *Macmillan's Magazine** (1868-1883). On appointment Grove was already fully conversant with *Macmillan's Magazine's* progressive philosophic slant, having been assistant editor on the journal since 1866, and his commissioning policy assured continuity. Even so, he shifted emphasis to reflect his own political*, social, ethical and cultural priorities, as with the journal's coverage of the 'Irish Question', parliamentary franchise reform, and deficiencies in the British education system. Grove was particularly concerned with the perceived threat of the newly unified Germany to peace and stability in Europe; accordingly, he commissioned articles that surveyed Britain's defence capabilities together with pieces that explored international co-operation and conflict resolution.

In cultural matters, Grove ensured that *Macmillan's Magazine* also reflected his own biblical, geographical and diverse cultural interests. Music* especially, a lifelong passion, was for the first time given coverage. Throughout his tenure at *Macmillan's Magazine,* a journal that was originally conceived as family* reading, Grove gave new prominence to poetry* and fiction written by women (Christina Rossetti, Margaret Oliphant* and Frances Hodgson Burnett), as well as articles about women and for female readers*. As for contributors, Grove blended youth with experience and proven distinction. While calling upon such eminent figures as Sir John Seeley (history* and politics), Clements Markham (geography) and Frances Martin (women's education), he also gave younger writers such as Arthur J. Evans (archaeology) and Edward Dannreuther (contemporary music) their chance to shine.

As an editor Grove was dependable, versatile, supportive and discriminating, and his success led Macmillan's to give him more responsibility within the firm; having acted as general literary advisor since the 1860s, he was appointed full-time general editor in 1873 while retaining the editorship of its *Magazine.* Grove left *Macmillan's Magazine* on his appointment as director of the newly created Royal College of Music (1883-1894), an institution for which he had lobbied long and hard. Away from magazine journalism, Grove was a distinguished lexicographer and musicologist, being best remembered as the editor of the serially produced *Dictionary of Music and Musicians* (Macmillan 1879-1889) a work that contributed hugely to the construction of the British 'musical renaissance'. MH

Sources: Graves 1903, Hughes and Stradling 2001, *New Grove*, *ODNB*, Worth 2003, Young 1980.

GRUB STREET Grub Street, in the City of London to the north of London Wall (now Milton Street), was an impoverished area of London that became renowned in the eighteenth century for its literary underworld of hack (i.e. for hire) journalists* and literati. Satirized by Alexander Pope in *The Dunciad* (1728) and by Jonathan Swift in *The Tale of a Tub* (1704), the expression 'Grub Street' became synonymous with low-level journalistic endeavour. As Samuel Johnson put it in *A Dictionary of the English Language* (1755), 'any mean production is called grubstreet'. By the nineteenth century, Grub Street, as a specific journalistic area, had ceased to exist, but George Gissing (1857-1903) used the expression in the title of his novel *New Grub Street* (1891) about aspiring but poverty stricken writers and journalists attempting to survive in the emerging cross currents of cultural commercialism. Although Gissing focuses some of the novel's literary activity on the Reading Room of the British Museum, he uses the expression in its colloquial rather than geographic sense. JRW

Source: Clarke 2004.

GRUNEISEN, CHARLES LEWIS (1806-79) The career and critical personality of music* critic Charles Gruneisen remain obscure for two reasons, because the bulk of his newspaper work was anonymous* and remains unattributed, and because sources of information for his biography are contradictory or uncorroborated.

According to an *Athenaeum** obituary* notice (8 Nov. 1879), Gruneisen began his journalistic life as subeditor of the Tory *Guardian** and editor* of the *British Traveller and Commercial and Law Gazette* in 1833, a few months later becoming foreign editor of the *Morning Post**. Rising to subeditor of the *Post*, he went as its war* correspondent to Spain (1837), and as foreign correspondent* to Paris (1839-1844), also cutting his teeth as a music critic writing notices for the *Post* about events in Paris and London.

On his permanent return to London in 1844, he settled into a career as a freelance music journalist and worked for several papers intermittently, including the *Britannia* (c1844-?1853), *Illustrated London News** (c1844-?1853), *Morning Post* (at least until 1846), *Morning Herald** (1845), *Morn-*

ing Chronicle* (1846-?1853) and *Maestro* (1844). He also served as editor* of the short-lived *Great Gun* (1844). Later in his career he wrote for the *Standard**, the *Queen** and the *Athenaeum* (from 1870). Authored publications include *The Opera and the Press* (1869).

Gruneisen was a competent, if not particularly original, writer on music. One of the first to champion the operas of Meyerbeer, Berlioz and Wagner in Britain, he was supportive of those who showcased European music and performers – a position that owed much to his continuing visits to Paris. Such a stance inevitably brought him into conflict with the partisan supporters of British music among London journalists, especially J. W. Davison*, who satirized him as 'Jenkins' (a conceit borrowed from *Punch**) in the *Musical World**. Gruneisen's activities outside his newspaper columns probably gave him greatest influence on London music: his support for the newly formed Royal Italian Opera (1847) and proximity to its manager Frederick Gye gave him a significant role in shaping repertoire and performance practices. CMB

Sources: *Athenaeum* 1879, Charlton and Ellis 2007, Dideriksen 1997, Langley 1983, *ODNB*.

GUARDIAN, A WEEKLY JOURNAL OF POLITICS, LITERATURE, MUSIC AND THE FINE ARTS, ECCLESIASTICAL, HOME, FOREIGN AND COLONIAL NEWS (1846-1951) A high church weekly* initially of 16 pages, the *Guardian* cost 6d and appeared on Wednesdays. It emerged from a crisis in the Oxford movement following the suppression of its organ the *British Critic** in 1843 and the conversion of its leader John Henry Newman to Roman Catholicism in 1845. Tractarianism had sought to stress the doctrinal continuities between the Catholic Church and the Church of England, but Newman's apostasy was a defining moment at which several of his key acolytes drew back from the brink. The foundating of the *Guardian* by Richard William Church (1815-1890), James Bowling Mozley*, Frederick Rogers and others was intended to steady the ship by propounding a more moderate High Anglicanism that would remain loyal to the national church.

While the *Guardian's* emergence must be understood in part as a repercussion of this theological schism, its contents are by no means confined to these issues. The lead article in its maiden issue, for example, is an attack on William Cobden's Land League, suggesting that the move away from radical theology was also conceived as a reengagement – on the Conservative side, and always through the lens of Christian morality – with the political* issues of the day. Domestic and foreign* news took up about half of the journal, with reports on parliamentary* debates and legal* cases usually a feature. Reviews* of books on a variety of subjects, correspondence* on theological or political matters, Ecclesiastical and University Intelligence (featuring lists of appointments and ordinations, as well as degrees awarded), lists of births, marriages and deaths, and brief reports on price fluctuations in the commodities markets* were also included. In contrast to more specialist religious* journals such as the *British Critic** or the *Christian Remembrancer** (where many Tractarians continued to publish), the *Guardian* appealed to laymen as well as to churchmen.

At the end of April in its first year of publication, a new series commenced in a larger format* (28cm x 41cm), which it retained for the remainder of the century. By 1855, the *Guardian* was frequently accompanied by a free supplement*, and by the end of the century this practice had developed to the point that the journal – now around 40 pages in length – was effectively divided into two sections separated by a wad of advertising*, the first containing the news* and leaders*, and the second (no longer referring to itself as a supplement) containing parliamentary* debates, reviews*, correspondence* and speeches by eminent clergymen. MaT

Sources: *ODNB, Waterloo.*

GUTCH, JOHN MATHEW (1776-1861) John Gutch, editor*, proprietor* and publisher* moved in 1803 from London, where he had been a law stationer, to Bristol. Here he became proprietor* of the Tory paper, *Felix Farley's Bristol Journal* until he died. Gutch achieved renown both as a newspaper editor and as a participant in local politics. During the 1820s he opposed corruption by the Bristol Corporation and wrote articles under the pseudonym* of 'Cosmo', citing heavy taxation and the lack of imaginative schemes for reviving the local economy as being the cause of Bristol's problems. In 1830 local radicals took up the war waged by *Felix Farley* on the corporation, and Gutch was forced to defend the status quo. His other newspaper enterprise was the founding of the London *Morning Journal* with Robert Alexander in 1828. In the following year, Gutch was arrested for libelling King George IV in addition to Lord Lyndhurst, resulting in the suppression of the *Journal* in 1830. Gutch's son, John Wheeley Gough Gutch (1809-1862), a surgeon, also followed

his father's journalistic path as editor of the *Literary and Scientific Register* (1842-1856) and editing the *Quarterly Journal of Meteorology and Physical Science* (1843) as well as contributing to *Felix Farley.* DHL
Sources: Harrison 1988, *ODNB.*

GYMNAST (1890-1899) A 2d publication of approximately 12 pages, the *Gymnast: A Monthly Journal of Gymnastics and Athletics* (Oct. 1890-March 1892) was edited* by J. W. Price until November 1891 when H. Parker took over the editorship. In February 1893, the magazine* was re-named the *Gymnast and Athletic Review: A Monthly Journal of Sport and Pastime* and the length of the periodical was increased to 16 pages although the price* remained constant. As its manifesto of 1890 states, *Gymnast* was founded as a British response to mass displays of foreign physical might as exhibited at German gymnastic festivals. Indeed, the contents and layout of the magazine indicate that the *Gymnast* was envisaged as an answer to concerns that Britain might be, as the piece describes, 'left behind in the race'.

The attempt to unify British gymnastics is apparent by the volume of articles and advertisements* featuring the activities of gymnasia and athletic clubs across the country. *Gymnast* contains diagrams and illustrations* for a variety of manoeuvres including figure marching and stretches with the Indian club and the wand. Suitable exercises for lady gymnasts were also amply covered. In its new guise as the *Gymnast and Athletic Review*, its expansion is indicated to the reader by the publication of a list of sports on the front cover of the magazine. These include antagonistics in the form of fencing, wrestling and boxing; athletic games such as hockey and football and pursuits such as fishing and indoor games. An annual rate of 5s (which included the subscription fee) was charged for the insertion of club advertisements*. Advertisements for fencing equipment were juxtaposed with articles arguing for the teaching of fencing in military schools, inviting the reader to draw the link between sporting pastimes and national defence. Although articles were largely unsigned*, the magazine did include contributions by physicians on the benefits of combining athletics and gymnastic training and on the hygienic construction of gymnasia.

Reasons behind the decision to cease publication remain obscure as the final issue of January 1899 has been classified unfit for public use. However, it is likely that *Gymnast* was eclipsed by competition from *Sandow's Magazine** and *Health and Strength** which appeared in 1898. While *Gymnast* attempted to broaden its range of interests, its pedagogical style may have discouraged the casual sports enthusiast. The Spartan format* of *Gymnast* was replaced by the photographic* journalism of its rivals which enjoyed greater success with professionals and the general public alike. Nevertheless, *Gymnast* constitutes a key step in the unification of athletics and gymnastics in the form of the sports journal. It is also a useful resource for the study of the development of sports in the context of late nineteenth-century nationalism in Europe. **EG**

Sources: Bartlett *et al.* 2006, *Gymnast* 1890-1898.

H

HALL, ANNA MARIA (1800-1881) Anna Maria Fielding, a prolific Irish journalist*, editor* and writer of fiction was generally known after her marriage in 1824 to Samuel Carter Hall* as Mrs S. C. Hall. Her career in the press is linked to his progress as an editor when he introduced her into literary life by publishing her Irish stories in the first volume of his annual* *Amulet* (1826-1837), and later in *Spirit and Manners of the Age* (1826-1829). These were collected and published as *Sketches of Irish Character* in 1829. But by this time she had already edited her own annual, the *Juvenile Forget-Me-Not* (1826-1834). She continued contributing to the *Amulet* until it closed, meanwhile writing further stories for the *New Monthly Magazine** (also later collected), miscellaneous articles, plays and four novels in the 1830s alone.

Hall published regular short fiction in the *Art Journal** during Samuel's editorship from 1839-1880; her other contributions include Irish stories for the *Irish Monthly Magazine** (1830), *Chambers's Edinburgh Journal** where one story, 'The Governess', gained approval from Dickens*, the *Irish Penny Journal* (1840-1841) the *Dublin University Magazine** (1835-1841), and an article on French manners in the *Westminster Review**(1839). Her editorial career continued with the *Finden's Tableaux* annual (1836) and later she took over for a short time the editorship of *Sharpe's London Magazine** (1852-1853), into which she introduced more serious material about and by women. She left, it seems, because she felt slandered by George Virtue, who was briefly its owner. She was the first editor of *St James's Magazine** (1861), where she also published serial* fiction. Despite some paternalism, her numerous periodical writings presented a somewhat benevolent image of Ireland to the British public. FB/AK
Sources: Crossland 1893, Hall 1883, Keane 1997, Morris 2002, *ODNB*, *Wellesley*.

HALL, SAMUEL CARTER (1800-1889) Samuel Carter Hall is a typical example of the energetic pragmatic nineteenth-century journalist*, editor* and writer, best known as the editor of the *Art Journal** and possibly partial model for Pecksniff in Dickens's* *Martin Chuzzlewit*. From an Irish military background, he entered literary life in 1822 as the secretary to the Italian romantic poet Ugo Foscolo, then exiled in London. Soon he was report-

ing parliament for several journals, including the dying *British Press* (1803-1826), the short-lived Murray* newspaper, the *Representative* (1825), and the *New Times* (1817-1828). He wrote the entire contents of the *Literary Observer* for six months in 1823 and three years later founded the annual* *Amulet: a Christian and Literary Remembrancer* (which he edited until 1837). He also edited with his wife the genteel – if irregularly published – *Spirit and Manners of the Age* (1826-1829) and its short-lived but more regular monthly successor, the *British Magazine* (1830). A conservative, he worked on several Tory papers although he was not always successful at keeping them alive. This included deputizing for the editor (who was imprisoned in 1830 for libelling Wellington and Peel) during the final year of the *Morning Journal* (1828-1830; a continuation of the *New Times*) and editing the weekly *Town* (1832-1834; this is not the same as Renton Nicholson's *Town**). Meanwhile, he contributed to the *Watchman and Wesleyan Advertiser* (1835-1884), and, between 1830 and 1836, alternately sub-edited and edited the *New Monthly Magazine**. In 1836, he subedited the Tory *John Bull** (now much more sedate) and the weekly *Britannia* (1836-1856). At the end of 1838, he accepted the editorship of a new magazine, the *Art-Union* (*Art Journal** from 1849) which he bought after a year and which, after overextending his resources to cover the Great Exhibition, he was forced to sell in 1851. However, he continued to edit it until 1880. This was to be the central activity for the rest of his life, although for a year from 1878 he also edited the earnest penny weekly *Social Notes* (1878-1881). His 1883 autobiography gives a valuable account of the London publishing scene. He was married to Anna Maria Hall*. AK
Sources: Hall 1883, Mancoff 1991, Morris 2002, *ODNB*.

HAMERTON, PHILIP GILBERT (1834-1894) Philip Gilbert Hamerton helped to shape late Victorian art criticism as both a didactic and opinionated discipline through his writings and editorship of the *Portfolio**.

In his memoirs, Hamerton recalled his early desire to become a painter in the manner of John Ruskin*, whom he met in 1853. The success of *A Painter's Camp in the Highlands* (1862) confirmed his decision to establish his career as a writer and shortly thereafter he began contributing to magazines such as *Macmillan's** and *Cornhill**. An article on 'Art Criticism' in the latter (Sept. 1863) confirmed his chosen career path and established a template for the emergent field of professional art criticism. In 1866, Hamerton succeeded Francis Palgrave as art critic for the *Saturday Review**, a position he held until 1868, when he found travel to London too difficult from France, where he had moved with his wife in 1861. His criticism reveals his gradual eschewal of the truth-to-nature dictums of John Ruskin in favour of more overt interpretation of the scene indicative of an artist's individual perception.

Rising interest in art criticism was reinforced by the establishment of specialist journals such as the *Fine Arts Quarterly Review*, to which Hamerton contributed. In 1870, Hamerton founded the *Portfolio*, a monthly*, with publisher* Richmond Seeley and served as its editor* until his death. Heavily illustrated* and featuring the work of both British and continental artists, *Portfolio* set a high standard of quality. His work for the *Portfolio* often became the basis of subsequent books, such as *Landscape* (1885), *Imagination in Landscape Painting* (1887), *Examples of Modern Etching* (1875) and the *Graphic Arts* (1882). The latter two volumes established Hamerton's considerable contribution to the etching revival traceable back to *Etching and Etchers* (1868). ALH

Sources: *Grove Dictionary of Art,* Hamerton 1896, Kissane 1972, *ODNB*, Prettejohn 1997.

HAMERTON, ROBERT JACOB (1809-1905) The Irish-born Robert Jacob Hamerton was one of the earliest lithographers* in this field. A significant contributor of illustrations* to *Punch** (1843-1848), he never seems to have consolidated his position on the magazine, perhaps because his main interest was in lithography and oil painting. He appears to have abandoned wood engraving* after his time at *Punch*. BM

Sources: AntiQbook online, Spielmann 1895.

HAMMOND, CHRISTIANA MARY DEMAIN (1861-1900); HAMMOND, GERTRUDE DEMAIN (1862-1952) Illustrators* of the 1890s, Christiana known as 'Chris' and Gertrude Hammond (later Mrs Henry McMurdie) attended Lambeth School of Art and the Royal Academy Schools.

As a student 'Chris' published illustrations in the *Detroit Free Press* and *Pick-Me-Up* and in 1894 her work appeared in the first issue of *St Paul's: an Illustrated Journal for the Home* (1894-1900) which guaranteed her future. She was inundated with work not only for magazines such as the *Illustrated London News** and the *Sketch**, but from book publishers Macmillan* and George Allen, among others. Praised by Alfred Foreman for their 'delicacy,

vigour, variety, subtlety of characterisation', her illustrations appeared in a variety of titles in the 1890s including the *Pall Mall Budget* (1891-1892), the *Ludgate Monthly* (1891/1895), the *Idler** (1892), the *English Illustrated Magazine** (1893-1896), the *Quiver** (1894-1895), *Madame* (1895), *Temple* (1896), *Pearson's Magazine* (1896), *Cassell's Family Magazine** (1898). Publication of Gertrude Hammond's work was similarly successful in the period in titles such as the *Quiver* (1890), *Ludgate Monthly* 1891), *Queen**, *Black and White**, the *Idler* (1892), *St Paul's Magazine** (1894), *Madame* (1895), the *Yellow Book** (1895), *Minister* (1895), the *Lady's Pictorial * and *Pick-Me-Up*. CL

Sources: Foreman 1900, Houfe 1978, Micklethwait and Peppin 1983, *Who's Who* 1929.

HANSARD, THOMAS CURSON (1776-1833) Best known for his publication of Hansard's Parliamentary Debates, widely known from the early nineteenth century as the standard record of the British Parliament's proceedings, Thomas Hansard began his career in the family parliamentary printing business as an apprentice to his father's business partner, Henry Hughes. In 1805 he purchased Thomas Rickaby's printing house, in Peterborough Court, Fleet Street* and by 1809 had begun publishing*, no doubt in part because of his sympathy for radical politics, William Cobbett's *Parliamentary Debates*, *Parliamentary History of England*, and *Complete Collection of State Trials*. In 1812 Hansard purchased the rights to publish the three publications from Cobbett, whose legal and financial difficulties left him unable to sustain them. While at first the text of the debates was extracted from newspaper reports, Hansard soon began to rely upon reporters. In 1829 Hansard added his name to the publication, and from the early 1830s 'Hansard's' became the colloquial way to refer to the records of Parliamentary debates. RSB

Sources: *DNB, ODNB*.

HAPPY HOURS, A WEEKLY JOURNAL OF INSTRUCTION AND RECREATION (1867-1877) A 1d weekly* and 'family* journal for all classes*', *Happy Hours* initially combined poetry*, short stories, trivia and serialized* fiction with a significant number of games and puzzles. Aimed at women and children, it had sections entitled 'Stories and Lessons for the Little Ones', 'Little Tales for Little Readers', and the fiction on offer was usually moralistic. Some content was reprinted from celebrated authors such as Hans Christian Anderson, but the majority was original, and there was a marked preponderance of female authors.

The purely entertaining elements of the magazine were always tempered by more serious articles such as the abridgements of De Quincey's* accounts of the Irish Rebellions of 1798, printed in 1867. But the balance arguably shifted from recreation to instruction. Chess problems were discontinued after the journal's first year, and the riddles, anagrams and puzzles that formed the backbone of the journal in its early years were increasingly directed at children, confined to the back pages, or completely absent. The final issue saw the conclusion of a debate, albeit a light-hearted one, on the question, 'Did Shakespeare mean to represent Hamlet as feigning madness all through the play, or that he really did become insane?' Whether it was a decline in readership* resulting from this more improving content that accounted for the journal's demise is pure speculation. **MaT**

Sources: *Happy Hours* 1867-1877, *Waterloo*.

HARDWICKE, ROBERT (1822-1875) Hardwicke's shop in Piccadilly was a focal point for natural history publishing* in the third quarter of the nineteenth century. Although Hardwicke's list mainly consisted of popular medical books, he also published four long-running natural history periodicals, *Hardwicke's Science-Gossip**, *Popular Science Review*, the *Journal of Botany* and the *Journal of the Quekett Microscopical Club*. Hardwicke obtained his articles as a printer in 1847, joining Salisbury and Bateman as partner at their business at 4 Clement Court, off Lincoln's Inn in London. By 1850 the firm had become Bateman and Hardwicke and moved to nearby Carey Street. In 1852 Hardwicke set up on his own at his premises at 192 Piccadilly. It was while he was trading from Piccadilly that Hardwicke was introduced to Edwin and Phebe Lankester*, and, through them, Mordecai Cubitt Cooke*. This prompted Hardwicke to develop his list of popular science* publications, beginning with the 2s 6d quarterly* *Popular Science Review* in 1861, with James Samuelson* as editor*. In 1865 he began *Hardwicke's Science-Gossip*, a 4d monthly with Cooke as editor. The shop became an informal meeting place for authors interested in natural history and, in 1865, Hardwicke, Cooke and his manager Thomas Ketteringham founded the Quekett Microscopical Club, publishing their journal from its foundation in 1868. **JEM**

Sources: English 1987, Lightman 2004a, *ODNB*.

***HARDWICKE'S SCIENCE-GOSSIP: AN ILLUS-TRATED MEDIUM OF INTERCHANGE AND GOSSIP FOR STUDENTS AND LOVERS OF NATURE* (1865-1902)** In 1864 the mycologist Mordecai Cubitt Cooke* alerted his publisher Robert Hardwicke*, who three years earlier had begun the quarterly* *Popular Science Review*, to a gap in the market for a cheap* monthly magazine on natural history, and, having abandoned Cooke's rather abstruse initial suggestion of the *Veil of Isis*, they instead opted for Hardwicke's stridently populist title *Science-Gossip*. With Cooke as editor* and Hardwicke publisher*, the first number appeared in January 1865, costing just 4d for 24 large octavo pages, and claiming to be the cheapest scientific journal yet published. Alongside numerous advertisements* which brought in a profit of £60 per month, its double-column* pages boasted Cooke's regular leaders*, signed articles with illustrations*, anecdotes, brief extracts from recent books and periodicals on subjects like entomology and zoology, and finally readers' letters*.

While *Science-Gossip* proved a success with readers*, many in the scientific community questioned the propriety of its informal title, and after the first year of publication Cooke proclaimed defiantly 'we again announce our name, however undignified it may be, and with it gain admission to the firesides of thousands, whilst the same talisman excludes us, we hope, from the drawing rooms of only a few' (quoted in English 1987:108). *Science-Gossip* certainly addressed itself principally to the growing ranks of amateur and plebeian naturalists, but Hardwicke and Cooke received assistance from professional experts at both the British Museum and Kew gardens, and occasionally published important articles by leading authorities such as the dermatologist William Tilbury Fox or up-and-coming naturalists like the young Ray Lankester*. The coverage of microscopy was particularly advanced, and the *Quarterly Journal of Microscopical Science* enthusiastically recommended *Science-Gossip* to its readers, who would 'all be interested in its contents'. Cooke even suggested that *Nature**, founded in 1869, was among the many imitators of his and Hardwicke's profitable journal. By this time, however, relations between editor and publisher had soured, and in 1872 Hardwicke replaced Cooke with John Ellor Taylor, who edited *Science-Gossip* for the next three decades – also assuming the proprietorship* following Hardwicke's death in 1875 – although never as successfully as Cooke.

By 1893 declining sales and poor health forced Taylor to close the journal. It was resurrected in the following year by John Carrington and Edward Step, who raised the price* to 6d and attempted, without much success, to attract contributions

from professional scientists. In 1902 *Science-Gossip* was subsumed into its rival *Knowledge*. **GD**
Sources: English 1987, Mussell 2007b, Sheets-Pyenson 1985, *Science-Gossip* 1865, *Waterloo*.

HARDY, PHILIP DIXON (1794-1875) Philip Dixon Hardy was a Dublin printer, publisher*, proprietor*, and editor*. After working in general printing, in 1830 he became editor and proprietor of the monthly* *National Magazine*, which closed in 1831 with losses of £250. In 1833 Hardy became the proprietor, editor and main contributor of the weekly *Dublin Penny Journal*. His pieces were anonymous*, and are therefore difficult to identify. He invested £3,000-£4,000 in the periodical, and purchased for it the first steam press* ever to be employed in Ireland. Hardy brought circulation* to 12,000 copies per week, including English sales of 4,000. Disputes with his staff led to ill-health and forced Hardy to close the *Dublin Penny Journal* in 1836, despite annual profits of £400-£500.

Hardy was interviewed by the Select Committee on Trades' Unions or Combinations of Workmen in 1838, providing valuable information on the printing and publishing trades in Ireland. In 1839-1840 he debated with Samuel Ferguson in the *Dublin University Magazine* and *Saunders' Newsletter* over an alleged decline of the *Dublin Penny Journal* under his management. Afterwards he continued to work as a publisher and author, mostly of tourist guides and religious works. Hardy was an innovator and keen businessman, and study of his contentious involvement with the *Dublin Penny Journal* is crucial for understanding the place of popular* periodicals in Ireland. **FB**
Sources: *Dublin Penny Journal* 1833, Hayley 1976, *Saunders's Newsletter* 1839, Select Committee on Trades' Unions 1837-1838, *Waterloo*.

HARDY, THOMAS (1840-1928) A major novelist, short-story writer and poet, Thomas Hardy first published most of his work in transatlantic* periodicals. He often wrote letters* to newspapers, on topics from animal welfare to the Boer War, and he participated in several round tables, principally on literary subjects, in journals including the *Fortnightly Review* and the *New Review*. In one such symposium, 'Candour in English Fiction' (Jan. 1890), Hardy complained that the convention of publishing novels in serial* form inhibited explicit treatment of sex and religion. Certainly this was his experience: from his first anonymous* serial, 'A Pair of Blue Eyes' (Sept. 1872-July 1873, in *Tinsleys' Magazine*), to his last, 'Hearts Insurgent' (Dec. 1894-Nov. 1895, in *Harper's New Monthly Maga-*

zine). Hardy self-censored* his fiction, reacting to, or anticipating, advice from editors such as Leslie Stephen*. Hardy's serial novels were illustrated* and he sometimes worked closely with artists like Thomas Macquoid (1820-1913). Of Hardy's occasional non-literary journalism, the most significant article is 'The Dorsetshire Labourer' (July 1883), in *Longman's Magazine*. A consumer of the press as much as he was a contributor to it, newspaper reports provided one source for Hardy's creative writing. **AC**
Sources: Greenslade 2004, Millgate 2001, *ODNB*, Wright 2003.

***HARMONICON* (1823-1833)** One of the first English-language periodicals to be devoted entirely to music*, *Harmonicon* was published monthly by the proprietors*William Clowes* and J. W. Parker*, and edited* by influential music administrator William Ayrton (1777-1858). It had an attractive format* and an accessible style, and included biographical sketches, reviews*, and news* of the musical world, with musical quotations and pictorial illustrations*. Each edition also contained a selection of printed music in performance editions. Readers learned much about British music as well as about continental masters.

In an age when Beethoven, Mendelssohn, Bellini and other early romantics were contemporary, the *Harmonicon* acquired a position of authority and influence, even though the views it expressed were sometimes idiosyncratic and old-fashioned. It was never anything other than lively, and its genuine magazine format* was futuristic. The reasons for its demise were financial, and in its reincarnation as the *Musical Library* (1834-1837) it was less discursive and shorterlived. Modern scholars find much in the *Harmonicon* about the reception of music and about musical life in London in the decades that preceded Victoria. **TH**
Sources: Langley 1989, Langley 1990, Langley 2001, Snigurowicz 1989

HARMSWORTH, ALFRED CHARLES WILLIAM (1865-1922) Alfred Harmsworth, Viscount Northcliffe, a journalist, editor* and newspaper proprietor*, was born in Dublin to an Anglo-Irish mother and English father. Beginning his career in journalism at 15, his first jobs included freelance reporting for the *Hampstead and Highgate Express*, cycling magazines (*Cyclist**, *Wheeling*) and magazines for boys and girls published by his early mentor, James Henderson.

He built up contacts through his freelance work for various London papers including the *Globe**,

*Morning Post**, *St James's Gazette**, and by writing articles and books for George Newnes'*, who proved to be an influential figure in Harmsworth's career. Newnes' understanding of the needs of a literate public craving entertaining reading material was shared by the young journalist. Harmsworth edited youth* in 1894 at the age of 19. After two years in Coventry working for the publishers Iliffe and Sons* (where he edited Bicycling News), he returned to London in 1897 with capital to start his own business. He established a chain of magazines over the next decade including the astonishingly successful* *Answers to Correspondents**, which he founded in 1888 as a rival to *Tit-Bits* and which eventually reached net weekly sales of more than a million copies. Other successful cheap periodicals* followed including Comic Cuts*, Illustrated Chips, and Forget-Me-Not. *Comic Cuts*, a pictorial magazine aimed 'at adults who had read little or nothing previously' (*ODNB*) was notable for its innovative use of the speech balloon, now a staple of comics (Taylor: 19). Harmsworth joined with his brother Harold Harmsworth*, a capable financial manager, to build the Amalgamated Press Company and their domination of the popular journalism market continued through magazines such as *Boys' Home Journal**, *Marvel, Home Sweet Home* and *Home Chat**. By 1892, the Harmsworths headed the largest magazine company in the world.

Harmsworth entered daily journalism when Kennedy Jones* persuaded him to purchase the failing *Evening News** in 1894. The paper was quickly turned into a successful enterprise and its distinctive pitch of less politics*, more sport*, eye-catching headlines and competitions for readers was perfected and enhanced in Harmsworth's new venture, the halfpenny *Daily Mail**, launched in 1896. The *Mail* targeted the commuter classes (one of its straplines was 'the busy man's daily journal') and it included an innovative page dedicated to women readers*. The newest advances in technology, including machines that printed, copied and folded papers at speed, were harnessed to ensure most efficient mass production and mass* sales.

Harmsworth set up a regional distribution* office in Manchester to make sure that his circulation* continued to grow and established a paper-producing enterprise in Newfoundland to guarantee steady supplies of cheap paper*. He launched a women's paper, the *Daily Mirror** in 1903 with an all female staff, and though it did not take off, it was successfully re-launched the following year as the *Illustrated Daily Mirror**. He branched into 'quality'

newspapers in 1905 in purchasing the *Observer** and in 1908 eventually secured for his empire the signature paper of Fleet Street*, *The Times**. It was a prestige purchase for Harmsworth but he did introduce changes when sales were dropping, such as eventually lowering its price* to a penny* and introducing illustrations*.

With his instinctive flair for 'getting inside the mind of the common man' (*ODNB*) the 'Napoleon of Fleet Street' was viewed with some wariness by government. Harmsworth's commentary on the profession, collected as a chapter, in Arthur Lawrence's *Journalism as a Profession* (1903) and his *Newspapers and Their Millionaires* (1922), offers insight into changes in the publishing industry. **FD/ ME**

Sources: Bourne 1990, *ODNB*, Pound and Harmsworth 1959, Taylor 1996.

HARMSWORTH, HAROLD (1868-1940) Harold Harmsworth, Viscount Rothermere, was the younger brother of the newspaper baron and pioneer of the popular* press, Alfred Harmsworth*. Like his brother, he left school early to help to support his family, working as a clerk in the mercantile marine office of the Board of Trade (*ODNB*). In 1888 he gave up his job to join his brother's growing magazine business and encouraged him to set up independently. Answers Company Ltd, named after Alfred's hugely successful magazine *Answers to Correspondents**, burgeoned into the Amalgamated Press Company – the biggest magazine firm in the world by 1892.

The business was carefully managed by the financial expert Harold while his brother, the more celebrated visionary, spearheaded the accumulation of popular, niche market and quality publications. Harold was more conservative than Alfred and often disagreed with him. His natural caution has seen him characterized as the 'uninteresting, sinister or comic addendum' to his brother (Bourne: 77). His astute management, however, was vital in turning the ailing *Evening News**, (purchased by Alfred in 1894), into 'our gold brick' (Pound and Harmsworth: 172). He was particularly effective in controlling advertising* revenue and in attending to peak distribution* points for the paper to catch the commuting classes (Taylor: 29). Though he and his brother had separate newspaper interests from the 1890s onwards, Harold Harmsworth has been credited as a key architect of the group's broader success (Bourne: 79).

Harold's money was behind the purchase of the *Glasgow Daily Record** in 1895: the paper served as a 'test bed' for the establishment in 1896 of the *Daily*

Mail, the enormously successful popular daily (Bourne: 80). He had accumulated a line of newspapers by 1921 including the *Glasgow Record and Mail*, *Sunday Pictorial*, *Daily Mirror**, *Glasgow Daily Record*, *Evening News** and *Sunday Mail*, some of which were originally owned by his brother, and some of which were in competition with Alfred's papers. Following Alfred's death in 1922, Harold took controlling interest in their media empire and by 1923 he owned three national morning, three national Sunday, and two London evening papers, four provincial* dailies*, and three provincial Sunday newspapers (*ODNB*). He sold the company to the Berry* brothers in 1926 and turned his attention to dominating the field of regional journalism by starting up evening newspapers in cities throughout Britain. Though never aligned with any political party, politicians regularly sought his support and he was made a peer in 1919. He became increasing critical of government policy through the 1920s, and tacitly supported fascist groups in Britain and across Europe in the 1930s. **FD**

Sources: Bourne 1990, *ODNB*, Pound and Harmsworth 1959, Taylor 1996.

HARMSWORTH MONTHLY PICTORIAL MAGAZINE (1898-1900) In the early 1890s, the Harmsworth brothers, Alfred* (later Lord Northcliffe) and Cecil, witnessed the success of George Newnes's* *Strand** and William Waldorf Astor's *Pall Mall Magazine**, and wanted to launch a competitor as early as 1893. But fiscal exigencies intervened, and it was not until the Harmsworths had launched the successful newspaper the *Daily Mail** in 1896 that their thoughts once again turned to the idea of a monthly* magazine. Although the *Harmsworth Monthly Pictorial Magazine* was more downmarket and sensational than the *Strand* or *Pall Mall Magazine*, its inauguration was prompted by the same sense of the emergence of a new style of journalism.

The *Harmsworth* appeared in July 1898 with the Canadian historian and journalist*, Henry Beckles Wilson, a fervent imperialist*, as its editor*, and it sold approximately 800,000 copies. With its emphasis on illustrations* and graphics, which often covered an entire page or the top half of a page, the *Harmsworth* was in the mainstream of 1890s taste for vogue drawing and the decorative arts. Just as the *Daily Mail* was famously 'a penny newspaper for a halfpenny', so the *Harmsworth* was a 6d magazine for 3d, although the second issue sold for 3 ½d. It was printed by new, giant rotary presses* located in Gravesend and Northfleet, but the first is-

sue sold so many copies that the printing presses could not handle the second run. The magazine's dimensions were six cm wide, 25 cm long, with an average length of 100 pages.

New writers were encouraged, both for their innovative appeal and their meagre demands for remuneration. The first few months included contributors such as Beatrice Heron-Maxwell, a prominent woman journalist who wrote tales of horror and the paranormal, Gerald Brenan and Winston Churchill (who was covering the Boer War* for the *Daily Mail*). Before the magazine was a year old, George Gissing had contributed a short story. In the early Edwardian period, H. G. Wells* and E. Phillips Oppenheim began to contribute. But the *Harmsworth* not only published conventional short fiction* but also short, purportedly non-fiction pieces about curiosities. The contributions were most often self-contained stories, not serials; even when the magazine, under a slightly different title, turned to publishing longer fiction in the 1910s, it featured complete novelettes* in one issue.

The *Harmsworth*'s stable included specialist genre writers: adventure, romance, gothic and orientalist were represented by Conan Doyle, Kipling and Flora Anne Steel; New Woman writers by Sarah Grand* and Grant Allen*; children's writers by E. Nesbit; maritime by Frank Bullen. Americans such as Bret Harte, 'O. Henry' and Jack London also contributed. Joseph Conrad, customarily more likely to be found in the *Pall Mall Magazine** or the *Strand*, tried to write in a populist style for the magazine. The official title for the first four issues was the *Harmsworth Pictorial Monthly Magazine*. In 1901, the title was changed* to the *Harmsworth London Magazine* before becoming the *London Magazine* by 1903; but it never attained the cultural position of either its predecessor or successor of that name. **NB**

Sources: *ODNB*, Thomas 1984.

HARNEY, GEORGE JULIAN (1817-1897) Largely self-educated, Harney became a shopman for Henry Hetherington* in 1833 and served three prison sentences for selling unstamped* newspapers. An avowed revolutionary (much of his Chartist* journalism* was anonymous*, and signed in the style of J-P. Marat, 'L'Ami du Peuple'), Harney was also influenced by the Spencean and socialist Allen Davenport*. His first venture into journalism (jointly with J. C. Coombe) was as printer and editor* of the *London Democrat* (April-June 1839), published for the ultra-radical East London Democratic Association of which Harney was a founder member. When this periodical failed, he concocted a living as a full-time political lecturer and occasional reporter* for *Northern Star**. In April 1841 he was appointed the paper's Sheffield staff reporter and in September 1843 deputy editor to Joshua Hobson*. The latter gave him increasing responsibility and Harney effectively edited the paper sometime before his official appointment (October 1845). Harney's editorship* (he resigned August 1850) was distinguished by increasing coverage of foreign* affairs and the case for a social programme complementing Chartism's central political* platform.

These were the central ground of Harney's own journals, *Democratic Review of British & Foreign Politics, History & Literature** (1849ff) and *Red Republican** (1850) the last issue of which (Nov. 1850), printed the first English translation of the *Communist Manifesto*. Retitling it *Friend of the People* Harney conducted the journal until 1852; he then merged* it into *Northern Star** (which he had purchased) under a new masthead*, the *Star of Freedom*. This was a failure, as was his *Vanguard* early the following year. That December Harney moved to Newcastle to work on the *Northern Tribune**. Shortly after its closure (March 1855) he accepted the editorship of the *Jersey Independent*, a post he held until 1862 when the proprietor* sacked him for outspokenly supporting the North in the American Civil War. He then emigrated to Massachusetts where, briefly, he edited the abolitionist *Commonwealth*. He remained in touch with British journalism, contributing to *Notes & Queries** and the *Newcastle Weekly Chronicle**. Returning to Britain in 1888, Harney became one of the *Chronicle*'s regular columnists* until his death. **MSC**
Sources: *DLB, ODNB*.

HARPER AND BROTHERS Harper, James (1795-1869); Harper, John (1797-1875); Harper, Joseph Wesley (1801-1870); Harper, Fletcher (1806-1877). A book and magazine publishing* company, J. & J. Harper was started by James and John Harper in New York, 1817. Joined by their younger brothers in the mid-1820s, the firm became Harper & Brothers in 1833.

*Harper's New Monthly Magazine** began in June 1850 as a general interest magazine, taking commercial advantage of the lack of international copyright*, it predominantly featured material already published in England, including prestigious writers such as Thackeray* and Dickens*. The magazine was a huge success with a circulation* of 50,000 after six months. However, jibes of anti-Americanism forced the company to revert to including American writers and artists. From 1880 to 1966 a Euro-

pean edition existed, usually referred to as the English edition. Initially, to avoid British copyright laws most of the magazine was printed in New York then shipped over for its London editor* (John Lillie 1880-1884 and Andrew Lang* 1884-1889) to add the editorial, news* and advertisements*. The sophistication of the publication with its high quality illustrations* challenged American editions of British periodicals, and created a market for Harper's books as well as recruiting British writers for Harper's publishing house. This successful publication was followed by *Harper's Weekly* in 1857 and *Harper's Bazar* in 1867. Financial problems in 1899 forced intervention by the banker J. Pierpoint Morgan, and the business was lost to the family in 1900. **CL**
Sources: Brake 1994a, *Harper's Magazine*, *Encyclopaedia Britannica*.

HARPER'S NEW MONTHLY MAGAZINE (1850-) Launched in 1850 and among the most popular American magazines of the mid- to late-nineteenth-century, *Harper's* took advantage of the lack of an international copyright* at mid-century. At first the magazine relied heavily on publishing material that had already been published in British publications and elsewhere. As the prospectus to the first issue notes, 'the Publishers of the New Monthly Magazine intend to remedy this evil, and to place everything of the Periodical Literature of the day, which has permanent value and commanding interest, in the hands of all who have the slightest desire to become acquainted with it. Each number will contain 144 octavo pages, in double columns*: the volumes of a single year, therefore, will present nearly 2,000 pages of the choicest and most attractive of the Miscellaneous Literature of the Age. The Magazine will transfer to its pages as rapidly as they may be issued all the continuous tales of Dickens*, Bulwer*, Croly, Lever*, Warren, and other distinguished contributors to British Periodicals…' It was a successful venture, with circulation* reaching 50,000 in about six months. As the popularity of the magazine increased, it began to rely less on British material and more on homegrown American literary talent. Among its most important editors* was the novelist W. D. Howells, whose 'Editor's Study' columns*, which began in 1886, provide an important extended discussion of American realism, among other things. **MWT**
Sources: Brake 1994a, Demoor 1988.

HARRIS, FRANK (1856?-1931) Frank Harris was born James Thomas Harris in Galway, Ireland as a British national and lived in London during his most successful period, though he eventually became a naturalized American citizen and died in France. Harris began as a French tutor at Brighton College, but spent most of his career as a journalist, serving as an editor* for a number of prominent and lesser publications including the *Evening News** (1883-1886), the *Fortnightly Review** (1886-1894), the *Saturday Review** for which he was also a partial proprietor*(1894-1898), the *Candid Friend* (1901-1902), *Motorist and Traveller* (1905 –1906), *Vanity Fair** (also a partial proprietor, 1907-1909), *Hearth and Home** (1911-1912), *Modern Society* (again a partial proprietor, 1913) and *Pearson's Magazine** (1916-1922).

Harris's most popular and productive work was done in the period 1883-1894. when he edited the *Evening News* and the *Fortnightly Review*, using Max Beerbohm* and George Bernard Shaw* as drama critics. During the 1880s, he focused on campaigning against poverty and critiquing both aristocracy and high society, continuing the latter throughout his life. A prolific writer, his success was impeded by his flamboyant personality and his controversial editorial decisions. He is also well known for his critiques of Britain during the First World War (published together in 1915 as *England or Germany?*) that marked him as a traitor and his salacious and sensational, if not entirely reliable, autobiography, *My Life and Loves*, which was published in three volumes (1923-1927). **SBA**
Sources: *Encyclopaedia Britannica* 2007, *ODNB*.

HARRISON, FREDERIC (1831-1923) Prolific essayist, jurist, historian and leading exponent of English positivism, Frederic Harrison was perhaps best known in his lifetime for precipitating one of the biggest theological uproars of the century. After graduating from Wadham College, Oxford, he was called to the bar in 1858 and began practising equity while writing polemics for the *Westminster Review**, with a notable early article appearing on the Italian question, and another, far more sensationally, on 'Essays and Reviews'. In 'Neo-Christianity' (1860), Harrison attacked the liberal-minded Essayists for appearing to abandon Christianity's major tenets without following this through by leaving the Church. Officially declaring himself a Positivist in 1870, Harrison was president of the English positivist Committee from 1880 to 1905, and co-founder of and contributor to the *Positivist Review**.

Harrison was also part of a group of influential writers, a 'male-dominated Positivist circle', who founded the *Fortnightly Review** in 1865, led by the journal's dynamic first editor*, G. H. Lewes*. Elsewhere, Harrison contributed to most of the serious-minded journals of his day: *Macmillan's Magazine**,

the *Contemporary Review**, the *Cornhill Magazine**, the *Nineteenth Century** and the *Pall Mall Gazette**. His far-reaching interests produced articles on a prodigious range of subjects from the extension of the franchise to the widening of primary education, the American Civil War*, Polish independence, Bismarckism, improving trade union laws and night-walking in London. **LL**
Sources: Harrison 1907, *ODNB*, Turner 2000a.

HARRISON, JANE ELLEN (1850-1928) Jane Harrison's career as a classical scholar and 'Cambridge Ritualist' can be charted through her extensive contribution to late nineteenth and early twentieth-century periodicals. Harrison was a regular reviewer* for the *Athenaeum**, although often anonymously*. She contributed extensively in the 1880s and 1890s on aspects of Greek myth and religion, although her input declined after 1901. Between 1879 and 1917 Harrison also wrote for the *Classical Review*, the *Edinburgh Review**, the *Spectator** and the *Journal of Hellenic Studies*, among others.

Her articles helped Harrison to develop her full-length works, finding inspiration in her reviews*. The journals provided a public forum where she could engage in academic debate, testing her hypotheses. In 1897 the *Edinburgh Review* published her review of Percy Gardner's *Sculptured Tombs of Hellas*. Her discussion of Greek funerary rites and perceptions of death prepared much of the ground for *Prolegomena to the Study of Greek Religion* (1903) and provides a deeply personal insight into her own loss of religious faith. Harrison's journal contributions were often personally revealing, and in 1891 she declared her support for the suffragist cause in the *Pall Mall Gazette**

Frequently uncompromising and controversial, her review of Lewis Farnell's the *Cults of the Greek States* in the *Cambridge Review* in 1907 ruffled feathers, with Percy Gardner jumping to Farnell's defence, claiming that Harrison's attack had been 'no review'. Many of Harrison's lectures were reproduced in the journals, including a series of lectures given at the Passmore Edwards Institute in Bloomsbury in 1898 on primitive matriarchal orders and mother-rule (a concept that underpinned Harrison's ideas on ancient culture). These were summarized in both the *Times** and the *Englishwoman's Review** in early 1898.

Towards the end of her career, Harrison focussed more closely on anthropology. Her reviews of W. H. R. Rivers and W. J. Perry in the *Nation and Athenæum* helped to shape her thoughts on the

GREEK MYTHS IN GREEK ART.   55

Choice, but far from being complete, the gathering of carriages at Cluny should form the nucleus of a collection that would be as good a means as exists of studying the out-door life of the last two centuries —a means whose interest is absolutely fresh and new. Even as that worn-out *désobligeant* which the author of "The Sentimental Journey" discovered in the innyard, and for whose misery he professed so much graceful pity, the wreck of many an interesting old vehicle might be unearthed in odd corners and out-of-the-way nooks. It should at least be possible to bring together all the carriages Roubo has described as existing in 1770:—The berlin; the diligence à l'Anglaise (answering to the English post-chaise), with its progenitor, the chaise de poste, in which the

coachman seems to be nearly on his horse's haunches; the calèche, open at the sides, with a roof and two seats; the diable, a similar vehicle with only one seat; and the grand cabriolet, shaped like a hansom without the driver's lofty perch. To these ought surely to be added a good specimen of that lumbering old caravan, the diligence; for although there are people still living who made the grand tour when there was one on every high road in France, it will soon become as curious as the megatherium — as impossible as the postillion's boots that are figured opposite the present writer's signature.   RICHARD HEATH.

GREEK MYTHS IN GREEK ART.—II.

HELEN OF TROY.

ABOUT the figure of Helen of Troy there plays a halo whose brightness no time may dim. In her image the beauty-worship of the Greeks culminates; she is peerless among women as Achilles among men; she is the mortal whom for her perfect loveliness none may criticise save to his own hurt. The poet Stesichorus dared in his "Destruction of Troy" to sing of her evil deeds and the sorrow she

wrought to Trojan and Greek; and for his impiety the gods smote him blind, nor restored him his eyes till he chanted his palinode "Not true is that word which I spake." Even Homer (so they fabled) was blind because he uttered blame of Queen Helen. In these modern days it is impossible—nay, perhaps it may not be wholly desirable—that we should so passionately worship this vision of beauty. Our

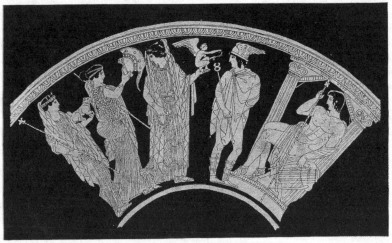

HELEN OF TROY.—I.: FROM A GREEK CYLIX. OBVERSE. (*Circ.* 400—300 B.C.)

Figure 26: Part II in a series of articles by J.E. Harrison on Greek art in the *Magazine of Art* , 1883: 55-62.

Orphic Mysteries, which she had examined in *Themis* (1912). Her death in 1928, however, prevented her from realizing these in print. **AS**

Sources: Ackerman 2002, Arlen 1990, Beard 2000, Demoor 2000, *ODNB*, Robinson 2002, Stewart 1959.

HART, ERNEST ABRAHAM (1835-1898) Hart was a key figure in British medical* journalism who edited* the *British Medical Journal** and prominently pursued a number of socio-medical reforms. Hart trained in medicine in London and subsequently held medical posts at several London hospitals. Soon after qualifying in 1856 he started contributing articles on medical topics to various periodicals and served on the staff of the *Lancet** from 1858 until he fell out with its editor, James Wakley, in 1866. He then moved to the *British Medical Journal*, serving as its editor* until his death in 1898, but with a short interruption in 1869-1870.

Through his energy, commitment and willingness to confront a wide range of social issues, Hart turned the *British Medical Journal* from an ailing weekly* into a highly respected and influential medical periodical*, increasing its circulation* about eightfold during his tenure. He also edited the *London Medical Record* (1873-1887) and the *Sanitary Record* (1874-1887), and contributed to the dailies* and such general periodicals as the *Fortnightly Review** and the *Nineteenth Century**. Through the *British Medical Journal* and other periodicals Hart tirelessly pursued such campaigns as sanitary reform, workhouse reform, medical education (including that of women), vaccination, vivisection, and the improvement of the conditions of naval surgeons. With equal commitment he also bitterly opposed hypnotism and mesmerism. **GC**

Sources: Bartrip 1990, *Jewish Chronicle* 14 Jan. 1898, Leighton 2001, *ODNB*.

HARVEY, WILLIAM (1796-1866) One of Bewick's most significant pupils, William Harvey abandoned wood* engraving early in his career and subsequently concentrated on designing for the wood engraving trade. His old-fashioned but elegant designs were produced in astonishing numbers – Engen calculates that he drew 3,000 book illustrations* within a single decade – and his work sought to establish wood engraving as a serious artistic medium as well as 'allowing for the first time the element of speed and impersonality in engraved illustration* that was to sweep the Victorian print world'.

Harvey was widely used as a source of images by Charles Knight* for the *Penny Magazine** and other of Knight's ambitious illustrated* projects in the 1840s, as well as producing decorative elements for *Punch** in its early years and, for 16 years (1843-1859), drawing for the *Illustrated London News**, which gave him a free hand to submit topographical and historical subjects. Harvey's highly polished work, which required to be engraved by Bewick's 'white line' technique, gave way to the more rapidly produced black line method in the 1840s as commercial considerations began to outweigh aesthetic ambition. But many of his periodical and book illustrations rank among the very best produced in the early Victorian period. **BM**

Sources: Engen 1990, Houfe 1978, *ODNB*.

HATTON, JOSEPH PAUL CHRISTOPHER (1841-1907) Journalist*, editor* and media historian, Joseph Hatton was the son of Francis Augustus Hatton, printer and bookseller at Chesterfield who, in 1854, founded the *Derbyshire Times*. Originally intended for the law, Joseph Hatton turned to journalism from around 1858. In 1861 he published a collection of tales and sketches entitled *Provincial Papers* and by 1863 he was editor* of the *Bristol Mirror**. Five years later, in 1868, tiring of provincial life, he moved to London. Here he tried to make a name for himself as a novelist and journalist, becoming editor of papers owned by the newspaper and magazine proprietors* Messrs. Grant and Company: the *Gentleman's Magazine**, the *School Board Chronicle* and the *Illustrated Midland News*. In 1871 he published reminiscences of Mark Lemon*, editor of *Punch**, entitled *With a Show in the North*. This was based on articles which had appeared in the *Gentleman's Magazine** A further series of articles entitled 'The True Story of Punch' appeared in the journal *London Society**, while his book *Journalistic London* (1882) was a collection of his pieces from *Harper's Magazine*.

In 1874 Hatton retired from editing. He became London correspondent* for the *New York Times*, the *Sydney Morning Herald* and the Berlin *Kreuz-Zeitung*. For a time he edited the *Sunday Times**. In 1881 the *Standard** sent him to New York to establish an independent telegraph* service, and he scooped the British press with news of the assassination of President Garfield. From 1892 he became editor of the *People*, a Conservative Sunday paper*, to which he contributed reminiscences, stories and interviews*. The publisher* William Tinsley recalled in his *Random Recollections of an Old Publisher* (1900) that he had never met a 'more energetic and reliable author' than Hatton. (Tinsley: 86) **DHL**

Sources: *ODNB*, Richards 2005, Tinsley 1900.

HAYDN, JOSEPH TIMOTHY (1788/1793?-1856) Joseph Timothy Haydn was born in Lisbon, the son of an expatriate Protestant Irishman. In 1809 he fled Napoleon's army and settled in Dublin where his first writing job was ghosting *A History of the Azores* for Thomas Ashe. In 1821, in collaboration with Frederick Conway, he founded the *Stage*. This was Haydn's first journalistic venture, and it contained reviews* of Dublin theatres.

After the journal folded, Haydn became a political* journalist*; between 1823 and 1838 he edited* and wrote for various Irish pro-government newspapers including the *Dublin Evening Mail**, the *Limerick Star* (1834-1838) and the *Limerick Times* (1837-c.1839). He made his name as a political journalist and in Dublin founded the *Statesman*, the *Patriot**, the *Morning Star* and the *Dublin Evening Mail**. Political journalism in Ireland could be hazardous: Haydn was physically assaulted for his views. In 1824 he was prosecuted for concealing his ownership of the *Mail* and the *Morning Star*, and banned from writing for the Dublin press in 1824. He continued to work in the Irish provinces where he contributed to the Cork *Bolster's Quarterly** which became the *Magazine of Ireland*. In 1839 Haydn moved to London where he became correspondent for the *Courier and Evening Gazette* (1839-c.1854). DHL

Sources: Myers 1983, *ODNB*.

HAYS, MATILDA MARY (1820?-1897) Matilda Mary Hays was an influential journalist associated with the mid-Victorian women's movement. Aiming to be a journalist as a young woman, she published in the 1840s in various magazines, including *Ainsworth's Magazine* and the *Mirror*. Early in her career, translating George Sand gave her an interest in women's issues which she explored in her novels, and in 1847 with Mary Howitt* she contemplated founding a women's journal, an ambition only realized when she became associated with Barbara Leigh Smith*, Bessie Rayner Parkes*, and other members of the Langham Place group in founding the *English Woman's Journal**.

Hays contributed poetry* to the group's first journalistic project, the *Waverley Journal,* and in 1858, she became a shareholder and co-editor of the *English Woman's Journal*. As a writer for the journal, Hays was industrious and controversial. George Eliot*, for example, privately referred to Hays's article on George Sand as a poorly written 'feminine rant'. Hays left the *English Woman's Journal* in 1864 because of personal conflicts with other members of the editorial team, who increasingly re-

garded her as a liability. Hay's cross-dressing and volatile romantic friendships tested the boundaries of radicalism within the nascent women's movement. ME

Sources: Hirsch 1998, Merrill 1999, *ODNB*.

HAZELL, WATSON AND VINEY LIMITED In the late 1860s the printers Hazell, Watson and Viney Limited had an established reputation as one of the leading printers of illustrated* magazines; by 1887 they were printing six weeklies*, 32 monthlies* and five quarterlies* (Keefe 1939).

George Watson, the founder, bought the p-rinting business of William Paul of Kirby Street, London, in 1843 acquiring a new Hopkinson & Cope press and five staff. On the strength of a contract to print the temperance* periodical the *Band of Hope Review**, he installed a steam press* in 1850. Five years later he doubled the size of his press on the basis of a second contract to print the monthly the *British Workman and Friends of the Sons of Toil** and later the *Eclectic and Congregational Review** (1863-1868) and the *Alexandra Magazine & Woman's Social and Industrial Advocate**. He founded the *Family Mirror* (1856-1857) which failed and Walter Hazell took charge of re-establishing a financially secure base for the firm. It launched the *Illustrated Photographer,* pioneering the use of photo-graphy* to produce its engravings*. This was followed later by the *Amateur Photographer* (1884-). The firm also printed the *Marylebone Mercury,* the *East London Observer* and the *Bucks Independent*.

In 1873 the partners bought Rogerson & Tuxford in the Strand and with it the *Mark Lane Express Agricultural Journal*. By 1879 the main premises had 31 machine presses and approximately 400 employees across its sites: Kirby Street, the Strand and in Aylesbury, where the partners had established a book works. George Watson's son brought the business of John Smith & Co. to the company in 1884. In the 1890s the firm was printing the *Pall Mall Gazette**, the *Lady's Realm**, the *Woman at Home**, the *Wide Wide World* and *Harmsworth Magazine**. Perhaps as a result of Walter Hazell's influence as a Liberal MP, social reformer and women's suffrage supporter, in 1896 the firm was employing women compositors in their Aylesbury works, on equal pay with men. The firm was also printing the *Woman's Signal** and the *Woman's Gazette*, papers dealing with female political* and economic interests. It undertook a range of reference book work including *Hazell's Annual Cyclopaedia* (1886-1922) and Letts' Diaries, and acquired other photographic and publishing* businesses. In the twentieth century the magazine business expanded and it printed many of Hearst's National Magazine Company's titles including *Nash's Magazine, Good Housekeeping, Harper's Bazaar* and the *Connoisseur*. AWe

Sources: Hazell 1919, Jowett 1887-1896, Keefe 1939, White 1897.

HAZLITT, WILLIAM (1778-1830) Hazlitt was arguably the only one of the English Romantics to keep faith with the ideals of the French Revolution throughout his life, and his journalism – which appeared in pamphlets and periodicals from around 1806 to the end of his life – is distinguished by its verve, erudition and political* commitment. Radical journalist*, essayist, portrait painter, lecturer and critic, Hazlitt sought to combine all these activities with affective personal opinion and close observation of quirky detail.

From a dissenting radical background (he followed his father by publishing with Joseph Johnson, friend of Wollstonecraft, Godwin and others), he spent part of his childhood in America. Having abandoned training for ordination, he turned to painting, achieving minor success with portraits. Simultaneously he published philosophical treatises, before announcing himself on the stage of political journalism with a generous portrait of Edmund Burke in William Cobbett's* *Weekly Political Register*. He began work in 1812 as a parliamentary reporter* for the *Morning Chronicle*, and within two years was its theatre critic; his passionate and involving accounts of contemporary performances of Shakespeare remain classics of the genre, though in May 1814 he was sacked for unreliable submission of copy. Having by now established an extensive network, including Leigh Hunt*, Wordsworth, Coleridge*, Lamb* and various publishers, Hazlitt was able to earn a living by writing for radical (or at least Whig) periodicals such as the *Examiner*, *Edinburgh Review*entre and the *Yellow Dwarf*. His political writing was fuelled by his anger at the defection of other Romantics – Wordsworth and Coleridge in particular – from the revolutionary cause.

Meanwhile the Tory press, most famously *Blackwood's* (but also the *Quarterly*), had begun to deem him worthy of attack as a member of the 'Cockney school', which included his friend Keats. Yet Hazlitt did not restrict himself to narrowly political subjects, taking a keen interest in contemporary popular culture, as his enthusiastic articles on sportsmen show. From 1820 he contributed the monthly series 'Table Talk' to the *London Magazine* which proved a turning point in his career. He

left on John Scott's* death in 1822 for the *New Monthly*. Two years later, still for the *New Monthly*, he began to write a series of brilliant biographical portraits of contemporary public figures, from Jeremy Bentham through William Godwin to Coleridge. These accounts were later published as *The Spirit of the Age, or, Contemporary Portraits* (1825). In 1824 he left on a tour of the continent, sending back letters to the *Morning Chronicle* (collected in 1826 as *Notes on a Journey through France and Italy*) and publishing, in the *New Monthly* under the pseudonym* 'Boswell redivivus', 'Conversations' with the artist Northcote. From then on his earnings declined as he moved to Paris, devoting his attention to a *Life of Napoleon*, though still contributing to the *New Monthly*, the *Atlas* and Colburn's* new *Court Journal* (1828-1925). AW/AK/MaT

Sources: Grayling 2000, Higgins 2005, *ODNB*, Parker 2000, Paulin 1998.

***HEALTH AND STRENGTH* (1898-)** Established in 1898 by the American dietician and exercise reformer Bernarr Macfadden, *Health and Strength* is one of the oldest physical culture journals in English. The monthly* magazine, priced* 1d for approximately 26 pages*, and 2d for approximately 36 pages from August 1900, was marketed as the 'national organ of physical fitness' and intended for a wide readership*. From September 1907, it appeared weekly*, repriced at 1d for 30 pages, in response to perceived demand. The magazine* was mainly directed towards the male consumer as indicated by the cover designs which offer popular interpretations of the Classical, Norse and Pre-historic muscular male. Articles on bodybuilding and weightlifting were complemented by advertising* on physical culture schools, energy drinks and gadgets to counteract weakness. Topics pertaining to general health such as diet (notably the practice of fasting, of which Macfadden was a keen advocate) and personal hygiene were designed to attract the casual sportsperson and average reader. Sexual overindulgence is obsessively discussed in the earliest issues and, vividly articulating 'Victorian' sexual anxiety, sport and hard work are constantly recommended as antidotes to the 'terrible vice'.

Turn-of-the-century editions of *Health and Strength* reflect a growing interest in defensive arts including boxing, jujitsu and Bartitsu, a martial art publicized by Edward William Barton-Wright in 1899 and misspelled as 'baritsu' in Arthur Conan Doyle's 'The Adventure of the Empty House' (*Strand Magazine* 1903). The advent of Bartitsu considerably changed the content of *Health and*

Strength. Barton-Wright and especially his protégés, Yukio Tani and Sadekazu Uyenishi, feature in the magazine, inspiring a flurry of articles on Japanese wrestling and mixed martial arts challenges. While manly fitness was prioritized, space was given to women readers*. Mary Nugent advised on beauty and women's health. Nugent also interviewed Barton-Wright in 1901. Throughout the Edwardian era, further articles appeared on female jujitsukas and women wrestlers. The early issues of *Health and Strength* are a helpful measure of anxieties and obsessions surrounding the male body during the time of the Boer War. At the same time, they also provide an indicator of women's involvement in the world of sports. **EG**

Sources: *Health and Strength* 1898-1914, *Waterloo*, *Willings Press Guide*, Wolf 2005.

HEARN, MARY ANNE (1834-1909) Mary Anne Hearn, one of the few Victorian women of humble birth to become a professional writer wrote under the pseudonym* of 'Marianne Farningham'. The daughter of a Kent postmaster, her career in journalism began when her Baptist minister Jonathan Whittemore invited Hearn to write for his periodical *Christian World** (1857ff). A 'cheap* family* magazine', the periodical took advantage of the repeal of the newspaper stamp* in 1855 to reach a broad and lowly, cross-denominational readership* by providing 'popular education', news*, and Christian literature in place of 'the debasing rubbish... of the ribald press'. In 1860 Hearn helped Whittemore establish the first magazine* aimed at the Sunday School and family readerships, the *Sunday School Times and Home Educator* (1860-1925), which featured lesson plans, hymns, and stories on 'family and educational subjects'. 'The first halfpenny paper on record', it hoped to reach 'the very poorest'.

In 1861 both the *Christian World* and *Sunday School Times* were taken over by James Clarke*, for whose large Christian publishing* house Hearn became a full-time writer in 1867. By 1871, the combined circulation* of these two magazines was 500,000. In 1885, Hearn became editor of the *Sunday School Times* with an annual salary of £50. Hearn's writings drew on her teaching, especially her Sunday School classes for girls who worked in the Northampton shoe factories, which inspired 'Girlhood', serialized in the *Sunday School Times* in 1868 and, like many of her magazine publications, reproduced in book form in 1869. Her affinity with readers was cemented by public lectures on topics like 'The Women of Today'. She knew leading female philanthropists like Mary Carpenter and Frances Power Cobbe*, but she was always conscious of the material difficulties faced by the poor, describing herself as 'half a socialist'. On her death she left an impressive £602. **HR**

Sources: *CBEL*, Farningham 1907, *ODNB*.

HEARTH AND HOME (1891-1914) Subtitled *An Illustrated* Weekly* Journal for Gentlewomen*, *Hearth and Home* was representative of one aspect of 1890s New Journalism*. It cost 3d, half the price* of *Queen**, the major competitor in the field of 'ladies' newspapers'. Broadsheet in format* and printed in three columns*, it was registered as a newspaper but had little in the way of conventional news*. Instead, as its title indicated, it included those genres* which had become the staple of journals targeted at middle-class women at home: advice on homes, gardens*, and household management; needlework and fashion; letters* pages, including one for 'Lassies and Laddies'; and short articles on servants, homes 'from castle to cottage, and similar topics. It was lavishly illustrated. Articles were often signed and the Editor*, Mrs. Talbot Coke*, contributed signed pieces, including the regular 'Home Advice' column*. **MRB**

Sources: Beetham 1996, *Hearth and Home*, *Waterloo*.

HEATH, WILLIAM (1794/5?-1840) Caricaturist* and illustrator*, William Heath's claim to attention in the history of periodicals is confined to two short-lived but nonetheless important ventures, both of which pioneered the reproduction of traditionally conceived caricature images in new periodical formats*. Using the relatively new medium of lithography* instead of the more conventional caricature modes of etching and engraving*, the *Glasgow Looking Glass** brought together a range of satirical* images on a large page, combining topical comment with satirical observation on contemporary manners. The *Glasgow Looking Glass*, for all its rather clumsy combination of contents, formed the first magazine* totally made up of caricatures.

Heath's subsequent magazine venture, projected and published* by Thomas McClean in London and called the *Looking Glass**, refined the caricature periodical into a successful and good-looking monthly magazine, using more traditional etched images in the place of lithographs. Launched in January 1830, and guaranteed respect by Heath's presence as the sole artist, the *Looking Glass provided* several decades of experimentation in adapting graphic satire to periodical formats*. But Heath's presence at the

magazine lasted for only the first seven issues before McClean brought in another distinguished comic artist, Robert Seymour* in his place. **BM**
Sources: Houfe 1978, *ODNB*.

HEDDERWICK, JAMES (1814-1897) James Hedderwick bridged the worlds of literature and journalism in nineteenth-century Scotland. Glasgow born and bred, Hedderwick's first exposure to publishing came while still a teenager, when he was employed in the printing shop of his father, who was the Queen's printer. After returning to Scotland from his studies in London University, he began his journalistic career proper in 1837, editing* and writing the *Saltwater Gazette*, a short-lived literary* periodical. It did not last the year, and on its demise he travelled to Edinburgh to work for the *Scotsman** as assistant editor, working under the direction of Charles MacLaren*. This position brought Hedderwick into contact with Edinburgh's literati and gave him a taste for highbrow writing that influenced the rest of his career.

In 1842 he returned to Glasgow to start up with his brother the weekly* *Glasgow Citizen**. The *Citizen* distinguished itself by featuring work of prominent Scottish authors such as William Black* David Gray, Hugh Macdonald, James Macfarlan, Alexander Smith, and David Wingate and, and proved a useful space for Hedderwick to develop his editing and management skills. Hedderwick expanded his journalistic presence in Glasgow over the next 40 years, founding literary journals such as *Hedderwick's Miscellany of Instructive and Entertaining Literature*, a short-lived compendium (1860-1862) similar to *Chambers's Journal** and the daily* 1/2d evening paper the *Glasgow Evening Citizen* in 1864.

The *Citizen* would prove his most successful venture, heralding the development of a substantial sector of cheap* late-edition journalism* in Britain. The *Citizen* was the best known and most successful of such inexpensive evening papers, leading to imitations across the border in England, including several masterminded by Hedderwick himself such as the *Echo** in London. Based on his initial success with the *Glasgow Evening Citizen*, Hedderwick, who was also a poet, established the *Glasgow Weekly Citizen*, a weekly* literary continuationof the original daily* broadsheet. He remained active as editor of both papers until 1882. **DF/MRH**
Sources: Boase 1912, Griffiths 1992, Hedderwick 1891, *ODNB*, Murdoch 1883.

HEMYNG, SAMUEL BRACEBRIDGE (1841-1901) A prolific and successful author of 'penny dreadfuls' for various English and American serials*, Samuel Bracebridge Hemyng created the mischievous and problematic character of young Jack Harkaway for Edwin J. Brett's* magazine *Boys of England** in 1871 and later took his character to the United States for Frank Leslie.

Hemyng became a barrister whose primary vocation was writing serials, first for the *Morning Star* and the *London Journal**. He also contributed to the prostitution section of Henry Mayhew's* *London Labour and the London Poor* (fourth volume, 1861). Jack Harkaway made Hemyng's fame and fortune, in spite of, or perhaps because of,Harkaway's boyish and careless bravado, characterized by support of imperialist* projects. After the success of the Jack Harkaway series in Britain, Hemyng travelled to the US in 1874 where he set Harkaway in America in Frank Leslie's the *Boys' and Girls' Weekly*, and in 1877, just before leaving the US (due apparently to an argument with Leslie), he also wrote two stories for the *Police Gazette*.

On his return to England in 1877, Hemyng continued the Harkaway series, as well as contributing to *Good News* and *Half Holiday* in 1897-1898. His Harkaway also made an appearance in *Jack Harkaway's Journal for Boys* (1893). The final volume of the Harkaway adventures was published in 1899 as *Jack Harkaway's War Scouts*, but Hemyng's authorship of this last volume is disputed. **KC**
Sources: Mitchell 1988, Sutherland 1989, House of Beadle, Adams online.

HENLEY, WILLIAM ERNEST (1849-1903) A robust editor* of various newspapers and periodicals, William Ernest Henley also published poetry* and criticism of literature*, music and art in the British and American press. From 1869-1876 he contributed poetry to the *Cornhill Magazine**, *St James's Magazine**, *Belgravia**, *Macmillan's Magazine** and Frederick Guest's comic weekly, the *Period* (1869-1871). During the late 1870s and early 1880s he reviewed* for the *Academy** and *Athenaeum**, with theatre and music* reviews* for the *Saturday Review**.

Henley's first serious enterprise was as staff writer and editor for the short-lived Conservative weekly *London** (1877-1879); Robert Louis Stevenson, Grant Allen*, Andrew Lang*, George Saintsbury* and Katharine De Mattos* were among his contributors. After the failure of the *London,* Henley reviewed books and plays for the *Pall Mall Gazette**. Not having any artistic experience, he was a surprising choice as editor of the *Magazine of Art** in 1881. He championed Rodin and Whistler* and decried the Royal Academy. Tired of editorial interference from his publishers Cassell & Co., he resigned in late summer 1886 and became consulting editor for the *Art Journal** until well into 1887. He also wrote the literary 'London Letter' for the New York *Critic* for two years from February 1886.

Henley's success with the *Magazine of Art* and his friendship with Stevenson's Edinburgh circle led in December 1888 to his appointment as editor of the recently established weekly* *Scots Observer** in Edinburgh. This was his most successful editorship where his strong political* views, literary judgment and encouragement of emerging literary talent were marks of the journal. The paper's Conservative and Imperialist* policy appealed despite its parochial interests. Among his many contributors (some of whom signed) were Stevenson, J. M. Barrie, William Archer, Lady Jeune*, Edmund Gosse*, Graham R. Tomson*, W. B. Yeats, Kipling, H. B. Marriott Watson, Gilbert Parker, George Bernard Shaw*, Thomas Hardy*, H. G. Wells* and Kenneth Grahame. Despite its masculine outlook the paper published essays and poetry by Alice Meynell, and poetry by May Kendall, Katharine Tynan and Edith Nesbit, with unsigned* fashion* articles from Graham R. Tomson and others. Henley placed his own imprimatur on the journal, revising many writers' work, notably Yeats. A title change* to the *National Observer* in November 1890 and a move to London in June 1892 failed to boost its circulation* and Henley resigned in March 1894.

Henley's final editorship, for the monthly *New Review**, lasted three years from January 1895. Again this was a Conservative journal suited to his style, but this time Henley's editorial control was limited by an editorial board. He published H. G. Wells's *Time Machine*, Henry James's* *What Maisie Knew* (under protest), Conrad and Arthur Morrison. Ill-health, other literary commitments and the journal's poor circulation* figures forced his resignation. He contributed book reviews and an article on Burns to its successor the *Outlook* between 1898-1903.

In his final years Henley reviewed for the *Pall Mall Magazine** and published Boer War* poetry in the *Sphere*. Many of his reviews were published in *Views and Reviews: Literature* (1890) and *Views and Reviews: Art* (1902). Henley is remembered for his forthright editorial control, his support for young artists and writers and his jingoistic outlook. The importance of literary content blinded him to financial concerns, limiting the life of his journals. **DA**
Sources: Atkinson 2000, *CBEL*, *ODNB*.

HENNESSY, WILLIAM JOHN (1839-1917)
William John Hennessy was Irish born, American trained, but resident in England from 1870, where he continued to develop his association with his American mentor W. J. Linton*. Hennessy contributed wood engraved* illustrations* to a wide variety of late Victorian magazines as well as maintaining his painting career. He worked for an eclectic mix of periodicals in the 1870s, ranging from *Punch** to the *Graphic**, from *Good Words** to the *Illustrated London News**, and continued to work for leading periodicals on into the 1880s and 1890s, when he contributed to the *English Illustrated Magazine**. **BM**
Sources: Engen 1990, Houfe 1978, Smith 1973.

HERBERT, HENRY WILLIAM (1807-1858)
Henry William Herbert was an English sports* writer and journalist* who spent his career in America. He fled to France and in 1831, to America, probably because of moral indiscretions and accumulated debts. Herbert remained in New York as a classics master for eight years, during which time he came into contact with sporting and literary men.

His first journalistic appointment was as co-editor* with James G. Bennett on the *Courier and Enquirer*. In 1833, Herbert founded the *American Monthly Magazine* (1833-1838) in collaboration with A. D. Patterson which was intended as a high-class magazine, focusing on literature, poetry*, biography, theatre reviews* and travel. Herbert's idealism made it difficult for Patterson to finance the project, and he resigned as co-editor in 1834, whilst Herbert continued as editor until 1835. This was because he feared that the sports writer Charles Fenno Hoffmann, who had replaced Paterson as co-editor, would turn the paper into a political organ. He then attempted to found a Sunday paper, the *Era*, which was the first American magazine aimed at a family* readership*, but it folded largely because of religious opposition to reading newspapers on Sundays. Herbert made many contributions to early American magazines, including translations of French and Greek literature, poetry and book reviews. While publication of his articles in regional American newspapers gave him a wide readership, he used the pseudonym* 'Frank Forester' when writing on sport and wildlife because he found writing for 'the common people' beneath him.

Despite a problematic personality, Herbert's contributions to early American periodicals made him an important figure in the development of journalism* in the United States where he saw himself as 'an American writer of English birth', who encouraged American writers and artists in his publications. **DHL**
Sources: Judd 1882, *ODNB*, Riley 1988.

HERSCHEL, JOHN FREDERICK WILLIAM (1792-1871) While still an undergraduate at Cambridge, Herschel contributed an anonymous* mathematical item to *Nicholson's Journal*, and subsequently published three important papers in the *Philosophical Transactions of the Royal Society* (1814-1818), which first brought him to the attention of the wider scientific community. The majority of his articles on various scientific* subjects appeared in specialist journals like the *Monthly Notices of the Royal Astronomical Society*, but throughout his long and distinguished career as a mathematician and astronomer, Herschel also wrote regularly for the general periodical press. In the 1830s and 1840s he contributed lengthy notices of recent scientific books to both the *Edinburgh Review** and the *Quarterly Review**, which were collected into a book (1857), and later wrote several popular articles on astronomy, physics and geology for the pious monthly *Good Words**. In 1862 George Smith* commissioned Herschel to contribute to the new *Cornhill Magazine**, and over the following year he co-wrote, with George Henry Lewes*, seven instalments of the shilling* monthly's regular science column. Smith considered Herschel's erudite contributions unsuited to the *Cornhill*'s readers*, although Lewes, when he became editor of the *Fortnightly Review** in 1865, included two articles by Herschel in the new review's first few numbers.
GD

Sources: Buttner 1970, Dawson 2004b, Lightman, ed. 2004, *ODNB*.

HETHERINGTON, HENRY (1792-1849) A compositor who had served his apprenticeship to Hansard*, the parliamentary printer, Hetherington was a seminal figure in London radical publishing* over three decades. A printer on his own account from 1822, his first venture into periodical publishing was the ephemeral *Political Economist and Universal Philanthropist* (1823). However, his unstamped* *Penny Papers for the People* (1830-31), the *Radical* (later the *Radical Reformer*, 1831-1832), *Republican* (1831-1832) and the mighty *Poor Man's Guardian* (1831-1835)* brought Hetherington prominence, numerous fines and three prison sentences. He was a resourceful, indeed wily, underground pressman. As a proprietor* and publisher, he had a knack for spotting talented young journalists, notably James Lorymer, Thomas Mayhew and James Bronterre O'Brien*. Hetherington's other unstamped publications were the '*Destructive*' & *Poor Man's Conservative* (1833-1834) and *Hetherington's Twopenny Dispatch & People's Police Register*

(1834-1836). In the latter, as in his later, legal *Halfpenny Magazine of Entertainment and Knowledge* (1840-1841) and the satirical* *Odd Fellow**, co-produced with W. J. Linton*, he experimented with more populist journalistic forms. However, he lacked the buccaneering verve necessary for success in commercial publishing. His stamped weekly* *London Dispatch* (1836-1839) developed many features adopted by the Leeds-based *Northern Star**, notably extensive reportage of local political* activities, but its circulation* was ground down by the *Star* and it closed with substantial losses.

Hetherington also placed his presses at the disposal of a number of radical movements, for minimal if any return. These included the [London] *Working Men's Association Gazette* (1839), the communitarian weeklies *Social Pioneer* (1839) and *Working Bee* (1839-1841), William Lovett's* *National Association Gazette* (1842) and the journal of the utopian socialist* Tropical Emigration Society, *Morning Star* (1844-1847). This was Hetherington's final periodical, as he died from cholera in 1849. His last years had included a major contribution to metropolitan* Chartism* and a fourth gaol sentence (1840-1841), for publishing the blasphemous serial *Letters to Clergy of all Denominations*.
MSC
Sources: *DLB, ODNB*.

HEYWOOD, ABEL (1810-1893) Abel Heywood, printer, publisher*, and newsagent*, established a small printers and news agency in 1831, having left school at nine to work as a warehouseman. A committed factory reformer, his first periodical publication was the *Workman's Expositor* (1832), aimed at cotton factory workers. However, publishing was a second string to newspaper distribution*. In 1831 Heywood took on the distribution of the *Poor Man's Guardian** throughout the Manchester region. From this he built a massive business handling popular periodicals. In evidence to the 1851 Parliamentary Select Committee on Newspaper Stamps, Heywood estimated that he handled 10 percent of the national output of popular* newspapers and magazines. His considerable business acumen was always balanced by strong political* commitment. He was imprisoned for four months in 1832, and fined in 1834, for selling *Poor Man's Guardian*, while in 1836 he was twice fined for refusing to pay stamp* duty on almanacs.

As a publisher he was responsible for some notable labour movement titles, several of them joint ventures with London publishers. He was a particularly active Chartist and his publications at this

time included the *Social Pioneer* (1839, published in London by Henry Hetherington* and John Cleave*, and in Leeds by Joshua Hobson*), the anti-capitalist *Herald of the Future* (1839-1840), the Friendly United Smiths' *Trades' Journal* (1840-1841) and the strident *McDouall's Chartist & Republican Journal* (1841). Subsequently Heywood published the factory reform *Champion of What is True and Right* (1849-1850), the *Trades' Unions' Magazine & Precursor of a People's Newspaper* (1850-1851), the *Trades Advocate & Herald of Progress* (published in London by James Watson*) and *Robert Owen's* Rational Quarterly Review and Journal* (1853). One of Manchester's leading Liberal politicians (and twice Lord Mayor), the politics of Heywood's later years were reflected in the titles his by-now substantial printing firm produced: the *Co-operator* (1860-1871) and the *Industrial Partnerships' Record* (1867-1869). By then the company's output ranged wider than politics, notably including *Ben Brierley's Journal* (1869-1891). **MSC**
Sources: *DLB, ODNB*.

HILL, WILLIAM (1806?-1867) In the mid-1830s, Hill was one of a group of Yorkshire radicals contemplating the launch of a regional newspaper. Their plans were overtaken by those of Feargus O'Connor*, whose plans materialized as the *Northern Star & Leeds General Advertiser*. William Hill became the founding editor* and under his management the paper achieved a circulation* larger than any other newspaper of the time. His main asset was a profound empathy with the interests and aspirations of the working-class* autodidacts who comprised the *Star*'s readership*. He treated these readers' reports of local* political activities with the same courtesy and care as those of Parliament. He balanced the paper's political* coverage with an eclectic mix of poetry*, reviews* and human interest stories; and he quickly steered it to truly national status. His leaders* were expressive rather than elegant, and he was prepared to dissent from O'Connor's opinions (for example, he consistently advocated temperance). After the pair parted company in July 1843, Hill never again ventured into journalism except for the sourly anti-O'Connor polemic *Lifeboat: A Weekly Political Pamphlet* (Dec. 1842-Jan. 1843), printed by Johnson of Hull and distributed by the unstamped* veterans Henry Hetherington*, John Cleave* and James Watson*. **MSC**
Sources: Chase 2007, Epstein 1976.

HINE, HENRY GEORGE (1811-1895) One of the many stalwart draughtsman/painters who filled the pages of early and mid-Victorian magazines

with their highly competent images, Henry George Hine's principal work was as an illustrator* for *Punch** in its earliest years, at a time when he and Newman* became its main illustrators in the years before Leech's* dominance. An early association with Landells*, which showed Hine's fluency in drawing direct on to the block, led to his association with *Punch*, for which he drew mainly social subjects, the so called 'Punch's Pencillings' and little silhouette 'blackies,' although he was occasionally responsible for the larger-scaled political* cartoons*. He also drew the first highly elaborated Almanack pages for *Punch*, drawing on the repertoire of Regency caricature*, and showing a special interest in the grotesque human body. The speed and quality of his work set benchmarks for subsequent *Punch* artists.

But by 1844 Hine fell out with *Punch*, leaving Leech as the presiding social cartoonist. He then worked for a range of comic magazines, the *Great Gun*, *Puck**, and the *Man in the Moon** among them, and, in a more serious idiom, for the *Illuminated Magazine** (1843-1845), a journal which brought together an assembly of the best early Victorian wood* block artists under its editor* W. J. Linton*, and, later, for the *Illustrated London News** and the *Welcome Guest**. By the mid-1860s Hine had given up drawing for the magazines to pursue his interests as a watercolour painter. **BM**
Sources: Engen 1990, Houfe 1978, Spielmann 1895.

HISTORY AND JOURNALISM Victorian historians were prolific contributors to Victorian periodicals, and nineteenth-century Britons of all classes* learned of their nation's past by reading periodical articles. Thomas Babington Macaulay's work was first circulated in his *Edinburgh Review** articles of the 1830s and only later in his *History of England* (1855-1861). J. R. Green, whose *Short History of the English People* (1874) was almost as popular as Macaulay's book, contributed often to periodicals, and might have served as editor* of a planned (but never published) popular periodical that was intended to present the work of serious historians to a wide audience. Several history books originated as articles in periodicals, and historians who are not remembered as journalists wrote extensively for weeklies*, monthlies* and quarterlies*.

This rich, though under-researched, body of writing was the context for the 1886 foundation of a dedicated journal for historical scholarship, the *English Historical Review*. Historians became increasingly attracted to an academic, even scientific, approach to their discipline, and grew dissatisfied with the literary and narrative expectations of existing periodicals. This discourse began in 1867 among the historians James Bryce, John Richard Green, Edward Augustus Freeman and the publisher* Alexander Macmillan*. Most of the historians wanted England to have a quarterly* devoted to brief, argument-driven accounts of contributions to historical knowledge derived from research in documentary sources – something like the German *Historische Zeitschrift* or the French *Révue Historique*. Macmillan cautioned that both format* and market would require consideration; he preferred an annual volume to the quarterly that Bryce and Freeman envisaged, while Green imagined a shilling* monthly. Macmillan warned that readers would expect to find coverage of subjects the historians hoped to avoid, such as biography, or offering the historical perspective on current events. His experience with *Macmillan's Magazine* and *Nature* seems to have shaped his perspective on planning what they all called 'a purely historical review'.

Green became aware that his own reputation for popular narrative history would prevent his acceptance by an increasingly academic discipline; he withdrew from the project in 1875. In the 1880s Oscar Browning, John Robert Seeley and Mandell Creighton revived the idea at Cambridge, but Cambridge University Press decided that a historical journal was inherently political* and hence undesirable. Meanwhile, existing periodicals continued to solicit, remunerate and publish a steady flow of articles on history. Creighton complained in 1883 that 'existing periodicals publish only popular* and sketchy articles' and that their editors imposed annoying restrictions on length. He became the first editor* of the *English Historical Review* when Charles J. Longman undertook to publish the journal in 1886. Early optimism about developing popular readership* was never warranted and after the first few years Longman stopped paying contributors; nevertheless, the journal flourished in the academic world. LKH

Sources: Brundage 1994, Goldstein 1986, Howsam 2004, Jann 1983, McKitterick 2004.

HOBSON, JOSHUA (1810-1876) A printer, editor* and political reformer, Hobson was born in Huddersfield, the son of a builder's labourer. Largely self-educated, he worked as a handloom weaver in Oldham in his teens, also writing in local* papers under the pen-name 'Whistler at the Loom'. In 1832, with financial backing from fellow reformers, he set up as a printer. After a brief period (Sept. 1832-Jan. 1833) producing the *Poor Man's Advocate, and People's Library*, in June 1833 he was instrumental in launching the weekly* *Voice of the West Riding*. This was the most influential of the provincial unstamped* papers and Hobson served six months' imprisonment for vending it from August 1833. On his release Hobson resumed managing the *Voice* until it closed in June 1834. Following his short-lived unstamped *Argus & Demagogue* (June-Aug. 1834), Hobson moved to Leeds. Further prison sentences for unstamped activities in 1835 and 1836 enhanced his reputation for gritty determination and personal integrity. His business benefited from his cordial relationship with London unstamped pressman John Cleave* and Manchester printer and bookseller Abel Heywood*.

The distribution* network this opened up was integral to the success of the *Northern Star*, which Hobson printed and managed from its inception in November 1837 until it moved to London in November 1844, and which he also edited from July 1843. During 1839-1841 he was also responsible for the production of the Owenite* socialist* weekly *New Moral World* and jointly published *Social Pioneer, or Record of the Progress of Socialism* (1839). Hobson sold his Leeds press when the *Northern Star* transferred to London, continuing in an editorial role until October 1845 when he opened a radical news agency* in Huddersfield. His rapidly deteriorating relationship with the paper's proprietor*, Feargus O'Connor* reached its nadir in 1847 when Hobson contributed a series of hard-hitting articles to the *Manchester Examiner* attacking O'Connor's darling, the Chartist land plan. Hitherto Hobson's journalism had been largely anonymous*: these signed articles marked an entry proper into journalism. From 1855 Hobson edited the weekly *Huddersfield Chronicle*. When it was relaunched as a daily* in 1871, he became founding editor of the *Huddersfield Weekly News*, a post he occupied until his death. MSC

Sources: *DLB*, Halstead 1991.

HODDER AND STOUGHTON (1868-) Founded by Matthew Hodder (1830-1911) and Thomas Stoughton (1840-1917) in 1868, this publishing* firm had an extensive list of serials* to complement their book list. Both partners grew up in dissenting families and had a particular interest in religious* publishing. From 1868-1886, for example, they published the *British Quarterly Review*, which has been called 'a vehicle for non-conformity', and the *Clergyman's Magazine* from the mid 1870s. One of the most successful of their enterprises was the *Expositor*, founded in 1875 as a non-sectarian monthly focused on biblical scholarship. The firm's religious book publications were sometimes lucrative as well, notably Henry Drummond's *Natural Law in the Spiritual World* (1883) which sold 70,000 copies during its first five years. Much of Hodder and Stoughton's early success can be attributed to Matthew Hodder's development of a strong international market* for the firm's list during his trips to the United States in the 1860s and 1870s.

In 1884, Hodder and Stoughton formed a partnership with a Kelso clergyman, W. Robertson Nicoll*, who was appointed editor* of the *Expositor*. Nicoll founded the *British Weekly* in 1886 as an organ of Christian and social progress and contributed to the firm's continuing success by introducing new writers (J. M. Barrie, for example) and by launching other successful journals, including *Woman at Home* (1893-1920), with Annie Swan* and Jane Stoddart*, and the *Bookman* co-edited by Annie Macdonell, J. E. Hodder Williams and Jane Stoddart. Nicoll mentored Matthew Hodder's grandson, J. Ernest Hodder Williams, who would become chief manager of the firm after his grandfather's death in 1911. **ME**

Sources: Attenborough 1975, *ODNB, Waterloo.*

HOEY, CHRISTOPHER CLINTON (1831-1885) Unlike most of his fellow journalists, Christopher Clinton Hoey came from a working-class background and entered journalism in the *Irish Builder* in Dublin in 1860, while still working as a benchhand for a Dublin builder, styling himself 'A Craftsman'. He wrote for the journal for the next 16 years, becoming its principal writer. He also contributed to the *Builder* in London and various other journals in England and Scotland on architecture and other technical subjects. His poetry* in the *Irish Builder,* which appeared under the pseudonym* 'Civis' and was collectively titled 'Civic Lyrics', comprised topical verses on civic issues, public health, etc. The *Irish Builder* 'exuded enthusiasm for improvement of every kind, not least in the provision of public services such as piped water and sewage', and was an example to R.V. Comerford of one of the better features of the Victorian outlook, both in its progressive, public spiritedness and in its assumption that 'the prose of a trade journal* should be as well-turned as that of a literary review.'

Hoey was a political animal and was one of the leaders of the National Brotherhood of Saint Patrick, becoming involved with their Dublin paper the *United Irishman and Galway American* and their London journal the *Irish Liberator*, also writing for the *Irishman*. His work, including histori-

cal* sketches, also appeared in journals in the USA, including the New York *Irish People,* and in Australia. In 1866, he became the last editor* of the Catholic *Universal News* in London, which expired at the end of 1869 in the midst of a row with the Catholic hierarchy over the paper's Fenian politics. He died in London of consumption aged 54. **AMcN**

Sources: Comerford 1989, *Irish Builder 27.609* 127, McNicholas 2007.

HOGARTH, GEORGE (1783-1879) George Hogarth is best known as a music* critic and editor*, and as Dickens's father-in-law. Initially a lawyer in Edinburgh, he knew Scott* and Lockhart*, and wrote for the *Edinburgh Evening Courant* (c. 1815-1830). In 1817, with Scott and his own brother-in-law James Ballantyne, he bought the *Edinburgh Weekly Journal* (1798-1847). Giving up the law and moving to London in 1830 (probably for financial reasons), he wrote briefly for the monthly music* journal the Harmonicon* before in 1831 going to Exeter to edit the Tory *Western Luminary* (1813-57). The following year he moved to Halifax as the first editor of the newly revamped *Halifax Guardian* (1832-1921). In 1834 he returned to London and was engaged by the *Morning Chronicle* as a writer on political* and musical subjects. A large share of the management of this paper devolved onto him, and it was here that he first encountered Dickens*.

In 1835 Hogarth, as co-editor, commissioned Dickens to write a series of 'Sketches' for the *Evening Chronicle,* an offshoot of the *Morning Chronicle.* The year after, Dickens married Hogarth's daughter Catherine; Hogarth actively promoted his son-in-law's career. Hogarth became editor of the weekly *Musical Herald* in 1846, and when Dickens founded the *Daily News*, Hogarth was appointed music critic, a post he held until 1866 when ill health caused his resignation. He was also music critic at the *Illustrated London News* from 1845 until his death, contributed to many other periodicals and edited various musical and literary works. **AK**

Sources: Adrian 1957, Carlton 1963, Dickens *Letters, Grove Music Online, ODNB.*

HOLL, FRANCIS MONTAGUE (1845-1888) A well-known oil painter with specialisms in portraits and urban realist scenes, Frank Holl's periodical work was relatively limited. However, like Herkomer* and Fildes*, he was one of the ambitious black and white artists who exploited the scale and editorial policy of the *Graphic* and the *Illustrated London News* to produce 20 or more spectacular detailed and naturalistic images of working lifeclass*. They were published in the *Graphic* in the decade 1872-1882. Along with Fildes's and Herkomer's contemporary illustrations* for the *Graphic*, these drawings influenced Van Gogh, who was deeply impressed by the social-realist strand of periodical illustration in Britain in the 1870s and 1880s. Holl also illustrated Trollope's*, *Phineas Redux* (1873), again in the *Graphic*. BM

Sources: Engen 1990, Houfe 1978, *ODNB*, Pickvance 1974.

HOLME, CHARLES (1848-1923)　Charles

Holme, editor* and proprietor* of the *Studio: an Illustrated Magazine of Fine and Applied Arts**, began his working life in his father's silk manufacturing business. He became a successful businessman in his twenties (trading in wool) and, as his trade extended across Europe towards the East, he married his interests in importing goods with his increasing passion for art. He became a collector and expert in Eastern art in his capacity as a buyer of designer craft work for the British domestic market.

Retiring in 1892, the following year he established the generously illustrated* *Studio*, 'to serve commercial interests and to promote good design' (*ODNB*). It included among its professional critics Marcus Huish (editor of the *Art Journal*), D. S. MacColl* and Aymer Vallance. Its readership* was middle class*, with a high number of women readers, and it reflected New Journalism's* more inclusive tendencies by running competitions for drawings, photographs*, etc and by its 'conversational style, human-interest stories, interviews*' (*ODNB*), though it maintained very high production values. Launched in the climate of the *Artist**, the *Hobby Horse* and the *Dial**, and soon in competition with Beardsley's* *Yellow Book** (1894ff) and the *Savoy**, the *Studio* long outlived its more literary* and avant-garde rivals. Holme's world-wide contacts saw the *Studio* achieve international distribution*; the journal had foreign correspondents* in America, Japan and throughout the British Empire. He withdrew from the business due to ill-health in 1922.

In addition to his journalism, Holme edited many books on art, design and painting, ranging in topics from peasant art in Sweden, Lapland, Hungary and Russia, old houses in Holland, sketching grounds and the art of book binding, to modern design in jewellery and fans. All were widely reviewed, and rooted in subjects addressed in his journal. FD

Sources: Brothers 1993, *ODNB, NSTC*.

HOLYOAKE, AUSTIN (1826-1874)　Austin

Holyoake, the younger brother of George Jacob Holyoake*, followed his brother's path, becoming an Owenite and working as a freethought* printer and publisher*. Yet his modesty meant that his efforts were not always acknowledged, as he was satisfied to dedicate his efforts quietly without recognition. In relation to this attitude seen with his brother at their business, a friend called him 'Jacob's Ladder'. Beginning work as a printer in 1842 in Birmingham and London on radical papers, from 1847 Austin Holyoake was to take charge of printing the *Reasoner**, George Holyoake's weekly* secularist periodical at the Clerkenwell premises. From 1849, Austin and his brother became partners at Holyoake and Co., based eventually in Fleet Street* with Austin taking responsibility for all printing including their monthly magazine, the *Secular World* (1862). After 1858 and until the company collapsed in 1862, he also acted as publisher*.

In 1864 Austin set himself up independently, naming his Fleet Street company Austin & Co. His radical political activities were integral to his press work, for in addition to working in the freethought movement, he was the last English printer to be indicted under the Newspaper Stamp Act for his work as a member of the Association for the Repeal of Taxes on Knowledge. Writing numerous pamphlets and lectures on secularism*, atheism, population control and republicanism, he was employed as the subeditor* and contributor on Charles Bradlaugh's* *National Reformer** from 1866 until his death. After Austin's death from consumption, his brother George made attempts to revive the *Reasoner*. From 1883 to 1886 the latter published a monthly* called the *Present Day* which has been considered an 'egocentric production of little importance'. (Royle 1980: 161) DHL

Sources: *ODNB*, Royle 1974, Royle 1980.

HOLYOAKE, GEORGE JACOB (1817-1906)　G. J.

Holyoake was one of the most prolific and well-known radical journalists in nineteenth-century England. A Birmingham engineer by trade, he became a lecturer for the Owenite movement and was imprisoned for blasphemy in August 1842. He moved to London after his release six months later and made a living as a radical publisher*, bookseller and writer. Holyoake took an active part in 'late' Chartism*, though more of his energies went into the Secularist movement. His greatest journalistic achievement was the *Reasoner**, the leading freethought periodical which he edited* (1846-1861).

Holyoake supported a myriad of agitations and

radical movements, though increasingly from the early 1860s most of his energies were directed to the rapidly expanding Co-operative movement. In 1868 he launched the *Social Economist* with E. O. Greening, but the paper was designed primarily to push the cause of profit-sharing and was soon displaced by the *Co-operative News* (1871ff). Holyoake's writings and impeccable Owenite credentials secured him an honoured place within the ranks of co-operators, but journalism remained Holyoake's bread and butter and he both edited and wrote for many radical newspapers, including Joseph Cowen's* *Newcastle Daily Chronicle*· As a subaltern author and journalist he often lived from hand to mouth, at least until the relative financial stability of his later years. He commented in 1861; 'Propagandism is not, as some suppose, a "trade", because nobody will follow a "trade" at which you may work with the industry of a slave and die with the reputation of a mendicant'. **PJG**

Sources: Blaszak 1988, Grugel 1976.

HOME AND FOREIGN REVIEW (1862-1864) The *Home and Foreign Review* was the successor to the *Rambler** and like its predecessor, it supported the Liberal Catholic movement. The quarterly* was founded in 1862 by the eminent historian Sir John Acton*, with Richard Simpson*, an Elizabethan scholar and man of letters, as co-proprietor*. Acton had brought the *Rambler* to an end in the spring of 1862, mainly in response to ecclesiastical censure, but also because he wanted to establish a more serious review that would bring the Roman Catholic Church closer to contemporary political and intellectual life.

Acton was editor* throughout the run. If the change of title signified a break with the *Rambler* and the offence which it had given to the Roman Catholic hierarchy by its liberal policies and implicit criticism of 'old' Catholics, the new title and format did not save the new journal from the wrath of the Church. The *Home and Foreign Review* was unapologetically liberal and differences between it and the Catholic hierarchy increased. In December 1863, a Papal brief to the Archbishop of Munich condemned the Liberal Catholic principle of scholarship being independent of ecclesiastical authority. Acton, faced with a conflict between his principles and church authority, decided to sacrifice the *Review*. In his article 'Conflicts with Rome' he gave his reasons for bringing the review to an end.

In his essay 'The Function of Criticism at the Present Time' (1864), Matthew Arnold* lamented

its passing, commenting that 'Perhaps in no organ of criticism in this country was there so much knowledge, so much play of mind; but these could not save it'. There was less emphasis on religious* issues in the *Home and Foreign* than in the *Rambler*. Contributors were not exclusively Roman Catholic and a high standard was maintained in its reviews* and articles which covered subjects as diverse as politics, economics, law, philology, archaeology and science*. **DHL**

Sources: Altholz 1962, Himmelfarb 1952, *Wellesley*.

HOME CHAT (1895-1958) Harmsworth's* earlier penny* magazines* for women, *Forget-Me Not* (1891-1918) and *Home Sweet Home*(1893-1901), were eclipsed by the success of *Home Chat*, which rivalled *Home Notes** and *Woman's Life** and was to prove a gold mine both in sales and advertising*. In the 1890s it offered serial fiction*, 'Chit Chat' or 'Society Small Talk' by Lady Greville, 'Chats with Celebrities', 'Dress and Fashion'* by Camilla and Lady Betty, lavish illustration*, competitions, and advice, 'tips' or 'wrinkles' on cooking and domestic* management, child-care, health, beauty and shopping. Advertisements* and editorial matter were visually inseparable and often merged in early examples of 'advertorials'. *Home Chat* was determinedly New Journalistic*. It made 'Chat' its central characteristic, offering its readers for the price* of a penny access on easy terms to aristocratic-sounding people and elements of the up-market ladies' journals, while recognizing that its readers needed 'tips' on how to manage with little money. It was a formula which proved successful well into the twentieth century. **MRB**

Sources: Beetham 1996, *Home Chat*.

HOME JOURNAL (1849) The *Home Journal* was a penny* weekly* founded during the cheap* literature movement of the 1840s. Focused on providing useful and entertaining knowledge to artisan and lower middle-class readers*, it published fiction, poetry* and short, non-political articles. The aim was to provide a wholesome alternative to contemporary penny dreadfuls and radical* political newspapers. The editors noted in their introductory address that the cheap price would enable the poor to read 'in their own homes, removed from the influence of dissipation to which book-societies and reading-rooms so often give rise'. The journal merged* with *Dipple's Miscellany* in October of 1849, bringing an unspectacular end to its brief four-month run. **ME**

Source: *Home Journal*.

HOME NOTES (1894-1957) Launched by Pearson* in a bid for the cheap* women's magazine readership*, *Home Notes* was a penny* monthly magazine with many of the characteristics of 1890s New Journalism*. It was lavishly illustrated*, informal in tone and consisted of short snippets of information, advice and gossip* under titles like 'Fire Side Chat', 'Household Hints' and 'Feminine Fancies'. It included short fiction and accounts of Paris fashions*, together with advice on home dress-making and a free dress pattern, an important selling point. Advertisements*, usually for national brands, were no longer confined to end papers but interspersed throughout and inseparable from editorial material. It was edited* by 'Isobel'* of *Pearson's Weekly* and among other regulars Ada Balin* contributed signed articles as well as the column*, 'Mothers in Council', attributed to 'The Editor of Baby'*. *Home Notes* together with its rivals, Harmsworth's* *Home Chat* and Newnes'* *Woman's Life (1895-1934)*, took the woman's magazine* even more downmarket* than the mid-century journals and provided the model for the mass magazines of the twentieth century. **MRB**
Sources: Beetham 1996, *Home Notes*.

HONE, WILLIAM (1779-1842) A radical editor*, journalist* and publisher*, Hone was hugely famous in the Regency period. Located at the centre of London's publishing trade at 45 Ludgate Hill, he was a prolific publisher, producing 175 titles (1815-1821). The focus of almost all these works was injustice and hypocrisy. A champion of the free press and a victim of censorship*, Hone was tried three times in 1817 for what was essentially the same charge: twice for blasphemous and seditious libel, and once for blasphemous libel. To the surprise of both the judiciary and his own supporters, Hone was found not guilty in each of his three trials, despite suffering a biased judge. His main contribution to radical-popular periodical culture was as editor of the *Critical Review* (1814-1815) and *Hone's Reformists' Register and Weekly Commentary* (Feb.-Oct. 1817)*. His most successful publication was his collaboration with George Cruikshank*, *The Political House that Jack Built* (1819). Written in response to the Peterloo massacre, this squib eventually sold over 100,000 copies. Hone was genuinely popular: his readership* encompassed the full range of society, from Cabinet ministers to the barely literate and disenfranchised. This success helped to consolidate the cause of popular and radical print culture into the 1820s and beyond. **JG**
Sources: Broughton Papers, Francis Place Collection, Hackwood 1970, *ODNB*, Rickword 1971, William Hone Papers, Wood 1994.

HONE'S REFORMISTS' REGISTER AND WEEKLY COMMENTARY (1817) In January 1817 William Hone* issued two numbers of *Hone's Weekly Commentary* at 6d per copy. This became *Hone's Reformists' Register and Weekly Commentary*, an octavo of 16 pages published every Saturday (1 Feb. 1817-25 Oct. 1817). Following the example of William Cobbett's* 'twopenny trash', the price* was soon reduced to 2d. Hone's paper, as the title suggests, featured articles pertaining to current reform issues such as universal suffrage, the Habeas Corpus Act, annual parliaments, the spy system, the judicial system and political* corruption. Five of its numbers were written by Francis Place*. The opening issue contained an article on the breaking of a window in the Prince Regent's carriage by a missile (many said it was a stone thrown by one of the jeering crowd), an incident used by the government as an excuse to suspend Habeas Corpus on 21 February 1817. An attempt at censorship* followed: in May 1817 Hone was arrested on three charges of blasphemous libel but continued to produce the *Register* from prison. He used the journal to claim that the government spy and agent provocateur William Oliver had attempted to entrap both himself and Thomas Wooler*, editor* of the *Black Dwarf*, while they were in prison (Wooler was acquitted on 5 June). Hone was released from prison, awaiting trial, in July 1817, and in the final issue of the *Register* he stated defiantly that he would return to his business as a publisher*, a promise which he fully realized after his acquittal in December 1817. **JG**
Sources: *DNB*, Grimes online, Hackwood 1970, Wood 1994.

HOOD, THOMAS (1799-1845); HOOD, TOM (1835-1874) Despite the sunny and genial nature of much of his writing, Thomas Hood's career was a long and losing battle against the literary market*. Apprenticed at 14 to an engraver*, and initially earning his living in that trade, he began to contribute occasional prose and poetry* to magazines as a teenager. His London literary career was launched early when he became subeditor* of the *London Magazine* in 1821 on its purchase by James Hessey and John Taylor (the latter had been an employee of Hood's father's bookselling firm). Hood published there some 30 pieces and networked widely. After he left, he engraved a little for the *New Monthly Magazine* and wrote some pieces for it, as for *Fraser's* and the *Retrospective Review* and edited the annual* *Gem* (1829). He was also involved in setting up the *Athenaeum*.

Hood was widely acknowledged as the leading exponent of the short humorous article or poem in the 1820s and his predisposition for punning, both visual and verbal, earned him further popularity. He turned his facility as a writer into a number of comic yet hard hitting social commentaries in verse of which 'The Song of the Shirt', published in the 1843 Christmas edition* of *Punch*, is the most famous. His sustained efforts in these fields were turned into the innovative *Comic Annual** (1831-1839), yet he was forced to reprint his occasional writing in book or serial formats like *Hood's Own* to eke out a living. In dire financial straits despite his labour, Hood left for Europe in 1835 and soon moved his wife and children (including his son Tom) to Koblenz and later to Ostend. He continued his contributions to the *Athenaeum* and started reissuing parts of the *Comic Annual* serially as *Hood's Own*. Five years later, he returned to London.

At the peak of his popularity he founded, largely wrote and edited the 2s 6d monthly *Hood's Magazine and Comic Miscellany* (1844-1849). It proved a financial disaster despite a glittering list of contributors who wished to help, including Mrs S. C. Hall*, Dickens*, Lewes*, Robert Browning and others. Hood's health, never good, was weakened by the strain and he died 16 months after its inception.

A deeply endearing if improvident figure, Hood's career gives an exemplary sense of the improvised, precarious and intermittent nature of the life of a literary* journalist*, however talented and popular, in the 1820s and 1830s. Along with Thackeray* and Forrester*, his life also reminds us of the widespread presence of writers who could draw and artists who could write in the emergent mass* markets of early Victorian periodicals.

Hood's son Tom, known as Thomas Hood the younger and best known as the editor of *Fun**, was also a comic writer of prose and poetry. Having left Oxford without a degree, he began his career in Cornwall where, 1856 to 1859, he wrote for and eventually edited the liberal *Liskeard Gazette* (1856-1889). When he found employment in the War Office, he moved back to London and published a variety of works. He contributed to *Fun** (1861ff) almost from its start and when he became editor in May 1865 he resigned from the War Office. Thereafter he succeeded in rendering it *Punch*'s principal rival. He also tried to capitalize on his father's reputation and revived *Tom Hood's Annual* in 1867. **BM/AK**

Sources: Morgan 1973, *ODNB*, Reid 1963.

HOOD'S MAGAZINE AND COMIC MISCELLANY (1844-1849) Initially published and edited by the poet and humorist Thomas Hood*, *Hood's Magazine and Comic Miscellany* was a monthly collection of usually light poetry* and fiction, costing 2s 6d, which included serialized* novels as well as short stories and witty fragments. Spoof letters* to the editor, for example, were a common feature. Comic pieces were occasionally complemented by sentimental skits in which elevated literary* subjects were adapted to fit contemporary tastes, as was the case in a dialogue dramatizing the final meeting between Dante and Beatrice. Although inevitably much of the comedy has lost its original lustre, Hood, the principal contributor in the early volumes, was genuinely funny, and a good poet* too. But perhaps more importantly, he was able to attract contributions from writers who had the popular touch, such as Charles Dickens* and Robert Browning, who could avoid the trite clichés and clumsy prosody that marred many other comic magazines of the period.

In a notice of May 1845 alerting readers to the impending death of Thomas Hood, the magazine celebrated 'the under-current of humour that often tinctured his gravest productions' and praised his 'almost Shakespearian versatility of genius'. If this was slightly hyperbolic, it cannot be doubted that the magazine lost much of its vitality and interest, along with its distinguished contributors, after his death. The comedy became less funny, and an increasing volume of serious and rather dull content was introduced. It was relaunched as *Hood's Magazine and Literary, Scientific and Dramatic Journal* in January 1849, but this proved to be the final number. **MaT**

Sources: Sullivan, *Waterloo*.

HOOK, THEODORE EDWARD (1788-1841) Theodore Hook, an editor* and author had three writing careers, as librettist, novelist and magazine editor. He edited *John Bull** and the *New Monthly Magazine**, as well as writing 'silver-fork' novels. Making his mark as a librettist, wit, and hoaxer in the Regency, he was appointed through connections treasurer of the colony at Mauritius in 1813. When an audit of 1817 revealed a massive shortfall, his possessions were seized and he returned to England disgraced. In 1820 he founded, with Daniel Terry and the printer Edward Shackell, a weekly* paper that took the king's side in the crisis concerning Queen Caroline. The Sunday* paper *John Bull* (17 Dec. 1820ff) was witty and libellous; it quickly became a sensation and reached a circulation* of

10,000 in six weeks. Its masthead* proclaimed 'For God, The King, and The People'. Rumours abounded as to the names of its writers and editors, and many suspected that Tory grandees such as John Wilson Croker* ruled *Bull* from behind the scenes. When pressed, Hook prevaricated. The paper is widely credited with turning the tide in the affair of the queen, partly through the publication of satirical* lyrics, but Hook made enough powerful Whig enemies that the Mauritius scandal was revived and he was imprisoned for debt (1823-1825). The paper, after the initial brouhaha, was gradually toned down, and regarded as the especial favourite of the Anglican clergy. Hook's most famous series of contributions were the 'Ramsbottom Papers'.

Hook was a celebrated society wit ('Mr Wagg' of Thackeray's* fiction), and improvisatore, but despite the popularity of his novels he outspent his means. In 1836 Henry Colburn*, worried about competition from former partner Richard Bentley's* proposed *Miscellany*, asked Hook to edit a new humorous journal; he took instead the editorship of the *New Monthly Magazine* in 1836 for a salary of £400 plus payment for contributions, while continuing with *John Bull*. Most of the routine work for the *New Monthly* was done by subeditor S. C. Hall*. Hook's serial* 'Gilbert Gurney' had appeared in the *New Monthly* in 1834-1835, and as editor he published writers such as Leigh Hunt*, Douglas Jerrold* and Thackeray*, while maintaining an apolitical stance. Hook died deeply in debt in 1841, and a subscription had to be mounted for his family. **DEL**
Sources: Barham 1853, *DNB*, Dunn 1996, Lockhart 1853, *Wellesley.*

HOOKER, WILLIAM JACKSON (1785-1865) In 1827, while professor of botany at Glasgow University, Hooker became editor* of the *Botanical Magazine* founded by William Curtis in the 1780s, a post that he would retain until the end of his life. With the *Botanical Magazine* specializing in representing ornamental foreign plants and each number featuring an elaborate coloured plate, Hooker personally nurtured the talented artist Walter Hood Fitch, who contributed more than 3,000 drawings to the magazine over a period of more than 40 years (1834-1878).

During the late 1830s Hooker also briefly assisted Richard Taylor* with the editing of the *Annals of Natural History*. The market* for botanical periodicals was expanding rapidly in this period and Hooker began a number of journals of his own,

most notably the *Journal of Botany* (initially called the *Botanical Miscellany*) in 1829, which, following Hooker's appointment in 1841 as director of the royal gardens at Kew, was from 1849 called *the Journal of Botany and Kew Garden Miscellany.* However, while the *Botanical Magazine* was the clear market leader, making Hooker a profit of £252 a year in the 1840s, his other ventures had only a limited circulation* and the various publishers he worked with, including John Murray* and Lovell Augustus Reeve, were unable to give contributors free copies of the journals or even offprints. Beset by such problems the Journal of Botany folded in 1857. Despite his onerous editorial responsibilities, Hooker never employed an assistant, instead relying on his wife Maria and their son Joseph Dalton Hooker, who would take over the editorship of the *Botanical Magazine* following his father's death, to help with reading proofs. **GD**
Sources: Allan 1967, Hooker 1902, Lightman, 2004, *ODNB.*

HOPE, ALEXANDER JAMES BERESFORD BERESFORD (1830-1887) A journalist, politician, architectural critic, and proprietor* of the *Saturday Review*, Hope entered Parliament at 21, inherited two fortunes and married the sister of the future prime minister, Lord Salisbury. A loyal supporter of Sir Robert Peel, he backed and contributed to the *Morning Chronicle*† in 1848, when it was taken over as a Peelite organ and briefly flourished under the editorship* of J. D. Cook*. In 1855 Hope provided a new outlet for Cook's talents when he financed the *Saturday Review,* which employed a number of the clever young university-educated writers Cook had recruited to the *Chronicle*. An ardent high churchman and energetic advocate of the Gothic style in architecture, Hope published in the *Transactions of the Cambridge Camden Society* [later the *Ecclesiological Society*], *The Times*†, the *Quarterly Review*†, the *Contemporary Review*† and the *Saturday Review* on his enthusiasms. He may also have contributed to the *Saturday Review* on other subjects, since he remarked towards the end of his life that 'even the success of the *Saturday* is in some respects failure since anonymous* journalism* involves self-effacement'.

Hope's 'Liberal-Conservative' politics* were reflected in his journal. His allegiance to the memory of Peel made him no admirer of Disraeli, and allowed the journal useful critical latitude on political matters. Although Cook is usually credited with the *Saturday's* success, Hope's role was not merely financial. Letters to Hope from Goldwin Smith, one of the journal's most brilliant writers, assuring him of his continuing

willingness to contribute when some of the staff were threatening to secede, suggests his importance. The *Saturday* prided itself on being written by, and for, university gentlemen. Cook was neither. Its leading writers didn't consider themselves professional journalists, which Cook was. Thus it was Hope, the gentleman scholar, the wealthy amateur, who exemplified the *Saturday's* distinctive social and intellectual tone and made his fellow contributors comfortable. It is difficult to imagine the future Lord Salisbury writing for that journal without the aegis of Beresford Hope. **CAK**
Sources: Bevington 1941, Law 1925, *ODNB*, *Waterloo*.

HOPKINS, ARTHUR (1848-1930)   Arthur Hopkins's career is characteristic of many relatively little known but enormously competent illustrators* of the second half of the nineteenth century who made a living primarily from periodical commissions in ways that allowed them to spend time on more 'serious' art; in Hopkins's case it was watercolour painting. Trained at the Royal Academy, he worked for many of the major illustrated weeklies* and monthlies*, including (for over 20 years) the *Illustrated London News*, the *Graphic*, the *Quiver*, and *Good Words*, where his work from the early 1870s was engraved by Joseph Swain*, with whom he formed a close if not always successful working relationship.

As a staff artist for *Belgravia*, Hopkins illustrated a broad range of fiction, most notably Thomas Hardy's* *Return of the Native* (1878), and became an indispensable member of the team M E Braddon* had assembled for the magazine. Hopkins was one of the social realist British periodical illustrators admired by Van Gogh, and while always relegated to the margins by historians of Victorian black and white illustration, his work remained consistently proficient and sought after by editors*. He even managed, late in his career in the 1890s, two comic illustrations for *Punch*. **BM**
Sources: Engen 1990, Reid 1928, Houfe 1978, Pickvance 1974, Spielmann 1895.

HORNE, RICHARD HENGIST (1802-1884) Richard Hengist (born Henry) Horne inadvertently entered the world of journalism in 1833 with the publication of his first book, *The Exposition of the False Medium and Barriers Excluding Men of Genius from the Public*. When W. J. Fox*, editor* of *the Monthly Repository*, favourably reviewed it, Horne sent Fox an article for the *Repository* in return. Fox published this and other articles by Horne, who eventually became editor and joint proprietor* of the magazine in July 1836.

Horne contributed reformist articles to the *Repository* on topics such as the growing threat of Irish famine and English trade policies with China. He also used the radical journal for his own benefit, contributing articles and reviews, often responding to negative reviews of his own works. He struggled with the *Repository's* declining sales until 1837, when, feeling he could not revitalize it, he sold it on to Leigh Hunt, at the same time straining his relationship with Fox. Horne rebounded from his troubles with the *Repository* by contributing articles to the *Monthly Chronicle*. He became editor of the *Chronicle* in 1838. As with the *Repository*, Horne used the *Chronicle* to publicize his own work, often incorporating favourable reviews in the periodical.

Horne earned limited literary success in 1843 with the publication of his epic poem *Orion*. He continued to rely on journalism, however, to make a living. In 1845, Charles Dickens* appointed Horne as a branch editor in Ireland for his new newspaper the *Daily News*. The paper focused on the Irish famine and the abolition of the Corn Laws. It was not a commercial success, and Horne left in 1846, after Dickens handed the paper over to John Forster*.

In 1850, Horne became one of the three full-time staff writers for Dickens's new magazine, *Household Words*. He covered topics as varied as education, public sanitation and emigration. His work with *Household Words* invigorated his literary career. By 1852, however, disputes with W. H. Wills*, the associate editor, and the promise of gold in Australia resulted in Horne's departure for Melbourne with William Howitt*. Even though Dickens allowed him to continue submitting articles to *Household Words* from Australia, his periodical readership* had long forgotten him by the time he returned to London in 1869. He nevertheless continued writing for magazines until his death. **AE**
Sources: Blainey 1968, *ODNB*.

HORNER, FRANCIS (1778-1817) One of the group of four young Edinburgh-based professionals who founded the *Edinburgh Review* in 1802, Francis Horner, like Francis Jeffrey*, the *Review's* first editor*, and Henry Brougham*, who joined the group after the first numbers had been published, was trained for the bar. His preference was for philosophy and science, but a legal career seemed more secure. Finding the Scottish bar not receptive to those with Whiggish principles, he switched to the English bar and entered Lincoln's Inn shortly after the establishment of the *Review*. According to Sydney Smith*, whose idea it was to found the *Review*,

his proposed motto 'Tenui musam meditamur ave-
na' [We cultivate literature upon a little oatmeal]
was vetoed by the humourless Horner who proposed instead 'judex damnatur cum nocens absolvi-
tur' from Publius Syrus, which was adopted. Although based in London almost from the beginning of the *Edinburgh's* history, Horner was a major
influence on editorial policy, particularly in establishing the *Review's* focus on political economy*,
which was one of its most distinctive features. He
contributed a substantial number of articles in its
first decade, but his developing political career
gradually took precedence, and he wrote only sparingly in the years leading up to his untimely death
in 1817. JS

Sources: Clive 1957, Fetter 1953, *ODNB, Wellesley.*

**HORSE AND HOUND (1884-); A JOURNAL OF
SPORT AND AGRICULTURE** This 16-page illustrated* magazine was originally printed and published*
in Middlesex by John Duncan MacFarlane. The paper adopted the motto: 'I freely confess that the
best of my fun, I owe it to Horse and Hound', by
George John Whyte-Melville (1821-1878), an
English sporting novelist who met his death while
hunting. The first issue, priced* 2d addressed high
and low classes*, stated neutrality on politics*,
promised to list full notices of past and future horse
sales, and to record subjects of interest faithfully. In
1884 the magazine's departments included advertisements*, racing, the programs of the week, turf
notes, the Lincoln spring meeting, horse sales,
hunting, breeding, agricultural gossip*, farm notes,
football, rowing, coaching, coursing, athletic
sports*, town and country gossip*, and turf nomi-
nations. AA

Sources: Case 1977, *Horse and Hound, Waterloo.*

**HOSPITAL: AN INSTITUTION, FAMILY AND
CONGREGATIONAL JOURNAL OF HOSPITALS,
ASYLUMS, AND ALL AGENCIES FOR THE CARE
OF THE SICK, CRITICISM AND NEWS (1886-
1924)** The *Hospital* appeared on 2 October 1886
as a 16-page 1d weekly*, 'to aid all to provide
against [disease], to face it happily, and to fight [it]
with the best weapons it can make available, by extending the area of public interest and knowledge
in the work of those who labour amongst sickness
and suffering' ('To Our Readers', 2 Oct. 1886:1). It
was the organ of the Hospitals Association to whose
members it was distributed free but aimed at a readership* beyond that to 'mothers and ministers', and
indeed the entire family*. To that end it carried
hospital-based or medical fiction (e.g. 'Sister Olive:
a Hospital Romance' by W. J. Eccott was one of the

first) as well as factual articles. Departments included Hospital Administration (designed to counter
unjust criticism in the press), Words of Consolation
(for reading to the sick), 'Flowers, Ferns and Ward
Decorations', 'Hospital Worthies' and 'The Editor's
Letter-Box'.

From the start there were prize competitions, series on hospitals, advice on which doctors and hospitals to go to with specific complaints. Advertising*, initially abundant, soon declined (down from
a regular supplement* of 12 pages to 6 by January
1888) and there was an admission that readership
was more limited than had been hoped – to 'medical
practitioners' says 'A Retrospect' (7 Jan. 1888: 2). At
the same time it refused to accept that its emphasis
on nursing specifically targeted (women) nurses –
'medical men' needed to know about nursing (by
implication nurses were not to know too much
medicine). Acknowledgement of this more defined
readership was reflected in a change of subtitle to 'a
weekly institutional journal of Science*, Medicine
and Philanthropy'.

In hostile anticipation of the birth of the radical
*Nursing Record** on 5 April 1888, *Hospital* started
the *Nursing Mirror* on 24 March, and included
'Nursing' in its own subtitle* – *after* 'Medicine' –
on 31 March. At first a mere column within the
body of the weekly, on 14 April the *Nursing Mirror*
appeared as a 4-page supplement with an article explaining the Hospital Association's alternative form
of registration to the British Nurses Association (see
Nursing Journals*). Vacancies, appointments and
correspondence were immediately introduced
along with a miscellaneous section called 'En Pas-
sant'. Soon examination questions and an Exchange and Mart were regular features as well. Over
the next few years advertising grew substantially in
the main magazine (16 pages by 1891), as did the
Nursing Mirror (six pages with six pages of its own
advertisements). Fiction by now was confined to
the supplement, and the whole periodical was displaying ever more the influence of the New Journalism*, with chatty, illustrated* feature articles
and a varied layout. The price* rose to 2d in 1892
but the format* remained much the same for the
rest of the century, despite several changes of publisher*. In 1921, it changed its title to *Hospital and
Health Review* but closed in 1924. AK

Sources: Abel-Smith 1960, McGann 1992, *Waterloo.*

HOUGHTON, ARTHUR BOYD (1836-1875) An
artist and illustrator* who was influenced by the
Pre-Raphaelite brotherhood, Arthur Boyd

Houghton was an immensely productive and hugely successful illustrator who drew for most of the major illustrated journals of the late 1860s and early 1870s. He worked for *Good Words** across a decade between 1862 and 1872, demonstrating a versatility that made him equally at home with poems about the countryside, child portraits (many of them rather disconcerting) and Russian stories. Other work appeared in *Tinsley's Magazine**, the *Sunday Magazine* (where he illustrated serialized* fiction) and *London Society**. If this work largely used the stylistic idiom established for wood engraved* illustration in the early 1860s, Houghton, in his work (1870-1872) for the *Graphic** moved on to more photographic* techniques, with tone largely replacing line, in order to complete an extended series called 'Graphic America' and a number of images of social and political* life in Britain and France. All the illustrations for the *Graphic* suggest that Houghton was an astute and somewhat disaffected commentator on contemporary manners, and his work, for all its accuracy of observation, was certainly more acerbic than that of contemporaries like Fildes*. **BM**
Sources: Engen 1990, Goldman 1994, Houfe 1987, Reid 1928, Suriano 2005, White 1897.

HOUSE MAGAZINES AND PUBLISHERS A prevalent arrangement throughout the nineteenth century was for a publishing house to finance a journal, usually a monthly, often in order to obtain authors, texts and publicity for the publishing house. The editing work was as a rule turned over to hired specialists. Archibald Constable* began the trend in 1805 with the monthly *Edinburgh Review**, edited* by Francis Jeffrey*. Others soon followed: John Murray* started the *Quarterly Review** in 1809, edited by William Gifford* and John Gibson Lockhart* successively; Henry Colburn* published the *New Monthly Magazine** from 1814 until his death in 1855; the Edinburgh publishers William Blackwood* Sons began their eponymously named *Blackwood's Edinburgh Magazine** in 1817; Robert* and William Chambers*, booksellers and publishers, inaugurated *Chambers's Edinburgh Journal** in 1832 to provide information for the newly literate middle classes and artisans. Other publishers of note in this arena included Richard Bentley, who published *Bentley's Miscellany** between 1837 and 1868; Alexander Macmillan*, who issued *Macmillan's Magazine** from 1859 onwards; and the Longman* firm, who established *Longman's Magazine** in 1882.

These and other such journals kept the names of their publishers firmly in front of the reading public. Reasons for sustaining such ventures, as William Tinsley declared on finding his losses for *Tinsley's Magazine** (launched in 1867) running at around £25 a month, were quite plain: 'What cheaper advertisement* can I have for twenty-five pounds a month? It advertises my name and publications; and it keeps my authors together'. (Schmidt: 143) The publishers* and editors* of such periodicals deliberately shaped contents to ensure their publishing brand and stable of authors were promoted to maximum effect. In return they offered literary journalists and creative writers space for expression and some financial reward for their efforts. **DF**
Sources: Finkelstein 2002, Finkelstein 2006, Schmidt 1984, Shattock and Wolff 1982.

HOUSEHOLD WORDS (1850-1859) Adorned with a combative motto from Shakespeare's *Henry V* ('Familiar in their Mouths as HOUSEHOLD WORDS'), Charles Dickens's* 2d weekly* magazine of original short fiction and crusading social journalism was launched to widespread publicity on 30 March 1850. Its subeditor was W. H. Wills*, a former assistant editor of *Chambers's Journal**, to which the new publication was typographically similar: two columns* of small type on relatively thin, acidic paper* (quad crown 12mo), no advertisements* or illustrations*, and the legend 'Conducted by Charles Dickens' as a running header on every spread of its 24 pages. Also, like *Chambers's*, *Household Words* was a hybrid, available in 9d monthly numbers with wrappers and handsome biannual volumes, aimed at affluent middle-class families and people of influence, no less than at working-class readers interested in 'trading up.'

Household Words was also a magazine with attitude. Dickens found *Chambers's* dull, and wanted his own weekly to distinguish itself through the freshness of its research, and stylistic flair. After an opening sale of 100,000, settling down to a steady 38,000 or so, Dickens rejoiced that it was 'playing havoc with the villainous literature' – by which he meant sensational penny* weeklies*, edited by the likes of Edward Lloyd* and G. W. M. Reynolds*. Its popular extra Christmas* supplements* regularly took sales over 100,000. As factual counterpoints to the clear partisanship of the weekly magazine on a wealth of issues, two spin-off publications emerged: the 2d monthly *Household Narrative of Current Events* (Jan. 1850-Dec. 1850), and a short-lived 4d annual* *Household Almanac* (1856-1857).

Dickens published *Hard Times* and *A Child's History of England* as serials in *Household Words*, as well as over 180 unsigned* solo and co-authored articles, short stories and 'chips' (short satirical* squibs). It has often been assumed that all the other anonymous* articles in *Household Words* voice Dickens's own opinions; this is not invariably the case. Of more than 380 contributors, some 90 were women – Elizabeth Gaskell, Harriet Martineau, and Eliza Lynn Linton* prominent among them – but the majority of the articles were written by a small corps of male staff writers (Wills, Henry Morley, Wilkie Collins* and R. H. Horne*) or by 'regulars' whom Dickens trained to write in a recognisably 'Dickensy' manner and who fell in with their editor's broadly Liberal agenda. The latter included G. A. Sala*, John Hollingshead*, William Moy Thomas, G. Walter Thornbury, Blanchard Jerrold*, Sydney Blanchard, James Payn* (a group dubbed Dickens's 'young men,' according to Sala) and Percy Fitzgerald.

Household Words ceased publication in acrimony, following Dickens's breach with publishers* Bradbury & Evans, over their reluctance to take his side publicly during his protracted separation (1858-1859) from his wife Catherine. In Chancery, Dickens successfully maintained his right to dissolve his press partnership unilaterally, no less than his marriage, and *Household Words* appeared for the last time on 28 May 1859, four weeks after Dickens's commencement of a look-alike journal called *All the Year Round**. JMD
Sources: Drew 2003, Edwards 1997, Huett 2005, Lai 2001, Lorhli 1973.

HOWITT, MARY (1799-1888) Mary Howitt was a journalist as well as a poet, novelist, children's writer and translator. Her literary life began as a joint one with her husband William* in the 1820s when they contributed poetry* to various periodicals. Howitt's sustained journalism began with the *People's Journal* (1846-1848)* part-edited* by John Saunders* and *Howitt's Journal* (1847-1848)*. Both periodicals demonstrate her political* ideals, tempered by her Quaker religious* background, in attempting to instruct 'the People' as she puts it. Her contributions were usually signed, and comprised short stories, articles on domestic topics, translations, a regular children's corner, biographical profiles and poems, as well as extracts from her previously published works. She also contributed on occasion to a range of monthly journals, including *Household Words** (at Dickens's* invitation). Howitt's fame resides in her enormous output, produced mostly under difficult and demanding circumstances. The volume of periodical reviews*

which her various publications attracted, however, suggests that her name carried a cachet which editors readily recognised. JEJ
Sources: Fraser 2003, Howitt 1889, Lohrli 1973, *ODNB*.

HOWITT, WILLIAM (1792-1879) Howitt began his career in the 1820s publishing in local journals and producing joint publications with his wife Mary Howitt*, a continuing partnership. He endorsed radical politics and his journalism always carried his by-line. He published articles in *Tait's** which indexed them under his name, indicating his standing. Howitt wrote for the *Constitutional* and other periodicals. His three major publications on English countryside (1838-1842) were very influential, promoting, it is argued, a 'national identity', material he reused in periodicals. He purchased a half-share in the *People's Journal** from John Saunders* seeking a voice for his radical politics and his writing on the countryside was also featured. A falling out with Saunders led to the establishment of *Howitt's Journal**, which only ran to three volumes before bankruptcy ensued. The marketplace was too tight for both journals to prosper given their identical readership*, size*, layout, illustrations* and content. Saunders then published* the *People's and Howitt's Journal*, to which Howitt never contributed. Returning from Australia in 1854 Howitt published articles in *Household Words** and weekly numbers for the *Illustrated History of England* (1856-1864) for John Cassell*. There is little evidence of further journalistic work before his leaving England permanently in 1870. JEJ
Sources: Howitt 1889, Lohrli 1973, *ODNB*, Ulin 1998, *Waterloo*.

HOWITT'S JOURNAL OF LITERATURE AND POPULAR PROGRESS (1847-1848) Only three half-yearly volumes of *Howitt's Journal* were published, (Jan.-June and July-Dec. 1847 and Jan.-June 1848,) yet it was in many respects the best conceived and most ambitiously pitched journal of those which sought to inform, elevate and interest artisan readers*. Edited* and owned by the Quaker journalists* and writers William and Mary Howitt*, it addressed the political* and cultural interests as well as the leisure needs of ambitious artisans. A weekly*, at the price* of 1 ½d., the 16-page double column* issues included a 'Weekly Record of facts and opinions connected with general interests and popular progress', so causing the magazine to be stamped*, at an additional cost of a 1d. The contents were varied, with lengthy articles on topical social issues and historical events as well as brief news* items, short narratives, reviews* and poetry*, all organized to further the Howitts' generous-spirited concept of what might support and encourage 'popular progress'.

The wood* engraved illustrations* included portraits, representations of significant events and versions of art works. Calling on their many friends and acquaintances, the Howitts built up an impressive list of contributors, all eager to be recognized as 'friends of the people', and accordingly offered space to such diverse figures as Samuel Smiles, Goodwyn Barmby and, in her earliest guises, Elizabeth Gaskell. Room was found for contributions by struggling but aspiring artisan writers, including the poet*, Henry Frank Lott. However, hampered by a very public dispute between William Howitt and John Saunders, who had set up the similarly oriented *People's Journal* in 1846 after detailed discussions with Howitt, *Howitt's Journal*, for all its seriousness of purpose and evident qualities, only ran for three volumes, although the name reappeared in the title of Saunders's revamped *People's Journal*, which Howitt co-edited for some of its life. **BM**
Sources: *ODNB, Waterloo.*

HUBBARD, LOUISA (1836-1906)   Louisa Maria Hubbard was the editor* and publisher* of a number of periodicals mainly concerned with women's employment, most notably the *Woman's Gazette* (1875-1879) which should not be confused with the *Women's Gazette* (1888-1891), a periodical of the Women's Liberal Federation. Her other major periodicals included *Work and Leisure* (1880-1893) and the *Year Book of Women's Work*, which in 1880 was renamed the *Englishwoman's Yearbook* (1875-1916). Although herself of independent means, her main concern was with lower-middle class* or even aspiring working-class women who needed to work for a living, and for the former she recognized the need to provide an alternative to governessing. Employments described ranged from the domestic to the professional, with increasing emphasis on the latter, and included such jobs as gardening, nursing, teaching and clerical work (including typewriting), as well as information on emigration.

The *Woman's Gazette* and *Work and Leisure* also gave occasional information for potential employers. The *Englishwoman's Yearbook* became an annual directory not only of employments for women, but of all sorts of women's organisations, including clubs, and is an invaluable resource for research on women at this period. Above all Hubbard was concerned to promote the professionalization of women's work, and to elevate its generally lowly status. In 1893 she gave up journalism for reasons of health, and editorship of the *Englishwoman's Yearbook* passed to Emily Janes. **DD**
Sources: Doughan and Sanchez 1987, *ODNB.*

HUDSON, EDWARD BURGESS (1854-1936)   At the age of 21, Edward Burgess Hudson, magazine publisher* and printer, took over the family printing business of Hudson & Kearns in London with great success. Hudson revitalized and expanded the company from printing books for other publishers to producing its own illustrated* magazines. Block-making and half-tone printing advances in illustration, in which Hudson took a technical interest, lay at the heart of his new venture, in partnership with George Newnes*, of *Famous Cricketers,* the *Navy and Army Illustrated* (1895-1914) and *Racing Illustrated* (1895-1896). There were also annuals such as the *Architect's Diary* (1884-1911?), the *Builder's Diary* (1884-1887), as well as *Famous Footballers and Athletes* (1895-1897) and the *Ladies' Field* (1896-1928).

In the face of the decline of *Racing Illustrated,* Hudson and Newnes amalgamated it with their new venture, initially called *Country Life Illustrated*. This was an up-market journal, aimed at an upper-class readership*. It contained articles on the countryside, country pursuits, society, fashion, and theatre and music reviews*, including a focus on country houses which enabled them to attract advertising* from estate agents. In 1903, the magazine was renamed *Country Life.* Two years later Hudson bought out Newnes, establishing Country Life Ltd as an independent publishing company. A meeting with Gertrude Jekyll in 1899, who already contributed to Hudson's magazine, the *Garden* (1871-1927), led to her writing a gardening column for *Country Life* as well as introducing Hudson to Edward Lutyens who influenced the architectural features in the magazine.

Hudson dominated the first thirty-five years of its history. Not a literary man, he rarely contributed articles*, but was concerned with the visual style of the journal, considering good quality print* and paper* as important as 'the excellence of the article.' (Maude: 59).The cultivation and direction of *Country Life* magazine by its proud owner set it on its firm course as a representative symbol of gracious living that has endured to the present day. **DHL**
Sources: Hussey 1936, Maude 1967, *ODNB,* Strong 1996, *Waterloo.*

HUEFFER, FRANCIS (1845-1889) As chief music* critic of *The Times**, and editor* of the *Musical Review* and *Musical World**, the German-born Francis Hueffer brought rare intellectual distinction and a new progressive spirit to British music journalism.

An internationalist and cultural radical at *The Times*, Hueffer promoted in his reviews* the continental *avant-garde*, that is, composers such as Berlioz, Liszt and especially Wagner and his 'music of the future'. Regarding British music, the anglophile Hueffer championed the national 'musical renaissance' and contemporary British composers, like Frederick Corder and Alexander Mackenzie, who embraced the progressivism of Liszt and Wagner. He also used his columns* to canvass public and political support for several causes, including the founding of a permanent national opera school and public funding for a new British music conservatory.

During the 1870s and 1880s, Hueffer acted as sometime music critic on the *Examiner** and editor of the *Musical Review* (1883), and wrote numerous articles for the *Fortnightly Review**, *Macmillan's Magazine**, and the *New Quarterly Magazine**. As editor of the *Musical World* (1885-1888), Hueffer had some success in reenergizing a failing journal by aligning it (for the first time) with the latest developments in music.

Hueffer was a key figure in shaping taste and canon formation in British musical life. He believed not only that musicians and journalists should join forces in search of musical reform and renewal, but also that music should be regarded as a spiritual, poetic and 'philosophical' art that must be harnessed to cultural and social transformation. A modernising presence of recognized integrity in British music journalism*, Hueffer was an uncompromising critic who looked to the past only to move music more confidently into the future. **MH**
Sources: Hueffer 1880, Hughes 2002, *New Grove*, obituaries *Musical Times* 1 Feb. 1889 and *Musical World* 26 Jan. 1889, *ODNB*, *The Times* 21 Jan. 1889.

HUGHES, ALICE MARY (1857-1939) Alice Hughes's initial motive to become a photographer was to record the work of her father, Edward Hughes, a portrait painter. Her success encouraged her to begin photographing people. She established her own business in1891 in Gower Street, London, where she employed women to process and develop her film, employing 60 assistants at best. Hughes began press work with photographs* of titled and society women, which appeared for instance, in the

*Woman at Home's** series of 'Brides and Bridegrooms' and included women such as Miss Borthwick (Countess of Bathurst), Miss Balmain (Mrs Cooper), and Lady Edith Ward (Lady Wolverton). Her photographs are distinguishable from those of male studios as she only photographed women and children, never men. Also, in contrast to the stiff, formality of other portraits, her sitters are more in relaxed poses, surrounded by or holding flowers, with decorated backgrounds, taken only in natural light.

As the foremost woman photographer in London, her work was used to illustrate articles in the *Woman's Signal* from 1894. By 1895 her photographs were also appearing in a series that *Hearth and Home** ran on the wives of members of parliament, followed by 'Our Empire Makers'. Towards the end of the century, Hughes' work dominated the society magazines particularly her cover portraits of fashionable and aristocratic women in *Country Life Illustrated**, full-length portraits against elaborate backdrops in the *Woman at Home* series, 'The Glass of Fashion', also in a wider range of magazines such as *Golf Illustrated* and the *County Gentleman*.

Hughes lamented the dearth of women photographers but acknowledged that hard work and application, endless practice and business acumen were all needed for success. She also promoted opportunities for women in photography in other roles such as developing and in the process of touching up finished work. **CL**
Sources: National Portrait Gallery, 19CUKP, *ODNB*.

HUGHES, ARTHUR (1832-1915) Artist and illustrator*, Arthur Hughes was one of several distinguished artists working in the Pre-Raphaelite manner whose careers coincided precisely with the heyday of wood engraved* periodical illustration in the 1860s and 1870s. Hughes benefited enormously from a long connection with the publisher*, Alexander Strahan*, whose stable of magazines included *Good Words**, the *Sunday Magazine* and *Good Words for the Young**. Hughes had a strong sense of the central importance of high quality wood engraved illustration for the success of these journals.

Hughes's work was widely published in all three journals in the late 1860s and early 1870s, and his collaboration with the editor* of *Good Words for the Young*, George Macdonald, was conspicuously successful, especially in the case of Macdonald's celebrated 'At the Back of the North Wind' (Nov.

1868-Nov. 1870). The reliably high quality of Hughes's designs is acknowledged by his long career as an illustrator that began in the 1850s in such magazines as the *Welcome Guest** and included contributions to *Queen** and the *Shilling Magazine** as well as his extensive work for Strahan. His work for periodicals was often reproduced in illustrated gift book reprints derived from the original magazine serialization*. BM

Sources: Engen 1990, Goldman 1994, Houfe 1978, Reid 1928, Suriano 2005, White 1897.

HULTON, EDWARD (1838-1904)   Edward Hulton was described in his obituary* note in *Sell's Dictionary of the World's Press* as, 'the most original and potent figure in Provincial* Journalism* in the last quarter of the nineteenth century'. From humble beginnings in Manchester, Hulton founded a newspaper group that catered for a growing demand for sports* news among the artisan and lower-middle classes* of the North and Midlands. Printer, racing tipster, editor* and proprietor*, Hulton saw his business expand from a racing sheet, or tissue, printed in a cellar and sold in public houses, to encompass a print centre in Manchester's Withy Grove that produced almost five million newspapers a week* for both a regional and national market*.

Hulton served an apprenticeship in a jobbing office before joining the *Manchester Guardian** as a compositor. A keen judge of horseracing, he made additional money by printing a racing sheet. In partnership with cotton broker Edward Overall Bleackley, Hulton launched the sports paper the *Sporting Chronicle** in 1871, specializing in racing, professional athletics and popular field sports such as coursing. The paper became a daily* in 1880, by which time Hulton had launched the *Athletic News**, a weekly* paper eschewing racing and gambling in favour of the increasingly popular and organised sports of cricket, cycling and the various football codes. Both papers claimed national circulations*, and Hulton continued his expansion, briefly owning *Bell's Life in London**, with further additions to Manchester's popular* press, the *Sunday Chronicle** (1885) and, together with his son Edward, the *Manchester Evening Chronicle* (1897) and *Daily Dispatch* (1899). At his death the net value of his estate was £509,000. His son oversaw a continued expansion until the group's sale in 1923. ST

Sources: *Lancashire Faces* 1901, *Manchester Evening Chronicle* 1904, Mason 1986, *Sporting Chronicle* 1971, *Sunday Chronicle* 1904.

HUNT, JAMES (1833-1869)   James Hunt was a controversial anthropologist, journalist*, editor* and proprietor*. Working as a speech therapist, he became interested in the diversity of human languages and their relation to the issue of racial differences. His increasingly outspoken views on race, including support for slavery, were frequently articulated in the *Transactions of the Ethnological Society*, although he diverged markedly from the more humanitarian approach of the Society's leaders. The dispute came to a head in 1862 over the use of derogatory images of Africans in a new *Journal of the Ethnological Society*, which had ceased publication in 1856 and for whose revival Hunt had been given responsibility. In 1863 Hunt founded the rival Anthropological Society, as well as editing, publishing and financing its official journal the *Anthropological Review*. While a subsidiary *Popular Magazine of Anthropology*, launched in 1866 and again personally superintended by Hunt, proved unsuccessful, the *Anthropological Review* became an effective forum for the avowedly racist, polygenist and anti-Darwinian views that Hunt adumbrated in the leader* of its opening number, and also attracted prominent contributions from Richard F. Burton and Edward Burnett Tylor. The *Anthropological Review's* circulation* was augmented by its distribution* to the more than 500 members of the Anthropological Society, although, as a controversy in *the Athenaeum** in 1868 revealed, many non-paying members received the *Review* for free and thus paying members were disproportionately subsidizing what was effectively Hunt's own personal organ. The acrimonious scandal damaged Hunt's health and he died in the following year. GD

Sources: Lightman, 2004, *ODNB*, Stocking 1987.

HUNT, JOHN (1775-1848)   Although John Hunt is best known as Leigh Hunt's brother, he was an influential publisher* in his own right. John Hunt founded his first weekly*, the *News* (1805-1808), in 1805 and in 1808 established the weekly newspaper the *Examiner** with himself as printer and Leigh as editor* and leader* writer. In 1810, he established a short-lived (1810-1811) quarterly* literary* and political* magazine called the *Reflector*. The successful *Examiner* lasted considerably longer, with the Hunts as publishers and editors until 1822. The paper tended towards liberal and reformist causes and featured contributions from talented writers, such as William Wordsworth, Charles Lamb*, William Hazlitt* and Charles Dickens*. John Hunt's willingness to publish provocative articles and literature often resulted in criminal charges against him, particularly during his most productive years (1805-1825). In 1812, when the *Examiner* printed a candid and essentially correct but highly critical assessment of the Prince Regent written by Leigh Hunt, both men were found guilty of libel, sentenced to two years' imprisonment and fined £500 pounds each. They could have had their sentences and fines commuted if they would promise not to attack the Prince Regent in their publications, but both men refused and from 1813-1815 were imprisoned, where John Hunt continued to manage the *Examiner*.

John Hunt published influential papers, periodicals, and texts for years to come; titles included the *Indicator* (1819-21), the *Yellow Dwarf* (1818), the *Literary Examiner* (1823), and the *Liberal* (1822-1823), which printed Lord Byron's 'Vision of Judgment' in its first issue. Byron's publisher declined the inflammatory piece, but John Hunt did not and he was again brought up on charges of libel against the King. He also took over publication of the later cantos of Byron's *Don Juan* and Byron's play *Heaven and Earth*. Throughout his career and despite considerable risk to himself, John Hunt made it possible for Leigh Hunt and many other major authors to disseminate important literary texts and to advocate reform and a free press. JNW

Sources: Drabble 2000, Fader and Bornstein 1972, *ODNB*.

HUNT, (JAMES HENRY) LEIGH (1784-1859) Leigh Hunt was one of the central figures in journalism of the first half of the nineteenth century. He knew almost everyone on the cultural scene, including Byron, Shelley, Keats and Dickens*, and his *Autobiography* (1850) and letters constitute important sources of information. Publishing first as a poet by subscription he later published poetry* in the *Morning Chronicle**, the *Monthly Mirror Magazine* (1822-1849), the *European Magazine* (1782-1826), the *Monthly Magazine* (1796-1843) and the *Poetical Register* (1802-1814). In 1804 he contributed to the *Traveller (1801-1822)*, and the following year he was writing for two papers edited* by his brother John, the *News* (1805-1835) and the *Statesman* (1806-1824). In 1808 Leigh Hunt began his most important periodical venture, the *Examiner**, which he edited and John published*. Leigh also edited the short-lived *Reflector* (1811-1812), again published by his brother, to which Lamb* and Barnes* contributed. In 1811 and 1812 two actions of libel were brought against the *Examiner*. As a result the brothers Hunt were fined £500 and imprisoned until 1815. They con-

tinued to publish the *Examiner* from their cells. From 1816, Shelley's work began to appear in the *Examiner*, where Leigh placed an important defence of 'the Young Poets'. These included Keats who later was to publish in Leigh's weekly* *Indicator* (1818-1821).

In 1821, Leigh was forced to give up editing both because of poor health and the lowered circulation* of *the Examiner* and *Indicator*. He and his family (including son Thornton*) left for Italy, eventually arriving in May 1822 where they were greeted by Shelley and Byron. After Shelley's drowning, four issues of the *Liberal* (1822-1823), a periodical previously projected by Shelley, Byron and Leigh, were published by John Hunt, with contributions by Leigh, Byron and Hazlitt*. Leigh and his family went to live in Florence from where he continued to write for the *Examiner* and began his series of contributions to the *New Monthly**. They returned to London in 1825, where Leigh tried to make money with four periodicals, all commercial failures – the *Companion* (1828), *Chat of the Week* (1830), *the Tatler* (1830-1832) and *Leigh Hunt's London Journal* (1834-1835). Besides continuing his journalistic labours, editing the *Monthly Repository** (1837-1838) and writing for journals and newspapers such as *Ainsworth's**, the *Atlas* (1826-1862), *Tait's**, the *True Sun (1832-1837)*, the *Monthly Chronicle** (1838-1841), *Fraser's** and the *Spectator**, for the remainder of his life Leigh supplemented his meagre income with a variety of literary labours, including playwriting. AK

Sources: Gates 1998, Hunt 1850, *ODNB*.

HUNT, THORNTON LEIGH (1810-1873) Thornton Hunt made a considerable contribution to the liberal intellectual press from the 1830s until his death. Best known as the influential second editor* of the *Daily Telegraph**, Thornton was the eldest son of Leigh Hunt*. Although Thornton kept up the family tradition of radical journalism, his career was not at all as controversial as his father's.

After deciding against a career as an artist, in 1836 Thornton was made subeditor* *of* the new *Constitutional* under Thackeray* by Blanchard*; he left when it closed the following year. In 1838 he turned to editing*, the *North Cheshire Reformer* (1836-1842) in Stockport and then the new *Glasgow Argus* (1839-1846). From 1840 he was based in London, engaged in two long-term journalistic commitments; first with Robert Rintoul's*, *Spectator**, the weekly* radical journal that Thornton, in part, edited, and then from 1855, he became part of the editorial team at Joseph Levy's* *Daily*

Telegraph. Thornton is credited with giving the *Telegraph* its early, if ultimately short-lived radical edge while the paper's owners were 'fumbling for editorial direction' (Burnham: 15). Thornton's leaders* for the *Telegraph* in particular were striking, shorter than usual for the time, direct and polemical, calling, among other things for the reform of the House of Lords and the banning of capital punishment. Under Thornton's direction, the paper was supportive of the Liberal* agenda generally, and he corresponded directly with W. E. Gladstone throughout the 1860s. In a memorandum to the paper's owners, he also insisted on the importance of reporting 'all striking events in science*, so told that the intelligent public can understand what has happened and can see its bearing on our daily life and our future' (Burnham: 8).

His own version of a radical agenda is most clearly evident, perhaps, in the liberal weekly paper, the *Leader**, which he conceived and co-edited with George Henry Lewes* in the early 1850s. In its first incarnation it was a strident, intellectual paper and an important addition to the radical press. Thornton edited the political* sections, Lewes the cultural section until financial* problems, personal differences, and political difficulties with the more conservative management team resulted in the gradual attenuation of his engagement with the paper, terminating in the mid 1850s. In 1851, he was instrumental in setting up the Association for the Promotion of the Repeal of the Taxes on Knowledge*.

Thornton wrote on a wide variety of topics in diverse publications including the *Morning Chronicle**, the *Globe**, *Atlas**, *Atlantic*, *Cassell's Illustrated Family Magazine** and the *Cornhill**. He was always over-extended by his many journalistic commitments: 'you could see leading articles in his corrugated expression' (Holyoake*, in Ashton: 89), and at his death he left an unfinished novel, an edition of William Maginn's* writings and a work on the progress of society. AK/FD
Sources: Ashton 1991, Burnham 1955, Bourne 1887, Holyoake 1872, *ODNB*, *Poole's*, Tatchell 1969, Thomas 1928.

HUNT, WILLIAM HOLMAN (1827-1910) Despite William Holman Hunt's fame as a Pre-Raphaelite artist and extensive output as a book illustrator, he contributed few illustrations* to periodicals. There were two etchings for the *Germ** in 1850, three designs for *Once a Week** ten years later, another for the *Queen* and a few images in *Good Words**. All are in the high Pre-Raphaelite manner.

Yet Hunt also contributed texts. In 1886 he had a series of three articles on 'Pre-Raphaelitism: A Fight for Art' published in the *Contemporary Review** (April, May, June 1886). He also contributed letters and articles to the *Athenaeum** (Aug. 1875, Oct. 1868), the *Musical World** (Feb. 1875, July 1890) and the *Magazine of Art** (Jan. 1891, Jan. 1893) which show him to be a committed artist and one who believes artistic production needs to be better defended by law. **BM**
Sources: Amor 1989, Engen 1990, Goldman 1994, Houfe 1978, Reid 1928, Suriano 2005.

HUNT'S UNIVERSAL YACHT LIST (1851-1934) *Hunt's Universal Yacht List* was an annual* publication by Hunt & Son, which in 1934 became *Norrie's Yacht List*. In 1853 the annual consisted of 146, 10 cm. pages, costing 4s. Contents included coloured illustrations* of ensigns and burgees of yacht clubs with a comprehensive guide to British yacht clubs, information on foreign royal yacht clubs such as the Imperial Yacht Club of St Petersburgh, (*sic*) and the Royal Netherlands and Belgian Yacht Clubs, as well as names of yachts and their owners. Also included were tide tables, weather forecasts, time tables, yacht race prize winners, addresses of yachting club secretaries, builders of yachts, with six pages of advertisements*. **DHL**
Sources: *Hunt's Universal Yacht List* 1853-1856, Waterloo.

HUTTON, RICHARD HOLT (1826-1897) Richard Holt Hutton – journalist*, editor* and proprietor* – was born in Leeds, the son of a Unitarian minister. Hutton's Unitarianism barred him from entering older universities, but in 1841 aged 15 he entered University College, London, where he met Walter Bagehot*, whose friendship and intellectual influence were to become a major force in his adult life. In 1847 he went to Manchester New College, where his teachers, James Martineau*, J. J. Tayler* and F. W. Newman helped to develop his strong, unconventional views. Illness forced him to abandon his post as vice principal and chaplain of University Hall, in London, and he turned to journalism.

From 1853 until 1855 he was joint editor of the Unitarian weekly *Inquirer**. He also contributed articles to the *Prospective Review**, joining the group which edited it in 1853. With Bagehot* he became co-editor (1855-1862) of the *National Review**, the successor to the *Prospective*. Hutton's contributions helped to make the *National Review* one of the most stimulating periodicals of its day. He was also assistant editor (1858-1860) on the *Economist**, as well as contributing to the *North British Review** and the *Saturday Review*. Hutton's growing reputation as a journalist led to his appointment, in 1861, as co-editor and proprietor of the *Spectator*. In this capacity he joined Meredith Townsend, who had bought the paper on returning from India. Hutton, as well as his other duties, managed the finances. His advocacy of the abolition of slavery and support for the Northern cause during the American Civil War proved disastrous for the *Spectator*. Subscriptions were cancelled and advertising* dwindled. Difficulties also arose in 1886 when Hutton supported Gladstone over the cause of Irish Home Rule. Meredith Townsend resigned and there was opposition to the *Spectator* from a powerful anti-Home Rule faction. In June 1897, Hutton ceased to take part in the management of the paper, and died in September.

Hutton was a prolific journalist and literary* critic. Estimates of his identifiable articles are in the thousands, with many others unsigned* and therefore unacknowledged. He republished some of his periodical essays in book collections. In addition he edited collections of the work of his colleague Bagehot and also that of his close friend and brother-in-law William Caldwell Roscoe*. Apart from journalistic activities, Hutton was, in 1869, one of the founders of the Metaphysical Society, with which the contents of the *Contemporary Review* and the *Nineteenth Century* were closely associated, and he wrote a history of the organization. **DHL**

Sources: Church 1908, Hogben 1899, *ODNB*, Orel 1984, Ward 1908, *Wellesley*.

HUXLEY, THOMAS HENRY (1825-1895) Lionized but impecunious after returning from the global voyages of HMS *Rattlesnake* in 1851, Huxley, who had contributed several papers to the *Philosophical Transactions of the Royal Society* while at sea, was commissioned by John Chapman* to write a regular science* column* for the radical *Westminster Review*, in which he honed an uncompromising rationalism matched by a razor-sharp wit and taste for provocation. After leaving the *Westminster* in the mid-1850's Huxley persuaded the *Saturday Review* to carry a similar fortnightly science column to which he not only contributed but also selected all the other contributors. Elevated into the limelight by his ardent defence of Charles Darwin's *Origin of Species* (1859), which he reviewed* for *The Times*, *Macmillan's Magazine* and the *Westminster*, and for his part in a long-running dispute over ape brains in the *Athenaeum*, Huxley became one of the most coveted contributors to general periodicals, writing on politics*, theology and education* as well as science, although he remained anxious to be perceived as an expert scientific practitioner rather than a mere journalist. In 1869 the number of the *Fortnightly Review* containing his article 'On the Physical Basis of Life' sold out an unprecedented seven editions.

However, Huxley's editorships* of the *Natural History Review*, which he took on in 1860 at the behest of its Irish founder Edward Perceval Wright in order to make it more cosmopolitan, and then the *Reader* were both *brief* and mostly unsuccessful, while his initial influence on the editorial line of *Nature*, for which he wrote the lead article of its opening number, was similarly short-lived. Even in old age, Huxley continued to write prodigiously for the press, especially for the *Nineteenth Century* where he engaged in heated theological disputes with William Gladstone, although he became increasingly exasperated by the New Journalistic* practices pioneered by William Thomas Stead*. **GD**

Sources: Dawson 2004, Desmond 1994-1997, Lightman 2004, *ODNB*, White 2003.

HYNDMAN, HENRY MAYERS (1842-1921) Though he is best known as the proprietor* and editor of the Social Democratic Federation's (SDF) flagship journal *Justice* (1884ff), Henry Hyndman first entered journalism as a war* correspondent for the conservative *Pall Mall Gazette* during the Italian/Austrian war (1866). He wrote about the British Empire for the *Nineteenth Century* and the *Pall Mall Gazette* during the 1870s, but it was his work during the 1880s and 1890s for the SDF which established his reputation. When Hyndman was accused by William Morris* of dictating SDF policy, the resulting split led to the formation of the Socialist League, the issuing body* of its own journal, the *Commonweal*. In 1887 Harry Quelch* was appointed editor* of *Justice*, though Hyndman continued to contribute articles. In addition to *Justice*, he also owned two monthlies*, *To-Day*, in which he published an overview of Marx's *Capital* under the name 'John Broadhouse', and the *Social Democrat* (1897-1913). He also wrote for non-socialist periodicals such as the *Contemporary Review* and *St James's Gazette*. There is some evidence to suggest that Hyndman was the author of one of the few *Justice* serializations of fiction*, 'A Working Class Tragedy' (1888-1889), under the pseudonym 'H. J. Bramsbury'. **DM**

Sources: Bevir 1991, Hyndman 1911, *ONDB*, Thompson 1955, Tsuzuki 1961.

I

IDLER (1892-1898) A 6d and then a 1s monthly targeted at the young male 'surburban' world of upwardly mobile clerks and other wage-earners, the *Idler* was originally the idea of Robert Barr, who had made considerable money as editor* of the British version of the *Detroit Free Press*. For the first three years Barr was co-editor with Jerome K. Jerome, who became proprietor* and editor* in 1895. Characterized by one critic as 'an adult version of extremely successful English juvenile publications such as *Boy's Own Paper*'* (Cox 17), the magazine was instantly successful. Lavishly illustrated*, its 'liberal, irreverent, and sentimental' tone was praised. Jerome attracted a wide array of excellent writers and illustrators such as Rudyard Kipling, Arthur Conan Doyle, George Bernard Shaw*, Andrew Lang*, Barry Pain, Israel Zangwill*, Rider Haggard, Hall Caine, George R. Sims*, R. M. Ballantyre, Richard Le Gallienne*, Bret Harte, H. G. Wells*, R. L. Stevenson and Aubrey Beardsley*

Figure 27: The cover of the bound *Idler* volume, 1893-1894.

When Barr sold the *Idler* to Jerome, the latter expanded the size* and introduced an even more lavish use of illustrations varying from high art to crude cartoon*. There was an average of 120-150 pages per issue. Fiction was the most prominent part of the letter press, but there were also the usual articles on theatre, books and exhibitions, interviews of celebrities and educational essays. One of the most popular departments was 'The Idler's Club' where a variety of well-known men, and ultimately women, wrote short, snappy paragraphs on set topics such as 'Duels and Duelling' and 'Are Clever Women or Stupid More Attractive?' but also some serious ones on giving women the vote and candidates for the greatest living British writer. The women contributors to the *Idler,* such as Eliza Lynn Linton*, Sarah Grand*, Ella Hepworth Dixon and John Oliver Hobbes, appeared most frequently in the 'Idler's Club' series.

In 1896 Jerome was in financial difficulties and had to sell the *Idler*. Edited by a hack writer, Arthur Lawrence, and a suddenly wealthy caricaturist* SidneySime, the quality of the magazine deteriorated rapidly and in two years it had disappeared. **AH**
Sources: Cox 1988, Humpherys 2005, *ODNB*.

ILIFFE FAMILY: ILIFFE, WILLIAM ISAAC (1843-1917); ILIFFE, EDWARD MAUGER (1877-1960) William Iliffe's father established the Iliffe Press, a prosperous stationary, wallpaper and printing business in Coventry which William joined in 1864, and developing a publishing* wing list for the firm. His predictive appreciation of Coventry's role in the growth of engineering manifested itself in the *Cyclist** in 1878, taking over two other periodicals to form the *Bicycling New* and in employing Alfred Harmsworth* in editing* and reporting work from 1885. William continued this theme with *Autocar* (1895), the *Motor Cycle* (1903) and in *Flight* (1909). In 1884, they launched *Amateur Photographer*.

The company was also in the forefront of Coventry newspapers with William purchasing the *Coventry Times* in 1879, followed by the *North Warwickshire Times* and the *Leamington and Warwick Times* while starting the *Midland Daily Telegraph* in 1891. The latter was advertised as an innovative paper, with four daily* editions; costing a ½d, it used telegraph* services to obtain the latest news* and, from 1897, supplied a special pink sporting Saturday edition. By 1906 it had a circulation* of 10,000.

Edward Iliffe joined the business in 1894; working on the *Coventry Evening Telegraph*, he took over management of Iliffe & Sons at his father William's death in partnership with his elder brother William Coker Iliffe. By 1924 together with William and Gomer Berry he had formed Allied Newspapers Ltd, a hugely successful enterprise which by the end of the 1920s owned both the *Daily Telegraph** and the *Sunday Times**. Although Allied Newspapers collapsed in 1937, Edward ensured that the family business continued its newspaper interests through the *Birmingham Post** and *Birmingham Mail*. Currently, Iliffe News & Media own 40 newspapers, 10 magazines, 24 related websites and a large share of a television company. **CL**

Sources: *ODNB*, British History online, Ketupa.net online.

ILLUMINATED MAGAZINE (1843-1845) The *Illuminated Magazine* was among the many illustrated* shilling* monthly* magazines which characterized the nascent entrepreneurship and rapid development of the periodical idea in the 1830s and 1840s. It was short lived, running to three volumes (1843-1844) under its first editor*, the playwright, journalist* and progressive thinker Douglas Jerrold*, before slipping into oblivion after two further, increasingly eccentric volumes under the guidance of the engraver, poet* and political activist, W. J. Linton*. Each monthly issue of between 50 and 60 pages used the squarish, double column* page popularized by *Punch**, a conspicuously versatile shape for a publication containing a wide variety of illustrations.

The contents of the *Illuminated Magazine* seem to conform to the expected template for such monthlies, comprising a mixture of fanciful or whimsical sketches, historical* anecdotes and legends, travel pieces, social commentary and investigation, poetry* and stories and, to a limited extent, reviews*. But the *Illuminated Magazine* often managed to be somewhat more progressive through translating the ambitions of the genteel monthly into something more usefully and progressively 'popular'*. Originally financed by Herbert Ingram* to recover authors like Mark Lemon* and Jerrold from their increasing affiliation with the *Pictorial Times*, Linton, as art editor, built an outstanding list of artists and engravers including Kenny Meadows*, H. G. Hine*, Ebenezer Landells* and John Leech*, who produced both full-page etchings and engravings and wood engravings dropped into the text. With its coloured wood-block title page and impressive illustrations, the *Illuminated Magazine* looked forward to such journals as *Once a Week** and *Good Words** in its pursuit of visual quality. **BM**
Sources: Slater 2002, Smith 1973, *Waterloo*.

ILLUSTRATED EXHIBITOR (1851-1852) The *Illustrated Exhibitor*, a profusely illustrated* weekly* magazine selling initially for 2d rising to 4d by December for 16-20 pages, was launched, unsurprisingly, in July 1851 to coincide with the opening of the Great Exhibition, and ran for 30 issues in a first series until December 1851. More unexpected was the success of a second series of 52 numbers issued in 1852 after the closure of the Exhibition. The *Illustrated Exhibitor* came at that moment when the innovative publisher* John Cassell*, who had already been involved in various commercial ventures to support relatively poor visitors to London, began to recognize aspiring artisans as an important potential niche market* for periodicals, and to think through the likely cultural needs and tastes of this increasingly significant social group. The outcomes were such important and successful periodicals as *Cassell's Illustrated Family Paper** as well as a variety of hugely successful educational and self-help manuals.

The *Exhibitor* combined a number of differing functions. While essentially a 'virtual' trip round the Exhibition for those unable to make the journey to London, it also developed a number of other features that became commonplace in later periodicals, most notably the 'visit' to a specialist factory to see how commodities were made and the extensive reproduction of art works through the medium of wood engraving*. It also largely avoided the chauvinistic celebration of commodities, inventiveness and imperial* power that was prevalent in many writings about the Exhibition and sought to offer at least some recognition of the importance of working men and women in industrial production. The *Illustrated Exhibitor* was, on the whole, progressive in its development of ways of addressing and interesting artisans through illustrated periodicals, and largely free of the condescension found in the *Penny Magazine**. The format* was revived for the International Exhibition of 1862. **BM**
Sources: Maidment 1996, Nowell-Smith 1958, *ODNB*.

ILLUSTRATED LONDON NEWS (1842-1989) The *Illustrated London News* was one of the great entrepreneurial and commercial triumphs of Victorian print culture, and ranks high on any list of successful nineteenth-century commodities. All three elements expressed in its title were necessary to its success. 'Illustration'* was key. The magazine's founding partnership comprised a printer, newsagent* and patent medicine salesman, Henry Ingram*, who largely capitalised the venture, and

Henry Vizetelly*, by 1842 an already successful London-based engraver who had undertaken publicity work for Ingram. Although the editor* was nominally F. W. N. Bayley, the driving force behind the weekly* magazine was the experienced John Timbs*, who had previously worked at the *Mirror of Literature*, one of the first weekly magazines to exploit the potential of wood* engraving.

Given Vizetelly's experience, contacts and eye for business, it was certain that the new magazine would capitalize upon the commercial appeal of wood-engraved illustration*, especially given the opportunities offered by the expanses of the chosen multi-column* broadsheet-sized* page, and the editorial team began to build spectacular spreads out of the combined illustration and text. Vizetelly and Timbs's extensive contacts within the newly dynamic London engraving trades enabled them to bring an astonishing gathering of talent to the *Illustrated London News*, and many artists took up the challenge of supplying images to Vizetelly's engravers including Sir John Gilbert*, Henry Anelay*, Birket Foster*, H. G. Hine* and Kenny Meadows*. The French artist Gavarni* was a particularly impressive contributor during the turmoil of 1848. The workshops of Ebenezer Landells* and Stephen Sly* provided many illustrations for early volumes, and the high quality was maintained under later art editors like Mason Jackson*. The magazine managed to adapt to photo-reprographic* methods of production in the 1880s without too much upheaval.

The *Illustrated London News* occupies a uniquely important role in the history of wood engraving, however, for reasons other than the profusion and

Figure 28: The masthead of the *Illustrated London News* and a picture illustrating the Irish Land League trials, 15 Jan. 1881

quality of the images it printed. The magazine continually insisted that wood engraving was an entirely immediate, unmediated and naturalistic way of representing the world. As the leader* to the first issue on 12 May 1842 put it , 'the public will have henceforth under their glance, and within their grasp, the very form and presence of events as they transpire'. Such an unequivocal yoking together of the wood engraved image with realism had never been asserted so forcefully before, and the *Illustrated London News* capitalized heavily on this assumption, making wood engraving synonymous with claims for documentary accuracy in reportage. The introduction of 'specials' reporters sent out to bring back vivid and immediate graphic and verbal reports from war*– confirmed the importance of the documentary idea to the magazine.

The second element of the magazine's title – 'London' – was also essential to its self-image in asserting the centrality of London as the commercial and imperial* knowledge capital of the world, as well as its major economic centre. The idea of London as the 'world city' was brilliantly incorporated into the Thames skylines used as emblematic mastheads* for the journal, and in the constant celebration of metropolitan street spectacle. The third title element – 'news' – was to some extent a polemical term in 1842 as it foregrounded the intense cultural debates about the advisability of giving the mass of the populace free access to current events. The *Illustrated London News* was, for over a decade, a stamped periodical, which raised its cover price* to 6d per weekly issue. Clearly such a high cost served to keep the magazine from a mass* working-class readership*, but in any case by the 1840s the progressive attitude – that incorporation was better than repression – had become the dominant ideological position with regard to print culture and current events. The *Illustrated London News* thus began to appear exactly at the moment when the intensity of contests over the nature and value of 'useful knowledge'* had largely receded. Furthermore the magazine was firmly aimed at the middle classes, and its presentation of news was highly mediated through the codes of melodrama, spectacle and sentimentality. Much of its news repertoire, indeed, comprised politically uncontentious subjects such as accidents, fires, street spectacles and technological triumphs. The *Illustrated London News* was, right from its inception, something much more than a 'news' magazine. It was also a brand, and as well as the famous give-away supplements* of massive engravings, it gave its name to such ventures as the

1850 *Illustrated London Instructor*, a self-educative handbook for aspiring artisans.

It is interesting that the magazine continued smoothly on after Ingram's death in 1860, saw out several editors who never became well known (indeed, the two most significant editors Timbs (1846-1852) and John Lash Latey (1859-1890) were both staffers who already knew the magazine intimately), and had no star writers. It was indeed a triumph of brand and corporate identity over individual achievement. It was also, too, in shape and structure as close to a family magazine* as it was to a newspaper. The organization of each weekly issue acknowledged a family readership catering for men, women and children in various columns* such as chess problems, fashion* notes, and games, and the magazine printed a considerable amount of fiction from the 1880s. It also commissioned both humorous illustration, especially for holiday seasons, printing full-page plates by the likes of Kenny Meadows* and John Leech*, and self-consciously ambitious art images which showed off the best qualities of the wood-engraved medium. The large pages with their many wood-engraved illustrations also gave the magazine an important afterlife as a source of scraps for albums, or even as material for covering furniture and walls. Like *Punch**, the *Illustrated London News* became enough of an institution to survive way past 1900, and reached beyond its 125th anniversary before finally declaring itself to be an anachronism in 1989. **BM**
Sources: Engen 1985, Sinnema 1998.

ILLUSTRATED POLICE BUDGET **(1893-1910)** 'The leading illustrated* police journal in England' according to its own account, this 16-page penny*'widely read' weekly* featured lurid full front page illustrations of sensationally violent crimes with more of the same inside. For particularly notorious crimes – like the Jack the Ripper murders or the Oscar Wilde trial – the paper published special grandly illustrated supplements*.

The publisher* and printer was Frank Shaw, and from 1899 the editor* was Harold Furniss, who was to become a well-known publisher of accounts of criminal cases. To complement the array of illustrations, the *Illustrated Police Budget* covered stories from the metropolitan and provincial courts, and paid particular attention to the divorce court. In addition to the sensationalized crime* stories, the paper also reported on sports* news (football and boxing in particular), theatrical gossip* and a section* called 'war of the week'.

In its first issue the paper nailed its flag to working-class* grievances: 'in addition to giving the latest and fullest information regarding every criminal case of interest powerfully portrayed by Artists exclusively engaged we shall endeavour to make this emphatically a *Journal of Justice*. Any real case of oppression of the Poor by the rich, or genuine grievance of the Masses against the Classes, will command full ventilation in our columns'.

The paper was particularly obsessed with the Oscar Wilde trial and while it was discreet about the details, it gave every attention to Wilde's looks and movements, the editor assigning a reporter to dog Wilde's every step. The paper continued its intense illustrated coverage of Wilde even after he had gone to jail. In 1910, its focus shifted to sport, and in its final years (1910-1912) it became the *Illustrated Sporting Budget and Boxing Record*, and in mid-1912 simply the *Sporting Budget*. **AH**
Sources: Diamond 2004, *Waterloo*, Wiener 2004.

ILLUSTRATED POLICE NEWS **(1864-1938)** Published* in London by John Ransom and George Purkess* and printed by Purkess and Richard Beard, the *Illustrated Police News* claimed to give attention to 'subjects of more than ordinary interest' ranging from gory murders to courtroom dramas. The sensational weekly*, priced* at 1d, contained 'all "news"* sufficient to satisfy any man who has but a few hours a week to spare from his toil' (Our Intentions no.1: p.2). The masthead* contained the title and subtitle, '*Law-court and weekly record*', and was surrounded by heavy decoration. It appeared atop a front page that was composed entirely of illustrations* with brief captions. Short articles, with more illustrations, appeared inside its 58-cm pages*. Its circulation* grew over its first 20 years of publication from 100,000 to 300,000.

The newspaper is most familiar for its coverage of the Jack the Ripper murders and it featured the Ripper story on 184 of its covers in the four years after the last murder. It also covered the trial of Oscar Wilde*, where early illustrations of a well-dressed Wilde gave way to the representation that the 'fortnight's confinement in Holloway Gaol has told severely on Wilde' (20 April 1895). While these famous cases were covered, as well as international crimes* and police work at home and abroad, the *Illustrated Police News* focused on the local crimes that reflect the often desperate lives of its working-class* readers. There are countless pieces on domestic violence, railway accidents, suicides, and riots, with occasional colour added by exotic crimes such as an account of a 'Novel and Fatal Balloon Duel' (1878) or 'A Burglar Bitten by a

Skeleton'. The newspaper became the *Sporting Record* in 1938. **CR**

Sources: De Vries 1971, *Waterloo*.

ILLUSTRATED SPORTING AND DRAMATIC NEWS (1874-1984) A periodical with a wide coverage of sporting, theatrical and miscellaneous topics, it underwent three title changes* and formats* during its lengthy career. It was continued as *Sport and Country* (Feb. 1943 to Oct. 1957), then *Farm and Country* until it folded in 1984. In the nineteenth century the paper was issued weekly* and fortnightly, providing a varied coverage of sporting* and theatrical topics. These included theatre, music* and music hall reviews*, a weekly betting calendar, principle turf fixtures, railway information, billiards, sporting intelligence, correspondence*, canoeing and poetry*. Priced* 6d, in 1875 the publisher* and printer was Thomas Fox, followed by R. Clay & Sons. By 1899 the journal was published by the Lady's Pictorial and Sporting and Dramatic Publishing Co. Ltd.

Contributors included Wallis and William Mackay, Montague Vizetelly and the illustrator* Alfred Bryan. *Mitchell's Newspaper Directory* in 1900 claimed that the journal aimed at 'justice and impartiality in describing sport, music and the drama. The illustrations are of the highest order. The articles are all characterised by freshness and talent'. **DHL**

Sources: Connolly & Wearing 1978, Layton 1912, *Mitchell's, Waterloo*.

ILLUSTRATED TIMES (1855-1872) The *Illustrated Times* was a 2d weekly* that promised at its launch to 'espouse no party, political, or religious questions, but confine its columns to the news* of the day, to literature*, science*, and art'. The proprietor* was David Bogue and the editor* Henry Vizetelly*. Their intention was to rival the mighty *Illustrated London News** and by employing respected contributors and using high-quality engraved* illustrations* the *Illustrated Times* achieved extremely impressive circulation* figures of 400,000 by 1856.

Contributors to the newspaper included Robert Brough*, Edward Draper, James Hannay, Frederick Greenwood*, George Augustus Sala* and Edmund Yates*. In its early years the newspaper was particularly strong on foreign reportage, especially on the Crimean War* and the Paris Exhibition of 1855. Domestic news included law* and crime*, the House of Commons and the money market. Poetry* was also a mainstay in the early years and there was serialized* fiction. Sala's 'Baddington Peerage'

ran from March to December 1857, and he also provided some engravings. In the fourth number Yates's series 'Lounger At The Clubs'* began'; an irreverent and gossipy* set of articles, they initiated a new style of 'personal' journalism. Yates wrote about the current whereabouts and employment of artists, theatrical people and fellow-writers. The dramatist T. W. Robertson* replaced Yates as the 'Theatrical Lounger' in May 1864.

Although the *Illustrated Times* could not match the quality or superiority of the *Illustrated London News*, within five years it sold sufficiently well to prompt the latter's owner, Herbert Ingram,* to buy out the *Illustrated Times* in 1859, in an attempt, characteristic of his methods, to 'clip the wings' of his rival. The price* was increased to 4d and circulation quickly fell. In 1872 in the 885th edition an announcement was made that the *Illustrated Times* was to be absorbed by *Zig-Zag* (1872-1881). **PB**

Sources: Edwards 1997, *Waterloo*, Yates 1885.

ILLUSTRATION Drawing on emergent reprographic media, initially wood engraving* (which allowed text and illustration to be printed together) and, to a more limited extent, lithography* and then a variety of photo-reprographic* techniques, illustration was a central attribute of many nineteenth-century periodicals. Indeed, some periodicals* like the *Illustrated London News** were pre-eminently defined by their dependence on illustration. Much of the dynamism and investment in periodicals in the early Victorian period derived from entrepreneurs who were engravers or printers by trade, and thus well attuned to the importance of illustration in defining and selling new magazines.

Established as central to the periodical market by such pioneering journals as the *Mirror of Literature** and the *Mechanic's Magazine** in the 1820s, wood* engraved illustration proved essential both to the development of the graphic account of the physical world which characterized the magazines of popular education and to the appeal of fiction serialized* in magazines. The cheapness and speed of wood engraving, as well as the rapidly developing technical skill of the new school of engravers, rapidly caused readers to forget the aesthetic limitations of an essentially linear monotone medium, and by the 1840s wood engraving was taken for granted as the most accurate and expressive way to visualise the material universe. Sectarian publishers*, drawing on a long tradition of tract literature, had immediately recognized the value of illustrations in increasing the attractiveness and effectiveness of devotional

Figure 29: Sensational photography of lightning in the *Leisure Hour*, Nov. 1888.

Figure 30: An illustration depicting the bust of the artist George Cruikshank in the *Illustrated London News*, 10 Sept. 1881.

magazines in which the combination of emblematic and naturalistic codes, as well as the allusion back to vernacular forms like the chap book, gave familiarity and reassurance to less well-educated readers.

As government anxiety about the dangers of a mass circulation* topical press receded in the 1840s and 1850s, and punitive taxes like the Stamp Duty* were rescinded, periodicals were able to draw heavily on the many workshops and jobbing engravers established in London in order to supply topical illustrations of political* and social happenings, and thus underpin the development of investigative journalism. Increasingly, too, the proprietors* of magazines gained an understanding of the value of images in negotiating social values, thus reinforcing such cherished ideas as the domestic*, temperance, and self-improvement through a range of visual tropes and codes available even to barely literate readers.

By the mid-century, ambitious magazines had begun to employ art editors* to commission and oversee their illustrations, and many magazines built up 'stables' of artists, and developed close, or even exclusive, relationships with their illustrators. Such 1860s magazines as *Good Words**, *Once a Week** and the *Cornhill Magazine**endorsed the aesthetic ambitions

of wood engraving by printing full-page images commissioned from leading artists, thus creating a collectors' market for images which were often reprinted in volume form. Both serialized* fiction and occasional contributions, especially poetry*, were illustrated in this way. Humorous and satirical* journals like the *Tomahawk**, building on the success of *Punch**, used the resources of both wood engraving and lithography to produce large-scale political cartoons*, although lithography never gained the widespread appeal that it enjoyed in French satirical and humorous periodicals. For most of the Victorian period colour reproduction was both too technically difficult and expensive for all but specialized small circulation journals, although two- or three-colour wood engravings were sometimes used, and many periodicals offered their regular readers free extra illustrations, often lithographs, to accompany Christmas* or other special issues. Exceptions to this general tendency were the fashion* plates reproduced in colour, often as fold-out illustrations, for many women's* magazines.

The introduction of 'process' reprographic techniques towards the end of the century formed another major shift in the ways in which the physical world was visualized. Process methods used photography to project original images of whatever kind on to metal plates. Subsequently etched, these plates enabled photographs to be printed alongside typeset material. Photomechanical reproduction made the visual content in newspapers and magazines of the late nineteenth century, in Beegan's words, 'more abundant, complex and increasingly hybrid'. He concludes 'the introduction of photomechanical technologies destabilized reproduction and representation so that the discrete categories of photograph, wood engraving and drawing took on a new fluidity', and certainly the use of half-tone engraving in particular accounts for the increasingly naturalistic and 'photographic' look of late nineteenth-century magazines and newspapers. The half tone was, despite some presence in book illustration, particularly the province of magazines and newspapers, where its ability to render detail was particularly useful. By the end of the century, illustration, largely carried out through photomechanical means, had become commonplace in almost every magazine except for specialist scholarly journals. By this stage, some periodicals like the *Dome** and the *Yellow Book** were even being used to expound aesthetic philosophies and thus draw together artwork, book design and literature*, offering space to such avant-garde and innovative artists as Beardsley* in the development of a Modernist aesthetic. As for the newspaper press, the *Daily Mirror* from 1904 was Britain's first 'picture paper' to make extensive use of photographic images as an integral component of editorial content, in particular in the reporting of sport*, politics*, war*, royalty and fashion. While this was generally resisted by the older broadsheets, illustration, both photographic and engraved, increased in scale and sophistication above all in newspaper advertising*. **BM/AGJ**

Sources: Anderson 1991, Beegan 2008, Evans 1978, Goldman 1994, Houfe 1981, James 1963, Reid 1928, Wakeman 1973, White 1897.

IMPERIALISM AND JOURNALISM The role of the press in British Imperialism was complex and dynamic, and recent scholarship has emphasized that any absolute distinction between metropole and Empire cannot be sustained. Debates about the Empire and representations of imperial subjects in both verbal and visual forms filled the press in Britain. British papers and journals were circulated* through the Empire, but the development of indigenous presses in English and other languages gave colonized peoples a space in which to talk back or create their own identities.

European imperialists encouraged the establishment of government presses in colonies as imperial rule was underpinned by the need to print administrative directives, gather and control colonial information, and engage in propaganda. The British convict ships bound for the Antipodes carried printing presses on board. The initial impetus to journalism, however, often came from religious proselytisation. For instance, Baptist missionaries* from England set up one of the first printing presses in Bengal to spread their Christian message which also produced the first Indian language newspapers in the beginning of the nineteenth century.

Technological improvement in communication was a crucial factor. The steam ship* revolution of the first half of the nineteenth century enabled the creation of a regular flow of news* as periodicals collated information passing to and from Britain, the colonies, and protectorates along the steam ship routes – such as from London to New South Wales via Aden, Karachi, Bombay, Ceylon, Calcutta and beyond.

The electric telegraph* from the 1850s (with the associated growth of news agencies* like the British Reuters*, French Havas and German Wolff), and the opening of the Suez Canal in 1869, revolutionised the speed of information flow linking far flung imperial peripheries to their European metropoles. This encouraged the public demand for news and the ability of European and colonial newspapers to satisfy this demand. This thirst for news was undoubtedly also influenced by the pace of imperial expansion throughout the nineteenth century, which witnessed the British consolidating their supremacy over India, South Africa, the Antipodes and Canada. Between 1870 and 1914 the African continent was carved up among Britain, France, Germany, Belgium, Italy, Spain and Portugal. The impetus to the growth of the modern newspaper press within these colonies was as a result of journalists from Europe exploiting the commercial opportunities that empire provided. Major newspapers in South Africa, Canada, India, Australia and New Zealand, for instance, were established and staffed by printers, editors* and reporters* from Britain. **ChK/MRB**

Sources: Innis 1986, Kaul 2003, Kaul 2006.

***INDIAN SPECTATOR* (1878-1913)** The colonial newspaper the *Indian Spectator* places itself within the context of British journalism through its title, which alludes to the eighteenth-century English *Spectator**, whereas the *Indian Spectator* began life in Bombay in 1878. In 1880, the Parsi social reformer Behramji Malabari bought and took over the editorship* of the paper. Printed by Dorabji Sorabji at the *Voice of India* printing press in Bombay, the newspaper was published every Sunday morning with an annual subscription rate of Rs.9 in Bombay and Rs.10 for the 'mofussil' (country edition). The rate for advertisements*, which were initially printed on the first and last pages of each issue, was one rupee for four lines or less.

The *Indian Spectator* merged* and split repeatedly with the newspapers the *Voice of India* and the *Champion*, publishing under a variety of combinations of these three titles over the course of its run: *Indian Spectator and the Voice of India* (1890-1900); *Indian Spectator* (1900-1901); *Indian Spectator and Champion* (1901); *The Voice of India, Indian Spectator, and Champion* (1901-1902); *Indian Spectator, Voice of India, and Champion* (1904-1913).

Malabari acted as editor from 1880 until 1901 at which point he sold the newspaper to Naoroji Dumasia, the former manager of the *Bombay Gazette*, in order to found and edit the periodical *East and West* (1901-1921). Malabari repurchased the newspaper in 1904 and acted as its editor until his death in 1912; the newspaper closed soon after.

Although addressed mostly to an educated Indian elite, the *Indian Spectator* aspired to reach a broader audience, advertising itself as the 'most acceptable Journal in the Country, With circulation also in England and elsewhere'. Malabari seems to have penned many of the articles, most of which reflected his active commitment to various social causes. Under his editorship, the *Indian Spectator* consistently advocated limited rights for Indian women*, whose uplift would mean the 'advancement' of the native community, and frequently criticized the British administration in India and the Anglo-Indian bureaucracy, while maintaining a rhetorical loyalty to the Empire*. SR

Sources: Burton 1998, Codell 2004, Gidumal 1888, Visram 1986.

INGRAM, HERBERT (1811-1860) Founder and proprietor* of the *Illustrated London News*, Herbert Ingram's exercised his belief in social reform both in the pages of the *Illustrated London News* and as a Member of Parliament for his native Boston, Lincolnshire. Apprenticed to a Boston* printer at the age of 14, Ingram moved to London at the age of 20 to work for two years as a printer before setting up a printing, stationer's and patent medicine business in Nottingham with his partner, Nathaniel Cooke.

According to most accounts, Ingram first conceptualized the *Illustrated London News* as a sensationalist publication illustrating stories of murder, arson, and poor-box burglary akin to the broadsheets he had printed or sold earlier in his career. But friends and associates helped to convince him that a respectable tone would be both more desirable and more profitable. Featuring articles and illustrations* rather than the standard advertisements* on its front page, the first issue of the *Illustrated London News*, published on 14 May 1842, was immensely popular. Priced* at 6d and including over 20 engravings, the issue went through five reprints and sold 26,000 copies, with circulation* increasing to 200,000 during the paper's coverage of the Great Exhibition in 1851.

Ingram installed new printing technology* in his London offices in 1843, and over the next five years began to acquire paper mills. He also added new publications, launching the short-lived *Comic News* in 1846 and acting briefly as proprietor of another *Punch** rival, the *Man in the Moon**. In 1848 he started the *London Telegraph* (Feb.-July), which quickly folded. Two cheap papers followed, the *Picture Times* (1855-1856), which merged* with the *Illustrated Times,* and the *People's Times.* They were Ingram's response to the imitative competitors of the *Illustrated London News* that had appeared after the abolition of the newspaper stamp, such as the *Illustrated Times** (1855ff) which Ingram himself finally bought out in 1859.

Ingram also published a series of books under the title, the *National Illustrated Library.* After his accidental death, his wife Ann Little became proprietor of the *News*, while it was managed by Edward Watkin until their sons were old enough to inherit and run the business. RSB

Sources: Bailey 1842, *ODNB,* Victorian Research Web.

INQUIRER (1838-1840) The *Inquirer* was launched in 1838 as an organ for the views of the hundreds of evangelicals who had withdrawn from the Society of Friends during the 'Beaconite Controversy' of 1835-1836. A monthly* of 32 pages in November 1838, its price* is unknown. Articles and poetry appeared in a single column, while reviews and intelligence appeared in two columns. Early articles were mostly on controversial topics related to the recent division, for example, evangelical views on justification by faith and baptism. Information was also provided regarding the state of the Friends as a denomination; the secession and baptism of Friends was also noted. With Vol. 2, the

anonymous* editors* decided to give a higher profile to topics they believed needed restating in view of the rise of Tractarianism, and they asserted that the monthly would 'no longer confine its animadversions to the errors of one denomination' but broaden its horizons as an 'unsectarian' evangelical periodical. The use of this term indicates that they were beginning to associate with the [Plymouth] Brethren, as does the switch to a publisher* and a printer who were each responsible for many Brethren works. Articles began to appear on topics of interest to that movement, such as biblical prophecy, and some articles offered defences of the Brethren. The magazine ceased publication suddenly at the end of 1840, without advance notice. **TG**
Sources: Grass 2006, Stunt 1970, *Waterloo,* West 2003.

INSTITUTE OF JOURNALISTS (1888-)   The Institute of Journalists is a professional organization established to promote the interests of the press as prior to this organization, journalists* lacked a corporate voice to defend their interests. In October 1884, a group of journalists meeting in Birmingham founded the National Association of Journalists 'to promote and advance the common interests of the profession'. In 1886, the National Association launched a regular journal for members and appointed the first salaried general secretary with offices in Fleet Street*. The organization changed its name to the Institute of Journalists in 1888 and received a Royal Charter from Queen Victoria on 19 April 1890. Early concerns of the organization included remuneration, access to information, allegations of misreporting and cases of financial hardship. An orphan fund was established in 1891, a benevolent fund for distressed journalists in 1898 and unemployment benefit in 1910.The Institute maintained an open membership to all working journalists, including women, despite initial disagreements about the use of entry examinations. The Institute's non-political stance led to the formation in 1907 of the National Union of Journalists*, the profession's first trade union. Unsuccessful attempts were made to merge the two organizations throughout the twentieth century. **MR**
Sources: Chartered Institute of Journalists online, Griffiths 1992, Jones 1996.

INTERVIEWS   The interview is a method of news-gathering first used during the second half of the nineteenth century. Interviewing was not accepted journalistic practice in America before the 1860s or in Britain before the 1880s. Prior to these dates, the term 'interview' was used to refer to any conversation between two people. From 1850 the meaning of the term evolved, and it began to refer to the published account of a meeting between a journalist and someone whose views were reported verbatim or through paraphrase.

The earliest news* stories did not include reported speech, whether direct or indirect. Before the use of the interview, newspapers published official documents and public speeches verbatim. The integration of direct quotation into news stories only became common practice towards the very end of the century. Interviewing was initially seen to be a social indiscretion or an invasion of privacy. Regarded by many as 'an American invention', interviewing by British journalists was considered to be less impertinent than that of their American counterparts.

The rise of the interview has been attributed to audience familiarity with court reports*, the development of a mass-market* press and growing interest in the personal lives of celebrities*. Although journalists such as William Beatty-Kingston (1837-1900), William Howard Russell* and George Augustus Sala* conducted interviews in the 1860s, the practice was still uncommon until editor* W. T. Stead* began to make regular use of interviews during the 1880s. His paper the *Pall Mall Gazette*™ employed Hulda Friederichs* as 'Chief Interviewer' from 1882. Interviews became a popular feature of the New Journalism* of the 1880s and 1890s through such series as Edmund Yates's* 'Celebrities at Home' for the *World*™ and George Newnes's 'Illustrated Interviews' for *Strand Magazine*™. The interview developed from a controversial technique to an integrated facet of journalistic practice. **MR**
Sources: Brown 1985, *ODNB*, Nilsson 1971, Schudson 1995, Silvester 1996.

INVERNESS COURIER (1817-DATE)   Initially twice weekly, then weekly*, and established by William Ettles, Roderick Reach and James Suter in rivalry to the *Inverness Journal*, its first issue (of four pages) appeared on 4 December gratis, with subsequent issues priced* at 7d. Printed by John Johnstone, it was edited* by his remarkable wife, Christian Johnstone*. After the Johnstones' move to Edinburgh in 1824 and a brief spell under James Mackay, Robert Carruthers took over, becoming sole proprietor* in 1831. Generally Liberal in its politics, it nonetheless remained loyal to the established church in the patronage battles of the 1840s. The paper had a noted London column* by Roderick Reach, then by his son A. B. Reach and then occasionally by Shirley Brooks*. Although the paper covered a period of Highland estate clearances, its criticism of the proceedings was fairly muted.

Walter Carruthers joined his father as editor in 1853, while another son, Robert, acted as business manager. Plans to move to a 1d daily* were abandoned, but it became thrice weekly (1880-1885) before reverting to bi-weekly. James Barron took over after Walter Carruthers' death in 1885 and soon after became sole proprietor*. A Whiggish Liberal in politics, although sympathetic to the Celtic movement, he became a Liberal Unionist after 1886. Barron continued to run the paper until 1919. **WHF**
Sources: Baron 1913, Baron 1927, Carruthers, 1878, Carruthers 1969, Noble 1903, *Waterloo Scotland.*

INVESTIGATIVE JOURNALISM While 'investigative journalism' is a twentieth-century term, this press strategy emerged in the latter half of the nineteenth century as a prominent (and early) element of New Journalism*. Associated at the time with sensationalism, its basic element involves a campaigning editor* or reporter personally embroiled with the subject at hand in order to expose its injustices or iniquities. It was enabled by the increasing independence of the press from the control of the government and political parties, most clearly signalled by the removal of the stamp* duty, taxes on advertising* and associated levies (1855-1861).

This new type of journalism was initially associated with the *Pall Mall Gazette*, started in 1865 by its first editor Frederick Greenwood*, who instigated innovative investigative journalism by his brother James, in a clear bid to stimulate sluggish circulation*. Greenwood sent his brother to spend a night in a workhouse: his dramatic, detailed and sententious account of the experience appeared in a sequence of articles beginning 12 January 1866 signed an 'Amateur Casual'. Probably the most celebrated nineteenth-century example of investigative journalism appeared in the same paper in 1885 when its then editor W.T. Stead* – sometimes rather generously credited with inventing the genre – bought a 12-year-old girl on the streets of London in an exposé of what became known as 'White Slavery'. His scoop, entitled 'The Maiden Tribute of Modern Babylon', claimed to expose a trade in young English girls who were being sold into prostitution, and combined sensationalist description with a high moral tone in a manner that has become a typical stylistic facet of investigative journalism. Arrested and imprisoned for his actions, he had his sentence curtailed, and his intervention is generally held to be a crucial contributing factor behind the

subsequent crackdown on child prostitution and the raising of the age of consent in Parliament from 13 to 16. 'Government by Journalism', Stead's article written from prison immediately followed, Writing in 1897 in the *Review of Reviews*, Stead praised William Randolph Hearst's type of American journalism in his *New York Journal* for its 'determination to supersede the journalism that chronicles by the journalism that acts'. The approach especially though its association with the New Journalism*– undoubtedly had its critics, but Stead's phrase still encapsulates the ambition of the investigative journalist. **MaT**
Sources: Brit Per online, De Burgh 2000, 19CBLN, *ODNB, OED.*

IRISH DAILY INDEPENDENT (1891-1904) A forerunner of the *Irish Independent*, which was to become the largest circulating Irish-owned daily* newspaper in Ireland in the twentieth century, the *Irish Daily Independent* was first published* by supporters of Parnell* in December 1891, two months after the death of their leader. Parnell had planned the newspaper and, indeed, had poached staff from *Freeman's Journal*. The *Journal* had formerly supported him but had backed his clerical opponents during the Kitty O'Shea scandal, an act that the new *Independent* described as 'the meanest act of political* and turncoat treachery in newspaper annals'.

The *Irish Daily Independent* espoused a radical, Parnellite programme, including not only 'national self-government' but also extension of the parliamentary and municipal franchises, and reinstatement of all tenants evicted from their holdings during the land agitation of the previous decade. It invoked the names of radical nationalists of the past such as Thomas Davis as its inspiration. In 1900 it absorbed the *Nation** and became the *Irish Independent and Daily Nation*. In 1904 it was bought by William Martin Murphy, later to become well known as the employers' leader in the Dublin lockout (1913), and was published from 2 January 1905 as the *Irish Independent*. **MJH**
Sources: Brown 1937, *Waterloo Irish.*

IRISH LIBERATOR (1863-1864) The *Irish Liberator* was one of series of short-lived weekly* journals addressed to post-famine Irish Catholic migrants to Britain. It was published in London from 3 October 1863, changed its name to the *National Liberator* in March 1864 and continued under that name until some time in July the same year when it folded. It was a political* journal, in its own words 'established by working men on principle, and by working men and principle it must stand or fall', the principle involved being the form of militant Irish nationalism known as Fenianism. It was the organ* in Britain of the National Brotherhood of Saint Patrick, an open cultural-cum-political organization which established an extensive network of branches in Britain and Ireland in the early to mid-1860s, holding lectures on historical and political subjects and reading from appropriate newspapers*. The NBSP was closely aligned with the secret Irish Republican (Fenian) Brotherhood. Many of those associated with the *Irish Liberator* were also, or became, Fenians. The NBSP had a sister paper in Dublin called the *United Irishman and Galway American*.

The *Irish Liberator's* first editor* was Denis Holland, who had previously owned and edited the *Irishman*, but he was quickly succeeded by David Bell, who had been a Presbyterian minister until he chose politics rather than religion and went on to become a leading political Fenian. He in turn was replaced by John Eugene O'Cavanagh, who had been associated with the London Catholic paper the *Universal News*. The paper, whose politics incorporated support for English radicals such as Richard Cobden as well as calls for Irish revolution, had a turbulent history characterized by internecine disputes and was eventually superseded by the Dublin *Irish People*. Some of those involved with the *Irish Liberator* and the NBSP, (Christopher Clinton Hoey* and J. P. McDonnell) went on to take over the *Universal News*, in 1867. **AMcN**
Sources: Bell 1968, Edwards and Storey 1985, McNicholas 2007.

IRISH LITERARY GAZETTE (1857-1861) The *Irish Literary Gazette*, began as a weekly* in August 1857, and became a monthly* from July 1858. Its initial intention to be a weekly journal of 'national literature, criticism, fiction, industry, science and art' recalled the (London-based) *Athenaeum*, though in November 1860 shortly before its demise it narrowed its purview to 'Literature, Science and the Arts', In its weekly format, it was issued on Saturdays and priced* 3d. In its monthly format*, adverts* survive in the 1861 volume in the NLI.

It was established with the express purpose of 'encouraging native talent and native literature of a high class', though its main sales pitch – stated in its third issue – was that Irish readers should support it 'in preference to the numerous periodicals necessarily imported from the other side of the Channel'. This was not an uncommon plea from Irish period-

ical publishers* but the *Irish Literary Gazette* was less successful than many of its contemporaries in including material of specifically Irish interest. In early volumes the 'Review'* section remained the main feature accompanied by smaller articles, stories* and miscellaneous vignettes. Some Irish interest material did appear, including accounts of the Irish flax industry (5 Sept. 1857) and an account of the mineral wealth of Ireland (14 Nov. 1857). One of the strongest Irish aspects of the content came in the form of topographical sketches, which included historical and descriptive accounts of Irish towns, with notices of geology and botany also common. From October 1857 many illustrations* within the text adorned these sketches and other content.

In later volumes the 'Review' department was replaced by a 'Literary Intelligence' column* as the opening section of the periodical, including gossip* and news* from Irish, British, European and American writers and publishers*. Lists of books recently published were also a staple feature, with segmented lists also often supplied for books recently published in Germany, France and America (e.g. Nov. 1860). In its final year the *Irish Literary Gazette* included a large amount of extracted material from other sources, though it made a point of acknowledging the authors. Prominent English authors whose work was regularly reprinted in its pages included John Hollingshed* on various literary topics, writer and critic William Michael Rossetti* on news* in the art world and George Walter Thornbury on eminent living artists. This shift in editorial policy led to a high standard of content with a wide variety of subjects and tastes catered for. The *Irish Literary Gazette* was successful in providing Irish material for some time but failed to distinguish itself as a specifically Irish literary periodical as it remained heavily reliant on reprinted texts from the major British titles of the day. **JCA**
Sources: au Casaide 1910, Clyde 2003, Hayley 1976, Hayley 1987, *ODNB*, *Waterloo Irish*.

***IRISH MONTHLY MAGAZINE* (1832-1834)** The *Irish Monthly Magazine* was a nationalist journal founded by the Irish Brigade, a splinter-group of the Comet Club, whose newspaper, the *Comet* attacked the tithe system and advocated the disestablishment of the Church of England in Ireland. Members of The Irish Brigade included the historian and journalist John Cornelius O'Callaghan and MP Maurice O'Connell, brother of Daniel O'Connell. They issued the *Irish Monthly Magazine* in May 1832, and later a newspaper, the *Repealer and Tradesman's Journal* (6 June 1832-18 May 1833). Lasting for 29 issues, the *Irish Monthly Magazine* was edited anonymously* by the club, including contributions from Daniel O'Connell, his eldest daughter Mrs Fitzsimmons and R. L. Sheil.

The stated aim of the *Magazine* was to provide a 'national vent' for Irish literary talents. Despite initial plans to eschew petty political controversies and partisan commentary, the magazine's content mirrored that of the *Comet* in its political* concerns. Its most radical content appeared in 1833, when it attacked restrictions on Catholics and the Act of Union; however, it always retained a miscellaneous mix of political, literary* and light material in the form of sketches, biographies, reviews*, extracts and poems*. The early issues of the *Irish Monthly Magazine* included material of Irish interest such as poems by 'Caorlan', 'Alfieri' or 'Conla', heroic legends and sketches and the serialization* of 'The Children of Usnach'. Original Irish literature was represented by Charles Lever* and Gerald Griffin in 1834, and articles relating to Irish literary figures such as William Carleton* ensured that the literary standard of the publication remained high throughout its lifetime. Other material of Irish interest appeared in the form of accounts such as 'Biographical account of the Dublin Magazine Periodicals who have lived and died since the union' (May 1832). The latter article was one of several interesting contemporary accounts of issues related to the Irish book trade dealing with government censorship*, and the copyright* laws in Ireland. **JCA**
Sources: Bowen 1942, Clyde 2003, Hayley 1976, Hayley 1987, Thuente 1994.

IRISH PEOPLE (1863-1865) The *Irish People*, launched in November 1863, was the Dublin journal of the Irish Republican Brotherhood, which sought to overthrow British rule in Ireland by force of arms. Its moving spirit was the 'Captain', James Stephens, but fellow 1848 veteran John O'Leary was the editor*, assisted by T. C. Luby, Charles J Kickham and Jeremiah O'Donovan Rossa. It was a foolhardy venture for a supposedly secret society, staffed by the leading members of the conspiracy and situated famously 'within a stone's throw of Dublin Castle', the British seat of power in Ireland. Inevitably the paper was suppressed on 15 September 1865 and those associated with it arrested and imprisoned, though Stephens himself later escaped. However, in its short existence it greatly increased the profile of the movement, outside Ireland as well as within. According to A. M. Sullivan of the *Nation**, who was no friend of the Fenians or their journal, 'it swept all before it amongst the Irish in England and Scotland'.

The *Irish People* was well written; Kickham and Luby were very able and O'Leary himself was a significant man of letters. Poetry* was a popular feature and R. D. Joyce, T. C. Irwin and John Francis O'Donnell all wrote for the paper. Women were well represented, including O'Leary's sister Ellen. His cousin Mary Kelly, Ellen Mary Downing (respectively known as 'Eva' and 'Mary' of the *Nation*), Parnell's teen-age sister Fanny and Mary O'Donovan Rossa also contributed.

Many of the liveliest controversies found in the pages of the *Irish People* were part of a conversation within Irish political* life, as much as between Ireland and Britain, as the IRB challenged both 'respectable' nationalism* as exemplified by the *Nation* and questioned the role of the Catholic Church in political life, leading its opponents to accuse it of being anti-religious. **AMcN**
Sources: Comerford 1985, McGee 2005, Sullivan 1877.

IRISH QUARTERLY REVIEW (1851-1860) The *Irish Quarterly Review* was a general-interest quarterly* periodical, published in Dublin by Catholic antiquarian bookseller W. B. Kelly, and owned and edited* by Patrick Joseph Murray. Its cover price* was 2s 6d, with annual subscriptions priced at 10s, or 12s by post. Octavo-sized*, it was wrapped in a brown paper cover, and contained eight pages of advertisements*, but no illustrations*.

The *Irish Quarterly Review* was inspired by the great London and Edinburgh quarterlies. It consisted mostly of long articles on general topics, many with Irish relevance, such as Irish politics*, literature*, and history. Literary reviews* were also prominent and carefully executed. Fiction by contrast was almost absent. Historian and archivist John Thomas Gilbert contributed an article on the 'Historical Literature of Ireland' in 1851, and another entitled 'Streets of Dublin' in 1852, which he later reworked in his *History of Dublin* (1861). **FB**
Sources: Clyde 2003, Hoey 1878, *ODNB*, *Waterloo*.

IRISH SOCIETY (1888-1924) *Irish Society* (1888-1901) was the leading journal of society and fashion* in Ireland. Appearing weekly* in an orange wrapper, it was published in Dublin and cost a penny. It included articles on fashion, gossip* about personalities, cookery, as well as short stories and serial* fiction. In 1901 it absorbed another Irish journal, *Social Review* (1893-1901) and became known as *Irish Society and Social Review* (1901-1924). Its first publisher* and printer was Robert Chapman, and its second Ernest Manico. Previous

to its acquisition, the *Social Review* had been published by R. J. Mecredy and S. Kyle. **FB**
Sources: Brown 1937, *Waterloo Irish*.

IRISH TIMES (1859-) The *Irish Times* was first published by Major Laurence E. Knox on 29 March 1859 as a political counter-weight to *Freeman's Journal*, its main competition* among the Dublin* newspapers. While aiming to be a national 1d daily* unionist* newspaper, its circulation was chiefly among the educated and influential. Claiming that politically it was independent and that its aim was to bring civilized, reasonable argument into Irish politics, its first leader asserted that 'As Irishmen we shall think and speak; but it shall be as Irishmen loyal to the British connection'.

The *Irish Times* was a conservative and unionist newspaper, though not without a liberal edge as it was in favour of extending the franchise 'to the more intelligent and well-conditioned portion of the working classes', of tenant right and of national education. As well as politics, its coverage included the arts, the Church of Ireland, the army and militia, and court affairs. Its perspective on the career of Parnell reveals something of its elitism, concluding that 'his errors were very great, and the injustice which he did to his own social class flagrant'. **MJH**
Sources: Brown 1937, *Waterloo Irish*.

IRISH TRIBUNE: AN IRISH NATIONAL JOURNAL FOR ENGLAND AND SCOTLAND. (1884-1897) The *Irish Tribune* was the first newspaper produced by the Catholic press baron and Irish nationalist MP Charles Diamond*. Launched on 13 December 1884 from Newcastle-upon-Tyne, it was an eight-page weekly*, with pages of five columns*. Its masthead* consisted of oversized Gothic for the main title, an ornament of an entwined shamrock and Irish harp, and a subtitle indicating its target readership*, the diaspora throughout England and Scotland. Priced* at just 1d, the *Tribune* was readily accessible and offered its readers a lively mixture of stirring political leaders*, Irish home news, 'Catholic intelligence', and British and American politics and literature. Diamond's debut editorial outlined the *Tribune's* mission 'to become the organ of Irish national thought in this country, to represent and possess the con– priest and laymen, labourers and merchants, rich and poor'. Diamond's proselytising agenda was conceived as a twin project to promote Irish nationalism and Roman Catholicism.

The *Tribune* was an instant success. Diamond claimed sales of 20,000 within the first few months and by the end of 1885 he was publishing separate and multiple* editions aimed at the major centres of Irish migration: Newcastle, Glasgow, Liverpool, Manchester and London. By 1886, the *Tribune* had expanded to 12 pages of newsprint and had an international circulation*. Diamond reproduced much of the news* content of the *Tribune* in other titles in his stable, notably the *Glasgow Observer*. In 1886 the *Tribune* claimed to reach an impressive 'four million Irish and Catholic people in England' and had become an effective tool for raising money for the Irish nationalist cause. The *Tribune* survived as an independent title until 1897 when it was absorbed into Diamond's nationally syndicated *Catholic Times*. **JA**
Sources: Allen 2005b, Allen 2007, Allen 2008, *DLB* 1987, Edwards 1979, Edwards and Storey 1985, *Waterloo Irish*.

IRVING, JOSEPH (1830-1891) Joseph Irving began a multi-faceted career as printer, journalist, compositor, editor*, bookseller* and publisher* in his birthplace, Dumfries. His first job was as an apprentice printer for the *Dumfries Standard*. Subsequently, he became a compositor and a journalist in Dumfries and Sunderland. He later moved to London where he was employed by the *Morning Chronicle and London Advertiser*. He returned to Scotland to became editor* of the *Dumbarton Herald* in 1854 and to start his own business as a bookseller* and publisher*. In 1867 he founded his own newspaper, the short-lived *Dumbarton Journal* (May-Nov. 1867). On the death of his wife in 1869, Irving left Dumbarton, eventually moving to Paisley where he contributed articles to the *Glasgow Herald* and other journals.

Irving was an excellent reviewer and had contributed a considerable number over the years. However, according to his obituary* in the *Lennox Herald*, Irving 'desired something more enduring than newspaper writing'(4) and became an authority on Scottish history, writing an 'exhaustive and reliable' *History of Dumbartonshire* (1857), which came to be regarded as the standard history of the county. In 1871 he published the first issue of *Annals of our Time*, which was reprinted periodically and augmented separately with a supplement* through 1897. *The West of Scotland in History* (1885) was a compilation of his journalism that had appeared in the *Glasgow Herald*. **DHL**
Sources: *Glasgow Herald* 1891, *Lennox Herald* 1891, *ODNB*, *Waterloo*, *Waterloo Scotland*.

ISIS. A LONDON WEEKLY PUBLICATION, EDITED BY A LADY (1832) Edited* (11 Feb.-15 Dec.) by the free thought lecturer Eliza Sharples*, the self-styled 'Lady of the Rotunda', this 6d weekly* was a quarto of 16 pages with double columns*. It marketed itself as unique in periodical history, with the 28-year-old Sharples claiming to be the first 'Editress'* of a publication peddling 'political*, moral, and philosophical instruction'. *Isis* successfully diffused Sharples' oral discourses on 'infidel' religion, female education and parliamentary reform, and these were bolstered by editorial attacks on the established radical demonology of 'kingcraft, lordcraft, and priestcraft'. Sharples was motivated by her desire to achieve 'female emancipation', dedicating the periodical to 'the young women of England', but her 500 or so subscribers were a non-specific audience of lower-middle reformers. This inability (or unwillingness) to carve out a female readership* was accompanied by a failure to penetrate to lower social levels, and plans to issue a 2d edition foundered.

Unadventurous in terms of format* and style, lacking illustrations* and relatively expensive, *Isis* was nonetheless notable for its highly original content, including poems*, book reviews*, essays and addresses, most of which were written by Sharples herself and engaged a range of anti-clerical, co-operative and radical political topics. *Isis* also offered its readers a series of letters from Sharples' paramour, the imprisoned radical pressman Richard Carlile*, and republished the lectures of Frances Wright and the 'infidel' preacher, Robert Taylor. Its continuities in content and argument with Carlile's periodical oeuvre located it in a decade-long tradition of free thought periodical literature, but *Isis* was significant as one of only a handful of journals edited by a woman in the early nineteenth century: its editorial voice was, therefore, almost unique. **DSM**

Sources: Harrison 1977, *Waterloo*.

ISSUING BODIES The confluence of mass literacy* and a massive newspaper and periodical press (more than 100 times the number and volume of printed books) both richly informed the broad populace of Great Britain and enabled social cohesion. Issuers of periodicals and newspapers brought state, church, business, trade and empire into the daily conversation of a large majority of the population. Issuing bodies generally represent smaller-scale social units established by more than 5,500 organizations across hundreds of subject areas. Here is a range from among those in the *Waterloo Directory* beginning with the letter 'D': the Dante Society; Davenport Academy of Natural Sciences; Devon and Cornwall Temperance League; Devon and Exeter Savings Bank; Devon Cattle Breeder's Society; Devon Congregational Union; Devon County Lunatic Asylum; Devon Longwoolled Sheep Breeders' Society; Derby Temperance Society; Devon and Exeter Architectural Society; Devon and Exeter Infant School Society; and the Devonshire Hospital and Buxton County Bath Charity. Scanning the issuing bodies listed in *Waterloo* suggests that more were concerned with social reform than with any other subject, and that in such cases cohesion has a moral more often than a monetary motive.

The press offered a voice, an identity and a means of developing a community of common interest to those who had the energy and funding to issue a publication. While larger bodies such as Cambridge University, a town council, or the Salvation Army, issued a variety of titles, in other cases a handful of students or sport fanciers put together a short-lived manuscript periodical. In each type, the requirements of regular frequency, of articulating purpose, defining audience and scope and the production of contributors provided self-affirmation, historical record, and a welcome to new adherents. Many issuing bodies provided annual reports containing executive and common membership lists, as well as details of finance and other activities. **JSN**

Source: *Waterloo*.

J

JACK AND JILL (1885-1887) *Jack and Jill; an Illustrated Weekly Journal for Boys and Girls* was the first comic specifically designed for children*. The ambitions of its proprietors* were clear at its launch, when the editor*, William Long, declared that 200,000 free copies had been distributed across the country, to popularize it in one fell swoop. The weekly*, heavily illustrated*, penny* journal offered 'high-class pictures and cheerful, wholesome literature', initially over eight pages (1885), eventually over 16 that same year and down to 12 in 1887, but apparently this was not enough to establish it, despite Edward Lear's presence on the back page. In May 1887, a title change* (to *Jack's Journal*) was announced. It was now no longer aimed squarely at children but carried the new subtitle *an Illustrated Weekly Miscellany for Everybody.* This strategy did not save it from meeting an early demise a month later. OD

Sources: Gifford 1976, *Waterloo.*

JACKSON, JOHN (1801-1848) One of the first generation of Bewick's pupils in wood* engraving, John Jackson, like so many other contemporary engravers, moved to London in 1824 at the end of his apprenticeship*. He quickly became locked into the dynamic network of contacts and collaborations that was driving the wood engraving trade into a central role in the development of print culture in the 1820s and 1830s.

Jackson worked with important engravers like William Harvey* and John Orrin Smith*, but it was his association with Charles Knight*, the publisher* for the Society for the Diffusion of Useful Knowledge*, that brought him into prominence. Among much other work for Knight, Jackson engraved frequently for the *Penny Magazine** from its inception in 1832, and was widely responsible for overseeing engravings for Knight's many other publications. Jackson's career, like that of his brother Mason Jackson* exemplifies the combined new role of engraver/entrepreneur/art director which was of central importance to the development of illustrated* periodicals and books in the 1830s and 1840s. Jackson also collaborated in the production of a *Treatise on Wood Engraving* with W. A. Chatto, published by Knight in 1839, with the costs mainly underwritten by Jackson. BM

Sources: Engen 1990, Houfe 1978, *ODNB.*

JACKSON, MASON (1819-1903) Two factors alone would justify Mason Jackson's place in the history of Victorian periodicals: after ten years of contributions as an engraver, he was appointed the art editor*(1860-1895) for the *Illustrated London News**. Secondly, in 1885, he published the *Pictorial Press: Its Origins and Progress*, the first extended study of the ways in which the development of mass* circulation* in the Victorian period had depended on its visual content.

These two emblematic achievements, however, need to be understood alongside Jackson's lengthy list of achievements as an engraver, which included a ten-year stint from 1850 as the principal engraver for the *Art Union of London,* early contributions to John Cassell's* innovative *Cassell's Illustrated Family Paper**, which combined the layout of a newspaper with the content of a magazine*, all at a remarkably low price*, and magazine work for eminent artists like John Gilbert* and Frederick Goodall. As with his brother John*, Mason's career suggests the importance of the engraver/entrepreneur to the development of early Victorian periodicals, not least for the long list of successful apprentices* that engravers like the Jacksons taught and then launched into artistic careers. BM

Sources: Engen 1990, Houfe 1978, *ODNB.*

JACKSON'S OXFORD JOURNAL (1753-1928) This weekly* paper was a Tory news sheet costing 2d when it was founded by the banker and Oxford University printer William Jackson (1724-1795), who had previously tried his hand at another weekly – the *Oxford Flying Weekly Journal and Cirencester Gazette* (1746-1748). Following his death in 1795, the paper – which remained Oxford's only newspaper until 1806 – was owned and edited by the physician John Grosvenor*.

In the early nineteenth century, like many regional papers of the time, *Jackson's Oxford Journal* engaged with local politics* and promoted local* interests, including those of the University, as well as providing its readers* with a regional angle on national and international news* stories. Sports* news, trade updates, advertisements*, information on agriculture and horticulture (including weather reports), lists of births deaths and marriages, with summaries of other notable local events that were often divided into subsections pertaining to the villages of Oxfordshire, also formed part of the paper. It maintained its broadly conservative stance, claiming on the occasion of its centenary in 1853 that its aim was 'to present a faithful mirror of the time, respecting the opinions of all, but at the same time cordially upholding all that we conceive to be dear to us as Englishmen, as lovers of order, and as faithful subjects'.

The price* rose to 5d in 1856, contrary to the general trend, falling again to 3d in 1882 when it hit a circulation* of 8,000. Towards the end of the century it began to cater increasingly for the women of Oxfordshire, including a regular 'Ladies' Letter', commencing in 1892, in which female correspondents* were invited to seek advice on 'dress, fashion*, the toilet, home decoration', advice duly dispensed by the paper's own 'Dorothy'. It was amalgamated with the *Oxfordshire County News* in 1898, renamed the *Oxford Journal Illustrated* in 1909, finally ceasing publication in 1928. **MaT**
Sources: 19CBLN, *Jackson's Oxford Journal* 1801-1899, *Waterloo*.

JAMES, HENRY (1843-1916) Renowned among readers of literature as a great novelist, Henry James was also deeply implicated in the nineteenth-century periodical press, as a versatile journalist in his early years, and as a literary* critic, travel writer and art and drama critic who brought a cosmopolitan outlook to bear on his work. Furthermore, his stories of the literary life are part of the cultural history of nineteenth-century publishing, that criticize its commercialization and consider its role in the public domain.

From 1864 to 1876, the year in which he took up permanent residence in England, James wrote primarily for the American periodical market. Important early articles on French and English literature appeared in the Boston-based monthly, the *Galaxy* countless reviews* appeared in the *Nation, North American Review* and the *Independent,* and his restless travels in Europe resulted in a large number of tales and travel pieces in the *Atlantic Monthly, Scribner's Monthly,* and the *Nation.* During this extended apprenticeship James became keenly sensitive to the dynamics of periodical publishing. He used the reviews to test the (middle-class*) market* for his fiction, but also grew suspicious as to its demand for 'newsy', 'gossipy'* journalism.

By 1876, James had developed a penchant for literary experiment in fiction and for subjective impressionism in criticism that may well have complicated his entry into the English publishing world, where he was still relatively unknown. His English launch was facilitated, however, by publisher Frederick Macmillan, who published *French Poets and Novelists* in February 1878, a collection of a dozen of his periodical reviews, despite the negative advice

of his reader John Morley*, and who ran 'Portrait of a Lady' in *Macmillan's Magazine* (Oct. 1880-Dec. 1881). George Smith* and Leslie Stephen* also helped, publishing 'Daisy Miller' (June-July 1978) and 'An International Episode' (Dec. 1878-Jan. 1879) in *Cornhill*. Meanwhile, 'The Europeans' was appearing serially in the *Atlantic Monthly* (July-Oct. 1878).

James's distaste for the periodical market became pronounced with the onset of the New Journalism* in the 1880s, but he continued to serialize* his fiction*, often catering for American and English journals simultaneously in an attempt to maximize serialization fees as well as the audiences he would reach. Criticism of overcommercialization and 'newspaperism', however, now grew conspicuous in his public utterances. In 1891 he asserted in the *New Review* that the practice of 'reviewing' in general 'has nothing in common with the art of criticism'. In the same vein he resisted paratextual* interference with his work (he was relieved to hear that his stories for the *Yellow Book** would not be illustrated*) and refused to give interviews*. What James called the 'age of trash triumphant' naturally entered his literary writings as well. His novel 'The Reverberator' in *Macmillan's Magazine** (1888)) and his stories for the *Yellow Book* ('The Death of the Lion', 'The Coxon Fund', 'The Next Time') in the 1890s thematized the New Journalism*, criticizing the way in which the mass media* encroached on people's privacy. However, 'The Art of Fiction' appeared in *Longman's Magazine* in 1884, and in 1900 he published eight separate titles in seven magazines. Even 'The Ambassadors' was serialized in the *North American Review* in 1903.

In Britain, James's journalism was collected additionally in *Partial Portraits* (1888), *Essays in London and Elsewhere* (1893) and *Notes on Novelists* (1914). In the United States it was collected in *The Art of Fiction* (1884) and *Views and Reviews* (1908). His pieces on visual artists and illustrators appeared as *Picture and Text* (1893). **MdW**
Sources: Brake 2001, Demoor 2004b, Edel and Laurence 1982, Fogel 1993, Freedman 1990, Moore 1993, Salmon 1997.

JAMESON, ANNA BROWNELL (1794-1860)
From the early 1820s, Anna Jameson (née Murphy) produced books and journalism covering a variety of genres*, but came to specialize in art criticism. Estranged early from her husband, she supported herself and various relatives through her writing, a recurrent theme of which is the nature, condition and potential of women. Jameson's first known

publication was a poem* 'Farewell to Italy', in the *London Magazine** for November 1822, later included in her first book, *The Diary of an Ennuyée* (1826). In the *New Monthly Magazine** for 1826 appeared her series 'The Windsor Beauties' and 'The Hampton Court Beauties', publicizing miniatures done by her father from Lely's paintings of seventeenth-century court beauties. To emphasize the scandalous aspects of the women's lives, Jameson adopted the persona of a gallant of the period; she modified her tone when adapting the series for a book published under her own name (1827).

She later wrote on miscellaneous artistic subjects for the *Monthly Chronicle** (1838-1839) and the *Art-Journal** (1849, 1850, 1852), and reviewed* a biography of B. R. Haydon (*Edinburgh Review** 1853), but her most significant periodical articles were for the *Penny Magazine** and the *Athenaeum**. For the first, she wrote, at £1 15s a page, a long series, 'Essays on the Lives of Italian Painters': 47 instalments (1843-1845), illustrated with woodcuts* by William Harvey and Harriet Clarke, and collected later as *Memoirs of the Early Italian Painters* (1845). Weekly* publication extended information not easily accessible elsewhere to a wide readership. In the *Athenaeum* (11 Jan. 1845-21 Feb. 1846) she published the first and most of the second volume of her most noteworthy work, *The Poetry of Sacred and Legendary Art* (5 vols.) a comprehensive 'guide to artistic representations of the sacred and legendary figures of Christianity' (Johnston: 183). The two serialized* volumes gave much attention to female saints and to Mary Magdalene. Also woman-centred was Jameson's *Athenaeum* article of 18 March 1843, its main emphasis being the need of middle-class women for paid employment. This was the last instance of Jameson's adopting a male persona, as the strategy offended both Harriet Martineau* and Lady Byron: the article was expanded for Jameson's *Memoirs and Essays Illustrative of Art, Literature and Social Morals* (1846), published under her own name. JCW

Sources: Holcomb 1983, Johnston 1997, Thomas 1967.

JEFFREY, FRANCIS (1773-1850) According to Walter Bagehot* in 1855, Francis Jeffrey 'invented the trade of editorship'. Before him, he insisted, 'an editor was a bookseller's drudge; he is now a distinguished functionary'. As one of three founders of the *Edinburgh Review** in 1802, Jeffrey was soon acknowledged as the de facto editor*. The crucial period in the history of the *Edinburgh* was the period of Jeffrey's editorship (1802-1829). Jeffrey had originally determined that the Review's ethos should be one of 'all gentlemen, and no pay'. Syd-

ney Smith*, one of the Review's co-founders, persuaded the publisher* Archibald Constable* that the editor as well as the contributors should be handsomely rewarded for their work. Jeffrey's editorial stipend rose from £200 to £700 during his tenure. Even the lower figure compared favourably with his earnings at the bar, which was the profession for which he had been trained.

Jeffrey wrote over 200 articles in the Review, on subjects ranging from biology, metaphysics, politics*, economics, history*, law* and biography, to the literary* criticism for which he became famous, if not notorious. There were acknowledged blind spots in his critical writing, the English 'Lake Poets', and Wordsworth in particular. His literary criticism was variously known as the 'beauty and blemish', the 'slashing' or 'damnatory' style of reviewing. His ruthlessness in revising the work of his colleagues, which Thomas Carlyle* once referred to as his 'light Editorial hacking and hewing to right and left' became part of the lore of nineteenth-century editing. But Jeffrey's most lasting achievement was to establish the *Edinburgh Review*'s cultural authority. Addressing its readers with a unified voice, its contributors adopted the corporate 'we' to which all, writing anonymously*, subscribed. It did not matter that within the *Review's* inner circles the authorship of many articles was a badly kept secret. Much of the political influence of the *Edinburgh* was mediated through Henry Brougham*, T. B. Macaulay and other eminent Whigs.

Jeffrey was assisted by William Empson*, later the review's editor, and by Macvey Napier* his immediate successor. But the architect of the *Edinburgh's* reputation in its period of greatest influence, between 1802 and 1830, when the Whigs came to power, was Jeffrey. He relinquished the editorship in 1829 on becoming Dean of the Faculty of Advocates, and later Lord Advocate. At his death in 1850, however, it was Francis Jeffrey, the reviewer and editor, rather than Lord Jeffrey, who was best remembered. He published four volumes of his contributions to the *Edinburgh* in 1844. JS

Sources: Bagehot 1855, Cockburn 1852, *ODNB*, Shattock 1989, Shattock 2007.

JENNINGS, LOUIS JOHN (1836-1893) The son of a London tailor, Louis Jennings, journalist, foreign* correspondent and editor*, started his career on provincial* newspapers in Derbyshire and Manchester. In 1854, he joined the Conservative *Morning Chronicle** under J. D. Cook*, and subsequently followed Cook to the *Saturday Review**. In 1863 he was engaged by *The Times** for a year to substitute for its correspondent in Calcutta, where he simultaneously edited the *Friend of India**, owned by Meredith Townsend. Jennings's graphic report of deaths under the Juggernaut was impressive, and on his return he was appointed *Times* correspondent in the United States, from June 1865.

Following the Civil War, *The Times*, which had supported the South, needed to mend fences. Jennings achieved this rapidly, not least with the help and guidance of Henry Raymond, founder of the *New York Times*. He reported extensively on the post-war South and on the Congressional debates on reconstruction; and secured an 'on-the-record' interview* with President Johnson. In 1867 he was recalled to assist with leader* writing (1867-1868). This was not a success, and when Raymond suddenly died in 1869, Jennings returned to take up a post with the *New York Times*. Within six months he had become editor, and achieved fame for bringing down the corrupt 'Boss' Tweed. In 1876, he failed in a bid to acquire the paper in collusion with supporters of President Grant, and returned to England, where he launched and edited the *Week* (1878-1879), a short-lived Saturday newspaper.

The remainder of his career was marked by variety, including journalism, scholarly editing and political work. Two tasks show his close relationship to the Tory *Quarterly Review*: his editorship of *The Croker Papers: the Correspondence and Diaries* of *J. W. Croker** (1885) and his publication there of over 30 political* articles. He also had a serialized* novel ('The Millionaire') in *Blackwood's Magazine* (1883), and an unhappy association, as MP for Stockport (1885-1893), with Lord Randolph Churchill. For a time he produced a weekly* 'London letter' for the *New York World*, owned by Jay Gould (the inspiration of the novel), and from 1889 edited a short-lived London edition of James Gordon Bennett's *New York Herald*. A champion of fair trade (protectionism) and 'Tory democracy', he was the author of several books. Jennings's transatlantic* career is testimony to the routine cross-fertilisation between British and American journalism in the period. **DIM**

Sources: Berger 1951, Morphet 2001, Morphet 2003, *ODNB*.

JERDAN, WILLIAM (1782-1869) Born in Scotland, William Jerdan, journalist and editor*, began his career in journalism in London in 1806 as a reporter, then editor, for the *Aurora*, an innkeepers' commercial newspaper. When this publication failed in 1807, Jerdan went to the *Pi-*

lot, an evening newspaper which had been founded that year. In 1808 he wrote editorials for the *Morning Post** and contributed to the *British Press* and the *Satirist, or Monthly Meteor**. He bought the copyright* of the latter from its previous owner and editor, George Manners. On 11 May 1813, Jerdan became editor of the *Sun,* a Tory newspaper. He left the post in 1817 after differences with the proprietor* John Taylor over editorial practices and ownership.

Jerdan then entered into his most important position – as editor of the *Literary Gazette**. He assumed this post in 1817, soon after after the founding of the journal, and remained until 1850. Slowly building up the journal, he supplemented his income from the *Gazette* by writing for provincial papers such as the *North Staffordshire Pottery Gazette* and the *Chelmsford Chronicle*. Apart from the *Literary Gazette* Jerdan edited the *Sheffield Mercury* and provided editorial features for other provincial* papers. In 1830 he helped to start and edit the *Foreign Literary Gazette* which was unsuccessful and ceased after 13 issues. Under the pseudonym* of 'Bushey Heath' he contributed for many years to *Notes and Queries**, as well as to *Fraser's** and the *Gentleman's Magazine**. Jerdan was also founder of the Royal Society of Literature in 1823. In 1826 he was elected a Fellow of the Royal Society of Antiquaries. He twice survived destitution, with the crash of Whitehead's Bank, and then in the panic of 1826. **DHL**

Sources: Graham 1930, Griffiths 1992, Jerdan 1852-1853, *ODNB*

JEROME, JEROME K. (1859-1927) Jerome K. (Klapka) Jerome was an actor before becoming a journalist and novelist. His first book, *On the Stage – and Off* (1885) was followed by *The Idle Thoughts of an Idle Fellow* (1886) and the classic *Three Men in a Boat* (1889). As a dramatist he was best known for 'The Passing of the Third Floor Back', a play (1910) developed from one of his short stories (1907). In 1892, the *Idler**, a 6d monthly, was founded by Jerome in partnership with Robert Barr and George Brown Burgin. Jerome was co-editor of the *Idler*, an illustrated* monthly, with Barr and was sole editor from 1895 to 1897. In 1893 he founded an illustrated literary* weekly*, *To-Day**. An 1893 advertisement in *Debrett's* for the *Idler* boasted that it contained 'The Best Work of the Best Writers and the Best Artists', in its '120 pages* 100 illustrations*' with contributors that included among others, Besant*, Zangwill*, and Conan Doyle.

Weekly teas at the *Idler* brought together both men and women* authors and the periodical's 'My

People I Have Never Met.

BY SCOTT RANKIN.

JEROME K. JEROME.

" Humour is not so much a peculiar way of looking at life, as of expressing what one sees and knows of life. Humourists see as clearly as anyone, and perhaps more clearly than many, the deep, true side of human life."

Figure 31: A cartoon of Jerome K. Jerome which appeared in the journal he edited himself, the *Idler* Jan. 1893:100.

First Book' series gave them a chance to recount their early years as writers. However, the loss of £9,000 to a libel action in 1897 in connection with *To-day* forced him to sell his share in both magazines. Twenty years later, Jerome revived *To-day* in the form of a monthly literary magazine which he edited himself (1817-1924). **FN**

Sources: *CBEL,* Connolly 1982, Humpherys 2005, *ODNB, The Times* 1927, Waller 2006.

JERROLD, (WILLIAM) BLANCHARD (1826-1884) Blanchard Jerrold was the oldest son of Douglas Jerrold*. Educated in London and Boulogne, in 1846 he joined the reporting staff of the newlyfounded *Daily News** and contributed a series of articles on 'The literature of the poor'. He wrote also for the *Illustrated London News**, the *Athenaeum** and *Douglas Jerrold's Weekly Newspaper**. Among his more notable contribution to the last-named was a series on emigration, 'The old woman who lived in a shoe'. In 1847 he married the daughter of his godfather Samuel Laman Blanchard*. Over the next decade he was a miscellaneous writer (novels, guidebooks, one travel book) and journal-

ist, contributing regularly to Dickens's* *Household Words**. In London he belonged to a set of *bon vivant* bohemian journalists including George Augustus Sala* and Peter Cunningham* which was much sneered at by the *Punch** staffers.

From the mid-1850s Jerrold lived much in Paris and published books and articles on various aspects of French life and culture. When his father died in 1857, Jerrold succeeded him as editor* of *Lloyd's Weekly Newspaper**, retaining this post until his own death, and maintaining the paper's strongly pro-Liberal stance. In the 1860s he began writing on gastronomic topics under the penname of 'Finbec' and in 1871 established a monthly* periodical called the *Knife and Fork* which became a 2d weekly* before ceasing publication in 1872. He also published* a series of pamphlets called *The Best of All Good Company* (1871-1873), each instalment describing an imaginary day spent with a famous author such as Dickens or Bulwer Lytton*.

Jerrold was friends with the French artist Gustave Doré* and in 1870-71 the two men collaborated on a travel book* *London: a Pilgrimage*, published first in monthly parts and then in volume form. Doré's powerful images of Victorian London have ensured that this work remains in print. **MS**
Sources: *ODNB,* Slater 2002.

JERROLD, DOUGLAS WILLIAM (1803-1857) Douglas Jerrold, journalist, editor* and dramatist was born into a family of strolling players. In 1813 he entered the Royal Navy as 'a volunteer of the first class' (equivalent to midshipman) and in 1815 served on a brig ferrying wounded soldiers back to England. This gave him a lasting horror of so-called 'military glory', just as seeing the brutalities of naval discipline made him a lifelong opponent of corporal, as well as capital, punishment and a champion of the ordinary British seaman, whom he saw very much in an heroic light. He left the Navy in 1815 to support his family and worked as a printer's apprentice in London. A worshipper of Shakespeare, he was ambitious to contribute to England's dramatic literature and began, in the early 1820s, writing farces and melodramas for the minor theatres. He also began his journalistic career, contributing dramatic criticism to the *Sunday Monitor**, the *Weekly Times** and the *Mirror of the Stage**.

In 1826 Jerrold started to contribute to the *Monthly Magazine**, then in 1829 scored an immense success with a nautical melodrama *Black Eyed Susan*'at the Surrey Theatre. It ran for 300 nights and was pirated by almost every other theatre in Britain for the rest of the century but earned Jerrold only £60 since dramatists had no copyright* protection and the royalty system did not yet exist. Despite the poor financial rewards he wrote many more plays over the next 20 years, graduating to the legitimate drama with five-act 'witty' comedies but, despite an occasional *succès d'estime*, had to rely upon journalism for his main income. He married young and had five children, one of whom married Henry Mayhew*.

Jerrold specialized as a journalist in satirical* sketches of occupational or social types, moral fables and anecdotes illustrative of human folly. He wrote for numerous journals, notably *Blackwood's* and the *New Monthly*, contributing to the latter under the name of 'Henry Brownrigg'. The appearance of *Punch* (1841) gave him an ideal outlet for his particular brand of Radical satirical journalism and he wrote regularly for the paper from its second number until his death. His 'Q papers', which were in effect *Punch* leaders*, were strongly Radical and he was accused of 'bitterness' (his *Punch* colleague Thackeray* once called him a 'savage little Robespierre'), but his most popular contributions, somewhat to his chagrin, were the comic 'Mrs Caudle's Curtain Lectures' (1845). In the 1850s, after Thackeray* became more dominant on the *Punch* team, the journal's Radical stance was much modified.

Jerrold was a close friend of Dickens* and wrote leaders for the *Daily News* under Dickens's brief editorship in 1846. His first venture into running a journal of his own was the short-lived monthly the *Illuminated Magazine*, financed by Herbert Ingram* and illustrated* by Kenny Meadows* and others. It was succeeded by another monthly*, *Douglas Jerrold's Shilling Magazine* and by *Douglas Jerrold's Weekly Newspaper*. In 1852 he was appointed by Edward Lloyd* to the editorship of *Lloyd's Weekly Newspaper* at a salary of £1,000, retaining this post until his early death when he was succeeded by his eldest son Blanchard Jerrold*. **MS**
Source: Slater 2002.

JEUNE, SUSAN MARY ELIZABETH (C.1849-1931) Born into an aristocratic Scottish family, Jeune used two signatures in her journalism, Lady Jeune or Mary Jeune. Socially known as Baroness St Helier (née Stewart-Mackenzie), Jeune was a society hostess with celebrity* guests, and a dedicated member of the London County Council; her journalism mirrored the three strands of her life.

On a suffrage committee with Millicent Fawcett*, she wrote articles analysing women's lives, such as 'A Century of Women' in the *Anglo-Saxon Review* (1900) or, reflecting the new freedoms, 'Cycling for Women' in the *Badminton Magazine of Sports and Pastimes* (1895). Others were co-written, including an item on marriage with Mary Braddon* *et al.* for the *Idler* (1896). Pieces on social issues, as in 'Saving the Innocents'(1885) and 'The Homes of the Poor' (1890) for the *Fortnightly Review*, contrasted with work reflecting her social position as Baroness St Helier, as did 'Conversation in Society' (1894) in the *English Illustrated Magazine*. A collection on social issues was published as 'Lesser Questions' in 1894; she was vice-president of the Women Writers' Club* and in 1925 awarded a DBE. **CL**
Sources: BritPer online, St Helier 1909, *Wellesley*, Wharton 1987.

JEWELLER AND METALWORKER: A FORTNIGHTLY REVIEW OF THE WATCHMAKING AND GOLD AND SILVERSMITH TRADES (1873-1972) The *Jeweller and Metalworker*, founded by William Allen, was an eight-page penny* fortnightly trade* journal intended to keep 'jewellers, watchmakers, goldsmiths and silversmiths' (and opticians) up to date with new developments in their fields and exchange information about available jobs and businesses for sale. While illustrations* appear in advertisements* from the first issue, the periodical itself was largely unillustrated, in keeping with its serious tone until the mid-1890s, when conversational pieces start to appear.

Although sales figures are lacking, its success can be gauged by how the price* of advertisements listed on the first page rose in line with the increased number of advertisements: a line cost 3d at first, but by May 1875 it cost 6d; soon thereafter prices are no longer listed though the number of advertisements continued to increase until around 1900 when they almost overwhelmed the text. The format* was never fixed, comprising a mixture of series on various topics (e.g. 'The International Inventions Exhibition' 1885, 'Practical Helps on Optics' 1895, 'Art Enamelling Upon Metals' by Henry Hardinge Cunyngham (1900) and individual items reporting new technologies or meetings of national associations of the relevant trades. There were occasional attempts to create regular departments such as 'Legal Notes and Queries' (which a qualified solicitor dealt with from May 1895), but these never lasted long. Recurrent, if irregular, features comprised lists of bankruptcies, patents, accounts of shoplifting and how to stop it (the use of mirrors in shops is advocated, for example), changes in fashion, and new methods of shop display. **AK**
Sources: *Jeweller and Metalworker* 1873-1900, *Mitchell's*.

JEWISH PERIODICALS One of the first pieces of Jewish journalism to emerge in Britain was the *Hebrew Intelligencer*, a short-lived monthly* publication (1823), priced* 6d. In 1834, the monthly *Hebrew Review and Magazine of Rabbinical Literature* appeared at the same price and was published regularly for three years. The reduction of Stamp Duty* in 1836 and developments within the Jewish community led to the emergence of two more significant Jewish publications in the 1840s, the *Voice of Jacob* (1841-1848, fortnightly) and the *Jewish Chronicle* (Nov. 1841-present). Difficulties following the launch of the *Jewish Chronicle* led to a break in publication from 1842-1844; it started again in 1844 on a fortnightly basis before being issued weekly* from 1847.

The success of the *Jewish Chronicle* invited competition, and a 1d weekly, the *Jewish Record*, appeared in 1868, causing the *Jewish Chronicle* to adapt and make changes. In addition to a new format* of the Third edition of the *Jewish Chronicle*, a 1d edition of the paper was launched, in an effort to win back readers who had moved their allegiance to the *Jewish Record*. The willingness of successive editors* of the *Jewish Chronicle* to adapt to commercial and cultural changes helped the paper fend off subsequent rivals, such as the *Jewish World* (1873), and remain the dominant organ of Jewish thought in Britain. Despite the success and influence of the *Jewish Chronicle*, it was far from being the only Jewish periodical of the nineteenth century. Others included the *Jewish Quarterly Review* (1888), the *Jewish Standard: the English Organ of Orthodoxy* (1888), the *Jewish Year Book* (1896) and the monthly children's* magazine, *Young Israel* (1897). **MK**

Sources: Altholz 1989, *Jewish Chronicle*.

JEWSBURY, GERALDINE ENDSOR (1812-1880) In a long career reviewing* for the *Athenaeum*￼ and working as publisher's reader, Geraldine Jewsbury exercised considerable influence over the fiction market. She had already written for *Douglas Jerrold's Shilling Magazine*￼ and published two novels, including her bestknown, *The Half-Sisters,* when Dickens* invited her to contribute 'papers or short stories' to *Household Words*￼. In her early periodical writing Jewsbury, like her elder sister Maria*, demonstrated independence of mind. Some of her social articles for Jerrold were overtly feminist, and her 'Religious faith and modern scepticism' (*Westminster Review*￼ 52, January 1850) reflected her personal religious struggles.

Her most significant journalistic contribution was as a critic. She wrote some 2,300 reviews*, mainly for the *Athenaeum,* under the various titles 'New Novels', 'Novels of the Week' and 'Our Library Table', sometimes contributing an entire section*. She sought psychological realism, and credible plots, occasionally expressing her contempt for weak fiction by revealing the ending. She deplored the moral ambiguity she found in Florence Maryatt's *Woman Against Woman* (*Athenaeum,* 17 Feb. 1866) and savaged Rhoda Broughton's lack of reticence in *Cometh Up as a Flower,* but could also be generous in her praise. Towards the end of her life, however, she was largely restricted to 'Christmas Books' and 'Books for Children'. She contributed to other journals, including the *Ladies' Companion at Home and Abroad*￼, the *New Monthly Belle Assemblée* and Anna Maria Hall's* *Juvenile Budget.*

Jewsbury was also a professional publisher's reader, first for Hurst & Blackett, and from 1858-1880 for Bentley & Sons*. **BMO**

Sources: Fryckstedt 1983, Ireland 1892, *ODNB*, Onslow 2000.

JEWSBURY, MARIA JANE (1800-1833) Maria Jane Jewsbury (later Fletcher) published her first poem* at 17 in the *Coventry Herald* (spring 1818), and contributed to the *Manchester Gazette* from 1821. Her book publications comprised a miscellany of poetry and prose, *Phantasmagoria* (2 vols, 1825), epistolary exhortations to piety (*Letters to the Young*, 1828), further poetry (*Lays of Leisure Hours*, 1829) and novellas (*The Three Histories*, 1830). She was also a prolific contributor (over 70 pieces) to the Annuals* of the 1820s and 1830s – some of her *Lays* first saw light there. Jewsbury's most significant achievement, however, was her many contributions to the *Athenaeum*￼ in 1830-1833.

For Jewsbury, anonymity* enabled a variety of authorial personae, while assuaging her self-doubt over overt female authorial ambition. In her *Athenaeum* writing, Jewsbury was analytical, sometimes satirical* and occasionally overtly masculine. One of the writers recruited by new editor Charles W. Dilke* in 1830, she reviewed* many books – poetry, fiction, memoirs and histories, conduct literature, writing for children. Many of her subjects were ephemeral, but they included Wordsworth, Ebenezer Elliott* and the controversial P. B. Shelley, whose work she defended. Particularly valuable is her treatment of women's writing and women's education. Her article on Jane Austen (27 Aug. 1831) is the first commentary on the novelist attributable to a woman, and the first to identify a discrepancy between the voice of the novels and the version of Austen offered by her family. Other notable literary* commentaries treat Jewsbury's close friend Felicia Hemans, where Jewsbury strives to define the specific qualities of men's and women's poetry (12 Feb. 1831), and Joanna Baillie (28 May 1831), where she highlights the 'power of mind' of Baillie and her contemporaries Elizabeth Inchbald, Ann Radcliffe and Mary Wollstonecraft. In her four articles 'On Modern Female Cultivation' (4, 11 and 25 Feb., 11 Aug. 1832), Jewsbury castigates male resistance to letting women develop vigorous and autonomous intellects. After marrying in August 1832 William Kew Fletcher, chaplain to the East India Company, she accompanied him to India, and sent to the *Athenaeum* extracts from her journal, plus the best poetry of her career, all published from December 1832 to December 1833. But Jewsbury herself died of cholera at Poona on 4 October 1833. JCW

Sources: Armstrong and Bristow 1996, Boyle 1967, Clarke 1990, Fryckstedt 1983-5, Marchand 1941, Ross 1989, Wilkes 2000, Wolfson 2006.

JOCKEY (1890-1914, 1919-1956)

The *Jockey* started as a penny* weekly* providing race reports, regional training reports, lists detailing the age, weight and form of horses entered in forthcoming races, guides to the odds on offer there and – perhaps most importantly for the punters who read it – expert tips. 'Art Notes', which often focused on equestrian portraiture and other sporting subjects, were included and there was also a section entitled 'Theatrical and Musical* Notes' that departed from the sporting* theme to provide information on upcoming concerts and productions and to convey theatrical gossip*. Advertisements* for a wide variety of products and services (including foodstuffs, household goods, medicaments, tailors, hotels, as well as a few items directly related to horses or horse racing) offered guidance to readers in the expenditure of their winnings. The *Jockey* quickly established itself as a broadsheet of four pages published on Saturdays. A Monday evening edition of four much smaller pages was available to subscribers at the higher price* of 1s, containing updated information on late entries, form, odds and conditions.

The paper's pundit-in-chief throughout the 1890s was known as 'The Admiral', and he seems to have had a reputation among the gambling public that preceded the first issue of the *Jockey*, where he bragged that 'I am pleased to be able to add an-

other winner [sic.] of a big event to the many I have already prognosticated'. That he was seen as a key asset of the paper is confirmed by its frequent assertions that he wrote 'for "The Jockey" only', and indeed in the paper's first year of publication one finds the repeated insistence that the Admiral 'has no connection whatever with any other person or paper using the same nom-de-plume', suggesting that a rival paper was attempting underhandedly to capitalize on the success of his prognostications. 'The Admiral's' most up-to-date tips were sent out by telegram* on the morning of the race to those who subscribed to this special service, which cost 10s per week in 1897. At this time there was also a weekly competition, where readers could fill in a coupon naming five horses. The first selection was free, but readers had to enclose a 1d stamp for every subsequent one: the prizes were an impressive £50 for picking four winners, and £100 for all five. The paper suspended publication at the beginning of the First World War in 1914, resuming again in 1919 after the suspension of hostilities. MaT

Source: *Waterloo.*

JOHN BULL (1820-1892)

A Conservative, anti-Catholic weekly of eight pages, *John Bull: For God, the King and the People* (1820-1837), was founded by Theodore Hook*. From 1837, when Victoria took the throne, the subtitle of the journal was adjusted to her gender by substituting the word 'Sovereign' for 'King': *John Bull: For God, the Sovereign and the People* (1837-1892). Its title was derived from a ruddy-faced personification of England that made its first appearance in a 1712 satire* by John Arbuthnot. Hook was also its editor* and principal contributor, and although he made strenuous efforts to maintain his anonymity* he was ultimately unsuccessful. The paper, initially costing 7d and later dropping to 6d, achieved an impressive circulation* of 10,000 within six weeks. While most of the press disapproved of the King's attempts to divorce Queen Caroline, *John Bull* backed the King, and its invective against his wife was a major selling point. It copied the *Courier* (1804-1842) in printing the names of ladies who called on the Queen, along with disparaging remarks: the flow of visitors soon dried up.

Queen Caroline's death in 1821 was reported with only the trappings of respect for the 'royal corpse'. Now that his principal enemy had 'paid the debt of nature', Hook diverted his attention to smearing prominent Whigs and Radicals. Joseph Hume (1777-1855) and William Hazlitt* came in for particularly savage attacks; indeed, it was *John*

Bull that first revealed that Hazlitt's *Liber Amoris* (published May 1823) was based on his affair with his landlord's daughter. Hook even managed to acquire – and print (22 June 1823) – a letter Hazlitt had sent to his lover.

As the paper toned down its vituperative approach to politics*, so its circulation and reputation declined. Hook began to focus on his novels and allowed others – among them his brother Dr John Hook, Thomas H. Bailey (1785-1856), Richard Dalton Barnham and Samuel Carter Hall* – to run the paper. Now relatively moderate – though it retained its allegiances to conservatism and Protestantism – *John Bull's* circulation was down to 1,600 in 1855, and 3,000 in 1870, eventually halting publication in 1892. **MaT**

Sources: BL Catalogue, *ODNB*, Sullivan, *Waterloo.*

JOHN MURRAY PUBLISHERS (1768-) The firm of John Murray was associated over its long life with two important nineteenth-century reviews, the *Edinburgh** and the *Quarterly**. It published other titles for shorter periods, such as the *Academy**, and attempted a short-lived house magazine*, *Murray's Magazine.*

Beginning as a bookseller and publisher* in 1768, John Murray I (1745-1793), had moved from Edinburgh to London to set up business as a bookseller. He became famous for editing* the *English Review* (1783-1797) which merged* with Joseph Johnson's *Analytical Review**. In 1803, John Murray II (1778-1843) became the Edinburgh publisher, Archibald Constable's London agent, taking over the London agency of the *Edinburgh Review** from Longman's. In 1809 together with George Canning and Walter Scott*, Murray launched the *Quarterly Review** with William Gifford* as its editor. This move proved the beginning of a remarkable series of publishing successes, which included the association with Byron, whose *Childe Harold* (1812) and other poetic works brought fame and fortune to the firm. Murray also published four of Jane Austen's novels. In addition to the *Quarterly*, Murray issued the *Journal of Science and the Arts* (1816-1819) for the Royal Institution, and the annual* *Admiralty*, thereafter the *Navy List* (1814-1964) and other annuals on diverse subjects. Murray took on William Blackwood* in 1814 as his Edinburgh agent, as they were both eager to share in the business of publishing the works of Walter Scott*. Although Murray tried his hand at publishing a daily* newspaper in 1826 (Jan.-July), with the youthful Benjamin Disraeli as its editor, the *Representative*, proved an expensive disappointment.

John Murray III (1808-92) was responsible for publishing the famous *Handbooks for Travellers*, the first of which was published in 1836. The firm's success continued to grow with the publication in 1859 of two best-sellers simultaneously, Charles Darwin's *The Origin of Species* and Samuel Smile's *Self-Help*. Murray also bought all the remaindered sheets and unpublished papers of the *Voyage of the Beagle* (1839), and the firm became the sole publisher of Darwin's books. Murray's ambition was to establish a periodical and in 1869 he financed a monthly literary* journal, the *Academy*, but after a year he withdrew as its editor refused to make the tone more accessible as Murray suggested. He achieved this style with his new 1887 journal, *Murray's Magazine,* which included serial* fiction; nevertheless it folded in 1891.

John Murray IV (1851-1928) assisted with the editing of the *Quarterly Review* as part of his apprenticeship, becoming a partner in 1878. He was also involved in setting up the Publishers' Association*, acting as president in 1899. In 1895 he published Prothero's edition of Byron, followed by the official nine-volume edition of Queen Victoria's letters, completed under the supervision of John Murray V (1884-1967) in 1932. These acquisitions were effective in making John Murray one of the most venerable publishing houses of its day. In 2002 John Murray was sold, but the imprint remains as a division of its new owner, Hodder Headline. **SGS**

Sources: *ODNB, Wellesley.*

JOHNSON, JAMES (1777-1845) A farmer's son from Northern Ireland, Johnson (originally Johnstone), a medical* journalist and editor*, joined the navy and worked as a surgeon's mate during the Napoleonic wars. Having taken up general practice in Plymouth, Johnson, working with Shirley Palmer and William Shearman launched the monthly *Medico-Chirurgical Journal* in 1816. He soon moved to London and established a private practice, and by 1818 he was both sole editor and proprietor* of the publication, changing its title to the *Medico-Chirurgical Review**. Johnson kept its costs down by producing the majority of the content himself, writing especially on his specialisms of public health and tropical medicine, and gained a considerable readership* with an American reprint published by R. & G. S. Wood of New York. He also contributed occasional articles on medical topics to general periodicals like the *Metropolitan Magazine** and the *New Monthly Magazine**, for which he briefly wrote a 'Medical Miscellanies' column* during 1818.

In 1836, however, the emergence of a rival publication, John Forbes's* *British and Foreign Medical Review*, led to a decline in the *Medico-Chirurgical Review*'s circulation*. Eventually Johnson's son, Henry James Johnson, also a doctor, became assistant editor of the *Review*. When Johnson retired from editing in 1844, Gavin Milroy became chief editor, and in 1848 Forbes's and Johnson's publications merged* to form the *British and Foreign Medico-Chirurgical Review*. CL

Sources: Johnson 1818, *ODNB*.

JOHNSON, THOMAS BURGELAND (C. 1778-1840) Thomas Burgeland Johnson was a printer, publisher* and distinguished writer on field sports*, whose career was dogged by ill-luck. He began his career as a printer in Liverpool. Using various pseudonyms* he published books on hunting dogs, guns and field sports throughout his life including, *The Shooter's Guide* (Liverpool 1809, by 'B. Thomas'), *The Complete Sportsman* (Liverpool 1817, by 'T H Needham'), *The Shooter's Companion* (Liverpool 1819, signed) and *The Hunting Directory* (London, 1826, signed). In the early 1820s, he was publisher, and printer of drama and entertainment titles such as the *Liverpool Theatrical Investigator and Review of Amusements,* which he also edited*; beginning as a daily* in 1821, the *Theatrical Investigator* became a weekly* in 1822, and collapsed later that year; additionally he printed and published the 2d weekly, the *Censor; or Review of Public Amusements in Liverpool* (Dec. 1821-Feb. 1822). In 1832, still in Liverpool, he tried his hand at the *Liverpool Examiner,* a monthly magazine, and the *Voice of the Country and General Provincial Politician,* another monthly. In 1831 he had published his most successful work, *The Sportsman's Cyclopedia,* which success led him to launch a journal, the *Sportsman's Cabinet and Town and Country Magazine.* This lasted for only 12 issues (Nov. 1832-Oct. 1833) and, having lost money through the failure of the magazine, Johnson moved to London. In an attempt to improve his prospects he published his last work, *Physiological Observations on Mental Susceptability* (1837), a mixture of anecdotes, quack science and chauvinism. Johnson died of consumption. Despite his talents as a sports and hunting journalist he was allegedly 'a difficult man, disappointed, cranky, vain, envious and ill-tempered' (Higginson: 33-34). DHL

Sources: *Gentleman's Magazine* 1841, Higginson 1951, *ODNB, Waterloo.*

JOHNSTONE, ARTHUR G. W. (1861-1904) As chief music* critic of the *Manchester Guardian** (1896-1904), Johnstone moulded British musical taste and shaped the national music canon. Educated at Oxford University and the Cologne Conservatorium, Johnstone was a modern and a liberal who, having been headhunted by C. P. Scott* brought a radicalism, intellectual breadth and vigour to the *Guardian*'s music coverage. Central to his journalism* was his support for the work of the Hallé Orchestra. As for Continental music, Johnstone was a 'progressive' who promoted the music of Berlioz ('the Columbus of music'), Wagner and especially Listz ('a master of life'). Among contemporary composers he advanced the work of Richard Strauss, whom he regarded as a 'great and typical modern'. Regarding British music, Johnstone considered Hubert Parry and Charles Stanford, the acknowledged pillars of the national 'musical renaissance', as worthy academics out of touch with the latest developments. In contrast, he judged Edward Elgar, whom he came to know personally, to be a 'thoroughly modern composer' and *the* key figure for the future of British music. Accordingly, he promoted a succession of new Elgar works in his columns*, *The Dream of Gerontius* especially benefiting from his advocacy.

Johnstone's importance to British music and journalism lay in the quality of his questing, informative reviews*, his championing of Elgar, and in his services to the Hallé and musical life of the north. Elgar, for his part, deemed Johnstone to be 'the best critic we have ever had'. MH

Sources: Elgar and Young 1965, Hughes 2002, Kennedy 1960, Reece and Elton 1905.

JOHNSTONE, CHRISTIAN ISOBEL (1781-1857) As a journalist and writer Christian Isobel Johnstone is an important but under-rated figure in the annals of nineteenth-century journalism. Her work as editor* and journalist on the monthly* *Tait's Edinburgh Magazine** accounts for that journal's steady success across a 12-year period, (1834-1846). Few, if any, women were editing a major journal for such a long time. Though politically radical herself, it was Johnstone's literary skills which toned down William Tait's* more aggressive editorial voice.

Her apprenticeship as editor* and journalist had been served in earlier newspaper and journal publishing ventures with her husband, John Johnstone (1779-1857), a teacher in Dunfermline who became a printer and the founder of the *Schoolmaster and Edinburgh Magazine* (1832-1834). Christian Johnson wrote most of the content of that magazine, later retitled *Johnstone's Edinburgh Magazine,* until it was incorporated with *Tait's* in June 1834 when she became its 'working editor'. Johnstone's most obvious political* impact, however, was the space accorded both to women journalists, and to reviews* of women's publications. She was not afraid to take up the cudgels on women's behalf either. In a piece on Captain Marryat's *Diary in America* (1839), using the editorial and ungendered 'we', she indicates scepticism regarding some of his pronouncements on women and quietly points out that other travellers, Anna Jameson* and Harriet Martineau*, have preceded him in his travels and that his rhapsodies over the Great Lakes can be verified by them.

In 1893 James Bertram* published his memoirs which included his working on *Tait's*. Johnstone was paid, says Bertram, £20 a month and he describes her as the journal's 'working genius', praising her reviews of 'important new books' as 'admirable' and declaring that her work brought prestige to *Tait's*. JEJ
Sources: Bertram 1893, *CBEL*, *ODNB*, *Wellesley.*

JONES, ALICE GRAY (1852-1943)   Editor*, temperance* activist, children's author and headmistress, Alice Jones (née Jones) became headmistress of her old school before marrying in 1881. However, her marriage did not restrict her public activity as a lecturer and organizer for the North Wales Women's Temperance Union (UDMGC). Using the pseudonym* of 'Ceridwen Peris', she began her writing career in 1874 by publishing her poetry, but by 1880 her work had appeared in several secular and religious* Welsh* periodicals, for adults and children, including Sarah Rees's* *Y Frythones.*

From October 1896 Jones became the editor* of a new magazine, *Y Gymraes* (the *Welshwoman*), an illustrated* non-denominational monthly* which by 1901 she had opportunely negotiated into becoming the official magazine for the UDMGC, ensuring a circulation* of 2,400 for Union branches. But Jones also ran features on biographies of Welsh women, present and past, advocated public roles for women, encouraged women's education, supported women's suffrage and largely encouraged women to contribute to the magazine. Jones was succeeded as editor by Mair Ogwen and *Y Gymraes* continued publication until 1934. AGJ/CL
Sources: Lloyd-Morgan 2004, Welsh Biography Online, *Y Goleuad* 1943.

JONES, STEPHEN (1763-1827)   Stephen Jones, printer and editor*, left home after quarrelling with his family and became a Fetter Lane printer's apprentice* in 1775. Subsequently he was employed by Thomas Wright as a journeyman press corrector and reader. On the death of Wright in March 1797, Jones took over as editor of the *White-*

hall *Evening Post.* After this paper closed in 1801, Jones moved to the *General Evening Post* (1801-1822) where he became manager and joint proprietor*. When it merged* with Charles Baldwin's* *St. James's Chronicle* in 1822, Jones went on to edit the *Spirit of Public Journals* (1797-1825), which was an annual* compilation of the best stories and articles from leading newspapers.

From 1807 Jones edited the *European Magazine* and, as an enthusiastic Freemason, the *Freemasons Magazine.* Among his literary works, Jones's most important achievement was the updated edition of the *Biographica Dramatica,* published in 1812, which gave details of British and Irish dramatists. DHL
Sources: BL Catalogue, Griffiths 1992, *Waterloo.*

JONES, WILLIAM KENNEDY (1865-1921)
William Kennedy Jones, editor* and newspaper manager, known as K. J., started working in newspapers at 16. He was reporter, then subeditor in his native city with the *Glasgow News* and *Glasgow Evening News* and, having worked shortterm as a reporter in Leicester and Birmingham, he joined the burgeoning London press trade in the early 1890s.

He helped start the *Morning* (1892-1900) in London in 1892 but the enterprise faltered, and after two years as news editor on T. P. O'Connor's* *Sun*, in 1894 he acquired, with Louis Tracy*, assistant editor of *Sun*, the *London Evening News*, then failing to make money despite its solid circulation* (about 100,000). Jones quickly sold on the paper to the media magnate Alfred Harmsworth*, while keeping a 7.5 per cent share, and remained editor until 1900. The paper was entirely redesigned along the innovative lines that promoted mass-market* readership*: eye-catching headlines, more sport* and competitions, and less politics*. The transformation was effective and Harold Harmsworth* approvingly called it 'our gold brick' (Pound and Harmsworth, cited in *ODNB*).

Jones encouraged Harmsworth to purchase the *Glasgow Daily Record* as the first of a series of regional investments, but Harmsworth's new 'flagship of popular* journalism' (*ODNB*), the *Daily Mail*, launched in May 1896, soon fully occupied Jones, who oversaw all content and style of the paper and helped to turn it into a 'voice of the Empire' (Taylor: 36). His 'blood and guts' formula, hooking readers with sensational crime* reports, further added to the success of the *Mail* (Taylor: 34). Harmsworth's 'right hand man' was also one of the 'most hated men in Fleet Street*' for his aggressive manner and 'acidulated humour' (Taylor: 27). He was 'completely cynical' (Taylor: 36) with a low opinion of his readers: 'don't forget you are writing for the meanest intelligence' (Kennedy Jones cited in Palmer: 217). Jones was credited with an instinct for news, however, and the ability to protect Harmsworth's best interests when required. He helped Harmsworth secure *The Times* in 1908 and went on to modernize methods of printing the paper, though he did not get the editorial chair.

Jones, elected as Unionist member for Hornsey in 1916, spent the rest of his life in politics. He wrote an important account of his career, *Fleet Street and Downing Street* (1919), which charts the developments of the popular press and relationship between the press and politicians (*ODNB*). **FD**

Sources: *ODNB*, Palmer 1978, Pound and Harmsworth 1959, Taylor 1996.

JOURNAL OF MENTAL SCIENCE (1853-)

The *Journal of Mental Science*, published by the Association of Medical Officers of Asylums and Hospitals for the Insane, began as the *Asylum Journal* in 1853. Its first editor*, John Charles Bucknill*, appended *of Mental Science* to the title in 1855 and then dropped *Asylum* in 1857. As Bucknill described it in the manifesto, the Journal would focus on practical issues such as mental physiology, mental disease and other matters important to 'medical* men who are engaged in the treatment of the insane'. Bucknill hoped to establish through the journal that physicians dealing with mental illness required specialized medical training. Henry Maudsley* began his contributions to the *Journal of Mental Science* in 1860 with an article on Edgar Allen Poe, as literary* works were then regarded as providing valuable insights into the workings of the mind. On Bucknill's stepping down, in 1862, Charles Lockhart Robertson was appointed editor, an unpaid position, and within a year Maudsley was elected as co-editor. After 1870 Maudsley co-edited with John Sibbald, and then with Thomas Smith Clouston (1871-1878).

The journal was divided into sections* of original articles on mental disease; clinical case descriptions; book reviews*, many of which were signed; asylum reports; abstracts of psychological literature; and notes on meetings and other events. Much of the journal appears to have been anonymously* written by the editors, in addition to the signed articles they contributed. Both Bucknill and Maudsley were interested in medico-legal issues, and Maudsley wrote on philosophical* questions. Prominent nineteenth-century specialists such as the psychologist Thomas Laycock and the neurologist John Hughlings Jackson published in the journal. Maudsley was pushed out of the editorship in 1878 by, among others, his brother-in-law, the psychiatrist Harrington Tuke, who attacked some of the views he believed Maudsley to be promoting, presumably his materialism. He may have also objected to Maudsley's speculative and literary leanings. Under the editorships of George Savage and Daniel Hack Tuke (1878-1894), the journal became increasingly clinical and continued in this direction into the twentieth century. **SA**

Sources: Collie 1988, Walk 1976.

JOURNAL OF THE WORKHOUSE VISITING SOCIETY (1859-1865)

With the establishment of the Workhouse Visiting Society in July 1858, this quarterly Journal* functioned as an information vehicle for the Society's aims of improving living conditions for workhouse inmates, as well as providing education and work. Published in London, free to members and on sale for 6d, it carried advertisements* on the inside and back covers. It embraced theory and action: papers given at the National Association for the Promotion of Social Science, statistics, government reports, book reviews*, annual accounts alongside campaign proposals, offers of help and requests for donations. With Louisa Twining's vigour, the *Journal* grew from a pamphlet to bi-monthly magazine. By January 1865, she declared it had created growth and an increase in visitors and would now cease. **CL**

Source: *Journal of the Workhouse Visiting Society* 1859-1865.

JOURNALISM SCHOOLS

In terms of the rise of journalism as a profession, the emergence of journalism schools late in the century was a landmark development. On 14 March 1887, the excitable *Pall Mall Gazette** asked rhetorically: '"A School of Journalism!" what next? How will it be worked; have we not journalists enough?' There followed an interview with the 'patentee of this new invention' – one David Anderson, a journalist of considerable experience, and a contributor to the *Daily Telegraph**, the *Weekly Dispatch** and *All the Year Round** – which revealed much about what appears to have been the first school of journalism in Britain, the London School of Journalism. In the interview, Anderson promised 'in the course of twelve months' practical tuition, to make any fairly well-educated young man a thoroughly trained and expert journalist, capable of earning from six to twenty pounds a week on the press'.

Anderson's pedagogical approach was to 'treat each of my pupils as if I were the editor* of a paper, and as if they were my staff'. Each day he would assign them tasks appropriate to the branch of the profession which they were interested in pursuing: some would be asked to write a leader* on the political events of the day, others would be dispatched to a gallery or theatre and asked to produce a review*, others would be assigned a piece of copy which they were instructed to condense into a shorter piece. Anderson also gave lectures and employed a small staff, teaching students libel law, interviewing* techniques, and how to use reference books, news agency* wires and other sources of information. Within a few months, the *Pall Mall Gazette* reported that Anderson's students were already being remunerated for articles published in society* journals. Anderson claimed that among his pupils were a number of Oxford and Cambridge graduates, and that five out of six of his students attained good posts.

Charging a fee of 100 guineas a year and apparently requiring a full-time commitment, Anderson's course was aimed squarely at young gentlemen. Over the next decade some cheaper options emerged. In 1889, the Southern School of Journalism, based in Bexhill on Sea, advertised a programme 'for the practical training of newspaper proprietors*, managers, or editors, authors, reporters, Press correspondents, publishers*, shorthand* writers, &c'. This induction into 'one of the most rising and desirable callings of the time' promised a salary from the beginning. Elsewhere, a postal school of journalism aimed particularly at aspiring female journalists was run by Eleanora Vynne run in the columns of *Atalanta** from 1896 to 1898. For 10s a year subscribers could enter monthly competitions and have their writing criticized by Vynne, who offered guidance on how to improve copy and sell it.

The English School of Journalism had commenced operations by 1896 at the latest, with D. F. Ranking as its principal. It began to publish its official organ – the *Authors' Circular** – in January 1898, when Charles Norris was secretary. This publication (which ran for only four months) printed syllabi which are highly informative guides to the constitution of the profession at the turn of the century. Composition, English literature and constitutional history were at the top of the billing, alongside the more practical arts of interviewing, subediting and so on. Also available by correspondence, the course prepared students for the official examinations of the Institute of Journalists*.

The establishment of journalism as an academic subject within universities came later. John Churton Collins began negotiations with Birmingham University in June 1907 about the foundation of a school of journalism, contributing an article on this subject to the *Nineteenth Century** in February 1908. This triggered a debate that culminated in 1919 with the University of London establishing a journalism course in conjunction with the Institute of Journalists. **MaT**

Sources: 19CBLN, Brake 2001, *ODNB*.

JOURNALIST Journalists struggled to achieve recognition as members of a legitimate profession throughout the nineteenth century. The word 'journalist' retained negative connotations from the previous century as a partisan hack employed by a patron or political* party. Not until advertisement revenue enabled newspapers to become independent of political control following the repeal of newspaper taxes (1836-1855) was the press able to establish its reputation as the 'Fourth Estate', a watchdog intent on bringing social issues to public attention. The appropriateness of this title was hotly debated, but journalism did become a political force at this time.

Factors contributing to the growing respectability of journalism included commercial success, improved technology and favourable publicity. Although the press was no longer associated with political sedition after the decline of the unstamped* radical newspapers in the 1840s, the policy of anonymous* contributions* continued in many publications until late in the century as a way of asserting the authority of the paper over the individual author. The division of labour into specialties including editor*, subeditor*, leader* writer, reporter* and correspondent was well established by mid-century. By the 1880s, the term 'journalist' had a pronounced association with the newspapers even as it continued to encompass writing for periodicals of all sorts.

Professional recognition was hindered by a lack of formal qualifications including entry requirements, qualifying examinations or certifying institutions. Journalists came from a wide range of backgrounds and learned most of their skills through informal apprenticeships in newspaper offices or, from the 1890s, journalism schools. The majority of journalists received little institutional support at this time to protect them from low pay and chronic job insecurity. Their professional identity was bolstered by the establishment of press clubs after 1870, the National Association of Journalists in 1884 (renamed the Institute of Journalists* in 1890) and the National Union of Journalists in 1907, the profession's first trade union. Early trade publications include the *Journalist** (1879-1881) and the *Journalist** (1886-1909). Journalism was exceptional among the professions in the contributions made by women despite long-standing prejudice. The establishment of the Society of Women Journalists* in 1895 sought to protect the interests of female members of the press. The journalist was no longer a pariah by the turn of the century. **MR**

Sources: Brown 1985, Conboy 2004, Jones 1996, Keating 1989, Tunstall 2001.

JOURNALIST: A MONTHLY PHONOGRAPHIC MAGAZINE FOR JOURNALISTS, SHORTHAND WRITERS AND REPORTERS (1879-1881)

A short-lived monthly* magazine* for journalists* costing 6d and edited* by Henry R. Evans, the *Journalist* was distinguished by being printed entirely in shorthand*, with the exception of the masthead*, titles of articles and department headings. By encrypting its articles – which seldom strayed from the topic of the practice of journalism – the journal constituted the journalistic profession as an impenetrable cabal. In doing so, however, it also drastically limited its readership*, and ran to only 21 issues. **MaT**

Source: *Journalist* 1879-1881.

JOURNALIST. A NEWSPAPER FOR ALL NEWSPAPER PRODUCERS (1886-1909)

The *Journalist* began as a weekly* trade* paper for journalists* costing 3d. Its aim was to keep readers abreast of the latest developments in the trade, reporting on significant appointments, providing biographies – often accompanied by illustrations* – of prominent or otherwise noteworthy journalists, and printing the proceedings of the National Association of Journalists, of which it was the semi-official organ. On top of this there were reports on key libel hearings, letters* to the editor, accounts of the successes and failures of given newspapers and periodicals and more discursive articles covering various aspects of the profession. As such it is a useful (and largely untapped) resource for the study of the late nineteenth-century press. Advertisements* – for situations vacant, typewriters*, machinery relating to the printing trade and other publications including its competition, the *Reporters' Magazine* – were also included.

By early1890 the *Journalist* had switched to monthly publication and its price* had fallen to 1d. The National Association of Journalists had altered its name to the Institute of Journalists* in 1888,

and received a Royal Charter to become the Chartered Institute of Journalists in April 1890, occasioning a change in the ownership of the *Journalist*. In May 1890, the new proprietors* raised the price to 2d and switched to fortnightly publication, adopting a smaller format* and doubling the number of pages to 16, also changing the title to the *Journalist and Newspaper Proprietor*.

When it ceased publication in 1909, it had shrunk to 8 pages, almost half of which were taken up with advertising, and reverted to monthly publication. It seems to have lost its connection with the Institute of Journalists, which was very close in the 1890s. The content – now largely reduced to gossip* and tittle-tattle – suffered as a consequence. **MaT**

Source: *Journalist* 1886, 1890, 1909.

JUDY: OR THE LONDON SERIO-COMIC JOURNAL (1867-1910)

As its name suggests, the long-lived satirical* weekly *Judy* set out its stall as competitor to *Punch**, to which its editor* Charles Ross in the first issue referred as 'our caitiff husband [...] who is wasting his substance in riotous living to the great discomfort of ourself, his lawful wife'. Aping *Punch* in size* and format*, the magazine cost 2d to *Punch's* 3d, aiming to capitalize on the fact that *Punch* had moved upmarket, and successfully exploiting the lower-middle-class* niche that had opened up as a result. It was also notable for its appeal to a female readership*, again signalled in its title. Together with several other comic weeklies,* *Judy* was at various times owned by the enterprising Dalziel* brothers.

Like *Punch*, *Judy* was made up of a variety of (usually illustrated*) comic skits, satirical political* sketches, creaky light verse and caricatures*, often including a large double-page etching*. Ross – himself a cartoonist* – was a key contributor, and it was in the pages of *Judy* that his most enduring creation first appeared, on 14 August 1867. Ally Sloper* became possibly the first celebrity cartoon character, and featured in countless spin-offs. In 1869, Ross's young wife Emilie de Tessier* took on the majority of the drawing of Ally Sloper under the pseudonym* 'Marie Duval'*. This was also the year of *Judy's* most significant innovation when it began the first ever serialized* comic strip, a series depicting Ally Sloper's exploits as the journal's war* correspondent. *Ally Sloper: A Moral Lesson* was issued by the *Judy* office in November 1873, arguably the world's first comic book.

The then unparalleled success of its most famous progeny probably stemmed more from his appeal to the public imagination than from the quality of the illustration, for in this respect *Judy* compared unfavourably with its rivals. Indeed, the illustrations seemed to get worse as time wore on, reflecting that the journal's failure to recruit a long-term illustrator of the quality of J. F. Sullivan at *Fun** or Matt Morgan* at the *Tomahawk**, let alone the trio of Leech,* Doyle* and Tenniel* at *Punch**. Morgan did make some contributions to *Judy*, but the magazine's political profile cannot have appealed to him. It proclaimed 'Conservatism of the Truest and Bluest', locating itself to the right of *Punch* on the political spectrum and in direct opposition to its liberal competitors *Fun* and *Tomahawk*. But this hardly tells the whole story about a magazine that had a subversive side, embodied by the heroic Ally Sloper whose name referred to the practice of sloping down alleys to evade a landlord's demands for rent. This irreverence also manifested itself in a knowing cynicism about Victorian sexuality, particularly that of high society. The distinction to be made between the paper's cultural identification with the lower-middle classes and its political identification with the Toryism of the ruling elite is therefore a crucial one. **BM/ KC/MaT**

Sources: Dalziel 1901, Houfe 1978.

JURIST (1837-1867) First appearing as a 6d 16-page weekly* 'intended to promote the diffusion of intelligence' (issue 1:1) among practising lawyers at a time of perceived rapid change in the legal world, the *Jurist* specialised in reports of the proceedings in the various courts*. There were always a few pages of commentary but the court reports were its main feature. A retrospective at the beginning of the second series (13 Jan. 1855) demonstrates the effects of the Newspaper Stamp Tax on the first series: by limiting the space available the usefulness of the journal to lawyers was restricted because adequate indexes could not be printed. This was now being remedied, the resultant annual volumes comprising several thousand pages each. Substantial supplements* ('The Second Part') priced* 1s were issued every week. These comprised leading articles, commentaries, book reviews*, news of the legal* profession in general and about individuals and relevant parliamentary intelligence. A full subscription was now a hefty three guineas. Advertisements* – which were numerous and included non-legal items (such as for the *Illustrated London News** and the *Family Friend*) – were handled by the Maxwell agency. In 1855 they already cost £2/10/- per column. The *Jurist* closed in 1867, having lost its audience to the *Weekly Law Journal**. **AK**

Sources: *Mitchell's*, *Waterloo*.

JUSTICE (1884-1925) *Justice, Organ of the Social Democracy*, can be regarded as the first English socialist* periodical. Founded and edited* in 1884 by Henry Mayer Hyndman*, it was funded by a donation of £300 from Edward Carpenter, although it was largely financed until 1889 by William Morris*. *Justice* was the weekly* journal of the *Social Democratic Federation*, the first Marxist organization in England. The decision of Hyndman, the Federation's chairman, to replace the first editor, Charles Fitzgerald, within weeks of the periodical's launch was interpreted by some as dictatorial control and was a factor in Morris breaking away from the party in 1884 to establish the Socialist League (taking with him a £10 weekly subsidy). In 1889, Harry Quelch* became editor and retained the post until his death in 1913, to be succeeded by H. W. Lee (1865-?1935). The broadsheet was launched by Henry Champion's* Modern Press; originally priced at 1d, the price* rose to 2d in 1896. Though it was criticized for its dry presentation, the periodical's mission to 'stir up' the workers and to educate the middle classes* in socialism drew an impressive range of contributors such as Eleanor Marx*, Edward Aveling, John Burns, Annie Besant*, George Bernard Shaw* and Walter Crane*. The periodical regularly published poetry* (including Morris's, 'Chants for Socialists'), political cartoons*, as well as some fiction.

Ostensibly guided by the Federation's manifesto, demanding better housing for industrial and agricultural workers, free compulsory education for all children, an eight-hour day and land nationalization, *Justice* also championed current political* issues. Morris, for example, attacked Herbert Spencer for urging laissez-faire capitalism as the safeguard for individualism. In leaders*, *Justice* called for demonstrations in support of the 1884 Franchise Bill and in November 1887 backing for the Trafalgar Square demonstration against unemployment and in demand of free speech that resulted in the violence of 'Bloody Sunday'. However *Justice* also reflected dissension among members of the Federation with conflicts over many issues, chief among them being the split over parliamentarianism. Hyndman believed socialists should further their agenda by standing for Parliament, while others, notably Morris, argued that socialists in Parliament would soon adopt middle-class values and attitudes. By the end of 1884, Morris, joined by Eleanor Marx, Edward Aveling and others, left the Federation and reformed as the Socialist League, dedicated to 'pure' socialism and international radicalism.

Poor sales meant that the periodical needed support from Champion's Modern Press and at one point Hyndman assisted the compositors in setting the type. In 1891 the Twentieth Century Press, whose shares were held by the Federation's executive council, bought *Justice* from Hyndman for £350. The periodical survived until January 1925, withstanding not only Morris's withdrawal of financial backing but also Hyndman's departure in the early twentieth century. **DM/ NK**

Sources: Barnes 2006, Bevir 1991, Thompson 1955, Tsuzuki 1961, *Waterloo*.

JUVENILE PRESS Children's* journals began in the eighteenth century with John Newberry's genteel *Lilliputian Magazine* (1751-1752). Early in the 1800s the genre* took a different turn, as Evangelical education of the poor coincided with the dramatic fall in the cost of printing and paper*, resulting in juvenile periodicals with a purpose. In 1805 the 19-year old William Lloyd, working for the interdenominational Sunday School Union, launched the penny* monthly* *Youth's Magazine; or Evangelical Miscellany.* Drawing on the format* of the popular chapbook, this combined dramatic woodcuts*, harrowing accounts of conversions and deathbeds, scriptural instruction, religious* exhortation and fearsome accounts of foreign (i.e. pagan) lands. The *Youth's Magazine*, which achieved a circulation* of 10,000 by its third series, elicited many imitations, including the *Children's Friend**, first edited* by the Rev. W. Carus Wilson, ('Mr Brocklehurst' in Charlotte Bronte's *Jane Eyre*). The most successful juvenile magazine was the Religious Tract Society's* *Child's Companion; or the Sunday Scholar's Reward**, which, largely bought by institutions for mass distribution*, in two years reached a circulation of 20,000. Much of the content was grimly Evangelical, but it did include general knowledge, natural history and geography, educational topics whose appeal was tapped by secular commercial magazines such as the American-inspired *Peter Parley's Magazine**.

In 1855 Samuel O. Beeton's* *Boy's Own Magazine**, starting as a 2d monthly, marked a dramatic shift in the form and content of juvenile periodicals. Beeton was the first to target a specific class*, sex and age group (the middle-class teenage male) and to shift its moral focus from the introspection of Evangelical religion to extrovert 'manly' activity. It offered stirring adventures, much historical* fiction, articles on physical sports*, scientific* experiments and prize essay competitions* on such subjects as 'True

Figure 32: Preaching to children all over the world, the cover of the *Juvenile Missionary Magazine*, Oct. 1847.

Courage'. By 1862 it boasted 40,000 readers*.

After the success of Beeton's *Boy's Own*, the majority of cheap* juvenile periodicals were aimed at boys, many of whom, with increased national prosperity, had pocket money to spend on such items. But, higher up the social scale, 6d monthlies designed for family* reading drew more liberally on the imaginative wealth of a golden age of children's literature, and appealed to both sexes. George MacDonald, Hans Andersen and Charles Kingsley wrote for *Good Words for the Young**. Andersen and Lewis Carroll were also popularized in Mrs Gatty's* labour of love, *Aunt Judy's Magazine* (1866-1885), a journal that put high literary* standards and fine illustrations* before popular* appeal, leaving its circulation low and profits vestigial.

Meanwhile the rapidly expanding working class readership* in the years surrounding the 1870 Elementary Education Act was creating rich pickings for the popular press. In 1866 Edwin J. Brett* began his penny* weekly*, *Boys of England**, whose violent, patriotic serials* and frenetic calls to activity put Beeton's failing publications in the shade. The popularity of Brett's 'Jack Harkaway' school stories helped his journal reach weekly circulation of 250,000 by 1879, and scores of rival periodicals appeared with names such as the *Young Englishman* (1873-1879) and the *Young Briton* (1869-1877). The respectable press reacted vigorously against the sadism and antisocial violence perceived in these 'penny packets of poison'. The Rev. Erskine Clarke published *Chatterbox* (1866-1955) to woo readers with more wholesome fiction. *Young Folks** featured both fairy stories and Robert Louis Stevenson's *Treasure Island*. But by far the most popular 'healthy' journal was the *Boy's Own Paper**, which in the 1890s reached sales of 650,000. Published by the Religious Tract Society, this offered a heady, extrovert mix of heroic adventure, strenuous sport* and industrious hobbies. A companion *Girl's Own Paper** achieved considerable success, reaching sales of 250,000 per week. But many girls preferred the *Boy's Own Paper.*

At the popular level, the press mogul Alfred Harmsworth* weighed into the moral crusade with *Marvel* (1893-1922), *Pluck* (1894-1924) and the *Boy's Friend* (1895-1927). Their modern illustrations and style made the 'penny dreadfuls' look old fashioned, and Harmsworth claimed the moral high ground for providing more wholesome fiction, and a closer engagement with the real life of his readers. But under the surface, the social values of his serials, which also came to feature outlaws and criminals, were equally questionable, and his success relied largely on his ability to sell his papers cheaply at a halfpenny. At the beginning of the century, children's magazines were dominated by moral issues; at its end, they were largely directed by commercial ones. **LJ**

Sources: Carpenter 1983, Drotner 1988, Egoff 1951, Hannabus 1983, Springhall 1994.

KANE, ROBERT JOHN (1809-1890) Robert
Kane, journalist and editor was the son of a Dublin
industrialist. Having trained as a chemist and phar-
macist in France and Germany, in 1832 he joined
the surgeon Robert J. Graves and the physician
William Stokes in founding and editing the *Dublin
Journal of Medical and Chemical Science* (later *Irish
Journal of Medical Science*), but resigned in 1834
upon appointment to a teaching post at the Royal
Dublin Society. Here he compiled the important
Industrial Resources of Ireland (1844) that led to
long-term reforms in Irish education. In 1840, having regularly supplied Richard Taylor* with contributions on organic chemistry for the *Philosophical
Magazine**, he was appointed a co-editor, thus consolidating its position as Britain's premier commercial journal of scientific research*. Kane's *Elements
of Chemistry* (1841) became a standard text in the
UK and The USA. His administrative responsibilities for education subsequently severely curtailed
his time for editing and publishing, though he continued to recommend Irish papers for publication
in the *Philosophical Magazine.* **WB**
Sources: Lightman 2004a, *ODNB,* Reilly 1955.

KEENE, CHARLES SAMUEL (1823-1891)
Charles Samuel Keene, along with Doyle*, Leech*
and Tenniel*, was one of *Punch** magazine's major
comic draughtsmen, working there for over 30
years, rising to become its leading social cartoonist*
after Leech's death in 1864, and subsequently
working alongside the political cartoonist, Tenniel
until 1890 to create a formidable and long lasting
partnership.

Trained as a wood* engraver in the workshops of
the Whymper brothers after failing to take to other
proposed careers, Keene began his new vocation
with the *Illustrated London News** where he worked
on drawings by Samuel Read*. By 1851 he was contributing his own drawings anonymously* to
Punch, and he had already made his reputation
through his depictions of London urban life before
he began to sign his work in 1854. While du Maurier* was predominantly the *Punch* artist most likely to revel in drawing room and salon scenes, Keene
preferred the streets as his subject. In all he produced somewhere near 3,000 images for *Punch*, all
drawn by means of his impulsive and improvisa-
tional methods, often directly on to the wood,

methods which tried the patience of even the most
skilful of his engravers.

Keene, like Doyle, published his *Punch* work in a
separate volume, *Our People,* in 1881, thus further
reminding the public of the quality of the magazine's visual elements. Despite a marked dislike for
the constraints of commissions, Keene also had
considerable success as an illustrator* of fiction in
the magazines, working extensively for the first few
volumes of *Once a Week** (1859ff), for which he
illustrated works by George Meredith and Mrs.
Henry Wood, and for *Good Words** in 1862 and the
*Cornhill** in 1864. **BM**
Sources: Engen 1990, Houfe 1978, Layard 1907,
ODNB, Spielmann 1895.

KEGAN PAUL (1877-) The firms owned by
Charles Kegan Paul, his predecessor, partner and
successors were associated with several Victorian
periodicals. Henry Samuel King (1817-1878), a
successful banker and India agent, began publishing* books in 1871. A loan to Alexander Strahan*
led to King's financial interest in a number of periodicals originally published by Strahan. These were
the *Contemporary Review**, *Good Words for the
Young**, and *Saint Paul`s Magazine**. For nearly two
years (c.1872-1874), these periodicals were published under King`s imprint and his wholesale net-
work handled their distribution*. King published
the new *Nineteenth Century** from its foundation in
1877, having worked with James T. Knowles* until
the latter lost editorial control of the *Contemporary*
and started the new journal. King and his successors published the *Nineteenth Century* until 1891
when Sampson Low* took over.

Charles Kegan Paul (1828-1902) joined King's
firm as literary adviser in 1873 and became its proprietor* in 1877. C. Kegan Paul & Co. published
the three volumes of a new series of the *New Quarterly Magazine** (Jan. 1879-April 1880) and Paul
served as editor* succeeding Francis Hueffer*. He
contributed six articles on subjects ranging from literature* to politics*. Earlier in his life, when Paul
was an Anglican clergyman, he contributed to *Fraser's Magazine** and the *Theological Review**. In his
later Positivist, and much later Roman Catholic periods, Paul contributed to the *British Quarterly Review**, the *New Review** and the *Fortnightly**. From
1881 the firm's imprint changed to Kegan Paul,
Trench & Co., when Alfred Chenevix Trench
(1849-1938) joined the firm.

After a financial crisis in 1889 the firm was amalgamated with those of the deceased Nicholas Trübner* and George William Redway (1859-1934) as

a limited company under the name Kegan Paul, Trench, Trübner & Co. Ltd. They continued Trübner's influential monthly *American and Oriental Literary Record* (1865-1891), which was widely used by scholars of Asian literature. In 1912 Kegan Paul, Trench, Trübner & Co. amalgamated with Routledge to form Routledge and Kegan Paul Ltd, which, after nearly 85 years, was bought out in turn by Taylor & Francis in 1998 at this point the Routledge imprint dropped 'Kegan Paul' which, however, remains as an independent imprint. Although remembered now as the predecessors of the prolific twentieth-century joint imprint, all of these nineteenth-century firms were implicated in both the financial and editorial management of periodicals. LKH

Sources: Howsam 1998, *ODNB*, Srebrnik 1986, *Waterloo, Wellesley.*

KELTIE, JOHN SCOTT (1840-1927) As a student in Edinburgh, Keltie supported himself through journalism, writing regular articles for the *Edinburgh Evening Courant** and, from 1861, working on the editorial staff of W. & R. Chambers*. At the beginning of the 1870s Keltie moved to London and joined the editorial staff of Macmillan & Co*., where he soon became subeditor* of the scientific* weekly *Nature**, working closely with its editor Norman Lockyer* and frequently contributing a quarter of the items in each issue. In 1875 he also began writing for *The Times**, particularly on the so-called 'Scramble for Africa'. African affairs were highly newsworthy in this period, and Keltie's journalistic focus on the continent, further augmented when he became editor of Macmillan's *Statesman's Year Book* in 1883, alerted him to the significance of the study of geography from a scientific perspective.

In the mid-1880s Keltie assisted Henry Walter Bates with editing the *Proceedings of the Royal Geographical Society*, before assuming the editorship himself in 1893 and changing the title to the *Geographical Journal*. Under Keltie, the *Geographical Journal* gained international renown in the nascent academic field of geography, and he remained as editor until 1917, also staying on as editor of the *Statesman's Year Book* until his death. GD

Sources: Jay 1986, *ODNB.*

KEMBLE, JOHN MITCHELL (1807-1857) Born into one of the most famous families of British actors, John Mitchell Kemble, journalist*, editor* and Anglo-Saxon scholar, was interested in the theatre, but instead of acting, he served, an appointment held previously by his father, as the examiner of stage

plays (1840-1857). After contributing to the third issue of the *British and Foreign Review; or, European Quarterly Journal**, Kemble became its editor (Dec. 1836-1844). Although the paper continued to publish political* articles during his tenure, Kemble made the *Review* more academic, publishing works about economics, philosophy*, art and literature*. He also covered publications of contemporary poets*, such as William Wordsworth, Samuel Taylor Coleridge* and Alfred Tennyson.

Unlike the proprietor* of the *Review*, Thomas Wentworth Beaumont*, Kemble believed the *Review* should publish less on Poland and more on European (and English) culture. Kemble also contributed to the *Athenaeum**, *Foreign Quarterly Review**, *Fraser's Magazine**, *Metropolitan Quarterly Review* and the annually published proceedings of the Archaeological Institute of Great Britain and Ireland. Notably, he was a leading expert on Teutonic languages and Anglo-Saxon literature, being the first English editor to translate *Beowulf.* BA

Sources: Block 1921, Dickins 1974, *ODNB*, *Waterloo, Wellesley*, Wiley 1979.

KEMPE, HARRY ROBERT (1852-1935) Having gained expertise in telegraphy* while working* with the telegraphic developers Charles Wheatstone, Samuel Canning and Robert Sabine, Harry Kempe began his first job in postal telegraphy under William Preece in 1872 and in November of the same year also began writing articles for the newly launched *Telegraphic Journal*. Although he was only 20 at the time, Kempe was one of the founders of the weekly*, which was renamed the *Electrical Review* in 1892, and he later became its editor* and proprietor*, retaining sole control until 1931. Many of his articles for the *Telegraphic Journal*, especially those on the sensitivity and accuracy of instruments used in telegraphy, were republished in the hugely influential *Handbook of Electrical Testing* (1876). In 1908 Kempe introduced and edited the important annual*, the *Engineers' Year-Book* which became *Kempe's Engineers' Year-Book* from 1950. CL

Sources: Armytage 1976, Gooday 2004b, *ODNB*, *Waterloo.*

KIDD, BENJAMIN (1858-1916) During the 1880s Kidd supplemented his modest income at the Inland Revenue by writing popular articles on natural history for *Longman's Magazine**. In 1890 Kidd's intimate and conversational interview* with the German biologist August Weismann was published in the *Review of Reviews** as a marked contrast to the rather abstract article on Weismann's germ plasm theory by Grant Allen* in an earlier number. The *Review*'s editor*, William Thomas Stead*, had quarrelled with Allen over methods of science* popularization, and clearly preferred Kidd's more vivid style, although Kidd himself became close friends of both men.

When, four years later, Kidd's book *Social Evolution* became an overnight sensation, Stead reminded the Review's readers that he had helped launch its author's career, and even claimed that the book's moderate Social Darwinism formed 'the scientific basis for the social gospel of the REVIEW OF REVIEWS' (Quoted in Dawson 2004a: 188). *Social Evolution* was widely reviewed and Kidd took the opportunity to respond to criticism in the *Nineteenth Century*. As well as Stead, Kidd also enjoyed the patronage of the radical journalist William Clarke, and by 1897 he had quit the civil service to become a full time writer. At the turn of the century Kidd was established as a leading sociologist, writing for the American *World's Work*, the *Daily News** and the *Spectator**, although he increasingly withdrew from metropolitan political and journalistic circles. He nevertheless maintained a close friendship with the journalist James Louis Garvin, and contributed regular articles to his sixpenny review the *Outlook* during the 1910s. **GD**

Sources: Crook 1984, Dawson 2004a, Lightman 2004b, *ODNB*.

KINGSLEY, HENRY (1830-1876) Kingsley, journalist* and editor*, was a serial* novelist and essayist who wrote for publications including the *Fortnightly Review**, *Macmillan's Magazine**, *Temple Bar**, the *New Quarterly Review** and the *North British Review**. Like several of his novels, his journalism frequently draws on his experiences of living in Australia, though he also published a range of literary* sketches on figures as diverse as Ben Jonson and Thackeray*.

He was editor of the Edinburgh-based *Daily Review* (1869-1871), a daily* penny* paper linked to the Free Presbyterian Church, but he never took to the daily pressures of editing, and, with the outbreak of the Franco-Prussian War, he went abroad and effectively became a kind of war correspondent*. His noteworthy accounts of the brutality of war were published in the *Daily Review* in September 1870. After resigning his editorship, he and his wife returned to London, where he continued to publish undistinguished fiction and to write miscellaneous pieces for a range of journals. He was never as acclaimed or as financially successful a writer or thinker as his brother Charles. **MWT**
Sources: Mellick 1983, *ODNB*, Scheuerle 1971.

KINGSTON'S MAGAZINE FOR BOYS (1859-1863) Although better known for his hardcover fiction, W. H. G. Kingston may also be counted among the pioneers of boys' magazines*, launching one of the genre's* very first, and finest examples.

Launched in 1859, *Kingston's Magazine for Boys* was similar in content and appearance to Samuel Beeton's* *Boy's Own Magazine**, although somewhat more light-hearted, notwithstanding its innately Christian tone, and slightly larger size*. Published monthly* at a cost of 6d (later rising to 8d) per number, it was aimed squarely at a middle-class* readership*. The journal was of a high quality: well written, profusely illustrated* to a good standard and accompanied by modest colour plates. Although Kingston did recruit other contributors, the majority of the paper's fiction was written by himself, and was characterized by the same themes which dominated his hardcover fiction, particularly the navy and the public schools. Non-fiction mainly focused on natural history; guides to the keeping of pets and notes on rambles were especially common. Annual* volumes boasted additional fiction and non-fiction bound up following the final number; one such supplement*, entitled 'My Travels in Many Lands', ran to a remarkable 304 pages, representing excellent value for money to boy readers.

Kingston's Magazine for Boys was discontinued after four volumes in 1863, much to the dismay of its proprietor*, disgruntled in his failure to secure lasting popularity despite considerable effort. At this point, Kingston joined Beeton's staff at the *Boy's Own Magazine*. Although he continued to write profusely for numerous boys' periodicals in the intervening years, and penned over 100 children's books, not until 1880 did Kingston launch another periodical of his own, *Union Jack**. **ChB**
Sources: Jay 1918-1921, *Waterloo*.

KIRLEW, GILBERT RICHARDSON (1858-1908) Gilbert Kirlew worked tirelessly to improve the conditions of sick and crippled children in Manchester through his editorship* of charity society periodicals. At the age of 21 Kirlew began his publicist career by assisting with the editing of *Delving and Diving*, the magazine* of the Manchester and Salford Street Children's Mission. In 1882 he was appointed joint honorary secretary to the Manchester Salford Boys' and Girls' Refuges Children's Aid Society and assumed editorship of their *Christian Worker** periodical. During the same year a children's society, the Band of Kindness was begun by the *Stockport Advertiser* and the *Children's*

Own Paper. Kirlew took over editorship of the *Children's Own Paper* in 1883, assuming the mantle of 'Uncle Gilbert' and steered the Band of Kindness away from its animal protection work to support the work of the refuges. Increasingly he relied on evangelical rhetoric to spur on Band members, who numbered nearly 50,000 in 1891, to distribute* his magazine and work for their society. Because of financial instability the *Paper* folded in 1892 and moved to become a constituent of the *Christian Worker* that was similarly suffering financially.

More tribulations followed. In June 1895 the satirical* paper *Spy*, edited by Henry Yeo, claimed that Kirlew was a 'preposterous being… [whose] love of street arabs is too real'. Yeo's paper was renowned for scurrilous allegations; nevertheless, paedophiliac allegations were disastrous for a renowned child-worker. Reprised in 1893, the *Children's Own Paper* ceased immediately, as did the *Christian Worker* and Kirlew resigned from the refuges. According to his wife, the source of the accusations was two former refuge inmates who held a grudge against Kirlew after he had dismissed them in 1894 for misconduct. After disastrous legal advice, Kirlew's immediate attempt to clear his name failed while *Spy's* attacks continued. A second libel attempt in 1898 led to Kirlew successfully restoring his reputation and Yeo gaoled. Kirlew began charitable work again, but the scandal broke his health and he died prematurely. **FSM**

Sources: Kirlew 1908, Mohr 1991, Mohr 1992.

KLEIN, HERMAN(N) (1856-1934) Hermann Klein, music* journalist, became London correspondent* for the *Norwich Argus*, his uncle's paper, in 1875 and was appointed music critic of the *Sunday Times* in 1881, for which he wrote for 20 years. In 1901 he left the *Sunday Times* and moved to New York, where he wrote music criticism for the *New York Herald*, taught singing and organized concerts. He returned to London in 1909, primarily to teach singing. He also contributed to the *Musical Times* and other titles, and, beginning in 1924, was a regular contributor to the *Gramophone* until shortly before his death.

Klein wrote most effectively about late nineteenth-century performances and performers, not composers, and at times assumed a celebratory tone about his subjects as if they were personal friends – as many of them were. He noted the difficulty of how 'to limit the use of superlatives' in writing about prima donna Adelina Patti (Klein 1920: ix). His journalism helped shape a view of late nineteenth-century operatic performance as 'the Age of Patti', though he also lavished praise on Teresa Tietjens,

Jean and Edouard de Reszke, and numerous others. His superlatives are generally well supported, and his reviews* show a keen musical sensitivity. A vivid memory of late Victorian performance practice informs his journalism in the *Gramophone*, making it a valuable link between Victorian and early twentieth-century musical sensibilities. **RTB**

Sources: Klein 1903, Klein 1920, Moran 1990, *New York Times* 11 March 1934, *The Times* 12 March 1934.

KLICKMANN, EMILY FLORA (1867-1958) Flora Klickmann's original choice of career was music, but on medical advice she relinquished it for journalism. Klickmann edited* the *Girl's Own Paper*, succeeding its founding editor* Charles Peters, and ran the magazine for 22 years.

Her training at Trinity College of Music and the Royal College of Organists proved valuable for writing a musical* column* for *Sylvia's Journal* in the early nineties, and for her 'Moments with Modern Musicians' series in *Windsor Magazine* (which she co-founded) from 1896 onwards. The chatty New Journalism* interview* style suited her, working as effectively with arctic explorers (*Windsor Magazine* Aug. 1895) as with musicians.

Figure 33: The first page of one of Flora Klickmann's articles on contemporary musicians, *Windsor Magazine*, Jan. 1896, 459.

She gained further editorial experience after 1904 in modernizing the Wesleyan missionary* journal the *Foreign Field,* and edited *Everybody's Story Magazine* (later *Everyone's*) 1909-1914. In 1908 Klickmann took on her most important editorial work, the renamed *Girl's Own Paper and Woman's Magazine.* Among the more significant changes she made were increasing the space devoted to needlework, and introducing a quarterly supplement* entitled *Stitchery.* She published numerous works based on material in *Girl's Own Paper,* on needlework, etiquette and, notably, her *Flower-patch* books published 1916-1948. **BMO**
Sources: Ashley 2006, Hughes 2005, *ODNB,* Onslow 2000, Ward 1992.

KNIGHT, CHARLES (1791-1873)   Charles Knight, publisher* and writer, was a key figure in the dissemination of low-cost print in the name of 'improvement' during the 1830s and 1840s. He was apprenticed to his father, a printer, and began his publishing career in August 1812, when he became joint-proprietor*, with his father, of the *Windsor and Eton Express* which he also edited* until 1827. During the early 1820s, Knight was involved in a series of short-lived journals such as *Knight's Quarterly Magazine* (1823-1824); from 1820-1823 he was also editor and part-proprietor of the London weekly*, the *Guardian*. In 1823 he sold the *Guardian* and moved to London. Knight's significance stems from his position as superintendent of publications for the Society for the Diffusion of Useful Knowledge*, a position he occupied from 1827, after his own business failed. His early activities for the SDUK included a Library of Entertaining Knowledge (1829-1837); however, his most influential venture was the *Penny Magazine*. Knight's adherence to popular improvement is also evident in the *Penny Cyclopedia* (1833-1844) published in penny parts: it swallowed up much time and expense, and was an ongoing financial loss.

Other notable serial* publications by Knight, which demonstrate his innovative use of illustration*, are the *Gallery of Portraits* (1832-4), *The Pictorial Bible* (1836-1838), *The Pictorial History of England* (1837?–1844) and the *Pictorial Shakespeare* (1838-1841). Knight was an author as well as publisher, his most substantial work being the eight-volume *Knight's Popular History of England* (1855-62) and a well-liked member of the London literary* scene. He contributed to *Household Words** and wrote several pamphlets against the Taxes on Knowledge, including *The Struggles of a Book Against Excessive Taxation* (1850) and *The*

Case of the Authors as Regards the Paper Duty (1851). His publishing activities declined after the dissolution of the SDUK in 1846, and he retired from publishing in 1855, although his literary output continued. Knight's career is particularly valuable because of his interest in publishing history, and the accounts he provided of his own publishing practices. These comprise a series for the *Penny Magazine* in 1833, *The Old Printer and the Modern Press* (1854), *Shadows of Old Booksellers* (1867) and his autobiography, *Passages from a Working Life* (1864-1865). **JSP**
Sources: Bennett 1982, Clowes 1892, Gray 2006, Mitchell 2004, Morbey 1979.

KNIGHT AND LACEY (FL. 1817-1828)   John Knight and Henry Lacey began their printing and publishing* business at 24 Paternoster Row, London in 1822. Prior to this, Knight had printed the Tory *Anti-Cobbett or the Weekly Patriotic Register* (1817), a fleeting publication. Within four years the two men were publishing 14 periodical titles as well as memoirs, novels, poetry*, prints and engravings* (one of their artists was Robert Seymour*, the *Pickwick Papers'* illustrator). Their largest group of periodicals was literary*, but they also catered for the growing interest in scientific development, publishing three journals: the *Chemist* (1824-1825), the *Lancet** (for 1824 only) and their most successful journal the *Mechanic's Magazine** (1823-1829). Responding to the growth in Mechanics' Institutes and artisan literacy, the latter sold 30,000 copies by 1826, but this success could not prevent the business failing in the great book trade crash of 1826.

However, Knight & Lacey resumed business in January 1827, repurchasing the *Mechanics' Magazine* and another successful title the *Pulpit*, but by November 1828 they had lost so much money on the *Library of the People* and other publications that they were again insolvent. Messrs Duckworth & Miers came to the rescue on condition that one of the partners should withdraw from the business, so Lacey assigned all the assets of the firm to Knight in order to pay off the creditors. Knight reneged on the agreement, stopped paying the creditors and sold the two successful journals and *Public Characters* for a large sum of money. As Lacey was legally equally liable to the creditors, he was forced to petition to be discharged by the Insolvency Court in 1829 to enable him to continue in business. **CL**
Sources: *The Times* 1829, *Waterloo.*

KNOWLEDGE (1881-1918)   *Knowledge: An Illustrated Magazine of Science, Plainly Worded – Exactly Described* was founded as a weekly* of 16 three-column* pages by the astronomer Richard Anthony Proctor* to counter what he saw as the increasingly inaccessibility of scientific research. Proctor had made a career out of science* popularization that refused to condescend to its audience and *Knowledge* was intended to participate in the debate over access to scientific knowledge. As a 2d weekly, with advertisements*, *Knowledge* was able to undercut the more established 4d *Nature*. Although the two journals appeared similar, each represented a different attitude to science. Whereas *Nature* was supported by the scientific establishment, *Knowledge*'s most vibrant feature was its extensive correspondence* columns. In foregrounding the contributions of readers*, *Knowledge* resembled another of its competitors*, the *English Mechanic*, also a 2d weekly. However, while the *English Mechanic* presented a forum that appeared free of editorial control, Proctor actively debated with his contributors in the pages of *Knowledge*.

In November 1885 Proctor turned *Knowledge* into a 6d monthly*. Although he claimed overwork, and Proctor often had to employ Edward Clodd as an assistant editor* while he was away on overseas lecture tours, this move also made financial sense as what was effectively a price* cut of half over a month (it was then 3d a week) was accompanied by a reduction in size* by three-quarters. As a monthly the journal phased out much of its correspondence* until, at the time of his death in 1889, Proctor was providing most of the content. *Knowledge* was continued by Proctor's friend Arthur Cowper Ranyard*, who solicited contributions from many of the leading science writers of the day. He also introduced full-page collotype reproductions of astronomical photographs* into the journal, making it an important vehicle for the dissemination of images of the stars. In 1891 H. F. Witherby succeeded W. H. Allen as publishers and, after Ranyard's death in 1894, it was Harry Forbes Witherby who took over the editorship. In 1902 *Knowledge* incorporated* *Science-Gossip* (Stardurcke's) and in 1904 merged* with *Illustrated Scientific News*, resulting in a new title, *Knowledge and Illustrated Scientific News; a Monthly Journal of Science* (1904-1910). It was then augmented to reflect both new stablemates, becoming *Knowledge; with which is incorporated Hardwicke's Science Gossip and the Illustrated Scientific News: a Monthly Record of Science* (1910-1918). **JEM**

Sources: Lancashire 1988, Lightman 2004a, Mussell 2007b, *Waterloo*.

KNOWLES, JAMES THOMAS (1831-1908) The founder of the *Nineteenth Century** and its owner-editor* until his death, Knowles followed his father into architecture and practised with modest success. His most important commission was to design Tennyson's house without charge to the idol who became his close friend. Largely self-educated, Knowles gave early evidence of his intellectual energy and curiosity in the high-minded *Clapham Magazine* (1850-1851) which he founded and co-edited. Knowles published a popular compilation from Malory's *Morte d'Arthur* that drew Tennyson's approval, and his disarming, reverential pushiness won him the reclusive poet's confidence. These same qualities enabled Knowles to found the Metaphysical Society in 1869, and to attract over 60 of the nation's leading intellectuals – including the prime minister, W. E. Gladstone – into that improbably successful body dedicated to the earnest discussion of 'Big Ideas'. The Society was a perfect pool of potential contributors to a serious review*, and Knowles took full advantage of it when he became editor of the *Contemporary Review** in 1870, taking over from Dean (Henry) Alford* who was himself a Society member.

The *Contemporary*'s policy of signed articles suited Knowles, who believed in the 'open platform' and had no particular axes of his own to grind. Controversy flourished under his editorship, and drew publicity. Signature brought further publicity, since his big name contributors could be identified. His type of intellectual celebrity* journalism was an interesting counterpart to the growing social celebrity journalism of the period. Religious differences with his publishers caused his departure from the *Contemporary* in January, 1877 and three months later he launched the *Nineteenth Century*, where as owner-editor he could exercise unfettered his talents as an intellectual lionhunter and impresario of debate. Knowles received Tennyson's blessing, and an introductory sonnet, while Gladstone – who would contribute 63 articles, reviews and letters – congratulated him for keeping 'the "Nineteenth Century" pot boiling'. When the Metaphysical Society quietly folded in 1880, the journal offered a convenient substitute forum. Knowles's own contributions to his journals were modest. He wrote nothing for the *Contemporary* but for the *Nineteenth Century* he wrote 12 reviews of 'recent science*' in its early issues, and several short introductions to debates over issues such as women's suffrage and the Channel Tunnel. **CAK**

Sources: Brown 1947, Metcalf 1980, *ODNB*.

KYDD, SAMUEL (1812-1892) A Chartist lecturer and later a successful barrister, Kydd contributed extensively to the Chartist press and to the journals of his mentor, Richard Oastler. His well-written accounts of his lecture tours appeared in the *Northern Star** in 1847-1849. Between 1849 and 1852, in *Reynolds Political Instructor**, *Cooper's Journal**, the *Star of Freedom* and Oastler's the *Home*, he argued for the regulation of imports, wages and factory conditions. These pieces were signed 'Gracchus' (confusingly a by-line also adopted by another contributor to radical journals called Bunney) or 'Alfred'. In 1857 Kydd was employed by *Reynolds's Weekly Newspaper** to write a series of reports on life in working-class* communities. The following year he entered Gray's Inn and his long legal career began, ending his journalistic career. **SFR**
Source: Roberts 1993.

L

LABOUCHÈRE, HENRY DU PRÉ (1831-1912) Henry Du Pré Labouchère, journalist*, proprietor*, editor*, politician, was born in London to a wealthy Huguenot family. Having lived abroad from the age of 21, he returned to England in 1865 and immediately embarked on standing for Parliament. He was elected in 1867, lost his seat in 1868 and was finally returned in 1880 (*ODNB*). In the intervals he established a successful and influential journalistic career, becoming a leading figure in the society* papers of the 1870s, and undertook ownership and management of the Queen's Theatre, London.

A series of his witty travel letters from Florence and Nice was published in the *Daily News**, of which he became part-proprietor, in 1868. He was in Paris in 1870 during the war, and his letters from a 'besieged resident' at the heart of the action, along with Archibald Forbes*' vivid dispatches, secured a huge increase in the circulation* of the *Daily News*. He was financial editor of the *World** – its co-owner was his friend Edmund Yates* – from its second number (July 1874) until 1876 when he left to establish his own weekly*, *Truth**, 'another and a better *World*' (Labouchère, cited in Thorold: 110).

Labouchère's commitment to exposing commercial fraud and social hypocrisy came to its fullest expression in *Truth*. His character pervaded its pages and his style, 'an idiosyncratic blend of lively satire*, colourful personal reminiscence and calculated outrage' (Sullivan: 425), amusing, informed and critical, set the tone. Serious political* articles sat alongside gossip* high society pieces; exposés of financial corruption earned him much praise, while also provoking numerous libel cases. Labouchère himself wrote the journal's financial* advice columns*, political editorials reflecting his radical Liberal views, dramatic criticism (under the name 'Scrutator') and many essays on varied topics derived from his catholic interests.

His return to formal politics in 1880 marked a gradual turning over of the management of *Truth* to Horace Voules, Labouchère's deputy since 1876. The generally liberal Labouchère, whose weekly was praised in 1904 as a champion of 'the oppressed, the unpopular, the unjustly judged' (J. H. McCarthy, cited in Sullivan: 430) had strong views on homosexuality and his name has become forever associated with the now notorious clause he had added to the Criminal Law Amendment Act of 1885 by which Oscar Wilde* was tried and sentenced in 1895. **FD**

Sources: *ODNB*, Sullivan 1984, Thorold 1921.

LABOUR ELECTOR (1888-1890, 1893-1894) The *Labour Elector* was an important socialist* periodical in the late Victorian period. Priced* at 1d, it was published* fortnightly for most of its existence and at its peak contained 16 pages. Edited* by Henry Hyde Champion*, it was published in London by Champion's Modern Press and partially funded by the soap manufacturer R. W. Hudson. It quickly acquired a reputation for hard-hitting reportage of the factory system: it exposed the deleterious conditions at Bryant and May's factory prior to the famous match-girls' strike, and it employed the trade unionist Tom Mann as an undercover reporter* to expose dangerous working practices at the Liberal MP J. T. Brunner's chemical plant. The paper's support for the 1889 London Dock Strike was a key moment: Champion's active involvement (which required handing over the editorship to Michael Maltman Barry) helped to boost circulation* to over 20,000; the paper absorbed the *Labour Leader** and added a new subtitle, 'The Organ of Practical Socialism'. Publication was suspended (April 1890-Jan. 1893) when Champion went to Australia but resumed on his return. At this point the paper made another shift in allegiance with a new subtitle, 'The Organ of the Independent Labour Party', despite protests from the Independent Labour Party itself. The serialization* of Margaret Harkness's novel 'Connie' began in June 1893, but the paper ceased publication before this was completed. Often combative in its journalism, the paper made an impact on the British socialist movement through its promotion of New Unionism and working-class parliamentary representation. **DM**

Sources: Barnes 2006, *DLB*, *ODNB*, Pelling 1952-1953, *Waterloo*, Whitehead 1983.

LABOUR LEADER (1894-1987) The version of the *Labour Leader* that has become acknowledged was that of the organ of the Independent Labour League, edited* originally by Keir Hardie, the Scottish socialist and leader of the Independent Labour Party who briefly changed the name of a periodical called the *Miner* to the *Labour Leader* before its termination in 1889. The Independent Labour Party was subsequently founded in Bradford in 1893 to represent the needs of working people in the light of the failure of the Liberal Party of the time and the *Labour Leader* changed from a

Glasgow-based Independent Labour Party monthly* to a London-based weekly* in March 1894, when Hardie had amassed the necessary share capital.

The paper vouched readers 'drawn from all ranks of people', but working-class* purchasers formed a significant part of the readership*, and it was proud to sell at a 'democratic penny'*. Hardie claimed a circulation* of 50,000 by 1895, but the paper was clearly struggling, for as both editor and proprietor* he was compelled to sell parts of his library and allegedly mortgaged his life-insurance to keep the title afloat. Among the editors* were Fred Henderson, W. B. Hodgson, J. B. Joyce and Philip Snowden. The paper was influenced by the *Clarion's* embrace of New Journalism*. Hardie famously wrote much of the *Labour Leader* himself, and his more imaginative alter egos included 'Daddy Time' of the children's page and sometimes 'Lily Bell' of the women's column*. It attracted key contributors from the socialist and trades union movements such as Ben Tillett (who provided regular 'Cycling Notes' as well as political* articles), H. C. Rowe, who contributed novels as well as non-fiction, Charles Allen Clarke* and Fred Brocklehurst, who wrote in the paper for both children and adults. Other contributors included W. A. Carlile, George Gissing, Bessie Rayner Parkes*, John Ruskin*, Robert Smillie and Frank Smith, who often signed their articles. Trade Union Labour, the *Labour Leader's* printer, altered the magazine's layout from two columns in 1891 to four columns by 1900. Editors classified letterpress by departments including 'Zig-zag Jottings', 'Chats with the Children', 'Our Woman's Page', 'Labour Diary', 'Answers to Correspondents*', 'Short Stories', 'Our Readers', Views', 'Among Trade Unions*', 'Poetry*', 'Parliament*', 'News'*, 'Comics' and 'Advertisements'*. Measuring 43 cm with 8 or 16 pages, this illustrated* magazine was issued on a Saturday.

The *Labour Leader* is particularly valuable for its fascinating insights into the birth of the Labour Party. Hardie grudgingly sold the paper in 1903, passing the editorship over to J. Bruce Glasier. It underwent several name changes in the twentieth century in line with its political commitments, but when the Independent Labour Party merged with the Labour Party in 1975 the paper reverted to its original name, ceasing publication in 1987. CRS/MDB

Sources: Benn 1997, Boos 1982, *Encyclopaedia Britannica,* Harrison 1974, Hopkin 1985, Morgan 1975, *ODNB, Waterloo, WGBLP* 1977.

LABOUR PROPHET (1892-1901) Published in Manchester and London, this 'Organ of the Labour Church' was a penny* socialist* monthly* edited* by John Trevor, who had founded the Labour Church in 1891. Trevor asserted in his first leader* that the journal sought to be a 'propagandist organ' and to 'represent the religious* life which inspires the labour movement'. With a circulation* of around 5,000, the paper struggled financially, but this did not prevent Trevor from including an illustrated* 'Cinderella Supplement*' for children. This promoted both socialist education and the philanthropic Cinderella Clubs pioneered by the *Clarion's* Robert Blatchford*. A number of the *Prophet's* contributors also wrote for Keir Hardie's *Labour Leader*, which provided a column* on Labour Church News from 1894. Both periodicals championed a 'religion' of socialism. A notable feature of the *Labour Prophet* was the encouragement it offered to the working-class autodidact. In the paper's Missionary* and Correspondence Classes, readers* were offered prizes for the pursuit of self-improving knowledge and 'personal development'. Retitled the *Labour Prophet and Labour Church Record* from 1895, it became the free quarterly* *Labour Church Record* in 1898 and was edited until its demise in 1901 by Charles Allen Clarke*. CRS

Sources: Bevir 1999, Inglis 1963, Mutch 2005, Summers 1958, *WGBLP* 1977.

LABOUR STANDARD (1881-1885) The driving force behind the *Labour Standard* was George Shipton, secretary of the London Trades Council (1871-1896) and the paper's first editor*. The *Labour Standard*, subtitled *An Organ of Industry,* was a trade union* paper published every Saturday at 1d, its 52 cm, eight pages with advertisements*, containing all manner of political* information and news* relating to the labour movement in Britain and America as well as women and children's sections. Shipton invited Friedrich Engels to contribute a series of articles on reformism and the labour movement to launch the paper. Engels wrote 11 articles in all in the form of anonymous* editorials but stopped contributing to the paper because of what he perceived as Shipton's allying himself too closely with middle-class* interests. Writing to Karl Marx*, Engels scathingly described the paper as, 'predominantly Gladstonian'. Shipton gave up his editorship* in 1884. CL

Sources: Harrison 1977, Kapp 1979, Lapides 1990, *Waterloo.*

LABOURER (1847-1848) The *Labourer: A Monthly Magazine of Politics, Literature, Poetry &c* was a Chartist* periodical, published in London at the *Northern Star** offices and in Manchester by Abel Heywood*. Nominally jointly edited* by Feargus O'Connor* and Ernest Jones*, the latter bore all routine editorial responsibilities. *Labourer* reflected O'Connor's strategy for Chartism, however, being conceived as a vehicle through which to promote his brainchild the Chartist Land Plan and, to a lesser extent, alliance with the organized trades. It was also intended to reinforce Chartism's claim to intellectual substance by publishing work of greater length than could be accommodated in the *Star**: all 48 pages of issue four, for example, were devoted to O'Connor's 'Treatise on the Small Proprietary System'. Mainly, though, *Labourer* was devoted to history*, serial* fiction and poetry*, the purpose of which was to provide appropriately elevated literature* for those aspiring to a new life on a Land Plan colony.

Each issue appeared in blue wrappers after the manner of a middle-class* journal, O'Connor enjoining readers to retain them all, 'handsomely bound and preserved in their cottage library'. His imaginative writing, however, never matched his political* journalism or platform rhetoric and it fell to Jones to supply most of the material in the journal's pages. This he did with considerable distinction, fine-tuning the talent evident in his subsequent periodical writing until he was imprisoned for two years in June 1848. Without Jones's assistance, O'Connor's increasingly frantic attempts to stave off the collapse of the Land Plan led him to neglect the journal. The July 1848 issue was postponed to August. When the double issue appeared it, and the next number, were occupied entirely by transcripts from a parliamentary enquiry into the Plan. The final three issues haphazardly mixed scraps left on Jones's desk and yet more Land Plan polemic. MSC

Source: Allen and Ashton 2005.

LADIES' CABINET OF FASHION, MUSIC, AND ROMANCE (1832-1870) This high-quality shilling monthly*, published* by George Henderson, offered its readers a diet of fiction poetry*, reviews*, fashion*, news* and beautifully engraved* fashion coloured plates. These were of high quality and lavish in quantity, up to eight per month. It carried a pre-Victorian model of the ladies' magazine into the new era, though by the 1840s it was defending its emphasis on dress and furniture as being consistent with 'elegance, refinement and delicate discernment in everyday affairs' and indeed claimed a moral purpose in its coverage of fashion. Edited* at first by Margaret and Beatrice de Courcy, its history is complicated because from 1852 its contents were identical with those of the *New Monthly Belle Assemblee** and the *Ladies' Companion**, which had themselves amalgamated and were issued under the title the *Ladies' Companion and New Monthly Belle Assemblee.* Later editorial arrangements are obscure, though possibly Camilla Toulmin* edited it for a while. MRB

Sources: *Ladies' Cabinet, Waterloo.*

LADIES' COMPANION (1849-1870) Launched by the publishers Bradbury & Evans* at the very end of 1849, this lively double-column* weekly* sold for 3d. It was edited* by Jane Loudon* and early contributors included Mary Howitt*, Mary Russell Mitford and Geraldine Jewsbury*. As well as serialized fiction*, it included poetry*, reviews* of books and theatre, articles, occasional letters and illustrated* needlework patterns. The full-size woodcuts* often accompanied poems, though it was not always clear which was primary. If this element looked back to earlier publication models, it was in advance of its time in its regular columns* on gardening* and on household 'hints and receipts', the latter written by Eliza Acton, whose work not only influenced Isabella Beeton* but also provided some of her copy. Despite this, the *Ladies' Companion* after just over two years was amalgamated with two older ladies' magazines, the *Ladies Cabinet** and the *New Monthly Belle Assemblee,* and became identical with their combined title. MRB

Sources: *Ladies' Companion, Waterloo.*

LADIES' JOURNAL: A NEWSPAPER OF FASHION, LITERATURE, MUSIC AND VARIETY (1847) As its name suggests, the *Ladies' Journal* was aimed by its publisher* Edward Lloyd* at a female audience, though the price* of just 1d (2d stamped) distinguished this periodical from its more polite rivals. Profusely illustrated*, the periodical was similar to many of the publications that Lloyd was putting out from his office in Salisbury Square*, off Fleet Street*. It combined romantic fiction with poetry* and articles about leading figures of the day such as Jenny Lind (8 May 1847). Features such as 'The Drunkard's Wife' (10 July 1847) suggest some engagement with temperance*, but this was not a persistent theme. Each issue contained articles about fashion* for women (with a particular emphasis on the latest styles from France). Other features included guides to dance steps and advice on domestic* economy. The periodical always featured a serial* fiction. There was at least one page of advertising* (usually for household goods, musical instruments and notices of Lloyd's other publications including his sheet music). Although most of the authors were male, there were a number of female contributors. Launched on 3 April 1847, it was incorporated with *Lloyd's Penny Sunday Times and People's Police Gazette* on 18 September 1847. RM

Source: *Ladies' Journal.*

LADIES' LITERARY DINNER (1889 – 1914) Honor Morten* acted as the honorary secretary, supported by co-writers, Sarah Grand* and L. T. Meade* in organizing the annual Ladies' Literary Dinner held from 1889 at the Criterion Restaurant. Morten explained the reason for this annual event being that, 'it helps that unity amongst our sex which gives strength, it provides experience in speech-making, and it provides the pleasure to be found in a purely feminine gathering'. From 1894 it was known as the Women Writers' Dinner. The Dinner was open to women journalists* and other writers, and at the 1894 dinner journalists were represented by among others Miss Billington from the *Daily Graphic**, Evelyn March-Phillipps* of the *Fortnightly Review**, Mrs Aitken from the *Gentlewoman* and Miss Bulley from the *Manchester Guardian**. Women who were members of the Women Writers' Club* also attended this event such as Mrs Stannard*, Annie S. Swan* and Mrs Humphry Ward. At the last dinner of the century 200 women were present, including Clementina Black*, Lady Jane Strachey and Beatrice Harraden, Eliza L. Linton's* protégée. As with so many other British fixtures, the dinner was abandoned after the outbreak of the First World War. CL

Sources: *Englishwoman's Review* 1900, *Hearth and Home* 1899, Hughes 2007, *Women's Penny Paper* 1890, *Women's Signal* 1894.

LADIES' TREASURY (1858-1895) The *Ladies' Treasury* is considered the longest-lasting general illustrated* monthly magazine of the Victorian period. Its subtitle – *An Illustrated Magazine of Entertaining Literature, Education, Fine Art, Domestic Economy, Needlework and Fashion* – reveals the emphasis on topics considered appropriate for middle-class* Victorian women. Initially 7d, for a 32-page issue published* by Ward & Lock*, it is generally portrayed as the chief rival of Samuel* and Isabella* Beeton's *Englishwoman's Domestic Magazine (EDM)**, aimed at the same audience, addressing similar subjects and sold at an equally cheap* price*.

All this made the *Ladies' Treasury* a principal competitor*, especially because of its popular supplement*, the *Treasury of Literature* (1868-1875). From the 1860s, fashion* plates and needlework patterns were also added regularly. Its editor* was

Eliza Warren, a journalist* and writer of advice books for the lower middle classes. Another famous name was the novelist Harriette Marie Smythies, who published fiction in its pages, as well as regular articles on the conduct of women. JDR

Sources: Beetham 1996, Cross 1985, White 1970.

LADY (1885-) This weekly* magazine, founded in 1885 by Thomas Gibson Bowles*, is still published and privately owned by the grandchildren of the founder. It was one of a group of 6d weeklies aimed at 'ladies' which appeared in the 1880s and 1890s, following the success of the *Queen**, and it contained much the same mix of contents aimed at the 'intelligent', but domestic*, upper-middle class woman. However, the *Lady* dropped its price* to 3d and built its subsequent success by developing one aspect of the general formula, namely the personal advertisements*, particularly those for domestic staff and country cottages, a niche it still occupies. It was at first edited jointly by Mr Tiller and Mr Hemyng but in 1895 Rita Shell (the governess of Bowles's children) was appointed editor*, remained in the post for 25 years, and is credited with the journal's success. AU

Sources: Beetham 1996, *Lady*, *Waterloo*, White 1970.

LADY CYCLIST (1895-1897) The *Lady Cyclist* was edited by Charles S. Sisley who intended that the material in the journal 'shall be almost entirely written by members of the fair sex'. A 54-page monthly selling for 3d and then weekly* (1897) at 1d, the journal was one of the signs of the bicycling craze of the 1890s and was owned by Cycling Press Ltd of Fleet Street*. It 'aimed to provide useful advice for the growing number of women who shared this enthusiasm' (British Library) As a monthly* it

Figure 34: A 'lady cyclist' ridiculed in *Punch*, 5 Oct. 1895: 159.

had a circulation* of 5,000. Each issue suggested particular rides, information about maintaining a bicycle and carried fiction and advertisements*. But it was more than an enthusiasts' technical magazine as the *Lady Cyclist* was one of the voices that campaigned against the corset and carried articles that reflected the way women were challenging their prescribed social roles. The first issue, for instance, carried an article on 'The New Woman and the Woman of Old'. Illustrated* with engravings* and photographs*, the front cover was inspired by the art nouveau influence of the period. J. C. Percy edited* it in 1897, at which point it was merged* with *Wheelwoman* (1897-1899), owned by Miss E. E. Palmer and edited by Mabel Edwards and Charles F. Rideal. **AH**

Sources: *BL Catalogue, Waterloo.*

LADY'S MAGAZINE (1770-1847) Claiming to be written 'by ladies for ladies', this important monthly established the mixed and heterogeneous genre* of the magazine* as appropriate for upper-class* ladies' reading and included several of the elements which came to define 'the woman's magazine'* for the next century. These included fiction, articles, poetry*, music*, exemplary biographies (often illustrated*), and dress and fashion*. Notably absent were those elements of domestic* advice which were later to become a staple, but the general tone was didactic. Its first title – the *Lady's Magazine; or Entertaining Companion for the Fair Sex, Appropriated Solely to their Use and Amusement* – lasted some 60 years until 1830, when it changed to *Lady's Magazine or Mirror of the Belles Lettres, Fine Arts, Music, Drama, Fashions, etc.* At 2s 6d in 1832, the magazine was expensive. It encouraged readers to contribute and those who did were addressed, rebuked and encouraged. However, most of the copy was written by professional or semi-professional writers, notably Mary Russell Mitford with her series of sketches on our 'Our Village', which appeared from 1819. In 1832 the *Lady's Magazine* amalgamated with the *Lady's Monthly Museum* (1798-1832*)*, and the title changed to *Lady's Magazine and Museum of the Belles Lettres, Fine Arts, Music, Drama, Fashions, etc* and in 1847 with the already amalgamated *Court Magazine and Monthly Critic*. However, the combined title folded in 1847, overtaken by the new kinds of publishing associated with the Victorian era. **MRB**

Sources: Beetham 1996, Hunter 1977, Pearson 1996.

LADY'S PICTORIAL (1880-1921) According to an 1895 interview* published in the *Sketch*,

Alfred Gibbons created the *Lady's Pictorial* as a rival to the *Queen*, bringing out the first number in September 1880 as a 3d monthly* illustrated* paper for ladies. Soon, in March 1881, it became a weekly*, still priced* 3d. Three years later, when Gibbons was joined by William and Charles Ingram of the *Illustrated London News*, the journal increased both in size* and cost, and remained at 6d until 1918.

At a time when periodicals flourished and perished rapidly, the *Lady's Pictorial* was remarkably long lasting, perhaps because it aimed from the beginning to be more than a fashion* and society* magazine, and regularly published articles on the enlargement of women's sphere, including several series on employment for women. The editors* also made a point of employing a large number of women on the staff. Many used pseudonyms*, but others such as Ella Hepworth Dixon* signed with their own names. Moreover, especially for its Summer and Christmas* numbers, the *Lady's Pictorial* could boast of prestigious pens such as Rhoda Broughton, Marie Corelli, Violet Hunt and Margaret Oliphant*. It also employed avant-garde artists such as Maurice Greiffenhagen, Dudley Hardy, Bernard Partridge and F. H. Townsend. **VF**

Sources: Fehlbaum 2005, Phillipps 1894, *Sketch* 30 Jan. 1895, *Waterloo, Woman at Home* 1898.

LADY'S REALM (1896-1915) The *Lady's Realm* was an upmarket, monthly* women's magazine* aimed at aspirational middle-class and upper-class* readers. Costing 6d, it was lavishly illustrated* with engravings and photographs* and featured popular authors such as Marie Corelli, Frances Hodgson Burnett, and M. E. Braddon*. Along with fiction, poetry* and fashion* reports, *Lady's Realm* addressed the relatively new interest in home decor and featured a regular society* column*. Participating in celebrity* journalism, the first issue advertised portraits and autographs on its cover. White notes that *Lady's Realm* was one of the magazines which allowed its name to be used for endorsements in advertising*. It was a staple of public library ladies' reading rooms*. **TD**

Sources: Ashdown 1971, Baggs 2005, Beetham 1996, Varty 2000, Versteeg 1981, White 1970.

LADY'S WORLD (1886-1887); WOMAN'S WORLD (1887-1890) The *Lady's World*, a shilling* illustrated* monthly* magazine published by Cassell & Co* was founded by general manager Sir Thomas Wemyss Reid. After six rather unsuccessful months, Oscar Wilde* was employed to take over as editor*. He suggested a change of title* to

Woman's World, a term which did not carry the same connotations of class* and referred obliquely to contemporary debates on the woman question. He also undertook a revamp, on the grounds that the magazine was 'too feminine and not sufficiently womanly'. Wilde's identity as editor was advertised* well in advance and appeared on the cover. Where signature of articles in the *Lady's World* had been infrequent, Wilde mostly insisted upon it, assembling a cast of well-known literary* figures including Olive Schreiner, Emily Faithfull* and Millicent Garrett-Fawcett*. Under his editorship the magazine carried articles on Sappho and cross-dressing and often advocated progressive views on gender* roles and on women's social and cultural achievements. Wilde resigned in August 1889 and the magazine continued with a new editor (probably Wilde's subeditor*, Arthur Fish) until it ceased publication in 1890. Though targeted at middle- and upper-class readers*, the price* may have been too high to make it a financially viable enterprise.
ALC
Sources: Clayworth 1997, Green 1997, Holland 2000, Nowell-Smith, 1958.

LAMB, CHARLES (1775-1834) Best known for his essays of 'Elia' in the *London Magazine** in the 1820s, and for his earlier *Tales from Shakespeare* (written for children with his sister Mary), Lamb was a playwright, novelist, poet and contributor to several other literary periodicals.

School proved an important opportunity for networking: at Christ's Hospital, which Leigh Hunt* also attended, Lamb formed a close friendship with Coleridge*, through whom he began publishing (four of his sonnets appeared in Coleridge's *Poems** in 1796) and entered literary circles (he met the Wordsworths at Coleridge's house the same year). Later he was to befriend William Godwin, R. H. Horne, John Horne Tooke, De Quincey*, Keats, Shelley and others. After unsuccessful experiments in drama, the much more successful *Tales from Shakespeare* (1807) and other volume-form works for children published by Godwin, Lamb's first periodical essays appeared in Leigh Hunt's *Reflector* in 1810. He also contributed political* poetry* to the *Examiner**, but no more essays appeared until 1819, again in the *Examiner*. From September 1820 to December 1823 the Elia essays appeared almost monthly in the *London*. While several more essays appeared in the *London* until May 1826, by January of that year Lamb was writing regularly for the *New Monthly**. After September, however, increasingly prey to drink, his major productive period was over, though he did go on to contribute pieces to William Hone's* *Table Book, Blackwood's**, the *Englishman's Magazine**, and *the Athenaeum**.
AK
Sources: Burton 2003, *Charles Lamb Bulletin*, *ODNB*, Parker 2000, Wu 1998.

LANCASHIRE CONGREGATIONAL CALENDAR (1866-1920) Started in 1866 as a 4d annual* octavo of around 240 pages, this superseded the *Annual Report of the Committee of the Lancashire Congregational Union*, which dated back to 1838. Though better produced, contents and pattern remained similar to the *Calendar*, apart from the inclusion of some advertisements* for stained glass windows, unfermented wine and local* publications. It was typical of the many annual reports produced by both religious* and secular bodies throughout the century. The *Calendar* was published* in Manchester first by John Heywood and then by Tubbs and Brook, and was edited* for over 35 years by the Rev. James McDougall. It contained rules of the Union, a list of officers, ministers and delegates, the Chairman's address, report for the current year, business of the annual meeting, treasurers' statements and statistics of and reports from local Churches. In addition it published reports of the Lancashire College, the London Missionary* Society, the Irish Evangelical Society, the Colonial Missionary Society, the Pastors' Retiring Fund and the Nottingham Congregational Institute. In 1881 the title was changed to the *Lancashire Congregational Year Book*, which continued until 1920.
MP/TW/MRB
Sources: *Annual Reports of the Committee to the Independent Churches and Congregations of Lancashire, Lancashire Congregational Calendar.*

LANCET (1823-) The *Lancet*, a general medical* weekly*, first published 5 October, was named after both the surgical instrument and pointed arch window, its purpose being both to excise dross and supply illumination. It was not the first medical weekly, but its predecessors soon failed whereas the *Lancet* achieved a circulation* of over 4,000 by the end of 1825 and some 8,000 by 1828. Until overtaken by the *British Medical Journal** in the 1870s, it had the largest circulation* of any medical periodical. The *Lancet* was founded by the redoubtable Thomas Wakley*. At first it was not purely a medical journal and carried columns* on chess, literature*, the theatre and other subjects. But by 1825 all non-medical material had been dropped.

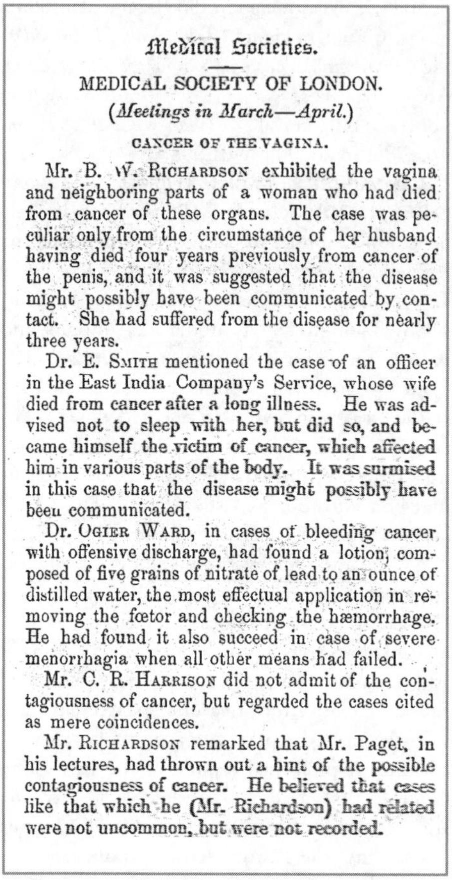

Medical Societies.

MEDICAL SOCIETY OF LONDON.

(*Meetings in March—April.*)

CANCER OF THE VAGINA.

Mr. B. W. RICHARDSON exhibited the vagina and neighboring parts of a woman who had died from cancer of these organs. The case was peculiar only from the circumstance of her husband having died four years previously from cancer of the penis, and it was suggested that the disease might possibly have been communicated by contact. She had suffered from the disease for nearly three years.

Dr. E. SMITH mentioned the case of an officer in the East India Company's Service, whose wife died from cancer after a long illness. He was advised not to sleep with her, but did so, and became himself the victim of cancer, which affected him in various parts of the body. It was surmised in this case that the disease might possibly have been communicated.

Dr. OGIER WARD, in cases of bleeding cancer with offensive discharge, had found a lotion, composed of five grains of nitrate of lead to an ounce of distilled water, the most effectual application in removing the fœtor and checking the hæmorrhage. He had found it also succeed in case of severe menorrhagia when all other means had failed.

Mr. C. R. HARRISON did not admit of the contagiousness of cancer, but regarded the cases cited as mere coincidences.

Mr. RICHARDSON remarked that Mr. Paget, in his lectures, had thrown out a hint of the possible contagiousness of cancer. He believed that cases like that which he (Mr. Richardson) had related were not uncommon, but were not recorded.

Figure 35: Detail of a page in the *Lancet* (May 1854: 457) summarizing the current research on cancer of the vagina as presented at the Medical Society of London.

Some have claimed that Wakley established the *Lancet* principally as a campaigning journal to press the case for medical reform. However, his principal goal was always to inform and educate by publishing the latest information for medical students and practitioners in Britain and beyond. The preface to the journal's first number carried no hint that Wakley had any goal but to disseminate knowledge. Only when the medical establishment obstructed his educational mission did Wakley become a committed and combative reformer. Even then, the bulk of the journal consisted of reprints of lectures and other educational matter; the calls for reform and the vituperation that are often viewed as synonymous with the early *Lancet* never occupied more than a quarter of each issue. There can be no doubt, however, that the early *Lancet* gave much offence in some quarters, not only through its scurrilous and often libellous attacks on individuals and institutions but also by its cavalier attitude towards copyright* law. Yet though sued ten times in its first decade, it incurred only modest damages verdicts and its legal costs were largely met through public subscription. Opinion varies about whether Wakley's forthright agitation for medical reform advanced or hindered the cause. James Fernandez Clarke*, who was associated with the *Lancet* for 30 years, considered his editor's* approach counterproductive and noted that Wakley later regretted the havoc he caused.

For a decade the *Lancet* had no regular staff aside from a subeditor*, George Mills. Clarke claimed that thereafter he was the journal's mainstay. Others associated with its early years included James Lambert, Sir William Lawrence and James Wardrop. William Cobbett was an inspiration to Wakley while financial backing and the idea for the *Lancet* may have come from an American, Walter Channing. In 1857 Wakley made his two medically qualified sons, Thomas* and James, his co-proprietors*. In 1862 James became editor* assisted by his older brother. When James died, the *Lancet* was jointly edited by Thomas and his son (also Thomas*). Altogether, the Wakley family exercised editorial control over the journal until 1909, when Squire Sprigge took over. From an early stage the *Lancet* campaigned on socio-medical issues; targets included food adulteration, poor law infirmaries and quackery. It also carried many major contributions to medical science. **PWB**

Sources: Bostetter 1985, Clarke 1874, *ODNB*, Sherrington 1973, Sprigge 1897.

LAND AND WATER (1866-1920) Launched and edited* (until 1880) by the natural historian and pisciculturalist, Francis Buckland* in 1866, *Land and Water* was an illustrated* weekly* journal aimed at country gentlemen for whom a knowledge of practical natural history was likely to be useful. Articles were anonymous*, though contributors' names may be found in the *Wellesley Index to Periodicals** and included John Keast Lord, a personal friend of Buckland's. The magazine, initially subtitled *A Journal of Field Sport, Sea, River Fisheries and Practical Natural History,* was initially conceived as a rival to *Field*, a field-sports magazine for which Buckland had written prolifically for almost ten years prior to 1866; it contained departments on sea and river fisheries, hunting and practical natural history alongside sporting* reports focusing on horseracing, polo, billiards, cricket, football, rowing and shooting, for example. During Buckland's editorship there were often articles, penned by the editor, on practical steps for improving British fish supplies, a subject dear to his heart as Inspector of Fisheries. Its title change in 1914 to *Country Gentleman and Land and Water* was followed in 1916 by another, a reversion to the stark *Land and Water*, but it folded five years later nevertheless. **AB**

Source: *Waterloo.*

LANDELLS, EBENEZER (1808-1860) The key to Ebenezer Landells's significant contribution to the development of the illustrated* periodical as an engraver*, illustrator and proprietor* lies in his apprenticeship to the famous engraver, Thomas Bewick. Moving from Newcastle-upon-Tyne to London in 1829, Landells's career began at Branston* and Vizetelly's* fine art engraving department as manager.

Launching his career at an exciting time marked by a growth in the use of wood engraving illustrations in books and the press, Landells had the energy and talent to recognize this confluence. Starting his own small engraving workshop with his brother, the enterprise evolved fostering talented young engravers, the Dalziel brothers*, Edmund Evans* and Birket Foster*. He was now able to provide illustrations for his own fashion* journal, *Cosmorama*, a brief venture preceding his major contribution to the world of Victorian periodical publication. Combining his inspiration from the French magazine *Le Charivari*, his involvement with journalists Douglas Jerrold*, Henry Mayhew* and William Thackeray*, and his illustrative and financial capacity, Landells published* the first issue of *Punch, or, the London Charivari** in July 1841. He was no businessman, and although *Punch* was a success, there were financial problems that were solved by a takeover by Bradbury & Evans*. However, the new owners reneged on their promise to retain Landells as head of engraving, replacing him with Joseph Swain*.

Having advised Herbert Ingram* on production issues for his new *Illustrated London News** in 1842, Landells was employed as art correspondent to illustrate Queen Victoria's Scottish visit for Ingram's *News*. But Landells' career as magazine proprietor and engraver was by no means over. He was associated with the *Illuminated Magazine**, the *Great Gun*, the *Lady's Newspaper, Diogenes* and the *Illustrated Inventor*. By combining high-quality engraving with technical invention suited to large-scale distribution*, Landells promoted the art of illustration in the periodical press but failed to accrue the financial reward that his enterprise seemed to warrant. **CL**

Source: *ODNB.*

LANDON, LAETITIA ELIZABETH (1802-1838) A ubiquitous presence in print culture from her debut in 1820 to her death, Laetitia Landon was an able poet, editor*, and critic. First appearing in the *Literary Gazette** at age 17, and later a frequent contributor of poetry* to the *New Monthly Magazine**, Landon became one of the best-known names in the literary* annuals*. She contributed to the *Forget-Me-Not* (1824-1833, 1835-1837, 1839, 1844), *Friendship's Offering* (1824-1828, 1836-1837, 1844), *Literary Souvenir* (1825-1828, 1831-1832, 1835-1837), *Amulet* (1826-1833, 1835-1836), and *Juvenile Forget-Me-Not* (1831-1833, 1826-1837). Additionally, she edited and single-handedly authored entire volumes of *Fisher's Drawing Room Scrapbook* (1832-1838), the 1832 *Easter Gift*, the 1833 *Book of Beauty* and the 1838 *Flowers of Loveliness*. Her anonymous* literary criticism appeared contemporaneously.

By 1828 Landon was the *Literary Gazette's* chief reviewer*. Her close working relationship with William Maginn*, as well as a professional and personal relationship with William Jerdan*, led to gossip that doomed Landon's marriage to the governor of Africa's Gold Coast. Her sudden death there, under suspicious circumstances, was widely reported and comprised her poignant, last contributions to contemporary journalism; some work in gift books and annuals* continued to appear for a few months after her death. Decades later, her affiliation with the *Keepsake* (1828-1829, 1831-1834, 1836-1837) was commemorated in *Middlemarch* (Chapter 27). **KF**

Sources: Lawford 2000, Renalds 1990, Stephenson 1995.

LANE, JOHN (1854-1925) John Lane, noted publisher* of books through his London firm of John Lane, the Bodley Head, gave nineteenth-century journalism two important magazines: the *Yellow Book** and the *Anglo-Saxon Review: A Quarterly Miscellany**. They embodied, respectively, two significant British *fin-de-siècle* currents – aesthetic experimentation and imperialist* triumphalism.

Although the Bodley Head was founded jointly in 1887 by Elkin Mathews and John Lane, the latter forced out his partner while launching the *Yellow Book*. Lane's involvement in the quarterly* went beyond merely publishing it, for he sometimes overrode decisions by Henry Harland, its literary* editor*, and Aubrey Beardsley*, the art editor. In April 1895, amidst the scandal of the Oscar Wilde* trials, he fired Beardsley. With Patten Wilson, he then oversaw the magazine's art contents. The *Yellow Book* was innovative in abjuring serial fiction*, reproducing visual works for their own sake (not as illustrations*), and featuring numerous women writers and artists. Lane also made it a transatlantic* success, distributing* it in both Britain and the United States.

Lane's other 1890s periodical was the brainchild of the American-born ('Jennie') Lady Randolph Churchill. While the *Yellow Book* avoided contemporary events, the *Anglo-Saxon Review* mixed art and literature with jingoistic politics*. Lane clashed with Jennie Churchill over business matters but supported her demand for an aesthetic format, with leather bindings modelled upon Renaissance originals. **MDS**

Sources: Lambert and Ratcliffe 1987, Lasner 1998, Mix 1960, Nelson 1970, Stetz and Lasner 1994.

LANG, ANDREW (1844-1912) Andrew Lang was one of the most prolific men of letters of the 1880s and 1890s. He contributed to journals such as *Dark Blue*, *Fraser's Magazine* and *Macmillan's Magazine* first as a student, later as a fellow at Oxford. At Oxford he also met Frederick William Longman, son of a Longman's* partner, thus becoming part of a network of Oxford and Cambridge alumnae that dominated print media in coming decades. Lang's friendship with the young Longman may also explain his life-long involvement with the firm as author, reader and consultant.

Lang's marriage in 1875 was incompatible with his Oxford fellowship and he moved to London. From then on he earned a livelihood by his pen. Edmund Gosse* described him emerging in 1876 as 'the finest finished product of his age, with the bright armour of Oxford burnished on his body to such a brilliance that humdrum eyes could hardly bear the radiance of it'. 'No editor', George Saintsbury* commented, 'could hesitate about annexing anything of Lang's that was offered to him and promptly demanding more'. Lang's success was instantaneous. He was invited almost at once to write non-political leaders* or middles* for the *Saturday Review* and the *Daily News*. His style became his trademark. Young authors like W. P. Ridge, C. K. Shorter* and G. B. Shaw* counted the day empty unless they had read an article by Lang. His leaders for the *Daily News*, described as 'fairy-tales written by an erudite Puck', appeared three or four times a week. Lang's prolificacy was extraordinary. He contributed historical* essays on a regular basis to *Bookworm*, he wrote on literature* and historical mysteries for *Cornhill Magazine*, he commented on literature for *Fortnightly Review*, *Academy* and *Dark Blue*, and contributed on anthropological

subjects for *Fraser's Magazine*. Lang also contributed occasionally to *Antiquary, Author, Century Magazine, Chapman's Magazine of Fiction, English Illustrated Magazine*, *Magazine of Art*, *Manchester Guardian*, *Morning Post*, *Nineteenth Century*, *Outlook in Politics, Life, Letters and the Arts, Portfolio*, *Scots Observer*, and the *Sketch*. His main platform after 1882 was 'At the Sign of the Ship', a monthly causerie* in *Longman's Magazine*.

Lang's influence as a literary critic can hardly be overstated. In the debate on the romance vs. the realistic novel he was firmly on the side of the romance. His reviews launched the careers of Robert Louis Stevenson, Henry Rider Haggard and Rudyard Kipling. Conversely, he attracted bitter reactions from authors whose work he could not appreciate in the form of unsympathetic fictional creations modelled on him and his career, in George Gissing's *New Grub Street* (as Jasper Milvain) and Corelli's *The Silver Domino*.

Lang was a well-paid writer. Apart from his journalistic work he published more than 80 books. His hope to become an editor* never materialized, although he was briefly the English editor of *Harper's Magazine* (1884-1885). **MD**

Sources: Demoor 1988, Green 1946, *ODNB*.

LANKESTER, EDWIN (1814-1874) Lankester had long combined his medical career with wider scientific interests and during the 1840s he began giving popular lectures and writing regularly for the *Daily News*, where he supported Thomas Wakley's* campaigns for medical* reform in the *Lancet*. He also contributed extensively to the *Athenaeum* (1845-1870), claiming that, until 1849, he was responsible for virtually every article on medicine, sanitation, physiology and natural history. In 1845 he married Phebe Pope*, whose own botanical interests led her towards journalism, and in the early 1860s both published a number of articles in their friend Robert Hardwicke's* *Popular Science Review*, he on public health and sanitation and she on wild flowers, while their eldest son Ray* wrote on entomology and fossils. Lankester shared the publisher's interest in microscopy, becoming president of the Quekett Microscopical Club in 1865, with Hardwicke as its treasurer.

In 1853 Lankester helped found the *Quarterly Journal of Microscopical Science*, which he co-edited* with George Busk until 1868, when he was joined by his son Ray, who then took over the editorship with Joseph Frank Payne in 1872. In 1865 Lankester also began a new *Journal of Social Science*, and used his editorship to expound his own views on sanitation and contagious diseases, although it folded in the following year after only two volumes. **GD**

Sources: English 1990, Lightman 2004a, *ODNB*.

LANKESTER, (EDWIN) RAY (1847-1929) Through his parents Edwin* and Phebe*, Lankester began contributing to the *Popular Science Review* while still in his teens, and in 1869 joined his father as co-editor* of the *Quarterly Journal of Microscopical Science*, then co-editing it with Joseph Frank Payne and others following his father's departure in 1871, before finally becoming sole editor* (1878-1920). Under Ray Lankester, the *Quarterly Journal* shifted from his father's emphasis on diffusion and instead became more attuned to professional* requirements, accepting contributions only from university researchers as well as leading foreign authorities. It also became more specialized, jettisoning botany to concentrate exclusively on zoology. In addition to editing it, Lankester contributed more than 70 articles, and wrote for numerous other scientific* periodicals like the *Annals and Magazine of Natural History*.

Despite his determination to reform and professionalize the study of science, Lankester never lost his original interest in popularization, and throughout his life contributed to a number of general periodicals, including the *Fortnightly Review* and the *English Illustrated Magazine*, where he published a sketch of his friend H. G. Wells* in 1904. Three years later Lankester began a popular and long-running weekly column* in the *Daily Telegraph* entitled 'Science from an Easy Chair', and earlier in the 1870s he had utilized *The Times* to engineer a public scandal over fraudulent spiritualists. **GD**

Sources: Bourne 1919, Lightman 2004a, Luckhurst 2002, *ODNB*.

LANKESTER, PHEBE (1825-1900) Renowned during her lifetime for her books on botany, Lankester (née Pope), was a prolific journalist*, who contributed to the popularization of scientific* issues, as well as a number of important late Victorian concerns about the place of women in society. Lankester, who also wrote under the pseudonym 'Penelope', has often been overshadowed by her more famous husband, Dr Edwin Lankester*, and her son, Sir Ray Lankester*, but her own writings are an apt example of the contribution women made to the dissemination of science from mid-century onwards.

Lankester wrote articles for the *Popular Science Review* (1861-1864), revealing her understanding of scientific language as well as the historical and cultural aspects of plants and flowers. In the 1870s Lankester turned increasingly to a consideration of women's health and sanitary conditions, publishing articles in the *Queen*, *Chambers's Journal* and *Magazine of the Arts*. Her interests in the female condition and in the popularization of science were united in a concern for the spread of formal scientific education for all children. For 20 years after the death of her husband, she used the pseudonym 'Penelope' to write a weekly column* in several provincial* newspapers on contemporary topics of concern to women, including employment and emigration. **CB**

Sources: Lightman 2004c, *ODNB*, Shteir 1997.

LARDNER, DIONYSIUS (1793-1859) A journalist*, editor*, proprietor* and encyclopaedist, Dionysius Lardner was an important figure in the early and mid-nineteenth-century 'march of mind'.

In residence at Trinity College, Dublin (1817-1827), Lardner devoted himself to writing on literary* and scientific* subjects for the *Encyclopaedia Edinensis* and the *Encyclopaedia Metropolitana*; he also contributed to the *Transactions of the Irish Academy* and wrote four treatises on mathematics for beginners. Elected to the new London University's Chair of Natural Philosophy and Astronomy in 1827, he held the professorship for four years, during which time he continued his efforts to educate in other venues as well. His course of lectures on the steam engine, first published in 1828, was termed by the *Athenaeum* 'the most popular mechanical treatise ever published'.

Although he wrote for the *Daily News*, *British and Foreign Review*, *Edinburgh Review*, and *Herapath's Railway Magazine*, Lardner's most significant journalistic venture was the *Monthly Chronicle*. He had conceived of such a journal in 1832, but it was not begun until 1838, with Edward Bulwer (later Bulwer Lytton*) as co-proprietor/editor for its first six months; Lardner was sole editor* (Nov. 1838-March 1839), during which the journal lived up to its subtitle, *A National Journal of Politics, Literature, Science, and Art*. Most issues began with or featured a substantial article by Bulwer on a pressing political* issue; literature was variously addressed, for instance in the monthly* 'Review* of Literature'; theatre, music, the opera, engraving* and the Royal Academy Exhibition (reviewed by Anna Jameson)* were among the arts covered. Not surprisingly given Lardner's background and interests, however, 'The Sciences and Useful Arts' were prominent. The Advertisement had promised coverage of science* topics for 'the general reader' unfamiliar with 'the technicalities of science,' and Lardner wrote on subjects ranging from the moon (March and Sept. 1838), comets (Aug. 1838), and meteors (Nov. 1838) to heating stoves (March and May 1838). He also promoted such pet projects as steam navigation (March and July 1838) and railways (Aug. and Sept. 1838, Jan. and Feb. 1839).

Because many of Lardner's longer works were published in numbers for a popular* audience, arguably as serials* they may be classed with his journalism. *Dr Lardner's Cabinet Library*, begun in 1830, was discontinued in 1832 after nine volumes, but he edited the 33-volume *Edinburgh Cabinet Library* from 1830 to 1844. His *magnum opus*, the 133-volume *Cabinet Cyclopaedia*, was published in parts at 6d per volume, and the 12-volume *Museum of Science and Art* (1852-1854) which he wrote, appeared in cheap* periodical volumes.

Lardner's critical reputation has fluctuated. While some contemporaries such as William Thackeray* mocked him, others and later commentators considered him a distinguished mathematician, an influential member of the William Whewell group of mathematical economists and an important contributor to mid-century debates about the government regulation of railways. Most scholars now agree that his journalism made him a crucial mediator between the public mind and the new sciences and technologies of early Victorian Britain. JMS

Sources: Allibone 1859, Henderson 1991, *ODNB*, *Wellesley*.

Last, Joseph William (1809?-1880) Joseph Last, master printer and journal proprietor*, came from Ipswich in Suffolk and established a business as a printer, dealer and chapman in Hampstead by 1839. He had created a reputation for himself within the trade, producing successful weeklies* such as *Clarke's Tales of the Wars* (1836-1840?), whose extensive circulation* rested on the superior quality of their illustration*. Last's high level of innovative technical expertise in illustration printing from a cylinder printing* press and his knowledge and execution in printing contributed to the success of these weekly periodicals. Among the papers he printed were *Cockney Adventures and Tales of London Life* (1837-1838), the *Pictorial Mirror* (1838) and *Tom Spring's Life in London and Sporting Chronicle* (1840-1843). Last's ability in poster and display printing was also suited to his success as a theatrical printer located at and near the Strand. After setting himself up as a printer, he launched his first magazine, the *Town**, in 1837. This weekly*

contained scurrilous articles aimed at men about town. It collapsed in May 1840, after 156 numbers. Other short-lived titles include the *Crown* (July 1838-April 1839), the *Squib,* a comic journal (29 May-17 Dec. 1842) and the *People's Police Gazette* (1841) which sought to cash in on the reporting of crime*, murder and execution.

Last was involved in a collaboration with Ebenezer Landells* to publish a journal envisaged as the *Cosmorama* and he introduced Landells to Henry Mayhew*. He was also associated with Mayhew in one of the most significant projects, retrospectively, of his career as one of the group in the initial meetings and plans for the magazine *Punch** (July 1841ff) together with Mark Lemon*; indeed, Last invested one-third of the initial capital (£600) with the first issue printed. However, disagreements as to the format* and design of the magazine, which Last thought ill-advised, led him to withdraw from further involvement. Yet, it was just this experience in illustrative printing that gained him his position as the managing printer involved with Herbert Ingram* in the launch of the *Illustrated London News** in 1842. Last's success was with his involvement with cheap* weekly periodicals, targeted at a new readership* due to the rising literacy levels, coupled with his specialism in illustrative reproduction. DHL/CL

Sources: Griffiths 1992, *ODNB*, Spielmann 1895, *Waterloo*.

Latimer, Thomas (1803-1888) Thomas Latimer, shorthand*-reporter, and Devon-based editor* and proprietor* was born in Bristol, and following a sparse education was apprenticed to a printer in London. There, he and a group of like-minded apprentices (including the future humorist and playwright Douglas Jerrold*) devoted themselves to self-education. Latimer studied at George Birkbeck's London Mechanics' Institute, but withdrew to form the London Gymnastic Society. After his apprenticeship he wrote briefly for the *Morning Post**, supplying jokes for 6d for seven lines, then wrote articles for the radical *Albion* until the government closed it down.

Latimer settled in Exeter, where he was introduced to the leading figures in the local Reform Club who wanted to make better use of the press in campaigning for parliamentary reform. They were prepared to subsidise a newspaper which would support their cause and offered Latimer, whose salary they would pay, as a reporter* to Thomas Besley, proprietor of the *Exeter News and Devon County Chronicle*. Besley probably took on Latimer because he knew shorthand, a rare accomplishment at the time. Latimer claimed to be the first shorthand reporter in the West Country, but after a year this arrangement with the *Chronicle* collapsed. Latimer was then engaged by the *Plymouth Journal,* and in the first six months of 1830 he also edited the *Philo-Danmonian,* a literary* periodical.

Later that year he joined the *Exeter and Plymouth Gazette,* eventually being made acting editor, writing articles exposing poverty and social injustice. These led to his dismissal, particularly his attack on the clergy for opposing asylum reform in the county. However Latimer was immediately hired by James Terrell, proprietor of the radical newspaper, the *Western Times.* In June 1835, Latimer became proprietor and improved the paper by introducing more modern printing machinery*, reducing the price*, and bringing in new features such as a weather forecast and reviews* of books and plays. On important occasions he issued free supplements* and in 1866 Latimer changed the *Western Times* from a weekly* to a daily* paper. During the same year he set up a branch office at neighbouring Tiverton and published the *Tiverton Times and East Devon Reporter.* Although by the mid-century Latimer moderated his journalistic vehemence, he remained committed to social* reform, becoming an overseer of the poor and improvement commissioner in 1849 and a magistrate in 1851. Increasing deafness led him, in the late 1850s, to hand the editorship to his younger son Hugh (1843-1920). DHL

Sources: Lambert 1939, *ODNB.*

LAW MAGAZINE (1828-1915) The *Law Magazine or Quarterly Review of Jurisprudence* (1828-1856), aimed at an audience that included both lawyers and the educated lay public. Edited initially by Abraham Hayward, it acted primarily as an organ of the legal* profession's demands for simplified procedure and abolition of abuses that were the rallying cries of Victorian law reform. It came, however, to represent in the public mind a voice favourable only to the narrow interests of practitioners. A new series began in 1844 with the same name in an attempt to broaden its appeal. The magazine eliminated its primary competitors in 1856 when it absorbed the *Law Review,* while the *Legal Observer* went out of business. The journal now became the *Law Magazine and Law Review* (1856-1872). By adding articles of more intellectual interest, particularly discussions of jurisprudence, the periodical now became the leading legal journal for three decades. In 1872 the magazine changed names again

by dropping the second Law, becoming monthly and starting another series, then another (1875-1898) and then a final series before its demise.

It continued after 1856 to attempt to combine theoretical articles with practical advice, its most famous contributors being Albert Venn Dicey, Thomas Erskine Holland and Sir Henry Maine. The inauguration of the *Law Quarterly Review** in 1885 sealed the journal's fate for the *Law Magazine* did not provide the inquiry into a science of law that legal academics of the 1880s deemed vital. The magazine limped on, but the fusion of law and equity in 1873-1875 had robbed it of its main crusading objective. The First World War presented the final challenge that the magazine could not overcome; in its day, however, it had been perhaps the most influential law journal of the mid-Victorian period. RC

Sources: Cosgrove 1994, Ibbetson 2006, *Waterloo.*

LAW QUARTERLY REVIEW (1885-) Legal periodicals in the nineteenth century usually had two discrete goals: to serve practitioners in their daily labours or to educate the public about the legal system in favour of or against reform. The foundation of the *Law Quarterly Review* in 1885 addressed both these issues and, in addition, aimed at fostering inquiry into law as a science. The editor* was Sir Frederick Pollock, Corpus Professor of Jurisprudence at Oxford, who held the position for nearly 35 years (1885-1919) and who wrote many of the case notes. The periodical reflected dissatisfaction with the structure and content of previous attempts to furnish a journal that fused legal practice and jurisprudence. In retrospect, the *Review* succeeded more in its appeal to the nascent profession of academic law than to barristers and solicitors. Even so, the magazine located its office in London rather than in Oxford, where most of its founders held academic positions.

From its inception the periodical earned a reputation for scholarly excellence that persists to the present. In the first volume alone, among the contributors were such luminaries of legal history and jurisprudence as Sir William Anson, Albert Venn Dicey, Thomas Erskine Holland, Oliver Wendell Holmes, Frederic William Maitland, Paul Vinogradoff and Pollock himself. The outpouring of quality legal scholarship in the *Review* sought to demonstrate the inner logic of the common law as a legal system and thereby establish the law as a worthy field of study at Oxford and Cambridge. In this purpose it triumphed. The case notes did not fare as well, for academic lawyers discovered that the judiciary rarely deigned to notice their efforts, especially when critical, and often rejected the suggestions of their academic colleagues. Nonetheless the *Review* set standards of scholarship and commentary that have perhaps been equalled but never surpassed. It continues today as a premier outlet for legal scholarship in addition to sustaining its reputation for excellence in guidance to contemporary case law. RC

Sources: Cosgrove 1994, Duxbury 2004, *ODNB*, Pollock 1935.

LAW REPORTING See Court and parliamentary reporting

LAWLESS, MATTHEW JAMES (1837-1864) Both artist and illustrator*, Matthew James Lawless only published work in periodicals for a few brief years between 1859 and his early death. His work appeared primarily in *Once a Week**, although he also drew for *Good Words**, *London Society** and the *Churchman's Family Magazine*. A few of his designs were published by *Punch** in 1860 and 1861. Firmly Pre-Raphaelite in mode, Lawless's work was admired sufficiently to be reprinted in several anthologies of illustrations published after his death. BM

Sources: Engen 1990, Goldman 1994, Houfe 1978, Reid 1928, Suriano 2005, White 1897.

LAWRANCE, HANNAH (1795-1875) An historian and journalist, Hannah Lawrance contributed anonymously* to a variety of periodicals (1831-1870), including *Blackwood's Edinburgh Magazine** (1836), *Tait's Edinburgh Magazine** (1841, 1847), *Fraser's** (1844, 1847), *Hood's Magazine** (1844) and *Household Words** (1854-1855). But her most extended commitments, mainly as a reviewer*, were to the *Athenaeum** (1831-1853), and especially to the heavyweight periodical which reflected her own Non-conformist leanings, the *British Quarterly Review** (1847-1870). It is her substantial contributions to this last which most reflect her considerable intellectual range: her subjects include art exhibitions, African exploration, educational and employment opportunities for women and contemporary writers such as Dickens*, Tennyson, Charlotte Brontë and Barrett Browning.

Lawrance's main subjects, however, were the history* and literature* of earlier eras – the Early Modern, and especially the medieval and pre-medieval periods. She knew Latin, Old French, Anglo-Norman, and Old and Middle English, and was committed to making early texts and the ways of life they disclosed more familiar to contemporary readers. In the *Athenaeum* Lawrance welcomed journals, letters, and memoirs relating to the seven-

teenth century and earlier, plus editions of early works, such as the successive parts of the Welsh *Mabinogion* as edited* by Lady Charlotte Guest, and the poetry* of Wyatt and Surrey. She also reviewed early English metrical romances (18 June 1842, 18 Jan. 1845); later in the *British Quarterly* she drew attention to modern editions of medieval histories, romances and ballads in a variety of languages (Feb. 1847, Aug. 1847, Jan. 1860, April 1861, July 1864), and pointed out the impact of Arthurian legends and values on contemporary literature (Oct. 1859). Among Early Modern writers, she covered Spenser (Oct. 1855), Jonson (Apr. 1857), and Sidney (Jan. 1863), and, having surveyed Shakespeare's dramatic predecessors (Aug. 1851), authored the *British Quarterly's* contribution to the Shakespeare tercentenary (April 1864). JCW

Sources: *Athenaeum* Index online, Korn 1981, Lohrli 1973, *ODNB*, *Wellesley*.

LAWSON, EDWARD LEVY (1833-1916) Lawson, first Baron Burnham, a newspaper proprietor*, was born in London in December 1833, the eldest child of Joseph Moses Levy*, printer and proprietor of the *Sunday Times** and *Daily Telegraph**. Educated at University College School, Lawson became a drama critic for the *Sunday Times* but found his most influential role as part of the editorial team (with Thornton Hunt* initially) at the pioneering penny* daily*, the *Daily Telegraph*.

Lawson was one of the committee that sought the repeal of the last of the paper* duties: its abolition in 1861 further facilitated the mass expansion of press readership*, with Lawson among those at the forefront of this historic transformation. Lawson was a hands-on overall manager (though never named editor*) long before his father's withdrawal from the business in the 1880s. Though judged not to have his father's business skill, he had a 'deeper knowledge of public affairs' and was 'much more politically minded' (Burnham: 166). He marshalled an impressive team including Edwin Arnold*, John Merry Le Sage*, Henry Sala* and T. P. O'Connor*, but he still read proofs of the leaders* in each morning's edition with an editorial pencil in hand, 'deleting, strengthening, building up' (W. L. Courtney* cited in Burnham: 163).

Lawson's team took full advantage of the increasingly efficient telegraph* system to provide coverage of national and international news*, and Lawson took personal interest in the paper's focus on art, music* and theatre criticism in particular. Lawson saw the *Telegraph* as an imperial* newspaper

(Koss, I: 203) and came into open conflict with the radical Henry du Pre Labouchère*, who libelled Lawson in 1879 over his holdings of Turkish Bonds. Lawson received a baronetcy from Gladstone in 1892 and a peerage from Alfred Balfour in 1903, the year he handed over the day-to-day running of the paper to his more Liberal-minded son, Harry. **FD**

Sources: Burnham 1955, Koss 1990, *ODNB*.

LAWSON, FRANCIS WILFRID (1842-1935) Primarily a painter, Lawson was also a prolific draughtsman for wood* engravings, and contributed to the major weeklies* and monthlies* of the 1860s and 1870s that specialized in ambitious full-page illustration*. He worked for all three of the literary* magazines with the highest reputation for their illustrations, *Once A Week*, *Good Words* and the *Cornhill Magazine* but also drew for the *Graphic*, a journal committed to combining topical reportage with aesthetically ambitious images, and for comic and satirical* journals like *Fun* and *Punch*. Such versatility was common enough among those jobbing artists who used periodical work, especially early in their careers while they were establishing a reputation, as a means to purchase the leisure to devote to their more ambitious painting. **BM**

Sources: Engen 1990, Houfe 1978, Spielmann 1895.

LAZENBY, WILLIAM (C.1825?-C.1888?) One of the primary publishers* of obscene literature in the 1870s-1880s in London, William Lazenby, like virtually all obscene publishers, used a number of aliases, including 'Duncan Cameron', 'Henry Ashford' and 'Thomas Judd'. In particular, Lazenby published erotic works depicting flagellation, the 'English vice'. He is perhaps best known as the publisher, editor* and occasional contributor to the *Pearl*, a pornographic* magazine* which remains one of the most well-known works of Victorian obscene literature. The *Cremorne; A Magazine of Wit, Facetiae, Parody, Graphic Tales of Love, Etc.* (1882, though backdated on the title page to 1851 to confuse prosecutors) and the *Boudoir* (1883-1884) were both short-lived sequels to the *Pearl*. The *Cremorne* was privately published in a run of 300 and each number sold for a guinea. Lazenby sold to a coterie of wealthy British men, including Monkton Milnes and Charles Algernon Swinburne* circle of pornography collectors. Having previously absconded and escaped imprisonment in the 1870s, in 1886, the 61-year old Lazenby was prosecuted and his stock of obscene literature seized. **MWT**

Sources: Colligan 2006, Mendes 1993.

LEACH, JAMES (C. 1806-1869) James Leach was a leading Manchester Chartist. In 1839, after the loss of his job as a spinner, he became opposed to wage reduction. Faced with an uncertain future, he established a bookselling and printing business in Manchester and in 1844 published* damning details of the ratio between workers and spinning machinery in the cotton mills. Also a committed supporter of the collaboration between English Chartists* and Irish confederates, he represented the Chartists in Dublin on 12 January 1848, at the first meeting between the two movements. In the same year he co-edited*, with fellow Chartists, George Archdeacon and George White, the *English Patriot and Irish Repealer*, which continued until mid-September 1848 as the *English Patriot and Herald of Labour and Co-operation*, with Leach as sole editor. Publication ceased in December when he was arrested for conspiracy and imprisoned with other Chartists in Kirkdale gaol.

Friedrich Engels described Leach as 'an honest, trustworthy and capable man.' (145) His integrity was evident in his capabilities as editor of the *English Patriot* and in the publication of polemical treatises. **DHL**

Sources: Engels 1845, Harrison and Thompson 1978, *ODNB*, Pickering 1995.

LEADER (1850-1860) The *Leader* was a 6d weekly* established in 1850 by Thornton Leigh Hunt* and George Henry Lewes*. Its politics* were progressive, and it set out to provide a forum for the 'most advanced opinions on the questions of the day'. Each issue opened with the 'News* of the Week' and included a 'Postscript' inserted the day before publication. Leading* articles and correspondence* ('Open Council') separated the portion devoted to current affairs from the literary* content at its rear. The latter section combined coverage of the arts (Lewes provided its theatre reviews* as 'Vivian') with original literary material. This was followed by market reports, and usually two pages of advertisements*.

The *Leader* published two editions a week, one for the 'country' on Friday, and one for 'town' on Saturday. Despite its small readership*, the *Leader* ran for almost 11 years. It sourced most of its news and market intelligence from other publications, a strategy that allowed it to avoid the Stamp Act* and survive a fire that burnt down its offices in 1853. In July 1858 its new publisher*, Frederick Tomlins, expanded the mercantile portions of the journal. The *Leader* merged* with the *Saturday Analyst* in January 1860 and ceased publication the following November. **JM**

Source: *ODNB*.

LEADING ARTICLES / LEADERS The *Oxford English Dictionary* records the first use of the term 'leading article' in 1807. The expression 'leader' may have derived not just from the prominence of the article but also from the custom of 'leading' the column* by using strips of lead to space the lines of type more widely. The 'Letters of Junius' which appeared in Henry Sampson Woodfall's *Public Advertiser* (1768-1772), and believed to have been written by Sir Philip Francis, are sometimes considered to be the prototype of the anonymous* leading article, representing the opinion of the newspaper and usually dealing with the major political* or foreign policy issues of the day. The use of a leader enabled editorial policy to be positioned with regard to a specific news item or theme. A newspaper could thus demonstrate some collective voice or identity, which was a valuable way to promote and capture its intended readership*. Whenever you locate its inception, the leading article certainly flexed considerable muscle by the Victorian period.

As Dallas Liddle has argued, 'the genre* [the leading article] denoted was the most important, authoritative, and characteristic mode of British journalism, a position it would hold powerfully through much of the nineteenth century, and formally until well into the twentieth century'. (Liddle: 5) Many of the most prominent journalists and editors* of the nineteenth century crafted their skills as leader writers. However, as the influence of the New Journalism* came to be felt in the daily* press, the weight of the leading article waned. Leslie Stephen*, for example, notes that the leading article of the *Pall Mall Gazette*, founded in 1865, 'took up a larger proportion of space than it does at the present day' (1895), adding that his brother, James Fitzjames Stephen* wrote between half and two-thirds of the leaders 1865-1869 (214). The newspapers linked to the New Journalism which emerged towards the end of the century tended to cut the leading article to a short pithy paragraph or two, more easily digested by the speed reader. **JRW**
Sources: Hindle 1937, Liddle 1999, Stephen 1895.

LEATHERLAND, JOHN AYRE (1812-1874) A widely-known poet in his native Northamptonshire, J. A. Leatherland turned to journalism after an accident made it impossible for him to continue making and selling silk vests. He became a local leader of Chartism and wrote pamphlets and in the early 1840s contributed poetry* to Thomas Cooper's* *Midland Counties Illuminator* (1841). In the late 1840s he also wrote articles on local* news* for the *Northampton Herald* and another local paper

the *South Midland Free Press,* but this work did not pay well. In the 1850s Leatherland earned no more than £50 a year from his newspaper work, although his articles were often interesting enough to win prizes and find their way into periodicals. His greatest success came in 1860 with the publication of a piece in John Cassell's* *Family Magazine*. In the last years of his life Leatherland experienced an extraordinary economic transformation. Having come into some money, he was able to buy the *Wellingborough News* for £100. This provided him with an annual income of £300. After his death in 1874, his widow sold the *Wellingborough News* for £650. **SFR**
Sources: Ashton and Roberts 1999, Leatherland 1862,

LEE, RAWDON BRIGGS (1845-1908) Rawdon Lee's father, a Unitarian minister, was also proprietor* and editor* of the *Kendal Mercury* and Rawdon learned journalism from him, whom he succeeded as editor, remaining in this post until 1883 when he went to London. Lee had a keen interest in field sports and dog breeding, and the latter interest led him to induce the *Field** to appoint him as Kennel Editor in succession to John Henry Walsh. Lee remained in this post for nearly 24 years, until June 1907. He had an intimate knowledge of nearly every breed of dog and was a reporter* of dog shows and field trials for 40 years. He was also well-known as a shower and judge of dogs – particularly fox terriers.

In addition to his writing for the *Field,* he contributed articles on angling, otter hunting, wrestling and dogs to other journals such as *Land and Water**, the *Fishing Gazette** and the *Stock-Keeper and Fancier's Chronicle*. He sometimes used the pseudonym* of 'Sprint' or his initials 'R. B. L.'. Lee's journalism established his reputation as an expert, and his book, *A History and Description of the Modern Dogs of Great Britain and Ireland, Non-Sporting Division* (2 vols 1894) was regarded as a classic. **DHL**
Sources: *Kendal Mercury* 1908, *ODNB*, *The Times* 1908, *Westmorland Gazette* 1908.

'LEE, VERNON' (1856-1935) Journalist and critic, Violet Paget was better known under her pseudonym of 'Vernon Lee'. A prodigious child, educated by her mother and half-brother the poet Eugène Lee-Hamilton, she was in her teens when she placed her first journal articles in the Swiss journal *La Famille* (1870) and the Italian journal (*La Rivista Europea*, 1875). Her first writings in English appeared in *Fraser's Magazine** in 1877. The publication of *Studies of the Eighteenth Century in Italy*

(1880), a book that earned her public acclaim and brought her to the attention of major writers and intellectuals of late nineteenth-century London, including Walter Pater*, Mary F. Robinson, William Michael Rossetti*, Robert Browning, Bertrand Russell, Henry James*, Bernard Berenson, George Moore, Arthur Symons*, John Addington Symonds and Oscar Wilde*. Her relationship with these writers and their networks opened new doors for her in the English and American periodical press. While associating with Aesthetes and Decadents, she emerged as their critic in her novel *Miss Brown.*

Together with Kate Field, Louise Chandler Moulton, A. Mary F. Robinson, and Helen Zimmern*, Lee was hired by Norman McColl as an anonymous reviewer* for the *Athenaeum*. She reviewed and contributed essays on aesthetics and short fiction to key journals such as the *Cornhill Magazine*, *Contemporary Review*, *Blackwood's Magazine*, the *Academy*, *Living Age* and the *Magazine of Art* (edited by poet W. E. Henley*) among others, utilizing these magazines to publicize and reprint her work. A prolific journalist, she was one of the women who contributed to the most famous periodical of the 1890s, the *Yellow Book*. APV
Sources: Colby 2003, Demoor 2000, Gunn 1964, Mannocchi 1983, Zorn 2003.

LEECH, JOHN (1817-1864) Nineteenth-century caricaturists* began their careers young, and John Leech was publishing his etched and lithographed* satirical* observations by 1835. He was taught to draw for wood* engravings by John Orrin Smith* contributing to *Bell's Life in London* while still in his teens, and establishing a public presence through Percival Leigh's two 'Comic Grammars'. By 1840 he was producing etched comic illustrations* for *Bentley's Miscellany*, and his prolific and popular output of book illustrations* meant that such ambitious illustrated journals as W. J. Linton's* *Illuminated Magazine* were commissioning full-page etchings from him in the early 1840s.

In spite of some technical deficiencies in his technique in drawing for wood, he was inevitably incorporated into the team of *Punch*** contributors when the magazine was launched in 1841. Leech first contributed to the fourth issue of *Punch* (7 August 1841), and he was, with Tenniel* in support, chief political* cartoonist* until 1861, when Tenniel took over. Leech published 3,000 of his drawings in the course of his tenure at the magazine. Spielmann asserts that between 1848 and 1884 Leech and Tenniel were more or less exclusively responsible for the

large-scale political cartoons that dominated each weekly issue, but he also contributed many other drawings. As well as political satire, Leech was responsible for some of *Punch's* spectacular humanitarian gestures, typified in his cartoon 'The Poor Man's Friend' (1845) which shows the appalling skeletal figure of death befriending a destitute social outcast. As well as *Bentley's Miscellany,* Leech contributed to a wide range of fiction-bearing magazines, including the *New Monthly Magazine*, *Once A Week* and the *Illustrated London News*, which commissioned a surprisingly large amount of comic illustration in its early years. BM
Sources: Engen 1990, *ODNB*, Spielmann 1895.

LEEDS INTELLIGENCER (1754-1866) The conservative *Leeds Intelligencer* was published under the motto 'The Altar, the Throne, and the Cottage'. A four-page weekly* founded in Leeds, Yorkshire by Griffith Knight in 1754, from 1819 it was known as the *Leeds Intelligencer and Yorkshire General Advertiser*. Attempting to unite the interests of the landed classes* and industrial workers against the middle classes, this powerful provincial* news* journal circulated well beyond Leeds, collecting political* news from the London press. After the 1790s, the *Leeds Intelligencer* became increasingly recognized as the leading Yorkshire Tory organ and as such was anti-Catholic. It decried Chartism* in 1838 and criticized the Anti-Corn Law League in the 1840s for betraying the interest of the labouring classes, and also supported child labour as 'essential,' providing 'excellent training, humane treatment and useful incomes'.

Departments included local* and foreign* news, cricket, poetry*, liberalism and the established church, advertisements*, health, sports*, commercial intelligence and market* news. During the late 1850s and early 1860s, the *Leeds Intelligencer* printed anti-slavery lectures by Sarah Parker Redmond and William Howard Day. The paper also included usually free supplements* for special occasions, such as on the Spa Field riots of 1817, the trials of Henry Hunt and Burdett in 1820 and the Newark election of 1829. A good medium for advertisements, the *Leeds Intelligencer* managed to maintain a solid if small circulation* in a largely liberal area of England. At times, its advertising space was exploited by the competing *Leeds Mercury*, whose manifestos would be published in the *Intelligencer* as advertisements. In 1855, when the *Mercury* became tri-weekly, the *Intelligencer* countered briefly by becoming bi-weekly, reverting in less than one year to weekly. In 1866, the *Leeds Intelligencer* was

bought out by a small group of conservatives, and became the daily *Yorkshire Post*, originally retaining the *Leeds Intelligencer* as a subheading. **KC**
Sources: *Encyclopaedia Britannica Online*, George 1956, University of Detroit Mercy Black Abolitionist Archive, *Waterloo*.

LEEDS MERCURY (1718-1939) Though there was a *Leeds Mercury* from 1718, it was only in 1801 when a group of Whig figures provided the funding for buying the newspaper for Edward Baines* that its distinguished history as a liberal and influential provincial* newspaper began. The size* of the paper was increased in 1803 and it continued to grow in size and legibility. Baines's son, also Edward, was essentially the editor* by the end of the 1820s. and under him the political* positions tended to be more doctrinaire. Contributors included John Forster* and Richard Oastler who in 1830 wrote a famous article 'Yorkshire Slavery' which was influential in the passing of the Ten Hours Bill in 1833. The Baines family owned the paper throughout the nineteenth century and the paper continued to represent their liberal views. Costing 7d in the 1840s, the newspaper had a readership* of between 9,000 and 10,000 through that decade.

A weekly* (it became a daily* in 1861), the *Leeds Mercury* was unabashed in the expression of its Whig-liberal political views. It supported parliamentary reform, Catholic emancipation, and the extension of civil liberties. It was vigorous in support of the Anti-Corn Law League and the Reform Bill. It also supported general education for the working classes, though not state sponsored, since the paper was leery for the first half of its existence of any government intervention including all the legislative reforms of the 1840s. Its most famous crusade in the early years was the effort to expose the government spy system which resulted in Baines's revelation of Oliver the Spy, an agent provocateur. However, Baines's close connections to the cotton industry may have made him unsympathetic to progressive working class demands; he and thus the paper were against the factory acts, the Charter, Anti-Poor Law reform and also universal suffrage. As result his paper did not have much influence among the working class. Charlotte Brontë used the files of the *Leeds Mercury* for *Shirley*; her family were subscribers and several letters from Patrick Brontë appeared in it. From 1859 into the 1860s, the newspaper published a number of articles attacking slavery in the United States.

In 1866 Thomas Wemys Reid became head of the reporting* staff of the *Mercury*. From autumn of 1867, he was its London representative and active in the movement that in 1881 opened the gallery to the provincial* press. Three years after he returned to Leeds (1870) to become editor of the *Mercury*, he opened a London office (1873), sharing it with the *Glasgow Herald*. Under his editorship the *Leeds Mercury* became the first provincial paper to rival the London press, and it supported Gladstone when he took up the cause of Home Rule. In 1887 Reid withdrew from the editorship though he continued a weekly contribution until his death in 1906. His leaving weakened the newspaper, and it limped along until 1900 at which point the Harmsworth* brothers reportedly gave £30,000 to transfer the paper to their control. It was absorbed by the *Yorkshire Post** in 1939. **AH**
Sources: Lee 1976, Koss 1981, *ODNB*, Read 1961, Rosengarten 1971, *Waterloo*.

LEES, FREDERICK RICHARD (1815-1897) A temperance publisher*, proprietor*, author, editor* and journalist*, Frederick Lees was involved in the Temperance movement, a member of the Debating Society and the Leeds Temperance Society. In January 1837, he founded with four other associates a temperance* journal which disappeared by the end of the year. In 1840, Lees became the editor and proprietor of the *British Temperance Advocate and Journal* (1840-1844), ceded to him by the British Temperance Associations. Under the management of the new editor, the journal became increasingly successful.

Lees wrote on subjects connected with the social welfare of the people, advocating total abstinence from alcohol or 'teetotallism'. He wrote 'The History of the Wine Question' (1841) and published supplements* to the *Advocate* in collective form titled the 'Standard Temperance Library' in 1843. He also published the 'Illustrated History of Alcohol', which included some telling pathological plates of a stomach in a state of disease through the consumption of spirits. Thanks to some articles, worthy of narration, Lees was awarded prizes: 'The Aberdeen Prize Essay on Deut. XIV., 25-20' and 'The Nature, Elements, and Rites of the Christian Eucharist'. Lees resigned from the journal in late 1844. He signed some of his articles under the name of the 'Pathfinder', 'the Truth Seeker' and also 'Flavius Raphael de Linde' (F. R. L). In the 50 years following, Lees published prodigious numbers of tracts and books on temperance questions, only occasionally returning to the periodical press, as in 1854-1855, when he was a contributor to the *Northern Tribune; a periodical for the People*. **CK**
Sources: Cubbon 1935, Lees 1904.

Le Fanu, Joseph Thomas Sheridan (1814-1873) An Irish novelist, editor* and newspaper proprietor*, Le Fanu was born in Dublin to a family of Huguenot descent. Studying at Trinity College (Dublin University) and the King's Inns, Le Fanu graduated in 1836 with a BA degree and was called to the Irish bar, though he never practised as a barrister. Acquainted with the founders of the *Dublin University Magazine* at Trinity, and a close friend of Isaac Butt*, editor of that journal 1834-1838, Le Fanu began contributing stories anonymously* to the *Dublin University Magazine* from 1838.

During the 1840s Le Fanu held an interest in the Dublin Tory paper the *Statesman* for which he wrote conservative political leaders* (the paper folded in 1846), and in the *Warder* (1820-1884), a more successful Orange weekly*, in which he remained a partner until 1870. In 1861 Le Fanu acquired an interest in the *Dublin Evening Mail*, and acted as co-editor of the paper. In the same year he bought the *Dublin University Magazine* and for the next eight years used it as a vehicle for his own fiction, as well as the work of other more obscure Irish and English writers, such as Annie J. Robertson, and his niece Rhoda Broughton.

However, as proprietor of the *Dublin University Magazine* Le Fanu was responsible for reinstating its Irish focus and raising its popularity at home. Editorials on political*, religious*, and cultural issues, fiction, poetry*, and general notices put Ireland at the centre of interest, and Le Fanu's own fictional contributions ensured that the increasingly precarious position of his class was examined from all angles. Le Fanu sold the *Dublin University Magazine*, reputedly for £1500, in 1870, and died a recluse in Dublin.

Despite Le Fanu's social position as part of Dublin's Protestant middle class, he was never particularly well off, and was constantly beset by financial worries. Writing was an essential way of making money, and Le Fanu's serial novels* and short fiction are to be found in English as well as Irish publications: *All the Year Round*, *Temple Bar*, *Belgravia* and *Dark Blue*, among others. His first two novels were published by Irish firms, but the majority of his fiction in volume form was published in England, and written with an English readership* in mind. The result is a peculiar tone in the stories in which the anxieties and obsessions of his haunted characters are clearly the result of the sort of garrison mentality one associates with the Anglo-Irish but transposed to an English landscape. **ET**
Sources: Brown 1937, Inglis 1954, McCormack

1991, *ODNB*, *PGIL*, Rafroidi 1980, *Wellesley, Waterloo*.

Le Gallienne, Richard Thomas (1866-1947) Poet, novelist, and journalist*, Richard Le Gallienne worked in England during the 1890s, then with decreasing success in America and France. In summer 1891, he became 'Books and Bookmen' columnist* for the *Star*. Though occasionally engaging in literary skirmishes, e.g., with the formidable William Ernest Henley*, he preferred to praise rather than denigrate. His literary* reviews* and articles tend toward personal appreciation, sometimes tinged with sentimentality, but almost always balanced and astute. Many of the aspiring writers he championed, including Francis Thompson, George Egerton and Lionel Pigot Johnson, are well regarded today. His work also appeared in the *Academy*, the *Century Guild Hobby Horse*, the *Daily Chronicle*, the *Illustrated London News*, the *Manchester Evening Times*, the *Nineteenth Century*, the *Pall Mall Budget*, the *Review of Reviews*, the *Sketch* and the *Yellow Book*.

Early in his career, Le Gallienne effectively exploited his roles as journalist and advisor to the Bodley Head to influence the reading public. Puffing* or logrolling, which could involve not only recommending a book for publication but reviewing it, entails a conflict of interest not uncharacteristic of the times, but he thereby launched the career of poet Francis Thompson. Due primarily to encroaching alcoholism and debt, his influence began to decline after 1900. **PC**
Sources: Le Gallienne 1896, Le Gallienne 1925, *ODNB*, Thornton 1993, Whittington-Egan and Smerdon 1960.

Leigh Hunt's London Journal (1834-1835) Leigh Hunt* entered the market of the cheap* press with his 1½d weekly* *London Journal* as a riposte to what he saw as the dour non-fiction *Chambers's Edinburgh Journal*, providing an imagined working-class* reader* with material 'a little more southern and literary'. Desirous of supplying 'the more ornamental part of utility', the journal put comfort at the heart of utilitarianism, distancing itself from the 'business-oriented' *Chambers's* and the 'authoritative' *Penny Magazine* ('Address' *Leigh Hunt's London Journal* 2 April 1834: 1), and avoiding satire* and politics*. While initially marketing itself as an 'English' literary* weekly, in practice the journal is international in scope, and a variation on what Edgecombe (1994) has called the Huntian 'rococo', an elaborate and intimate focus on the 'off-centre' pleasurable, here in the intimate tone of a blithely confident, eighteenth-century-gentlemanly internationalism that can accommodate praise for *Legends and Scenes of the North of Scotland* and for Carlyle's* translations of Goethe as well as poems* on the virtuosity of Paganini and a series on classical authors.

Hunt wrote almost all of it himself and the strain of this shows in the large number of extracts printed (although there are also a good many original essays). Attempting to cover two markets at once, the journal was published weekly* and monthly*, the latter with a supplement*, 'The Streets of the Metropolis'. Nonetheless, it was not a success and advertising* disappeared early on, which must have created financial difficulties. Hunt initially owned the *Journal* jointly with Thomas Littleton Holt and it was published* by Sparrow and Co. from the office of *Bell's* Weekly Magazine*; but H. Hooper bought the journal in June 1834, and Hunt received a salary thereafter. When Charles Knight* merged* it with his *Printing Machine* in June 1835, he felt neither was making enough money to warrant a continuation on its own. While it ran for less than two years (1834-1835), Hunt claimed that it was still available at 'a good, steady price'* on second-hand book-stalls, 'in request ... for sea voyages' in the late 1840s (Hunt: 1850, 428). He started a second *Leigh Hunt's Journal* in 1850 which lasted a mere 17 weekly numbers. **AK**
Sources: Edgecombe 1994, Gates 1998, Hunt 1850, Sullivan.

LEIGHTON, CHARLES BLAIR (1823-1855) A painter of portraits and historical subjects, in 1849 Charles Blair Leighton joined his brothers, George Cargill and Steven, to form Leighton Brothers, a firm that printed coloured illustrations* for books and serials*. Leighton Brothers specialized in using multiple, separately tinted, wood and metal blocks to develop large subtly hued prints. This method was well suited to serial* publication, as it was much faster than the intaglio process popularized by George Baxter, under whom George Leighton had been apprenticed. One of their first published prints reproduced Edwin Landseer's *Hawking Party*, in *Art Journal**, in 1851. For the next 33 years, Leighton Brothers provided illustrations for numerous periodicals and books, many of which owed their success to such illustrations.

The firm's collaboration with the *Illustrated London News** is perhaps its most influential achievement, as it popularized the use of full-page colour illustrations in serial publications. In 1855, the journal published three full-page Leighton Brothers

prints in its Christmas* supplement*. As Courtney Lewis suggests, in *The Story Of Picture Printing in England During The XIX Century*, they could barely print it fast enough to satisfy public demand (83). In 1857, Leighton Brothers began printing the serial in its entirety. For the next 30 years, the *Illustrated London News* continued to publish Leighton Brothers prints, mostly in occasional supplements. Like their first published print, many of them reproduced paintings currently on exhibition. As Anthony Hamber notes, in *A Higher Branch of the Art: Photographing the Fine Arts in England, 1839-1880*, many of these prints were so popular as to be reproduced, and sold separately, in great numbers (49). Long after Charles Leighton's death in 1855, Leighton Brothers continued to establish colour printing as a popular means of making art accessible to a growing periodical readership*. **PG**
Sources: Gascoigne 1997, Hamber 1996, Lewis 1928, *ODNB*.

LEISURE HOUR (1852-1905) The *Leisure Hour*, subtitled *A Family Journal of Instruction and Recreation*, was issued weekly* by the Religious Tract Society (RTS)*. Absorbing its earlier *Visitor, or Monthly Instructer* (1833-1851), the RTS launched the *Leisure Hour* as a competitor to the popular* 1d weeklies* that were dominated by melodramatic fiction, and sought to 'catch the attention of peer and peasant, of master and man'. The magazine was initially edited* by William Haig Miller, one of the RTS'S regular writers; later editors* included James Macaulay (1858-1895) and William Stevens (1895-1899).

With a handful of fine engravings*, the penny* paper quickly achieved a circulation* of around 80,000-100,000 copies. Much of the material was not overtly religious*, and the *Leisure Hour* was even printed without the RTS'* imprint so that it would not be dismissed as a tract. From the beginning, the *Leisure Hour* featured regular articles on popular science*, history*, biography, and poetry* of an uplifting character. Later, there were columns* devoted to domestic and moral advice for housewives or servants, and prize competitions in composition or needlework. Throughout its history the periodical maintained a steady focus on overseas travel, colonial life and foreign mission fields. The most prominent and lengthy attraction, however, was always serial fiction* of a self-improving nature, often anonymous*; the blind Irish author Frances Browne contributed tales regularly for over 20 years. Prominent contributions included fiction by Margaret Oliphant* and Ellen Wood*, articles

Figure 36: The lavishly decorated cover of the *Leisure Hour*, 1888.

by Henry William Massingham* as well as John Keast Lord (1818-1872), with illustrations* by George Du Maurier* together with John Gilbert*.

In 1881 the *Leisure Hour* shifted to monthly publication, at the same time increasing illustration and reducing evangelical zeal. By the turn of the century the magazine was struggling and it eventually ceased publication in 1905. **AJL/GL**

Sources: Altholz 1989, Billington 1986, Fyfe 2004, Green 1899, Scott 1992.

LEMON, MARK (1809-1870) Mark Lemon was the founder editor* of *Punch*, working for the paper from its creation in 1841 until his death in 1870. Though also a prolific dramatist, 'Uncle Mark', as he was known to the Punchites, was 'made for *Punch*' and it was for his time on this periodical that he is most renowned. Lemon's early career was in the brewing trade though he already wrote small sketches for both the *New Sporting Magazine* and *Bentley's Miscellany*ature the pen name 'Tom Moody'. In 1836 his first play *The P. L., or, 30, Strand* was produced at the Strand Theatre. His work in theatre was to prove key to the success of *Punch* as Lemon had to publish a number of plays in the periodical's early years to keep it financially viable.

While Lemon wrote a variety of pieces for *Punch* (e.g. 'The Moral of Punch', 'The Heir of Applebite' and 'Songs for the Sentimental'), his editorial skills were more important. His decision to go against the editorial board and publish Thomas Hood's* 'Song of the Shirt' in 1843, the same year that John Leech's* 'cartoon'* 'Substance and Shadow' was first published, marked both a turning point in the humanistic rhetoric of the periodical and in establishing the terms of his editorial role. It was his decision to pay contributors a weekly salary, allotting them a percentage of column* space to fill each week. This more systematic approach to running the periodical contributed to the continuity of style and tone which was to make the periodical a national institution. Despite his successes with *Punch*, he failed when editing the *London Journal*, with his decision to serialize* the Waverley Novels dramatically lowering circulation*. Other work in nineteenth-century journalism includes acting as advisor to Herbert Ingram*, founder of the *Illustrated London News* in 1842, and being editor of the *Field* in 1853. **CH**

Sources: Adrian 1966, *ODNB*, Prager 1979, Price 1957, Spielmann [1895] 1969.

LENG, JOHN (1828-1906) John Leng's interest in the press began at Hull grammar school where he co-edited a magazine with Charles Cooper who became editor* of the *Scotsman*. Leng started as a reporter and subeditor's* assistant at the *Hull Advertiser* in 1847, rapidly becoming subeditor, chief reporter, drama and music* critic combined. He became editor of the ailing bi-weekly *Dundee Advertiser* in 1851 and made it one of the most successful Scottish papers. But his talents also extended to a keen business sense and an appreciation of the economic benefits of innovation, both of which he used when he was made a partner in the *Advertiser*. He moved to larger premises, installed new presses to improve production from 350 to 20,000 copies an hour. He introduced illustrations* into the daily* paper and forged a direct telegraphic* link between Dundee and London to promote news* immediacy.

Leng's next step was to broaden the range and extent of his publications so that by 1858 the weekly* *People's Journal* ran ten local editions with a 250,000 circulation*. Part of its success lay in Leng's positive attitude to its working-class* readership* which he also fostered in his illustrated* *People's Friend* that contained shortened modern

novels. His concern was to provide sound improving copy for his working-class readers. From 1861 the *Dundee Advertiser* became a daily and from 1877 Leng & Co. also published the *Evening Telegraph* in Dundee. The Liberal politics* he fostered in his papers were transformed into a parliamentary seat in Dundee which he held for 16 years. **CL**
Sources: Bell 2007, *ODNB*.

LENO, JOHN BEDFORD (1826-1894) Leno (pseudonym* 'J. Bonel') was an important radical printer, proprietor*, editor* and journalist*. Beginning with a small printing business* in Uxbridge in the late 1840s, he moved on to become foreman printer for the Working Printers' Association, a co-operative venture sponsored by Charles Kingsley's group of Christian Socialists. Leno's contribution to the world of radical journalism was impressive. With fellow Chartist* leader Gerald Massey*, he started in February 1849, a monthly* journal of literature* and general information, the *Uxbridge Pioneer*, price* 3d; it was the offspring of an earlier manuscript newspaper, the *Attempt*, of which seven issues were produced (1846-1849).

Shortly after the second issue of the *Pioneer* had been published, political differences alienated the more radical Leno and Massey from the other editors. They therefore started a new paper and 1,000 copies of the ultra-radical* *Uxbridge Spirit of Freedom: A Working Man's Vindicator*, price 1d, went on sale in April 1849. The journal ran until December with the publication of nine monthly issues. While working for the cooperative printers, Leno contributed both prose and verse in 1850 to its monthly *Christian Socialist*, and he also wrote (May-Dec. 1858) for the *National Union: a Political and Social Record*, a London-based Chartist newspaper. During the 1860s his involvement in journalism became more varied: he was proprietor-editor of the *Westminster News* (1863-1864), and of *St Crispin* (1868-1874), a shoemakers' trade journal*; editor in 1865 of the International Working Men's Association's newspaper, the *Workman's Advocate*, and of the Reform League's the *Commonwealth* (1866). For a short while in 1880 he was subeditor* of Henry Solly's labour monthly, *Common Good*, proprietor-editor of the short-lived *Anti-Tithe Journal* (1881) and a contributor in prose and verse to William Morris's* the *Commonweal** (1889). Much of Leno's presswork was informed by a profound commitment to the cause of labour, the struggle against privilege in church and state and to the exposure of capitalist greed. **OA**
Sources: Ashton 2003b, Ashton and Roberts 1999,

Breuilly 1995, Burnett, 1984, Leno papers (Brotherton Library), Obituaries.

LE SAGE, JOHN MERRY (1837-1926) Journalist* and newspaper editor*, Le Sage worked on local* papers in Torquay and Plymouth before taking a position in 1863 with the *Daily Telegraph** as personal assistant to Edward Levy Lawson*. For the next 60 years he remained loyal to that newspaper, working alongside three generations of the Levy family. He served for a time as a special foreign* correspondent for the *Telegraph* and in this capacity, among other things, interviewed Sitting Bull, reported on the death of Napoleon III, received an audience with Pope Leo XIII and Sultan Abdul Hamid and scored a memorable coup by getting news of the German army's entry into Paris in 1871 ahead of his rivals by using a special train to Lille where telegraph* wires were open (Burnham: 49; *ODNB*).

In general, however, Le Sage's reporting was more solid and straightforward than distinctive, and his newspaper talents are adjudged to have been best 'displayed in an executive capacity': 'the autocrat of Peterborough Court' (*ODNB*) worked for 40 years as the *Telegraph*'s decisive, unflappable and very traditional managing editor. His fellow worker on the *Telegraph*, T. P. O'Connor*, summed him up as 'a man who took everything seriously, but nothing tragically' with 'sober and realistic common sense' (cited in Burnham: 50). He struggled to maintain the *Telegraph*'s status as a particular type of middle-class* newspaper in the transforming decades of the late nineteenth and early twentieth century, finding it difficult to adapt to the new pace and style of modern journalism. He was knighted for his services to journalism in 1918. **FD**
Sources: Burnham 1955, *ODNB*.

LETTERS/ CORRESPONDENCE Across the vast range of newspapers and journals of the nineteenth century, which catered for various market* niches in every branch of practical and theoretical knowledge, letters to the editor served a variety of functions. As a literary form, the letter – whether real or fictional – had come to the fore in the eighteenth century as a means of framing personal, intellectual and political concerns, with the epistolary novels of Samuel Richardson, Alexander Pope's epistles, and Steele's (often pseudonymous*) letters to the editors of various periodicals indicative of the most celebrated examples. The periodical press also published readers' letters, often mixed with (and indistinguishable from) letters from entirely fictional or allegorized characters, as in Edward Moore's (1712-1757) the *World* (1753-1756), which featured letters (penned by Moore) from 'Rebecca Blameless' and 'Toby Frettabit'. To reflect on the role of the letter in eighteenth century print culture is to be reminded that while the form might represent itself as conveying the private outpourings of the individual soul, it is often a highly artificial public performance. This is a salutary lesson in any consideration of letters columns* in the nineteenth century press.

One complicating factor is that while the first use of 'correspondent' – in the sense of one who writes letters into a newspaper or periodical – that the *OED* records is in 1711 (used by Steele), but it is sometimes difficult to distinguish between the paid employees of a newspaper – such as a 'war correspondent'* in the special sense that developed in the nineteenth century – and unpaid members of the public writing – sometimes at length and with detailed specialist knowledge – for other reasons. Some publications made a clear distinction, others not. A trade paper* such as the *Mining Journal*, for example, featured a large section composed entirely of regular correspondence from mine owners and engineers that was intended to alert investors and technicians of extraction rates or any problems encountered. Were they paid for their copy? It is difficult to tell. Letters to other specialist journals were equally ambiguous in their status. For example, James Prescott Joule's (1818-1889) first contributions (around 1840) to the *Annals of Electricity, Magnetism and Chemistry*, reporting on his experiments with electromagnetic engines, were addressed and printed as letters to the editor.

It is possible to divide letters to the editor into two broad categories that serve different functions: those from the general public, and those from notable public figures. The former saw readers either responding to a slight (real or perceived) on their way of life, correcting factual errors, praising or disputing with articles in previous issues or asking for the opinion or advice of the editor or other readers. It is in this context that the parallel tradition of advice to readers developed, in which lengthy advice was given in response to an often entirely fictitious or absent epistolary prompt. In some cases, as is made clear by the example of the *British Controversialist*, correspondents were given more space to develop their own arguments and continue disagreements with other readers. But it is the expansion and institutionalization of letters to the editor in the mainstream press that is perhaps the most notable development, with its inevitable connotation of opening up the pages of the papers to the public to create a putatively free forum for debate. Thomas Barnes* is usually credited with developing the 'Letters to the Editor'* page of *The Times* into something of a national institution when he edited the paper (1817-1841). Subsequently, correspondence columns became particularly popular in the popular Sunday* papers of the 1850s onwards such as *Reynolds's*, *Lloyd's* and the *Weekly Times* (1847-1912): the *Weekly Times* answered an average of 167 readers' queries per week in 1886. In some areas – notably in the *British Controversialist*, which included extensive epistolary debates between readers (largely from the self-improving lower-middle class*) on a variety of topical and intellectual issues – there was a free exchange of ideas, though even the *Controversialist* had an agenda of its own. Generally, however, editors printed only the letters that they wanted to print, and in some cases penned a significant proportion of them themselves. So while the very existence of the letters page boasted of a two-way relationship in which readers' views were fully represented, this characterization was only partly true. Apart from excluding letters that would reflect badly on the periodical or its editorial line, there were also cases where editors published letters from notable correspondents that were intended solely for private consumption, such as the mischievous publication of some rather pompous letters by Coleridge* in *Blackwood's Magazine*.

Letters from public figures, well-known journalists or writers, on the other hand, were an opportunity for them to throw their weight behind important issues. Walter Scott* wrote three letters to the editor of the *Edinburgh Weekly Journal* (1800-1848) in 1826, in which he argued (at a time of financial crisis) that Scottish banks should be able to issue their own notes without restriction. Now known as *The Letters of Malachi Malagrowther*, their popular, nationalistic tone caused a sensation. In another context, seeking to publicize an important issue affecting public health, the eminent physician Henry Leach (1836-1879) wrote a series of eight letters to *The Times* in 1866 on his experience of treating scurvy, in response to an anonymous* leader* on the subject. The use of specialist scientific* knowledge in the popular media to advocate a particular stance foreshadows debates about the role of the public intellectual in the twentieth century.

Since public figures were apt to use the letters pages of newspapers and journals to influence public opinion (and derogate the names of their rivals), it is unsurprising that these pages played host to countless high-profile literary* spats. This was already an established tradition in the eighteenth century, as in the case of a feud over plagiary between two female dramatists, Hannah Cowley (1743-1809) and Hannah More, which played itself out in the pages of the *St James's Chronicle* and was thought interesting enough to be reprinted in the *Gentleman's Magazine** in 1779. The gladiatorial aspect of such exchanges was not lost on the editors of the nineteenth century. The letters pages of *The Times* played host to many public disputes, including a beef between Thomas Newby (1797/8-1882) and G. H. Lewes* in 1859 over Newby's fraudulent publication of *Adam Bede, Junior: a Sequel*, and countless other literary and political controversies.

In general, letters columns* suggest that nineteenth-century readers were not passive consumers of print but active respondents who wanted to be in dialogue with the publications they read and with other readers. One must always be mindful, however, of the motives of editors in printing such material. To be seen to reflect and to accommodate the opinions of the reading public was a great selling point. But by vetting these opinions and adding ones of their own, editors created their own images of what that public thought and believed. **MaT**

Sources: Berridge 1978, BritPer, *ODNB, OED, The Times.*

LEVER, CHARLES (1806-1872) Novelist and magazine* editor*, Charles Lever was born in Dublin to an English father and Anglo-Irish mother. He attended Trinity College Dublin, and qualifying as a doctor (1831), he practised for a time in County Clare, where the poverty and disease endemic in the West profoundly affected him. A subsequent period as local physician in Co. Derry allowed more time for writing, and he submitted occasional pieces to *Saunder's**, the *Cork Quarterly Magazine,* the *Dublin Literary Gazette* and others. His early contributions to the *Dublin University Magazine**, chiefly the serial novel* 'The Confessions of Harry Lorrequer' (1837-1840), are credited with establishing the popularity of the magazine, and the serial's success convinced him that he might make a living as a writer. When he was then offered the editorship of *Bentley's Miscellany** at a salary of £800 per annum, he used the offer to negotiate a better deal with rival Irish publishers* McGlashan* & Curry* in 1842, whereby he would edit their *Dublin University Magazine* for £1,200 per annum, in addition to half-profits on his own writings.

Before Lever, the identity of the *Dublin University Magazine* most closely resembled that of the class from which its contributors and readers were drawn: educated, privileged, overwhelmingly Protestant in religion and conservative in politics. With Lever as editor, the magazine began to foreground fiction rather than polemic: a new instalment of one of Lever's serial novels typically fronted each issue. Work from popular – and politically inoffensive – writers (see Hall 118), was solicited. Fiction by G. P. R. James, Catherine Gore, and Mortimer and Samuel O'Sullivan* joined poetry* by J. C. Mangan* and essays by Harriet Martineau*, John Fisher Murray, and Eliot Warburton, whose travel pieces on Asia were later collected to make a highly successful travel book.

Ultimately, controversy could not be kept out of the pages of the *Dublin University Magazine*, and essays lauding Protestantism as a remedy for all of the ills plaguing Irish society garnered strong criticism from Catholic readers*. Lever's own easy-going character left him unprepared for the personal abuse he received whenever the *Dublin University Magazine* printed an article or story deemed insulting to one group or another. His praise for Thackeray's* *Irish Sketch Book* (dedicated to Lever in 1843) left him open to the outrage of nationalists. William Carleton* in particular saw Lever's fiction as perpetuating Irish stereotypes, and he roundly attacked both editor and magazine in articles in the *Nation**. By 1845 Lever had had enough. He left Ireland for Brussels in March, though he continued to edit the *Dublin University Magazine* until the end of May.

Though his managerial duties ceased, Lever contributed fiction to the *Dublin University Magazine* until 1859; his other novels were published in parts or appeared as serials in *All the Year Round**, *Blackwood's**, *Cornhill**, and *St Paul's Magazine**. Lever's editorship of the *Dublin University Magazine* coincided with its highest circulation* figures (4,000 copies per month) ever. **ET**

Sources: Bareham 1991, Deane 1991, Haddelsey 2000, Hall 1999, *ODNB*, Rafroidi 1980, Stevenson 1939.

LEVINSTEIN, IVAN (1845-1916) A German-born journalist*, editor*, proprietor*, chemist and dye manufacturer, Ivan Levinstein became a British subject in 1873. He was an enormously successful businessman and head of a large public company, and became president of the Society of Chemical Industry, publishing technical articles in its organ the *Journal of the Society of Chemical Industry.* He also contributed to more general business periodicals such as the *Manchester Chamber of Commerce*

Monthly Record, as well as producing articles in German for publication in his native country. His most substantial contribution to the chemical press was the founding of the *Chemical Review* in 1871, a monthly* periodical which he edited* for several years, contributing numerous articles on technical and industrial matters.

Levinstein's initial leader* expressed surprise that 'the first commercial country of the world does not have a single journal which deals with the practical application of chemical science* to different branches of Art and Industry'. William Crookes's* *Chemical News** was either strategically ignored or adjudged to be too purely theoretical to fulfil this brief. In any case, the *Chemical Review,* which continued until 1891, reflected Levinstein's solid business acumen, and focused on the industrial and commercial implications of developments in theoretical chemistry. **MaT**

Sources: Donnelly 1986, *ODNB, Waterloo.*

LEVY, JOSEPH MOSES (1812-1888) Levy was a newspaper proprietor*. Born in London's East End, he left England for Germany when he was 14 to work as an apprentice to a printer. He established his own printing business in Fleet Street* on his return to London in his early twenties, and quickly became both printer and main proprietor of the *Sunday Times**. Father of Edward Levy Lawson*, Baron Burnham, the first press peer, the family's entrepreneurial skill was clearly displayed in Joseph Levy's ability to recognize and take opportunities: he rescued the ailing *Daily Telegraph and Courier** from mismanagement by its founder Col. Arthur Burroughes Sleigh, by first agreeing to print the paper for its troubled owner and taking it over when Sleigh defaulted on his bills. He soon dropped the word 'Courier' from the title, took on his own son Edward and Thornton Hunt* as an editorial team and relaunched the paper in September 1855 as the first cheap* double-sheet, eight-page morning daily*, selling at the 'sensationally low price' of 1d (*ODNB*). The *Telegraph* absorbed the *Morning Chronicle** in 1860 and soon the paper was outstripping its rivals, the *Daily News** and *Morning Post**. The *Telegraph* eventually reached an unrivalled circulation* of 300,000 (its slogan boasted: 'the largest, best and cheapest newspaper in the world') and maintained its leading status until the arrival of Alfred Harmsworth's* *Daily Mail** in 1896.

Levy was involved in the day-to-day production of the paper until the 1880s. He also helped to campaign for the successful repeal of the last of the paper duties in 1861. Under Levy the paper, particularly in its early decades, was Liberal in its politics* and contained regular art and theatre reviews* (Levy was one time owner of the Gaiety Theatre). Notably, it was also deliberately sensationalist in its reporting of crime*- based and unusual stories (e.g., 'Shocking occurrence: Five Men Smothered in a Gin Vat') – a key to its mass readership*. *Punch** acknowledged Levy's business sense in this regard, claiming Levy's was 'a name that all will link with the Cheap Press.... /the Proletariat pence he found would build/A fortune for the shrewd and the strong willed' (cited in Burnham: 165). Levy was nonetheless singled out for praise by Matthew Arnold* in his *Friendship's Garland* for producing the very first popular* daily 'conducted with a high tone...without Americanisms in layout or republicanism along American lines' (*ODNB*). **FD**

Sources: Burnham 1955, *ODNB.*

LEWER, ETHEL HARRIET COMYNS (1861-1946) Daughter of an Anglo-Indian officer, born in India and educated privately, Ethel Lewer (née Garrett) was a proprietor* and editor* of a trade journal*. In October 1884, she was involved in an innovative venture of establishing and running the Ladies' Typewriting Office (LTO) opened in Chancery Lane in connection with the Society for the Employment of Women. The LTO also had links with the Women's Printing Society*. Garrett made over the LTO to her partner when she married Alexander Comyns in c.1887; when he died in 1890, Ethel Comyns inherited the magazine of poultry husbandry, the *Feathered World,* that her husband had started shortly before his death.

Becoming the only woman in the UK who was proprietor, editor and manager of a periodical, she continued to build on its initial success, increasing the weekly* circulation* from 12,000 to 20,000 in a few years. The magazine's 36 illustrated* pages dealt with poultry, pigeons and cage birds. In 1896, she married the publisher* and editor Sidney H. Lewer with whom she also co-wrote books on poultry. Comyns-Lewer also worked with the Cambridge geneticist R. C. Punnett to produce a bibliography for his book, *Notes on Old Poultry Books,* which was published in the *Feathered World* (1930). She continued to edit the *Feathered World* until her retirement in 1935. **CL**

Sources: 19CUKP, Harvey and Ogilvie 2000, Onslow 2000.

LEWES, GEORGE HENRY (1817-1878) In a diverse career that spanned 40 years, G. H. Lewes, journalist*, editor* and author, published over 500 articles in a wide range of journals, often under ironic pseudonyms* (including 'Frank Churchill'; 'Professor Wolfgang von Bibundtüker'; 'Slingsby Lawrence'; 'Vivian Latouche'). A novelist, playwright, amateur actor and biographer of Goethe, Lewes's informed and engaging criticism of leading writers of the nineteenth century (Arnold*, Austen, Balzac, Charlotte Brontë, the Brownings, Darwin*, Dickens*, Dumas, Elizabeth Gaskell, Macaulay, George Sand, Thackeray*, Tennyson*) and on emerging critical discourses such as literary realism, remains influential. His extraordinarily wide range of interests led him to publish original articles (often later turned into books) on natural history, psychology and philosophy and important reviews* on British and European literary* culture in most of the leading heavyweight journals of the day including the *Westminster Review** and the *Edinburgh Review**. His drama criticism, mostly for the *Leader**, in the witty, sarcastic persona of 'Vivian' in the 1850s and for the *Pall Mall Gazette** in the 1860s (the latter reprinted in volume form as *On Actors and Acting*, 1875), demonstrates the persuasive mixture of lucid style, penetrating critique and humour that defined his journalism. G. B. Shaw* nominated him as an important influence (Ashton, 2000, 105) and Lewes's balance of instruction and entertainment in his early scientific* writings in particular was a key feature of the broad appeal of his three series on natural history published in the popular miscellanies, *Blackwood's Magazine** and *Cornhill Magazine**. Such work, though, meant many of his contemporaries dismissed him as a mere 'bread and butter scholar' (Haight: 44), suspicious of his lack of formal education, his populist conversational style and the display of too wide a range of interests in his journalism in an age of increasing specialism.

Lewes had a brief stint as co-editor of the short-lived *National Magazine and Monthly Critic* at the beginning of his career in 1837. He was the literary editor and co-founder with Thornton Hunt* of the *Leader** in 1850, the 'best liberal weekly* newspaper to be published in the Victorian period' (Ashton: 1992). Lewes withdrew from his involvement in the management of the *Leader* when he travelled to Germany with Marian Evans* in the summer of 1854 at the beginning of their life-long relationship. His contacts with John Blackwood* were used to good effect in bringing the first fiction of the still unnamed 'George Eliot' to Blackwood in 1856 when he sent 'Amos Barton,' the first part of her 'Scenes of Clerical

Life' for consideration by *Blackwood's Magazine*, just as his own popular science series*, 'Sea-side Studies', was appearing in that journal. He acted in an advisory editorial capacity at the *Cornhill Magazine* from 1862-1864, following Thackeray's departure. His position as the first editor of the *Fortnightly Review** in 1865, at Trollope's* request, was a significantly high-profile role, and a mark of the increasing respect with which he was held. Ill-health forced his resignation the following year.

A 'prince of journalists' in the words of a contemporary (Espinasse: 276), with an ability to turn his hand to any subject, 'so versatile was he, so lucid, so sparkling and adept' (Robertson Scott: 148), Lewes died in 1878 just days after he sent George Eliot's last work, *Impressions of Theophrastus Such,* for publication, a series of essays that sharply criticized the media that had sustained Lewes all his life. **FD**

Sources: Ashton 1991, Ashton 1992, Espinasse 1893, Haight 1969, Scott 1950, *Wellesley*.

'LEWIS, AMELIA' (1824/5-1881) 'Amelia Lewis' advocated women's rights* through several journals that she founded and edited* in the 1870s. Born Amelia Louisa Rudiger in Prussia, she married Dr J. C. H. Freund (1808-1879), founder and director of the German Hospital in London. She wrote numerous leaders* promoting female suffrage, equal education for women and labour reform. In 1872 she created *Woman*, later titled *Social Review**, which lasted only a few months, and she edited *Women's Opinion* for much of 1874. Both journals included articles on the arts, music* and theatre. The purpose of her next newspaper, the weekly* *National Food and Fuel Reformer* (Nov. 1874-May 1876), was to educate the public in home economics. In May 1876, she began a similar journal, *Housekeeper: A Domestic Journal*, but, like the *National Food and Fuel Reformer*, it folded. Indomitable, she tried again in 1879, with *Food and Health Leaves*, which folded after eight months. **BA**

Sources: Doughan 1987, Jaffé 2003, *ODNB*, Wright 2004.

LIBRARY (1888-) Although the *Library* is now subtitled 'Transactions of the Bibliographical Society', it predates the organization by four years. Originally subtitled 'A Magazine of Bibliography and Literature', the periodical was established by John Young Walker McAlister (1856-1925) in December 1888 as the organ of the Library Association. Published monthly* on large octavo and 'handsomely printed on antique paper'* at a price* of 8d, its original aims were 'to advance the objects of the Association... advocate the Free Library movement, and deal with the many important questions affecting the management and administration of public and private libraries'.

The prospectus promised articles by leading librarians and bookmen, including Walter Besant*, Andrew Lang* and Richard Garnett (1835-1906). Its content was to reflect a strong antiquarian interest and a taste for the arcane, in its own words, 'waifs and strays, chips from literary workshops, so often lost for ever for lack of a fitting Storehouse'. The first issue included Austin Dobson (1840-1921) on the travel accounts of C. P. Moritz (1757-1793), H. R. Tedder (1850-1924) on the bibliography of French history*, Willam Blades (1824-1890) on parish libraries in the late seventeenth century and Arthur Bullen (1857-1920) on an American private press.

The *Library*'s close association with the Bibliographical Society began with the founding of the Society in 1892, initiated by an article in the January issue by Walter Copinger (1847-1910) entitled 'On the Necessity for the Formation of a Bibliographical Society for the United Kingdom'. With the establishment of the *Library Association Record* in 1899, the *Library* gained its independence from the Association, its second series commencing in December, published by Kegan, Paul, Trench, Trübner & Co.*, and printed at the Chiswick Press. It continues today as an imprint of Oxford University Press. **BB**

Sources: Pollard 1930, *ODNB*.

LIGHT ON THE WAY (1892-1896) A Manchester-based Unitarian monthly, it described itself as, 'A magazine of liberal faith for home reading'. It addressed 'Liberal' and 'Free Christians' as well as 'members of the Presbyterian and other non-subscribing churches' and was clearly designed for Sunday reading. It included short illustrated* biographies of notables like Rev. Martineau, progressive articles on social and theological questions, reviews*, hymns with their tunes and a regular section for children called 'Uncle William's Sunbeam Circle', which was often illustrated. Most of its contributors were clergy and included Canon Barnett, but other contributors were Mrs Ormiston Chant, Keir Hardie, 'A Rabbi' and local writers like W. E. A. Axon. It favoured northern and Lancashire topics. Despite certain concessions to popular journalism*, such as its 'Chats about Churches', which focused on the locality of Manchester, its editors* were 'disappointed at the indifference to their venture' where they expected more enthusiasm. This

presumably accounted for its relatively short run. TW/MRB

Source: *Light on the Way.*

LIMBIRD, JOHN (C.1796-1883) During the 1820s and 1830s Limbird enjoyed brief but notable success as a publisher* of cheap printed works. Trading as a stationer and bookseller on the Strand, he issued several volumes of his 'British Novelist' series of weekly fiction instalments (1823-1846) – but his career was defined by the production of low-priced periodical and newspaper titles between the late 1810s and the early 1850s. Limbird's ownership and publication of the *Mirror of Literature, Amusement, and Instruction*ered (1822-1847) – a 2d weekly* illustrated* miscellany*, calculated to 'afford the greatest quantity of "Amusement and Instruction" at the lowest possible expense... [for] readers in the humblest circumstances' – ensured that his name was well known to readers*, philanthropic improvers and contemporaries in the book trade.

In 1808 Limbird moved from his native Huntingdonshire to London, entering the employment of the radical bookseller-publisher Thomas Dolby. In 1819 he turned away from the politicized and pornographic* literary subculture of the Strand, experimenting with respectable 6d weekly titles like the *Literary Journal* (1818-1819), the *Literary Chronicle** and the monthly *Cambro-Briton and General Celtic Repository*. His abortive attempt in 1820 to establish the 2d weekly *Londoner* was followed in November 1822 by the publication of the *Mirror*, which boasted an enormous, and doubtful, circulation* of between 80,000 and 150,000 numbers a week during the 1820s (15,000 a week has been suggested as a more realistic figure). Claims made by the editor*, Thomas Byerley (1788-1826), that the journal was 'to be found in the cottage of the peasant, on the loom of the manufacturer... and in the carriages of the nobility' were also exaggerated: the majority of its readership* came from the lower-middling and artisan classes. This relatively humble audience had rarely been targeted by periodical publishers, and only the cheap radical press of the 1790s and the post-war period had previously done so on any large scale (and Limbird duly copied their weekly, 16-page and 32-column* octavo format*). By fusing literary, satirical and scientific* content – communicated through reviews*, excerpts from original and pirated literature*, poetry*, biographies and (more innovatively) woodcut* illustrations – the *Mirror* also carried an eighteenth-century miscellany* tradition into the changed market* of the early 1820s. Limbird's early success had thus grown from his ability to capitalize on previous experimentation with periodical readership, price* and format.

Throughout the 1820s Limbird produced other periodicals, including the weekly *Cabinet of Curiosities* (1823-1824) and the annual *Arcana of Science and Art* (1828-1879), but his publication of Joseph Clinton Robertson's (1788-1852) 7d *Trades' Newspaper and Mechanics' Weekly Journal* (1825-1827) represented his most significant attempt to reach a 'new' readership; this time of skilled metropolitan* working men. His later output was less impressive, comprising a couple of musical titles, including the 3d weekly *Musical Journal* (1840), and the *Traveller* (1841-1845), a 3d weekly carrying information about mail-coach, steamboat and railway schedules. When Limbird died on 30 October 1883, the successful days of the *Mirror* had long since passed, but for some historians, his reputation as one of the prime movers in the attempt to forge a mass* audience for cheap*, apolitical literature is secure. Limbird was motivated by profit rather than by any such mission – but his credentials as a print popularizer* are compromised more by the reality that his publications were rarely read by the very lowest levels of society. **DM**

Sources: *Mirror of Literature* 21 May 1823 and 1 Jan. 1826, James 1963, Lightman 2004a, Topham 2004, *Waterloo*.

LINK, A JOURNAL FOR THE SERVANTS OF MAN (1888) The *Link,* which first appeared 4 February, originated in the aftermath of Bloody Sunday, the unprovoked attack by police and soldiers on unarmed demonstrators in and around Trafalgar Square. The Law and Liberty League was formed to defend and represent those caught up in the proceedings and the *Link* was its paper, representing Annie Besant's* idea for what she, as an atheist, termed 'a new Church', one that would unite people in a humanitarian drive to work for improvements in the economic and social conditions of the poor. As a first attempt in this unity, Besant and W. T. Stead* contrived and edited* the *Link* as a ½d weekly* , inspired by words from Victor Hugo, 'The people are silence. I will be the advocate of this silence'.

The paper focused on activism, exposing sweated industries, starvation wages and their results. It attacked unjust landlords and workhouse scandals, as well as enforcing legislation such as the Employers' Liability Act. Neighbourhood Vigilance Circles were formed to detect cruelty to children, and a legion of injustice, reporting the findings directly to Besant. Sidney Webb wrote on the paper's campaign to improve the dockers' wages, Josephine Butler* and Herbert Burrows also contributed. But it was Burrows who worked with Besant on the *Link's* legendary campaign, when they interviewed the Bryant and May match girls and Besant revealed the appalling exploitation in her article, 'White Slavery in London' (23 June). Threatened with a libel action by the company, Besant was also visited by a deputation of match girls in her Fleet Street* office and together they instigated the direct action which resulted in unionization of the works. The paper closed in December that year when Besant began her exploration of Theosophy. **CL**

Sources: Besant 1893, *Waterloo*.

LINTON, ELIZABETH LYNN (1822-1898) Eliza Lynn Linton was one of the most prolific and notable journalists* of the century, and the first woman to obtain a salaried post on an English national* newspaper. She educated herself while housekeeping for her clergyman father and motherless siblings, but escaped from Cumberland by obtaining permission to go to London to prove herself as a novelist.

Her well-received second novel *Amymone: A Romance in the Days of Pericles*, a plea for women's rights, brought valuable contacts in Walter Savage Landor, George Bentley and John Douglas Cook*, editor* of the *Morning Chronicle*, which she joined in 1848 and for which she wrote leaders*. She left in 1851 after quarrelling with Cook, though she freelanced for him from Paris where she stayed until 1854, living somewhat precariously as correspondent* for the *Leader* and contributor to *Household Words*. For that magazine she produced 60 articles and stories, and continued writing for Dickens* in *All the Year Round*.

The early 1860s, following her ill-starred marriage in 1858 to the radical engraver* William Linton*, were thin journalistically. In the late 1860s, however, her lively, controversial *Saturday Review* articles on the faults and follies of modern girls determined her career, establishing her as the scourge of the 'Girl of the Period', a topic she was still exploiting in the 1890s when she opposed the 'Wild Women', her interpretation of the New Woman.

Linton published in an astonishing number and range of periodicals including *Ainsworth's*, *Tinsley's*, *St Paul's* and *Fraser's* magazines, the *Athenaeum*, the *Cornhill*, the *Nineteenth Century*, the *Fortnightly*, *National*, *New* and *Universal* reviews, *London Society**, *Good Words**, the *Queen** and *Temple Bar**.

Linton never became the great novelist she once aspired to be, but in her final decade was acknowledged as a doyenne of literary* life, and was one of the first women members elected to the governing council of the Society of Authors. A thorough professional, her claim that she 'never "scamped" a paper' in her life is probably near the truth. Her novels *Sowing the Wind* and *Christopher Kirkland* draw upon her journalistic experiences. **BMO**
Sources: Anderson 1987, Layard 1901, Linton 1885, *ODNB*, Onslow 2000.

LINTON, WILLIAM JAMES (1812-1897) Born in London, the radical journalist* and engraver* William James Linton was apprenticed to the renowned engraver George Wilmot Bonner* (1796–1836), whose workshop provided ample opportunity for Linton to read the writings of radical authors. In 1839 Linton and the radical printer James Watson* produced a short-lived weekly*, the *National*, which promoted European nationalism. In 1842 Linton's reputation received a major boost when in partnership with his former master John Orrin Smith* he secured the principal engraving rights for the newly launched *Illustrated London News**.

As Chartism declined in the 1840s, Linton transferred his radical energies to producing his own periodicals. In 1852 the radical Newcastle newspaper owner Joseph Cowen* helped Linton acquire Brantwood house on Lake Coniston (later the home of John Ruskin*). Here Linton set up his first private press, recruiting a group of like-minded printers and journalists, including W. E. Adams*, to produce a range of radical pamphlets and journals. Between January 1851 and April 1855, he published his most impressive periodical, the *English Republic**, a lavishly illustrated* monthly* and weekly* journal, with a tricolour on the front cover which blazoned its nationalist credentials. Though he secured contributions from Mazzini, Alexander Herzen and Karl Stolzman, the *Republic* struggled to pay its way. Neither Cowen nor Linton were daunted by this failure and in 1854 they launched the *Northern Tribune** which campaigned, among other things, for the removal of the tax on newspapers. It, too, had a short shelf life and was sold on to George Jacob Holyoake* in 1855, appearing thereafter as the *Reasoner and London Tribune.* Eventually, Linton's financial difficulties caught up with him and he departed for America, leaving his estranged third wife Eliza Lynn* behind. Beginning

with a post on the prestigious *Frank Leslie's Illustrated Newspaper* (1858-1878), Linton's contribution to American cultural life led to his admission to the Century Club, though his noisy criticism of American politics* offended many. His career culminated in his election to the American National Academy of Arts in 1882 and the production of his *Masters of Wood Engraving* (1889), 'the most sumptuous book on wood-engraving in the English language'. He died in New Haven. **JA**
Sources: W. E. Adams papers, Allen 2007, Amsterdam Institute of Social History, Ashton 1991, Joseph Cowen papers, Tyne and Wear archives service, *ODNB*, Smith 1973.

***LITERARY CHRONICLE AND WEEKLY REVIEW* (1819-1828)** With its intention to review* weekly* all significant publications in *Literature, Philosophy, the Fine and Useful Arts, History, the Drama, etc'* the *Literary Chronicle* set itself a task that it accomplished with a satisfactory degree of objectivity. It prided itself on aiming to keep its price* down so that all sections of society could enjoy it and on not being a tool of the bookselling trade, unlike its rival the *Literary Gazette* (1817ff)*, that it dismissed as merely puffing* forthcoming publications. The price ranged from 6d for 16 pages in 1819 to 1s in 1828.

Published on Saturday with 16 quarto pages, it was issuing by 1820 a tenpage country edition launched by special request. The *Chronicle* tried to encourage new authors and included foreign and English literature*, music*, theatre and art in its reviews; original writing included poetry*, and coverage of science* and biography. From 1819 to 1826 it was edited* by Thomas Byerley, who also edited the *Mirror of Literature**. When John Watson Dalby took over in 1826, there was an increased interest taken in theological debate and expressed support of anti-Catholicism. Contributors were substantial in number and largely anonymous*, though they sometimes used initials or pseudonyms*. The stint of Frederick Denison Maurice (1805-1872) as editor (May-July 1828), aged 23, was as liberal as it was short lived, lasting only until the merger* with the *Athenaeum** in August 1828, which resulted in the *Athenaeum and Literary Chronicle.* **CL**
Sources: Sullivan 1983, *Waterloo.*

***LITERARY GAZETTE, AND JOURNAL OF BELLES LETTRES, ARTS, SCIENCES &CT* (1817-1863)** The *Literary Gazette* was launched on 25 January by Henry Colburn*, newspaper speculator and publisher* of 'fashionable novels'.

Six months later William Jerdan*, one of Colburn's contributors, was appointed editor*. He was to hold this influential position until 28 December 1850, first as shareholder and from 1842 as sole proprietor*.

Aiming at a general readership*, the *Gazette* supplied literary news* and reviews*, as well as articles on the fine arts and philosophy*, British economy, biographical memoirs, and the latest scientific* inventions. As a weekly*, it was considerably ahead of more sophisticated quarterlies* like the *Edinburgh Review** and the *Quarterly Review** in terms of reviewing new books; reviews of books published by Colburn & Richard Bentley* appeared even before they were available in the shops. The entanglement of interests between the *Gazette* and Colburn's publishing house, particularly in the early years, led to many accusations of puffing*, and Colburn was blamed for withholding new titles from other periodicals until the *Gazette* had covered them first.

Despite this controversial reviewing* practice, the *Gazette* became a literary* authority to the extent that Jerdan's reviews could make or break a novel's fortune. As Jerdan and his contributors aimed their reviews at the larger novel-reading public, they were seldom analytical; instead, they often included large sections of a new book, ignoring any concern on the part of writers and publishers that this practice might bring down sales figures.

Stylistic similarities between the majority of articles suggest that Jerdan wrote most of them himself. Nevertheless, he assembled a number of well-known contributors (although lack of documentation makes it difficult to attribute all articles), such as William Blackwood*, Edward Bulwer-Lytton*, Thomas Hood*, Walter Scott* and Robert Southey. As regards his editorial tasks, Jerdan preferred to have sole responsibility. He made an exception for the popular poet Letitia Landon*, who shared his tastes and joined him in the late 1820s.

The *Literary Gazette* was remarkably successful until about 1830. At the initial price of 1s it sold 4,000 copies a week in 1823, standing up to the *Edinburgh Review* and the *Quarterly* (7,000 and 17,000 a month respectively). A first price* change, from 1s to 8d, occurred in 1826 to remain in the competition* with the other periodicals, and a second one, from 8d to 4d, in 1846. When the *Athenaeum** (1828ff) and *Fraser's Magazine** (1830ff) appeared on the market and became instant hits, the success of the *Gazette* started to wane. Never recovering, it held a minor position for another 33 years, a period which was marked by Jerdan's bank-

ruptcy in December 1850 and 12 years under nine successive editors. It eventually merged* with the *Parthenon* in 1862 and issued its last copy in 1863. KL
Sources: *CBEL 3*, Griffiths 1992, *ODNB*, Sullivan 1983, *Waterloo*.

LITERARY GUARDIAN, AND SPECTATOR OF BOOKS, FINE ARTS, PUBLIC AMUSEMENTS, AND FASHIONS (1831-1832) Although the *Literary Guardian* was only produced from 1 October 1831 until 4 August 1832, its importance as a literary* periodical far outweighs its lifespan, laying the foundation for the likes of the *Saturday Review**. Edited* by the anonymous* Messrs Book-Worm, Glow-Worm and Silk-Worm and priced* 2d, it targeted an inclusive and large readership*. Its 16 quarto pages included reviews* of contemporary works, the format* of which was limited to anonymous analysis followed by extensive extracts. Books ranged across the arts and sciences*, from fiction and travel writing to psychology and medicine.

Mapping the intellectual and cultural climate of the time, its weekly* contents sometimes featured selections from British and American periodicals or appraisals of other journals. It estimated its circulation* at 3,000 with a monthly compilation of four previous editions distributed* across Britain, Paris and some parts of America reaching 12,000. Predominantly featuring new work, its political* stance was reflected in its publication of complete versions of five of Byron's letters to John Hunt, while publishing one of the first reviews of *Principles of Geology* by George Lyell. Despite its facility for detecting intellectual and scientific trends, its pages of advertisements* reflecting modern tastes and halving its price, it failed to survive. CL
Source: Sullivan 1983.

LITERARY REPLICATION A term coined by historian of science James Secord in his major study of Robert Chambers's* *Vestiges of the Natural History of Creation*, it describes the various processes by which a text is reproduced beyond its first publication. The study of the literary replication of a text involves paying attention to all of the material forms in which it is has been made available to readers and the exploration of how these different forms, in altering the reading experience, may have affected the text's meaning and reception. Secord argues that knowledge of *Vestiges*, along with other works of nineteenth-century science*, was spread not simply through the reading of the book itself, but by wider discussion of its contents, particularly in periodicals. Excerpts, summaries, supplements*, reviews* and advertisements* gave those who had not read the book an idea of its main concepts and possible implications, significantly widening its influence.

The idea that the reception history of a nineteenth-century text can be traced through its 'literary replication' recognizes the interdependency of the periodical press and the book publishers in this period. While this has long been acknowledged by media historians working on the relationship between literature* and the periodical press, particularly serial* fiction and the novel, it has been less evident in studies of non-fiction. The idea of 'literary replication' offers a loose model for studying the press in relation to a range of disciplines, and seems to be encouraging new studies which recognize the vital importance of journalism* to our wider understanding of nineteenth-century intellectual history. CCF

Sources: Brake 2001, Secord 2000.

LITERATURE (1897-1902) A weekly* literary paper priced* 6d and published* by *The Times*, *Literature* was intended to be the 'organ of the literary classes', a new type of publication that would provide an impartial platform for literary criticism, and report goings on in the literary* world. Its editor*, the erudite H. D. Traill*, argued in the first issue that literary criticism must become tougher: it was right to praise genuine talent, but this appreciation was 'necessarily deprecated in value by association with a too liberal complaisance of attention to all writers whatsoever'. This kind of self-examination became typical of the paper, and many articles dealt with the function of criticism, arguing for the rigorous and scientific analysis and against the 'orgie of superlatives' that was contemporary criticism.

The introductory section contained a leader* by Traill, and often a poem* or a short story. Following this were around 25 anonymous* reviews* of new fiction, biographies, art books and others. Obituaries*, notices of literary events and lists of books published that week took up the latter part of the magazine. Contributions by Henry James*, Jerome K. Jerome*, George Gissing and Rudyard Kipling, among others, ensured that the content was diverse and often of the highest quality.

Traill's death in 1900 caused *Literature* to drift from its initial remit. Portraits of literary celebrities* now took the place of the articles, and these occasionally verged on hagiography, far from the tough critical analysis that the paper had originally aspired to. In 1902, it was absorbed by the *Academy*, with a change of title*, to form the *Academy and Literature: A Weekly Review of Literature and Life*. This publication lost direction and petered

out, but *Literature*'s true heritage is the *Times Literary Supplement* (1902-), which began six days after the final issue of *Literature* and adopted its approach. MaT

Sources: *ODNB*, Sullivan, *Waterloo*.

LITERATURE AND JOURNALISM Debate about the 'right' relation of journalism* to literature pervades the critical discourses of the century, with an increasing tendency to polarise them as the growth of new, common readers accelerated after the repeal of Stamp* Duty and the Education Act of 1870. However, as George Saintsbury* alleges in 1895 much if not all of the century's literature had its origins in the periodical press. This included not only fiction, but poetry* and the essay. The incidence of poetry in newspapers and periodicals was high, and its writers included anonymous, new and well-established poets of both genders.

The relationship between Literature and Journalism is represented in four main models by nineteenth-century writers: that literature and journalism overlap as Saintsbury suggests; that journalism 'carries' literature in its pages, from which it is however distinct; that journalism is a subset of Literature in its widest sense, as intimated by Innes Shand in his series, 'Contemporary Literature' (*Blackwood's Magazine** 1878); and that journalism and literature are patently distinct and adversarial. In this last reading, journalism is associated with mean conditions of production – addressed to the undiscerning populous and produced in haste against a pressing deadline, while literature is associated with Art, its text produced at leisure, without 'compromise' to well-educated readers*. This is the view of George Gissing, who juxtaposes Literature with Journalism in his novel *New Grub Street* (1891): Jasper Milvain, the journalist not only thrives economically while Reardon, the artist/novelist starves personally and professionally, but Milvain survives to inherit the impoverished novelist's wife. Other newspaper novels* such as those by George Moore (*Drama in Muslin*) and Thackeray* allowed for more overlap, although certainly Henry James's* was not among them.

Although Gissing's novel widely disseminated this exaggerated denial of productive traffic between journalism and literature, Saintsbury's interpretation swiftly followed. Authors such as Doyle, Thomas Hardy*, Oliphant*, and Henry James continued to serialise* their fiction in periodicals as their predecessors had done. Moreover, a high proportion of criticism had originated in the newspaper and periodical press, and continued to do so, being only subsequently collected into volume form. In these ways, authors, publishers* and editors* alike fostered traffic between literature and journalism, for their own gain and that of the industry. Arguably (cf Brake), the symbiotic relationship of literature and journalism from the shilling* monthlies* to the gradual collapse of the three volume novel (1860-mid 1890s) fostered both, with the journals showcasing, delivering, reviewing* and advertising* fiction to its increasing readership while fiction sustained the periodical and eventually newspaper press, resulting in their unprecedented efflorescence in these years. **LRB**

Sources: Brake 2001, Brake 2009, Hughes 2004, Hughes 2007, Saintsbury 1895, Shand 1878-1879.

LITHOGRAPHY Invented early in the nineteenth century, lithography is a popular reprographic medium that sought to suggest the aesthetic effects of drawing or wash through the use of crayons and varnish 'stopping' on a prepared stone plate. However, it never found in Britain the widespread success it enjoyed in France and the United States. While the spontaneity of line and direct contact of the artist with the plate made it a medium much used for artists' prints, the technical difficulty and expense of printing the cumbersome plates made it less suitable for periodicals.

Nonetheless, lithography enjoyed a brief moment of popularity as a reprographic medium for periodicals among the emergent caricature* magazines of the 1820s and 1830s. Defining the typical page of the first caricature magazine was the *Glasgow Looking Glass**, before finding a more widespread audience through McClean's *Looking Glass* of 1830 and the various periodical experiments of C. J. Grant*. Even the double-page centre-fold caricatures of such comic periodicals as *Punch** and *Will O' the Wisp** remained firmly attached to the wood engraved* medium, despite the vivid potential that coloured lithographed cartoons* demonstrated in American journals like *Puck*. Matt Morgan's* spectacular foldout satirical plates for the *Tomahawk** in the late 1860s used tinted wood engravings to approximate to the effects of lithography rather than lithographs themselves. Although various art journals used lithography occasionally for one-off illustrations and there were a number of printing trade* journals devoted to the craft late in the century, lithography remained something of a poor relation to wood engraving within British periodicals of the nineteenth century. **BM**

Sources: Pound 1998, Twyman 2001, Wakeman 1970.

LIVERPOOL COURIER AND COMMERCIAL ADVERTISER (1808-1863); DAILY COURIER, THE (1863-1882); LIVERPOOL COURIER(1882-1922); LIVERPOOL DAILY COURIER (1922); DAILY COURIER(1922-1929) The *Liverpool Courier* began life in 1808 as a weekly* political newspaper of four pages that came out on Wednesdays, priced* 6d , and published and printed by Thomas Kaye. The 'Introductory Remarks' in its first issue declared that '[n]eutrality is, in the present posture of our affairs at home and abroad, wholly out of the question', and went on to expound an intelligent but strident conservatism, based on an unshakeable allegiance to the crown and to the national church. This was most likely penned by the paper's first editor Rev. Richard Watson (1781-1833), who held the post for some time. Political news* and comment predominated, but – since Liverpool was at the time one of the busiest ports in the world – there were also lists of ships departing for the colonies and for Europe, detailed inventories of cargo ships arriving in port, tide times, and a 'Naval Intelligence' section providing updates on the progress and whereabouts of various ships. Lists of births, deaths, marriages and bankruptcies, and – increasingly as time went on – poetry* and literary reviews*, were also included.

The paper doubled in size* to eight pages, with its price gradually declining (4d following the abolition of the Stamp* Duty in 1855). It moved to biweekly publication on Saturdays and Wednesdays, before switching to daily* publication – and changing its name to the *Daily Courier* – in April 1863. A leader* in the first issue of the *Daily Courier* – now printed and published by Charles Tinling – reflected on the first 55 years, and (with another bellicose Bonaparte ruling France) concluded that the conservative patriotism advocated at the paper's inception was now more vital than ever. By 1882 – by which time it had followed the market in dropping its price to 1d – it had established a London office from where it received up-to-date political news by telegraph*. That year it reverted to its former title, but continued to go out daily. **MaT**

Sources: Koss 1981, Lee 1976, *ODNB*, *Waterloo*.

LIVERPOOL DAILY POST (1855-) The 1851 Select Committee on Newspaper Stamps asked a witness, Michael James Whitty, whether abolition of newspaper taxes would allow papers as good as *The Times** to be published for a penny. 'Yes … I would publish one myself instantly,' he replied. Whitty, editor* of the weekly* *Liverpool Journal* (1830-84), kept his promise. On Monday 11 June 1855, three weeks before Stamp Duty* was abolished, he launched the *Daily Post*, one of the first penny* dailies* in the UK. More Radical and less sectarian than its local* rivals, the *Daily Post* succeeded in Tory-dominated Liverpool thanks to its writing, its commercial dynamism and its clear stance. It gave unequivocal support to the North in the American civil war – despite losing readers* and advertisers* – and to Irish Home Rule.

Whitty made Edward Richard Russell editor in 1869. Russell was an accomplished drama critic and political* journalist, whose deferential relations with Gladstone and Chamberlain, and position in London literary life, enhanced the paper's prestige. He was editor until 1919, and part-proprietor* after 1872. His was one of the first provincial* papers to commission its own war* correspondents. Contributors included Unitarian scholar and journalist Charles Beard, statistician Thomas Ellison, Welsh writer Beriah Gwynfe Evans, the judge Arthur Greer (Baron Fairfield), Liberal MP Samuel Smith and founding editor of the *East Anglian Daily Times* Frederick William Wilson.

The paper's circulation* area eventually encompassed Liverpool's city region: west Cheshire, south-west Lancashire and north Wales. Its politics* attracted a broader readership than other Liverpool dailies, and the launch of the more s-ensational *Liverpool Weekly Post* (1878-1940) and the halfpenny evening *Liverpool Echo* (1879-) increased profits, thanks in part to Alexander Grigor Jeans, manager from 1879 to 1924. In 1889 the *Liverpool Daily Post* and *Echo* claimed a combined daily circulation of about 95,000, rising to 165,000 in 1892, although most of this growth was probably due to the *Echo*. In 1904 the *Daily Post* bought its rival, the Liberal *Liverpool Mercury*, to create the *Liverpool Daily Post and Mercury*.

Founded at the height of Liverpool's commercial power, the newspaper set out to show that 'this town is now large enough to compete with London in literature* and politics, as it does already in trade and commerce' (*Liverpool Journal*). The paper's links with national politics and metropolitan journalism made it the leading journal of a de facto city state well into the twentieth century. AJH

Sources: *Liverpool Daily Post* 'Centenary Supplement', 11 June 1955, *Mitchell's*, ODNB, *Waterloo*.

LIVERPOOL JOURNAL OF COMMERCE, DAILY SHIPPING, AND MERCANTILE ADVISOR (1861-1873); JOURNAL OF COMMERCE (1873-1880); LIVERPOOL JOURNAL OF COMMERCE (1880-1911); JOURNAL OF COMMERCE AND SHIPPING TELEGRAPH (1911-1984) Published daily* at 1d,

the *Liverpool Journal of Commerce*, a shipping paper of four pages (later expanding to eight) that achieved an international distribution, was started in 1861 by its printer and proprietor* Henry Greenwood, and initially published by Walter Henry Peat. It set out to be 'the Representative of the interests of the enterprising and intelligent Bankers, Merchants, Shipowners, Brokers and Traders of this great Northern Metropolis'.

One of its main functions was to convey data on the departure times for steamships* to Philadelphia, Bombay, Hamburg and countless other destinations, for freight or passage. It also carried a great deal of financial* and economic information on the markets and on customs and excise, served as a place to advertise vessels for sale, and published a daily 'Alphabetical Dock Directory', listing all the vessels currently in the various docks of the Liverpool area. Lists of ships loading at London were also included, and according to *Hubbard's Newspaper Directory* of 1882, the paper was published in both cities simultaneously. News* items, leaders* and editorials were usually shipping-related, but this remit was broadly defined, and the paper's coverage of a variety of geopolitical developments reflected an understanding that these could in various ways disrupt or facilitate colonial trade. After changing its title* to the *Journal of Commerce* in 1873, it reverted to its original title in 1880, by which time Charles Birchall had taken over as proprietor, printer and publisher*. MaT

Sources: *Hubbard's Newspaper Directory* 1882, Lee 1976, *Waterloo*.

LIVERPOOL STANDARD (1832-1856) Published by Samuel Franceys on Tuesday and Friday mornings and initially costing 7d, the eight page *Liverpool Standard and General Commercial Advertiser* began in November 1832 as a conservative, Protestant voice, railing against the groundswell of liberal sentiment that surrounded the Reform Bill of that year. A leader* in the first issue was a plea directed at 'the electors of the United Kingdom' – many of whom were newly enfranchised – advising them to ignore the propaganda of the Anti-Slavery Society, whose behaviour was 'quite inconsistent with the freedom of Election for a Reformed Parliament'. The *Standard* doubted the 'Negroes' actual progress towards civilisation', and argued for the continuation of colonial slavery. This set the tone for future editorials, which usually took the side of the conservative establishment on the major debates in national and international politics*.

The *Standard*'s political coverage was generally

orientated towards Westminster and the colonies, and – unless the extensive listings of ships departing the city's docks are counted – there was scant interest at the beginning in local* news. In 1854, by which time Robert Pearson Thacker had taken over as proprietor and publisher, the price* had dropped to 5d, and it changed its title* to the *Liverpool Standard and General Advertiser*, there was more local news, but the political emphasis remained on national and international issues. It also carried poetry* and literary reviews*, alongside complete price lists for raw materials and commodities traded at the docks.

The *Standard* neither advocated nor applauded the repeal of the Stamp* Duty in 1855, and feared that the inevitable 'large and sudden crop of cheap newspapers' would have a deleterious effect on British culture. It cut its price, but only to 3 ½d – expensive in the context – and refused to compromise its principles or 'bid for mob patronage'; its title also changed once again, to the *Liverpool Standard and General Commercial Advertiser.* These tactics did not serve it well and it ceased publication in the following year. MaT

Sources: Black 2001, *Waterloo.*

LIVESEY, JOSEPH (1794-1884) A lack of formal education did not dampen Joseph Livesey's voracious appetite for reading and writing ('I had a strong inclination for scribbling', he later recalled), or hinder his later career as a journalist, editor*, publisher*, lecturer and writer. Having established his reputation as a public campaigner for teetotalism, his first journalist endeavour was the *Moral Reformer* (1831-1833). This was succeeded by the *Preston Temperance Advocate* (1834-1837) which featured woodcut* illustrations* and a populist* style. Considered to be the first teetotal periodical in Britain, it was characterized according to Livesey by 'clear reasoning, strong arguments, powerful facts, and interesting narratives'.

After a short-lived revival of the *Moral Reformer*, Livesey commenced what was arguably his most important and influential journal. The *Struggle* (1842-1846) was established to promote repeal of the Corn Laws and what Livesey called 'collateral subjects', including a wide range of reforms from teetotalism to complete suffrage. The approach begun in the *Temperance Advocate* was developed in the *Struggle.* Aimed specifically at a working-class* readership*, the journal included rough woodcuts that were 'well adapted to influence the public mind', interspersed with articles in Livesey's direct, categorical prose. Each issue was published without

a date – its message was not meant to go out of date – and offered a clear, uncompromising vision of a reformed Britain in which 'monopoly' in all its guises was in retreat. In 1844 Livesey commenced the *Preston Guardian* (1844-1964) which became a successful local* newspaper (with liberal sympathies) in Lancashire and continued as such long after he had sold it in 1859. Livesey continued to publish and write for self-help and teetotal newspapers, many of them ephemeral, until his death. **PAP** Sources: Harrison, 1971, Livesey 1868, *ODNB*, Pearce 1885, Pickering and Tyrrell 2000.

LLOYD, EDWARD (1815-1890) Edward Lloyd was one of the most important pioneers of mass* publishing and journalism in the nineteenth century. He was born into a poor background in Wales but at an early age came to London where he became a publisher* notorious for the production of cheap* penny* dreadfuls aimed at a working-class* readership*. No respecter of the rights of authors, he published plagiarisms of Dickens* such as the serials* *Nikelas Nickelbery* (1838) and *Oliver Twiss* (1839). Other stories such as 'The String of Pearls' (which introduced the character of Sweeney Todd) catered to the popular delight in horror and the gothic. They became part of the 'Salisbury Square School of Fiction', named after the location of Lloyd's office and notorious for the use of bloodcurdling narratives.

In 1842, Lloyd moved into journalism with his unstamped* newspaper, *Lloyd's Illustrated London Newspaper*. Lloyd was compelled to pay the newspaper stamp and he relaunched the paper the following year as *Lloyd's Weekly London Newspaper* (known as *Lloyd's Weekly Newspaper* 1849ff, *Lloyd's Weekly News* from 1902, *Lloyd's Sunday News* from 1918 and *Sunday News* from 1930. Following the abolition of the Stamp Duty, the price* of the paper was reduced to from 2d to 1d in 1861. It lasted until 1931 (as the *Sunday News*) and became (in 1896) the first newspaper to sell more than one million copies. The paper's Liberal politics* appealed to a wide range of lower-middle and working-class readers. Lloyd increasingly concentrated on his role as a newspaper proprietor*, which he considered to be more respectable than publishing cheap fiction. He bought the *Daily Chronicle* (1872-1930) in 1876 and turned it into a major London paper that campaigned for local government reform in the metropolis. Lloyd was a pioneer in newspaper production, introducing Hoe's rotary press* to Britain in 1856 and the web press in 1873. He also concentrated on paper* manufacturing, establishing several paper mills and leasing land in Algeria to grow grass for paper production. **RM**

Sources: Hatton 1882, Hoggart 1984, *ODNB*.

LLOYD'S PENNY ATLAS AND WEEKLY REGISTER OF NOVEL ENTERTAINMENT (1843-1845) *Lloyd's Penny Atlas* was one of the cheap* popular* papers published by Edward Lloyd*, aimed at a working-class* readership*. A weekly*, it was illustrated* with woodcuts*, and advertised as 'Sixteen Large Quarto Pages for One penny!!!' (Cranfield: 171) Like Lloyd's other penny* weeklies, it was a mixture of Gothic and sensational fiction, much of it serialised. Authors, 'not of high literary repute', were paid ten shillings for each instalment. Its similarity to *Lloyd's Penny Weekly Miscellany* (1843-1846) leads James to speculate that the simultaneity of the two journals was Lloyd's way of accommodating a superfluity of suitable copy, which led James Rymer, editor of the weekly *Miscellany*, to publish more than one number a week on occasion (James: 43-44).

The first issue of the *Penny Atlas* contained stories of vampires, hunchbacks, cannibalism and murder. Behind this sensationalism lay a purported moral purpose. A leader* in the first number expounded the belief that 'True morality – sound reasoning – and exalted sentiments may be more easily, more effectively and more pleasantly conveyed to the mind through…works of fiction than by any other means' (Cranfield: 171). Lloyd was a shrewd businessman and saw the commercial value of not only expressing moral sentiments, but also including exposés of issues such as government corruption, greedy employers and upper-class immorality. With their heady mix of sensationalism and morality, papers such as *Lloyd's Penny Atlas* provided an escape from drudgery for its readers*. **DHL**

Sources: Altick 1957, Cranfield 1978, Bourne 1887, James 1963, *Waterloo*

LLOYD'S WEEKLY NEWSPAPER (1842-1931) Edward Lloyd* published* the first issue of his Sunday* weekly*, *Lloyd's Illustrated London Newspaper*, on 27 November 1842 as a fiction paper to avoid the newspaper stamp tax. The paper's first issues cost 1d, but the price* quickly rose to 2d when the 'fictional' stories bore closer resemblance to fact, requiring a stamp. Its initial issues sold 30,000 copies, a circulation* that dipped temporarily with the price jump. In January 1843, after the eighth issue of the paper, it merged* with the *Illustrated Sunday Herald* and became *Lloyd's Weekly Newspaper*, dropping the illustrations*, changing from eight to twelve pages, and increasing its price to 3d. In

1856, *Lloyd's* revolutionized the newspaper industry by installing the first Hoe rotary press*, which allowed for faster and cheaper printing. In 1861, with the removal of the duty on papers, sales rose to more than 170,000, and *Lloyd's* broke new records in 1896 when the readership reached a million.

The newspaper appealed to a largely lower-middle class* readership*, which gave it a more radical bent than the strictly working-class oriented papers of the time. It was edited* variously by William Carpenter, Douglas Jerrold*, a prominent figure in the 1850s world of print publication* and thereafter by his son William Blanchard Jerrold*. The paper was always aimed at a rather wide audience, lending itself more to topics of general interest than particular politics*. Its mass* appeal and circulation caused increasing production costs, despite the Hoe press innovation. To defray these costs, Edward Lloyd increasingly included advertising* material, and, by 1886, advertising made up almost 40 per cent of the paper. Lloyd also self-published the paper, which helped financially. He was eventually supplying Algerian raw materials to his own paper* mill and factory by 1877. In 1918, a syndicate acquired the paper, changing its name to *Lloyd's Sunday News* and in 1923 to the *Sunday News*, a move headed by Henry Dalziel*. Finally, in 1931, Allied Newspapers purchased the *Sunday News* and incorporated it into the *Sunday Graphic*. **SBA**

Sources: Griffiths 1992, Koss 1981, Lee 1976, Sullivan 1984, Vann 1989.

LOCAL PRESS Increasingly ubiquitous yet always low status, local papers became the most common form of nineteenth-century newspaper, typically serving a market town or borough, sometimes even smaller areas. The *Essex Road and Balls Pond Advertiser* boasted that 'every person reading an announcement in its pages would be within walking distance of the advertiser'. Numbers grew rapidly after Stamp Duty* was reduced in 1836 and abolished in 1855, although London's local press only dates from the 1850s.

Between 1855 and 1861, 137 papers were launched in 123 English towns previously without one. In 1871, Hastings (population 30,000) published nine papers, illustrating the intense competition*, usually along political* lines. Content developed from early digests of London papers into comprehensive miscellanies of parliamentary*, foreign* and British news*, alongside detailed reporting of local public bodies. Other staples were fiction (including local themes), agricultural and market news, railway timetables and advertising* (the main source of income). Some non-local content was obtained as stereotypes* from London agencies*, or shared with papers owned by the same proprietor* (local weeklies pioneered chain ownership). Large readerships*, and therefore much advertising, made some local papers very profitable. They moved towards the political middle ground in later decades to placate advertisers and protect the capital now necessary to enter the market.

From 1868, the Press Association's* cheap telegraphed* news, and cheaper newsprint, made halfpenny evening papers viable even in small towns, with growth from 13 titles in 1870 to 68 in 1880. Aimed at working-class* readers, the evening papers were central to the development of gambling and professional football. Although the mouthpieces of local elites, local papers were open to amateur contributions, including dialect poetry* and prose, and letters* columns* served as miniature public spheres.

In addition to those publications which designated themselves 'papers', there was a flourishing of local periodicals and journals particularly in the latter part of the century. Parish magazines, yearbooks from religious* and philanthropic organizations, satiric* and comic squibs, literary* publications featuring national* and local writers, publications from local learned societies like the Literary and Philosophical Societies which had been founded in urban centres – all these provided a rich and varied diet of periodicals with a particular provenance and appeal. Large urban centres like Manchester with its satellite townships sustained a range of local journals, but such publications were not confined to major urban centres. Little researched by scholars, these are a potentially important resource for historians. Together with the local papers, they helped to assemble the canon of the local, and turned peripheral places into their own small centres. **AJH/MRB**

Sources: Brown, L. 1985, Grant 1871, Harris 1990, Jones 1993, Lee 1976.

LOCKHART, JOHN GIBSON (1794-1854) John Gibson Lockhart, journalist and editor* was educated at Glasgow and Oxford and thereafter qualified as an Edinburgh advocate. In 1817 he visited Germany, funded by an advance by William Blackwood* for a translation of Schlegel's *Lectures on the History of Literature*, published in 1818. Though he wished above all to be known as an author – he published four novels and other works before he was 30 – he was drawn into journalism via *Blackwood's Edinburgh Magazine*, which he joined

shortly after its foundation in Edinburgh in 1817. There, together with John Wilson* he established a reputation for keen satire*. Known as 'the Scorpion', he lampooned Edinburgh figures and (as 'Z') attacked the 'Cockney School of Poetry'* – Leigh Hunt*, Hazlitt* and Keats, in the issue for October 1817. A dispute over his role in *Blackwood's* led in 1821 to the death in a duel of John Scott*, the editor* of the *London Magazine*, at the hands of his friend J. H. Christie.

In 1825, he moved to London on appointment by John Murray* as editor* of the *Quarterly Review*, despite reservations by J. W. Croker* and others about his involvement with *Blackwood's*. In 1828, he seriously misread the government's approach to Roman Catholic emancipation. Responsibility for the political* side of the *Quarterly* was in practice taken out of his hands in 1832 via an agreement between Murray and Croker. Lockhart was nevertheless an active editor and wrote over 100 articles for the *Quarterly* on literary* and other matters, including an (adverse) review of Tennyson's *Poems* in 1833, and an article of 1841 on copyright* which had a significant effect on the development of copyright law. In 1854, he resigned as editor due to ill-health. **DIM**

Sources: Jennings 1884, Lang 1897, Lockhead 1954, *ODNB*, Oliphant 1897, Shattock 1989, *Wellesley.*

LOCKYER, JOSEPH NORMAN (1836-1920) Norman Lockyer, journalist* and editor* moved to London from the Midlands in the late 1850s to work in the War Office. Living in Wimbledon, he became acquainted with members of the Christian Socialist group, especially Thomas Hughes. He had already written some popular science* articles for journals like the *London Review*, so, when Hughes became involved in establishing a new journal – the *Reader* – in 1863, Lockyer was invited to become a regular contributor. This literary* work brought him into contact with the group advising Alexander Macmillan, including Thomas Henry Huxley*. The *Reader*'s finances soon proved shaky, and it was sold in 1865.

Huxley and Lockyer had, however, become convinced that a general science journal designed to aid communication between scientists and with the general public would be valuable. They persuaded Macmillan, and this led to the appearance, on 4 November 1869, of the first issue of *Nature*, with Lockyer as editor. By this time, he was becoming renowned as an astronomer, and, in the latter part of the 1870s, he took charge of a new observatory at South Kensington. His research assistants there were expected to help with *Nature*. One, Richard Gregory*, became so involved that he was appointed assistant editor. Although the journal was not profitable until 1899, it soon established itself as a leading science journal, abroad as well as at home. Lockyer became an eminent scientist in his own right, but his involvement with *Nature* also led to him being seen as a spokesman for science, and as a much sought-after contributor by a range of journals. Lockyer only resigned as editor of *Nature* in 1919, after 50 years, though his input in the final years was limited. **AJM**

Sources: Lightman 2004a, Meadows 1972, *ODNB*.

LONDON: THE CONSERVATIVE WEEKLY JOURNAL OF POLITICS, FINANCE, SOCIETY AND THE ARTS (1877-1879) This short-lived weekly* was founded, financed and edited* by the Scot Robert Glasgow Brown, with the first issue on 3 February 1877. As there 'is no weekly Conservative organ at present', the *London,* was designed to fill the gap. Its Conservative policy was clear, and news* was to be discussed 'from the standpoint of a belief in historical England and its traditions'. The paper was a broadsheet, similar in layout to the *Pall Mall Gazette** and the *World**.

London consisted of six sections: politics*, finance, stories/novels, 'rumours, gossip*, scandals', society* news and the arts. Brown was not a strong editor and much of the work fell to W. E. Henley* and Robert Louis Stevenson, with Henley becoming editor from 15 December 1877. No circulation* figures are available, but Stevenson's mother claims they were small. The main contributors were Robert Brown, R. L. Stevenson, W. E. Henley, Andrew Lang*, George Saintsbury*, James Runciman*, Katharine De Mattos*, James Walter Ferrier and Grant Allen*. Articles and reviews* were anonymous* with rare exceptions, and there were a few pseudonyms in 1878. There were two types of poetry*: political verse (trite) and literary, some of which were 'fillers' written by Henley. A few poems were signed by Henley (W. E. H). The journal's remaining claim to fame was the publication of Stevenson's signed *Latter-Day Arabian Nights* in 1878. Stevenson claimed in early 1877 that Brown was too demanding in asking for copy and it was not until Henley became editor that Stevenson was a more regular contributor.

Brown's health declined and in 1878 (probably early on) the solicitor Gerard Coke Meynell bought the journal but did not change the format*. The journal ceased with the issue of 5 April 1879. *Lon-*

don's small circulation and outspoken Tory views led to its failure. **DA**

Sources: Atkinson 2000, *London*, Saintsbury 1922.

LONDON AND PARIS LADIES' MAGAZINE OF FASHION (1828-91) Focusing on fashion*, the *London and Paris Ladies' Magazine* was a luxuriously produced monthly magazine priced* 1s. Each issue contained colour plates of several figures set in leisured surroundings described in detail, with accompanying black and white plates showing back views, as well as poetry* and fiction. Its editor* was Mrs Edward Thomas, then from 1847 Hon. Mrs Ford.

During its long run it experienced mergers*, title and subtitle changes* and contained the same content as other journals with different titles. In 1832 *Le Beau Monde* (1806-1831) was absorbed by it, followed by the *Ladies' Museum* (1828-1832) in 1833. It was the same as the *World of Fashion* (1824-1851) and *Townsend's Monthly Selection of Parisian Fashions* (1823-1888). From 1828-1834, it was also known in its caption titles by variants on the cover title: as the *Ladies' Magazine of Fashion* from 1828-1834, in 1835 as *Robertson's Monthly Fashions* and in later additions its main title was sometimes extended to the *London and Paris Ladies' Magazine of Fashion, Literature and Arts*. These modifications were evident in numerous fashion* and women's* journals of the period, and reflected the constant changes characteristic of the fashion industry itself. In a saturated market*, publishers constantly sought ways to prolong a magazine's run. **RA**

Source: Beetham and Boardman 2001.

LONDON COMMERCIAL RECORD (1844-1940) The *London Commercial Record* was one of the longest-lasting minor commercial weeklies* of the nineteenth century. It began as a continuation of the third *Nicholson's Weekly Register of Useful Knowledge. Commercial, Temperance and Monetary Barometer* (1842) which passionately sought to help 'the Middle and Working Classes'* through providing basic information about prices, economics and trading methods. For John Nicholson, a tea dealer, this was his second periodical venture after *Nicholson's Commercial Gazette and Grocers' Register of Useful Knowledge* (1832-1835), a combination of opinionated general newspaper and early trade* paper which, because it unashamedly carried news* and was decidedly radical, was closed immediately after it dared appear unstamped*. *Nicholson's Weekly Register* was even more unsuccessful: by issue 54 it had been sold to Charles Smith, who had been publishing* the *London Mercantile Journal* since 1831.

Smith aimed to make the journal into 'the organ the shopkeepers require' and devoted more space to markets, reviews of the corn trade, lists of bankrupts, public sales and correspondence* – matters, however, that engaged the merchant rather than the shopkeeper. It was now only available through subscription at 3s 3d per quarter in advance. By 22 June 1844, Smith openly admitted to subscribers that he had never made a profit and to do so wanted to raise the subscription to 5s a quarter and change the name to the *London Commercial Record*. If hitherto advertisements* had been very scarce indeed, they started coming regularly by 1850, and the identity of the journal as a wholesale-dealers' and merchants' paper was confirmed. Articles on merchant law became more prominent, though under the firm of Charles Smith (which owned it for the rest of the century) the paper was always mainly a facts and figures publication. In 1889, subscription changed to £1 a year in advance, suggesting a continued need to minimize risk. **AK**
Sources: Mitchell *et al.* 1994.

LONDON ENTR'ACTE (1869-1907) The illustrated* weekly* *London Entr'acte: the Illustrated Theatrical and Musical Critic and Advertiser: a Consulting Paper for all Amusements* was launched in July 1869 to give 'at one view a complete statement of the entertainment provided at each of the principal London Theatres … accompanied by criticisms and other appropriate original matter', as editor* Samuel Albert Barrow announced in its first issue. Priced* 1d in 1869 for eight pages, it had expanded to 16 pages by 1900. The journal's tone was generally light-hearted and mildly satirical and rather approached that of a comic paper. Its most prominent features were the lively full-page cartoons* of, mostly, stage figures by caricaturist* Alfred Bryan (1852-1899). The *Entr'acte* also published court* reports, as well as boasting columns* on politics* and art, but its main focus remained on the gossip* side of the London theatre and music* world. The title was changed to *Entr'acte and Limelight* in March 1871; then to *London and Provincial Entr'acte* in February 1872; and finally reverted back to *Entr'acte and Limelight* in May 1875. **OD**
Sources: Vann and VanArsdel 1994, *Waterloo*.

LONDON JOURNAL; AND WEEKLY RECORD OF LITERATURE, SCIENCE AND ART (1845-1928) The *London Journal* was a penny* illustrated* fiction weekly* which, achieving sales of over 500,000 in the early 1850s, is key to understanding the development of the cheap press*. Begun by George Stiff* as a cross between the *Illustrated London*

Figure 37: The fashion supplement in the *London Journal*, March 1895.

*News** and the *Family Herald**, it was initially edited* by G. W. M. Reynolds* who left in 1847 to found *Reynolds's Miscellany**. It published (1848-1855) six long serial* novels by J. F. Smith that came to typify the highly commercial 'London Journal school' of fiction: complex plots of many characters, rapid action, extreme emotion and always a final re-establishment of moral equilibrium.

In 1857 the *Journal* was bought by Herbert Ingram* and Bradbury and Evans* who put Mark Lemon* in charge. He sought to educate its readership* by serialising Walter Scott* novels. The result was a dramatic fall in circulation* that in 1859 caused the sale of the *Journal* back to Stiff who recovered its popularity by combining it with his magazine the *Guide* and running novels by Emma D. E. N. Southworth, a very successful American writer. Financially strained, Stiff was forced to sell the magazine to the printer W. S. Johnson in 1862, who continued Stiff's policies and success. Pierce Egan the Younger* was editor* (1860-1880) and himself contributed 24 novels. In later years Smith's novels were twice reserialized in attempts to regain dwindling circulation, once under the editorship of Herbert J. Allingham* (1890-1909). The effects were temporary and in 1912 the *Journal* was combined with *Spare Moments*. It eventually died altogether in 1928. Other notable contributors to the *Journal* include M. E. Braddon*, Percy B. St John*, Charles Reade, John Wilson Ross* and John Parsons Hall. **AK**

Source: King 2004.

LONDON MAGAZINE (1820-1829) The *London Magazine* was founded by Robert Baldwin* to counteract the success of *Blackwood's Edinburgh Magazine*, with its first monthly* issue in January 1820. Priced* 2s 6d, it was between 110-120 pages initially. Liberal in its outlook, it concentrated on original literary* and critical articles without *Blackwood's* habit of attacking and praising personalities. It was known as Baldwin's *London Magazine* (1821-1824) to avoid confusion with the short-lived Gold's *London Magazine* (1820-1821).

John Scott*, the first editor*, established a group of distinguished writers including William Hazlitt*, Charles Lamb*, Carlyle*, Allan Cunningham and Horace Smith, during his short editorship (Jan. 1820-Feb. 1821). Scott was also a contributor. Acrimony between Scott and *Blackwood's* over Scott's attacking *Blackwood's* abuse of writers resulted in Scott being killed in a duel by J. H. Christie. Baldwin was probably the interim editor with help from J. H. Reynolds until the journal was sold to Taylor and Hessey, with John Taylor becoming editor. According to Taylor the circulation* for July 1821 was 1,700, an insignificant figure compared with *Blackwood's* circulation of around 14,000 per issue. Taylor delegated some of his work to others, notably Thomas Hood*.

Taylor carried on Scott's good editorial work and added some new contributors, among whom were Thomas De Quincey*, George Darley*, John Clare, Mary Shelley, Thomas Griffiths Wainewright, Charles Wentworth Dilke*, Walter Savage Landor and Henry Francis Cary, who wrote on foreign literature*. The peak year for the journal was 1823, after which, despite some new blood, the standard declined. Taylor's interference with contributions and his delegation of work led to some contributors quitting, Hazlitt and Lamb among them.

Henry Southern became editor in 1825, inaugurating a new series with the January issue, increasing the number of pages with now a single column* per page. With a decline in literary quality and subsequently a declining circulation*, the owners sold to Southern in September 1825. His Utilitarian outlook and his pragmatic approach to contributors' pay led to further decline, and by April 1828

he sold it to Charles Knight* and Barry St Leger. From January 1829 a *Journal of Facts* was included in the magazine. Falling circulation and the loss of contributors, many to the *New Monthly Magazine*, saw the *London* absorbed by it in July 1829. **DA**

Sources: Bauer 1953, *ODNB*, Parker 2000, Riga and Prance 1978, Sullivan, *Waterloo*.

LONDON MECHANICS' REGISTER (1824-1828) Marketed as a 'cheap scientific* periodical' for 'the humble Mechanic', the *Mechanics' Register* was launched on 6 November 1824. Published* by George Cowie* and William Strange*, it sold for 3d weekly* (Saturday), 1s monthly*, and 7s 6d as an annual* in boards. Its aim was 'to encourage the efforts of incipient genius', a mission echoed in its motto from Dr Johnson: 'He that enlarges his curiosity after the works of nature, demonstrably multiplies his inlets to happiness'. It reported the lectures of George Birkbeck's (1776-1841) London Mechanics' Institution, abridged works on 'Natural and Experimental Philosophy*, Practical Mechanics, Astronomy, Chemistry, Literature* and the Arts,' inserted communications from men of 'scientific experience' and published letters* from its 'Operative Artisan' readers. Presenting itself as 'a light and agreeable companion... as well as a vehicle of useful information', it included non-technical articles ranging from the history of coffee to animal cruelty and Voltaire's philosophy.

There are no circulation* figures, though agents are listed in London, Paris, New York and Rio Janeiro. Although it issued 2s supplements* illustrated* with woodcuts*, and despite being relaunched in 1827 as the *New London Mechanics' Register and Magazine of Science and the Useful Arts*, the periodical was less successful than the rival it so closely imitated, the *Mechanic's Magazine*, and publication ended in 1828. Despite its commercial failure, the *Mechanics' Register* reflects the overlapping print strategies of elite social reformers, opportunistic cheap* publishers and artisan self-improvers in the 1820s. **DSM**

Sources: BL Catalogue, Francis Place collection, Sheets-Pyenson 1985, *Waterloo*.

LONDON MEDICAL GAZETTE, BEING A WEEKLY JOURNAL OF MEDICINE AND THE COLLATERAL SCIENCES (1827-1852); MEDICAL TIMES AND GAZETTE, A JOURNAL OF MEDICAL SCIENCE, LITERATURE, CRITICISM, AND NEWS (1852-1885) The *London Medical Gazette* was founded by Sir Benjamin Brodie, John Abernethy and others in explicit opposition to the *Lancet**, and continued to be a major rival throughout its life. The 'Address' on the opening of the *Gazette* complains of the invasion of 'literary plunderers' into the 'peace and quiet' of doctors' professional and private lives. Now the lectures they had worked so hard to generate and deliver were 'suddenly snatched from them, and published for the profit of others', while physicians and surgeons 'were held up to public scorn for errors to which, even if actually committed, the ablest men are occasionally liable'. Roderick Macleod left the august *Medical and Physical Journal* (see *British and Foreign Medical Review**), into which he had introduced hospital reports in imitation of the *Lancet*, in order to edit* the *Gazette*. The latter was even more obviously modelled on the *Lancet*, and included leading* articles on general topics such as the state of medical* education, original papers (lectures or essays) on medical topics, reviews* ('analyses') of books, relevant extracts from various sources, hospital reports and a miscellaneous section. There were over 30 direct attacks on the *Lancet* in the first year alone or on its proprietor* Thomas Wakley*, mainly for lapses of taste or grammatical error. Wakley responded in kind, open war between the two medical weeklies* lasting three years before more subtle methods were used, such as milking connections in order to publish lectures first. Nonetheless, its circulation* remained small despite the efforts of the notable surgeon and writer James Paget, who was subeditor* 1837-42. In 1852, the *Gazette* was amalgamated with the *Medical Times*, which Frederick Knight Hunt had begun in 1839, as another weekly rival to the *Lancet**.

The *Medical Times* was edited initially by the Edinburgh anatomist Robert Knox (who had fled Edinburgh after it had been discovered that he had dissected murder victims). Its proprietor*, Hunt, had been forced to sell to T. P. Healey in 1841 after actions for libel. Then (perhaps) Marshall Hall edited the journal for a while until its owner took over. In 1846 Healey attacked Wakley and the *Lancet* for supporting an investigation into a soldier flogged to death; Wakley went to court for libel and won considerable damages. In 1849 John Stevenson Bushnan became editor and the following year the medical publishing magnate John Churchill bought the journal. Two years later he bought the *Gazette* as well and combined the two, upon which Bushnan left to become senior physician of the Metropolitan Free Hospital. Under its new title, the combined *Medical Times and Gazette, a journal of medical science, literature, criticism and news* (1852ff)it was edited by a series of notables,

including Thomas Spencer Wells (dates uncertain); Robert Druitt (1862-1872) and Francis Cornelius Webb (1873-1883). Its final years were edited by Joseph Henry Philpot. **AK**
Sources: Bartrip 1990, Bynum *et al.* 1992, Clarke 1874, *ODNB*, Sprigge 1897, *Waterloo*.

LONDON QUARTERLY REVIEW (1853-1968); CHURCH QUARTERLY REVIEW (1968-1971) Emanating from the Methodist Connexion, the *London Quarterly Review* first appeared in September 1853, based on the characteristic quarterly* review* model. James Harrison Rigg, when still a Methodist theological student, had mooted the idea of such a publication as early as 1839, but he had to wait for more propitious times. More progressive than might have been anticipated, the review steered a middle course with regard to Methodist divisions.

First edited* by Thomas M'Nicoll until 1859, the *London Quarterly Review* was intent on upholding the high standards of intellectual theological discourse that its editors felt was lacking in both church and society. Editors William Burt Pope (1859-1886) and James H. Rigg (1883-1898) were both Methodist clergymen and teachers. Rigg, whose early vision had finally been realized, was able to enlist financial support for the quarterly from the laymen and theologians of Westminster Training College of which he was principal.

Although reviews of religious* publications dominated, science* and literature* were also well represented, the former from an objective stance. The first issue, for example, integrated a discussion of Christianity and Islam into a review of a travel book on Turkey while including a substantial number of natural history books as well as discussions emanating from reviews of Wesleyan and Methodist texts. While its circulation* approximated a modest 1,200, it gained a reputation for quality as when the artist and writer James Smetham reviewed Alexander Gilchrist's *Life of William Blake*, a piece which was praised by Dante Gabriel Rossetti for its perspicacity. Toward the end of the century, original articles were also featured.

For four years from 1858, it became the *London Review*, before reverting to its original title. In the following century, it merged with the *Holborn Review* in 1932 to become the *London Quarterly and Holborn Review*, before being merged* in 1968 with the *Church Quarterly Review*, which itself ceased publication four years later. **CL**
Sources: Altholz 1989, Sullivan, *Wellesley*.

LONDON SOCIETY (1862-1898) *London Society* was a shilling* monthly* launched in 1862 by the publisher* James Hogg. Its first years were marked by anonymity* and, to a certain degree, mediocrity. The move towards accreditation was speeded up when Richard Bentley* bought the magazine in 1870 and initially employed Henry Blackburn as editor*. It followed the model set by *Cornhill Magazine** and achieved a circulation* of 20,000 by the mid-1860s through its high-profile contributors such as Wilkie Collins*, Charles Reade and 'Ouida'*. The novelist Florence Marryat* was brought in to act as editor in 1872. She also serialised* her fiction in its pages. Alongside serial* fiction the publication included short articles and stories covering a wide range of themes (holidays and travel, the arts and the pursuits of high society*: hunting, balls, dinner parties, the marriage market and London life.)

The magazine prided itself on its illustrations* provided by a bank of artists. By the 1870s, George Cruikshank's* cartoons* – their frequency and variety ranging from coloured fold-out folios to tiny emblems – made *London Society* more interesting graphically than many of its shilling monthly competitors. After Marryat left in 1876, *London Society* failed to attract any authors of similar popularity, and readership* tailed off gradually during several changes of publisher. Sampson, Low* continued publishing the magazine from 1872 until 1880 when it was bought by F. V. White, who published it for nine years before a final move to Arliss Andrews in its last year of publication (1897-1898). BP

Sources: *ODNB, Poole's,* Sutherland 1990, *Waterloo.*

LONDONDERRY STANDARD (1836-1964) Published as a 4d bi-weekly from 1836 under the motto, 'our faith, our firesides', the *Londonderry Standard's* masthead* of a cannon pointing out from crenellated walls under a flag emblazoned with '1688', the year the Apprentice Boys closed the city gates against Catholic troops, indicated it was a unionist newspaper. The *Londonderry Standard* proclaimed that it was conservative but not intolerant or bigoted, aiming to promote the 'commercial and social advantage of the City of Londonderry'. The *Standard* aligned itself with Presbyterianism, noting that few transported convicts were Presbyterians and asserting that in its agriculture, manufacturing and commerce, Ulster was a place apart from the rest of Ireland. This 'intellectual and moral grandeur' was a consequence of 'the presence and workings of Presbyterianism'. By 1855 the price* had risen to 5d.

In 1887 the *Standard* was bought by William Glendinning and Co. and thenceforth published three times weekly*. It continued as a staunchly Presbyterian publication, although the 1688 masthead was dropped and in 1888 the title changed to the *Derry Standard*, taking up the campaign for 'tenant right', which had previously been lampooned as 'tenant wrong'. By this time, it cos 1d. Its obituary* on Parnell admonished British politicians for their complaisance with Home Rule, lamenting that 'the 'loyal minority' in Ireland were the only people who understood its consequences. MJH
Source: *Waterloo Irish.*

LONGMAN Longman, Thomas Norton (1771-1842); **Longman, Thomas** (1804-1879); **Longman, William** (1813-1877); **Longman, Thomas Norton** (1849-1930); **Longman, Charles James** (1852-1934); **Longman, William** (1882-1967); **Longman, Robert Guy** (1882-1971).

The history of the Longman family publishing* dynasty began with the first Thomas Longman (1699-1755) in Bristol and ended with Mark Frederick Kerr Longman (1916-1972) in London. The premises of the firm from 1770 were 38-41 Paternoster Row. Its insignias – the Black Swan and the Ship – though quite well known, only appeared occasionally on title pages until well into the twentieth century. The enduring success of the company lay in its combination of business acumen and sufficient capital to realize a publishing vision, as with Thomas Norton Longman who left over £200,000 in 1842 to two of his sons, Thomas IV and William, to continue company expansion. A third son, Charles (1809-1873), was apprenticed to John Dickinson in the paper*-making business. And one of his daughters, Mary (1801-1870), married Andrew Spottiswoode, a member of the famous printing firm. Thus the Longman family connections extended into two businesses that were key to a successful publishing company. An obituary* acknowledged Thomas Norton Longman as a Leviathan of nineteenth-century publishing. His youngest son, William, was the mastermind of the firm in the mid-nineteenth century. He, among other things, founded the *Publishers' Circular** in 1837, which published a weekly* list of new books (thus publicizing Longman's list among others), and he bought the company of J. W. Parker* in 1863. In the last decades of the nineteenth century, Charles James Longman (well known under the initials C. J. L.), a son of William, was the most dominant partner. Both he and his older brother Frederick were close friends of Andrew Lang* and they were to rely on the latter's literary advice for many of their publishing decisions.

The number and variety of Longman's London imprints are extensive, changing from Longman to Longmans on occasion, and publishing with a number of partners, in a huge diversity of combinations such as Longman and Co; Longman and Orme and Co; Longman, Brown Green, and Longmans; Longman, Brown, Green, Longmans and Roberts; Longman Rees, Orme, Brown, Green and Longman; Longman, Hurst, Rees, Orme and Brown; Longman, Green, Reader and Dyer; Longman, Simpkin and Stanford – to name but a few!

Longman's contribution to periodical publication was significant. With Constable* as publisher*, Longman was the proprietor* of the Whig quarterly, the *Edinburgh Review** from 1802, and became sole proprietor from 1826. *Fraser's Magazine** became part of the Longman list with their takeover of J. W. Parker's. Their house* monthly, *Longman's Magazine**, was launched in 1882. Literary* in character, it published fiction by Thomas Hardy*, Rudyard Kipling and Elizabeth Nesbitt*. Nominally edited* by Charles James Longman, Andrew Lang for many years actually did the job. In 1886 Longman initiated one of the earliest specialist journals for historians, the *English Historical Review*. It was edited by one of Longman's authors, Mandell Creighton, Professor of Ecclesiastical History at Cambridge and later Bishop of London. These three are only a selection from the most well known of their periodical list, which also includes the *Athenaeum* (1807), the *Keepsake*, the *London Medical Review*, the *Monthly Magazine and British Register**, John Loudon's* *Magazine of Natural History* and the *Naturalist*.

As book publisher* and bookseller, Longman's boasted a massive range of authors covering an impressive intellectual base such as John Stuart Mill*and John Henry Newman, books destined to become classics such as P. M. Roget's *Thesaurus*, *Gray's Anatomy*, Johnson's *Dictionary* and Wordsworth's *Lyrical Ballads,* and the medical reforms of Florence Nightingale. In 1968, Mark Longman negotiated a takeover resulting in Pearson* Longman Ltd, which terminated in 1994; Longmans is now an imprint of Pearson Education. **CL/MD/LB**
Sources: *ODNB*, Wallis 1974, *Waterloo*.

LONGMAN'S MAGAZINE (1882-1905) Established by Charles Longman*, *Longman's Magazine* was a 6d monthly* that catered to the family* magazine* market. By pricing Longman's below the shilling* magazines such as *Argosy** and *Temple*

Figure 38: Andrew Lang's causerie in Longman's Magazine (1886-1905) was called 'At the Sign of the Ship', referring to the symbol over the Longman imprint.

Bar*, Longman hoped to reach the new class of readers that had emerged following the 1870 Education Bill. However, the price* of the journal made it primarily accessible to middle-class* readers.

The first issue sold well, reaching a circulation* of 74,000, but thereafter it declined. *Longman's Magazine* was in many ways a successor to *Fraser's Magazine**, which Charles Longman* had acquired in 1863. Yet *Longman's*, unlike *Fraser's*, was dedicated to a non-partisan political* stance and studiously avoided controversy, favouring light, entertaining fiction and informative articles. Andrew Lang*, Longman's chief literary advisor, was largely responsible for the middle-class appeal of the magazine. His causerie*, 'At the Sign of the Ship', was a distinctive selling point and his dislike of realistic and psychological fiction guided the journal's literary* offerings, which primarily included adventure and romance serials*.

Beginning in 1883, *Longman's* sponsored a food cart, the 'Donna,' which was intended to relieve poor dock workers. The magazine solicited contributions from readers and acknowledged supporters by name in the journal. Following a policy of signed publication, *Longman's* also advertised the names of literary contributors on the cover of each issue. This list included J. A. Froude*, Robert Louis Stevenson, Rudyard Kipling, Margaret Oliphant*, Jean Ingelow, W. D. Howells and Grant Allen*. The magazine folded due to changes in market forces that favoured illustrated* popular newspapers over old-style literary magazines. In an editorial note published in the last number of the magazine, Longman noted that 'competition for the patronage of the sixpenny public has become very severe, and the mere endeavour to keep up a high literary standard is nowadays not sufficient'. **ME**

Sources: Demoor 1988, *ODNB*, Tye 1974, *Wellesley*.

LOOKING GLASS (1830-1836) Published* by the established London print dealer, Thomas McClean, the *Looking Glass* gave a metropolitan gloss to the format* established a few years before by the *Glasgow Looking Glass**. Caricature* magazines, using a large format multi-image page which combined political* commentary with social satire*, were a characteristic product of the London periodical marketplace in the 1830s, and the *Looking Glass*, successively drawn by three major caricaturists of the time (William Heath*, Robert Seymour* and Henry Heath*) was the most widely distributed example, drawing heavily on the reputation of its artists for its success.

Like Grant's* *Every Body's Album**, McClean wanted to use lithography* as the mode of production, and this seems to have led to a dispute with William Heath which resulted in Seymour taking over the illustrations* after the first seven monthly issues. McClean seems to have increasingly imposed his will on the magazine, retitling it as *McClean's Monthly Sheet of Caricatures Or the Looking Glass* in January 1831, changing the layout, with Seymour and William Heath using fewer larger images and moving steadily towards social rather than political satire. **BM**

Source: Pound 1998.

LOUDON, JANE (1807-1858) Jane Loudon (née Webb), magazine editor*, journalist*, and botanical and natural history writer, started as a writer of poetry* and science fiction in the 1820s; her anonymous* first novel, *The Mummy! A Tale of the Twenty-Second Century*, appeared in 1827. Informally educated, and acquiring modern languages partly through trips to Europe with her father after her mother died, she had been writing fiction and poetry from the age of 17. Her father, a Birmingham businessman and engineer who had suffered financial loss, died in 1824 leaving her an orphan. She became a salaried contributor to the *Literary Gazette* under the auspices of its editor* William Jerdan*. When she married in 1830, she had been about to set up *Tabby's Magazine* with Elizabeth Spence (and Laetitia E. Landon* and Jerdan as advisors).

Her marriage to John Claudius Loudon*, journalist, editor, publisher*, proprietor*, horticultural-

ist and garden designer altered the trajectory of Webb Loudon's career, as her skills were subsumed into his projects for almost a decade. From the occasion of his near bankruptcy in 1838, she authored gardening* publications under her married name 'Mrs Loudon'. During 1841, she edited the short-lived 1s 6d monthly the *Ladies' Magazine of Gardening*, published by William Smith and printed by Bradbury & Evans*. Driven by science* like John Loudon's *Gardener's* Magazine*, containing edited and re-written extracts from it and sharing its wood engravings*, her magazine informed readers about botany, ornithology, garden visits and the maintenance of suburban gardens and plants in the home. After John Loudon's death in 1843 she continued with her informative illustrated* *Ladies' Flower-Garden* series, also serially* published by William Smith, and printed by Bradbury and Evans. By the late 1840s 'Mrs Loudon' had became a well-established brand for middle-class* women's* publications.

This may have been a factor in her appointment as the first editor of the *Ladies' Companion at Home and Abroad** (1849-1851), a 3d (4d stamped) weekly*, published by Bradbury and Evans. Under her editorship the magazine offered an alternative to what was currently available to middle-class woman readers by means of its relatively large size* (19 × 27cm), its plentiful use of illustration and varied typographic devices; its wide range of departments included art and science as well as fiction, poetry*, fashion*, domestic management and reviews* of current cultural events. Loudon subscribed to 'separate spheres' for men and women; however, she also campaigned to support women who worked and the 'class of maligned and despised females whose rights have hitherto been scoffed at, and who have scarcely been considered members of the great human family', otherwise known as the 'old maid' (*Ladies' Companion*, 1, 22 June 1850: 406). She was fired after six months. Her short tenure and the merging* in 1852 of the magazine with the *New Monthly Belle Assemblée* (1834-1870) suggest that the audience for the magazine failed to materialize in sufficient numbers for it to continue in its original form.

Despite an award from the Royal Literary Fund (1844) and a civil-list pension of £100 from 1846, Loudon was in financial difficulties after the loss of her editorship She published two more educational books for children, and another on the management of pets. However, she was also obliged to travel to Europe with her daughter and let her house in

Porchester Terrace (designed by John Loudon), in order to survive financially. **SD**

Sources: Howe 1961, Jerdan 1852, *ODNB,* Simo 1988.

LOUDON, JOHN CLAUDIUS (1783-1844) John Claudius Loudon (1783-1843), journalist*, editor*, proprietor*, publisher* and landscape gardener was born in Scotland, the son of a farmer; he attended Edinburgh University while apprenticed to a market gardener. In 1803, he was introduced to Jeremy Bentham in London, and a combination of the Scottish Enlightenment's anti-aristocratic ideal of scientific knowledge and Bentham's utilitarian philosophy underlies much of his work. His first article appeared in 1803, and journalism and many books followed, interspersed with landscape projects. Having made a fortune from farming, he lost it in 1815 through speculation. That and the progression of debilitating illness which damaged his foot and led to the amputation of his right arm in 1825 meant that he turned increasingly to writing

The *Gardener's Magazine** (1826ff), was the first of the periodicals he established and edited. This was followed by the *Magazine of Natural History* (1828-1836) and the *Architectural Magazine* (1834-1839). The same size* and containing illustrations* like the *Gardener's Magazine,* both publications were inclusive of male and female readership*. The *Magazine of Natural History,* initially a bi-monthly, priced* at 3s 6d but reduced by 1835 to 2s on becoming a monthly*, was both cheaper and more regularly issued than the elite quarterlies* of the Royal Societies. Its price however, limited it to a middle-class* readership, even if a poorer audience was targeted, and may have had access through the myriad 'library' systems of coffee houses, pubs and the Mechanic's Institutes. Subjects covered ranged from zoology, botany and minerology to geology and meteorology. The *Architectural Magazine* (a monthly, priced at 2s), was likewise pioneering: the first periodical devoted to architecture, it provided a forum for debate, exemplified by that concerning the competition for the design for the new palace of Westminster (1835). Interestingly, it published an early piece by John Ruskin*, later to become a distinguished writer on architecture. Anticipating William Morris* and harking back to Joshua Reynolds, Loudon argued for the connection between society and art; improving domestic buildings 'for the great mass of society'(*Architectural Magazine* 1: 1) was one of his aims. For one year (Nov. 1840-Nov. 1841) he was also editor of the

Gardeners' Gazette (1837-1844), the first weekly* horticultural newspaper.

Loudon was a designer of landscapes, a number of which were intended for use by the public, including cemeteries, as well as of private estates. However, it is through the 'book manufactory of Bayswater', his home-based publishing enterprise in which his sisters Jane and Mary Loudon, as well as his wife Jane (Webb) Loudon* participated as writers and wood* engravers, that he may have exerted greatest influence. Apart from his editorial activities, he also produced five encyclopaedias in order to augment and codify professional knowledge in architecture, agriculture, landscape gardening, horticulture and botany. The strategy of publishing serially*, as well as in 'complete' volumes reduced his costs and ensured that his work reached diverse audiences. He was also an influential figure in the shaping of domestic ideology through gardens and architecture, exemplified in another serial publication, the *Suburban Gardener and Villa Companion* (1838). His volume of work and perhaps over-ambition led to large debts from a sumptuous survey of trees in Britain (he owed the engravers and printers £10,000), and although at his death the sum was reduced, it left his family in financial difficulties. **SD**

Sources: Leathlean 1993, *ODNB,* Rennie 1834, Schenker 2002, Sheets-Pyenson 1981b, Simo 1988, *The Times, Waterloo.*

LOVER, SAMUEL (1797-1868) Samuel Lover was a Dublin painter, illustrator*, novelist and songwriter. He is mostly known as a miniature and landscape painter, but he also provided fiction and illustrations for periodicals. Lover published his first short story in the *Dublin Literary Gazette* (Jan.-June 1830), the only time he was not paid for his literary* work. He remained involved with the journal after new editor* Philip Dixon Hardy renamed it the *National Magazine* (1830-1831). Lover went on to work as an illustrator for the weekly* *Irish Penny Magazine* (1833), providing the landscape engravings* that opened every issue. Barbara Hayley identifies Lover as its editor*.

Lover also contributed fiction to the first four issues of the *Dublin University Magazine** from January to April 1833. After moving to London in 1835, he befriended Charles Dickens* and became involved with *Bentley's Miscellany**. He published there the initial chapters of his most famous novel, *Handy Andy* (1837-1839).

From 1844 on Lover developed a one-man show entitled 'Irish Evenings'; it consisted of recitations, songs and dramatizations of his own works and was apparently very well received during a tour of America in 1846. A short-lived stint (Nov.1849-Jan. 1850) as editor of the Dublin fine arts magazine *Amateur* marks his last foray into journalism. During the 1860s Lover collected and published to general acclaim his songs, poetry and plays in both Irish and English editions. Oscar Wilde's* comment on Lover as one of those who 'came from a class that did not – mainly for political reasons – take the populace seriously [...] of its passion, its gloom, its tragedy, they knew nothing' (Wilde, quoted in Kiberd, 1995: 49) encapsulates the way Lover's work has been seen by subsequent generations. **FB**

Sources: Bernard 1874, Brown 1937, Hayley 1976, Kiberd 1995, *ODNB*, PGIL-*Eirdata,* Sullivan 1984, *Waterloo Irish.*

LOVETT, WILLIAM (1800-1877) A central figure within London artisan politics, Lovett's involvement in periodical publication began with the monthly *Co-operative Magazine* and its several successor titles (1826-1830) of which, with James Watson*, he was the mainstay. A cabinetmaker by trade, Lovett's involvement in journalism was sporadic but significant. He was a critically important activist in the unstamped* press, 'one of the most important political movements that I was ever associated with', he later wrote. Lovett was a close friend of Henry Hetherington*, helping manage *Poor Man's Guardian** during Hetherington's absence in 1831-1832, and entering into fictive ownership arrangements of the latter's presses in 1834-1835 to evade their confiscation. Lovett served as a trustee of the *Charter* (1839-1840) and on the management committee of the *Gazette of the Working Men's Association*. He managed the *National Association Gazette*, was joint publisher* (with John Cleave*) of the *Educational Circular and Communist Apostle* (1841-1846) and sole publisher of *Howitt's Journal of Literature and Popular Progress** (1847-1851), the third volume of which he also printed.

Lovett was an indefatigable correspondent* with editors and contributed substantial pieces to both the *Scottish* and *English Chartist Circulars* and many of Hetherington's periodicals, notably *London Dispatch*. In his old age he contributed both to the trade unionist* weekly* *Bee-Hive** (1862-1876) and the teetotal *Alliance News* (1862-1905). Most of Lovett's published work took the form of closely argued addresses, written anonymously* on behalf of organizations in which he was involved – often as secretary – notably the London Working Men's Association. Many of these (*The People's Charter* of 1838 was effectively one of them) enjoyed a mass circulation* in the radical press of the 1830s and 1840s. **MSC**

Sources: *DLB*, Lovett 1876, *ODNB*.

LOW, SAMPSON (1797-1886) Sampson Low was apprenticed to several booksellers and publishers* before starting his own business at 42 Lamb's Conduit Street in 1819. By 1837, as a successful publisher of schoolbooks, religious tracts and general literature, he was asked by a committee of about 20 London publishers to edit* a new trade journal*. He thus became a part owner, and later full owner, of the *Publishers' Circular**, a bi-monthly, which continued well into the twentieth century.

In 1850 the Booksellers' Association was revived in order to discourage the sale of books at large discounts, and Low became its secretary. However, two years later a committee of distinguished writers and jurists ruled in favour of the undersellers, effectively dissolving the Association. In London, Low became the leading publisher of American works, facilitated in part by being the agent for Harper Brothers* of New York. He distinguished himself from many British publishers by trying to secure valid copyrights* for American books in England and paying American authors for their writings.

Low also was one of the early British publishers to incorporate photographic* illustrations* in his publications, and in the early 1860s he included photographs of Wilkie Collins* and Edward Bulwer Lytton* as frontispieces in his editions. By the 1870s he published elaborate volumes of art work, travel literature and nature studies, all based on photographs. The firm of Sampson Low & Co. continued in business until 1964, and was known especially for writers such as Jules Verne, Henry Morton Stanley, R. D. Blackmore, Harriet Beecher Stowe and Louisa May Alcott. **JJB**

Sources: Hamber 1996, Marston 1904, *ODNB*.

LUCAS, WILLIAM (DATES UNKNOWN) As far as can be ascertained, William Lucas began his publishing* career in 1885. He only appears to have published three books, which were offshoots from his business of periodical publishing in London. He worked with the editor/proprietor* T. Harrison Roberts, sharing the same London office addresses (1886-1899), in Essex Street, Fleet Street* and Dean Street off New Fetter Lane.

Lucas first appears in the trade directories as publisher of the Primrose Library, a series of 'railway' novels published from May 1885 at 3d per month. His business was based on publishing 'complete stories' in novelettes*, and miscellanies*, and his publications ran stories bought from both the Tillotson's and Leng's* syndication agencies* (Law 2000). In 1886, the Primrose Library changed from book series to novelette periodical and supplement*, merging with the *Family Novelist Monthly Supplement* and the *Illustrated Family Novelist*. This became simply the *Family Novelist* in 1888, disappearing in 1890. This complex fluidity of title and property is typical of Lucas's career, which shows a repetitive pattern of acquisition, merger*, namechanges and supplements.

A few years after Lucas took over *Illustrated Tit-Bits* (1886-1891), it disappeared for a few years and reappeared as *Illustrated Bits* (1895-1899). *The Illustrated Family Novelist* had had a long history with Roberts before Lucas became its proprietor in 1885, while *the Illustrated Fireside Novelist* and the *Fireside Novelist* (both associated with Lucas from 1886, and disappearing in 1897 and 1899 respectively) appear to have been almost indistinguishable in appearance and content, and probably exchanged tales indiscriminately. The boys' magazine *Ching-Ching's Own*, acquired in 1888, was renamed the *Best for Boys: Ching-Ching's Own* in 1890, and then *the Best for Merry Boys: Ching-Ching's Own* in 1891, ceasing publication in 1893, although Lucas does not appear to have been associated with its last incarnation. His the *Book for All*, acquired in 1890, also underwent serial name changes, becoming the *May Flower Complete Novelettes* in 1892, and the *Mayflower* in 1893, surviving until 1899. The *Lady's Own Novelette & Weekly Supplement* was a more stable, and possibly more successful publication (1890-1899), when it was presumably sold to another proprietor, since it continued to be published until 1906. *Sporting Bits* (acquired 1892) seems to have been another malleable property, changing its name to *Sporting Sketches* in 1896, and then being passed on to another owner in 1898, surviving until 1907. The pattern persisted with the new fiction title *Lazy-Land* (1893) which transmuted itself into the supplement of its own former supplement *Good Company* in 1895. The conjoined titles then turned into *Home Stories* in 1898, finally disappearing at the end of 1899. Another fiction magazine, *Silver Chimes*, was extremely short-lived, existing only in 1894; its promotion is a good example of heavy advertising* for sister properties within the Lucas empire. Lucas then moved into new technologies, using improved photo reproduction printing for *Photos* (1895-1896), quickly renamed *Photos and Sketches* within

the start year so as not to lose the *Tit-Bits* readership. He then bought the gossip* magazine *In Town* in 1896, but this only lasted a year.

Confusingly, Lucas was publishing another fiction magazine called *Good Company* in 1894, a year before *Lazy-Land* changed its name, and the 'first' *Good Company* changed its name to *Home Stories* in 1897, disappearing in 1899. The relatively long-lived *Dorothy's Home Journal* was bought by Lucas in 1897, and lasted until 1899, when it became a supplement of another proprietor's *Home Journal*. The last periodicals published by Lucas that have been traced were the *Boys' Stories of Adventure and Daring* and the *Cigarette*, both 1898-1899. **KM Sources**: *Mitchell's* 1889, *Sell's* 1888, *Waterloo*, *Willings'* 1886.

LUCY, HENRY WILLIAM (1843-1924) A political* journalist, Lucy was born in Crosby, Lancashire, and began writing for newspapers while still a junior clerk to a hide merchant in Liverpool. He published poetry* in the *Liverpool Mercury* and secured a post as a local reporter, having taught himself shorthand* (*ODNB*). He was chief reporter for the *Shrewsbury Chronicle* by 1864 and contributed to the local* *Observer* — of which he was editor* and part proprietor* for a time in 1865, and to the *Shropshire News*.

His only attempt at establishing a journal of his own, the *Mayfair* (Dec. 1877-1879), failed and his work as editor (for Henry Labouchère* at the *Daily News* in 1885) was equally unsuccessful. He was an industrious, 'fluent, if essentially lightweight' writer (Brown: 115); he had the advantage of close contact with the Liberal leaders, however, and was knighted for his services. As the *ODNB* notes, he left £250,000 at his death, making him 'probably the wealthiest Victorian journalist who was not a proprietor'.

Lucy built up contacts working as a freelance journalist for the latter part of the decade while he travelled as secretary to the railway contractor Richard Samuel France. His first period of work on a metropolitan* journal was a six-month stint (Jan.-June 1870) as subeditor* on the short-lived morning edition of the *Pall Mall Gazette**, followed by a period as assistant editor with the *Exeter Gazette*. He returned to London journalism in October 1872 to head the parliamentary* reporting team at the *Daily News** on John Richard Robinson's request and wrote a regular 'London letters' column that was published in eight provincial papers (Lucy 111). His hugely successful journalistic career was built on parliamentary reporting, most notably with the *Observer**, where he wrote the 'Cross bench' column* for 29 years from 1880, and from 1881 with *Punch** where he succeeded Shirley Brookes* writing the 'Essence of Parliament' as 'Toby, MP', until 1916. His 'remarkable flair for politics* and parliamentary affairs' (*ODNB*), and his commitment – he reputedly stayed in the House of Commons 'from the time the Speaker takes the Chair 'till he leaves it' (Koss: 55) – saw him become a leading political writer of his day; his journalistic experiences were the basis of his many book publications, including popular political handbooks, two studies of Gladstone (1885; 1895), personal reminiscences including *The Diary of a Journalist* (3 vols. 1920-1923) and many volumes compiled from his *Punch* parliamentary sketches. FD

Sources: Brown 1985, Koss 1973, Lucy 1911, *ODNB*.

LUDLOW, HENRY STEPHEN (1861-1925)
Henry Stephen Ludlow's output as an illustrator* was characteristic of those many little- known figures who supplied countless images for the late Victorian press. Trained by the Dalziel* Brothers as an engraver*, his employers quickly realised his talents were more suited to illustration* and, over several decades, he drew for major illustrated weeklies* like the Dalziels's own *Pictorial World* and the *Illustrated London News* (1882-1889)*. Ludlow also held a post at *Judy** in the late 1880s, and worked on into the 1890s for journals as various as *Ally Sloper's Half Holiday**, *Cassell's Family Magazine**, and *Queen**. BM

Sources: Engen 1990, Houfe 1978.

LUDLOW, JOHN MALCOLM FORBES (1821-1911) John Ludlow was the co-founder of the Christian socialist movement and joint editor*, with F. D. Maurice, of the short-lived *Politics for the People**, which ran from May to July 1848, and which he wrote for under the pseudonym* 'John Townsend'. An early life spent in France was highly significant: Ludlow transported French ideals of workers' co-operatives to England and influenced a generation of thinkers, including the novelists Charles Kingsley and Thomas Hughes. In 1850, he founded and edited the 1d weekly*, the *Christian Socialist* (Nov.1850-Dec.1851), but resigned as editor because of internal disputes with working men's associations. The journal limped on for a further six months under Hughes's editorship and the newly secularized title of *Journal of Association* (previously, the dominant subtitle) before folding because of financial problems. Ludlow was, throughout a very long life, prolific as contributor and edi-

tor of social and literary* weeklies, monthlies and quarterlies* in addition to his city job as a legal conveyancer. His many articles appeared in the *Edinburgh Review**, *Fraser's Magazine**, *Macmillan's Magazine**, the *Contemporary Review**, and the *Fortnightly Review**. Fluent in French and a lifelong worshipper at the French Protestant Church in London, Ludlow never lost the sense of being an exile in both countries, 'the odd man of the household', but probably possessed more genuinely democratic instincts than many of his contemporaries. LL

Sources: Ludlow 1981, Norman 1987, *ODNB*, *Waterloo*.

LUNN, HENRY C. (1817-1894) As a music* journalist and editor* of the *Musical Times**, Henry C. Lunn was a pioneer in the renewal of British musical life.

Lunn's career began in 1845-1846 with a weekly column*, 'Musings of a Musician', in the *Musical World** that set out a radical reform programme. In this series, Lunn, a cultural democrat whose targets included grasping publishers and the 'gentlemanly ignorant', took up causes such as 'music for the multitude' and the creation of a 'national school of music' and 'Grand National English Opera'.

As editor of the *Musical Times*, Lunn transformed the journal into the leading music periodical of the day, tripling its content and doubling its circulation* (to 14,000) by 1870. Ever the enemy of 'musical conservatism', he ensured that the *Musical Times* robustly though not uncritically promoted new British music while serving as a vehicle for his reforming ideas. Alongside his editorial duties, he covered major music events for the journal, writing reviews* that reflected his own Mendelssohnian preferences while supporting contemporary British composers such as George Macfarren, William Sterndale Bennett and Arthur Sullivan.

Lunn, a self-styled 'musical patriot' whose journalism was hard-hitting and polemical, was an influential voice in canon and taste formation in British music. MH

Sources: Brown and Stratton 1897, Hughes 2002, Hurd 1981, Lunn 1846, *Musical Times* 1894.

LUXFORD, GEORGE (1807-1854) George Luxford specialized in publishing* botanical journals and literature*. In 1837 he came from Birmingham to London where he set up as a printer. It was not long before he was contracted by Longmans* to print *Loudon's Magazine of Natural History*. In 1841 Luxford's printing business was bought out by the entomologist and journalist Edward Newman, whose book on ferns Luxford had printed. After a rift with the Entomological Society, Newman decided on a partnership to print other books by him. In 1841 he appointed Luxford as editor* of the *Phytologist* a monthly* botanical magazine*. Although this journal was not commercially successful, it survived for 13 years, only ceasing publication with Luxford's death. **DHL**

Sources: Allen 1986, Allen 1996, Newman 1876, *ODNB*, Trimen 1876.

M

MACAULAY, THOMAS BABINGTON (1800-1859) A prominent historian, essayist and poet, Macaulay entered the peripheries of the literary scene in 1824, writing for *Knight's Quarterly Magazine*. In January 1825, he made his debut as a reviewer for the *Edinburgh Review**, where all of his most significant journalism* appeared. Here, during the 1820s, he published important articles on Milton, West Indian slavery, Dryden and several on the theory of history, including a famous attack on James Mill's* *Essay on Government*. Macaulay's view of history, indeed, was deliberately ranged against that of Mill and his utilitarian circle. He scorned the idea that political justice could be arrived at by deductive, scientific means, and held the Romantic view that history should somehow take account of the lives of ordinary people, using the creative resources of the novelist rather than the dry chronologies of the constitutional historian. The spat with Mill is revealing in the context of a broader conflict between the liberal *Edinburgh Review* and one of its major competitors*, the radical and Benthamite quarterly* the *Westminster Review**, to which Mill contributed.

Such political rivalries became a determining feature of Macaulay's journalistic career, as he became a Whig MP and a passionate and vociferous advocate of the Reform Bill. He withdrew from the *Edinburgh Review* in 1830 when Henry Brougham* – who had long been a co-contributor and political rival – exerted his increasing influence over the periodical to block the publication of an article by Macaulay on the French Revolution. Macaulay continued to contribute to the *Review* thereafter, however, so his self-imposed exile from its pages was temporary. His views on the French Revolution were aired in an appreciative review of Dumont's *Souvenir sur Mirabeau* in 1832. He also continued to use the *Edinburgh Review* to publish savage attacks on rivals like J. W. Croker* and M. T. Sadler (1780-1835), who stood against him as a Tory candidate in the first elections of the reformed parliament.

Macaulay spent four years from 1834 in India, during which time his contributions to the *Edinburgh Review* slowed to a trickle, with only two coming in those years. While in India he asked that he be paid for his articles in books so that he could keep abreast of current publications. Another spate of essays for the *Edinburgh* followed his return to England and his appointment to the cabinet. In 1843 he was persuaded by Longman, the *Edinburgh's* publisher, to collect and republish his articles from the review. The phenomenal success of the *Essays* persuaded several of his colleagues, including Francis Jeffrey*, and later Sydney Smith and Brougham, to follow suit. His contributions tailed off in 1844 as he focussed his energies on his *chef d'oeuvre*, the *History of England*. **MaT**
Sources: *ODNB*, Shattock 1989, *Wellesley*.

MACCOLL, DUGALD SUTHERLAND (1859-1948) D. S. MacColl was one of the most prominent proponents of the 'New Art Criticism' in the 1890s. Writing in the *Spectator** (1890-1896) and the *Saturday Review** (1896-1906, 1921-1930), MacColl vigorously championed modern art and argued that the formal properties of a work of art were more significant than its subject matter.

MacColl's journalistic defence of modern art was punctuated by important public controversies. In 1893, MacColl and John Alfred Spender*, critic for the *Westminster Gazette**, had a long and contentious debate over the relative importance of moral and aesthetic considerations in the evaluation of Edgar Degas's painting *L'Absinthe*. The debate spilled over into the pages of other journals and magazines in articles, leaders* and letters* to the editor*; MacColl's contributions played a significant role in explaining and justifying both Impressionist art and new formalist standards of criticism. In 1903, he once again did battle with the art establishment, writing an article in the *Saturday Review* charging the Royal Academy with misusing the Chantrey Bequest. The funds were intended for the purchase of modern art for the national collection, and MacColl accused the administrators of favouring inferior work by Academicians over more important avant-garde art. Appointed Keeper of the Tate Gallery only three years later, MacColl was keenly aware of the irony of his position, and resigned from the *Saturday Review*. He then served as curator of the Wallace Collection (1911-1924), and returned to journalism in the 1920s and 1930s, writing for the *Saturday Review* and the *Week-End Review*.

MacColl was one of the most important defenders and interpreters of the French Impressionists and their British followers in the New English Art Club, and his criticism was a critical factor in the acceptance of modern art in Britain. **PF**
Sources: Borland 1995, Lago 1996, *ODNB*, Stokes 1989.

MacColl, Norman (1843-1904) Norman MacColl edited* the *Athenaeum** for nearly 30 years from 1871 to 1900, restoring the journal to the eminence it had enjoyed under Charles Wentworth Dilke*. Soon after Dilke's grandson Sir Charles Dilke inherited the journal in 1869 from his father, he appointed MacColl as joint-editor, his red-bearded Cambridge friend whom he proclaimed 'the Scotch Solomon'. Because of Dilke's political commitments, he soon made Maccoll the sole editor, a position MacColl held (1871-1900) until he was succeeded by Vernon Rendall.

MacColl opened the *Athenaeum* to new ideas, choosing reviewers who responded positively to such movements as Darwinism and Pre-Raphaelitism. Under him the journal was noted for its scholarship and fairness. *The Times** acclaimed him for being 'in full and perfect sympathy' with the day's major literary and scientific movements, while the *Athenaeum* praised him as a 'wonderfully accurate, wonderfully fair' editor who sent books not to friends or enemies of an author but to 'the competent and dispassionate stranger'. MacColl recruited reviewers for their expertise and their willingness to criticize books rather than praise them indiscriminately. Among them were numerous women. This is not surprising since he was one of 661 members of the Cambridge Senate to vote in 1898 to admit women to degrees (versus 1707 opposed). MacColl's policy is evident from the significant decline in women contributors after Rendall became editor*.

Though MacColl wrote fewer reviews* than his predecessors, he paid particular attention to the *Athenaeum's* annual reviews of foreign literature*. Extensively involved in day-to-day operations, he heavily corrected proofs and modified the layout of the journal to make it more attractive and readable. In addition to his work on the *Athenaeum*, he occasionally served as editorial consultant to *Notes and Queries**, which was also owned by Dilke. EC
Sources: *Athenaeum* 24 Dec. 1904, Demoor 2000, *DNB*, *ODNB*, *The Times* 16 Dec 1904.

McConnell, William (1831-1867) A career illustrator*, William McConnell provided a broad range of satirical* and comic images for the magazines of the 1850s and 1860s. Trained by Joseph Swain* at *Punch** on the strength of early promise as a cartoonist*, he drew for the magazine until 1852, but left after financial disputes. He made his living from a combination of book and magazine illustration*, working for such magazines as the *Illustrated London News** (1851-1860) the *Illustrated Times** (1855-1861), where he was the staff car-

toonist, and *Town Talk* (1858-1859). His best-known work comprised the paired images of London scenes organized on an hour by hour survey of street life which he drew to illustrate G. A. Sala's* *Twice Round the Clock* published in the opening issues of the *Welcome Guest** in 1858-1859. In a career cut short by tuberculosis, McConnell showed a versatility and talent which never reached its full potential. BM
Sources: Engen 1990, Houfe 1978, *ODNB*, Spielmann 1895.

Macdonell, James (1841-1879) James Macdonell was introduced to William McCombie, editor* of the liberal newspaper *Aberdeen Free Press* in 1858. Macdonell's precocious literary talent led to his appointment as leader* writer and it was while working for the paper that he formulated his interest in ecclesiastical history. In 1862 Macdonell moved to Edinburgh, where he worked for the sectarian *Edinburgh Daily Review*, yet after less than a year he moved to Newcastle-on-Tyne to become editor of the *Northern Daily Express*. When William Saunders bought out the paper in 1865, Macdonell regretfully left for London. His salary was only £150 a year and although Saunders offered him more money, he objected to Saunders's managerial interference in editorial matters, particularly his insistence on the leader being sent down daily from London.

Macdonell declined a senior post with the *Scotsman** in favour of becoming an assistant editor on the *Daily Telegraph**. While working for the paper he became a confidential assistant to Edward Levy (1833-1916), son of the principal proprietor*. His first article for the *Daily Telegraph** appeared on 8 July 1865 and he wrote six leaders a week for the paper, as well as others for the *Leeds Mercury** and *Levant Herald*. Macdonell's interest in France led to his appointment as the *Daily Telegraph's* special correspondent there from December 1871 until May 1872. On 25 March 1875 he joined *The Times** for a trial period as a leader writer and worked on the paper until his death, although his views led to conflict with the editor, John T. Delane*. As well as writing for *The Times* he contributed articles (1865-1873) to the *Spectator**, *Fraser's Magazine** and the *North British Review**. As a journalist Macdonell was held in high regard by his contemporaries; a posthumous volume of collected articles entitled *France since the First Empire* appeared in 1879. DHL
Sources: Griffiths 1992, Nicoll 1890, *ODNB*.

MACFARLANE, HELEN (C.1820-?) Born in Scotland, it is believed that Helen Macfarlane was politically radicalized through her experience of the February 1848 revolution in Vienna. Returning to London, she became an active Chartist through the Fraternal Democrats.

With German-language skills and knowledge of literature and history, she began to contribute articles to George Harney's* Chartist* paper, the *Democratic Review**. They included a three-part series (April-June 1850) on Thomas Carlyle's 'Latter-Day Pamphlets' and a withering essay on the British constitution (Sept. 1850), which attacked the Whig interpretation of history. She also translated some of Hegel's work for the *Democratic Review*.

Macfarlane then went on to write for Harney's *Red Republican**. Throughout her articles in 1850, her strong political* commitment is reflected in the style of her journalism, for example in her response to George Henry Lewes* about his accusations against the Red Republicans in a *Leader** editorial: 'violent, audacious and wrathfully earnest, I should think we are', she contended. Equally combative was her article, 'Fine Words (Household or Otherwise) Butter no Parsnips' attacking Dickens* and other 'rosewater political sentimentalists of the Boz school' for an article in *Household Words** about his observations on child beggars. No sentimentality for her, she wrote of the degradation of the poor in London, the abuse of women, 'thirty-thousand women...starving at shirtmaking' and of the masses of women forced into prostitution in the capital.

She also contributed to the *Red Republican* using the pseudonym, 'Howard Morton'. Her real journalistic coup was to produce the first English translation of Karl Marx's* *Communist Manifesto* for the *Republican*, published in four parts (9 Nov. 1850ff). Marx described her as the most original writer in the Chartist press. CL
Sources: Black, D. 2004, *Waterloo*.

MACFARREN, WALTER CECIL (1826-1905) Appointed music critic of the *Queen** in 1862, Macfarren contributed regularly to the paper until his death. He was, like most music* journalists of the period, a respected practitioner, being appointed sub-professor of the piano at the Royal Academy of Music in 1846, where he remained on the staff for 57 years. He enjoyed a close professional and personal affiliation with James Davison*, musical critic of *The Times** and the *Saturday Review**.

Macfarren's regular 'Music and Musicians' column* in the *Queen* combined concert reviews*, reviews of new sheet music and a 'Musical Doings' section, which collected short music-related* news* stories and advertised forthcoming events. His reviews – in keeping with the general timbre of the *Queen* – were perhaps more concerned with delineating the boundaries of acceptable good taste than elaborating a critical lexicon. Keeping readers in touch with the latest developments, and keenly noting which celebrities* attended which concerts, Macfarren directed his female readership* towards music that was fashionable and even sophisticated, but never too exotic to be compatible with polite respectability. While this attitude sometimes appears in the guise of a narrow parochialism, it could more charitably be construed as a passionate advocacy of English music. Macfarren complained that 'it is found cheaper ... to adapt foreign operas than to pay for original scores' and that consequently 'English opera is to be snubbed and sneered at'. This perception led him to make the case for the formation of a National Opera House. Macfarren also contributed to *Musical Society* (1886-1889), the *Leeds College of Music Quarterly News* (1897-1906) and the *Yorkshire Musical Age* (1890). MaT
Sources: *Musical Times*, ODNB, *Queen*, *Waterloo*.

MCGEE, THOMAS D'ARCY (1825-1868) Thomas D'Arcy McGee was a journalist and newspaper editor* active in Ireland, the United States and Canada. McGee began his career as a journalist for the *Boston Pilot* in 1842-1845. When in 1845 he became London parliamentary correspondent for the Dublin *Freeman's Journal**, he was soon dismissed when it emerged he had also been writing for the Dublin nationalist newspaper *Nation**. McGee then moved to this paper, where he became one of the main contributors of political* articles and poetry*. He held moderate views on Irish independence, like *Nation* editor Charles Gavan Duffy*.

McGee's participation in the 1848 Young Ireland* uprising forced him to flee to the United States. He returned to journalism there, founding and editing the *New York Nation*, in 1848-1850, and then the *American Celt* in Boston (1850-1851), Buffalo (1852-1853) and New York (1854-?). He emigrated to Canada in 1857, and edited the *New Era* in Montreal in 1857-1858. His subsequent political career and his support for Canadian confederation resulted in his murder in 1868 at the age of 43 at the hands of the Fenian Brotherhood. McGee also published books on Irish history and politics, and volumes of verse. FB
Sources: Duffy 1880-1883, *ODNB*.

McGLASHAN, JAMES (1800?-1858) A publisher*, editor* and bookseller, James McGlashan was born in Scotland and first worked for William Blackwood* publishing in Edinburgh. He then moved to Dublin around 1830, joining as a partner the publishing firm of William Curry Jnr*, and becoming a committee member of the Dublin Booksellers' Society. He persuaded Curry to purchase the *Dublin University Magazine*, of which they were already the publishers, in 1833. He succeeded Isaac Butt* as editor of the *Dublin University Magazine* (Dec. 1838-April 1842), when his friend Charles Lever* took over.

McGlashan brought to the *Dublin University Magazine* a more conciliatory tone than Butt's strenuous Unionism. Main contributions under his editorship included serial* fiction from Charles Lever, short stories from William Carleton*, poetry* from James Clarence Mangan* and Mary Anne Browne, and theatre reviews* from Henry Robert Addison. In 1846, McGlashan opened his own publishing and bookselling firm. His catalogue included the works of many Irish contributors of the *Dublin University Magazine*. He continued to publish the *Magazine* until ill-health forced him to sell his business to Michael Henry Gill* in 1856 for £3,000. 'Utterly ruined in health and fortune' (as he told Lever), he died in Edinburgh in 1858. **FB**
Sources: Anderson 1991, Hall 1999, Kinane 1994.

MACLAREN, CHARLES (1782-1866) Born in East Lothian, the son of a farmer, Charles Maclaren's education was limited and he was largely self-taught. As a young man he moved to Edinburgh where he became an official in the Custom House, and joined a debating society where he made the acquaintance of men with advanced Whig views. In 1816 he was approached by William Ritchie with a view to founding a Scottish radical newspaper. The first number of the *Scotsman** appeared on 25 January 1817. It was edited* by Maclaren with John Ramsay McCulloch (1817-1818). McCulloch acted as editor* only until the paper was established, during which period Maclaren remained a custom-house clerk. Eventually, he was fully employed by the paper (1820-1845).

Initially a weekly* paper, the *Scotsman* appeared twice weekly from 1823 and Maclaren wrote its leaders*. This was unusual as most Scottish newspapers reprinted leaders from London papers. Supporting radical ideas, Maclaren argued for political* reform in Scotland, even fighting a duel with the editor of the conservative *Caledonian Mercury** in *1829*. He forecast the value of railways, publishing

articles on their advantages, as well as researching mechanical problems. As editor of the *Scotsman* Maclaren formed its style, steering the paper through periods of national struggle and reform. As well as occasionally writing for other periodicals like the *Foreign Quarterly Review**, Maclaren was also a renowned geologist and in the final year of his editorship he made the *Scotsman* an important forum for discussion of Robert Chambers's* c-ontroversial *Vestiges of the Natural History of C-reation* (1844). **DHL**
Sources: Cowan 1946, Magnusson 1967, *ODNB*, Secord 2000.

MACLEOD, NORMAN (1812-1872) A prominent and popular evangelical minister in the Church of Scotland, Norman Macleod edited* and wrote for several magazines. Born in Argyll, he studied divinity at Edinburgh University, becoming an ordained minister in 1838. In 1849 he was appointed editor of the *Edinburgh Christian Magazine*. A decade later, approached by the young publisher*, Alexander Strahan* who was looking for an editor for a new family* magazine, Macleod left his position at the *Edinburgh Christian Magazine* to become editor of *Good Words** in 1860. The new magazine quickly achieved success under his editorship, becoming one of the most popular monthlies in Britain.

When Strahan started a new magazine for children* in 1868 called *Good Words for the Young**, Macleod was initially advertised as its editor. However, it is doubtful that Macleod, in declining health following a trip to India in 1867, had much to do with the new publication. In addition to his duties as editor and his active career as a minister, Macleod wrote non-fiction and fiction, most of which was published in the periodicals he edited. **AL**
Sources: Macleod 1876, *ODNB*, Srebrnik 1986, Sullivan, Turner 2000c.

MACMILLAN, ALEXANDER (1818-1896) A distinguished Victorian publisher* of books, Alexander Macmillan also made his mark as the founder of, and guiding spirit behind, *Macmillan's Magazine** and other influential nineteenth-century periodicals. The youngest son of an Ayrshire crofter who died when the boy was four, Macmillan had a difficult start in life. Despite the taste for literature and the thirst for learning that he acquired from his mother, a university education was out of the question for him. Forced to leave the Irvine Academy at the age of 15 in order to earn money, he held a succession of humble jobs for the next half-dozen years: teaching at various little schools, working in shops, going on one voyage as a sailor to America from which he returned to Glasgow with virtually no money. Not until he joined his brother Daniel in a Fleet Street* bookseller's business on his 21st birthday was he embarked on his life's work in the world of the written word.

Alexander and Daniel Macmillan opened the first bookshop of their own in Cambridge in 1843 and almost immediately began publishing, as well as selling, books, chiefly academic in nature. In 1855 Macmillan & Co. had brought out their first work of fiction, Charles Kingsley's *Westward Ho!*, and the firm grew and prospered, despite Daniel's death in 1857. A London branch, which soon became the firm's headquarters, was established in 1858, and *Macmillan's Magazine**, a shilling* monthly*, was launched in 1859. By that year, Macmillan & Co. was generally recognized as one of the most important English publishing houses.

Throughout the editorships* of David Masson* (1859-1867) and George Grove* (1868-1883), Alexander Macmillan did more than anyone else to shape the policies and determine the contents of *Macmillan's Magazine*. His grip loosened during John Morley's* brief tenure (1883-1885) and he finally let go altogether while Mowbray Morris*, the last editor, was in charge from November 1885. Of the other periodicals published by Macmillan & Co. during his lifetime, the most enduring was *Nature**, founded in 1869 and still going strong today. The *English Illustrated Magazine** (begun in 1883) was broader in its appeal and more attuned to contemporaneous fashion than *Macmillan's* but did not prosper long. There were also several nineteenth-century Macmillan scholarly journals that enjoyed various degrees of longevity: the *Cambridge Mathematical Journal* (1846), the *Journal of Classical and Sacred Philology* (1878), *Brain* and the *Economic Journal* (1891).

Although not primarily a writer, Alexander Macmillan himself occasionally contributed to periodicals: to the *Christian Socialist* in 1851 and to *Macmillan's Magazine* (1859,1876). It is, however, as the facilitator of other people's work, not only in books but also in periodical journalism of various kinds, that his primary significance lies. **GW**

Sources: Ainger 1896, Graves 1910, Macmillan 1908, *ODNB*, Worth 2003.

MACMILLAN'S MAGAZINE (1859-1907) *Macmillan's Magazine*, a monthly* catering for a middle-class* family* readership, was launched by the Macmillan publishing firm as an 'organ of opinion rather than purveyor of fiction'. Its aim was to provide first-class literary matter at a keen price, and this house* magazine was the first of the new generation of 'shilling monthlies'*. During its first two decades its founder and proprietor*, Alexander Macmillan*, was closely involved in guaranteeing its quality as well as in shaping its liberal, Christian, ethical outlook and determining its contents. First appearing on 1 November 1859, an issue (size* 22 cm) of *Macmillan's Magazine*, priced* at 1/0, comprised 80 double-column* pages* and typically contained a political* article, a serial*, a literary* or philosophical* article, an historical* or travel article, and a poem* or short story. It eschewed illustrations* throughout its existence and advertising* appeared only on the end papers (3pp).

Macmillan's Magazine adopted a progressive stance on political, social and cultural matters. In British domestic politics, it took a Liberal position on such issues as parliamentary reform, educational and public health improvements, national defence, the relationship between church and state, and the Irish 'land question'. While in foreign affairs, although it supported peace and stability (as over the Franco-Prussian conflict), due to its antipathy to slavery it strongly favoured the Union side during the American Civil War. As for culture, although the journal's content ranged far and wide (archaeology, biblical studies, geography and music*), it reserved a special place for literature and literary discussion, publishing much new poetry and serializing fiction of distinction. True to its remit as a 'family' journal, *Macmillan's Magazine* regularly contained articles by women, and about women and their interests (for example, female suffrage).

Macmillan's editors* were David Masson* (1859-1868), George Grove* (1868-1883), John Morley* (1883-1885) and Mowbray Morris* (1885-1907), while its distinguished contributors included Frances Martin (women's education), F. D. Maurice (religion), Sir John Seeley (history and politics) and the writers Henry James*, Rudyard Kipling and Margaret Oliphant*. By the end of the century it was suffering from increasing financial constraints, a changing market* and complacent editorial leadership, and despite being revamped (1905) with – the introduction of a new single-column* format* and larger font – and having its price halved, it ceased publication in October 1907. **MH**

Sources: *Waterloo*, Worth 2003.

MacRae, Douglas Gordon (1861-1901) Born in Aberdeenshire, Scottish publisher* and editor* Douglas Gordon MacRae used his energy and occasionally reckless behaviour to establish the *Financial Times** (1888-) as a pre-eminent London newspaper in the 1890s. After beginning his career in Scotland as a printing apprentice and an occasional writer about cricket, MacRae moved to London, where he established his own printing works. He initially printed newspapers owned by Horatio Bottomley's* publishing association, but in 1887 he combined his company with others to form MacRae, Curtice & Company. This merger* allowed him to expand into publishing and editorial work.

At first, he merely published Bottomley's *Financial Times*, but within a few months his press controlled the newspaper, to the extent that MacRae became its director in July 1888 and its editor by the end of the year. Around this time, Bottomley created a company with the intention of taking over Macrae's firms; MacRae responded by breaking away, taking the *Financial Times* and *Draper's Record* (1887-) with him. The two men maintained a professional rivalry, particularly as Bottomley's *Financial News* competed with MacRae's paper, but they eventually agreed on a truce. Although under MacRae, the *Financial Times* prided itself on its ability to protect the public, the editor was not always seen as benevolent; in 1889, company promoter Alfred Green attacked MacRae after the paper repeatedly criticized him. In 1889, MacRae became managing editor of the Financial Times Limited and its primary shareholder. This did not save the paper from experiencing financial difficulties during the first half of the 1890s, but MacRae pulled the company through. His innovations often signified an advance in newspaper publishing, as when, in 1893, he made the paper the first London morning paper to be composed on a Linotype machine. MacRae's most famous and lasting experiment was to print his newspaper on salmon-coloured pages. **TR**

Sources: Kynaston 1988, *ODNB*.

MADDEN, RICHARD ROBERT (1798-1886) Born in Dublin, Richard Madden trained as a doctor but spent most of his life working as a colonial arbitrator and advocate for aboriginal rights in such countries as Jamaica (implementing anti-slavery legislation), Cuba, Egypt, Africa and finally in Western Australia. At the same time he managed to act as special correspondent for the *Morning Herald** in Italy in the 1820s, and (1843-1846) in Lisbon as correspondent for the *Morning Chronicle**. Madden also contributed articles to the *Nation** under the name 'Ierne' in 1842-1843, and to the *Citizen** as 'RRM'. He finally returned to Ireland in 1848 and took up a position as Secretary to the Loan Fund Board at Dublin Castle (1850-1880). **ET**

Sources: Madden 1867, Madden 1891, Ó Broin 1972, *ODNB*, PGIL-*Eirdata*, Rafroidi 1980.

MAGAZINE DAY A term within the publishing industry for the penultimate day of the month on which monthlies were supplied from their printers and publishers for distribution* by the wholesale and retail trades. Special carriers were hired for the day to transport the journals to agents and publishers in Paternoster Row; in turn they deployed additional staff to make up orders for bookshops, newsagents*, circulating libraries and other subscribers nationwide. Publishers* who issued monthly book lists and part-issues also took advantage of this day to supply agents with new titles. Magazine Day defines the period in the nineteenth century when monthlies had taken over from quarterlies*, and monthly publishing rhythms dominated the industry. James Bertram*, a pioneer of popular journalism, reports that by 1893 Magazine Day 'of the old kind' no longer existed, but that formerly, probably by the late 1840s, 'it was a sacred institution'. Charles Manby Smith provides a full and colourful account of Magazine Day in the 1850s. **LRB**

Sources: Bertram 1893, Smith 1857.

MAGAZINE OF ART (1878-1904) The Paris International Exhibition of 1878 was the spur to Cassell's* introduction of this magazine, echoing the company's original art publication inspired by the 1851 Great Exhibition, the *Illustrated Exhibitor and Magazine of Art**. Conforming to the company's aim of providing access to good quality educational publications for the majority, Cassell's intended the *Magazine of Art* to present an alternative to the elitist *Art-Journal**. A significant way in which it made the subject more accessible was its adoption of the style of the New Journalism*. Yet it managed to fulfil more than its popularist* mission, as the *Academy** dubbed it 'the only Art Magazine which at all keeps pace with the moving current of Art'. Beginning modestly with brief articles accompanied by wood engravings* as well as pen and ink drawings, it was originally priced* at 8d, then 7d. By 1880 it had become larger and more sophisticated: the price rise to 1s did not deter sales; rather, circulation* rose. Contents displayed a breadth of interests, embracing photography*, theatre, design,

Japanese art and architecture. The distinctive note was struck when it introduced photogravure art reproductions in colour to each edition; a wealth of illustrations*, plus annual supplements* such as 'European Pictures of the Year' (1892-1894) and 'Royal Academy Pictures' (1889-1893) completed its comprehensive view.

Published in London, Paris and New York as a monthly, originally sized* 27cm later increasing to 30cm, printed in large type on good paper*, its departments featured art exhibitions, current artists, essays and notices of art books. One of its editors* (1881-1886), was William E. Henley*, poet and journalist, who was a prodigious contributor to the periodical press. He was able to elicit articles from his good friend, R. L. Stevenson, the first being, 'Byways of book illustrators'. Julia Cartwright, art historian and biographer, contributed art criticism; the painter Millais in his 'Thoughts on our art of today' (1888) provided an exceptional insight to the painter's mind; 'Sculpture in the Home' (1895) by the writer Edmund Gosse* and

Mabel Robinson's (pseudonym, 'W. R. Gregg') writing on Italian art were typical of the breadth of content. The decorative artist and industrial designer, Lewis Foreman featured frequently, with illustrations from, among others, William Symons and Herbert Railton*, a specialist in the 'black and white school'. The quality of its contributors, illustrators and presentation ensured its success in fulfilling its publisher's intention of popularity in this field. **CL**

Sources: *ODNB, Waterloo.*

MAGAZINES The word 'magazine' had first been applied to a periodical publication in the 1730s but it only gradually emerged during the first half of the nineteenth century as a preferred term against such rivals as 'repository', 'museum' or 'mirror', though it remained largely interchangeable with 'journal'. Retaining elements of its original meaning of 'storehouse', the term referred to publications characterized by the variety and heterogeneity of their constituent genres* and by a diversity of voices. Unlike newspapers, magazines did not carry 'news'*,

Figure 39: A war scene of 1870 drawn by special artist, Sydney Hall, to illustrate the Franco-Prussian war, *Magazine of Art*, Jan. 1883: 164.

though they might include political* comment. Unlike the great Reviews of the early century, they did not consist entirely of one genre, though they often included reviews* of books, periodicals, theatre and art. Eighteenth-century titles including the *Monthly Magazine**, *Gentleman's Magazine** and *Lady's Magazine** carried the name into the new century, but the launch of *Blackwood's Edinburgh Magazine** in 1817 marked an important cultural milestone. This title, which continued publishing until 1981, moved the miscellany* form into the centre of literary culture where it remained throughout the century.

The arrival of three rival weeklies*, *Chambers's Journal**, Charles Knight's *Penny Magazine** and the *Saturday Magazine** all sold at 1d or ½d, all launched in 1832, established the magazine in popular* reading. The genre flourished throughout the 1840s and 1850s. with titles like *Eliza Cook's Journal** and Dickens's* *Household Words** providing magazine reading, despite not carrying the word in their titles, while *Punch** remade the tradition of satiric* journalism. The magazine was transformed again in 1859-1860 with the launch of *Macmillan's Magazine** and the sumptuously illustrated* *Cornhill Magazine**. These established as an important publishing genre, the shilling* monthly aimed at the middle class* and offering quality serialised* fiction. With the New Journalism* of the 1890s, the magazine emerged as a dominant journalistic genre. It encompassed elite literary* journals like the *Academy*, penny women's* magazines like *Woman**, cheap* weekly miscellanies like *Pearson's**, popular illustrated monthlies like the *Strand**, specifically religious* publications like the *Free Churchman* (1897-), unillustrated fiction publications like *Longman's**, family* journals suitable for Sunday reading like *Good Words**, publications for children* and young people like *the Boy's Own Paper** and the *Girl's Own Paper**, and sporting* journals like *Sporting Bits* (1892-1908). **MRB**

MAGINN, WILLIAM (1794-1842) William Maginn was a prolific writer and editor* of magazines and newspapers, most with a strong Tory bias. Born in Cork, Ireland, by 1819 he had been awarded the LL.D. (whence his sobriquet 'The Doctor'). He was also writing for the London *Literary Gazette** and *Blackwood's Edinburgh Magazine**, where he collaborated with John Wilson* and John Gibson Lockhart* on the 'Noctes Ambrosianæ' and wrote under shared pseudonyms such as 'Sir Morgan O'Doherty' and 'Timothy Tickler'. In January 1824 he moved to London to assist Theodore

Hook* with the Sunday newspaper *John Bull**, and edit the short-lived *John Bull Magazine* (1824). Late in 1825 at Lockhart's suggestion John Murray* hired him as Paris correspondent for a new daily* instigated by Benjamin Disraeli, the *Representative*, at a salary of £500 per annum. When it struggled he was brought back as editor, and was on board when it merged* with the *New Times* in the Fall of 1826. Next, he wrote and edited for the Sunday *English Gentleman** and the *Literary Chronicle**, was involved with the *Age** after it was taken over by Charles Molloy Westmacott* and, most lastingly, joined fellow Irish Tory Stanley Lees Giffard at the *Standard**, helping it to become the leading Tory evening paper. Maginn's political* leaders* were noted for their range and incisiveness, and his squibs and parodies for their barbs.

Late in 1829, Maginn and a group of his friends (including Hugh Fraser and William Fraser) planned a new magazine; they found an eager publisher* in James Fraser (all Frasers unrelated). *Fraser's Magazine** was launched in February 1830 and Maginn was the guiding light of its first decade. In 'Regina' he was perhaps most celebrated for the text accompanying fellow Corkman Daniel Maclise's lithographs* in the 'Gallery of Illustrious Literary Characters'; of more significance may have been *Fraser's* aid in the transformation of the disarrayed Tories into a modern 'Conservative' party.

While writing scores of articles for *Fraser's* Maginn continued to serve with the *Standard* and the *Age*, and also wrote for the *True Sun* (1832-1833), collaborated on *Fraser's Literary Chronicle* (1835-1836), edited the *Lancashire Herald* (1839) and helped Thackeray with the *National Standard** (1833). When *Bentley's Miscellany** was launched with Dickens* at the helm (1837), Maginn wrote the introductory poem*, followed by papers on Shakespeare.

A young Benjamin Disraeli accurately described Maginn as 'a very prosopopeia of the Public Press'. The full extent of his press activities will never be known, but their range and number indicate the level of employment required for a journalist* to earn a living before 1855 and the proliferation of regular staffing positions at new weeklies and dailies, after the repeal of the newspaper stamp. **DEL**
Sources: Kenealy 1844, Latané 2005a, *ODNB*, Oliphant 1897, Thrall 1934.

MAGNET (1837-1888) The *Magnet* was published* originally by Charles Willey Corfield as a general 4d weekly* folio of eight pages. It was designed to have broad appeal. 'Our's [sic] is the

CAUSE OF THE PEOPLE... WE ARE REFORMERS, but we are not destructives', it declared in its first issue (13 March) and went on to stake a fundamentally conservative position, 'desirous of preserving the prerogative and just privileges of the three estates' and both favouring the Church and welcoming dissenters. Its straplines were 'The Largest of the Largest, the cheapest of the cheapest, forwarded to all parts of the world free of postage' (in reality subscription outside the UK was higher: 5s or 7s 6d per quarter). It contained the usual news* of debates in Parliament*, the money market*, theatres, extracts from new publications, news of criminal* proceedings, bankruptcies, partnerships dissolved, dividends and the latest corn and produce prices. To these it added departments called 'The Physician' offering advice on illnesses and how to stay healthy, and 'The Lawyer' on general legal points. It was soon was bought by J. B. Bell*, the founder of the *News of the World**, and provided a 4½d conservative counterpart to that paper (although Mitchell remarks that most of its matter derives from Bell's other papers).

Bell redirected the paper to the farming and agricultural constituency, adding the subtitle *Agricultural, Commercial and Family Gazette*. In addition to the general news, there were reports on corn, produce and cattle markets all over the UK, and a column* entitled 'The Practical Farmer'. With minor variations this format* was retained until the paper's demise on 27 August 1888, when readers were recommended to turn to the *News of the World*. What is surprising about the *Magnet* is the low quantity of advertising* throughout its run: often there is a column or less (out of 48) and never did it rise above three. Even the local *South London Chronicle* (1857-1907) – a similar eight-page folio weekly – had 4.5 pages of adverts in 1888. With a circulation* of over 20,000 in the early 1850s it might have been possible not to rely on adverts, especially if most of the material was being recycled from other publications, but an advert in *Mitchell* in 1864 claims a mere 6,000 readers. Later adverts claim 10,000, but this was still very low. It seems very likely that Bell subvented this publication to the end. AK

Sources: *Mitchell's, Waterloo.*

MAHONEY, J. (FL.1865-1876) From humble beginnings as an uneducated lithographer's* assistant, J. Mahoney was trained by Edward Whymper as an illustrator*, proving to be an able but feckless apprentice. Nonetheless he found wide employment in the 1860s and 1870s, working for both magazines and books, gaining the admiration of the Dalziel* brothers in the process who employed him as an illustrator on the Household Editions of many of Dickens's* books. He drew on commission for a characteristically wide variety of publications including comic magazines like *Fun** and *Judy**, family* weeklies* like the *Leisure Hour**, children's* journals including *Good Words for the Young** and *Little Folks* and established fiction-bearing magazines like the *Quiver**. Quite how far his dissolute lifestyle affected the severe judgments of his work by Forrest Reid and Gleeson White* is difficult to say, but Mahoney's skills were widely enough acknowledged by publishers* and editors* to give his work considerable prominence for the decade 1865-1875. BM

Sources: Dalziel 1901, Engen 1990, Houfe 1978, Reid 1928, White 1897.

M. A. P. – MAINLY ABOUT PEOPLE (1898-1911) Founded by T. P. O'Connor* and edited* by him (1898-1909), *Mainly About People* was subtitled, *A Popular Penny Weekly* of Pleasant Gossip, Personal Portraits, and Social News* and published* by Arthur Pearson*. The paper originated in a gossip* column* of the same name that O'Connor wrote for his earlier publishing venture*, the *Star* (1888-1924). O'Connor described *Mainly About People* as 'a sort of penny *Truth* with a dash of *Modern Society*' (Waller: 86). He intended its focus to be 'social journalism'*, carrying short stories, interviews*, gossip of people in society, in politics*, sport*, and abroad, in Paris; there were fashion* items, and under the heading of 'In the Days of my Youth', autobiographical essays by authors such as George Bernard Shaw (Sept.1898), Mary Kingsley (May 1899) and others. Illustrated* with engravings, it also carried advertisements* and was firmly placed in the New Journalism* camp. FN

Sources: Gibbs 2000, *ODNB*, Waller 2006.

MAITLAND, JOHN A. FULLER (1856-1936) As chief music* critic of *The Times** (1889-1911) and editor* of the second edition of Grove's *Dictionary of Music and Musicians* (5 vols 1904-1910), Cambridge-educated Fuller Maitland exercised great influence over the 'renaissance' of British music.

Early in his career Fuller Maitland worked as a critic on the *Pall Mall Gazette** (1882-1884) and as London critic on the *Manchester Guardian** (1884-1889), and was a supporter of the J. S. Bach revival and Folk Song and Early Music movements. At *The Times* Fuller Maitland, a conservative, supported the 'classical' Schumann-Brahms tradition that for him represented the purest artistic aims.

Conversely, his reception of late-Romantic progressivism, for example the work of Richard Strauss, was generally condemnatory. He was also a critic-patriot committed to the construction of a national 'musical renaissance' so long as it conformed to his own m-usical doctrines. Accordingly, he promoted the music of composers like Hubert Parry, Charles Stanford and Ralph Vaughan Williams, whom he cast as the leaders of the new British school, while decrying the music of Arthur Sullivan, Frederick Delius and Edward Elgar. Fuller Maitland relished his power as a journalist. Styling himself a 'doorkeeper of music', he zealously guarded the citadel of public taste and kept the door of the musical canon with conviction. **MH**

Sources: Hughes 2002, Maitland 1902, Maitland 1929, *Musical Times* 1 May 1936, *New Grove*, *ODNB*.

MAN IN THE MOON (1847-1849) *Man in the Moon* was a satirical* weekly* and one of the most successful rivals to *Punch** in the 1840s. It contained fold-out cartoons* and single-page illustrations* drawn by a number of illustrators including 'Phiz'* and George Augustus Sala*. It offered parodies of literature* and drama, and was particularly proficient at burlesques of melodramatic writing and drama such as that found in the series 'Drawing room Theatricals'. It also reviewed* theatrical productions and new books. Comic poems* were usually accompanied by an illustration. It was edited* by Angus Reach (who had been an investigative* journalist for the *Morning Chronicle*)* and Albert Smith (whose journalistic experience included work for the *Illustrated London News** and *Punch*).

Its small size* meant that it was convenient for reading while travelling and its front page proudly announces that it is 'sold at every railway station in the kingdom'. The *Man in the Moon* made its enmity with *Punch* clear by commenting on its competitor's inferiority throughout its pages. It differed from *Punch* in its format* but also in its less overtly political* satires, so it is not clear that their readerships* would have entirely overlapped. However, the rivalry was also a useful way of garnering publicity. Angus Reach joined the staff of *Punch* at the conclusion of *Man in the Moon*. **BP**

Sources: Garlick 1998, *ODNB*, Poole's, *Waterloo*.

MANCHESTER GUARDIAN (1821-) The *Manchester Guardian* originated after the government attempted to censor* accounts of the Peterloo Massacre and a group of Manchester Dissenters decided to start a weekly* paper that would support liberal causes and provide complete, accurate news* coverage for a local* market*. The editor* was John Edward Taylor (1791-1844), a wealthy cotton merchant who had written pamphlets advocating reform, as well as the first unbiased report of the Peterloo Massacre. With experienced printer and publisher* Jeremiah Garnett*, formerly of the Tory *Manchester Chronicle*, respected contributors Archibald Prentice and John Shuttleworth and a £1,000 start-up fund from a dozen subscribers, Taylor launched the *Manchester Guardian*, publishing its first issue on Saturday, 5 May 1821. The paper was Whiggish rather than radical, not supporting the strikes of 1820-1821, but its reporting of them was far more evenhanded than that of the London press. The paper was four pages long, one sheet of newsprint, folded, carrying advertisements* on the front page, plus occasional woodcut* illustrations*. Because the paper's price* was high, its readers* were prosperous Manchester merchants who did not necessarily agree with its progressive politics, which led to a rightward shift.

Circulation* rose rapidly from 1,000 copies in 1821 to 2,000 copies in 1823 and over 3,000 by 1825. Growth was bolstered by the failure of the *Manchester Observer*, which on shutting down in 1821 recommended the *Guardian* to its readers. In 1825, the *Manchester Guardian* took over the *British Volunteer*, and until 1828 the paper ran as the *Manchester Guardian and British Volunteer*. In 1836, the paper became bi-weekly, starting a Wednesday edition, and began to be printed on eight pages of the largest paper* size* available. When John Edward Taylor died in 1844, circulation was at 8,000 copies bi-weekly*. As the paper expanded in size and circulation, its price dropped from 7p weekly in 1821 (4d of this was tax), to 4d bi-weekly in 1836, 2d daily in 1855 and 1d daily in 1857.

John Edward Taylor left the *Guardian* in the hands of his son, Russell Scott Taylor, who edited the paper, with considerable assistance from Jeremiah Garnett* when Garnett took over (1848-1861). Under his management, the *Manchester Guardian* began publishing daily* in 1855. Russell's brother, John Edward Taylor Jnr, returned the paper to Taylor family control in 1861 and to its radical roots, with investigative reporting into social problems and advocacy of the Parliamentary Reform Act (1867) and the Secret Ballot Act (1872). In 1868, the *Manchester Evening News* was founded, and Taylor snapped it up with his brother-in-law Peter Allen. In that same year, he secured a seat for a *Guardian* parliamentary* reporter in the House of

Commons, also opening a London office for the paper. Over the next three years, J. E. Taylor Jnr edited the paper from London, with much of the work carried out by the paper's Manchester-based writers, including H. M. Acton, Robert Dowman, and J. M. Maclean. This system did not work well, so in 1871 Taylor appointed his cousin, Charles Prestwich Scott, to the paper and within a year, Scott was editor. Magisterial even in his youth, he brought the paper into its glory, moving the paper's editorial slant further to the left while recruiting the best arts and science* writers available, including James Bryce, C. E. Montague, Arnold Toynbee and A. W. Ward. By the late 1880s, the *Guardian's* circulation was over 40,000 copies a day. After J. E. Taylor Jnr died in 1905, Scott bought the paper in 1907 for £240,000. **LB**

Sources: Ayerst 1971, Mills 1922, Nichols 1946.

MANCHESTER PRESS The nineteenth century saw Manchester emerge as England's second city for print culture, with imprints of books and periodicals, including newspapers, journals and magazines*, far in excess of other provincial* cities.

For newspapers, however, Manchester remained so far behind the metropolis, with possibly less than a twentieth of the publications of London, that its title of 'the other Fleet Street*' is hardly justified until the twentieth century. There were a number of important newspapers, of which the *Manchester Guardian** remains the best example, though the conservative *Manchester Courier* (1825-) and liberal *Manchester Examiner and Times* (1848-) were hardly less significant. Indeed, the *Guardian's* longevity and popularity has possibly distorted our historical understanding. Perhaps the most characteristic feature of the city's nineteenth-century newspaper production was its sporting* press rather than its political weeklies* or dailies*. In 1871 Ned Hulton* began to publish the *Sporting Chronicle**, the first of a huge empire which he established in Manchester, which included the *Sunday Chronicle*, the *Daily Dispatch* and *Athletic News**. Hulton's new premises in Withy Grove in the heart of the city became the biggest printing house in Europe.

But, as with other major industries, notably cotton, Manchester's importance in the newspaper trade lies less in terms of manufacture and production than in wholesale and distribution*. The creation in 1842 of the London-Birmingham-Manchester railway made Manchester the major provincial hub from which London papers could reach the north of England and beyond that, Wales and Scotland. By this means newspapers became truly na-

tional. In the early 1850s, thanks to the improved railway network, the Manchester publisher* Abel Heywood* could estimate to Parliament that he handled as much as 10 per cent of the whole national issue of popular* publications, including the main London papers, a testament to the role of railway transport* in distributing print in nineteenth-century Britain. The interaction of national and indigenous titles was underscored towards the end of the century by the establishment of offices in Manchester to bring out northern editions of London papers. These were distributed throughout Yorkshire and the rest of the north by a new network of newspaper trains.

Alongside this national role, Manchester and its satellite townships were home to a proliferation of local* journals and papers. Magazines ranged from church magazines, through scientific and literary titles like *Country Words** and the *Manchester Magazine* to the satiric *Momus/Comus* on which W. G. Baxter*, the major creator of Ally Sloper*, began. Most were in standard English but some, like *Ben Brierley's Journal**, fostered dialect writing. **MP/ TW/MRB**

Sources: *Manchester Region History Review* 2006, *Waterloo.*

MANGAN, JAMES (1803-1849) One of the nineteenth-century's most enigmatic but influential Irish poets, Mangan wrote nearly a thousand poems* for the Irish periodical press, using both his own name and a variety of pseudonyms; he was also known as 'J. C. M.', 'Clarence' and 'The Man in the Cloak'. Born into a family of Catholic Dublin shopkeepers, he was trained as a scrivener, though alcoholism and depression in his later years meant only irregular employment, and he often relied on the payment from his periodical contributions for survival. He was a skilled author of puzzle poems for the popular Dublin almanacs* of the 1820s, and of satirical* work for several pugnacious newspapers of the early 1830s, including the *Comet* and the *Dublin Satirist*. He became an important contributor to the more conservative *Dublin University Magazine** throughout the 1830s, supplying it with regular articles on German and 'oriental' poetry* and accompanying his translations and pseudo-translations with mercurial prose commentaries. In the 1840s he became interested in the Irish-language poetry then being collected and edited by antiquarians like George Petrie*, and published popular translations and adaptations of these in nationalist newspapers like the *Nation**, the *United Irishman** and the *Irishman**. 'Dark Rosaleen' (from the *Nation* 1846) is the most well known of these lyrics. Too solitary and eccentric in his habits to become personally involved in the Young Ireland* movement, he was nevertheless befriended and supported in his last years by prominent Irish nationalist editors like Charles Gavan Duffy*, John Mitchel* and Joseph Brenan. He died from the effects of cholera and malnutrition in the summer of 1849. SMR

Sources: *ODNB*, Ryder 2004, Shannon-Mangan 1996.

MARKET Although in the nineteenth century the press was recognized as being organised in terms of a market, What the 'market' was and how it was to be regulated were much debated. Early on there were two main political positions: one, mindful of the perceived effects of print in causing the French Revolution, was that print media should operate in a controlled economy which kept prices* high. Seditious matter would, according to this model, circulate only with difficulty. A development of centralised state organization of the media that had been in force since the early years of print in Britain, this model is most clearly exemplified by the 'Taxes on Knowledge'. The other, newer, position held that a free market economy would result in socially responsible material driving out seditious, according to the natural laws of progress. This indeed proved to be the case, although not for the idealistic reasons discussed at the time. The commercial organization of the press meant that periodicals relied on subvention by advertising*. Advertisers did not wish to address readers who could not buy their products, with the result that the oppositional and alternative press with their poorer readerships found it difficult to survive.

If the idea of the free market won out in theory, in practice the market for print never became completely free, for it continued to be regulated directly by laws of copyright*, libel, obscenity, the Official Secrets Act (from 1889) and the complicated area of employment relations. Indirectly, Government intervention such as the 1870 Education Act and state-declared wars also affected the market, for both massively stimulated demand. Loose centralized control meant that the industry became much more fragmented and its participants more numerous and more competitive. Although on the whole still reflecting the values of individual owners and editors (rather than the more corporate identities of the twentieth century), periodicals and newspapers aimed to distinguish themselves from competitors* with their own 'characters', and so attract particular

kinds of advertisers. The market for periodicals and newspapers was also recognized as different from that for books. As J. S. Mill* pointed out, periodicals require immediate and regular sales, with a high turnover ratio, whereas capital can be tied up for substantial periods in books and still turn a profit.

Throughout the century the market organization of print media was questioned not only on political but also on moral and aesthetic grounds (Wordsworth's 1800 'Preface' to the *Lyrical Ballads* has a famous early example of the latter). From mid-century onwards, opposition gained force and socialist* papers and journalists such as Eleanor Marx* sought alternatives. Often the risks of a male-dominated industry that manufactured desire in women were explored (see e.g. Mary Braddon*'s 1864 serial 'The Doctor's Wife'). At other times the market was seen to threaten the artist's integrity, a concern highlighted by the romantics: in their different ways, Tennyson's letters, Gissing's 1891 novel *New Grub Street* and the 1889 Vizetelly* trial over the publication of Zola all explore the relation of the artist to the market. AK

Sources: Curran and Seaton 2003, Ledbetter 2007, Mill 1824.

MARRYAT, FLORENCE (1837-1899) Known primarily as a romance novelist of over 70 titles, Florence Marryat served as editor* of *London Society: Light and Amusing Literature for the Hours of Relaxation* from 1872-1876. *London Society* targeted the middle and upper classes* with engravings, poetry*, articles, and serialized* novels by many of the most popular authors of the time; contributors included Charles Reade, Jules Verne, Mrs J. H. (Charlotte) Riddell, Arthur Conan Doyle (pre-Sherlock Holmes), Alan Muir, Eleanor Catharine Price and Henry Kingsley*. Marryat serialized* three of her own novels during her tenure and published articles on topics of popular interest.

The daughter of novelist and former naval officer Captain Frederick Marryat* and Catherine Shairp Marryat, Florence Marryat, although married, used her maiden name as her signature, linking herself with her famous father. JN

Sources: Delaney and Tobin 1961, Dickerson 1988, Neisius 1992, *ODNB*.

MARRYAT, FREDERICK (1792-1848) Usually referred to as 'Captain Marryat' because of his prior career as naval officer, Marryat wrote numerous nautical novels that were immensely popular with the readers of his time. Almost all of his writing was first published in serial* form in the *Metropolitan*

*Magazine**, of which he was both proprietor* and editor* (1832-1836).

Marryat started to get fully involved in the *Metropolitan** when he succeeded Thomas Campbell as editor*, whom he thought unfit for a position that demanded a quick mind and communicative skills. At the same time J. G. Cochrane, the former proprietor* of the *Metropolitan*, got into financial difficulties and cleared the stage for Marryat, who soon became chief proprietor. In the following years, Marryat succeeded in endowing the magazine with a perceptible nautical touch, as he assembled a number of contributors who, like himself, had a naval past (or present) and literary ambitions. Among them were Captain Walter Glascock, Captain Basil Hall, Captain Frederick Chamier and Lieutenant the Honourable Edward Howard, who became Marryat's assistant editor.

The nautical theme appealed to the contemporary public, who enjoyed stories about sea battles of the past. In turn, this line of trade provided some of the contributing writers with some much-needed income. Nevertheless, as contributions did not come regularly or in large numbers, the *Metropolitan* was mainly Marryat's product; there were times when he was not only the editor, but also the author of all the articles of an issue.

Fiction first published in the *Metropolitan*, includes 'Newton Forster' (1832),' Peter Simple' and 'Jacob Faithful' (both 1834), 'Mr. Midshipman Easy' and 'Japhet in Search of a Father' (both 1836). Apart from these longer works, Marryat printed miscellaneous shorter writing in the magazine (including plays, short stories, travel journalism and essays), which were later reissued in one volume with the title *Olla Podrida* ('hotchpotch') in 1840. 'The Pacha of many Tales (1835), a collection of short stories inspired by the *Arabian Nights*, was also first published in the *Metropolitan*.

The opinions of his reviewers differed; while some criticized him for the carelessness with which he wrote (and which allowed him to produce such a vast number of novels in rapid succession) and his formulaic plots, others admired the vivacity of his stories. Drawing on personal experiences of life at sea, Marryat knew how to add colour and humour to his adventures. The firm hand with which he had transformed the *Metropolitan* into a nautical magazine* had not only provided him with a platform for his real and fictional adventures but had turned the naval novel into a fashionable genre*. **KL**

Sources: *Cardiff Corvey, Encyclopedia Britannica, ODNB*, Pocock 2000, Warner 1953.

MARTINEAU, HARRIET (1802-1876) Harriet Martineau made one of the most significant contributions to nineteenth-century journalism as a writer of leaders*, reviews* and articles. A specialist in economics and sociological issues, unusually for a woman journalist of her time, she did not eschew political* issues.

She received a particularly enlightened education for a girl, but was afflicted by deafness. Thus, when forced to earn her living, following the death of her father, she chose writing rather than the more usual governessing. Her earliest work was as unpaid contributor to the theological journal the *Monthly Repository** (1822), but her sustained journalistic career began in the 1850s when she was already renowned for her books, like *Illustrations of Political Economy* (1832-1834), which employed a narrative format to popularize its subject. Though she declined to contribute fiction, she published over 40 articles in Charles Dickens's* *Household Words**, for which the narrative format* was ideally suited. She was also producing more substantial, heavyweight essays and reviews* for the *Westminster Review** in which she made a financial investment. In 1858 when her cousin, Henry Reeve*, was editor* of the *Edinburgh Review**, she associated herself, instead, with that quarterly*, which published her final essay (1868).

In 1852 she became a leader* writer for the *Daily News** and despite, a couple of years later, suffering a near-fatal illness, wrote over 1,600 leaders (1855-1866). The efficiency of the postal system, and Martineau's ability to mine some pamphlet or report for a topical nugget as the basis of a trenchant polemic, enabled her to be a consummate journalist from her rural Ambleside retreat. Her tour of America in the 1830s had made her a life-long abolitionist and in 1861 she became a correspondent of the New York *Anti-Slavery Standard*. Though her strong views earned her the soubriquet 'the Sheradical', she could adapt herself to the journal, and Florence Fenwick Miller* thought some of her best 'political papers' appeared in *Once a Week** in 1863, 'best' precisely because they eschewed party* politics. Martineau also contributed to other journals including the *Cornhill**, *Dublin University Magazine**, *Macmillan's Magazine**, the *New Monthly**, and *Tait's Edinburgh Magazine**. Her reputation was such that in the latter decades of the century she was cited as a model for women journalists. When Martineau died on 27 June 1876, a piece she wrote herself for the *Daily News* appeared as her obituary. BMO

Sources: Arbuckle 1994, Miller 1884, *ODNB*, Onslow 2000, Webb 1960.

MARTINEAU, JAMES (1805-1900) During his period in Liverpool as minister of the Paradise Street Chapel (1832-1857), James Martineau became joint editor* of the *Prospective Review**, a significant journal of liberal Unitarian theology and literature* that explored the formative ideas of the day. His fellow editors (1845-1855) were John J. Tayler*, John H. Thom* and Charles Wicksteed. In 1840 Martineau was appointed as professor of mental and moral philosophy at Manchester College when it returned to Manchester, and he combined this post with his Liverpool ministry.

A leading intellectual figure, he not only wrote influential theological works but many significant articles for journals such as the *Inquirer**, the *Monthly Repository of Theology and General Literature**, the *Sunday School Penny Magazine* and the *Theological Review**. He also made a substantial contribution as co-founder of the Unitarian journal, the *National Review**. Of his many intellectual concerns were the conflicts between science and religion*, ethics and theology*, forging philosophical* links to religious discourse utilizing philosophical methodology and the claim of religion for a central position within rational discourse.

Martineau was known for becoming embroiled in controversial debates, one of which originated with his article in the *National Review*, critiquing Herbert Spencer's position on agnosticism (Oct. 1862). His long estrangement from his sister Harriet Martineau* was the result of an ideological quarrel. Prevented from taking up the chair of philosophy of mind and logic at University College London because of his position as a minister of religion, in 1869 he became principal of Manchester College. CL

Sources: *ODNB*, *Waterloo*.

MARX, ELEANOR (1855-1898) Eleanor Marx was the youngest child of the revolutionary socialist philosopher Karl Marx. After her father's death in 1883, Eleanor's struggle to forge an independent identity began through her major work as a political activist in the cause of socialism and women's rights where journalism, translation, lecturing and teaching work were interwoven as a paradigm of the emerging 'New Woman'.

Eleanor Marx's writing life was divided between working as an unpaid political* journalist and locating enough paid work to live on. From 1881 she had précised articles at £2 a week for a scientific*

journal and contributed to Henry Massingham's* evening paper, the *Star**. The difficulty of finding regular paid work meant that she also did 'hack' work and 'devilling' where she undertook research at the British Museum in order to write articles and reviews as a proxy for Miss Zimmerman who, while she received 30-35s for them, only paid Eleanor between 5s and 7s 6d. Marx explained to her sister, 'I don't half like writing articles for other people to sign, but necessity knows no laws and 5/- is 5/-...'

Among her ceaseless political work, journalism was a vital activist tool, integral to her professional existence. Her articles were signed Eleanor Marx, E. Marx, the adopted Marx-Aveling or E. M. A*., Edward Aveling, journalist and editor*, being the man she lived with. From January 1884 Marx contributed a regular column* on international news for *To-Day**, later called the *Monthly Magazine of Scientific Socialists*, and in the same year she began a similar column, 'Record of the Revolutionary International Movement' for the Socialist League's, *Commonweal** and also for the *Labour Elector**. The London International Workers' Educational Club's paper *Arbeter Fraint* was another outlet for her campaigning. She and Aveling had joined the Democratic Federation in 1883 and from the following year they co-wrote for its paper, *Justice**, while from 1897 they wrote for the *Social Democrat*. She had been contributing to the secularist monthly *Progress* (which Aveling had edited since 1883), beginning with two articles on her father's life and work.

Marx and Aveling also worked together on paid work: from 1887 they had been contributing joint articles to the cultural monthly *Time**, and from January 1890 they worked as assistant editors for its owner Ernest Belfort Bax*, as well as writing drama notes and theatre reviews* during the 1890s. CL

Sources: Kapp 1979, Meier 1982, Mutch 2005, Pykett 2000.

MARX, KARL HEINRICH (1818-1883) Karl Marx, revolutionary socialist, took his doctorate in philosophy at Berlin University and it was in Berlin in 1841 that he was offered his first employment as a journalist, writing on economic and political* issues for a new journal, the *Rheinische Zeitung*. Becoming editor* after six months, this work lasted until the journal was terminated by the censor and Marx left for Paris at the end of 1843 to become joint editor of the *Deutsche-Französiche Jahrbucher*. The following year, Frederick Engels submitted an article to the *Jahrbucher* and their lifelong working relationship began. In the same year, the Prussian government accused the editors of treason, the journal was forced to close and Marx became a stateless, political refugee.

Against the background of the 1848 Revolution, Marx lived and travelled between Belgium, Britain and Paris, before Engels funded a newspaper in Cologne to be edited by Marx, with Engels as his assistant. So the *Neue Rheinische Zeitung: Organ der Democratie*, a daily* newspaper as a voice for the democratic left, was launched. As a highly-regarded daily, it provided Marx with an opportunity to develop the talent of elucidating complex intellectual arguments at speed. Expelled from Prussia after the failure of the revolution, Marx settled with his family in London in 1849. With hopes for a successful revolution crushed, he nevertheless published six issues of the *Neue Rheinische Zeitung: Politisch-Ökonomische Revue* in London, hoping for a revolutionary revival that did not materialize. Left in a political vacuum with lack of hope compounded by financial distress, Marx's journalism now had to provide additional income supplementing Engels' generosity. In 1855 he wrote for the Breslau *Neue Oder-Zeitung*, but throughout the 1850s he was receiving a regular income of up to £2 an article as London correspondent for the liberal *New York Daily Tribune*, a post which ceased with the outbreak of war in America. From October 1861, Marx was then able to contribute 35 articles on the American Civil War, with Engels' assistance, to the Vienna *Presse* for a year

Not all Marx's journalism was for publications abroad. In previous years, he had contact with the British Chartist movement and now had the opportunity to write for the Chartist* paper, the *Northern Star*. In 1852 he wrote for and was joint editor with the Chartist, Ernest Jones, of a new publication, *Notes to the People; the champion of political justice and universal right*, which later became the successful *People's Paper*. In the year from 1855, he contributed to the liberal *Free Press; journal of the Foreign Affairs Committee*. With the formation of the International Working Men's Association in 1864, Marx's links with the trade union movement swept him into the forefront of public activism and writing for the developing socialist movement and his days of 'continual scribbling' could be left behind. CL
Sources: Blumenberg 1998, Kapp 1979, *ODNB*, *Waterloo*.

MASS JOURNALISM AND THE NINETEENTH-CENTURY PRESS The development of mass journalism was part of the broader shift towards mass culture, as the forces of modernity, including indus-trialization, urbanization, and globalization, came to shape the contemporary world. It is difficult to say exactly when mass journalism emerged – some critics have suggested it was the arrival in 1896 of the 'Penny Newspaper for One Halfpenny', the *Daily Mail*, which, through aggressive advertising* and a focus on increased circulation*, challenged the dominance of the leading morning newspaper, the *Daily Telegraph*.

While the arrival of the *Daily Mail* marks the beginning of the 'Northcliffe Revolution' in media history, that story arguably has more to do with the twentieth century than the nineteenth. In fact, there is no original moment of inception for mass journalism, and it should be thought of as an ongoing process – a long revolution, to borrow from Raymond Williams – in which technological, social, and political events overlap. Consider this partial list of important milestones in gradual unfolding nineteenth-century press history: the emergence of the railway as a primary mode of distribution* from the 1830s; the invention of the rotary press in 1846, which could print 20,000 newspapers per hour; the founding of Sunday papers like *Lloyd's Weekly Paper*, which sought to corner the market* on working-class readers*; the gradual spread of the telegraph* around the world in the 1850s, which made global contact quicker and more immediate than ever before; the repeal of the final 'taxes on knowledge' in 1861, which led to a freer but more fiercely commercial press; the Education Act of 1870, which led to far higher rates of literacy in the generation that followed; the introduction of wood-pulp processes in the 1880s which made paper* cheaper than ever; the emergence of the New Journalism*.

All of these are significant parts of how mass journalism came to be; however, the meaning of mass journalism is more complicated and ambivalent, since the concept of 'mass' or 'popular'* press was one that many cultural critics (Matthew Arnold*, to name just one) resisted. Implicit for many who looked askance at mass journalism was a belief that culture itself was dumbing down. According to detractors, the values of the factory line – speed, efficiency, continual production – had come not only to define the workings of the press industry, but also to define the culture of the press, its writing and its content. So at the heart of debates about the cultural values of an increasingly mass society was its chief, most exemplary literature – the popular press. MWT
Sources: Lee 1976, Ward 1989, Williams 1961.

MASSEY, (THOMAS) GERALD (1828-1907) A Chartist journalist* and editor*, Massey's career began in 1849 with J. B. Leno's* *Uxbridge Pioneer* and *Uxbridge Spirit of Freedom*. In the next few years Massey (pseudonyms* 'Bandiera' and 'Armand Carrel') contributed to a number of short-lived radical and reforming journals: Thomas Cooper's* *Cooper's Journal*, Charles Kingsley's* *Christian Socialist* and George Julian Harney's* *Red Republican* which became *Friend of the People* (1850-1852). When Harney incorporated the latter with the moribund *Northern Star* to form the *Star of Freedom* (1852), he appointed Massey as literary editor. Following the demise of this paper, Massey moved to Edinburgh where he edited the *Edinburgh News* (1848-1863) and wrote for Hugh Miller*'s *Witness* (1840-1864). He returned to London in 1858 where he worked for the *Daily Telegraph** and as a poetry* reviewer* for the *Athenæum** (1858-1869), contributing also to the *North British Review** and *Quarterly Review** (1858-1867). He then virtually abandoned journalism for a lecturing and writing career. **DS**

Sources: Leno 1892, Massey papers, Shaw 1995.

MASSINGHAM, HENRY WILLIAM (1860-1924) When his education at King Edward VI's Grammar School in Norwich ended, Henry Massingham went to work in the newspaper group that was one of his family's business interests. Starting as a trainee reporter* on the *Eastern Daily Press*, he eventually became its editor* as well as contributing to the National Press Agency. In 1883 he became the columnist* for the 'London Letter' on the *Norfolk News,* a provincial* paper which his father, a Methodist minister, had helped to found.

Five years later he moved to an evening newspaper, the *Star**, and became its editor in 1890 for a short-lived six months, leaving after an altercation with its owner, T. P. O'Connor*, not, however, before he had succeeded with George Bernard Shaw* and Ernest Belfort Bax* in increasing the *Star's* radical profile. After working briefly on the weekly *Labour World* as editor, he left for the *Daily Chronicle** where he was by turns, leader* writer, literary* editor, and parliamentary correspondent*, before being promoted to assistant editor after a year. Becoming its editor in 1895, his talents in the literary and political* fields enhanced the paper. However, his nonconformist background emerged when he opposed the government position on the Boer War, a move which damaged the *Chronicle's* circulation* and revenue; Massingham resigned in 1899. This was followed by yet another short-lived

appointment from March 1900 of less than a year as a London correspondent providing parliamentary* profiles for the *Manchester Guardian**.

Pursuing his attraction to political journalism*, he became parliamentary correspondent on the *Daily News** before editing the Liberal publication, the *Nation** (1907-1923), when a change of ownership and political alignment forced him to resign. After joining the Labour Party in 1923, Massingham then favoured freelance work, with his 'Wayfarer's Diary' in the *New Statesman**, London correspondence for *Haagsche Post* and the *Christian Science Monitor,* together with occasional pieces for the *Observer**, *Daily Herald, New Leader,* and the *Spectator**. **CL**

Sources: Havighurst 1974, *ODNB*.

MASSON, DAVID (1822-1907) David Masson produced an impressive body of other writings during a career as journalist, critic, historian, editor* and university teacher that spanned more than half a century. After having abandoned his intention of becoming a minister in the Church of Scotland, he became the editor of an Aberdeen weekly*, the *Banner,* in 1842 and two years later turned to writing as a profession, first for the Edinburgh publishing house of W. and R. Chambers* and then as a freelance, contributing to various periodicals, starting with *Fraser's Magazine** (1844-1858).

In 1847 Masson moved from Aberdeen to London, where he made many literary* acquaintances, and by 1853 his own reputation as a man of letters was such that he was appointed Professor of English Literature at University College London while continuing his work for periodicals, including the *North British Review**(1848-1856), *the British Quarterly Review** (1849-1857), the *Dublin University Magazine** (1851), the *National Review** (1856), the *Westminster Review** (1856) and the *Quarterly Review** (1858).

Masson also agreed to edit two important new periodicals as they began publication in an increasingly crowded and competitive* market*: the monthly* *Macmillan's Magazine** (Nov. 1859) and the weekly* *Reader** (1863-1864). In 1865 Masson became Professor of Rhetoric and English Literature at the University of Edinburgh. Although he continued to write for *Macmillan's* until 1883, he had given up his editorship under some pressure from its publisher, his good friend Alexander Macmillan*, at the end of 1867, remaining nominally in charge until the end of the volume in April 1868. His attempt to edit the *Magazine* from 400 miles away had not turned out to be feasible. Other periodicals to which Masson contributed occasionally in his later years included the *Contemporary Review* (1873), the *Edinburgh Review* (1882), the *Nineteenth Century* (1892) and *Blackwood's Magazine* (1893). **GW**

Sources: Eigner and Worth 1985, *ODNB, Wellesley,* Worth 2003.

MASTER HUMPHREY'S CLOCK (1840-1841) Following the resounding success of the serialization of *Pickwick Papers* (April 1836-Nov. 1837) and *Nicholas Nickleby* (April 1838-Oct. 1839) in illustrated* monthly parts, publishers Chapman & Hall* were anxious to fall in with the scheme of their star author, Charles Dickens*, who wished to found and edit a new weekly* miscellany*, based on the model of the eighteenth-century British Essayists (Addison, Steele, Johnson, Goldsmith *et al.*) and incorporating the notion of a club* of eccentric gentlemen meeting periodically to exchange stories, by turns queer and satirical*, Gothic and modern, of London life.

The result was an innovative 'weekly periodical of One Sheet Royal Octavo to sell for three pence a number; each … to contain twelve pages of Original Literary* matter' (*Letters*, Appendix C: 681). Dickens received £50 a week to supply this, and originally thought of hiring his old friend from the Reporters' Gallery, Thomas Beard, as subeditor*, and of commissioning contributions from other writers. But (among other factors) the production costs of the whimsical woodcuts*, designed by George Cattermole and three other prominent artists and cut by leading engravers*, drove Dickens to contribute all the material himself. Instead of being able, as he and his literary adviser John Forster* hoped, 'for a time to discontinue the writing of a long story with all its strain on his fancy', Dickens found himself having to write two, end-to-end, namely the serial* fictions republished in volume form as *The Old Curiosity Shop* and *Barnaby Rudge* (both 1841). Of the 88 weekly* numbers of the *Clock,* only six contained no instalment of these serials*. However, they helped raise the magazine's circulation*, at times well above the 50,000 per week anticipated; it peaked at something over 100,000 at the close of the first serial, declining from 70,000 at the start of *Barnaby Rudge* to nearer 30,000 by its close. Further sales were generated by monthly numbers of the *Clock* priced* at 1s or 1s 3d, and three unequal bi-annual volumes, selling for between 8s and 10s 6d. The various modes, formats* and frequencies* of the *Clock* were intended, Dickens told Cattermole, 'to baffle the imitators

and make it as novel as possible' (*Letters* 2: 7). Few other Victorian authors or publishers either cared to, or could, follow its example. **JMD**

Sources: Chittick 1982, Forster 1872-1874, House & Storey 1965 and 1969, Patten 1978, Schlicke 1998.

MASTHEADS A common feature of many Victorian periodicals and newspapers, mastheads, along with the title pages of volume reissues and part-issue wrappers and covers, sought to establish an instant 'brand image' for the journals they represented. Indeed, mastheads drew together several constituent elements of a magazine's textual and paratextual make-up, to establish and advertise a precise identity, often combining emblems and graphic devices such as the lamp of knowledge held by a neo-classical figure on the title page of the volumes of the *Penny Magazine*. Many titles exploited allusions to geographical locations as with the *Cornhill*, the *London Journal*; or elements of content, especially illustration*, as in the *Illuminated Magazine*, as well as definitions of audience such as the *Boy's Own Magazine*, the *British Workman* and the *Family Economist*.

Mastheads were of particular use to magazines that presented themselves as combining a complex range of attributes. Thus the *Illustrated London News*, a title that included concepts of visuality, topicality and metropolitan cachet, offered each issue under a sophisticated and apparently naturalistic large-scale wood* engraving of the Thames and its skyline that also sought figurative meanings to do with trade, prosperity, Empire and nationhood. Many other magazines*, particularly those aimed at less sophisticated readers*, took advantage of the emblematic potential of the masthead, notably *Cassell's Illustrated Family Paper*, which, using the structures of old master paintings, was published under an elaborate masthead of a family engaged in 'useful leisure' activities, including the reading of appropriate magazines. Perhaps most spectacular of all was the *British Workman*, where the various mastheads offered a serial celebration of the contribution made to British society by hard-working trades people and artisans, again drawing on a combination of naturalistic and symbolic motifs.

Newspapers too furnished their mastheads with a variety of tropes. Some sought to inscribe visual representations of democracy, or the free press or constitutional loyalty as signifiers of their editorial positions. Others emphasized speed and novelty by means of commonly understood classical allusions, for example to Mercury, or projected journalism's capacity to cast light into the darkness of social ignorance with illustrations of lamps, the sun, the stars or the all-seeing eye, which often ideographically reinforced the organ's title. **BM/AGJ**

Sources: Harling 1950, Jones 1993, Jones 2005, Murray 2007, Murray 2008.

MAUDSLEY, HENRY (1835-1918) Psychiatrist, asylum director, founder of the Maudsley Hospital in London and editor* of the *Journal of Mental Science**, Maudsley published 54 signed articles (besides reviews*, books, and pamphlets) on psychology. Additionally, he contributed much anonymous* journalism to the *Journal of Mental Science*, while editor (1863-1878). Maudsley was particularly concerned with the physical nature of the mind, insanity and criminal responsibility, heredity, degeneration, and evolutionary theory in his writing. He wrote as well on literary* topics, publishing, for instance, a piece on *Hamlet* (1865) in the *Westminster Review**, and his own style was frequently described, sometimes denigrated, as literary rather than scientific*. Roughly half of his articles appeared in the *Journal of Mental Science*. His role as editor of the journal almost certainly made it easier for him to publish on controversial topics, although he was asked to step down from the editorship in 1877.

Maudsley also wrote for general journals such as the *Fortnightly Review** on gender and mind, hallucination, and materialism, as well as for specialized medical* journals such as the *Lancet** on aphasia, insanity and medical psychology. He was drawn to philosophical* questions, writing several articles on consciousness and brain physiology for *Mind**. Over the course of his prolific 60-year writing career, Maudsley established himself as one of the most influential psychiatrists of the Victorian period. **SA**

Sources: Collie 1988, *ODNB*, Walk 1976.

MAUND, BENJAMIN (BAP. 1790-1863) Editor* of the *Botanic Garden* (1825-1851), the *Auctuarium* (1833), the *Floral Register* (1834-1836) and the *Botanist* (1836-1842), titles which contributed to the 1820s and 1830s boom in botanical magazines. Benjamin Maund was the son of a farmer in Tenbury, Worcester. Little is known about him until in 1813 he bought a printing and bookselling firm in Market Place, Bromsgrove. From 1818 in the High Street, Bromsgrove he had a bookseller, stationer, printer, bookbinder, publisher* and chemist business. Alongside his editorship of the long-running *Botanic Garden* his name appears as joint editor on the title page of the first volume of the *Naturalist* (1837-1839), though his specific

contribution to it is unknown and he did not author any of its articles.

Though Maund was admitted to the Linnean Society in 1827 he had little specialist scientific* knowledge. But his titles were known for their quality of production, and Maund often boasted about the detailed artistic plates which graced the pages of his magazines and the first-rate status of the artists who produced them. Over 100 of the 250 plates in the *Botanist* were contributed by Mrs Withers, a leading floral illustrator*. Other illustrators included the artist, Edwin Dalton Smith (fl. 1823-1846) and two of Maund's daughters. Botanical descriptions and analyses were provided by, among others, Dr Robert Dickson, Robert Graham and Frederick Westcott, whom Maund instructed to indulge 'in the elegancies of literature* when science was exhausted' in order to appeal to more readers than 'the professional botanist'. In his time Maund was credited with innovating the practice of adding extraneous material to botanical periodicals such as guides, introductions, and glossaries of terms, making them accessible to a wider readership*. **AB**

Sources: Blunt and Stearn 1994, *Gardener's Magazine* 1839, *Journal of Botany*, ODNB.

MAXSE, LEOPOLD JAMES (1864-1932) Leopold Maxse, editor* and proprietor*, was born in London, the second son of Admiral Frederick Augustus Maxse and his wife Cecilia Steel, and educated at Harrow and Cambridge. Financial support from his family enabled his travels around the world to Canada, the USA, Australia, New Zealand and India, which laid the foundation for his journalistic career, providing him with both a first-hand understanding of colonial affairs and international contacts. His father purchased the *National Review** on his behalf in 1893. Maxse dismissed its then editor, the poet Alfred Austin*, took full editorial control, and with unchallenged authority over the paper's content, shaped the review around his own political* interests. He waged campaigns against political corruption and Liberal hypocrisy (wealthy politicians, living in luxury, supposedly championing the cause of the poor); he was determinedly pro-France and anti Germany and wrote persistently of his fears of war with Germany both before 1914 and after 1918 (later collected as *Germany on the Brain or the Obsessions of 'a Crank': Gleanings from the National Review 1899-1914*). His avid imperialist* stance was clear from his attacks on nationalist movements in Ireland, India and Egypt. He edited the evening daily* *Globe**

(1917-1921) and, as with the *National Review*, doubled its sales within a short period. He resigned his post when the *Globe* was absorbed by the *Pall Mall Gazette*.

His long-term achievement was to turn a lacklustre *National Review* into a lively organ of the Conservatives. It was influential and widely read within the party; he attracted leading Conservative voices to the journal; and his own 'Episodes of the Month' was a consistent review of important international and domestic concerns. He was involved in the Tariff Reform League and his entire career was grounded in the belief that the press, in its capacity to reach grass-root activists, could help to shape politics. Maxse, like many of his contemporaries, was also alert to the value in rousing his reading audiences* with colourful rhetoric and sensationalist stories. His writing, 'although invariably dogmatic and repetitive' was 'lively and entertaining' (*ODNB*) at its best; his 'genius was political rather than literary' (Sullivan: 245). For some, the review under Maxse became a publication that 'gave vent to the obsessions of its owner editor' (Koss: 9); nonetheless for almost 30 years, Maxse was for others 'one of Britain's foremost Conservative journalistic spokesmen' (Sullivan: 244). **FD**

Sources: Hutcheson 1989, Koss 1973, *ODNB*, Sullivan 1984.

MAXWELL, JOHN (1824-1895) John Maxwell was a controversial publisher* and proprietor*. In the late 1850s and 1860s he published magazines intended for working-class* readers*, while simultaneously trying to imitate the success of the *Cornhill** with 1s-monthly publications for the middle classes.

Born in Ireland, Maxwell came to London at the age of 18 to publish an edition of the works of the Irish poet and novelist Gerald Griffin. He went on to work as a newsagent* before becoming an advertising* agent for various newspapers. While working as an agent for the *Illustrated Times**, Maxwell met bohemian journalists like Edmund Yates* and George Augustus Sala*. Maxwell's first publishing venture was a weekly gossip-sheet* called *Town Talk* (1858-1859). Edmund Yates wrote his inflammatory remarks about W. M. Thackeray* in it, resulting in the Garrick Affair. In 1859 Maxwell bought the 1d weekly* *Welcome Guest** from Henry Vizetelly*, losing £2,000 on the venture. The price* was raised to 2d and the name changed to *Robin Goodfellow* in 1861. The early chapters of M. E. Braddon's* most famous novel, 'Lady Audley's' Secret, were published within its pages. In

December 1860 Maxwell established *Temple Bar**, a shilling* monthly* with Sala as editor*. In 1861 Maxwell founded three magazines, the monthly *St. James's Magazine* * and two weeklies serializing* lower-class* fiction, the *Halfpenny Journal* (1861-1864) and the *Sixpenny Magazine* (1861-1868). Maxwell was declared bankrupt in 1862 and turned to his partner, Mary Braddon for financial help. In the same year he started *Twice A Week* (1862) and *Every Week* (1862-1863). His most successful venture was the monthly *Belgravia**, with Braddon as editor and main contributor.

Maxwell was influential in disseminating good quality fiction to a working-class readership* and breaking the monopoly held by G. W. M. Reynolds* and Edward Lloyd*. But he was criticized by many for riding the bandwagon of sensationalist fiction and for his sharp business practices. He was perceived as epitomizing the 'brash new hustler' of the publishing industry, of whom 'profits and publicity were of prime importance', with his contributors often poorly paid and feeling exploited. Sala criticised his practice of paying contributors by the weight of their copy, rather than the content. Without Braddon's financial and literary help, Maxwell's many magazine ventures would have been even less successful. **PB**

Sources: Carnell 2000, Edwards 1997, McKenzie 1993, Sutherland 1989.

MAXWELL, WILLIAM HAMILTON (1792-1850) William Hamilton Maxwell's best-known works were *Wild Sports of the West* (1832) and *The Fortunes of Hector O'Halloran* (1842-1843). Maxwell contributed short stories to the *New Monthly Magazine** (1829-1830), to the *Dublin University Magazine** (1833-1834) and to *Bentley's Miscellany** (1837-1838). The *New Monthly Magazine* serialised* his novel *Lights and Shades* (collected as *Captain O'Sullivan*) in 24 parts (1844-1846), and he published another novel, 'Brian O'Linn', in 23 instalments (1845-1847) in *Bentley's Miscellany*, to which he also contributed frequent articles and sketches (1848-1850).

Maxwell's picaresque and humorous stories were quite successful at the time of publication. His periodical contributions further established him as the popular author of military* novels and Irish tales. Charles Lever is generally acknowledged as his literary successor. **FB**

Sources: Maginn 1859, *ODNB*, *Wellesley*, Wolff 1979a.

MAYHEW, HENRY (1812-1887) A London-based journalist, playwright and novelist, Mayhew's major contribution to journalism were his investigative reports on skilled and unskilled labour in London which, as the metropolitan* correspondent, he wrote for the series 'Labour and the Poor' in the *Morning Chronicle** (1849-1850). After a dispute with the publishers*, he continued his investigations in a separate weekly* publication, *London Labour and the London Poor* (1851-1852), which, in spite of the title, covered only the people who made their living in a variety of ways on the London streets. He covered this subject exhaustively over two years, but the whole did not reach book publication until 1863 when additional information was added to complete four volumes.

Under the newspaper pressures of time and space, Mayhew devised a unique method of reporting his interviews*; he absorbed the questions into the answers and reported the results in the voice of the interviewee. These 'biographies', one of the few sources of first-hand accounts of working-class* life and work, made Mayhew's reputation both in his own time and later. Earlier Mayhew and Gilbert À Beckett* founded *Figaro in London** (1835-1838), based on the famous French periodical. Mayhew was also one of the founders of *Punch** in 1841 and supposedly contributed the journal's name and one of its most famous jokes, 'Attention Persons about to Marry! Don't!' His connection with that journal lasted only a few years, but in the *Punch* vein he also wrote for the *Comic Almanack** (1850-1851) and contributed articles to *Bentley's Miscellany**, and the *Edinburgh News and Literary Chronicle*. He wrote a few articles after *London Labour and the London Poor* was interrupted by a lawsuit in 1852, but essentially disappeared from the journalistic scene after 1862. **AH**

Sources: Humpherys 1977, *ODNB*.

MEADE, ELIZABETH THOMASINA (1844-1914) Born in Ireland, novelist, editor*, and journalist* L. T. Meade moved to London to pursue a literary career. She published as 'Mrs' L.T. Meade, continuing to do so after marrying Alfred Toulmin Smith. Meade was already established as a novelist of family stories when she became editor of the girls'* paper *Atalanta** in 1887. For six years, she maintained a productive tension between progressive and conservative elements in *Atalanta*. As a prolific author and editor of a popular periodical, Meade became a journalistic celebrity*. Active in the New Journalism*, Meade not only wrote self-referential articles about journalism and editing but was a frequent subject of interviews* in periodicals like *Girl's Realm* and *Young Woman**. She was a

Figure 40: Christina Rossetti's poem 'Exultate Deo', with a reproduction of her signature, on the title page of *Atalanta*, Oct. 1888, during L. T. Meade's editorship.

member of the Pioneer Club, which catered to professional women, and also presided over the Ladies' Literary Dinner* (later the Women Writers' Dinner) in 1890 and 1891. Meade participated in the formation of a network of professional women writers. **TD**

Sources: Bilston 2004, Hughes 2007, Mitchell 1995, *NCBEL*, Onslow 2000, Reimer 1994, *Waterloo*.

MEADOWS, JOSEPH KENNY (1790-1874) Joseph Kenny Meadows's large output of illustrations* for the Victorian press was characteristic of those jobbing but relatively successful artists trained in both wood engraving* and the Regency caricature* tradition but forced to adapt to the new requirements of mid-century magazines. A contributor of comic images to *Bell's Life in London** relatively early in his career, Meadows continued to be commissioned by a broad range of journals to produce numerous observations of urban life and manners.

In the 1840s he contributed a series of wood engraved urban 'sketches', much in the manner of his well-known *Heads of the People* (1841), to middlebrow magazines like the *Illuminated Magazine** and

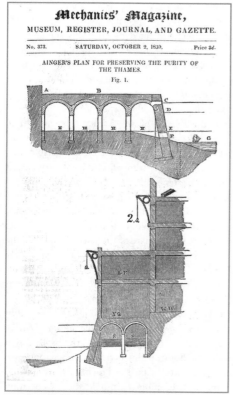

Figure 41: The title page of the *Mechanics' Magazine*, 2 Oct. 1830.

the *People's Journal**. Through the 1840s and 1850s he provided such well-known publications as the *Illustrated London News**, *Cassell's Illustrated Family Paper**, the *Illustrated Times** and the *Welcome Guest** with both small-scale comic images and more carefully worked through full page drawings, which proved especially useful for Christmas* or other special issues. An early contributor to *Punch** in his middle age, contemporaries, according to Spielmann, thought of Meadows as a ' "general utility" man' rather than an artist of true note or talent. Yet the wide range and geniality of his published work, and the prominence with which it was displayed, suggests that his comic images proved a considerable asset to many journals. **BM**

Sources: Engen 1985, Houfe 1978, *ODNB*.

MECHANICS' MAGAZINE, MUSEUM, REGISTER, JOURNAL AND GAZETTE (1823-25 SEPT. 1824); MECHANICS' MAGAZINE, MUSEUM, REGISTER, JOURNAL AND GAZETTE (2 OCT. 1824-1857); MECHANICS' MAGAZINE (1858ff) The original cheap scientific* weekly*, the *Mechanics' Magazine*, carried the motto 'knowledge is power' and the subtitle, *Museum, Register, Journal, and Gazette*. It was aimed at a new kind of readership*, 'intelligent mechanics', epitomizing the culture of artisan self-improvement in the 1820s. These were the technocratic artisans who had become more widely responsible for managing, improving and repairing the increasingly complex machinery on which industrialisation depended. Such recognition of ambitious artisans, with newfound cultural and economic aspirations, provided a significant market* for periodical literature and was crucial to the development a decade later of the *Penny Magazine** and the *Saturday Magazine**, and to publishers like John Cassell* who attempted to inform, address and influence the industrial working-classes through cheap informative serial publications.

Sold each Saturday for 3d (4d stamped) and in monthly and annual volumes, illustrated* with small-scale wood engravings*, it quickly achieved a circulation* of 16,000 per number in 1824. Founded by the patent agent, Joseph Clinton Robertson (1788-1852) and the radical political economist, Thomas Hodgskin (1787-1869), it was edited* by Robertson until his death. Published* by John Knight and Henry Lacey* of Paternoster Row until April 1829, thereafter by Robertson in Fleet Street*, it employed a succession of printers, notably Thomas Curson Hansard*. In October 1852, Richard Brooman became editor and publisher, assisted by Edward James Reed (1830-1906) between July 1857 and December 1872.

The *Mechanics' Magazine* offered readers scientific* material with a bias towards practical discoveries in chemistry, mineralogy and engineering, and generally eschewed theoretical discussion. The insertion of letters* from 'humble' mechanics cultivated a dialogue with its audience, and articles on issues affecting journeymen tradesmen were included alongside 'that lighter matter, which those who toil... most need' (stories, poetry* and biographical narratives). The proportion of this 'lighter' content declined over time, as more complex scientific and mathematical problems began to dominate. In its use of wood* engraving rather than the traditional eighteenth-century mode of copper plates to illustrate often complex industrial and mechanical processes and machinery, its use of the double-column* octavo page pioneered by such 'knowledge' journals as the *Hive* and the *Mirror of Literature**, its cheapness*, and its often progressive championing of new scientific inventions and discoveries, the *Mechanics' Magazine* was a leader in the democratization of scientific periodicals*, in what had previously been largely genteel modes of understanding. It enlightened working people on their own terms, for their own benefit and in their own language. DSM/BM

Sources: Brock 1988, Mussell 2006, Francis Place Collection, *Waterloo*.

MEDICAL JOURNALS: ALTERNATIVE, COMPLEMENTARY, FRINGE The notions of the 'alternative/ complementary' or (the term usually used) 'fringe' are, of course, a retrospectively formed classification from the position of the victor. While there are several studies of the orthodox *British Medical Journal** or *Lancet**, for example, the selection of journals mentioned here – the phrenological, the dietetic, the homeopathic, the hydropathic, the mesmeric – have received almost no study, as Peterson noted in 1994 (see Lefanu 1984 for a more complete list). When journals devoted to fringe medicine* began to appear in the 1820s – the *Transactions of the Phrenological Society* (1820-1823) and *Phrenological Journal and Miscellany* (1823-1847) seem the first – it was still possible that phrenology and homeopathy at least might have become mainstream, the very titles being modelled on publications of orthodoxy. Especially, Phrenology had a long life, feeding into the work of Lombroso in the 1880s and 1890s – the *Popular Phrenologist* (1896-1904) shows his influence. Besides an enormous number of articles devoted to phrenology in professional medical journals and lay periodicals (for the latter, see Palmegiano, 1998), there were at least 12 phrenological magazines between 1823 and 1900. A few, such as *Zadkiel's Magazine, or Record and Review of Astrology, Phrenology, Mesmerism and other sciences* (1849), one of several publications by the astrologer Richard James Morrison, contributed to phrenology's outsider status by linking it with archaic forms of knowledge in ways that echo the chapbook. But most, like the *People's Phrenological Journal and Compendium of Mental and Moral Science Weekly* (1843), were earnestly devoted to popular improvement (and Harrison, 1987, has noted fringe medicine's links to radical politics). Despite a sensational title (*The Forbidden Book*) added when the periodical came out in volume form to mark the orthodox journals' opposition to the notion that 'all disorders are repetitive and accompanied by changes of temperature', the *Chrono-Thermalist or the People's Medical Enquirer* (1850-1851) was of this sort, as was Spencer T. Halls's *Phreno-Magnet and Mirror of Nature* (1849). Both were shilling* monthlies* that seem composed by one person, the former finishing, so it

claims, because the author needs a rest.

All long-lasting specialist journals appeal to a lifestyle or well-defined identity in constant need of reinforcement or redefinition through updating. Of these, the *Vegetarian Messenger** (1849-) is an outstanding example, as the wider implications of vegetarianism, social, moral and political, keep changing both in their specifics and in general around a core set of well-defined behaviours. The *Hygeian Journal* (1832-1835) and *Hygeian Almanac* (1855-1867) similarly centre on a vegetable diet, though selling the regimen of the colourful quack James Morison (see Porter 2000). Related to dietetic periodicals are, of course, temperance* magazines. More of a threat to mainstream medicine than either phrenology or dietetics, homeopathy also attracted its share of specialist periodicals, the earliest being the 28 numbers of the *Annals of the London Homeopathic Medical Dispensary* (1840-1844), the *British Journal of Homeopathy* (1843-1884) and the *Homeopathic Times* (1849-1856). After the *Monthly Journal of Homeopathy* (1850-1852, a continuation of the *Journal of Health and Disease*, 1846-1850), the early 1850s saw a flurry of homeopathy periodicals in response to concerted attacks by the Provincial Medical and Surgical Association (British Medical Association from 1856) which culminated in the 1858 Medical Act establishing an official Medical Register and the exclusion of homeopaths from it (Nichols, 1988 charts the *Lancet*'s* repeated assaults; see also Porter, 1989). The periodicals included several from the regions: the *Norwich Homeopathic Journal* (1852-1853), when, amalgamated with the *Northampton Homeopathic Record*, it became the *Manchester Homeopathic Lancet and Provincial Homeopathic Gazette*, and later *Homeopathic Record*, which survived until 1860); *Homeopathist* (1853-1854); *Sheffield Homeopathic Lancet* (1853); *Notes of a New Truth, a Monthly Journal of Homeopathy* issued by English Homeopathic Association (1856-1869); *Monthly Homeopathic Review* (1856-1907, soon the *British Homeopathic Review*) and longest-lasting of all, the rival to the *British Journal of Homeopathy*, *Homeopathic World* (1866-).

Hydropathy, closely linked to local commercial interests in spa towns, is the third area which generated a decent amount of comment in the press, though few dedicated periodicals: all were short lived. Of these, the *Water Cure and Hygenic Magazine* (a 6d monthly, 1847-1849) stands out, not least since in 1849 it was edited by the notorious murderer Dr Smethurst. More typical, however, is the 1d sanitary-reforming *Aberdeen Water-Cure Journal* (1859-1860), and Malvern's *Hydropathic Record* (1868-1869). Even fewer journals concentrated on mesmerism and animal magnetism, the most ridiculed by orthodox medicine: the 1839 *Zoo-Magnetic Journal* had only two issues and the *Magnetic Review* only five annual ones (1874-1878). The *Zoist* (1843-1856), which supported mesmerism, managed to survive, as Ruth (1999) explains, by articulating the changing tensions between professional and popular, radical and liberal. Finally, precisely because it indicates the permeability of categories, mention must be made of the *Malthusian*, a 1d monthly* begun by the Malthusian League dedicated to birth control in 1879. Contributors included, unsurprisingly, Annie Besant* and Charles Bradlaugh*. **AK**

Sources: Bynum *et al.* 1992, Harrison 1987, Lefanu 1984, Nichols 1988, Palmegiano 1998, Peterson 1994, Porter 2000, Ruth 1999.

MEDICINE AND JOURNALISM Health was (and still is) a major preoccupation not only of the specialist medical press but of a wide range of periodicals from *All the Year Round** to the *Westminster**. Besides any consideration of content, however, medicine and journalism are complexly interwoven in ways that here shall be unpicked to form five main strands. In descending order of perceived status they comprise first, the orthodox professional* medical journals run by doctors for doctors. Then there are contributions by the medical profession written in general magazines for a lay audience; these may not necessarily centre or indeed ever engage with medical topics. Third, there are pieces on medical or medicine-related matters by lay writers for a lay audience. Fourth, there is the 'fringe' medical press whose contributors were usually heterodox medical practitioners. Enjoying the lowest status of all, but very important to the economics of the press in general, there is material provided by or concerned with quacks which comprises mainly, but not exclusively, advertising*.

That the specialist press was central to the definition and professionalization of medicine is well known. Through initially annual transactions, then quarterlies*, monthlies and weeklies*(see also frequency), standards were set and the identities, epistemologies and practices of orthodox medicine developed: without the organized pressures brought to bear on government by the medical press it is doubtful that the Medical Register would have been formed in 1858, for example. For many doctors, writing for the specialized press provided extra

income as well as a professional identity. Very few devoted themselves entirely to publication. If Wakley* may be well known, his single-minded dedication to the *Lancet** was rare; most editors* of and contributors to the specialist medical press (e.g. Arthur Jacob and Henry Mansell of the *Dublin Medical Press** or George Ross of the *Medical Press and Circular*) were first and foremost practising doctors. They engaged in periodical publication not only for the immediate income it brought: like lawyers, many did so with a view to increasing their status and extending their network, as well as being enabled to keep abreast – and control the dissemination – of the latest research. Having made their names through the specialist press, doctors would often leave to take up prestigious posts at universities, hospitals or asylums.

Such career progression was by no means helped by contribution to the general press, however. While John Leech* trained in medical school for only a year, Percival Leigh* qualified in medicine but is remembered for his work in *Punch**. Conan Doyle sought to combine specialization in ophthalmics with writing for the *Strand**; the latter won. Andrew Wynter* edited the *Association Medical Journal* (later *British Medical Journal**) 1855-1860, having written for periodicals such as *Ainsworth's** and *Fraser's** before that. He continued to write for the *Quarterly Review** during his editorship and the *Edinburgh** after it, as well as for *Cassell's Magazine**, *Good Words** and *Once a Week**. He probably left the *British Medical Journal* in order to pursue what had become for him a more lucrative literary career, writing on non-medical topics. Some doctors improved their income (but not their social standing) by composing medical series* for cheap* magazines such as *Reynolds's Miscellany** (*The Anatomy and Physiology of Ourselves Popularly Considered* by James Johnson, M. R. C. S., 1846-1847) or the *London Journal** (*The Wonders of Anatomy and Physiology* by J. A. Clarke, Esq., Surgeon, 1848). Henry Morley wrote many articles on health-related topics for *Household Words* (1850-1859). Pieces by lay writers on matters medical cover a huge range. Palmegiano (1998) has conveniently listed articles and series in many general periodicals. There we learn that G. H. Lewes* wrote a piece on 'The Effect of Railways on Health' for the *Cornhill* in 1862; Christian Johnstone* wrote several articles on lunatic asylums for *Tait's**; Harriet Martineau* wrote a series on the health of various workers for *Once a Week** (1859-1860). An overlooked source of popular medical information lies in the many anonymous Answers to correspondents* (on e.g. how to get rid of skin blemishes).

Sometimes, periodicals launched campaigns such as *Punch's*￼ in the 1850s on public health which involved many different resources of the journal: artists as well as journalists of all kinds. 'People's medicine' and political* radicalism (such as Chartism*; see Harrison) have links with the fringe medical press which provided a topic for discussion in both medical and lay press as an other against which the orthodox was defined. While interest by the medical press tailed off in the latter part of the century (as the orthodox became more established*, such matters became *infra dignitatem*), the popular lay press kept up a lively interest in homeopathy. Finally, the importance of patent medicines to journalism cannot be overlooked. While there is a good number of articles on quack medicines, more important for journalism is the indirect effect products such as Holloway's, Morison's or Beecham's Pills had in providing a considerable proportion of advertising* revenue over a very wide spectrum of the press. **AK**
Sources: Bynum 1992, Harrison, J. 1987, Helfand 1977, Lefanu 1984, Palmegiano 1998, Peterson 1994, Porter 2000, Porter 2001.

MEE, ARTHUR (1875-1943) Arthur Mee's long journalistic* career started at the age of 14 when he was employed as a copyholder on the *Nottingham Evening Post*. Mee taught himself Pitman's shorthand* and this knowledge gained him employment, at 16, as a trainee reporter* on the *Nottingham Daily Express*. After four years, he was promoted to editor* of the *Nottingham Evening News* where he formed a life-long friendship with the fellow journalist and editor, John Hammerton. At this time, Mee also learned typewriting*, and was able to produce typewritten rather than the customary handwritten copy, which meant he could work faster than other reporters and journalists on the paper. Mee augmented his salary by submitting articles to journals such as *Tit-Bits*. His success as a journalist allowed him to try his luck in London where he joined the staff of *Tit-Bits*, and also contributed to the *Morning Herald*￼ and *St James's Gazette*.

Mee edited the 6d weekly* *Black and White* (1901-1904), where his friend Hammerton was literary and drama critic*. In 1898, Mee had been invited to join the *Daily Mail*￼ by its proprietor* Sir Alfred Harmsworth* and was appointed literary editor in 1903. The idea for a series* entitled *Who's Who this Week* led to several collaborations* between Mee and Hammerton for Harmsworth's

publishing syndicate*. The first of these was the *Self-Educator* which ran for 48 issues* (1905-1907), followed by the *Harmsworth History of the World* (1907-1909) and the 'World's Great Books' (1909-1910). His *Children's Encyclopaedia* as first published in 50 fortnightly parts (1908-1910), and other publications including *My Magazine* (1910-1935) and the weekly, *Children's Newspaper* (1919-1964), which was read throughout the British Empire. **DHL**
Sources: Hammerton 1946, *ODNB*, Robson 2002.

MELBOURNE AGE (1854-) Founded in 1854 during the gold rush in Victoria, Australia, the *Melbourne Age* took a radical stand against the interests of landowners and traders. In 1856, David Syme and his brother purchased it and 'King David' agitated for land reform, constitutional reform and tariff protectionism. Circulation* grew from 22,000 in 1874 to 152,000 in 1916, although the paper had become more conservative after Syme's death in 1908, failing effectively to modernize. Increasing competition* led the Syme family to merge the company with Fairfax, owners of the *Sydney Morning Herald*, allowing expansion. In 1991 Fairfax was taken over by US and Canadian interests, including Conrad Black. **SJP**
Sources: Holden 1961, Mayer 1964, Walker 1982.

MENNONS, JOHN (1747-1818) John Mennons, proprietor*and publisher*, is believed to have served an apprenticeship in the printing office of the *Edinburgh Courant*. Establishing his own business in 1778, he published the short-lived* *Scots and County Magazine,* followed by several periodicals such as the *Town and Country Almanack* and the *Weekly Mirror.* In 1782, after moving to Glasgow, and purchasing a previously owned printing press, he published the *Glasgow Advertiser*, the first number of which appeared on 27 January 1783. Despite ensuring political* impartiality, Mennons was arrested for publishing a seditious article.

In 1802 Mennons sold the *Glasgow Advertiser* and went into an industrial venture which failed. Returning to publishing, he launched the *Caledonian*, a weekly* paper which folded in October 1807, and was replaced by the *Western Star*. Mennons was prosecuted for bankruptcy when his involvement with the *Western Star* ended (1809). His last venture, the *Scotchman* (1812-March 1813), was probably the first newspaper aimed at the week-end reader, but this also ceased publication quickly. With remarkable resilience, Mennons opened yet another title, the *Irvine and County of Ayr Miscellany*￼ (1814-1815). His second son, also called John

(c. 1786-1843), worked for his father in publishing and was later editor of the *Greenock Advertiser*. Mennons's own contribution to the press lies in his foundation of the *Glasgow Advertiser*, the city's longest running newspaper. **DHL**
Sources: Gourlay 1949, *ODNB*.

MENZIES, JOHN (1808-1879) Newsagent* and distributor, John Menzies intended to pursue a publishing* career in London, but family responsibilities contributed to his position as one of the most influential nineteenth-century Scottish distributors. After his apprenticeship with an Edinburgh bookseller, Menzies moved to London, where he worked for the Fleet Street* bookseller Charles Tilt as well as a variety of publishers, in order to gain as broad a view as possible of the publishing industry. This career plan ended abruptly in 1833, when his father died; Menzies returned to Edinburgh to support his stepmother and two sisters.

He initially set up shop as a bookseller in Princes Street but soon realized that Edinburgh lacked a wholesale distributor*, and that London booksellers would appreciate a Scottish bookseller who could handle both wholesale and retail sales. Menzies soon became the agent for several important London firms, including Chapman & Hall*, who gave him rights to handle all of Charles Dickens's work in eastern Scotland, and Bradbury & Evans*, for whom he handled *Punch*. Although Menzies maintained a publishing sideline, his business most notably explored a variety of distribution possibilities. In 1855, he began retail newspaper distribution for the *Scotsman*, thereby accelerating and increasing the volume of transactions previously undertaken since the eighteenth century by newsmen and agents*. Although he toyed briefly with the export market*, this did not succeed and was soon abandoned. His most dramatic venture was to open railway bookstalls, after noting that existing bookstalls in Edinburgh were owned by non-local companies. His bookstalls became heavily influential in directing the taste of public reading, and he was considered responsible for the distribution of authors such as William Wordsworth and William Makepeace Thackeray* among crofters and shepherds of the Scottish highlands. His success came about in spite of his preference for good-natured business over single-minded ambition. **TSR**
Sources: Gardiner 1983, Menzies 1958, *ODNB*.

MERGERS As with title changes*, mergers between journals were a constant feature of the nineteenth-century press, and occurred for a variety of reasons. A journal might be bought out and con-

sumed by a rival, consolidated by joining with a like-minded publication, or splinter and regroup as the coterie behind a publication evolves over time.

The *Westminster Review* stands as an example of this latter category, as changes in editorship* led James and John Stuart Mill* to leave the publication in 1828. After the Reform Bill of 1832, the political* spectrum in which the *Westminster* had formed itself altered, and the Mills took part in the formation of a rival to the *Westminster*, with the broader political framework inherent in the title of the *London Review* (1835-1836). Eventually, with their differences laid aside, the two journals merged to become the *London and Westminster Review* (1836-1840) though under the editorship of the *Londoners*. Reverting to its original title in 1840, the *Westminster* merged again, this time with the *Foreign Quarterly Review*. In the renamed *Westminster and Foreign Quarterly Review* of 1846 another form of merger occurs, namely that of two periodicals that were under the same ownership being merged into one by their proprietors*, Chapman* and Hall. Though keeping the *Quarterly*'s title for a while, the intrinsic qualities of this journal were soon lost in the new venture.

Indeed the merging of journals in terms of ownership, so rampant in the twentieth century, begins to gather momentum during the nineteenth century, with the predatory George Newnes* being described as the first British 'Press Baron'*. Within the Scottish press*, the demise of the *Caledonian Mercury* was a result of it being sold to its rival the *Scotsman* in 1867. Though technically a merger in terms of ownership, this predatory move resulted in the *Scotsman*'s most established rival over the last 50 years being eliminated. Within the sphere of provincial* and more specialised journals, mergers could, however, offer the chance of consolidating a weakening periodical and increasing its longevity. The Catholic *Ulster Observer* is one such example, as its 'manager' A. J. M'Kenna, after having looked 'in vain for a resting place' since the broadsheet's closure in 1868, was able to join forces with the Belfast *Northern Star* in 1870. This gathering together under the banner of Catholicism is a marked feature of the resulting *Northern Star and Ulster Observer*, as the two individual papers held opposing political views, being Whig and Tory respectively. **MBT**
Sources: Bell 2007, *Northern Star* (Belfast), *ODNB*, Wellesley, *Westminster Review*, *Ulster Observer*.

MERRY ENGLAND (1883-1895) Launched in May 1883, *Merry England* was an illustrated* literary* monthly magazine published in London and priced* 1s. It was run by the husband and wife team of Alice* and Wilfred Meynell (1852-1948). Wilfred undertook much of the editorial* work and Alice contributed a significant number of articles. While the manifesto published at the end of the first issue offered a religiously inspired vision of the renewal of joy and merriment in England, 'we shall seek to revive in our own hearts, and in the hearts of others, the enthusiasm of the Christian Faith'*, the Catholic vision of the magazine was broad, with a particular focus on literature* and art. Prominent writers were encouraged to write for the magazine by the charisma and friendship of the Meynells, including Katharine Tynan (1859-1931), R. D. Blackmore (1825-1900), Andrew Lang*, Coventry Patmore (1823-1896) and Francis Thompson (1808-1895). The latter first published 'The Hound of Heaven' in the pages of *Merry England*. **MK**

Sources: Knight and Mason 2006, *ODNB, Waterloo*.

METEYARD, ELIZA (1816-1879) A prolific writer in the periodical press, Eliza Meteyard was a surgeon's daughter. She helped her brother compile reports for the Tithe Commission in the 1830s and this training in social investigation underpinned her subsequent fiction and journalism. She moved to London from Shrewsbury in 1842 where, as a single middle-class* woman, she struggled to support herself as a writer. The challenges facing women writers were the subject of 'Scenes in the Life of an Authoress' (*Tait's Edinburgh Magazine**, Dec. 1843-April 1844), republished as *Struggles for Fame* (1845), the first of eight novels. Her serial* fiction and novels tended to rework the social issues that preoccupied her journalism and social commentary. In 1846 Meteyard adopted the pseudonym* 'Silverpen' given to her by Douglas Jerrold* when she wrote for his *Weekly Newspaper** (1846-1848), though she often used it in conjunction with her own name. A close friend of the editor* Mary Howitt, in the 1840s and 1850s she became a prolific contributor of fiction and essays to the 'improvement' press, including the *People's Journal**, *Chamber's Journal**, *Home Companion* (1852-1854), *Howitt's Journal**, *Eliza Cook's Journal**, *Sharpe's London Magazine* (1845-1849) and the *Ladies' Cabinet** (1852-1870).

Meteyard's writings link two phases in feminism: the predominantly intellectual debate on the Woman Question of the 1830s and 1840s, fostered by radical Unitarianism, and the liberal women's movements of the 1850s and 1860s. More of an activist than many in the earlier generation,

Meteyard's practical proposals for female education and employment, including design schools for women, anticipated later discussions in the *English Woman's Journal** (1858-1864), to which she contributed occasionally. With Jerrold, she sat on the Council of the Whittington Club, an organization which aimed to provide rational recreation to both sexes and all classes, and on its Women's Committee. Cross-class* dialogue was dramatized in fictions like 'John Ashmore of Birmingham' (*Eliza Cook's Journal*, 1849) which drew explicitly on writings about political* economy and working-class associations to imagine the future of a co-operative iron works. With other stories mixing social science and domestic fiction, it was republished in support of the Early Closing Association as *The Nine Hours Movement: Industrial and Household Tales* (1872), a volume which exemplifies the crossover between Meteyard's journalism, fiction and activism. Meteyard won some acclaim, yet often her work was rejected for being too radical, and she complained of having to tone down her writing to win commissions. Despite grants from the Royal Literary Fund and a government pension, she left less than £200 when she died. **HR**

Sources: Boardman 2004, Gleadle 1995, *ODNB*, Rogers 2000.

METROPOLITAN MAGAZINE (1831-1850)

One of the earliest nineteenth-century monthly* magazines to publish serial* fiction, the *Metropolitan Magazine* was a true miscellany*. Reviews* of art, books, music*, and drama; articles on science*, commerce, and politics*; serial* fiction; poetry*; and even articles on the weather all appeared in the pages of the *Metropolitan Magazine*, originally entitled the *Metropolitan: A Monthly Journal of Literature, Science, and the Fine Arts*. Captain Frederick Marryat*, who previously had a financial interest in the journal, renamed it after buying out his business partners in 1832.

The magazine built its reputation around its serial fiction. Marryat was one of the first to recognize the aesthetic and financial necessity of retaining audience interest from issue to issue. Although other magazines published long fiction in the 1830s, the stories tended to be self-contained. Marryat himself wrote two complete serials for the magazine, 'Jacob Faithful' and 'Japhet, in Search of a Father', and published portions of three other full-length works. While he was not as skilled as Charles Dickens* in structuring narratives, Marryat's nautical tales gripped audiences.

Liberal in its political orientation – it favourably

reviewed Shelley's poems – the magazine was an advocate of reform, 'hailing the cause of liberty everywhere' (Schachterle: 305), and it closely followed the debates around the First Reform Bill. The *Metropolitan Magazine* was also an early advocate of women's suffrage* with a May 1838 article 'An Outline of the Grievances of Women' averring that 'there is no post of trust, no important office, for which women are not naturally as well qualified as men' (Killham: 145). Despite the magazine's early success, it declined after Edward Howard took over as editor* in 1836. Seen as too tied to older writing styles, the magazine could not compete with modern titles like the *New Monthly Magazine*. **LML**
Sources: Killham 1958, *ODNB*, Schachterle 1983, *Waterloo*.

METROPOLITAN PRESS The continued growth of London in the nineteenth-century enhanced its role as a national and global hub of information gathering and dissemination. News* flowed into, through and out of the capital in increasing volumes through the century, driven by political* reporting, the growth of empire*, the commercial and financial power of the City and the variety and energy of a news-hungry urban population. Fleet* Street became uniquely placed to act as a central lightning rod for this constant stream of activity, and was home to titles that served not only the metropolitan elites but were also distributed widely throughout the British Isles and beyond. The London press thus served its own internal social and regional readerships, contributed substantially to a national British news media, and provided a service, and set a standard, to the English-speaking world.

If London was trailed closely by Edinburgh in the first quarter of the century as a centre of periodical publications, it gradually drew such titles south, but after the repeal of taxes 1855-1861, daily* and weekly* provincial* newspapers in cities such as Aberdeen, Birmingham, Cardiff, Dublin, Glasgow, Liverpool, Manchester, Sheffield, Newcastle and Leeds proliferated, also altering the balance. Nevertheless, until 1870 the provincial press – urban, regional and local* – remained heavily dependent on metropolitan papers and sources for news, still largely deploying scissors* and paste journalism. Access in 1870 to affordable telegraph* services through the campaigns of the Provincial Newspaper Society* bolstered their independence from the 'centre'. While study of the press has tended to focus on single titles, or locations, or niches ('provincial'*, 'metropolitan', or 'local'), research on

the national profile is now greatly facilitated by the electronic dissemination of full runs of many nineteenth-century titles across the UK. **AGJ/LRB**
Sources: Asquith 1978, Brown 1985, Lee 1978.

MEYNELL, ALICE (1847-1922) Known equally for her spare, disciplined style and often esoteric topics, Alice Meynell found a wide readership* through such periodicals as the *Dublin Review*, the *Scots Observer* and the *Pall Mall Gazette*. Meynell's career in journalism was fuelled by her marriage to fellow Catholic Wilfrid Meynell, with whom she collaborated on several magazines – drafting leaders*, reading proofs and reviewing* books. Their most extensive joint venture was *Merry England* (1883-1895), yet she simultaneously advanced her independent career, eventually writing for the *Bookman*, the *Spectator*, the *Atlantic Monthly* and other magazines. She contributed regularly to the unsigned columns* known as 'the Wares of Autolycus' in the *Pall Mall Gazette* and also used its 'Occasional Verse' feature to publish some of her poetry*.

Meynell gathered many of her *Pall Mall Gazette* essays in *The Colour of Life* (1896), *The Spirit of Place* (1899) and *Ceres' Runaway* (1909), and her substantial body of literary* criticism forms the basis of *Hearts of Controversy* (1917) and *Second Person Singular* (1921). Significantly, Meynell rejected the opportunity to contribute to the *Yellow Book*; the gesture underscores her uneasy relationship to the *fin de siècle*, at least as epitomized by figures such as Beardsley*, Wilde* and Beerbohm*. While G. K. Chesterton long ago concluded that 'it was an accident she found fame in the days of the decadents' (*Dublin Review* Jan. 1923: 5), recent revisionary scholarship has proffered a more heterogeneous model of *fin de siècle* literary culture. Meynell helped to revitalize the familiar essay, using it to posit new understandings of subjectivity and autonomy. Her experimental approach to her subjects – including women's experiences and contributions to history – helped to imbue her journalism with a progressive edge that, while 'less politically overt than others', was no less instrumental to the development of female aestheticism. In 1897 she became president of the Society of Women Journalists*. **MF**
Sources: Badeni 1981, Meynell, 1929, Schaffer 2000, Schaffer 2003, Seeley 1998.

MIDDLES ' Middles' are articles appearing after political leaders* and before book reviews*, typically in weeklies*, and notably in the *Saturday Review*. Leslie Stephen* in his biography of his brother describes James Fitzjames Stephen's* artful and anticipated middles as akin to lay sermons (*Life* 178). Their author collected his *Saturday Review* middles in *Essays by a Barrister* (1862) and *Horae Sabbaticae* (1892). **LR**

Sources: *ODNB*, Smith 1988, Stephen 1895.

MILES, EUSTACE HAMILTON (1868-1948) Eustace Hamilton Miles, journalist, author and athlete, was the son of a bookseller who was later associated with publishers* Simpkin, Marshall & Co. Eustace Miles was educated at Marlborough College where he became a close friend of the future novelist E. F. Benson. Together they edited* the college magazine the *Malburian*. After Cambridge, Miles became an amateur athletic champion, but he published over many years a prodigious number of primers and popular how-to volumes on topics ranging from athletics to classics to food to essay writing. Among these, for example, are sporting books for Hurst & Blackwell's Imperial Athletic Library (1902-1905) that he edited with Benson. More elusive but nevertheless indicative of similar prolific contributions to the press under various combinations of his name and initials are pieces largely on athletics and travel-related topics in *Badminton Magazine* (1898), *Outing: the Gentleman's Magazine of Sport, Travel, and Outdoor Life* (1900,1902-1903), the *Windsor Magazine* (1900), the *Humane Review* (1901), *Literary World* (1901) and *Outlook: a Family Paper* (1901). There is evidence of the recycling of their contents into later volumes, although it seems unlikely from the sporadic evidence found that all, or even most, of Miles's turn-of-the century books appeared initially in the press. In 1903 Miles became assistant editor* of the *Magazine of Sport and Health*. **DHL/LRB**

Sources: Masters 1991, C19 Masterlist online, *ODNB*.

MILITARY PERIODICALS Periodicals devoted to the armed services emerged primarily before 1850. The first of these, the *Military Register*, was short-lived (March 1814-April 1823). The *United Service Gazette*, however, lasted out the century and beyond (Feb. 1833-Dec. 1921). Its less successful rival, the *Naval and Military Gazette*, ran from February 1833 to February 1886; the *Broad Arrow*, begun later, also persisted into the new century (July 1868-April 1917). At mid-century others were added to the chief early periodicals: the *Civil Service Gazette* (Jan. 1853-Nov. 1926) and the *Army and Navy Gazette* (Jan. 1860-Sept. 1957). A late addition was the *Admiralty and Horse Guards' Gazette* (Nov. 1884-Jan. 1901). Promotions and transfers

in the army were officially recorded in the *London Gazette* (1665-1877) from 1762.

In addition to these specialist journals, more general publications were also important for the armed services. These general titles, which ran many service-related advertisements*, recorded ship sailings, provided information about career changes, discussed social and political issues affecting the armed forces*, invited correspondence*, played a part in urging service reform, especially in the army and some even published poetry* and illustrations*. The *Metropolitan*, later the *Metropolitan Magazine*, under the editorship* of Captain Frederick Marryat*, published a number of naval adventure serials*, including his own. *Blackwood's Magazine* was hospitable to stories and articles about the army throughout the century. Aside from battle reports during wartime, which at the beginning of the century were subject to significant delays, the daily* and weekly* papers rarely reported on the services, though bad behaviour of enlisted men might make the news. William Russell*, reporting* the Crimean War for the London *Times*, is credited with changing journalism about the services, especially since his reports indicted army administrators for incompetence and sympathized with the conditions of common soldiers. Subsequent reporting of wars* throughout the empire received greater attention, climaxing with coverage of the Boer War* at the end of the century, when the young Winston Churchill served as a correspondent for the *Morning Post*. **JRR**

Sources: *CBEL*, Lalumia 1984, Tucker 1994.

MILL, JOHN STUART (1806-1873) Journalist, editor*, proprietor*, political philosopher and reformer, John Stuart Mill had a prodigious appetite for disseminating his passions through political* journalism. Between 1822 and his death he contributed to over 32 periodicals and newspapers. Mill's output can be divided between political and philosophical* theory, disseminated in monthly and quarterly* periodicals, and radical political activism channelled through newspapers. He used 28 different signatures in his writing, from 'A' signifying 'Antiquus', to 'Friend of Science', his initials or his full name.

Mill regarded his full-time work as a clerk at the East India Company, a post which he held for 35 years, as a rest from his 'own pursuits' as a philosopher, political reformer, journalist, editor and periodical proprietor, all undertaken in addition to his employment. At 16 his first letter on politics appeared in the *Traveller*. He went on to write over

420 items in 13 newspapers, the most significant in the *Examiner**, the *Morning Chronicle** and the *Daily News**. Seeking new principles for political reform, he was inspired by the 1830 revolution in Paris and wrote on French politics for Fonblanque's *Examiner*, producing a series of articles on 'The Spirit of the Age'. Mill's support for the Radical members of the 1832 Parliament also appeared in the *Examiner*.

Mill contributed to 19 periodicals, the bulk of his work (103 items) appearing in the *Fortnightly Review**, *Fraser's Magazine**, the *Westminster Review** and the *Edinburgh Review**. In 1824, the utilitarian philosopher Jeremy Bentham had launched the *Westminster Review** with Mill contributing articles on politics, history* and economics plus book reviews*. Ten years later he became unofficial editor of Sir William Molesworth's new *London Review**, a replacement for the previous *Westminster Review* which Molesworth subsequently bought in 1836, forming the *London and Westminster Review*. That Mill's father, James Mill, also wrote articles for the *Review*, which were outside his editorial control, forced Mill into a new policy of permitting signed or initialled contributions which recognized their adherence to the periodical's aims but signalled that they did not necessarily concur with the editor's opinion. After his father's death in 1836, Mill felt free to improve the *Westminster's* political influence by extending the variety of issues and writers. With the *Review* running at a loss, he took over as proprietor for three years in 1837 and his last article, on the philosophical implications of Coleridge, coincided with the transfer of ownership to William Hickson* on condition that the original name of the *Westminster Review* be reinstated. After his marriage to Harriet Taylor in 1851, and with his new parliamentary career, Mill's focus shifted increasingly from journalism to philosophical writing and to his political campaigns, such as the enfranchisement of women. Yet even after his retirement to Avignon in 1868, articles still found their way to the *Fortnightly Review*. CL
Sources: Britton 1969, Mill 1969, Online Library of Liberty, *Wellesley*.

MILLAIS, JOHN EVERETT (1829-1896) While the majority of the leading Pre-Raphaelite artists, including Burne-Jones, Ford Madox Brown, Holman Hunt* and Dante Gabriel Rossetti, published little of their work in magazines*, the prodigiously talented artist and illustrator* John Everett Millais contributed widely to the periodical press. His drawings in magazines were immediately praised

and prized, and as early as 1866 a volume called *Millais's Collected Illustrations* had been published* by Alexander Strahan*. One of his series of illustrations*, 'The Parables of the Lord', originally produced in book form, showed such a mastery of the wood engraved* medium that the plates were sold to *Good Words**, where the designs were triumphantly republished in 1863 before further reissues in book form.

Millais was fortunate to have found favour with such outstanding engravers as the Dalziel brothers*, who commissioned the 'Parables' after successful early collaborations*, and Joseph Swain*, who worked with him on illustrations for a number of periodicals. Millais's high reputation as an illustrator had originally depended on his work for *Once a Week** beginning in 1859 and the *Cornhill** in the early 1860s, where he had published both single illustrations and series of images to accompany Trollope's* *Framley Parsonage* (1860-1861) and the *Small House at Allington* (1863-1864). *Good Words**, *London Society** and *St. Paul's Magazine** (a further set of Trollope illustrations, this time for *Phineas Finn*) all used his work in the early 1860s, and even the *Illustrated London News** and *Punch** published single examples of his work. Millais's many drawings for magazines in the 1860s represented both for contemporaries and for subsequent critics some of the highest achievements of monochrome wood engraving as an expressive medium. BM
Sources: Engen 1990, Houfe 1978, Goldman 1994, *ODNB*, Reid 1928, Suriano 2005, White 1897.

MILLER, FLORENCE FENWICK (1854-1935) Florence Fenwick Miller, whose career as columnist, editor* and leader* writer spanned 40 years, was one of the most prolific and influential women journalists of her day. Her introduction to journalism came fortuitously in her teens while being coached in Edinburgh for matriculation by a tutor who happened to be a news editor for the *Edinburgh Courant**. Though trained in medicine, she practised only briefly. Instead she used her specialist knowledge in early articles in the 1870s, and finally for the *Fortnightly Review** on 'Pioneer Women in Medicine' (1924).

Between 1883 and 1890 her 'Filomena's Letter' column* was syndicated* in provincial* newspapers. During this period she was also writing leaders for two dailies*, producing freelance articles and books, notably her biography of Harriet Martineau*, serving as a School Board member, as well as establishing her reputation as a talented platform speaker, and embarking on what were to be her two most significant journalistic achievements, her widely-praised column in a metropolitan* weekly* and her role as a campaigning editor.

In 1886 the *Illustrated London News** launched her 'Ladies' Column', later called the 'Ladies' Page. It was to run for 32 years. Though she covered the staples of a women's column and was acutely aware of her paper's core middle-class* readership*, she lost no opportunity to promote those feminist politics* and women's causes, particularly women's suffrage, for which she fought on the platform.

At the end of the eighties she took on the editorship of *Outward Bound*, and later its companion *Homeward Bound*, both intended for circulation* in the colonies. As well as contributing letterpress herself, she recruited other writers, including James Payn*, a fellow *Illustrated London News* columnist, and Henrietta Stannard*. Practical experience of what editorship involves must have proved useful when in 1895 she acquired the failing *Woman's Signal** to which she had contributed, turning it into an effective, persuasive voice for the suffrage cause by drawing on the best strategies of New Journalism*. She increased advertising* and rewarded readers who recruited new subscribers. True to her desire for influence rather than profit, she had no objection to provincial* editors plagiarizing it for copy. When she finally closed the paper in 1899, a contributory factor to its demise was surely the sheer amount of unpaid work involved.

Though her style could be acerbic, whether as columnist or editor, she was rarely strident, winning praise from writers as disparate as journalist Mary Billington* and Oscar Wilde*. She was elected to the Institute of Journalists*. **BMO**

Sources: *ODNB*, Onslow 2000, Onslow 2005, Van Arsdel 2001.

MILLER, HUGH (1802-1856) Hugh Miller, born in Cromarty on the Scottish coast, contributed articles on the herring fishery and other topics to local* papers such as the *Inverness Courier**. He also worked as an amateur geologist, discovering fossil fishes in the Old Red Sandstone at Cromarty. Miller belonged to the evangelical, 'non-intrusionist' wing of the Church of Scotland, who were devoted to restoring the Church's freedom from secular interference. He was recruited to edit* the Edinburgh-based *Witness**, a bi-weekly paper founded in support of the non-intrusionist cause. The first issue appeared on 15 January 1840. Through his editorship and later proprietorship* of the *Witness*

Miller became a distinguished and influential journalist and a leading figure in the so-called 'Disruption' which led to the establishment of the Free Church of Scotland in 1843.

Under Miller the circulation* of the *Witness* rose rapidly and soon had the highest readership* among Edinburgh newspapers. The paper blended news* with comment and criticism on a wide range of topics. His phenomenally successful book *The Old Red Sandstone* (1841), by which he became a leading popular exponent of geology, was first serialized* in the *Witness*. Miller's success as an editor was based on his passionate belief in the cause of freedom for the Scottish church, but his influence on Free Church policy diminished after 1843. Many of his articles on natural science*, and his contributions to the public debate on pre-Darwinian evolutionary ideas, were combined into popular and substantial books. **DHL**

Sources: Bayne 1871, Leask 1896, Mackenzie 1905, *ODNB*, Shortland 1995, Shortland 1996.

MILNER, ALFRED (1854-1925) Alfred Milner, journalist, and public servant, was born in Germany. His life-long commitment to public service was fostered while he was a student at Oxford. It was reinforced, among other continuing Oxford influences, by his early years as a staff journalist at the *Pall Mall Gazette**, which he joined in 1882, having worked for a time as a free-lance journalist on political* and foreign affairs. The *Pall Mall Gazette*, then edited* by John Morley*, included in its pages the influential journalism of W. T. Stead*, who later succeeded Morley as editor*. Stead was an outspoken advocate of social reform and imperialism* and these 'formative years' (*ODNB*) at the *Gazette* helped to shape Milner, the future colonial administrator and political economist.

Milner withdrew as Stead's assistant editor in 1885 to concentrate on his political career, for which he is best remembered (Saxon-Mills: 41, 67). E. T. Cook*, who took over his role at the paper, had originally been invited by Milner to join the staff full-time in that year, and the two men remained life-long correspondents. Their friendship no doubt influenced the pro-war position on South Africa – 'Milner's war', as it was termed (*ODNB*)– in the *Daily News**, which Cook edited from 1896.

Milner's growing distance from Stead's style and political positions, however, gave Milner further reasons for leaving the *Pall Mall Gazette* in 1885. He was increasingly embarrassed by Stead's crusades in its pages: 'it is bad enough while one agrees with Stead, but when one differs violently about

three things out of every four', he complained to Cook in July 1885. Stead recalled Milner's role with more equanimity in 1899, noting that Milner functioned as an effective guardian 'armed with ruthless pen', tempering inflammatory rhetoric and editing out needlessly offensive material: 'he was always putting water in my wine' Stead notes, 'always combing out the knots in the tangled mane of the P. M. G'. (Stead, cited in Saxon-Mills: 55). **FD**
Sources: *ODNB*, Porter 1973, Saxon-Mills 1921.

MILNER, MARY (1797-1863) Mary Compton Milner's career as an editor* began in 1844 with the *Christian Mother's Magazine*. It reflected Milner's maternal experience combined with her theoretical and Christian background and gave expression to her extensive scholarly interests in the sciences* and the arts. When it was re-formed as the *Englishwoman's Magazine and Christian Mother's Miscellany* (1846-1854), it took on a feminist flavour discussing women and literature* and featuring biographies of notable women such as Maria Edgeworth. Finally it reverted to the more acceptable formula of Christian content with the *Christian Lady's Magazine* (1855-1857). In 1850 Milner took on editing *Fisher's Juvenile Scrapbook,* a mixed bag of 'amusement' for children* within a Christian context. Her final stint as editor was for Joseph Milner's *Essentials of Christianity* in 1855. **CL**
Source: *ODNB*.

MIND: A QUARTERLY REVIEW OF PSYCHOLOGY AND PHILOSOPHY (1876-) *Mind: A Quarterly Review of Psychology and Philosophy* was Britain's first philosophical* journal, founded and subsidized by the Scottish psychologist Alexander Bain*. Before launching the journal, Bain gained the support of prominent British philosophers and psychologists such as Herbert Spencer*, and he appointed George Croom Robertson*, his former student at Aberdeen University, as its first editor* (1876-1891). *Mind* aimed to be impartial and representative. In its first decades, the journal published articles by an impressive roster of writers: Charles Darwin, William James, George Henry Lewes*, Francis Galton, Josiah Royce and F. H. Bradley, among others, and even a piece by James Sully* on 'George Eliot's'* philosophy. *Mind* helped to advance professional academic psychology but its principal importance lay increasingly in the field of philosophy. It was also one of the early intellectually specialist journals along with *Nature** (1869ff) and *English Historical Review* (1886ff).

After Robertson's resignation, the philosopher Henry Sidgwick began funding the journal, organizing, before his death, a Mind Association to support the periodical with income from subscriptions. When the Association took over in 1900, some members hoped to bring *Mind* under the control of Oxford University, resulting in a period of tension among those involved. George Frederick Stout, editor from 1892 until 1920, began a new series, but made only minor changes to the journal. The *Proceedings of the Aristotelian Society,* which had been founded in 1887, became an important rival to the journal during Stout's editorship, although for a brief period (1896-1899) *Mind* published the *Proceedings.* Stout, like Robertson, envisaged a journal that would integrate psychology and philosophy, but with the appearance of the *British Journal of Psychology* in 1904, articles on scientific* psychology began to disappear from *Mind.* The word 'psychology', however, was not dropped from the title until 1974, when the journal was renamed *Mind: A Quarterly Review of Philosophy.* **SA**
Sources: Bain 1893, Hamlyn 1976, Passmore 1976, Quinton 1976, Sorley 1926.

MINING JOURNAL AND COMMERCIAL GAZETTE (1835-) Founded by Henry English in 1835, the *Mining Journal and Commercial Gazette* was begun as an illustrated* weekly* providing technical information, share prices and comment to mine owners, technicians and investors. By 1837 – as the *Magazine of Natural History* (1828-1870) affirmed – it was in 'undisputed possession of the field', beating off inferior imitators and establishing a 'very considerable' circulation*. Its pre-eminence continued throughout the nineteenth century, as it grew from eight pages to 16 and then 28, with its price* fluctuating around the 6d mark. Its title changed to *Mining Journal, Railway and Commercial Gazette* in 1844 and, again, to *Mining Journal* in 1980.

Central to the *Mining Journal* was its large correspondence* section where mine* managers in Britain and across the globe reported on ground quality, the standard of ores extracted, drainage problems and the efficacy of new techniques and technologies. Useful to managers of other mines, such reports also provided valuable inside information to the investor, since all of these factors had a bearing on the cost of extraction. Listings of share prices were a weekly fixture, alongside market* prices of metals, coal and other minerals. The journal also provided an overview of new patents and carried advertisements* for machinery, shares and analytical chemists offering to assess the quality and composition of ores. That the *Mining Journal* was the organ of capital rather than of labour was reflected in its attitude towards strikes, shut-outs and industrial disputes. A leader* of 1 February 1890 argued that agitations in favour of a 10 to 15 per cent pay increase 'show a lack of sagacity and discretion, but they are not so hurtful as the proposal for an eight hours' day'. Yet while it was critical of the militant tendency, the *Mining Journal* was not altogether blind to workers' rights. It found sympathy with the 'calm and moderate' attitude expressed by the trade unionist Thomas Burt and endorsed his motto, 'conciliate and arbitrate'. It is still considered one of the world's foremost sources of information on mining. MaT

Sources: BL Catalogue, *ODNB*, Vann and Van-Arsdel 1994, *Waterloo*, Mining Journal online.

MINING PRESS The massive demand for raw materials generated by the industrial revolution created a wealth of opportunities for entrepreneurs, and heavy investment in mining both at home and abroad – encouraged by impressive returns – became one of the key elements of industrial expansion in nineteenth-century Britain. In contrast to trades such as building or electrical engineering, where skilled and semi-skilled labourers worked in collaboration with professionals and the periodical literature often attempted to address all these groups, the mining business was from the beginning characterized by a stark opposition of capital and labour, which was reflected in the mining press. Aside from a number of technical journals – like *Mining Engineering* (1896-1912) and *Iron Trade Exchange* (1847-1905) – which, being aimed at mine managers and engineers, sat somewhere in between, mining periodicals tended to cater either for capitalists or for labourers. Journals directed at proprietors* and speculative capitalists offered comprehensive listings of share prices alongside reports on mineral deposits discovered, technical developments in mining and smelting and new patents. Henry English's *Quarterly Mining Review* (1830-1835) and his (weekly) *Mining Journal*＊ attained an early prominence, but later examples such as the *Mining World and Engineering and Commercial Record* (1871-1962) were also significant. At the level of the investor, the nature of the business did not matter so much as the likelihood of its profitability, and there was therefore scope for considerable crossover with other industries. Transport* journals such as John Robertson's *Railway Record* (1844-1901) and George Bradshaw's *Railway Gazette*＊ (1845-1882) survived the collapse in the fortunes of railway speculation that began in 1846 partly by adding coverage of mining, changing

their names to *Railway Record, Mining Register and Joint Stock Companies' Reporter* and the *Railway Gazette and Mining Chronicle* respectively. Financial periodicals* like the *Bankers' Circular*＊ and the *Financial News*＊ carried information on mining alongside other industries. There was also a branch of periodical literature dedicated to mining in the colonies, with the *British Colonist* (1896-1899) touting itself as 'a reliable review of colonial mining and commercial securities', and a variety of often short-lived publications – like *Australian Gold Fields* (1894-1895) and the *British Columbia Review and North American Mining Journal* (1898-1901), both published in London – dedicated to mining prospects in one specific colony.

The mining press looked very different to those actually digging minerals out of the dirt. Miners, often set to work while still children, were among the least-educated sections of the proletariat. Attempts by middle-class* Owenites, socialists or trade unionists to turn this group into first a readership* for periodical literature, and then an historical agency capable of shaking capitalism out of its disregard for human life, tended to stutter and fail. The *British Miner and General Newsman* (1862-1867), 'a publication devoted to the interests of the working miners of the United Kingdom', was a pro-trade unionist weekly that changed its name first to the *Miner* (1863), then to the *Miner and Workman's Advocate* (1863-1865), then to the *Workman's Advocate* (1865-1866) and finally to the *Commonwealth* (1866-1867), before disappearing completely. The trade unionist, potter and editor William Owen – a relative of Robert Owen* and arguably the most important advocate of the labour newspaper system – founded and edited the West Midlands-based *Labour Press, Miner's and Workmen's Examiner* (1873-1879) (which also changed its name to the *Miner* from 1875) as an 'organ of underground labour' intended to be the working-class answer to *The Times*＊. Conflicting pressures from trade union* leaders, more extreme radicals and printers prevented it from gaining the distribution* and readership that might have allowed it to shape the development of British industrial relations. It was absorbed into the *Wolverhampton Times and Midland Examiner* and the *Evening Echo* before folding in 1879. At this stage, at least, trade union organization was more effectively prosecuted through large-scale congresses than through journalistic endeavour. MaT

Sources: Harrison, 1974, Jones 1982, Thompson 1963, *Waterloo*.

Figure 42: An instructive title page of the *Mirror*, 2 Nov. 1822.

MIRROR OF LITERATURE, AMUSEMENT, AND INSTRUCTION (1822-1847) The *Mirror of Literature*, as it was commonly known, was begun by the stationer, publisher*, printer and entrepreneur John Limbird*, whose cut-rate editions of novels such as *The Mysteries of Udolpho* and *The Vicar of Wakefield* had already brought him financial success. Following in the footsteps of such popular miscellanies* as the *Hive*, the 2d *Mirror* was intended to provide quality reading material for the lower middle classes*, those who, disdaining the more sensational penny* papers, might wish to buy something like the *Gentleman's Magazine* but could not afford it. It was almost immediately successful, quickly achieving a circulation* of 80,000 and above, and was the first of the cheap* periodicals to last more than two years.

Though it was comprised mainly of excerpts and clippings from novels and other periodicals, the 16-page* *Mirror*, published weekly* in a compact 21cm format*, also contained original articles and advertised, among other things, its 'historical* narratives, sketches of society', pieces on 'discoveries in the arts and sciences'* and 'useful domestic* hints', along with serial fiction* and poetry. The magazine was notably apolitical*. Contributors included Hector Berlioz, Mrs Bushby, the Countess of Blessington*, Douglas Jerrold*, Fanny E. Lacy and Frank Marryatt. The *Mirror* was distinguished from some of its competitors, such as the *Cheap Magazine*, by being printed on good paper*, as well as by having numerous illustrations* of a fairly high quality, which contributed greatly to its success.

The *Mirror*'s first editor*, Thomas Byerley, has been referred to as a hack, but certainly saw himself as a serious and important journalist. The magazine's popularity, and its position as the first of its kind to really succeed, later led him to claim that he had 'created a new era in the history of periodical literature'. His editorship was followed by that of John A. Heraud, Percy B. St John*, and John Timbs*, who had begun as Limbird's shop boy and had then worked as the magazine's principal compiler before editing it in two separate stints. After its 15-year run as a weekly, the *Mirror* briefly became a monthly* called the *Mirror Monthly Magazine* (Oct. 1847-Dec. 1849), and in its last year, 1849 to 1850, was published as the *London Review*. In each incarnation it was not only popular* but generally well respected, and when its originator, Limbird, died in 1883, his obituary* designated him 'the father of our periodical literature'. FCA

Sources: Altick 1957, King and Plunkett 2005, *Waterloo*.

MIRROR OF THE STAGE, OR THE NEW DRAMATIC CENSOR (1822-1824) This short-lived monthly* focused on the publication of 'memoirs of the principal actors; criticisms of the new pieces and performers as they appear; anecdotes, original essays, &c'. (12 Aug. 1822). At 6d, it offered its readers an engraved* coloured title page and colour plates. In the fourth issue, it was announced that the entire copyright* to the *New Theatrical Inquisitor* had been acquired by the present owners, and that the staff of that journal would now join forces with the writers on the *Mirror*. This did not, however, prevent the journal from suffering an early demise. OD

Source: *Waterloo*.

MISCELLANY Deriving from *miscellanea*, a Latin culinary term for a hash or stew, the word 'miscellany' was employed in early English print culture for collective works such as the poetic anthology, *Tottel's Miscellany* (1557). Since most serials are miscellaneous in both content and authorship, the term sometimes occurred simply as a synonym for a periodical.

But from the early eighteenth century, periodicals principally intended to inform, such as newspapers, were followed by those designed variously to instruct and amuse, reviews* and journals, for example. The word 'miscellany' tended to imply lighter and less serious fare. The *Monthly Miscellany; or, Memoirs for the Curious* (1707) was a typical title.

In the nineteenth century, 'miscellany' continued to imply diversity of content as well as authorship, and it differed little in connotation from 'magazine'*. Indeed, many serials, including both weeklies* and monthlies, contained both terms in their long titles, the *Scots Magazine, and Edinburgh Literature Miscellany* (1804-1817), for example. *Bentley's Miscellany**, initially edited by Charles Dickens*, was perhaps the best-known Victorian periodical to use the term prominently. The title originally advertised had been the *Wits' Miscellany*, which prompted Bentley's enemies to jest that he had gone to the opposite extreme in making the change. The following list of contemporary short titles gives an indication of the range of possible conjunctions: the *Asiatic Miscellany*, the *Botanical Miscellany*, the *Christian Miscellany*, the *Halfpenny Miscellany*, the *Lady's Miscellany*, the *Oxford Miscellany*, the *Secular Miscellany* and the *Weekly Miscellany*. Common collocations indicating sub-genre* are: 'literary miscellany', typically fiction, verse, essays, and reviews; 'news miscellany', usually a summary of the week's news* with literary* features and entertainment material. It was only after the turn of the twentieth century that the term lost its currency. GL

Sources: *Waterloo, Wellesley.*

MISSIONARY CHRONICLE (1813-1836); MISSIONARY MAGAZINE AND CHRONICLE (1837-1866); CHRONICLE OF THE LONDON MISSIONARY SOCIETY (1867-1935); WORLD MISSION (1966-1967) The *Missionary Magazine and Chronicle* and its succeeding titles were the organ of the London Missionary Society, a mainly Congregationalist organization which, despite its name, had branches, or 'Auxiliary Societies', throughout Britain. In 1813 the *Evangelical Magazine* had become the *Evangelical Magazine and Missionary Chronicle*, the *Missionary Chronicle* being appended at the back of the magazine, apart from a few separate copies which were sent to the Auxiliary Societies.

Then in June 1836 the *Missionary Chronicle* became the *Missionary Magazine and Chronicle*, and began to be published separately as well as continuing to appear as an appendix to the *Evangelical Magazine and Chronicle*. (In fact, the January 1837 issue carried the title *Missionary Magazine*, and the new name was only used consistently from February 1837 onwards.) As well as enjoying its own sales (by subscription at the price* of 1d), it thus also continued to share the *Evangelical Magazine and Chronicle's* circulation*. This stood at 13,000 in 1837, although a notice soliciting advertisers* in 1817 had boasted that 'at a moderate computation' the *Evangelical Magazine and Missionary Chronicle* was 'read by a hundred thousand individuals'.

Starting out with 16 pages, by 1865 the *Missionary Magazine and Chronicle* had grown to 24 pages. Its reports of missionary* activity were peppered with sensational accounts, and lurid illustrations, of human sacrifice, torture and attacks by wild animals, although the editors* claimed they included such material with 'unfeigned reluctance'. Like other missionary magazines it was preoccupied by 'idolatry' and the enthrallment of non-European peoples to 'puerile and degrading superstition'. Each May the magazine* published the agenda of the upcoming General Meeting of the London Missionary Society, and each June it carried a report on the Meeting.

In January 1867 the magazine was relaunched as the *Chronicle of the London Missionary Society* (1867-1935). Edited by the Rev. Joseph Mullens (who was still in place in 1879), its 20 monthly pages cost 1d, a price that remained stable to the end of the century. Mullens's leader in the first issue under the new title acknowledged that some progress had been made in 'explaining to heathen people the design, the doctrine and the fruit of Christianity' since the launch of the journal, and claimed for its issuing body much of the credit for this. But there was still work to be done, particularly in India and China, and Mullens appealed for greater generosity on the part of the donors who supported the Society. The *Chronicle* itself, it was acknowledged, was run at a loss.

In January 1892 the 'New Series' began with a switch to a larger format* and an increase in size* to 24 pages. The larger dimensions meant that it could no longer be parcelled with the *Evangelical Magazine*, so that this date marks the end point of the relationship with that publication. The Rev. George Cousins was now editor, though by 1900 – while Cousins remained joint foreign secretary of the Society – The Rev. D. H. Gaunt had taken over as editor. **SdB/MaT**

Sources: 19CBLN, 19CUKP, *Waterloo.*

MISSIONARY HERALD (1819-1911) The *Missionary Herald* was the organ of the Baptist

Missionary Society* (from January 1884 onwards the masthead* reads 'The Missionary Herald of the Baptist Missionary Society') with Edward Bean Underhill, the Society's long-standing secretary, contributing regular articles. For most of the nineteenth century it comprised 16 pages, increasing to 40 by the 1890s, measuring 14.6 cm by 22.5 cm, and priced* 1d, apart from a brief rise to 2d from December 1880 to January 1881. Sold by subscription and distributed* by post, at the end of 1876 circulation* stood at 5,500, rising to 28,500 by 1886 and with a reported 37,000 distributed copies in the months prior to January 1890. Issues in the 1850s and 1860s might have only one or two illustrations*, but they could be of somewhat sensational subjects, such as a tiger attack, or a scantily clad female peasant. Alternatively there might be a fold-out map. By the 1880s there were more illustrations, many engraved* from photographs*.

In 1859 the *Missionary Herald* reported a Baptist Missionary Society resolution to establish a mission to China, providing another topic for the magazine in addition to reported missionary* work in India, Ceylon, Africa, and the Caribbean, detailing types of 'idolatry' and the 'depravity' it entailed. Most issues carried a list of letters received from overseas, acknowledgements of items donated to the Society and ending with detailed accounts of financial contributions to the Society. In 1896 the *Zenana Missionary Herald*, 'Being the Monthly Report of the Work of the Ladies' Association', merged with the *Missionary Herald* and appeared at the back of each issue. In 1912 the *Missionary Herald* became the *Herald*. SdB

Sources: *ODNB, Waterloo*.

MISSIONARY PRESS The missionary press flooded Britain with morally improving texts in the nineteenth century. The archetypal religious* magazine emerged in 1760 and, according to Altholz, 'immediately established itself as the dominant type of publication for over a century' (1989: 5). It retained this dominance until the mid-nineteenth century when it was succeeded by the temperance* press. Established by highly competitive* missionary societies, and funded by donations, these periodicals were a key means of uniting religious communities throughout Britain and beyond. The London Missionary Society, the 'largest evangelical institution peddling its spiritual wares in the arena of empire' (McClintock: 261), was the dominant figure in the market. The London Missionary Society generated an extraordinary amount of written and visual material to publicize their evangelical activities and to foster support – financial and moral – for missionary work at home and abroad.

From its inception, the London Missionary Society published annual* reports and the occasional *Transactions of the Missionary Society* (1804-1818), although official communication initially issued from the non-denominational *Evangelical Magazine** (1793-1904). Later, annual reports were recycled in the Society's *Missionary Sketches* (1818-1865), the series of titles which made up the *Missionary Chronicle* (1813-1967) and the *Report of the Directors ... to the General Meeting of the Missionary Society* (1815-1940). As the century progressed, the London Missionary Society diversified its publications for different markets*. Each periodical had a clearly defined audience – women, children, youth groups, and so forth – and ranged from cheap pamphlets to formally published magazines. Children's* magazines were keenly sought after; Topham notes that all the successful juvenile magazines 'of the first three decades of the century* were issued either by evangelical organizations or by prominent evangelical clergy' (2004: 60). Like other religious tracts, missionary publications became 'a ubiquitous part of the social landscape' (Altick: 103). They were distributed in great quantities through schools, travelling missionary caravans, and charitable organizations. Often ideologically crude, moralistic and frankly imperialist*, the missionary press influenced evangelical Britons in numbers of which more sophisticated journalists could only dream. AnJ

Sources: Altholz 1989, Altick 1957, Barringer 1997, McClintock 1995, Topham 2004.

MITCHEL, JOHN (1815-1875) John Mitchel was an Irish journalist* and newspaper editor*. Born a Presbyterian in the north of Ireland, he nonetheless embraced Irish nationalism. After Thomas Davis's* death in 1845, Charles Gavan Duffy* persuaded Mitchel to write for his newspaper the *Nation**. His articles involved the paper in a trial for seditious libel in 1846, but Mitchel remained the *Nation*'s main contributor and a pivotal member of Young Ireland* until December 1847. Having embraced more radical views, and founded the weekly newspaper *United Irishman** in February 1848, he was arrested in May 1848 for advocating armed rebellion against British rule, and sentenced to transportation.

He escaped Australia in 1853 and fled to the United States, where he edited or contributed to numerous newspapers, including the pro-slavery *Southern Citizen* (Knoxville, 1857-1859), the

Confederate *Richmond Enquirer* (1862-1864) and *Richmond Examiner* (1864), and the *Irish Citizen* (New York, 1867-1872). He was also Paris correspondent of the *Irishman** in 1860-1862. Ireland remained the main subject of his journalism, especially of his influential political* essays, such as 'Jail Journal' (1854) and 'The Last Conquest of Ireland. (Perhaps)' (1861), which he serialized in the New York *Citizen** and the Dublin *Nation* respectively. He died in Ireland. Mitchel was a compelling and controversial writer who shaped modern Irish identity through his journalism. **FB**

Sources: Duffy 1898, *ODNB*, PGIL *Eirdata*.

MITCHELL'S NEWSPAPER PRESS DIRECTORY (1846-) Charles Mitchell, an advertising* agent, began publishing the *Newspaper Press Directory* (sometimes with subtitle *and Advertiser's Guide*) in 1846 in order 'to form a guide to advertisers in their selection of journals as mediums more particularly suitable for their announcements'. The descriptive entries of the individual newspapers vary in length and characterize the publications in terms of points likely to be salient to advertisers*, listing the title, day and place of publication, price*, area of circulation*, publisher or proprietor*, and the political*, religious*, economic, and class* advocacy of the paper. Motivated by commercial concerns, the descriptions of the papers, though supposedly impartial, are generally friendly. The directory was published intermittently in 1846, 1847, 1851 and 1854, but from 1856 it was published annually. The early octavo volumes are primarily geographical indexes covering London, the provinces, the Channel Islands and the Isle of Man, Scotland, Ireland and Wales, with alphabetical cross-listing and listing by counties. The first change in format* came in 1854 when the size was increased to 'extra imperial' and the price* reduced to one florin.

When Mitchell died in 1859, editorship* passed to his adopted stepson Walter Wellsman. In the 1860 volume, Wellsman expanded the scope of the directory by adding an index of magazines* and periodicals and a national newspaper map. Subsequent additions include an index of continental papers (1878), an index of class papers and periodicals (1879), an index of American papers (1880), an index of the daily* press (1881) and a colonial supplement* (1886). Along with the listings and indexes, the directory also contained essays concerning the history of the press* in articles such as 'The Newspaper Press – its Origin and Progress' (1846-1856, 1859), and 'The Power and Character of the Press' (1851-1854); legal matters in articles such as 'The

Law of Newspapers' (1854-1863, 1873-1876) and 'The Law of Copyright and Libel' (1896); and social issues such as 'Women's Work in the London Provincial Press' (1897), and 'The Development of Class Journalism' (1899). In 1949 the directory was bought by the Benn publishing* house, and its title was changed to *Benn's Press Directory* in 1978. It is still published as *Benn's Media Directory*. **PZ**

Sources: Gliserman 1969, Jones 1996, Linton 1987, *ODNB*.

MODERN REVIEW: A QUARTERLY MAGAZINE (1880-1884) The *Modern Review* was an unusual attempt to create a new, serious, quarterly* intellectual review*, excluding the fiction and other entertainment prominent in the monthly* magazines* and excluding the socio-political debates in periodicals such as the *Fortnightly Review**, *Contemporary Review** and *Nineteenth Century**.

Edited* first by Richard Acland Armstrong, then by Robert Crompton Jones, the *Modern Review* focused on the ongoing intellectual struggle between science* and religion*, between a world of rational positivism and a world of faith. Articles were for the most part signed and writers wrote from both denominational and non-denominational positions, ensuring a spirit of open and free inquiry. Indicative of the material published is William Binns's 'Science, Theology, and the Evolution of Man' (April 1880) and William B. Carpenter's 'The Doctrine of Evolution in its Relation to Theism' (Oct. 1882). Contents also touch on married women's debts, medicine and morality, and the history* of religion. Of particular note for the history of journalism* was an article published by Armstrong in the first issue, 'The Story of Nineteenth Century Reviewing' (Jan. 1880) which provides an interesting overview of the development of reviewing* culture and of the centrality of periodical discourse to the formation of public opinion in the nineteenth century. Only lasting four years, the *Modern Review* never made a significant challenge to the established monthly reviews of opinion or to the old quarterlies. **MWT**

Source: *Wellesley*.

MOIR, DAVID MACBETH (1798-1851) After a grammar school education, magazine writer David Macbeth Moir was apprenticed to medicine and entered practice in 1817. By then he was contributing anonymously* to local* journals and soon sent poems* and squibs to the new *Blackwood's Edinburgh Magazine**, concealing his identity so as not to damage his medical career. After revealing himself to William Blackwood* in 1821, he became a valued advisor to the magazine and frequent contributor, especially of verse under the signature (thus he was generally known as 'Delta'). A series of yarns about a Scottish tailor named Mansie Wauch began to appear in 1824, and became Moir's best-known work.

Moir was recruited by his friend William Maginn* to write for *Fraser's Magazine** in 1830, and in addition to poems wrote several pieces on medical* issues. But his primary allegiance was always to *Blackwood's* and to the Blackwood family, to whom he was a trustworthy man of letters and personal physician. He contributed about 370 items over 35 years to *Blackwood's*, supplemented by some lengthy biographies of agronomists for Blackwood's *Quarterly Journal of Agriculture*. Despite this output he spent most of his hours in medical labour and was an authority on cholera. Though his poems were frequently reprinted in compilations and newspapers, their reputation was ephemeral. **DEL**
Sources: Aird 1852, Nolte 1955, *ODNB*, Oliphant 1897.

***MONEY MARKET REVIEW. A WEEKLY RECORD OF TRADE AND FINANCE* (1860-)** The *Money Market Review* is one of the longest-running financial newspapers. It appeared on 9 June 1860 advertising itself as 'a high-class weekly journal exclusively devoted to the consideration of Commercial and Financial topics', intended to appeal to an audience wider than those targeted by the 'Railway, Mining and Shipping Journals' (issue 1: 3). Comments in *Mitchell's Press Directory** suggest a preference for subscription by 'the highest class'* (the *Review* cost 26s a year, or 6d per issue, a price* maintained throughout its 54 years of independent existence). It quickly passed through several owners but was consistently published* over its first decade by John Atter. Its offices were in the City (Birchin Lane, and from 1874, the Royal Exchange) and it boasted insider knowledge displayed in detailed articles on stocks, shares and the finances of various public companies, including railways, banks and mines.

Correspondence* was a regular feature. The first page was given over to three columns* of advertising*, a format* maintained to the end of 1936 (May's agency handled the advertising). There were also numerous advertisements* on its back pages. On 1 March 1870 the 2d daily *Financier* ('the Business Paper for Business Men' – especially designed for commuters) began publication from the same offices. On 1 August 1914 the *Money Market Review* merged* with the *Investor's Chronicle and*

Journal of Finance, becoming the *Money Market and Investor's Chronicle*. The then editor* Geoffrey J. Holmes kept the paper going despite difficulties caused by the First World War and continued to edit the paper until his death in 1937. In 1928 the proprietors* of the paper, Holmes and Lamert, sold their stakes to a newly formed company called Financial Newspaper Proprietors. In July 1967 the *Investors Chronicle* merged with the *Stock Exchange Gazette*. **JB**
Sources: *Investment Chronicle* archives, *Mitchell's*.

***MONTH, ILLUSTRATED MAGAZINE OF LITERATURE, SCIENCE AND ART* (1864-1939)** A Roman Catholic magazine, published in London and comparable with the *Cornhill Magazine**, the *Month* was launched by Fanny Margaret Taylor, proprietor* and editor* of another Catholic journal, the *Lamp*. In its first year, the *Month* contained poetry*, fiction and articles on history*, art, and literature*. However, the direction changed when the *Month* was sold to the Jesuits of the Farm Street community in London. Taylor sold the magazine for various reasons, including a lack of profit and the belief that her spiritual advisor, Father Peter Gallwey, who had assisted in its foundation, should take charge of it.

From 1865, the *Month* became a serious periodical under the gifted editorship of the Catholic convert Henry Coleridge, great-nephew of the poet Samuel Taylor Coleridge, who was followed by another Catholic convert, R. F. Clark. The quality of the editors attracted learned writers such as the historian John Morris and the scientist Herbert Thurston, while Fanny Taylor continued her connection by contributing fiction. Issues contained reviews*, articles on topics of current concern, philosophy*, travel* and education. Illustrations* included engravings* from Walter Crane*, maps, photographs* of art works, and diagrams. Until 1882, the cover depicted St George and the Dragon, which was replaced by a table of contents until 1897 when St George returned. In 1873 the title changed to the *Month and Catholic Review* and continued as the *Month, a Catholic Magazine and Review* until 1939. **CL**
Sources: Altholz 1989, Sullivan 1984.

***MONTHLY CHRONICLE, A NATIONAL JOURNAL OF POLITICS, LITERATURE, SCIENCE AND ART* (1838-1841)** The *Monthly Chronicle* was the brainchild of Dionysius Lardner*, who founded the magazine and was its principal editor*. A monthly 'miscellany'* of around 100 pages costing 2s 6d, it attempted to bring together the diverse branches of human knowledge, alleged to be a novelty at the time, for a predominantly *national* (a word emphasized on its volume title page) and middle-class* readership*. Lardner – whose principal training was scientific – brought on board as co-proprietor* and co-editor the writer Edward Lytton Bulwer* (later Bulwer-Lytton), who was intended to oversee the magazine's coverage of art and culture, but resigned from both positions after seven months. The variety of the *Chronicle*'s content was impressive, its first year seeing the publication of an article on 'various influences on animal and vegetable bodies erroneously attributed to the moon', a piece on Handel, one on meteors and Bulwer's essay on 'Art in Fiction', a pioneering attempt to articulate an aesthetics of prose fiction.

The magazine's dedication to the dissemination of useful knowledge* was Utilitarian in origin, a fact reflected in the style and approach of the articles. These were shorter than was usual in monthly* periodicals of this kind at the time, and made the attempt to eschew technical jargon, even when dealing with potentially complicated scientific* issues. Contributors included W. J. Fox*, Baden Powell (1796-1860) and Richard Henry Horne*, but articles were anonymous* so that these well-known names could not boost the *Chronicle*'s generally poor circulation*. It was no help, either, that the magazine was considered by many to be rather dull. It initially contained no fiction except for serializations* of Bulwer's novels, one of which, *Zicci*, was abandoned in mid-flight as Bulwer lost faith in it. Robert Bell became editor in 1839 and introduced regular short stories and an increasing volume of poetry* in an attempt to invigorate the journal. But apart from this minor innovation, Bell did little to change an ailing format* and the journal's inevitable demise came under his stewardship. MaT

Sources: *ODNB, Waterloo, Wellesley.*

MONTHLY MAGAZINE (1796-1843) The *Monthly Magazine* was an influential monthly* founded and published* for its first 28 years by Richard Phillips (1767-1840). Its title changes over its lifetime – *Monthly Magazine and British Register* (1796-1825), *Monthly Magazine or, British Register of Literature, Science, and Belles Lettres* (1826-1838), *Monthly Magazine of Politics, Literature, Science, and Belles Lettres* (1839-1843) – suggest an uncertainty about the relative balance among arts, science* and politics* in its contents, and Kenneth Curry in Sullivan suggests that its contents are more political and social science-related than literary.

Phillips, its proprietor*, was an advocate of Parliamentary Reform who had been imprisoned for 18 months in 1793 for selling Thomas Paine's *Rights of Man*. A bookseller* and newspaper proprietor at the time, he continued to publish the *Leicester Herald*, which he had founded, from prison, and defiantly continued to invoke Paine later in his contributions to the *Monthly Magazine*, which he signed 'Common Sense'. The first editor, John Aikin was succeeded after a decade in 1806 by George Gregory, who only lasted until 1808. According to Aikin, quoted in Sullivan, Phillips took an active role in producing the journal, and always acted as literary* editor.

Dissenting in religion, and liberal in politics* and economics, the magazine reached a circulation* of 5,000, a healthy total, but although it was cheaper than most other monthlies at the time – 1s initially and 2s from 1800 – its sales remained just below later arrivals like *Blackwood's Edinburgh Magazine*, the *Quarterly Review*, the *Edinburgh Review*, and equal with the *New Monthly Magazine and Universal Register*, which Henry Colburn* established as a Tory alternative in 1814. In format*, Phillips' journal aped the long-established *Gentleman's Magazine*, publishing short articles on a diverse variety of topics – including issues in medicine*, theology, the various branches of science*, literature*, politics and travel – alongside correspondence*, poetry* and 'Register' contents such as lists of births and deaths, obituaries* and statistical analyses of population and weather patterns. It was liberally illustrated*, unlike the *Gentleman's Magazine* at this time. In its early days the Original Poetry section attracted contributions from Samuel Taylor Coleridge*, Robert Southey and Charles Lamb*. Critically, its reviews* stood out for their appreciation of Byron's work without 'moral' blinders, and for their translations of continental and Far Eastern poetry.

Phillips sold the magazine to Cox and Baylis in 1824, and after this the magazine became less stable and its influence went into decline. It absorbed the *European Magazine* (1782-1826) in 1826, and – circulation* having declined to around 600 – was again sold to a Captain J. B. Holland, who also became editor, in 1833. Following the political furore surrounding the passage of the reform bill in 1832, the *Monthly* complained – in a notice of January 1834 – of the 'destructive and overwhelming effects of political excitement' in literary matters. Holland was ardent in his liberalism, but he wanted to carve out a niche for fiction away from the hurly burly of party politics. Accordingly, the magazine began to publish short stories, including Charles Dickens's* first published works, the short character pieces later to be collected as *Sketches by Boz*. The briefly resurgent *Monthly* also carried pieces by William Hazlitt* and G. M. W. Reynolds*.

In 1839, now under the editorship of J. A. Heraud (1799-1887), the *Monthly Magazine* became the organ of the Syncretic Association, endeavouring to 'display the divine protheitc doctrine of *unity* as the highest point of intellectual ambition'. This esoteric turn seems likely to have contributed to the magazine's final demise. MaT

Sources: Chittick 1984, *ODNB*, 'Prospectus' 1796, Sullivan, *Waterloo*.

MONTHLY MAGAZINES The launch, in 1814, of the *New Monthly Magazine**, by the ambitious and commercially minded publisher Henry Colburn*, heralded a succession of monthly publications which sought to capture a middle-class* audience, with a new style of reviewing* and some innovative features. The magazines' readership* was larger and more diverse than that of the quarterly* reviews which dominated the reviewing scene from 1802, with the establishment of the *Edinburgh Review**. William Blackwood*, the Edinburgh bookseller, founded *Blackwood's Edinburgh Magazine** in 1817 as a direct challenge to the *Edinburgh's* Whiggish politics and to its monopoly north of the border. The *London Magazine**, in turn, under the charismatic John Scott*, was founded in 1820 in response to *Blackwood's*. In 1830 *Fraser's Magazine for Town and Country** was launched by the publisher* William Fraser, with a Tory agenda and sharing many of *Blackwood's* contributors. And in 1832, the radical publisher William Tait* founded *Tait's Edinburgh Magazine* as another challenge to William Blackwood on his home territory.

The magazines of the 1820s and 1830s deliberately targeted a growing readership which included women. Literary reviews* in the magazines, like all of their features, were shorter and more informal in tone than those in the quarterlies. The emphasis on the literary* was often a deliberate antidote to the magazines' political* agendas. With their octavo format*, the magazines resembled the quarterlies in appearance, but numbers were shorter, from 100 to 120 pages. Many magazines used double columns*, a signal that they were not to be regarded as multiple parts of a book, which was the image projected by the quarterlies.

The range of subjects for review was narrower than that of the quarterlies, the magazines again

deliberately eschewing theology, ancient literatures, and other scholarly subjects in favour of poetry, drama, history*, art, and the novel, in acknowledgement of the tastes of their readers. Selling at between 2s and 3s 6d, they paved the way for the shilling* monthlies of the 1850s and 1860s, which even more successfully blended publishers' interests and readers' demands.

*Macmillan's Magazine**, established in November 1859 by the Cambridge publishing house of Macmillan*, and the *Cornhill Magazine**, founded in January 1860 by George Smith* of Smith, Elder and Co*, revolutionized the role of the monthly magazine. Fiction featured prominently as entire novels by eminent contemporaries were serialized* in successive issues. This was combined with criticism of current publications, avoiding politics, and in the case of the *Cornhill*, religion, in tacit recognition of the family* and in particular the female readership of the new style magazines. The most significant feature of the new magazines was their price of a shilling. With the emergence of *Macmillan's* and the *Cornhill* it became possible to identify a culture of serious 'literary' reviewing in the monthly magazines, as distinct from the more wide-ranging, mandarin cultural criticism offered by the quarterlies, and the free-wheeling, personality-driven experiments of the magazines of the 1830s. JS

Sources: Parker 2000, *Wellesley*.

MONTHLY MUSICAL RECORD (1871-1960) The *Monthly Musical Record*, a leading British music* journal of the nineteenth century, was founded by the German music-publishing firm Augener in 1871. Small quarto in form, the size*, layout and typeface of the *Monthly Musical Record* changed little over time. A typical 20-page issue consisted of two substantial articles, 'foreign correspondence*', 'reviews*', 'concerts', 'musical notes' and advertisements*. The journal increased in size* in February 1880 when four pages of printed music were added. Its launch price* of 2d remained unchanged until the end of the century, and its circulation*, recorded at 6,000 copies in 1876, persisted into the mid-1890s.

Proudly displaying a medallion of Beethoven on its masthead*, the *Monthly Musical Record* set out to be a 'high-class' publication that impartially covered British and foreign music possessed of 'real artistic merit'. With its thorough, scholarly approach, the journal gave prominence to articles of general music history* and criticism, often in serial* form, together with analyses not only of the established repertoire but also of little-known works, for example, by Joachim Raff (symphonies) and Schubert (masses). Despite its avowed objectivity, however, it appeared at times to concentrate on German music, both canonical and contemporary, while being relatively indifferent to that of other European nations. Certainly although it was generally supportive of the 'renaissance' in native British music, it occasionally seemed to report on its progress from the height of an assumed German musical superiority.

It was edited* by Ebenezer Prout* (1871-1874), C. A. Barry (1874-1876), W. A. Barrett* (1877-1887) and others, while among its many distinguished British and German contributors were E. A. Baughan, Frederick Niecks and Edward Dannreuther. MH

Sources: Hughes 2002, *New Grove*, *Waterloo*.

MONTHLY PACKET OF EVENING READINGS FOR YOUNGER MEMBERS OF THE CHURCH OF ENGLAND (1851-1899) The *Monthly Packet of Evening Readings for Younger Members of the Church of England* was launched as a religious* monthly* with a professed aim to assist girls between the ages of 15 and 25 'to bring your religious principles to bear upon your daily life'. It addressed the issue of girlhood in such a way as to sympathize with the potential conflict between duty and desire but also to reinforce the need for traditional hierarchies like the family and the church. From the outset Charlotte M. Yonge* was the editor*, and she regularly contributed fiction*, editorials and book reviews*. Regular features included cameos from English history*, conversations on the Catechism, non-fiction generally excerpted from other sources and a variety of fiction, either part of a serial* or standalone.

Initially priced at 6d per issue, its price* rose to 8d in 1857. In 1866, at the beginning of the second of the four series of the journal, the word 'Younger' was removed from the title of the magazine, suggesting that it was not solely girls who were reading the magazine, but mothers as well. At this date too, the size* of its pages were enlarged and the price increased to 1s. Publishers* included John and Charles Mozley and J. H. Parker among others for over 20 years until 1874 when Walter Smith replaced Parker, and worked with Mozley for five years until Mozley died, leaving Walter Smith the sole publisher 1879-1887, when he was joined by Innes. Smith withdrew in 1891.

Yonge continued to edit the magazine with success, regularly serializing her own novels and including contributions by people like Amy Herbert,

Elizabeth M. Sewell and later Christabel Coleridge. By the 1890s, however, the magazine's popularity was waning, in part because the increasing secularization* of England meant that the magazine's High Anglican rhetoric was no longer as appealing. Yonge accepted that the magazine was losing readers, noting that competitors* like *Atalanta*" were supplanting it. Its final years were marked by an increasing tension between attempts at modernization and those readers who wished the 'dear old Packet' to stay the same. In 1891, Arthur D. Innes became its sole and final publisher, and Yonge accepted Christabel Coleridge as a co-editor. Changes followed, including an increased focus on women and work. In a further attempt to modernize the magazine*, Innes forced Yonge to resign except as a contributor in 1894, and he and Coleridge acted as co-editors until the final issue in June 1899. Although there was some talk of reviving the magazine at a cheaper price, nothing came of it, probably because of Innes's financial difficulties. KLM

Sources: Altholz 1989, Coleridge 1903.

MONTHLY REPOSITORY (1806-1837) After taking over the ailing *Universal Theological Magazine* (1802-1805) in 1805, the Unitarian minister Robert Aspland (1782-1845) founded the *Monthly Repository of Theology and General Literature*, a monthly octavo of around 60 pages that first appeared in February 1806. Under his editorship* the magazine combined radical nonconformist politics* with theological controversy, and was in effect the principal organ of the Unitarian movement, attracting contributions from Henry Crabb Robinson (1775-1867), John Bowring* and Harriet Martineau*. This did not make it a commercial prospect, however, and subscriptions hovered unprofitably around the 1,000 mark.

Aspland transferred ownership of the *Repository* to the British and Foreign Unitarian Association in 1826, where it was edited by committee until W. J. Fox* was appointed editor in 1827, when the title was enhanced to include the word review (*Monthly Repository and Review*, 1827-1831). Fox purchased the periodical in 1831, assuring readers* that 'the principles it advocates, and the objects to which it is devoted, remain the same'. His editorship, however, saw the magazine develop into a literary* periodical of more general interest, in which reviews* and poetry* became more prominent. Fox attempted to shift the journal's theoretical Unitarianism into a short-lived sister journal the *Unitarian Chronicle* (1832-1833), but Aspland's *Christian Reformer*" effectively took over as the focus of the

Unitarian movement. In the *Repository*, Fox praised young poets such as Alfred Tennyson (1809-1892) and Robert Browning (1812-1889), and his influence allowed him to attract contributions from John Stuart Mill* (1806-1873) among others. As Fox's religious* militancy gave way to a political one, the *Repository* campaigned for the Reform Bill, and for more sweeping political reforms.

This drift in message led to a fall in Unitarian subscriptions, and Fox sold the *Repository* to R. H. Horne* in 1836, who also became editor. He was succeeded in 1837 by Leigh Hunt*, who oversaw the journal's demise. **MaT**
Sources: BL Catalogue, ncse, *ODNB*, *Waterloo*.

MOONSHINE (1879-1902) Launched on 1 March, *Moonshine* was an illustrated* weekly comic paper, based in London. Its first editor* was Charles Harrison, who was succeeded in 1883 by Arthur Clements. Its political* orientation was conservative. In the first issue, the journal announced itself in the following self-confident manner: 'This important journal is started for the benefit of the public; but no one will believe it. ... While there is a single wrong unremedied, we shall continue to write...' The editor's bold claim that the journal would persist to write 'even until the day of judgment' proved too optimistic when the journal was forced to close in 1902.

Each issue consisted of 16 pages, illustrated* with various engravings, sketches and cartoons*. The journal set out to rival *Punch** in its format*, but towards the end of the century it tended to provide more room for straight political comment and theatre reviews*. An advertisement* published in 1891 boasted that *Moonshine* could claim the 'largest and most influential circulation* of any constitutional paper', but there is no proof to corroborate this statement. **OD**
Source: *Waterloo*.

MOORE, THOMAS STURGE (1870-1944) A poet, translator, dramatist and book illustrator as well as a wood* engraver, Thomas Sturge Moore's career was significantly shaped by his acquaintance with Charles Shannon* and Charles Ricketts*, who employed Moore to help in many ways with their work at the Vale Press. He studied wood engraving at the Lambeth School of Art, and contributed major work to Ricketts's and Shannon's periodical the *Dial** from 1895 on. Most of his subsequent wood engravings were published as book illustrations* and he became an important figure in the private press movement. **BM**
Sources: Engen 1990, *ODNB*.

MORE, HANNAH (1745-1833) Despite her importance in fields including the abolition of slavery and Evangelical moral reform, Hannah More produced little actual journalism. Her political and moral conservatism was expressed in the *Strictures on Female Education* (1799), yet More's own writing empowered women campaigners and philanthropists, making an indirect but significant contribution to nineteenth-century journalism. The *Cheap Repository Tract* series which More edited* from 1795-1798 used the quasi-journalistic form of monthly publication. Richard Porteus, the Bishop of London, called on More because of her ability to mimic familiar vernacular forms of ballad, recipe or news*; the lack of originality that had earlier led to an accusation of plagiarism from Hannah Cowley now stood her in good stead. The aim was to displace popular* radical works with loyalist moral literature offered at cut-price rates to hawkers or purchased by middle-class* supporters for cheap* resale. The unwitting achievement may have been to develop a taste for reading and a network of circulation* available to writers of any political* persuasion.

In 1804 More responded to Wilberforce's request for a contribution to the Evangelical *Christian Observer** with a piece on 'The White Slave Trade', which adapted the rhetoric of abolition to an attack on the world of fashion*. Wilberforce viewed More as able to provide the sprightly tone much needed by a journal defined by moral earnestness. **SM**
Sources: *ODNB*, Stott 2003.

MORGAN, MATT SOMERVILLE (1836-1890) Artist, illustrator* and caricaturist*, Matt Morgan's wood engraved* illustrations for periodicals comprised two major strands: documentary reportage for mid-Victorian illustrated weeklies*, and, later in his career, caricatures and cartoons* for satirical* magazines. Both modes of his work were informed by a strong sense of social responsibility, which perhaps derived from his early experiences in Italy as a war* artist for the *Illustrated Times** (1859-1861). He drew extensively for the *Illustrated London News** (1859-1886) as well as continuing to work for the *Illustrated Times* in the 1860s, specializing in images of the urban poor and of political meetings.

Morgan evolved a powerful realist technique to convey his social concerns, and this, together with his radical politics, served him well when he turned to caricature late in the 1860s. He became the cartoonist* for the *Tomahawk** in 1867, for which he produced a sequence of large-scale foldout cartoons which made striking and distinctive use of tinted wood engraved techniques. In one image, (23 Nov. 1867) for example, called 'Couleur de Rose!' he places two roundels tinted pink and showing an imagined benevolent treatment of the poor in the centre of a mass of black and white images showing 'true' accounts of urban suffering and oppression. All these images are contained within an emblematic thick black border. The originality and outspokenness of his work, as well as its technical excellence, gave him considerable scope to express his views, and he produced work for several other satirical* journals including *Judy** and *Will o' the Wisp**. His work offered some continuation of the early radicalism of *Punch** into the mid- and late Victorian period, and combined technical innovation with outspoken and unwavering social criticism. BM

Sources: Engen 1990, Houfe 1978, *ODNB*.

MORLEY, JOHN (1838-1923) Perhaps the most distinguished journalist of his era, Morley took up that profession on leaving Oxford after his father withdrew support because he wouldn't take holy orders. The young Morley worked hard, largely avoided the temptations of Bohemia, and soon became a reader for Macmillan*. He was briefly editor* of the short-lived *Literary Review* around 1861, and of the Cobdenite *Morning Star* in 1869, but it was his earnest, intelligent 'middles'* in the *Saturday Review** that attracted the notice of John Stuart Mill*, and his talent for intellectual friendships that brought him the editorship of the *Fortnightly Review** in 1867. He succeeded in making that journal, in which he wrote extensively on both contemporary politics* and Enlightenment intellectual history*, the leading organ of advanced thought, and made himself a force in the political and intellectual vanguard. Accepting the *Fortnightly's* policy of signed articles, having laboured under the yoke of anonymity* at the *Saturday*, Morley supported the principle of authorial responsibility and was skilful in conducting his team of talented, independent-minded contributors such as Frederic Harrison*.

Morley became increasingly sensitive to the ways in which signature impaired the power of an editor to maintain a coherent editorial line, especially as his own ambitions pushed him closer to a political career. He ceased editing the *Fortnightly* in 1882, having become in 1880 editor of the *Pall Mall Gazette*, where he enjoyed exercising serious political influence from the editorial pulpit and controlling

a team of bright young journalists like E. T. Cook* and Alfred Milner*. In addition, mainly for financial reasons, he edited *Macmillan's Magazine** (May 1883-1885). In 1883 Morley finally realized his ambition of entering Parliament, and by 1886 was a minister in Gladstone's third government. He ceased to be a professional journalist, and ended up a political peer, though he contributed to journals like the *Speaker**. where he was something of a hero to young Liberal intellectuals. Morley's career exemplified the French saying: 'Journalism can lead you anywhere – provided you leave it', but his political achievements did not equal his journalistic achievements, and he is probably best remembered for his great biography of his own hero, W. E. Gladstone. CAK

Sources: Hamer 1968, Kent 1969, Kent 1978, Knickerbocker 1943.

***MORNING CHRONICLE* (1770-1862)** Founded as the *Morning Chronicle and Daily Advertiser* (1770-1800) by William Woodfall to serve as a Whig 'principal mouthpiece', its political* orientation shifted at various times in its history. With James Perry at the editorial helm in 1789, the paper flourished with the contributions of radical-minded writers such as William Hazlitt* and Albany Fonblanque. Perry rattled the government authorities sufficiently to be charged three times with seditious libel. London's leading daily* at the beginning of the nineteenth-century, the *Morning Chronicle* ran two, three-column* sheets on broadsheet rag paper*. It was the first newspaper to offer parliamentary* reports, which it supplemented with literary and theatrical reviews*, foreign* letters and news, fashion*, crime reports* and mercantile news. By 1810, the *Morning Chronicle* achieved a circulation* of 7,000 and by 1820 it made an annual profit of £12,000.

Under the next editor*, John Black (1817), its claims upon newspaper fame included employing John Stuart Mill* and Charles Dickens* (1834), who wrote under the penname 'Boz', reporting on Parliament and writing short stories later collected in *Sketches by Boz* (1836), hiring Eliza Lynn Linton*, the first woman on a reporting staff in 1848 and sponsoring Henry Mayhew's* investigations into the lives and circumstances of the poor of London, part of a larger investigation of 'Labour and the Poor' throughout the country. Generally considered abler than Perry with the public questions of the day, Black was apostrophized by Jeremy Bentham as the greatest publicist that the country had ever seen.

By 1834, the faltering paper was bought by bankers and stockbrokers headed by John Easthope, an ardent Whig who used the *Morning Chronicle* to wage a war against *The Times**. However, one commentator asserted that 'everyone agreed that the *Morning Chronicle* was a most unsatisfactory Opposition newspaper' (Aspinall: 281). In spite of this, the paper remained the 'most famous' morning daily during the first half of the nineteenth-century, attracting such contributors as William Thackeray*, who published 35 articles (1844-1848). A thrice-weekly offshoot of the *Morning Chronicle* called the *Evening Chronicle* appeared 1835-1855, edited by George Hogarth, Charles Dickens's father-in-law. Dismissed by Mitchell's *Newspaper Press Directory* as identical to its parent paper, it is called a second edition by James Grant. Four pages and costing 7d in 1836, it mirrored the type of contents of the morning title, with some updated elements designed to attract a second wave of consumers. The *Chronicle* was absorbed by the *Daily Telegraph and Courier* in 1862. KC

Sources: Aspinall 1973, *Cambridge History of English and American Literature* 1916, *Spartacus online*, *Waterloo*.

MORNING HERALD (1780-1869) The *Morning Herald and Daily Advertiser* was launched in 1780 by Henry Bate, the 'fighting parson' (1745-1824), in opposition to the *Morning Post**, of which Bate had previously been an editor* and proprietor*. The paper was one of the first to contain parliamentary* reports, but its success may have owed more to its penchant for scandal, gossip* and virulent attacks on politicians and public figures. Bate left the paper in or about 1805 and control passed to the Thwaites family, from whom the paper was purchased by the Baldwin* Family, who already owned the *Standard**. Initially, it was run successfully by Edward Baldwin, with Stanley Lees Giffard as its editor. However, ill-judged dealings in the railway boom brought about Baldwin's bankruptcy in 1857, and the *Morning Herald* and the *Standard* were purchased by James Johnstone*, who closed the paper in 1869. JRW

Sources: Griffiths 1992, *ODNB*.

MORNING POST (1772-1937) The *Morning Post* was founded in 1772 as a morning daily*, in part to be a medium for advertising*, the alternative interests of its founders, who included the bookseller John Bell, James Christie the auctioneer, Richard Tattersall, founder of Tattersall's and Joseph Richardson, playwright. Initially called the

Morning Post and Daily Advertising Pamphlet (1772), then the *Morning Post and Daily Advertiser* (1773-1803) and finally the *Morning Post* (1803), it was edited*, until 1780, by Henry Bate, 'the fighting parson', who was later to found and edit the *Morning Herald**. In 1795 it was purchased by Daniel Stuart*, already its printer. Changing its politics* from Whig to Tory, Stuart employed writers of ability including James Macintosh, Samuel Taylor Coleridge* (who wrote leaders*), Robert Southey, William Wordsworth and Charles Lamb*. Coleridge, Southey and Wordsworth all contributed poetry*.

In 1798, Stuart bought the *Telegraph* and merged* it with the *Morning Post*, selling the paper in 1803 having increased its circulation* to 4,500. For the next 30 years, its editor was Nicholas Byrne, under whom the paper declined, displaying sycophancy toward the Prince Regent, and opposing parliamentary reform. Byrne, who was murdered at his desk in 1833, was succeeded as editor by C. Eastland Michele who continued the paper's reactionary stance, opposing the abolition of the Corn Laws. During his editorship, prominent leader* writers were Winthrop Mackworth Praed and Benjamin Disraeli. The editorship was taken over by Peter Borthwick in 1849, the start of a family connection that was to last until 1924. On Borthwick's death in 1852, the editorship passed to his son Algernon Borthwick, who bought the paper in 1876, and consolidated its imperialist* and conservative tone. He also continued its interest in sporting* matters, particularly racing. When he took over the paper, its circulation had declined to under 3,000 (compared to a circulation of *The Times* of 40,000.) He reduced the price* from 3d to 1d and increased its circulation. During his editorship, leader writers included Andrew Lang* and Alfred Austin*. William E. Henley*, Thomas Hardy* and Rudyard Kipling contributed verse while George Meredith was its special correspondent during the Italian wars* of liberation from Austria. Borthwick, now Lord Glenesk, died in 1908 and his family sold the paper in 1924. It merged* with the *Daily Telegraph** in 1937. JRW

Sources: Griffiths 1992, Hindle 1937, *ODNB*.

MORRIS, MOWBRAY (1847-1911) Mowbray Morris began his journalistic career in England, after a three-year stay in Australia (1869-1873), when he joined the staff of *The Times**, of which his father, also named Mowbray Morris, was manager. The younger Morris was appointed the paper's drama critic in 1877, and his forthright work in that capacity was collected in *Essays in Theatrical Criticism* (1882). He began contributing to periodicals in the 1880s: the *Fortnightly Review** (1882), the *Quarterly Review** (1880-92), *Temple Bar** (1878-87) and most notably and most frequently *Macmillan's Magazine** (1882-1900). He became editor* of *Macmillan's* in 1885, carrying on until it ceased publication in 1907, and performing other editorial and administrative duties for the house of Macmillan*.

Perhaps Morris's greatest achievement as editor of *Macmillan's* was his recruitment of the young Rudyard Kipling as a contributor: a dozen of his stories and poems* appeared in the *Magazine* (Nov.1889-Jan.1893), effectively launching his career in England. Morris also maintained productive relations with two long-time contributors, Henry James* and Walter Pater*, and attracted other estimable writers. On the other hand, he was not sympathetic to Thomas Hardy*, whose *Tess of the d'Urbervilles* he reviled in the *Quarterly Review*, although he did print a serialized*, somewhat bowdlerized version of his *The Woodlanders*, which John Morley*, his predecessor as editor, had secured; nor was he favourably disposed toward the poetry of George Meredith and Alfred Tennyson, although both were Macmillan and Co. authors.

Always outspoken in expressing his literary* and political* judgments and rigorous in his vetting of manuscripts, Morris did show signs of blind spots and prejudices, principally what Charles Morgan called an 'anti-realistic bias', which tended to impair his work as an editor and a critic. Although he did not really feel at home in the late nineteenth-century and early twentieth-century world, Morris should not be held responsible for the demise of the magazine* on which he played the leading role during more than two decades, for the market* and the reading* public were changing in ways that also doomed other established periodicals. **GW**
Sources: Bolitho 1950, Gwynn 1926, Morgan 1944, Whibley 1911, Worth 2003.

MORRIS, WILLIAM (1834-1896) An important figure in the history of socialist* journalism, William Morris has been credited with bringing a literary* and aesthetic dimension to the British socialist movement. Throughout his professional life (1852-1896) as an author, designer socialist and fine-press publisher*, William Morris contributed to, edited* and financed journalism in Oxford and London. Because he had so many spheres of activity, his journalistic endeavours cannot be separated from his other pursuits. Morris addressed a wide audience, proselytizing about design, beauty, peace and racial and social equality. After taking his degree from Oxford in 1855, he supported and contributed to the *Oxford and Cambridge Magazine* (1 Jan.-Dec. 1856). Although he gave up the editorship after only nine days, his contributions to this literary 'little magazine' foreshadow his later lifelong interests including 'The Story of the Unknown Church' (architecture), reviews* of Browning and Ruskin (poetry* and literature), 'Svend and his Brethren' (Nordic lore) and 'A Night in a Cathedral' (socialism).

Between 1869 and 1888, Morris contributed signed articles to the *Fortnightly Review**, importantly 'The Revival of Architecture' (June 1888) and 'The Revival of Handicraft' (Dec. 1888). Together, Morris contributed to 58 newspapers and journals throughout the United Kingdom on subjects as diverse as the 'Eastern Question', proposed destruction of historical buildings, Pre-Raphaelite poetry and the need for social equality in England.

During his brief membership of the Social Democratic Federation, Morris helped to found the movement's periodical *Justice** and kept the publication afloat by regular financial contributions. *Justice* helped to establish Morris's reputation as a socialist writer with his 33 articles for the journal, publishing commentary such as 'Socialism in England in 1884' (1884) and 'A Factory As It Might Be' (1884), short stories such as 'An Old Fable Retold' (1884) and poetry such as 'The Voice of Toil' (1884). At the end of 1884 Morris broke with the Federation and its leader Hyndman* to found the Socialist League and a new periodical, the *Commonweal**. Morris's journalism for *Commonweal* is especially prolific; 433 articles include the serialized works* with Morris's most famous socialist work including 'How We Live and How We Might Live' (1887), 'Pilgrims of Hope' (1885-1886), 'A Death Song' (1889), 'A Dream of John Ball' (1886-1887) and 'News from Nowhere' (1890).

When Morris was ousted as editor in 1890, he continued his financial support of the periodical, and his final contribution was 'Where Are We Now' (Nov. 1890). As the Socialist League disintegrated under Anarchist pressures, Morris worked towards building socialist unity in Britain, refusing to join any group and writing for various periodicals including the *Labour Leader**. **DM/TT**
Sources: *CBEL* 2000, Faulkner 1973, Mitchell 1987, Morris online, Mutch 2005, *ODNB*, Thompson 1955, Tobin 2002, *Wellesley*.

MORTEN, THOMAS (1836-1866) A gifted but troubled artist, talented enough to be exhibiting at the Royal Academy at the age of 19, Morten is one of the less known but also one of the most gifted of the black and white artists who drew for the illustrated* magazines of the 1860s. The bulk of his output was in periodical illustration, and he worked with distinction for *Good Words*, *London Society*, *Once a Week* and the *Quiver* between 1861 and his suicide in 1866. Morten worked at a moment of high intensity and achievement for periodical illustration, and his work stands comparison with that of his better-known contemporaries like Millais*, Pinwell* or Lawless*. **BM**

Sources: Engen 1990, Goldman 1994, Houfe 1978, *ODNB*, Reid 1928, White 1897.

MORTEN, VIOLET HONNOR (1861-1913) Violet Morten was a nurse whose concern for the medical welfare of women and children fuelled numerous publications on nursing and child welfare. Her articles for the *Globe** and the *Daily News* were published* as *Sketches of Hospital Life* by Sampson Low* in 1888, followed by 'The Story of a Nurse' (1892), illustrated* by Mary L. Gow and serialized* in the *Graphic*. The following year, 'Tales of the Children's Ward', co-written with Miss H. F. Gethen of the London Hospital was also serialized. She was on the staff of the *Hospital* as subeditor* and also wrote for *Clinical Sketches*, the *Humane Review* and the *National Review**. Additionally, Morten worked for the Manchester Press Company.

As a regular contributor to the *Daily News** and the *Glasgow Herald** (her Scottish connection came through her uncle, the journalist* and writer William Black*), she publicized and promoted her extensive activities from London County Council hygiene lecturer to her political work on the London School Board. As a campaigner for equal pay for nurses and women teachers, she supported other working women, writing for the *Woman's Signal*. Of the generation of single women who dedicated their lives to an impressive interplay of achievements, another of her innovations was the Ladies' Literary Dinner* with colleagues such as Sarah Grand* and L. T. Meade*. Like her associate Clementina Black*, Morten's awareness of the value of the press meant that her journalism had a dual purpose, as a career and in the service of her many social causes. **CL**

Sources: 19CBLN, 19CUKP, *The Times* 1913.

MOTHERS' COMPANION (1887-1896) ' An illustrated* monthly* magazine* for the home', the *Mothers' Companion* offered popular general coverage of domestic* topics such as dressmaking, childcare, children's fiction and bible lessons, but also provided frequent items of political* and economic interest to women from high profile contributors such as Clementina Black* and Millicent Fawcett*. Published* by Partridge & Co. in London, costing 1d for a 16-page magazine (2s for the yearly volume) including advertisements* on the back page, with plentiful, attractive drawings and engravings, it had a regular gardening* feature from Jane S. Clarke, medical* advice from a woman doctor, Mrs Atkins and serialized* fiction, sometimes with a social edge as in Eliza Clarke's, 'Bread-Winners' (1888). Fawcett contributed widely with biographical sketches on accomplished women and Black provided information on women's union and employment activities. **CL**

Sources: *Mothers' Companion* 1888, *Waterloo*.

MOTHER'S MAGAZINE (1834-1862) Reprinted from the American edition with British material inserted, the *Mother's Magazine* was a sober evangelical monthly for 'Christian mothers'*. Edited* by Mrs A. G. Whiteley and published* in Britain by James Paul, it eschewed fiction as dangerous, offering instead a diet of moral tales, essays, exhortations, poems* and advice on bringing up children. Like *The British Mothers' Magazine** with its link to 'Maternal Meetings', the *Mother's Magazine* was the vehicle for the Maternal Associations pioneered in the United States. Reports of meetings and letters* from members in the United States and Britain, as well as from missionaries* around the world, assumed women had an important social role, based on a maternal spirituality. **MRB**

Sources: Beetham 1996, *Mothers' Magazine*, *Waterloo*.

MOTHERS' MAGAZINES For most of the century mothers were held responsible for supervising children's reading and, indeed, for ensuring that family reading, particularly of daughters, was 'healthy'. This expectation crossed class* divides. Hannah More* and Sarah Trimmer* were important pioneers here and the latter's *Family Magazine* (1788-1789) and the *Guardian of Education* (1802-1806) emphasized the importance of these family responsibilities among the lower classes. At the same time expensive ladies' magazines* like the *Lady's Monthly Museum* (1798-1832) assured aristocratic mothers that the journal provided suitable reading for 'the rising generation'.

In the mid-century the rapid development of a popular* press included such titles as the *Family Friend* and the *Magazine of Domestic Economy* which assumed the role of mothers in the homes of the 'poor but industrious classes'. However, magazines which specifically targeted 'mothers' grew out of the tradition of serious religious* journalism exemplified by Trimmer. The *Mother's Magazine* and the *British Mothers' Magazine* were unillustrated monthlies which carried an evangelical message about the importance of mothers to the spiritual well-being of their children. Both these journals were linked to the Maternal Associations which had come to Britain from America.

After 1850, and particularly in the 1880s and 1890s, general magazines for women* often included regular columns* of advice to mothers along with special pages for children, as did *Home Chat*. Middle-class women's magazines took up debates about what to do with 'our daughters', while girls' magazines sometimes included an address to mothers, as was made explicit when the *Girl's Own Paper* carried the subtitle 'For Young Women and their Mothers'. New Journalism*, with its concomitant identification of more specific target groups of readers, brought a second wave of magazines addressed specifically to mothers. The *Mothers' Union Church Journal* (1888-1925) continued the religious tradition of the early magazines, but titles like *Baby** and *Babyhood* (1884-1892), which became the *Mother's Nursery,* offered a secularized* model of child development and identified mothers as potential consumers of advertised* goods. Instead of the Bible, *Baby* referred mothers to the work of scientists* and medical* men in relation to child development. The importance of mothers as readers* and managers of family reading persisted across such changes. MRB

Sources: *Baby,* Beetham 1996, *British Mothers' Magazine, Mother's Magazine, Waterloo.*

MOZLEY, ANNE (1809-1891) Anne Mozley's writings mostly comprised anonymous* contributions to highbrow periodicals. She liked the latitude enabled by anonymity, as it allowed her at times to adopt a male persona, or to discuss topics considered outside women's ken.

Mozley edited* the High Anglican *Magazine for the Young* for several years from the mid-1840s, and in 1844 began literary* reviewing* for the similarly orientated *Christian Remembrancer** (co-edited by James Mozley till 1855), which she continued till the periodical's demise in 1868. James's co-editor William Bell Scott* gave her the entrée to the *Saturday Review**, in which she published (1861-1877). Unfortunately many of her writings cannot be identified with certainty, but she produced for the *Christian Remembrancer* important reviews of Charlotte Brontë's *Villette* (April 1853) and Elizabeth Gaskell's *Life of Charlotte Brontë* (July 1857).

For the *Saturday Review** she wrote 'middles'* – a wide variety of articles on social life and the moral issues it raised. She brought out two volumes of these (*Essays on Social Subjects*, 1864, 1865), although still anonymously. Their publication by Blackwood fostered her writing for *Blackwood's Edinburgh Magazine**, and this continued till 1880. As well as social mores, her subjects included the works of Catholic converts (including Newman, Sept. 1866), 'Clever Women' (Oct. 1868), and J. S. Mill's* *Subjection of Women* (Sept. 1869). In discussing the 'Woman Question', Mozley championed women's intellectual capacities, while accommodating *Blackwood's* social conservatism.

Mozley's most notable review, nonetheless, was one of four for the short-lived *Bentley's Quarterly Review**, on *Adam Bede* (July 1859). Here she identified 'George Eliot'* as female on internal evidence, notably the narrator's 'stand of observation rather than more active participation': it was the review that Eliot herself most appreciated. After Mozley's death, her sister and nephew republished this review, plus some of her contributions to *Blackwood's* (*Essays from Blackwood's* 1892); their 'Memoir' disclosed the extent, if not the details, of Mozley's journalistic career – 'another world of her own, which for a great part of the day was indeed the world that interested her' ([vii]). JCW

Sources: Jordan 2004, Mozley 1892, *ODNB, Wellesley,* Wilkes 2005.

MOZLEY, JAMES BOWLING (1813-1878) James Mozley was a religious* journalist and academic whose career as a writer and editor* was shaped by his involvement with Tractarianism, also known as the Oxford Movement. This was an affiliation of High-Church Anglicans, initially centred around Mozley's good friend John Henry Newman, who believed – broadly – that there was no essential theological conflict between the Church of England and the Catholic church. Mozley contributed 11 articles on historical and theological issues to the movement's organ the *British Critic**, which was edited by Newman and then by Mozley's brother Thomas Mozley.

Following the suppression of the *British Critic* and Newman's conversion to Roman Catholicism, Mozley – who was never a radical by temperament – adopted a more mainstream High Anglicanism, which was reflected in his journalistic activities. He was active in the foundation of the *Guardian**, a High-Church weekly*, and became co-editor of the *Christian Remembrancer**. This quarterly* review attracted contributions from other veterans of the

Oxford movement, but in reality it was a moderate voice, and Mozley's contributions reflected his increasingly orthodox perspective. He was frankly critical of Newman's apostasy, and left the *Christian Remembrancer* in 1855, effectively severing his last link with Tractarianism. He increasingly focused his attention on publishing sermons and tracts, which remained doctrinally High Anglican, but equally insisted upon the validity and importance of the Church of England. During this period, he contributed to such magazines as the *Contemporary Review** and the *Quarterly Review**, where he published a generous review of Newman's *Grammar of Assent* in 1870, choosing to 'call attention to agreement rather than differences' and praising it as a 'powerful defence ... of a common Christianity'. MaT

Sources: *ODNB*, *Waterloo*, *Wellesley.*

MOZLEY, THOMAS (1806-1893) A High Church clergyman, editor* and journalist* from Lincolnshire, Thomas Mozley graduated from Oriel College, Oxford, in 1825, where he was acquainted with John Henry Newman, his professor and later his friend and brother-in-law. Mozley married Newman's sister Hariett in 1836. Mozley's father was a bookseller and a publisher* and his brother, James Bowling Mozley*, was well known for his theological works.

Owing to his familiar connection to Newman, Mozley was associated with the Oxford movement. It was chiefly as a contributor to the *British Critic** that he supported the Tractarian movement. In 1841, he acted as editor* (1841-1843) and succeeded Newman, the founder of the paper. After diverging views concerning the editorial perspective, Mozley resigned the position. Although Newman converted to Roman Catholicism, Mozley decided to remain Anglican, which probably widened the gap between them. In 1844, Mozley contributed articles to *The Times**, being for a while a correspondent to Rome. He is also the author of a testimony of his experience as a former Oxford movement supporter, *Reminiscences, Chiefly of Oriel*, and the *Oxford Movement*, published in 1882. CK

Source: *ODNB.*

MRS. ELLIS'S MORNING CALL: A TABLE BOOK OF LITERATURE AND ART (1850-1852) This lavishly produced monthly* was edited by Mrs. Ellis (Sarah Stickey), famous for books such as *The Women of England*. Her experience as editor* of *Books of Beauty and Annuals** was evident in the wide margins, high-quality engravings* and heavy paper* as well as the gold-embossed covers of the

bound volumes. It was intended to have aesthetic as much as literary* appeal. However, Ellis's serious message for middle-class* women on their moral and social responsibilities was evident also in the tone of the serial* fiction, the poetry* on domestic themes and in articles, for example, on 'Poor Women' and on the Frankfurt Peace Congress. MRB

Sources: Beetham 2001, *Mrs. Ellis's Morning Call* Vol. 1-4, *Waterloo.*

MULLER, HENRIETTA FRANCES (c.1845/46-1906) Henrietta Muller was a journalist, editor* and proprietor*, perhaps best known for founding and editing the *Women's Penny Paper** in 1888.

In 1881 she had one of her first articles published in *Macmillan's Magazine**. Several others on women's issues appeared in the *Westminster Review** (1884-1888), based on personal experience and on her political* ideals, such as 'The Woman Question in Europe' (1884). In that year, a series of her articles from the *Westminster Review* was published in book form as *The Future of Single Women*.

Frustrated by the lack of coverage for women's issues in the press, Muller decided to start a paper that would adequately represent women's rights* and in 1888 the *Women's Penny Paper* went on sale, marketed as 'The only Paper Conducted, Written, Printed and Published* by Women'*. In order to protect the paper from possible damage due to her notoriety she adopted the pseudonym*, 'Helena B. Temple' for her editorship*. Muller decided to take a politically non-sectarian stand with regard to the paper, imbuing it with a radical and feminist ethos. After three years the name of the paper changed to the *Woman's Herald* (later the *Woman's Signal*), with Muller remaining as editor until April 1892, when she sold the paper.

In 1891 she became a member of the Theosophical Society, eventually going to live in India to work with Annie Besant*. She wrote a short story based on her journey to Bombay, 'That Theosophist', for the *Woman's Signal* (1894). CL

Sources: 19C UKP, *ODNB*, *Wellesley*, *Woman's Herald* 1891.

MULTIPLE EDITIONS Daily* newspapers and some weeklies* had multiple editions in the nineteenth century, that is successive editions, usually with the same date. For metropolitan* dailies, new editions are usually issued to take account of buying patterns (e.g., commuters at both ends of the day), and to accommodate up-to-date news, some of it foreseeable such as closing (stock market) prices, and some of it opportunistic (to scoop breaking news). The number of editions is often related to the nature of current events. For example, war* time is likely to result in a higher number of editions per day; so are special events such as the Great Exhibition, which involved a great influx of visitors to the capital, and train travel. Some weeklies*, such as the *Leader*, had town and country editions; others like the *Northern Star*, which was initially published in Leeds, had a number of editions customized for particular geographical readerships*, Ireland, Manchester, etc. The first editions were often for 'country' readers: that is, they are published early (sometimes the night before) to meet distribution* timetables that would deliver the paper outside of its place of publication at optimum moments of sale on the date on the masthead*. Other stimuli to multiple editions included opportunities for sales, such as Market Days or political meetings. New copy might appear in later editions, displacing previous stories, and advertising* might vary in town and country editions.

Although such multiple editions repay attention from the scholar, they are seldom accessible. An even less acknowledged form of multiple editions is the edition that appeared as the text for annual* or semi-annual bound volumes issued by publishers of periodicals. These almost invariably filled out the covers and advertisements attached to issues and are thus incomplete, and sometimes reprinted new sheets with different pagination the original. Certain libraries, such as the British Library from collected and bound multiple copies of some titles during some periods of the century, and some of these are available electronically in the British Library 19C Newspaper collection and ncse (nineteenth-century serials edition), but these are exceptions to the general rule multiple editions are all but invisible, and seldom figure in scholarly investigation of newspaper material. **LRB**

Source: ncse 2008.

MURRAY, DAVID CHRISTIE (1847-1907)

David Murray contributed to British journalism on a regional, national, and international scale, although remembered today chiefly as a novelist.

Born and raised in West Bromwich, Staffordshire, he began writing (unpaid) as a teenager for the *Wednesbury Advertiser*, a weekly* local* paper. His first paying job as a journalist came when he joined the *Birmingham Morning News*, newly founded under the direction of George Dawson. For reporting on crime*, inquests, and coal-mine accidents, Murray received 25s a week and a reputation that extended beyond the West Midlands. About the same time Murray published his first

newspaper poetry*, on the Franco-Prussian war, in Joseph Hatton's* *Illustrated Midland News*.

In 1865 Murray moved to London, and in 1871 he began working as a parliamentary* reporter* for the *Daily News*. In 1877 he got his first taste of foreign reporting. That year Murray received a £40 advance to cover the Russo-Turkish War for the *Chicago Herald*. Unable to make contact with his employer once he arrived, Murray spent 'an adventurous year in Turkey' as special war correspondent for the *Scotsman** and *The Times**. Travels through Australia and New Zealand led to articles in the *Contemporary Review** in 1891, and his trip through the United States and Canada in 1894-1895 generated pieces in the *New York Herald*. Between those two journeys he assumed the editorship of the *Morning*, a short-lived London daily, and wrote a great deal for the *Referee*.

Fiction was clearly Murray's preferred genre of writing. He had an acute sense, however, of the link between news* reporting and creative literature; as he remarked in his memoir *Recollections*, 'I have always held that there is no training for a novelist like ... that boiling, bubbling, seething cauldron called journalism'. **MRH**

Sources: Kirk 1891, Murray 1908, Nash 2002, *ODNB*, *The Times* 1907.

MURRAY, EUSTACE CLARE GRENVILLE (1824-1881)

A journalist and diplomat, Murray was the illegitimate son of Richard Grenville, second Duke of Buckingham and Chandos. His early years in the dual capacities of diplomat and journalist* were marked by controversy: unsurprisingly, given the incompatible nature of the roles in the eyes of the Foreign Office. He blatantly broke the Office's conventions when as an attaché to the British Embassy in Vienna 1851, he also worked as the *Morning Post*'s* Vienna Correspondent. Lord Palmerston's patronage meant he was saved from dismissal, but he was moved through a series of lesser posts across Europe and the Middle East, and, always in conflict with authority, Murray was eventually dismissed in 1868.

His experiences fuelled his journalism in content and tone. His 'Roving Englishman' series of travel pieces, notably satirizing* the Turkish ambassador Sir Stratford Canning as Sir Hector Stubble, was published in *Household Words** from 1854 and was hugely successful. On his return to London in 1868 he wrote for *Cornhill**, *Vanity Fair**, and in 1869 started the weekly* *Queen's Messenger**, a 'prototype of the later Society Paper' (*ODNB*), though he denied that he had full authority over the contents of the *Messenger* when the paper was accused of slandering Lord Carrington. Charged with perjury, Murray jumped bail and fled to Paris where he remained for the rest of his life, living under his Spanish wife's title as Count de Rethel d'Aragon while producing fiction and journalism on such a prodigious scale that it was suspected some of his work was in fact produced by a team of writers (Lohrli: 382).

He was Paris correspondent for the *Daily News** and *New York Herald* and wrote for the *Pall Mall Gazette**, *Truth** and the *Illustrated London News**, among others. His forte was the humorous, acerbic article on politics* and culture. 'One of the most irreverent and witty journalists of his day' (*ODNB*), he shamelessly brought gossip* into his political pieces, changing the nature of political commentary in the mainstream press with both this tendency and his frankness. In 1874, he established the weekly the *World** with Edmund Yates*, boasting a 'new and striking' format* for advertisements*. The form did not succeed; nor did the relationship with Yates, who bought out Murray in early 1875 when the two clashed over Murray's tendency to attack old enemies through the pages of the press. **FD**

Sources: Lohrli 1973, *ODNB*, Yates 1885.

MUSIC AND JOURNALISM Some 200 dedicated music journals were launched in England, Scotland or Wales between 1800 and 1900, including scholarly quarterlies*, polite monthlies, weekly* trade* papers and music society annuals*. They hold only a portion of the writing on music in the nineteenth-century British press. The larger part consists of articles in general and literary periodicals, as well as review* columns* in many weekly (from the 1820s) and daily* (from the 1840s) newspapers. This plethora reflects unprecedented growth in the British music industry, already highly internationalized by 1800. It also documents music's gradual rise in national cultural esteem, its diffusion among varying social levels, and, from the 1880s, a virtual explosion of public interest in the subject. Specialist coverage became ever more specialized – for Gregorianists, Wagnerians, brass players, piano dealers and bellringers – while high-circulation* papers, including the *Daily Telegraph**, routinely carried prominent advertising* for concerts and popular songs. The press expanded and diversified ahead of the music business, but links between them were always symbiotic.

Promoting a musical product or point of view went hand in hand with disseminating information. Music publishers'* house* magazines* are the obvious examples: Wessel, Novello, Curwen, Cramer and Augener each utilized serials* to attract readers and stimulate a market* for their wares in, respectively, imported sheet music, choral works, Tonic Sol-fa, concert culture and educational keyboard editions. Booksellers, too, such as Alexander Macmillan* and William Reeves, used music articles in their literary* magazines, or even whole music journals, to test the market for music books. Journals with music supplements* meanwhile advanced music printing technology – and the affordability of all music – by experimenting with large edition sizes*: William Clowes'*'s *Harmonicon** (from 1823) and J. Alfred Novello's *Musical Times** (from 1844) led the way with improvements in music typesetting, later stereotype. Well-targeted literary periodicals offered serious intellectual discourse on music, from R. M. Bacon's* *Quarterly Musical Magazine and Review** (from1818) to the Wagner Society's *Meister* (1888-1895).

Journalistic opportunity undoubtedly created professional musical writers. Some were excellent, many not; those in the newspaper trade known as 'critics' might be authoritative or ignorant. A prevailingly freelance environment encouraged peripatetic work and multiple reporting, often anonymous*, of which the outstanding exponent was George Hogarth*. English criticism's generally conservative reputation sprang from a handful of long-serving journalists with fixed tastes, among them Henry Chorley*, J. W. Davison* and Joseph Bennett*, though their representativeness is doubtful: Beethoven, Berlioz, Verdi, Schumann, Liszt and Wagner, all musical innovators, found favour with plenty of British listeners despite critical reserve. Journalists were more often influential in performers' careers, and in generating discussion of topical issues – education, the state of cathedral music, the need for all-sung English opera, the claims of indigenous composers and musical women, aesthetic style change, advances in musical knowledge and the construction of an English musical past. Music scholarship indeed flourished through a range of serial publications, not least George Grove's* *Dictionary of Music and Musicians* (1878-1889), showing that keen readers, not universities or the state, were the ultimate paymasters of research. **LeL**

Sources: *Grove Music* online, Langley 1983, Langley 1989, Langley 1990, Langley 1994, Langley 2003.

MUSICAL STANDARD (1862-1933) The *Mu-*

York Minster, St. Paul's Cathedral, and Durham Cathedral, in the early part of the 17th century. Before the art of organ building had reached the standard of the age in which these English builders flourished, there had been a re-action in several of the countries of the European continent against the use of organs in churches. This resulted in their banishment from the musical services of the church for some considerable time. They however began to return into favour in the 16th century, so were re-admitted, but many improvements were made in their construction compared with those in use before the crusade against them.

We may well begin the next portion of our consideration on the History of the Organ with a brief glance at some of the improvements which were introduced into organs about this time.   *(To be Continued.)*

Inauguration of the Riga Organ.

BEFORE the commencement of divine service on Sunday in the Cathedral at Riga, the dedication of the new organ by Walcker took place. After the singing of the 100th Psalm by the Cathedral choir, and the Introit sung by the assembled parishes, to the accompaniment of trumpets, the three preachers of the Cathedral, Superintendent Jentsch, Werbatus, and Hellmaun, ascended the altar steps, the congregation arose to its feet, and Supt. Jentsch formally dedicated the new organ to the service of the parish in an eloquent address. Towards the close of his speech, the organ began in the faintest tones to be heard, and as the speaker concluded, the new instrument burst forth in all its imposing splendour in the old Lutheran hymn, "A Strong Fortress," joined immediately by the mighty chorus of the congregation, which thus took a share in the solemn act of dedication, with visible emotion and thankful elation. After service the congregation was dismissed with the Toccato by Bach, played for a postlude, in a masterly manner by the organist, Wilhelm Bergner. Both he and Herr Walcker were overwhelmed with congratulations in the organ loft. This organ, which is destined to take a first rank among the great "kings of instruments," has really been dedicated and begun its work ere its completion. None surely could have guessed that the magnificent display on that day was not the whole capacity of the organ; but the truth is there remains fully a quarter of the work to be finished, a portion which would compose a really respectable organ by itself. Thirty-six additional speaking stops have yet to be added, and a number of additional mechanical accessories. The Riga organ was built at the manufactory of Walcker and Co., Ludwigsburgh, Germany. It is the largest in the world, and will contain 7,000 pipes, 124 voices with 174 stops, couplings, draughts, and treads, and several swells of powerful effect. The wind is supplied by a continuous self-regulating mechanical blast, driven by a gas-engine of 4-horse power. The organ has a height of 66ft., a breadth of 36ft., and a depth of 33ft. The largest wooden pipe is 33ft long, and has a cubic contents of 440 gallons, whilst the smallest pipe is scarcely a 0.6in. long.

Rudiments of Music

FOR PIANOFORTE STUDENTS.

Being an exposition of music, viewed from the standpoint of the new method.

That portion of any composition included between two double bars with dots, is to be repeated. When the dots precede the first Double-bar in the composition, the repeat is to be from the beginning.

REPEATS.

The *termination* of a repeated portion is sometimes altered; this is indicated by the bar or measure at the end of the repeated portion being marked 1st and 2nd time; and on the repetition, the bar marked 2nd time is to be substituted for that preceding it, marked 1st time.

The words DA CAPO indicate that a return is to be made to the beginning, and the repetition continued till the word FINE occurs, or a pause.

The letters and sign D.C. &c. which are sometimes used, indicate that the return is to be made to the sign, either at the beginning or at some other point in the piece. In all such cases, the repeated portion is to be performed *without the observance of any repeat* marks that may occur in it.

ORNAMENTS.

The ornaments or embellishments in modern use are the SHAKE, the TRILL, the TURN, the inverted TURN, the APPOGGIATURA, and the ACCIACATURA; they are written and played as follows:—

Abbandone,	With abandonment.
A Capriccio,	Capriciously; in free, irregular time.
Ad libitum,	At the pleasure of the performer.
Agitato,	In an agitated manner.
Amabile,	Amiably.
Amarezza,	Bitterness, grief.
Appassionato	Impassioned.
Arioso,	In a melodious, singing, agreeable manner.
Bravura,	Bravery, spirit.
Brilliante,	Brilliant.
Calando,	Literally, falling away, and applicable to tone.
Cantabile,	In a singing manner.
Con Amore,	Lovingly.
Con Anima,	With soul.
Con Fuoco,	With fire.
Con Leggerezza	With lightness and agility.
Cres.,	Crescendo, increasing in tone.
Deciso,	Decided.
Decres.,	Decrescendo, decreasing in tone.
Dolce,	Softly, sweetly.
Espressivo,	With expression.
Gaio, or Gajo,	Gaily.
Grandioso,	Grandly.
Grazioso,	Gracefully.
Gustoso,	With taste.
Impetuoso,	Impetuously.
Languido,	In a languid manner.
Maestoso,	In a majestic manner.
Morendo,	Sad, pensive.
Mesto,	Placidly.
Placidamente,	Dying away.
Pomposo,	Pompously.
Risoluto,	In a resolute manner.
Scherzando,	Playfully.
Semplice,	Simply—without ornament.
Sforzando,	Force, especially to a particular note or chord.
Singhiozzando,	In a sobbing manner.
Smorzando,	Smotheringly.
Soave,	Sweetly, agreeable.
Sostenuto,	In a sustained manner.
Sotto Voce,	With subdued tone.
Staccato,	Notes to be played in a short, crisp, disconnected manner.
Mezzo-Staccato, Dashes or Dots,	Notes to be detached but not crisp. Placed over or under notes indicate they are to be played staccato or mezzo-staccato.
Stentando,	Holding back the time.
Teneramente,	Tenderly.
Tranquillo,	Tranquilly.
Vibrato,	With much vibration of tone.
Vivace,	In a lively manner.
Volante,	In a light flying manner.
P,	Piano, soft.
PP,	Pianissimo, very soft.
MF,	Mezzoforte, half loud.
F,	Forte, loud.
FF,	Fortissimo, very loud.
FP,	The first note soft the others loud.

However carefully a composer may mark his compositions by time signatures or words, it should never be forgotten that musical compositions, to a large extent, tell their own tale—indicate their own character; it is by careful study alone that the performers will be able to enter into the meaning of the composer, and it must be left to the executants to render it accordingly.

(To be Continued.)

Figure 43: Some basic musical concepts as explained in one of the many nineteenth-century music magazines, *Magazine of Music*, May 1884: 19.

sical Standard's first leader* cited the routine provocation for its launch, the 'inadequacy of the present literary productions of the periodical music press'. Beginning as a twice-monthly publication of 16 pages, priced* 2d, it went weekly* in 1866, and by 1868 it claimed to be 'the principle and only independent representative of Music in the London weekly press'. The issue of independence was taken seriously, and the *Musical Standard* was rare among nineteenth-century music* journals in that it was not produced by a music publisher or other music issuing body*. A new illustrated* series, starting in 1894, featured a price reduction, to a penny.

The 'Reviews'* section carried detailed and well-informed critiques of contemporary performances and publications, but the *Musical Standard* was addressed primarily to learned amateurs, and – crucially – church musicians. Indeed, if the ecclesiastical foundations of nineteenth-century music were in doubt, then one need look no further than an issue of the *Musical Standard* to have them reconfirmed. Advertisements*, occupying around a quarter of the journal, listed vacancies for organists, choir boys and volunteers for amateur choral societies as well as organs for sale. Sections entitled 'Organ News' and 'Campanology' reinforced the journal's image as a trade* paper for the army of musicians in the employ of the established Church.

The journal adopted an inclusive attitude to this audience, providing sheet music for organ or choir, and often printing a poem* for readers to set to music themselves. The correspondence* section played host to debates over controversial appointments of organists, or the state of the industry in general, and technical questions on issues ranging from organ design to theories of harmony. Notable contributors included William Howard Glover*, George French Flowers 1811-1872) and musicians Henry John Gauntlett (1805-1876) and Henry Hiles (1826-1904). **MaT**

Source: *Musical Standard*.

MUSICAL TIMES AND SINGING CLASS CIRCULAR (1844-) Established by J. Alfred Novello as a continuation of Joseph Mainzer's publication of the same name (1842-1844), the *Musical Times and Singing Class Circular* has the longest continuous lineage of all music periodicals (becoming simply the *Musical Times* from 1903). Initially aimed at the amateur and working-class* audience provided by the Victorian choral movement, this monthly* journal, originally priced* at 1½d, was notable for cheapness. The price* also included a

choral music supplement*. The formula was successful, and the journal was enlarged from eight to 12 pages in 1848, and to 16 pages in 1849. By the early 1870s its monthly circulation* was 15,000 – a huge figure for a music periodical.

In its first five years it was overwhelmingly the journal of choral societies, but it subsequently developed a focus on Anglican Church music and gradually broadened its scope to include more music criticism and a wider range of musical topics. It was probably unique among music* journals of the period in having a woman, Mary Cowden-Clarke*, Novello's sister, as editor* (1853-1856). Its contributors included the poet and essayist Leigh Hunt* and music critic Edward Holmes*, who is largely credited with establishing it as an exemplar of serious music journalism. The *Musical Times* has sometimes been criticized for insularity, but its approach was influenced by a concern to reflect the musical experience of its readership*. Its popularity testifies to the success of this strategy. **HB**

Sources: Cooper 2003, Langley 1990, 'Our Jubilee' June 1894, Scholes 1947, Temperley 1969.

MUSICAL WORLD (1836-1891) The weekly *Musical World* was one of the most successful and influential British music* journals of the nineteenth century. With its broad appeal, cosmopolitan approach, range and depth of coverage, and bold, controversial treatment of British musical life, it gave a lead to other British music journals and overshadowed its rivals until well into the 1860s. Founded by J. A. Novello in March 1836, it quickly passed to Henry Hooper & Co in 1838; it was taken over by Hugh Cunningham & Co. (1841-1842) and had several proprietors* thereafter, before being bought by Boosey & Co. in 1853. A decade later it was acquired by the Duncan Davison firm, which ran it until the late1880s.

From 1842 its size* and format* changed from small octavo of Novello's launch to quarto under Hooper. A typical issue was 16 pages (two of adverts*); it usually featured a humorous illustration* as well as a mix of performance reviews*, feature articles, foreign and provincial news*, readers' correspondence* and a leader* page. The journal appeared on Saturdays and was priced* at 4d for most of its existence.

Editors* included Charles Cowden Clarke* and Desmond Ryan, among others, before passing into the lengthy editorial control of J. W. Davison* (1843-1885). His successor Francis Hueffer* (1885-1888) attempted to modernize the journal and move its coverage closer to the mainstream of contemporary musical life. Edgar Jacques became the *Musical World*'s last editor and proprietor (1888-1891) after Hueffer's death. Its many distinguished contributors included Joseph Bennett*, H. J. Gauntlett and Edward Rimbault. **MH**

Sources: Cooper 2002, Hughes 2002, Hurd 1981, *New Grove, Waterloo.*

MYRA'S JOURNAL OF DRESS AND FASHION (1875-1912) Matilda Browne*, with the publisher* Samuel Beeton*, set up the monthly* women's* magazine, *Myra's Journal of Dress and Fashion.* She had previously written for the *Young Englishwoman** as 'Myra', and the 'Spinnings' column* for the *Englishwoman's Domestic Magazine**, as 'The Silkworm'. The first-person style she employed in these latter columns, discussing shops she had visited, pioneered the advertorial. This tone was extended in her new venture, which addressed a wide readership*, mainly in the middle class*. The magazine cost 3d, with supplements* of fashion* plates and patterns at 3d. Her advice on health, beauty and dress proved so popular that in 1876 a further supplement was added to include the growing number of readers' letters*.

Both its graphic and reporting style reflected the ideals of the New Journalism*. Women were addressed as consumers. Fashion advice and dressmaking instruction were regular features, as were Paris fashion reports, at the start by Madame Marie Goubaud, who also advertised in the magazine. Large fashion plates were a key feature, usually two colour examples per issue, and approximately 14 reproductions of plates by Jules David, whose work in the important French fashion magazine *Le Moniteur de la Mode* was reproduced in many European women's journals and in the *Englishwoman's Domestic Magazine.* **RLA**

Sources: Beetham 2001, Breward 1994, Holland 1988, White 1971.

N

NAPIER, MACVEY (1776-1847) Like many university-educated lawyers of his generation, Macvey Napier preferred literature to the law. He became a contributor to the newly established *Edinburgh Review** in the third year of its existence, in 1805, and through his friendship with its publisher* Archibald Constable* became editor* of the supplement* to the sixth edition of the *Encyclopaedia Britannica* and eventually editor of the seventh edition. Napier balanced his academic responsibilities as Professor of Conveyancing at Edinburgh University with his editorial labours for the encyclopaedia until 1829 when, to the surprise of many of his colleagues, he succeeded the legendary Francis Jeffrey* as editor of the *Edinburgh*.

Napier's style and temperament differed markedly from his predecessor. He was not a public man of affairs, nor were his instincts particularly political*. But ironically it fell to him to lead the Whiggish *Edinburgh* from nearly 30 years as an opposition journal to become a 'government' review* when Charles Grey and the Whigs came to power in 1830. Napier's allies were William Empson*, who acted unofficially as sub-editor*, and T. B. Macaulay, the *Review*'s star contributor in the 1830s and 1840s. Like Jeffrey, Napier was an interventionist editor, reducing the length of the individual articles in order to increase their number in each issue, and attempting to curb the extravagant styles of some of the contributors. Of these one, of the most irascible was Carlyle*, who referred to him on one occasion as 'Naso the blockhead', an unkind reference to Napier's prominent nose. He had the goodwill of most of the *Edinburgh*'s regular contributors apart from Henry Brougham*, one of the original founders, who attempted to turn the review into a personal organ in his war with the Whig ministry.

The 1840s were a calmer time editorially, but the political influence of the quarterlies* and their cultural impact were on the wane. On his death in 1847 Napier was succeeded as editor by William Empson. His contemporary Henry Cockburn reflected on Napier's achievement that 'the habit of merely delivering others is apt to impair or at least to supersede, the power of one's own creation. If Napier had not given his best years to the editing of these works [the review and the encyclopaedia], he would probably have produced something worthy

of his own'. John Morley*, reviewing a selection of Napier's posthumously published letters, likened the role of editor to the manager of an opera house, requiring 'tact, resolution, patience, foresight, tenacity, flexibility, as are only expected from the great ruler or the great soldier'. JS

Sources: Cockburn 1874, Morley 1878, Napier 1879, *ODNB*, Shattock 1989.

NATION (1842-1900) The *Nation; A Weekly Journal of Politics, Literature and the Arts* was the mouthpiece of Young Ireland*, the romantic, cosmopolitan nationalist group led by the charismatic Thomas Davis*. The newspaper was in some senses typical of the cultural and physical force nationalism that was spreading across Europe.

Davis's initial mission for his 6d Saturday weekly* was to make the *Nation* 'racy of the soil'. However, its nationalism* was not exclusively Catholic or Gaelic and the poetry* published in its pages could be said to be part of the emergence of an Anglo-Irish nationalist tradition that was to find expression later in Yeats and Gregory.

The newspaper continued to publish articles of historical*, political*, literary* and cultural commentary after Davis's death in 1845 and fostered the early journalistic career of John Mitchel. It was suppressed during the revolutionary agitation of 1848, but soon revived under Charles Gavan Duffy* and in 1855 was sold to A. M. Sullivan.

Under Sullivan's control the character of the *Nation* changed significantly. It became moderately nationalist in outlook, a mouthpiece for the parliamentary focus and manoeuvrings of the Home Rule movement. Sullivan was succeeded by his brother Timothy.

The *Nation* contains many significant examples of the discourses through which Irish national identity was constructed in the mid-nineteenth century. MJH

Source: *Waterloo*.

***NATIONAL* (1839)** The *National; a library for the people* was an illustrated* weekly* published* by James Watson* that, running for just 23 issues (5 Jan.-29 June), was both traditional and subversive. Using the wood* engraved title page and 16-page octavo format* of the cheap*, information-based miscellanies* that had drawn their inspiration from the *Mirror of Literature** in the 1820s, the *National* replaced uncontentious miscellaneity with a declared socio-political purpose. It aimed to offer a progressive educative programme to 'the millions' through words and pictures, and sought to democratize the literary and intellectual tradition through carefully selected extracts from a range of free-thinking authors.

The editor*, W. J. Linton*, as a renowned engraver, artist, cultural entrepreneur and radical sympathizer, was in an ideal position to mount such a project, and, in addition to his editorial activities, he drew and engraved many of the illustrations*, which were often based on major art works. The last of the magazines to use this format* for the dissemination of 'useful knowledge*', Linton's *National* represented an important attempt to offset the definitions of knowledge offered by the *Penny Magazine** and to provide a cheap and attractive weekly* journal for working people that made them better educated, more thoughtful and, Linton hoped, more radical. **BM**

Sources: *ODNB*, Smith 1973.

NATIONAL IDENTITY AND THE PRESS IN THE UNITED KINGDOM The extent to which the press contributed in fashioning and disseminating collective identities in the UK cannot be overestimated. From 1793 to 1815 the French wars provided the stage on which national 'characters' were attributed, performed and appropriated not only through cartoons* and pamphlets but also the newspaper press, whose role was celebrated in Sir David Wilkie's *Chelsea Pensioners Reading the Gazette of the Battle of Waterloo* (1822). This painting was also a reminder of the variety and meaning of Britishness, that the 'free-born Englishman' had defeated Napoleonic despotism with the help of his 'Celtic' partners in the Union. The Scots, Irish and Welsh claimed a stake in the Empire, whose pluralist nature was to be celebrated rather than suppressed.

Meanwhile the influential periodical press, including the *Edinburgh**, the *Westminster** and *Fortnightly** reviews, canvassed the values of a dynamic, increasingly urbanized and comparatively tolerant society, a pervasive Protestant culture and the associated creeds of political economy* and utilitarianism. An emphasis on Parliament as the guarantor of liberty characterized both the respectable newspapers and the 'unstamped'* radical and Chartist press and, in Ireland, both the Unionist and the

"LA GLOIRE!"

FRENCH SOLDIER. "I SUFFER—I DIE! NO MATTER!—OUR VICTORY WILL ANNOY JOHN BULL!" (*Vide French Press.*)
"What the French have to consider is the balance of advantages for France, not the balance of disadvantages for England."—*Times, Oct. 9.*

Figure 44: A portrayal of the tensions between France and Britain based on remarks published in *The Times*, reproduced in *Punch*, 19 Oct. 1895.

Repeal newspapers (with the former celebrating the country's role within the Westminster system and the latter demanding a return to Dublin's parliamentary autonomy). Such attachment to Parliamentary government remained the common ground between the often-conflicting identities of the peoples and parties of these Isles throughout the century, despite dramatic constitutional and social changes and the devastating impact of the famine in Ireland (1845-1850).

From the 1860s a large number of newspapers, including the metropolitan* *Daily Telegraph** and *Daily News**, the *Manchester Guardian** and the *Newcastle Daily Chronicle** rivalled *The Times** in their ability to report and discuss news* both from Europe and the wider world. In 1876 the 'Bulgarian Atrocities' became the first systematic violation of human rights to be exposed by the media. It resulted in the famous Agitation, which affirmed human rights as a feature of Britishness, in contrast to the allegedly 'barbaric' Ottomans. From 1886 the 'claims of humanity' became the Gladstonian and Home Ruler battle cry against government repression in Ireland, although both Irish and British Unionists claimed that coercion was necessary to protect individual rights against mob rule. At the turn of the century the imperialist* fervour which characterized the early stages of the Boer War (1899-1902) reflected a further dimension of this Unionist vision of coercion as the first step towards British freedom (in this case, freedom for the *Uitlanders* and the 'coloureds', against *Afrikander* oppression). However, it also marked its crisis and rapid decline in the wake of the 'methods of barbarism' and 'Chinese slavery' scandals, which enabled the radical press to revive the Gladstonian demand that Britishness not be separated from 'fair play' and humanity. **EB**

Sources: Biagini 1992, Biagini 2007, Hutchinson 1986, Koss 1981, Lee 1976, Legg 1999, Potter 2004, Williams 1979.

***NATIONAL REFORMER* (1860-1891)** Founded in 1860 by Charles Bradlaugh* and Joseph Barker*, and based in London, the *National Reformer* was, for a time, the most important radical periodical in England. Appealing to the British working class*, this paper sought to inform and mobilize labourers over important issues. Published weekly* at a price* of 2d, its issuing body* was the National Secular Society. The two founders co-edited* the paper, but held diverging views, especially over issues of religion* and birth control. This resulted in a novel editorial arrangement, in which Barker edited the

content of the first half and Bradlaugh the second. This understanding proved unsustainable as Barker could not tolerate Bradlaugh's insistence on publishing articles dealing with birth control and he left in August 1861 to found a more conservative reform paper.

After Bradlaugh became the full proprietor* in 1862 and with the exception of a brief hiatus (1862-1863), Bradlaugh worked quite closely with the paper until his death in 1891. Other major contributors to the paper included William Edwin Adams* who wrote a column* on free thought* in the press under the pseudonym* 'Caractacus' and Annie Besant* who worked with Bradlaugh in an editorial capacity (1874-1891). The paper also encountered a number of legal problems for its publication of radical views as in 1867 when it was prosecuted for sedition. During the trial, Bradlaugh's refusal to testify under oath, as he was an atheist, resulted in the Evidence Amendment Act of 1869. The *National Reformer*'s advocacy of birth control in the 1870s resulted in the prosecution of both Bradlaugh and Besant, with Bradlaugh imprisoned briefly in 1876 before his appeal succeeded. **SBA**

Sources: Griffiths 1992, Vann 1989, *Waterloo*.

***NATIONAL REVIEW* (1855-1864)** The quarterly* *National Review* was founded by the Unitarian minister James Martineau* as a more intellectually upbeat successor to his periodical the *Prospective Review**. Richard Holt Hutton* and non-Unitarian Walter Bagehot* were appointed editors*, and the first number of 250 pages appeared in July 1855. It described itself in an advert in the *Athenaeum** (30 June) as 'A New Quarterly Journal of General Literature*, Politics*, and Social and Religious* Philosophy*, priced* at 5s per issue. In addition to Unitarian topics, the new title contained a wide range of subjects, including politics, literature and social affairs. Maintaining this balance between an editorial obligation to the journal's Unitarian supporters and the demands of a wider readership* proved to be difficult. Another difficulty arose through Hutton's growing Anglican sympathies. He resigned in June 1862, and was replaced by Charles Henry Pearson.

Despite the introduction of new contributors, the journal could not survive the transfer of Unitarian financial backing to a new periodical, the *Theological Review**. The last regular number of the *National Review* appeared in April 1864. Bagehot brought out another issue in November of that year, but reader support had evaporated. Despite its difficulties, the *National Review* made a notable contribution to Victorian thought. It contained some of the most brilliant essays of Walter Bagehot, as well as articles by eminent figures such as Matthew Arnold*, David Brewster, W. R Greg*, Florence Fenwick Miller, Coventry Patmore, Mark Pattison and Baden Powell. **DHL**

Sources: Shattock 1983, Sullivan 1984, Tener 1974, *Waterloo*, *Wellesley*.

NATIONAL REVIEW (1883-1960) A Conservative monthly* journal, the *National Review* was more or less explicitly designed to fill a partisan gap in the market. Initially edited* by Alfred Austin* and William Courthope*, the *National Review* claimed in its first number that it was 'not a Party organ'. This declaration of political* independence should not be taken at face value however, as in the same leader*, Austin wrote that the *National*'s 'pages will be open to all Conservatives who have anything to say, and who know how to say it'. The quarterlies* that had operated as an outlet for the Conservative party, such as the *Quarterly Review**, were losing their influence, and the booming market for monthlies was dominated by the liberal *Fortnightly Review** and the politically noncommittal *Nineteenth Century**.

Climbing from an initial 160 pages, including advertisements*, and costing 2s, the *National* was clearly modelled on monthlies like these, and as a party man, Austin counted among his contributors many of the prominent Conservatives of the day. Alongside political comment, the *National* included articles on art and literature*, often commissioned or written by Courthope, a poet and a literary scholar. In 1893, Leopold James Maxse* took over the editorship, his father having supplied the capital to purchase the magazine* from Austin. Despite Maxse's reassurances that the *National* would remain solidly Conservative, he was a more independent and energetic editor than his predecessor. While the journal retained its conservative inclinations, it emerged as an influential political journal with a populist* style and a much-improved circulation*, due to his determination to appeal to the Tory grass roots. **MaT**

Sources: *National Review* 1883-1899, *ODNB*, *Waterloo*, *Wellesley*.

NATIONAL UNION OF JOURNALISTS (NUJ) (1907-) The National Union of Journalists (NUJ) is the largest trade union for journalists in Britain and Ireland. Today, membership includes 'the whole range of editorial work: staff and freelance, writers and reporters, editors* and subeditors*, photographers and illustrators, working in broadcasting, newspapers, magazines, books, on the internet and in public relations', although entitlement to membership was a contentious issue at its founding.

The NUJ began as an off-shoot of the first professional* association for journalists in Britain, initially called the National Association of Journalists (NAJ), which was inaugurated in Birmingham in October 1884. The NAJ aimed to redress grievances regarding information access, particularly exclusion from the courts and from government meetings, and wrongful accusations of libel, and to assist journalists and their families who were in financial distress. In the March 1886 meeting in London, the NAJ appointed its first general secretary and launched its journal (*Journalism*, 1887-1889). In 1888, the Association changed its name to the Institute of Journalists*, and in 1890 the Institute received a royal charter and became the Chartered Institute of Journalists. The Institute established a number of funds to benefit members, including an orphan fund (1891), a benevolent fund (1898) and a fund to provide unemployment benefits (1910), and a periodical, the *Journalist and Newspaper Proprietor**.

From its inception, the Institute's members disagreed over who should be permitted to join, particularly whether it was appropriate for editors and proprietors* to participate in discussions of working conditions and salaries alongside their employees. Though only a few members, such as the *Manchester Guardian*'s* C. P. Scott, were proprietors, these were disproportionately influential. In 1921, the Institute created a Salaries and Conditions Board that excluded anyone in management.

Long before the Institute arrived at this solution, in 1907, a conference of journalists led by J. H. Haslam, R. C. Spencer, T. K. Sledge, and W. N. Watts voted to form a union to supplement the Institute of Journalists. The National Union of Journalists (NUJ) was registered under the Trade Union Acts, 1871 and 1876, on 15 August 1907, and the first issue of the Union *Journal** (renamed the *Journalist* in 1917), edited by H. M. Richardson, came out in November 1908. Also in 1908, the National Union of Journalists elected G. H. Lethem its first president and achieved its first parliamentary* victory, convincing the House of Commons to pass the Local Authorities (Admission of the Press to Meetings) Act, which restricted the extent to which local governments could exclude reporters* from proceedings. **LB**

Sources: Bainbridge 1984, Bundock 1957, Mansfield 1943, NUJ Website, *Waterloo*.

NATURAL HISTORY REVIEW (1854-1865)
Founded in 1854, the *Natural History Review; A Quarterly Journal of Biological Science* was set up by faculty members of Dublin University in order to publish the transactions of scientific* societies from across Ireland. It was published from Dublin by Hodges and Smith and edited* by Edward Perceval Wright, William Henry Harvey, Samuel Haughton and Arthur Riky Hogan. Its exclusively Irish focus restricted the review's circulation*, especially in the more profitable English market*, and it veered irregularly from quarterly* to annual publication.

In 1860 Wright sought the assistance of Thomas Henry Huxley* in making the unprofitable journal more cosmopolitan and agreed to shift production to England, where Williams and Norgate took over as publishers, as well as allowing Huxley to become general editor. Dismayed at what he considered the 'low condition of natural history journalisation' and swept up in the controversies prompted by the publication of Charles Darwin's *Origin of Species* a year earlier, Huxley set out to transform the *Natural History Review* into a forum, modelled on influential general quarterlies like the *Westminster Review**, for the critical discussion of current biological issues that would appeal to both scientific specialists and general readers. Huxley handpicked a panel of co-editors from the rising generation of naturalists who supported Darwinism, including George Busk and William Benjamin Carpenter*, and wrote privately that the review, which had broadly opposed Darwinism in its Irish incarnation, would now give Darwin an opportunity to slay his adversaries.

Huxley's ambitious agenda was short-lived however. His editorial role was not only massively time-consuming but also failed to deliver a general audience, with circulation* never getting beyond 1,000, and the avowedly inclusive and open-minded *Natural History Review* became both increasingly specialist and narrowly partisan. The review's use of detailed and expensively produced anatomical plates which offended prudish general readers exemplified the tensions involved in presenting professional scientific journalism to a broad audience. The *Natural History Review* folded in 1865 with Huxley losing £25 of his own money. **GD**
Sources: Barton 1998, Burkhardt 1983, Desmond 1994-1997, Huxley 1900, *Waterloo*.

NATURE (1869-) Founded in 1869, *Nature* quickly became the most prestigious scientific* journal in Britain. In the circular sent out in advance of the first number, its editor*, Joseph Norman Lockyer*, stated that the new journal had two specific aims: 'First, to place before the general public the grand results of Scientific Work and Scientific Discovery, and to urge the claims of Science to a more general recognition in Education and in Daily Life; and Secondly, to aid Scientific men themselves, by giving early information of all advances made in any branch of Natural Knowledge throughout the world, and by affording them an opportunity of discussing the various Scientific questions which arise from time to time'.

In 1870 Lockyer declared the journal a success, steering a middle course between being a barely read specialist scientific journal and an overly sensational popular science journal. However, although Lockyer boasted of *Nature*'s 5,000 subscribers and 15,000 readers*, this was still markedly less than other scientific weeklies* such as *Chemical News**, *Knowledge** and the *English Mechanic**. What distinguished *Nature* from its competitors* was the calibre of its contributors. Lockyer's previous editorial experience had been as science editor of the *Reader** during the period in which it was taken over by the group of scientists associated with the X Club. Although it was sold in 1865 as it was losing money, Lockyer – and the various contributors to the *Reader* – believed that a general scientific weekly could pay. It was periodicity that was important: the failure of Thomas Henry Huxley's* earlier experiment in periodical publishing with the quarterly* *Natural History Review* persuaded Lockyer and the publisher* of *Nature*, Alexander Macmillan* that a weekly journal would provide a prompt medium for the publication of scientific research while also serving as a vehicle for scientific news*.

The form of *Nature* resembled existing non-scientific weeklies such as the *Athenaeum**. Each number opened with leading articles and scientific papers, followed by more miscellaneous articles and notices. Although Lockyer only contributed a minority of the leaders*, they often focused on the place of science within culture and many were devoted to what was seen as his pet topic, the endowment of scientific research. 'Notes', reviews* of recent books and journals, reports from scientific societies (from London, elsewhere in Britain and around the world), and a lively correspondence* column* allowed *Nature* to keep abreast of current controversies. There was a list of the week's forthcoming meetings printed on the final pages or in the advertising* wrapper.

When its price* rose from 4d to 6d in 1878, *Nature* was twice the price of the *Athenaeum* and more expensive than most other scientific weeklies. Both

Lockyer and Macmillan were well connected within the scientific community, and so could draw upon their contacts to provide content and a ready market* for the journal. These same contacts were also used to attract talented young office staff, including John Scott Keltie* and Richard Arman Gregory*, who could assist Lockyer with editing the journal. However, the rather select audience for *Nature* was not sufficient to make it profitable, and it did not turn a profit until 1899. Macmillan nevertheless bore the costs both out of sympathy for the journal's goals and for the advertising opportunities afforded by such an influential niche publication. JEM

Sources: Anon 2007, Barton 2004, Macleod 2000, Meadows 1970, Roos 1981.

NEW AGE (1894-1938) Founded as a 1d weekly* in October 1894 by Frederick A. Atkins with the subtitle *A Weekly Record of Christian Culture, Social Service, and Literary Life*, the journal aimed to 'combine the highest uses of a newspaper with the more instructive services of a magazine'. Reflecting its subtitle, its 20 pages included topical commentary on religious* issues, mixed with interviews* and book reviews*, and interspersed with advertisements*, in particular for books likely to appeal to its late nineteenth-century Christian readership*. Its early contributors included Richard Le Gallienne*, Israel Zangwill*, Katharine Tynan and Jerome K Jerome*. A. E. Fletcher became editor* in 1895 and the journal progressively became more socialist*, changing its sub-title to *A Journal for Thinkers and Workers*; at the same time Ramsay MacDonald became a regular contributor. Fletcher was succeeded as editor by Arthur Compton-Rickett and then Joseph Clayton.

By 1907, the journal was severely in debt to its printers, Bonner & Co, and was acquired by A. R. Orage and Holbrook Jackson with funding provided, in part, by the Fabian socialist George Bernard Shaw*. Orage and Jackson began a new series of the journal, which, under Orage, went on to become

Figure 45: The masthead of the *New Age*, 4 Oct. 1894.

an important source of and platform for socialist and modernist ideas. 'The *New Age* has been honourably associated in the past with the enthusiastic advocacy of the ideals of life. It is therefore fitting that the *New Age* should now become the critical friendly exponent of the practical steps towards the realisation of those ideals' wrote Orage in 1907, in the introductory leader* to the new series of the journal. JRW

Sources: Martin 1967, *ODNB*.

NEW BON-TON MAGAZINE OR THE TELESCOPE OF THE TIMES (1818-1821) In October 1818 the first issue of the satirical* monthly* *New Bon-Ton Magazine or The Telescope of the Times* (subtitled *Microscope of Fashion and Folly*) appeared. It made no reference to the *Bon-Ton Magazine* of two decades earlier, into whose satirical footsteps it supposedly followed. In comparison with the near-contemporary *Satirist*, the *New Bon-Ton* adopted a much milder tone, even rejecting contributors for offering immoderate or inflammatory material. The proprietors*, in fact, wished the magazine* to be both 'a monitor of moral instruction' and 'an agreeable companion', hence the motto on its title page: 'To lash the follies and vices of mankind;/ To mend the moral, and instruct the mind; / this is our object, this our sole endeavour;/ By this we hope to keep in public favour'.

The periodical concentrated on political* and social* satire and found its main interest in royalty, the church and the law. Articles also covered such topics as the Revolution in Haiti, Catholic emancipation, the Queen Caroline controversy and the Irish question. Last but not least, the English aristocracy in society received a good deal of attention. The *New Bon-Ton* made the bold claim that vice flourished more abundantly in the higher than in the lower echelons of society, and saw it as its duty to bring this to light. Not surprisingly, contributors preferred to write under cover of anonymity* and use pseudonyms, so as to avoid prosecution. The only literary* criticism of note that appeared in the journal was an attack on the dubious moral foundation of Byron's *Don Juan*.

The magazine was edited by J. Johnston (also the publisher*) and John Mitford. The latter (not to be confused with the editor of the *Gentleman's Magazine*) led a turbulent, alcohol-drenched life which came to a tragic end in St Giles Workhouse on 24 December 1831. Before starting work on the *New Bon-Ton*, he had edited* *Scourge, or Monthly Expositor of Imposture and Folly* (1811-1814), and shortly before his death, he had been at work on the *Quizzical Gazette*.

Each issue of the *New Bon-Ton* opened with a coloured cartoon*. In appearance and layout, the magazine was attractive and readable, with its pages appearing in single-column*, with clear print and bold-faced captions. **OD**

Sources: *ODNB*, Sullivan, *Waterloo*.

NEW JOURNALISM The term 'New Journalism' refers to a set of typographical and textual innovations that transformed the press in the late nineteenth century. It was made notorious in an article by Matthew Arnold* entitled 'Up to Easter' published in the *Nineteenth Century** in 1887. Although Arnold claimed that the new journalism 'has much to recommend it', its one fault, he wrote, was that 'it is *feather-brained*'. For Arnold the new journalism represented the worst elements of democratic levelling, bringing periodical publishing down to the level of journalism rather than up to literature or criticism. In particular, Arnold viewed William Thomas Stead*, then editor* of the *Pall Mall Gazette**, as a well-intentioned but misguided demagogue. What Stead represented was a certain campaigning form of journalism. While editor of the *Northern Echo (1871-1880)* and *Pall Mall Gazette (1883-1889)* he conceived the editor's role as marshalling the public, and drew upon techniques from American dailies*, such as cross heads, interviews*, bold headlines, illustration*, indices and specials, in order to reach them better. In the aftermath of one of the defining incidents associated with the New Journalism, the scandal stirred up by his 'The Maiden Tribute of Modern Babylon' in 1885, Stead wrote two essays in the *Contemporary Review** that set out to define journalism as the medium for democracy. However, these essays, 'Government by Journalism' and 'The Future of Journalism', were written while the circulation* of the *Pall Mall Gazette* was in decline as both readers and advertisers* became increasingly wary of its editor's campaigning zeal.

There were those, however, who did succeed in making New Journalism profitable. In 1881, while Stead was working under John Morley* at the *Pall Mall Gazette, George Newnes** – a schoolmate of Stead's* – launched *Tit-Bits**, a penny weekly* that consisted of short snippets of morally-sound content aimed squarely at the lower middle classes*. Selling between 400-600,000 copies a week, *Tit-Bits* avoided alienating its readers with light content that could be consumed both on the journey to work or read in the home. Newnes employed a range of gimmicks, including providing travel insurance to readers and running elaborate competitions, in order to attract readers. These techniques were so effective that not only did *Tit-Bits* rapidly gather a number of imitators such as *Answers to Correspondents** and *Pearson's Weekly** but its techniques spread to journals with quite different ideological positions such as the evangelical penny weekly *Great Thoughts*.

Although Arnold identified Stead as the archetypal editor of the New Journalism, the changes with which the genre* was associated had more to do with changes in the market*. The 1870 Education Act prompted the recognition of new readers – and correspondingly new places and tunes of reading – that coincided with shifts in ideology in more established periodical publications. The foundation of the *Fortnightly Review** (1865) and the *Nineteenth Century* (1877) marked a move from the editorial 'we' to a recognition of the star quality of named authorities. Equally, the various typographical innovations of the new journalism had long existed in the advertising* pages of the press. What Arnold objected to was the adoption of such trends in publications that conceived of the public in the largest possible terms: the serious reader studied texts in private; the New Journalism was explicit about selling itself to 'the busy man' or 'busy woman' to read whenever they could. **JEM**

Sources: Arnold 1887, Baylen 1972, Brake 1994, Jackson 2001, O'Connor 1889.

***NEW MONTHLY MAGAZINE* (1814-1884)** The *New Monthly Magazine and Universal Register* was founded by the publisher* Henry Colburn* as a Tory counter to the more liberal journals of the period. With the first issue in February 1814, it aimed to be 'bound to no party either in literature* or politics*'. For six years the journal covered subjects as diverse as its 'Chemical Report' and 'New Acts of Parliament', together with the standard magazine contents and a format* similar to the *Gentleman's Magazine** and the *Annual Register*.

In January 1820 Colburn changed the title to the *New Monthly Magazine and Literary Journal*, improved the format and increased the number of literary articles. The poet Thomas Campbell* became a figurehead editor* and much of the work was undertaken by Cyrus Redding. Contributors included William Hazlitt*, Leigh Hunt*, Mary Russell Mitford, W. H. Ainsworth*, Eliza Lynn Linton*, Thackeray*, Ugo Foscolo and Horace Smith. In July 1829 the *New Monthly* absorbed its main competition* the *London Magazine**. Redding and Campbell resigned over differences with Colburn in 1830 and were replaced by S. C. Hall* for a short period, followed by the novelist E. L. Bulwer* (Nov. 1831-Aug. 1833). As a publisher and proprietor* Colburn achieved notoriety for 'puffing'* his own authors and the practice was attacked by Macaulay in the April 1830 *Edinburgh Review**. Colburn continued the practice nevertheless.

Bulwer advocated political reform (especially the 1832 Reform Bill) through the journal, and Thomas Carlyle*, Harriet Martineau*, Elizabeth Barrett Browning, John Forster* and Benjamin Disraeli became contributors. Bulwer resigned through ill-health and Hall again took control with less emphasis on politics. Theodore Hook* became editor (Jan. 1837-Aug. 1841) with a change in title to the *New Monthly and Humorist.* Frances Trollope and William Makepeace Thackeray* upheld the literary standard. A period of editorial instability ended with W. H. Ainsworth's* acquisition and editorship of the journal (June 1845-Dec. 1870). In January 1853 the title was shortened to the *New Monthly Magazine.* Contributors included both W. H. Ainsworth and his cousin William Francis Ainsworth, R. S. Surtees, Ellen Wood*, John Oxenford* and Mary Anne S. Bushby. From January 1871 to 1879 W. F. Ainsworth was both proprietor and editor, with Chapman and Hall* owning it in its final years. In 1883 only three issues were published with the last issue at 1s in January 1884. **DA**
Sources: *ODNB,* Parker 2000, Sullivan, *Waterloo, Wellesley.*

NEW MORAL WORLD (1834-1845)

The *New Moral World* was the national organ of Owenism. The longest-enduring early socialist* periodical, the *New Moral World* was launched in November 1834 as popular interest in Owenism was at its height. This phase of early socialism emphasized general unionism and labour exchanges, keenly anticipating peaceable revolution. But this mood swiftly ebbed away, replaced by greater emphasis upon establishing socialist communities. The change was encapsulated by Robert Owen's* decision to close the weekly* *Crisis**, replacing it with *New Moral World: A London Weekly Publication, Developing the Principles of the Rational System of Society.* The title had already been used by one of the many ephemeral Owenite periodicals, *New Moral World & Official Gazette of the National Association of Industry, Humanity, and Knowledge* (30 Aug. 1834). *Crisis* had been given away in large numbers by wealthy supporters, and *New Moral World* never matched its circulation*. Blending branch news, policy directives, correspondence*, poetry* and extensive comment pieces, the *New Moral World* and its Chartist

equivalent the *Northern Star** were distributed by the same network of radical newsagents*, while production also often overlapped.

In 1837 Owen handed routine editorial matters over to George Fleming (editor of the *Star**, 1850-1852), while between 1839 and 1842, Joshua Hobson* produced both papers from Leeds. This move coincided with a subtitle change to, the *Gazette of the Universal Community Society of Rational Religionists,* reflecting the recent opening of the official Owenite community, Harmony Hall, in Hampshire. For seven months in 1845 the *World* was printed at Harmony, but the community and the paper failed simultaneously. As contemporary wits observed, Harmony Hall was 'all owin', no payin', an allusion to debts of £315. Owen had already walked away from both Harmony and the paper which was then sold to James Hill, one of Owen's fiercest socialist critics. Hill published the three final issues, overlapping Fleming's attempted revival, as the *Moral World* (Aug.-Nov. 1845). **MSC**
Sources: Harrison 1969, Royle 1998.

NEW QUARTERLY MAGAZINE (1873-1880)

The *New Quarterly Magazine* was a curious anomaly. Offering complete works of fiction in each issue, it tried to compete with existing essay-laden quarterlies* and the monthly* or weekly* magazines that used serial* fiction as a draw. Its founder, Oswald Crawfurd*, was a diplomat whose light duties allowed ample time for writing. He had clear ideas about the sorts of things the *New Quarterly Magazine* was interested in; the prospectus in the *Athenaeum** (6 Sept. 1873: 319) lists 'Papers on Topics of Social and General Interest', travel, biography, and of course in each issue 'Two or more Tales of considerable length by Eminent Writers. The tales will invariably be completed in the Number in which they appear. In fact the first tale offered, 'Olivia Tempest: A Novel', written by one 'John Dangerfield', was by Crawfurd himself, and he continued to write a substantial amount of the magazine's fiction.

The intended audience of the *New Quarterly Magazine* was clearly defined: literary, discerning, educated, like its editor*. At 2s 6d (11s per annum), each issue of the magazine was substantial at 220 pages, and the venture was clearly successful, at least initially. The *Athenaeum* for 11 October 1873 carries a notice from the editor to the effect that reprints of the first issue (published on 1 Oct.) will be available from 13 October. In January 1876 Crawfurd inaugurated a new section called 'Current Literature* and Current Criticism'. The idea was to gather critical opinion about a particular work; the publication intervals between issues of the magazine would allow for this, and for any controversy about a book to die down. So that the *New Quarterly Magazine* could be seen to be impartial, advertisements* from publishers were declined. The *Academy** thought it clever, though they also joked that the readers of the *New Quarterly Magazine* prefer to be 'a quarter behind the world' (*Academy*, 8 Jan. 1876: 32).

At the end of 1877 Crawfurd sold the magazine to Francis Hueffer*, previously assistant editor of the *Academy* and contributor to the *New Quarterly Magazine*. The proprietorship* passed similarly from Ward, Lock & Tyler* to Chatto and Windus*, Hueffer arranging to edit the magazine for Chatto & Windus for £10 per issue, 'with 'a further sum of £5 for every 500 copies sold beyond 2000 of each number' (*Wellesley*). Crawfurd had been careful to exclude controversial subjects from the pages of the magazine. Under Hueffer articles on politics* appeared, and the quality of literary contributors was raised. R. L. Stevenson, Thomas Hardy* and Edmund Gosse* all wrote for the *New Quarterly Magazine*. Hueffer also kept the 'Current Literature and Current Criticism' section, similarly declining advertisements from publishers. In 1878 Hueffer became music* critic for *The Times** and sold his interest in the magazine to Kegan Paul*, at which point the impartiality of the magazine disappeared. Circulation* appeared to be a problem, and the issue for April 1880 was its last. ET

Sources: *Athenaeum* 1873, *Athenaeum* 1878, *ODNB*, *The Times* 1 Feb. 1909 (Crawfurd obituary), *Waterloo*, *Wellesley*.

NEW REVIEW (1889-1897) Founded by Archibald Grove*, the Liberal MP for West Ham, the *New Review* aimed to be a critical journal on 'Politics, Science, and Art'. It was edited by Grove, assisted by Gerard Yorke Twisleton-Wykeham Fiennes and, later, Arthur Waugh, and published by Longmans, Green*. From the beginning an impressive group contributed signed articles, including Charles Bradlaugh*, Thomas Carlyle*, Charles W. Dilke*, Millicent Fawcett*, Rider Haggard, G. J. Holyoake*, Henry James*, Andrew Lang*, Eliza Lynn Linton*, Cardinal Manning, Max Müller and Leo Tolstoy. Taking its cue from its competitor*, the *Nineteenth Century*, symposia were soon a featured format*, with some – 'Candour in English Fiction' – becoming important documents of their time, as did certain articles such as T. P. O'Connor's on the New Journalism*.

Priced* at just 6d, the monthly* initially sold 39,000 copies per issue, four times the circulation* of the *Nineteenth Century* selling for 2s. However, almost immediately there were financial difficulties. In 1891 the price rose to 9d, then to 1s in 1894. Despite this, in January 1894 Grove announced that the *New Review* would begin a new series, aiming to be a 'review of tomorrow'. Later that year, though, Grove retired as editor* and proprietor* and a group of his friends, including the publisher William Heinemann, briefly took over. As assistant editor, Waugh increasingly ran the journal, but the contents began to drop in quality and sales declined.

At the beginning of 1895 it was purchased for the jobless William Ernest Henley* by his friends who installed him as the nominal editor. Henley's extensive literary contacts were of considerable importance for the journal. He brought with him H. G. Wells's* 'The Time Machine' (1895) and later published Joseph Conrad's first novel 'The Nigger of the Narcissus' (1897) as well as some of W. B. Yeats's occult stories. But Henley's advanced literary tastes were often out of line with those of the *New Review*'s readers*, and after the publication of an 'indiscreet' story with sexual overtones, sales dropped sharply. George Wyndham*, who tried to salvage the wreckage of the *New Review*, was unable to rescue it. Even the publication of Henry James's 'What Maisie Knew' did nothing to help and the issue for December 1897 was its last. ML

Sources: Gross 1969, Koss 1981-1984, Sullivan, *Wellesley*.

NEW SPORTING MAGAZINE (1831-1870) The *New Sporting Magazine* was founded by the journalist and writer Robert Smith Surtees* in collaboration with the publisher* Rudolph Ackerman and the sporting* journalist, C. J. Apperley ('Nimrod')*. A monthly* magazine, it consisted of 50 to 60 pages of double-column* print, illustrated* with engravings* and lithographs*. The subject matter was mainly devoted to hunting and field sports, but it also covered Parliament*, the fine arts and anatomy.

Surtees, a gifted and hard-working editor*, had left his post as hunting correspondent with the *Sporting Magazine** to found the rival New Sporting Magazine, and it was an immediate success. However, as the *New Sporting Magazine* was 'established by gentlemen who carried it on more for amusement than for profit' (Watson: 56), it was launched with little capital and no revenue, making it difficult to procure contributors. Surtees solved the problem by writing the whole journal himself under different pseudonyms*. Despite financial difficulties, Surtees did manage to attract other notable contributors including Mark Lemon* (who signed himself 'Tom Moody' for the journal) and Thomas Hood*. Illustrators* included Francis Grant, J. F Henning and Edwin Landseer. Surtees created the immensely popular character 'John Jorrocks', grocer, huntsman and squire, (1831-1834). Surtees's novel 'Handley Cross' was serialized* (1840-1841), after his departure as editor in 1836, when he left after a disagreement with Apperley. The journal was offered for sale, and W. A. Chatto became editor in 1837. The first series of the *New Sporting Magazine* continued until 1840, with the second series1841-1870. **DHL**

Sources: Gregory 2003, Sutherland 1988, *Waterloo*, Watson 1933, Welcome 1982.

NEWCASTLE CHRONICLE (1764-1858); NEWCASTLE DAILY CHRONICLE (1858-)

The *Newcastle Chronicle* was founded in 1764 by Thomas Slack and then came under the proprietorship* of the Hodgson family, first Sarah and then her sons Thomas and James, who were owners and editors* until December 1849. The Hodgson brothers, both Unitarians, invested heavily in the paper and succeeded in making the *Chronicle* 'the leading political* organ between York and Edinburgh'. It was a highly influential paper, especially among local Whigs and secured a stable advertising* base from its middle-class* readers. It roundly condemned the Peterloo massacre and became a staunch advocate of political reform. The Hodgsons were well connected, not least to Earl Grey's family, and the *Chronicle*'s support during the reform crisis of 1832 helped the Northern Political Union to create a mass platform.

The launch of a Tory newspaper, the *Newcastle Journal*, in May 1832 placed the Hodgsons under great pressure from local Liberals to circulate the *Chronicle* twice weekly. Then, and later when other newspapers appeared, they outwitted their competitors by investing in new technology and a robust distribution* system which facilitated its circulation* beyond the North-East, into Yorkshire and Cumberland. In 1850 the *Chronicle* was sold on to Mark William Lambert and his two associates. They installed new machinery, including a hydraulic press* from William Armstrong, and recruited an able team of journalists. With this new infrastructure in place, the paper was relaunched on 1 May 1858 as the *Newcastle Daily Chronicle*, a four-page 1d paper. The pressures of daily* publication,

however, proved too much and in late 1859 the paper was sold to the famous Newcastle radical Joseph Cowen Jnr (1829-1900) whose entrepreneurial talents secured its long-term future.

Cowen was already convinced that the 'paper pulpit' was the best way to promote his radical creed. He invested upwards of £40,000 in technological and stylistic improvements in a bid to make the *Chronicle* 'The Times of the North'. He launched the *Newcastle Weekly Chronicle** and installed the new rotary press; in the face of considerable criticism, he introduced sports* reports, serialized* literature, local gossip* and special features on mining villages and co-operative stores. With the veteran journalist W. E. Adams* as editor of the *Weekly*, and Richard Bagnall Reed as manager of the *Daily*, Cowen soon had a formidable team. In 1871 he acquired a London office and it became the first provincial* newspaper to have its own private telegraph*, and the first to install a Linotype. With daily sales of over 40,000 by 1873, it claimed to be the largest selling regional* newspaper of its kind. Other innovations followed, four double-web printing presses* in 1878, a Paris office, the introduction of illustrations* and the launch of the *Evening Chronicle* in 1885.

After Cowen's death in 1900 the *Chronicle* press was managed by Cowen's daughter Jane, who expanded the paper to ten pages. The *Chronicle* came under strong competition at the beginning of the twentieth century, not least from the *North Mail*, which was founded in 1901. Nevertheless, the 'pitmen's' bible' survived the vicissitudes of two world wars and other commercial threats. As with many other provincial titles it passed out of family hands, first of all to the Thomson Press and eventually, in company with its old rival the *Newcastle Journal*, into the hands of Trinity Mirror plc. **JA**

Sources: Allen 2007, Ashton 1991, Brett 1924, Hodgson 1908, Read 1961.

NEWCASTLE COURANT: WITH NEWS FORREIGN AND DOMESTICK (1711-1902)

The *Newcastle Courant*, one of the earliest eighteenth-century provincial* newspapers, was founded on 29 July 1711 by John White Jnr. (1689-1769), who also had business interests in the *York Mercury* and the *York Courant*. Initially it was published as a tri-weekly of four quarto pages before moving to a weekly* format*. White capitalized on Newcastle's burgeoning economy and printed an unusually high volume of advertisements*. Its success was largely attributable to White who circumvented the tax in 1712 by presenting the paper as a periodical and doubling its size* to provide extensive coverage of the Peace of Utrecht. He provided a balance of news* and entertainment, and after the mid-century he published a regular fashion* column*. The *Courant*'s brand of high Tory* respectability ensured that it retained the loyalties of the local elite and rising middle classes After White's death in 1769 the paper passed to Thomas Saint who introduced the 'General Hue and Cry' to the front page in 1772. Successive proprietors* John Hall (1788) and Edward Walker (1796) maintained the paper's conservative stance. Walker enlarged the paper and introduced a heraldic motif to the *Courant*'s masthead*.

In the first decades of the nineteenth century the paper firmly denounced the 'dangerous spirits' advocating reform and criticized other newspapers for encouraging dissent. Its price* fell in these years from 6d (Nov. 1806) to 3½d (May 1807) to 2d (1832). Still competitively* priced at 4½ d in 1838, it offered readers the full spectrum of commercial, agricultural and shipping intelligence as well as news* and parliamentary* reports. Regular sporting* columns helped to anchor its position as the most popular* newspaper in the region with a claimed weekly circulation* of more than 5,000 copies in 1848. After 1855 the paper struggled and was repeatedly sold on. John Henry Rutherford, who acquired the *Courant* in 1869, reduced the price and launched an evening edition in April 1870, but to no avail. In February 1876 it was bought out by the *Newcastle Daily Journal* who initially published it as the *Newcastle Courant, with which is incorporated the North of England Farmer.* In 1884, under Robert Redpath's proprietorship*, the paper was rebranded as the *Newcastle Weekly Courant.* After 1902 it appeared variously as the *Newcastle Weekly Journal and Courant*, the *Newcastle Daily Journal and Courant* (1915-1924) and the *Newcastle Journal, North Star and Courant (1924-1930)*. The title finally disappeared in March 1939. JA

Sources: Barker 1998, Black 1987, Clephan 1859, Milne 1971, Isaac 1999.

NEWCASTLE WEEKLY CHRONICLE (1864-1953)

The *Newcastle Weekly Chronicle* was an influential, innovatory and widely read radical newspaper edited* by the ex-Chartist* W. E. Adams and owned by Joseph Cowen Jnr. Its promotion of universal suffrage, trade unionism, working-class self-help institutions and internationalism earned it a reputation as the 'pit-men's bible'. But it was also a family* newspaper, broadened its appeal with illus-

trations*, a Ladies' Column*, a Children's Corner, a Doctor's Department, a Lawyer's Corner, poetry* and essay competitions. The *Weekly Chronicle* also developed a strong regional identity with features on north-east history, folk lore and legend. A Literary* Supplement* was launched in 1885, the same year that the paper halved its price* to 1d and doubled its size* to 16 pages. The paper's continuing success was underlined by the steady rise in its circulation* figures: from 2,000 in 1864, the paper claimed 45,000 readers* in 1875 drawn both from within and beyond the region.

By this time the *Chronicle* benefited from Cowen's investment in state of the art machinery, a London office in Essex Street, the Strand and a nation-wide distribution* network (copies were also made available for purchase in New York, Paris and Antwerp). Staff included James Annand (later the editor of the *Pall Mall Gazette*) and a number of veteran Chartist and radical journalists including R. G. Gammage, G. J. Harney*, G. J. Holyoake*, Lloyd Jones and George Howell. The paper won considerable praise in America with one Chicago editor calling it the 'the best paper in the world'. Adams retired in 1900 and was succeeded by his son Ernest. The *Chronicle* was published continuously (interrupted only by the Second World War) until 5 April 1953, when it was absorbed into the *Newcastle Evening Chronicle*. OA

Sources: Allen 2007, Ashton 1991, Milne 1971, Todd 1991.

NEWMAN, EDWARD (1801-1876)

Newman pursued an interest in natural history while working as a wool-stapler and then a rope-maker, and in 1831 began contributing to the *Magazine of Natural History*° under the pseudonym* 'Rusticus'. In the following year he *helped* found and became editor* of the *Entomological Magazine,* which ran until 1838. In 1840 Newman became the partner of George Luxford*, an East London printer who had the contract for the *Magazine of Natural History,* before buying Luxford out only a year later. This arrangement enabled Newman to start a number of natural history periodicals, beginning with the *Entomologist* in 1840, which he merged with the *Zoologist* in 1843 and edited until his death, having earlier resurrected *the Entomologist* as a separate title in 1863. Additionally, in 1841 he set up and contributed to the *Phytologist,* which was edited by Luxford and ran until 1863 although it was never a commercial success.

Newman used his journals to advance his anti-evolutionary views and to encourage greater

amateur participation in science*. Newman was also the natural history editor of the *Field* (1858-1876). **GD**
Sources: Lightman 2004a, *ODNB*, Sheets-Pyenson 1985.

NEWMAN, WILLIAM (FL.1832-1864) Although William Newman's dates are unknown, he was of the generation of Robert Seymour* and Cruikshank*, all artists who came to periodical illustration* by way of the single-plate caricature* tradition. He was drawing satirical* alternative title pages for periodicals in direct imitation of C. J. Grant* in the early 1830s, but only reappears in periodical illustration in the early 1840s, by which time he was working in wood for the short-lived *Squib* (1842). An uncouth and ill-educated man, he was introduced to *Punch** by Ebenezer Landells*, drawing several hundred cuts for the magazine in the second half of the 1840s. Despite his prolific output, he never gained access to the inner circle at *Punch*, and spent much of his time drawing the tiny silhouettes or 'blackies' that maintained the punning Regency mode of Hood* and his contemporaries on into the early Victorian period. An important link between an earlier caricature tradition and the increasingly whimsical cartooning* of the 1840s, Newman became disillusioned with his treatment at *Punch*. As he was paid only 18s for 12 silhouettes, he resented Leech's* higher rates of pay, and decided to emigrate to America*, working there for a wide variety of comic magazines. **BM**
Sources: Engen 1990, Houfe 1978.

NEWNES, GEORGE (1851-1910) George Newnes, editor*, publisher*, and proprietor*, was one of the most influential figures in British publishing during the late Victorian and Edwardian periods, especially in the development of the New Journalism* which laid the foundations for modern journalistic practice. He established a vast number and variety of periodicals in the years 1881 to 1910, pioneering new styles, formats* and journalistic techniques and accessing new audiences.

With the weekly *Tit-Bits** (1881), financed by a vegetarian restaurant he had opened in Manchester, Newnes established the first widely circulating* penny* miscellany* paper. The *Million* (1892) pioneered colour illustration* in the cheap* popular* press. The *Westminster Gazette** was a Liberal evening newspaper which straddled the ground between the political press and the commercial press, combining the traditions and attachments of the old journalism with the modernizing techniques of New Journalism*. The *Strand Magazine** was a pro-

totype of the 6d short-story magazine in which illustrations* were featured prominently and frequently, and the *Ladies' Field* (1898) set new standards in pictorial printing. Newnes used new techniques of photographic* reproduction extensively in the *Wide World Magazine* – the original 'true story magazine' which was much copied in the twentieth century. The *Captain* (1899) was an early and successful example of the 'respectable' boys' paper, with its use of acknowledged authorities and real sporting heroes a new technique in soliciting readers. And *C. B. Fry's Magazine* (1904) was one of the first magazines to employ the sportsman-editor, writing under his own name, to produce an authoritative sporting* journal.

Politically, Newnes was a firm Liberal, holding a parliamentary seat for the Newmarket division of Cambridgeshire (1885-1895), and again for Swansea (1900-1910). He was awarded a baronetcy in recognition of his services to the party. In journalism, Newnes was an innovator and an entrepreneur, balancing the potentially conflicting imperatives of old and new journalism to become one of a handful of 'press barons' that dominated late-nineteenth century journalism. As the *Daily Graphic** commented in its obituary*, 'An innovator has gone, though he has left his influence behind…'. **KJ**
Sources: Jackson, *ODNB*, *Waterloo*.

NEWS The difficulty of defining 'news' was well known in the nineteenth century even though it was key for the legal classification of newspapers and class publications*. The term was current in fourteenth-century English, when it was more or less synonymous with 'novelties'. The emergence of its specialised sense – where it refers to reported recent events of special interest or importance – was bound up with the printing revolution. The industrialization of printing in the nineteenth century amplified many of the early effects of Gutenberg's invention, and wholesale changes in the nature and function of news resulted. 'News' – who has the right to define, produce and read it and the regulation of these acts – was a site of intense political struggle during the period that the Taxes on Knowledge* were in force, while the effective triumph of the market* in 1855 when the Stamp Duty became optional only meant that the market had proved itself a more effective form of social control. Resistance to news as a product in a marketplace took place thereafter only sporadically, e.g. with some socialist newspapers*. It is also important to recognize that news never existed unfettered, as it was closely regulated by libel, blasphemy

Figure 46: A cartoon of the 1830s literally portraying the blow which Henry Brougham hoped Stamp Duty reduction would deal to *The Times*.

and obscenity laws and, from 1889, by the Official Secrets Act.

If what news comprises is hard to pin down, it is nonetheless a defining characteristic not just of newspapers but, in a more subtle form, of periodicals in general. The latter, according to Mill (1824), depend on an organization of capital which is based on rapid turnover (even quarterlies*, as he points out, are ruled by this logic); the book by contrast is an investment which requires capital to be tied up for perhaps indefinite periods. The rapid turnover of periodicals is generated by a concentration on the topical – necessarily temporary in its interest – which might comprise, in the case of the Reviews*, the latest issues one ought to discuss socially or the books one ought to read. Weekly* satirical* journals such as *Punch** were based largely on events reported in the daily* press. Fashion* news, shipping news, literary news, sports results, theatrical notices and countless other subcategories of news might find their way into newspapers and periodicals depending on the outlook, the function and the readership* of the publication in hand. Specialist journals usually carried news sections (under various headings) with their own implicit definitions of what constituted news for their readers: the

*Builder** reported on architectural competitions and technological advances in building techniques, while the *Musical Times and Singing Class Circular** relayed to its readers information about the doings of composers, conductors, musicians, orchestras, and choirs. Across most genres* of periodical, advertising* was an important component that was often itself news, drawing attention to the latest inventions, forthcoming theatrical performances or job vacancies (*Mitchell's**, amongst others, noted the potential legal confusion of news and advertisements).

For newspapers, 'news' might cover such diverse items as speeches in parliament, the latest horrid murder, natural disasters or the current price of corn. Different models of what constituted news existed: was news out there waiting to be found, or – as was the case in the investigative journalism* that developed in the latter part of the century as an element of the New Journalism* – were newspapers under an obligation to make the news rather than simply register it? W. T. Stead* of the *Pall Mall Gazette** famously advocated the latter. There are also important distinctions to be made between the national and local press. The processes of news gathering in the metropolitan press – with its focus on political and foreign news – is well documented (the bibliography to this volume provides an extensive secondary literature, and see Journalists, Reporters, News Agencies*, Foreign correspondents*, Foreign news*, Global Journalism*). The provincial press* contained stories of local* interest that would not necessarily be picked up by the nationals, while it raided metropolitan* newspapers for stories (often reprinting entire articles several days later). The nationalization of the telegraph* system in 1870 and the formation of the Press Association* and Reuters* effectively gave the provincial press equal access to national and international news, but it also meant that what constituted news was no longer decided solely by the editor* of a given paper but also by the anonymous and only purportedly impartial operatives of news agencies*. The selection of news by each paper from the hundreds or even thousands of Press Association wires that arrived daily was itself a highly charged ideological activity.

It is in the periodical's agenda-setting function with its inevitable sell-by date that news becomes a defining feature of periodicals. In the whirl of modernity of which the press is a part, readers over centuries learnt that they could never have enough news, that they were always already out of date. The news cycle itself became shorter and shorter throughout the nineteenth century as the drive to be the first with the news (by both producer and consumer) was aided by developments in communications and printing technologies. News – and with the advent of the *Illustrated London News**, news illustration* – fed into a manufactured desire for what metaphysicians would call 'presence', allowing readers to imagine that they were face to face with events or actors of social importance (a definition which allows a variety of uses and gratifications, or social contextual approaches to news consumption: see Ang 1995). Multiple editions* of a single issue of a newspaper enabled key events to be added as the day (or the week) wore on, and the New Journalism pioneered the use of headlines to give an eye-catching typographical emphasis to the latest piece of important news. That possession of the news – engagement in the public sphere – is presented as a necessary component of the good citizen does not detract from its nature as a magical commodity. While from a consumer's view news might have a metaphysical dimension, from the perspective of an investor , news is a hook to make people buy regularly and increase capital turnover, a particular approach to handling the risks of capital investment in the print industry. This was certainly the reasoning of *The Times** editor Delane* who determined to keep intact the reputation of his paper as the first with news when he sent W. H. Russell to the Crimean front after the *Morning Chronicle** had beaten it by 48 hours with news that the Turks had crossed the Danube in October 1853 (*History of the Times*, vol.2:167-168). AK/MaT
Sources: Ang 1995, Baldasty 1992, Boyce, Conboy 2004, Curran and Wingate 1978, Hampton 2004, Jones 1996, Kellner 1992, King and Plunkett 2005.

NEWS AGENCIES As the demand for national and international news* grew, and the speed with which a newspaper was able to inform its readers of the latest developments at home and abroad became a crucial factor for sales, the necessity for a network of reporters controlled by news agencies who would supply reports to many newspapers became increasingly apparent. It was impossible for newspapers – particularly small regional ones – to employ correspondents in every corner of the globe that their readers wanted to know about, and many smaller papers had to rely on rehashing, often days later, stories gathered by wealthy London papers who could afford to employ foreign* correspondents, such as *The Times**.

The first agency was Havas in Paris in 1832, but this operated against a broader market* for the news supported by penny-a-liners, freelancers, moonlighting salaried staff, reciprocal arrangements between papers and outright plagiarism. The later development of the news agencies was closely connected to the development of communication technologies, particularly the telegraph*. As the network developed, the relationship between major cities and the provinces was reconfigured. For instance, the formation of the Press Association* in Britain in 1868 – a powerful advocate for the nationalization of the telegraph network – provided an alternative source of international news to that of the London papers. After the network was nationalized in 1870 and the rates were dropped, the provincial* press was able to compete with the London papers by offering readers* local content complemented by an up-to-date international perspective. International news was mainly provided by agencies such as Havas, Associated Press (1848), Wolff (1849) and Reuters* (1851).

In 1868 a deal was struck whereby Reuters would supply the Press Association with international news in return for an annual subscription of £3,000. The Press Association also supplied

Reuters with UK news for sale to newspapers overseas, and so a mutually beneficial relationship developed between the two principal news agencies that continue to dominate the market.

An essential part of the work of the agencies was to prepare the news into a form suitable for their customers. This editorial role was well recognized: in Britain the Central Press (1863) was sold to the Conservative Party in 1871, and its proprietor*, William Saunders set up an independent agency, Central News. The Liberal Party responded by establishing the National Press Agency in 1873. Sporting* and market* news provided an important income stream for the agencies, and subscribers to these services included clubs, hotels and institutes as well as newspapers. JEM/MaT
Sources: Brown 1985, Lee 1976, Read 1999, Scott 1968.

NEWS OF THE WORLD (1843-) The first number of John Browne Bell's *News of the World* entered the field of mid-Victorian, mass-circulation* Sunday* papers on 1 October 1843. It was aimed at the same lower-middle-class* and working-class readership* as *Lloyd's Weekly Newspaper*, and sold for 3d like its competitor. Declaring, 'our motto is truth. Our practice is the fearless advocacy of the truth', the *News of the World* published an entertaining blend of crime*, scandal and sensationalism that quickly earned it the largest circulation* of any British weekly*. It sold 109,000 copies in 1855, but went into decline following Bell's death that same year. The paper's circulation continued to dwindle for the next five decades.

A consortium of families led by George Riddell, Lascelles Carr, and Charles Jackson purchased the ailing paper from the Bell family in 1891. Carr appointed his nephew Emsley Carr as editor of the *News of the World*, a title he held for the next 50 years. Emsley Carr had been political correspondent to the *Western Mail*, and he remained its chief political* correspondent into the 1930s. George Riddell, also connected to the *Western Mail* as its London solicitor, had been the consortium's legal counsel, but he increased his shareholding in the *News of the World* until by 1903 he was managing director.

Riddell worked ardently to boost circulation, establishing a network of his own newsagents* to sell the paper directly throughout the country. He improved the paper in many ways, though it remained devoted to crime coverage and news of the sensational and titillating variety. The *News of the World* became decidedly Liberal under Riddell's manage-

ment, and he was knighted for its value to the party in 1909.

The *News of the World* absorbed the *Empire News* in 1960, and remained a family business until acquired by Rupert Murdoch's News Group in 1969. It retains its original flavour to this day. JK
Sources: Boyce 1978, Fyfe 1949, *ODNB*, *Waterloo*.

NEWSAGENTS 'Newsagent' is a term that is first recorded in 1844 (*OED*), 'news vender' being an earlier term (from 1805). 'Newswalk' referring to the exclusive right to sell newspapers to established customers in a specific area, precedes both, being recognized in law by the late eighteenth century as an asset. The owner of the retail business, or often his son, would either deliver the papers to certain addresses or, as a newsboy*, would hawk them on the street. By the end of the nineteenth century the 'newswalk' seems to have effectively disappeared as a legal right. Bookstalls in railways stations (of which the first was Marshall's at Fenchurch Street in 1841) were not of this order since they were entered into contractually rather than established by custom and use.

Newsagents over the course of the nineteenth century came to be divided into two categories. One, concerned with the distribution* of newspapers over long distances, is closely linked (but not limited) to wholesale distribution. The most famous newsagent in this sense is W. H. Smith*, though John Menzies (founded in 1833) was dominant in Scotland and Eason (who started as Smith's Irish representative) in Ireland from 1886. The second, concerned with the retail trade, may be a small private enterprise or, like the railway stalls* of Smith's, the end point of a wholesale distribution network. While the histories of wholesale and retail are intimately linked in the case of the large firms, they are nonetheless separate. The rise of the wholesale newsagent is covered in detail by Wilson (1985), who shows its complex interaction from when they began in the third quarter of the eighteenth century both with changing government policies regarding news distribution (not least the 'free' transmission of newspapers which paid the newspaper stamp duty) and with the increasing importance given to morning dailies* by the provincial commercial classes who required the news* earlier than the Post Office, previously the usual distributor, could transmit it.

The history of the retail trade outside the major players remains much more obscure. Certainly, retail newsagents were not widespread outside large conurbations until the end of the nineteenth century. In 1900 an anonymous Scottish newsagent recalled that as late as the 1850s the entire daily news intake of his town comprised three or four merchants sharing a single *Times** between them. In 1858 he started a magazine library, renting out a dozen of the 'top magazines' of the day, so beginning what became a small newsagent's retail business (*Newsagent and Advertisers' Record*, 9 June 1900). His commencement with a lending library is indicative of how selling newspapers alone was not viable: Wright (1867:194) refers to a newsagent coupled with an outfitters; an advert in *The Times* (24 June 1844) records for sale a newsagent's business which included a cigar and tobacco outlet, a small library and a 'newswalk'. Some, such as George Berger*, combined publishing*, bookselling and a retail newsagency. However, by the end of the century the trade had grown so much that retailers had become sufficiently distinct as an occupational category to be able to support a trade* periodical (*the Newsagent and Advertisers' Record**). Wholesalers, meanwhile, had become so powerful as to be able to affect the entire industry as witnessed by the Net Book Agreement (1900) and the demise of the three-volume novel. **AK**

Sources: King and Plunkett 2005, Wilson 1985, Wright 1867.

***NEWSAGENT AND ADVERTISERS' RECORD: THE TRADE JOURNAL FOR NEWSPAPER DISTRIBUTORS, STATIONERS, PRINTERS AND ADVERTISERS* (1889-1950)** Set up initially to provide 'a means of communication between newspaper proprietors*, publishers*, stationery manufacturers, &c and the wholesale and retail houses which, directly or indirectly, deal with them', the *Newsagent and Advertisers' Record* underwent several metamorphoses and title changes*, all of them interesting to the student of late nineteenth-century journalism. There were illustrated* interviews* with a variety of trade celebrities* such as the business manager of the *Star** William O'Malley, in issue 1 and later Fitzroy Gardner, the founder of *Woman** (31 Jan. 1891); details of the material production of periodicals (e.g. 'What it costs to bring out a newspaper' and the 'Production of the *Daily Graphic**', both in Dec. 1890); a wealth of photographs* and line drawings* of the interiors and exteriors of relevant buildings; material useful for women's position in the trade (not only 'The Experiences of a Lady Journalist' but on the skills of women advertising* canvassers or the excellent weather forecasts in the *Graphic* by 'a school of lady clerks'); and even let-

ters* from literary* luminaries such as Oscar Wilde* (on the origins of *Dorian Gray* in the October 1890 issue).

The beginning of the *Newsagent and Advertisers' Record* was not auspicious. It was intended by its publishers Lambert & Co as a 6d quarterly* in July 1889, but its second number is dated October and its third December. Thereafter it continued monthly, being sold to G. F. Goulder in September 1890, until it became a 1d weekly* on 31 January 1891 as the *Newsagent, Advertiser, and Bookseller's Record*. It now announced itself as the 'Official Organ of the Newsagents and Booksellers' Union' (whose inaugural meeting had been 3 January), though leaders* stress the independence of the journal from the union. The *Newsagent* soon dropped 'Advertiser' from its title and replaced 'Record' with 'Review'. In *Willing's Press Guide* for 1891, an advert claimed 'the largest circulation* of the trade journals*': figures given are 10,000 and 7,500. The *Newsagent* gradually became more focused on the retail trade and came closer to a conventional trade journal, so that by 1900 it was advertising business sales and exchanges, advice for keeping shop accounts in order, as well as issuing various advertising supplements* such as for Christmas goods (which came out in June so that the colonial trade could order it in time). It survived until April 1950, changing its title in April 1940 to the *News and Book Trade Review and Stationers' Gazette*. The Newsagents and Booksellers' Union still survives as the National Federation of Retail Newsagents. **AK**

Sources: Kamper 2004, *Newsagent and Advertisers' Record*, *Willing's*.

***NEWSAGENT'S CHRONICLE* (1896-1898)** *Newsagent's Chronicle* was advertised as 'A Journal for all Engaged in the Production and Distribution of Newspapers and Serial Literature'. The first issue appeared on 20 June 1896. It was published by William Dawson and Sons Limited. The price* was ½d and it was quarto size*. Originally, *Newsagent's Chronicle* was issued weekly* and then from 11 December 1897 it appeared fortnightly. Until that date it was a supplement* to the *Publishers' Circular**. It continued as an independent paper for a further year. Then it merged with the *Book and News Trade Gazette* on 17 December 1898. **DHL**

Sources: Growoll 1903, *Waterloo*.

NEWSBOY The rise of the newsboy correlates directly with the demise of the 1d newspaper stamp tax in 1855. With limited circulation*, most papers in the first half of the century were sold either at the newspaper office or by subscription. In the 1830s and 1840s, popular papers frequently had 20 or more readers per copy (Hampton: 27). The cheap* presses, however, needed mass circulation* to succeed and relied on newsboys to sell their product.

'Newsboys' were not necessarily children or even males, though boys seemed to prevail as the century progressed. Speed was an element in the sale of the daily* papers, and children with their 'extreme alacrity' could rush more readily from one corner to the next (*Chambers's Journal* 1874: 114). Newsagents* complained bitterly because they believed these agile children, these 'street arabs', were unfair competition (Lee: 66). To further enhance their marketing, the *Daily Telegraph* used uniformed boys while the *Echo* employed 500 boys wearing 'Echo' caps.

The *Manchester Guardian* along with others addressed concerns in the 1870s about the newsboy's future. The use of the newsboy on a semi-contractual basis, however, changed very little throughout the century (Lee: 66). Though the job offered no security and an uncertain future on the streets, many viewed the newsboy's life as superior to that of the child in the factory or mine. As late as 1901, editors* argued that street selling was necessary to the trade and to the public and that it did not contradict the Cruelty to Children Act (Lee: 66). Though an unlikely occurrence, *Chambers's Journal* sites several examples of newsboys hired off the street by businessmen and publishers* ('Street News-Boys': 114).

By 1911, the newsboy had surpassed all other street vendors in numbers, with 23,000 boys in England and Wales (Rose: 70). **BJ**
Sources: *Chambers's Journal* 1874, Hampton 2004, Lee 1976, Rose 1991.

NEWSGATHERING While most regional* newspapers relied on other titles or 'split-printing' syndication* agencies for their news* items, reporters and local 'penny a liner' stringers were tasked to cover both routine and unexpected events for publication. In practice, large proportions of local*, and some early regional newspapers were researched, written and set by the editor*. The growth of news agencies* in Britain from 1863 and the Press Association's acquisition of the telegraph* in 1868 further stimulated demand for news and led to the greater professionalization* of newsgathering and the specialization of news. This in turn impacted on the format* of newspapers, with, principally, local, national*, foreign*, financial* and sport* sections. **AGJ**
Sources: Boyce 1978, Lee 1976.

NEWSPAPER DIRECTORIES The seminal press guide was advertising* agent Charles Mitchell's* *Newspaper Press Directory*, initially issued in 1846 but appearing annually only from 1856. It was founded to facilitate producers' desires to expand the sale of goods and services through syndicated advertising, that is, the broadcasting of publicity in a wide range of periodical publications. Early issues listed newspapers only by region, providing basic information concerning each journal's price*, character, affiliation, and readership*.

With the huge stimulus to serial publication provided by the abolition of the substantial taxes on advertising and newspapers in 1853 and 1855 respectively, the size* and scope of the press directory also increased. The *Newspaper Press Directory* soon began to list magazines* as well as newspapers, to cover English-language serials in the British Colonies and the United States, to feature specialist articles on new developments and to compile general data revealing past and current trends. Significant competitors to emerge were May's *British and Irish Press Guide* from 1871, Deacon's *Newspaper Handbook* from 1877 and Sell's *Dictionary of the World's Press* from 1884; May was bought out by Willing in 1890. Though such press directories were originally created to serve nineteenth-century commercial advertisers, today they represent a vital resource for academic research into transformations in the Victorian media. **GL**
Sources: *CBEL*, Gliserman 1969, Linton 1979, Linton 1987.

NEWSPAPER NOVELS Given the increasing prominence and sheer number of periodicals and newspapers throughout the century and given that so many novelists, playwrights and poets* both contributed to periodicals and newspapers and, indeed, edited* them, it is perhaps unsurprising that the print trade and representations of periodical culture entered the fictional imagination. Among the two most well-known novels of the nineteenth century that depicted the often precarious world of periodicals and the print trade were W. M. Thackeray's* *History of Pendennis* (serialized* in monthly parts, 1848-1850), an autobiographical novel in which the hero Pendennis finds his way into journalism and writes for the *Pall Mall Gazette* (which provided the title for the daily evening paper established in 1865) and George Gissing's* *New Grub Street* (1891), a novel about aspiration in the context of the cynical world of journalism. Anthony Trollope's* *An Editor's Tales* (serialized in 1869-1870) is interesting for its focus on the trials of editing. Journalists figure in many stories and novels by Henry James, notably in 'The Death of the Lion' (1894) and *The Reverberator* (1888).

Other novels, stories and plays feature the press variously. In M. E. Braddon's *Aurora Floyd* (serialized 1862-1863), Aurora reads an advertisement* in *Bell's Life in London**, which pushes the sensation plot forward. In Trollope's *The Way We Live Now* (serialized in monthly numbers in 1874-1875), the Lady Cardew subplot implicitly condemns the cutthroat world of contemporary publishing by suggesting that good reviews* of bad books are paid for through sex, and in Bulwer-Lytton's play *Money* (1840), the circulation* of news* and gossip* in the press mirrors the circulation of money in an increasingly money-obsessed culture. **MWT**

Sources: Brake 2001, Davis 1998, Saintsbury 1913, Salmon 1997.

NEWSPAPER TAXES, TAXES ON KNOWLEDGE, STAMP TAXES The 'Taxes on knowledge', as they came to be known, were first imposed in 1712. They consisted of stamp duty on newspapers, taxes on both advertisements* and paper*, and were primarily intended to curb the circulation* of cheap* periodicals. Initially the sums involved were small, although the tax on newspapers, the most controversial of the three, was increased substantially in 1797 and in 1815 to 4d per sheet. Radical workingmen referred to this tax as a 'slave-mark', particularly after one of the 'Six Acts' of 1819 extended the impost to virtually all periodicals published more frequently than monthly* and selling for less than 6d. This drove cheap political* papers out of the market* and made it difficult for a provincial* press with limited resources to compete against powerful London dailies* like *The Times**.

Beginning in 1830 a significant movement against the 'Taxes on knowledge' commenced, which involved large numbers of reformers in London and the provinces. Many were radical workingmen who viewed a penny press as a means to achieve economic and political change. Others sought repeal as a way of spreading education among the poor or promoting free trade. Of the three taxes under attack the advertisement duty was the first to go. It was reduced by 50 per cent in 1833 and abolished in 1853. Likewise, the excise duty on paper was halved in 1836 and then repealed in 1861. Smaller, less controversial duties on pamphlets and almanacs were ended in 1833 and 1834. But it was the newspaper duty that evoked the fiercest response among reformers during the 1830s. Between 1830 and 1836 more than 400 il-

legal unstamped* periodicals, many of them selling at a 1d, were published* in defiance of the law. Some went out of business quickly, while others fought a continuing battle against attempts to suppress them. Henry Hetherington* published his *Poor Man's Guardian** for more than four years and led the campaign for repeal, which became known as the War of the Unstamped. Hundreds of vendors were imprisoned, and Hetherington and two close associates, James Watson* and John Cleave*, were repeatedly incarcerated. Finally, in 1836, the Whig government brought the agitation to an end when it reduced the Stamp Duty to 1d.

After 1836 most of the unstamped newspapers disappeared, while some of a non-political nature were allowed to publish. Many radicals became embittered by the failure to abolish the tax and turned to Chartism* and other forms of political protest. Finally, in 1855 the government of Lord Palmerston repealed the Stamp Duty and established a 'free trade in newspapers'. In that year the *Daily Telegraph* became the first 1d daily* newspaper to be published successfully in Britain. This was the starting point for an unprecedented expansion of journalism* that culminated in the emergence of a mass* press in the final decades of the century. **JHW**

Sources: Hollis 1970, Weiner 1969.

NEWSPAPER TRAINS Speed of delivery was essential to the growth of the newspaper trade. In 1872 the *Scotsman** was the first newspaper to employ a 'newspaper train' to speed up distribution* by sorting the bundles destined for individual retailers en route rather than at the wholesaler's warehouse. As the *Graphic** claimed, this allowed the paper to be 'published almost simultaneously in Edinburgh and Glasgow'. The train left Edinburgh at 4.20am with a 'packing carriage' from which parcels were dispatched while the train was still in motion. It arrived in Glasgow some 70 minutes later with 400 parcels.

This 'complete revolution' in newspaper distribution, as the *Graphic* called it, spread to England in 1875 when *The Times** began to use the same principal to deliver newspapers between London and Birmingham. *The Times* express was quickly replaced by a number of early morning services offered by the Midland, Great Northern and the London and North Western Railway (LNWR) that were open to all the newspapers. This method of distribution was fairly straightforward if the packages consisted only of a single title, and in order to compete with this new service W. H. Smith & Son* transferred some of their packing of mixed parcels to the rail. In 1875 they used two 'sorting carriages' on the two-hour journey from St Pancras to Leicester. In 1876 the 5.15am London North Western Railway service, including several of Smith's vans, dropped packages at six stations before reaching Birmingham at 8.20am. Some of these packages were transferred to express trains that sped them to large towns such as Crewe, Chester, Manchester and Liverpool, while others arrived in Glasgow, Edinburgh and Dublin by the early evening. This innovation meant that the newspapers were arriving some four hours earlier than they had in the 1850s. The use of newspaper trains continued into the twentieth century. SC

Sources: *Graphic* 1875, Shaw 1876, *Story of the Scotsman* 1886.

NICHOLS FAMILY (1745-1939) For three generations (1778-1856) the Nichols family were responsible for editing*, printing and publishing* the monthly *Gentleman's Magazine**. In June 1778, John Nichols (1745-1826), printer and writer, bought half the proprietorship* of the *Gentleman's Magazine* from the sister of its founder Edward Cave, who had published the first issue in 1731. At first Nichols was responsible for half the printing and all the folding and stitching of each issue. In 1778 he became joint editor* with Cave's brother-in-law, David Henry, also a printer. Shortly before his death in 1792, Henry gave entire editorial control to John Nichols, who had already expanded the magazine. From 1783 he had doubled the number of pages* and created extra space for articles from prolific correspondents*. He introduced full-scale memoirs into the obituary* columns, while parliamentary* debates became a feature of the news* of the month. In 1812, John Nichols entered into partnership with his nephew, Richard Bentley*. The firm became known as Nichols, Son and Bentley, until Bentley's retirement in 1818. It was operated by the Nichols family throughout the remainder of the nineteenth century, with their descendents retaining an interest in the firm until 1939.

John Nichols's eldest child of his second marriage, John Bowyer Nichols (1779-1863), was also involved with the *Gentleman's Magazine*. He joined the business in 1796, and from an early age assisted in editing the journal. He also made contributions under the signature 'N. R. S'*. In 1833 he became sole proprietor of the *Gentleman's Magazine*. A year later he transferred to William Pickering* a share in the journal, which he repurchased in 1856 when he sold the *Gentleman's Magazine* to J. H. Parker at

Oxford, but continued to be a contributor. From the 1830s John Bowyer Nichols expanded the magazine to include reviews* of art exhibitions, musical performances and learned societies. There was no longer a separate poetry* section as poems and translations were distributed among the articles. His son John Gough Nichols (1806-1873) assisted his father in the printing works before he left school. After his grandfather John Nichols's death in 1826, John Gough Nichols helped to edit the *Gentleman's Magazine*, and he was sole editor (1850-1856), as well as author, printer and compiler of archaeological and heraldic works. DHL

Sources: *Gentleman's Magazine* 1863, Kuist 1982, Nichols 1874, *ODNB*, Smith 1963.

NICHOLSON, RENTON (1809-1861) Known as the 'Lord Chief Baron', Renton Nicholson was a gambler, impresario, pornographer*, man about town and sometime editor*, who frequently found himself on the wrong side of the law. As a journalist, he is best known for editing the *Town* (1836-1840), an unstamped*, semi-pornographic* and sensational weekly* paper, printed by Joseph Last*, which Nicholson described in his autobiography as 'a weekly necessity with the fast community of London'. The prospectus gleefully notes that 'we have assumed the title of 'The Town', because we treat upon the vices and follies of this great metropolis in the age we live in'. During this period he also helped to found the *Crown*, a weekly* paper with a sporting and drinking bent. From the 1840s, Nicholson made his name in devising and leading humorous, sometimes lead theatricals – the witty, sensationalist mock trials he presented, the *tableaux vivants* he staged, the *poses plastiques*– which focused mostly around the Garrick's Head and Town Hotel in Covent Garden and the Coal Hole in Fountain Court. Renton's publications and readership* immediately precedes the similar 'flash' press in New York City in the early 1840s. MWT

Sources: Cohen et al. 2008, Gray 1982, McCalman 1988, *ODNB*, [Renton] 1860.

NICHOLSON, WILLIAM (1753-1815) William Nicholson, editor* and proprietor*, was typical of those who found career opportunities in 'public science*' during Britain's first wave of industrialization. As secretary of the London Chapter Coffee House, he translated a number of French texts concerning the new oxygen-based chemistry and published his own *First Principles of Chemistry* (1790) and *Dictionary of Chemistry* (1795). In April 1797 he began the monthly *Journal of Natural Philosophy, Chemistry and the Arts** (1773-1793), usually known as *Nicholson's Journal*, based on the model of the French monthly *Observations sur la physique*. Priced* 2s 6d, Nicholson's 46-page quarto journal contained a dozen articles, two engravings* and an annual index. Wide margins containing brevier side notes and abstracts were imposed 'at great expense'.

In 1802, after publishing* five such luxurious quarto volumes of the monthly numbers, Nicholson switched to octavo, the favoured format* for commercial science journals throughout the nineteenth century. In 1813, after 36 volumes of the second series, Nicholson sold the journal to Alexander Tilloch*, who had begun the monthly* *Philosophical Magazine* as a direct and ultimately more successful competitor. *Nicholson's Journal* is consulted by historians because of its excellent coverage of developments in electrochemistry and technology. **WB**

Sources: *DSB*, Lilley 1948, *ODNB*.

NICOLL, WILLIAM ROBERTSON (1851-1923) A prominent Free Church proprietor*, journalist and editor*, William Robertson Nicoll was licensed to preach in his native Aberdeenshire at the age of 21. Ill-health necessitated a move to London and journalism became his occupation and surrogate pulpit. Nicoll became editor of the *Expositor* (1884) beginning a long and significant relationship with the publishers* Hodder and Stoughton*. In 1886 he helped to found the *British Weekly: a Journal of Social and Christian Progress* for which he operated as proprietor, editor and prolific contributor. Nicoll was also instrumental in founding the *Bookman*, *Woman at Home*, the *Christian Budget* (1898) and the *British Monthly* (1900). He acted as literary advisor to Hodder and Stoughton from 1886 and was linked to the founding of the Kailyard school of Scottish writing. However it was as editor of the *British Weekly* that Nicoll exercised his greatest influence. Set up to promote the issues which mattered most to the Free Churches, the *British Weekly* became a central force in shaping and promoting the 'nonconformist conscience'. **RH**

Sources: Darlow 1925, Stoddart 1938.

NINETEENTH CENTURY: A MONTHLY REVIEW (1877-1901) One of the most important and distinguished monthlies of serious thought in the last quarter of the nineteenth century, the *Nineteenth Century* took its place alongside such distinguished periodicals as the *Fortnightly Review*. Founded in 1877 by the editor*-proprietor* James Knowles* who had been editing the similarly thoughtful *Contemporary Review*, this liberal periodical was strikingly fresh in establishing an open forum for serious discussion in the 'Modern Symposium' section which ran frequently. This engaged, energetic, dialogic, symposium-style discourse allowed contributors to exchange opinions and to disagree, around topics such as 'the influence upon morality of a decline in religious belief' (April 1877) and 'the soul and future life' (Oct. 1877).

The journal counted among its signed contributors most of the major public intellectuals and opinion-makers of the day, including W. E. Gladstone, Alfred Tennyson, James Fitzjames Stephen*, Matthew Arnold*, T. H. Huxley*, Walter Bagehot*, Frederic Harrison*, Oscar Wilde* and Algernon Swinburne* – arguing against proposals for such things as the Channel tunnel and women's suffragism – and addressed a range of the most important topics of the day (the Irish Question and Home Rule, agnosticism and belief, trades unions and the emerging labour movement, to name only a few). In the 1890s, the periodical became increasingly topical, though still committed to an open-forum style debate. A periodical with a long life, it changed its title to the *Nineteenth Century and After* in 1901 and to the *Twentieth Century* in 1951. **MWT**

Sources: Brake 1994a, Brake 2004a, Small 2003, *Wellesley*.

NONCONFORMIST (1841-1900) The *Nonconformist* was first published in April 1841 as a religiously-based political* protest against the national establishment of religion. Editors* W. Freeman (1856) and Edward Miall (1841, 1854) focused on rousing their middle-class*, politically liberal readers, as well as Dissenters, to act for a peaceful severance of church and state. Its motto was 'the dissidence of dissent and the Protestation of the protestant religion*'. Although it was associated with the temperance movement and had a high moral tone, its pages devoted more space to politics than religion. It was affiliated with the British Anti-State Church Association and the Society for the Liberation of Religion from State Control.

Published in London and owned by Miall Lloyd and Edward Miall, contributors included Mary Steadman Aldis, W. E. Gladstone, Gawin Kirkham, F. Fox Thomas and A. J. Wookey. Its departments included: ecclesiastical affairs, correspondence*, general news*, literature*, trade and commerce, advertisements*, religious intelligence, politics, excerpts from the *Globe*, *The Times* and the *Examiner*. Its circulation* was estimated at 3,200 in 1853, but it shrank to 3,000 by 1855. Each copy, measuring 37 cm and 16 pages in 1845 and 24 pages in 1874, was illustrated* with tables, charts, photographs* and sketches. Weekly proceeds from advertisements* averaged £8 to £10, while the price* fluctuated between 4d and 6d (1845-1890). Published weekly*, it appeared on Wednesdays (1841-1879), thereafter on Thursdays.

In 1880, it merged* with the *English Independent and Free Church Advocate*, formerly the *Patriot**, to become the *Nonconformist and Independent* (Jan. 1880-Sept. 1890). This was the first of many mergers and title changes* for its last 25 years, as it responded to the dynamics of new markets*. The editors reversed the publication's title to the *Independent and Nonconformist* (26 Sept. 1890-30 Dec. 1897). Becoming the *Independent* (6 Jan. 1898-29 March 1900), it was finally incorporated into the *Examiner** (April 1900-July 1906). **MDB**
Source: *Waterloo.*

NORMAN, HENRY (1858-1939) Henry Norman's early interest in the church was replaced by a life-long career as a journalist, specializing in cultural and political* commentary. In 1884 Norman moved to London and began contributing articles to the New York paper *Nation* and to the *Daily News**. In 1885 he interviewed* W. T. Stead*, and the meeting led to Norman being appointed to the editorial staff of Stead's *Pall Mall Gazette** that same year. While on its staff, Norman continued to write on political and literary* topics for American newspapers, being described by the New York *Evening Post* as their 'cable correspondent'. In the style of Stead, Norman was seen as a crusading journalist.

Norman frequently gathered in book form his newspaper articles and first-hand accounts of English behaviour abroad. Articles for the *Fortnightly Review**, the *Contemporary Review**, the *Nineteenth Century** and other journals accompanied such longer works as *Bodyke: A Chapter in the History of Irish Landlordism* (1887), which detailed Norman's eye-witness reports of the brutal evictions of tenants in Ireland by their English landlords. It was followed by several books chronicling his sponsored travels in places as diverse as Canada, the far East, and Siberia. In 1892 Norman joined the editorial staff of the London *Daily Chronicle**. For the next three years he had charge of the literary page of the paper, and was subsequently appointed assistant editor* in 1895.

Norman had a reputation for daring and tenacious investigation* and over the next few years was sent by the *Chronicle* as war* correspondent to areas of conflict in the East and in 1898 to Washington to cover the Spanish-American War. Having retired from journalism in 1899, he was elected to Parliament as a Liberal (1900-1923). **ET**
Sources: French 1995, *ODNB, Wellesley.*

NORTH BRITISH REVIEW (1844-1871) Founded by adherents of the newly established Free Church of Scotland in 1844, the prospectus of the *North British Review* declared that the new quarterly*, without being a theological journal, would take into account the 'strong religious* feelings of the age'. A later editor*, W. G. Blaikie, remarked that it had been established because neither the *Edinburgh Review** nor the *Quarterly** had seemed satisfactory to 'Edinburgh men', the former being too secular and the latter too conservative. Its earliest contributors were drawn from the evangelical wing of the Church of Scotland, including the Free Church, from among the Scottish legal profession and from Scottish universities. It soon outsold the *Edinburgh Review* in Scotland, although its total print run of 3,000 in 1846 lagged behind the *Edinburgh's* circulation* of 5,000.

By 1850, under the editorship of Alexander Campbell Fraser, an academic philosopher, it acquired a national reputation, and became a serious rival to both the *Edinburgh* and the *Quarterly* in the quality of its literary reviewing*. Fraser recruited a large number of English reviewers, among them Charles Kingsley, Thomas de Quincey*, W. R. Greg*, J. M. Ludlow*, Edward Freeman, J. W. Kaye, A. P. Stanley, Herbert Spencer* and Richard Whately. These joined Scotsman like David Masson*, Gerald Massey*, John Tulloch and David Brewster*, who collectively maintained the high standard of reviewing. Fraser's editorship (1850-1857) steered the review in a secular* direction, as did that of W. G. Blaikie (1860-1863), and the publisher* David Douglas (1863-1869). The review's last period marked another change in direction. In 1869 it was acquired by Sir John, later Lord Acton*, as the organ of the liberal Catholic movement, a de facto successor to the *Home and Foreign Review**. The contributions of Richard Simpson* and others in this last period maintained the *North British's* reputation for innovative and independent criticism to the end of its life. **JS**
Sources: Shattock 1973, Shattock 1977, Sullivan, *Wellesley.*

NORTHERN ECHO (1870-) Founded in 1870 by Liberal Scotsman John Hyslop Bell at the behest of local industrial Quaker magnates – the Pease family and others – who wanted a counter to various conservative northern periodicals, the *Northern*

Star was a morning daily* priced* at a halfpence. The newspaper emanated from Darlington, the railway hub, and was unusual in not being located in a major urban center. Bell appointed Jonathan Copelston as editor*, but by late April 1871 Copleston wanted to emigrate to the United States to look at its journalism first hand. By August 1871 the then unknown 23-year old W. T. Stead*, who had been an unpaid but regular contributor of letters* and leaders* to the *Northern Echo,* was its editor; gradually he turned this small provincial paper (circulation* 13,000) into one of the best known daily newspapers outside of London. In 1876 Stead wrote a series of articles about the atrocities committed by the Ottoman Empire during the suppression of the Bulgarian uprising which first brought the newspaper to wide notice. He also invited Mme. Olga Novikoff to write regularly on Anglo-Russian affairs.

Under Stead's editorship the paper supported the causes of the radical Liberals, championed Gladstone, advocated compulsory education, universal male (and female) suffrage, and Home Rule for Ireland. Stead introduced colorful and forceful reporting, including interviews* with well-known people, and lively commentary, all characteristics that would be associated with the New Journalism* (as Matthew Arnold* later called it) and which Stead is conventionally credited with advocating and developing in the world of Victorian newspapers.

Gladstone thought the 1870s *Echo* was 'admirably got up in every way'. John Bright in 1882 used the paper as a model of the way the news* – drawn from other sources as well its own – insured the democratic spread of information: 'This ½ Daily Paper comes for a whole week into the house of every pitman in that country who chooses to take it in. It comes there, bringing all the news, concisely but accurately reported, from all parts of the world, and he has it in his pitman's house just as early and as certain as the News reaches the grand ducal mansion of Raby Castle' (Brown: 126).

Stead edited and wrote for the paper for a decade and then left to become assistant editor of the *Pall Mall Gazette* under John Morley*. Bell had left the *Northern Echo* in 1889, and Charles Starmer became editor in 1895.The paper steadily lost circulation and just survived until in 1904 when it was on the verge of bankruptcy. At that point it was saved when it was acquired by the North of England Newspaper Company, owned by the Rowntrees. It remains today one of the oldest newspapers in north-eastern England. In 2003 it was the North

East Newspaper of the Year. It changed from broadsheet to compact format* in January 2006. **AH**
Sources: Brown 1985, Chapman 1998, Koss 1981, *ODNB, Waterloo,* Wiener 1988.

NORTHERN LIBERATOR (1837-1840) The *Northern Liberator* was 'one of the longest lived and liveliest' of the many Chartist* newspapers, first published on 31 October 1837, a few weeks before the launch of the more famous *Northern Star*, as a large format* stamped weekly* of four pages. Initially it was owned by the Anglo-American radical Augustus Hardin Beaumont and his brother Arthur. When Augustus died suddenly in January 1838 the paper was purchased for £500 by Robert Blakey*, a seasoned writer who had contributed to a number of radical journals including *Black Dwarf*. Blakey edited* the *Liberator* jointly with Thomas Doubleday* until its demise in December 1840.

The *Liberator* quickly outsold the other established Tyneside papers, including the *Newcastle Courant*, with a claimed circulation of 4,000 copies at the end of January 1838. With agents across England and Scotland and a strong advertising* base, Blakey expanded the editorial team by appointing the Irish journalist Thomas Ainge Devyr as roving reporter and London correspondent. Blakey dressed up his biting analysis of the political* inequities in satirical* form and for a time their scurrilous writings enabled them to escape prosecution. The innovative use of engraving* to illustrate the evils of the capitalist system was as commercially successful as it was an effective educative tool. Some of these images, such as the 'Tree of Taxation', were subsequently produced as Chartist handbills. In addition, Blakey and Doubleday penned some lengthy satirical works, such as 'The Political Tale of a Tub' and 'The Political Pilgrim's Progress' that were serialized* before being published separately at a handsome profit. The latter publication proved to be a great money-spinner and was reprinted in New York for circulation* across America.

By 1839, three separate editions of the *Liberator* were published every week and a home delivery service had been introduced. With a stable income from the large membership of the Northern Political Union, the paper's financial future seemed assured. The Whig owners of the *Gateshead Observer* (1837-1849) were so unnerved that they offered the Chartist Dr John Taylor £300 to edit a rival organ. Blakey's bullish response was to relaunch the *Liberator* in July 1839 in an extended format* of 48

columns*. As the Chartist struggle moved into its most dangerous phase, the *Liberator's* editors advised its readers* on the right to bear arms and even its advertisements* were couched in physical force rhetoric. Its last days were dogged by a bad tempered dispute with the printers over working practices. Although it was swiftly resolved, Blakey was prosecuted for sedition and bound over to keep the peace. In May 1840 loss of revenue forced the *Liberator* to merge* with the *London Champion*. JA
Sources: Allen 2007, Haywood 1999, Hugman 1999, Maehl 1969, Thompson 1984.

NORTHERN STAR (1837-1852) For all the liveliness of the Chartist* press, the *Northern Star* was the only broadsheet paper to enjoy sustained success and the only Chartist periodical to achieve genuinely mass* circulation* as the pre-eminent newspaper of the Chartist movement. A stamped* weekly* newspaper to serve northern radicalism had been mooted since 1836, but credit for driving the initiative forward and assembling its shareholder base was entirely due to Feargus O'Connor*. He recognized that the burgeoning radical movement would remain atomized without a paper that reflected the national impetus and reported local activities in that context. Just as Chartism subsumed a variety of grievances into one demand for universal male suffrage, local* political* activity became in the pages of the *Northern Star* part of a unified movement. The *Northern Star*, unlike its unstamped* predecessors, spent hundreds of pounds yearly on reporting, providing publicity to local leaders and events, and its national distribution* helped co-ordinate Chartist strategy in the place of a strong central organization.

Completely unversed in the practicalities of newspaper publishing*, O'Connor initially planned to install second-hand print equipment in the back room of a Barnsley pub. However, in May 1837 Joshua Hobson* persuaded him otherwise and introduced him to the existing circle interested in starting a stamped weekly, notably William Hill, who became the *Northern Star & Leeds General Advertiser's* founding editor*. Hobson produced the paper from his works in Market Street, Briggate. Within a few weeks the *Northern Star* returned a profit and it prospered further as its fortunes, and O'Connor's, became linked to the emerging movement for parliamentary and social reform to be known as Chartism. At its peak (April-Sept. 1839), priced* at 4½d, stamp returns suggest average weekly sales of around 43,000, an unprecedented number for a working-class* newspaper and more

than any provincial* journal, even exceeding those of *The Times*. Right up to its final year, this six-column*, eight-page broadsheet was consistently politically potent. It was also read avidly for its reportage* of local meetings, its book reviews*, poetry* column, and, from March 1849, serial* fiction. The paper celebrated Chartism's cultural side, giving considerable attention to the radical schools, churches, reading clubs and temperance societies that flourished throughout the 1840s and in its turn, the paper was honoured at banquets and meetings, praised in poems, speeches, and toasts. More than most newspapers at this time, though, the *Northern Star* enjoyed a mass audience as well as a mass readership*, with accounts of its being read aloud in pubs, workshops and political meetings, as well as in Chartist homes. Many scholars believe its readership* exceeded its circulation by as much as a factor of 10 to 20. Throughout most of the 1840s, the circulation of the *Northern Star* remained between 7,000 and 13,000, but sales declined sharply after the rejection of the third Chartist petition in 1848.

Though the *Star's* early success depended on the militant northern centres of the West Riding, the conception of the paper was national and in November 1844, O'Connor moved production of the paper to London, changing its title to *Northern Star & National Trades' Journal* to strengthen its appeal to trade* unionists. These constituted, he believed, a less volatile readership than the working class at large. Yet the *Northern Star* had a multi-sided relationship with the movement upon which it reported, with its journalists doubling as organizers. Profits went to fund further agitation, pay the costs of political trials and support the families of Chartist prisoners. All this suggests the *Northern Star* was not simply the vehicle of Feargus O'Connor, which distinguished it from earlier radical imprints. Though O'Connor published a weekly letter and his speeches received significant attention, the *Star's* proprietor* gave substantial freedom to his editors. The paper tapped the rich resources of the journals of the 1830s, relying on veterans of the 'War of the Unstamped' for its writers, editors, and vendors. Bronterre O'Brien* contributed frequently in 1838.

O'Connor had broken with Hill in July 1843, since when Hobson had edited the paper with the assistance of G. J. Harney. Hobson sold his business in Leeds to follow the paper south but was increasingly disenchanted with Chartism and O'Connor in particular. Harney, previously a newsboy* for the

*Poor Man's Guardian**, became editor de facto until officially appointed in October 1845. To O'Connor's consternation, Harney considerably increased the paper's coverage of international politics although foreign news* had appeared in the paper from the beginning. However, much of the popular interest in, and support for, the continental revolutions of 1848 (and thus Chartism's reviving fortunes that year) can be ascribed to the *Northern Star*. Its fortunes after 1848, however, reflected those of the broader movement, a sorry saga of sectarian tension played out against sharply diminishing popular commitment.

Harney became estranged from O'Connor during 1849 and much of the responsibility for managing the *Northern Star* passed to his assistant, the Owenite George Fleming, and to William Rider (an old ally of O'Connor). Fleming, the full editor from May 1851, purchased the paper from the ailing O'Connor early the following year. A relaunch (March 1852) as the *Star & National Trades' Journal* failed to revive the paper. Harney fared no better when he bought it two months later, changed the title to the *Star of Freedom* and the format* and content to a political journal, but publication ceased on 27 November 1852. GV/MSC

Sources: Chase 2007, Epstein 1976, Goodway 1982, Jones 1975, Saville 1987, Schoyen 1958.

NORTHERN TRIBUNE: A PERIODICAL FOR THE PEOPLE (1854-1855) The radical monthly* journal, the *Northern Tribune* was launched by the Newcastle press entrepreneur and activist Joseph Cowen*. With its stablemate, the *English Republic**, the paper was published in the Lake District by the republican engraver* William James Linton* and W. E. Adams* (the latter subsequently edited* Cowen's *Newcastle Weekly Chronicle**). Linton supplied the fine quality illustrations* and a number of eminent British and European radicals, including George Julian Harney*, Thomas Cooper*, Louis Kossuth and Giuseppe Mazzini contributed articles.

Although the *Northern Tribune* offered a balanced mix of articles on political reform (the motto was 'Light! More Light!'), it was widely condemned for its extremist views. Nevertheless, Cowen refused to modify the paper's tone, insisting that the *Tribune* would 'write neither for pay nor pastime and to forego one principle of our democratic creed would be to play traitor to our conscience'. The first issue is reputed to have sold 4,000 copies and in December 1854 the paper switched to weekly* publication and enlarged its pool of writers to include George J.

Holyoake*, Samuel Kydd* and Gerald Massey*. Ironically, the abolition of the Newspaper Stamp Duty in 1855, a cause strongly supported by the paper, led to an adversely competitive climate and in March 1855 Cowen sold the *Tribune* to Holyoake at a loss of about £1,150. Holyoake incorporated the paper into his own anti-clerical publication, the *Reasoner**. JA

Sources: W. E. Adams Papers, Allen 2005, Allen 2007, Ashton 1991, Cowen Papers, Smith 1973.

NORTHERN WEEKLY LEADER (1884-1919), NEWCASTLE DAILY LEADER (1885-1903) & EVENING LEADER (1899-1903)' In February 1884 the *Northern Weekly Leader* (*NWL*) was begun in South Shields as the Gladstonian Liberal riposte to the *Newcastle Chronicle's** estrangement from the party over the 'Eastern Question'. The coal-owner James Joicey took over the new paper in September 1885, moved its production to Newcastle and introduced a morning daily* edition, the *Newcastle Daily Leader*. James Annand*, a former editor* of the *Newcastle Daily Chronicle** and forced to resign by its proprietor* Joseph Cowen* over the Eastern Question, edited both newspapers. Annand modelled the *NWL* on the successful *Newcastle Weekly Chronicle**, including instigating his children's Golden Circle society and column* that constantly vied with the *Chronicle's* Dicky Bird Society* for the affection of Newcastle's children.

Annand resigned his editorship in 1885. Aaron Watson took over and revamped his papers' contents. The introduction of the *Evening Leader* in 1899 suggests Watson was successful, but his decision to take a pro-Boer stance during the South African War undid this good work. This standpoint caused a loss in valuable advertising* revenue, which proved catastrophic in Newcastle's overcrowded newspaper market and Watson left in 1901. Arthur Pearson* bought all three papers in 1903. The *Daily Leader* ceased, the *Evening Leader* was re-titled the *Evening Mail**, but the Saturday issued *Northern Weekly Leader* survived, albeit now aligned to Pearson's imperialist tariff reform politics. The *Leader* increasingly raised the profile of its 'Golden Circle' feature that often filled two pages of the newspaper with readers' letters and had now extended its reach to adults. It undertook widespread philanthropic work including Christmas collections, financial handouts to the poor, social evenings for readers and even formed a football team. The *Northern Weekly Leader* changed hands again in 1917 when the *Newcastle Chronicle's* owner, Colonel Joseph Cowen*, purchased it. Paper* shortages caused by the ongoing war* saw the *Northern Weekly Leader* reduced to just six pages in 1918, leaving its Golden Circle as its only redeeming feature. Cowen had a cluttered stable of newspapers, including two Saturday publications and he dispensed with the *Northern Weekly Leader* in December 1919. **FSM**

Sources: Allen, 2007, Milne 1971, Gliddon 2000.'

NORTHERN WHIG (1824-1963) A 'political*, commercial and literary* miscellany*', the *Northern Whig* was at the outset a subscription journal. Published in Belfast from 1824, it evolved into a bi-weekly (1834), a tri-weekly (1839) and a daily* newspaper by 1886. The paper was published* and edited* by Francis Dalzell Finlay* from inception until his death in 1857, when it passed to his son. Finlay was a protégé of the former United Irishman William Drennan* and under Finlay's control the *Northern Whig* supported Catholic emancipation (1829), tenant rights and electoral reform. Publication was suspended (1826-1827) after Finlay was imprisoned following a libel case. The *Northern Whig* addressed the serious political issues of its time from a liberal perspective, and its correspondents included major political and religious figures of the day. **MJH**

Sources: *ODNB, Waterloo.*

NORTON, CAROLINE ELIZABETH SARAH (1808-1877) A gifted and serious writer from an early age, Caroline Norton (*née* Sheridan) became a professional journalist, author, poet and playwright. Initially acclaimed, her good reputation was subsequently overshadowed by her advocacy of the rights of married women.

Motivated by a compulsion to write, Norton was also fuelled by the necessity to sustain an appropriate lifestyle for herself, her children and her shiftless husband. While she made considerable sums of money from the publication of fiction in the periodical press, for example in *Blackwood's Magazine*, she found that her poetry* and journalism were more lucrative. *Macmillan's Magazine*, *New Monthly Magazine* and *Fraser's Magazine* were some of the periodicals to which she contributed.

Her poetry resulted in the invitation to edit* the *Belle Assemblee and Court Magazine* (1832-1837), and she also contributed articles such as 'The Invisibility of London Husbands'. Further editorial positions were at the *English Annual* (1834-1837), the *Keepsake* (1836) and *Fisher's Drawing Room Scrap-Book* (1846-1849). Despite the often enforced intensity of her work, she confessed that 'The power of writing has always been to me a source of intense pleasure'. **CL**

Sources: Forster 1984, *ODNB, Waterloo, Wellesley.*

NOTES AND QUERIES (1849-) *Notes and Queries* was a prestigious scholarly weekly* established by antiquarian William J. Thoms (1803-1885) to serve, according to its initial subtitle, as 'a medium of inter-communication for literary men, artists, antiquaries, genealogists, etc'. With the encouragement of Charles Wentworth Dilke*, the project grew out of Thoms's folklore column* running from 1846 in the *Athenaeum*. Articles, generally signed, were factual and brief, and each issue concluded with even briefer 'Notices to Correspondents'*. Though the initial circulation* measured only in the hundreds, the journal quickly stimulated animated exchanges between scholars in many fields of historical* enquiry. It went on to provide a significant impetus to national projects like the *Dictionary of National Biography* (1882-), the *Oxford English Dictionary* (1884-) and the *English Dialect Dictionary* (1898-1905). The journal also encouraged new research methods such as the use of photography* in manuscript studies, and more systematic indexing, exemplified by the journal's own periodic General Indexes.

Thoms resigned as editor* in 1872, succeeded in turn by John Doran*, H. F. Turle (1878-1883) and Joseph Knight (1883-1907). The journal still thrives today as a quarterly* issued in both paper and digital form by Oxford University Press, 'for readers and writers, collectors and librarians'. **GL**

Sources: Thoms 1867-1876, *ODNB*, Sullivan.

NOTES TO THE PEOPLE (MAY 1851-MAY 1852) The first of a series of periodicals edited* by the Chartist* poet Ernest Jones, *Notes to the People* sought to establish Jones as the pre-eminent leader of late Chartism. Published weekly* by J. Pavey, the journal began with a flourish as Jones included in the early issues his most recent verse, 'The New World', 'Beldagon Church', 'The Painter of Florence' and poems* written during his imprisonment for sedition in 1848-1850. The journal is also notable for the serialization* of two of Jones's novels, the semi-autobiographical 'De Brassier', and his disquisition on the status of women, 'Women's Wrongs'.

Apart from periodic contributions airing trades' grievances and, in later issues, some reports of Chartist activity, the journal was wholly the work of Jones. As he intended the content to be mentally uplifting, poetry* was placed next to political* columns* seeking to resuscitate Chartism* under his leadership. Typical content included histories* of

Rome and Florence, an inspiring essay on Hereward the Wake and information on the geography of the colonies.

Jones repeatedly complained that posters sent to newsagents* to advertise the journal mysteriously did not arrive or, if displayed, were removed by the police or his Chartist enemies. In this, rather than the existence of other rival radical journals, Jones found the explanation for the disappointing sales of *Notes to the People*. That the journal kept going as long as it did owed much to his relentless promotion on his lecture tours. However, long before the journal had closed, Jones's attention and interest had turned to a new and more ambitious venture, the *People's Paper*. **SFR**

Source: Taylor 2003.

NOVELETTES The late nineteenth-century explosion in the penny* domestic fiction market brought forth the novelette. These weekly magazines surged into ubiquity after 1875, becoming a byword for cheap* and disposable fiction. In 1858 Wilkie Collins* called them 'penny-novel Journals', identifying their low price* and low-quality content as the principal factors which made them a new publishing* phenomenon. The novelettes, consisting of a 'complete story' rather than serialized episodes, began to rise in numbers after the 1880s. At their peak, in 1897, the market* was swamped with over 35 titles. In 1883, in the *Nineteenth Century* Thomas Wright contradicted the prevalent view that the novelettes were read by the female domestic servant, citing rather the semi-educated daughters of the genteel classes, who had too much leisure time but not much money

Novelette stories were formulaic and predictable, but their clear profitability ensured their continuance into the twentieth century. Their leading publishers* and editors* included Edwin J. Brett, Charles Shurey, William Lucas* and T. Harrison Roberts, but the authors who wrote for the novelettes are largely forgotten, and most wrote either anonymously* or under pseudonyms*. Those who can be identified who had earlier or later successes include Mary Elizabeth Braddon*, Emma Watts Phillips, M. P. Shiel and Frederick Merrick White. **KM**

Sources: Macdonald and Demoor 2007, Macdonald and Demoor 2008, Repplier 1891, Wright 1883.

NURSING PRESS Long before Florence Nightingale's famous establishment of the training school for nurses at St Thomas's Hospital, London, in 1860, Mary Aikenhead had founded the Irish Sis-

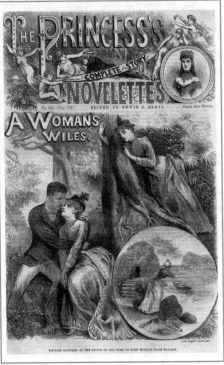

Figure 47: 'A Woman's Wiles', one of the tales published in the *Princess's Novelettes*.

ters of Charity in Dublin in 1815, and St John's House in London had begun training nurses in 1848. However, the specialist nursing press appeared surprisingly late in the nineteenth century for two reasons: the small number of trained nurses until the twentieth century offered a small consumer base, with *Nursing Notes* in December 1887 estimating only 5,000; also, complex and changing class* and gender prejudices against nurses remained, both among the lay public and medical men. As Mrs Bedford Fenwick, the founder of the British Nurses Association in 1887, famously put it: 'The Nurse Question is the Woman Question…We have to run the gauntlet of those historic rotten eggs' (quoted by Moore 1988: ix-x).

The well-documented shift from an occupation drawn from domestic servants, paupers and prostitutes to a preponderance of educated middle- and upper-class women also meant that the identity of nursing was fraught from within its ranks as well as pressurized from without. While there is a good deal of material revealing attitudes towards nurses and the techniques and organization of nursing in both the general press (see, e.g. Palmegiano 1998) and the medical press*, the first periodical devoted to nursing was *Nursing Notes* (1887-; *Midwives' Chronicle* from 1940). It was founded by the suffragist and midwife Rosalind Paget as the organ of the Midwives' Institute (later Royal College of Midwives) which she had set up in 1881 to argue for the official registration of midwives (resisted by Parliament until 1902). It is particularly interesting in that its first appearance was as part of a general feminist 1d 8-page weekly* called *Woman* (1 June-20 July 1887), founded to promote support for the Women's Suffrage Bill and which only lasted until the reading of the Bill. Quite in accord with the statement of Fenwick, *Woman* sought to offer women of all classes inspiring examples of 'the big-brained and large-hearted women who are the path-finders and champions of the weaker' ('To our Readers' 1: 4). 'Nursing Notes' comprised its second and third pages (after the front-page adverts*).

From the first, 'Nursing Notes' was keen to promote the idea of a nursing 'profession*'. The second and last time it appeared (July 6), it offered readers the chance to purchase *Nursing Notes* alone, on the first Wednesday of every month. When it appeared as a separate publication, it cost 2d, was edited by Mrs Nichol at 15 Buckingham Street and brought out by the same publisher* as *Woman*, George Hill at 154 Westminster Bridge Road. The New Series which began on 1 January 1888 added the subtitle 'A Practical Journal for Nurses' and the colophon reveals that it was being printed by the Women's Printing Society, 21b Great College Street, Westminster. By the following month there was a noticeable focus on the situation of midwives; by August there was a notice to the effect that matrons were requested to encourage their nurses to take in this 'professional paper', suggestive that its dull, unillustrated format was not widely appreciated. Even the few advertisements*, being personals, were short and verbal. While always remaining the organ of midwives, over the 1890s *Nursing Notes* gathered together a series of other organizations devoted to nursing specialisms including the Workhouse Infirmary Nursing Association, the Incorporated Society of Trained Masseuses and the Colonial Nursing Association.

The drive for registration was key for general nurses as well, and two associations and their journals were founded around rival conceptions of what registration meant. The *Nursing Record**, initially the organ of Bedford Fenwick's British Nurses' Association, argued that nursing should become a profession* (the word is repeated polemically several times in the opening 'To Our Readers') and that

to do this the many different bodies of nurses should federate. Great stress was laid both on the importance of state registration (achieved only in 1919) and technical knowledge – and, less explicitly, on how nurses should come from the ruling classes and disassociate themselves from untrained nurses and from earning money. Given this, it cannot be surprising that its readership* was small, though powerful. In 1891, the British Nurses' Association was granted a royal charter and in February that year began a quarterly* *Nurses' Journal* (1891-1918), named as 'the only official organ' of the Association, and full of polemic for the distinction between registered professional and unregistered amateur nurses. While 6d was printed on its cover, it was nonetheless distributed free to members. By 1896, Fenwick had been ousted from the council of the Royal British Nurses' Association, and she took the *Nursing Record* with her. Fenwick's main opponents comprised Henry Burdett and his Hospital Association and, behind the scenes, Florence Nightingale. The Hospital Association had its journal *Hospital** and, later, an annual (*Burdett's Hospital Annual*, 1890-1967, with changes of title), but in 1888 Burdett issued the *Nursing Mirror* (1888-1907), a supplement to *Hospital* (1886-1924; changes of title). It deliberately opposed Fenwick's *Record*. The *Nursing Mirror* became the proponent of a different, more commercial, form of registration, one open to all who had worked for at least one year in a hospital and had been trained, could provide a good character reference, 2s 6d joining fee and 1s annually thereafter. It went on to enjoy the largest circulation* of any nursing journal over the first half of the twentieth century, but was then overtaken by *Nursing Times* (1905-), which bought it in 1985.

At least half of trained nurses went into private practice and many went to work in the colonies. Such nurses were not in direct contact with the latest advances found in the training hospitals. The journals were of particular value to them not only for the information in the body of the text and the controversies they record, but for the adverts, keeping them up to date with new products and service: from Hartmann's complete set of equipment for childbirth and Allen & Hanbury's pocket case for examination of urine to Bovril, diet charts and Wright's Coal Tar Soap. Thus the large number of advertisements in *Hospital* as compared to the others not only indicated its popularity but contributed to it. From the early 1890s, all three journals used repeated full-page illustrated* advertisements as their front pages, each journal associated with a different product. This procedure granted them a striking appearance while receiving income for so doing, benefiting the advertiser by implied endorsement by a professional publication, an ethical issue that many professional journals had to face. **AK**

Sources: Abel-Smith 1960, McGann 1992, Moore 1988, Palmegiano 1998, Thomson 2005.

NURSING RECORD (1888-1956) The *Nursing Record* was first published as a weekly* journal written by nurses for nurses. It was closely associated with the establishment of the first professional* organization for nurses, the (Royal) British Nurses' Association, the same year. The journal's objectives were to protect the interests of trained nurses and to promote their state registration. From the start, the *Record* was regarded as radical by the hospital medical establishment and to counter its impact Henry Burdett, founder and editor* of *Hospital,* started the *Nursing Mirror.* In 1893 the *Nursing Record* was taken over by Mrs Bedford Fenwick, a former matron of St Bartholomew's Hospital, and her husband Dr Bedford Fenwick. Mrs Fenwick became the editor* and for the next 25 years she pursued the cause of state registration with single-minded fanaticism, developing a style of journalism which was passionate, aggressive and at times libellous.

She was active in the women's movement, which is reflected in the journal, and she founded the International Council of Nurses in 1899. In 1901 she renamed her journal the *British Journal of Nursing* and it was adopted as the official journal of the Council.

Through the journal Fenwick influenced the development of professional awareness among nurses in the English-speaking world. However, at home her readership* was small, appealing to the intellectual and professionally minded nurse, while the *Nursing Mirror* had a more populist approach and was more widely read. Having achieved state registration in 1919, and having had to swallow the marriage of the (Royal) College of Nursing, which she violently opposed, with the *Nursing Times* (started in 1905 by Macmillan's), Fenwick was forced to reduce the *British Journal of Nursing* to a monthly edition in 1925. She continued to edit the journal until a few months before her death in 1947. It survived her by nine years, ceasing publication in 1956. She had used her personal money to finance the journal for many years. She was president of the Society of Women Journalists* (1910-1911). **SYM**

Sources: *Hospital,* McGann 1992, *Nursing Record, ODNB.*

O

OAKELEY, HERBERT STANLEY (1830-1903) Music* critic of the *Manchester Guardian** (1858-1868), Oakeley was a prominent figure in British music* journalism, as well as being a composer and an organist. In the period when Oakeley was a contributor, the *Manchester Guardian* championed efforts by the Manchester Choral Society and others to provide concerts for the working class*, and celebrated the opening up of musical knowledge to a wider audience. It also advocated the maintenance of high musical standards against a wave of 'trashy novelties'.

Oakeley was Reid professor of the theory of music at the University of Edinburgh (1865-1891), where he strove with only limited success to develop music as an academic subject, but he continued to contribute articles to the *Musical Times** and the *Organist and Choirmaster* (1893-1919), among others. He travelled widely and wrote dispatches from abroad, covering festivals and other music-related events, reporting* for example, on the unveiling of a statue of Beethoven in Vienna in 1880 for the *Musical Times*.

As a Scottish resident (later attaining the title of 'Composer of Music to Her Majesty in Scotland'), his Continental orientation – manifested in both his journalism and in the concerts he programmed – was a contentious issue for nationalists who would perhaps have preferred to see a Scot in the Reid chair. In 1876, he was attacked by John Stuart Blackie in the *Scotsman** as a representative of the 'idolatry of foreign music', and the neglect of Scottish song. The accusation sparked an impassioned exchange of letters in the *Scotsman** involving many correspondents*, and the row also spilled into the pages of the *Musical Times*, where both sides of a fascinating debate about the relation of music to nationalism* were represented. **MaT**
Sources: *Musical Times* 1876, 1880, New Grove, *ODNB*, *Scotsman* Digital Archive, *Guardian* and *Observer* Digital Archive.

OBITUARIES Formal obituary notices, in terms of being measured judgements on the lives of deceased persons of note, were not a regular feature of the national newspaper press for much of the nineteenth century. *The Times** had no 'Obituary' heading until very late in the century, with the sporadic coverage of notable deaths, such as that of Sir Robert Peel, 1850, being covered as an item of news* on first reporting, with articles reflecting on his career following in leaders* the following day. Each issue of the *Gentleman's Magazine**, however, included a full section headed 'Obituary' as one of its six or seven major categories. These included lengthy obituaries of notable soldiers, aristocrats, clergy, MPs, and even booksellers, often several pages long each, with the total coverage regularly running from 12 to over 20 pages.

A landmark in journalism obituaries occurred in 1832 when *Chambers's Edinburgh Journal** issued a supplement* dedicated to the memory of Sir Walter Scott. This substantial work sold 180,000 copies initially and was expanded and reprinted many times throughout the century, becoming a standard biographical work on Scott and ensuring the financial future of the journal. Twenty years later, the death of the Duke of Wellington in September 1852 was reported as a monumental national loss, forging anew the definition of the patriotic Englishman. *The Times* dedicated entire pages of six columns* to this 'very type and model of an Englishman' in an unprecedented act of journalistic remembrance throughout the week following the initial announcement. The more jingoistic weekly* *Illustrated London News** devoted several front pages to this 'greatest of living men' and Britain's 'mightiest soldier' (Sept.-Nov. 1852), also issuing four illustrated* supplements celebrating the life and military works of the Duke in great detail. Similarly, the *Glasgow Herald's* editor* Samuel Hunter advanced the fortunes and reputation of his journal by exploiting the story of Nelson's death for almost a month.

Throughout the 1800s, specialized journals regularly included obituaries of notable persons within their own particular field. These are sometimes much more partial than the generally objective and fact-based accounts in the *Gentleman's Magazine* and *The Times*, such as the emotionally charged reminiscences of Dante Gabriel Rossetti and Matthew Arnold* found in the *Century Guild Hobby Horse**. By the end of the century, the heading 'Obituary' was in occasional use in *The Times*, such as on 1 December, 1900, where the life of Count Yorck von Wartenburg is remembered, and the following, unheaded paragraph gives a terse and judgemental account of the recently deceased Oscar Wilde*. **MBT**
Sources: Bell 2007, Brake 2006, *Century Guild Hobby Horse*, Chambers 1871, Demoor 2005, *Gentleman's Magazine*, *Illustrated London News*, Sinnema 2006, *The Times*.

O'BRIEN, JAMES (1804-1864) The radical journalist James O'Brien arrived in London from Ireland in 1829, intending to become a barrister, but was swiftly attracted to the unstamped* press. His pen name 'Bronterre' was a romantic melding of the Gaelic *bron* (sorrow) with the French *terre* (earth), matching the attractive earnestness of his journalistic style and political* beliefs. Contributions to William Carpenter's *Political Letters & Pamphlets* led to an offer of editing the *Midland Representative & Birmingham Herald* (1831-1832). Upon its incorporation into the *Birmingham Journal*, O'Brien returned to London to succeed Thomas Mayhew as editor* of the *Poor Man's Guardian*. With its proprietor* Henry Hetherington*, O'Brien went on to develop two further unstamped weeklies*, *Destructive* (1833-1834) and *Hetherington's Twopenny Dispatch* (1834-1836).

Always restless, O'Brien departed to the short-lived *Bronterre's National Reformer* (1837) before joining John Bell as joint-editor of the *London Mercury* (1836-1837). Established to undermine the *True Sun* (which Bell previously edited), The *London Mercury* was soon in conflict with Hetherington's *London Dispatch*. This was for both commercial and political reasons, as O'Brien and his allies sought to out-manoeuvre the London Working Men's Association (of which Hetherington was a leading member). Among O'Brien's allies was Fargus O'Connor* and when the *London Mercury* failed, Bronterre became a prominent contributor to the *Northern Star*, sealing his reputation as a leading Chartist*.

O'Brien also conducted two papers of his own, *Operative* (1838-1839) and *Southern Star* (1840), a title indicative of rivalry with O'Connor. Subsequent ventures met indifferent fortunes: the *British Statesman* (1842-1843) lasted eight months, the *Poor Man's Guardian & Repealer's Friend* traded on past glories, the *National Reformer* depended on relaxed Manx taxation and postage regulations; *Power of the Pence* (1848-1849), *Social Reformer* (1849) and *Bronterre O'Brien's European Letters* (1851) were ephemeral. Thereafter he depended on freelance work as London correspondent of the *Glasgow Sentinel*, for *Reynolds's Political Instructor*, *Reynolds's Newspaper* and the general weekly *Empire* (1853-1856). Bronterre's last articles appeared in the *Morning Star* (1856-1869), an avowed Liberal daily*, closely associated with Richard Cobden. It was an inauspicious end for a journalist O'Connor once dubbed, 'the schoolmaster of Chartism'. **MSC**
Sources: Chase 2007, *ODNB*, Plumber 1971.

OBSERVER (1791-) Britain's oldest Sunday paper, the *Observer*, was founded in 1791 by W. S. Bourne who promised a paper '– uninfluenced by party … whose principle is independence'. Despite this declaration, it was in part funded by government subsidy, and effectively became a mouthpiece for the ruling party. During its early years, it approved twice weekly, on Monday as well as Sunday, for example in 1834. Priced* at 4d for four pages in 1793, its price fluctuated in the ensuring century – from 7d (1821, 1834) to 6d (1846) to 5d (1856) to 3d (1868) to 1d (1912). In 1814 it was acquired by William Innell Clement, the proprietor* of other titles (including the *Morning Chronicle*), under whom it flourished. It gained a reputation for serious coverage of politics* and literature*, supporting the reform of the franchise slowly but progressively from the 1820s. It also pioneered the use of woodcuts* to illustrate* its articles, in particular its reporting of the Cato Street Conspiracy in 1820, an early illustrated crime story, allegedly the first, but certainly part of the early history of crime* reporting. Illustrated supplements*, such as that for the coronation (22 July 1821) were also an early feature. Its coverage of drama in 1846 is noted in *Mitchell's*.

Clement died in 1852, and the paper declined, not least because of its allegiance to the Northern States in the U.S. Civil War. It was revived by Julius Beer who acquired the paper in 1870, appointing Edward Dicey as editor*. Frederick Beer inherited the paper on the death of his father in 1880, and in 1891 installed his wife as editor. Rachel Beer, the aunt of Siegfried Sassoon, also edited the *Sunday Times*. It was acquired by Lord Northcliffe* in 1905, by which time its circulation* was a mere 5,000, and revived again by J. L. Garvin who became a distinguished editor in 1908. **JRW**
Sources: *History of the Observer, ODNB, Waterloo*.

O'CONNOR, FEARGUS EDWARD (1796-1855) As the owner and presiding genius of the Chartist* newspaper, the *Northern Star*, Feargus O'Connor made a considerable impact on newspaper history. Completely without prior newspaper experience, O'Connor depended heavily on his editor* William Hill* and his printer-manager Joshua Hobson*. However, it was O'Connor who decisively shaped the weekly* paper. First, he placed the paper wholly at the movement's service; second, O'Connor's weekly letters to readers became one of the *Northern Star*'s most compelling features. Often dictated, these were strident and deeply personal commentaries on contemporary politics*. Third, his extensive speaking tours raised the profile of the paper. Support for the *Northern Star* effectively became synonymous with a personal political commitment to Chartism and O'Connor himself. Relations with Hill and Hobson became strained when O'Connor took over the daily* London paper, the *Evening Star* in August 1842 only to sell it five months later at a considerable loss. This venture adversely affected the circulation* of the *Northern Star* and O'Connor moved the paper to London in 1844 partly to revive sales, but his relations with Hobson and his successor, G. J. Harney* were never stable. After Harney's resignation in 1849, O'Connor retreated from active involvement in the paper and eventually sold it in March 1852.

O'Connor also contributed occasionally to the *English Chartist Circular* (1841-1843), run by John Cleave*, and he enjoyed some commercial success with the *Labourer: A Monthly Magazine of Politics, Literature, Poetry &c.*, though his co-editor Ernest Jones shouldered most responsibility for it. O'Connor's last venture into periodical publishing* was a weekly magazine, the *National Instructor* (1850-1851), now chiefly of interest for the unfinished autobiography he contributed to it. O'Connor's involvement in journalism was always secondary to his political career. Yet it is difficult to disentangle the two. Chartism was a movement on the cusp between a largely oral and an increasingly print-based popular political culture and O'Connor did more than any other person to ensure it successfully bridged the two. **MSC**
Sources: Chase 2007, Epstein 1976, Epstein 1982, *ODNB*.

O'CONNOR, THOMAS POWER (1848-1929)
Thomas Power O'Connor, also known as 'Tay Pay', was a journalist and MP from 1880 until his death. After graduating from Queen's College, Galway in 1866 he became a reporter for the conservative *Saunder's Newsletter* in Dublin. In 1870, after moving to London, he reported on the Franco-Prussian War* for the *Daily Telegraph*, which he also served briefly as a subeditor*, and then worked, again only temporarily, for the *New York Herald*. Subsequently, as a freelancer, he reported on parliamentary* debates from the press gallery of the House of Commons and became involved with radical politics* and Irish nationalism*. He wrote an unflattering biography of Disraeli (*Lord Beaconsfield: a Biography*) that was serialized* anonymously* in 1876 and published under his own name in 1879. Its popular reception paved the way for his entry into politics as a radical Parnellite in 1880. His career as a politician was closely intertwined

with his journalism when he later wrote a nightly report* on Parliament* proceedings in the *Pall Mall Gazette*; he was first elected to a seat from Galway in 1880 and subsequently from Liverpool in 1885.

In 1888 O'Connor raised sufficient financial backing to found the radical evening paper, the *Star*, a ½d newspaper with a daily* circulation* of over 162,000, which helped inaugurate the New Journalism*. O'Connor was the first editor* of the *Star* but was dismissed in July 1890 by the directors and given a payment of £15,000 on condition that he did not start another evening paper for three years. O'Connor then purchased the *Sunday Sun* in May 1891, and in 1893, after the expiration of the three-year prohibition, it was divided into the *Weekly Sun* (1893-1901), issued on Saturday and Sunday*, and the *Sun* (1893-1906), an evening daily*. The *Star* and the *Sun* were noted for pioneering 'new journalism'* and aimed at a popular* and populist market. They featured gossip* in O'Connor's 'Mainly about People' column* in the *Star*, racing tips, and coverage of divorce* and murder cases, but were also favourable to women's issues and to literature*, with a 'Book of the Week' column by O'Connor on the front page of the *Sunday Sun*.

In an 1889 essay in the *New Review*, O'Connor defined New Journalism as having a more personal tone, one that gave faces and personalities to the speakers behind the Parliamentary speeches recorded in Hansard and in the older newspapers, and that gave readers* gossip* because people had an interest in other people, what they wore, what they said, and what they experienced. In 1898 he started *M. A. P. (Mainly about people)*, a gossipy* *weekly* which had developed from his column of the same name in the *Star*. In 1902 he launched his best-known paper, *T. P.'s Weekly*, a literary paper for the general public. As a long-serving member of the House of Commons, O'Connor became Father of the House, and in later life returned to the *Daily Telegraph* where he specialized in writing obituaries*. **ML/FN**
Sources: *Men and Women of the Time* 1899, *ODNB*, Power, 1929, *The Times* 1929, Waller 2006.

OCCASIONAL NOTES This was a genre* of writing and format* created by the *Pall Mall Gazette* under its first editor* Frederick Greenwood* and further developed by W. T. Stead*, whereby a department of the paper of this name was regularly devoted to a series of successive, mostly unrelated, topical and well-written anonymous* paragraphs on diverse subjects comprising information, speculation, opinion and interpretation, separated from each other only by leading and a rule, and not by headers. Like leaders*, they appeared to represent the paper while being written by diverse hands. This extension in the *Pall Mall Gazette* of the ruminative space to afforded leaders in other dailies* related to the publication space it gained as an evening paper relieved of the pressure to report Parliament and the courts verbatim but also to the intention of its founders to combine the qualities of a review and a newspaper. LRB

Sources: Schults 1972, Stead 1893.

ODD FELLOW (1839-1842) A satirical*, illustrated 'seriocomic' 1d weekly* that supported Chartism* and other working-class* issues, *Odd Fellow* was started by the early working-class publisher* and activist, Henry Hetherington*. Disappointed by the lack of success of his *London Dispatch*, Hetherington designed his new journal for popular* consumption by including fiction and poetry*, theatrical information, cartoons* and political* squibs. According to Louis James, although the journal 'claimed to be concerned with the Society of Odd Fellows, it was entirely a literary* magazine' (26-27)

The first editor* was the dramatist James Cooke, whose *The Bachelor Club* was serialized* in the journal. The well-known working-class artist and writer W. J. Linton was a contributor and became editor in 1842.

The puns in the opening editor's column* give a sense of its tone: i.e. 'though it may appear strange to cut a friend, yet we are determined to give our readers a cut every week... when we find there is nothing to write about, why we shall right about face'. As Ian Haywood has said, *Odd Fellow* 'acted as a bridge between the unstamped* graphic satire of C. J. Grant, Seymour and *Figaro in London,* and the polite, inconsistently radical satire of *Punch'* (2004: 145).

Hetherington published 32 complete 'Sketches by "Boz"' in the *Odd Fellow* but he was forced to publish an apology and was stopped from further such piracies by threat of a law suit. *Odd Fellow* merged* with the *Fire-side Journal, and Penny Miscellany of Wit, Humour, Literature, Amusement and Romance* in December 1842. AH

Sources: Haywood 2004, James 1963, *ODNB*, *Waterloo*.

ODNB DICTIONARY OF NATIONAL BIOGRAPHY (1885-2003); OXFORD DICTIONARY OF NATIONAL BIOGRAPHY (2004-) Conceived by the periodical publisher* George Smith*, it was initially published serially in 63 quarterly parts

between 1885 and 1900. Coupled with its most recent incarnation as the paper and online *ODNB* of 2004, it is a unique work of scholarship without which the present volume of *DNCJ* would be close to unimaginable.

The *Dictionary of National Biography* was deeply involved with the periodical press from the outset. Smith's original ambition was to produce a 'dictionary of universal biography' of international scope, but he was talked out of his hubris by Leslie Stephen* – editor* of Smith's *Cornhill Magazine* – who became the *Dictionary*'s first editor. The coverage of the resulting work was national only, but the interweaving levels of social, political, intellectual and cultural history that it made accessible to its readers gave it just claim to be the most important single work of humanities scholarship since Johnson's *Dictionary*. When Smith (who lost around £70,000 in producing the dictionary) dubbed it a 'gift to English letters', it was no idle boast.

Unlike Johnson's dictionary, however, but like so much of the contemporary periodical literature which its two guiding lights were engaged in producing, the *Dictionary of National Biography* was a profoundly collaborative project. On the editorial side, apart from Smith and Stephen, Sidney Lee (1859-1926) was appointed subeditor* and played a key role, complementing Stephen's expertise in eighteenth-and nineteenth-century literature with a profound knowledge of the Elizabethan period. His fastidious proof-reading and fact-checking did much to ensure the accuracy of the entries, and his insistence on clear, unornamented prose made them a pleasure to read. Lee himself contributed 820 entries, including an entry on the dictionary's founder George Smith and a book-length life of Queen Victoria, both of whom died in 1901 with the entries therefore appearing later in supplements. He also took on the responsibility for ensuring that the many other contributors met copy deadlines. Lee became joint editor with the overworked and ailing Stephen from volume 21, and then sole editor from volume 27 to the end. Under this editorial core there was a second tier of assistants – including (at various times) C. L. Kingsford (1862-1926), Thomas Seccombe (1866-1923) and A. F. Pollard (1869-1948) – who spent three hours every morning in the British Museum, and four hours every afternoon in the dictionary's office at 14 Waterloo Place, often followed by evening proofreading. Beyond this circle were a much larger group of contributors, many of whom – like Francis Espinasse*, Alfred Ainger (1837-1904), Edward

Dutton Cook (1831-1883) and William Hunt (1842-1931) – were themselves noted journalists or writers.

The original project has had a substantial after-life and an immeasurable impact on humanities research. Lee published a concise version in 1903, and a substantial volume of errata to accompany the first edition in 1904. Subsequent volumes produced throughout the twentieth century added the lives of recently deceased notables. It was not until 1992 that work began on a second edition, which became the *Oxford Dictionary of National Biography*, published in sixty volumes and online in 2004. This monumental work of modern scholarship rests on nineteenth-century foundations that owed much to the working methods – and indeed the personnel – of the contemporary periodical press. **MaT**

Sources: Amigoni 1993, Brake 1975, Faber and Harrison 2002, Matthew 1997, *ODNB*.

O'DONOVAN, JOHN (1806-1861) John O'Donovan, a foremost Irish-language scholar began writing for periodicals through his work colleague at the Irish Ordnance Survey, antiquarian George Petrie*, who was editor*of the *Dublin Penny Journal* (1832-1833)*. O'Donovan contributed 19 articles to that *Journal*, mostly translations from the *Annals of the Four Masters* and other Irish-language texts. He also wrote seven articles on Irish surnames for Petrie's later periodical, the *Irish Penny Journal* (1840-1841). Subsequently, O'Donovan contributed a dozen articles to the *Journal of the Kilkenny Archaeological Society* (1850-1860), 11 to the *Ulster Journal of Archaeology* (1857-1861) and seven to *Duffy's Hibernian Magazine** (1860-1861). As a Catholic scholar who earned respect for his studies of Irish-language material, O'Donovan was an uncommon figure in early and mid-nineteenth-century Ireland. His contributions to popular* periodicals are especially significant as an attempt to disseminate the results of his research to a larger Irish audience. **FB**

Sources: Andrews 1975, Boyne 1987, *ODNB*.

OLIO, OR MUSEUM OF ENTERTAINMENT (1828-1833) Published by Joseph Shackell, the *Olio* was a weekly* illustrated* miscellany* whose watchwords were 'interest, spirit and raciness'. An unstamped*, compact, 16-page octavo, it offered, at the affordable (if not actually rock-bottom) price* of 3d, a combination of original articles and stories with material excerpted from more expensive, upmarket publications such as the *Quarterly Review** or the *Edinburgh Literary Journal* (1828-1831). In seeking out a lower-middle-class* audience for such material, the *Olio* was attempting to replicate the success of such papers as the *Mirror of Literature**. It was half-hearted at best in its dedication to instruction and improvement, however, and while it touted its interest in history* and natural history, they were used primarily as sources of *outré* or mildly titillating material. Aside from a reverent curiosity about the activities of the royals, contemporary events were rarely discussed: the *Olio* was gleefully apolitical.

It specialized instead in humorous and exotic tales such as 'The Reminisces of an Old Monkey', 'Ghertrude Bremmel, or, the Harpooner of Fish Hook Bay', or 'The Nymph of the Lurlei Berg', and also carried poetry* of dubious literary merit. The 'Diary and Chronology' section that occupied the back page mixed – almost at random – religious instruction pertaining to given dates in the Christian calendar, gnomic wisdom about the progression of the seasons, useful information such as tide times or the phases of the lunar cycle, and anniversaries of the births or deaths of saints, historical figures, or recent celebrities*.

Its demise in 1833 can probably be attributed to the success of a new wave of cheap* periodicals that began in 1832 with *Chambers's Edinburgh Journal** and the *Penny Magazine**. **MaT**

Sources: James 1963, *Waterloo*, Wiener 1970.

OLIPHANT, MARGARET OLIPHANT WILSON (1828-1897) For the majority of her career (1849-1897), Scottish-born Margaret Oliphant relied upon literary* journalism to supplement the income she made as a prolific novelist and biographer, believing that the two activities complemented one another. In 1851 her mother obtained an introduction, through 'Delta' (David Macbeth Moir*), to John and Major William Blackwood*, whose house* periodical, *Blackwood's Edinburgh Magazine** (*Maga*), had formed staple reading in the Wilson household despite its Tory stance. From 1852 *Maga* provided her major outlet. When she came to write the first two volumes of the publishing firm's history, *Annals of a Publishing House* (1897-1898), she described her role as that of 'general utility woman' (2: 349,475), ready, as reviewer* and commentator, to speak for the common reader on a range of topics, which, especially in her later series, 'The Old Saloon' (Jan. 1887-Dec. 1892) and 'A Looker-On' Oct. 1896), ranged well beyond the purely literary.

Her ready agreement to *Maga*'s principle of anonymous* reviewing and her calculated adoption of a male persona, concealed that, on occasion, she

Figure 48: The cover of *Once a Week*, March 1872.

Figure 49: The cover of *Once a Week*, Sept. 1872.

supplied up to a third of the month's copy. In later years, when *Maga*'s format as a family* periodical came to seem dated, she questioned the price her loyalty had exacted, envying fellow writers the lucrative editorships* that a patriarchal firm such as Blackwoods would never offer. Nevertheless she attempted to revamp her reviewing persona to accord with the clubland* literary atmosphere of the late 1880s.

Although she occasionally wrote for other periodicals, in particular the *Spectator** for which she wrote 55 articles (March 1874-Feb. 1897), including the series 'A Commentary in an Easy Chair', occasional articles usually reflected her expertise as a biographer or travel writer. Only in her last years, driven by financial need, did she undertake larger commitments such as her series of 'A Fireside Commentary' (Jan.-Aug. 1888) for *St James's Gazette* and *St James's Budget*.

Henry James's assertion in her obituary*, that 'no woman had ever, for half a century, had her personal "say" so publicly' ('London Notes', *Harper's Weekly* 41: 1897) revealed something of the antagonism of her male peers to her prodigious output and influence. **EJJ**

Sources: Clarke 1997, Jay 1995, *ODNB*, Oliphant 1897.

***ONCE A WEEK* (1859-1880)** After breaking with their partner Charles Dickens*, with whom they had published *Household Words**, Bradbury and Evans*, proprietors* of *Punch**, launched their new periodical *Once a Week* in 1859. It was edited* by Samuel Lucas. The new journal, competing with Dickens's *All the Year Round**, featured work by popular *Punch** contributors, including illustrators* John Leech*, John Tenniel*, Charles Keene*, Hablot K. Browne*, George Du Maurier* and John Everett Millais*, and writers Mark Lemon*, Shirley Brooks* and Tom Taylor*. Early issues also included serialized* novels by Charles Reade and George Meredith.

In spite of its literary* and artistic merits, however, the journal did not succeed commercially. Although it was very popular* initially, circulation* declined through the years. Lucas died in 1865, and in 1867 *Once a Week* was acquired by James Rice. Financially, the journal was a losing venture for Rice, but after meeting journal contributor Walter Besant*, Rice formed a successful literary partnership with him and the two went on to publish a series of novels together. **CJM**

Sources: Sullivan, *Wellesley.*

ONWARD: THE ORGAN OF THE BAND OF HOPE MOVEMENT (1865-1910) As the title suggests, *Onward* was a journal for juveniles*, intended to promote temperance* instruction, the work of the Sabbath school and, in particular, the Band of Hope movement, throughout the whole country. Each issue contained a number of 'short, interesting tales, anecdotes and facts, with original and select songs, music* and recitations' ('To Our Readers' No. 1:1). From 1872 onwards each monthly number was illustrated* with wood* engravings by artists such as Mary Ellen Edwards* and John Dawson Watson, with letterpress provided by well-respected temperance authors including Clara Lucas Balfour and the Rev, John William Kirton. During the course of publication there were a number of modest increases in page size*, although the price* remained constant at 1d per month.

The journal was issued as *Workers Onward* in January 1910 and ceased publication in December of the same year. **FM**
Sources: Altholz 1989, Harrison, Niessen 1994, *Waterloo*.

ONWHYN, THOMAS (1814-1886) Best known as a prolific illustrator* of serial* fiction, Thomas Onwhyn produced a number of series of extra illustrations for Dickens's* work which brought down the wrath of the author. His talents lay in the full-plate etched caricatures* he produced for novels and in a series of satirical* lithographed* 'panoramas' or 'pull-out' works from the 1850s. Belonging to the generation of Seymour* and George Cruikshank*, sharing their satirical vision and caricature training, Onwhyn inevitably gravitated towards *Punch**, although he only produced a few illustrations for the magazine mainly published (1847-1848). **BM**
Sources: Engen 1990, Houfe 1978, *ODNB*, Spielmann 1895.

ORAL AND PRINT CULTURE: RELATIONSHIP Although the relation between oral and print culture was long construed as antithetical, both cultures are now rather perceived as intersecting areas that have been engaged in a dynamic and productive process of transfer and communication.

From John Brand's *Popular Antiquities* (1777) and J. G. Herder's *Volkslieder* (1778) onwards, collecting folk tales and folk songs was in fashion throughout Europe. Collectors gathered their material in interviews with local populations as well as by consulting broadsides and chapbooks. While classic efforts in the genre* like Walter Scott's* *Minstrelsy of the Scottish Border* (1802) were motivated by the perception

that oral culture was in decline (and hence in need of transmission to print), they were at the same time seen as accelerating that decline. Romantic antiquarianism continued unabated in the nineteenth century, the study of 'folklore' (a term coined by William Thoms* in the *Athenaeum**, 22 Aug. 1846) being absorbed in the new discipline of history* as it developed. Thoms founded *Notes and Queries** in 1849 as a forum of exchange for antiquarians. In 1878 the Folklore Society was established in order to systematise antiquarian knowledge.

The received impression that the 'oral tradition' properly so called declined with the rise of print culture and literacy levels needs qualification on several counts. First, with the Industrial Revolution the composition of folk songs, rather than disappearing, was displaced from the countryside to factories and mines, as many labourers were keen to preserve a sense of history and of continuity with their pre-industrial roots and culture. In addition, new forms of popular culture developed such as variety, circus and the music hall tradition, which began in the 1830s and blossomed in the 1850s. Some of those new forms were in fact enabled by the ascent of print culture and periodical reading: among them authorial readings (Dickens)* and the practice of reading literature*, including serial* fiction, aloud in the middle-class* family. Finally, as new means of transport revolutionized England's political culture, oratory – speaking from the hustings – became a prominent feature of national politics; subsequently, speech reporting become an important feature of daily* newspapers (verbatim in some). What those different developments underline is that the antithesis between oral and literate cultures was not sharp or absolute, but that modern print culture continued elements of orality (e.g. performance) in new forms. **MdW**
Sources: Altick 1957, Vincent 1982, Vincent 1989, Williams 1978.

O'SULLIVAN, MORTIMER (1791-1859) A Church of Ireland clergyman and writer, O'Sullivan was born at Clonmel, and converted to Protestantism before entering Trinity College in 1813. He began his literary career with *Captain Rock Detected (1824)*, a response to Thomas Moore's indictment of Irish landlords in *Memoirs of Captain Rock* (1824). When Moore published another defence of Catholicism, *Travels of an Irish Gentleman in Search of a Religion* (1833), O'Sullivan countered again with *A Guide to an Irish Gentleman in His Search for a Religion* (1833). The political*, religious* and social concerns of these works were the subject of over 30 of

O'Sullivan's contributions to the *Dublin University Magazine** (1834-1850), though his early contributions were more focused on literary* and historical* topics. With his brother Samuel, he published a 12-part series, 'By-ways of Irish History', which aimed to provide a history of Ireland that was not written with a British bias (Aug. 1837-March 1839) (Hall 1999: 66). In the British press, his six articles for the *Quarterly Review** (1828-1852), generally offered views of Ireland as from an 'Irish correspondent' and dealt with the 'State of Ireland' and issues of religion in Ireland. Similarly two articles in *Blackwood's Magazine** related to the Orange Lodges of Ireland (Feb. 1836), and 1790s Ireland under the triple alliance (Feb.-March 1839).

From 1842 O'Sullivan contributed numerous book reviews* to the *Dublin University Magazine,* covering religious and political titles. Reflecting the rise of nationalist politics as articulated by the *Nation** newspaper and the Young Irelanders*, O'Sullivan's writings became more politically engaged in the *Dublin University Magazine* with articles on 'Old Ireland and Young' (Jan. 1843), 'Repeal agitation' (June-Nov. 1843), 'How should Irish Protestants meet their dangers?' (July 1845) and 'Life and times of O'Connell' (Sept. 1848).

Charles Gavin Duffy* noted that Mortimer O'Sullivan was the first Protestant since Wolfe Tone who not only sympathized with the wrongs of the Celts, but accepted and embraced the whole volume of their hopes and sympathies. (Duffy cited in Hall: 77). By the end of his career O'Sullivan was considered much more of a controversialist when he collaborated with R. J. McGhee in the provocative two-volume work *Romanism as it Rules in Ireland* (1840) (Bowen: 119-120). O'Sullivan's journalistic output reflects this move from conservative to radical beliefs and the increasingly polarised religious attitudes in Ireland in the mid-nineteenth century. JCA

Sources: Bowen 1978, *Dublin University Magazine* 1851: 504-08, Hall 1991, Hall 1999, Martin and O'Sullivan 1853, Whelan 2005.

O'SULLIVAN, SAMUEL (1790-1851) A Church of Ireland clergyman and writer, he was the elder brother of Mortimer O'Sullivan*, also a clergyman and writer. Like his brother, he converted to Protestantism at school.

O'Sullivan began his journalistic career contributing to *Blackwood's Magazine** (1829-1838) mainly on subjects of religion in Ireland. His most sustained literary connection was with the *Dublin University Magazine*. Hall (1999) has suggested that O'Sullivan may have given £10 to £15 in 1833 to establish the periodical. Samuel O'Sullivan was responsible for the very first article in the *Dublin University Magazine,* 'The Present Crisis' (Jan. 1833), which articulated the concerns of the Protestant ascendancy in Ireland, themes that were throughout the magazine's* long life. From the beginning of his association with the *Magazine* his writings included political* and historical* essays, such as 'Discourse on general politics' (Feb. 1833), '[Robert] Emmet's insurrection' (May 1833), and 'Political prospects' (Jan. 1836), though the majority of his contributions discussed the religious issues of the country.

From 1837-1839 he published, with his brother, a 12-part series, 'By-ways of Irish History', which aimed to provide a history of Ireland from an Irish perspective (Aug. 1837-March 1839) (Hall 1999: 66). The social issues of Ireland dominated his articles in the 1840s: poor laws, tenant rights, famine and the conditions of the poor in general. Despite this turn to issues of social interest in his later writings, Samuel was noted by Charles Gavin Duffy* for 'furious bigotry', though he did sympathize with the Catholic peasantry and the abuses they suffered (Duffy, cited in Hall: 77). Through their journalistic careers both Samuel and his brother Mortimer O'Sullivan were instrumental figures in the most successful Irish literary periodical of the mid-nineteenth century, the Dublin University Magazine. JCA

Sources: Bowen 1978, *Dublin University Magazine* 1851, Hall 1991, Hall 1999, Martin and O'Sullivan 1853, Whelan 2005.

OTWAY, CAESAR (1780-1842) Born into an Anglo-Irish family, Caesar Otway, proprietor*, editor* and journalist, took a BA degree from Trinity College, Dublin in 1801, and became a Church of Ireland clergyman. In 1825 he set up, with Joseph Henderson Singer, the long-running monthly*, the *Christian Examiner and Church of Ireland Magazine**. It was through Otway that William Carleton* published*, in the *Christian Examiner**, the first of his Irish stories. In 1832 Otway, together with printer/publisher John Folds*, founded the weekly* *Dublin Penny Journal**, soon bringing in George Petrie* as co-editor*. Otway wrote articles on Irish topography and antiquities for the magazine, signing himself with a pseudonym*, 'Terence O'Toole'. After about 20 numbers of the *Journal*, Otway seems to have ceased his editing duties.

He appears again in 1833 as one of the group of Trinity men who established the monthly* *Dublin University Magazine**. Otway contributed at least two articles to it while continuing his association with the *Christian Examiner.* One (published in Jan.

1841) was an appreciation of the work of William Carleton for the *Dublin University Magazine*'s 'Our Portrait Gallery' illustrated* series. Otway himself was honoured as the first of the Gallery's subjects in October 1839. Otway's anti-Catholic stance permeated the *Christian Examiner*, and his conservative principles were mirrored in the *Dublin University Magazine*, but his devotion to Irish subjects and promotion of Irish authors remained paramount. **ET Sources:** Clyde 2003, Hall 1999, *ODNB*, Rafroidi 1980, *Wellesley.*

'OUIDA' (1839-1908) Although known today for her novels in book form, Maria Louisa Ramé, best known under the pseudonym* of 'Ouida', was a prolific contributor to periodicals. Born in Bury St Edmunds she moved to London in 1857, was introduced to Harrison Ainsworth* through her family doctor, and in 1859 published a tale in *Bentley's Miscellany** (April-May) which Ainsworth then edited. For the next two years hardly a number of *Bentley's* was without one of her tales. Her first serial* novel 'Held in Bondage, or Granville de Vigne', appeared in the *New Monthly** (Jan. 1861-June 1863). She now turned to serials full-time, the last of which was her most famous, *Under Two Flags* (*British Army and Navy Review* Aug. 1865-June 1866).

Figure 50: 'Ouida' (Maria Louisa Ramé), in a fairly unknown portrait, *Idler,* Oct. 1893: 273.

Thereafter Ouida published fiction mainly in book form, though over 1871-1872 she returned to single-episode tales for the American *Lippincott's*. By now she was living in Tuscany. In 1878 Ouida's journalism proper began, with articles in the *Whitehall Review*. The following year she started writing letters* to *The Times** on subjects such as the state of fiction, and the state of Italy. Later she sent poems on topical subjects, some too politically* scandalous to be published. In 1882 she contributed articles on vivisection, Italian land ownership and Charles Reade to the *Gentleman's Magazine**. From 1885 she wrote a series of commentaries for the *North American Review* on topics such as female suffrage, the fallacies of science*, the state of literature* and Italian cities, and also wrote three pieces in 1888 for Oscar Wilde's* *Woman's World**. In 1892 she began to publish in the *Fortnightly Review** and later in the *Nineteenth Century** on a similar range of topics (her distaste for the 'New Woman' led to that figure's famous defence by Sarah Grand* and others in this period). She also published a few pieces in the Italian periodical, the *Nuova Antologia*, which had previously serialised several of her novels in translation. Much of her later journalism* Ouida collected in *Views and Opinions* (1895), *An Altruist, and Four Essays* (1897), and *Critical Studies* (1900). Her last piece was an account of Richard Burton, a friend, for the *Fortnightly* in 1906. Not having retained her copyrights*, Ouida died, in Viareggio, penniless. **AK Sources:** Jordan 1995, Stirling 1957, Weedon 2003

OUR CELEBRITIES: A PORTRAIT GALLERY (1888-1895) The monthly* *Our Celebrities* was launched in 1888 and included three biographical sketches with accompanying photographic* portraits in each issue. Part of the interest in celebrity* and personality* in the late nineteenth century, this was a lavish publication, with photos by Stanislaus Walery, photographer to the Queen, reflected in the hefty price* of 2s 6d. Portraits of aristocrats mingled alongside artists including Frederic Leighton and even writer-journalists such as Edmund Yates*. T. H. Huxley* appeared in May 1889, though he chose to write his own profile, noting that 'I could not see what business the public had with my private life'. But by this time, private lives were an important feature of the New Journalism*. **MWT Sources:** Turner 2000c, *Waterloo.*

OUR YOUNG FOLKS (1871-1897) James Henderson's *Our Young Folks' Weekly Budget* was among the longest-running of all Victorian children's* periodicals.

Launched in 1871, the eight-page miscellany* was priced* competitively* at just one halfpenny per weekly* number. While it went through numerous title changes* (*Our Young Folks' Weekly Budget* (1871-1876), *Young Folks' Weekly Budget* (1876-1879), *Young Folks' Budget* (1879); *Young Folks* (1879-1884), *Young Folks' Paper* (1884-1891), *Old and Young* (1891-1896), *Folks at Home* (1896-1897)), it was aimed at boys and girls alike, and a somewhat older and higher class of reader* than many of its contemporaries. In 1873 the paper was expanded to 16 pages, and its price raised to 1d.

Its motto professing 'To Inform, To Instruct, To Amuse', *Our Young Folks' Weekly Budget* carried serial* fiction, short stories and factual articles, plus puzzles and correspondence*. With a keen eye on developments in the periodical market, Henderson strived to stay ahead of his competition, regularly revising the paper's title, content and appearance. Although editorial duties were often delegated to others, such as Clinton Leighton, Robert Leighton and Richard Quittenton, Henderson remained proprietor* throughout the paper's existence.

Our Young Folks' Weekly Budget specialized in publishing series of adventure stories featuring popular lead protagonists. Henderson was doubtless inspired by the 'Jack Harkaway' series, published in Edwin J. Brett's* *Boys of England* (1866-1899)*, which had proven that stalwart characters could help a paper maintain a strong sale. The 1870s saw the commencement of several such serials*, including Richard Quittenton's 'Tim Pippin', S. Holland's 'Wonderland', Walter Villiers's 'Silverspeare' and Alfred R. Phillips's 'Prince Goldenwings'.

Our Young Folks' Weekly Budget is perhaps most significant for being the paper which first serialised Robert Louis Stevenson's *Treasure Island*. The story (1881-1882), credited to the pseudonymous* 'Captain North', unceremoniously occupied the back pages, and was sparsely illustrated*. Stevenson had intended for the tale to be entitled 'The Sea Cook', but was persuaded by Henderson to adopt a more marketable alternative. Two further Stevenson tales, *The Black Arrow* and *Kidnapped*, appeared in the paper in the 1880s. **CMB**
Sources: Jay 1918-1921, Rollington 1913, *Waterloo.*

OWEN, DAVID (1795-1866) Journalist, editor* and writer, David Owen was born in Wales, the son of an Anglican shoemaker and a Baptist mother. Locally educated as an Anglican, he became a Baptist while pursuing a medical apprenticeship. After a year studying for the Baptist Ministry in England, he returned to Wales as a school-master and lay preacher before taking charge of the Baptist churches on the Lleyn peninsula. There he was ordained and married. Living and working almost entirely among Welsh-speakers, in 1824 he shocked his literate contemporaries by publishing, in Welsh, an excoriating article on 'The poverty of the Welsh language' in the journal *Seren Gomer* (the star of Gomer) under the signature 'Brutus, Lleyn' (Brutus from Lleyn). In it he berated the Welsh for being a 'nation of thieves', reliant on the literary culture of England. The article triggered a long and lively public debate, and 'Brutus' continued to play a similarly provocative role in Welsh intellectual life for the rest of his career.

Following theological tensions closer to home, he was expelled from the Baptist Church and migrated to the Independents, but abandoned the cloth for journalism in January 1828, becoming editor of *Lleuad yr Oes* (Moon of the Age; 1828-1835), a non-denominational monthly published in Aberystwyth. In it he attacked child baptism (1828) and Catholicism (1829),but becoming increasingly conservative in both politics and theology, he alienated even the Independents, who closed the journal in May 1835 and three months later launched a radical, anti-Tory and anti-Anglican magazine *Y Diwygiwr (the reformer)*, in Llanelli, under the editorship of David Rees *(y Cynhyrfurr 1801-1869)*. A month earlier Owen, now returned to the Anglican fold, began to edit a new monthly* periodical, *Yr Haul* (The Sun; 1835-1866). The two journals, locked in permanent conflict, defined Welsh* religious, political, and cultural life for the next decade. His acerbic and prolific contribution to Welsh-language journalism invigorated public discourse in Wales for almost half a century, and he was recognized in the 1880s as 'the first Welsh writer who made politics* popular'. **AGJ**
Sources: Davies 1962, Davies 1963, Davies 1866, *DWB,* Jones 1993, Jones 1867, Owen 1855, Williams 1914.

OWEN, RICHARD (1804-1892) Thomas Wakley's* campaigning against the ineptitude of the Royal College of Surgeons in the *Lancet** prompted Richard Owen's initial appointment at the College's museum in 1827, from where he was able to establish himself as one of the foremost scientific* figures of the century. Owen's astonishingly prodigious output of over 600 scientific papers, on subjects ranging from palaeontology to medical education, were mostly published in specialist journals like the *Proceedings of the Zoological Society of London,* but he also skilfully utilized the general periodical press to promote his scientific standing and expound his functionalist and idealist approaches to anatomy, including writing overtly popular articles for Charles Dickens's* *Household Words**. In particular, Owen exploited the conventions of anonymity*, and, with the apparent acquiescence of editors* like John Gibson Lockhart* of the *Quarterly Review** to such egregious puffing*, frequently reviewed his own work while referring to himself in the third person, an underhand practice that did not go unnoticed amongst indignant rivals.

In 1860 Owen's anonymous* but identifiably intemperate notice of Charles Darwin's *Origin of Species* (1859) in the *Edinburgh Review** estranged him from many former colleagues and his persistent antipathy to Darwinism damaged his standing with the public. The eventual realization in 1881 of his longstanding plan for a Natural History Museum was nevertheless widely celebrated in the press. **GD**
Sources: Lightman 2004a, *ODNB*, Rupke 1994.

OWEN, ROBERT (1771-1858) Political reformer and one of the founders of socialism, Robert Owen, having become an educated and successful industrialist from a humble start in life, began his involvement in journalism modestly in 1817, editing* the short-lived *Mirror of Truth* to publicize his ideas. But Owen's inspirational influence on the production of 'Owenite' periodicals extended far beyond those Owen conducted himself, and over 80 British journals promoted aspects of Owenite political* ideals. Owen's own weekly* paper, the *Crisis* (1832-1834), also co-edited by Owen, assisted by his son Robert Dale Owen and James 'Shepherd' Smith, reflected this popularity. Trade unionist enthusiasm was such that in April 1833 Owen changed its subtitle to the *National Co-operative Trades' Union & Equitable Labour Exchange Gazette*. However, sustained mass support proved elusive. In August 1834, frustrated that Smith kept the *Crisis* afloat largely by including 'heterogeneous opinions, some... opposed to, my principles', Owen closed it.

The more successful *New Moral World** (1834ff), which centred upon promoting social-ist* communities, took its place. Some elements of the Owenite press criticized the 'Social Father' as with the *Social Pioneer* (1839), for example, issued by dissident communitarians, which was critical of Owen's domineering paternalism. The collapse of 'Harmony Hall' (1839-1845), the only British community which Owen sanctioned, took *New Moral World* with it. Owenite ideas now permeated many aspects of secularism and reform, but Owen enjoyed diminishing acclaim. His subsequent periodicals were, even by his standards, remarkably sanctimonious: *Robert Owen's Weekly Letter to the Human Race* (1850 – second editions titled *Letters to the Human Race on the coming Universal Revolution*); *Robert Owen's Journal, Explanatory of the Means to Well-Place, Well-Employ, and Well-Educate the Population of the World* (1850-1852); *Robert Owen's Rational Quarterly Review & Journal* (1853); and, finally the irregular, *Robert Owen's Millennial Gazette* (1856-1858). **MSC**
Sources: Harrison 1969, *ODNB*.

OXENFORD, JOHN (1812-1877) Writer of over one hundred plays, John Oxenford's theatre success led to his gaining the position of drama critic for *The Times** (1840s-1870s). Dynamically involved in London's theatre world, he often reviewed* his friends' plays and, sometimes, even reviewed his own work. His reviews were marked by a benign tone, and several contemporaries recalled that his reputation gained him a private box in every theatre. Oxenford was a versatile contributor as well as reviewer; his catholic interests were reflected in the myriad of articles he wrote for periodical publications throughout his career, producing serious, scholarly articles for the *Foreign Quarterly Review** and the *Westminster Review**, as well as translations of French, Spanish and German literature*. His translation of Johann Wolfgang von Goethe's (1749-1832) works were serialized* in the *Musical World**. Oxenford also demonstrated a more playful side to his literary character in his contributions to *Punch** and other comic miscellanies*. **BP**
Sources: *ODNB*, Stierstorfer 1996, *Waterloo, Wellesley.*

P

PAE, DAVID (1828-1884) As a result of his serialized* fiction that emerged as a staple of weekly* provincial* newspapers, David Pae, novelist and editor*, transformed the fortunes of several press titles, including the Dundee *People's Journal** that moved from an obscure provincial to a true national* newspaper with a six-figure circulation*. Pae was greatly affected by millenarianism and published several pamphlets in the 1850s and 1860s that promulgated his vision of the end of the world. This belief affected his first novel, *George Sandford; or, the Draper's Assistant* (1853) which exposed the murkiness of commerce. During the 1850s the Scottish* newspaper press began publishing instalment fiction and this convention gave Pae his first success as an author. 'Jessie Melville; or the Double Sacrifice' was first published in the *North Briton* in 1855; further serials* subsequently appeared (1856-1863) in the *Berwick Journal, Falkirk Herald* and the *Glasgow Times*, among others.

Pae's career accelerated; he was appointed editor of the Dunfermline *Saturday Press* in 1859-1860, then given a contract in 1863 by John Leng* to write novels for the *Dundee Advertiser* group. This was marked by Pae with *Lucy the Factory Girl* again attacking the capitalist culture and was initially published in the *People's Journal** (1863-1864), proving immensely popular. Donaldson suggests it made Pae 'the leading serial novelist in Scotland'. Law calculates that Pae might have produced 50 or more such works, although Pae was extremely reticent about personally attributing his own work*. Leng's contract ensured Pae's novels were exclusively first published in the *People's Journal*, but the Leng family ties with other newspapers led to Pae's writings being reproduced south of the border. This included the *Sheffield Daily Telegraph*, a relationship that began in 1865 and lasted nearly a decade. Noteworthy also was the decision by W. F. Tillotson* to make *Jessie Melville* the first novel in his new *Bolton Weekly Journal** in 1871 which effectively established Tillotson's new paper. Pae resumed his editing role in 1870, when he was offered the post at the newly independent *People's Friend*, a position he held until his death. Before the Tillotson era, Pae may have been responsible for half the full-length serial novels in British newspapers. FSM

Sources: Donaldson 1986, Law 2000.

PAGAN REVIEW (1892) The sole issue of the *Pagan Review* was published on 15 August 1892 by William Sharp*, who used the pseudonym* of 'Fiona Macleod'. Sharp was a Scottish writer who was part of the Celtic Revival and a member of the magical association known as the Hermetic Order of the Golden Dawn. Uninterested in 'the general reader', Sharp aimed for 'thorough-going unpopularity'. The journal was to publish only writers who identified themselves with 'the younger men'. It is unclear whom Sharp meant by this as he alone authored all the contributions to the issue. The stories, poetry* and articles reveal the influence of the Aesthetic and Decadent Movements as Sharp had met most key participants and written a book on Dante Gabriel Rossetti, while his leader* includes a discussion of 'copartnery' that somewhat superficially taps into the spirit of the women's suffrage movement. Sharp's interest in diverse forms of paganism is apparent in the journal's use of classical myth, Celtic folklore and African animism. Relations between paganisms and other religions* are also addressed in pieces such as 'The Black Madonna' and 'Dionysos in India,' reflecting the rising British interest in world paganisms during the latter half of the century. DND

Sources: Alaya 1970, Cevasco 1993, Tye 1974, *Waterloo*.

PAGEANT (1896-1897) This successful art and literature* annual* is a good example of the potential popularity of the artistic avant-garde of the 1890s. Called 'the best gift-book for the ordinary reader' in *Review of Reviews**, the two issues of the *Pageant* offered a respectable version of more controversial 'Decadent' periodicals notorious for their (often uncalled-for) association with Oscar Wilde*. Its editors* were Gleeson White* (for literature) and Charles H. Shannon* (for art), both of whom had acquired editorial experience with earlier little magazines*. Shannon, alongside his companion Charles Ricketts*, was still involved with his coterie publication the *Dial**, and White had been the *Studio's** founding editor. No doubt they viewed the *Pageant* more or less as a continuation of these previous ventures. With Shannon, Ricketts, Reginald Savage, John Gray and Thomas Sturge Moore*, the circle of friends that had been previously associated with the *Dial* is reconstituted here. The *Pageant* even features some illustrations* that were previously printed in its predecessor, and some of the contributions are excerpts from publications by Ricketts's own Vale Press.

The first issue (Dec. 1896) contained an eclectic mix of all that was fashionable at the time. It contained reproductions of well-known works by D. G. Rossetti, J. E. Millais* and Edward Burne-Jones. It paid homage to Swinburne* by means of a portrait by William Rothenstein, and the publication of the exclusive 'Roundel of Rabelais' by his own hand. The Impressionist trend is represented by Charles Conder and James Whistler*. The contributions by two prominent foreign poets*, Maeterlinck and Verlaine (a poem on Rossetti's painting 'Monna Rosa'), are left in the original French.

In the second issue (1897) Maeterlinck and Villiers de l'Isle-Adam are featured in English translation. There is a lavishly illustrated* article by Gleeson White on the paintings of Gustave Moureau. Rothenstein is present with a portrait of J. K. Huysmans, and there are two reproductions after Puvis de Chavannes. Rossetti is also featured twice, as is George Watts. Of the younger generation, we find mostly the same names as in the previous issue, as well as a poem by Michael Field and illustrations by Walter Crane* and William Strang*. The first issue has a leading* article on medieval Florentine religious plays, and the second has a brief history of engraving by Ricketts. The two boarded issues were published* by H. Henry & Co* and have luxurious designs by Ricketts and end papers by Lucien Pissarro. KNC

Source: Sullivan.

PAGET FAMILY The three Paget brothers, Henry Marriott (1856-1936), Sydney Edward (1860-1908) and Walter Stanley (1863-1935), were well-known periodical and book illustrators* in the late nineteenth and early twentieth centuries. All three were educated at the Royal Academy Schools, Henry winning an award there in 1877 and Walter in 1887. The brothers were known both for their black and white illustrations and for their portraits. Walter, known as 'Wal', was employed as a war* artist by the *Illustrated London News** in 1884 to cover the expedition to relieve General Gordon at Khartoum. He also provided illustrations for other periodicals, including *Black and White**, the *Sphere**, and the *Sporting and Dramatic Mirror*. As a book illustrator he was best known for the 120 illustrations he did for the 1891 Cassell edition of *Robinson Crusoe* and for illustrating Rider Haggard's novels. Sidney, who died at 47, also worked for the *Illustrated London News* and the *Sphere* and is best known for his *Strand Magazine** illustrations of Sherlock Holmes. Although *The Times** obituary* for Wal Paget states that he was the model for Sherlock Holmes, the *ODNB* emphatically states that no one person served as the model. Henry also contributed to periodicals, was a war artist during the Balken War of 1912-1913 and served as an officer in France during The First World War, designing camouflage. FN

Sources: *ODNB, The Times* 1908/1935/1936.

'PAID PARAGRAPHS' 'Paid paragraphs' were a covert form of advertising* new books in the guise of ordinary book reviews*, resorted to by some publishers*, largely pre-1850, keen to ensure favourable reviews for their list. A form of puffing*, which exploited the hegemonic policy of anonymity* in the press before 1860, these advertorials were widely associated at the time with Henry Colburn*, a book and periodical publisher. Colburn not only employed inhouse staff to write the paragraphs and paid other journals to include them, but he insisted on their inclusion in his own periodicals as well. Thomas Hood*, trying to edit* Colburn's *New Monthly Magazine** in 1843, complained both against the practice under his watch but also about the poor quality of the paragraphs: 'I undertook to review all books except Colburn's own with the puffing of which I of course desired to have no concern. They are *done* [Peter George] Patmore, [Robert Folkestone or David E] Williams or [William] Shoberl (Frederic's son). If you see the Mag. you will know what wretched things these reviews are… I am ashamed of them at present or should be were it not pretty well known that I have no hand in them' (Jerrold: 369-370). By naming their authors, he indicates how implicated in the practice the industry was – not only Colburn and his writers but his editors (like Hood, who soon quit) and the publisher/editors of the other newspapers and periodicals who accepted the fee and inserted the 'paragraphs'. That the practice extended beyond Colburn is suggested by the vigorous measures taken by principled editors and publishers such as Dilke* in the *Athenaeum** under his watch to avoid puffing by his staff. LRB

Sources: Brake 1994a, Jerrold 1907, Sutherland 1986, *Wellesley*.

PALL MALL GAZETTE (1865-1923) Like its fictional namesake in W. M. Thackeray's* *Pendennis*, the *Pall Mall Gazette* prided itself on being 'written by gentlemen for gentlemen'. Established in 1865 by George Smith*, this elegant little two-column* daily* evening (briefly morning, 1870) tabloid was printed on good paper* and sold for 2d, later 1d. Its elite readership* was concentrated in clubland* and its early contributors were among the most distinguished practitioners of higher journalism*. Under its founding editor*, Frederick Greenwood*, it published the innovative investigative* journalism of his brother James, the 'Amateur Casual', Matthew Arnold's* witty 'Friendship's Garland', social sketches by Leslie Stephen* and Anthony Trollope*, trenchant leaders by Fitzjames Stephen* and Sir Henry Maine, off-beat Occasional* Notes by Matthew Higgins ('Jacob Omnium')*, literary reviews* by George Meredith and letters from John Ruskin*. In many respects it resembled a daily version of the *Saturday Review** or *Cornhill Magazine**. Smith indulged Greenwood's increasing Toryism but in 1880 gave the paper to his son-in-law Henry Yates Thompson*, who required his editor to align the paper with Gladstone's* government. Greenwood refused and resigned, taking many staff with him to found the rival *St James's Gazette**.

Under the intensely political* editorship of John Morley* the *Gazette* became a leading liberal paper. When he became an MP in 1883, his assistant W. T. Stead* took over and ably assisted by Edward T. Cook* and Alfred Milner* pursued the editorial crusading and celebrity* interviewing* characteristic of the 'new journalism'*. Although Stead's sensational exposé of child prostitution in London in 1885 raised the paper's circulation* to 12,000, it also brought a social odium that distressed Thompson, who finally dismissed him in 1890, promoting Cook to editor.

Thompson sold the *Pall Mall Gazette* in 1892 to William Waldorf Astor, a rich American conservative and future press baron* seeking political and social influence. He dismissed Cook, replacing him with the glamorous Henry Cust*, whom he fired in 1896 for failing to follow his directions. More amenable were Sir Douglas Straight, editor until 1909, and F. J. Higginbottom, under whom the paper duly plodded downhill. The *Gazette* enjoyed a last brief flare of political influence under the brilliant editorship of J. L. Garvin, who doubled its circulation during his four-year tenure, 1911-1915, but it relapsed into pedestrianism under its last editor, D. M. Sutherland. With a new owner, Sir Henry Dalziel, it absorbed the *Globe** in 1921 only to be dissolved in 1923 into Lord Beaverbrook's *Evening Standard*. CAK

Sources: Koss 1984, *ODNB*, Scott 1950, Scott 1952, *Waterloo*.

PALL MALL MAGAZINE (1893-1914) Begun in 1893 by William Waldorf Astor, the monthly *Pall Mall Magazine* commenced just when literary* magazines like the *Cornhill**, and *Macmillan's** were de-

clining in popularity and circulation*. Astor intended the magazine, a companion to the *Pall Mall Gazette**, to be a high quality literary publication, but its quality ebbed and flowed over its 21-year run.

Its first editors*, Lord Frederick Spencer Hamilton and Sir Douglas Straight (May 1893-Nov. 1896), designed it as a 'periodical aimed at securing and maintaining a high and refined literary and artistic standard'. It began as a shilling* monthly* of 120 pages per issue, which by 1895 had extended to 160 pages; signature* and celebrity* were highlighted, with prefaces to volumes largely taken up with lists of forthcoming authors' names. Best known for its fiction and illustrations*, Hamilton and Straight also published a variety of articles on current political* and social issues as well as military history* and travel essays. Most of these articles were superbly illustrated*, such as Lord Ernest Hamilton's May 1900 piece, 'The Passage to the Great North-west', which included 17 illustrations from photographs* of the Pacific Northwest.

After Straight's departure in 1896, the quality noticeably declined. According to Mike Ashley, Straight had been responsible for commissioning most of the articles and fiction while Hamilton had been in charge of the magazine's 'artistic presence'. Though it continued to publish fiction by popular writers such as 'Ouida'* and H. Rider Haggard, its articles suffered, emphasizing sports*, art collectibles and aristocratic lifestyles more than political or social issues. Both F. A. Roller's, 'Otter Hunting' in England' and Elizabeth J. Savile's 'Audley House, House of the Earl of Suffolk' of 1897 were typical of the magazine's non-fiction under Hamilton. George Halkett, who became editor in 1900, revitalized the magazine, publishing articles on science* and literary debates and embracing controversial issues. Nevertheless, it was unable to compete with magazines like the *Strand**, and was forced to close, merging* with *Nash's* in September 1914. LML

Sources: Ashley 2006, Rutenberg 1984, Sullivan, *Waterloo*.

PAMPHLETS FOR THE PEOPLE (1835-1836) Strictly speaking, *Pamphlets for the People* was not a journal at all, but a series of cheap* (1½ to 2d) undated pamphlets with different titles issued irregularly. It came into being at the instigation of its editor*, John Arthur Roebuck, a barrister and MP, specifically to frustrate the purpose of the Stamp Act*, in the middle of a campaign – the war of the Unstamped against the Taxes on Knowledge – and in the wake of publications of the SDUK and the SPCK as well as the example of the *Poor Man's*

Guardian. Roebuck had founded what he called 'A Society for the Diffusion of Moral and Political Knowledge'*, as citizens of a democratic country, and *Pamphlets for the People* was designed to address these points. Thirty-six unstamped*, weekly* (if undated) issues covered everything from support for paper* makers, hand-loom weavers, the Irish Question, to the Reform Bill and, of course, a denunciation of the Stamp Act. Newspapers came under attack as well: *The Times**, for its practice of accepting anonymous* leaders*, the *Examiner** and especially the *Morning Chronicle**, which Roebuck declared was simply an organ of the Whigs. In fact, John Black, editor of the *Chronicle*, challenged Roebuck to a duel in 1835 to defend his honesty; neither party was injured.

Issues of *Pamphlets for the People* were generally 16 pages in length, in double columns* and written in a remarkably fresh style, mostly by Roebuck himself, and by his associates H. S. Chapman and T. Falconer. Allegedly, they were financed by Francis Place, Joseph Hume and others, as well as Roebuck. **ET**

Sources: *ODNB, Waterloo.*

PAPER Paper is composed essentially of pulped fibres and a binding agent, the fibres being derived from rags, grasses and/or wood. Paper for journals, and especially newsprint, must be both tough enough to withstand the printing process and reader usage, and absorbent enough to facilitate the speedy drying of ink. The nineteenth century saw many great developments in paper production, in terms of both quality and speed of production, but changes in paper technology and usage were also driven by costs, especially taxation. Since 1712, Stamp Duty* was applied to paper produced for newsprint, and increases in taxation had the result of reducing borders, headings and font sizes of newspapers such as *The Times** during the early nineteenth century.

The 1861 remission of the paper tax allowed *The Times* to lower its town price*, but the costs for national* and imperial postage were still problematic, leading *The Times*' manager to offer a £1,000 reward for the development of thinner, lighter paper than the traditional rag-pulp. The use of esparto grass was key to this further development of newsprint paper, in terms of its suitability and ready supply from southern Europe and North Africa during the 1860s. The radical nature of this change in production may be seen in the fact that in 1850 the fastest paper presses produced 8,000 unperfected sheets per hour, whereas the rotary presses of 1901 could produce 52,000 larger, perfected sheets. Advances in machinery obviously played a large part in this change, but the presses could only function in tandem with the new papers. *Printing* The Times notes that 'the newspaper's political significance in the Victorian age' depended greatly upon its 'mechanical efficiency', demonstrating the importance of reliable and suitable paper supplies for Victorian society en masse.

Inks, originally made from Lamp Black, had to be 'married' with specific papers, necessitating the careful selection of both by publishers and printers. Matters such as absorption, discolouration and 'set-off' (smudging) depend upon the correct selection of paper and ink. 'Total Art' journals such as the *Century Guild Hobby Horse** and the *Dial** carefully selected handmade papers and specific inks for their publications, resulting in a self-conscious fusion of form with content. Equally the abandonment of finely made paper for thinner, cheaper, mass-produced paper, such as that which occurs in the *Yellow Book** at volume eight, demonstrates the changing fortunes of a publication within its physical matter. **MBT**

Sources: *The History of* The Times, *A Newspaper History* 1935, *Printing* The Times 1953, Weatherill 1974.

PAPER AND PRINTING TRADES JOURNAL (1872-1896) The quarterly* *Paper and Printing Trades Journal* was conceived as 'A Medium of Intercommunication Between Stationers, Printers, Publishers and Booksellers and the Manufacturers'. Edited* by Andrew White Tuer, the journal was published by Field & Tuer Ye Leadenhalle Presse, well-known for its high-quality printing and facsimile publication of decorative eighteenth-century texts. The journal included short articles such as 'Our Supply of Paper' (1872) and 'Standard Sizes and Cut of Papers' (1872), and included regular columns* on 'Home' and 'Foreign'* news* related to the book trade, 'New Books', 'Notes on Periodicals', 'Trade Notices' and readers' comments in the form of 'Chit Chat'. Each issue, however, primarily comprised advertisements* for representatives from every aspect of the print industry. A directory of manufacturers was introduced in September 1873 in which, for 1gn per annum, manufacturers could have their name and addresses listed.

Though it was originally intended to be financed solely through advertising and sent free to all stationers, printers, publishers and booksellers in Great Britain and in some of the larger cities throughout the world, a subscription fee of 1s was introduced in March 1874. This issue also marked the introduction of perforated tables, which could be removed and mounted, on a variety of trade-related topics such as a 'Table of Paper Mills' (Sept. 1876), 'Table of Sizes of Millboards' (March 1879), and a 'Table of Classical Phrases' Translated (March, June, Sept. and Dec. 1883). The journal was a success, increasing in size* from an average of around 20 pages in its early issues to well over 100 pages in later numbers. By 1888 it cost 2s/annum. An index containing the references for all the articles, items of information, contributors of specimens, advertisers and directory of manufacturers from the first 32 issues was published in 1881. **PZ**

Sources: *ODNB*, *Paper and Printing Trades Journal*, *Waterloo*.

PARADE (1897) Lasting only for one issue, *Parade* stands alone in its genre* as the subtitle announces: *an illustrated gift-book for boys and girls,* styled in a typically 'Nineties' fashion. The attractively boarded annual*, published* by the prominent firm of H. Henry & Co* and priced* at 6s, was among the last editorial ventures of Gleeson White*. It is therefore not surprising that *Parade* closely resembles the contemporary *Pageant** in layout, and to some extent even in rationale. In his editorial preface, the ever-ambitious Gleeson White states that he wanted to create a children's* gift book that would be unlike traditional publications of this type by not being patronizing, and encouraging its young readers to form their own opinions about the included stories, illustrations*, poems* and songs: 'For if one is not quite an infallible critic before one has left one's teens, when is there any hope of being so?'

Contributors included Aubrey Beardsley*, Laurence Housman*, Max Beerbohm* and Richard Le Gallienne*, who at the time were still controversial for their involvement with periodicals such as the *Yellow Book** and the *Savoy**. Although several of its contributors were commonly associated with the phenomenon of 1890s Decadence, the magazine itself cannot be called iconoclastic. Some short stories and drawings are nostalgic about boyish mischief, but all seems to have remained well within the margins of what the late-Victorian mainstream deemed respectable. The ideal to develop the tastes of the young is apparent from a poem* by Robert Herrick set to music, and the 'Stories to read to the young', which are summaries of the literary classics *Undine* by Friedrich de la Motte Fouqué and *Rip Van Winkle* by Washington Irving, apparently intended as bedtime stories. **KNC**

Source: *Waterloo*.

PARATEXTS Gérard Genette's notion of the paratext, the unusual collection of verbal statements and illustrations*, which includes the title*, the author's name, advertisements*, the cover ornaments, the masthead* etc., that are extraneous to the text but integral to the manner in which that text is presented to the world, has a particular resonance for the nineteenth-century press. At the beginning of the twenty-first century, we are perhaps increasingly inclined to focus on the text, since it is often accessible digitally, stripped of all its surrounding paraphernalia and in fully searchable form. It is not only the digital media that have created this bias, however: the binding of periodicals for storage in libraries* has generally entailed the removal of their wrappers, a process replicated as periodicals were transferred to microfilm, and then more recently digitally scanned.

Though the paratextual matter, which inhabits the text, has often been neglected by scholars, there is little doubt that it formed a crucial element of the way in which serials and periodicals were experienced by their first readers. Wrappers were often decorative and colourful, offering an enticement to buy, and they were generally dominated by advertisements* for a wide variety of products and services, including those for other periodicals and serial* publications. These can give us a valuable insight into the interrelation between different publications: for instance, it is surprising, but instructive, to see the Society for the Propagation of Christian Knowledge's* populist and staunchly Christian *People's Magazine* advertised on the wrapper of the *Fortnightly Review**.

Moreover, these materials provide an important reminder of the thoroughly commercial nature of print in the nineteenth century. It may suit us to imagine that 'George Eliot's' *Middlemarch* was an object of high culture divorced from the supposed corruption of the marketplace, but each part came wrapped in a healthy wad of advertising, some of which, such as an advertisement for the Scottish Widow's Fund appearing on the wrapper facing the end of Book VII, bore a direct thematic relation to the events described in the novel. At least to an extent, text and paratext engaged with similar discourses. The final, double number of Dickens's* novels (nos. 19 and 20) could contain up to 70 pages of advertisements, as was the case in the concluding part of *Our Mutual Friend*. Advertisements in a weekly* like the *Athenaeum** or a daily* like the *Morning Post** comprise part of the news*. Attention to paratextual matter, where considerable overlap between different fields of print culture can be observed, can help to challenge the easy distinctions that historians have tended to make between serialized* fiction, periodicals and newspapers in the nineteenth century. MaT

Sources: Brake 2001, Cachin *et al* 2007, Genette 1997.

PARKE, ERNEST (1860-1944) A journalist and newspaper editor*, Ernest Parke began his career as a reporter for the *Birmingham Gazette* in 1882. He was brought to the notice of T. P. O'Connor*, who hired Parke in 1887 as chief subeditor* for his new venture, the *Star*. Ultimately, Parke became editor* of the paper, at the same time managing to edit the *Morning Leader*. His reporting of the Jack the Ripper murders vastly increased circulation* figures of the *Star*. Parke's radical politics* informed his leaders* in 1889-1890 in the *North London Press*, and his condemnation of the preferential treatment being accorded to well-connected suspects in the Cleveland Street affair led to a libel suit being brought against him, and he was jailed. Like W. T. Stead*, Parke was an earnest campaigner for justice, one of the founders of the 'new journalism'* and a respected reporter. ET

Sources: Brake 2001, O'Connor 1929, *ODNB*, *The Times* 25 Nov. 1889, 23 June 1944.

PARKER, JOHN WILLIAM (1792-1870) John William Parker worked in printing from childhood; apprenticed at 14 to the printer William Clowes*, he remained with him, eventually becoming an accountant in the firm. In 1828, Clowes sent Parker to become a superintendent at the Cambridge University Press, where he modernized all aspects of its operation. Having been appointed official publisher* for the Society for Promoting Christian Knowledge* in 1832, Parker left Clowes to form his own publishing firm but retained his Cambridge assignment. For this organization Parker inaugurated the 1d *Saturday Magazine* (1832-1845), which was intended to counteract the cheap*, licentious magazines aimed at the lower classes. Instead, it offered a useful and entertaining compendium of facts. The magazine also contained illustrations* by Parker's son, Frederick. The *Saturday Magazine* was replaced by *Parker's London Magazine,* which lasted for only two issues; also unsuccessful was Parker's earlier attempt, the *Magazine of Popular Science and Journal of Useful Arts* (1836-1837).

On 15 November 1836 Parker was elected official printer to the University of Cambridge, mostly publishing Bibles, Testaments and the *Book of Common Prayer*. In 1843, Parker's son, also John

William Parker (1820-1860), joined his father's publishing firm as general manager. Five years later, in 1848, the firm became John W. Parker and Son. Under Parker junior, the firm was in the forefront of promoting liberal Christianity, and eventually Christian socialism*. As editor* of *Fraser's Magazine*, Parker junior redirected it in 1847 to embrace the Christian policies of the publishing company. The journal became deeply concerned with the social* utility of the Church of England and the condition of English society. In May 1848 Parker launched the first issue of *Politics for the People*, a monthly* journal intended for middle and lower-class* readers. Its appearance marked the beginning of the Christian Socialist movement, but it folded after one month owing to a lack of subscribers. Significantly, the only novels taken on by Parker and Son were by Charles Kingsley, a supporter of 'muscular Christianity', and in 1860 the controversial 'higher criticism', rationalist critique of Anglicanism, *Essays and Reviews,* appeared under its imprint. After John William Parker the younger died in 1860, the firm became Parker, Son and Bourn, which was sold three years later to Longmans*. DHL

Sources: Curwen 1873, Dean 1991, *ODNB*.

PARKES, BESSIE RAYNER (1829-1925) A descendant of Joseph Priestley, Bessie Rayner Parkes became a journalist* and editor*. Parkes was born into a prosperous Unitarian family with pronounced liberal views. In her early twenties, she began a career in journalism, writing for local* newspapers and radical journals. In the 1850s she contributed to the National Association for the Promotion of Social Science, and in 1854 published anonymously* *Remarks on the Education of Girls.*

In 1858, with financial backing from her friend Barbara Leigh Smith Bodichon*, she started the monthly *English Woman's Journal* which rapidly became the first real British feminist* periodical, concentrating particularly on middle-class* women's education and employment, married women's property, female emigration and eventually the vote, although it also included travel writing, stories and even poetry*. Isa Craig and Adelaide Ann Procter were contributors, the latter's famous 'Lost Chord' first appearing in the journal. It was the organ of the early feminist group that became known as the Langham Place Circle, from the address of the Women's Employment Bureau, and soon attracted other contributors such as Emily Faithfull*, Jessie Boucherett* and Maria Rye. In 1862 Parkes gave up the editorship, mainly for health reasons. In 1864 she was received into the Roman Catholic Church, and in 1867 married Louis Belloc. Thereafter although she occasionally wrote for the press, her journalistic career was effectively over. However, both her children went on to earn much of their living through journalism. **DD**

Source: Crawford *et al.* 1983, *ODNB*.

PARLIAMENTARY REPORTING   See Court and parliamentary reporting

PARRY, JOHN (1776-1851) As 'concert critic' on the *Morning Post** (1834-1849), the Welsh composer John Parry (fl.1819-1849) helped to set new standards in British music* journalism

Parry, a professional musician who worked as a part-time critic during the London 'season', supported the capital's burgeoning musical life while giving music an enhanced presence in the *Morning Post*. In his substantial, erudite and thought-provoking reviews* he privileged musical expression (over 'science'), while combining reverence for Beethoven with support for contemporary composers (Mendelssohn, Spohr) and an ambivalence towards some of the leading lights of the virtuoso school (Moscheles). His notices, distinctive for their stylistic clarity and polished resonance, were balanced, forthright and free of partisanship and chauvinism.

Parry was a thoroughgoing modern who energetically promoted the ideal of musical progress in Britain. He also wrote articles on Welsh music for the *Cambro-Briton** (1819-1822), contributed to the *Musical World** in its earliest years and was sometime 'music editor'* of the *Sunday Times** (dates unknown). In the Welsh* press Parry wrote under the pseudonym* 'Bardd Alaw' ('Master of Song'). Away from journalism, he was a composer for the stage, an editor and publisher of the national music of Wales, and the author of several books on music. **MH**

Sources: *DWB*, Grove, *ODNB*.

PATER, WALTER (1839-1894) Although Walter Pater was an Oxford academic and aesthete, he constructed most of his books from his journalism*. Pater's lifelong involvement with the press was not anomalous, but typical of a generation of nineteenth-century 'university men', and of periodicals that attracted and accommodated them.

Pater served his apprenticeship in the journals. Between 1866-1868 he published anonymous*, article-length reviews* in a single liberal quarterly*, the *Westminster Review**. In 1869 he began a sustained association with the high-culture, monthly* reviews* and magazines*. There he published his careful and considered prose, now signed, in the *Fortnightly Review**, the *Contemporary Review**, the *Nineteenth Century**, the *Bookman**, *Harper's New Monthly Magazine**, the *New Review** and in the magazine of his publisher, *Macllan's Magazine**, which he largely confined to his short stories and novella. He also contributed anonymously to the weekly* (Church) *Guardian* (1886-1890), where he published some anonymous reviews of French fiction but mainly of work by friends. This common form of puffing* was a two-way process, and friends reviewed his books as well: Wilde's* favourable review of *Appreciations* in 1890 was repaid by Pater's 1891 obligatory review of *The Picture of Dorian Gray*.

Pater's use of anonymity in the 1860s is also telling. His anonymous reviews for the *Westminster Review* were among the most explicit of his career, on (Coleridge*and) religion, homosexual culture (Winckelmann) and hedonism (William Morris*). Once launched, and released from the terms of writing anonymous (and probably unpaid) reviews on disparate subjects for the *Westminster Review*, Pater published in the *Fortnightly Review* a succession of four signed articles on the Renaissance, a single subject of his choice. Having thus 'found' the subject of his controversial and exquisite first book, *Studies in the History of the Renaissance* (1873), he produced the volume largely from unsigned* and signed published work from the two journals. Repeating this process for three of his four subsequent books, Pater gathered four short stories from *Macmillan's Magazine* (1885-1887) to constitute *Imaginary Portraits* (1887), articles written over 20 years to make up *Appreciations* (1889) and university lectures on Plato, some of which first appeared in the *Contemporary Review** and *Macmillan's Magazine* (1891, 1892) to comprise *Plato and Platonism* (1893).

Macmillan produced three additional volumes posthumously, the bulk of which were uncollected journalism. Regarding *Greek Studies* (1895), Pater found that although he could publish articles on this subject in a number of journals without censure*, he could not risk collecting them into a volume. Even Pater's prose – risky, homosocial, highly finished, and demanding* was safely accommodated by the proliferation and diversity of nineteenth-century journalism, whereas books were subject to the notice and castigation of reviewers. Serial* publication in journals allowed Pater to work up a subject over time, remunerated him piecemeal, trailed the contents of his book and his name to readers before book publication, advertised* them, and reviewed them once they appeared. Almost all of

Pater's volumes were thus implicated in journalism from conception to realization, their very structure (articles or 'chapters') included. **LRB**

Sources: Inman 1980, *ODNB*, Wright 1975.

PATERSON, EMMA ANNE (1848-1886) Emma Anne Paterson was a pioneering women's trade* unionist who breached the male domination of the trade union movement and furthered the cause by publishing activist articles, eventually founding and editing* the monthly *Women's Union Journal*. Born in London, Paterson became involved in trade union work at the age of 18 and in the women's suffrage movement in 1872. She began utilizing periodicals in April 1874, publishing 'The Position of Working Women, and How to Improve It' in *Labour News* to call for the establishment of affiliated women's trade unions. The article stimulated much discussion, including a conference in July of 1874 which resulted in the fruition of Paterson's initiative of the Women's Protective and Provident League (WPPL) as a central society to benefit working women and to link societies specific to different trades. Launched in 1874, Paterson founded the Women's Printing Society* as an employment and printing concern, which among others, published the League's *Women's Union Journal*. **KC**

Sources: Mitchell 1988, *ODNB*.

PATRIOT (1832-1866) Established by a committee of Baptists and Congregationalists (the latter outnumbered the former and were more influential), the *Patriot* began life in February 1832 as a weekly*. The prospectus announced that the paper would be 'devoted to the maintenance of the great principles cherished by the Evangelical Nonconformists' and the *Patriot* enjoyed considerable respect among moderate dissenters in the middle of the nineteenth century. Positioning itself as a family* and general newspaper, it covered a range of material, including literature*, denominational news*, foreign* notes and leading* articles.

Its most important editor* was Josiah Conder (1789-1855), an influential figure who also edited the *Eclectic Review** from 1814-1837. Conder was asked to take over the editorship at the end of 1832 and he agreed, with some reluctance. His editorship was a success and he remained in the role until his death in 1855. Circulation* rose to 2,400 copies in 1833 and to 3,500 copies by 1840; the paper was published twice a week from 1836, following the reduction of stamp duty. The *Patriot* spawned and later absorbed the *British Banner* (1848-1858), a cheap* weekly Congregationalist paper. In 1867 the *Patriot* merged with the *British Standard* to create the *English Independent and Free Church Advocate*, later becoming the *Nonconformist and Independent* (1880-1889), and finally, the *Independent and Nonconformist* (1890-1900). **MK**

Sources: Conder 1857, Cooper 1981, Sullivan 1984.

PAUL, CHARLES KEGAN (1828-1902) Charles Kegan Paul, publisher*, proprietor*, editor* and journalist, was ordained an Anglican priest in 1852 after graduating from Oxford in 1849. After nine years as chaplain at Eton he became a vicar in Dorset until, dissatisfied with the Church, he moved to London in 1874, where he joined the publishing firm H. S. King & Co., a publisher* of science, religion and literature.

In 1877 he bought the business, renaming it C. Kegan Paul & Co*. Among the new firm's authors were Tennyson, George Meredith, Thomas Hardy* and Robert Louis Stevenson*. Paul also owned, edited and published the *New Quarterly Magazine** (Jan. 1879-April 1880) and he published the *Nineteenth Century** (Jan. 1878-June 1891). In 1881 the firm became Kegan Paul, Trench & Co. and in 1889 was sold as Kegan Paul, Trench, Trübner & Co. Ltd., with Paul as a director. Paul encouraged the publication of poetry*, especially that of Andrew Lang*, Wilfrid Blunt and Austin Dobson, but religion* was his mainstay. Falling profits led to his resignation in 1895 and he left the firm after an accident the same year. Although establishing a strong firm in the 1880s, Paul's failure was a lack of financial acumen. Wilfrid Meynell believed that after Stevenson had left the firm, he based the character of Jekyll and Hyde on Paul.

Paul took a great interest in book production and in a *Fortnightly Review** article (1883) he stressed that authors should be well educated, with something to say. Royalties should be accepted, rather than commission, and copyright* should be the author's unless the work was a novel. Spelling should be left to the author and not corrected by the printer; otherwise the American way might predominate. He attacked circulating libraries for encouraging the publishing of second-rate novels. Other journals to which Paul contributed include *British Quarterly Review**, the *Contemporary Review**, the *New Quarterly Magazine**, *Merry England**, and the *Theological Review**. **DA**

Sources: Howsam 1998, Meynell 1902, *ODNB*, *Wellesley*.

PAUL PRY Like Mr Punch and John Bull, Paul Pry was one of the invented personae through which Regency and early Victorian society explored its own social personality. As with the renowned

Tom and Jerry, who investigated London's pleasures both in fiction and on the stage, the origins of the Paul Pry persona lay in the theatre. *Paul Pry* by John Poole (1825) was a play that became famous in the late 1820s, with the central role most famously played by the celebrated comic actor John Liston. The same title was used for a periodical in Britain (1826) and a gossipy* magazine published in Washington DC (1831-1836) edited* by the pioneering woman journalist Anne (sometimes given as Ann) Royall. It entered popular consciousness in many ways, becoming a pseudonym* for both the caricaturist* William Heath* and for the author of two volumes of *London Oddities* (1838). Both Hull (*Paul Pry in Hull* 1832) and Liverpool (*Paul Pry in Liverpool* 1834-1835) can boast satirical* periodicals looking at the social scene as the inquisitive Paul Pry might have seen it. **BM**

PAYN, JAMES (1830-1898) Ill-health forced James Payn, editor* publisher's reader and writer of fiction, to leave the Royal Military Academy at Woolwich in 1847, but he gained a Cambridge degree in 1853. Payn's first journal contribution was a poem* in *Leigh Hunt's Journal*￼ (15 March 1851), followed by an account of his Woolwich experiences in *Household Words*￼ (9 April 1853). This resulted in a friendship with Charles Dickens* and many years contributing to *Household Words*. Self-publication of his *Stories from Boccaccio and other Poems* (1852) decided him to pursue literature as a career. He contributed to many journals in the 1860s and 1870s, including *All the Year Round*￼, *Harper's New Monthly Magazine*, *Belgravia*￼ and *Chambers's Journal*￼, and he started on a prolific story and novel-writing career. Many of his novels and stories first appeared in journal form, notably 'Lost Sir Massingberd' in *Chambers's Journal* in 1864, which greatly increased the journal's circulation*.

On Leslie Stephen's* invitation Payn became editor of *Chambers's Journal* (1859-1874) when he became a reader for the publishers Smith, Elder & Co* for about 20 years. Payn's main contribution to *Chambers's* was his support of Conan Doyle. In January 1883 Payn succeeded Stephen as editor of the *Cornhill Magazine*￼ until ill-heath forced his resignation in June 1896. Circulation* was falling; Payn reduced the price* with a new series in July 1883 and attempted to broaden the journal's scope by increasing the fiction content at the expense of literary articles, and adding articles on popular science*. Payn's editorship was in contrast to the strict, non-controversial and narrow one of Stephen. However, he failed to retain the readership and the journal's reputation declined. Payn was basically a prolific but minor novelist with his novels appearing in magazine form prior to book publication. **DA**
Sources: *CBEL*, *ODNB*, Payn 1894, *Wellesley.*

PEARL: A JOURNAL OF FACETIA VOLUPTUOUS READING (1879-1880) The most well-known periodical of Victorian pornography*, the monthly* *Pearl*, published and edited by William Lazenby*, ran to three volumes (six months per volume) (1879-1880), and was privately published* under the auspices of the fictitious 'Society of Vice'. The actual number of private copies printed was about 150, and the target market was wealthy British men who could afford the exceptionally high price* £ 18 for the set of three volumes according to one account, £25 according to another. One issue is said to have sold for two guineas, but it is difficult to determine since the publication was effectively underground and circulation* was largely through coterie connections.

The magazine included serialized* stories, short tales, anecdotes, poetry* and chromolithographs, and while flagellation narratives were something of a favourite, a range of often complex and overlapping sexual fantasies (interracial slave narratives, lesbianism, threesomes, homosexual male encounters, among others) were depicted, drawing on common stereotypes about gender and race. Titles of serial narratives include 'Sub Umbra, or Sport Among the She Noodles' (July 1879-Feb. 1880), 'Lady Pokingham, or They all Do It' (July 1879-Sept. 1880), and 'Flunkeyana, or Belgravian Morals' (July 1880-Nov. 1880). Linked to the publication of the *Pearl* was a series of special Christmas* numbers, parodying the convention of many Victorian periodicals for special annual* issues. The Christmas* numbers with colour chromolithographs had distinct titles, and ran to more than 60 pages: *Swivia*, 1879; *The Haunted House*, 1880; *The Pearl Christmas Annual*, 1881; *The Erotic Casket Gift Book*, 1883. Few complete copies of the original run of the *Pearl* still exist, though a slightly later reprint can be found in the British Library. **MWT**
Sources: Colligan 2006, Mendes 1993.

PEARSON, CYRIL ARTHUR (1866-1921) Arthur Pearson, journalist and newspaper proprietor*, was an influential force in the development of the New Journalism* at the end of the nineteenth century. He got his start in journalism in 1884 when he won a *Tit-Bits*￼ general knowledge competition and was awarded a clerkship with the journal. A year later, he was manager of *Tit-Bits* and in 1890 was appointed business manager of George Newnes'* and W. T. Stead's* *Review of Reviews*. The same year he parted ways with his mentors and founded his own popular journal, *Pearson's Weekly*.

In his introductory address, Pearson claimed that the journal's intent was 'To Interest, to Elevate, to Amuse' but also to assume a 'higher tone than at present exists in the class of literature to which it belongs'. Its prize competitions made it immediately popular. The first number achieved a circulation* of 250,000, and by 1897 sales surpassed one million. During the 1890s, Pearson founded a number of other periodicals, including *Home Notes*, *Pearson's Magazine* and the *Royal Magazine*, but he achieved even greater success in 1900 with the founding of the *Daily Express*, a half penny newspaper. During this period, Pearson developed a number of joint ventures with American publishing firms, including *Everybody's Magazine* and an American edition of *Pearson's Magazine*, both of which were established in 1899. During the first years of the twentieth century, Pearson expanded his newspaper holdings significantly. In 1903, he assumed a controlling interest in the *St James Gazette** and in 1904 acquired the *Standard* and the *Evening Standard*. In 1908 he made an unsuccessful bid for *The Times**, losing the battle to Alfred Harmsworth*, his long-time rival. Two years later Pearson sold the *Standard* and the *Evening Standard*. Due to impending blindness, he retired from active interest in the newspaper industry after 1912 and devoted himself to philanthropic pursuits. **ME** Sources: Dark 1922, *DNB*, *ODNB*.

***PEARSON'S MAGAZINE* (1896-1939)** *Pearson's Magazine* soon became the crown jewel in a publishing* empire that also included the *Daily Express*. Initiated in January 1896 by C. Arthur Pearson*, it was intended for a popular* rather than a highbrow audience; each monthly issue contained serialized* and complete fiction, poetry*, satire*, personal reflections and society news, as well as articles on art, history*, science* and contemporary social issues. However, the journal's signature feature was its frequent use of illustrations*, cartoons*, paintings and photographs*. Taking advantage of new image-reproduction technologies, almost every sheet of the 120-page journal had graphics in order to entice potential readers. Highly successful, the magazine reached a circulation* of over a million copies by the late 1890s. This wide and diversified readership* did much to create a mass* culture that blurred regional and class* divisions. Priced* at 6d, it appealed to rich and poor alike, although its primary audience was

the lower and middle classes*. Like many other family* magazines*, *Pearson's* was patriotic, royalist and imperialistic* and appealed to these sentiments through articles that trumpeted the bravery of British soldiers, the might of the military and the wonders of the ever-expanding Empire.

In the early years of its publication, *Pearson's* serialized both Rudyard Kipling's *Captain Courageous* and H. G. Wells'* *War of the Worlds*. Other contributors included, Marie Belloc, Walter Besant*, W. F. Calderon, Ernest Dowson, Conan Doyle, Winifred Graham, W. W. Jacobs, May Kendall and Jack London. By 1901 approximately one-third of the pages in each number were taken up by advertisements* for such products as patent medicines, weight loss powders and 'get-rich-quick' schemes. Drawing on this history, James Joyce mentions that *Pearson's* is one of the publications Gerty MacDowell reads in the 'Nausicaa' episode of *Ulysses*. Pearson served as editor* until 1900 and proprietor* until his death in 1921. His firm continued to publish the magazine until 1939. **EFO** Sources: Mitchell 1988, Richards 1985, *Waterloo*.

PELLEGRINI, CARLO (1839-1889) An Italian caricaturist* whose drawings appeared in *Vanity Fair** under the pseudonym* 'Ape', Pellegrini was a key figure in the development of modern English caricature despite not having attended art school. He arrived penniless in London from Italy in 1864 but moved in bohemian circles, becoming acquainted with aristocrats and royals whom he would depict in amusing caricatures. In 1969 Thomas Gibson Bowles* spotted his talent and commissioned cartoons* of the politicians Disraeli and Gladstone, reproduced as full-page lithographs* for *Vanity Fair*. Save for two brief hiatuses in which he attempted unsuccessfully to transfer his skills to serious portraiture, Pellegrini continued at *Vanity Fair* until his death, caricaturing 322 prominent figures of the day, drawing on the work of Melchiorre Delfico (1825-1895) as well as on that of Honoré Daumier (1808-1878) and the French school. Pellegrini was highly influential, inspiring Leslie Ward ('Spy')* and Max Beerbohm*, who considered him to be the greatest caricaturist of the period. **MaT** Sources: *ODNB*, *Waterloo*.

PENNELL, ELIZABETH ROBINS (1855-1936) Transatlantic* journalist Elizabeth Robins Pennell* was born in Philadelphia, where she also began a lifelong collaboration with fellow Philadelphian and illustrator*, Joseph Pennell*. They married in 1884 and travelled to London as the *Century*'s European correspondents, where they remained for over 20 years. Best known as James McNeill Whistler's* co-biographer (with Joseph), Elizabeth Pennell was a prolific journalist whose collaborative and solo efforts ranged across travel articles and art, music*, and literary* criticism for publications including *Harper's**, *St. Nicholas*, the *Daily Chronicle*, *Woman** and the *Fortnightly Review**.

From 1893 to 1896 Pennell anonymously* wrote a weekly food column* for the *Pall Mall Gazette's** 'Wares of Autolycus', and she also had a long-running cycling column in the same paper. A selection of her food columns was published in 1896 as *The Feasts of Autolycus*; other themed collections appeared in books, including *French Cathedrals* (1909). As an art critic, Pennell was a well regarded New Critic: anti-Ruskin*, anti-Royal Academy, pro-French and English Impressionists, and a supporter of other avant-garde painters affiliated with the New English Art Club, Whistler and Rodin among them. In 1888, she assumed her husband's post as art critic of the *Star** under the pseudonym of 'A. U.' Other art pieces were published in the *Nation** under the pseudonym 'N. N'. JT

Sources: Clarke 2005, Hughes 2005, Onslow 2000, Pennell 1916, Schaffer 2000, Williams 2000.

PENNELL, JOSEPH (1857-1926) Illustrator*, printmaker and art critic, Philadelphia-born Joseph Pennell began his career in 1881 by selling drawings of American cities to *Scribner's Monthly**. After collaborating on assignments with budding journalist Elizabeth Robins*, they married (1884) and became lifelong working partners. Joseph was appointed the *Century*'s European correspondent, and when they were not travelling throughout England and on the Continent, particularly Paris and the French countryside, they lived in London. In addition to illustrating a multitude of travel and architecture articles, they championed the New English Arts Club and its progressive artists when it was formed in 1885, in reaction to the Royal Academy.

The Pennells particularly befriended and promoted fellow American James McNeill Whistler*, who entrusted Joseph to work on many of his finest prints. Pennell illustrated for a number of publications, including the *Yellow Book**. In 1888 he became art critic for the *Star** under the pseudonym 'A. U'. He soon relinquished the column* to Elizabeth, which helped her make her own reputation as an incisive art critic. Pennell contributed several articles to the *Studio**, including 'Aubrey Beardsley*, A New Illustrator' (1893), which helped launch

Beardsley's career; in other *Studio* articles he heralded 'Robert Louis Stevenson*, Illustrator' (1896), and wrote and illustrated 'The Truth About Photography' (1899). He also contributed to the *London Daily Chronicle**, *Modern Illustrator*, the *Graphic**, the *London Illustrated News**, the *Art Journal** and the *Magazine of Art**. Pennell later went on to edit the magazine the *Whistler Journal* and became famous for his poster for the fourth Liberty Loans campaign of 1918. JT

Sources: Clarke 2005, Hughes 2005, Pennell 1916, Pennell 1930, Williams 2000.

PENNY MAGAZINE (1832-1845); KNIGHT'S PENNY MAGAZINE (1846) The organ of the Society for the Diffusion of Useful Knowledge (SDUK), the *Penny Magazine* along with *Chambers's Edinburgh Journal* and the *Saturday Magazine* was one of the periodicals at the centre of the explosion in the size and character of the reading* public in the 1830s. As proprietor*, publisher* and editor*, Charles Knight* took much of the credit for the journal's rapid rise to prominence, calling it 'the most successful experiment in popular literature the world has ever seen'. An unstamped* journal costing 1d, as its name proudly advertised, it hit an unprecedented weekly circulation* of 200,000 in its first year. This feat would have been impossible without Knight's wholesale adoption of the latest mechanical printing* technology. The journal was aware of its own importance in the history of media with Knight's 'The Commercial History of a Penny Magazine' issued as four monthly supplements* in 1833, staking a claim that the *Penny Magazine* was placing recent technological developments in the service of enlightenment.

Its aim was to provide information and improving instruction to the working class*, although the evidence suggests that its readership* was largely composed of artisans and members of the emerging middle* class. Articles on science*, art, literature and history* formed the backbone of the magazine, while potentially controversial subjects such as theology and politics* were avoided. That it contained no topical comment was used to justify the refusal to pay the Stamp Duty that was liable on newspapers. It also carried poetry* and its engravings were a major selling point: Knight was again ahead of the competition in adopting wood* engraving, a cheaper and faster technique than the steel-engraving that was the norm.

For its staunchly religious rival the *Saturday Magazine*, the *Penny Magazine* epitomized a dangerous trend towards popular secularism, and indeed the Society for the Diffusion of Useful Knowledge was driven by a utilitarian ideology according to which the moral improvement of the lower orders was perfectly feasible without the help of God. This secular* tendency may have allowed the magazine to avoid the longwinded theological debates and the sermonizing that sometimes marred the religious* periodicals of the period, but the magazine arguably replaced these with its own pieties. Its lengthy descriptions of the marvels of nature and of civilization, impressive plants or exotic monkeys, the construction and provenance of castles, boats or stately homes, were often sententious and dull. Declining readership* eventually led to the demise of the *Penny Magazine* after just over 12 years, but not before it had played an instrumental role in a revolution in periodical publishing. MaT

Sources: Altick 1998, Gray 2006, Knight 1864, *ODNB, Penny Magazine, Waterloo*.

PENNY NOVELIST (1832-1834)   The *Penny Novelist* lasted a mere 18 months (Aug. 1832-Feb. 1834). An illustrated* weekly* costing 1d, it contained both original and reprinted 'tales, fiction, poetry*, and romance', and printed on quarto pages (four sheets, roughly 19 x 12.5 inches each). Published* by George Berger* and printed by G. G. Davidson, the *Penny Novelist* was started by Benjamin Steill amid an explosion of similar newspapers which aimed to give the working-class* light, pleasurable, affordable reading. All costing 1d or ½d, these papers, including the *Half-Penny Magazine*, the *London Penny Journal*, the *Penny Comic Magazine*, and the *Penny Story-Teller**, quickly drew disapproval and even horror from reformers, clerics and other moral authorities. This general handwringing was a response not only to the magazines' sensational stories but also to the poor quality of their writing, which critics thought would degrade readers both intellectually and spiritually. Today, the term 'penny* novel', which did not become current until the 1860s, a generation after the *Penny Novelist* and its competitors flooded the market, still connotes an embarrassing lack of taste. It refers to popular material with overblown characters, wooden dialogue and wildly improbable plots.

The swift demise of the *Penny Novelist* seems not to have been mourned. Though some consider it a precursor to better remembered cheap* Victorian serial* fiction, such as Dickens's* *Pickwick Papers*, it is mainly thought of as an example of the ephemeral penny papers of the early 1830s. An obituary* of sorts was written for these in 1833 by Edward

Bulwer-Lytton*, '[They] seem, Pigmy-like, of a marvellous ferocity and valour; they make great tread against their foes – they spread themselves incontinently – they possess the land – they live but a short time'. FCA

Sources: Altick 1957, Etherington *et al.* 2005, *OED online, Waterloo*.

PENNY PAPERS The often used 'Penny' in magazine titles suggests that something more than cheapness was at stake, and indeed the concept of the totemic penny formed a battleground between competing ideologies and commercial motives from the 1830s. The 35 titles listed by Wiener that use 'penny' as the first word in their title range from the Society for the Diffusion of Useful Knowledge's celebrated mass* circulation weekly* *Penny Magazine**. which tried to equate cheapness with respectability and celebrate a self-help ethic, through various down-market self-help journals produced by radical publishers*, like William Strange's the *Penny School-Book* (1832) to the increasingly despised yet perennially popular* penny fiction of the *Penny Novelist* (1832-1834). The diversity of serialized 'penny' publications in the 1830s suggests the range of meanings ascribed to the term by anxious metropolitan commentators, many of whom were alarmed equally by the populist appropriations of the term in radical political* journals and by the increasing availability of sensational illustrated* fiction in penny formats. Either way, many critics, in spite of the appropriation of the term by the S.D.U.K. and other sectarian organizations, sought to associate the concept of 'penny' issue serial literature with a range of social threats, exemplified by journals like the *Penny Satirist* (1837-1846), which took considerable delight in attacking public figures with scurrilous and, often, invented stories.

Penny issue fiction, which gave rise to the term 'Penny Dreadful', was similarly absorbed by the many but despised by the influential few, who believed such cheap* literature inflamed ill-educated emotions and wasted potentially socially useful time. In a famous article published in *Fraser's Magazine** in March 1838, ('Half a Crown's Worth of Cheap Knowledge') Thackeray* offered a not entirely jaundiced overview of the variety to be found in the penny press. Four of the 15 journals he reviewed had 'Penny' in their title. The competing meanings implicit in the 'penny' tag were never resolved in the Victorian period, and penny journals included weekly* papers, often religious* in orientation, fiction-led miscellanies* like the *London Journal** and useful knowledge publications.

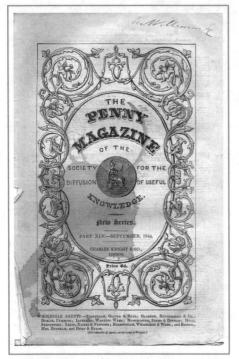

Figure 51: The cover of the *Penny Magazine*, Sept. 1844.

The launch of Newnes's* *Tit-Bits** in 1880, followed by *Answers** and *Pearson's Weekly**, began a new era in the penny press. The press barons of the New Journalism* claimed to be able to reconcile cheapness with the provision of 'healthy' reading. Penny magazines for women were at the heart of Harmsworth's* publishing* empire, and Newnes* and Pearson* followed. Domestic* magazines like *Home Notes**, *Home Chat**, *Woman's Life** and *Woman** competed for the pennies of woman readers* along with novelettes* and new style fiction serials* like *Sweethearts*. Penny papers for the young included the Religious Tract Society*'s hugely successful *Girl's Own Paper** and *Boy's Own Paper** which were designed to combat the influence of sensational serials. The huge expansion of these titles modified, but did not allay, middle-class* anxieties about the cheap press, though the totemic importance of 'the penny' was diminishing by 1900. MRB/ BM

Sources: Altick 1957, Anderson 1991, Wiener 1969.

PENNY STORY-TELLER (1832-1837) The *Penny Story-Teller*, a 1d Wednesday weekly* begun by the editor* William Strange* and his collaborator, the aptly named Charles Penny*, is credited with having been the first of the illustrated* penny*

newspapers. However, its appearance was almost simultaneous with that of a number of other similar periodicals such as the *Penny Novelist**, the *Penny Comic Magazine* and the *True Half-Penny Magazine*, all begun within a few months of each other. These papers, aimed at the lower classes*, were popular in pubs and coffee houses, suitable for a short read. The *Penny Story-Teller* was small (28 cm), only eight pages long, and illustrated* with black-and-white engravings. Strange, who also published in the 'useful knowledge'* vein, covering topics such as politics*, popular science* and current events, proclaimed in the *Penny Story-Teller*'s opening issue that the magazine would 'avoid everything which is indelicate, improper, or foolish... the object is to afford a pleasing and innocent amusement to the families of the Gentleman and Christian'. The *Penny Story-Teller*, however, along with many of its imitators, was deplored by reformers and clerics, among others. The problem was not merely with content; even seemingly innocent plots drew fire for their poor writing quality and especially their sensationalism. Though the *Penny Story-Teller* was short-lived, it nevertheless outlasted a number of its competitors*, many of which ran for less than a year. FCA

Sources: Altick 1957, Edgell 1838, Haywood 2004, Thackeray 1838, *Waterloo*.

PENNY SUNDAY TIMES AND PEOPLE'S POLICE GAZETTE (1840-1849?) In April 1840, Edward Lloyd, an established publisher* of cheap*, entertaining fiction, launched his first sensationalist Sunday 'newspaper', the *Penny Sunday Times and People's Police Gazette*, a four-page weekly* printed at his offices in Shoreditch. Its rather patchy survival, including that of its secondary, spin-off publications, (*Lloyd's Companion to the Penny Sunday Times and People's Police Gazette* Sept.1841-Jan.1847, the *People's Police Gazette* Nov.1841-Dec.1841) combined with conflicting evidence provided by nineteenth-century commentators, mean that it is difficult to provide precise details about this newspaper. Much confusion, for example, has centred on whether the so-called news* printed in the *Penny Sunday Times* was factual or fictional, as it is known that Lloyd successfully avoided paying the stamp tax for the newspaper, thereby managing to maintain its low 1d price*. In reality, the paper's sensational reportage probably liberally blended fact and fiction.

Modelled closely on John Cleave's* unstamped* *Weekly Police Gazette*, the paper included graphic front-page woodcuts* of violent crimes* and human tragedies (as Lloyd instructed his illustra-

tor*, George Augustus Sala*, 'The eyes must be larger, and there must be more blood– much more blood!'). Predictably, the *Penny Sunday Times* attracted much concern and condemnation from the respectable classes*. However, it proved popular with its intended readership* of the lower classes, as reflected in the various estimated circulation* rates from 20,000 (Catling, Berridge) to 95,000 (James). Although printed in London for a metropolitan* audience, there is also substantial evidence to suggest that it reached provincial* audiences in towns such as Ipswich and Preston. **RHC**
Sources: Berridge 1972, Catling 1911, James 1963, Sala 1895, *Waterloo*.

PEOPLE'S FRIEND (1869-) A family paper* with a predominantly working-class readership*, the *People's Friend* began as a monthly* published on the first Wednesday of the month in Dundee by John Leng*, and announcing in its subtitle a connection with Leng's hugely popular *People's Journal*. A light miscellany* of 16 pages that sought to marry instruction and entertainment, the *People's Friend* went weekly* by 1876 and was priced* 1d throughout its nineteenth-century run. It contained a mixture of short stories, poetry*, summaries of the plots of popular novels, light biographical and literary* articles, and a short 'Scientific* Jottings' section (later called 'Scientific and Useful', then – by 1888, when illustrations* had become a feature – 'Monthly Notes on Science and Invention') which contained interesting facts and useful information. Puzzles, jokes, recipes and other domestic* advice were also included by 1888. **MaT**
Sources: *ODNB*, *People's Friend* 1869-1897, *Waterloo*.

PEOPLE'S JOURNAL (1846-1848); PEOPLE'S JOURNAL IN WHICH IS INCORPORATED HOWITT'S JOURNAL (1848-1849); PEOPLE'S AND HOWITT'S JOURNAL (1849-1851) The jointly conceived project of two self-declared 'Friends of the People', John Saunders and William Howitt,* the *People's Journal*, in its various incarnations, survived a very public row between the two men to form one of the more sustained and successful journals of popular progress. Entirely similar in format* to *Howitt's Journal*, the *People's Journal* gives testimony to the hopes and ambitions that concerned metropolitan* journalists* had of the power of periodicals to elevate, encourage and educate the urban working classes*.

An illustrated* weekly*, 1 ½d. unstamped* and a penny* dearer stamped, the magazine contained extensive and thoughtful articles on contemporary issues and political* thought (including progressive Continental thinking) as well as news* snippets and a weekly series of 'Annals of Industry and Progress' which gathered together accounts of developments and events in the industrial cities. With contributors of the calibre of Harriet Martineau*, the Howitts*, Eliza Meteyard* and even Mazzini, and artists of the stature of Kenny Meadows*, W. J. Linton* and William Harvey*, Saunders and Howitt, when they could put their differences on one side, put together an impressive gathering of progressive ideas and images, and Saunders boasted of a circulation* of 20,000 in the Preface to the third volume. **BM**
Source: *DNB*, *Waterloo*.

PEOPLE'S JOURNAL (1858-1990) The first number of the *Dundee, Perth and Forfar People's Journal* appeared in January 1858. It was published* by John Leng* who, since 1851, had been editor* and proprietor* of the *Dundee Advertiser*. It was intended to encourage 'intellectual and social advancement' among a working-class* readership*. In 1863 an Aberdeen, Banff and Kincardine edition was launched, with local news* and advertisements* printed on the recto pages of the Dundee edition. By the end of the 1860s circulation* had exceeded 100,000. Other district editions followed, until, by the 1890s, there were 11, and with over 220,000 copies it had the largest circulation of any Scottish* paper.

The *Journal's* editor (1861-1898) was William Latto who published a good deal on social conditions and reported sympathetically on the emerging independent labour movement. National and local news* coverage was interspersed with anecdotes, often in Scots, as well as competitions. There was a Sunbeam Club for children*, an 'Aunt Kate's' recipes and domestic advice and occasional free offers in return for tokens. Encouragement was given to readers* to produce short articles and there was a substantial section devoted to popular fiction. Such was the supply of this material that a separate *People's Friend* was launched in 1869. Leng was Liberal in politics* and his papers stayed loyal to Gladstone in the Home Rule crisis. Leng publications merged* with D. C. Thomson & Co. in 1906*. **WHF**
Sources: Bell 2007, Donaldson 1986, Ferguson 1984, Leng & Co. 1898, Miller 1901, *ODNB*.

PEOPLE'S PAPER (1852-1858) The *People's Paper* was a 12-page weekly* political* organ which expressed 'extreme Chartism'* and was published* and edited* by Ernest Jones with contributions by Karl Marx*. 'Chartism, which emerged partly out of the struggle for a free press, made its last stand in Jones's magnificent newspaper' (Harrison: 139).

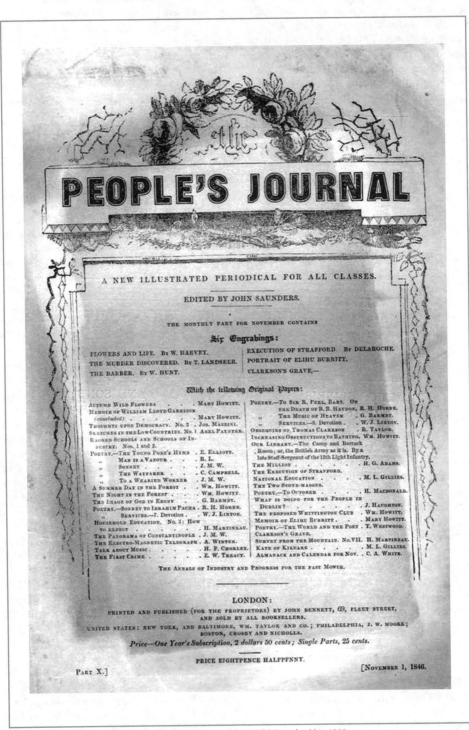

PEOPLE'S JOURNAL

A NEW ILLUSTRATED PERIODICAL FOR ALL CLASSES.

EDITED BY JOHN SAUNDERS.

THE MONTHLY PART FOR NOVEMBER CONTAINS

Six Engravings:

FLOWERS AND LIFE. By W. HARVEY.
THE MURDER DISCOVERED. By T. LANDSEER.
THE BARBER. By W. HUNT.

EXECUTION OF STRAFFORD. By DELAROCHE.
PORTRAIT OF ELIHU BURRITT.
CLARKSON'S GRAVE,—

With the following Original Papers:

AUTUMN WILD FLOWERS . . . . MARY HOWITT.
MEMOIR OF WILLIAM LLOYD GARRISON
   (concluded) . . . . MARY HOWITT.
THOUGHTS UPON DEMOCRACY. No. 2 . JOS. MAZZINI.
SKETCHES IN THE LOW COUNTRIES. No. 1 ABEL PAYNTER.
RAGGED SCHOOLS AND SCHOOLS OF IN-
   DUSTRY. Nos. 1 and 2.
POETRY.—THE YOUNG POET'S HYMN . E. ELLIOTT.
   "   MAN IS A VAPOUR . . . R. L.
   "   SONNET . . . . . J. M. W.
   "   THE WAYFARER . . . C. CAMPBELL.
   "   TO A WEARIED WORKER . J. M. W.
A SUMMER DAY IN THE FOREST . . WM. HOWITT.
THE NIGHT IN THE FOREST . . . WM. HOWITT.
THE IMAGE OF GOD IN EBONY . . G. BARMBY.
POETRY.—SONNET TO IBRAHIM PACHA . R. H. HORNE.
   "   SERVICES.—7. Devotion . . W. J. LINTON.
HOUSEHOLD EDUCATION. No. 3; How
   TO EXPECT . . . . . . H. MARTINEAU.
THE PANORAMA OF CONSTANTINOPLE . J. M. W.
THE ELECTRO-MAGNETIC TELEGRAPH . A. WINTER.
TALK ABOUT MUSIC . . . . . H. F. CHORLEY.
THE FIRST CRIME . . . . . E. W. TREACY.

POETRY.—TO SIR R. PEEL, BART. ON
   THE DEATH OF B. R. HAYDON, R. H. HORNE.
   "   THE MUSIC OF HEAVEN . G. BARMBY.
   "   SERVICES.—8. Devotion . W. J. LINTON.
OBSEQUIES OF THOMAS CLARKSON . R. TAYLOR.
INCREASING OBSTRUCTIONS TO BATHING, WM. HOWITT.
OUR LIBRARY.—The Camp and Barrack
   Room; or, the British Army as it is. By a
   late Staff-Sergeant of the 13th Light Infantry.
THE MILLION . . . . . . H. G. ADAMS.
THE EXECUTION OF STRAFFORD.
NATIONAL EDUCATION . . . . M. L. GILLIES.
THE TWO STONE-MASONS.
POETRY.—TO OCTOBER . . . . H. MACDONALD.
WHAT IS DOING FOR THE PEOPLE IN
   DUBLIN? . . . . . . J. HAUGHTON.
THE PROPOSED WHITTINGTON CLUB . WM. HOWITT.
MEMOIR OF ELIHU BURRITT. . . MARY HOWITT.
POETRY.—THE WORLD AND THE POET . T. WESTWOOD.
CLARKSON'S GRAVE.
SURVEY FROM THE MOUNTAINS. No. VII. H. MARTINEAU.
KATE OF KILDARE . . . . . M. L. GILLIES.
ALMANACK AND CALENDAR FOR NOV. . C. A. WHITE.

THE ANNALS OF INDUSTRY AND PROGRESS FOR THE PAST MONTH.

LONDON:

PRINTED AND PUBLISHED (FOR THE PROPRIETORS) BY JOHN BENNETT, 69, FLEET STREET,
AND SOLD BY ALL BOOKSELLERS.

UNITED STATES: NEW YORK, AND BALTIMORE, WM. TAYLOR AND CO.; PHILADELPHIA, J. W. MOORE;
BOSTON, CROSBY AND NICHOLLS.

Price—One Year's Subscription, 2 dollars 50 cents; Single Parts, 25 cents.

PRICE EIGHTPENCE HALFPENNY.

PART X.]   [NOVEMBER 1, 1846.

Figure 52: Contents page of the *People's Journal*, 1 Nov. 1846.

Priced* at 5d (3 ½ d in 1854), it had a circulation* somewhere short of 3,000. It grew out of Jones's previous publication, *Notes to the People**, which he shared with Julian Harney* (1851-1852), but also was meant to take the place of the *Northern Star**, which had ceased publication in 1852. The *People's Paper* bore the slogan on its masthead* 'The champion of political* justice & universal right'. In addition to Marx, who contributed some five articles plus one co-authored with Frederick Engels, there were many contributions, particularly poetry*, written by the journal's working-class readers as well as on international events. On the big issues of the 1850s, the paper took a consistent stand. It solicited funds and support for the Preston weavers' strike of 1852 and the Hyde Park demonstration against the Sunday trading laws in 1855, and Jones wrote sympathetically about the Indians' cause in the wake of the uprising in 1857.

Its literary* content was high, including a department called 'Gleaner' consisting of wide-ranging literary extracts, original fiction – much of it by Jones himself and reviews* of both British and international poetry and fiction. Always short of money to run it, Jones closed it (Sept. 1858). **AH**

Sources: Harrison 1973, Murphy 1989, *ODNB*, *Waterloo*.

PEOPLE'S PERIODICAL AND FAMILY LIBRARY (10 OCT. 1846-2 OCT. 1847) The *People's Periodical and Family Library* was typical of the range of cheap* 1d weekly* publications published* by Edward Lloyd. The periodical was similar to many popular miscellanies* aimed at the working classes* but made no attempt to comment on current affairs. Instead, it offered a diet of sensational fiction ('penny dreadfuls'), domestic romance, historical curiosities and reviews* of contemporary literature*. It reported on the serialization of Dickens's *Dombey and Son*, featuring several extracts from it. Some articles, such as 'The First Offer of Marriage' (29 May 1847), make it clear that Lloyd had a female readership* in mind. The *People's Periodical* is mainly remembered for the serial 'The String of Pearls' (21 Nov. 1846-20 March 1847), as the story marked the first appearance in fiction of the popular folk-devil, Sweeney Todd. **RM**

Sources: Haining 1993, Smith 2002, Turner 1948.

PERSONALITY AND THE PRESS By the end of the nineteenth century, there is little doubt that the cult of personality had become a mainstay of the popular* press. The widespread, sometimes lurid coverage of the trials of Oscar Wilde* in 1895 suggest both the press's hunger for celebrity* and the human cost to a life led in the public eye, but, by

then, there was no turning back. Human interest stories about individual achievement and failure; interviews* with people of note (from actresses to acrobats, scientists to sports figures); sensational stories covering divorce; society* journalism focusing on the 'upper ten thousand' all of these were features of the so-called New Journalism* which Matthew Arnold* both defined and objected to in 1887 and which form the context for understanding personality and the press.

When precisely the shift to an identifiable personality-led journalism took place is difficult to determine, not least because an interest in biography and the lives of the great and good were a feature of periodical literature since the eighteenth century: one thinks of colourful William Maginn's* editorship* of *Fraser's Magazine** or Charles Dickens's* conducting of *Household Words**. In both cases, the powerful presence of the editor ought to be seen as part of a gradual, unfolding story of how the press mediates social changes more broadly. **MWT**
Source: Wiener 1988.

PETER PARLEY'S MAGAZINE (1839-1863) Starting as a monthly* illustrated* magazine* for children* in imitation of the immensely successful American series written by Samuel Griswold Goodrich under the pseudonym 'Peter Parley', this juvenile* magazine had independent success in Britain. The English 'Peter Parley' was William Martin (1801-1867), a prolific and successful writer of books and magazines for children and adults. Martin took Goodrich's idea of short, explanatory and entertaining stories for school and home and adapted them to his English audience. *Peter Parley's Magazine* was published* by Darton and Clark; they also bound up the monthly magazine parts at Christmas* and sold it as *Peter Parley's Annual* at 5s. The magazine ceased publication in 1863, but the *Annual* continued until 1892. **AH**
Sources: *ODNB*, *Waterloo*.

PETRIE, GEORGE (1790-1866) Petrie was proficient in a huge range of diverse fields: painting, music, topography, archaeology, ethnography, journalism, and there is no other name in early nineteenth-century Ireland that so completely typifies the prevailing mood of the time. He enquired into everything, was unfailingly generous to fellow scholars and attempted to make his findings available to all levels of society.

Born in Dublin and trained as a painter, Petrie's love of Ireland was based on romantic notions of the connection between the landscape and the country's ancient Gaelic heritage. His efforts to make this understood, however, took advantage of new technology in publishing. Caesar Otway's* *Dublin Penny Journal*, produced by steam press*, proved the perfect medium for the education of the Irish public about their own past. Petrie edited* the journal with Otway throughout 1832, writing numerous articles on landscape, architecture and antiquities, and illustrating* them with his own woodcuts*.

Petrie's travels throughout Ireland made him invaluable to the Irish Ordnance Survey (he was Head of the Topographical Department during the 1830s), and his reports on the archaeology of all 32 counties made him a prominent member of the Royal Irish Academy, to which he had been elected in 1828. As part of the Committee of Publication for the RIA, Petrie was one of those responsible for the production of the Academy's two publication series*: the *Transactions*, in which his own papers on Tara and the origin of the round towers of Ireland appeared, and the *Proceedings*, which offered information in a more user-friendly format. Petrie's work also found an outlet in the short-lived *Irish Penny Journal*, which he edited and wrote for during 1842. During the 1830s Petrie developed a new design for an Irish typeface, and in 1856 Cardinal Newman asked that he produce a variation of this that could be employed by the recently established Catholic University. The resulting type was still in use well into the twentieth century.

Petrie's journalism and scholarship are remembered for their lucidity, meticulous attention to detail and appeal to all classes* of reader. ET
Sources: Leerssen 1996, McGuinne 1992, Murray 2004, *ODNB*, Stokes 1868.

PHARMACEUTICAL JOURNAL (1841-)

The *Pharmaceutical Journal* is among the oldest professional* journals in the world, having first appeared as the monthly* *Transactions of the Pharmaceutical Meetings* in July 1841. It was a private venture by Jacob Bell, a founder of the Pharmaceutical Society (now the Royal Pharmaceutical Society of Great Britain) two years later. The title *Pharmaceutical Journal and Transactions* was adopted in January 1842 and within a year it contained all the features of an orthodox professional journal: leading* articles, meeting reports, critical commentaries, letters* to the editor, book reviews* and personal notices about members of the profession.

Bell edited* the *Journal* until his death in 1859 and bequeathed it to the Pharmaceutical Society on his deathbed. The Society has published it ever since, although financial pressures on the Society

nearly brought about its sale after only two years. However, one of the Society's Council members was as enough to realise that if two publisher's – one of them the publisher of *Chemist & Druggist*, the *Journal*'s chief competitor* – were keen to acquire the *Journal* because of its potential for advertisement* revenue, the Society should be able to make money from it too. And it did, benefiting hugely from its relationship with the Pharmaceutical Society. Weekly* publication replaced monthly issues in July 1870 and the *Journal* has appeared weekly ever since, adopting the title the *Pharmaceutical Journal* in July 1895. Editors have generally occupied their chairs for many years. The current editor is only the 10th, although Jacob Bell's successor was a triumvirate put in place to prevent a single person altering the original vision. MPT
Source: Archives of the *Pharmaceutical Journal*

PHILLIPPS, EVELYN MARCH (?-1915)

Born in Devonshire, and the eldest daughter of a barrister, March Phillipps was a journalist* and woman activist. There were two strands to her writing and lecturing career in London: women's employment and Italian art.

Her articles on the economics of women's employment concerned both middle and working-class* women, as with 'The Working Lady in London' (1892) and 'The New Factory Bill: As It Affects Women' (1894); these and other articles were largely published in the *Fortnightly Review*. Her writing also reflected her commitment to women's organizations in the women's movement as in 'The Progress of Women's Trade Unions' (March 1893).

Phillipps belonged to the Women's Industrial Council, formed in 1894, and was active in the National Union of Women Workers from its establishment in 1895, speaking at the 1896 Women Workers' Conference on 'Openings for the Employment of Educated Women'. Her interest in journalism as a career for women and her appreciation of the need for women-only networks were demonstrated in her membership of the Society of Women Journalists*; speaking at their annual meeting in 1895 on 'Women in Journalism', she published on 'Women's Newspapers' in the *Fortnightly Review* (1894) and on 'The New Journalism' in the *New Review* (1895). In 1895 she co-edited* the *Englishwoman's Year Book*.

She was also an active member of the emancipationist women's Pioneer Club, the International Congress of Women and attended meetings of the Central National Society for Women's Suffrage. In 1899 she contributed a six-article series to the *Monthly Packet* on 'Women of Other Nations' that described the status of women abroad, having previously published there a series on 'Women's Industrial Life' (1897 and 'Women's Public Work' (1898)).

March Phillipps'* four books on Italian art, such as *Frescoes on the Sistine Chapel* and *Tintoretto* were all published at the beginning of the twentieth century along with some articles in the *Monthly Review* and the *Fortnightly Review*. Her final publication in the year she died was a biography of the woman writer Lanoe Falconer (Mary Hawker) on whom she had published an article in the *Cornhill** in 1912. **CL**
Sources: BritPer, 19CBLN, 19CUKP, *The Times* 1913, *Wellesley*.

PHILLIPS, CLAUDE (1846-1924) After an early career in law, Claude Phillips became a notable art critic, writer and curator in his later years. As art critic for the *Daily Telegraph** (1897-1924), Phillips interpreted the challenges of modern art to a large popular audience.

While specializing in international law Phillips travelled widely across Europe, devoting his leisure to the study of art and music and contributing articles on art to the *Manchester Guardian**. He rapidly acquired a public reputation as a connoisseur as London correspondent for the *Gazette des Beaux Arts* (1884-1891) and author of monographs on Watteau (1893), Frederick Walker* (1894) and Titian (1897-1898) for the *Portfolio**. In 1897 he became the regular art critic for the *Daily Telegraph,* which was owned by his first cousin, Edward Levy-Lawson*. In lengthy reviews* of the Royal Academy and other exhibitions, Phillips upheld traditional artistic values of sincerity, emotion and beauty. He was nonetheless open-minded in his appraisals of modern art, and his reviews of the controversial Post-Impressionist exhibitions of 1910 and 1912 cautiously appreciated the work of Cézanne, Matisse and Van Gogh. Phillips also wrote for specialized art periodicals including the *Art Journal**, *Magazine of Art** and the *Burlington Magazine*, and regularly contributed reviews of major art exhibitions across Europe to the *Quarterly Review**, *Edinburgh Review**, *Fortnightly Review** and *Nineteenth Century**.

Like many in the turn-of-the-century art world, Phillips moved easily between the roles of critic and curator, acting as the Keeper of the Wallace Collection (1897-1911). A voice of the older generation at a time of rapid change in the art market, Phillips's scholarship on the Old Masters and his knowledge of European museums added weight to his conservative but balanced assessments of modern art. **PF**
Sources: Brockwell 1925, Lago 1996, *ODNB*, Sutton 1982.

PHILLIPS, SAMUEL (1814-1854) Samuel Phillips's reputation as a literary reviewer* for *The Times** can be gauged by his successor E. S. Dallas's* comment to John Blackwood that, 'the *Times* doesn't mean to give to any one again such power as Phillips had' (Dallas to Blackwood, Jan. 1856). Phillips, a journalist, editor* and proprietor*, was initially trained for the stage but went on to study briefly at the University of London, the University of Göttingen and Sidney Sussex College, Cambridge. By 1841, an unsuccessful attempt to revive his father's chandelier business and economic necessity led him to journalism. A long relationship with *Blackwood's Edinburgh Magazine** ensued, after the serial* publication of his single novel *Caleb Stukely*. With the help of members of the Blackwood* family, Phillips learned to write leaders* for the *Berwick Warder*. By 1845, Philips was writing for the *Morning Herald**, the *Albion*, the *Literary Gazette**, and was in the process of becoming a powerful reviewer* for *The Times* while continuing his contributions to *Blackwood's*.

An 1846 letter to John Blackwood offers a picture of his journalistic working habits: 'At the present moment my table is literally covered with books for review from Delane; two articles are in hand for *Maga*; and the working part of three days weekly is taken up by the 'Albion' and the 'Warder' (Oliphant II: 316). Some of Phillips's work reappeared in volume form when John Murray* published two selections of literary reviews from *The Times* as *Essays from 'The Times'* (1851) and *A Second Series of Essays from 'The Times'* followed (1854). Originally published anonymously*, they were reissued by Murray in 1871 with Phillips's authorship attributed.

Phillips was also briefly both editor* and proprietor* of *John Bull** (1845-1846), but sold the paper in 1846 because of a combination of financial and health reasons. Plagued by illness, Phillip's private and business correspondence records his constant struggle to deliver copy in the deadline-oriented context of London journalism*. **RSB**
Sources: Blackwood Correspondence, *ODNB*, Oliphant 1897.

PHILOSOPHICAL MAGAZINE (1798-) The *Philosophical Magazine, comprehending the various branches of science, the liberal and fine arts, agriculture, manufactures, and commerce,* priced* at 2/6d, was founded as a monthly journal of science* by Alexander Tilloch*. Its agenda was 'to diffuse philosophical knowledge among every class* of society'. From 1800 it was printed by Richard Taylor* who joined Tilloch as editor* in 1822. It amalgamated with William Nicholson's* *Journal of Natural Philosophy* in 1814 and with Thomas Thomson's* *Annals of Philosophy* in 1826, when Richard Phillips joined Taylor as editor. David Brewster* became a co-editor in 1832 when his *Edinburgh Philosophical Journal* (1819-1832) was sold to Taylor. By adding the Irish chemist Robert Kane* to the editorial board in 1840, Taylor justifiably retitled the journal as the *London, Edinburgh and Dublin Philosophical Magazine and Journal.* The science-trained printer William Francis* joined the board in 1851, and from 1852 the journal was printed and published* by Taylor* & Francis. The journal regularly began a new series after 50 volumes for the supposed convenience of new subscribers, the sixth series beginning in 1901. Print runs were 500 copies in the 1820s, 1,000 in the 1890s, 2,500 in the 1960s.

Until the mid-nineteenth century Tilloch's format of original papers and letters, reprints and translations from other journals, notices of books and proceedings of learned societies remained largely unchanged. However, as other specialized journals in mathematics, chemistry, geology and biology emerged, the *Philosophical Magazine* became less a general journal of science* than a periodical specializing in physics. This tendency was encouraged by Francis's appointment of John Tyndall*, William Thomson*, J. J. Thomson and many other physicists to the editorial board from the 1850s onwards. The *Philosophical Magazine* published more of the important advances in practical and theoretical physics than all other Victorian science journals combined. **WB**

Sources: Brock and Meadows 1998, *Waterloo.*

PHILOSOPHY AND JOURNALISM For most of the nineteenth century, philosophical discourse formed part of the mainstream of Anglophone culture in a way it no longer does today, with intellectually significant philosophical debate being carried out in periodicals aimed at the general reader. This was in part because the category of philosophy itself included topics which nowadays are the province of different disciplines such as neuroscience and sociology. However, this meant that articles on subjects not obviously philosophical to the current reader were often approached in the nineteenth-century periodical press from a philosophical angle. The most extreme example of this tendency was the journalism of William Hazlitt*, whose opinion and colour-pieces often invoked issues directly addressed in his early philosophical work. An intermingling of philosophy and social commentary was

also characteristic of Thomas Carlyle's* contributions to periodicals.

Philosophical argument was frequently linked with religious issues. A good example can be found in the reception of J. S. Mill's* *A System of Logic,* which was the subject of a lengthy attack by W. G. Ward* in the *British Critic* (inspired by the religious thought of J. H. Newman) and was reviewed* in a number of other journals with religious* affiliations. Philosophical and religious issues also mingled together in pages of the *Contemporary Review*, as W. A. Knight's contributions make clear. More exclusively philosophical articles were published in mainstream journals such as J. F. Ferrier's series on the philosophy of consciousness in *Blackwood's Edinburgh Magazine*. But it was not until the foundation of the exclusively philosophical journal *Mind** in 1876 that more specialized forms of philosophical discourse emerged which no longer attempted to address the general public*. **GB**

Sources: Budge 2007, *DNCBP,* Jessop 1997.

PHILP, ROBERT KEMP (1819-1882) Robert Kemp Philp, printer, editor* and publisher* was born into a Falmouth Unitarian family. Initially (1835) apprenticed to printing, he soon left to start a radical newsagency* in Bath where he was arrested (1840) for distributing* the *Western Vindicator*, implicated in the disastrous Welsh Chartist* rising of 1839. Philp avoided prosecution, and played a leading role in regrouping Chartism. He printed and published* the weekly* *Executive Journal of the National Charter Association* (1841); but the executive's decision to abandon it unsettled Philp, who espoused a more class-conciliatory outlook than the *Northern Star** (which became the National Charter Association's principal mouthpiece). He became one of a small minority of Chartists favouring active co-operation with middle-class* suffragists, a stance actively promoted through the *People's Journal* (1½d weekly*, 1846-1851), which he sub-edited* until 1848.

Philp now turned to compiling household journals and periodicals for Houlston & Stoneman (hitherto specialists in religious literature), commencing with the ground-breaking, *Family Friend* (2d monthly 1849; fortnightly* 1850-1852). Boasting 75,000 subscribers, its content and format were shrewdly shaped to working-class readers (blatantly imitated by Samuel Beeton*). In gross circulation* terms Philp probably had the edge, especially when he turned to compiling periodical reference works. The earliest, *Family Tutor* (1851-1853), *Home Companion* (1852-1856) and *Family*

Treasury (1853-1854), were spin-offs from *Family Friend*. The most enduring, *Enquire Within Upon Everything** (1856), initially appeared fortnightly: by 1882 the complete work had sold a million copies and the final, 125th edition (much of it still Philp's work) appeared in 1973. In all he was responsible for 33 reference works, mostly monthly serials*, including the *History of Progress in Great Britain* (1858-1860), a *Dictionary of Medical & Surgical Knowledge* (1862-1864) and finally, *Domestic World* (1878). Philp boosted circulation by presenting lottery tickets to regular subscribers and encouraged extensive correspondence* (sometimes paying readers whose domestic 'receipts' he printed). Throughout, he promoted the notion that his readers were a close-knit family. **MSC**
Sources: *ODNB, The Times* 1882.

***PHOTOGRAPHIC QUARTERLY* (1889-1892)** In the crowded marketplace for photographic periodicals at the end of the 1880s, advertisements* in trade books proclaimed that the *Photographic Quarterly*, which first appeared in October 1889, would be 'The only publication devoted exclusively to original articles on Photography'. It was, its own pages later suggested, 'a digest of all matters of interest to workers in photography' which, unlike more narrowly defined rivals such as the technical *Photographic News* or the *Photographic Art Journal*, was concerned equally with 'the advance of the Science of Photography, and its progress as an Art' (1, 2, :200). Under the editorship* of Charles William Hastings, who also edited the *Amateur Photographer* and the *Photographic Reporter*, the *Photographic Quarterly* was published* by Hazell, Watson & Viney*, and carried articles by many prominent photographers including the impressionist George Davison, who wrote, for instance, on 'The Limits and Possibilities of Art Photography' in 1890.

Costing 1s 6d, and then 2s from October 1891, the *Photographic Quarterly* was a high-quality publication initially illustrated* with black-and-white photographs, as well as occasionally featuring mounted photographs. It was also pioneering in it use of colour photography, and in 1890 H. Snowden Ward noted in the *Review of Reviews** that 'in the July issue of the *Photographic Quarterly* is published a photo-chrome, or photo-mechanical print in natural colours, which is interesting as being the first photo-chrome from solid objects issued to the public in England, if not the world'. Despite its distinctiveness and innovation, the *Photographic Quarterly* closed in July 1892. **DHL**
Sources: Bolton 1897, Ward 1890, *Waterloo*.

Figure 53: 'Photoshop' effects to prove the existence of ghosts in the *Idler*, Dec. 1893, 519.

PHOTOJOURNALISM Photojournalism has no exact beginning; it emerged from the convergence between advances in photographic technology and the growth of illustrated* newspapers. Aspirations for photo journalism are certainly evident from the early stages of the illustrated press. As early as 1843, the *Illustrated London News** was claiming that its artists provided a 'daguerreotypic fidelity' (30 Sept.: 212.). The *Illustrated London News* also introduced engravings of photographs from its early years such as of Roger Fenton's photographs from the Crimea. However, it was only with the advent of half-tone process engraving in the 1880s that the illustrated press was able to directly reproduce significant numbers of photographs. The first half-tone process block used by the *Graphic** was on 6 September 1884: The Midnight Sun, photographed at the North Cape' (22).

Defined as the reportage* of contemporary events, photojournalism was also held back by the inability of cameras to take instantaneous images. Photographs marking events were taken in the 1850s and 1860s, with the London Stereoscopic Company, for example, paying nearly 2,000 guineas for rights to photograph the 1862 International

Exhibition. However, these pictures were predominantly of the exhibits and do not necessarily count as reportage. Photographers were constrained because the dominant 'wet-plate' method required the glass negative slide to be coated with collodion only a short time before use, and developed almost immediately, thereby requiring them to carry inordinate amounts of equipment. The wedding of the Prince of Wales in March 1863 was one of the first events where photographers felt confident enough to attempt pictures of the moving procession; however, poor weather meant that the *Photographic News* described the results as 'comparatively useless' (2 April 1863: 169). Their failure is in marked contrast to the popularity of the official photographic portraits by J. E. Mayall, taken under more favourable studio conditions.

The 1870s saw the advent of gelatine 'dry-plate' negatives, which made the use of photography for reportage more feasible. Thanks in part to this, the late 1880s and 1890s saw the advent of a large number of illustrated newspapers that included photographs. These included the *Graphic*, the *Sketch**, *Black and White**, the *Gentlewoman* (1890-1926) and the *Daily Graphic**. The spread of photojournalism was further encouraged by the advent of cinematography. Early cinema made much of its ability to record contemporary events such as the 1896 Derby, and Queen Victoria's 1897 Diamond Jubilee. During the Boer War, William Kennedy Laurie Dickson took his film camera to South Africa, where he successfully recorded scenes such as troop movements and war* damage. These national and international reportage films were extremely popular. JSP

Sources: Dickson 1901, Gernsheim 1969, Plunkett 2003, Shorter 1899.

PHRENOLOGICAL JOURNAL AND MISCELLANY (1823-1847) Intended to both legitimize and popularize Franz Joseph Gall's controversial theories of the relation between brain and character, the *Phrenological Journal and Miscellany* was founded in December 1823 by George and Andrew Combe and other members of the Edinburgh Phrenological Society, superseding the Society's *Transactions* established earlier in the same year. The opening item of its first number proclaimed that phrenology was the 'most important discovery of modern times', with the establishment of 'scientific truth' as its main objective. The quarterly* publication cost 4s for c.164 pages and was modelled on the proceedings of elite scientific* institutions like the Royal Society of London, distinguishing it from

other phrenological journals of the period like the monthly *Phreno-Magnet and Mirror of Nature* (1843) or the Glasgow-based *Phrenological Almanac* (1842-1844).

The *Phrenological Journal* was published* in Edinburgh by John Anderson and initially edited* by the Combe brothers along with James Simpson, Richard Poole, who left in 1824, and William Scott*. Following Scott's departure in 1829 the Combes's nephew Robert Cox became the most active member of the editorial panel, although after his own resignation in 1836 production of the journal's second series was moved to London and, under the new editor Hewett Cottrell Watson, its subtitle was altered from *Miscellany* to *Magazine of Moral Science*. As well as aiming to raise the journal's scientific standards, Watson also lowered the price to 2s 6d and by 1839 the circulation* reached 550, with perhaps as many as 3,000 actually reading each number. However, the *Phrenological Journal* rarely broke even and relied on financial contributions from supporters of its aims, while Watson's caustic manner frequently upset both contributors and readers. Cox returned to replace Watson in 1841, but the journal lasted only another six years and folded following the death of Andrew Combe in 1847. **GD**

Sources: Cooter 1984, 'Introductory Statement' 1823, Kurshan 2006, *ODNB*, Van Wyhe 2004.

PINWELL, GEORGE JOHN (1842-1875) The short-lived but prolific artist and illustrator*, George J. Pinwell drew for most of the key illustrated journals of the 1860s and early 1870s, especially *Once a Week**, the *Sunday Magazine* and *Good Words**. Unusually for an illustrator at this time the bulk of his work appeared in periodicals rather than books. A contributor to *Good Words* (1863-1875), his last work for the magazine* comprised a major series of illustrations for Jean Ingelow's, 'Fated to be Free' which showed his acknowledged skill at figure drawing. He also worked occasionally for such journals as the *Graphic**, the *Quiver** and *London Society**. **BM**

Sources: Engen 1990, Goldman 1994, Houfe 1987, *ODNB*, Reid 1928, Suriano 2005, White 1897.

PLACE, FRANCIS (1771-1854) With his deep involvement as a writer in metropolitan* print culture, Francis Place exerted his radical convictions and organizational talents for many decades in the early nineteenth century. In 1817, he edited* five numbers of *Hone's Reformists' Register*, claiming to have put it 'fairly on its legs', and in 1818 lent assistance to the radical weekly* *Gorgon**. In the 1820s he wrote articles for the *Republican, Traveller, Morning Chronicle** and *Scotsman**, but it was his attempt to popularize political* economy in the *Trades' Newspaper and Mechanics' Weekly Journal* that encouraged his best writing. Place contributed over 30 articles on the Combination Laws (the repeal of which he assisted in 1824-1825), the Corn Laws, currency, wages, population, the Irish poor and machine-breaking. His foray into elite literary* circles was less successful, though he did make contributions to the *Westminster Review** (1826-1827).

In 1831, Place founded the National Political Union, and although his efforts to launch a *Political and Moral Magazine* failed, he achieved success with articles on the 'taxes on knowledge' and municipal reform in J. A. Roebuck's *Pamphlets for the People*. Place was also an assiduous compiler of metropolitan and provincial* periodicals. His notebooks and letters reveal a conflicted attitude towards the press as he invoked articles as evidence, yet frequently denounced their truth-value; castigated the press as a 'demoralizer' of the people, but simultaneously argued that its growth would precipitate their intellectual, moral and political reformation. The powerful image in Place's autobiography of an elderly man carefully cutting out newspaper articles that 'might be useful at some future time, in relation to the working-classes', demonstrates his belief that the press had a key role to play in improving people's lives. **DSM**
Sources: Miles 1988, *ODNB*, Francis Place Collection, Rowe 1973, Thale 1972, Wallas 1918.

POETRY Poems in periodicals were vehicles of high culture, patriotic and domestic sentiment, religious piety, satire*, political* commentary, class* identity, humour, as well as fillers. Major Victorian poets, published original work in periodicals, underscoring the close relationship between canonical poetry and periodicals. Once printed as original verse or in reviews*, poems could be republished in other journals without violating copyright*. That 'Sonnet XIV' of *Sonnets from the Portuguese* (1850), by Elizabeth Barrett Browning, appeared in the 26 December 1857 *London Journal**, demonstrates the convergence between an ostensibly 'high culture' genre* and mass* popular medium, and the ready availability of poetry to mass readerships*. High culture, celebrity* and marketing also converged when *Macmillan's Magazine** and the *Cornhill Magazine** featured works by the Poet Laureate Alfred Tennyson (Jan.-Feb. 1860) to impart prestige to these new 1s monthlies* and attract buyers.

Original poems sometimes overlapped with news*. Thomas Hood's* 'The Song of the Shirt' (*Punch** 16 Dec. 1843) took the public by storm and was immediately reprinted in the 16 December 1843 issues of the *Athenaeum** and *The Times**, with other periodicals following suit. Hood's poem, itself prompted by periodical coverage of the *Second Report of the Children's Employment Commission* (1843), also functioned as political commentary, as did Tennyson's 'Charge of the Light Brigade' (*Examiner**, 9 Dec. 1854) and Barrett Browning's 'A Tale of Villafranca' (*Athenaeum*, 24 Sept. 1859). Poetic political commentary extended well beyond canonical poets. In Chartist* and other radical journals such as the *Northern Star**, many poems were contributed by readers (a practice also common to many women's* periodicals). Fostering political community and a sense of personal agency, such poems also protested official policy and shored up class identities and readerships. Across class formations and periodical titles, verse both serious and humorous repeatedly commented on wars, social wrongs and the pros and cons of governance and empire. Humour as an entertaining end in itself also characterized many poems appearing in *Punch*, *Bentley's Miscellany** and even some daily* papers.

Through its ties to hymns and meditation, poetry was also closely associated with religion*, a link enforced by the Oxford Movement. Pious verse, which ranged from John Henry Newman's 'Lead, Kindly Light' (first published as 'Faith' in the *British Magazine*, Feb. 1834) to a host of signed and unsigned poems in monthlies* and weeklies*, intersected with broader coverage of religion and counterbalanced an ephemeral commercial medium and its sometimes sensational contents. Domestic* and sentimental poetry played key roles in annuals*, women's magazines* and the popular* press as well as high-prestige titles. Examples of the latter include poems by Adelaide Procter in *Household Words** and *All the Year Round**, or by Dinah Mulock Craik in *Macmillan's*. Obituary* was another journalistic function of poetry; examples include 'Haworth Churchyard' (*Fraser's Magazine**, May 1855), Matthew Arnold's* tribute to Charlotte Brontë and 'A New Year's Eve' (*Nineteenth Century**, Feb. 1895), in which A. C. Swinburne* memorialized Christina Rossetti. Poetry also functioned visually in periodicals through its distinctive stanzaic layout and its embellishment with numerous illustrations*. **LH**
Sources: Bratton 1975, Hughes 2007b, Janowitz 1998, Ledbetter 2007, Scheinberg 2002.

POLITICAL ECONOMY AND JOURNALISM The triple tasks of political economy in the eighteenth and nineteenth centuries were: to theorize the economic/political/social systems (Adam Smith, Thomas Malthus), to educate the social classes (James and John Mill, Jane Marcet, Harriet Martineau*), and to employ this knowledge in practical terms for the good of all in society (Jeremy Bentham, Malthus). Most political economists saw themselves, at least in part, as educators of the public or even popularizers. Often they were neither academics nor associated with formal economic institutions. That fact and the presence of an enlightened bourgeois culture meant that ideas were publicized and exchanged through the journalistic media: periodicals (the *Monthly Repository*, *London and Westminster Review*, *Fortnightly Review*, *Quarterly Review*, *Edinburgh Review*), serialized* stories and penny-books (certain editions of Martineau's *Illustrations of Political Economy*, for example), newspapers (the *Daily News*, *The Times*, *Daily Telegraph*), encyclopaedias (*Encyclopaedia Britannica*), private and public correspondence, lectures and courses in Mechanics Institutes and other public venues, and discussions at the Athenaeum and other literary clubs*, as well as books and monographs. Political economy, therefore, became insinuated into the public discourse via a wide spectrum of journalistic media.

The term political economy has been defined in numerous contexts to signify (1) the natural laws that explain the relationships between capital, labour, and land; (2) the fundamental principles of the workings of the economy and the polity and their consequences for society; (3) the effects of public policy on economic and social issues; (4) the scientific study of the natural interrelationships among economic, political and social formations, including production, distribution, exchange, and consumption. A basic principle in political economy theory concerns the *natural identity of interests in society*, a principle that seemed in the nineteenth century to reflect social and economic realities in the transition from mercantilism to bourgeois capitalism. Classical political economy emerges as one of the earliest, if not *the* earliest, of the social sciences in the writings of Adam Smith, Adam Ferguson, Bentham, David Ricardo, James Mill, Hannah More*, Marcet, Harriet Martineau, John Stuart Mill*, Malthus, John R. McCulloch, J.E. Cairnes, J.B. Say, Dugald Stewart and Robert H. Patterson, a journalist*.

In contrast to the classical school, critical political economy denied the natural identity of interests in bourgeois capitalism as it was evolving and emphasized the inherent opposition of social class interests, as seen in the writings of such figures as Thomas Carlyle*, Karl Marx* and Friedrich Engels. During particular periods of their lives, these individuals authored articles in journalistic publications. Indeed, middle class periodicals generally carried articles supportive of the new industrial capitalism to be built on new financial institutions, technology and a population holding to a strong work ethic.

Writings in political economy included treatises or text-like monographs, fictional presentations, and illustrative tales of political economy theory, often didactic in form, and periodical articles by and about these theorists and their writings. Although writings on political economy were directed toward intellectuals and political figures in society, particularly in the middle classes (Marcet's *Conversations on Political Economy* 1816 and James Mill's *Elements of Political Economy* 1821), they were framed for readerships* in all social classes. Martineau's 25-volume *Illustrations of Political Economy* (1832-1834) were aimed at both middle and working classes and were published in leather-bound library editions as well as single volume penny books. These theorists of political economy assumed that if the members of society understood the natural principles inherent in the economic, social and political worlds, they would act more effectively and cooperatively as individuals to actualize these natural laws in daily life. In the nineteenth century, political economy carried a moral mission to instruct the various social classes of their specific responsibilities and obligations within the economic and social organism, conceptualized in sociology, for instance, as organicism (Auguste Comte). Finally, these authors defined political economy as a science and worked to develop rational and systematic explanations of these phenomena. Their aim was to establish the natural principles at work, to explain them, and to educate members of society to understand and live according to them.

Journalism served a critical function in the political economy discourse, as in numerous other social and economic issues (see Social* science and the press). Political economists contributed regularly to the *Fortnightly*, the *Edinburgh Review* and the *Westminster Review*, which were 'active propagandists' for their ideas (Webb: 98). The *Monthly Repository*, a Unitarian publication begun in 1805 by Robert Aspland, was an important forum in the first half-century for Dissenters and other middle-class intellectuals' exchanges and analyses of the rapidly changing and often conflictual industrial England. The range of genres included essays on political economy by James Mill, Harriet Martineau, John S. Mill and others. For over a century, generations of political economists and organizations such as the Society for the Diffusion of Useful Knowledge*, the British Association for the Advancement of Science, and the National Association for the Promotion of Social Science used the press, periodicals, penny books, and oral presentations to inform the public about political economy and to encourage the enactment of its principles.

In writing 'On The Duty of Studying Political Economy' (1831) in the *Monthly Repository*, Martineau decries the ignorance of the public in all social classes of political economy and its absence in all public institutions: 'The press alone is open to them; and that they have obtained for our nation such a reputation as the American Professor innocently assigns us, is a proof which is exhilarating to receive of the greatness and stability of the power they have won, in opposition to the blind prejudices of the people, and the haughty irrationality of the aristocracy'. (Martineau 1832: 25) **SH-D**
Sources: Altick 1957, Blaug 1958, Halevy 1928,1934, Marcet 1816, Martineau 1832, Martineau 1832-1834, Webb 1955, Yeo 1996.

POLITICAL PARTIES AND THE PRESS The emergence of modern political parties was a process intertwined with the development of the press in the nineteenth century, as political leaders were enabled to communicate with their followers and with the electorate as a whole in fundamentally new ways. Throughout the period, the interaction between political parties and the press was a vitally important element of political life. The newspaper press enabled parties to promote and popularize their programmes and help shape public debate, and was also used to raise funds, or to personalize politics around the celebration of the lives and images of political leaders: Disraeli and Gladstone being among the first to be represented in this manner on a mass scale.

Liberals, who had already adopted a free trade position in relation to popular communication, were arguably the most aggressive in their overtures to editors* and journalists. Many of the key editors of the century, in particular those in provincial* cities, were not only firm supporters of the Liberal Party but also became MPs and established political dynasties. However, leading Conservatives, notably Disraeli, also acknowledged the political benefits that accrued from friendly coverage in the daily* and weekly* press, and by the mid-1890s, dominance over the printed media had shifted in the direction of the Conservative Party. **AGJ/MaT**
Sources: Brown 1985, Koss 1981, Lee 1976.

POLITICS AND THE PRESS The potential of printed communication to affect political thought and behaviour had been grasped by civil and religious authorities even in Gutenberg's day. By the start of the nineteenth century, political organizations, whether more or less formal pressure groups or political factions and parties, were obliged to contend with the many forms of journalism* as unavoidable features of the political landscape. Historically speaking, politics and the press can be regarded in two separate but connected ways. The first major campaign waged by the printed word in the early nineteenth century was for press freedom itself. The War of the Unstamped* challenged fiscal constraints on readers' access to news*, an aim largely achieved by 1855. The Repeal of the Stamp Duty led to further speculative growth in the number of titles and in the scale of their ambition. This process was intensified when the reform of the electoral system became the subject of renewed public interest, especially in the years before and after the 1867 Reform Act. The crystallization of older political factions into modern political parties in significant part involved the ability of political leaders to communicate directly with a reshaped electorate, one that was also rapidly urbanizing and whose prosperity and social* aspirations were also rising.

Structurally, the political functioning of the press can be seen in two nearly antithetical ways. On the one hand, the press was seen as the bulwark of political power, an organ used by the state to manipulate public opinion to its advantage. In the early part of the century, the Secret Service Fund was used by the government to support sympathetic papers. William Innell Clement's *Observer*receivedpayments in return for its support of the government, and free copies were distributed as propaganda. On the other hand, there was the notion of the press as guardian of the people or 'Fourth Estate'. Frederick Knight's book *The Fourth Estate* argued in 1850 that 'where Journals are numerous the people have power, intelligence, and wealth; where Journals are few, the many are in reality mere slaves'. Whether or not they subscribed to this rather utopian view of print, small political organizations and social movements produced a hugely diverse range of newspapers and magazines* to promote their political programmes, from suffrage or socialist* societies to temperance* groups and trade unions*.

In reality, a view of the press as either sinister state propaganda or Fourth Estate is over-simplistic. Throughout the nineteenth century (and beyond), government and its radical critics alike strove for mastery of the mechanisms by which information and ideology could effectively be disseminated in print. But the complex power of the press was always difficult to harness by legislative means while it remained subject to commercial pressures and changing markets and technologies. Furthermore, the political capacities of the press extended far beyond the reach of the explicitly partisan titles, and publications intended as pure entertainment and without obvious political programmes could exert a profound impact on the political sphere. AGJ/MaT

Sources: Brown 1985, Koss 1981, Lee 1976.

POLITICS FOR THE PEOPLE (6 MAY 1848-29 JULY 1848) *Politics for the People,* a Christian Socialist* weekly*, appeared in the immediate aftermath of the mass Chartist* demonstration on Kennington Common on 10 April 1848. Though Charles Kingsley and his Christian Socialist associates campaigned against poverty, their new periodical was opposed to both universal suffrage and the perceived confrontational or 'physical force' element in Chartism.

In the first number, John M. Ludlow, who edited* the journal and contributed a substantial amount of the content, condemned the events of 10 April, and in subsequent issues mounted a sustained assault on Chartism's Six Points. Kingsley ('Parson Lot') wrote a series of three 'Letters to the Chartists,' recommending the wisdom of the Bible, while F. D. Maurice ('A Clergyman'), who was the senior figure in the enterprise, contributed philosophical dialogues and some pieces on education. Public health reform was tackled by W. A. Guy, as well as interest in the ideas emanating from revolutionary France being reflected on in reports of lectures by A. J. Scott. Additionally, four supplements* were produced. Although it sold for 1d, with sales peaking at around 2,000 copies a week, and none of the contributors was paid, the journal lost money and, after just three months, Maurice announced the closure of the Christian Socialists' first periodical. SFR

Source: Chitty 1974.

POOLE'S INDEX TO PERIODICAL LITERATURE In 1847 William Frederick Poole noticed 'that the sets of standard periodicals with which the library was well supplied were not used, although they were rich in the treatment of subjects about which inquiries

were made in vain every day'. His first effort to remedy this situation, undertaken when he was a student at Yale University in connection with the library of the Society of Brothers in Unity, resulted in his *Index to Subjects Treated in the Reviews and Other Periodicals* (1848), which was followed by the more extensive *Index to Periodical Literature* (1853). Yet *Poole's Index's* actual inception dates to 1876, when at the first meeting of the American Library Association, Poole introduced a plan for cooperatively sharing the ongoing work of periodical indexing among member libraries, offering to act as editor*, and accepting the help of associate editor William I. Fletcher. In 1877, the Library Association of the United Kingdom joined the indexing project, which was a voluntary enterprise, and in 1882 the first volume of *Poole's Index to Periodical Literature* appeared.

In his introduction to the first volume, Poole explains the *Index's* principle of inclusion and indexing arising from the needs of generalists and journalists*. He explains that 'the main purpose in the work has been to meet the average wants of students, literary men, and writers for the press, in other words, to help general scholars, who are many, in preference to the few who give their whole attention to a single topic'. Quoting from the indexing rules, Poole insisted on the highest standards so that 'All references must be made from the inspection and, if necessary, the perusal of each article'.

The massive first volume was published in 1882, covering periodicals published between 1802 and 1881, followed by supplements* issued in five-year intervals as follows:volume 2 (first supplement), covering 1882-1887, published 1888; volume 3, second supplement, covering 1887-1892, published 1893; volume 4, third supplement, covering 1892-1896, published 1897; volume 5, fourth supplement, covering 1897-1902, published 1903; volume 6, fifth supplement, covering 1902-1907, published 1908.

The main volume, and the five, five-year supplements to the *Index* are indexed and cross-referenced by subject only, and not by author. However, a *Cumulative Author Index for Poole's Index to Periodical Literature, 1802-1906* (1971) was later compiled and edited by C. Edward Wall. RSB

Sources: *Poole's Index, Waterloo, WorldCat.*

POOR MAN'S GUARDIAN: A WEEKLY NEWSPAPER FOR THE PEOPLE, ESTABLISHED CONTRARY TO 'LAW' TO TRY THE POWERS OF 'MIGHT' AGAINST 'RIGHT' (1831-1835) This radical London weekly* 1d newspaper was published* and printed by Henry Hetherington* (July 1831-Dec. 1835). It was preceded by a series of weekly 'pamphlets', also issued by Hetherington, referred to as the *Penny Papers for the People, Published by the Poor Man's Guardian* (Oct. 1830-July 1831). The *Poor Man's Guardian* was the best-known and most important of the political* illegal newspapers of the 1830s, with an estimated peak circulation* of 15,000. Its editors* included Thomas Mayhew* (until Dec. 1831), Bronterre O'Brien* (from Nov. 1832) and Julian Hibbert.

The paper championed working-class* demands such as universal suffrage, factory legislation, trade* union rights, repeal of the Poor Law Amendment Act of 1834 and an end to the evils of a competitive economic system. Most importantly, it was in the forefront of the struggle to repeal the tax on newspapers, which became known as the War of the Unstamped*. Hetherington was gaoled three times and fined repeatedly for publishing the *Poor Man's Guardian*, and several hundred of the newspaper's vendors and agents* were imprisoned. The paper was largely given over to accounts of radical and working-class meetings in London and the provinces, as well as attempts to organize political unions. It contains some poetry* and miscellaneous literary* material but no illustrations*. **JHW**
Sources: Hollis 1970, Wiener 1969.

POPULAR PRESS A truly 'popular press' did not emerge in England until the 1840s when, as the government's prohibitive newspaper stamp tax and paper duty were gradually reduced and eventually removed, a number of cheap* weekly* newspapers designed to appeal to a large readership* appeared in the market place: *Lloyd's Weekly London Newspaper*, *News of the World*, *Weekly Times* and *Reynolds's Weekly Newspaper*. As demonstrated by their individual circulation* rates, of around 50,000 by the early 1850s, these newspapers quickly captured an unprecedented share of the market, their dominance continuing as their prices* continued to fall all the way down to 1d in 1861.

Prior to this period, access to newspapers with comprehensive coverage was, for many, very limited. Daily* papers, such as *The Times** and the *Morning Chronicle**, and weekly papers, such as the *Observer** and the *Weekly Chronicle*, were not only firm supporters of the Establishment, but were also expensive, and could only be purchased regularly by the upper class* and the more affluent sections of the middle class. However, it must also be remembered that access was considerably increased through newspaper lending operating in public houses and coffee houses, as well as community sharing networks. An alternative, cheap, unstamped* press had emerged

during the early nineteenth century as a counter-weight to the establishment press, yet the appeal of these newspapers was also limited as they were largely mouthpieces for numerous radical groups around the country. A number of publishers* attempted to rectify this with some success during the 1830s, as, following in the tradition of the broadsides, they appended more sensational news such as police intelligence to their political* commentaries, as with Hetherington's *Twopenny Dispatch* (1834-1836) and *Cleave's Weekly Police Gazette**.

The popular press of the mid-nineteenth century thus filled the yawning gap between these two camps with an eye focused on profits rather than political causes. Proprietors* such as Edward Lloyd* and G. W. M. Reynolds* founded successful papers by combining news*, such as parliamentary* and foreign* intelligence, with a large quantity of sensational content including criminal intelligence and human tragedy. Editors* began to experiment with different formats* and the layout of the news, altering text size*, including prominent sub-headings and cross heads, in order to increase the appeal to new readers*. Except in the case of *Reynolds's Weekly Newspaper* (its political tone later hampered its circulation*), political radicalism was mostly toned down. As a result, the newspapers generally attracted readers from a variety of occupational backgrounds, predominantly of the working and lower-middle classes. Their sales soon dwarfed those of the competition* and they became mass* circulation newspapers.

Elements of this successful formula were subsequently fed into the New Journalism* of the latter part of the nineteenth century, demonstrating the taste for sensationalism among the more affluent classes. Yet more notable in this context is the continued expansion of the popular press throughout the second half of the century. While the weekly newspapers maintained their popularity (*Lloyd's Weekly Newspaper* was the first newspaper to circulate one million copies in 1896), they were joined by a number of 1d and ½d morning and evening papers, a development facilitated by falling costs in printing and a corresponding rise in lower-class incomes. These new newspapers included the *Echo**, the *Star** and the *Daily Mail**. The triumph of the popular press in England is perhaps most evident in Benjamin Seebohm Rowntree's poverty budget of 1901, which declared that doing without a ½d Sunday newspaper was one indication of deprivation. **RHC**
Sources: Altick 1957, Berridge 1972, Lee 1976, Rowntree 1901, Vincent 1989.

POPULAR SCIENCE MONTHLY (1872-1915) After failing to secure a sufficient readership* as editor* of *Appleton's Journal of Popular Literature, Science and Art* (1869-1870), the American science* writer Edward Livingston Youmans became editor* of the *Galaxy's* 'Scientific Miscellany' as well as scientific advisor to the New York publisher* D. Appleton. On Appleton's behalf, he negotiated for an Anglo-American monograph series with leading British men of science such as Thomas Henry Huxley* and Herbert Spencer*, and also arranged for the serialization of Spencer's contribution to the series in the *Galaxy* alongside its British serial* publication in the *Contemporary Review*. However, difficulties with the timing of the simultaneous transatlantic* publication prompted Youmans to begin a new monthly journal of his own that would enable him to accommodate Spencer's demands as well as furthering his longstanding aims for the diffusion of evolutionary science.

In May 1872 Youmans began the *Popular Science Monthly*, which was published and printed in America by Appleton, and then, from November 1895, also published in Britain by Kegan Paul, Trench, Trübner*, making it the most significant example of transatlantic science* journalism of the nineteenth century. Costing 2s 6d for 128 to 158 octavo pages, the *Popular Science Monthly* carried numerous articles from prominent British scientific practitioners as well as popularizers like Grant Allen*, while Spencer was by far its most regular contributor. These articles, often illustrated by high-quality woodcuts*, were supplemented by extensive extracts from books and periodicals and the miscellaneous 'Editor's Chair' column*, all of which addressed aspects of science relevant to the general public. The print run was 12,000 in 1872, rising to 18,000 by 1886, rendering the *Popular Science Monthly* a considerable financial success. Youmans described himself as the journal's 'Conductor', as would Richard Proctor* in *Knowledge*￿ founded later in 1872, and virtually every element of the *Popular Science Monthly* adhered to his doctrinaire evolutionism and opposition to religion*. From the start Youmans was assisted by his younger brother William Jay, who assumed the sole editorship in 1887, before being replaced by James McKeen Cattell in 1900. In 1915 the rights to the *Popular Science Monthly* were sold to a New York publisher who began a different journal under the same title. GD

Sources: Fiske 1894, Haar 1948, Leverette Jnr 1965, Lightman 2007, *Science* 8 November 1895, *Waterloo*.

PORNOGRAPHIC AND EROTIC LITERATURE The trade in obscene literature centred around Holywell Street off the Strand in central London, where bookshops carried a range of illicit material, often using the window displays to lure in potential customers. The extent of obscene periodical literature is difficult to determine, however, since print runs were small (often aimed at specific coteries of male buyers) and information on title pages is often purposefully and playfully misleading (to avoid prosecution). The murky world of underground publishing relied on pseudonyms and aliases, further complicating our ability to trace the major figures involved in the pornographic press (see, for example, William Lazenby*), although by the end of the century, overtly erotic literature was more above ground (see Leonard Smithers*). Magazines ranged from the semi-pornographic weekly* periodical of 'fast life' in London, such as the *Town*￿ to the more overtly pornographic and most well-known magazine, the *Pearl*￿. MWT

Sources: Colligan 2006, Mendes 1993, Nead 2000.

PORTFOLIO (1870-1907) The monthly* *Portfolio* was founded and edited* by Philip Gilbert Hamerton* to promote British and Continental printmakers and publish original engravings and etchings, including works by painter-etchers like James MacNeill Whistler* and Seymour Haden. Each volume included a monograph on an artist (e.g., Rembrandt, Turner) or group of artists, frequently written by Hamerton in the sophisticated language of an art criticism based on impressions rather than aesthetic presumptions, and addressed primarily to connoisseurs and scholars. *Portfolio* was published* in London by Seeley, Jackson and Halliday up to 1894, when Hamerton died, and then by Seeley and Co. The publishers occasionally republished *Portfolio* articles in book form, e.g., much of Hamerton's book on J. M. W. Turner first appeared in the magazine. After 1894, the magazine* became an annual series of artists' monographs written by major art critics and scholars. JC

Sources: Codell 1987, Collins 1976, Hamerton 1897, Roberts 1970.

POTTER, THOMAS ROSSELL (1799-1873) Thomas Potter was a sporting* journalist and editor* of at least four provincial* newspapers. Using the pseudonym* 'Old Grey' (the name of his favourite horse), he regularly contributed to the *Sporting Magazine* (1827-1840) writings that were 'remarkable for their pungency, raciness and pleasantry' (Jewitt: 17). His witty poem* the 'Meltonians' was so successful that the proprietor* of the *Sporting*

Magazine presented Potter with a valuable hunting horse. He subsequently wrote for the *Sporting Review**. In 1849 he began his new career as an editor of local* newspapers, first the *Leicester Advertiser**, a county weekly with a large circulation*. In 1856, he also took on the editorship of the *Ilkeston Pioneer,* and when the ownership of the *Leicester Advertiser* changed in 1858, he moved to the editorship of the *Leicester Guardian.* By 1865 he was editor of the *Loughborough Monitor,* which subsequently amalgamated with the *Loughborough News.* Potter also contributed articles on local history* to the latter journal. While a prolific contributor to the local press he was also a Fellow of the Royal Society of Literature and 'a frequent and eloquent lecturer' at Literary and Mechanics' Institutions. DHL
Sources: Jewitt 1873, *Leicester Advertiser* 1873, ODNB.

POWER, JOHN (1820-1872) Information about John Power comes primarily from the first issue of the *Irish Book Lover* (1909), where he is described as Ireland's first bibliographer. Power established the *Irish Literary Enquirer* in 1865; four issues of the journal were published, containing important material on Irish periodicals, some of it previously published in *Notes and Queries**. In 1866, after the journal folded, Power further edited* and gathered all of this material together as *A List of Irish Periodical Productions (Chiefly Literary) from 1729 to the Present Time; Reprinted from 'Notes and Queries', March and April, 1866, and 'The Irish Literary Enquirer', No. IV, with Additions and Corrections* (London 1866). Titles and dates of periodicals are often accompanied by Power's assessment of their worth (not always complimentary), and later writers on Irish publishing* in the nineteenth century often use Power's comments as emblematic of the difficulties encountered by firms after the Act of Union in 1802. Power begins his list with the following (unattributed) quotation from 1840: 'Never was there a more fragile history than that of Irish periodical literature: like that of our ancient monarchs, it comprises little more than a narrative of untimely deaths'. ET
Sources: Crone 1909, PGIL *Eirdata.*

PRAGNELL, KATE (C.1851-?) Kate Pragnell, a press photographer*, opened a London studio in the 1890s when Alice Hughes* was the only female professional photographer in London. Pragnell's work differed from Hughes's in that she also photographed male sitters, unusual at the time because the general antagonism toward women usually precluded men from employing them; but statesmen,

soldiers and artists had all been among her clients. Her work appeared in many of the same magazine series as Hughes, such as 'Brides and Bridegrooms' in *Woman at Home**, but Pragnell photographed the bridegrooms as well as the brides. The magazine* *Hearth and Home** was where Pragnell had a virtual monopoly. Being in competition with Hughes, Pragnell displayed great ingenuity with her marketing having a regular, advertisement* in *Hearth and Home* to their mutual advantage: 'Any Ladies wishing to be photographed in their Drawing Room dresses for publication in *Hearth and Home* can have a free sitting at Kate Pragnell & Co'. Two years later, it was for photographs in their court dresses. In the same magazine, they aped *Woman at Home*'s wedding feature by introducing their own series, 'Marriage and Giving in Marriage', using Pragnell's photographs.

Pragnell attempted to use the camera to produce an effect as much like a painted portrait as possible, with another distinguishing feature being her use of light and shade. Her studio backgrounds, all designed by her, were constantly changing with only the most expensive artificial flowers from Paris deployed. Although she had an assistant, a Miss Stewart, Pragnell took all the shots herself, and, like Hughes, only employed women at her studio to undertake the printing. With the demand for photography increasing, in March 1897 Pragnell was advertising in *Hearth and Home* for women trainee photographers for her studio. She was aware from colleagues that women journalists going on assignments now wanted women photographers to accompany them, but there were none. She was hoping to provide those photographers.

By 1901, Pragnell had moved to another studio at 39 Brompton Square; her work had developed to include news* photography for outlets such as the *Illustrated London News**, which published, for instance, photographs she had taken of the suffragette procession of June 1908. CL
Source: 19CUKP.

PRESS AGENCIES See Associated Press, Press Association, and Provincial Newspaper Society

PRESS ASSOCIATION Founded in 1868, the Press Association was a newspaper co-operative intended to supply papers with domestic and foreign* news that developed into the principal news* agency* for British news. The prime movers behind its formation were proprietors of regional newspapers – especially those in the Provincial* Newspaper Society* – who complained of the monopoly that the three telegraph* companies held over the ness to make their first start where they are already known. There are certainly openings for lady photographers in many of the great provincial towns, and there, in many cases, a young lady would find herself backed up by many old family friends; still, valuable as is a good connection, any woman who wishes to take up photography as a business knows that, though her friends are generally willing enough to give her one sitting, they will not continue to patronize her studio, still less recommend it to their friends, unless the work done is thoroughly satisfactory. Take my own case. When I first opened my studio, my friends were all very kind to me; but I did not lose sight of the fact that one of my photographs was from the first a better advertisement, as regards strangers, than even the warmest and kindest of recommendations.

"In one matter the latter-day photographer is to be congratulated. In old days even very rich people were only photographed once in three or four years; now the same woman will often come to sit to me three or four times a year. Many people, again, have their children photographed every three or six months; several mothers of my acquaintance have thus a charming gallery, showing their children at every age and, it may almost be said, in every mood.

"Of course, delightful as it is to have the same sitter returning to my studio, it makes it necessary for me to be perpetually inventing and investing in new accessories. By the way, I never employ those who design backgrounds by the hundred; everything in my studio is made entirely from my own designs; and, to take but one item, all the artificial flowers used by me are the best that Paris can produce, and this, again, as you can easily understand, means a considerable and ever-recurring expenditure."

Perhaps one of the most interesting and valuable features about Miss Kate Pragnell's photographs is the extraordinarily clever manipulation of light and shade. Many of the beautiful full-lengths, which are a speciality of the studio, give one the impression of having been taken out of doors. It should, however, be added that Miss Pragnell does not remain, as do so many photographers, entirely faithful to the full-length poses, and she is especially successful with her groups.

"Lighting and posing are all important, for

From Photo by]   [*Miss Kate Pragnell.*
SIR HARRY JOHNSTON.

Figure 54: An extract from an interview with Kate Pragnell published in *Woman at Home*, April 1899.

transmission of news. These companies (operating as a cartel) offered an in-house service for the gathering and supply of news, sending out up to 4,000 words a day. The so-called Intelligence Department of the companies included editorial and reporting staffs, but they were an inexpert crew, many of whom had no prior experience of journalism. Its output was notoriously variable in quality, its transmission was unpredictable, and it often contained basic inaccuracies, yet because this was the only means of obtaining up-to-date news, newspapers were effectively held to ransom, paying between £150 and £250 for an annual subscription.

The Press Association – whose early meetings were chaired by John Edward Taylor (1830-1905), proprietor* and editor* of the influential *Manchester Guardian** – was formed following the passage of the Telegraph Bill in 1868, which empowered the Government to acquire the telegraph* system. The consequent nationalisation of the telegraph network in 1870, from which time it came under the control of the Post Office, ushered in a new era in the transmission of news, and the Press Association was at the heart of the new system. '[T]he Association is formed on the principle of co-operation', reported the committee following its inauguration, 'and can never be worked for individual profit, or become exclusive in its character'.

While John Edward Taylor provided much of the impetus for the formation of the Association, it was John Jaffray of the *Birmingham Daily Post**, Frederick Clifford (1828-1904) of the *Sheffield Telegraph* (1855-) and George Harper of the *Huddersfield Chronicle* (1850-1916) who ran it in the early years. The latter was responsible, as president of the Provincial Newspaper Society*, for ensuring the co-operation of the regional weeklies* in the new enterprise. The London papers were not involved in the setting up of the Press Association, but by the end of its first year of operations all of the London morning and evening papers as well as some weeklies and sporting papers were buying news from the agency. How the agency was going to source its foreign* news was a potential sticking point: Reuters* had been the key source of such information since 1851, with the telegraph companies paying an annual £3,000 subscription to receive it. The Press Association struck a deal with Reuters, agreeing to confine its activities to the UK and paying Reuters £3,000 annually for its foreign coverage, as well as helping Reuters with UK news to supply to its foreign clients. A closely symbiotic relationship between the two agencies developed.

Despite teething problems, with the Post Office initially unable to handle the load, the Press Association established itself as a countrywide network of reporters and editorial staff whose reports were more accurate and timely than those of the Intelligence Department of the telegraph companies. Their reporters* were properly trained and sometimes even talented journalists. By 1880, 436 messages adding up to 39,000 words were received by the Press Association in one day, some of which were foreign stories channelled from Reuters, with the remainder made up by the Association's own reporters. After processing these messages and parcelling them up, the Association sent out 7,897 separate addresses, totalling 262,000 words.

The agency liberated the provincial newspapers from their dependence on the London press, and inaugurated what was arguably the first national news broadcasting network. Its influence today is more pervasive than ever and also arguably more malign, as cash-strapped newspapers cut back on their own reporting staff and increasingly rely on uncorroborated wire copy. **MaT**
Sources: *ODNB*, Scott 1968, Storey 1951, *Waterloo*, Whorlow 1886.

PRESS HISTORY Alongside the expansion of the newspaper press as an institution and the development of journalism* as a profession, the later nineteenth century witnessed a burgeoning interest in the history of the press itself. At the turn of the nineteenth century, journalism was considered a less than dignified profession*, with the majority of those who wrote for the 'daily* prints' remaining anonymous*, and the press itself was not considered a subject worthy of sustained historical enquiry. By the 1840s, however, there had arisen a marked interest in quantifying and defining the character of the British newspaper press and its writers. One of the most significant products of this began in 1846, with the initial publication of Charles Mitchell's, *Newspaper Press Directory**, a periodical guide published four times (1846-1854), and annually after 1856. Intended primarily as a guide to advertisers* rather than a historical record, Mitchell's *Directory* nonetheless contained valuable information on the scope and history of the nineteenth-century press, along with notes on the political* and religious* affiliations of individual papers. Although it was presented as an unbiased, empirical account of the press, the *Newspaper Press Directory* tended to privilege the more 'respectable' newspapers at the expense of papers aimed at a popular* readership*, such as the unstamped* press.

From the 1850s, detailed histories of the newspaper press in Britain, usually written by journalists, began to appear. The first comprehensive history of the press was Frederick Knight Hunt's *The Fourth Estate: Contributions Towards a History of Newspapers, and of the Liberty of the Press* (2 vols 1850). The form of Hunt's work, which traced the origins and history of the newspaper press by concentrating on major publications and noted journalists, was certainly influential on succeeding press histories such as Alexander Andrews', *History of British Journalism: From the Foundation of the Newspaper Press in England, to the Repeal of the Stamp Act in 1855 with Sketches of Press Celebrities* (2 vols 1859). In 1871-1872, James Grant published *The Newspaper Press: its Origins, Progress and Present Position* (3 vols.), an influential if somewhat inaccurate account of the development of the press up to the later nineteenth century, which incorporated reminiscences from Grant's own long career in journalism and editing. The following decade, histories with an even more contemporary and anecdotal focus appeared such as Charles Pebody's *English Journalism and the Men Who Have Made It* (1882), Joseph Hatton's *Journalistic London: Being a Sketch of the Famous Pens and Papers of the Day* (1882) and Mason Jackson's *The Pictorial Press: its Origins and Progress* (1885). The later 1880s also saw the publication of the most significant and enduring nineteenth century press history, Henry Fox Bourne's* *English Newspapers: Chapters in the History of Journalism* (2 vols 1887). Fox Bourne's work is still widely used today as a historical source, but like its antecedents it concentrated primarily on constructing a history of literary journalism focused on major writers and 'respectable' newspapers, which Fox Bourne saw as under threat from the sensationalism of the so-called New Journalism. In the midst of the self-conscious New Journalism, the indexing of the contents of the periodical press by William Pede* (1891ff.) opened up its contents – retrospectively and in the present – for journalists and press historians.

It is possible concentrating on 'press celebrities*' and major publications of all eras, the nineteenth-century histories of the press presented an imbalanced picture of the workings of the press, and the lives and careers of the majority of journalists, in the nineteenth century itself. Certainly, the rise of the popular* press in the century was often dealt with in a cursory manner, if not entirely omitted, from these works. Since these histories were generally written by career journalists, however, it is hardly surprisingly that the authors dwelt on what they took to be the outstanding achievements in their field, and the increasing popularity of press histories in the latter part of the century can be seen to be related to the solidifying sense of journalism as a respectable profession. **JG**

Sources: Andrews 1859, Aspinall 1945, Bourne 1885, Hampton 1999, Hatton 1882, Hunt 1850, Linton 1979.

PRICE AND COVER PRICE For the first half of the century, the price of newspapers was driven by three considerations, costs of production* and distribution*, competitive pricing and fiscal legislation. However, even then, advertising* was often a more important source of income than the sale price. Furthermore, many newspapers were resold at a declining cost, or were rented by the hour by street hawkers. The cover price also included stamp, paper and advertising duties. These were reduced in 1836 after the 'war of the unstamped'*, and were abolished between 1853 and 1861, leading the way to the 1d dailies* of the 1870s such as the *Daily Telegraph** and the ½d *Daily Mail** of 1896. The price of a title is a crucial factor at the time and for press historians in determining the economic and cultural niches of its readership*. **AGJ**

Sources: Boyce 1978, Lee 1976, Read 1961.

PRIMITIVE METHODIST MAGAZINE (1821-1932) The *Primitive Methodist Magazine* was edited* by Hugh Bourne. After ill-health forced Bourne to interrupt his editorship of a *Methodist Magazine* soon after its debut in 1819, it was relaunched as the *Primitive Methodist Magazine*. The Primitive Methodists, or Ranters, were the only major nonconformist denomination whose roots and support were almost entirely drawn from the working classes*, with many of their members being farm workers, miners and artisans. Yet, despite this, the Primitive Methodists were the most 'sophisticated producers of periodicals among the Wesleyan secession' (Altholz: 84), publishing*, in addition, titles such as the *Primitive Methodist* (a 1d weekly*, 1868-1905) and the *Primitive Methodists' Children's* Magazine* (1824-1851). The emphasis of the *Primitive Methodist Magazine* was interpersonal and narrative-driven, consisting of travelling preachers' journals, anecdotes about 'providences' or miraculous events, obituaries*, poetry*, records of camp meetings or 'lovefeasts', and morally improving tales of salvation or damnation such as 'The Awful Death of A Backslider'. It became the *Aldersgate Primitive Methodist Magazine* in 1898 and continued until 1932, when the Primitive Methodists merged with the main Methodist body. **LL**

Sources: Altholtz 1989, *Waterloo*.

PRINGLE, THOMAS (1789-1834) Born to a family of farmers near Kelso, Scotland and educated at Edinburgh University, Thomas Pringle emerged as an unlikely candidate to edit* the *Edinburgh Monthly Magazine*, the first incarnation of *Blackwood's Magazine*. A Whig by temperament, while the owner William Blackwood I* stood along Tory lines, Pringle was nevertheless brought aboard, along with his friend John Cleghorn, to edit the magazine's original 1817 launch. The initial numbers, which sold poorly, introduced material later critics have called 'dull and decent' and a 'meek and mild miscellany'. Looking for a more topical, perhaps sensational, approach, Blackwood terminated the editors' contract and was later 'infuriated' to discover both had secretly taken on positions at the rival *Edinburgh Magazine* (1817-1826). The second editorial body at Blackwood's, which included James Hogg, John Gibson Lockhart* and John Wilson*, ruthlessly parodied the original editors – as well as the entire Whig establishment of Edinburgh – in the 'Translations from an Ancient Chaldee Manuscript'. Composed in mock biblical form, this infamous satire which skewered the bland editorial sensibility and physical disability of Pringle (crippled during an accident in his early years), offended established taste yet ensured future sales, as readers gravitated to the trenchant sensibility of the new editorial group.

Pringle, unable to support his new wife with his income, sought opportunities abroad. With the help of Walter Scott*, who wrote letters on his behalf, Pringle was elected as one of the leaders of the government's 1820 emigration scheme to South Africa's eastern Cape. After four years in the colonial interior, he moved to Cape Town, where his interest in journalism was rekindled. Pringle helped establish the *South African Commercial Advertiser*, the first independent English newspaper in the region in January 1824, and South Africa's first literary magazine, the bilingual *South African Journal*, in March (*ODNB*). The newspaper quickly ran into trouble with Lord Charles Somerset, the Cape's governor, who objected to the *Advertiser's* Whiggish editorial position and forced its closure. Pringle returned to England in 1826. Partly as a response to 'The State of Slavery at the Cape', an article printed in the *New Monthly Magazine**, as well as his editorial involvement with Mary Prince (a Caribbean writer, former slave and one-time servant in his household), Pringle was asked to become Secretary of the Anti-Slavery Society. In 1834, a year after signing the Act of Emancipation, effectively abolishing slavery in the British empire, he died of a lung hemorrhage. **TJ**

Sources: Mackenzie 1867, *ODNB*, Pereira and Chapman 1989, Tredrey 1954.

***PRINTING MACHINE* (FEB. 1834-MAY 1835)**
Charles Knight* began the *Printing Machine: a Review for the Many* as a Saturday 4d monthly*, which he changed to fortnightly from the fourth (April) number and to weekly* from 6 September. The name was chosen as a sign of modernity, marking the difference between the advanced printing machine and the old-fashioned printing press: Applegath and Cooper's* printing machine appeared in its masthead*. From issue three the subtitle changed to *or, Companion to the Library,* an alteration which tied it to the accretion of 'universal knowledge' through collecting serial issues of a larger volume of information.

To some extent the *Printing Machine* was a house* journal in that it reviewed Knight's own publications such as the SDUK's* *Poor Laws and Paupers Illustrated* by Harriet Martineau*, but it also reviewed* works issued by other publishers. Implicitly attacking the *Athenaeum**, an address to readers in four claimed that it was not interested in novelty for its own sake but preferred 'accuracy and impartiality, which commonly result from a patient and diligent consideration of the plan and execution of any individual book'. The reviews* are indeed long and analytic, eschewing on the whole both the reproduction of long extracts or dissertations upon some topic suggested by the works in question as found in the quarterlies*, although there is an attempt to give a brief abstract of every new book. Its focus can be on high-status works such as translations of Dante, or the *Westminster Review's** commentary on Bentham's *Deontology, The Life and Correspondence of Henry Salt* (Bentley 1834).

Never a commercial success, the journal soon combined with Knight's monthly *Companion to the Newspaper** (which continued to come out once a month while the *Printing Machine* was fortnightly). A major reason for turning weekly was to directly rival the *Athenaeum*, which, it was claimed, is the effete voice of a corrupt aristocracy, set up solely to attack the SDUK. By 3 January 1835 the price* had been reduced to 3d and the last two pages had advertisements* (before there were none previously that survive). On 6 June it combined with *Leigh Hunt's London Journal** to form a curious publication of two distinct halves, separated with a double bar across the page. The last issue of this joint publication seems to be 26 December 1835 with a final 2d supplement* dated 31 December. **AK**
Sources: Sullivan, *Waterloo*.

PRINTING PRESSES The mechanization of printing in the nineteenth century played an essential part in a media revolution that transformed British society. During the century, the basic framework of Johannes Gutenberg's (1400-1468) moveable type printing press, imported into Britain by William Caxton (d. 1492) in the 1470s, was improved – almost beyond recognition – by automation and mechanization. Increases in the speed and efficiency of production were amplified by innovations in paper* production and typesetting*. Without these developments, the unprecedented boom in mass* circulation* newspapers and periodicals would not have been possible.

The situation at the end of the eighteenth century was much as Caxton had left it: the wooden screw press, manually operated by two men, produced around 200 impressions an hour. Demand for print vastly exceeded the capacity of printers to supply it. In 1798 the Earl of Stanhope (1753-1816) patented an iron press which produced 250 better quality impressions an hour. Its weight doubled the printing surface of each impression, effectively doubling the rate of production.

The definitive development, though, was the application of steam power to printing. Friedrich Koenig (1774-1833) – a German engineer based in London – patented in 1810 a steam-powered flatbed press based on the Stanhope model, quickly abandoned in favour of a rotary press, as mooted in 1790 by William Nicholson*. Assembled in April 1811, Koenig's steam-powered machine had its type arranged on a drum and inked by rollers, and it was soon capable of printing 1,000 sheets per hour. Offered initially to the *Morning Chronicle**, where it was declined, John Walter* of *The Times** saw its potential and installed it secretly at night on 29 November 1814. His printers arrived at work to find that they were obsolete, and were told to seek alternative employment. *The Times* hailed 'the greatest improvement connected with printing, since the discovery of the art itself'. *The Times* established itself as the most influential newspaper of its day, rising from a circulation of 5,000 in 1815 to around 50,000 in the middle of the century: the *Morning Chronicle**, by comparison, lost its way and petered out in 1862.

From this point, the success of a mass circulation publication partly depended on its proprietor's* willingness to embrace cutting-edge technology, despite opposition from printers who feared for their jobs. As publisher for the Society for the Diffusion of Useful Knowledge (SDUK), Charles Knight* achieved a circulation of 200,000 a week with the *Penny Magazine** in the 1830s. For Knight, the rotary steam press hailed a new era in the democratization of knowledge, like the Gutenberg press four centuries before. By 1839 William Clowes*, the SDUK's printer, had 19 steam presses, each churning out 1,000 sheets an hour.

Applegath and Cowper* had by 1825 developed a press capable of 2,000 impressions per hour, and the Applegath cylinder machine – exhibited at the 1851 Great Exhibition – raised the bar to 5,000. In 1856, *Lloyd's Weekly Newspaper** was the first to adopt the American high-speed Hoe press, which became the industry standard, increasing the rate of production to 20,000 impressions an hour: 100 times faster than had been possible at the beginning of the century. The example of *Lloyd's* strengthens the argument that the adoption of state-of-the-art printing technology engendered commercial success: in the 1890s it became the first newspaper to hit a circulation of a million. **MaT**
Sources: Berridge 1978, Dudek 1960, Jones 1996, *ODNB*, Rummonds 2004.

PROCEEDINGS OF THE SOCIETY FOR PSYCHICAL RESEARCH (1882-) The Society for Psychical Research (SPR: 1882ff) quickly established itself as the most intellectually respectable face of a growing interest in mesmerism, apparitions, spiritualism, multiple personality and other 'psychical' phenomena. The Society's *Proceedings*, published* quarterly* by Trübner* and Co, was the principal forum for SPR members' experimental researches, and also featured the SPR presidential addresses, book reviews* and lists of members. From 20 to 500 pages, the *Proceedings* was an expensive purchase (from 2s 6d to 7s) and was typically aimed at the same bourgeois and aristocratic individuals who dominated the Society's membership.

Until the early 1900s, it was largely edited* by, and filled with the researches of, F. W. H. Myers, Henry Sidgwick, Edmund Gurney and other members of a small coterie of distinguished i-ntellectuals who effectively ran the SPR. It presented the society's most formidable arguments for the reality of 'telepathy', the survival of the soul following bodily death, and the existence of the 'subliminal self', and featured more sensational investigations of the physical phenomena of spiritualism and theosophy. From 1884, the SPR issued a sister periodical, the *Journal*, which was issued privately to members and which allowed more controversial researches and views to be presented. **RN**
Sources: Fodor 1934, Gauld 1968, Grattan-Guinness 1982.

PROCTOR, RICHARD ANTHONY (1837-1888)

Although Richard Proctor, science* journalist, editor* and proprietor* trained for the Bar, the death of his eldest son in 1863 caused him to abandon the law for astronomy and immerse himself in science writing. His first article, 'Colours of the Double Stars', was published in the *Cornhill Magazine** in 1863, and his first book, *Saturn and its System*, came out two years later. Initially these publications were unremunerative, but a failed business speculation in 1866 forced him to turn to writing as his main source of income. A prolific journalist, Proctor contributed over 500 articles to publications including the *Popular Science Review, Harper's New Monthly Magazine**, the *English Mechanic* and *Scribner's Magazine*. Until he distanced himself from the Royal Astronomical Society in 1874, Proctor was a frequent contributor to their *Monthly Notices*, even acting as its temporary editor.

In 1881 Proctor founded *Knowledge**, a 2d weekly* scientific* journal, intended as a cheap* competitor* to *Nature**. A vocal opponent of the endowment of research and scientific cliques of all kinds, Proctor conceived of *Knowledge* – with its motto 'Exactly Described' – as a vehicle for amateur scientific endeavour, making much of the contributions of his readers and publishing writers with similar views to his own. In 1885 Proctor, pleading overwork, transformed *Knowledge* into a 6d monthly. In the previous year Proctor had moved to Florida in order to concentrate on his magnum opus, *Old and New Astronomy*, appointing Edward Clodd as a subeditor* in London. In 1888, while en route to Britain for a lecture tour, he was taken ill in New York. Wrongly suspected of having yellow fever, he was ejected from his hotel and died. Both *Knowledge* and *Old and New Astronomy* were continued by his friend Arthur Cowper Ranyard*.

JEM

Sources: Lightman 2000, Lightman 2004a, Lightman 2004c, *ODNB*, Sheehan 1995.

PROFESSIONAL JOURNALS

A great range of professional journals sprang up and evolved throughout the nineteenth century, beginning in or around the 1820s and taking flight in the last quarter of the century. In many cases, these journals first allowed a certain professional discourse or knowledge community to differentiate and branch out into different directions, before acting as a conduit leading to greater standardization and to the accreditation of only a small selection of journals within the profession or discipline. A key feature in this respect, common to all professional journals, is the correspondence* column, which acts as a forum for exploration, communication and ultimately standardization of ideas within a particular discipline.

This development of a discipline through diverse journalism* is well illustrated within the medical field. General medical* periodicals like the *Lancet**, the *Medico-Chirurgical Review** and the *British Medical Journal** for a long time coexisted alongside journals devoted to specific areas of practice and expertise (e.g. dentistry, nursing, magnetism, phrenology, herbalism or even narcotism). In law, journals of a practical bent like the *Solicitor's Journal and Reporter* (1857-1900+) flourished alongside periodicals making inquiries of a broader intellectual type (important here was the *Law Magazine and Law Review*, 1856-1872, then continued as *Law Magazine and Review**). Legal journals took an academic turn with the foundation of the *Law Quarterly Review** by its first editor* Frederick Pollock in 1885. While bridging the gap between academic lawyers and practitioners, the *Law Quarterly Review* established strict scholarly standards and commanded an authority hitherto unknown. Not in all cases did those journals lead to recognized specialties: the estimated 458 medical journals published in the course of the century thus had a filtering function, ultimately resulting in more rather than less homogeneity. This dual process of growing differentiation followed by standardization is reflected in professional journals in the fields of law, physical and social science, history, architecture, the military, transport, finance and trade, and agriculture.

The standardization of disciplines is discernable within the evolution of the professional journal itself, for example in the changes in professed intended readership*. Added to this, the functional role of many journals reflects developments in society among the professional classes. Though a purely research-orientated journal at the close of the century, at its inception the stated aim of the *Lancet* was to make reports of the Metropolitan Hospital Lectures accessible to the general public, as well as to students and practitioners. Alongside the medical lectures, early contents include political* articles, theatrical reviews*, a defence of Poet Laureate Robert Southey in the wake of his drubbing from Byron and problems and solutions in chess. Though eventually dropped by the *Lancet*, this broader 'gentleman's magazine' format* remained popular among professional journals such as the *Law Gazette* (1890-1894), which included along with its case studies weekly portraits of notables from the profession, chess and whist problems/solutions and a very broad array of advertising* aimed more towards the reader's private and social, rather than professional, life. The *Accountant** also shares this feature of being a journal largely dedicated to professional matter within its letterpress but including a wide variety of third-party advertising aimed at the individual, irrespective of profession. Many professional journals were weeklies*, and in terms of the extra-professional material, share aspects of the 'magazine*' quality of the broader weekly press. One exception is the weekly *Schoolmaster* (1872-1900+), whose format follows *The Times** almost exactly (despite its smaller size*), with opening pages of short classified adverts and dense, text-only articles with headings such as 'Educational Intelligence' within.

The apex of growth in professional journals was around mid-century, when there were some 1,000 scientific journals, of which 60 per cent were commercial. Thereafter, the interdisciplinary nature of Victorian professional discourse was turned into a rather more compartmentalized disciplinary landscape, journals playing a key role in the institutional regulation of the professions. **MdW/ MBT**
Sources: *Accountant, Lancet, Law Gazette*, Perkin 1989, *Schoolmaster*, Vann and VanArsdel 1994.

PROFESSIONS AND THE PRESS That the British professions made enormous use of journals and journalism* to establish their collective identities in the nineteenth century is hardly contentious. But how, why and when different professions used journals and journalism is still a matter for detailed investigation. Some individuals used publication for professional advancement, others merely to supplement income, but the systemic patterns of such use across the various occupation groups has yet to be investigated (Altick 1989, is useful here, and see Medicine and Journalism*, Science and Journalism*). Rather than try to untangle the narrative skeins of the various professions, however, this entry seeks to establish a theoretical framework and suggest directions for further work.

The sociological consensus is that a profession may be defined by: (1) command of esoteric skills and/or knowledge expressed in an exclusive language, usually aimed at solving problems (2) processes of exclusion so as to generate a monopoly over the relevant domain (3) autonomous control over members of the profession and what that profession comprises and (4) a meritocratic service ideal which prioritises the execution of the task in hand over the interests of the individual professional. This definition applies just as much to the traditional profes-

sions – clerical, legal*, medical, and the military* – as it does to those who strategically usurped the term in the nineteenth century to gain prestige and moral authority, groups as diverse as accountants (*Accountant*, 1874-1986; *Accountants' Journal*, 1883-1936), architects (Building Press*), bankers (Financial Journals*), engineers (*Engineer*, 1856-), teachers (e.g. *Schoolmaster*, 1872-1962 (changes of title); *Schoolmistress*, 1881-1935; *Teacher*, 1879-1881; *Board Teacher*, 1883-1904; *Head Teacher*, 1894-1908), telegraphists (Electrical Journals*), even dance instructors (see Buckland 2007) and journalists. Although the above definition can accommodate artists and performing musicians and the term was regularly applied to both by the 1780s to distinguish them from amateurs, and although music at least had its own technical periodicals (see Music* and Journalism*), the sociological literature does not generally consider them as 'professionals' in the same way as others.

Part of the process of becoming a profession was the public roping off, justification and advertisement of the specialist domain, combined with a more introspective exploration of the limits of professional identity, a double impulse outwards to a lay audience and inwards to members that can be seen at every turn in professional journals*. While sometimes the two audiences are explicitly addressed at the same time (e.g. the *Builder**), more often the lay is marked through its exclusion, usually through specialist vocabulary, reference and activities (by e.g. examination papers). While professions are sometimes described as networks of equals, in each professional journal hierarchy is always established by an editor* who, at the most basic level, decides who has the right to representation and to what extent. Given the early use of signature in professional journals to ensure reliability of data, 'stars' emerge whose work and (through obituaries*, reports of meetings and, more rarely, interviews*) whose lives become authoritative models. In this, professional journals overlap with trade journals*. At the same time, a feature of many professional journals is correspondence* with ordinary members. It is here that the image of parity is clearest.

Although promoting the self-regulation of the professions, journals could also either directly or indirectly hail the state to ask for legal recognition and protection in the face of threats. Calls for the formation of the medical register by the orthodox medical press are well known; parallel is the work towards the state registration of nurses in the Nursing Press*. That such invitations to state intervention and resistance to them spilled out into the general press is only to be expected, either through the lifting from, or debate of, material inspired by the professional journals, or through interventions professionals wrote in the general press to bring their case to wider notices (see medicine and journalism*). Even the spats between journals in the same profession such as between the *Lancet** and *London Medical Gazette** or the founding of a new journal either in opposition to others (e.g. the *Law Quarterly Review**) or dedicated to a new specialism in an established profession (e.g. *Journal of Mental Science**) only served to reinforce the legitimacy of the profession as a whole by demonstrating that the domain was worthy of investment and debate.

While the traditional professions were set up as exclusively masculine, and there was a strong patrilineal element in professional recruitment (sons either following fathers or entering a neighbouring profession, as many entries on journalists here show), their commitment to an impersonal knowledge- and skills-based meritocracy proved, as Corfield (1995:212-213) suggests, the Trojan horse that let women in: this seems the reasoning behind the *Nursing Record's** initial stress on the knowledge economy of nursing and its rival the *Hospital*s* resistance to it. We see the same in the many similar claims in journals dedicated to women educators (e.g. *Governess**) and women 'professionals' in general periodicals (see Young 2007; feminist press*).

An area that awaits exploration (though see Thomson 2005) is the place of advertisements* in professional journals. While doctors and lawyers were forbidden from advertising themselves by their professional associations, their journals were nonetheless subvented by advertising. Thus for many years Van Houten's took out adverts for cocoa in the *British Medical Journal**, *Lancet**, *Edinburgh Medical Journal** and *Hospital*, exploiting appropriately recherché medical vocabulary and testimonials from these journals. Such adverts not only reminded professionals of favourite products in the pursuance of their calling and informed them of new ones but called on them to be advocates for the product. That this might compromise professional dedication to the service ideal through false claims was always a danger. Other advertisements reinforced professional identity as a consumer group, not only for specialist equipment (surgical appliances, instruction manuals, office furniture) but for the signs of an appropriate lifestyle beyond work (pianos, furniture, clothes, rest homes). Clerical (a pensions and investment company dating from 1824) Medical is a notable example of a company originally and early tailored to specific professions. **AK**

Sources: Altick 1989, Buckland 2007, Burrage 1990a, Burrage 1990b, Corfield 1995, Perkin 1989, Thomson 2005, Young 2007.

PROPRIETORS Proprietors of nineteenth-century British newspapers and journals were capable of exerting enormous power and influence. Many were extremely innovative and nurtured journalistic and editorial talent. Several also edited* the papers they owned. Families were also important as dynastic proprietors, notably of *The Times** of which the Walter* family were chief proprietors, 1788-1908 and 1922-1967. The Rivington family* were periodical publishers from the 1770s. Their most successful journal, the *British Critic** commenced in 1793, survived until 1843. The *Manchester Guardian** boasted the century's most notable new dynasty, the* Taylors. The family exercised a light hand on editorial matters from the 1870s, but in the absence of clear proposals to secure its future, John Edward Taylor Jnr's death (1905) plunged the paper into crisis. Not all proprietors, however, were successful: numerous papers failed after a few issues, while owners of the unstamped* press could face imprisonment and sequestration of their printing equipment.

Most proprietors aimed to increase profits by reaching as wide a readership* as possible, especially with the gradual reduction of stamp tax and paper duty (1833-1861). Newspaper owners such as Edward Lloyd* and the radical George Reynolds* started 'penny* weeklies*' aimed at the lower classes*. A low price* and a large circulation* could increase profits. The emergence of popular 'dailies'* in the late nineteenth-century led to the rise of new dynasties ('press barons') who dominated newspaper and magazine* publication far into the next century. These proprietors were highly competitive. Rival papers were often launched in a bid to outdo other successful owners, while failing papers were taken over and made financially viable. Ownership often inter-twined with political* activities. The *Manchester Evening News* was launched in 1868 to support its owner's bid to become the city's MP (when that failed he sold it to the Taylors). John Walter II and III were both MPs, as were Sir George Newnes* and Joseph Cowen, republican proprietor of the *Newcastle Chronicle*. No proprietor, however, was elevated to the peerage in the nineteenth century. Alfred Harmsworth* became the first 'press baron'* in 1905 as Baron Northcliffe, and the term itself only emerged in the 1920s. **DHL/MBT/MSC**

Sources: Altick 1957, Brendon 1982, Jackson 2001, Lee 1976, Rivington 1919, Teich 1983.

PROSPECTIVE REVIEW: A QUARTERLY JOURNAL OF THEOLOGY AND LITERATURE (1845-1855) The *Prospective Review* was one of a number of distinguished periodicals supported by the English Unitarians throughout the nineteenth century. Its direct predecessor was the *Christian Teacher** (1835-1844) edited* by John Hamilton Thom* which became the *Prospective Review* in 1845. Published* by John Chapman*, the *Prospective* was edited by a committee including Thom, J. J. Tayler*, James Martineau* and Charles Wicksteed*, progressive Unitarian ministers in the North of England who regarded managing and writing for the periodical as an extension to their ministerial role. They were also the major contributors, each being responsible for his own 'department'. Individual issues were substantial in length (129 pages by 1855), and advertisements* have survived in some copies.

As the 'Prefatory Note' to Issue 1 (1 Feb. 1845) explained, the title of the periodical described its philosophy: 'prospective' indicated a Unitarian interest in meditating upon change and continuity, and free inquiry as opposed to dogma, and 'review' indicated a departure from strict 'teaching' and showed its catholicity of interests. The first number dealt mainly with religious* and theological issues, including a review* of Robert Chambers's* anonymous and controversial *Vestiges of the Natural History of Creation* by F. W. Newman, but from the second number onwards, its contents were broadened to include history*, linguistics and politics*. To appeal to a national readership*, local* issues were weeded out, and each number consisted of several lengthy, thorough and impartial review articles. While theology and philosophy* remained its major concerns, the arts, music* and English and foreign literature* were also covered. Contributors included John Kendrick, F. W. Newman, Walter Bagehot* and Richard Holt Hutton*.

The circle of editors increased in 1852 to include William Caldwell Roscoe*. Hutton joined the group from August 1853. The 1850s also saw the publication of two reviews of considerable literary historical interest. Harriet Martineau's* *Letters on the Laws of Man's Nature and Development* was unfavourably reviewed (May 1851) by James Martineau*, causing a final break in the relationship between brother and sister. Charles Beard's review of *Uncle Tom's Log Cabin* (Nov. 1852) issue appreciated the qualities of the novel and took the opportunity to condemn the practice of slavery. The periodical's demise was partly due to financial difficulties and the absence of continuous sponsorship but also because its contents appeared too liberal to Unitarians and too partisan to the general public. Nevertheless, prominent writers and intellectuals like Arthur Hugh Clough and George Eliot* were numbered among its supporters. The tradition of liberal Unitarian journalism that the *Prospective* established was continued by its direct descendant the *National Review**(strongly influenced by the editorial board of the *Prospective*), and later by the *Theological Review** and the *Modern Review**. ZV

Sources: *ODNB*, Sullivan, *Wellesley.*

PROTESTANT WOMAN (1894-1958); PROTESTANT GIRL (1895-1900). The *Protestant Woman* and the *Protestant Girl** were the monthly* publications of the Protestant Union and its daughter group, the Girls' Protestant Union, both instigated by Mrs W. Reirson Arbuthnot, vice-president of the Women's Total Abstinence Union and president of the Gospel Temperance Work. Alarmed by 'the encroachments of Ritualism and Romanism', Arbuthnot launched the Women's Protestant Union in 1891, at the annual meeting of the Association of Female Workers. Seeking a method of communication among its members, she started a *Monthly Letter*, initially only available to members. Gradually, it expanded to become the *Protestant Woman* magazine*. As membership steadily grew, a junior branch (the Girls' Protestant Union), was formed (1895) with its own magazine, the *Protestant Girl*. Both publications were produced and edited* at Mrs Arbuthnot's home and published* by Marshall Brothers of Paternoster Row, London. Free for members, they were also on sale at booksellers for 1d.

Each magazine began with an address from the Unions' presidential editor, in which Arbuthnot discussed contemporary issues, many of which had been raised by the members. The *Protestant Girl* consisted of eight illustrated* pages of poetry*, articles on Protestant heroines, competitions and proverbs. Its mother paper was narrowly focused on the members and the Union, building an intimacy through letters*, shared experiences, notices of the Union's events, prayer and religious* items, illustrated with engravings. It grew in size* with its membership, from an original 16 to 20 pages by 1899. The *Protestant Girl* ceased publication in 1900; the *Protestant Woman* continued until 1958. CL

Sources: Gordon and Doughan 2001, *Waterloo, Wings* 1899.

PROUT, EBENEZER (1835-1909)   Ebenezer Prout was the first editor* of the *Monthly Musical Record** (1871 to 1875). A celebrated conductor, organist and composer in his own right, he became a significant figure in the development of music* criticism in England, importing the ideas of German theorists like Hugo Riemann (1849-1919) and developing a critical idiom that would do much to shape the genre*. At the *Monthly Musical Record*, he championed then scarcely known works by Continental composers such as Wagner, Schubert and Schumann. His leaders* were richly European in flavour, and his admiration of continental musical culture was coupled with a perception that the English scene was wan by comparison.

Prout went on to become music critic at the *Academy** (1874-1879) and the *Athenaeum** (1879-1889). His *Athenaeum* contributions stressed the need for 'true musical progress', praised Beethoven's late quartets and railed against the star system, 'one of the greatest curses of music in this country' (21 Jan. 1882). An eminent Handel scholar, he became embroiled in a spat over Franz's controversial edition of the *Messiah* in 1891. His impassioned defence of the work appeared in the *Monthly Musical Record*, and Joseph Bennett* retaliated in the *Musical Times**.

He increasingly moved away from journalism, but the critical perspectives he developed in his journalistic writing found a more systematic expression in a series of definitive treatises on musical topics, notably *Harmony, its Theory and Practice* (1889), *Musical Form* (1893) and *The Orchestra* (1897). **MaT**
Sources: C19Masterfile, *Athenaeum* 1882/1885, *Monthly Musical Record* 1871/1910, *Musical Times* 1891/1899/1910, *New Grove, ODNB, Pall Mall Gazette* 1878, *The Times* 1909.

PROVINCIAL MEDICAL AND SURGICAL JOURNAL (1840-1852); ASSOCIATION MEDICAL JOURNAL (1853-1857)   As the first manifestation of the *British Medical Journal** (1857ff), the *Provincial Medical and Surgical Journal* – whose title was a provocation to those who sought to keep medicine and surgery apart – appeared as a 16-page octavo weekly* on 3 October 1840. Although its editors*, Dr Hennis Green and Dr R. J. Streeton, did not claim an official connection to the Provincial Medical and Surgical Association, in their opening address they refer to promoting the interests of medical associations in general and 'more especially' those of the Provincial Medical and Surgical Association: Streeton, indeed, as physician to the

Worcester Infirmary, was in constant contact with Charles Hastings, who had founded the Association at the Infirmary in 1832. After a year as the *Provincial Medical Journal and Retrospect of the Medical Sciences* (9 Apr. 1842-23 March 1844) on 3 April 1844 the journal reverted to its original title, began a new series and the Provincial Medical and Surgical Association became its official issuing body*, and Streeton its sole editor. Five years later he was replaced by John Henry Walsh and William Harcourt Rankin, who had been appointed foreign editor in 1847. In 1853, the *Provincial Medical and Surgical Journal* was amalgamated with the *London Journal of Medicine* which had been founded by John Rose Cormack* in January 1849. Rose Cormack became editor of the new periodical in late 1852 and marked his editorship – and the establishment of the journal in London – with a change of title* to the *Association Medical Journal* in January 1853. The following year he became secretary of the Association as well.

The *Provincial Medical and Surgical Journal* encountered problems common to many professional* periodicals, as revealed by the minutes of the Association meetings. In 1846 branch members called for it to become fortnightly to save costs. This it did the following year, though the size* of the fortnightly was larger than two previous weekly* numbers combined. The collection of subscriptions caused a financial headache, but the most heat was generated by the perceived exclusionary and political* editorial practices of Rose Cormack. He was forced to resign when it was decided that the offices of editor of the journal and the secretary of the Association could not be held by the same person. Andrew Wynter* took over the editorship in October 1855. **AK**
Sources: Bartrip 1990, Bynum 1992, *Waterloo*.

PROVINCIAL NEWSPAPER SOCIETY (1836-)   The Provincial Newspaper Society held its first meeting in Fleet* Street in April 1836, and became an extremely influential force in the provincial* press, representing a model of mutual co-operation between the newspapers of different regions. Called by the society's founder J. Buller, the meeting was chaired by John Matthew Gutch* of *Felix Farley's Bristol Journal* (1752-1864), who became the Society's first president. Also in attendance were the proprietors* of 17 other regional papers, including Robert Perring of the *Leeds Intelligencer* (1754-1866), John Blackwell of the *Newcastle Courant** and C. E. Brown of the *Cambridge Chronicle. It* was formed to 'promote the general interests of the provincial press'. Business interests were put ahead of any ideological mission, and neutrality with regard to politics and religion was enshrined in the Society's constitution.

In the year of the Society's formation, it is estimated that London produced as many newspapers as all of the provinces combined. But over the next few decades the relative position of the provincial press strengthened, with the Provincial Newspaper Society playing a key role. Its membership grew rapidly from 23 papers in 1837 to 123 in 1842, and continued to expand steadily thereafter, reaching 268 in 1885. The majority of the major regional newspapers of the nineteenth century, including the Manchester Guardian*, were members. The society campaigned on a variety of issues, but its two most significant achievements were its role in the reform of the libel laws and the formation in 1868 of the Press Association*.

The libel laws of the first part of the century were generally seen by newspaper proprietors* as draconian, and they undoubtedly operated as a barrier to the accurate reporting of the news. For one thing, when reporting on parliamentary* debates or legal* cases the newspaper could be held responsible for any defamatory words printed, even though they were actually spoken in Parliament or in court. From its inception the Society applied continuous pressure on the government about this issue through petitions and lobbying. This resulted in Lord Campbell's Libel Act in 1843 (which introduced among other things the power for the defendant to plead the truth and public benefit of an alleged libel) and later the Newspaper Libel and Registration Act of 1881, which finally removed newspapers' liability for reporting defamatory remarks made at public meetings. J. D. Hutchinson, MP for Halifax, proprietor of the Halifax Courier (1853-1967) and president of the Provincial Newspaper Society (1880-1881) can take much of the credit for pushing the bill through opposition in parliament.

The formation of the Press Association can be partly attributed to the agency of the Provincial Newspaper Society, which in 1864 began to petition against the monopoly held by the three telegraph* companies over the transmission of news. Four years later, when the first committee of the Press Association was formed, it consisted largely of members of the Provincial Newspaper Society, and operated in the same spirit of co-operation. The nationalization of the telegraph system (following pressure from the Society and the Press Associa-

tion*) meant that news could be transmitted more efficiently and cheaply, improving the reporting of national and international news* in the provincial newspapers, and ultimately helping to raise their circulation*.

In 1886 the London newspapers joined the Society, which was thereafter known as the Newspaper Society. The London papers left in 1916, but the Newspaper Society continues to protect the interests of local* newspapers to this day. **MaT**
Sources: Boorman 1968, *ODNB*, Scott 1968, *Waterloo*, Whorlow 1886.

PROVINCIAL NEWSPAPERS Before the nineteenth century, newspaper journalism in Britain was strongly represented in the industrially developed provinces outside London. While the *London Gazette* was established in 1665, other key early newspaper titles such as Berrow's *Worcester Journal* (c.1690) or the *Lincoln, Rutland and Stamford Mercury* (1695) were started in county towns to serve their immediate regions. The provincial press witnessed strong growth throughout the eighteenth century, but the emergence during the nineteenth century of national titles edited* and printed in London brought with it a new newspaper economy to which the English provincial titles were obliged to adjust, and which lent to the term 'provincial' an increasingly derogatory tone. Nevertheless, provincial titles continued to play a dynamic role in the development of British journalism* throughout the century, and remain valuable sources of historical evidence.

The provincial newspapers of Scotland*, and to a lesser extent Wales*, continued to serve national markets, but in England too the newspapers of the larger industrial towns served as hubs for powerful political* dynasties, such as the Cowen family in Newcastle, or support bases for political leaders such as Joseph Chamberlain in Birmingham. During the second half of the century, most provincial towns and cities enjoyed a vibrant and comparatively diverse periodical press that included weekly* and even daily* newspapers. It was also well organized through the Provincial Newspaper Society, established in 1836. Although the wealthier proprietors* could access national and foreign* news from the telegraph* companies from 1845, most had to rely on scissors-and-paste* journalism from London sources, until 1870 when the telegraph was nationalized.

These newspapers provided an apprenticeship for large numbers of aspiring national journalists, W. T. Stead* being perhaps the most celebrated example, while some provincial titles, such as the *Northern Star** or, later, the *Manchester Guardian**, became London-based nationals. Some major national* newspaper owners such as the Berry brothers (cf Lords Buckland, Camrose and Kemsley) also emerged from the provincial press. The continued engagement of powerful proprietors such as these with the press of Britain's provinces led in the early twentieth century to the greater regionalization of ownership, the circulation* wars and the reduction of the rich diversity of the provincial press of the preceding 250 years. **AGJ**

Sources: Lee 1976, Read 1961.

PSEUDONYMS See Anonymity and signature

PUBLIC LIBRARIES AND READING ROOMS The provision of a reading room* for the perusal of newspapers was a characteristic of public libraries in Britain and elsewhere from their inception in the mid-nineteenth century. As public libraries multiplied, independent subscription-based institutions for the reading of newspapers and magazines came under pressure. Symbolic of this shift in patronage was the taking over, in 1852, of the premises of the Union News Room in Duke Street, Liverpool, to house the city's first rate-supported free library. Being the most popular aspect of public library provision, newspapers rooms were generally located on the ground floor of libraries and close to the entrance, thereby preserving greater peace and quiet in other rooms, such as the reference department, reserved for more serious study. Newspapers were mostly displayed, securely, on large reading slopes, around which a number of readers* might congregate. Slopes often carried a sign with the name of the newspaper it housed, providing a vista of the newsroom as a 'public sphere' space symbolic of a democratic society in which rational debate was tolerated and encouraged. This is not to say, however, that the reading room was not subjected to occasional censorship* by librarians and library managers. Some newspapers, for example those of various late nineteenth-century socialist* societies, were excluded, while even mainstream publications could be the subject of the library censor*, as was the case in respect of the 'blacking out' of racing news* and gambling information. There were libraries that opened magazine* rooms in addition to newsrooms and, as readers underwent increased categorization, separate reading rooms were provided for women and children, each stocking newspapers and magazines deemed appropriate to its occupants.

The public library reading room was the culmination of a long process of historical development.

A notable development in the eighteenth and nineteenth centuries was the circular reading room, emblematic of a new openness to knowledge. From the eighteenth century onwards, reading rooms were also linked to popular commercial ventures such as taverns, coffee houses and booksellers. Though access to reading was by definition not free, as the patron was a customer first and a reader second, the success of these establishments confirmed the importance of the reading room for the ideology of self-improvement and the diffusion of knowledge. In libraries of poorer means the reading room was no less valuable in terms of fulfilling the purpose of the institution. This was the case in regard to the reading rooms that sprang up in connection with Chartism*, Britain's first working-class* movement which campaigned in the 1830s and 1840s for political rights, most notably the right to vote. Recognizing the importance of education for working-class emancipation, local Chartist* reading rooms were established as co-operative lending libraries, offering books and access to newspapers and magazines for members of radical organisations. Other voluntary libraries were established in the nineteenth century to meet the reading requirements of the working class, including a network of libraries and reading rooms in the Miners' Institutes of South Wales, largely funded by the miners, which survived into the 1950s.

Autonomous working-class libraries were a cultural outcome of working-class identity and political agitation. In public libraries too, not least through the newspapers they provided, the working-class found a useful vehicle for expressing their consciousness and satisfying their thirst for education and entertainment. Public libraries were initiated partly as a means of control, to divert workers away from radical reading, yet reading was, in itself, a means of advance and emancipation. This was certainly understood by an emergent middle class in search of its identity, who also made good use of public libraries, including the pluralistic and well-stocked newspaper reading rooms. **AMB**

Sources: Black 1966, Black and Hoare 2006, Kelly 1977, Munford 1951, Snape 1995.

PUBLISHERS AND THE PRESS Periodicals and newspapers alike have origins inside and outside the industry, but within the former category, newspapers tend to spring from printers and periodicals from publishers. To nineteenth-century publishing houses, the periodical was one publishing genre* among others, deriving part of its interest from its intersection with the novel, books and other publications in the market for general literature* and news*.

In the early nineteenth century, prices* of books and periodicals alike were high, making the common reader dependent on lending and circulation* schemes. Periodicals, then, had not yet been discovered as a commercially interesting publishing format*. This situation altered with idealistic efforts outside the circle of established publishing firms to bring cheap* but edifying reading to the masses*: bookseller W. Chambers's* initiative, *Chambers's Edinburgh Journal**, only later established its founder as a lucrative publisher, while the *Penny Magazine** was not commercial but depended on private sponsors. Both were launched in 1832 to great success, showing what a ready market there was to be explored.

It is one of the ironies of Victorian print culture that publishers' continuing resistance to publishing cheap* books incited a thriving periodical and serial* fiction market after the 1830s. The great firms of the early and mid-nineteenth century all entered the competition, partly because periodicals provided a free forum for advertisements* and 'puffing'*. Bentley*, Blackwood*, Bradbury and Evans*, Chapman and Hall* and Macmillan* all added at least one periodical to their 'publisher's list', often underlining their status as publisher-proprietor* in the title: e.g. *Blackwood's Edinburgh Magazine**; *Bentley's Miscellany**; *Macmillan's Magazine**; *Tinsley's Magazine**; and *Longman's Magazine**. Publishers did not, however, retain their proprietorship* as a rule: *Bentley's Miscellany* was owned by novelist W. H. Ainsworth* (1854-1868).

As publishing houses (e.g. Macmillan, Tinsley) developed into fiction-publishing concerns after mid-century, they also began to use periodicals for serializing novels (hitherto published in part-issue instalments). Fiction became dominant in family* magazines from 1860 onwards, when the firm of Smith, Elder* launched the *Cornhill Magazine**. This development entailed a further commercialization of the press to advance publishers' interests: periodicals were now used to test the market for fiction and attract potential novelistic talent to add to their list of profitable volumes. Another development that affected the relations between publishers and the press was the advent of signed writing in the late 1860s and 1870s. On the face of it, this weakened publishers' ideological hold over their titles, as it introduced a free market principle to periodical writing. Political differences between publishers, proprietors and editors were not, however, easy to cancel out. A vanguard review like the *Fortnightly Review** set out with private proprietors in 1865 before financial strains necessitated that it be handed over to a commercial publisher (Chapman and Hall*) two years later. In the end, the history of the relations between publishers and the press in nineteenth-century England shows a constant tension between innovation and conservatism.

The publishing trade had its own trade* journals as well as annual* catalogues: *Bent's Monthly Literary Advertiser**, the fortnightly *Publishers' Circular**, and the monthly *Bookseller**. **MdW**

Sources: Altick 1957, Anderson and Rose 1991, Feltes 1986, *ODNB*, Sutherland 1976, Weedon 2003.

PUBLISHERS' CIRCULAR (1837-1959) The *Publishers' Circular and General Record of British and Foreign Literature* was a trade* fortnightly intended to advertise* new books to the retail trade and bulk buyers of books. Originally developed by a group of 14 publishers*, the journal was edited* by Sampson Low*, who also held the post of the manager of the Publishers Group, a society established in the late 1830s for the protection of retail booksellers against underselling. The journal was distributed free to professionals in the book trade (1837-1843), with an initial price* for others of 2d, rising to 3d in 1843. Alongside the list of books published in the previous fortnight and an index to authors and titles, it also contained regular columns* on trade-related matters such as businesses for sale and job vacancies, obituaries* and American books. From 1841 its leading item was a section on 'Literary Intelligence', which featured recent book-trade news*. One of the most important supplements* to the journal was the *English (or British) Catalogue* (1842ff) an annual* digest derived from the fortnightly issues. Other important innovations include the introduction of a book review* section in the 1870s, which described the content of new publications, and the publication of special issues. A special 'Education Issue' was begun in 1840, and by 1842 had become bi-annual. Also, though the journal did not generally include illustrations*, in 1851 an 'Annual Illustrated Christmas* Number' was introduced. This special issue continued for 70 years and provides a visual record of changing styles and techniques of book illustration and periodical graphics. The journal also regularly included a number of advertisements, originally priced at 8d a line, £2 a column and £4 a page but quickly lowered to 3gns a page and 6d a line.

In 1867 Low bought the journal outright from its managing committee. He continued as editor until 1883 when management of the journal passed to Edward Marston, who, from 1846, had been responsible for the journal's regular compilation of detailed statistical data. Under Marston's management, the journal became decidedly more opinionated, campaigning for further ordering and regulation of the book trade and continuing the journal's conservative approach to issues such as underselling and book imports. In 1900 Marston's son Robert took over the editorship (1900-1926). Throughout its nineteenth-century publication, the arrangement of the journal remained relatively stable. It was published in octavo format*, usually on the first and fifteenth of the month, from 1837 until 1891, when the size* of the pages was increased slightly, publication became weekly*, its price halved, and its advertising* rates increased. **PZ**

Sources: Eliot and Sutherland 1988, ncse, *ODNB*.

PUCK (JAN. 1889-JUNE 1890); ARIEL OR THE LONDON PUCK (JULY 1890-FEB. 1892) A satirical* comic paper with illustrations* and caricatures*, *Puck* began as a 1d weekly*. The figure of Shakespeare's mischievous sprite was subsequently frequently invoked as a vector of good-natured satire. *Puck* developed a standard format* with the front page given over to a large caricature. Inside could be found a mixture of smaller illustrations, short stories, spoof interviews* and dialogues, phoney diary entries by politicians and statesmen, doggerel and (usually absurd) correspondence*. Advertisements* for all manner of household goods, financial services and medicaments generally took up one or two pages.

In June 1889, the paper's failure to attract a significant readership* led to the inclusion of four colour pages, the considerable expense of which was to be partly offset by raising the cover price* to 2d. Puck predicted that this innovation would 'produce an earthquake in Fleet Street*', but colour printing was not the panacea it was hoped. When in December 1889 the price was dropped again to 1d, it was claimed that the 'public clears out our whole edition at twopence'. Yet in March 1890, when Israel Zangwill* took over as editor*, a change in format* suggested that four colour pages could not be supported at a cover price of 1d: a single colour portrait was now included every week as a supplement*. In July 1890, the periodical changed its name to *Ariel or the London Puck* (purportedly to avoid confusion with the American *Puck*), shifted from a quarto to a smaller format and abandoned colour printing al-

together. *Ariel*, which under Zangwill's editorship became increasingly literary*, fizzled out in February 1892. **MaT**

Sources: Rochelson, Spielmann, *Waterloo*.

PUFFING; LOGROLLING The practice of puffing or logrolling, giving excessive or unmerited praise to a performance or work of art or literature*, is as old as criticism itself, and the proliferation of periodicals in the nineteenth century gave it plenty of scope. The overlap of book publishers and magazine proprietors* allowed a publisher* like Henry Colburn* not only to ensure that reviews* of books on his list were favourably noticed in his own 'house'* journal, the *New Monthly Magazine** but to commission 'paid paragraphs' on books on his list, reviews which he paid other journals to insert.

Writing art, theatre, music* and book reviews for a minor publication was a common first step of a career in journalism*, and progress in such a career created bonds of friendship, obligation and mutual support. Anonymity* was defended as a means of insulating the critic from such pressures, but the identities of regular art, music* and drama critics for major publications were often an open secret. Critics who were also practitioners like *The Times*'s drama critic John Oxenford*, himself a prolific but mediocre playwright, gave further hostage to judgement. Gossip* columnists* were notorious puffers: the correspondence of G. A. Sala* includes numerous letters from puff-seekers, and he admitted to 'rolling the dramatic log' of his favourite actress, Genevieve Ward. Journals like the *Athenaeum**, *Spectator** and *Academy** prided themselves on their critical independence, but authors of considerable repute were not above promoting their friends, as did Swinburne*, for instance, in his reviews of William Morris* and D. G. Rossetti in the *Fortnightly Review**.

The late Victorian period saw the emergence of mass*-circulation periodical reviewing in which the puffs of influential tastemakers like T. P. O'Connor* and Clement Shorter* could make a best seller. The ubiquity of debates in the press on Colburn's practices earlier in the period, and on the relative evils and merits of anonymity* and signature in the 1860s and 1890s, indicate the longevity of the problem, attested to by Richard le Gallienne's* pseudonym* 'Logroller' in the 1890s. **CAK**

Sources: Kent 1980, Kent 1986, Sala 1993, Waller 2006.

PUNCH (1841-2002) A Victorian institution, *Punch* was published weekly* right through the

Figure 55: The cover of *Punch*, Aug. 1841.

assembled a number of requisite elements for success. Not least of these was the versatile squarish, double-columned page, which was especially well adapted to the kind of interplay between visual and textual elements that *Punch* required. To such prerequisites were added an experienced and well-connected staff and an ability both to sustain the traditions of Regency mockery and to develop a newer whimsical mode of comedy that focused on the trials and aspirations of the still emergent middle classes.

Such little financial backing as the nascent *Punch* had was supplied largely by the engraver Ebenezer Landells* and the printer James Last, who underwrote Mark Lemon* and Henry Mayhew's* uncertain editorial venture. Early sales, while they reached the substantial level of 6,000 copies, could not sustain *Punch* for long, but more permanent support was supplied by the firm of Bradbury and Evans* who were able not only to capitalize the new magazine properly but also supplied both its printing and publishing needs. If its early years were somewhat chaotic, *Punch* nonetheless rapidly developed some remarkably stable characteristics over the following 60 years. It had very few editors*, several of whom enjoyed lengthy tenancies: Henry Mayhew was joint editor with Mark Lemon from 1841 to 1842, but then Lemon became sole editor until 1870, to be followed by Shirley Brooks (1870-1874), Tom Taylor*(1874-1880) and Francis Burnand* (1880-1906). After Ebenezer Landells, one of the founding figures of the magazine, was sacked in 1843, Joseph Swain* took over the crucial role of overseeing the engraving of the many illustrations and, building his business on his agreement with *Punch*, remained in that role until 1900. His promptness and efficiency formed a crucial element in *Punch's* subsequent development. The coterie of slightly bohemian and sometimes politically radical journalists, authors and writers who formed the inner circle of early contributors, which included Douglas Jerrold, Gilbert À Beckett*, Henry Mayhew, Thomas Hood* and William Makepeace Thackeray* among its writers and Leech*, Doyle*, Tenniel*, Keene and du Maurier* among its artists, remained, apart from occasional rows and defections, coherent and famously sociable.

nineteenth century from its first issue of 17 July 1841, and remains one of the key sources for elucidating the opinions of nineteenth-century middle England. The 12-page double column* issues, each costing 3d in the first instance, comprised text, full-page wood* engraved cartoons*, a variety of wood-engraved vignette comic illustration* dropped into the text and a range of visual embellishments, including elaborate capital letters and tiny silhouettes which ran over from the weekly parts into the index of the reprinted volumes and the yearly supplementary* Almanack.

There was no good reason in its early days why *Punch* should have been any more successful than the many short-lived satirical* journals that failed all around it. But in bringing together the tradition of wood engraved politically* radical illustration derived from the Hone*/Cruikshank* pamphlets of 20 years before and Seymour's* images for *Figaro in London* from the 1830s, the use of a highly evolved persona drawn from popular culture to serve as a satirical presiding spirit (as well as 'Figaro', 'Punch' had already been used in such a role by Douglas Jerrold* for the short-lived 1832 *Punch in London*), and the example of French satirical periodicals (Phillipon's Paris-based magazine *Charivari* gave *Punch* its subtitle, 'The London Charivari'), *Punch*

But there were other factors at work in sustaining *Punch's* success, more to do with its understanding of business practice and the marketplace for periodicals than the quality of its contributors. *Punch* made itself available in a tempting variety of formats*: weekly* single issues, monthly compilations which came in decorative wrappers and carried a considerable amount of advertisement* and half-yearly volumes, which included an elaborate and often highly decorative index. Additionally, later in the century, *Punch* was reissued in stereotype* versions, usually with five half-yearly volumes bound up in cloth to form huge single volumes, thus becoming one of what must be one of very few periodicals from the nineteenth century to sell its early volumes all over again. Ever astute in making use of its famous brand name, *Punch issued* a yearly pocket-book, volumes collecting together the almanacks, volumes of drawings drawn from its pages by individual artists (Doyle's cartoons were particularly popular), the volume reprinting of *Punch* contributions by well-established authors like Jerrold and Thackeray and the compilation of 'histories' drawn from *Punch* commentaries.

Famous in its early years for outspoken criticism of various social ills, *Punch* lost much of its radical energy in its later history but remained a broad-based repository of social and political* commentary. It continued to attract artists of the calibre of Tenniel, du Maurier and Samborne* to draw its cartoons and a range of now relatively little known humorous writers including Shirley Brooks, Gilbert a Beckett, George Augustus Sala*, George and Weedon Grossmith and Andrew Lang*. Long outliving the nineteenth century, there were several attempts to sustain the magazine into the twenty-first century, but it finally expired in 2002. **BM**
Sources: Altick1997, Burnand 1904, Engen 1990, Price 1957, Spielmann 1895.

PURKESS, GEORGE (c.1802-1862?); PURKESS, GEORGE (c.1832-1892) George Purkess, sometimes spelled 'Purkiss' and his son of the same name were two important figures positioned on the margins of nineteenth-century journalism as their publications, while popular*, were, for the most part, a challenge to the respectable establishment.

According to the 1841 census, George Purkess (senior) was born c.1802. Certainly from the early 1830s, Purkess had begun to operate a bookselling and publishing* business out of his residence at 59/60 Dean Street, Soho. Purkess was part of the younger generation of printers turned radical pressmen, including George Vickers, William Strange*, Benjamin Cousins and, to a lesser extent, Edward Lloyd*. Links between these men were important as often several banded together to compose and circulate radical, violent and sometimes bawdy 'bon ton' periodicals such as the *New Moral World*

(1834-1835)*, the *Girls' and Boys' Penny Magazine* (1832-1833) and the *Lives of the Most Notorious Highwaymen, Footpads and Murderers* (1836-1837). Purkess continued in this business right up to his death.

Purkess was succeeded in the business by his son and the common themes which guided their publications meant that the transition was almost seamless. George Purkess (junior) had entered the publishing industry by the 1850s and during that decade worked alongside his father at their offices in Compton Street, Soho, publishing penny bloods, the titles of which appeared weekly* in the advertisement* columns* of *Reynolds's Newspaper* (1850-1967). Yet Purkess was of a different generation from that of his father, and, as a member of the 'old Unity Club', had important links with the bohemian journalists of the 1860s and 1870s. By 1858, Purkess had acquired retail premises in St Alban's Place, Edgware Road, and by the mid-1860s had moved his publishing business to the Strand where he took control of the famous *Illustrated Police News** (1863-1938). A reporter for the *Pall Mall Gazette** in 1886 described Purkess's publishing offices as dark, diminutive and dismal, and could not fail to draw attention to the crowd of persons gathered outside every day gazing at the front page illustrations of the current issue pasted on a placard. In addition to the weekly* newspaper, Purkess simultaneously published short biographies of famous murderers and a rather risqué periodical, the *Family Doctor and People's Medical Advisor* (1885-1918). Purkess junior died unexpectedly from tuberculosis. **RHC**
Sources: British Book Trade Index, Census 1841, Census 1891, McCalman 1988, *Waterloo*.

PYNE, WILLIAM HENRY (1770-1843) London-based William Henry Pyne forged his career as an art critic and journalist (fl. 1812-1841) through the contacts made and experiences gained in his primary work as a watercolour artist and illustrator*. He wrote and illustrated a number of books but also contributed articles, art criticism, and illustrations to the *Literary Gazette**, *Fraser's Magazine** and other periodicals largely to balance the financial losses suffered through his private publishing ventures.

Pyne was closely associated with publisher* Rudolph Ackermann, contributing the illustrated series 'Observations on the Rise and Progress of Painting in Watercolours' (Nov. 1812-April 1813) to Ackermann's monthly* *Repository of Arts, Literature, Commerce, Manufactures, Fashions and Politics* (1809-1828). He also wrote for *Arnold's Magazine* *of the Fine Arts* (1831-1834), furnished *Fraser's Magazine* with the series 'The Greater and Lesser Stars of Old Pall Mall' (Nov. 1840-Dec. 1841), and had a short-lived proprietorship* and editorship* of the weekly* miscellany* the *Somerset House Gazette* (1823-1824). From 1820-1822 Pyne supplied gossipy*, anecdotal narratives of London life to the *Literary Gazette* under the pseudonym* 'Ephraim Hardcastle' which were collected in two volumes entitled *Wine and Walnuts* (1823). **CW**

Sources: *Grove Art Online*, Jos 1883, Myers 1996, *ONDB*, Roget 1891.

Q

QUAKER PERIODICALS Quaker periodicals of the nineteenth century reflect the often stormy changes that shook this historically insular denomination as it responded to evangelical and then liberal theology. Quaker periodicals offer a window onto many of the century's reform movements, in which Quakers exerted an influence greatly exceeding what might be expected from their relatively small numbers (14,000 to 17,000).

The insularity of the Quaker community at this time is reflected in the content of the first Quaker periodical publication, William Alexander's *Annual Monitor**, consisting of the obituaries* of all British Quakers from the previous year. The *Friends' Monthly Magazine* (1830-1831) was the first Quaker monthly*, while the literary annual* *Aurora Borealis* (1833), with contributions from early Quaker liberals like Bernard Barton and William Howitt*, briefly foreshadowed the turn that Quakerism would take later in the century. Encouraged by evangelicalism elsewhere, some Quakers had begun to recognize scripture as a higher authority than the inner light and even to advocate sacraments proscribed by traditional Quaker practice. The Manchester 'Beaconites', responding to Isaac Crewdson's evangelical *Beacon to the Society of Friends* (1835), separated from the Society and began publishing the monthly* *Inquirer**. Another more moderate evangelical monthly was the *Yorkshireman,* edited* and owned by Luke Howard and published* by Alexander from 1832 to 1837.

In 1837, William Bell, an abolitionist and temperance advocate, inaugurated the monthly *Irish Friend*, which ran until 1842, when its place was taken simultaneously by the *Friend** of London and the *British Friend* of Glasgow (the former taking a more evangelical stance in contrast to the latter's traditional position). All three publications combined articles on Quaker history, biography and doctrine with articles on religious and political reform. By the 1890s, the *British Friend* was leading a reconciliation of traditional Quaker doctrine with the liberal theology emerging across Britain's religious landscape.

In 1867, William Westlake began the *Friends' Quarterly Examiner**. This first Quaker review, though run entirely on a volunteer basis, allowed a more thorough examination of Quaker ideas and drew contributions from most major Quaker intellectuals. More polemical was the *Manchester Friend* (1871-1873), in which the Free Friends' movement of David Duncan promoted a freethinking theology informed by new scientific ideas and Biblical criticism. While liberalism was slowly displacing evangelicalism in the Society of Friends, the growth of Quaker missionary* work both at home and abroad was evident in several late nineteenth-century periodicals, including the *Monthly Record* (1869-1891) and *Our Missions* (1897-1917). The more liberal but short-lived monthly, *Essayist and Friends' Review* (Jan.-March 1893) focused on art and literature*. The monthly *Quakeriana,* subtitled 'books, antiques, prints', survived for two years (1894-1896) before becoming *Quaker Notes and Queries* for one issue and folding. The most significant Quaker periodical of the 1890s was John Wilhelm Rowntree's review, *Present-Day Papers*, published irregularly (1898), then monthly (1899-1902). Here Rowntree and other leading Quaker liberals urged Friends away from biblical literalism, reclaiming the priority of the 'inner light' over scripture, and renewing the liberal movement begun 25 years earlier in the *Manchester Friend*. **DU**
Sources: Altholz 1989, Bronner 1990, Isichei 1970, Kennedy 2001, Mortimer 1963.

QUARTERLY JOURNAL OF SCIENCE (1878); MONTHLY JOURNAL OF SCIENCE (1879); JOURNAL OF SCIENCE (1879-1885) At the end of 1863, James Samuelson* resigned his editorship* of the *Popular Science Review* (1861-1876) and joined one of its regular contributors, William Crookes*, in founding the more elite *Quarterly Journal of Science* in January 1864. He then purchased the copyright* of the ailing *Edinburgh New Philosophical Journal* (1826-April 1864) and amalgamated the two periodicals in July 1864. Published by John Churchill, the *Quarterly Journal of Science* was modelled on the religious* and political* quarterlies* as a 'review of the progress of science in all parts of the world', and aimed at practising scientists, science students and the general reading public. Priced* at 5s, issues were 112 pages. with advertisements* at £2 a page. With a circulation* of ca. 2,000, the journal contained signed commissioned and beautifully illustrated* articles by both major and minor scientists, reports on the progress of science and technology, on scientific societies, and signed book reviews*. The masthead* motto, *Post Terebras Lux* (light after shadow), identified its natural theological tone. Leaders* focused on science and religion, public health and science* education.

When Samuelson resigned in 1870 to study law, Crookes took over as proprietor*, editor and printer with a new series, using it to promote his work on spiritualism. A subtitle was added: *Annals of mining, metallurgy, engineering, industrial arts, manufactures and technology*. After issuing 15 volumes, and to speed up reporting, in February 1879 Crookes turned it into the *Monthly Journal of Science* (1879), 48 pp, price* 1s 6d. Later in 1879 Crookes passed the editorship to a business associate, John W. Slater, who dropped 'monthly' from the title. Crookes retained a position on the editorial board and remained the printer. Reasons for closure in December 1885 are unclear, though references to abuse from anti-vivisectionists offer a clue. **WB**

Sources: Barton 1998a, Brock 2008, Knight 1996.

QUARTERLY MUSICAL MAGAZINE AND REVIEW (1818-1830) With backing from the London music publisher*, Samuel Chappell, an expository approach modelled on the *Edinburgh Review*, and the clear editorial voice of the Norfolk newspaperman Richard Mackenzie Bacon*, the *Quarterly Musical Magazine and Review* attempted a bold experiment in autumn 1818, the union of music* and literature* in one periodical. Especially striking was its elevation of music aesthetics, history*, manners and society over the treatment of music as a commodity. There was no printed music section. Remarkably, the magazine* lasted nearly 12 years, four times longer than any previous English music journal. It appeared first under the imprint of the London bookseller Baldwin, Cradock & Joy, and then under Hurst, Chance & Co (mid-1827-spring 1830, despite 'December 1828' on its final number, No. 40). The quarterly* publication interval, always erratic, was deliberately lengthened in mid-1826.

From his provincial base near Norwich, Bacon, an informed musical amateur, wrote or compiled, then printed, most of the *Musical Magazine* himself, drawing on his Handelian tastes, knowledge of singing, library of English and foreign books, desire for *rapprochement* between amateurs and professionals, and flair for crafting pseudonymous* letters* 'To the Editor'. Meanwhile he built up a range of real correspondents, composers, organists and other practitioners, some local, some from London or abroad, offering news* and inside information for the journal's intelligence pages and reviews*. Among the most notable were George Smart, William Ayrton, Henry Bishop, Cipriani Potter, Ferdinando Paer, Marie Henri Beyle ('Stendhal') and

William Horsley, the last a regular (anonymous*) reviewer and musical adviser to Bacon. Despite its failure, *Musical Magazine* deepened the level of British enquiry into music while also advocating major national improvements, from the founding of the Royal Academy of Music and the spread of provincial festivals to the artistic value of through-sung opera in English. **LeL**

Source: Langley 1983.

QUARTERLY REVIEW (1809-1967) The high Tory *Quarterly Review* was launched on the initiative of publisher John Murray* – encouraged by Foreign Secretary George Canning – to counter the Whig *Edinburgh Review*, deemed to be dangerously unpatriotic. Canning and his friend George Ellis secured William Gifford*, former editor of the *Anti-Jacobin*, as editor*, and further support came from Walter Scott* and others, including Robert Southey. The *Quarterly* was published by the house of Murray throughout the century. Priced at 6s in 1824, issues were hefty, typically 250-300pp in that year.

From the outset, it covered a range of topics – travel, biography, literature*, arts, science*, medicine*, theology – and a regular 'political'* article provided a Tory line on current issues. Articles (conventionally anonymous* and normally up to 40 pages long) were prefaced by one or more titles of books or pamphlets which were the subject of review, either specifically or obliquely. Each issue contained a dozen or so articles, and ran to some 300 closely-printed pages. Circulation* grew rapidly. In 1817, when some 10,000 copies were printed, Southey considered that the actual readership* was five times that number. It became standard reading for Tory squires and clergy country-wide.

Under Gifford (1809-1824), it attacked Whigs and radicals fiercely, and was hostile to any kind of innovation – a notorious adverse review of Keats's *Endymion* in 1818 is a case in point. Where, exceptionally, it addressed social issues, as in articles by Southey on the Poor Laws in 1812, its tone was paternalistic.

On Gifford's retirement, Murray engaged John Taylor Coleridge, nephew of the poet, for a short period, replacing him with John Gibson Lockhart*, who served 1826-1854. Following the passage of the Reform Bill in 1832, the political articles were written for over 20 years by John Wilson Croker* until the appointment of a new editor, Whitwell Elwin* (1854-1860), who for a year or two secured Gladstone – at that time a Peelite – and, following him, Lord Robert Cecil as the review's main political contributor. Cecil's more than 30 articles constitute the single most impressive body of political writing in the *Quarterly*, though the political articles (1881-1892) of Louis Jennings*, attacking Chamberlain and Gladstone, are noteworthy successors to the anti-radical tradition which began under Gifford.

With the growth of the daily* press, the *Quarterly* declined in political influence, but continued to enjoy considerable prestige in Tory circles, and was a prominent feature of the Victorian literary and intellectual scene. Notable contributors included Matthew Arnold*, Bulwer Lytton*, Lord Acton* and J. A. Froude*. **DIM**

Sources: Morphet 2003, John Murray Archives, Shattock 1989, Shine 1949, Smiles 1891, *Waterloo, Wellesley.*

QUARTERLY REVIEWS Quarterly reviews were serious, general reviews*, published four times a year, which included all forms of literature, from history*, philosophy*, economics and mathematics, to science*, art, theology and travel writing, in their remit. The quarterlies' approach to knowledge was non-hierarchical and non-specialized. Contemporary poetry*, fiction and drama occupied a relatively small proportion of their contents. The *Edinburgh Review**, founded in 1802, established itself as a model, and became the review against which all subsequent quarterlies were measured. The 'great triumvirate' of early quarterlies, the Whig-affiliated *Edinburgh*, the Tory *Quarterly Review**, founded in response to the *Edinburgh* in 1809, and the Radical *Westminster Review**, established in 1824, all had clear political* agendas. The next generation of quarterlies often had sectarian affiliations, or at least a specific focus, among them the *Foreign Quarterly** (1827), devoted to European literature* and thought; the *Dublin Review** (1836), the organ of the Catholic revival; the short-lived Oxford-supported *London Review** (1829) and its namesake the *London Review* (1835) which amalgamated with the *Westminster* in 1836 and the *British and Foreign Review** (1835), with its focus on contemporary European politics. Other quarterlies were founded at mid-century: the *North British** (1844), initially the organ of the Free Church of Scotland; the nonconformist *British Quarterly** (1845); the High Church *Christian Remembrancer**(1845); the Methodist *London Quarterly** (1853); the Unitarian-affiliated *National Review* (1855); the liberal Catholic *Home and Foreign** (1862).

Each quarterly number was approximately 250 octavo pages in length, containing between eight and ten articles. Their price* ranged between 4s and 6s. The price was indicative of their middle and upper-middle class* readership*. With their generous margins, clear type and good quality paper* the bound volumes of the quarterlies resembled books rather than periodical publications. Unlike their predecessors, the eighteenth-century monthly reviews, the quarterlies were selective in the books they chose to review and often robust and opinionated in their judgments. And again unlike the earlier reviews, they were independent of their publishers* in terms of the books they selected.

The bulky quarterlies dominated the first four decades of the nineteenth century in terms of critical and political* influence. But the emergence of a responsible newspaper press in the 1840s began to erode their political power, and the length of their articles proved unattractive when set against the shorter reviews of the new monthly* magazines*. Nevertheless, quarterlies remained a feature of the reviewing scene until the end of the century, and the *Edinburgh Review*, which Walter Bagehot claimed 'began the system' at the beginning of the nineteenth century continued into the twentieth, ceasing publication only in 1929. **JS**

Sources: Bagehot 1884, Klancher 1987, Shattock 1989, *Wellesley.*

QUEEN (1861-1967) Started in 1861 as the *Queen: the ladies' newspaper* by Samuel Beeton*, this became one of the most important magazines* of the late nineteenth and early twentieth centuries. At first Beeton intended it to be simply an up-market weekly newspaper, reporting mainly on social events, employment, artistic and cultural matters, as well as entertainments; in its first few years it also contained much information about Queen Victoria. It was of broadsheet format* but used heavier, and eventually glossier, paper* than was usual for newspapers. However, in 1862 Beeton sold it to William Cox, who aimed it at a more precise market*. The social events now almost exclusively referred to such upper-class* concerns as The London Season and fashionable weddings. As well as romantic serial* fiction, Cox introduced Parisian fashion*– an important development.

By the 1880s the *Queen* had become the preferred weekly* of ladies of the 'upper ten-thousand', and although much of its circulation* was doubtless due to celebrity* fantasies, it did reflect a wide range of matters of interest to upper-class women, so that alongside reviews* of premieres by composers such as Tchaikovsky and hints on where to lodge one's servants when estivating at Biarritz can be found reports of the activities of such organizations as the Women's Co-operative Guild and various philanthropic bodies, especially those for females in reduced circumstances. Its success and claim to be read by 'the upper ten-thousand' made it a favoured title for advertisers* and in the 1880s and 1890s, Queen typically carried as many pages of advertisements as of editorial matter.

As well as pages of commercial advertisements, it had huge success with its 'Exchange' or 'Exchange and Mart' columns in which readers offered to sell or exchange goods. This led Cox to launch a separate publication, Exchange and Mart*, consisting entirely of these. In Queen's heyday, from (c.1880-1914), it was the glossy to end all glossies, and saw off competition* from such less exalted titles as the Lady* or the Gentlewoman*. Although it was more than a fashionable magazine*, this was ultimately its function. After the First World War, however, it faced stiff competition, especially from Vogue, and in 1967 merged* with Harper's Bazaar. **DD**
Sources: Beetham 1996, Queen, White 1970.

QUELCH, HENRY (HARRY) (1858-1913) Harry Quelch, journalist* and editor*, was one of the few working-class* contributors to the Social Democratic Federation's weekly paper, Justice*. Quelch gave up his job as a meat porter when Henry Hyndman passed the editorship of Justice to him in 1887, a position he held almost continuously until his death. His journalism, often published under the pseudonym* 'The Tattler', exposed working-class hardships unblinkingly, contemporaries describing his political* polemic as incisive. One measure of the success of his reportage is that his vivid reports on London's unemployment problems may have inspired Charles Booth's research into the London poor.

In other political areas Quelch was more reactionary, as in his criticism of the women's suffrage movement, with Ernest Belfort Bax*, in the pages of Justice. Beyond his work for Justice, Quelch was editor of the monthly Social Democrat, wrote for the British Socialist (1911-1913) and was managing director of Twentieth-Century Press from 1891 to 1909 (where he briefly shared an office with Lenin). After his death, Bax published a selection of his journalism as a tribute, Harry Quelch: Literary Remains (1914). **DM**
Sources: Bax 1914, Hunt 1996, Lenin 1913, ODNB.

QUILTER, HARRY (1851-1907) After receiving his BA (1874) and MA (1877) from Cambridge University, Harry Quilter –journalist*, editor* and proprietor*– trained for a career in law as well as studying at the Slade School of Art. He began his journalist's* career by contributing art criticism to the Spectator* (1876-1887). A prolific writer, Quilter also contributed articles throughout the 1880s and 1890s to the Contemporary Review*, the Cornhill Magazine*, Fraser's*, the Fortnightly Review*, Macmillan's Magazine*, the National Review*, the New Review*, the Nineteenth Century* and his own Universal Review*. Quilter is primarily known as the founding editor* of the influential but short-lived Universal Review*, which blended high quality illustrations*, political* articles, and literature*.

Throughout his career, Quilter reviewed* art, interior design, theatre*, and literature. He also wrote on contemporary politics*, education and women's rights*, which he opposed.

In his book, Is Marriage a Failure? (1888), Quilter famously perpetuated a newspaper controversy created by the Daily Telegraph* which had invited correspondence* on this question, as a riposte to allegations against contemporary marriage by 'Mona Caird' in the Westminster Review*. By selecting from the 27,000 letters received by the Telegraph and provocative editing, Quilter tapped into conservative reactions to this aspect of the woman question and created a bestseller by recirculating repackaged journalism. While a supporter of Pre-Raphaelitism, Quilter was an outspoken opponent of aestheticism, arguing that it embodied 'the lowest theory of art-usefulness, and the most morbid and sickly art-results'. Such criticism led him to support John Ruskin* in Ruskin's dispute with James McNeill Whistler*. **LML**
Sources: Fisher 1984, ODNB, Quilter 1880.

QUIVER (1861-1926) An addition to the list of periodicals published by Cassell & Co.*, notably the Cassell's Popular Educator (1852-1855) and the Cassell's Family Paper*, the Quiver began as an unillustrated 1d weekly* of a dozen pages. The paper took up a strongly evangelical stance, without denominational affiliation. According to the subtitle, the journal's aims were the Defence of Biblical Truth and the Advancement of Religion in the Homes of the People*. 'The Half-Hour Bible Class', 'Our Pulpit' and 'Our Missionary Corner' were among the regular columns*. But there was also an entertaining 'Youths' Department' and a generous supply of fiction: 'The Channings' (1861-1862) was the first of a number of best-selling novels by Ellen Wood* to be serialized* in the Quiver.

After the death of John Cassell* in 1865, the

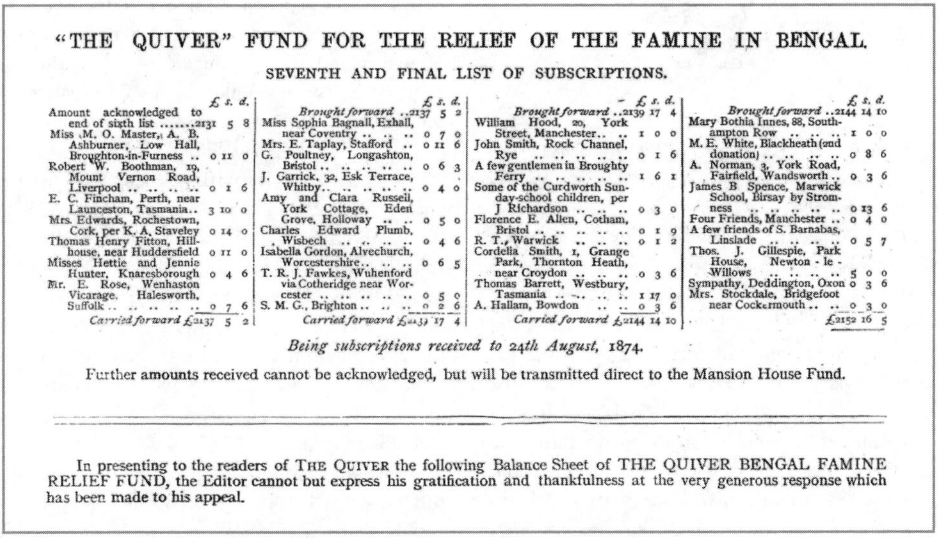

"THE QUIVER" FUND FOR THE RELIEF OF THE FAMINE IN BENGAL.

SEVENTH AND FINAL LIST OF SUBSCRIPTIONS.

	£ s. d.		£ s. d.		£ s. d.		£ s. d.
Amount acknowledged to end of sixth list	2131 5 8	Brought forward ..	2137 5 2	Brought forward ..	2139 17 4	Brought forward ..	2144 14 10
Miss M. O. Master, A. B. Ashburner, Low Hall, Broughton-in-Furness ..	0 11 0	Miss Sophia Bagnall, Exhall, near Coventry	0 7 0	William Hood, 20, York Street, Manchester.. ..	1 0 0	Mary Bothia Innes, 88, Southampton Row	1 0 0
		Mrs. E. Taplay, Stafford ..	0 11 6	John Smith, Rock Channel, Rye	0 1 6	M. E. White, Blackheath (2nd donation)	0 8 6
Robert W. Boothman, 19, Mount Vernon Road, Liverpool	0 1 6	G. Poultney, Longashton, Bristol	0 6 3	A few gentlemen in Broughty Ferry	1 6 1	A. Norman, 3, York Road, Fairfield, Wandsworth ..	0 3 6
E. C. Fincham, Perth, near Launceston, Tasmania.	3 10 0	J. Garrick, 32, Esk Terrace, Whitby	0 4 0	Some of the Curdworth Sunday-school children, per J Richardson	0 3 0	James B Spence, Marwick School, Birsay by Stromness	0 13 6
Mrs. Edwards, Rochestown, Cork, per K. A. Staveley	0 14 0	Amy and Clara Russell, York Cottage, Eden Grove, Holloway	0 5 0	Florence E. Allen, Cotham, Bristol	0 1 9	Four Friends, Manchester ..	0 4 0
Thomas Henry Fitton, Hillhouse, near Huddersfield	0 11 0	Charles Edward Plumb, Wisbech	0 4 6	R. T., Warwick	0 1 2	A few friends of S. Barnabas, Linslade	0 5 7
Misses Hettie and Jennie Hunter, Knaresborough	0 4 6	Isabella Gordon, Alvechurch, Worcestershire.. ..	0 6 5	Cordelia Smith, 1, Grange Park, Thornton Heath, near Croydon	0 3 6	Thos. J. Gillespie, Park House, Newton - le - Willows	5 0 0
Mr. E. Rose, Wenhaston Vicarage, Halesworth,		T. R. J. Fawkes, Wuhenford via Cotheridge near Worcester	0 5 0	Thomas Barrett, Westbury, Tasmania	1 17 0	Sympathy, Deddington, Oxon	0 3 6
Suffolk	0 7 6	S. M. G., Brighton	0 2 6	A. Hallam, Bowdon	0 3 6	Mrs. Stockdale, Bridgefoot near Cockermouth	0 3 0
Carried forward £2137	5 2	Carried forward £2139	17 4	Carried forward £2144	14 10	£2152	16 5

Being subscriptions received to 24th August, 1874.

Further amounts received cannot be acknowledged, but will be transmitted direct to the Mansion House Fund.

In presenting to the readers of THE QUIVER the following Balance Sheet of THE QUIVER BENGAL FAMINE RELIEF FUND, the Editor cannot but express his gratification and thankfulness at the very generous response which has been made to his appeal.

Figure 56: Fund raising in the *Quiver*, Aug. 1874, 832.

subtitle changed to *An Illustrated* Magazine for Sunday and General Reading*, reflecting not only the introduction of pictures, but also a more general shift in the balance between instruction and amusement. Lavish special Christmas* numbers were created, like *Golden Arrows* in 1869. Around this time the editorial* team seems to have been joined by the young G. H. Bonavia Hunt, who was ordained in 1878 and remained in charge of the journal until 1905. **GL**

Sources: Altholz 1989, Cutt 1979, Nowell-Smith 1958, *ODNB*, Sullivan 1984.

R

RACING CALENDAR (1773-1912) *Containing an account of the plates, matches, and sweepstakes, run for in Great Britain and Ireland* as its subtitle claimed, the *Racing Calendar* was published* by five members of the Weatherby family during the nineteenth century. Edward Weatherby was also a contributor. However, it was John Cheney who originated and published the *Racing Calendar* (1727-1750) as the official organ of the Jockey Club. The *Calendar* functioned as a 'gentleman's guide' to betting by providing all the required information on form and breeding. Cheney's name and his part in this publication were lost as a consequence of James Weatherby purloining all the findings from Cheney's original publication without any acknowledgement in the new *Racing Calendar*. Printed in London by C. W. and H. Reynell, it consisted of 365 pages at 17 cm. In 1846 it was issued twice annually, to subscribers only, at 21s per annum.

As the *Calendar* provided a comprehensive coverage of all matters relating to the turf, detailing forthcoming races, results, betting rates, pedigree and description of runners, it was an important advertising* medium for all those interested in the turf and field world. **DHL**
Sources: *ODNB, Waterloo.*

RACING TIMES (c.1836-1868) The *Racing Times* was a 38 cm weekly* of eight pages with a circulation* of approximately 1,120 in the 1860s. Its price* ranged from 1d to 4d at various times throughout its run. It was published* from 1851 onwards by Thomas Storr Parr and Henry Wilde in their Grub Street, London offices and by James Collins and Thomas Hollingsworth in 1868. While not an illustrated* broadsheet, the *Racing Times* had a striking masthead*.

As part of its news* reporting of the British turf, 'Priam' offered predictions for the coming racing week in a popular weekly column*, 'Priam's Chant' (1851-1864). Offering the gentleman reader* a catalogue of possible horses to back in future races, the column maintained a light-hearted tone and catchy rhyme scheme. For example, in the 3 December 1860 number 'Priam' offers his predictions for the Innkeeper's Plate with the lines 'With *Heads or Tails* I'll try to win,/And stick to that through thick and thin;/Next I will to *Roscommon* go,/And there the *Magenta* colour show'.

In 1866 the paper changed to include coverage of London amateur dramatics, along with publication of poetry*and short, comedic sketches; this expanded contents was reflected in a title change* to the *Racing Times and Amateur Dramatic Chronicle* and the end of 'Priam's Chant'. Thereafter a broadening of the paper's sporting* focus reflected the growth of sport and recreation culture since 1850, though its advertisements* did not change. Regular columns reporting on rugby, aquatics, inter-University sporting contests between Oxford and Cambridge, and pedestrian contests now appeared, as did a larger number of advertisements, alongside extant columns with a racing focus, including lists of meetings and acceptances, Derby reports, and racing intelligence.

While not as widely circulated* as other popular turf papers such as the *Racing World** and the *Racing Calendar**, the *Racing Times* was a solid example of the periodical appealing to the gentleman sportsman that went into decline in the latter part of the century. **SRS**
Sources: Huggins 2000, *Waterloo.*

RACING WORLD AND NEWMARKET SPORTSMAN (1887-1929) The *Racing World and Newmarket Sportsman*, a 1d weekly*, was edited* by H. Ross. Reflecting an expanding definition of sport*, it was one of a number of specialist sports titles that emerged after 1870 and it coincided with the inclusion of racing tips in New Journalism* papers such as the *Star**. Although its subtitle claimed that it was a *journal of sporting, theatrical and general intelligence,* there was little for the theatre-goer or indeed for the seeker of general intelligence. This was a paper dedicated to betting on horses, often boasting in its masthead* of the winners it had picked the previous week. It reported on races all over Britain and sometimes beyond, as well as conveying information about forthcoming races and offering tips purportedly based on insider knowledge. Out every Saturday, a special midnight edition also appeared on Mondays, initially at the price* of 1s. That anyone was willing to pay so much suggests that the up-to-date information it carried on the form and weight of runners and the jockeys likely to be riding them, betting information, as well as conditions at the track, was held in high esteem. Even more up-to-date tips were occasionally available by telegram. Readers* who paid the reply for 36 words could receive the final selection from the paper's expert the morning of the race. Not illustrated* at first, by 1890 it carried a weekly 'portrait gallery' carrying engravings of jockeys, owners, trainers and anyone related to the racing world.

Although the *Racing Times** had folded in 1868, the *Racing World* did face some considerable competition*, which it largely fought off. The *Racing Times* was revived twice: first in 1883 to be absorbed by *Racecourse* in 1886, and then in 1891, this time being incorporated by the *Racing World* in 1893, which even outlived the *Racing Calendar**. MaT

Sources: BL Catalogue, Goodbody 1988, Mason 1994, *Racing World* 1887-1900, Waterloo.

RAILTON, HERBERT (1857-1910) A prolific if sometimes repetitive illustrator*, Herbert Railton used his training as an architectural draughtsman to construct a version of English topography and history* that found widespread favour in late Victorian periodicals. His style of pen drawing using a broken line technique was well adapted to the new forms of line-block printing which came to dominate magazine illustration from the late 1880s on, and he worked extensively for many prominent journals especially the *English Illustrated Magazine**, the *Graphic**, *Good Words**, and the *Magazine of Art**. His evocation of a picturesque and historic nation exemplified in its heritage of ancient buildings became popular enough to sustain the reprinting of much of his magazine work in volume form and to influence a whole generation of graphic chroniclers of British architecture. **BM**
Sources: Engen 1990, Houfe 1978.

RAILWAY BOOKSTALLS See W. H. Smith.

RAILWAY PRESS Almost as soon as the first major railway, the Liverpool & Manchester, was completed in 1830, a new branch of the press emerged to report on the progress of the industry and publicize potential projects for investment (see also Transport press*). The first railway journal was the *Railway Gazette* (1835), a fortnightly which only survived a few issues and is not to be confused with later publications of the same name. That same year, the most prominent journal of the nineteenth century, initially called the *Railway Magazine and Annals of Science* began, changing its name to the *Railway Journal*. It quickly became known as *Herapath*, after its editor*, John Herapath who was an able writer but prone to strong and rather eccentric views such as his ill-founded dislike of excursion services and express trains. *Railway Magazine's* most prominent rival was the *Railway Times* which was particularly fervent in its opposition to any government interference in the railways and claimed a circulation* of 27,000 by 1842.

The railway mania (1842-1845) involved hundreds of railway schemes being put forward by promoters, not all of them genuine or honest. Publishers seized on the opportunity by creating their own obsession with a proliferation of railway journals which, like the railways themselves, could not possibly all be viable. By October 1845, there were 29 railway periodicals in England, so many that the obvious names were soon taken and less likely ones appeared, such as *Railway King*, *Railway Chart* and *Railway Engine*. There was a further two each in Scotland and Ireland. The *Iron Times* published daily* and *Steam Times,* three times per week; a further seven appeared twice weekly while the rest were weekly*.

This vast press was aimed at investors and its quality was variable. Publications provided copious amounts of information on railway bills and projects, but their proprietors* or editors* were wont to express their opinions forcibly, however ignorant or misguided. Their finances tended to be dependent on advertising* from railway promoters which made them liable to editorial interference, nor were they always impartial. Herapath, on his masthead*, claimed his was the only journal that was 'neither the property of an engineer, nor under the control of a railway company'. This may have been a relatively accurate if rather sweeping statement, but Herapath himself could not claim detachment since he invested heavily in railway schemes and frequently turned up at shareholders' meetings to shout abuse at the directors. Therefore the thousands of ordinary people who were putting their meagre life savings in an industry that was experiencing a huge speculative boom were not served well by the railway press. In 1846, the mania collapsed and most of these publications disappeared that year. By the end of the decade, only *Herapath*, the *Railway Times*, the *Railway Gazette* (the second publication of that name) and the *Railway Record* survived.

Some more specialized journals, providing technical details, began to appear rather later, notably the *Railway Engineer* (1860-1935). Towards the end of the century, the contemporary type of railway press began to emerge. Two monthly* journals aimed at enthusiasts and trainspotters started publication in the 1890s, *Moore's Monthly Magazine* (subsequently renamed the *Locomotive*) in 1896 and the *Railway Magazine* the following year, and they were to form the basis of the popular railway press serving the growing number of enthusiasts. **CTW**
Sources: Freeman 1999, Simmons 1995, Wolmar 2007.

RAMBLER: A WEEKLY MAGAZINE OF HOME AND FOREIGN LITERATURE, POLITICS, SCIENCE, AND ART (1848-1862) Following the ecclesiastical chaos and estrangement that accompanied John Henry Newman's conversion to Roman Catholicism in 1845, John Moore Capes* founded the *Rambler* as a unifying and healing focus for the new community of Catholic converts. Capes wrote of his vision to Newman in 1846, explaining that the journal would be 'entering into all subjects of literary*, philosophic* and moral interest, treating them as a person would who believes Catholicism to be the only true religion'. Capes also intermittently was its editor* (1848-1852, 1854-1857; etc.).

Capes directed the *Rambler*'s policy and content, writing a large amount of the copy, assisted by his brother Frederick and his friend James Spencer Northcote (1821-1907). Home and foreign literature*, politics*, science*, music* and the fine arts were included. Starting in January as a weekly* with 16 quarto pages, by August it had became a monthly. Although successful, financial concerns and the weight of responsibility led Capes in 1850 to give it more of a review* format*, which included moving to octavo size* and abandoning its double columns*. By 1852 Capes's ill-health prompted him to relinquish the editorship to Northcote. Richard Simpson* became assistant editor in 1854, his controversial articles upsetting some of the Catholic authorities in England and marking a style that continued with his later editorship. When the *Rambler* folded in 1862, Simpson and fellow proprietor* (and previous editor (1859-1862)) Sir John Acton*, launched a quarterly* review with a new title, the *Home and Foreign Review*, that continued the debates of its parent. CL

Sources: Altholz 1962, Sullivan, *Wellesley, Waterloo.*

RAMÉ, MARIA LOUISA See 'Ouida'

RANYARD, ARTHUR COWPER (1845-1894) Although a barrister and member of the London County Council, Ranyard was better known for his scientific* activities and it was in this direction that his journalistic activity was directed. Ranyard was an astronomer, and closely connected with the Royal Astronomical Society (RAS) since his nomination as Fellow in 1863. Ranyard worked as a sub-editor* (1871-1873) on *Nature*, and as Secretary to the RAS (1874-1880) he was involved in preparing papers for publication in its *Monthly Notices*. From 1871-1879 Ranyard worked on and eventually oversaw the production of the eclipse edition of the *Memoirs of the Royal Astronomical Society,* a special issue of the Society's annual *Memoirs* that

summarized the information for every eclipse between 1715 and 1871.

In 1888 Ranyard succeeded his friend Richard Anthony Proctor* as editor and proprietor* of *Knowledge*. Ranyard brought his expertise in photographic reproduction to the magazine and, under his editorship, *Knowledge* became well-known for its high-quality collotype reproductions of photographs*. A popular figure within the scientific community, Ranyard drew on his personal connections to solicit contributions to *Knowledge*. JEM

Sources: *ODNB*, RAS Ranyard MS 1-10, Wesley 1895.

RATIONAL DRESS SOCIETY'S GAZETTE (1888-1889) The quarterly* *Rational Dress Society's Gazette* was published at a price* of 3d per number by the reformist Rational Dress Society. The Society's mission was to counter the 'tyranny of fashion*' by reducing the weight of clothing that women had to wear to no more than 7 pounds. 'The aim…of the Rational Dress Society is', we're told in the Editorial Note to the first number, 'to suggest a dress that shall give at the same time a minimum of weight, an even distribution of warmth, and perfect freedom of movement, and we hope, through the pages of the little Magazine, to express to our readers the dangers and inconveniences attendant upon our present system of dress and to point out such suggestions for its reform, as may prove of practical use'. Although some attention was focused on children's and men's clothing, the journal was primarily aimed at an audience of middle and upper-class* women, precisely those who wore the tight-laced corsets, heavy skirts, and narrow, high-heeled shoes at which the majority of the articles took aim. As a single-topic publication, the *Gazette* was a small magazine, each number comprising eight pages of letterpress, a cover and three full pages of advertisements*, mostly for shoemakers, fabrics, yarn, undergarments and other materials that might aid the aspiring rationally dressed woman.

While articles were anonymous*, Constance Wilde, Charlotte Carmichael Stopes and Laura McClaren were among the contributors. Editorship* is commonly attributed to Constance Wilde; both she and Oscar* supported the parent organization and its aims, and she also gave a number of public lectures on the topic of dress reform. The secretary of the organization (Mrs Carpenter-Fenton, for the first issue, and Mrs Hall for subsequent issues) was the only official identified by name, although various drawing room meetings were described at which

Viscountess Harberton, Mrs Stopes, Mrs Sharman Crawford and Mrs Oscar Wilde are identified as speakers.

The focus of articles is on health and the perception of beauty, as well as practical ways to achieve rational dress. Particular concerns centre around corseting with its potential ill-effects on health, the weighty encumbrance provided by women's clothing, including the health and safety concerns that arise from it, as well as the promotion of divided skirts, which are seen as a liberating benefit to women. Actual discussion of clothing styles is surprisingly abstract. The first issue contains several sketches of rational dress outfits for female children, but subsequent discussion of clothing is by description only. After six issues, the *Gazette* ceased publication; declining membership in the organization as well as the amateur status of its staff led to its demise. CAS/MWT

Sources: Belford 2000, Boardman at Fathom online, Fraser 2003.

REACH, ANGUS BETHUNE (1821-1856) Renowned for his vivid descriptive writing, comic inventiveness and prodigious powers of work, Angus B. Reach at mid-century had become one of London's best known literary* men. In addition to a vast output of miscellaneous writing, he made signal contributions to two of the most characteristic periodical genres* of the 1840s: detailed social* investigation* and illustrated* comic journalism. His illness and death at an early age removed from the literary scene one of its most popular and promising talents, and was universally construed as a warning against the dangers of authorial overwork.

Reach was born in Inverness and briefly attended the University of Edinburgh. While still in his teens, he wrote a variety of well-regarded descriptive articles for the *Inverness Courier*, then edited by Robert Carruthers. Coming to London in 1841, he joined the staff of the *Morning Chronicle*, where he would remain for the rest of his life. Beginning as a shorthand* court* and parliamentary* reporter, first at the Old Bailey and then in the House of Commons, he soon came to be relied upon for descriptive news*, pioneering a first-person 'picturesque' style of reporting that was widely imitated. In December 1849, as part of the same investigative series that employed Henry Mayhew and others as 'special correspondents', Reach reported on the condition of the labouring poor in the textile manufacturing districts of Lancashire and Yorkshire. Thereafter, he served as the *Chronicle's* principal reviewer* of drama and art, while also writing a week-

ly 'London Letter' for the *Inverness Courier* as well as the 'Town and Table Talk' column* for the *Illustrated London News*.

Concurrently with his newspaper work, Reach wrote articles and sketches for many periodicals, including *Ainsworth's Magazine* *Bentley's Miscellany*, *Fraser's Magazine* and *Chambers's Edinburgh Journal*. An early mentor was Douglas Jerrold*, who in 1844 featured regular contributions from Reach in his new *Illuminated Magazine*, and later in his *Weekly Newspaper* and *Shilling Magazine*. Reach's insistence on having his name, or at least his initials, attached to as much of his periodical work as possible helped to create a market* for his writing. His greatest success came in exploiting the 1840s craze for illustrated comic serials*, most conspicuously as co-editor* with Albert Smith* of *Punch* rival the *Man in the Moon*, of which he served as sole editor and principal contributor for most of 1848. Pointed but good-natured satire* of middleclass* types ('The Natural History of Humbugs') and the vagaries of railway travel and the railway investment mania ('The Comic Bradshaw') formed the staple of much of Reach's humorous writing, which was also published in book form by his friend David Bogue. Two short novels, also published by Bogue, were well received but not as popular as his comic work.

In the winter of 1854-1855, Reach was struck down by what appears to have been a cerebral hemorrhage ('softening of the brain'. in contemporary accounts), which left him completely incapacitated. His many friends in the London literary world raised funds for his support, and his best friend, Shirley Brooks*, quietly took over Reach's weekly newspaper work so that his salary would continue to be paid. Reach never recovered, and died the following year at the age of 35, leaving a wife in straitened circumstances. Because of his reputation within the literary fraternity for his strenuous writing schedule, Reach's illness and early death called forth much commentary in the newspapers about the dangers of over-taxing the brain by an excess of literary work, commentary whose echo can be heard in the brief accounts of Reach to be found in later nineteenth-century memoirs of the period. PL

Sources: *Lady's Newspaper* 1851, Mackay 1877, Simpson 1905.

READ, SAMUEL (1815-1883) Primarily a water colour painter, nonetheless Samuel Read has a place in the history of nineteenth-century periodicals largely through a long association with the *Illustrated London News*. Trained in wood*

engraving by J. W. Whymper, Read first drew for the *Illustrated London News* in 1844, and over many years contributed work in a number of genres* characteristic of the new illustrated* papers, topographical and landscape subjects, factory interiors and manufacturing processes and large-scale celebratory images of public events. In 1851 he became the first 'special artist' to be sent out by the magazine*, travelling first to Constantinople to draw for on the spot reports*, after which he travelled extensively through Europe. Read thus has some claim to have established the credentials of the detailed naturalistic graphic reportage for which the *Illustrated London News* became renowned. Eventually Read became art editor* for the magazine, and continued to contribute illustrations into the 1880s. **BM**
Sources: Engen 1990, Houfe 1978, *ODNB*.

READER: A REVIEW OF LITERATURE, SCIENCE, AND ART (1863-1867) The *Reader* was an attempt 'to supply the long-felt want of a first-class literary* newspaper, equal in literary merit and general ability to the political* press of London' (Prospectus). It was a combination of the *Athenaeum** and the *Publishers' Circular*– that is, a weekly* review of recent publications, but including a complete list of all works published, with particular attention to foreign literature, though its early years were marked by the influence of Christian Socialists including F. D. Maurice and Thomas Hughes. Other contributors included John Stuart Mill*, Michael Rossetti*, Charles Kingsley, Mark Pattison, Elizabeth Gaskell, Frances Power Cobbe* and many more of the most significant writers of the 1860s. Each issue cost 4d for 24 pages, and the weekly boasted that it was not connected to any specific publishing firm; that is, it was not in the business of puffing* writers on its own list, as other periodicals were wont to do. The *Academy**, founded in 1869, was influenced by the *Reader*. **MWT**
Sources: Sullivan, *Waterloo*.

READERS AND READERSHIP: REAL OR HISTORICAL READERS Discovering who actually read the many thousands of different newspapers, magazines and periodicals produced during the nineteenth century is a difficult task. Title and price* are guides to readership*: for example, Dickens's* *Household Words** at 2d was twice as expensive as the penny* journals and apparently aimed at middle-class* families rather than at the working-class readers of the *London Journal** at 1d. However, as most contemporary discussions of Victorian print culture noted, price did not necessarily restrict access. Expensive texts such as *The Times**

were often shared by groups of readers in commercial newsrooms, or coffee shops, and yet more read them a few days after publication when they were often redistributed through the post in order to recover something of their initial cost. Many readers also heard texts being read aloud, and such groups could include both literate and illiterate members.

The most famous investigation of the real readers of the periodical press written during the nineteenth century is Wilkie Collins's* essay 'The Unknown Public', which first appeared in *Household Words** in 1858. Collins explored the 'Answers to Correspondents'* columns* of 'the penny-novel Journal' in order to discover more about the kinds of readers that they attracted. Such columns provide some insight into the way in which actual readers made sense of texts and Collins argues that they show a profound ignorance on the part of many – but, as recent research into the women's magazines* of the later century suggests, such columns are controlled by the editor* and are often used to construct an ideal reader for the text. Evidence for those 'real readers' who did not write in is more difficult to find, but recent work by Kate Flint and other historians of reading practices has shown just how much detailed information about readers can be recovered from diaries, letters and other autobiographical sources. **SC**
Sources: Colclough 2007, Collins 1858, Flint 1993, Gerrard 1998, Report from the Select Committee on Newspaper Stamps 1851, Warren 2000.

READING Newspapers and magazines have become the subject of a spirited debate within the history of reading, and work in this area can be described as genuinely eclectic. Statistical research that explores mass* readerships* has been joined by qualitative attempts to recover the reading practices of individuals and communities. Recent scholarship has viewed these inquiries in tandem with wider concerns, including the construction of reading spaces, contemporary conceptualisations of periodical reading, the question of 'serial time', and relationships between reading and textual form. It is only possible to give a flavour of such work here, but the following critics provide useful introductions to debates in the field.

Richard Altick's long classic *English Common Reader* offers a contextualisation of the expansion of the periodical press within the broader framework of the rise of popular literacy. Nevertheless, calculating readerships from sales of newspaper stamps*, publishers' print runs or newsagents'* sales figures has particular difficulties, as Altick acknowledged.

The multiple readers of each copy of a newspaper or magazine – in gentleman's clubs, coffee houses, pubs and railway* carriages, as well as in library reading rooms* and upstairs and downstairs in the domestic circle – means accurate estimates of readership are notoriously difficult to come by.

David Vincent's attempts to place the spread of literacy within the context of changes to the postal service and other modes of distribution have been joined by studies which explore particular reading communities and spaces (such as Stephen Colclough's work on libraries* and railway* bookstalls). Of course, the presence of a magazine in a library catalogue rarely sheds light on actual readers or distinctive reading experiences. The attempt to recover individual or communal reading practices – from letters, diaries, autobiographies or commonplace books – has been a major development in recent years. Jonathan Rose includes some accounts of serial reading among working-class individuals, while correspondence* columns have been employed (by Margaret Beetham and others) to offer insights into women's and popular reading.

The Open University/University of London *Reading Experience Database 1450-1945* includes hundreds of entries on particular experiences of magazine, newspaper, and serial reading. It is searchable online and continues to expand. Research on individual reading practices creates an interesting dialogue with work that has tackled broader conceptualisations of reading in the nineteenth century. Debates over female periodical reading have been addressed by Kate Flint, while Brian Maidment has explored visual images of the dustman as newspaper reader. The imagined dangers and social benefits of newspaper reading have been discussed by Aled Jones, while Kelly Mays has focused on concerns over magazine reading. Perhaps equally significant, however, have been the attempts to rethink serial reading through engagement with more recent theoretical approaches. Linda K. Hughes and Michael Lund have discussed the 'progress and pause' of serial reading; Beetham has explored the periodical's 'open and closed' traits, while Mark W. Turner has also focused on relationships between time and textual form. Some of these questions were first opened up in 1989, in Laurel Brake and Anne Humpherys' Critical Theory Special Issue of *Victorian Periodicals Review*. **CRS**

Sources: Altick 1957/1998, Beetham 1990, Beetham 2000, Colclough 2007, Flint 1993, Hughes and Lund 1991, Jones 1996, Maidment 2001b, Mays 1995, Reading Experience Database 2007, Rose 2001, Turner 2006, Vincent 1989, *Victorian Periodicals Review* 12: 1989.

READING AND GENDER, READING AND CLASS
Throughout the nineteenth century, literacy rates rose, printing technologies* improved, taxes* on periodicals were revoked, circulating library* access spread, and cheap* books appeared in railway* bookstalls making reading a commonplace pastime that transcended gender and class. While these changes helped educate women and workers, many saw the expansion of reading as dangerous.

The consolidation of middle-class power gave its women both the leisure time and disposable income to devote themselves to reading. It was assumed that novel-reading was the primary focus of women readers; most novels were serialized in the new shilling* monthlies* delivered directly to the home each month or obtained in three-volume form from circulating libraries*. Anxious critics implied that reading sensation novels and other unsavoury narratives would infect women with romanticized expectations that would leave them dissatisfied with their mundane domestic lives or with impure notions that could lead to immoral behaviour. It was often assumed that women were uncritical readers* whose choices had to be regulated. While working class women also read more as the century progressed – especially servants who had access to journals and books owned by their employers – they were usually excluded from the public outcry against the indiscriminate spread of reading. Servant reading was often the butt of jokes about the intermingling of classes, but did not seem to pose as big a threat as the reading of working-class men.

With the gradual shortening of working hours, working men also had more time to read. Cheap* magazines such as the *Chambers's Edinburgh Journal** (1832ff) were aimed specifically at readers with little disposable income. The founding of the Society for the Diffusion of Useful Knowledge* put forth an educational agenda for working audiences. Focused on practical, mechanical, and scientific knowledge, Charles Knight's* publications for the society the *Penny Magazine** and the *Penny Cyclopaedia** were appealing partly because of their lavish illustrations. The sensational Penny Dreadfuls were endlessly popular and inspired the same fears expressed about middle-brow sensation novels for women. Working men's collectives also promoted reading by purchasing reading materials for the use of their members. The communal nature of reading among working class males in clubs and public houses highlighted middle-class fears of collective action that could potentially result from increased literacy and education inculcated by access to printed materials.

In the last decides of the century there was a flood of cheap print aimed ostensibly at those who had come out of the Board Schools set up by the 1870 Education Act, which culminated in the launch in 1896 of the *Daily Mail**, the first ½d daily paper. Middle-class anxiety about the reading of women and the working class was then focused not so much on its potential for subversion as on its triviality and sensationalism. **JJP**

Sources: Altick 1957, Flint 1993, Phegley 2004a, Rose 2001.

READING ROOMS See Public libraries

REASONER (1846-1860); SECULAR WORLD (1862-1863) Launched and edited* by the free-thinking secularist* George Jacob Holyoake*, with a modest budget of £50, the *Reasoner: and 'Herald of Progress'* (1846-1847), was dedicated to 'reasoning our way to the conclusions we proclaim, and testing speculative as well as practical subjects by the tangible standard of utility' (3 June 1846). Its allegiances were also clear: 'The *Reasoner* will be Communistic in Social Economy – Utilitarian in Morals – Republican in Politics – and Anti-theological in Religion' and its primary goal throughout is the exclusion of poverty from contemporary Britain'.

A weekly* of 16 pages, divided into two ruled columns*, the *Reasoner* cost 2d initially; by No 14 its price had fallen to 1½d. Volume II (1847) is announced as a New Series, associated with The Society of Theological Utilitarians, whose manifesto it publishes, and which supercedes the now defunct Rational Society. While the volume title has altered to the *Reasoner and Utilitarian Record* (1847), individual issues are simply called the *Reasoner.* In volume II (Nos 27-38), the size* of the page is smaller, and the columns have disappeared, and from No 38, the price reverts to 2d. Its contents range widely, though it covers predictable ground for a broadly Chartist*, secularist journal – short, often signed essays on materialism, enfranchisement, atheism, 'socialist errors and rationalist remedies', communism, brief sketches of thinkers or radicals like Thomas Paine, Hegel and Shelley and one page of advertisements*. Volume VII contains a lengthy explanation by Holyoake about why the journal is to end, but Volume VIII (1850) does appear, again at a reduced price* of 1d, but with half the pagination, at eight pages. To amend for this, the monthly 'Tract or Lecture' issue and the monthly issue compendium appear with a four-page supplement*, 'because what we propose to print on the Wrappers

has increased so much, that we must give a monthly supplement'. From 1847, the periodical went through a number of title changes*, which accelerated after 1860. **MWT/LRB**

Sources: Altick 1957, *ODNB, Waterloo.*

RECORD (1828-1948) Founded in 1828, the *Record* was a Church of England broadsheet newspaper of four pages promoting the interests of conservative evangelicals. Originally published weekly*, it was soon published twice (and, later, three) times a week before reverting to weekly publication in the 1880s. Like many newspapers its price* fell over the century, from 7d (1828) to 5d (1836) to 3d (1855) to 1d (1912), reflecting the gradual reduction of newspaper taxes (1833-1861) and competition*. Its contents are typical of broadsheets of its day, including coverage of domestic and foreign* news, commerce, prices and the law, as well as the Church and religious questions. Proposed by Andrew Hamilton as an evangelical newspaper, the *Record* quickly encountered financial difficulties and underwent significant changes in its first year, the most important of which was the appointment of Alexander Haldane (1800-1882) as editor*. Haldane, who eventually became its main proprietor*, was instrumental in the formation, through the paper, of a new group of evangelicals called the 'Recordites', who looked rigorously to the Bible, and defended sabbatarianism.

Under Haldane's influence, the *Record* quickly became one of the loudest and most extreme voices of conservative evangelicalism in the Church of England. The *Record* was the first to denounce the Tractarians in 1833, and it targeted several other persons, publications and trends throughout the nineteenth century, among them *Good Words**, a moderate evangelical magazine. In the 1860s the *Record* complained of *Good Words*'s failure to treat the Sabbath seriously, protesting against the magazine's alleged '"mingle-mangle" ... of persons, and of things'.

During the mid-nineteenth century the *Record* shifted the emphasis of its attacks from the High Church towards the Broad Church. This shift partly reflected changes in the religious scene and partly reflected the influence of Edward Garbett (1817-1887), who assisted Haldane in editing the *Record* from 1854 to 1867. When Haldane died, the *Record* lost much of its energy. It became a more moderate publication and eventually merged* with the *Church of England Newspaper*, becoming the *Church of England Newspaper and the Record* from 1949. **MK**

Sources: Altholz 1987, Knight and Mason 2006, *ODNB*, Palmer 1991, *Waterloo.*

RECORD OF THE MUSICAL UNION (1845-1881)

The *Record of the Musical Union* was an annual* compilation of concert pamphlets assembled, mostly authored, and edited* by John Ella. It targeted his Musical Union, a high-status concert society for the performance of chamber music* that met fortnightly in the West End of London during the season (April-July) under his artistic direction. Initially published* by Cramer, Beale & Co. (later by Ridgway), it was distributed* to subscribers gratis, usually during January of the following year.

The publication's significance lies in its principal content, 'analytical' programme notes for the works performed in the concerts, complete with music* examples of important themes set in music type. These represent the first sustained attempt in Europe to introduce this form of journalism and music* appreciation to a concert audience. Composer Hector Berlioz was among many who were favourably impressed by what Ella attempted; this included distributing the notes ahead of each concert so that audience members could prepare themselves for the performance.

News*, features and opinion on topics of current interest in the musical world were also included; selected contents were republished in Ella's *Musical Sketches, Abroad and at Home* (1869). Companion publications from the same stable were the *Record of the Musical Winter Evenings* (1852-1855) and the *Musical Record* (1857). **CMB**

Sources: Bashford 2008, Vann and Van Arsdel 1993, Wagstaff 1998.

RED DRAGON: THE NATIONAL MAGAZINE OF WALES (1882-1887)

The *Red Dragon* was a monthly* miscellany* launched by its first editor* Charles Wilkins, a frequent contributor to South Wales weeklies*. Unusual within the Welsh press* for targeting Anglophone readers, it included biographies of 'notable' Welsh figures, poetry*, serial fiction*, folklore, literary* and art reviews*, parliamentary reports* from 'Our "Red Dragons" at Westminster', gossip* from Welsh colleges, correspondence* and jokes. Though not overtly radical, the magazine challenged English stereotypes of Wales and heightened Welsh national consciousness. As such, like *Wales* and *Young Wales*, the *Red Dragon* functioned as a seedbed for both Welsh writing in English and the Young Wales movement. Under James Harris (its editor as of July 1885), the magazine* became primarily antiquarian and ceased publication after June 1887. **SY**

Sources: Ballin 2004, Jones 2000, Mathias 1985, Walters 2003, Williams 1959.

RED REPUBLICAN (JUNE-NOV. 1850); FRIEND OF THE PEOPLE (DEC. 1850-APRIL 1852)

Established by George Julian Harney in June 1850 as a Chartist* weekly* magazine*, the *Red Republican* declared 'Equality, Liberty, Fraternity' as its motto on the cover, echoing its intention of militant internationalism. Harney changed the title* in December 1850 to the *Friend of the People* because he was under threat of arrest due to the magazine's violent tone, as well as newsagents* refusing to sell a paper with *Red* in its title, especially amid the threat from mid-century European revolutions. Mottoes for the retitled magazine were, 'The Charter and Something More' and 'Abolition of Classes and Sovereignty of Labour'. Harney with his other editors*, W. H. Ainsworth* and Ernest Jones, also used poetry* to provide the language of reform.

The magazine was published* in London, owned, published and printed by Harney and several associates. Prominent socialists*, including Friedrich Engels, contributed articles regularly and the last four numbers of the magazine printed the first English translation of Karl Marx's* 'Communist Manifesto'. Among other contributors were Alfred Fennell, G. J. Holyoake*, Ernest Jones, William James Linton*, Helen MacFarlane*, Servo Malden, Gerald Massey*, Joseph Mazzini, Ledru Rollin, Eliot Warburton and Joseph Wood. A typical issue of the magazine began with 'Letters of L'Ami du Peuple', notices to correspondents*, institutions and laws of republican America, life in London, propositions of the National Reform League, republic and royalty in Italy, reviews*, foreign* affairs, labour records, songs and advertisements*.

Circulation* is estimated at approximately 250 readers per number, mostly working class*. It was issued each Saturday and sold for 1½d, or 1d while unstamped* in November 1850. Printed with three columns* per page, the magazine's size varied from 27 to 39 cm; and from 8 to 94 pages. It was illustrated* with engravings and sketches, to include a cover and masthead* design of a workman's cap placed atop an axe and spear, with the magazine's title slashed prominently above it. In 1852, the *Friend of the People* merged* with Harney's other paper the *Northern Star*, resulting in the *Star of Freedom*, a 'journal of political progress, trades' record, and co-operation chronicle'. **MDB**

Sources: Fulton and Colee 1955, Harrison 1977, *Waterloo*.

REES, SARAH JANE (1839-1916)

Sarah Rees was the founder and the first woman to edit* (1878-1889) a Welsh* language women's magazine,

Y Frythones (the *British Woman*), a monthly* magazine* (1878-1891) 'devoted to the women* of Wales'. Modelled on the *Englishwoman's Domestic Magazine* with Hannah More* and Elizabeth Fry represented as ideals, it aimed to promote women's secular and religious education. Intended for working-class* women, the magazine was illustrated*, and contained features, fiction, poetry*, an advice* page and included articles on women's suffrage and women's employment. Rees herself was a primary contributor, and provided opportunities for other Welsh women writers such as Alice Gray Jones*. AGJ/CL
Sources: Beddoe 2004, Jones 1932, Welsh Biography Online.

REEVE, HENRY (1813-1895) As editor* of the *Edinburgh Review** for 40 years (1855-1895), Henry Reeve was the longest serving editor of a quarterly* review* in the nineteenth century. His preparation for a career in journalism, like that of many men of letters without connections, was one of effective networking, reinforced by native ability. After a period of Continental travel and residence in Paris, he began by writing for the *British and Foreign Review**. In 1840 he joined the staff of *The Times** as a leader* writer and foreign* correspondent, using his European political contacts, and those made at home to good effect. In 1843 he was appointed to the post of registrar of the Privy Council. Reeve wrote as many as four or five articles a week for *The Times* in the 1840s and 1850s, gaining considerable influence as a result. Of his period at the paper he remarked, 'I question whether there was any person out of the Cabinet more correctly acquainted with the course of affairs; indeed some things reached me which the bulk of the Cabinet did not know'.

In 1855 Reeve took over the editorship of the *Edinburgh Review* from George Cornewall Lewis, for some months combining work for the *Edinburgh* with writing for *The Times*. He resigned from the latter after a quarrel with the acting editor G. W. Dasent, and, as he put it, 'fell back on the *Edinburgh Review*, which is a sort of peerage as compared with the tumult of the Lower House'. Had the quarrel not occurred, he claimed he would probably have stayed with newspaper in preference to the review, enjoying 'the power it conferred of governing public opinion'. He gained a reputation, as an editor, for rejecting articles irrespective of the distinction of the contributors, and for excessive alterations to much of what he accepted. One injured contributor commented that there must be few people who hold 'like Reeve that they know more of all branches of human knowledge than the people who have severally got them up'. The *Edinburgh's* policy of anonymity* continued under Reeve's editorship, long after most of its contributors had gone over to signed articles. Reeve himself did a large number of the reviews on politics* and on cultural affairs, and it was largely due to his connections that the political* influence of the *Edinburgh* remained high in a period in which the power of the quarterlies in general was waning. JS
Sources: Laughton 1898, *ODNB*, Shattock 1985.

REIS AND RAYYET (1882-1910) The colonial weekly* *Reis and Rayyet* (1882-1910), or 'Prince and Peasant', began life in Calcutta and continued uninterrupted until its demise. The newspaper's founder and editor*, Babu Sambhu Chunder Mookerjee, was a public figure and a prolific writer, as well as the editor of the periodical *Mookerjee's Magazine* (1861-1876). Issued every Saturday, *Reis and Rayyet's* rate of subscription was Rs.12 annually. Advertising* rates were 'charged by the space taken up, at the rate of four annas a line' and each issue included several pages of advertisements at the end of each issue. Printed and published* by Mutty Lall Ghose at the Bee Press in Calcutta, its pagination was continuous from issue to issue within the year. As a self-proclaimed 'review of politics*, literature* and society' invested in English notions of 'taste', the newspaper frequently included poetry*, stories and reviews* of literature and art within its pages.

Reis and Rayyet announced its mission in an editorial statement in the first issue: 'The name fixes the platform. It will be an Indian Paper for all India. Unconnected with party, and independent of persons, it will be loyal to the backbone, to the Crown and the Constitution'. The paper declared itself sympathetic to all natives whether they be Hindu or Muslim, prince or peasant, as long as he is a 'man, brother, and fellow-citizen'. Targeted on the educated native male (the reader is presumably man, brother, and fellow-citizen), the newspaper also assumed an Anglo-Indian and English audience. *Reis and Rayyet* proclaimed a 'nationalist'* agenda but remained loyal to Queen and Empire* despite its incisive critiques of Anglo-Indian bureaucracy and imperial policy. SR
Sources: Paul 2004, Ray 1993, Skrine 1895.

RELIGIOUS PRESS The importance of religious journalism for the development of the periodical press in the nineteenth century can hardly be overstated. Altholz argues that for a century from 1760, when the pioneering *Christian's Magazine* (1760-1767) was launched, religious periodicals dominated the British press. He identifies some 3,000 titles in the Victorian period, and while most of these related to the Christian faith, other faiths, such as Judaism, were also represented. Religious titles included national journals and local* parish or regional titles; those addressed to specific denominational or sectional readerships, like the 'High' Anglican *English Churchman* (1843-) or the Wesleyan *Methodist Recorder* (1861-); and those titles produced by religious organizations which addressed general readerships*, including the 'secular publishing with a religious tone' of the Religious Tract Society* (whose publications included the *Leisure Hour** and juvenile* publications such as the popular *Boy's Own Paper** and *Girl's Own Paper**). The religious press overlapped with the journalism of the missionary* and temperance* movements, each of which was responsible for journals with vast circulations*.

However, even beyond these specific titles, religious journalism was important in the press through the work of men and women who worked across both secular and religious publications, men like William Robertson Nicoll*, who not only edited* the non-conformist *British Weekly** but also, through his connection with the evangelical publishing house of Hodder and Stoughton*, founded and edited such secular titles as the *Bookman** and *Woman at Home**. As important were publishers and entrepreneurs whose religious convictions shaped their business practice, as was the case with the nonconformist and temperance* campaigner John Cassell*, and, one might argue, W. T. Stead*, the 'enfant terrible' of the New Journalism*.

The importance of the religious press declined as the century went on. During the first 25 years, religious journals dominated. Topham shows that not only were a quarter of the leading journals in 1807 religious but also that the circulation* (and the much greater readership*) of such titles as the *Evangelical Magazine** or the relatively cheap* Methodist *Child's Companion** was far greater than secular journals from across the price range. By the end of the century, religious publications had been overtaken by the mass* periodicals of the New Journalism, although the Catholic *Universe,* the non-conformist *Christian World**, and the Anglican *Church Times** (to name only select newspapers) each had six figure readerships* and remained extremely influential. It is difficult, however, to ascertain whether the apparent decline in the religious press was the result of secularisation. The decline might also be attributed to an intentional diffusion of religious beliefs and practices throughout nineteenth-century culture the evangelical editor of *Good Words**, for

instance, made it clear that employing a style that was not always overtly religious was an important part of his effort to propagate the Christian faith.

The religious press was neither homogeneous nor consistently didactic. All the major periodical genres* from the yearbook and quarterly* review through the weekly* and monthly* magazine to the weekly* or bi-weekly newspaper were deployed. As Thomas Carlyle* famously complained, the religious press was divided along sectarian lines, with every denomination or grouping within the Church wanting its own publication(s). These differences were a major shaping influence, with the religious press following the non-religious press in thinking carefully about how it might attract more readers. Periodicals targeted specifically at children*, like their adult counterparts, became more varied and interesting as the century went on, both visually and in terms of print matter. Subsidy and/or large sales enabled some religious publishers to use the latest forms of print technology and high quality illustration*. Other religious journals experimented with different forms of writing (including sensational tales) to carry their message. **MRB/MK Sources**: Altholz 1989, Butts 2006, Knight and Mason 2006, Topham 2004.

RELIGIOUS TRACT SOCIETY The Religious Tract Society (RTS) was founded by a group of evangelicals in 1799 headed by the Congregationalist minister George Burder (1752-1832). It aimed to provide morally improving Christian literature for the labouring classes* by printing and distributing bibles, pamphlets and tracts. Beginning as a small volunteer organization, the RTS grew rapidly to become a worldwide publisher and one of the largest issuers of periodicals in the nineteenth century. The RTS began producing religious periodicals in the 1820s, and by 1861 it was said to be producing 13 million copies of periodicals per year, as well as 20 million tracts. From the 1840s the RTS shifted its exclusively theological focus to cover subjects such as history*, science* and biography from a Christian angle. The RTS focused its efforts on the popular* periodical market* and was remarkably adept at adjusting to meet the needs of changing markets. It overcame its evangelical dislike for fiction when it became apparent that readers wanted serialized* novels and the RTS provided suitable stories in the *Leisure Hour** and *Sunday at Home**. The RTS is perhaps best remembered now as a publisher of long-running children's* periodicals including the *Boy's Own Paper** and the *Girl's Own Paper**. **BP Sources**: Alderson and Garnett 1999, Altholz 1989, Altick 1957, Fyfe 2004, *Waterloo.*

REPORTER The reporter should be seen as a subset within the developing profession of journalism*, and a result of the division of labour within this new occupation. In the early nineteenth century the term reporter began to be used in a general sense to describe someone employed by a newspaper or magazine* to report on debates, elections, sporting events, speeches and meetings. Factual, impersonal reports provided a record of events with minimal analysis. After the Battle of Waterloo in 1815, it became increasingly common for newspapers to use paid or staff reporters to describe public occasions rather than relying on letters sent by amateur correspondents.

However, in two specialized areas, those of law* reporting and parliamentary* reporting, the concept of the reporter had an older provenance (the first parliamentary* reporter, Sir Simon D'Ewes, reported on the parliaments of Elizabeth I), and these forms of reporting formed the blueprint for the later development of the profession. Over the course of the nineteenth century, the structure of the Houses of Parliament developed to accommodate parliamentary reporters, with the enlargement of the press galleries and the designation of 'writing-out-rooms' fitted with desks and inkstands, where reporters converted their shorthand* transcriptions of parliamentary debates into longhand. War* reporting, the practice of newspapers sending representatives with armies to report on events in the field, began in the early 1850s during the Crimean War. Before this date, whatever stories from the battlefield contained in the newspapers relied entirely on official dispatches for information. Technical developments such as shorthand and the telegraph* impacted on the reporter's craft significantly during the century.

During the course of the New Journalism*, with its introduction of investigative* reporting, editors* such as Frederic Greenwood* and W. T. Stead* on the *Pall Mall Gazette** (1865ff) raised the profile of the reporter who was to make his own news, disguising himself as an 'Amateur Casual' to report on the doss house, or procuring a child to expose under-age prostitution. Stead's later essays on journalism* (1891ff) placed reporters heroically over the globe as 'scouts', on the lookout not only for 'news' but for political* trends which editors might use to govern by journalism. The figure of the reporter today is both lionized as a heroic figure, standing apart from the otherwise venal journalistic profession in its disinterested pursuit of the facts, and demonized as the grasping, stone-hearted hack who salivates at the thought of another gruesome murder, and is already writing copy as it hounds the bereaved for a quote. Both ways of thinking about the reporter circulated in Victorian Britain. Above all, as an article in *Chambers's Journal** in 1868 argued, the reporter came to play a crucial role in the functioning of the Victorian media, acting as the 'eyes and ears for the world at large'. **MaT**

Sources: Brake 2004b, Brake 2008, BritPer, *Chambers's Journal* 1868, Gratton 1860, MacDonagh 1895, MacDonagh 1898.

RESEARCH SOCIETY FOR VICTORIAN PERIODICALS [RSVP] (1968-) RSVP was founded in 1968 by Michael Wolff as an organization of scholars from across disciplines – history, art history, and literature – and across countries who are interested in researching the vast field of Victorian periodicals. More or less simultaneously, he and others interested in periodical research started the first scholarly periodical devoted to publication of this research, the *Victorian Periodicals Newsletter* which became the official publication of RSVP. Both of these developments were part of a burgeoning scholarly interest in Victorian culture, marked by the founding of *Victorian Studies* in 1956 with many of the same scholars involved in the beginnings of both journals. Also a sign of the interest in Victorian periodicals at this time was the publication of the first volume of the *Wellesley Index of Victorian Periodicals** (1965), edited* by Walter Houghton and the *Waterloo Directory of Victorian Periodicals**, whose first volume, published in 1976, was co-edited by Michael Wolff and John North and supported in part by RSVP.

RSVP has held a yearly conference every year since 1968, alternating locations in the USA, the UK and Canada with one conference in Ghent, Belgium. A significant number of books on Victorian periodicals has resulted from these conferences. The organization also gives a number of awards and prizes every year. RSVP has a website (www.RS4VP.org) that contains information about conferences, other related meetings and publications and current research projects.

Victorian Periodicals Newsletter underwent several format*, editor, and title* changes as well as publishers. With its final title, *Victorian Periodicals Review*, it took its current shape as a quarterly* publication, publishing articles and information on all aspects of the Victorian periodical press. The journal also publishes yearly a comprehensive bibliography of articles, reviews and books on the Victorian periodical press which has been periodically gathered into multi-year formats published as part of the journal. The journal and its annual bibliography are currently being digitized by JSTOR.

The 40th anniversary issue of *Victorian Periodicals Review* (41:1 Spring 2008) contains a full history of RSVP and *VPR* with essays by the founding members of the organization as well as by the editors of the journal. Over this period RSVP has been instrumental in stimulating research and developing the field of 'periodical studies' through its conferences, publications, prizes and projects, and not least in the support and stimulus it has offered to individual scholars in their pioneering work. **AH**
Source: *Victorian Periodicals Review* 41 (spring 2008): 1-60.

REUTERS (1865-) This news agency* originated in Paul Julius Reuter's arrangements to send news* between Aachen and Berlin in 1850 by telegraphy*. A year later, Reuter was in London to take advantage of the telegraph connecting France and England under the English Channel. By the end of 1851 he was providing stock prices and other financial information from across continental Europe* to brokers in London and Paris, and Reuters was the first agency to report in Europe the assassination of Abraham Lincoln in 1865. Becoming a British subject in 1857, Reuter launched Reuter's Telegram Company in 1865, just as the expansion of British journalism* was beginning. **AGJ**
Source: Read 1992.

***REVIEW OF REVIEWS* (1890-1936)** Founded by W. T. Stead* and George Newnes* in 1890, the *Review of Reviews* set out to make 'the best thoughts of the best writers universally accessible' by sifting through the mass of periodical literature for those articles that merited republishing. The journal was to be an index to the 'mighty maze of periodical literature' that would aid 'the busy man' to read the best that was contained in the magazines* and periodicals. For Stead there was no contradiction in echoing Mathew Arnold's* definition of culture while employing the New Journalism* that Arnold so opposed in order to communicate it better. Stead intended the *Review of Reviews* to provide a digest of the heterogeneous content of the periodicals: at 6d a month it was not only more affordable than many of its predecessors but also attempted to present content in a more accessible style. Stead eschewed the policy of using named authorities within the *Review of Reviews*, instead offering himself (as the editor*) as abstractor, mediator and moral guide for his readers

The first number appeared on 6 January 1890,

Figure 57: The cover of the *Review of Reviews*.

just four weeks after Newnes and Stead had agreed to collaborate on the new monthly*. Within three months, Newnes, recognizing that Stead's evangelical campaigning might attract a readership* but would not necessarily make money, decamped to found a monthly of his own, the *Strand Magazine**. Stead, with financial support from the Salvation Army, bought out Newnes's share of the title, and relocated it from the *Tit-Bits** office to his own premises at Mowbray House. Stead for the first time was editor*, proprietor* and publisher*, but although the sole voice within the journal was his, he built up a talented staff who could produce content in his manner even when he was absent in person.

A supporter of female suffrage, Stead ensured that the relatively large number of women that he employed in the *Review of Reviews* office were on the same salaries as the men. Although the strategy of abstracting from other titles was certainly not unique – it was a staple of 'scissors and paste' Stead's adoption of it for the *Review of Reviews* remained controversial. Although Stead presented the title as above party politics*, he advocated a Christian, radical, democratic, imperialist* politics through his comments on world affairs in the opening department, 'Progress of the World', and his editorial glosses on the words of others in 'Leading Articles in the Reviews' and 'The Reviews Reviewed'. Such a stance, coupled with his own notoriety, meant that some writers objected to his use of their texts and, although he attempted to obtain permissions, publishers saw his techniques as little more than piracy. Characteristically, Stead argued that he provided free publicity for the various publications from which he took content and a much wider audience for the writers who published within them.

The *Review of Reviews* was the focus of Stead's publishing activity for the rest of his life, producing Australasian, French and American editions, various supplements* (including his Christmas* annuals* and the spiritualist quarterly *Borderland**) and was the medium through which he launched his *Daily Paper* in 1893 and 1904. **JEM**
Sources: Baylen 1972, Baylen 1979, Brake 2004a, Brake 2007, Brake 2008, Dawson 2004a, Eckley 2007.

REVIEWING Thomas Carlyle's* comment in 1831, that reviewing 'spreads with strange vigour' and that soon literature* would 'become one boundless self-devouring Review' reflected his irritation with contemporary literary life, in which reviewing paid so well that no man (or woman) of letters could afford to ignore it. By the 1830s there were a significant number of quarterly* reviews, monthly* magazines* and weekly* papers that offered opportunities for reviewing all forms of 'literature', from history*, philosophy*, political* economy, theology, science*, through to the poetry*, art, drama and the novel. George Henry Lewes*, the prototype of the mid-Victorian reviewer, argued that the healthy state of the newly-established 'profession'* of literature was owing to 'the excellence and abundance of periodical literature' which offered so many opportunities for earning a living by one's pen. Reviewing, which was well remunerated by the mid-century, offered an adjunct career to university dons, civil servants, lawyers, the clergy and other professionals, who combined it with their other responsibilities. Women made inroads into this masculine preserve, although in far fewer numbers.

The reviews in the quarterlies, which dominated the early decades of the nineteenth century, were often scholarly, sometimes opinionated and on occasion politically driven. Reviewing in the magazines of the early decades of the century, from the establishment of *Blackwood's Edinburgh Magazine** in 1817 until the 1830s, was dominated by personalities, and could be scurrilous, but it evolved into a more polite and scholarly mode by the end of the decade. Reviews in the quarterlies and magazines*

were unsigned, although some contributors were identifiable by an initial or a pseudonym*. *Macmillan's Magazine**, established in 1859, took an important step in allowing a large proportion of articles to be signed. Three reviews established in the 1860s and 1870s, the *Fortnightly** (1865), the *Contemporary** (1866), and the *Nineteenth Century** (1877) operated from the outset on the principle of signed reviews. The *Nineteenth Century* so traded on the celebrities* it attracted as reviewers that James Knowles*, its proprietor*, was accused of 'lion-hunting', and it was acknowledged that a 'star system' in reviewing had emerged. According to the precedent set by the *Edinburgh Review**, nineteenth-century reviewing was largely independent of booksellers, unlike the eighteenth-century reviews, which had existed to promote the lists of their proprietors.

'Puffing'*, or the blatant promotion of a bookseller's lists, was an acknowledged feature of some publications, but the practice largely died out by the beginning of the 1840s. The other determining factor in reviewing was space, or the size* of review articles. Those in the quarterlies were leisurely and discursive, sometimes extending to 40 octavo pages or more, and containing lengthy quotations from the works under review. Those in the monthly magazines and reviews were shorter, between 10 and 15 pages, and those in the multi-columned* weekly papers shorter still. Literary reviewing was not a feature of the newspaper press until later in the century. Apart from *The Times**, the daily* press* was slow to institute regular features on contemporary literature until the 1890s. **JS**
Sources: Brake 1994a, Carlyle 1831, Kent 1969, Lewes 1847, Shattock 1989.

REVIEWS Throughout the nineteenth-century there were a significant number of periodical publications*, appearing quarterly* (at intervals of three months), monthly, and weekly*, which offered a range of criticism on 'literature'* in its broadest sense, all published forms of knowledge from history*, philosophy*, political economy*, theology, and science*, through to the more popular forms of poetry*, art, drama and the novel. The term 'review' was applied to both the periodical and to the essays or articles within it. In a famous article on 'The First Edinburgh Reviewers' published in 1855, the critic Walter Bagehot* referred to 'the review-like essay and the essay-like review' which characterized the contents of the quarterly reviews. These discursive articles, 40 pages or more in length, frequently used the book under review as a pretext or 'peg' on which to hang a more wide-ranging discussion, hence their 'essay-like' qualities. The reviews in monthly magazines* were shorter and often less formal in tone. The quarterlies prided themselves on being selective in the books they reviewed, and robust and opinionated in their critical judgments, in contrast to the encyclopaedic model of their predecessors, the *Monthly* (1756), *Critical* (1757) and the *Analytical* (1788) reviews, whose purpose was to keep readers abreast of the state of knowledge in all fields.

The quarterly reviews sold for between 4s and 6s per number. The price* of monthly magazines in the 1830s ranged from 3s to 3s 6d. The monthly magazines of the 1850s and 1860s, of which *Macmillan's** and the *Cornhill** were the best known, sold for 1s and contained a large number of reviews of current publications. The weekly* reviews were different in format* – usually four and five columns* per page, selling for as little as 4d or 6d per issue. Their review articles were shorter still. Weekly* reviews increased in popularity throughout the nineteenth century, their succinct formats* and low price attracting the same readers who responded favourably to the gradual introduction of literary reviews into the daily* newspaper press. **JS**

Sources: Bagehot 1855, Brake 1994a, Shattock 1989.

REYNOLDS, GEORGE WILLIAM MACARTHUR (1814-1879) G.W.M. Reynolds was a radical novelist and journalist* who became an important pioneer of the mass* press and editor* of several important popular periodicals. A committed republican and, from 1848, a leading Chartist*, Reynolds was the first editor of the *London Journal** in 1845, raising its circulation* to 50,000, and went on to launch a number of popular periodicals in association with the publisher* John Dicks*. *Reynolds's Miscellany** serialized* many of Reynolds's romantic novels but also provided informative articles about current affairs and matters of household economy. Reynolds developed a strong relationship with his readers* and would post answers* to queries sent to him on political* or often mundane matters.

His involvement with Chartism led to the more narrowly political *Reynolds's Political Instructor** which was essentially a dry run for a mass*-circulation national newspaper, *Reynolds's Weekly Newspaper** which became the most successful working-class* newspaper in the mid-Victorian period. It championed the cause of labour but combined this with an emphasis on crime*, scandal and stories about horrific accidents that appealed to a mass au-

dience. By 1872 its circulation* was estimated at 350,000 (*ODNB*). Reynolds owed his success to the way he applied the melodramatic approach he had developed in his fiction (notably in *Mysteries of London*), to his journalism, thus developing the language of sensational narrative that became an integral feature of the mass press. **RM**

Sources: Haywood 2004, Humphreys and James 2008, McWilliam 1996, *ODNB*.

REYNOLDS, JOHN HAMILTON (1794-1852) John Hamilton Reynolds, journalist* and editor* became a clerk in a newspaper office at 15 and, after a year, in an assurance company in Fleet Street*. In his spare time Reynolds read and wrote poetry*, mingling with leading writers, artists and editors. On 13 July 1815 two of his sonnets appeared in the *Champion*,* a Sunday newspaper on which, from later that year, Reynolds was employed until December 1817. During the first five months of this post Reynolds remained with the assurance office. Mainly writing theatre and literary reviews*, he also did general articles and contributed to other journals, including the *Repository of Arts, Literature and Fashions*, the *Gentleman's Magazine**, and the *Inquirer**. In 1816 he resigned from his job as a clerk to become a full-time journalist and poet.

In 1818 Reynolds contributed to the short-lived periodical* the *Yellow Dwarf* edited by Leigh Hunt's brother, John. It was through Leigh Hunt that Reynolds met John Keats and became a close friend and champion of the poet. Realizing he could not match the genius of Keats, and concerned about the lack of financial security, Reynolds studied to become a lawyer. While completing his legal apprenticeship he continued to write for periodicals, especially the *Athenaeum**, also spending any time he could spare from legal work in assisting John Scott with the editorship of the *London Magazine**. In the 1830s he contributed to *Bentley's Miscellany** edited by Charles Dickens* and, later in the 1830s, financial difficulties led Reynolds to become editor of the *New Sporting Monthly Magazine* (1836-1840). He began to drink heavily, and by 1838 he was declared bankrupt. In 1847 he retired from London to the Isle of Wight, where he became assistant clerk at the Newport county court. **DHL**

Sources: Jones 1984, Marsh 1928, *ODNB*.

REYNOLDS'S MISCELLANY (1846-1869) The republican figure and journalist, G. W. M. Reynolds* founded this journal as *Reynolds's Magazine*; its subtitle, *of romance, general literature*, science**, defined the intended scope to be targeted at the lower middle and working classes*. Priced* at 1d and published* by John Dicks*, who was later to be the most important publisher of cheap* literature of the century, the journal's name was changed within months to *Reynolds's Miscellany*. Within a year its circulation* was reported as 30,000 and by 1855 perhaps as much as 300,000. A popular* weekly* magazine that featured a sensational woodcut* and serial fiction* in the front, frequently written by Reynolds, the *Miscellany* also included a wide range of politically* tinged commentary such as Reynolds's 'Letters to the Industrious Classes' in which he tried to educate cotton spinners and needlewomen, schoolmasters and governesses, to the ways in which an aristocratic hierarchy oppressed them. Reynolds later introduced a popular department, the 'Notices to Correspondents'*, in which the editor* answered a wide range of requests for information and personal questions, as well as propagandizing his republican views. In 1846 the *Miscellany* also published a series of articles on 'The Provincial* Press of the United Kingdom' which covered 38 papers with brief accounts of their history*, political* news*, circulation* and advertising importance.

In his initial 'To Our Readers', Reynolds wrote that, 'convinced that the readers of Cheap Literature are imbued with a profound spirit of inquiry in respect to Science*, Art, Manufacture, and the various matters of social or national importance, the Projector of this 'Miscellany'* has determined to blend Instruction with Amusement, and to allot a fair proportion of each Number to Useful Articles, as well as to Tales and Light Reading'. The journal underwent some modifications in format* in the early years, increasing page size, but the nature and quality of the contents remained fairly consistent. Contributors included Gabriel Alexander and Edwin Roberts; Reynolds stopped contributing fiction in the late 1850s. In 1869, Dicks having bought the rights to Reynolds's work, the *Miscellany* was merged* with another Dicks's penny journal, *Bow Bells**. AH
Sources: Humphreys 1983, King 2007, *ODNB*, Waterloo.

REYNOLDS'S POLITICAL INSTRUCTOR (10 NOV. 1849-11 MAY 1850)

Reynolds's Political Instructor was launched after the defeat of the third wave of Chartism* in 1848. Edited* by the radical journalist* and novelist G. W. M. Reynolds* and published* by John Dicks*, the *Instructor* took over the political* content of *Reynolds's Miscellany*, which had featured articles denouncing the conditions of the labouring classes. Costing 1d (unstamped*), each weekly* eight-page issue of the *Instructor* featured radical commentaries on the week's events by Reynolds and other contributors including Bronterre O'Brien*. The *Instructor* was essentially a Chartist periodical arguing for universal manhood suffrage but Reynolds employed it to argue for 'the Charter and Something More'. To the six points of the People's Charter, the *Instructor* added the recognition of the rights of labour (defined as 'a fair day's wage for a fair day's work, and that every man willing and able to work should have work found for him') and the abolition of the law of primogeniture. (The latter reflected Reynolds's belief that most social ills arose from the domination of the aristocracy.)

The paper was part of the culture of radical internationalism, supporting revolutionary and liberal movements in Europe, and as such was also published in Paris by the Galignani* brothers. On its front cover the paper featured admiring portraits of Louis Blanc, Joseph Mazzini, 'George Sand' and British Chartists. Reynolds closed the paper in 1850 to embark on the more enduring *Reynolds's Weekly*, a newspaper aimed at the working classes* that maintained the *Instructor*'s political analysis. RM
Sources: Haywood 2004, Humpherys and James 2008, McWilliam 1996.

REYNOLDS'S WEEKLY NEWSPAPER (1850-1851); REYNOLDS'S NEWSPAPER (1851-1967)

Reynolds's Weekly Newspaper, which began publication on 5 May 1850 as *Reynolds's Weekly Newspaper*, changed its title* in February 1851 to *Reynolds's Newspaper*. A Sunday* broadsheet, it appealed to republicans, Chartists* and other radicals, and only ceased publication as the *Sunday Citizen* in 1967, having maintained a consistently leftist stance. Founded by novelist and journalist G. W. M. Reynolds*, it replaced his more polemical weekly* paper, *Reynolds's Political Instructor**, which he folded on the launch of the *Newspaper*. On his death in 1879 his brother Edward became editor*, followed by William Thompson on Edward's death in 1894.

Reynolds's Newspaper was published* and printed in London by Reynolds and John Dicks* in four editions, on Thursday, Friday, Saturday, and Sunday, the first three for shipment beyond London; all carried the official Sunday publication date. Sold initially at a price* of 4d, the price was briefly raised to 5d in July in response to Lord Ashley's bill prohibiting newspaper delivery on Sundays, and then lowered in mid-August to 2½d. It remained at that price until the repeal of the newspaper stamp regulations, when it was lowered to a penny*. It was laid out on 16 pages in four columns* (changed to eight larger pages and eight columns in 1861), and carried a core set of sections that appealed to radical readers. The front page carried a lead opinion article on news of the day from a republican perspective; until August 1853, it was written and signed by Reynolds himself. Two other columns of fairly straightforward news* stories ran on the front page, and were sometimes continued inside. Another front-page staple was 'Foreign* Intelligence', which devoted itself to other countries' politics.

G. W. M. Reynolds was his newspaper's most prolific writer, and the only one, save for the authors of occasional special and limited features, with a named byline. It is unclear how many reporters* worked for the paper and who they were. James Bronterre O'Brien* wrote there briefly, but not after August 1850. The pseudonymous* columnists 'Northumbrian' and 'Gracchus', whose offerings ran on facing interior pages, addressed political* issues different from those addressed by the front-page leader*. 'Northumbrian' was later identified as 'Mr Macintosh', while 'Gracchus' was the publisher's brother Edward Reynolds, who wrote the column possibly from its inception until 1894.

Other regular features were common to Victorian newspapers: Police News, which highlighted lurid crimes*, especially if committed by an aristocrat; Literary Miscellania, which excerpted stories from other papers; Court* News, which ran next to the Sports* News; Book Reviews*, which regularly reviewed books from a radical perspective; and Notices to Correspondents*, in which Reynolds provided answers to correspondents' questions on a wide range of subjects.

A mixture of radical politics, practical advice, and gossip*, Reynolds's Newspaper established a personal relationship with its readers, giving them a forum for their interests. Widely circulated at home and abroad (its claimed circulation* was over 200,000 by the 1870s, with a readership* greater than that), it was the most popular post-Chartist radical newspaper until at least the twentieth century, long after Reynolds's death in 1879. MiS
Sources: Humphreys 1983, ODNB, Shirley 2007, Waterloo.

RICHARDS, (FRANKLIN THOMAS) GRANT (1872-1948) Though Richards made his name as a literary publisher in the twentieth century, his early work as a book reviewer* provided him a critical entrée into the trade. He obtained a clerical position with the Review of Reviews* (1890-1936) in its fledgling months. Assigned by editor* W. T. Stead* to write a survey of Christmas* literature for the December 1890 issue, Richards soon thereafter assumed responsibility for the book section, for which he wrote numerous reviews and articles covering the London literary world. He also contributed to Great Thoughts from Master Minds (1884-1937), and edited the 1895 issue of Phil May's Illustrated Winter Annual (1892-1905).

Richards remained with the Review of Reviews until the end of 1896, when he left to open his own publishing house, where before the end of the century he had issued works by Grant Allen*, G. B. Shaw* and A. E. Housman. The congenial voice with which he reviewed current books presaged the anecdotal advertising* columns* he later contributed to the Times Literary Supplement (1902-1968), and his appreciation for popular literature inspired his writing of several novels. Richards maintained that his years with Stead were of 'incalculable value' (Richards, 145) in introducing him to a wide range of authors and the publishing trade. WSB
Sources: Anderson 1991, ODNB, Richards 1932.

RICHARDSON, BENJAMIN WARD (1828-1896) Working as a physician in London, Benjamin Richardson, journalist*, proprietor* and editor*, became acquainted with Douglas Jerrold* and became a member of 'Our Club' alongside bohemian literary* journalists like Mark Lemon*. His own journalism initially appeared in professional* journals such as the Lancet* and the British Medical Journal*, but from the 1870s he also wrote on public health issues, particularly temperance*, for general periodicals including Fraser's Magazine* and the Fortnightly Review*. In 1855 he founded and edited the Journal of Public Health and Sanitary Review, reversing the order of the title* a few months later at the suggestion of John Chapman*.

The Sanitary Review, which published the transactions of the Epidemiological Society on the proviso that the Society's Fellows became subscribers, was the first journal to deal exclusively with public health, although Richardson closed it in 1859 due to pressure of work. Five years later he started a new weekly* journal* the Social Science Review, which again closed due to Richardson's numerous other commitments in 1866, while in 1884 he began the quarterly* Asclepiad, having originally published it as a single annual* volume in 1861. The Asclepiad, as its lengthy subtitle indicated, was dedicated to Science, Art and Literature of Medicine, and Richardson contributed many literary articles on subjects like Keats's medical training, as well as publishing his own plays in the Social Science Review (he also published a triple-decker historical novel). Richardson remained as editor of the Asclepiad until his death, when the journal ceased publication. GD
Sources: MacNalty 1950, ODNB, Richardson 1897.

RICHARDSON, JOSEPH HALL (1857-1945)
Joseph Richardson, journalist* and editor*, was educated in France and at the City of London College. After a period working in the City, he started working as a journalist in 1874 by contributing to the London *Figaro** and *Tomahawk**. In 1879, he founded and became editor of the *Mid-Surrey Mirror*. In 1881, he joined the *Daily Telegraph** as a reporter, acting as a foreign correspondent* for the paper in France, Belgium, Holland, Italy, Morocco and Canada. He became the *Telegraph's* assistant editor in 1906, and in 1923, its general manager, retiring from the paper in 1928. JRW
Sources: Richardson 1927, *Who Was Who*.

RICKETTS, CHARLES DE SOUSY (1866-1931) Working as a painter, illustrator*, printer, critic, short story-writer and engraver, Charles Ricketts was one of the most influential artists of the nineteenth century. He spent the first few years of his life in France, retaining, like many of his artistic contemporaries, a preference for this country throughout his life. As he considered himself fit for hardly anything except an artistic vocation, he entered the apprenticeship of wood* engraver, Charles Roberts at 16, where he also met his lifelong collaborator and rumoured lover, Charles Hazlewood Shannon*. The pursuit of this kind of artistic artisanship in an age where image reproduction was already taken over by automatic machines quickly positioned him in the avant-garde scene, upholding the heritage of the Arts & Crafts and Aesthetic movements. A long cherished wish to found a magazine resulted in 1889 in the *Dial**.

Ricketts partly did the engravings for the *Dial* himself in the old way of his former teacher, but some illustrations were assigned to an electric engravers' company. Many of his most praised early drawings and paintings were featured in the magazine, but he also contributed some slightly grotesque fairytales, and wrote literary* and art criticism under the pseudonym* 'Charles Sturt'. Especially before the advent of the *Dial*, he had worked as an illustrator for a range of other periodicals, including *Atalanta**, *Alarum*, *Woman's World**, *Magazine of Art**, *Universal Review** and *Harper's Magazine**. KNC
Sources: *ODNB*, Ricketts 1939, Sullivan 1983, Watry 2004.

RINTOUL, ROBERT STEPHEN (1787-1858)
Scottish editor*, printer and publisher*, Robert Rintoul served his printer's apprenticeship in Edinburgh, becoming a printer for the *Dundee Advertiser* in 1809; two years later he was its editor. From

1811 to 1825 he edited, printed and published the *Dundee Advertiser*, and wrote on reform issues. Having gained a political* profile with the paper, he was persuaded by leading London Liberals to leave Dundee for London where he took over as editor of the weekly *Atlas** in 1826. Contact with *Blackwood's** journalists in Edinburgh had prompted him to consider the interesting potential of a weekly* publication, so demands for him to lower standards at the paper resulted in his departure. The radical Joseph Hume together with other supporters wanted an advocate for their cause in the press and funded Rintoul to found the *Spectator** in 1828, where he was editor and publisher.

Rintoul could now employ his ambitious and novel plans for the *Spectator's* content to include news* coverage, analysis of current politics, book, drama and music* criticism plus scientific* and sundry information. Consisting of 16 pages, priced* 9d, including 4d tax, by 1831 the number of pages had risen to 24, priced at 1d. Although supporting the Whig government the *Spectator* adhered to a non-party line, opposing the Corn Laws, supporting colonial change and the Reform Bill. As a dedicated Abolitionist, Rintoul opposed the gradualist agenda on anti-slavery. His dedication, hard work and integrity gained support for the journal and attracted quality writers of the class of John Stuart Mill*. Driven by his sense of duty to the reform agenda, after 30 years of devotion to his paper, deteriorating health caused the sale of the *Spectator*.

Robert Rintoul's legacy lay in the political influence that his paper had delivered and in the respect in which he was held as its mentor. CL
Sources: Herd 1952, *New York Times*, *ODNB*, Sullivan.

RIVINGTON FAMILY Rivington, Francis (1745-1822); **Rivington, Charles** (1754-1831); **Rivington, John** (1779-1841); **Rivington, George** (1801-1858); **Rivington, Francis** (1805-1885); **Rivington, Francis Hansard** (1834-1913); **Rivington, Septimus** (1846-1926).

From its inception by Charles Rivington (1688-1742), who was apprenticed to a London bookbinder in 1703, the family printing and publishing* business involved complex permutations of the Rivington family. At the death of their father John in 1792, brothers Francis and Charles Rivington continued their bookselling and publishing business as F. and C. Rivington. In 1793 they started the monthly*, *British Critic**, a Tory and High Church periodical, edited* by Robert Nares and William Beloe, later known as the *British Critic*,

Quarterly Theological Review, and Ecclesiastical Record.

In 1810, Francis's eldest son John joined the firm. With Francis's death in 1822, it became C. and J. Rivington until 1827 when, with Charles's two sons, George and Francis, it became, C., J., G., and F. Rivington. Francis was occupied in the Oxford and Tractarian movement to reform the Church of England. A series of pamphlets, 'Tracts for the Times', by the leaders of the movement was printed, published and circulated by Rivington's (1833-1841). This involvement identified the firm as a High Church publisher and business accordingly prospered. In 1765, John Rivington (1720-1792) had become publisher and bookseller for the Society for the Promotion of Christian Knowledge (SPCK), custom that the firm retained for the next 70 years. However, as the theological debate intensified, the SPCK disassociated itself from Rivington's in 1835, and published its own materials in direct competition. In conjunction with this rift, the *British Critic* was attacked for its radical position and closed in 1843, replaced by the *English Review* that continued until 1853. Finding itself estranged from the evangelical church and distanced from the Church of England, Rivington's fortunes continued to deteriorate.

By the 1860s, the firm was in the hands of Francis Hansard and Septimus who divided the company, Francis taking theology and Septimus creating a new educational branch. However, they dissolved the partnership in 1889, and in 1890 Francis sold the family business to Longmans* bringing the Rivington publishing reign to a close. **CL**

Source: *ODNB*.

ROBERTSON, GEORGE CROOM (1842-1892) Robertson was appointed editor* of *Mind: A Quarterly Review of Psychology and Philosophy** by its founder Alexander Bain*. Robertson shaped the journal for the first 16 years of its existence (1876-1891) until illness forced him to resign the editorship a year before his death. His contemporaries, Leslie Stephen* among them, noted that Robertson devoted painstaking attention to *Mind*, scrupulously editing each submission and taking part in all stages of its production to the detriment of his own philosophical writing. His earliest work in philosophy* was published in the 1860s in *Macmillan's Magazine**, the *British and Foreign Evangelical Review** and the *Contemporary Review**, his other articles appearing in *Mind* during his tenure as editor.

Robertson was respected for his willingness to publish contributions from a wide range of philo-

sophical perspectives. Regarding psychology as essential to philosophy – as the name he chose for the journal indicates – he believed that *Mind* should help determine whether psychology was a science. In his introductory essay to the first number, Robertson expressed the hope that *Mind* would usher in a new era of professional* philosophy, and his work as editor is now regarded as having played an important role in transforming philosophy into an academic discipline. **SA**

Sources: Bain 1893, *ODNB*, Quinton 1976, Sorley 1926.

ROBIN GOODFELLOW (1861) A 'Weekly* Journal of Fact and Fiction' selling at 2d, whose only claim to fame was that the opening episodes of the best-selling sensation novel 'Lady Audley's Secret' by Mary Elizabeth Braddon* appeared unsigned* in its pages. It was among the flurry of precarious periodicals launched around the time of the abolition of the 'taxes on knowledge'* by Braddon's companion, the Irish entrepreneur John Maxwell*. Others were the *Train* (1856-1858), *Town Talk* (1858-1859), the *Welcome Guest**, *Temple Bar**, the *Halfpenny Journal* (1861-1865) and the *Sixpenny Magazine* (1861-1867), in which 'Lady Audley's Secret' ran in its entirety throughout 1862. Edited* by Dr Charles Mackay (1814-1889), formerly with the *Illustrated London News**, *Robin Goodfellow* survived only 12 issues (6 July-21 Sept). Over five pages of the opening issue were given over to a discussion of the choice of title, though there were also poems* by Samuel Lover and the editor*, plus the opening chapters of a second serial* novel. Sir Frederick Charles Lascelles Wraxall also seems to have carried out editorial duties. **GL**

Sources: Carnell 2000, Wynne 2001.

ROBINSON, DAVID (1787-1849) David Robinson was the chief political* writer in *Blackwood's Edinburgh Magazine** for nearly eight years (1824-1831). He contributed 93 articles, generally of one 'sheet', viz. 16 pages octavo of c.9,000 words. Moving to *Fraser's Magazine** (c.1832-36), where attributions are less certain, he wrote 30 to 40 articles. His total output was thus well over one million words.

Born into a modest farming family, at Garton in Yorkshire, and leaving school aged 12 (although continuing to educate himself), Robinson changed course, after the failure of a family business, to embark on periodical journalism. Thereafter he was exclusively dependent on his pen for his living.

Robinson's contributions were invariably to Tory journals, first to the *New Times*, c. 1821-1823, notably in his 'Cato' letters. An article for the *Quarterly Review** on 'The Opposition' received a friendly notice in *Blackwood's*, in the 'Noctes Ambrosianae' for March 1823, prompting Robinson to contact William Blackwood*, who thus acquired his chief political contributor. An intensely private man, who jealously sought to preserve his anonymity – usually adopting the pseudonym* 'Y.Y.Y.', but never giving his own – Robinson succeeded all too well. He has almost disappeared from history, other than in the writings of a handful of economic historians. The most widely-read tribute to his ability comes from Harold Perkin, who describes Robinson as 'by far the most brilliant and original' of the *Blackwood's* contributors on economic topics, developing in his articles a 'proto-Keynesian economics'. For an example, see Robinson's article on 'Public Distress' (*Blackwood's* April 1826).

Although harsh and uncompromising in his views on Whigs, political economists, and 'liberal' Tories, Robinson showed heartfelt, paternalistic concern for the victims of economic fluctuation (see his fierce onslaught on Mathusianism, 'Poor Laws', *Blackwood's*, June 1828). This anticipates some of the points made, with equal force, in Thomas Carlyle's* 'Chartism' (Dec. 1839). The two were contemporaries at *Fraser's*, although there was no contact between them. Robinson's article, 'Reforms and Reformers', *Fraser's*, March 1834, became the base-article whereby the revisions to the *Wellesley Index* at last recognised his *Fraser's* work, from internal evidence. Robinson's advocacy of a measure of parliamentary reform, coming round to this view from the ultra-Tory side (see 'The Reform of the House of Commons', *Blackwood's*, April 1830) was utilised in a seminal article by D. C. Moore, without being aware of Robinson's authorship.

Obscure to the last, sick and in penury, Robinson died just over a year after a failed application to the Royal Literary Fund: denied because he had failed to publish a free-standing book. **MM**
Sources: Blackwood Papers NLS, Fetter 1960, Gordon 1979, Moore 1961, Perkin 1969, Rashid 1978, *Wellesley*.

ROCK (1868-1905) The *Rock* was a cheap*, long-lived Church of England weekly*, initially priced* at 1d for a four-page broadsheet. Established partly as a response to the *Church Times** and partly as an attempt to restore the conservative evangelical voice offered by the *Record** during the editorship* of Alexander Haldane, the *Rock* pursued an extreme Protestant line and opposed every trace of Roman Catholicism in the Anglican Church. Considerable energy went into early publicity for the paper and circulation* initially varied between 25,000 and 30,000 copies a week. However, the *Rock* quickly encountered problems and the owners, W. H. and L. Collingridge, briefly tried publishing the paper twice a week before changing the editor* and returning to weekly publication and a new format* of 16 smaller pages. By the 1880s, the *Rock* had become a more moderate paper. **MK**
Sources: Grant 1872, Palmer 1991, Reed 1996, *Waterloo*.

ROLLASON, ANN (1768/9-1846) Ann Rollason was the wife of Noah Rollason, printer, bookseller and proprietor* of the *Coventry Mercury**. After her husband's death in 1813, Rollason was able to continue the business in her own right as the city of Coventry allowed master craftsmen's widows to do so and she became proprietor of the *Coventry Mercury*. Rollason was assisted in the work by several journeyman printers in the firm, but especially by William Reader (1782-1852), a partner since 1808, who remained as manager until 1833 after his partnership agreement ceased in 1822.

Rollason did not renew the partnership with Reader, in order to protect her and her family's financial position. Her son Charles joined the business in 1820 as manager of the *Coventry Mercury*, but the paper merged* with the *Coventry Standard* in 1836. In addition to her work as printer, bookseller and binder, Rollason expanded the business to encompass the sale of magazines, stationery, stamps and patent medicines. She maintained her position running the business until her death, leaving an estate of £14,000. Only after her death did ownership pass to her eldest son. Rollason's astute business decisions and retention of control until her death indicate commercial experience that predates her husband's death. **DHL/CL**
Source: *ODNB*.

'ROLLINGTON, RALPH' (1844-1922?) ' Ralph Rollington', pseudonym* of Herbert John Allingham, was a journalist*, editor* and proprietor*. Although not a dominant figure in the world of boys' penny* weeklies*, he was a central witness to its workings during the 1870s and 1880s. His *Brief History of Boys' Journals with Interesting Facts about the Writers of Boys' Stories* was published by a collector in 1913, and Rollington was also a primary source for Frank Jay's *Peeps into the Past* (1918-1920) which details the 'fierce' boys'* papers.

Rollington was a printer who was involved with his brother James W. Allingham's Christian *Globe**.

Rollington founded the *Boy's World* (1879-1886) and other publications in the sensational style popularized by Edwin Brett's *Boys of England** and the Emmett family. As well as owning and editing his paper, Rollington was usually its main contributor, taking his pseudonym from his own most successful fictional character. The blurring of boundaries and the multiplicity of roles were characteristic of an age of small masters and could not survive the centralisation of capital and specialization of function that was characteristic of the Harmsworth's* Amalgamated Press*. A disapproving insight into Rollington's business methods can be found in the 1886 diary of his nephew Herbert Allingham which records the founding of the *New Boys' Paper*. **JJ**

Sources: Boyd 2000, Jay 1918-1921, Jones 2006, Lofts, 1970, Rollington 1913.

ROSCOE, WILLIAM CALDWELL (1823-1859) William Caldwell Roscoe, journalist* and poet, was born in Liverpool and educated at University College, London. He spent a brief period as a barrister before embarking on his twin alternate careers. From 1852-1855 he was one of a group who edited* the Unitarian *Prospective Review**, the forerunner of the *National Review**. Roscoe then went on to contribute literary* and political* review articles and poetry* to the Unitarian affiliated *National Review**, a quarterly* which was established in 1855 by Walter Bagehot* and others, and edited by his brother-in-law R. H. Hutton*. Roscoe contributed an article to virtually every number until his untimely death at 36 from typhoid fever.

Roscoe's standard of intellectual rigour helped to safeguard the *National Review*'s reputation for consistently high-quality reviews*. His piece 'W. M. Thackeray*, artist and moralist' (Jan. 1856) established him, according to a modern scholar, as Thackeray's 'first great substantial critic'. Like many of the close knit group involved in the running of both the *Prospective* and the *National*, Roscoe was involved with the weekly* press, and in particular the conduct of the Unitarian *Inquirer** (1851-1855). A selection of his journalism together with his plays and poetry were collected into a volume, with a memoir, by Hutton, in 1860. **CL/JS**

Sources: *ODNB*, *Waterloo*, *Wellesley*.

ROSS, JANET ANNE (1842-1927) Janet Ross (née Duff-Gordon) came from a long line of 'unconventional' women. Her literary efforts were often overshadowed by her outsize personality, nevertheless she produced lively works marked by the same sense of mischief and adventure with which she approached her life in general. She contributed travel writing to the *English Illustrated Magazine**, *National Review** and *Macmillan's Magazine** which was eventually published as *Italian Sketches* (1887) and *Old Tuscany and Modern Florence* (1904).

Married in 1860, Ross moved to Alexandria, where her many social connections and essential nosiness positioned her as an ideal observer of foreign* affairs; she was briefly the Egyptian correspondent for the *Evening Mail,* and for The *Times** (1863-1866). In 1867, the Rosses moved to Italy where her writing flourished. When she died in Italy, Ross's obituary* in The *Times* was full of wild, though true, stories and studded with the names of her famous friends and admirers. **FCA**

Sources: C19, Benjamin 2006, Duff Gordon 1902, *ODNB*, Ross 1888, *The Times* 1927

ROSS, JOHN WILSON (1818-1887) Editor*, short-story writer and polemicist, John Wilson Ross's most sustained engagement with journalism was with the *London Journal**. Son of a prominent member of the colonial administration of St Vincent, he was educated at King's College, London. He began his literary* career with a tale in *Bentley's Miscellany** in 1844 before becoming the first named contributor in the *London Journal* (1845), in which he went on to publish many tales and articles on a wide variety of subjects. He became its second editor in October 1846 when G. W. M. Reynolds* left, and Ross redirected the *Journal's* focus onto art and translations of French novels. It is not certain when he left the *Journal* (perhaps as early as autumn 1848), but in 1851 he placed a second tale in *Bentley's*. Although described as 'an acute thinker, a versatile writer and a first rate scholar' (Dix 1854: 287), this tribute was penned by an alcoholic friend and colleague.

Ross was in fact not successful in the literary world and no more is heard of him until 1860, when he is known to have edited the *Universal Decorator* – the series lasted only a few issues. Thereafter his work rebelled against the market and became recherché, with an anti-Darwinian pamphlet, *The Biblical Prophecy of the Burning of the World'* (1869), and 'The Doctrine of the Chorizontes (*Edinburgh Review**, 1871 – on the authorship of the *Iliad* and *Odyssey*). His career closed with an historiographical volume, *Tacitus and Bracciolini* (1878), which sought to prove that the Roman historian's work was a Medici forgery. In typical Bohemian fashion, Ross left just £26 on his death. **AK**

Sources: Dix 1854, King 2004, *ODNB*, *The Times*.

ROSSETTI, WILLIAM MICHAEL (1829-1919) Editor*, journalist*, critic, career civil servant, and one of seven original Pre-Raphaelite 'Brothers', William Michael Rossetti wrote hundreds of articles on fine art and literature* for periodicals. His criticism aimed at critical impartiality and was admired by John Ruskin* and George du Maurier*. His frank dislike of anonymous* reviews* also won the praise of Henry James*.

First in the *Critic*, then as art critic of the *Spectator*, Rossetti promoted contemporary artists, especially the Pre-Raphaelites. From 1850-1878 he wrote nearly 400 art reviews for journals and newspapers including the *Academy*, *Saturday Review*, *Fraser's Magazine*, *Edinburgh Weekly Review, London Review*, *Pall Mall Gazette*, *Reader*, *Weldon's Register, Liverpool Post*, *Fine Arts Quarterly Review* and the New York *Crayon*. Rossetti collected his best work, including a seminal article 'Præraphaelitism' (*Spectator* 4 Oct. 1851), in *Fine Art, Chiefly Contemporary* (1867). His critical acumen remained attuned to the new. One of the first advocates in London of oriental art, he championed Whistler's* new aestheticism and contributed to Mackmurdo's, *Century Guild Hobby Horse*.

Rossetti's literary reviews were equally avant-garde. As editor* of the *Germ*, the Pre-Raphaelites' experimental magazine, Rossetti contributed 'critiques' of Clough, Arnold* and Browning. He defended Swinburne* against mid-Victorian prudery and was one of the first British commentators to acclaim Walt Whitman's 'entire originality' (*Chronicle* 6 July 1867). He wrote about 60 articles (1878-1895) for the *Athenaeum*, mostly on Shelley, but also on the Italian literature of his dual heritage. A taxman who thought like a radical, Rossetti's admiration for Shelley and Whitman underpinned his egalitarian politics. He voiced his opposition to slavery in 'English Opinion on the American War' (*Atlantic Monthly*, Feb. 1866). A lifelong democrat, Rossetti's achievement in journalism* was to popularize the arts for all sections of the Victorian public. AGT
Sources: L'Enfant 1999, *ODNB*, Peattie 1975, Thirlwell 2003.

ROUTLEDGE, GEORGE (1812-1888) George Routledge was founder of the prominent and influential publishing* house Routledge and Sons. Following an apprenticeship in Carlisle, he moved to London in 1833 and after brief employment with Baldwin and Craddock, he went into the publishing business with his brother-in-law William Henry Warne. Their business grew quickly, and from the 1830s they moved to premises of increasing sizes around the capital, eventually settling in Ludgate Hill. They were particularly successful with Routledge's Railway* Library from 1849, a vast series of regularly issued shilling volumes that included authors such as Stowe, Irving and Disraeli. In the 1860s they embarked on some juvenile* titles, issuing them monthly and then bound as annuals*. Titles of this kind included *Every Boy's Magazine* (1862-1879) which continued until 1889 under a number of changing titles* including Routledge's *Magazine for Boys* (1865-1868), *Young Gentleman's Magazine* (1869-1873), reverting to the original *Every Boy's Magazine* (1874-1889). There was a female counterpart in the 1870s, *Every Girl's Magazine* (1878-1885). By 1898, when the Railway Library ended, there were 1,277 volumes.

In 1858, Routledge took his eldest son into partnership, at which time the business became George Routledge and Sons. Once described as 'a man of uncommon modesty and generosity of spirit', Routledge was well known and well liked in the publishing industry. His business model of providing small, cheap* editions of classic texts had prefigured the shape of the publishing industry in the twentieth century. KJH
Sources: Maidment 1973, *New York Times* 15 Dec.1888, *ODNB*, Routledge 1875.

ROYAL IRISH ACADEMY: *TRANSACTIONS OF THE ROYAL IRISH ACADEMY* (1787-1907) AND *PROCEEDINGS OF THE ROYAL IRISH ACADEMY* (1836-1901) The Royal Irish Academy received its charter in 1785 as a Society for promoting the study of science, polite literature and antiquities', and from the outset publication of its members' scholarly papers was highly important its *Transactions*, appearing irregularly (1787-1907) and its *Proceedings* (1836-1901), for both of which it was the issuing body*. The *Transactions* were expensive, specialized productions: quarto size*, with wide margins and large type, lavishly illustrated*. In volume form, the *Transactions* could run from 500 to 600 pages, with papers averaging about 50 pages in length. Individual parts of the *Transactions* were priced* from 15s to 20s each, depending on the length of the papers, and usually in print runs of about 500 copies.

Transactions were offered for sale in quite a long list of newspapers and journals – from the *Athenaeum** to *Saunders' Newsletter** – but most were intended as gifts to philosophical or scientific societies outside Ireland. The pattern of publication follows roughly the pattern of activity in the Academy itself; that is, the initial enthusiasm of Academy members led to one volume per year until about 1803. From then on until the 1820s, gaps appear in the publication schedule.

In 1836 the Academy Council decided to embark on a new publishing venture, largely for the benefit of its own members, but also to keep general readers abreast of developments in science* and related literature. The result was the *Proceedings*: cheaper than the *Transactions* to produce, and employing a more user-friendly format that presumably would appeal to the less academically-inclined reader. Individual parts of the *Proceedings* were octavo, with fewer woodcuts* and engravings than the *Transactions*, and its pages included non-scholarly material. Items in the new *Proceedings* included lists of papers read to the Academy, abstracts of papers, and occasionally full texts of papers. News*, such as notices of new members elected, resolutions passed, and lists of council members elected began each relevant part. Unlike the *Transactions*, the *Proceedings* appeared at regular monthly* intervals and were free to members of the Academy and for sale to the public at a price* that varied with the length of each issue; the first part was a mere 2s.

The split in Academy publications inevitably meant that material reserved for the *Transactions* was (or was perceived to be) of higher quality than that published in the *Proceedings*. Minute Books record the battles between members over space in the Academy's publications, and neatly duplicate a similar clash between late eighteenth-century antiquarianism and Victorian utilitarianism in the scientific community. George Petrie* was Chair of the Publications Committee in the late 1830s, and his style of research, meticulous and historically-based, led the way. In 1902 the *Proceedings* were split into three sections: A) Mathematical and Physical Sciences, B) Biology and Environment, C) Archaeology, Linguistics and Literature. ET

Sources: Andrews 2002, Leerssen 1996, *RIA* Minute Books 1837.

RUFF, WILLIAM (1801-1856) William Ruff, sports'* journalist*, was born in London and had a legal education. Around 1820 he became general sports' reporter* for London newspapers as well as racing reporter for *Bell's Life in London and Sporting Chronicle**, a position he inherited from his father. His connection with *Bell's Life* extended over 25 years and at a period noted for dishonest dealings in the racing world, Ruff was noted for the accuracy and honesty of his reporting; Henry Dixon wrote that his racing reports 'were marvellous specimens

of pithy condensation'. (Dixon:174).

Priding himself on the swiftness of news* delivery, Ruff also pioneered the use of pigeons to carry his reports from provincial race courses to London newspapers. This meant results could be brought to readers with greater speed. Ruff's enduring racing legacy was his *Guide to the Turf, or Pocket Racing Companion* which was initially an annual publication (1843ff.) that brought him 'world-wide celebrity*' and is still published today by *Sporting Life*. In 1854 Ruff retired due to ill-health attributed to overwork, and according to his obituary* in *Bell's Life in London* he never visited a racecourse again. DHL

Sources: *Bell's Life in London* 1857, Dixon 1880, *ODNB*.

RUNCIMAN, JOHN F. (1866-1916) As music* critic for the *Saturday Review**, John F. Runciman was reputed to be forceful at best and libellous at worst. His dismissal of academic pretentiousness and common hypocrisy was thought to originate from his northern roots and may explain his column's* popularity with a general audience. Yet his writing style was deemed 'vigorous' and 'picturesque', and his acerbity was informed by an extensive knowledge of his subject: he was a musician of catholic tastes.

He also contributed music criticism to the *Fortnightly Review** and the *New Review** as well as literary criticism to the *Saturday Review*. Runciman edited* the *Chord*, a short-lived quarterly*, wrote for the *Dome** and placed articles in several American papers, including the *Musical World* (Boston). Though his erudition was confirmed by the series of books he produced on composers such as Haydn, Purcell and Wagner, his most popular book was a compilation of his *Saturday Review* articles, *Old Scores and New Readings: Discussions on Music and Certain Musicians* (1899). CL

Sources: *Musical Times* 1916, Runciman 1895, *The Times* 1916.

RUSKIN, JOHN (1819-1901) Ever alert to the need for lively engagement with his potential readers, and despite his repeatedly expressed contempt for journalism* and sensationalism, John Ruskin published much of his work in periodicals. His heterodox views on economics and the challenging individuality of his style brought him into repeated conflict with editors*, notably Thackeray* at the *Cornhill** (where Ruskin published 'Unto This Last' in 1860) and Froude* at *Fraser's Magazine**, who brought 'Munera Pulveris' to a premature conclusion after four instalments had been published

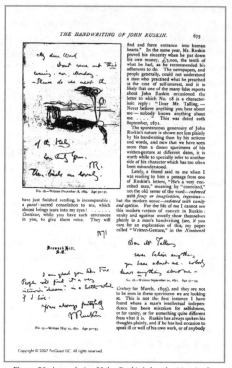

Figure 58: An analysis of John Ruskin's handwriting in the *Strand*, July 1895: 675.

in 1862. As well as his persistent use of periodicals for the publication of his new work in serial* form after 1860, Ruskin wrote nearly 20 articles for a range of periodicals from the *Magazine of Natural History* to such established journals as the *Contemporary Review** and the *Nineteenth Century**. He was also an enthusiastic and endlessly polemical contributor to the correspondence* pages of newspapers and magazines*, gathering his letters to the press into several occasional volumes, such as *Arrows of the Chace* (1880).

Ruskin's extraordinary late work, *Fors Clavigera* (1871-1884), was conceived and published as a combination of a diary and a periodical. While never popular or, indeed, understood at the time, *Fors* was nonetheless a unique experiment in the confessional genre that owed much to Ruskin's understanding of how to construct dialogues with the public through the use of serial form. **BM**
Sources: Cook and Wedderburn 1899, Maidment 1982.

RUSSEL, ALEXANDER (1814-1876) Alexander Russel was a newspaper editor* and journalist* unafraid to pursue his own research for a story and the public good, though he was also known as a task-

master who found it difficult to praise his colleagues' work. Following an apprenticeship to a printer, Russel became editor of the *Berwick Advertiser** in 1839, doubling as a reporter* because he knew shorthand*. Having edited both the *Fife Herald* and the liberal *Kilmarnock Chronicle* (1842-1845), Russel came to the attention of John Ritchie, one of the founders of the *Scotsman**, who invited him to become the assistant to *Scotsman* editor Charles Maclaren*. Russel took up this position in March 1845 in Edinburgh, primarily subediting* and writing leaders*, but soon took over editorial duties when Maclaren was abroad. By the end of 1845, Russel had effectively become the paper's editor, though he was not officially made so until 1849.

His work could be identified even when printed anonymously* because of his individualistic style. (It was known that if he romped with his children while writing a piece, the exuberance would show in his article.) His interest in investigating* a story personally prompted him to explore Highland destitution in 1847; he toured the Highlands and Islands and published articles both in the *Scotsman* and the *Edinburgh Review**. His reports prompted government assistance and public subscriptions, and thus played a major role in relieving poverty. In 1851, Russel was the only Scottish journalist who travelled to London in order to argue against the abolition of Stamp Duty* on newspapers. When stamp duty was repealed in 1855, leaving smaller liberal papers to expand their readership* and threaten advertising* revenue for more established papers, Russel countered by increasing the *Scotsman's* frequency* from twice weekly* to daily*, a bold move which helped develop it from a local* city newspaper into a national one with a circulation* of 50,000 by 1877. Additional to his editorial success, Russel was a pioneer in angling journalism, contributing many articles some of which were reprinted in the *Salmon* (1864). **TR**
Sources: Magnusson 1967, *ODNB*.

RUSSELL, WILLIAM CLARK (1844-1911) Following a privileged upbringing, William Clark Russell, journalist* and editor*, made the surprising choice in 1858 to become a British merchant seaman. His eight years in the Merchant Navy furnished him with the material for a successful writing career. After a false start as a playwright, he turned to journalism, becoming editor* in 1868 of the *Leader* (1867-1869), a 2d weekly* paper originating in Liverpool, before writing for the *Kent County News* (1871ff). Utilizing his experiences as a merchant seaman, he contributed articles to several journals before becoming a member of staff at the *Newcastle Chronicle** in 1880 and then working briefly as editor of *Mayfair*. Under the pseudonym* 'A Seafarer', he wrote for the *Daily Telegraph**, where he was on the staff (1882-1889); his articles were published in collections such as *Round the Galley Fire* (1883). Other pseudonyms were 'Sydney Mostyn' and 'Eliza Rhyl Davies'.

In tandem with his journalism, Russell wrote successful fictional sea adventures, 57 novels in total. Russell's experiences at sea were also the basis for numerous campaigning articles that urged parliamentary reform* to the hardships and dangers that were a routine part of merchant seamen's lives. The future George V acknowledged the influence of Russell's journalism on the continuation of legislative reform after the 1876 'Plimsoll Line' Act. **CL** Source: *ODNB*.

RUSSELL, WILLIAM HOWARD (1820-1907) A gifted and energetic descriptive reporter*, William Howard Russell achieved celebrity* status as the best known and one of the most influential of all Victorian newspapermen. Propelled to prominence by his path-breaking reports for *The Times** from the scenes of battle, Russell is best remembered as the world's first war* correspondent*, a term he himself disliked. His journalism* was marked by colourful and vigorous narrative as well as pointedly critical reporting, the latter often reflecting his reformist and somewhat idiosyncratic Conservative views.

Born in Ireland, where he was raised by his Protestant grandparents and attended Trinity College without taking a degree, Russell was hired in 1841 as a reporter for *The Times* by his cousin Robert Russell, who covered the Irish general election for the paper. Following the election, Russell travelled to London where he learned shorthand* and continued to write for *The Times*, whose editor John T. Delane* sent him back to Ireland in 1843 to cover the repeal agitation. Delane was impressed with Russell's work and handed him some plum assignments (including O'Connell's 1844 trial and the 'railway mania') as well as putting him to work in the press gallery of the House of Commons.

In 1845 he moved to the *Morning Chronicle**, before returning to *The Times* in 1848. His first work as a war correspondent came for that paper in 1850 when he followed the conflict between the Schleswig-Holstein forces and the Danish army. His daily dispatches from the field of battle gave readers gripping accounts of the realities of war as they unfolded, listing hourly developments and attempting to gauge the effects of the conflict on the civilian population of the region as well as providing detailed accounts of military manoeuvres and citing examples of courage in the face of the deadly firepower of the Danes.

These skills were put to more sustained use when Delane dispatched him to cover the Crimean War in 1854, an assignment that lasted two years and made his name. His reports of the siege of Sebastopol and other key battles dwelt on the heroism of the British army, but also sought to expose the military, logistical and medical blunders that contributed to the suffering of the troops. He was overtly critical of Lord Raglan and other leading officers, and his reports had a profound influence on public attitudes toward the war, playing a large role in the fall of Aberdeen's ministry and in bringing Florence Nightingale to the Crimea. Russell's description of the charge of the doomed Light Brigade at Balaclava inspired Tennyson's poem and helped enshrine the event in British memory. By the time Russell returned to Britain, his Crimea reporting had made him a hero to many of his readers, and a sought-after author and speaker.

Russell was dispatched to India in 1857 to report on the Sepoy rebellion, where he advocated a conciliatory approach, criticising the harsh treatment meted out to the Indians. Returning from India in 1859, he was sent to America in 1860, where his support for the north and his contempt for the slave-owning traditions of the Confederacy initially won him adulation. But his criticisms of the Union army following their retreat in the first battle of Bull Run led to withdrawal of official permission for him to accompany the Federal forces, and he returned home in April 1862. The following year he published *My Diary North and South* (1863) with Bradbury and Evans*, through whom he enjoyed a close association with the *Punch** circle. Initially ambivalent about writing war stories under the time limitations of filing by telegraph, Russell published a book in 1865 on the *Atlantic Telegraph*. In 1860, Russell had founded the successful service periodical, *Army and Navy Gazette*, of which he remained editor and chief proprietor for over forty years.

Russell later reported for *The Times* on the Austro-Prussian War in 1866 and the Franco-Prussian war in 1870-1871. In 1879 his attempt to cover the Anglo-Zulu war for the *Daily Telegraph** (*The Times* was not interested this time) was scuppered when he arrived after the war was over, but he still managed to print some provocative depictions of the misconduct of the British troops. This occasioned a public spat with Wolseley, who subsequently prevented him from accompanying British troops on a campaign in Egypt in 1882. Russell's marked ability to enrage prominent generals owed something to his tendency to indulge personal grudges, as well as to his altruism and crusading zeal. Russell had qualified as a barrister in 1850, although he rarely practised at the bar. In 1895 a knighthood was added to his many honours. **MaT**

Sources: *ODNB, Times Digital Archive, Waterloo*

RYMER, JAMES MALCOLM (1814-1884) James Malcolm Rymer was one of the three most popular writers of sensation fiction for the mid-Victorian penny press*. Yet, unlike his rivals, G. W. M. Reynolds* and J. F. Smith, he guarded his middle class respectability behind anonymity*, issuing his fiction as 'by the author of ...' (listing his previous novelistic successes), or under pseudonyms*, the most common being 'M. J. Errym' or 'James Malcolm Merry'.

Rymer was born in London to a well-to-do family, and became a civil engineer and engraver, with social aspirations. Engraving brought him into contact with Edward Lloyd*, and he became the foremost author of Lloyd's luridly illustrated* penny* issue fiction. For Lloyd he wrote 'Adeline; or the Grave of the Forsaken' (1841); edited* *Lloyd's Penny Weekly Miscellany* (1843-1846), leading with his own sensation 'Ada the Betrayed; or, the Murder at the Old Smithy' besides contributing over 25 other novels, ranging from traditional Gothic ('The Black Monk', 1844) to social melodrama ('The White Slave: a Romance for the Nineteenth Century', 1845), and including 'Varney the Vampyre; or the Feast of Blood' (1845-1847), which is still (2008) in print.

As Lloyd's serials became dated in the 1850s, Rymer moved to *Reynolds's Miscellany**, and with 'The Life Raft; a Tale of the Sea' (1856) became one of John Dicks's* most popular authors. His last fiction appears to have been for the short-lived *London Miscellany* in 1866, which included 'A Mystery in Scarlet', a tale that delighted Robert Louis Stevenson. From the 1860s his novels were repeatedly pirated in America under a bewildering variety of titles and attributions. Rymer did acknowledge editorship of the *Queen's Magazine; or Monthly Miscellany* (5 numbers, 1842), poems, short stories and essays written for 'ladies and gentlemen', one of which advised the would-be popular writer 'to study the animals for whom he had to cater'. Rymer's own success with this formula pioneered a new market-based professionalism* in constructing fiction for the new periodical mass* readership. **LJ**

Sources: Catling 1911, James 1963, Jay 2008, Johannssen 1950, Rymer 1842, Stevenson 1888, *ODNB*.

S

S.H. BENSON   A circuitous career path brought Samuel Herbert Benson (1854-1914) to his eventual success as founder of S.H. Benson, an advertising agency*. Invalided out of the Royal Navy, in 1885 Benson attempted his first entrepreneurial venture in competition* with the Post Office, a unit of messenger boys making up his Express Courier Corps. Conceding Post Office hostility, Benson went into management when this business failed. Now, in the Bovril company, came an opportunity to develop new skills as its advertising agent.

In 1893 he established his own agency, S. H. Benson, becoming known for honour in a dishonourable business. With imagination and flair, utilizing the latest technology such as electric signs, his business flourished, and the Advertisers' Exhibition of 1899 in London, organized by Benson, supported his contention that advertising was inevitable in the business world. Despite hostility to his ideas from the publisher* and editor*, George Newnes* and disputes over financial issues and circulation* claims, the representative presence of Fleet Street* at the Exhibition's inaugural lunch proclaimed the veracity of Benson's assertion as to advertising's life-giving essence in the world of print.

Benson delivered his ground-breaking advertising* concepts in his books, *Wisdom in Advertising* (1901) and *Force in Advertising* (1904) and, from 1905, *Benson's Facts* that included various categories of information (e.g. figures) on press advertising. S. H. Benson's legacy lay in the depth of his understanding of the market*, his treatment of his staff and his attempt to establish an Association of Advertising Agents, demonstrating his desire to regulate and professionalize* a business often marred by sharp practice.

S. H. Benson's son, Phillip, took over in 1914, and established the agency as one of the most successful in the UK. In 1948 it helped fund David Oglivy in New York who created Hewitt, Oglivy, Benson and Mather. In 1953 Hewitt was dropped, and in 1964 the New York agency merged* with Mather and Crowder of London, changing its title to Oglivy and Mather, and losing Benson. **CL**
Source: Corporate Watch online, *ODNB.*

ST JAMES'S GAZETTE: AN EVENING REVIEW AND RECORD OF NEWS (1880-1905)   *St James's Gazette* was a conservative daily* broadsheet*, started by Henry Hucks Gibbs for Frederick Greenwood*, who had resigned from his previous editorship of the *Pall Mall Gazette** on seeing that it had moved in the liberal direction. In his eight years as editor*, Greenwood imitated the format of his former paper in the new one, which appeared as a 16-page, 1d evening paper every weekday. From 3 July 1880 a weekly* edition, the *St James's Budget*, appeared, offering 40 large pages in two-column* format* for 6d each Saturday. Sidney Low took over the editorship in 1888, and finally passed it over to Hugh Chisholm. It was bought by Cyril Pearson* in 1903.

The daily *St James's Gazette* offered ten pages of social, political* and literary* commentary, news*, marriage announcements, stock market prices and about two pages of advertisements*. Contributors included J. M. Barrie, Edmund Gosse* and Sidney Low. It effected J. M. Barrie's literary breakthrough by publishing his humorous sketch 'An Auld Licht Community' (14 Nov. 1884), a success that encouraged Barrie to write a series based on Scottish life. Margaret Oliphant's* series of articles 'A Fireside Commentary' (11 Jan.-8 June 1888) provides an example of elegant commentary on everyday life and historical reminiscence that was characteristic of this publication. **ZV**
Sources: Altick 1957, *ODNB, Wellesley.*

ST JAMES'S MAGAZINE (1861-1900)   The *St James's Magazine* was launched as a literary* monthly* simultaneously with the *Cornhill**, *St Paul's**, *Temple Bar* and *Belgravia** during the fad of capitalizing on a fashionable corner of London to market a new periodical. It was intended to be the main rival of the *Cornhill*. Initiated by John Maxwell* and published by W. Kent and Co. in 1861, its first editor* (1861-1868) was Anna Maria Hall*, an established editor, writer and playwright. As Hall put it in the first issue, she intended to 'promote the Interests of the Home, the Refinements of Life, and the Amusement and Information of All Classes*', and indeed, refinement was evident in the first leading article discussing the Court of St James. Circulation* was around 15,000 copies in 1884.

Hall's best novel, 'Can Wrong be Right?' was the opening serial; it was followed by good serial* fiction during her editorship, including Mary E. Braddon's* 'Only a Clod' (Aug. 1864-July 1865). There were articles on astronomy, travel, literature* and science*, with a series on 'Historical misrepresentations' (April 1865-Dec. 1865). Foreign issues and literature were often tackled in the mid-1860s, when the Abyssinian question was discussed (Aug. 1865), in the company of 'Early Spanish Playwrights' (Aug. 1865) and 'Danish Romances' (Nov. 1865). The periodical also carried poetry* by Thomas Hood*, Dinah Craik, and Adelaide Procter. Social questions were addressed, philanthropic enterprises described, and leisured women's interests were met by hints at the servant problem*. Hall also introduced a children's column*, 'For the Young of the Household' (April 1861-Jan. 1863).

St James's Magazine also provided training for one of the most effective female periodical editors of the century, Mary Braddon*, who was to become editor of *Belgravia** in 1866. In 1867, Hall was joined by the novelist Charlotte E. Riddell as co-editor and proprietor*, and then replaced by Riddell, who edited the magazine from 1868 for some years, continuing to publish articles on a diverse range of topics. In 1872, the title* changed to the *St James's Magazine and United Empire Review* (1872-1877), but in 1878 reverted to its original form. **ZV/MBT**
Sources: Altick 1957, *ODNB*, Onslow 2000, *Waterloo*.

ST JOHN, BAYLE FREDERICK (1822-1859) Bayle St John, a bohemian writer on the Middle East, translator from French and Paris correspondent for the *Telegraph** (1855-1858), was the son of James Augustus St John* and brother of Percy* and Horace. He spent much of his childhood with his family in France and Switzerland, returning to London when he was 11. His first article was accepted by a monthly* magazine* two years later and he was soon contributing to the *Sunday Times**, the *Penny Magazine**, and the *Foreign Quarterly Review**. In 1842 he wrote the series 'De re vehiculari, or a Comic History of Chariots' for *Fraser's Magazine**. When he was 24, following in his father's footsteps, he travelled via France and Italy to Egypt, where he learnt Arabic over two years. Returning to Paris in June 1848 he wrote a series of books and articles on his experiences, including *Two Years' Residence in a Levantine Family* (1850) based on the diary he had kept in Alexandria. Various other books and articles followed a second visit to Egypt (1850-1851), including 40 pieces for *Household Words**.

Suffering from tuberculosis and in dire poverty, with a wife and two daughters to support, he resettled in London in 1858 where he began 'Violet Davenant', a serial novel for the *London Journal** which remained unfinished at his death. Dickens* organized his widow's charity performance. St

John's writings were 'characterized by shrewdness, animation, and vigour of style, and were deservedly popular' (*Annual Register 1859*, 1860), though recent critics have rightly noted both a commitment to liberal republicanism in common with his brothers and father and a powerful current of racism. **AK**
Sources: *Annual Register 1859*, *Athenaeum* 1859, *Atlas* 1859, Lohli 1973, *ODNB*.

ST JOHN, JAMES AUGUSTUS (1795-1875) Prolific initially in radical journalism and editing*, and from the mid-1820s in writing and editing mainstream publications – and in fathering 11 children, four of whom (Percy*, Bayle*, Horace Roscoe and Vane Ireton) followed in their father's journalistic footsteps – St John was from a humble background in Wales. Largely self-educated, he constitutes an excellent example of energetic Victorian self-fashioning through print. Born simple James John, he early employed the more impressive 'Julian Augustus St John' when contributing to *Sherwin's Weekly Political Register* and its continuation the *Republican** (editing the latter for a few months in 1819 while Carlile* was in prison).

St John edited a radical newspaper, the *Patriot** (1820-1822), but then, reverting to 'James' (though keeping the Augustus and St), he became subeditor on James Silk Buckingham's* monthly* *Oriental Herald and Colonial Review* (1824-1829). With David Lester Richardson, he founded the *London Weekly Review* in 1827 which sought to combine the virtues of a weekly* and quarterly*. It attracted contributors such as Mary Howitt* and Shelley. In 1829 it was purchased by Henry Colburn* and renamed the *Court Journal*. The same year St John and his growing family went to live in France and Switzerland while he continued to publish in England (including in the *Westminster** and for the SDUK*). In 1832 he left for Egypt, returning to London after two years to capitalize on his experiences in factual and fictional works. He specialized in overseas areas, especially the Orient. A few pieces by him occur in the *Monthly Chronicle* (1838-1841) in 1838. In the 1840s, he wrote for the *Foreign Quarterly Review**, and for the *Sunday Times** as 'Greville Brooke'. In the late 1850s, now blind, he wrote political* leaders* for the *Daily Telegraph**, helped by his son Horace. An isolated article appeared in the *Edinburgh Review** in the 1860s. He died, as so many like him did, destitute. **AK**
Sources: *ODNB*, *Wellesley*, Wiener 1983.

ST JOHN, PERCY BOLINGBROKE (1821-89) The eldest son of James Augustus St John*, Percy Bolingbroke St John was a key contributor to penny* family* weeklies*. He travelled extensively in America in his youth, contributed a few pieces to *Bentley's** and *Ainsworth's** in 1843-1844 and 1844-1845 respectively, some stories to *Hood's Magazine and Comic Miscellany** in 1845 and one piece to the *Foreign and Quarterly Review** (Jan. 1845), before editing* the final years of the *Mirror of Literature** (1846-1850). Meanwhile, he was writing a good deal for *Tait's Edinburgh Magazine**, and in 1847 published his first of four tales for the *London Journal** in this period; it may be that he also acted as Paris correspondent* of the *North British Daily Mail* and *Lloyd's Weekly News**: in 1850 letters appeared from him in *The Times** with a French address.

In 1853 St John became the first front-page novelist for *Cassell's Illustrated Family Paper**, while contributing the odd tale to the *London Journal*. He was persuaded to move, as front-page novelist, to the latter in early 1856. St John briefly attempted to run his own penny* fiction weekly in 1861-1863, the *London Herald*, before returning as contributor of serials* and tales to the *London Journal*. Simultaneously, he was employed to 'revise and edit' at least 16 translations (1858-1868) by George Vickers. He stayed with Vickers and the *Journal* until 1883, pirated all the while in America. St John died in apparently wretched circumstances. **AK**
Sources: *Bookseller* 1861, King 2004, *ODNB*, *The Times*.

SAINT PAUL'S: A MONTHLY MAGAZINE (1867-1874)

Saint Paul's was a shilling* monthly* launched by the printer James Virtue*, with the novelist Anthony Trollope* as editor*. Establishing a new magazine* in January 1867 was no easy task, as the relatively short lifespan of *Saint Paul's* suggests. Since the repeal of the final taxes on knowledge in 1861, periodical publishing was cheaper than ever before, so the market* into which new publications ventured was more competitive*. Virtue approached Trollope, one of the giants of the circulating libraries* and a contributor to a range of periodicals, with an offer of £1,000 to edit the new title, which he hoped to name after Trollope – perhaps 'Trollope's Monthly'. Virtue was hoping to capitalize on a brand name, but Trollope balked at this level of self-promotion, and also warned Virtue 'that the chances of an adequate return to him of his money were very small'. Still, Trollope was won over and became yet another novelist-editor (like Thackeray*, Mary E. Braddon* and, in the same year, Ellen Wood*) in the shilling* monthly market. Following a well-established convention, the magazine adopted an instantly recognizable London place name for its title, like the *Cornhill**, *Temple Bar**, and *Belgravia**.

As might be expected, there was serial* fiction alongside a range of miscellaneous articles, although, pointedly, not literary criticism, which Trollope felt was an area in which high quality could not easily be maintained. In fact, the editor, who had recently unsuccessfully campaigned to become an MP, emphasized mostly Liberal politics*. The lead serial, Trollope's own 'Phineas Finn, the Irish Member', followed a young man's entrance into Parliament, and a number of articles addressed the Second Reform Bill of 1867 and the Irish Question. The high-quality writers included figures such as Leslie Stephen*, G. H. Lewes*, Edward Dicey and Eliza Lynn Linton*. Like all shilling monthlies, *Saint Paul's* aimed at a wide, general, middle-class* readership*, though the magazine never brought in sufficient numbers to make it pay. Virtue sold the title on to Alexander Strahan* in May 1869, and Trollope resigned as editor in 1870. While the editor regretted that he could not make the magazine succeed, he did find in his experience food for the imagination, and his revealing series of short stories about the world of periodicals – 'An Editor's Tales' – was serialized in *Saint Paul's* (1869-1870). **MWT**
Sources: Turner 2000c, *Waterloo*, *Wellesley*.

SAINTSBURY, GEORGE EDWARD BATEMAN (1845-1933)

From his first major essay, on the French poet Charles Baudelaire, published in the *Fortnightly Review** in October 1875, to his important *Short History of English Literature* in 1898, Saintsbury was both a man of the press and someone who understood the significance of the impact of journalism in contemporary society. His period of greatest productivity as a journalist was between the 1870s and the 1890s, during which he wrote reviews, literary* essays and political* journalism extensively for *Macmillan's Magazine**, the *Pall Mall Gazette**, *St. James's Gazette** and especially the conservative *Saturday Review**, among the most important journals for literary criticism at the time and of which he was assistant editor* (1883-1894).

Saintsbury's career as prolific journalist was brought to a near halt in 1895 when he took up the Regius Professorship of Rhetoric and English Literature at University of Edinburgh. From then on, he concentrated mostly on writing an astonishing number of often multi-volume histories of literature covering all periods.

In 1895, in his *History of Nineteenth-Century Literature*, Saintsbury gave an assessment of the place of journalism in the period that located it as the pre-eminent aspect of contemporary literature: 'Perhaps there is no single feature of the English literary history of the nineteenth century, not even the enormous popularisation and multiplication of the novel, which is so distinctive and characteristic as the development in it of periodical literature' (Saintsbury: 166). MWT

Sources: Jones 1992, Orel 1984, Saintsbury 1896.

SALA, GEORGE AUGUSTUS (1828-1895) George Augustus Sala, journalist*, editor* and illustrator*, was one of the most prolific contributors to newspapers and periodicals in the nineteenth century. His personal style of writing and the exuberance of language in his articles, short stories and serialized novels won him many followers. His critics thought he was vulgar, uneducated and believed his name was synonymous with all that was negative about the professionalization* of journalism.

Sala's first published work was a short story satirizing* George Hudson. Entitled 'Choo-Lew-Kwang; Or The Stags of Pekin', it appeared in the *Family Herald* (1842-1940) on 13 December 1845. Sala was also at this time an illustrator, working for *Man In The Moon**, the *Lady's Newspaper* (1847-1863) and *Lloyd's Weekly London Newspaper**. Sala began to contribute essays and short fiction to *Chat* (1847-1849) and towards the end of the run became its editor. Sala's big break into journalism arrived when Charles Dickens* accepted an essay entitled 'The Key Of The Street' for inclusion in *Household Words** (6 Sept. 1851). Sala would go on to contribute 158 essays for Dickens's weekly* over the next six and a half years – only Henry Morley wrote more for the magazine – and would finally renounce illustration* for a career in journalism.

Despite living in a dissolute fashion in the 1850s and surrounding himself with fellow bohemian journalists, Sala managed to contribute articles to *Punchinello* (1854-1855), *Train**, *Illustrated Times**, the *Critic* (1843-1863), *Everybody's Journal* (1859-1860), the *Leader** and the *Welcome Guest** (1858-1861). His first novel, 'Baddington Peerage' was serialized* in the *Illustrated Times* and the *Welcome Guest* published his second, 'Make Your Game', along with a series of articles chronicling London life entitled 'Twice Round The Clock'. In 1860 Sala began a series of weekly columns* for the *Illustrated London News** entitled 'Echoes Of The Week' (1860-1887). He also contributed nine on William Hogarth to *Cornhill**. In December 1860 he assumed the role of editor of the shilling* monthly *Temple Bar** which aimed to emulate the success of *Cornhill*. Edmund Yates* took over editorial

duties in 1863 when Sala was sent by the *Daily Telegraph** to report on the American Civil War*.

Sala had begun writing for the *Daily Telegraph* in 1857 and his successful association with the newspaper lasted until his death. He became its Special Correspondent* (1860-1890) and wrote lively, personal accounts of the inhabitants and customs of such far flung countries as Algeria, Australia, New Zealand and the USA, as well as reporting on many European countries. Sala also contributed during this period to *All The Year Round**, *Belgravia**, *Bow Bells**, *Banter* (1867-1868), *Truth**, *Touchstone* (1878-1879), *Mirth* (1877-1878), *Fun**, *Gentleman's Magazine** as well as editing his own title, *Sala's Journal* (1892-1894), which had initial circulation* figures of 200,000.

Sala's reputation as an innovative and influential journalist lies in his series 'Twice Round the Clock', the articles he contributed to *Household Words* and his travel reportage. He was an influence on the New Journalism* of the 1880s and his leaders* for the *Daily Telegraph* significantly contributed to its massive circulation* figures. To Matthew Arnold* and the critics of the *Saturday Review** however, his 'Telegraphese' was representative of the philistinism of the middle class. PB

Sources: Blake 2006, Edwards 1997, Sala 1895, Straus 1942.

SAMBOURNE, EDWARD LINLEY (1844-1910) A largely self-taught illustrator* and cartoonist*, Edward Linley Sambourne fell by chance out of a potential career as an engineering draughtsman when some of his early drawings were shown to Mark Lemon* at *Punch**. Sambourne's subsequent career was indissolubly associated with that magazine*, his first drawing appearing in April 1867. Although his distinctive style emerged only slowly, he became a regular staff member of *Punch* in 1871, and, at the end of John Tenniel's* long occupancy in 1901, its chief cartoonist.

Unusually for a black and white artist, Sambourne used a huge library of photographic* images to give accuracy to his work, which was characterized by a vivid and decisive linearity as well as an artistic inventiveness that took his images far beyond the simple concept of a cartoon* or 'comic cut'. The quality of his work for *Punch* was acknowledged by the Royal Academy, which exhibited his drawings over a 20-year period. While his work for *Punch* occupied most of his energy, he also drew occasionally for a range of magazines in the 1890s, *Good Words**, *Black and White** and the *Sketch** among them. BM

Sources: Engen 1990, Houfe 1978, Spielmann 1895.

SAMPSON, HENRY (1841-1891) The career of Henry Sampson embraced the full gamut of potential and risk surrounding the growth of popular* journalism in the second half of the nineteenth century. From boy compositor to proofreader, contributor, subeditor*, leader* writer*, sports* columnist, then on to editor* and proprietor*, it was a career punctuated by the collapse of short-lived titles amid a dizzying round of appointments. In 1877, Sampson helped found the 1d Sunday sporting* newspaper, the *Referee*, where his sporting journalism under the signature* 'Pendragon', proved a popular feature until his death.

Born in Lincoln, the son of a schoolmaster who later took up journalism*, Sampson's family moved to London where, upon his father's death, he entered a printing office, aged 12. He excelled at sport, but at 23 he was forced to give up competition through injury; by the time he was 25, Sampson was writing occasional pieces for the press, before securing work on the *Glow-worm* and *Weekly Dispatch*. Joining the staff of the *Illustrated Sporting and Theatrical News*, he was appointed editor in 1869, briefly working on the *Latest News*. He worked on *Fun*, as subeditor* and later editor of the *Fun Comic Annual*, and at the *Morning Advertiser* as leader* writer.

His enthusiasm for games saw him contribute a sporting column* to the *Weekly Dispatch* (1872-1877) and, in partnership with *Dispatch* owner Ashton Dilke, he launched the *Referee* in August 1877, acting as editor and transferring his 'Pendragon' column to the new title. Upon Dilke's death in 1883 Sampson became sole proprietor. Sampson helped produce the *Slang Dictionary* (1873) for Chatto and Windus* and in the following year wrote *A History of Advertising* for the same publishers. In 1879 he was the author of *Modern Boxing*, by 'Pendragon'. **ST**
Sources: Boase 1908, Simonis 1917, *Sporting Mirror* 1881, *The Times* 1891.

SAMPSON LOW & CO. (1825-1964) This publishing* house had its origins in Sampson Low (1797-1886), who set up business in 1819 as a bookseller and stationer based at 42 Lamb's Conduit Street. Previously apprenticed to Lionel Booth, proprietor of a circulating library, Low then worked for Longman & Co*. In the *Morning Chronicle* of 27 June 1822 Low advertised the opening of a subscription library and reading room* at the same address 'which will be regularly supplied with the Morning and Evening Newspapers, the Periodical Publications, and all New Works of interest'. In 1837 he was installed as editor* and publisher* of the *Publishers' Circular*, a new trade* paper for the publishing industry. His editorship of the *Publishers' Circular* lasted many years, and he eventually became sole proprietor* in 1867.

Though Low published quite a few books before 1848 (including Oliver Wendell Holmes's *One Hundred Days in Europe* and religious titles such as Elizabeth Maria Lord's *Exercises in the Gospel Narrative of the Life of Our Lord*), the *Publisher's Circular* seems to have been the focus of his publishing activities until he opened a dedicated publishing company in that year on the corner of Red Lion Court, Fleet Street* in partnership with his son Sampson Low Jnr. Edward Marston became a partner in 1856, followed by Samuel Warren Searle in 1872, then William John Rivington, and Marston's son Robert in 1883. 'Sampson Low, Son, and Marston' was the company's principal name during this period: the elder Low retired in 1875. The company's principal line of business was book publishing, and it became the leading publisher of American works, facilitated in part by Low's role as the agent for Harper Brothers* of New York which had begun in 1844. The company distinguished itself from many British publishers by trying to secure valid copyrights* for American books in England and paying American authors for their writings. Marston's extensive connections with the Australian publishing scene were also used to good effect. On top of its international list, the firm published popular British authors* like Wilkie Collins* and Edward Bulwer Lytton*, and was notable for embracing the latest printing technology, particularly when it came to illustrations*.

Like many nineteenth-century publishing houses, Sampson Low published a range of periodicals and journals alongside its book publication business, and as well as the long-running *Publishers' Circular*. Among these were several titles such as the *Etcher* (1879-1883) and the *Picture Gallery* (1872-1880) where illustration* was the focus, supplying readers with fine art prints in the form of etchings or photographic* reproductions. The diverse range of other titles at some time published by the firm included the *Union Jack*, *Index to Current Literature* (1859-1861), the *Dark Blue* and the *Fishing Gazette*. The company continued to expand its periodical publishing arm after Low's retirement and subsequent death, acquiring the *Nineteenth Century* in 1891 and *Scribner's Magazine* in 1892 (both according to *Waterloo*). Sampson Low & Co. continued in business until 1964. **JJB/MaT**
Sources: Hamber 1996, Marston 1904, ncse, *ODNB*, *Waterloo*.

SAMUELSON, JAMES (1829-1918) In 1861, following experience as a writer on microscopy and as a science teacher for the Department of Science and Art, the Liverpool industrialist Samuelson founded the quarterly* *Popular Science Review* (1861-1876) with the natural history publisher Robert Hardwicke*. Priced* at 2s 6d and modelled on the cheaper *Recreational Science* (1860-1871) edited* by Shirley Hibberd, it contained long articles that aimed to both entertain and instruct. It also reported on scientific* activities in the provinces as well as in academic centres. After selling the journal to the medical* writer Henry Lawson in 1864, Samuelson and William Crookes* launched the more academic *Quarterly Journal of Science* modelled on the elite reviews. This broke with the tradition of anonymity* in the political and theological quarterlies.

Following a decision to study law, Samuelson sold the journal to Crookes in 1870 and took up political and social causes. In 1890 he returned to periodical editing* with the highly original thematic quarterly* *Subjects of the Day* (1890-1891), but despite attracting writers like William Gladstone, Routledge* closed the periodical after only four issues. In retirement, Samuelson continued to write on 'subjects of the day' such as temperance* and trades unionism*. **WB**

Sources: Barton 1998, Lightman 2004, Samuelson 1907.

SANDYS, FREDERICK (1832-1904) Although Frederick Sandys, artist and illustrator*, published relatively few designs in periodicals, some of them in obscure journals, his work was generally understood to be original and of outstanding quality. In particular, Sandys brought an interest in German art, especially Dürer, Holbein and Rethel, to his work, and, through his close if sometimes awkward association with the circle of major Pre-Raphaelite artists, he influenced many contemporaries, including D. G. Rossetti, and William Morris*. His work appeared occasionally in the early 1860s in the great trio of illustrated journals from that decade, the *Cornhill*, *Once a Week* and *Good Words*. There were also one-off, but outstanding, contributions to the *Shilling Magazine*, and the *Churchman's Family Magazine* in the same period. **BM**

Sources: *Engen* 1990, Goldman 1994, Houfe 1978, *ODNB*, Reid 1928, Suriano 2005, White 1897.

SATIRICAL MAGAZINES Hundreds of magazines claiming to be satirical appeared during the nineteenth century, from the cleverly conservative *Anti-Jacobin* onwards. During the politically and socially tense opening decades, satire more usually cloaked radical journalism*, its classical credentials lending generic dignity to political* and social critique. Satire's rhetorical deployment of scorn and ridicule to claim the moral high ground made prosecution somewhat more embarrassing, but did not stop the authorities from attempting to suppress William Cobbett's *Political Register*, Thomas J. Wooler's* *Black Dwarf* and other organs of radical satire during their long and ultimately unsuccessful wars against the cheap*, unstamped* press. Meanwhile pungent satirical writing could be found in the early *Blackwood's* and *Fraser's* magazines, but internecine warfare among the literati hardly threatened the established order. Nor did, at a different level, the satirical journalism of periodicals like the *Age*, *John Bull* and the *Satirist*, which specialized in highly personal and scurrilous scandal-mongering – even blackmail – parading as righteous censure of immorality. They were not regarded as seriously subversive, being politically conservative and – priced* at 7d a copy – too expensive for the dangerous classes.

The appearance of *Figaro in London* in 1831 was an important development in satirical journalism. Its motto 'Satire should, like a razor keen,/ Wound with a touch that's scarcely felt or seen' points the direction most subsequent satirical magazines would take – good-humoured commentary on the political* and social* scene from a mildly reformist perspective. Its successor *Punch* further refined the formula, offering a fairly reliable barometer of political and social tensions as the fraught 1840s gave way to calm. Such satirical bite as Thackeray* and Jerrold* gave it in its first decade was dulled and steered away from dangerous topics like labour unrest towards safer realms like mocking aestheticism by cautiously genial editors* like Tom Taylor* and Francis Burnand*. *Punch's* success encouraged countless imitators. The majority of the titles in Donald Gray's invaluable list of over 360 'comic periodicals' described themselves as satirical in their subtitle or editorial statement, though in most cases the satire they offer is notably benign. A combination of quiet times, the libel laws and the Obscene Publications Act of 1857 were a disincentive to satire of the more acrid sort. Significantly, when *Mitchell's Press Directory* began to classify periodicals from 1879 onwards, it employed the category 'Satirical' to include all magazines* of humour. Among the journals that stand out as offering satire beyond the anodyne are *Tomahawk* with its angry,

gentleman-radical criticism of upper-class* social corruption, the inadequacy of the Poor Laws and, most notoriously, Queen Victoria's relationship with her Highland servant John Brown. Matt Morgan's* tinted two-page cartoons* were the most effective means of delivering its satirical message, as indeed was frequently the case with the best Victorian satirical magazines. The satire of middle-class social aspirations embedded in W. G. Baxter's* cartoons for *Ally Sloper's Half-Holiday**, and in the milder cartoons of Charles Keene* and George Du Maurier* in *Punch*, offer other examples. Britain's provincial* press also produced a number of satirical magazines, of which Liverpool's *Porcupine* is perhaps the most notable. **CAK**
Sources: Altick 1997, Bailey 1998, Gray 1972, Kent 1998, *Waterloo*.

***SATIRIST* (1831-1849)** The *Satirist* was the *Town's** closest rival among the scandal and gossip* centred metropolitan* journals of the 1830s, a group that also included the *Age** and the early volumes of *John Bull**. Its editor*, Barnard Gregory*, like C. M. Westmacott* at the *Age*, used, or rather misused, the power of the press to publish scurrilous allegations not just to increase his circulation* but also to blackmail those unfortunates whom he threatened to denounce or disgrace in his columns*.

Gregory developed the voice of a genteel if dissipated man about town to guide his publication, while at the same time expressing constant disbelief at the wickedness and corruption of all he saw. Consequently, his publication was as cynically scandalous, often about relatively insignificant individuals, as such a tone and manner suggests. The entertainments of the 'town' provided much of his other material, drawing on the legacy of Pierce Egan's* fictionalized wandering urban transgressors described in his 1821 novel *Life in London*. Never firmly established financially, and at the high (stamped*) price* of 7d an issue, the *Satirist*, like its rivals, became a victim of an increasing distaste for the sleaziness and muckraking of scandalous journalism in the early Victorian period. **BM**
Source: Gray 1982.

***SATURDAY MAGAZINE* (1832-1844)** The organ of the Society for Promoting Christian Knowledge (SPCK; see SDUK*), the *Saturday Magazine* was, along with Charles Knight's* *Penny Magazine** and *Chambers's Edinburgh Journal**, one of the key players in the development of a mass* readership* for periodicals in the 1830s. Like these rival publications, the *Saturday Magazine* was an unstamped*

penny* weekly* of eight pages, comprising a series of short articles on literary*, historical* and moral topics, some poetry*, brief articles on natural history, and a variety of other trivia. The front page generally carried an engraving, often of a church or of some exotic location. Published* by John William Parker*, it was explicitly aimed at counteracting 'cheap* pamphlets, of the most dangerous and deplorable tendency', similarly to the *Penny Magazine* and *Chambers's Edinburgh Journal**. It was the policy of the SPCK to discriminate between two varieties of knowledge: the good, improving, Christian material, and that which was 'not sanctified nor directed by Christian belief and principle'. Along with the perceived secularism of the popular press, the atheistic tendencies of Voltaire, Hume and Gibbon were seen as a threat to the whole edifice.

One remarkable aspect of the magazine was its self-conscious regard for the possibilities – and particularly the pitfalls – of a mass-circulation* periodical press. A series of articles on 'Newspaper Literature' which appeared in 1836 developed a nuanced argument which balanced the advantages of mass literacy against the knowledge that 'the pen is sometimes a dangerous instrument in the hands of designing men', developing this into an informed critique of legislation relating to the press. In the first number, the leader* sententiously eulogized Gutenberg's invention of moveable type which had brought 'the learning of the learned, and the wisdom of the wise, within reach and possession of all classes of the community'. The development of the periodical press was the next phase: 'our little magazine will go forth every Saturday morning, like a skilful gardener, to plant in every corner of the land, within sight of every man's door, and within reach of every man's arm, a tree of true knowledge'. This two-headed biblical allusion – to the Parable of the Sower and the Tree of Knowledge – shifts a discourse of enlightenment into the dimension of Christian allegory, a rhetorical move that might sum up the mission of the *Saturday Magazine*. **MaT**
Sources: Bennet 1982, BL Catalogue, BritPer, James 1963, *Waterloo*.

***SATURDAY REVIEW OF POLITICS, LITERATURE, SCIENCE, AND ART* (1855-1938)** The *Saturday Review* positioned itself between established quarterlies* like the *Edinburgh Review** and the *Quarterly Review**, both of which by 1855 were past their prime, and the monthly* magazines* like *Blackwood's** and *Fraser's**. The quarterlies were authoritative but required patience on the part of readers*; the monthlies, though certainly containing reviews*, were primarily organs of entertainment. There seemed room for a weekly*, alongside the *Athenaeum** and the *Spectator**, that would keep pace with a rapidly expanding readership* interested in debating critical issues of the day – political*, social and cultural. By 1855, its first year of production, both the stamp* duty and advertisement* duty had been abolished, and at 5d (6d stamped) per 16-page issue, the *Saturday Review* offered value for money. By 1858 each issue contained 24 pages, and from 1864 on the usual number was around 44 pages, the price* having been increased to 6d (7d stamped).

The founder of the *Saturday Review* was the Cambridge-educated, Anglo-Catholic A. J. B. Beresford Hope* who then brought on board J. D. Cook*, his former co-worker at the *Morning Chronicle*, to edit the paper. Cook in turn employed well-educated, serious young men, largely from Cambridge and Oxford, as contributors: James Fitzjames Stephen*, Vernon Harcourt, Henry Sumner Maine, as well as Eliza Lynn Linton*, the first woman in England to draw a regular salary from journalism*. Linton pronounced Cook, under whom she worked both at the *Morning Chronicle** and at the *Saturday Review** 'the best constructive editor of his time, [one who] knew how to choose his staff and apportion his material with a discrimination that was almost another sense' (Bevington: 15).

From the outset its columns* were unsigned*, a circumstance that allowed the review to offer what appeared to be a unified voice, the voice of the educated upper middle class. The *Saturday* had a substantial look; there were no brief articles or notices of books, and no letters from correspondents*. Leading articles were generally two to four columns* in length, and were set in larger type than what were called 'middles'* (articles on general subjects) and substantial book reviews*. The editorial line was cautiously liberal, mindful of class privilege and conscious of its own authority. The robust, at times rambunctious nature of its prejudices and reviews* led to its nickname, the *Saturday Reviler*. Estimations of the authors of the day were predictable: Eliot*, Thackeray* and Tennyson were lauded, Dickens* was warned about his amateurish call for social reform (Sullivan: 380), Browning and Swinburne* were both frowned upon. Not surprisingly, the bulk of the advertising* space was taken by publishers. Circulation* grew steadily, so that by 1858 5,000 copies were being sold weekly; by 1868 circulation was in excess of 10,000 (Bevington: 24).

Philip Harwood became editor of the *Saturday Review* at Cook's death (1868-1883), followed by Walter Herries Pollock (1883-1894). Frank Harris* moved from the *Fortnightly Review** to succeed Pollock as editor (1894-1898), and was responsible for bringing George Bernard Shaw* on board as drama critic. The *Saturday Review* had its heyday during the middle years of the nineteenth century, and its longevity was due largely to the reputation it garnered during those years. **ET**
Sources: Bevington 1941, Cohen 1996, Scott 1950, Sullivan, *Waterloo.*

SAUNDERS'S NEWSLETTER (1755-c.1793); SAUNDERS'S NEWS-LETTER AND DAILY ADVERTISER (1793-1827); SAUNDERS'S NEWS-LETTER AND IRISH DAILY NEWS (1828-1878); SAUNDERS'S IRISH DAILY NEWS (1878-1879) In 1755, Dublin printer and bookseller Henry Saunders purchased the newspaper *Esdall's Newsletter* (1754-1755). Renamed *Saunders's Newsletter*, it was published three times a week, consisted of four pages and retailed for three half-pence, increased to 4d with stamp duty. In 1773, it was sold to printer James Potts, who turned it into a daily* in 1777. His descendants owned *Saunders's* for over a century, selling it only in 1875. Its last proprietor* was William A. Murray (1878-1879).

Saunders's was the main Dublin newspaper for daily advertisements*, which occupied at least half of its pages, beside parliamentary, financial and foreign intelligence. It did not contain original leading articles, quoting instead from the main English newspapers. R. R. Madden* stated that 'if it had been published in Iceland, it could not have been more destitute of Irish news*' (Madden: 255). *Saunders's* news content, both Irish and general, increased to three pages during the 1840s, but its reliance on scissors* and paste journalism persisted until the late 1860s. T. P. O'Connor* began his journalistic career as a *Saunders's* reporter* (1867-1870).

In mid-century it was Ireland's best-selling daily newspaper, purchasing 804,000 stamps in 1848. Though considered moderate by contemporaries, *Saunders's* political* stance was clearly Conservative, Unionist and Protestant. **FB**
Sources: Brown 1937, Hoey 1877, Madden 1867, *Waterloo.*

SAVAGE, JAMES (1767-1845) Born in Yorkshire, James Savage, editor* and antiquary, contributed articles to local* periodicals before going into a bookselling and printing business in 1790 with his brother, printer and engraver, William Savage (1770-1843). James followed his brother to London in 1803 where he took work with a series of publishers*, writing for the *Monthly Magazine** and the *Universal Magazine* in addition to editing books on commerce and architecture. In 1806 he was appointed clerk to the librarian of the London Institution and in 1808-1809 he edited the *Librarian*, printed by his brother. Having been involved in embezzling funds from the London Institution, he made his escape to Birmingham in 1810 where he edited a local* newspaper and in 1811 wrote, *An Account of the London Daily Newspapers* which provided information on their circulation* and political* stance, whilst outlining a plan for a provincial paper. Making it known on his return to London that he was seeking the editorship of just such a paper, he received an invitation to manage the *Taunton and Bridgewater Journal** (1811-1816). He and his wife, Margaret Luckfield, had also set up a bookshop, circulating library* and reading* room in Taunton, which she managed while Savage established several presses in London.

Savage went on to write historical* publications, *Memorabilia* (1820), plus a reworking of the *History of Taunton* by Joshua Toulmin (1822), and *A History of the Hundred of Carhampton* (1830). In 1822 he had taken the post of librarian of the Somerset and Taunton Institution and in connection with his research amassed a collection of manuscripts. Savage's fraudulent behaviour surfaced once more in 1829 and he was committed to a London debtors' prison. Not without friends, he was found another newspaper editing job on the *Dorset County Chronicle and Somersetshire Gazette*, also producing an historical work on Dorchester in 1833. Despite his dishonesty, Savage's obituary* in the *Dorset County Chronicle* described him as having 'a high sense of integrity', and praised him as 'a sincere and devout Protestant churchman… pious without ostentation'. **DHL**
Sources: Brooke 1960, *Dorset County Chronicle* 1845, *ODNB*.

SAVOY (1896) The *Savoy* is undoubtedly one of the most noted art and literature* periodicals from the 1890s, only second in fame to its direct competitor*, the *Yellow Book**. During the commotion produced by the Wilde* affair, its publisher*, Leonard Smithers* managed to secure several of the more controversial authors and artists of the British avant-garde such as Arthur Symons* and Aubrey Beardsley*, who had been ousted from the *Yellow Book*. The new magazine* was named for the Strand hotel that had been the scene of several recent scandals. Although Symons, its editor*, stated in the prospectus that for them 'all art is good

which is good art', in its contents at least the magazine clearly resembles the early issues of the *Yellow Book*.

Beardsley dominated the art section of the magazine, providing half its contributions. Other visual artists with original work included Charles H. Shannon*, Charles Conder, and Joseph Pennell*. Beardsley's unfinished serialized* novella, 'Under the Hill', Joseph Conrad's 'The Idiots' and some haunting tales from W. B. Yeats formed the *Savoy's* most interesting short fiction. Havelock Ellis provided lengthy articles, while Symons, Max Beerbohm* and G. B. Shaw* contributed often fanciful causeries*. Except for forgotten offerings from Ford Madox Ford and Ernest Dowson, and some translations of Mallarmé and Verlaine, the magazine's poetry* was mostly unremarkable. Reproductions of Impressionist and Pre-Raphaelite paintings indicate the magazine's primary inspiration.

Only two quarterly* (Jan. and April 1896) and six monthly* (July-Dec. 1896) issues were published, at the competitive price* of 2s 6d for the quarterly and 2s for the monthly. In the final issue, Symons himself suggests as the main reasons for this failure: 'giving so much for so little money' as well as 'abandoning a quarterly for a monthly issue'. It obviously did not help that W. H. Smith* quite unexpectedly refused to continue stocking the magazine after an illustrated* article on Blake in the third issue. There indeed seemed to be not 'very many people in the world who really cared for art… really for art's sake'. **KNC**
Sources: Beckson 1987, Brake 1994, Nelson 2000, Sullivan.

SCIENCE AND JOURNALISM As a prominent part of nineteenth-century culture, science was frequently in the news* throughout the period. But journalism was also an integral part of the economy of science, providing a much needed income for scientists as well as an essential medium for the exchange of information and the consolidation of scientific communities. The constant stream of scientific results produced by scientists meant that the practice was an ideal source of news. This was reinforced by the location of science within newsworthy institutions. For instance, the daily* and weekly* press reported the activities of scientific societies alongside those of non-scientific societies; scientific lectures were reported whether they were delivered in scientific institutions such as the Royal Institution or non-scientific institutions like the Victoria Institute, Society of Arts or Sunday Lecture Society; and, because they were often funded by subscription and functioned as markers of civic or national pride, the scientific activities of museums, universities and public laboratories were interpreted as in the public interest. Science then, regardless of its content, was reported as part of the cultural life of the nation. Some of these institutions – for example the activities of the Royal Society, or those of the Botanical Gardens, the Royal Observatory or the Royal Mint – were newsworthy because of their cultural status. However, the status of science as a discourse was contested.

The use of science for ideological means ensured that scientific content filled the publications of societies such as the Society for the Diffusion of Useful Knowledge* and was a staple of many 'improving' publications aimed at distinct groups such as children and the working classes*. The demand for scientific content and the difficulties that were associated with understanding it ensured that there was a demand for writers who could summarize and, if necessary, translate scientific news into the more general discourse of a particular journal. As there was no established career path for the scientific worker, such opportunities provided a necessary source of income for scientists. However, the sums that could be earned by writing were not considerable. In 1873 the clergyman and amateur astronomer the Reverend Thomas William Webb complained to Arthur Ranyard* about the low rates *Nature** – then the most well-respected scientific publication in Britain – paid its reviewers*. Although some scientists such as Richard Anthony Proctor* did support themselves entirely through writing, most combined journalism with paid positions elsewhere. Thomas Henry Huxley* and John Tyndall* held scientific positions at the School of Mines and the Royal Institution while also being paid for contributions to the *Westminster Review**; and Joseph Norman Lockyer* supplemented the salary he received as editor* of *Nature* with positions at the War Office and then the School of Mines.

Although the remuneration for journalism was poor, it offered the potential to wield substantial influence. Science depended upon its textual base for the announcement of discoveries, the archiving of research, the distribution of representations of scientific practice and scientists, and – crucially – to provide a medium for their intercommunication. Journalism* provided access to the most timely products of print culture: the very places where results were announced, work was discussed, and esteem was awarded. JEM
Sources: Brock 1980, Cantor and Shuttleworth 2004, Cantor *et al* 2004, Henson *et al* 2004, Mussell 2007a.

SCIENCE POPULARIZATION Journalism sustained the energetic movements for the popularization of science in the nineteenth century. Although there was a substantial market for scientific books – whether sold in parts by organizations such as the Society for the Diffusion of Useful Knowledge* (SDUK) or in series such as the International Scientific Series – it was through newspapers and periodicals that writers believed they could reach readers beyond recognizable scientific communities. The diffusionist model of scientific popularization, which was widespread in the nineteenth century and continues to be influential today, describes popularization as the practice of describing scientific research for a non-scientific audience. This top-down, diffusionist model often conceals an ideological purpose. For the SDUK, science provided a rational recreation that avoided divisive topics such as politics* or religion*. For Thomas Henry Huxley*, who gave lectures to working men and contributed widely across the press, popular science would establish science more broadly as a valid means of understanding the world. The diffusionist model of science popularization also obscures the roles played by authors, publishers*, illustrators, printers and editors* in determining the form in which science is encountered. Equally, it takes little account of readers' interpretations of popular science. What was perceived as a non-scientific audience was actually a mixed set of readers with differing interests who often belonged to scientific communities of their own.

Much popular science therefore found an eager readership* who often used it for their own ends. This was exemplified by miscellanies* such as the *Mechanics' Magazine** and the *English Mechanic** which largely consisted of contributions from readers. This type of publication, which was often cheap to produce and capable of reaching a large audience, juxtaposed readers' contributions with those of acknowledged experts and so emphasized dialogue and conflict rather than demonstrating scientific truths. As both an important province of knowledge and a relatively harmless source of amusement, there was a demand for those who could write about science in an accessible form. Although popular science books, especially those dealing with sciences founded on observation such as natural history or astronomy, could sell in substantial numbers, this market only sustained a handful of authors. However, the existing audience for science, coupled with the shifting nature of amateurism fostered by the development of leisure among the middle classes*, made scientific content desirable to editors* and proprietors* of general periodicals. For editors, scientific content presented serious matter, often masculine in tone, that could complement other forms of content. For contributors, publication in the press provided a valuable income for scientific work with the possibility that articles could be republished as books. Although the presence of articles like George Henry Lewes's* 'Studies in Animal Life' in the *Cornhill Magazine* might be taken as evidence of a common intellectual context, in which science sat alongside literature* in a family* magazine, it is important to acknowledge the specific rhetoric of popular science articles, the role that they played in the publication as a whole and the differing ways in which they were received. JEM

Sources: Cantor *et al* 2004, Cooter and Pumfrey 1994, Fyfe 2004, Lightman 2007, Sheets-Pyenson 1985.

'SCISSORS-AND-PASTE' JOURNALISM A contemporary term, often used pejoratively, for the widespread practice of excerpting from or recycling of articles from other publications, this term actually covered a number of different editorial strategies, ranging from agreed syndication* to unacknowledged piracy. A staple newsgathering technique of provincial* newspapers, which often filled their pages with stories from national papers in the eighteenth and early nineteenth centuries, 'scissors-and-paste' became a favourite tool of the radical unstamped* press in the 1820s and 1830s. The practice was not limited to news* and, encouraged by confused and ambiguous copyright* law, many cheap* literary* miscellanies* were founded on the premise of extracting 'useful knowledge'* from prohibitively expensive books, monthlies and quarterlies* to make it more accessible to the lower classes*. Examples include the *Hive* (1822-1824), the *Mirror of Literature, Amusement and Instruction**, the *Spirit of the Times* (1825-1828) and the *Cab* (1832). Others such as the *Thief* (1832-1834); known as the *London Weekly Magazine* (March 1833-Nov. 1833), before reverting to the *Thief* (until March 1834) and the *Penny Pirate* (1832), both published by William Strange*, particularly drew attention to the ambiguous legal and moral status of their editorial strategy; it was their defining feature.

Later in the century, the term was regularly levelled at the 'snippet' papers and periodical digests that were characteristic of the New Journalism*, particularly George Newnes's* *Tit-Bits** and even W. T. Stead's* *Review of Reviews**, with varying degrees of accuracy, as Stead's *Review* both acknowledged and paid for its sources, while *Tit-Bits* did neither. CCF

Sources: Barker 2000, Brown 1985, Topham 2005, Wiener 1969.

SCOTS OBSERVER (1888-1890); NATIONAL OBSERVER (1890-1897) The weekly* *Scots Observer: a Record and a Review*, founded by Edinburgh businessman Robert Fitzroy Bell, was advertised not only as a 'Record and Review of Current Politics*, Literature*, Science*, Art, &c' but also as a 'Scottish* National Journal, dealing with Imperial* and General Affairs, and giving a hearty support to Constitutional Principles'.

James Nicol Dunn* was the initial editor* until replaced by W. E. Henley* in 1889. Consisting of 38 pages, originally priced* at 6d, reducing to 3d in March 1896 and finally 2d from July of that year, the paper was published every Saturday. Contributions were generally unsigned*, although among the signatories were J. M. Barrie, William Archer, Robert Louis Stevenson, Alice Meynell*, Edmund Gosse*, Graham R. Tomson*, W. B. Yeats, Kipling, H. G. Wells*, T. E. Brown, May Kendall, Katharine Tynan and Edith Nesbit. Mallarmé contributed in French. Fiction came from Murray Gilchrist, H. D. Lowry, Gilbert Parker and H. B. Marriott Watson. Under Henley and the assistant editor Charles Whibley*, the journal forthrightly endorsed Conservative* and imperial policies and attacked anything resembling cant. Gladstone's Irish home rule was condemned, and Kipling's poem 'Cleared' attacked the acquittal of Charles Stewart Parnell, MP of involvement in conspiracy and murder. Socialism was duly abhorred. The journal also attacked Oscar Wilde's* artistic morality in *The Picture of Dorian Gray* in July 1890, though Henley published the seduction scene in Thomas Hardy's *Tess* as 'Saturday Night in Arcady' when it was refused for the *Graphic**. An interesting feature was 'Modern Men', a series of assessments of renowned men (26 Jan. 1889-30 Sept. 1893, revived late 1897).

The Scottish connection and the failure to increase circulation* resulted in a title change* to the *National Observer* (Nov. 1890). Bell failed to form a limited company and in June 1892 the journal moved to London before suffering increasing financial losses resulting in its sale in March 1894 to James Edmund Vincent, who became the new editor. The journal staggered on with an 'improved and enlarged form' in January 1895, but it lacked the bite of Henley's editorship. Between 20 March and 22 May 1897 it amalgamated with the *British*

Review to become the *National Observer and British Review*, edited by W. H. Mallock; it then changed its title for two months (29 May-7 Aug. 1897) to the *British Review and National Observer*, only to be revived as the *National Observer* for one issue (16 Oct.). A similar format* was published as the *National Critic* with pagination following from the *National Observer*, but with a different printer and publisher*.

Unquestionably the journal's high point was Henley's editorship and the established and emerging young writers he recruited. Its forthright stance on politics narrowed its circulation*, and Henley's failure to appreciate the finances of a journal doomed its profitability. **DA**
Sources: *ODNB*, *Scots Observer*, *Scotsman*, 'Draft Agreement' 1890.

SCOTSMAN (1817-) The *Scotsman or Edinburgh Political and Literary Journal* was launched by a group of Whigs: Charles Maclaren*, a customs-house official, William Ritchie, a solicitor and John Robertson, a bookseller. Challenging the existing Tory press, it vigorously pressed laissez-faire arguments when John Ramsay McCulloch took over from Maclaren as editor* at the end of 1817. Maclaren resumed the editorship in 1821, moving the paper to twice weekly. Unlike most Scottish papers at the time, the *Scotsman's* leaders* under Maclaren were original pieces, rather than scissors-and-paste* extracts from London papers (*ODNB*). It campaigned for modest political* reform and Benthamite radicalism. Although hostile to those who were pressing for an end to church patronage, it became more sympathetic to the Free Church after the 1843 Disruption. Its unwavering loyalty to the Whigs* lost it readers after 1832, but its support for the Anti-Corn Law League in the 1840s began to win them back.

Maclaren's deputy (1845-1849) Alexander Russel*, officially became editor in 1849. His Liberalism was Palmerstonian and the paper got caught up in bitter wrangles with the more radical Liberal elements in the city. Russel's articles on destitution in the Highlands in the aftermath of the potato famine showed little empathy with the Gaels and he was vituperatively hostile to trade unionism*. James Bruce's pieces on social conditions in Edinburgh contributed to the campaign for city improvements. Unlike the *Glasgow Herald*, the *Scotsman* gave no support to the nationalism of the National Association for the Vindication of Scottish Rights.

On the repeal of the Stamp Act*, it became the *Daily Scotsman*, retaining the adjective until 1860;

circulation* nearly doubled to around 10,000. Under the business management of James Law, who retained that position for 64 years, the paper's distribution* was extended beyond Edinburgh. By 1887, circulation exceeded 60,000. When Russel retired in 1876, the editorship – inexplicably – was given to the minister Robert Wallace, not Charles Cooper, Russel's assistant since 1868. Cooper eventually became editor (1880-1905).

After Maclaren's death in 1866, sole ownership of the paper was in the hands of John Ritchie. Russel and Ritchie's nephew, John Ritchie Findlay, became partners in 1860, and were joined by Law in 1868. Findlay inherited his uncle's shares when John Ritchie died in 1870 and when Findlay died in 1898 these passed to his son, also John Findlay. At the end of the 1870s the paper was very much in admiration of Lord Rosebery, giving extensive coverage to Gladstone's Midlothian campaign and campaigning for a Scottish Secretary of State. However, after 1886, like many Scottish Liberals, it moved into the Liberal Unionist camp, despite an antipathy towards Joe Chamberlain, and became increasingly enthusiastic for Empire*, adopting a strongly jingoistic stance during the Boer War*. **WHF**
Sources: 'C. M.' 1831, Cooper 1896, Cox 1869, Magnusson 1967, *ODNB*, *Waterloo*.

SCOTT, CLEMENT WILLIAM (1841-1904) Clement Scott was a prominent drama critic at a time when theatre came into its own as a serious art. His defence of 'natural acting', free adaptation and 'dramatic free-trade' – allowing more foreign actors onto English stages – was instrumental in helping find theatre a respectable, professional voice ca. 1860-1890. His conception of drama as a new 'religion of the people', however, also added a moralistic and patronizing touch to his work.

Scott began his career at the *Era** and the *Sunday Times**, which he was forced to leave in 1865 because the 'acerbity' of his drama criticism upset actor-managers. He then contributed to *Fun** and, as 'Almaviva', to the *London Figaro**, where he sharpened his satirical* wit. His career was fully launched when he started writing for the *Daily Telegraph** in 1871, where in 1878 he became the principal drama critic as successor to E. L. Blanchard. In 1879 he bought the signed monthly* review* the *Theatre** from the Shakespearean actor-manager Henry Irving, editing it (1880-1889) until it ran him into financial difficulties. It was in this decade that, according to *The Times**, Scott created for himself 'a position that was for a time unique and threatened to be autocratic'.

This position is reflected in Scott's double-sided presentation of himself. On the one hand he courted popularity as a first-night critic: he modestly called his pieces 'notices' or 'reports', presented himself as a mere 'playtaster' and cemented his relationship with theatre audiences – who often recognized and greeted him – by mentioning theatregoers in his columns*. On the other hand he was keen to exert pressure to steer drama away from literary experiment and 'pessimism'. His intervention in the *Daily Telegraph* in an argument between Oscar Wilde* and actor-manager George Alexander (of St James's Theatre) led to the replotting of *Lady Windermere's Fan* in 1892. In the same year he influenced Edward Pigott, examiner of plays, to censor* Edward Brandes's play *A Visit*. In 1893 he doubted whether the stage could 'be retained for the people'. As the literary theatre of Wilde*, Ibsen and Shaw* gained ground, Scott's criticism – focusing on performance and actors rather than dramatic texts – marched increasingly out of step.

Scott was forced to resign from the *Daily Telegraph* in 1897. A brief spell in the United States followed, during which he wrote for the *International Monthly* and the *New York Daily Herald*. He started the short-lived weekly* the *Free Lance* in 1901. His lifelong criticism of Henry Irving was collected in *From 'The Bells' to 'King Arthur'* (1896). He also wrote travel essays for the *Daily Telegraph*, which were collected in *Round about the Islands* (1873), *Poppy Land-Papers* (1886) and *Pictures Round the World* (1894). MdW

Sources: Hapgood 1967, Kaplan 1992, *ODNB*, *The Times* 1904.

SCOTT, JOHN (1784-1821) John Scott's entry into the world of journalism was through his friendship with Leigh Hunt*, who appointed him editor* of the *Statesman*, a radical newspaper which he had founded in 1806. Scott left the paper after a year in order found his own radical weekly*, the *Censor*, which collapsed after several months. He then moved to Lincolnshire to edit the weekly *Drakard's Stamford News* which he transformed into an influential liberal paper. He returned to London in 1813 as owner and editor of *Drakard's Paper*, modelled on the Hunt brothers' *Examiner**, and in effect the London edition of the *Stamford News*. In 1814 he changed its name to the *Champion**, and recruited William Hazlitt* and Charles Lamb* as contributors, writing much of the copy himself. An attack on Byron in the paper in 1816 led to a parting of the ways with Hunt, and in 1817 he disposed of the *Champion*. In 1819 he was invit-

ed by the publisher* Robert Baldwin* to edit a new monthly magazine, projected as a liberal and metropolitan* rival to the Tory *Blackwood's Edinburgh Magazine**.

The first number of the *London Magazine** appeared in January 1820, its contributors including B. W. Procter ('Barry Cornwall'), De Quincey*, Hazlitt and Lamb, who wrote the first of his 'Essays of Elia' for the magazine. As well as its high profile contributors, the magazine had a number of innovative features including 'the 'Lion's Head' series, a kind of literary gossip* column. Scott's attacks on *Blackwood's*, in response to the latter's infamous attacks on the so-called 'Cockney School' of poets* led J. G. Lockhart* to brand Scott a 'liar and a scoundrel'. The quarrel escalated into a challenge by Scott to J. H. Christie, Lockhart's London agent. A duel took place at Chalk Farm in which Scott was fatally wounded and died some days later. In an age of personality-dominated, and often libellous reviewing*, this became a celebrated fatality. Scott's innovative editorship of the *London Magazine* and his talents as a journalist were for a time eclipsed by the manner of his death. JS

Sources: Leary 1983, *ODNB*, Parker 2000.

SCOTT, JOHN WILLIAM ROBERTSON (1866-1962) Born in Wigton in Cumberland, his father's early death obliged Scott to support his family while still in his teens. As a freelance journalist, Scott contributed to the *Manchester Guardian** and several other journals until he was invited to join the staff of the *Birmingham Gazette*. As a Liberal, Scott had an aversion to writing in support of the Conservatives, and he left the paper. In 1887 W. T. Stead* asked Scott to write for the *Pall Mall Gazette**. When the *Pall Mall's* later editor*, E. T. Cook*, left the paper to found the *Westminster Gazette** in 1893, Scott moved with him. He ended his career in London as a writer for the *Daily Chronicle**, resigning with H. W. Massingham* over the paper's support of the Boer War*.

Scott's activities as founder of a Tokyo journal (the *New East*) and of the *Countryman* in the Cotswolds (1927-1947) were undertaken in addition to his many volumes of reminiscences of London journalism and articles on agriculture, politics* and cultural understanding. Scott's book, *The Story of the Pall Mall Gazette* (1950) is a great source of anecdotal information about a fascinating period. ET

Sources: Scott 1950, *ODNB*, Sullivan.

SCOTT, WALTER (1771-1832) Sir Walter Scott, the Scottish author of the bestselling Waverley Novels, was also a proprietor* of printing and publishing concerns, a regular contributor to many literary reviews* such as the *Athenaeum* and the *British Critic**, as well as writing miscellaneous articles for two of the most prominent periodicals of the time. In 1805, Scott became a partner in James Ballantyne's* printing business, Border Press, while a regular contributor to the *Edinburgh Review**. By 1808, stung by a critical review of his own work, *Marmion*, in the periodical, and thoroughly dissatisfied with the *Edinburgh Review*'s liberal and reformist leanings, he helped set up its Tory rival the *Quarterly Review** and contributed four articles to its first number in 1809. He remained a primary contributor from 1809-1811, going on to write reviews, articles, and historical* notes discussing a wide range of topics for many years to come, also selecting other contributors who often reviewed his verse and novels.

In 1809, Scott quarrelled with his literary publisher* Archibald Constable*, and set up his own publishing concern, Ballantyne & Co., with James and John Ballantyne. Scott largely financed its establishment and funnelled all his own writing through the firm. As the primary source of income for the firm, Scott exercised considerable control over the company's publishing decisions which, unfortunately, were largely unsound. Scott insisted the company publish many authors whose work did not sell well and the firm lost money. Later, Scott repaired his friendship with Constable, who became involved with Ballantyne & Co. What followed was a series of convoluted and injudicious business arrangements. Scott should have profited handsomely from arrangements in which he was not only the author but also part owner of the printing and publishing venture, but poor decisions resulted in the 1826 crash of the printing and publishing business, and Scott spent the rest of his life writing constantly to pay off debts. JNW

Sources: Drabble 2000, *ODNB*, Sutherland 1995.

SCOTT, WILLIAM BELL (1811-1890)   A painter, poet, and art critic, William Bell Scott contributed chiefly to art periodicals in London and Edinburgh from 1834 until his death. His poetry* first appeared in the *Monthly Repository** (1846) and the seminal 'little magazine' the *Germ** ('Morning Sleep' and 'Early Aspirations' Jan.-April 1850), after which he became closely associated with members of the Pre-Raphaelite movement, especially John Everett Millais* and Dante Gabriel Rossetti.

Best known as a painter and poet, Scott was master of the Newcastle-on-Tyne design school (1843-1864) and art examiner at South Kensington (1864-1885). In his role as a painter, teacher and

art critic, he helped to foster a resurgence of interest in the history of England and the revival of disused techniques from earlier times. In his journalism, Scott reported on mural decoration, art copyright*, and the work of his fellow artists in specialized organs such as the *Sessional Papers of the Royal Academy of British Architects* (1867-1868), as well as writing for more general periodicals including *Blackwood's Edinburgh Magazine** and the *Athenaeum**. He also published five books of poetry and 12 monographs. **TT**

Sources: *DNB*, *ODNB*, Rowley *et al* 1883, Scott 1867, Scott 1892.

SCOTTISH MOUNTAINEERING CLUB JOURNAL (1890-)   The Scottish Mountaineering Club was founded in 1889 in response to a series of letters* in the *Glasgow Herald** by several men who wondered why Scotland lacked a club devoted to its own mountains. The *Scottish Mountaineering Club Journal** was initially edited* by Joseph Gibson Scott, who had had to argue and convince members of the necessity of a publication in which to record and distribute information about the Scottish highlands. The editorship was taken over by William Douglas in 1892 for the following 18 years and in 1898, the identifying insignia of the axes and rope first appeared on the *Journal*'s cover.

From its inception, the *Journal* had two primary purposes, to introduce climbers to areas of Scotland which had previously been unknown to them, and to create a community among Scottish climbers. This reflected the wide-ranging interests of Club members, which included mountaineers who courted danger, hill-walkers who preferred less risky climbs and people such as artists who loved the hills primarily for aesthetic reasons. *Journal* articles emphasized exploration of lesser-known routes, descriptions of the 'wilder and more picturesque' parts of Scotland, and acknowledgments of the rights of others who used the mountains, including farmers and deerstalkers.

The *Journal* was published in January, May and September until 1918 when this was reduced to twice yearly, becoming an annual* from 1942. Club members, including Sir Hugh Munro, collected information that was published in the *Journal*'s 'guidebook' section. The *Journal* therefore appears to have played an essential role in familiarizing Scottish mountaineers with the local landscape and urging them not to consider continental Europe as holding a monopoly on challenging climbs. It also acted as a guide for spurring climbers on to greater feats, as mountains, which

could be tackled easily, might subsequently be mastered by more difficult routes. **TR**
Sources: Ramsay 1896, *Scottish Mountaineering Club Journal* 1896, Scottish Mountaineering Club online.

Scottish press The Scottish press played an important role in underpinning Scottish civil society throughout the century. Several major urban papers had their start in the eighteenth and early nineteenth century: the *Edinburgh Evening Courant** began in 1718; the *Aberdeen Press and Journal**, one of the world's oldest surviving newspapers, launched in 1748; the *Glasgow Herald** appeared from 1783; and the Edinburgh-based *Scotsman** was founded in 1817. Other towns and regions equally benefited from a local paper as part of their social infrastructure. In 1845 25 Scottish burghs had a newspaper; by 1860 this had doubled, and by 1900 had doubled again. (Donaldson: 3)

Scottish press circulation* and influence during first half of century was inhibited by punitive taxes on paper*, print and ads, the so-called 'taxes on knowledge', many of which were repealed in the late 1850s. Most only came out weekly or twice weekly*. News* reporting in the first half of the century was also parochial: most papers were content to copy foreign and English news* from London journals, with regional correspondents filing reports of local interest. The repeal of the Stamp Duty* in 1855 in particular created a fresh impetus for commercial developments including the launch of many daily* newspapers. These entrants also benefited from the introduction of new technologies (steam railway* networks, telegraph* systems*, cheaper and faster production systems). Several established papers converted to daily* imprint to compete with new rivals: the *Scotsman*, for example, changed from twice-weekly to daily in 1855; the *Glasgow Herald* followed suit in 1859 and the *Dundee Advertiser* in 1861. In 1854 Scotland had 85 newspapers; in 1856 this had risen to over 105; by 1910 the number of papers of all kinds (daily, weekly, monthly) is said to have increased threefold (Cowan: 275; Donaldson: 3). At the end of the century Scotland's press was a robust presence in local* and regional terms. **DF**
Sources: Cowan 1946, Donaldson 1986, Magnusson, Moulton, et.al. 1967, Reid 2006, Thomson 2000.

Scottish Review (1882-1900) The *Scottish Review* was a quarterly* journal begun by William Musham Metcalfe (editor*) and Alexander Gardner (proprietor*) with the explicit aim of promoting

Scottish Home Rule and disproving the claim that Scotland was incapable of supporting a literary journal of its own. It inaugurated the practice of providing summaries of foreign reviews* and keeping contributors anonymous*, at least in the beginning. In 1886 Gardner sold the journal at a loss to J. P. Crichton-Stuart (Lord Bute), already a frequent contributor. Under Crichton-Stuart the tone of the journal changed, with more articles on antiquarian and historical* subjects replacing the general essays and reviews that previously filled its pages. Articles were solid, respectable, some said ponderous, but the journal did try to be cosmopolitan in its efforts to include work on Europe, North America and articles on science* and technology as well as on literature*. Circulation* was always low: 300 of 600 copies printed in 1886, for example, were sold. Crichton-Stuart died in 1900 and the *Review* appeared to have died with him. A second series (1914-1920) was launched, however, after a 14-year interval, with issues initially costing 1s. **ET**
Sources: *Waterloo, Wellesley.*

SDUK Society for the Diffusion of Useful Knowledge (1826-1846); **SPCK** Society for Promoting Christian Knowledge (1698-). A number of technological and social developments in the nineteenth century, especially the explosion of print culture and the democratization of knowledge, led to the emergence of religious and secular societies devoted to making knowledge cheaply available in print to as wide a readership* as possible. Some of these groups, such as the Church of England-linked Society for Promoting Christian Knowledge (SPCK), were established well before the nineteenth century, but the growth of cheap* publishing revolutionized the work that such groups undertook. Spurred into renewed activity by the work of the Religious Tract Society (RTS)*, SPCK produced a range of material including, from 1832, the *Saturday Magazine** and, from 1878-1928, the ½d monthly* miscellany*, *Dawn of Day.*

In 1826 a group of liberals led by Henry Brougham* established the Society for the Diffusion of Useful Knowledge (SDUK), a non-religious alternative to organizations such as RTS* and SPCK. Charles Knight* was closely involved with the SDUK, acting as superintendent of publications, and he edited* the *Penny Magazine** when it was launched by the SDUK in 1832. The *Penny Magazine* achieved early sales of 200,000 a week, but like the *Saturday Magazine**, its popularity declined in the 1840s. While many of the

publications of the SDUK sold well, a lack of commercial acumen led to significant losses and the demise of the SDUK in 1846. MK
Sources: Altholz 1989, Altick 1997, Brantlinger 1998, Fyfe 2004.

SECULAR PRESS In 1841, Charles Southwell*, with the help of the compositor William Chilton*, began the *Oracle of Reason* in an attempt to build popular opposition to Robert Owen's* rejection of democracy within the Owenist movement. Bold attacks on religion won popular support and famously earned Southwell, and then his replacement Thomas Paterson, sentences for blasphemy. The *Oracle of Reason* (1841-1843) was only the first of many titles which together mixed wide-ranging religious*, philosophical*, ethical, political*, social and scientific discussion with literature*, humour, miscellany, and blasphemous cartoons*. Despite broadly polarizing in the second half of the nineteenth century around two key strands of secularism, the sober, agnostic and respectable variety associated with George Jacob Holyoake*, and Charles Bradlaugh's* more militant, atheist and popular version, they all aimed to unite and recruit support for the cause of secularism at home and abroad.

Two titles acted as the organ of the National Secular Society, Bradlaugh's *National Reformer* from 1866 to 1890, and then George William Foote's *Freethinker*. Because of their content secular periodicals often had a precarious existence and regularly resorted to unconventional distribution* methods, although they typically achieved circulations* of between 1,000, for Holyoake's rather dry and reserved *Reasoner* in 1849, and 10,000, for Foote's humorously impious *Freethinker* in 1882. These publications were chiefly sold in London, Lancashire, the Midlands and Yorkshire for between 1d and 2d, providing readers* with genuine enlightenment, entertainment and a sense of belonging. Decline began in the 1890s as secularists reoriented around a less radical ethical movement and split over new sexual and Socialist* politics. SP
Sources: Paylor 2002, Royle 1981.

SECULAR REVIEW (1876-1888); AGNOSTIC JOURNAL AND SECULAR REVIEW (1888); AGNOSTIC JOURNAL AND ECLECTIC REVIEW (1889-1907) The *Secular Review: A Journal of Daily Life* was launched in August 1876 by George Jacob Holyoake*, after he and George William Foote found difficulties with their collaborative* editorship* of the *Secularist: A Liberal Weekly Review* (1876-1877). A well-set Sunday weekly* selling for 1d, the *Secular Review*'s stance was repre-

sentative of a relatively moderate style of Secularism, sympathetic to socialism and aligned against the individualism and militant atheism of Charles Bradlaugh* and his *National Reformer*. In its discussion of religion*, philosophy*, ethics, science* and history*, and in reviewing Secularism and 'what purports to be so, and is not', the title's stated domain of inquiry was 'this world, without implying disregard or denial of another' (Holyoake 1876). When, in February 1877, Bradlaugh disowned Charles Watts for admitting his part in the republication of an 'obscene' book on birth control – thus exposing Bradlaugh – Holyoake handed over the *Secular Review* to Watts's editorship. Four months later the title merged* with the *Secularist* to become the Saturday-published *Secular Review and Secularist* and Watts was joined, until March 1878, by Foote as co-editor.

Under the editorship of William Stewart Ross, who served as co-editor with Watts from January 1882 and took over sole editorship in July 1884 under the pseudonym 'Saladin', the journal's content gradually shifted from directly addressing the business of the Secularist movement and the rivalry between Holyoake and Bradlaugh that had split it over the last decade. Ross, who raised the price* of the publication in April 1887 from 1d to 2d, and in December 1888 changed the title to the *Agnostic Journal and Secular Review*, had a successful textbook publishing business and did not need the paper to be a popular success. This allowed Ross, in the name of true free-thinking, to explore a full and somewhat eccentric range of controversial subjects from his staunchly agnostic perspective in a playful yet 'darkly cynical' and 'piercingly witty' style, and from January 1889 he renamed it the *Agnostic Journal and Eclectic Review* accordingly. Ross died in November 1906 and the last issue appeared in June 1907. SP
Sources: Holyoake 1876, Marsh 1998, Nash 1999, Paylor 2002, Royle 1981.

SERIALIZED SOCIALIST FICTION Socialist periodicals which flourished in the 1880s and 1890s often followed the Chartist* lead by including polemical fiction. Published on Friday or Saturday to take advantage of Sunday leisure time, serialized fiction was seen as an effective way to maintain readership* and to present a different perspective on the periodical's version of socialism. Moreover, the reader had a week or month to contemplate the issues raised before the next instalment.

The importance placed on fiction as a vehicle for polemic varied across the socialist* movement. The

Social Democratic Federation's *Justice** published only four serialized fictions between 1884 and 1914. This implies a low opinion of their political* use, although one story, 'A Working Class Tragedy' (1888-1889), may have been written by Henry Hyndman* under the pseudonym* ' H. J. Bramsbury'. Robert Blatchford's* *Clarion** and Charles Allen Clarke's* *Teddy Ashton's Journal/Northern Weekly** gave a great deal of space to creative literature, often overlapping serializations, though they both questioned the efficacy of fiction during times of international crisis. (Blatchford ceased to write fiction when concerned about the impending First World War, and Clarke delayed the publication of his serial 'The Cotton Panic' (1900-1901) at the start of the Boer War.) Many stories were written by members of the group publishing the periodical: William Morris's *Commonweal* serialized 'News from Nowhere' (1890) and 'A Dream of John Ball' (1886-1887); Henry Hyde Champion's* *Labour Elector** serialized Margaret Harkness's 'Connie' (1893) after the two worked together during the 1889 London dock strike. Clarke wrote much of the fiction in *Teddy Ashton's Journal*, alongside colleagues such as James Haslem and Fred Plant, and the *Clarion* published serializations by most of the *Clarion* team including Blatchford, his brother Montague, Edward Fay and A. Neil Lyons. The publication of James Skipp Borlase's 'Darker than Death' (1885) in *Justice* suggests that some editors also bought in fiction, as Borlase was not a member of the Federation and had a number of fictions published through Tillotson's* newspaper library.

The aesthetic standard of the serializations in socialist periodicals has been criticized, but this view underestimates the attempt to create an alternative to the bourgeois novel, not least through the ways in which these periodicals embedded fiction within a radical political* context of commentary and analysis. **DM**

Sources: Barnes 2006, Law 2000, Mitchell 1987, Mutch 2005, Thompson 1951, Tzusuki 1961.

SERIALS AND THE NINETEENTH-CENTURY PUBLISHING INDUSTRY The category of 'serial publications' embraces three groups: periodicals with miscellaneous contents, including both magazines and newspapers; unified texts issued at intervals in independent fascicles or parts; books in uniform series, often, but not necessarily, numbered. Both parts and periodicals were typically formatted* so that either the purchaser or the vendor could bind them into volumes when the sequence was complete, so that the uniform series is not the only overlap between instalment and book publication. Serial publication was not a Victorian invention, as all three of these print formats had clear precedents in the eighteenth century if not earlier. The principal motivations underlying the rise of serial publication were speed and economy. Serial issue itself, and the more dispersed channels for the distribution* of serials (canvassers, general stores, the postal service), offered the reader* an immediacy of access to written information that traditional booksellers could not match. At the same time, publishers* were able to spread the cost of production*, and readers the purchase price*, painlessly over the period of issue, while either side could withdraw from a publication that proved unpopular.

Yet it is equally clear that from around the second quarter of the nineteenth century, serial publication underwent a revolution that was both qualitative and quantitative. In the Victorian period, as the balance shifted from the predominance of reprinted to that of original material, aesthetic considerations took on a much larger role in motivating instalment publication, so that it then becomes important to recognize not only new mechanisms of serial publishing such as fiction syndication* but also developments in the art of serial composition and the psychology of serial reading*. The early Victorian serial boom is the clearest evidence of the emergence of print-capitalism in Britain, that is, of the shift from petty-commodity-text to commodity-text production (Feltes). Also, the symptoms of this profound change can also be found in the increasing 'trepidation of the spheres' of serial and volume publication (Brake). Economic history is here also supported by etymology. Though 'number', 'part' and 'fascicle', or 'miscellany'*, 'journal', 'magazine' and 'periodical' have a rather longer history, the term 'serial' itself, whether as adjective or noun, only comes into common usage around the beginning of the Victorian era. In Dickens's* correspondence, for example, the noun 'number' tends to be used indifferently to refer to a single fascicle or an issue of a miscellany, while the adjective 'periodical' is employed to characterize the publication of either. At first the term 'serial' is employed *only* to refer to a uniform series of books such as Bentley's Standard Novels, though Dickens soon extends the usage to cover both modes of publication in instalments. The emergence of this new word thus also serves to justify the use of the concept of 'revolution' to define the changes taking place in serial publication in the mid-nineteenth century. **GL**

Sources: Altick 1957, Brake 2001, Feltes 1986, Hughes and Lund 1991, Law 2000.

SERVANT'S MAGAZINE (1838-1869) The *Servant's Magazine* first appeared when the 'March of Intellect' was at its height 'under the supervision of the London Female Mission' to provide improving reading for servant girls. The tone was patronizing and austerely evangelical throughout. A column* by 'Grandfather Jonathon' admonished his readers* to persevere in their duties, regularly study the Bible, and observe absolute obedience to those placed over them. 'The Servant's Hall' advised on how to improve housework, and suggested simple recipes, while a woodcut* temporarily adapted as the magazine's motif idealized the neatly dressed servant as part of the happy family. Fiction was forbidden, and servants were warned against reading any novel they noticed in their master's study. A chance visit to a fair was shown to be a dire (if unspecified) disaster. Servants should be faithful: 'Servants who often change their situation are always poor'.

Competition* from other cheap* periodicals forced changes on the editors*. In 1842 steel engravings were introduced, and illustrations* became a feature of the magazine. By mid-century it included articles on botany and the history* of the Holy Land. Although in 1853 readers* were instructed 'Let nothing ever induce you to read novels', in 1855 'The Three Sisters' by 'Sally Meanwell' introduced fiction under the guise of moral instruction, and such stories became a staple of the periodical. Nothing, however, softened the authoritarian tone, and in 1869, shortly before its closure, it was still advising servants never to change their employment, 'unless the Lord tells you it will be for your soul's good', a context the editor left tantalizingly indefinite.

Although it was published monthly*, cheaply at a penny, and it survived for over 30 years, the magazine's contents indicate that the mistress of the house bought it for her servants: few would have bought it for themselves. **LJ**
Sources: Adburgham 1972, Burnett 1972, James 1982, *Waterloo*.

SEYMOUR, ROBERT (1798-1836) The caricature* illustrations* of Robert Seymour became the defining presence of two important and innovative satirical* magazines, *Figaro in London** and the *Looking Glass**. In a career dogged by the uncertainties of the literary market* in the 1820s and 1830s, Seymour learnt his trade working for the illustrated journals published* by Knight and Lacey*, many of which had begun to use wood* engraved vignettes to broaden their appeal. On the failure of his publishers in 1827, Seymour, like many of his contemporaries, broadened his work to include etching, engraving and lithography*. His new found versatility paid immediate dividends in developing an association with the publisher Thomas McClean, and in 1830 Seymour began to produce the four pages of lithographs required for each issue of the *Looking Glass*, a monthly* publication that depended entirely on graphic satire*. In taking over from William Heath*, Seymour rejected etching in favour of the faster, more impressionistic lithograph, and continued to shift the weight of the magazine's content from political* satire* to contemporary manners.

In 1831 Seymour became the illustrator for a more overtly political* journal, *Figaro in London*, for which he drew small wood* engraved images as well as the title page image of Figaro. In 1834 a row with *Figaro's* editor*, Gilbert À Beckett* ended Seymour's connection with the magazine, but he continued to produce the *Looking Glass* up to his death. As well as his well-known work for these two journals, Seymour also produced extended serialized works comprising his caricatures. The 26 monthly issues of *New Readings of Old Authors*, produced in the early 1830s, in particular brought an innovative seriality to the publication of comic images. **BM**
Sources: Everitt 1893, Houfe 1978, *ODNB*.

SHAFTS (1892-1899) *Shafts*, variously subtitled *Light comes to those who dare to think*, *A paper for women and the working classes*, and *A monthly journal of progressive thought*, was an important feminist* periodical with a strong 'new morality' emphasis. Initially a penny* weekly*, it was edited* by Margaret Shurmer Sibthorp and strongly reflected her interests. These included not only by now traditional feminist campaigns as those for the vote, women's employment and education, but radical attitudes to social purity, dress reform, women's control of their own sexuality, child care, anti-vivisectionism, vegetarianism, opposition to cruelty to animals and Theosophy. Classes for readers were held in the periodical's office.

Contributors included Elizabeth Elmy*, Dora Montefiore, Edith Ward and Charlotte Carmichael Stopes (Shakespeare specialist and mother of Marie Stopes). In many ways, it was ahead of its time; for example, in addition to the coverage above, the editor avoided using masculine pronouns to express general statements. It also reported regularly and in detail on the activity of progressive women's clubs, most notably the Pioneer Club, the ultimate 'New Woman' organization, and the Grosvenor Crescent

Club. It started out as a weekly*, but soon became a monthly* and eventually bi-monthly. One reason lies in its precariousness funding, mainly from individual anonymous* donors, which resulted in shaky finances; and in 1899 it had gaps in production, due apparently to its editor's health. Together these seem to have led to its demise after October 1899, although it announced it was to become a quarterly*. **DD**

Sources: Beaumont 2006, Brady 1978, Dougan and Sanchez 1987, *ODNB*, Schuch 2001, *Shafts* 1829-1899.

SHAMROCK (1866-1919?) The *Shamrock* was a weekly* illustrated* penny* journal published in Dublin every Saturday. Its editor* and proprietor* was journalist Richard Pigott, who also controlled another weekly, the *Irishman*.

The *Shamrock* was composed mostly of fiction, with four serials* running in each issue, but it also contained articles on Irish history* and the Irish language. Contributors included novelist William Carleton*, journalists Denis Holland and John Augustus O'Shea and poet John Francis O'Donnell. Notable illustrators* include Harry Furniss*, and Royal Hibernian Academy members Edward Shiel and Edmund Fitzpatrick. William F. Lynam's stories on comic character Mick McQuaid proved its most popular and enduring series. The serial ran 1867-1919, being continued by different authors after Lynam's death in 1894.

In 1881 Pigott was forced to sell the *Shamrock* and his other periodicals to the Irish National Newspaper and Publishing Company, owned by the Land League. Articles in favour of Irish nationalism* increased under new editor, but the format* of the *Shamrock* remained stable under the new management. The *Shamrock* absorbed the entertainment journal the *Irish Emerald* (1892-1912) in 1912, and changed its title* to *The Shamrock and Irish Emerald* (1912-1919?), but its marked decline in literary quality led to its demise. **FB**

Sources: Brown 1937, Carleton and O'Donoghue 1896, Clyde 2003, COPAC, National Library of Ireland Catalogue, *ODNB*, *Waterloo Irish*.

SHANNON, CHARLES HASLEWOOD (1863-1937) Frequently portrayed as the lesser figure in a lifelong working and perhaps romantic partnership with Charles Ricketts*, Shannon was, during their lifetimes at least, the more famous of the two. Shannon was an expert engraver and lithographer*, but he was mostly known for his paintings. The traditionalism of his engraving techniques and the conspicuous influence of French Impressionism, Symbolism and the Pre-Raphaelites on his paintings and illustrations* made him a fashionable artist during the 1890s. Reproductions and original illustrations of his were published in periodicals such as the *Hobby Horse*, *Universal Review*, the *Sketch*, the *Savoy*, the *Studio* and the *Venture* (an early twentieth-century annual* edited* by Laurence Housman and W. Somerset Maugham). Together with Ricketts, he edited the coterie publication the *Dial* to which he also contributed several illustrations and even a bizarre impressionistic short story. Later on, he became art editor* (the literary editor being Gleeson White*) for the *Pageant*, a commercially more ambitious version of the *Dial*. **KNC**

Sources: *ODNB*, Robinson 1987, Sullivan.

SHARP, WILLIAM (1855-1905) Sharp was a jobbing journalist* who wrote for a number of periodicals including *Harper's Magazine*, and he enjoyed being a part of literary* London in the 1870s and 1880s, counting such writers as Algernon Swinburne*, William Morris* and Walter Pater* among his acquaintances. He became the art critic for the *Glasgow Herald* in 1883, and not long after, held the same position simultaneously for the *Art Journal*, though his critical work was increasingly hampered by continued ill health. After spending four years travelling, Sharp and his wife, the writer Evelyn Sharp, returned to Britain to live in Sussex, and, in 1892 he began editing and largely writing pseudonymously the *Pagan Review*, the chief organ of the 'new paganism'. Among the ideas he espoused here was the view that man and woman should not be considered as distinct, something he took on board personally in developing the pseudonymous female writing persona 'Fiona MacLeod', which was indebted to myths linked to contemporary Celticism. He took this dual, feminine part of himself so seriously that it likely added to his ill-health, leading to a near nervous breakdown in the late 1890s. **MWT**

Sources: *ODNB*, Sharp 1910.

SHARPE'S LONDON MAGAZINE (1845-1870) Promising 'Entertainment and Instruction for General Reading', *Sharpe's London Magazine* was one of a number of literary miscellanies* (including *Douglas Jerrold's Shilling Magazine* and *Household Words*) trying to capture the reading public among the 'middle and lower walks of society'*. *Sharpe's London Magazine* began as a 16-page* weekly* at ½d, in small print and with a single woodcut*, but changed to a shilling* monthly* with steel engravings from 1848. The title became *Sharpe's London Journal* (March 1849-June 1852).

Control of the magazine was also unstable: the original proprietor* was the publisher* T. B. Sharpe; ownership transferred to Arthur Hall in mid-1848; and by 1853 the editorship* had passed through the hands of Frank Smedley, W. H. Bartlett and Anna Maria Hall*.

The magazine* typically included biographical and travel sketches, as well as literary reviews*, but pride of place was given to verse and serial* fiction. Three Smedley novels ran consecutively in the magazine (1846-1853), with 'Phiz' (Hablot Knight Browne*) among the illustrators*. From the late 1850s the magazine cultivated a female audience and survived until 1870; it could not, however, compete with the new wave of illustrated 1s monthlies* led by the Cornhill*. GL

Sources: Bede 1879, Boase 1879, Mitchell 1981, Onslow 2000.

SHARPLES, ELIZA (1804-1852) Elizabeth Sharples (later Carlile) occupies an unusual position in histories of feminism and radical publishing. When women's involvement in radical culture was largely supportive and anonymous*, she was a principal lecturer at the freethinking Rotunda theatre in Blackfriars, a venue of radical instruction and entertainment run by her common-law husband, the infidel publisher Richard Carlile*. Following the imprisonment of Robert Taylor and Carlile, in 1832, she continued their radical agenda, lecturing on social justice at the Rotunda. Those lectures were the centrepiece of the Isis*. A London Weekly Publication, Edited by a Lady of which Sharples proudly proclaimed herself 'Editress'.

The Isis (11 Feb.-15 Dec. 1832), the only contemporary radical journal edited by a woman, was aimed at the capital's freethinkers and supporters of the Reform Bill. Sharples intended it as 'a mild, philosophical publication' (11 Feb 1832: 6) with contributions from Frances Wright, Carlile and other freethinking* celebrities. At 6d, it was aimed at a 'respectable' audience and though Sharples campaigned against the taxes on knowledge she refused to lower the price to reach readers of the unstamped press: 'I pity but cannot appeal to poverty and misery for assistance' (11 Feb 1832: 5).

Sharples visited Carlile in gaol daily to prepare lectures, edit the Isis, and consummate their 'moral marriage'. The extent of Sharples's authorship of the Isis has been questioned. Her daughter claimed that Carlile 'outlined' all her lectures (Carlile Campbell: 159). However, the Isis devotes more attention to gender politics than Carlile's other publications and frequent references to her own experience suggest

Sharples's input (Rogers: 52-53). Sharples's feminist* discourse was in part inspired by Mary Wollstonecraft. Her 'Discourses to the People' urged readers to embrace free thought, controversially employed anti-church rhetoric and called for women to be included in public life. She also spoke for a group called 'The Female Society, The Friends of the Oppressed' which campaigned for the unstamped* press. Deploying the flamboyant guises of Eve, Isis, and Hypatia both on the stage and in her journal, Sharples encouraged women to be producers of radical knowledge but her idiosyncratic personae may have lost her potential followers.

Sharples had little head for business and the Isis proved unprofitable. Plans for a cheaper edition came to nothing, though in 1834 the 'Editress' brought out a folio edition. Attempts to revive her career after Carlile's death in 1843 were thwarted by poverty, although a public subscription enabled her to continue her work on women's rights and radical freethought for a time at the Warner Street Temperance Hall run as a coffee and discussion room. This was where she gave lodgings to the young Charles Bradlaugh*. But the reluctance of radical men to allow women to take up prominent positions as speakers, writers and editors proved a consistent obstacle. HR/DeM

Sources: Carlile 1899, Frow 1989, McFarlane 2005, ODNB, Rogers 2000, Waterloo, Wiener 1983.

SHAW, FLORA (1852-1929) Flora Shaw, later Lady Lugard, journalist* and author, was raised in Dublin and Woolwich. Her family was immersed in military and political life: her father was a Captain in the Royal artillery and her grandfather, Sir Frederick Shaw, MP, a leader of the Irish conservatives. Shaw considered herself Irish-French (her mother was French), but she was nonetheless a lifelong advocate of what she presented as responsible British imperial* expansion. She has the distinction of being the first woman on the permanent staff of The Times*, initially as a foreign* correspondent and later, from 1893-1900, as its colonial editor* at an annual salary of £800 per annum.

She was encouraged by John Ruskin*, whom she met in 1869, to write children's fiction: two of her novels were serialized* in Aunt Judy's Magazine*: 'Hector' (1880-1881) and 'Phyllis Brown' (1882-1883). Her break into high-profile journalism followed from an interview in Gibraltar with Zobehr Pasha, the exiled political prisoner; she sent a piece charting his life story to W. T. Stead* (whom she had met through George Meredith) at the Pall

*Mall Gazette**, openly criticizing British justice in a front page coup (28 June 1887) and Zobehr was later released. Further commissions followed and Shaw, excluded from directly participating in politics because of her gender, came to view journalism as a form of 'active politics'* (Shaw, qtd Callaway and Helly: 81).

She was foreign correspondent* based in Egypt for the *Manchester Guardian** and the *Pall Mall Gazette* (1888-1889) and there met Moberly Bell, correspondent for *The Times**, who persuaded her to work for that paper, initially concealing the fact that she was a woman from his proprietor* (Onslow: 235-236) while acknowledging that if she were a man she 'would be Colonial Editor of the *The Times* tomorrow' (Bell: 92). In 1890 she began writing 'The colonies', a fortnightly column* that ran for a decade and for which she travelled widely, filing over 500 articles on a range of colonial issues from labour conditions in South Africa to official corruption in the Yukon, all characterised by her 'incisive intellect', solid research and cogent style (Callaway and Helly: 79). She reputedly coined the name 'Nigeria' in an 1897 *Times* article. She was a close friend of leading colonial politicians including Cecil Rhodes and Joseph Chamberlain. Her correspondence with the former was subject to official scrutiny during a House of Commons inquiry into military incursions into the Transvaal in 1897.

Shaw retired from *The Times* in 1900, married Sir Frederick Lugard in 1902, then high commissioner of north Nigeria. She was a 'crusader' with a 'powerful mind and compelling personality'; she is said to have 'directly influenced policies and statesmen', and helped revive the reputation of *The Times* in the last decade of the century (Woods and Bishop, qtd *ODNB*). **FD**
Sources: Bell 1947, Callaway and Helly 1992, *ODNB*, Onslow 2000, Woods and Bishop 1985.

SHAW, GEORGE BERNARD (1856-1950) Controversial and prolific playwright, formidable political* activist, art and music* critic, anti-vivisectionist, vegetarian, feminist, socialist and pacifist, there was not an issue Bernard Shaw did not write about in his phenomenally prolific career as a journalist*. He was born in Dublin to an amateur mezzo-soprano and to an alcoholic grain merchant. In 1876 he left his father and followed his mother to Britain, where he gained an unusual knowledge of classical music from attending his mother's singing lessons with Vandeleur Lee. His first writings for the periodical press were in fact as a music critic for the *Hornet* (he was Lee's ghostwriter). In London, Shaw socialised with

various radical groups of aesthetic writers and thinkers interested in social and political questions. He joined the Fabian Society in 1884 to become the voice of the movement, taking advantage of the periodical press to publish the movement's political and social manifestoes. Inspired by Henrik Ibsen, he started to write plays for the theatre.

Through the influence of William Archer, Shaw became the principal reviewer* of music and art for major periodicals such as the *Dramatic Review*, the *Star**, the *World** and the *Pall Mall Gazette**, and became a great supporter of Wagner's music. He openly used his articles to explore many of the political and social issues of the day, including the New Woman, prostitution and the Irish question, publishing in a huge variety of periodicals and newspapers, from *Animal's Friend* to the *Fabian News*, *Lady** to the *Contemporary Review**, the *Daily Mail** to the *The Times**. For a full list of his contributions to the periodical press see Laurence 1983 (vol. 2, section C) and Shaw (2005) (Part 3). **APV**
Sources: Laurence 1983, Shaw 2005.

SHEFFIELD IRIS (1794-1848) The *Sheffield Iris* had its origins in the radical weekly newspaper the *Sheffield Register*, started by the Unitarian Joseph Gales in 1787. In 1794 Gales fled to America and sold the paper to his clerk and bookkeeper, James Montgomery. The change of name to the *Sheffield Iris* in July 1794 denoted a change of politics*. Under Montgomery's editorship, the *Iris* became primarily a mouthpiece of the new evangelical middle-class* reform movement.

Montgomery was a lead player in the development of an interdenominational middle-class network of evangelical reform societies in Sheffield, including the Society for Bettering the Condition of the Poor, the Aged Female Society, the Sunday Schools' Union, missionary societies, the Literary and Philosophical Society, Mechanics' and Apprentices' Library and the Anti-Slavery Society. These societies formed a middle-class movement which sought to reform the poor at home and the 'heathen' overseas. The *Iris* supported this movement, in leaders*, poetry* and extensive reporting of meetings and events. In journalistic terms, Montgomery was neither dynamic nor exciting, seeing himself rather as a poet, hymnologist and philanthropist. He remained editor* of the *Iris* until 1825, when the paper was bought by John Blackwell, who appointed as his editor* John Holland (1794-1872), a friend and admirer of Montgomery who later became one of his biographers, but Holland was similarly lacking in journalistic flair. In 1832, the paper was sold again, to Anthony Whitaker, John Bridgeford and James L. Leek. During the 1830s it achieved relative success as a radical newspaper, and supported the Chartists*. By this time, however, the paper was increasingly overshadowed by the successful *Sheffield Independent* (1819-1938) and the *Sheffield Iris* was finally absorbed by the *Sheffield Times* in 1848. **AAT**

Sources: Holland and Everett 1855-1856, King 1858, Knight 1857, Read 1961, Twells 2008, Wigley 1975.

SHEFFIELD WEEKLY TELEGRAPH (1862-1887); WEEKLY TELEGRAPH (1887-1951) The

*Waterloo Directory** places the start date for the *Sheffield Weekly Telegraph* in January 1884. This accords with the only known run of the paper, held in the British Library, but (following a few unnumbered supplements* from earlier in January 1884) the first numbered issue is No. 1131 (26 Jan. 1884), and it states that the paper was established in April 1862. Consequently, little is known about the life of the paper before 1884, by which time it was a weekly illustrated* broadsheet priced* at 1d and published* by William Christopher Leng. Though it had the look and format* of a serious newspaper, the emphasis was firmly on fiction and light entertainment: on 26 January 1884 readers would have had to turn to page 6 of an eight-page paper to get to anything resembling news*, and then it was delivered in the most peremptory fashion. They would encounter on the way: a comic story by Mark Twain; a medical treatment of the latest fashion quandary 'Knee Breeches v. Trousers' excerpted from the *Lancet**; advice to readers* suffering from corns; chapters from a serial by F. W. Robinson entitled 'The Man She Cared For' and another entitled 'The Black Hand: a tale of the secret societies' by an anonymous author; a historical sketch of the times of Martin Luther; many other short stories, jokes, humorous poems* and vignettes; and a section describing 'Feminine Fancies, Foibles and Fashions'.

On 1 October 1887 the paper switched to a smaller format*, halving in size to a tabloid and doubling the number of pages to 16 at the same time. Two weeks later it changed its name to the *Weekly Telegraph*, retaining the basic formula whereby humour and entertainment took up the bulk of the paper, accompanied by synoptic and light coverage of national and local news towards the back of the paper. By 1895 (when Leng was still the publisher) it had again adopted a smaller format and increased to 24 pages with a regular eight-page supplement* bound in to what now had the feel of a comic magazine*. The front page was made up of short jokes, and inside there was a mixture of short stories, serialised* fiction, humorous verse, fashion*, gossip*, recipes, interesting facts ('Amazing! Interesting! Instructive!'), excerpts from the popular London press (including the *Pall Mall Gazette**, *St. James's Gazette** and others), advice on personal fitness, gardening, and other domestic issues, correspondence, and a mutual-aid column* in which readers responded to other correspondents' queries on a variety of topics. **MaT**

Source: *Waterloo.*

SHERARD, ROBERT HARBOROUGH (1861-1943) A close friend and first biographer of Oscar Wilde*, Sherard made his living as a journalist*, starting as Paris correspondent* for the *Bombay Gazette* in 1884 and getting his big break with the *New York World* and *Pall Mall Gazette** in 1887. He did not co-operate with the *World's* policy of 'tomahawking the aristocrats' and was fired twice before moving over to the *New York Morning Journal* in 1890. Between firings he kept busy with trade* journals like the *Caterer* (1884-1932), his columns* rich with the social history of Paris street life. In the 1890s he was Paris correspondent for the *Author* (1892-1897) and the *Bookman** (1895-1897), and also worked as an undercover investigator* of pauperism for the *Daily Graphic** (1891), and, for *Pearson's Magazine** (1896), of health problems in the lead industry that prompted government reform.

Sherard was an excellent interviewer* and scene setter, although he often had an agenda: to rehabilitate the reputation of society's pariahs like Wilde*, or to defend controversial figures like Émile Zola or Henrik Ibsen from crusading moralists. His best work appeared in the *Pall Mall Gazette* and *McClure's Magazine* (1893-1899). Industrious, passionate and courageous, Sherard was not a man of sound judgement and made more enemies than friends, never backing down from a pub brawl or a controversy in the newspapers. **KO'B**

Sources: O'Brien 1985, O'Brien 1987, O'Brien 1993, Sherard 1940.

SHERIDAN, LOUISA HENRIETTA (?-1841) Louisa Sheridan (later Lady Wyatt) was one of the first women caricaturists* in the British periodical press and, in the competitive field of the annual*, the first woman* to bring out her own comic annual, as editor*, author and illustrator* of the *Comic Offering or ladies' melange of literary mirth* (1831-1835). As a rival to Hood's* *Comic Annual**, it was well received in the press; its woodcuts* from Sheridan's designs gained commendation as the *Literary Ex-*

aminer enthused 'We have had many hearty laughs over it' (13 Nov. 1831). Published* by Smith, Elder and Company*, the *Comic Offering* was over 300 pages of caricatures, fiction and poetry*. Sheridan's other talent as a musician and songwriter was reflected in the inclusion of music* scores. There were contributions from others, such as the poet Maria Abdy, and Isabel Hill, the poet and playwright.

In 1838, Sheridan edited another annual, rather more lavish in production, the *Diadem, a Book for the Boudoir. The Times** rhapsodized over it: 'the perennial of ornamental literature. The embellishments are truly beautiful'. Bound in maroon morocco, embossed in gilt with 13 engravings, at £1 11s 6d its exterior was worthy of its internal dignitaries, past and present, the Earl of Chesterfield, the Duchess of Devonshire, Lady Blessington*, Count Pepoli and 'the fair authoress herself'.

Sheridan also contributed widely to other publications, both comic* and otherwise. A large number of her engravings appeared in the *Comic Magazine,* whereas her witty verses, limericks and comic songs appeared in the *Court Journal,* the *Morning Chronicle**, the *Ipswich Journal,* the *Champion and Weekly Herald*, the *Hampshire Telegraph and Sussex Chronicle*. She wrote for *Forget-me-Not, La Belle Assemblee**, the *New Monthly Magazine* and Humorist* and for Mrs Baron Wilson's* *La Ninon*. She was in correspondence with Lady Blessington*, sending contributions to her publications, the *Keepsake* and the *Book of Beauty.*

In her letters to Blessington she confides the limitations her ill-health is placing on her writing, having to cease publishing the *Comic Offering* in 1836. By 1839 she was reported as being 'alarmingly ill'. The following year she married in Paris, dying there a year later from consumption, a woman of 'playful humour and talent…taken from us in the flower of life' (*Literary Gazette** 21 Oct. 1841). **CL**
Sources: Alexander Street Press, BritPer, *The Times* 1838, *Waterloo*.

SHIELD (1870-1933) The *Shield; the Anti-Contagious Diseases Act Associations' weekly circular* was launched in response to the government's Contagious Diseases Acts, as part of a political* campaign backed by the Ladies' National Association and led by the feminist, Josephine Butler* who edited* the paper. Although the *Shield* was a single-issue paper, it was significant in terms of the fight to establish an equal moral standard, publicly discussing matters which were deemed unfit for 'ladies'. Debates relating to the criminalization of prostitutes but not their clients, the provision of prostitutes for the British army, the definition of prostitution, women's freedom of movement, the class* system's relation to the moral categorization of women and the expression of women's sexuality were all integral strands.

Published* by William Dagleas Learmount and printed by Frederick Charles Banks, it was a 28 cm, 16-page paper* priced* at 1d. As a campaigning paper to abolish the Contagious Diseases Act, it dealt principally with parliamentary* reports and news* items relating to the cause and those incidents emanating from the districts controlled by the Act. When in 1886 the campaign succeeded in its goal, the paper was terminated. However, in response to the attempt to extend the application of state regulation of vice in India to Britain, the paper was reinstated in May 1897 under the aegis of the Josephine Butler Society and the British Committee of the International Federation for the Abolition of the State Regulation of Vice.

During the First World War it fought the Defence of the Realm Act regulating prostitution, extending its remit to support the fight for women's suffrage. With no issues published in February-March 1916, it was reissued in April 1916 as the paper of the Association for Moral and Social Hygiene. Retaining its core strategy as part of the coalition for the political, social and economic protection and advancement for wartime women workers, it continued in the post-war struggle for women's full equality. **CL**
Sources: Law 1997, *Waterloo*.

SHILLING MONTHLIES A phenomenon that appeared first in 1859, shilling monthlies were periodicals aimed at a middle-class* family*-oriented audience, costing less than half of extant middle-class monthlies such as *Blackwood's**. Principal titles were *Macmillan's Magazine**, then *Cornhill**, *Temple Bar**, *St James's Magazine* and *Belgravia**. An emphasis on serial* fiction and, with the exception of *Macmillan's*, a general refusal to engage with politics* or religion*, enabled shilling monthlies to offer readers regular, respectable amusement at an attractive price*. Shilling monthlies cemented the link between new fiction and the regular publication of extant serials that *Blackwood's**, the *London Journal** and *Household Words** had already noted, leading to the popular fiction papers and newspaper novels that followed, as well as assuring the health of the periodical press for the remainder of the century.

Publishers* were not slow to see the advantages

of the new form: George Smith*, writing about his *Cornhill Magazine*, noted that: 'the existing magazines were few, and when not high-priced were narrow in literary range, and it seemed to me that a shilling magazine which contained, in addition to other first-class literary* matter, a serial novel by Thackeray* must command a large sale' (Sullivan: 82). Other publishers followed suit, anchoring their magazines* to the reputations of well-known writers or trading on the trust the public already held in their products. As a result, the monthlies became a source of free advertising* for their publishers, as well as offering space at a price to competitors. Many monthlies were very successful; for instance, 120,000 copies of the first number of the *Cornhill* were sold, though as titles proliferated and competition for readers grew, the circulation* figures of most shilling monthlies never exceeded 15,000 copies (Altick: 359). ET

Sources: Altick 1957, Sullivan, *Wellesley.*

SHOBERL (SCHOBERL), FREDERIC (1775-1853) Although his parents were German, Frederic Shoberl was born in London and then sent to Fulneck, the Moravian school in Leeds, before returning to London to live and work. Many years of his journalistic and editorial career were spent working on three of the German publisher*, lithographer* and inventor Rudolph Ackermann's publications. He edited* Ackermann's *Repository of Arts* (1809-1828), managed the annual* *Forget-Me-Not* (1822-1834) and edited the *Juvenile Forget-Me-Not* (1828-1832). In addition to Ackermann's periodicals, in 1814 Shoberl was in partnership with the publisher Henry Colburn*; they devised and owned the *New Monthly Magazine and Universal Register** to which Shoberl contributed. As well as his periodical work, for a year he published and printed the Tory paper the *Cornwall Gazette, Falmouth Packet and Plymouth Journal* (1818).

Apart from his journalism, Shoberl was a prolific writer, predominantly of history and travel books and worked with John Watkins* on the 1816 *Biographical Dictionary of Living Authors*. Both sons followed their father's example, William becoming a publisher and Frederic a printer. CL

Source: *ODNB.*

SHORTER, CLEMENT KING (1857-1926) A proponent of the New Journalism*, Clement Shorter was the most influential editor* of pictorial papers at the turn of the twentieth century. After a decade and more as a clerk at Somerset House, Shorter began to write weekly book columns* for the *Star** and the *Queen**. His talent was quickly recognized by Sir William Ingram of the *Illustrated London News**, and he took over the editorship of that paper from John Latey in 1891. In 1893 he took editorial control of two further Ingram periodicals, the *English Illustrated Magazine**, purchased from Macmillan*, and the newly founded *Sketch**. This light illustrated* weekly* journal devoted to 'art and actuality' was Shorter's brain child.

On the flotation of Ingram's company, Shorter broke with his boss but soon found a new patron in the shipping magnate Sir John Ellerman. With his financial backing, Shorter made a success of the *Sphere* (1900) and the *Tatler* (1901), new weekly* photographic* papers 'for the home' and 'of society and the stage' respectively. The former he edited almost until his death, contributing a literary column where he was free to pursue his personal interests in writers like the Brontës. GL

Sources: Beegan 2001, *ODNB*, Shorter 1899, Shorter 1927.

SHORTHAND Systems of shorthand, or stenography as it is sometimes called, have been used since the time of the Greeks. Julius Caesar was an accomplished shorthand writer; Pepys recorded his diary in shorthand; sermons by famous clerics were often recorded surreptitiously by reporters* sitting in the congregation and later reproduced in pirate editions. During the Industrial Revolution shorthand simplified the copying of business documents. In the nineteenth-century shorthand as a method of reproducing parliamentary* debates and speeches came into its own.

Parliament objected, at first, to what it called 'strangers' in the gallery being admitted, but eventually bowed to public pressure and not only allowed notes of speeches to be taken, but by 1835 provided special areas in the gallery for parliamentary reporters*. Macaulay, writing in the *Edinburgh Review** in 1828, saw public support for the reporters as akin to lack of support for the Constitution (Chittick: 10) and thus a material contribution towards change. In the 1830s *Fraser's Magazine** (Chittick: 14) singled out the *Morning Chronicle**, *The Times** and the *Morning Herald** as the newspapers whose reporters had perfected the art; it was the staff of the *Chronicle* that Dickens*, as a young parliamentary reporter*, was most anxious to join. Most practitioners seem to have been law students and used shorthand, like Dickens, as a means of making money.

A good shorthand reporter could also raise the profile and reputation of a paper. Politicians were not slow to realize this, and often, say *Fraser's,* would address their remarks not to the Speaker's Chair but to the reporters in the gallery. Similarly, the move from ambitious shorthand reporter to respected barrister or full-time author was frequently made. Mastery of the technique, therefore, became associated with ambition and is allied with the nineteenth-century debate about reading for pleasure versus reading for improvement. By the end of the century everything from Plutarch to Sherlock Holmes stories could be bought in shorthand editions, aimed particularly at male office clerks interested in social mobility. **ET**

Sources: Chittick 1990, 'Shorthand' *Encyclopaedia Britannica* 2007, Price and Thurschwell 2005.

SIMCOX, EDITH (1844-1901) Prodigious journalist*, businesswoman, social reformer and author, Edith Simcox (pseudonym* 'H. Lawrenny') contributed to leading periodicals (1869-1900). Beginning with its first issue in 1869, she wrote more than 70 articles for the *Academy**. Her topics for reviews* and articles included economic reform, philosophy*, autobiographies, the Australian family, myths and fairytales, George Eliot*, Robert Browning, Charles Dickens*, John Henry Newman, John Stuart Mill*, Charles Darwin, William Morris* and John Morley*. Her work appeared in *Fraser's Magazine**, the *Fortnightly Review**, the *Nineteenth Century**, *Macmillan's Magazine**, *North British Review**, *St Paul's Magazine** and *Longman's Magazine**.

Simcox's major articles promoted education and employment for women*, women's suffrage and the formation of trade unions*. As a representative to the International Trades Union Congress and similar groups, she frequently contributed daily reports to the *Manchester Guardian** and other newspapers, as well as writing articles for the *Co-operative News,* the *Labour Tribune,* the *Women's Union Journal** and *The Times**. She detailed her own success as a businesswoman in 'Eight Years of Co-Operative Shirtmaking' in *Nineteenth Century** (June 1884). She was an independent woman who not only advocated economic and intellectual opportunities for women but also worked to provide them. **CMF**

Sources: Barfield and Fulmer 1998, Fulmer 1998, McKenzie 1961, Simcox 1884.

SIMPKIN AND MARSHALL (1815-1955); SIMPKIN, WILLIAM (1772-1854); MARSHALL, RICHARD (1788-1863) The bookseller and publisher* Simpkin and Marshall embodied the explosion in demand for printed matter during this period, managing the successful symbiosis of cultural need with commercial delivery. Unlike some oth-ers, their enterprise coped with expansion in response to demand.

William Simpkin's working life began as a hatter and bookseller; he became an assistant to Benjamin Crosby, a bookseller and stationer, whose premises were at 4 Stationers' Court between 1874-1815. When Crosby retired in 1815, Simpkin together with Richard Marshall took over the business off Ludgate Street. In 1834, Simpkin and Marshall became Simpkin, Marshall and Co., and various imprints with changing partners ensued. Particularly in its first 25 years, the firm was engaged with a cornucopia of periodicals touching every dimension of the market. By 1900 it had been involved with nearly 90 journals including the esoteric *Zadkiel's Almanac and Herald of Astrology,* the highly regarded *Westminster Review**, the popular *Ackermann's Repository of Fashions,* the *Dublin University Magazine**, the *Anti-Infidel and Religious Advocate,* the *Electrical Magazine,* the *Greenhouse and Gardener,* the *Magazine of Science and School of Arts,* the *Musical Magazine* and the *North of England Magazine.*

The firm also printed and published an array of books, pamphlets and essays, mirroring the engagement with the growth in knowledge. The business was still operating from its original premises into the late 1920s, and the imprint survived until 1955. **CL**

Sources: Glasgow 1998, *Notes & Queries* 1908/ 1943, *Waterloo.*

SIMPSON, RICHARD (1820-1876) Having converted to Roman Catholicism in 1846, Richard Simpson began contributing articles to the *Rambler** in 1850. Here he started a close association and friendship with another convert, the editor* and proprietor* John Moore Capes*. In April 1854 Capes offered Simpson the post of assistant editor*, which Simpson declined, mainly because of differences with the then editor James Spencer Northcote. However, after Northcote's retirement later that year, Simpson became subeditor*. When Capes resigned as editor (Oct. 1857) his post was temporarily assumed by Simpson; in February 1858 Simpson became editor under Sir John Acton*, who had recently joined the *Rambler* as contributor and part owner. In 1859, Simpson, because of his liberal views, was forced to resign and was replaced as editor by John Henry Newman. Nevertheless Simpson, Acton and Capes remained contributors and proprietors.

In 1862 Acton founded the *Home and Foreign Review** as a successor to the *Rambler*. Simpson became co-proprietor of this new liberal Catholic journal. However his association proved prejudicial to the paper. Acton relied increasingly on the assistance of Thomas Wetherell as subeditor, and Simpson gradually became disenchanted with the secondary role allotted to him. After the termination of the *Home and Foreign Review* in 1864, he retreated into Shakespearean studies. He contributed articles on Shakespeare and contemporary events to the *Chronicle*, a journal which lasted for just a year (1867-1868). Simpson also made financial contributions when Acton took over the *North British Review** in 1869. It survived until 1871, with Simpson contributing a number of noteworthy articles.

Simpson was versatile and his articles covered a wide variety of subjects. His main interest, however, was in theological themes, and he could not reconcile himself to ecclesiastical disapproval of a layman writing on such matters. Nor could he completely reconcile himself to Papal infallibility. He died while in Rome, where he was buried. DHL
Sources: Altholz 1962, Altholz and McElrath 1971, *ODNB*, *Wellesley.*

SIMS, GEORGE ROBERT (1847-1922) George Sims was a journalist*, columnist*, social campaigner and popular dramatist. Born in London in comfortable circumstances, Sims worked for his father's manufacturing business after leaving school. He began writing copy for such journals as *Fun**, *Woman** and *Dark Blue* as a distraction from his dull office job, and soon found himself contributing a regular column* called 'Mustard and Cress' under the pseudonym* 'Dagonet' to the weekly* *Referee* (1877-1928), a journal of sport* and drama. Collected editions of his work for this paper were republished frequently from the 1880s.

Sims was deeply interested in social reform, and articles on London's working class*, housing conditions for the poor, white slavery, etc., appeared under his name in the *Daily News**, *Pictorial World, Sunday Dispatch* and the *Daily Telegraph**, and led to his active campaigning for change. Sims's impact as a social* journalist is partly overshadowed by his great success as a writer of stage melodramas, a success that some felt belittled his attempts to effect change. ET
Sources: *ODNB*, Sims 1901-1903, Sims 1917.

SIZE AND FORMAT Broadsheet newspapers are the most homogenous group of nineteenth-century journals in terms of their format, size and general appearance. *The Times**, the *Daily News** and the *Morning Chronicle** are typical of the daily broadsheet, having either six or seven columns* to a page with densely set news* items. This is common to both national and local* broadsheet newspapers

such as the *Derby Mercury.* As Newspaper* Stamp Duty applied only to paper* upon which news was to be printed, advertisement* pages were used to 'bulk out' newspapers and were often used as 'wrappers' within which the newspaper proper was protected. The removal of Stamp Duty changed the broadsheet in the second half of the century, as these 'wrappers' gave way to advertisements* within news pages throughout the paper. The removal of tax, coupled with lower printing costs through advanced technology, also led to newspapers having considerably more pages for a greatly reduced cover price*; the *Daily News* was 3d for four sheets in 1834, but only 1d for eight by 1880. This broadsheet format applied to much of the weekly* news press, with the six-column *Reynolds's Weekly Newspaper** being a largely advertisement-free affair in the early 1850s, but offering the same number of pages, liberally strewn with advertisements, for a quarter of the price by 1900. Weeklies* were also more often illustrated*, such as the sumptuous *Illustrated London News** (1842ff).

*Lloyd's Weekly Newspaper** followed the broadsheet format, and it also spawned the part-illustrated *Lloyd's Weekly Miscellany,* typified by its smaller format and three-column pages of articles covering science*, literature* and art. The weekly miscellanies* and literary periodicals are a much more varied category in terms of their size, but are typically much smaller than the newspaper press, with their pages laid out in either two or three columns and more frequently illustrated or decorated. The smaller format weeklies such as *Household Words**, *All the Year Round** and *Chambers's Journal** are printed with continuous pagination, demonstrating the intent for these pages to transcend the ephemeral nature of journalism* by being more conveniently bound as bookish volumes. Annual indices were added to the likes of *Lloyds, Chambers's* and *Dickens's** journals when bound, and advertising pages were removed, eradicating the commercial aspect of many of the journals endowed with greater longevity. Quality monthlies* such as the 2s 6d *Blackwoods**, as well as the later shilling* monthlies like the *Cornhill**, also share these qualities with the smaller format weekly press, whereas the hybrid news-and-literary *Spectator** shows its liminal nature in its form as well as content. Though the pages are printed in two columns with continuous pagination, it is inconveniently large when bound and has no overall index.

The duality of form inherent in bound volumes of journalism is central to the far smaller *Yellow*

Book: An Illustrated Quarterly*. Dispensing with columns and continuous pagination, this journal was created as a series of self-contained books of art and literature at once uniform and individual. **MBT**

Sources: *All the Year Round, Chambers's Journal, Daily News, Derby Mercury*, Finkelstein 2006, *Household Words, Illustrated London News, Lloyd's Weekly Miscellany, Lloyd's Weekly Newspaper, Morning Chronicle, Reynolds's Weekly Newspaper, Spectator, The Times, Yellow Book*.

SKELTON, JOHN (1831-1897) Like many Victorian writers, John Skelton successfully combined the career of a civil servant with that of a man of letters. It was by his contributions to major magazines* of the period that Skelton made his name. He began to write for *Fraser's Magazine** in 1855, and contributed over 60 articles (1855-1880). His contributions to *Blackwood's Magazine** (1869-1897) amounted to more than 40 pieces. His pseudonym* 'Shirley,' derived from Charlotte Brontë's novel (1849), was not meant to conceal his identity; rather, it served as an established trademark. Most of his articles in these journals contained topical criticism of a range of contemporary literature* and the arts. In *Fraser's* (1855-1880) he focused on important, often controversial, figures of his age. He discussed Ruskin's* view of ancient and modern poets, Homer and Tennyson in particular (1856), and *Modern Painters* (1857), Macaulay's historiography (1860), and Robert Browning's and Swinburne's* poetry* (1863, 1866).

From 1869, *Blackwood's Magazine* became his primary outlet. In *'Maga'*, Scottish themes and authors (Margaret Oliphant* (1883, 1888), Jane Welsh Carlyle's letters (1883) and Scott (1893) were predominant, but his work also included a wider range of topics (historiography and politics*, such as home rule in Scotland [1886]). He regularly returned to the controversy surrounding Mary Queen of Scots in which he ably defended her from her accusers (1888). **ZV**

Sources: *ODNB, Wellesley*.

SKETCH (1893-1959) As originally conceived by C. K. Shorter*, the *Sketch* was a copiously illustrated* 6d weekly* journal of 'art and actuality'. With the *Illustrated London News** and the *English Illustrated Magazine** (purchased from Macmillan* in 1893), it made up the trio of leading pictorial periodicals operated by the Illustrated London News Co. Until 1900 all three were edited* by Shorter, who, in the first issue of the *Sketch* (1 Feb. 1893), imagined the new paper as a liberated youth

chasing 'that sudden and slippery worm, the popular whim', while 'our venerable parent [the *ILN*] pursues her stately flight down the broad avenues of public life'. The *Sketch* thus concerned itself with the latest trends in drama, painting, literature*, music*, sport*, fashion* and high society. In-depth articles gave way to titbits and anecdotes*. In place of serial* fiction there were short stories, with Gissing's grim sketches of 'Human Odds and Ends' appearing from autumn 1895. By the end of the century each issue contained nearly a hundred pictures, all photographs* apart from the cartoons*, fiction illustrations, and fashion* plates, many devoted to the female form. In brief, Shorter's new paper encapsulated the impact of the New Journalism* on the pictorial press. **GL**

Sources: Beegan 2001, *ODNB*, Shorter 1899, Shorter 1927.

SKUES, GEORGE EDWARD MACKENZIE (1858-1949) George Edward Mackenzie Skues attended Winchester College before spending his entire career as a solicitor with the same firm until his retirement at 81. Skues was regarded as one of the greatest practitioners of and writers on fly-fishing; his accumulated knowledge, especially on the behaviour of the trout and insects, also made his writing valuable to natural history and biology specialists. Skues's achievement was to perfect fly-fishing with the nymph, but his expertise on all aspects of the art of fly-fishing was expounded in his prolific articles in the *Fishing Gazette** and the *Flyfishers' Journal* often under different pen names. His first article appeared in the press in 1888 under the pseudonym*, 'Val Conson'. A number of these articles were reprinted in the twentieth century from the first of his many books on the subject, *Minor Tactics of the Chalk Stream* (1910). In the fishing fraternity he has come to be known as 'the father of the nymph'. **DHL**

Source: *ODNB*, Overfield 1977, Skues 1951.

SLACK, HENRY JAMES (1818-1896) Brought up as a Unitarian and with a keen interest in science, Slack began his long journalistic career working for the provincial* press, particularly the *North Devon Journal*, in the mid-1840s. After a brief and unsuccessful stint editing* just one number of the *Westminster Review** in April 1851, Slack took over as both proprietor* and editor of the *Atlas** in the following year, finally selling it back to the former editor Robert Bell at the end of the decade. During the same period he also wrote regularly for the *Weekly Times**, where he adopted the pseudonym* 'Little John'.

In 1862 Slack became editor of the *Intellectual Observer*, a journal of natural history and microscopy that superseded James Shirley Hibberd's *Recreative Science*, although Hibberd continued to contribute many of the new periodical's lead articles. Under Slack the *Intellectual Observer* shifted away from the religious* overtones and overt emphasis on science* as an amateur pastime of Hibberd's *Recreative Science*, and in 1867 he even asked Charles Darwin to contribute to the journal. A year later the journal changed its title to the *Student*, signalling an attempt to cover art and literature* alongside science. Slack also wrote extensively for other scientific journals like *Knowledge*, the *Popular Science Monthly* and the *Meteorological Journal*, as well as contributing articles on science to general periodicals such as *Ainsworth's Magazine* and *Belgravia*. **GD**
Sources: Barton 1998, Burkhardt and Smith 1994, *ODNB*, *Wellesley*.

SLY, STEPHEN (FL.1836-1847) A pupil of Henry Vizetelly*, Sly and his frequent collaborator Henry Anelay* were two of the prolific wood* engravers who supplied the increasingly voracious appetite for small but well produced images that derived from the rapid development of new mass* circulation* illustrated* journals in the 1830s and 1840s. Sly worked most notably for Charles Knight's* *Penny Magazine* and for the *Illustrated London News*. He engraved the famous view of the London skyline across the Thames that formed the first masthead* for the *Illustrated London News,* and his name appears frequently on a wide variety of illustrations throughout the early years of the magazine. **BM**
Sources: Engen 1990, Houfe 1978, Vizetelly 1893.

SMALL, WILLIAM (1843-1929) Small was a frequent contributor of illustrations* to an immensely wide range of periodicals in the 1860s and early 1870s. He illustrated a number of serialized* novels, including Charles Reade's 'Griffith Gaunt' in the *Argosy** (1865-1866) and Wilkie Collins's* 'Man and Wife' in *Cassell's Magazine** in 1869. But his versatility was such that he contributed to the *Boy's Own**, the *Children's Hour,* the *Friendly Visitor, Good Words**, *Once a Week**, the *People's Magazine,* the *Quiver**, *Sunday at Home* and the *Sunday Magazine**. In quite a different idiom he contributed satirical* images to *London Society** in 1871 and, in a further extension of his range, topographical images to the *Graphic**. Less celebrated than many of his contemporaries and never commissioned to draw a major serialized novel, nonetheless Small was high-

ly enough regarded for his magazine work to be reprinted in a number of anthologies. **BM**
Sources: Engen 1990, Forrest Reid 1928, Gleeson White 1897, Goldman 1994, Houfe 1978, Suriano 2005.

SMALLEY, GEORGE WASHBURN (1833-1916) A newspaper journalist, known as 'GWS' to his readers, Smalley graduated from Yale University in 1853 and studied Law at Harvard, later being admitted to the Massachusetts bar. Smalley contributed intimate reports of the American Civil War to the *New York Tribune*, eventually becoming their representative in London (1867-1895). Smalley is often credited with being instrumental in furthering Anglo-American relations following the war. He covered the Austro-Prussian War and the Franco-Prussian War*, finally moving to the post of London *Times** correspondent* in the US (1895-1906).

Opinionated, anti-Irish, often in conflict with his editors, Smalley's views altered as he grew older and his youthful reputation as a radical was replaced by his standing in the 1880s as a staunch Tory*. Smalley was among the first to see the potential for newspaper circulation* growth in the increase in American tourists to Europe from the 1870s on; he was central in the strategic selling of advertisements* and in the placement of American newspapers in European hotels and on board ship to meet the demand for the comforts of home. **ET**
Sources: *Oxford Companion to American Literature*, Mathews 1973, Smalley 1891, Smalley 1895, Smalley 1911-1912.

SMITH, ALBERT RICHARD (1816-1860) Albert Smith followed his father into the medical profession, and from 1838 was employed in his father's practice in Surrey. Three years later he established his own practice in London's Tottenham Court Road but soon abandoned his profession to become a journalist, writer and entertainer.

Smith's expansive personality and penchant for the comic and absurd found expression in the publications he wrote for and edited*. He contributed to the *Comic Almanack**, *Punch** and its offshoot *George Cruikshank's Table Book*, the *Comic Times*, the *Illuminated Magazine**, and *Joe Miller the Younger*. Smith's longest lived editorship (1847-1849) was with Angus B. Reach* at the *Man in the Moon**. Others were rather briefer, the *Wassail Bowl* (1843), *Puck** (1844), the *Town and Country Miscellany* (1850) and the *Month** (1851). Smith's journalism also seemed to provide a training ground for ideas and interests that were later to

inhabit his novels and his 'lectures', such as 'A Mark of Snobbism' and 'Sunset and Night on Mont Blanc' for the *London Journal**. His pieces sometimes employ medical terminology to comic effect as in 'The Prevailing Epidemic' in the *North of England Magazine** (1842) and he evidently enjoyed studying the foibles of human behaviour for most contributions, as with *Reynolds's Miscellany** and *Chambers's Edinburgh Journal**. His love of theatrical display he put to good use as drama critic of the *Illustrated London News**. He published nearly 30 successful books, with the *Natural History of the Gent* (1847) a best-seller and the first in a series. **CL**
Sources: BritPer, *ODNB*, *Waterloo*.

SMITH, GEORGE MURRAY (1824-1901) George Smith, publisher* and businessman, started his working life in his father's bookselling business, Smith and Elder where he received an invaluable introduction to the benefit of canny niche-market publications and of high-quality book production. Smith is perhaps best known for two very diverse reasons: as the founder of the *Dictionary of National Biography* and as the person who brought Charlotte Brontë's *Jane Eyre* (1847) into print. Between the massive *Dictionary of National Biography* (see *ODNB**) project towards the end his life and the cultivation of one remarkable author in the early stages of his career, Smith ran a range of successful business enterprises and provided publication outlets in periodicals (and book format) for most of the leading writers of the century including Arnold*, Browning, 'George Eliot' (Marian Evans), Gaskell, Hardy*, Henry James*, Tennyson, Thackeray*, Trollope* and Ruskin*.

Smith used the contacts secured through his successful trading ventures to various parts of the Empire to run two successful newspapers in the 1850s. The weekly* *Overland Mail* (launched in 1855), with John William Kane as editor*, brought news to India and its counterpart, *Homeward Mail* (1857), with E. B. Eastwick as editor sent news of the colony to Britain. In 1860, he established one of the first hugely successful shilling* monthlies, the *Cornhill Magazine** 'perhaps the great tour de force of Smith's publishing career' (*ODNB*). Smith persuaded Thackeray, a major draw for the magazine*, to edit the journal. Thackeray used his literary* connections to attract leading writers while Smith provided finances, which proved substantial enough, for instance, to allow him to lure 'George Eliot' from John Blackwood* to publish Romola in the *Cornhill* in serial form (1862-1863) with one of the highest payments for such work ever offered (£10,000), and to insist on high-quality illustrations*

for the magazine in its early years that included work by Leighton, Millais* and Du Maurier*.

In 1865 he launched a new daily*, the *Pall Mall Gazette**, that took its name from the fictional journal in Thackeray's *The History of Pendennis*. Smith took advantage of the abolition of the last of the taxes on knowledge to keep the price* of the paper low at 2d. Frederick Greenwood*, formerly subeditor* of the *Cornhill* took the editorial chair to carry out Smith's professed purpose: 'to bring into Daily Journalism that full measure of thought and culture which is now found only in a few Reviews' (Prospectus). It was 'unashamedly highbrow' (Glynn: 151) but, like the *Cornhill*, maintained its focus on general middle-class* readership* with popular 'Occasional Notes'* taking up over a quarter of its eight pages to ensure it held onto the leisure readers, commuters and club men for the most part. A four-month experiment in 1869 to establish a morning daily to complement the evening edition failed but by then, the *Pall Mall Gazette* had established a reputation for high-quality, non party-focused journalism. Always alert to new developments in the field of publishing, the 1870s saw Smith's business expanding to capture the niche market in medical* publications, including the *London Medical Record* and the *Sanitary Record*.

He withdrew from hands-on engagement with the running of both *Cornhill* and *Pall Mall Gazette*, and by the 1880s Smith was investing more time and his considerable energy into his other businesses, in particular into the *Dictionary of National Biography* (edited by Leslie Stephen*, who previously edited the *Cornhill*), the final volume of which appeared in the year of Smith's death. **FD**
Sources: Glynn 1986, *ODNB*, Robertson Scott 1950.

SMITH, HERBERT GREENHOUGH (1855-1935) Smith, who was born in Gloucestershire, and educated at St John's College, Cambridge, was one of the late nineteenth-century 'University men' who made journalism a career. Having served on the staff of *Temple Bar** and of George Newnes's* *Tit-Bits**, in 1891 Smith became Literary* Editor* of the *Strand Magazine** under the general editorship of Newnes, and held the position until 1930. A writer of novels himself, Smith is often credited with understanding the potential for periodical sales in A. C. Doyle's Sherlock Holmes stories, and with safeguarding the standards and respectability of the *Strand* for most of its long history. **ET**
Sources: Ashley 2006, Jackson 2006, Pound 1966, Sullivan 1984.

SMITH, JOHN ORRIN (1799-1843); SMITH, HARVEY ORRIN (FL. 1850-1870) John Orrin Smith, after c.1836 known as John Orrinsmith, was a prolific engraver with a high reputation for the fine finish of his work. Smith worked mainly as a book illustrator* until 1842 when he entered a partnership with W. J. Linton* to act as engravers for the newly established *Illustrated London News**. Engen notes that the firm 'quickly gained a reputation for quick, accurate press work', a necessity given the extremely demanding schedule of production and the broad range of work required for the magazine. Smith and Linton employed several assistants, often commissioning work for engraving from well-known artists. Smith, like many other engravers of his generation, was also responsible for mentoring and sponsoring the work of other engravers. Henry Vizetelly* was his apprentice, and John Leech* was among the many welcomed at his hospitable workshops. John's son, Harvey Orrin Smith (later Orrinsmith), also worked as an engraver for the *Illustrated London News*, establishing a partnership with Linton in the 1860s, and working on commissions for Charles Knight's* various publishing* ventures. **BM**

Sources: Engen 1990, *ODNB*, Vizetelly 1893.

SMITH, SYDNEY (1771-1845) Educated at Winchester and New College, Oxford, Sydney Smith became a clergyman, his tutorial duties taking him to Edinburgh in 1798 where his literary life began. Stimulated by his new social circle of the philosopher Dugald Stewart and Henry Brougham*, Francis Horner*, and Francis Jeffrey* (all of whom were Whigs), Smith proposed that he, Horner and Jeffrey should launch a literary* review*. Financed by the Edinburgh bookseller Archibald Constable*, the *Edinburgh Review** was published in October 1802. The first three issues were co-edited* by Smith, Horner and Jeffrey, when Smith recommended to Constable that Jeffrey should be appointed full-time editor. According to Jeffrey he was a timid co-editor, insisting that meetings took place in secret, and that the participants arrived singly and by back lanes, so that their identity should not be known. Smith worked hard to establish the *Edinburgh Review*, contributing 19 articles to the first four issues on a catholic range from travel to theology and drama; his work was flavoured with the distinctive wit that was to become his trademark.

In 1803 Smith left Edinburgh for London, where he graced the Holland House social set. His friendship with Lord and Lady Holland yielded a prosperous living from a parish near York while he remained in London. All the while he continued with his articles, books and lectures; *Peter Plymley's Letters*, an artful, anonymous, defence of the 1807 political crisis, went into 16 editions. Leaving London to undertake his clerical duties, he put into practice his social justice ideals. His articles for the *Edinburgh Review* continued, promoting his ideas on issues such as mental health, legal procedure and the importance of educating women.

In 1828 on being made a canon at Bristol Cathedral, Smith decided that in order to further his ambitions he would have to relinquish writing for the *Edinburgh Review*, although he still became involved in the campaign for the Reform Bill and wrote political* pamphlets. In 1831 he was made a canon at St Paul's, resuming his life of literary sociability in the metropolis. His *Collected Works*, containing many of his reviews for the *Edinburgh*, were published in 1854. **CL**

Sources: Clive 1957, *ODNB*.

SMITH, WILLIAM HENRY (1825-1891) The young William Henry Smith wanted to go to Oxford and become a clergyman, but his hard-nosed father insisted that his son entered the news agency* business of W. H. Smith* that he had built to distribute* London newspapers nationwide using the latest transportation. Smith was soon running the company and in 1854 acquired sole rights to distribute *The Times** outside London for an annual fee of £4,000. By 1862 he held a virtual monopoly over railway bookstalls throughout Britain, having recognized railway travellers' need for 'something to read on the train'. He quickly expanded into bookselling, creating an extensive circulating library*, and for a time published cheap editions of fiction. He further captured the minds of travellers by leasing the walls of railway stations and selling the space for advertising*. The extent of his influence caused Smith to take very seriously the self-assigned role of censor*, excluding from his bookstalls material he considered immoral. Although to be stocked by Smith's was considered vital to a journal's success, the salacious *Illustrated Police News** managed to sell 100,000 copies a week despite being banned from its shelves. Some even suggested that being banned by Smith's could bring profitable notoriety.

Smith's precocious business success gave him political* ambitions. Those in media-related businesses were usually Liberal, but anti-'trade' snobbery caused him to be blackballed by the Reform Club and drove him into the arms of the Conservative Party. His rapid ascent to a cabinet position as first lord of the Admiralty ('Ruler of the Queen's Navee') was lampooned by W. S. Gilbert in *H. M. S. Pinafore*, but his business skills made him an effective minister. He finally burned himself out in the demanding job of leader of the House of Commons under Lord Salisbury. Selling periodicals and books made him one of Britain's richest men, with an estate of nearly £2,000,000* when he died. CAK

Sources: Chilston 1965, *ODNB*, Wilson 1985.

SMITHERS, LEONARD CHARLES (1861-1907) Before becoming the most controversial publisher* of the second half of the so-called 'Yellow Nineties', Leonard Smithers worked as a solicitor in his native Sheffield. He entered the literary* scene as a translator of classical erotic literature, in close collaboration with Sir Richard Burton*. Still home in Sheffield, he met his future printer H. S. Nichols*, who like him soon became prominent in the underground world of illicit erotica. After moving to London Smithers ran an infamous bookstore specializing in rare items and pornography*, and gradually started up his eponymous publishing firm soon renowned for its luxurious editions of literary* classics and risqué new releases.

Smithers owed his pivotal position in the artistic avant-garde to the characteristic boldness that allowed him to publish 'Decadent' authors who had become pariahs after the Wilde* affair. When several of these were ousted from the *Yellow Book*, Smithers took advantage of this situation, and founded his first and only periodical the *Savoy* (1896). Although existing for a year only, this magazine edited by Arthur Symons* and Aubrey Beardsley* is still credited as one of the best and most representative of the British fin-de-siècle. Through the journal, Smithers consolidated his professional relationship with many of its choice contributors for his book list. KNC

Source: Nelson 2000.

SMITHIES, THOMAS BYWATER (1817-1883) As a dedicated temperance* and humanitarian worker, Thomas Smithies devoted his publishing* career to producing periodicals that promulgated his evangelical* values. In 1851 he began the *Band of Hope Review and Sunday Scholar's Friend* that supported the fledgling children's temperance* movement. This started a lifelong association with his publishing* company, S. W. Partridge & Co., which Smithies was later accredited with founding.

The content of *Band of Hope Review* typified much of Smithies's later publications. This mediated primarily on the ills of drink and the persuasive benefits of abstinence, but also the evils of animal cruelty, and the benefit of living a God-fearing life directed by the scriptures. This formula was transferred to the 1d monthly* paper, the *British Workman, and Friend of the Sons of Toil* that launched in 1855 and reached a circulation* of 250,000 copies by 1862. This improving periodical, which was translated for export abroad, was especially noted for its high-class illustrations*. These were undertaken by John Gilbert*, John Knight* and Harrison Weir, among others. Decorated scriptural texts were specifically designed for posting on 'cottage walls'. Smithies was a prodigious editor*; his output included the *Children's Friend*, *Friendly Visitor* (both taken over from William Carus Wilson), the *Family Friend*, *Infant's Magazine*, *Servant's Magazine*, and *Weekly Welcome*, as well as numerous tracts, handbills and almanacs. He had a keen eye for meeting readers'* needs. Mountjoy records how the *Children's Friend* was transformed from a morbidly pious tract to one that became warmer in tone, and most importantly, 'desirable' to young readers.

Smithies was also an industrious Sunday school worker and served on the London school board. He supported the Lord's Day Observance Society, the Drinking Fountain Association and the Royal Society for the Prevention of Cruelty to Animals. His committee work for this latter cause led him to advise on establishing the *Animal World* in 1869, and then launch the *Band of Mercy Advocate* in 1879. This last periodical supported the children's* animal welfare movement that was formed in 1875 by his mother. FSM

Sources: Mountjoy 1985, *ODNB*, Rowe 1884.

SOCIAL SCIENCE AND THE PRESS Victorian social science was only slowly and partially institutionalised in academic institutions and was therefore more closely associated with the press than might be imagined. Newspapers and journals carried reports of the meetings of learned societies, reviewed* the latest literature and even editorialized on the likelihood that a usable social science would be developed. Contemporaries generally thought of social science as a guide to public policy and as a 'science of reform' in the public sphere rather than the academy.

The most important journals included a number that emerged in the early 1830s, encouraged by and coincident with Whig social reforms. The *Journal of the Statistical Society of London* appeared from 1834; the *Reports of the British Association for the Advancement of Science*, which founded a Statistical

Section at its 1833 meeting, carried social scientific matter through the rest of the century despite attempts in the 1880s to exclude the social sciences from the Association's remit; the Manchester Statistical Society, founded in 1833, published social research in its *Transactions**. From 1857 to 1886 the *Transactions of the National Association for the Promotion of Social Science*, a large and influential policy-making forum, provided a voluminous commentary on all the social questions of the age. Other more short-lived periodicals included the *Social Science Review* (1862-1866) and *Meliora*, 'a quarterly* review of social science' (1858-1869), which was the mouthpiece of the temperance campaign of the United Kingdom Alliance.

Meetings of the Social Science Association were covered extensively by metropolitan* daily* newspapers including *The Times**, the *Daily Telegraph** and the *Daily News**. Even greater detail was offered by the provincial* press in the major cities where the Association held its annual congresses, including the *Birmingham Daily Post**, the *Liverpool Daily Post**, the *Bradford Observer*, the *Manchester Guardian** and *Leeds Mercury**. They published verbatim reports of lectures and debates, subjected new ideas to scrutiny in leading articles and entertained readers with accounts of the entertainments and soirees at each meeting. The proceedings of these organizations were sometimes reviewed in mainstream periodicals, including *Blackwood's Edinburgh Magazine**, *Macmillan's Magazine** and the *Fortnightly Review**. These journals, and others like the *London and Westminster Review**, also carried essays on the most important social-scientific treatises of the age including the works of Comte, Mill* and Herbert Spencer, treated in each case not as the specialized works of practitioners in the social sciences but as thinkers of interest to an intelligent, general readership*.

More specialized publications also emerged. From its first publication in 1843 the *Economist** became the guardian of laissez-faire liberalism and the hard science of political* economy, often treating the professions of the more inductive and descriptive social sciences then struggling for attention with amused contempt. The *Bee-Hive**, the weekly* newspaper for the skilled workmen of mid-Victorian Britain, treated social science as it affected the emerging organized labour movement. Women's participation in the Social Science Association, and in ventures like the Ladies Sanitary Association and Louisa Twining's Workhouse Visiting

Society*, was dealt with in the first years of the *English Woman's Journal** following its inception in 1858. The *British Medical Journal** and the *Lancet** dealt with socio-medical questions, and the mid-century *Law Magazine and Law Review** covered the legal profession's role in providing the legislative and administrative expertise for social reform.

The wide readership of dailies attracted social investigators: 'Outcast London' and its analogues in other Victorian cities was made known to the Victorian public through the press. Henry Mayhew*, co-editor of *Punch** (which often deflated the pretensions of social science) published his remarkable portrait of London's poverty in the *Morning Chronicle** in 1849-1850 (republished in 1851 as *London Labour and the London Poor*). The *Pall Mall Gazette** developed a reputation for sponsoring social investigation, and James Greenwood's* exposé, 'A Night in the Workhouse' was serialized* there in 1866. George R. Sims's* 'How the Poor Live' was first published serially in the *Pictorial World* in 1883.

One of the greatest social research projects, Charles Booth's study of living standards in late-Victorian London, demonstrates the inter-dependence of various media. Articles like Sims's in the press and periodicals of the early 1880s drew middle-class* attention to the so-called 'rediscovery of poverty' among the inhabitants of cities, especially London. Booth's attempts to assess and quantify this social deprivation led to the publication of his first results, based on surveys in east London, in the *Journal of the Royal Statistical Society* in 1886-1888, and then to volumes of his larger survey of poverty and religious life in the capital, *Life and Labour of the People in London* (1902-1903).

Print media of the nineteenth century carried much that would later crystallize into the discrete academic social sciences, with their specialized journals. But from the 1830s, when different social sciences were gradually laying claim to their disciplinary independence, social science appeared across the media as a whole. **LG**

Sources: Abrams 1968, Goldman 2002, Keating 1976, O'Day and Englander 1993, Thompson and Yeo 1971.

SOCIAL-DEMOCRAT (1897-1911); BRITISH SOCIALIST (1911-1913) The *Social-Democrat, a monthly socialist** review* was published* by Henry Mayers Hyndman*, the founder of the Social Democratic Federation until December 1911, when it became the *British Socialist* after the foundation of the

British Socialist Party. Like Hyndman's other socialist paper *Justice**, much of the hands-on editing* and unattributed writing was done by Henry (Harry) Quelch*, with the largely anonymous* contributors including some notable socialists of the day, such as Eleanor Marx* and George Lansbury.

Typically, each issue was an amalgam of new articles and reviews*, biographies of leading figures past and present, sketches, poetry*, transcribed material from other sources, short stories and editorial notes provided primarily by Quelch. Originally a 32-page monthly*, costing 2d, the magazine doubled in size* in 1903, with longer issues printed on higher-quality paper*, costing 6d. Decreasing sales brought a price* cut to 3d in 1908, but the sales of the renamed *British Socialist* continued to fall, and in December 1913 the magazine published its final issue. **LAR**

Sources: Lee 1913, *ODNB, Waterloo.*

SOCIALIST NEWSPAPERS Between 1880 and 1900 approximately 250 periodicals and newspapers were published in broad support of the socialist and labour movement, quite apart from those which were published by the trade* union movement. The majority of these publications were published weekly* or monthly* by the branches or supporters that began to develop from 1881 onwards. Many, however, were infrequent and irregular and until 1911 there was no daily socialist or labour newspaper in Britain.

The majority appear to have lasted for relatively short periods of time, although there were some notable exceptions. The Social Democratic Party's (SDF) weekly *Justice** (later *Social -Democrat*) appeared continuously between 1884 and 1933, while the *Labour Leader**, originally published as a semi-private venture by Keir Hardie, the leader of the Independent Labour Party (ILP), was acquired by the party itself and published in various forms until the 1980s. Some local* newspapers were published over a number of years, especially in Yorkshire where the socialist movement was particularly strong. Often a newspaper in a remote area might bridge political divisions within the labour movement such as the Plymouth *Socialist,* shared between the local branches of the moderate ILP and the Marxist SDF. Indeed, in several cases, syndicated* material appeared simultaneously in newspapers ostensibly claiming very different political* affiliations. As the socialist movement evolved, divided and reformed, so newspapers often followed suit. *Commonweal**, for instance, marked the political evolution of its editor* William Morris* from utopian socialism to anarchism through its change of subtitle. Many of the newspapers were produced by experienced and professional editors, typographers or printers. However, the political leaders of the emerging socialist movement were often directly involved in editorship including H. M. Hyndman*, William Morris*, Tom Mann, Keir Hardie, Bruce Glasier, Ramsay MacDonald, Philip Snowden and F. W. Jowett.

Local socialist newspapers appeared in many parts of Britain, not always in the most obvious places. Yorkshire and Lancashire produced the largest number, closely followed by London. Scotland published a number, clustered around the Clyde and the mining communities of Lanarkshire and Fife. Occasional titles appeared in East Anglia, the West Country and the North-East but some prominent industrial and working class areas, notably South Wales, had no local socialist newspaper until after 1900. The socialist newspapers of this period were generally unsuccessful in economic terms. Many were distributed* freely with occasional advertisements*, circulation* was usually small and uncertain. The main source of income was the local political branch itself whose strength was therefore a key determinant of a paper's survival. The most enduring periodicals were published by very well-organized and funded branches such as the *Bradford Labour Echo* or the *Huddersfield Worker.* Most demonstrated little business planning or awareness of commercial considerations as their main purpose was to mobilize political support and counter the hostility of the conventional newspaper press. Only one socialist paper in this period became in any sense a mass*-circulation paper when Robert Blatchford* surrendered a lucrative career as a Fleet Street* journalist to launch the *Clarion** in 1891. Its clever use of typography*, and stylish headlining, as well as its populist message, generated a wide-spread national readership*, spawning its own Clarion 'Movement' with the paper lasting for 43 years. It was not until the turn of the twentieth century and the emergence of the Labour Party that it became possible to contemplate much larger enterprises such as the *Daily Citizen.* As in politics, the 1880s and 1890s was largely a period of small-scale trial and experiment for the socialist press. **DH**

Sources: Harrison 1977, Hopkin 1977, Hopkin 1996, Mutch 2005, Wingate 1997.

SOCIALIST PERIODICALS The rise to prominence of socialist ideology in the final two decades of the nineteenth century produced an explosion of socialist periodicals. Almost all were broadsheet or pamphlet-sized, prices* ranged from free to 3d and most were published weekly* or monthly*. Although rarely profitable, and often a drain on the resources of the sponsoring group or the proprietor*/editor*, the periodicals were driven by a missionary zeal best expressed by Ferdinand Lassalle, contemporary of Karl Marx*, who saw the periodical as a vital educational medium. Each variety of socialism, ranging from the Socialist League's shift from revolutionary socialism to anarchy, the Social Democratic Federation's Marxism, the Independent Labour Party's ethical socialism and trade unionism, or Fabian permeation policies, produced a corresponding periodical.

Socialist periodicals were characterized by agitation not reflection. William Morris's* *Commonweal* announced in its first number in February 1885 that it sought to 'awaken the sluggish, to strengthen the waverers [and] to instruct the seekers after truth', and during an economic depression (1886-1889), *Justice** organized demonstrations and marches to stimulate government responsibility for the unemployed. The importance of the periodical for the socialist movement is evident in the drafting of two of the most important documents in the history of the labour movement which took place under the auspices of two prominent periodicals. Robert Blatchford* drew up the constitution for the Manchester Independent Labour Party in the offices of the *Clarion** eight months before the founding of the national party in Bradford in 1893, and in the offices of the *Labour Leader**, Keir Hardie drafted the motion for the 1899 Trades* Union Conference which created the Labour Representation Committee, later the Labour Party.

The focus on education rather than profit ensured that socialist periodicals did not always have to achieve commercially viable circulations*, and they were often personally funded by the editor and/or proprietor. Comparisons are revealing: while George Newnes's* *Tit-Bits** regularly sold between 400,000 and 600,000 copies weekly, the best-selling socialist periodical the *Clarion* peaked around 90,000 and averaged between 40,000 to 50,000, while *Justice* sold as few as 2,500 in 1891, but both periodicals continued to be published into the twentieth century. Often using union labour and British-made paper*, production of socialist periodicals was expensive, but the low sales figures mask a greater reading public as the periodicals were often shared or read communally in clubhouses and meeting rooms.

Socialist periodicals were not exclusively working class*. Pricing policy, style and content indicates a varied targeted readership*. For example, the 3d price* for the monthly Social Democratic Party's pe-

riodical *To-Day** suggests it was aimed at the wealthier middle classes, rather than the working-class reader that its sister periodical *Justice** attracted at 1d. The implied middle-class* reader* of *To-Day* is also evident in its content: it carried long, densely written, time-consuming articles by heavyweight political* commentators such as Michael Davitt, Marx's son-in-law Paul Lafargue and George Bernard Shaw*. *Justice*, on the other hand, often adopted the livelier, chattier, more informal tone of New Journalism*. The *Clarion* also harnessed New Journalism to the socialist cause with its humorous style, prolific use of illustrations*, fiction and poetry*. There were some accusations that such populism pandered to vulgarity, but the tone and lay-out of the New Journalism were not adopted wholesale by socialist periodicals and a didactic tone and a focus on economic analysis usually remained.

Two other aspects of this genre* of the press are often overlooked by commentators. Serialized* socialist fiction was a significant presence in many periodicals: the *Clarion* serialized* eight novel-sized works of fiction before the turn of the century, including Robert Blatchford's 'No.66' (1893), and Leo Tolstoy's 'Resurrection' (1899-1900). Advertising* was another vexed source of income. *Justice* made an early and unsustainable claim to be independent of advertisements, while Allen Clarke* stated in 1898 that his paper the *Northern Weekly** would only carry the advertisements of 'those whom we believe are genuine and honest'. Hence advertising for Cadbury, Rowntree and Hudson's soap was included because of the manufacturers' radical views; those for Hayman's Balsam and Mother Siegel's Syrup reflected working-class medical needs, while commercials for the Liverpool Victoria Legal Friendly Society encouraged long-term financial planning. Closer to home, the *Clarion*'s advertisements for bicycle companies reflected the thriving Clarion Cycle Club. These were significant features helping to sustain the popular appeal of socialist periodicals. **DM**

Sources: Mutch 2005, Waters 2004.

SOCIETY JOURNALISM Society journalism denotes a genre* usually associated with weekly* papers in the 1870s and later in the century that relied on a diet of gossip* about the aristocracy – their parties and events, fashions, guests and general comings and goings – alongside sensational stories about divorce, financial scandal and the like. The *World** (1874ff) and *Truth** (1877ff) were two papers particularly linked to society news. **MWT**

Source: Gray 1982.

SOCIETY OF WOMEN JOURNALISTS (1893-)
Founded by Joseph Snell Wood, editor of the *Gentlewoman,* in response to the rising number of women journalists, membership of the Society was open to female journalists who had worked as paid contributors for two years. With Mrs Arthur Stannard* as the first of its illustrious women presidents, the Society was scornful of dilettantes damaging its serious intention of supporting professionals* and by 1899 it also provided 'probationer' and 'associate' memberships.

Services included a lecture programme, typewriting*, legal assistance, medical advice, information about publications, plus a benevolent fund. The yellow membership card proved invaluable as verification of women journalists' credentials, while an arrangement with the manager of the London Shoe Company provided important members' facilities for 'reading, writing and toilet rooms' at 117 New Bond Street. By 1900 the Society was firmly established with an increasing membership. **CL**
Sources: Gordon and Doughan 2001, Rubinstein 1986, SWJ Annual Reports 1897-1900.

SOLICITORS' JOURNAL (1857-) Launched in January 1857 by solicitor William Shaen, the *Solicitors' Journal and Reporter,* as it was then, was the first weekly* publication for lawyers in England. 'This *Journal* owes its origin [...] to the conviction long entertained by solicitors in town and country, that their branch of the legal profession ought to be represented by a newspaper established and conducted by themselves, reflecting their opinions, watching over their interests and reputation, and urging upon the legislature and the nation their just and reasonable demands', said Shaen in his opening lines of the first issue. The *Journal* was published every Saturday at an annual subscription price* of £2 12s.

The *Journal* remained a weekly, and successive editors* have remained faithful to the original owners' goal to act as an independent voice representing the interests of the legal profession. Over the years, the *Journal* increased its coverage of legal developments, providing critical comments on cases and legislation, and lobbying for changes in the law where appropriate. Initially owned by The Law Newspaper Society, of which Shaen was the secretary, the *Journal* was acquired by Henry Villiers in 1880. He brought on board William Mitchell Fawcett as editor, and the two men worked together for nearly 40 years until their deaths, in 1912 and 1913 respectively. Since then the Journal has moved and been bought several times. It is now owned by Waterlow Professional Publishing, a publishing business set up in 1844 which, quite appositely, had been an advertiser* in the very first issue of the *Journal.* **J-YG**
Sources : Archives of the *Solicitors' Journal.*

SOLOMON, SIMEON (1840-1905) Simeon Solomon's high reputation as a magazine illustrator* depends almost entirely on a series of ten 'Illustrations of Jewish Customs' which were published in the *Leisure Hour*** in 1866. Described by one recent critic as 'elaborately tonal, relentlessly cross-hatched, mysteriously lit miniature masterpieces', these illustrations extended the Pre-Raphaelite illustrative repertoire on towards modernism, and represent a high moment in mid-Victorian wood* engraving. Solomon produced a few other less intense but still highly spiritual illustrations for *Good Words*** and *Once a Week*** in 1862. **BM**
Sources: Engen 1990, Goldman 1994, Houfe 1978, *ODNB,* Reid 1928, Suriano 2005, White 1897.

SOMERVILLE, ALEXANDER (1811-1885) The first contribution of Alexander Somerville, a radical journalist*, to a newspaper led to national notoriety and earned him 100 lashes. As a young soldier he had written to London's *Weekly Dispatch*** at the height of the Reform Bill crisis in 1831 to claim provocatively that the army would not prevent citizens from undertaking peaceful protest in support of reform. He was subsequently court-marshalled and flogged. After a public subscription secured his release from military service, Somerville resolved to capitalize on his celebrity* and embark on a literary career. Over the next 20 years or more Somerville wrote several books and countless articles for a plethora of journals across the spectrum of liberal and radical politics in Britain such as the *Manchester Temperance Reporter and Journal of Progress.* He was one of the editors* of the fleeting *Cosmopolite* (1832-1833) and the even briefer *Somerville's Manchester School of Political Economy* (June-Aug. 1850).

His best-known work as a journalist was his writing on rural affairs, which was undertaken in support of the cause of Corn Law repeal. Employed by Richard Cobden, he was in the pay of the Anti-Corn Law League, touring rural Britain (and later Ireland at the height of the famine) extensively (1842-1847), publishing regular letters* in the *Morning Chronicle*** and the *Manchester Examiner*** under the signature 'One Who Has Whistled at the Plough'. Somerville's vivid descriptions of rural life and his Cobbett-like eye for a good tale with a political sting in it meant that his articles were both popular and influential. In 1852, Somerville published a selection of his articles in a popular book, *The Whistler at the Plough*. By this time he had fallen out with the leadership of the League, publishing a vicious attack on Richard Cobden in 1854. Somerville migrated to Canada in 1859, contributing articles about his new home to several British newspapers and editing the *Canadian Illustrated News* (1862-1864) and the *Church Herald* (1873-1875). PAP

Sources: Carswell 1951, *ODNB*, Snell 1989, Somerville 1848, Somerville 1852, *Waterloo*.

SOMERVILLE, MARY FAIRFAX GREIG (1780-1872) Although known primarily for books on the sciences* which were enormously popular from the 1830s until her death, Somerville contributed to a number of periodicals. Indeed, and ironically, given the concern over female participation in scientific study, it was a fashionable women's journal which first introduced her to the 'mystery' of algebra. After the death of her first husband in 1807, Somerville returned from London to her native Scotland and became acquainted with some of the founders of and contributors to the *Edinburgh Review** who shared her staunchly liberal principles such as Henry Brougham* (who would later commission her to translate Laplace's *Mechanism of the Heavens*) and John Playfair*.

Between 1811 and 1816, Somerville offered five solutions (one medal-winning) to questions in Thomas Leybourn's *New Series of the Mathematical Repository* (1806-1835), under the pseudonym* of 'A Lady'. Somerville's later contributions were both to specialist and to popular periodicals, exemplifying the division in her career between devotion to abstract science and pressing economic needs. Original experiments on sunlight and magnetism were published in the Royal Society's *Philosophical Transactions* in 1826 and 1845, while an article on comets was published in the *Quarterly Review** in 1835. CB

Sources: Brock 2006, McMillan 2001, Neeley 2001, Patterson 1983, Secord 2004.

SONS OF BRITANNIA (1870-1877) Although brothers William Laurence Emmett and George Emmett issued numerous boys' magazines* throughout the 1860s and the 1880s, *Sons of Britannia* was arguably their most successful. It launched as a 1d weekly* following the demise of William Laurence Emmett's *Young Englishman's Journal**. In common with boys' periodicals of the time, sensational fiction and educative non-fiction were its key constituents, though it was known for being somewhat more bloodthirsty than many of its rivals. The journal was initially edited* by William Emmett, although George took over after a matter of months, a step perhaps made necessary by the elder brother's bankruptcy.

Many of the established authors of boys' periodical fiction contributed stories to *Sons of Britannia*: E. Harcourt Burrage, William Stevens Hayward, Bracebridge Hemyng*, Charles Stevens and Percy B.* and Vane St. John. As with *Young Englishman's Journal*, the Emmett brothers contributed a great many stories themselves, including in 1873 'The Lads of Englewood', the final story penned by William Laurence prior to his death. Sibling Harry Emmett also supplied several stories under the pseudonym* of 'Captain Harry', while American showman P. T. Barnum was recruited to pen two 1876 tales, 'Lion Jack' and a sequel, 'Jack in the Jungle; a Tale of Land and Sea'. Illustrations* were provided by Fleet Street* stalwarts 'Phiz'*, Harry Maguire and John Proctor.

'Tom Wildrake's Schooldays', published in 1870, was without doubt *Sons of Britannia's* most significant tale. Begun by George Emmett and completed by E. Harcourt Burrage, the anarchic public school story consolidated the formula first conceived in the *Young Englishman's Journal* tale 'Boys of Bircham School', establishing the blueprint not only for Bracebridge Hemyng's* 'Jack Harkaway' tales, published in *Boys of England** in the 1870s, but for a host of imitators for decades to come.

Sons of Britannia was read predominantly by boys of the working class*. Although circulation* figures have not survived, it was long-lived in comparison with many of its rivals, a sure indicator of a good weekly sale. Nevertheless, after a slow and steady decline, the paper was sold in June 1877 to London publishers* Ritchie and Son, who relaunched it as the *Champion Journal* (1877-1879) the following September. Although George Emmett continued to write prolifically, he would never achieve the success he had enjoyed through the *Young Englishman's Journal* and *Sons of Britannia*; indeed, a downturn in his fortunes brought about bankruptcy in 1879, and worse still, necessitated a spell authoring for bitter rival Edwin J. Brett*. ChB

Sources: Jay 1918-1921, Rollington 1913, Springhall 1991, Springhall 1994, *Waterloo*.

SOUTHWELL, CHARLES (1814-1860) Born in London, the 33rd and last child fathered by an irreligious piano maker, Southwell had been a rebellious yet bookish boy and in his early 20s abandoned the family trade to set up an ultra-radical bookshop in Westminster. From here he became involved in the burgeoning Secularist* movement, helping to found a 'rational school' and supporting the radical press. In November 1841, after his service in the British Legion in Spain and a brief return to piano finishing, Southwell, with the help of the compositor William Chilton* and others, began the pro-evolutionary, and almost certainly the first atheistic penny* weekly, the *Oracle of Reason* (1841-1843). By 1842 its deliberately provocative attacks on religion had earned Southwell a £100 fine and a year's imprisonment for blasphemy.

Although on his release he refused to resume the editorship* of the *Oracle* and instead launched the more moderate and short-lived *Investigator* in 1843, Southwell continued to be closely involved with the secularist movement. He published numerous secularist pamphlets and was employed variously as a very popular speaker, proprietor of a free-thought coffee house, manager of the Manchester Hall of Science and a London lecture hall, and editor of the *Lancashire Beacon* until his emigration to Melbourne in 1855. After a year on tour with a theatrical company in Australia, he settled in Auckland and founded the *Auckland Examiner* in 1856. The paper folded in 1860 and Southwell died shortly afterwards. **SP**

Sources: Cook 1998, *ODNB*, Royle 1974, Smith 2007, *Waterloo*, Wheeler 1889.

SOWERBY, AMY MILLICENT (1878-1967) Millicent Sowerby, artist and illustrator*, was born in Gateshead, where her father was a designer and illustrator employed in the family glass works. She was largely self-taught as her attendance at art school was spasmodic. With a decline in business, the family moved to Colchester in 1896 where, as a means of supplementing the family's income, she illustrated the books that her sister Githa wrote. As well as being a prolific children's book and picture postcard illustrator, Sowerby 'worked in black and white' in the periodical press, contributing to the *Illustrated London News**, the *Pall Mall Magazine**, the *Tatler**, the *Windsor Magazine**, the *Ladies' Field* and children's annuals* such as the *Tiny Folks' Annual**. **CL**

Sources: Micklethwait and Peppin 1983, *Rutherford & Son* Study Guide online, Wee Web, *Who's Who* 1929.

SPEAKER (1890-1907) The *Speaker: A Review of Politics, Letters, Science and the Arts* was launched as a 6d Gladstonian Liberal intellectual weekly* to fill the gap left by the defection of the *Spectator** to Unionism. The *Speaker* was founded with the financial backing of the radical industrialist Sir John Brunner by the influential journalist* Wemyss Reid*, who was the manager of the paper's publisher*, Cassell & Co*. Reid edited* it until 1899,

when Brunner's private secretary J. L. Hammond took over as editor, assisted by F. W. Hirst and R. Barry O'Brien. As contributors, Hammond recruited an outstandingly talented and committed corps of ardent young liberal intellectuals including G. K. Chesterton, R. C. K. Ensor, L. T. Hobhouse, Rudolph Lehman, C. F. G. Masterman, H. W. Massingham*, Nora Vynne and G. H. Perris who supported the Liberal Party's 'pro-Boer' wing during its divisive years and helped steer it through the post-Gladstonian trauma towards the emerging 'New Liberalism'. Hobhouse's *Democracy and Reaction* first appeared as articles in the *Speaker*.

The paper was never a financial success with its circulation* hovering below 4,000 and it continued to need subsidises. Frank Swinnerton pronounced it 'dull', perhaps on account of its political* righteousness, yet it had some distinguished contributors on the arts. Arthur Quiller-Couch, an early assistant editor, published a short story each week. Arthur Clutton-Brock was a later literary* editor, and Edward Garnett and Chesterton were on the staff. Gladstone had a standing invitation to contribute, and a review of British poetry* he wrote for it in 1890 helped make the reputation of the young philosopher-poet, Constance Naden. In the same year Oscar Wilde* published one of his last critical reviews* there. Edward Clerihew Bentley contributed regularly, as did John Davidson*, Henry Dawson Lowry, Lionel Johnson and less, regularly, Hubert Crackanthorpe. A. B. Walkley was its drama critic. In 1907 it was renamed and revivified under Massingham as the *Nation**. **CAK**

Sources: Freeden 1978, Havighurst 1974, Koss 1970, Koss 1981, *ODNB*.

SPECTATOR (1828-) 'There is no cant in the *Spectator*, no indecency, no impiety, may I say no trash, and not much dullness', proclaimed its first editor*, Robert Rintoul*. Funded by radicals Joseph Hume (1777-1855) and Douglas Kinnaird (1788-1830) to launch a new London weekly* paper, given complete autonomy and taking the title from Addison and Steele's eighteenth-century predecessor, Rintoul dedicated 30 years of his life to making the *Spectator* his 'household* paper'.

Mindful of the high cost of such publications, Rintoul determined that the *Spectator* would deliver a full range of material including coverage of the week's news*, with a front page summary, a comprehensive account of political* events, international issues, literature* through reviews* and extracts, and finally, criticism relating to music* and drama. Consisting of 16 pages, priced* 9d

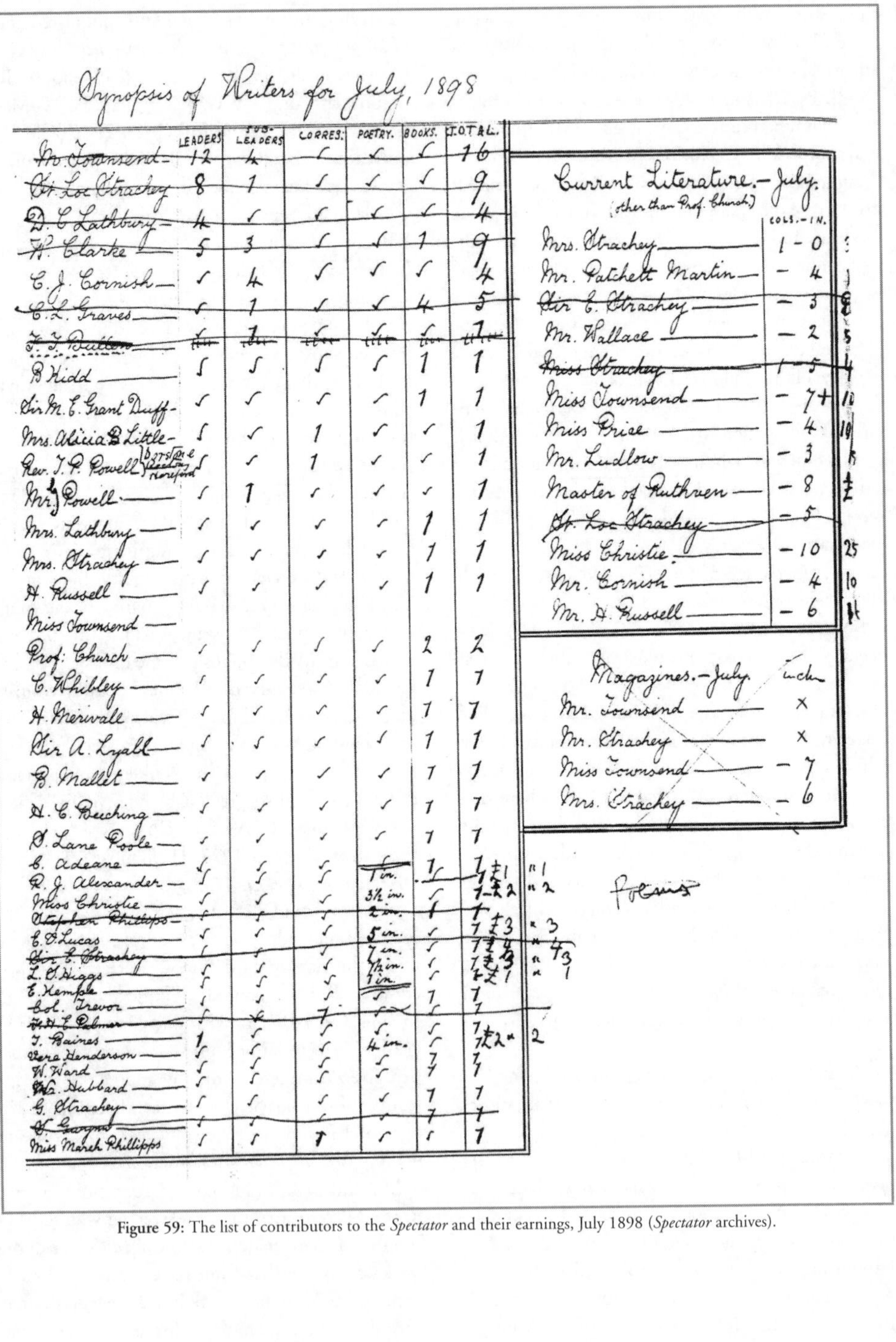

Figure 59: The list of contributors to the *Spectator* and their earnings, July 1898 (*Spectator* archives).

(including 4d tax), the paper resulted in a deficit estimated at between £7,000 to £8,000 for the first two years. By 1831 the number of pages had risen to 24 and the price to 1s, the amount, Rintoul admitted, it should always have been (though by 1837 it had dropped again to 9d). Rintoul was constantly begging free publicity from his friend William Blackwood*, and although circulation* was never expected to be high, by 1832 it was calculated to be second only to *John Bull**. Circulation stood at 3,500 by 1840. Yet sales did not equal readership* (estimated at being much higher in clubs and reading* rooms) and the *Spectator's* profile was measured not in sales but in its level of political influence and the stature of its readership.

By February 1858 Rintoul's deteriorating health forced a sale to Leigh Hunt's* son Thornton Hunt*, whose editorial failings saw the paper's fortunes slide, leading to a further sale in 1861, this time to Meredith Townsend (1831-1911) who shortly afterwards took Richard Holt Hutton* as his partner. By this time the cover price had dropped to 7d stamped or 6d unstamped*, though the format* was* unchanged. Hutton and Townsend's advocacy of the North in the American Civil War was a contributing factor in a rather unsure start for the pair, which saw circulation drop from 3,000 in 1860 to 2,000 in 1865. Their resurgence followed shortly after this, however, and a doubling in circulation to 4,000 by 1870 was only the first phase of an impressive reign that lasted until Hutton's death in 1897, shortly followed by Townsend's retirement.

Hutton and Townsend maintained the tradition of anonymity* in the *Spectator* at a time when many periodicals of its kind were switching to signed contributions, but a strong editorial line – accompanied by a distinctive style – was in evidence. Hutton – who became widely known for his books on literary*, religious* and political* matters as well as the signed articles he published elsewhere – was widely recognised as its originator. His passion for literature led to a shift of emphasis in the periodical from politics to literary reviews (though the journal retained its independent liberal orientation), and his Broad Church sympathies pushed the discussion of religion to the fore. The *Spectator's* hostility to science*, meanwhile, was made manifest in its staunch opposition to the evolutionists in the furore that followed the publication of Darwin's *Origin of Species*: Hutton's religious attitudes undoubtedly helped to define the periodical's stance on this issue. In literary matters, the *Spectator* was somewhat conservative, reflecting Victorian tastes rather than

challenging them, and generally regarding the innovative work of writers like Browning, Pater*, Carlyle*, Wilde* and even sometime contributor Algernon Charles Swinburne* with scepticism. While Hutton's preference for a literature grounded in Christian ethics perhaps goes some way to explaining the *Spectator's* resistance to literary innovation during this period, the articles he published were never so simplistic as to endorse a bland moral didacticism. Hutton's theatre criticism for the *Spectator* – amounting to over 30 unsigned articles – is particularly astute, and in his appraisals of contemporary acting he consistently valued freshness over conventionality.

Following Hutton's death in 1897, John St Loe Strachey (1860-1927), who had been employed as assistant editor over ten years previously, took over, reviving the *Spectator's* political focus and increasing circulation, providing a basis for the periodical's twentieth-century success. Leigh Hunt* attributed the *Spectator's* longevity to editorial strength, and this, along with the calibre of its contributors, including John Stuart Mill*, James Martineau*, Margaret Oliphant*, Octavia Hill (1838-1912), Harry Quilter* and Swinburne, ensured a solid base for its survival. Now essentially a conservative organ, it continues as an influential voice in contemporary politics. **CL/MaT**

Sources: *ODNB*, Sullivan, Tener and Woodfield 1989, Tener 1998, Thomas 1928.

SPENCER, HERBERT (1820-1903) Whilst working as an engineer during the railway boom of the 1830s and 1840s, the autodidactic Spencer became increasingly involved with the radical provincial* press, writing regularly for *the Nonconformist** and briefly serving as subeditor of the *Pilot*. In 1848 he was appointed, through a family connection, as subeditor* of the *Economist**, where the laissez-faire perspective of his leaders* largely accorded with the editorial line of Thomas Hodgskin. Living initially at the *Economist's* offices in London, Spencer joined the group of dissident intellectuals, including George Henry Lewes*, Marian Evans* and Thomas Henry Huxley*, brought together by John Chapman* to write for the newly revamped *Westminster Review**, and Spencer began contributing to the *Westminster* even before leaving the Economist in 1853.

Spencer's early articles for the *Westminster*, as well as for the *Leader**, outlined the emerging doctrine of progressive development, especially in its relation to human society, and were read and admired by Charles Darwin as he formulated his own evolutionary theory. During the controversy prompted by Darwin's *Origin of Species* (1859) Spencer became a much coveted contributor to numerous periodicals, and, although never a practising natural scientist, he wrote widely on evolutionary biology and psychology, as well as his own particular field of sociology. Much of Spencer's subsequent career was taken up with writing the lengthy books that comprised his mammoth *System of Synthetic Philosophy (1862-1896), but he still found time to respond* to critics in leading journals like the *Fortnightly Review**, the *Contemporary Review** and the *Nineteenth Century**, while the American *Popular Science Monthly** was set up in 1872 partly in order to publish his writings. **GD**

Sources: Lightman 2004a, *ODNB*, Peel 1971.

SPENDER, JOHN ALFRED (1862-1942) Spender was one of the 'University men' who became journalists*. After Oxford, Spender had a short stint on the *Echo,* but his first job of note was as editor* (1886-1891) of the *Eastern Morning News and Hull Advertiser,* a paper owned by his uncle William Saunders. He learned to manage all aspects of the business until his uncle sold the paper under him, and Spender returned to London as a freelance journalist. E. T. Cook* hired Spender as his assistant on the *Pall Mall Gazette** in 1892, and Spender then moved with Cook to George Newnes's* *Westminster Gazette** in 1893, being appointed editor in 1896. Considered a moderate Liberal whose leaders* were objective and fair, Spender's stint on the paper was largely untroubled. The *Gazette* always had an influence far greater than its circulation*, and Spender is widely credited with its appeal to what he called 'the serious reader'.

When Newnes sold the paper to a group of businessmen heavily involved in Liberal politics, Spender found independence from the board and its agenda difficult to maintain, and he resigned in 1922. In the ensuing years he continued to contribute to the *Gazette,* its successor the *News Chronicle* (until 1935) and the *Sunday Times**. Broadcasting and writing actively filled his life, with more than 12 books: essays on social and political topics, biographies of political figures and two titles in 1925 and 1927 particularly informative about journalism, *The Public Life,* and *Life, Journalism and Politics.* **ET**
Sources: Griffiths 2006, Jackson 2001, *ODNB*, Spender 1925, Spender 1927.

SPHINX (1868-1871) The *Sphinx* was an illustrated*, penny* weekly* paper, launched in July 1868 in Manchester. Its editor*, J. H. Nodal, had previously been editor of the *Free Lance** from its launch in 1866. When a dispute arose regarding the conduct of that paper, Nodal, and the entire literary staff of the *Free Lance,* walked out and formed the *Sphinx* as a direct rival, announcing in the first issue that it would be 'a Journal of criticism and humour, by the late editor and contributors of the *Free Lance*, all of whom are engaged in the New Paper'.

Published every Saturday, the paper was intensely local* in focus; for instance, critical of London papers, *Sphinx* saw the *Daily Telegraph** as infinitely superior to *The Times**, noting that 'The *Daily Telegraph* is amply compensated for the unfriendliness of the press and the neglect of snobbish cockneys by the enormous popularity and influence which it possesses in the country' (15 Aug. 1868). Three, shortly to become two columns* of short articles on Manchester politics* and cultural events, along with snippets of news* from other papers made up each ten-page issue, supplemented* with four to six pages of advertisements*. Eventually Nodal left the paper in 1871 to become editor of the *Manchester City News,* and the *Sphinx* ceased publication on 28 October of that year. **ET**

Sources:*ODNB,* Leeds Trinity online.

SPIELMANN, MARION HARRY (1858-1948) Editor*, art critic and connoisseur of art, Marion Harry Spielmann introduced New Journalism* into the art press, interviewing* artists and provoking them into press debates on art nouveau, copyright*, photography* and advertising*. A London journalist* his entire life, Spielmann wrote for the illustrated* weekly* newspaper the *Graphic** as its art critic, commencing shortly after critic Tom Taylor* died. In 1883 he joined the *Pall Mall Gazette**, learning new journalism from its editor W. T. Stead*. Spielmann succeeded William Henley* as editor of the *Magazine of Art** (1886-1904), also editing the *Magazine's* supplement*, *European Pictures of the Year,* to which critics throughout Europe contributed. Unlike Henley's avant-garde predisposition, Spielmann's taste was populist, international and eclectic across all styles and media, including 'high' and commercial arts: painting, sculpture, crafts, posters, advertising, illustration* and photography.

Spielmann was educated as an engineer but began collecting art in the 1880s while beginning his journalism career writing for *Black and White**, the *Daily Graphic**, *Illustrated London News**, *Westminster Gazette**, and the *Morning Post**. He published widely in mainstream periodicals such as the *Contemporary Review**, the *Nineteenth Century**, *Pall Mall Magazine**, the *National Review**, the *New Review**. His work also appeared in specialist periodicals such as *Book Buyer, Bookman**, *Journal of the*

Society of Arts, the *Speaker**, and in many American titles (*Harper's Bazaar*, *American Architect and Building News*, the *Critic*, the *Dial*, *Scribner's Magazine*).

Spielmann's articles on Charles Keene*, Linley Sambourne*, Phil May, Harry Furniss* and John Tenniel* were collected as a book on *Punch** in 1895. He promoted many professional illustrators and artist-illustrators, as well as British and Continental engravers who worked for the press. Bibliophile, art historian, critic, Spielmann introduced new topics into art criticism such as notes on works in progress and reports on activities of societies, museums and galleries. He demystified Victorian art institutions, describing the rituals of the beleaguered Royal Academy, the workings and reforms of the National Gallery and South Kensington (later the Victoria and Albert Museum) and the prominent public collections of Richard Wallace and Henry Tate. He advocated the professionalization* of artists through honorary degrees, art in university curricula, copyright* protection for artists and a ministry of culture. He used the press to link middle-class* buyers and artists, especially for artists in the New Sculpture movement, promoting small bronze sculpture for modest flats. The press was Spielmann's tool to acknowledge the business of art and promote artists' economic and social status, about which many artists sought his counsel and his favour. However, he was not an avant-garde New Critic and never liked modern art. **JC**
Sources: Codell 1989a, Codell 1989b, Collins 1976, Roberts 1970, Spielmann 1895.

SPIRITUAL MAGAZINE (1860-1877) The journal began life as the weekly* *British Spiritual Telegraph* (1857-1859), published in Keighley, Yorkshire, where dissenters and secularists* followed their intellectual leader Robert Owen* into Spiritualism after contact with American mediums and millenarians. The *Spiritual Magazine* remained a dissenting Christian journal but moved to London, became a monthly* and was edited* by the Christian socialist and active spiritualist Thomas Shorter. It reported on star mediums (such as D. D. Home and Henry Slade), published religious* and philosophical* articles by prominent Spiritualists such as William Howitt*, and also angrily denounced the mockery of the movement by the mainstream press (*All the Year Round**, *Punch* and *Cornhill** came in for particular criticism). Later issues tracked the impact of scientific naturalism on religious thought. The journal attacked the physicist John Tyndall's* 'Belfast Address' for demanding that science replace religion, but it was also anxious to acquire the authority of scientific 'proof' for its evidences of the afterlife.

In the last years of the journal, changes of editor reflected factionalism in the Spiritualist movement. George Sexton resigned, complaining of the anti-Christian tenor in Spiritualism as it aimed for scientific* empiricism over pious belief. The magazine* became marginal, noting with pain that it had not been represented at the meetings that formed the National Association of Spiritualists in 1873. By then, the Spiritualist weeklies* the *Spiritualist* (1869-1882) and *Medium and Daybreak* (1870-1895) had stolen most of the market*. **RL**
Sources: Barrow 1986, Oppenheim 1985, Prothero 1997.

SPIRITUALIST PRESS Periodicals played crucial roles in the spread of 'Modern Spiritualism' from its birth in America in the late 1840s. Enterprising journalists*, often supported by wealthy spiritualist converts, exploited falling costs of periodical production and the growing fascination for 'spirit-rapping', to launch journals promoting spiritualism as a religious*, scientific*, philosophical*, political* and social enterprise. During spiritualism's heyday (1850-1900), a plethora of spiritualist journals were published (principally in the United States, Britain, France, and Germany) and these ranged from cheap* weeklies* for plebeian spiritualists to more expensive monthlies* catering to bourgeois and aristocratic interests in the subject. Some, such as the *Spiritual Messenger* (1858-59), enjoyed only brief lives, while others, such as *Light* (1881-), continue to this day. Distinctive aspects of these periodicals included reports of domestic séances, transcripts of 'trance' addresses and reproductions of 'spirit' photographs*.

Spiritualist periodicals reflected the wide variety of uses to which spiritualism was put. Thus, in Britain, the *Medium and Daybreak* (1869-1895) promoted spiritualism as an alternative to Christianity, while the *Spiritual Magazine** used spiritualism as weapon against Christian unbelief. The *Spiritualist* (1869-1881) was one of many that placed more emphasis on spiritualism as the basis of a new science of the mind. The spiritualist press was the place where many key nineteenth-century figures – including the journalists Samuel Carter Hall* and William Howitt* and the scientists William Crookes* and Alfred Russel Wallace* – expressed some of their profoundest views on the relationship between body and mind, and matter and spirit. **RN**
Sources: Barrow 1986, Braude 1989, Fodor 1934, Podmore 1902.

SPORTING CHRONICLE (1871-1983) The Manchester-based *Sporting Chronicle* was launched as the *Prophetic Bell* (1871-1873) to meet a demand among the artisan and lower-middle classes* for reliable racing information and news*. Its primary selling point was the provision of accurate and prompt pre-race details of horses and their form in training, plus racing results, to enable the reader to make an informed choice when placing a bet. Proprietor* and publisher* Edward Hulton* oversaw a circulation* expansion for his 'journal of turf prophecy', from city centre Manchester to national prominence, with daily* sales variously put at 30,000 in 1883, rising to150,000 in 1898.

The *Chronicle* competed* with the *Sporting Life*, the *Sportsman*, and *Bell's Life in London* for a share of a developing market* for sports* news in the closing decades of the nineteenth century, prompted by the remarkable growth of organized sports. Pedestrianism, coursing, cricket and the various football codes were among an array of sports covered, but with racing always a priority. Along with its rivals, the paper played an active role in the promotion of sport, including holding stake money, offering prize competitions and providing judges and referees for important contests.

The *Chronicle* survived intense early competition* in Manchester from a host of short-lived sporting titles. Developing from the *Prophetic Bell*, which was printed each race day, and edited* by Hulton under the byline, 'Kettledrum', the 1d, four-page paper expanded to daily production by 1880, with financial backing from cotton broker Edward Overall Bleackley, and with minor title* changes to *Prophetic Bell and Sporting Chronicle* (1873ff) and *Sporting Chronicle* (1880ff). Its success underpinned the establishment of the Withy Grove print works, producing almost five million newspapers a week by the close of the century. Editors* up to the inter-war years included Duncan McArthur, Harry Mounsey, James Catton*, W. L. Sinclair, and Dick Reading. Hulton's son sold the newspaper group in 1923. ST
Sources: Leary 1896, Mason 1986, *Sporting Chronicle* 1971, *Sunday Chronicle* 1904.

SPORTING CLIPPER (1872-1897) The *Sporting Clipper* was a weekly* London newspaper addressing the rise in interest for horse racing. It was 'published every Saturday in time for the early trains' in order to fulfil its specific objective of 'the more successful and rapid transmission of Turf Intelligence and Important Communications to all parts of the United Kingdom'. As its publishers* were racehorse owners who appreciated the necessity for fast intelligence from the racetrack, they employed agents at a range of courses across the country who could utilize the latest telegraph* network.

Published* by J. Clave, Thomas Narburgh (1872) and E. H. Wood (1897) over its lifetime, and printed by Thomas Narburgh (1872) and then the Fleet Printing Works (1897), it varied in size* from four pages at 51 cm. in 1872 to 58 cm. in 1897. In 1872 it cost 2d, but it was reduced to 1d by 1897 when it was illustrated* with engravings. In 1872 it included advertisements*, racing notes and special training notes, but by 1897 it had broadened its appeal to include a theatrical section, as well as extending its racing information to cover reports on Newmarket, specific personnel and their horses, training information, the latest news* and a 'code-key programme'. According to H. R. Fox Bourne*, the *Sporting Clipper* had a certain facility for providing tips (Bourne: 322). DHL
Sources: Bourne 1887, *Waterloo*.

SPORTING GAZETTE (1862-1879); COUNTRY GENTLEMAN (1880-1915) London based, the 3d *Sporting Gazette* was published weekly* on Saturday by Foster, going out on early morning trains to be distributed* countrywide by the afternoon. In its first edition on 1 November its opening address promised the readers* a 'class' journal established by a group of 'Noblemen and Gentlemen'.

Encouraged by the proliferation of sport, the journal would cover the turf, steeple-chasing, coursing, hunting, cricket, shooting, fishing, aquatics, chess and archery. Contributors, 'of eminence' would be contracted and the popular 'Rhyming Richard' would write exclusively for the *Gazette*. Fair play and independence would be its editorial watchword. Book reviews* would be included, as would notices of opera, music* and the theatre. Book notices related to sporting* and agricultural matters as did miscellaneous items of interest to the country person, such as the weather and harvests, diseases in various animals, legislative matters and so on. Correspondence* columns* followed the leader*.

In 1862 the 16-page* three column* paper carried numerous advertisements* on the first two and back pages, with detailed coverage of horse racing and betting. In January 1864 it announced a price* rise to 4d, an increase in pagination and an extension of coverage of domestic and foreign* news, with more agriculture and horticulture. It also shared its pleasure at having become a favourite of the higher ranks in society.

The history of the titles of the *Sporting Gazette*

provides insight into changing markets and the protean shape of a title trying to maintain its extant readers while attracting new ones. The *Sporting Gazette* had only minor changes of subtitle for nearly 20 years until 1879, when a title* change – *Sporting Gazette and Agricultural Journal* – signalled a broader readership was sought. The following year it became the 6d *County Gentleman, Sporting Gazette and Agricultural Journal. A Newspaper for Country Families,* but in 1888 it tried to attract city men with the addition: *and 'The Man about Town'.* Several more alterations followed: it lost the *Sporting Gazette and Agricultural* tail in 1903, merged* with *Land and Water* in 1905 (*Country Gentleman and Land and Water*) and became simply *Land and Water* in 1915, before being incorporated into the *Field** in 1920. **CL/LRB**
Sources: 19CUKP, *Waterloo.*

SPORTING JOURNALISM By the end of the nineteenth century, Britain had laid the foundations of many of the world's major sports including cricket, boxing, football, rugby, bowls and lawn tennis. In 1800, however, the scene was very different. The first British journal to have 'sport' in its title was the *Sporting Magazine** (1792ff), which originally catered for a largely rural readership*, and reported on traditional field sports. Then, in the Regency period, Pierce Egan Snr's* seminal serial *Life in London* (1821-1822) celebrated the emergence of a new, vibrant urban culture. The leading historian of boxing, Egan pioneered sporting journalism as a distinct genre* with its own style and language. His success inspired *Bell's Life in London and Sporting Chronicle**, which absorbed his own *Pierce Egan's Life in London and Sporting Guide* (1824-1827) and remained a major sporting journal for over half a century. Another distinctive (and also highly mannered) sporting voice was 'Nimrod' (Charles Apperley*), an expert on all things equestrian. Poached from the *Sporting Magazine,* he established the popularity of its rival, the monthly *New Sporting Magazine**.

The sports scene was changing with the advancing century. The old, unregulated and often brutal contests such as bare-knuckle 'mills' and dog fighting were falling out of favour. Sports took their place alongside other urban recreations, notably drama. The *Era**, the leading chronicler of the stage, also reported on sporting events; the *Racing Times** included theatre reviews, while the long-running *Illustrated Sporting and Dramatic News** advertised its interest in both. The tone of sporting journalism became more sophisticated. Besides publishing Apperley, the *New Sporting Magazine* serialized the fiction of R. S.

Surtees*, who satirized 'Nimrod' as 'Pomponius Ego', and mocked sporting cockneys in *Jorrocks Jaunts and Jollities* (1841-1844). The *Field** emerged as a quality monthly*, reflecting the country gentry's interest in hunting, fishing, croquet and lawn tennis. The new interest in mountaineering was recorded in the *Alpine Journal**. Women increasingly took a role in sport. *Bicycling News* (1876-1897), the *Cycle* (1893ff) and the *Illustrated Sporting and Dramatic News* (1874-1943) all introduced a ladies' column* in the early 1890s.

The 1860s brought a massive increase in sporting activities, with a concomitant expansion of sports journalism. Increasing prosperity had brought more time and money for sport. But more importantly, the purposeful dynamic of the mid-Victorian era expressed itself in competitive games, and the conviction that a healthy body created a healthy mind focused society's energies on physical activity. This spirit was particularly evident in the public school ethos, but it affected all classes and many types of activity. The popular *Athletic News** covered a wide range from football to track events, swimming and gymnastics. Cricket brought together teams from the upper and lower classes*, and by the 1870s had gained a national status. But it was Association Football, mobilizing local loyalties in the industrial north, and benefiting from the establishment of Saturday afternoons as a sporting half-holiday, that in the 1880s emerged as the most popular British sport.

Journalism had a symbiotic relationship with these developments. From the times of Vincent Dowling*, the editor of *Bell's Life in London* from 1824, press reports made local events national. Dowling was the first to employ knowledgeable reporters*, adjudicate rules through the correspondence* columns and bank wagers for major events. Journals had a direct impact on the formation of individual sports. The English Football Association was founded in 1863 in response to a letter printed in *Bell's Life.* In 1875 John Henry Walsh*, as editor of the *Field,* founded the all-England Croquet Club, and the magazine awarded the trophy for the first Wimbledon Open Lawn Tennis Championship in 1877. Journals recorded histories and records of individual sports, and created their heroes. From 1864, *Wisden's Cricketers' Almanack** became the 'cricketer's Bible'. Press coverage, and the betting activity that went with it, made national events out of Ascot, the St Leger and the Derby, and the Oxford and Cambridge Boat Race.

With the widening audience and plummeting

costs, the sales of sporting periodicals rocketed. Sold at a penny*, the *Sporting Life** by 1880 was selling 300,000 copies a week. Provincial* papers such as the Manchester-based *Sporting Chronicle** reflected the sporting interest of northern readers*. But the major change came with the electric telegraph*, first introduced in London by Paul Reuter in 1851, and organized nationally under the Post Office in 1870. This made all results simultaneously available to the press wherever its locale. By the end of the century, with all newspapers throughout the country devoting substantial space to such activities, 'sporting journalism' could no longer be seen as a separate genre. LJ

Sources: Bourne 1887, Grant 1872, Harvey 2004, Huggins 2004, *ODNB*.

SPORTING LIFE (1859-1998) George Maddick and Samuel O. Beeton launched the first 1d paper to concentrate on sporting news* as *Penny Bell's Life and Sporting News* (24 March-27 April 1859). Although this new paper challenged the supremacy of *Bell's Life in London** as a provider of sporting* news, *Bell's* successfully sought an injunction to end the use of its name and *Penny Bell's* became the *Sporting Life* (30 April ff).

While horse racing dominated the coverage in the *Sporting Life*, virtually the entire sporting world received attention. The paper appeared on Wednesdays and Saturdays and by 1876, it boasted of a weekly* circulation* of 200,000. Competition* from other penny* sporting papers, the *Sportsman** and the *Sporting Chronicle**, and its increasing popularity prompted its expansion to Tuesdays and Thursdays in 1881, and in 1883 it became a daily* paper. By this time, the paper covered athletics, aquatics, angling, cricket, cycling, billiards, boxing, coursing, football, golf, hunting and lacrosse, as well as issuing reports on American, French and Australian sport.

Anchored by the journalism* of editor* Henry M. Feist, who had written the 'Hotspur' racing column* for the *Daily Telegraph**, the coverage of horse racing was central to the *Sporting Life*. Feist wrote under the pseudonym* 'Augur' until his death in 1874 and was central to the development of racing news. The paper provided the vital information of training reports, probable starters and jockeys, starting price odds and racing tips, which enabled the betting public to handicap races. Feist's successor as editor, Charles Blake, whose tenure lasted until 1891, had written for the paper since 1868 and was trained as a veterinary surgeon. In 1886, the *Sporting Life* acquired *Bell's Life in Lon-*

don, and eventually became the leading sporting paper in Britain when it merged* with the *Sportsman* in 1924. MJM

Sources: Boase 1965, Bourne 1887, Mason 1986, Moore 1903, *Sporting Mirror* 1881.

SPORTING MAGAZINE, OR MONTHLY CALENDAR OF THE TRANSACTIONS OF THE TURF, THE CHASE &C. (1792-1870) The *Sporting Magazine* was founded by proprietor* Walter Gilbey, and the publisher* Vinton and Co. Robert Smith Surtees** was its editor* and hunting correspondent until 1831, when he left the journal to found the rival *New Sporting Magazine**. Contributors included Henry Braddon (who wrote for the paper under the pseudonym* 'Gilbert Forrester'), John Lawrence, William Pitt Lennox, Eric Parker, Thomas R. Potter, Hacker Thomas, Scott Thomas and George John Whyte-Melville. An important aspect of this periodical was the reproduction of steel engraved illustrations* by well-known artists, such as the animal painters John Fernley, Thomas Woodward and Engleheart Thomas. An index of engravings was issued in 1892. The *Sporting Magazine* appeared monthly*, and its price* varied from 1s to 2s 6d. From July 1846 it was issued, with different title* pages, as the *New Sporting Magazine*, the *Sportsman* and the *Sporting Review**. DHL

Sources: Cooper 1872, Sutherland 1988, *Waterloo*.

SPORTING REVIEW, A MONTHLY CHRONICLE OF THE TURF, THE CHASE, AND RURAL SPORTS IN ALL THEIR VARIETIES (1839-1870) The *Sporting Review* was devoted to racing and field sports*. Between 1845 and 1870, this monthly* journal was identical to the *Sportsman* (1838-1870) and *New Sporting Magazine**, and from July 1846 with the *Sporting Magazine**, while retaining its own distinctive cover. John William Carleton* who used the pseudonym* 'Craven' edited* the paper from 1856. Contributors included the sporting journalist* Charles Bindley* who wrote as 'Henry Hieover'. His last article 'Riding to Hounds' appearing in March 1859. Thomas Rossell Potter*, the antiquary, also wrote 'pungent' articles and poems*, and its illustrators* included the well-known artist Sir Edwin Landseer. DHL

Sources: COPAC, *ODNB*, *Waterloo*.

SPORTING TIMES: A CHRONICLE OF RACING, LITERATURE, ART AND THE DRAMA (1865-1931) The *Sporting Times*, published weekly* for over 60 years, was founded by Dr Joseph Henry Shorthouse, whose hobby was horse racing; he was proprietor* and, in 1865 and 1872, also its editor*. The first publisher* and printer was Frederick

Farrah; in 1872 it was printed by S. Taylor. The sporting journalist* John Corlett* bought the *Sporting Times* for £50 in 1874 and was the proprietor until 1912, as well as editor* and printer in 1900. Contributors included Owen Hall writing as 'James Davis' who, as well as having a passionate interest in horse racing, was the paper's drama critic. Lt-Col. Nathaniel Newnham-Davis was a contributor and assistant editor.

The size* of the paper varied: in 1865 it was 8 pages of 40 cm.; from 1872 the size increased to 45 cm; by 1890 it was 50 cm. The paper appeared weekly* every Saturday, and, in 1865, cost 2d. When Corlett became proprietor in 1874 he increased the circulation* from three figures to around 20,000, mainly due to his energy, enthusiasm and good relations with his staff. By 1880-1881 the circulation had increased to 49,000. As its subtitle suggests, the *Sporting Times* covered a fairly broad range of subjects besides racing, particularly drama. It also contained sections on art, literature*, finance, notes and queries, 'the woman about town', gossip* columns*, current events, 'Northern cracks' and 'social America'. The paper carried advertisements* and was illustrated* with sketches and engravings. In the late nineteenth century, it was popularly known as the *Pink'un*, due to it being printed on pink paper, as an economy measure from April 1876. In 1887, the journalist and editor H. R. Fox Bourne, criticized the *Sporting Times* for having 'thriven less upon its racing news than a profusion of coarse and scurrilous scraps of tittle-tattle, representing "society journalism" in its most degraded form' (Fox Bourne: 322). **DHL**

Sources: Fox Bourne 1887, Grant 1871, Mason 1986, *ODNB*, *Waterloo*.

SPORTSMAN (1865-1924) The core journalism of the *Sportsman* was its racing news. It analysed the betting market's movements, reported from training centres, provided racing predictions and published starting price odds for the benefit of the gambling public. 'Vigilant's Note Book'* anchored its racing news, and its authors included John Corlett* and his successor as 'Vigilant', J. Mitchell. Charles Hitchen Ashley was the journalist* responsible for the success of the *Sportsman*. Ashley became the lead racing reporter* soon after its debut, following his service on the racing staff of the *Sporting Life** and numerous Sheffield newspapers. In 1874, he became a partner in the paper.

Ashley & Smith, then Rogerson & Tuxford, published* the broadsheet newspaper with varying frequency throughout its run. The *Sportsman* appeared thrice weekly* in 1865, four times a week in 1872 (including a Saturday double edition of eight pages) and in 1876 it moved to daily* publication, thus becoming perhaps the first daily sporting paper in the world. Though the frequency* of its appearance changed, along with its price* (1871: 2s 6d; 1912: 1d)*, its masthead*, lack of illustrations*, and advertising* pages did not.

Though in the first number the editors* staunchly affirmed that, 'racing has always formed, and must continue to form, the most prominent feature in an English newspaper', the *Sportsman's* broad coverage of a variety of sports, both old and new, was indicative of the diversity of the sport and recreation culture developing after 1850. 'Our creed in sport is catholic', the editors proclaimed, 'our position independent, and our resources as large as enterprise and research can make them'. Thus the paper's coverage included reporting on sports other than the Turf that were regarded by the readership* as contributing to a cohesive English national identity with shooting, hunting and coursing, cricket and pedestrian contests, as well as yachting, rowing, and swimming. In keeping with this unity of coverage, the *Sportsman* also maintained a cross-class* appeal, touting itself as a 'new experiment in sporting literature [suitable for tastes] high and low'. After the *Sportsman's* founding in 1865, Football Association meetings were often held at its offices. Its connection to the Football Association included Charles W. Alcock*, who began his journalism career as an athletics subeditor* and football reporter at the paper in the late 1860s.

The paper also published a variety of guides and annuals* for dedicated followers of sport to supplement its daily coverage. These included the *Sportsman's Pocket Book: A Complete Record and Handy Work of Reference for the World of Sport* and periodic handbooks covering racing, the *Sportsman Special*, available every race day, the *Sportsman's Weekly Guide to the Turf* and the *Sportsman's Monthly Guide to the Turf*.

Over the century, the cluster of major sporting papers, of which the *Sportsman* was a part, began to shrink as older papers such as *Bell's Life in London*° were taken over by publications such as the *Sporting Life*°. In part because of the massive social and cultural changes following the First World War, the *Sportsman* was taken over by the *Sporting Life* in 1924. **SRS/MJM**

Sources: Football Association 1953, Mason 1986, *Sporting Mirror* 1881, *Waterloo*.

SPOTTISWOODE, WILLIAM (1825-1883)

William Spottiswoode, in partnership with George Edward Eyre, founded the publishing* and printing firm of Eyre & Spottiswoode. This was a separate company from the printing house of Spottiswoode & Company, which was under the proprietorship* of William's younger brother George Andrew Spottiswoode. As printers, Eyre & Spottiswoode produced a huge list of diverse magazines, many of them trade* journals such as the *Anglo-Indian and American Traders' Journal*, the *Board Teacher*, the *Parish Councils Journal* and the *World's Printers*, but there were also more general recreational titles such as *After Work* and *Fashions and Fancies*. The firm of Eyre & Spottiswoode held Royal letters patent for printing the authorized version of the Bible, as well as the Book of Common Prayer and Acts of Parliament.

Both brothers were concerned for the welfare of their employees, and the companies combined to form the Spottiswoode Institute which aimed to provide both amusement and intellectual stimulus for those employed by the two firms. Activities included a library, rowing and cricket clubs, a choral society and a volunteer corps. Clergymen held services, and classes for boys were held in rooms rented by the firms, who also paid for a schoolmaster.

These activities gave the Institute the impetus to publish the *Spottiswoode Magazine* (March-Oct. 1881). Edited* by John Malcolm Isbister, it contained moralizing general interest articles interspersed with news* of the activities of the Spottiswoode Institute. Unfortunately, Isbister found the task of editing for both firms too arduous and the magazine folded after only four numbers. **DHL**
Sources: Bigmore and Wyman 1880-1886, *Waterloo*.

SPY; THE SERIO-COMIC AND FREE LANCE FOR MANCHESTER, SALFORD AND DISTRICT (1891-1898) *Spy* was an 8-page, illustrated*, comic penny* weekly* paper. Like many similar weekly papers of amusement, it was a combination of cartoons*, articles, commentary on various issues and interviews*. As it proclaimed, '"Spy" is the "organ" of no political party, and will, therefore, exercise a perfectly independent attitude, so far as politics* are concerned; either side being subject to praise or criticism, as "Spy" thinks fit'. Regular departments included Press Notices, Ladies' Letters, At the Bazaar, the Sporting World, Prizes and Sports* and Pastimes. **MWT**
Source: *Waterloo*.

STAGE DIRECTORY/STAGE (1880-1959) *Stage Directory* was the original title of what is now *Stage*

and Television Today. This theatrical journal, initially a monthly* publication costing 3d, was founded jointly by the editor* Charles Lionel Carson and his business manager Maurice Comerford. From 25 March 1881, the title* changed to the *Stage* and it was published weekly*. The size* of the journal was expanded from 33 to 37 cm, and from 12 to 16 pages. By reducing the price* to 1d, Carson and Comerford undercut rival theatrical journals such as the *Era*. But the price rose again to 2d on 5 October 1883. *Stage Directory* (or *The Stage*) was an important point of contact for those employed in theatres and music halls. Actors and other performers placed advertisements* for the benefit of managers and agents, as well as in the hope of future employment. They gave information regarding their addresses, or where they were playing if on tour. Some included favourable reviews* of their own performances. The paper also carried advertisements for performers and back stage staff, and letterpress included items of 'chit-chat', play competitions, biographies, sport* and notes on provincial productions. It claimed to have 'the largest circulation* of all dramatic journals'. In February 1959 the title* changed* to *Stage and Television Today*, though it remained under the ownership of the Carson and Comerford families. **DHL**
Sources: Arnott 1970, Graham 1930, Lowe 1888, Stratman 1972, *Waterloo*.

STAMP DUTY See 'Unstamped' Press, Newspaper taxes.

STANDARD (1827-1916) The *Standard* was founded in 1827 as an evening daily* with a price* of 7d by Charles Baldwin*, who already owned the *St James's Chronicle*. With Stanley Lees Giffard as editor and assisted by Alaric Alexander Watts and William Maginn*, and its slogan 'Plant here THE STANDARD: here we shall best remain', it set itself up as 'old tory', opposing Catholic emancipation, parliamentary reform and the repeal of the Corn Laws. By 1832, it had a circulation* of 1,500. Following the bankruptcy in 1857 of Edward Baldwin, who had succeeded his father as proprietor*, the paper was purchased by James Johnstone*. He reduced the price from 4d to 2d and converted it into a morning paper. By the following year, when its price was reduced further to 1d, its circulation was 30,000, to be boosted by its support of the Southern States in the American Civil War. The *Evening Standard* was issued as a sister paper in 1860.

After the death of Johnstone in 1878, the paper passed into the control and editorship of William Heseltine Mudford and by the mid-1880's the

Standard had become a powerful force in conservative journalism* with a circulation of 250,000. Its leader* writers included Alfred Austin* and Thomas Escott*. George Alfred Henty, the author of stories for boys, was its war* correspondent*.

Under the challenge from the New Journalism* the paper declined and following Mudford's death in 1899, the paper, together with the *Evening Standard*, was acquired by C. Arthur Pearson* in 1904, when its circulation was 80,000. The *Standard* ceased publication in 1916, but the *Evening Standard* continued. JRW

Source: Griffiths 1996.

STANNARD, HENRIETTA ELIZA (1856-1911) Stannard (née Palmer) was an editor*, journalist* and novelist who published initially in periodicals from April 1874. Early fiction appeared in the *Family Herald* under her pen-name 'Violet Whyte', with articles in the *Cornhill* and the *Temple Bar*.

There was a history of military service in the family which formed the basis for much of her fiction. While her early novels, such as *The Old Love or the New* (1880) also appeared under her pen-name, her publisher suggested she should adopt a male pseudonym* as sales of military novels would suffer under a woman's name. As 'John Strange Winter' her phenomenal output of close to 100 novels and books of short stories began, with *Bootles' Baby* (1885) selling two million copies in the first ten years. By 1889, the extent of her popularity led to the exposure of her identity* but her reputation was undiminished and praise for the accuracy of her portrayals was unstinting.

Some of her novels were serialized* in the *Graphic*, and Stannard continued to write for periodicals and papers with work appearing in the 1890s in *Children*, the *Chimes, Good Company*, the *Hour Glass* (later *Lazy Land*), the *Sunday Daily Telegraph*, the *Surrey Magazine, Sword & Chatelaine*, and the *Wednesday Journal*. In April 1891, as Mrs Arthur Stannard, she published* and edited* her own weekly* 1d magazine *Golden Gates*, which became *Winter's Weekly* (1892-1895). In both this magazine* and in her later novels she started to address women's rights* in terms of legal and social independence and the equal moral standard. Hypocrisy in the church and the patronising attitude of publishers toward women writers were other targets in later novels. She was president of the Writers' Club (1892), Fellow of the Royal Society of Literature (1893) and president of the Society of Women Journalists* (1901-1903). CL

Sources: Adam Matthew Publications, *Gentlewoman* 1906, Rutgers & Schlueter 1998, *Waterloo, Who Was Who* 1991.

STAR (1888-1960) The *Star* was founded as a London ½d evening daily* under the editorship* of T. P. O'Connor*. It was the first of O'Connor's New Journalism* publications, intended to be 'animated, readable and stirring' with news* on the front page. It was politically* radical and became the first daily* newspaper to feature a regular political cartoon*. The first issue was said to have sold 142,600 copies.

O'Connor left the paper in 1890 after a disagreement with its owners, who included the Norfolk Colman family. H. W. Massingham* was O'Connor's assistant at the start but became editor in 1890 before leaving to join the *Daily Chronicle* in 1891. Under Massingham's influence it acquired contributors of great talent. George Bernard Shaw*, initially a leader* writer, was its music* critic, under the pseudonym* 'Corno di Bassetto' (Feb. 1889-May 1890), in succession to E. Belfort Bax*. Drama critics included A. B. Walkley* and Gilbert Cannan. Joseph Pennell* contributed art criticism. Richard Le Gallienne* ('Log-Roller') contributed on literary* matters. Ernest Parke's* energetic reporting of the Jack the Ripper crimes* greatly increased its circulation* in its early years. Parke succeeded to the editorship after Massingham and remained editor until 1908. Acquired in 1909 by a syndicate* that included the Cadbury family who owned the *Daily News*, it merged* with the *Evening News* in 1960. JRW

Sources: Linton and Boston 1987, Symons 1914.

STATIST; A JOURNAL OF PRACTICAL FINANCE AND TRADE (1878-1967) The *Statist* was founded as a 6d weekly* by Robert Giffen, a notable government statistician and former assistant editor* of the *Economist*, probably when Giffen, on financial grounds, turned down the editorship* of the *Economist* after Bagehot* died. Giffen did not, it seems, edit the paper but contributed extensively to it; the editor throughout the nineteenth century was Thomas Lloyd, also an important economics author. Launched during a period of long-term price* drops and a slow economic collapse which it sought to analyse and remedy, the *Statist* quickly became the main rival of the *Economist* both in its assiduous support of free trade and self help and in its use of statistics as a basis for economic analysis (hence its title). Indeed, it published a price index designed by Augustus Sauerbeck, based on *Economist*-related statistical work, and the two price indexes had no competition* until 1903 when the official wholesale price index was published.

Unlike many financial* journals*, the *Statist*

resolutely refused to side with any political* party. Its particular concern was not only economic record but in-depth analysis of that record. Many of its articles discuss the effects of the money supply, and from 1899 it made a feature of analysing gold supply, which in turn meant a new focus on mining and exploration which it continued into the twentieth century. When it closed, owned by International Publishing Co and a run-of-the-mill investment weekly, it was making a small loss with a circulation* of 20,000-30,000. The *Statist* was the second periodical of this title, the first being a bi-monthly published (1854-1855) by the advertising agent* Charles Mitchell of which only two issues are known. **AK**
Sources: Edwards 1993, Vann and VanArsdel 1994, *Waterloo*.

STEAD, WILLIAM THOMAS (1849-1912) Despite having received only two years of formal schooling, Stead, imbued with a Puritan sense of destiny and irrepressible energy, forged a career in provincial* journalism at the *Northern Echo**, a Liberal daily* based in Darlington. In 1871 he was made the youngest newspaper editor* in the country, and set about transforming the *Northern Echo* into a campaigning organ of national renown which, in 1880, contributed greatly to William Gladstone's triumphant return to power at the Midlothian election.

Stead's success gained him entry to the journalistic purlieus of London, and, following the election and on Gladstone's recommendation, he became subeditor* of the *Pall Mall Gazette**, forming an uneasy but effective partnership with its more high-minded editor John Morley*. In 1883 Stead succeeded Morley as editor and, with his assistant Edward Tyas Cook*, immediately introduced a number of innovative journalistic and typographical* devices, including bold headlines and interviews*, to the hitherto rather staid evening paper. Under Stead's editorship, the *Pall Mall Gazette* also became notorious for journalistic crusades on behalf of various political* and moral causes, with Stead himself being sensationally imprisoned in 1885 during a lurid exposé of the trade in child prostitution in the 'Modern Babylon' of London that prompted Parliament to raise the age of consent. While in gaol, from where he continued editing the *Pall Mall Gazette*, Stead set out his agenda for an evangelistic and demotic journalism* that would supersede parliamentary democracy in two articles for the *Contemporary Review**, although his self-aggrandizing stance, as well as his apparent ob-

session with sexual morality, increasingly provoked criticism, even from Gladstone, while Matthew Arnold* famously dubbed his vivid and sensational style the '*featherbrained*...New Journalism'*. The *Pall Mall Gazette*'s proprietor* Henry Yates Thompson* also became concerned with his editor's penchant for controversy, and in 1889 Stead resigned and set up, initially in collaboration with George Newnes* and then with financial assistance from the Salvation Army, a new monthly journal, the *Review of Reviews**, that, with him as editor, publisher* and proprietor*, would entirely reflect his own idiosyncratic dissenting and radical imperialist* outlook. However, soon he was restless with a position outside daily* journalism, and attempted to launch the morning *Daily Paper* in November 1893. Again, using the platform of his monthly*, Stead published a succession of *Review of Reviews* annuals* and standalones such as *If Christ Came to Chicago* (1894) to sustain his moral and sensational journalism agenda.

In 1891 Stead became a spiritualist, and material relating to the occult soon began to monopolize the *Review of Reviews* to such an extent that Stead felt impelled, in 1893, to launch a further monthly journal, *Borderland**, wholly dedicated to the supernatural. *Borderland* lasted only four years and in 1904 a second abortive attempt to establish the *Daily Paper* almost ruined Stead financially, but it was only his death aboard the *Titanic* in 1912, while still editor of the *Review of Reviews*, that finally ended his lifelong crusade to turn journalism into a potent political and moral force. **GD**
Sources: Brake 2004, Baylen 1972, Baylen 1979, Dawson 2004, *ODNB*, Whyte 1925.

STEAMSHIP NEWSPAPERS The development of regular steamship mail services between Britain and English-speaking settler communities across the globe was accompanied by the establishment of steamship newspapers published in Liverpool or London especially for these overseas markets. These newspapers structured their periodicity and production deadlines according to steamship mail schedules. Published on the eve of the departure of each mail, they reported news* covering the period since the last mail departure to the relevant destination. These adjuncts to global steamship mail services became large business enterprises and were an important news and advertising* medium of the British Empire.

The first such newspaper, established in London in January 1840 by Bradbury & Evans*, appears to have been the *London Mail* published twice monthly on the eve of the departure of the Indian mail. This was followed by the *Monthly Times* and the *Atlas for India*, both also for the Indian market, established in 1842. Another rival, the *European Times*, was established in Liverpool in 1843. By 1855 this was published in four editions catering to different shipping routes and readerships*. The two most important such papers were *Home News* established in 1847 (which incorporated the *London Mail*) and the *European Mail* established in 1868 (which incorporated the *European Times*). Initially described as a 'summary of European intelligence for India, China and the colonies', *Home News* was later published under more specific titles including *Home News for Australia* which commenced in 1853. The *European Mail* was initially targeted at the South African market*, but by the end of 1870 was published as eight separate titles including the *European Mail for Australia and New Zealand* and the *European Mail for India*. There were also editions (some monthly and others bi-monthly or weekly* depending on the frequency of mail services to a particular region) for the West Indies, North America, Brazil and the River Plate, China and Japan, South Africa and the West Coast of Africa. While the editions had considerable common content, they also carried substantial material of special interest to the various readerships. The publishers described them as 'eight totally distinct newspapers'. They provided a 'summary of Universal Intelligence and exact Commercial Statistics from Mail to Mail, specially prepared for the Colonies and the Transoceanic World Generally'. Steamship newspapers declined as the telegraph* became cheaper and came to dominate international news flow. Both *Home News* and the *European Mail* ceased publication in 1898. **PP**

Source: Putnis 2007.

STEED, HENRY WICKHAM (1871-1956) A journalist and newspaper editor*, Steed was originally destined for the City, but early on found his strength lay in reporting* and interpreting world events. While studying economics, philosophy, sociology and history in Berlin, and later at the Sorbonne, Steed submitted work to the New York *World*, for which he became Paris correspondent*, and to *The Times*, which appointed him Berlin correspondent in 1896. In 1897 Steed moved to the position of Rome correspondent, still for *The Times*, and in 1902 he became its Vienna correspondent. By 1913 Steed was back in London as head of *The Times*'s European department for

Lord Northcliffe*, though, as Steed notes in his autobiography, Northcliffe seemed to have no idea about what he was supposed to do, except that the job would involve travel.

Steed's deep knowledge of European politics* and trends informed his leading articles; for instance, he spearheaded the campaign to move public opinion against what he saw as the imminent attack by Austria-Hungary on Serbia. By 1919 Steed had been appointed editor of *The Times*. Steed was Northcliffe's advisor on foreign policy at a particularly delicate time, but the relationship between the two was always rather precarious. When Northcliffe died in 1922, and *The Times* changed hands, Steed was dismissed.

In 1923 he bought the *Review of Reviews** and acted as its editor-in-chief until 1930, using the journal as a platform for his ideas, especially his conviction that another war with Germany was inevitable. Steed's later years were spent writing, lecturing on European history at King's College, London and broadcasting on world affairs for the BBC. **ET**

Sources: Koss 2 1984, *ODNB*, Steed 1913, Steed 1924, *The Times* 14 January 1956.

STEEVENS, GEORGE WARRINGTON (1869-1900) After a brilliant academic career at Oxford and London University, George Warrington Steevens turned to journalism*, eventually becoming a war* correspondent. While living in Cambridge he wrote for the *Cambridge Observer* for a short period, and then for the *Scots Observer**, on Zola (12 Aug. 1893). He later wrote reviews*, 'middles'* and leaders* when it became the *National Observer*. He was also on the staff of the *Pall Mall Gazette** and the *Pall Mall Budget**. He resigned, with Harry Cust* and Iwan-Müller, from these two Astor-financed newspapers in February 1896. He joined the *Daily Mail** and travelled to America in 1896 to report the presidential election. The next year he became the *Daily Mail's* war* correspondent during the war between Greece and Turkey. Starting in September 1897 he published a series of 16 articles in the *Daily Mail*, 'Under the Iron Heel', warning about the political and military rise of Germany. He covered Kitchener's Anglo-Egyptian army campaign in the Sudan in 1898. He reported the Dreyfus retrial at Rennes in September 1899 for the *Daily Mail*, *McClure's Magazine* (Oct. 1899), and *Harper's Magazine* (Oct. 1899). Steevens contributed to *Blackwood's** (Jan. 1895-Feb. 1899), *Current Literature*, the *Eclectic Magazine*, *Frank Leslie's Popular Monthly*, the *Living Age* and the *New Review** (Jan 1895 to Nov. 1897).

His final assignment was the Boer War. Trapped in Ladysmith during the siege he was the founding editor of the *Ladysmith Lyre*, a humorous and light-hearted parody of the siege. He died of typhoid and was posthumously awarded the Queen's South Africa medal on 23 February 1903. Steevens published volumes of his travels and adventures, the best known of which were *With Kitchener to Khartoum* (1898) and *From Capetown to Ladysmith* (1900).

Steevens was a reporter* in the imperialist* vein and Kitchener commented that 'I wish all correspondents were like him'. **DA**
Sources: Davies 2006, Griffiths 1992, *ODNB*, Street 1900, Thompson 2000.

STEPHEN, JAMES FITZJAMES (1829-1894) Well known as a legal historian (*History of the Criminal Law of England*, 1883) and High Court justice (1879-1890), James Fitzjames Stephen (elder brother of Leslie Stephen*) had a significant journalistic career, contributing numerous articles to periodicals, particularly the *Saturday Review** and the *Pall Mall Gazette**. His contributions not only served to develop the approaches to the English criminal law that he would later enunciate in his *History* and legal digests, but they also manifest the intensity with which those publishing in the 'higher journalism' at mid-century launched attacks on what they identified as the cant of the day.

Educated at Trinity College, Cambridge, Stephen was called to the bar of the Inner Temple in 1854 and began his career as a barrister on the Midland Circuit. Eager for additional income, he had already started placing a few articles in the *Morning Chronicle** and *Christian Observer** as early as 1851-1852, but it was while he was on the Circuit that he embarked more fully on his work as a journalist. On occasion, he would draft his articles in court, as he waited for cases. In the late 1850s and early 1860s, Stephen's most sustained journalistic commitment was to the *Saturday Review*. His first contribution to the *Review* appeared in its second number. Stephen attended not only to legal topics but also to the works of philosophers, novelists and historians. His no-nonsense style and controversial attacks on received wisdom are said to have defined the *Saturday Review*. In addition to book reviews*, Stephen, along with Thomas Collett Sandars, produced what came to be known as middles*, that is, articles appearing after the political leaders* and before the book reviews*. Leslie Stephen in his biography of his brother describes

his brother's middles* as a kind of 'lay sermon' (*Life* 178). Stephen reprinted a selection of his *Saturday Review* middles in *Essays by a Barrister* (1862). At about this same time, he had a falling out with the *Review*'s editor John Douglas Cook over the right to contribute to other journals, and he stopped writing for the *Review* altogether. Shortly before his death, he published a second collection of his *Saturday Review* pieces, *Horae Sabbaticae* (3 vols, 1892).

During the late 1850s and throughout the 1860s, Stephen also contributed articles to the *Edinburgh Review** (where he famously got into a row with Charles Dickens* over negative comments on *Little Dorrit*), *Fraser's Magazine** and the *Cornhill Magazine**. Stephen contributed most frequently to the *Cornhill*, during which time he became acquainted with George Smith* of Smith, Elder & Co*., the magazine's publisher*. Stephen felt constrained by the lighter tone of the *Cornhill*, and in 1865 he started his association with Smith's newly founded *Pall Mall Gazette*. The *Pall Mall* welcomed his attacks on sentimentalism and political pandering. Although Leslie Stephen reports that Fitzjames Stephen wrote in excess of 800 articles and 200 notes for the *Pall Mall*, few have been definitively attributed to him.

Stephen left for India in 1869, having been appointed as the legal member of the Indian viceroy's council. Upon his return in 1872, he resumed his work with the *Pall Mall Gazette* and continued for the next three years, using it to launch one of his most important works, *Liberty, Equality, Fraternity* (1873), his response to John Stuart Mill's* *On Liberty*. Thereafter he produced less journalistic work, though he did contribute articles to the *Nineteenth Century** in the late 1870s (often these were papers emerging from the Metaphysical Society) and on into the early 1890s, of which his last was 'Gambling and the Law' (July-Dec. 1891). **LR**
Sources: *ODNB*, Radzinowcz 1957, Smith 1988, Stephen 1895.

STEPHEN, LESLIE (1832-1904) Leslie Stephen is best known now as the first editor* of the *Dictionary of National Biography*, as an important literary critic, and as father of Virginia Woolf and Vanessa Bell, but he edited magazines* and wrote widely for the periodical press for much of his life. Beginning in the 1860s, and despite his own committed Liberal politics, he wrote for two conservative journals, the weekly* *Saturday Review** and the evening *Pall Mall Gazette**, while also contributing a fortnightly 'London Letter' to the American weekly the *Nation*, and writing for the shilling* monthly* *Cornhill Magazine**, the Liberal *Fortnightly Review** and others. In short, he undertook regular journalistic work, including reviews* and longer articles on topics as various as alpine walking, art and morality, Wordsworth's ethics, Darwinism and agnosticism, and education reform.

Having declined the editorship of *Fraser's Magazine**, Stephen accepted the editorship of the prestigious *Cornhill* in 1871, at a salary of £500 per annum. In addition to being a regular *Cornhill* writer by this time, there were significant family connections, since Stephen married the youngest daughter of W. M. Thackeray*, founding editor of the *Cornhill*. The *Cornhill* was known for its policy of not courting controversy and Stephen towed the line in not espousing particular political* or religious* positions. He continued to publish articles here and elsewhere, which he often collected and published in volume form.

While Stephen ensured a steady pair of hands in editing the *Cornhill*, circulation* steadily declined, but the publisher* George Smith* had the inspired idea of giving Stephen a large, new project, editing the first *Dictionary of National Biography*, the first volume of which appeared in 1885. While his heyday in the world of the periodical press was behind him, he continued to publish articles, for example his series of biographical essays in the *National Review** on literary* figures including his contemporaries John Ruskin*, Matthew Arnold* and Walter Bagehot*. **MWT**

Sources: Annan 1984, *ODNB*, *Wellesley*.

STEPHENS, FREDERIC GEORGE (1827-1907) Frederic George Stephens's long career as an art critic began in 1848 when he joined the Pre-Raphaelite brotherhood and was sustained by his position as art critic for the *Athenaeum** (1861-1901) which included an unsigned* 'Fine Arts Gossip'* column*. Before this appointment Stephens contributed to the *Dublin University Magazine**, *Fraser's Magazine** and *Macmillan's Magazine** among others. Stephens and his contemporary, J. B. Atkinson, 'seem to have been the first English writers to earn a living from periodical art criticism' (Prettejohn: 76). However, the *Athenaeum* provided insufficient income and Stephens also wrote for specialist art serials such as the *Art Journal**, *Magazine of Art**, the *Germ** and *Portfolio**.

Although Stephens briefly studied painting at the Royal Academy Schools in 1844 and taught drawing at University College School (1870-1902), he was better known as a writer. Stephen's

offered important analyses of Pre-Raphaelitism, and continued to support his former colleagues but he could also be highly critical, as he was of William Holman Hunt's* late work, which launched a public debate between artist and critic. Stephen's penchant for severity led his *Athenaeum* editor* Norman MacColl* to recommend that he temper his remarks.

Nonetheless, Stephens maintained close ties with important Victorian artists such as Ford Madox Brown, J. W. Inchbold and William Richmond, as revealed through his correspondence, his position as secretary of the Hogarth Club* and numerous biographies, essays and monographs; he produced as well an illustrated book, *Artists at Home* (1884). His 90-part series on Victorian art collectors for the *Athenaeum* likewise took readers into the private realm and created an important preliminary catalogue of these collections. **ALH**

Sources: Flint 2000, Grove, MacLeod 1986a, MacLeod 1986b, Prettejohn 1997.

STEREOTYPES Stereotyping is a method of making perfect facsimiles in type-metal of the faces of pages composed in moveable types. The earliest stereotype plates are thought to be the invention of the Dutch printers Mueller and Van der Mey in 1701. In Britain the first successful stereotype plates were made around 1727 by William Ged, a goldsmith in Edinburgh. In 1781 another Scotsman, Alexander Tilloch, conceived the idea of stereotype printing without knowledge of his predecessors. He set up a stereotype business in 1782 in partnership with Messrs Foulis of Glasgow. By 1819 stereotyping techniques were used for printing tables in low-price publications such as *Ready Reckoners* and *Logarithms*. Thomas Allan, another Edinburgh printer, made improvements to stereotype printing and introduced a system where a number of plates could be cast at once.

The process of using papier mâché moulds was introduced into England in 1846 by an Italian named Vanour. Around the same time, the brothers James and Tommaso Bartolomeo Dellagana fled from Paris to London and set up a factory for making stereotype plates. Stereotyping had become established for book printing, but it was not considered suitable for printing large pages of newspapers. However, in 1857 the Dellagana brothers succeeded in casting the first whole page stereotype for a British newspaper, *The Times**. By 1863 they were successfully using a curved casting box, enabling them to produce convex plates which could be fitted directly onto the cylinder of a rotary press*. The

full potential for newspapers of this method of printing, where increased machine speed was of primary importance*, was recognized. A later development by Henry Wise Wood of New York saved time and labour by eliminating the hot press and by forming 40 to 50 plates simultaneously. **DHL**
Sources: Berry and Poole 1966, Clair 1976, Hansard 1841, Timperley 1842.

STEVENSON, GEORGE JOHN (1818-1888)
Stevenson, publisher*, proprietor*, bookseller and journalist*, was born in Chesterfield, and became a Methodist in 1831 while apprenticed to a printer. From 1841 he managed a printing business in Great Yarmouth where he established a lending library* in connection with the local Methodist Sunday school, also occasionally preaching. In 1844 he moved to London where he trained as a teacher at St John's College, and by 1848 he had become Headmaster of the endowed parochial school in Lambeth.

In this position, he helped to launch the *School and Teachers**, aimed at primary school teachers, and in 1855 Stevenson resigned from teaching to establish a printing and bookselling business in Paternoster Row, remaining the proprietor* of this firm until a few years before his death. His interest in education led to the publication of a number of journals such as the *Pupil Teacher* (1857), the *Christian Chronicle** (1857-1858), the *Youth's Instructor* (1858) and the *English Journal of Education* (1859) which incorporated the *School and Teachers*. In the same year, he purchased the *Wesleyan Times* to which he contributed articles on hymnology. In 1872 came the *Hebrew Christian Witness*, and the *Prophetic News*.

Stevenson also published cheap schoolbooks, sermons, pamphlets and religious tracts. Another interest was Methodist history, on which he published in books and articles. Despite having given publishing up in 1873 to concentrate on writing, in 1882 he edited* the short-lived *Union Review and Chronicle of Wesleyan Methodist Literary and Mutual Associations*. **DHL**
Sources: Julian 1892, *ODNB*.

STEVENSON, ROBERT ALAN MOWBRAY (1847-1900) As an art critic, Robert Alan Mowbray Stevenson (cousin to Robert Louis Stevenson) helped fuel interest in Britain in the work of the Old Masters as well as that of contemporary art, particularly new directions in French painting. As 'the leader of a new school of art criticism in England'(*ODNB*), he belonged to the school of New Critics comprised of George Moore, Elizabeth Robins Pennell*, Joseph Pennell*, Walter Sickert, and Frederick Wedmore.

Stevenson first took his university degrees at Cambridge (1871,1882) and then trained as a painter, studying at the École des Beaux-Arts, Antwerp, and then in the studio of Carolus-Duran (Charles-Emile-Auguste Durand) degrees at Cambridge, Stevenson trained as a painter, a decisive experience, as after a brief exhibiting career in the early 1880s, Stevenson turned to art criticism. He first began writing on art and music for the *Saturday Review**. In 1889, he ceased his regular contributions in order to take the Roscoe Chair of Fine Art at University College, Liverpool, where he remained for four years before becoming art critic for the *Pall Mall Gazette**. He also contributed to the *Magazine of Art**, *New Review** and *Portfolio**. **ALH**
Sources: Clarke 2005, Flint 2000, *ODNB*, *Wellesley.*

STIFF, GEORGE (1807-1873) George Stiff was an important yet obscure entrepreneur in the development of cheap* illustrated* periodical literature in the mid Victorian period. He emerged into notice as an engraver in charge of illustration production at the *Illustrated London News**. By 1847 he had become the proprietor* of the *Weekly Times** and began to develop a large-scale publishing* business based on illustrated cheap mass* circulation journals, the most celebrated of which was the *London Journal**. At one point he was employing a staff of 80. In serializing* the sensational* fiction of such authors as G. W. M. Reynolds* and Percy B. St John*, Stiff brought in outstanding illustrators of the calibre of John Gilbert*, Hablot Browne* and John Proctor, and the *London Journal* remained extremely successful despite various financial* escapades in the late 1850s.

Later in his career Stiff bought an interest in the *Morning Chronicle** in 1860, and on his death in 1873 he had been the proprietor* of the *Weekly Dispatch** for several years. Other ventures, including a magazine* called the *London Reader** launched by Stiff in 1864, struggled to repeat the success of the *London Journal*. Stiff died, as he had largely lived, in considerable obscurity despite pursuing one of the emblematic career paths found in Victorian journalism, from an engraver's apprenticeship to the status of the proprietor of an extensive publishing operation. **BM**
Sources: James 1963, King 2004, *ODNB*.

STIRLING OBSERVER (1836-) The *Stirling Observer* was first published by the Liberal bookseller Ebenezer Johnstone, in order to challenge the Tory *Stirling Journal* which had failed to publish Johnstone's criticisms of the established Church. Its perspective on politics was that of the evangelical dissenting groups in Scotland. A four page broadsheet of 6 columns*, it began as a 4d weekly*. Broad coverage of Parliament, foreign, Scottish, local, Irish, and general news* as well as business, agriculture, religion and the Free Church of Scotland, local advertisements* and a letters column seem to have assured its survival. George Murray, who changed his name to James Bolivar Manson, succeeded Johnstone as editor* in 1852 and the paper became more openly radical, sympathetic to Cobden and Bright*, and this, along with financial malfeasance may have led to his dismissal in 1855.

Johnstone's ownership* of the paper ended in 1860 and Samuel Cowan took over, with James Manners as editor. Cowan sold to Robert Gray in 1866, but five years later, Messrs Duncan and Jamieson bought the paper. From 1877 John Jamieson was sole proprietor* and after W. B. Cook retired as editor in 1886, Jamieson edited the paper himself with his nephew J. J. Munro dealing with the business side. In 1895 David Lindsay, Jamieson's assistant, became editor, a position he held until 1928. Politically, it retained a mild radicalism, remaining loyal to Liberalism after 1886. The paper became twice weekly* in 1873 with the publication of a Saturday edition and, reputedly, was popular among the local textile workers*. It has survived until the present day. **WHF**
Sources: Cowan 1946, Ferguson 1946, *Waterloo* 1989.

STOCKDALE, JOHN JOSEPH (C. 1776-1847) John Joseph Stockdale set up his own bookselling concern in Pall Mall in 1806, focusing on erotic publications. The son of John Stockdale, a prosperous influential bookseller in Piccadilly, for most of his career Stockdale traded in a financially precarious state, and by the mid 1820s his main publishing interests were in scandalous and pornographic* works, many of which he is thought to have written or edited himself under the pseudonym* 'Thomas Little'. However, he seems to have published some short-lived periodicals, including the *True Briton*, a 1d daily* in aid of Queen Caroline's cause (1821-1822), *Stockdale's Budget*, which he edited (13 Dec. 1826-6 June 1827), the *Probe* (31 Aug. 1833ff.?), in which as editor*, printer and publisher he discusses his legal entanglements of 1828-1829, and possibly the *Comet*, a mock newspaper (1806).

Stockdale was frequently involved in legal disputes, both as a defendant and as a litigant. His most famous legal entanglement occurred 1836-1840, after he was named in a parliamentary* report as the publisher* of an indecent work found among the belongings of a prisoner in Newgate. Stockdale commenced a series of libel actions against the Hansard family which eventually spiralled into a legal crisis over the extent of parliamentary privilege. In contrast to the majority of nineteenth-century publishers of erotica, who generally carried on their trade in clandestine fashion, Stockdale was a relentless self-promoter who seems to have deliberately courted notoriety. He published accounts of his various legal actions, and attached appendices of letters and other personal material to some of his more popular works. **NG**
Sources: Bourne 1975, Stockdale 2005, Todd 1972, *Waterloo*.

STODDART, JANE THOMPSON (1863-1944) Born in Scotland and setting out as a teacher, Jane Stoddart ventured first into print as a novelist. However, in 1890 Robertson Nicoll* invited her to come to London to work with him at Hodder & Stoughton* on the *British Weekly* which he edited. She spent the rest of her long working life assisting Nicoll in various capacities on the *British Weekly* and as assistant editor* on *Woman at Home*, where Annie S. Swan* (another of Nicoll's associates) was the chief journalist. All three were steeped in the Scottish non-conformist tradition which shaped their journalism. It is likely that behind the scenes Stoddart did much of the editorial work on both these journals as well as the *Bookman*, another Hodder and Stoughton* publication. At the *British Weekly*, she also developed the New Journalistic* device of the interview* to good effect often under the pseudonym* 'Lorna'. In the early twentieth century she wrote a series of influential articles on socialism. She retired from the *British Weekly* in 1937. **MRB**
Sources: Darlow 1925, *ODNB*, *Woman at Home*.

STRAD: A MONTHLY JOURNAL FOR PROFESSIONALS & AMATEURS OF ALL STRINGED INSTRUMENTS PLAYED WITH THE BOW (1890-) The *Strad: A Monthly Journal for Professionals & Amateurs of all Stringed Instruments played with the Bow* was established in London to serve a specialist readership* of professional and amateur string players. From 1891 it was published* by D. R. Duncan; its ownership*, editorship* and management initially focused around Harry Lavender and Eugene Polonaski, a violin connoisseur who was briefly named as editor. In December 1893 co-publication began in New York, in 1896 this spread to Sydney, Melbourne, and Adelaide in Australia.

The *Strad*'s content was always a well-judged mix of reviews* of concerts and recently published music*, news*, correspondence* columns*, articles on string technique and organological matters, features on celebrated* players (often illustrated* with portraits), analyses of musical works, and even short stories. As the magazine became established, its contributor base grew to include many experts: performers, teachers, critics, and organologists such as John Tiplady Carrodus, Carl Courvoisier, Robin Legge, and Edmund van der Straeten. From the outset, trade advertisements* for instruments, accessories, tuition, music, and the miscellaneous were prominent and numerous.

The magazine's* foundation was timely, the number of people (including, for the first time, women) taking and giving formal violin lessons had been growing since the 1870s, as had outlets for public performance. The *Strad* was able successfully to serve and corner this booming market*. By 1893 the magazine had become the official journal for the College of Violinists, a national examination board under the presidency of Carrodus, a tie-in that was probably crucial to ensuring commercial viability. The title continues today as the *Strad*. **CMB**

Sources: Vann and Van Arsdel 1993, Wagstaff 1998.

STRAHAN, ALEXANDER STUART (1833-1918) The Scot Alexander Stuart Strahan joined the Edinburgh publishing firm Johnstone and Hunter in 1853, and in 1858, with William Isbister, he founded Strahan & Co. The firm published* religious works, children's books, and reprinted American titles and in 1862 it moved to London, adding novels, essays and poetry. On its list were Eliza Lynn Linton*, Charles Kingsley, Frederick Locker-Lampson and George MacDonald. Probably Strahan's greatest acquisition was securing the rights to publish Tennyson*.

Strahan's strict religious upbringing played a major part in his career. He founded and published the *Christian Guest* in 1859, an amalgam of stories and articles from writers of differing religious* persuasions, which became *Good Words*ered* the following year. It was one of the successes of mid-Victorian journalism, with a readership* of over 160,000 by 1864. He founded the secular* *Argosy*er* in 1865 but sold it in October 1867 after a story about bigamy proved unacceptable. *Good Words for the Young*er* was founded in 1869, but Strahan sold it in 1872 as a financial failure. He acquired *Paul's Magazine*er* in May 1869 with Anthony Trollope* as editor*, but it too made a loss and he sold it in October 1872.

Despite his failures Strahan founded and published the enormously successful *Contemporary Review*er* in 1866 as a religious counter to the secular *Fortnightly Review*er*. Contributors were of differing religious backgrounds and included the Shakespearian scholar Edward Dowden, John Tulloch, Henry Alford* (Dean of Canterbury) and James Thomas Knowles*. Strahan was editor from February 1877 to 1882.

Strahan's lack of financial acumen led to his forced resignation from the firm in 1872 although he retained the copyright* of the *Contemporary*, which he then published from December 1873 to May 1876. Strahan & Co. Ltd. was formed in 1876 with Strahan as a director, but his resignation was forced in 1881 with the company declared bankrupt in 1882. **DA**

Sources: *ODNB*, Srebrnik 1986, *Waterloo*, *Wellesley*.

STRAND MAGAZINE (1891-1950) The *Strand Magazine*, at 6d per monthly* issue, represented excellent value to its readers*: profusely illustrated*, entertaining, solidly middle class* in tone. Indeed, the first issue, at 112 pages, sold 300,000 copies, and with sales in America as well, circulation* soon climbed to 500,000.

The *Strand* was founded by George Newnes* with profits from his weekly paper *Tit-Bits*er*. The emphasis on illustration and entertainment was Newnes's idea, though based on American illustrated magazines of the same era (*Harper's*, *Scribner's*). H. Greenhough Smith* was its first editor* (1891-1930). It was Smith who saw the potential for circulation* figures for the *Strand* in Arthur Conan Doyle's 'Sherlock Holmes' stories. Each story formed a discreet unit yet was linked through characterization with the one previous. The formula was a departure from the traditional Victorian serialization of the novel, though it performed the same functions, increasing circulation and creating a body of avid readers*. Sidney Paget's* illustrations for the stories were similarly influential, so much so that later film and television adaptations habitually employed actors who resembled Paget's drawings of Holmes. Doyle's stories (1891-1927) contributed greatly to the lasting popularity of the magazine, though the *Strand* also benefited from the work of the best writers of the day: Kipling, Wells, Huxley, Greene, and others. Reginald Pound, coming to the *Strand* as editor towards the end of its life (1941-1946), wrote a history of the magazine which said: 'the middle-classes of England never cast a clearer image of themselves in print than they did in the *Strand Magazine*. Confirming their preference for mental as well as physical comfort, for more than half a century it

62 THE STRAND MAGAZINE.

that you have been getting yourself very wet lately, and that you have a most clumsy and careless servant girl ? "

" My dear Holmes," said I, " this is too much. You would certainly have been burned, had you lived a few centuries ago. It is true that I had a country walk on Thursday and came home in a dreadful mess; but, as I have changed my clothes, I can't imagine how you deduce it. As to Mary Jane, she is incorrigible, and my wife has given her notice ; but there again I fail to see how you work it out."

He chuckled to himself and rubbed his long nervous hands together.

" It is simplicity itself," said he ; " my eyes tell me that on the inside of your left shoe, just where the firelight strikes it, the leather is scored by six almost parallel cuts. Obviously they have been caused by someone who has very carelessly scraped round the edges of the sole in order to remove crusted mud from it. Hence, you see, my double deduction that you had been out in vile

" THEN HE STOOD BEFORE THE FIRE."

Figure 60: One of the popular 'Adventures of Sherlock Holmes', *Strand Magazine*, July 1891, 62: 'A Scandal in Bohemia' with a typical Sidney Paget illustration.

faithfully mirrored their tastes, prejudices, and intellectual limitations. From them it drew a large and loyal readership that was the envy of the publishing world' (Pound: 7). **ET**
Sources: Ashley 2006, Jackson 2001, Pound 1966, Sullivan 1984.

STRAND MUSICAL MAGAZINE (1895-c.1899) The *Strand Musical Magazine* was launched by George Newnes* Ltd in an attempt to repeat the success of its *Strand Magazine** with a musical monthly* for young ladies. Priced* at 6d, it was 80 pages (29cm in size), 20 pages of which were text and 60 pages printed music*. A typical issue began with an illustrated* article (4 pages) on a musical institution (usually written by its principal), or an illustrated interview* with an 'eminent musician' or a biographical sketch of a 'great composer'. Two shorter illustrated features (2 pages) on a living performer, a band, or musical club (for example, the Stock Exchange Orchestral Society) came next, followed by a short story (4 pages) that invariably involved a young female musician and a romantic attachment. Full-page portrait photographs* and a printed music supplement* were essential, while humorous sketches and prize competitions appeared from time to time. Advertising* was confined to the end papers (3 pages).

With its attractive format*, easy-going prose, cheerful emphasis on celebrity* and quality fiction, the *Strand Musical Magazine* aimed to be a serious-minded and respectable, yet entertaining, inexpensive and up-to-the-minute publication in tune with its youthful middle-class* readership*. A unique venture in its market* segment, the journal aimed to exploit commercially its own claim that the British were an increasingly 'music-loving people', while popularizing music, supporting the efforts and publicising the achievements of the national 'musical renaissance'.

The *Strand Musical Magazine* was edited* throughout its existence by E. Hatzfeld, and its many distinguished contributors included George Grove*, Charles Hallé, Ignaz Paderewski and Arthur Sullivan. After 36 issues (Jan. 1895-Dec. 1897), Newnes sold the journal to Musical Magazines Ltd, a subsidiary of Stanley Lucas, Weber, Pitt and Hatzfeld Ltd, music publishers*. The new owners desultorily brought out five issues before ceasing publication (probably in 1899). **MH**
Source: *Waterloo*.

STRANG, WILLIAM (1859-1921) Primarily an etcher and intaglio printmaker in his early career and a painter in his later years, William Strang was none-theless a technically innovative artist on wood whose work pushed the tonal effects of wood* engraving to new levels of sophistication and complexity. Associated with the late century revival of wood engraving, which was in turn related to a developing awareness of the politics of craft manufacture, Strang published in a range of prominent progressive or experimental illustrated* periodicals, notably the *Yellow Book** (1895), the *Dome** (1898-1900) and the *English Illustrated Magazine** (1898). His massive foldout woodcut plate of 'The Plough', published in the *Dome* in 1900, found wider fame when distributed by the Art for Schools Association. **BM**
Sources: Engen 1990, Houfe 1978, *ODNB*.

STRANGE, WILLIAM (1801-1871) An important London bookseller, publisher* and cheap* periodical proprietor*, William Strange, along with George Cowie, established a retail and publishing business in 1822 in Fetter Lane, from where they produced a range of technical, religious*, literary* and satirical* periodicals costing between 1d and 4d. In 1830, Strange opened a shop in Paternoster Row and became publisher to the radical journalist William Carpenter, whose *Political Letters* (1830-1831) signalled the beginning of the putative 'war of the unstamped'* press. This partnership ensured Strange's notoriety as a radical publisher, but his output was diverse, mixing politics* with populist literary and bawdy genres. His greatest success was the 1d *Figaro in London**, a comic weekly* that in 1832 boasted a circulation* of 70,000.

Over the next 30 years Strange produced many periodicals including some which advocated physical education and mesmerism, but he continued to publish mainstream popular titles including *Chambers's London Journal*, the *Penny Illustrated News* (1849-1850) and the *Bookbinders' Trade Circular* (1850-1877). Strange's opportunism was demonstrated by his unauthorized publication of a catalogue of sketches made by Queen Victoria and Prince Albert (*The Royal Victoria and Albert Gallery of Etchings* [1848]), abandoned only after the Prince himself secured an injunction. In 1852, Strange relocated to Amen Corner, and in 1861 was still trading as a bookseller with his son. His bankruptcy in 1860 and rumours about the 'indecent' content of his latest periodical, *Fast Life* (1859-1860), served as a reminder of his tendency towards controversy and predilection for risqué literature. Reporting on one of his many legal wrangles, *The Times* described Strange as 'old and crafty', but following his death, the *Bookseller* noted that he was 'one of the early pioneers of literature in the then unpalatable form of periodicals, especially those of a political kind'. The *Athenaeum** observed that he was 'much respected in [Paternoster] Row' and commended 'his unwearied perseverance'. These were all realistic judgements of a pressman who had throughout his career indiscriminately championed cheap* literature and straddled both rough and respectable print cultures. **DSM**

Sources: *Athenaeum* 1871, *Bookseller* 1871, Haywood 2004, James 1963, McCalman 1988, *The Times* 1829-1860.

STUART, DANIEL (1766-1846) Printer and newspaper proprietor*, Daniel Stuart was born in Edinburgh and moved to London in 1778. Stuart bought the *Morning Post** in 1795, having been its printer since at least 1788. Under his ownership the *Morning Post* thrived and he sold it in 1803 reputedly for £25,000. During this period he also acquired the *Telegraph* and the *Gazetteer* and associated himself and the *Morning Post* with the campaign for parliamentary reform. In about 1801, Stuart bought the *Courier* with T. G. Street, which was as successful, but which, against the background of the Napoleonic Wars, pursued a patriotic and much more conservative line than the *Morning Post*. He progressively distanced himself from the daily affairs of the *Courier*, though he still owned an interest in 1823. **JRW**

Source: *ODNB*.

STUDIO: AN ILLUSTRATED MAGAZINE OF FINE AND APPLIED ART (1893-1993) By a happy coincidence, the publisher John Lane* introduced Charles Lewis Hind to Charles Holme* in 1892 to discuss their common dream: launching an art magazine*. Hind (1862-1928) had been a subeditor* at the *Art Journal** (1887-1892), and Holme had just retired from his lucrative business importing textiles and decorative arts from Asia and the Far East. The first issue of their collaboration*, the *Studio: an illustrated magazine of fine and applied art*, appeared in April 1893, copiously illustrated and priced* 4 ½d. It entered a competitive* market* crowded with magazines* that addressed art and design, including the *Artist and Journal of Home Culture**, the *Art Journal*, the *Dial**, the *[Century Guild] Hobby Horse**, the *Magazine of Art**, the *Savoy** and the *Yellow Book**. But before the first issue of the *Studio* was published, Hind left to edit* the *Pall Mall Budget*, and was replaced as editor by Gleeson White*, a regular contributor to the *Artist*. In just over a year White also left, in June 1894, after which time Charles Holme edited the magazine himself until 1921.

As proprietor*, Holme intended the *Studio* to be an illustrated* international monthly* for all art lovers, a very broad readership* indeed: artists, designers, tradespeople, students, teachers, collectors, professionals* and amateurs. His concept worked, for although the price later rose to 1s, the magazine flourished for 167 volumes, and 853 issues, until May 1964. From June 1964, (vol. 167, no. 854), the title changed to *Studio International*, and was published bi-monthly in London and New York, and edited by Charles Holme's son, Charles Geoffrey Holme.

The success of the *Studio* was the result of its timing, its international content, and the quality and quantity of its illustrations (Holme 1978: 1). Holme's insistence on world-wide distribution* helped as well. Holme and White used the latest techniques to showcase the work of Aubrey Beardsley* in their first issue, which brought the new magazine immediately to the attention of the public and existing art magazines. The mix of material on decorative art, industrial design and fine art, with the inclusion of many new media and techniques such as photography, posters and Japanese art, immediately popularized the *Studio* (Johnson: 198).

Contributors were specialists in their field. Fine art critics included R. A. M. Stevenson*, Charles W. Furse, Walter Shaw Sparrow and Frederick Wedmore, while Eve Blantyre Simpson (EBS), Aymer Vallance, Gleeson White*, William T. Whitley and Gabriel Mourey (alias 'Gil Blas', who also edited the Paris edition of the *Studio*) covered the crafts.

Charles Holme expanded the Studio Publications, adding Special Numbers of the *Studio* from 1896, annuals* such as *The Year Book of Decorative Art* from 1905, and many books on topics ranging from toys to housing design to fine art. **HVH**

Sources: Charles Holme Archive 2003, De Laszlo 1933, General Index *Studio* [1901], Holme 1978, Holme 1933, Johnson 1970, Levetus 1933.

STURMEY, JOHN JAMES HENRY (1857-1930) As a keen cyclist, Henry Sturmey resigned from a teaching post in 1877 to complete the *Indispensable Bicyclist's Handbook*, which sold out within a month of its publication in that year. Spending his vacations in Coventry and other centres of the bicycle industry researching for the second edition of his bicyclists' handbook, he met the publisher* William I. Iliffe* whose family printed the *Bicycling World*. Having suggested a new weekly* periodical called the *Cyclist** to replace the *Bicycling World*, he was appointed at 22 as editor* of the journal*, with one-third of the profits. The first issue (22 Oct. 1879) was published under the partnership of Il-iffe* Sons & Sturmey. Having moved to Coventry, Sturmey then combined his teaching and journalism careers. His diverse technical interests led him to found other journals* including *Photography* (later *Amateur Photographer*) in 1888, *Autocar* (1895) and the quarterly* *Flying* (1917-1919), which proved in advance of its time.

After breaking with Iliffe, Sturmey became a contributor to *Motor* (1903ff), but eventually gave up journalism to concentrate on commercial projects, mainly relating to cars and motor accessories. As an editor* Sturmey did not welcome criticism and was impatient with interference from anyone he regarded as not having the same grasp of technical subjects as himself. Nevertheless he became one of the best-known cycling journalists and steered the *Cyclist* into the front rank of cycling journals. DHL

Sources: *Coventry Herald* 1930, *Coventry Standard* 1930, Hadland 1987, *ODNB*, *The Times* 1930.

STUTFIELD, HUGH EDWARD MILLINGTON (1858-1929) A barrister, sportsman, mountaineer, and fervent Protestant, Stutfield contributed articles on a notably diverse variety of topics to periodicals such as the *Living Age*, *Blackwood's Magazine**, the *National Review**, the *Review of Reviews**, and *Longman's Magazine**. Called to the Bar in 1884, he began to write for periodicals in the late 1880s, his early work focussing on his travel and mountaineering experiences. A narrative entitled 'A Big Buck Chamois' appeared in *Longman's* in December 1889, in which Stutfield relates the story of a hunting trip during which he bagged a 75 lb chamois, concluding that 'it was a fine head, and I look forward to seeing it shortly in the place of honour over my chimneypiece'. An avid explorer and sportsman, such yarns were a continuing theme of Stutfield's writing, a seam he mined at greater length in his book *Climbs and Explorations in the Canadian Rockies* (1903) (co-authored with John Norman Collie (1859-1942)). Stutfield also contributed a number of articles on financial* and other topics to the conservative *National Review*.

Staunchly traditional in his social views, Stutfield's response to a mantinée performance of Ibsen's *Little Eyolf* appeared in *Blackwood's Magazine* in January 1897 under the title 'The Psychology of Feminism', and it is a fascinating example of *fin-de-siècle* anti-feminism at its most embittered. Disgusted as much by the audience as by the play itself, he denounced the women present as 'self-centred, neurotic, and egotistical', their narcissism being fuelled by 'the Ibsenite theory of female individualism' that was playing itself out onstage. Feminism, for Stutfield, was a pathology spread by an upstart cabal of hysterical women, whipped up into a frenzy by the radically egalitarian and amoral ideas with which Ibsen's name was so strongly associated in late-Victorian England. If anything Stutfield's deep antipathy towards Catholicism exceeded even his hatred of feminism, and this similarly found expression in his journalism. He perhaps never made his views so clear as in 1922 when he argued in the *National Review* that the malign influence of the Church explained the Irishman's 'enormous cruelty and his inordinate lust of blood, English blood in particular'. Indeed, with characteristic bombast, Stutfield estimated that 'Roman Catholics are, on a rough average, about *four times* as wicked as other people'. MaT

Sources: Obituary *The Times* April 1929, Stutfield Jan. 1897, Stutfield Aug. 1922.

SUBEDITING For F. J. Mansfield, writing in 1932, the newspaper subeditor was a product of the New Journalism* of the late nineteenth century, and the medium for importing the beneficial influence of the American 'yellow press'* on the accessibility of the British daily* and Sunday* newspaper. Subeditors converted 'the mass of undigested and ill-assorted matter into a connected, readable and fascinating story' by refining the art of the narrative headline, the structuring of news* values and the deliberate design of layout*, typography* and illustration* to conform to the editorial house style that defined a title's identity. AGJ

Source: Mansfield 1932.

SULLY, JAMES (1842-1923) Sully became John Morley's* assistant at the *Fortnightly Review** in 1871, on Alexander Bain's* recommendation. After three unsuccessful applications for chairs in philosophy, Sully turned to freelance journalism to supplement his income. He wrote on psychology, aesthetics, and other philosophical topics for the *Cornhill Magazine**, the *Fortnightly*, the *Nineteenth Century**, the Westminster Review* and *Mind**. In his memoirs, Sully described his work for the *Cornhill* under Leslie Stephen's* editorship as 'the pleasantest stadium of my literary activity'. His association with Morley continued in the 1880s as a reviewer* for the *Pall Mall Gazette**.

Sully wrote an obituary* article in 1879 on his friend George Henry Lewes* for the *New Quarterly Magazine**, which George Eliot* deemed the best of the obituaries* but nonetheless inadequate. All told, Sully published more than 60 articles on topics such as child development, evolutionary psychology, music*, literary* imagination (influenced by conversations with Robert Louis Stevenson), German philosophy, and perception, many of which were further developed in his books. Sigmund Freud acknowledged the influence of Sully's 1893 *Fortnightly Review* article 'The Dream as Revelation'. Sully was appointed to the Grote chair of the philosophy of mind and logic at University College, London in 1892, on George Croom Robertson's* resignation, after which his contributions to serials slackened. **SA**

Sources: Block 1984, Gurjeva 2001, *ONDB*, Sully 1918, *Wellesley.*

SUNDAY AT HOME (1854-1940) *Sunday at Home* (1854-1940), subtitled 'A Family* Magazine for Sabbath Reading', was an illustrated*, non-denominational religious* magazine issued by the Religious Tract Society (RTS)*. In 1852 the Society launched its first general penny* weekly*, *Leisure Hour*. Apparently pleased with *Leisure Hour*'s sales, it launched *Sunday at Home* as a sister periodical – also a penny weekly – in May 1854. While the varied content of *Sunday at Home* (featuring fiction, poetry* and articles) resembled its forebear, it was more overtly religious. Indeed, the primary purpose of *Sunday at Home* was to provide suitable reading for all classes* of people for those hours on Sunday* not devoted to worship or reading scriptures – the sanctity of Sundays was a sensitive subject among evangelicals during this period. *Sunday at Home* achieved a circulation* of 130,000 by 1865. By the 1890s, however, it was struggling and was transformed into a 6d monthly* in 1895. Nevertheless, it survived another 45 years.

Initially edited* by William Haig Miller, one of the Religious Tract Society's regular writers. Later editors included James Macaulay (1858-1895) and William Stevens (1895-1899). Prominent contributions included fiction by Sarah Smith (pseudonym 'Hesba Stretton'), articles by Frances Browne and illustrations by George John Pinwell. **AL**

Sources: Altholz 1989, Billington 1986, Fyfe 2004, Green 1899, Scott 1992.

SUNDAY PAPERS The typical Sunday paper of the nineteenth century combined serious political* news* items with sensationalism. Started by W. S. Bourne in 1791, the *Observer** was the first successful Sunday paper, setting a precedent by fluctuating between scurrility and respectability. It had radical leanings, but was bought in 1814 by the venal William Innell Clement (1779/80-1852), who took payments from the government in return for his support. By 1819, circulation* stood at 10,850 stamped copies, as well as a further 2,000 of the Monday print. It was estimated that a further 10,000 unstamped* copies were given away as propaganda. The rival *New Observer* (1821) was set up in 1821, and became the *Sunday Times** the following year when it was bought by Daniel Whittle Harvey (1786-1863), blending similar material.

In the 1840s, an extension of the readership* among the working class*, compared with the predominantly middle-class readership of the *Observer* and the *Sunday Times,* saw a flurry of new titles came onto the market*. Foremost among these were John Browne Bell's *News of the World**, George Stiff's* *Weekly Times** and the two Sundays that would dominate the latter half of the century, *Lloyd's Weekly Newspaper** and *Reynolds's Newspaper**. G. M. W. Reynolds* had Chartist* sympathies, and Edward Lloyd*, although a Liberal, employed the more radical William Carpenter* as his first editor*. Yet while these papers inclined to the left, commercial ends took precedence over political ones. Sensationalist crime* reporting dominated over political comment, with the populist Douglas Jerrold*, followed by his son Blanchard Jerrold* becoming editors of *Lloyd's.*

After the removal of the Paper Duty in 1861, most Sundays sold for 1d, but those that did not suffered declining readership*. Both *Reynolds's* and *Lloyd's* had circulations* far exceeding the best-selling dailies*, with *Lloyd's* becoming the first paper to sell a million copies in 1896. **MaT**

Sources: Berridge 1978, *ODNB*, *Waterloo.*

SUNDAY TIMES (1821-) Founded as a Sunday* paper by Henry White as the *New Observer* (Feb.-March 1821) and, then, the *Independent Observer* (April 1821-Oct. 1822) to attract readers from the *Sunday Observer**, the paper's name was changed in 1822 to the *Sunday Times*. In the same year it was acquired, in settlement of a debt, by David Whittle Harvey, who despite being imprisoned for libel for suggesting that George IV was mad like his father, made a success of the paper. During the 1850s, the paper came for a short time under the control of Joseph Moses Levy*, better known for his ownership of the *Daily Telegraph**.

Generally the *Sunday Times* had a somewhat chequered history during the mid part of the century, but did build up a reputation for its coverage of the arts and theatre. In the early 1860s Clement William Scott* was its theatre critic (1863-1865). In 1877, it was acquired by Alice Cornwell ('Princess Midas'), whose fortune derived from Australian gold mining, so that she could confer the editorship* on her future husband, Frederick Stannard Robinson, a war correspondent*. Under Cornwell's ownership, the paper consolidated its conservative stance and developed from what she described as 'a scissors and paste* affair'. The female influence was continued when, in 1893, Cornwell sold the paper to Rachel Beer* of the Sassoon family, whose husband Frederick Beer already owned the *Observer**. Rachel Beer edited both papers concurrently until a mental collapse, following the death of her husband, forced her to relinquish the editorship. In 1904, the *Sunday Times* was sold by her trustees. **JRW**

Sources: Griffiths 1992, Hobson *et al.* 1972, *ODNB*.

SUPPLEMENTS Supplements sustained their parent titles, contributed to their formal organization and enhanced their editorial contents. This form of nineteenth-century journalism was supplementary to a prior text, but was not always preserved with its parent, nor was it always evident that the primary text was accompanied by a supplement. Sometimes they were bound in, and sometimes not. Supplements were frequently lost and many, even most, remain unpreserved or unrecognized.

Perhaps the dominant meaning of 'supplement' is the notion of its defining status as 'extra', and, with luck, 'free'. They were supplementary in physical terms as well in content. As structural elements they were related to the organizational units of serial publications, defined by their position outside the serial. They may have later broken away completely from the parent but retained its title, such as with the *Times Literary Supplement*. Supplements could simply be an intensification of a subject already well established in the parent title, providing more coverage than the weekly* issue could normally offer. Supplements were also associated with topicality, for example the guides to the Great Exhibition that the *Illustrated London News** published in conjunction with its issues, and for separate sale.

Supplements might have attempted to raise the consciousness of readers to a cause associated with the parent periodical, for example Chartist* heroes in the *Northern Star**. Supplements also gave editors* and contributors more space and a way of experimenting with an increase in pagination. Supplements could have been used to launch new journals safely, by distribution* with an established title before going independent, for example with the *Unitarian Chronicle*, which initially was issued with the *Monthly Repository**.

Supplements were calculated to raise revenue from the cover price*, by selling more copies or by charging more. After initial distribution with the parent publication, they could escape their original date of issue, and be sold again elsewhere. Supplements could attract advertisers*, or encourage subscriptions. Supplements needed to pay their way. **LRB**

Source: Macdonald and Demoor 2007.

SURTEES, ROBERT SMITH (1803-1864) Robert Smith Surtees is best known for his creation of the popular sporting Cockney grocer and fox-hunter, Jorrocks. This character's appearance in the novels Jorrocks's *Jaunts and Jollities* (1838), *Handley Cross* (1843), and *Hillingdon Hall* (1845) ensured their success. But Surtees was also a contributor and editor* of a variety of periodicals and his innovative and experimental development of the Jorrocks character within the periodical format* would influence comic journals like *Punch**.

Surtees's journalistic career began in 1829 as a contributor to the *Sporting Magazine**, before taking over the position of hunting correspondent in 1830 when C. J. Apperley* ('Nimrod') withdrew his services. Surtees wrote under the pseudonyms* 'Nim South' and 'a Durham Sportsman'. After being refused a share in the *Sporting Magazine*, Surtees started the *New Sporting Magazine** in conjunction with the art publisher Rudolph Ackermann, and was editor* and chief contributor until 1836. He wrote under numerous pseudonyms*, 'the Yorkshireman', 'Jorrocks', 'Simpkins', 'Nimrod' and 'the Editor'. The majority of his novels were serialised in the *New Sporting Magazine, Bell's Life in London** and the *New Monthly Magazine**. Surtees's later journalism* consisted of articles about London life and mores with biographical details of 'Nimrod'. These articles were featured in *Ainsworth's Magazine**, the *New Monthly Magazine** and *Field**. Surtees was also editor of the *New Anti-Jacobin* (1833).

Surtees's reputation as an innovative journalist* rests on the experiments in form he conceived for the *New Sportsman's Magazine*. Whereas the older periodical (*Sporting Magazine*, afterwards dubbed the *Old Sporting Magazine*) had chronicled real events and personalities* from the sporting* world, Surtees's new venture featured a variety of fictional and comic sporting characters. Uniquely, the 64-page monthly* was practically written by himself until 1836, and Surtees used this freedom to create a more subtle type of humour than would otherwise have been expected from a sporting publication. Jorrocks, who appeared in the third number of the magazine, is used as a type of anti-hero who ironically attacks the other fictional contributors as well as real-life personalities. This use of Jorrocks within the periodical format* greatly influenced Mark Lemon* when he established *Punch*. Surtees's use of multiple voices in dialogue with themselves was perfectly suited to the periodical form and not surprisingly, given the unusual amount of freedom he had on the *New Sportsman*, his subsequent journalism was never able to achieve the same innovative qualities. **PB**

Sources: Cooper 1952, Gregory 2003, Noakes 1952, *ODNB*.

SWAIN, JOSEPH (1820-1909) Joseph Swain was one of the few prominent mid-Victorian wood* engravers not to stray beyond his profession into other aspects of the print trade or to attempt to display his own artistic talents. Nonetheless, he became an influential and respected figure much trusted by the major black and white artists to do justice to their drawings, partly because of his early training in 'facsimile' techniques which aimed to transfer the drawn line directly into the printed image without adding tonality and texture.

Inextricably associated with *Punch** in 1843, after Ebenezer Landells's* fall from favour, Swain was offered the chance to engrave one of John Leech's* cartoons* and the result found such favour that he immediately replaced Landells as the exclusive engraver for the magazine, a post which he held until 1900. Spielmann, writing five years after Swain's retirement from the management of his business (although he continued to engrave images for *Punch* up to 1900), described him as 'one of *Punch's* most faithful, loyal and talented servants'. Pointing out to *Punch* the advantages of an expanded business, Swain developed his firm beyond the six or eight staff fully employed on work for the magazine. His meticulousness and promptness as an engraver and his ability to bring out the best in a drawing, as well as his reluctance to embellish the artist's drawings, ensured that his firm gained and sustained an extremely large amount of business.

Swain worked extensively for the *Cornhill Magazine** as well as *Good Words**, *Once A Week**, the *Argosy**, and, inevitably, the *Illustrated London News**. As a commercially extremely successful firm at a time when engravers were often left free to employ those artists they thought appropriate for the work in hand, Swain had considerable influence in introducing new artists, and there is evidence of the help he gave to young artists like Helen Allingham*. Swain had insisted for

many years that wood blocks offered the only satisfactory ways to reproduce art images, but late in his career he accepted the introduction of photo*-mechanical engraving methods and even invested in them. **BM**

Sources: Engen 1990, Houfe 1978, *ODNB*, Spielmann 1895.

'SWAN, ANNIE' (1859-1943) Writing under the pseudonyms* 'Annie S. Swan' or 'David Lyall', Mrs Burnett Smith was a prolific novelist and journalist*. She wrote over 100 novels, 40 under her male pseudonym*, as well as a good deal of journalism, a feat she attributed to working before breakfast, writing 3,000 words a day and never redrafting.

Though she spent much of her working life in London, she was born in Scotland, was early linked with the Kailyard School and retained a strong sense of her Scottish identity. Winning a short story competition in the *People's Friend** encouraged her to persist with a career as a writer. Her main journalistic venture was the 6d monthly *Woman at Home* (1893-1920)*, launched by her friend Robertson Nicoll* and subtitled *Annie Swan's Magazine*. Here she not only contributed fiction, but wrote two regular columns* of answers to correspondents*. These, particularly 'Over the Tea Cups', made her famous and she claimed thousands of women wrote to her about their problems. Her sympathetic persona made her a pioneer of the women's magazine* 'agony aunt'. **MRB**

Sources: Beetham 2000, Darlow 1925, Nicoll 1945, *ODNB*, *Woman at Home*.

SWINBURNE, ALGERNON CHARLES (1837-1909) Although best known for his poetry*, Algernon Charles Swinburne produced dozens of articles in a broad spectrum of periodicals, most in the *Fortnightly Review**, *Athenaeum** and *Spectator**. A secondary figure in the Pre-Raphaelite movement influenced by his close intellectual and personal connections with D. G. and W. M. Rossetti*, Swinburne advocated aestheticism in literature*, art and culture as in his review* of Baudelaire's *Les Fleurs du Mal* in the *Spectator* (6 Sept. 1862). In this way he paved the way for similar rhetorical studies by aesthetes such as Walter Pater* and Oscar Wilde*. Often he engaged in debates with other nineteenth-century critics such as Robert Buchanan, and cultural institutions such as the Royal Academy.

Swinburne's championing of art as an end in itself challenged the social and political conventions of Victorian culture. He also produced a significant body of work examining Renaissance drama and frequently advocated Republicanism in the political* turmoil in France and Italy, using both poetry and prose to praise leaders in Italian political struggles like Mazzini as well as to memorialize key figures in French aesthetics such as Victor Hugo and Charles Baudelaire. According to his letters, most of his periodical work was undertaken for money. **CLM**

Sources: Lang 1957, Meyers 2004-2005, Rooksby 1997, C19, Welby 1968.

SYMONS, ARTHUR WILLIAM (1865-1945) Journalist*, editor*, poet* and literary theorist, Arthur Symons wrote on literature* and the theatre for popular* newspapers and high culture magazines alike. First published in the *Wesleyan Methodist Magazine** ('Robert Browning as a Religious Poet', Dec. 1882), Symons wrote for over 35 periodicals between 1885-1934 including the *Academy**, *Art Journal**, *Bookman**, *Contemporary Review**, *Critic**, *Dial**, *English Review, Forum, International Quarterly, Journal of Gypsy Folklore, Lamp, Lippincott's, Macmillan's**, *National Review**, *New Review**, *Outlook, Sketch**, *Speaker**, *Westminster Review** and *Vanity Fair**. As 'Silhouette'*, Symons was the music* hall critic for the *Star** in the early 1890s and replaced A. B. Walkley as drama critic in 1900.

His most substantial contributions, including important analyses of literary Decadence, appeared in the *Fortnightly Review**, *Harper's New Monthly Magazine** and the *Saturday Review**. In 1896 Leonard Smithers* appointed Symons editor of the short-lived *Savoy**, to which he also contributed along with Joseph Conrad, Havelock Ellis, Selwyn Image, Max Beerbohm*, W. B. Yeats, Ernest Dowson, Aubrey Beardsley*, James McNeill Whistler* and Will Rothenstein. In 1908 Symons suffered a complete mental breakdown and never fully regained his creative energy and acumen. Nonetheless, Symons's criticism influenced his own generation as well as that of Conrad, Woolf and Eliot. **MA**

Sources: Beckson 1987, BritPer, *Poole's, Wellesley.*

T

TABLET (1840-) The *Tablet* was founded by Frederick Lucas, a recent convert from the Society of Friends to Roman Catholicism. Published weekly*, priced* 6d, the *Tablet* focused on politics* and religion* but included book reviews*, foreign notices and legal news*. In 1842 Lucas fell out with his co-proprietor* John Cox, a Protestant publisher. For a brief period there were two versions of the Catholic weekly*, the *Tablet* (issued by Cox) and the *True Tablet* (issue by Lucas). Although Lucas quickly regained control of the original title and enjoyed considerable support from Catholics at large, he was a controversial editor* whose support for Ireland upset several leading figures. In 1849 he announced that he was moving to Dublin, a move that his brother would later claim brought the *Tablet* to the attention of English newspapers such as *The Times*.

When Lucas died in 1855, he was succeeded as editor by John Wallis, who moved the paper back to England. Wallis enjoyed good relations with Cardinal Nicholas Wiseman* and during his tenure the *Tablet* published a number of papal documents. The closeness of the *Tablet* to Catholic authorities in England and abroad was strengthened when Herbert Vaughan bought it in 1868. Vaughan was heavily involved with editing the paper and he oversaw a shift from a newspaper format* to a serious magazine* or 'Weekly Review'. While Vaughan was committed to freedom of speech, his conservative beliefs increasingly shaped the *Tablet* and the newspaper became a strong supporter of Papal Infallibility. When other commitments curtailed Vaughan's involvement with the *Tablet*, George Elliot Ranken took over, followed, in 1884, by John George Snead-Cox. MK

Source: Walsh 1990.

TAIT, WILLIAM (1793-1864) William Tait was well known both as an Edinburgh-based publisher* and a periodical editor* of radical leanings. Inspired by ideas of utilitarianism and radicalism, William Tait formed close ties with Jeremy Bentham (whose collected works he published), John Bowring* and J. S. Mill*, and launched a periodical that represented the same radical tradition as the *Westminster Review*, of which he was the sole distributor* in Scotland. As a publisher*, Tait favoured Scottish authors such as Thomas Carlyle* and George Gilfillan* and subjects, such as Tytler's

multi-volume *History of Scotland* (1828-1845). *Tait's Edinburgh Magazine* first appeared in April 1832. Its main emphasis was on politics, economics, legislation and jurisprudence rather than fiction, literary essays and poetry* which constituted the main offering of the other monthly magazines*. Its political convictions are particularly well exemplified in an article in its first issue called 'The Revolution', which recommended the founding of elementary schools in every district, the disestablishment of the Church, *laissez-faire* principles in trade and the repeal of the Corn Laws. Its 'Monthly Register' contained reflections on leading events in art, literature*, politics and trade.

Tait's relationship to the magazine changed in 1834, when it absorbed *Johnstone's Edinburgh Magazine*, giving Christian Johnstone* half the property of the magazine. While Johnstone made the editorial decisions, Tait corresponded with authors, solicited new writers and managed the business, resulting in a transformation of the magazine to a predominantly literary publication. Contributors included Catherine Gore, Mary Russell Mitford, John Galt, Harriet Martineau*, Leigh Hunt*, J. S. Mill* and Thomas de Quincey*. Tait also contributed over 50 articles to his magazine (1832-1843). His main contributions discussed foreign and domestic political topics expressing his radical commitment. His 'State of the Radical Party' (Nov. 1833) argued for the participation of Radicals in government. He also published reviews* of '[Richard] Cobden's *Russia*' (Aug. 1836), of the works of Jeremy Bentham (Sept. 1836), and discussed international politics and the Repeal of the Corn Laws (1843). Tait and Johnstone retired in 1846, selling the magazine to a Glasgow firm managed by George Troup. Surviving until 1861, it was not successful. ZV
Sources: *ODNB, Wellesley.*

TAIT'S EDINBURGH MAGAZINE (1832-1861) *Tait's Edinburgh Magazine* was the project of William Tait*, an Edinburgh bookseller with known radical sympathies. Its first number (31 March 1832), published a month before the passage of the Great Reform Bill, announced that the magazine* was to be 'the fearless and uncompromising advocate' of reform, and its object, 'the good of the PEOPLE'. Although the prospectus did not state it, *Tait's* was also determined to rival *Blackwood's* as an Edinburgh-based magazine*. Articles advocating tax and legal reforms, the removal of duties on newspapers and foreign books, and the abolition of tithes were interspersed with short fiction by Catherine Gore and Harriet Martineau* and articles by Leigh Hunt*. The first number concluded with a 'Monthly Register', which became a regular feature, and included current events, commercial news* and short reviews* of new publications. The reviews of poetry*, fiction and biography were written by Christian Isobel Johnstone*, who later became the magazine's editor* and co-proprietor*.

Contributors to early numbers included J. S. Mill*, Thomas Perronet Thompson, John Bowring* and J. A. Roebuck, all with impeccable radical connections, and known to Tait through his role as the distributor of the *Westminster Review** in Scotland. Tait wrote many of the early political articles himself. Scottish contributors included Thomas Dick Lauder and John Galt, and in 1833, Thomas De Quincey*, who remained a contributor until 1851. Circulation* was estimated at 4,000 per month, nearly three-quarters in England. The magazine claimed to outsell *Blackwood's* in Scotland. Its price* of 2s for 130 pages was standard for monthly magazines* aimed at a middle-class* audience. In 1834, two years after its launch, the price dropped to 1s, making *Tait's* the first of the shilling* monthlies* that were to dominate the periodical market* from the late 1850s.

Under the 12-year editorship of Christian Johnstone*, which began in 1834, the magazine's focus moved from politics* to that of a more general literary* magazine. Writers like R. H. Horne*, John Hill Burton, Willliam Howitt* and George Gilfillan* contributed during this period. Theodore Martin and W. E. Aytoun collaborated on a number of articles, often under the signature 'Bon Gaultier'. Johnstone wrote over 400 articles during her editorship, an estimated 20 per cent of the review, most of them on literary topics. She encouraged the work of women contributors, among them Mary Russell Mitford, Amelia Opie, Eliza Meteyard* and Hannah Lawrance*. Johnstone's editorship is regarded by many as the highpoint of the magazine's history. She and Tait, who had continued to oversee the production of the journal, retired together in 1846.

The magazine was purchased by George Troup*, one of Tait's staff, and its headquarters moved to Glasgow. A period of English ownership (1850-1855) saw a return to the standards achieved by Tait and Johnstone, although the magazine could no longer claim to be either a Scottish or an Edinburgh publication. In 1855 Troup resumed the editorship, and later the proprietorship*. The magazine once again moved to Glasgow, and reflected Troup's allegiance to the Free Church of Scotland. Its core Scottish readership*, however, drifted away,

as its English readers had done before them, and it folded. JS

Sources: Bertram 1893, Shattock 2007, *Wellesley.*

TALLIS'S DRAMATIC MAGAZINE AND GENERAL THEATRICAL AND MUSICAL REVIEW (1850-1853) *Tallis's Dramatic Magazine* was a theatrical monthly founded in mid-century by the publisher* John Tallis. The first issue announced the journal's intention to defend modern drama against its detractors, as well as voicing a firm belief in the advent of a 'new era of the stage'. It was not, however, concerned with speculative literary criticism or philosophizing about the future of the drama, but ranged itself firmly on the side of the average theatregoer. It typically printed biographies of popular actors like John Kemble Phelps and William Charles Macready, as well as notices of current productions, with occasional comments on such issues as dramatic censorship*. The journal ran for a total of 34 issues and underwent two title* changes, first to *Tallis's Drawing Room Table Book of Theatrical Portraits, Memoirs and Anecdotes* in 1851, and one year later to *Tallis's Shakespeare Gallery*, which remained the title until the final issue. OD

Sources: Vann 1994, *Waterloo.*

TATLER (1830-1832) The *Tatler, A Daily Journal of Literature and the Stage* was one of the many journals writer, essayist and dramatic critic James Leigh Hunt* edited*. It superseded his *Chat of the Week* (1830) and was launched as a daily journal, containing mostly playbills, criticisms on literature* and performances* and poetry*. Until June 1831, its publisher* was J. Onwhyn, who was succeeded by Robert Seton. Although Hunt was acquainted with young poets like Shelley and Byron and although he initiated most projects with his brother John Hunt*, like the successful *Examiner**, the *Tatler* was written and edited solely by him. Hunt declared the journal was 'a companion to daily newspapers' and it even had the appearance of a newspaper, consisting of four folio pages. Its motto read 'veritas et varietas'. Hunt wanted the *Tatler* to be a political* and literary weapon, but its public scope did not reach much further than the theatregoing public. The paper mainly served a practical purpose and was sold at theatre doors, such as those of the Drury Lane theatre.

Hunt's editorship of the *Tatler*, of which he said 'it almost killed him', ended with number 452 (13 Feb. 1832). The paper went into decline, indicated by numerous changes in frequency* (from daily* to thrice weekly), format* (quarto) and price* (from 2d to 1d and finally 3d). Variations in the subtitle show that the paper was broadening its contents and tried to reach a wider audience, but subscribers were hard to find and the *Tatler* kept struggling. The *Tatler* evolved into *Leigh Hunt's London Journal** and *Leigh Hunt's Journal**. JoS

Sources: Houtchens 1949, Hunt 1948, *ODNB*, Stratman 1962, *Waterloo*.

TAXES ON KNOWLEDGE See Newspaper taxes.

TAYLER, JOHN JAMES A Unitarian minister, theologian, and professor of ecclesiastical history at the Unitarian Manchester College before becoming its principal, John James Tayler's literary involvement spanned an impressive catalogue of theological, philosophical and literary works of which his contributions to several quarterly* reviews and editing* the *Prospective Review**, formed a vital component of his ecumenical vision.

Tayler was one of a group of four liberal Unitarian ministers, joint founders and editors* of the *Prospective Review**, close friends as well as editorial colleagues; the group comprised James Martineau*, a fellow tutor at Manchester College when it was still in Manchester, John H. Thom*, Charles Wicksteed and Tayler. Along with his colleagues, Tayler had contributed to the *Prospective Review*'s forerunner, the *Christian Teacher**. Yet the *Prospective Review* was not used as a narrow vehicle for delivering the strictures of a determined creed, but as a liberating platform investigating the complexities that humanism and Romanticism interpolated into faith, involving history, philosophy and reflections on foreign ideas and institutions. Tayler remained an editor* for the life of the journal (1845-1855), and his anonymous* articles treated politics ('Socialist and communist theories', July 1848), reviews* of non fiction and fiction ('Miss Martineau's* *Eastern Life*', Nov. 1848 and Gaskell's *Mary Barton*, Feb. 1849) as well as theology ('The harmony of the intuitional and logical elements in the ultimate grounds of religious belief, Nov. 1851). However, as Tayler's duties as the principal of Manchester College in London from September 1853 increased, so his output and participation in managing the *Prospective Review* diminished.

While Tayler had made weighty contributions to the *Prospective Review*, he also published important pieces in the *Prospective Review*'s successor, the *National Review** (1855-1864), including 'The mutual relation of history and religion' (April 1857) and 'The church and theology of Germany during the nineteenth century' (Jan. 1864). By spring 1863, Tayler was again involved in discussions about the establishment of a new periodical to succeed the

*Christian Reformer**. Although this time Tayler was not actually an editor, he was part of the board determining editorial policy for the new *Theological Review**. Using the pseudonym* 'T.', 'J.J.' or 'T.' for submissions (1864-1869), Tayler wrote reviews*, philosophy, theological analysis and articles such as the 'Narrative of a visit to the Unitarian churches in Transylvania' (Jan. 1869). CL

Sources: *ODNB*, *Wellesley*.

TAYLOR, RICHARD (1781-1858) A member of the well-connected Presbyterian-Unitarian dynasty of Norwich Taylors, Taylor was apprenticed to the London printer Jonas Davis in 1797. Davis's printing portfolio included the Linnaean Society's *Transactions* (1787-) and the *Philosophical Magazine** edited* by Alexander Tilloch*. Despite his natural bent towards antiquarianism, Taylor was drawn to scientific* printing and publishing when he acquired Davis's business in 1802. A man of striking business acumen, Taylor's firm rapidly acquired a reputation for printing and publishing scientific periodicals and textbooks. He played a major role in supporting the mechanization of printing from 1809 onwards. Following Tilloch's death in 1825, Taylor became proprietor*, printer, publisher* and co-editor* of the *Philosophical Magazine*, which he nurtured into a major organ of scientific communication. He did the same for biological studies with the *Annals of Natural History**, which he also co-edited. Together with his natural son William Francis*, Taylor sponsored translations of significant papers by continental scientists* through the seven volumes of *(Taylor's) Scientific Memoirs* (1837-1852). In 1852 he took Francis into partnership. As Taylor & Francis from 1858, the business held a virtual monopoly of printing learned society journals for much of the nineteenth century. **WB**

Sources: Brock and Meadows 1998, Lightman 2004a, *ODNB*.

TAYLOR, TOM (1817-1880) Tom Taylor was a polymath critic, equally adept in art criticism, drama and humour, and an emerging professional critic with a university education; he also did more general journalism work, such as leader* writing and editing. Taylor took his degrees at Trinity College, Cambridge, where he became a fellow in 1842. His first professional position was a professorship in English literature and language at London University (1845-1847); he was called to the bar in 1846; and in 1850 he was appointed assistant secretary of the Board of Health at Whitehall, subsequently becoming secretary of the Sanitary

Department. Concurrently, he was a leader writer for the *Morning Chronicle** and *Daily News** and also contributed articles on diverse topics to *Tait's Edinburgh Magazine** (1851-1853) and other journals. From 1857 until his death, he was 'in effect the art critic of *The Times* although the official history of that paper notes that 'his position was never regularized' (439). His art criticism also appeared in specialist journals, including the *Graphic** and the short-lived *Fine Arts Quarterly Review*. His journalism helped to consolidate the notion of a 'British School' of art, but his lasting significance in art may be his role as witness on behalf of John Ruskin* in the trial of James McNeill Whistler* v. Ruskin in 1878. His criticism was the subject of Whistler's ire in *The Gentle Art of Making Enemies* (1890), Whistler's riposte to critics.

Taylor's penchant for humour fuelled his long-standing association with *Punch**. He contributed comical poems* and columns* from 1844 until his death, and a series on the misadventures of the 'unprotected female'* (1849-1851). He became editor* (1874-1880), though his editorship attracts scant praise from historians of *Punch*. **ALH**
Sources: Altick 1997, *History of the Times* 1939, Merrill 1992, Price 1957, West 1990.

TEDDY ASHTON'S JOURNAL/NORTHERN WEEKLY (1896-1908) Costing just ½d, *Teddy Ashton's Journal* was the most successful venture of the socialist* journalist Charles Allen Clarke*. The weekly* periodical was published in Bolton by the Tillotson* family, who had given Clarke his first post on the *Bolton Evening News* (1868). Though Clarke blamed the failure of his previous periodical the *Labour Light* on his working-class* readers' preference for entertainment over political* education, he was determined to make the new paper a success. The bias towards serializations*, short stories, poetry* and dialect literature* at the expense of political commentary ensured a circulation* averaging 30,000 per week, and the yearly Christmas* annual* continued publication until 1940 – five years after Clarke's death.

Clarke's famous 'Bill Spriggs' series of comedy dialect sketches formed part of the regular content along with other dialect characters such as 'Georgie Greensauce' and 'Patsy Filligan'. Alongside Clarke, the periodical published work by other northern socialists such as Fred Plant, James Haslem and George S. Band. The paper took advertising* but Clarke stated from the beginning that he would only carry adverts for ethical and socialist manufacturers. There were several title* changes: *Teddy Ash-*

ton's Journal (1896-1899); *Northern Weekly and Teddy Ashton's Journal* (Jan.-May 1899); *Teddy Ashton's Northern Weekly* (1899-1908). **DM**
Sources, *DLB*, Frow 1971-1972, Mutch 2005.

TEGETMEIER, WILLIAM BERNHARDT (1816-1912) After failing to find a career in medicine, Tegetmeier combined teaching domestic economy with journalism, writing on natural history, and especially on pigeon fancying, for the *Poultry Chronicle* and the *Cottage Gardener*. In the mid-1850s Tegetmeier began corresponding with Charles Darwin, at whose behest he placed enquiries in the *Cottage Gardener* requesting information from readers* on different aspects of the breeding of birds. Tegetmeier also published in more specialist scientific* periodicals, and his 1859 article on the construction of bee's cells in the *Entomological Society Transactions* formed the basis of Darwin's treatment of the subject in the *Origin of Species* later that year. However, journalism remained considerably more remunerative than science* for Tegetmeier, and, again in 1859, he began contributing extensively to the *Field**, soon becoming its poultry editor* and maintaining his connection with the journal until 1909.

Old Teg, as he was known, also wrote for numerous other periodicals such as the *Intellectual Observer*, to which he contributed a monthly 'Proceedings of Learned Societies' section, and even the satirical journal *Fun**, becoming a celebrated eccentric and bohemian in metropolitan* journalistic circles. In the 1870s Darwin noted Tegetmeier's miscellaneous 'never-ending, always beginning editorial cares', among which were his general editorship* of *Ibis*, the journal of the British Ornithologists' Union, and his position, from 1882, as chief leader* writer for the women's newspaper the *Queen**, where he maintained a resolutely anti-feminist line. **GD**
Sources: Barton 1998b, Lightman 2004a, *ODNB*, Secord 1981.

TELEGRAPH While experimental electric telegraphs date from the early 1800s, their practical application for railway signalling and the transmission of text messages arose from the inventions of William F. Cooke and Charles Wheatstone in Britain in the late 1830s and from the concurrent development in America, by Samuel Morse, of a coding system which represented letters of the alphabet via electrical impulses. In August 1844, a telegraph link between Windsor and London was used to announce the birth of Queen Victoria's second son, prompting *The Times**, which was first to publish the news*, to declare itself 'indebted to the extraordinary power of the Electro-Magnetic Tele-graph'.

Britain's telegraph networks were initially built by private companies, as was the first international submarine cable, between Dover and Calais, which opened in November 1851. From the late 1840s these telegraph companies provided news services to Britain's provincial* newspapers, thus combining the roles of carrier and content provider. By 1854, more than 120 subscribing papers were receiving regular political*, financial* and sporting* news* in this way. However, these arrangements, which involved the telegraph companies employing their own reporters* and editors and excluding other news traffic, were increasingly resented by the larger provincial papers which supported moves in the 1860s to nationalize the telegraph. Britain's domestic telegraph network system was in fact nationalized with the Post Office taking over its operation in 1870. This brought the separation of the roles of news gathering and news transmission desired by the newspapers. Henceforth, the Press Association*, a provincial press co-operative formed in 1865, provided telegraphic news services to papers outside London. For its part, the Post Office encouraged the circulation* of telegraphic news throughout Britain as a matter of national interest by setting a favourable press tariff, particularly for identical messages sent to multiple destinations.

Press traffic expanded enormously from 32 million words weekly in 1871 to some 110 million words weekly in the early 1900s. Low domestic press rates subsidized the massive press expansion of these decades while also leading to large financial losses for the Post Office. While Britain's domestic telegraphs were nationalized, international cables remained in private hands, with British companies playing the dominant role in their development.

After unsuccessful attempts in the late 1850s, a telegraph connection between Europe and America was established in 1866, while Australia was connected to Britain via India in 1872. The international telegraph network enabled speedy collection of news from around the globe and its sale to multiple newspaper subscribers by international news agencies* such as Reuters*, which, although established in 1865, had its origin in London from 1851 in Reuter's private Submarine Telegraph Co., which by the late 1850s regularly supplied both the London and provincial press. The telegraph played a role in the reporting of the Crimean War* (1854-1856), though the Franco-Prussian War of 1870 was the first major conflict whose progress was rou-tinely and extensively reported from the seat of battle by telegraph. From its earliest days the telegraph was regarded as a powerful mechanism which, it was said, 'annihilated space and time'. As well as transforming news timeliness and distribution*, it had a profound impact on news style, encouraging brevity and factual reporting. PP

Sources: Brown 1985, Kieve 1973, Read 1999.

TEMPERANCE ADVOCATES During the second quarter of the nineteenth century there was a proliferation of magazines* and journals dedicated to the promotion of temperance and total abstinence principles. Numerous titles professed to be advocates for the cause, but many, such as the three issues of the *North of England Temperance Advocate and Register* (1832), and the *Total Abstainer and Liverpool Temperance Advocate* (1840), were parochial, dull and short lived. Of the 63 titles issued between 1831 and 1850, 39 per cent failed within the first year of publication and 71 per cent within five years (*Waterloo*).

However, two journals originally established and edited* by Joseph Livesey* stand out as being of particular significance: the *Preston Temperance Advocate* (1834-1837), later the *British Temperance Advocate and Journal* (1839-1841), and the *National Temperance Advocate and Herald* (1843-1850), which was finally issued as the *British Temperance Advocate* (1850-1949), the official journal of the British Temperance League. Initially the *Preston Temperance Advocate* was issued weekly* priced* 1 ½d and the early editions were illustrated*. By 1840 it had become a 1d monthly* with a circulation* of around 10,000 copies per month, minus illustrations. The staple matter consisted of temperance intelligence, the effects of intemperance, varieties, notices and editorials.

Until the 1860s most temperance publications were issued by secular bodies with a few, like the *Alliance* (1854-1905), adopting an overtly political* stance on temperance issues. The Anglican Church was largely opposed to the temperance movement on ideological grounds, but, through the efforts of evangelical reformers, it began to adopt a more proactive stance. The *Church of England Temperance Magazine* (1862-1872), later the *Church of England Temperance Chronicle* (1873-1888), finally the *Temperance Chronicle* (1888-1914), as the official organ of the Church of England Temperance Society was primarily designed to convert Anglican clergy to abstinence. Originally issued monthly, it was issued weekly* from 1878 and grew into one of the four major late Victorian temperance periodicals.

Although women were interested in temperance issues from the beginning of the movement, the number of mixed groups was limited. This changed radically with the foundation of the British Women's Temperance Association in 1876, which had 570 branches and a reputed 50,000 members by 1892. The Women's Association published its own journal, *Wings* (1892-1910). But the Association divided in 1893 over the inclusion of the suffrage campaign onto its agenda, and the new Women's Total Abstinence Union kept *Wings* as its publication while the British Association started a new paper in 1896 called the *White Ribbon*. There was a separate group in Wales, Undeb Dirwestol Merched Gogledd Cymru (North Wales Women's Temperance Union), with two papers dealing with temperance matters. The paper started by Sarah Jane Rees*, *Y Frythones* (the *British Woman*) (1879), included relevant articles from its inception and *Y Gymraes* (the *Welshwoman*) (1896), edited by Alice Gray Jones*, was more rooted in the temperance cause. FM/CL

Sources: Gordon and Doughan 2001, Harrison 1969, Harrison 1994, Lloyd-Morgan 1991, Olsen 1973, *Waterloo*.

TEMPERANCE MAGAZINES   In 1860-1861, William Tweedie, a temperance publisher*, reported that there were more than 13 large temperance associations in the UK, producing three weekly* newspapers with a combined subscription of over 25,000, six monthly* papers with over 20,000 subscribers, two quarterly* reviews with over 10,000, magazines with over 10,000 subscribers and two papers for young subscribers, the Scottish *Advisor* (50,000) and the *Band of Hope Review** (circulation* of over 250,000). The latter was an illustrated* ½d monthly, begun in 1851 and published by the Band of Hope Union. The *Review* targeted England's lower classes*, emphasizing self-help and encouraging poor children to find work. Its motto was 'It is better to work than to beg'. The *Band of Hope Review** became the Union's paper and was distributed* in the South of England. In 1865 it found a counterpart in *Onward**, a magazine circulated in the North of England. *Onward** was published by the Manchester-based Lancashire and Cheshire Band of Hope Union. A third paper, the *Temperance Lighthouse*, began in 1870, published by the Yorkshire Band of Hope Union, but it was not as successful as the other two. The *Band of Hope Review** spawned many imitators and encouraged temperance workers to write temperance novels for adolescents. Two journals written mostly for adult

women had a particularly wide circulation: *Wings; The Official Organ of the Women's Total Abstinence Union* and *White Ribbon: The Journal of the National British Women's Total Abstinence Union*.

Getting churches to support temperance was extremely difficult. Despite its resistance, the Church of England put out the *Church of England Temperance Magazine* in 1862, later renaming it the *Church of England Temperance Chronicle* (1873-1914). Subscribers increased when the queen became the patron of the Church of England Temperance Society in 1875. Although the *British Temperance Advocate** boasted that there were four million teetotallers in the UK in 1841, shoemakers alone served 187,943 drinks in 1841 and licences to sell alcohol increased 15 per cent from 1841 to 1851. For all their newspapers and magazines, teetotallers had little hope of bringing about national prohibition and the main result of their attempts to promote temperance was the formation of an alternate culture where people could refrain from drinking without social recrimination. BA

Sources: Bordin 1981, Harrison 1971, Longmate 1968, Shiman 1988.

TEMPLE BAR (1860-1906)   *Temple Bar: A London Magazine for Town and Country Readers*, a shilling* monthly* published by Ward and Lock* and aimed at the same middle-class* readership* that had made *Cornhill** so successful, was one of John Maxwell's* stable of periodicals. Its editor* George Augustus Sala* promised 'a domestic romance'*, a 'fair review'* of a popular book, social, biographical*, philosophical* and travel essays, but no politics. Its bright purple cover was dominated by an illustration* of Christopher Wren's gateway, the Temple Bar, and the title page carried the spurious quotation: 'Sir' said Dr Johnson 'Let us take a walk down Fleet Street*'. Against the fashion for illustrating* magazines of light literature*, it was decided to include additional letterpress instead of etchings and woodcuts*. With rare exceptions, this policy prevailed throughout the life of the magazine. Both the title and the format* – two serialized* novels interspersed with a variety of essays and poetry* – directly imitated *Cornhill*, although *Temple Bar* did not have illustrations and would never attain anything like the same circulation* figures as its rival. In its heyday, 1860-1863, *Temple Bar* regularly commanded 30,000 readers.

Maxwell remained *Temple Bar*'s proprietor* until 1866. Apart from installing Sala as its editor* he appointed Edmund Yates* as subeditor*. Yates would perform most of the editorial duties due to

Sala's many work commitments. Sala and Yates brought with them the bohemian journalists they had been working with for the past decade: writers like Blanchard Jerrold*, Mortimer Collins, Charles Kenney, W. S. Austin and Robert Buchanan. The December 1860 edition of *Temple Bar* featured a respectable, anonymous* serialized novel of domestic realism, 'For Better, For Worse', and articles praising Giuseppe Garibaldi and philanthropy, and criticizing the French press. But as the magazine progressed, the more bohemian and radical side of the contributors came to the fore. Sala serialized his novel attacking bourgeois obsession with capitalist greed, 'The Seven Sons of Mammon', and Yates wrote articles exposing the conditions in workhouses and of the homeless. Buchanan wrote poetry* detailing child death in the metropolis. *Temple Bar* was also one of the first shilling* monthlies to include women writers on its staff. Notable among early writers were Eliza Lynn Linton*, who contributed from 1860 to1898, and Mary Braddon*, who began serializing* 'Aurora Floyd' in January 1862; three other novels followed. Sensational fiction, short stories and essays became a staple of *Temple Bar* in the Sala and Yates years. In November 1863 Yates took over full editorial duties while Sala travelled to America to cover the Civil War for the *Daily Telegraph**. Sala returned in 1864 to commence his popular 'Streets of the World' series. During Sala's editorship and that of Yates's contributions were usually unsigned or pseudonymous*.

While the distinct *Temple Bar* flavour of early issues, with articles about the press, 'London poems'* and Sala's series on tours of Middlesex, faded over time, and the subtitle reference to London was dropped in 1899, the core mixture of fiction, chatty topographical, and biographical essays, interspersed with serious discussions of current social issues such as canteens for the poor, survived.

In 1866 *Temple Bar* was bought by the publishing* firm of Richard Bentley* & Son, and in 1868 it incorporated *Bentley's Miscellany**. George Bentley took over as editor when Yates assumed the same office for *Tinsley's Magazine**. Bentley would stay in the role for nearly 30 years, and introduced a more conservative and less sensational element to the magazine. Among novelists published during Bentley's reign (1867-1895) were Wilkie Collins* ('The New Magdalen'), Ellen Wood*, Rhoda Broughton, Jessie Fothergill and Annie Edwardes (notably 'A Girton Girl'). Non-fiction writers included Walter Besant* and Emily Eden ('Letters from India').

The magazine* carried advertisements*. In March 1875, for instance, there were seven numbered pages of the 'Temple Bar Advertiser' at the front as well as advertisements on the inside cover and unnumbered pages at the back. Judged by circulation* figures, the journal was successful, initially reaching about 30,000, stabilizing about 13,000 in 1868, though by 1896, when Richard Bentley succeeded on his father's death, sales had fallen to 8,000. Despite attracting contributors like George Gissing and Arthur Conan Doyle, the paper was sold to Maurice Macmillan* in 1898, and edited by Gertrude Townshend Mayer. **PB/BMO**

Sources: Blake 2006, DeBaun 1955, Gettmann 1960, Sullivan, *Wellesley*.

TENNIEL, JOHN (1820-1914) John Tenniel's outstanding contribution to periodical literature was his 50-year association with *Punch* as an illustrator*. A precocious young painter, Tenniel had already met two of the artists, Charles Keene* and John Leech* who, together with himself and Doyle*, formed *Punch's* front rank of cartoonists* in the nineteenth century, before he joined the magazine's* staff in 1850. Tenniel had met Keene while studying life drawing in London in the mid-1840s, and he shared special constable duties with Leech in the political turmoils of 1848. Doyle's acrimonious split with *Punch* in 1850 allowed Tenniel to join the staff as a jobbing artist, but in 1861 he became junior partner to Leech, employed on the considerable annual salary of £500. On Leech's death in 1864, Tenniel became *Punch's* senior staff artist, and produced a staggering output of work for the magazine, nearly all of it engraved by Joseph Swain*, until Tenniel finally retired at an advanced age in 1901.

Tenniel's work combined a knowledge of, and respect for, classical painting together with his encyclopaedic visual memory. He developed a speciality in comic versions of history, and showed a particular relish for savage accounts of the Irish. He was given to claiming that only five weekly* numbers of *Punch* lacked some of his work over the 50 years he had been a contributor, and he certainly drew over 2,000 full-page cartoons for the magazine. Apart from his work for *Punch,* Tenniel made few illustrations for other periodicals, although he was a prolific book illustrator. *Once a Week** used a number of his images, and a few illustrations appeared in *Good Words**, and the *Illustrated London News**, but it was his considerable contribution to *Punch* that gave him his reputation as one of the most important comic artists of the century. **BM**

Sources: Engen 1990, Houfe 1978, *ODNB*, Simpson 1994, Spielmann 1895.

TEXTILE RECORDER; A MONTHLY JOURNAL OF THE TEXTILE INDUSTRIES (1883-1967); TEXTILE MONTH (1968-) The long-running monthly*, the *Textile Recorder* supplied its readers* with crucial information on the textile industry. Topics covered typically in this trade* journal ranged from technological advances to various social developments, with issues of 24 pages supplemented by advertising*. The first number, for example, contained articles on the decline of cotton spinning in Glasgow, as well as reports on political events relevant to the industry. In its nineteenth-century incarnation, the *Textile Recorder*** was edited by Joseph Nasmith, the author of various publications on modern cotton spinning and engineering. Incorporated into the *Textile Month* in 1968, it is still in print. Over the years, the journal always retained its focus on the comprehensive coverage of all aspects of international textile manufacturing. **OD**

Source: *Waterloo.*

THACKERAY, WILLIAM MAKEPEACE (1811-1863) With the origins of his career rooted in early journalistic struggles, Thackeray came to inhabit the world of Victorian periodicals in the fullest imaginable way as an illustrator*, a prolific contributor of both comic and serious journalism, an author of hugely popular fiction serialized* in a variety of magazines* and as the editor* of a major monthly* journal. His output was prodigious – Spielmann's 100-year-old account of Thackeray's *Punch*** contributions based on the magazine's daybooks lists several hundred pieces, many of them illustrated by the author. In the mid-1840s Thackeray was producing over 40 articles a year for this one magazine alone.

As a young man with an inheritance Thackeray was drawn early to the opportunities offered by the periodical press, buying the *National Standard* newspaper in 1833, and largely writing it himself. The venture failed in 1834, at a moment when Thackeray had lost his financial base, and he thus launched himself on an uncertain literary career without security. He worked for the progressive newspaper the *Constitutional* from 1836 after a spell as correspondent for the *Paris Literary Gazette* in 1835, where he contributed in a variety of genres and began to evolve his writing towards narrative, especially through the use of the first of many literary* personae, 'Augustus Wagstaff' to sign his contributions. A foreign correspondent*, Philip Firman, was to form the central character of Thackeray's later novel 'The Adventures of Philip' which was serialized* in the *Cornhill Magazine*'* in 1861. Under a second pseudonym*, 'Michael Angelo

Titmarsh', Thackeray began exploring the relatively undeveloped field of art reviews* for *Fraser's Magazine* in 1838, and this magazine and *Punch* became the major outlets for his work over the next decade. Some of his articles and sketches were reorganized for publication as *The Paris Sketch-Book* (1840). While much of Thackeray's major fiction was published in monthly serial parts, a number of his works were serialized in magazines – 'The Newcomes' (1853-1855) and 'The Virginians' (1857-1859) in *Harper's Magazine*, and 'Lovel the Widower' (1860), 'The Adventures of Philip' (1861) and 'Denis Duval' (1864) in the *Cornhill Magazine* (1864).

In late 1859 Thackeray's publisher* George Smith* had asked his author to edit a prestigious new monthly, the *Cornhill Magazine*, and Thackeray, who had since 1852 been free of any association with periodicals and published very little journalism, held the editorship until March 1862. The *Cornhill*, with its starry list of contributors, gave Thackeray a place to publicize his own work, and became one of the most significant monthlies of the mid-Victorian period. As well as fiction Thackeray contributed the 'Roundabout Papers' (1860-1863), and he remained a contributor to the magazine up to his death in 1863, even after he had resigned the editorship after a series of disagreements with his publisher. Thackeray's writing career offers one of the most complex and interesting examples of the ways in which Victorian freelance writers engaged with the periodical press in sustaining their careers in a highly competitive* environment. **BM**

Sources: Buchanan-Brown 1979, *ODNB*, Pearson 2000, Spielmann 1899.

THEATRE. A MONTHLY REVIEW OF THE DRAMA, MUSIC AND THE FINE ARTS (1880-1897) *Theatre* was launched in its most durable form in 1880 as *Theatre: A Monthly Review of the Drama, Music and the Fine Arts* (published* by Charles Dickens & F.M. Evans*). From 1880-1897 four editors* directed the journal: Clement Scott*, Bernard E. J. Capes (1889-1890), Charles Eglington (with Capes, 1891-1892; on his own, 1893), and Addison Bright (1894-1897). Of these four, Scott was by far the most influential. He combined his editorship for *Theatre* with a position as drama critic for the *Daily Telegraph*, which gave him 'immense power' in London journalism. His work for the *Telegraph* and *Theatre* 'gave theatrical journalism a stability it had never previously achieved'.

In December 1882, after six volumes, Scott announced a relaunch of *Theatre*: 'The January number for 1883 will be my fourth anniversary as an editor, and I propose to start what is virtually a new series.' He set out to change the journal's style, publisher (now David Bogue), printer and management. Of the new series 30 volumes were published (Jan. 1883-Dec. 1897). These provide a valuable overview of late nineteenth-century English drama. The January 1896 issue opened with: 'The year 1895 will not be marked as an annus mirabilis in the history of the English stage. It has seen the production of a number of plays of average merit, acted with average talent' and commented on the failure of Henry James's* *Guy Domville* and 'the sudden and shameful interruption' of Oscar Wilde's* career. Mainly due to Scott's guidance, *Theatre* became an authoritative medium in theatrical journalism. Scott was a reactionary critic, who responded violently to Henrik Ibsen's realist drama in articles such as 'Why do we go to the play?' (March 1888).

Compared to its contemporaries *Era** and *London Entr'acte and Limelight**, *Theatre* is said to have given 'the most consistent, if conservative, evaluation of issues'. The journal also contributed to the coming of age of professional dramatists by giving them as much exposure as actors. UW

Sources: *CBEL*, Jenkins 1991, Roswell 1956, Sullivan.

THEATRICAL INQUISITOR (1812-1820)   As even one of its editors* admitted, the *Theatrical Inquisitor* had a 'chequered existence' ('Preface', vol. 15). Frequent changes of editor*, title* and focus indicate a journal that often lost its way.

The *Theatrical Inquisitor, or Literary Mirror* debuted in September 1812 under the proprietorship* of 'Cerberus' (actor and printer William Oxberry). He dropped out after the first month, and several changes of editorship followed, from 'H' (vol. 4) to 'GS' (vols 5-6) to 'J' (vol. 8); internal evidence suggests a single editor for volumes 10-13 and 15-16 and the one volume of the new series (July-Nov. 1820). Shifts of focus were frequent too. In addition to its *raison d'être*, a 'Theatrical Inquisitions' section reviewing* performers and productions, the journal published contributions on various theatrical issues. After 'Cerberus' departed, a new focus on topics of general interest provided 'entertainment with instruction' for 'scholar' and 'lounger' alike ('Preface', vol. 2). At this point the journal's content depended heavily on readers*, and this new direction seems designed to accommodate 'miscellaneous communications' from 'several valuable correspondents'. But another shift of focus soon followed – towards a 'miscellany'* of dramatic and literary* criticism and biography, to inform the

man of letters and 'purify the taste of the student' ('Preface', vol. 3) – and this and subsequent editors also rejected submissions, on grounds of politics as well as taste. In short, the *Theatrical Inquisitor* displays a tension between openness to correspondents' interests and efforts to shape the periodical's identity.

A similar tension emerges in the journal's relation to the theatre. Each issue opened with a short, celebratory biography of a player and an engraving of her or him in costume; the journal's true opinions of performers, however, are to be found in the 'Theatrical Inquisitions' section ('Address to the Reader', vol. 5). Several later 'Prefaces' defend against charges of 'unjustifiable severity' (vol. 12) and reiterate the journal's duty to provide 'manly and impartial criticism' (vol. 16). By the final volume the defiant tone has disappeared, as have the engravings – due to financial difficulties, a further sign of the journal's unresolved conflicts.

Like the editors, many of the writers remain unidentified. While a few signed their contributions (M. G. Lewis, Andrew Becket, Andrew More), others used pseudonyms* and many used initials ('ENB' and 'EH' were frequent correspondents). Women's contributions were sometimes identified by name (Mrs [Elizabeth] Hamilton's tale), sometimes not ([Anna Barbauld's] 'Washing Day'). One editor policed correspondents to spare 'the delicacy of our female readers' (Sept. 1814), and others actively encouraged women contributors. One such, M[argaret] H[arries], went on to edit several fashion* periodicals during the 1830s and 1840s under her married name of Mrs Cornwall Baron Wilson*.

For students of women's writing then, the *Theatrical Inquisitor* may yield information about women's contributions to nineteenth-century journalism. For students of theatre, of course, the notices of London and regional theatres contribute to performance history, while the engravings of players form an invaluable record of staging and costuming practices. JMS

Sources: Onslow 2000, *Waterloo*.

THEATRICAL JOURNAL (1839-1873)   The main emphasis of this weekly* stage periodical was on amateur dramatic clubs and performances, and it is therefore not surprising that the presence of Shakespeare loomed large in its pages. In fact, each issue was headed pictorially by a bust of the Bard, accompanied by some of his most popular creations. *Theatrical Journal* also published reviews* of professional performances (often reprinted from other sources), and ran series on topics such as

'Early Dramatists' and 'Popular Actresses'. Its long-time proprietor*, editor* and chief contributor was William Bestow, who wrote under the pen name 'Beta', and also published his own dramatic blank verse in the journal. He was later assisted by Benjamin William Watkins, who serialized* his biography of Bestow in the journal's pages in 1862-1863.

Like many of its competitors*, *Theatrical Journal* aimed to counteract the widely perceived decline in standards of quality and – no less importantly – decency on the British stage, campaigning actively against 'filth and double-entendre, semi-nudity, and the like' (14 July 1869). Watkins's early death in 1871 and Bestow's increasing ill-health were probably the main causes behind the journal's closure. **OD**

Sources: Vann and VanArsdel 1994, *Waterloo*.

THEATRICAL TIMES (1846-1851) This wide-ranging illustrated* weekly* theatre periodical promised, in its first issue (13 June 1846), to provide 'fair and impartial notice of everything connected with the stage'. Its breadth of coverage is evident from the attention the journal paid to provincial* and continental theatre. In addition to original articles, it contained familiar gossip* and correspondence* columns. It also featured so-called Thespian biography, as well as portraits of contemporary actors. *Theatrical Times* was priced* at 1d and contained illustrations*. **OD**

Sources: Vann and VanArsdel 1994, *Waterloo*.

THEATRICAL 'WORLD' (1893-1897) *Theatrical 'World'* comprises a series of five annual* hardcover volumes, each of which reprints William Archer's reviews* for the *World** for the year in question. Introductions to each volume were provided by noted playwrights such as Sidney Grundy, Arthur Wing Pinero and George Bernard Shaw*. In addition, each volume from 1894 onwards contained a synopsis of the year's playbills, compiled by Henry George Hibbert. **OD**

Sources: Vann and VanArsdel 1994, *Waterloo*.

THEOLOGICAL REVIEW (1864-1879) Liberal-minded, earnest and scholarly, the *Theological Review* (published four to six times a year) was conceived as a discursive mouthpiece for the most up-to-date and diverse Unitarian thinking. The *Review*'s Prospectus, which preceded the first issue in March 1864, championed the 'freest of discussion of controverted topics in theology'*, provided that such debate was 'at once scientific in its method and reverent in its tone'. Two main problems resulted. The first of these arose from the relentlessly progressive and open-minded policy of the journal's

editor* the Rev. Charles Beard; he encountered strident opposition from conservative Unitarians, suspicious of any system of religious thinking based on a 'scientific approach'. Unitarian traditionalists like Samuel Bache focused on such issues as maintaining the supernatural character of Christ and the acceptance of biblical miracles as a test of faith.

The *Review*'s second predicament concerned its aims and ethos in an increasingly secularizing and heterogeneous marketplace. The first issue of the journal, priced* at 2s, contained just four very lengthy essays, each ranging from 24 to 36 pages, because Beard had professed himself not keen on 'frittering away strength and interest on short articles'. Yet such extended disquisitions, no matter how learned and reverent, could only ever find a limited interest and while Beard adjusted this initial style, by the early 1870s he was quietly predicting 'a slow death' for the journal. **LL**

Sources: McLachlan 1934, *Waterloo*, *Wellesley*.

THEORY AND JOURNALISM (1900-PRESENT) In the USA the First Amendment to the Constitution and, in the UK, the concept of a press free from state interference as embedded in John Stuart Mill's* *On Liberty* (1859) dominated debates. The stress on the right of the citizen, in this case acting as a journalist, to publish without fear of state-initiated suppression or punishment was central to this view.

The practice of journalism in the press and broadcasting, including public service broadcasting was theorised in relation to the importance of impartiality, accuracy and objectivity as legitimising standards for journalism. Considerable thought was also expended on developing theories about how culture, organisational practice, economics and workplace routines influenced journalism and also on the applicability of Western models of press freedom to non-Western societies.

Jürgen Habermas's concept of the public sphere, a set of institutions, including the media, accessible to all citizens, in which rational debate about matters of public concern took place, added a theoretical norm against which journalism could be assessed. Robert Darnton's concept of the circuit of communications in which journalism is one part of the flow of information in society, complemented Habermas's by stimulating analysis of the production and circulation of information.

In the late twentieth century the revival of liberal economic thought influenced government's attitude to media markets*, and encouraged a greater degree of support for a view that the marketplace in ideas, unencumbered by state – supported public service media, was the best guarantor of journalistic freedom. Critics of this view, including Edwin C. Baker and James Curran, argued that market pressures in fact inhibited independent critical journalism. It is, however, notable that theories about journalism at the start of the twenty-first century remain dominated by thinking about the press articulated in the eighteenth and nineteenth centuries. TPO

Sources: Baker 2002, Curran 2000, Curran 2002, Dahlgren and Sparks 1991, Darnton 2007, Habermas 1990, Harvey 2007, O'Malley and Soley 2000.

THOM, ALEXANDER (?1801-1879) Like the publisher* James McGlashan*, Alexander Thom was a Scot who set up business as a printer/publisher in Dublin in the early nineteenth century. His father Walter was proprietor* from 1817 of the venerable *Dublin Journal* newspaper (1725-), originally published by George Faulkner, the famous eighteenth-century Dublin publisher, and Alexander helped run the paper until his father's death in 1824. Thom was subsequently granted a contract for printing for the Post Office and then for the Irish Railway Commission in 1838 – the first time an Irish printing firm had been awarded such a privilege.

Thom was one of the few serious competitors* of the Dublin University Press from the 1830s on. He is most well known for *Thom's Irish Almanac and Official Directory*, published from 1844. In 1878 his conduct during a Dublin printer's strike (he was sending work to be finished in Scotland) led to questions being asked about the crisis in the House of Commons. ET

Sources: Hancock 1879-1880, Kinane 1994, Madden 1867.

THOM, JOHN HAMILTON (1808-1894) As well as being a Unitarian minister and advocate of liberal Unitarian theology, John Thom was a periodical editor* and reviewer*. Thom was an associate of James Martineau* and J. J. Tayler* and Thom's most significant contribution to Victorian journalism was his editorship of the leading liberal Unitarian review, the *Christian Teacher* from 1838 to 1844. After its demise, Thom became one of the co-editors of its successor the *Prospective Review*. Thom was partly responsible for the 'Prefatory Notes' published in the first issue, defining the shift in the periodical's profile from a proselytizing purpose towards a catholicity of interests. He contributed many articles to the *Prospective Review* (1845-1854), primarily reviewing theological subjects including Charles Hennell's *An Inquiry Concerning the Origin of Christianity* (Feb. 1845) and *The Life and Writings of Dr Chalmers* (Nov. 1850; July 1852). He also reviewed literature from the theological viewpoint as manifested in his review of Kingsley's social problem novel *Yeast* (Nov. 1851).

From 1864 onwards, Thom actively contributed to the *Theological Review** which carried on the theological interest of the *Prospective*. He wrote primarily on religious subjects including Tayler's *Retrospect of the Religious Life of England* (1876) but also published a literary* review of Arnold's *Literature and Dogma* (July 1873). ZV

Sources: *ODNB, Wellesley.*

THOMAS, WILLIAM LUSON (1830-1900) Yet another example of the wood* engraver turned entrepreneur, William Luson Thomas is principally celebrated for his role as the founder and publisher* of the *Graphic**, which from its first publication in 1869 combined reportage* with a rapidly developing tradition of naturalistic image making which was hugely influential on the visual culture of late nineteenth-century Europe. With his brother George Thomas, William had early experience of running newspapers in America before setting up business in London as a wood engraver. In the 1850s he worked largely with W. J. Linton* in preparing blocks for publication by the *Illustrated London News** often from drawings by his brother. He also engraved extensively for books and the periodical press throughout the 1860s and 1870s.

Working with Linton on the reproduction of art images for the *Illustrated London News* caused Thomas to think through the possibility of a periodical which drew much of its energy from contemporary painting, a vision that found form in the *Graphic*. The *Graphic*'s great and consistent achievement was to reconsider and then exploit the relationship between fine art painting (and indeed all available visual media) and the topical interests of the weekly* press, especially in finding ways of bringing the realism of oil painting into mass circulation* graphic form. Against common practice, he commissioned his team of artists directly rather than asking his engravers to supply images, and put together an assembly of high stature contributors, including Pinwell*, Herkomer*, Allingham* and Fildes*, who contributed his famous social realist image of 'Houseless and Hungry' in response to an invitation from Thomas to draw whatever he wanted. In 1890 Thomas went on to establish the *Daily Graphic** as the first London-based illustrated* daily* newspaper. BM

Sources: Engen 1990, Houfe 1978.

THOMPSON, HENRY YATES (1838-1928)
Thompson was proprietor* of the *Pall Mall Gazette**. Its previous owner, publisher* George Smith*, made the paper over to Thompson in 1880, two years after Thompson married Smith's daughter Elizabeth. Thompson is largely remembered for those editors* he employed: John Morley*, W. T. Stead* and E. T. Cook*. Under Thompson's proprietorship the paper supported Gladstone's government, while its tone reflected the crusading zeal of Stead and his reporters. However, Thompson regretted the scandal attached to Stead's 'Maiden Tribute' campaign in 1885 with the ensuing drop in circulation*, and Stead was forced to resign in 1889. In 1892 Thompson sold the newspaper to William Waldorf Astor, under whose stewardship it supported the Conservatives. ET
Sources: Clarke 2004, Griffiths 2006, *ODNB*.

THOMSON, DAVID COUPER (1861-1954) A Scottish shipping manager turned newspaper proprietor*, Thomson took control of a handful of mass-market* newspapers in the 1880s and in the early twentieth century built them into a regional and national corporation publishing more than 20 titles. Born in Dundee to shipowner William Thomson, he joined his father's business in 1877, and then was apprenticed to a marine engineer in Glasgow before becoming his father's partner in 1884. In 1886 he became manager of W. and D. C. Thomson, operating the *Dundee Courier and Argus** and *Weekly News* (1855-), newspapers his father had acquired.

Thomson expanded his offices to Manchester and Glasgow early in the twentieth century, starting the Glasgow *Sunday Post* (1915) and a boy's paper* the *Adventure* (1920), and acquiring other properties. His firm's local importance is reflected in the 'three Js' traditionally used to describe Dundee: 'jute, jam and journalism'. Politically conservative, Thomson was a strong opponent of trades unions, especially with respect to his own papers, and a political* antagonist of Winston Churchill when Churchill was member of Parliament for Dundee.

In the twentieth century Thomson controlled popular Scottish* newspapers and periodicals including the *Dundee Courier**, *Evening Telegraph and Post* (1877-), *Weekly Welcome* (1896-1917), *Wizard of the North* (1879-1916), and the *Sunday Post*, and became nationally known for children's comics including *Oor Wullie* and *The Beano*. He was deputy lieutenant for the city of Dundee for 54 years, and a governor of the university college for 62 years. Contemporary reputation portrayed him as aloof and au-

tocratic but fair to his workers. DHL/CL
Sources: *Chambers*, *ODNB*, *The Times* 7 April 1892, *Waterloo*, *WWW.*

THOMSON, DAVID CROAL (1855-1930) David Croal Thomson, best known as an art dealer, was also an important art editor*. After early training in commercial art in his native Edinburgh, Thomson moved to London in 1880 to work as subeditor* of the *Year's Art*, a subsidiary of the *Art Journal**. In 1881, he was appointed subeditor* of the *Art Journal*, a position he held until 1888. In 1885 he also became London branch manager of Goupil Maison, owned by a Paris-based print publisher and commercial gallery.

He succeeded Marcus Huish as editor* of the *Art Journal* (1893-1902) and brought new critics, including Frederick Wedmore, to the journal. His taste as an art dealer overlapped strongly with that as editor; he promoted the work of the French Barbizon school and English modernists, particularly James McNeill Whistler*, George Clausen and Philip Wilson Steer. At the end of 1897, he left Goupil for Thomas Agnew's & Sons; in 1908 he became partner in the French Gallery, remaining until he opened his own firm Barbizon House in 1918, which he operated until his death.

Thomson also contributed to specialist art journals including the *Magazine of Art**, *Scotsman** and the *Studio**. Many of these articles were expanded into books as with the *Barbizon School of Painters* (1890, 1902) and *Corot* (1892). ALH
Sources: Helmreich 2005, Houfe 1984, Thomson Papers, *The Times* 1930, Weil 1975.

THOMSON, HUGH (1860-1920) Hugh Thomson was an immensely popular book illustrator* of the late nineteenth and early twentieth century who quickly learnt to exploit the new colour printing techniques made available by photomechanical line block printing. He was enduringly associated with the illustration of eighteenth century literature and social life, themes that he drew in a nostalgically precise and courteous manner. His popularity was established by his work for the *English Illustrated Magazine** to which he contributed 1883-1892. His series of drawings for 'Days with Sir Roger de Coverley' became the template for much of his later work. Thomson did not demonstrate great awareness of the more experimental and ambitious artists who also worked for the magazine, preferring to sustain his own version of eighteenth-century taste through many commissions for illustrated books. BM
Sources: Engen 1990, Houfe 1978, *ODNB*.

THOMSON, THOMAS (1773-1852) Until 1818, when he was appointed Regius Professor of chemistry at the University of Glasgow, Thomson earned his living as a writer, editor* and private teacher. In 1796, while a medical student in Edinburgh, he was made scientific* editor for the third edition of the *Encyclopaedia Britannica,* to which he contributed a long entry on chemistry that became the basis of his highly successful textbook *System of Chemistry* (1802; six editions).

In 1813, aware that William Nicholson's* *Journal of Natural Philosophy** was ailing (it was amalgamated with the *Philosophical Magazine** in 1814), Thomson and the London printer and publisher* Robert Baldwin launched the lively monthly *Annals of Philosophy* (1813-1826). Although primarily a vehicle for research on the new chemical atomic theory, it also carried detailed annual surveys of the progress of all the sciences. In Glasgow, Thomson's editorial standards dropped and in 1826 Baldwin sold *Annals* to Alexander Tilloch*, who amalgamated it with the *Philosophical Magazine.* In 1835, together with his nephew Robert Dundas Thomson (1810-1864), Thomson edited the monthly* *Records of Science* (1835-1836) using it as a vehicle for research in inorganic chemistry when interest was primarily directed at organic chemistry. The journal was unprofitable and Thomson spent the remainder of his career fighting the cause of Scottish university reform. **WB**

Sources: *DSB*, Lightman 2004a, Morrell 1972, *ODNB*.

THOMSON, WILLIAM (1824-1907) Strenuously schooled in science* in Glasgow, William Thomson, Baron Kelvin, published his first paper in the *Cambridge Mathematical Journal* even before entering Cambridge as an undergraduate in 1841. Within four years he had become editor* of the *Journal,* which endeavoured to modernize Cambridge mathematical practice by keeping readers abreast of the very latest developments detailed in foreign scientific periodicals. Thomson sought to turn it into a publication of national importance, adopting the more expansive title the *Cambridge and Dublin Mathematical Journal,* and encouraging leading professional mathematicians to contribute their original researches to its pages. The majority of these contributions, however, were on pure mathematical subjects and Thomson became exasperated by his inability to steer the *Journal* more towards his own interests in physical mathematics, relinquishing the editorship in 1852.

Thomson adhered to the Whig ideal of the diffu-

sion of knowledge, but only seldom ventured into the general press. Nevertheless, a brief article in the *Philosophical Magazine** in 1852 first brought the ideas of the conservation and dissipation of energy to public attention, while a co-written piece for the pious *Good Words** in 1862 spelt out the theological implications of the new energy physics. Later in the same year, Thomson's influential article for *Macmillan's Magazine**, 'On the Age of the Sun's Heat', dramatically curtailed the timescale available for the operations of Darwinian evolution. In 1871 a further commission from Norman Macleod* to write on compasses for *Good Words* led Thomson to make a number of important improvements to maritime navigational instruments. **GD**

Sources: Lightman 2004a, *ODNB*, Smith and Wise 1989.

THURSFIELD, JAMES RICHARD (1840-1923) Forced to resign from an Oxford fellowship after marrying in 1881, Thursfield moved to London and began a career in journalism when he was offered a staff position as a leader* writer on *The Times** by the editor* Thomas Chenery. Thursfield's articles were infused with the breadth of his knowledge as well as a profound sense of integrity which led him to refuse to write supportively on issues with which he disagreed. When he was assigned coverage of the annual naval manoeuvres in 1887, his interest in naval history operated in tandem with his exceptional abilities as a journalist and he was made *The Times*'s naval correspondent in the same year. Writing on political* as well as naval matters resulted in his often being consulted by the Admiralty. *The Times*'s 'Books of the Week' section became his domain from 1891 until it developed, at the instigation of Charles Frederic Moberly Bell, into the *Times Literary Supplement* in 1902.

Thursfield served as the *Times Literary Supplement*'s first editor until 1905, and also contributed regularly. Although Lord Northcliffe* commissioned Thursfield to write a history of *The Times,* he discarded his attempt after three years. Thursfield also sporadically wrote for the *Athenaeum**. His wife Emily, however, frequently reviewed* children's literature and light fiction for the weekly*. **CL**

Sources: Demoor 2000, May 2001, *ODNB*.

TILLOCH, ALEXANDER (1759-1825) Dr Alexander Tilloch was an inventor and publisher* whose interests ranged from mechanical sciences to biblical prophecy. Like William Nicholson*, Tilloch (born Tulloch) seized upon the career opportunities offered by Britain's first wave of industrialization. After matriculating at the University of Glasgow,

Tilloch worked as a printer and bookseller in the city, using his spare time to devise improvements to heavy machinery. Working with Andrew Foulis, he 'reinvented' the process of stereotyping*, later learning they had improved upon a process first promulgated by William Ged in 1725. In 1790, he devised a means of printing banknotes that would render forgery virtually impossible. In 1797 he moved to London where he became part owner and served as editor* of the daily *Star*, an evening newspaper. He raised the paper's profile by publishing anonymous*, controversial verses that Londoners knew were contributed by Robert Burns, then near the peak of his fame. Under the pseudonym* 'Biblicus', Tilloch also contributed a series of articles to the *Star* exploring the Book of Revelation.

In 1798, having joined several improvement societies such as the Askesian Society, where original papers were read, he began a monthly journal where they could be printed. The *Philosophical Magazine**, which by 1802 was printed by Richard Taylor*, was in direct competition with William Nicholson's *Journal of Natural Philosophy, Chemistry, and the Arts* (1797-1813) and Thomas Thomson's* *Annals of Philosophy* (1813-1826). It aimed, in the spirit of the Scottish Enlightenment, to diffuse scientific knowledge among all nations and all classes* of society. Editor, as well as proprietor*, Tilloch capitalized on the public's interest in popular science* and stocked the magazine with accounts of scientific lectures and news* of the latest discoveries and inventions. Eventually, Tilloch bought out Nicholson and combined the two ventures into the *Philosophical Magazine and Journal*, remaining sole owner until 1822.

By that time, when Taylor became a co-editor, the *Philosophical Magazine* had become the primary vehicle for the rapid dissemination of new scientific work. In 1824, sensing new markets in the Mechanics' Institutes movement, Tilloch edited the weekly double-columned* *Mechanic's Oracle* (1824-1825) but died before it could be adequately developed, leaving the market open for Joseph Robertson's rival weekly* *Mechanics' Magazine**.

While Tilloch's printing innovations advanced the art, his astute understanding of the demand for popular science* and his determination to make science accessible to the common reader* has had far greater effect. His *Philosophical Magazine* paved the way for the scientific periodicals of today. **WB/JNW**
Sources: Brock and Meadows 1998, *DSB*, *Gentleman's Magazine* 1825, Hamblyn 2002, Lightman 2004a, *ODNB*.

TILLOTSON, WILLIAM FREDERIC (1844-1889) Despite his early death, William Tillotson's reputation and fortune was made by devising the pioneering Tillotson's Newspaper Literature Syndicate. This piece of commercial inspiration secured his position as a newspaper proprietor* and publisher*, put his home town of Bolton, Lancashire on the publishing map and impacted on newspaper history.

Tillotson had received a business education, with evident benefits, before being apprenticed at his father John's printing works. With his father's help, he founded the *Bolton Evening News* in 1867, edited* by William Brimelow and the first daily* evening ½d paper to be published outside London. He followed this in 1871 with the *Bolton Journal**. Tillotson went on to launch the Lancashire Journal series in the early 1870s with the *Eccles and Patricroft Journal*, the *Farnworth Journal and Observer*, the *Leigh Journal*, the *Swinton and Pendlebury Journal* and the *Tyldesley Journal*.

The inspiration for his Newspaper Literature Syndicate was twofold; commercially he intended it to increase sales of his newspapers and he wanted to provide good fiction to a mass* market*. Tillotson began what developed into an international fiction distribution network in 1873 with the expedient of engaging Mary Elizabeth Braddon* to write 'Taken at the Flood' which he serialized* in his own and other people's papers. He then sold the stereotyped* serial novel plates together with a 'London letter' and a 'Woman's page' to UK regional daily* and weekly* papers. But Tillotson's vision spread further as sales became international, embracing America, Australia and other British colonies and in translation to German and French newspapers. In this way the work of Arnold Bennett*, Walter Besant*, Thomas Hardy*, 'Ouida*' and many others went worldwide as did Tillotson's Syndicate idea which became a model for others in many countries. **CL**
Sources: *ODNB*, Law, 2000.

TIMBS, JOHN (1801-1875) Timbs was a significant editor* and prolific author whose writing covers an extremely wide variety of subjects. His first work was produced following the completion of his apprenticeship, a collection of papers entitled 'A Picturesque Promenade around Dorking', published in 1820 in the *Monthly Magazine**. Timbs was a central figure in mass*-market periodicals, in which much of his work was published. Beginning as amanuensis to Sir Richard Phillips, editor* of the *Monthly Magazine**, Timbs himself edited several periodicals including the *Mirror of Literature**

Figure 61: Eagerly reading *The Times* in Benjamin Haydon's painting 'Waiting for *The Times*' (*A Newspaper History* 1935: 10).

(1827-1838), the *Harlequin* (1829) and the *Literary World* (1839-1840). He also spent a significant period as subeditor* of the *Illustrated London News** (1842-1858), and was originator and editor of the *Year-Book of Science and Art* which began in 1839.

Non-fiction came to typify Timbs's writing, which extends to over 150 volumes (pseudonyms include 'Harold Foote' and 'Horace Welby'). His best-known work includes publications on contemporary city life, notably *Curiosities of London* (1855) and *Club Life of London with Anecdotes* (1865), which provide 'valuable illustrations of the social manners and morality of various periods' (*Spectator** 1870: 670). He also published widely on areas of artistic, cultural, domestic, historical* and scientific* interest, and edited several books, including *Pepys's Memoirs* (1871). Despite this success, however, like many authors of his time he gained little financial reward for his efforts, and died destitute. **AW**
Sources: Allibone 1859, *ODNB*, *Spectator*, Ward 1883.

THE TIMES (1785-) *The Times* was founded by John Walter I as the *Daily Universal Register* on 1 January 1785, initially comprising parliamentary* reports, foreign news* and advertisements*. Published daily* from Printing House Square in Blackfriars, the name was changed to *The Times* on 1 January 1788 with the expansion of its coverage. By 1800, when its price* was 6d, it had a circulation* of nearly 5,000. John Walter II*, who became principal proprietor* in 1803, appointed Thomas Barnes* as editor* in 1817. Barnes, who remained editor until 1841, has been described as the person who 'created the nineteenth-century English news-

paper'. Barnes developed the paper as a radical force in the context of the liberalizing reforms of the early part of the century. Positioning itself as the champion of middle-class* opinion and 'thundering for reform', *The Times* supported under his editorship Catholic emancipation and parliamentary reform. In 1832, Sir Robert Peel described the paper as 'the great, the principal and most powerful advocate of Reform', in Britain. Much of its success during this period can be attributed to the establishment of its own speedy methods of obtaining news*, particularly foreign* news*, largely organized by Thomas Massa Alsager*, which, together with its ability to access the inner sanctums of government while remaining largely independent, became a major distinguishing feature of the paper. Alsager also acted as City correspondent, and established the paper as a force in financial circles. By Barnes's death in 1841, the circulation* had reached 28,000.

Barnes was succeeded as editor by John Thaddeus Delane*, who was appointed at the age of 24. Under Delane, the paper continued to exert a considerable radical influence and, in particular, campaigned for the repeal of the Corn Laws. Delane and his principal leader* writers Henry Reeve* and Robert Lowe moved in influential political circles but continued to maintain the papers independence from government. Barnes and Delane between them presided over the paper during the major European conflicts which dominated the nineteenth century. They employed a succession of highly influential foreign* correspondents including Henry Crabb Robinson, William Howard Russell*, whose reporting* of the Crimean War is legendary, Thomas Chenery and Henri de Blowitz. By 1855, when its price was 5d, its circulation had reached a peak of 60,000. Thomas Chenery, formerly a foreign* correspondent, was appointed editor in 1878 and was succeeded by George Buckle in 1884, under whose editorship the paper became increasingly conservative and 'Empire'* orientated. The paper remained in the ownership of the Walter family throughout the nineteenth century, and continued to be printed by them. John Walter II introduced new Koenig and Bauer steam-driven printing* presses in 1814. In 1866, new 'Walter' presses were introduced which speeded the production process by enabling both sides of the page to be printed at the same time from a continuous roll.

Financially weakened by the costs of its defence in the publication of the forged Parnell letters, it also suffered a decline in circulation in the last part of the century when it was under pressure from the

Figure 62: An illustration showing the small steam engine used to drive one of the Applegath and Cowper presses at *The Times* in 1814 (*A Newspaper History,* 1935: 138).

new press emerging in the wake of the repeal of stamp tax on newspapers. Despite the reduction in the cover price to 3d in 1861 which continued until 1913, it continued to lose ground and by 1904 the circulation had declined to 32,000. All this was exacerbated by divisions within the younger generation of the Walter family, and *The Times* passed into the control of Lord Northcliffe (A. C. Harmsworth*) in 1908. **JRW**
Sources: *History of The Times* 1935/1939/1947, *ODNB*, Monopolies Commission 1966, Woods and Bishop 1983.

***TIMES OF INDIA* (1838-)** The colonial newspaper, the *Times of India*, was established in 1838 as the bi-weekly *Bombay Times and Journal of Commerce,* edited* by J. E. Brennan. Its front page consisted of advertisements*, a common practice at the time, which endured until 1939. In 1846 George Buist became editor*, and in 1850 it became a daily*. After merging* with the *Bombay Telegraph and Courier* in 1861, the newly christened *Times of India* began publishing as a broadsheet of 4 pages under a new editor, Robert Knight.

Alongside local* and international news*, the paper included in the 1860s a commercial section with lists of colonial share prices and dividends, and a small section of telegraphic* news provided data on exchange rates and securities from further afield, as well as reporting the safe landing of steamships.

Another section reported the movements and activities of military units and garrisons. Detailed statistics on mortality rates – broken down according to race, caste and location – were provided in the form of charts. The paper also included excerpts from the English press, although it depended on these being delivered by steamer* so they were substantially delayed: the issue of 1 January 1869, for example, carried excerpts from the English press up to 8 December 1868. Parliamentary reports* appearing on 4 January 1869 were similarly out of synch, providing coverage of debates that took place on 10 and 11 December of the previous year. Advertisers* included merchants touting wines, beers and spirits, landlords with accommodation to let and steamers offering to transport goods and passengers between the colonies, providing lists of dates and times of departure from India's various ports.

In 1879 the *Times of India* reported on the assumption by Queen Victoria of the Imperial Crown of India, welcoming the development despite concerns that the Indians were not as yet sufficiently enamoured with their Imperial masters. A leader* put it this way: 'no Empire, and least of all an Empire of foreign conquerers, is secure, unless it can win the affection and cordial cooperation of its subjects. On this day, however, instead of dwelling on the causes and the symptoms of this defect [the failure of the Empire fully to win over the populace], we prefer to look on the brighter augeries: and to believe that the new relations into which England this day enters with India will increase the feeling of union among all classes of Her Majesty's subjects'. The *Times of India* was a newspaper that strongly supported the Empire*, then, but it was one that also saw the wellbeing of its subjects as a barometer of its health.

A weekly* edition was launched in 1880, and by 1885 the daily edition had expanded to eight pages. The newspaper was bought by the editor Henry Curwen, with Charles Kane, in 1890, but following Curwen's death in 1892, the new editor and owner, T. J. Bennett*, went into partnership with F. M. Coleman to form Bennett, Coleman & Co. Ltd. The establishment of a more modern system of journalism* is attributable to Stanley Reed (editor 1907-1923).

In its efforts to bind together imperialism and journalism* more closely, the British government tried to collaborate to a greater degree with the Anglo-Indian press. By 1900, more news* was exchanged between Fleet Street* and the colonial press*, especially the Anglo-Indian press, with a cheaper and more efficient telegraph system (which began in earnest with its nationalisation in 1870) enabling this exchange to happen much more quickly. However, the *Times of India* was unusual in its sympathies for 'Indian political aspirations' (Kaul: 102). The title remained in British ownership until 1946, when Bennett Coleman sold the *Times of India* to Seth Ramakrishna Dalmia, a leading Indian industrialist, on the eve of Indian independence. The newspaper continues to this day. SR/ChK/MaT

Sources: Hirschmann 2004, Kaul 2003, Televisionpoint online, *Times of India* 1861, 1869, 1885.

TIMPERLEY, CHARLES HENRY (1794-1861) Charles Timperley, a printer and writer born in Manchester, began his career with an apprenticeship to an engraver and copperplate printer. In 1810, he enlisted in the 33rd Regiment of Foot and suffered a leg wound at the Battle of Waterloo. He then became a letterpress printer in 1821, indentured to Messrs Dicey & Smithson, proprietors* of the *Northampton Mercury*.

When his indenture ceased, he moved from job to job, eventually becoming foreman to T. Kirk, printer of the *Nottingham Mercury*. In 1830, while working for Kirk, he started a monthly* magazine* called the *Nottingham* (or *Nottinghamshire*) *Wreath*. Around this time, he left Nottingham for London where he published books concerned with printing.

Timperley produced the unique *Songs of the Press* (1833), the only collection of printers' songs in English, later publishing the *Printer's Manual* (1838) and *A Dictionary of Printers* (1839). Unfortunately, he became indebted to an unscrupulous publisher* and to pay his debts he disposed of his stock to a crooked auctioneer who ran off with the proceeds. 'Broken-hearted by misfortune', he accepted a post with the publishers Fisher & Jackson, where he became an editor*, dying while in their service. DHL

Sources: Bigmore and Wyman 1886, Curwen 1873, *ODNB*, Timperley 1839.

***TINSLEY'S MAGAZINE* (1867-1892)** This illustrated* monthly*, 'conducted' by Edmund Yates*, and published* by the Tinsley Brothers on the Strand, was launched into a competitive* monthly magazine* market* in 1867. The prospectus noted 'our aim will be essentially amusement, though topics of current interest will occasionally be treated by competent writers'. It was true to its word, with serial* fiction (the bedrock of all monthly magazines at the time), articles about Paris fashions, yachting and the 'male flirt' put alongside more heavyweight discussions of Irish Fenianism and the Woman Question, making it more willing to take on controversial topics than some of its competitors. Contributors to *Tinsley's* included Thomas Hardy*, Frances Power Cobbe*, Sheridan Le Fanu, G. A. Sala* and Ellen Wood*. MWT

Source: *Waterloo*.

TIPSTERS The predictions of horse racing tipsters began to appear in periodicals after the birth of the penny* press in the late 1850s. In their columns*, these prophets described and analyzed the racing action and betting movements at race meetings throughout Britain. Tipsters offered their predictions for probable winners by evaluating an array of information concerning horses, jockeys, trainers and course conditions. These experts' proximity and connections to the racing world enabled them to provide the information or insight that might win their readers a bet. Betters consulted racing prophets for a variety of reasons: some might not have had time to study form to make their own selections, while others used tipsters to reinforce their own choices.

Henry M. Feist, who later wrote the 'Augur' column* and edited* the *Sporting Life** until his death in 1874, appears to have been the first regular tipster in a daily* newspaper, writing the 'Hotspur' column for the *Daily Telegraph** in the late 1850s. At the *Sportsman**, 'Vigilant's Note Book' provided the tips and one of its numerous authors was John

Corlett*. In 1871, Edward Hulton* began publishing* and editing a Manchester paper, the *Prophetic Bell* which later became the *Sporting Chronicle**, in which he also handicapped races as the prophet 'Kettledrum'.

By the late 1880s, morning and evening papers seeking a mass* audience recognized that reliable racing news, especially predictions from a tipster, heralded a rise in circulation*. Even while the anti-gambling movement criticized the publication of racing news in the 1890s, turf intelligence remained the foundation of sporting news. Many of the prominent tipster columns established by daily newspapers during the nineteenth century, including 'Hotspur' and 'Robin Goodfellow' of the *Daily Mail**, remain features in the twenty-first century. **MJM**
Sources: Bissell 1899, Cox 1892, Griffiths 1992, McKibbin 1990, Watson 1904.

TIT-BITS (1881-1984) The weekly* 1d paper *Tit-Bits* was part of the sensationalist aspect of 'new journalism**'. It was launched by George Newnes*, who claimed to have formulated the idea of providing brief eye-catching stories when reading a piece about 'A Runaway Train' in the *Manchester Evening News*. Aimed at the reading needs of the upper working and lower middle classes whose literacy levels had significantly increased during the second half of the century, it found its niche in the market* very soon and quickly reached a circulation* of 500,000 which it managed to retain. Its main characteristics were the concentration on drama, the publication of shorter, disconnected news* items, and also the startling mode of advertising*, prize contests and insurance schemes.

From its inception *Tit-Bits* was denounced as the offspring of the commodification of literature, and as an indication of the degree to which high Victorian journalism* was giving way to cheap mass* culture. However, it also served the need for self-improvement by printing excerpts from canonical authors including Grant Allen* who in 1891 won a prize of £1,000 for his novel 'What's Bred in the Bone', which was serialized* in the magazine*. 'Titbits' from prominent literary* authors were also included, and readers were offered the payment of one guinea for finding a suitable quotation from writers that would best illustrate the title of any recent article from the magazine.

Departing from traditional journalism, which normally offered a standardised product largely written by permanent staff and editors*, *Tit-Bits* represented participatory journalism with readers and editors* exchanging queries, with Newnes often answering readers' letters*. Questions ranged from the historical to the whimsical, from 'Which archbishop killed a man?' to 'Do birds teach each other to sing?' The combination of 'reader-generated' content, lucrative competitions and insurance schemes kept the sales high, developed a loyal readership and created a strong bond among its readers. The title alone remains in *Titbits International*, after *Tit-Bits* was incorporated into *Weekend* in 1984. **ZV**
Sources: Altick 1957, Jackson 2001, *ODNB*, *Waterloo*.

TITBITS The term 'titbit' refers to a genre* often used in the popular press of late nineteenth-century journalism*. Titbits themselves were snippets of information, short stories, pieces of advice, jokes, correspondence*, which, in the company of prize contests and insurance schemes, secured the commercial success of cheap weeklies*. The genre started in 1881, when George Newnes* had an inspiration when reading an article on 'A Runaway Train' in the *Manchester Evening News*, which generated the launch of his 16-quarto-page 1d weekly*, under the title *Tit-Bits**, which also gave the name to the genre.

The formula thus established was so successful that *Tit-Bits* soon found its niche in the market* and reached an average circulation* of 500,000 copies a week. Its main readership* consisted of the members of the lower middle and upper working classes*. The genre was characterised by two-inch long articles, plus short pieces carefully converted for publication by the process of editorial synthesis. Eye-catching headlines and the skilful application of the new technology of picture reproduction belonged to the innovative nature of the titbit type of periodical. Illustrations* were amply used, but sexual innuendo was carefully avoided in the nineteenth century. *Tit-Bits* established a formula that was soon imitated by other magazines. Alfred Harmsworth*, who published *Answers to Correspondents**, first followed the formula described in its title, but soon converted to the *Tit-Bits* formula resulting in the paper reaching net weekly sales of a million copies in the early 1890s. The third editor adopting the new genre was Cyril Pearson*, formerly business manager to George Newnes, who started his own *Pearson's Weekly** in 1890 which soon reached the publication of 250,000 copies. In this way, Newnes, Harmsworth and Pearson revolutionised popular journalism*. **ZV**
Sources: Beetham 1996, Jackson 2001, *ODNB*, *Waterloo*.

TITLE CHANGES Title changes are endemic within the world of nineteenth-century journalism. Variations within a given journal, such as changes of editor*, publisher* or principal contributors, and changes in the wider society to which a journal targets itself, such as class* movement, increased wealth and the development of popular sciences*, frequently lead to changes in title. The dominance of *Chambers's Edinburgh Journal** within the cheap*, popular weekly* miscellanies* who avoided Stamp Duty by not including news*, was facilitated in no small part by changes in title. In 1854 it became 'less Scottish'* and removed 'Edinburgh' from its title, in order to appeal more to an English market. In addition, though being closely associated with the working class initially, *Chambers's* rebranded itself in order to appeal to the more affluent and educated middle classes, adding a pricier* monthly* edition entitled *Chambers's Journal of Popular Literature, Science and Arts*.

The *Leader* and *Athenaeum** both made frequent changes of title, under various editors*, in their attempts to reflect changing editorial preoccupations and to win new readership* groups. From its wide subtitle, *A Political and Literary Review, Mercantile Journal and Record of Joint Stock Companies, Banks, Railways, Mines, Shipping, etc.*, the *Leader* changed under Charles Nuttal's editorship in 1860 to become the *Leader and Saturday Analyst: A Review and Record of Political, Artistic and Social Events*. Alfred Whitty changed the title variously to *A Journal of Politics, Literature, Art*, the *Leader of Fashion, Literature, Art* and the *Leader of Literature, Theology, Art* before T. R. Threlfall's radical changes in political* specificity of the *Leader: For Social, Political, and Industrial Advancement of the Masses* and eventually the *Leader and Workers' Advocate*. After several minor subtitle changes, the *Athenaeum* became the *Athenaeum and Literary Chronicle* under J. S. Buckingham's* editorship, and more specifically the *Athenaeum and London Literary Chronicle* during 1828. Under James Holmes, it spawned almost 20 changes in title, championing its low price the *Penny, Twopenny* and *Fourpenny Athenaeum*, and changes in frequency were also heralded with *Daily, Weekly,* and *Monthly Athenaeum*s, and titles specifying each day of the week bar Monday.

Attempts to widen readership may be discerned in geographical changes of title, such as the *Glasgow Looking Glass** which made a bid for broader appeal by becoming the *Northern Looking Glass*. Title changes can also reflect the consolidation of a journal within a particular niche market, such as the *London, Provincial, and Colonial Press News: A Literary and Business Journal* which eventually

dropped the subtitle as it specialized solely on the press trade. In addition, though keeping the prefatory globe-straddling geographical references, these were gradually reduced in size* on the title page after more succinct titles had established themselves within the industry. **MBT**

Sources: Bell 2005, *Waterloo*.

TOBACCO, A MONTHLY TRADE JOURNAL FOR THE IMPORTER, EXPORTER, MANUFACTURER AND RETAILER OF TOBACCO (1881-1929) Published by E. S. Caton, *Tobacco* was a 4d monthly trade* journal. Unlike *Cigar and Tobacco World**, jokes and humour comprised a small proportion of its contents (though never excluded altogether); like *Tobacco Trade Review**, however, against which it started as a direct rival, *Tobacco* was a predominantly serious publication that sought to dignify the trade though the dissemination of detailed information. *Mitchell's Press Directory** reports it as aimed at dealers and manufacturers (rather than retailers, the target of *Cigar and Tobacco World*). Throughout, *Tobacco* claimed to have international as well as national correspondents, though such reports were initially not as regular as they were to become in the early 1890s. Indeed for its first ten years, substantial use was made of extracts from other publications (e.g. the *Havana Daily News* or the *Daily Telegraph**). There were always reports of relevant police news*, 'business failures and arrangements' – which discursively offered much more detail than the bare 'Gazette' of bankruptcies and dividends also included – a 'Register of Patents' (e.g. in improved tobaccopipes), and an illustrated department called 'Applications for the Registration of Trade Marks during the Month'. Other regular departments included tobacco markets at home and abroad, reports of various tobacconists' associations around the UK, bills of sale of businesses and board of trade returns (like the *Tobacco Trades Review**, the paper lamented that tobacco provided Customs with its highest revenue for a single product).

In 1894, having already introduced the odd line drawing, the periodical began to be illustrated* – sparsely – with photographs*. It also gave away separate photolithographs on sturdy paper of tobacco luminaries or other relevant images such as 'Group of coolies on a Sumatra tobacco plantation' (March 1895), 'Bullfight in Havana' (July 1895). While the price* had risen temporarily to 6d in the late 1880s, even though furnished with a decent proportion of advertisements* from the beginning (averaging c. 23 per cent of space in 1880 and 1885), in the

1890s adverts began to far outnumber the body of the periodical, and the price returned to 4d. Indeed, so many were the advertisements that indexes to advertisers were being published by 1895, when there were three times as many pages of adverts as text (78 pages as opposed to 26). AK

Sources: Hilton 2000, *Waterloo*.

TOBACCO TRADE REVIEW: A MONTHLY TRADE JOURNAL (1868-1937); THEN TOBACCONIST AND CONFECTIONER (1938-1968)

The *Tobacco Trade Review* was the first trade* journal devoted to tobacco. Significantly the periodical was started, by William Reed, who specialized in trade publishing (he had launched the *Grocer**), at the end of the American Civil War: its initial issues repeatedly considered the effects of the cultivation of tobacco no longer being done by slaves. It was founded as a 6d monthly (though it preferred the risk-minimising 5s annual subscription) to fight the cause of the tobacco trade, which it presented for many years as fettered by unfair duties.

Initially it was aimed at the whole trade – grower and exporter, importer and merchant, manufacturer and trader – but until the mid-1890s its unremittingly serious tone and the information it provided seem more appropriate for the former three categories. Illustration* began in 1869, confined to the department 'Novelties' with images of pipes, machinery, tobacco pouches and so on. Throughout its life in the nineteenth century the periodical covered reports of shareholders' meetings, national and international laws relative to tobacco, the markets, imports, deliveries and stock and bankruptcies. From the first, it was provided with advertising* revenue: of the 16 pages of its first issue, six comprised adverts. Advertising remained strong: by January 1881 when its rival *Tobacco** was launched, it could boast 16 pages of adverts against 20 pages of 'matter' plus one page comprising a cumulative 'Trade Marks and Labels Directory'; by January 1894 it had 38 pages of ads in supplements*, plus six pages within the 30 pages of 'matter'. By this time, however, its audience had markedly changed to tobacco retailers rather than merchants, growers or manufacturers, its rival thus becoming *Cigar and Tobacco World**. It maintained a distance from that periodical by retaining its serious voice and two-column* format*, and claimed a boosted circulation* and increased number of adverts. Indeed, besides many full-page display adverts for tobacco brands, there were also now numerous personals from men and women looking for work. In 1898, so great was the advertising revenue (and no doubt competition* from its rival), it lowered its price to a 1d. AK

Sources: Hilton 2000, *Waterloo*.

TO-DAY: A WEEKLY MAGAZINE-JOURNAL (1893-1905)

Founded by Jerome K. Jerome in 1893, *To-Day* was a 2d illustrated*, weekly*, 'magazine-journal', literary* in tone, up to date and urban. Jerome was editing* the *Idler** at the same time, and he managed to employ many of his *Idler* contributors on the new magazine: Kipling, Stevenson, Bret Harte, Gissing, and illustrators Aubrey Beardsley* and Phil May. Stories were interspersed with often racy review articles and editorials. Watkins in Sullivan connects its style with the 'clique journalism'* of the 1890s.

In December 1894 Jerome denounced as 'an outrage to literature' the *Chameleon*, an undergraduate journal* for which Oscar Wilde and Alfred Douglas had written, his statement contributed to their destruction in the trials that followed in spring 1895. Another such review* in May 1894, written by Jerome's city editor, involved the paper in a libel suit; *To-Day* lost the suit, and Jerome was forced to sell the paper in 1897 in order to pay court costs. Barry Pain took over as editor, and the magazine was eventually incorporated with *London Opinion* in 1905. ET

Sources: Ashley 2006, Nichols 2005, *ODNB*, Sullivan.

TOMAHAWK (1867-1870)

The editor* of the *Tomahawk*, Arthur William À Beckett*, was a civil servant turned journalist, and he was able to mobilize a group of similarly sophisticated contributors including his better-known brothers Gilbert and Albert, along with the future poet laureate Alfred Austin*, who brought a considerable knowledge of institutional politics* to the magazine. From unusually genteel backgrounds for journalists, À Beckett's men together represented a principled, and sometimes even a radical conservatism, and were unafraid of controversy. Described by one recent critic as an 'organ of embattled gentlemanliness', the *Tomahawk* became notorious for its criticism of Queen Victoria's withdrawal from public life as well as its opposition to social change, especially when the traditional class* structure was challenged.

The essential component for a weekly* satirical* journal of a versatile and hard-hitting cartoonist* was fortunately supplied by Matt Morgan*. Interested in social reportage as well as satire, he produced a stunning series of large-scale images for the magazine, depicting social deprivation as caustically as the antics of politicians. The cartoon, in the form of tinted wood* engravings, was alone worth the weekly price* of 2d. After a successful three-year run, the magazine came to an abrupt conclusion in July 1870. **BM**

Sources: Kent 1998, ncse, *Waterloo.*

TONNA, CHARLOTTE ELIZABETH (1790-1846) Charlotte Elizabeth Tonna, editor* of several religious* periodicals, was motivated throughout her literary* career by her devout Protestantism. She began writing for the Dublin Tract Society in the early 1820s, and continued to be a prolific producer of religious tracts, short stories and poetry* throughout her life. But a conversion experience in the mid-1820s galvanized her into a career of religious activism on behalf of the pre-Millenarian evangelical cause.

Tonna achieved most public influence through her work as an editor* particularly on the *Christian Lady's Magazine**, which she edited from 1834 until her death, and wrote largely in its entirety from 1836. Tonna's spiritual stance informed the tone and content of the magazine, which simultaneously asserted women's rightful social and political subordination to their menfolk while urging their active participation in social and political debate. Tonna sought to engage her readers in a number of causes including a Ten Hours Factory Bill and the conversion of the Jews, but she was against slavery, liberalism and mesmerism. Tonna's dominant note was one of extreme anti-Catholicism. Her work as editor of the *Protestant Annual* in 1840 drew her to the attention of the anti-Catholic Protestant Association, and she was the anonymous editor (June 1841-Dec. 1844) of their primary publication the *Protestant Magazine.* Here she wrote an anonymous* monthly leader*, 'The Watchman' which she used to propagandize on behalf of the Tory ultra-Protestant cause. **ED**

Sources: Altholz 1989, Dzelzainis 2003, Fryckstedt 1980, Gleadle 2007, *ODNB.*

TOOLEY, SARAH ANNE (1857-1946) Studies at University College, London led Sarah A. Tooley (born Southall) to a literary* career: she published several books, but most of her work was in journalism, specializing in biographies and interviews*. She published regularly throughout the 1890s in the *Humanitarian*, the *Woman at Home**, the *Young Woman** and the *Woman's Signal**. Later a member of the Women Writers' Suffrage League, Tooley interviewed many women's rights activists, like Clementina Black*, Beatrice Harraden and Sarah Grand*. Tooley contributed to professionalizing women in journalism. She was a

Member of the Council of the Society of Women Journalists*, serving as vice-chairman and vice-president. **TD**

Sources: Lawrence 1896, Richardson 2003, *WWW.*

TOULMIN, CAMILLA DUFOUR (1812-1895) Camilla Toulmin (Mrs Newton Crosland) made a distinctive contribution to the early annuals*, which she defended in her lively memoir *Landmarks of a Literary Life.* Her writing career was launched when Lady Blessington* accepted some poetry for the *Book of Beauty* in 1837. From then until her marriage in 1848 she supplemented her meagre wages as a daily governess with modest earnings from poetry*, fiction and articles for annuals and other journals.

Her most sustained connection was with *Chambers's Journal** to which she contributed for over 50 years. She assisted Marguerite Power* when she edited the *Keepsake*, corresponding with authors and doing most of the proofreading. As Leitch Ritchie's assistant on *Friendship's Offering,* she took on virtually the editor's* role since she additionally read and commissioned manuscripts. She probably also edited the *New Monthly Belle Assemblée** and the *Ladies' Companion**. Throughout her life she wrote for periodicals, alongside publishing novels and other books. **BMO**

Sources: Crosland 1893, *ODNB.*

TOWN (1837-1842) With its weekly diet of gossip*, innuendo and salacious stories about London personalities, the *Town* was both a throwback to the scurrilous weeklies* of the Regency and a precursor of a tradition of scandalous journalism* that persisted through the Victorian period despite considerable and vocal opposition. It was also important in its success in attracting to the periodical market a new audience of relatively low-status male readers, especially clerks, shop-men and apprentices, keen to be included in the version of urban adventure and metropolitan* pleasures offered by the *Town.*

Gray estimates that at its peak the journal may have sold up to 10,000 copies a week. The *Town* was cheap* at 2d, thus vastly undercutting the cost of a stamped weekly* newspaper and several of its immediate rivals, but, as it was for most of its existence unstamped*, it could not directly publish topical or political* journalism. Instead it offered a diet of fiction, descriptions of London nightlife, accounts of criminal and subcriminal life, with racy anecdotes. Crude puns were a staple of the magazine. One column* was called 'Facts and Rumours', although the 'facts' seemed every bit as much rumours as the 'rumours'. The *Town's* editor Renton

Nicholson*, became embroiled in various slanging matches with rival editors, notably Barnard Gregory* at the famously scurrilous *Satirist**. Of scandalous journals of this kind, one of the best-known titles was C. M. Westmacott's* *Age**, which ran with some success until the end of the 1840s, by which time their fantasized vision of metropolitan adventures and pleasures lying just short of criminality became outmoded. They are comparable to the 'flash' press of New York City at this time. Among them, the *Town* was unusual in seeking, and finding, a predominantly working-class* readership*.
BM
Source: Gray 1982.

TRADE PRESS For the purposes of this *Dictionary*, the 'trade press' refers to a subset of class journals that celebrates and forwards specific identities based on the production and distribution* of particular classes of goods, almost always accompanied by abundant advertising*. Although a vast field employing enormous numbers of journalists, the field suffers from almost total neglect. Neither Fox Bourne's* nor Grant's* histories of the press mention the trade press (though they describe examples of the older kind of class journal* such as the *Builder**, *Economist** and *Lancet**). Despite Elliott (1982) and Moss and Hosgood (1994), what is offered here must necessarily be a tentative exploration.

Shipping, insurance and other forms of finance, besides being covered by general newspapers, early had periodical publications devoted to them (*Lloyd's List* dates from 1726) but they never developed into trade papers in the sense defined above. The *Morning Advertiser** was started in 1794 by the Society of London Licensed Victuallers, every member of which was obliged to subscribe. This is a closer ancestor, but because of its circulation* in public houses and consequent wide readership*, it attracted diverse advertisers and was in effect a general newspaper (Grant 1871, vol: 55-64; newspapers, while carrying trade news, are excluded from this definition). Even closer were the various *Farmer's Magazines*, especially the several from the SDUK* from 1832 on, which, like the *Farmer's Journal* (1807-1832), relied heavily on advertising*. These must be discounted from this entry as farming, while certainly commercial, is not a *trade*. Significant as a pioneer in trade journalism is the radical William Nicholson*: his periodicals were aimed at shopkeepers to ensure equitable trading and thereby political liberation. He seems, however, more linked more to figures such as Cobbett* or Reynolds* and to publications like the *Trades'*

*Newspaper** than to my definition of trade journals. The weekly *Wine Trade Circular* (1852), on the other hand, is an early and isolated example of a trade journal proper, but seems to have survived for only 17 issues. Other forerunners (in terms of function, not format) include periodicals comprising lists of products, such as *Bent's Literary Advertiser** or the *Publishers' Circular**, and professional periodicals such as the *Builder** (which nonetheless overlap with the trade press). However, it was not until January 1858 and the *Bookseller** that trade journalism can truly be said to have begun. In May of the following year *Morgan's Monthly Circular* and the *Draper and Clothier* were simultaneously founded. These offered instructive models for later periodicals in a wide variety of fields and will accordingly be compared her.

It was not clear what social group the title of *Morgan's* was aimed at and thus in the 4th (monthly) issue it was renamed the *Ironmonger*. It became successful so rapidly (circulation rose from 2,000 to 10,000 in its first seven months alone) that it inspired the *Chemist and Druggist* and the *Stationer* to emerge less than four months after it began, and, indeed, provided the template for later trade journals. Edited by John Cargill Brough and backed by the Morgan family (who would be come the in-laws of another famous trade publisher, William Reed of the *Grocer** and *Tobacco Trade Review**), it celebrated ironmongery through advertising*, information, humour and heroics. By 1865 it comprised 16 pages sandwiched between 40 pages of adverts, with regular correspondents in the major manufacturing centres and occasional contributors in the minor. It kept the reader up to date with relevant developments in technology, law, gossip*, accidents, crime* in the trade and how to prevent it, and other salient news* market prices for raw materials might be affected by wars or new treaties, for example. Besides offering amusing sketches like '"Myself and My Ancestors" by a Chamber Candlestick (31 Jan 1860)', it also made celebrities* out of major* players, both narrating their paths to success and describing in detail the current operation of their firms. Both these helped to create a common mythology for the trade and hence a common identity. Mindful that it was a channel of communication between members of a specific class of readers, not just a centre-periphery communication, there was always a substantial correspondence section.

The *Draper and Clothier*, probably started with the subvention of its publishers, Houlston and Wright, took a different, destructive and equally instructive course. While lists of bankruptcies were a special characteristic of trade journals – it was important to know who in the trade was credit-worthy – the *Draper and Clothier* also published the names of bankrupts' creditors, an unhelpfully humiliating practice criticised heavily by correspondents without effect. Championing old-fashioned hard work and honesty by individuals, the periodical attacked large establishments that undercut smaller rivals. Refusing modern business practices and promoting too obviously the perspective of an individual rather than the trade, it failed to attract advertising and folded in April 1862, after a year of revealing complaints by the editor.

For the rest of the century the trade press flourished as publishers identified new potential audiences, helped by census reports that detailed the number of people occupied in a trade. See also e.g. *Book World**, *Bookman**, *British and Foreign Confectioner**, Building Press*, Fashion Journals*, *Grocer**, *Jeweller**, *Lewer**, Mining Press*, *Newsagent**, *Paper and Printing Trades Journal**, Publishers and the Press*, *Tobacco**. AK

Sources: Cook 1984, Elliott 1962, Bourne 1887, Grant 1871-1872, Moss and Hosgood 1994.

TRADE UNIONS AND THE PRESS With the repeal of the Combination Laws in Britain (1824) and the ever-increasing need for a representative voice for the working classes, trade unions found themselves the unofficial protectors of the workers of Britain. Trade union journals, and the parallel, but not necessarily synonymous radical press, became a vehicle for political* agitation, tackling subjects including factory legislation, wages, child and female labour, universal suffrage, working conditions and the truck system.

Trade union journals proliferated during the era of the 'taxes on knowledge*' and 'war of the unstamped'*. Among the most widely read were John Gast and William Carpenter's* *Trades' Newspaper and Mechanics Weekly Journal*; the unstamped *United Trades Cooperative Journal* (1830), published by John Doherty's* National Association for the Protection of Labour; the *Voice of the People* (1831-1834); James Morrison's trade unionist *Pioneer* (1833-1834); Robert Owen's* co-operative *Crisis**; and the Rev George Stringer (Parson) Bull's Christian *British Labourer's Protector, and Factory Child's Friend* (1832-1833). The Owenite* mouthpiece of the London Co-operative Society, the *Co-operative Magazine**, edited* by James Watson* and Henry Hetherington*, advocated the independence of the Mechanics' Institutes.

Among the multitude of trade union journals published at the height of Chartism* were R. K. Philp's* *Executive Journal of the National Charter Association* (1841), the *National Association Gazette* (1842), and the *Labourer*, whose joint editors Fergus O'Connor* and Ernest Jones showed considerable support for the National Association of United Trades. Trade union journals were often region-specific, such as the pro-Chartist* *Sheffield Working Man's Advocate* (1841), the profits of which were designated for the construction of a workers' meeting hall in Sheffield. The trade union press also supplied accounts of current union activity. The *National United Trades' Association Report* and *Labourer's Advocate* (1848), which was succeeded by the *Labour League; or, Journal of the National Association of United Trades* (1848-1849), provided details of the programme and progress of the Association, and supported the 'right to work'.

Journals were often published by specific trades; radical publisher* William Strange's* bi-monthly *Bookbinders' Trade Circular* (1850-1877), published by the London Consolidated Society of Journeymen Bookbinders, contained articles on labour conditions and law, philosophies of trade unionism, and workers' wages. However, by the turn of the century, many of the journals specific to location and trade gave way to burgeoning socialism, with journals such as the *Labour Leader** participating in the growing Labour movement of the late nineteenth and early twentieth century. MT

Sources: Harrison 1977, Haywood 2004, Hollis 1970, Wiener 1969.

TRADES' NEWSPAPER AND MECHANICS' WEEKLY JOURNAL (1825-1831) The London-based weekly* *Trades' Newspaper and Mechanics' Weekly Journal* was launched on 17 July 1825 as one of the first stamped Sunday* newspapers owned and managed exclusively by and for artisans and mechanics. Its second number announced that 'the working classes* laid hold of a means of mutual enlightenment', and this mission was reflected in its two Banner mottos, 'They helped everyone his neighbour; and every one said to his brother, BE OF GOOD COURAGE' (*Isaiah* xii. 6) and 'To protect industry'. Selling at the high price* of 7d, it achieved a modest weekly circulation* of 628 (1827) and around 1,000 in 1829. Fusing radical, trade union and self-improving rhetoric with coverage of political* events, scientific* discoveries, inventions and literary and theatrical news, it was characterized by repeated engagement with political* economy, radical reform and co-operative principles.

Established by a trades' committee led by the shipwright John Gast, it was edited* until February 1826 by the patent agent Joseph Clinton Robertson (1788-1852) and published* by John Limbird* (c.1796-1883) at his *Mirror** office on the Strand. In March 1826 the paper moved to Fleet Street*, but in 1827 financial problems precipitated an appeal to Francis Place* for assistance, and a merger* with the *London Free Press* was arranged to create the *Trades' Free Press* (29 July 1827-23 Aug. 1828). In December 1827, the religious compiler and radical William Carpenter* became editor, bringing with him the radical pressman John Cleave* and employing a succession of minor publishers. The paper's identity as a vehicle of artisan independence was eroded by Carpenter's drive to create a more socially inclusive readership* and by alliances with new loci of popular politics in the capital. Under its new title, the *Weekly Free Press and Co-operative Journal* (5 Dec. 1829-2 April 1831), the paper represented the British Association for Promoting Co-operative Knowledge and the Radical Reform Association, but these shifts undermined artisan control over content.

The significance of the *Trades'* lies in the careers of its editors, the importance of its contributors (in particular the serialization* of Thomas Hodgskin's [1787-1869] 'Labour defended against the claims of capital' [1825]), its fusion of demands for radical reform with schemes for self-improvement and its unique record of the intellectual world and cultural praxes of London's skilled working population. **DSM**

Sources: Harrison 1977, Prothero 1979, Thompson 1963, *Waterloo*.

TRAILL, HENRY DUFF (1842-1900) A literary* and political* journalist* and satirist* of some note, Traill's first forays into journalism (after dabbling with law) were for the *Yorkshire Post* (1754-). Settling in London in the early 1870s, he contributed to the *Observer**, and in 1873 got a job on the staff of Frederick Greenwood's* *Pall Mall Gazette**, leaving with Greenwood for the *St James's Gazette** when it was founded in 1880. In 1876 he had published the 'Israelitish Question', an anonymous* pamphlet in which he parodied the newspaper press. He also contributed a variety of reviews*, articles and essays to the *Saturday Review**, and wrote satirical verse for the press that was republished later in book form. In 1882 he left the staff of the *St James's Gazette* and became chief political leader* writer (1882-1897) at the *Daily Telegraph**, and also edited the weekly* *Observer* (1889-1891).

Books in the 1880s include *English Men of Letters*, biographies of literary figures Coleridge and Laurence Sterne, and in the 1890s he edited six volumes on *Social England*, a range of work reflecting his journalism competencies as well.

His politics, as his obituary* in *The Times** put it, were 'those of a sceptical and cool-headed conservative' and this demeanour was reflected in his political journalism, which was penetrating and sometimes quietly scathing but generally dispassionate. In 1897, writing a commemorative piece for the 10,000th issue of the *Pall Mall Gazette*, he complained that the average standard of the evening paper had declined markedly: there was no time for considered political speculation or truly accomplished literary journalism in an age when evening papers were competing* to convey early sporting intelligence and filling their pages with vapid 'Society Journalism'. That same year he became editor of *Literature**, the new literary supplement* published by *The Times*. Advocating a new, tougher form of literary criticism, *Literature* was erudite and lively, with Traill's contributions combining wit and learning to good effect. Traill's editorship ended with his sudden death and the journal petered out two years later, but its enduring legacy is the *Times Literary Supplement* (1902-) which replaced it, and which adopted many of the values that Traill had instilled in the earlier publication. **MaT**

Sources: *Daily News* 22 Feb. 1900, *ODNB*, *Pall Mall Gazette* 14 April 1897, *The Times* 22 Feb. 1900, *Waterloo*.

TRAIN (1856-1858) The *Train: A First Class Magazine* was launched as a seriocomic 1s monthly*. Its motto was *Vires Acquirit Eundo* and it soon established itself as the 'fast' magazine* of the day. The editor* was Edmund Yates* and because nearly all of his contributors had previously worked together on the *Comic Times* they became known as the 'Trainband'. The contributors were bohemian journalists specializing in light, satirical* and literary* short stories, essays and poems*. Of particular bohemian interest were the contributions by George Augustus Sala*, namely 'Parisian Nights' Entertainments', and the ballad 'Caviar and Rudesheimer'. Robert Brough's* autobiographical novel *Marston Lynch* was sporadically serialised* when Sala's intended work 'Fripanelli's Daughter' failed to materialize. Yates contributed a series called 'Men Of Mark' which was a forerunner to his 'Celebrities At Home' articles for the *World**.

Yates was chosen as editor because 'his ways of life were less erratic than those of most of his friends'.

Those friends and contributors also included William McConnell (who provided illustrations*), William Brough, William P. Hale, John Hollingshead, Frank Scudamore and James Hain Friswell. Other contributors outside the 'Trainband' were also welcome and the *Train* is chiefly remembered and sought after today because of Lewis Carroll's poems; Frank Smedley and John Oxenford* also wrote for it. All articles, unusually for the time, were signed by the authors, who unanimously agreed that 'anonymity* was the bane of literature'. The *Train* declined in quality during its last ten months once initial interest had subsided. **PB**

Sources: Edwards 1997, Straus 1942, Yates 1885.

TRANSACTIONS Transactions – the publication of papers read at the meetings of a learned society – comprise one of the oldest periodical forms. The term is consequently loaded with the status of antiquity, although the first British example, the *Philosophical Transactions of the Royal Society* (1665-), like its models the German *Erbaüliche Monaths-Unterredungen* ['Edifying monthly discussions, 1663-1668] and the French *Journal des Scavants* (1665-1753), started by providing abstracts of books and anecdotes of new discoveries rather than publishing proceedings (how or if 'Transactions' differ from 'Proceedings' is moot). By the nineteenth century 'Transactions' had established itself as a title for the repeated publications of a society with pretensions to learning. They were usually distributed free on payment of the annual subscription to an association such as the Medical Society of London (whose *Transactions* began in 1810). They thus constitute an important part of a society's declaration of identity to its members who are often geographically widespread, forming a closed discourse community with its own codes, narratives and practices.

By no means all learned societies issued transactions, however, some publishing not at all and others intermittently (the *Transactions of the Royal College of Physicians* were issued only six times between 1772 and 1820, for instance). Others again, such as the Royal Agricultural Society, preferred to communicate through the more regular channel of journals, usually quarterlies* or monthlies*. Transactions were always both less frequent and less regular than other periodicals. The term also has a more exclusive aura, even though a few were available for sale to the public: Longmans' annual* *London Catalogue of Periodicals, Newspapers and Transactions of Various Societies* listed 29 such in 1859. Interestingly, the number did not vary greatly (in

1885, the *Catalogue* lists only 4 more learned society publications on general sale than in 1859).

Transactions of many major societies were issued serially. The price* was almost always high – as much as 40s for just a single part of the *Linnaean Society Transactions* for 1870- though there were cheaper ones: the entire *Transactions of the Cornwall Geological Society* cost 28s in 1858, and one part of those of the Pomological Society (1854-1864) cost 1s 6d. Some were issued in two forms, with and without illustrations*. In 1868, Part 2 of the Zoological Society's *Transactions*, known for its splendid engravings since its first issue in 1835, cost 15s with illustrations and 4s without. The latter price was nonetheless still high. Such pricing may be considered part of the societies' exclusionary practices, the extent and purposes of which varied enormously. The use of the term for the proceedings (1859-1907) of the all-male Obstetrical Society in the face of traditionally female midwifery is telling (on the struggles of female midwives, see nursing* journals). The 12s price tag of the 700-plus pages of the *Transactions of the National Association for the Promotion of Social Science* (1857-1886), dedicated to liberal principles and on general sale, is more ambiguous in intention, if not in effect, for it maintains the study of society in the hands of an elite (even if it famously welcomed the participation of women). High prices coupled with high production values suggest the aspiration of many transactions to permanent encyclopaedic and historical record. They enabled the subscriber literally to display his learning and perhaps professional identity on his walls. In this they are the original models for professional journals (see Professions* and the press).

Characteristic of many (but not all) transactions is the enumeration of the rules of the society and lists of officers and members. This is not found in professional journals unless, as organs of specific bodies, they combine the status and exclusivity of transactions with more inclusive periodical forms. Sometimes, 'transactions' form part of the subtitle of such publications (e.g. the monthly *Journal of the Photographic Society of London, containing the Transactions of the Society and a General record of Photographic Art and Science*, 1853-1999, with changes of title).

Finally, it must be remembered that not all transactions were published by grand metropolitan* or even urban groups. Nonetheless, the general description above holds good even for publications such as the *Transactions of the Woolhope Naturalists' Field Club* (1852-) begun by a small group of Herefordshire gentry to record their field trips. **AK**

TRANSATLANTIC JOURNALISM Nineteenth-century journalism* was inextricably linked to a transatlantic literary* publishing industry. The lack of an international copyright* law until the passage of the Chace Act (1891) encouraged a rampant culture of reprinting, especially of British publications in America. Periodicals like *Harper's New Monthly Magazine** and *Littell's Living Age* were dependent upon copying selections from British magazines* and repackaging them for an American audience. Copies of entire British magazines were also printed in cheap* editions by fledgling American publishing companies, with or without permission from the original publishers*. However, many of the 'piratical' practices in the United States began to decline in the 1860s with an increase in American literary* nationalism*, which encouraged the payment and promotion of new American writers rather than a reliance on tried and true British imports. Newspaper bureaus and fiction syndicates* also began to branch out from the British provincial* press to form alliances with regional American papers in the early 1880s. The spread of literary syndicates such as Tillotson's* Newspaper Fiction Bureau facilitated the brokering of deals that provided adequate compensation to authors for the transatlantic publication of their works.

Transatlantic exchange was by no means a one-way street. British publications such as the *London Journal** and the *Family Herald** benefited from the publication of American writers without remuneration or permission, publishing serial* fiction from the likes of Fanny Fern, E. D. E. N. Southworth and Harriet Beecher Stowe. In the 1860s, *Harper's* had an impact in England as its format* (increasingly filled with original contributions) served as a model for shilling* monthly magazines such as the *Cornhill** and *Macmillan's**. The influence of the United States was also felt in England through the establishment of foreign* correspondents. Harriet Martineau* became one of the first unofficial foreign correspondents by writing a series of articles for British periodicals such as the *Daily News**, the *Spectator** and *Once a Week**, covering topics related to the slave trade and the Civil War. Many American and British journalists* followed Martineau's lead, venturing, for example, to the Crimea to cover the war* for news outlets back home. In 1870 the *New York Tribune* was one of the first papers to take advantage of the transatlantic telegraph* cable, established in 1866, to transmit news* across the Atlantic. By the turn of the century, the founding of foreign news services such as the

Associated Press* and Reuters* had fostered a permanent corps of transatlantic reporters.

In the 1880s the emergence of New Journalism* with its increased reliance on eye-catching layout, bold headlines, informal language and sensationalism* presented in short, easily digestible selections was seen as a potentially dangerous American import. The market* for this kind of reporting was rapidly expanding and the ability to reach a mass* audience was further facilitated by other American innovations including the linotype machine and the Hoe rotary press, which greatly increased typesetting and printing speeds. From the 1890s, the annuals* (1891-1902) of W. T. Stead* indicated the professional fascination of British journalism with its American counterpart, and the two-way traffic of journalists across the Atlantic. The development of transatlantic journalistic exchange went hand in hand with the establishment of journalism* as a commercial, technologically innovative, and professional* endeavour. JJP/DM

Sources: Heald 1998, Johanningsmeier 1997, King 2004, Law 2000, Phegley 2004b.

***TRANSPORT; A WEEKLY REVIEW OF DOCKS, HARBOURS, CANALS AND RAILWAYS, SHIPPING AND SHIPBUILDING** (1892-1935) Transport* was a form of trade* weekly which boasted a national and international readership* and it claimed it was available in more than 300 ports and places in England and abroad. Published in London at 6d, its aim was to review 'in a comprehensive manner' all events and incidents relating to the transport industry: from policy and management of corporations to proposals for the construction of new means of communication. As a specialist journal, its intended readership* was notably broad: 'chairmen, trustees, directors, officials, and principal stock- and share-holders of harbour and dock trusts and Companies; railway, tramway, shipping, marine insurance, and telegraph* companies, engineers, contractors, foreign and colonial merchants; shipbuilders, ship-owners, shipbrokers, freight agents, consulates, Lloyds' agencies, and the chambers of commerce'. Its departments included 'A Word from the Editor' and 'Financial Notes' and 'Directories'. One of its most interesting sections was 'Legal Notes', which discussed topics such as new parliamentary laws on transport both at home and abroad (eg 'The Railway and Canal Traffic Act, 1888' and 'Railway French Law'), or court cases relevant to the trade – the incident of the boat *The Aladdin*, where seamen refused to travel due to a cholera outbreak in the port destination, for instance. Finances figured heavily in the journal. A feature was the publication of the closing prices of docks, harbours and canals (both in the UK and abroad) as quoted on the London Stock Market (cf financial* journals). From 1905 onwards, the journal focused more on railways. **APV**

Source: *Waterloo.*

TRANSPORT PRESS Britain's advances in transportation technology (railways, trams, omnibuses, underground trains and steamships) and the development of new transport networks were subjects treated by the nineteenth-century press on a daily basis, whose readership* was boosted by the appearance and development of railway bookstalls such as W. H. Smith's*. Newspapers like *The Times** or the *Illustrated London News** reported extensively on Britain's first transport revolution, devoting pages and pages to news* such as the opening of a new railway line or railway station, the discovery of new forms of traction and power, the formation and dissolution of railway companies and corporations, parliamentary* laws on transportation and accidents. Monthlies* and weeklies* also reported the news, adapting them for their readerships*. The financial speculation railway companies during the railway mania years, for example, detailed in the financial* press, was often satirized* by *Punch**, while etiquette, dress code, safety and information on routes for travel, work or pleasure figured extensively in the *Queen**. Passengers often used periodical literature (usually in the forms of 'Letters* to the Editor') to express their views on issues such as punctuality, price of tickets, respectability of conductors, codes of conduct, security and service. Publishers responded to the new reading spaces created by trains not only by generating volume formats* suitable for the commuter (the 'Railway Libraries' of the 1860s) but periodical formats with clearly defined layout which included headlines and short paragraphs (see New Journalism* and e.g. *Financial** *News, Answer to Correspondents**).

As a specialized subject, the nineteenth-century transport press took three main directions. The first focused on the trade itself. Created for and written by people associated with transport technology, it had a distinct, specialist readership* in mind (engineers, workers, managers, investors, etc). This first group includes journals such as: *Railway Review* (a penny* weekly* edited* by J. Greenwood and issued by the National Union of Railwaymen, 1880-1994); *Tramway and Railway World* (1892-1968, with title* changes); *On the Line: the Journal of the United Kingdom Railway Temperance Union* (1882-1963, edited by Frederick Sherlock and published by the United Kingdom Railway Temperance Union); the *Coach Builders and Saddlers' Journal* (1863-1864); the penny journal *Cab and Omnibus News* (1875); the *Whip and Cab and Omnibus Guardian* (1867); the *Railway Chart and Advertiser* (1845); the *British and Foreign Railway Journal* (1845; a short-lived 4d weekly incorporating the *Railway Engine* and *Wetenhall's Share Guide*); the *Railway Argos* (1845-6d); *Railway Standard* (1846-6d); and *Bradshaw's Railway Gazette* (1845-1882; with various changes of title). One of the most successful journals in this group was *Transport**.

The second type focused on the publication of timetables and guides to facilitate and attract passenger travel. There were literally hundreds of periodicals of this kind. They advertised companies' timetables in the UK and abroad, and as such they were key for passenger and goods mobility in the British Isles and the British Empire. A tiny selection might include *Croydon Review Railway Time Tables* (1880-1896); *Chapman's British Railway Guide; and Steam Packet Directory for England, Ireland, Scotland, & Wales* (railway timetables 1854-1892); *Monthly Telegraph and Commercial Advertiser; or Guide to Railways, Steam boats, Mail and Stage Coaches* continued as *Harthill's Monthly Telegraph, or Railway, Coach & Steam-boat Guide* (Lothian, Edinburgh) (1844-1846); and the most famous, *Bradshaw's Railway, &c., Through Route and Overland Guide to India, Egypt and China; or the Traveller's Manual, etc.* (with changes of title 1857-1913).

Finally, the third type focused on entertainment. It not only offered reading material for passengers to pass the time while travelling, but also gave advice on travel and tourism (places of interest, hotels, restaurants, curiosities etc). Some of the most interesting examples are: the bi-monthly 2s 6d *British and Foreign Railway Journal* (1845) which included contributions by Sarah Taylor Austin* and Henry Samuel Chapman; the *Traveller; An International Weekly Journal for Rail, River, Ocean and Road* (1885-1886) which was a 2d weekly magazine whose aim was to indicate 'those about to roam amid the multitudinous beauty-spots of the Continent the hotels, restaurants, and pensions where they may depend upon being well looked after'; and *Travel; an Illustrated Monthly Magazine* (1896-1905) a 3d monthly devoted 'to that large and important section of society who in their summer, autumn, and winter migrations to the Continent, surely need some guide, philosopher, and friend'. Edited by Henry Simpson Lunn, *Travel* counted among its contributors S. Baring-Gould, Dean Farrar, Frederick W. W. Howell and Joseph Pennell*. APV

Sources: Freeman 1999, Schivelbusch 1977, Vadillo 2005.

TREWMAN FAMILY Robert Trewman, printer and newspaper proprietor*, was apprenticed to Andrew Brice, proprietor of the *Exeter Journal* for seven years. After a quarrel with Brice he left, with the foreman William Andrews, to establish the *Exeter Mercury*, with the first issue appearing on 2 September 1763. The paper underwent several title* changes; on 11 July 1765 it became the *Exeter Evening Post or the West Country Advertiser*, then on 25 July the title changed again to the *Exeter Evening Post or Plymouth and Cornish Courant*. It underwent other changes of title until it became known preponderantly if intermittently as *Trewman's Exeter Flying Post* (1770-1779, 1804-1807, etc).

Trewman's eldest son, also called Robert, (1767-1816), became a partner in his father's firm. After the death of the elder Trewman in 1802, his son continued the *Flying Post* as a Tory paper, supporting the cause of Reform. As well as editing* the newspaper, Robert Trewman Jnr ran a bookshop which became a meeting point for Exeter literati. His son, Robert John Trewman, did not edit the paper but continued as proprietor until his death in 1860. By the late nineteenth century, *Trewman's Exeter Flying Post* was the oldest newspaper still being published in Devon, continuing until April 1917. DHL

Sources: Dymond 1886, *ODNB*, *Waterloo*.

TRIMMER, SARAH (1741-1810) Sunday School founder Sarah Trimmer established herself as an authority on education with two periodicals she edited* and wrote largely herself: the *Family Magazine* (1788-1789) and the *Guardian of Education* (1802-1806). In 1793 Trimmer also began an association with the Society for Promoting Christian Knowledge (SPCK, see SDUK*), which issued several of her books. Staunchly Anglican and anti-Jacobin, Trimmer worked to counter what she described in the *Guardian* as a 'conspiracy against CHRISTIANITY and all SOCIAL ORDER'.

Often, though erroneously, credited as the first to review* children's books, Trimmer was the first to do so systematically and professionally; unlike other authors of the day, she did not puff* her own books. Trimmer is critiqued for her reactionary values, and especially her negative reviews of fairy tales, but recently scholars have found nuances in her conservatism. A respected female editor, Trimmer established a model for the evangelical mothers' magazines* of the 1830s and 1840s. TD

Sources: Beetham 1996, *DNB*, Grenby 2005, Immel 1990, Yarde 1971.

TROLLOPE, ANTHONY (1815-1882) Anthony Trollope's presence in mid-Victorian journalism can be felt in three ways. First, he was a prolific serial* novelist, who made his name as a popular author of realist fiction aimed at the circulating library* reader. Although he had published several novels previously, his first serialized* novel, the hugely popular 'Framley Parsonage', helped launch and ensure the success of Thackeray's* *Cornhill Magazine* in 1860. From this point on, he conceived of and wrote all of his fiction in serial form, even if they were not always published in parts. Among the periodicals who carried his fiction were *Blackwood's**, the *Graphic** and the *Fortnightly Review**, in addition to newspapers and periodicals in America, Australia and elsewhere.

Second, Trollope had some experience as a proprietor* and editor*, and in 1865, he was on the founding proprietorial board of the *Fortnightly Review*, with his friend G. H. Lewes* as editor. Two years later, he launched his own title, *St Paul's Magazine**, published by James Virtue*, which he edited until 1870. This shilling* monthly offered Trollope the opportunity he was denied in his failed bid to enter Parliament, namely, to discuss politics* publicly. As his Palliser novels about London political life attest, Trollope was keenly interested in contemporary politics, and his political novel, 'Phineas Finn', about a young Irish M. P. launched *St Paul's*, though it didn't have the same success as his previous serials in *Cornhill* and elsewhere. Although Trollope described himself as a 'conservative Liberal', *St Paul's* was largely dedicated to the Liberal cause, and questions related to Irish Home Rule are especially noticeable.

Finally, Trollope was himself a journalist, contributing a range of articles, often literary*, to contemporary periodicals. Of particular interest to the history of journalism* is his article 'On Anonymous Journalism' (*Fortnightly Review*, July 1865), which contributes to mid-1860s debates about signature, and his series of short stories about the often trying life of a magazine editor (first published in *St Paul's* and collected in volume form as *An Editor's Tales* in 1870) make engaging reading on the milieu of mid-nineteenth-century journalism. MWT

Source: Turner 2000c.

TROUP, GEORGE WILLIAM DAVID (BAPTIZED 1810-1879) George Troup was a member of the evangelical branch of the Church of Scotland, supporting anti-slavery and the temperance movement. As a journalist and publisher*, he had a long association with *Tait's Edinburgh Magazine**, first as a journalist in the 1830s, then as joint owner with Alexander Alison, editing* it from 1847 to 1849, when Troup, the sole proprietor*, moved it to Glasgow. He contributed to the magazine on politics* and literature* but was forced to sell it out of financial necessity in 1850. In 1853 he was once again writing for *Tait's*, editing it by 1855, proprietor by 1858, forced to close it by 1861.

In between the vicissitudes of *Tait's*, Troup was briefly editor of the *Liverpool Weekly Telegraph* and the *Montrose Review*. As editor at the evangelical *Aberdeen Banner* while editing the *Scottish Temperance Herald* (1840-1842) and writing anti-Corn Law pamphlets, editorial intrusion from the clergy in the *Banner* forced Troup out. In Belfast he became editor, printer and part owner of the *Banner of Ulster* which appeared twice a week. But his journeying continued: leaving Belfast in 1846 he returned to Glasgow.

As editor and printer in 1847 of the *North British Daily Mail*, Scotland's first daily*, financed by the industrialist Alexander Alison, Troup used the paper as a campaigning vehicle to attack the problems of Glasgow's slums. Alison's bankruptcy saw the *Mail* taken over by local businessmen, but Troup retained his editorial position. After writing from 1857 for the 1d daily the *Glasgow Bulletin,* the first of its kind in Scotland, Troup bought and edited it, and with his usual economic problems was forced to incorporate it with the *North British Daily Mail.*

Continuing his editorial passion, he briefly took on the *Witness**, a Free Church paper in 1860. In 1861 through his political* intervention in the campaign for a nine-hour working day he met the trade unionist George Potter and became financially and editorially embroiled in Potter's weekly* the *Bee-Hive**. However, his stewardship was made untenable due to his position over slavery, although he continued to contribute articles and work with Potter. He returned to Aberdeen in the late 1860s. **CL**
Source: *ODNB*.

TRÜBNER, JOHANN NICHOLAS (1817-1884) Born in Heidelberg, Nicholas Trübner, publisher* and philologist, served an apprenticeship at a university bookseller's in that town. While working in a Frankfurt bookshop, he met William Longman* from the London publishing house who gave him work and Trübner moved to London in 1843.

After working for Longmans, he established a bookselling agency, Trübner, in 1851 in partnership with Thomas Delf for American publications. They were later joined by David Nutt and based on Trübner's own expertise added oriental publications to their list. To this end Trübner started a monthly periodical in 1865, *Trübner's American and Oriental Literary Record*. Trübner imported books and published scholarly works from all over the world, the range and nature of their specialization facilitating the role of agent, publisher* and bookseller to numerous government departments and intellectual circles in England and Europe.

The company also fostered radical philosophical thought, publishing George Holyoake's* periodical the *Reasoner** and the *Westminster Review** (1862-1889). As a sympathizer with the women's cause, he published, on commission, the *Englishwoman's Review** and from 1870 the *Women's Suffrage Journal**. He also printed and published pamphlets and articles for women's groups, reprinting J. S. Mill's* 1867 parliamentary* speech supporting women's suffrage for the Enfranchisement of Women Committee, and issuing works by radical women writers such as 'Mona Caird*'.

After Trübner's death, Horatio Bottomley* brokered a merger* for Trübner's with Charles Kegan Paul* and Alfred Trench in 1889. Trübner and Company is now an imprint of Kegan Paul. **CL**
Sources: Crawford 1999, Ketupa online, *ODNB*.

TRUTH (1877-1957) *Truth* was a 6d weekly* launched in 1877 by the editor*-proprietor* Henry Du Pre Labouchère*. It was a cheekily playful, witty, often radically Liberal periodical that was also part of the new 'society* journalism' in the 1870s. Somewhat in the manner of his friend Edmund Yates's* *World**, *Truth* combined gleeful paragraphs of gossip* about the aristocracy and celebrities* (party comings and goings but also adultery and other social transgressions in a section entitled 'Entre Nous') with columns* dedicated to literature*, art, fashion*, theatre and politics*, though none of the literary material has been much remembered for its quality.

A great deal of the copy in the early years was produced by Labouchère himself, who, until he entered Parliament in 1880, put an enormous amount of energy into making his venture work. And work it did – arguably the most successful of the society weeklies at the end of the century, it remained in publication 80 years. **MWT**
Sources: Sullivan, *Waterloo*, Weber 1993.

TYMMS, SAMUEL (1808-1871) Antiquarian and topographical author, editor*, printer and publisher*, Samuel Tymms was born in Camberwell, Surrey. His earliest contribution to journalism was an essay on 'peg tankards' for the *Gentleman's Magazine** in 1827. By 1851 he was living in Bury-St-Edmunds where he worked on the staff of the *Bury Post*. In 1857 Tymms moved to Lowestoft where he worked as a bookseller and stationer, and a year later he began editing, printing and publishing the *East Anglian, or Notes and Queries on Subjects Connected with the Counties of Suffolk, Cambridge, Essex, Norfolk* (1858-1871), priced* 3d for 12 pp in 1858. As the subtitle suggests, the issues focused on local* history*, and were generally very highly regarded. Although the journal ceased publication following Tymms's death in 1871, it was revived (1885-1910). Alongside this new series, Tymms's original publication was reissued (1885-1887) by the Committee of the Suffolk Institute of Archaeology, Statistics, and Natural History, on account of the high quality of Tymms's original work. **MBT**
Sources: Boase, *ODNB, Poole's, Waterloo*.

TYNDALL, JOHN (1820-1893) In the late 1840s Tyndall helped fund his scientific education in Germany by translating articles for the *Philosophical Magazine**, where he also published his first papers on mathematics and diamagnetism, as well as later serving on its editorial board. In London a decade later the rising Irish physicist assisted Thomas Henry Huxley* with his regular science* articles for the *Westminster Review**, and in 1859 began a jointly written column* with him for the *Saturday Review**. Even after becoming professor of natural philosophy at the Royal Institution, Tyndall continued to write regularly for leading liberal periodicals like the *Fortnightly Review** and the *Nineteenth Century**.

The belligerent rationalism and penchant for controversy that characterized Tyndall's journalism were epitomized by the so-called prayer-gauge debate of 1872, prompted by his proposal in the *Contemporary Review** for a comparative survey of the mortality rates of hospital patients treated by medicine and those who were prayed for. Tyndall also engaged in acrimonious disputes with fellow scientists in *Nature**, but later refused any further contributions to the scientific weekly* after falling out with its editor* Norman Lockyer*. The famously explosive controversy sparked by Tyndall's avowedly materialistic Belfast Address of 1874 was likewise largely fought out in various sectors of the press. **GD**
Sources: Barton 2004, Lightman 2004a, Lightman 2004d, *ODNB*.

TYPESETTING The first British typesetting machine was invented in 1822 by Dr William Church, a New Yorker living in London. His ideas were adopted by a number of other inventors of typesetting machines during the early nineteenth century. However the first really effective machine was that of David Bruce, patented in America in 1838. Britain, however, lagged behind other countries in making use of typesetting machinery. Most type was set by hand and many founders feared trouble with their workmen if they introduced machines.

In 1823 Louis Jean Pouchée in France invented a machine calculated to cast from 150 to 200 types. But it could not be marketed in England, owing to certain type-founders who had bought one of the machines and destroyed it. The early type-setting machines were not completely successful, but in 1857 Robert Hattersley (1829 – 1867) patented a type composing machine which was an improvement on its predecessors. It proved to be one of the longest-lived typesetting machines made in England, still in use up to the First World War. Ten years after Hattersley, Alexander Mackie (1825-1894), proprietor* of the *Warrington Guardian*, invented a steam driven machine, which he used for setting the text of his own newspaper. However, it was Frederick Wicks's rotary casting machine, invented in 1878 and patented in 1881, which improved the speed of newspaper printing. *The Times**, which employed Wicks, used his machine in conjunction with the Kastenbein composing machine. This meant that fresh type could be used every day, saving the labour of distribution. Rotary printing was superseded by the linotype composing machine, invented by Ottmar Mergenthaler (1854 – 1899), a German residing in the USA. This automated the selection and setting process of reusable metal type – a labour-saving device which led to an 85 per cent reduction in printing times. Mergenthaler's first machine was completed in 1885, and by 1886 it was in use at the *New York Tribune*. By 1890 an improved model was available in America and Britain. The linotype machine accelerated circulation*, and by 1900 20 London dailies* and over 200 other British papers were composed by this machine. Other typesetting systems included monotype (1887), the Paige compositor (1894), and Intertype (1914). The latter was simpler than linotype, and more versatile. **DHL**
Sources: Berry and Poole 1966, Clair 1976.

TYPEWRITING Typewriting was among those technological practices (like stenography or, somewhat differently, telegraphy*) that transformed the shape of journalism in the nineteenth century, particularly with regard to the speed with which text could be produced. When exactly the first typewriter was invented is a matter of debate, and there are precursors to the typewriter as far back as the early eighteenth century, but it was in the nineteenth century that the typewriter was perfected. In 1829 the 'typographer' was patented by William Austin Burt in America, and in 1855, the Italian Giuseppe Ravizza's *macchina da scrivere a tasti* ('writing machine with keys') was unveiled. But the typewriter did not become practical and commercially successful until E. Remington and Sons, the American manufacturer of sewing machines, purchased a patent and began selling the 'Scholes and Glidden Type-Writer', with its now-standard QWERTY arrangement of the alphabet, emphasizing not alphabetical order but the frequency with which letters are used in writing. The typewriter was used mostly for dictation and became associated with female labour and the creation of the secretariat by the end of the nineteenth century (depicted popularly as 'The Typewriter Girl', in Grant Allen's 1894 novel of the same name).

By the end of the century, copy was increasingly submitted to journals in typewritten form. By June 1895, Donald MacLeod, editor* of *Good Words** stated, in an interview* published in the *Review of Reviews**, that 'nearly all the stories and a great many of the articles' were submitted to his journal as typescript. In 1898 it was reported in the same journal that *Cassell's Family Magazine**, *Pearson's Magazine**, the *New Review**, the *Windsor Magazine**, *Pall Mall Magazine**, *Idler**, *Chapman's Magazine of Fiction* (1895-1898), *Cornhill Magazine**, the *Fortnightly Review**, and the *National Review** all insisted upon typewritten copy. *Blackwood's Magazine**, *Harper's New Monthly Magazine*, *Longman's Magazine**, and the *Magazine of Art* all preferred it, while *Chambers's Journal**, the *Badminton Magazine of Sports and Pastimes* (1895-1923), *Boy's Own Paper**, *Scribner's Magazine* (1887-1939), and the *Gentlemen's Magazine** were indifferent. 'In no case does any important journal say that it prefers handwriting', the *Review of Reviews* concluded.

The production of typed copy by journalists was done in a number of ways. Relatively eminent writers like George Sims* – whose 'Mustard and Cress' column* appeared in the *Referee* (1877-1928) – would employ a 'lady typist', as he revealed in the *Idler* (Dec. 1897). In an interview with the *Bookman** (Nov. 1897), Gerald Massey* related that his manuscripts were typed by his eldest daughter: this strategy of utilizing an otherwise economically inactive female member of the household seems to have been a popular one. Other journalists would either have to rely on having their copy typewritten by one of the many agencies (such a service is advertised at 10d per 1,000 words in the *Review of Reviews*, Aug. 1897), or learn to use the Remington themselves, as an anonymous editor recommended in the 1899 handbook *How to Write for the Press*. **MWT/MaT**

Sources: 'An Editor' 1899, *ODNB*, Price 2003, Wershler-Henry 2005.

TYPOGRAPHY Typefaces or fonts came in a variety of styles in nineteenth-century Britain, from the elaborate gothic medievalism of Old English through new decorative fonts based on to the classical simplicity of Times Old Roman, developed and used by *The Times** until 1932, or the plain sans-serif of such radical artisan titles as the *Charter* (1839) to the new typefaces of aesthetic periodicals of the 1890s. It may in many cases be plausibly inferred that editors* chose fonts that visually represented the core editorial or even political values of their titles. Genre* was evidently a significant consideration: thus comic journalism and advertising tended to use a broader range of styles than serious Parliamentary reporting. Helpful is the dichotomy between what Drucker has called marked texts – those with highly noticeable typographic features and which are typically commercial, aiming to sell a particular message – and unmarked texts with 'invisible' typography that seeks to efface the materials and the labour that has gone into the text's production. This invisibility in turn lends the text the authority and seeming truth value of 'pure Word' (Drucker 1994: 95).

Marked text could, however, be used not to sell anything directly but for comic effect, its humour deriving from how it drew attention to its material, as in *Punch's* 'Comic Alphabet'. In practice, however, most titles combined different typefaces for the masthead*, the advertising* and editorial sections, the key determinants being visual impact, legibility and the economic use of limited page space. The increased use of machine typesetting*, improvements in inking and newsprint production technologies and changing fashions in layout* increasingly affected font choice, though not always offering greater freedom: the new technologies of monotype and linotype along with a zeal for economically efficient standardization of line size and ease of justification for unmarked text restricted the possibilities of type design. Printers' periodicals (e.g. *Paper and Printing Trades Journal*, *British Printer*) are particularly valuable sources of information on changing typographical trends. **AGJ/AK**

Sources: Allen 1940, Drucker 1994, McGann 1991, Southward 1898-1900.

U

ULSTER MAGAZINE AND MONTHLY REVIEW OF SCIENCE AND LITERATURE (1860-1864)

The *Ulster Magazine and Monthly Review of Science* and Literature** (1860-1864) was a monthly* family* journal, published* in Belfast by C. H. McCloskie. Focused on fiction, poetry* and articles of local* Ulster interest, its main objective was the popularization of literary and scientific information. Notable contributors included self-taught poet Francis Davis, a sympathizer of Young Ireland* and writer for the Nation* and David Herbison an Ulster poet writing in both English and Ulster Scots. **FB**
Sources: Brown 1937, Clyde 2003, *ODNB, Waterloo Irish.*

ULSTER OBSERVER (1862-1868); NORTHERN STAR AND ULSTER OBSERVER (1870-1872)

The *Ulster Observer** was a Catholic broadsheet, founded by A. J. M'Kenna as an 'Organ devoted to the exposition of [Catholic] views and the vindication of their rights'. It appeared three times per week for a 1d, with a six-column* page and advertisement* 'wrappers'. Alongside Catholic editorial matter, the paper covered national and international news*. Particularly notable for its regular literary* section, it included poetry* and fiction, some of which was serialized* from issue to issue, and a literary gossip* column. These literary items were original compositions for the paper rather than copied from national papers in scissors* and paste journalism, as had been the case with the earlier *Protestant Ulster Times**. That the layout of the *Observer* closely follows that of the *Ulster Times* invites comparison of the two, which draws attention to the lack of the Catholic voice within the broader northern Irish Press.

In 1868 the paper closed, but in 1870 it reappeared, merged* with the *Belfast Northern Star*, surviving as the *Northern Star and Ulster Observer* until 1872. **MBT**
Sources: *Ulster Observer, Ulster Times.*

ULSTER TIMES (1836-1842)

The *Ulster Times* was a thrice-weekly evening broadsheet in advertisement* 'wrappers' costing 5d, varying between four and seven pages in length and often including free supplements*. In general its appearance was modelled on *The Times**. Stridently patriotic*, the *Ulster Times* carried an emblem of a crown and sceptre atop a heavy bound book, pre-

sumably the Bible, and took upon itself the 'proud office of representing the public opinion of the Province of Ulster'. In doing so it announced that 'the standard we unfurl is that of PROTESTANTISM and CONSERVATISM. Its contents covered national and international news* and politics* as well as local* items. Its regular literature* section of poetry* and reviews* was almost entirely taken from other sources such as the *Athenaeum** and the *Morning Herald**. **MBT**
Source: *Ulster Times.*

ULSTERMAN (1852-1858); IRISHMAN (1858-1885)

The *Ulsterman* (1852-1858) was a bi-weekly Belfast newspaper, published on Wednesdays and Saturdays. It was founded in 1852 by journalist Denis Holland, and advocated Catholic rights. The paper was renamed the *Irishman* in 1858, removed to Dublin in 1859 and changed to a weekly*, managed by Holland and journalist Richard Pigott.

Among its contributors were former members of Young Ireland*: John Mitchel,* John E. Pigot and journalist John Augustus O'Shea. Holland suffered financial losses in two libel cases in 1861-1862 and formed a personal rivalry with A. M. O'Sullivan, editor* of the other leading nationalist weekly, the *Nation**. In 1863 Holland sold the *Irishman* to journalist Patrick James Smyth, but due to low sales, he in turn sold it to Richard Pigott in 1865 for £700. The suppression of another competitor*, the *Irish People*, allowed the *Irishman* to raise its circulation* to 50,000 copies per week (1865-1869).

Under Pigott the paper supported the Fenian Brotherhood, which led to more lawsuits and imprisonment. As doubts over Pigott's professional conduct increased, he was forced in 1881 to sell for a total of £3,000 both the *Irishman* and his other magazines, the *Flag of Ireland* and the *Shamrock**, to the Irish National Newspaper and Publishing Company, owned by Charles Stewart Parnell's Land League. The *Irishman* was then edited* briefly by scholar, Dr George Sigerson, until its closure. **FB**
Sources: Brown 1937, Comerford 1985, Lyons 1977, *ODNB, Waterloo Irish.*

UNION JACK (1880-1883)

The *Union Jack* was a weekly magazine of 'stirring literature'* aimed at boys and young men. An imperialist* and jingoistic rhetoric coloured much of the writing, which aimed to foster ideals of manliness and duty in its young readers. The children's writer and promoter of colonization, W. H. G. Kingston founded *Union Jack* but died within eight months of its first number. The editorship* was passed on to George

Alfred Henty, who had served in the Crimea, and become a war* correspondent and highly successful writer of stories for boys. He serialized* much of his own work in the magazine as well as stories from writers such as Jules Verne, R. M. Ballantyne and Robert Louis Stevenson. Henty also brought in prize competitions for his readers and addressed them sympathetically as 'My Dear Lads'. He hoped that *Union Jack*'s 'lessons' had 'taught such as would help its readers to be honest, straightforward and manly' ('Preface', vol. IV).

The magazine* was well illustrated* and sometimes used colour. The *Union Jack* had three publishers* in as many years and each failed to make the venture as profitable as its high initial circulation* had promised among increasingly fierce competition* for the boys' market. **BP**
Sources: Dixon 1999, Harris and Lee 1986, James 1973, *ODNB*, *Waterloo*.

UNITED IRISHMAN AND GALWAY AMERICAN (JULY 1863-APRIL 1864) The *United Irishman and Galway American* (motto: 'Faith, Fortitude, Fatherland'), the Dublin organ of the issuing* body the National Brotherhood of Saint Patrick, was published weekly* in Dublin at 2d, 3d stamped. It had begun life in Galway in April 1862 as the plain *Galway American*, dedicated to advocating 'the National Rights and development of the Industrial Resources of Ireland'. However, when Denis Holland's *Irishman**, which had been sympathetic, was sold in 1863, on failing to launch a newspaper entirely under their control, the Brotherhood persuaded the proprietor* of the *Galway American* Thomas O'Neil Russel (along with Holland, one of the movement's founders) and editor* James Roche, to move the paper to Dublin and to change its name.

The somewhat strange title is explained by Roche's personal history and political* philosophy. An émigré returned from America, he had been one of the originators of the Fenian Brotherhood there, editing their paper the *Phoenix* in New York. The new journal's masthead* (a star-spangled banner, a Fenian sunburst flag, a French cap of liberty, Irish pikes and an American eagle rising phoenix-like from the flames) reflected his transatlantic* and revolutionary interests, combining iconic references to French, American and Irish revolutions. Publicity material stressed the plebian character of the Brotherhood: 'The National Brotherhood has removed to a great extent the fallacious notion that none but the "higher classes" could think for Ireland. They can think and only await the opportunity to act'. Christopher Clinton Hoey* of the Cen-

tral Council and Joseph P. McDonnell, the Brotherhood secretary, both worked on the paper.

However, the association with the National Brotherhood was not to last. Roche fell out with the more militantly minded members when in March 1864 he condemned as an attack on free speech a violent disturbance at a meeting in the Rotundo Dublin at which A. M. Sullivan of the Dublin Nation was speaking. This led the Brotherhood to sever its connection with his paper, which folded soon afterwards. **AMcN**
Sources: Joyce 1995, Joyce 1996, McNicholas 2007.

UNITED SERVICES GAZETTE (1833-1854) The *United Service Gazette* was a weekly paper begun in 1833 by Alaric Watts, journalist* and editor*. It was launched in the same year and indeed on the same day as Henry Colburn's* *Naval and Military Gazette* (1833-1886). This seeming coincidence is to be accounted for by the fact that the rival proprietors* engaged in a race as to which publication should be first in the field, the result of which was that they appeared simultaneously. Watts claimed that his intent was to include more writing about the navy, particularly about the Royal Marines, and to criticize the scale of family patronage in the services; his sympathies, however, were fundamentally Tory and supportive of the status quo. He eventually ran into financial difficulties and lost the *United Service Gazette* in 1843, when the paper was auctioned to Andrew Spottiswoode*, who appointed J. H. Stocqueler as editor* in 1846.

Stocqueler had spent the years from 1826 to 1841 as a journalist in India, and on his return to Britain he became a writer on military affairs. As editor of the *United Service Gazette* he entered into competition* with John Phillipart of the *Naval and Military Gazette*, although they were fundamentally in agreement in their advocacy of military reforms and in welcoming correspondence from officers sympathetic to their ideas. The naval editor for the *United Service Gazette* M. H. Barker was known as 'the Old Sailor'; he was a former Royal Navy officer who had for some years served as a mercenary before settling down to a career in journalism. Circulation* for the *United Service Gazette* came to 1,300 copies per week, though the number of readers was undoubtedly larger, as many subscriptions were held by regimental and garrison messes where each copy might be read by 30 to 50 readers. **MaK**
Sources: Vann 1994, *Waterloo*.

UNIVERSAL NEWS (1860-69) The *Universal News* (motto 'Our Faith, Our Fatherland') was published weekly* between December 1860 and December 1869, a long career for a secular* paper aimed at an Irish Catholic readership*. It began as a joint venture between English and Irish Catholics, with a mission to 'supersede the low-priced, dangerous and profligate publications' then current among the working classes*. It was not to be a religious* journal though but 'a thoroughly useful general newspaper,' one however 'conducted in a moral and truly Catholic spirit'. It quickly became an Irish paper but in its politics* had to negotiate a delicate course between the aspirations of the majority of its readers and what was acceptable to its remaining English backers and readers and to the Catholic hierarchy. By 1867 it had become 'a Fenian paper masquerading as a Catholic journal' and this eventually led to its demise, following a public row with Bishop Ullathorne of Birmingham.

Its first editor* was A. W. Harnett of the *Tipperary Advocate*, assisted by John F O'Donnell, who succeeded him and edited the paper at various times over the next decade and also contributed poetry*. John Eugene O'Cavanagh also edited the paper. The last editor was Christopher Clinton Hoey*, who with fellow Fenian J. P. McDonnell ran the paper until its demise. Historical sketches, poetry, drama and prose fiction featured, especially under C. C. Hoey*. Michael Davitt contributed poetry. Other notable contributors include Arthur M. Forrester*, James Owen O' Connor, Charles P. O'Connor ('Cairn Thierna'), Elizabeth Willoughby Treacy ('Finola'), Thomas Neilson Underwood ('Celt') and Robert J. Grannell. **AMcN**

Sources: Dudley Edwards and Storey 1985, McNicholas 2007.

UNIVERSAL REVIEW (1888-1890) An illustrated monthly* magazine*, Harry Quilter's* *Universal Review* published substantive reviews* on art, artists, and art exhibits, complete with high-quality illustrations* and reproductions of paintings by prominent artists such as Sir Frederick Leighton, Alfred Hunt, Laurence Housman and Walter Crane*. The magazine was innovative in its blend of art criticism, politics*, international affairs and literary* reviews. It emphasized art criticism and the study of art as a separate element of its editorial purview. Every issue featured several full-page facsimiles of the paintings being discussed as well as other illustrations. Quilter wrote a majority of the art criticism, and his advocacy of Pre-Raphaelitism saturates these reviews.

The *Universal Review*, however, was not solely devoted to art criticism. A true miscellany*, it published literary reviews and political and social* essays from influential writers such as Charles Wentworth Dilke, Eliza Lynn Linton*, Grant Allen* and Annie Besant*. As Benjamin F. Fisher IV claims, the magazine stood in the middle of the day's debates. The magazine addressed current political and social issues ranging from Anglo-Indian relations to women's suffrage, but it was not always consistent in its handling of an issue. For example, George Fleming's 'On a Certain Deficiency in Women' (July 1888) argues that women are incapable of independent rational thought while Emilia Dilke's* 'The Next Extension of the Suffrage' (July 1889) and Allen's 'Girl of the Future' (May 1890) support an open debate on women's suffrage. Despite its innovations and stable of writers and artists, a lack of financing forced the magazine to fold after two and half years. **CL**

Sources: Sullivan, *Waterloo*.

UNIVERSITY MAGAZINES British university periodicals date back at least to 1643 and Oxford's Civil War newsbook, the *Mercurius Aulicus* (1643-1648), although it was the nineteenth century that contributed most to what we think of today as 'university magazines'. Dominated by Oxford and Cambridge, these may be divided into two main types: that closest to the core meaning, periodicals published by students, and the type published by university authorities. A third, commercial, kind, is rare, the *Dublin University Magazine** and Oxford's *Isis* (1892-) being the few with commercial backing, though others such as *Granta* became commercially successful in the twentieth century. It should be noted that many journalists referred to in this Dictionary (Pater* for example) belonged to networks formed at university; some went on to generate periodicals derived largely from these networks, such as the *Contemporary Review**. The limits of the 'University magazine' are, then, to some extent arbitrary and uncertain.

It is unsurprising that student magazines, since they rely on specific networks that are transitory and are produced outside a commercial nexus which can support them, tend to be extremely ephemeral. The earliest student magazine seems to have been Oxford's *Student* (1750-1751), to which Christopher Smart contributed, but it was not until the late 1820s and 1830s that they began to appear in any number: thus, the *Cambridge Snob* (1829) and its continuation the *Gownsman* (1830) in which Thackeray* published his earliest works, the

Freshman, the *Fellow* (both 1836) and *Tripos* (1838-1839); and the Oxford *Isis* (1829) and *Oxford University Magazine* (1834-1835). Most were scurrilous and lasted only a few months, sometimes suppressed for obscenity. Much more serious were the *London University Magazine* (1829), *Chronicle* (1830) and *Examiner* (1833), none of which, however, survived beyond a very few issues. The earliest example of Scottish student journalism known is the *Edinburgh College Magazine* (1822), and indeed Edinburgh generated several similar in the 1820s and 1830s, including the *Lapsus Linguae* (1824-1826; irregular, change of title). Interesting as the training ground for figures who would later become famous are the *Cambridge University Magazine* (1839-1843; there are several others of the same name) edited* by C. B. Willox and later by W. M. W. Call who was to become a friend of George Eliot* and prolific contributor to the *Westminster Review**; the *Edinburgh University Magazine* (in a manifestation which lasted a few months in 1871), edited by Robert Louis Stevenson; the *Oxford Spirit Lamp* (1892-1893), founded as a literary* magazine and later edited by Lord Alfred Douglas who turned it 'decadent'; and the *Oxford and Cambridge Magazine* (12 issues, 1852), founded and written by William Morris*, edited by William Fulford and to which Burne-Jones, Rossetti and Vernon Lushington contributed. Not all university magazines might be regarded as innocently undergraduate or progressive: one, the *Moslem*, appeared for three issues in 1870 as supposedly advanced and liberal but in reality a vicious protest against the admission of overseas students. There was a second major wave of student magazines in the 1880s and 1890s which included periodicals such as *Granta* (1889-) and the revived *Oxford Review* (1885; originally *Oxford Undergraduates' Journal* and other titles from 1866) and many more short-lived ones. The arrival of women's student magazines comprises part of this wave (the *Girton College Review* was the first, starting in 1882), but they were corralled into a separate space, mirroring the geographical separation of women's university education. Most differentiated themselves from men's publications by using the names of flowers: thus the *Iris* (Owens College, Manchester, 1887-1894), the *Daisy* (1890-1899, Lady Margaret's College, Oxford) and *Fritillary* (1893-1931, Oxford Women's Colleges). *King's College Magazine (Ladies Dept)* (1896-1914) more defiantly marks its difference.

Unsurprisingly, periodicals published or sanctioned by university authorities were longerlived.

The *Cambridge University Reporter* (1870-) publishes notices and reports, calendars, examination papers and so forth; the *Oxford University Gazette* is similar except that the examination papers are published separately. Other universities published similar periodicals. The *Oxford Magazine* (1883-1970) had few contributions by undergraduates, while the *Cambridge Review* (1879-), ostensibly run by students, was heavily subvented by the authorities – Marillier suggested in 1898 that it survived only by printing the university sermons. **AK**

Sources: Marillier 1902, Rice 1924, Sullivan, VanArsdel *et al.* 1994.

'UNSTAMPED' PRESS The term 'unstamped', as applied to a newspaper avoiding the stamp duty levied on sheets of newsprint, had existed since the early eighteenth century. It acquired a radical political* association in November 1816, when William Cobbett circumvented the existing 4d duty by re-issuing editorials from his weekly*, *Political Register* in a cheap* 2d format*. This strategy established the unstamped press as a vehicle of radical expression: Cobbett's example was quickly followed by Richard Carlile's* *Republican*, Thomas J. Wooler's* *Black Dwarf*, William Hone's* *Hone's Reformists' Register* and John Wade's *Gorgon*.

The 1819 Stamp Act (one of the repressive 'Six Acts' passed in the immediate wake of the Peterloo massacre) targeted the radical unstamped press by defining any periodical containing news or comment as a 'newspaper' (and thus subject to stamp, paper and advertisement* duties), commencing a period of legal-political repression that stifled the radical press. Despite this clampdown on freedom of expression, the cheap periodical market continued to diversify and expand in the 1820s. Costing between 1d and 3d (and 'unstamped'), this new generation of cheap periodicals was produced by a combination of veteran radical, entrepreneurial and philanthropic bookseller-publishers* and encompassed a diversity of literary, political, scientific and religious genres*. The cultivation of the infrastructure, content and form of the cheap periodical by publishers in the 1820s enabled the rapid mobilization of the radical press during the 'war of the unstamped' between 1830-1836. In the context of this campaign against the 'taxes on knowledge'*, the term 'unstamped' continued to connote illegal radical newspapers, of which William Carpenter's* *Political Letters* (1830-1831), Henry Hetherington's* *Penny Papers for the People* (1830-1831) and *Poor Man's Guardian**, and James Watson's* *Working Man's Friend** were the quintessential examples.

These were succeeded by John Cleave's* broadsheet, the *Weekly Police Gazette**, James Morrison's trade* unionist Pioneer (1833-1834), Robert Owen's* co-operative *Crisis**, Carlile's republican *Gauntlet*, Richard E. Lee's Spencean Man (1833-1834) and scores of other political weeklies*, for the dissemination of which hundreds of publishers, printers and vendors were fined or imprisoned. Even so, the unstamped press of the 1830s reflected the diversity of the cheap market forged in the previous decade.

Metropolitan* and provincial* publishers including William Strange, George Cowie, Benjamin Cousins, Benjamin Steill, George Purkess, George Berger, Effingham Wilson, Charles Penny, Abel Heywood, James Mann and Joshua Hobson produced hundreds of different unstamped titles including the medical* *Doctor* (1832-1837), the newspaper-style *National Omnibus* and Hetherington's *Two-Penny Dispatch* (1836), the literary* *Parterre* (1834-1837), the *Penny Satirist* (1837-1848) and the penny comic weekly *Figaro** in London. Strange was also involved in publishing the *Penny Cyclopaedia* (1833-1843) of the Society for the Diffusion of Useful Knowledge*, and Charles Knight* invoked the 'unstamped' label for his celebrated *Penny Magazine*. The Society for Promoting Christian Knowledge likewise issued its *Saturday Magazine** as an unstamped 1d weekly*, demonstrating how pressmen external to radical print culture appropriated this cheap format. The proliferation of the unstamped press and pressure from across the political and social spectrum forced the reduction of the stamp duty to a penny in 1836, although it was not finally repealed until 1855. In the context of political crisis the term 'unstamped' functioned as a synonym for a radical press deemed to be an 'unsafe' species in an otherwise 'safe' cheap periodical genus. This distinction was arbitrarily drawn, and the overlap in personnel, ideas and readership* was considerable. Moreover, cheap satirical*, literary, co-operative*, sensationalist, 'useful* knowledge' and religious periodicals were all technically unstamped, and ultimately the growing market for cheap periodical literature between 1815 and 1836 bore testimony to the increasing production and consumption of all these forms. **DSM**

Sources: Harrison 1977, Haywood 2004, Hollis 1970, *Waterloo*, Wiener 1969.

UPTON, FLORENCE KATE (1873-1922) Florence Upton's British parents were living in New York at the time of her birth. When her father died in 1889, Florence began working as a magazine illustrator* to help the family's finances. In 1893 the family returned to Hampstead where Upton continued her career as an illustrator in order to fund her younger's brother's education.

Upton contributed cartoons* to the magazine *Punch** and in 1894 started an association with *Strand Magazine** which continued until 1903. In 1895 she also had work published in the *Idler**, but 1895 was the year which saw the creation that brought her the greatest financial success. *The Adventures of Two Dutch Dolls* featured Upton's iconic Golliwogg, a character based on a black doll that she and her sister had owned. Stories featuring this character were produced annually until 1909 with Upton's drawings in stories woven around episodes from bicycles to airships.

Using the proceeds from these books to pursue her art training, and after many years of struggle, Upton gained a significant European reputation as a portraitist. **CL**

Sources: Lyttelton 1926, Micklethwaite and Peppin 1983, *ODNB*.

USEFUL KNOWLEDGE Useful knowledge was a label applied to predominantly scientific* and technical content intended for a non-specialist, mainly working-class* readership* in the early nineteenth century. The existence of an audience for print among the working class was well recognized, and the desire for education seemed to unite artisans with the interests of middle-class philanthropists. However, the provision of educative material by one class for another was necessarily political* and produced different notions of what was, in fact, useful.

The ideological underpinnings of useful knowledge were set out in Henry Brougham's* pamphlet 'Observations on the Education of the People' in 1825. Dedicated to George Birkbeck, whose mechanics' class at Glasgow had been successfully imitated in the foundation of the London Mechanics' Institution in 1823, the pamphlet took for granted that the people wanted to be instructed, and suggested instead that the issue was how this was to be achieved. As artisans were short of time and money, it argued that the role of the middle classes was to provide cheap* and accessible material. This was not to be given away however: Brougham cautioned against charity, arguing that the expenses of such a project must be defrayed by the working classes in order to avoid them becoming dependent on those he calls 'their superiors'. The establishment of the Society for the Diffusion of Useful Knowledge (SDUK*) in 1826 provided an institutional base from which to put into practice Brougham's suggestions.

The phrase 'Diffusion of Useful Knowledge' was from an article in Charles Knight's* *Plain Englishman* in 1823. Knight, whose publishing business had failed in 1826, joined the SDUK and became their official publisher* in 1829. The SDUK produced a large number of books, pamphlets and serials*, on a wide range of subject matter. Knight was instrumental in this, using his knowledge of the market to produce well-presented content in innovative formats. Most successful of the Society's ventures was the *Penny Magazine*, which began in 1832 and reached 200,000 readers a month.

Although useful knowledge was primarily intended as practical scientific and technical content, the range of subjects encompassed by the SDUK was diverse. The SDUK, following the practice of many clubs and societies, banned religion* and politics* from its publications and, as it required large readerships* to pay for its cheap publications, was forced to find subjects of interest to all. As the pages of the *Penny Magazine* showed, these tended to be eclectic and often far-removed from the actual world of its readers. It was its irrelevance, coupled with the well-known political orientation of its supporters, that prompted much of the opposition to useful knowledge.

However, although the SDUK was disbanded due to financial reasons in 1846, there were enterprising publishers who were using useful knowledge to turn a profit. Whereas radical artisans dismissed its publications as little more than paternalistic propaganda, the activities of the SDUK demonstrated a market for serials*, miscellanies* and compilations that offered information on a wide range of subjects. Such reference works were to become staple publications of many firms and provided much of the content of other books, periodicals and newspapers throughout the century. **JEM**

Sources: Brougham 1825, *ODNB*, Prothero 1981, Rauch 2001.

V

VANITY FAIR (1868-1929) The best and most successful 'society journal', *Vanity Fair: A Weekly* *Show of Political, Social, and Literary Wares?* was established by Thomas Gibson Bowles*and took its name and motto from John Bunyan's *Pilgrim's Progress*. Aimed at an educated and politically aware audience, early issues of the 12-page, two-column*, folio-sized*journal were primarily devoted to national and world events, government news* and social topics. Book and drama reviews*, a letter from Paris, letters*to the editor and a word games page were also included. From January 1869, the journal incorporated full-page, chromo-lithograph caricatures*of well-known government, social, literary and religious figures, a feature that helped to make the magazine famous contributed by the most prestigious caricaturists such as Max Beerbohm*, Carlo 'Ape' Pellegrini* and Leslie 'Spy' Ward*. In the 1870s, the journal expanded to an average of 18 pages per week and commenced each issue with brief, often satiric*items of political* or social news variously called 'Notes', 'Chronicle' and, finally, 'Vanities'. In the 1880s and 1890s, *Vanity Fair* averaged 22 pages and, in addition to its core political and society content, contained serial*and complete fiction, extensive reviews, arts profiles, and sports*coverage. Contributors included Matthew Arnold*, Robert Browning, Lewis Carroll, Lady Florence Dixie*, Ashley Dukes, Charles Kingsley, Grenville Murray*, Henry Pottinger Stephens and William Wilde.

Originally priced*at 2d, it was raised to 6d in 1870 and remained at that level until 1912, with the exception of a brief, failed price rise to 1s in 1874. Although the first issue only sold 619 copies, circulation*increased to over 2,500 by March 1869. Advertisements*were a key source of revenue for the journal and even early issues contained an average of three pages of advertisements at the back. Later issues contained even more advertisements dispersed throughout the magazine. In April 1869, a full-page ad cost £12, and a column, £4.

Bowles, who served as editor*and proprietor*(1869-1889), was succeeded by A. G. Witherby. In 1914, *Vanity Fair* merged* with the women's magazine *Hearth and Home*, and nothing remained of its original format in the new journal except its title *Vanity Fair and Hearth and Home,* which folded fifteen years later. **EFO**
Source: *Waterloo.*

VEGETARIAN MESSENGER (1849-1859); DIE-TETIC REFORMER AND VEGETARIAN MESSENGER (1860-1886); 1887, VEGETARIAN MESSENGER AND HEALTH REVIEW (1887-1961); THE VEGE-TARIAN (1962-) The *Vegetarian Messenger* was begun as a penny*, unillustrated 16-page. demi-octavo monthly by the Vegetarian Society to commemorate their first annual meeting. The Society had been founded in 1847 by the alliance of a midlands group of radical Swedenborgians known as the Bible Christians (or Cowherdites, after their founder William Cowherd) and a school in Richmond (outside London), known as the Concordium dedicated to celibacy, raw food, fresh air and loose clothing. It espoused notions of popular progress though regulation of the diet and hence behaviour – like alcohol, meat was considered to stimulate the body in an unnatural and unhealthy way (cf. Medical Journals: Alternative/Complementary Fringe*). As Spencer (2000: 254-255) reports, much was made in the *Messenger* of the horrors of slaughtering animals and meat eating, which could readily lead to murder.

The *Messenger* was initially published* by William Bremner and William Horsell (who ran a vegetarian hydropathic infirmary at Ramsgate), though Abel Haywood*and Fred Pitman joined them from the second (December) number when the periodical took a recognizable shape, with around 12 pages of essays, lectures and reviews*, two pages for Notices to Correspondents* and advertisements* (at first mainly for the Vegetarian Society itself, with a few vegetarian books, though later water-cure establishments also took out space) and 2 pages of miscellaneous paragraphs known as the 'Supplement*'.

There is no indication of the editor*, though from volume 2 (Jan. 1851) correspondence and contributions are to be addressed to Bremner in Manchester. The format* changes here too, being split up into various sections with separate pagination: eight pages for the main body comprising articles and so on; two pages of the Vegetarian Treasury (= miscellaneous); two pages of the Vegetarian Controversialist (= correspondence) and two pages (actually four half-sized ones) on the question of land management. This curious form was maintained until 1852 when it took over as the official organ of the Society after the *Vegetarian Advocate* (1848-1851) closed.

Circulation* was always a problem – in 1853 there were only 889 members of the Society and in 1870 only 125 – and no doubt for economic reasons the new version of the periodical in 1861 was a 3d 64-page quarterly*. It seems that the Rev. James Clark, secretary of the Society, ran the periodical, and while other publishers were also involved, Pitman and Bremner remained faithful.

By the New Series in 1887 and the restoration of the original title, vegetarianism was much more popular, as testified by the 12-16 pages of advertisements where restaurants and foodstuffs had become more prominent than publications. The *Messenger* was a monthly again, costing 2d, of 32 pages and some confidence, with accounts of local and foreign meetings and news, correspondence, recipes, reviews, 'Scraps from the Press' and series on dietetics and 'The Vegetable Garden' as well as official announcements of the Society and interviews* with prominent vegetarians (Shaw*was interviewed in January 1898). **AK**
Source: Spencer 2000, *Waterloo*.

VERSCHOYLE, JOHN STUART (1853-1915)
Born in Ireland, John S. Verschoyle, a friend of Frank Harris*, became Harris's subeditor* on the *Fortnightly Review*in 1889 and probably resigned when Harris did in 1894. Verschoyle was a curate of the Church of the Holy Trinity, Marylebone, but he helped Harris with his writing and editing for around eight years. He also wrote a number of articles for the *Fortnightly Review* on local* and literary* topics, and one in 1896 defending Cecil Rhodes. Esther Houghton thought he might have been 'Imperialist*' who wrote three further articles in 1896, 1897 and 1898 which took 'an enthusiastic view of the great Empire builder.' **AH**
Source: Houghton 1968.

VICTORIA MAGAZINE (1863-1880)
The monthly *Victoria Magazine* was launched by Emily Faithfull*and Emily Davies, although Davies soon left to pursue other interests. Faithfull remained as editor* and her company, the Victoria Press*, published and printed the magazine* from the beginning. Like the other magazines produced by the women of Langham Place, including the *English Woman's Journal*and the *Alexandra Magazine*, the *Victoria Magazine* was a committed supporter of and advocate for women's* rights. Named after Queen Victoria, it used the figure of the Queen to endorse feminine domesticity at the same time that it emphasized her position in the public sphere as monarch.

One of the strengths of the *Victoria Magazine* lay in its coverage of the women's movement, though it had literary* objectives as well. It differed from its competitors* by including serialized* fiction, short stories and poetry* by contributors such as Isa Craig, Adelaide

Procter, Christina Rossetti, Thomas Trollope, Tom Hood* and George MacDonald. In addition, a strong focus on women's education, employment, suffrage and property rights contributed to its relatively long run, with articles by Frances Power Cobbe* and Margaret Oliphant*. Regular features included 'Literature of the Month,' which tended to review* books relevant to the women's movement, and a 'Social Science*' section that covered events related to the women's movement. In later years 'Correspondence*' and 'Victorian Discussion Society' features provided an excellent view of readers'* perspectives and a history of the women's movement in the 1860s and 1870s. **KLM**
Sources: Fraser 2003, Frawley 1998, Nestor 1982, Sullivan.

VIRTUE, JAMES SPRENT (1829-1892)
Often remembered in media history as the publisher* of Anthony Trollope's failed *St Paul's Magazine*, James Virtue was for the most part a successful printer and publisher of first-quality illustrated* books and periodicals including the *Art Journal*. Born in London, the son of serial* part-issue publishing specialist George Virtue, James was apprenticed to his father at 14 and went to New York in 1848, rising to lead Virtue & Co.'s American branch by 1851. In 1855 he took over the business when his father retired because of ill-health. He continued to support his father's expensively illustrated* *Art Journal*, publishing important engraved collections in it including the Royal, J. M. W. Turner, Landseer and other galleries, as well as illustrated volumes and annuals* including the *Fine Art Annual* (1872-1873), illustrated editions of Shakespeare and the Holy Bible and a collection called 'Picturesque Palestine' that reportedly turned a profit despite production costs of £ 25,000. In 1862 he formed Virtue Brothers & Co. with elder brother George Henry Virtue, and started the short-lived *Parthenon: A Weekly Journal of Literature, Science, and Art* (1862-1863).

The first printer of the *Fortnightly Review*, Virtue attended early board meetings and may have been an investor. The company became Virtue & Co. again at George Henry's death in 1866. In 1867 Virtue funded the launch of a new shilling* monthly, recruiting Anthony Trollope*as editor* with full control and a budget for editorial salaries of 1,000 per year. Although Virtue sold the underperforming *St Paul's* to Strahan* & Co. in May 1869, he continued as its printer until the magazine folded in 1874. A partnership of Virtue, Spalding & Daldy was formed with other Strahan creditors in 1873; in 1875 it became a limited company with

Virtue as chairman. Trollope's *Autobiography* (1883) praises Virtue's 'wide liberality' and 'perpetual good humour'. **DHL**
Sources: Boase, *ODNB*, Srebrnik 1982, Trollope 1883, *Wellesley.*

VIZETELLY, FRANK (1830-1883) Artist and journalist*, Frank Vizetelly, was the youngest and most well travelled of the three English Vizetelly brothers who worked in periodicals in the second half of the nineteenth century, spending long periods as a foreign* correspondent. Having previously contributed to the *Pictorial Times*, which his brother Henry*had founded in 1843, he helped establish *Le Monde Illustré* in Paris in 1857, editing*it for two years. In 1859 he returned to England and began work for the *Illustrated London News**. Vizetelly became one of the first war*correspondents and artists, and was frequently named or referred to as 'our special artist'. He sent drawings back to be engraved by the *Illustrated London News* team, a system which was capable of great speed and preserved the immediacy of many of his illustrations*, often emphasized by the term 'sketch' in the attribution.

Vizetelly followed Garibaldi on his *Risorgimento* campaigns in Sicily and the mainland of Italy in 1860, greatly contributing to the popular esteem of Garibaldi in England. Following this, he went to America to cover the Civil War, originally with access to the Northern forces, but lost favour with the Union Army after his unflattering portrayal of the 'Stampede from Bull Run' (21 July 1861). Thereafter he accompanied the Confederate forces, sending back over 100 drawings to be published and even on occasion acting as a courier for General J. E. B. Stuart. The *Illustrated's* coverage of the conflict thus became more pro-Confederate. Returning to England in 1865, Vizetelly then became a war correspondent in Spain, reporting on the revolution in 1868. In 1883 he travelled as the paper's war correspondent in Egypt and was believed to have died there in the Sudan, at the Kashgil massacre. **AM**
Sources: Engen 1990, Houfe 1978, *ODNB*, Vizetelly 1893.

VIZETELLY, HENRY RICHARD (1820-1894)
Henry Richard Vizetelly was a wood* engraver, printer, editor*, journalist* and publisher*. The son of a printer and engraver, he had publishing and the print trade in his blood. He was apprenticed to John Orrin Smith*, one of the most prominent wood* engravers of the day, which is one reason why Vizetelly eventually became a leading figure in the pictorial press. He encountered Herbert In-

gram*when they collaborated on an illustrated*advertising*booklet for a popular nostrum, 'Parr's Life Pills', Vizetelly supplying a portrait. This project met with such success that the partners were encouraged to move into illustrated* publishing.

Ingram and Vizetelly founded the *Illustrated London News**in May 1842, and although Frederick Naylor was appointed editor*for the text, Vizetelly directed the illustrations, which often took innovative forms. For example, the 'special Colosseum Print of London' (7 Jan. 1843), which was offered to subscribers for the first six months, took the form of a foldout panorama. When Vizetelly left Ingram later that year to found the rival *Pictorial Times* with his brother James (1817-1897) and Andrew Spottiswoode*, he offered an even more impressive panorama of the Thames as an incentive to subscribers of the new publication (eventually published 11 Jan. 1845). This was printed as four sections which, when joined up, measured over 12 feet, and carried his name.

Vizetelly went on to edit (in partnership with David Bogue) the hugely successful 2d weekly *Illustrated Times**, publishing without a stamp for some weeks but escaping prosecution. It had a circulation*of over 200,000 and many of the late-nineteenth century's most prominent journalists were among those who partly learned their trade writing for the title, including Edmund Yates*, G. A. Sala*and James Hannay*. Among the Vizetelly Brothers' great successes were the engravings of Bogue's editions of Henry Wadsworth Longfellow's poems, and the engraved National Illustrated Library series (published by Ingram) in the 1850s.

Vizetelly established the *Welcome Guest** in 1858 but sold this after two years. While Vizetelly lived in Paris (1865-1877) he was a correspondent* for the *Illustrated London News*, while also contributing to the *Pall Mall Gazette**, *All the Year Round** and *Once a Week**. Returning to Britain in 1877, he founded Vizetelly & Company, which was known for its publications of translations of French and Russian literature, often considered outré and unconventional at the time. His championing of Emile Zola's novels in the late 1880s, for which he was imprisoned in 1889, marks a significant point in the history of the fight against literary* censorship*.

Vizetelly's autobiography, *Glances Back through Seventy Years*, offers considerable information on the Victorian press. **MWT/AM**
Sources: Engen 1990, *ODNB*, Vizetelly 1893.

W

W. H. ALLEN W. H. Allen is first noted in business in 1817, with Messrs Alexander Black, Thomas Kingsbury, Charles Parbury and William H. Allen as booksellers in Leadenhall Street, London dealing predominantly in oriental publications. By 1822, the firm is without Alexander Black and by 1825 with the publication of the *General East India Guide*, they are noted to be 'Official booksellers to the East India Company'. In 1827, Parbury & Allen alone began publishing the periodical the *Bengal Almanac for the Year* (1827-1844). In 1830, Wm. H. Allen & Co. took over publication from Allen Parbury and Co. of the *Asiatic Journal and Monthly Register for British and Foreign India, China, Australasia*, which encompassed literary*, philosophical* and historical* content, domestic news*, with news from the East India Company. However, in September 1837, the partnership of (Charles) Parbury & Allen was dissolved and Wm. H. Allen & Co, still of Leadenhall Street, began expanding its English and oriental publishing* business, with the *Statesman* Series, *Scenes and Characteristics of Hindostan* (sic) and the *East India Year Book* (1841).

In 1843, the *Asian Journal* was separated into two parts: the *Asian Journal* continued, with 'original Papers, Home Intelligence, etc' published on the first of the month, price* 2s 6d. The second part became the *Indian Mail; a monthly register for British and foreign India, China and Australasia*, containing 'Asiatic Intelligence, Appointments, Deaths, etc', published 'immediately after the arrival of each month's mail', priced 1s. Meeting the needs of the readers* was Allen's explanation: news, not cultural essays, was what interested those in Britain with families in the Empire. By separating the content, Allen could expand the news section and target his markets* more effectively. The *Indian Mail* took its proprietor's* name (1845-1891), becoming *Allen's Indian Mail* 'to distinguish it more effectively than before from any other journal of similar character'. This oblique reference to George Allen, a publisher in India who founded the *Lahore Civil and Military Gazette*, indicates the competition*.

William Allen died in January 1855, but the company continued, publishing the *National Review** from 1883, the *Asiatic Quarterly Review* in 1886, as well as specializing in Indian language texts. In that year, the partnership of W. H. Allen & Co., booksellers and publishers, now of Waterloo-place, Pall-Mall, was dissolved. A reconfigured company took over the *Illustrated Naval and Military Magazine* in 1888, while in October 1890, Messrs W. H. Allen & Co., English and Oriental publishers, became a limited liability company with shares being taken by the company and their friends. **CL**

Sources: 19CBLN, *Waterloo*.

W. H. SMITH & SON (1790s-) W. H. Smith & Son were one of the major nineteenth-century wholesalers, distributors* and retailers of newspapers, periodicals and books. Founded as a London news-walk in the 1790s, it was under the management of William Henry Smith I (1792-1865) that the company first came to prominence as a distributor of London newspapers to the provinces. From the 1820s, Smith I used the fast day-coach system to deliver newspapers to agents*, newsrooms and individual subscribers throughout the British Isles. This method of distribution was significantly faster than the mail coaches that had previously been used to make overnight deliveries.

Smith began to shift newspaper distribution to the emerging railway* system when his son William Henry Smith II (1825-1891) joined the business. The company* became W. H. Smith & Son in 1846. One of Smith II's earliest decisions was to take over all of the bookstalls on the London and North-Western Railway when they were put out to tender in August 1848. During the 1850s their bookstall business expanded throughout the British Isles, although they lost their last Scottish stall in 1857, never to return. The bookstalls were particularly important to the development of Victorian print culture for as well as being important retail sites they acted as distribution centres for Smith's wholesale trade. In 1854 they entered into a deal with *The Times* that gave them effective control of distribution outside London. As the number of ½d papers multiplied in the late nineteenth century, much of their wholesale business was transferred from the stalls to a series of large provincial wholesale houses, and their retail interests began to include shops, although it was not until 1905 that a major move to the high street occurred.

Despite W. H. Smith's II's reputation as a puritanical individual (his nicknames included 'Old Morality'), during the mid-Victorian period their stalls stocked a vast range of texts, including the *London Journal**, that were frowned upon by middle-class* commentators. From 1860 they also included a circulating library* from which both books and magazines could be rented. Advertisements* placed in periodicals during the 1890s reveal that ex-library magazines could be bought from the Library Department six weeks after first publication. Smith's thus gave many Victorian readers access to the new, proliferating periodical culture, but their control over the market* could sometimes be used to limit the number of titles available if material was thought offensive or unprofitable. SC

Sources: *Belgravia* 1892, *ODNB*, Wilson 1985.

WAKLEY, THOMAS (1795-1862)   Although Wakley trained as a surgeon, his decision at the age of 28 to begin the *Lancet** resulted in his becoming instead one of the most formidable reforming editors* of the age. Wakley's future father-in-law had enabled him to purchase a lucrative practice in the West End in 1819, but the following year he was assaulted and his house burnt down. While engaged in a legal dispute with his insurers he practised near the Strand, becoming a close associate of William Cobbett* and developing an interest in journalism*.

In 1823 he commenced his highly innovative *Lancet*, a small weekly* medical* journal, priced at 6d, which aimed to reach a wide readership* with medical information in the form of hospital lectures and case histories. The journal flourished (earning its editor* a good income), but, encountering resistance from the vested interests of London's medical elite, Wakley rapidly made it a tool for the reform of British medicine, a role it continued to fulfil throughout his long editorship. His implacable hostility to all abuses – whether they were the result of self-interest or incompetence – led him into a number of legal cases in the early years but also helped to bring about significant changes in medical organization, education and practice.

During the reform crisis, Wakley produced a radical weekly* entitled the *Ballot* (1831-1832), and as MP for Finsbury (1835-1852) he continued to champion the cause of equality, as well as taking a leading role in medical legislation. Wakley involved numerous writers and subeditors* in the *Lancet* over the years and, following his wife's death in 1857, two of his sons, James and Thomas Henry Wakley*, joined him in the journal's management, continuing (in turn) to edit it after his death. JRT

Sources: Bostetter 1985, Clarke 1874, *ODNB*, Richardson 2006, Sprigge 1897.

WAKLEY, THOMAS HENRY (1821-1907); WAKLEY, THOMAS (1851-1909)   Thomas Henry Wakley was the eldest of the three sons of Thomas Wakley*, founder and first editor* of the general medical* weekly the *Lancet*. He studied medicine at Oxford and London universities as well as in Paris. After qualifying in 1845 he practised medicine with distinction but published little. In 1857, as his father's health declined, he and his youngest brother James joined the *Lancet* as part proprietors* and managers. When their father died, James became its editor*. Thomas continued his interest in the journal but was mainly occupied by his medical* career. Only when he retired from surgical work in 1882 did Thomas Henry Wakley assume a fuller role on the *Lancet*. Little is known about his personal contribution to the *Lancet* except that he was a fair-minded, efficient and conscientious editor

Between 1886 and his death he jointly edited the journal with his only son Thomas Wakely, who qualified in medicine in 1883 after studying at Cambridge University and St Thomas's Hospital, London. Instead of embarking on medical practice, the youngest of the Wakleys immediately joined the *Lancet* which, since 1862, had been edited by his uncle James Wakley, assisted by his father. On James's death, Thomas and his father became editors of the journal. Under their guidance it continued to hold a leading position among medical journals, though losing ground to the *British Medical Journal**, then under the dynamic editorship of Ernest Hart*, formerly of the *Lancet*. Relations with the *British Medical Journal* reverted to friendly rivalry rather than the open hostility that had previously prevailed, especially during James Wakley's regime. Their joint editorship lasted until 1907 when, on his father's death, Thomas briefly assumed sole editorial control.

He was the last member of the Wakley dynasty to edit the *Lancet*. Alone or with his father and uncle, he presided over a flourishing periodical that remained at the forefront of medical journalism. Obituary* notices apart, he wrote little for the journal, but the late-Victorian *Lancet* carried the work of some of the leading medical scientists and practitioners of the day. Quiet, fair and unassuming, he strove to ensure that *Lancet* contributions gave no personal offence. PWB

Sources: *British Medical Journal* 13 April 1907: 903-904, 13 March 1909: 697-698, *Lancet* 13 April 1907:1025, 1048-1053, 13 March 1909: 772, 800-804, 857, *ODNB*.

THE LANCET.

A Journal of British and Foreign Medicine, Physiology, Surgery, Chemistry, Criticism, Literature, and News.

No. X.
Vol. I. 1867.

LONDON, SATURDAY, MARCH 9, 1867.

Price Sevenpence.
Stamped, Eightpence.

THE LANCET SANITARY COMMISSION FOR INVESTIGATING THE STATE OF THE INFIRMARIES OF WORKHOUSES.

In THE LANCET of Saturday next, March 16th, will be Published the SECOND REPORT of the

Changes Effected in the Management of London Workhouse Infirmaries since the Opening of "The Lancet" Commission.

Figure 63: The front page of the *Lancet* of 9 March 1867 during James Wakley's editorship.

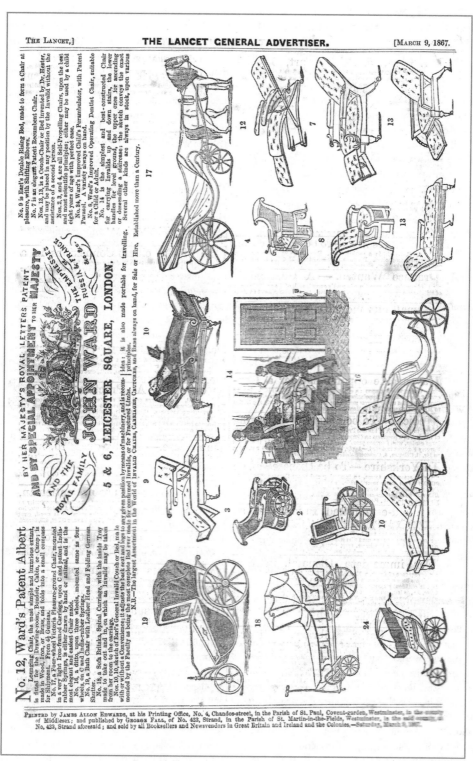

Figure 64: The back page of the *Lancet* of 9 March 1867.

WALES: A NATIONAL MAGAZINE FOR THE ENGLISH-SPEAKING PARTS OF WALES (1894-1897) A monthly* literary* miscellany*, it was founded in May 1894 by Owen Morgan Edwards, a prolific scholar and educator who served as the magazine's sole editor* and, arguably, the father of Welsh cultural nationalism. Responding to the nineteenth-century decline in Welsh-language fluency, *Wales* wooed a growing Anglophone Welsh readership*, especially targeting Edwards's ideal audience, the cultured working class* or *gwerin* ('folk'). Like *Cymru*, Edwards's Welsh-language monthly, *Wales* worked to bridge political, religious, and linguistic differences within Wales by popularizing tales and images from a shared national past.

Though *Wales* had mixed success, with circulation* falling from 3,700 to 1,100 by December 1897, and was not as directly involved in Welsh nationalism as *Young Wales* would be, it helped spread national consciousness while avoiding the sectarian divisions characteristic of the Welsh* press. Its illustrations* were progressive for their time, and Edwards's patronage supported contributing artists such as David John (Dyer) Davies as well as writers such as Allen Raine and Ernest Rhys. SY
Sources: Ballin 2004, Davies 1988, Jones 2000, Thomas 1979, Walters 2003.

WALKER, FREDERICK (1840-1875) Frederick Walker contributed to all three of the monthlies* of the 1860s best known for illustration*, *Good Words**, the *Cornhill** and *Once a Week**. Although his reputation was established by his work for the *Cornhill* serialization* of its editor* Thackeray's* 'Philip' *(Dec. 1861-Aug. 1862), his ability as a fiction illustrator was acknowledged in the commission to draw for Mrs Henry Wood's 'Oswald Cray', published in *Good Words* (1864). Quotidian rather than poetic, Walker's work was nonetheless highly regarded at the time as an accurate depiction of contemporary manners. BM
Sources: Engen 1990, Forrest Reid 1928, Goldman 1994, Houfe 1978, Suriano 2005, White 1897.

WALKLEY, ARTHUR BINGHAM (1855-1926).
A notable literary* and dramatic critic, Walkley had a parallel career as a civil servant in the postal service from which he did not retire until 1919 despite a successful literary* career. When the *Star** was founded in 1888, he was appointed its first theatre critic, writing under the pseudonym* 'Spectator' and continuing in the post until 1900. Alongside reviews* of the latest theatrical attractions, he wrote occasional, more general pieces on the state of the theatre (where he developed his skills as an essayist)

and a series of light-hearted, mildly satirical* 'Fly leaves'. He was theatre critic of the *Speaker** from 1890-1899, and his books *Playhouse Impressions* (1892) and *Frames of Mind* (1899) collected reviews* and papers written for the *Star*, the *Speaker*, the *National Observer** and others. He also contributed during the 1890s to the *Fortnightly Review**, *Theatre**, the *New Review** and *Cosmopolis**.

In 1899 he began to contribute theatre reviews to *The Times**, starting with a review of Herbert Beerbohm Tree's production of *King John* that praised its 'rapidity and vitality', arguing that the production benefited by eschewing 'the accumulating burden of "Shakespearian traditions" of performance. The following year he was officially appointed the paper's theatre critic, also contributing to *Literature** and then the *Times Literary Supplement*, both literary papers published by *The Times*.

As suggested by his review of Tree's production of *King John*, Walkley was receptive to modern dramaturgy. Describing his approach as 'impressionist', he sought to focus on the sensory experience of theatre rather than judging it according to preordained aesthetic categories. Early in his career he was unusual for championing Ibsen not as a social reformer but as a playwright, attempting to rescue his plays from the maelstrom of moral advocacy and condemnation which their first performances occasioned. Perhaps inevitably, he became a less vigorous champion of the new and developed a taste for a rather more 'safe' genre of light, comic drama. Following his retirement from the Post Office in 1919, he began a series of articles published in *The Times* on Wednesdays which treated an eclectic range of literary and theatrical topics. MaT
Sources: *ODNB*, *Poole's*, *Times Digital Archive*, *Waterloo*.

WALLACE, ALFRED RUSSEL (1823-1913)
Brought up in poverty after the collapse of his father's short-lived literary* magazine*, during the late 1830s Wallace trained as a surveyor and first encountered socialist politics*, reading the radical *Constitutional* newspaper. By the early 1840s Wallace himself aspired to write political* journalism, penning an overwrought article on insurrectionary Welsh farmers for which he was unable to find a publisher. However, Wallace's rural surveying work had also turned his attention to the natural world, and beginning in 1847 he began contributing observations to the *Zoologist* and other scientific* journals. Wallace's global voyages (1848-1862) afforded plentiful material for many more articles in the scientific press, as well as occasionally in more

general periodicals like the *Literary Gazette** and *Chambers's Journal**.

In 1855 an article by Wallace on new species for the *Annals and Magazine of Natural History** alerted Charles Darwin to Wallace's similar conception of evolution, and three years later they jointly published papers on natural selection in the *Journal of the Proceedings of the Linnaean Society*. Now fêted as a leading evolutionary naturalist, Wallace's writing nevertheless remained his main source of income. In 1866 Wallace declared himself an adherent of spiritualism, vigorously defending the scientific credibility of occult phenomena in the *Fortnightly Review** and *Fraser's Magazine**. In old age Wallace returned to the political journalism* of his youth, and an overtly socialist article for the *Contemporary Review** in 1880 led directly to the formation of the Land Nationalisation Society. **GD**
Sources: Lightman 2004a, Moore 1997, *ODNB*, Wallace 1905.

WALSH, JOHN HENRY (1810-1888) Also known as 'Stonehenge', Walsh qualified in medicine in 1832. He briefly practised and taught in London before moving to Worcester, where (1849-1852) he jointly edited* the *Provincial Medical and Surgical Journal* with William Harcourt Ranking at an annual salary of £125. Although an early history of the *Journal* referred to its 'marked improvement' under Ranking and Walsh (*PMSJ* 5 Jan. 1856: 14), others questioned its merit. Ranking resigned in August 1852, but Walsh, fearing the journal would be irreparably damaged if both editors departed simultaneously, remained until the end of the year. During his final months as editor he repeatedly attacked his critics and their plans for the *Provincial Medical and Surgical Journal*.

Walsh settled in London in 1852 and began contributing articles on greyhounds to *Bell's Life**, which were later published in book form. He went on to write many other books, mainly on sport, dogs and guns but also on cookery and domestic management. In 1856 he began to write for the *Field** (1853-), and in the following year he ceased medical practice on being appointed its editor. He took up the editorship in 1858 and retained it for 30 highly successful years. **PWB**
Sources: Boase, *Field* 18 Feb. 1888: 205-206, 231, *ODNB*, Rose 1953, *The Times* 14 Feb. 1888.

WALTER FAMILY (1739?-1910) The Walter family founded and owned *The Times** newspaper from its inception in 1785 until its sale in 1908. John Walter I (1739?-1812) began as a successful coal merchant but moved into insurance and joined

Lloyd's in 1781. His insurance business soon failed and in 1782 he acquired the patent to the logographic method of printing which involved setting type with fonts comprised of whole words. In 1784 he set up the Logographic Press at the King's Printing House in Blackfriars which began by printing *Lloyd's List*, but in 1785 launched the *Daily Universal Register* which became *The Times* in January 1788. The following year, Walter also established the *Evening Mail*.

John Walter II (1776-1847) was educated at Oxford and in 1797 joined his father's printing business, becoming a master printer while gradually acquiring a half share in the business. On his elder brother William's retirement in 1803, John took over, managing the entire operation of the printing venture, as well as *The Times* and the *Evening Mail*. In the face of poor business practices by both his father and his elder brother, Walter II set out to reverse the company's fortunes through expanding *The Times*, developing its printing capability with the introduction of new presses and establishing methods for collecting and disseminating news*, particularly foreign news, more speedily via a network of correspondents throughout Europe. However, he also devised a system which attempted to circumvent the Post Office charges for handling foreign newspapers which led to an acrimonious dispute resulting in a charge of and conviction for libel levelled at Walter and his father. Even this did not blunt Walter's ambition and *The Times* was still publishing news far in advance of any other source, resulting in escalating sales and increased power.

Walter capitalized on this ascendancy for another of his other innovations, a revised attitude toward theatre reviews and theatre advertising* in the paper, which required his reviewers to maintain their independence from theatre managements and thereby preserve their integrity. Contrary to custom, Walter insisted on full payment for advertisements instead of the previous stamp tax only regime, and the paper's dominance ensured compliance from theatres. Walter's business acumen coupled with ruthless ambition was evident in his introduction of the new Koenig printing* presses, both in the terms and conditions on which he acquired the presses and the way in which he instituted them to subvert the protests of his workforce, many of whom he had previously prosecuted for attempting to protect their rights by challenging their wages. With the clear-sighted drive that Walter demonstrated in running the business, it was entirely complementary that he should detach himself from the convention of party political partiality, and assert the political* independence of his newspapers. This attitude resulted in the loss of a valuable government contract, and in such sensitive times made him vulnerable to accusations of treachery and partiality toward the French. His business disputes were not confined to the government, but the complexities of family loyalties and rivalries also confused inheritance issues although he retained sole control over *The Times* at his father's death. Despite the contests throughout his management, it was John Walter II who had secured the undisputed success and status of *The Times*. In 1846, he appointed his son John Walter III sole manager of the paper, previously shared with John Delane and Thomas Alsager*.

John Walter III (1818-1894) combined his proprietorship* of *The Times* with a parliamentary career. Having been judiciously schooled by his father in continuing the family legacy, he was more than competent in balancing the competing demands on a proprietor to maintain and improve on *The Times's* reputation. Walter III was particularly responsive to new technology and oversaw further successful innovation with the introduction of the Walter printing press in 1866, which had been in development since his father's day. Walter also had to negotiate the difficult task of any accusations of partiality within the overlap of the political power of the paper and his personal position as a member of Parliament. *The Times* continued to prosper under Walter III's ownership and on his death in 1894 control of the paper passed to his son Arthur Fraser Walter (1846-1910). However, declining fortunes and family disputes with regard to fragmented ownership arrangements led to the paper's sale to Lord Northcliffe* in 1908. JRW

Source: *ODNB*.

WAR AND JOURNALISM 'War, to put it frankly, is good for media business' (Taylor 1995) is a statement that both stresses and summarises a complex synergistic relationship between the state, the military, and the press* that is borne out throughout the nineteenth century, from the wars with France onwards. Early in the century accounts of foreign campaigns in the British press relied on two main sources: foreign newspapers and correspondents*. The latter were often army officers who would send letters to the newspaper, either commissioned or gratis, or local residents. Sometimes families would send in letters they had received from relatives at the front. In both cases the ideological charges of the accounts were considerable: it was hardly to be

expected that army officers should report impartially. Newspapers might make synthetic accounts or publish each source separately, a practice which continued throughout the century.

William Howard Russell's* coverage of the Crimean War for Delane's* *The Times** is often regarded as the first war reportage in the modern sense, a notion encouraged by Russell's own self-promotion in later years – he came to call himself 'the miserable parent of a luckless tribe'. His significance is nonetheless indubitable: he went on to cover numerous campaigns for Delane, including the Indian Uprising in 1857, the American Civil War, the Franco-Prussian War of 1871 and the Zulu War of 1879. He received a knighthood for his achievements in 1895 and was buried in St Paul's when he died in 1907.

But there had been earlier wars covered by reporters (Russell himself had reported the 1850 war between Denmark and Schleswig-Holstein) just as there were at least four other reporters* at the Crimean front, including Edward Lawrence Godkin of the London *Daily News**. The standard story is that an 'elite corps of journalists' arose in the wake of Russell, who reported from the fronts of various imperial wars, and who became heroic, even romantic, figures. Their activities and eccentricities made the period 1865 to 1914 a 'Golden Age' of war reporting*. But this is a version of news* history that is highly problematic in its failure to take into account continuing technological limitations, state and military interference with reportage either officially through censorship* or unofficially through military prevention of access to sources, the complexities of systems (including syndication and news agencies*), and ideological partiality culminating in 1890s imperialist* propaganda (which was later to feed into World War I reportage). Furthermore, while it might be said that the young Winston Churchill's experience as a war correspondent in the Boer War exemplified the reporter as imperial hero, Henry Nevinson's coverage of the same war from 1899, as Angela John argues, turned the conventions of war reporting 'to fit an alternative voice of opposition'. However, this oppositional stance needs to be contextualised with the many anti-war and anti-imperial voices, such as 'Ouida's*', that had appeared in the periodical press for many years before this.

Even if not really the first reported war, the Crimean War remains a turning point in many ways. Not only did Russell's reportage help the government to topple, bringing an end to the Stamp

Duty* and showing the power of the 'Fourth Estate' that W. H. Stead* was to remember, it is also significant for the technologies of reportage. The *Illustrated London News** sent artists to the front (including Constantin Guys, Baudelaire's 'Artist of Modern Life') and photography* was used for the first time in a war (Roger Fenton's photograph albums were part of a commercial and royal imperative to counter Russell's words, but he was only the most famous of several photographers, and no photograph appeared in the press). Despite the telegraph*, news still took weeks to arrive. While Russell* made use of the telegraph to send messages to *The Times*, the military* and the state also made use of it to generate news.

The following account of how one item of news from the Crimea came to appear in the press illustrates many of the factors in the business of war reporting that need to be taken into account when analysing war and journalism in nineteenth-century Britain, from multiple editions of newspapers and synthesis of various accounts, to misunderstood telegrams and oral relay.

The first news of the Battle of the Alma on 23 September 1854 reached Britain on 7 November through a telegraph from the Ambassador at Constantinople to the Minister of War. The latter informed the staff of the *London Gazette* – the official government newspaper – who were required to make up copy immediately at any time of day or night. They generated an *Extraordinary Gazette*. Usually the morning and evening journals were then supplied with copies of the *Gazette*, followed by ministers of state, then ambassadors and clubhouses. Copies were also sent by special post and trains to major postal towns with instructions that they be displayed in prominent places. The *Extraordinary Gazette* with first news of the Alma is marked '8pm Downing Street'. Being a Saturday, the *Gazette* could not go directly to the dailies*, as they did not publish on a Sunday. Instead a copy was sent to the Lord Mayor of London in Mansion House, who received it only after 9 pm. He immediately went to the London Tavern (where the inauguration of the new Sheriffs of London and Middlesex was being celebrated) and announced the news. After toasts he went to the Royal Exchange accompanied by several members of the Corporation. The civic trumpeter sounded several times and a crowd gathered before which the Mayor read out the news. The *Extraordinary Gazette* now went round the theatres where it was read out to the audiences. On Monday morning canons

were fired in both St James's Park and the Tower at 6am to acknowledge receipt by the Government of the despatch about the battle written by Lord Raglan on 23 September. *The Times* quoted the *Gazette* quoting Raglan, and also added some information from the Paris *Moniteur* of the previous Saturday. There was an announcement that this news had appeared in the second and third editions of the Saturday *Times*. These initial reports from the front were ambiguous and it was believed that Sebastopol had fallen; only from 9 October was the news reported less joyfully as 'The Battle of the Alma'. **AGJ/ AK**

Sources: John 2006, Knightley 2000, McLaughlin 2002, Taylor 1995, *The Times* 24 Oct. 1854, *Weekly Times* 7 Oct.14 Oct. 21 Oct. 1854, *Illustrated London News* 7 Oct. 14 Oct. 21 Oct. 1854.

WAR CRY (1879-) The official newspaper of the Salvation Army, the *War Cry* first appeared in December 1879 with General William Booth making the clarion call, 'Why a weekly war cry? Because the Salvation Army means more war!' Employing many of the most inventive aspects of modern journalism*, including bold, eye-catching headlines, large newspaper format* and numerous illustrations*, the paper combined traditional forms of working-class* entertainment such as broadside and rhyme with conversion narratives. Priced* at ½d, the *War Cry's* first print run was 17,000, but by 1881 the Army was printing over 200,000 with circulation* rising by 100,000 in one year. So popular was it that by 1882 it was being published twice-weekly, with the *Little Soldier*, the magazine for Army children, also flourishing.

Unashamedly populist* and repeatedly accused of irreverence and vulgarisms, the newspaper nonetheless resisted journalistic commercialism. In September 1882, an Army leader based in Sunderland stated that he had refused to sell advertising* space to a medical firm, which would have earned £100, in order that he could leave 'every paragraph' free for salvation. Column* inches meant steps to heaven, yet the *War Cry* freely adopted the language of the advertising* industry to describe conversion experiences, a trend begun by its predecessor the *Christian Mission Magazine* (1870-1878). It also led the way in creating brand loyalty by marketing Salvation Army products such as tea, *cartes de visites*, and bedspreads, linking its readers commercially and spiritually both to the newspaper and to a life of salvation. **LL**

Sources: Hattersley 1999, Salvation Army Heritage Centre, Walker 2001.

WARD, LESLIE MATTHEW (1851-1922) With both parents prominent painters, being well placed in society, and having been educated at Eton, Leslie Ward was by background and heredity advantageously sited to become a caricaturist of the political and *beau monde*. Having evaded his father's attempts to turn him into an architect, he studied at the Royal Academy Schools under W. P. Frith and exhibited portraits in oil and watercolour. But it was his talent for the caricature*, which emerged while still at school, that was to be the basis of his professional life.

John Everett Millais*, an illustrious family friend, showed some of Ward's work to the founder and editor* of the magazine *Vanity Fair* Thomas Gibson Bowles*, thus initiating Ward's career. From 1873 until his retirement in 1909, Ward worked for *Vanity Fair*, alongside his colleague, the famous caricaturist Carlo Pellegrini*. Ward adopted the pseudonym 'Spy' as representative of the function of the caricaturist, although his work varied from the witty and insightful to more acceptable and less critical representations, especially in the case of royalty. His watercolours, which displayed his ability and training, formed the basis of the estimated 1,325 coloured lithographs that appeared in *Vanity Fair*, although he also contributed to the *Graphic**, *World** and *Mayfair*. CL

Sources: Bryant and Heneage 1994, *ODNB*.

WARD, THOMAS HUMPHRY (1845-1926) Art critic and journalist*, Thomas Humphry Ward was a fellow and tutor of Brasenose College (1870-1880). His earliest journalism* was as one of the authors of the undergraduate journal, the *Oxford Spectator* (1867-1868). He also contributed to *Macmillan's Magazine**, the *Dark Blue**, *Edinburgh Review** and the *Quarterly Review**. In 1872 he married Mary Arnold, Matthew Arnold's* niece, who became a celebrated novelist.

Ward moved to London in 1881, where he joined the staff of *The Times**, contributing leaders* and becoming its principal art critic in 1884, a position he held for over 25 years. In addition to regular anonymous* art reviews*, of which detailed notices of Royal Academy exhibitions were a primary feature, Ward's publications included the illustrated* *English Art in the Public Galleries of London* (1886-1888); fine art catalogues, such as that of the J. Pierpont Morgan collection (1907), and the two volume *Romney: a Biographical and Critical Essay, with a Catalogue Raisonné of his Works*, co-authored by William Roberts (1904). His art journalism was to become best known for its conserva-

tism in the face of modern developments in Britain and France. However, Ward's extensive *Times* journalism indicates the crucial importance of the Academy to turn-of-the-century metropolitan culture. MEC

Sources: *ONDB*, *The Times* 1926, Ward 1918, *Wellesley*.

WARD, WILLIAM (1769-1823) William Ward was apprenticed to John Drewry, a printer and bookseller in Derby. At the expiration of his apprenticeship, Ward stayed on for two more years, during which he assisted Drewry with editing* the *Derby Mercury**, a conservative family* journal (1753-). In due course Ward edited the paper himself. Around 1794 or 1795 he moved to Stafford where he helped Joshua Drewry the proprietor* and relative of his former master to edit the *Staffordshire Advertiser* (1795-1973).

At the end of 1795, Ward moved to Hull where he opened a printing business. For nine months in 1796, he was editor of the relatively new *Hull Advertiser and Exchange Gazette* (1794-1844; then the *Hull Advertiser*). In 1796 Ward was baptized into the Baptist church, eventually becoming a missionary in India. Arriving in Bengal in October 1799, he superintended the printing press at Serampore, which published the Bible translated into Hindi. Ward also wrote books on India and the Hindus, as well as producing a number of other publications. DHL

Sources: Marshman 1859, *ODNB*, Stanley 1992, Stennett 1825.

WARD, LOCK & CO. A London publisher of middlebrow educational and reference works, fiction and periodicals, Ward & Lock was established 1854 at 158 Fleet Street* by former apprentice chemist George Lock and Ebenezer Ward who had been apprenticed at publisher Henry G. Bohm and previously managed the book department of Herbert Ingram & Co. The two purchased the failed Ingram's stock in 1856, acquiring *Webster's Dictionary* and other titles, and built a diversified trade in low-priced editions of standard works. Samuel Beeton* joined them as an editor* after his bankruptcy in 1866, when the firm acquired Beeton periodicals including the *Boy's Own Magazine** (1855-1890), the *Englishwoman's Domestic Magazine** (1852-1881), *Young Englishwoman** (1-865-1877, later *Sylvia's Home Journal* 1878-1894) and *Beeton's Christmas Annual* (1860-1898), and book copyrights including the *Book of Household Management*. Their popular mid-century novelists included G. A. Sala*, Mary Elizabeth Braddon*, and

Charles Reade; a line of American writers included James Russell Lowell and Oliver Wendell Holmes.

The house acquired E. Moxon, Son and Co. in 1871 and W. H. Smith's* *Select Library of Fiction* in 1885, and by the early 1890s published 12 magazines* and serials* monthly including British editions of *Lippincott's* and *Atlantic Monthly*. In 1895 it launched the successful *Windsor Magazine**. The house traded as Ward, Lock & Tyler (1865-1873), became Ward Lock, Bowden & Company in 1890, Ward Lock and Bowden Ltd in 1893, and Ward Lock & Co., Ltd in 1897. It continued an independent publisher through most of the twentieth century. CL

Sources: Healey 1989, Liveing 1954, McDonald 1997, *Waterloo*, Weedon 2003.

WATERLOO DIRECTORIES OF THE UNITED KINGDOM AND IRELAND NEWSPAPERS AND PERIODICALS The *Waterloo Directory of English Newspapers and Periodicals, 1800-1900* is a multiseries, enumerative, descriptive and analytical bibliography providing access to nineteenth-century British newspapers and periodicals published in all subjects and all languages. Its momentous decision to include both newspapers and periodicals echoes nineteenth-century press directories, but cuts across the customary twentieth-century tendency to separate them, and its template for recording detailed information has proved exemplary and invaluable, not least to *DNCJ*.

The first volume appeared in 1976 as the *Waterloo Directory of Victorian Periodicals 1824 – 1900*. The editor*, John North of the University of Waterloo, was assisted by Michael Wolff and Dorothy Deering. The first edition contained 28,995 entries with minimal data on each, gathered solely from secondary sources. Two geographically specific and much more detailed volumes followed, the product of shelf checks, and edited by North alone: The *Waterloo Directory of Irish Newspapers and Periodicals 1800-1900* (1986), listing 3,972 Irish titles, including indexes of people, places, issuing bodies* and subjects; and *The Waterloo Directory of Scottish Newspapers and Periodicals 1800-1900* (1989) in two volumes, covering 7,320 titles. The Scottish volumes featured illustrations* of title pages for many of the publications. All volumes include UK locations as well as North American finding lists.

Published by North Waterloo Academic Press, *Waterloo* appears in a rolling ten-volume series whereby each new series adds an additional 25,000 titles, alphabetically integrated with the titles of the previous series, each of those earlier entries being

enriched as the data collection throughout UK libraries proceeds. The first electronic version of the English press appeared on CD-Rom in 1994, and two print editions have followed, Series 1 of ten volumes (1998) and Series 2 of 20 volumes (2003). The current Series 2 on-line edition first appeared in 2001, and has since been greatly enlarged and improved. Series 3 is to appear soon.

The *Directory* lists more than 50,000 newspapers and periodicals, with facsimile title pages for most. Up to 30 categories of information are provided in an ambitious and exacting template for each title, including: the main, later and generic titles; the issuing* and subissuing body; numbering, volume and date; place of publication; editors, proprietors* printers and publishers*; contributors; size*; price*; illustrations; circulation*; indexes; mergers*; subject categories; political and religious affiliation; and locations. Secondary sources are listed and quoted for many of the entries, directing scholars to further historical and biographical information. In effect these provide a concise history of scholarly research on entries. Almost all relevant titles held by the British Library in its newspaper and periodical collections are included, supplemented by titles from the university libraries of Oxford, Cambridge, London, Glasgow, Edinburgh, Trinity College Dublin, Queens Belfast, and the national libraries of Ireland, Scotland and Wales, as well as numerous smaller public and private, general and specialized libraries.

Over the last decades, the *Waterloo Directory* has become one of the fundamental reference works on the nineteenth-century British press, unique in both its scope and its detail. A first port of call for researchers, it provides an overview of print journalism, its variety, density and numbers, as well as the minutiae of media history. DHL/LRB

Source: *Waterloo*.

WATERLOW, SYDNEY HEDLEY (1822-1906) In 1836 Sydney Waterlow was apprenticed through the Stationers' Company to his uncle Thomas Harrison the government printer. By the fourth year of his apprenticeship he was in sole charge of Foreign Office printing with full responsibility for its confidentiality. On finishing his apprenticeship in November 1843, Waterlow went to Paris where he was employed in printing the catalogue of the library of the publisher* Galignani*. On returning to London he joined his brothers Alfred, Walter and Albert in forming a printing branch of the family stationery business, Messrs Waterlow and Sons.

In March 1844 Sydney Waterlow began printing the first number of the *Banker's Magazine*. It appeared

a month later, edited* by J. S. Dalton, a clerk in the Provincial Bank of Ireland. Waterlow and Sons acquired a good share of printing and stationery work from the expanding railway companies. It also printed the *Banking Almanac*, the *Solicitor's Diary* and the *Solicitor's Pocket-Book*. The firm of Messrs Waterlow and Sons became known throughout the world for printing paper money for home and colonial banks, as well as for foreign governments. **DHL**
Sources: *ODNB*, Smalley 1909.

WATKINS, JOHN (1808-1858) From a Whitby gentry family, John Watkins enjoyed modest success as a topographical writer and contributor to local* papers, but by 1838 was lamenting the absence of a 'truth-telling Newspaper' in the town. Politicized* by the Chartist* press, Watkins consciously used Chartism to forge a literary* career, initiating a frequent correspondence* with the *Northern Star* during 1839. A weekly salary of £1 from the paper prompted him to move to London, and he contributed poetry* and comment (March 1840-Nov. 1842) to the *Northern Star* almost weekly, under his own name and the pseudonyms* 'Junius Rusticus' and 'Chartius'. He probably also complied the regular 'Chartist Shakespeare' feature. A combative champion of Feargus O'Connor*, Watkins sought the transfer of the main London agency for *Northern Star*, held by John Cleave*, to his own 'depot for the vend of true Chartism' near Temple Bar. O'Connor, respecting the unstamped* press veteran Cleave and his business acumen, declined. Watkins's news agency* floundered, heavily reliant on credit from O'Connor. In 1843 his relations with O'Connor plummeted after he commented acerbically on the internal politics* of Chartism. O'Connor swiftly severed every link.

Watkins commenced a new journal, the *London Chartist Monthly Magazine* (1843). Each issue included political essays, fiction and historical material; but 1843 was an unpropitious time to launch a new Chartist journal, when monthly magazines* were a relatively untried format* in radical publishing. It survived only four issues. Watkins strongly supported William Hill* after his acrimonious exit from editing the *Star*, contributing to Hill's *Lifeboat* (1843-1844). He also wrote a steady stream of articles (mostly as 'Lictor' or 'An Old Chartist') denouncing O'Connor in *Lloyd's Weekly Newspaper**. One of the most regular and prolific contributors to *Northern Star* during its period of greatest influence, by 1849 Watkins was completely alienated from Chartism. He left journalism for a life as a gentleman of independent means. **MSC**
Sources: Chase 2007, *DLB*.

WATSON, JAMES (1799-1874) James Watson was important as a prolific printer and publisher* of political* books, pamphlets and over 20 periodicals. Initially a shopman employed by Richard Carlile* James Watson was imprisoned for 12 months (1823-1824) for selling seditious literature. On his release, Watson trained as a compositor, working on Carlile's *Republican* (1817-1826) before setting up on his own as a bookseller, printer and publisher. He was also a leading figure on the monthly* *Co-operative Magazine* and its various successor titles* (1826-1830). From 1830, Watson was one of the main distributors of the *Poor Man's Guardian** which resulted in a six-month jail term in 1833. This, in turn, meant that his own earliest publishing venture, that of the *Working Man's Friend**, was largely conducted by his partner in the business, John Cleave*. Watson served a further six-month sentence in 1834 for distributing Hetherington's* *Destructive*.

One of the most self-effacing of 'the heroes of the unstamped*', his periodicals conveyed the flavour of their politics*, for example the *Anti-Persecution Gazette*, the *Christian Socialist*, the *Deist*, the *Free-thinker's Magazine**, the *Model Republic* and the *Trades' Advocate & Herald of Progress**. He enjoyed a close working relationship with G. J. Harney* and W. J. Linton*, respectively printing for them the *Democratic Review** and the *English Republic**. The leading freethinker* George Holyoake* was another colleague, whom he encouraged to produce the *Reasoner**, which Watson himself printed and published. He also distributed numerous political periodicals, especially nominally Manx publications which enjoyed immunity from taxation and free carriage to mainland agents, circulating extensively among British radicals. **MSC**
Sources: Linton 1880, *ODNB*, *Warwick Guide*.

WATSON, JOHN DAWSON (1832-1892) Although John Dawson Watson's drawings were widely published in the most highly regarded illustrated* magazines of the 1860s, he also worked extensively for less glamorous journals aimed at artisan readers, notably the *British Workman** and the *Servant's Magazine**. Frequently used by the Dalziel* brothers for their various projects, Watson seemed to have suffered somewhat from the facility of his technique which led him to take on a huge variety of commissions. His work is found across the spectrum of magazines* from *Good Words** to the *Graphic**, from *London Society** to the *Infant's Magazine*. **BM**
Sources: Engen 1990, Goldman 1994, Houfe 1978, Reid 1928, Suriano 2005, White 1897.

WATSON, ROSAMUND MARRIOTT (1860-1911) Poet, journalist*, critic, and editor* Rosamond Tomson, alias 'Graham R. Tomson', co-edited *Art Weekly* (Feb.-July 1890), aimed at professional artists, and edited *Sylvia's Journal* (Dec. 1892-April 1894), which merged aestheticism and New Woman* articles with the standard features of a monthly* woman's magazine*. Publishing her earliest journalism* as 'Mrs. G. Armytage*' in *Fortnightly Review* ('Modern Dress', Sept. 1883), Tomson later contributed an anonymous* fashion* column* to W. E. Henley's* *Scots Observer* (Jan. 1889-March 1892). Her signed poetry* reviews* appeared in the *Academy* (Jan. 1892-June 1894) and *Illustrated London News* (July 1891-Dec. 1892), her signed articles on art in the *Woman's World* (July-Aug. 1889), *Longman's Magazine* (Sept. 1888) and the *Scottish Art Review* (Feb.-July 1889). A staff art critic under the pseudonym* 'N. E. Vermind' for the *Morning Leader* (May 1892-May 1894), she also wrote anonymous articles on interior decoration for 'Wares of Autolycus' in the *Pall Mall Gazette* (June 1893-Nov. 1894).

After a second divorce, Tomson adopted the signature Rosamund Marriott Watson (fl.1894-1911), writing numerous anonymous fiction reviews* and serving as staff critic for the *Athenaeum* (June 1903-Dec. 1909). Her signed pieces on gardens* also appeared in the *New Liberal Review* (Sept. 1901-Jan. 1902) and the *Daily Mail* (22 May-28 Dec. 1901). **LH**
Sources: Demoor 2000, Hughes 1996, Hughes 2005, Schaffer 2000.

WATTS, (WALTER) THEODORE (1832-1914)
Theodore Watts (after 1896, when he added his mother's name to his own, known as Watts-Dunton), trained as a solicitor but gave up his practice to take up the life of a literary critic. He started as a reviewer* for the *Examiner* in 1874 and soon after began to write for many of the most influential reviews such as the *Nineteenth Century*, the *New Quarterly Magazine* and the *Fortnightly Review*. His current reputation, however, as that of a formidable poetry critic, rests mainly on the anonymous poetry reviews which he was believed to have contributed to the *Athenaeum* in the last three decades of the nineteenth century. Yet this reputation was to a large extent created by Hake and Compton-Rickett in a biography published two years after Watts's death. In reality, Watts was just one of a number of poetry reviewers for the *Athenaeum* with several of his colleagues – Augusta Webster, Westland Marston, Mathilde Blind* and Arthur Symons, to

name only a few – being poets themselves. Yet the myth that Watts was the unique powerful voice of the *Athenaeum's* poetry section has persisted, in spite of the fact that the 'marked copy' of the *Athenaeum* has been available for years (City University Library, London) and that the online partially digitized index to the *Athenaeum* (Ghent University) shows poetry reviews to be a task he shared.

Watts's name is further mainly associated with that of C. A. Swinburne*, as the friend who took care of the poet's life when the latter's dissolute life style was bound to take him to an untimely death. **MD**
Sources: Athenaeum Index online, Demoor 2000, Hake and Compton-Rickett 1916, *ODNB*, *Wellesley*.

WAY, THOMAS (1837-1915); WAY, T. R. (1861-1913) Lithographer*, engraver and general printer, Thomas Way was born, baptized and worked in Covent Garden. For over 50 years, he worked as a lithographer, mostly from a building in Wellington Street. In 1859 he had acquired the well-established lithography business of George Edward Madeley (1798-1858). The premises was shared with Sotheby's, and in 1865 a disastrous fire destroyed the building, resulting in the loss of Way's equipment, stock and records.

Thomas Way specialized in lithographed plans and views for property auctioneers. He also printed art gallery catalogues, fashion* plates for the monthly *West End Gazette* (1861-1929) as well as illustrations* for various publications including the *Studio*. Way's principle contribution to lithography however was in his encouragement of well-known artists, especially James McNeill Whistler*, to turn to making prints. This interest in art and artists influenced his son Thomas Robert, known as T. R. Way. Way the younger not only gained experience from his father in appraising works of art but also learned about the printing processes for their reproduction. During the 1890s he played an important role in the collaboration with Whistler in the firm of Thomas Way and Son, as well as in the revival of lithography in England.

The firm printed the catalogues for the Fine Arts Society shows where Whistler was exhibited. It also printed large editions of original lithographs for periodicals such as the *Whirlwind* (1890), the *Albermale* (1892), the *Art Journal*. It printed lithographs by well-known artists in the *Studio* (1894-1897). The 1890s also saw the development of T. R. Way both as lithographic artist and author, and he contributed articles on Whistler and on

lithography to the *Studio* (1894-1903). His most important published work was the catalogue of Whistler's lithographs (March 1894-spring 1896). He also published books and lithographs concerning London's architectural heritage, and in 1910 he was commissioned to produce the iconic advertisements* for the London underground. **DHL**
Sources: *ODNB*, Smale 1987, Smale 1998.

WEDDERBURN, ROBERT (1762-1835/6?) One of the earliest black British journalists was Olaudah Equiano, a contributor to the *Public Advertiser* in 1788, but Robert Wedderburn, a radical and Unitarian preacher, followed closely after, as well as being an early black British editor*. His weekly* *Axe Laid to the Root, or A Fatal Blow to Oppressors* (Oct. 1817-Dec. 1817) was issued from Covent Garden and was printed nearby by Arthur Seale, whom Wedderburn had met through the revolutionary circle around Thomas Spence. A distinguishing feature of Spence's philosophy was its respect for non-white peoples, but Wedderburn's engagement was not limited to anti-slavery. 'I am a West Indian, a lover of liberty, and would dishonour human nature if I did not show myself a friend to the liberty of others', he wrote in the first *Axe*. *Axe* succeeded the *'Forlorn Hope', or a Call to the Supine* (Oct 1817), written by Wedderburn and edited by the Spencean (later socialist and Chartist*), Charles Jennison.

Axe followed its predecessor in offering a mix of epistolary journalism and poetry*, to which Wedderburn added a strong autobiographical content. It is an appealing work, but its circulation* was slight. Always impoverished, Wedderburn was forced to concentrate upon tailoring to survive. He remained a close associate of the Spencean writer Allen Davenport and in 1828 contributed to Richard Carlile's* *Lion* (1828-1829), a parody of Anglican liturgy 'upon the principles of PURE CHRISTIAN DIABOLISM'. Wedderburn's book *The Horrors of Slavery* was published in 1824. **MSC**
Sources: *DLB*, McCalman 1988, McCalman 1991, *ODNB*.

WEDGWOOD, FRANCES JULIA (1833-1913) Julia Frances Wedgwood (pseudonym* 'Florence Dawson'), great-granddaughter of Josiah Wedgwood and niece of Charles Darwin, was a journalist*, writer, and novelist. Although greatly influenced by family discussions about religion versus scientific* knowledge, she first wrote two moderately successful novels before *Macmillan's Magazine* published three articles, 'Boundaries of Science' (1860-1861), 'Origin of Language' (1862) and the 'Antiquity of Man' (1863). She also contrib-

uted single articles to the *Westminster Review** (1867), the *British Quarterly Review** (1884) and the *National Review** (1891).

The balance of her journalism*, 30 articles (1870-1900), appeared in the *Contemporary Review**. Subject matter ranged from classical topics to Shakespeare, ethical and scientific concerns, plus women's issues*, as well as studies of her contemporaries such as J. A. Froude*, Carlyle*, George Eliot*, Tolstoy and Ruskin*. Although Wedgwood ultimately wrote books on *John Wesley*, the *Moral Ideal,* and the *Message of Israel,* journalism remained a focus of her life as she sought to reconcile the difficulties of the great debate of the age concerning scientific knowledge and religious belief. Wedgwood was widely considered, along with George Eliot, as one of the significant female* intellects of her time. **RV**
Sources: Curle 1937, *ODNB*, Sutherland 1989, VanArsdel 2000, Wedgwood and Wedgwood 1980.

WEEKLIES Weekly issue encouraged a straddling of the divide between newspaper and magazine. Though dailies* typically take the form of broadsheet newspapers paginated by the issue, and monthlies* that of magazines* that can be bound into book-like volumes, weeklies cover the spectrum in between.

As regards newspapers proper, successes in the struggle against the 'taxes on knowledge*' in particular had an impact on the character of the weekly edition. During the 1830s significant tax reductions gave rise to a boom in metropolitan Sunday* journals, led by new titles like the *News of the World**. Before the abolition of the taxes at the mid-century, daily papers enjoyed a secure existence only in the metropolis, though soon afterwards major provincial* cities typically hosted at least two competing dailies. Then many established local weeklies were transformed into miscellaneous papers like the *Newcastle Weekly Chronicle**, containing a wealth of feature material as well as an overview of recent events, while, with the help of a variety of syndicated* material, new weekly papers began to emerge in relatively small communities both urban and rural.

Among the many new genres of weekly serial that flourished during the nineteenth century are seminal examples of: radical* journals (*Cobbett's Political Register**), critical and literary reviews (the *Athenaeum**), pictorial papers (the *Illustrated London News**), comic* papers (*Punch**), journals of fiction and popular entertainment (the *London*

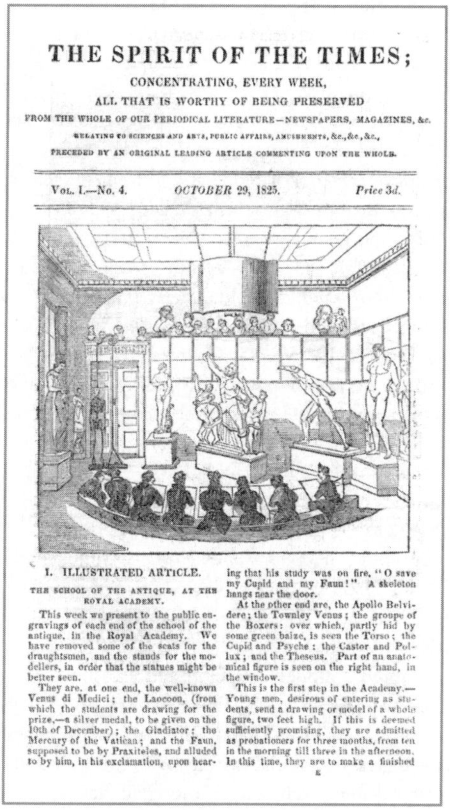

THE SPIRIT OF THE TIMES;

CONCENTRATING, EVERY WEEK,

ALL THAT IS WORTHY OF BEING PRESERVED

FROM THE WHOLE OF OUR PERIODICAL LITERATURE—NEWSPAPERS, MAGAZINES, &c.

RELATING TO SCIENCES AND ARTS, PUBLIC AFFAIRS, AMUSEMENTS, &c., &c., &c.,

PRECEDED BY AN ORIGINAL LEADING ARTICLE COMMENTING UPON THE WHOLE.

VOL. I.—No. 4. *OCTOBER* 29, 1825. *Price* 3*d*.

I. ILLUSTRATED ARTICLE.

THE SCHOOL OF THE ANTIQUE, AT THE ROYAL ACADEMY.

This week we present to the public engravings of each end of the school of the antique, in the Royal Academy. We have removed some of the seats for the draughtsmen, and the stands for the modellers, in order that the statues might be better seen.

They are, at one end, the well-known Venus di Medici; the Laocoon, (from which the students are drawing for the prize,—a silver medal, to be given on the 10th of December); the Gladiator; the Mercury of the Vatican; and the Faun, supposed to be by Praxiteles, and alluded to by him, in his exclamation, upon hearing that his study was on fire, "O save my Cupid and my Faun!" A skeleton hangs near the door.

At the other end are, the Apollo Belvidere; the Townley Venus; the groupe of the Boxers: over which, partly hid by some green baize, is seen the Torso; the Cupid and Psyche: the Castor and Pollux; and the Theseus. Part of an anatomical figure is seen on the right hand, in the window.

This is the first step in the Academy.—Young men, desirous of entering as students, send a drawing or model of a whole figure, two feet high. If this is deemed sufficiently promising, they are admitted as probationers for three months, from ten in the morning till three in the afternoon. In this time, they are to make a finished

E

Figure 65: The *Spirit of the Times,* 29 Oct. 1825, an early nineteenth-century weekly.

*Journal**), religious* papers (the Anglican *Guardian**), society* papers (*Vanity Fair**), family* papers (D-ickens's* *Household Words**), papers for women (the *Lady's Newspaper**), and children's papers (*Boys of England**). Additionally, many specialized weekly organs emerged in the second half of the century to serve the followers of particular professions*, trades*, and hobbies.

Whether in terms of character of readership*, editorial content or physical format*, weekly issue probably represents the most diverse mode of nineteenth-century serial* publication. **GL**

Sources: Altick 1957, Brown 1985, Lee 1976, Vann and VanArsdel 1994.

***WEEKLY CHRONICLE* (1836-1867)** The *Weekly Chronicle*, an illustrated broadsheet, was owned and edited by Henry George Ward (1797-1860), a successful diplomat and colonial administrator who was governor of Ceylon (1855-1867). Henry Ward was a staunch liberal and founded the *Weekly Chronicle* as a means to present his political* views to the general public. Despite his predominantly political aims, the *Weekly Chronicle* featured a variety of material, such as foreign* and national news*, London news, outlines of the week, law intelligence, court* reports, insurance reports, book reviews* and literary criticism. Costing 6d in 1846, its price fell as taxes were removed (4d [1856] and 3d [1860]).

Although owned and edited* by the same person, the *Weekly Chronicle* was published by a succession of different publishers*. It appeared with varying frequency*: three times a week during 1846 (Friday, Saturday and Sunday), twice a week during 1851 and 1856 (Saturday and Sunday) and once a week during 1860 (Saturday). The *Weekly Chronicle's* sales also varied considerably: 17,000 to 21,000 copies were sold during the early 1840s, whereas in 1848 its circulation* peaked at 152,000 issues. After 1848 the numbers dwindled, although 1851 still saw the sale of 50,000 copies. **OD**

Sources: *ODNB*, *Waterloo.*

***WEEKLY DISPATCH* (1795-1961)** This newspaper became renowned as the *Weekly Dispatch*, although it underwent numerous title changes* in its first three decades. Founded by Robert Bell* as *Bell's Weekly Dispatch**, it became the *Weekly Dispatch* in 1801, reverted to *Bell's Weekly Dispatch* in 1812, changed to *Kent's Weekly Dispatch and Sporting Mercury* (1814-1823), reverted to the *Weekly Dispatch* for over a century (1823-1928), ending up as the *Sunday Dispatch*. Robert Bell was the first proprietor*, and sometime editor* (1815, 1824), as well as publisher* (1813, 1824). Later proprietors included Ashton Dilke (1875), George Kent, Alderman Harmer, Alfred Charles Harmsworth* and George Newnes*. Pierce Egan* (1825), William Cox Bennett, George Gissing, John Stuart Mill* and Eliza Orme are among many notable contributors. As a Sunday* paper, aimed at working-class readers*, it specialized in sensational news* and sport* in its early phase, from vivid crime reports such as the supposed involvement of the preacher John Church in the London Vere Street homosexual brothel to Pierce Egan's noted boxing reports.

In 1840, with a circulation* of over 60,000, three times that of its closest rival, the *Weekly Dispatch* was clearly the most powerful metropolitan* newspaper in terms of sales. According to the journalist James Grant circulation rose 'with rapidity which probably had no previous parallel in the history of the Weekly World Newspaper Press' (Grant: 43). This was largely due to the proprietorship of Alderman Harmer who 'lost no time in greatly enlarging its size*, and adding new and attractive features to it' (Grant: 41). The *Weekly Dispatch* was a survivor of the first generation of Sunday* papers, when publishing on the Sabbath was a declaration of secularism* and radicalism. But unlike *Bell's Weekly Messenger**, which had opposed the Reform Bill and transformed into the *Country Gentleman and Farmer's Journal*, the *Dispatch* maintained its rebellious spirit into the Victorian era. Alongside its sensational crime reporting*, lively sports coverage, and timely reviews* (of contemporary serial stories, for example), salty political attacks on government and church were a particular attraction. All the same, the *Weekly Dispatch* was disapproving of the 'physical force' Chartism* of Feargus O'Connor's* *Northern Star**.

In the mid-1840s, the *Dispatch* was overtaken by several new metropolitan weekly* titles. Though the best-seller was by then the up-market *Illustrated London News**, which offered attractive features and copious cuts, the main rivals were cheaper offerings targeting a proletarian audience, like *Lloyd's Weekly Newspaper** or the *News of the World**. Even after the abolition of the 'taxes on knowledge'*, the *Dispatch* was slow to reduce its cover price* to the 1d charged by its competitors*. Under the editorship* of H. R. Fox Bourne* (1876-1887), the paper retained its radical independence but cultivated a more sedate, middle-class* readership*. The paper then began to feature serial* fiction with a socialist* flavour, notably by 'Fabian Bland', that is, Edith Nesbit with her husband Hubert Bland. By the final decade of the century, the circulation* was around 180,000, less than a third that enjoyed by *Lloyd's Weekly**. The paper was eventually absorbed into the *Sunday Express* in 1961. **GL/DHL**
Sources: Altick 1957, Bourne 1887, Grant 1871, Harrison 1974, Law 2005, Morison 1932, *Waterloo*.

WEEKLY LAW JOURNAL (1866-) The *Weekly Law Journal: A Weekly Publication of Notes of Cases and Legal News* began in 1866 and became the most successful periodical to capitalize on those legal* professionals who required swift access to the decisions of the appellate courts. It swept away all competitors* (e.g. the *Jurist**) by a combination of rapidity and accuracy, covering in a timely fashion analyses of recently passed legislation and the legal issues that might arise from the application of the statutes. The transmission of such knowledge served the interests of all who came into contact with the law. Appellate decisions made new law and those in the legal system needed to keep abreast of such changes.

An influential speech by Lord Brougham in 1828 had raised the cry of law reform and, although five decades passed before a comprehensive scheme passed through Parliament in 1873-1875, the topic provoked much discussion in law periodicals. The *Journal*, in professing to safeguard the interests of practitioners, took a moderate position on reform while many other law journals failed because, by opposing the issue altogether, they were perceived to represent only the narrow agenda of the legal profession without public benefit. The *Weekly Law Journal* changed its name to the *Law Journal* in 1917 and later became the *New Law Journal* in 1965. Its continuing success still rests on the prompt provision of information as well as responsible editorials on contemporary legal issues of importance to the profession and to the general public. **RC**
Sources: Cosgrove 1975, Cosgrove 1994.

WEEKLY TIMES (1847-1912) George Stiff*, proprietor* of the *London Journal**, launched the *Weekly Times: a London Newspaper of History, Politics, Literature, and Art* as a rival to *Lloyd's Weekly Newspaper** and the *News of the World**. It was an illustrated* Sunday* paper published* by George Vickers and sold for 3d, like its competitors*. True to its subtitle, the *Weekly Times* mixed its news* coverage with original writing on a variety of topics, both cultural and literary* although it gravitated toward the sensationalism* associated with other 1d weeklies* after removal of the paper duty in 1861. The *Weekly Times's* politics* were radical, and it featured a long-running column* of political commentary on the leading events of the week signed 'Littlejohn'. This column was collaborative and was written by numerous writers over the years, Shelton Mackenzie and F. G. Tomlins among them. Tomlins penned the column for nearly two decades, and became the *Weekly Times's* political editor* in 1865. Pierce Egan*, prolific contributor to Stiff's *London Journal**, also wrote for the *Weekly Times* and served as its editor for a time.

In 1884, *Echo** proprietor* John Passmore Edwards* bought the *Weekly Times* and merged* it with the *Weekly Echo*, a Sunday paper he had established during the brief time that the *Echo* was controlled by the Carnegie/Storey syndicate. Edwards hired Ebeneezer Job Kibblewhite as editor of the *Weekly Times*, a position that he held for 25 years. Bought by Progressive Newspapers Ltd in 1912, the *Weekly Times* printed its final issue on 29 December of that year. **JK**
Sources: Bourne 1966, Boyce 1978, Griffiths 1992, *ODNB*, *Waterloo*.

WELCOME GUEST (1858-1861) The *Welcome Guest* was a weekly* penny* dreadful established by Henry Vizetelly* in 1858 and purchased by John Maxwell in 1860. It aimed to be 'recreative reading for all', with the Shakespearean motto, 'A Guest That Best Becomes the Table'. In 1858, priced* at 2d, the circulation* was 120,000 copies. The *Welcome Guest* was published* by Houlston and Wright and printed by J. and W. Rider.

In Vizetelly's original incarnation, the *Welcome Guest* included illustrations*, but Maxwell got rid of the illustrations as well as issuing the periodical at a higher price. The *Welcome Guest* was edited* by Robert P. Brough and, after his untimely death, Robert Buchanan* took over. Contributors included Mary Elizabeth Braddon* (whose first stories were published there and who met John Maxwell* through the journal), Frederick Greenwood*, Arthur Boyd Houghton* and the illustrator* Arthur Hughes*.

Maxwell lost £2,000 in two years of publishing the *Welcome Guest*. He then created *Robin Goodfellow** (July 1861-Sept. 1861) as its successor, at double the price. Ultimately, in December of 1864, Maxwell incorporated the *Welcome Guest* into the *Halfpenny Journal* (1861-1866). **KNH**

Sources: Berridge 1976, *CBEL*, *ODNB*, Sullivan, Sutherland, *Waterloo*.

WELDON'S LADIES' JOURNAL (1879-1954) Charles Weldon, who had been an associate of Samuel Beeton's*, launched this as an illustrated* 3d monthly*. Subtitled: *of Dress, Fashion**, *Needlework, Literature** and *Art*, it was devoted mainly to dress and needlework, though it also carried reviews* and, like Beeton's journals, offered tempting prizes to subscribers. Edited* by 'Madame Bayard' and 'The Busy Bee', who also wrote a column*, modelled perhaps on Myra's 'Silkworm' column in the *Englishwoman's Domestic Magazine**, its main aim was to enable women to make fashionable clothes at home. It therefore offered paper patterns and practical advice.

Weldon had identified an expanding market* and rapidly developed a whole range of other journals and spin-offs priced from 1d upwards, several of which continued well into and sometimes beyond the twentieth century. In the 1880s and 1890s, *Weldon's Ladies' Journal* carried 20 pages of editorial matter and 18 of advertisements*, many of them puffs* for his other ventures. These included: *Weldon's Home Dressmaker* (1895-), *Weldon's Home Milliner* (1895-1928), *Weldon's Illustrated Dressmaker* (1880-1935), *Weldon's Bazaar of Children's Fashions*, *Weldon's Ladies' Quarterly* (1885), *Weldon's Practical Needlework* (1885-1829), as well as series of booklets such as 'Weldon's Practical Needlework Series', launched in 1881. **MRB**

Sources: Hughes 2005, *Waterloo*, *Weldon's Ladies' Journal*.

WELLESLEY INDEX TO VICTORIAN PERIODICALS (1824-1900) The *Wellesley Index to Victorian Periodicals* was first published in five volumes (1965-1988) by the University of Toronto Press. Its chief editor* was Walter Houghton, assisted by a board of editors, a staff team, as well as an international array of librarians and scholars. The *Wellesley Index* was originally a multi-volume work whose aim was to provide better and more comprehensive information for researchers of Victorian periodicals than earlier compilations such as *Poole's Index to Periodical Literature**. Uniquely, it focused on the contents of whole issues, succesively, and drew attention to the composition and architecture of serial numbers, and the runs they made up. Among its innovations was the inclusion of a badly needed index of authors of nineteenth-century articles, the first detailed published index of its kind. This was a monumental undertaking, since the vast majority of contributions were either pseudonymous or anonymous*.

The *Wellesley Index* not only lists periodicals but also provides a seamless linking between records of articles, contributors, pseudonyms and periodical introductions. This includes: a comprehensive history of each item; an index of pseudonyms* for British periodicals; a bibliography of articles written by each contributor, with each pseudonym; as well as evidence supporting attributions of authorship, biographical and vocational details. The index covers 45 important monthly* and quarterly* journals. An exception is the *Edinburgh Review** which is indexed from its first issue in 1802. Poetry* was initially excluded from the *Index*. Routledge published a CD-Rom edition in 1999 which incorporated corrections and additions published in the *Victorian Periodicals Review* up to the end of 1997. Currently, an up-to-date edition of the *Wellesley Index to Victorian Periodicals* is accessible online, and an RSVP project is under way to index the missing poetry. **DHL**

Source: *Wellesley*.

WELLS, HERBERT GEORGE (1866-1946) Although prolific as a writer of science fiction, realist novels and popular textbooks on history, biology and economics, H. G. Wells began his writing career as a journalist for popular* periodicals, the educational press and science* magazines*. His journalism began at the Normal School of Science, South Kensington, when he founded and edited the student magazine *Science Schools Journal* (1886-1887). From student journalism, Wells began publishing a mixture of comical and educational essays in journals such as *Answers to Correspondents**, the *Family Herald**, the *Journal of Education, Education* and the *Educational Times* (1888-1891).

Although teaching was Wells's primary career (1888-1895), ill-health kept him from the classroom and channelled his efforts towards profitable writing. His first major breakthrough occurred in 1891 with the publication of 'The Rediscovery of the Unique' in the *Fortnightly Review**, a speculative essay which was clearly the kernel of Wells's later success as a science-fiction writer. Wells's journalism eventually took primacy over teaching when in 1893 he became a regular contributor to the *Pall Mall Gazette** (and its companion paper, the *Pall Mall Budget*) of serio-comic articles on everyday life and, later, theatre criticism. He was chief literary* critic for the *Saturday Review** 1895-1897. During this time Wells also began applying his biological knowledge to popular science essays and reviews in *Nature** (1893- 1944). Although from 1895, after the publication of *The Time Machine*, Wells no longer relied upon periodical publishing, he nonetheless remained a prolific journalist, serializing* most of his early fiction and publishing prophetic pieces in the *Fortnightly Review* (1900-1903), writing on social and political* issues in the *Daily Mail* (1905-1912), publishing in dozens of journals during The First World War and having his work syndicated* worldwide during the 1920s. Wells published his last piece of writing, 'That Mosley Money!', in the *Socialist and New Leader* (6 July 1946). JP

Sources: Parrinder and Philmus 1980, Partington 2008, Smith 2008.

WELSH NEWSPAPERS The growth of the newspaper press in Wales, from its inception in 1804, followed closely that of the rest of the United Kingdom, but with two important exceptions. These were the prevalence of two languages, Welsh and English, and the proliferation of newspapers associated with the main nonconformist denominations. Most religious* organs were in Welsh, and while Thomas Gee* published* the successful *Baner ac Amserau Cymru** from Denbigh, the journalism of the major towns was increasingly English. Hence the first dailies*, the *Cambria Daily Leader* (1861), the *Western Mail** and the *South Wales Daily News*

(1872) were all in English. Together with newspapers from Liverpool and Manchester, they came to dominate the Welsh market during the last 20 years of the nineteenth century. **AGJ**

Source: Jones 1993.

WESLEYAN METHODIST MAGAZINE (1778-1969) The *Wesleyan Methodist Magazine* was a monthly* periodical that began as the *Arminian Magazine* (1778-1797). John Wesley's (1703-1791) commitment to securing the Methodist faith through social structures resulted in the establishment of a publishing house or Book Room to issue and control the theological material issued. The initial choice of title was an attempt by Wesley to reclaim a term of abuse aimed at him, of being a follower of the freewill theology advocated by the Dutch theologian Jacobus Arminius (1560-1609). Issues of the *Arminian Magazine* proclaimed the doctrine of the faith through inspiring accounts of devotional lives with some poetry*; the periodical was sold at chapels to increase revenue.

In 1798 the title* was changed to the *Methodist Magazine*. Joseph Benson (1749-1821), the editor* (1804-1821), shared Wesley's belief in the importance of education and the format* of the periodical changed accordingly. Benson successfully increased the circulation* to 20,000, but the *Methodist Magazine* underwent further change when Benson died in 1821. In an attempt to reassert the Wesleyan heritage, the hardliner of the Methodist Connexion, Jabez Bunting (1779-1858) added *Wesleyan* to the title in 1822 and brought in Thomas Jackson as editor. Bunting's authoritarianism was stamped on the *Magazine*'s conservative religious*, literary* and political* content. Despite Methodism's increasingly liberal political stance on theological matters, the *Magazine* maintained its conservative position. After 1818 the separate *Missionary** *Notes* was included within the *Magazine*, and when after 1914 its title continued to change, the masthead* proclaimed its enduring appeal as 'The Oldest Religious Magazine in the World'. **CL**

Source: Altholz 1989, Topham 2004.

WESTERN MAIL (1869-) The *Western Mail* was established in Cardiff by John Crichton Stuart (1847-1900), Third Marquess of Bute, as a conservative 1d daily* paper. Although its focus was on regional* news, it also reported national and international news*, sports* events and stock market fluctuations. Its editorial policy was to combine serious political* news with more sensational items focusing on the latest murder. From the start, it touted itself as the national newspaper of Wales, and by 1878 it claimed that within Wales it circulated* 'more extensively than all the other papers put together'.

Lascelles Carr (1841-1902) edited* the paper from the beginning, and along with Daniel Owen (1836-1895) he purchased it from Bute in 1877. Published in English, and orientated towards Westminster as the seat of political power, whatever patriotism the paper expressed towards Wales was framed by a strong support for the constitutional values of the United Kingdom and indeed the British Empire. Though the paper acknowledged the right of the Welsh miners to union representation, it deplored the radical tactics – the 'disgraceful intimidation' – used by some in the trades* union movement, those who would erroneously 'look upon the capitalist as their natural enemy'. It adopted the line – popular among industrialists – that conciliation was key. Similarly, any attempt to convert the groundswell of national identity into separatism was met with scorn, and the paper's mocking treatment of 'those enthusiastic personages who set up a claim for the Welsh language to be considered the primitive language of paradise' demonstrated its acceptance of the hegemony of English.

In the 1890s it published a separate women's supplement*, carrying a variety of articles on issues affecting women (such as one on 'men flirts v. women coquettes'), fashion* tips, stories and domestic advice. Now owned by Trinity Mirror, it remains one of the largest newspapers in Wales. **MaT**
Sources: Cayford 1992, 19CBLN, *Mitchell's*, *ODNB*.

WESTERN VINDICATOR (23 FEB. TO 14 DEC. 1839)

An unstamped* weekly* Chartist* newspaper circulating across South Wales and the West of England, the *Western Vindicator* was published* and edited* from Bristol by Henry Vincent. Invaluable financial support was provided by John Miniken, Vincent's London-based cousin. Selling for 2d, the four-page paper was extended to 16 columns* after two weeks. The average weekly sale was 2,000, though this figure rose to 3,400 in mid August. After the Newport Rising in early November 1839, in which the *Vindicator* was heavily implicated, the price* was reduced to 1d but the paper had to be printed covertly in Bath, as the authorities were determined to confiscate all copies.

The *Vindicator* provides a conspicuous example of the resourcefulness and variety of early radical journalism. Unstamped papers were not legally allowed to report news*, so Vincent used a range of devices to comment on politics*, the most prominent of

which was his 'Life and Rambles' column. Facetiously dedicated to the new Queen Victoria, it was carefully designed to reflect the results of his missionary zeal in arousing mass Chartist support in the provincial* regions in which the *Vindicator* circulated. Despite the success of this subterfuge, Vincent was sentenced to a year in prison in August 1839, from where he continued to both edit and contribute to the paper. Other features of the paper included debates and digests, correspondence* (some in Welsh), historical* surveys, satirical* sketches, inspirational poetry* and dream narratives.

Notable local Chartists who wrote for the paper included William Prowting Roberts, William Edwards and John Frost. Many articles were devoted to the new trade unions*, Irish coercion and the anti-truck agitation. Coverage of the New Poor Law, temperance* and educational issues ensured considerable female support. Its political columns* were further enlivened by extracts from the writings of Paine, Wooler, Cobbett and the Comte de Volney. **OA**
Sources: Ashton 2005, Herbert 1988, Jones 1985, *ODNB*, Pugh 1965, Vincent-Miniken Papers, Wilks 1984, Williams 1969.

WESTMACOTT, CHARLES MOLLOY (1788?-1868)

While Charles Molloy Westmacott was a satiric poet, playwright, novelist, art collector and art critic, he is chiefly remembered as a newspaper proprietor*/editor* and reputed blackmailer. He was born in London and claimed to be the natural son of the sculptor Richard Westmacott. At St Paul's school, which he attended from 1800, he was known as Charles Molloy. After working at the Adelphi theatre as a machinist, Westmacott acquired his first weekly* paper the *Observer of the Times*phur in 1821; the following year he moved on to the *Gazette of Fashion*, which attempted to make its name by exposing gambling hells and attacking Walter Scott's Waverley novels. The *Gazette* also published Westmacott's songs, complete with music*, fashion* plates, and author portraits. In 1824 he published his most famous book, *The English Spy*, a deluxe farrago of gossip* in prose and poetry* with illustrations* by Robert Cruikshank* and Thomas Rowlandson.

In 1825 he was working with William Maginn* on the *English Gentleman*, and in July 1827, through a devious financial transaction, secured the scandal-mongering paper the *Age*, which he owned and edited through 1838, with Maginn writing, most probably, many of the political leaders*. The *Age*, a true forerunner of the modern tabloids, was rabidly Tory in politics*, satiric in perspective, and for a time had the highest circulation* of any London weekly. Westmacott was widely, though not respectably, known within the Tory aristocracy, and by theatrical performers and the literati. The *Age* was read by all within those orbits, who when skewered claimed it was a paper read only by valets and chambermaids. If one wanted to know with whom Madame Vestris was sleeping, or whether Bulwer was still beating his wife, one read the *Age*. What stayed out was sometimes as lucrative as what stayed in; in 1829 in what the press called 'The Mysterious Affair' he was paid £5,000 in a scandal involving the royal family. Westmacott was no stranger to the law courts, and was physically assaulted on occasion, most notably by Charles Kemble in the lobby of Drury Lane (1830).

Westmacott sold a half interest to the theatre impresario Captain Polhill in 1834, and in 1838 transferred the property to Albert Bunn. At the end of the year, however, he was induced by prominent Tories to launch a new paper the *Argus** (3 Jan. 1839ff), with Maginn once more on board. The *Argus* merged* back with the *Age* in 1843, and expired in 1845. Westmacott's last known contributions to the press were, oddly enough, to the *New Sporting Magazine* (1846-1848). He died in Paris. **DEL**
Sources: Bates 1873, Latané 2007, *ODNB.*

WESTMINSTER GAZETTE (1893-1928) Founded by George Newnes*, the *Westminster Gazette* was a 'clubland' 1d evening daily*, politically* liberal and printed on green paper*, known as 'the pea-green incorruptible'. Following the purchase of the *Pall Mall Gazette** by Tory interests in 1892, Newnes recruited Edward Tyas Cook* as editor*, and John Alfred Spender* as assistant editor, together with Francis Carruthers Gould the cartoonist*, to establish the *Westminster Gazette* as its radical liberal successor.

Cook resigned as editor in 1895, and Spender assumed the editorship, a position he held with great distinction until 1922. Notwithstanding its influence and the respect in which it was held, the paper never made a profit and its circulation* did not exceed 25,000. In 1908, Newnes sold the title to a liberal syndicate* headed by Sir Alfred Mond. It became a morning paper in 1921 and in 1928 it was merged* with the *Daily News**. **JRW**
Sources: Brown 1985, *ODNB*, Linton and Boston 1987.

WESTMINSTER REVIEW (1824-1914) The *Westminster Review*, conceived by Jeremy Bentham and James Mill* and co-edited* initially by Henry Southern and John Bowring*, began as a liberal quarterly* alternative to the Whig *Edinburgh Review** and the Tory *Quarterly Review**. Early in its existence, the *Westminster Review* faced financial difficulties as well as conflicts between Bowring*, James Mill and his son John Stuart Mill. In 1829, Thomas Perronet Thompson* paid off its debts and joined Bentham as co-proprietor*, while Southern resigned as editor and Bowring remained, although from 1829 to 1836, Thompson assumed principal editorial control.

Two years later, William Molesworth's newly formed *London Review** took over the older publication to form the *London and Westminster Review* with a price* of 6s. Thomas Falconer in April 1837 and John Robertson were named as editors, but they were actually controlled by J. S. Mill. All articles were to be signed, and, though a signature might be pseudonymous*, it would remain constant. The 1830s was a productive decade for the *Review*, with contributors such as W. M. Thackeray*, Leigh Hunt* and Harriet Martineau*. However, in January 1838, a changing political climate led Molesworth to sell the *Review* to J. S. Mill, who in 1840 sold it to Henry Cole and William Edward Hickson* on condition that the title of the journal revert to the original title of the *Westminster Review*. Although Cole left after the first issue, Hickson continued in both capacities for the next 11 years; he perpetuated Mill's policy of representing a range of reformist ideas, while history* and the arts achieved new prominence with the contributions of George Henry Lewes*.

In October 1846, the *Review* merged* with the *Foreign Quarterly Review** to become the *Westminster and Foreign Quarterly Review*, or, less frequently, the *Foreign Quarterly and Westminster Review*, with the *Foreign Quarterly* reduced to a brief section at the end of each issue. In 1851, the shorter title was restored, even though individual issues retained the longer title until 1887. In January 1852 John Chapman* purchased the *Review* and elevated its stature with a rich selection of science*, religion*, literature*, politics, and philosophy* from such leading thinkers as G. H. Lewes, W. R. Greg*, J. A. Froude*, Thomas Huxley* and John Tyndall*. Realizing the need for an editorial assistant, Chapman employed Marian Evans* (later 'George Eliot'), who worked with him for the first two years. Chapman found himself losing money, though contributors and editors continued to receive little or no recompense. In 1860, he declared bankruptcy, selling his publishing business to George Manwaring, retaining, however, the editorship and ownership of the *Review* until 1887, when it was sold to the newly formed Westminster Review Company. Chapman continued as editor, with the *Review* becoming a monthly* with shorter articles. Following his death in 1894, his wife Hannah Hughes Chapman managed and edited the *Review* into the following century. **DU**

Sources: Mill 1961, Nesbitt 1934, Sullivan, Van Arsdel 1961, *Wellesley*.

WHEELER, THOMAS MARTIN (1811-1862)
Thomas Martin Wheeler, journalist and novelist, was closely associated with the important Chartist* newspaper the *Northern Star**. His first articles were for the Owenite* *New Moral World** in 1839, but his journalistic* career took off when Feargus O'Connor* invited him to become the London correspondent of the *Northern* Star, a paid position he held in 1841-1843 and 1850.

Wheeler was deeply involved with the Chartist Land Plan, writing extensively on the subject for the *Northern Star*. Typical of his contributions was 'Walks and Wanderings around O'Connorville' (April 1848), which reflected his admiration for this new Chartist community where he lived (1847-1849). He spent his time there tending his livestock and writing a novel, 'Sunshine and Shadow', which was serialized* in the *Northern Star* (March 1849-Jan. 1850). Another novel, 'A Light in the Gloom', appeared in Ernest Jones's periodical the *People's Paper** in the 1850s. Wheeler was also involved with the financial management of this newspaper, but Ernest Jones's financial affairs were complicated and the £50 of his own money which Wheeler put up for the enterprise eventually led to a brief imprisonment for debt. In the late 1850s, Wheeler was also a contributor to *Reynolds's Weekly Newspaper**. **SFR**

Sources: Goodway 1982, Saville 1982, Taylor 2003.

WHIBLEY, CHARLES (1859-1930) Cambridge-educated Charles Whibley worked for the publishers Cassell & Co*, where he met W. E. Henley* who persuaded him to write for the *Scots Observer** (later the *National Observer*) from 1889.

Whibley was the mainstay of the newspaper in its first years, writing leaders*, 'middles*' and book reviews*, although he was a lethargic contributor. His high Tory politics and imperial leanings were ideally suited to the newspaper. His forthright views were highlighted in his anonymous* attack on the immorality of Wilde's* *The Picture of Dorian Gray* in July 1890. On the few occasions of Henley's ab-

sence he edited* the paper.

After the *National Observer* changed hands in 1894, Whibley became the Paris correspondent for the *Pall Mall Gazette** until 1897. From March 1898 he wrote for *Blackwood's Magazine**, in particular the unsigned monthly column* 'Musing without Method' (Feb. 1900-Dec. 1929).

Whibley was also a prolific contributor to the *Academy**, *Art Journal**, *Bookman* (USA), *Cornhill**, *Country Life*, *Criterion*, *Current Literature*, *Current Opinion*, *Daily Graphic**, *Daily Mail**, *Eclectic Magazine*, *English Review*, *Fortnightly Review**, *Harper's Magazine**, *Literary Opinion*, *Literature*, *Living Age*, *McClure's Magazine*, *Macmillan's Magazine**, *Magazine of Art**, *New Review**, *Nineteenth Century**, *North American Review*, *Outlook*, *Pall Mall Gazette** *Quarterly Review**, *Speaker**, *Spectator**, *Strand**, and the *Mercure de France*.

Whibley's later writings echoed his early *Scots/National Observer* work. His *Nineteenth Century* articles (1894 and 1897) were against the 'encroachment' of women and the 'farce of university extension'. Whibley wrote on a vast range of topics but always with a strong and often biased voice. He was never satisfied with the present but delighted in the virtues of the past as he saw them. In later life his even more entrenched views were out of fashion with the times. **DA**

Sources: *CBEL*, Donovan 2006, Finkelstein 1995, *ODNB*, *Wellesley*.

WHISTLER, JAMES ABBOTT MCNEILL (1834-1903) Whistler's claims for a place in an account of nineteenth-century journalism are small but insistent. His two drawings for *Good Words** in 1862, accompanying a story called the 'Trial Sermon' and four more for *Once a Week** from the same year, have been widely regarded by commentators as among the best black and white illustrations* of the nineteenth century, leading Reid to state that 'had we nothing of Whistler's but his six wood* engravings I think we might still claim that he was a great artist'. **BM**

Sources: Engen 1990, Houfe 1978, *ODNB*, Reid 1928, White 1897.

WHITAKER, JOSEPH (1820-1895); WHITAKER, JOSEPH VERNON (1845-1895)
The Whitakers, father and son, are best known for their involvement with the *Bookseller**, *Whitaker's Almanack* (1869-) and *Whitaker's Books in Print* (1874-). Joseph started in the book trade aged 14 as an apprentice to a Fleet Street* booksellers and in 1849 moved towards publishing* when he started the *Penny Post* (1849-1896), a Church of England

monthly* initially edited* by Frederick George Lee and published by John Henry Parker*. Soon there was *Whitaker's Penny Alamanack* (1850-1852) and *Whitaker's Clergyman's Diary*, both published by Parker. In 1854 Whitaker began his own theological publishing house and brought out the 6d *Artist* in 1855. This was unsuccessful, lasting only seven issues. To supplement his income, he edited the *Gentleman's Magazine** (1856-1859). To do so he compiled a commonplace book of newspaper cuttings, notes and material from government publications. In January 1858, he spotted a gap in the market* and launched the pioneering trade* journal, the *Bookseller**. This was so successful that after two years it absorbed its only rival, the now tired *Bent's Literary Advertiser**. In December 1868, Whitaker returned to his commonplace book by using it as the basis for *Whitaker's Almanack*, supplementing his own work with astronomical information obtained with the help of the Astronomer Royal, Sir George Biddell Airey (1801-1892). The *Almanack's* first print run was 40,000, of which 36,000 were sold before publication: total sales of the first edition reached 60,000. Whitaker continued to publish devotional works, but in 1874 he produced the *Reference Catalogue of Current Literature* (*British Books in Print* 1965-1987, and since then, *Whitaker's Books in Print*).

Joseph's eldest son Joseph Vernon joined his father on the *Bookseller* from c.1870. Soon after, invited by G. W. Childs, the young man went to Philadelphia to edit the *American Literary Gazette*. The paper was taken over in 1872 by the New York *Publishers' Weekly,* but Joseph Vernon remained in Philadelphia where he subedited* the *Public Ledger*. His father recalled him to London in 1875, finding his own work on both the *Almanack* and *Bookseller* too great: Joseph Vernon now took over the editorship of the latter. Subsequently, he was also to edit the *Reference Catalogue*. In 1880, at his instigation, his father began the *Stationery Trades' Journal* (1880-1939), another success. Like his father, who had been campaigning against underselling since the 1850s and had set up a fund for Paris booksellers in 1871, Joseph Vernon was very energetic within the trade, instituting annual trade dinners for booksellers, campaigning against a rise in the railway distribution* rates for publications in 1889 and the same year helping found the London Booksellers Society (later the Associated Booksellers of Great Britain and Ireland) which

eventually arrived at the Net Book Agreement of 1900. The *Almanack* belonged to the family until 1997. **AK**

Sources: Altholz, 1989, *Bookseller* 1908, *Bookseller* 1958, *ODNB*.

WHITE, JOSEPH WILLIAM GLEESON (1851-1898) The multi-talented Gleeson White was one the most prominent artists, critics and editors* of the late nineteenth century, working primarily from an Arts and Crafts rationale. He was an accomplished book designer associated with the Art Workers Guild, and also in his critical writings proved himself an authority on the subject. However, he also contributed to the popular fiction paper the *Argosy**, the *Band of Hope Review**, the *British Workman** and the *Photogram*. His articles on book design and illustration*, interior decoration, art history and literary criticism were published in aesthetic/decadent journals such as the *Art Journal**, the *Artist**, the *Dome**, the *Quarto**, the *Scottish Art Review** and the *Studio**.

During a stay in New York (1890-1893) he actively participated in the local cultural life, among other things editing the *Art Amateur* (1891-1892). Back in London, he became the first editor of the *Studio** (1893), leaving his mark on both its stylish

Figure 66: The *Pageant* (1897) edited by Gleeson White, with a cover designed by Charles Ricketts.

Figure 67: The endpapers of the *Pageant* designed by Lucien Pissaro.

appearance and the wide scope of its contents. Together with the like-minded Charles Shannon* he edited the *Pageant**, a lavishly decorated annual* mostly focused on Pre-Raphaelite art and continental literature*. In 1897 he also edited *Parade**, an attractive 'illustrated gift book for boys and girls' that can be seen as a successful application of his aesthetic principles to a children's periodical*.

The love of aesthetically pleasing publications permeated White's every venture; he even compiled an anthology called *Book-Song* (1893) consisting entirely of poetry* devoted to books. White died of typhoid fever at the age of 47. **KNC**

Sources: *New York Times* (obituary), Sullivan.

WHITE, (WILLIAM) HALE (1831-1913) Hale White published his literary prose as 'Mark Rutherford' and 'Reuben Shapcott'; yet his little-known but voluminous journalism appeared under his own name if not published anonymously*.

Moderately successful as a civil servant in the Registrar General's office, Hale White sought to supplement his income by writing for provincial newspapers of a liberal and nonconformist bent, such as the *Aberdeen Herald*, the *Birmingham Post and Journal*, the *Morning Star*, the *Nonconformist**, the *Norfolk News*, the *Rochdale Observer* and the *Scotsman**. He had already had an early taste of the publishing market* when John Chapman* employed him as personal assistant and 'subscription tout' at the *Westminster Review** and lodged him at 142 Strand ('George Eliot*' being a fellow lodger). The idea to use his own pen came when his father, William White, who was Doorkeeper to the House of Commons, started to give him access to the House, enabling him to write as a parliamentary* reporter* or London correspondent. Not all of

Hale White's contributions to the provincial* press had longevity, but his 'Sketches in Parliament' for the *Birmingham Post and Journal* ran for 14 years.

Among the prestigious literary* reviews, the *Contemporary Review** and *Macmillan's Magazine** published occasional essays by Hale White (on 'Byron, Goethe, Arnold' and 'Shelley's Birthplace' respectively). They were reprinted in collections which he signed as 'Mark Rutherford': *Pages from a Journal* (1900) and *Last Pages from a Journal* (1915). Hale White also wrote for the *Athenaeum** (especially on Dorothy Wordsworth), the *Spectator** the literary monthly the *Bookman** and the Non-Conformist penny* weekly* the *British Weekly**. The last two periodicals were edited* by W. Robertson Nicoll*, who later issued a memoir of 'Mark Rutherford'. Hale White's very last papers appeared in the *Nation*.

There is no reason to suppose that Hale White saw his journalism as related to his novelistic work. He largely restricted himself to political* reporting, his only personal political statement being an early pamphlet called *An Argument for the Extension of the Franchise: A Letter Addressed to George Jacob Holyoake, Esq.* (1866). **MdW**

Sources: Nicoll 1913, *ODNB*, Stone 1954, White 1924.

WHITE, WILLIAM HALE (1857-1949) William Hale-White, editor*, medical writer and physician, was born in London, the eldest son of William Hale White, known as 'Mark Rutherford', author of autobiographical novels. Sir William hyphenated his own surname at the time of his father's death. Hale-White trained at Guy's Hospital from 1875, and served as an administrator there before becoming a physician.

Hale-White wrote prolifically on medical* subjects: case reports published in the *Transactions of the Pathological Society* covered almost all branches of medicine. Making his name with the textbook *Materia Medica, Pharmacology and Therapeutic* (1892), he was one of the two editors* of *Guy's Hospital Reports* (1886-1893), also contributing many papers to the journal. For almost 20 years (1907-1927), he was editor of the *Quarterly Journal of Medicine*. Hale-White gave up his medical practice in 1927 as he was also interested in the poet John Keats, and in 1925 published* in *Guy's Hospital Reports* an account of Keats as a medical student. An article on Oliver Goldsmith was published in the *Lancet** in 1929. Hale-White enjoyed writing and also produced several books on medical history. **DHL**

Sources: Campbell 1949, *ODNB*.

WHITEING, RICHARD (1840-1928) Whiteing was a journalist and novelist, beginning his career in 1866 writing articles for the *Evening Star*. He covered the Paris Exhibition in 1867 for the *Morning Star* and the job led to his becoming Paris correspondent for the London and New York branches of the *World**. Whiteing was on the staff of the *Manchester Guardian** (Jan.1874-May 1875), the paper which sent him to France again in 1880 as its Paris correspondent. Back in London by 1886, Whiteing served as journalist at the *Daily News** until 1899 when he retired.

Whiteing published a collection of his satirical* articles from his time at the *Evening Star* under the title *Mr Sprouts, His Opinions* (1867) as well as six works of fiction (1876-1907) and an autobiography, *My Harvest* (1915). ET
Source: *ODNB*.

WILDE, JANE FRANCES AGNES (1821-1896) Born in Wexford, 'Speranza', the pseudonym by which Jane Wilde was usually known, was an Irish nationalist writer and poet who contributed to many of the most popular* magazines* of her day. She was active in the Young Ireland* movement of the 1840s, publishing poetry* and leaders* in the *Nation**, the *Dublin University Magazine** and in *Duffy's Hibernian Magazine**. Indeed, when Charles Gavan Duffy*, editor* of the *Nation* was imprisoned in 1848, Speranza wrote a lead article (29 July) calling for an armed uprising. Not surprisingly, the article led to the suppression of the paper for sedition.

In Ireland 'Speranza' became famous as a reteller of traditional tales, and, like William Carleton*, of stories of the Famine. A skilled linguist, she published translations of French and German tales to great acclaim. Over a long career, she contributed articles and poems to the *Pall Mall Gazette**, *Queen**, the *Burlington Magazine*, *Lady's Pictorial** and to *Gentlewoman*, supporting the new Married Women's Property Act in 1883. Speranza remained a strong advocate of her son Oscar Wilde* throughout his life, and occasionally contributed to his magazine *Woman's World**. She influenced generations of Irish writers: Carleton called her an 'extraordinary prodigy'; Joyce, Yeats and later Seamus Heaney have all paid tribute to her ability to transform the raw materials of Irish history into living testaments of a brutal past. ET
Sources: Melville 1994, *ODNB*, Rafroidi 1980, PGIL eirdata.

WILDE, OSCAR (1854-1900) Oscar Wilde's first piece of journalism – an extended review* of the newly opened and highly fashionable G-rosven-or Gallery – was published in the *Dublin University Review** in July 1877 when he was still at Oxford. In late 1879 he moved to London and embarked on a life as a freelance writer with theatrical and poetic aspirations but prepared throughout the coming decade to produce brief anonymous* notices for the papers. Although his output slackened when he ceased reviewing* books for the *Pall Mall Gazette** in 1890 (probably because the editor* W. T. Stead* had recently resigned), he contributed major critical essays to the *Nineteenth Century**, and the *Fortnightly Review** in 1889 and 1890. His short fictions appeared in the *World**, *Blackwood's Magazine** and elsewhere, while an early version of *The Picture of Dorian Gray* was published in the Philadelphia-based *Lippincott's Magazine* in June 1890.

Had his career as a writer not effectively come to an end following his arrest and imprisonment in 1895, it is likely that Wilde would have continued contributing to periodicals but probably not as a regular reviewer. Although the bulk of his output in the 1880s was for the *Pall Mall Gazette*, he also wrote important pieces on the then controversial topic of scenic 'archaeology' for the *Dramatic Review**, a short-lived but for its time 'advanced' semi-professional journal, and various features for the *Court and Society Review** which combined moderately high literary standards with aristocratic gossip* and topical comment.

Wilde's greatest involvement with the world of periodical publication came when he became editor of the *Woman's World** in November 1887. By changing its name from the previous *Lady's World** Wilde signalled new ambitions and the refurbished journal paid great attention to the professional and literary* achievements of women. The commissions were adventurous though often drawing upon Wilde's many contacts in London. His own lengthy leaders*, however, are by no means confined to social events in the United Kingdom, and the overall contents of the periodical include items on fashion* (a subject which Wilde had always taken with considerable seriousness), classical scholarship, current books, plays and poetry* as well as more domestic matters. By 1889 the regular duties of editorship seem to have proved too great a burden and in July he stood down.

Wilde's career as a journalist* was both idiosyncratic in its attention to style and entirely typical of its period in its versatility and its familiarity with the current cultural scene. Certain personal preoccupations do shine through – Irish heritage (myths, crafts, politics*), the visual arts (book design, interior furnishings as well as painting) and poetry of every kind. His manner can be surprisingly pedantic and portentous. Often amused yet never discourteous, he was the consummate professional. JAS

Sources: Ellmann 1987, Guy 2007, Raby 1997, Stokes 2003, Wilde 2004.

WILLIAM DAWSON William Dawson started his news agency* business in 1809 at 74 Cannon Street, London, where he also functioned as bookseller and stationer. As the century progressed, trading as William Dawson & Sons Ltd, wholesale and retail newsvendors and booksellers, he was supplying stamped and unstamped London newspapers, including *The Times**, with periodicals such as the *Illustrated News*. Capitalizing on the developments in railway* transportation and steamships, as well as the advent of a cheaper postal system, the firm supplied all London newspapers throughout the country as well as dispatching them globally, twice a day. Recognizing the power of advertising*, Dawson assured his prospective customers that he took advertisements* in all London and country newspapers. The business also published* catalogues relating to its various services, listing magazines and periodicals together with its *Standard English Authors, Ancient and Modern* that provided details of books it carried for sale. Dawson also published the *Publishers' Circular Newspaper, Magazine and Periodical Supplement** from 1898. By 1911 it was producing the *Dawson Little Red Book-Guide to the Press of the World*.

The current incarnation of the business is that of Dawson Holdings, third in line behind W. H. Smith* and John Menzies*. CL

Sources: Brake 2001, Dawson Holdings online, ncse online, *The Times* Digital Archive

WILLIAM PICKERING (1820-1854); PICKERING AND CHATTO (C. 1887-1893) The entry of William Pickering (1796-1854), bookseller, publisher and proprietor*, into the publishing* trade came when he was apprenticed to the Quaker booksellers and publishers* John and Arthur Arch in 1810. He subsequently worked for Longmans* and then John Cuthill before setting up his own bookshop in 1820 at 31 Lincoln's Inn Fields. He began to publish a series of clothbound (and therefore very affordable) miniature reprints of classic English, Italian, Latin and Greek literature* called 'Diamond Classics' and printed by Charles Corrall. Following his move to Chancery Lane in 1823, he continued to produce editions of the classics that were notable for their design and illustrations*.

Book publishing was perhaps the backbone of his business, but he also published several well-known and high-circulation* periodicals, entering the market in earnest in 1828 with the popular literary annual* *Bijou*. In 1834, in conjunction with J. B. Nichols*, he took over the *Gentleman's Magazine**, and – a supporter of the Church of England – started the *Church of England Quarterly Review** in 1837. He also published the *Rugby Magazine* (1835-1837) and the *Oxford and Cambridge Review* (1845-1847).

Pickering moved to 177 Piccadilly in 1842, and his last years were plagued by illness and financial problems caused by his tendency to amass excessive stock. Following his death his creditors were paid off by the sale of his stock, and James Toovey took over the business. Pickering's son Basil Montague Pickering (1835-1878) was apprenticed to Toovey and set up his own business in 1858 at 196 Piccadilly. He republished editions published by his father and other, new titles, seeking always to maintain his high standards, but his main activity was as an antiquarian book dealer. Thomas Chatto, son of the publisher Andrew Chatto (1840-1913) of Chatto & Windus*, joined the firm to form Pickering & Chatto which began publishing books on antiquarian subjects in the 1880s. A descendent of Basil Montague Pickering's bookshop – also called Pickering & Chatto – still exists as a rare book dealership at 144-146 Bond Street. The exact genealogy of the two firms is rather unclear. MaT

Sources: *ODNB*, Pickering & Chatto website, *Waterloo*.

WILL O' THE WISP (1867-1871) *Will o' the Wisp* was one of several satirical* magazines of the later Victorian period that struggled to find a clear identity. Starting as a fortnightly of eight 30 cm* pages for 4d, it became a weekly* from 1868 of 12 pages, selling by 1871 for 2d. Initially, it concentrated on politics* and was akin to the *Owl*. But *Will o' the Wisp* became extremely dependent on the ability of its lead cartoonist* John Proctor, who produced a sequence of large-scale *Punch**-style foldout images which formed the central attraction of the magazine. While never able to reach the heights of Matt Morgan* at the *Tomahawk**, Proctor was nonetheless an experienced and capable draughtsman who had been lead illustrator* at *Judy** just before joining the newly launched *Will o' the Wisp*, later taking up similar roles at *Moonshine**, the *Sketch** and *Fun**. Under the editorship* of Hamilton Hume, *Will o' the Wisp* offered a predictable combination of social satire, facetious political*

comment and Proctor's weekly cartoon, but it failed to prosper in a highly competitive market*. **BM**
Sources: Engen 1990, Houfe 1987.

WILLIAMS, DAWSON (1854-1928) In 1881, the year he obtained his MD degree, Dawson Williams, wishing to supplement his income through medical* journalism, obtained an introduction to Ernest Hart*, editor* of the *British Medical Journal**. His appointment as a contributor marked the beginning of an association with the medical weekly* that continued to within weeks of his death. While still practising medicine, mainly as a paediatrician, he became, successively, the journal's hospital reporter* (1884), principal sub-editor* (1886) and assistant editor (1895).

As Hart's health deteriorated during the 1890s, Williams was, effectively, editing the *British Medical Journal*. On his predecessor's death in 1898, Williams succeeded to the editorship at an annual salary of £650 plus payments for contributions. The vacancy was not advertised and no other candidate was considered. Hence Williams was the first *British Medical Journal* editor appointed through internal promotion rather than open competition. He occupied the post until January 1928 when he reluctantly retired. No other editorial tenure of the *Journal* has lasted as long. In 1902, at the insistence of the British Medical Association, the journal's proprietor*, Williams relinquished his hospital appointments and became the *Journal's* first full-time editor. His 47-year association with the journal coincided in large part with its years of pre-eminence.
PWB
Sources: Bartrip 1990, *British Medical Journal* 10 March 1928: 414-425, *Lancet* 3 March 1928: 476-478, *ODNB*, *The Times* 28 Feb. 1928.

WILLIAMS FAMILY (1800-1877?) Spanning two generations of engravers, the Williams Family include some of the most highly respected names in book and periodical illustration* during the nineteenth century. Samuel Williams (1788-1853), draughtsman, wood* engraver, oil painter and natural history illustrator, was born in Colchester and worked there as an apprentice to the printer J. Marsden from 1802. During this apprenticeship, Samuel taught himself to etch and engrave on copper as well as how to draw and engrave on wood. Having established his own business in Colchester, Samuel moved to London in 1819 where he became a prolific illustrator, aided by his sister Ann Mary Williams (c.1788-?). Ann also worked independently, predominantly on book illustration, especially noted for the guidebooks on Hampton

Court and Westminster Abbey.

Alongside the illustration of highly prized books, Samuel Williams 'played a leading role in the embellishment of illustrated periodicals' (*ODNB*). His engraved illustrations grace the pages of the radical William Hone's* *Every-Day Book* (1825-1827) and are a particular feature of the weekly* journal the *Olio, or, Museum of Entertainment**. He also illustrated the monthly *Parterre of Fiction, Poetry, History, Literature, and the Fine Arts* (1834-1835), the title page of which bears his name. Jackson's *A Treatise on Wood Engraving* (1861) cites Samuel Williams and his brother Thomas Williams (1798-?) as being among the 'English wood engravers ... best entitled to honourable mention'. As well as quality book illustration, including collaborations with his brother and sister, Thomas Williams contributed illustrations for the *Penny Magazine** and also designed the emblem for the Chiswick Press.

The second generation of Williams's family engravers comprised Samuel Williams's four sons and daughter, Alfred Mayhew Williams, Emma Williams, Frederick George Williams, Joseph Lionel Williams and John Manning Williams (all five siblings baptized 1832, but only Joseph Lionel has a date of death, 1877). They frequently worked in collaboration with each other and their father.

Of these, Joseph, John and Alfred made the biggest contribution to journalism*. Joseph Williams is noted for his drawings of architectural subjects and machinery. He contributed to the *Art Journal** and was a regular and critically acclaimed contributor to the *Illustrated London News** during the 1840s and 1850s. Alfred Williams also worked as an engraver for the same journal during the 1850s and 1860s, including many illustrations in collaboration with his brother John Williams. Throughout the second-generation's three-decade involvement with the *Illustrated London News*, Joseph, Alfred and John Williams contributed a number of highly acclaimed engravings.

The known signatures* of the Williams Family engravers are as follows: Samuel Williams:'S. Williams' or 'S. W'.; Thomas Williams: 'Thos Williams sc' or 'T Williams' or 'T W' or 'TW'; Mary Ann Williams: 'M. A. Williams, sc' or 'MARY ANN WILLIAMS SC'; Alfred and John Williams: 'J. & A. W'. or 'J. & A. Williams'. **MBT**
Sources: Boase 1965, Houfe 1996, Jackson 1861, *ODNB*.

WILLS, WILLIAM HENRY (1810-1880) William Henry, or 'Harry', Wills was a well-known and popular figure in mid-Victorian press circles, known for his meticulous subbing skills and pleasant if amusingly pedantic manner of relaying factual information. Born in Plymouth, Wills moved with his family to a working-class area of Somers Town in North London and on the death of his father became responsible for the upkeep of the family. Trained as a wood* engraver, he drifted into journalism, contributing to the *Penny Magazine**, the *Saturday Magazine**, and becoming a subeditor of the *Monthly Magazine** in 1835. He was one of the original literary staff of *Punch**, contributing satirical* prose, verse and acting as drama critic in 1841 before moving to Edinburgh to become assistant editor* of *Chambers's Journal**(1842-1845), where he met and later married Janet Chambers, sister of William* and Robert Chambers*.

His first contact with Charles Dickens* came when the latter accepted his contributions to *Bentley's Miscellany** (1837); contact improved into acquaintance in 1845-1846 when he was hired as subeditor and secretary to the *Daily News**, in which role he continued until 1849. John Forster* then recommended him to Dickens as an ideal subeditor for *Household Words**, and Wills became a versatile, conscientious and indispensable complement to Dickens in every aspect of the conduct of his journals, *All the Year Round** included, until he was forced into early retirement following a riding accident in 1868. **JMD**
Sources: *DNB*, Lehmann 1912, *ODNB*, Schlicke 1999, Spencer 1988.

WILSON, CHARLOTTE MARY (1854-1944)

Charlotte Mary Wilson was an influential middle-class journalist* and activist in the early British male-dominated anarchist movement. Born in Kemerton, Worcestershire, she attended Newnham College, Cambridge (1873-1876) and in 1884 joined both the Social Democratic Federation and the Fabian Society, contributing articles to the societies' papers *Justice** and the *Fabian Society* as well as giving lectures. Wilson went on to contribute to Henry Seymour's *Anarchist*, Britain's first English-language anarchist paper (March 1885). With Seymour she founded the English Anarchist Circle, and she also contributed to the short-lived *Practical Socialist*, listed as C. M. Wilson. She became publisher*, editor*, and main contributor of the anarchist paper *Freedom** (1886-), which she and Peter Kropotkin co-founded.

Wilson was involved with *Freedom* intermittently until 1895, after which, due to illness, she withdrew. Her last contribution, written in 1896 and

published in 1901, was 'A Short History of Freedom'. During this period of intense involvement, Wilson was also concerned in the production of a series of Freedom Pamphlets. After 1906, Wilson turned her political attentions to the women's movement, founding the Fabian Women's Group in 1908. **KC**
Sources: Freedom Press online, *ODNB*, Sutherland 1988.

WILSON, JOHN (1785-1854)

Following a brilliant university career at Glasgow and Oxford, John Wilson, the son of a Paisley manufacturer, was forced by major financial losses in 1815 to turn to writing for a living. He contributed briefly to the *Edinburgh Review**, then found his niche in the rival pages of the monthly *Blackwood's Edinburgh Magazine**. Wilson pseudonym* 'Christoph North' played a major role in the journal's infamous relaunch in September 1817, joining John Gibson Lockhart* and James Hogg in editing* and writing significant pieces that offered readers a literary* journal with a witty yet sharp critical bite.

Wilson's prodigious journalistic work (1817-1854) for *Blackwood's* (over 500 pieces in 37 years) made him the pre-eminent critic of his day. His distinctive, personalized, critical prose style defined and shaped British critical periodical discourse for over a generation. As one critic astutely noted, 'The Age of Wordsworth turned to him in magazine* writing as it turned to Byron in poetry and to Walter Scott in the novel' (Strout: 9). His contributions in particular to the ongoing series 'Noctes Ambrosianae' in *Blackwood's Magazine* (1822ff) gained him lasting recognition, allowing him the opportunity to create a conversational narrative style that incisively analysed and dissected pre-Victorian culture and literary tastes. The series ran until 1835, with Wilson in sole charge of the monthly column* from 1825 onwards. He would return to the commentary format* for a less successful series for *Blackwood's*, 'Dies Boreales' (1849-1854).

In the 1830s Wilson slowed in his periodical output, in part due to personal losses of friends and family. He also suffered ill-health. In 1851 he resigned the professorship in moral philosophy and political economy he had held at the University of Edinburgh since 1820, and though he continued to write for *Blackwood's Edinburgh Magazine*, his contributions were less effective than in earlier times. **DF**
Sources: Alexander 1992, Craig 1988, *ODNB*, Oliphant 1897, Strout 1959, Swann 1934, Tredrey 1954.

WILSON, MARGARET CORNWELL BARON (1797-1846) Principally known as a poet, Mrs Baron Wilson (née Harries) was extensively published in weekly* and monthly* periodicals such as the *Mirror of Literature** and the *New Monthly Magazine and Humorist** as well as many literary* annuals*. In 1833 she launched the *Weekly Belle Assemblée* which the following year became the *New Monthly Belle Assemblée, a Magazine of Literature** *and Fashion*. As well as working assiduously as the journal's editor* and writing book reviews*, it provided her with an additional outlet for her poetry*. Baron Wilson's other talent was as a composer and she founded and edited the short-lived periodical *La Ninon, or Leaves for the Album, consisting of original music***, poetry and romance* (1833). CL
Sources: *ODNB, Waterloo*.

WINDSOR MAGAZINE (1895-1939) The *Windsor Magazine* published articles and stories buttressing traditional Victorian middle-class family* values and gender* roles for over 40 years in consistently high-quality monthly issues, while also offering escapist literature. The *Windsor* opposed the New Woman, women's suffrage and socialism and tacitly supported the expanding British Empire* and all traditional aspects of Englishness. It managed to maintain moral rectitude without high-minded preaching and appealed to both men and women readers.

The first issue announced its purpose was to 'illuminate the hearth with genial philosophy' and 'make it crackle with the good humour which is born of true tolerance and puts to flight the exaggerated self-consciousness of aggressive virtue'. For male readers, the *Windsor Magazine* offered both educative and informative articles together with escapist adventure fiction. For female readers*, the magazine* covered educational issues, housekeeping, fashion*, celebrity* and royalty gossip*, romance stories and sentimental poetry*. Pieces also reflected the interest in society figures with articles such as 'Homes of Notable People'.

The first editor* Stanhope Sprigg was quickly followed by David Williamson in 1896, under whose direction the magazine dropped the women's columns*. In the January 1896 issue, Williamson introduced 'The Editor's Scrap-Book', a mix of humour, *bon mots*, poems and vignettes which lasted for the rest of the magazine's life. He also introduced 'The Editor's Post-Bag' (Sept. 1896) – the first time that readers' letters* were published in a British popular monthly. Articles on technology and scientific* achievements proliferated alongside

pieces on expeditions to the North Pole, regular sporting* features and interviews* with authors and artists. In the *Windsor Magazine's* history, many articles were also republished from American* magazines, mostly *McClure's*. The *Windsor* also published American writers such as Jack London and Josephine Dodge Daskam. The magazine is perhaps best remembered for its fiction with two of the best-known and most lasting detective characters that emerged being Guy Boothby's Dr Nikola and Arthur Morrison's Holmesian detective Martin Hewitt.

The editor following Williamson, Arthur Hutchinson, took the helm in 1898, and built on the existing model of escapist amusement for the next 30 years. At this point, circulation* was claimed to be 150,000-170,000 with 200,000 for Christmas* issues, but a later historian suggested a more modest 110,000-115,000 and 150,000 for the Christmas issue. One consistent characteristic of the magazine's high-quality production was the beautiful illustrations* that accompanied the fiction, plus the works of art regularly included as part of its educational content. KC
Sources: Ashley 2006, Sullivan, *Waterloo*.

WISDEN CRICKETERS' ALMANACK (1864-) The annual* editions of *Wisden Cricketers' Almanack*, providing a review of the previous season's matches from the English first-class game to public school fixtures, and featuring lengthy and comprehensive sections of cricket records, developed to become an essential reference work and respected arbiter in matters of cricket fact. Brighton builder's son John Wisden, a noted bowler in both county and national representative teams, opened a 'cricket and cigar depot' in London in 1855 from where he launched the almanack in 1864, priced* 1s. From an initial 116 pages the annual* grew consistently, numbering 236 pages in 1880, and 646 by 1900. Regular statistical features were accompanied by a variety of articles including comment and advice.

By 1887, the editorial work was being undertaken by the staff of the London-based Cricket Reporting Agency, with the editor* generally a partner in the agency. Charles Pardon, his brother Sydney Pardon and Charles Stewart Caine, renowned as three of the leading sports' journalists* of their generation, succeeded each other as editors. The almanack recruited some of the finest authorities on the game such as cricket historian and author, F. S. Ashley-Cooper, who compiled both the 'Births and Deaths' of cricketers and 'Cricket Records' sections for more than 30 years, until his death in 1932. Sydney Southerton, known as 'Figure Fiend' in the agency, compiled the match statistics from 1894.

Independent of cricket's administrators, *Wisden* voiced an opinion on many contentious issues surrounding the game. Sydney Pardon, for example, campaigned against suspect bowling actions, or 'throwing', in the 1890s, with a more formal editorial platform created in 1901 with the introduction of the influential 'Notes by the Editor'. Advertisements* were carried from 1867, with their number and range expanding to cover the full spectrum of cricketing requisites, from bats and gloves to marquees, and later including fashion* goods, hobby accessories and equipment for other sports such as cycling, golf and billiards. The performance of touring teams abroad remained a constant feature, as did obituaries*, details of the laws of the game and rules of county cricket and, from 1889, photographs* of a handful of players who, in the almanack's opinion, were the stars of the previous season. Primarily though, as the major statistical work concerned with cricket, *Wisden* became a byword for accuracy, detail and comprehensive coverage of the game. ST

Sources: Green 1979, Gutteridge 1963, *ODNB*, *Wisden* 1926, *Wisden* 1933, *Wisden* 2000.

WISEMAN, NICHOLAS (1802-1865) As the first Archbishop of Westminster, Cardinal Wiseman was the spiritual leader of British Roman Catholics, and his efforts to guide this community included work for the *Dublin Review**. Although of Irish descent, Wiseman's boyhood was spent at Ushaw College, near Durham, England, and he considered himself English.

Having become a priest and scholar in Rome, it was while giving a lecture series in London in 1836 that Wiseman became a founding proprietor* of the London-based Catholic quarterly* the *Dublin Review*. From 1847-1862 he was the sole proprietor*, and for much of the period between 1836 and 1862, Wiseman was viewed as the journal's real editor*, with the official one being more akin to a managing editor. Wiseman hoped that the *Dublin Review* would aid the Catholic revival in Britain and, in terms of intramural tensions, bolster the conservative, Ultramontane side. He contributed many articles himself, including an article in the August 1839 issue which John Henry Newman credited with being the first piece of Roman Catholic polemics that rattled his Anglican complacency. Several years later, in an article in the December 1856 issue, Wiseman attacked

the English liberal Catholic publication the *Rambler**. TL

Sources: Altholz 1989, *ODNB*, Schiefen 1984, Ward 1897, *Wellesley.*

WOMAN (1890-1912) Launched in a decade which saw a proliferation of new magazines* for women* readers, *Woman* was a well illustrated* penny* weekly* intended to appeal to the modern woman. The first editor* Fitzroy Gardner targeted a broad cross-class* readership* and secured a wide circulation*. *Woman* included articles on fashion*, royal gossip*, domestic* advice and the new professions for women, as well as interviews* and letters* from readers. Contributors ranged from anti-feminist figures such as Eliza Lynn Linton* to those more sympathetic to the New Woman such as Clementina Black*. Articles were predominantly signed and pseudonyms* were also used, for example Arnold Bennett* appeared as 'Sal Volatile' and 'Barbara'.

The magazine employed many of the techniques of New Journalism*, including short, chatty 'titbits', supplements*, increased illustrations and prize competitions for readers. Unusually, it did not include as much serialized* fiction as other contemporary women's magazines. It relied heavily on advertising* in order to keep the price* down and the dominance of advertisements* annoyed some readers, and tended to detract from its potentially progressive agenda.

The magazine was ambiguous in espousing both advances for women and the traditional domestic virtues, an ambiguity signalled in its motto from 1890 to 1899, 'Forward but not too fast'. Articles on woman's entry into the professions advised readers never to forget their womanliness, reflecting this editorial ambivalence. When Arnold Bennett took over as editor in 1896, the magazine became less interested in the New Woman and her concerns. Fashion* items, household management and gossip* were given additional space. The stress on readers* remaining 'womanly' increased in the early twentieth century, by which time the periodical had become a fashionable lady's magazine. By 1912 its popularity had waned. EL

Sources: Beetham 1996, de Stasio 1995, *Waterloo.*

WOMAN AT HOME (1893-1920) *Woman at Home*, subtitled '*Annie S. Swan's* Magazine', was a 6d monthly* which specifically targeted the middle-class* woman. It was quarto-size, printed in double columns* on glossy paper*. It included articles, biographies, domestic* advice and fashion* but most of its 80 pages were given over to fiction, mainly serialized* or linked short stories, a model made popular by the Sherlock Homes stories in Newnes's* *Strand** magazine*. One such series centred on a woman doctor, another on a woman school teacher. Both these were by Annie Swan but her most important contributions to the magazine were her advice columns*, 'Over the Tea-Cups' and 'Love, Marriage and Courtship', where she printed extracts from readers' letters* and commented on them. Like later 'agony aunts', she adopted a sympathetic tone and persona, responding to the dilemmas of those trapped in loveless marriages or working in situations for which their upbringing had not prepared them.

The publisher* Hodder and Stoughton* was known for its religious publications and Swan shared a Scottish nonconformist background with the editors* Robertson Nicoll* and Jane Stoddart*. However, the journal's religious* tone was muted. It had some characteristics of the New Journalism*: for example, like the *Strand,* it had a picture on every double spread. In 1910 Newnes bought the title and issued a new series but this was subsumed into *Girls' World* in 1920. **MRB**

Sources: Beetham 1996, *Waterloo, Woman at Home.*

WOMANHOOD (1898-1907) *Womanhood* was the creation of the journalist Ada Ballin*, whose intention was to provide a monthly* magazine* to 'appeal to intellectual and highly-educated women*' like herself. The target of the 'New Woman' was acknowledged in the masthead* where the title appeared in dramatic art nouveau script. With its subtitle *the magazine of woman's progress and interests, political, legal, social, and intellectual, and of health and beauty culture,* Ballin was acknowledging the arrival of sophistication and independence combined. Contents included fiction, drama, health, social, political* and industrial issues, biographical profiles, foreign* news* and travel, pets, sport* – particularly cycling, health and beauty, letters* and advice; the range was broad and focused on a woman's life and needs. Articles were predominantly signed, a few anonymous*. Echoing the masthead, illustrations* were modern and there were no advertisements*; at 6d for a lengthy issue, it represented value.

Having started her journalism at 16, Ballin's experience enabled her to make *Womanhood* inclusive, cleverly melding traditional attractions with the new; as well as her own beauty articles there was serialized* fiction, for example, from Marie Corelli. Yet most prominent were the regular articles on women's clubs in London, accounts of single work-

ing women and successes by women in new fields. By 1906, the magazine* contained five pages of advertisements* additional to the front page, thus maintaining its price*, and still managing its appeal, balancing the regular section on suffrage events (Ballin was a supporter) with cookery competitions. Strongly edited* by Ballin, the magazine could not survive her death in 1906 and folded the following year. **CL**

Sources: Gerritsen Collection, *Waterloo.*

WOMAN'S AGRICULTURAL TIMES (1899-1906). Lady Frances Warwick founded the Agricultural Association for Women in February 1899 with 140 members as part of a trend to promote employment opportunities for educated middle-class women. The 1d monthly* *Woman's Agricultural Times* was part of her scheme for women to earn a living in horticulture and 'light' farming.

A large-format journal of 16 pages, it deployed the cover to attract readers with a drawing of Ceres, to list the contents, and on the verso to accommodate advertisements*. The paper gave accounts of the courses and activities established in association with the Reading University Extension College and the hostels Warwick opened for the students. The meetings and work of other women's movement groups such as the Society for Promoting the Employment of Women and the International Council of Women were also included. **CL**

Sources: *Waterloo, Woman's Agricultural Times* 1899.

WOMAN'S LIFE (1895-1934). Subtitled *An Illustrated Weekly* for the Home,* this was George Newnes's* bid for the penny* woman's magazine* market* which emerged as a major element in popular* periodical publishing in the 1890s. Like its rivals, Harmsworth's* weekly *Home Chat** and Pearson's* monthly *Home Notes*, Woman's Life* offered a mixture of old and new in the chatty style of the New Journalism*. Fiction, advice on dress and fashion*, domestic* 'tips' including the relatively new area of home furnishing, 'chats' with aristocratic ladies or other celebrities*, baby-lore and advertisements* were mixed together and seasoned with information about, or interviews* with, 'advanced women' or women working in the newly opened professions. Boasting '70 Illustrations*' in every 62-page issue and offering one, and sometimes two, complete stories each week, *Woman's Life* was extremely successful and claimed to have sold 200,000 copies in 1897. **MRB**

Sources: Altick 1957, Beetham 1996, *Woman's Life.*

Figure 68: Women compositors working at the Victoria Press, *Women and Work*, 10 Oct. 1874: 6.

WOMEN AND WORK, A WEEKLY INDUSTRIAL, EDUCATIONAL, AND HOUSEHOLD REGISTER FOR WOMEN **(1874-1876)** *Women and Work* was one of Emily Faithfull's* Victoria Press periodicals. Edited* by her, it was part of the women's movement campaign to forge openings for necessitous middle-class women in respectable employment, aiming to 'alleviate one of the most painful and delicate problems of the nineteenth century'.

Available every Saturday, this eight-page 1d publication emanated from the Industrial and Educational Bureau which addressed these 'painful problems'. The paper carried practical information and advice: on possible employment avenues and job application procedures, training and educational opportunities, funding assistance, employment legislation, book reviews* and reassuring editorials. There were general advertisements* and a job-seekers' column*. It ceased publication with no prior warning. CL

Sources: Banks 1985, Crawford *et al* 1983, Doughan and Sanchez 1987, *Women and Work* (1874-1876).

WOMEN'S INDUSTRIAL NEWS **(1895-1919)** The quarterly* paper of the politically independent union the Women's Industrial Council (WIC) was edited* by trade* unionist and suffragist Clementina Black*. The WIC was the 1894 successor to the 1889 Women's Trade Union Association; it sought to protect and promote the interests of women working in industrial trades and this house journal was one of its tools. It publicized the Council's findings, campaigned for improved conditions and supported and informed the membership. As such it included reports of WIC's business, information on committee proceedings, progress on campaigns*,

announcements of special events, plus information on essential publications. Beginning with a four-page issue at 1d, it expanded by 1899 to 16 pages carrying an additional four of advertising*, costing 3d. As a pragmatic publication from an organization with limited funds, it was simple and unembellished. CL

Sources: Gordon 2001, Mappen 1985, *Waterloo.*

WOMEN'S PENNY PAPER **(1888-1890);** *WOMAN'S HERALD* **(1891-1893)** Debuting in London, the *Women's Penny* Paper* asserted: 'we claim for women* a full share of power with all its duties, responsibilities and privileges in public and private life'. Scholars consider it to be 'the most vigorous feminist* paper of its time', as Doughan puts it. Founded and edited by prominent women's rights advocate Henrietta B. Muller* under the pen name 'Helena B. Temple', the paper was published weekly* and sold for 1d. It covered local*, national and international news* of interest to women, correspondence* and community notices, information about women's groups, reviews* of literature* and theatre and lengthy biographical interviews* with feminist activists, for which it was renowned.

In 1891, the paper changed its title* to the *Woman's Herald* – a move intended to echo larger societal trends and 'herald the New Womanhood' (3 Jan. 1891). Originally, the paper aspired to a broad readership*, 'open to all shades of opinion, to the working woman as freely as to the educated lady; to the conservative and the radical' (27 Oct. 1888). Muller's departure in April 1892 led to a shift in editorial policy under successor Christina S. Bremner, and the paper became a 'Woman's Liberal paper' (30 April 1892). The paper's final editors* Lady Henry Somerset and Edwin H. Stout (23 Feb. 1893) focused coverage on their own interests, and temperance* became a dominant theme. The final issue was published 28 December 1893, after which the *Women's Herald* was superseded by Somerset's own *Woman's Signal*. EW

Sources: Doughan 1987, Pidduck 1997.

WOMEN'S PERIODICALS From its inception in the early eighteenth century, periodical publishing had acknowledged 'the fair sex' both as readers and contributors and this persisted through the nineteenth century. Women were often the implicit targets of periodicals whose titles included words like 'Family'*, 'Home' or 'Domestic*' and periodical publishing remained, like the novel, a forum in which women were able to enter public print – sometimes anonymously* or disguised but often in their own person. Periodicals specifically targeted at 'women', at 'mothers', or at 'girls', as well as specifically feminine genres* like the novelette*, all arose within that general context.

The *Lady's Magazine** was the first to identify 'ladies' as its readers and writers. It also installed the magazine* as a particularly appropriate form for such a venture because its heterogeneous nature enabled the mixture of fiction, poetry*, advice, gossip*, fashion* and illustration* which were defined as appropriate feminine reading. This set the pattern for the development of the 'woman's magazine'. The early nineteenth-century titles like the *Lady's Monthly Museum* (1798-1832) and *La Belle Assemblée** were illustrated*, expensive and defined their readers by class as much as gender*. By the early Victorian period, other kinds of periodicals for and by women were appearing. Some, like the *Christian Lady's Magazine** and the *Mother's Magazine**, were religious* publications and attacked the fashion and fiction of ladies' journals. However, fashion and dress remained an important component of most women's periodicals, as well as being concentrated in specific fashion magazines.

The 1850s and 1860s saw the eclipse of the older ladies' journals and the emergence of the magazine for middle-class* women. Titles like the *Englishwoman's Domestic Magazine**, the *Ladies' Companion** and the *Ladies' Treasury** continued in cheaper form a commitment to fashion and fiction, but made advice and answers to readers' letters* important features. The latter were often combined in columns* where advice on marriage, home and fashion was dispensed along with needlework patterns and dress patterns. This became the model for the proliferation of domestic magazines for women, especially in the 1880s and 1890s. Development of commercial advertising* towards the end of the century was particularly significant, as women increasingly became defined as 'shoppers'. Some titles, like *Woman**, depended on advertisements to keep prices* low. The press barons of the New Journalism*, Harmsworth*, Newnes* and Pearson*, all recognized the importance of the cheap* women's magazines and made central to their publishing business such titles as *Home Notes**, *Home Chat**, and *Woman's Life** (which sold 200,000 in the mid-1890s).

As magazines, none of these titles carried 'news' in the conventional sense. However, in the second half of the century 'ladies' newspapers' began to appear, broadsheets, printed in columns. The first of these was the *Lady's Newspaper** which merged* with the *Queen**, the most successful of these papers. The news* they offered was mainly fashion and gossip but they did include information on women's campaigns, on work, and on women in the public eye. Other important developments of the second half of the century included publications which campaigned for women's rights*, adopted specifically feminist* agendas or addressed particular issues affecting women and work. These included the *English Woman's Journal** and the *Women's Penny Paper**. **MRB**

Sources: Beetham 1996, Beetham and Boardman 2001, Palmegiano 1976.

WOMEN'S PRINTING SOCIETY (1876-1935?) Emma Paterson*, suffragist and trade* unionist, was the force behind the creation of the Women's Printing Society (Ltd) (WPS) in London with the objective of expanding the opportunities of employment for women and girls within the printing trade, largely as compositors. The fundraising appeal was launched in spring 1874 with shares available at £2. For parents concerned at young women being employed in an all-male environment, Mrs Paterson guaranteed that although some instructors would necessarily be male the advantage of the Society was that it was run by women and it would take on printing work to enable young women to train and work there.

By the summer of 1876 the venture was operating from temporary premises at 38 Castle Street in Holborn and in its first annual report it claimed that 212 shares had been taken, seven trainees were apprenticed, there were two women workers and it was printing one weekly* and two monthly journals, a play by suffragist Helena Swanwick and a number of pamphlets. Henrietta Muller*, proprietor* and editor* of the *Women's Penny Paper**, printed by the Society, was now a director of the firm. Space and equipment restrictions that prevented taking on more apprentices and work were resolved with a move to larger, permanent premises at 21B Great College Street, Westminster, together with the purchase of a Cropper Minerva compositing machine. In 1878, they took on the *Women's Kalendar* (sic), detailing the events of the women's movement, several Church of England publications and more fiction and by 1880 there was a new training departure on offer, lessons in proofreading.

When Paterson died in 1886, her assistant of 16 years, Miss M. Weede, a printer's daughter, took over as manager. By 1893 further expansion took the firm to 66 Whitcomb-street, with increased production from 30 girls and women, two composing rooms for magazines, books and reports, plus a room for 'jobbing work' on circulars, programmes, cards, note and bill headings, plus display work. The Society's development was allied to the growth in women's professional activity in publishing and in political* organisations, for which most of the WPS's work was conducted such as the Women Liberal Federation's monthly, the *Women Liberal Federation News* and its annual reports, the feminist literary periodical the *Gatherer* and the *Women's Union Journal**. By 1897, pay was an average 24s a week, the company had 11 women directors and the 1896 figure for work undertaken was £4,138.12s 11d. The 1905 annual meeting noted that sustained success ensured that a 15 per cent bonus was to be shared among the employees. **CL**

Sources: Doughan 1987, Gerritsen Collection, Gordon 2001, *ODNB*, C19.

WOMEN'S RIGHTS' JOURNALS The expression of women's rights within discrete journals often reflected the individual experience and dedication of those middle-class* women who founded, financed and edited them as tools to investigate the critical basis for women's emancipation. Such periodicals provided a focused public voice in the creation of a critical mass for activism by disseminating information and discussion of the arguments.

The *Englishwoman's Journal**, printed by Emily Faithfull*, was principally the creation of Barbara Bodichon*; it held economic participation as the key. Briefly merging* with Bessie Rayner Parkes's* *Alexandra Magazine**, it was revived by Jessie Boucherett* as the *Englishwoman's Review** with a broadened subject scope, completing its transformation as the *Englishwoman's Review of Social and Industrial Questions**. The cream of the women's movement participated as joint editors* and contributors in these ventures, including Emily Davies, campaigner on higher education, and Elizabeth Garrett Anderson, pioneer for entry into medicine and the professions.

Many of these women had been signatories to the 1866 parliamentary suffrage petition and the *Women's Suffrage Journal**, financed and edited by Lydia Becker*, unified the work of the branches of the National Society for Women's Suffrage. Helen Blackburn* edited the annual *Women's Suffrage Calendar* (1885-1898) while Henrietta Muller* aimed 'to further the emancipation of women in every direction and in every land' in her *Women's Penny Paper**. These journals were the basis for the explosion of publications for 'the Cause' in the Edwardian period. **CL**

Sources: Banks 1985, Crawford 1999, Doughan and Sanchez 1987, *Waterloo*.

WOMEN'S SUFFRAGE JOURNAL (1870-1890) The *Women's Suffrage Journal*, a monthly edited* and largely written by Lydia Becker for its duration, began as the *Manchester National Society for Women's Suffrage Journal*. Originating from the Society Committee, it made clear its intention to be a medium of communication among the members and a record of the regional societies of the national organization. It was the first suffrage journal, and as Becker's *ODNB* entry remarks, an indispensable record of the movement. After six months 'Manchester' (as well as the Society's name) was dropped from the title, though retained in the dateline. Its belief that spreading knowledge of the issues and of the activism of others would increase support for the movement was reflected in the journal's success – in terms of size* (from 12 pages to over 30) – and variety of advertising*, which by 1890 included cover advertisements for household names like Reckitt's Blue, Benger's Food and Fry's cocoa. In its early years it cost a penny*.

Most of the articles were unsigned. Early emphasis was on the Women's Disabilities Bill, though the bill to amend the Married Women's Property Act (1873) was also highlighted. There were occasional double issues following a vital parliamentary* debate. Thus the loss of the motion for the Women's Disabilities Bill was not only given a detailed report in the June 1871 issue but MPs' votes were listed, together with a letter to *The Times* from an embarrassed member claiming to have voted against the bill by mistake. Leading* articles encouraged readers to persevere in their efforts, for example by analysing voting patterns (May 1873) to demonstrate how support for the bill was increasing on both sides of the house. The paper provided an informal space for readers' input as correspondents* expressed views on topics ranging from the unfairness of charitable schemes which helped indigent working men but not equally destitute women working at home, to strategies for supporting the movement without upsetting one's husband. Throughout its existence the *Journal* published reports from regional societies including, in later decades, 'Drawing Room meetings', but also items on other causes, such as university access, and obituaries* of prominent supporters like John Stuart Mill* (June 1873) and Emily Pfeiffer (March 1890).

In June 1890 a tiny note below the leading article announced that Miss Lydia Becker was in Aix-les-Bains for the benefit of her health. With her death the *Journal* ceased. **BMO**

Sources: Doughan and Sanchez 1987, *ODNB*.

WOMEN'S UNION JOURNAL (1876-1890) The *Women's Union Journal* was founded by the printer Emma Anne Paterson with the express purpose of promoting trades* union organizations for women workers. It was published quarterly* by the Women's Protective and Provident League (later the Women's Trades Union League), printed by the Women's Printing Society* and edited* by Paterson from its first issue until her death in 1886. Until 1890 its subtitle identified it as the organ of the League: 'the organ of the Women's Protective and Provident League'. Costing 1d an issue, it carried advertising*, mainly for League publications and occasionally small ads.

Leaders* presented arguments for unionism and other issues of interest to working women, for instance one on rational dress (Feb. 1882). The paper carried announcements and reports of the League's own meetings, but also encouraged unionism more broadly by noting prominently the work of other women's trade societies like those for bookbinders and upholsterers. While most of the pieces were published without signature, initials for poetry* or 'Author of" for fiction did appear. Through scissors-and-paste* journalism it covered industrial news such as the china clay workers' strike (*Royal Cornwall Gazette*), and alerted women to successful compensation claims for industrial injuries (national dailies*). Relevant issues debated in Parliament* were reported, as were occasional coroners' reports on deaths where poor working conditions or starvation wages were factors. Women's participation in school boards was a recurrent topic. By the late 1880s the *Journal* was publishing lists of 'Employers who pay fair Wages' under different trade headings, lists which encouragingly lengthened over the years.

The League supported women workers in improving their health and minds, so its campaign for women's swimming facilities was given considerable prominence in the journal, and notes of books acquired for the library featured regularly. The *Journal* also reflected these aims by including book reviews* and, particularly in the early years, poetry*. In 1887 it began a series of 'Sketches of Eminent Women' including Ann Flaxmann, Grace Darling, Caroline Herschel, Mrs Somerville and Harriet Beecher Stowe. Perhaps in an attempt to attract less politically minded readers, from the start it carried serial* fiction by J. W. Overton, who also contributed light-hearted short items. The death of this consistent contributor in 1890 following the earlier loss of Paterson may have influenced the decision to announce a change of format*. The promised 'details', however, consisted of a statement of its demise, arguing that trades unionism was now covered in the general press and the *Journal* had never achieved wide circulation* among working women. Its replacement was to be a *Quarterly Report and Review*. After one issue this became the *Women's Trades Union Review* (July 1891-July 1919). **BMO**

Sources: BL Catalogue, Doughan and Sanchez 1987.

WOMEN WRITERS' CLUB Variously known as the Women Writers' Club and the Writers' Club, it was founded by women for women but allowed men to attend as guests. Founded in 1892 with Mrs Arthur Stannard* as its first President, it was open to 'Women Authors and Journalists* and Artists in Black and White' at one guinea for town membership and half a guinea for those from the country. Its aim was to assist professional* women with networking and provide them with a secure and comfortable environment in the centre of London where they could work and socialise. The first 'humble' premises were at 190 Fleet Street* but with membership in excess of 200 by 1894, it moved to larger premises in Hastings House, Norfolk Street, the Strand. Here members enjoyed a library and writing room for working, with a wide range of newspapers and periodicals, as well as typewriters plus a dining-room where inexpensive meals were provided. 'House teas' were held on the first Friday in the month both as a social and business opportunity where many male literary figures would be seen alongside the 'rank and file of feminine journalism'. These proved so popular that in 1899 house dinners were also introduced.

Lady Jeune* and Mrs Humphry Ward were among the early Presidents and Florence Routledge (also chairwoman of the Women's Trade Union League) was the honorary secretary for many years. By 1900 the Club was the only one of the women's clubs* in London that remained in the complete ownership of its members. **CL**

Sources: *Monthly Packet* 1893, *Hearth and Home* 1894, *Woman's Signal* 1898), *Englishwoman's Review* 1900, *The Times* 1937, Vicinus 1985.

WOOD, ELLEN (1814-1887) Better known as the author 'Mrs. Henry Wood', Wood published many short stories, mostly anonymously*, in periodicals including *Bentley's Miscellany* before her serial* novel 'East Lynne', published in 1860 in the *New Monthly Magazine*, became a massive popular hit with readers* and a bestseller when published in volume form in 1861. A number of morally improving serial novels followed, in periodicals including *Once a Week**, the *Quiver** and the *New Monthly Magazine*. In 1867, she became editor* of the *Argosy**, a monthly* magazine founded by Alexander Strahan* two years earlier, remaining editor until her death.

In addition to writing numerous often fashionably sensational serial novels for the magazine, emphasizing women's voices and issues related to marriage, she likely wrote up to half of the contents in her early years as editor and penned a long series of quiet tales of provincial life, narrated by Johnnie Ludlow. MWT

Sources: *ODNB*, Phegley 2005, Wood 1894.

WOOD, JOSEPH SNELL (1853-1920) Proprietor* and editor* of the *Gentlewoman* (1890-1916) and the *Young Gentlewoman* (1892-1915) magazines*, in the latter part of the century Joseph Wood appears to have been supportive of women's emancipationist intent. The *Gentlewoman* carried information on suffrage events, features on women writers and how to make money. In 1893 he founded the Society of Women Writers and Journalists* and took the post of honorary director which he resigned three years later, remarking that he was doing so as he believed that now the Society was established, a woman's group ought to be run by women.

Wood also worked tirelessly in a philanthropic capacity, and published the *Social Review, a monthly record of industrial, sanitary and social progress* (Jan. 1875-June 1877). Many of these charities were in relation to women and children and in total raised nearly £500,000 by the time of his death. He was a member of the council of the Conservative Party women's group, the Primrose League and secretary of the Chelsea Hospital for Women, requesting that on his death in lieu of flowers, donations should be given to the Hospital. CL

Sources: Beetham 1996, *The Times* 1920, *Woman's Signal* 1896.

WOOD ENGRAVINGS AND WOODCUTS The wood engraving, properly differentiated from the woodcut by the use of the end-grain of a hard wood tree rather than the plank from a softer wood, is so central to the development of the mass circulation periodical in the nineteenth century that its presence is often taken for granted. Emerging in the wake of Thomas Bewick's reinvention of the technique in the first two decades of the nineteenth century and despite some initial qualms about both the aesthetic credentials and representational power of the medium, wood engraving began to dominate the periodicals market in the 1820s.

Magazines* like the *Mirror of Literature**, which sought to democratize the appeal of genteel eighteenth-century miscellanies* typified by the *Gentleman's Magazine** and the *Mechanic's Magazine**, which translated the visual delineation of mechanical and scientific information from copper engraving into the cheaper and more rapidly achieved form of the wood engraving, demonstrated the versatility and efficacy of the wood engraving. The emergence of groundbreaking periodicals like the *Penny Magazine** in the 1830s saw the scale and versatility of the wood engraving established as a naturalistic medium for representing the visible world in all its aspects, and led to the rapid development of the London engraving trade through the establishment of large workshops which took on many apprentices. Several leading wood engravers including W. J. Linton*, Ebenezer Landells* and the Dalziel brothers* became major figures in London print culture, acting not just as a source of engraved images but also as art editors* or financiers for periodicals.

In the 1840s, the success of magazines like the *Illustrated London News** and *Punch** saw the uses of the wood engraving expand still further into reportage* and comic journalism*, aided by the ability of the medium to produce print-ready images rapidly and to almost any shape. That wood-engraved images could be printed off together with accompanying typeset* copy was a major factor in the success of the medium, and the ability to build large-scale images through pulling together smaller blocks in the form also led to some brilliant experimental page layouts. At the same time that wood engraving was beginning to be fully exploited as an essentially representational or diagrammatic medium in the 1840s, there was also developing recognition of its aesthetic potential. A journal like the *Illuminated Magazine** in the early 1840s depended on its use of wood engraving to differentiate it from the fiction-bearing monthlies, where etched or engraved full page plates remained the norm.

By the 1860s, a range of monthlies* was beginning to emerge that made much of the quality of their wood engravings, which were often commissioned from major artists like Millais* to illustrate serial* fiction or one-off poems*. The leaders in this field were *Good Words**, *Once A Week** and the *Cornhill Magazine**, but there were many others including the *Welcome Guest** and the *Leisure Hour** that combined cheap price*, substantial content and excellent wood-engraved illustration*. The illustrations produced for the periodical press during the 1860s are still regarded as one of the high points of the British artistic tradition, and few ambitious artists failed to use this medium alongside a vast

number of less well-known specialist illustrators. From the 1860s photo-reprographic* media began to evolve which processed wood engraved drawings for publication. Yet the medium never completely lost its popularity in the nineteenth century, especially for comic journals. **BM**
Sources: Anderson 1991, de Mare 1980, Fox 1988, Reid 1928, Wakeman 1970, White 1897.

WOODGATE, WALTER BRADFORD (1840-1920) In its obituary*, *The Times** described Walter Woodgate (pseudonym* 'Wat Bradwood') as being 'one of the last of the Bohemians', who could be encountered wearing 'a low-crowned top hat, an Inverness cape, and knee breeches with box-cloth leggings'.

As a journalist* he had a varied career, helping to launch the journals *Vanity Fair** and *Land and Water**, and was associated with the *Pall Mall Gazette** at its foundation in 1865. For nearly half a century, he was among 'the most constant contributors' to the *Field**, and 'could write anything from a curate's sermon to a leading article on the Torts of Landlords, or a racy description of a prize fight or a sculling match' (Higginson: 258). An outstanding oarsman, his knowledge of rowing inspired him to write the textbook *Oars and Sculls, and How to Use Them* (1872). Woodgate also wrote novels as 'Wat Bradwood'. His autobiography *Reminiscences of an Old Sportsman* was published in 1909. Like several of his other journalistic contemporaries, Woodgate remained a bachelor. According to the *Field,* he 'was not inclined to rule his life, or his attire, by the ordinary fashion of the day'; nevertheless, he was 'a man of great ability and vast information'. **DHL**
Sources: Dodd 1981, *Field* 1920, Higginson 1951, *ODNB*, *The Times* 1920.

WOODWARD, ALICE BOLINGBROKE (1862-1951) Daughter of an eminent scientist who worked at the Natural History Museum, Alice Woodward earned money by illustrating* her father's scientific papers and lectures in order to fund her art training at schools in London and Paris. Her subsequent career in illustration had two strands, general and scientific*, in periodicals and books. The precision and delicacy of her scientific drawings are a measure of her talent. Woodward signed her name to her scientific illustrations, but for all others she adopted a butterfly monogram. An early achievement was as successor to Aubrey Beardsley*, illustrating the final two volumes of Dent's *Bon-Mots*. Her work appeared in *Blackie's Annuals**, *Cassell's Magazine**, the *Daily Chronicle** (1895), the *Daily Graphic**, the *Illustrated London News**

(1895), *Quarto* (1890) and the *Strand Magazine** (1905). The Glasgow publisher* Blackie & Son Ltd was her most significant employer for her book illustrations (1896-1900), when she worked on a series of children's literature. **CL**
Sources: Micklethwaite and Peppin 1983, Natural History Museum online.

WOOLER, THOMAS JONATHAN (1787-1853) Thomas Jonathan Wooler was a printer, radical journalist*, editor* and publisher*. Wooler was closely associated with, and may have taken some editorial part in the literary journal the *Reasoner**, also editing the *Republican: A Weekly Historical Magazine* (22 issues, 1813), but abandoned it to launch the *Stage*. Here Wooler developed his journalistic style, at once comedic and melodramatic, through a mixture of theatrical criticism and attacks on the management of metropolitan theatre. In January 1817, Wooler began *Black Dwarf** the unstamped* weekly* with which he became synonymous; its circulation* of over 12,000 made it one of the most successful radical periodicals of the day. Wooler's courageous, and ultimately successful, defence against charges of seditious libel in June 1817 attracted widespread admiration which encouraged him to publish a weekly, *Wooler's British Gazette* (1819-1823). His name was mooted as a parliamentary candidate and the *Manchester Observer* even proposed a subscription to purchase a 'rotten borough' from which to send Wooler to Westminster. When, after a hiatus from December 1820, the *Manchester Observer* was relaunched (Aug. 1821-Sept. 1822), it took *Wooler's British Gazette* as its subtitle, drawing heavily for content on its London namesake.

Wooler played a prominent part in the reform movement of 1818-1820, leading to a 15-month prison sentence (1820-1821). Financial support from the veteran reformer Major Cartwright enabled him to continue publishing *Black Dwarf.* Released on sureties of good behaviour for five years, Wooler's conduct on his release was understandably more cautious. Shortly after Cartwright's death in 1824, *Black Dwarf* closed. Wooler cut loose from radicalism, developing a successful legal career. The Chartist* movement briefly revived his publishing career when Benjamin Steill (who printed the first volume of *Black Dwarf*) enlisted him to edit the weekly *Plain Speaker* (1849) with the Chartist Thomas Cooper*. Although Cooper later described Wooler as ineffective, he nonetheless enlisted him to assist with early issues of *Cooper's Journal: or Unfettered Thinker & Plain Speaker*. He also wrote pamphlets and books on parliamentary and legal reform. MSC

Sources: Kelly and Applegate 1996, *ODNB*.

WORKING-CLASS PERIODICALS The relationship of working-class men and women to the periodical press of the nineteenth century can only be understood in connection with working-class culture, including the rise of literacy*, and the rise and decline of a politicized working-class consciousness. Initially, it was probably the desire for news* of battles and movements in the Napoleonic wars that drove a rise in literacy, but newspapers and periodicals remained financially out of reach for most working-class readers until November 1816, when William Cobbett slashed the price* of his *Political Register** by almost 90 per cent to 2d. The following year saw the introduction of Thomas Wooler's* *Black Dwarf**, Richard Carlile's* *Sherwin's Political Register** (the *Republican**, 1819) and William Hone's* short-lived *Reformists' Register**.

In 1819, the Newspaper Stamp Act turned the stamp tax into a form of censorship* by singling out publications with reportage or commentary on the news* costing less than 6d, issued more frequently than every 26 days and printed on two sheets or less. Nevertheless, working-class readership* continued at levels far beyond what newspaper sales data would suggest, as readers clubbed together for subscriptions, shared copies or read aloud to family and friends.

In 1832, another response to working-class literacy emerged with the beginning of the 'useful knowledge*' publications, aimed at providing general, non-political information in geography, science*, history* and other areas. The first issue of *Chambers's Edinburgh Journal** appeared in February 1832 with the *Penny Magazine** debuting in March under the auspices of the Society for the Diffusion of Useful Knowledge. Similar publications to appear over the next two decades included *Eliza Cook's Journal**, the *People's Journal** and *Howitt's Journal**. The latter provided not only a safer outlet for working-class literary desires but valuable venues for working-class writers and artists, whose interests frequently coincided with those of the radical middle class on such matters as anti-Corn Law legislation and electoral reform. Robert Owen's* co-operative* ideas spawned another set of periodicals (1820s-1830s) aimed at and produced by members of the working class. The rise of Chartism* at the end of the 1830s ushered in a new wave of radical working-class journalism*. Most successful in circulation* and longevity among the Chartist periodicals was probably the *Northern Star**.

Perhaps recognizing the growth of working-class literacy in other areas, by the 1830s periodicals also began to take a more tolerant view of imaginative writing. These journalists recognized the emotional power of poetry* as a vehicle for the furtherance of working-class ideals, and it was that standard against which literature* was usually measured. Fiction was slower in gaining acceptance in the Chartist and working-class press, but by the 1850s Ernest Jones* was making room in the *People's Paper** for his own fiction along with reviews* and serializations* of contemporary writers.

With rising incomes and cheaper* publications, newspapers were no longer beyond the means of working-class readers, but the closing of the *People's Paper* in 1858 marked the end of the Chartist press and the end of the golden age of class-conscious working-class periodicals. In 1861, the paper duty was repealed, paving the way for even cheaper periodicals, with a host of penny* periodicals. Yet in spite of the cheap daily*, it was the weekly* that most attracted working-class readers throughout the nineteenth century. Most of the popular weekly newspapers like *Reynolds's Weekly Newspaper**, *Lloyd's Weekly Newspaper** and the *Weekly Dispatch** remained politically left of centre (the *Illustrated London News** was an exception), but without the fervent politics* of their predecessors. Catering to a rapidly expanding market, publishers relied on illustrations*, a practice begun in the 1830s with Charles Knight's* *Penny Magazine*, sensational fiction and humorous* or sensational non-fiction.

It is difficult at the end of the century to speak of a working-class press in so far as the elimination of taxes and the increase in wages had brought many more publications within reach of working-class readers, while creating a lucrative new market* for publishers* ready to supply on those readers' interests. Price* could no longer define a working-class periodical, nor could editorial policies, since the imperative to entertain had largely eclipsed the class-consciousness of earlier publications. **DU**

Sources: Altick 1998, Klancher 1987, Murphy 1994, Vicinus 1974, Webb 1955.

WORKING MAN'S FRIEND; AND POLITICAL MAGAZINE (1832-1833) This radical London weekly* 1d newspaper was published* and printed by H. Wills (numbers 1-9) and James Watson* (numbers 10-33). Its editor* for much of the time was John Cleave*, who wrote many of its articles. Notwithstanding a circulation* that did not exceed

5,000, the *Working Man's Friend* was one of the foremost illegal newspapers of the decade in the struggle against the 'taxes on knowledge'. It repeatedly attacked factory abuses, the competitive economic system and inequality of taxation, as well as fund holders, churchmen and others who allegedly profited from their privileged position in society. It also printed a large amount of Irish news* and campaigned forcefully for repeal of the Union with Ireland.

Watson was the driving force behind the paper, both politically* and financially, and he and Cleave worked closely with Henry Hetherington* and his *Poor Man's Guardian** throughout these turbulent years. For one thing, the two newspapers never printed identical reports of meetings or speeches and participated in a system of mutual distribution*. Watson was incarcerated in Clerkenwell Prison for six months in 1833 as a result of his association with the journal. JHW

Sources: Hollis 1970, Wiener 1969.

WORKMAN'S TIMES (1890-1894) The *Workman's Times* was an off-shoot of John Andrew's other trade* union papers, the *Cotton Factory Times* and *Yorkshire Factory Times* (1889-1926). Edited* by Joseph Burgess* and published in Huddersfield, the 1d broadsheet was not marketed as predominantly political, nor confined to men. Attempting to attract a wider audience, with references to its being a family* paper, the *Workman's Times* also included romantic fiction serials* and a domestic* advice* column* to attract women readers, with support for the women's franchise. Weekly circulation* in the first year was a respectable 10,000, increasing to over 62,500 by October 1891, rising to its maximum by 1892. But independent regional* editions such as the *Birmingham Workman's Times* (1890) were a drain on resources, and the paper struggled to maintain a viable circulation with constant financial challenges.

Early changes in staffing shifted the paper's politics* from Liberal to socialist*; however, in its short history the paper was overshadowed by its rivals the *Clarion** and *Labour Elector**. An office was opened in Fleet Street*, London in 1891 in an attempt to build a national profile and increase sales, but the effect was limited. The paper's major political campaign was to support the foundation of the Independent Labour Party. Contributors included J. Keir Hardie, John Trevor of the Labour Church, Katherine Conway and Robert Blatchford*. Despite this support, Keir Hardie refused to adopt the paper for the Independent Labour Party and used his own *La-bour Leader** instead. Popular socialist Carolyn Martin was hired in February 1894 to raise the paper's sales, but it ceased publication the following month. DM

Sources: Barnes 2006, McPhilips 2005, Mutch 2005, Ugolini 1997.

WORLD (1874-1922) This weekly* newspaper was founded in partnership with Grenville Murray* by Edmund Yates*, a playwright and novelist who had previously been editor* of *Temple Bar** and *Tinsley's Magazine**. Grenville Murray withdrew early on, having made a sizeable profit since the *World* was immediately popular, partly because it deliberately sought a readership* of women as well as men. Yates claimed that its secret was 'to be found in its loyalty to the full scope of its title. It has never been unmindful of the wants and interests of every section of the English community.' Having virtually invented the society gossip* column in 1860s, he introduced the feature 'What the World says' signed by 'Atlas', his *nom de plume*, and launched a long-running series, 'Celebrities* at Home', which he capitalized upon with three volumes of collected interviews* (1877-1879).

Yates's boast that he recorded 'the social and private as well as the political and public life of our times... without offence, with advantage to all and injury to none' did not always protect him, and in 1885 he served a short prison sentence for criminal libel. He is said to have gone out his way to recruit Oscar Wilde* (as a poet* and writer of short fiction rather than as a columnist) much as he made a point of attracting other lively young writers such as William Archer* who wrote on drama and Bernard Shaw* who wrote on music* as well as on the visual arts. Other contributors included J. Comyns Carr*, W. L. Courtney*, Richard Jefferies and Richard Whiteing*. By the mid-eighties the *World* was strongly rivalled by the *Pall Mall Gazette**, which had introduced its own gossip column in 1865. The *World* was later edited by Arthur C. F. Griffiths* and taken over by Harmsworth Brothers. JAS

Sources: Edwards 1997, Yates 1884.

WORLD OF FASHION (1824-1851) The *World of Fashion*'s contents focused upon fashion* and fashionable living. In 1852 it was renamed the *Ladies' Monthly Magazine and World of Fashion*, and was the same as *Townsend's Monthly Selection* and the *London and Paris Ladies' Magazine of Fashion*. From 1880-1891, its name changed again to *Le Monde Elegant or The World of Fashion*.

Published monthly, it drew upon the model of *La Belle Assemblée** and *Ackerman's Repository*. From

1824 until the 1840s, it employed Mrs Mary Ann Bell, who had established the fashion credibility of the former journal in the 1810s. Mrs Bell also ran a shop, which was advertised* in the magazine, and by 1830 both her shop and the magazine's publisher* Mr Bell had moved to the same establishment in St James's, London. Sold in Great Britain, Paris and New York, it could be forwarded to the East and West Indies.

It included fashion plates with up to six figures, usually copies of French examples, the best engraved by William Wolfe Alais during the 1820s. The plates were very detailed, and in the 1860s-1870s it still issued its own plates rather than French imports. From the 1850s it included full-size patterns, an innovation which was to become standard in later fashion journalism. RLA
Sources: Adburgham 1972, Beetham 2001, Holland 1988.

WRITER AND READER (AUG.-OCT. 1888) The *Writer and Reader*, a literary monthly* that lasted a mere three issues, is interesting for being one of the few journals explicitly aimed at all three parties involved in the literary* process: authors, readers* and publishers*. Each issue was about 20 pages long, and cost 2d. The (unknown) editor* stated in the maiden issue that many authors lacked the financial means to properly advertise* their work. The periodical consequently aimed to improve or extend the ways in which writers and publishers could 'bring books under the notice of readers', and to make it easier for 'the Reader' to 'find out those books which are worth reading'. OD
Source: *Waterloo*.

WYNDHAM, GEORGE (1863-1913). Educated at Eton and Sandhurst, George Wyndham pursued a short military career before becoming Tory MP (1889-1913). His brief foray into journalism* was an addendum to his political career. He contributed to the *Contemporary Review*, the *Fortnightly Review*, the *New Review*, the *Eclectic Magazine* and the *Dublin Review*, writing on his two main interests, literature* and the Irish question.

In early 1890 he contributed a political* article for the *Scots Observer* and began a lifelong friendship with the editor* W. E. Henley*. He continued to write when it became the *National Observer*. In 1894 Wyndham, Harry Cust*, Ernest Iwan-Müller and Sir Herbert Stephen acquired the failing monthly* *New Review*, making Henley editor. With falling sales by the end of 1896, a board of directors was formed, with Lord Windsor as chairman, and Wyndham a member of an editorial sub-committee which managed the daily work. Wyndham remarked, 'I have got more control than anyone else over the *Review*'. He also supplied funds. Wyndham managed to get Gladstone to contribute an article for July 1896 and was instrumental in persuading Henley to publish Henry James's* 'What Maisie Knew' (1897).

Wyndham was not consulted on the announcement of Henley's resignation in December 1897. However, the *New Review* became the weekly *Outlook* and was relaunched in February 1898 with Wyndham's choice of Percy Hurd as editor. Wyndham decided on the title as late as 23 January and saw the journal as 'pledged to an Imperial* British trade policy' and 'fair criticism and no stabbing'. Pressure of parliamentary work forced Wyndham to withdraw from the *Outlook* in 1904. DA
Sources: Biggs-Davison 1951, Mackail and Wyndham 1925, Murtagh 1981, *ODNB, Wellesley*.

WYNTER, ANDREW (1819-1876) Wynter, a practising physician, probably published his first article in *Ainsworth's Magazine* in October 1846. In the 1850s and 1860s he published articles in the *Fortnightly*, *Edinburgh*, *London* and *Quarterly* reviews, *Cassell's Magazine*, *Good Words* and *Once a Week*. His journalistic output was a mixture of extended reviews* on medical* and scientific* subjects, together with sketches of modern metropolitan life. His 12 articles for the *Quarterly* (March 1853-Jan. 1858), for example, cover lunatic asylums, human hair, rats, the Crystal Palace and the Zoological Gardens.

Wynter's literary and medical careers significantly overlapped. While continuing to practise at his London home, in October 1855 he became editor* of the *Association Medical Journal* (*British Medical Journal* from 1857). He remained as editor until 1860, when he resigned following criticism from members. He continued to publish on medical subjects. In his most substantial contribution, *The Borderlands of Insanity and Other Allied Papers* (1875), he advocated the treatment of mental illness without the use of physical restraint. Many of his articles were collected and reissued in book form. Published volumes include *Odds and Ends from an Old Drawer* (1855), *Pictures of Town from my Mental Camera* (1855), *Fruit Between the Leaves* (1875), *Curiosities of Civilization* (1860), *Subtle Brains and Lissom Fingers* (1863) and *Peeps into the Human Hive* (1874). His two 1855 books were published with his name rendered in reverse (as 'Werdna Retnyw'). JSP
Sources: *British Medical Journal, Medical Times and Gazette, ODNB, Wellesley*.

YACHTING WORLD (1894-1976) Published in London, *Yachting World* appeared monthly initially and weekly* by 1912, when its price* was 3d. In 1903 it consisted of 20, 36 cm pages. Contents included 'the skipper's column*', 'sea breezes', tide tables, local yachting news*, a section for marine mechanics, advertisements* and illustrations* in the form of tables and photographs*. An index was published in 1903. *Yachting World* remained under that title until 1976 when it became the *Yachting World and Marine Motor Journal*, and later the *Yachting World and Motor Boating Journal*. DHL
Sources: Layton 1912, Waterloo.

YATES, EDMUND HODGSON (1831-1894) E-dmund Yates, son of actors Elizabeth and Frederick Yates, worked as a clerk at the General Post Office from 1847 for 25 years. Inspired by Thackeray's* work he began to submit his writing to periodicals in 1852, assisted by the journalist and writer Albert Smith*. Yates's first editorial opportunity came on the *Comic Times* (1855) and at the *Train* of which he was joint proprietor*. Appropriately, he became the theatre critic for the *Daily News** (1855-early 1860s). But his innovative contribution to journalism* was made when he devised a gossip* column in the *Illustrated Times* (1855-1863): 'The lounger at the clubs' began a new form of personal journalism in the popular press. Inhabiting his role as a gossip rather too literally, Yates committed two indiscretions that exposed his violation of confidences relating to Thackeray and Trollope* that he used in pieces in *Town Talk* (1858) and the *New York Times**. Both episodes resulted in ruptures with the men involved, and damaged Yates's reputation considerably.

Yates had a parallel career as a West End playwright and as the author of 19 novels. His first novel was serialized* in *Temple Bar**, where he became editor*. His fiction appeared in many periodicals and in newspapers such as the *Birmingham Morning News*. In 1867 Yates took up the editorship of *Tinsley's Magazine**; yet again controversy followed him with accusations of salary irregularities. Declared bankrupt in 1868, on retiring from the Post Office in 1872, he utilized his notoriety, friendship with Dickens* (he had contributed to *All the Year Round**), novels and presentational flair to embark on an American lecture tour which revived his finances and landed him the post of foreign* correspondent on the *New York Herald**. In 1874, with Grenville Murray*, he launched the *World**, which was such a success that he bought Murray's share after only six months. Repeating an old but popular formula, Yates, signing as 'Atlas', indulged in creating a gossip feature – 'What the world says', which made his fortune. But repeating more than the formula, he failed to edit a scurrilous item that saw him imprisoned for criminal libel with damage to his health as well as his reputation. CL
Sources: *ODNB, Waterloo.*

YELLOW BOOK (1894-1897) The *Yellow Book*, edited* by the American expatriate writer Henry Harland, and the young British decadent artist Aubrey Beardsley* (dandies, both), was the centre of the 'new art' and the 'new literature'* in the mid-1890s. It was a product of its experimental, provocative moment in time and was largely a venture linked to the writers and artists on the list of publishers* John Lane* and Elkin Mathews. Ella D'Arcy* and 'George Egerton', some of Lane's 'New Woman' writers, featured prominently in the magazine, alongside other now-renowned writers and artists including writers Max Beerbohm*, Baron Corvo, Hubert Crackanthorpe, Henry James*, Richard Le Gallienne*, Evelyn Sharp, Arthur Symons, Rosamund Mariott Watson* and artists Walter Crane*, Kenneth Grahame, Frederick Leighton, Will Rothenstein and Walter Sickert. Beardsley's graphics were its brand, and pervaded the first four numbers.

It was published quarterly*, in cloth-bound volumes, at the serious price* of 5s per volume. At a time when books were getting cheaper, the *Yellow Book* was an expensive commodity, blending the category of the art book with a quarterly, high-quality literary review* and signalling that it was an artefact to keep rather than ephemera. Its layout suggested luxuriousness, with wide margins and blank pages before images. As the editors noted in the prospectus, 'we feel that the time has come for an absolutely new era in the way of magazine* literature....Distinction, modernness – these, probably, so nearly as they can be picked out, are the two leading features of our plan'. From the beginning, then, the editors were audacious in their retrogressive decision to publish quarterly at a moment when time was speeding up; and to combine a provocative and commercial get up high-quality art and literature*, to create a hybrid periodical-book.

Whether or not the periodical was as daring as it suggested was a matter of debate. The *Critic** found

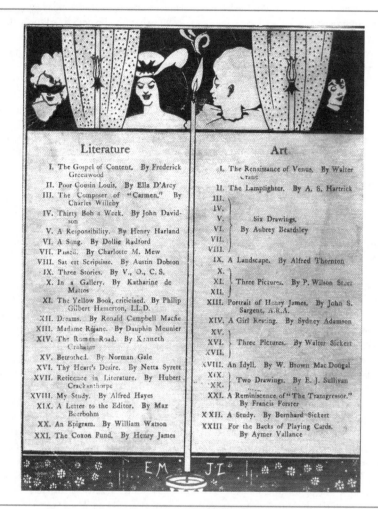

Figure 69: The back cover of the *Yellow Book* for July 1894 bearing the Beardsley stamp.

the contents of the first issue challenging, commenting of Beardsley that 'his genius is so grotesque that it is beyond the understanding of ordinary mortals', and calling later volumes of the *Yellow Book* a 'Yellow Impertinence'. The *Athenaeum** found it less outré, commenting that it 'aims at novelty' but has more in common with children's periodicals like *Chatterbox*. The *Times** described it as 'a combination of English rowdyism and French lubricity', referring implicitly to the yellow covers which alluded to the yellow covers of French novels at the time. In fact, the *Yellow Book* was unconventional in some ways – the prominence it gave to art, the content of some of Beardsley's cheeky, sexually suggestive drawings, the high-profile given to New Women writers, its innovative form, its aestheti-

cism – and conventional in other ways – its leading writer in the first issue was Henry James*, and other more established writers such as Edmund Gosse* and William Watson were also among its pages. The *Yellow Book* was linked in the public's mind to Oscar Wilde*, though he never contributed to it. When Wilde was arrested in 1895, it was erroneously but widely reported that he was carrying with him a copy of the *Yellow Book*, and as a result Beardsley was sacked, again erroneously, as a supposed close associate with Wilde. Still, after the fall of Wilde, there seemed to be less popular tolerance for the *Yellow Book*'s dandiacal strain, and while its run continued for 13 volumes, it did so without Beardsley and allegedly without the energetic exuberance that characterized its first year of publication. But the establishment of the *Savoy** (1896), fuelled by breakaway contributors who followed Beardsley's expulsion to a new rival, edited by Beardsley and Symons and published* by Leonard Smithers, cut into the limited market niche of the *Yellow Book*, and they both folded within months of each other. MWT

Sources: Brake 1995b, Brake 2001, Jackson 1913, Ledger 2007, Turner 2005.

YELLOW JOURNALISM The term 'yellow journalism' refers to the corrupt and sensational journalism* popular for a brief period of time at the turn of the twentieth century. The term is most closely associated with the New York newspaper rivalry between Joseph Pulitzer and William Randolph Hearst. In the 1890s, Pulitzer's *New York World* had pushed New Journalism* to extremes, promoting an activist stance against special interest and scandal-ridden reportage. Hearst's *New York Journal*, Pulitzer's rival publication, prided itself on a similar style. As the competition* intensified, Pulitzer's style shifted toward what would eventually be called yellow journalism, featuring compelling elements such as numerous illustrations,* sensational headlines and ostentatious Sunday magazines*, with news* stories that were increasingly fanciful. The term itself arose from a comic* strip called 'Yellow Kid', originally published in Pulitzer's newspaper that mocked Hearst's tactics and portrayed a rumbustious, working-class* existence.

Historians hold yellow journalism's inaccurate reporting practices responsible for stimulating popular support for American intervention in Cuba that started the Spanish-American War. Though predominantly an American fin-de-siècle phenomenon due to general European resistance, reporting of the yellow journalism genre* did make its way to France due to James Gordon Bennett, Jnr, and to England through Viscount Northcliffe, Alfred Harmsworth*, Harmsworth's distinctive adaptation of yellow journalism taking the form of the *Daily Mail**. In W T Stead's* journalism manifestos, in the *Review of Reviews* and its annuals, Stead first defends and then critiqued the yellow journalism of the American press, ending by defining an allegedly British (Stead) version. SBA

Sources: Brake 2004b, Marzoff 1983, *ODNB*.

YONGE, CHARLOTTE MARY (1823-1901) Charlotte Mary Yonge, one of the most successful British popular novelists of the nineteenth century, was also the editor* of the long-running journal for young Christian girls, the *Monthly Packet**. She launched the journal and remained sole editor until 1890, when she became co-editor with Christabel Coleridge, and her journalistic career is primarily associated with this periodical, which reflected her Tractarian beliefs.

After contributing to Ann Mozley's* *Magazine for the Young* (1842-), Yonge acquired a knowledge of the juvenile* market* and religious* magazines, which she used to good effect in her own journal. Signed articles covered literary* criticism, advice on reading, female authorship, historical* sketches and religious topics such as missionary* work, though it is likely that she also wrote much of the material in the early volumes. She also contributed an article on 'Children's Literature of the Last Century' to *Macmillan's Magazine** in 1869.

While her brand of Christian journalism aimed at middle-class* girls has been seen as 'clearly uncontroversial', like other female novelist-editors of the mid-century including Mrs Henry Wood* and Mary Elizabeth Braddon*, she was also able to include in her journal articles which questioned women's domestic* roles or supported spinsterhood. EL

Sources: *DNB*, Hayter 1996, Sanders 1996.

YOUNG ENGLISHMAN'S JOURNAL (1867-1870) Launched in 1867 by William Laurence Emmett, the *Young Englishman's Journal* was the first in a long series of boys' magazines which appeared in the wake of Edwin J. Brett's* pioneering *Boys of England**. Aimed at the working classes*, the penny* weekly* was issued from the offices of the Temple Publishing Company, established purveyors of penny dreadful serials including *Poor Boys of London* (1866) and *Tom Turpin* (1867).

Characterized by its bloodthirsty fiction, informative non-fiction, free gifts and prize competitions, so striking were the similarities between the *Young Englishman's Journal* and *Boys of England* that many readers* believed that the two were issued by the same publisher. Brett was aggrieved by what he perceived as an imitation of his work. A fierce and bitter competition* soon developed between the two publishers*, who publicly exchanged insults and innuendo via the correspondence* columns of their papers.

Emmett himself penned many of the most popular tales in *Young Englishman's Journal*, while his brother George was also a prolific contributor. Several of the paper's remaining authors such as Percy B. St John*, Captain Mayne Reid, William Stephens Hayward and original *Boys of England* editor Charles Stevens, were drawn from the same pool of men who wrote for Brett. Charles Dickens's* illustrator* 'Phiz'

(Hablot Browne*) and Harry Maguire numbered among the paper's illustrators.

The most significant achievement of the *Young Englishman's Journal* was that it pioneered the boys' public school story. George Emmett's 'Boys of Bircham School', an exhilarating story of schoolboy hi-jinks which commenced in the paper's earliest weeks, acted as prototype for Bracebridge Hemyng's* hugely successful 1870s 'Jack Harkaway' tales in *Boys of England* and myriad successors. Other noteworthy *Young Englishman's Journal* stories include George Emmett's long running 'Shot and Shell' series of military tales.

Despite purportedly securing a circulation* of 125,000, William Laurence Emmett went bankrupt towards the end of the run of *Young Englishman's Journal*. Legal restrictions necessitated that brother George assumed editorship which he undertook under the pseudonym of 'George Brent'. William Laurence Emmett's bankruptcy may have been a factor behind the incorporation of *Young Englishman's Journal* into a new periodical, *Sons of Britannia**, in 1870. **ChB**

Sources: Jay 1918-1921, Rollington 1913, Springhall 1991, Springhall 1994, *Waterloo*.

YOUNG ENGLISHWOMAN (1864-1894) One of Samuel O. Beeton's* most successful titles, the *Young Englishwoman: A Magazine of Fiction and Entertaining Literature, Music, Poetry, Fine Arts, Fashions, and Useful and Ornamental Needlework* commenced publication with a promise to parents in its introduction that it 'may be placed without the slightest fear in the hands of girls of tender age'. Initially edited* by Beeton and his wife Isabella*, the magazine capitalized on the relatively new identification of adolescent girls* as an untapped market of readers and, along with titles such as the *English Girls Journal and Ladies' Magazine* (1863-1864) and the *Young Ladies' Journal** published by Edward Harrison, marked the 1860s as a period of transition in girls' periodical publishing.

The *Young Englishwoman's* focus was on practical and domestic* topics in the mode of the *Englishwoman's Domestic Magazine** and contained serialized* fiction, poetry*, hand-coloured fashion* engravings from Paris, patterns for crafts and needlework, and a correspondence* column* entitled 'Our Drawing Room'. The Beetons commissioned innocuous material that reinforced the middle class emphasis on domesticity for girls who would grow into middle-class women. A matter of weeks after Isabella Beeton's death in 1865 the Beetons' neighbour Matilda Browne* (later known as 'Myra') as-

sumed an editorial role with the *Young Englishwoman* and the *Englishwoman's Domestic Magazine*, her association with both magazines* continuing until they ceased publication under those titles in 1877.

When Overend and Gurney, the financial institution from which Samuel Beeton borrowed heavily to fund the publication of his seven magazines collapsed in 1866, Beeton's copyrights*, including that for the *Young Englishwoman,* were transferred to Ward, Lock & Tyler* in a debt settlement. Under Ward, Lock & Tyler the *Young Englishwoman's* name was changed in 1870 to *Beeton's Young Englishwoman,* but changed very little in other respects aside from a new two column*-per-page format*.

After Samuel Beeton's departure from Ward, Lock & Tyler and his death in 1877, *Beeton's Young Englishwoman* underwent a change of title* in 1878 to *Sylvia's Home Journal*. In 1881 the editor, Miss Graham, oversaw a female staff including manuscript reader Alice Hoatson and contributor E. Nesbit. In 1892, the title was streamlined to *Sylvia's Journal* in keeping with the agenda of new editor, Graham R. Tomson; (Dec. 1892-Apr. 1894), who retained features on fashion*, the toilet, needlework and gardening*, but, like Oscar Wilde* before her in *Woman's World**, infused a woman's magazine with aestheticism and New Woman writing. Black-and-white art by Robert Anning Bell*, a New Woman novel by May Kendall, a series of articles on women's* colleges and poets' heroines, with articles on the decorative arts by Gleeson White* exemplified the new editorial tone. Other contributors included Violet Hunt, Katharine Tynan, Richard Garnett and Flora Klickmann*.

In April 1894 Graham R. Tomson, a remarried divorcée, abruptly ended her editorship two months before leaving her second husband to become Rosamund Marriott Watson*. No editor was named to replace her and the magazine ceased publication in December. **SMcn/LH**

Sources: Drotner 1988, Hughes 1996, Hughes 2005, Hughes, 2006.

YOUNG IRELAND The term refers to a group of mainly middle-class Irish nationalist writers and activists associated with the *Nation** and several other newspapers (1842-1848). From the beginning, the Young Ireland movement recognized the utility of journalism* as a means of articulating and disseminating political* ideas and cultural values, and viewed the press as a necessary instrument for the creation of an inclusive and progressive public sphere in Ireland. Young Ireland journalism was distinguished by its diverse range of material: each of its newspapers published poetry*, literary* reviews* and historical* articles in addition to news*, analysis and political* polemic. The name 'Young Ireland' was originally coined by the English press in recognition of the group's resemblance to similarly named movements in Europe; it was later used pejoratively by Daniel O'Connell when tensions emerged between him and Thomas Davis* and Charles Gavan Duffy*. As a coherent group it effectively dissolved after a failed rebellion in the summer of 1848 and the death or exile of many of its leaders.

Its founding figures were Thomas Davis, Charles Gavan Duffy and John Blake Dillon, who established the *Nation** newspaper in October 1845. Other notable members included John Mitchel,* Thomas Francis Meagher, William Smith O'Brien and James Fintan Lalor. Influenced by both utilitarian and romantic ideas, the Young Irelanders were committed to the creation of a national consciousness through education, cultural production and political agitation, and sought to move beyond the sectarian and class* divisions that had damaged Irish politics and culture since the seventeenth century. Politically, the movement began as a supporter of Daniel O'Connell's non-violent Repeal movement. By 1848, however, the frustration and increasingly radical thinking of Young Irelanders like Mitchel and Lalor, as well as the inspiration provided by the 1848 uprisings elsewhere in Europe, led to the establishment of more revolutionary Young Ireland newspapers such as the *United Irishman*,* the *Irish Felon*, the *Irish Tribune* and the *Irishman** which called for insurrection if necessary.

Although unsuccessful in achieving their immediate political aims, the ideals of the Young Ireland writers had a profound effect on subsequent generations of Irish nationalists. **SMR**
Source: Davis 1987.

YOUNG LADIES' JOURNAL (1864-1920)   Edward Harrison founded the weekly* *Young Ladies' Journal* to compete* with Samuel Beeton's* *Young Englishwoman**. At a cost of 6d in 1864, 9d in 1868, and 1d in 1894, it provided value for money, as the lengthy subtitle from the first issue attests: *an illustrated Magazine of Entertaining Literature**, *Original Music**, *Toilet and Household Receipts, every description of Paris Fashions** *and Needlework, with magnificent supplementary** *volume containing full-size Patterns for Ladies' and Children's dresses, etc., and coloured plates of Fashion and Berlin Work direct from Paris.* This mix of contents set a standard followed in later girls'* magazines* such as the *Girl's*

Own Paper* and *Atalanta**. Contributions were generally signed.

The *Young Ladies' Journal* catered to a middle-class* audience. Like other girls' magazines, it addressed both girls in their mid-teens and young women into their twenties. The 'household receipts' and fashion* supplements* with full-size patterns for ladies' and children's clothing were likely to appeal more to housewives than to young girls. In keeping with the increased importance of advertising* in the women's* periodical press in the 1880s, the *Journal* actively courted advertisers, promising 'Our old advertisers say it pays to advertise in the *Young Ladies' Journal*'. Staying abreast of his competitors made Harrison's magazine one of the first successful girls' magazines. **TD**
Sources: Baggs 2005, Beetham 1996, Beetham and Boardman 2001, Drotner 1988, *Waterloo*, White 1970.

YOUNG MEN OF GREAT BRITAIN (1868-1888) Boys' magazine *Young Men of Great Britain* was the successful and long-lived companion to Edwin J. Brett's* *Boys of England**.

Launched by Brett in 1868 from the Fleet Street* offices of the Newsagents' Publishing Company, *Young Men of Great Britain* was intended to quell demand for *Boys of England* to be issued twice-weekly. While visually identical to *Boys of England*, and adopting the same size* of paper, *Young Men of Great Britain* began in a shorter, 12-page format*, before expanding to a standard 16 pages later. Sensational fiction, edifying non-fiction and lurid illustrations* formed the paper's familiar repertoire, although *Young Men of Great Britain* tended to carry a higher proportion of serial* fiction than *Boys of England*. Early numbers also boasted a prize competition, a purse of ten guineas being its lead attraction. Costing just a 1d per weekly* number, it sought to cater for an increasingly eager working-class* audience.

Young Men of Great Britain's stories were generally penned by the same group of authors who wrote for *Boys of England*: Bracebridge Hemyng*, William Hillyard, James Greenwood*, Captain Mayne Reid, Charles Henry Ross, Vane and Percy B. St John*. Many of the paper's tales rivalled *Boys of England's* in popularity, especially the 'Scapegrace' series (1872-1873), which followed the escapades of boy hero Dick Lightheart, and the 'Ned Nimble' series (1879-1882); several were reissued as complete 1s volumes. Although *Young Men of Great Britain* was overseen by Brett himself, routine editorial duties were delegated to Vane St John in the paper's earliest years.

In 1869, publication moved to Brett's new *Boys of England* office. At around this time, the circulation* of *Young Men of Great Britain* reached an impressive 170,000; it is entirely plausible that by the 1870s the paper may have enjoyed a sale approaching the 250,000 claimed by *Boys of England*. A weekly reissue of *Young Men of Great Britain*, which appeared around a decade after the original issue, also fared well.

However, the late 1880s witnessed the beginning of a general waning in the popularity of periodicals of the type published* by Brett. Consequently, *Young Men of Great Britain* was merged* in 1888 with Brett's full-colour *Boys of the Empire* (1888-1893) after 42 volumes, in an attempt to boost the prospects of the new venture. ChB
Sources: Banham 2006, Jay 1918-1921, Rollington 1913, *Waterloo*.

YOUNG WALES (1895-1904) *Young Wales* was a monthly miscellany* founded and edited* by John Hugh Edwards, supporter of the Liberal Young Wales movement and future MP. Inspired by *Young Ireland** and the Irish press, Edwards 'preach[ed] the gospel of the national unity of Wales' to Anglophone readers and publicized the early career of David Lloyd George, who also contributed to the magazine. Undeterred by the defeat of *Young Wales*'s Home Rule platform in January 1896, the monthly served as a vehicle for the nationalist movement's ongoing life in the Welsh* press, publishing political* and educational news, including parliamentary* reports, history*, fiction, poetry*, literary* reviews* and editorials. Contributors included Allen Raine, later a bestselling novelist, Ernest Rhys, William Llewelyn Williams, journalist* and future MP and 'Y Ddau Wynne', the sisters Mallt and Gwenffreda Williams, whose serialized* novel 'A Maid of Cymru' dramatized the nationalist* loyalty of Welsh women. SY
Sources: Ballin 2004, Jones 2000, Knight 2004, Walters 2003.

YOUNG WOMAN (1892-1915) The *Young Woman*, a serious monthly* publication, presented itself as a 'journal and review'; it began as a companion to the *Young Man*, a moralistic, if not specifically religious magazine aimed at lower middle class* readers such as shop assistants. Edited* by Frederick A. Atkins, who was also its proprietor*, the *Young Woman* was published* by S. W. Partridge and Co. in octavo pages (16 pages, roughly 12.5 x 9.5 inches each), priced* 3d. The magazine title's emphasis on youth was typical of New Journalism*, specifying a target audience rather than

appearing to be for a general readership*. Described by one regular contributor as being for 'girls who think', *Young Woman* was aimed at young women working mainly in the clerical and generally lower-status professions. Though it did not identify itself as a feminist magazine *per se*, the *Young Woman* attempted to educate its readers about how to better their own and other women's lives monetarily, socially, and politically. Its stated goal was to 'cut right across the limits imposed by social stratification' and unite 'like-minded women … in churches, business houses, the mills, public and high schools … who read, who think, and who have a real interest in social effort, religious truth, and for whom the fashion* plate and the novelette* have little charm'. The magazine did contain serial* fiction, but focused more on articles, usually by women journalists*, on such topics as women's clubs*, education, and spinsterhood, and the new kinds of paid work opening to women. In 1894, it ran a series on the theme 'How Can I Earn My Living?' Nursing, child care (for example, the Norland Institute) and clerical work all received attention, as did professions such as medicine.

The first issue contained a piece by W. T. Stead* on young women in journalism*. Barry Pain contributed pieces focused on female working-class characters. Florence Fenwick Miller* reported for *Young Woman* on the 1893 Columbia Exposition, having offered her services to the magazine specifically for this assignment. An important feature was a monthly interview* or biographical sketch of a prominent woman, such as Frances Willard, Josephine Butler and Mrs Oliphant, where the magazine demonstrated its broadly progressive though not explicitly feminist approach. Among other departments were an advice column*, very practical for the time, written by Mrs Esler, and 'Our Sisters across the Sea', which reported on women's achievements and behaviour in American and Europe. Religious themes were also regularly discussed and typical articles focused on women in Christianity and young women of the Bible. Its advertisements* supported such thinking, listing some of the newer white-collar jobs for women: shorthand, teaching, and press cutting, for example. Other subjects such as travel notes and 'chats with famous ladies' show how *Young woman* hovered between a genteel and a more feminist* tone, balancing 'ladies' with 'sisters across the sea'.

Contributors included Sarah Grand*, L. T. Meade*, Hulda Friederichs*, and feminist figures

Clementina Black* and Josephine Butler. In 1915, *Young Woman* merged* with *Young Men* to form the *Young Man and Woman*; it was a relatively successful marriage lasting until 1919, but *Young Woman* was at its liveliest in the 1890s. **FCA/DD/EL**

Sources: Beetham 1996, Beetham and Boardman 2001, Doughan and Sanchez 1987, Mitchell 1995, *ODNB, Waterloo*.

Z

ZANGWILL, ISRAEL (1864-1926)
Israel Zangwill, writer of fiction, journalist* and editor*, is best known for his writings on Jewish subjects. On occasion, he used the pseudonyms; 'J. Freeman Bell and 'Baroness von S'. Zangwill was reputedly the anonymous* editor of *Purim*, a Jewish* annual* (1883-1885), and in 1889 he contributed an important article on contemporary Judaism to the *Jewish Quarterly Review*. As 'Marshallik', or jester, he wrote a satirical* column* for the weekly* *Jewish Standard* (11 May 1888-27 Feb. 1891), and soon became the paper's subeditor*, possibly its editor (Oct. 1888-early 1891). In March 1890 Zangwill assumed the editorship of a general interest, humorous weekly, *Puck**, increasing its size* from eight to 12 pages and strengthening its editorial content. Soon Zangwill changed the paper's name to *Ariel, or the London Puck* (5 July 1890-Feb.1892) to distinguish it from an American comic paper and to compete* with *Punch**, the format* of which *Ariel* now adopted.

In 1892 Zangwill began contributing stories to the *Idler** and commentary to its 'Idler's Club' (1892-1897). He also began a series of columns entitled 'Without Prejudice' (1893-late 1896) in the *Pall Mall Magazine**, cautiously supporting the *fin de siècle* avant-garde in reviews*, literary* and social commentary, travel essays, and miscellaneous causeries*. Zangwill's twentieth-century contributions to newspapers, magazines* and intellectual periodicals reflected his active role in the British women's suffrage movement, Zionism and the Jewish Territorialist Organization. **MJR**
Sources: Rochelson 2000, Rochelson 2008, Udelson 1990, Winehouse 1970.

ZIMMERN, HELEN (1846-1934)
Born in Germany in 1846, Helen Zimmern emigrated with her parents and sister Alice (1855-1939) to Britain in 1850. Both sisters had unusual language skills, but Helen was possibly the most prolific writer of the two. She was fluent in four and possibly five European languages, and translated the work of writers such as Lessing, Goldoni, Schopenhauer and Nietzsche. Helen Zimmern contributed short stories and reviews* to a variety of journals on a regular basis; these included the *Argosy**, *Athenaeum**, *Blackwood's Magazine**, *Cornhill Magazine**, *Fortnightly Review**, *Fraser's Magazine**, *National Re-*

view*, *Spectator** and *Temple Bar**. Upon first meeting Zimmern in 1881, 'Vernon Lee' described her as 'a pleasant, intelligent, little black woman, quite capable of doing good work but who has to do hack reviewing to support her people' (Willis: 65).

In 1887, Zimmern emigrated to Florence, Italy, but she continued to contribute to several British periodicals. She became associated with the *Corriere della Sera* and edited the *Florence Gazette*. Alice Zimmern was an educationist and a suffragette, and she contributed a fair number of reviews to the *Athenaeum*, mainly on educational subjects and French literature. **OM**
Sources: Demoor 2000, *ODNB*, Willis 1937.

ZOOLOGICAL JOURNAL (1824-1834)
Frustrated by the Linnean Society's outmoded system of classification and especially the slowness, irregularity and expense of its *Transactions*, in 1822 Nicholas Aylward Vigors, William Sharp Macleay and other proponents of Quinarian taxonomy formed the breakaway Zoological Club. Although the Club remained uneasily as part of the Linnean Society, within two years its members had utilized new steam-printing technologies to produce their own cheap* and fast in-house organ, the *Zoological Journal*, the first purely zoological periodical to appear in Britain, which was published at variable intervals three or four times a year

The upcoming contents of the *Zoological Journal*, mostly made up of papers presented to the Club along with analytical notices of books and reports of the proceedings of learned societies, were controversially withheld from the Linnean Council, enabling the journal to become a forum for open discussion of taxonomic issues as well as trumpeting the exotic discoveries, particularly in entomology, of the career zoologists who dominated the Club. It also opposed the evolutionary accounts of organic descent emerging from France. The *Zoological Journal* was initially edited* by Thomas Bell along with John George Children and James and George Sowerby, who described themselves as the journal's conductors, the latter also acting as its English distributor* with W. Phillips serving as printer and publisher*.

In 1827 Vigors took over as principal editor, and immediately sought out high-profile contributions from William Kirby and Charles-Lucien Bonaparte. By this time, however, most of the Zoological Club's leading members, including Vigors, had switched allegiance to the new, independent and socially well-connected Zoological Society of London, the *Proceedings* of which, founded in 1830, and then the *Transactions*, which began five years later, featured the same contributors and largely superseded the purposes of the *Zoological Journal*, which then ceased publication. **GD**

Sources: Desmond 1985, Fish 1976, Freeman 1852, *Waterloo*.

Bibliography

A

À Beckett, Arthur William, *The à Becketts of 'Punch': Memories of Fathers and Sons* (New York: E. P. Dutton, 1903)

Abel-Smith, Brian, *A History of the Nursing Profession in Great Britain* (London: Heinemann, 1960)

The Aberdeen Journal, Our 150th Year: A Unique Journalistic Record (Aberdeen: Aberdeen Journals, 1897)

Abrams, Philip, *The Origins of British Sociology 1834-1914; an Essay with Selected Papers* (Chicago: University of Chicago Press, 1968)

Ackerman, Robert, *The Myth and Ritual School: J.G. Frazer and the Cambridge Ritualists* (New York and London: Routledge, 2002)

Adams, Eric, *Francis Danby: Varieties of Poetic Landscape* (New Haven: Yale University Press, 1973)

Adams, W. E., *Memoirs of a Social Atom*, 2 vols., repr. with Introduction by John Saville (New York: Augustus M. Kelley Publishers, 1968)

------, *Our American Cousins, Being Personal Impressions of the People and Institutions of the United States*, London, 1883, repr. with intro. by Owen R. Ashton and Alun Munslow (New York: Edwin Mellen, 1992)

Adburgham, Alison, *Women in Print: Writing Women and Women's Magazines from the Restoration to the Accession of Victoria* (London: Allen and Unwin, 1972)

Adrian, Arthur A., *Georgina Hogarth and the Dickens Circle* (Oxford: Oxford University Press, 1957)

------, *Mark Lemon: First Editor of Punch* (London: Oxford University Press, 1966)

Aghasy, Husni Samira, *William Allingham: An Annotated Bibliography* (Beirut: The Lebanese Establishment for Publishing and Printing Services, 1984)

Agnew, Robin A. L., *The Life of Sir John Forbes (1787-1861)* (Bramber: Bernard Durnford, 2002)

Ainger, Alfred, 'Alexander Macmillan (A Personal Reminiscence)', *Macmillan's Magazine,* 73 (1896), 397-400

Ainslie, Rosalynde, *The Press in Africa: Communications Past and Present* (London: Victor Gollancz, 1966)

Ainsworth, W. H., 'Prologue to the Hundredth Volume', *New Monthly Magazine,* 100 (Jan. 1854), 1-5

Aird, Thomas, ed., *The Poetical Works of David Macbeth Moir, with a Memoir by Thomas Aird,* 2 vols (Edinburgh: William Blackwood and Sons, 1852)

Alaya, Flavia, *William Sharp. 'Fiona MacLeod', 1855-1905* (Cambridge, MA: Harvard University Press, 1970)

Alcock, Charles W., ed., *The Football Annual 1873* (London: Virtue, 1874)

Alderson, Brian and Pat Garnett, *The Religious Tract Society as a Publisher of Children's Books* (Hoddesdon: Children's Books History Society, 1999)

Alethea, Cherry, 'A Life of Charles Knight 1791-1873, with Special Reference to his Political and Educational Activities' (unpublished MA dissertation, University of London, 1943)

Alexander, J.H., ed., *The Tavern Sages: Selections from the 'Noctes Ambrosianae'* (Aberdeen: Association for Scottish Literary Studies, 1992)

Allan, Mea, *The Hookers of Kew, 1785-1911* (London: Michael Joseph, 1967)

Allan, Stuart, *News Culture* (Buckingham, Philadelphia: Open University Press, 1999)

Allen, David, *The Naturalist in Britain: A Social History* (London: Allen Lane, 1976)

------, *The Botanists: a History of the Botanical Society of the British Isles through a Hundred and Fifty Years* (Winchester: St. Paul's Bibliographies, 1986)

------, 'The Struggle for Specialist Journals: Natural History in the British Periodicals Market in the First Half of the Nineteenth Century', *Archives of Natural History,* 23 (1996), 107-123

[Allen, Grant], 'The Trade of Author', *Fortnightly Review,* n.s. 45 (1889), 261-274

Allen, Joan, *Joseph Cowen and Popular Radicalism on Tyneside, 1829-1900* (London: Merlin Press, 2007)

------, ' "Keeping the Faith": the Catholic Press and the Preservation of Celtic Identity in Britain in the Late Nineteenth Century', in *Irelands of the Mind,* ed. by Richard C. Allen and Stephen Regan (Newcastle: Cambridge Scholars Press, 2008), 32-49

------, ' "Resurrecting Jerusalem": The Late Chartist Press in the North-East of England, 1852-1859', in Allen and Ashton (2005), 168-189

Allen, Joan and Owen R. Ashton, eds, *Papers for the People. A Study of the Chartist Press,* (London: Merlin Press, 2005)

Allen, John E., *The Modern Newspaper: Its Typography and Methods of News Presentation* (New York and London: Harper & Bros, 1940)

Allibone, S. A., ed., *A Critical Dictionary of English Literature and British and American Authors, Living and Deceased* (London: Trübner and Co., 1859); *A Supplement to Allibone's Critical Dictionary of English Literature and British and American Authors* (Philadelphia: J. B. Lippincott, 1891)

Allingham, Helen and D. Radford, eds, *William Allingham: Diary* (Sussex: Centaur Press, 1967)

Allingham, Margery, *Dance of the Years* (London: Michael Joseph, 1943)

Allingham, William, *Letters to William Allingham* (London: Longman and Green, 1911)

Altholz, Josef L., *The Liberal Catholic Movement in England:* The Rambler *and its Contributors 1848-1864* (London: Burns and Oates, 1962)

------, and Damian McElrath, eds, *The Correspondence of Lord Acton and Richard Simpson* (Cambridge: Cambridge University Press, 1971)

------, 'Alexander Haldane, the *Record*, and Religious Journalism', *VPR*, 20.1 (Spring, 1987), 23-31

------, *The Religious Press in Britain, 1760-1900* (New York: Greenwood Press, 1989)

Altick, Richard D., *The Cowden Clarkes* (Oxford: Oxford University Press, 1948)

------, *The English Common Reader: A Social History of the Mass Reading Public, 1800-1900* (Chicago: University of Chicago Press, 1957; 1988, 2nd edn, 1998)

------, *Victorian Studies in Scarlet* (London: Dent, 1972)

------, *The Shows of London: A Panoramic History of Exhibitions, 1600-1862* (Cambridge, MA: Belknap, 1978)

------, *Deadly Encounters: Two Victorian Sensations* (Philadelphia: University of Pennsylvania Press, 1986)

------, 'The Sociology of Authorship: The Social Origins, Education, and Occupations of 1,100 British Writers, 1800-1935', in *Writers, Readers, Occasions: Selected Essays on Victorian Literature and Life*, ed. by Richard Altick (Columbus: Ohio State University Press, 1989), 95-112

------, *Punch, The Lively Youth of a British Institution 1841-1851* (Columbus: Ohio State University Press, 1997)

Ames, Alfred C., 'Contemporary Defence of Wordsworth's "Pedlar"', *Modern Language Notes*, 63.8 (1948), 543-545

Amigoni, David, *Victorian Biography: Intellectuals and the Ordering of Discourse* (New York and London: Harvester Wheatsheaf, 1993)

Amor, Anne Clarke, *William Holman Hunt: The True Pre-Raphaelite* (London: Constable, 1989)

Anderson, Alan, ed., *Ella D'Arcy: Some Letters to John Lane* (Edinburgh: Tragara, 1990)

Anderson, N. F., *Woman against Women in Victorian England: A Life of Eliza Lynn Linton* (Bloomington, IN: Indiana University Press, 1987)

Anderson, Patricia, *The Printed Image and the Transformation of Popular Culture 1790-1860* (Oxford: Clarendon Press, 1991)

Anderson, Patricia J. and Jonathan Rose, eds, *British Literary Publishing Houses, 1820-1880, Dictionary of Literary Biography*, v. 106 (Detroit: Gale Research, 1991)

Anderson, William, *The Scottish Nation; or, the Surnames, Families, Literature, Honours, and Biographical History of the People of Scotland*, 8 vols (Edinburgh and London: A. Fullarton & Co., 1882), II, 481

Andrews, Alexander, *A History of British Journalism from the Foundation of the Newspaper Press in England, to the Repeal of the Stamp Act in 1855, with Sketches of Press Celebrities* (London: R. Bentley, 1859, repr. Routledge/ Thoemmes Press, 1998)

Andrews, John H., *A Paper Landscape: The Ordnance Survey in Nineteenth-Century Ireland* (Oxford: Clarendon Press, 1975; Dublin: Four Courts Press, 2002)

Ang, Ien, 'The Nature of the Audience', in *Questioning the Media*, ed. by John Dowling, Ali Mohammadi and Annabelle Szreberny-Mohammadi (London: Sage, 1995), 207-220

Angus-Butterworth, L. M., *Lancashire Literary Worthies* (St Andrews: W.C. Henderson, 1980)

Annan, Noel, *Leslie Stephen: the Godless Victorian*, 2nd edn (London: Weidenfeld and Nicolson, 1984)

Annual Register, or a View of the History and Politics of the Year 1859 (London: Longman & Co., 1860)

Anon., 'Long Odds', *Horse Racing and Winners* (London: Horace Cox, 1892)

Appleton, J. H. and A. H. Sayce, *Dr. Appleton: his Life and Literary Relics* (London: Trübner and Co. 1881)

Arbuckle, E.S., (ed.), *Harriet Martineau in the London Daily News: Selected Contributions, 1852-1866* (New York; Garland Publishing Inc., 1993)

Ardis, Ann L., 'The Dialogics of Modernism(s) in *The New Age*', *Modernism/Modernity*, 14.3 (Sept. 2007), 407-434

Arlen, Shelley, *The Cambridge Ritualists: An Annotated Bibliography of the Works by and about Jane Ellen Harrison, Gilbert Murray, Francis M. Cornford and Arthur Bernard Cook* (Metuchen, NJ: Scarecrow, 1990)

Armstrong, Arthur. C., *Bouverie Street to Bowling Green Lane: Fifty-Five Years of Specialized Publishing* (London: Hodder and Stoughton, 1946)

Armstrong, Isobel, and Joseph Bristow with Cath Sharrock, eds, *Nineteenth-Century Women Poets: An Oxford Anthology* (Oxford: Clarendon Press, 1996)

Armytage, W. H. G., *Sir Richard Gregory: his Life and Work* (London: Macmillan 1957)

Arnold, Julian B., *Giants in Dressing Gowns* (London: Macdonald and Co., 1945)

Arnold, Matthew, *Friendship's Garland* (London: Smith. Elder & Co., 1871)

------, 'Up to Easter', *Nineteenth Century*, 21 (1887), 629-643

Arnold, Thorpe, 'The President of the Football League: A Talk with Mr. J. J. Bentley', *Windsor Magazine* 15 (1902), 665-670

Arnott, James Fullarton and John William Robinson, *English Theatrical Literature 1559-1900* (London: Society for Theatre Research, 1970)

Ashdown, Dulcie M., ed., *Over the Teacups: An Anthology in Facsimile* (London: Cornmarket Press, 1971)

Ashley, Mike, *The Age of the Storytellers: British Popular Fiction Magazines, 1880-1950* (London and New Castle, DE: British Library and Oak Knoll Press, 2006)

Ashton, Owen R., *W. E. Adams: Chartist, Radical and Journalist. 'An Honour to the Fourth Estate'* (Tyne and Wear: Bewick Press, 1991)

------, R. Fyson and S. Roberts, eds, *The Chartist Movement: A New Annotated Bibliography* (London: Mansell, 1995)

------, and Stephen Roberts, eds, *The Autobiography of William Farish: The Struggles of a Handloom Weaver* (published privately, 1889; repr. London: Caliban Books, 1996)

------, 'W. E. Adams, Chartist and Republican in Victorian England' in David W. Howell and Kenneth O. Morgan, eds., *Crime, Protest and Police in Modern British Society: Essays in Memory of David J. V. Jones* (Cardiff: University of Wales Press, 1999), 120-148

------, and Stephen Roberts, *The Victorian Working Class Writer* (London: Cassell, 1999)

------, (2003a) 'Benjamin Brierley, Chartist, Radical, Author' in Gildart, Howell and Kirk (2003)

------, (2003b) 'John Bedford Leno, Chartist, Radical, Poet' in Gildart, Howell and Kirk (2003)

------, 'The *Western Vindicator* and early Chartism' in Allen and Ashton (2005), 54-81

Ashton, Rosemary, ed., *Versatile Victorian: Selected Critical Writings of George Henry Lewes* (London: Bristol Classical Press, 1992)

------, *The Life of Samuel Taylor Coleridge: A Critical Biography* (Oxford: Blackwell, 1996)

------, *George Henry Lewes: An Unconventional Victorian* (Oxford: Oxford University Press, 1991; London: Pimlico, 2000)

------, *142 The Strand: A Radical Address in Victorian London* (London: Chatto and Windus, 2006)

Aspden, Hartley, *Fifty Years a Journalist* (Clitheroe: Advertiser and Times, 1930)

Aspinall, Arthur, 'The Social Status of Journalists at the Beginning of the Nineteenth Century' *Review of English Studies*, 21(1945), 216-232

------, *Politics and the Press 1780-1850* (New York and London: Harper and Rowe, Home & Van Thal Ltd, 1949)

------, 'Statistical Accounts of London Newspapers, 1800-1836's', *English Historical Review, 65* (April 1950), 222-234

Asquith, Ivor, 'The Whig Party and the Press in the Early Nineteenth Century', *Bulletin of the Institute of Historical Research*, 49(1976), 283

------, 'The Structure, Ownership and Control of the Press, 1780-1855', in Boyce, Curran and Wingate (1978), 98-116

Astore, William J., *Observing God: Thomas Dick, Evangelicalism, and Popular Science in Victorian Britain and America* (Aldershot: Ashgate, 2001)

Athenaeum (22 Dec. 1838), 914, 'Melaia and Other Poems'

Athenaeum (24 Dec. 1904), 874-875, 'Norman Maccoll'

Atkinson, Damian, ed., *The Selected Letters of W. E. Henley* (Aldershot: Ashgate, 2000)

Attenborough, John, *A Living Memory: Hodder & Stoughton Publishers, 1868-1975* (London: Hodder and Stoughton, 1975)

Au Casaide, Seamus, 'Irish Literary Gazette,' *Irish Book Lover*, 10: 3-5 (1910), 42-43

Austin, Alfred, *The Autobiography of Alfred Austin*, 2 vols (London: Macmillan, 1911)

Ayerst, David, Guardian: *Biography of a Newspaper* (London: Collins, 1971)

B
—

Back, W.J., 'The First Half-Century of *The Accountant*', *Economic Journal*, 35 (Sept. 1925), 493-495

Badeni, June, *The Slender Tree; A Life of Alice Meynell* (Cornwall: Tabb House, 1981)

Bagehot, Walter, 'The First Edinburgh Reviewers', *Literary Studies*, 2 vols (London: Longmans, Green & Co., 1884) 1, 1-40 (orig. *National Review*, 1 (1855))

Baggs, Chris, ' "In the Separate Reading Room for Ladies are Provided Those Publications Specially Interesting to Them": Ladies' Reading Rooms and British Public Libraries 1850-1914', *VPR*, 38.3 (2005), 280-306

Bailey, Isabel, *Herbert Ingram Esq., M.P., of Boston: Founder* of The Illustrated London News, *1842* (Boston: R. Kay, 1996)

Bailey, Peter, *Popular Culture and Performance in the Victorian City* (Cambridge: Cambridge University Press, 1998a)

------, (1998b), '*Ally Sloper's Half-Holiday*: Comic Art in the 1880s' in Bailey (1998a), 47-79

Bain, Alexander, 'George Croom Robertson', *Mind*, n.s. 2.5 (1893), 1-14

------, *Autobiography* (London: Longmans, Green, 1904)

Bainbridge, Cyril, *The Chartered Institute of Journalists: History* (London: Constable, 1902)

Baines, Edward, Sir, *The Life of Edward Baines* (London: Longman & Co., 1859)

Baker, C. Edwin, *Media Markets and Democracy* (Cambridge: Cambridge University Press, 2002)

Baker, J.H., *An Introduction to English Legal History*, 3rd ed. (London: Butterworths, 1990)

Baker, William and John C. Ross, eds, *George Eliot: A Bibliographical History* (Delaware and London: Oak Knoll Press and the British Library, 2002)

Baldwin, Arthur D., 'Anstie's Alcohol Limit: Francis Edmund Anstie, 1833-1874', *American Journal of Public Health*, 67.7 (July 1977), 679-681

Ballaster, Ros, Margaret Beetham, Elizabeth Fraser and Sandra Hebron, *Women's Worlds: Ideology, Femininity and the Woman's Magazine* (London: Macmillan, 1991)

Ballin, Ada, 'Rational Dress for Children', *Baby: the Mothers' Magazine* (Dec. 1887)

------, 'Introduction', *Womanhood* (Dec. 1898)

------, *From Cradle to School* (London: Constable, 1902)

Ballin, Malcolm, 'Welsh Periodicals in English 1880-1965: Literary Form and Cultural Substance', *Welsh Writing in English: A Yearbook of Critical Essays*, v. 9 (Llandysul, Wales: Gomer, 2004), 1-32

Bamford, Samuel, *Poems* (London: Simpkin Marshall & Co., 1864)

------, *Passages in the Life of a Radical* (Oxford: Oxford University Press, 1984)

------, *The Diaries of Samuel Bamford*, ed. by Martin Hewitt and Robert Poole (New York: St. Martin's Press, 2000)

Banham, Christopher M., 'Boys of England and Edwin J. Brett', 1866-1899 (unpublished PhD thesis: University of Leeds, 2006)

Banks, Olive, *The Biographical Dictionary of British Feminists, Volume One: 1800-1930* (New York: New York University Press, 1985)

Bareham, Tony, ed., *Charles Lever: New Evaluations* (Gerard's Cross, Buckinghamshire: Colin Smythe, 1991)

Barham, R. H. Dalton, *The Life and Remains of Theodore Edward Hook*, new ed. (London: Bentley, 1853)

Barker, Hannah, *Newspapers, Politics and Public Opinion in late Eighteenth Century England* (Oxford: Oxford University Press, 1998)

------, *Newspapers, Politics and English Society, 1695-1855* (Harlow: Longman, 2000)

Barker, J. T., *Life of Joseph Barker, Written by Himself* (London: Hodder & Stoughton, 1880)

Barlow, Monica, 'The Clouded Face of Truth: a Review of the South African Newspaper Press Approaching Union' (unpublished D.Phil. thesis: University of Bristol, 1988)

Barnes, John, *Socialist Champion: Portrait of the Gentleman as Crusader* (Melbourne: Australian Scholarly Publishing, 2006)

Barron, Evan MacLeod, *A Highland Editor: Selected Writings of James Barron of the* Inverness Courier (Inverness: R. Carruthers and Sons, 1927)

Barron, James, *The Northern Highlands in the Nineteenth Century: Newspaper Index and Annals* (from the *Inverness Courier*) (Inverness: Robert Carruthers and Sons, 1913)

Barrow, Logie, *Independent Spirits: Spiritualism and English Plebeians, 1850-1910* (London: Routledge, 1986)

Barton, Ruth, 'Just before *Nature*: the purposes of sciences and the purposes of popularization in some English popular science journals of the 1860s', *Annals of Science*, 55 (1998a), 1-33

------, '"Huxley, Lubbock, and a Half Dozen Others": Professionals and Gentlemen in the Formation of the X Club, 1851-1864', *Isis*, 89 (1998b), 410-444

------, 'Scientific Authority and Scientific Controversy in *Nature*: North Britain against the X-Club' in Henson, Cantor, et al. (2004), 223-235

Bartrip, P.W.J., *Mirror of Medicine. A History of the British Medical Journal* (Oxford: British Medical Journal and Clarendon Press, 1990)

Bashford, Christina, *The Pursuit of High Culture: John Ella and Chamber Music in Victorian London* (Woodbridge: Boydell Press, 2008)

Baskin, Jonathan Barron and Paul J. Miranti, *A History of Corporate Finance* (Cambridge: Cambridge University Press, 1997)

Bate, William, ed., *A Gallery of Illustrious Literary Characters (1830-1838) Drawn by the Late Daniel Maclise, R.A., and Accompanied by Notices Chiefly by the Late William Maginn* (London: Chatto & Windus, 1873)

Bateson, F.W., ed., *Cambridge Bibliography of English Literature* (Cambridge: Cambridge University Press, 1940)

Bauer, Josephine, *The London Magazine, 1820-29* (Copenhagen: Rosenkilde and Bagger, 1953)

Bax, Ernest Belfort, 'Leaders of Modern Thought: XXIII. Karl Marx', *Modern Thought*, 3.12 (Dec. 1881), 349-584

------, 'The Woman Question', *Justice* (12 Jan. 1885), p.6

------, Preface to *Harry Quelch: Literary Remains* (London: Grant Richards, 1914)

Baylen, Joseph O., 'W. T. Stead's *Borderland: A Quarterly Review and Index of Psychic Phenomena*, 1893-97', *VPN*, 1 (1969), 30-35

------, 'The "New Journalism" in Late Victorian Britain', *Australian Journal of Politics and History*, 18 (1972), 367-385

------, 'W. T. Stead as Publisher and Editor of the *Review of Reviews*', *VPR*, 12 (1979), 70-84

------, and Norbert J. Gossman, eds, *Biographical Dictionary of Modern British Radicals*, 2 vols (Sussex, England: Harvester Press, 1979, 1984)

Bayne, Peter, *The Life and Letters of Hugh Miller*, 2 vols (London: Strahan, 1871)

Baynes, Peter, *John Passmore Edwards, 1823-1911: An Account of his Life and Works* (London: P. A. Baynes, 1994)

Beard, Mary, *The Invention of Jane Harrison* (Cambridge, MA: Harvard University Press, 2000)

Bebbington, D. W., *Evangelicalism in Modern Britain: A History from the 1730s to the 1980s* (London: Unwin Hyman, 1989)

Beckman, Linda Hunt, *Amy Levy: Her Life and Letters* (Athens: Ohio University Press, 2000)

Beckson, Karl, *Arthur Symons: A Life* (Oxford: Clarendon Press, 1987)

'Bede, Cuthbert' [pseud. Edward Bradley], 'Sharpe's London Magazine', *Notes & Queries*, s. 5, v. 11 (26 April 1879), 330-331

Beegan, Gerry, 'The Up-to-Date Periodical: Subjectivity, Technology and Time in the Late Victorian Press', *Time and Society*, 10.1 (2001), 113-134

------, *The Mass Image: A Social History of Photomechanical Reproduction in Victorian London* (Basingstoke: Palgrave Macmillan, 2008)

Beetham, Margaret, ' "Healthy Reading": The Periodical Press in Late Victorian Manchester' in *City, Class and Culture: Studies of Cultural Production and Social Policy in Victorian Manchester*, eds A.J. Kidd and K. W. Roberts (Manchester: Manchester University Press, 1985), 167-187

------, 'Towards a Theory of the Periodical as a Publishing Genre' in Brake, Jones and Madden (1990), 19-32

------, *A Magazine of their Own? Domesticity and Desire in the Woman's Magazine, 1800-1914* (London: Routledge, 1996)

------, 'The Agony Aunt, the Romancing Uncle and the Family of Empire: Defining the Sixpenny Reading Public in the 1890s' in Brake, Bell and Finkelstein (2000), 253-270

------, and Kay Boardman, *Victorian Women's Magazines: An Anthology* (Manchester: Manchester University Press, 2001)

Belchem, John, Alan Crosby, G. Alan and J.R. Lowerson, eds, *Oxford Dictionary of National Biography* (Oxford: Oxford University Press, 2004)

Belford, Barbara, *Oscar Wilde: A Certain Genius* (New York: Random House, 2000)

Bell, Bill, 'From Parnassus to Grub Street: Matthew Arnold and the House of Macmillan' in *Macmillan: A Publishing Tradition*, ed. by Elizabeth James (Basingstoke: Palgrave, 2002), 52-69

------, ed., *The Edinburgh History of the Book in Scotland*, v. 3. *Ambition and Industry 1800-1880* (Edinburgh: Edinburgh University Press, 2007)

------, 'The Age of the Periodical' in Bell (2007), 340-342

Bell, E.M., *Flora Shaw (Lady Lugard, DBE)* (London: Constable, 1947)

Bell, Thomas, 'The Reverend David Bell', *The Clogher Record*, 6.2 (Monaghan: Cumann Seanchais Chlochair, 1968)

Bell's Life in London and Sporting Chronicle (4 Jan. 1857), 4, 'Death of W. Ruff, Esq.'

Bellamy, Joyce M., and John Saville, eds., *Dictionary of Labour Biography*, 9 vols (London: Macmillan, 1972-1993)

Bellanger, Claude, ed., *Histoire générale de la presse française*, vols. I-III (Paris: Presses Universitaires de France, 1969-1972)

Benn, Caroline, *Keir Hardie: A Biography* (London: Metro, 1997)

Bennett, B. & Hamilton, A., *Edward Arnold, 100 Years of Publishing* (London: Edward Arnold, 1990)

Bennett, Joseph, *Forty Years of Music, 1865-1905* (London: Methuen, 1908)

Bennett, Scott, 'Revolutions in Thought: Serial Publication and the Mass Market for Reading' in Shattock and Wolff (1982), 225-257

Berger, Meyer, *The Story of the New York Times* (New York: Simon and Schuster, 1951)

Berkeley Jr, Edmund, ed, *Autographs and Manuscripts: a Collector's Manual* (New York: Scribner, 1978)

Bernard, William Bayle, *The Life of Samuel Lover R.H.A., Artistic, Literary, and Musical, with Selections from his Unpublished Papers and Correspondence* (London: H.S. King, 1874)

Berridge, Virginia, 'Popular Journalism and Working-Class Attitudes, 1854-1886: A Study of *Reynolds's Newspaper, Lloyd's Weekly Newspaper* and the *Weekly Times*' (unpublished PhD thesis: University of London, 1972)

------, 'Popular Sunday Papers and mid-Victorian Society', in Boyce, Curran and Wingate (London: Constable, 1978), 247-264

Bertram, James Glass, 'An Exposition of Betting and Bookmaking', *Fraser's Magazine for Town and Country*, 96 (July 1877), 75-84

------, 'The Fisher Folk of the Scottish East Coast', *Macmillan's Magazine*, 6, (Oct. 1862), 501-512

------, 'Pisciculture: its Progress and Utility', *Blackwood's Edinburgh Magazine*, 131 (May, 1882), 593-608

------, *Some Memories of Books, Authors and Events* (London: Constable & Co., 1893)

Besant, Annie, *Annie Besant: an Autobiography* (London: T. Fisher Unwin, 1893)

Bettesworth, W. A., *Chats on the Cricket Field* (London: Merrit and Hatcher, 1910)

Bevington, Merle Mowbray, *The Saturday Review 1855-1868: Representative Educated Opinion in Victorian England* (New York: Columbia University Press, 1941)

Bevir, Mark, 'H. M. Hyndman: A Rereading and a Reassessment', *History of Political Thought*, 12 (1991), 125-145

------, 'The Labour Church Movement, 1891-1902', *Journal of British Studies*, 38 (1999), 217-45

Biggs-Davison, John, *George Wyndham: A Study in Toryism* (London: Hodder and Stoughton, 1951)

Bigmore, Edward Clements and Charles William Henry Wyman, *A Bibliography of Printing*, 3 vols (London: Quaritch, 1880-1886)

Billington, Louis, 'The Religious Periodical and Newspaper Press 1770-1870' in Harris and Lee (1986), 113-132

Bilston, Sarah, *The Awkward Age in Women's Popular Fiction 1850-1900: Girls and the Transition to Womanhood* (Oxford: Clarendon, 2004)

Bindley, Charles (Harry Hieover), *Sporting Facts and Sporting Fancies* (London: Thomas Cautley Newby, 1853)

Binns, John, *The Trial of John Binns, Deputy of the London Corresponding Society, for Sedition* (Birmingham: John Binns, 1797)

------, *Recollections of the Life of John Binns: Twenty-Nine Years in Europe and Fifty-Three in the United States* (Philadelphia: Parry and M'Millan, 1854)

Binstead, Arthur M., *A Pink 'Un and a Pelican* (London: Bliss, Sands, 1898)

------, *Pitcher in Paradise* (London: Sands and Co., 1903)

Biograph and Review, 4 (1880), 456, 'Edwin J. Brett'

Birrell, Augustine, 'Finland and Russia', *Contemporary Review*, 78 (July 1900), 16-27

------, *The Collected Essays and Addresses of Augustine Birrell*, 3 vols (London: J.M. Dent & Sons, 1922)

Bishop, F. P., *The Economics of Advertising* (London: Robert Hale, 1944)

Bissell, H., *Modern Racing Tipsters* (Tipton: Hall Street, 1899)

Black, Alistair and Peter Hoare, eds, *The Cambridge History of Libraries in Britain and Ireland. Volume III: 1850-2000* (Cambridge: Cambridge University Press, 2006)

Black, David, *Helen Macfarlane: A Feminist, Revolutionary Journalist and Philosopher in Mid-Nineteenth-Century England* (Lanham, MD: Lexington Books, 2004)

Black, F.G., and R. Métivier Black, eds, *The Harney Papers* (Assen: Van Gorcum & Co., 1969)

Black, J., *The English Press in the Eighteenth Century* (London: Croom Helm, 1987)

Blackburn, H., *Randolph Caldecott: a Personal Memoir of his Early Art Career* (London: Sampson Low, Marston, Searle, and Rivington, 1886)

Blackwood's Magazine, 78 (Dec. 1855), 757-758, 'Death of the Rev. John Eagles'

Blain, Virginia et al., *The Feminist Companion to Literature in English: Women Writers from the Middle Ages to the Present* (New Haven: Yale University Press, 1990)

Blainey, A., *The Farthing Poet: A Biography of Richard Hengist Horne 1802-84* (London: Shenval Press, 1968)

Blake, Peter, 'The Paradox of a Periodical: *Temple Bar* Under The Editorship Of George Augustus Sala' (unpublished MA dissertation: Sussex University, 2006)

Blaszak, Barbara, J., *George Jacob Holyoake and the Development of the British Cooperative Movement* (Lewiston, NY: Edwin Mellon Press, 1988)

Blatchford, Robert, *My Eighty Years* (London: Cassell, 1931)

Blathwayt, Raymond, *Interviews* (London: A.W. Hall, 1893)

------, *Through Life and Around the World* (London: E.P Dutton, 1917)

------, *Looking Down the Years* (London: Allen and Unwin, 1935)

Blaug, Mark, *Ricardian Economics: A Historical Study* (New Haven and London: Yale University Press, 1958)

Bledsoe, Robert T., *Henry Fothergill Chorley: Victorian Journalist* (Aldershot: Ashgate, 1988)

Block Jr, ed, 'Evolutionist Psychology and Aesthetics: *Cornhill Magazine*, 1875-1880', *Journal of the History of Ideas*, 45.3 (1984), 465-475

Block, Maurice, *The British and Foreign Review; or, European Quarterly Journal* (Göttingen: Druck von L. Hofer, 1921)

Blumenberg, Werner, *Karl Marx: an Illustrated Biography* (London: Verso, 1998)

Blumenfeld, R.D., *All in a Lifetime* (London: Ernest Bern, 1931)

Blunden, Edmund, *Leigh Hunt's* Examiner *Examined* (North Haven: Archon Books, 1967)

Blunt, William, *The Art of Botanical Illustration* (London: Collins, 1950)

------, *The Art of Botanical Illustration*, new ed., rev. and enl. by William T. Stearn (Woodbridge, Suffolk: Antique Collectors' Club, 1994)

Boardman, Kay, 'The Ideology of Domesticity: The Regulation of the Household Economy in Victorian Women's Magazines', *VPR*, 33.2 (Summer 2000), 150-164

------, 'Eliza Meteyard's Principled Career', in *Popular Victorian Women Writers*, ed. by Kay Boardman and Shirley Jones (Manchester: Manchester University Press, 2004), 46-65

Boas, Louise Schutz, ' "Erasmus Perkins" and Shelley', *Modern Language Notes*, 70.6 (June 1955), 408-413

Boase, Frederic, *Modern English Biography: Many Thousand Concise Memoirs of Persons Who Have Died Since the Year 1850* (Truro: Netherton and Worth, 1892, 1908, repr. London: Frank Cass & Co. Ltd, 1965)

Boase, George C., 'Sharpe's London Magazine', *Notes & Queries*, s.5, v.11 (1879), 293

Bolitho, Hector, *A Biographer's Notebook* (New York: Macmillan, 1950)

Bolton, Henry Carrington, *A Catalogue of Scientific and Technical Periodicals 1665-1895* (Washington, DC: Smithsonian Institution, 1897)

Bompas, George C., *Life of Franck Buckland* (London: Smith Elder, 1885)

Bookman, 4.2 (Oct. 1896), 97-112, 'Chronicle and Comment'

Bookseller (24 Jan. 1908), 9-43, 'Fifty Years of the *Bookseller* and Bookselling'

Bookseller (3 May 1958), 1530, 'Joseph Whitaker: Founder of the *Bookseller* 100 Years Ago'

Bookseller (3 May 1958), 1532-1652, 'One Hundred Years of the Book Trade'

Boos, Florence S., ' "Spasm" and Class: W. E. Aytoun, George Gilfillan, Sydney Dobell, and Alexander Smith', *Victorian Poetry*, 42.4 (2004), 553-583

Booth, J. B., 'Foreword', in *The Works of Arthur M. Binstead*, v. 1, ed. by Arthur M. Binstead (London: T Werner Laurie, 1930)

------, Sporting Times. *The 'Pink 'Un' World* (London: T. Werner Laurie Ltd., 1938)

Booth, Keith, *The Father of Modern Sport: The Life and Times of Charles W. Alcock* (Manchester: Parrs Wood Press, 2002)

Bordin, Ruth, *Woman and Temperance: The Quest for Power and Liberty 1873-1900* (Philadelphia: Temple University Press, 1981)

Borland, Maureen, *D. S. MacColl: Painter, Poet, Art Critic* (Harpenden: Lennard Publishing, 1995)

Bostetter, M., 'The Journalism of Thomas Wakley', in Wiener (1985), 275-292

Bostick, Darwin F., 'An Account of the *Examiner*', *VPN*, 11 (1978), 19-21

Bourne, Gilbert C., 'Fifty Years of the *Quarterly Journal of Microscopical Science* under the Editorship of Sir E. Ray Lankester', *Quarterly Journal of Microscopical Science*, s. 2, v. 64, (1919), 1-17

Bourne, Henry R. Fox, *English Newspapers: Chapters in the History of Journalism*, 2 vols (London: Bentley, 1887; repr. New York: Russell & Russell, 1966; repr. London: Routledge/Thoemmes, 1998)

Bourne, Kenneth (ed.), *The Blackmailing of the Chancellor: Some Intimate and Hitherto Unpublished Letters from Harriette Wilson to her Friend Henry Brougham, Lord Chancellor of England* (London: Lemon Tree Press, 1975)

Bourne, Richard, *Lords of Fleet Street: the Harmsworth Dynasty* (London: Unwin Hymen, 1990)

Bowen, B. P., 'The *"Comet"* Newspaper (1831-1833)', *Irish Book Lover*, 28 (1942), 120-127

Bowen, Desmond, *The Protestant Crusade in Ireland, 1800-70* (Dublin: Gill and Macmillan, 1978)

Bowring, Sir John, *A magyarok költészete/Poetry of the Hungarians* (Budapest: Allprint, 2006)

Boyce, George, James Curran and Pauline Wingate, eds, *Newspaper History from the Seventeenth Century to the Present Day* (London: Constable and Company, 1978)

Boyd, Kelly, *Manliness and the Boys' Story Paper: a Cultural History, 1855-1940* (Basingstoke: Palgrave Macmillan, 2003)

Boylan, Henry, *A Dictionary of Irish Biography*, 3rd ed. (Dublin: Gill and Macmillan, 1998)

Boyle, Andrew, *An Index to the Annuals. By the Late Andrew Boyle. v. I. The Authors 1820-1850* (Worcester: Andrew Boyle Booksellers Ltd., 1967)

Boyne, Patricia, *John O'Donovan, 1806-1861: A Biography* (Kilkenny: Boethius, 1987)

Brady, Norman, '*Shafts* and the Quest for a New Morality' (MA dissertation: Centre for Social History, University of Warwick, 1978)

Braithwaite, Helen, *Romanticism, Publishing and Dissent: Joseph Johnson and the Cause of Liberty* (Basingstoke: Palgrave Macmillan, 2003)

Brake, Laurel, 'Problems in Victorian Biography: The DNB and the DNB "Walter Pater"', *Modern Language Review*, 70.4 (Oct., 1975), 731-742

------, 'The Old Journalism and the New', in. Wiener (1988a), 1-24

------, and Anne Humpherys, eds, *VPR*, 12 (1989), Critical Theory Special Number

------, Aled Jones and Lionel Madden, eds, *Investigating Victorian Journalism* (Basingstoke and London: Macmillan, 1990)

------, *Subjugated Knowledges, Journalism, Gender and Literature in the Nineteenth Century* (London: Macmillan, 1994a)

------, 'Theories of Formation: the *Nineteenth Century*' in *Subjugated Knowledges* (London: Macmillan, 1994b), 51-62

------, (1995a) 'The "Wicked Westminster", The *Fortnightly*, and Walter Pater's Renaissance' in Jordan and Patten (1995), 289-305

------, 'Endgames: The Politics of *The Yellow Book* or, Decadence, Gender and the New Journalism', *Essays and Studies*, 48 (1995b), 38-64

------, Bill Bell and David Finkelstein, eds, *Nineteenth-Century Media and the Construction of Identities* (Basingstoke: Palgrave, 2000)

------, *Print in Transition, 1850-1910: Studies in Media and Book History* (New York: Palgrave, 2001)

------, 'Writing Women's History: "the sex" debates of 1889' in *New Women Hybridities*, ed. by Ann Heilmann and Margaret Beetham (London: Routledge, 2004a), 51-73

------, (2004b) ' "Who is 'We'?" The "Daily Paper" Projects and the Journalism Manifestos of W.T. Stead', in Demoor (2004), 54-72

------, and Julie Codell, eds, *Encounters in the Periodical Press: Editors, Authors, Readers* (London: Palgrave, 2005)

------, 'The Deaths of Heroes: Biography, Obits and the Discourse of the Press, 1890-1900' in *Life Writing and Victorian Culture*, ed. by David Amigoni (Aldershot: Ashgate, 2006), 165-194

------, 'The Popular "Weeklies"' in Bell (2007), 358-369

------, ' "Fiction of Another Sort": News and the Novel in W.T. Stead's Journalism' in Cachin and Parfait (2007), 179-192

------, 'Journalism and Modernism, Continued: the Case of W.T. Stead' in *Transatlantic Print Culture*, ed. by A. Ardis and P. Collier (Basingstoke: Palgrave, 2008)

------ and Marysa Demoor, eds, *The Lure of Illustration* (Basingstoke: Palgrave, 2008)

Brantlinger, Patrick, *The Reading Lesson: The Threat of Mass Literacy in Nineteenth-Century Fiction* (Indiana: Indiana University Press, 1998)

Bratton, J. S., *The Victorian Popular Ballad* (London: Macmillan Press, 1975)

Braude, Anne, 'News from the Spirit World: A Checklist of American Spiritualist Periodicals, 1848-1900', *Proceedings of the American Antiquarian Society*, 99 (1989), 339-462

Bray, John, *Innovation and the Communications Revolution: From the Victorian Pioneers to Broadband Internet* (Stevenage: Institution of Engineering and Technology, 2002)

Brendon, Piers, *The Life and Death of the Press Barons* (London: Secker and Warburg, 1982)

Brett, Peter, 'Early Nineteenth-Century Reform Newspapers in the Provinces: The *Newcastle Chronicle* and the *Bristol Mercury*' in *Studies in Newspaper and Periodical History*, ed. by Michael Harris and Tom O'Malley (Westport, CT: Greenwood Press, 1997)

Breuilly, John, Gottfried Niedhart and Antony Taylor, eds, *The Era of the Reform League: English Labour and Radical Politics 1857-1872* (Mannheim: Palatium, 1995)

Breward, Christopher, 'Femininity and Consumption: The Problem of the Late Nineteenth-Century Fashion Journal', *Journal of Design History*, 7.2 (1994), 71-89

------, *The Hidden Consumer; Masculinities,, Fashion and City Life 1860-1914*, Manchester: Manchester University Press, 1999

Brice, A.W.C. and K.J. Fielding, 'Dickens and the Tooting Disaster', *Victorian Studies*, 12.2 (1968), 227-244

Brierley, Ben, *Home Memories and Recollections of a Life* (Manchester: Heywood, 1886)

Brightfield, Myron, *John Wilson Croker* (London: Allen & Unwin, 1940)

Briggs, Asa, *Press and Public in Early Nineteenth Century Birmingham* (Oxford: Dugdale Society, 1949)

Bristow, Joseph, 'Reassessing Margaret Veley's Poetry: The Value of *Harper's* Transatlantic Spirit' in *Victorian Women Poets*, ed. by Alison Chapman (Woodbridge, UK: Brewer, 2003), 165-194

Britton, Karl, *John Stuart Mill, Life and Philosophy* (New York: Dover Publications, 1969)

Brock, Claire, 'The Public Worth of Mary Somerville', *British Journal for the History of Science*, 39.2 (June 2006), 255-272

Brock, William H., 'The Development of Commercial Science Journals in Victorian Britain' in *Development of Science Publishing in Europe*, ed. by A.J. Meadows (Amsterdam: Elsevier, 1980), 95-122

------, 'Brewster as a Scientific Journalist' in *Martyr of Science: Sir David Brewster 1781-1868*, ed. by A. D. Morrison-Low, J. R. Christie, et al. (Edinburgh: Royal Scottish Museum, 1984), 37-42

------, 'British Periodicals and Culture: 1820-50', *VPR*, 21.2 (1988), 47-55

------, 'The *Chemical News*, 1859-1932', *Bulletin of the History of Chemistry*, 12 (1992), 30-35

------, and Arthur Jack Meadows, *The Lamp of Learning. Two Centuries of Publishing at Taylor & Francis* (London: Taylor & Francis, 1998)

------, 'The Making of an Editor: the Case of William Crookes' in Henson, Cantor et al. (2004), 189-198

------, *William Crookes (1832-1919) and the Commercialization of Science* (Aldershot: Ashgate, 2008)

Brockwell, Maurice W., 'Preface' in *Emotion in Art*, by Claude Phillips (London: W. Heinemann, 1925)

Brooke, Leslie, and Ernest John, *Somerset Newspapers 1725-1960* (Yeovil: published by the author, 1960)

Brooks, Michael, '*The Builder* in the 1840s: The Making of a Magazine, the Shaping of a Profession', *VPR*, 14.2 (summer 1981), 86-93

Bronner, Edwin B., 'Moderates in London Yearly Meeting', *Church History*, 59.3 (1990), 356-371

Brothers, Ann, *A Studio Portrait: the Marketing of Art and Taste 1892-1918* (Parkville: University of Melbourne, 1993)

Brougham, Henry, *Observations of the Education of the People, Addressed to the Working Classes and Their Employers* (London: Richard Taylor, 1825)

Brown, Alan Willard, *The Metaphysical Society: Victorian Minds in Crisis, 1869-1880* (New York: Columbia University Press, 1947)

Brown J. D. and S. S. Stratton, *British Musical Biography; A Dictionary of Musical Artists, Authors and Composers born in Britain and its Colonies, 1897* (London: S.S. Stratton, 1897; repr. New York: Da Capo Press, 1971)

Brown, Lucy, 'The Treatment of the News in Mid-Victorian Newspapers', *Transactions of the Royal Historical Society*, 27 (1977), 23-39

------, *Victorian News and Newspapers* (Oxford: Clarendon, 1985)

Brown, Monika, 'Literacy and the Reading Public' in Mitchell (1988), 457-458

Brown, Stephen J.M., *The Press in Ireland: A Survey and Guide* (Dublin: Browne and Nolan, 1937)

Brownson, Siobhan Craft, ' "On the Western Circuit": The Success of a Bowdlerized Story', *PostScript*, 17.3 (2000), 29-43

Bruce, Charles, *News and the Southams* (Toronto: Macmillan of Canada, 1968)

Brück, Mary, 'Agnes Mary Clerke, Chronicler of *Astronomy*', *Quarterly Journal of the Royal Astronomical Society*, 35 (1994), 59-79

------, *Agnes Mary Clerke and the Rise of Astrophysics* (Cambridge: Cambridge University Press, 2002)

Brugmans, Linette F., *The Correspondence of André Gide and Edmund Goss 1904-1928* (Westport, CT: Greenwood, 1959)

Brundage, Anthony, *The People's Historian: John Richard Green and the Writing of History in Victorian England* (Westport, CT: Greenwood Press, 1994)

Bryant, Mark, and Simon Heneage, *Dictionary of British Cartoonists and Caricaturists 1730-1980* (Aldershot: Scolar Press, 1994)

Buchan, Alistair, *The Spare Chancellor: The Life of Walter Bagehot* (London: Chatto and Windus, 1959)

Buchanan, Robert [Thomas Maitland], 'The Fleshly School of Poetry: Mr. D.G. Rossetti', *Contemporary Review*, 18 (Oct. 1871), 334-350

Buchanan-Brown, John, ed., *The Illustrations of William Makepeace Thackeray* (London: David and Charles 1979)

Buckland, Francis Trevelyan, *Land and Water* (14 Dec. 1872), 387-395

Buckland, Teresa Jill, ' "Crompton's Campaign": The Professionalization of Pedagogy in late Victorian England', *Dance Research: The Journal of the Society for Dance Research*, 25.1 (2007), 1-34

Budge, Gavin, *Charlotte M. Yonge: Religion, Feminism and Realism in the Victorian Novel* (Bern and New York: Lang, 2007)

Bundock, Clement J., *The National Union of Journalists: A Jubilee History 1907-1957* (Oxford: Oxford University Press, 1957)

Buress, G.H, *The Curious World of Frank Buckland* (London: John Baker, 1967)

Burgess, Joseph, *A Potential Poet? His Autobiography and Verse* (Ilford: Burgess Publications, 1927)

Burkhardt, Frederick H. et al, eds, *The Correspondence of Charles Darwin*, 15 vols (Cambridge: Cambridge University Press, 1983)

------, and Sydney Smith, eds, *A Calendar of the Correspondence of Charles Darwin, 1821-1882, with Supplement* (Cambridge: Cambridge University Press, 1994)

Burnand, Francis Cowley, *Records and Reminiscences, Personal and General* (London: Methuen and Co., 1904)

Burnett, John, ed., *Useful Toil* (London: Allen Lane, 1972)

------, David Vincent and David Mayall, eds, *The Autobiography of the Working Class*, v. 1: 1790-1900 (New York: New York University Press, 1984)

Burnham, Lord [Edward Frederick Lawson], *Peterborough Court: The Story of* The Daily Telegraph (London: Cassell, 1955)

Burrage, Michael and Rolf Torstendahl, eds, *Professions in Theory and History* (London: Sage, 1990a)

------, *The Formation of Professions: Knowledge, State and Strategy* (London: Sage, 1990b)

Burton, Antoinette, *At the Heart of the Empire: Indians and the Colonial Encounter in Late-Victorian Britain* (Berkeley: University of California Press, 1998)

Burton, Sarah, *A Double Life: a Biography of Charles and Mary Lamb* (London: Viking, 2003)

Buttner, Günther, *The Shadow of the Telescope: A Biography of John Herschel* (New York: Scribner, 1970)

Butts, Dennis, *From the Dairyman's Daughter to Worrals of the WAAF: Children's Literature and the Religious Tract Society* (Cambridge: Lutterworth Press, 2006)

Buzzard, Thomas, 'The Late Dr. Anstie', *The Practitioner*, 16 (1876), 1-43

Bynum, W.F., S. Lock and R. Porter, *Medical Journals and Medical Knowledge: Historical Essays* (London: Routledge, 1992)

------, and Janice C. Wilson, 'Periodical Knowledge: Medical Journals and their Editors in Nineteenth-Century Britain' in Bynum, Lock and Porter (1992), 29-48

C

C. L., Review of *The Ideals of Painting* by J. Comyns Carr, *The Burlington Magazine for Connoisseurs*, 31 (Dec.1917), 247

Cachin, Marie-Francoise, Diana Cooper-Richet, Jean-Yves Mollier and Claire Parfait, eds, *Au bonheur du feuilleton* (Paris: Créaphis, 2007)

Calcutta Review, no.1, May-Aug. 1844 (Calcutta: Thacker, 1846, 3rd ed.)

Calcutta Review Index to the First Fifty Volumes (Calcutta: Thos. S. Smith, 1873)

Calendar of Horrors, a Series of Romantic Legends, Terrific Tales, Awful Narrations and Supernatural Adventures, ed. by T. P. Prest, 91 nos. (London: G. Drake, 1835-6)

Callaway, Helen and Dorothy O. Helley, 'Crusader for Empire: Flora Shaw/Lady Lugard' in *Western Women and Imperialism: Complicity and Resistance*, ed. by Napur Chaudhuri and Margaret Strobel (Indiana: University Press, 1992), 79-118

Campbell, James Dyke, 'Englishman's Magazine', *Athenaeum* (7 Dec., 1889)

Campbell, Kate, ed., *Journalism, Literature and Modernity: From Hazlitt to Modernism* (Edinburgh: Edinburgh University Press, 2004a)

------, (2004b) 'Matthew Arnold and Publicity: A Modern Critic as Journalist' in Campbell (2004a), 91-120

Campbell, Maurice, 'Sir William Hale-White', *Guy's Hospital Reports*, v. 98, Nos. 1 & 2 (1949), 1-17

Campbell, Theophilia Carlile, *The Battle of the Press as Told in the Story of Richard Carlile* (London: A. & H. B. Bonner, 1899)

Cantor, Geoffrey, 'Quaker Responses to Darwin', *Osiris* 16 (2001), 321-342

------, Gowan Dawson, Graeme Gooday, Richard Noakes, Sally Shuttleworth and Jonathan R. Topham, *Science in the Nineteenth-Century Periodical: Reading the Magazine of Nature* (Cambridge: Cambridge University Press, 2004)

------, and Sally Shuttleworth, eds, *Science Serialized: Representations of the Sciences in Nineteenth-Century Periodicals* (Cambridge, MA: MIT Press, 2004)

Carleton, William and D.J. O'Donoghue, *The Life of William Carleton* (London: Downey, 1896)

Carlile, Theophilia Campbell, *The Battle of the Press as Told in the Story of Richard Carlile* (London: A. & H. B. Bonner, 1899)

Carlisle Journal (27 March 1896), 'Farish, William'

Carlton, W. J., 'George Hogarth: a Link with Scott and Dickens', *The Dickensian*, 59 (1963), 78-89

Carlyle, Thomas, 'Characteristics', *Essays*, 4 vols (London: Chapman and Hall, 1857; orig. *Edinburgh Review*, 54, Dec. 1831), 351-383

------, Thomas, Jane Welsh Carlyle and Clyde de L. Ryals, *The Collected Letters of Thomas and Jane Welsh Carlyle*, 35 vols (Durham and London: Duke University Press, 1970-present)

Carnell, Jennifer, *The Literary Lives of Mary Elizabeth Braddon: A Study of Her Life and Work* (Hastings: Sensation Press, 2000)

Carpenter, Humphrey and Mari Prichard, eds, *The Oxford Companion to Children's Literature* (Oxford: Oxford University Press, 1984, repr. 1999)

Carpenter, J. Estlin, 'William Benjamin Carpenter' in *Nature and Man: Essays Scientific and Philosophical*, ed. by William B. Carpenter (London: Kegan, Paul, Trench, 1888), 3-152

Carpenter, Kevin, *Penny Dreadfuls and Comics* (London: Victoria and Albert Museum, 1983)

[Carruthers, Robert], 'In Memoriam: Robert Carruthers, LL.D' (Inverness: Robert Carruthers and Sons, 1878) (Glasgow: private circulation, 1888)

------, *A Highland Newspaper. The Inverness Courier 1817-1967* (Inverness: Robert Carruthers & Sons, 1969)

Carter, Brian, 'Controversy and Conciliation in the English Catholic Enlightenment 1790-1840', *Enlightenment and Dissent*, 7 (1988), 1-24

Case, Walter, *Ninety Years of Horse and Hound* (London: Country Life Books, 1977)

Catholic Encyclopedia: An International Work of Reference on the Constitution. Doctrine, Discipline, and History of the Catholic Church (New York: The Encyclopedia Press, 1913)

Catling, Thomas, *My Life's Pilgrimage* (London: John Murray, 1911)

Catton J. A. H., *Wickets and Goals. Stories of Play* (London: Chapman and Hall, 1926)

Cayford, Joanne Mary, '*The Western Mail* 1869-1914: a Study in the Politics and Management of a Provincial Newspaper' (unpublished PhD thesis: Aberystwyth, 1992)

Census Returns of England and Wales (Kew, Surrey: The National Archives, Public Record Office)

Cevasco, G. A., ed., *The 1890s: An Encyclopedia of British Literature, Art and Culture* (New York: Garland, 1993)

Chambers, Deborah, Linda Steiner and Carole Fleming, *Women in Journalism* (London: Routledge, 2004)

Chambers, Robert, *Life of Sir Walter Scott* (Edinburgh and London: W. & R. Chambers, 1871)

------, ed., *A Biographical Dictionary of Eminent Scotsmen,* 9 vols (Glasgow: Blackie, 1853-5)

Chambers, William, *Story of a Long and Busy Life* (Edinburgh and London: W. & R. Chambers, 1882)

------, *Memoir of William and Robert Chambers,* 13th ed. (Edinburgh and London: W. & R. Chambers, 1884)

Chambers's Journal 'Extra Double Christmas Number' (Dec. 1865), 1, 'Waiting for the Host' [by Leitch Ritchie?]

Chambers's Journal, 4.11 (1874), 113-115, 'The Street News-Boys of London'

Chandler, John H. and H. Dagnell, *The Newspaper and Almanac Stamps of Great Britain and Ireland* (Saffron Waldon: Great Britain Philatelic Publications, 1981)

Chapman, Jane, *Comparative Media History* (Cambridge: Polity Press, 2005)

Chapman, M. W, ed., *Harriet Martineau's Autobiography,* 3 vols (London: Macmillan, 1877)

Chapman, Peter, 'Developing "This is The Northeast"', *Aslib Proceedings*, 50.9 (Oct. 1998), 264

Charlton, David, and Katharine Ellis, eds, *The Musical Voyager: Berlioz in Europe* (Frankfurt am Main: Peter Lang, 2007)

Chase, Malcolm, *Early Trade Unionism: Fraternity, Skill and the Politics of Labour* (Aldershot: Ashgate, 2000)

------, *Chartism: A New History* (Manchester: Manchester University Press, 2007)

Chattopadhyay, G., P. Chaudhuri, M. Chakraborty and B. Chattopadhyay, eds, *Classified Subject Index to the* Calcutta Review *1844-1920* (Calcutta: India Book Exchange, 1974)

CHC [Christopher Clinton Hoey], 'The Rise and Progress of Printing and Publishing in Ireland', *Irish Builder* (1 March, 1878), 67-68

------, 'Notes on the Rise and Progress of Printing and Publishing in Ireland', *Irish Builder* (15 Dec., 1877), 362

Cheltenham Free Press (5 December 1846), 'Biography of Henry Vincent'

Chester Courant (25 March 1896), 'Farish, William'

Chester Chronicle, (28 March 1896), 'Farish, William'

Chilston, Viscount, *W.H. Smith* (Toronto: Routledge, 1965)

Chittick, Kathryn, 'The Idea of a Miscellany: *Master Humphrey's Clock*', *Dickensian*, 78 (1982), 156-164

------, 'Pickwick Papers and the *Sun*, 1833-1836' in *Nineteenth-Century Fiction*, 39.3 (Dec. 1984), 328-335

------, *Dickens and the 1830s* (Cambridge: Cambridge University Press, 1990)

Chitty, Susan, *The Beast & the Monk: A Life of Charles Kingsley* (New York: Mason/Charter, 1974)

Chorley, Henry Fothergill, *An Autobiography, Memoir and Letters*, ed. by H. G. Hewlett, 2 vols (London: Richard Bentley & Son, 1873)

Church, Alfred John, *Memories of Men and Books* (London: Smith Elder, 1908)

C. K. [Charles Kent], 'Bindley, Charles better known as HARRY HIEOVER (1795-1859)', *DNB*, 2 (1973), 507

Clarke, Bob, *From Grub Street to Fleet Street: An Illustrated History of English Newspapers to 1899* (Aldershot: Ashgate, 2004)

Clarke, J. F. *Autobiographical Recollections of the Medical Profession* (London: J. & A. Churchill, 1874)

Clarke, John Stock, *Margaret Oliphant (1828-1897). Non-Fictional Writings: A Bibliography*, Victorian Fiction Research Guide, 26 (University of Queensland, 1997)

Clarke, M.C., *My Long Life, an Autobiographical Sketch* (London: T. Fischer Unwin, 1896)

------, *Letters to an Enthusiast* (Chicago: McClurg & Co., 1902)

------, *World Noted Women* (New York: Appleton & Co., 1858)

Clarke, Meaghan, *Critical Voices: Women and Art Criticism in Britain, 1880-1906* (Aldershot: Ashgate, 2005)

Clarke, Norma, 'Feminism and the Popular Novel of the 1890s: A Brief Consideration of a Forgotten Feminist Novelist', *Feminist Review*, 19-21 (1985), 91-104

------, *Ambitious Heights: Writing, Friendship, Love: The Jewsbury Sisters, Felicia Hemans, and Jane Welsh Carlyle* (London: Routledge, 1990)

Clayton, Ellen C., *English Female Artists* (London: Tinsley Bros, 1876)

Clayworth, Anya, 'The Woman's World: Oscar Wilde as Editor', *VPR*, 30.2 (1997), 84-101

Clephan, J., *Half-an-Hour with the Newcastle Courant* (Gateshead: Gateshead Observer, 1859)

Clive, John, *Scotch Reviewers. The Edinburgh Review, 1802-1815* (London: Faber and Faber, 1957)

Clowes, Alice, *Charles Knight: A Sketch* (London; R. Bentley and Son, 1892)

Clyde, Tom, *Irish Literary Magazines: An Outline History and Descriptive Bibliography* (Dublin: Irish Academic Press, 2003)

'C. M.' [William Cosmo Monkhouse], 'Landseer, Sir Edwin Henry (1802-1873)', *DNB*, *11* (1973), 505-509

------, *Biographical Notice of William Ritchie* (Edinburgh: The Scotsman Office, 1831)

Coad, Roy, *A History of the Brethren Movement*, 2nd edn (Exeter: Paternoster, 1976)

Cobbett, Martin, *The Man on the March* (London: Bliss, Sands, 1896)

------, *Wayfaring Notions* (London: Sands, 1906)

Cockburn, Henry, *Life of Lord Jeffrey*, 2 vols (Edinburgh: Adam and Charles Black, 1852)

------, *Journal of Henry Cockburn 1831-1854*, 2 vols (Edinburgh: Edmonston and Douglas, 1874)

Codell, Julie F., 'Moderate Praise: Art Criticism of *The Portfolio*', *VPR*, 20.3 (Autumn 1987), 83-93

------, ' "The Artist's Cause at Heart": Marion Harry Spielmann and the Late Victorian Art World', *Bulletin of the John Rylands University Library of Manchester*, 71 (1989a), 139-163

------, 'M. H. Spielmann and the Press in the Professionalization of Artists', *VPR*, 22 (1989b), 7-15

------, ed. *Imperial Co.-Histories: National Identities and the British and Colonial Press* (Madison: Fairleigh Dickinson University Press, 2003)

------, ' "Getting the Twain to Meet": Global Regionalism in *East and West: A Monthly Review*', *VPR*, 37. 2 (Summer 2004), 141-160 ('The Nineteenth-Century Press in India', ed. by Julie F. Codell, Special Issue)

Cohen, Deborah, 'Why did the House Fail, or, Demand and Supply Before the Modern Home Magazine, 1880s-1900s', *Journal of Design History*, 18.1 (2005), 35-42

------, *Household Gods: The British and Their Possessions* (New Haven: Yale University Press, 2006)

Cohen, Lewis Lennard, 'Towards Modernism: the *Saturday Review* under Frank Harris' (unpublished PhD thesis: University of London, 1996)

Cohen, Patricia Cline, Timothy J. Gilfoyle and H. L Horowitz, *The Flash Press: Sporting Male Weeklies in 1840s New York* (Chicago: University of Chicago Press, 2008)

Cohn, Albert M., *George Cruikshank: A Catalogue Raisonné of Works 1806-1877* (London: Bookman's Journal, 1924)

Coke, Mrs Talbot, *The Gentlewoman at Home* (London: Henry and Co., 1892)

Colby, Vineta, *Vernon Lee: A Literary Biography* (Charlottesville and London: University of Virginia Press, 2003)

Colclough, Stephen, *Consuming Texts: Readers and Reading Communities 1695-1870* (Basingstoke: Palgrave Macmillan, 2007)

Cole, G. D. H. *The Co.-ops and Labour* (London: London Co.-operative Society, 1945)

------, *Chartist Portraits* (London: Cassell, 1941; repr. Cassell History, 1989)

Coleridge, Christabel, *Charlotte Yonge: Her Life and Letters* (London: Macmillan, 1903)

Collet, Collet Dobson, *History of the Taxes on Knowledge* (London: T. Fisher Unwin, 1899)

Collie, Michael, *Henry Maudsley: Victorian Psychiatrist. A Bibliographical Study* (Winchester: St Paul's Bibliographies, 1988)

Colligan, Colette, *The Traffic in Obscenity from Byron to Beardsley: Sexuality and Exoticism in Nineteenth-Century Print Culture* (London: Palgrave, 2006)

Collins, Irene, *The Government and the Newspaper Press in France, 1814-1881* (Oxford: Oxford University Press, 1959)

Collins, Michael, 'English Art Magazines Before 1901', *Connoisseur*, 191 (March 1976), 198-205

Collins, Ross F., and E.M. Palmegiano, *The Rise of Western Journalism, 1815-1914* (Jefferson and London: McFarland and Company Inc., 2007)

[Collins, Wilkie], 'The Unknown Public', *Household Words*, 18 (21 Aug. 1858), 217-222 in King and Plunkett (2005), 207-216

------, *The Woman in White*, 3 vols (London: Sampson Low, Son, & Co., 1860)

Colloms, Brenda, *Charles Kingsley: the Lion of Eversley* (London: Barnes and Noble, 1975)

Coltham, S., 'George Potter, the Junta, and the *Bee-Hive*', *International Review of Social History*, 1.9 (1964), 2.10 (1965)

Colquhoun, Kate, *A Thing in Disguise: The Visionary Life of Joseph Paxton* (London: Fourth Estate, 2002)

Colvin, Sidney, *Memories and Notes of Persons and Places, 1852-1912* (London: Edward Arnold, 1921)

Comerford, Richard V., *The Fenians in Context. Irish Politics and Society 1848-1882* (Dublin: Wolfhound, 1985)

------, 'Ireland 1850-70: Post Famine and Mid-Victorian', in *A New History of Ireland*, v. 5, *Ireland under the Union 1801-70*, ed. by William E. Vaughan, 9 vols; (Oxford: Clarendon Press, 1989)

Conboy, Martin, *Journalism: A Critical History* (London: Sage Publications, 2004)

Conder, Eustace, *Josiah Conder: A Memoir* (London: John Snow, 1857)

Connolly, J., *Jerome K. Jerome* (London: Orbis Publishing, 1982)

Connolly, L. W and J. P. Wearing, eds, *English Drama and Theatre 1800-1900: a Guide to Information Sources*, v. 12, in *The American Literature, English Literature and World Literatures in English Information Guide Series* (Detroit, Michigan: Gale Research Company, 1978)

Constable, Memoir [of Archibald] (London and Edinburgh: W. & R. Chambers, [ca. 1870])

Constable, Thomas, *Archibald Constable and his Literary Correspondents*, 3 vols (Edinburgh: Edmonston & Douglas, 1873)

Constable, T. & A. Ltd., *Brief Notes on the Origins of T. & A. Constable Ltd* (Edinburgh: T. and A. Constable Ltd, 1937)

Cook, Bernard, H., 'Agriculture' in Vann and VanArsdel (1994), 235-248

Cook, Eliza, *Jottings from my Journal* (London: Routledge, Warne & Routledge, 1860)

Cook, E.T. and A.D.O. Wedderburn, *The Works of John Ruskin,* 39 vols (London: George Allen, 1902-1912)

Cooney, Sondra Miley, 'Publishers for the People: W. & R. Chambers: The Early Years, 1832-1850' (unpublished PhD thesis: Ohio State University, 1970)

Cooper, Charles A., *An Editor's Retrospect: Fifty Years of Newspaper Work* (London: Macmillan & Co., 1896)

Cooper, Charles A., *An Editor's Retrospect. Fifty Years of Newspaper Work* (London: Macmillan & Co., 1896)

Cooper, J. Nicoll, 'Dissenters and National Journalism: *The Patriot* in the 1830s', *VPR,* 14.2 (1981), 58-66

Cooper, Leonard, *R.S. Surtees* (London: Arthur Baker Ltd, 1952)

Cooper, Thomas, *Life of Thomas Cooper* (Leicester: Leicester University Press, 1872; rprt. 1971)

Cooper, Thompson, *Men of the Time: A Dictionary of Contemporaries, Containing Biographical Notices of Eminent Characters of Both Sexes*, 8th edn (London: Routledge, 1872)

Cooper, Victoria L., *The House of Novello: Practice and Policy of a Victorian Music Publisher, 1829-1866* (Aldershot: Ashgate, 2003)

Cooter, Roger, *The Cultural Meaning of Popular Science: Phrenology and the Organization of Consent in Nineteenth-Century Britain* (Cambridge: Cambridge University Press, 1984)

------, and Steven Pumfrey, 'Separate Spheres and Public Places: Reflections on the History of Science Popularization and Science in Popular Culture', *History of Science*, 32 (1994), 237-267

Copinger, W. A., *The Law of Copyright in Works of Literature and Art,* 4th edn, ed. by J. M. Easton (London: Stevens and Haynes, 1904)

Cordery, Simon, 'Joshua Hobson', in Bellamy and Saville, v. 8 (1987), 113-119

Corfield, Penelope, *Power and the Professions in Britain 1700-1850* (London: Routledge, 1995)

Cormack, Alexander A., *The Chalmers Family and Aberdeen Newspapers* (Peterculter: Alexander A. Cormack, 1958)

Cosgrove, Richard A, 'Victorian Legal Periodicals', *VPN,* 7.1 (1975), 21-25

------, 'Law' in Vann and VanArsdel (1994), 11-21

Coulling, Sidney M. B., 'Matthew Arnold and the *Daily Telegraph*', *Review of English Studies,* (1961), 173-179

Couper, W.J., 'A Bibliography of Edinburgh Periodical Literature', *Scottish Notes & Queries,* s.2, v. 6 (Dec. 1904), 85-87

Courtney, W.L., *The Making of an Editor: W.L. Courtney, 1850-1928* (London: Macmillan and Co. Ltd, 1930)

Courtney, Winifred, 'The Englishman's Magazine' in Sullivan (1983), 144-150

Coventry Herald (Jan. 10 and 11, 1930), 7, 'Mr. H. Sturmey, Cycle and Motor Industry Pioneer'

Coventry Standard (Jan. 10 and 11, 1930), 8, 'Death of Mr. Henry J. Sturmey: a Pioneer of Cycle and Motor Industries'

Cowan, R.M.W., *The Newspapers in Scotland: A Study of its First Expansion, 1815-1860* (Glasgow: George Outram & Co., Ltd, 1946)

Cowley, John, *The Victorian Encounter with Marx: A Study of Ernest Belfort Bax* (London: British Academic Press, 1992)

Cox, Alison Janice Minoff, 'Robert Barr' in *Dictionary of Literary Biography*, v. 70, ed. by Bernard Benstock and Thomas F. Staley (Detroit: Gale Research, 1988), 14-21

Cox, Jack, *Take a Cold Tub, Sir! The Story of the Boy's Own Paper* (Guildford: Lutterworth, 1982)

Cox, Robert, and James Nicol, eds, *Selected Writings, Political, Scientific, Topographical and Miscellaneous of the Late Charles Maclaren* (Edinburgh: 1869)

Crackanthorpe, David, *Hubert Crackanthorpe and English Realism in the 1890s* (Columbia: University of Missouri Press, 1977)

Craig, C., ed., *The History of Scottish Literature*, v. 3: *Nineteenth Century*, general ed. D. Gifford, (Aberdeen: Aberdeen University Press, 1988)

Cranfield, G. A., *The Press and Society From Caxton to Northcliffe* (London/ New York: Longman, 1978)

Crawford, Anne et al., eds, *Europa Biographical Dictionary of British Women* (London: Europa, 1983)

Crawford, Elizabeth, *The Women's Suffrage Movement: a Reference Guide 1866-1928* (London: University College London, 1999)

------, *Enterprising Women: The Garretts and their Circle* (London: Francis Bootle Publishers, 2002)

Crawson, N.J., *Fleet Street, Press Barons and Politics: the Journals of Collin Brooks, 1932-1940* (London: Royal Historical Society, 1998)

Crilly, Tony, *Arthur Cayley: Mathematician Laureate of the Victorian Age* (Baltimore: Johns Hopkins University Press, 2006)

Crone, John S., 'Our Forerunner', *Irish Book Lover*, 1.1 (1909)

------, *A Concise Dictionary of Irish Biography* (Dublin: Talbot Press, 1928)

Cronin, Richard, 'The Spasmodics' in *A Companion to Victorian Poetry*, ed. by R. Cronin, Alison Chapman and Antony Harrison (Oxford: Blackwell, 2002), 291-304

Crook, D. P., *Benjamin Kidd: Portrait of a Social Darwinist* (Cambridge: Cambridge University Press, 1984)

Cross, Nigel, *The Common Writer: Life in Nineteenth-Century Grub Street* (Cambridge: Cambridge University Press, 1985)

Crossland, N., *Landmarks of a Literary Life 1820-92* (New York: Charles Scribner's Sons, 1893)

Croydon Advertiser and Surrey County Reporter (5 Oct. 1956), 13, 'Notable Croydonians Number 19: Birthday Party for a Born Inventor'

Cubbon, W., *A Bibliographical Account of Works Relating to the Isle of Man*, v. 2. (Douglas: Manx Museum and National Trust, 1935)

Cumming, Mark, ed., *The Carlyle Encyclopedia* (Madison, NJ: Fairleigh Dickinson University Press, 2004)

Curle, Richard, *Robert Browning and Julia Wedgwood: A Broken Friendship as Revealed in Their Letters* (New York: Stokes, 1937)

Curran, James, *Media and Power: Communication and Society* (London: Routledge, 2002)

------, and Myung-Jin Park, eds., *De-Westernizing Media Studies* (London: Routledge, 2000)

------, and Jean Seaton, *Power without Responsibility: the Press, Broadcasting and New Media in Britain,* 6th ed. (London: Routledge, 2003)

Curtis, L. Perry, *Jack the Ripper and the London Press* (New Haven: Yale University Press, 2001)

Curwen, Henry, *A History of Booksellers, the Old and New* (London: Chatto and Windus, 1873)

Cutt, Margaret Nancy, *Ministering Angels: A Study of Nineteenth-Century Evangelical Writing for Children* (Wormley: Five Owls Press, 1979)

D

Dahlgren, P. and C. Sparks, eds., *Communication and Citizenship. Journalism and the Public Sphere in the New Media Age* (London: Rooutledge, 1991)

Daily News (22 Feb. 1900), 4, 'Death of Mr. H.D. Traill'

D'Albe, E. E. Fournier, *The Life of Sir William Crookes, OM, FRS* (London: T. Fisher Unwin, 1923)

Dalziel, George and Edward Dalziel, *The Brothers Dalziel* (London: Methuen, 1901)

Damrosch, David, *The Buried Book: The Loss and Rediscovery of the Great Epic of Gilgamesh* (New York: Henry Holt, 2007)

Dan, H. Laurence, *Bernard Shaw: A Bibliography,* 2 vols (Oxford: Clarendon Press, 1983)

D'Arcy, Ella, *Some Letters to John Lane*, ed. by Alan Anderson (Edinburgh: Tragara Press, 1990)

Dark, Sidney, *The Life of Sir Arthur Pearson* (London: Hodder and Stoughton, 1922)

Darlow, T.H., *William Robertson Nicoll: Life and Letters* (London: Hodder and Stoughton, 1925)

Darren Wershler-Henry, *The Iron Whim: A Fragmented History of Typewriting* (Ithaca, NY: Cornell University Press, 2005)

Darnton, Robert, '"What is the History of Books?" Revisited', Modern Intellectual History, 4.3 (2007), 495-508

Davies, James A., *John Forster: a Literary Life* (Leicester: Leicester University Press, 1983)

Davies, Laurence, ' "A sideways ending to it all": G. W. Steevens, Blackwood, and the *Daily Mail*, in Finkelstein (2006), 236-258

Davis, Kenneth W., 'Literary Guardian' in Sullivan (1983), 246-251

Davis, Lloyd, 'Journalism and Victorian Fiction' in Garlick and Harris (1998) 197-211

Davis, Paul, *The Penguin Dickens Companion: The Essential Reference to His Life and Work* (Harmondsworth: Penguin, 1999)

Davis, Richard, *The Young Ireland Movement* (Dublin: Gill and Macmillan, 1987)

Davison Henry, ed., *Music in the Victorian Era: from Mendelssohn to Wagner, being the Memoirs of J. W. Davison* (London: W. Reeves, 1912)

Dawson, Gowan, (2004a) 'The *Review of Reviews* and the New Journalism in Late Victorian Britain' in Cantor et al., (2004), 172-195

------, (2004b) 'The *Cornhill Magazine* and Shilling Monthlies in Mid-Victorian Britain' in Cantor et al., (2004), 123-150

------, (2004c) 'Victorian Periodicals and the Making of William Kingdon Clifford's Posthumous Reputation' in Cantor and Shuttleworth (2004), 259-284

Dean, Dennis R., 'John W. Parker' in Anderson and Rose (1991), 233-236

Deane, Seamus, *The Field Day Anthology of Irish Writing*, v. 1 (Derry: Field Day Publications, 1991)

De Baun, Vincent, Temple Bar*: Index of Victorian Middle-Class Thought* (Rutgers University: Journal of the Rutgers University Library v. 19, Dec. 1955)

De Burgh, Hugo, *Investigative Journalism: Context and Practice* (London: Routledge, 2000)

De la Motte, Dean, and Jeannene M. Przyblyski, eds, *Making the News: Modernity and the Mass Press in Nineteenth-Century France* (Amherst: University of Massachusetts Press, 1999)

Delaney, John and James Tobin, eds, *Dictionary of Catholic Biography* (Garden City, New York: Doubleday, 1961)

De Laszlo, P.A., 'The Founder of *The Studio* As I Knew Him', *Studio*, 105 (April 1933), 211-212

Dell'Orto, Giovanna, *Giving Meaning to the World: The First US Foreign Correspondents, 1838-1859* (Westport, CT: Greenwood Publishing, 2002)

De Maré, Eric, *The Victorian Woodblock Illustrators* (London: Gordon Fraser, 1980a)

------, *The Canals of England* (Oxford: Architectural Press, 1980b)

Demata, M. and D. Wu, eds, *British Romanticism and the Edinburgh Review: Bicentenary Essays* (London: Palgrave, 2002)

Demoor, Marysa, 'Andrew Lang's *Causeries* 1874-1912', *VPR*, 21.1 (Spring 1988), 15-22

------, 'Men of Letters, their Clubs and "At Homes" in London in the 1880s and 1890s', *Belgian Association of Anglicists in Higher Education*, Papers 1987-1988 (Belgium: Université de Liège 1989), 24-36

------, 'Where No Woman Fears to Tread: the Gossip Columns in the *Athenaeum*', *Essays from ESSE: proceedings of the Women's Studies Section at the European Society for the Study of English Conference, Bordeaux 1993* (Barcelona: 1996, *Bells no. 7*), 33-42

------, *Their Fair Share: Women, Power and Criticism in the* Athenaeum*, from Millicent Garrett Fawcett to Katherine Mansfield, 1870-1920* (Aldershot: Ashgate, 2000)

------, ed., *Marketing the Author: Authorial Personae, Narrative Selves and Self-Fashioning, 1880-1930* (Basingstoke: Palgrave Macmillan, 2004a)

------, ' "The Flesh-tints of Rubens": Henry James's Contribution to the Construction of English-ness', *Nineteenth Century Prose*, 31.1 (April 2004b), 101-120

------, 'From Epitaph to Obituary: the Death Politics of T.S. Eliot and Ezra Pound', *Biography*, 28.2 (Spring 2005), 255-275

------, 'In the Beginning there was the *Germ'* in *Modernist Magazines: A Critical and Cultural History*, v. I, part 1.2, ed. by Andrew Thacker and Peter Brooker, (Oxford University Press, 2008)

Dempster, John A.H., *The T. & T. Clark Story* (Edinburgh: Pentland Press, 1992)

Denney, Colleen, *At the Temple of Art: The Grosvenor Gallery, 1877-1890* (Madison, NJ: Fairleigh Dickinson University Press, 1999; London: Associated University Presses, 2000)

Desmond, Adrian, 'The Making of Institutional Zoology in London 1822-1836', *History of Science*, 23 (1985), 153-185 and 223-250

------, 'Artisan Resistance and Evolution in Britain, 1819-1848', *Osiris*, 3 (1987), 77-110

------, *Huxley: From the Devil's Disciple to Evolution's High Priest* (London: Michael Joseph, 1994-1997)

Desmond, Ray, 'Victorian Gardening Magazines', *Garden History: The Journal of the Garden History Society*, 5.3 (1977)

------, 'Loudon and Nineteenth Century Horticultural Journalism' in *John Claudius Loudon and the Early Nineteenth Century in Great Britain*, ed. by Elizabeth B. MacDougall (Washington, DC: Dumbarton Oaks, 1980), 79-103

Desmond, Robert A., *The Information Process: World News Reporting to the Twentieth Century* (Iowa City: University of Iowa Press, 1978)

De Stasio, Clotilde, 'Arnold Bennett and late-Victorian *Woman'*, *VPR*, 28.1 (1995), 40-53

De Vries, Leonard, *'Orrible Murder: An Anthology of Victorian Crime and Passion Compiled from the* Illustrated Police News (London: Macdonald, 1971)

Diamond, Marion, *Emigration and Empire: The Life of Maria S. Rye* (London: Garland, 1999)

Diamond, Michael, *Victorian Sensation* (London: Anthem Press, 2004)

Dickens, Charles, *Letters*, ed. M. House, G. Storey, et al., 12 vols (Oxford: Clarendon Press, 1965-)

------, *Charles Dickens: Selected Journalism 1850-1870*, ed. by David Pascoe (London: Penguin, 1997)

Dickerson, Vanessa, 'Florence Marryat' in Mitchell (1988)

Dickins, Bruce, *Two Kembles, John and Henry* (Cambridge: Cambridge University Library, 1974)

Dicks, Guy, *The John Dicks Press* (Lulu.com, 2006)

Dickson, W. K. Laurie, *The* Biograph *in Battle: its Story in the South African War* (London: T.F. Unwin, 1901)

Dideriksen, Gabriella, 'Repertory and Rivalry: Opera at the Second Covent Garden Theatre, 1830 to 1856' (unpublished PhD thesis: University of London, 1997)

Diedrick, James, 'A Pioneering Female Aesthete: Mathilde Blind in the *Dark Blue*', *VPR*, 36.6 (2003), 210-241

Dillane, Fionnuala, 'Before George Eliot: Marian Evans and the Periodical Press' (unpublished PhD thesis, Trinity College Dublin, 2004)

Dix, John, *Lions: Living and Dead; or, Personal Recollections of the 'Great and Gifted'* (London: Tweedie, 1854)

Dixon, Diana, (1986a) 'Children and the Press, 1866-1914' in Harris and Lee (1986), 133-148

------, 'From Instruction to Amusement: Attitudes of Authority in Children's Periodicals Before 1914', *VPR*, XIX/2 (Summer 1986b), 63-67

------, 'Bradbury and Evans' in Anderson and Rose (1991), 62-67

------, 'Children and the Press, 1866-1914' in *The Oxford Companion to Children's Literature*, ed. by Humphrey Carpenter and Mari Pritchard (Oxford: Oxford University Press, 1999)

Dixon, Ella Hepworth, 'My Faith and My Work', *Woman* (23 Sept.1896)

------, *As I Knew Them* (London: Hutchinson and Company 1930)

Dixon, Henry Hall (pseud. 'The Druid'), *The Post and the Paddock* (London: Warne, 1880)

Dobson, William. T., *The Ballantyne Press and its Founders 1796-1908* (Edinburgh: Ballantyne, Hanson, 1909)

Dodd, Christopher, *Henley Royal Regatta* (London: Stanley Paul, 1981; repr. 1989)

Donaldson, William, *Popular Literature in Victorian Scotland: Language, Fiction and the Press* (Aberdeen: Aberdeen University Press, 1986)

Donnelly, J. F., 'Representations of Applied Science: Academics and Chemical Industry in Late Nineteenth-Century England', *Social Studies of Science*, 16 (1986), 195-234

Donovan, Stephen, 'The Muse of Blackwood's: Charles Whibley and Literary Criticism in the World' in Finkelstein (2006), 339-378

Dorrington, William (Dorrington Bros), ed., *London, Provincial, and Colonial Press News: A Literary and Business Journal* (London: Dorrington, 1866-1912)

Dorset County Chronicle and Somersetshire Gazette (27 March 1845) (back page; unnumbered), 'The Late Mr. James Savage'

Doughan, David, *Feminist Periodicals 1855-1984: An Annotated Critical Bibliography of British, Irish, Commonwealth and International Titles*, ed. by David Doughan and Denise Sanchez (New York: New York University Press, 1987)

Doughty, Terri, 'Introduction', *Selections from the 'Girl's Own Paper' 1880-1907* (Peterborough: Broadview Press, 2004)

Drabble, Margaret, ed., *The Oxford Companion to English Literature* (Oxford: Oxford University Press, 2000)

Drew, John M. L., *Dickens the Journalist*, (Basingstoke: Palgrave Macmillan, 2003)

------, 'Dickens's Evolution as a Journalist' in *A Companion to Charles Dickens*, ed. by David Paroissien (Oxford: Blackwell, 2008)

Drinkwater, John, 'Eneas Sweetland Dallas' in *The Eighteen-Sixties*, ed. by John Drinkwater (Cambridge: Cambridge University Press, 1932), 201-223

Drotner, Kirsten, *English Children and Their Magazines, 1751-1945* (New Haven: Yale University Press, 1988)

Drower, G., *Garden Heroes and Villains* (Stroud: Sutton Publishing Ltd, 2006)

Drucker, Johanna, *The Visible Word: Experimental Typography and Modern Art, 1909-1923* (Chicago: Chicago University Press, 1994)

Dublin University Magazine, 38 (1851), 504-508 'The late Rev. Samuel O'Sullivan'

Dudek, Louis, *Literature and the Press: a History of Printing, Printed Media and their Relation to Literature* (Toronto: Ryerson Press, 1960)

Duff Gordon, Lucie, *Letters from Egypt,* ed. Janet Ross (London: R. Brimley Johnson, 1902)

Duffy, Charles Gavan, *Young Ireland, of Four Years of Irish History, parts I and II* (London: Cassell, 1880-1883)

------, *My Life in Two Hemispheres* (London: Fisher Unwin, 1898)

Duffy, Patrick, *The Skilled Compositor 1850-1914: an Aristocrat among the Working Man* (Aldershot: Ashgate, 2000)

Dunae, Patrick A., '*Boy's Own Paper*: Origins and Editorial Policies', *The Private Library*, s.2, 9.4 (1976), 121-158

------, "Penny Dreadfuls: Late Nineteenth Century Boys' Literature and Crime", *Victorian Studies*, 22.2 (1979), 133-150

Dunn, B. N., *The Man Who Was John Bull: The Biography of Theodore Edward Hook* (London: Allendale, 1996)

Duxbury, Neil, *Frederick Pollock and the English Juristic Tradition* (New York: Oxford University Press, 2004)

Dyck, Ian, *William Cobbett and Rural Popular Culture* (Cambridge: Cambridge University Press, 1992)

Dymond, Robert, 'Trewman's Flying Post', *The Western Antiquary*, 8.5 (January 1886), 163-166

Dzelzainis, Ella, 'Charlotte Elizabeth Tonna, Pre-Millenarianism, and the Formation of Gender Ideology in the Ten Hours Campaign', *Victorian Literature and Culture*, 31 (2003), 181-191

E

Eatwell, John, Murray Milgate and Peter Newman, eds, *The New Palgrave: A Dictionary of Economics*, 4 vols (London: Macmillan, 1987)

Eberle-Sinatra, Michael, *Leigh Hunt and the London Literary Scene: A Reception History of his Major Works, 1805-1828* (New York: Routledge, 2005)

Eckley, Grace, *Maiden Tribute: A Life of W. T. Stead* (Philadelphia: Xlibris 2007)

Eddy, Spencer L., *The Founding of The* Cornhill Magazine (Muncie, IN; Ball State University Press, 1970)

Edel, Leon, and Dan H. Laurence, *A Bibliography of Henry James*, 3rd edn (Oxford: Clarendon, 1982)

Edgecombe, Rodney Stenning, *Leigh Hunt and the Poetry of Fancy* (London: Associated University Presses, 1994)

Edgell, Wyatt Edgell, 'Moral Statistics of the Parishes of St. James, St. George, and St. Anne Soho, in the City of Westminster. Supplementary to the Third Report of the Education Committee of the Statistical Society of London', *Journal of the Statistical Society of London*, 1.8 (Dec. 1838), 478-492

'Editor, An': *How to Write for the Press: A Practical Handbook for Beginners in Journalism* (London: H. Cox, 1899)

Edwards, Charles, 'The New Football Mania', *Nineteenth Century*, 32 (1892), 622-631

Edwards, Eliezer, *Personal Recollections of Birmingham and Birmingham Men* (Birmingham: Midland Educational Trading Co., 1877)

Edwards, John Passmore, *A Few Footprints*, 2nd edn (London: Watts & Co., 1906)

Edwards, Owen Dudley, 'The Catholic Press in Scotland since the Restoration of the Hierarchy', in *Modern Scottish Catholicism 1878*-1978, ed. by David McRoberts (Glasgow: Burns, 1979), 156-182

------, and Patricia J. Storey, 'The Irish Press in Victorian Britain' in *The Irish in the Victorian City*, ed. by Roger Swift and Sheridan Gilley (London: Croom Helm, 1985), 158-178

Edwards, P. D., I.G. Sibley, and M. Versteeg, *Indexes to Fiction in* Belgravia *(1867-1899)*, Victorian Fiction Research Guide, v. 14 (St Lucia: University of Queensland: 1989)

------, *Dickens's 'Young Men': George Augustus Sala, Edmund Yates, and the World of Victorian Journalism* (Aldershot: Ashgate, 1997)

Edwards, Ruth Dudley, *The Pursuit of Reason: The* Economist *1843-1993* (London: Hamish Hamilton, 1993)

Egoff, Sheila, *Children's Periodicals of the Nineteenth Century: A Survey and Bibliography* (London: Library Association, 1951)

Eigner, Edwin, and George J. Worth, eds, *Victorian Criticism of the Novel* (Cambridge: Cambridge University Press, 1985)

Elgar, E., and P. M. Young, eds, *Letters to Nimrod: Edward Elgar to August Jaeger, 1897-1908* (London: D. Dobson, 1965)

------, and P.M. Young, eds, *A Future for English Music and Other Lectures* (London: D. Dobson, 1968)

Eliot, Simon, and John Sutherland, eds, *The* Publisher's Circular *1837-1900: Guide to the Microfiche Edition* (Cambridge: Chadwyck Healey, 1988)

------, *Some Patterns and Trends in British Publishing 1800-1919* (Occasional Papers of the Bibliographical Society, 8 (London: The Bibliographical Society, 1994)

------, 'Hotten: Rotten: Forgotten? An Apologia for a General Publisher', *Book History*, 3 (2000), 61-93

Ellegård, Alvar, *The Readership of the Periodical Press in Mid-Victorian Britain* (Göteborg: Göteborgs universitets årsskrift, 1957), repr. *VPN*, 13 (1971), 3-22

Elliott, Blanche B., *A History of English Advertising* (London: Arrow Books Ltd, 1962)

Ellis, Marie, 'The English Illustrated Magazine' in Cevasco (1993), 190-191

Ellis, S. M., *William Harrison Ainsworth and His Friends*, 2 vols (London: John Lane, 1911)

Ellis, III, Ted R., 'Victorian Comic Journals', Appendix G in Sullivan (1984), 501-518

Ellis, Theodore R., 'Another Broadside into *Mardi*', *American Literature*, 41.3 (November 1969), 419-422

Ellmann, Richard, *Oscar Wilde* (London: Hamish Hamilton, 1987)

Elwin, Malcolm, *Victorian Wallflowers: A Panoramic Survey of the Popular Literary Periodicals* (London: Cape, 1934; repr. New York: Kennikat Press, 1966)

Elwin, Warwick, 'Memoir of Whitwell Elwin' in Whitwell Elwin, *Some XVIII Men of Letters* (London: J. Murray, 1902)

Engels, Friedrich, *The Condition of the Working Class in England* (1845), ed. by David McLellan (Oxford: Oxford University Press, 1993)

Engen, Rodney K., *Randolph Caldecott, 'Lord of the Nursery'* (London: Oresko Books Ltd, 1976)

------, *Dictionary of Victorian Engravers, Print Publishers and Their Works* (Cambridge: Chadwyck-Healey, 1979)

------, *Richard Doyle* (Stroud: Catalpa Press, 1983)

------, *Dictionary of Victorian Wood Engravers* (Cambridge: Chadwyck-Healey, 1985; Aldershot: Scolar Press, 1990)

English, Mary, *Mordecai Cubitt Cooke: Vegetarian, Naturalist, Mycologist, Teacher and Eccentric* (Bristol: Biopress, 1987)

English, Mary P., *Victorian Values: The Life and Times of Dr Edwin Lankester* (Bristol: Biopress, 1990)

Epstein, James, 'Feargus O'Connor and the *Northern Star*', *International Review of Social History*, 21 (1976), 51-97

------, *The Lion of Freedom: Feargus O'Connor and the Chartist Movement, 1832-42* (London: Croom Helm, 1982)

------, *Radical Expression: Political Language, Ritual and Symbol in England, 1790-1850* (Oxford: Oxford University Press, 1994)

Erickson, Lee, 'The Economy of Novel Reading: Jane Austen and the Circulating Library', *Studies in English Literature, 1500-1900*, 30.4 (Autumn, 1990), 573-590

Escott, T. H. S. [Thomas Hay Sweet], *The Masters of English Journalism: a Study of Personal Forces* (London and Leipsic: T. Fisher Unwin, 1911)

------, *Club Makers and Club Members* (New York: Sturgis & Walton, 1914)

------, 'What the Newspaper Owes to the Magazine', *London Quarterly Review*, 128 (July 1917), 62-71

Espinasse, Francis, *Literary Recollections and Sketches* (London: Hodder, 1893)

Espinasse, Margaret, '(Charles) Allen Clarke', in Bellamy and Saville, v. 8 (1987)

Eustace Miles Monthly Booklet (Jan. 1916)

Evans, Joan, *A History of the Society of Antiquaries* (Oxford: Oxford University Press, 1956)

Everett, Edwin M., *The Party of Humanity,* The Fortnightly Review *and Its Contributors, 1865-1874* (Chapel Hill: University of North Carolina Press, 1939)

Everitt, Graham, *English Caricaturists and Graphic Humourists of the Nineteenth Century* (London: Swan Sonnenschein & Co., 1893)

Ewing, A. McLaren, *A History of the Glasgow Herald 1783-1948* (Glasgow, private circulation, 1948)

F

Fader, Daniel, and George Bornstein, *British Periodicals of the 18th and 19th Centuries* (Ann Arbor: University Microfilms, 1972)

Faithfull, Emily, 'The Victoria Press', *English Women's Journal* (Oct. 1860) in Lacey (1987), 281-286

------, 'Women Compositors', *English Woman's Journal* (Sept.1861) in Lacey (1987), 287-292

Farish, William, *Thirty One Years Ago: My First Visit to Chester* (Chester: 1887; pamphlet sold in aid of the Christian Temperance Hall), 1-11

------, *Occasional Articles on Temperance, Politics and Other Subjects, Reprinted form Various Sources* (Liverpool: J. R. Williams, 1890)

Farningham, Marianne, *A Working Woman's Life: An Autobiography* (London: James Clarke, 1907)

Faulkner, Peter, ed., *William Morris: The Critical Heritage* (London: Routledge, 1973)

Fawcett, Millicent Garrett, *What I Remember* (London: T. Fisher Unwin Ltd, 1924)

Faxon, Frederick W., *Literary Annuals and Gift Books: A Bibliography 1823-1903, reprinted with Supplementary Essays by Eleanore Jamieson and Iain Bain* (Boston, MA and Middlesex: Boston Book Co., 1912; Private Libraries Association, 1973)

Fehlbaum, Valerie, *Ella Hepworth Dixon: The Story of a Modern Woman* (Aldershot: Ashgate 2005)

Feltes, N.N., *Modes of Production of Victorian Novels* (Chicago: University of Chicago Press, 1986)

Fennell, Francis, 'George Gilfillan: A Biographical and Critical Study' (unpublished PhD thesis: Northwestern University, 1968)

Fenner, Theodore, *Leigh Hunt and Opera Criticism: The* Examiner *Years, 1808-1821* (Lawrence: University Press of Kansas, 1972)

Fenstermaker, John J., *John Forster* (Boston: Twayne, 1984)

Fenwick Miller F., *Harriet Martineau* (London: WH Allen, 1884)

Ferenczi, Thomas, *L'invention du journalisme en France* (Paris: Plon, 1993)

Ferguson, Joan P.S., *Directory of Scottish Newspapers* (Edinburgh: National Library of Scotland, 1984)

Fetter, F.W., 'The Authorship of Economic Articles in the *Edinburgh Review*, 1802-1847', *Journal of Political Economy*, 61 (June 1953), 232-259

------, 'The Economic Articles in *Blackwood's Edinburgh Magazine* and their Authors, 1817-1853', *Scottish Journal of Political Economy*, 7 (1960), 85-107 and 213-231

Field (23 March 1867), 207, 'Angling: Mr. Ffennell and Mr. Shaw of Drumlanrig'

Field (13 Nov. 1920), 694, 'Rowing: W. B. Woodgate'

Finkelman, Paul, ed., *Encyclopedia of the United States in the Nineteenth Century*, v. 2 (New York: Charles Scribner's Sons, 2001)

Finkelstein, David, *An Index to* Blackwood's Magazine, *1901-1980* (Aldershot: Scolar Press, 1995)

------, *The House of Blackwood: Author-Publisher Relations in the Victorian Era* (University Park, PA: Pennsylvania State University Press, 2002)

------, ed., *Print Culture and the Blackwood Tradition* (Toronto: University of Toronto Press, 2006)

Finn, M., *After Chartism. Class and Nation in English Radical Politics, 1848-1874* (Cambridge: Cambridge University Press, 1993)

Fish, R., 'The Library and Scientific Publications of the Zoological Society of London' in *The Zoological Society of London 1826-1976 and Beyond*, ed. by S. Zuckerman (London: Academic Press, 1976), 233-252

Fisher IV, Benjamin F. 'The Universal Review' in Sullivan (1984), 432-436

------, 'Ella D'Arcy: A Commentary with a Primary and Annotated Secondary Bibliography', *English Literature in Transition 1880-1920*, 35.2 (1992), 179-211

------, 'Ella D'Arcy Reminisces', *English Literature in Transition 1880-1920*, 37.1 (1994), 28-37

------, 'D'Arcy, Ella' in Hammill, et al. (2006), 64-65

Fisher, Judith L., ' "In the Present Famine of Anything Substantial": "Portraits" and the Construction of Literary Celebrity; or "Personality, Personality is the Appetite of the Age"', *VPR*, 39.2 (Summer 2006), 97-135

Fishing Gazette (17 Jan. 1885), 25, 'Death of Mr. Greville Fennell'

Fiske, John, *Edward Livingston Youmans: A Sketch of His Life* (New York: D. Appleton, 1894)

Fitzgerald, Percy H., *Memories of Charles Dickens: With an Account of* Household Words *and* All The Year Round *and of the Contributors Thereto* (Bristol: J. W. Arrowsmith, 1913)

Fitzsimmons, Raymond, *The Baron of Piccadilly: The Travels and Entertainments of Albert Smith, 1816-1860* (London: Bles, 1967)

Fladeland, Betty, *Abolitionists and Working Class Problems in the Age of Industrialization* (London: Macmillan, 1984)

Fleishman, A., *The English Historical Novel: Walter Scott to Virginia Woolf* (Baltimore: John Hopkins University Press, 1971)

Fletcher, Ian, *Rediscovering Herbert Horne: Poet, Architect, Typographer, Art Historian* (Greensboro, NC: ELT Press, 1990)

Fletcher, J. R., 'Early Catholic Periodicals in England', *Dublin Review*, 198 (1936), 284-310

Fletcher, W.G.D., 'Potter, Thomas, Antiquary', *DNB*, 14 (1896, repr. 1973), 223

Flint, Kate, *The Woman Reader 1837-1914* (Oxford: Oxford University Press, 1993)

------, *The Victorians and the Visual Imagination* (Cambridge: University of Cambridge, 2000)

Fodor, Nandor, *Encyclopedia of Psychic Science* (London: Arthurs Press, 1934)

Fogel, Daniel Mark, ed., *A Companion to Henry James Studies* (Westport, CT and London: Greenwood Press, 1993)

Football Association, *The History of the Football Association* (London: Naldrett Press, 1853)

Forbes, Athol, 'My Impressions of Sarah Grand', *Lady's World* (1900), 880-883, repr. in Heilmann and Forward (2000), v.1, 881-883

Foreman, Alfred, 'Chris Hammond: In Memoriam', *Argosy*, 71 (July 1900), 343

Forrest Reid, *Illustrators of the Sixties* (London: Faber and Gwyer, 1928)

Forrester, Wendy, *Great Grandmama's Weekly: A Celebration of the* Girl's Own Paper, *1880-1901* (Guildford and London: Lutterworth Press, 1980)

Forster, John, *The Life of Charles Dickens*, 3 vols [1872-1874], ed. by J. W. T. Ley, (London: Cecil Palmer, 1928)

Forster, Margaret, *Significant Sisters, the Grassroots of Active Feminism 1839-1939* (Harmondsworth: Penguin, 1984)

Forsyth, William, *Selections from the Writings of the late William Forsyth, Editor of the* Aberdeen Journal (Aberdeen: L. Smith, 1882)

Fox, Celina, *Graphic Journalism in England during 1830s and 1840s* (London: Garland, 1988)

Fox, William J., *Lectures, Addressed Chiefly to the Working Classes*, 4 vols (London: 1845-1849)

Francis, John C., *John Francis: A Literary Chronicle of Half a Century*, 2 vols (London: Richard Bentley & Son, 1888)

Fraser, Hilary, Stephanie Green and Judith Johnston, *Gender and the Victorian Periodical* (Cambridge: Cambridge University Press, 2003)

Frawley, Maria, 'The Editor as Advocate: Emily Faithfull and the *Victoria Magazine*', *VPR*, 31.1 (Spring 1998), 87-104

Fredeman, W.E., 'Review of "*The Germ: A Pre-Raphaelite Magazine*", edited and with an introduction by Robert Stahr Hosman', *Victorian Poetry*, 10.1 (1972), 87-94

Freeden, Michael, *The New Liberalism: An Ideology of Social Reform* (Oxford: Clarendon Press, 1978)

Freedman, Jonathan, *Professions of Taste: Henry James, British Aestheticism, and Commodity Culture* (Stanford: Stanford University Press, 1990)

Freeman, John, *Life of the Rev. William Kirby* (London: Longman, Brown, Green, 1852)

Freeman, Michael, *Railways and the Victorian Imagination* (New Haven: Yale University Press, 1999)

Freeman, Sarah, *Isabella and Sam: the Story of Mrs Beeton* (London: Gollancz, 1977)

French, Patrick, *The Life of Henry Norman* (London: Unicron Press, 1995)

Freund, John C., 'Address to the Public', *Dark Blue*, 2 (Feb. 1872), iii-v

Friederichs, Hulda, *The Life of Sir George Newnes, Bart* (London: Cassell and Co., 1911)

Frost, Peter, 'The Literary Periodicals of the Nineties', *Antiquarian Book Monthly Review*, 6 (1979), 467-474

Frost, Thomas, *Forty Years' Recollections: Literary and Political* (London: Samson Low, 1880)

Frost, Thomas, *Reminiscences of a Country Journalist* (London: Ward and Downey, 1886)

Frow, Ruth and Edmund Frow, 'C. Allen Clarke, Lancashire Author', *Eccles and District History Society Newsletter* (1971-1972)

------, eds, *Political Women 1800-1850* (London: Pluto Press, 1989)

Fryckstedt, Monica Correa, 'Charlotte Elizabeth Tonna: A Forgotten Evangelical Writer', *Studia Neophilologica*, 52 (1980), 79-102

------, 'Charlotte Elizabeth Tonna and the *Christian Lady's Magazine*', *VPR*, 14.2 (Summer 1981), 43-51

------, *Geraldine Jewsbury's Athenaeum Reviews: Mirror of Mid-Victorian Attitudes to Fiction* (Uppsala: University of Uppsala, 1983)

------, 'The Hidden Rill: the Life and Career of Maria Jane Jewsbury', *Bulletin of the John Rylands University Library of Manchester*, 66 (1983-1984), 177-203, and 67 (1984-1985), 450-473

Fulmer, Constance M., 'Edith Simcox: Feminist Critic and Reformer', *VPR*, 31.1 (Spring 1998), 105-121

------, and Margaret E. Barfield, eds, *A Monument to the Memory of George Eliot: Edith J. Simcox's Autobiography of a Shirtmaker* (New York: Garland, 1998)

Fulton, Richard D. and C. M. Colee, eds, *A Union List of Victorian Serials available in United States and Canadian Libraries* (New York and London: Garland, 1985)

Furniss, Harry, *The Confessions of a Caricaturist* (London: T. Fisher Unwin, 1901)

Fyfe, Aileen, *Science and Salvation: Evangelical Popular Science Publishing in Victorian Britain* (Chicago: University of Chicago Press, 2004)

------, 'Information Revolution: William Chambers, the Publishing Pioneer', *Endeavour*, 30.4 (2006), 120-125

Fyfe, Hamilton, *Sixty Years of Fleet Street* (London: W.H. Allen & Co., 1949)

G

Galtung, J. and Ruge, M., 'The Structure of Foreign News: the Presentation of the Congo, Cuba and Cyprus Crises in Four Norwegian Newspapers', *Journal of International Peace Research*, 1 (1965), 64-91

Gardham, Julie, *The World of Chaucer: Medieval Books and Manuscripts: Catalogue of an Exhibition of Manuscripts and Early Printed Books from Glasgow University Library* (Glasgow: Glasgow University Library, 2004)

Gardener's Magazine, 14, (1838), 'The Botanical Periodicals and their Illustrations'

Gardener's Magazine, 15 (1839), 90-91, 'The Botanical Periodicals'

Gardiner, Leslie, *The Making of John Menzies* (Edinburgh: John Bartholomew and Son, 1983)

Garlick, Barbara and Margaret Harris, eds, *Victorian Journalism: Exotic and Domestic: Essays in Honour of P.D. Edwards* (St Lucia: Queensland University Press, 1998)

Garnett, Richard, concluded by Edward Garnett, *The Life of W. J. Fox, Public Teacher and Social reformer, 1786-1864* (London and New York: John Lane, John Lane Co., 1910)

Garratt, Morris, *Samuel Bamford Portrait of a Radical* (Littleborough: Kelsall, 1992)

Garrett, Albert, *A History of Wood Engraving* (London: Midas Books, 1978)

Garrett, William, *Charles Wentworth Dilke* (Boston: Twayne, 1982)

Gascoigne, Bamber, *Milestones in Colour Printing, 1450-1850* (Cambridge: Cambridge University Press, 1997)

Gasson, Andrew, *Wilkie Collins: An Illustrated Guide* (Oxford: Oxford University Press, 1998)

Gates, Eleanor M., ed., *Leigh Hunt: a Life in Letters* (Essex, CT: Falls Rivers Publications, 1998)

Gatty, Margaret, *Parables from Nature* (London: Bell and Daldy, 1880)

Gauld, Alan, *The Founders of Psychical Research* (London: Routledge, 1968)

Gavine, David, 'Thomas Dick, LL.D., 1774-1857', *Journal of the British Astronomical Association*, 84 (1974), 345-350

Gennard, John, *A History of the National Graphical Association* (London: Unwin Hyman, 1990)

Gentleman's Magazine (26 Jan. 1825), 'Obituary-Tilloch, Alexander' LL.D.'

------, 441 (Sept.1855), 322-323, 'Obituary-James Silk Buckingham, Esq.'

George, M.D., review of F. Beckwith, *Account of the Leeds Intelligencer, 1754-1866* in *English Historical Review*, 71 (Jan. 1956), 165-166

Gernsheim, Helmut with Alison Gernsheim, *The History of Photography from the Camera Obscura to the Beginning of the Modern Era* (London: Thames and Hudson, 1969)

Gerrard, Teresa, 'New Methods in the History of Reading: "Answers to Correspondents" in the *Family Herald*, 1860-1900', *Publishing History*, 43 (1998), 52-69

Gettmann, Royal A., *A Victorian Publisher. A Study of the Bentley Papers* (Cambridge: Cambridge University Press, 1960)

Gibbs, A.M., *A Bernard Shaw Chronology* (Basingstoke: Macmillan, 2000)

Gibson, Alfred and William Pickford, *Association Football and the Men who Made It*, 2 vols (London: Caxton, 1906)

Gidumal, Dayaram, *The Life and Life-Work of Behramji M. Malabari* (Bombay: Education Society's Press, 1888)

Gifford, Dennis, *The British Comic Catalogue, 1874-1974* (Westport, CT: Greenwood Press, 1975a)

------, *Happy Days: a Century of Comics* (London: Jupiter, 1975b)

------, *Victorian Comics* (London: George Allen and Unwin, 1976)

------, 'Ally Sloper: The Legendary Cartoon Character Celebrates the 100th Anniversary of his Comic this Year', *Book and Magazine Collector*, 3 (May 1984), 37-43

Gilbert, Pamela, Aeron Haynie and Marlene Tromp, eds, *Beyond Sensation: Mary Elizabeth Braddon in Context* (Albany: State University of New York Press, 2000)

Gildart, Keith, David Howell, Neville Kirk, eds, *Dictionary of Labour Biography*, v. 11 (Basingstoke: Palgrave Macmillan, 2003), 17-24

Gilfillan, George, 'Tennyson', from *A Gallery of Literary Portraits* (London: J. M. Dent and Co., 1909), xxx

Gillespie, C.C., ed., *Dictionary of Scientific Biography*, 16 vols (New York: Charles Scribner's Sons, 1970-1980)

Glage, Liselotte, *Clementina Black* (Heidelberg: Carl Winter, 1981)

Glanville, Williams, *Learning the Law* (London: Stevens & Co., 1963)

Glasgow, Eric, 'Publishing in Victorian England', *Library Review*, 47.8 (1998), 395-400

Glasgow Herald (5 Sept. 1891) 4, 'Death of Mr. Joseph Irving, F. S. A. Scot'

Gleadle, Kathryn, *The Early Feminists: Radical Unitarians and the Emergence of the Women's Rights Movement, 1831-51* (Basingstoke: Macmillan, 1995)

------, 'Charlotte Elizabeth Tonna and the Mobilization of Tory Women in Early Victorian England', *Historical Journal*, 50.1 (2007), 97-117

Gliddon, Paul Martin, 'The North of England Newspaper Company, 1903-1939: the Declining Political Importance of a Liberal Newspaper Company' (unpublished PhD thesis: University of Newcastle, 2000)

Gliserman, Susan, 'Mitchell's Newspaper Press Directory: 1846-1907', *VPN*, 4 (1969), 10-30

Glynn, Jennifer, *Prince of Publishers: A Biography of George Smith* (London and New York: Allison and Busby, 1986)

Goldman, Lawrence, *Science, Reform and Politics in Victorian Britain. The Social Science Association 1857-1886* (Cambridge: Cambridge University Press, 2002)

Goldman, Paul, *Victorian Illustrated Books 1850-1870* (London: British Museum Press, 1994)

------, *Victorian Illustration: The Pre-Raphaelites, the Idyllic School and the High Victorians* (Aldershot: Scolar Press, 1996)

Goldstein, D. S., 'The Role of Historical Journals in the Professionalization of History in England, 1886-1923', *Tijdschrift voor Geschiedenis*, 99 (1986), 591-605

Gooday, Graeme, ' "I never will have the electric light in my house": Alice Gordon and the Gendered Periodical Representation of a Contentious New Technology' (2004a) in Henson, Cantor, et al. (2004)

------, 'Profit and Prophecy: Electricity in the Late Victorian Periodical' (2004b) in Cantor, Dawson, Gooday, et al. (2004), 238-254

Goodbody, John, 'The *Star*' in Wiener (1988a), 143-163

Goodway, David, *London Chartism, 1838-1848* (Cambridge: Cambridge University Press, 1982)

Gordon, B.J., *Economic Doctrine and Tory Liberalism 1824-1830* (London: Macmillan, 1979)

Gordon, Margaret Maria, *The Home Life of Sir David Brewster* (Edinburgh: Edmonston and Douglas, 1869)

Gordon, Peter and Doughan, David, *Dictionary of British Women's Organizations 1825-1960* (London: Woburn Press, 2001)

Gourlay, James, 'Notes on the life of John Mennons' in Ewing (1948)

Graham, Walter, *English Literary Periodicals* (New York: Nelson, 1930)

Grant, James, *The Great Metropolis* (London: Saunders and Otley, 1837)

Grant, James, *The Newspaper Press: its Origin, Progress, and Present Position.* 3 vols (London: Tinsley Bros, 1871-1872)

Grass, Tim, *Gathering to His Name: The Story of Brethren in Britain and Ireland* (Milton Keynes: Paternoster, 2006)

Grattan-Guinness, Ivor, ed., *Psychical Research. A Guide to its History, Principles and Practices* (Wellingborough: The Aquarian Press, 1982)

Gratton, Charles J., *The Gallery: a Sketch of the History of Parliamentary Reporting and Reporters* (London: Pitman, 1860)

Graves, Alfred Percival, *To Return to All That* (London: Jonathan Cape, 1930)

Graves, Charles. L., *The Life and Letters of Sir George Grove* (London: Macmillan, 1903)

Gray, Donald J., 'A List of Comic Periodicals Published in Great Britain, 1800-1900, with a Prefatory Essay', *VPN*, 15 (March, 1972), 2-39

------, 'Early Victorian Scandalous Journalism: Renton Nicholson's *The Town* (1837-1842)' in Shattock and Wolff (1982), 317-348

Gray, Valerie, *Charles Knight: Educator, Publisher, Writer* (Aldershot: Ashgate, 2006)

Grayling, A. C., *The Quarrel of the Age: The Life and Times of William Hazlitt* (London: Weidenfeld & Nicolson, 2000)

Green, Benny, ed., *Wisden Anthology 1864-1900* (London: Queen Anne Press, 1979)

Green, Roger Lancelyn, *Andrew Lang: A Critical Biography with a Short-Title Bibliography of the Works of Andrew Lang* (Worthing, West Sussex: Littlehampton Book Service (LBS), 1946)

Green, Samuel G., *The Story of the Religious Tract Society* (London: Religious Tract Society, 1899)

Green, Stephanie, 'Oscar Wilde's *The Woman's World*', *VPR*, 30.2 (1997), 102-118

Greenslade, William, ed., *Thomas Hardy's 'Facts' Notebook: A Critical Edition* (Aldershot: Ashgate, 2004)

------, and Terence Rodgers, *Grant Allen: Literature and Cultural Politics at the Fin de Siècle* (Aldershot: Ashgate, 2005)

Greenwood, James ('Amateur Casual'), *The Seven Curses of London* (London: Stanley Rivers, 1869)

Gregory, Troy, 'Mr. Jorrock's Lost Sporting Magazine', *VPR,* 36.4 (Winter 2003), 331-349

Grenby, M. O., '"A Conservative Woman Doing Radical Things": Sarah Trimmer and the Guardian of Education' in *Culturing the Child 1690-1914: Essays in Memory of Mitzi Myers, Donelle Ruwe,* ed. by Donelle Ruwe (Lanham: Children's Literature Association & Scarecrow Press, 2005), 137-161

Grenier, Janet E., 'Clementina Black: Working Women and the Trade Board Act of 1909' (unpublished MSc. dissertation: London School of Economics, 1986)

Griest, Guinevere L., 'A Victorian Leviathan: Mudie's Select Library', *Nineteenth-Century Fiction,* 20.2 (1965), 103-126

Griffiths, Dennis, *The Encyclopedia of the British Press: 1422-1992* (Basingstoke: Macmillan, 1992)

------, *Plant Here The Standard* (Basingstoke: Macmillan, 1996)

------, *Fleet Street: Five Hundred Years of the Press* (London: British Library, 2006)

Grimstone, Mary Leman (pseud. 'Oscar'), *A Spanish Tale in Three Cantos; and Other Poems, Stanzas and Canzonets* (London: Whittaker, 1820)

------, *Cleone, Summer's Sunset Vision, The Confession: with Other Poems & Stanzas* (London: Whittaker, 1821)

------, *Woman's Love, a Novel* (London: Saunders & Otley, 1832)

------, *Characters; Or, Jew and Gentile; a Tale in Two Volumes.* (London: Fox, 1833)

------, *Cleone, a Tale of Married Life* (London: Wilson, 1834)

Gross, John, *The Rise and Fall of the Man of Letters: English Literary Life since 1800* (London: Weidenfeld & Nicolson, 1969)

[Grove] *New Grove Dictionary of Music and Musicians,* ed. by Stanley Sadie, 29 vols (London: Macmillan, 2001)

Growoll, Adolf and Wilberforce Eames, *Three Centuries of English Book Trade Bibliography* (New York: The Dibdin Club, 1903)

Grugel, Lee E., *George Jacob Holyoake: A Study in the Evolution of a Victorian Radical* (Philadelphia: Porcupine Press, 1976)

Gullette, Margaret Morganroth, 'Afterword' to Mona Caird, *The Daughters of Danaus* (New York: Feminist Press, 1980), 493-539

Gunn, Peter, *Vernon Lee: Violet Paget, 1856-1935* (London: Oxford University Press, 1964)

Gunn, S., *The Public Culture of the Victorian Middle Class: Ritual and Authority and the English Industrial City, 1840-1914* (Manchester: Manchester University Press, 2000)

Gurjeva, L. G., 'James Sully and Scientific Psychology, 1870-1910' in *Psychology in Britain: Historical Essays and Personal Reflections,* ed. by G. C. Bunn, A. D. Lovie, and G. D. Richards (Leicester: British Psychological Society, 2001), 72-94

Gurney, Peter, *Co.-operative Culture and the Politics of Consumption in England, 1870-1930* (Manchester: Manchester University Press, 1996)

------, 'Working-Class Writers and the Art of Escapology in Victorian England: The Case of Thomas Frost', *Journal of British Studies*, 45 (2006), 51-71

Gutch, J. M., 'Memoir of the Late Rev. John Eagles' in *A Garland of Roses*, ed. by John Eagles (Worcester: Blackwood & Sons, 1857)

Gutteridge, L. E. S., 'A History of Wisden', *Wisden Cricketers' Almanack Centenary Edition* (London: Sporting Handbooks, 1963)

Gwynn, Stephen and Gertrude M. Tuckwell, *The Life of the Rt. Hon. Sir Charles W. Dilke*, 2 vols (London: John Murray, 1917)

------, *Experiences of a Literary Man* (London: Butterworth, 1926)

H

Haar, Charles M., 'E. L. Youmans: A Chapter in the Diffusion of Science in America', *Journal of the History of Ideas*, 9 (1948), 193-213

Habermas, Jürgen, *The Structural Transformation of the Public Sphere* (Cambridge: Polity Press, 1989)

Hackwood, F.W., *William Hone: His Life and Times* (New York; Augustus M. Kelley, 1970)

Haddelsey, Stephen, *Charles Lever: The Lost Victorian* (Gerard's Cross, Bucks: Colin Smythe, 2000)

Hadland, Tony, *The Sturmey-Archer Story* (Birmingham: Pinkerton Press, 1987)

Haight, Gordon S., *George Eliot and John Chapman* (London: Archon Books, 1940 and 1969, 2nd rev. edn)

------, ed., *George Eliot Letters*, 9 vols (Yale: New Haven University Press, 1954-1978)

Hailstone, Alf, *The British Bandsman Centenary Book: A Social History of Brass Bands* (Baldock, Herts.: Egon Publishers, 1987)

Haining, Peter, *Sweeney Todd* (London: Boxtree, 1993)

Halévy, Elie, *The Growth of Philosophic Radicalism*, trans. by Mary Morris (London: Faber & Faber Ltd, 1928, 1934)

Hall, S. C., *Retrospect of a Long Life, from 1815 to 1883*, 2 vols (London: Richard Bentley and Son, 1883)

Hall, Wayne E., 'Attribution Problems: the *Wellesley Index* vs. the *Dublin University Magazine*', *Long Room*, 36 (1991), 29-34

------, *Dialogues in the Margin: a Study of the* Dublin University Magazine (Washington, DC: Catholic University of America Press, 1999)

Halstead, John, ' "*The Voice of the West Riding*": Promoters and Supporters of a Provincial Unstamped Newspaper, 1833-34' in *On the Move: Essays in Labour and Transport History Presented to Philip Bagwell*, ed. by C. Wrigley and J. Shepherd (London: Hambledon Press, 1991)

Hamber, Anthony J., *'A Higher Branch of the Arts': Photographing the Fine Arts in England, 1839-1880* (Australia and United Kingdom; Gordon and Breach, 1996; New York: Routledge, 1996)

Hamblyn, Richard, *The Invention of Clouds: How an Amateur Meteorologist Forged the Language of the Skies* (New York: Farrar, Straus and Giroux, 2002)

Hamburger, Lotte and Joseph, *Contemplating Adultery: The Secret Life of a Victorian Woman* (New York and London: Fawcett Columbine, 1991, 1992)

Hamer, David Allan, *John Morley: Liberal Intellectual in Politics* (Oxford: Clarendon Press, 1968)

Hamerton, Eugénie, *Philip Gilbert Hamerton; An Autobiography, 1834-1858, and a Memoir by his Wife, 1858-1894* (Boston: Roberts Brothers, 1896; London: Seeley and Co., 1897)

Hamerton, John Alexander, *The Child of Wonder: an Intimate Biography of Arthur Mee* (London: Hodder and Stoughton, 1946)

Hammill, Faye, Esme Miskimmin and Ashlie Sponenberg, eds, *Encyclopedia of British Women's Writing 1900-1950* (Basingstoke: Palgrave Macmillan, 2006)

Hamilton, Susan, *Frances Power Cobbe and Victorian Feminism* (Basingstoke and New York: Palgrave Macmillan, 2006)

Hamlyn, D. W., 'A Hundred Years of Mind', *Mind,* n.s. 85.337 (1976), 1-5

Hampton, Mark, 'Journalists and the "Professional Ideal" in Britain, 1884-1907', *Historical Research,* 72 (1999), 183-201

------, *Visions of the Press in Britain, 1850-1950* (Chicago: University of Illinois Press, 2004)

Hancock, William Neilson, 'Obituary Notice of the Late Alexander Thom, Esq. J. P., Queen's Printer in Ireland, a Vice-President of the Statistical and Social Inquiry Society of Ireland', *Journal of the Statistical and Social Inquiry Society of Ireland,* 7.56 (1879/1880), 5-8

Hannabus, C. Stuard, 'Nineteenth Century Religious Periodicals for Children', *British Journal of Religious Education,* 6.1 (1983), 20-40

Hansen, Peter H., 'Albert Smith, the Alpine Club, and the Invention of Mountaineering in Mid-Victorian Britain', *Journal of British Studies,* 34 (1995), 300-24

Hapgood, R., ' "His Heart Upon His Sleeve": Clement Scott as a Reviewer of Shakespearean Productions', *Jahrbuch Deutsche Shakespeare-Gesellschaft West* (1967), 70-82

Harcup, T. and D. O'Neill, 'What is News? Galtung and Ruge Revisited', *Journalism Studies,* 2.2 (2001), 261-280

Harle, W. L. 'John Forster, a Sketch', *Monthly Chronicle of North Country Lore and Legend,* 2 (1888), 50-54

Harling, Philip, 'Leigh Hunt's *Examiner* and the Language of Patriotism', *English Historical Review,* 111.444 (1996), 1159-1187

Harper, Norman, *Press and Journal: The First 250 Years 1848-1998* (Aberdeen: Aberdeen Journals, 1998)

Harris, Janice Hubbard, *Edwardian Tales of Divorce* (New Brunswick, JN: Rutgers University Press, 1996)

Harris, M., 'London's Local Newspapers: Patterns of Change in the Victorian Period' in Brake, Jones and Madden (1990), 104-119

Harris, Margaret and Judith Johnstone, eds, *Journals of George Eliot* (Cambridge: Cambridge University Press, 1998)

Harris, Michael and Alan Lee, eds, *The Press in English Society from the Seventeenth to the Nineteenth Centuries* (Rutherford, NJ: Farleigh Dickinson University Press, 1986)

Harrison, Brian, 'A World of which we had no Conception', *Victorian Studies*, 13 (Dec. 1969), 125-158

------, *Drink and the Victorians: the Temperance Question in England, 1815-1872* (London: Faber & Faber, 1971)

Harrison, Frederic, *The Creed of a Layman: Apologia Pro Fide Mea* (London: Macmillan, 1907)

Harrison, J. F. C., *Robert Owen and the Owenites in Britain and America* (London: Routledge and Kegan Paul, 1969; New York, Scribner, 1969)

------, and Dorothy Thompson, eds, *Bibliography of the Chartist Movement* (Hassocks: Harvester, 1978)

------, 'Early Victorian Radicals and the Medical Fringe' in *Medical Fringe and Medical Orthodoxy 1750-1850*, ed. by W.F. Bynum and R. Porter (London: Croom Helm, 1987), 198-215

Harrison, Mark, *Crowds and History: Mass Phenomena in English Towns 1790-1835* (Cambridge: Cambridge University Press, 1988)

Harrison, Royden, Gillian B. Woolven, and Robert Duncan, *The Warwick Guide to British Labour Periodicals, 1790-1970: A Checklist* (Sussex: Harvester Press, 1977)

Harrison, Stanley, *Poor Men's Guardians: A Record of the Struggles for a Democratic Newspaper Press, 1763-1973* (London: Lawrence and Wishart, 1974)

Hart, James D. and Philip Leininger, *Oxford Companion to American Literature* (Oxford: Oxford University Press, 1995)

Harvey, Adrian, *The Beginnings of a Commercial Sporting Culture in Britain, 1793-1850* (Aldershot: Ashgate, 2004)

Harvey, David, *A Brief History of Neoliberalism* (Oxford: Oxford University Press, 2005)

Harvey, Joy and Marilyn Ogilvie, *The Biographical Dictionary of Women in Science* (London: Taylor and Francis, 2000)

Harvey, William, *Printing in Stirling. Charles Randall and His Successors. The Story of the* Stirling Observer (Stirling: Jamieson and Munro, 1923)

Hattersley, Roy, *Blood & Fire: William and Catherine Booth and their Salvation Army* (London: Little, Brown, 1999)

Hatton, Joseph, *Journalistic London. Being a Series of Sketches of Famous Pens and Papers of the Day, Profusely Illustrated with Engravings from Drawings by M.W. Ridley; together with Many Original Portraits of Distinguished Editors, and Writers for The Press*, (London: Sampson, Low1882; repr. Routledge/ Thoemmes Press, 1998)

Havighurst, Alfred F., *Radical Journalist: H.W. Massingham (1860-1924)* (Cambridge: Cambridge University Press, 1974)

Hawes, Donald, 'Thackeray and the *National Standard*', *Review of English Studies*, n.s. 23.89 (Feb. 1972), 35-51

Hayley, Barbara, 'Irish Periodicals from Union to the Nation', *Anglo-Irish Studies*, 2 (1976), 83-108

------, *A Bibliography of the Writings of William Carleton* (Gerrards Cross: Colin Smythe, 1985)

------, 'A Reading and Thinking Nation: Periodicals as the Voice of Nineteenth-Century Ireland' in *300 years of Irish Periodicals*, ed. by Barbara Hayley and Enda McKay (Dublin: Association of Irish Learned Journals, 1987), 29-47

Hayter, Alethea, *Charlotte Yonge* (Plymouth: Northcote House, 1996)

Haywood, Ian, *The Revolution in Popular Literature: Print, Politics, and the People, 1790-1860* (Cambridge: Cambridge University Press, 2004)

Hazell, R. C., *Walter Hazell, 1843-1919* (London: Hodder & Stoughton, 1919)

Hazlitt, William, *A Letter to William Gifford Esq.* (London: John Miller, 1819)

------, *The Spirit of the Age, or, Contemporary Portraits* (London: Henry Colburn, 1825)

Head, F.B., 'The Printer's Devil', *Quarterly Review*, 65 (Dec. 1839), 1-30

Heald, Morrell, *Transatlantic Vistas: American Journalists in Europe, 1900-1940* (Kent, Ohio: Kent State University Press, 1988)

Healey, R.M., 'Ward, Lock and Company' in Anderson and Rose (1991), 321-327

Hedderwick, James, *Backward Glances, or, Some Personal Recollections* (Edinburgh, William Blackwood, 1891)

Heilmann, Ann, ed., *Marriage and Motherhood*, v. 1 of *The Late-Victorian Marriage Question: A Collection of Key New Woman Texts* (London: Routledge Thoemmes, 1998)

------, and Stephanie Forward, eds, *Social Purity and Sarah Grand*, 4 vols (London: Routledge, 2000)

------, *New Woman Strategies: Sarah Grand, Olive Schreiner, Mona Caird* (Manchester: Manchester University Press, 2004)

Held, David, Anthony McGrew, David Goldblatt and Jonathan Perraton, 'The Shape of Contemporary Globalisation' in *Global Transformations* (Oxford: Polity Press, 1999), 414-444

Helfand, W. H., 'James Morison and his Pills', *Transactions of British Society for the History of Pharmacy*, 1 (1970-77), 101-35

Helmreich, Anne, 'The Art Dealer and Taste: The Case of David Croal Thomson and the Goupil Gallery, 1885-1897', *Visual Culture in Britain*, 6 (2005), 31-49

Henderson, James P., 'The Whewell Group of Mathematical Economists' in *William Whewell (1794-1866), Dionysius Lardner (1793-1859), Charles Babbage (1792-1871)*, ed. by Mark Blaug (Aldershot: Edward Elgar, 1991), 228-255

Hendrix, Richard, 'Popular Humor and *The Black Dwarf*', *Journal of British Studies*, 16.1 (1976), 108-128

Henson, Louise, Geoffrey Cantor, Gowan Dawson, Richard Noakes, Sally Shuttleworth and Jonathan R. Topham, eds, *Culture and Science in the Nineteenth-Century Media* (Aldershot: Ashgate, 2004)

Herbert, Trevor, ed., *The British Brass Band: A Musical and Social History* (Oxford: Oxford University Press, 2000)

Herbert, T., and G. E. Jones, eds, *People and Protest: Wales 1815-1880* (Cardiff: University of Wales Press, 1988)

Herd H., *The March of Journalism: the Story of the British Press from 1622 to the Present Day* (London: George Allen & Unwin Ltd, 1952)

Herlihy, David V., *Bicycle: The History* (New Haven: Yale University Press, 2004)

Herstein, Sheila, *A Mid-Victorian Feminist, Barbara Leigh Smith Bodichon* (New Haven: Yale University Press, 1985)

------, 'The Langham Place Circle and Feminist Periodicals of the 1860s', *VPR*, 26.1 (1993), 24-27

Higgins, David, *Romantic Genius and the Literary Magazine: Biography, Celebrity and Politics* (London: Routledge, 2005)

Higginson, A. Henry, *British and American Sporting Authors: Their Writings and Biographies* (London: Hutchinson, 1951)

Higgit, Rebekah, ' "*Newton dépossédé!*": The British Response to the Pascal Forgeries of 1867', *British Journal for the History of Science*, 36 (2003), 437-453

Hiller, Mary Ruth, '*The Eclectic Review*: 1805-1868', *VPR*, 27 (1994), 179-278

Hilton, Matthew, *Smoking in British Popular Culture 1800-2000: Perfect Pleasures* (Manchester: Manchester University Press, 2000)

Himmelfarb, Gertrude, *Lord Acton: a Study in Conscience and Politics* (London: Routledge & Kegan Paul, 1952)

Hindle, Wilfred, *The* Morning Post: *1772-1937, Portrait of a Newspaper* (London: Routledge, 1937)

Hindley, Charles, *Curiosities of Street Literature* (London: Reeves and Turner, 1871)

Hirsch, Pam, *Barbara Leigh Smith Bodichon, 1827-1891: Feminist, Artist and Rebel* (London: Chatto and Windus, 1998)

Hirshfield, Claire, '*Truth*', in Sullivan (1984), 423-432

Hobsbawm, E. J., *Labour's Turning Point, 1880-1900* (Brighton: Harvester, 1974)

Hobson, Harold, Phillip Knightly and Leonard Russell, *The Pearl of Days: An Intimate Memoir of the* Sunday Times, *1822-1972* (London: Hamish Hamilton, 1972)

Hodgson, G.B., *From Smithy to Senate: The Life Story of James Annand* (London, Cassell, 1908)

Hodgson, W.B. and H.G. Slack, eds, *Memorial Edition of Collected Works of W. J. Fox*, 12 vols (London: C. Fox and Trubner & Co., 1865-1868)

Hoey, Christopher Clinton, 'Notes on the Rise and Progress of Printing and Publishing in Ireland', *Irish Builder* (15 April 1878)

Hogan, Robert, ed., *Dictionary of Irish Literature* (Basingstoke: Macmillan, 1980)

------, ed., *Dictionary of Irish Literature: Revised and Expanded Edition*, 2 vols (Westport, CT: Greenwood Press, 1996)

Hogben, J., *Richard Holt Hutton of* The Spectator: *a Monograph* (Edinburgh: Oliver and Boyd, 1899)

Hoggart, P. R., 'Edward Lloyd, the Father of the Cheap Press', *The Dickensian,* 80 (1984), 33-38

Holcomb, Adele M., 'Anna Jameson: The First Professional English Art Historian', *Art History,* 6 (1983), 171-187

Holden, W. Sprague, *Australia Goes to Press* (Detroit: Wayne State University Press, 1961)

Holland, John and Everett, James, *Memoirs of the Life and Writing of James Montgomery,* Vols 1-7 (London: Longman, Brown, Green and Longmans, 1855-1856)

Holland, Merlin and Rupert Hart-Davis, *The Complete Letters of Oscar Wilde* (London: Fourth Estate, 2000)

Holland, Vyvyan, *Hand Coloured Fashion Plates, 1770-1899* (London: Batsford, 1988)

Hollingshead, John, 'Fifty Years of Household Words', *Household Words* 'Jubilee Number' (May 1900)

Hollis, Patricia, *The Pauper Press, A Study in the Working-Class Radicalism of the 1830s* (Oxford: Oxford University Press, 1970)

Holme, Bryan, 'Introduction', *The* Studio: *A Bibliography. The First Fifty Years, 1893-1943* (London: Sims & Reed Ltd., 1978)

Holme, Charles Geoffrey. 'Art History in the Making. The Pioneer Work of the *Studio* – for Forty Years the World's Art Magazine', *Studio,* 105.481 (April 1933), 207-209

Holmes, Richard, *Shelley: The Pursuit* (London: Weidenfeld & Nicolson, 1974)

Holyoake, George J., *60 Years of an Agitator's Life* (London: Unwin, 1872)

------, 'The Field of Action', *Secular Review* (6 Aug. 1876)

Hone, William, *The Three Trials of William Hone, for Publishing Three Parodies* (London: William Hone, 1818)

Hooker, J. D., 'A Sketch of the Life and Labours of Sir William Jackson Hooker', *Annals of Botany,* 16 (1902), lx-ccxxi

Hopkin, Deian, 'The Socialist Press in Britain, 1880-1910' in Boyce, Curran and Wingate (1977), 295-306

------, 'The Labour Party Press' in *The First Labour Party 1906-14,* ed. by K. D. Brown, (Beckenham: Croom Helm, 1985), 105-28

------, 'The Left-Wing Press and the New Journalism' in Wiener (1988a)

------, 'The Price of Politics: Financing the Left Wing Press, 1880-1914' in *Recognitions: Essays presented to Professor Edmund Fryde, FBA,* ed. by Colin Richmond and Isobel Harvey (Aberystwyth: National Library of Wales, 1996), 537-574

Hosmon, Robert Stahr, ed., *The Germ: A Pre-Raphaelite Little Magazine* (Coral Gables: University of Miami Press, 1970)

Houfe, Simon, *Dictionary of Nineteenth-Century British Book Illustrators* (Woodbridge: Antique Collectors' Club, 1978)

------, *The Dictionary of British Book Illustrators and Caricaturists 1800-1914* (Woodbridge: Antique Collectors' Club, 1978; revised edn 1981, 1996)

------, 'David Croal Thomson's Whistler's Aid-de-Camp', *Apollo,* 119 (February 1984), 112-119

------, *Fin de Siècle: The Illustrators of the Nineties* (London: Barries and Jenkins, 1992)

Houghton, Bernard, *Scientific Periodicals: Their Historical Development, Characteristics and Control* (London: Clive Bingley, 1975)

Houghton, Ester, 'John Verschoyle and the *Fortnightly Review*', *VPN*, 3 (Nov. 1968), 17-21

Houghton, Walter E. et al., eds, *The Wellesley Index to Victorian Periodicals, 1824-1900* (Toronto: University of Toronto Press, 1966)

Houseman, Lorna, *The House that Thomas Built: The Story of De La Rue* (London: Chatto and Windus, 1968)

Houtchens, L.H. and C.W. Houtchens, eds, *Leigh Hunt's Dramatic Criticism 1808-1831* (New York: Columbia University Press, 1949)

Howe, Bea, *Lady with Green Fingers, the Life of Jane Loudon* (London: Country Life, 1961)

Howitt, Harold, *The History of the Institute of Chartered Accountants in England and Wales 1870 to 1965* (London: Heinemann, 1966; repr. New York/London: Garland, 1984)

Howitt, Margaret, ed., *Mary Howitt. An Autobiography* (London: Wm Isbister, 1889)

Howsam, Leslie, *Kegan Paul: A Victorian Imprint: Publishers, Books and Cultural History* (London: Kegan Paul 1998)

------, 'Academic Discipline or Literary Genre? The Establishment of Boundaries in Historical Writing', *Victorian Literature and Culture*, 32 (2004), 525-545

Huddleston, Joan, comp., *Sarah Grand: A Bibliography*, Victorian Fiction Research Guides, 1 (St Lucia, Queensland: Dept. of English, University of Queensland, 1979)

Hudleston, C. Roy, 'John Evans of Bristol', *Transactions of the Bristol and Gloucester Archaeological Society* (1939), 61

Hudson, Derek, *Thomas Barnes of* The Times (Cambridge: University Press, 1943)

Hudson, Frederic, *Journalism in the United States* (New York: Harper & Bros, 1873)

Hueffer, Francis, *Musical Studies* (Edinburgh: Adam and Charles Black, 1880)

Huett, Lorna, 'Among the Unknown Public: *Household Words, All the Year Round* and the Mass-Market Weekly Periodical in the Mid-Nineteenth Century', *VPR*, 38 (2005), 61-82

Huggins, Mike, *Flat Racing and British Society, 1790-1914: A Social and Economic History* (London: Frank Cass, 2000)

------, and J. A. Mangan, *Disreputable Pleasures: Less Virtuous Victorians at Play* (London: Routledge, 2004)

------, *The Victorians and Sport* (London: Hambledon and London, 2004)

Hughes, Kathryn, *The Short Life and Long Times of Mrs. Beeton* (London, Fourth Estate, 2005)

Hughes, Linda K., 'Textual/Sexual Pleasure and Serial Publication' in Jordan and Patten (1995), 143-164

------, 'A Female Aesthete at the Helm: *Sylvia's Journal* and "Graham R. Thomson", 1893-1894', *VPR*, 29.2 (1996), 173-192

------, 'Women Poets and Contested Spaces in the *Yellow Book*', *Studies in English Literature*, 44.4 (2004), 849-872

------, and Michael Lund, *The Victorian Serial* (Charlottesville: University Press of Virginia, 1991)

------, and R. Graham, *Rosamund Marriott Watson, Woman of Letters* (Athens, OH: Ohio University Press, 2005)

------, ' "A Club of Their Own": New Women Writers, and Fin-de-siècle Authorship', *Victorian Literature and Culture*, 35 (2007a), 233-260

------, 'What the *Wellesley Index* Left Out: Why Poetry Matters to Periodical Studies', *VPR*, 40.2 (Summer 2007b), 91-125

Hughes Meirion, and Robert A. Stradling, *The English Musical Renaissance 1840-1940: Constructing a National Music* (Manchester: Manchester University Press, 2001)

------, *The English Musical Renaissance and the Press, 1850-1914: Watchmen of Music* (Aldershot: Ashgate, 2002)

Hugman, Joan, ' "A Small Drop of Ink": Tyneside Chartism and the *Northern Liberator*' in *The Chartist Legacy*, ed. by Owen R. Ashton, R. Fyson and S. Roberts (London: Merlin Press, 1999), 24-47

------, 'Print and Preach: The Entrepreneurial Spirit of Newcastle upon Tyne' in *Newcastle upon Tyne: A Modern History*, ed. by R. Colls and B. Lancaster (Chichester: Phillimore Press, 2001), 113-132

Huk, David, *Ben Brierley, 1825-1895* (Manchester: Neil Richardson Publications, 1995)

Humpherys, Anne, *Travels into the Poor Man's Country: The Work of Henry Mayhew* (Athens, GA: University of Georgia Press, 1977)

------, 'G.W.M. Reynolds: Popular Literature and Popular Politics', *VPR*, 16 (Fall and Winter 1983), 79-89

------, 'Coming Apart: The British Newspaper Press and the Divorce Court' in Brake, Bell and Finkelstein (2000), 220-231

------, 'The Journal that Did: *The Adult* (1897-1899)', *Media History*, 9.1 (April 2003), 63-78

------, and Louis James, *G. W. M. Reynolds, Nineteenth-Century Fiction, Politics and the Press* (Aldershot: Ashgate, 2008)

Hunisett, Basil, *A Dictionary of British Steel Engravers* (Leigh-on-Sea: F. Lewis, 1980)

Hunt, Frederick Knight, *The Fourth Estate: Contributions Towards a History of Newspapers, and of the Liberty of the Press*, 2 vols (London: Bogue, 1850; repr. London: Routledge/ Thoemmes Press, 1998)

Hunt, Karen, *Equivocal Feminists: The Social Democratic Federation and the Woman Question, 1884-1911* (Cambridge: Cambridge University Press, 1996)

Hunt, Leigh, *The Autobiography of Leigh Hunt; with Reminiscences of Friends and Contemporaries*, ed. with an introduction and notes by J.E. Monpurgo (London: Smith, Elder and Co., 1850; repr. Cresset Press, 1949)

Hunt, William Holman, *Pre-Raphaelitism and the Pre-Raphaelite Brotherhood*, 2nd edn, 2 vols (London: Chapman and Hall, 1913)

Hunter, J., 'The *Lady's Magazine* and the Study of Englishwomen in the Eighteenth Century' in *Newsletters to Newspapers; Eighteenth-Century Journalism*, ed. by H. B. Donavon and W. R. MacLeod (Morgantown: West Virginia Newsletter, 1977)

Hurd, Michael, *Vincent Novello & Company* (London: Granada, 1981)

Hurwitz, Brian and Ruth Richardson, 'The *Penny Lancet*', *The Lancet*, 364 (2004), 2224-2228

Hussey, Christopher, 'Edward Hudson: an Appreciation', *Country Life*, 80 (26 Sept. 1936), 318-319

Hutcheson, J. A., *Leopold Maxse and the* National Review, *1893-1914: Right-Wing Politics and Journalism in the Edwardian Era* (New York: Garland, 1989)

Huxley, Leonard, *Life and Letters of Thomas Henry Huxley*, 2 vols (London: Macmillan, 1900)

Hyman, Alan, *The Rise and Fall of Horatio Bottomley: Biography of a Swindler* (London: Cassell, 1972)

Hyndman, H. M., *The Record of an Adventurous Life* (London: Macmillan, 1911)

I

Ibbetson, David J., 'Legal Periodicals in England 1820-1870', *Zeitschrift für Neuere Rechtsgeschichte*, 28 (2006), 175-194

Illustrated Police News (24 Dec. 1892), 2, 'The late Mr Purkess'

Immel, Andrea, *Revolutionary Reviewing: Sarah Trimmer's* Guardian of Education *and the Cultural Politics of Juvenile Literature: An Index to* The Guardian (Los Angeles: Department of Special Collections, University Research Library, University of California, 1990)

Inglis, Brian, *The Freedom of the Press in Ireland: 1784-1841* (London: Faber and Faber, 1954)

Inglis, K. S., *The Churches and the Working Classes in Victorian Britain* (London: Routledge and Kegan Paul, 1963)

Inglis, Simon, *League Football and the Men who Made it* (London: Willow Books, 1988)

Innis, Harold A., *Empire and Communications* (Toronto: University of Toronto Press, 1986; 1st edn, 1950)

Ireland, A.M.A., ed., *Selections from the Letters of Geraldine Endsor Jewsbury to Jane Welsh Carlyle* (London: Longmans Green & Co., 1892)

Irish Book Lover, 18.6 (Nov., Dec. 1930), 168, 'How James Duffy Rose to Fame'

Irish Monthly, 23 (Nov. 1895), 596, 'Contributions to Irish Biography. No. 29: James Duffy the Publisher'

Isaac, P., ed., *Newspapers in the North East: The 'Fourth Estate' at Work in Northumberland and Durham* (Wylam: Allenholme Press, 1999)

Isichei, Elizabeth Allo, *Victorian Quakers* (London: Oxford University Press, 1970)

Israel, K., *Names and Stories: Emilia Dilke and Victorian Culture* (Oxford: Oxford University Press, 1999)

Iusová, Iveta, *The New Woman and the Empire* (Columbus: Ohio State University Press, 2005)

J
—

Jack, Thomas C., *Scottish Newspaper Directory and Guide to Advertisers. A Complete Manual of the Newspaper Press* (Edinburgh; T.C. Jack, 1855)

Jackson, Holbrook, *The Eighteen Nineties: A Review of Art and Ideas at the Close of the Nineteenth Century* (London: Grant Richards, 1913)

Jackson, John, *A Treatise on Wood Engraving, Historical and Practical, with Upwards of Three Hundred Illustrations Engraved on Wood* (London: Henry G. Bohn, 1861)

Jackson, Kate, 'The *Tit-bits* Phenomenon: George Newnes, New Journalism and the Periodical Texts', *VPR*, 30 (1997), 201-226

------, *George Newnes and the New Journalism in Britain, 1880-1910, Culture and Profit* (Aldershot: Ashgate, 2001)

Jackson, Kenneth T., ed., *Encyclopedia of New York City* (New Haven: Yale University Press, 1995)

Jackson, Mason, *The Pictorial Press* (Hurst and Blackett, 1885; repr. New York: Burt Franklin, 1969)

Jaffé, Deborah, *Ingenious Women: From Tincture of Saffron to Flying Machines* (Stroud: Sutton, 2003)

James, Elizabeth, ed., *Macmillan: A Publishing Tradition* (Basingstoke: Palgrave, 2002)

James, Frank A. J. L., ed., *The Correspondence of Michael Faraday*, 4 vols (London: Institution of Electrical Engineers, 1991)

James, Louis, *Fiction for the Working Man 1830-1850: A Study of the Literature Produced for the Working Classes in Early Victorian Urban England* (London: Oxford University Press, 1963)

------, 'Tom Brown's Imperialist Sons', *Victorian Studies,* 17 (1973), 80-99

------, *Print and the People, 1819-51* (London: Allen Lane, 1976)

------, ' "The Trouble with Betsy": Periodicals and the Common Reader in Mid-Nineteenth-Century England' in Shattock and Wolff, (1982), 349-366.

James, Philip. *Introduction to English Law*, 10th edn (London: Butterworths, 1979)

Jann, Rosemary, 'From Amateur to Professional: The Case of the Oxbridge Historians', *Journal of British Studies,* 22 (1983), 122-147

Janowitz, Anne, *Lyric and Labour in the Romantic Tradition* (Cambridge University Press, 1998)

Jay, Elisabeth, *Mrs Oliphant: 'A Fiction to Herself'. A Literary Life* (Oxford: Clarendon Press, 1995)

Jay, L. J., 'John Scott Keltie', *Geographers: Bibliographical Studies,* 10 (1986), 93-98

Jenkins, Anthony, *The Making of Victorian Drama* (Cambridge: Cambridge University Press, 1991)

Jennings, Louis, J. ed., *The Croker Papers: The Correspondence and Diaries of J W Croker* (London: John Murray, 1884)

Jerdan, William, *Autobiography,* 4 vols (London: Hall, Virtue, 1852)

[Jerdan, William], 'The Grand Force!', *Fraser's Magazine,* 79 (March 1869), 380-383

Jeremy, David T., ed., *Dictionary of Business Biography: a Biographical Dictionary of Business Leaders Active in Britain in the Period 1860-1980* (London: Butterworths, 1984)

Jerrold, Blanchard, 'Shirley Brooks', *Gentleman's Magazine*, 236 (1874), 561-569

Jerrold, Walter, *Thomas Hood: His Life and Times* (London: Alston Rivers, 1907)

Jessop, Ralph, *Carlyle and Scottish Thought* (Basingstoke: Macmillan 1997)

Jewish Chronicle 1841-1941: A Century of Newspaper History (London: The Jewish Chronicle, 1949)

Jewitt, Llewellyn, 'Thomas Rossell Potter – A Memory', *Antiquary*, 14 (1873-74), 17-20

Johanssen, Albert, *The House of Beadle and Adams* (Norman, OK: University of Oklahoma Press, 1950, 1962)

Johanningsmeier, Charles, *Fiction and the American Literary Marketplace: The Role of Newspaper Syndicates in America, 1860-1900* (Cambridge: Cambridge University Press, 1997)

John, Angela, V., *War, Journalism and the Shaping of the Twentieth Century* (London: I.B. Tauris, 2006)

Johnson, Diane Chalmers, '[The Studio] A Contribution to the '90s', *Apollo*, 91 (March 1970), 198-203

Johnston, Judith, *Anna Jameson: Victorian, Feminist, Woman of Letters* (Aldershot: Scolar Press, 1997)

Johnstone, A. G. W., *Musical Criticisms* (Manchester: Manchester University Press, 1905)

Jones, Aled, 'Workmen's Advocates: Ideology and Class in a mid-Victorian Newspaper System' in Shattock and Wolff, (1982), 297-316

------, *Press, Politics and Society: A History of Journalism in Wales* (Cardiff: University of Wales Press, 1993)

------, *Powers of the Press: Newspapers, Power and the Public in Nineteenth-Century England* (Aldershot: Scolar, 1996)

------, 'The Nineteenth-Century Media and Welsh Identity' in Brake, Bell and Finkelstein (2000), 310-325

------, 'Chartist Journalism and Print Culture in Britain, 1830-1855' in Allen and Ashton (2005), 1-24

Jones, David, *The Last Rising* (Oxford: Clarendon Press, 1985)

------, *Chartism and the Chartists* (London: Allen Lane, 1975)

Jones, David Glanaman, *Cofiant Cranogwen* (Caernarfon: Undeb Dirwestol Merched y De, 1932)

Jones, Dorothy Richardson, *King of Critics: George Saintsbury, 1845-1933* (Ann Arbor: University of Michigan Press, 1992)

Jones, Julia, 'Family Fictions: the Working Life of Herbert Allingham' (unpublished PhD thesis: University of Surrey, 2006)

Jones, Leonidas M., *The Life of John Hamilton Reynolds* (Hanover/London: University Press of New England, 1984)

Jones, Philip Henry, 'A Nineteenth-Century Welsh Printer; Some Aspects of the Career of Thomas Gee, 1815-1898' (London: Thesis for the Fellowship of the Library Association, 1977)

------, and Eiluned Rees, eds, *A Nation and its Books. A History of the Book in Wales* (Aberystwyth: National Library of Wales, 1998)

Jordan, Ellen, 'Sister as Journalist: The Almost Anonymous Career of Anne Mozley', *VPR*, 37 (2004), 315-341

------, and Anne Bridger, ' "An unexpected recruit to feminism": Jessie Boucherett, the Society for Promoting the Employment of Women, and the Importance of Being Wealthy', *Women's History Review*, 15.3 (July, 2006), 385-412

Jordan, J.T., 'The writings of "Ouida"' (unpublished PhD Thesis: University of London, 1995)

Jopling, Louise, *Twenty Years of My Life 1867-1887* (London: John Lane, 1928)

Jordan, John O. and Robert L. Patten, eds, *Literature in the Marketplace: Nineteenth-Century British Publishing and Reading Practices* (Cambridge: Cambridge University Press, 1995)

Jos, J. J., 'Wine and Walnuts', *Notes & Queries*, 8.6 (1883), 411-412

Joseph, Michael Scott, 'Randolph Caldecott' in *Dictionary of Literary Biography*, v.163: *British Children's Writers 1800-1880*, ed. Meena Khorana (Detroit: Gale Group, 1996), 37-47

Journal of Botany, British and Foreign, n.s. 5 (1876), 223-224, 'Botanical News'

Jowett, H., ed., *Hazell's Magazine: A Monthly Journal* (London: Hazell, Watson & Viney Ltd, 1887)

Joyce, Toby, 'The Galway American 1862-3. Part One: James Roche and the American Civil War' and 'Part Two: Politics and Place in a Fenian Newspaper', *Journal of the Galway Archaeological and Historical Society*, 48 (1996), 104-136; 47 (1995), 108-137

Judd, David W., ed., *Life and Writings of Frank Forester (Henry William Herbert)* (London: Frederick Warne, [1882])

Julian, John, ed., *A Dictionary of Hymnology* (London: John Murray, 1892)

K

Kaiser, David, *Pedagogy and the Practice of Science: Historical and Contemporary Perspectives* (Cambridge, MA: MIT Press, 2005)

Kamen, Ruth H., *British and Irish Architectural History: a Bibliography and Guide to Sources of Information* (London: Architectural Press, 1981)

Kamper, David Scott, 'Popular Sunday Newspapers', in *Disreputable Pleasures*, ed. by Mike Huggins and J. A. Mangan (London: Routledge, 2004), 83-102

Kaplan, Joel H., 'A Puppet's Power: George Alexander, Clement Scott, and the Replotting of *Lady Windermere's Fan*', *Theatre Notebook*, 46.2 (1992), 59-73

Kapp, Yvonne, *Eleanor Marx: Family Life 1855-1883* (London: Virago, 1979)

Kaul, Chandrika, *Reporting the Raj, the British Press and India* (Manchester: Manchester University Press, 2003)

------, ed., *Media and the British Empire* (London/New York: Palgrave Macmillan, 2006)

Keane, Maureen, *Mrs S.C. Hall: A Literary Biography* (Gerrards Cross, Bucks: Colin Smythe, 1997)

Keating, Peter, ed., *Into Unknown England 1866-1913. Selections from the Social Explorers* (Lanham, MD: Rowman and Littlefield, 1976)

------, *The Haunted Study: A Social History of the English Novel, 1875-1914* (London: Secker & Warburg, 1989)

Keefe, H. J., *A Century in Print: The Story of Hazell's 1839-1939* (London: Hazell, Watson & Viney Ltd, 1939)

Keenan, Dennis, *Smith and Keenan's English Law*, 8th edn (London: Pitman, 1986)

Keir, David, *The House of Collins: the Story of a Scottish Family of Publishers from 1789 to the Present Day* (London: Collins, 1952)

Kellner, Douglas, *The Persian Gulf TV War* (Boulder, CO.: Westview Press, 1992)

Kelly, G., and E. Applegate, eds, *British Reform Writers, 1789-1832* (Detroit: Gale Research Inc., 1996)

Kelly, Thomas, *A History of Public Libraries in Great Britain, 1845-1975* (London: Library Association, 1977)

Kendal Mercury (6 March 1908), 5, 'Deaths: Lee'

Kenealy, Edward Vaughan, 'William Maginn, LL.D.', *Dublin University Magazine*, 23 (Jan. 1844), 72-101

Kennedy, M., *The Hallé Tradition – A Century of Music* (Manchester: Manchester University Press, 1960)

Kennedy, Thomas C., *British Quakerism, 1860-1920: The Transformation of a Religious Community* (Oxford: Oxford University Press, 2001)

Kenneth, W., *Annals of Aberdeen* (Aberdeen: A. Brown & Co., 1818)

Kent, Christopher, 'Higher Journalism and the Mid-Victorian Clerisy', *Victorian Studies*, 13 (Dec. 1969), 181-198

------, *Brains and Numbers: Elitism, Comtism, and Democracy in Mid-Victorian England* (Toronto: University of Toronto Press, 1978)

------, 'Critics of Drama, Music and Art 1830-1914: A Preliminary List', *VPR*, 13 (Spring/Summer 1980), 31-54

------, 'Of Woods and Trees; a Review', *VPR*, 15, (Winter 1982,), 4

------, '*The Academy*' in Sullivan (1984), 3-7

------, 'The Editor and the Law' in Wiener (1985), 99-119

------, 'More Critics of Drama, Music and Art 1830-1914', *VPR*, 19 (Autumn 1986), 99-105

------, 'The Angry Young Gentlemen of *Tomahawk*' in Garlick and Harris (1998), 75-94

------, 'British Bohemia and the Victorian Journalist', *Australasian Victorian Studies Journal*, 6 (2000), 25-35

------, 'Depicting Gentlemen's Fashions in the *Tailor and Cutter*, 1868-1900' in Laurel Brake and Demoor (2008).

Kersley, Gillian, *Darling Madame: Sarah Grand & Devoted Friend* (London: Virago, 1983)

Kesterton, W. H., *A History of Journalism in Canada* (Toronto: McClelland and Stewart, 1967)

Kiberd, Declan, *Inventing Ireland: The Literature of the Modern Nation* (London: Cape, 1995)

Kieve, Jeffrey, *The Electric Telegraph: A Social and Economic History* (Newton Abbot: David & Charles, 1973)

Killham, John, *Tennyson and* The Princess: *Reflections of an Age* (London: University of London, Athlone Press, 1958)

Kinane, Vincent, *A History of the Dublin University Press, 1734-1976* (Dublin: Gill & Macmillan, 1994)

------, and Michael Gill, 'McGlashan and Gill' in Anderson and Rose (1991), 203-5

King, Andrew, *The London Journal 1845-1883: Periodicals, Production and Gender* (Aldershot: Ashgate, 2004)

------, and John Plunkett, eds, *Popular Print Media, 1820-1900*, 3 vols (London: Routledge, 2004)

------, and John Plunkett, eds, *Victorian Print Media: A Reader* (Oxford: Oxford University Press, 2005)

------, '*Reynolds's Miscellany* 1846-1849: Advertising Networks and Politics' in Humpherys and James (Aldershot: Ashgate, 2007), 53-74

King, J. W., *James Montgomery: a Memoir, Political and Poetical* (London: Partridge and Co., 1858)

Kirby, R. G. and A. E. Musson, *The Voice of the People: John Doherty 1798-1854* (Manchester: Manchester University Press, 1975)

Kirlew, E., *Gilbert R. Kirlew: A Brief Memoir By His Wife* (London: Morgan & Scott, 1908)

Kissane, James, 'Art Historians and Art Critics – IX. P. G. Hamerton, Victorian Art Critic', *Burlington Magazine*, 114 (Jan. 1972), 22-29

Klancher, Jon P., *The Making of English Reading Audiences, 1790-1832* (Madison: University of Wisconsin Press, 1987)

Klein, Hermann, *Thirty Years of Musical Life in London 1870-1900* (London: William Heinemann: The Century Co., 1903)

------, *The Reign of Patti* (New York: The Century Co., 1920)

Knelman, Judith, *Twisting in the Wind: The Murderess and the English Press* (Toronto: University of Toronto Press, 1998)

Knight, Charles, ed., *London* (London: Charles Knight & Co., 1841)

------, *Passages of a Working Life During Half a Century*, 3 vols (London: Bradbury and Evans, 1864-1865)

Knight, David M., 'Science and Culture in mid-Victorian Britain: The Reviews and William Crookes', *Quarterly Journal of Science*, 11 (1996), 43-54

Knight, Helen C., *Life of James Montgomery* (Boston: Gould and Lincoln, 1857)

Knight, Mark and Emma Mason, *Nineteenth-Century Religion and Literature: An Introduction* (Oxford: Oxford University Press, 2006)

Knight, Stephen, *A Hundred Years of Fiction: Writing Wales in English* (Cardiff: University of Wales Press, 2004)

Knightley, Phillip, *The First Casualty: The War Correspondent as Hero and Myth-Maker from the Crimea to Kosovo* (1975; revised edn, London: Prion, 2000; 3rd revised edn., Andre Deutsch, 2003)

Korey, Marie Elena, Yannick Portebois, Dorothy E. Speirs and Richard Landon, *Vizetelly & Compan(ies): A Complex Tale of Victorian Printing and Publishing*, Exhibition Catalogue (Toronto: University of Toronto, 2003)

Korn, Frederick, 'An Unpublished Letter by Thomas Hood: Hannah Lawrance and Hood's Magazine', *English Language Notes*, 18 (March 1981), 192-194

Koss, Stephen, *Sir John Brunner: Radical Plutocrat* (Cambridge: Cambridge University Press, 1970)

------, *Fleet Street Radical; A. G. Gardiner and the* Daily News (London, Allen Lane, 1973)

------, *The Rise and Fall of the Political Press in Britain: The Nineteenth Century* (London: Hamilton, 1981)

Koven, Seth, *Slumming: Sexual and Social Politics in Victorian London* (Princeton: Princeton University Press, 2004)

Krueger, Christine, *The Reader's Repentance: Women Preachers, Women Writers, and Nineteenth-Century Social Discourse* (Chicago: Chicago University Press, 1992)

Kuhn, William M., *Democratic Royalism: The Transformation of the British Monarchy, 1861-1914* (Basingstoke: Macmillan, 1996)

Kuist, James M., *The Nichols File of the* Gentleman's Magazine (Madison: University of Wisconsin Press, 1982)

Kunzle, David, 'Between Broadsheet Caricature and *Punch*: Cheap Newspaper Cuts for the Lower Classes in the 1830s', *Art Journal*, 43. 4 (1983), 339-346

------, 'Marie Duval: A Caricaturist Rediscovered', *Woman's Art Journal*, 7 (Spring/Summer 1986), 26-31

------, *The History of the Comic Strip*, v. 2: *The Nineteenth Century* (Berkeley and Oxford: University of California Press, 1990)

Kurshan, Ilana, 'Mind Reading: Literature in the Discourse of Early Victorian Phrenology and Mesmerism' in *Victorian Literary Mesmerism*, ed. by Martin Willis and Catherine Wynne (Amsterdam: Rodopi, 2006), 17-38

Kynaston, David, *The Financial Times: A Centenary History* (London: Viking, 1988)

L

Lacey, Candida Ann, ed., *Barbara Leigh Smith Bodichon and the Langham Place Group* (London: Routledge and Kegan Paul, 1987)

Lady Newspaper (28 June 1851), 362-365, 'Mr. A.B. Reach'

Lago, Mary, *Christiana Herringham and the Edwardian Art Scene* (Columbia: University of Missouri Press, 1996)

Lai, Shu-Fang, 'Fact or Fancy: What Can We Learn about Dickens from his Periodicals *Household Words* and *All the Year Round*?', *VPR*, 34 (2001), 41-53

Lalumia, Matthew Paul, *Realism and Politics in Victorian Art of the Crimean War* (Ann Arbor, MI: UMI Research Press, 1984)

Lamb, Charles, *The Letters of Charles Lamb*, ed. by E. V. Lucas, 3 vols (London: J. M. Dent & Sons Ltd, 1935)

Lambert, J. W. and Michael Ratcliffe, *The Bodley Head, 1887-1987* (London: The Bodley Head, 1987)

Lambert, John, '"The thinking is done in London": South Africa's English Language Press and Imperialism' in *Media and the British Empire*, ed. by Chandrika Kaul (New York: Palgrave Macmillan, 2006)

Lambert, Richard S., *The Cobbett of the West: A Study of Thomas Latimer and the Struggle Between Pulpit and Press at Exeter* (London: Nicholas & Watson, 1939)

Lancashire Congregational Calendar /Annual Reports of the Committee to the Independent Churches and Congregations of Lancashire (1807-?1868)

Lancashire, Julie Ann, 'An Historical Study of the Popularization of Science in General Science Periodicals in Britain 1890-1939'(unpublished PhD thesis: University of Canterbury, NZ, 1988)

Land and Water (16 March 1867), 173, 'William Joshua Ffennell'

Landow, George P., 'The *Art-Journal*, 1850-1880: Antiquarians, the Medieval Revival, and the Reception of Pre-Raphaelitism', *The Pre-Raphaelite Review*, 2 (1979), 71-76

Lang, Andrew, *The Life and Letters of John Gibson Lockhart*, 2 vols (London: J.C. Nimmo, 1897)

Lang, Cecil Y., *The Swinburne Letters*, 6 vols (New Haven: Yale University Press, 1959-1962)

Langford, John Alfred, *A Century of Birmingham Life: or, a Chronicle of Local Events from 1741 to 1841*, 2 vols (Birmingham: W.G. Moore & Co., 1871)

Langley, Leanne, 'The English Musical Journal in the Early Nineteenth Century' (unpublished PhD thesis: University of North Carolina, 1983)

------, 'The Life and Death of the *Harmonicon*', *Research Chronicle of the Royal Musical Association*, 22 (1989), 137-163

------, 'The Musical Press in Nineteenth-Century England', *Notes*, s. 2, 46.3 (March 1990), 583-592

------, 'Music' in Vann and VanArsdel (1994), 99-126

------, (2001a) 'Ayrton, William' in [Grove] (2001)

------, (2001b) 'Bacon, Richard Mackenzie' in [Grove] (2001)

------, 'Roots of a Tradition: The First *Dictionary of Music and Musicians'* in *George Grove, Music and Victorian Culture*, ed. by Michael Musgrave (Basingstoke: Palgrave Macmillan, 2003), 168-215

Lapides, Kenneth, ed., *Marx and Engels on the Trade Unions* (New York: International Publishers, 1990)

Larson, T., *Crisis of Doubt* (Oxford: Oxford University Press, 2006)

Latané, David E., (2005a), ' "Perge, signifer," – or, Where did William Maginn stand?' in *Structures of Belief in Nineteenth-Century Ireland*, ed. by James Murphy (Dublin: Four Courts Press, 2005), 61-72

------, (2005b), 'Two Letters from Caroline Norton to Charles Molloy Westmacott', *Notes & Queries*, 52.1 (March, 2005), 65-68

------, 'Charles Molloy Westmacott and the Spirit of *The Age*', *VPR*, 40.1 (2007), 44-71

Laughton, J.K., *Memoirs of the Life and Correspondence of Henry Reeve* (London: Longman's, Green and Co., 1898)

Lauster, Martina, *Sketches of the Nineteenth Century: European Journalism and its Physiologies, 1830-50* (Basingstoke: Palgrave, 2007)

Law, Cheryl, *Suffrage and Power: The Women's Movement 1918-1928* (London: I. B. Tauris, 1997)

Law, Graham, *Serializing Fiction in the Victorian Press* (Basingstoke: Palgrave, 2000)

------, 'Periodicals and Serialization' in *A Companion to the Victorian Novel*, ed. by William Baker and Kenneth Womack (Westport, CT: Greenwood Press, 2002)

------, ' "Nothing but a Newspaper": Serializing Fiction in the Press in the 1840s' in Brake and Codell (2005), 29-49

------, and Andrew Maunder, *Wilkie Collins: A Literary Life* (Basingstoke: Palgrave Macmillan, 2008)

Law, Henry William and Irene Law, *The Book of the Beresford Hopes* (London: Heath Cranton Ltd., 1925)

Lawford, Cynthia, 'Diary', *London Review of Books* (21 September 2000), 36-37

Lawrence, Arthur H., 'Interviewing as Women's Work: A Chat with Mrs. Sarah A. Tooley', *The Young Woman*, 5 (1896), 441-447

Layard, George Somes, *The Life and Letters of Charles Samuel Keene* (London: Sampson Low, Marston & Co., 1892)

------, *Mrs. Lynn Linton: her Life, Letters and Opinions* (London: Methuen, 1901)

------, *Shirley Brooks of* Punch: *His Life, Letters, and Diaries* (London: Henry Holt and Co., 1907)

Layton, Charles and Edwin, *A Handy Newspaper List* (London: Charles and Edwin Layton, 1912)

Leary, Patrick, '*Fraser's Magazine* and the Literary Life, 1830-1847', *VPR*, 27.2 (Summer 1994), 105-126

Leask, W. Keith, *Hugh Miller* (Edinburgh: Oliphant, Anderson and Ferrier, 1896)

Leatherland, J. A., *Essays and Poems with a Brief Autobiographical Memoir* (London: Tweedie, 1862)

Leathlean, Howard, 'Loudon's Architectural Magazine and the Houses of Parliament Competition', *VPR*, 26.3 (Fall 1993), 145-153

Ledbetter, Kathryn *Tennyson and Victorian Periodicals: Commodities in Context* (Aldershot: Ashgate, 2007)

------, and Terence Hoagwood, *'Colour'd Shadows': Contexts in Publishing, Printing, and Reading Nineteenth-Century British Women Writers* (New York: Palgrave/Macmillan, 2005)

Ledger, Sally, 'Wilde Women and *The Yellow Book*: The Sexual Politics of Aestheticism and Decadence', *English Literature in Transition, 1880-1920*, 50.1 (2007), 5-26

Lee, Alan J., *The Origins of the Popular Press in England, 1855-1914* (London: Croom Helm, 1976)

Lee, Alan, 'The Structure, Ownership and Control of the Press, 1855-1914' in Boyce, Curran and Wingate (1978), 117-129

Leerssen, Joep, *Remembrance and Imagination: Patterns in the Historical and Literary Representation of Ireland in the Nineteenth Century* (Cork: Cork University Press, 1996)

Lees, Dr. F.R., *A Biography by Frederick Lees* (London: H. J. Osborn, 1904)

Lefanu, W.R., *British Periodicals of Medicine: a Chronological List 1640-1899*, revd edn (Oxford: Wellcome Unit for the History of Medicine, 1984)

Le Gallienne, Richard, *Retrospective Reviews: A Literary Log*, 2 vols (London: John Lane; NewYork: Dodd Mead and Company, 1896)

------, *The Romantic '90s* (Garden City, New York: Doubleday, Page & Company, 1925)

Lehmann, R. C., ed., *Charles Dickens as Editor* (London: Smith, Elder, 1912)

Leicester Advertiser (26 April 1873), 7, 'The Late T. R. Potter, Esq.'

Leighton, Mary Elizabeth, ' "Hypnosis Redivivus": Ernest Hart, the *British Medical Journal*, and the Hypnotism Controversy', *VPR*, 34 (2001), 104-127

Le-May Sheffield, Suzanne, *Revealing New Worlds: Three Victorian Women Naturalists* (London: Routledge, 2001)

L'Enfant, Julie, *William Rossetti's Art Criticism: the Search for Truth in Victorian Art* (Lanham, MD: University Press of America, 1999)

Leno, John Bedford, *The Aftermath* (London: Reeves and Turner, 1892)

Lennox Herald and Weekly Advertiser (5 Sept. 1891), 4, 'Death of Mr. Joseph Irving, F. S. A., Scot'

Le Pla, J., 'Collecting Series No.2 – The Beeton Boy's Own Library', *Imaginative Book Illustration Society Newsletter*, 16 (2000), 15-22

Leverette Jr., William E., 'E. L. Youmans' Crusade for Scientific Autonomy and Respectability', *American Quarterly*, 17 (1965), 12-32

Levetus, Amelia S, 'The European Influence of the *Studio*', *Studio*, 105 (1933), 257-258

Levey, Judith S. and Agnes Greenhall, eds, *The Concise Columbia Encylopedia* (Irvington, NY: Columbia University Press, 1983)

Levy, D. B., 'Thomas Massa Alsager, Esq.: A Beethoven Advocate in London', *Nineteenth-Century Music*, 9.2 (1985), 119-127

Levine, Philippa, ' "So Few Prizes and So Many Blanks": Marriage and Feminism in Later Nineteenth-Century England', *Journal of British Studies*, 28.2 (1989), 150-174

Lewes, George H., 'The Condition of Authors in England, Germany and France', *Fraser's Magazine*, 35 (March 1847), 285-295

------, *The Letters of George Henry Lewes*, ed. W. Baker, 2 vols (Victoria, BC: University of Victoria, 1995)

Lewis, Charles Thomas Courtney, *George Baxter, Colour Printer: His Life and Work* (London: Sampson Low Marston, 1908)

Lewis, Courtney, *The Story Of Picture Printing in England During the XIX Century, or Forty Years of Wood And Stone* (London: Sampson Low, 1928)

Liddington, Jill and Norris, Jill, *One Hand Tied Behind Us: The Rise of the Women's Suffrage Movement* (London: Virago, 1978)

Liddle, Dallas, 'Who Invented the Leading Article?', *Media History*, 5.1 (1999), 5-18

Lightman, Bernard, 'The Visual Theology of Victorian Popularizers of Science: From Lilley, Samuel. 'Nicholson's Journal 1797-1813', *Annals of Science*, 6 (1948), 78-101

------, 'Ideology, Evolution and Late Victorian Agnostic Popularizers' in *History, Humanity and Evolution*, ed. by James R. Moore (Cambridge: Cambridge University Press, 1989), 285-309

------, ed., *Victorian Science in Context* (Chicago: The University of Chicago Press, 1994)

------, 'Victorian Popularizers of Science: From Reverent Eye to Chemical Retina', *Isis*, 91 (2000), 651-680

------, ed., *The Dictionary of Nineteenth-Century British Scientists*, 4 vols (Bristol: Thoemmes Continuum, 2004a)

------, '*Knowledge* Confronts *Nature*: Richard Anthony Proctor and Popular Science Periodicals', (2004b) in Henson, Cantor, et al. (2004), 199-210

------, ed., *Science Writing By Women* (Bristol: Thoemmes Continuum, 2004c)

------, (2004d) 'Scientists as Materialists in the Periodical Press: Tyndall's Belfast Address' in Cantor and Shuttleworth (2004), 199-237

------, *Victorian Popularizers of Science: Designing Nature for New Audiences* (Chicago: University of Chicago Press, 2007)

Lilley, Samuel, 'Nicholson's Journal 1797-1813', *Annals of Science*, 6 (1948), 78-101

Lindley, Nathaniel, 'The History of the Law Reports', *Law Quarterly Review*, 1 (1885), 137-149

Linton, David, 'Mr. Mitchell's "National Work" ', *Journal of Advertising History*, 2 (Jan. 1979), 29-31

------, and Ray Boston, eds, *The Newspaper Press in Britain: An Annotated Bibliography* (London and New York: Mansell, 1987)

------, 'Mitchell's, May's and Sell's: Newspaper Directories of the Victorian Era', *Journal of Newspaper and Periodical History*, 3.2 (1987), 20-28

Linton, E. L., *The Autobiography of Christopher Kirkland* (London, Richard Bentley & Son, 1885)

Linton, W. J., *James Watson: A Memoir* (Manchester: A. Heywood and Son, 1880)

Liveing, Edward, *Adventure in Publishing: The House of Ward Lock 1854-1954* (London and Melbourne: Ward, Lock & Co., 1954)

Livesey, Joseph, *Autobiography of Joseph Livesey* (London: National Temperance League Publication Depot, 1868)

Lochhead, Marion, *John Gibson Lockhart* (London: John Murray, 1954)

Lockhart, John Gibson, *Theodore Hook: A Sketch*, 4th edn (London: John Murray, 1853)

Lodge, Sara, *Thomas Hood and Nineteenth-Century Poetry: Work, Play and Politics* (Manchester: Manchester University Press 2007)

Lofts, W. O. G., and D. J. Adley, *The Men Behind Boys' Fiction* (London: Howard Baker, 1970)

Lohrli, Anne, ed., *Household Words: A Weekly Journal Conducted by Charles Dickens: Table of Contents, List of Contributions* (Toronto: University of Toronto Press, 1973)

London Figaro (6 Jan. 1892), 11, 'Figaro's Fancies and Facts'

Longmate, Norman, *The Waterdrinkers: A History of Temperance* (London: Hamish Hamilton, 1968)

Lovett, William, *Life and Struggles of William Lovett in his Pursuit of Bread, Knowledge and Freedom* (London: Trubner, 1876)

Low, Sidney J., 'Newspaper Copyright', *National Review,* 19 (1892), 648-666

Lowe, Robert W., *A Bibliographical Account of English Theatrical Literature from the Earliest Times to the Present Day* (London: Nimmo, 1888)

Lower, Mark Antony, *The Worthies of Sussex* (Lewes: privately printed, 1865)

Lowndes, W. T., *British Librarian* (London: Thomas Rodd, 1842)

Luckhurst, Roger, *The Invention of Telepathy* (Oxford: Oxford University Press, 2002)

Lucy, Henry, *Sixty Years in the Wilderness* (London: Smith, Elder and Co., 1911)

Ludlow, John, *The Autobiography of A Christian Socialist*, ed. by A. D. Murray (London: Frank Cass, 1981)

Lunn, Henry. C., *Musings of a Musician* (London: Simpkin, Marshall, and Co., 1846)

Lyttelton, Edith, *Florence Upton, Painter* (London: Longmans, Green and Co. Ltd, 1926)

M

McAleer, Joseph, *Popular Reading and Publishing in Britain, 1914-1950* (Oxford: Clarendon Press, 1992)

McCalman, Iain, *Radical Underworld: Prophets, Revolutionaries, and Pornographers in London, 1795-1840* (Cambridge: Cambridge University Press, 1988)

------, ed., *The Horrors of Slavery and Other Writings by Robert Wedderburn* (Edinburgh: Edinburgh University Press, 1991)

McCarthy, Justin and John Robinson, *The* Daily News *Jubilee; a Political and Social Retrospect of Fifty Years of the Queen's Reign* (London: S. Low, Marston, 1896)

McClintock, Anne, *Imperial Leather: Race, Gender, and Sexuality in the Colonial Contest* (London: Routledge, 1995)

McCormack, W.J., *Sheridan LeFanu and Victorian Ireland* (Dublin: Lilliput Press, 1991)

McCulloch, Andrew, *The Feeneys of the Birmingham Post* (Birmingham: University of Birmingham Press, 2004)

McCutcheon, Bob and Alan C. Rennie, *Stirling Observer: 150 Years On* (Stirling: Stirling Observer, 1986)

MacDonagh, Michael, 'A Night in the Reporters' Gallery', *Nineteenth Century*, 37 (March 1895), 516-526

------, 'Can We Rely On Our War News?' *Fortnightly Review*, 63 (April 1898), 612-625

------, *The Reporters' Gallery* (London and New York: Hodder and Stoughton, 1913)

Macdonald, Kate and Marysa Demoor, 'The *Dorothy* and its Supplements: a Late-Victorian Novelette (1889-1899)', *Publishing History*, 61 (Spring 2007), 71-101

McDonald, Peter D., *British Literary Culture and Publishing Practice, 1880-1914* (Cambridge: Cambridge University Press, 1997)

McFarlane, Delphine, 'Politicising Gender in the 1830s British Periodical' (unpublished PhD thesis: University of Western Australia, 2005)

McGann, Jerome, *The Textual Condition* (Princeton: Princeton University Press, 1991)

McGann, Susan, *The Battle of the Nurses* (London: Scutari Press, 1992)

McGee, Owen, *The IRB: The Irish Republican Brotherhood from the Land League to Sinn Fein* (Dublin: Four Courts Press, 2005)

McGuinne, Dermot, *Irish Type Design: A History of Printing Types in the Irish Character* (Dublin: Irish Academic Press, 1992)

Mackail, J. W. and Guy Wyndham, *Life and Letters of George Wyndham*, 2 vols (London: Hutchinson, 1925)

Mackay, Charles, *Forty Years' Recollections* (London: Chapman & Hall, 1877)

Mackay, H., 'Buckingham, James Silk' in Baylen and Grossman, v. 2 (1984), 105-106

Mackenzie, Ian, *British Prints: Dictionary and Price Guide* (Woodbridge: Antique Collectors' Club, 1987)

McKenzie, Judy, *Letters of G.A. Sala to Edmund Yates* (Brisbane: University of Queensland, 1993)

McKenzie, K. A., *Edith Simcox and George Eliot.* (Oxford: Oxford University Press, 1961)

Mackenzie, Shelton, 'Memoir' in *Miscellaneous Writings of the Late Dr. Maginn*, 5 volumes (New York: Redfield, 1855-1857), v. 5, ix-cx

------, 'History of *Blackwood's Magazine*' in John Wilson, *Noctes Ambrosianae* (New York: W. J. Widdleton, 1867)

Mackenzie, W. M., *Hugh Miller: A Critical Study* (London: Hodder and Stoughton, 1905)

McKibbin, Ross, ed., *The Ideologies of Class: Social Relations in Britain, 1880-1950* (Oxford: Oxford University Press, 1991a)

------, (1991b) 'Working-class Gambling in Britain, 1880-1939' in McKibbin (1991a), 101-138

McKitterick, David, *A History of Cambridge University Press: New Worlds for Learning* (Cambridge: Cambridge University Press, 2004)

McLachlan, Herbert, *The Unitarian Movement in the Religious Life of England: Its Contribution to Thought and Learning 1700-1900* (London: George Allen and Unwin, 1934)

McLaughlin, Greg, *The War Correspondent* (London: Pluto Press, 2000)

MacLeod, Dianne Sachko (1986a), 'F. G. Stephens, Pre-Raphaelite Critic and Art Historian', *Burlington Magazine,* 128 (June, 1986), 398-406

------, (1986b), 'Mid-Victorian Patronage of the Arts: F. G. Stephens's "The Private Collections of England" ', *Burlington Magazine,* 128 (Aug. 1986), 597-607

------, *Art and the Victorian Middle Class: Money and the Making of Cultural Identity* (Cambridge: Cambridge University Press, 1998)

Macleod, Donald, *Memoir of Norman Macleod* (London: Daldy, Isbister, 1876)

Macleod, Roy M., *The 'Creed of Science' in Victorian England* (Aldershot: Ashgate, 2000)

McMillan, Dorothy, ed., *Queen of Science: Personal Recollections of Mary Somerville* (Edinburgh: Canongate, 2001)

Macmillan, George A., ed., *Letters of Alexander Macmillan* (Glasgow: privately printed, 1908)

MacNalty, Arthur Salusbury, *A Biography of Sir Benjamin Ward Richardson* (London: Harvey & Blythe, 1950)

McNicholas, Anthony, *Politics, Religion and the Press: Irish Journalism in Mid-Victorian England* (Oxford: Peter Lang, 2007)

McPhillips, Kevin, *Joseph Burgess (1853-1934) and the Founding of the Independent Labour Party* (Lampeter: Edwin Mellen Press, 2005)

McWilliam, Rohan, 'The Mysteries of G.W.M. Reynolds' in *Living and Learning: Essays in Honour of J. F. C. Harrison,* ed. by Malcolm Chase and Ian Dyck (Aldershot: Scholar Press, 1996), 182-198

------, *The Tichborne Claimant* (London: Hambledon Continuum, 2007)

Madden, Richard Robert, *The Literary Life and Correspondence of the Countess of Blessington,* 3 vols (London: T. C. Newby, 1855)

------, *The History of Irish Periodical Literature, from the End of the 17th to the Middle of the 19th Century,* 2 vols (London: T. C. Newby, 1867)

Madden, T.M., ed., *Memoirs of Richard Robert Madden* (London: Ward and Downey, 1891)

Maehl, W.H., 'Augustus Hardin Beaumont: Anglo-American Radical (1798-1838)', *International Review of Social History,* 14 (1969) 237-250

------, 'The Dynamics of Violence in Chartism: A Case Study in North-East England, 1839', *Albion,* 7 (1975), 101-119

Maginn, William, *Biographical Sketch of William Hamilton Maxwell* (London: Richard Bentley, 1859)

Magnusson, Magnus, et al., *The Glorious Privilege: The History of the Scotsman* (Edinburgh: Nelson 1967)

------, Matthew J. Moulton, William R. Munro, et al., *The Glorious Privilege: The History of the Scotsman* (Edinburgh: Thomas Nelson and Sons, 1967)

Maidment, Brian, *The Archives of George Routledge & Co.. 1853-1902* (London: Chadwyck-Healy, 1973)

------, 'Readers Fair and Foul: John Ruskin and the Periodical Press' in Shattock and Wolff (1982), 29-58

------, ed., *The Poorhouse Fugitives: Self-Taught Poets and Poetry in Victorian Britain* (Manchester: Carcanet, 1987)

------, (2001a) 'Entrepreneurship and the Artisans: John Cassell, the Great Exhibition and the Periodical Idea' in *The Great Exhibition of 1851: New Interdisciplinary Essays*, ed. by L. Purbrick (Manchester: Manchester University Press, 2001), 79-113

------, (2001b) *Reading Popular Prints* (Manchester and New York: Manchester University Press, 1996, 2001)

Maitland, J. A. Fuller, *English Music in the Nineteenth Century* (London: Grant Richards, 1902)

------, *A Door-Keeper of Music* (London: Murray, 1929)

Manchester, A. H., *A Modern Legal History of England and Wales 1750-1950* (London: Butterworths, 1980)

Manchester Region History Review, 17.2 (2006), Special Issue on Nineteenth-Century Manchester Literary Culture and Periodical Press

Mancoff, D.N., 'Samuel Carter Hall: Publisher as Promoter of the High Arts', *VPR*, 24 (1991), 11-21

Mander, W. J. and Alan P. F. Sell, eds, *Dictionary of Nineteenth-Century British Philosophers* (Bristol: Thoemmes Press, 2002)

Mangum, Teresa, *Married, Middlebrow and Militant: Sarah Grand and the New Woman Novel* (Ann Arbor: University of Michigan Press, 1998)

Manocchi, Phyllis F., ' "Vernon Lee": A Bibliography and Primary Reintroduction', *English Literature in Transition*, 26.4 (1983), 231-267

Mansfield, Elizabeth, 'The Victorian Grand Siècle', *Victorian Literature and Culture*, 28 (2000), 133-147

Mansfield, F.J., *Sub-Editing. A Book Mainly for Young Journalists* (London: Pitman and Sons Ltd., 1932)

------, *'Gentlemen, The Press!' Chronicles of a Crusade (Official History of the National Union of Journalists)* (London: W.H. Allen & Co., 1943)

Marcet, Jane Haldimann, *Conversations on Political Economy, in which the Elements of that Science are Familiarly Explained* (London: Longman, Hurst, Rees Orme and Brown, 1816)

Marchand, Leslie A., *The* Athenaeum: *A Mirror of Victorian Culture* (Chapel Hill: University of North Carolina Press, 1941; New York: Octagon Books, 1971)

Marcus, Steven, *The Other Victorians: A Study of Sexuality and Pornography in Mid-Nineteenth-Century England*, 2nd edn (New York: W. W. Norton, 1985; orig. London, Book Club Associates, 1966)

Marillier, H.C., *University Magazines and their Makers* (London: H. W. Bell, 1902)

Markus, Julia, *J. Anthony Froude: The Last Undiscovered Great Victorian, A Biography* (New York: Scribner, 2005)

Marsh, George L., 'Introduction' and notes, *John Hamilton Reynolds: Poetry and Prose* (London: Humphrey Milford, 1928), 9-48

Marsh, Joss, *Word Crimes: Blasphemy, Culture and Literature in Nineteenth-Century England* (Chicago: University of Chicago Press, 1998)

Marsham, John Clark, *The Life and Times of Carey, Marsham and Ward, Embracing the History of the Serampore Mission*, 2 vols (London: Longman, Brown, Green, Longmans and Roberts, 1859)

Marston, Edward, *After Work: Fragments from the Workshop of an Old Publisher* (London: William Heinemann, 1904)

Marston, R. B., 'The Late John Greville Fennell', *Fishing Gazette* (31 Jan. 1885), 51

Martin, Carol, *George Eliot's Serial Fiction* (Columbus: Ohio State University Press, 1994)

Martin, Henri-Jean, and Roger Chartier, eds, *Histoire de l'édition française. v. 3, Le Temps des éditeurs: du Romantisme à la Belle Époque* (Paris: Promodis, 1985)

Martin, J.C. and M. O'Sullivan, eds, *Remains of the Rev. Samuel O'Sullivan, DD* (Dublin: J. McClashan, 1853)

Martin, Ralph G., *Jennie: The Life of Lady Randolph Churchill: The Dramatic Years, 1875-1921* (Englewood Cliffs, NJ: Prentice Hall, 1971)

Martin, Wallace, *The New Age under Orage: Chapters in English Cultural History* (Manchester: Manchester University Press, 1967)

Martineau, Harriet, *Illustrations of Political Economy*, 9 vols (London: Charles Fox, 1832-1834)

------, *Poor Laws and Paupers Illustrated*, 2 vols (London: Charles Fox for SDUK, 1833-1834)

------, *Illustrations of Taxation*, 2 vols (London: Charles Fox, 1834)

------, 'On the Duty of Studying Political Economy', *Monthly Repository*, 7 (Jan.1832), 24-34

Mason, John, 'Monthly and Quarterly Reviews, 1865-1914' in Boyce, Curran and Wingate (1978), 281-293

Mason, Nicholas, ed., *Blackwood's Magazine, 1817-25: Selections from Maga's Infancy*, 6 vols (London: Pickering and Chatto, 2006)

Mason, Tony, *Association Football and English Society, 1863-1915* (Brighton: Harvester Press, 1980)

------, 'Sporting News 1860-1914' in Harris and Lee (1986), 168-186

------, 'Sport' in Vann and VanArsdel (1994) 291-297

Massingham, H. W., *The London Daily Press* (London: Fleming H. Revell Company, 1892)

Masters, Brian, *The Life of E. F. Benson* (London: Chatto and Windus, 1991)

Mathews, Joseph, J., *George W. Smalley: Forty Years a Foreign Correspondent* (North Carolina: University of North Carolina Press, 1973)

Mathias, Roland, 'The Lonely Editor: A Glance at Anglo-Welsh Magazines' in *A Ride Through the Woods: Essays on Anglo-Welsh Literature* (Bridgend: Poetry Wales Press, 1985)

Matthew, H. C. G. and B., Harrison, eds, *ODNB: from the Earliest Times to the Year 2000* (Oxford: Oxford University Press, 2004)

Maude, Pamela, 'Portrait of a Perfectionist: Edward Hudson the Founder of *Country Life*', *Country Life*, 141 (12 January 1967), 58-60

Maunder, Andrew, 'Ellen Wood as a Writer: Rediscovering Collins's Rival', *Wilkie Collins Society Journal*, 3 (2000), 17-31

------, ed., *Mary Elizabeth Braddon*, v. 1 in *Lives of Victorian Literary Figures Part 5*, 3 vols, ed. by William Baker, Judith L Fisher, Andrew Gasson and Andrew Maunder (London: Pickering and Chatto, 2007)

Maurer, Oscar E., 'Anonymity vs. Signature in Victorian Reviewing', *University of Texas Studies in English*, 27 (June 1948), 1-27

------, 'Andrew Lang and *Longman's Magazine*', *University of Texas Studies in English*, 24 (1965), 152-178

Maurice, Arthur Bartlett, 'Dickens as an Editor', *Bookman*, 30 (1909), 111-114

Maxwell, William Hamilton, *Erin-Go-Bragh: Or, Irish Life Pictures* (London: R. Bentley, 1859; repr. New York: Garland, 1979)

May's British and Irish Press Guide and Advertiser's Handbook and Dictionary (1874, 1877-1880, 1883-1889)

Mayer, Henry, *The Press in Australia*, (London: Angus & Robertson, 1964)

Mayhew, Henry, *London Labour and the London Poor* (London: Griffin Bohn, 1861)

Mays, Kelly J., 'The Disease of Reading and Victorian Periodicals' in Jordan and Patten (1995), 165-194

Meadows, A. J., *Science and Controversy: A Biography of Sir Norman Lockyer* (London: Macmillan, 1972)

Meier, Olga, ed., *The Daughters of Karl Marx* (London: Deutsch, 1982)

Mellick, J.S.D., *The Passing Guest: A Life of Henry Kingsley* (St Lucia: University of Queensland Press, 1983)

Melville, Joy, *Mother of Oscar: The Life of Jane Francesca Wilde* (London: John Murray, 1994)

Melville, Lewis, ed., *Stray Papers: Being Stories, Reviews, Verses, and Sketches (1821-1847)* (London: Hutchinson and Co., 1901)

Mendes, Peter, *Clandestine Erotic Fiction in English, 1800-1930: A Bibliographical Study* (Aldershot: Scolar Press, 1993)

[Menzies, John], *The House of Menzies* (Edinburgh: John Menzies and Company, 1958)

Merriam, Harold G., *Edward Moxon, Publisher of Poets* (New York: Columbia University Press, 1939)

Merrill, Linda, *A Pot of Paint, Aesthetics on Trial in Whistler v. Ruskin* (Washington DC: Smithsonian Institution Press, 1992)

Merrill, Lisa, *When Romeo was a Woman: Charlotte Cushman and Her Circle of Female Spectators* (Ann Arbor: University of Michigan Press, 1999)

Metcalf, Priscilla, *James Knowles, Victorian Editor and Architect* (Oxford: Oxford University Press, 1980)

Metford, J. C. J., 'An Early Liverpool Hispanist: John Rutter Chorley', *Bulletin of Hispanic Studies*, 25 (1948), 247-259

Meyers, Terry L., ed., *The Uncollected Letters of Algernon Charles Swinburne*, 2 vols (London: Pickering & Chatto, 2004-2005)

Meynell, Viola, *Alice Meynell: A Memoir* (New York: Charles Scribner's Sons, 1929)

Micklethwait, John and Adrian Woolridge, *The Company* (London: Phoenix, 2003)

Micklethwaite, Lucy and Brigid Peppin, *Dictionary of British Book Illustrators: the Twentieth Century* (London: John Murray, 1983)

Miles, D. *Francis Place, 1771-1854: The Life of a Remarkable Radical* (London: St Martin's Press, 1988)

Mill, James, 'Periodical Literature', *Westminster Review*, 1 (Jan.1824), 206-268, in King and Plunkett (2005), 14-21

Mill, John Stuart, *The Early Draft of John Stuart Mill's Autobiography*, ed. by Jack Stillinger (Urbana: University of Illinois Press, 1961)

------, *Autobiography* (London: Oxford University Press, 1969)

------, *On Liberty* (London: Longman's, Green and Co., 1865), reptd. in *On Liberty and Other Essays,* ed. by John Grey (Oxford: Oxford University Press, 1998)

Miller, A.H., *The* Dundee Advertiser, *1801-1901: A Centenary Memoir* (Dundee: John Leng & Co., 1901)

Miller, Anita, *Arnold Bennett: An Annotated Bibliography, 1887-1932* (New York: Garland, 1977)

Miller, Rev. Henry, ed., *Memoirs of Dr Robert Blakey* (London: Trubner & Co., 1879)

Miller, T.Y., ed., *Dundee Past and Present* (Dundee: William Kidd & Sons, 1909)

Millgate, Michael, ed., *Thomas Hardy's Public Voice: The Essays, Speeches, and Miscellaneous Prose* (Oxford: Clarendon Press, 2001)

Mills, J. Saxon, *Sir Edward Cook, KBE: a Biography* (New York: Dutton, 1921)

Mills, William Haslam, *The Manchester Guardian: A Century of History* (New York: Henry Holt, 1922)

Milne, Maurice, *The Newspapers of Northumberland and Durham: A Study of their Progress during the 'Golden Age' of the Provincial Press* (Newcastle-upon-Tyne: Frank Graham, 1971)

------, 'The "Veiled Editor" unveiled: William Blackwood and his Magazine', *Publishing History,* 16 (1984), 87-103

------, 'The Management of a Nineteenth-Century Magazine: William Blackwood and Sons', *Journal of Newspaper and Periodical History*, 1.3 (Summer 1985), 24-33

Mineka, Francis, *The Dissidence of Dissent: the* Monthly Repository *1806-1838* (Chapel Hill: University of North Carolina Press, 1944)

Minney, R. J., *Viscount Southwood* (London: Odhams, 1954)

Mitchell, Jack, 'Tendencies in Narrative Fiction in the London-Based Socialist Press of the 1880's and 1890's' in *The Rise of Socialist Fiction*, ed. by H. Gustav Klaus (Brighton: Harvester Press, 1987), 49-72

Mitchell, Sally, *The Fallen Angel: Chastity, Class and Women's Reading 1835-1880* (Bowling Green, Ohio: Bowling Green University Popular Press, 1981)

------, *Victorian Britain: an Encyclopaedia* (London: St. James Press, 1988)

------, *The New Girl: Girls' Culture in England, 1880-1915* (New York: Columbia University Press, 1995)

------, *Frances Power Cobbe: Victorian Feminist, Journalist, Reformer* (Charlottesville and London: University of Virginia Press, 2004)

[Mitchell's] Newspaper Press Directory and Advertisers' Guide (London: C. Mitchell, 1846-)

Mix, Katherine Lyon, *A Study in Yellow: The Yellow Book and Its Contributors* (Lawrence: University of Kansas Press, 1960)

Mohr, Peter D., 'Philanthropy and the Crippled Child: the Band of Kindness and the Crippled Children's Help Society in Manchester and Salford 1882-1948' (unpublished MSc. dissertation: Manchester, 1991)

------, 'Gilbert Kirlew and the Development of Crippled Children's Societies in Victorian Manchester and Salford', *Manchester Region History Review*, 6 (1992), 42-48

Moleyns, Clara E. de, 'Interview. Miss F. Henrietta Muller', *Woman's Herald* (28 November 1891), 916

Molony, John N., *A Soul Came into Ireland: Thomas Davis 1814-1845* (Dublin: Geography Publications, 1995)

Montluzin, Emily Lorraine de, 'William Blackwood: the Human Face behind the Mask of "Ebony" ', *Keats-Shelley Journal*, 36 (1987), 158-189

------, 'Attributions of Authorship in the *British Critic* during the Editorial Regime of Robert Nares, 1793-1813', *Studies in Bibliography* 51 (1998), 241-258

------, 'The *Anti-Jacobin* Revisited: Newly Identified Contributions to the *Anti-Jacobin Review* during the Editorial Regime of John Gifford, 1798-1806', *Library*, 4.3 (2003), 278-302

Moore, D. C., 'The Other Face of Reform', *Victorian Studies,* 5 (1961), 7-34

Moore, James, 'Wallace's Malthusian Moment: The Common Context Revisited' in Lightman (1997), 290-311

Moore, James Robert, 'Progressive Pioneers: Manchester Liberalism, the Independent Labour Party, and Local Politics in the 1890s', *Historical Journal,* 44.4 (2001), 989-1013

Moore, Judith, *A Zeal for Responsibility: The Struggle for Professional Nursing in Victorian England 1868-1883* (Athens, G.A.: University of Georgia Press, 1988)

Moore, Rayburn S., ed., *The Correspondence of Henry James and the House of Macmillan, 1877-1914* (London: Macmillan, 1993)

Moran, James, *Printing Presses: History and Development from the Fifteenth Century To Modern Times* (London: Faber & Faber, 1973)

Moran, William R., ed., *Herman Klein and* The Gramophone (Portland, OR: Amadeus Press, 1990)

Morbey, Charles, *Charles Knight: an Appreciation and Bibliography of a Great Victorian Publisher* (Birmingham: Birmingham Polytechnic Department of Librarianship, 1979)

Morgan, Charles, *The House of Macmillan 1843-1943* (London: Macmillan, 1944)

-Morgan, Kenneth O., *Keir Hardie: Radical and Socialist* (London: Weidenfeld and Nicolson, 1975)

Morgan, P.F., ed., *The Letters of Thomas Hood* (Edinburgh: Oliver and Boyd, 1973)

Morison, Stanley, *A Memoir of John Bell, 1745-1831* (Cambridge: Cambridge University Press, 1930)

------, *The English Newspaper* (Cambridge: Cambridge University Press, 1932)

Morley, John, 'Memorials of a Man of Letters', *Fortnightly Review*, n.s. 136 (April 1878), 596-610)

Morpurgo, J.E., ed., *The Autobiography of Leigh Hunt* (London: The Cresset Press, 1948)

Morrell, J. B., 'The Chemist Breeders: the Research Schools of Liebig and Thomas Thomson', *Ambix*, 19 (1972), 1-46

Morris, Hazel, *Hand, Head and Heart: Samuel Carter Hall and the* Art Journal (Norwich: Michael Russell, 2002)

Morris, Lewis, 'Proem', *The Universal Review*, 1.1 (May 1888), 1-4

Morphet, David, *Louis Jennings, MP, Editor of the* New York Times *and Tory Democrat* (London: Notion Books, 2001)

------, 'Political Comment in the *Quarterly Review* after Croker', *VPR*, 36. 2 (2003), 109-134

Morison, Stanley, *The English Newspaper: Some Account of the Physical Development of Journals Printed in London Between 1622 & The Present Day* (Cambridge: Cambridge University Press, 1932)

Morrison, R., 'John Wilson and the Editorship of *Blackwood's Magazine*', *Notes & Queries*, 244 (March 1999), 48-50

Mortimer, Russell S., 'Quaker Printers, 1750-1850', *Journal of Friends' Historical Society*, 50.3 (1963), 100-133

Morton, Peter, *The Busiest Man in England: Grant Allen and the Writing Trade, 1875-1900* (New York: Palgrave MacMillan, 2005)

Moss, Arthur W., *Valiant Crusade: The History of the RSPCA* (London: Cassell, 1961)

Moss, David, '*Circular to Bankers:* The Role of the Proto-Typical Trade Journal in the Evolution of the Middle Class Professional Consciousness', *VPR*, 25: 3 (1992), 129-136

------, and Chris Hosgood, "The Financial and Trade Press" in Vann and VanArsdel (1994), 199-218

Mountjoy, Peter Roger, 'Thomas Bywater Smithies, Editor of the *British Workman*', *VPR*, 18.2 (Summer 1985), 46-56

Mozley, Fanny, and Frank Mozley, 'Memoir', in *Essays from Blackwood's by the Late Anne Mozley*, (Edinburgh and London: Blackwood, 1892) [vii]-xx

Munford, William, *Penny Rate: Aspects of British Library History, 1850-1950* (London: Library Association, 1951)

Murphy, Paul Thomas, *Toward a Working-Class Canon: Literary Criticism in British Working-Class Periodicals, 1816-1858* (Columbus: Ohio State University Press, 1994)

Murray, Bill, *The Old Firm: Sectarianism, Sport and Society in Scotland*, rev. edn (Edinburgh: John Donald, 2000)

Murray, David Christie, *Recollections* (London: John Long, 1908)

Murray, Frank, 'Thomas Bywater Smithies and the *British Workman*: Temperance Education and Mass-Circulation Graphic Imagery for the Working Classes 1855-1883' (unpublished PhD thesis: University of Salford, 2007)

------, 'Often Taken Where a Tract is Refused: T.B. Smithies, the *British Workman*, and the Popularisation of the Religious and Temperance Message' in Brake and Demoor (Houndsmill: Palgrave, 2008)

Murray, Janet Horowitz and Myra Stark, 'The *Englishwoman's Review*: An Introduction' in *The English Woman's Review of Social and Industrial Questions: An Index* (New York and London: Garland, 1985)

Murray, Padmini Ray, 'Newspapers' in Bell (2007), 370-381

Murray, Peter, *George Petrie (1790-1866): The Rediscovery of Ireland's Past* (Cork: Crawford Municipal Art Gallery; Kinsale: Gandon Editions, 2004)

Murphy, Martin, *Blanco White: Self-Banished Spaniard* (New Haven and London: Yale University Press, 1989)

Murphy, Patricia, *Time is of the Essence: Temporality, Gender, and the New Woman* (Albany: State University of New York Press, 2000)

Murtagh, Anne, 'The *New Review*: A Glimpse at the Nineties', *VPR*, 14.1 (1981), 11-21

Musical Times and Singing Class Circular, 35 (June 1894), 369-377, 'Our Jubilee. Reflections and a Retrospect'/'The Musical Times. Points of Interest in its Journalistic and Literary Career'

Musical Times, 57 (1 May 1916), 250, 'Obituary: John F. Runciman'

Mussell, James, '"This is ours and for us": the *Mechanic's Magazine* and Low Scientific Culture in Regency London' in *Repositioning Victorian Sciences*, ed. by D. Clifford (London, New York: Anthem Press, 2006)

------, 'Nineteenth-Century Popular Science Magazines', *Journalism Studies*, 8 (2007a), 656-666

------, *Science, Time and Space in the Late Nineteenth-Century Periodical Press* (Aldershot: Ashgate 2007b)

Musson, A.E., 'Newspaper Printing in the Industrial Revolution', *The Economic History Review*, n.s. 10.3 (1958), 411-426

Mutch, Deborah, *English Socialist Periodicals, 1880-1900: A Reference Source* (Aldershot: Ashgate, 2005)

------, ' "A Working Class Tragedy": The Fiction of Henry Hyndman', *Nineteenth-Century Studies*, 20 (2006), 99-112

Myers, Harris, *William Henry Pyne and his 'Microcosm'* (Stroud: Sutton, 1996)

Myers, Robin, 'Writing for Booksellers in the Early Nineteenth Century: a Case Study' in *Author/ Publisher Relations during the Eighteenth and Nineteenth Centuries*, ed. by Robin Myers and Michael Harris (Oxford: Oxford Polytechnic Press, 1983)

N

Nahin, Paul J., *Oliver Heaviside: Sage in Solitude, the Life, Work and Times of an Electrical Genius of the Victorian Age* (New York: IEEE Press, 1988)

Nalbach, Alex, ' "The Software of Empire": Telegraphic News Agencies and Imperial Publicity, 1865-1914' in *Imperial Co.-Histories: National Identities and the British and Colonial Press*, ed. by Julie F. Codell (Teaneck, NJ: Fairleigh Dickinson University Press, 2003), 68-94

Napier, M, ed., *Selections from the Correspondence of Macvey Napier* (London: Macmillan, 1879)

Nash, Andrew, 'A Publisher's Reader on the Verge of Modernity', *Book History*, 6 (2003), 175-195

------, 'Life in Gissing's New Grub Street: David Christie Murray and the Practice of Authorship 1880-1900', *Publishing History*, 51 (2000), 23-60.

Nash, David S., *Blasphemy in Modern Britain: 1789 to the Present* (Aldershot: Ashgate, 1999)

Naylor, Leonard E., *The Irrepressible Victorian; The Story of Thomas Gibson Bowles* (London; Macdonald, 1965)

Nead, Lynda, *Victorian Babylon* (New Haven and London: Yale University Press, 2000)

Neeley, Kathryn A., *Mary Somerville: Science, Illumination and the Female Mind* (Cambridge: Cambridge University Press, 2001)

Neisius, Jean Gano, 'Acting the Role of Romance: Text and Subtext in the Work of Florence Marryat' (unpublished PhD thesis: Texas Christian University, 1992)

Nelson, James G., *The Early Nineties: A View from the Bodley Head* (Cambridge, MA: Harvard University Press, 1970)

------, *Publisher to the Decadents: Leonard Smithers in the Careers of Beardsley, Wilde, Dowson* (University Park: Pennsylvania State University Press, 2000)

Nesbitt, George Lyman, *Benthamite Reviewing; the First Twelve Years of the Westminster Review, 1824-1836* (New York: Columbia University Press, 1934)

Nestor, Pauline, 'A New Departure in Women's Publishing: The *English Woman's Journal* and the *Victoria Magazine*', *VPR*, 15 (1982), 93-106

Nevett, Terence R., 'The Development of Commercial Advertising, 1800-1914' (unpublished PhD thesis: University of London: 1979)

------, *Advertising in Britain: a History* (London: Heinemann, 1982)

------, 'Media Planning in Nineteenth Century Britain' in *Marketing in the Long Run*, ed. by Stanley Hollander and Terence Nevett (East Lancing, MI: Graduate School of Business Administration, Michigan State University, 1985), 18-29

------, 'Advertising' in Vann and VanArsdel (1994), 219-234

New York Times (18 Aug.1922) 8

Newman, Thomas Prichard, *Memoir of the Life and Works of Edward Newman by his Son* (1876); facs., with a new introduction by E. W. Classey, Classica Entomologica, no. 6 (Farringdon: Classey, 1980)

Newmann, Kate, *Dictionary of Ulster Biography* (Belfast: Queen's University, 1993)

[Newspaper Stamps] *A Return of the Number of Newspaper Stamps* (House of Commons Papers, 1852-1856)

Nightingale, Benjamin, *The Story of the Lancashire Congregational Union 1806-1906* (Manchester: John Heywood, 1906)

'Nimrod' [Charles James Apperley], *The Life of a Sportsman* (New York: D. Appleton & Co., 1903)

------, *My Life and Times*, ed. by E. D. Cuming (Edinburgh: William Blackwood, 1927)

Nichols, H.D., 'The *Guardian* before Scott' in *C.P Scott (1846-1932): The Making of the* Manchester Guardian (London: Frederick Muller, 1946)

Nichols, Phillip A., *Homeopathy and the Medical Profession* (London: Croom Helm, 1988)

Nichols, Robert Cradock, *Memoir of the late John Gough Nichols, F. S. A.* (London: Westminster, 1874)

[Nicholson, Renton] *The Lord Chief Baron Nicholson: An Autobiography* (London: G. Vickers, 1860)

Nicoll, Mildred Robertson, ed., *The Letters of Annie S. Swan* (London: Hodder and Stoughton, 1945)

Nicoll, W. Robertson, *James MacDonnell, Journalist* (London: Hodder and Stoughton, 1890)

------, 'Ten Years of the *Bookman*', *Bookman*, 20 (1901), 174-175

------, *A Bookman's Letters* (London: Hodder and Stoughton, 1913)

Niessen, Olwen C., 'Temperance' in Vann and VanArsdel (1994), 251-227

Nilsson, Nils Gunnar, 'The Origin of the Interview', *Journalism Quarterly*, 48 (1971), 707-713

Noakes, Aubrey, *The World of Henry Alken* (London: H.F. & G. Witherby Ltd., 1952)

Noble, James Ashcroft, 'A Pre-Raphaelite Magazine', *Fraser's Magazine*, o.s. 105, n.s. 25 (May 1882), 568-580

Noble, John, *Bibliography of Inverness Newspapers and Periodicals* (Stirling: Eneas Mackay, 1903)

Nockles, Peter Benedict, *The Oxford Movement in Context. Anglican High Churchmanship, 1760-1857* (Cambridge: Cambridge University Press, 1994)

Nolte, Eugene A., 'The Letters of David Macbeth Moir to William Blackwood and His Sons in the National Library of Scotland' (unpublished PhD Thesis: Texas Technological College, 1955)

Norman, Edward, *The Victorian Christian Socialists* (Cambridge: Cambridge University Press, 1987)

North, John S., ed., *The Waterloo Directory of English Newspapers and Periodicals, 1800-1900*, series 1, 10 vols; series 2, 20 vols (Waterloo: North Waterloo Academic Press, 1997, 2003)

-------, ed., *The Waterloo Directory of Irish Newspapers and,Periodicals, 1900-1900*, 2 vols (Waterloo: North Waterloo Academic Press, 1986)

-------, ed., *The Waterloo Directory of Scottish Newspapers and Periodicals, 1900-1900*, 2 vols (Waterloo: North Waterloo Academic Press, 1989)

North Wales Chronicle (26 Dec. 1868), review of S. W. Partridge and Co.s Publications

Nossiter, T. J., *Influence, Opinion and Political Idioms in Reformed England. Case Studies from the North East 1832-1874* (Brighton: Harvester Press, 1975)

Notes & Queries, 184.4 (1943), 99-100, 'The Annual Register'

Nowell-Smith, Simon, *The House of Cassell 1848-1958* (London: Cassell, 1958)

------, *International Copyright Law and the Publisher in the Reign of Queen Victoria* (Oxford: Clarendon Press, 1968)

Nurse, Bernard, 'George Cruikshank's *The Antiquarian Society* and Sir Henry Charles Englefield', *Antiquaries Journal*, 80 (2000), 316-320

O

O'Brien, Kevin H.F., 'Robert Sherard: Friend of Oscar Wilde', *English Literature in Transition*, 48 (1985), 3-29

------, 'Irene Osgood, John Richmond Limited and the Wilde Circle', *Publishing History*, 22 (1987), 73-93

------, 'Robert Harborough Sherard' in Cevasco (1993), 548-549

Ó Broin, Léon, 'R. R. Madden, Historian of the United Irishmen', *Irish University Review*, 2.1 (1972), 20-33

O'Connor, T. P., 'The New Journalism', *The New Review*, 1 (1889), 423-434 in King and Plunkett (2004) v. 3

------, *Memoirs of an Old Parliamentarian*, 2 vols (London: Ernest Benn, 1929)

O'Day, Rosemary and David Englander, *Mr. Charles Booth's Inquiry: Life and Labour of the People in London Reconsidered* (London: Hambledon Press, 1993)

O'Leary, Patrick, *Regency Editor: The Life of John Scott* (Aberdeen: Aberdeen University Press, 1983)

Oliphant, Margaret, *Annals of a Publishing House: William Blackwood and his Sons*, 2 vols, (Edinburgh and London: Blackwood, 1897; continued with v. 3 by Mrs Gerald Porter, 1898)

------, 'The Byways of Literature: Reading for the Million', *Blackwood's Edinburgh Magazine*, 84 (1858) 200-216 in King and Plunkett (2005), 198-206

Olsen, Donald J., 'The Changing Image of London in *The Builder*', *VPR*, 19 (March 1973), 4-9

Olsen G. W., 'Anglican Temperance Movements in England, 1859-1873: An Example of Practical Ecumenism', in *Canadian Catholic Historical Association Study Sessions*, 40 (1973), 41-51

O'Malley, Tom and Clive Soley, *Regulating the Press* (London: Pluto, 2000)

Onslow, Barbara, *Women of the Press in Nineteenth Century Britain* (Basingstoke, Hampshire: Macmillan Press Ltd, 2000)

------, 'Sensationalising Science: Braddon's Marketing of Science in Belgravia', *VPR*, 35: 2 (Summer 2002), 160-177

------, 'Preaching to the Ladies' in Brake and Codell (2005), 88-102

Oppenheim, Janet, *The Other World: Spiritualism and Psychical Research in England, 1850-1914* (Cambridge: Cambridge University Press, 1985)

Ordish, T. Fairman, '*Chambers's Journal*', *Bibliographer*, 4.3 (1883), 57-65

Orel, Harold, *Victorian Literary Critics: George Henry Lewes, Walter Bagehot, Richard Holt Hutton, Leslie Stephen, Andrews Lang, George Saintsbury and Edmund Gosse* (London: St. Martin's Press, 1984)

Osborne, John W., 'Robert Blatchford: Neglected Socialist', *Journal of the Rutgers University Libraries*, (1997), 62-67

Osbourn, R. V., 'The British Quarterly Review', *Review of English Studies*, 1.2 (April, 1950), 147-152

Ostrom, Hans, 'Edward Moxon' in Anderson and Rose (1991), 213-218

Ousby, Ian, *The Cambridge Guide to Literature in English* (Cambridge: Cambridge University Press, 1993)

Overfield, T. Donald, *The Way of a Man with a Trout* (London and Trowbridge: Benn, 1977)

P

Pall Mall Gazette (23 Nov. 1886), 1-2, 'The Worst Newspaper in England'

Palmegiano, E.M., 'Women and British Periodicals 1832-1876', Toronto, *VPN*, 9 (1976), 3-36

------, *Health and British Magazines in the Nineteenth Century* (Lanham MD and London: Scarecrow Press, 1998)

Palmer, Bernard, *Gadfly for God: A History of the* Church Times (London: Hodder and Stoughton, 1991

Palmer, H.J., 'The March of the Advertiser', *Nineteenth Century*, 41 (Jan. 1897), 135-141

Palmer, Michael, 'The British Press and International News 1851-99: of Agencies and Newspapers' in Boyce, Curran and Wingate (1978), 204-219

Pantazzi, Sybile, 'Elliot Stock', *Book Collector*, 20 (Spring 1971), 25-46

Parker, Mark, *Literary Magazines and British Romanticism* (Cambridge: Cambridge University Press, 2000)

Parnaby, Margaret Rachel, 'William Johnson Fox and the *Monthly Repository* Circle of 1832-1836' (unpublished PhD Thesis: Australian National University, 1979)

Paroissien, David, *An English Lady in Paris: the Diary of Frances Anne Crewe 1786* (Oxford: Blackwell, 2007)

Parrinder, Patrick and Robert M. Philmus, eds, *H. G. Wells's Literary Criticism*, (Brighton: Harvester Press, 1980)

Parry, Melanie, ed., *Chambers Biographical Dictionary* (London: Chambers Harrap Publishers, 1997)

Partington, John, S., *H. G. Wells in Nature, 1893-1946* (Oxford: Peter Lang, 2008)

Passmore, J. A., 'G. F. Stout's Editorship of Mind (1892-1920)', *Mind*, n.s. 85 (1976), 17-36

Patten, Robert L., *Dickens and his Publishers* (Oxford: Oxford University Press, 1978)

------, *George Cruikshank's Life, Times and Art*, 2 vols (Cambridge: Lutterworth Press, 1992, 1996)

------, and David Finkelstein, 'Editing *Blackwood's*; or, What Do Editors Do?' in Finkelstein (2006) 146-183

Patterson, A. Temple, *Radical Leicester: A History of Leicester 1780-1850* (Leicester: University College, 1954)

Patterson, Elizabeth Chambers, *Mary Somerville and the Cultivation of Science, 1815-1840* (Boston, MA and The Hague: Martinus Nijhoff Publishers, 1983)

Paulin, Tom, *The Day-Star of Liberty: William Hazlitt's Radical Style* (London: Faber, 1999)

Paylor, Suzanne, 'Scientific Authority and the Democratic Intellect: Popular Encounters with Darwinian Ideas in Later Nineteenth-Century Britain, with Special Reference to the Secularist Movement' (unpublished D.Phil. thesis: University of York, 2002)

Payn, James, *Gleams of Memory* (London: Smith, Elder & Co., 1894)

Paz, D.G., *Popular Anti-Catholicism in Mid-Victorian England* (Stanford: Stanford University Press, 1992)

Pearce, J., *The Life and Teachings of Joseph Livesey Comprising His Autobiography with an Introductory Review of his Labours as Reformer and Teacher* (London: National Temperance League, c. 1885)

Pearson, J., ' "Books, my greatest joy": Constructing the Female Reader in *The Lady's Magazine* 1770-1800', *Women's Writing*, 3 (1996), 3-16

Pearson, Richard, *W. M. Thackeray and the Mediated Text: Writing for Periodicals in the Mid-Nineteenth Century* (Aldershot/ Vermont: Ashgate, 2000)

Peattie, Roger W., 'William Michael Rossetti's Art Notices in the Periodicals, 1850-1878: An Annotated Checklist', *VPN*, 8 (June 1975), 79-92

Pebody, Charles, *English Journalism, and the Men who have Made it* (London: Cassell, Petter, Galpin & Co., 1882)

Peel, J.D.Y., *Herbert Spencer: The Evolution of a Sociologist* (London: Heinemann, 1971)

Peiris, William, *Edwin Arnold: A Brief Account of his Life and Contribution to Buddhism* (Kandy: Buddhist Publication Society, 1970)

Pelling, Henry, 'H. H. Champion: Pioneer of Labour Representation', *Cambridge Journal*, 6 (1952-1953), 222-238

Pennell, Elizabeth, *Nights. Rome. Venice in the Aesthetic Eighties; Paris in the Fighting Nineties* (London: Heinemann, 1916)

------, *Life and Letters of Joseph Pennell*, 2 vols (London: Benn, 1930)

Penzler, Otto and Chris Steinbrunner, *Encyclopedia of Mystery and Detection* (New York: McGraw Hill, 1976)

Pereira, Ernest and Michael Chapman, *Introduction to African Poems of Thomas Pringle* (Durban and Pietermaritzburg: Killie Campbell Africana Library and University of Natal Press, 1989)

Perkin, Harold, *The Origins of Modern English Society, 1780-1880* (London: Routledge and Kegan Paul, 1969)

------, *The Rise of Professional Society: England Since 1880* (London: Routledge, 1989)

Peters, Catherine, *The King of Inventors* (London: Secker & Warburg, 1991)

Peterson, M. Jeanne, 'Medicine' in Vann and VanArsdel (1994), 22-44

Phegley, Jennifer, *Educating the Proper Woman Reader: Victorian Family Literary Magazines and the Cultural Health of the Nation* (Columbus: Ohio State University Press, 2004a)

------, 'Literary Piracy, Nationalism, and Women Readers in *Harper's New Monthly Magazine*, 1850-1855' in *American Periodicals: A Journal of History, Criticism, and Bibliography*, 14.1 (2004b), 63-90

------, 'Domesticating the Sensation Novelist: Ellen Price Wood as Author and Editor of the *Argosy Magazine*', *VPR*, 38.2 (Summer 2005), 180-198

------, 'Mary Elizabeth Braddon' in *Kindred Hands: Letters on Writing by Women Authors, 1860-1920*, ed. by Jennifer Cognard-Black and Elizabeth MacLeod Walls (Iowa City: University of Iowa Press, 2006), 87-106

Phillips, Alastair, *Glasgow's Herald: Two Hundred years of a Newspaper 1783-1983* (Glasgow: Drew, 1982)

Phillips, Evelyn March, 'Women's Newspapers', *Fortnightly Review*, o.s. 62, n.s. 58 (1894), 661-670 in King and Plunkett (2004), v. 3

Pickering, Paul A., *Chartism and Chartists in Manchester and Salford* (London/Basingstoke: Macmillan, 1995)

------, and A. Tyrrell, *The People's Bread: A History of the Anti-Corn Law League* (London: Leicester University Press, 2000)

Pickering, Samuel, Jr., *The Moral Tradition in English Fiction 1785-1850* (Hanover, NH: The University Press of New England, 1976)

Pickvance, Ronald, *English Influences on Vincent Van Gogh* (London: Arts Council of Great Britain, 1974)

Pidduck, William, 'Introduction', *Women's Journals of the Nineteenth Century. Part One:* The Women's Penny Paper *and* Woman's Herald, *1888-1893* (Marlborough: Adam Matthew Publications, 1997), 1-4

Piesse, G.W. Septimus. 'Young's Type Composing-Machine', *Notes & Queries*, s.3, v. 49 (5 July, 1862), 19

Pike, Godfrey Holden, *John Cassell* (London: Cassell, 1894)

Pinks, William J., *The History of Clerkenwell* (London: J. T. Pickburn, 1865)

Pinney, Thomas, ed., *Essays of George Eliot* (London: Routledge and Kegan Paul, 1963)

Plarr, Victor, G, ed., *Men and Women of the Time: A Dictionary of Contemporaries*, 15th edn (London: Routledge, 1899)

Plume, W.T., 'Memoir of T. Raffles Davison', *Journal of the Royal Institute of Architects*, 44 (22 May 1937), 753

Plummer, A., *Bronterre* (London: Allen & Unwin, 1971)

Plunkett, John, *Queen Victoria: First Media Monarch* (Oxford: Oxford University Press, 2003)

Pollard, A.W., '*The Library*, A History of Forty Volumes', *Library*, s.4, 10.4 (1930), 398-417

Poole, William F. and William I. Fletcher, eds, *Poole's Index to Periodical Literature*, 5 Supplements (Boston: James R. Osgood, 1882-1908)

Pollock, Sir Frederick, 'Our Jubilee', *Law Quarterly Review*, 51 (1935), 5-10

Pocock, Tom, *Captain Marryat: Seaman, Writer and Adventurer* (London: Chatham Publishing, 2000)

Podmore, Frank, *Modern Spiritualism: A History and a Criticism*, 2 vols (London: Methuen, 1902)

Porter, A. N., 'Sir Alfred Milner and the Press, 1897-1899', *Historical Journal*, 16.2 (June1973), 323-339

Porter, Dilwyn, ' "Trusted Guide of the Investing Public": Harry Marks and the *Financial News*, 1884-1916', *Business History*, 28 (1986), 1-17

Porter, Roy, *Quacks: Fakers and Charlatans in English Medicine* (Stroud: Tempus, 2000)

------, *Bodies Politic: Disease, Death and Doctors in Britain, 1650-1900* (London: Reaktion Books, 2001)

Potter, Elaine, *The Press as Opposition: The Political Role of South African Newspapers* (London: Chatto & Windus, 1975)

Potter, Simon, J., *News and the British World: The Emergence of an Imperial Press System, 1876-1922* (Oxford University Press, Oxford, 2003)

Potts, R. A. J., 'Early Cornish Printers, 1740-1850', *Journal of the Royal Institution of Cornwall*, n.s., 4.3 (1963), 264-325

Pound, Reginald J., ed., *C. J. Grant's Political Drama: A Radical Satirist Rediscovered* (London: University College London, 1998)

------, and Geoffrey Harmsworth, *Northcliffe* (London: Cassell and Co., 1959)

------, *The Strand Magazine: 1891-1950* (London: Heinemann, 1966)

Pound, Richard, 'Serial Journalism and the Transformation of English Graphic Satire 1830-1836' (unpublished PhD thesis: University College London, 2002)

Prager, Arthur, *The Mahogany Tree: An Informal History of* Punch (New York: Hawthorn Books, 1979)

Prance, Claude A., 'Elliot Stock and Some Old Book-Collecting Magazines', *Private Library*, 3rd ser., 2 (1979), 42-48

------, 'The *Englishman's Magazine*', *Charles Lamb Bulletin*, 37 (Jan.1982), 98-101

Prettejohn, Elizabeth, 'Aesthetic Value and the Professionalization of Victorian Art Criticism 1837-78', *Journal of Victorian Culture*, 2 (Spring 1997), 71-94

Price, Leah, 'From Ghostwriter to Typewriter: Delegating Authority at the Fin de Siècle' in *The Faces of Anonymity: Anonymous and Pseudonymous Publications from the Sixteenth to the Twentieth Century*, ed. by Robert J. Griffin (Basingstoke: Palgrave, 2003), 211-232

------, and Pamela Thurschwell, eds, *Literary Secretaries/Secretarial Culture* (Aldershot: Ashgate, 2005)

Price, R. G. G., *A History of* Punch (London: Collins, 1957)

Private Wire, Centenary Issue, (Sept. 1971), 'Frederick George Creed 1871-1957. The Man, The Inventor, The Company'

Prothero, Iorwerth J., *Artisans and Politics in Early Nineteenth-Century London: John Gast and his Times* (London: Methuen, 1981)

------, *Radical Artisans in England and France 1830-70* (Cambridge: Cambridge University Press, 1997)

Pugh, R. B., 'Chartism in Somerset and Wiltshire' in *Chartist Studies*, ed. by Asa Briggs (London: Macmillan, 1959; repr. 1965), 174-219

Pursglove, Glyn, 'George Gilfillan' in *Dictionary of Literary Biography*, v. 144: *Nineteenth-Century Literary Biographers*, ed. by Steven Serafin (Detroit: Gale, 1994), 117-126

Putnis, P., 'The British Transoceanic Steamship Press in Nineteenth-Century India and Australia: an Overview', *Journal of Australian Studies*, 91 (2007), 69-79, 183-186

Pykett, Lyn, 'Reading the Periodical Press: Text and Context' in Brake, Jones and Madden (1990), 3-189

------, 'The Cause of Women and the Course of Fiction: The Case of Mona Caird' in *Gender Roles and Sexuality in Victorian Literature*, ed. by Christopher Parker (Aldershot: Scolar, 1995), 128-42

------, ' "A Daughter of Today": the Socialist-Feminist Intellectual as Woman of Letters' in *Eleanor Marx: Life, Work, Contacts,* ed. by John Stokes (Aldershot: Ashgate, 2000), 13-23

Q

Quilter, Harry, 'The New Renaissance; or, The Gospel of Intensity', *Macmillan's Magazine*, 42 (Sept. 1880), 391-400

Quinn Schmidt, Barbara, 'Novelists, Publishers, and Fiction in Middle-Class Magazines: 1860-1880', *VPR*, 17.4 (Winter 1984), 142-152

Quinton, Anthony, 'George Croom Robertson: Editor 1876-1891', *Mind*, n.s. 85 (1976), 6-16

R

Radford, Ernest, 'The Life and Death of *The Germ*', *Idler*, 13 (1898), 227-233

Radzinowicz, Leon, *Sir James Fitzjames Stephen, 1829-1894, and his Contribution to the Development of the Criminal Law* (London: Qauritch, 1957)

Rafroidi, Patrick, *Irish Literature in English: The Romantic Period, 1789-1850* (Dublin: Colin Smythe, 1980)

Raghavan, G.N.S., *The Press in India: a New History* (New Delhi: Gyan Publishing House, 1994)

Ramsay, G.G., 'The Formation of the Scottish Mountaineering Club', *Scottish Mountaineering Club Journal*, 4 (1896), 73-91

Rantanen, Terhi, 'The Globalisation of Electronic News in the Nineteenth Century', *Media, Culture and Society*, 19.4 (1997), 605-620

Rashid, Salim, 'David Robinson and the Tory Macro-Economics of *Blackwood's Edinburgh Magazine*', *History of Political Economy*, 10.2 (1978), 258-270

Rauch, Alan, *Useful Knowledge: The Victorians, Morality, and the March of Intellect* (Durham, NC: Duke University Press, 2001)

Ray, Ujjal, *From Diffidence to Reliance: Journey of a Colonial Intellectual* (India: Minerva Associates, 1993)

Read, Donald, *Press and People 1790-1850: Opinion in Three English Cities* (London: Edward Arnold, 1961)

------, *The Power of News: The History of Reuters, 1849-1989* (Oxford: Oxford University Press, 1992)

[Redivivus] 'Brunel Redivivus', 'Special Newspaper Trains', *Railway Magazine*, v. 5 (Nov.1899), 410-412

Reece, H. and O. Elton, eds, *Musical Criticisms by Arthur Johnstone* (Manchester: Manchester University Press, 1905)

Reed, David, *The Popular Magazine in Britain and the United States of America, 1880-1960* (London: British Library, 1997)

Reed, John Shelton, *Glorious Battle: The Cultural Politics of Victorian Anglo-Catholicism* (Nashville: Vanderbilt University Press, 1996)

Reid Charles, *The Music Monster: A Biography of J. W. Davison, Music Critic of* The Times *of London* (London: Quartet Books, 1984)

Reid, Forrest, *Illustrators of the Eighteen Sixties: An Illustrated Survey of the Work of 58 British Artists* (London: Faber and Gwyer, 1928; Toronto: Dover Reprints, 1975)

Reid, Harry, *Deadline: The Story of the Scottish Press* (Edinburgh: St Andrews Press, 2006)

Reid, John Cowie, *Thomas Hood*, (London: Routledge Kegan Paul, 1963)

------, *Bucks and Bruisers: Pierce Egan and Regency England* (London: Routledge Kegan Paul, 1971)

Reid, Stuart J., *Memoirs of Sir Wemyss Reid 1842-1885* (London: Cassell & Co., 1905)

Reid, T.W., *William Black: Novelist* (London: Cassell, 1902)

Reilly, Desmond, 'Robert John Kane (1809-90): Irish Chemist and Educator', *Journal of Chemical Education*, 32 (1955), 404-406

Reimer, Mavis, 'L. T. Meade' in Zaidman and Hunt (1994), 186-198

------, 'Worlds of Girls: Educational Reform and Fictional Form in L. T. Meade's School Stories' in *Culturing the Child 1690-1914: Essays in Memory of Mitzi Meyers*, ed. by Donelle Ruwe (Lanham, MD: Children's Literature Association, Scarecrow Press, 2005), 199-217

Renalds, Brenda H, 'Letitia Elizabeth Landon' in *Dictionary of Literary Biography*, v. 96, *British Romantic Poets, 1789-1832, Second Series*, ed. by John R. Greenfield (Detroit: Gale, 1990), 220-228

Rendall, Jane, ' "A moral engine"? Feminism, Liberalism and the *English Woman's Journal*' in *Equal or Different? Women's Politics, 1800-1914*, ed. by Jane Rendall (Oxford: Basil Blackwell, 1987), 112-138

Renier, Anne, *Friendship's Offering: An Essay on the Annuals and Gift Books of the Nineteenth Century* (London: Private Libraries Association, 1964)

Rennie, James, 'Book Manufactory of Bayswater', *Magazine of Botany and Gardening*, 2 (June 1834), 8

Repplier, Agnes, 'English Railway Fiction', *Points of View* (Cambridge, MA: Riverside Press, 1891), 209-239

Rice, F.A., *The* Granta *and its Contributors 1889-1914* (London: Constable & Co., 1924)

Richards, Grant, *Memories of a Misspent Youth, 1872-1896* (London: Heinemann, 1932)

Richards, Jeffrey, *Sir Henry Irving; A Victorian Actor and His World* (London and New York: Hambledon and London, 2005)

Richards, Thomas Karr, 'Gerty McDowell and the Irish Common Reader', *English Literary History*, 52.3 (Autumn 1985), 755-756

Richards, Thomas, *The Commodity Culture of Victorian England: Advertising and Spectacle, 1851-1914* (Stanford, CA: Stanford University Press, 1990)

Richardson, Angelique, *Love and Eugenics in the Late Nineteenth-Century: Rational Reproduction and the New Woman* (Oxford: Oxford University Press, 2003)

Richardson, Benjamin Ward, *Vita Medica: Chapters of a Medical Life and Work* (London: Longmans, Green, 1897)

Richardson, Joseph Hall, *From the City to Fleet Street: Some Journalistic Experiences* (London: Stanley Paul, 1927)

------, *Who Was Who: 1941-1950* (London: Adam and Charles Black, 1952)

Richardson, Rev. J., *Recollections, Political, Literary, Dramatic and Miscellaneous of the Last Half Century*, 2 vols (London: Savill and Edwards, 1855)

Richardson, Ruth, *Vintage Papers from the* Lancet (Edinburgh: Elsevier, 2006)

------, and Robert Thorne, *The* Builder: *Illustrations Index* (London: Builder Group and Hutton, 1994)

------, and Robert Thorne, "Architecture" in Vann and VanArsdel (1994), 45-61

Ricketts, Charles, *Self-Portrait* (London: Richard West, 1939)

Rickword, Edgell, *Radical Squibs and Loyal Ripostes* (London: Adams & Dart, 1971)

Riga, Frank P., and Claude A. Prance, *Index to the London Magazine* (New York and London: Garland Publishing Inc, 1978)

Riley, Sam G., ed., 'American Magazine Journalists 1741-1850' in *Dictionary of Literary Biography*, v. 73 (Detroit, Mich.: Gale Research Co., 1988)

Rivington, Septimus, *The Publishing Family of Rivington* (London: Rivington, 1919)

Roberts, Helene E., 'British Art Periodicals of the Eighteenth and Nineteenth Centuries', *VPN*, 9 (July 1970), 2-56

Roberts, Stephen, *Joseph Barker and the Radical Cause 1848-51* (Leeds: Publications of the Thoresby Society (Leeds Historical Society), 1991)

------, *Radical Politicians and Poets in Early Victorian Britain* (New York: E. Mellen Press, 1993)

------, *The Chartist Prisoners. The Radical Lives of Thomas Cooper (1805-92) & Arthur O'Neill (1819-96)* (Oxford: Peter Lang, 2008)

Robertson, David, *Sir Charles Eastlake and the Victorian Art World* (Princeton NJ: Princeton University Press, 1978)

Robinson, Annabel, *The Life and Work of Jane Ellen Harrison* (Oxford: Oxford University Press, 2002)

Robinson, Judith, *At The Sign of The Dial: Charles Haslewood Shannon and His Circle* (Lincoln: Usher Gallery, 1987)

Robinson, Solveig, 'Editing Belgravia: M E Braddon's Defence of "Light Literature" ', *VPR*, 28.2 (Summer 1995), 109-122

------, '"Amazed at our success": The Langham Place Editors and the Emergence of a Feminist Critical Tradition', *VPR*, 29.2 (1996), 159-172

Robson, John, *Marriage or Celibacy? The* Daily Telegraph *on a Victorian Dilemma* (Toronto: University of Toronto Press, 1995)

Robson, Maisie, *Arthur Mee's Dream of England: The Story of the Man who Edited the Children's Encyclopedia and the King's England Series* (Barnsley: Eynsford Hill Press, 2002)

Rochelson, Meri-Jane, 'Israel Zangwill's Early Journalism and the Formation of an Anglo-Jewish Literary Identity' in Brake, Bell and Finkelstein (2000), 178-194

------, *A Jew in the Public Arena: The Career of Israel Zangwill* (Detroit: Wayne State University Press, 2008)

Roe, Michael, 'Grimstone, Mary Leman (1796?-1869)', *Australian Dictionary of Biography*, Supplementary Volume, (Carlton, VIC: Melbourne University Press, 2005), 156-157

Rogers, Helen, *Women and the People: Authority, Authorship and the Radical Tradition* (Aldershot: Ashgate, 2000)

Roget, John Lewis, *A History of the 'Old Water-Colour' Society* (London: Longmans, 1891)

Rolleston, H. and W.A.R. Thomson, *The Practitioner*, 201 (1968) 246-249

Roll-Hansen, Diderik, *The Academy: 1869-1879* (Copenhagen: Rosenkilde and Bagger, 1957)

Rollington, Ralph, *A Brief History of Boys' Journals with Interesting Facts about the Writers of Boys' Stories* (Leicester: H. Simpson, 1913)

Rooksby, Rikky, *A.C. Swinburne: A Poet's Life* (Aldershot: Scolar Press, 1997)

Roos, David, 'The Aims and Intentions of *Nature*' in *Victorian Science and Victorian Values*, ed. by J. G. Paradis and T. Postlewait (New York: New York Academy of Sciences, 1981)

Rose, Andrea, 'Preface', *The Germ: The Literary Magazine of the Pre-Raphaelites*, ed. by Andrea Rose, (Oxford: Ashmolean Museum, 1992), v-xxiii

Rose, John Holland, 'The Unstamped Press, 1815-1836', *English Historical Review*, 12.48 (1897), 711-726

Rose, Jonathan, *The Intellectual Life of the British Working Classes* (New Haven: Yale, 2001)

Rose, Lionel, *The Erosion of Childhood: Child Oppression in Britain 1860-1918* (London: Routledge, 1991)

Rose, R.N., *The* Field, *1853-1953. A Centenary History* (London: Michael Joseph, 1953)

Rosen, Judith, 'A Different Scene of Desire: Women and Work in Penny Magazine Fiction', *Pacific Coast Philology*, 27 (1-2) (Sept. 1992), 102-109

Rosenberg, Sheila, 'John Chapman, George Eliot and the *Westminster Review*, 1852-60' (unpublished MA dissertation: University of Birmingham, 1963)

------, 'The Financing of Radical Opinion: John Chapman and the *Westminster Review*' in Shattock and Wolff (1982), 167-192

------, 'The "wicked *Westminster*": John Chapman, his Contributors and Promises Fulfilled', *VPR*, 33.3 (Fall 2000), 225-246

Rosengarten, Herbert, 'Charlotte Brontë's *Shirley* and the *Leeds Mercury*', *Studies in English Literature, 1500-1900*, 16.4 (Autumn 1976), 591-600

Ross, Janet, *Three Generations of Englishwomen: Memoirs and Correspondence of Mrs. John Taylor, Mrs. Sarah Austin, and Lady Duff Gordon*, 2 vols (London: John Murray, 1888)

Ross, Marlon B., *The Contours of Masculine Desire: Romanticism and the Rise of Women's Poetry* (Oxford: Oxford University Press, 1989)

Rossetti, William Michael, 'Introduction', repr. from 1901 Elliot Stock facsimile *The Germ* ed. Rose (1992), 5-30

------, *The P.R.B. Journal: William Michael Rossetti's Diary of the Pre-Raphaelite Brotherhood 1849-1853, Together with Other Pre-Raphaelite Documents*, ed. by William E. Fredeman (Oxford: Clarendon Press, 1975)

Routledge, George, *Routledge's Manuel of Etiquette* (London: George Routledge & Sons, 1875)

Rowdon, Harold H., *The Origins of the Brethren 1825-1850* (London: Pickering & Inglis, 1967)

Rowbotham, Judith and Kim Stevenson, eds, *Criminal Conversations: Victorian Crimes, Social Panic, and Moral Outrage* (Columbus: Ohio State University Press, 2005)

Rowe, D. J., 'Francis Place and the Historian', *History Journal*, 16 (1973)

------, Review of *The Pauper Press: A Study in Working-Class Radicalism of the 1830s* by Patricia Hollis (London: Oxford University Press, 1970) in *Historical Journal*, 14.2 (1971), 448-450.

Rowe, G. Stringer, *T. B. Smithies: A Memoir* (London: Partridge, 1884)

Rowell, George, *The Victorian Theatre, 1792-1914: A Survey* (Oxford: Oxford University Press, 1956)

Rowlette, Robert J., *Medical Press and Circular* (London: Medical Press and Circular, 1939)

Rowley, Charles, Jr., George P[rice] Boyce and William Bell Scott, 'Art Copyright, ' *Athenaeum* (24 Feb. 1883), 254-255

Rowntree, Benjamin Seebohm, *Poverty: A Study of Town Life* (London: Macmillan and Co., 1901)

Royden, Harrison, Gillian Woolven and Robert Duncan, eds, *The Warwick Guide to British Labour Periodicals 1790-1970* (Hassocks, Sussex: Harvester Press, 1977)

Royle, Edward, *Victorian Infidels: The Origins of the British Secularist Movement 1791-1866* (Totawa NJ: Rowman and Littlefield, 1974)

------, *Radicals, Secularists and Republicans: Popular Freethought in Britain 1866-1915* (Manchester: Manchester University Press, 1980)

------, *Religion, Radicalism and Free Thought in Victorian and Edwardian Britain: Collection of Periodicals, 1834-1916* (Wakefield: E.P. Microfilms, 1981)

------, *Robert Owen and the Commencement of the Millennium* (Manchester: Manchester University Press, 1998)

Rubinstein, David, *Before the Suffragettes, Women's Emancipation in the 1890s* (Brighton: Harvester Press, 1986)

Rummonds, Richard-Gabriel, *Nineteenth-Century Printing Practices and the Iron Handpress; with Selected Readings* (London: British Library, 2004)

Runciman, John F., 'The Gentle Art of Music Criticism', *New Review*, 73 (June 1895), 622

Rupke, Nicholaas A., *Richard Owen: Victorian Naturalist* (New Haven: Yale University Press, 1994)

Ruskin, John, *The Works of John Ruskin*, ed. by E.T. Cook and A. Wedderburn, 39 vols (London and New York: George Allen and Longmans, Green, and Co., 1903-1912)

Russell, Dave, 'Yearbooks', in *Encyclopedia of British Football*, ed. by Richard Cox, Dave Russell and Wray Vamplew (London: Frank Cass, 2002)

Russell, Matthew, 'Contributions to Irish Biography. No 29 – James Duffy the Publisher', *The Irish Monthly*, 23 (Nov 1895), 596

Ruth, Jennifer, 'Gross Humbug or the Language of Truth? The Case of the *Zoist*', *VPR*, 32.4 (1999), 299-323

Rutherford, Paul, *A Victorian Authority: The Daily Press in Late Nineteenth-Century Canada* (Toronto: University of Toronto Press, 1972)

Ryder, Sean, ed., *James Clarence Mangan: Selected Writings* (Dublin: University College Dublin Press, 2004)

Rylance, Rick, *Victorian Psychology and British Culture 1850-1880* (Oxford: Oxford University Press, 2000)

Rymer, James Malcolm, 'Popular Writing', *Queen's Magazine*, 1 (1842), 99-100 in King and Plunkett (2005), 170-175

S

Sage, Lorna, *The Cambridge Guide to Women's Writing in English* (New York: Cambridge University Press, 1999)

St Helier, Lady, *Memories of Fifty Years* (London: Edward Arnold, 1909)

St John-Stevas, Norman, ed., *The Collected Works of Walter Bagehot*, 15 vols (London: The Economist, 1965-1986)

Saintsbury, George, *A History of Nineteenth Century Literature, 1780-1895* (London: Macmillan & Co., 1896)

------, *The English Novel* (London: Dent, 1913)

------, *A Scrap Book* (London: Macmillan and Co. Ltd, 1922)

Sala, G.A., *The Life and Adventures of George Augustus Sala* (London: Cassell, 1895)

------, *Letters of George Augustus Sala to Edmund Yates*, ed. by Judy McKenzie, Victorian Fiction Research Guides, 19-20 (St Lucia, Australia: Dept. of English, University of Queensland, 1993)

Salmon, Richard, *Henry James and the Culture of Publicity* (Cambridge: Cambridge University Press, 1997)

Sampson, Henry, *The History of Advertising* (Chatto and Windus, 1874)

Samuels Lasner, Mark, *The Yellow Book: A Checklist and Index* (London: The Eighteen Nineties Society, 1998)

Samuelson, James, *Recollections: Being Some Experiences and Reflections Mainly on Subjects of the Day* (London: Simpkin, Marshall & Co., 1907)

Sanders, A., *The Victorian Historical Novel 1840-1880* (London: Macmillan, 1978)

Sanders, Valerie, *Eve's Renegades: Victorian Anti-Feminist Women Novelists* (Basingstoke: Macmillan, 1996)

Saunders, David, *Authorship and Copyright* (London: Routledge, 1992)

Savage, William, *A Dictionary of the Art of Printing* (London: Longman, Brown, Green and Longmans, 1841)

Saville, John, 'Introduction', The Red Republican *and* The Friend of the People, 2 vols (London: Merlin Press, 1966)

------, *1848, The British State and the Chartist Movement* (Cambridge: Cambridge University Press, 1987)

------, 'Introduction', *W. E. Adams Memoirs of a Social Atom*, 2 vols in 1, Reprints of Economic Classics (New York: Augustus M. Kelley, 1968)

Saxon-Mills, J., *Sir Edward Cook, KBE: a Biography* (London: Constable, 1921)

Schachterle, Lance, '*The Metropolitan Magazine*', Sullivan (1983), 304-308

Schaffer, Talia, *The Forgotten Female Aesthetes: Literary Culture in Late-Victorian England* (Charlottesville, VA: University Press of Virginia, 2000)

------, 'Writing a Public Self: Alice Meynell's "Unstable Equilibrium" ' in *Women's Experience of Modernity*, ed. by Ann L. Ardis and Leslie W. Lewis (Baltimore, MD: Johns Hopkins University Press, 2003), 13-30

Scheinberg, Cynthia, *Women's Poetry and Religion in Victorian England: Jewish Identity and Christian Culture* (Cambridge: Cambridge University Press, 2002)

Schenker, Heath, 'Women, Gardens and the English Middle Class in the Early Nineteenth Century' in *Bourgeois and Aristocratic Cultural Encounters in Garden Art, 1550-1850*, ed. by Michael Conan (Washington, DC: Dumbarton Oaks, 2002), 337-60

Scheuerle, W.H., *The Neglected Brother: A Study of Henry Kingsley* (Gainesville, FL: Florida State University Press, 1971)

Schiefen, Richard J, *Nicholas Wiseman and the Transformation of English Catholicism* (Shepherdstown, WV: Patmos Press, 1984)

Schivelbusch, Wolfgang, *The Railway Journey. Trains and Travel in the Nineteenth Century*, trans. by Anselm Hollo (New York: Urizen Books, 1977)

Schlicke, P.V.W., 'The Impact of Sketches by Boz', *Dickens Quarterly*, 22 (2005), 3-18

------, ed., *Oxford Reader's Companion to Dickens* (Oxford: Oxford University Press, 1999)

------, 'Barnaby Rudge' and 'Old Curiosity Shop,' in Schlicke (1999)

Schlueter, Paul and June, eds, *An Encyclopedia of British Women Writers* (New York: Garland, 1988)

Scholes, Percy, *The Mirror of Music 1844-1944: A Century of Musical Life in Britain as Reflected in the Pages of the* Musical Times, 2 vols (London and Oxford: Novello & Company Ltd and Oxford University Press, 1947)

Scholnick, Robert J., ' "The Fiery Cross of Knowledge": *Chambers's Edinburgh Journal*, 1832-1844', *VPR*, 32 (1999), 324-358

Schoyen, A.R., *The Chartist Challenge, A Portrait of George Julian Harney* (London: Heinemann, 1958)

Schuche, Elke, ' "Shafts of Thought": New Wifestyles in Victorian Feminist Periodicals in the 1890s', *Nineteenth Century Feminisms* 4 (2001), 118-134

Schudson, Michael, *The Power of News* (Cambridge, MA: Harvard University Press, 1995)

Schults, Raymond, *Crusader in Babylon: W. T. Stead and the* Pall Mall Gazette (Lincoln, NA: University of Nebraska Press, 1972)

[*Scotsman*], *The Story of the* Scotsman: *A Chapter in the Annals of British Journalism* (Edinburgh: Private Circulation, 1886)

Scott, George, *Reporter Anonymous: The Story of the Press Association* (London: Hutchinson, 1968)

Scott, J.W. Robertson, *The Story of the* Pall Mall Gazette, *of its First Editor Frederick Greenwood and of its Founder George Murray Smith* (London: Oxford University Press, 1950)

------, *The Life and Death of a Newspaper; An Account of the Temperaments, Perturbations and Achievements of John Morley, W.T. Stead, E.T. Cook, Harry Cust, J.L. Garvin, and Three Other Editors of the* Pall Mall Gazette... (London: Methuen, 1952)

Scott, Rosemary, 'The Sunday Periodical: *Sunday at Home*', *VPR,* 25 (1992), 158-162

Scott, W[illiam] B[ell], 'Mural Decorations at the Mansion of Sir Walter Trevelyan', *Sessional Papers of the Royal Academy of British Architects,* 18.3 (2 Dec. 1867), 31-46

Scottish Printing Archival Trust, *A Reputation for Excellence: A History of the Dundee and Perth Printing Industries* (Edinburgh: Merchiston Publishing, 1996)

Scull, Andrew, Charlotte MacKenzie and Nicholas Hervey, *Masters of Bedlam: The Transformation of the Mad-Doctoring Trade* (Princeton: Princeton University Press, 1996)

Secord, James A., 'Nature's Fancy: Charles Darwin and the Breeding of Pigeons', *Isis,* 72 (1981), 163-186

------, 'Behind the Veil: Robert Chambers and *Vestiges*' in *History, Humanity, and Evolution,* ed. by James R. Moore (Cambridge: Cambridge University Press, 1989), 165-94

------, *Victorian Sensation: the Extraordinary Publication, Reception, and Secret Authorship of 'Vestiges of the Natural History of Creation'* (Chicago: University of Chicago Press, 2000)

------, ed., *The Collected Works of Mary Somerville* (Bristol: Thoemmes Continuum, 2004)

Seeley, Tracy, 'Alice Meynell, Essayist: Taking Life "Greatly to Heart" ', *Women's Studies,* 27 (1998), 105-130

Sell's Dictionary of the World's Press (London: H. Sell, 1883/4-1921)

Serafin, Steven, ed., *Dictionary of Literary Biography,* v. 144: *Nineteenth-Century Literary Biographers* (Detroit: Gale, 1994)

Sessa, Anne Dzamba, *Richard Wagner and the English* (London: Associated University Presses, 1979)

[Shand, Innes], 'Contemporary Literature, I-VIII', *Blackwood's Magazine,* vols 124-125 (1878-1879) in King and Plunkett (2004), v. 3

Shannon, Brent, *The Cut of His Coat: Men, Dress, and Consumer Culture in Britain 1860-1914* (Athens OH: Ohio University Press, 2006)

Shannon-Mangan, Ellen, *James Clarence Mangan: A Biography* (Dublin: Irish Academia Press, 1996)

Sharp, Elizabeth Amelia, *William Sharp (Fiona MacLeod): A Memoir* (New York: Duffield and Company, 1910)

Shattock, Joanne, 'A Study of the *North British Review* (1844-1871); Its History, Policies and Contributors' (unpublished PhD Thesis: University of London, 1973)

------, 'Editorial Policy and the Quarterlies: the Case of the *North British Review*', *VPN,* 10 (1977), 130-139

------, 'Showman, Lion-Tamer or Hack: The Quarterly Editor at Mid-Century', *VPR,* 16.3/4 (1983), 89-103

------, *Politics and Reviewers: the* Edinburgh *and the* Quarterly *in the Early Victorian Age* (Leicester: Leicester University Press, 1989)

------, *The Oxford Guide to British Women Writers* (Oxford: Oxford University Press, 1993)

------, *The Cambridge Bibliography of English Literature*, v. 4 (1800-1900), 3rd ed. (Cambridge: Cambridge University Press: 1999)

------, 'Reviews and Monthlies' in Bell (2007), 343-357

------, and Michael Wolff, ed., *The Victorian Periodical Press: Samplings and Soundings* (Leicester: Leicester University Press, 1982)

Shaw, Bernard, *Shaw: The Papers of Bernard Shaw (1856-1950) from the British Library,* Adam Matthews Publications (2005), 'Part 3: Journalism, Lectures and Autobiographical Material' (17 microfilm reels) (Editorial Introduction by L.W. Conolly)

Shaw, David, *Gerald Massey: Chartist, Poet, Radical and Freethinker* (London: Buckland, 1995)

Shaw, G., ed., *The Official Tourists' Picturesque Guide to the London and North-Western Railway* (London: Norton and Shaw [1876])

Shaw, Gerald, *Some Beginnings: The* Cape Times, *1876-1910* (Cape Town: Oxford University Press, 1975)

------, *The* Cape Times: *an Informal History* (Cape Town: David Philip Publishers, 1999)

Sheehan, William, *The Immortal Fire Within: The Life and Work of Edward Emerson Barnard* (Cambridge, Cambridge University Press, 1995)

Sheehy, Noel, Antony J. Chapman, and Wendy A. Conroy, eds, *Biographical Dictionary of Psychology* (London: Routledge, 1997)

Sheets-Pyenson, Susan, 'Darwin's Data: His Reading of Natural History Journals, 1837-1842', *Journal of the History of Biology,* 14 (1981a), 231-248

------, 'A Measure of Success: The Publication of Natural History Journals in Early Victorian Britain', *Publishing History,* 9 (1981b), 21-36

------, 'Popular Science Periodicals in Paris and London: The Emergence of a Low Scientific Culture, 1820-75', *Annals of Science,* 42 (1985), 549-572

Sheffield Daily Telegraph, 1855-1925: a Record of Seventy Years (Sheffield: W.C. Leng & Co., [1925])

Shepard, Leslie, *The Broadside Ballad* (London: Herbert Jenkins, 1962)

Sherbo, Arthur, 'The Bibliographer, Book-Lore, and the Bookworm', *Studies in Bibliography,* 40 (1987), 207-219

Sherrington, E., 'Thomas Wakley and Reform' (unpublished D.Phil. thesis: Oxford University, 1973)

Shiman, Lilian Lewis, *Crusade against Drink in Victorian England* (New York: St. Martin's Press, 1988)

Shine, Hill and Helen, *The* Quarterly Review *under Gifford: Identification of Contributors, 1809-24* (Chapel Hill, NC: University of North Carolina Press, 1949)

Shorter, Clement King, 'Illustrated Journalism: Its Past and its Future', *Contemporary Review,* 75 (April 1899), 481-494 in King and Plunkett (2004), v. 3

------, *C. K. S.: An Autobiography*, ed. by J. M. Bulloch (Edinburgh: privately printed, 1927)

Shortland, Michael, ed., *Hugh Miller's Memoir: From Stonemason to Geologist* (Edinburgh: Edinburgh University Press, 1995)

------, ed., *Hugh Miller and the Controversies of Victorian Science* (Oxford: Clarendon, 1996)

Shortt, John, *The Law Relating to Works of Literature and Art*, 2nd edn (London: Reeves & Turner, 1884)

Shteir, Ann B., 'Elegant Recreations? Configuring Science Writing for Women' in Lightman (1997), 236-255

Shuttleworth, Sally, 'Tickling Babies: Gender, Authority and 'Baby Science' in Cantor, Dawson, et al. (2004), 199-215

Silvester, Christopher, *The Norton Book of Interviews: An Anthology from 1859 to the Present Day* (New York: W. W. Norton & Co. Inc, 1996)

Simcox, Edith, 'Eight Years of Co.-operative Shirtmaking', *Nineteenth Century*, 15 (June 1884), 1037-1054

Simmons, Jack, *The Victorian Railway* (London: Thames & Hudson, 1995)

Simo, Melanie, *Loudon and the Landscape, From Country Seat to Metropolis 1783-1843* (New Haven and London: Yale University Press, 1988)

Simonis, H., *The Street of Ink. An Intimate History of Journalism* (London: Cassell, 1917)

Simpson, Roger, *Sir John Tenniel: Aspects of His Work* (Madison, NJ: Fairleigh Dickinson University Press, 1994)

Simpson, William, *Two Famous Correspondents: The Reachs – Father and Son* (Inverness: Courier Office, 1905)

Sims, G.R., ed., *Living London*, 3 vols (1901-1903) (London: Cassell, 1901)

------, *My Life: Sixty Years Recollections of Bohemian London* (London: Eveleigh Nash, 1917)

Sinclair, Alexander, *Fifty Years of Newspaper Life, 1845-1895: Being Chiefly Reminiscences of that Time* (Glasgow, printed for private circulation, 1896)

Singleton, Frank, *Tillotsons 1850-1950* (Bolton, Lancashire: Tillotson and Son, 1950)

Sinnema, Peter, *Dynamics of the Printed Page* (Aldershot: Ashgate, 1998)

------, *The Wake of Wellington: Englishness in 1852* (Athens GA, Georgia: Ohio University Press, 2006)

Sketch (30 Jan. 1895), 23, 'Journals and Journalists of Today, XXXII: Mr Gibbons and the *Lady's Pictorial*'

Skingsley, T. A., 'Technical Training and Education in the English Printing Industry: A Study of Late-Nineteenth-Century Attitudes', *Journal of the Printing Historical Society*, Part I, 13 (1978/79), 1-25; Part II, 14 (1979/80), 1-58

Skrine, Francis Henry Bennett, *An Indian Journalist: Being the Life, Letters and Correspondence of Dr Sambhu C. Mukerjee* (Calcutta: Thacker, Spink and Co., 1895)

Skues, George Edward Mackenzie, *Itchen Memories* (London: Herbert Jenkins, 1951)

Sladen, Douglas, *Twenty Years of My Life* (London: Constable, 1914)

Slater, Michael, ed., *Uniform Edition of Dickens' Journalism*, 4 vols (v. 4 with John Drew) (London: J. M. Dent, 1994-2000)

------, *Douglas Jerrold 1803-1857* (London: Duckworth, 2002)

Smale, Nicholas, 'Thomas R. Way: his Life and Work', *The Tamarind Papers; a Journal of Fine Print*, 10.1 (Spring 1987), 16-27

------, 'Whistler, Way and Wellington Street' in *The Lithographs of James McNeill Whistler*, ed. by Harriet K. Stratis and Martha Tedeschi, 2 vols (Chicago: Art Institute of Chicago, in association with the Arie and Ida Crown Memorial, 1998)

Small, Helen, 'Liberal Editing in the *Fortnightly Review* and the *Nineteenth Century*,' *Publishing History*, 53 (2003), 75-96

------, 'Science, Liberalism, and the Ethics of Belief: The *Contemporary Review* in 1877' in Cantor and Shuttleworth (2004), 239-257

Smalley, George Washburn, *London Letters* (New York: Harper and Brothers, 1891)

------, *Studies of Men* (New York: Harper, 1895)

------, *The Life of Sir Sydney H. Waterlow, Bart.; London Apprentice, Lord Mayor, Captain of Industry and Philanthropist* (London: Edward Arnold, 1909)

------, *Anglo-American Memories*, 2 vols (New York and London: G. P. Putnam's Sons, The Knickerbocker Press, 1911)

Smiles, Samuel, *A Publisher and his Friends. Memoir of John Murray*, 2 vols (London: John Murray, 1891)

Smith, Albert H., 'John Nichols, Printer and Publisher', *Library*, s.5, 18.3 (Sept. 1963), 169-190

Smith, Charles Manby, *The Little World of London; or, Pictures in Little of London Life* (London: Arthur Hall, Virtue, and Co., 1857)

Smith, Crosbie and M. Norton, *Wise, Energy and Empire: A Biographical Study of Lord Kelvin* (Cambridge: Cambridge University Press, 1989)

Smith, David C., ed., *The Definitive Bibliography of Herbert George Wells* (Oss, Netherlands: Equilibris Publishing, 2008)

Smith, F., *The Band of Hope Jubilee Volume* (London: United Kingdom Band of Hope Union, 1897)

Smith, F.B., *Radical Artisan: William James Linton 1812-97* (Manchester: Manchester University Press, 1973)

Smith, Helen R., *New Light on Sweeney Todd, Thomas Peckett Prest, James Malcolm Rymer and Elizabeth Caroline Grey* (London: Jarndyce, 2002)

Smith, I. Norman, *The Journal Men: P. D. Ross, E. Norman Smith and Grattan O'Leary of the Ottawa Journal* (Toronto: McClelland and Stewart, 1974)

Smith, James V., 'Reason, Revelation, and Reform: Thomas Dick of Methven and the "Improvement of Society by the Diffusion of Knowledge"', *History of Education*, 12 (1983), 255-270

Smith, K.J.M., *James Fitzjames Stephen: Portrait of a Victorian Rationalist* (Cambridge: Cambridge University Press, 1988)

Smith, Olivia, *The Politics of Language 1791-1819* (Oxford: Clarendon Press, 1984)

Smith, Timothy d'Arch, *Love in Earnest: Some Notes on the Lives and Writings of English 'Uranian' Poets from 1889-1930* (London: Routledge and Kegan Paul, 1970)

Snape, Bob, *Leisure and the Rise of the Public Library* (London: Library Association, 1995)

Snell, W.E., 'Frank Buckland – Medical Naturalist', *Proceedings of the Royal Society of Medicine*, 60 (1967), 291-296

Snigurowicz, Diana, compiler, *The Harmonicon: 1823-1833*, 4 vols (data processed and edited at the Center for Studies in Nineteenth-Century Music, University of Maryland. Ann Arbor, Mich.: UMI, 1989)

Somerville, A., *The Autobiography of a Working Man* (1848), edited and intro. by John Carswell (London: Turnstile Press, 1951)

------, *The Whistler at the Plough* (1852), ed. and intro. by K.D. M. Snell, (London, Merlin Press, 1989)

Sorley, W. R, 'Fifty Years of *Mind*', *Mind*, n.s. 35 (1926), 409-418

Sotiron, Minko, *From Politics to Profit: The Commercialization of Canadian Daily Newspapers, 1890-1920* (Montreal and Kingston: McGill-Queen's University Press, 1997)

Southward, John, *Modern Printing, A Handbook Of The Principles And Practice Of Typography And The Auxiliary Arts.* (London: Raithby, Lawrence & Co., 1898-1900)

Sparrow, Andrew, *Obscure Scribblers: A History of Parliamentary Journalism* (London: Politicos, 2003)

Spater, George, *William Cobbett, the Poor Man's Friend* (Cambridge: Cambridge University Press, 1982)

Spencer, Colin, *Vegetarianism: A History* (London: Grub Street, 2000)

Spencer, Sandra, 'The Indispensable Mr. Wills', *VPR*, 21 (1988), 145-151

Spender, J A., *The Public Life*, 2 vols (London: Cassell, 1925)

------, *Life, Journalism and Politics*, 2 vols (London: Cassell, 1927)

Sper, Felix, *The Periodical Press of London Theatrical and Literary (Excluding the Daily Newspaper)* (Boston: Faxon, 1937)

Spielmann, M.H., *The History of* Punch (London: Cassell and Company 1895; New York: Greenwood Press, 1969)

------, *The Hitherto Unidentified Contributions of W. M. Thackeray to* Punch (London and New York: Harper Brothers, 1899)

Spiers, C. H., 'William Thomas Brande, Leather Expert', *Annals of Science*, 25 (1969), 179-201

Sporting Review (March 1859), 155, 'The Omnibus'

Sprigge, Sir Samuel Squire, *The Life and Times of Thomas Wakley* (London: Longmans, Green and Co., 1897)

Springhall, John O., ' "A Life Story for the People?" Edwin J. Brett and the London "Low-Life" Penny Dreadfuls of the 1860s', *Victorian Studies*, 33 (1989-1990), 223-246

------, ' "Boys of Bircham School": the Penny Dreadful Origins of the English School Story, 1867-1900', *History of Education*, 20.2 (1991), 77-94

------, ' "Disseminating Impure Literature": the "Penny Dreadful" Publishing Business Since 1860', *Economic History Review*, 47.3 (1994), 567-584

------, *Youth, Popular Culture and Moral Panics. Penny Gaffs to Gangsta Rap 1830-1996* (Basingstoke: Macmillan Press, 1998)

Sproat, Thomas, *The History and Progress of the Amalgamated Society of Lithographic Printers and Auxiliaries of Great Britain and Ireland 1880-1930: Jubilee Souvenir* (Manchester: ASLP, 1930)

Srebrnik, Patricia, 'Trollope, James Virtue, and *Saint Paul's Magazine*', *Nineteenth Century Fiction*, 37.2 (1982), 443-463

------, *Alexander Strahan: Victorian Publisher* (Ann Arbor: University of Michigan Press, 1986)

Stanley, Brian, *The History of the Baptist Missionary Society 1792-1992* (London: T.&T. Clark, 1992)

Stead, William, Jr, *The Art of Advertising* (London: T.B. Browne, 1899)

Stead, W. T., 'Character Sketch: February. *The Pall Mall Gazette*', *Review of Reviews* (Feb. 1893), 139-156

------, 'The Novel of the Modern Woman', *Review of Reviews*, 10 (1894a), 64-74

------, 'Preface', *Borderland*, 1 (1894b), iii-iv

Stearn, Roger T., 'Archibald Forbes, Special Correspondent', *Journal of Newspaper and Periodical History*, 8.2 (1992)

Steed, Henry Wickham, *The Hapsburg Monarchy* (New York: Charles Scribner's Sons, 1913)

------, *Through Thirty Years, 1892-1922: A Personal Narrative,* 2 vols (London: Heinemann, 1924)

Steevens, G.W., ed., *Things Seen: Impressions of Men, Cities, and Books* (Edinburgh: Blackwood, 1900)

Stennett, Samuel, *Memoirs of the Life of the Reverend William Ward, Late Baptist Missionary in India* (London: J. Haddon, 1825)

Stenton, Michael and Stephen Lees, eds, *Who's Who of British Members of Parliament. Volume II: 1886-1918* (Sussex: Harvester Press, 1978)

Stephen, Leslie, *The Life of Sir James Fitzjames Stephen, bart., K.C.S.L., a Judge of the High Court of Justice.* 2nd ed (London: Smith, Elder, 1895).

Stephens, Ian, *A Brief History of the Statesman* (Calcutta: Statesman Printing Press, 1947)

Stephens, John Russell, *The Profession of the Playwright: British Theatre 1800-1900* (Cambridge: Cambridge University Press, 1992)

Stephenson, Glennis, *Letitia Landon: The Woman Behind L.E.L.* (Manchester: Manchester University Press, 1995)

Stetz, Margaret D. and Mark Samuels Lasner, *The* Yellow Book: *A Centenary Exhibition* (Cambridge, MA: The Houghton Library, 1994)

Stevenson, Lionel, *Dr Quicksilver: The Life of Charles Lever* (London: Chapman and Hall, 1939)

Stevenson, Robert Louis, 'Popular Authors', *Scribner's Magazine*, 4 (July 1888) 122-128, repr. in Vailima edition (London: Heinemann), 26 vols., v.12, *Random Memories*, (1922) 326-344

Stewart, Jessie, *Jane Ellen Harrison: A Portrait From Letters* (Merlin Press, 1959)

Stewart, M and L. Hunter. *The Needle Is Threaded* (London: Heinemann and Newman Neame for the National Union of Tailors and Garment Workers, 1964)

Stierstorfer, K., *John Oxenford (1812-1877) as Farceur and Critic of Comedy* (Frankfurt: Peter Lang, 1996)

Stillinger, Jack, ed., *The Early Draft of John Stuart Mill's Autobiography* (Urbana: University of Illinois Press, 1961)

Stirling, Monica, *The Fine and the Wicked: The Life and Times of Ouida* (New York: Coward-McCann, 1957)

Stockdale, Eric, *'Tis Treason My Good Man! Four Revolutionary Presidents and a Piccadilly Bookshop* (New Castle, DE.: Oak Knoll, 2005)

Stokes, John, *In the Nineties* (Chicago: University of Chicago Press, 1989)

------, 'Wilde the Journalist' in *The Cambridge Companion to Oscar Wilde*, ed. by Peter Raby (Cambridge: Cambridge University Press, 1997), 69-79

------, 'Wilde's World: Oscar Wilde and Theatrical Journalism in the 1880s' in *Wilde Writings: Contextual Conditions*, ed. by Joseph Bristow (Toronto: University of Toronto Press, 2003), 41-58

Stokes, William, *The Life and Labours in Art and Archaeology of George Petrie L.L.D., M.R.I.A.* (London: Longman Green & Co., 1868)

Stocking, Jr., George W., *Victorian Anthropology* (New York: Free Press, 1987)

Stoddart, J.T., *The Harvest of My Years* (London: Hodder and Stoughton, 1938)

Stone, Wilfred, 'Bibliography' in *Religion and Art of William Hale White* (Stanford: Stanford University, 1954), 215-232

Storey, Graham et al., eds, *Letters of Charles Dickens*, 'Pilgrim Edition', 12 vols (Oxford: Clarendon Press, 1965-2002)

Stott, Anne, *Hannah More: The First Victorian* (Oxford: Oxford University Press, 2003)

Strachey, Ray, *Millicent Garrett Fawcett* (London: John Murray, 1931)

Stratman, Carl. J., *A Bibliography of British Dramatic Periodicals 1720-1960* (New York: The New York Public Library, 1962)

Straus, Ralph, *Sala: The Portrait of an Eminent Victorian* (London: Constable & Co., 1942)

Strong, Roy, *Country Life 1897-1997: The English Arcadia* (London: Country Life, 1996)

Stuart, Daniel, 'Anecdotes of Coleridge and London Newspapers', *Gentleman's Magazine*, n.s. 10, (July 1838), 23-27

Stunt, T. C. F., *Early Brethren and the Society of Friends* (Pinner: Christian Brethren Research Fellowship, 1970)

Stutfield, H.E.M., 'The Psychology of Feminism', *Blackwood's Magazine*, 161 (January 1897), 104-117

------, 'The Ethics of Assassination', *National Review*, 474 (Aug. 1922)

Straus, R., *Sala: The Portrait of an Eminent Victorian* (London, Constable & Co., 1942)

Street, G.S. ed., *G. W. Steevens, Things Seen: Impressions of Men, Cities, and Books.* (Edinburgh: Blackwood, 1900)

Strout, A.L., *A Bibliography of Articles in Blackwood's Magazine, 1817-1825* (Lubbock TX: Texas Technical College, 1959)

Stuart, Daniel, 'Anecdotes of Coleridge and London Newspapers', *Gentleman's Magazine,* 10 (1838), 23-27

Studio 1893-1901, General Index to First Twenty-one Volumes (London, Paris, New York: Offices of 'The Studio' [1901])

Sullivan, Alexander M., *New Ireland: Political Sketches and Personal Reminiscences of Thirty Years of Irish Public Life* (London: Burns Oates and Washbourne Ltd, 1877)

Sullivan, Alvin, ed., *British Literary Magazines,* 4 vols, v. 2, *The Romantic Age, 1789-1836,* (Westport, CT.: Greenwood Press, 1983)

------, *British Literary Magazines,* 4 vols, v. 3, *The Victorian and Edwardian Age, 1837-1913,* (Westport, CT.: Greenwood Press, 1984)

Sully, James, *My Life & Friends: A Psychologist's Memories* (London: T. Fisher Unwin, 1918)

Summers, David, 'The Labour Church and Affiliated Movements' (unpublished PhD thesis: University of Edinburgh, 1958)

Suriano, Gregory R., *The Pre-Raphaelite Illustrators: The Published Graphic Art of the English Pre-Raphaelites and their Associates* (Delaware and London: Oak Knoll Press and British Library 2000, 2005)

[Surtees, Robert Smith], *Handley Cross, or, Mr. Jorrock's Hunt* (London: Bradbury and Evans, 1854)

Sutherland, John, *Victorian Novelists and Publishers* (London: Athlone Press, 1976)

------, *The Longman Companion to Victorian Fiction* (Harlow: Longman, 1988; repr. 1990; also as *The Stanford Companion to Victorian Fiction*, Stanford University Press, 1989, repr. 1990)

------, *Victorian Fiction: Writers, Publishers, Readers* (Basingstoke: Macmillan, 1995)

------, *The Life of Sir Walter Scott: a Critical Biography* (Oxford: Blackwell, 1995)

Sutton, Denys, 'Sir Claude Phillips: First Keeper of the Wallace Collection', *Apollo,* 116 (1982), 322-332

Sutton-Ramspeck, Beth, *Raising the Dust: The Literary Housekeeping of Mary Ward, Sarah Grand, and Charlotte Perkins Gilman* (Athens: Ohio University Press, 2004)

Swann, E., *Christopher North (John Wilson)* (Edinburgh: Oliver and Boyd, 1934)

Swinburne, Algernon Charles, 'Notes on the Text of Shelley', *Essays and Studies,* (London: Chatto and Windus, 1875), 184-237

------, *The Swinburne Letters,* ed. by Cecil Y. Lang, 6 vols (New Haven: Yale University Press, 1959-62)

Symon, James D., *The Press and its Story* (London: Seely, Service, 1914)

T

Taffe, Thomas Gafney, 'Andrews, William Eusabius' in *The Catholic Cyclopedia*, ed. by C. G. Herbermann (New York: Appleton, 1907), 475

Tanselle, G. Thomas, 'Bibliographical History As a Field of Study', *Studies in Bibliography*, 41 (1988), 33-63

Tarr, Rodger L., *Thomas Carlyle: A Bibliography of English Language Criticism, 1824-1974* (Charlottesville: University Press of Virginia, 1976)

------, *Thomas Carlyle: A Descriptive Bibliography* (Pittsburgh, PA: University of Pittsburgh Press, 1989)

Tatchell, M., 'Thornton Hunt', *Keats-Shelley Journal*, 20 (1969), 13-20

Tate, Steve, 'James Catton, "Tityrus" of the *Athletic News* (1860 to 1936): A Biographical Study', *Sport in History*, 25.1 (Abingdon: Routledge, 2005), 98-115

Taylor, Debra, 'Epitaphs', *Jolly*, 1, 303-304

Taylor, Jenny, 'The Eighteen-Sixties: London', *Literature and History*, 10 (Autumn 1984), 189-203

Taylor, Miles, *Ernest Jones: Chartism and the Romance of Politics: 1819-1869* (Oxford: Oxford University Press, 2003)

Taylor, S.J., *The Great Outsiders, Harmsworth, Rothermere and the* Daily Mail (London: Weidenfeld & Nicolson, 1996)

Teich, 'The *British Critic*' in Sullivan (1983), 57-62

Temperley, Nicholas, '*MT* and Musical Journalism', *Musical Times*, 110, 125th Anniversary Issue (June 1969), 583-586

Tener, Robert H., 'R. N. Hutton's Editorial Career: II. *The Prospective* and *National Reviews*', *VPN*, 8.4 (Dec. 1974), 6-13

------, 'R.H. Hutton's Editorial Career: III. The *Economist* and the *Spectator*', *VPN*, 8 (1975), 6-17

------, and Malcolm Woodfield, *A Victorian Spectator: The Uncollected Writings of R.H. Hutton* (Bristol: Bristol Press, 1989; repr. Calgary: University of Calgary Press, c.1998)

Tennyson, Jesse F., *The Trial of Madeleine Smith* (London: William Hodge, 1927)

Thackeray, W.M., 'Half a Crown's Worth of Cheap Knowledge', *Fraser's Magazine*, 17 (March, 1838) 279-290, in King and Plunkett (2004), v. 1

------, *The Letters and Private Papers of William Makepeace Thackeray*, ed. by Gordon Ray, 4 vols (Oxford: Oxford University Press, 1945-1946)

Thale, Mary, ed., *The Autobiography of Francis Place, 1771-1854* (Cambridge: Cambridge University Press, 1972)

Thesing, William, B., ed., *British Short-Fiction Writers, 1880-1914: The Realist Tradition*, Dictionary of Literary Biography, v. 135 (1994)

Thirlwell, Angela, *William and Lucy: The Other Rossettis* (New Haven and London: Yale University Press, 2003)

Thomas, Clara, *Love and Work Enough: The Life of Anna Jameson* (Toronto: University of Toronto Press, 1967)

Thomas, C. Jack, *Scottish Newspaper Directory and Guide to Advertisers: A Complete Manual of the Newspaper Press* (Edinburgh: T.C. Jack, 1855)

Thomas, Deborah, *Dickens and the Short Story* (Philadelphia: University of Pennsylvania Press, 1982)

Thomas, Joan, *An Index to* Wales *1894-1897* (Caernarfon: Welsh Library Association, 1979)

Thomas, Sue, *Indexes to Fiction in the* Harmsworth Magazine, *Later the* London Magazine *(1898-1915)*, Victorian Fiction Research Guides, 10 (St Lucia, Queensland: Dept. of English, University of Queensland, 1984)

Thomas, William, *The Quarrel of Macaulay and Croker: Politics and History in the Age of Reform* (Oxford: Oxford University Press, 2000)

Thomas, William Beach, *The Story of the Spectator 1828-1928* (London: Methuen & Co. Ltd, 1928)

Thompson, Alex M., *Here I Lie* (London: Routledge, 1937)

Thompson, Dorothy, *The Chartists: Popular Politics in the Industrial Revolution* (London and New York: Temple Smith and Pantheon Books, 1984)

Thompson, E. P., *William Morris, Romantic to Revolutionary* (New York: Pantheon, 1955)

------, *The Making of the English Working Class* (London: V. Gollancz, 1963; New York: Vintage, 1966)

------, and Eileen Yeo, eds, *The Unknown Mayhew. Selections from the* Morning Chronicle *1849-50* (New York: Pantheon, 1971)

Thompson, J. Lee, *Northcliffe: Press Baron in Politics, 1865-1922* (London: John Murray, 2000)

Thompson, James R., *Leigh Hunt*, Twayne's English Authors Series, v. 210, ed. by Sylvia E. Bowman (Boston: G.K. Hall, 1977)

Thompson, John B., *Media and Modernity* (Cambridge: Polity Press, 1995)

Thompson, Laurence, *Robert Blatchford: Portrait of an Englishman* (London: Gollancz, 1951)

Thompson, Nicola Diane, *Victorian Women Writers and the Woman Question* (Cambridge: Cambridge University Press, 1999)

Thomson, Elaine, ' "Beware of worthless imitation": Advertising in Nursing Periodicals, c.1888-1945' in *New Directions in the History of Nursing: International Perspectives*, ed. by Barbara Mortimer and Susan McGann (London: Routledge, 2005), 158-178

Thomson, Robert, *A Reputation for Excellence: A History of the Aberdeen and Northern Counties Printing Industries* (Edinburgh: Merchiston Publishing, 2000)

Thornton, Kelsey, 'Le Gallienne, Richard (1866-1947)' in Cevasco (1993), 348-349

Thorold, Algar Labouchere, *Life of Henry Labouchere* (New York: JP Putnam and Sons, 1913)

Thrall, Miriam M. H., *Rebellious* Fraser's*: Nol Yorke's Magazine in the Days of Maginn, Thackeray, and Carlyle* (New York: Columbia University Press, 1934)

Thuente, Mary Helen, *The Harp Re-Strung: The United Irishmen and the Rise of Irish Literary Nationalism* (New York: Syracuse University Press, 1994)

Thussu, Daya Kishan, *International Communication* (London: Arnold, 2000)

Thwaite, Ann, *Edmund Gosse. A Literary Landscape, 1849-1928* (Oxford: Oxford University Press, 1985)

Timbs, John, *Anecdote Lives of the Later Wits and Humourists*, 2 vols (London: Bentley, 1874)

[*Times, The*], 'History of *The Times*', 5 vols (London: The Office of *The Times*, 1935-52)

------, *Printing since 1785: Some Account of the Means of Production and Changes of Dress of the Newspaper* (London: Times, 1953)

------, *A Newspaper History 1785-1935: Reprinted from the 150th Anniversary Number of* The Times *(1 Jan. 1935)* (London: The Times Publishing Co., 1935)

Times, The (26 May 1853), 6, 'Death of F.W.Conway'

------, (1 Feb. 1855), 3, 'The Patriotic Fund Journal'

------, (15 Oct. 1855), 4, 'Royal Commission of the Patriotic Fund'

------, (18 Aug. 1868), 5, 'The Late Mr. John Douglas Cook'

------, (7 Sept. 1876), 7, 'Death of John Forster'

------, (31 Dec. 1891), 6, 'Obituary: W.H. Davenport-Adams'

------, (22 Feb. 1900), 7, 'Death of Mr. H.D. Traill'

------, (Aug. 2, 1907), 6, 'Obituary: David Christie Murray'

------, (2 March 1908), 9, 'Obituary: Mr. Rawdon B. Lee'

------, (10 July 1908), 13, 'Mr. C. J. Dunphie'

------, (2 Nov. 1920), 15, 'Sportsman and Bohemian: Death of Mr. W. B. Woodgate'

------, (Oct. 29, 1928), 17, 'The First Hansard'

------, (4 April 1929), 17, 'Mr. H.E.M. Stutfield'

------, (10 Jan. 1930), 14, 'Mr. Henry Sturmey'

------, (21 Nov. 1933), 17, 'Augustine Birrell'

Timperley, Charles Henry, *A Dictionary of Printers and Printing with the Progress of Literature Ancient and Modern* (London: Timperley, 1839)

------, *Encyclopaedia of Literary and Typographical Anecdote* (London, Bohn, 1842; repr. New York: Garland Publishing Company, 1977)

Tinsley, William, *Random Recollections of an Old Publisher*, 2 vols (London: Simpkin, Marshall, Hamilton, Kent, 1900)

Tjaden, Will, '*The Gardener's Gazette* 1837 and Its Rivals', *Garden History: The Journal of the Garden History Society*, 11.1 (1983) 70-78

Tobin, Thomas J., *Pre-Raphaelitism in the Nineteenth-Century Press* (Victoria, BC: English Literary Studies, 2002)

Todd, Nigel, *The Militant Democracy: Joseph Cowen and Victorian Radicalism* (Whitley Bay, UK: Bewick Press, 1991)

Todd, William B., *A Directory of Printers and Others in Allied Trades, London and Vicinity 1800-1840* (London: Printing Historical Society, 1972)

Topham, Jonathan R., (2004a), 'The *Wesleyan-Methodist Magazine* and Religious Monthlies in Early Nineteenth-Century Britain' in Cantor, Dawson et al., (2004), 67-90

------, 'Periodicals and the Making of Reading Audiences for Science in Early Nineteenth-Century Britain: *The Youth's Magazine*, 1828-1837' (2004b) in Henson, Cantor et al. (2004), 57-69

------, 'John Limbird, Thomas Byerley, and the Production of Cheap Periodicals in the 1820s', *Book History*, 8 (2005), 75-106

Toye, Francis, *For What We Have Received: An Autobiography* (London: Heinemann, 1950)

Traill, H.D., 'The Evening Newspaper 1872-1897', *Pall Mall Gazette* No. 10000 (14 Apr. 1897)

Treasure, J.A.P., *The History of British Advertising Agencies 1875-1939* (Edinburgh: Scottish Academic Press, 1977)

Tredrey, F.D., *The House of Blackwood, 1804-1954* (Edinburgh: Blackwood, 1954)

Trewin, John Courtenay, *Printer to the House, the Story of Hansard* (London: Methuen, [1952])

Trexler, Adam, 'Economic Ideas and British Literature, 1900-1930: The Fabian Society, Bloomsbury, and *The New Age*', *Literature Compass*, 4.3 (May 2007), 862-887

Triggs, Kathy, *The Stars and the Stillness: A Portrait of George MacDonald* (Cambridge: Lutterworth, 1986)

Trimen, H., 'Edward Newman', *Journal of Botany*, 14 (1876), 223-224

Trollope, Anthony, *An Autobiography* (London: Blackwood, 1883; repr. Oxford: Oxford University Press, 1980)

Tsuzuki, Chushichi, *H. M. Hyndman and British Socialism* (Oxford: Oxford University Press, 1961)

Tucker, Albert, 'Military' in Vann and VanArsdel (1994), 62-80

Tunstall, Jeremy, *Media Occupations and Professions: A Reader* (Oxford: Oxford University Press, 2001)

Turner, E. S., *Boys Will Be Boys* (London: Michael Joseph, 1948)

Turner, Mark W., 'Defining Discourses: The *Westminster Review*, *Fortnightly Review*, and Comte's Positivism', *VPR*, 33.3 (Autumn 2000a), 273-282

------, 'Hybrid Journalism: Women and the Progressive *Fortnightly*' in Campbell (2000b), 72-91

------, *Trollope and the Magazines* (Basingstoke: Macmillan, 2000c)

------, 'Periodical Time in the Nineteenth Century', *Media History*, 8.2 (2002), 183-196

------, 'Urban Encounters and Visual Play in the *Yellow Book*' in Brake and Codell (2005), 138-160

------, 'Time, Periodicals, and Literary Studies', *VPR*, 39 (2006), 309-316

Turner, Michael L., 'The Syndication of Fiction in Provincial Newspapers, 1870-1939: The Example of the Tillotson "Fiction Bureau"' (unpublished B.Litt. Dissertation: Oxford University, 1968)

Tusan, Michelle Elizabeth, 'Inventing the New Woman: Print Culture and Identity Politics during the Fin-de-Siècle', *VPR*, 31 (1998), 169-182

Twells, Alison, *The Civilising Mission and the English Middle Class: the 'Heathen' at Home and Overseas, 1792-1850* (Basingstoke: Palgrave, 2008)

Twyman, Michael, *Early Lithographed Books* (Williamsburg, VA and London: The Book Press Ltd. and the Private Libraries Association, 1990)

------, *Breaking the Mould: the First 100 Years of Lithography* (London: British Library, 2001)

Tye, J. R., *Periodicals of the Nineties* (Oxford: Oxford Bibliographic Society, 1974)

Tyrell, Alex, 'Samuel Smiles and the Woman Question in Early Victorian Britain', *Journal of British Studies*, 39 (2000), 185-216

Tyson, Gerald P., *Joseph Johnson: A Liberal Publisher* (Iowa City: University of Iowa Press, 1979)

U

Udelson, Joseph, *Dreamer of the Ghetto: The Life and Works of Israel Zangwill* (Tuscaloosa, AL: University of Alabama Press, 1990)

Uglow, Jenny, *A Little History of British Gardening* (London: Pimlico, 2005)

Ugolini, Laura, 'The *Workman's Times*, Independent Labour Representation and Women's Suffrage, 1891-4' in *The Men's Share? Masculinities, Male Support and Women's Suffrage in Britain, 1890-1920*, ed. by Angela John and Claire Eustace (London: Routledge, 1997)

Ulin, Donald, 'The Making of the English Countryside: Tourism and Literary Representation in Nineteenth-Century England' (unpublished PhD Thesis, Indiana University, 1998)

V

Vadillo, Ana Parejo, *Women Poets and Urban Aestheticism: Passengers of Modernity* (Basingstoke: Palgrave, 2005)

VanArsdel, Rosemary, 'The Westminster Review, 1825-1837: With Special Emphasis on Literary Attitudes' (unpublished PhD Thesis: Columbia University, 1961)

------, '*Macmillan's Magazine* and the Fair Sex 1850-1874', *VPR*, 33.4 (Winter 2000), 374-396

------, *Florence Fenwick Miller: Feminist* (Aldershot: Ashgate, 2003)

------, and John S. North, 'Student Journals' in Vann and VanArsdel (1994), 311-331

Van Wyhe, John, *Phrenology and the Origins of Scientific Naturalism* (Aldershot: Ashgate, 2004)

Vanden Bossche, Chris R., ed., *Carlyle, Thomas: Historical Essays* (Berkeley and Los Angeles: University of California Press, 2002)

Vann, J. Don and Rosemary T. VanArsdel, eds, *Victorian Periodicals: A Guide to Research*, 2 vols (New York: Modern Language Association, l978/ 1989)

------, *Victorian Periodicals and Victorian Society* (Aldershot, Hants; Toronto: Scolar Press; University of Toronto Press, 1994)

------, *Periodicals of Queen Victoria's Empire: An Exploration* (Toronto: University of Toronto Press, 1996)

Varty, Anne, ed., *Eve's Century: A Sourcebook of Writing on Women & Journalism 1895-1918* (London: Routledge, 2000)

Versteeg, Margaret, Sue Thomas and Joan Huddleston, *Index to Fiction in the* Lady's Realm, Victorian Fiction Research Guides, 5 (St Lucia: Queensland University, Department of English, 1981)

Vicinus, Martha, *The Industrial Muse: A Study of Nineteenth Century British Working-Class Literature* (New York: Barnes & Noble Books, 1974)

Victor, Carol de Saint, '*Anglo-Saxon Review – A Quarterly Miscellany*' in Sullivan (1883), 14-22

Vincent, David, 'On the Decline of the Oral Tradition in Popular Culture' in *Popular Culture and Custom in Nineteenth-Century England*, ed. by R.D. Storch (London and Canberra: Croom Helm, 1982), 20-47

------, *Literacy and Popular Culture: England, 1750-1914* (Cambridge: Cambridge University Press, 1989)

Visram, Rozina, *Ayahs, Lascars and Princes: The History of Indians in Britain, 1700-1947* (London: Pluto Press, 1986)

Vizetelly, Henry, *Glances Back Through Seventy Years: Autobiographical and Other Reminiscences* (London: Kegan Paul, Trench, Trubner, and Co. Ltd, 1893)

Vogler, Richard A., *The Graphic Works of George Cruikshank* (New York: Dover Publications, 1979)

W

Wadsworth, A. P., 'Newspaper Circulations, 1800-1954', *Transactions of the Manchester Statistical Society* (1955), 1-41

Wagstaff, John, ed., *British Union Catalogue of Music Periodicals* (Aldershot: Ashgate, 1998)

Wakeman, Geoffrey, *Aspects of Victorian Lithography: Anastatic Printing and Photozincography* (Wymondham: Brewhouse Press, 1970)

------, *Victorian Book Illustration: The Technical Revolution* (Newton Abbot: David & Charles 1973)

Wallace, Alfred Russel, *My Life: A Record of Events and Opinions* (London: Chapman & Hall, 1905)

Wallas, G., *The Life of Francis Place*, revd. edn (London: George Allen & Unwin, 1918)

Waller, Philip, *Readers, Writers, and Reputations: Literary Life in Britain 1870-1918* (Oxford: Oxford University Press, 2006)

Walk, Alexander, 'Medico-Psychologists, Maudsley and the Maudsley', *British Journal of Psychiatry*, 128 (1976), 19-30

Walker, Martin, *Powers of the Press: the World's Great Newspapers* (London: Quartet Books, 1982)

Walker, Pamela J., *Pulling the Devil's Kingdom Down: The Salvation Army in Victorian Britain* (Berkeley: University of California Press, 2001)

Waller, Philip, *Writers, Readers, and Reputations: Literary Life in Britain 1870-1918* (Oxford: Oxford University Press, 2006)

Wallis, L.W., *A Concise Chronology of Typesetting Developments 1886-1986* (Aldershot: Lund Humphries, 1988)

Wallis, P., *At the Sign of The Ship, 1924-1974* (London: Longman, 1974)

Walsh, Michael J., *The* Tablet *1840-1890: A Commemorative History* (London: The Tablet, 1990)

Walters, Huw, *Llyfryddiaeth Cylchgronau Cymreig 1851-1900 / A Bibliography of Welsh Periodicals 1851-1900* (Aberystwyth: National Library of Wales, 2003)

Ward, Bernard, *The Dawn of the Catholic Revival in England*, 2 vols (London: Longmans Green, 1909)

Ward, E. Honor, *The Girl's Own Guide* (Colne: A.&B. Whitworth, 1992)

Ward, H. Snowden, 'Our Scientific Causerie. Photography in Natural Colours', *Review of Reviews*, 2 (1890), 187-188

Ward, Ken, *Mass Communications and the Modern World* (Basingstoke: Macmillan, 1989)

Ward, Mrs Humphry, *A Writer's Recollections* (London: W. Collins Sons and Co., 1918)

Ward, T. H., ed., *Men of the Reign: A Biographical Dictionary of Eminent Persons of British and Colonial Birth who have Died During the Reign of Queen Victoria* (London: Routledge and Sons, 1883)

Ward, W., *The Life and Times of Cardinal Wiseman* (London: Longmans, Green, and Co., 1897)

------, *Ten Personal Studies* (London: Longmans Green, 1908)

Warner, Alan, *William Allingham: An Introduction* (Dublin: Dolman Press, 1971)

Warner, Oliver, *Captain Marryat: A Rediscovery* (London: Constable, 1953)

------, *Chatto & Windus: A Brief Account of the Firm's Origin, History and Development* (London: Chatto and Windus, 1973)

Warren, Lynne, ' "Women in Conference": Reading the Correspondence Columns in *Woman* 1890-1910' in Brake, Bell and Finkelstein (2000), 122-133

Waterhouse, Robert, *The Other Fleet Street: How Manchester Made Newspapers National* (Altrincham: First Edition, 2004)

Waterloo Directories, see North, John S.; Wolff, Michael, et al.

Waters, Chris, *British Socialists and the Politics of Popular Culture* (Stanford: Stanford University Press, 1990)

Watry, Maureen, *The Vale Press: Charles Ricketts, A Publisher in Earnest* (London: British Library, 2004)

Watson, Aaron, *A Newspaper Man's Memories* (London: Hutchinson & Co., 1925)

Watson, Alfred E.T., ed., *The Racing World and Its Inhabitants* (London: Macmillan, 1904)

Watson, Frederick, *Robert Smith Surtees: A Critical Study* (London: Harrap, 1933; repr. Frome, Somerset: The R. S. Surtees Society, 1991)

Watson, G., ed., *New Cambridge Bibliography of English Literature*, 5 vols (Cambridge: Cambridge University Press, l969-77)

Watson, Robert A. and Elizabeth S. Watson, *George Gilfillan: Letters and Journals with Memoir* (London: Hodder and Stoughton, 1892)

Watson, Robert Patrick. *Memoirs of Robert Patrick Watson* (London: Smith, Ainslie, 1899)

Watts, Charles A., 'Introductory', *Agnostic Annual*, 1 (1884), 3-4

Waugh, Arthur, *One Man's Road* (London: Chapman & Hall, 1931)

Weatherill, Lorna, *One Hundred Years of Papermaking: An Illustrated History of the Guard Bridge Paper Company Ltd 1873-1973* (Guard Bridge: privately printed, 1974)

Webb, Maurice Everett, and Herbert Wigglesworth, eds, *Raffles Davison...: a Record of his Life and Work from 1870 to 1926* (London: Batsford, 1927)

Webb, R.K., *The British Working Class Reader, 1790-1848; Literacy and Social Tension* (London: Allen & Unwin, 1955)

------, *Harriet Martineau: a Radical Victorian* (London: Heinemann, 1960)

Weber, Gary, 'Henry Labouchere, *Truth* and the New Journalism of Late Victorian Britain', *VPR*, 26.1 (Spring 1993), 36-42

Webster, Christopher and John Elliott, eds, *A Church as it Should Be: The Cambridge Camden Society and its Influence* (Stamford: Shaun Tyas, 2000)

Wedgwood, Barbara, and H. Wedgwood, *The Wedgwood Circle, 1730-1897: Four Generations of a Family and Their Friends* (London: Studio Vista, 1980)

Weedon, Alexis, *Victorian Publishing: The Economics of Book Production for a Mass Market 1836-1916* (Aldershot: Ashgate, 2003)

Weil, Al, 'David Croal Thomson: Spokesman for Art', *Scottish Art Review*, 14 (1975), 1-27

Weintraub, Stanley, 'Shaw's Goddess: Lady Colin Campbell', *SHAW: The Annual of Bernard Shaw Studies*, 25 (2005), 241-256

Welby, T. Earle, *The Victorian Romantics, 1850-70: The Early Works of Dante Gabriel Rossetti, William Morris, Burne-Jones, Swinburne, Simeon Solomon and their Associates* (London: G. Howe, 1929)

------, *A Study of Swinburne* (London: Faber and Gwyer, 1926; repr. Port Washington: Kennikat Press, 1968)

Welcome, John, *The Sporting World of R. S. Surtees* (Oxford: Oxford University Press, 1982)

Welford, Richard, *Men of Mark 'Twixt Tyne and Tweed,* 3 vols (London: Walter Scott, 1895)

Welsh, Robert, ed., *Concise Oxford Companion to Irish Literature* (Oxford: Oxford University Press, 2000)

Wesley, W.H., 'Arthur Cowper Ranyard and His Work', *Knowledge*, 18 (1895), 25-27

West, Paul, 'The Dome: An Aesthetic Periodical of the 1890's', *Book Collector*, 6 (1957), 160-169

West, Shearer, 'Tom Taylor, William Powell Frith, and the British School of Art', *Victorian Studies*, 33 (Winter 1990), 307-326

Westmorland Gazette (7 March 1908), 3, 'Death of Mr. Rawdon Lee'

Westwater, Martha, '*Victoria Magazine*' in Sullivan (1984), 443-446

Wharton, Edith, *A Backward Glance* (London: Century, 1987)

Whates, H.R.G., *The Birmingham Post 1857-1957: A Centenary Perspective* (Birmingham: The Birmingham Post and Mail Ltd, 1957)

Wheeler, J.M., *A Biographical Dictionary Of Freethinkers* (London: Progressive Publishing Co., 1889)

Whelan, Irene, *The Bible War in Ireland: The 'Second Reformation' and the Polarization of Protestant-Catholic Relations, 1800-1840* (Dublin: Lilliput Press, 2005)

Whibley, Charles, 'Musings without Method', *Blackwood's Magazine*, 190 (1911), 265-276

White, Cynthia, *Women's Magazines 1693-1968* (London: Michael Joseph Ltd, 1971)

White, Gleeson, *English Illustration 'The Sixties': 1855-70* (London: Constable, 1897; Bath: Kingsmead Reprints, 1970)

White, James F., *The Cambridge Movement: The Ecclesiological and the Gothic Revival* (Cambridge: University Press, 1962)

White, Paul, *Thomas Huxley: Making the 'Man of Science'*, (Cambridge: Cambridge University Press, 2003)

White, Terence de Vere, *The Road to Excess: A Biography of Isaac Butt* (Dublin: Browne & Nolan, 1946)

White, William Hale, *Letters to Three Friends* (Oxford: Oxford University Press, 1924)

Whitehead, Andrew, ' "Quorum Pars Fui": The Autobiography of H. H. Champion', *Society for the Study of Labour History*, 47 (1983), 17-35

Whittington-Egan, Richard and Geoffrey Smerdon, *The Quest of the Golden Boy: The Life and Letters of Richard Le Gallienne* (London: The Unicorn Press, 1960)

Who's Who: An Annual Biographical Dictionary (London: Adam and Charles Black, 1849-)

Who Was Who? (London: Adam and Charles Black, 1897-)

Whorlow, H., *The Provincial Newspaper Society, 1836-1886: 'A Jubilee Retrospect'* (London: Page, Pratt, 1886)

Whyte, Frederick, *The Life of W. T. Stead*, 2 vols (London: Jonathan Cape, 1925)

Wickham, D. E., 'Thomas Massa Alsager (1779-1846): An Elian Shade Illuminated', *Charles Lamb Bulletin*, 35 (1981), 45-62

Wickwar, W. Hardy, *The Struggle for the Freedom of the Press, 1819-1832* (London: Allen and Unwin, 1928)

Wiener, Joel H., *The War of the Unstamped: The Movement to Repeal the Newspaper Tax, 1830-1836* (Ithaca: Cornell University Press, 1969)

------, *A Descriptive Finding List of Unstamped British Periodicals, 1830-1836* (London: The Bibliographical Society, 1970)

------, *Radicalism and Freethought in Nineteenth-Century Britain: The Life of Richard Carlile* (London: Greenwood Press, 1983)

------, (1985a) ed., *Innovators and Preachers: the Role of the Editor in Victorian England* (Westport, CT: Greenwood Press, 1985)

------, (1985b) 'Edmund Yates: The Gossip as Editor' in Wiener (1985), 259-274

------, ed., *Papers for the Millions: The New Journalism in Britain 1850s to 1924* (Westport, CT: Greenwood Press, 1988a)

------, (1988b) 'Press, Radical and Unstamped' in Mitchell (1988)

------, 'The Radical and Labor Press' in Vann and VanArsdel (1989), 45-57

Wiener, Martin J., *Men of Blood: Violence, Manliness and Criminal Justice in Victorian England* (Cambridge: Cambridge University Press, 2004)

Wigley, J., 'James Montgomery and the Sheffield *Iris*, 1792-1825: a Study in the Weakness of Provincial Radicalism', *Transactions of the Hunter Archaeological Society,* 10.3 (1975), 173-181

Wilde, Oscar, *Selected Journalism*, ed. by Anya Clayworth (Oxford: Oxford World's Classics, 2004)

------, *Critical Essays*, v. 4 ed. by Josephine Guy, in *The Complete Works of Oscar Wilde*, general eds Russell Jackson and Ian Small, 4 vols (Oxford: Oxford University Press, 2007)

Wiley, Raymond A., 'Anglo-Saxon Kemple: The Life and Works of John Mitchell Kemble, 1807-1857: Philologist, Historian, Archaeologist' in *Anglo-Saxon Studies in Archaeology and History,* v. 1, ed. by Sonia Chadwick Hawkes, David Brown, and James Campbell (Oxford: British Archaeological Reports, 1979), 165-173

Wilks, Ivor, *South Wales and the Rising of 1839: Class Struggle as Armed Struggle* (London: Routledge, 1984)

Williams, David, *John Frost: A Study in Chartism* (Cardiff: University of Wales Press Board, 1939; repr. London: Evelyn Adams and Mackay, 1969)

Williams, Edward Ivor, 'Wilkins, Charles (Catwg; 1831-1913)', *The Dictionary of Welsh Biography Down to 1940*, ed. by R.T. Jenkins (Oxford: B.H. Blackwell, 1959) 1019

Williams, Jacqueline Block, ed., 'Introduction' to *The Delights of Delicate Eating,* first published as *The Feasts of Autolycus. The Diary of a Greedy Woman* by Elizabeth Robins Pennell (London: repr. from the *Pall Mall Gazette,* 1896; Urbana: University of Illinois Press, 2000), vii-xxv

Williams, Raymond, *The Long Revolution* (New York: Columbia University Press, 1961)

------, 'The Press and Popular Culture: An Historical Perspective' in Boyce, Curran, and Wingate (1978), 41-50

Willing's British and Irish Press Guide (1890-1892, 1894-1898); continued as *Willing's Press Guide* (1899-1905, 1907-1909, 1911-)

Wilkes, Joanne, ' "Only the Broken Music"? The Critical Writings of Maria Jane Jewsbury', *Women's Writing,* 7 (2000), 105-118

------, '"Clever Women": Anne Mozley, Jane Austen, and Charlotte Brontë' in *New Windows on Women's Writing: A Festschrift for Jocelyn Harris,* 2 vols (Dunedin, New Zealand: University of Otago Press, 2005), 297-308

Willison, I. R., ed., *The New Cambridge Bibliography of English Literature*, 5 vols (Cambridge: Cambridge University Press, 1972)

Wilson, Charles, *First With the News: The History of W.H. Smith 1792-1972* (London: Cape, 1985)

Wilson, Keith M., *A Study in the History and Politics of the* Morning Post*, 1905-1926* (Lampeter: Mellon Press, 1990)

Windholz, Anne M., 'The Woman Who Would Be Editor: Ella D'Arcy and the *Yellow Book*', *VPR*, 29.2 (Summer 1996), 116-130

Winehouse, Bernard, 'The Literary Career of Israel Zangwill from its Beginnings Until 1898' (unpublished PhD thesis: University of London, 1970)

Wohl, Anthony S., ' "Dizzi-Ben-Dizzi": Disraeli as Alien', *Journal of British Studies* (July 1995), 375-411

Wolf, Tony, ed., *The Bartitsu Compendium*, v.1, *History and Canonical Syllabus* (Lulu Publishing.com, 2005)

Wolff, Michael, 'The British Controversialist', *VPN*, 2 (June 1968), 27-45

------, 'The *British Controversialist and Impartial Inquirer*, 1850-1872: A Pearl from the Golden Stream' in Shattock and Wolff (1982), 367-392

------, John S. North and Dorothy Deering, *Waterloo Directory of Victorian Periodicals, 1824-1900*, Phase 1 (Waterloo, Ontario: Wilfrid Laurier University Press, [1976])

Wolff, Robert Lee, 'Devoted Disciple: the Letters of Mary Elizabeth Braddon to Sir Edward Bulwer-Lytton, 1862-1873', *Harvard Library Bulletin*, 22 (April 1974), 5-35, 129-61

------, Introduction, 'The Irish Fiction of William Hamilton Maxwell (1792-1850)', *Erin-go-bragh: or, Irish Life Pictures* by William Hamilton Maxwell (1859; New York and London: Garland, 1979a)

------, *Sensational Victorian: The Life and Fiction of Mary Elizabeth Braddon* (New York: Garland, 1979b)

Wolfson, Susan J., *Borderlines: The Shiftings of Gender in British Romanticism* (Princeton: Princeton University Press, 2006)

Wolmar, Christian, *Fire & Steam* (London: Atlantic Books, 2007)

Woman at Home, (1898), 561-565, 'Two Great Ladies' Papers: 1. *The Lady's Pictorial*'

Woman's Signal (19 Nov. 1896), 330, 'Signals from Our Watchtower'

Wood, Charles W., *Memorials of Mrs. Henry Wood* (London: Richard Bentley & Son, 1894)

Wood Jnr, Charles W., 'John Doherty' in Baylen and Gossman (Sussex: Harvester Press, 1979)

Wood, Marcus, *Radical Satire and Print Culture 1790-1822* (Oxford: Clarendon Press, 1994)

Woods, Oliver and James Bishop, *The Story of The Times: Bicentenary Edition 1785-1985* (London: Michael Joseph, 1985)

Wooler, T.J., *The Black Dwarf*, 12 vols (Westport, CT: Greenwood Reprint Corporation, 1970)

Worth, George J. James Hannay, *His Life and Works* (Lawrence: University of Kansas Press, 1964)

------, *Macmillan's Magazine, 1859-1907: 'No Flippancy Or Abuse Allowed'* (Burlington, VT and Aldershot: Ashgate, 2003)

Wright, T. R., *Hardy and his Readers* (Basingstoke: Palgrave Macmillan, 2003)

Wu, Duncan, 'Charles Lamb, *Elia*', in *A Companion to Romanticism*, ed. by Duncan Wu (Oxford: Blackwell, 1998), 277-282

Wynne, Deborah, *The Sensation Novel and the Victorian Family Magazine* (New York and London: Palgrave, 2001)

Y

Yarde, Doris M., *The Life and Works of Sarah Trimmer* (Bedfont: Hounslow & District Historical Society, 1971)

Yates, Edmund, *Edmund Yates: his Recollections and Experiences*, 2 vols (London: Richard Bentley and Son, 1884)

Yeo, Eileen, *The Contest for Social Science: Relations and Representations of Gender and Class* (London: Rivers Oram Press, 1996)

Young, Arlene, 'Ladies and Professionalism: The Evolution of the Idea of Work in the *Queen*, 1861-1900', *VPR*, 40.3 (2007), 189-215

Young, G.M., 'The Greatest Victorian' in *Today and Yesterday: Collected Essays and Addresses* (London: Rupert Hart-Davis, 1948), 237-243

Young, Percy M., ed., *A Future for English Music and Other Lectures, by Sir Edward Elgar* (London: Dobson, 1968)

------, *George Grove 1820-1900: A Biography* (London: Macmillan, 1980)

Z

Zaidman, Laura, M. and Caroline C. Hunt, eds, *Dictionary of Literary Biography*, v. 141, *British Children's Writers 1880-1914* (Detroit: Gale, 1994)

Zieger, Susan, ' "How far am I responsible?" Women and Morphinomania in Late Nineteenth-Century Britain', *Victorian Studies*, 48: 1 (Autumn 2005), 59-81

Ziegler, Arthur P., Jr, 'The *Dome* and its Editor Publisher: An Exploration', *American Book Collector*, 15 (1965), 19-21

Zorn, Christa, *Vernon Lee: Aesthetics, History and the Victorian Intellectual* (Athens: Ohio University Press, 2003)

Archives and Electronic Resources

19th Century Masterfile, http://poolesplus.odyssi.com/19thcentWelcome.htm

C19 Nineteenth Century Index, http://c19index.chadwyck.com

Victorian Research Web, http://www.thevictorianweb.org

Aberdeen Press and Journal Archive, http://www.pressandjournal.Co.uk/

'Aberdeen Journal', Headnote, British Library Nineteenth-Century Newspapers, 2008, http://www.jisc.ac.uk/whatwedo/programmes/digitisation/bln.aspx

Adams, W. E., Papers, International Institute of Social History, Amsterdam

Allingham, Helen, Society, http://www.helenallingham.com/Helen_Biography.htm

Allingham, Philip V., 'Charles Dickens, the Examiner, and "The Fine Old English Gentleman"', Victorian Research Web, http://www.victorianweb.org/authors/dickens/pva/pva351.html

--------, *An Introduction to the* 'Illustrated London News', Victorian Research Web, http://victorianweb.org/periodicals/pva160.html

Anarchist Archives, http://dwardmac.pitzer.edu:16080/Anarchist_Archives/index.html

AntiQbook Website, http://www.antiqbook.com

Allen, Grant, Website, http://ehlt.flinders.edu.au/english/GA/GAHome.html

Archive of Art and Design, Blythe House, 23 Blythe Road, London W14 0QX, UK

Associated Press Archive, http://www.ap.org/aparchive/index.html

Athenaeum Index of Reviews and Reviewers: 1830 to 1870, http://athenaeum.soi.city.ac.uk/reviews/home.html

Barringer, Terry, David Seton, and Rosemary Seton, eds, 'Currents in World Christianity: Missionary Periodicals Database', http://research.yale.edu:8084/missionperiodicals

Beadle and Adams Dime Novel Digitization Project, http://www.ulib.niu.edu/badndp

Beaumont, Matthew, 'Influential Force: *Shafts* and the Diffusion of Knowledge at the *Fin de Siecle*', 19, *Interdisciplinary Studies in the Long Nineteenth Century*', 3 (2006), http://www.19.bbk.ac.uk

Beddoe, Deirdre, 'Sarah Jane Rees' in *ODNB,* http://www.oxforddnb.com/view/article/48648

Black Abolitionist Archive, University of Detroit Mercy, http://www.dalnet.lib.mi.us/

Blackwood Papers, National Library of Scotland, 57 George IV Bridge, Edinburgh, EH1 1EW, UK

Bledsoe, Robert, "Chorley, Henry F." in *Grove Music Online. Oxford Music Online*, http://www.oxfordmusiconline.com/subscriber/article/grove/music/05678

Boardman, Kay, *The Spectacular Female Body: Dress, Fashion and Modernity in Victorian Women's Magazines,* http://www.fathom.com/course/21701733/session3.html

British Library, http://www.bl.uk/

BL e-Collections, http://www.britishlibrary.uk/collections/early/victorian/magazin/magaz9.html

British Library Newspaper Project, http://newspapers.bl.uk/

Bob Speel, http://myweb.tiscali.Co.uk

Bookseller archive, Endeavour House, 189 Shaftesbury Avenue, London, WC2H 8TJ, UK

British Annuals and Giftbooks, http://www.britannuals.com

British History Online, http://www.british-history.ac.uk

British Library Catalogue, http://catalogue.bl.uk

British Periodicals, http://britishperiodicals.chadwyck.Co.uk

Brotherton Library, Leeds University, Special Collections, Leeds University Library, Woodhouse Lane, Leeds, West Yorkshire, LS2 9JT, UK

Broughton Papers, http://www.proni.gov.uk/introduction__murray_papers_d2860-2.pdf

Cambrian Index online, http://www2.swansea.gov.uk/_info/cambrian/

Cardiff Corvey Index, http://www.cf.ac.uk/encap/corvey

Centre for the History of the Book/Scottish Book Trade Archive Inventory, http://www.hss.ed.ac.uk/chb/sbtai-db/recordT.htm Papers 3

Chartered Institute of Journalists Website http://www.cioj.Co.uk/

Clark, Robert, 'Circulating Libraries', *The Literary Encyclopedia*, http://www.litencyc.com/php/stopics.php?rec=true&UID=189

Cooke, Bill, 'Charles Southwell: New Zealand's First Freethinker', *The New Zealand Rationalist & Humanist*, (Spring 1998), http://www.nzarh.org.nz/document/southwell.htm

Copac Academic and National Library Catalogue, http://copac.ac.uk/

Cowen, Joseph, Papers (Tyne and Wear Archives, Newcastle upon Tyne)

'Draft Agreement between Robert Fitzroy Bell, Esq., and The Scots Observer, Limited, May 1890', PPMS Box 145, File 45, The Library, School of Oriental and African Studies Library, University of London

Eastbourne Heritage Centre, http://www.eastbourneheritagecentre.Co.uk

Encyclopaedia Britannica, http://www.britannica.com

England's Poor Law Commissioners, http://www.mdx.ac.uk

Ewing, Juliana Horatia, 'Margaret Gatty' (1809-1873), *Parables From Nature by Margaret Gatty, With a Memoir by her Daughter. Series 1* (London: George Bell and Sons, York Street, Covent Garden, 1885), ix-xxi, in "A Celebration of Women Writers", http://digital.library.upenn.edu/women/ewing/parables/memorial.html

Fairplay, http://fairplay.Co.uk

Freedom Press, http://www.freedompress.org.uk/

Gardham, Julie, 'Curtis's Botanical Magazine', Glasgow University Special Collections Department, http://special.lib.gla.ac.uk/exhibns/month/oct2004.html

Germ, The, Rossetti Archive, http://www.rossettiarchive.org

Getty Research Institute, David Croal Thomson Papers, 1879-1931, Accession no. 910126

Glasgow University Library Special Collections Website, http://special.lib.gla.ac.uk

Grimes, Kyle, 'The William Hone bio-text', www.uab/edu/english/hone/

Grove Art Online, http://www.oxfordartonline.com/public/

Grove Music Online, http://www.oxfordmusiconline.com/public

Guardian and *Observer* digital archive, http://archive.guardian.Co.uk

[Guardian], 'History of the Guardian', *Guardian Unlimited* (6 June 2002), http://www.guardian.Co.uk/newsroom/story/0,,728443,00.html

Harper's Magazine, http://www.harpers.org/harpers/about

Harris, Katherine D., 'Forget Me Not: A Hypertextual Archive of Ackermann's 19th-Century Literary Annual', http://www.orgs.muohio.edu/anthologies/FMN/Index.htm

Hawkins, Roger. *Northumbriana, Morpeth Antiquarian Society,* http://www.northumbriana.org.uk/antiquarian

Hertfordshire Mercury, http://www.hertfordshiremercury.Co.uk

Hoagwood, Terence and Kathryn Ledbetter, 'L.E.L.'s "Verses" and *The Keepsake* for 1829', *Romantic Circles,* http://www.rc.umd.edu/editions/lel/keepsake.htm

Hone, William, papers at Washington State University Libraries, Manuscripts, Archives, and Special Collections, Pullman, WA 99164-5610 USA, (509) 335-6691, http://www.wsulibs.wsu.edu/Holland/masc/finders/cg136.htm

The 1890s Hypermedia Archive, http://www.ryerson.ca/1890s/

Humpherys, Ann, 'Putting Women in the Boat in *The Idler* (1892-1898) and *TO-DAY* (1893-1897)', *Interdisciplinary Studies in the Long Nineteenth Century,* 19.1 (2005), http://www.19.bbk.ac.uk

--------, 'The Journals that Did: Writing about Sex in the late 1890's', *Interdisciplinary Studies in the Long Nineteenth Century,* 19.3 (2006), http://www.19.bbk.ac.uk

International Institute of Social History, Amsterdam, P.O. Box 2169, 1000 CD Amsterdam, The Netherlands

Jay, Frank, 'Peeps into the Past', *The London Journal* as supplement to *Spare Moments* v. 60-61 (26 October 1918-17; May 1919), http://www.geocities.com/justingilb/texts/PEEPS.htm

Jenkins, Stephanie, Oxford History, http://www.headington.org.uk/oxon/index.htm

Ketupa.net, a Media Industry Resource, http://www.ketupa.net

Labour History Archive & Study Centre: see People's Museum

Lam, Siobhan, 'Evangelical Tracts and Magazines for Children', Victorian Web, http://www.victorianweb.org/genre/childlit/mag-evangelical.html

Landow, George P., 'Mudie's Select Library and the Form of Victorian Fiction', 1972, Victorian Web, http://www.victorianweb.org/economics/mudie.html

Leanne Langley, "Hogarth, George", *Grove Music Online. Oxford Music Online*, http://www.oxfordmusiconline.com/subscriber/article/grove/music/13181

Lee, Elizabeth (rev. Sayoni Basu). "Murray, David Christie." *ODNB*, http://www.oxforddnb.com/view/printable/35157

Lee, H.W., 'The 'Social Democrat' and British Socialist,' 1897-1913', *The British Socialist*, (Dec. 1913), http://www.marxists.org/history/international/social-democracy/social-democrat/1913/12/overview.htm

Leary, Fred, "History of the Manchester Periodical Press" (MS in Manchester Central Reference Library, 1896)

Lenin, V. I., Obituary of Harry Quelch, *Pravda Truda*, (11 Sep.1913), 369-371, http://www.marx2mao.net/Lenin/HQ13.html

J. B. Leno papers, Brotherton Library, Leeds University, http://www.leedstrinity.ac.uk/depart/history/mh/Resources/Resources/Press/Sphinx/Sphinx.htm

Library of Liberty online, http://oll.libertyfund.org

Literary Heritage, http://www.LiteraryHeritage.org.uk

Lloyd's Maritime Register, http://www.lrfairplay.com/About/About_lrf.html

Ceridwen Lloyd-Morgan, 'Jones, Alice Gray [Ceridwen Peris] (1852-1943)', *ODNB*, Oxford University Press, 2004, http://www.oxforddnb.com/view/article/55220

Making of the Modern World, http://www.galeuk.com/trials/mome

Manchester Central Reference Library, http://www.manchester.gov.uk/libraries/central/

Marzolf, Marion, 'The American "New Journalism" and the Europeans', paper presented at the Annual Meeting of the Association for Education in Journalism and Mass Communication (66th, Corvallis, Oregon, Aug.6-9, 1983), Education Resources Information Centre, CUNY Libraries at http://web.ebscohost.com.ezproxy.gc.cuny.edu

Massey, Gerald, Papers, Upper Norwood Library, 39 Westow Hill, London SE19 1TJ

Menzies, John, http://www.johnmenziesplc.com

Mill, J.S. Collected Works, Online Library of Liberty, http://oll.libertyfund.org

Mining Journal, http://www.mining-journal.com

Missionary Periodicals Database, http://research.yale.edu:8084/missionperiodicals

Morris. William Internet Archive, http://www.marxists.org/archive/morris

John Murray Archives, National Library of Scotland, http://www.nls.uk/jma/index.html

National Archives, UK Government Records and Information Management,
 http://www.nationalarchives.gov.uk/

National Archives Learning Curve, http://www.learningcurve.gov.uk

National Library of Scotland, Scottish Book Trade Index,
 http://www.nls.uk/catalogues/resources/sbti/

National Portrait Gallery, Search the Collection, http://www.npg.org.uk

National Secular Society, http://www.secularism.org.uk

National Union of Journalists, http://www.nuj.org.uk

Natural History Museum, http://www.nhm.ac.uk

[Nature], 'History of the Journal *Nature*', http://www.nature.com/nature/history/index.html

The New Grove Dictionary of Music and Musicians, http://www.grovemusic.com/index

Newsplan, British Library, http://www.bl.uk/concord/linc/newsplan.html

Nichols, Jeremy 23 March 2005, Jerome K Jerome Forum,
 http://www.jeromekjerome.com/forum/viewtopic.php?t=42

ncse, 'Nineteenth Century Serials Edition', www.ncse.kcl.ac.uk/redist/pdf/016.pdf

Nineteenth Century Short Title Catalogue (NSTC), CD-ROM. Series III, 1870-1919, Newcastle-on-
 Tyne: Avero Publications Ltd.

Nineteenth Century British Library Newspapers,
 http://www.jisc.ac.uk/whatwedo/programmes/digitisation/bln.aspx

Nineteenth Century UK Periodicals,
 http://www.gale.cengage.com/DigitalCollections/products/ukperiodicals/

[Observer], *History of the Observer*,
 http://www.guardian.Co.uk/newsroom/story/0,,728445,00.html#article_continue

People's History Museum, 103 Princess Street, Manchester, M1 6DD, United Kingdom
 (formerly National Museum of Labour History)

Periodicals Index Online, http://gateway.proquest.com/openurl?url_ver=Z39.88-2004&res_dat=xri:
 c19index&rft_dat=xri:c19index:screen:pci

Princess Grace Irish Library (Monaco), http://www.pgil-eirdata.org/

Pickering and Chatto online, http://www.pickeringchatto.com/

Pharmaceutical Journal, Archives of, 1 Lambeth High Street, London SE1 7JN

Place, Francis, Collection, British Library Newspapers at Colindale, http://www.bl.uk/reshelp/findhelprestype/microform/francisplace/francisplace/index.html

Poole's Index (19th Century Masterfile), http://poolesplus.odyssi.com/19centWelcome.htm

Punch Archive, British Library, http://www.bl.uk/puncharchive.html

Pye, Dennis, 'The Clarion Movement, 1891-1914', *Working Class Movement Library*, http://www.wcml.org.uk/group/clarion.htm

Quarterly Musical Magazine and Review (1818-1828), http://www.ripm.org/pdf/Introductions/QMMintroEnglish.pdf

Quekett Microscopical Club, http://www.nhm.ac.uk/hosted_sites/quekett/

Reading Experience Database 1450-1945, http://www.open.ac.uk/Arts/reading/

Retrospective Index to Music Periodicals, http://www.ripm.org

Rossetti Archive, http://rossettiarchive.org

Rossijskij Centr Chranenija i Izucenija Dokumnentov Novejsej Istorii, Moscow; microfilm copy at International Institute of Social History, Amsterdam

Rutherford & Son Study Guide, http://www.artsalive.ca/pdf/eth/activities/rutherford_guide.pdf

Sabin, Roger, 'Ally Sloper: The First Comic's Super Star?', *Image & Narrative*, 7 (Oct. 2003) http: //www.imageandnarrative.be/graphicnovel/rogersabin.htm

Science in the Nineteenth Century Periodical, http://www.sciper.org/

Scoop, http://www.scoop-database.com

Scotsman Digital Archive, http://archive.scotsman.com

Scott Trust: Timeline, http://www.gmgplc.Co.uk/ScottTrust/Timeline/tabid/279/Default.aspx

Scottish Book Trade Index, http://www.nls.uk/catalogues/resources/sbti

'Scottish Clarks, http://www.scottishclarks.com/7html

Scottish Mountaineering Club, http://www.smc.org.uk/

Sell, Henry, *The Philosophy of Advertising* (Item SL09 in the History Of Advertising Trust Sell Collection, 1886), The History of Advertising Trust Archive, 12 Raveningham Centre, Raveningham, Norwich, NR14 6NU, Norfolk, UK

SHARP web (Society for the History of Authorship, Reading, and Publishing), http://www.sharpweb.org

Sherard, Robert H., 'The Adventures of a Journalist', *The Border Standard*, (10 Aug. to 16 Nov.1940) [completed in April 1912] (University of Reading MS 1047/3/9), The University of Reading, Redlands Road, Reading, Berkshire, RG1 5EX, UK

Simkin, John, '*Manchester Guardian*' Spartacus Educational, http://www.spartacus.schoolnet.Co.uk/PRguardian.htm

Smith, F.B., 'Southwell, Charles 1814-1860', *Dictionary of New Zealand Biography* (1990, updated 2007), http://www.dnzb.govt.nz/dnzb/

Society for Promoting the Training of Women Archives, Girton College Library, Girton College, Cambridge, CB3 OJG, UK

Spartacus Educational, http://www.spartacus.schoolnet.Co.uk

Speel Bob, Website of, http://myweb.tiscali.Co.uk

The Sphinx online, http://www.leedstrinity.ac.uk/depart/history/mh/Resources/Resources/Press/Sphinx/Sphinx.htm

Spielmann, Percy, 'Art, Books, and Friendships of Marion H. Spielmann, FSA, 1858-1948', typescript, (ref: MSL/1976/6348), National Art Library, Victoria and Albert Museum, Cromwell Road, London SW7 2RL, UK

Stead, W.T. Resource Site, http://www.attacking.Co.uk

'Studio: Aims of the Magazine in Detail', Charles Holme Archive File 1, 4-5, AAD/2003/10 (Archive of Art and Design)

Taylor, Philip M., 'War and the Media', Sandhurst Keynote, 1995, http://ics.leeds.ac.uk/papers/vp01.cfm?outfit=print&folder=258&paper=47

Televisionpoint.com, http://www.televisionpoint.com/

Times Digital Archive, http://www.timesonline.Co.uk

Together Trust, http://www.togethertrust.org.uk

Tyne and Wear Archives, Blandford House, Blandford Square, Newcastle upon Tyne, NE1 4JA, UK

Ulster History Circle, http://ulsterhistory.Co.uk/williamdrennan.htm

University of Detroit Mercy Black Abolitionist Archive, http://www.dalnet.lib.mi.us/gsdl/cgi-bin/library?p=about&c=baa

Victorian Fiction Research Guides, http://www.canterbury.ac.uk/arts-humanities/media/victorian-fiction-research-guides/index.asp

Victorian Women Writers Project, http://www.indiana.edu/~letrs/vwwp

Waterloo Directory of English Newspapers and Periodicals 1800-1900, http://www.victorianperiodicals.com/series2

Wee Web, Authors and Illustrators Archive, http://www.theweeweb.Co.uk

Wellesley Index to Victorian Periodicals 1824-1900, http://wellesley.chadwyck.Co.uk

Welsh Biography Online, http://yba.llgc.org.uk/en/index.html

West, Gerald, 'From Friend to Brother: The Spiritual Migration of Luke Howard and his Family, and the Meetings of Friends and Brethren at Tottenham' (unpublished MS, 2003)

Ward, A.W. et al, eds., *The Cambridge History of English and American Literature in 18 Volumes* (1907-1921), http: //www.bartleby.com/224/0420.html

[Whitaker], 'A History Of Whitaker's Almanack',
http://www.whitakersalmanack.co.uk/history.asp

Wilson, David, *The Complaynt of Scotland*,
http://www.scotsindependent.org/features/scots/complaynt/intro.htm

WorldCat, http://www.worldcat.org

Women Children's Book Illustrators, http://www.ortakeles.com/illustrators/Greenaway.html

Women's Library Catalogue, http://www.londonmet.ac.uk

Wright, Jane, *Review of Ingenious Women* by Deborah Jaffé,
http://www.camdennewjournal.Co.uk/2004%20archive/080104/r080104_6.htm

Yesterday's Papers, http://yesterdays-papers.blogspot.com

Headword Index by Category

Individuals, groups and companies have been grouped according their main occupation (journalist/editor, publisher, etc). When they have other areas of interest these are mentioned in brackets after the name: (e) for editor, (i) for illustrator, (j) for journalist, (p) for publisher, (prin) for printer, (prop) for proprietor.

Illustrators
Aldin, Cecil Charles Windsor
Allingham, Helen Mary Elizabeth
Andrews, George Henry
Anelay, Henry
Archer, John Wykeham
Attwell, Mabel Lucie
Barnard, Frederick
Baxter, William Giles
Beardsley, Aubrey Vincent (e)
Beerbohm, Henry Maximilian (j)
Bell, Robert Anning
Bennett, Charles Henry
Bonner, George Wilmot
Brandard, Robert/Edward Paxman
Branston, Robert/Robert Edward/Frederick William
Browne, Hablot Knight
Claxton, Florence A./Adelaide
Coode, Helen Hoppner (j)
Corbould, Astor Chantrey
Costello, Dudley/ Louisa
Cowham, Hilda Gertrude
Craig, Edward Henry Gordon
Crane, Walter
Cruikshank, George
Dadd, Frank
Dalziel family
Dickes, William
Doré, Paul Gustave Louis Christophe
Doyle, Richard
Du Maurier, George
'Duval, Marie'
Edwards, Mary Ellen
Fennell, John Greville
Fildes, Samuel Luke
Forrester, Alfred Henry
Foster, Myles Birket
Furniss, Henry

Gardner, W. Biscombe
Gavarni, H. G. S. Chevalier
Gilbert, John
Grant, Charles Jameson
Greenaway, Catherine
Greenaway, John
Hamerton, Robert Jacob
Hammond, Christine E Demain & Gertrude Demain
Harvey, William
Heath, William
Hennessy, William John
Hine, Henry George
Holl, Francis Montague
Hopkins, Arthur
Houghton, Arthur Boyd
Hughes, Alice Mary
Hughes, Arthur
Hunt, William Holman
Jackson, John
Jackson, Mason (e)
Keene, Charles Samuel
Landells, Ebenezer (prop)
Lawless, Matthew James
Lawson, Francis Wilfred
Leech, John
Leighton, Charles Blair
Linton, William James
Lover, Samuel (j)
Ludlow, Henry Stephen
McConnell, William
Mahoney, J.
Meadows, Joseph Kenny
Millais, John Everett
Moore, Thomas Sturge
Morgan, Matt Somerville
Morten, Thomas
Newman, William
Onwhyn, Thomas

Paget family
Pellegrini, Carlo
Pennell, Joseph (j)
Petrie, George (e)
Pinwell, George John
Pragnell, Kate
Purkess, George
Pyne, William Henry (j)
Railton, Herbert
Read, Samuel
Ricketts, Charles de Sousy
Sambourne, Edward Linley
Sandys, Frederick
Scott, William Bell (j)
Seymour, Robert
Shannon, Charles Haslewood
Sheridan, Louisa Henrietta
Sly, Stephen
Small, William
Smith, John Orrin/Harvey Orrin
Solomon, Simeon
Sowerby, Amy Millicent
Strang, William
Swain, Joseph
Tenniel, John
Thomson, Hugh
Upton, Florence Kate
Vizetelly, Henry Richard (e)
Walker, Frederick
Ward, Leslie Matthew
Watson, John Dawson
Whistler, James Abbot McNeill
Williams family
Woodward, Alice Bolingbroke

Inventor
Creed, Frederick George

Journalists/Editors
A Beckett, Arthur William (e)
Adams, William Edwin (e)
Adams, William Henry Davenport (e, prop)
Ainsworth, William Harrison (e, prop)
Alcock, Charles William (e)
Alford, Henry (e)
Allen, (Charles) Grant Blairfindie
Allingham, William
Alsager, Thomas Massa (prop)
Ansted, David Thomas
Anstie, Francis Edmund
Apperley, Charles James
Arnold, Edwin
Arnold, Matthew
Austin, Alfred (e)
Austin, Sarah (e)
Bacon, Richard Mackenzie (prop)
Bagehot, Walter (e)
Bain, Alexander
Bakewell, Mrs J. (e)
Balfour, Clara Lucas (e)
Bamford, Samuel
Barker, Joseph (e)
Barnes, Thomas (e)
Barrett, William A. (e)

Bax, Ernest Belfort (e)
Bayley, Frederick William Naylor (e)
Becker, Lydia Ernestine (e)
Beeton, Isabella Mary (e)
Bennett, Arnold (e)
Bennett, Joseph
Bennett, Thomas Jewell (prop)
Bentley, John James (e)
Besant, Annie (e)
Besant, Walter (e)
Bevington, Louisa Sarah
Biggs, Charles Henry Walker (e)
Billington, Mary Frances
Bindley, Charles
Binns, John (prop)
Binstead, Arthur Morris (e)
Birrell, Augustine
Black, Clementina Maria
Black, Helen C.
Black, William (e)
Blackburn, Helen
Blackwood, John (e)
Blakey, Robert (prop)
Blanchard, (Samuel) Laman
Blatchford, Robert Peel Glanville
Blathwayt, Raymond
Blessington, Marguerite (e) DEL Countess of; ADD
     Marguerite
Blind, Mathilde
Blumenfeld, Ralph David (e)
Bodichon, Barbara Leigh Smith (prop)
Bourne, Henry Richard Fox
Bowles, Thomas Milner-Gibson (prop)
Bowring, John (e)
Braddon, Mary Elizabeth (e)
Bradley, Edward
Brande, William Thomas (e)
Brewster, David (e)
Brierley, Benjamin (e)
Brooks, Charles William Shirley (e)
Brough, John Cargill (e)
Brough, Robert Barnabas (i)
Brougham, Henry (e)
Browne, Matilda (e)
Buchanan, David (e)
Buckland, Francis (e)
Bucknill, John Charles (e)
Bulwer Lytton, Edward (e)
Burgess, Joseph (e)
Burnand, Francis Cowley (e)
Burnett, George
Butler, Josephine Elizabeth (e)
Butt, Isaac (e)
Caird, Mona
Caldecott, Randolph
Campbell, Lady Colin
Campbell, Thomas (e)
Cannon, George (p)
Capes, John Moore (e, prop)
Carleton, William
Carlyle, Thomas
Carpenter, William Benjamin (e)
Carr, Joseph William Comyns
Catling, Thomas (e)

White, Joseph William Gleeson (e)
White, (William) Hale
White, William Hale- (e)
Whiteing, Richard
Wilde, Jane Frances Agnes
Wilde, Oscar (e)
Williams, Dawson (e)
Wills, William Henry
Wilson, Charlotte Mary
Wilson, John
Wilson, Margaret Cornwell Baron (e)
Wood, Ellen
Woodgate, Walter Bradford
Wooler, Thomas Jonathan (prin), (p)
Wyndham, George
Wynter, Andrew (e)
Yates, Edmund Hodgson (e, prop)
Yonge, Charlotte Mary (e)
Zangwill, Israel (e)
Zimmern, Helen

Newsagents/Distributors
Menzies, John
S. H. Benson
Smith, William Henry
W. H. Smith & Son
William Dawson

Printers
Applegath & Cowper
Ballantyne, James(e, p)
Baxter, John
Bradbury & Evans (p)
Bradbury, William
Chalmers family (p)
Clowes family
Dorrington, William
Dunkin, Alfred John (e, prop)
Evans, Edmund
Evans, Frederick Moule
Evans, Frederick Mullet (p, prop)
Evans, John (prop, e)
Finlay, Francis Dalzell (p)
Folds, John S.
Garnett, Jeremiah (e)
Gill, Michael Henry (p)
Grosvenor, John (e)
Hardy, Philip Dixon (prop)
Harney, George Julian (e)
Hazell, Watson & Viney Limited
Heywood, Abel (p)
Hobson, Joshua (e)
Holyoake, Austin (p)
Johnson, Thomas Burgeland (p)
Jones, Stephen (e)
Last, Joseph William (prop)
Leno, John Bedford (prop), (e), (j)
Nichols family (e), (p)
Philp, Robert Kemp (p)
Spottiswoode, William (p)
Taylor, Richard (e, p)
Thom, Alexander (p)
Timperly, Charles Henry
Waterlow, Sidney Hedley

Watson, James (p)
Way, Thomas/T. R. (p)

Publishers/Proprietors
Acton, John Emerich Edward Dalberg (e)
Andrews, William Eusebius (e)
Appleton, Charles Edward Cutts Birchall (e, j)
Baines, Edward/Edward Jnr (prin)
Baldwin family (prin)
Ballin, Ada Sarah (e, j)
Beaumont, Thomas Wentworth
Beer, Rachel (e)
Beeton, Samuel Orchart
Bell, John (prin)
Benbow, William
Bennett, Alfred William (e)
Bentley, Richard (prin)
Berger, George
Bertram, James Glass (e, j)
Blackwood, William
Bottomley, Horatio William (j)
Boucherett, Emilia Jessie (j)
Bradlaugh, Charles (e)
Braithwaite, John, the younger (e)
Brett, Edwin J.
Buckingham, James Silk
Carlile, Richard
Carpenter, William (e)
Cassell & Co.
Cassell, John (e)
Chambers, Robert
Chambers, William
Champion, Henry Hyde (j)
Chapman & Hall
Chapman, John (e)
Chatto & Windus
T & T Clark
Cobbe, Frances Power
Colburn, Henry
Collins family
Constable & Co.
Constable, Archibald
Cook, Eliza (e)
Corlett, John (j)
Cormack, John Rose (e)
Cowen, Joseph
Cowie, George (prin)
Cox, Edward William (j, e)
Curry, William
Dangerfield, Edmund (prin)
Davison, Thomas (prin, j)
De La Rue family
Diamond, Charles
Dicks, John
Doherty, John
Duffy, James
Dugdale, William
Elias, Julius Salter (prin)
Elliot Stock
Faithfull, Emily (e)
Ffennell, William Joshua
Francis, John
Galignani, (John) Anthony/Giovanni Antonio/William
Gee, Thomas

Gregory, Barnard
Grove, Archibald Newcomen
Gutch, John Mathew (e)
Hansard, Thomas Curson (prin)
Hardwicke, Robert
Harmsworth, Alfred Charles William (e)
Harmsworth, Harold
Harper & Brothers
Hetherington, Henry (prin)
Hodder & Stoughton
Holme, Charles (e)
Hope, Alexander James Beresford Beresford (j)
Hudson, Edward Burgess (prin)
Hulton, Edward (e)
Hunt, John
Hyndman, Henry Mayers (j, e)
Iliffe, family
Ingram, Herbert
John Murray publishers
Jones, William Kennedy (newspaper manager)
Kegan Paul
Kempe, Harry Robert (e)
Knight, Charles
Knight, John and Lacey, Henry
Knowles, James Thomas
Labouchère, Henry Du Pré (e), (j)
Lane, John
Lawson, Edward Levy
Lazenby, William
Le Fanu, Joseph Thomas Sheridan (e)
Levy, Joseph Moses
Lewer, Ethel Harriet Comyns (e)
'Lewis, Amelia' (e)
Limbird, John
Lloyd, Edward
Longman family
Lovett, William (j)
Low, Sampson
Lucas, William
Luxford, George
McGlashan, James (e)
Macmillan, Alexander
MacRae, Douglas Gordon (e)
Maxwell, John
Mennons, John
Morris, William (j, e)
Newnes, George (e)
Nicholson, William (e)
O'Connor, Feargus Edward
Parker, John William
Paul, Charles Kegan
Pearson, Cyril Arthur (j)
Power, John (e)
Richards, (Franklin Thomas) Grant (j)
Rivington family (prin)
Rollason, Ann
Routledge, George
Sampson Low & Co
Samuelson, James
Scott, Walter (j)
Simpkin & Marshall
Smith, George Murray
Smithers, Leonard Charles
Smithies, Thomas Bywater

Southwell, Charles (e)
Stevenson, George John (j)
Stiff, George
Stockdale, John Joseph
Strahan, Alexander Stuart
Strange, William (+ bookseller) Stuart, Daniel (prin)
Tait, William (e)
Thomas, William Luson (i)
Thompson, Henry Yates
Thomson, David Couper
Tilloch, Alexander
Tillotson, William Frederic
Trewman family (e)
Trübner, Johann Nicholas
Virtue, James Sprent (prin)
W. H. Allen
Walter family
Ward, Lock & Co.
Westmacott, Charles Molloy (e)
Whitaker, Joseph/Joseph Vernon
William Pickering
Wisemen, Nicholas (e)
Wood, Joseph Snell (e)

Titles

Aberdeen Journal
Academy
Accountant
Actors by Daylight
Adult
Age
Agnostic Annual
Ainsworth's Magazine
Alexandra Magazine
All the Year Round
Ally Sloper's Half-Holiday
Alpine Journal
Analytical Review
Anglo-Saxon Review
Annals and Magazine of Natural History
Annals of Electricity, Magnetism and Chemistry
Annals of Sporting and Fancy Gazette
Annual Monitor
Answers to Correspondents
Anti-Jacobin Review and Magazine
Archaeological Journal
Argosy
Art Journal
Artist and Journal of Home Culture
Atalanta
Athenaeum
Athletic News and Cyclists' Journal
Atlantis
Atlas
Auction Register and Law Chronicle
Author's Circular
Baby: The Mother's Magazine
Bachelors' Buttons
Bachelors' Papers
Baily's Monthly Magazine
Band of Hope Review
Band of Mercy Advocate
Baner ac Amserau Cymru (Banner and Times of Wales)
Beacon

Bee-Hive
Belfast News-Letter
Belfast Vindicator
Belfast Weekly News
Belgravia
Bell's Life in London, and Sporting Chronicle
Bell's Weekly Messenger
La Belle Assemblée
Bentley's Miscellany
Bent's Monthly Literary Advertise
Bicycling Times and Tourist's Gazette
Birmingham Argus
Birmingham Daily Post
Birmingham Journal
Black and White
Black Dwarf
Blackwood's Edinburgh Magazine
Bolster's Quarterly
Bolton Weekly Journal
Book World
Bookman
Bookseller
Borderland
Botanical Magazine
Bow Bells
Boy's Journal
Boys' Miscellany
Boy's Own Library
Boy's Own Magazine
Boy's Own Paper
Bradshaw's Railway Gazette
British and Foreign Confectioner
British and Foreign Evangelical Review
British and Foreign Review
British Architect
British Bandsman
British Chess Magazine
British Controversialist
British Critic
British Medical Journal
British Mothers' Magazine
British Quarterly Review
British Stage and Literary Cabinet
British Weekly
British Workman
British Workwoman
Builder
Builders' Weekly Reporter
Bullionist
Calcutta Review
Caledonian Mercury
Calender of Horrors
Cambrian
Cambro-Briton
Cape Argus
Cape Times
Caricaturist
Cassell's (Illustrated) Family Paper; Cassell's Magazine
Celebrities of the Day
Century Guild Hobby Horse
Chambers's (Edinburgh) Journal
Champion
Chemical News
Children's Friend

Children's Own Paper
Child's Companion
Christian Examiner and Church of Ireland Magazine
Christian Globe
Christian Guardian and Church of England Magazine
Christian Lady's Magazine
Christian Mother's Magazine
Christian Observer
Christian Reformer
Christian Remembrancer
Christian Teacher
Christian Witness
Christian Worker
Christian World
Church of England Quarterly Review
Church Times
Cigar and Tobacco World
Circular to Bankers
Citizen
City Jackdaw
Civil Engineer and Architect's Journal
Clarion
Cleave's Weekly Police Gazette
Clerkenwell News
Cobbett's Political Register
Comic Almanack
Comic Cuts
Commonweal
Companion for Youth
Companion to the Newspaper
Contemporary Review
Co-Operative Magazine and Monthly Herald
Cooper's Journal
Cork Examiner
Cornhill Magazine
Cosmopolis: An International Review
Cottager and Artisan
Country Life
Country Words
Crisis
Criterion
Critic
Cyclist
Daily Graphic
Daily Mail
Daily News
Daily Telegraph
Dark Blue
Democratic Review
Dial
Dome
Domestic Servants' Journal
Douglas Jerrold's Shilling Magazine
Douglas Jerrold's Weekly Newspaper
Dramatic Notes
Dublin Builder/Irish Builder
Dublin Evening Mail
Dublin Evening Post
Dublin Medical Press
Dublin Penny Journal
Dublin Review
Dublin University Magazine
Duffy's Hibernian Magazine/Duffy's Hibernian Sixpenny
    Magazine

Dundee Courier
Ecclesiastical Gazette
Ecclesiologist
Echo
Eclectic Review
Economist
Edinburgh Evening Courant
Edinburgh Medical and Surgical Journal
Edinburgh Review
Eliza Cook's Journal
Engineer
Engineering
English Gentleman
English Illustrated Magazine
English Mechanic
English Republic
English Woman's Journal
Englishman's Magazine
Englishwoman
Englishwoman's Domestic Magazine
Englishwoman's Review
Era
Evangelical Christendom
Evangelical Magazine
Evening News
Everybody's Album and Caricature Magazine
Examiner
Exquisite
Fairplay
Family H
Field
Figaro in London
Financial and Commercial Record
Financial News
Financial Times
Fishing Gazette
Le Follet
Football Annual
Foreign Quarterly Review
Fortnightly Review
Fraser's Magazine
Free Review
Freedom
Freeman's Journal
Freethinker
Friend of India
Friend/British Friend
Friends' Quarterly Examiner
Fun
Funny Folks
Gardener's Chronicle and Agricultural Gazette
Gardener's Magazine
Gentleman's Magazine
Germ
Girl's Own Paper
Glasgow Herald
Glasgow Looking Glass
Glasgow Sentinel
Globe
Golf
Good Words
Good Words for the Young
Gorgon
Governess

Grocer and Oil Trade Review
Guardian
Gymnast
Happy Hours
Hardwicke's Science Gossip
Harmonicon
Harmsworth Monthly Pictorial Magazine
Harper's New Monthly Magazine
Health and Strength
Hearth and Home
Home Chat
Home and Foreign Review
Home Journal
Home Notes
Hone's Reformists' Register and Weekly Commentry
Hood's Magazine and Comic Miscellany
Horse and Hound
Hospital
Household Words
Howitt's Journal
Hunt's Universal Yacht List
Idler
Illuminated Magazine
Illustrated Exhibitor
Illustrated London News
Illustrated Police Budget
Illustrated Police News
Illustrated Sporting and Dramatic News
Illustrated Times
Indian Spectator
Inquirer
Inverness Courier
Irish Daily Independent
Irish Liberator
Irish Literary Gazette
Irish Monthly Magazine
Irish People
Irish Quarterly Review
Irish Society
Irish Times
Irish Tribune
Isis
Jack and Jill
Jackson's Oxford Journal
Jeweller and Metalworker
Jockey
John Bull
Journal of Mental Science
Journal of the Workhouse Visiting Society
Journalist: A Monthly Phonographic Magazine
Journalist: A Newspaper for All Newspaper Producers
Judy
Jurist
Justice
Kingston's Magazine for Boys
Knowledge
Labour Elector
Labour Leader
Labour Prophet
Labour Standard
Labourer
Ladies' Cabinet of Fashion, Music and Romance
Ladies' Companion
Ladies' Journal: A Newspaper of Fashion, Literature, Music

Patriot
Pearl
Pearson's Magazine
Penny Magazine/Knight's Penny Magazine
Penny Novelist
Penny Story-Teller
Penny Sunday Times and People's Police Gazette
People's Friend
People's Journal (1846)
People's Journal (1858)
People's Paper
People's Periodical and Family Library
Peter Parley's Magazine
Pharmaceutical Journal
Philosophical Magazine
Photographic Quarterly
Phrenological Journal and Miscellany
Politics for the People
Poole's Index to Periodical Literature
Poor Man's Guardian
Popular Science Monthly
Portfolio
Primitive Methodist Magazine
Printing Machine
Proceedings of the Society for Psychical Research
Prospective Review
Protestant Woman/Protestant Girl
Provincial Medical and Surgical Journal/Association
    Medical Journal
Publisher's Circular
Puck/Ariel or the London Puck
Punch
Quarterly Journal of Science
Quarterly Musical Magazine and Review
Quarterly Review
Queen
Quiver
Racing Calendar
Racing Times
Racing World and Newmarket Sportsman
Rambler
Rational Dress Society's Gazette
Reader
Reasoner/Secular World
Record
Record Of The Musical Union
Red Dragon
Red Republican
Reis and Rayyet
Review of Reviews
Reynolds's Miscellany
Reynolds's Political Instructor
Reynolds's Weekly Newspaper/Reynolds's Newspaper
Robin Goodfellow
Rock
Royal Irish Academy: Transactions/Proceedings
St James's Gazette
St James's Magazine
St Paul's
Satirist
Saturday Magazine
Saturday Review
Saunders's Newsletter
Savoy

Scots Observer/National Observer
Scotsman
Scottish Mountaineering Club Journal
Scottish Review
Secular Review
Servant's Magazine
Shafts
Shamrock
Sharpe's London Magazine
Sheffield Iris
Sheffield Weekly Telegraph
Shield
Sketch
Social-Democrat
Solicitors Journal
Sons of Britannia
Speaker
Spectator
Sphinx
Spiritual Magazine
Sporting Chronicle
Sporting Clipper
Sporting Gazette/Country Gentleman
Sporting Life
Sporting Magazine
Sporting Review
Sporting Times
Sportman
Spy
Stage Director/Stage
Standard
Star
Statist
Stirling Observer
Strad
Strand Magazine
Strand Musical Magazine
Studio
Sunday At Home
Sunday Times
Tablet
Tait's Edinburgh Magazine
Tallis's Dramatic Magazine
Tatler
Teddy Ashton's Journal/Northern Weekly
Temple Bar
Textile Recorder
Theatre
Theatrical Inquisitor
Theatrical Journal
Theatrical Times
Theatrical 'World'
Theological Review
The Times
Times of India
Tinsley's Magazine
Tit-Bits
Tobacco, a Monthly Trade Journal
Tobacco Trade Review: a Monthly Trade Journal
Tomahawk
Town
Trades' Newspaper and Mechanics' Weekly Journal
Train
Transport

General Index

The main point of entry for each name or journal is via each name, journal or topic. These are indicated in bold type in the index. References to a particular name, journal or topic in other entries are listed as subheadings to the main entry. Page numbers in the index refer to whole entries; a or b following the page number refers to the first (a) or second (b) column.

editor, *Blackwood's* 60
and Lewes 361-2
and S. Phillips 493b
proprietor, *Blackwood's Edinburgh Magazine* 469-70
and G. M. Smith 579
Blackwood, Robert 58-9
Blackwood, William **59-60**
and Coleridge 132a-b
contributor, *Literary Gazette* 365-6
and Lockhart 372
and Moir 420-1
and Murray 322
proprietor, *Blackwood's Edinburgh Magazine* 423, 469-70
and Rintoul 587-9
support for *Spectator* 587-9
Blackwood, William I, proprietor, *Edinburgh Monthly Magazine* 507a
Blackwood, William III, editor, *Blackwood's* 60, 191-3
Blackwood family 420-1
Blackwood's (Edinburgh) Magazine 58-9, 59-60, **60**
anonymity of authors 193
attack on Braddon 45-6
and Carleton 95-6
and class 125-6
Coleridge and 132a-b
Coleridge's letters 358-60
collaborations 132-3
colonial distribution 170-2
columns 134-5
contributor(s): A. Austin 29-30; Bertram 52a-b; Courthope 148a-b; D'Arcy 161a; De Quincey 165; Eagles 187a; Escott 206-7; Evans 361-2; Marian Evans 209-10; Ferrier 494; Gilfillan 248b; F. Greenwood 259; Jennings 316-17; D. W. Jerrold 318-19; Lamb 343a; Lawrance 350a-b; V. Lee 352-3; Lever 360; Lewes 361-2; Lockhart 372, 392; Maginn 392; Masson 400-1; Moir 420-1; A. Mozley 430; Norton 461a-b; Oliphant 469-70; M. O'Sullivan 471-2; S. O'Sullivan 472; S. Phillips 493b; Robinson 543-4; W. B. Scott 564; Shand 367-8; Skelton 577a; Steevens 599-600; Stutfield 608a-b; Trollope 640b; Whibley 673a-b; J. Wilson 372, 392, 679b; Zimmern 699a-b
cover price 573-4
editors: J. Blackwood 58-9; Hogg 679b; Lockhart 679b; J. Wilson 679b
establishment 391-2
military stories 412a-b
position of 'Editor' 59-60
precursors 507a
proprietors, W. Blackwood 422-3
publishers' status 515-16
reviewing 538
and Rintoul 542a-b
rivals 213a-b, 229-30, 375a, 557-8, 563a-b
role of editor 191-3
satire 556-7
serialization of Bulwer Lytton's work 87
size and format 576-7
and social sciences 581-2
and *Tait's Edinburgh Magazine* 613-14
and typewritten copy 642-3
views on Gifford 246-7

Blackwoods (publishers)
London office 58-9
McGlashan at 388a
A. Mozley 430
publishers, periodicals 515-16
Blades, William
contributor, *Library* 362-3
and Elliot Stock 198
Blaikie, W. G., editor, *North British Review* 123, 457b
Blake, Benjamin, publisher, *Family Herald* 213-14
Blake, Charles, editor, *Sporting Life* 594a-b
Blake, William 103-4, 559
W. Allingham on 12-13
Blakey, Robert **60-1**
contributor, *Black Dwarf* 458-9
and Doubleday 176b
editor, *Northern Liberator* 458-9
proprietor, *Northern Liberator* 458-9
Blanc, Louis
contributor, *Democratic Review* 164b
in *Reynolds's Political Instructor* 540
Blanchard, E. L., contributor, *Daily Telegraph* 562-3
Blanchard, (Samuel) Laman 9-10, **61**, 318
and *Constitution* 297-8
editor, *Court Journal* 131-2
Blanchard, Sydney, contributor, *Household Words* 292-3
Bland, Edith *see* Nesbit, Edith
'Bland, Fabian' (E. Nesbit and H. Bland) 667-8
Bland, Hubert, contributor, *Weekly Dispatch* 667-8
blasphemy 231-2
Foote's conviction 231-2
Hetherington 281a-b
G. J. Holyoake 285-6
legal challenges against 232-3
and news 448-50
Paterson 566a
secular press 566a
Southwell 112b, 566a, 586-7
trial of Bradlaugh 72b
Wedderburn 93a-b
see also libel, blasphemous
Blatchford, Montague
contributor, *Clarion* 122-3
serialized socialist fiction 566-7
Blatchford, Robert Peel Glanville **61**
and Burgess 87-8
and *Clarion* 122-3, 339b, 566-7, 583, 583-4
contributor: *Daily Mail* 157-8; *Manchester Sunday Chronicle* 122-3; *Workman's Times* 690a-b
serialized socialist fiction 566-7
Blatchford, Winnie, editor, *Clarion* 122-3
Blathwayt, Raymond **61-2**
Blavatsky, Madame, and Annie Besant 52b
Bleackley, Edward Overall
and *Bell's Life in London* 46-7
financer, *Prophetic Bell* 592a
Hulton 296a
Bleakley & Co. 46-7
Blessington, Marguerite, Countess of (née Gardiner) **62**
annuals 17-18
contributor, *Mirror of Literature* 417a-b
proprietor: *Book of Beauty* 572-3; *Keepsake* 572-3
and Toulmin 633b
Blind, Mathilde **62**

and secular press 566a
and Watts 566a-b
see also National Reformer
Bradley, Edward **72-3**
Bradley, F. H., contributor, *Mind* 414a-b
Bradley, Richard
  editor, *A General Treatise of Husbandry and Gardening* 242-3
  proprietor, *A General Treatise of Husbandry and Gardening* 242-3
Bradshaw, George, proprietor, *Railway Gazette* 73a, 416
Bradshaw's Monthly Railway Guide 73a
Bradshaw's Railway, &c., Through Route and Overland Guide 639-40
Bradshaw's Railway Almanack 73a
Bradshaw's Railway Companion 73a
Bradshaw's Railway Gazette **73**, 639-40
Bradshaw's Railway Timetables 73a
Brahms, Johannes
  Barrett on 39a-b
  J. Bennett on 49a-b
  Freemantle on 231a-b
Braille edition, *Daily Mail* 157-8
Brain
  editor, Bucknill 84-5
  publisher, Macmillan 388-9
Braithwaite, John, the younger **73**
Braithwaite, Joseph Bevan, contributor, *Friends' Quarterly Examiner* 236-7
Brake, Laurel 530-1
Brame, Charlotte Mary, contributor, *Bow Bells* 67a-b
'Bramsbury, H. J.' (H. M. Hyndman) 299b
brand identity, comic annuals and 135b
Brandard, Edward Paxman **73**
Brandard, Robert **73**
Brande, William Thomas **73-4**
Brandes, Edward, and C. W. Scott 562-3
Branston, Frederick William **74**
Branston, Robert **74**
Branston, Robert Edward **74**, 258b
Branston and Vizetelly, and Landells 345a
Brasenose College, T. W. Ward at 662a-b
Bremner, Christina S., editor, *Woman's Herald* 683b
Bremner, William, publisher, *Vegetarian Messenger* 651-2
Brenan, Gerald, contributor, *Harmsworth's* 271
Brenan, Joseph, and Mangan 395-6
Brennan, J. E., editor, *Bombay Times and Journal of Commerce* 628-9
'Brent, George' (G. Emmett) 694-5
Brentano Brothers, publishers *British Chess Magazine* 77a-b
Brereton, Austin, editor, *Dramatic Notes* 178a-b
Brett, Edwin J. **74**, 329-30
  and *Boys of England* 69, 329-30, 544-5
  and *Boys' Miscellany* 68-9
  and Emmett 586a-b
  founder, *Young Men of Great Britain* 696-7
  Hemyng 279a-b
  and novelettes 462
  and *Young Englishman's Journal* 694-5
Brewer, Emma, contributor, *Girl's Own Paper* 249a
Brewster, David **75**
  contributor: *National Review* 439-40; *North British Review* 457b
  editor, *Philosophical Magazine* 493-4
  proprietor, *Edinburgh Philosophical Journal* 493-4
Brice, Andrew, proprietor, *Exeter Journal* 640a
Brick and Tile Gazette 86
Bridgeford, John, proprietor, *Sheffield Isis* 571-2
Brierley, Benjamin **75**
  contributor, *Country Words* 146-7
Bright, Addison, editor, *Theatre* 620-1
Bright, Charles, contributor, *Electrician* 195-7
Bright, John
  and *Stirling Observer* 602-3
  views on *Northern Echo* 457-8
Bright, Mary Dunne *see* 'Egerton, George'
Brighton, *Evening Argus* 157a
Brimelow, William, editor, *Bolton Evening News* 626
Bristol Cathedral, S. Smith at 580
Bristol Corporation 264
Bristol Mercury
  Chilton at 112b
  proprietor, J. Evans 209
Bristol Mirror, editor, J. P. C. Hatton 275b
Bristol Observer and Gloucester, Monmouth, Somerset and Wilts Courier 209
Bristol papers, J. Evans and 209
Bristol Riots 228-9
Britannia
  contributor(s): A. Austin 29-30; Gruneisen 263a-b
  subeditor, S. C. Hall 266a-b
British, *see also* United Kingdom
British and Foreign Confectioner(, Baker and Restaurateur) 75-6
British and Foreign Evangelical Review 76
  contributor(s), Robertson 543a-b
British and Foreign Mechanic 203-4
British and Foreign Medical Review 375-6
  proprietors: Connolly 224b; J. Forbes 224b, 322-3
British and Foreign Medico-Chirurgical Review 322-3
  contributor(s), W. B. Carpenter 98a
British and Foreign Railway Journal
  contributor(s): Austin 639-40; Chapman 639-40
British and Foreign Review 76, 523
  and Beaumont 42a-b
  contributor(s): Sarah Austin 30; Lardner 347-8; Reeve 534a-b
  editor, Kemble 332a-b
  proprietor, T. W. Beaumont 332a-b
  rivals 226-7
British Archaeological Association 22-3
  printer, Dunkin 185-6
British Architect 76-7, 86
British Army and Navy Review, contributor(s), Ouida 473
British Association for the Advancement of Science 260-1
  political economy 498-9
  Statistical Section 581-2
British Association for Promoting Co-operative Knowledge 635-6
British Bandsman (and Orchestral Times) 77
British Banner, mergers 483a-b
British Bookmaker, printers, Clowes 128-9
British Books in Print 673-4
British Catalogue (annual) 516-17
British Chess Magazine 77
British Churchman, editor, Christmas 118a-b

Lewes on 361-2
publishers, G. M. Smith 579
re-appraisal 237b
reviews 428
Saturday Review and 557-8
Simcox on 575a
Skelton on 577a
Spectator and 587-9
'Brownrigg, Henry' (Jerrold) 318-19
Bruce, David, typesetting machine 642b
'Bruce, Edward' (Bulwer Lytton) 87
Bruce, James, contributor, *Scotsman* 562
Bruce, John Thackray, editor, *Birmingham Daily Post*
55-6
Brunner, J. T., chemical plant 338b
Brunner, John, financer, *Speaker* 587a-b
Brunner Mond 106b
'Brutus' (*Black Dwarf*) 57-8
'Brutus' (David Owen) 474
Bryan, Alfred
illustrator: *Illustrated Sporting and Dramatic News*
304; *London Entr'acte* 374
Bryant & May
matchgirls 364
working conditions 338b
Bryce, James
contributor, *Manchester Guardian* 394-5
history 282-3
Bryerley, Thomas, editor, *Mirror of Literature* 417a-b
Bubble Act (1720) 219-20
Buchan, John, contributor, *Blackwood's Edinburgh
Magazine* 60
Buchanan, David 83-4
editor, *Edinburgh Evening Courant* 189-90
Buchanan, Robert
contributor: *Contemporary Review* 26-8; *Temple Bar*
618-19
editor, *Welcome Guest* 669a
and Swinburne 611-12
views on *Germ* 246-7
Buck, Henry, proprietor, *Bell's Life in London* 46-7
Buckingham, James Silk 84
editor, *Athenaeum* 630-1
proprietor, *Oriental Herald and Colonial Review* 552b
Buckland, Francis T. 84
editor, *Land and Water* 344-5
proprietor, *Land and Water* 217b
Buckle, George, editor, *The Times* 625b
Bucknill, John Charles 84-5
editor: *Asylum Journal* 325a-b; *Journal of Mental
Science* 325a-b
Bucks Independent, printers, Hazell, Watson & Viney
Limited 276-7
BUCOP 663
Budd, Edward, editor, *West Briton* 222
Budd, John, publisher, *Cobbett's Political Register* 130-1
Buggy, Kevin T., editor, *Belfast Vindicator* 45a
Builder 85, 121-2, 126, 510-11
contributor(s), Hoey 284a-b
mergers 76-7
news in 448-50
Owenite philosophy 86
and trade press 634-5
Builder's Journal and Architectural Record 86

Builder's Reporter and Engineering Times 85-6
Builders' Weekly Reporter 85-6, 86, 121-2
building, separation from architecture in 19th C 86
Building and Engineering Times 86
absorbed by *Builders' Weekly Reporter* 85-6
building materials, prices 121-2
Building News, publisher, J. P. Edwards 194
Building press 86
Buist, George, editor, *Times of India* 628-9
Bulgarian Atrocities 438-9
Daily News on
Northern Echo on 457-8
Bull, George Stringer, proprietor, *British Labourer's
Protector, and Factory Child's Friend* 635
Bull Run 549-50
Bullen, Arthur, contributor, *Library* 362-3
Bullen, Frank, contributor, *Harmsworth's* 271
Buller, J., founder, Provincial Newspaper Society 514-15
Bulley, Miss, and *Manchester Guardian* 341a
Bullionist 86-7
readership 219-20
Bullionist Publishing Co. 86-7
Bullock rotary press, *Daily Telegraph* 158-9
Bulwark, or Reformist Journal, printers, Constable 138-9
Bulwer Lytton, Edward 87
Age and 671-2
contributor: *Foreign Quarterly Review* 226-7; *Literary
Gazette* 365-6; *Quarterly Review* 522-3
editor, *New Monthly Magazine and Literary Journal*
131-2, 443-4
financial support, *Examiner* 211-12
B. Jerrold on 318
photographs 381b
plays 453-4
proprietor, *Monthly Chronicle* 347-8, 421-2
publishers, Sampson Low & Co. 555a-b
serialized fiction in *All the Year Round* 11a-b
views on journalistic impersonality 18-19
views on penny newspapers 487
Bunn, Albert, proprietor, *Age* 671-2
Bunting, Jabez, proprietor, *Wesleyan Methodist Magazine*
670b
Bunting, P. W. *192*
Bunting, Percy, editor, *Contemporary Review* 139a-b
Burder, George
editor, *Evangelical Magazine* 208a
founder, Religious Tract Society 535
Burdett, Henry
and Fenwick 462-4
proprietor: *Hospital* 462-4, 464; *Nursing Mirror*
462-4, 464
Burdett's Hospital Annual 462-4
Burgess, Henry, proprietor, *Circular to Bankers* 119
Burgess, Joseph 87-8
editor, *Workman's Times* 690a-b
proprietor, *Workman's Times* 106b
Burgin, George Brown, proprietor, *Idler* 317-18
Burlington Magazine
contributor(s): C. Phillips 493a; J. F. A. Wilde 676a
views on Carr 98a-b
Burnand, Francis Cowley 88
editor, *Punch* 517-19
satirical journalism 556-7
Burne-Jones, Edward

caricaturists
Beerbohm 43b
C. H. Bennett 49a
Bryan 304, 374
Cruikshank 155a-b
Duval 186b
Furniss 238-40
C. J. Grant 211a, 257b
Heath 278-9
Leech 353
Meadows 404-5
Morgan 425-6
W. Newman 448a
Pellegrini 485b, 662a
Seymour 218-19
Sheridan 572-3
Sime 57b, 300
L. M. Ward 662a
Carl Rosa Opera Co 231a-b
Carleton, John William, editor, *Sporting Review* 594b
Carleton, William 95-6
contributor: *Christian Examiner* 472-3; *Christian Examiner and Church of Ireland Magazine* 113b, 155-6; *Citizen* 120-1; *Dublin University Magazine* 89, 183-4, 388a; *Duffy's Hibernian Magazine* 185; *Nation* (Irish) 360; *Shamrock* 569a
in *Irish Monthly Magazine* 310-11
views on J. F. A. Wilde 676a
Carlile, Alfred 96
Carlile, Elizabeth Sharples *see* Sharples, Eliza
Carlile, Jane 96
Carlile, Richard 96
contributor, *Isis* 312-13
and T. Davison 163
imprisonment 570
proprietor, *Lion* 666a
publisher: *Gorgon* 255a; *Republican* 232-3, 552b, 689
and E. Sharples (Carlile) 570
unstamped press 648-9
and James Watson 664b
Carlile, Thomas 96
Carlile, W. A., contributor, *Labour Leader* 338-9
Carlile's Political Register, publishers, Carlile 96
Carlisle Journal, contributor(s), Farish 215
Carlisle Patriot, and Chartism 108-9
Carlton Club, first journalist admitted 62-3
Carlyle, Jane Welsh
letters 96-7
Skelton on 577a
Wedgwood on 666a-b
Carlyle, Thomas 96-7
biography 237b
and J. R. Chorley 113a-b
contributor: *Examiner* 211-12; *Foreign Review* 226-7; *Fraser's Magazine* 229-30; *London Magazine* 375a; *New Monthly Magazine and Literary Journal* 443-4; *New Review* 445
Macfarlane on 387a
and Napier 437
philosophy and journalism 494
and political economy 498-9
Spectator and 587-9
translations 355-6
views on Chartism 543-4

views on Jeffrey 316
views on religious press 534-5
views on reviewing 538
Carmarthen Journal 92a
Carmichael, Richard 181-2
Carnegie, Andrew, co-proprietor, *Echo* 194, 668b
Carnie, Ethel, and co-operative press 142-3
Caroline, Queen
controversy 442-3
and divorce 106-7
Flindell and 222
and *John Bull* 321-2
Stockdale and 603a-b
Carpenter, Edward 4, 328-9
Carpenter, Mary 278a
Carpenter, William (1797-1874) 97-8
editor: *Lloyd's Weekly Newspaper* 371a-b, 609a-b; *Political Letters* 606-7; *Trades' Free Press* 635-6; *Weekly Free Press* 126-7, 635-6
Political Letters 648-9
proprietor, *Trades' Newspaper and Mechanics' Weekly Journal* 635
publisher: *Political Letters & Pamphlets* 126-7; *Slap at the Church* 126-7
Carpenter, William Benjamin (1813-1885) 98
contributor: *Agnostic Annual* 8-9; *Modern Review* 420b
editor, *Natural History Review* 441
Carpenter-Fenton, Mrs, and Rational Dress Society 528-9
Carpenter's London Journal, publishers, W. Carpenter 97-8
Carpenter's Monthly Political Magazine, publishers, W. Carpenter 97-8
Carpenter's Political and Historical Essays, publishers, W. Carpenter 97-8
Carr, Emsley, editor, *News of the World* 451
Carr, J. W. Comyns, editor, *English Illustrated Magazine* 201-3
Carr, Joseph William Comyns 98
contributor, *World* 690b
Carr, Lascelles
co-proprietor, *News of the World* 451
editor, *Western Mail* 670-1
proprietor, *Western Mail* 670-1
carrier pigeons
and foreign news 225-6
and horse-racing press 547a-b
Carrington, John, *Science-Gossip* 268-9
Carrington, Lord 432-3
Carrodus, John Tiplady, contributor, *Strad* 603-4
'Carroll, Lewis' *see* Dodgson, Charles L.
Carruthers, Robert, and *Inverness Courier* 308-9, 529
Carruthers, Robert (Jnr.), manager, *Inverness Courier* 308-9
Carruthers, Walter, editor, *Inverness Courier* 308-9
cars *see* motoring
Carson, Charles Lionel, proprietor, *Stage Directory* 596a-b
Carton, James, editor, *Athletic News* 241a
cartoons/cartoonists 98, 100
Ally Sloper's Half-Holiday 12-13
anti-Christian movement 232-3
Baxter 40-1, 556-7
F. Claxton 126a-b

and rural affairs 585-6
unstamped press 648-9
and T. Wakley 343-4, 655a
Western Vindicator and 671
Cobbett's Political Register 93a-b, **130-1**
    Benbow as agent 48a-b
    and cheap journalism 109-10
    contributor(s): Blakey 60-1; Buchanan 83-4
    proprietors, Cobbett 556-7, 689
    read out loud 170-2
    as weekly 666-7
Cobbett's Twopenny Trash 130-1
Cobden, Richard 426
    and *Irish Liberator* 309-10
    and A. Somerville 585-6
    and *Stirling Observer* 602-3
Cobden, William, Land League 263-4
Cochrane, J. G., proprietor, *Metropolitan Magazine* 396-7
Cochrane, John George, editor, *Foreign Quarterly Review* 226-7
Cochrane's 226-7
Cockburn, Henry 437
cocking 17a
Cockney Adventures and Tales of London Life, printer, Last 348
Cockney School of Poetry 372
    Blackwood's on 60
    C. W. Dilke and 169-70
    Hazlitt 277
    Lockhart and 372, 563a-b
    J. Scott and 563a-b
coffee shops
    as journal distributors 170-2
    reading rooms 515
Cohen, Chapman, editor, *Freethinker* 231-2
Coke, Charlotte H. Talbot (née Fitzgerald) **131**
    and *Hearth and Home* 20, 131a, 278b
Colam, John, editor, *Band of Mercy Advocate* 37-8
Colburn, Henry **131-2**
    and R. Bentley 50a-b
    and Galignani family 241a-b
    Hook 288-9
    house magazines 292
    Naval and Military Gazette 646b
    and paid paragraphs 477b
    proprietor: *Court Journal* 552b; *Literary Gazette* 365-6; *London Weekly Review* 552b; *New Monthly Magazine and Universal Register* 422-3, 443-4, 574a
    publishers, *New Monthly Magazine* 92-3, 423
    puffing 517b
    see also New Monthly Magazine
Colburn, Zerah
    editor, *Engineer* 200-1
    founder, *Engineering* 201
Colclough, Stephen 530-1
Cole, Henry, proprietor, *Westminster Review* 672-3
Coleman, F. M. (printer) 49-50, 628-9
Coleridge, Christabel
    contributor, *Monthly Packet* 424
    and Yonge 694a-b
Coleridge, Christabel Rose, editor, *Guardian* 132a
Coleridge, Henry, editor, *Month* 421b
Coleridge, John Taylor, editor, *Quarterly Review* 522-3
Coleridge, Mary Elizabeth **132**

Coleridge, Samuel Taylor **132**, 421b
    Anti-Jacobin Review on 20-1
    contributor: *Gentleman's Magazine* 245-6; *Monthly Magazine* 422-3; *Morning Post* 427a-b
    Hazlitt 277
    and Lamb 343a
    letters, in *Blackwood's Magazine* 358-60
    J. S. Mill on 412-13
    and the press 32
    reviews 482-3
    and Thelwell 106-7
    Traill on 636
    collaboration **132-3**, 408a-b
Collard, William (engraver) 23a
College Magazine (Edinburgh University) 647-8
College of Violinists, and *Strad* 603-4
Collie, John Norman 608a-b
Collingridge, L., proprietor, *Rock* 544a-b
Collingridge, W. H., proprietor, *Rock* 544a-b
Collins, James, publisher, *Racing Times* 526a-b
Collins, John Churton 325-6
    contributor: *Nineteenth Century* 325-6; *Quarterly Review* 255b
Collins, Mortimer, contributor, *Temple Bar* 618-19
Collins, William & Co.
    historical background 133
    output 133
Collins, William I 133
Collins, William II 133
Collins' Cheer-Me-Up, publishers, Collins 133
Collins' Directory of Trowbridge, publishers, Collins 133
Collins family **133**
Collins, William (Wilkie) 32, **133-4**
    and Christmas issues 117-18
    contributor: *Bow Bells* 67a-b; *Cassell's Magazine* 578a-b; *Cornhill Magazine* 145; *Globe* 253a; *Household Words* 292-3, 530a-b; *London Society* 376-7; *Temple Bar* 618-19
    fiction serialized 11a-b, 45-6
    as journalist 32
    novelettes 462
    photograph in Low's editions 381b
    photographs 381b
    publishers, Sampson Low & Co. 555a-b
    views on class 125-6
Collinson, James, illustrator, *Germ* 246-7
Colman family, proprietors, *Star* 597b
Colman's Magazine, contributor(s), Brierley 75a-b
Cologne 398-9
Cologne Conservatorium 323a-b
colonial distribution of journals 170-2
Colonial Intelligencer and Aborigines' Friend, editor, Bourne 67a
colonial market for periodicals 170-2
Colonial Missionary Society, reports 343b
Colonial Nursing Association 462-4
colonial press **134**
    Bradbury & Evans and 208-9
    Times of India 628-9
    see also imperialism
colonial social life, in *Blackwood's* 60
colonies
    expansion 306
    fiction distribution 626

publishers: Cleave 381a; Lovett 381a
educational features of journals, *Atalanta* 26
*Educational Magazine and Journal of Christian
Philanthropy and of Public Utility*, editor, Dick 166-7
educational manuals 301b
Educational Times, contributor(s), Wells 669-70
Edward, Prince of Wales
    and gossip 256
    marriage 213a-b; photographs 495-6
Edward Arnold (publishers), publisher, *English Illustrated
Magazine* 201-3
Edwardes, Annie, contributor, *Temple Bar* 618-19
Edwards, (Samuel Jules) Celestine **193-4**
Edwards, John Hugh, founder/editor, *Young Wales* 697
Edwards, John Passmore **194**
    proprietor: *Echo* 188a-b, 668b; *English Mechanic*
    203-4; *Weekly Echo* 668b; *Weekly Times* 668b
    recruitment of Billington 54a
Edwards, Lewis, editor, *Y Traetodydd* 244a-b
Edwards, Mabel, editor, *Wheelwoman* 341-2
Edwards, Mary Ellen **194-5**
    illustrator: *Belgravia* 45-6; *Cassell's Illustrated Family
    Paper* 101; *Girl's Own Paper* 249a; *Onward* 471a
Edwards, Owen Morgan, proprietor, *Wales* 658a
Edwards, William, contributor, *Western Vindicator* 671
Egan, Pierce **195**, 557a
    contributor: *London Journal* 668b; *Weekly Dispatch*
    667-8; *Weekly Times* 668b
    editor, *Weekly Times* 668b
    influence on *Bell's Life in London* 46-7
    sporting journalism 593-4
Egan, Pierce, the Younger, editor, *London Journal* 374-5
Egan, Pierce James **195**
    editor, *London Journal* 374-5
Egan, Pierce (son of P J Egan), editor, *London Journal*
195b
'Egerton, George' (Mary Dunne Bright)
    contributor, *Yellow Book* 692-4
    and Le Gallienne 355b
Eglington, Charles, editor, *Theatre* 620-1
Egypt 549-50
    St. John in 552, 552b
electoral reform
    and *Glasgow Sentinel* 251-2
    and *Northern Whig* 461a
    and the press 499-500
Electric Light 195-7
electric lighting, journals for skilled workers 195-7
electric telegraph 306
electric typesetting machines, Hooker's 128-9
Electrical Engineer 53-4
Electrical Engineering 195-7
electrical journals **195-7**
    Annals of Electricity 16-17
    professional 510-11
Electrical Magazine 195-7
    publishers, Simpkin, Marshall & Co. 575a-b
Electrical News & Telegraphic Reporter, proprietors,
    Crookes 155a
Electrical Review, editor, Kempe 332b
electrical science and technology 254-5
    journals for amateur enthusiasts 195-7
*Electrician: A Weekly Journal of Theoretical and Applied
Electricity and Chemical Physics* (1878-1952) 195-7

editor, Biggs 53-4
*Electrician, A Weekly Journal of Telegraphy, Electricity and
Applied Chemistry* (1861-1864) 195-7
Electricity, and Electrical Engineering 195-7
electrochemistry 455-6
Elementary Education Act (1870) 329-30
Elgar, Edward 393-4
    J. Bennett on 49a-b
    A. Johnstone on 323a-b
    Maitland on 393-4
    musical contributions, *Dome* 174-5
Elgin Courier, editor, J. Grant 257-8
Elias, Julius Salter **197**
Eliot, George *see* Evans, Marian
elite journals 391-2
elitism 312a
Eliza Cook's Journal **197-8**, 391-2
    contributor(s), Meteyard 410
    editor, Eliza Cook 140
    and feminist press 216a-b
    proprietors, Eliza Cook 140
    as working-class periodical 689
Eliza Eliza Cook's Journal, contributor(s), Eliza Cook 140
Elizabeth I, Queen 536
Ella, John, editor, *Record Of The Musical Union* 533a
Ellerman, John
    financer: *Sphere* 574a-b; *Tatler* 574a-b
Elliot, Arthur Ralph Douglas **198**
    editor, *Edinburgh Review* 190-1
Elliot Stock **198**
Elliott, Ebenezer, M. J. Jewsbury on 320-1
Ellis, George
    contributor, *Anti-Jacobin or Weekly Examiner* 246-7
    and *Quarterly Review* 246-7, 522-3
Ellis, Havelock 4
    contributor, *Savoy* 559, 5598
'Ellis, Mrs.' (Sarah Stickey) 431a-b
    annuals 17-18
    contributor, *British Workman* 80a-b
    editor, *Mrs. Ellis's Morning Call* 431a-b
'Ellis Ethelmer' (Elmy, E & B) 198b
Ellison, Thomas, contributor, *Liverpool Daily Post* 368-9
Elmy, Benjamin **199**
Elmy, Elizabeth Clarke Wolstenholme **199**
    contributor, *Shafts* 568-9
Elwin, Whitwell **199-200**
    editor, *Quarterly Review* 522-3
Ely and Wisbech Advertiser, contributor(s), T. J. Bennett
49-50
Emerson, Ralph Waldo
    and Appleton 22
    proprietor, *Dial* 107
Emigrant's Almanack and Directory for 1849, publishers,
    Cassell & Co. 100, 100-1
Emmett, George
    contributor: *Sons of Britannia* 586a-b; *Young
    Englishman's Journal* 694-5
    editor: *Sons of Britannia* 586a-b; *Young Englishman's
    Journal* 694-5
    proprietor, *Sons of Britannia* 586a-b
Emmett, Harry, contributor, *Sons of Britannia* 586a-b
Emmett, William Laurence
    contributor: *Sons of Britannia* 586a-b; *Young
    Englishman's Journal* 694-5

editor: *Evening News* 210-11; *Fortnightly Review* 227-8, 557-8, 652a; *Saturday Review* 557-8
Harris, James, editor, *Red Dragon* 533a
Harris, James Lampen, editor, *Christian Witness* 116b
Harris, William, contributor, *Birmingham Daily Post* 55-6
Harris, William Snow, and *Annals of Electricity* 16-17
Harrison, Charles, editor, *Moonshine* 425a
Harrison, Edward
    and *Boys' Miscellany* 68-9
    founder, *Young Ladies' Journal* 696
    proprietor, *Young Ladies' Journal* 249-50, 695
Harrison, Frederic **273**, 426
    contributor, *Nineteenth Century* 456a-b
Harrison, Jane Ellen **273-5**
    contributor, *Athenaeum* 26-8
Harrison, Joseph
    contributor, *Black Dwarf* 57-8
    editor, *Florist Magazine* 242-3
Harrison, Thomas, and Waterlow 663-4
'Harry Hie'over/Hieover' (C. Bindley) 54a-b
Hart, Ernest Abraham **275**
    at *Lancet* 655b
    editor, *British Medical Journal* 78-9, 655b, 678a
Harte, Bret
    contributor: *Harmsworth's* 271; *Idler* 300; *To-Day* 632b
Harthill's Monthly Telegraph 639-40
Hartwell, Robert, editor, *Bee-Hive* 42-3
Harvard, Smalley at 578b
Harvey, Daniel Whittle, proprietor, *Sunday Times* 609-10, 609a-b
Harvey, William **275**
    and Gatty 244a
    illustrator: *Illustrated London News* 489a-b; *Penny Magazine* 315-16
    and J. Jackson 314a
Harvey, William Henry, editor, *Natural History Review* 441
Harwood, Philip
    editor: *Morning Herald and Daily Advertiser* 140-1; *Saturday Review* 557-8
Haslam, James
    and co-operative press 142-3
    contributor, *Teddy Ashton's Journal* 616a-b
    and National Union of Journalists 440
    serialized socialist fiction 566-7
Hastings, local papers 63a-b, 371-2
Hastings, Charles William
    editor: *Amateur Photographer* 495; *Photographic Quarterly* 495; *Photographic Reporter* 495
Hastings and St Leonard's News, contributor(s), Bodichon 63a-b
Hattersley, Robert, type composing machine 642b
Hatton, Francis Augustus, *Derbyshire Times* 275b
Hatton, Joseph Paul Christopher **275**
    editor, *Gentleman's Magazine* 245-6
    press history 505-6
Hatzfeld, E., editor, *Strand Musical Magazine* 606a
Haughton, Samuel, editor, *Natural History Review* 441
Havana Daily News, extracts 631-2
Havas, Charles 252-3
    see also Agence Havas
Hawker, Mary (Lanoe Falconer) 492-3
Haydn, Joseph (composer) 14a, 253b, 547b

Haydn, Joseph Timothy **276**
    founder, *Dublin Evening Mail* 181
Haydon, Benjamin, paintings *20.47*
Hayley, Barbara 380-1
Hayman's Balsam, advertising in *Northern Weekly* 583-4
Hays, Mary, contributor, *Analytical Review* 15a
Hays, Matilda Mary **276**
    assistant editor, *English Woman's Journal* 204-5
Hayward, Abraham, editors, *Law Magazine* 349
Hayward, William Stephens
    contributor: *Boy's Journal* 68a-b; *Sons of Britannia* 586a-b; *Young Englishman's Journal* 694-5
Haywood, Abel, publisher, *Vegetarian Messenger* 651-2
Hazell, Walter, Hazell, Watson & Viney Limited 276-7
Hazell, Watson & Viney 276-7
    publishers, *Photographic Quarterly* 495
Hazlewood, Colin Henry, contributor, *Bow Bells* 67a-b
Hazlitt, William **277**
    collaborations 132-3
    contributor: *Atlas* 28-9; *Champion* 106-7, 563a-b; *Examiner* 211-12; *Gentleman's Magazine* 245-6; *London Magazine* 375a, 563a-b; *Monthly Magazine* 422-3; *Morning Chronicle* 426-7; *New Monthly Magazine and Literary Journal* 443-4
    Examiner 296-7
    and Gifford 246-7
    and *John Bull* 321-2
    Liberal 297
    and Lockhart 372
    philosophy and journalism 494
    views on Cobbett 130-1
    views on the *Edinburgh Review* 190-1
Head, F. B., contributor, *Quarterly Review* 128-9
Head Teacher, as professional journal 510-11
headlines
    Harmsworth's policy 269-70, 324-5
    news 448-50
Healey, T. P., proprietor, *Medical Times* 375-6
Health: A weekly journal of Sanitary Science, contributor(s), Ballin 36b
health
    alternative, complementary, fringe medicine **406-7**, 407-8
    Ballin on 36b
    see also medical journalists; medical journals; public health
Health and Strength **277-8**
    rivals 264-5
Heaney, Seamus, views on J. F. A. Wilde 676a
Hearn, Mary Anne ('Marianne Farningham') **278**
Hearst, William Randolph
    proprietor, *New York Journal* 309a-b
    and yellow journalism 694a
Hearth and Home **278**, 651a
    advice supplement 20
    and Coke 20, 131a, 278a-b
    contributor(s), Arnold Bennett 48-9
    illustrators, A. M. Hughes 295a-b
    merger with *Vanity Fair* 651a
    photographers, Pragnell 503a-b
'Heath, Bushey' (Jerdan) 317
Heath, Henry, illustrator, *Looking Glass* 379a
Heath, William ('Paul Pry') 251a, **278-9**, 483-4
    illustrator: *Glasgow Looking Glass* 95a-b, 251a;

ILP *see* Independent Labour Party
Image, Selwyn
    contributor, *Savoy* 612
    proprietor, *Century Guild Hobby Horse* 103-4
impartiality
    and anonymity of reviewers 18-19
    and journalism 622-3
Imperial Dictionary of Universal Biography, contributor(s),
    Espinasse 207
imperialism
    anti-imperialism 139-40
    Borthwick and 427a-b
    Daily Mail 157-8
    Edinburgh Medical and Surgical Journal articles 190
    endorsement by *Boy's Own Paper* 70-1
    and journalism 134, **306**, 628-9

Manchester Literary Club 146-7
  Brierley and 75a-b
Manchester Magazine 395
Manchester National Society for Women's Suffrage 685b
  Becker and 42b
Manchester National Society for Women's Suffrage Journal
  685b
Manchester Observer 394-5
  and Wooler 688-9
Manchester press 395
Manchester Press Company 429a
Manchester and Salford Boys' and Girls' Refuges and
  Homes, and *Christian Worker and Cry of the Children*
  116-17
Manchester Spectator, contributor(s), Brierley 75a-b
Manchester Statistical Society 581-2
Manchester Sunday Chronicle
  contributor(s), Blatchford 122-3
  editor, Hulton 122-3
Manchester Temperance Reporter and Journal of Progress,
  contributor(s), A. Somerville 585-6
Manchester Weekly Times
  children's columns 111a-b
  contributor(s), Brierley 75a-b
Manea Fen, socialist community 162a
Mangan, James Clarence **395-6**
  contributor: *Belfast Vindicator* 45a; *Dublin Penny
  Journal* 182-3; *Dublin University Magazine* 89,
  177a, 209-10, 360, 388a
Manico, Ernest, publisher, *Irish Society* 311-12
Mann, James, unstamped press 648-9
Mann, Tom
  and C. A. Clarke 123b
  and socialist newspapers 583
  as undercover reporter 106b, 338b
Manners, George, proprietor, *The Satirist, or Monthly
  Meteor* 317
Manners, James, editor, *Stirling Observer* 602-3
Manning, Cardinal
  contributor, *New Review* 445
  V. M. Crawford and 151b
Mansell, Henry, editor, *Dublin Medical Press* 407-8
Mansfield, F. J., on subediting 608b
Manson, James Bolivar, editor, *Stirling Observer* 602-3
Manson, Patrick, contributor, *British Medical Journal*
  78-9
manufacturers, directories 479
Manwaring, George 672-3
Marcet, Jane, and political economy 498-9
March-Phillips, Evelyn, and *Fortnightly Review* 341a
marine subjects in illustrations, G. H. Andrews 15a
Marischal College (Aberdeen), Chalmers at 104
Mark Lane Express
  contributor(s), H. H. Dixon 173-4
  proprietors, Hazell, Watson & Viney Ltd 276-7
Mark Twain *see* Twain, Mark
market for periodicals **396**
  and 'class' publications 126a
  and competition 137-8
Markham, Clements, contributor, *Macmillan's Magazine*
  262-3
Markham, W. O., editor, *British Medical Journal* 78-9
Marks, Harry, founder, *Evening News* 210-11
Marks, Harry Hananel

  editor, *Daily Mining News* 220
  and *Financial and Mining News* 220
Marlborough College 412a
Marlborough's (news agency), J. Francis at 229a
Marlburian
  editors: Benson 412a; Miles 412a
Marnock, Robert, proprietor, *Floriculture Magazine*
  242-3
marriage
  Adult debates 4
  Matrimonial Causes Act (1857) and divorce news
  172a
  opposition to 33a-b
Married Women's Property Act (1870), amendment bill
  685b
Married Women's Property Act (1882) 676a
Marryat, Florence **396**
  contributor, *Belgravia* 45-6
  criticisms 320a-b
  editor, *London Society* 376-7
Marryat, Frank, contributor, *Mirror of Literature* 417a-b
Marryat, Frederick **396-7**, 396b
  criticisms 323-4
  proprietor, *Metropolitan Magazine* 410-11, 412a-b
Marryat, Shairp 396b
Marsden, J., and Williams 678a-b
Marsden, John Buxton, editor, *Christian Observer* 115a-b
Marshall, Richard 575
Marshall, Simpkin & Co *see* Simpkin & Marshall
Marshall Brothers
  publishers: *Protestant Girl* 512b; *Protestant Woman*
  512b
'Marshallik' (Israel Zangwill) 699a
Marshman, Joshua, editor, *Friend of India* 236
Marston, Edward
  and Low 555a-b
  manager, *Publisher's Circular* 516-17
Marston, J. W., letter to W. H. Dixon *174*
Marston, R. B., editor, *Fishing Gazette* 221b
Marston, Robert, and Low 555a-b
Marston, Westland, contributor, *Athenaeum* 665a-b
martial arts 277-8
Martin, Carolyn, and *Workman's Times* 690a-b
Martin, Frances
  contributor: *Macmillan's Magazine* 262-3, 389;
  *Monthly Repository of Theology and General
  Literature* 228-9
Martin, Theodore, contributor, *Tait's Edinburgh
  Magazine* 613-14
Martin, William, proprietor, *Peter Parley's Magazine* 491b
Martineau, Harriet **397-8**
  biography 413-14
  contributor: *Daily News* 158, 638; *Dublin University
  Magazine* 360; *Household Words* 71-2, 292-3;
  London and Westminster Review 672-3; *Monthly
  Repository* 398a, 424-5; *New Monthly Magazine and
  Literary Journal* 443-4; *Once A Week* 407-8, 638;
  People's Journal 489a-b; *Spectator* 638; *Tait's
  Edinburgh Magazine* 613-14, 613a-b; *Westminster
  Review* 107
  estrangement from brother 398a
  and Jameson 315-16
  C. I. Johnstone on 323-4
  and political economy 498-9

editor, Robertson 543a-b
establishment 494
proprietors, Bain 543a-b
publisher, Bain 34a-b
Mind Association 414a-b
Miner 338-9, 416
minerology, in *Annals of Natural History* 16a-b
Miners' Institutes, reading rooms 515
Miniken, John, financier, *Western Vindicator* 671
mining
    and *Cape Argus* 94a
    colonies 416
    coverage in *Engineer* 200-1
    and labour press 416
    and trade union movement 415-16, 416, 670-1
Mining Engineering 416
Mining Journal 358-60, **415-16**, 416
mining press 415-16, **416**
Mining World and Engineering and Commercial Record
    416
Minister, illustrators, G. D. Hammond 267a-b
Minto, William, proprietor, *Examiner* 211-12
Le Miroir Politique 164
Mirror 417a-b, 417b
    contributor(s), Hays 276a-b
    and miscellany tradition 363-4
    proprietor, Limbird 363-4
'mirror', use of term 391-2
Mirror of Literature 301-3, **417**
    and cheap journalism 109-10
    contributor(s): Alford 11a; T. Campbell 92-3; M.
        Wilson 680a
    editors: Byerley 365b; P. B. St. John 552-3; Timbs
        626-7
    illustration 304-6
    illustrators, Forrester 227
    influences 437-8
    layout 405-6
    proprietors: Limbird 363-4, 635-6; Timbs 227, 301-3
    scissors-and-paste journalism 561
    wood engravings 687a-b
Mirror Monthly Magazine 417a-b
Mirror of Parliament, contributor(s), Dickens 167
Mirror of Science 203-4
Mirror of the Stage 417
    contributor(s): Blanchard 61a-b; D. Jerrold 61a-b,
        322
Mirror of Truth, editor, Robert Owen 475
Mirth, contributor(s), Sala 554
miscellanies **417-18**
    contributors, Forrester 227
    signed articles 18-19
    size and format 576-7
'Miss X' (Freer) 231b
missionaries 306, 429b
    Baptist 236
    and colonial press 134
    Methodist 134
    Quaker 521
    and religious press 534-5
    W. Ward 662b
Missionary Chronicle **418**, 419
Missionary Herald **418-19**
Missionary Magazine 418, 419

Missionary Magazine and Chronicle 418, 419
Missionary Notes, and *Wesleyan Methodist Magazine* 670b
missionary press 418-19, **419**
    Eclectic Review 188-9
Missionary Sketches 419
missionary societies 418-19
    annuals 17-18
    and *Sheffield Iris* 571-2
'missions', E. Arnold 24
missions, China 418-19
Mistletoe Bough, Christmas annual, editor, Braddon 72a
Mitchel, John **419-20**
    and *Cork Examiner* 144a
    and Mangan 395-6
    and *Nation* (Irish) 184, 437b
    Ulsterman/Irishman 645b
    and Young Ireland 695-6
Mitchell, Charles (advertising agent)
    proprietor, *Newspaper Press Directory* 420a, 453b
    publisher: *Chemical News* 110-11; *Newspaper Press
        Directory* 505-6; *Statist* (1854-5) 597-8
Mitchell, J., contributor, *Sportsman* 595
Mitchell's Newspaper Press Directory 7-8, 392-3, **420**, 663
    circulation data 120
    on *Evening Chronicle* 426-7
    on *Fairplay* 213a
    on *Fishing Gazette* 221b
    on *Illustrated Sporting and Dramatic News* 304
    on *Money Market Review* 421a-b
    on potential confusion between news and
        advertisements 448-50
    proprietor, Mitchell 453b
    satirical category 556-7
    on *Tobacco* 631-2
Mitford, John
    and Benbow 48a-b
    editor, *Gentleman's Magazine* 442-3
Mitford, John (II)
    editor: *New Bon Ton Magazine or The Telescope of the
        Times* 442-3; *Quizzical Gazette* 442-3; *Scourge, or
        Monthly Expositor of Imposture and Folly* 442-3
Mitford, Mary Russell
    annuals 17-18
    contributor: *Chambers's (Edinburgh) Journal* 106a-b;
        Ladies' Companion 340b; *Lady's Magazine* 342a;
        New Monthly Magazine and Literary Journal 443-4;
        Tait's Edinburgh Magazine 613-14, 613a-b
Mitton, Henry (printer) 21-2
M'Kenna, A. J.
    manager, *Ulster Observer* 409a-b
    Ulster Observer 645a
M'Nicholl, Thomas, editor, *London Quarterly Review*
    376b
Model Republic, publishers, James Watson 664b
Modern Illustrator, contributor(s), J. Pennell 486
Modern Press (Champion) 106b, 328-9, 338b
Modern Review **420**, 512a
    contributor(s): Bevington 53a-b; W. B. Carpenter 98a
Modern Society 393b
Modern Thought, contributor(s), Bax 40a-b
Mogridge, George ('Old Humphrey'), contributor,
    British Workman 80a-b
Mohammedan religion 376b, 534b
Moir, David Macbeth **420-1**

proprietor, Bradlaugh 72b, 232-3, 566a, 566a-b
publisher, J. O'Brien 466
National Review (1855-1864) **439-40**, 512a, 523
  contributor(s): M. Arnold 24; Bagehot 33-4; W. B.
    Carpenter 98a; Marian Evans 209-10; Greg 260a; J.
    Martineau 398a; Masson 400-1; Roscoe 545a; J. A.
    Ross 545a-b; Spielmann 590-1; L. Stephen 600-1;
    Symons 612; Tayler 615a-b
  editors: Bagehot 298-9; R. H. Hutton 298-9, 545a
  precursors 545a
  proprietors, Bagehot 545a
  publisher, Chapman & Hall 107-8
National Review (1883-1960) **440**
  contributor(s): Cust 156; Escott 206-7; E. L. Linton
    364-5; Low 143; V. Morten 429a; Quilter 524a-b;
    Stutfield 608a-b; Wedgwood 666a-b; Zimmern
    699a-b
  editor: A. Austin 29-30, 402-3; Courthope 148a-b
  proprietors: Austin 148a-b; Maxse 402-3
  publishers, W. H. Allen 654
  and typewritten copy 642-3
National Secular Society 8-9, 52b, 72b, 232-3
  and *Freethinker* 231-2, 566a
  and *National Reformer* 439, 566a
National Secular Society Almanack 72b
National Society for Women's Suffrage 685a
  and Becker 42b
  Blackburn and 58b
National Standard
  contributor(s): Maginn 392; Thackeray 392, 620a-b
  proprietors, Thackeray 620a-b
National Temperance Advocate and Herald
  editor, Livesey 617-18
  proprietors, Livesey 617-18
National Temperance Movement, Cassell and 100
National Union, contributor(s), Leno 358a
National Union of Journalists **440**
  establishment 308
National Union of Railwaymen 639-40
National Union of Women Workers 492-3
National United Trades' Association Report 635
National Vigilance Association 139a-b
nationalism 387
  Anglo-Irish 437b
  British 438-9
  w. J. Linton and 365a-b
  Maxse and 402-3
  and music 465a
  Scottish 358-60, 562
nationalization, of telegraph 616-17
natural history 361-2
  Cooke 141a
  W. Francis 229b
  Hardwicke 268-9, 268a
  and *Intellectual Observer* 577-8
  journalists, Buckland 84b
  journals 241-2, 441; *Annals of Natural History* 16a-b,
    see also science journals
  Kidd 332-3
  Kingston's Magazine for Boys 333b
Natural History Museum 688a-b
Natural History Review **441**
  editor, Huxley 299, 441-2
natural selection

Darwin and 658-9
Wallace and 658-9
Naturalist
  editor, Maund 402a-b
  publishers, Longman 377-8
Nature 414a-b, **441-2**
  compared with *Knowledge* 335-6
  contributor(s): A. W. Bennett 48b; Clerke 127-8;
    Huxley 299; Keltie 332a; Tyndall 642a; Wells
    669-70
  editors: R. A. Gregory 260-1, 372-3, 441-2; Lockyer
    260b, 332a, 372-3, 559-60, 642a; Ranyard 528a-b
  publisher, Macmillan 388-9
  publishing rates 559-60
  rivals 509
  subeditor, J. C. Brough 81-2
nautical themes, in *Metropolitan Magazine* 396-7
naval journalism, Thursfield 625b
Naval and Military Gazette 412a-b
  editor, Phillipart 646b
  proprietors, Colburn 131-2
  publishers, Colburn 646b
Naval and Military Magazine, editor, À Beckett 1a
navigational aids, W. Thomson and 625a-b
Navy and Army Illustrated, publishers, Hudson 294b
Navy List, publishers, John Murray Publishers 322
NBSP *see* National Brotherhood of Saint Patrick
Neale, John Mason, contributor, *Ecclesiologist* 188a
needlework, *Weldon's Ladies' Journal* 669a-b
Neighbourhood Vigilance Circles 364
Neil, Samuel, contributor, *British Controversialist* 77-8
Nelson & Sons 3-4
neo-Malthusianism
  National Reformer as advocate 72b
  see also Malthus, Thomas
Nesbit, Edith 32
  collaborations 132-3
  contributor: *Atalanta* 26; *Athenaeum* 26-8;
    Harmsworth's 271; *Pall Mall Gazette* 156; *Scots
    Observer* 279-80, 561-2; *Sylvia's Home Journal* 695;
    Weekly Dispatch 667-8
Nesbitt, Elizabeth, contributor, *Longman's Magazine*
  377-8
Net Book Agreement (1900) 451-2, 673-4
  Bookseller campaign 65a
Neue Oder-Zeitung, contributor(s), Marx 398-9
Neue Rheinische Zeitung: Organ der Democratie 398-9
Neue Rheinische Zeitung: Politisch-Ökonomische Revue
  398-9
Neue Rheinische Zeitung 398-9
neuropsychiatry, Bucknill 84-5
Nevinson, Henry W.
  war correspondent: Boer War 660-1; *Daily Chronicle*
    128a
New Age **442**
  contributor(s): Arnold Bennett 48-9; Elmy 198b
New Anti-Jacobin, editor, Surtees 610-11
New Art Criticism 385b
  E. R. Pennell 485-6
New Bon-Ton Magazine **442-3**
New Boys' Paper, proprietors, Rollington 544-5
New Casket, publishers, Cowie 149b
New Clarion, publishers, Clarion Fellowship 122-3
New Comic Annual, illustrators, Brown 135b

H. M. Paget 477a-b
W. S. Paget 477a-b
war correspondents 660-1
  À Beckett 1a
  Beckett 253a
  Bennett 48-9
  W. Black 57a-b
  Churchill 660-1
  Cormack 144-5
  Daily News 158
  Dixie 172b
  employment status 358-60
  A. Forbes 224a
  'Golden Age' of 660-1
  Gruneisen 263a-b
  Henty 596-7
  historical background 536
  H. Kingsley 333a
  D. C. Murray 432
  Nevinson 128a, 660-1
  Norman 457
  W. H. Russell 549-50, 660-1
  Sala 618-19
  Steevens 599-600
  F. Vizetelly 653a
War Cry **661**
War Office 372-3, 559-60
War Telegraph, as 'class' publication 126a
War of the Unstamped
  concept of 499-500
  and cover price 506b
  origin of term 454, 500-1
Warburton, Eliot
  contributor: *Dublin University Magazine* 360; *Red Republican* 533b
Ward & Lock 662-3
  Beeton's assets sold to 44, 69-70, 70
  establishment 662-3
  proprietor, *Englishwoman's Domestic Magazine* 205-6
  publisher: *Ladies' Treasury* 341a-b; *Temple Bar* 618-19
Ward, A. W., contributor, *Manchester Guardian* 394-5
Ward, Ebenezer, proprietor, Ward & Lock 662-3
Ward, Edith, contributor, *Shafts* 568-9
Ward, Genevieve, and puffing 517b
Ward, H. Snowden, contributor, *Review of Reviews* 495
Ward, Harriet, foreign correspondent, *United Service Magazine* 224-5
Ward, Henry George
  editor, *Weekly Chronicle* 667
  proprietor, *Weekly Chronicle* 667
Ward, Mrs Humphrey (Mary Augusta Ward) 662a-b
  and Women Writers' Club 341a, 686b
Ward, Leslie Matthew 485b, **662**
  illustrator, *Vanity Fair* 651a
Ward, Mary, contributor, *Atalanta* 26
Ward, Mary Augusta *see* Ward, Mrs Humphrey
Ward, Thomas Humphry **662**
Ward, William **662**
  proprietor, *Friend of India* 236
Ward, William George
  contributor, *British Critic* 494
  editor, *Dublin Review* 183
Ward, Lock & Co. **662-3**
Ward, Lock & Tyler 662-3

proprietors: *Beeton's Young Englishwoman* 695; *New Quarterly Magazine* 444-5
Ward Lock & Bowden Ltd. 662-3
Ward Lock & Co., Ltd. 662-3
Ward Lock, Bowden & Company 662-3
Warder
  contributor(s), Le Fanu 355a
  merger with *Protestant Guardian* 89
Wardrop, James, contributor, *Lancet* 343-4
Warne, William Henry, and Routledge 546a-b
Warren, Eliza, editor, *Ladies' Treasury* 341a-b
Warrington Guardian
  proprietors, Mackie 215
  typesetting machine 642b
Warsaw, Russian capture of 92-3
Warwick, Frances, proprietor, *Woman's Agricultural Times* 682b
Warwick, Sidney, contributor, *Daily Mail* 157-8
Wassail Bowl, editor, A. R. Smith 578-9
'Wat Bradwood' (Woodgate) 688a
watchmakers 319-20
Watchman, proprietors, Coleridge 132a-b
Watchman and Wesleyan Advertiser, contributor(s), S. C. Hall 266a-b
Water Cure and Hygienic Magazine, editor, Smethurst 406-7
watercolourists
  Archer 23a
  A. Claxton 126a-b
  Read 529-30
Waterloo, Battle of (1815) 536
  Timperley at 629a-b
Waterloo (Canada) University, publications 663
Waterloo Directories of the United Kingdom and Ireland Newspapers and Periodicals **663**
Waterloo Directory of English Newspapers and Periodicals, 1800-1900 230b, 313, **663**
  circulation data 120
Waterloo Directory of Irish Newspapers and Periodicals 663
Waterloo Directory of Scottish Newspapers and Periodicals, 1800-1900 663
Waterloo Directory of Victorian Periodicals 1824-1900 536-7, 663
Waterlow & Sons 663-4
  printers, *Banking Almanac* 663-4
Waterlow, Albert 663-4
Waterlow, Alfred 663-4
Waterlow, Sidney Hedley **663-4**
Waterlow, Walter 663-4
Waterlow Professional Publishing 585a-b
Watford University Press 230
Watkin, Edward, manager, *Illustrated London News* 307
Watkins, Benjamin William, contributor, *Theatrical Journal* 621-2
Watkins, John **664**
  and Chartist press 108-9
  and Shoberl 574a
Watkinson, John, editor, *British Chess Magazine* 77a-b
Watson, Aaron
  editor: *Evening Leader* 460-1; *Northern Weekly Leader* 460-1
Watson, George, Hazell, Watson & Viney Ltd 276-7
Watson, H. B. Marriott, contributor, *Scots Observer* 279-80, 561-2